ACPL ITEM
DISCARDED

SO-BWV-008

JUL 19 1948

6-10-49

The Gramophone Shop
ENCYCLOPEDIA OF
RECORDED MUSIC

THE

Gramophone Shop

ENCYCLOPEDIA

OF

RECORDED MUSIC

THIRD EDITION, REVISED AND ENLARGED

CROWN PUBLISHERS

NEW YORK · 1948

Copyright, 1936, 1942, by The Gramophone Shop, Inc.

Copyright, 1948, by The Gramophone Shop, Inc.

PRINTED IN THE UNITED STATES OF AMERICA

Contents

641847

Baker & Taylor 3.30

JUL 2 6 1949

Preface

The Gramophone Shop Encyclopedia of Recorded Music is a reference tool bringing together in one compact volume, and in as concise a form as possible, all listings of serious music currently to be found in the catalogues of the world's record manufacturers. Designed with the needs of the amateur music lover paramount in mind, the encyclopedia has also been found an indispensable adjunct in the record shop, and graces the shelves of public libraries the world over.

This edition includes all records issued up to and including January of 1948. In addition, it catalogues the major portion of all records placed on the market through June 1st and contains, as well, listings of many important sets which—though in some cases already manufactured—have yet to be released to the public.

The organization of this completely revised and enlarged third edition does not differ essentially from the two which have preceded it, albeit its newest feature should prove to be a most useful and welcome one. For those music lovers partial to the creative efforts of certain performing artists, an alphabetical index will be found at the back of the volume which will cite the pages and columns upon which all recordings of these artists will be found. In addition to this novel feature, this edition employs a new typographical arrangement and a simplified and uniform style, designed to assure easy reference and readability. In one sense, however, this volume complements but does not supersede the two previous editions, for listings of recordings withdrawn from current catalogues will not be found in these pages. To those interested in an historical survey of recorded music, or those attempting to identify and procure any specific "cut-out" item, the suggestion is made that the three editions be consulted side by side.*

Needless to say, the laborious task of correct identification, numbering of works and the arrangement of material often so confusing in manufacturers' catalogues, a task courageously assumed by the editor of the original edition, continues apace in this one. However, since some of the problems encountered by the editors compiling this volume still remain open questions in the more lofty realm of musicology, it is hoped that such discrepancies as are found by specialists will be viewed charitably, and the appropriate corrections sent in to

---

* At this writing copies of the first (1936) edition are still available and may be ordered from *The Gramophone Shop.*

this office for our edification. All such contributions, addressed to *The Gramophone Shop, Inc., 18 East 48th Street, New York 17, N. Y.,* will be gratefully received and acknowledged.

The preparation of this volume has not been as simple a task as it on first blush might seem. Dismissing as a comparatively minor matter the ever-present and vexing problem of mis-labeling by manufacturers, there still remain two factors which proved to add greatly to the difficulties. First, the repercussions of World War II are still with us, and the resultant confusion in the record industry almost defies description. In many cases, European companies have not issued catalogues since the early war years; in such catalogues as have appeared recently—and here in the United States this is also the case—large segments of the recorded repertoire have been suppressed. Record factories have been bombed out and many masters destroyed. Manufacture of German records especially has been slowed by the time-consuming litigations involved in reconstituting these companies. And worst of all, much of the information reaching us from Europe on these and allied matters is fragmentary. Time is still needed to restore the record business to a firm and stable footing.

The second complicating factor arises from the transformation of the record industry from a luxury to a mass basis, in the course of which another measure of confusion has been superimposed upon that which already exists. Manufacturers' numbers of discs and albums have been countlessly revised; catalogues, no sooner issued, become obsolete; the recorded repertoire has been dangerously overextended in the most popular categories, and at the same time seriously curtailed in areas that are not of mass appeal.

We cite these factors not as an excuse for such errors as are inescapable in an undertaking of this scope, but rather to urge patience upon the user of this volume in his attempt to procure items listed herein. All entries have been culled from the most reliable sources, and all recordings listed are therefore theoretically available. Yet the sheer bulk of the recorded repertoire, machine and material shortages, mass distribution methods, importing difficulties, combined with unprecedented demand, will undoubtedly conspire to limit for some time the availability of many desired recordings.

The supervising editor has incurred the pleasant obligation of acknowledging the assistance he has received in the preparation of this volume. Without doubt he is heavily in debt to R. D. Darrell for his pioneering work on the 1936 edition and to G. C. Leslie's efforts in behalf of the more recent second edition of 1942. He must take this opportunity again to express his long-standing gratitude to those numerous—and therefore necessarily anonymous—individuals whose written corrections and suggestions have, over a period of years, been received here at *The Gramophone Shop*. The indebtedness to manufacturers' catalogues, notwithstanding their many shortcomings, is too obvious to be dwelt upon, but those of *His Master's Voice* & *Columbia (England)* might here be acknowledged as models of accuracy, completeness and concision. Likewise, great use has been made of the domestic and foreign record periodical literature and in this regard special mention should be made of the English *Gramophone* and the Italian journal, *Musica e Dischi*.

Special thanks for European record information must be rendered to Eugene Hartkoff and Herbert Rosenberg of Scandinavian HMV, Jürgens Balzer of Copenhagen, James Gray of English Decca, W. Hamburger of Danish Decca, Cecil Pollard of the *Gramophone Magazine*, Valentine Britten of the BBC and Bengt Pleijel of *Musik Revy*. Among the many here in the United States who have given freely of their time and knowledge, the editor is especially grateful to Philip L. Miller and the staffs of the Music Division and the 58th Street Branch of the *New York Public Library*, and to Herman Adler and David Hall. To Charles Hoffman and Byron Goode the editor offers his thanks for their steady assistance in the preparation of the typescript and the correction of proofs. Lastly, the undersigned is deeply indebted to the members of the staff of *The Gramophone Shop*, and in particular to its proprietor, Mr. Joseph Brogan, without whose vision, patience and wholehearted support this volume could not have appeared.

ROBERT H. REID, *Supervising Editor*.

Explanation of Plan and Symbols

1. *The Gramophone Shop Encyclopedia of Recorded Music* is organized alphabetically by composers' surnames listed according to the most authentic and widely accepted spelling. This is the case with the exception of two categories, *Anonymous* and *Gregorian Chant* in the body of the text, and the performer's index and list of collections contained in the last sections of the volume.

2. Under each composer's name, his works are arranged alphabetically by original title with the exception that certain well defined forms—concertos, masses, motets, songs, symphonies, etc.—are grouped together and listed numerically by opus, edition or date, or alphabetically by text or key, according to the nature and dictates of the material under consideration. Recorded collections of a composer's works are listed either above the alphabetical entries or under that category—songs, quartets, madrigals, etc.—to which they most properly belong.

3. All works and recordings are (subject to the availability of the records in question, and/or the presence of adequate information in manufacturers' catalogues) identified according to the best information currently available and so described to the maximum degree of clarity consistent with the exigencies of space and the plan of this *Encyclopedia.*

4. The ensembles, instruments and/or voices printed following each listing of a composition are those specified by the composer. In most cases performances listed below employ the indicated instrumentation within certain limits, unless alternate media are indicated in parentheses following the individual performers' names.

5. Arrangements are grouped either among the DUPLICATIONS or, if musically legitimate and meritorious, in a separate category prefixed by a long dash, and followed by the kind of arrangement and the arranger's name (when ascertained).

6. Recordings of parts of a composition follow those which are complete. These are also prefixed by a long dash, and followed by the specific part excerpted from the composition.

7. The order in which performing artists are entered is as follows: soloist(s), accompanist or accompanying instrument(s), ensemble(s), orchestra, and last, the name of the conductor prefixed by a long dash.

8. The main entries of composers' names, main entries of titles and generic titles of their works, translations (when necessary), headings of arrangements, and parts thereof, and the major record numbers are, for clarity, printed in **bold face** characters. In addition, main entries of composers' names, their operas, the more important works and generic titles are printed in **CAPITALS**. Brief notes which follow the main composer entry to identify him (when necessary) in time, place and musical importance, and those notes necessary to clarify certain entries are printed in *italics*.

9. Record numbers listed in **bold face** characters are domestic (USA) whenever available; those found in parentheses are generally duplications on imported surfaces of the performance indicated immediately above. The list of all record makes herein employed will be found on the pages immediately following these explanatory remarks.

10. Composers and titles enclosed in brackets [   ] are those coupled to recordings which require an odd number of sides. Where no bracketed entry is to be found, all sides of the listed records are used for the work in question. Where an odd side is left blank by the manufacturer, this fact is so noted.

11. In the case of compositions which are issued by the manufacturer as parts of a record set not available separately or only procurable on special or replacement order (and then with difficulty), the album numbers are printed in light face characters and prefixed by the word *in*. In the case of Society sets, this fact is often specifically stated.

12. A dagger (†) following record or set numbers indicates the availability of these records in drop-automatic coupling. In the case of domestic Columbia records, the dagger also indicates the non-availability of these records in manual sequence. As changes in these policies are announced, notices will be inserted in *The Gramophone Shop Record Supplement*.

13. An asterisk (*) following a record number signifies that the listed item is an acoustical (non-electric) recording.

14.   The order in which recordings of any specific work are listed is governed by a variety of criteria. Among these may be mentioned completeness, authenticity of the performance, acoustical quality and age of the recording, use of the original language in vocal compositions, ready availability in the United States, and lastly the editorial opinion of *The Gramophone Shop* as contained in its *Record Supplement*. Where the number of recordings is judged to be more than sufficient to provide ample freedom of selection by most users, the residue are, in accordance with the above-mentioned criteria, enumerated in short entries under the heading: DUPLICATIONS.

15.   This verbal explanation cannot detail all the minor adjustments necessitated by the vicissitudes of organizing the material at hand. Special problems have been disposed of in the most practical fashion possible. It is the belief of the editor that entries in *The Gramophone Shop Encyclopedia of Recorded Music* will for the most part be self-explanatory, and that the success of his efforts will in part be inversely proportionate to the necessity of consulting the above explanations.

Record Makes

Listed alphabetically below are the code letters used to identify the manufacturers whose records are represented in *The Gramophone Shop Encyclopedia of Recorded Music.* These code letters are prefixed to the record order numbers. Where no code letter is indicated below, the full name has been employed in the body of the Encyclopedia.

ADAM	Adam (Italy)
AL	Allegro (USA)
ALCO	Alco (USA)
ARIA	Aria Disc (USA)
ART	Artist (USA)
AS	(L')Anthologie sonore (International)
ASCH	Asch (see also DISC) (USA)
B	Brunswick (England)
BAM	Boîte à Musique (France)
	Bibletone (USA)
C	Columbia (USA & Europe)
CAP	Capitol (USA)
CdM	Chant du Monde (France)
CET	Cetra (Italy & USA)
CH	Concert Hall (USA)
CM	Columbia Masterworks Set (USA)
CODA	Coda (USA)
COMP	Compass (USSR)
CON	Continental (USA)
	Concord (USA)
COSMO	Cosmo (USA)
CRS	Collectors' Record Shop (USA)
CX	Columbia two-record Sets (USA)
D	Decca (England & USA)
DF	Discophiles Français (France)
DISC	Disc (See also ASCH) (USA)
ELEC	Electro (Finland)
ELITE	Elite (Switzerland)
ESTA	Esta (Czechoslovakia)
FLOR	Florilege (France)
FON	Fonit (Italy)
G	Gramophone (HMV) (Europe)
GM	Gramophone Masterworks Sets (England)
GRCH	Canadian Gregorian Chants (USA)
GSC	Gramophone Shop Celebrities (USA)

GSV	Gramophone Shop Varieties (USA)
IMP	Imperial (Austria)
INT	International (USA)
K	Keynote (USA)
KYR	Kyriale (USA)
LUM	Lumen (France)
MC	Musicraft (USA)
MIA	Musiche Italiane Antiche (Italy)
MW	Hargail (USA)
NP	Nordisk Polyphon (Danish Decca Agency)
	Night Music (USA)
O	Odeon (Germany, Sweden & France)
OL	(L')Oiseau Lyre (France)
OLY	Olympia (Belgium)
P	Parlophone (England)
PD	Polydor (France, Germany & Switzerland)
PAR	Paraclete (USA)
PAT	Pathé (France)
PIL	Pilotone (USA)
RAD	Radiola (Hungary)
RJ	Swedish Radiotjanst
SEMS	Société de l'Edition de Musique Sacrée (Includes: Musique au Vatican) (Italy & France)
SEVA	Seva (USA)
STIN	Stinson (USA)
SYM	Symfoni (Sweden)
T	Telefunken (Germany, Italy, Sweden & Switzerland)
TC	Technicord (USA)
TONO	Tono (Danish)
U	Ultraphon (Czechoslovakia)
USSR	USSR (Compass) (Russia)
V	Victor (USA)
VM	Victor Masterworks Set
VOX	Vox (USA)
YPR	Young People's Records (USA)

ABACO, Evaristo Felice dall' (1675-1742)

Italian by birth, dall'Abaco spent his mature years in Germany serving the Electoral Court at Munich. One of countless Baroque composers whose merits are obscured by their numbers, his works include church and chamber sonatas and concerted music for strings.

Concerto, B flat major Strings
Edwin Fischer Chamber Orch.
12"—G-DB3175

Sonata, F major, Op. 3, No. 2 (c1714) 2 Violins & Basso continuo
Jean Fournier & Jean Pasquier (vls), Etienne Pasquier (vlc), & Ruggero Gerlin (harpsichord) (in Vol. V)
12"—AS-46

l' ABBE, Joseph Barnabé Saint Sevin (1727-1802)

A violinist at the "Concerts spirituels" and the "Opéra" during the late Rococo period, l'Abbé wrote extensively for the violin.

Aria, Chasse & Minuetto
Alfred Dubois (vl) & Marcel Maas (pf)
12"—C-DFX199
[Debussy: Sonata, Pt. 3]

ABEL, Karl Friedrich (1725-1787)

A pupil of J. S. Bach and an accomplished performer on the viola da gamba, Abel won an outstanding place in the musical life of London when he migrated there in 1759.

Symphony, E flat major, Op. 10, No. 3 (arr. Adam Carse)
Boyd Neel String Orch.   12"—D-K944

ACHRON, JOSEPH (1886-   )

Hebrew Dance Violin & Piano (arr. Heifetz)
Bronislaw Gimpel & Artur Balsam, in VOX-616

Hebrew Melody Violin & Piano (arr. Leopold Auer)
Jascha Heifetz & Emanuel Bay
12"—V-11-9572
[Schubert: Rondo, arr. Friedberg]
[Debussy: La plus que lente on G-DB-6469] (Older version on G-DB1048)
Mischa Elman & Leopold Mittman
12"—V-11-9111
[Sibelius: Mazurka, Op. 81, No. 1]
Ida Haendel & Adela Kotowska
12"—D-K1047
[Wieniawski: Scherzo tarantelle, Op. 16]

ACQUA, Eva dell' (1856-   )

Villanelle (J'ai vu passer l'hirondelle) Soprano
Lily Pons (G-DB3939)   12"—V-15610
[Strauss: Le Beau Danube Bleu]
(in VM-599)
Miliza Korjus (in German) 12"—G-C2784
[Strauss: 1001 Nights]
Gwen Catley (in English) 12"—G-C3638
[Strauss: Frühlingsstimmen]
Mado Robin   10"—G-DA4940
[Grieg: Peer Gynt-Solvejg's Song]
DUPLICATION: Erna Sack (in German), PD-561119

ADAM, Adolphe Charles (1803-1856)

Having studied with Boieldieu, Adam composed many successful "opéras-comiques" and ballets. His ballet "Giselle" the popular "Noël" and the opera "Le Postillon de Longjumeau" are excellent samples of his work.

Giselle Ballet Suite (arr. Lambert)
Giselle's Dance; Mad Sc.; Pas de deux, Act II; Closing Scene
Royal Opera House Orch., Covent Garden-Constant Lambert   2 12"—CX-277
(C-DX1270/1)

Noël (Cantique de Noël: "Minuit, Chrétiens")
Christmas Song in French
Georges Thill (t)   12"—C-9097M
[Bizet: Agnus Dei] (C-LFX275)
Karl Erb (t) (in Ger.)   10"—G-DA4426
[Loewe: Des fremden Kindes Heiliger Christ]
DUPLICATIONS: E. Caruso, G-DB139*; L. Morturier, G-K5717; A. Baugé, PAT-X93117; Pactat, LUM-30059; Roger Bourdin, O-123513; Paul Franz, C-DF253; L. Lynel, O-166209; M. Medus & Chorus, LUM-30031; Robert Couzinou & Raoul Gilles with Chorus, PD-521813; Cantorum Chorus, PAT-X93038. Also: Paul Godwin Orch., PD-22073; Marek Weber Orch., G-HN602

OPERAS-COMIQUES In French

(LE) CHALET 1834

Arrêtons-nous ici—Recit.,
Vallons de l'Helvétie Aria, Pt. 1 Bass
Louis Morturier   12"—G-W889
[Flégier: Le Cor]

(LE) FARFADET

On m'a dit dans le village
Personne en bas dans le moulin Baritone
André Baugé   10"—PAT-PG6

(LE) POSTILLON DE LONGJUMEAU 1836

Je vais le revoir Soprano
Ger. Ich soll ihn wiedersehen
Felicie Hüni-Mihacsek (In German)
12"—PD-66616
[Flotow: Alessandro Stradella-Alles teile unser Glück]

Mes amis, écoutez l'histoire, Act I Tenor (Rondo du Postillon)
Ger. Postillonlied: Freunde, vernehmet die Geschichte
Miguel Villabella   10"—PAT-PG27
[Romance du Postillon]
Helge Roswaenge (in German) with Berlin State Opera Orch.—Seidler-Winkler
10"—G-DA4414
[Auber: Fra Diavolo-Pour toujours]
Peter Anders (in German) & German Opera Orch., Schultze   10"—T-A10131
[Strauss: Nacht in Venedig-Gondellied]
(Also on T-A1901)
Kolomon von Pataky   12"—PD-66648
[Nicolai: Die lustigen Weiber von Windsor-Horch, die Lerche]

Romance du postillon
Miguel Villabella   10″—PAT-PG27
[Mes amis, écoutez l'histoire]

(LA) POUPEE DE NUREMBERG
Overture Orchestra
Künstler Orch.—Dobrindt 10″—O-25629

SI J'ETAIS ROI 1852—Ger. Wenn ich König wär; Eng. If I Were King
Overture Orchestra
Concert Orch.—Seidler-Winkler
12″—G-EH1086
Berlin State Opera Orch.—Blech
12″—G-EJ307
Lamoureux Orch.—Cariven
10″—PAT-PD69
Vienna State Opera Orch.—Reichwein
12″—O-7876
Berlin Philharmonic—Schleger
(U-B18056)   10″—T-A1095
Berlin-Charlottenburg Orch.—Melichar
12″—PD-27176
Symphony Orch.—Bigot 12″—C-DFX89
Symphony Orch.—Szyfer 12″—G-L838

Individual excerpts In alphabetical order

Dans le sommeil: Si vous croyez (Cavatine)
Baritone
André Baugé (PAT-X90069)
10″—PAT-PG73
[Varney: Les Mousquetaires au Couvent-
Pour faire un brave mousquetaire]
(Also G-P447)
Pierre Deldi   10″—C-RF72
[Thomas: Hamlet-Chanson Bachique]

Des souverains du rivage
Eng. **Nemea's Aria** Soprano
Hjördis Schymberg (in Swedish) & Orch.
—Grevillius   10″—G-X6010
[Gounod: Faust-Jewel Song]

Elle est princesse! Tenor
Miguel Villabella   10″—PAT-PG26
[Auber: La Dame Blanche—Rêverie de
Georges Brown]
Marcel Claudel (PD-524064)
10″—PD-62702
[Maillart: Les Dragons de Villars—Ne
parle pas]

J'ignorais son nom, sa naissance Tenor
Miguel Villabella   12″—PAT-PAT6
[Maillart: Les Dragons de Villars—Ne
parle pas]
Jean Planel   10″—PAT-X90037
[Flotow: Marta—M'apparì]

Vous m'aimez & Je vous cherchais Duo:
Soprano & Tenor
Germaine Féraldy & Villabella
10″—PAT-PD12

Zéphoris est bon camarade Tenor
André Noël   10″—PAT-X91019
[Offenbach: La Fille du Tambour-Major
—Couplets de l'uniforme]

(LE) TOREADOR 1849
Ah! vous dirai-je maman Soprano
(These bravura variations were adapted
from Mozart's Variations for Piano,
K.265)

Miliza Korjus (in German) 12″—V-13826
[Donizetti: La Zingara-Aria]
[Rossini: Barbiere—Una voce, on
G-C2688]
[Alabiev: Russian Nightingale, on
G-EH876]
Erna Sack (in German) & Berlin State
Opera Orch.—Czernik 12″— T-E3063
[Czernik: Chi sa, Tarantella]
DUPLICATION: A. Galli Curci, G-DB262*

Oui! la vie! Bass
Narçon   10″—C-RF17
[Meyerbeer: L' Etoile du Nord—Romance
de Pierre le Grand]

ADAM DE LA HALLE (c1230-1287)
A trouvère, Adam de la Halle arranged pastoral plays for the French court at Naples where he had accompanied his patron the Comte d'Artois.

(LE) JEU DE ROBIN ET MARION
Pastorale in French
Motets on "Robin m'aime" (Rondeau de
Marion) & **"Hé! réveille-toi"**
Psallette Notre-Dame Chorus
10″—LUM-30058
[Anon: 13th Century Danseries]
Minnelied (unspecified) Sung in German
Basler Liedertafel—Münch
10″—G-FK159
[Huber: Härz, wohin zieht es?]
Rondeau: Li dous regars de ma dame
La Société Pro Musica Antiqua, Brussels
—Cape   12″—AS-71
[Virelai & Examples of 13th Century Ars
Antiqua] (in Vol. VIII)
(6) Rondeaux Chorus
**Or est Bayars; Bone amourette; Fines
amourettes; Diex comment pourroie;
Hareu li maus d'aimer; Diex soit en cheste
maison**
Psallette Notre-Dame Chorus—
J. Chailley   10″—LUM-30057
Rondeau et Virelai:
**Je meurs, je meurs d'amourette; Fines
amourettes aie**
La Psallette de Notre-Dame—J. Chailley
12″—G-DB5116
[Anon: 13th Century—Belle Ysabelot]
(in French Masters of the Middle Ages
Set)

ADAMS, Stephen Michael Maybricke (1844-1913)
The Holy City (Weatherley)
Gladys Ripley (c) & Herbert Dawson
(org.)   12″—G-C3549
[Handel: Serse-Largo]
A. Piccaver (t) & Gerald Moore (pf)
10″—D-F8153
[Liszt: Liebestraum]
Richard Crooks (t) & Orch.—Barbirolli
12″—V-7854
[Star of Bethlehem] (G-DB1796)
Webster Booth (t) & Organ
12″—G-C3196
[Star of Bethlehem]

DUPLICATIONS: Josef Locke,
C-DX1437; Oscar Natzke, P-E11430;
Peter Dawson, G-C3038; Clara Butt &
Chorus, C-DX812
The Star of Bethlehem
Richard Crooks (t) & Organ 12"—V-7854
[The Holy City] (G-DB1798)
Webster Booth (t) & Organ
12"—G-C3196
[The Holy City]
Josef Locke (t) 12"—C-DX1437
[The Holy City]

ADDINSELL, Richard (1904-)

*One of the most promising of the younger
British composers, Addinsell is known in the
United States for his scores composed for films
("Blithe Spirit" and "Suicide Squadron") and
for the LeGallienne repertory production of
"Alice in Wonderland." Working with British
films during wartime he contributed musical
scores for documentaries.*

BLITHE SPIRIT Music for the Film
Prelude & Waltz
London Symphony Orch.—Muir Mathie-
son (C-DX1186) 12"—C-7441M
—**Waltz only**
Mantovani & his Orch. 10"—D-F8541
[Tune in G]
Also: V. Sokoloff (pf) & Henri René
Orch., V-46-0003
SUICIDE SQUADRON Music for the Film
(British title: **Dangerous Moonlight**)
Warsaw Concerto Piano & Orchestra
Leo Litwin & Boston "Pops" Orch.—
Fiedler 12"—V-11-8863
Harry Kaufman & Philharmonic Orch.
of Los Angeles—Wallenstein
12"—D-29150
London Symphony Orch.—Mathieson,
with pf. (C-DX1062) 12"—C-7409M
André Kostelanetz & his Orch., with pf.
12"—C-7443M
Ellen Gilberg & Tivoli Concert Orch.—
Felumb 12"—TONO-X25047
Mantovani & his Concert Orch.
10"—D-F8021
—**Arr. 2 Pianos**
Rawicz & Landauer, C-DB2096; Hatzfeld
& Strong, D-F8094
Tune in G
Mantovani & his Orch. 10"—D-F8541
[Blithe Spirit—Waltz]

(L') AFFILARD, Michel
(Early 18th Century)

Iris
G. Micheletti (t) & R. Gerlin
(harpsi.) 12"—AS-98
[Airs Sérieux et à Boire] (in Vol. X)

AGERBY, Aksel

*A contemporary Scandanavian composer of art
songs.*

SONGS In Danish
Havren
Majnat (J. Aakjaer)
Aksel Schiøtz (t) & Aksel Agerby (pf)
10"—G-X6348

Havren (J. Aakjaer)
Edith Oldrup-Pedersen (s) & Folmer
Jensen (pf) 10"—G-DA5219
[Weyse: Der er en øi Livet]
Jeg ved g'hvorfra du kommer (Anders V.
Holm)
Lille Konval (Helge Rode)
Aksel Schiøtz (t) & Aksel Agerby (pf)
10"—G-X6347
Kløver
College Mens Choral Union—Hye-
Knudsen G-X6689

AIBLINGER, Johann Kaspar (1779-1867)

*A Bavarian composer of choral works sung
largely in the Catholic Churches of South Germany.*

Jubilato Deo (Offertorium) Chorus in Latin
Aachen Cathedral Choir—Rehmann
10"—PD-27125
[Jaspers: Christus ist auferstanden,
Basilica Choir]

AICHINGER, Gregor (c.1565-1628)

*One of the great composers of his time, the
Bavarian Aichinger bridges between the Renaissance Venetian Gabrieli and the Baroque German Schütz.*

CHORUS Unacc. choral works in Latin
Factus est repente de coelo
Manécanterie des Petits Chanteurs à la
Croix de Bois 10"—G-K7155
[Victoria: Domine non sum]
Intonuit de Coeli
Munich Cathedral Cho.—Berberich
10"—PD-22588
[Anon. Es gingen drei heilige Frauen,
Paderborn Cho.]
Maria uns tröst (in German)
Dortmund Anthem Cho.—Holtschneider
12"—PD-27152
[Lemacher: Salve Mater Salvatoris,
Aachen Cathedral Cho.]
Regina Coeli
Manécanterie des Petits Chanteurs
10"—G-K7205
[Victoria: O vos omnes]
Schola St. Léon IX Cho.—Gaudard
12"—PAT-X93053
[Nanini: Diffusa est & Victoria: Vere
languores]
Salve Regina
Schola St. Léon IX Cho.—Gaudard
12"—PAT-X93054
[Anon.: 3 French Noëls]
Ubi est Abel
Dijon Cathedral Cho.—Samson
(in VM-212) 12"—V-11679
[Joao IV: Crux fidelis] (G-DB4895 in
GM-189)

ALABIEV, Alexander Nikolaevich
(1787-1851)

*A contemporary of Dargomijsky and Glinka,
this lesser-known Russian composer wrote "The
Nightingale" which is often heard in the "Lesson Scene" from Rossini's opera "Il Barbiere
di Siviglia."*

Russian Nightingale Song
Fr. Le Rossignol   Ger. Die Nachtigall
Lily Pons (s) & André Kostelanetz Orch.
(in CM-484)   12"—C-71305D
[Rimsky-Korsakov: Sadko—Song of
India]
Josephine Antoine (s) & S. Ross (pf)
12"—C-71025D
[Bishop: Lo, Hear the gentle lark]
Amelita Galli-Curci (s) (in English)
10"—V-1440
[Valverde: Clavelitos & Ponce:
Estrellita] (G-DA1095)
Miliza Korjus (s) (in German) & Orch.
—Müller   12"—V-11831
[Proch: Variations]
[Adam: Mozart Variations, on G-EH876]
Erna Sack (s) (in German) & Orch.—
Schroeder   10"—T-A2900
[Denza: Funiculi, Funicula]
DUPLICATIONS: Don Cossack Cho.,
C-17136D; Karin Munk (in Danish),
G-X6256; Pantofel-Nechetzkaiu (in Rus-
sian), USSR-10035/6

ALAIN, Albert
Cantate Domino
Lyons Cathedral Choir   12"—C-D11028
[Bach: Little G minor Fugue, Commette]
Le Paradis Breton Melody
Lyons Cathedral Choir   12"—C-D11030
[Noyon: Chant du triomphe]

**ALBENIZ, Isaac Manuel Francisco
(1860-1909)**

*An excellent pianist, having studied with Liszt
and Pedrell, Albéniz helped establish the newer
school of Spanish national composers.*

Aragon (Jota) See under Suite Española,
No. 6
CANTOS DE ESPANA, Op. 232 Piano
1. Preludio   2. Oriental
3. Sous le palmier (Bajo la Palmera)
(Tango Flamenco)
4. Cordoba (Nocturne)
5. Seguidillas (Castilla)
Note: The Seguidillas is the same as the
Castilla, No. 7, in the Suite Española.
No. 2, Oriental
Ricardo Viñes   10"—C-LF42
[Seguidillas]
No. 3, Sous le palmier (Tango Flamenco)
Alfred Cortot   10"—V-1271
[Brahms: Wiegenlied]
Suzanne Gyr   12"—G-DB10068
[Cordoba]
No. 4, Cordoba (Nocturne)
José Iturbi (G-DA1611)   10"—V-4373
Suzanne Gyr   12"—G-DB10068
[Sous le palmier]
C. Guilbert   12"—C-LFX607
[Mussorgsky: Pictures at an Exhibition
—Great Gate of Kiev]
Also: La Argentinita (castanets) & Orch.,
G-GW600; La Argentina (castanets) &
Orch., O-188682
No. 5, Seguidillas (same as Suite Española
No. 7)

Alfred Cortot   10"—G-DA1121
[Malagueña]
Andor Foldes, in CON-34
Ricardo Viñes   10"—C-LF42
[Oriental]

IBERIA, Book I, Piano Suite
Evocación, El Puerto, El Corpus en Sevilla
No. 1, Evocación only
William Kapell   12"—V-11-9457
[Liszt: Mephisto Waltz, Pt. 3] (in VM-
1101†)

IBERIA, Book II, Piano Suite
Rondeña, Almería, Triana
No. 3, Triana only
Artur Rubinstein   12"—G-DB1762
[Villa-Lobos: A Prole do Bébé—3 Pieces]
Cyril Smith   12"—C-DX1214
[Liszt: Paganini Etude No. 3, La
Campanella]

IBERIA, Book III, Piano Suite
El Albaicín, El Polo, Lavapiés
No recordings available

IBERIA, Book IV, Piano Suite
Málaga, Jérez, Eritaña
No. 1. Málaga only
Alexander Borowsky (PD-27343)
12"—PD-516613
[Liszt: Au bord d'une source]
Malagueña (Rumores de la Caleta) Op. 71,
No. 6 Piano
A. Benedetti Michelangeli
10"—G-DA5432
[Mompou: Canción y danza]
Alfred Cortot   10"—G-DA1121
[Seguidilla]
—Arr. Violin & Piano
Fritz Kreisler & Carl Lamson
10"—G-DA1354
[Tango, Op. 165, No. 2]
Ida Haendel & pf. acc.   12"—D-K1073
[Falla: La Vida Breve]
Jacques Thibaud & T. Janopoulo
12"—G-DB2011
[Desplanes: Intrada]
—Arr. 'Cello & Piano (J. Stutschewsky &
I. Thaler)
Raya Garbousova & Erich-Itor Kahn
(in VM-1017)   12"—V-11-8871
[K. P. E. Bach: Concerto, A major-Largo]
M. Amfitheatrof & Orch.   12"—G-DB5414
[Grazioli: Adagio]
Also: I. Presti (guitar), G-K7957;
G-X4924
Navarra (completed by Déodat de Séverac)
Piano
Artur Rubinstein (arr. Rubinstein)
12"—V-11-8622
[Brahms: Ballade No. 5, G minor, Op.
118, No. 3] (Earlier recording on G-
DB1257, with Sevillana)
—Arr. Orch.
Madrid Symphony Orch.—E. F. Arbós,
(in CM-146†)   12"—C-67821D

PEPITA JIMENEZ Opera in Spanish 1895/6
Intermedio (Intermezzo) Orchestra
Madrid Symphony Orch.—E. F. Arbós,
12"—C-67820D

[Bretón: Polo Gitano] (in CM-146†)

SUITE ESPANOLA Piano
1. Granada 2. Cataluña 3. Sevillanas
4. Cádiz 5. Asturias
6. Jota de Aragon, Op. 164, No. 1
7. Seguidillas 8. Cuba
Complete recording Arr. 2 Pianos
Rawicz & Landauer 3 10"— C-DB2132/4
1. Granada (Serenata)
Marie Panthès　　　　　12"—C-DFX169
[Mozart: Pastorale variée]
Ricardo Viñes　　　　　12"—C-LFX73
[Blancafort: Parc des Attractions]
—Arr. Orch.
Albert Locatelli Orch.　10"—C-DF2043
[Gossec: Gavotte]
[Sarasate: Romanza Andaluza,
C-DQ2400]
—Arr. Guitar
Andres Segovia
　　　　　　(in D-A384) 12"—D-29154
[Granados: La Maja de Goya] (B-0159)
Also: Prof. Mozzani, G-GW1754
3. Sevillana (Seville)
José Iturbi　　　　　12"—V-11562
[Granados: La Maja y el Ruiseñor]
Andor Foldes, in CON-34
Artur Rubinstein　　　12"—G-DB1257
[Navarra]
Magda Tagliaferro　　12"—PAT-PAT22
[Chopin: Fantaisie Impromptu]
—Arr. Vl. & Pf.
Jascha Heifetz & Arpad Sandor
　　　　　　　　　　12"—G-DB2220
[Dohnanyi: Ruralia Hungarica—Gypsy
andante]
—Arr. Castanets
La Argentina　　　　10"—O-188755
[Falla: Serenata Andaluza]
La Argentinita & Orch.　10"—G-K5497
[Cádiz] (G-GW598)
—Arr. Guitar
Andres Segovia, in D-A384
Also: Saxophone Quartet of Paris,
C-DF1461
4. Cádiz (Saeta) (same as Serenade
Espagnole, Op. 181)
Ricardo Viñes　　　　10"—G-DA4885
[Tango, A minor]
—Arr. Orchestra
Albert Locatelli Orch., C-DF2000
—Arr. 'Cello & Piano
Gaspar Cassadó & Michael Raucheisen,
T-A2127
—Arr. Castanets
La Argentinita & Orch.　10"—G-K5497
[Sevillanas] (G-GW598)
5. Asturias (Leyenda)
G. Gourevitch, PAT-X9957
7. Seguidillas (See under Cantos de España,
No. 5)
Tango, A minor (Danza Española, Op.
164, No. 2) Piano
Ricardo Viñes　　　　10"—G-DA4885
[Cádiz]
Tango, D major, Op. 165, No. 2 Piano
Oscar Levant, in CM-568
Andor Foldes, in CON-34
Eileen Joyce　　　　10"—P-R2738

[Liszt: Valse oubliée, No. 1]
Ida Perin (arr. Godowsky)
　　　　　　　　10"—PAT-X98153
[Mendelssohn: Spring Song & Spinning
song]
DUPLICATION: William Murdoch,
D-F3584
—Arr. Violin & Piano
Fritz Kreisler & Carl Lamson
　　　　　　　　10"—G-DA1009
[Falla: La Vida Breve-Danza]
G. Kulenkampff & Franz Rupp
　　　　　　　　10"—T-A2551
[Tchaikovsky: Neapolitanisch]
Jacques Thibaud & T. Janopoulo
　　　　　　　　10"—G-DA1339
[Poldini: Poupée valsante]
DUPLICATIONS: Alfredo Campoli, D-
F2512; Simone Filon, PD-524288;
Manuel Quiroga, PAT-X9938; Miguel
Candela, C-LF32
—Arr. 'Cello & Piano
Emanuel Feuermann & Gerald Moore
　　　　　　　　10"—C-17158D
[Cui: Kaleidosçope, Op. 50, No. 9—
Orientale]
—Vocal arrangement
Beniamino Gigli (t)　　10"—G-DA1295
[Sandoval: Eres tu]
Ninon Vallin (s) & Pierre Darck (pf)
　　　　　　　　10"—O-281037
[Hollman-Grandmougin: Chanson
d'amour]
Torre Bermeja (Serenata) Piano (from
Piezas Características)
Ricardo Viñes　　　　12"—C-D15245
[Debussy: La Soirée dans Grenade]
—Arr. Guitar
Andres Segovia, in D-A384
—Arr. Castanets
Manuela del Rio (castanets) & J. Roca
(guitar) with L. Compolieti (pf),
G-K7116

ALBERT, Eugene d' (1864-1932)
*Born in Glasgow, Scotland, Eugene d'Albert
achieved international reputation as a pianist,
teacher and editor. He was closely connected
with German musical life and it is there that
his compositions are best known.*

OPERAS In German
TIEFLAND 1903
Vocal & Orchestral selections (Querschnitt)
Anita Gura (s), Carla Spletter (s), Peter
Anders (t), Hanns-Heinz Nissen (b) with
Berlin Philharmonic Chorus & Orch.—
Schmidt-Isserstedt　　　12"—T-E1873
Orchestral Selections (Fantasias, etc.)
Concert Orch.　　　　12"—G-EH1290
Grand Orch.　　　　　12"—G-EH394
Symphony Orch.—Manfred Gurlitt
　　　　　　　　　12"—PD-19974
Berlin Philharmonic-Schleger
(U-B18068)　　　　　10"—T-A1194
Individual Excerpts
Hülle in die mantille Baritone
Theodor Scheidl　　　10"— PD-90165
[Mascagni: Cavalleria Rusticana—Il
cavallo scalpita]

Ich grüss noch einmal Tenor
Franz Völker & Berlin State Opera Orch.
—Steeger   12"—PD-67685
[Wolfserzählung]
Mein Leben wagt' ich drum See under
Wolfserzählung
Schau her, dast ist ein Taler See under
Wolfserzählung
Traumzählung: Zwei Vater unser bet' ich
Tenor
Hugo Meyer-Welfing & German Opera
House Orch.—Dobrindt   12"—O-7963
[Wolfserzählung]
Torsten Ralf   12"—G-DB5697
[Wolfserzählung]
Wolfserzählung, Act I Tenor
(The Meyer-Welfing version begins with
"Schau her, dast ist ein Taler," the Völker ver-
sion begins a little further along with "Mein
Leben wagt")
Hugo Meyer-Welfing & German Opera
House Orch.—Dobrindt   12"—O-7963
[Traumzählung]
Torsten Ralf   12"—G-DB5697
[Traumzählung]
Franz Völker & Berlin State Opera Orch.
Steeger   12"—PD-67685
[Ich grüss noch einmal]
(DIE) TOTEN AUGEN 1916
Psyche wandelt durch Saülenhallen (Air
of Psyche) Soprano
Lotte Lehmann   10"—P-P0158
[Mozart: Nozze di Figaro-Deh vieni]
SONGS In German
Möchte wohl gerne ein Schmetterling sein,
Op. 27, No. 2
Zur Drossel sprach der Fink, Op. 9, No. 4
Erna Sack (s) & Michael Raucheisen (pf)
10"—T-A2202

ALBERT, Heinrich (1604-1651)
A nephew of Heinrich Schütz, Albert was a
well-known organist, poet and composer of
vocal music.

SONGS In German
Festlied: Auf! mein Geist nur erhebe
Yves Tinayre (b) & Alex. Cellier (organ)
(in Yves Tinayre Album No. 1)
12"—LUM-32014
[Bach: Cantata No. 85—No. 5; Franck:
Passionlied]
O der rauhen Grausamkeit
Raffet auch der Tod die greisen Haare
Jacques Bastard (b) & Ars Rediviva
Ensemble   12"—BAM-19
[Bach: Sonata, D minor, 2 violins, Pt. 3]
Todeslied: Ach, lasst uns Gott doch einig
leben
Yves Tinayre (b) & organ (in Yves
Tinayre Album No. 2) 12"—LUM-32022
[Hammerschmidt: Danklied; Mozart:
Laudate Dominum]

ALFANO, Franco (1876-   )
A follower of "verismo," Alfano is known outside Italy chiefly by his opera "La Risurrezione," based on Tolstoi's novel. He also completed Puccini's "Turandot" from sketches of

the final scenes left by the composer at his
death.

Nostalgie Piano
Nino Rossi   10"—G-DA5365
[Pick-Mangiagalli: La Ronda di Ariele]

OPERA In Italian
RISURREZIONE 4 Acts 1904
Dio Pietosa
Gianna Pederzini (s) 12"—CET-BB25027
[Cilea: L'Arlesiana-Esser madre]
Symphony No. 2, C major
EIAR Orch.—Fernando Previtali
4 12"—CET-CB20306/9

ALFVEN, Hugo (1872-   )
A violinist, Alfven is one of Sweden's outstand-
ing contemporary composers.
Brutenfeld Orchestra
Stockholm Orch.—Grevillius
12"—T-E19031
Festspel, Op. 25 Orchestra
Göteborg Symphony Orch.—Tor Mann
12"—G-Z203
[Svendsen: Festpolonaise, Op. 12]
Gustave Adolf II Suite Orchestra
—Elegy only
Stockholm Concert Association Orch.—
Grevillius   12"—G-C3483
[Midsommarvaka, Pt. 3] (G-Z260)
Hjalmar Brantings March
Military Band   12"—G-Z158
[Hjalmar Branting—recitation]
Midsommarvaka (Swedish Rhapsody)
Op. 19 Orchestra Eng. Midsummer Vigil
Stockholm Concert Association Orch.—
Grevillius   2 12"—G-C3482/3
[Gustav Adolf II Suite—Elegy]
(G-Z259/60)
Stockholm Symphony Orch.
2 10"—G-X2426/7

SONG In Swedish
Skogen sofver
Jussi Björling (t) & H. Ebert (pf)
12"—G-DB5787
[Chlof: Morgen; Schubert: An die Leier]
Sveriges Flagga Orchestra
Stockholm Symphony Orch.
[Stenhammer: Sverige]   10"—G-X2409

ALLENDE, Humberto (1885-   )
A Chilean composer and pedagogue, Allende's
style can be traced to his European training.

Tonadas Chileñas Piano
Ricardo Viñes   10"—G-DA4910
[Lopez-Buchardo: Bailecto & Troiani:
Milonga]

ALNAES, Eyvind (1872-1932)
A Norwegian organist and choir director, Alnaes
is best known for his songs, reminiscent in style
of Grieg and Sibelius, but original in their
atmospheric charm.

SONGS In Norwegian
A leva (A. Vesbotn)
Randi Heide Stenn (s) & Robert
Levin (pf)   10"—G-AL2929
[Grieg: Lengs en å]

Der du gjekk Jyre (A. O. Vinge)
Eva Gustavson (ms) & Amund
Rakserud (pf)　　　　10"—G-DA11901
[Jensen: Alter]
Lykken mellem to Mennesker (Viggo Stuckenberg)
Eva Gustavson (ms) & Armund
Rakserud (pf)　　　　10"—G-DA11900
[Nu brister i alle de klöfter]
Kirsten Flagstad (s) & Edwin
McArthur (pf) (in VM-342) 10"—V-1816
[Grieg: Et Hab]
Nu brister i alle de klöfter (Viggo Stuckenberg)
Eva Gustavson (ms.) & Armund
Rakserud (pf)　　　　10"—G-DA11900
[Lykken mellem to Mennesker]
Traditional Song Arr. Alnaes
Anne Knutsdatter
Randi Heide Stenn (s) & Robert
Levin (pf)　　　　10"—G-AL2931
[Backer-Grøndahl: Efter er sommerfugl
& Grieg: Kveldsang for Blakken]

ALTENBURG, Michael (1584-1640)
A contributor to German chorale literature, Altenburg was a Lutheran pastor.
CHORALE Sung in French
Gloire Eternelle au Dieu Puissant
Chorale du Petit Séminaire de Paris
　　　　10"—LUM-30054
[Mermety-Bach: Louons le Dieu Puissant;
Perruchot: L'adorable mystère]

ALWYN, William (1905-　)
A British composer who has contributed several scores for the films and made settings of traditional and folk melodies.
(2) Folk Tunes (Norwegian & Irish)
Watson Forbes (vla) & Maria Korchinska (harp)　　　　12"—D-K943
[Bax: Viola Sonata, Pt. 5]
(3) Negro Spirituals (arr.)
You'll hear the trumpet sound
Didn't my Lord deliver David
I'm travelling to my grave
Watson Forbes (vla) & Etienne de
Chevalier (pf)　　　　10"—D-M577

(THE) NOTORIOUS GENTLEMAN (or, The Rake's Progress) Music for the Film
Calypso Music
London Symphony—Muir Mathieson
　　　　12"—D-K1544
[Parker: Seascape—from the film "Western Approaches," or "The Raiders"]

AMBROSE, Saint (340-397)
A bishop of Milan who sponsored the singing of types of plainsong which differed from the Gregorian chant. Works often attributed to him may not always be his own compositions.
AMBROSIAN CHANTS In Latin
Tantum ergo
O Salutaris
O sacrum Convivium
Choir of S. Vittore, Milan
　　　　10"—G-HN1593
[Hymn: Dio sia benedetto]

AMFITHEATROFF, Daniele (1901-　)
A Russian-Italian conductor and composer for films both here and abroad, Amfitheatroff is not well represented on discs at the present time. The orchestral work listed below reflects Hawaiian and American rhythms.
Panorama Américain
Pasdeloup Orch.—Amfitheatroff
(C-GQX10855/6) 2 12"—PAT-PDT40/1

ANERIO, Felice (1560?-1614)
A pupil of Palestrina, Anerio succeeded him as composer to the Papal Chapel. He wrote both sacred and secular works.
Missa pro Defunctis Eng. Requiem Mass
Unacc. Chorus in Latin
—Introitus: Requiem aeternum
Sistine Chapel Choir—Rella (In GM-139)
[Victoria: Tenebrae]　12"—G-DB1572
Factum est silentium
Julian Chapel Choir—Boezzi
　　　　12"—SEMS-39
[Refice: Alma redemptoris Mater]

ANONYMOUS
10th CENTURY
Hymn of St. Adalbert
Choir of the Pius X School of Liturgical
Music (in VM-739)　　12"—V-13555
[Anon: Angelus Domini; Leoninus:
Easter Gradual—Haec Dies]
11th CENTURY
Alleluia—Angelus Domini (Chartres Ms.)
Choir of the Pius X School of Liturgical
Music (in VM-739)　　12"—V-13555
[Leoninus: Easter Gradual & Anon:
Hymn of St. Adalbert]

DANISH MEDIAEVAL SONGS
Dronning Dagmars Død (Queen Dagmar's Death); Lave og Jon; Ebbe Skamelsûn; Ulver og Vaenelil
Aksel Schiøtz (t) & Choir (a cappella)
　　　　12"—G-DB5266
Knud Lavard Hymne (Hymn to the St. Knud Lavard)
Copenhagen Boys Choir (a cappella)—
Mogens Wöldike (in preparation)
Danish HMV

13th CENTURY
Minor Forms of the Ars Antiqua
(Gymel-Conduct, Motets, Rondeau, Virelai, Instrumental Music)
La Société Pro Musica Antiqua, Brussels-
Cape (in Vol. VIII)　　12"—AS-71
Transfretasse 2 voices 2 instruments
Deus Misertus 4 voices a cappella
Mm. Bonté, Deniau, Rousselon, Bousquet
—G. de Van (in Vol. X)　12"—AS-99
[Instrumental music]
Alleluia—Psallat
(Worcester Mediaeval Harmony)
Choir of the Pius X School of Liturgical
Music　(in VM-739)　12"—V-13559
[Obrecht: Missa sine Nomine-Credo]
13th Century Motets
J. Archimbaud (s) & R. Bonté (t) with
Trumpet—G. de Van　12"—OL-109

Dances of the Middle Ages—13th & 14th Century
(13th Century English Dance, French Dance, English Stantipes, 14th Century French Estampie, Italian Ballo)
Crunelle (piccolo), Debondue (musette), Clayette (tambour) (in Vol. II)
12"—AS-16

Juggler's Music & Learned Music
En may la rosée. Mairy Kuhner (medieval harp), Motet sacré (a cappella). Vocal trio—Cape (in Vol. X) 12"—AS-91
[Beginnings of Swiss Polyphony]

Laudi a San Lorenzo
(Motet: Ave gloriosa Mater Salvatoris)
Yves Tinayre (in Yves Tinayre Album No. 2) 12"—LUM-32018
[Franco of Cologne: Motet—Ave Gloriosa Mater]

Belle Ysabelot (Motet in 3 parts) Trans. Pierre Aubry (Teneur, Motet, Tripli: Contre-point des 3 parties)
La Psallette de Notre Dame, (unacc.)— Chailley 12"—G-DB5116
[Adam de la Halle: Rondeau et Virelai]

Crucificat Omnes (Conductus Triplum) (Ecole de Paris)
La Psalette de Notre-Dame—J. Chailley (in French Masters of the Middle Ages set) 12"—G-DB5119
[Perotin: Organum triplum: "Difusa est"]

O Miranda dei Caritas (from Aubry's "Cent Motets")
Choir of the Pius X School of Liturgical Music (in VM-739) 12"—V-13556
[Puellare Gremium & Dunstable: Quam Pulchra es; c.1349: Flagellants' Hymn]

Puellare Gremium (from Worcester Mediaeval Harmony)
Choir of the Pius X School of Liturgical Music (in VM-739) 12"—V-13556
[O Miranda dei Caritas; Dunstable: Quam Pulchra es; c.1349: Flagellants' Hymn]

14th CENTURY

A vous, Vierge de Douçour; Ad te Virgo Clamitans Venio
J. Archimbaud (s) & R. Bonté (t) with trumpet, trombone & hurdy gurdy—G. de Van 12"—OL-2
[Jacopo da Bologna: Lux Purpurata Padus & Diligito Justiciam]

Virelai: Or sus vous dormes trop
J. Archimbaud (s) with 2 trumpets & trombone—G. de Van 12"—OL-3
[Guillaume de Machaut: Hoquetus David]

Ave Mater
Yves Tinayre (t) with 3 bowed instruments (in Yves Tinayre Album No. 2)
[Dufay: Vergine Bella] 12"—LUM-32019

Lauda de Noël (Gloria in cielo)
Max Meili (t) & Fr. Seidersbeck (viol) (in Vol I) 12"—AS-1
[with Italian Ballads and Religious songs of the 14th Century]

Chace "Se je chant mains que ne suel"
F. Anspach & E. Jacquier (tenors) (in Vol. VI) 12"—AS-59
[with examples of the Chace & Caccia—

the "canon" in the 14th Century]

French Chansons of the 14th Century for Six Instruments
Les Paraphonistes de Saint-Jean-des-Matines—G. de Van
(in Vol. XI) 12"—AS-110

Descent of the Holy Ghost (Catalan Folk Song)
Choir of the Pius X School of Liturgical Music (in VM-739) 12"—V-13557
[Dufay: Flos Florum; Obrecht: Qui cum]

Flagellants' Hymn (Year of the Plague)
Choir of the Pius X School of Liturgical Music (in VM-739) 12"—V-13556
[Dunstable: Quam Pulchra es & 13th c.: Miranda dei Caritas; Puellare Gremium]
Schola Cantorum Pontificale
[Vecchi: Il Grillo] 12"—SEMS-1120

Beginning of Swiss Polyphony
Benedicamus trope (for 2 voices); Motet (for 2 voices)
Bousquet & Rousselon
(in Vol. X) 12"—AS-91
[Juggler's Music & Learned Music]

15th CENTURY

Popular Fifteenth Century Frottole
(Dal letto levava; Rusticus; Rende l'arme al fiero amore)

Fifteenth Century Italian Laude
(Sancta Maria; Anima Christi; Poichè)
Les Paraphonistes de Saint-Jean-des-Matines—G. de Van
(in Vol. VIII) AS-77

Penitential Motets of the Fifteenth Century
(Parce Domine)
Les Paraphonistes de St.-Jean-des-Matines—G. de Van
(in Vol. IX) 12"—AS-80

Déploration sur la Mort de Binchois
Yvonne Gouverné Choir, unacc.
12"—OL-62
[Binchois: O solis Ortu Cardine; Sanctus]

L'Âmour de Moy
La Psallette Notre Dame Chorus (in French) with viols & recorders—Chailley (in French Masters of the Middle Ages set) 12"—G-DB5117
[Dufay: Omnes amici ejus; Bon jour bon mois]
Roland Hayes (t) & Boardman (pf) (in CM-393) 12"—C-17176D
[Massenet: Manon-Le Rêve]

Laude de l'Annunciazione (words by Poliziano)
Schola Cantorum Pontificale
12"—SEMS-1119
[Palestrina: I vaghi fiori]

16th CENTURY

French Dances of the 16th Century
(Bassedanse; Tourdion; Allemande; Pavane; Gaillarde; Pavane; Branle simple; Branle double; Branle de Bourgogne; Branle de Champagne)
String Orch.—Curt Sachs
(in Vol. I) 12"—AS-6

Court Airs & Songs
Il me suffit
Mlle. M. Vhita (c) & H. Leeb (lute) (in Vol. IV) 12"—AS-36

[with music of Nicolas de la Grotte, Clemens non Papa, Jean-Baptiste Besard]

Pavane "Lequercardes;" Gaillarde "La Fanfare," Fantaisie & Passomezza "La Doulce"
Margaret Riedel (harpsichord) with recorders   10"—G-EG6098
[with Gervaise: Allemande]

Resonet in laudibus & In dulci jubilo Organ (2 pieces from Fridolin Sicher's Tablature Book)
Carl Weinrich (Westminster Choir School organ) (in MC-9)

Suite of Dances Harpsichord
Italiana; 2 Danses d'étudiants; Passamezzo; Saltarello
Ruggero Gerlin   12"—LUM-35017
[Gerlin: Divertissement sur des Airs Vénitiens]

Trois Versets du "Te Deum" Organ 1531
Joseph Bonnet (Gonzalez Organ)
12"—PAT-PAT67
[in 3 Centuries of Organ Music collection]

17th CENTURY

Son come farfalletta
Margherita Voltolina (s) & Mario Salerno (pf)   12"—CET-IT582
[Monteverdi: Lasciatemi morire; Bellini: L'abbandono]

Aria fiamminga (arr. Renzo Bossi)
Poltronieri String Quartet
[D. Scarlatti: Scherzo] 10"—C-GQ7199

Sonata for Violin, Viole d'amour, bass (Ger.)
Ensemble of Viols—Curt Sachs
(in Vol. II)   12"—AS-19

Le bon vin chasse le chagrin
Gaston Micheletti (t) & R. Gerlin (harpsichord)
(in Vol. X)   12"—AS-98
[with Airs Sérieux et à Boire]

18th CENTURY

Concerto (Harpsichord solo) B minor (transcribed from the work of an anonymous composer by J. S. Bach)
(No. 8 of the 16 "Vivaldi" concertos)
Ruggero Gerlin (harpsichord)
12"—LUM-35018

Air anonyme (arr. Crussard)
Leila Ben Sedira (s) with harpsichord & strings   12"—G-DB5023
[A. Scarlatti: Ariette]

Sonata for 3 Flutes
3 Flutes   10"—OL-127

Dolce Madonna
Giuseppe De Luca (b) & Pietro Cimara (pf), (in D-U1)

ARBEAU, Thoinot (Jehan Tabourot) (1519-c.1595)
A French priest who, taking a great delight in dancing, wrote a book called Orchésographie *devoted to detailed instructions for the performance of the dances of the times, together with many dance tunes. The book was published in 1588, and in recent years the tunes were orchestrated by Peter Warlock (Philip Heseltine) for his "Capriol Suite." For recordings of this music see under Warlock. Since Arbeau's book was dedicated to a patron and pupil of*

the dance, a gentleman surnamed Capriol, his name is used by Warlock for the title of the modern Suite.

L' ORCHESOGRAPHIE
Pavane—Belle qui tient ma vie
Isabelle French (s) & harpsichord acc. (in TC-2)

ARCADELT, Jacob (c.1514-1575)
A member of the Netherland contrapuntal school and many years an organist at St. Mark's Cathedral in Venice.

Ave Maria Unacc. Chorus in Latin
(From the St. Gregory Hymnal, Proper Offertory for the Fourth Sunday in Advent and other occasions; setting attributed to Arcadelt)
Sistine Chapel Choir—A. Rella
(in GM-139) 12"—G-DB1570
[Palestrina: Sicut Cervus]
—Arr. Organ
Charles M. Courboin (St. Patrick's Cathedral Organ)
(in VM-1091) 12"—V-11-9403
[McGrath: Adoration]
—Arr. Orchestra McDonald
Boston "Pops" Orch.—Fiedler
10"—V-10-1070
[Bach-Cailliet: Fugue à la Gigue]

ARCHANGELSKY, Alexander (1846-1924)
A Russian choral director who composed many works for the Russian liturgy.

CHORUS Unacc. Choral Works in Russian
The Creed   Credo: Liturgica Domestica
Russian: **Verooyou**
Feodor Chaliapin (bs) & Russian Metropolitan Church Choir—Afonsky
12"—V-7715
[Gretchaninov: Glory to Thee]
(G-DB1701)

Blest is the Man (1st Psalm of David)
A. Zakharova & Russian Metropolitan Church Choir—Afonsky 12"—G-EL10
[Tchessnokoff: Litany]

Green Pasture   Russian: Zelyony Loog
Aristoff Choir   10"—G-EV7
[Anon.: Song of the Volga]

Lord, Hear My Prayer (Psalm 55) Russian: **Gospodi uslyshi moleetvu Moyu**
Don Cossack Chorus—Jaroff
[Lvovsky: Requiem] 12"—C-7352M
General Platoff Don Cossack Chorus
(in VM-768) 12"—V-17918
[Bakhmetiev: Requiem]
Metropolitan Russian Church Choir—Afonsky   12"—G-C2206
[Gretchaninoff: Credo] (G-EL7)
(G-L880)

ARDITI, Luigi (1822-1903)
A well known operatic conductor during his time, Arditi is represented today by the bravura vocal works listed below.

SONGS In Italian
Il Bacio—Vals   Eng. The Kiss

Lucrezia Bori (s) 10"—V-1262
[Pestalozza: Ciribiribin] (G-DA900)
Isobel Baillie (s) In English
12"—C-DX165
[Offenbach: Contes d'Hoffmann—Doll
Song]
Miliza Korjus (s) 12"—V-12588
[Parla] (G-EH908)
[Denza: Funiculi, Funicula on G-C3152]
DUPLICATIONS: Clara Clairbert, PD-
62704; Gwen Catley (in English),
G-C3214; Adele Kern (in German),
PD-27226; Millicent Phillips, P-R2589
Parla—Vals
Amelita Galli-Curci (s) 10"—G-DA928
[Benedict: The Gypsy and the Bird]
[Yradier: La Paloma, on G-DA5400]
Adele Kern (s) 12"—PD-27226
[Il Bacio]
Clara Clairbert (s) 10"—PD-561080
[Benedict: Capinera]
Miliza Korjus (s) 12"—V-12588
[Il Bacio] (G-EH908)
Erna Sack (s) (in German)
12"—T-E1772
[Flotow: Marta-Den Teuer zu versöhnen]
Leggiero invisibile Bolero
Ernestine Schumann-Heink
(Recorded 1907) 12"—V-15-1012*
[Donizetti: Lucrezia Borgia—Brindisi]

ARENSKY, Anton (1861-1906)

One of the lesser-known composers of the Russian cosmopolitan school.

CONCERTO, A minor Violin & Orchestra
—Tempo di valse only Arr. Heifetz
Jascha Heifetz & Emanuel Bay (pf)
(in VM-1158) 10"—V-10-1344
[Mendelssohn: Piano Trio No. 1—
Scherzo]
Serenade, G major, Op. 30, No. 2
Violin & Piano
Mischa Elman & Josef Bonime
[Beethoven: Minuet in G] 10"—V-1434
DUPLICATION: Alfredo Campoli,
D-F7533
Suite No 1, Op. 15 2 Pianos
—Romance only
Ethel Bartlett & Rae Robertson
10"—C-17198D
[Beethoven: Ruins of Athens—Turkish
March]
—Waltz only
Ethel Bartlett & Rae Robertson
12"—C-71398D
[Mendelssohn: Midsummer Night's
Dream—Scherzo]
Vitya Vronsky & Victor Babin
(in CM-576) 12"—C-71672D
[Babin: Russian Village]
Trio, D minor, Op. 32 Piano, Violin & 'Cello
Eileen Joyce, H. Temianka & A. Sala
3 12"—P-E11386/8†
**Variations on a Theme of Tchaikovsky,
Op. 35a** String Orchestra
(Theme: Tchaikovsky song "Christ had
a garden" Opus. 54, No. 1)
(Orchestral version of 2nd Mvt. of String
Quartet, A minor, Op. 35)

Philadelphia Chamber String Sinfonietta
—Fabien Sevitzky 2 12"—VM-896†
Boyd Neel String Orch.—Neel
2 12"—D-X261/2

ARNE, Michael (1741-1786)

The son of the famous Dr. Arne, Michael was a curious man whose expensive dabblings in alchemy led him to debtor's prison. He is known expressly for the song listed below and for other airs of this type.

The Lass with the Delicate Air
Song in English
Ada Alsop (s) & Boyd Neel String
Orch. 12"—D-K1686
[Boyce: Tell me, lovely shepherd]
Also: Josh White (vocal) with guitar,
in D-A447

ARNE, (Dr.) Thomas Augustine (1710-1778)

A very talented musician who introduced the use of women's voices into the oratorio. His most successful works were musical productions for the London stage.

COMUS Masque 1738
Preach not me your musty rules
Richard Crooks (t) & Fred Schauwecker
(pf) (in VM-846) 10"—V-2175
[Haydn: Serenade & Handel: Floridante
—Alma mia]

JUDGEMENT OF PARIS Masque after
Congreve
Scene—O ravishing delight
Arr. Cummings
Isobel Baillie (s) & Gerald Moore (pf)
[Where the bee sucks] 10"—C-DB2121

SULEIMAN AND ZAIDE Opera
On the transport of possessing
Isabel French (s), Hugues Cuenod (t),
Claude Jean Chiasson (harpsichord) &
Chamber Orch., (in TC-2)
Rule Britannia (Originally finale of the
masque "Alfred")
—Arr. Orchestra
BBC Orch.—Sir Adrian Boult
10"—G-B8553
[British Grenadiers & God Save the King]
(Also on G-B9420)

SONGS
Under the Greenwood Tree
Leslie French, on C-DX927
Where the Bee Sucks (from Shakespeare's
"Tempest") Ariel's song
Isobel Baillie (s) & Gerald Moore (pf)
[O ravishing delight] 10"—C-DB2121
Elsie Suddaby (s) & Gerald Moore (pf)
10"—D-M510
[Loch Lomond & Morley: It was a lover]
Also: Leslie French, (in C-DX928)

Sonatas
No. 3, G major
Ruggero Gerlin (harpsichord)
10"—C-BQ6015

ARRIETA y CORRERA, Pascual Juan Emilio (1823-1894)

A successful composer of the popular "zarzuelas," Correra also wrote religious music.

MARINA Zarzuela in Spanish
Complete recording
Mercédes Capsir (s), Hipólito Lázaro (t), José Mardones (bs), Marcos Redondo (b), with Chorus and Orch.—Monterio
12 12"—C-OP11†
(There are undoubtedly additional recordings listed in Spanish catalogues.)

ATTERBERG, Kurt (1887-   )

A Swedish composer, critic and conductor, Atterberg won the international prize in the Schubert Centennial with his Sixth Symphony.

BAECKAHASTEN, Op. 24 Opera
Prelude (Förspel)
Symphony Orch.—A. Järnefelt
12"—O-D6024
[Sinfonia Piccola: 4th Movement]

CONCERTO Horn & Orchestra
—Adagio only
Axel Malm (horn) & Stockholm Broadcasting Orch.—Atterberg 12"—C-13603

FANAL Opera
I männer över lag och rätt Aria Tenor
Jussi Björling (t) 10"—G-X4436
[Puccini: Fanciulla del West—Ch'ella mi creda libero, in Swedish]
En Svensk Midsommarnatt Orchestra
Symphony Orch.—Järnefelt
12"—O-D6033
De Fåvitska Jungfrurna, Op. 17 Orchestra
Stockholm Broadcasting Orch.—
Atterberg 12"—C-13602
Symphony Orch.—Järnefelt (O-7699)
12"—O-D6023
Gathenhielmavalsen Song in Swedish
(Söderblom)
Harry Brandelius 10"—G-X4131
[Hanon: Ensjomansdans]
String Quartet Op. 11
Garaguly Quartet 2 12"—G-DB11014/5

SYMPHONIES Orchestra
No 6, C major, Op. 31
Berlin Philharmonic Orch.—Atterberg
3 12"—PD-95193/5
Sinfonia Piccola
4th Mvt. (Rondo) only
Symphony Orch.—Järnefelt
12"—O-D6024
[Baeckahaesten—Prelude]
Suite Pastorale, Op. 34 Orchestra
Prelude, Aria, Serenata, Giga
Chamber Orch.—Atterberg
2 10"—G-X4966/7

ATTEY, John (c.1640)

An Elizabethan lutenist, Attey published a volume of Ayres in 1622. These may be sung either as polyphonic madrigals or as solo Ayres with lute realizations of the lower voices.

Sweet was the song (arr. Rokseth from lute tablature First Book of Ayres, 1622)
Yves Tinayre (t) with virginal
(in Tinayre Album No. 2)
12"—LUM-32020
[Benet: Pleni sunt coeli & Torre: Adoramus Te, Señor]

ATTWOOD, Thomas (1765-1838)

Patronized by George IV, Atwood was a friend and pupil of Mozart. Later he was recognized as an organist of renown and held various positions in English churches. He was also a close friend of Mendelssohn and a founder of the Philharmonic Society in London.

Canticle: Magnificat (ed. Walford Davies)
BBC Singers—Leslie Woodgate
10"—G-B9308
[Walmesley: Nunc Dimittis; Kelway: Psalm 15; Pye: Psalm 16]

AUBER, Daniel François Esprit (1782-1871)

A witty person and a clever composer, Auber was, with Offenbach, one of the last composers of "opéra-comique" in the school of Boieldieu.

OPERAS & OPERAS-COMIQUES In French
(LE) CHEVAL DE BRONZE 1835
Eng. The Bronze Horse
Overture Orchestra
London Philharmonic Orch.—Lambert
(G-C3061) (G-L1068) 12"—V-12511
National Symphony Orch.—Olof
12"—D-K1325

(LES) DIAMANTS DE LA COURONNE
1841 Eng. The Crown Diamonds
Overture Orchestra
London Philharmonic Orch.—Lambert
12"—G-C3071
London Philharmonic—Cameron
12"—D-K1458

(LE) DOMINO NOIR 1837
Overture Orchestra
Thalia Orch.—Puchelt 12"—O-7979
[Le Maçon—Overture]
Individual Excerpts
Act II
Ne craignez rien, Milord—Recit.
Quel bonheur (Cavatina)—Aria Soprano
It. Or son sola, alfin respiro
Ger. Nur unbesorgt, Mylord
Lina Pagliughi (in Italian)
12"—P-DPX14
[Bellini: Sonnambula—Come per me sereno] (CET-PP60002)
Erna Berger (in German)
10"—PD-10285
[Bizet: Pêcheurs des Perles—Air de Leila]
Act III
Pour toujours, disait-elle, je suis à toi
Tenor
Helge Roswaenge (in German) & Berlin State Opera Orch.—Seidler-Winkler
10"—G-DA4414
[Adams: Postillon de Longjumeau—Postillionlied]

FRA DIAVOLO 1830 3 Acts

Overture Orchestra
London Philharmonic Orch.—Lambert
12"—G-C3084
London Philharmonic Orch.—Fistoulari
12"—D-K1489
Italian Radio Orch.—Basile
12"—CET-CB20369
DUPLICATIONS: Berlin State Opera
Orch.—Lutze, T-E2832: U-F14404; Berlin State Opera Orch.—Melichar, PD-57031; Orch. of the Suisse Romande—Blech, in preparation: Swiss Decca; German Opera House Orch.—Grüber, O-7964; Milan Symphony Orch.—Molajoli, C-GQX10027; Hastings Municipal Orch.—Harrison, D-K577; Vienna Philharmonic Orch.—Krauss, G-S10158

(LE) MACON Ger. Maurer und Schlosser
Overture Orchestra
Symphony Orch.—Gustave Havemann
10"—PD-25218
Thalia Orch.—Puchelt 12"—O-7979
[Le Domino Noir—Overture]

MANON LESCAUT 1856

L'Eclat de rire: C'est l'histoire amoureuse
Soprano
Yvonne Brothier 12"—G-W845
DUPLICATION: Elynne Celys, G-K7813

(LA) MUETTE DE PORTICI 1828

Eng. Masaniello
Ger. Die Stumme von Portici
Ital. La Muta di Portici
Overture Orchestra
London Symphony Orch.—Olof
12"—D-K1314
BBC Symphony Orch.—Boult
12"—G-DB2364
Berlin Philharmonic Orch.—Schmidt-Isserstedt (U-F18076) 12"—T-E2686
DUPLICATIONS: Berlin State Opera
Orch.—Blech, G-EJ304; Polydor Symphony Orch., PD-19673; Berlin State Opera Orch., PD-15248; Milan Symphony Orch.—Molajoli, C-GQX10013
Barcarolle. Act II
Wilhelm Strienz (bs) In German
12"—G-EH1083
[Flatow: Marta—Solo, profugo, with W. Ludwig]

AUBERT, Louis (1877-   )

A pupil of Fauré, Aubert is best known as a conductor and orchestrator. His compositions tend toward the academic.

Habañera Orchestra
Paris Conservatory Orch.—Münch
12"—G-DB11109
(La) Nuit Ensorcelée Orchestra
(Ballet based on Chopin selections)
Paris Conservatory Orch.—Münch
3 12"—G-DB11100/2
Symphony Orch.—Aubert
(C-LFX223/4) 2 12"—CX-76†

AULIN, Tor (1866-1914)

A Swedish violinist and composer, conductor of the Stockholm Kunstverein and founder of the Aulin String Quartet. Although he wrote several works in large forms, he is known today for his short violin pieces which have been popularized by leading virtuosi.

Humoresque Violin & Piano
Endré Wolff & pf. acc. 10"—G-X7379
[Bach: Sarabande]
Charles Barkel & pf. acc.
[Sinding: Alte Weise] 10"—O-D1002

AURIC, Georges (1899-   )

A member of the famous French "Les Six," Auric has composed very polished music in the lighter forms and scored for several films both in France and England.

Impromptus, E major & G major Piano
Jacques Février 10"—CdM-519
[Honegger: Petite Suite]

SONGS
(Le) Gloxinia
Pierre Bernac (b) & Francis Poulenc (pf)
10"—G-DA4893
[Satie: Statue de Bronze; Le Chapelier]
Printemps (from "Margot")
Yvonne Printemps (s) 10"—G-DA4879
[Poulenc: A Sa Guitare]

Trio for Oboe, Clarinet & Bassoon
Trio d'Anches de Paris
2 10"—OL-103/4
(La) Vie Privée d'Adam et Eve
(Fable written by Claude Roy with music by Auric)
Anonymous Cast & Orch.
3 12"—DISC-S53

FOLKSONG SETTINGS
Chanson de Marin: Valparaiso
Yvonne George (s) & pf. acc.
[Lenoir: Paris] 10"—C-D12022
Chantons pour passer le temps—Chant des Marins
Mme. O. Ortaud & J. Peyron with Orch.
—Désormière 10"—CdM-522
[Drappier: Les regrets de la vieille]
Chantons jeunes Filles
Chorale de la Jeunesse & Orch.—
Désormière 10"—CdM-501
[Honegger: Jeunesse]
(La) Corvée d'eau
Chorus & Orch.—Désormière
10"— CdM-504
[Shostakovich: Au devant de la vie]
(Le) Fils du Cordonnier
Yvonne Gouverné Chorus & Orch.—
Désormière 10"—CdM-511
[arr. Delannoy: La Mort de Jean Renaud]
(Le) Roi a fait battre tambour (Poitou)
Mme. M. T. Holley & Orch.—
Désormière 10"—CdM-512
[arr. Jaubert: Les Cloches de Nantes]

BACH, Johann Christian (1735-1782)

The youngest son of Johann Sebastian, J. C. Bach spent many years in England.

CONCERTOS—Harpsichord & Strings

C major—Rondo only
Marguerite Roesgen-Champion & Paris Symphony—Gaillard 12"—PAT-PGT25
[Mozart: Concerto No. 1, K. 37—Rondo]

E flat major, Op. 7, No. 5
Ralph Kirkpatrick (harpsichord), Hildegarde Donaldson (vl), Lois Porter (vl) & Aaron Bodenhorn (vcl)
2 12"—MC-38

—Allegro only
Marguerite Roesgen-Champion & Lamoureux Orch.—Wolff
12"—G-W1522
[Bach: Concerto No. 7 in G minor, Pt. 3]

G major, Op. 7, No. 6
Marguerite Roesgen-Champion & String Trio 2 10"—G-K6423/4

A major
Li Stadelmann & Berlin State Opera Orch.—H. Wirth 3 12"—PD-57096/8S
[Last side blank]

F major, Op. 13, No. 3
—Rondo only
Marguerite Roesgen-Champion (pf) & Lamoureux Orch.—Wolff
12"—C-RFX76
[Mozart: Concerto No. 4, G major, K. 41, Pt. 3]

Quintet, D major, No. 6
Flute, Oboe, Violin, Viola & 'Cello Chamber Ensemble
(in Vol. V) 12"—AS-50

Serenata Notturna, E flat major
H. Merckel & Schwartz (vls) & Navarra (vcl) 2 10"—OL-118/9

Sonata, E major, Opus 5, No. 3 Clavier
—Rondo only
Harold Samuel (pf) (in Columbia History of Music, Vol. III: CM-233)
10"—C-DB830
[K. P. E. Bach: Sonata, F minor 1st Mvt.]

Sonata, E flat major Clavier
Jacques Février (pf)
(in Vol. VII) 12"—AS-68

Sonata, G major, Op. 16, No. 2
Flute & Harpsichord
Verne Q. Powell (fl) & Claude Jean Chiasson (harpsichord)
12"—TC-1538

SYMPHONIES

B flat major (Overture to "Lucio Silla")
Berlin State Opera Orch.—Walter Gmeindl 2 12"—PD-67552/3
(Fonit-91142/3)
New York Philharmonic Symphony Orch. Mengelberg 2 12"—G-D1988/9
[J. S. Bach: Suite No. 3, D major—Air]

—1st 2 Mvts. only
Amsterdam Concertgebouw Orch.— Mengelberg 12"—C-GQX10488

B flat major
—Abridged Version
Boyd Neel Orch.—Neel 10"—D-M486

BACH, Johann Christoph Friedrich (1732-1795)

J. S. Bach's ninth son composed chamber music and many cantatas.

QUARTETS—String

No. 4, D major
—Allegro moderato only
Calvet Quartet 12"—C-LFX213
[Debussy: Quartet, Pt. 7]

BACH, Johann Michael (1648-1694)
No recordings available.

BACH, Johann Sebastian (1685-1750)

Widely renowned in his own day as a performer and improviser on the clavier, Johann Sebastian Bach was a prolific craftsman in his compositions. His consummate skill and inexhaustible fund of inspiration contrive to synthesize the whole wealth of Baroque music in all its intimate details and evoke the spirit of that deeply religious period.
Despite the fact that there is a great wealth of recorded music from Bach's compositions, there is a need for complete recordings of many of the cantatas, the Christmas Oratorio, the St. John Passion and miscellaneous organ works.

Adagio See under Toccata, Adagio & Fugue
Air & 30 Variations See under Goldberg Variations
Air on the G String See under Suite (Orch.) No. 3, 2nd Mvt.
Arioso See under Cantata No. 156 - Sinfonia also under Concerto No. 5 for Clavier & Orch. - 2nd Mvt.
Art of the Fugue See under Kunst der Fuge
Ave Maria See under GOUNOD
Brandenburg Concertos See under Concertos—I

CANTATAS In German

I. Church Cantatas (Kirchenkantaten)
(Bach Gesellschaft numbering)
4, Christ lag in Todesbanden ("Easter Cantata")
Eng. Christ lay in the bonds of death
Complete recording
Victor Chorale & Orch.—Robert Shaw
4 10"—VM-1096†
—No. 1, Sinfonia Orchestra
Boston Symphony Orch.—Koussevitzky
(In VM-1050†) 12"—V-11-9156
[Brandenburg concerto No. 3, 1st Mvt.]
—No. 3, Den Tod Sop. & Alto
Martha Angelici & Germaine Cernay (in French) N. Pierront (organ)
[Schütz: Erhöre mich] 12"—LUM-32059
—No. 4, Jesus Cristus, Gottes Sohn
—Arr. Orch. Stokowski
Philadelphia Orch.—Stokowski
(in VM-401†) 12"—V-14583
[Sonata for Unaccomp. Violin, No. 2— Sarabande]

6, Bleib' bei uns
—No. 1, Bleib' bei uns Chorus
Copenhagen Academy Chorus & Orch.—
Walter Mayer-Radon　　　12″—PD-67061
[Handel: Psalm 100]
12, Weinen, Klagen, Sorgen, Zagen
—No. 4, Kreuz und Krone Contralto
Marian Anderson & Victor Orch.—
Robert Shaw
　　　　(in VM-1087)　　12″—V-11-9378
[Cantata No. 81, No. 1—Jesus schläft]
20, Ach wie flüchtig, ach wie nichtig
—No. 1, Ach wie flüchtig Opening Chorus
—Arr. Orch. Walton
Sadler's Wells Orch.—Walton (G-C3179)
　　　　(in VM-817)　12″—V-13753
21, Ich hatte viel Bekümmerniss
—No. 3, Seufzer, Tränen, Kummer, Not
Soprano
Margherita Perras & Organ
　　　　　　12″—G-DB10093
[Cantata No. 68-No. 2, Mein gläubiges
Herze]
Mme. Malnory-Marseillac (in French)
with oboe & pf. acc.　　12″—LUM-32005
[Cantata No. 68-No. 2, Mein gläubiges
Herze]
22, Jesus Nahm zu sich die Zwölfe
—No. 5, Ertöt' uns durch dein' Güte
—Arr. Piano
Dorothea Salmon　　　　10″—G-JK31
[Prelude, E minor]
Harriet Cohen　　　　　10″—C-LB21
[Liebster Jesu]
**29. Wir danken dir, Gott (Rathswahlkan-
tate)**
—No. 1, Sinfonia Orchestra
(Another version of the Sonata for unac-
companied violin, No. 6, in E—Preludio)
—Arr. Pf. Wilhelm Kempff
Wilhelm Kempff　　　　10″—PD-90189
[Das Wohltemperierte Clavier: Prelude
& Fugue No. 5, D major]
39. Brich dem Hungrigen dein Brod
—No. 5, Höchster, was ich habe Sop.
Margherita Perras with flute & organ
　　　　　　12″—G-DB10094
[Johannes-Passion-Ich folge dir
gleichfalls]
A. Noordewier-Reddingius with flute &
organ　　　　　　　　12″—C-DHX37
[Handel: Süsse Stille]
50. Nun ist das Heil und die Kraft
(one movement only)
Berlin Philharmonic Cho. & Orch.—
Schuricht　　　　　　12″—T-E1709
[Cantata No. 104, No. 1—Du Hirte
Israel, höre]
51. Jauchzet Gott in allen Landen
—No. 1, Jauchzet Gott in allen Landen Sop.
Martha Angelici (in Fr.) & Orch.—
Cébron　　　　　　　10″—LUM-30096
**53. Schlage doch, gewünschte Stunde (one
movement only) Alto**
Lina Falk (in Fr.) & Orch.
　　　　　　12″—LUM-32028
[Christmas Oratorio—Bereite dich Zion]
65. Sie werden aus Saba Alle kommen
—No. 1, Sie werden aus Saba Cho.
—No. 2, Die Könige aus Saba Cho.

—No. 6, Nimm mich dir zu eigen hin Ten.
—No. 7, Ei nun, mein Gott Cho.
Max Meili with Basel Chamber Choir &
Orch.—Sacher (in Vol. VII) 12″—AS-61
68. Also hat Gott die Welt geliebt
—No. 2, Mein gläubiges Herze Sop.
Eng. My heart ever faithful
Margherita Perras & organ
　　　　　　12″—G-DB10093
[Cantata No. 21—No. 3, Seufzer,
Tränen]
Isobel Baillie (in Eng.) & City of Bir-
mingham Orch.—B. Cameron
　　　　　　12″—C-DX1022
[Handel: Rodelinda—Art Thou
troubled]
Germaine Lubin (in Fr.) & Pf.
　　　　　　12″—O-123641
[Chopin: Etude No. 3—Vocal arr.]
Mme. Malnory-Marseillac (in Fr.) with
Pascal Quartet　　　12″—LUM-32005
[Cantata No. 21—No. 3, Seufzer,
Tränen, Kummer, Not]
78. Jesu, der du meine Seele
Eng. Jesus, Thou my wearied spirit
Complete recording (Sung in English)
Bach Choir of Bethlehem & Orch.—Ifor
Jones with Lucius Metz (t) & Mack
Harrell (b)　　　4　12″—VM-1045†
—No. 2, Wir eilen Sop. & Alto
Martha Angelici & Germaine Cernay (in
Fr.) with N. Pierront (org.)
　　　　　　10″—LUM-30079
Reinhardt Cho., with Hélène Glassman
(harpsichord) 'cellos & String Orch.—
Reinhardt (C-DNX1598)　12″—C-8858
81, Jesus schläft, was soll ich hoffen?
—No. 1, Jesus schläft Contralto
Marian Anderson & Victor Orch.—
Robert Shaw
　　　　(in VM-1087)　12″—V-11-9478
[Cantata No. 12—No. 4, Kreuz und
Krone]
85, Ich bin ein guter Hirt
—No. 5, Seht! was die Liebe tut! Tenor
Yves Tinayre (b) & Orch. with organ-
Cellier　　　　　　12″—LUM-32014
[J. W. Franck: Passionslied; Albert:
Festlied]
(in Yves Tinayre Album No. 1)
—Arr. Orchestra Walton
Sadler's Wells Orch.—Walton (G-C3178)
　　　　(in VM-817)　12″—V-13752
99, Was Gott tut, das ist wohlgetan
—No. 1, Was Gott tut Opening Chorus
—Arr. Orchestra Walton
Sadler's Wells Orch.—Walton (G-C3178)
　　　　(in VM-817)　12″—V-13752
104, Du Hirte Israel, höre
—No. 1, Du Hirte Israel, höre Chorus
Berlin Philharmonic Chorus & Orch.—
Schuricht　　　　　12″—T-E1709
[Cantata No. 50, Nun ist das Heil und die
Kraft]
106, Gottes Zeit ist die allerbeste Zeit
(Actus tragicus) Eng. God's Time is the
Best
Complete recording Sung in English
Harvard Glee Club & Radcliffe Choral
Society, with Chamber Orch.—

Woodworth 3 12"—TC-T6
—No. 1, Sonatina (Prelude) Orchestra
Symphony Orch.—Bret (G-S10448)
12"'—G-L964
[Concerto for four Claviers & Orch.,
Pt. 3]
112, Der Herr ist mein getreuer Hirt
—No. 2, Zum reinen Wasser Contralto
Marian Anderson & Victor Orch.—
Robert Shaw
(in VM-1087) 12"—V-11-9379
[Christmas Oratorio—No. 4, Bereite
dich, Zion]
129, Gelobet sei der Herr
—Finale only. Arr. Orchestra Walton
Sadler's Wells Orch.—Walton (G-C3178)
(in VM-817) 12"—V-13753
140, Wachet auf, ruft uns die Stimme
Eng. Sleepers, Wake!
Complete recording Sung in German
Victor Chorale & Orch.—Robert Shaw,
with Suzanne Freil (s), Roy Russell (t),
Paul Matthen (b) 4 10"—VM-1162†
—No. 1, Wachet auf Chorus
—No. 4, Zion hört die Wächter Chorus
—No. 7, Gloria sei dir gesungen Chorus
Bach Society Chorus (in French) with
Orch. & Organ—G. Bret (abridged)
2 12"—G-DB4983/4
Orfeó Catalá, Barcelona (in Catalonian)
—L. Millet (abridged)
2 12"—G-AW276/7
—No. 1, Wachet auf
—Arr. Orch. Bantock
City of Birmingham Orch.—Weldon
12"—C-DX1388
—No. 7, Gloria sei dir gesungen
Eng. Now let every tongue adore Thee
—Arr. O'Connell
Dorothy Maynor (s) & Philadelphia
Orch.—Ormandy 12"—V-18166
[Matthäus-Passion—No. 3, Herzliebster
Jesu]
[Mass in B minor—No. 5, Laudamus te,
on V-11-9108, in VM-1043]
142, Uns ist ein Kind geboren
Fr. Cantate de la Nativité
—No. 2, Uns ist ein Kind geboren Chorus
St. Léon IX Chorus—Gaudard
10"—PAT-X93050
(Matthäus-Passion—No. 63, O Haupt
voll Blut]
147, Herz und Mund und Tat und Leben
—No. 10, Jesu bleibet meine Freude
Chorale
(Chorus, String Orchestra & Oboe)
Eng. Jesu, joy of man's desiring
Bach Chorus (in English), Cantata Club
Orch., with Leon Goossens (ob)—
K. Scott (C-DF1089) 10"—C-DB507
[Suite No. 2—Rondeau & Badinerie]
(in Columbia History of Music, Vol. II:
CM-232)
Choir (in French), Oboe, String Orch. &
Organ-Cellier 12"—LUM-32026
[Aus tiefer Noth, organ only]
—Arr. Orchestra Cailliet
Philadelphia Orch.—Ormandy
12"—V-14973
[Sonata No. 6 for Unacc. Violin-Preludio]

—Arr. Organ Biggs
E. Power Biggs 12"—V-18292
[Brahms: Chorale Prelude—Es is ein
Ros' entsprungen]
—Arr. Piano Hess
Myra Hess (G-B9035) 10"—V-4538
[Scarlatti: Sonata, G major, L. 387]
[French Suite No. 5—Gigue, on
C-4084M: C-D1635]
Walter Gieseking 10"—C-17150D
[French Suite No. 5—Gigue]
—Chorus arrangement (Based on the Hess
arrangement)
Temple Church Choir (in English) with
Leon Goossens (ob) & pf.—G. T. Ball
10"—G-B8123
[Spohr: Last Judgement—Lord God of
Heaven]
Choir of H. M. Chapel Royal (in English)
& Organ 10"—G-E445
[Arr. Pettman: Gabriel's message; Born
this day]
—Arr. Piano Levêque
Albert Levêque 10"—G-K7502
[Das Wohltemperierte Clavier-Prelude &
Fugue No. 3]
—Arr. 2 Pianos Horne
Ethel Bartlett & Rae Robertson
10"—C-17240D
[Gluck: Gavotte]
151. Süsser Trost, mein Jesus kommt
—No. 1, Süsser Trost, mein Jesus kommt
Sop.
A. Noordewier-Reddingius, with flute &
organ 12"—C-DHX38
Margherita Perras, with flute & organ
12"—G-DB10096
156. Ich steh' mit einem Fuss im Grabe
—No. 1, Sinfonia ("Arioso") Orch.
Bach Cantata Club String Orch. & Leon
Goossens (oboe)—K. Scott
10"—C-DB506
[Chorales: Herzlich tut & Vater unser]
(in Columbia History of Music, Vol. 2:
CM-232) (C-DF1946)
NBC Symphony Orch.—Stokowski
(Arr. Stokowski) 12"—V-18498
Boyd Neel String Orch.—Neel (arr.
Franko) 12"—D-X237
[Lekeu: Adagio for String Orch., op. 3]
—Arr. Violin & Piano
Alfredo Campoli & Eric Gritton
12"—D-K1532
[Tartini: Sonata, G minor, Pt. 3]
—Arr. Organ Virgil Fox
Virgil Fox 12"—V-11-8236
[Vivaldi: Concerto Grosso No. 11, D
minor—3rd Mvt.]
159. Sehet, wir geh'n hinauf gen Jerusalem
—No. 4, Es ist vollbracht (Bass, with oboe
obbl.)
Elisabeth Schumann (s), Leon Goossens
(oboe), & Orch.—Karl Alwin (Arr.
Alwin) 12"—G-D1410
[Matthäus-Passion: Aus Liebe will mein
Heiland sterben] (G-W980)
189, Meine Seele rühmt und preist
(Tenor solo with Chamber Orchestra)
Complete recording
—No. 1, Meine Seele Aria

—No. 2, Denn, seh' ich mich—Recit.
—No. 3, Gott hat sich hoch gesetzet—Aria
—No. 4, O, was vor grosse Dinge
—No. 5, Deine Güte, dein Erbarmen
Pierre Bernac & Chamber Orch.—Münch
  2   12"—G-DB5193/4
—Nos 1 (abridged), 4 & 5 only
Max Meili, with Chamber Ensemble—
Curt Sachs   (in Vol. III)   12"—AS-23
II. Secular Cantatas (Weltliche Kantaten)
201, Der Streit zwischen Phoebus und Pan
—No. 3, Patron, das macht der Wind Sop.
Eng. Ah, yes, just so!
Lily Pons (s) (in French) & Renaissance
Quintet   (in VM-756)   10"—V-2152
[Pergolesi: Se tu m'ami]
Isobel Baillie (s) (in English)
  10"—C-DB2067
[Schubert: An die Musik]
205, Der zufriedengestellte Aeolus
—No. 7, Können nicht die roten Wangen
(Pomona's Air)   Contralto
Germaine Cernay (in French) & Cham-
ber Orch.—Bret   12"—C-RFX55
[Christmas Oratorio—No. 4, Bereite
dich, Zion]
206, Schleicht, spielende Wellen
("Birthday Cantata" for August III)
—No. 9, Hört doch! der sanften Flöten
Chor Soprano
Hedwig von Debicka & Orch.—
Prüwer   12"—PD-95422
[Gluck: Paride ed Elena—O del mio
dolce ardor]
208, Was mir behagt, ist nur die
munt're Jagd ("Birthday Cantata")
—No. 9, Schafe können sicher weiden
Soprano
Eng. Sheep may safely graze
Elisabeth Schwarzkopf with flutes, vlc.
& harpsichord   12"—C-LCX115
Isobel Baillie (in English) with flutes,
vlc., & pf.   12"—C-DX1103
Katherine Harris, with recorders, gamba
& harpsichord   10"—Hargail-MW-104
—Arr. Piano Levêque
Kathleen Long   12"—D-K1066
[Fantasia, C minor]
—Arr. 2 pfs. Howe
Ethel Bartlett & Rae Robertson
  12"—C-68918D
[Handel: Solomon—Entrance of the
Queen of Sheba] (C-DX992)
—Arr. Orch. Barbirolli
Philharmonic Symphony Orch. of N. Y.—
Barbirolli
  (in CX-200†)   12"—C-11575D
[Brahms: Academic Festival Overture,
Pt. 3]
—Arr. Orch. Walton
Sadler's Wells Orch.—Walton
(G-C3179) (in VM-817)   12"—V-13753
(Also on G-B9380: 10")
—Arr. Organ Biggs
E. Power Biggs
  (in VM-1048†)   12"—V-11-9146
[Fugue in C]
211. Schweigt stille, plaudert nicht
("Coffee Cantata")
William Hain (t, narrator), Benjamin

de Loache (b), Ethyl Hayden (s) & In-
strumental Ensemble—Ernst V. Wolff
(harpsichord)   4   12"—MC-5
[Song, So oft ich meine Tabakspfeife]
212, Mer hahn en neue Oberkeet
Fr. Nous avons un nouveau Gouverneur
("Peasant Cantata")
(for Soprano, Baritone & Orch., without
Chorus)
Abridged version Sung in French
Jeanne Guyla (s), Martial Singher (b) &
Chamber Orch.—Bret
  2   12"—G-DB4939/40
—No. 24, Wir geh'n nun, wo der Dudelsack
Eng. Come let us to the Bagpipe's sound
—Arr. Orch. Victor Orch., in V-E81; Older
recording, V-24793

CHORALES Chorus in German
In alphabetical order by German title

NOTE: *The majority of the chorales are for unaccompanied voices and the recorded performances below may be assumed to be a cappella
unless orchestral or other accompaniments are
specified. While Bach wrote some of his own
chorale tunes, the majority of his works in this
form are settings of old German hymn tunes by
other composers. Many tunes were set in several
different versions, sometimes with different
texts.*

Dir, dir, Jehova will ich singen
  (B. G. Vol. 39, No. 46; also Anna Magda-
lena Bach Notebook No. 39A. For solo
version see Songs)
St. Thomas Church Choir—Straube
  12"—PD-66708
[Motet: Singet dem Herrn—Alles was
Odem hat]
Ein' feste, Burg ist unser Gott
Eng. A Mighty Fortress, or Stronghold
Sure

NOTE: *This famous chorale is usually more
closely associated with the author of the text
and probable composer of the melody, Martin
Luther, than it is with Bach. The Stokowski
transcription, while credited to Bach, is simpler
than any of his settings and is based largely on
the original Luther setting.*

—Arr. Orch. Stokowski
Philadelphia Orch.—Stokowski
  10"—V-1692
[Anon.: Russian Christmas Music]
All-American Orch.—Stokowski
  (in CX-219†)   12"—C-11758D
[Toccata & Fugue, D minor, Pt. 3]
Es ist das Heil uns kommen her

NOTE: *Sung here to the words "O Tod, wo ist
dein Stachel nun" The setting used is that for
the Schlusschoral "Die Hoffnung wart't" from
Cantata No. 86, "Wahrlich ich sage euch."*

St. George's Choir, Berlin & organ
  10"—PD-22105
[Matthäus-Passion—Wenn ich einmal
soll scheiden]
Herzlich tut mich verlangen See under
Matthäus-Passion—No. 53

In dulci jubilo
St. Martin's Choral Society—
Goldsbrough   10"—D-F2640
[Sears-Willis: While Shepherds
Watched]
Trapp Family Choir   10"—V-2184
[Wer nu den lieben Gott lässt walten]
Lobe den Herren Fr. Louez le Dieu puissant
NOTE: *There are two Bach settings of a tune,
composed by Johann Gottfried Walther, in
Cantatas 57 and 137, but we have been unable
to hear the recorded version for exact iden-
tification.*
Chorale du Petit Séminaire de Paris—
Vallet   10"—LUM-30054
[Altenburg: Gloire éternelle au Dieu
puissant]
Die Sonn' hat sich mit ihrem Glanz
NOTE: *Not heard for identification.*
Chorale Scoute unacc.—Jacques Chailley
10"—LUM-30037
[Scout Melody: Les fleurs du chemin]
Vater unser im Himmelreich

NOTE: *There are several Bach settings of this
tune. The one used below is that in the
Johannes-Passion—"Dein Will' gescheh', Herr
Gott"—sung here in an English version, "Our
Father in Heaven."*

London Bach Cantata Club Chorus—
Scott   10"—C-DB506
[Chorale: Herzlich tut & Cantata No.
156—Sinfonia]
(in Columbia History of Music Vol. II:
CM-232)
Wer nur den lieben Gott lässt walten
Trapp Family Choir   10"—V-2184
[In dulci jubilo]

CHORALE-PRELUDES Organ
Collections

**An Wasserflüssen Babylon; Christ lag in
Todesbanden; Christum wir sollen loben
schon; Christus der uns selig macht; Da
Jesus an dem Kreuze stund; Erschienen
ist der herrlich Tag; Jesus Christus un-
ser Heiland; Liebster Jesu wir sind hier;
Mit Fried und Freud ich fahr' dahin; O
Lamm Gottes unschuldig; O Mensch be-
wein' dein Sünde gross; Schmücke dich,
o liebe Seele; Sei gegrüsset, Jesu gütig.**
Albert Schweitzer (Organ of Ste. Aurélie,
Strasbourg)   7 12"—CM-310†
(in Bach Society, Vol. II)
**Ach bleib' bei uns; An Wasserflüssen Baby-
lon; Ein' feste Burg ist unser Gott;
Kommst du nun, Jesu, vom Himmel her-
unter; Meine Seele erhebt den Herren;
Valet will ich dir geben; Wachet auf;
Wer nur den Lieben Gott lässt walten;
Wo soll ich fliehen hin.**
Carl Weinrich (Westminster Choir
School, Princeton, N. J.)
5 10"—MC-22
NOTE: *Bach arranged several of the chorale-
preludes in collections: Schübler Chorales;
Das Orgelbüchlein; Eighteen "Great" Preludes;
Clavierübung III (Catechism Chorales). In
the following alphabetical list, Schübler Chor-
ales are identified as Sch, followed by the*

*number; Das Orgelbüchlein as OB, etc.; the
Eighteen Preludes by 18; the Clavierübung
by CU.*

In alphabetical order
Ach, bleib' bei uns, Herr Jesu Christ Sch. 5.
(Peters Vol. VI, No 2)
Carl Weinrich, in MC-22
Ach wie nichtig, ach wie flüchtig O.B. 45
(Peters Vol. V, No. 1)
E. Power Biggs (Germanic Museum organ,
Harvard), on V-17334, in VM-697
**Allein Gott in der Höh' sei Ehr (C. U. 1st
version)**
(Peters Vol. VI, No. 5)
Fritz Heitmann (Charlottenburg organ)
12"—T-E2710
[Kyrie: Gott Vater in Ewigkeit]
Hans Vollenweider (unidentified)
10"—G-JK30
[Ein' feste Burg]
Alle Menschen müssen sterben O.B. 44
(Peters Vol. V, No. 2)
E. Power Biggs, on V-17334 in VM-697
Das Alte Jahr vergangen ist O.B. 16
(Peters Vol. V, No. 10)
E. Power Biggs, on V-17458 in VM-711
Gustave Bret (Fréjus Cathedral)
12"—G-DB4949
[Liebster Jesu; Lasso: Benedictus,
Dijon Chorus]
Edouard Commette (Lyons Cathedral)
10"—C-DF681
[Christ lag in Todesbanden]
—**Arr. 'Cello & Piano** Fournier
Pierre Fournier & Gerald Moore
12"—G-DB6372
[O Mensch bewein dein Sünde gross &
Wenn wir in höchsten Nöten sein]
An Wasserflüssen Babylon
(Peters Vol. VI, No. 12a)
Carl Weinrich, in MC-22
An Wasserflüssen Babylon "18" No. 3
(Peters Vol. VI, No. 12b)
Albert Schweitzer, in Bach Organ So-
ciety, Vol. II: CM-310†
Aus der Tiefe rufe ich
(Peters Anh. 1, No. 12)
—**Arr. Orch.** Stokowski
Philadelphia Orch.—Stokowski
(G-DB1789) 12"—V-7553
Aus tiefer Not (De Profundis) C.U.
(Peters Vol. VI, No. 13)
Fritz Heitmann (Charlottenburg Palace
organ)   12"—T-E2712
[Christ unser Herr & Vater unser im
Himmelreich]
Alexander Cellier (St.-Sulpice Organ) &
Trombones   12"—LUM-32026
[Cantata No. 147-No. 10, Jesu bleibet
meine Freude, in French]
Christe, du Lamm Gottes O.B. 21
(Peters Vol. V, No. 3)
E. Power Biggs, on V-15889 in VM-652
Christ ist erstanden O.B. 29
(Peters Vol. V, No. 4)
—**Verse I**
E. Power Biggs, on V-15890 in VM-652
—**Verse II & Verse III**
E. Power Biggs, on V-17332 in VM-697

Christ lag in Todesbanden O.B. 27
  (Peters Vol. V, No. 5)
  E. Power Biggs, on V-15890 in VM-652
  Albert Schweitzer, in Bach Society, Vol.
  II: CM-310†
  Charles Hens (Gonzalez organ)
  12″—PAT-PAT66
  [Purcell: Trompette et air] (in 3 Centuries of Organ Music album)
  Edouard Commette (Lyons Cathedral)
  10″—C-DF681
  [Das alte Jahr vergangen ist]
  L. Vierne, O-166147
—Arr. Orchestra Stokowski
  Philadelphia Orch.—Stokowski
  12″—V-7437
  [Little Fugue, G minor] (G-DB1952)
Christ, unser Herr, zum Jordan kam C.U.
  (Peters Vol. VI, No. 18)
  Fritz Heitmann (Charlottenburg Palace
  organ) 12″—T-E2712
  [Vater unser & Aus tiefer Not]
Christum wir sollen loben schon O.B. 13
  (Peters Vol. V, No. 6)
  Albert Schweitzer, in Bach Society,
  Vol. II: CM-310†
  E. Power Biggs, on V-17459 in VM-711
Christus, der uns selig macht O.B. 22
  (Peters Vol. V, No. 8)
  E. Power Biggs, on V-15889 in VM-652
  Albert Schweitzer, in Bach Organ
  Society, Vol. II: CM-310†
Da Jesus an dem Kreuze stund O.B. 23
  (Peters Vol. V. No. 9)
  Albert Schweitzer, in Bach Organ
  Society, Vol. II: CM-310†
  E. Power Biggs, on V-15889 in VM-652
Dies sind die heil'gen zehn Gebot' O.B. 36
  (Peters Vol. V, No. 12)
  E. Power Biggs, on V-17332 in VM-697
Dies sind die heil'gen zehn Gebot' C.U.
  (Peters Vol. VI, No. 19)
  Fritz Heitmann (Charlottenburg Palace
  organ) 12″—T-E2711
  [Wir glauben all']
Durch Adams Fall ist ganz verderbt O.B. 38
  (Peters Vol. V, No. 13)
  E. Power Biggs, on V-17333 in VM-697
Ein' feste Burg ist unser Gott
  (Peters Vol. VI, No. 22)
  Carl Weinrich, in MC-22
  E. Power Biggs on V-11-9145 in
  VM-1048†
  Hans Vollenweider 10″—G-JK30
  [Allein Gott in der Höh']
Erschienen ist der herrlich Tag O.B.31
  (Peters Vol. V, No. 15)
  E. Power Biggs, on V-15890 in VM-652
  Albert Schweitzer, in Bach Organ
  Society, Vol. II: CM-310†
Erstanden ist der heil'ge Christ O.B. 30
  (Peters Vol. V, No. 14)
  E. Power Biggs, on V-15890 in VM-652
Es ist das Heil uns kommen her O.B. 39
  (Peters Vol. V, No. 16)
  E. Power Biggs, on V-17333 in VM-697
Gelobet seist du, Jesu Christ O.B. 6
  (Peters Vol. V, No. 17)
  E. Power Biggs, on V-17458 in VM-711

Gottes Sohn ist kommen O.B. 2
  (Peters Vol. V, No. 19)
  E. Power Biggs, on V-17335 in VM-697
Helft mir Gottes Güte preisen O.B. 15
  (Peters Vol. V, No. 21)
  E. Power Biggs, on V-17479 in VM-711
Herr Christ, der ein'ge Gottes Sohn O.B. 3
  (Peters Vol. V, No. 22)
  E. Power Biggs, on V-17335 in VM-697
—Arr. Orchestra Hodge
  Boyd Neel String Orch.—Neel
  12″—D-K1543
  [Brandenburg Concerto No. 1, Pt. 5]
Herr Gott, nun schleuss den Himmel auf
  O.B. 19 (Peters Vol. V, No. 24)
  E. Power Biggs, on V-15888 in VM-652
Herr Jesu Christ, dich zu uns wend O.B. 34
  (Peters Vol. V, No. 25)
  E. Power Biggs, on V-17322 in VM-697
Herzlich tut mich verlangen
  (Peters Vol. V, No. 27)
  Fritz Heitmann (Berlin Dom organ)
  12″—T-E2682
  [Passacaglia, C minor, Pt.3]
  Charles M. Courboin 12″—V-14927
  [Suite No. 3, D major—Aria]
  Fernando Germani 12″—SEMS-1137
  [Daquin: Noel X]
Heut' triumphieret Gottes Sohn O.B. 32
  (Peters Vol. V, No. 28)
  E. Power Biggs, on V-15890 in VM-652
Hilf Gott, dass mir's gelinge O.B. 26
  (Peters Vol. V, No. 29)
  E. Power Biggs, on V-15890 in VM-652
Ich ruf' zu dir, Herr Jesu Christ, O.B. 40
  (Peters Vol. V, No. 30)
  E. Power Biggs, on V-17333 in VM-697
—Arr. Piano Busoni
  Egon Petri 12″—C-71463D
  [Wachet auf, etc.]
  Edwin Fischer 12″—G-DB5688
  [Toccata, D major, Pt. 3]
  Carlo Zecchi 12″—CET-CB20353
  [Wohltemperierte Clavier-Prelude &
  Fugue No. 14]
—Arr. Orchestra Stokowski
  Philadelphia Orch.—Stokowski
  (in VM-963) 12″—V-11-8577
  [Little Organ Preludes-No. 3, E minor]
  [Wagner: Tannhäuser, Prelude Act III,
  Pt. 3 on V-15314 in VM-530†]
  (Older version: V-6786: G-D1465;
  G-AW19 with Wohltemperierte Clavier-
  Prelude No. 8)
In dich hab' ich gehoffet, Herr O.B. 41
  (Peters Vol. V, No. 33)
  E. Power Biggs, on V-17333 in VM-697
In dir ist Freude O.B. 17
  (Peters Vol. V, No. 34)
  E. Power Biggs, on V-15888 in VM-652
  Louis Vierne, O-166147
—Arr. Piano Busoni
  Egon Petri 12″—C-71463D
  [Ich ruf zu dir, etc.]
In dulci jubilo O.B. 10
  (Peters Vol. V, No. 35)
  E. Power Biggs, on V-17458, in VM-711
In dulci jubilo
  (Straube Collection, Peters, 1904)
  E. Power Biggs, on V-15729 in VM-616

Jens Laumann (Compenius Organ
Frederiksborg Castle Church)
10″—G-X4975
[Walther: Meinen Jesum lass ich nicht]
In dulci jubilo
(version unidentified)
Fernando Germani   12″—SEMS-1139
[Handel: Prelude & Fugue, F minor]
Jesu, meine Freude O.B. 12
(Peters Vol. V, No. 31)
E. Power Biggs, on V-17459 in VM-711
Jesus Christus, unser Heiland, der den Tod
O.B. 28 (Peters Vol. V, No. 32)
E. Power Biggs, on V-15890 in VM-652
Jesus Christus, unser Heiland, der von uns
den Zorn Gottes wandt C.U
(Peters Vol. VI, No. 30)
Fritz Heitmann (Charlottenburg Palace
Organ)   12″—T-E2713
[Duetto No. 2, F major]
Friedrich Mihatsch (Gonzalez Organ)
12″—PAT-PAT73
[Liebster Jesu]
(in 3 Centuries of Organ Music set)
Jesus Christus, unser Heiland, der von uns
den Zorn Gottes wandt "18" No. 16
(Peters Vol. VI, No. 31)
Albert Schweitzer, in Bach Organ
Society, Vol. II; CM-310†
Komm, Gott Schöpfer, heiliger Geist O.B.
33 (Peters Vol. VII, No. 35)
E. Power Biggs, on V-17332 in VM-697
Kommst du nun, Jesu, vom Himmel Sch. 6
(Peters Vol. VII, No. 38)
Carl Weinrich, in MC-22
—Arr. Orchestra Gui
Orch. of the "Maggio Musicale"—Gui
12″—CET-BB25170
[Beethoven: Leonore Overture No. 3,
Pt. 3]
Kyrie, Gott Vater in Ewigkeit C.U.
(Peters Vol. VII, No. 39a)
Fritz Heitmann (Charlottenburg Palace
Organ)   12″—T-E2710
[Allein Gott in der Höh']
Liebster Jesu, wir sind hier O.B. 35a
(Peters Vol. V, No. 37, variant)
E. Power Biggs, on V-17332 in VM-697
Liebster Jesu, wir sind hier O.B. 35b
(Peters Vol. V, No. 37)
E. Power Biggs, on V-17332 in VM-697
Friedrich Mihatsch (Gonzalez Organ)
12″—PAT-PAT73
[Jesus Christus, unser Heiland]
(in 3 Centuries of Organ Music set)
Gustave Bret (Fréjus Cathedral Organ)
12″—G-DB4949
[Das alte Jahr & Lasso: Benedictus,
Dijon Cathedral Choir)
Liebster Jesu, wir sind hier
(Peters Vol. V, No. 36)
Friedrich Mihatsch on PAT-PAT73
Liebster Jesu, wir sind hier
(Augener Vol. VIII, p. 1101)
Friedrich Mihatsch on PAT-PAT73
Liebster Jesu, wir sind hier
(Peters Vol. V, Anh. No. 5)
Albert Schweitzer, in Bach Organ
Society, Vol. II: CM-310

—Arr. Piano Cohen
Harriet Cohen   10″—C-LB21
[Cantata No. 22, No. 5, Ertödt uns]
Lob sei dem allmächtigen Gott O.B. 4
(Peters Vol. V, No. 38)
E. Power Biggs, on V-17335 in VM-697
Lobt Gott, ihr Christen, allzugleich O.B. 11
(Peters Vol. V, No. 40)
E. Power Biggs, on V-17459 in VM-711
Meine Seele erhebt den Herren Sch. 4
(Peters Vol. VII, No. 42)
Carl Weinrich, in MC-22
Mit Fried und Freud' ich fahr dahin O.B.
18 (Peters Vol. V, No. 41)
E. Power Biggs, on V-15888 in VM-652
Albert Schweitzer, in Bach Organ Society,
Vol. II: CM-310†
Nun freut euch, lieben Christen g'mein
(Peters Vol. VII, No. 44)
E. Power Biggs, on V-15729 in VM-616
André Marchal (Gonzalez Organ)
12″—PAT-PAT72
[Toccata, Adagio & Fugue, C major,
Pt. 3]
(in 3 Centuries of Organ Music album)
—Arr. Piano Busoni
Egon Petri, C-71463D
Nun komm', der Heiden Heiland O.B. 1
(Peters Vol. V, No. 42)
E. Power Biggs, on V-17335 in VM-697
Nun komm', der Heiden Heiland "18" No. 9
(Peters Vol. VII, No. 45)
E. Power Biggs, on V-15729 in VM-616
—Arr. Orchestra Stokowski
Philadelphia Orch.—Stokowski
in VM-243†)   12″—V-8494
[Sonata for unacc. violin No. 4-Chaconne,
Pt. 5]
[Komm, süsser Tod on G-DB2274]
—Arr. Orchestra Klemperer
Pro Musica Orch.—Klemperer, in
VOX-618
[With Brandenburg Concerto No. 1]
O Lamm Gottes unschuldig O.B. 20
(Peters Vol. V, No. 44)
E. Power Biggs, on V-15888 in VM-652
O Lamm Gottes unschuldig "18" No. 6
(Peters Vol. VII, No. 48)
Albert Schweitzer, in Bach Organ
Society, Vol. II: CM-310†
O Mensch, bewein dein' Sünde gross O.B. 24
(Peters Vol. V, No. 45)
E. Power Biggs, on V-15889 in VM-652
Albert Schweitzer, in Bach Organ Society,
Vol. II: CM-310†
—Arr. String Orch.—Reger
String Orch.—Edvard Fendler
12″—G-L999
—Arr. 'Cello & Piano Fournier
Pierre Fournier & Gerald Moore
12″—G-DB6372
[Das alte Jahr & Wenn wir in höchsten
Nöten sein]
Puer natus in Bethlehem O.B. 5
(Peters Vol. V, No. 46)
E. Power Biggs, on V-17458 in VM-711
Schmücke dich, o liebe Seele "18" No. 4
(Peters Vol. VII, No. 49)
Albert Schweitzer, in Bach Organ Society,
Vol. II: CM-310

Der Tag, der ist so freudenreich O.B. 7
(Peters Vol. V, No. 11)
E. Power Biggs, on V-17458 in VM-711
Valet will ich dir geben
(Peters Vol. VII, No. 50)
Carl Weinrich, in MC-22
Vater unser im Himmelreich O.B.37
(Peters Vol. V, No. 48)
E. Power Biggs, on V-17333 in VM-697
Vater unser im Himmel'reich C.U.
(Peters Vol. V, No. 47)
Fritz Heitmann (Charlottenburg Palace
Organ)   12"—T-E2712
[Christ unser Herr & Aus tiefer Not]
Vom Himmel hoch da komm' ich her O.B. 8
(Peters Vol. V, No. 49)
E. Power Biggs, on V-17458 in VM-711
Vom Himmel Kam der Engel Schar O.B. 9
(Peters Vol. V, No. 50)
E. Power Biggs, on V-17458 in VM-711
Wachet auf, ruft uns die Stimme Sch. 1
(Peters Vol. VII, No. 57)
Carl Weinrich, in MC-22
E. Power Biggs, on V-15729 in VM-616
(Also in TC-T1)
Gustave Bret (Fréjus Cathedral Organ)
                          10"—G-DA4802
[Wenn wir in höchsten Nöten]
Edouard Commette (Lyons Cathedral
Organ)   12"—C-DFX239
[Fugue, B minor]
[Prelude, E minor on C-D11079]
—Arr. Piano Busoni
Egon Petri, C-71463D
—Arr. Piano Kempff
Wilhelm Kempff (PD-516696)
                          12"—PD-67086
[Beethoven: Piano Concerto No. 5, Pt. 9]
Wenn wir in höchsten Nöten sein O.B. 42
(Peters Vol. V, No. 51)
E. Power Biggs, on V-17334 in VM-697
Gustave Bret (Fréjus Cathedral Organ)
                          10"—G-DA4802
[Wachet auf]
—Arr. 'Cello & Piano Fournier
Pierre Fournier & Gerald Moore
                          12"—G-DB6372
[Das alte Jahr & O Mensch bewein' dein
Sünde gross]
Wenn wir in höchsten Nöten sein "18",
No. 18 (Peters Vol. VII, No. 58)
E. Power Biggs, on V-18229 in VM-883
Wer nur den lieben Gott lässt walten O.B.
43 (Peters Vol. V, No. 53)
E. Power Biggs, on V-17334 in VM-697
Wer nur den lieben Gott lässt walten Sch. 3
(Peters Vol. VII, No. 59)
Carl Weinrich, in MC-22
Wir Christenleut' O.B. 14 (Peters Vol. V,
No. 55)
E. Power Biggs, on V-17459 in VM-711
Wir danken dir, Herr Jesu Christ O.B. 25
(Peters Vol. V, No. 56)
E. Power Biggs, on V-15890 in VM-652
Wir glauben all' an einen Gott, Schöpfer.
C.U. (Peters Vol. VII, No. 60) ("Giant
Fugue")
Fritz Heitmann (Charlottenburg Palace
Organ)   12"—T-E2711

[Dies sind die Heiligen]
Noëlie Pierront   10"—LUM—30084
[Sonata No. 1, E flat, Pt. 3]
—Arr. Orchestra Stokowski
Philadelphia Orch.—Stokowski
(G-W1063)   (G-AW102)
                    (in VM-59 12"—V-7089
—Arr. Boessenroth
Minneapolis Symphony Orch.—
Mitropoulos
                    (in CX-244) 12"—C-11994D
[Fantasia & Fugue, G minor]
Wo soll ich fliehen hin Sch. 2
(Peters Vol. VII, No. 63)
Carl Weinrich, in MC-22

CHORALE VARIATIONS Organ

Sei gegrüsst, Jesu gütig
(Peters Vol. V, Section II, No. 3)
—Variation XI only
Albert Schweitzer, in Bach Organ
Society, Vol. II: CM-310†

Chromatic Fantasia & Fugue, D minor
(Peters Vol. IV, No. 1) Clavier
Ralph Kirkpatrick (harpsichord), in
MC-25
Wanda Landowska (harpsichord)
                    2 12"—G-DB4993/4
[Präludium 1, 2 & 3]
Paul Baumgartner (piano)
                    2 12"—G-DB10100/1
Marcelle Meyer (pf), in DF-A22
Edwin Fischer (pf)
                    2 12"—G-DB4403/4

CLAVIERUEBUNG

See Partitas, Italian Concerto, Ouverture à
la Manière Française, Prelude & Fugue
E flat major, Chorale Preludes, 4 Duets,
Goldberg Variations.

CONCERTOS FOR CHAMBER ORCHESTRA

I. (6) BRANDENBURG CONCERTOS
1. F major 2. F major 3. G major
4. G major 5. D major   6. B flat major
Busch Chamber Players—Busch
(C-LX436/49) (C-GQX10790/803)
CLFX434/6; 439/40; 480/8)
           14 12"—CM-249† & CM-250†
Side 6, left blank in the American set, is
occupied by the Siciliano—Largo (from
Vl. Sonata No. 4, C minor) played by
Busch and Serkin, in the British set
(C-LX438).
Soloists: Adolf Busch (vl), E. Rothwell
(ob), Aubrey Brain (horn), F. Bradley
(horn), G. Eskdale (trum), Marcel Moyse
(fl), L. Moyse (fl), Rudolf Serkin (pf)
Individual Brandenburg Concertos
—No. 1, F major (violin, 3 oboes, bassoon,
2 horns, strings)
Busch Chamber Players—Busch
   (in CM-249†) 3 12"—C-68434/6DS
(Side 6 blank)
[Vl. Sonata, No. 4—Siciliano, on
C-LX436/8; C-LFX434/6]
Ecole Normale Orch.—Alfred Cortot
                    2 12"—G-DB2033/4

Berlin Philharmonic Orch.—Alois
Melichar 3 12″—PD-27313/5
[Prelude, E minor, Alfred Sittard, organ]
Pro Musica Orch.—Klemperer
3 12″—VOX-618
[Nun komm, der Heiden Heiland]
Boyd Neel Orch.—Neel
3 12″—D-K1541/3
[Herr Christ, der ein'ge Gottes Sohn]
—No. 2, F major (flute, violin, oboe, trumpet, strings)
Busch Chambers Players—Busch
(in CM-249†) 2 12″—C-68437/8D
(C-LX439/40) (C-LFX439/40)
Ecole Normale Orch.—Alfred Cortot
2 12″—G-DB2035/6
Chamber Orch.—F. Oubradous
2 12″—O-123868/9
[Suite No. 1—Minuet & Bourrée]
Boston Symphony Orch.—Koussevitzky
(in VM-1118†) 2 12″—V-11-9538/9
[No. 5, Pt. 1]
Pro Musica Orch.—Klemperer
2 12″—VOX-619
Boyd Neel Orch.—Neel
(D-K1550/1) 2 12″—D-ED27
Soloists: Arthur Cleghorn (fl), Evelyn
Rothwell (ob), George Eskdale (trump),
Frederick Grinke (vl)
Berlin Philharmonic Orch.—Melichar
2 12″—PD-27293/4
Soloists: S. Goldberg (vl), P. Spörri (tr),
A. Harzer (fl), G. Kern (ob)
Edwin Fischer Chamber Orch.
2 12″—G-DB7612/3
Philadelphia Orch.—Stokowski
(in VM-59) 3 12″—V-7087/90
[Wir glauben all'] (G-AW101/3)
—No. 3, G major (strings)
Busch Chambers Players—Busch
(in CM-249†) 12″—C-68439D
(C-LX443) (C-LFX480)
Ecole Normale Orch.—Alfred Cortot
2 10″—G-DA1259/60
Berlin Philharmonic Orch.—Furtwängler
2 12″—PD-95417/8
[Schubert: Rosamunde—Entr'acte]
Boston Symphony Orch.—Koussevitzky
(in VM-1050†) 2 12″—V-11-9156/7
[Partita No. 3 for unacc. violin—
Prelude, arr. Pick-Mangiagalli]
[Sinfonia from Cantata No. 4 used as a
slow movement] (with Concerto No. 4)
Boyd Neel String Orch.—Neel
12″—D-K1619
Pro Musica Orch.—Klemperer
[Bist du bei mir] 2 12″—VOX-620
British Symphony Orch.—Wood
12″—C-LX173
—No. 4, G major (violin, 2 flutes, strings)
Busch Chamber Players—Busch
(in CM-249†) 3 12″—C-68440/1D
(C-LX441/2) (C-LFX481/2)
Ecole Normale Orch.—Alfred Cortot
2 12″—G-DB2037/8
Soloists: Bouillon (vl), Cortet &
Morseau (fl)
Berlin Philharmonic Orch.—Melichar
3 12″—PD-27307/9

Soloists: Goldberg (vl), Harzer &
Breiden (fl),
[Reger: Concerto in Olden Style—
Allegro]
Boston Symphony Orch.—Koussevitzky
(in VM-1050†) 2 12″—V-11-9158/9
Soloists: Burgin (vl), Laurent & Madsen
(fl)
[with Concerto No. 3]
Hamburg Philharmonic Chamber Orch.—
Schmidt-Isserstedt 2 12″—T-E2956/7
Soloists: Prick (vl), Brinckmann &
Knobber (fl)
Curtis String Ensemble
3 12″—Hargail-MW105
Soloists: Marian Head (vl), Alfred Mann
& Anton Winkler (recorders)
[Telemann: Bourrée, Edith Weiss-Mann,
harpsichord]
Pro Musica Orch.—Klemperer
2 12″—VOX-621
—No. 5, D major (clavier, flute, violin,
strings)
Busch Chamber Players—Busch
(in CM-250) 3 12″—C-68442/4D
Soloists: Adolf Busch (vl), Marcel
Moyse (fl), Rudolf Serkin (pf.)
(C-LX444/6) (C-LFX483/5)
Ecole Normale Orch.—Alfred Cortot
(G-DB1783/4) 2 12″—V-7863/4
Soloists: Thibaud (vl), Cortet (fl) &
Cortot (pf.)
Berlin Philharmonic Orch.—Melichar
4 12″—PD-15073/6
Soloists: Rupp (harpsichord), Börries
(vl), Thomas (fl)
[Bach-Vivaldi: Concerto, D minor—
Allegro, Sittard, organ]
EIAR String Orch.—Previtali
(O-7884/6) 3 12″—CET-CB20159/61
Soloists: Carlo Zecchi (pf), G. de Vito
(vl) & A. Tassinari (fl) (O-50003/5)
Boston Symphony Orch.—Koussevitzky
(in VM-1118) 3 12″—V-11-9539/41
Soloists: Lukas Foss (pf), Richard
Burgin (vl), Georges Laurent (fl)
[No. 2, F major, Pt. 3]
Pro Musica Orch.—Klemperer
3 12″—VOX-622
—No. 6, B flat major (violas, violas da
gamba, cello, bass)
Busch Chamber Players—Busch
(in CM-250†) 3 12″—C-68445/7D
(C-LX447/9) (C-LFX486/8)
Ecole Normale Orch.—Cortot
2 12″—G-DB1626/7
Berlin Philharmonic Orch.—Melichar
2 12″—PD-15066/7
Pro Musica Orch.—Klemperer
3 12″—VOX-623

II CLAVIER CONCERTOS
IIa. Solo Clavier & Orchestra
1. D minor
Edwin Fischer (pf) & his Chamber
Orchestra (G-DB4420/2)
3 12″—VM-252†
Eugene Istomin (pf) & Busch Chamber
Players—Busch 3 12″—CM-624†
Harriet Cohen (pf) & Philharmonia

Orch.—Süsskind   3   12″—C-DX1312/4
Marguerite Roesgen-Champion (pf) &
Lamoureux Orch.—Bigot
       3   12″—G-W1581/3
Alexander Borovsky (pf) & Lamoureux
Orch.—Eugène Bigot (PD-566201/2)
(Arr. Busoni)   2 12″—VOX-162
—Arr. Violin
Joseph Szigeti (vl) & New Friends of
Music Orch.—Fritz Stiedry
       3   12″—CM-418†
4. A major
Edwin Fischer (pf) & his Chamber Orch.
       2   12″—G-DB3081/2
Marguerite Roesgen-Champion (pf) &
l'Orchestre des Concerts—Marius
François Gaillard   2 12″—G-DB5150/1
[English Suite No. 1—Sarabande &
Bourrées]
5. F minor
Edwin Fischer (pf) & his Chamber
Orch.   2   12″—VM-786†
[Mozart: Contretanz-Das Donnerwetter,
K. 534]
(G-DB4679/80)
Alexander Borovsky (pf) & Lamoureux
Orch.—Bigot   12″—PD-566203
(Arr. Busoni)
—1st Mvt. only (labeled Allegro, F minor)
Yvonne Arnaud (pf) & String Orch.—
Barbirolli   12″—G-C2456
[Raff: La fileuse]
—2nd Mvt. only
Alfred Cortot (arr. Cortot)
       12″—G-DB3262
[Bach-Vivaldi: Concerto, D minor]
—Arr. Orch. Stokowski (labeled Arioso)
All American Orch.—Stokowski
     (in CM-541†)   12″—C-11976D
7. G minor (Same as Violin Concerto No. 1, A minor)
Anna Linde (harpsichord) & String
Orch.   2   12″—P-DPX2/3
Marguerite Roesgen-Champion (pf) &
Lamoureux Orch.—Wolff
       2   12″—G-W1521/2
[J. C. Bach: Concerto in E flat, Op. 7,
No. 5—Allegro]
IIb. 2 Claviers & Orchestra
1. C minor
Scheck-Wenzinger Chamber Orch.
(G-HEX2/3)   2   12″—G-EH1296/7
—Arr. 2 Violins & Orchestra
Dominique Blot & Sonia Lovis with Ars
Rediviva Ensemble—Claude Crussard
       2   12″—BAM-38/9
—Arr. Violin, Oboe & Orchestra
Else Marie Brunn & Waldemar Wolsing
with Chamber Orch. of Palace Chapel,
Copenhagen—Wöldike
       2   12″—G-DB5286/7
Manuel Compinsky & G. Schonberg with
Orch. (Transposed to D minor)
       2   12″—ALCO-AC202
2. C major
Ruggero Gerlin, Marcelle Charbonnier
(harpsichords) with String Orch.—
Curt Sachs
     (in Vol. IV)   2   12″—AS-41/2

Artur & Karl Ulrich Schnabel (pfs)
with London Symphony Orch.—Boult
(G-DB3041/3)   3   12″—VM-357†
3. C minor (Same as Concerto for 2 Violins, D minor)
No recording available
IIc. 3 Claviers & Orchestra
2. C major
Anonymous soloists with Orch.—Ducasse
       2   12″—O-7508/9
IId. 4 Claviers & Orchestra, A minor
(Original—Vivaldi concerto for four vio-
lins and orchestra, B minor, Op. 3, No.
10)
H. Pignari, Leroux, Rolet, Piero Coppola
& Orch.—Bret (G-S10447/8)
       2   12″—G-L963/4
[Cantata No. 106—Sinfonia] G-S10447/8

III VIOLIN CONCERTOS
IIIa. Solo Violin & Orchestra
1. A minor (same as Clavier Concerto No. 7, G minor)
Max Strub & Collegium Musicum—
Fritz Stein   2   12″—G-DB5527/8
Yehudi Menuhin & Paris Symphony Orch.
—Enesco   2   12″—G-DB2911/2
Yvonne Astruc & Orch.—Gustave Bret
       2   12″—PD-516636/7
Bronislaw Hubermann & Vienna
Philharmonic Orch.—Dobrowen
       2   12″—C-GQX10737/8
Roman Totenberg & Musicraft Chamber
Orch.   2 12″—MC-78
—Andante only
J. Pasquier & Orch.—Cébron
       10″—LUM-30088
2. E major (Same as Clavier Concerto No. 3, D major)
Yehudi Menuhin & Orch.—Enesco
       3 12″—G-DB2003/5
[Sonata for unaccompanied violin No. 2
—Sarabande]
Adolf Busch & Busch Chamber Players
       3   12″—CM-530†
[Corelli-Busch: Sonata, F major—
Preludio]
Louis Kaufman & Santa Monica
Symphony—Rachmilovich (in
preparation)   **DISC**
Bronislaw Huberman & Vienna
Philharmonic—Dobrowen
       3   12″—C-LFX411/3
[Sonata No. 3—Andante]
—1st Mvt. only
Y. Bratza & Orch.—Scott
       10″—C-DB504
(in Columbia History of Music Vol. II: in
CM-232)
—2nd Mvt. only
George Kulenkampff & Berlin Philhar-
monic Orch.—Kletzki   12″—T-F1193
D minor (Arrangement of Concerto for Clavier & Orchestra, D minor)
Joseph Szigeti & New Friends of Music
Orch.—Stiedry   3 12″—CM-418†
IIIb. Two Violins & Orchestra
D minor (same as Concerto for two claviers and Orchestra, C minor, No. 3)

Else Marie Bruun & Julius Koppel with
Chamber Orch. of the Palace Chapel,
Copenhagen—Wöldike
2 12"—G-DB5289/90
Yehudi Menuhin, Georges Enesco &
Paris Symphony—Monteux
(G-DB1718/9) 2 12"—VM-932†
Herman Diener, Charlotte Hampe &
Collegium Musicum
2 12"—G-EH1217/8
Arthur Grumiaux & Jean Pougnet &
Philharmonia String Orch.—Süsskind
(Boris Ord, harpsichord)
2 12"—C-DX1276/7
Adolf Busch & Frances Magnes with
Busch Chamber Players
2 12"—CX-253†
Joseph Szigeti, Carl Flesch & Orch.—
Goehr 2 12"—CX-90†
(C-LX659/60) (C-GQX10887/8)
Jascha Heifetz (playing both solo parts)
with Victor Chamber Orch.—Waxman
2 12"—VM-1136†
C minor (Same as Concerto No. 1 for 2
Claviers & Orch. in C minor & Concerto
for Violin, Oboe & Orch.)
Dominique Blot & Sonia Lovis (vls)
with Ars Rediviva Ensemble—
Crussard 2 12"—BAM-38/9

IV. MISCELLANEOUS CONCERTOS

Concerto for Violin, Oboe & Orch.
C minor (Same as Concerto No. 1, C minor
for 2 Claviers and also 2 Violins)
Else Marie Bruun (vl), Waldemar
Wolsing (ob.) & Chamber Orch. of
Palace Chapel, Copenhagen—Mogens
Wöldike 2 12"—G-DB5286/7
—Transposed to D minor
Manuel Compinsky (vl), Gordon
Schonberg (ob) & Pacific Sinfonietta—
William van den Berg
2 12"—ALCO-AC202

CONCERTOS FOR SOLO HARPSICHORD

a. Italian Concerto, F major
Wanda Landowska (harpsichord)
2 12"—G-DB5007/8
[2 Preludes, C major; Prelude &
Fugue, C minor]
Pauline Girard (harpsichord)
2 12"—C-LFX718/9
Sylvia Marlowe (harpsichord) in D-DAU4
Artur Schnabel (pf) (G-DB3732/3)
2 12"—VM-806
Walter Gieseking (pf)
2 10"—C-LW33/4
Marcelle Meyer (pf) in DF-A13
—Arr. Orchestra
Berlin Philharmonic Orch.—Schmidt-
Isserstedt 2 12"—T-E2079/80
[Gluck-Gevaert: Armide-Gavotte;
Iphigénie en Aulide-Tambourin]
—1st Mvt. only
Wilhelm Kempff (pf) 10"—PD-90188
[Flute Sonata No. 2: Siciliano, arr.
Kempff]
b. Concertos after Vivaldi
No. 1, D major
Wanda Landowska (harpsichord) on

V-12-0001 in VM-1181
Ruggero Gerlin (harpsichord)
(in Vol. III) 12"—AS-38
Sylvia Marlowe (harpsichord) in D-DAU4
No. 3, D minor (after Marcello: Oboe Con-
certo, C minor)
Ruggero Gerlin (harpsichord)
12"—MIA-9
—2nd Mvt. (Adagio) only
Edwin Fischer (pf) 10"—G-DA1339
[Mozart: Minuet, K. 1]
Nino Rossi (pf) 12"—G-DB5353
[Das Wohltemperierte Clavier—Prelude
& Fugue No. 10]
No 8, B minor (original composer un-
known)
Ruggero Gerlin (harpsichord)
12"—LUM-35018
No. 14, G minor (after Telemann: Violin
Concerto)
Ruggero Gerlin (harpsichord)
12"—C-BQX2534
No. 15, G major
Ruggero Gerlin (harpsichord)
12"—C-BQX2533
[Partita No. 3, A minor, Pt. 3]

CONCERTOS FOR ORGAN

A minor
(After Vivaldi Concerto Grosso, Op. 3,
No. 8) (Peters Vol. VIII, No. 2)
E. Power Biggs, in TC-T1
D minor (Peters 3002)
(After Vivaldi Concerto Grosso, D minor,
Op. 3, No. 11)
Alfred Cortot (pf)
2 12"—G-DB3261/2
[Concerto No. 5, F minor-Largo]
Alexander Brailowsky (pf)
2 12"—G-DB3703/4
—Finale only
Alfred Sittard (St. Michael organ)
12"—PD-66553
["Cathedral" Prelude, E minor]
[Brandenburg Concerto No. 5, Pt. 1 on
PD-15073]
Duets Keyboard (Clavierübung III)
No. 2, F major
Fritz Heitmann (Charlottenburg Palace
Organ) 12"—T-E2713
[Jesu Christus]
E minor; F major; G major; A minor
—Arr. Violin & Viola
Frederick Grinke & Watson Forbes
12"—D-K1072

English Suites See under Suites I a

FANTASIAS Clavier
See also Fantasias & Fugues
C minor (Peters Vol. IX, No. 7)
Wanda Landowska (harpsichord)
10"—G-DA1129
[English Suite No. 5—Passepied only]
Kathleen Long (pf) 12"—D-K1066
[Cantata 208 No. 9—Sheep may safely
graze]
Marcelle Meyer (pf) in DF-A13
José Iturbi (pf) 12"—V-18126
[Beethoven: Concerto No. 3, Pt. 9]
(in VM-801†)

C minor (Peters Vol. 1X, No. 10)
Wanda Landowska (harpsichord)
in VM-1181†
G minor (Peters Vol. XIII, No. 5)
Yella Pessl (harpsichord)
(in CX-70†) 12"—C-68746D
[Fugue, C major; Toccata in D, Pt. 3]
A minor (Peters Vol. XIII, No. 1)
Edwin Fischer (pf) 12"—G-DB3287

FANTASIAS Organ
C major B.G. Vol. 38
—Arr. Orchestra L. Bedell
Boston "Pops" Orch.—Fiedler
12"—V-13809
[Sonata No. 3 for Unacc. Violin—
Adagio]

FANTASIAS & FUGUES Clavier
D minor (see Chromatic Fantasia & Fugue)
A minor (Peters Vol. IV, No. 6)
Marcelle Meyer (pf), in DF-A17

FANTASIAS & FUGUES Organ
(See also under Toccatas)
C minor (Peters Vol. III, No. 6)
Edouard Commette (St. Jean de Lyon
organ) 12"—C-70087D
—Arr. Orchestra
Wiesbadener Collegium Musicum—E.
Weyns (Arr. Schmell) 12"—T-E3064
London Symphony Orch.—Coates
(Arr. Elgar)
12"—G-AW51
—Fantasia only
Edouard Commette 12"—C-DFX222
[Fugue, G minor, Book 4, No. 5]
[Prelude & Fugue, G major, Book 8 on
C-DFX94]
D major, see Toccata in D
G minor ("Great" G minor)
(Peters Vol II, No. 4)
Albert Schweitzer, in Bach Organ
Society, Vol. I: CM-270†
G. D. Cunningham (St. Margaret organ
Westminster) 12"—G-C1812
—Arr. Orchestra Mitropoulos
Minneapolis Symphony Orch.—
Mitropoulos 2 12"—CX-244†
[Wir glauben all' an einen Gott]
—Arr. Piano Liszt
Alexander Borovsky (PD-67074)
12"—PD-516617
—Fantasia only
Edouard Commette (St. Jean de Lyon
organ) 10"—C-DF2638
(Earlier version on C-D11027—12")
—Fugue only
Marcel Dupré (Saint-Sulpice organ)
12"—LUM-32024
Edouard Commette (Lyon Cathedral
organ) 10"—C-D19199
—Fugue only Arr. Orch. Stokowski
Philadelphia Orch.—Stokowski
10"—V-1728
French Suites, See under Suites 1b

FUGUES Clavier
C major (Peters Vol. IX, No. 8)

Yella Pessl (harpsichord)
(in CX-70†) 12"—C-68746D
[Fantasia, G minor & Toccata in D
major, Pt. 3]
C minor (Peters Vol. VII, No. 2]
Wanda Landowska (harpsichord)
12"—G-DB5008
[1st 3 of 12 Little Preludes & Italian
Concerto, Pt. 3]
A minor (Peters Vol. IX, No. 15)
Ernst Victor Wolff (harpsichord)
(in CM-357†) 12"—C-69465D
[Ouverture à la manière Française, Pt. 7]
Marcelle Meyer (pf), in DF-A17
Julia Menz (harpsichord)
[Prelude, G major] 10"—PD-62822
—Arr. Orchestra Boyd Neel String Orch.,
D-X247

FUGUES Organ
C major ("Fanfare") (B.G. Vol. 38, Anh. II)
E. Power Biggs
(in VM-1048†) 12"—V-11-9146
[Cantata 208, No. 9—Sheep may safely
graze]
G major ("à la gigue") (Peters Anhang I,
Series 5, No. 5)
Virgil Fox (organ)
(in VM-1177†) 12"—V-11-9970
—Arr. Orch. Cailliet
Boston "Pops" Orch.—Fiedler
10"—V-10-1070
[Arcadelt: Ave Maria]
G minor ("Little") (Peters Vol. IV. No. 7)
Albert Schweitzer, in Bach Organ
Society, Vol. I: CM-270†
Edouard Commette (Lyons Cathedral
Organ) 12"—C-DFX222
[Fantasia, C minor, Book 3, No. 6]
[Alain: Cantate Domino, Lyons Cathedral
choir on C-D11028]
E. Power Biggs, on V-11-9145 in
VM-1048†
H. Vollenweider 12"—G-FKX69
[Handel: Organ Concerto No. 10—
Allegro]
—Arr. Orchestra Stokowski
Philadelphia Orch.—Stokowski
(G-DB1952) 12"—V-7437
[Christ lag in Todesbanden]
All-American Youth Orch.—Stokowski
(in CM-451†) 12"—C-11547D
[Beethoven: Symphony No. 5, Pt. 9]
[William Grant Still: Afro-American
Symphony—Scherzo on C-1192D]
Pittsburgh Symphony—Reiner (arr.
Cailliet), in CM-695†
(with Suite No. 2)
—Arr. Piano
Chailley-Richez 12"—PAT-PG68
[Das Wohltemperierte Clavier, Fugue No.
12]
A major (unidentified)
Hans Vollenweider (organ)
12"—G-HEX104
[Buxtehude: Toccata & Fugue, F major]

FUGUES Miscellaneous
Violin & Continuo
G minor (Peters Vol. VII, No. 3)
—**Arr. String Quartet & Piano** Crussard
 Ars Rediviva Ensemble 12"—**BAM-10**
 [Funk: Suite, G minor]
Gavotte for Lute See under Sonata No. 6
 for Unacc. Violin—Gavotte

GOLDBERG VARIATIONS Clavierübung IV
Wanda Landowska (harpsichord)
 6 12"—**VM-1022**†
(recorded in N. Y., June 1945)
(Also earlier recording for H. M. V.
Goldberg Variations Society)

INVENTIONS 2-Pt & 3-Pt Clavier
Complete
Alexander Borovsky (pf)
(PD-62807/10 & 12/3)
 6 10"—**PD-561128/33**
—**2-Pt. only**
Erno Balogh (pf)
 4 10"—**ASCH-DM102**
[6 Little Preludes—No. 5, E major]
—**3-Pt. only**
Erno Balogh (pf) 3 12"—**DISC-770**
Italian Concerto, See Concertos, Solo, I a
Jesu, Joy of Man's Desiring See under
 Cantata No. 147
Komm, süsser Tod See under songs

DIE KUNST DER FUGE
—**Arr. Orch.** Diener
 Collegium Musicum—Hermann Diener
 10 12"—**G-EH1007/16**
—**Arr. String Quartet** Roy Harris & M.
 D. Herter Norton
 Roth Quartet (19 sides)
 10 12"—**CM-206**†
 (Society release in England)
—**Arr. Organ** (based on Graeser Edition)
 E. Power Biggs Vol. I 4 12"—**VM-832**†
 Vol. II 6 12"—**VM-833**†
 [Chorale Prelude—Wenn wir in höchsten
 Nöten sein]
Contrapuncti 1-8, Arr. Orchestra Roger
 Vuataz
 Beromünster Drch.— H. Scherchen
 4 12"—in preparation Swiss Decca

Magnificat, D major
Complete recording
 Victor Chorale & Orch.—Robert Shaw
 5 10"—**VM-1182**†
 Soloists: Suzanne Freil (s), Blanche
 Thebom (ms), Ernice Lawrence (t),
 Paul Matthen (bs)
—**No. 2, Et Exultavit**
 Carol Brice & Columbia Concert Orch.—
 D. Saidenberg, in CX-283†
—**Nos. 3 (Quia respexit), 4 (Omnes
 generationes), 7 (Fecit potentiam), & 12
 (Gloria) only**
 Terront (s), Bach Society Cho., with
 orch.—Gustave Bret 2 12"—**G-W882/3**
—**No. 9, Esurientes implevit bonis**
 Lina Falk (c), Crunelle & Manouvrier
 (fl), & Ruggero Gerlin (harpsichord)
 12"—**LUM-32051**

[Mass, B minor—No. 23: Agnus Dei]
Carol Brice & Columbia Concert Orch.—
Saidenberg, in CX-283†

MARCHES (from Anna Magdalena Bach
Notebook)
D major (Peters Anhang I, No. 11)
Edwin Bodky (clavichord)
 (in Vol. II) 12"—**AS-24**
[Miscellaneous clavier pieces & K. P. E.
Bach: Abschied]
—**Arr. Orch.** MacDowell
Victor Orchestra, V-24793

MASSES
A major
—**No. 2, Qui tollis** Orig. for Sop.
Yves Tinayre (b), Blanquart & Morseau
(fl), with String Orch.—A. Cellier
 12"—**LUM-32044**
B minor
Complete recordings
Elisabeth Schumann (s), Margaret Bal-
four (c), Walter Widdop (t), Friedrich
Schorr (bs), Royal Choral Society, Lon-
don Symphony Orch.—Albert Coates
 17 12"—**VM-104**†
(G-C1710/28 in GM-87†)
Anne McKnight & June Gardner (s),
Lydia Summers (c), Lucius Metz (t),
Paul Matthen (bs), Victor Chorale &
Orch.—Robert Shaw
 17 12"—**VM-1145/6**†
Individual Excerpts
—**5. Laudamus te** Sop., vl. solo & Orch.
Dorothy Maynor, Joseph Fuchs & Victor
Orch.—Levin
 (in VM-1043) 12"—**V-11-9108**
[Cantata No. 120—No. 7, Gloria sei dir
gesungen—Let every tongue]
—**9, Qui Sedes** Contralto
Carol Brice & Columbia Orch.—
Saidenberg, in CX-283†
—**22. Benedictus** Tenor
Georges Thill & Orch.—Bigot
 10"—**C-LF151**
—**23. Agnus Dei** Contralto
Lina Falk (c) & String Orch. & Harpsi-
chord—Gerlin **LUM-32051**
[Magnificat in D minor—No. 9,
Esurientes]
Carol Brice & Columbia Concert Orch.—
Saidenberg, in CX-283†
Matthäus-Passion—See under Passions

MINUETS
F minor (B.G. Vol. 36, p. 210)
Erwin Bodky (clavichord)
 (in Vol. III) 12"—**AS-24**
[Miscellaneous pieces & K. P. E. Bach:
Abschied]
G major (Peters Anhang I. No. 2)
Erwin Bodky (clavichord)
 (in Vol. III) 12"—**AS-24**
[Miscellaneous pieces & K. P. E. Bach:
Abschied]
—**Arr. Vl. & Pf.** Winternitz (combined with
 G minor, No. 3)
Fritz Kreisler (vl) & Carl Lamson (pf)
[Beethoven: Gavotte] 10"—**V-1136**

G minor (Peters Anhang I, No. 3)
See above: Kreisler, combined with G
major Minuet
(3) Minuets: G major, minor, major
(Peters Vol XIII, No. 11)
Suzanne Gyr (pf)   12"—G-DB10070
[Toccata in D major, Pt. 3]
Erno Balogh (pf), in DISC-771
(with 12 Little Preludes)

MOTETS B.G. Vol. 39 (1)
1. Singet dem Herrn (Peters No. 6)
Die Kantorei der Staatlichen Hochschule
für Musik, Berlin—Kurt Thomas
2 12"—T-E2958/9
Cercle J. S. Bach de Genève—Francis
Bodet (in French)
2 12"—LUM-32046/7
Vocal Ensemble—M. Couraud
DF (in preparation)
—No. 3, Alles was Odem hat Final Fugue
Chorus
St. Thomas Church Choir—K. Straube
[Dir, Dir Jehovah]   12"—PD-66708
2. Der Geist hilft uns'rer Schwachheit auf
(Peters No. 2)
—No. 2 Der aber die Herzen forschet
Staats-und-Domchor, conducted by
Rüdel   10"—P-R1025
[Schütz: Psalm III]
(in 2000 Years of Music)
St. Thomas' Church Choir—K. Straube
12"—PD-66706
[No. 3—Du heilige Brunst]
—No. 3, Du heilige Brunst
St. Thomas' Church Choir—Straube
12"—PD-66706
[No. 2—Der aber die Herzen forschet]
3. Jesu, meine Freude (Peters No. 1)
Vocal Ensemble—M. Couraud
DF (in preparation)
5. Komm, Jesu, komm (Peters No. 4)
Cercle J. S. Bach de Genève—Bodet
(in Fr.)   2 12"—LUM-32048/9
—No. 2 Baldrufst du mich
St. Thomas Choir, Leipzig—Ramin
10"—PD-47574
[Kommt Seelen, dieser Tag; Hassler: All
mein Gedenken]

DAS MUSIKALISCHE OPFER
Complete—Edited Hans T. David
Chamber Ensemble—Pessl
6 12"—G-DB10014/9
Complete—Arr. Orch. Oubradous
L'Oiseau Lyre Orch.—Oubradous
(11 sides)   6 12"—OL-130/5
—Fuga—Ricercare a 6 voci
—Arr. String Orch.—Fischer
Edwin Fischer Orch.   12"—V-8660
(G-DB4419)
—Arr. Orch.—Schmell
Wiesbaden Collegium Musicum—
Weyns   12"—T-E2996
—Arr. Orch.—Lenzewski
Boyd Neel String Orch.—Neel
12"—D-K903
—Canones diversi super thema regium
Canon perpetuus; Canon a 2 (Ascendente
modulatione ascendat Gloria Regis);

Canon a 2 (Per augmentationem con-
trario motu)
Wiesbaden Collegium Musicum—
Weyns   12"—T-E3082
—Canon perpetuus
A. Jaunet (fl), R. Baumgartner (vl),
with harpsichord & viola da gamba
10"—ELITE-4489
—Sonata (Trio) C minor
Danish Quartet (Flute, Violin, 'Cello &
Piano)   2 12"—G-DB5215/6
A. Jaunet (fl), R. Baumgartner (vl),
with harpsichord & viola da gamba
2 10"—ELITE-4487/8
—Arr. Violin, 'Cello & Piano Casella
Poltronieri, Bonucci, Casella
2 12"—G-DB2168/9

ORATORIOS
Oster-Oratorium "Kommt, eilet und laufet"
Eng. Easter Oratorio
—2. Adagio Oboe & Orchestra
Arr. W. G. Whittaker
Leon Goossens & Liverpool Philharmonic
—Sargent   12"—C-DX1138
[Cimarosa: Oboe Concerto, Pt. 3]

Weihnachts-Oratorium
Eng. Christmas Oratorio
—4. Bereite dich Zion   Contralto
Marian Anderson & Victor Orch.—
Robert Shaw
(in VM-1087)   12"—V-11-9379
[Cantata No. 112—No. 2, Zum reinen
Wasser]
Lina Falk (in French) with strings &
harpsichord—Cellier   12"—LUM-32028
[Cantata No. 53—Schlage doch]
Germaine Cernay (in French) & Orch.—
Bret   12"—C-RFX55
[Cantata No. 205—No. 7, Pomona's Air]
—10. Sinfonie   Orchestra
Eng. Shepherd's Christmas Music, or
Pastorale
Philadelphia Orch.—Stokowski
12"—V-7142
—Arr. Piano Lucas
Wilhelm Backhaus
(G-DB2406)   12"—V-8736
[Beethoven: Moonlight Sonata, Pt. 3]
—15. Frohe Hirten, eilt Tenor
Aksel Schiøtz w. Johan Bentzon (fl),
Mogens Wöldike (harpsichord) &
Alberto Medici (vcl)   12"—G-DB5240
[Buxtehude: Was mich auf dieser Welt
betrübt]
—Unidentified solo
Claire Chalandon (s), in French, with
Orch.—Tokayère   12"—G-DB5098
[Caccini: Amarilli]

ORCHESTRAL TRANSCRIPTIONS
Bach 250th Anniversary Album (Freely
transcribed for orchestra by Leopold
Stokowski)
Chaconne (Unacc. Violin Sonata No. 4)
Chorale-Prelude: Nun komm' der
Heiden Heiland
Adagio (from Toccata, Adagio & Fugue,
C major)
Siciliano (Clavier & Violin Sonata No. 4)
Song: Komm süsser Tod

Sarabande (English Suite No. 3)
Philadelphia Orch.—Stokowski
5 12″—VM-243†
(A) Program of Bach (Freely transcribed
for orchestra by Stokowski)
Organ Passacaglia & Fugue, C minor
Matthäus-Passion—Chorale: O Haupt
voll Blut und Wunden
Song: Mein Jesus, was für Seelenweh
Cantata No. 4—Jesus Christus Gottes
Sohn
Sarabande (Unacc. Violin Sonata No. 2)
Air (Orchestral Suite No. 3)
Philadelphia Orch.—Stokowski
1 10″ & 4 12″— VM-401†
Transcriptions for Orchestra—Stokowski
Trio Sonata, E flat—1st Mvt.
Chorale-Prelude: Ich ruf' zu dir, Herr
Jesu Christ
Prelude & Fugue, E minor (No. 3 from "8
Little Preludes & Fugues")
Johannes-Passion—Es ist vollbracht
Philadelphia Orch.—Stokowski
3 12″—VM-963
[Palestrina: Adoramus Te]
Bach-Stokowski Album No. 1 (Columbia)
Song: Komm süsser Tod
Air (Orchestral Suite No. 3)
All American Orch.—Stokowski
2 12″—CX-220†
Bach-Stokowski Album No. 2 (Columbia)
Arioso (Largo)—Clavier Concerto No. 5,
F minor) Prelude No. 8, E flat minor
(Wohltemperiertes Clavier Bk. 1) An-
dante sostenuto (Unacc. Violin Sonata
No. 3)
All American Orch.—Stokowski
3 12″—CM-541†

ORGAN COLLECTIONS

Bach Organ Society
Volume I—Fantasia & Fugue, G minor;
"Little" Fugue, G minor; Preludes &
Fugues in C major, F minor, G major;
Toccata & Fugue, D minor
Albert Schweitzer (All Hallows, Barking,
Organ) 7 12″—CM-270†
Volume II—(13) Chorale-Preludes
Albert Schweitzer (Ste. Aurélie, Stras-
bourg, Silbermann Organ)
7 12″—CM-310†
Volume III—Preludes & Fugues in C minor,
C major, E minor; Fugue, A minor
Albert Schweitzer (Ste. Aurélie, Stras-
bourg, Silbermann Organ)
7 12″—CM-320†
Organ Collection (from the 3rd Volume of
the Clavierübung)
Prelude, E flat major
Chorale-Preludes:
Kyrie, Gott Vater in Ewigkeit
(greater version)
Allein Gott in der Höh' sei Ehr
(first version)
Dies sind die heil'gen zehn Gebot'
(greater)
Wir glauben all' an einen Gott (greater)
Vater unser in Himmelreich
(lesser version)

Christ, unser Herr, zum Jordan kam
(lesser)
Aus tiefer Not schrei ich zu dir (greater)
Jesus Christ, unser Heiland (greater)
Duetto No. 2, F major
Triple Fugue, E flat major
Fritz Heitmann (Schnitger Organ, Char-
lottenburg Palace, Berlin)
6 12″—T-E2709/14
Organ Recital
Vivaldi Concerto No. 2, A minor
Chorale-Prelude: Wachet auf!
Prelude & Fugue, E flat major (St. Ann
Fugue)
Trio-Sonata No. 1, E flat major
E. Power Biggs (Baroque Organ of the
Germanic Museum—Harvard University,
Cambridge, Mass.) 5 12″—TC-T1
Organ Music
Fugue, G minor ("Little")
Chorale-Prelude: Ein' feste Burg ist unser
Gott
Fugue, C major ("Fanfare")
Sheep may safely graze (from Cantata No.
208)
Passacaglia & Fugue, C minor
E. Power Biggs (Skinner Organ of Me-
morial Church, Cambridge, Mass.)
4 12″—VM-1048†
See also under—Chorale Preludes; Preludes
& Fugues; Toccatas & Fugues

(DAS) ORGELBUECHLEIN

Eng. The Little Organ Book
E. Power Biggs (Germanic Museum—
Cambridge, Mass.)
Nos. 17 to 32 (Victor Vol. I)
3 12″—VM-652
No. 29, 33 to 45 and 1 to 4 (Victor
Vol. II) 4 12″—VM-697
Nos. 5 to 16 (Victor Vol. III)
2 12″—VM-711
Ouverture à la manière Française (Partita
No. 7, B minor)
Ernst Victor Wolff (harpsichord)
[Fugue, A minor] 4 12″—CM-357†
Overtures See Suites (Orch.)
PARTITAS Clavier
No. 1, B flat major
Wanda Landowska (harpsichord)
2 12″—G-DB4995/6
[Praeludien 4, 5 & 6]
Marcelle Meyer (pf), in DF-A18
Blanche Selva (pf) 2 12″—C-D15234/5
—1st, 4th, 5th & 6th Mvts. only
(Praeludium, Sarabande, Menuets I &
II, Gigue)
Walter Gieseking (pf) 12″—C-LWX336
—5th Mvt. (Menuets 1 & 2) & 6th Mvt.
(Gigue) only
Walter Gieseking (pf)
(CM-243†) 12″—C-69533D
[Beethoven: Concerto No. 5, Pt. 9]
(C-LX346) (C-LFX363) (C-GQX10768)
—5th Mvt. (Menuetto) only
Friedrich Gulda
in preparation Dutch Decca
—6th Mvt. (Gigue) only
Percy Grainger (pf) 12″—C-7134M

[Guion: Sheep 'n Goat; Liszt: Liebes-
traum No. 3]
No. 2, C minor
Harold Samuel (pf)   2 12″—**CX-5**†
Marcelle Meyer (pf), in DF-A22
Emma Contestabile (pf)
   2 10″—**C-GQ7220/1**
No. 3, A minor
Ruggero Gerlin (harpsichord)
   2 12″—**C-BQX2532/3**
[Concerto, G major]
Marcelle Meyer (pf), in DF-A18
No. 5, G major
Walter Gieseking (pf)   2 12″—**CX-208**†
Marcelle Meyer (pf), in DF-A18
No. 6, E minor
Walter Gieseking (pf)   2 12″—**CX-135**†
Marcelle Meyer (pf), in DF-A23
**No. 7, B minor—See under Ouverture à la
manière Française**
**Partitas for Unaccompanied Violin—See
under Sonatas for Unaccompanied Violin
—Nos. 2, 4, 6**
Passacaglia & Fugue, C minor
(Peters Vol I, No. 2)
Carl Weinrich (Westminster Choir
School organ)   2 12″—**MC-10**
Fritz Heitmann (Berlin Dom Organ)
   2 12″—**T-E2681/2**
[Herzlich tut mich verlangen]
E. Power Biggs
(in VM-1048†)   2 12″—**V-11-9147/8**
—**Arr. Orchestra** Stokowski
Philadelphia Orch.—Stokowski
(G-DB3252/3)
(in VM-401†)   2 12″—**V-14580/1**
Older version: V-7090/1, in VM-59†;
G-W1189/90
All-American Orch.—Stokowski
   2 12″—**CX-216**†

PASSIONS

JOHANNES-PASSION

Eng. St. John Passion
—**1. Herr, unser Herrscher; 7. O grosse
Lieb'; 9. Dein Will' gescheh'; 44. Weg,
weg mit dem; 67. Ruht wohl** Chorus
Brussels Royal Conservatory Orch.
Chorus & Organ—Désiré Defauw (in
French) (C-GQX10762/3)
   2 12″—**C-D15015/6**
—**7. See No. 1 above**
—**9. See No. 1 above**
—**13. Ich folge dir gleichfalls** Soprano
Margherita Perras, Flute & Organ
   12″—**G-DB10094**
[Cantata No. 39, No. 5—Höchster, was
ich habe]
—**19. Ach, mein Sinn** Tenor
Julius Patzak & Berlin State Opera
Orch.—Melichar   10″—**PD-62791**
—**44. Weg, weg mit dem See No. 1 above**
—**52. In meines Herzens Grunde** Chorus
State Music Academy Chorus & Berlin
Instrumental College—Stein
   10″—**G-EG6010**
[No. 68, Ach, Herr, lass' dein lieb'
Engelein]

—**58. Es ist vollbracht** Contralto
Lina Falk (in French), Clerget (gamba),
Noëlie Pierront (organ) with strings—
Gerlin   12″—**LUM-32052**
[Pergolesi: Stabat Mater—Fac, ut
portem]
Marian Anderson & Victor Orch.—
O'Connell (in English)
(in VM-850)   12″—**V-18326**
—**Arr. Orchestra** Stokowski
Philadelphia Orch.—Stokowski
(in VM-963)   12″—**V-11-8578**
(Older version, V-8764, G-DB2762)
—**67. Ruht wohl** Chorus
State Music Academy Cho—Berlin
Instrumental College—Stein
   12″—**G-EH1062**
See also No. 1 above
—**68. Ach, Herr, las dein lieb' Engelein**
Chorus
State Music Academy Cho.—Berlin
Instrumental College—Stein
   10″—**G-EG6010**
[No. 52.—In meines Herzens Grunde]
Himmel reisse, Welt erbebe
(Aria with Chorale originally intended
for the St. John Passion; B.G. Vol. 12
(1), p. 135)
Jacques Bastard (b), Jacqueline Heuclin
(vcl), Cho. of Yvonne Gouverné, Claude
Crussard & Ars Rediviva Ensemble
   10″—**G-DA4933**

MATTHAEUS-PASSION

Eng. St. Matthew Passion
Abridged recording (Recorded in St.
Thomas Church, Leipzig)
Tiana Lemnitz (s), Friedel Beckmann
(c), Karl Erb (t), Gerhard Hüsch (b),
Siegfried Schulze (bs) with Chorus of
St. Thomas, Leipzig & Gewandhaus Orch.
—Günther Ramin
(31 sides)   16 12″—**G-DB6516/23
G-DBS6524; G-DB6525/31**
NOTE: *This set was issued in Germany with the
following numbers:* G-DB7625/40, G-DBS7638
being a single-faced record.

Abridged recording
Tilla Briem (s), Gusta Hammer (c),
Walter Ludwig (t), Hans Herman Nissen
(b), Fred Drissen (bs), with Bruno Kittel
Choir & Berlin Philharmonic Orch.—
Bruno Kittel   18 12″—**PD-67951/68**
(35 sides) (CET-RR8040/57)
(FONIT—96101/18)

Excerpts (Sung in English)
Elsie Suddaby (s), Kathleen Ferrier (c),
Eric Greene (t), William Parsons (bs),
Bruce Boyce (bs) with Bach Choir &
Jacques Orch. (Thornton Lofthouse, harp-
sichord & Dr. Peasgood, organ)
   7 12″—**D-K1673/9**
Individual Excerpts
—**1. Kommt, ihr Töchter** Chorus
Berlin Philharmonic Chorus & Orch.—
S. Ochs   12″—**G-EJ195**
—**3. Herzliebster Jesu Chorale**

—**Arr. Orchestra O'Connell**
Philadelphia Orch.—Ormandy
12″—**V-18166**
[Cantata No. 140—No. 7, Gloria sei dir
gesungen, Arr. O'Connell, with Dorothy
Maynor]
—**12. Blute nur** Soprano
Dorothy Maynor (in English) & Victor
Orch.—S. Levin
(in VM-1043) **V-11-9107**
[Mozart: Exsultate Jubilate—Alleluia]
—**25. O Schmerz**
—**26. Ich will bei meinen Jesu wachen**
Ten. & Cho.
Aksel Schiøtz with Cho. & Orch.—
Wöldike 12″—**G-DB5267**
—**26 only**
Julius Patzak w. Favre Cho. & Berlin
State Opera Orch.—Melichar
10″—**PD-62790**
—**33. So ist mein Jesus nun gefangen**
Sop., Alto & Cho.
Lotte Leonard, Emmi Leisner, Bruno
Kittel Cho.—Berlin Phil. Orch.—Kittel
(No. 44 & 63) 12″—**PD-66721**
—**44. Wer hat dich so geschlagen** Chorale
Bruno Kittel Cho.—Kittel
(No. 33 & 63) 12″—**PD-66721**
—**47. Erbarme dich, mein Gott** Contralto
Marian Anderson, with Joseph Fuchs
(vl) & Victor Orch.—Robert Shaw
(in VM-1087) 12″—**V-11-9380**
—**51. Gebt mir meinen Jesum wieder** Bass
Norman Cordon (in English) & Victor
Orch.—S. Levin
(in VM-1094) 12″—**V-11-9431**
[Mendelssohn: St. Paul—No. 18, O God,
have mercy]
—**53. Befiehl du deine Wege**
London Cantata Club—Scott (in Eng-
lish) 10″—**C-DB506**
[Chorale: Vater unser & Cantata 156—
Sinfonia]
(in Columbia History of Music, Vol. II:
CM-232)
—**58. Aus Liebe will mein Heiland sterben**
Sop.
Elisabeth Schumann & Orch.—Alwin
(John Amadio, flute)
(G-W980) 12″—**G-D1410**
[Cantata No. 159: No. 4—Es ist
vollbracht]
—**63. O Haupt voll Blut und Wunden**
Chorale
Berliner Solisten Vereinigung
10″—**G-EG3188**
[No. 72; Hassler: Christ ist erstanden]
Bruno Kittel Cho.—Kittel
[No. 33 & No. 44] 12″—**PD-66721**
Paderborn Cathedral Choir
12″—**PD-22589**
[Brahms: In stiller nacht]
St. Leon IX Choir (in French)
10″—**PAT-X93050**
[Cantata No. 142—No. 2, Uns ist ein
Kind geboren]
—**72. Wenn ich einmal soll scheiden**
Chorale only
Berliner Solisten Vereinigung
10″—**G-EG3188**

[No. 63; Hassler: Christ ist erstanden]
St. George's Choir, Berlin & Organ
10″—**PD-22105**
[Cantata No. 9—Es ist das Heil uns
kommen her]
—**Arr. Orchestra Stokowski**
[Labeled My Soul is Athirst]
Philadelphia Orch.—Stokowski
(G-DB3405)
(in-VM-401†) 12″—**V-14582**
[Schemelli Gesangbuch: Mein Jesu was
für Seelenweh]
—**74. Am Abend, da es kühle war** Bass
recit.
Paul Sandoz & Hans Vollenweider (org)
[No. 75] 12″—**G-DB10061**
—**75. Mache dich, mein Herze rein** Bass
aria
Paul Sandoz & Hans Vollenweider (org)
[No. 74] 12″—**G-DB10061**
—**78. Wir setzen uns mit Tränen nieder**
Final Chorus
Bruno Kittel Cho. & Berlin Philhar-
monic Orch.—Kittel 12″—**PD-66720**

Polonaise, G minor (Clavier)
(Peters Anhang I, No. 14)
Erwin Bodky (clavichord)
(in Vol. II) 12″—**AS-24**
[Miscellaneous clavichord pieces & K. P.
E. Bach: Abschied von meinem Clavier]

PRELUDES Clavier

(6) Little Preludes
(Peters Vol. VII, No. 1)
Erno Balogh (pf), in DISC-772
—**Nos. 1, 2 & 3 only**
Wanda Landowska (harpsichord)
12″—**G-DB4994**
[Chromatic Fantasy & Fugue, Pt. 3]
—**Nos. 4, 5 & 6 only**
Wanda Landowska (harpsichord)
.. 12″—**G-DB4996**
[Partita No. 1, B flat major, Pt. 3]
(12) Little Preludes
(Peters Vol. IX, No. 16)
Erno Balogh (pf), in DISC-771
—**1, 2 & 3 only**
Wanda Landowska (harpsichord)
12″—**G-DB5008**
[Fugue, C minor & Italian Concerto, Pt.
3]
—**5, E major only**
Erno Balogh (pf), in DISC-102
G major (possibly Peters Vol. III, No. 11)
Julia Menz (harpsichord)
[Fugue, A minor] 10″—**PD-62822**

PRELUDES Organ

C major (unidentified)
Hans Vollenweider 10″—**G-JK9**
[Handel: Bourrée, F major]

PRELUDES AND FUGUES Clavier

A minor
(Peters Vol. IV, No. 2)
Eileen Joyce (pf) 12″—**P-E11354**
[Paradies: Toccata]
See also under Wohltemperiertes Clavier

PRELUDES AND FUGUES Organ
Collections
Preludes & Fugues, Vol. I
A major (Peters Vol. II, No. 3)
C major (Vol. IV, No. 1)
A minor (Vol. II, No. 8)
Carl Weinrich 3 12"—MC-80
(8) **Little Preludes & Fugues**
(Peters Vol. VIII, No. 5)
Ernest White (Studio Organ, St. Mary the
Virgin, New York) 4 12"—TC-T10
Individual recordings
C major (Peters Vol. II, No. 1)
Albert Schweitzer in Bach Organ Society
Vol. 1, CM-270†
—Fugue only
Günther Ramin 12"—O-7913
[Handel: Messiah-Hallelujah Chorus,
Bruno Kittel Choir]
C major (Peters Vol. II, No. 7)
Albert Schweitzer in Bach Organ Society
Vol. 3, CM-320†
C major (Peters Vol. IV, No. 1)
Carl Weinrich, in MC-80
C major (Little Prelude No. 1)
Ernest White, in TC-T10
C minor (Peters, Vol. II, No. 6)
Albert Schweitzer, in Bach Organ Society
Vol. III: CM-320†
—Prelude only
Edouard Commette (St. Jean Cathedral,
Lyons) (C-DFX229) 12"—C-71366D
D major (Peters Vol. IV, No. 3)
N. O. Raasted 12"—TONO-K8033
D minor (Peters Vol. III, No. 4)
—Prelude only Arr. Orchestra Pick-
Mangiagalli
EIAR Symphony Orch., Turin—Willy
Ferrero 12"—CET-BB25042
[Violin Sonata No. 6—Prelude]
D minor (Little Prelude No. 2)
Ernest White, in TC-T10
E flat major (known as "St. Ann")
(Peters Vol. III, No. 1)
(Clavierübung III)
Fritz Heitmann (Charlottenburg Palace
Organ) 2 12"—T-E2709 & E2714
E. Power Biggs, in TC-T1
—Arr. Orchestra Stock
Chicago Symphony Orch.—Frederick
Stock 2 12"—VM-958†
—Arr. Orchestra Schönberg
Berlin Philharmonic Orch.—Kleiber
2 12"—U-E463/4
—Arr. Piano Busoni
Edwin Fischer 2 12"—G-DB1991/2
—Prelude only
Fernando Germani 12"—SEMS-1136
—Fugue only
Joseph Bonnet (Hammond Museum
organ) 12"—V-11-8528
Karl Linder 10"—PD-10302
E minor (Peters Vol. II, No. 9) ("Great"
with "Wedge" fugue)
Albert Schweitzer, in Bach Organ Society,
Vol. III: CM-320†
E minor (Peters Vol. III, No. 10)
("Cathedral")
Edouard Commette (St. Jean Cathedral,
Lyons)

(C-DF2545) 10"—C-17243D
E. Power Biggs (Germanic Museum,
Harvard) 10"—V-10-1121
Albert Schweitzer 12"—G-S10129
—Prelude only
Edouard Commette (St. Jean Cathedral,
Lyons) 12"—C-D11079
[Wachet auf]
Alfred Sittard (St. Michael organ,
Hamburg) 12"—PD-66553
[Bach-Vivaldi: Concerto, D minor—
Allegro]
[Brandenburg Concerto No. 1, Pt. 5 on
PD-27315]
E minor (Little Prelude No. 3)
Ernest White, in TC-T10
—Arr. Orchestra Stokowski
Philadelphia Orch.—Stokowski
(in VM-963) 12"—V-11-8577
[Ich ruf' zu dir]
[Bloch: Schelomo, with E. Feuermann, on
V-17338 in VM-698]
F major (Little Prelude No. 4)
Ernest White, in TC-T10
F minor (Peters Vol. II, No. 5)
Albert Schweitzer, in Bach Organ Society
Vol. I: CM-270†
—Arr. Orchestra Cailliet
Philadelphia Orch.—Ormandy
12"—V-14382
G major ("Great") (Peters Vol. II, No. 2)
Albert Schweitzer, in Bach Organ Society
Vol. I: CM-270†
Marcel Dupré 12"—G-W1146
G major (Little Prelude No. 5)
Ernest White, in TC-T10
Edouard Commette 12"—C-DFX94
[Fantasia, C minor]
G minor (Little Prelude No. 6)
Ernest White, in TC-T10
A major (Peters Vol. II, No. 3)
Carl Weinrich, in MC-80
A minor ("Great")
(Peters Vol. II, No. 8)
Carl Weinrich, in MC-80
—Arr. Piano Liszt
Solomon 12"—G-C3376
André Collard 12"—C-DFX212
—Prelude only
Edouard Commette (St. Jean Cathedral,
Lyons) 12"—C-DFX227
[Je suis comblé & Par toi nous, Bk. V]
—Fugue only
Albert Schweitzer in Bach Organ Society
Vol. III: CM-320†
A minor (Little Prelude No. 7)
Ernest White, in TC-T10
B flat major (Little Prelude No. 8)
Ernest White, in TC-T10
Fritz Heitmann 12"—U-E815
[Rossi: Toccata]
B minor ("Great")
(Peters Vol. II, No. 10)
Fernando Germani (Westminster
Cathedral Organ) 2 12"—G-C3604/5
—Fugue only
Edouard Commette 12"—C-DFX239
[Wachet auf]

Prelude, Fugue & Allegro, E flat major
(Peters Vol. III, No. 4)
Wanda Landowska (harpsichord)
(in VM-1181†)   2 12"—**V-11-9996/7**

SONATAS

The Bach Sonatas are arranged as follows:
I. Unaccompanied Sonatas
   a. Sonatas & Partitas for Violin
   b. Suites (Sonatas) for 'Cello
   c. Sonata for Flute
II. Sonatas for Harpsichord & 1 Instrument
   a. Harpsichord & Violin
   b. Harpsichord & Viola da Gamba
   c. Harpsichord & Flute
III. Sonatas for 1 Instrument & Continuo
   a. Flute & Continuo
   b. Violin & Continuo
IV. Trio Sonatas (2 Instruments & Continuo)
V. Trio Sonatas for Organ
   (2 Manuals & Pedal)

1. UNACCOMPANIED SONATAS

I. a) SONATAS—Unacommpanied Violin

*Strictly speaking these six works are divided
into 3 Sonatas and 3 Partitas arranged alter-
nately but for convenience they are usually all
referred to as sonatas. Record labels, unfortunately, are not consistent in listing these works.*

No. 1, G minor (Sonata No. 1)
Yehudi Menuhin   2 12"—**V-8361/2**
Joseph Szigeti
(C-GQX10694/5)   2 12"—**CX-1†**
—**1st Movement (adagio or prelude) only**
Henri Merckel   12"—**C-DFX81**
[Sonata No. 6—Minuettos 1 & 2]
—**2nd Movement (Fugue) only**
—**Arr. Guitar** Segovia
Andrés Segovia, G-W1035
No. 2, B minor (Partita No. 1)
Yehudi Menuhin   4 12"—**VM-487†**
—**3rd Movement (Sarabande) only**
Bronislaw Hubermann   12"—**C-LX513**
[Beethoven: Violin Concerto, Pt. 9]
[Sonata No. 4—Sarabande, Milstein, on
C-GQX10992]
Yehudi Menuhin   12"—**G-DB2005**
[Violin Concerto No. 2, E major, Pt. 5]
[Sonata No. 6, Pt. 5, on V-15126 in
VM-488†]
—**Arr. Orchestra** Stokowski
Philadelphia Orch.—Stokowski
    (in VM-401†)   12"—**V-14583**
[Cantata No. 4: No. 4—Jesus Christus]
—**4th Mvt. (Bourrée) only**
Joseph Szigeti
    (in CX-202†)   12"—**C-71186D**
[Corelli: La Folia, Pt. 3]
No. 3, A minor (Sonata No. 2)
Joseph Szigeti   2 12"—**CX-2†**
Ruggiero Ricci   2 12"—**VOX-187**
—**3rd Mvt. (Andante) only**
Yehudi Menuhin (G-DB1738)
    (in VM-231)   12"—**V-7737**
[Mozart: Concerto No. 7, K. 271, Pt. 7]
Bronislaw Hubermann   12"—**C-LFX413**
[Violin Concerto No. 2, Pt. 5, with
Vienna Philharmonic]

—**Arr. Orchestra** Bachrich (mislabeled
Adagio)
Arthur Fiedler's Sinfonietta—Fiedler
    12"—**V-13809**
[Fantasia, C, arr. Bedell]
—**Arr. Orchestra** Stokowski (labelled:
Andante sostenuto)
All American Orchestra—Stokowski
    (in CM-541†)   12"—**C-11978D**
—**Arr. 'Cello & Piano** Siloti
Pablo Casals & Blas-Net
    12"—**G-DB1404**
[Suite No. 3—Air]
No. 4, D minor (Partita No. 2)
Yehudi Menuhin   4 12"—**VM-232†**
(G-DB2287/90 in GM-226†)
Nathan Milstein   3 12"—**CM-276**
(C-GQX10990/2, with Sarabande from
Sonata No. 2—Hubermann)
Adolf Busch   3 12"—**G-DB1422/4**
Louis Kaufman, in DISC album (in
preparation)
—**3rd Mvt. (Sarabande) only**
Endre Wolff (vl)   10"—**G-X7379**
[Aulin: Humoresque]
—**5th Mvt. (Chaconne) only**
Gerhard Taschner
(O-50532/3)   2 12"—**O-8764/5**
—**Arr. Piano** Busoni
Erik Then-Bergh   2 12"—**G-EH1207/8**
Ernst Victor Wolff   2 12"—**CX-91†**
—**Arr. Orchestra** Stokowski
Philadelphia Orch.—Stokowski
    3 12"—**VM-243†**
[Nun komm' der Heiden Heiland]
(Ein' Feste Burg & Fugue in C minor on
G-DB2451/3)
—**Arr. Guitar** Segovia
Andrés Segovia   2 12"—**MC-85**
[Sonata No. 6—Gavotte]
No. 5, C major (Sonata No. 3)
Yehudi Menuhin
(G-DB2284/6)   3 12"—**VM-284†**
—**1st Mvt. (Adagio)** arr. Clavier Bach
(Transposed to G major)
Dennis Matthews (pf)
    12"—**C-DX1166**
[Beethoven: Trio No. 4, Op. 11, Pt. 5]
No. 6, E major (Partita No. 3)
Yehudi Menuhin   3 12"—**VM-488†**
[Sonata No. 2—3rd. Mvt., Sarabande]
—**1st Mvt. (Preludio) only**
This movement is variously listed as Prae-
ludium, Prelude, etc. It was also used by
Bach as the Sinfonia to the Cantata No.
29.
Yehudi Menuhin
    (in VM-987†)   12"—**V-11-8785**
[Brahms: Sonata No. 1, G major, Pt. 7]
(with Air from Suite No. 3—Marcel
Gazelle, pf., on G-DB6156)
C. F. Cillario   12"—**G-DB5409**
[Veracini, arr. Corti—Largo]
Zino Francescatti   12"—**C-LFX726**
[Lalo: Symphonie espagnole, Pt. 7]
—**Arr. Violin & Pf.**
Denise Soriano & Magda Tagliafero
    12"—**PAT-PAT10**
[Fauré: Andante, Op. 75]

—**Arr. Viola & Piano** Richardson
Watson Forbes, with pf. 10"—**D-M499**
[Gavotte]
—**Arr. Pf.**
Sergei Rachmaninoff 12"—**V-11-8607**
[Gavotte, Rondo & Giga]
—**Arr. Orch.** Cailliet
Philadelphia Orch.—Ormandy
(G-DB3693) 12"—**V-14973**
[Jesu, Joy of Man's Desiring]
—**Arr. Orch.** Pick-Mangiagalli
Boston Symphony Orch.—Koussevitzky
(in VM-1050†) 12"—**V-11-9157**
[Brandenburg Concerto No. 3, Pt. 3]
[Beethoven: Symphony No. 2, Pt. 7 on
V-15774 in VM-625†]
[Strauss: Also sprach Zarathustra, Pt. 9,
on V-8623 in VM-257†]
BBC Symphony Orch.—Boult
12"—**G-DB1965**
[Suite in D, Pt. 5]
EIAR Symphony Orch.—Ferrero
12"—**CET-BB25042**
[Prelude & Fugue, D minor—Prelude]
—**Arr. Orchestra** Stokowski
All American Orch.—Stokowski
12"—**C-11983D**
[Mendelssohn: Midsummer Night's
Dream—Scherzo]
—**Arr. Orch.** Sir Henry Wood
New Queen's Hall Orch.—Wood
(in CM-459†) 12"—**C-71144D**
[Haydn: Symphony No. 101, Pt. 7, CBS
Orch.—Barlow]
[Liszt: Hungarian Rhapsody, Pt. 3 on
C-DX10]
—**3rd Mvt. (Gavotte & Rondo) only**
Georg Kulenkampff 12"—**T-E2398**
[Schumann: Violin Concerto, D minor,
Pt. 7]
—**Arr. Violin and Pf.** Kreisler
Fritz Kreisler & Franz Rupp
(G-DA1628) 10"—**V-10-1022**
[Kreisler: Rondino]
—**Arr. Viola & Pf.** Richardson
Watson Forbes, with pf. 10"—**D-M499**
[Prelude]
—**Arr. Piano**
Sergei Rachmaninoff 12"—**V-11-8607**
[Preludio & Giga]
—**Arr. Guitar** (from Bach's lute arrange-
ment)
Andrés Segovia
(G-AW4416) 12"—**G-D1255**
[Sor: Thème varié]
(with Sonata No. 4—Chaconne, in
MC-85)
—**Arr. String orch.** Sir Henry Wood
British Symphony Orch.—Wood
(C-DX475) 12"—**C-7324M**
[Suite, D major—Air]
—**4th Mvt. (Minuettos 1 & 2) only**
Henri Merckel 12"—**C-DFX81**
[Sonata No. 1—Adagio]
—**7th Mvt. (Giga) only**
—**Arr. Piano**
Sergei Rachmaninoff 12"—**V-11-8607**
[Prelude & Gavotte]

I. b) (6) SONATAS—Unaccompanied
'Cello (Suites)
No. 1, G major
Pablo Casals 3 12" (in Bach Society,
Vol. VII, VM-742†)
No. 2, D minor
Pablo Casals 3 12" (in Bach Society,
Vol. VI, VM-611†)
No. 3, C major
Pablo Casals 3 12" (in Bach Society,
Vol. VI, VM-611†)
—**5th Mvt. (Bourrée) only**
—**Arr. Orch.**
CBS Orch.—Barlow 12"—**C-71411D**
[Suite No. 3—Air; Beethoven: Minuet &
Contra-Dance]
No. 4, E flat major
Pablo Casals 3 12"—**G-W1528/30**
No. 6, D major (originally for 'Cello piccolo)
Pablo Casals 4 12" (in Bach Society,
Vol. VII, VM-742†)
—**3rd (Courante), 4th (Sarabande), 5th
(Gavottes 1 & 2) Mvts. only**
Van Leeuven Boomkamp (5 stringed
Violoncello Piccolo)
(in Volume VII) 12"—**AS-76**
—**4th Mvt. (Sarabande) only**
—**Arr. String Quartet**
Quatuor à Cordes "In Cimbalis Bene
Sonantibus" 12"—**SEMS-1144**
[Von Stainlen: Quartet No. 2, Op. 2—
Andante Religioso]
—**5th Mvt. (Gavottes 1 & 2) only**
Arr. Lifschey
Samuel Lifschey (vla)
(in CM-487†) 12"—**C-71316D**
[Brahms: Sonata No. 1 for vla. & pf.,
Pt. 5]
I. c) SONATA—Unaccompanied Flute
A minor
René Le Roy 2 12"—**MC-32**
—**3rd Mvt. (Sarabande) only**
Marcel Moyse 10"—**C-DF1801**
[Ibert: Pièce pour flûte]

II. SONATAS—Harpsichord & 1 Instrument

II. a) (6) SONATAS—Harpsichord & Violin
Complete recording
Ralph Kirkpatrick (harpsichord) &
Alexander Schneider (vl)
14 12"—**CM-719†**
No. 1, B minor
Ralph Kirkpatrick & Alexander
Schneider, in CM-719†
No. 2, A major
Ralph Kirkpatrick & Alexander
Schneider, in CM-719†
No. 3, E major
Ralph Kirkpatrick & Alexander
Schneider, in CM-719†
Wanda Landowska (harpsichord) &
Yehudi Menuhin (vl)
3 12"—**VM-1035†**
Hepzibah Menuhin (pf) & Yehudi
Menuhin (vl) 2 12"—**VM-887†**
—**3rd Mvt. (adagio ma non tanto) only**
Blanche Selva (pf) & Joan Massia (vl)
12"—**C-LFX108**
[Beethoven: Violin Sonata No. 5, Pt. 7]

No. 4, C minor
Ralph Kirkpatrick & Alexander
Schneider, in CM-719†
Marcel Maas (pf) & Alfred Dubois (vl)
2 12"—C-LFX267/8
—1st Mvt. (Siciliano) only
Rudolf Serkin (pf) & Adolf Busch (vl)
(C-LFX436) 12"—C-LX438
[Brandenburg Concerto No. 1, Pt. 5]
—Arr. Orchestra Stokowski
Philadelphia Orch.—Stokowski
(In VM-243†) 12"—V-8495
[Toccata, Adagio & Fugue, C major—
Adagio]
—1st Mvt. (Siciliano) & 3rd Mvt.
(Adagio) only
Günther Ramin (harpsichord) & Licco
Amar (vl) 12"—PD-19869
No. 5, F minor
Ralph Kirkpatrick & Alexander
Schneider, in CM-719†
No. 6, G major
Ralph Kirkpatrick & Alexander
Schneider, in CM-719†
Marcel Maas (pf) & Alfred Dubois (vl)
2 12"—C-LFX272/3

II. b) (3) SONATAS—Harpsichord & Viola
da Gamba
No. 1, G major See under Trio-Sonatas for
earlier version—2 Flutes & Continuo
Isabelle Nef (harpsichord) & Antonio
Tusa (vla. da gamba)
2 12"—OL-94/5
Denise Lassimonne (pf) & Watson
Forbes (vla) 2 12"—D-K10412
Galina Werschenska (pf) & Louis
Jensen (vlc) 2 12"—G-DB5224/5
No. 2, D major
Isabelle Nef (harpsichord) & Antonio
Tusa (vla. da gamba)
2 12"—OL-96/7
[French Suite No. 4, E flat—Allemande
& Courante, Nef solo]
Ernst Victor Wolff (harpsichord) & Janos
Scholz (vla. da gamba)
2 12"—CX-111
Denise Lassimonne (pf) & Watson
Forbes (vla) 2 12"—D-K1043/4
[No. 3, Pt. 1]
No. 3, G minor
Isabelle Nef (harpsichord) & Antonio
Tusa (vla. da gamba)
2 12"—OL-98/9
Denise Lassimonne (pf) & Watson
Forbes (vla)
2 12"—D-K1044/5
[No. 2, Pt. 3]
II. c) (3) SONATAS—Harpsichord & Flute
No. 2, E flat major
—2nd Mvt. (Siciliano) only Arr. Pf.
Wilhelm Kempff 10"—PD-90188
[Italian Concerto—1st Mvt.]

III. SONATAS—1 Instrument & Continuo
III. a) (3) SONATAS—Flute & Continuo
No. 2, E minor (Peters No. 5)
René Le Roy (fl) Albert-Levêque
(harpsichord) Lucien Kirch (vcl), in
MC-16

—3rd Mvt. (Andante) only
H. Kuttruff (fl) & Hans Vollenweider
(organ) 12"—G-HEX105
[Vinci: Sonata, D major]
No. 3, E major (Peters No. 6)
René Le Roy (fl), Albert-Levêque
(harpsichord), Lucien Kirsch (vcl), in
MC-16

III. b) SONATAS—Violin & Continuo
Sonata, E minor (Peters Vol. VII, No. 2)
Dominique Blot (vl) & Claude Crus-
sard (pf) 12"—BAM-9
Adolf Busch (vl) & Artur Balsam (pf)
12"—C-71582D
Sonata, G major
(N.B.G. Vol. 30, publ. 1928)
NOTE: *The bass of this work is identical with
that of the Trio-Sonata for Flute, Violin and
Figured Bass in G major.*
Adolf Busch (vl) & Rudolf Serkin (pf)
12"—G-DB1434

IV. TRIO SONATAS—2 Instruments &
Continuo
C major (2 Violins & Figured Bass)
(Peters Vol. VIII, No. 1)
Dominique Blot & Edmée Ortmans-Bach
(vls), Jacqueline Alliaume (vlc), Claude
Crussard (harpsichord)
2 12"—BAM-28/9
D minor (2 Violins & Figured Bass)
(*A newly discovered Trio-Sonata published by
A. Nagel, Hannover, 1929*)
Edmée Ortmans-Bach & Dominique Blot
(vls), Yvonne Thibout (vlc), Claude
Crussard (pf) 2 12"—BAM-18/9
[Albert: 2 Songs, Jacques Bastard & acc.]
G major (Flute, Violin & Figured Bass)
(Peters Vol. VIII, No. 2)
(*The bass is identical with that of the Sonata
in G major for violin & Continuo*)
Danish Quartet (Flute, Violin, 'Cello
Piano) 12"—G-DB5221
Moyse Trio (Flute, Violin & Piano)
(G-DB5076) 12"—G-C3671
G major (2 Flutes & Figured Bass)
(*Earlier version of Sonata No. 1 for Clavier &
Gamba*)
René LeRoy & André Musset (fls) &
Claude Crussard (harpsichord)
2 10"—BAM-11/2

V. (6) TRIO SONATAS FOR ORGAN
(2 Manuals & Pedal)
No. 1, E flat major
E. Power Biggs, in TC-T1
Noëlie Pierront 2 10"—LUM-30083/4
[Wir glauben all']
—1st Mvt. only
—Arr. Orch. Stokowski
Philadelphia Orch.—Stokowski
(in VM-963) 12"—V-11-8576
[Palestrina: Adoramus Te]
No. 4, E minor
Günther Ramin (St. Thomaskirche,
Leipzig, organ) 2 10"—O-4732/3
—Arr. 2 Pfs. Babin
Vitya Vronsky & Victor Babin
(in VM-778) 2 12"—V-13626/7
[Sonata No. 5, 1st Mvt.]

No. 5, C major
Carl Weinrich, in MC-6
—Arr. 2 Pfs. Babin
Vitya Bronsky & Victor Babin
(in VM-778) 2 12"—V-13627/8
[Sonata No. 4, Pt. 3]
No. 6, G major
Carl Weinrich, in MC-6

SONGS (Sacred & Secular)
(Solo Voice and Figured Bass)

*Bach's sacred songs (or airs or hymns) are
mostly drawn from Georg Christian Schemelli's
"Musikalisches Gesangbuch," 1736. Bach edited
this book, composing some of the songs himself and arranging the others. Only one is
signed with his name ("Vergiss mein nicht"),
but of the others some 24 are generally considered to be Bach's own composition. A few
other songs, including "Bist du bei mir," come
from the Anna Magdalena Bach Notebook. All
these songs, including those not generally
thought to be Bach's own work, are published
in the Bach Gesellschaft Vol. 39. The Schemelli
Nos. given below are those in the B. G. edition.*

Bist du bei mir (Anna Magdalena Bach Note-
book, No. 25)
Jo Vincent (s) with harpsichord & 'cello
[Ich halte treuliche still] 10"—C-DH132
Paul Sandoz (b) & H. Vollenweider
(organ) 10"—G-DA6007
[Komm süsser Tod]
(Same, in French, on G-DA6008)
Roland Hayes (t) & Reginald Board-
man (pf) (in CM-393) 10"—C-17177D
[Anon: L'Amour de moy]
Elisabeth Schumann (s), with orch.
(G-DB2291) 12"—V-8423
[Schubert: Ave Maria]
Isobel Baillie (s) (in English) & Bertram
Harrison (organ) 12"—C-DX1133
[Komm süsser Tod & Ich halte
treulich still]
Mme. Malnory-Marseillac (s) with pf.
[O Jesulein süss] 10"—LUM-30018
Brich entzwei mein armes Herze
(probably not by Bach)
(Schemelli No. 6)
Mme. Malnory-Marseillac (s) in French,
with Gustave Bret (org.)
10"—G-K7344
[Dir, dir, Jehova & Ich halte treulich
still]
Dir, dir, Jehova, will ich singen
(Schemelli No. 14)
Mme. Malnory-Marseillac (s) in French,
& G. Bret (organ 10"—G-K7344
[Ich halte treulich & Brich entzwei mein
armes Herze]
—4 Pt. Cho. (AMB No. 38)
St. Thomas Church Choir—Straube
12"—PD-66708
[Motet: Singet dem Herrn—No. 3, Alles
was Odem hat]
Gedenke doch, mein Geist zurück
(AMB No. 40)
Jacques Bastard (b) with Ars Rediviva
ensemble—Crussard 12"—G-DB5191
[Lully: Alceste-Air de Caron, Act IV;

Anon. 17th Century—O nuit plus belle
que le jour]
Gib dich zufrieden und sei stille
(AMB Nos. 12/4)
Dresdner Kreuzchor—Mauersberger
[Liebster Herr Jesu] 10"—PD-10280
Ich halte treulich still
(Schemelli No. 30)
Jo Vincent (s) with harpsichord & vlc
[Bist du bei mir] 10"—C-DH132
Isobel Baillie (s, in Eng.) & Bertram
Harrison (organ) 12"—C-DX1133
[Bist du bei mir & Komm süsser Tod]
Mme. Malnory-Marseillac (s, in Fr.) &
Bret (organ) 10"—G-K7344
[Dir, dir, Jehova & Brich entzwei]
—Arr. Chorus
Dresdner Kreuzchor—Mauersberger,
G-EG3638
Jesus, unser Trost und Leben
(probably not by Bach)
(Schemelli No. 39)
Theodora Versteegh (c) & organ
[Liebster Herr Jesu] 10"—C-D10043
Komm, süsser Tod (Schemelli No. 42)
Eng. Come sweet death
Fr. Viens douce Mort
Ingeborg Steffensen (ms) with M.
Wöldike (harpsichord) & Louis Jensen
(vlc) 10"—G-DA5205
[O Jesulein süss]
Theodora Versteegh (c) & organ
[Kommt Seelen] 10"—C-D10042
Marian Anderson (c) & Kosti
Vehanen (pf) (G-DA1529) 10"—V-1939
[Handel: L'Allegro—Let me wander]
Paul Sandoz (b) & H. Vollenweider
(org.) 10"—G-DA6007
[Bist du bei mir]
(in French on G-DA6008)
Isobel Baillie (s, in Eng.) & Bertram
Harrison (org.) 12"—C-DX1133
[Bist du bei mir & Ich halte treulich
still]
Yves Tinayre (b, in Fr.)
12"—LUM-30022
[De Bréville: Prières d'enfant]
Hulda Lashanska (s) with cho. & orch.
12"—V-7085
[Brahms: Wiegenlied & Sapphische Ode]
—Arr. Orchestra Stokowski
Philadelphia Orch.—Stokowski
(in VM-243†) 12"—V-8496
[English Suite No. 3—Sarabande]
[Nun komm' der Heiden Heiland on
G-DB2274]
[Beethoven: Symphony No. 9, Pt. 17 on
V-8432 in VM-236†]
All American Orch.—Stokowski
(in CX-220†) 12"—C-11773D
—Arr. Organ Fox
Virgil Fox (Girard College, Philadelphia,
organ) 12"—V-18495
—Arr. Viola
William Primrose with organ
[Schubert: Litanei] 12"—V-11-9117
[Smetana: Quartet No. 1, Pt. 7, on
V-16316 in VM-675†]

—Arr. 'Cello & Piano Siloti
 Pablo Casals & Blas-Net 12"—G-DB1400
 [Tartini: Concerto—Grave]
Kommt, Seelen, dieser Tag
 (Schemelli No. 43)
 Theodora Versteegh (c) with organ
 [Komm, süsser Tod] 10"—C-D10042
Arr. Cho.—St. Thomas Cho., Leipzig—
 Ramin, PD-47574
Liebster Herr Jesu, wo bleibst du so lange?
 (Schemelli No. 48)
 Theodora Versteegh (c) with organ
 [Jesus unser Trost] 10"—C-D10043
—Arr. Chorus F. Wagner
 Dresdner Kreuzchor—Mauersberger
 [Gib dich zufrieden] 10"—PD-10280
Mein Jesu, was für Seelenweh
 (Schemelli No. 51)
 Eng. My Jesus in Gethsemane
—Arr. Orchestra Stokowski
 Philadelphia Orch.—Stokowski
  (in VM-401†) 12"—V-14582
 [Matthäus-Passion: Wenn ich einmal
 soll scheiden] (G-DB3405)
 All American Youth Orch.—Stokowski
  10"—C-19004D
O Jesulein süss, O Jesulein mild
 (probably not by Bach)
 (Schemelli No. 58)
 Ingeborg Steffensen (ms), M. Wöldike
 (harpsichord) & Louis Jensen (vlc)
 [Komm, süsser Tod] 10"—G-DA5205
 Karl Erb (t) & Bruno Seidler-Winkler
 (pf) 10"—G-EG3184
 [Schubert: Litanei]
 Mme. Malnory-Marseillac (s) & Pascal
 String Quartet 10"—LUM-30018
 [Bist du bei mir]
So gehst du nun (probably not by Bach)
 (Schemelli No. 66)
 French: Le Calvaire
 Arr. F. A. Gevaert, in French for cho.
 in unison
 Chorale du Petit Séminaire de Paris,
 with organ—Vallet 10"—LUM-30053
 [Praetorious: Chantons sur terre]
So oft ich meine Tabakspfeife
 (Erbauliche Gedanken eines Taba-
 krauchers—Tobacco Song)
 (AMB No. 21)
 Benjamin de Loache (b), Ernst Victor
 Wolff (harpsichord), Sterling Hunkins
 vlc), in MC-5
 [with Coffee Cantata]

641847

SUITES

The Bach Suites are listed as follows:
I. Solo Clavier Suites
 a. English b. French
II. Orchestral Suites
 *For the Suites for Unacc. Violin & for Unacc.
 'Cello, see under Sonatas. For other solo clavier
 Suites, see under Partitas & Ouverture à la
 Manière Française.*

I. a) (6) ENGLISH SUITES Clavier
No. 1, A major
—5th Mvt. (Sarabande) & 6th Mvt.
 (Bourrées I & II)

—Arr. Piano & Orchestra
 M. Roesgen-Champion & Orchestre des
 Concerts—M. F. Gaillard
  12"—G-DB5151
 [Concerto No. 4, A major, Pt. 3]
No. 2, A minor
 Wanda Landowska (harpsichord) in
 Bach Society Vol. V: VM-447†
—1st Mvt. (Prelude) only
 Alice Ehlers (harpsichord), in D-A62
No. 3, G minor
 Isabelle Nef (harpsichord)
  2 12"—OL-122/123
 Alexander Borovsky (pf)
  3 10"—VOX-170
 (PD-62758/9 & 62785)
 (PD-561097/8 & 561103)
—1st Mvt. (Prelude) & 4th Mvt.
 (Sarabande) only
 Alexander Borovsky (pf)
  10"—PD-561094
—1st Mvt. (Prelude) only
 Johanne Stockmarr (pf)
  10"—G-DA5248
 [Scarlatti-Tausig: Pastorale]
—4th Mvt. (Sarabande) only
—Arr. Orchestra Stokowski
 Philadelphia Orch.—Stokowski
  (in VM-243†) 12"—V-8496
 [Komm, süsser Tod]
—5th Mvt. (Gavotte) & 6th Mvt.
 (Gigue) only
—Arr. cl., oboe, & bassoon Oubradous
 Trio d'Anches de Paris 10"—OL-120
—5th Mvt. (Gavotte) only
 Wanda Landowska (harpsichord)
  10"—G-DA1014
 [Byrd: Woolsey's Wilde]
 Raoul von Koczalski (pf) 10"—O-4761
 [Chopin: Prelude No. 7, & Waltz No. 6]
No. 5, E minor
—5th Mvt. (Passepied) only
 Wanda Landowska (harpsichord)
 [Fantasia, C minor] 10"—G-DA1129
No. 6, D minor
—5th Mvt. (Gavotte) only
 Erno Balogh (pf), in DISC-772
 [with 6 Kleine Praeludien]
—Arr. Violin & Piano Heifetz
 Jascha Heifetz & Emanuel Bay
  (in VM-1158) 10"—V-10-1342
 [Beethoven: Folk Dance]

I. b) (6) FRENCH SUITES Clavier
No. 1, D minor
—1st Mvt. (Sarabande) only
 Alice Ehlers (harpsichord)
  (in D-A61) 10"—D-23090
 [J. C. F. Fischer: Passepied & Loeillet:
 Suite, G minor—Gigue]
 (D-M494)
No 3, B minor
—1st Mvt.. (Allemande) & 5th Mvt.
 (Menuet) only
—Arr. cl., oboe, & bassoon Oubradous
 Trio d'Anches de Paris 10"—OL-121
No. 4, E flat major
—1st Mvt. (Allemande) & 2nd Mvt.
 (Courante) only
 Isabelle Nef (harpsichord) 12"—OL-97

[Sonata for Viola da gamba & harpsichord, No. 2, D major, Pt. 3—with Antonio Tusa]
—1st Mvt. (Allemande) only
Alice Ehlers (harpsichord) in D-A62
No. 5, G major
Wilhelm Kempff (pf) 12"—PD-67066
—3rd Mvt. (Sarabande) & 4th Mvt. (Gavotte) only
Erwin Bodky (clavichord)
(in 2000 Years of Music) 10"—P-R1027
[Rameau: La Poule]
—4th Mvt. (Gavotte) only
Alice Ehlers (harpsichord)
(in D-A61) 10"—D-23089
[Byrd: Earl of Salisbury; Frescobaldi; Gagliarda; Lully; Courante]
(D-F7726)
—7th Mvt. (Gigue) only Arr. Hess
Myra Hess (pf) (C-D1635)
10"—C-4084M
[Jesu, Joy of Man's Desiring]
Walter Gieseking (pf) 10"—C-17150D
[Jesu, Joy of Man's Desiring]
No. 6, E major
Wanda Landowska (harpsichord)
(G-DB5005) 12"—V-14384

II. ORCHESTRAL SUITES (Overtures)

No. 1, C major
Busch Chamber Players—Adolf Busch
(G-DB3012/4)
(in VM-332†) 3 12"—V-11993/5
—5th Mvt. (Menuet) & 6th Mvt. (Bourrée) only
Chamber Orch.—Oubradous
12"—O-123869
[Brandenburg Concerto No. 2, Pt. 3]
No. 2, B minor (Flute & Strings)
Busch Chamber Players—Adolf Busch, with Marcel Moyse (G-DB3015/7)
(in VM-332†) 3 12"—V-11996/8
Amsterdam Concertgebouw Orch.—
Mengelberg 3 12"—CM-168†
(C-GQX10589/91) (C-LFX243/5)
Boston Symphony Orch.—Koussevitzky, with Georges Laurent
(in VM-1123†) 3 12"—V-11-9583/5
[Suite No. 3, Pt. 1]
Pittsburgh Symphony—Reiner, with S. Caratelli 3 12"—CM-695†
[Fugue, G minor, arr. Cailliet]
—2nd Mvt. (Rondeau) & 7th Mvt. (Badinerie) only
String Orch.—K. Scott & R. Murchie (fl)
(C-DF1089) 10"—C-DB507
[Cantata No. 147-No. 10]
(in Columbia History of Music Vol. II: CM-232)
—5th Mvt. (Polonaise) only
Boston Symphony Orch.—Koussevitzky
(in VM-730†) 12"—V-17518
[Brahms: Symphony No. 4, Pt. 9]
—Arr. Flute & Piano
A. Tassinari & A. Quadri, C-CQ750
No. 3, D major (with the celebrated air)
Busch Chamber Players—Adolf Busch
(in VM-339†) 3 12"—V-12009/11
[Suite No. 4, Pt. 1] (G-DB3018/20)

Paris Conservatory Orch.—Weingartner
(C-LX874/6) 3 12"—CM-428†
[Boccherini: Minuet]
Boston Symphony Orch.—Koussevitzky
(in VM-1123†) 3 12"—V-11-9585/7
[Suite No. 2, Pt. 5]
BBC Symphony Orch.—Boult
3 12"—G-DB1963/5
[Sonata No. 6 for Unacc. Violin-Preludio]
Brussels Conservatory Orch.—Defauw
3 12"—C-D15229/31
[Corelli: Sarabande, Madrid Symphony Orch.—Arbós]

—2nd Mvt. (Air) only
NBC Symphony Orch.—Toscanini
(in VM-1080†) 12"—V-11-9344
[Mozart: Symphony No. 41, Pt. 7]
Amsterdam Concertgebouw Orch.—
Mengelberg 12"—T-SK2402
[Vivaldi: Concerto, A minor, Op. 3, No. 8, Pt. 3]
Boston "Pops" Orch.—Fiedler
12"—G-C3239
[Schubert-Wilhelmj: Ave Maria]
CBS Symphony Orch.—Barlow
12"—C-71411D
[Bourrée, from Cello Suite No. 3 & Beethoven: Minuet in G & Contra-Dance No. 1]
Boston Symphony Orch.—Koussevitzky
(in VM-581†) 12"—V-15530
[Brahms: Violin Concerto, Pt. 9, with Jascha Heifetz]
British Symphony Orch.—Wood
(C-DX475) 12"—C-7324M
[Sonata for unaccompanied violin No. 6—Gavotte]
Berlin Philharmonic Orch.—Furtwängler
12"—PD-66935
[Schubert: Rosamunde-Ballet Music No. 2]
[Mendelssohn: Midsummer Night's Dream—Overture, Pt. 3, on PD-66926]
New York Philharmonic Symphony Orch.—Mengelberg (arr. Mahler)
12"—G-D1989
[J. C. Bach: Sinfonia, Pt. 3]
Lamoureux Orch.—Albert Wolff
(PD-566027) 12"—PD-67006
[Schubert: Ave Maria]
Philadelphia Orch.—Stokowski (arr. Stokowski (in VM-401) 10"—V-1843
All American Orch.—Stokowski
(in CX-220†) 12"—C-11774D
[with Komm, süsser Tod]
Vienna Philharmonic Orch.—Böhm
12"—G-DB7651
[Mozart: Symphony No. 35, Pt. 5]
DUPLICATIONS: Liverpool Philharmonic Orch.—Sargent, in CM-703; New Symphony Orch.—Sargent, G-B2913; Bournemouth Municipal Orch.—Birch, D-F7969

—Arr. Violin & Piano (in original key)
Yehudi Menuhin & Marcel Gazelle
12"—G-DB6156
[Sonata No. 6, E—Praeludium unacc.]

—Arr. Violin & Piano Wilhelmj ("Air on the G String")
Mischa Elman & R. Baumann
    12"—**V-7103**
[Schubert-Wilhelmj: Ave Maria]
Ellen Birgithe Nielsen & Carl Browall
    12"—**G-DB5284**
[Schubert-Wilhelmj: Ave Maria]
DUPLICATIONS: Jacques Thibaud & H. Craxton, G-DB1017; Ferenc Vecsey, PD-10413; Emil Telmanyi, TONO-A108; Jewssey Wülf, G-HN212; Ettore Gandini & String Orch., SEMS-1151; Richard Heber & organ, PD-21842; Jenö Hubay, G-AN418; Bronislaw Hubermann, O-8746; C-LX107, C-GQX10302

—Arr. Cello
Pablo Casals   12"—**G-DB1404**
[Violin Sonata No. 3, A minor—Andante]
H. Bottermund, with organ
[Handel: Largo]   12"—**PD-19973**
DUPLICATION: André-Lévy, O-166046

—Arr. Organ
Charles Courboin   12"—**V-14927**
[Herzlich tut mich verlangen]
H. Schimmelpfennig   10"—**PD-10433**
[Handel: Largo]

No. 4, D major
Busch Chamber Players—Adolf Busch
    (in VM-339†) 3 12"—**V-12011/3**
[Suite No. 3, Pt. 5] (G-DB3020/2)

Suite, A minor—Flute, Strings & Figured Bass (Ed. W. Hinnenthal)
—Sarabande only
Scheck-Wenzinger Chamber Orch.
(G-S10495)   12"—**G-EH1220**
[Pergolesi: Concerto for Flute, Strings & Bass, G major, Pt. 3]

TOCCATAS

TOCCATAS & FUGUES Clavier
Toccata & Fugue, C minor
(Peters Vol. IV, No. 5)
Marcel Maas (pf) 2 12"—**C-LFX197/8**
[Toccata & Fugue, E minor—Fugue]
Marcelle Meyer (pf), in DF-A17

Toccata, D major (Fantasia & Fugue)
(Peters Vol. IX, No. 3)
Wanda Landowska (harpsichord)
    2 12"—**G-DB5047/8**
[Pachelbel: 2 Magnificats]
Yella Pessl (harpsichord)
    2 12"—**CX-70†**
[Fantasia, G minor; Fugue, C major]
Edwin Fischer (pf)
    2 12"—**G-DB5687/8**
[Ich ruf' zu dir]
Suzanne Gyr (pf)
[3 Minuets] 2 12"—**G-DB10069/70**
Marcelle Meyer (pf), in DF-A17

Toccata & Fugue, D minor
(Peters Vol IV, No. 10)
Marcelle Meyer (pf), in DF-A13

Toccata & Fugue, E minor
(Peters Vol. IV, No. 3)
Rudolf Serkin (pf)   12"—**C-71594D**

—Fugue only
Marcel Maas (pf)   12"—**C-LFX198**
[Toccata & Fugue, C minor, Pt. 3]

TOCCATAS & FUGUES Organ
Complete recording
Carl Weinrich (Praetorius Organ of the Westminister Choir College, Princeton, N. J.) 4 12"—**MC-36**
    3 12"—**MC-37**
(Vol. I contains Toccatas & Fugues, D minor; F major; & E major—with 2 fugues.)
(Vol. II contains Toccata, Adagio & Fugue, C major & "Dorian" Toccata & Fugue, D minor.)

Toccata, Adagio and Fugue in C major
(Peters Vol. III, No. 8)
Carl Weinrich, in MC-37
André Marchal (Gonzalez organ)
    2 12"—**PAT-PAT71/72**
(in 3 Cent. of Organ Music)
[Nun freut euch]

—Arr. Piano Busoni
Alexander Borovsky 2 12"—**VOX-193**
(PD-27344/5) (PD-516641/2)
Artur Rubinstein 2 12"—**G-DB2421/2**

—Arr. Orchestra Weiner
Minneapolis Symphony Orch.—
Mitropoulos 2 12"—**CX-195**

—1st Mvt. (Toccata) only
Hans Vollenweider (Organ)
    10"—**G-JK35**

—2nd Mvt. (Adagio) only
—Arr. Orchestra Stokowski
Philadelphia Orch.—Stokowski
    (in VM-243) 12"—**V-8495**
[Sonata for Clavier & Violin No. 4—Siciliano]
[Beethoven: Symphony No. 9, Pt. 17, on G-DB2335]

—Arr. Cello & Piano Siloti & Casals
Pablo Casals & Blas-Net 12"—**V-6635**
[Granados: Goyescas—Intermezzo] (G-DB1067)

"Dorian" Toccata & Fugue, D minor
(Peters Vol. III, No. 3)
Carl Weinrich, in MC-37
—Toccata only
Alfred Sittard   10"—**PD-10286**

Toccata & Fugue, D minor
(Peters Vol. IV, No. 4)
Carl Weinrich, in MC-36
Albert Schweitzer, in Bach Organ Society Vol. I: CM-270†
Günther Ramin   12"—**G-DB5634**
Gustave Bret (Fréjus Cathedral)
    12"—**G-DB4812**
Hans Vollenweider 12"—**G-FKX70**
Fritz Heitmann (Berlin Dom)
(older version: U-E216) 12"—**T-E2780**
E. Power Biggs 12"—**V-18058**
[Germanic Museum, Cambridge, Mass.]
Jeanne Demessieux (St. Mark's Church, London)   12"—**D-K1635**
Edouard Commette (St. Jean-Lyons)
(C-DFX218)   12"—**C-69490D**
Marcel Dupré (St. Sulpice)
    12"—**LUM-32023**

G. D. Cunningham (Cent. Hall,
Westminster) 12"—C-DX515
Alfred Sittard (St. Michael, Hamburg)
12"—PD-95159

DUPLICATIONS: G. T. Ball, G-C2610;
Arnold Goldsbrough, D-K585; Julio Per-
ceval, O-6971
—Arr. Orchestra Melichar
Berlin Philharmonic Orch.—Melichar
(PD-566204) 12"—PD-15243
—Arr. Orchestra Stokowski
Philadelphia Orch.—Stokowski
(G-DB2572) 12"—V-8697
(Also V-11-9235 in VM-1064)
All American Orch.—Stokowski
[Ein' feste Burg] 2 12"—CX-219†
Symphony Orch.—Stokowski
12"—V-11-9653
—Arr. Orchestra "Klenovsky" (Wood)
Queen's Hall Orchestra—Sir Henry J.
Wood
(PD-516673) 12"—D-K768
Toccata & 2 Fugues, E major
(Peters Vol. III, No. 7)
(also extant in C major)
Carl Weinrich, in MC-36
Toccata & Fugue, F major
(Peters Vol. III, No. 2)
Carl Weinrich, in MC-36

(DAS) WOHLTEMPERIERTE CLAVIER
(48 Preludes & Fugues—Books I & II)
Eng. The Well-Tempered Clavier

*The famous "Forty-Eight" were issued in two
books, separated by an interval of some twenty-
two years. Only the first book bears the title
"Wohltemperierte Clavier" but it is customary
to ascribe that title to the complete collection.
All recordings listed are piano performances
unless otherwise noted.*

COLLECTIONS
Bach Society (Complete recording) (HMV)
Vol. I (Preludes & Fugues Nos. 1 to 12)
Vol. II (Preludes & Fugues Nos. 13 to 24)
Vol. III (Preludes & Fugues Nos. 25 to 34)
Edwin Fischer (Each of the 1st Vols.
contains 7 12" records.)
Vol. IV (Preludes & Fugues Nos. 35 to 43)
incl.)
Edwin Fischer 7 12"—VM-334†
Vol. V (Preludes & Fugues Nos. 44 to 48)
Edwin Fischer 6 12"—VM-447†
(with English Suite No. 2, A minor—
Landowska—harpsichord)

Preludes & Fugues Nos. 1 to 9
Isabelle Nef (harpsichord)
6 12"—OL-160/5
Preludes & Fugues Nos. 10 to 48
Isabelle Nef (harpsichord)
(in preparation) 24 12"—OL
Preludes & Fugues Nos. 1 to 5
Dorothy Lane (harpsichord)
3 12"—CONCORD-1
Preludes & Fugues Nos. 1 to 9
Harriet Cohen 6 12"—CM-120†

INDIVIDUAL PRELUDES & FUGUES
*All recordings which are part of the above col-
lections are omitted from the following list.*

BOOK I
No. 1, C major 4-pt. fugue
NOTE: *It is the Prelude of this work that served
as the basis for Gounod's "Ave Maria."*
Arnold Dolmetsch (clavichord)
10"—C-DB505
[No. 21] (in Columbia History of Music,
Vol. II, CM-232)
—Prelude only
Paul Brunold (harpsichord) PD-522585
[Prelude No. 8]
Liselotte Selbiger (harpsichord)
(in preparation) Danish Columbia

No. 2, C minor 3-pt. fugue
—Fugue only Arr. Orchestra Stokowski
Philadelphia Orchestra—Stokowski
[Frescobaldi: Gagliarda] 10"—V-1985
[Ein' feste Burg & Sonata for unacc.
violin, No. 4—Chaconne Pt. 5, on
G-DB2453]

No. 3, C sharp major 3-pt. fugue
Harold Bauer in SCH-1
Wilhelm Kempff 12"—PD-95107
[No. 5]
[Beethoven: Symphony No. 7, Pt. 9, on
PD-67166; PD-516751]
Albert-Levêque 10"—G-K7502
[Jesu, Joy of Man's Desiring]
Alexander Borovsky 10"—G-DA1308
[Rimsky-Korsakov: Flight of the
Bumble Bee]
—Prelude only
Yvonne Loriod 12"—PAT-PDT110
[No. 4]

No. 4, C sharp minor 5-pt. fugue
Yvonne Loriod 12"—PAT-PDT110
[Prelude No. 3]

No. 5, D major 4-pt. fugue
Edwin Fischer 12"—G-DB4404
[Chromatic Fantasia & Fugue]
Wilhelm Kempff (pf) 10"—PD-90189
[Cantata No. 29—Sinfonia, arr. Kempff]
[No. 3 on PD-95107]
[Beethoven: Vlc. Sonata, No. 3, Pt. 5, on
PD-67099; PD-516712]

No. 8, E flat minor 3-pt. fugue
—Prelude only
Paul Brunold (harpsichord)
10"—PD-522585
[No. 1—Prelude only]
—Arr. Orchestra Stokowski
All American Orch.—Stokowski
(in CM-541†) 12"—C-11977D
Philadelphia Orch.—Stokowski
(G-D1464) (G-AW19) 12"—V-6786
[Ich ruf' zu dir]
—Fugue only Arr. Mozart, (in D minor, vl,
vla, vlc, K.404a—No. 1)
Pasquier Trio, in DF-A4 (with Mozart:
Adagio, D minor)

No. 10, E minor 2-pt. fugue
Nino Rossi 12"—G-DB5353
[Concerto after Marcello, D minor—
Adagio]

No. 12, F minor 4-pt. fugue
Mme. Chailley-Richez 10"—PAT-PG68
["Little" G minor fugue]

No. 13, F sharp major 3-pt. fugue
Soulima Stravinsky 12"—BAM-27
[Stravinsky: Two Etudes, Op. 7]

No. 14, F sharp minor 4-pt. fugue
Carlo Zecchi 12"—CET-CB20353
[Ich ruf' zu dir]

No. 15, G major 3-pt. fugue
Friedrich Gulda
in preparation Dutch Decca

No. 16, G minor 4-pt. fugue
Liselotte Selbiger (harpsichord)
Danish Columbia (in preparation)

No. 20, A minor
—Fugue only. Arr. Orchestra Fischer
Edwin Fischer & Chamber Orch.
10"—G-DA4461

No. 21, B flat major 3-pt. fugue
Arnold Dolmetsch (clavichord)
10"—C-DB505
[No. 1] (in Columbia History of music,
Vol. II, CM-232)

No. 22, B flat minor 5-pt. fugue
Wilhelm Backhaus (pf) 12"—G-DB2408
[Beethoven: Sonata, Op. 81a, Pt. 3]

No. 24. B minor 4-pt. fugue
—Prelude only Arr. Orchestra Stokowski
Philadelphia Orch.—Stokowski
(G-AW219) 12"—V-7316
[Handel: Messiah—Pastoral Symphony]
[Haydn: Quartet in F, Op. 3, No. 5—
Serenade, on G-D1995]

BOOK II

*The numbers given in parentheses are those
of the individual works in Book II.*

No. 37 (13), F sharp major 3-pt fugue
—Fugue only Arr. Mozart (in F major,
Vl., vla. & vlc. K. 404a No. 3)
Pasquier Trio (in DF-A4) 12"—DF-19
[Mozart: Adagio in F major]

No. 38 (14), F sharp minor 3-pt. fugue
—Fugue only Arr. Mozart (in G minor, Vl.,
vla. & vlc. K. 404a No. 2)
Pasquier Trio (In DF-A4) 12"—DF-18
[Mozart: Adagio in G minor]

No. 48 (24), B minor 3-pt. fugue
—Arr. Oboe, Clarinet, Bassoon Oubradous
Trio d'Anches de Paris 10"—OL-8

B flat minor (unident.)
Walter Rummel 12"—PD-67933

ARRANGEMENT OF MISCELLANEOUS SELECTIONS

Trio, E minor (arr. Pillney)
(Adagio-Vivace, Andante)
(Possibly first 2 mvts. of Trio Sonata f.
Organ No. 4)
Kölner Kammertrio (Pillney, harpsichord; Fritzsche, flute; Schwamberger,
viola da gamba) 12"—O-7947

THE WISE VIRGINS—Ballet (arr. William
Walton)
(Including: No. 3—Opening Chorus of
Cantata No. 99: Was Gott tut das ist
wohlgetan; No. 4—Herzlich tut mich
verlangen; No. 5—Air for tenor from
Cantata No. 85; No. 6—Opening Chorus
from Cantata No. 26; No. 7—Schafe
können sicher weiden; No. 9—Chorale
finale to Cantata No. 129)
Sadler's Wells Orchestra—Walton
(G-C3178/9) 2 12"—VM-817

BACH, Karl Philipp Emanuel (1714-1788)

*The second son of Johann Sebastian, who codified existing instrumental practices and developed the sonata form to the point where
Haydn and Mozart took over. Known as the
Berlin or Hamburg Bach, his fame eclipsed,
for many years, that of his illustrious father.*

Abschied von meinem Silbermannischen
Claviere in einem Rondeau
Erwin Bodky (clavichord)
(in Vol. III) 12"—AS-24
[J. S. Bach: Miscellaneous Clavier
Pieces]

CONCERTO—'Cello & Orchestra

No. 3, A major
—Largo Mesto only
Etienne Pasquier (vlc) & Orch.—
Cébron 10"—LUM-30087
Raya Garbousova (vlc) & Erich-Itor
Kahn (pf)
(in VM-1017) 12"—V-11-8871
(Albéniz: Malagueña]

Rondo (unidentified)
Gunnar Johansen (pf) 10"—C-XJ5
[Kreisler-Rachmaninoff: Liebesleid]
Solfeggietto
—Arr. Primrose
William Primrose (vla) & Joseph Kahn
(pf) 10"—V-10-1098
[Rameau: Tambourin & Kreisler:
Allegretto in the Style of Boccherini]

SONATAS Clavier

F minor (No. 3, 3rd Collection of sonatas
"für Kenner und Liebhaber")
—1st Mvt. only
Harold Samuel (pf) 10"—C-DB830
[J. C. Bach: Sonata, E major—Rondo
only]
(in Columbia History of Music, Vol. 3,
CM-233)

G major (No. 3, 1st Collection of sonatas
"für Kenner und Liebhaber")
—Slow Mvt. (Rondo expressivo) only
Harold Samuel (pf) 10"—C-DB831
[Clementi: Sonata No. 13, 1st Mvt.]
(in Columbia History of Music, Vol. 3,
CM-233)

SUITE (Concerto) D major

—Arr. for modern orchestra Maximilian
Steinberg
Boston Symphony Orch.—Koussevitzky
2 12"—VM-559

SYMPHONIES

No. 1, D major
Winterthur Municipal Orch.—Scherchen
2 12"—**G-DB6095/6**
[Purcell: Dido & Aeneas—Overture]
No. 5, B minor 1773
Zürich Collegium Musicum—P. Sacher
2 12"—**C-LZX8/9**
[Purcell: Four Part Fantasia, A minor]

TRIOS

A minor
K. P. Pillney (harpsichord), R. Fritzsche
(fl), & K. Schwamberger (vla da gamba)
12"—**O-3606**

BACH, Wilhelm Friedemann (1710-1784)

Air
Ginette Neveu (pf) 12"—**G-DB4577**
[Suk: Un poco triste]
Concerto, D minor (after Vivaldi, Op. 3,
No. 11—Transcription possibly by J. S.
Bach)
Alexander Brailowsky (pf)
2 12"—**G-DB3703/4**
Kein Hälmlein wächst auf Erden
Wolfgang Kieling & Choir
10"—**G-EG6426**
[Reger: Mariä Wiegenlied]
Polonaise IV, D minor
Alice Ehlers (harpsichord)
(in D-A62) 10"—**D-23112**
[Mozart: German Dance, C major K.536,
No. 1; Rameau: Suite, E minor—
Musette & Rondeau; Couperin:
Rigaudon]
Symphony, D minor
Hamburg Philharmonic Chamber Orch.—
Schmidt-Isserstedt 12"—**T-E2599**

BACHELET, Alfred Georges (1864-   )

*French composer who won the Prix de Rome
in 1890 with his cantata "Cléopatre," Bachelet
has written many operas and arranged scores of
early music for the ballet in his own country.
He is best known here for his songs.*

Chère Nuit Song in French
Lily Pons (s) & Andre Kostelanetz Orch.
(in CM-689) 12"—**C-72048D**
[Fauré: Les Roses d'Ispahan]
Ninon Vallin (s) with Vl. & Pf. acc.
10"—**O-123583**
[Saint-Saëns: Le bonheur est chose
légère]

BACKER-GRONDAHL, Agathe (1847-1907)

*A notable Norwegian pianist herself, having
studied with Kullak, Liszt and Von Bulow,
Backer-Grondahl composed music in the lighter
forms.*

Ballade, Op. 36
Fridtjof Backer-Grøndahl (pf)
12"—**C-DNX4**
[Konsertetyde, B major, op. 11]
Efter er sommerfugl
Randi Heide Stenn (s) & Robert Levin
(pf) 10"—**G-AL2931**
[Trad. arr. Alnaes: Anne Knutsdatter &
Grieg: Kveldsang for Blakken]

Huldreslaat
String Quartet 10"—**G-X2330**
[Mot Kveld]
Klovereng Arr. Vuillermoz
Eide Norena (s) & Orch.—Coppola
10"—**G-DA4855**
[Mot Kveld]
Konsertetyde, B major, Op. 11
Fridtjof Backer-Grøndahl (pf)
12"—**C-DNX4**
[Ballade, Op. 36]
Mot Kveld, Op. 42, No. 7
Kirsten Flagstad (s) 10"—**G-DA1520**
[Grieg: Jeg elsker dig]
Erling Krogh (t) & Qt. 10"—**G-X3862**
[Sommervise]
Eidé Noréna (s) & Orch.—Coppola
[Klovereng] 10"—**G-DA4855**
Ebba Wilton (s) 10"—**G-V181**
[Swedish folksong: Fjorten ar tror jag]
—Arr. Orchestra
Columbia Salon Orch.
[Olsen: Solefallssang] 10"—**C-GN47**
Sommervise
Erling Krogh (t) & Qt. 10"—**G-X3862**
[Mot Kveld]
—Arr. Piano
Fridtjof Backer-Grøndahl (pf)
10"—**C-GN408**
[Svalenes flukt & Trollhallen]
Svalenes flukt
Fridtjof Backer-Grøndahl (pf)
10"—**C-GN408**
[Sommervise & Trollhallen]
Trollhallen, Op. 44
Fridtjof Backer-Grøndahl (pf)
10"—**C-GN408**
[Svalenes flukt & Sommervise]

BAKHMETIEV (1807-1891)

Requiem
General Platoff Don Cossack Choir
(in VM-768) 12"—**V-17918**
[Archangelsky: Inspire my prayer, O
Lord]

BALAKIREV, Mili (1837-1910)

*The driving spirit of the famous Russian na-
tionalist group "The Five," Balakirev stimulated
the use of native sources in the rest of the
group which consisted of Cui, Borodin, Mussorgsky and Rimsky-Korsakov.*

Islamey Piano
Louis Kentner 12"—**C-DX1175**
Claudio Arrau 12"—**PD-95112**
Mazurka No. 6 Piano
Louis Kentner 12"—**C-DX1237**
[Rêverie]
Rêverie Piano
Louis Kentner 12"—**C-DX1237**
[Mazurka No. 6]
Russia Orchestra
London Philharmonic Orch.—Harty
(C-DF1479/80) 2 12"—**C-DB1236/7**
(in Columbia History of Music, Vol. 4,
CM-234)

Oh, come to me Song—Arr. A. Volpi
Mischa Elman (vl) & Leopold Mittmann
(pf)   12″—V-11-9423
[Hubay: Hejre Kati, Op. 32]
Tamar Symphonic Poem   Orchestra
Paris Conservatory Orch.—Coppola
2 12″—G-DB4801/2

BALBASTRE, Claude (1727-1799)

Noëls variés
Ruggero Gerlin (harpsichord)
12″—LUM-33161

BALFE, Michael (1808-1870)

"The Bohemian Girl," Balfe's best remembered opera, has achieved international reputation. His compositions, in the melodramatic operatic style of the nineteenth century, are excellent theatre, and his melodies frequently have great beauty.

OPERAS   In English
(THE) BOHEMIAN GIRL 3 Acts 1843
It. **La Zingara**   Ger. **Die Zigeunerin**
Overture
Symphony Orch.—John Barbirolli
12″—G-C2635
Bournemouth Municipal Orch.—Birch
10″—D-F7946
Then You'll Remember Me   Act III   Tenor
Christopher Lynch & Orch.—Pilzer
10″—V-10-1276
[Marshall: I hear you calling me]

(THE) SIEGE OF LA ROCHELLE   1835
Travelers of Every Station
Peter Dawson (bs) & pf.   12″—G-C1442
[Molloy: Kerry Dance]

SONGS

Come into the garden, Maud (Tennyson)
Webster Booth (t) & Gerald Moore (pf)
12″—G-C3418
[Strauss: Morgen]
Excelsior (Longfellow) Tenor-Baritone duet
Webster Booth & Dennis Noble, with
male Cho.   12″—G-C3124
[Sarjeant: Watchman, what of the night?]
(The) Harp that once through Tara's Halls
John McCormack (t) & pf.
(G-DA1171)   10″—V-1553
[arr. Liddle: The garden where the praties grow]
Killarney
Eileen Farrell (s) & Columbia Concert
Orch.—Lichter
(in CM-662)   10″—C-4444M
[Claribel: Come back to Erin]
John McCormack (t)   12″—G-DB342*
[Crouch: Kathleen Mavourneen]
Richard Crooks (t)   12″—G-DB2337
[Tosti: Goodbye]

BANTOCK, Granville (1868-)

A conservative British composer who has written profusely in all forms, whose arrangements of folksongs are well known outside of England.

FOLKSONGS   Arr. Bantock
O can ye sew cushions? (Lullaby)
Glasgow Orpheus Choir—Roberton
10″—G-B9464
[Stanford: The Blue Bird]
Scots wha' hae with Wallace bled
Glasgow Orpheus Choir—Roberton
10″—G-E409
[Arr. Roberton: Eriskay Love Lilt]
Song to the Seals
John McCormack (t) & Edwin Schneider
(pf)   10″—G-DA1851
[Dunhill: The Cloths of Heaven]
Sea Sorrow (A choral arrangement of one
of Marjorie Kennedy-Fraser's **"Songs of
the Hebrides"**)
Glasgow Orpheus Choir—Roberton
12″—G-C3639
[Arr. Grant: Crimond—Scottish Psalm
Tune]
Miscellaneous arrangements   Orchestra
Bach: Cantata No. 140—Wachet auf!
Opening Chorus
City of Birmingham Orch.—Weldon
12″—C-DX1388

BARVALLE, Vittorio

ANDREA DEL SARTO   Opera

Introduction   Orchestra
EIAR Orch.—Tansini
12″—CET-CB20285
[Parelli: La Giornata di Marcellina—La
fontana delle ninfe]

BARBER, Samuel (1910-)

One of the young American composers, Barber has remained aloof from the more radical and experimental groups.

Adagio for Strings
NBC Symphony Orch.—Toscanini
(G-DB6180)   12″—V-11-8287
"Capricorn" Concerto, Op. 21
Saidenberg Little Symphony (Limited
edition)   2   12″—CH-A4
Essay for Orchestra, Op. 12
Philadelphia Orch.—Ormandy
12″—V-18062
Overture to "School for Scandal" Orchestra
Janssen Symphony of Los Angeles—
Werner Janssen   12″—V-11-8591
Sonata for 'Cello & Piano
Raya Garbousova & Erich-Itor Kahn
(Limited edition)   4   12″—CH-B1
Symphony No. 1, Op. 9
New York Philharmonic-Symphony Orch.
Walter   2 12″—CX-252†

BARLOW, Wayne (1912-)

A graduate of the Eastman School of Music and a pupil of Schönberg, Barlow has used Franco-Flemish methods with interesting results.

Rhapsody "The Winter's Past"
Oboe & String Orchestra
Robert Sprenkle & Eastman-Rochester
Symphony—Howard Hanson
(in VM-802)   12″—V-18101
[Rogers: Soliloquy]

BARRAUD, Henry (1900-   )

A contemporary French composer, pupil of Louis Aubert, he has composed in all forms and is best known by his chamber music.

Trio à vent (oboe, clarinet, bassoon) 1936
    Trio d'Anches de Paris   2 10″—OL-6/7

BARRE, Michel de la (1647?-1743)

A flutist at the court in Paris, de la Barre composed ballet-operas, songs and chamber music.

Bien que l'amour
    Micheletti (t) & Ruggero Gerlin
    (harpsichord)
                    (in Vol. IX)   12″—AS-98
    [Airs sérieux et à boire]

BARTOK, Béla (1881-1945)

An outstanding composer in all forms, Bartók also achieved fame as a teacher and collector of folksongs of his native Hungary. Discovering that Liszt had barely scraped the surface of the enormous wealth of Magyar folk music, Bartók developed his own expression of these sources with remarkable originality. His association with Zoltan Kodaly proved most beneficial and stimulating. There are probably additional recordings in Hungarian catalogues. Since Bartók's death, previously unrecorded works are now appearing for the first time in domestic catalogues.

COLLECTIONS Piano

Este a Szekelyeknel; Medvetane; Children's Pieces—15 Selections
    Béla Bartók   2 12″—VOX-625
Allegro Barbaro Piano
    Béla Bartók   10″—G-AM2622
    [Bagatelle & Kicsit Azottan]
    Hans Leygraf   10″—G-X7330
    [Rondo No. 1]
Bagatelle, Op. 6, No. 2 Piano
    Béla Bartók   10″—G-AM2622
    [Allegro barbaro & Kicsit Azottan]
Bear Dance Piano   Hung. **Medvetane**
    Béla Bartók (also in VOX-625)
                    12″—G-AN469
    [Este a Szekelyeknel & Romanian Dance]
Children's Pieces Piano (15 Selections)
    Béla Bartók   12″—in VOX-625

CONCERTOS

Piano & Orchestra No. 3
    Gyorgy Sandor & Philadelphia Orch.—
    Ormandy   3 12″—CM-674†
Violin & Orchestra
    Yehudi Menuhin & Dallas Symphony
    Orch.—Dorati   5 12″—VM-1120†

Contrasts
    Joseph Szigeti (vl), Benny Goodman (cl),
    & Béla Bartók (pf)   2 12″—CX-178†
Este a Szekelyeknel Piano
    Béla Bartók   12″—G-AN469
    [Bear Dance & Romanian Dance]
    (Also in VOX-625)
Kicsit Azottan Piano
    Béla Bartók   10″—G-AM2622
    [Bagatelle & Allegro Barbaro]

MIKROKOSMOS Piano

A collection of 153 short piano pieces employed in teaching the young pianist.
—Staccato & Ostinato only
    Béla Bartók   10″—C-DB1306
    [Stravinsky: Les Noces, excerpt]
    (in Columbia History of Music, Vol. V:
    CM-361)

QUARTETS String

No. 1, A minor, Op. 7
    Pro Arte Quartet   4 12″—VM-286†
No. 2, A minor, Op. 17
    Budapest Quartet   4 12″—VM-320†
No. 4
    Guilet Quartet   6 12″—CH-A8
    (Limited Edition)
No. 5
    Hungarian Quartet
                    4 12″—G-C3511/4†

ROMANIAN FOLK DANCE SETTINGS

Nos. 1 - 7
    Lily Kraus (pf)   12″—P-PXO1026
    [3 Rondos on Folk Tunes, Pt. 3]
—Arr. Willner
    Philharmonia String Orch.—Lambert
                    12″—C-DX1221
    Residentie Orch.—Fritz Schuman
                in preparation **Dutch Decca**
No. 1 - 6 only Arr. **Violin & Piano** Szekely
    Joseph Szigeti & Béla Bartók
                    10″—C-17089D
    Yehudi Menuhin & Marcel Gazelle
                    12″—G-DB6178
    Bronislaw Gimpel & Artur Balsam
                    10″—in VOX-616
Nos. 1 - 4 & 6 only
    Zoltan Szekely & Geza Frid 12″—D-K872
    [Manén: Chanson adagietto]
Nos. 1 - 4 only
    Tossy Spivakowsky & Artur Balsam, in
    CH-AA (with Violin Sonata No. 2)

RONDOS Piano

(3) Rondos on Folk Tunes
    Lili Kraus   2 12″—P-PXO1025/6
    [Romanian Folk Dances]
—No. 1 only
    Hans Leygraf   10″—G-X7330
    [Allegro barbaro]

SONATAS Violin & Piano

No. 2
    Tossy Spivakowsky & Artur Balsam
    [4 Romanian Dances]   3 12″—CH-AA

SONGS

Enchanting Song
    Morriston Boys' Choir   12″—D-K1157
    [Britten: A Ceremony of Carols, Pt. 5 &
    Kodaly: Ave Maria]
Hungarian Folksong Settings
Elindultam szep hazambol, Altal mennek en a Tiszen, A gyulai kert allat
    Vilma Medgyaszay (s) & Béla Bartók (pf)
                    10″—G-AM1676
    [Kodalý: Zold erdoben]

Feketefold, Asszonyok asszonyok, Istenem Istenem, Ha kimegyek arr' a magas tetore
Maria Basilides (s) & Béla Bartók (pf)
10″—G-AM1671

Nen messze van ide Kismargitta, Vevig mentem a tarkanyi sej-haj nagy utcan
Vilma Medgyaszay (s) & Béla Bartók (pf)
10″—G-AM1678
[Kodalý: Most jottem Erdelybol]

Toltik a Nagy Erdo Utjat, Eddig valo Dolgom, Olvado a ho
Ferencz Szekelyhidy (t) & Béla Bartók (pf)
12″—G-AN215
[Kodalý: Kadar Istvan]

Suite, Op. 14 Piano
Béla Bartók 12″—G-AN468
Marcella Barzetti 12″—G-S10491

BATE, Stanley (1912-   )
Young British composer and pianist, a pupil of Vaughan-Williams and Nadia Boulanger.

Sonata Flute & Piano
Marcel Moyse & Louise Moyse
2 10″—OL-25/6
[Naudot: Sonata for 2 Flutes]

BATH, Hubert (1883-1946)
British composer and conductor who has written comic operas, cantatas, songs and smaller orchestral works. He had prepared several scores for films (including the excerpt below) at the time of his sudden death.

Cornish Rhapsody (Music for the film— "Love Story") Piano & Orchestra
Harriet Cohen & London Symphony Orch.—Bath 12″—C-7440M
(C-DX1171)
Monia Liter & Concert Orch.— Mantovani 10″—D-F8484

BAX, Sir Arnold Trevor (1883-   )
A British composer of many technical achievements, Bax has written much pleasant and interesting music, showing the definite influence of Wagner and French Impressionism.

ENGLISH MUSIC SOCIETY, Volume II
Sonata for viola & piano
William Primrose & Harriet Cohen
Nonet for String Quartet, with Bass, Flute, Clarinet, Oboe & Harp
Griller String Quartet & Ensemble
Mater ora Filium
BBC Chorus—Leslie Woodgate
7 12″—CM-386†
(A) Hill Tune Piano
Harriet Cohen 12″—C-DX1109
[A Mountain Mood]
Mater ora Filium Carol for unacc. double choir
BBC Chorus —Woodgate, in English Music Society, Vol. II, CM-386†
Mediterranean Piano
—Arr. Orchestra Bax
New Symphony Orch.—Goossens
[Tintagel, Pt. 3] 12″—G-C1620
—Arr. Violin & Piano Heifetz
Jascha Heifetz & Emanuel Bay
(in VM-1126) 10″—V-10-1293
[Castelnuovo-Tedesco: Tango]

Morning Song ("Maytime in Sussex")
Harriet Cohen (pf) & Orch.—Sargent
12″—C-DX1361

(A) Mountain Mood - Theme & Variations Piano
Harriet Cohen 12″—C-DX1109
[A Hill Tune]

Nonet
Griller Quartet & Ensemble, in English Music Society, Vol. II; CM-386†

Overture to a Picaresque Comedy Orchestra
London Philharmonic Orch.—Harty
12″—C-LX394

Paean Piano
Harriet Cohen 10″—C-DB1786
[Vaughan-Williams: Kyrie, Westminster Abbey Choir—Bullock]
(in Columbia History of Music, Vol. V, CM-361)

Quartet (String) No. 1, G major
Griller Quartet 4 12″—D-K1009/12

Sonata ("Phantasy") Viola & Harp
Watson Forbes & Maria Korchinska
3 12″—D-K941/3
[Alwyn: Two Folk Tunes]

Sonata Viola & Piano
William Primrose & Harriet Cohen, in English Music Society, Vol. II, CM-386†

SONGS

I Heard a Piper Singing
Astra Desmond (c) & Gerald Moore (pf)
10″—D-M522
[Vaughan-Williams: Linden Lea]

The White Peace (MacLeod)
John McCormack (t) & Gerald Moore (pf) 10″—G-DA1791
[Vaughan-Williams: Linden Lea]

Symphony No. 3
Hallé Orch.—Barbirolli
6 12″—G-3380/5†

Tintagel Orchestra
New Symphony Orch.—Goossens
[Mediterranean] 2 12″—G-C1619/20

BAZZINI, Antonio (1818-1897)
An Italian violinist and composer, known chiefly for the popular work listed below. As a professor of composition at Milan Conservatory, he was known abroad for his opera scores, cantatas and chamber music.

La Ronde des lutins, Op. 25 Violin & Piano
Jascha Heifetz & Emanuel Bey
(G-DB3535) 12″—V-15813
[Falla: La Vida Breve—Danza Española]
[Beethoven: Violin Sonata No. 3, Pt. 5, on V-18329, in VM-852†]
Yehudi Menuhin & M. Gazelle
(G-DB5395) 12″—G-DB2414
[Sarasate: Rondo Andaluza]
Ida Haendel & Adela Kotowska
10″—D-F7659
[Massenet: Thaïs—Méditation]
DUPLICATION: Vasa Prihoda, PD-25703;

BEACH, Mrs. H. H. A. (1867-1944)
A brilliant concert pianist who also composed numerous songs.

Ah, Love, But a Day
Gladys Swarthout (ms) & Lester
Hodges (pf)   10"—V-10-1050
[Brahe: Bless This House]

BEETHOVEN, Ludwig Van (1770-1827)

Although a tremendous amount of Beethoven's music has been recorded in complete form (the Society albums, etc.) there still remain to be recorded such works as "Fidelio" and many works now dropped from current catalogues.

Adelaide See under Songs
Ah, Perfido! Op. 65 Soprano
Kirsten Flagstad & Philadelphia Orch.
—Ormandy   1 10" & 1 12"—VM-439
Andante Favori, F major Piano
(Grove's No. 170)
Elly Ney   12"—G-DB4676
Dirk Schäfer   12"—C-DHX11

BAGATELLES Piano

A minor, "Für Elise" (Grove's No. 173)
Artur Schnabel, in Beethoven Society
Vol XV
Artur Schnabel
(in VM-158†)   12"—V-7673
[Concerto No. 1, Pt. 9]
(G-DB1694 in GM-156†)
[Schubert: Sonata, A major, Op. Posth.,
Pt. 9, in VM-580†]
Eileen Joyce   12"—C-DX974
[Bagatelle, Op. 33, No. 2]
Johanne Stockmarr   10"—G-DA5241
[Sonata No. 7, D major, Op. 10, No. 3—
Minuet only]
(7) Bagatelles, Op. 33 Piano
Artur Schnabel, in Beethoven Society,
Vol. XV
—No. 1, E flat major
Walter Gieseking
(in CM-358†)   12"—C-69478D
[Sonata No. 21, C major, Pt. 5]
(C-LX783) (C-LWX265) (C-GQX11009)
Eileen Joyce   12"—D-K1555
[Sonata No. 8, Pt. 5]
Erik Then-Bergh   10"—T-A10510
[Bagatelle No. 4]
—No. 2, C major
Eileen Joyce   12"—C-DX974
[Für Elise]
—No. 4, A major
Erik Then-Bergh   10"—T-A10510
[Bagatelle No. 1]
—No. 5, C major
Wilhelm Kempff   10"—PD-24795
[Ecossaises] (PD-62630)
(13) Bagatelles, Op. 119 Piano
—No. 1
Denis Matthews   12"—C-DX1061
[No. 11 & 32 Variations, Pt. 3]
—No. 11
Denis Matthews   12"—C-DX1061
[No. 1 & 32 Variations, Pt. 3]
Myra Hess   10"—C4083M
[Scarlatti: 2 Sonatas & Brahms:
Capriccio, Op. 78, No. 2]
(6) Bagatelles, Op. 126 Piano
Artur Schnabel, Beethoven Sonata
Society, Vol. XIV

—Nos. 1 & 2
Guido Agosti   12"—G-AW297
[Sonata No. 31, Pt. 5]
"Battle" Symphony See under Symphonies

BEETHOVEN "SOCIETIES"
See: Sonatas (Piano; Violin & Piano)

CONCERTOS

Piano & Orchestra
No. 1, C major, Op. 15
Ania Dorfmann & NBC Symphony
Orch.—Toscanini   4 12"—VM-1036†
Artur Schnabel & London Symphony
Orch.—Sargent   5 10"—VM-158†
[Für Elise] (G-DB1690/4 in GM-156†)
Walter Gieseking & Berlin State Opera
Orch.—Rosbaud   4 12"—CM-308†
(C-LX631/4) (C-LFX494/7)
(C-LWX229/32) (C-GQX10879/82)
No. 2, B flat major, Op. 19
Artur Schnabel & Philharmonia Orch.—
Dobrowen   4 12"—G-DB6323/6†
William Kapell & NBC Symphony Orch.
—Golschman   4 12"—VM-1132†
[Brahms: Intermezzo, Op. 116, No. 6
E major]
Artur Schnabel & London Philarmonic
Orch.—Sargent   4 12"—VM-295†
(G-DB2573/6 in GM-238†)
Elly Ney & Landesorchester—
Fritz Zaun   12"—G-DB4503/6
No. 3, C minor, Op. 37
Solomon & BBC Orch.—Boult
4 12"—G-DB6196/9†
Artur Rubinstein & NBC Symphony—
Toscanini   4 12"—VM-1016†
Artur Schnabel & London Philharmonic
—Sargent   5 12"—VM-194†
[Rondo, Op. 51, No. 1] (G-DB1940/4).
Lubka Kolessa & Saxon State Orch.
Böhm   5 12"—G-DB5506/10
[Hummel: Rondo, E flat major, Kolessa
solo]
José Iturbi & Rochester Philharmonic
Orch.—Iturbi   5 12"—VM-801†
[Bach: Fantasia, C minor]
Eduard Erdmann & Berlin Philharmonic
Orch.—A. Rother   4 12"—T-E1889/92
—1st Mvt. (Condensed)
Jesús María Sanromá & Symphony Orch.
—O'Connell, in VM-818
No. 4, G major, Op. 58
Artur Schnabel & Philharmonia Orch.—
Dobrowen   4 12"—G-DB6303/6†
Artur Schnabel & Chicago Symphony
Orch.—Stock   4 12"—VM-930†
Walter Gieseking & Saxon State Orch.—
Böhm   4 12"—CM-411†
(C-LX847/50) (C-BQX3000/3)
(C-LWX288/91)
Wilhelm Backhaus & London Symphony
—Barbirolli   4 12"—GM-105†
(G-DB1425/8)
No. 5, E flat major, Op. 73 ("Emperor")
Artur Schnabel & Chicago Symphony
Orch.—Stock   5 12"—VM-939†
(G-DB6184/8)
Rudolf Serkin & New York Philharmonic-

Symphony Orch.—Walter
5 12"—CM-500†
Edwin Fischer & Saxon State Orch.—
Böhm 5 12"—G-DB5511/5
Conrad Hansen & German Opera House
Orch.—Jochum 5 12"—T-SK3203/7
Marguerite Long & Paris Conservatory
Orch.—Münch 5 12"—C-LFX679/83
Walter Gieseking & Vienna Philharmonic
Orch.—Walter 5 12"—CM-243†
[Bach: Partita No. 1—Menuets &
Gigue] (C-LX342/6)
(C-GQX10764/8) (C-LFX359/63)
Benno Moiseiwitsch & London Philhar-
monic Orch.—Szell 5 12"—GM-321†
(G-C3043/7)
Wilhelm Kempff & Berlin Philharmonic
Orch.—Raabe 5 12"—PD-516692/6
(PD-67062/6)
[Bach-Kempff: Wachet auf]
Victor Schiøler & Danish State Radio
Symphony Orch.—Garaguly
5 12"—TONO-X25098/102
Violin & Orchestra, D major, Op. 61
Joseph Szigeti & Philharmonic-Symphony
of N. Y.—Bruno Walter
5 12"—CM-697†
Jascha Heifetz & NBC Symphony Orch.
—Toscanini 5 12"—VM-705†
[Quartet No. 16, Scherzo only]
(G-DB5724/8S: last side blank)
[Schubert-Friedberg: Rondo, on
G-DB11110/4]
Yehudi Menuhin & Lucerne Festival
Orch.—Furtwängler
6 12"—G-DB6574/9S†
Bronislaw Hubermann & Vienna Phil-
harmonic Orch.—Szell
5 12"—C-LX509/13†
[Bach: Partita No. 1—Sarabande &
Double]
Fritz Kreisler & London Philharmonic—
Barbirolli 6 12"—VM-325†
[Kreisler: Tambourin Chinois]
[G-DB2927/32S: last side blank]
Max Strub & Saxon State Orch.—Böhm
6 12"—G-DB5516/21S
Georg Kulenkampff & Berlin Philhar-
monic Orch.—Schmidt-Isserstedt
5 12"—T-E2016/21
[Mozart: Adagio, K. 261]
Karl Freund & Berlin Philharmonic Orch.
—Davisson 5 12"—PD-15205/9
Henri Merckel & Lamoureux Orch.—
Bigot 5 12"—G-W1508/12
Joseph Szigeti & British Symphony Orch.
—Walter 5 12"—CM-177†
(C-LX174/8) (C-LFX293/7)
(C-GQX10667/71)
L. Zimmermann & Amsterdam Concert-
gebouw Orch.—Rudolf Mengelberg
5 12"—C-DHX20/4
—3rd Mvt. (Rondo) only
Jascha Heifetz & NBC Symphony Orch.
Toscanini
(in VM-1064) 12"—V-11-9236
C major, Op. 36 ("Triple") Violin, 'Cello,
Piano & Orchestra
Richard Odnoposoff, Stefan Auber,
Angelica Morales & Vienna Philharmonic
Orch.—Weingartner 5 12"—CM-327†

(C-LX671/5s) (C-LFX518/22s)
(Last side blank)
[Mozart: Nozze di Figaro-Overture,
Symphony Orch. on C-GQX10915/9]
**(12) Contretänze Orchestra (Grove's
No. 141)**
*Contretänze is commonly but incorrectly An-
gelicized as "Country Dances"; the correct
English form is "Contra-Dances." Exact dis-
tinctions are not always made between "Con-
tretänze," "Ländler" and "Deutsche Tänze."*
CBS Orch.—Barlow 2 10"—CX-184†
—No. 1
CBS Orch.—Barlow 12"—C-71411D
[Minuet, G major & Bach: Suite No. 3—
Air on G String & Vlc Suite No 3—
Bourrée]
Victor Orchestra 10"—onV-20451
—No. 6
Victor Orchestra 10"—onV-24795
Consecration of the House
See under Die Weihe des Hauses
Coriolan Overture, C minor, Op. 62
Orchestra Eng. Coriolanus Overture
NBC Symphony Orch.—Toscanini
12"—V-11-9023
London Symphony Orch.—Walter
(G-DB3638) 12"—V-12535
EIAR Orch.—Geri 12"—CET-BB25100
Berlin State Opera Orch.—Schuricht
12"—PD-67939
Munich Philharmonic Orch.—Kabasta
12"—G-DB5636
DUPLICATIONS: Amsterdam Concertge-
bouw Orch.—Mengelberg, C-LX167:
C-GQX10371: O-8595: C-LFX261;
Minneapolis Symphony Orch.—Mitro-
poulos, C-11175D; Berlin State Opera
Orch.—Klemperer, PD-516635; Berlin
Philharmonic Orch.—Kleiber, U-E653;
London Symphony Orch.—Pablo Casals,
G-D1409; Symphony Orch.—Ruhlmann,
PAT-X96132
Creation's Hymn—See under Song —
Ehre Gottes
**(12) Deutsche Tänze Orchestra (Grove's
No. 140)**
—No. 11 & 12
Berlin Symphony Orch.—Fritz Zaun
12"—O-7966
[Mozart: Serenade No. 6, Pt. 3]
Minuet, E flat major Piano
Artur Schnabel in Beethoven Society,
Vol. XIV (not available separately)
DUOS—Clarinet & Bassoon
No. 1, C major (Grove's No. 147)
Pierre Lefèbvre & Fernand Oubradous
2 12"—OL-79/80
[Weber: Concerto, F major, Op. 75—
Adagio, Oubradous & Paris Orch.]
No. 2, F major
Pierre Lefèbvre & Fernand Oubradous
12"—OL-4
No. 3, B flat major
Pierre Lefèbvre & Fernand Oubradous
12"—OL-78
DUOS—Viola & Cello
E flat major
("for viola, 'cello & two obbligato eye-
glasses" written as a joke in 1796) (not

included in complete works) (Peters Edition, 1912)
William Primrose & Emanuel Feuermann
12"—V-11-8620

(6) Ecossaises (B. & H. Series 25, No. 302)
Piano
Wilhelm Kempff 10"—PD-24795
[Bagatelle, Op. 33, No. 5]

EGMONT, Op. 84 Incidental Music (To Goethe's Drama)

Overture, F minor Orchestra
Philharmonia Orch.—Alceo Galliera
(C-GQX11100) 12"—C-DX1273
Vienna Philharmonic Orch.—Weingartner
(C-LX690) 12"—C-69195D
NBC Symphony Orch.—Toscanini
12"—G-DB5705
BBC Symphony Orch.—Boult
12"—G-DB1925
Dresden State Opera Orch.—Böhm
(G-EH919) 12"—G-C2780
Berlin Philharmonic Orch.—Jochum
12"—T-E2683
Dresden Philharmonic—Van Kempen
12"—PD-15309
Amsterdam Concertgebouw Orch.—
Mengelberg 12"—C-LX161
(O-8300) (C-GQX10349)
(C-LFX260)
Zurich Tonhalle Orch.—Georg Solti
(in preparation)—Swiss Decca
DUPLICATIONS: N. Y. Philharmonic-Symphony Orch.—Mengelberg, V-7291; G-AW216; Berlin Philharmonic Orch.—Furtwängler, PD-67055
No. 3—Entr'acte No. 2
London Philharmonic Orch.—Weingartner
(in CX-133†) 12"—C-69596D
[Eleven Viennese Dances, Pt. 3]
(C-LX771) (C-LWX298)
(C-GQX10997)
No. 7—Clärchens Tod
London Philharmonic Orch.—Weingartner
(in CX-140†) 12"—C-69657D
[Weihe des Hauses, Pt. 3] (C-LX812)

Fantasia, G minor, Op. 77 Piano
Artur Schnabel, Beethoven Sonata Society, Vol. XIV
Farewell to the Piano Piano
Arr. Werschenska
Galina Werschenska 12"—G-Z249
[Brahms: Waltz, E minor, Op. 39, No. 1 & Schubert: Waltz, A flat major, Op. 9a]

FIDELIO, Op. 72
Opera in 2 Acts In German
Overture Orchestra
London Philharmonic Orch.—Weingartner 12"—C-69545D
(C-LX784) (C-LFX562)
(C-GQX11006)
BBC Symphony Orch.—Bruno Walter
(G-DB2261) 12"—V-11809
Symphony Orch.—C. Raybould
(C-DF1947) 10"—DB835
(in Columbia History of Music, Vol. III, CM-233)

Berlin Philharmonic Orch.—Abendroth
(O-188150) 12"—O-4617
DUPLICATIONS: Berlin State Opera Orch.—von Zemlinsky, PD-62667; Berlin State Opera Orch.—Blech, G-EW19

ACT I

No. 3, Ach wär' ich schon mit dir vereint
Sop.
Adele Kern & Berlin-Charlottenburg Orch.—Prüwer 12"—PD-66946
[Meyerbeer: Les Huguenots—Nobles Seigneurs]
No. 4, Mir ist so wunderbar Quartet
Erna Berger (s), H. Gottlieb (s), Marcel Wittrisch (t), Willi Domgraf-Fassbaender (b) [No. 16] 12"—G-DB4417
No. 10, Abscheulicher, wo eilst du hin? (Recit.) & Komm, Hoffnung (Aria)
Soprano
Kirsten Flagstad & Philadelphia Orch.—Ormandy 12"—V-14972
Hilde Konetzni & Berlin Opera Orch.—Schmidt-Isserstedt 12"—T-E2290
Rose Bampton & NBC Symphony Orch.—Toscanini 12"—V-11-9110
Helena Braun & Berlin State Opera Orch.—Ludwig 12"—PD-67929
Lotte Lehmann & Orch.—Gurlitt
(Recit. omitted) 12"—P-PXO1013
Elisabeth Ohms 12"—PD-66904

ACT II

No. 13, Gott! welch' Dunkel hier (Recit.) & In des Lebens Frühlingstagen (Aria)
Tenor
Helge Roswaenge & Berlin State Opera Orch.—Seidler-Winkler
12"—G-DB4522
Franz Völker & Berlin State Opera Orch.—Melichar 12"—PD-27311
René Maison & Orch.—Leinsdorf
12"—C-71410D
No. 16, Er sterbe, doch er soll erst wissen
Quartet
H. Gottlieb (s), W. Ludwig (t), Willi Domgraf-Fassbaender (b) & W. Grossmann (bs) [No. 4] 12"—G-DB4417

Für Elise See: Bagatelle, A minor
Gavotte, F major Piano 4-hands
—Arr. Violin & Piano Kramer
Fritz Kreisler & Carl Lamson
10"—V-1136
[Bach-Winternitz: Gavotte]

(DIE) GESCHOEPFE DES PROMETHEUS, Op. 43 Ballet Eng. The Men of Prometheus or, Prometheus
Overture Orchestra
NBC Symphony Orch.—Toscanini
(in VM-1098†) 12"—V-11-9449
[Leonore Overture No. 3, Pt. 3]
[Symphony No. 3, Pt. 11, on V-17858 in VM-765†]
Vienna Philharmonic Orch.—Weingartner 12"—C-68560D
[Symphony No. 7, Pt. 9] (in CM-260†)
(C-LX488) (C-LFX428)
(C-GQX10781)

London Philharmonic Orch.—
Weingartner
(in CM-197†)   12″—C-68220D
[Symphony No. 4, Pt. 7]
(C-LX277) (C-DFX173)

Grosse Fuge See under Quartet—String
Op. 133

**(Das) Heiligenstadter Testament vom. 6.
10. 1802**
Elly Ney (reading in German)
12″—G-DB4460
[Sonata No. 8—Adagio cantabile only]

**Introduction & Variations on "Ich bin der
Schneider Kakadu" op. 121a** (Theme by
Wenzel Müller—**Die Schwestern von
Prague**) Piano, Violin & Cello
Holger Lund Christiansen, Erling Bloch
& Torben Svendsen of Danish Quartet
2 12″—G-DB5229/30

König Stefan Overture, E flat major, Op. 117
Orchestra
Janssen Symphony of Los Angeles—
Werner Jenssen   (In Artist-JS14)
[with Battle Symphony: Wellington's
Victory]

Ländler unspecified
—**Arr. Violin & Piano** Heifetz
Jascha Heifetz & Emanuel Bay
(in VM-1158)   10″—V-10-1342
[Bach: English Suite No. 6—Gavottes
I & II]

LEONORE OVERTURES Orchestra

No. 1, C major, Op. 138
BBC Symphony Orch.—Toscanini
(G-DB3846)   12″—V-15945

No. 2, C major, Op. 72a
Amsterdam Concertgebouw Orch.—
Beinum (D-K1431/2)   2 12″—D-ED4†
London Symphony Orch.—
Weingartner   2 12″—CX-96†
(C-LX712/3) (C-LFX531/2)

No. 3, C major, Op. 72a
NBC Symphony Orch.—Toscanini
[Prometheus Overture] 2 12″—VM-1098†
NBC Symphony Orch.—Toscanini
2 12″—G-DB5703/4
Minneapolis Symphony Orch.—
Mitropoulos   2 12″—CX-173†
Saxon State Orch.—Böhm
2 12″—G-DB4558/9
Orch. of the "Maggio Musicale"—Gui
2 12″—CET-BB25169/70
[Bach—Gui: Chorale Prelude—Kommst
du nun, Jesu]
Vienna Philharmonic Orch.—Walter
2 12″—VM-359†
[Ruins of Athens—Overture, cond. by
A. Rosé] (G-DB2885/6)
Berlin Philharmonic Orch.—Jochum
(U-F18021/2)   2 12″—T-E2278/9
Berlin Philharmonic Orch.—Ludwig
2 12″—PD-15195/6
[Ruins of Athens—Turkish March]
Tivoli Concert Orch.—Thomas Jensen
2 12″—TONO-X25006/7
DUPLICATIONS: Berlin State Opera
Orch.—Blech, G-EJ131/2; Amsterdam

Concertgebouw Orch.—Mengelberg,
C-LX129/30; C-LFX187/8

MARCHES

**Yorkscher Marsch (Marsch des Yorkschen
Korps, 1813)**
Polydor Band—Snaga   10″—PD-21817
[Neumann: Petipa Marsch]
See also Funeral Marches in Sonata No. 12
& Symphony No. 3

MASSES

Missa Solemnis, D major, Op. 123
Jeanette Vreeland (s), John Priebe (t),
Anna Kaskas (c), Norman Cordon (bs),
Harvard Glee Club, Radcliffe Choral So-
ciety, E. Power Biggs (organ), Boston
Symphony Orch.—Serge Koussevitzky
12 12″—VM-758/759†
Lotte Leonard (s), Emmy Land (s), Elea-
nor Schlosshauer-Reynolds (c), Anton
Maria Topitz (t), Eugen Transky (t),
Wilhelm Guttmann (bs), Herman Schey
(bs), Wilfred Hanke (vl), Bruno Kittel
Choir, Berlin Philharmonic Orch.—Bruno
Kittel.
(PD-95146/56)   11 12″—VOX-466
[Die ehre Gottes, arr. Chorus]

Minuet, G major Piano   (No. 2 of 6,
Grove's No. 167)
Mark Hambourg   10″—G-B3798
[Chopin: Valse, Op. 64, No. 2 & Gossec:
Tambourin]

—**Arr. Orchestra**
CBS Orchestra—Barlow 12″—C-71411D
[Contra-Dance No. 1 & Bach: Suite No.
3—Air & Cello Suite No. 2—Bourrée]
Albert Sandler Orchestra 12″—C-DX759
[Minuet Medley]
Marek Weber Orchestra   10″—G-B4466
(G-EG2703) (G-HE2305) (G-HN620)
DUPLICATIONS: Mandoline Orchestra,
PD-21622; Geczy Orch., G-EG7082

—**Arr. Violin & Piano**
Mischa Elman & J. Bonime 10″—V-1434
[Arensky: Serenade]
DUPLICATIONS: Albert Sammons,
D-F7529; Pablo Casals (vlc), G-DB1419

Polonaise in C major, Op. 89   Piano
Edward Kilenyi   12″—C-71968D
[Mendelssohn: Scherzo a capriccio]
Friedrich Wührer   10″—G-EG7024

Prometheus—See **(Die) Geschöpfe des
Prometheus. Op. 43**

QUARTETS—String

No. 1, F major, Op. 18, No. 1
Budapest Quartet   4 12″—CM-444†
Busch Quartet   3 12″—G-DB6300/2†
(Also on G-DB2102/4)
Calvet Quartet   4 12″—T-SK2142/5
(U-F18026/9)
Lener Quartet   3 12″—C-GQX10365/7

No. 2, G major, Op. 18, No. 2
Budapest Quartet   3 12″—VM-601†
Stross Quartet   4 12″—PD-15315/18

Lener Quartet   3 12"—CM-66
(C-GQX10422/4)

No. 3, D major, Op. 18, No. 3
Pascal Quartet   3 12"—O-123874/6
Lener Quartet   3 12"—C-GQX10425/7

No. 4, C minor, Op. 18, No. 4
Budapest Quartet   3 12"—CM-556†
Paganini Quartet 3 12"—G-DB6488/90†
Lener Quartet   3 12"—C-GQX10903/5
(Also: C-GQX10368/70)
Stross Quartet   3 12"—PD-15312/4

No. 5, A major, Op. 18, No. 5
Lener String Quartet 3 12"—CM-301†
Stross Quartet   3 12"—PD-15297/9
Calvet Quartet   3 12"—T-E2923/5
Capet Quartet   4 10"—C-D1659/62

No. 6, B flat major, Op. 18, No. 6
Lener Quartet 3 12"—C-GQX10428/30
—3rd Mvt. only
Prisca Quartet   12"—PD-10539
[Quartet No. 8, Pt. 11]

**No. 7, F major, Op. 59 ("Rasoumovsky")
No. 1**
Philharmonia Quartet
    5 12"—C-DX1067/71†
Coolidge Quartet   4 12"—VM-804†
Paganini Quartet   5 12"—VM-1151†
[Mozart: Quartet No. 17—Menuetto
only]
Busch Quartet   6 12"—CM-543†
[Haydn Quartet, B flat major, Op. 103—
Minuetto only]
Roth Quartet   5 12"—CM-256†
Lener Quartet   5 12"—C-GQX10360/4

**No. 8, E minor, Op. 59 ("Rasoumovsky")
No. 2**
Budapest Quartet   4 12"—VM-340†
Paganini Quartet   4 12"—VM-1152†
Calvet Quartet   4 12"—T-E2595/8
Coolidge Quartet   4 12"—VM-919†
Prisca Quartet   5 12"—PD-10534/9
[Quartet No. 6, 3rd Mvt. only]
Lener Quartet   4 12"—C-GQX10377/80

—4th Mvt. only
Guarneri Quartet   12"—PD-67140
[Haydn: Quartet, G minor, Op. 74, No. 3
—2nd Mvt.]

**No. 9, C major, Op. 59 ("Rasoumovsky")
No. 3**
Budapest Quartet   4 12"—CM-510†
Paganini Quartet   4 12"—VM-1153†
[Mozart: Quartet No. 21—Menuetto only]
Calvet Quartet   4 12"—T-E3066/9
Strub Quartet   4 12"—G-DB5599/602s
Busch Quartet   4 12"—G-DB2109/12
Lener Quartet   4 12"—C-GQX10381/4

No. 10, E. flat major, Op. 74 ("Harfen")
Budapest Quartet   4 12"—VM-467†
Gabriel Bouillon Quartet
    4 12"—G-DB5127/30

No. 11, F minor, Op. 95 ("Serious")
Budapest Quartet   3 12"—CM-519†
Busch Quartet   2 12"—G-DB1799/800
Calvet Quartet   3 12"—T-E2960/2
Lener Quartet 3 12"—C-GQX10439/41

No. 12, E flat major, Op. 127
Budapest Quartet   5 12"—CM-537†
Lener Quartet   5 12"—C-GQX10434/8

No. 13, B flat major, Op. 130
NOTE: *This Quartet—as published—contains 6
movements, the last of which is an "Allegro."
Beethoven originally intended the finale to be
a gigantic fugal movement. This was withdrawn at the publisher's request and later issued separately as the "Grosse Fuge" Op. 133.
For recordings of this work see entry following
Quartet No. 16.*

Budapest Quartet   5 12"—VM-157†
(G-DB2239/43, in GM-274†)
Busch Quartet   5 12"—CM-474†
Lener Quartet   5 12"—C-GQX10442/6
—5th Mvt. (Cavatina) only
Berlin Philharmonic Orch.—
Furtwängler   12"—T-SK3104

No. 14, C sharp minor, Op. 131
Budapest Quartet   5 12"—CM-429†
Busch Quartet   5 12"—G-DB2810/4
Calvet Quartet
(U-F18084/8)   5 12"—T-E2590/4
Capet Quartet
(C-L2283/7)   5 12"—C-D15097/101

**No. 15, A minor, Op. 132 ("Heiliger
Dankgesang")**
Budapest Quartet   5 12"—CM-545†
Busch Quartet
(G-DB3375/80)   6 12"—VM-490†
[Sonata No. 14—1st Mvt., Wilhelm
Backhaus, pf. solo]
Lener Quartet   5 12"—C-GQX10811/5
No. 16, F. major, Op. 135
Budapest Quartet   3 12"—CM-489†
Busch Quartet   4 12"—G-DB2113/6
Lener Quartet   3 12"—C-GQX10431/33
—2nd & 3rd Mvts. only
—Arr. String Orchestra
NBC Symphony Orch.—Toscanini
(G-DB3904 & G-DB3858)
    2 12"—VM-590†
[Paganini: Moto perpetuo]
—Scherzo only
NBC Symphony—Toscanini
    (in VM-705†)   12"—V-17445
[Violin Concerto, with Heifetz, Pt. 9]
Grosse Fuge, Op. 133
Budapest Quartet 2 12"—G-DB1559/60
Lener Quartet   2 12"—CX-6†
Kroll Quartet   2 12"—MC-73
Pascal Quartet   2 12"—O-123880/1
—Arr. Chamber Orchestra Weingartner
Busch Chamber Players
    2 12"—CX-211†
Edwin Fischer & Chamber Orch.
    2 12"—G-DB5547/8

QUARTETS Piano and Strings
No. 2, D major
—Rondo only
Reginald Paul Piano Quartet
    12"—D-X241
[Walton: Piano Quartet, Pt. 5]

QUINTETS
Quintet, C major, Op. 29 2 vls., 2 vlas., vlc
(1801)

Milton Katims (vla) & Budapest
Quartet 4 12"—CM-623†
William Primrose (vla) & Lener
Quartet 4 12"—CM-294†
(C-GQX10822/5)

Quintet E flat major, Op. 16
Piano, Oboe, Clarinet, Bassoon, Horn
Ernst Victor Wolff & Berlin State Opera
Orch. soloists 4 12"—PD-27302/5
[Trio, Op. 11, 2nd Mvt. with Munich
Chamber Music Ensemble]

ROMANCES Violin & Orchestra

No. 1, G major, Op. 40
Siegfried Borries & Berlin Philharmonic
Orch.—Schüler 12"—G-DB4662
Georg Kulenkampff & German Opera
House Orch.—Rother 12"—T-E2904
Mischa Elman & Symphony Orch.—
Collingwood 12"—G-DB1846
—Arr. Violin & Piano Flesch
Ibolyka Zilzer & pf. 10"—PD-27132
No. 2, F major, Op. 50
Siegfried Borries & Berlin Philharmonic
Orch.—Schüler 12"—G-DB4661
Georg Kulenkampff & Berlin Philhar-
monic Orch.—Kletzki 12"—T-F1142
Emil Telmanyi & Tivoli Orch.
12"—TONO-X25004
Mischa Elman & Symphony Orch.—
Collingwood 12"—G-DB1847
—Arr. Violin & Piano
Paul Kaul & G. Andolfi 12"—PAT-PAT47
Ibolyka Zilzer & pf. 12"—PD-27077
Jacques Thibaud & pf. acc.
12"—G-DB904
**Rondino in E flat (Grove's No. 146) 2 Oboes,
2 Clarinets, 2 Horns, 2 Bassoons**
(Early composition: published 1829)
Société des Instruments à vent—
Oubradous 10"—G-DA4926

RONDOS Piano

C major, Op. 51, No. 1
Benno Moiseiwitsch 12"—G-C3291
[Sonata No. 21, C major, Op. 53, Pt. 5]
G major, Op. 51, No. 2
Frederic Lamond 12"—G-EH975
A major (Grove's No. 164) 1784
Artur Schnabel, in Beethoven Society,
Vol. XIV
**Rondo a Capriccio, G major, Op. 129 ("Die
Wut' über den verlor'nen Groschen")**
Piano Eng. **Fury over the lost penny**
Artur Schnabel, in Beethoven Society,
Vol. XIV
Alexander Brailowsky 12"—V-15407
(G-DB3705)
[Scarlatti: Pastorale & Capriccio]
Wilhelm Kempff 10"—PD-62802
Friedrich Wührer 10"—G-EG6905

RONDO Violin & Piano
G major
Yehudi & Hephzibah Menuhin
(in VM-1008†) 12"—V-11-8843
[Sonata No. 7, C minor, Op. 30, No. 2
Pt. 7]

(DIE) RUINEN VON ATHEN, Op. 113
Incidental Music
Eng. **The Ruins of Athens**
Overture
Vienna Philharmonic Orch.—Arnold Rosé
(in VM-359†) 12"—V-11959
[Leonore Overture No. 3, Pt. 3]
(G-DB2886)
London Philharmonic Orch.—
Weingartner 12"—C-LX898
[Liszt: Mephisto Waltz, Pt. 3]
DUPLICATION: Casals Orch. of Barce-
lona, G-AW133
Chor der Derwische (Chorus of Dervishes)
—Arr. Violin & Piano
Ruggiero Ricci & Louis Persinger, in
VOX-196
Marcia alla Turca (Turkish March)
Vienna Philharmonic Orch.—Karl
Alwin 10"—G-B3188
[Mozart: Rondo alla Turca] (G-K7174)
Berlin Philharmonic Orch.—Ludwig
12"—PD-15196
[Leonore Overture No. 3, Pt. 3]
Amsterdam Concertgebouw Orch.—
Mengelberg 12"—C-LX130
[Leonore Overture No. 3, Pt. 3]
(C-LFX188)
—Arr. Piano Beethoven (with 6 variations)
as Op. 76
Wilhelm Kempff 10"—PD-62762
[Schumann: Träumerei]
Sergei Rachmaninoff 10"—V-1196
[Schubert-Rachmaninoff. Wohin?]
Emil von Sauer 10"—O-4762
[Sauer: Espenlaub]
—Arr. 2 Pianos Thern
Ethel Bartlett & Rae Robertson
10"—C-17198D
[Arensky: Suite No. 1, Op. 15—Romance]
—Arr. Violin & Piano Auer
Yehudi Menuhin & Marcel Gazelle
10"—G-DA1494
[Kreisler: "La Chasse" in the Style of
Cartier]

Septet, E flat major, Op. 20 Violin, Viola,
'Cello, String Bass, Clarinet, Bassoon,
Horn
Lener Quartet members, Hobday, Draper,
Hinchcliffe, Brain
5 12"—C-GQX10486/510/11/12/18

SERENADES (Trios)

D major, Op. 8 Vln., Vla., Vlc.
Pasquier Trio 3 12"—PAT-PAT58/60
Simon Goldberg, Paul Hindemith &
Emanuel Feuermann 3 12"—CM-217†
D major, Op. 25 Flute, Vln., Vla.
Klingler Trio 3 12"—G-EH1073/5

SONATAS Piano

Beethoven Piano Sonata Society
Artur Schnabel
Vol. 1—No. 24, F sharp major, Op. 78; No.
27, E minor, Op. 90; No. 32, C minor,
Op. 111 (unobtainable)
Vol. II—No. 9, E major, Op. 14, No. 1; No.
13, E flat major, Op. 27, No. 1; No. 30,
E major, Op. 109 (unobtainable)

Vol. III—No. 15, D major, Op. 28 ("Pastorale"); No. 19, G minor, Op. 49, No. 1; No. 31, A flat major, Op. 110

Vol. IV—No. 2, A major, Op. 2, No. 2; No. 14, C sharp minor, Op. 27, No. 2 ("Moonlight"); No. 26, E flat major, Op. 81a ("Lebewohl")

Vol. V—No. 11, B flat major, Op. 22; No. 20, G major, Op. 49, No. 2; No. 28, F minor, Op. 57 ("Appassionata") ²³

Vol. VI—No. 18, E flat major, Op. 31, No. 3; No. 6, F major, Op. 10, No. 2; No. 8 C minor, Op. 13 ("Pathétique")

Vol. VII—No. 1, F minor, Op. 2, No. 1; No. 10, G major, Op. 14, No. 2; No. 28, A major, Op. 101

Vol. VIII—No. 3, C major, Op. 2, No. 2; No. 17, D minor, Op. 31, No. 2; No. 22, F major, Op. 54

Vol. IX—No. 12, A flat major, Op. 26 ("Funeral March"); No. 21, C major, Op. 53 ("Waldstein")

Vol. X—No. 29, B flat major, Op. 106 ("Hammerklavier")

Vol. XI—No. 4, E flat major, Op. 7; No. 16, G major, Op. 31, No. 1

Vol. XII—No. 5, C minor, Op. 10, No. 1; No. 7, D major, Op. 10, No. 3; No. 25, G major, Op. 79

Vol. XIII—Diabelli Variations, Op. 120

Vol. XIV—Six Bagatelles, Op. 126; Fantasia in G minor, Op. 77; Rondo a Capriccio, G major, Op. 129; Rondo, A major, Grove's No. 164; Variations, F major, Op. 34

Vol. XV—Seven Bagatelles, Op. 33; Für Elise; Minuet, E flat major; Variations in E flat major, Op. 35 ("Eroica")

Individual Sonatas

No. 1, F minor, Op. 2, No. 1
  Artur Schnabel (Beethoven Society, Vol. VII, not available separately)

No. 2, A major, Op. 2, No. 2
  Artur Schnabel (Beethoven Society, Vol. IV, not available separately)
  Wilhelm Kempff   3 12"—PD-67590/2

No. 3, C major, Op. 2, No. 3
  Artur Schnabel (Beethoven Society, Vol. VIII, not available separately)
  Arturo Benedetti-Michelangeli
     3 12"—G-DB5442/4

No. 4, E flat major, Op. 7
  Artur Schnabel (Beethoven Society, Vol. XI, not available separately)
  Elly Ney   4 12"—G-DB4582/5s
  Wilhelm Kempff   4 12"—PD-67806/9S

No. 5, C minor, Op. 10, No. 1
  Artur Schnabel (Beethoven Society, Vol. XII, not available separately)
  Wilhelm Kempff   2 12"—PD-67810/1

No. 6, F major, Op. 10, No. 2
  Artur Schnabel (Beethoven Society, Vol. VI, not available separately)
  Wilhelm Kempff   2 12"—PD-67812/3S

No. 7, D major, Op. 10, No. 3
  Artur Schnabel (Beethoven Society, Vol. XII, not available separately)
  Wilhelm Kempff   3 12"—PD-67814/6

—Minuet only
  Johanne Stockmarr   10"—G-DA5241
  [Für Elise]

No. 8, C minor, Op. 13 ("Pathétique")
  Artur Schnabel (Beethoven Society, Vol. VI, not available separately)
  Benno Moiseiwitsch 2 12"—G-C3246/7
  Edwin Fischer 2 12"—G-DB3666/7
  Wilhelm Backhaus 2 12"—G-DB1031/2
  Rudolph Serkin 3 12"—CM-648†
  Artur Rubinstein 2 12"—VM-1102†
  Paul Baumgartner
     2 12"—G-DB10029/30
  Wilhelm Kempff 2 12"—PD-67113/4
  Ernö Balogh 2 12"—VOX-611
  Eileen Joyce 3 12"—D-K1553/5
  [Bagatelle, E flat, Op. 33, No. 1]
  William Murdoch 2 12"—C-9362/3

—2nd Mvt. (Adagio) only
  Elly Ney   12"—G-DB4460
  [Heiligenstädter Testament, read by Elly Ney]
  Oscar Levant   10"—C-17403D

—Arr. Orchestra
  Berlin Philharmonic Orch. 12"—T-E2544
  [Sonata No. 14, 1st Mvt. only]
  New Light Symphony Orch.—
  Sargent   12"—G-C2234
  [Sonata No. 14, 1st Mvt. only—Arr. Weninger]
  Also: Albert Sandler Trio, C-DB2033

No. 9, E major, Op. 14, No. 1
  Artur Schnabel (Beethoven Society, Vol. II, not available)
  Wilhelm Kempff 2 12"—PD-67817/8S

No. 10, G major, Op. 14, No. 2
  Artur Schnabel (Beethoven Society, Vol. VII, not available separately)
  Wilhelm Kempff 2 12"—PD-67819/20

No. 11, B flat major, Op. 22
  Artur Schnabel (Beethoven Society, Vol. V, not available separately)
  Wilhelm Kempff 3 12"—PD-67821/3

No. 12, A flat major, Op. 26 ("Funeral March")
  Artur Schnabel (Beethoven Society, Vol. IX, not available separately)
  Wilhelm Kempff
  (PD-95465/7)   3 12"—VOX-457
  (Also PD-67824/6)

—3rd Mvt. (Marcia funebre) only
  Arr. Orchestra
  Berlin Philharmonic Orch.—
  Meyrowitz   10"—U-B14499
  [Chopin: Sonata, B flat minor, Funeral March only]
  Victor Orch., on V-24795

No. 13, E flat major, Op. 27, No. 1
  Artur Schnabel (Beethoven Society, Vol. II, not available)
  Wilhelm Kempff 2 12"—PD-67858/9

No. 14, C sharp minor, Op. 27, No. 2 ("Moonlight")
  Artur Schnabel (Beethoven Society, Vol. IV, not available separately)
  Solomon 2 12"—G-C3455/6
  Benno Moiseiwitsch 2 12"—G-C3259/60
  [Schumann: Romance, F sharp minor, Op. 28, No. 2]
  Egon Petri   2 12"—CX-77†

[Liszt: Concert Etude, D flat major]
(C-LX602/3)
Vladimir Horowitz 2 12"—VM-1115†
Wilhelm Backhaus 2 12"—V-8735/6
[Bach: Christmas Oratorio—Pastorale
only] (G-DB2405/6)
Ignaz Friedman 2 12"—C-L1818/9
Rudolf Serkin 2 12"—CX-237†
Ignace Jan Paderewski 2 12"—VM-349†
[Paderewski: Minuet, G. major]
(G-DB3123/4)
Wilhelm Kempff
(PD-90191/2) 2 10"—VOX-462
(Also PD-67856/7: 2-12")
Victor Schiøler 3 10"—C-DC15/7
[Scarlatti: Pastorale & Capriccio]
[Mendelssohn-Schiøler: Scherzo, on
TONO-A105/6; Sonora-K9503/4)
Paul Baumgartner 2 12"—G-DB10007/8
[Schubert: Impromptu, A flat, Op. 142,
No. 2]
Oscar Levant 2 12"—CX-273†
[Sonata No. 20—Minuet only]
—1st Mvt. (Adagio sostenuto) only
Wilhelm Backhaus, in VM-490, with Quartet No. 15, A minor, Op. 32—Busch
Quartet
Ignace Jan Paderewski 12"—V-16250
[Paderewski: Minuet, G major]
(Earlier recording, G-DB1090)
—Arr. Orchestra
Berlin Philharmonic Orch.
12"—T-E2544
New Light Symphony Orch.—Sargent
12"—G-C2234
[Sonata No. 8, 1st Mvt. only—
Arr. Weninger]
Also: Albert Sandler Trio, C-DB2033
No. 15, D major, Op. 28 ("Pastorale")
Artur Schnabel (Beethoven Society, Vol.
III, not available separately)
Wilhelm Kempff 3 12"—PD-67860/2
No. 16, G major, Op. 31, No. 1
Artur Schnabel (Beethoven Society, Vol.
XI, not available separately)
No. 17, D minor, Op. 31, No. 2 ("Tempest")
Artur Schnabel (Beethoven Society, Vol.
VIII, not available separately)
Walter Gieseking 2 12"—CX-39†
(C-DFX132/3) (C-GQX16605/6)
Boris Zadri 2 12"—PAT-PAT147/8
René Gianoli 3 12"—BAM-41/3
[Brahms: Rhapsody, Op. 79, No. 2]
No. 18, E flat major, Op. 31, No. 3
Artur Schnabel (Beethoven Society, Vol.
VI, not available separately)
Wilhelm Kempff 3 12"—PD-67069/71
[Haydn: Trio—Rondo all' ungarese, Elly
Ney Trio]
—Minuet only
Artur Rubinstein
(in VM-1018†) 12"—V-11-8882
[Sonata No. 23, "Appassionata," Pt. 5]
(Also in V-V3†)
No. 19, G minor, Op. 49, No. 1
Artur Schnabel (Beethoven Society, Vol.
III, not available separately)
No. 20, G major, Op. 49, No. 2
Artur Schnabel (Beethoven Society, Vol.
V, not available separately)

Walter Gieseking 10"—C-LW39
—2nd Mvt. (Minuet) only
Oscar Levant, in CX-273
No. 21, C minor, Op. 53 ("Waldstein")
Artur Schnabel (Beethoven Society Vol.
IX, not available separately)
Benno Moisiewitsch 3 12"—G-C3289/91†
[Rondo, C major, Op. 51, No. 1]
Walter Gieseking 3 12"—CM-358†
[Bagatelle, E flat major, Op. 33, No. 1]
(C-LX781/3) (C-LWX263/5)
(C-GQX11007/9)
Wilhelm Kempff 3 12"—VOX-463
(PD-66678/80) (PD-95474/6)
No. 22, F major, Op. 54
Artur Schnabel (Beethoven Society, Vol.
VIII, not available separately)
No. 23, F minor, Op. 57 ("Appassionata")
Artur Schnabel (Beethoven Society, Vol.
V, not available separately)
Edwin Fischer 3 12"—G-DB2517/9†
Artur Rubinstein 3 12"—VM-1018†
[Sonata No. 18, E flat major, Op. 31,
No. 3—Minuetto only]
(Also in V-V3†, vinylite pressing)
Nicolas Medtner 3 12"—C-C3551/3†
Suzanne Gyr 3 12"—G-DB10081/3
Galina Werschenska
3 12"—TONO-A118/20
Wilhelm Kempff 3 12"—VOX-460
(PD-95471/3)
Rudolf Serkin 3 10"—CM-711†
(Also on G-FKX52/4)
Ormella Paliti Santoloquido
3 12"—G-AW308/10
A. de Barentzen 3 12"—G-DB11150/2
—2nd Mvt. (Andante con moto) only
—Arr. Voice Höhne
Ger. Hymne an die Nacht
Regensburger Domchor 10"—G-EG2897
[Reichardt: Heil'ge Nacht]
Ida Harth (c) 10"—T-A1248
[Anon.: Herbei o ihr Gläubigen]
Coro di Trento (in Italian)—Mingozzi
[Schubert: Die Nacht) 10"—T-A9145
No. 24, F sharp minor, Op. 78
Artur Schnabel (Beethoven Society, Vol.
I, not available)
Wilhelm Kempff 10"—PD-90193
Egon Petri 12"—C-68939D
(C-LWX162) (C-GQX10902)
No. 25, G major, Op. 79
Artur Schnabel (Beethoven Society, Vol.
XII, not available separately)
No. 26, E flat major, Op. 81a ("Das
Lebewohl" or "Les Adieux")
Artur Schnabel (Beethoven Society, Vol.
IV, not available separately)
Artur Rubinstein 2 12"—VM-858†
Johanne Stockmarr 2 12"—G-DB5272/3
Wilhelm Backhaus 2 12"—G-DB2407/8
[Bach: Prelude & Fugue No. 22]
Robert Casadesus 2 10"—C-LF97/8
Wilhelm Kempff 2 12"—PD-66687/8
Albert Ferber 2 12"—D-K1569/70
Paul Baumgartner 2 12"—G-DB10054/5
No. 27, E minor, Op. 90
Artur Schnabel (Beethoven Society, Vol.
I, not available)

Egon Petri 2 12"—CX-71†
Wilhelm Kempff
1 10" & 1 12"—PD-62639 & PD-66712
No. 28, A major, Op. 101
Artur Schnabel (Beethoven Society, Vol.
VII, not available separately)
Walter Gieseking 2 12"—CX-172†
Erik Then-Berg 3 12"—G-EH1257/9
Leonard Shure 2 12"—VOX-612
**No. 29, B flat major, Op. 106 ("Hammer-
klavier")**
Artur Schnabel (Beethoven Society, Vol.
X) 6 12"—VM-403†
Louis Kentner 5 12"—C-DX912/6†
Wilhelm Kempff 5 12"—VOX-456
(PD-516697/701) (PD-67077/81)
No. 30, E major, Op. 109
Artur Schnabel (Beethoven Society, Vol.
II, not available)
Wilhelm Kempff (PD-67091/2)
(PD-516756/7) 2 12"—VOX-461
Boris Zadri 2 12"—PAT-PAT130/1
Nino Rossi 2 12"—G-DB5411/2
Walter Gieseking 2 12"—C-LWX327/8
No. 31, A flat major, Op. 110
Artur Schnabel (Beethoven Society, Vol.
III, not available separately)
Edwin Fischer 2 12"—G-DB3707/8
Wilhelm Kempff 3 12"—PD-67088/90
[Variations on Nel cor più]
Guido Agosti 3 12"—G-AW295/7
[Bagatelles, Op. 126, Nos. 1 & 2]
Leonard Shure 2 12"—VOX-613
No. 32, C minor, Op. 111
Artur Schnabel (Beethoven Society, Vol.
I, not available)
Egon Petri 3 12"—CM-263†
Wilhelm Kempff 3 12"—PD-67093/5
(PD-516743/5)
Elly Ney 4 12"—G-DB4476/9
[Variations on Nel cor più]

SONATAS Violin & Piano
HMV Beethoven Violin Sonata Society
(Individual records from volumes are not
available separately)
Fritz Kreisler & Franz Rupp
Vol. I—No. 1, D major, Op. 12, No. 1; No.
2, A major, Op. 12, No. 2; No. 3, E flat
major, Op. 12, No. 3
Vol. II—No. 4, A minor, Op. 23; No. 5, F
major, Op. 24 ("Spring"); No. 8, G
major, Op. 30, No. 3
Vol. III—No. 7, C minor, Op. 30, No. 2;
No. 9, A major, Op. 47 ("Kreutzer")
Vol. IV—No. 6, A major, Op. 30, No. 1;
No. 10, G major, Op. 96
Individual Sonatas
No. 1, D major, Op. 12, No. 1
Fritz Kreisler & Franz Rupp
(Beethoven Violin Society, Vol. I,
not available separately)
Joseph Szigeti & M. Horszowski
2 12"—C-LX1018/9
No. 2, A major, Op. 12, No. 2
Fritz Kreisler & Franz Rupp
(Beethoven Violin Society, Vol. I,
not available separately)
No. 3, E flat major, Op. 12, No. 3
Fritz Kreisler & Franz Rupp

(Beethoven Violin Society, Vol. I,
not available separately)
Jascha Heifetz & Emanuel Bay
3 12"—VM-852†
[Bazzini: La ronde des Lutins]
Yehudi & Hephzibah Menuhin
3 12"—G-DB5802/4S
Ferenc Vecsey & Guido Agosti
3 10"—PD- 10318/20
(PD-62717/9) (CET-LL205/7)
Adolf Busch & Rudolf Serkin
2 12"—G-DB1519/20
No. 4, A minor, Op. 23
Fritz Kreisler & Franz Rupp
(Beethoven Violin Society. Vol. II,
not available separately)
**No. 5, F major, Op. 24 ("Frühling" or
"Spring")**
Fritz Kreisler & Franz Rupp
(Beethoven Violin Society, Vol. II,
not available separately)
Jeno Lener & Louis Kentner
3 12"—CM-404†
Adolf Busch & Rudolf Serkin
3 12"—G-DB1970/2
Erling Block & H. Lund Christansen
3 12"—G-DB14/6
Hugo Kolberg & Franz Rupp
3 12"—O-7771/3
Georg Kulenkampff & Siegfried
Schultze 3 12"—T-E3124/6
S. Borries & Rose Schmid
3 12"—G-DB5610/2
Joan Massia & Blanche Selva
4 12"—C-LFX105/8
[Bach: Violin Sonata No. 3—Adagio]
No. 6, A major, Op. 30, No. 1
Fritz Kreisler & Franz Rupp
(Beethoven Violin Society, Vol. IV,
not available separately)
No. 7, C minor, Op. 30, No. 2
Fritz Kreisler & Franz Rupp
(Beethoven Violin Society, Vol. III,
not available separately)
Yehudi & Hephzibah Menuhin
4 12"—VM-1008†
[Rondo in G major]
Isaac Stern & Alexander Zakin
4 12"—CM-604†
[Handel: Sonata in D major, Op. 1,
No. 13—Allegro]
Alfred Dubois & Marcel Maas
3 12"—C-DFX195/7
Adolf Busch & Rudolf Serkin
3 12"—G-DB1973/5
No. 8, G major, Op. 30, No. 3
Fritz Kreisler & Franz Rupp
(Beethoven Violin Society, Vol. II,
not available separately)
Nathan Milstein & Arthur Balsam
2 12"—CX-137†
Erling Block & H. Lund Christiansen
2 12"—G-DB5280/1
Ida Haendel & Noel Mewton-Wood
2 12"—D-K959/60
Fritz Kreisler & Sergei Rachmaninoff
2 12"—G-DB1463/4
—3rd Mvt. (Allegro vivace) only
Joseph Szigeti & K. Ruhrseitz, C-GQ7207

Yehudi & Hepzibah Menuhin, on
G-DB2834
No. 9, A major, Op. 47 ("Kreutzer")
Fritz Kreisler & Franz Rupp
(Beethoven Violin Society, Vol. III,
not available separately)
Adolf Busch & Rudolf Serkin
4 12"—CM-496†
Yehudi Menuhin & Hephzibah Menuhin
4 12"—VM-260†
(G-DB2409/12, in GM-228)
Georg Kulenkampff & S. Schultze
4 12"—T-E3108/11
Erling Block & H. Lund Christiansen
4 12"—G-DB10/3
Georg Kulenkampff & Wilhelm Kempff
(PD-67062/5) 4 12"—PD-516621/4
Simon Goldberg & Lili Kraus
4 12"—P-P34
(O-123828/3) (P-R20478/81)
Bronislaw Huberman & Ignaz Friedmann
4 12"—C-LFX95/8
Emil Telmanyi & Victor Schiøler
4 12"—TONO-X25011/4
Georg Kulenkampff & Georg Solti
4 12"—(in preparation) Swiss Decca
A. Sammons & W. Murdoch
5 12"—C-9352/6
Jacques Thibaud & Alfred Cortot
4 12"—G-DB1328/31
No. 10, G major, Op. 96
Fritz Kreisler & Franz Rupp
(Beethoven Violin Society, Vol. IV,
not available separately)
Simon Goldberg & Lili Kraus
3 12"—P-P50
(P-R20383/5) (O-123825/7)

SONATAS 'Cello and Piano

No. 1, F major, Op. 5, No. 1
Pablo Casals & Mieczyslaw Horszowski
3 12"—VM-843†
No. 2, G minor, Op. 5, No. 2
Gregor Piatigorsky & Artur Schnabel
3 12"—G-DB2391/3
No. 3, A major, Op. 69
Pierre Fournier & Artur Schnabel
3 12"—G-DB6464/6
Pablo Casals & Mieczyslaw Horszowski
3 12"—G-DB3914/6
Emanuel Feuermann & Myra Hess
3 12"—CM-312†
[Weber: Konzertstück—Andantino]
Paul Grummer & Wilhelm Kempff
3 12"—VOX-459
[Bach: Prelude & Fugue, D major—
Kempff]
(PD-67097/9) (PD-516710/2)
Pablo Casals & Otto Schulhof
[Minuet in G] 3 12"—G-DB1417/9
No. 4, C major, Op. 102, No. 1
Pablo Casals & Mieczyslaw Horszowski
2 12"—G-DB3065/6
No. 5, D major, Op. 102, No. 2
Gregor Piatigorsky & Ralph Berkowitz
2 12"—CX-258†
**Sonata for French Horn (or Cello) &
Piano, F major, Op. 17**
Dennis Brain (horn) & Dennis
Matthews (pf) 2 12"—C-DX1152/3

**Sonatine in C minor (Grove's No. 150—
Ser. 25, No. 245)**
(Originally for mandoline & cembalo)
(Arr. Vlc. & pf. by J. Stutschewsky &
I. Thaler)
Edmund Kurtz & Emanuel Bay
12"—V-11-8815
[Glazunov: Chant du ménestrel]

SONGS
Collections
An die ferne Geliebte, Op. 98 (Jeitteles)
1. **Auf dem Hügel sitz' ich**
2. **Wo die Berge so blau**
3. **Leichte Segler in den Höhen**
4. **Diese Wolken in den Höhen**
5. **Es kehret der Maien**
6. **Nimm sie hin denn, diese Lieder**
Gerhard Hüsch (b) & Hanns Udo
Müller (pf) 2 12"—V-12246/7
(G-DB4496/7) [Andenken]
Heinrich Schlusnus (b) & S. Peschko
(pf) 2 12"—PD-67544/5
Charles Panzéra (b) & Mme. Panzéra-
Baillot (pf) 2 12"—G-DB5081/2
[In questa tomba]

Gellert Lieder, Op. 48
Bitten; Die Liebe des Nächsten; Vom
Tode; Gottes Macht; Busslied; Die Ehre
Gottes
Paul Sandoz (b) & K. Matthaei (organ)
2 12"—G-DB10091/2
[Handel: Dank sei dir Herr]
Individual Songs
Adelaide, Op. 46 (Matthisson)
Jussi Björling (t) & Harry Ebert (pf)
(G-DA1705) 10"—V-2195
Karl Erb (t) & Bruno Seidler-
Winkler (pf) 10"—G-DA4428
Heinrich Schlusnus (b) & Pf.
12"—PD-95391
Roland Hayes (t) in English, & R.
Boardman (pf)
(in CM-393) 10"—C-17175D
Marthe Angelici (s) in French & Jean
Hubeau (pf) 12"—LUM-32064
[Bitten]
An die Hoffnung
Heinrich Schlusnus (b) & Sebastian
Peschko (pf) 10"—PD-62797
Andenken (Ich denke dein) (Matthisson)
(Grove's No. 240)
Gerhard Hüsch (b) & Hanns Udo
Müller (pf) (G-DB4497) 12"—V-12247
[An die ferne Geliebte, Pt. 3]
Heinrich Schlusnus (b) & Sebastian
Peschko (pf) 12"—PD-67251
[Der Wachtelschlag]
Bitten, Op. 48, No. 1 (Gellert) Fr. Prière
Paul Sandoz, on G-DB10091
Alice Raveau (c) in Fr. & Chorus
12"—PAT-X93097
Marthe Angelici (s, in Fr.) & Jean
Hubeau (pf) 12"—LUM-32064
[Adelaide]
Wilhelm Strienz (b) & Chorus
[Die Ehre Gottes] 12"—G-EH912
Busslied, Op. 48, No. 5 (Gellert)
Paul Sandoz, G-DB10091

Die Ehre Gottes aus der Natur, Op. 48, No. 4 (Gellert)
Paul Sandoz (b) & organ, on
G-DB10091
Kirsten Flagstad (s) & Edwin Mc-
Arthur (pf) (in VM-342)   10"—**V-1815**
[Ich liebe dich]
Eva Liebenberg (c)   12"—**T-E1443**
[Schubert: Die Allmacht]
DUPLICATIONS: Alice Raveau, (in Fr.),
PAT-X93096; Heinrich Schlusnus,
PD-67467: PD-95421; Wilhelm Strienz &
Cho., G-EH912; Richard Tauber, P-PO165

—Arr. Chorus
Basilica Chorus, with orch. & organ
(PD-66560; PD-66896) 12"—**PD-95156**
[Missa Solemnis, Pt. 21]
DUPLICATIONS: Berlin State Opera
Chorus, G-FKX19: G-EH408

Das Geheimnis
Karl Erb (t) & Bruno Seidler-Winkler
(pf)   12"—**G-DB4677**
[Der Wachtelschlag & Ich liebe dich]

Gottes Macht und Vorsehung, Op. 48, No. 5 (Gellert)
Paul Sandoz, on G-DB10091
Alice Raveau (c) in Fr., PAT-X93097

Ich liebe dich (Herrosen) (Grove's No. 235)
Kirsten Flagstad (s) & Edwin Mc-
Arthur (pf) (in VM-342)   10"—**V-1815**
[Die Ehre Gottes]
Karl Erb (t) & Bruno Seidler-Winkler
(pf)   12"—**G-DB4677**
[Der Wachtelschlag & Das Geheimnis]
DUPLICATIONS: Walter Ludwig,
G-EG4016; Aulikki Rautawaara,
T-A2781; Heinrich Schlusnus, PD-90198;
Karl Schmitt-Walter, T-A1885

In questa tomba oscura (Carpani) (Grove's No. 239)
Charles Panzéra (b) & Mme. Panzéra-
Baillot (pf)   12"—**G-DB5082**
[An die ferne Geliebte, Pt. 3]
Heinrich Schlusnus (b) & pf.
[Ich liebe dich]   10"—**PD-90198**
Tancredi Pasero (bs) & Rome Opera
Orch.—Ricci   10"—**G-DA5440**
[Stradella: Pietà, Signore]
Feodor Chaliapin (bs)   12"—**V-6822**
[Trad.: Song of the Volga Boatman]
(G-DB1068)
John Charles Thomas, on V-15857
in VM-645

(Der) Kuss, Op. 128 (Arietta) (Weisse)
Walter Ludwig (t) & Ferdinand
Leitner (pf)   10"—**G-EG4016**
[Ich liebe dich]

(Die) Liebe des Nächsten, Op. 48, No. 2 (Gellert)
Paul Sandoz, on G-DB10091
Alice Raveau (c) in Fr., PAT-X93097
[Bitten & Gottes macht]

Irish Songs Voice & Piano Trio Obbligato
(Settings by Beethoven of Traditional
Irish Songs)
Collection (Selections)
**The Pulse of the Irishman; Once More I
Hail Thee; The Return to Ulster; Oh!**

**Who, My Dear Dermott; The Morning
Air Plays on My Face; Morning a Cruel
Turmoiler Is**
Richard Dyer-Benett (t) with Ignace
Strassfogel (pf), Stefan Frenkel (vl) &
Jascha Bernstein (vlc) 3 10"—**CH-AG**

Scottish Songs Voice & Piano Trio
Obbligato   (1809/23)
Collection (Selections)
**Faithful Johnnie; O Sweet Were the
Hours; O How Can I Be Blithe and Glad;
The Lovely Lass of Inverness; Could This
ild World Have Been Contriv'd; Sunset;
Again My Lure; On the Massacre of Glen-
coe; The British Light Dragoons; O Mary,
at Thy Window Be; Bonnie Laddie; High-
land Laddie**
Richard Dyer-Benett (t) with instru-
mental ensemble
(Limited edition)   4 12"—**CH-A9**

Vom Tode, Op. 48, No. 3 (Gellert)
Paul Sandoz, on G-DB10091
Alice Raveau (c) in Fr. & Organ,
PAT-X93096

(Der) Wachtelschlag
Karl Erb (t) & Bruno Seidler-Winkler
(pf)   12"—**G-DB4677**
[Ich liebe dich & Das Geheimnis]
Heinrich Schlusnus (b) & Sebastian
Peschko (pf)   12"—**PD-67251**
[Andenken]

SYMPHONIES

No. 1, C major, Op. 21
BBC Symphony Orch.—Toscanini
in **VM-507†**
[Brahms: Tragische Ouvertüre, 3 sides]
(G-DB3537/40S: Last side blank)
Cleveland Orch.—Rodzinski
3 12"—**CM-535†**
Concertgebouw Orchestra Amsterdam—
Mengelberg   3 12"—**T-SK2270/2**
(U-G14701/3)
Philadelphia Orch.—Ormandy
(G-DB3179/82)   4 12"—**VM-409†**
Vienna Philharmonic Orch.—
Weingartner   3 12"—**CM-321†**
(C-LX677/9)   (C-LFX523/5)
—Minuet only
BBC Symphony Orch.—Toscanini
12"—**G-DB3350**
[Brahms: Tragische Ouvertüre, Pt. 3]

No. 2, D major, Op. 36
London Philharmonic Orch.—Beecham
(C-LX586/9)   4 12"—**CM-302†**
(C-LXW277/80)   (C-LFX474/7)
Boston Symphony Orch.—Koussevitzky
4 12"—**VM-625†**
[Bach: Violin Sonata No. 6—Preludio]
(G-DB3919/22S: Last side blank)
Belgian National Orch.—Kleiber
(U-G14704/7)   4 12"—**T-E2485/8**
Pittsburgh Symphony Orch.—Reiner
4 12"—**CM-597†**
Berlin Philharmonic—P. van Kempen
5 12"—**PD-67608/12S**
[Chopin: Etudes No. 14 & No. 5, with
Brailowsky, on CET-OR5078/82]
London Symphony Orch.—Weingartner
(C-LX725/8)   4 12"—**CM-377†**

Berlin State Opera Orch.—Kleiber
(PD-516585/8)   4 12"—PD-66905/8
Brussels Radio Orch.—Fritz Lehmann
                5 12"—O-50220/4
Orch. of the Suisse Romande—
Schuricht   4 12"—D-K1610/3
Vienna Philharmonic Orch.—Krauss
                4 12"—G-S10246/9

No. 3, E flat major, Op. 55 ("Eroica")
NBC Symphony Orch.—Toscanini
                6 12"—VM-765†
[Die Geschöpfe des Prometheus—
Overture]
(G-DB5946/51S: Last side blank)
Vienna Philharmonic—Weingartner
                6 12"—CM-285†
(C-LX532/7)   (C-LFX444/9)
(C-GQX10823/9)
New York Philharmonic-Symphony
Orchestra—Walter   6 12"—CM-449†
Boston Symphony Orch.—
Koussevitzky   6 12"—VM-1161†
(Also on V-V8†: vinylite pressing)
London Philharmonic—de Sabata
(D-K1507/13)   7 12"—D-ED19†
Berlin Philharmonic Orch.—Jochum
(U-G18001/6)   6 12"—T-E2311/6
Amsterdam Concertgebouw Orch.—
Mengelberg   6 12"—T-SK3117/22
Berlin Philharmonic—Knappertsbusch
                6 12"—G-DB7666/71
Berlin Philharmonic Orch.—Pfitzner
                6 12"—PD-66939/44
Berlin Philharmonic—Schuricht
                6 12"—PD-67793/8

No. 4, B flat major, Op. 60
BBC Symphony Orch.—Toscanini
(G-DB3896/9)   4 12"—VM-676†
London Philharmonic Orch.—Beecham
                4 12"—VM-1081†
London Philharmonic Orch.—
Weingartner   4 12"—CM-197†
[Die Geschöpfe des Prometheus—
Overture] (C-LX274/7)
(C-DFX170/3) (C-DCX57/60)
Concertgebouw Orch. Amsterdam—
Mengelberg   4 12"—T-SK2794/7
(U-G14708/11)
Cleveland Orch.—George Szell
                4 12"—CM-705†

No. 5, C. minor, Op. 67
NBC Symphony Orch.—Toscanini
(G-DB3822/5)   4 12"—VM-640†
Berlin Philharmonic Orch.—
Furtwängler 5 12"—G-DB3328/32S†
[Last side blank]
Concertgebouw Orch. Amsterdam—
Mengelberg   4 12"—T-SK2210/3
(U-G14712/5)
London Philharmonic Orch.—
Weingartner   4 12"—CM-254†
(C-DX516/9)   (C-DFX150/3)
(C-GQX10716/9)
New York Philharmonic-Symphony
Orch.—Walter   4 12"—CM-498†
(C-LZX207/10)
Dresden Philharmonic Orch.—P. van
Kempen   5 12"—PD-67635/95S
[Chopin: Waltz No. 7, Brailowsky, on
CET-OR5073/7]

Queen's Hall Orch.—Sir Henry J. Wood
                4 12"—PD-516666/9
Berlin State Opera Orch.—Richard
Strauss   4 12"—PD-66814/7
All-American Youth Orch.—Stokowski
                5 12"—CM-451†
[Bach: Fugue, G minor, Arr. Stokowski]
DUPLICATIONS: National Symphony
Orch.—Sargent, D-K1126/9; Berlin Phil-
harmonic Orch.—Abendroth,
P-E11434/7: O-7898/901
—1st Mvt. only (Abridged)
Victor Symphony Orch.—O'Connell, in
V-G15

No. 6, F major, Op. 68 ("Pastorale")
BBC Symphony Orch.—Toscanini
                5 12"—VM-417†
(G-DB3333/7 in GM-295)
Philadelphia Orch.—Bruno Walter
(C-LX963/7)   5 12"—CM-631†
New York City Symphony—Stokowski
                5 12"—VM-1032†
Vienna Philharmonic Orch.—Bruno
Walter (G-DB3051/5) 5 12"—GM-272†
Concertgebouw Orch. Amsterdam—
Mengelberg   5 12"—T-SK2424/8
(U-G14716/20)
Minneapolis Symphony Orch.—
Mitropoulos   5 12"—CM-401†
Symphony Orch. of the Augusteo, Rome-
De Sabata   5 12"—G-DB6473/7†
DUPLICATIONS: Berlin State Opera
Orch.—Pfitzner, PD-95378/83; Colonne
Orch.—Paray C-BFX8/12:
C-GQX10730/44: C-DCX63/7

No. 7, A major, Op. 92
New York Philharmonic-Symphony
Orch.—Toscanini   5 12"—VM-317†
(G-DB2986/90 in GM-266)
Philadelphia Orch.—Ormandy
                5 12"—CM-557†
Berlin State Orch.—H. von Karajan
                5 12"—PD-67643/8S
(PD-68006/10) (Last side blank)
[Chopin: Etude No. 25, Brailowsky on
CET-RR8024/9)
Vienna Philharmonic Orch.—
Weingartner   5 12"—CM-260†
[Die Geschöpfe des Prometheus—
Overture]   (C-LX484/8)
(C-LFX424/8) (C-GQX10777/81)
Berlin Philharmonic Orch.—Jochum
(U-G18007/11)   5 12"—T-SK2763/7
Berlin Philharmonic Orch.—Schuricht
                5 12"—PD-67162/6
[Bach: Prelude & Fugue, C sharp major,
W. Kempff] (PD-516747/51)
Philadelphia Orch.—Stokowski
                5 12"—VM-17†

No. 8, F major, Op. 93
Vienna Philharmonic—von Karajan
                3 12"—C-LX988/90†
NBC Symphony Orch.—Toscanini
(G-DB6160/2)   3 12"—VM-908†
Munich Philharmonic Orch.—Kabasta
                3 12"—G-DB5639/41
New York Philharmonic-Symphony
Orch.—Walter   3 12"—CM-525†
Vienna Philharmonic Orch.—Weingart-
ner   3 12"—CM-292†

(C-LX563/5) (C-LFX457/9)
(C-GQX10831/3)
Berlin Philharmonic Orch.—van Kempen
(CET-OR5083/5) 3 12"—PD-67662/4
Berlin Philharmonic Orch.—Pfitzner
3 12"—PD-15020/2
Boston Symphony Orch.—Koussevitzky
(G-DB3172/4) 3 12"—VM-336†
Concertgebouw Orch. Amsterdam—
Mengelberg 3 12"—T-SK2760/2
(U-G14721/3)
Vienna Philharmonic Orch.—Schalk
3 12"—G-AW16/8
—2nd & 3rd Mvts. only
Reichs-Symphonie Orchester—Franz
Adam 12"—PD-15159
—2nd Mvt. only
Concertgebouw Orch., Amsterdam—
Mengelberg 12"—O-8398
[Weber: Oberon-Overture, Pt. 3]
[Cherubini: Anacreon Overture, Pt. 3,
on C-GQX10461]

No. 9, D minor, Op. 125 ("Choral")
Vienna Philharmonic Orch., Vienna State
Opera Cho., with Luise Helletsgrüber (s),
Rosette Anday (c), Georg Maikl (t),
Richard Mayr (b), conducted by Felix
Weingartner 8 12"—CM-227†
(C-LX413/20) (C-LFX393/400)
(C-LWX134/41) (C-GQX10782/9)
Philadelphia Orch.—Ormandy, with
Westminster Choir, Stella Roman (s),
Enid Szantho (c), Frederick Jagel, (t),
Nicola Moscona (bs) 8 12"—CM-591†
Hamburg State Philharmonic Orch.,
Hamburg State Opera Cho., with Helene
Fahrni (s), Gusta Hammer (c), Walther
Ludwig (t), Rudolf Wagle (bs), con-
ducted by Eugene Jochum
(U-G18012/20) 9 12"—T-SK2615/23
Berlin State Opera Orch., Bruno Kittel
Choir, with Lotte Leonard (s), Jenny
Sonnenberg (c), Eugene Transky (t),
Wilhelm Guttmann (bs), conducted by
Oskar Fried 7 12"—PD-66657/63
Philadelphia Orch. & Cho. with Agnes
Davis (s), Ruth Carhart (c), Robert
Bett (t), Eugene Löwenthal (b), in
English, conducted by Leopold Stokowski
9 12"—VM-236†
[Bach: Komm süsser Tod]
[Bach: Toccata, C major—Adagio on
G-DB2327/35 in GM-223†]
Saxon State Orch. & Dresden State Opera
Cho., with Margaret Teschemacher (s),
Elisabeth Hoengen (c), Torsten Ralf (t),
Josef Hermann (bs)—Karl Böhm
9 12"—G-DB5652/60S
[Last side blank]
—Finale (Excerpts: "Freude, schöner Göt-
terfunken")
Berlin State Opera Orch. & Chorus—
Schmalstich (G-FKX19) 12"—G-EH408
[Die Ehre Gottes]
"Battle" Symphony—Wellingtons Sieg,
oder die Schlacht bei Vittoria Op. 91
Eng: Wellington's Victory at the Battle of
Vittoria Orchestra

Jansen Symphony of Los Angeles—
Werner Janssen 3 12"—Artist-JS14
[with König Stephen—Overture]
"Jena" Symphony
NOTE: Attributed to Beethoven but authentic-
ity doubted.
Janssen Symphony of Los Angeles—
Werner Janssen 3 12"—VM-946†

TRIOS—Violin, Viola, Cello

No. 2, G major, Op. 9, No. 1
Pasquier Trio (PAT-PAT121/3)
3 12"—CM-384†

No. 4, C minor, Op. 9, No. 3
Pasquier Trio 3 12"—CM-397†
(PAT-PAT7/9) (C-CQX16597/9)

TRIOS—Violin, Cello, Piano

No. 3, C minor, Op. 1, No. 3
Benvenuti (pf), Benedetti (vl), Navarra
(vlc) 3 12"—PAT-PGT33/5
—Menuetto only
Elly Ney Trio 12"—G-DB4590
[Trio, D major, Op. 70, No. 1, Pt. 7]
No. 4, B flat major, Op. 11 (See B flat
Clarinet Trio)
No. 5, D major, Op. 70, No. 1 ("Geister" or
"Spirit")
Yehudi Menuhin, Maurice Eisenberg,
Hephzibah Menuhin 3 12"—VM-370†
(G-DB2879/81)
Elly Ney Trio 4 12"—G-DB4587/90
[Trio, C minor, Op. 1, No. 3—Minuet]
Bern-Hirt Trio 4 12"—PD-95346/9
(PD-27261/4)
[Schubert-Liszt: Lindenbaum]
Poltronieri, Bonucci, Casella
2 12"—C-GQX10132/3

No. 6, E flat, Op. 70, No. 2
Frederick Grinke, Florence Hooton,
Kendall Taylor 3 12"—D-K1069/71

No. 7, B flat major, Op. 97 ("Archduke")
Jascha Heifetz, Emanuel Feuermann,
Artur Rubinstein 5 12"—VM-949†
Henry Holst, Anthoni Pini, Solomon
5 12"—G-C3362/6†
Jacques Thibaud, Pablo Casals, Alfred
Cortot 5 12"—G-DB1223/7
Sammons, Squire, Murdoch
5 12"—C-GQX10372/6

TRIOS—Clarinet, 'Cello, Piano

B flat major ("Gassenhauser"), Op. 11 (See
also Trio. Op. 11 above)
Denis Matthews (pf), Reginald Kell (cl),
Anthony Pini (vlc)
3 12"—C-DX1164/6†
[Bach: Unacc. Violin Sonata No. 3—1st
Mvt.]
Munich Chamber Music Ensemble
3 12"—PD-95222/4
[Haydn: Minuet, E flat, played by Charlotte Kaufmann on Mozart Piano from
1790]
Luigi Amodio (cl), Siegfried Schultze
(pf), Hans Schrader (vlc)
3 12"—CET-OR5095/7

—2nd Mvt.
Munich Chamber Music Ensemble,
PD-27305: PD-95383

TRIO, G major—Flute, Bassoon, Piano
Marcel Moyse, Fernand Oubradous, Noël
Gallon 2 12"—OL-81/2

VARIATIONS

**(15) Variations in E flat major ("Eroica")
Op. 35** Piano
Artur Schnabel (Beethoven Piano Society,
Vol. XIV, not available separately)
Claudio Arrau 5 12"—VM-892†
[with Variations, Op. 34]
Lili Krauss 3 12"—P-PXO1040/2
**(33) Variations on a Waltz by Diabelli, Op.
120** Piano
Artur Schnabel (Beethoven Piano Society,
Vol. XIII, Not available separately)
(32) Variations, C minor, Grove's No. 191
Piano
Dennis Matthews 2 12"—C-DX1060/1
[Bagatelles Nos. 1 & 11]
DUPLICATION: V. Horowitz,
G-DA1387/8
(6) Variations, F major, Op. 34 Piano
Artur Schnabel (Beethoven Society, Vol.
XIV, not available separately)
Claudio Arrau 5 12"—VM-892†
[with Variations, E flat major, Op. 35—
"Eroica"]
Leonard Shure 2 12"—VOX-602
**Variations on "Nel cor più" from Paisiello's
La Molinara, Grove's No. 180**
Elly Ney 12"—G-DB4479
[Sonata, Op. 111, Pt. 7]
Wilhelm Kempff 12"—PD-67090
[Sonata, Op. 110, Pt. 5]
**Variations on "Ein Mädchen oder Weib-
chen" from Mozart's "Zauberflöte," Op.
66.** Cello & Piano
André Navarra & Joseph Benvenuti
12"—PAT-PDT107
**Variations on "Bei Mannern" from Mozart's
"Zauberflöte" Grove's No. 158** 'Cello &
Piano
André Navarra & Joseph Benvenuti
12"—PAT-PDT108
Pablo Casals & Alfred Cortot
2 10"—G-DA915/6
**Variations on "La ci darem la mano" from
Mozart's "Don Giovanni"**
Lois Wann (ob), Ferdinand Prio (ob),
Engelbert Brenner (Eng. horn)
2 10"—MC-34
**Variations on "Ich bin der Schneider
Kakadu," Op. 121a**
See: Introduction & Variations
(11) Viennese Dances (Wiener Tänze)
London Philharmonic Orchestra— Felix
Weingartner (C-LX770/1)
2 12"—CX-133†
[Egmont, Op. 84—Larghetto]
(C-GQX10996/7) (C-LWX297/8)
(Die) Weihe des Hauses—Overture. Op. 124
Eng. Consecration of the House
London Philharmonic Orch.—
Weingartner 2 12"—CX-140†
[Egmont: Clärchens Tod] (C-LX811/2)

Wellington's Victory See under Symphonies

BEGUE, Nicolas Antoine De (1630?-1702)
*At one time organist to Louis XIV, Bégue pro-
duced a great body of courtly music.*
Les Cloches
Finn Viderø (Organ of Frederiksborg
Castle) 10"—G-DA5207
[Cabezon: Tiento del Primer Tono &
Tomas de Sancta Maria: Fantasia Tertii
Toni]

BELLINI, Vincenzo (1801-1835)
*Born in Sicily, educated in music at Naples,
Bellini was a contemporary of Donizetti and
Mercadante. His operas, requiring great singers,
have recently fallen into decline.*

OPERAS in Italian

NORMA 4 Acts 1831
Complete Recording
Soloists, Chorus & EIAR Symphony Orch.
—Vittorio Gui 18 12"—P-P20/1†
(P-R20349/66) (0-7750/67)
(CET-CB20010/27)
The Cast:
Norma .... Gina Gigna (s)
Adalgisa .... Ebe Stignani (c)
Pollione .... Giovanni Breviario (t)
Oroveso .... Tancredi Pasero (bs)
Clotilde .... Adriana Perris (c)
Flavio .... Emilio Renzi (t)
Overture Orchestra
National Symphony Orch.—Anatole
Fistoulari 12"—D-K1291
[Tchaikovsky: The Oprichnik—Over-
ture]
La Scala Orch.—Marinuzzi (U-G18112)
12"—T-SKB3265
Milan Symphony Orch.—Molajoli
10"—C-D12271
La Scala Orch.—Sabajno 12"—G-S10045
[Puccini: Manon Lescaut—Intermezzo
Act III]
[Mascagni: L'Amico Fritz—Intermezzo
on G-S10336]

ACT I
Ite sul colle, O Druidi! Bass & Chorus
Ezio Pinza & Metropolitan Opera Chorus
—Setti 12"—G-DB1203
[Verdi: Forza del Destino—Il santo
nome]
[Puritani-A te, o cara, Lauri-Volpi on
G-DB2396]
Tancredi Pasero & Chorus
12"—C-GQX10736
[La Sonnambula-D'un pensiero]
[Verdi: Trovatore-Di due figli, on
C-GQX10159]
Sediziose voci—Recit.
Casta Diva che inargenti (Cavatina)
Ah! bello, a me ritorna—Air Soprano &
Chorus
Rosa Ponselle with Metropolitan Chorus
& Orch.—Setti (G-DB1280)
12"—V-8125
Ebe Stignani (ms) with EIAR Chorus &

Symphony Orch.—Ugo Tansini
    (in CET-9)   12″—CET-BB25097
Dusolina Giannini, with La Scala
Chorus & Orch.—Sabajno
               12″—G-DB1576
Ina Souez, with Chorus & Orch.—
Barbirolli   12″—V-36286
—Casta Diva only
Claudia Muzio, with Chorus & Orch.—
Molajoli   (in CM-259)   12″—C-9165M
[La Sonnambula-Ah, non credea]
[Refice-Ombra di nube, on C-LCX23:
C-BQX2502]
[Verdi: Forza-Pace, on C-BQX2520]
Toti Dal Monte, with La Scala Chorus &
Orch.   12″—G-DB2125
[Rossini: Barbiere-Dunque io son, with
Montesanto]
[Sonnambula-Ah, non credea, on
G-DB2395]
Zinka Milanov, with Victor Chorale &
Orch.—Weissman   12″—V-11-9293
[Ponchielli: Gioconda-Suicidio!]
Gina Cigna (no chorus) & Orch.
            12″—C-GQX10663
[Catalani: La Wally-Ne mai dunque]
Giannina Arangi-Lombardi
            12″—C-GQX10277
[Mascagni: Cavalleria Rusticana-Voi lo
sapete]
[Sonnambula-O fosco cielo, Quartet on
C-GQX10735]
DUPLICATIONS: Maria Pedrini, CET-
CC2214; I. Pacetti, C-DQ684; Ninon Val-
lin, (in Fr.) O-123709; Wanda Bardone,
G-S5442
Meco all' altar di Venere Tenor
Giacomo Lauri-Volpi   10″—G-DA983
[Puccini: La Tosca—E lucevan le stelle]
[Ah! del tebro, Pinza, on G-DA1412]
Francesco Merli   10″—C-GQ7197
[Me protegge me difende]
DUPLICATIONS: P. Pauli, G-HN736; G.
Chiaia, C-DQ261: C-DQ1186
Sgombra è la sacra selva Contralto
Irene Minghini-Cattaneo (ms)
            12″—G-DB1749
[Bizet: Carmen-Parle-moi, Cortis &
Rozsa]
[Sonnambula-Son geloso, Galli-Curci &
Schipa on G-DB2397]

ACT III (Act II in some versions)

Mira, O Norma!
Si, fino all'ore Duo: Soprano & Contralto
Rosa Ponselle & Marian Telva
(G-DB1276)   12″—V-8110
Zinka Milanov & Margaret Harshaw
            12″—V-11-8924
Giannina Arangi-Lombardi & Ebe
Stignani   12″—C-GQX10160
ACT IV (Act II, Scene 2, in some versions)
Non parti
Metropolitan Chorus & Orch.—Setti
            12″—G-AW166
[Verdi: Trovatore—Soldier's Chorus]
Ah! del Tebro al giogo indegno Bass &
Chorus
Ezio Pinza & Metropolitan Opera Chorus
& Orch.—Setti   10″—V-1753

[Gounod: Faust-Le Veau d'or]
[Meco all'altar di Venere, Lauri-Volpi, on
G-DA1412]
Tancredi Pasero & EIAR Chorus &
Orch.—Gui   12″—CET-BB25109
[Verdi: Nabucco-Va pensiero, Chorus
only, dir. Tansini]
Guerra, guerra! Soprano & Chorus
Lella Gaio & Chorus   10″—C-GQ7188
[Verdi: Nabucco-Coro di Leviti]
[Puritani-A te, o cara, Solari, on
C-DQ1185]
Deh! non volerli vittime Trio & Chorus
Poli Randacio, Ezio Pinza, Boscacci &
Chorus   12″—G-DB729*
[Mascagni: Cavalleria Rusticana-Voi lo
sapete, Poli Randacio]
—Soprano part only
Iva Pacetti   10″—C-DQ1159

**(I) PURITANI 3 Acts 1835 Eng. The
Puritans**

ACT I

Or dove fuggo io mai Baritone
Ah! per sempre
Carlo Tagliabue & La Scala Orch.—
Berrettoni   12″—G-DB11303
[Verdi: Ernani-Oh de'verd'anni miei]
A te, o cara, amor talora Tenor
Giacomo Lauri-Volpi   12″—G-DB1438
[Gomes: Lo Schiavo-Quando nascesti]
[Norma-Ite sul colle, Pinza on G-DB2396]
[Giordano: Andrea Chênier-Improviso,
on G-DB5391]
Cristi Solari & Orch.   10″—C-DQ1185
[Norma-Guerra, guerra, L. Gaio &
Chorus]
[Donizetti: Elisir d'amore-Una furtiva
lagrima, on C-D5699]
DUPLICATION: Aureliano Pertile,
G-DA1183; Miguel Fleta, G-DA445*;
Borghetti, G-HN736; A. Gentilini,
C-DQX2985
Son vergin vezzosa Soprano
Lina Pagliughi & EIAR Symphony Orch.
—Tansini   12″—P-DPX19
[Qui la voce] (CET-BB25003)
Elda Ribetti   12″—G-DB5446
[Mozart: Don Giovanni-Vedrai carino,
Favero]
DUPLICATION: A. Galli-Curci,
G-DB641*

ACT II

Qui la voce sua soave Soprano ("Mad
Scene")
Lina Pagliughi, & EIAR Symphony Orch.
Tansini   12″—P-DPX19
[Son vergin vezzosa] (CET-BB25003)
Mercedes Capsir   12″—C-GQX10696
[Vien diletto]
Vien diletto Soprano (**Part 2 of Qui la voce**)
Mercedes Capsir   12″—C-GQX10696
[Qui la voce]
DUPLICATION: E. di Veroli, C-DQ230
Il rival salvar tu puoi Baritone & Bass
Gino Vanelli & Tancredi Pasero
            12″—C-GQX10248
[Suoni la tromba]

Suoni la tromba Baritone & Bass
G. Manacchini & L. Neroni, with EIAR
Symphony Orch.—Tansini
    12″—CET-CC2150
[Gounod: Faust-Dio possente,
Manacchini]
Gino Vanelli & Tancredi Pasero
    12″—C-GQX10248
[Il rival salvar tu puoi]

ACT III

Vieni fra queste braccia Tenor
Hipolito Lazaro   10″—CRS-18*
[Verdi: Trovatore-Di quella pira]

(LA) SONNAMBULA 3 Acts 1831
Fr. La Somnanbule Ger. Die Nachtwand-
lerin

ACT I

Come per me serena (Cavatina) & **Sovra il
sen la man mi posa** Soprano
Lina Pagliughi   12″—P-DPX14
(CET-PP60002)
[Auber: Fra Diavalo-Or son sola]
Prendi l'anel ti dono Soprano, Tenor &
Chorus
Toti Dal Monte, Tito Schipa & La Scala
Chorus & Orch.—Ghione 10″—G-DA1351
[Donizetti: Don Pasquale-Tornami a
dir]
—Tenor part only
Ferruccio Tagliavini
 (in CET-1) 18″—CET-BB25022
[Verdi: Falstaff-Dal labbro il canto]
Nino Ederle   10″—C-DQ245
[Donizetti: Elisir d'amore-Una furtiva
lagrima]
Enzo De Muro Lomanto 10″—C-DQ1101
[Massenet: Manon-Le Rêve]
G. Manuritta (in French)
    12″—PAT-X15755
[Rossini: Barbiere-Se il mio nome]
DUPLICATIONS: D. Borgioli, C-DQ1184,
C-D5037; C-GQ7104
Vi ravviso, o luoghi ameni Bass
Tancredi Pasero & EIAR Symphony—
Tansini   12″—CET-BB25065
[Verdi: Vespri Siciliani-Tu Palermo]
[Also on C-GQ7086]
Tancredi Pasero 12″—G-DBO5356
[Rossini: Barbiere-La calunnia]
Umberto di Lelio 10″—C-D5749
Feodor Chaliapin 10″—G-DA962
[Boito: Mefistofele-Ave Signor]
Tu non sai Bass & Cho.
Tancredi Pasero 10″—C-DQ1103
[Thomas: Mignon-Berceuse]
A fosco cielo Chorus
Salvatore Baccaloni, E. Cheni, I. Man-
narini, E. Venturini & Chorus
    12″—C-GQX10273
[Verdi: Rigoletto-Zitti, zitti]
[Norma-Casta Diva, Arangi Lombardi, on
C-GQX10735]
Oh ciel—che tento? Soprano & Bass
G. Bernelli & T. Pasero 12″—G-DB11306
[Verdi: Rigoletto—Quel vecchio male-
divami, Bechi & Pasero]

Son geloso del zefiro Soprano & Tenor
Maria Gentile & Enzo de Muro Lomanto
    10″—C-DQ1097
A. Galli-Curci & Tito Schipa
    12″—G-DB811*
[Donizetti: Lucia di Lammermoor-
Verranno a te]
[Norma-Sgombra è la sacra selva,
Minghini-Cattaneo on G-DB2397*]

ACT II

D'un pensiero Quartet & Chorus
Maria Gentile, Dino Borgioli, G. Pedrini,
I. Mannarini & Chorus 12″—C-GQX10154
[Donizetti: Lucia-Sextet]
[Norma-Ite sul colle, Pasero, on
C-GQX10736]

ACT III

Ah! non credea mirarti Soprano
(The brief choral passages are invariably
omitted)
Claudia Muzio
  (in CM-259) 12″—C-9165M
[Norma-Casta Diva]
[Refice: Ave Maria, on C-LCX27:
C-BQX2506]
[Verdi: Traviata-Addio del passato, on
C-BQX2522]
Lina Pagliughi (CET-BB25001)
    12″—P-DPX18
[Donizetti: Figlia del Regimento-Convien
partir]
[Rigoletto-Caro nome on CET-BB25073]
Bidù Sayão & Metropolitan Opera Orch.
—Cleva (in CM-612) 12″—C-72093D
[Puccini: Bohème-Addio]
Lina Aimaro 12″—C-GQX10982
[Rossini: Barbiere-Una voce poco fa]
Anna Maria Guglielmetti
    12″—C-GQX10177
[Verdi: Rigoletto-Caro nome]
Margherita Carosio & Royal Opera Orch.,
Covent Garden—Patanè
    12″—G-DB6388
[Ponchielli: Lina-La Madre mia]
Toti Dal Monte 12″—G-DB1317
[Verdi: Falstaff-Sul fin d'un soffio
etesio]
[Norma-Casta Diva on G-DB2395]
DUPLICATION: Luisa Tetrazzini,
G-DB533*
Ah! non giunge Soprano & Chorus
(The brief choral passages are invariably
omitted)
Anna Maria Guglielmetti
    12″—C-DQ1110
[Verdi: Traviata-Sempre libera]
[Prendi l'anel ti dono, on G-DQ1184]
DUPLICATION: Luisa Tetrazzini,
G-DB533*

SONGS

L'Abbandono
Margherita Voltolina (s) & Mario
Salerno (pf) 12″—CET-IT582
[Monteverdi: Lasciatemi morire &
Anon: Son come farfalletta]

BELLMAN, Carl Michael (1740-1795)

Swedish poet and composer, living at the court of Gustave III, who wrote a series of lyrics, "Fredmans Epistlar and Sänger," set principally to popular French melodies. He has been called the "last of the troubadours."

SONGS In Swedish
Blasen nu alla (Fredmans Epistel No. 25)
  College Men's Choral Union—J. Hye-
  Knudsen   10"—**G-X6898**
  [Villa vid denna källa]
Fjäriln vingad syns pa Haga (Fredmans
  Sang No. 64)
  Aksel Schiøtz (t) & Lute acc.
                  10"—**G-X6404**
  [Ulla, min Ulla]
Gubben är gammal (Fredmans Epistel No.
  27)
  Aksel Schiøtz (t) & Ulrik Neumann
  (guitar)   10"—**G-X6998**
  [Käraste bröder, systrar och vänner]
Hör klokorna med ängsligt dan (Fredmans
  Sang No. 6)
  Aksel Schiøtz (t) & Ulrik Neumann
  (guitar)   10"—**G-X6999**
  [Sa lunka vi sa smaningom]
Joachim uti Babylon (Fredmans Sang No.
  44)
  Aksel Schiøtz (t) & Ulrik Neuman
  (guitar)   10"—**G-X7200**
  [Vila vid denna källa]
Käraste bröder, systrar och vänner
  (Fredmans Epistel No. 9)
  Aksel Schiøtz (t) & Ulrik Neumann
  (guitar)   10"—**G-X6998**
  [Gubben är gammal]
Sa lunka vi sa smaningom (Fredmans Sang
  No. 21)
  Aksel Schiøtz (t) & Ulrik Neumann
  (guitar)   10"—**G-X6999**
  [Hör klokorna med ängsligt dan]
Ulla, min Ulla (Fredmans Epistel No. 71)
  Aksel Schiøtz (t) & Lute acc.
                  10"—**G-X6404**
  [Fjäriln vingad syns pa Haga]
Vila vid denna källa (Fredmans Epistel No.
  82)
  Aksel Schiøtz (t) & Ulrik Neumann
  (guitar)   10"—**G-X7200**
  [Joachim uti Babylon]
  College Men's Choral Union—J. Hye-
  Knudsen   10"—**G-X6898**
  [Blasen nu alla]

BENDA, Jan Jiri (1722-1795)

A Czech-German composer, at one time chamber musician in Berlin, and court Kapellmeister at Gotha, best known for his concert pieces and numerous operas. Benda is credited with originating the idea of the music drama with spoken words, with the music handled by the orchestra alone—pure melodrama.

Concerto, G major Violin & Orchestra
—Grave only
  Karel Moravec & J. Zich (pf)
              12"—**U-G12933**
  [O. Zich: Elégie]
Presto Harpsichord
  J. Langer   10"—**U-B12385**
  [Myslevecek: Rondo]

BENEDICT, Sir Julius (1804-1885)

A German conductor and intimate friend of Weber, Benedict was well known as an impressario. He composed bravura works which coloraturas still sing.

OPERAS

THE LILY OF KILLARNEY In English
1862
Eily Mavourneen
  Heddle Nash (t) & pf. acc.
                  10"—**C-DB863**
  [Clutsam: I know of two bright eyes]

SONGS
La Capinera Eng. The Wren
  Amelita Galli-Curci (s)   10"—**V-1338**
  [Yradier: La Paloma] (G-DA1002)
  Lily Pons (s) & Orch.—Kostelanetz
        (in VM-599)   10"—**V-1905**
  [Debussy: Green & Mandoline]
  Claire Clairbert (s, in French)
                10"—**PD-561080**
  [Arditi: Parla valse]
  Lucienne Dugard & Orch.—Briez
                10"—**PAT-PA1369**
  [Arditi: Parla]
  DUPLICATION: Milicent Phillips,
  P-R2641
Il Carnevale di Venezia Eng. Carnival of
  Venice
  Toti Dal Monte (s)   12"—**G-DB1001**
  Claire Clairbert (s, in French)
  (PD-566155)   12"—**PD-67045**
  Miliza Korjus (s, in German) & Orch.—
  Seidler-Winkler
  (G-EH997) (in VM-871) 12"—**V-13806**
  [Taubert: Der Vogel im Walde]
  Erna Sack (s) & Zurich Tonhalle Orch.—
  Reinshagen (in preparation) Swiss Decca
The Gypsy and the Bird
  Amelita Galli-Curci (s) 10"—**G-DA928**
  [Arditi: Parla]
  DUPLICATION: Mado Robin (in
  French), G-DA4960

BENET, John (early 15th century)

A contemporary of Chaucer and Dunstable, Benet probably traveled extensively on the continent, for his music shows the influence of the Ars Nova.

Pleni sunt coeli
  Yves Tinayre (t) & M. Mondain (English
  horn)   12"—**LUM-32020**
  [Attey: Sweet was the song & Torre:
  Adoramos, te, Señor]
  (in Yves Tinayre album No. 2)

BENJAMIN, Arthur (1893-   )

An Australian by birth, Benjamin has taught both in the Sydney State Conservatory and the Royal College of Music, London.

Elegy, Waltz & Toccata
  William Primrose (vla) & Vladimir
  Sokoloff (pf)
  (in VM-1061†) 2 12"—**V-11-9210/1**
  [with Harris: Soliloquy & Dance]

Jamaican Rhumba; Matty Rag; Cookie;
From San Domingo (arr. Primrose)
William Primrose (vla) & Vladimir
Sokoloff (pf)   12"—V-11-8947
—Jamaican Rhumba only
Jascha Heifetz (vl) & Milton Kaye (pf)
        (in D-A385)   10"—D-23385
[Godowsky: Wienerisch]
Overture to an Italian Comedy Orchestra
Chicago Symphony Orch.—Stock
        12"—V-11-8157

BENNETT, Robert Russell (1894-   )

*Although Bennett has composed much original
music, he is best known for his orchestral arrangements of Broadway musical comedies and
operettas.*

Hexapoda Violin & Piano
Jascha Heifetz & Emanuel Bay
        2 10"—D-DA454
[Dyer: An Outlandish Suite—Florida
Night Song]
Song Sonata Violin & Piano
Louis Kaufman & Theodore Saidenberg
        (in preparation) DISC
(A) Symphonic Picture (from "Porgy and
Bess"—Gershwin)
Pittsburgh Symphony Orch.—Reiner
        3 12"—CM-572†
Indianapolis Symphony Orch.—Sevitzky
        3 12"—VM-999†
Also: Philharmonic Orch., Los Angeles-
Wallenstein, D-DA397

BENTZON, Jørgen (1897-   )

*A Danish composer, pupil of Carl Nielson, who
writes in a modern contrapuntal style, and
whose music has often been heard at Chamber
Music Festivals abroad.*

Racconto, No. 3, Op. 31
W. Wolsing (ob), P. Allin Ericksen (cl),
Kjell Roikjer (bsn)   12"—G-DB5285

SONG in Danish
Lyse Land (Alex Garff)
College Men's Choral Union—Hye-
Knudsen   10"—G-X6681
[Hoffding: Purpurprikken]

BENTZON, Niels Viggo (1919-   )
Toccata Piano
Niels Viggo Bentzon   12"—G-Z276

BERCHEM, Jachet Van (16th century)

*A member of the Franco-Flemish school of
polyphony, little is known of his life but that
he was organist to the Duke of Ferrara in 1555.
His works consist of numerous masses, motets,
capriccios and chansons.*

Jehan de Lagny
Marcelle Gerar (s) with viols & flutes &
guitar   (in Vol. II) 12"—AS-15
[Que feu craintif]
Que feu craintif
Marcelle Gerar (s) with viols, flute &
guitar   (in Vol. II) 12"—AS-15
[Jehan de Lagny]

O Jesu Christe 4-Pt. Unacc. Motet
Chorale de la Cathédrale de Strasbourg—
Hoch   12"—C-RFX57
[Victoria: O quam gloriosum]
Sainte-Chapelle Choir—Delépine
        12"—C-DFX18
[Victoria: O vos omnes]
St. Gervais Chorus   10"—LUM-30002
[Rameau: Laboravi]

BERG, Alban (1885-1935)

*A pupil of Schönberg who manifested a remark-
able talent for handling the duodecuple system.
His work is gradually becoming more widely
appreciated although at the present time not
much of it is represented on discs.*

Concerto for Violin & Orchestra
Louis Krasner & Cleveland Orch.—
Rodzinski   3 12"—CM-465†
Suite Lyrique String Quartet or Orchestra
Galimir Quartet (PD-516659/62)
        4 12"—VOX-181

WOZZECK Opera
Excerpts
Charlotte Boerner (s) & Janssen
Symphony Orch. of Los Angeles
        2 12"—ARTIST-JS12

BERGER
Legend of Prince Eugene
Munich Philharmonic Orch.—Kabasta
        12"—G-DB7652

BERLIOZ, Hector (1803-1869)

*A man with an unusually imaginative sense of
instrumental coloring. Berlioz is also known
for his witty and fascinating autobiography.*

BEATRICE ET BENEDICT Comic Opera 2
Acts
Overture Orchestra
National Symphony—Sargent
        12"—D-K1416
Liverpool Philharmonic—Cameron
        12"—C-DX1145
London Philharmonic Orch.—Harty
        12"—C-LX371
Berlin Philharmonic Orch.—Kopsch
        12"—PD-27163

BENVENUTO CELLINI, Opus 23 Opera 3
Acts
Overture Orchestra
Lamoureux Orch.—Bigot
        12"—PAT-PDT133
Paris Symphony Orch.—Monteux
        2 12"—G-W1141/2
[Les Troyens-Overture]
Berlin Philharmonic Orch.—Prüwer
        2 12"—PD-95252/3
[Rakoczy March]
Berlin Philharmonic Orch.—Kleiber
        2 12"—T-E532/3
[Rakoczy March]

(LE) CARNAVAL ROMAIN Overture, Op. 9
Boston Symphony Orch.—Koussevitzky
        12"—V-11-9008
London Philharmonic Orch.—De Sabata
        12"—D-K1552

London Philharmonic Orch.—Wood
　　　　　　　12″—**C-DX982**
London Philharmonic Orch.—Beecham
　　(in CM-552) 12″—**C-71623D**
(C-LX570) (C-LWX158) (C-68921D)
National Symphony Orch.—Beer
　　　　　　　12″—**D-K1312**
DUPLICATIONS: New York Philharmon-
ic-Symphony Orch.—Barbirolli,
C-11670D; Symphony Orch.—Eugène
Bigot, G-DB5037; Hallé Orch.—Harty,
C-LFX285: O-9422; BBC Symphony
Orch.—Boult, G-DB2078; Concertge-
bouw, Mengelberg, T-SK2489: U-F14265;
Colonne Orch.—Pierné, O-123524/5;
Berlin State Opera Orch.—Kleiber,
PD-516626: PD-66647; Also: Aily Mathe
& Gypsy Orch., PD-524172

(LE) CORSAIRE Overture, Op. 21
Royal Philharmonic Orch.—Beecham
(G-DB6357)　　　　　12″—**V-11-9955**
London Philharmonic—De Sabata
　　　　　　　12″—**D-K1552**
London Philharmonic—Harty
(C-DFX201)　　　　　12″—**C-DX664**

(LA) DAMNATION DE FAUST Opera
(Dramatic Legend) 4 Acts Op. 24
Slightly abridged recording in French
Soloists, Emile Passani Choir, Radio
Paris Orch.—Jean Fournet
　　　　　15 12″—**C-LFX614/28**
The Cast:
Marguerite .... Mona Laurena (s)
Faust .... Georges Jouatte (t)
Méphisto .... Paul Cabanel (b)
Brander .... M. Pactat (bs)
Slightly abridged recording in French
Soloists, St. Gervais Chorus, & Pasdeloup
Orch.—Coppola　　10 12″—**G-L886/95**
The Cast:
Marguerite ...... Mireille Berthon (s)
Faust .... José de Trevi (t)
Méphisto .... Charles Panzéra (b)
Brander .... Louis Morturier (bs)

ACT I
Marche hongroise (Rakoczy March)
　Orchestra
Boston Symphony Orch.—Koussevitzky
　　　　　　　12″—**V-14230**
[Danse des sylphes]
[Also on V-11-9232 in VM-1063]
[Minuet—Will o' the Wisps on
G-DB3009]
Amsterdam Concertgebouw Orch.—
van Bienum　　　　　12″—**D-K1648**
[Minuet—Will o' the Wisps]
London Philharmonic Orch.—Beecham
(C-LX702) (in CX-94†) 12″—**C-69173D**
Saxon State Orch.—Böhm
　　　　　　　12″—**G-DB5559**
[Schubert: Marche Militaire]
Berlin State Opera Orch.—Weissmann
(O-170140)　　　　　12″—**P-E11077**
[Wagner: Walküre—Ride of the
Valkyrs]
National Symphony Orch.—Fistoulari
　　　　　　　12″—**D-K1281**

[Glière: Red Poppy—Sailors' Dance]
DUPLICATIONS: Berlin Philharmonic
Orch.—Furtwängler, PD-95411; Ber-
lin Philharmonic—Kleiber, T-SK1215:
U-F14385; Amsterdam Concertgebouw
Orch. — Mengelberg, C-GQX10352:
O-171004: O-8303; CBS Symphony
Orch.—Barlow, C-71287D; Covent Gar-
den Orch.—Goossens, G-C1279: G-S8834;
Italian Radio Orch.—Basile, CET-
CB20365; Lamoureux Orch.—Wolff, PD-
66955: PD-566010; Paris Conservatory
Orch.—Gaubert, C-LFX530; Philadel-
phia. Orch. — Stokowski, V-6823:
G-D1807; G-AW160; Pittsburgh Sym-
phony Orch.—Reiner, C-11709D in CM-
491; Symphony Orch.—Heward, D-K513;
Also: BBC Military Band, C-DB1087;
Garde Républicaine Band, C-DFX147

ACT II
Chanson de la puce Baritone
Martial Singher & Metropolitan Opera
Orch.—Breisach
　　(in CM-578) 12″—**C-72086D**
[Sérénade & Voici des Roses; & Gounod:
Roméo-Ballade de la Reine Mab]
DUPLICATIONS: E. Billot, O-188745;
Vanni-Marcoux, G-DA1158
Voici des roses (Air des Roses) Baritone
Martial Singher & Metropolitan Opera
Orch.—Breisach
　　(in CM-578) 12″—**C-72086D**
[Chanson de la puce & Sérénade; &
Gounod: Roméo-Ballade de la Reine
Mab]
Artur Endrèze & Orch.—Ruhlmann
　　　　　　　12″—**PAT-PDT26**
[Saint-Saëns: Samson-Maudit à jamais
soit la race]
[Older version on PAT-PD18]
[Wagner: Tannhäuser-Recit. of Wolfram
on PAT-X90073]
DUPLICATIONS: Alex Sved (in Italian),
G-DA5388; José Beckmanns, PD-561010;
Willy Tubiana, G-P714
Danse des sylphes Orchestra
Boston Symphony Orch.—Koussevitzky
　　　　　　　12″—**V-14230**
[Rakoczy March]
[Also on V-11-9232 in VM-1063]
[Handel: Concerto Grosso No. 12—
Larghetto, on G-DB3010]
London Philharmonic Orch.—Beecham
　　(in CX-94) 12″—**C-69173D**
[Rakoczy March]
(C-LX702) (C-LWX236)
Italian Radio Orch.—Basile
　　　　　　　12″—**CET-CB20365**
[Rakoczy March]
Amsterdam Concertgebouw Orch.— Van
Bienum　　　　　　　12″—**D-K1649**
[Les Troyens-Marche Troyenne]
Amsterdam Concertgebouw Orch.—
Mengelberg　　　　　12″—**O-171004**
[Rakoczy March]
(C-GQX10352) (O-8303)
DUPLICATIONS: Lamoureux Orch.—
Wolff, PD-66954: PD-566009; "Maggio

Musicale" Orch. — Markevitch, CET-CB25157

ACT III

Autrefois un roi de Thule (Chanson gothique or Ballade) Soprano
Germaine Martinelli
(PD-66969) 12"—PD-566040
[D'amour l'ardente flamme]
Mireille Berthon 12"—G-L891
Merci, doux crépuscule Tenor It. A te grazie, o crepuscolo
Henri Saint-Cricq 12"—PAT-X7236
[L'Enfance du Christ: Le Repos de la Sainte-Famille]
Giovanni Malipiero (in Italian)
12"—G-DB5445
[Nature immense]
Menuet des Feux-Follets Orchestra
Eng. Minuet of the Will o' the Wisps
Boston Symphony Orch.—Koussevitzky
12"—V-14231
[Handel: Concerto No. 12—Larghetto]
[Rakoczy March on G-DB3009]
London Philharmonic Orch.—Beecham
(in CX-94) 12"—C-69174D
(C-LX703) (C-LWX237)
Amsterdam Concertgebouw Orch.—van Beinum 12"—D-K1648
[Rakoczy March]
DUPLICATIONS: Lamoureux Orch.—Wolff: PD-66954: PD-566009; Paris Conservatory Orch.—Gaubert, C-LFX530
Sérénade de Méphisto Baritone
Martial Singher & Metropolitan Opera Orch.—Breisach
(in CM-528) 12"—C-72086D
[Chanson de la puce & Voici des Roses; Gounod: Roméo-Ballade de la Reine Mab]
Alexander Sved (in Italian)
10"—G-DA5388
[Voici des roses]
DUPLICATIONS: José Beckmans: PD-561010; J. Claverie, P-29560; Vanni-Marcoux, G-DA1158
In Italian: T. Ruffo, G-DA164*

ACT IV

D'amour l'ardente flamme (Romance)
Soprano
Rose Bampton & Victor Orch.—Pelletier 12"—V-12-0015
Yvonne Gall 12"—C-LFX5
Germaine Martinelli 12"—PD-66969
[Chanson gothique] (PD-566040)
Nature immense (Invocation à la nature)
Tenor It. Natura immensa
Raoul Jobin
(in CM-696) 12"—C-72138D
[Meyerbeer: L'Africaine—O Paradis]
G. Malipiero (in Italian)
12"—G-DB5445
[Merci, doux crépuscule]
DUPLICATIONS: René Maison, O-123502; Henry Saint-Cricq, PAT-X7221

L'ENFANCE DU CHRIST, OP. 25 Oratorio
Prelude—The Flight into Egypt
Symphony Orch.—F. Cébron
10"—LUM-30082

Part I
—No. 3.—Recit. Toujours ce rêve. & Air: O misère des Rois Bass
Louis Morturier 12"—G-W1137
[Haydn: Seasons—Schön eilet froh]
Narçon, & Orch.—Szyfer 12"—C-RFX8
[Saint-Saëns: Le pas d'armes]

Part II
—No. 2—L'Adieu des bergers Chorus
Strasbourg Cathedral Choir—Hoch
12"—C-69693D
[Josquin des Près: Ave vera Virginitas]
(C-LX767) (C-LWX296)
[Mozart: Ave Verum, on C-RFX60]
Paris Teachers' Chorus—Roger-Ducasse 12"—C-DF1184
[Schumann: Zigeunerleben]
—No. 3—Le Repos de la Sainte Famille
Tenor
Jean Planel & Paris Symphony Orch.—Ruhlmann 12"—PAT-X93102
DUPLICATION: Henri Saint-Cricq, PAT-X7236

(LES) FRANCS JUGES Overture, Op. 3
Orchestra
Eng. The Judges of the Secret Court
BBC Symphony Orch.—Boult
2 12"—G-DB3131/2
[Tchaikovsky: Eugene Onegin—Polonaise]

GRANDE MESSE DES MORTS
Georges Jouatte (t) & Emile Passani
Choir & Radio Paris Orch.—Fournet
11 12"—C-LFX659/69

HAROLD EN ITALIE, Op. 16 Orchestra with Viola obbligato
(Symphony for Viola & Orchestra)
William Primrose & Boston Symphony—Koussevitzky 5 12"—VM-989†
(G-DB6261/5)

Marche funèbre (for the last scene of Hamlet) Op. 18, No. 3
London Philharmonic—Harty
12"—C-LFX414

(LES) NUITS D'ETE, Op. 7 (Songs, to texts by Theophile Gautier)
1. Villanelle
Ninon Vallin (s) & pf.
[Canal: Roses de Saadi] 10"—PAT-PG62
2. Le Spectre de la rose
Maggie Teyte (s) & London Philharmonic Orch.—Heward
12"—(In Gramophone Shop Album)
4. L'Absence
Maggie Teyte (s) & London Philharmonic Orch.—Heward
12"—(In Gramophone Shop Album)

REQUIEM See Grand Messe des Morts

Rêverie et Caprice (Romance for Violin
& Orchestra) Op. 8
Joseph Szigeti & Philharmonia Orch.—
Lambert   12"—C-LX946

ROI LEAR Overture, Op. 4 Orchestra
London Symphony Orch.—Harty
  2 12"—PD-516685/6
[Les Troyens—Marche]

ROMEO ET JULIETTE, Op. 17 Dramatic
Symphony, with Chorus

Part II

Excerpts: Roméo seul; Tristesse; Concert et
Bal; Grand Fête chez Capulet; Scene
d'amour
NBC Symphony Orch.—Toscanini
(V-V7†-Plastic) 3 12"—VM-1160†
—Roméo seul; Tristesse; Concert et Bal;
Grande Fête chez Capulet only
London Philharmonic Orch.—Harty
  2 10"—C-DB1230/1
(in Columbia History of Music, Vol.
III: CM-234)

Part IV

La Reine Mab, ou la Fée des songes
(Queen Mab Scherzo)
No recording available.

SYMPHONIE FANTASIQUE, Op. 14a
Orchestra
San Francisco Symphony—Monteux
  6 12"—VM-994†
Paris Conservatory Orch.—Bruno
Walter 6 12"—G-DB3852/7†
Cleveland Orch.—Rodzinski
  6 12"—CM-488†
Hallé Orch.—Barbirolli
  7 12"—G-C3563/9†
Concertgebouw Orch. of Amsterdam—
van Beinum 6 12"—D-K1626/31†
Paris Symphony—Meyrowitz
  6 12"—PAT-PDT10/15
DUPLICATION: Paris Symphony Orch.
Monteux, G-W1100/5
—2nd Mvt. (Un bal); 4th Mvt. (Marche au
supplice); 5th Mvt. (Songe d'une Nuit
de Sabbat) only
Colonne Orch.—Pierné
  5 12"—O-123536/9
[Chabrier: Marche Joyeuse]
—2nd Mvt. (Un bal) only
Berlin Philharmonic Orch. Kleiber
  12"—U-E808

(LES) TROYENS Opera in 2 Parts
 Part I—La Prise de Troie (Acts I & II)
 Part II—Les Troyens à Carthage
 (Acts III, IV, & V)
Part II—Les Troyens à Carthage Overture
Paris Symphony Orch.—Monteux
  12"—G-W1142
[Benvenuto Cellini—Overture, Pt. 3]

Act III
Chasse royale et orage
 Eng. Royal Hunt & Storm
 London Philharmonic Orch.—
 Beecham 12"—G-DB6241
 [Also in VM-1141; with Trojan March &
 Borodin: Prince Igor Overture]
 Hallé Orch.—Harty 12"—C-DFX117
Marche (Arr. concert by Berlioz as Marche
Troyenne)
 London Philharmonic Orch.—
 Beecham 12"—G-DB6238
 [Borodin: Prince Igor—Overture, Pt. 3]
 [Also in VM-1141, with Chasse royale et
 orage & Borodin: Prince Igor—
 Overture]
 Paris Conservatory Orch.—Weingartner
 (C-LX861)
  (in CX-169†) 12"—C-70089D
 [Wagner: Rienzi—Overture, Pt. 3]
 London Symphony Orch.—Harty
   12"—PD-516686
 [Roi Lear Overture, Pt. 3]
 Amsterdam Concertgebouw Orch.—
 van Beinum 12"—D-K1649
 [La Damnation de Faust—Danse des
 sylphes]
Inutiles regrets
En un dernier naufrage Tenor & Chorus
 Georges Thill & Chorus 12"—C-LFX358

MISCELLANEOUS:
Harmonization of "La Marseillaise"
 La Chorale Populaire de Paris, with
 Orch.—Rosset, O-281114
—Arrangement: Weber's Aufforderung zum
Tanz: See under Weber

BERNABEI, Gioseffo Antonio (1649-1732)
*A court musician at Munich who composed
masses, motets and nearly 20 operas.*
Alma Redemptoris Mater 4-Part
 Milan Cathedral Chorus—Perosi
 (Adolfo Bossi, organ) 12"—G-HN1380
 [Marziano Perosi: Resurrexit]
 (G-EG6289)

BERNARD, Jean-Emile (1843-1902)
*A French organist and composer of chamber
music, concertos, oratorios.*
Ça fait peur aux oiseaux Song
 Jane Bathori (s) with self piano acc.
   10"—C-LF74
 [Darcier: Souvenirs de jeunesse]
 Mary Marquet (s) & Lily Laskine
 (harp) 10"—G-DA4836
 [Sévérac: Le roi a fait battre]
Divertissement (or, Suite ancienne)
 Woodwinds
 Garde Républicaine soloists
 [Letorey: Scherzo] 2 10"—C-D6261/2

BERNERS, Lord (Gerald Hugh Tyrwhitt-
 Wilson) (1883-)
*Berners is inclined to be a bit sardonic in his
music, though always restrained by good taste
and a delightful sense of what makes interesting listening. Recently he has turned to writing
background music for films in England.*

Nicholas Nickleby—Incidental music from
the film
Philharmonia Orch.—Ernest Irving
12"—C-DX1362
(The) Triumph of Neptune Ballet Suite
Schottische; Hornpipe; Polka—Sailor's
Return; Harlequinade; Dance of the Fairy
Princesses; Sunday Morning—Intermez-
zo; Apotheosis
London Philharmonic Orch.—
Beecham 2 12"—C-LX697/8

BERNIER, Nicolas (1664-1734)
*One of the earliest French cantata composers,
a choirmaster whose seven volumes of church
music make him one of the outstanding musicians of his time.*

Motets In Latin
Lauda Jerusalem Tenor, Violins, Harpsi-
chord
Laudate Dominum Tenor, Violins, Flute,
Harpsichord
Jean Planel & Instr. acc., with R.
Gerlin (harpsichord) 10"—LUM-30077

BERNSTEIN, Leonard (1918-   )
*A young American conductor and composer
who has met with success here and abroad for
his ballet and musical comedy scores.*

FANCY FREE Ballet Suite
Big Stuff (Prologue); Opening Dance;
Scene at the Bar; Pas de Deux; Competi-
tion Scene; Waltz Variations; Danzón
Variations; Galop Variations; Finale
Ballet Theatre Orch.—Bernstein, with
Billie Holliday (vocal)
4 10"—D-DA406
—Three Variations (Galop, Waltz &
Danzón) only
Boston "Pops" Orch.—Fiedler
12"—V-11-9386

FACSIMILE—A Choreographic Essay
Ballet Suite Orchestra
Victor Orch.—Bernstein
2 12"—VM-1142†

"JEREMIAH" SYMPHONY
St. Louis Symphony Orch.—Bernstein,
with Nan Merriman (ms)
3 12"—VM-1026†

ON THE TOWN Selections from musical
comedy
Victor Chorale & "On the Town" Orch.—
Bernstein & Robert Shaw
4 10"—VM-995†
Nancy Walker, Betty Comden, Adolph
Green & Mary Martin with Orch.—
Leonard Joy 3 10"—D-A416
Sonata for Clarinet & Piano
David Oppenheim & Leonard Bernstein
2 12"—Hargail MW-501
[Three Anniversaries]
Three Anniversaries
For my sister Shirley
In Memorium—Natalie Koussevitzky
For William Schuman
Leonard Bernstein (pf)
in Hargail MW-501

BERTRAND, Antoine De (fl. 1576-1580)
*A friend of Ronsard, Bertrand is best known
for his four-voice settings of that French poet's
sonnets.*

Las, je me plainds Unacc. Chorus in French
Chantérie de la Renaissance—Expert
12"—C-DFX54
[Claude le Jeune: Belle aronde]

BERWALD, Franz (1796-1868)
*A Swedish violinist friend of Mendelssohn who
composed music for Jenny Lind and who devoted the latter part of his life to teaching at
the Academy of Music in Stockholm. In recent
years a great deal of his music has been recorded
by his fellow countrymen.*

Collections:
Album I—Symphony, G minor (Singulière)
Göteborg Radio Orch.—Tor Mann
Symphony, D major (Capricieuse)
Stockholm Radio Orch.—Sten Bromann
7 12"—RD-501/7
(Swedish Radiotjänst)
Album II—Symphony, E flat
Göteborg Radio Orch.—Tor Mann
The Queen of Golconda—Overture
Göteborg Radio Orch.—Eckerberg
Estrella di Soria—Overture
Estrella's 1st Aria (B. Nilsson, s);
Muza's Vengeance Aria (S. Nillson, bs)
with Göteborg Radio Orch.—S.
Eckerberg 7 12"—RD-508/14
(Swedish Radiotjänst)
Album III—Symphony, G minor (Sérieuse)
Tales from Norwegian Mountains
Earnest and Happy Fancies
Göteborg Radio Orch.—Tor Mann
6 12"—RD-515/20
(Swedish Radiotjänst)
Album IV—Piano Trio, D minor
String Quartet, A minor
Piano Quintet, C minor
8 12"—Swedish Radiotjänst
(in preparation)
Estrella di Soria—Overture
Stockholm Royal Opera Orch.—Sten
Frykberg 12"—G-Z310
String Quartet, E flat
Kyndel Quartet 3 12"—G-DB11001/3
[Roman: Church Sonata—Trio, G minor,
Pt. 3 on G-DB11001]

**BESARD, Jean-Baptiste (Giovanni Battista
Bessardo) (1565-1625)**
*French amateur composer and lutenist, also
known for two books "Thesaurus harmonicus"
and "Novus partus musicae." His dance tune
"Branle de village" is used by Respighi as the
"Danza Rustica"—No. 2 of the second suite of
Antique Airs and Dances.*

16th Century Lute Music
Branle gay, Les Cloches de Paris, Danse
Anglaise, Villanelle
Hermann Leeb
(in Vol. IV) 12"—AS-36

BEYDTS, Louis

A contemporary French composer of songs and light musicales.

A l'aimable Sabine Excerpts
Jacques Jensen (t) & Germaine Roger
(s)   2 12"—G-DA5012/3
A Travers Paris
Instrumental Ensemble—Beydts
                2 10"—G-K7811/2
SONGS in French
C'est moi
En Arles
Un Ceri
Mme. Geori-Boué (s)   10"—O-188947
Lyre et amour Song Cycle
Le bracelet; L'écho; La belle esclave noir;
Le baiser de Dorinde
Pierre Bernac (b) & Orch.—Beydts
                2 12"—G-W1586/7

BIBER, Heinrich Ignaz Franz von (1664-1704)

Kapellmeister at Salzburg at the end of the 17th century, Biber wrote both operas and devotional music. He was knighted in 1690.

Sonata, C minor Violin & Harpsichord
["Leiden Christi am oelberg"]
Mme. G. Strauss & Pauline Aubert
                (in Vol. X) 12"—AS-94

BILLINGS, William (1746-1800)

The composer of "Psalms and Fuguing Tunes" was originally a tanner by profession who turned to music when he became dissatisfied with the slow-paced hymn tunes of his day and exerted considerable influence on the church music in Colonial America. He published many books of tunes, is said to have introduced the pitch pipe for use in church services and in singing societies, and is the first native American to become a professional musician.

Chester 1770 (See also collection below)
Madrigal Singers—Lehmann Engel
                (in CM-329) 10"—C-4400M
[Brave Wolfe; American Hero; Burman Lover]
—Arr. Orchestra Maganini
Boston "Pops" Orch.—Fiedler
                10"—V-4502
[Arr. Guion: Arkansas Traveler]

PSALMS & FUGUING TUNES

Be Glad Then, America; New Plymouth; When Jesus Wept; Creation; Judea; Dying Christian's Farewell; Chester
The Madrigalists   3 10"—CM-434
Shepherd's Carol
Victor Chorale—Robert Shaw, in VM-1077

BINCHOIS, Egidius (or Gilles) (1400-1460)

One of the great 15th century Netherlanders, Binchois composed many excellent religious and secular chansons.

A Solis ortu Cardine
Sanctus
Yvonne Gouverné Chorus (in Latin)
                10"—OL-62
[Anon: Déploration sur la mort de Binchois]

De plus en plus—Rondeau
Mlle. H. Guermant & F. Anspach with Medieval viols, Lute, Little Harp & Recorder—Cape
                (in Vol. IV) 12"—AS-39
[Grossin de Paris: Va t'en soupir & Lantins: Puisque je voy]
Files a marier
Yvonne Gouverné Chorus (in French)
                10"—OL-63
[Ghizeghem: Les Grans Regrez & Morton: Trois Chansons]
Inter Natos Mulierum
R. Bonte (t) with flute & vlc.
                10"—OL-126
[Morton: Trois Chansons]
Je loe amours
Lise Daniels (s, in French) & Pasquier Trio   10"—OL-42
[Vide: Las, j'ay perdu mon espincel & Vit encore ce faux dangier]

BINET, Jean (1893-   )

A Swiss composer who has spent much of his life in America and is known for his instrumental works, chamber music and music for the ballet.

Chansons (C. F. Ramuz)
Chanson devant la guérite; Complainte; Petite fille; Chanson du route
Huguès Cuenod (t) & Chamber Orch. of the Suisse Romande—J. Binet
                2 10"—ELITE-4469/70

BINGHAM, Seth (1882-   )

American organist, teacher and composer who has held positions at Yale and Columbia Universities.

Chorale, Op. 9, No. 4 Organ
Joseph Bonnet (Hammond Organ, Gloucester, Mass)
                (in VM-835) 12"—V-18214
[Shelly: Spring Song]

BISHOP, Sir Henry Rowley (1766-1855)

A British composer of ballad-operas, Bishop was remarkably successful in his day. Today he is chiefly remembered by "Home Sweet Home" which is from the opera, "Clari, Maid of Milan" and for various virtuosi solos for coloratura soprano.

SONGS

Echo Song
Lily Pons (s) & Renaissance Quintet
                (in VM-756) 10"—V-2150
A. Galli-Curci (s)   12"—G-DB258*
[Lo! here the gentle lark]
Home, Sweet Home
A. Galli-Curci (s) & H. Samuels (pf)
(G-DA1011)   10"—V-1355
[Flotow: Marta—Last Rose of Summer]
Gwen Catley (s) & Orch.—Robinson
                10"—G-B9574
[Flotow: Marta—Last Rose of Summer]
Helen Traubel (s) with Male Chorus & Orch.—O'Connell
                (in CM-639) 12"—C-72102D
[Bayly: Long, long ago]

Lily Pons (s) & Orch.—Kostelanetz
 (in CM-484) 12"—**C-71307D**
[Poldini—La Forge: Poupée valsante]
Raymond Dixon (t) & Orch.
    10"—**V-21949**
[Barnby: Sweet and low]
Lo! Here the Gentle Lark
Josephine Antoine (s), with J. Henry
Bove (fl) & Stuart Ross (pf)
    12"—**C-71025D**
[Alabiev: The Russian Nightingale]
Lily Pons (s) & Gordon Walker (fl) with
Orch. (G-DB2502) 12"—**V-8733**
[Mozart: Zauberflöte-Ach, ich fühls]
Gwen Catley (s) & G. Burrows (fl) with
Orch. 12"—**G-C3214**
[Arditi: Il bacio]
A. Galli-Curci (s) & M. Berenguer (fl)
with Orch. (G-DB1278) 12"—**V-6924**
[Grieg: Peer Gynt-Solvejg's Song]
[Echo Song, on G-DB258*]
Marie Huston (s), with fl. & pf. acc., in
V-P39
My Pretty Jane (The bloom is on the rye)
Heddle Nash (t) 10"—**C-DB720**
[Trad: Bonnie Mary of Argyle]
Pretty Mocking Bird
Lily Pons (s) with flute & Orch.
 (in VM-702) 12"—**V-17231**
[Flotow: Marta—Last Rose of Summer]
Gwen Catley (s) & Gerald Moore (pf),
with fl. obb. 12"—**G-C3233**
[Braga: Angel's Serenade]

BIZET, Georges (1838-1875)

*Bizet's "Carmen" not only influenced the
French school of "opera seria," but also im-
pressed its stamp on Puccini, Mascagni and
other composers who made up the school of
"verismo" in Italy. Bizet was one of the many
French composers who incorporated "Spanish
atmosphere" into his scores.*

(L') ARLESIENNE Incidental music to
Alphonse Daudet's drama
Collection:
 Prélude (Based on Marche des rois);
Pastorale (L'Etang de Vaccarés) Act II,
Scene 1; Choeur suivant la pastorale; In-
termezzo (La Cuisine de Castelet), Act
II, Scene 2; Minuetto No. 1 (Intermezzo)
between Acts II & III; Le Carillon
(Entr'acte), Act II, Scene 2; Adagietto
(Balthazar & Mère Renaud love music);
Farandole, Act III, Scene 1; Marche des
rois (with chorus)
Odeon Theatre Chorus & Symphony
Orch.—Pierre Chagnon
(C-4988/92) 5 10"—**C-D6293/7**

**SUITE NO. 1 (Prelude; Minuetto No. 1;
Carillon; Adagietto)**

**SUITE NO. 2 (Pastorale; Intermezzo; Min-
uetto No. 2; Fandarole)**
Berlin Philharmonic Orch.—Schreker
 5 12"—**PD-66703/4 & PD-66799/801**
(PD-516601/5)
DUPLICATIONS: Symphony Orch.—Ing-
helbrecht, PAT-X96226/7 & PAT-
X96263/5

SUITE NO 1 only
Hallé Orch.—Sargent
   3 12"—**C-DX1085/7**
[Vaughan-Williams: Greensleeves
Fantasia]
Philadelphia Orch.—Stokowski
(G-AW143/5) 3 12"—**VM-62**
(G-D1801/3) (G-W1089/91)
[Suite No. 2—Pastorale]
Berlin Philharmonic—Schuricht
   2 12"—**T-E1850/1**
Symphony Orch.—Inghelbrecht
  2 12" & 10"—**PAT-X96263/5**
[Carmen: Entr'acte, Act III]
—Prelude; Adagietto & Minuetto only
London Philharmonic Orch.—Beecham
(C-LX541/2) 2 12"—**CX-69**
National Symphony—Beer
 (in D-ED42†) 2 12"—**D-K1278/9**

SUITE NO. 2 only
Boston "Pops" Orch.—Fiedler
(G-C3206/7) 2 12"—**VM-683**
Berlin Philharmonic—Schmidt-Isserstedt
(U-F14408/9) 2 12"—**T-E3061/2**
Italian Radio Orch.—Basile
   3 12"—**CET-CB20362/4**
[Carmen—Prelude Act I]
London Symphony Orch.—Goossens
  2 12"—**G-EH1239/40**
[The Farandole from this set is included
on V-11-8379 in VM-916: Vaughan-
Williams: London Symphony]
—Minuetto & Farandole only
London Philharmonic Orch.—Beecham
    12"—**C-68882D**
(C-LX614) (C-LFX490) (C-LWX201)
**Miscellaneous collection from Suites 1
& 2**
**Prélude, Pastorale, Intermezzo, Adagiet-
to, Carillon, Minuetto, Farandole**
Colonne Orch.—Pierné
   4 12"—**O-123685/8**
Opéra-Comique Orch.—Cloëz
   4 10"—**O-165051/4**
Individual numbers (in alphabetical
order)
Adagietto (Suite No. 1)
—Arr. Violin
D. Soriano, PAT-PG31
Farandole (Suite No. 2)
London Symphony Orch.—Goossens
 (in VM-916†) 12"—**V-11-8379**
[Vaughan-Williams: London Symphony,
Pt. 9]
New York City Symphony Orch.—
Stokowski, in VM-1002†
National Symphony—Beer, D-K1280, in
D-ED42†
Minuetto No. 1 (Suite No. 1)
New York City Symphony Orch.—
Stokowski, in VM-1002†
—Arr. Flute
Marcel Moyse, G-K5165
Pastorale (Suite No. 2)
—Andantino (middle section) only
Philadelphia Orch.—Stokowski
 (in VM-62) 12"—**V-7126**
(G-D1803) (G-W1091) (G-AW145)
[Suite No. 1, Pt. 5]

Berlin State Opera Orch. & Chorus—
Weigert 12"—**PD-27191**
[Carmen—Selections]
Unspecified Excerpts: Symphony Orch.—
Segna, ESTA-D2022
Jeux d'enfants See under Petite Suite

OPERAS in French

CARMEN 4 Acts 1875

Complete recording in French
Soloists, Chorus & Orch. of Opéra-
Comique, Paris-Elie Cohen
15 12"—**C-OP1†**
(C-D14222/36) (C-9527/41)
The Cast:
Carmen ...... Raymonde Visconti (ms)
Micaëla .... Marthe Nespoulos (s)
Don José .... Georges Thill (t)
Escamillo .... M. Guénot (b)
Frasquita .... Andrée Vavon (s)
Mercédès .... Andrée Bernadet (s)
La Dancaïre .... M. Roussel (b)
Le Remendado .... M. Mathyl (t)

Complete recording in Italian
Soloists, Chorus & Orch. of La Scala,
Milan—Carlo Sabajno
19 12"—**VM-128†**
(G-C2310/28) (G-S10300/18)
The Cast:
Carmen ..... Gabriella Besanzoni (ms)
Micaëla ...... Maria Carbone (s)
Don José .... Piero Bauli (t)
Escamillo ...... Ernesto Besanzoni (b)
Frasquita .... Nerina Ferrari (s)
Mercédès .... Tamara Beltacchi (s)
Le Dancaïre .... Nello Pauli (b)
Le Remendado ..... E. Venturini (t)

Complete recording in Italian
Soloists, Chorus & Orch. of La Scala,
Milan—Molajoli
19 12"—**C-GQX10641/59**
The Cast:
Carmen .... Aurora Buades (ms)
Micaëla .... Ines Alfani Tellini (s)
Don José .... Aureliano Pertile (t)
Escamillo ..... Benevenuto Franci (b)
Frasquita .... Irma Mion (s)
Mercédès .... Ebe Ticozzi (s)
Zuniga .... Bruno Carmassi (bs)
Morales } ... Attilio Bordonalli (b)
Le Dancaïre }
Le Remendado .... Giuseppe Nessi

Complete recording in French
Soloists, Chorus & Orch. of Opéra-
Comique, Paris—Coppola
17 12"—**G-L695/711**
The Cast:
Carmen .... Lucy Perelli (ms)
Micaëla .... Yvonne Brothier (s)
Don José .... José de Trevi (t)
Escamillo .... Louis Musy (b)
Frasquita .... Lebard (s)
Mercédès .... Fenoyer (s)
Zuniga .... Louis Morturier (bs)
Le Dancaïre .... Payen (b)
Le Remendado .... Cornellier (b)

Abridged recording in French
Soloists and Chorus of Opéra-Comique
with Lamoureux Orch.—Wolff
5 12"—**PD-566033/7**
The Cast includes: Mmes. Brohly, G.
Corney, Lebard, A. Bernadet & Mm. H.
Saint Cricq, J. Beckmans, Payen, Vieulle,
Roussel & Herent

Abridged recording in Italian
Soloists, Chorus & Orch. of La Scala,
Milan—Molajoli 6 12"—**C-DX492/7**
(A condensed version of the Molajoli-
Columbia complete set listed above)

Selections in French
Soloists of the Metropolitan Opera, with
Victor Chorale—Robert Shaw, & Victor
Symphony Orch.—Erich Leinsdorf
6 12"—**VM-1078†**
The Cast:
Carmen ...... Gladys Swarthout (ms)
Micaëla .... Licia Albanese (s)
Don José .... Ramon Vinay (t)
Escamillo .... Robert Merrill (b)
with Thelma Votipka, Lucielle Browning,
Anthony Amato & George Chehanovsky.

Selections in French
Soloists & Chorus of Metropolitan Opera,
with Orch.—Sebastian
5 12"—**CM-607†**
The Cast:
Carmen .... Risë Stevens (ms)
Micaëla .... Nadine Conner (s)
Don José .... Raoul Jobin (t)
Escamillo .... Robert Weede (b)

Vocal & Orchestral Selections (Potpourris, etc.)
Noel Eadie, Nancy Evans, Webster Booth,
Dennis Noble, with Sadler's Wells
Chorus(in English) & Orch.—
Braithwaite 12"—**G-C2143**
Anni Frind, Eva Leibenberg, Helge Ros-
waenge, Wilhelm Guttmann with Chorus
(in German) of Berlin State Opera, and
Berlin Philharmonic Orch. 12"—**T-E1158**
M. Satta (s) & A. Laffi (b), with Milan
Symphony Orch.—Molajoli
10"—**C-GQ7189**

CARMEN SUITES Orchestra

Prelude, Act I; Aragonaise; Intermezzo, Act
III; Dragoons of Alcala, Act II; Nocturne
(Micaëla's Air); Bullfight; Habañera &
Changing of the Guard, Act I; March of
Smugglers; Chanson Bohème, Act II
New York City Symphony—Stokowski
4 12"—**VM-1002†**

Prelude, Act I; Aragonaise, Act IV; Dragoons of Alcala, Act II; Changing of the
Guard, Act I; Intermezzo, Act III; Chanson Bohème, Act II
London Philharmonic—Beecham
2 12"—**CX-144†**
(C-LX823/4) (C-LWX305/6)

Prelude, Act I; Dragoons of Alcala; Chang-
ing of the Guard; Habañera; Chanson
Bohème; Prelude, Act III; March of
Smugglers; Micaëla's Air
National Symphony—Fistoulari
(D-K1286/8) 3 12"—**D-ED41†**

Miscellaneous

Prelude Act I, and Entr'acte Act II, III & IV

Czech Philharmonic Orch.—Kleiber
(U-F14398/9)   2   12"—T-E2041/2
Symphony Orch.—Inghelbrecht
         2   10"—PAT-PG49/50
Dresden Philharmonic Orch.—Paul van
Kempen   12"—PD-15191
(PD-516774) (CET-OR5060)
(This version lacks Prelude Act I)

Entr'actes Unspecified

Beromünster Radio Orch.—Scherchen
         12"—D-K1614
Symphony Orch.—Segna
         10"—ESTA-D2021

Selections (Potpourri) Orchestra

Berlin-Charlottenburg Opera Orch.—
Melichar   12"—PD-27169
Royal Opera Orch.—Barbirolli (arr.
Gilbaro)   12"—G-C2056
Also: Marek Weber Orch., G-L961:
G-S10374: G-C2596: G-Z225: G-EH777;
Creatore Band, G-S8442 & G-S8444
See under Miscellaneous for Violin, Piano
fantasias on themes from "Carmen" by
Sarasate, Busoni, Horowitz, etc.
(See under Suites, etc., above)

Individual Excerpts

ACT I
Prelude

Czech Philharmonic Orch.—Kleiber
(U-F14398)   12"—T-E2041
[Entr'Acte, Act II]
Italian Radio Orch.—Basile
         12"—CET-CB20364
[L'Arlésienne Suite No. 2, Pt. 5]
DUPLICATIONS: Berlin Philharmonic
Orch.—Wolff, PD-66723: PD-66726:
PD-516654; Symphony Orch.—Inghel-
brecht, PAT-PG49; Milan Symphony
Orch.—Molajoli, C-D12275; Berlin State
Opera Orch.—Weigert, PD-27190;
London Philharmonic Orch.—Beecham,
in CX-144†: C-LX823/4
New York City Symphony Orch.—
Stokowski, in VM-1002†

**Sur la place (Opening Chorus) Soprano,
Baritone & Chorus**
Felicie Hüni-Mihacsek, Willi Domgraf-
Fassbaender & Berlin State Opera
Chorus, in German   12"—PD-95451
[Parle-moi de ma mére]

Avec la garde montante Boy's Chorus
Children's Chorus of La Scala, in Italian
[Les voici]   12"—C-GQX10263
—Arr. Orchestra (Changing of the Guard)
(See Suites above)
Paris Philharmonic—Cloëz
         10"—O-249000
[Smugglers' March, Act III]

**Dans l'air (Choeur des cigarières) Eng.
Cigarette Girl's Chorus**
—Arr. Orchestra
Pasdeloup Orch.—Inghelbrecht
[Les voici]   12"—PAT-X5488

Habañera: L'Amour est un oiseau rebelle
Soprano
It. E l'amore uno strano augello
Ger. Ja die Liebe hat bunte Flügel
Conchita Supervia   12"—P-R20278
[Rossini: L'Italiana in Algeri—O che
muso, with Scattola]
[Non, tu ne m'aimes pas, with Micheletti,
on O-123773]
Ninon Vallin with Chorus & Orch.—
Andolfi (PAT-PAT52)   12"—C-P9152M
[Chanson Bohème]
[Séguedille on PAT-X90030]
[Messager: Fortunio-Air du chandelier,
with Bourdin, on O-188541]
Gladys Swarthout, with Victor Chorale &
Orch.—Leinsdorf
      (in VM-1074)   12"—V-11-9289
[Gounod: Faust-Soldier's Chorus with
Victor Chorale—Shaw]
Gladys Swarthout & Orch.—Smallens
[Séguedille]   12"—V-14419
Jeanne Gerville-Réache (Recorded 1910)
         12"—V-15-1008*
[Masse: Paul et Virginie-Chanson du
Tigre]
Risë Stevens & Orch.—Weissman
         12"—C-71192D
[Thomas: Mignon-Connais-tu le pays?]

DUPLICATIONS: A. Bernadet, PD-
521896; Emma Calvé, V-18144* in VM-
816; Else Brems, TONO-X25030
In Italian: Aurora Buades, C-GQX10061;
Gianna Pederzini, G-DA5385; Ebe Stig-
nani, C-DQ1042; G. Zinetti, C-D12317;
Irene Minghini-Cattaneo, G-DB1303
In German: Margarete Klose, PD-67789;
Emmi Leisner, PD-66738; Karin Bran-
zell, CRS-23*
In Swedish: Gertrud Wettergren,
G-X2644
In Czech: Marta Krasova, U-G12732

—Arr. Orchestra Stokowski
New York City Symphony Orch.—
Stokowski, in VM-1002†

Parle-moi de ma mère;
Qui sait de quel démon Soprano & Tenor
It. La tua madre Ger. Ich seh' die Mütter
Ninon Vallin & Villabella
         12"—PAT-PDT18
Jane Rolland & Charles Friant
         12"—O-123807
Fanny Heldy & Fernand Ansseau
         12"—G-DB1115
G. Corney & Lens   12"—PD-516600
In Italian: B. Gigli & R. Gigli, G-DA5416;
Antonio Cortis & Anna Rozsa, G-DB1749;
In German: Aulikki Rautawaara & Peter
Anders, T-E2654; Margherita Perras &
Walter Ludwig, G-DB4498; H. von De-
bicka & Helge Roswaenge, PD-95451;
In Czech: M. Budikova & J. Gleich,
U-G12903; S. Jelinkova & B. Blachut,
ESTA-H5122

Séguedille: Près des remparts de Séville
Ger. Draussen am Wald It. Presso il
bastion di Siviglia

NOTE: *The brief duo with José following the Séguedille proper is omitted in most of the isolated recordings.*

(See also Collections)
Conchita Supervia & Micheletti
(O-123714) 12″—P-R20127
[Chanson bohème, Act II]
Ninon Vallin & Villabella
12″—PAT-X90030
[Habañera]
[Messager: Fortunio-Lorsque je n'étais, on O-188521]
Gladys Swarthout & Orch.—Smallens
[Habañera] 12″—V-14419
Risë Stevens & Raoul Jobin (also in CM-607) (in CM-676†) 12″—C-71974D
[Saint-Saëns: Samson et Dalila-Mon coeur s'ouvre à ta voix]
DUPLICATIONS: Alice Raveau, PAT-X90025; A. Bernadet, PD-521896; Else Brems & Otto Svendsen, TONO-X25030;
In Italian: Gianna Pederzini, CET-BB25025; G. Zinetti, C-D12317; Aurora Buades, C-GQX10509;
In German: Friedel Beckmann, G-DB5693; Rosette Anday, PD-66779
In Swedish: Gertrud Wettergren, G-X2644
In Czech: Marta Krasova, ESTA-H5120

ACT II

Prelude (Entr'acte) (Les Dragons d'Alcala)
See also Orchestral Suites
Czech Philharmonic Orch.—Kleiber
(U-F14398) 12″—T-E2041
[Prelude to Act I]
Dresden Philharmonic Orch.—Paul van Kempen (PD-516774) 12″—PD-15191
[Entr'actes, Acts III & IV]
Philadelphia Orch.—Stokowski
12″—G-D1816
[Entr'acte, Act. III & Danse Bohème, Act II]
DUPLICATIONS: Berlin State Opera Orch.—Weigert, PD-27190; Symphony Orch.—Inghelbrecht, PAT-PG49
Introduction (Danse bohème) & Chanson bohème: Les Tringles des sistres tintaient —Arr. Orchestra
Philadelphia Orch.—Stokowski
12″—G-D1816
[Entr'actes, Acts II & III]
Chanson bohème only
Conchita Supervia, with Chorus & Orch.
—Cloëz (O-123714) 12″—P-R20127
[Séguedille]
Ninon Vallin & Chorus—Andolfi
(PAT-PAT52) 12″—C-P9152M
[Habañera]
[Air des cartes, Act III, on PAT-X90031]
Chanson du Toréador: Votre toast Baritone & Chorus
Eng. Toreador Song Ger. Euren Toast
Lawrence Tibbett & Metropolitan Opera Cho.—Setti (G-DB1298) 12″—V-8124
[Puccini: Tosca-Te Deum]
[Rossini: Barbiere-Largo al factotum, on V-14202 in VM-329]

Leonard Warren & Victor Orch.—
Tarrasch 12″—V-11-8744
[Rossini: Barbiere-Largo al factotum]
Artur Endrèze, with Cho. & Orch.—
Defosse 12″—O-123776
[Je suis Escamillo, Act III with Micheletti]
Martial Singher
(in CM-578) 12″—C-72088D
[Offenbach: Contes d'Hoffmann-Scintille diamant]
Carlo Tagliabue with EIAR Chorus (in Italian)—Parodi 12″—CET-BB25102
[Verdi: Otello-Credo]
Hans Hotter with Chorus (in German) & Berlin Opera House Orch.—Rotter
12″—PD-67854
[Leoncavallo: Pagliacci-Prologue]
Nelson Eddy & Orch.—Armbruster
(C-DX990) 12″—C-70349D
[Massenet: Herodiade-Vision fugitive]
DUPLICATIONS: Guénot, C-D14211; Roger Bourdin, O-171013; C. Cambon, PD-516524; André Baugé, PAT-X90015; Lovano, PD-521903;
In Italian: Riccardo Stracciari, C-L2129: C-D18036: C-GQX10174; L. R. Morelli, C-DQ259; Carlo Galeffi, C-GQ7044; Titta Ruffo, G-DB406*; G-DB5386*
In German: Karl Schmitt-Walter, T-E2119; Heinrich Schlusnus, PD-73086; Josef Hermann, G-DB5678
In English: Peter Dawson, G-C1400; Harold Williams, C-9873;
In Czech: Z. Otava, U-G12711: ESTA-H5123; A. Wolkov, ESTA-F5212

Nous avons en tête une affaire Quintet
Conchita Supervia, Appolini, Ida Mannarini, Baracchi, Nessi (in Italian) with Orch. 10″—O-188691
Je vais danser en votre honneur Soprano & Tenor
Conchita Supervia & Micheletti
12″—P-PXO1019
[Non, tu ne m'aimes pas]
[Air de la fleur, Micheletti, on O-123772]
Air de fleur: La fleur que tu m'avais jetée Tenor
It. Il fior che avevi a me tu dato
Ger. Blümenarie: Hier am Herzen treu geborgen
Eng. Flower Song
Jussi Björling & Orch.—Grevillius
(G-DB3603) 12″—V-12635
[Massenet: Manon-En ferment les yeux]
Enrico Caruso & re-recorded Orch.
12″—V-14234
[Meyerbeer: L'Africana—O Paradiso]
[In Italian, with Mascagni: Cavalleria Rusticana-Addio, on G-DB3023]
[In Italian, with Handel: Serse-Largo on G-DB5388]
(Original version: G-DB117*)
José Luccioni, with Orch.—Bigot
12″—G-DB5006
[Massenet: Werther—O nature]
Richard Tauber 12″—P-R20550
[Mozart: Zauberflöte-Bildnisarie]

James Melton & Orch.—Morel
10″—**V-10-1324**
[Flotow: Marta-M'Apparì]
DUPLICATIONS: Charles Friant,
O-171028; Otto Svendsen, TONO-
X25021; Sydney Rayner, D-K677; P. H.
Vergnes, O-123806; Jan Kiepura,
C-71397D; René Maison, G-DB4938; Vil-
labella, PAT-X90064; M. Lens, PD-
521938; Gaston Micheletti, O-123772:
O-123650; Charles Dalmores (rec. 1907),
V-18141* in VM-816 & (rec. 1912), V-15-
1013*
In Italian: Dino Borgioli, C-D5107; An-
tonio Cortis, G-DB1363; Beniamino Gigli,
G-DB2531; Aroldo Lindi, C-CQ690;
Francesco Merli, C-GQ7050; A. Melandri,
C-GQX10592; Paolo Civil, CET-CB20277;
Augusto Ferrauto, CET-CB20282; Ales-
sandro Valente, G-HN768; Miguel Fleta,
G-DB1071: G-DB524*; G. Chiaia,
C-CQ355
In German: Peter Anders, T-E1761; Jul-
ius Patzak, PD-90183; Helge Roswaenge,
G-DB4524; Gino Sinimberghi, PD-27432;
Franz Völker, PD-95037: PD-67105;
Marcel Wittrisch, G-DB4408;
In English: Webster Booth, G-C3030;
Charles Kullman, C-DX442; Heddle
Nash, G-C3405
In Icelandic: Pjetur Jonsson, G-Z182
In Czech: Jaroslav Gleich, U-G12732;
Beno Blachut, ESTA-H5121

Non, tu ne m'aimes pas (A continuation of
the duo above, **"Je vais danser"** which
was interrupted by the **"Air de la
Fleur"**)
Conchita Supervia & G. Micheletti
12″—**P-PX01019**
[Je vais danser]
[Habañera, Supervia on O-123773]
Friedel Beckmann & Torsten Ralf (in
German) 12″—**G-DB5693**
[Séguedille]

ACT III

Entr'acte (Prelude)
See also orchestral Suites
Philharmonic-Symphony of New York—
Rodzinski
(in CM-596†) 12″—**C-12250D**
[Symphony, C major, Pt. 7]
Czech Philharmonic Orch.—Kleiber
(U-F14399) 12″—**T-E2042**
[Entr'acte, Act IV]
Dresden Philharmonic Orch.—Van
Kempen 12″—**PD-15191**
(PD-516774) (CET-OR5060)
[Entr'actes, Acts II & IV]
Berlin State Opera Orch.—Weigert
12″—**PD-27190**
[Entr'actes, Acts I & II]
DUPLICATIONS: Philadelphia Orch.—
Stokowski, G-D1816; Symphony Orch.—
Inghelbrecht, PAT-PG50: PAT-X96265

Ecoute, compagnon! Sextette & Chorus
Eng.**March of the Smugglers**
—**Arr. Orchestra**

Paris Philharmonic Orch.—Cloëz
10″—**O-249000**
[Garde montante, Act I]
Mêlons! Coupons! (Trio des cartes) 3
Sopranos
Eng. **Card Scene** (Part 2 of this trio is the
"Card air"
Conchita Supervia, Vavon, Bernadet,
with Orch.—Cloëz
(O-123713) 12″—**P-PXO1017**
Air des cartes: En vain pour éviter Soprano
It. **Andiam, la mia sorte**
Germaine Pape (ms) & Opéra-Comique
Orch.—Cloëz 10″—**C-LF192**
[Massenet: Werther-Les larmes]
Ninon Vallin 12″—**PAT-X90031**
[Chanson bohème, Act II]
Dusolina Giannini 12″—**G-DB1792**
[Habañera]
DUPLICATION: Alice Raveau, PAT-
X90025
In Italian: Gianna Pederzini, CET-
BB25025; Aurora Buades, C-GQ7186;
Ebe Stignani, C-DQ1105
In German: Emmi Leisner, PD-67738;
Karin Branzel, CRS-23*; M. Klose, PD-
67789
In Czech: Marta Krasova, ESTA-H5120
C'est des contrebandiers—Recit.
Je dis que rien ne m'épouvante—**Air de
Micaëla** Soprano
It. **Io dico no, non son pauroso** Ger. **Ich
sprach, das ich furchtlos mich fühle**
Eidé Noréna, & Orch.—Coppola
(G-DB4922) 12″—**V-14742**
[Gounod: Roméo et Juliette—Valse]
Lina Pagliughi (in Italian) & EIAR
Orch.—Parodi
(in CET-8) 12″—**CET-BB25110**
[Rossini: Semiramide-Bel raggio]
Licia Albanese & Victor Orch.—
Leinsdorf 12″—**V-12-0014**
[Verdi: Traviata-Addio del passato]
[Also on V-11-9321 in VM-1078]
Eleanor Steber & Philharmonia Orch.—
Süsskind 12″—**G-DB6514**
[Charpentier: Louise-Depuis le jour]
H. Ranczak (in German)
12″—**T-SK1273**
[Verdi: Otello-Ave Maria]
A. Perris (in Italian) 12″—**G-GQX11080**
[Puccini: Bohème-Musetta's Waltz]
DUPLICATIONS: Joan Taylor (in Eng-
lish), D-K1087; Edith Oldrup-Pedersen,
TONO-X2502; S. Jelinkova (in Czech),
ESTA-H5122
Je suis Escamillo Baritone & Tenor
Artur Endrèze & G. Micheletti
12″—**O-123776**
[Chanson du Toréador, Act II]
Roger Bourdin & C. Friant
12″—**O-171013**
[Chanson du Toréador, Bourdin]

ACT IV

Entr'acte (Prelude)
See also orchestral Suites
Czech Philharmonic Orch.—Kleiber
(U-F14399) 12″—**T-E2042**
[Prelude, Act III]

Dresden Philharmonic Orch.—Paul van Kempen
(PD-516774)　　　　　12″—PD-15191
[Prelude, Act II & Prelude, Act III]
(CET-OR5060)
DUPLICATIONS: Berlin State Opera Orch.—Weigert, PD-27191; La Scala Orch.—Molajoli, C-D12280; Symphony Orch.—Inghelbrecht, PAT-PG50

Ballet Music—Act IV

Bizet composed no specific ballet music for this opera, but used several dance numbers from other compositions, i. e. the music from "L'Arlésienne."

Les voici! (Choeur du cortège) Chorus
Eng. **March & Chorus.** Ger. **Ha, sie naht**
It. **Ecco vieni**
Hamburg State Opera Cho. (in German) & Orch.—Schmidt-Isserstedt
　　　　　　　　　　12″—T-E3042
[Verdi: Forza del Destino-Madre pietosa, with M. Wulf]
Berlin State Opera Chorus & Orch.—Weigert　　　　　12″—PD-27191
La Scala Chorus (in Italian)
　　　　　　　　　12″—C-GQX10263
[Avec la garde montante]
—**Arr. Orchestra**
Pasdeloup Orch.—Inghelbrecht, PAT-X5488

Finale Soprano, Baritone, Tenor & Chorus
—**Abridged version**
Margarete Klose, Marcel Wittrisch, Walther Grossmann, Gerson, Fischer & Berlin State Opera Chorus (in German)
　　　　　　　　　　12″—G-DB4418
—**Final duet only** Soprano & Tenor only
C'est toi? C'est moi!
It. **Sei tu? Son io!** Ger. **Du bist? Ich bin's!**
Conchita Supervia & G. Micheletti, with Orch.—Cloëz　　　12″—O-123774
Ninon Vallin & Villabella
　　　　　　　　　12″—PAT-X90061
Ninon Vallin & Charles Friant
　　　　　　　　　12″—O-171024
Emmi Leisner, Helge Roswaenge (in German) & Chorus　12″—PD-66818
DUPLICATIONS: Pederzini & Zanelli, (in Italian) G-DB1539; Orens & Ansseau, G-DB1384

Miscellaneous Transcriptions
Carmen—Concert Fantasia (Busoni) Piano
Michael von Zadora　　12″—PD-27171
—**Arr. Piano Horowitz**
Vladimir Horowitz　　　10″—V-1327
[Chopin: Mazurka, Op. 30, No. 4]
Fantasia on Themes from "Carmen"—
Violin & Piano Sarasate
Ida Haendel & pf. acc.
　　　　　2　10″—D-M501/2
I. Zilzer & pf. acc.　　12″—PD-27059
—**Arr. Orchestra** Waxman (as used in the film "Humoresque")
Jascha Heifetz & Victor Orch.—Voorhees
　　　　　　　　　12″—V-11-9422
Isaac Stern & Orch.—Franz Waxman
(in CM-657)　12″—C-71884D

"Carmen Jones" arr. Robert Russell Bennett
English text by Oscar Hammerstein II
Muriel Smith, Carlotta Franzell, Luther Saxon, Glyn Bryant with Carmen Jones Chorus—Robert Shaw & Carmen Jones Orch.—Joseph Littaw
　　　　　6　12″—D-DA366
—**Beat out dat rhythm on a drum**
(Adapted from Chanson bohème, Act II)
Gladys Swarthout (ms), with Chorus & Orch.—Blackton　　10″—V-10-1128
[Arlen: Bloomer Girl—Right as the rain]

(LA) JOLIE FILLE DE PERTH 4 Acts 1867
Eng.The Fair Maid of Perth
Orchestral Suite
Prélude, Aubade, Sérénade, Marche, Danse bohèmienne
London Philharmonic Orch.—Beecham
(C-LFX368/9)　　2　12″—C-LX317/8
—**Danse bohèmienne only**
(This excerpt is occasionally used as part of the ballet music for "Carmen" in Act IV)
London Philharmonic—Münch
[Symphony, Pt. 7]　　12″—D-K1784
London Philharmonic Orch.—Goehr
(in VM-721†)　12″—V-13504
[Symphony, Pt. 7] (G-C2989)
Berlin State Opera Orch.—Weigert
　　　　　　　　　12″—PD-27191
[Carmen—Prelude, Act 4]
Individual Excerpts
A la voix d'un amant fidèle ("Sérénade")
Tenor
Jean Planel　　　10″—PAT-X90046
[Godard: Jocelyn-Berceuse]
Heddle Nash (in English)
　　　　　　　　　12″—C-DX540
[Puccini: La Bohème-Che gelida manina]
Quand la flamme d'amour Bass
André Balbon　　10″—PAT-X90075
[Thomas: Mignon-Berceuse]
L. van Obbergh　　12″—PD-516647
[Rossini: Barbiere—La Calunnia]

(LES) PECHEURS DE PERLES 3 Acts 1863
It. I Pescatori di Perle
Ger. Die Perlenfischer　Eng. The Pearl Fishers
Individual Excerpts

ACT I
C'est toi, toi qu'enfin je revois!—Recit.
Au fond du temple saint Tenor & Baritone
It. **Del Tempio al limitar**
Villabella & André Baugé
　　　　　　　　　12″—PAT-PGT14
[Puccini: Bohème—Ah! Mimì]
José Luccioni & Pierre Deldi
　　　　　　　　　12″—C-BFX16
[Leoncavallo: Pagliacci—Prologue, Deldi solo]
Paul-Henri Vergnes & Artur Endrèze
　　　　　　　　　12″—O-123803
L. Dister & L. Richard　12″—C-D14255
[J. B. Faure: Le Crucifix]
Franz Kaisin & Robert Couzinou
　　　　　　　　　12″—PD-516589

[Gounod: Faust-Salut, ô mon dernier matin, Kaisin]
Beniamino Gigli & Giuseppe De Luca (in Italian) (G-DB1150)   12"—V-8084
[Ponchielli: Gioconda—Enzo Grimaldo]
DUPLICATIONS: Borgioli & Vanelli (in Italian), C-GQX10250; Borgioli & Franci (in Italian), C-D5173: C-D5127; Stephen Islandi & Henry Skjaer (in Danish), G-DB5268; L. Fort & L. Piccioli (in Italian), C-CQ1393

A cette voix quel trouble agitait tout mon être—Recit.
Je crois entendre encore Tenor
It. **Mi par d'udire ancora**
(Romance de Nadir)
Enrico Caruso, with re-recorded orch.
(G-DB1875)   12"—V-7770
[Verdi: Aida—Celeste Aida]
(original version G-DB136*)
Tino Rossi   10"—C-4212M
(C-BF31) (C-GN414) (C-DB1765)
[Godard: Jocelyn—Berceuse]
Giuseppe Lugo   12"—PD-566139
(PD-95478)
[Puccini: Bohème—Che gelida manina]
César Vezzani   10"—G-P733
[Meyerbeer: Huguenots—Pif, Paf, Louis Morturier]
Miguel Villabella   12"—PAT-X90026
[Rossini: Barbiere—Ecco ridente]
DUPLICATIONS: Enrico Di Mazzei, O-188512; Gaston Micheletti, O-188898; In Italian: Beniamino Gigli, G-DA1216; Richard Crooks, V-15544 in VM-585: G-DB3926; Tommaso Alcaide, C-LFX291: C-GQX10063; Robert D'Alessio, C-GQX10226; Dino Borgioli, C-D4963; Luigi Fort, C-OQX8001; Lionello Cecil, C-D16411; Hipolito Lazaro, C-GQX11066; Costa Milona, P-DPX7; Miguel Fleta, G-DB1071: G-DB5392; In English: Heddle Nash, G-C3409

ACT II

Me voilà seul—Recit.
Comme autrefois dans la nuit sombre Soprano
It. **Siccome un dì caduto il sole**
Ninon Vallin & Orch.—Cloëz
    10"—O-188742
Claire Clairbert   12"—PD-566157
[Delibes: Lakmé—Dans la forêt]
Janine Micheau   12"—D-K1672
Germaine Féraldy   12"—C-LFX25
[Gounod: Mireille—Allons, me voilà reposée]
Lina Pagliughi (in Italian)
(CET-BB25060)   12"—P-E11406
[Rossini: Guillaume Tell—Sombre forêt]
DUPLICATION: A. Galli-Curci, G-DB255*
In Italian: T. Tashko, C-DQ2366; Toti Dal Monte, G-DB1316
In German: Erna Berger, PD-10285
De mon amie, fleur endormie Tenor
It. **Della mia vita**
Joseph Rogatchewsky   10"—C-D13041
[Massenet: Werther—Chant d'Ossian]

Giuseppe Lugo (also in VOX-176)
    10"—PD-561083
[Puccini: Tosca—E lucevan le stelle]
Dino Borgioli (in Italian)
    10"—C-DQ1108
[Wagner: Lohengrin—Mercè, mercè]
G. Manuritta (in Italian)
    10"—C-DQ1069
[Rossini: Barbiere—Se il mio nome]
DUPLICATION: Enrico Caruso, G-DA114*

O Dieu Brahma It. **Brahma, gran Dio**
Toti Dal Monte & La Scala Chorus (in Italian)   12"—G-DB1316
[Comme autrefois]

ACT III

L'Orage s'est calmé Baritone
It. **Il Nembo si calmò**
Charles Cambon   12"—PD-516524
[Carmen—Chanson du Toréador]
Carlo Tagliabue (in Italian)
    12"—G-DBO5359

PATRIE Overture

Paris Conservatory Orch.—Cluytens
    2   12"—G-W1609/10

PETITE SUITE Jeux d'enfants, Op. 22

Marche, Berceuse, Impromptu, Duo, Galop
London Philharmonic Orch.—Dorati
(G-C2940/1)   2   12"—VM-510
Orch. of the Maggio Musicale—Gui
    2   12"—CET-T17047/8
—No. 1 (Marche) & No. 3 (Impromptu) only
Victor Concert Orch.   10"—V-19730
[Pierné: Marche des petits soldats de plomb]
—No. 5 (Galop) only
Symphony Orch.—Goehr
    (also in V-630)   12"—G-C2983

SONGS in French (except where noted)

Adieux de l'hôtesse arabe, Op. 21, No. 4
(Victor Hugo)
Conchita Supervia (ms)   12"—O-121160
[Grieg: Peer Gynt—Solvejg's Song]

Agnus Dei In Latin
This song is a vocal arrangement of the Intermezzo (La Cuisine de Castelet) from Bizet's incidental music to "L'Arlésienne." See under Arlésienne for recordings of instrumental versions.

Enrico Caruso (t) with re-recorded orchestra   12"—V-17814
[Granier: Hosanna] (original version: G-DB120*)
[Puccini: La Tosca—Recondita armonia on G-DB2644]
Beniamino Gigli (t)   10"—G-DA1488
[Bach-Gounod: Ave Maria]
Webster Booth (t) with chorus, organ, orchestra—Reeves (in English)
    10"—G-B8990
[Sullivan: The Lost Chord]
Astra Desmond (c) with Gerald Moore

(pf) & Edward Silverman (vl)
12″—D-K1014
[Bach-Gounod: Ave Maria]
Pierre Giannotti (b)   12″—LUM-32061
[J. B. Faure: Sancta Maria]
Richard Tauber (t) with chorus and
orchestra   10″—P-RO20501
[Schubert-Geehl: Ave Maria]
Georges Thill (t) with orch. & organ
12″—C-9097M
[Adam: Nöel] — (C-LFX275)
DUPLICATIONS: René Maison,
O-188546; Villabella, PAT-X93041;
Alexander Sved, PD-47094; Heinrich
Schlusnus, PD-30005; Karl Schmitt-
Walter, T-E2521; E. Salazar, C-CQX-
16512; Fernando Busso, D-K999; Di
Mazzei, O-188566; Jeanette MacDonald,
in VM-996
Chanson d'Avril, Op. 21, No. 1 (Bouilhet)
Maggie Teyte (s) & Gerald Moore (pf)
[Chausson: Le Colibri] 10″—G-DA1833
Eglogue   (Victor Hugo)
Conchita Supervia (ms) 10″—O-184220
[Delibes: Les Filles de Cadix]
Ouvre ton coeur (Boléro, or Sérénade espagnole)
Georges Thill (t) & pf.   10″—C-LF118
[Massenet: Nuit d'Espagne]
Jeanette MacDonald (s) & Victor Con-
cert Orch.—Stothart
(in VM-847)   12″—V-18316
[Molloy: Kerry Dance]
—**Arr. Orchestra:** Victor Symphony
Orch., V-10521
Pastorale
Maggie Teyte (s) & Gerald Moore (pf)
10″—G-DA1840
[Godard: Chanson d'Estelle]

SUITES

See: **Arlésienne, Carmen, Jolie Fille de
Perth, Pêcheurs de Perles, Petite Suite**

SYMPHONY

C major
London Philharmonic—Münch
4   12″—D-K1781/4
[La Jolie Fille de Perth—Danse bo-
hèmienne]
New York Philharmonic Symphony—
Rodzinski   4 12″—CM-596†
[Carmen—Act 3, Entr'acte]
London Philharmonic Orchestra—
Walter Goehr   4 12″—VM-721†
[La Jolie Fille de Perth—Danse
bohèmienne]
(GM-305: G-C2986/9) (G-L1074/7)

BJORKANDER, Niels Fredrik (1893-   )
*A Swedish composer and teacher & the director
of the Piano Institute at Stockholm for a num-
ber of years.*
Sketches from the Archipelago Arr. Tor
Mann
Radio Orch.—Sten Frykberg
2   12″—RA-112/3
(Swedish Radiotjanst)

BLACHER, Boris (1903-   )
Concertante Musik
Berlin Philharmonic Orch.—J. Schüler
12″—G-DB4618

BLAMONT, François Colon de (1690-1760)
*Court composer and superintendent of the
royal music at Versailles, who composed ballets,
operas and many miscellaneous pieces.*

CIRCE 2 récits et Air
Mlle. G. Epicaste (s) & Mme. Pauline
Aubert (harpsichord) with orch. de la So-
ciété des Concerts de Versailles—Cloëz
(in Vol. IX) 12″—AS-86
[Destouches: Callirhoë]

BLAND, James
*A member of the Haverly Minstrels with which
he toured the United States, Bland wrote many
successful songs for that organization.*
Carry me back to old Virginny
Ger. Heimweh nach Virginia
Marian Anderson (s) & Victor Sym-
phony orch.—O'Connell 12″—V-18314
[Foster: My old Kentucky Home]
Helen Traubel (s) with male cho. &
orch.—O'Connell
(in CM-639) 12″—C-72104D
[Foster: Old Folks at Home]
Wilhelm Strienz (b, in German) with
cho. & orch.   10″—G-EG6228
[Mackeben: Traume nur]

BLAVET, Michel (1700-1768)
*One of the first French flute virtuosi, Blavet
composed many sonatas and concertos.*

**SONATA—Flute & Harpsichord, No. 2 ("La
Vibray")**
Marcel Moyse & Pauline Aubert
(in Vol. I) 12″—AS-9

BLISS, Arthur (1891-   )
*One of the first "radical modernists" to be
represented on discs, Bliss is a sound craftsman
in his art. He has been closely connected with
the British film industry since his remarkable
score for "Things to Come" strongly influenced
the method of screen writing.*
**Baraza (Music for the film "Men of Two
Worlds")**
Eileen Joyce (pf) & National Symphony
with male cho.—Muir Mathieson
12″—D-K1174

Concerto—Piano & orchestra
Solomon & Liverpool Philharmonic orch.
—Boult   5 12″—G-C3348/52

Fanfare Jubilante;

Fanfare for a Dignified Occasion
(for the wedding of T. R. H. Princess
Elizabeth and the Duke of Edinburgh,
1947)
Trumpeters of the Royal Military School
of Music—Roberts   10″—G-B9616
[with Fanfares by Bax, Benjamin &
Curzon]

March "The Phoenix" (in honor of France)
Philharmonia orch.—Constant Lambert
12″—G-C3518

Miracle in the Gorbals—Ballet Suite
Royal Opera House orch.—Lambert
2 12″—C-DX1260/1

Music for Strings
Strings of BBC Symphony orch.—Boult
3 12″—G-DB3257/9

Polonaise Piano
Cyril Smith 12″—D-K780
[Clarinet Quintet, Pt. 1]

QUARTET—Strings, B flat major
Griller Quartet 4 12″—D-K1091/4

QUINTET—Clarinet & strings
F. Thurston & Griller Quartet (Dir.
Bliss) 4 12″—D-K780/3
[Polonaise—Cyril Smith, pf.]

SONATA—Viola & Piano
Watson Forbes & Myers Foggin
3 12″—D-X233/5

THINGS TO COME (Incidental music to
H. G. Well's film)
**Ballet for Children; Melodramas—Pesti-
lence & Attack; The World in Ruins**
London Symphony Orch.—Bliss
2 12″—D-K810/1
[March; Epilogue—with Chorus]
London Symphony Orch.—Muir
Mathieson 12″—D-K817

BLITZSTEIN, Marc (1905-   )
*A contemporary composer, Blitzstein has re-
jected the sophistication of the greater part of
American composers in favor of a directness—
making it obvious that he is addressing his art
to the "man in the street."*

Dusty Sun
Walter Sheff (b) & Leonard Bernstein
(pf)   (in VM-1117†)   12″—V-11-9530
[Symphony—"The Airborne," Pt. 13]

Freedom Morning
Czech Broadcasting Orch.—H. Weisgall
12″—U-H18130

Music for "Show"
Mark Blitzstein (pf), in CH-B9 (Limited
edition)

(The) Purest Kind of a Guy
Paul Robeson (b) & Lawrence Brown
(pf)   (in CM-534)   10″—C-17457D
[Robinson: Joe Hill]

SYMPHONY—"The Airborne"
**Theory of Flight; Ballad of History &
Mythology; Kittyhawk; The Airborne;
The Enemy; Threat & Approach; Ballad
of the Cities; Morning Poem; Ballad of
the Hurry Up; Night Music; Ballad of the
Bombardier; Open Sky**
New York City Symphony Orch.—Leon-
ard Bernstein, with Victor Chorale, Rob-
ert Shaw (narrator & choral director),
Charles Holland (t) & Walter Sheff (b)
7 12″—VM-1117†
[Dusty Sun, W. Scheff & L. Bernstein]

BLOCH, Ernest (1880-   )
*Born in Switzerland and now a naturalized
American, Bloch is conscientiously Jewish in
his compositions. Sensuously beautiful and intensely emotional, they tend to be rhapsodic
and oriental in character.*

Abodah (Adoration de Dieu) 1929
Yehudi Menuhin (vl) & Hendrick Endt
(pf)   12″—V-15887
[Ravel: Kaddisch]
Ida Haendel (vl) & Adela Kotowska (pf)
12″—D-K1076
[Dinicu-Heifetz: Hora Staccato]

BAAL SHEM (3 Pictures of Chassidic Life)
Violin & Piano
1. Vidui (Contrition)
2. Nigun (Improvisation)
3. Simshas Torah
Joseph Szigeti & A. Farkas
2 12″—CX-188†
[Milhaud: Saudades do Brazil—Sumare
& Falla: Three-Cornered Hat—
Miller's dance]
Yfrah Neaman & I. Newton
2 12″—D-K1192/3
—No. 1
Francis Koene & Van Ijzer
12″—C-D17187
[Falla: Asturiana & Nin: Tornada
Murciana]
—No. 2
Mischa Elman & Vladimir Padwa
12″—V-11-8575
Yehudi Menuhin & A. Persinger
12″—G-DB1283

Concerto Grosso—String Orch. & Pf
Curtis Chamber Music Ensemble—Louis
Bailly 3 12″—VM-563†
[Sibelius: Canzonetta for string orch., op.
62a]

CONCERTO—Violin & orchestra (1939)
Joseph Szigeti & Paris Conservatory
Orch.—Charles Münch
4 12″—CM-380†

QUARTETS—String
No. 1 1916
Stuyvesant Quartet 6 12″—CM-392†
No. 2 1945
Stuyvesant Quartet 4 12″—INT-IM302

QUINTET Piano & Strings
Alfredo Casella & Pro Arte Quartet
4 12″—G-DB1882/5

**SCHELOMO Hebrew Rhapsody for 'Cello
& Orchestra**
Emanuel Feuermann & Philadelphia
Orch.—Stokowski 3 12″—VM-698†
[Bach-Stokowski: Prelude & Fugue in E
minor]
[G-DB5816/8s last side blank]
[Rimsky-Korsakov: Ivan the Terrible—
Prelude, Act II, on G-DB6055/7]

SUITE—Viola & Piano
William Primrose & Fritz Kitzinger
4 12″—VM-575†

BLONDEL (de Nesles) (12th Century)

A noted French trouvère and crusader, friend of Richard Coeur-de-Lion, Blondel de Nesles was the author of many songs, about twenty of which survive.

A l'entrant d'esté Trouvère song in French
Max Meili (t) & Fr. Seidersbeck (viol)
(in Vol. II)   12″—**AS-18**
[with group of French Trouvère & German Minnesänger songs]

BLUM, Robert (1906-   )

A Swiss composer and conductor who was a pupil of Busoni.

Lamentatio angelorum
Zurich Radio Orch.—Blum
2   12″—**ELITE-7010/1**

BOATNER, Edward (1897-   )

An American Negro singer and arranger, Boatner is the son of a minister. His arrangements of Negro spirituals are well known. See current catalogues for further examples.

Oh, what a Beautiful City
Marian Anderson (c) & Franz Rupp (pf)
(G-DA1846)   10″—**V-10-1040**
[arr. Lawrence: Let us break bread together]

Trampin' (Tryin' to make Heaven my home)
Marian Anderson (c) & K. Vehanen (pf)
10″—**V-1896**
[Trad.—I know the Lord laid His hands on me]

BOCCHERINI, Luigi (1743-1805)

An Italian violincellist who spent the latter part of his life in Spain, Boccherini was a contemporary of Haydn. His music, sadly neglected in recent years, is of excellent quality and deserves more than the obscurity to which it has been relegated.

Adagio See Trio, op. 38
Allegretto Actually by Kreisler
For recordings see Kreisler

CONCERTO—'Cello & Orch. B flat major

Pablo Casals & London Symphony—Sir
Landon Ronald   3   12″—**VM-381**†
[with Casals cadenza] (G-DB3056/8)
—**Arr. Grützmacher**
Tibor von Machulla & Berlin Philharmonic—Von Benda
2   12″—**T-E2778/9**
—**2nd Mvt. (Adagio non troppo) only Arr. Vlc. & Piano**
A. Bonucci & S. Fuga 12″—**CET-CC2057**
[Veracini: Largo]
Minuet (This is the Tempo di Minuetto movement in A major from String Quintet in E major, Op. 13, No. 5)
—**Arr. Orchestra**
Paris Conservatory Orch.—Weingartner
(in CM-428†)   12″—**C-70674D**
[Bach: Suite No. 3, Pt. 5]
Philadelphia Orchestra—Stokowski
(G-AW181)   12″—**V-7256**
[Haydn: Quartet, Op. 3, No. 5—Serenade]

Winterthur Municipal Orch.—H.
Scherchen   12″—**G-DB6090**
[Haydn: Quartet, Op. 3, No. 5—Minuet]
Berlin Philharmonic Orch.—Borchard
10″—**T-A1711**
[Haydn: Symphony No. 88, G major—Finale only]
Grand Orchestre Symphonique, Paris—
Ruhlman   10″—**PAT-X96259**
[Rameau: Les Fêtes d'Hébé—Musette et Tambourin]
DUPLICATIONS: Victor Concert Orch.,
V-20636: G-B9036: G-K5488; BBC
Orch.—Pitt, C-9092
—**Arr. Instrumental ensembles, etc.**
C. Kolessa (vlc), G-EG7103; Saxophone
Quartet C-DF1724; Zilzer, Hopf, Gurlitt
Trio, PD-22542
—**Arr. Harpsichord**
Corradina Mola   10″—**G-DA5394**
[Scarlatti: Sonatina, C major]

QUARTETS—String

Op. 1, No. 2 Pascal Quartet
(in Vol. XIII)   2   12″—**AS-129/3**
D major, Op. 6, No. 1
Poltronieri String Quartet (arr. Polo)
2   12″—**C-GQX10877/8**
Roma String Quartet
2   12″—**G-DB4462/3**
[Quartet, E flat, Op. 6, No. 3—Allegro con brio]
E flat major, Op. 6, No. 3
—**3rd Mvt. only (Allegro con brio)**
Roma Quartet   12″—**G-DB4463**
[Quartet, D major, Op. 6, No. 1, Pt. 3]
A major, Op. 33, No. 6
Belardinelli Quartet
2   12″—**G-AW322/3**
A major, Op. 39, No. 1—Allegro giusto only
G minor, Op. 27, No. 2—Minuetto only
Veneziano del Vittoriale Quartet
[1 side each]   10″—**C-D5840**
Unspecified Quartet
—**Allegro con brio & Siciliano only**
Poltronieri String Quartet
10″—**C-GQ7015**

QUINTETS—String

E major, Op. 13, No. 5
—**Tempo di Minuetto** See **Minuet**
D major, Op. 37
—**Pastorale only**
EIAR Symphony Orch.—Previtali
12″—**CET-CB20175**
[Handel: Messiah—Pastoral Symphony]
C major, (Arr. Lauterbach)
String Orchestra—Carlo Zecchi
2   12″—**CET-BB25114/5**
Rondo (Unspecified) Arr. Cello & Piano
Bezelaire
Ludwig Hoelscher & Elly Ney
10″—**G-EG3041**
[Gluck: Orfeo—Mélodie]
DUPLICATION: Marcelli-Herson,
G-K5234

SONATAS—'Cello & Piano
No. 2, C major
Pierre Fournier & Ruggero Gerlin
(in Vol. VII) 12"—AS-66
Gregor Piatigorsky & Valentin Pavlovsky
12"—C-71785D
No. 3, G major (excerpt only)
Gilberto Crepax & pf. acc.
10"—C-D5442
[Galuppi: Sonata]
No. 6, A major
William Primrose (vla) & Joseph Kahn
12"—V-17513
Pablo Casals & Blas-Net
12"—G-DB1392
André Navarra & pf. acc. 12"—O-123873
Amedeo Baldoveno & M. Raucheisen
12"—C-DWX1625
DUPLICATION: Caruana & Maffezzoli,
G-GW1418

TRIOS—String
Op. 38—Adagio only
Pasquier Trio   12"—PAT-PAT30
[Haydn: Minuet]
Trio Concertante No. 6 Vl., Vla., vlc.
Pasquier Trio
(in Vol. XI) 12"—AS-119

MISCELLANEOUS:
Scuola di Ballo Ballet Suite (Arr. Jean
Françaix)
London Philharmonic Orch.—Dorati
2 12"—CX-157†
(C-DX944/5) (C-GQX11033/4)

BODART   (1905-   )
A German conductor and opera composer.
Spanish Night—Overture
Leipzig Radio Orch.—Rheinhold Merten
12"—G-EH1312
[Pick-Mangiagalli: Little Suite—Olaf's
Dance]

BODENSCHATZ, Erhard (c. 1570-1638)
A German theologian and composer and a
collector and editor of sacred music. The carol
listed below was used by Brahms, Reger and
many other composers.
Joseph, lieber Joseph mein Cho. in German
(14th Cent. Trad. German Christmas
Song)
St. Thomas Leipzig Choir—Straube
10"—PD-90160
[Trad.: In dulci jubilo]

BOEDDECKER, P. J.   (17th Century)
A theorist of Stuttgart who wrote a treatise on
thorough-bass which he published in 1701.
Christmas Cantata (Partly in Latin &
partly in German)
(Incorporates the carol, "Josef lieber,
Josef mein")
Jo Vincent (s)   12"—C-DHX40

BOELLMANN, Leon (1862-1897)
An Alsatian and a pupil of Gigout, Boellmann
became organist at St. Vincent de Paul in Paris.

Suite Gothique, Op. 25 Organ
Introduction & Choral, Menuet, Prière à
Notre Dame, Toccata
—2nd Mvt. only
Edouard Commette (St. Jean, Lyons)
10"—C-DF682
[Pierné: Prelude]
—4th Mvt. only
Edouard Commette (St. Jean, Lyons)
12"—C-D11026
[Gigout: Toccata]
Alfred Sittard (St. Michael's, Hamburg)
12"—PD-95157
[Schmid: Gaillard; & van den Ghehen:
Fugue in G]
—Arr. 'Cello: R. Meimberg, U-E649
Variations Symphoniques, Op. 23 Vlc. &
Orch.
Maurice Maréchal (vic) & M. Faure (pf)
12"—C-LFX209

BOEZI, Ernesto (1856-   )
Choral conductor at the Julian Chapel for
many years and a composer of Catholic church
music in the approved liturgical style.

Ave Regina Coelorum   12"—SEMS-1123
[Magnificat, Pt. 3]
Beatus vir   12"—SEMS-1124
Credidi   12"—SEMS-12
Dominus, Probasti me 2 12"—SEMS-6/7
Gradual   12"—SEMS-1108
[Antonelli: Antiphon]
Magnificat   2 12"—SEMS-1122/3
[Ave Regina Coelorum]
Missa Solemnis   4 12"—G-AW134/7
Miserere   3 12"—SEMS-32/4
[Refice: Ecce sic benedicitur—A Dado]
All by Julian Chapel Choir—E. Boezi
O Cor Amore
A. Dado (b)   12"—SEMS-50
[Marenzio: Innocentes, Julian Chapel
Choir]

BOEHM, Karl (1844-1928)
A pupil of Bischoff, Löschhorn and Russinau
and for many years professor of theory and
composition at the Berlin Royal Academy of
Music.

SONGS
Lacrimae Christi
Heinrich Schlusnus (b) & F. Rupp (pf)
10"—PD-62682
[Hill-Dippel: Herz am Rhein]
Still wie die Nacht, Op. 326, No. 27
Elizabeth Schumann (s) & Orch.
12"—G-DB3641
[Offenbach: Tales of Hoffmann—Bar-
carolle]
Helge Roswaenge (t) & Hedwig von
Debicka (s)   10"—PD-24615
[Ries: Wo du hingehst]
Marcel Wittrisch (t)
(G-EG6780)   10"—G-EG3175
[Aus der Jugendzeit]
DUPLICATIONS: Karl Schmitt-Walter,
T-A2633; Charles Kullmann (in Eng-
lish), C-4143M: C-DB1400; Also: Marek
Weber Orch., G-B8768: G-EG3609

BOIELDIEU, François (1775-1834)

A member of the French "opéra-comique" composers, Boieldeau composed many successful stage works. His music is melodious and sprightly and still enjoys popularity in Europe.

OPERAS-COMIQUES in French

LE CALIFE DE BAGDAD 1800
Overture
London Symphony—Muir Mathieson
12"—C-72237D
Vienna Symphony—Paul Kerby
12"—C-69065D
[Gounod: Mireille—Overture]
[Strauss-Korngold: Eine Nacht in Venedig, on C-DFX86]
Symphony Orchestra—Melichar
12"—PD-27164
Berlin State Opera Orch.—Schmalstich
10"—G-B3482
(G-EG1536) (G-HN797)
Symphony Orch.—Gurlitt
12"—O-170093

LA DAME BLANCHE 1825
Overture
Boston "Pops" Orch.—Fiedler
12"—V-11-9569
Berlin State Opera Orch.—Blech
12"—G-EJ306
Paris Symphony Orch.—Ruhlmann
12"—PAT-X96260
German Opera House Orch.—Lutze
(U-F14405)   12"—T-E2872
Individual Excerpts
Ah! quel plaisir d'être soldat! Tenor
André d'Arkor   12"—C-RFX26
[Viens, gentille Dame]
Déjà la nuit plus sombre Tenor
Villabella   10"—O-188586
[Viens, gentille Dame]
Rêverie de Georges Brown Tenor
(introducing the folk song "Robin
Adair")
Villabella   10"—PAT-PG26
[Adam: Si j'étais roi—Elle est princesse]
David Devries   12"—O-123548
[Gounod: Faust—Salut demeure]
Viens, gentille Dame Tenor
Villabella   10"—PAT-PG7
[Also on O-188586]
André d'Arkor   12"—C-RFX26
[Ah! quel plasir]
In Italian: Alessando Ziliani, G-DA1450

LES VOITURES VERSEES 1808
Au clair de la lune
Apollon toujours préside Duos: Soprano &
Baritone
Marie T. Gauley & José Beckmans
10"—PD-561068
Boléro (unspecified)
Leila Ben Sedira (s) with flute & harp
acc.   10"—G-DA4938
[Ravel: La flûte enchantée]

BOITO, Arrigo (1842-1918)

OPERAS in Italian

MEFISTOFELE Prologue, 4 Acts, Epilogue
1868
Complete recording sung in Italian
Soloists, La Scala Chorus & Orchestra
(C-GQX10619/35)   17   12"—C-Op17†
Margherita .... Mafalda Favero (s)
Elena .... G. Arangi-Lombardi (s)
Faust .... Antonio Melandri (t)
Mefistofele ... Nazareno de Angelis (bs)
Pantalis .... Rita Monticone (a)
Nereo .... Emilio Venturini (t)
Wagner .... Giuseppe Nessi (t)
Marta .... Ida Mannarini (a)
Lorenzo Molajoli, conductor
Vittorio Veneziani, chorus master
Individual Excerpts
Prologue
Complete recording
N. De Angelis, La Scala Chorus & Orch.—
Molajoli   3   12"—C-D14470/2
—Ave Signor only Bass
Feodor Chaliapin   10"—G-DA962
[Bellini: Sonnambula—Vi ravviso]
DUPLICATIONS: T. Pasero, C-DQ1087;
N. De Angelis, C-GQX10179
—Salve Regina only Chorus
La Scala Chorus—Bellezza
12"—G-S10139
[Ridda e fuga, Act II]

ACT I
Il bel giovanetto Chorus
La Scala Chorus—Molajoli 10"—C-4802
[Verdi: Traviata—Coro della zingarelle]
Dai campi, dai prati Tenor
Beniamino Gigli   10"—G-DA883
[Giunto sul passo]
Giovanni Malipiero   10"—G-DA5382
[Giunto sul passo]
Aureliano Pertile   10"—C-D4948
[Giunto sul passo]
[Puccini: Tosca—Recondita armonia, on
C-GQ7183]
Hipolito Lazaro   10"—C-GQX10144
[Giunto sul passo]
DUPLICATIONS: P. Civil, CET-CC2213:
C-DQ666; R. D'Alessio, C-DQ1091
Son lo spirito che nega (Ballata del fischio)
Bass
Feodor Chaliapin (Recorded at actual
performance)   12"—G-DB942
[Ridda e fuga]
Tancredi Pasero & Orch.—Marzollo
12"—G-DB11304
[Ecco il mondo]
[Older recording: C-DQ1085]
DUPLICATION: N. De Angelis,
C-GQX10179
Peasant Waltz Orchestra
Cincinnati Summer Opera Orch.—Cleva,
in D-A491
Se tu mi doni un'ora Tenor & Bass
Beniamino Gigli & C. Scattola
10"—G-DA223*
[Puccini: Tosca—E lucevan le stelle]

ACT II, Scene 1 (Scena del Giardino) (Garden Scene)

Complete scene
Gina Cigna (s), P. Civil (t), Tancredi
Pasero (bs), Ida Mannarini (a)
2 12″—**C-D14581/2**
[Gounod: Faust—Trio finale]
—Colma il tuo cor only Tenor
L. Cecil, C-DQ225

ACT II, Scene 2 (La Notte del Sabba)

Ecco il mondo Bass
Tancredi Pasero (bs) & Orch.
12″—**G-DB11304**
[Son lo spirito]
[Older recording: C-DQ1085]
DUPLICATION: N. De Angelis,
C-GQX10183
Riddiamo (Ridda e fuga infernale) Chorus
La Scala Chorus—Molajoli
12″—**C-GQX10281**
[Rossini: William Tell—Selva opaca,
Arangi-Lombardi]
Royal Opera Chorus—Bellezza
12″—**G-DB942**
[Son lo spirito, Chaliapin]
(Recorded at an actual performance,
1926)
La Scala Chorus—Bellezza
12″—**G-S10139**
[Salve Regina, Prologue]

ACT III

L'Altra notte in fondo al mare Eng. **Marguerite's aria** Soprano
Claudia Muzio & Orch.—Molajoli
(in CM-259) 12″—**C-9168M**
[Cilea: Arlesiana—Esser madre]
[Donaudy: O del mio amato ben on
C-LCX25: C-BQX2504]
[Puccini: Bohême—Mi chiamano Mimì
on C-BQX2514]
Ninon Vallin & Orch. 12″—**O-123709**
[Bellini: Norma—Casta Diva]
Magda Olivero & EIAR Orch.—La Rosa
Parodi 12″—**CET-BB25049**
[Cilea: Adriana Lecouvreur—Poveri
fiori]
Pia Tassinari 12″—**G-DB1932**
[Puccini: Bohême—O soave fanciulla—
with Pauli]
Licia Albanese 12″—**V-11-9848**
[Leoncavallo: Pagliacci—Ballatella]
DUPLICATIONS: L. B. Rasa,
C-CQX16514; B. Scacciati, C-DQ1077;
M. Zamboni, C-GQX10260
Lontano, lontano Duo: Soprano & Tenor
G. Arangi-Lombardi & A. Melandri
12″—**C-D14585**
[Act IV—Complete version, Pt. 5]
DUPLICATIONS: Bosini & Gigli,
G-DB271*; Pavoni & Pertile, C-D4949
Spunta l'aurora pallida Soprano, Tenor,
Bass & Chorus
(Most versions of Marguerite's death
scene omit the brief parts for Tenor, Bass
& Chorus.)
Augusta Otrabella & Orch.—Capuana
10″—**G-DA5351**
[Verdi: Traviata—Addio del passato]

Bianca Scacciati 10″—**C-DQ1077**
[L'altra notte]

ACT IV (La Notte del Sabba Classico)

Complete version
G. Arangi-Lombardi, A. Melandri, M. Vasari, S. Baccaloni, E. Venturini, & La
Scala Chorus & Orchestra—Molajoli
3 12″—**C-D14583/5**
[Lontano, lontano]
Forma ideal purissima
Amore! Misterio! Sop., Ten., Bass &
Chorus
Fanelli, Pauli, Masini & La Scala Chorus
& Orch. 12″—**G-DB1440**
Amore! Misterio! only Arr. Orchestra
La Scala Orch.—Sabajno
10″—**G-HN788**
[Catalani: La Wally—Prelude Act III]

EPILOGUE

Giunto sul passo estremo Tenor
Beniamino Gigli 10″—**G-DA883**
[Dai campi]
Giovanni Malipiero 10″—**G-DA5382**
[Dai campi]
[Puccini: Tosca—E lucevan le stelle, on
P-DPX29]
[Also on CET-BB25052 & CET-BB25063]
Aureliano Pertile 10″—**C-D4948**
[Dai campi]
[Wagner: Lohengrin—Atmest du nicht,
on C-GQ7182]
DUPLICATION: R. D'Alessio, C-DQ1114;
L. Cecil, C-DQ253; L. Marini, C-DQ1093;
D. Borgioli, C-D5107

NERONE 4 Acts 1924

Ecco il magico, Act II

Vivete in pace, Act III Tenor
Enrico Molinari 10″—**C-D12305**

BOLZONI, Giovanni (1841-1919)

*An Italian composer, violinist and conductor
whose works include operas, orchestral music,
chamber works and violin pieces.*

Minuet (Minuetto)
EIAR Orchestra—Tansini
10″—**CET-CB20276**
[Paisiello: Serva Padrona—Introduction]
Barnabás von Géczy Orch.
10″—**G-EG7082**
[Beethoven: Minuet]
Lucien Schwartz, on G-K6632
Also: Saxophone Quartet of Paris,
C-DF1558

BONNAL, Ermend

Trois Noëls (Poems of the 16th Century)
Janine Micheau (s) with Cho. & Marcel
Cariven (pf) 2 10″—**G-DA5004/5**
[Noël from Poèmes Franciscains, Micheau
& H. B. Etcheverry]
Noël (Poèmes Franciscains)
Janine Micheau (s) & H. B. Etcheverry
(b) & pf. acc. 10″—**G-DA5005**
[Trois Noëls, Pt. 3]

Trio (Strings)
1. Bidossoa 2. Navarra 3. Rhapsodie du
Sud
Pasquier Trio 3 12"—**PAT-PAT124/6**
[Purcell—Arr. Warlock: 2 Pt. Fantasia,
F major]

BONNET, Joseph (1884-1946)
*French organist, pupil of Tournemire and
Guilmant, Bonnet was well known as a recitalist
and editor.*

In Memoriam (To the Titanic's Heroes) Op.
10 (No. 1 of 12 pieces)
Joseph Bonnet (Organ in the John Hays
Hammond Museum, Gloucester, Mass.)
(in VM-835) 12"—**V-18216**
Matin Provençal (No. 2 from Trois Poèmes
d'Automne) Op. 3, No. 2
Romance sans Paroles
Joseph Bonnet (Organ in John Hays
Hammond Museum, Gloucester, Mass.)
(in VM-835) 12"—**V-18215**

BONPORTI, F. A. (1660-1740)
*Choirmaster of the private chapel of the Em-
peror of Austria who wrote many concerted
works for violin.*

Concerto, F major, Op. 10, No. 15
—Recitativo only (Arr. Barblan)
Arrigo Pelliccia (vl) & Chamber Orch. of
the Conservatory, San Pietro a Majella,
Naples—A. Lualdi 12"—**G-DBO5352**
[Pergolesi—Concerto, B flat, Pt. 3]

BORMIOLI, Enrico
Allegro da Concerto Piano & Orchestra
Enrico Bormioli & EIAR Chamber Orch.
—Petralia 10"—**CET-PE111**
Suite of Dances
Zingaresca; Tarantella; Gitana
Mario Salerno (pf) & Chamber Orch.—
Gallino 2 10"—**CET-PE78 & 74**
[Amadei: Oriental Impressions—In the
Bazaar]
Symphonic Variations for Piano & Orches-
tra on a Theme of Paganini
Enrico Bormioli & EIAR Chamber Orch.
—Petralia 2 12"—**CET-IT1117/8**

**BORODIN, Alexander Porfirievich (1833-
1887)**
*This brilliant composer is best remembered for
his too-seldom performed opera "Prince Igor."*

In the Steppes of Central Asia Symphonic
Sketch
Fr. Dans les steppes de l'Asie centrale
Orchestra
Philharmonia Orchestra—Constant
Lambert (C-DX1449) 12"—**C-71956D**
Amsterdam Concertgebouw Orch.—
Mengelberg 12"—**T-SK3198**
London Symphony Orch.—Coates
(G-D1885) 12"—**V-11169**
Lamoureux Orch.—Albert Wolff
(PD-566005) 12"—**PD-66951**
DUPLICATIONS: Colonne Orch.
Pierné, O-123576; Pasdeloup Orch.—
Inghelbrecht, PAT-X5489; Paris Conser-
vatory Orch.—Gaubert, C-12534,

C-GQX10921; EIAR Orch.—Failoni,
CET-BB25101

PRINCE IGOR 4 Act Opera in Russian 1890
NOTE: *"Prince Igor" was completed and edited,
after Borodin's death, by Rimsky-Korsakov and
Glazunov. The Overture was written and
scored by the latter, remembering as best he
could a piano performance by the composer.)*
Collection
No. 5 (Scene: Jaroslavna & Vladimir
Galitsky); No. 7 (Girl's Chorus); No. 15
(How goes it, Prince?); No. 17 (Polovt-
sian Dances); No. 27 (Duet: Jaroslavna
& Prince Igor)
Soloists, Bolshoi Theatre State Choir &
Orch., Moscow, USSR
5 12"—**ASCH-M-800**
Individual Excerpts
Overture Orchestra
London Philharmonic Orch.—Beecham
2 12"—**G-DB6237/8**
[Berlioz: Les Troyens—Marche
Troyenne]
[Also in VM-1141† with Berlioz: Les
Troyens—Chasse Royale & Marche
Troyenne]
Hallé Orch.—Heward
2 12"—**C-DX1078/9**
[Tchaikovsky: Sleeping Beauty—
Waltz]
EIAR Orch.—Amfitheatrof
12"—**CET-P56545**
Symphony Orch.—Coates
(G-AW189) 12"—**G-W847**
Prologue
No. 1 To the sun in his glory Chorus
Russian Opera Cho. & Orch.—
D'Angreneff 12"—**P-DPX5**
[No. 17, Dances, Pt. 1]
No. 2b I hate a dreary life Bass (Galitsky)
Alexander Kipnis
(in VM-1073) 12"—**V-11-9285**
[Mussorgsky: Boris Godunov—Inn
Scene]
Feodor Chaliapin 10"—**G-DA891**
[Mussorgsky: Boris Godunov—In the
town of Kazan]
—Arr. M. Fiveisky
S. Slepoushkin (Bs) & Gen. Platoff Don
Cossack Choir—Kostrukoff
12"—**V-11-9118**
[Trad.: Kaleenka]

ACT I
No. 5 Scene—Jaroslavna & Vladimir Galit-
sky
K. Derjinskaya (s) & A. Pirogiv (bs) &
Orch. of Bolshoi Theatre—A. Melik
Pashayev 12"—in **ASCH-M-800**
(D-X265) (G-DB4150)

ACT II
No. 7 The prairie floweret Girl's Chorus
E. Antonova (s) & Bolshoi Theatre State
Choir & Orch.—L. Steinberg
12"—in **ASCH-M-800**
—Arr. Orch. Stokowski
Philadelphia Orch.—Stokowski
(in VM-499) 12"—**V-15169**

[No. 8 & Dance No. 17] (G-DB3232)
No. 8 Girl's Dance Orchestra
Philadelphia Orch.—Stokowski
(in VM-499) 12"—**V-15169**
[No. 7 & Dances No. 17] (G-DB3232)
London Philharmonic Orch.—Goehr
(C-DFX214) 12"—**C-DX828**
[Mussorgsky: Fair at Sorotchinsk—Act
III, Gopak]
—**Part only**
Symphony Orch.—Goehr (in "Nights at
the Ballet" album), in V-C30
(G-C2983)
Berlin Philharmonic Orch.—Grüber
(O-250024) 12"—**O-7975**
[No. 17, Pt. 1]
No. 11 Daylight is fading away Tenor
(Vladimir's Cavatina)
Jussi Björling (in Swedish) & Orch.—
Grevillius 12"—**G-X4108**
[Laparra: Illustre Fregona—Serenade]
Joseph Rogatchewsky (in Russian)
12"—**C-D15012**
[Rimsky-Korsakoff: May Night—Recit.
& Romance of Lowko]
Charles Kullman (in German)
(C-LWX97) 12"—**C-GQX10914**
[Tchaikowsky: Eugen Onegin—Lenski's
Aria]
No. 13 No sleep, no rest Bar. (Prince Igor)
Ger. Umsonst nach Rube sucht das trübe,
schwere Herz
Fr. Hélas! mon âme est triste, adieu, le
doux repos
Eng. No sleep, no rest, for my afflicted
soul
G. M. Youreneff 12"—**G-EL8**
[Glinka: Russlan & Ludmilla—Russlan's
Air]
Heinrich Schlusnus (in German) &
Berlin Orch.—Melichar
12"—**PD-67057**
[Mussorgsky: Song of the Flea]
A. Baturin (in Russian) & Bolshoi
Theatre Orch. 12"—**D-X280**
John Hargreaves (in English) & Phil-
harmonia Orch.—Braithwaite
12"—**G-C3561**
No. 15 How goes it, Prince? Bass (Khan
Konchak)
M. Mikhailov & Orch. of Bolshoi Theatre
—Orlov
(D-X266) 12"—**in ASCH-M-800**
C. E. Kaidanoff & G. M. Youreneff (b)
12"—**G-EL9**
[Glinka: Russlan & Ludmilla—Farlaf's
Rondo]
Raphael Arie & Suisse Romande Orch.—
Karr 12"—**(in preparation)**
Swiss Decca
Feodor Chaliapin 12"—**G-DB1104**
[Rimsky-Korsakov: Sadko—Song of the
Viking Guest]
No. 17, Polovtsian Dances Chorus &
Orchestra
Bolshoi Theatre Orch. & Cho.—A. Melik
Pashayev 2 12"—**in ASCH-M-800**
(G-DB4150/1: D-X267/8)
[No. 27, Duet: Jaroslavna & Igor]
Leeds Festival Cho. & London Philhar-

monic Orch.—Beecham (in English)
(C-LFX421/2) 2 12"—**CX-54†**
[Mozart: Mass in C minor—Qui tollis]
(C-LX369/70)
London Symphony Orch. & Cho.—Coates
(in English) 12"—**G-D1528**
(G-W1003) (G-AW52)
Russian Opera Cho. & Orch.—
D'Angreneff 12"—**P-DPX5**
[Prologue, No. 1] (Part only)
—**Concert arrangement** Rimsky-Korsakov
London Philharmonic Orch.—Fitelberg
(D-K1536/7) 2 12"—**D-ED34†**
Philadelphia Orch.—Stokowski
(G-DB3232/3) 2 12"—**VM-499†**
[Nos. 7 & 8]
Berlin Philharmonic—Grüber
(O-250024/5) 2 12"—**O-7975/6**
[Nos. 8 & 18]
Lamoureux Orch.—Albert Wolff
(PD-566082/3) 2 12"—**PD-95434/5**
[Rimsky-Korsakov: Tsar Saltan—March]
—**2 Sided versions**
Philadelphia Orch.—Ormandy
(C-LX1027) 12"—**C-12269D**
Symphony Orch.—Goehr (Part only), in
V-C30: G-C2982
—**Arr. 2 Pianos**
Rawicz & Laudauer 10"—**C-DB2112**

ACT III

No. 18 Prelude Polovski March Orch.
London Philharmonic—Beecham
(in CX-123†) 12"—**C-69414D**
(C-LX769)
[Wagner: Tannhäuser—Overture, Pt. 3]
Berlin Philharmonic Orch.—Grüber
(O-250025) 12"—**O-7976**
[Polovtsian Dances, Pt. 3]
DUPLICATION: London Symphony
Orch.—Coates, G-DB1683

ACT IV

No. 27, Duet—Jaroslavna & Igor
K. Derjinskaya (s) & A. Baturin (b) &
Bolshoi Theatre Orch.—Steinberg
12"—**in ASCH-M-800**
(G-DB4151:D-X268]
[No. 17, Polovtsian Dances, Pt. 3]

QUARTETS String

No. 2, D major
Poltronieri Quartet
3 12"—**C-D14633/5**
—**3rd Mvt. (Notturno) only**
Lener Quartet
(C-GQX10911) 12"—**C-LX169**
Budapest Quartet 12"—**G-AW4386**
—**Arr. Violin & Piano:** Karel Sroubek,
U-G14234

QUINTET C minor Piano & Strings

Niklaus Aeschbacher & Jacques Mottier
Quartet 2 12"—**C-LZX13/4**
Scherzo Piano
Sergei Rachmaninoff 10"—**G-DA1522**
[Rachmaninoff: Serenade]

SYMPHONIES Orchestra

No. 2, B minor
Minneapolis Symphony—Mitropoulos
4   12"—CM-528†
[Glière: Red Poppy—Sailor's dance]
Hallé Orchestra—Lambert
4   12"—C-DX1125/8
[Mozart: Divertimento No. 11: K251—
Andantino only, Lawrence Turner]

BORRESEN, Hakon (1876-   )
A contemporary Danish composer.

Olympic Hymn
Danish State Radio Symphony—Georg
Hoeberg   10"—G-DA5215

Quartet, C minor
**—Intermezzo pizzicato (Scherzo molto
vivace) only**
Erling Bloch Quartet   12"—G-DB5282
[Schubert: Quartetsatz]

SONG in Danish

Hvis du har varme
Helge Roswaenge (t) & B. Seidler-
Winkler (pf)   10"—G-DA5224
[Heise: Aften paa Loggiaen]

BORTNIANSKY, Dimitri (1752-1825)
*A Ukrainian composer, student of Galuppi both
in St. Petersburg and Italy, Bortniansky was for
many years director of Empress Catherine's
church choir. He composed both operas and
sacred works, later edited by Tchaikovsky.*

Gloria in Excelsis Unacc. Chorus
Eng. **Glory to God in the Highest**
Ger. **Ehre sei Gott in der Höhe**
Russian Cathedral of Paris Cho.—
Afonsky (in Russian)   10"—G-K7992
[Allemanov: Christmas Hymn]
St. Caecilia Cho.—Pius Kalt (in German)
12"—PD-27208
[Crüger: Nun danket alle Gott, Neukölln
Teachers' Cho.]
[Praetorius: Es ist ein Ros' Entsprungen
on PD-23486]
Church Choir (in German)
12"—PD-24783
[Ritter-Charlie: Gross Gott wir loben
dich, Polydor Männerchor with org. &
orch.]
**How Glorious (or, How Greatly our Lord is
Glorified)** Unacc. Chorus
Ger. **Ich bete an die Macht der Liebe**
Rus. **Kolj Slavenj**
Russian Metropolitan Church Choir—
Afonsky (in Russian)   10"—G-EK131
[Trad.: Many years]
Don Cossacks Cho.—Jaroff (in Russian)
12"—C-7220M
[Gretchaninov: 2 old Wedding songs]
DUPLICATIONS: (German) Berliner
Solistenvereinigung & Orch.,
G-EG3735; Russian Military Orch.,
G-EK122.
Hymn of the Cherubims, No. 7 Unacc.
Chorus
Russian Cath. Cho., Paris—Afonsky
12"—G-L1005
[Tchesnokov: Prayer during Lent]

[Tchaikovsky: Pater Noster, on G-EK91
—older version]
Hymn of the Cherubim for Lent Unacc.
Chorus
Rus. **Nyne Sily nebesyja**
Russian Metropolitan Church Cho., Paris
—Afonsky   10"—G-K8154
[Savadsky: Pater Noster]
Je vois la salle du festin
Rus. **Tchertog twoy vijou, Spasee**
Russian Metropolitan Church Cho., Paris
—Afonsky   10"—G-EK142
[Ivanov: Oh! mon âme, lève-toi]
The Lord will rise again Unacc. Chorus
**Te Deum Laudamus (We Praise Thee, O
Lord)**
Russian Metropolitan Church Cho., Paris
—Afonsky   10"—G-EK89
Who can equal Thee? Rus. Kto bog velij
Don Cossack Cho.—Jaroff
12"—C-7325M
[Gretchaninov: Responsory XI]

BOSSI, Marco Enrico (1861-1925)
*A famous Italian organist, also known as a
composer of organ music and works in larger
forms.*

**Concerto—Organ & Orchestra, A minor,
Op. 100**
**—2nd Mvt. (Adagio) & 3rd Mvt. (Allegro)
only**
Kurt Grosse & Orch.—M. Gurlitt
2   12"—PD-95326/7

BOTTACCHIARI   (1879-   )
*A pupil of Mascagni and a composer of operas
and symphonies.*

L'OMBRA Opera
O tu ch'el sai Soprano
Mafalda Favero & harp acc.
10"—G-DA11301
[Gounod: Faust—Mephisto's Serenade,
T. Pasero]

BOUGHTON, Rutland (1875-   )
*A prolific British composer of many music-
dramas and large scale choral works who is
little known outside England.*

(THE) IMMORTAL HOUR Keltic Drama in
2 Acts

Faery Song Tenor
Webster Booth & harp acc.
10"—G-B8947
[German: The English Rose]
Walter Glynne & pf. acc.
10"—G-B3905
[Trent: June Music]
—Arr. Chorus
Glasgow Orpheus Choir—Roberton
10"—G-B9608
[Trad.: Bonnie Dundee]
Also: Albert Sandler Trio, C-FB1769

BOULANGER, Lilli (1893-1918)
*Creator of many artistic scores, Lilli Boulanger,
sister of Nadia, was the first woman in France
to win the Grand Prix de Rome.*

Nocturne Violin & Piano
Frederick Grinke & Ivor Newton (pf)
10"—D-M570
[Novacek: Perpetuum mobile]
DUPLICATION: V. Bratza, C-DQ3389

BOWLES, Paul (1911-   )
A student of Aaron Copland and Virgil Thom-son, Paul Bowles is one of the young American composers who has also made a career as a critic.

NIGHT WITHOUT SLEEP and other songs
(Massey & C. H. Ford)
Includes: Night without sleep; Song for my sister (from "The Garden of Disor-der"); You can't trust in love; You're right, the day ain't mine; Think of all the hair dressing (from "Denmark Vesey"); When rain or love began; Sailor's song; They can't stop death.
Romolo de Spirito (t) & Carrington
Welch (pf)   3 10"—DISC-730
Sonata for Two Pianos (1943/4)
Arthur Gold & Robert Fizdale
(Limited edition)   4 10"—CH-A5

BOYCE, William (Dr.) (1710-1779)
An English organist and composer of much sacred and instrumental music who worked on Greene's collection of English Cathedral music.

(THE) PROSPECT BEFORE US Ballet
Suite (Arr. Constant Lambert)
Sadler's Wells Orch.—Lambert
(G-C3181/3)   3 12"—VM-857

SONGS
(The) Song of Momus to Mars
Roy Henderson (b) & Eric Gritton (pf)
10"—D-M583
[Vaughan-Williams: Orpheus with his lute]
Tell me, Lovely shepherd
Ada Alsop (s) & Boyd Neel String Orch.
—Neel   12"—D-K1686
[M. Arne: The lass with the delicate air]

BOZZA, Eugene
Concertino for Saxophone & Orchestra
Marcel Mule & Orch.—Bozza
12"—FLOR-HP2053
Rhapsodie Violin & Orchestra
H. Merckel & Orch.—Bozza
12"—FLOR-HP2051/2
Scherzo
Saxophone Quartet of Paris
(C-DW4626)   10"—C-DF2239
[Françaix: Sérénade Comique]

BRAGA, Gaetano (1829-1907)
An Italian violincellist and composer of operas, vocal music and a method for 'Cello, who is known today chiefly by his "Angel's Serenade" originally for voice with 'Cello obbligato.
Angel's Serenade
It. Leggenda valacca Ger. Der Engel Lied
James Melton (t) with Zayde (vl) &
Kritz (pf)   12"—V-13431
[Massenet: Elégie]

Charles Kullman (t)   12"—C-DX458
[Gounod: Ave Maria]
Ninon Vallin (s)   12"—O-123582
[Hollman: Chanson d'amour]
Elsie Ackland (s)   10"—G-B8537
[German: Merrie England—O peaceful England]
Gwen Catley (s) & Gerald Moore (pf)
12"—G-C3233
[Bishop: Pretty Mocking Bird]
DUPLICATION: John McCormack & Kreisler, V-8033*
Instrumental Versions: Celeste Instru-mental Trio, C-FB2064; Willy Steiner Konzert Orch. PD-47135

BRAHMS, Johannes (1833-1897)

Abschiedslied ("Ich fahr' dahin") Chorus
(Deutsche Volklieder, Vol. II, No. 2)
Berlin Chamber Chorus   10"—C-DZ18
[In stiller Nacht]

Akademische Festouvertüre, Op. 80
Orchestra
Eng. Academic Festival Overture
Vienna Philharmonic Orch.—Walter
(G-DB3394)   12"—V-12190
London Symphony Orch.—Weingartner
12"—C-LX886
London Symphony—Krauss
12"—D-K1726
New York Philharmonic-Symphony Orch.
—Barbirolli   2 12"—CX-200†
[Bach: Cantata 208—Sheep may safely graze, arr. Barbirolli]
Amsterdam Concertgebouw Orch.—
Mengelberg 2 12"—C-GQX10299/300
(C-LWX246/7)
[Symphony No. 1—3rd Mvt. only]
Liverpool Philharmonic—Sargent
2 12"—C-DX1447/8
[Hungarian Dance No. 5, 6 minor]

Alto Rhapsody See: Rhapsody

BALLADES Piano
No. 1, D minor, Op. 10, No. 1 ("Edwarde")
Anatole Kitain
(in CM-342†) 12"—C-69280D
[Waltzes, Op. 39, Pt. 5] (C-DX861)
No. 5, G minor, Op. 118, No. 3
Artur Rubinstein   12"—V-11-8622
[Albéniz: Navarra]
Edwin Fischer   12"—G-DB6437
[Rhapsody No. 2, G minor]
Margaret Good   12"—D-K933
[Sonata No. 2, F major, Op. 99, Pt. 7—
Wm. Pleeth, vcl. & M. Good, pf.]

CAPRICCIOS Piano
No. 2, B minor, Op. 76, No. 2
Myra Hess   12"—G-B9189
[Intermezzo No. 1]
Artur Rubinstein
(G-DB1258)   12"—V-36289
[Debussy: La Cathédrale engloutie]
Wilhelm Backhaus
(in VM-774) 12"—V-17984
[Intermezzo No. 18 & Serenade No. 2, Pt. 7]

No. 5, D minor, Op. 116, No. 1
Leonard Shure, in VOX-178

No. 6, G minor, Op. 116, No. 3
Leonard Shure, in VOX-178

No. 7, D minor, Op. 116, No. 7
Leonard Shure, in VOX-178
Myra Hess   12"—G-C3226
[Intermezzi, Op. 117, No. 1 & Op. 119,
No. 3]

Chorale-Preludes, Op. 122 Organ

No. 8, Es ist ein' Ros' entsprungen
Eng. Lo, how a rose e'er blooming
E. Power Biggs (Memorial Church, Harvard University Cambridge, Mass.)
         12"—V-18292
[Bach: Cantata 147—Jesu, Joy of Man's
Desiring]
—Arr. Orchestra Leinsdorf
Cleveland Orch.—Leinsdorf
    (in CM-617) 12"—C-12356D
[Schumann: Symphony No. 1, Pt. 7]
—Arr. Piano
Ray Lev, in CH-A7 (Limited edition)

No. 11, O Welt, ich muss Dich lassen
—Arr. Piano
Ray Lev, in CH-A7 (Limited edition)

CONCERTOS Piano and Orchestra

No. 1, D minor, Op. 15
Artur Schnabel & London Philharmonic
—Szell   6 12"—VM-677†
Rudolf Serkin & Pittsburgh Symphony
—Reiner   6 12"—CM-652†
Wilhelm Backhaus & BBC Symphony
—Boult (G-DB1839/43) 5 12"—GM-174†
Clifford Curzon & National Symphony
—Jorda   6 12"—D-ED47†
(D-K1491/6)

No. 2, B flat major, Op. 83
Vladimir Horowitz & NBC Symphony—
Toscanini (G-DB5861/6 in GM-362)
        6 12"—VM-740†
Artur Schnabel & BBC Symphony—Boult
(G-DB2696/701)   6 12"—GM-245†
Solomon & Philharmonia Orch.—
Dobrowen   6 12"—G-C3610/5†
Rudolf Serkin & Philadelphia Orch.—
Ormandy   6 12"—CM-584†
Elly Ney & Berlin Philharmonic—
Fiedler   6 12"—PD-67566/71
Wilhelm Backhaus & Saxon State Orch.—
Böhm (Also G-DB5500/5)
      6 12"—G-DB3930/5
Boris Zadri & Lamoureux Orch.—Bigot
      6 12"—PAT-PDT52/6

CONCERETO Violin and Orchestra

D major, Op. 77
Joseph Szigeti & Philadelphia Orch.—
Ormandy   5 12"—CM-603†
[Sonata No. 3, D minor, Adagio only, with
Leonid Hambro, pf.]
(C-LX983/7s—last side blank)
Jascha Heifetz & Boston Symphony—
Koussevitzky   5 12"—VM-581†
[Bach: Suite No. 3—Air]
(G-DB5738/42s in GM-360—last side
blank)

Joseph Szigeti & Hallé Orch.—
        5 12"—CM-117†
[Violin Sonata No. 3—Adagio]
(C-L2265/9) (C-GQX16952/6)
Fritz Kreisler & London Philharmonic—
Barbirolli   5 12"—VM402†
[Kreisler: Chanson Louis XIII et Pavane,
with Victor Orch.—Voorhees]
(G-DB2915/9s in GM-261—last side
blank)
Georg Kulenkampff & Berlin Philharmonic—Schmidt-Isserstedt
        5 12"—T-E2074/8
[Max Reger: Sonata No. 1—Andante
sostenuto only]
Wolfi Schneiderhan & Saxon State Orch.
—Böhm   5 12"—C-LWX331/5
Ginette Neveu & Philharmonia Orch.—
Dobrowen (last side blank)
        5 12"—G-DB11145/9s
—2nd Mvt. (Adagio) only
Georg Kulenkampff & Berlin Philharmonic—Van Kempen   12"—T-F1423

CONCERTO Violin, 'Cello and Orchestra

(Double Concerto)
A minor, Op. 102
Jascha Heifetz, Emanuel Feuermann &
Philadelphia Orch.—Ormandy
(G-DB6120/3)   4 12"—VM-815†
Jacques Thibaud, Pablo Casals with
Casals Orch.—Cortot
        4 12"—G-DB1311/4
Georg Kulenkampff, Enrico Mainardi
with Orch. of the Suisse Romande—
Schuricht
    4 12"—in preparation Swiss Decca
Cradle Song See: Songs—**Wiegenlied**

DEUTSCHE VOLKSLIEDER
(German Folk Songs)

NOTE: *Brahms' German folk song settings are
divided into three groups:*

**1. Deutsche Volkslieder (Solo voice and
Piano acc.)**
(7 Books of 49 songs
**2. Deutsche Volkslieder (Unacc. 4 pt.
Cho.)** (2 Books of 14 songs)
**3. Volkskinderlieder (Solo voice and
Piano acc.)** (14 songs)
For recordings of works in Groups 1 &
3 see under Songs; for recording of
works in Groups 2 see: Abschiedslied & In
stiller Nacht.
(Ein) Deutsches Requiem. See: Requiem
Double Concerto See: Concerto—Violin,
'Cello & Orchestra
Duos—Instrumental See: Sonatas (Violin,
'Cello, Clarinet), Waltzes, Op. 39
Duos—Vocal See: Songs: Es Rauschet;
Der Jäger und sein Liebchen; Die Meere;
Klänge; Die Nonne und der Ritter; Die
Schwestern; Vor der Thür
(4) Ernste Gesänge, Op. 121 See Songs
Fahr' wohl, o Vöglein, Op. 93a, No. 4
Chorus
Dresden Kreuzchor-Mauersberger
        10"—PD-10282

[Mendelssohn: Immer wenn die Marz-
wind weht]
[In stiller Nacht on PD-10726]
Festival Overture See under—Akademische
Festouvertüre, Op. 80
Folksongs (arrangements) See: Deutsche
Volkslieder

FANTASIEN, Op. 116 Piano

No. 1, Capriccio, D minor
No. 2, Intermezzo, A minor
No. 3, Capriccio, G minor
No. 4, Intermezzo, E major
No. 5, Intermezzo, E minor
No. 6, Intermezzo, E major
No. 7, Capriccio, D minor
Complete recording
Leonard Shure   4 10"—**VOX-178**
See also under individual titles

HUNGARIAN DANCES Piano 4-Hands

No opus number   Ger. **Ungarische Tänze**
Fr. **Danses hongroises**
Collections
—**Arr. Violin & Piano** Joachim
No 1, G minor; No. 5, G minor; No. 6, B
flat major; No. 7, A major; No. 8, A
minor; No. 17, F sharp minor
Erica Morini & Arthur Balsam
                    3 10"—**VM-1053**
No. 1, G minor Arr. Orchestra
Indianapolis Symphony—Sevitzky
[Nos. 3 & 7]   12"—**V-11-8223**
Vienna Philharmonic—Krauss
[No. 3]   (G-HN481)   10"—**G-B3145**
Berlin Philharmonic—Furtwängler
[No. 3]   10"—**PD-90190**
—**Arr Stokowski**
Hollywood Bowl Symphony Orch.—
Stokowski   10"—**V-10-1302**
[Dolan: Lady in the Dark—A Message
for Liza]
Philadelphia Orch.—Stokowski
                   10"—**V-1675**
[Glière: Red Poppy—Russian Sailor's
Dance]
—**Arr. Violin & Piano** Joachim
Erica Morini & Arthur Balsam
[No. 8]   (in VM-1053) 10"—**V-10-1215**
Yehudi Menuhin & Marcel Gazelle
[No. 17]   (G-DA1491)   10"—**V-2010**
Grisha Goluboff & Ivor Newton
                   10"—**C-DW4529**
[Debussy-Hartman: La Fille aux
Cheveux de Lin]
Bronislaw Hubermann & S. Schultze
                   10"—**C-LF108**
[Chopin: Waltz No. 7]   (C-GQ7175)
Toscha Seidel & Eugene Kusmiak
[Provost: Intermezzo]   10"—**V-4458**
DUPLICATION: E. Pierangeli, CET-P-
56107
—**Arr. Telmanyi**
Emil Telmanyi (vl) & G. v. Vasarhelyi
(pf)   12"—**G-DB2798**
[Sibelius: Danse Champêtre]
—**Arr. 2 Pianos**
Rawicz & Landauer   10"—**C-DB2169**
[No. 2]

No. 2, D minor
(Many recordings labelled "Hungarian
Dance No. 2" are actually No. 6, origin-
ally in D flat major, but often transcrib-
ed to D major)
—**Arr. Piano**
Winifred Wolf   10"—**G-EG3496**
[Schubert: Moment Musical, No. 3]
—**Arr. Violin & Piano** Joachim
Nathan Milstein & Arthur Balsam
                   10"—**C-17352D**
[Rimsky-Korsakoff: Flight of the
Bumble Bee]
DUPLICATION: Issay Mitnitzky,
C-DN244
—**Arr. 2 Pianos**
Rawicz & Landauer   10"—**C-DB2169**
[No. 1]
No. 3, F major Arr. Orchestra
Indianapolis Symphony—Sevitzky
[Nos. 7 & 1]   12"—**V-11-8223**
Vienna Philharmonic—Krauss
[No. 1]   (G-HN481)   10"—**G-B3145**
Berlin Philharmonic—Furtwängler
[No. 1]   10"—**PD-90190**
No. 4, F minor
Artur Rubinstein   12"—**V-11-9732**
[Rhapsody No. 2]
—**Arr. Violin & Piano** Joachim
(Transcribed to B minor)
Yehudi Menuhin & Marcel Gazelle
                   12"—**V-14905**
[Dvořák: Slavonic Dance No. 10, E minor
—Arr. Kreisler]   (G-DB2922)
Vocal Arr. "Violon du Soir" P. Darck
(Text: Jean Calmes)
Ninon Vallin (s) & Instr. acc.
                   10"—**O-281277**
[Chopin: Valse de l'adieu, arr. Darck]
No. 5, F sharp minor
(sometimes labelled No. 1)
—**Arr. Orchestra** (Transcribed to G minor)
Philadelphia Orch.—Ormandy
        (in GM-588)   12"—**C-12607D**
[Straus: Wein, Weib und Gesang waltz]
Saxon State Orch.—Böhm
[No. 6]   10"—**G-DA4443**
Boston "Pops" Orch.—Fiedler
[No. 6]   (G-B8571)   10"—**V-4321**
DUPLICATIONS: Liverpool Philharmonic
—Sargent, C-DX1448; Orch. of "Maggio
Musicale"—Gui, CET-T17046; Hallé
Orch.—Harty, C-5466; Berlin Philhar-
monic—Prüwer, PD-21643; Hastings
Municipal Orch.—Harrison, D-F2307;
Milan Symphony—Molajoli, C-D14459;
Royal Opera Orch.—Sargent, G-C1415:
G-L672; Symphony Orch.—Cloëz,
O-170053; Berlin State Opera Orch.—
Blech, G-EW79; Lajos Kiss Orch.,
T-A10126: T-A1764; Symphony Orch.—
Ferruzzi, C-DQ2899; Dresden Philhar-
monic—van Kempen, PD-11056: CET-
LL3014; Rode & his Tziganes,
C-FB1622: PAT-PA834; Gypsy Orch.,
PD-24497
—**Arr. Band**
Garde Républicaine Band
[No. 6]   10"—**C-D19316**
Savoie Band   10"—**PAT-X96131**

—**Arr. Violin & Piano** Joachim
Erica Morini & Artur Balsam
      (in VM-1053)   10"—**V-10-1214**
[No. 7]
Josef Szigeti & Andor Földes
      (in CM-513)   10"—**C-17340D**
[Kodaly-Szigeti—Hary Janos—
Intermezzo]
DUPLICATIONS: E. Telmanyi, TONO-
A101; A107
No. 6, D flat major
(Sometimes labelled No. 2)
—**Arr. Orchestra** (Transcribed to D major)
Boston "Pops" Orch.—Fiedler
[No. 5] (G-B5571)   10"—**V-4321**
Dresden Philharmonic—van Kempen
                10"—**PD-11056**
[No. 5] (CET-LL3014)
Orch. of "Maggio Musicale—V. Gui
[No. 5]   10"—**CET-T17046**
Hallé Orch.—Harty   10"—**C-5466**
[No. 5]
DUPLICATIONS: Berlin Philharmonic
Prüwer, PD-21643; Milan Symphony—
Molajoli, C-D12273; Symphony Orch.—
Cloëz, O-170053; Berlin State Opera
Orch.—Blech, G-EW79; Royal Opera
Orch.—Sargent, G-C1874; Hastings
Municipal Orch.—Harrison, D-F2307;
Kiss Orch., T-A1764; Symphony Orch.—
Ferruzzi, C-DQ2899; Gypsy Orch.,
PD-24497
Also: Garde Républicaine Band,
C-D19316
—**Arr. Violin & Piano** Joachim
Erica Morini & Artur Balsam
[No. 17] (in VM-1053) 10"—**V-10-1213**
Yehudi Menuhin & Marcel Gazelle
                12"—**V-8866**
[Paganini: Moto pepetuo]
[Sarasate: Romanza Andaluza on
G-DB2413]
No. 7, A major Arr. Orchestra
Indianapolis Symphony Orch.—
Sevitzky   12"—**V-11-8223**
[No. 3 & No. 1]
—**Arr. Violin & Piano** Joachim
Yehudi Menuhin & Marcel Gazelle
[Sarasate: Zapateado] 10"—**G-DA1482**
Erica Morini & Artur Balsam
[No. 5] (in VM-1053) 10"—**V-10-1214**
Georg Kulenkampff & Franz Rupp
              10"—**PD-62749**
[Smetana: From my home]
No. 8, A minor
—**Arr. Violin & Piano** Joachim
Erica Morini & Artur Balsam
[No. 1] (in VM-1053) 10"—**V-10-1215**
(Older version: PD-67023, with M.
Raucheisen, pf., coupled with Waltz,
Op. 39, No. 15)
Yelli D'Aranyi & pf. acc.
[DeFalla: Jota]   10"—**C-DF251**
No. 11, D minor
—**Arr. Violin & Piano** Joachim
Yehudi Menuhin & George Webster
             12"—**G-DB3500**
[Granados: Spanish Dance No. 5]

No. 17, F sharp minor
—**Arr. Violin & Piano** Joachim
Yehudi Menuhin & Marcel Gazelle
[No. 1] (G-DA1491)   10"—**V-2010**
Erica Morini & Artur Balsam
[No. 6] (in VM-1053) 10"—**V-10-1213**
No. 18, D major Arr. Orchestra Dvořák
Minneapolis Symphony Orch.—
Ormandy   10"—**V-1796**
[Nos. 19, 20, 21] (G-DA1543)
No. 19, B minor Arr. Orchestra Dvořák
Minneapolis Symphony Orch.—
Ormandy   10"—**V-1796**
[Nos. 18, 20, 21] (G-DA1543)
BBC Symphony Orch.—Boult
             12"—**G-DB1804**
[Nos. 20, 21 & Tragic Overture, Pt. 3]
[Mozart: Così fan tutte-Overture,
on G-DB3814]
No. 20, E minor Arr. Orchestra Dvořák
Minneapolis Symphony Orch.—
Ormandy   10"—**V-1796**
[Nos. 18, 19, 21] (G-DA1543)
BBC Symphony Orch.—Boult
             12"—**G-DB1804**
[Nos. 19, 21 & Tragic Overture, Pt. 3]
[Mozart: Cosi Fan Tutte-Overture,
on G-DB3814]
No. 21, E minor Arr. Orchestra Dvořák
Minneapolis Symphony Orch.—
Ormandy   10"—**V-1796**
[Nos. 18, 19, 20] (G-DA1543)
BBC Symphony Orch.—Boult
             12"—**G-DB1804**
[Nos. 19, 20 & Tragic Overture, Pt. 3]
[Mozart: Cosi Fan Tutte-Overture,
on G-DB3814]
In stiller Nacht (Deutsche Volkslieder,
Vol. II, No. 1) Chorus in German
(Brahms also set this melody for solo
voice and piano—Deutche Volkslieder
No. 42)
Dresdener Kreuzchor   10"—**PD-10726**
[Fahr' wohl o Vöglein]
St. Thomas', Leipzig, Cho.—
Straube   10"—**PD-90158**
[Sandmännchen]
Glasgow Orpheus Choir—Roberton
             10"—**G-B9549**
[Trad.: Kedron] (In English)
DUPLICATION: Berliner Solistenvereini-
gun, G-EG3749

INTERMEZZOS Piano
Collections
No. 1, A flat major, Op. 76, No. 3
No. 2, B flat major, Op. 76, No. 4
No. 5, E major, Op. 116, No. 4
No. 15, E flat major, Op. 118, No. 6
No. 17, E minor, Op. 118, No. 2
Walter Gieseking   2 12"—**CX-201**

No. 4, A minor, Op. 76, No. 7
No. 9, E flat major, Op. 117, No. 1
No. 10, B flat minor, Op. 117, No. 2
No. 13, A major, Op. 118, No. 2
No. 15, E flat minor, Op. 118, No. 6
No. 18, C major, Op. 119, No. 3
(with Rhapsodies No. 1, B minor & No.
3, E flat major)

Artur Rubinstein 4 12″—**VM-893**
No. 6, E major, Op. 116, No. 4
No. 9, E flat major, Op. 117, No. 1
No. 10, B flat minor, Op. 117, No. 2
No. 16, B minor, Op. 119, No. 1
No. 17, E minor, Op. 119, No. 2
(with Waltzes, Op. 39, 1/16)
Wilhelm Backhaus 4 12″—**VM-321**
No. 1, A flat major, Op. 76, No. 3
Walter Gieseking
(in CX-201) 12″—**C-72117D**
[Nos. 2 & 15]
Myra Hess 10″—**G-B9189**
[Capriccio No. 2]
Elly Ney 10″—**G-DA4438**
[Waltz, Op. 39, No. 15 & Romance in F]
No. 2, B flat major, Op. 76, No. 4
Walter Gieseking
(in CX-201) 12″—**C-72117D**
[No. 1 & No. 15]
No. 4, A minor, Op. 76, No. 7
Artur Rubinstein
(in VM-893) 12″—**V-11-8140**
[No. 18 & Rhapsody No. 3]
No. 5, A minor, Op. 116, No. 2
Leonard Shure, in VOX-178
Theo van der Pas (in preparation)
Dutch Decca
No. 6, E major, Op. 116, No. 4
Walter Gieseking
[No. 17] (in CX-201) 12″—**C-72118D**
Wilhelm Backhaus
(in VM-321) 12″—**V-14132**
[Waltzes, Op. 39, Nos. 12/16]
Leonard Shure, in VOX-178
No. 7, E minor, Op. 116, No. 5
Leonard Shure, in VOX-178
No. 8, E major, Op. 116, No. 6
Leonard Shure, in VOX-178
William Kappell
(in VM-1132†) 12″—**V-11-9621**
[Beethoven: Concerto No. 2, Pt. 9]
No. 9, E flat major, Op. 117, No. 1
Edwin Fischer 12″—**G-DB6478**
[No. 10]
Artur Rubinstein
[No. 10] (in VM-893) 12″—**V-11-8138**
Wilhelm Backhaus
[No. 10] (in VM-321) 12″—**V-14133**
Myra Hess 12″—**G-C3226**
[No. 18 & Capriccio No. 7]
Elly Ney 12″—**G-DB4426**
[Rhapsody No. 3]
Geza Anda 12″—**BAM-46**
[No. 10]
No. 10, B flat minor, Op. 117, No. 2
Edwin Fischer 12″—**G-DB6478**
[No. 9]
Artur Rubinstein
[No. 9] (in VM-893) 12″—**V-11-8138**
Wilhelm Backhaus
[No. 9] (in VM-321) 12″—**V-14133**
Solomon 12″—**G-C3406**
[Rhapsody No. 2]
Walter Gieseking 12″—**C-LWX337**
[Romance, F major, Op. 118, No. 5]
DUPLICATIONS: Yves Nat, C-LFX555;
Stell Andersen, PD-516782; Myrtle C.
Eaver, V-24799; Geza Anda, BAM-46;
William Murdoch, D-K698

No. 11, C sharp minor, Op. 117, No. 3
Geza Anda 12″—**BAM-47**
[No. 17]
No. 13, A major, Op. 118, No. 2
Artur Rubinstein
[No. 15] (in VM-893) 12″—**V-11-8139**
Oscar Levant 12″—**C-72372D**
[Waltz, Op. 39, No. 15 & Schumann:
Träumerei]
No. 15, E flat minor, Op. 118, No. 6
Artur Rubinstein
[No. 13] (in VM-893) 12″—**V-11-8139**
Walter Gieseking
(in CX-201) 12″—**C-72117D**
[No. 1 & No. 2]
No. 16, B minor, Op. 119, No. 1
Wilhelm Backhaus
[No. 17] (in VM-321) 12″—**V-14134**
No. 17, E minor, Op. 119, No. 2
Walter Gieseking
[No. 6] (in CX-201) 12″—**C-72118D**
Wilhelm Backhaus
[No. 16] (in VM-321) 12″—**V-14134**
Geza Anda
[No. 11] 12″—**BAM-47**
No. 18, C major, Op. 119, No. 3
Artur Rubinstein
(in VM-893) 12″—**V-11-8140**
[No. 4 & Rhapsody No. 3]
Walter Gieseking 10″—**C-17079D**
[Chopin: Waltz No. 6, Prelude No. 23, &
Schubert: Moment Musical No. 3]
(C-LW15) (C-DQ7208)
Wilhelm Backhaus
(in VM-774) 12″—**V-17984**
[Capriccio No. 2 & Serenade No. 7, Pt. 7]
Myra Hess 12″—**G-C3226**
[No. 9 & Capriccio No. 7]
(also on C-4083M)
Liebeslieder Waltzes, Op. 52 See under
Waltzes
Lieder See Songs
Magelone Romances, Op. 33 See Songs—
Ruhe, Süssliebchen & Wie froh und
frisch
Motet See: O Heiland, reiss, die Himmel
auf, Op. 74, No. 2
Nänie, Op. 82 Chorus & Orchestra
Aachen Cathedral Choir (Irmgard See-
fried, soprano soloist) & Prussian State
Orch.—Rehmann
[Bruch: Jubilate] 2 12″—**G-DB7654/5**
**O Heiland, reiss, die Himmel auf Op. 74,
No. 2**
Motet, Unacc. Cho., in German Eng. O
Savior, Throw the Heavens wide
Westminster Choir—Williamson (in
Eng.)
(in CX-223†) 12″—**C-11802D**
[Schicksalslied, Pt. 3]
Overtures See: Akademisches & Tragische
Ouvertüren

PIANO

See under: Ballades, Capriccios, Concertos,
Hungarian Dances, Intermezzos, Rhapsodies, Romance, Sonatas, Songs (arrangements), Variations & Waltzes.

QUARTETS—Vocal
See Songs: Wiegenlied; Waltzes—Liebeslieder, Op. 52; Zigeunerlieder

QUARTETS—String
No. 1, C minor, Op. 51, No. 1
Busch Quartet   4 12″—VM-227†
Brenonal Quartet 4 12″—PD-67785/8
(CET-OR5123/6)
No. 2, A minor, Op. 51, No. 2
Busch Quartet 4 12″—C-LX1022/5†
Belardinelli Quartet
            4 12″—G-AW334/7
—3rd Mvt. only
Buxbaum Quartet   12″—PD-95361
[Symphony No. 4, Pt. 11]
No. 3, B flat major, Op. 67
Guilet Quartet   4 12″—VOX-208

QUARTETS—Piano & Strings
No. 1, G minor, Op. 25
Artur Rubinstein & Members of Pro Arte
Quartet   4 12″—VM-234†
Edwin Fischer, Vittorio Brero, Rudolf
Nel & Theo. Schurgers
            5 12″—G-DB5532/6S
(Last side blank)

QUINTETS—Strings
No. 1, F major, Op. 88
Budapest Quartet, with Alfred Hobday
(vlc)   3 12″—VM-466†
No. 2, G major, Op. 111
Budapest Quartet, with Hans Mahlke
(vlc)   3 12″—VM-184†

QUINTET—Clarinet & Strings, B minor,
Op. 115
Reginald Kell & Busch Quartet
            4 12″—VM-491†
(G-DB3383/6 in GM-311)
Luigi Amodio & Poltronieri Quartet
            4 12″—C-GQX11092/5

QUINTET—Piano & Strings, F minor, Op.
34
Rudolf Serkin & Busch Quartet
            5 12″—VM-607†
Olga Loeser-Lebert & Léner Quartet
            5 12″—C-GQX10947/51

REQUIEM: Ein deutches Requiem, Op. 45
Soloists, Chorus & Orchestra In German
Eng. A German Requiem
Individual Excerpts
No. 1, Selig sind, die da Leid tragen
Eng. Blest are they that mourn
Berlin Singakadamie Cho. & Orch.—
Schumann   2 12″—G-EH257/8
[Haydn: Jahreszeiten—Komm, holder
Lenz]
No. 2, Denn alles Fleisch, es ist wie Gras
Eng. Behold all flesh is as the grass, or,
All mortal flesh
Berlin Singakadamie Cho. & Orch.—
Schumann   2 12″—G-EH265/6
No. 3, Herr, lehre doch mich
Eng. Lord, make me to know
Albert Fischer (b) with Cho. & Orch.—
Dobrindt   12″—O-26530

No. 4, Wie lieblich sind deine Wohnungen
Eng. How lovely is Thy dwelling place
Irmler Choir & Orch.—Dobrindt
            12″—O-25102
Temple Church Cho. & Organ (in Eng-
lish)   10″—G-B3453
No. 5, Ihr habt nun Traurigkeit Soprano &
Chorus Eng. Ye that now are sorrowful
Hildegard Erdmann, Chorus & Orch.—
Seidler-Winkler   12″—G-EH1253
Emmy Bettendorf, Chorus & Orch.—
Dobrindt   12″—O-6882
No. 6, Denn wir haben hier Eng. Here on
earth
No. 7, Selig sind die Todten Eng. Blessed
are the dead
No recordings available.

(ALTO) RHAPSODY, Op. 53 Alto, Male
Cho. & Orch.
(after Goethe's "Harzreise im Winter")
Marian Anderson, Municipal Cho. & San
Francisco Orch.—Monteux
        2 12″—VM-1111†

RHAPSODIES Piano

(3) Rhapsodies for Piano, Op. 79 & 119
Egon Petri   2 12″—CX-183
No. 1, B minor, Op. 79, No. 1
Artur Rubinstein
        (in VM-893) V-11-8141
Egon Petri (in CX-183) 12″—C-70681D
No. 2, G minor, Op. 79, No. 2
Artur Rubinstein (G-DB3217)
            12″—V-14946
[Schumann: Romance No. 2]
(Also on V-11-9732 in VM-1149)
Egon Petri   12″—C-70682D
[No. 3] (in CX-183)
Edwin Fischer   12″—G-DB6437
[Ballade No. 5]
Solomon   12″—G-C3406
[Intermezzo No. 10]
Reine Gianoli   12″—BAM-43
[Beethoven: Sonata No. 17, D minor,
Pt. 5]
No. 3, E flat major, Op. 119, No. 4
Artur Rubinstein 12″—V-11-8140
[Intermezzos No. 4 & 17] (in VM-893)
Egon Petri (in CX-183) 12″—C-70682D
[No. 2, G minor]
DUPLICATIONS: Elly Ney, G-DB4426;
William Murdoch, D-K698
Romance, F major, Op. 118, No. 5 Piano
Elly Ney   10″—G-DA4438
[Waltz No. 15]
Walter Gieseking   12″—C-LWX337
[Intermezzo No. 10]
Sandmännchen See under Songs
Schicksalslied, Op. 54 Cho. & Orch.
Eng. Song of Destiny
Westminster Choir (in English), Phil-
harmonic-Symphony Orch. of New York—
Bruno Walter 2 12″—CX-223†
[O Heiland, reiss' die Himmel auf, West-
minster Choir—Williamson, only]
Serenade See under Songs—Ständchen

SERENADES Orchestra

No. 1, D major, Op. 11
—Minuet (G major) only
Chicago Symphony—Stock
      (in CX-214†)   12"—**C-11682D**
[Tragic Overture, Pt. 3]
No. 2, A major, Op. 16
Alumni Orch. of National Orchestral Association—Richard Korn
          4   12"—**VM-774†**
[Capriccio No. 2; Intermezzo No. 18, Backhaus]
Serious Songs See under Songs—Ernste Gesänge

SEXTETS—String

No. 1, B flat major, Op. 18
Pro Arte Quartet, A. Hobday (vla) & A. Pini (vlc.)   4   12"—**VM-296†**
(G-DB2566/9)
No. 2, G major, Op. 36
Budapest Quartet, A. Hobday (vla), & A. Pini (vlc)   4   12"—**VM-371†**

SONATAS—Piano

No. 1, C major, Op. 1
Ray Lev, in CH-A7 (Limited edition)
(with 2 Choral Preludes, Op. 122)
No. 3, F minor, Op. 5
Harold Bauer   4   12"—**SCH-14**
Shura Cherkassky   4   12"—**VOX-626**
Percy Grainger 4   12"—**C-GQX10451/4**

SONATAS—Violin & Piano

No. 1, G major, Op. 78 ("Regen")—(Rain Sonata)
Yehudi & Hephzibah Menuhin
          4   12"—**VM-987†**
[Bach: Sonata No. 6 for Unacc. Vl.—Praeludium only]
[Mozart: Sonata No. 25, G major, K. 301—Allegro only, on G-DB5798/801]
Emil Telmanyi & Georg Vasarhelyi
        3   12"—**G-DB4633/5**
Georg Kulenkampff & Georg Solti
        3   12"—**D-K1705/7**
Adolf Busch & Rudolf Serkin
        3   12"—**G-DB1527/9**
No. 2, A major, Op. 100 ("Thun")
Jascha Heifetz & Emanuel Bay
        3   12"—**VM-856†**
[Wieniawski: Scherzo Tarantelle, Op. 16]
Adolf Busch & Rudolf Serkin
        2   12"—**G-DB1805/6**
Emil Telmanyi & Georg Vasarhelyi
        2   12"—**G-DB4640/1**
No. 3, D minor, Op. 108
Yehudi & Hephzibah Menuhin
        3   12"—**G-DB6441/3**
[Older version on G-DB2832/4]
Joseph Szigeti & Egon Petri
(C-LWX233/5)   3   12"—**CM-324†**
—2nd Mvt. (Adagio) only
Joseph Szigeti & Leonard Hambro
    (in CM-603†)   12"—**C-12285D**
[Violin Concerto, Pt. 9]
[Older version, with Ruhrseitz, pf. on C-67621D in CM-117†]
(C-L2269) (C-GQX10956)

Sonatensatz Allegro (Scherzo) Movement in C minor
(From a Sonata for Violin & Piano composer jointly by Dietrich—1st Mvt.—Schumann—2nd & 4th Mvts.—& Brahms —3rd Mvt.)
Emil Telmanyi & Georg Vasarhelyi
          10"—**G-DA4464**
David Oistrakh & L. Oborin
          10"—**USSR—13249/50**

SONATAS—Clarinet—or Viola—& Piano.
(While Brahms wrote his two Op. 120 sonatas with the clarinet foremost in mind, he also provided Viola-Piano versions)
No. 1, F minor, Op. 120, No. 1
William Primrose (vla) & William Kapell (pf)   3   12"—**VM-1106†**
Samuel Lifschey (vla) & Egon Petri (pf)
        3   12"—**CM-487†**
[Bach: Suite No. 6, D minor for unacc. vlc.—Gavottes 1 & 2—Lifschey, vla., only]
Luigi Amodio (cl) & S. Schultze (Pf)
        3   12"—**CET-OR5106/8**
[Chopin: Valse No. 7, Brailowsky]
No. 2, E flat major, Op. 120, No. 2
Frederick Thurston (cl) & Meyers Foggin (pf) (PD-516735/7)
        3   12"—**D-X171/3**
Benny Goodman (cl) & Nadia Reisenberg (pf)   3   12"—**CM-629†**
William Primrose (vla) & Gerald Moore (pf) (G-DB3314/6) 3 12"—**VM-422†**

SONATAS—'Cello & Piano

No. 1, E minor, Op. 38
Gregor Piatigorsky & Artur Rubinstein (G-DB2952/4)   3   12"—**VM-564†**
Emanuel Feuermann & Theo. van der Pas   3   12"—**CM-236†**
(Last side blank)
No. 2, F major, Op. 99
William Pleeth & Margaret Good
          4   12"—**D-K930/3**
[Ballade No. 5]

SONGS (Lieder) In German

Collections
Brahms Song Society
Vol. I—Von ewiger Liebe; Erinnerung; Vier ernste Gesänge; Die Mainacht; Ein Sonett; Sonntag; O wüsst' ich doch den Weg zurück; Ständchen; Vergebliches Ständchen; Verrath; An die Nachtigall.
Alexander Kipnis (bs) & Gerald Moore (pf)   6   12"—**VM-522**
Vol. II—In stiller Nacht; Mein Mädel hat einen Rosenmund; Sandmännchen; Vor dem Fenster; Ruhe, Süssliebchen; Der Gang zum Liebchen; O kühler Wald; Dein blaues Auge; Meine Liebe ist grün; Geheimniss; Am Sonntag Morgen; In Waldeseinsamkeit; Wir wandelten; Wie Melodien zieht es mir; Wiegenlied; Auf dem Kirchhofe; Der Ueberläufer; Ein Wanderer.
Alexander Kipnis (bs) & Ernst Victor Wolff (pf)   5   12"—**VM-751**
Brahms Song Recital
Wie bist du, meine Königin; Wir Wandel-

ten; An die Nachtigall; Auf dem Kirch-
hofe; Erlaube mir, fein's Mädchen; Da
unten in Thale; Feinsliebchen, du sollst
mir nicht barfuss gehn; Die Mainacht;
Sonntag; O liebliche Wangen.
Lotte Lehmann (s) & Paul Ulanowsky
(pf)	2	10" & 2	12"—CM-453
Part Songs for Female Voices with 2 Horns
& Harp Op. 17
No. 1, Es tönt ein voller Harfenklang
No. 2, Komm' herbei, Tod
No. 3, Der Gärtner
No. 4, Gesang aus Fingal
Nottingham Oriana Choir (in English)—
Roy Henderson, with Dennis Brain &
Norman Del Mar (horns) & Gwendolyn
Mason (harp)	3	10"—D-M560/2
[Holst: Hymn to the Waters]
Vocal Quartet & 3 Vocal Duets In German
Der Gang zum liebchen, Op. 31, No. 3
(Quartet) Die Schwestern, Op. 61, No. 1
(Polignac & I. Kedroff)
Klänge, Op. 66, No. 2 & Die Meere, Op.
20, No. 3 (N. & I. Kedroff)
Jeanne de Polignac & Nathalie Kedroff
(sops.), Irene Kedroff (a), Hughes
Cuenod (t) & Doda Conrad (bs) with
Nadia Boulanger (pf)	12"—G-DB5060
Individual Songs—with piano accompani-
ment (unless noted)
Am Sonntag Morgen, Op. 49, No. 1 (Heyse's
Italianische Liederbuch)
Alexander Kipnis (bs) & Ernst V. Wolff
in Brahms Song Society Vol. II: VM-751
Heinrich Schlusnus (b) & Sebastian
Peschko	10"—PD-62783
[Der Gang zum Liebchen, Op. 48, No. 1
& Die Mainacht]
Irène Joachim (s) & Ludwig Bergmann
12"—G-L1055
[Wie melodien zieht es mir & O wüsst'
ich doch den Weg zurück]
An die Nachtigall, Op. 46, No. 4 (Holty &
Voss)
Alexander Kipnis (bs) & Gerald Moore,
in Brahms Song Society Vol. I: VM-522
Lotte Lehmann (s) & Paul Ulanowsky
(in CM-453)	10"—C-17439D
[Auf dem Kirchhofe]
Nancy Evans (a) & Meyers Foggin
12"—D-X166
[Zigeunerlieder, Pt. 3]
An die Tauben, Op. 63, No. 4 (von
Schenkendorff)
Heinrich Schlusnus (b)
10"—PD-30004
[Wenn du nur zuweilen lächelst & Tam-
bourliedchen]
Auf dem Kirchhofe, Op. 105, No. 4
(Lilencron)
Alexander Kipnis (bs) & Ernst V. Wolff,
in Brahms Song Society Vol. II: VM-751
Lotte Lehmann (s) & Paul Ulanowsky
(in CM-453)	10"—C-17439D
[An die Nachtigall]
Auf dem Schiffe, Op. 97, No. 2 (Reinhold)
Eng. On the river boat
Dorothea Helmrich (s, in Eng.) & Hu-
bert Foss	10"—C-DB1233
[Die Schwestern & Schumann: Du bist

wie eine Blume & An dem Abendstern]
(in Col. History of Music, Vol. 4: CM-
234)
Auf dem See, Op. 59, No. 2 (Simrock)
Heinrich Schlusnus (b) & Sebastian
Peschko	10"—PD-62782
[Botschaft]
Auf die Nacht in den Spinnstub'n See:
Mädchenlied, Op. 107, No. 5
(Die) Botschaft, Op. 47, No. 1 (Daumer)
Lotte Lehmann (s) & Erno Balogh
(in VM-419)	10"—V-1857
[Das Mädchen spricht & Mein Mädel]
Heinrich Schlusnus (b) & Sebastian
Peschko	10"—PD-62782
[Auf dem See]
Ria Ginster (s) & Paul Baumgartner
[Immer leiser]	10"—G-DA6017
Heinrich Rehkemper (b) & M. Rauch-
eisen	10"—PD-23148
[Nicht mehr zu dir zu gehen]
Cradle Song See—Wiegenlied
Da unten im Thale (Deutsche Volkslieder
No. 6)
Lotte Lehmann (s) & Paul Ulanowsky
(in CM-453)	12"—C-71979D
[Erlaube mir & Feinsliebchen' du sollst]
Dein blaues Auge, Op. 59, No. 8 (Groth)
Alexander Kipnis (bs) & Ernst V. Wolff,
in Brahms Society, Vol. II: VM-751
Denn es gehet dem Menschen See: Ernste
Gesänge No. 1
Erinnerung, Op. 63, No. 2 (von Schenken-
dorf)
Alexander Kipnis (bs) & Gerald Moore,
in Brahms Song Society Vol. I: VM-522
(4) Ernste Gesänge, Op. 121 (Biblical text)
Eng. Four Serious Songs
No. 1, Denn es gehet dem Menschen (Ecc.
III, 19-22)
No. 2, Ich wandte mich und sahe (Ecc.
IV, 1-3)
No. 3, O Tod, wie bitter bist du (Ecc.
XLI, 1-2)
No. 4, Wenn ich mit Menschen (Cor. I:
XIII, 1-3 & 12-13)
Alexander Kipnis (bs) & Gerald Moore,
in Brahms Song Society Vol. I: VM-522
Doda Conrad (bs) & Erich Itor Kahn
2	12"—G-DB5052/3
Emmi Leisner (c) 2	12"—G-DB5561/2
Erlaube mir, Fein's Mädchen (Deutsche
Volkslieder No. 2)
Lotte Lehmann (s) & Paul Ulanowsky
(in CM-453)	12"—C-71979D
[Da unten im Thale & Feinsliebchen, du
sollst]
Es tönt ein voller Harfenklang, Op. 17, No.
1, (Ruperti)
Eng. Whene'er the sounding harp is
heard
Nottingham Oriana Choir (in English)
with horns & harp	10"—D-M560
Feinsliebchen, du sollst mir nicht barfuss
geh'n
(Deutsche Volkslieder No. 12)
Lotte Lehman (s) & Paul Ulanowsky
(in CM-453)	12"—C-71979D
[Erlaube mir & Da unten im Thale]

Ursula van Diemen (s) & Arpad Sandor
          10"—G-EG1063
[Schumann: Lotusblume]
Feldeinsamkeit, Op. 86, No. 2 (Allmers)
Elena Gerhardt (ms) & C. van Bos
          12"—V-7793
[Nachtigall & Ständchen]
Heinrich Schlusnus (b) & Franz Rupp
          12"—PD-30009
[Wie bist du, meine Königin]
Karl Schmitt-Walter (b) & Franz Rupp
          10"—T-A2040
[Grieg: I love thee]
Gerhard Hüsch (b) & Hans Udo Müller
          10"—G-EG3308
[Wie bist du, meine Königin]
DUPLICATIONS: Leo Slezak, PD-19977;
Petre Montenou, CET-PE128
Der Gang zum Liebchen, Op. 31, No. 3
Quartet
Jeanne de Polignac, Irène Kedroff,
Hughes Cuenod, Doda Conrad, w. Nadia
Boulanger   12"—G-DB5060
[Die Schwestern; Klänge & Die Meere]
Der Gang zum Liebchen, Op. 48, No. 1 (Es
glänzt der Mond nieder)
(Slavonic folk-song text)
Alexander Kipnis (bs) & Ernst V. Wolff,
in Brahms Song Society Vol. II: VM-751
Heinrich Schlusnus (b) & Sebastian
Peschko   10"—PD-62783
[Am Sonntag Morgen & Die Mainacht]
Elena Gerhardt (ms) & Gerald Moore
(Private HMV recording)
(Der) Gärtner, Op. 17, No. 3 (Eichendorf)
Eng. **The Gardner**
Nottingham Oriana Choir (in English)
with horns & harp   10"—D-M561
[Komm herbei, Tod]
Geheimniss, Op. 71, No. 3
Alexander Kipnis (bs) & Ernst V. Wolff,
in Brahms Song Society, Vol. II: VM-751
Gesang aus Fingal, Op. 17, No. 4 (Ossian)
Eng. **The Death of Trenar**
Nottingham Oriana Choir (in English)
with horns & harp   10"—D-M562
[Holst: Hymn to the Waters]
Gestillte Sehnsucht, Op. 91, No. 1
(from Two Songs for Alto Voice, Viola &
Piano)
Marian Anderson (c), William Primrose
(vla) & Franz Rupp
     (in VM-882†) 12"—V-18507
Nancy Evans (a), Max Gilbert (vla) &
Meyers Foggin   12"—D-K901
Ria Ginster (s), Oskar Karmer (vla) &
Paul Baumgartner   12"—DB10098
Friedel Beckmann (ms), Karl Reitz (vla)
& B. Seidler-Winkler
[Geistliches Wiegenlied]
Geistliches Wiegenlied, Op. 91, No. 2
(from Two Songs for Alto Voice, Viola &
Piano)
(This is a setting of the medieval German
Christmas Carol, "Joseph, lieber Joseph
mein" used by other composers.)
Marian Anderson (c), William Primrose
(vla) & Franz Rupp
     (in VM-822†) 12"—V-18508
Nancy Evans (c), Max Gilbert (vla) &

Meyers Foggin   12"—D-K902
Ria Ginster (s), Oskar Kramer (vla) &
Paul Baumgartner   12"—G-DB10099
Friedel Beckmann (ms) & Karl Reitz
(vla) & B. Seidler-Winkler
          12"—G-EH1245
[Gestillte Sehnsucht]
Ich fahr' dahin See: Abschiedslied (without
opus number)
Ich wandte mich und sahe See: Ernste
Gesänge No. 2
**Immer leiser wird mein Schlummer, Op.
105, No. 2** (Lingg)
Elisabeth Schumann (s) & Orch.
[Wiegenlied]   10"—G-DA1562
Ria Ginster (s) & Paul Baumgartner
[Botschaft]   10"—G-DA6017
Tiana Lemnitz (s)   12"—G-DB5540
[Von ewiger liebe]
In stiller Nacht (Deutsche Volkslieder No.
42)
(For recordings of the choral version of
this song see: In stiller Nacht—Deutsche
Volkslieder for Chorus, Vol. II, No. 1)
Alexander Kipnis (bs) & Ernst V. Wolff,
in Brahms Song Society, Vol. II: VM-751
In dem Schatten meiner Locken (Span-
isches Lied, Op. 6, No. 1)
Margaret Klose (c)   10"—G-DA4473
[Nicht mehr zu dir zu gehen]
In Waldeseinsamkeit, Op. 85, No. 6
(Lemcke)
Alexander Kipnis (bs) & Ernst V. Wolff,
in Brahms Song Society, Vol. II: VM-751
Der Jäger, Op. 95, No. 4 (Halm)
Elisabeth Schumann (s) & Georges
Reeves   10"—V-1756
[Die Nachtigall, Vergebliches Ständchen
& Wiegenlied] (G-DA1417)
Klänge, Op. 66, No. 2 (Duo for Soprano &
Alto)
Irène & Nathalie Kedroff (s & a) &
Nadia Boulanger   12"—G-DB5060
[Die Meere; Der Gang zum Liebchen &
Die Schwestern]
Komm herbei, Tod, Op. 17, No. 2 (Shakes-
peare) Eng. **Come away Death**
(from Part Songs for Women's Voices, 2
Horns & Harp)
Nottingham Oriana Choir—Henderson
(in English), with Dennis Brain & Nor-
man Del Mar (horns) & Gwendolyn Ma-
son (harp)   10"—D-M561
[Die Gärtner]
Lerchengesang, Op. 70, No. 2 (Candidus)
Karl Erb (t) & Bruno Seidler-Winkler
          10"—G-EG3687
[Schubert: An Sylvia]
(Das) Mädchen spricht, Op. 107, No. 3
(Gruppe)
Lotte Lehmann (s) & Erno Balogh
     (in VM-419) 10"—V-1857
[Mein Mädel & Die Botschaft]
Mädchenlied, Op. 107, No. 5
Aulikki Rautawaara (s) & Ferdinand
Leitner   10"—T-A2538
[Sapphische Ode]
(15) Magelone Romanzen, Op. 33 (Tieck)
See—No. 9, Ruhe, Süssliebchen & No. 14,
Wie froh und frisch

Die Mainacht, Op. 43, No. 2 (Hölty & Voss)
  Alexander Kipnis (bs) & Gerald Moore,
  in Brahms Song Society, Vol. I: VM-522
  Marian Anderson (c) & Kosti Vehanen
                              12"—V-14610
  [Schumann: Der Nussbaum]
  Lotte Lehmann (s) & Paul Ulanowsky
      (in CM-453)   12"—C-71980D
  [Sonntag & O liebliche Wangen]
  Heinrich Schlusnus (b) & Sebastian
  Peschko   10"—PD-62783
  [Am Sonntag Morgen & Der Gang zum
  Liebchen]
  In Italian: Anzelotti, G-AV48

(Die) Meere, Op. 20, No. 3 (Duo for So-
  prano & Alto)
  Irène & Nathalie Kedroff, with Nadia
  Boulanger   12"—G-DB5060
  [Klänge; Der Gang zum Liebchen & Die
  Schwestern]

Meine Liebe ist grün, Op. 63, No. 5 (Felix
  Schumann) ("Junge Lieder I")
  Alexander Kipnis (bs) & Ernst V. Wolff,
  in Brahms Song Society, Vol. II: VM-751
  Lotte Lehmann (s) & Erno Balogh (pf)
      (in VM-292)   10"—V-1733
  [Therese & Tod das ist die kühle Nacht]
  Julius Patzak (t) & Franz Rupp
                              10"—PD-25014
  [Sonntag & O wüsst' ich]

Mein Mädel hat einen Rosenmund (Deutsche
  Volkslieder No. 25)
  Alexander Kipnis (bs) & Ernst V. Wolff,
  in Brahms Society, Vol. II: VM-751
  Lotte Lehmann (s) & Erno Balogh
      (in VM-419)   10"—V-1857
  [Das Mädchen spricht & Die Botschaft]
  Walther Ludwig (t)   10"—G-EG3329
  [Anon: Drauss' ist alles]

Minnelied, Op. 71, No. 5 (Hölty & Voss)
  Heinrich Schlusnus (b)   10"—PD-90177
  [Ständchen]
  Karl Schmitt-Walter (b) & Ferdinand
  Leitner   10"—T-A2539
  [Ständchen]

(Die) Nachtigall, Op. 97, No. 1 (Köstlin)
  Elisabeth Schumann (s) & George
  Reeves   10"—V-1756
  [Der Jäger; Vergebliches Ständchen &
  Wiegenlied] (G-DA1417)
  Elena Gerhardt (s) & Conrad von Bos
                              12"—V-7793
  [Ständchen & Feldeinsamkeit]

Nicht mehr zu dir zu gehen, Op. 32, No. 2
  (Daumer)
  Marjorie Lawrence (s) & Ivor Newton
                              10"—D-M598
  [So willst du des Armen & Der Schmied]
  Margaret Klöse (a)   10"—G-DA4473
  [In dem Schatten meiner Locken]
  Heinrich Rehkemper (b)
  [Die Botschaft]   10"—PD-23148

O kühler Wald, Op. 72, No. 3 (Brentano)
  Alexander Kipnis (bs) & Ernst V. Wolff,
  in Brahms Song Society, Vol. II: VM-751
  Karl Erb (t) & Bruno Seidler-Winkler
  [O wüsst' ich doch]   10"—G-DA4429

O liebliche Wangen, Op. 47, No. 4 (Fleming)
  Lotte Lehmann (s) & Paul Ulanowsky
      (in CM-453)   12"—C-71980D
  [Sonntag & Die Mainacht]

O Tod, wie bitter bist du See: Ernste
  Gesänge No. 3

O wüsst' ich doch den Weg zurück, Op. 63,
  No. 8 (Groth)
  Alexander Kipnis (bs) & Gerald Moore,
  in Brahms Song Society, Vol. I: VM-522
  Karl Erb (t) & Bruno Seidler-Winkler
  [O kühler Wald]   10"—G-DA4429
  Irène Joachim (s) & Ludwig Bergmann
                              12"—G-L1055
  [Am Sonntag Morgen & Wie Melodien
  zieht es mir]
  Julius Patzak (t)   10"—PD-25014
  [Meine Liebe ist grün & Sonntag]
  —In English "O Golden Age of Innocence"
  Richard Tauber (t) & Percy Kahn
                              10"—P-R020530
  [Vergebliches Ständchen]

Regenlied (Walle Regen, walle nieder)
  Heinrich Schlusnus (b)   12"—PD-67538
  [Von ewiger Liebe]

Ruhe, Süssliebchen, im Schatten, Op. 33,
  No. 9 (Tieck)
  [Magelone Romanzen No. 9]
  Alexander Kipnis (bs) & Ernst V. Wolff,
  in Brahms Song Society, Vol. II: VM-751
  Heinrich Schlusnus (b)   12"—PD-35032
  [Wie bist du, meine Königin]

Sandmännchen (Volkskinderliedern No. 4)
  Eng. Little Sandman, or Little Dustman
  Elisabeth Schumann (s) & Gerald Moore
                              10"—G-DA1526
  [Schubert: Hark, Hark the Lark]
  Alexander Kipnis (bs) & Ernst V. Wolff,
  in Brahms Song Society, Vol. II: VM-751
  DUPLICATION: Betty Martin (in Eng-
  lish), in C-J17

—Arr. Chorus
  St. Thomas, Leipzig, Cho.—Straube
  [In stiller Nacht]   10"—PD-90158
  Arr. Instrumental Ensemble: V-22160

Sapphische Ode, Op. 94, No. 4 (Schmidt)
  Kerstin Thorborg (c) & Leo Rosenek
                              12"—G-DB5766
  [Wolf: Gesang Weylas & Schubert: Hark,
  Hark the Lark]
  Aulikki Rautawaara (s) & F. Leitner
  [Mädchenlied]   10"—T-A2538
  Friedel Beckmann (ms) 10"—G-EG6846
  [Pfitzner: Ist der Himmel]
  Hulda Lashanska (s) & Orch
                              12"—V-7085
  [Wiegenlied & Bach: Komm süsser Tod]

(Der) Schmied, Op. 19, No. 4 (Uhland)
  Marjorie Lawrence (s) & Ivor Newton
                              10"—D-M598
  [So willst du des Armen & Nicht mehr zu
  dir zu gehen]
  DUPLICATION: Piroska Anday, RAD-
  RZ3011

Schöner Augen (Deutsche Volkslieder No.
  39)

—Arr. Chorus
  Berlin Chamber Cho.—Kreis
    [In stiller Nacht]   10"—C-DZ18
(Die) Schnur, die Perl' an Perle, Op. 57, No. 7
  Marian Anderson (a) & Franz Rupp
    (in VM-986) 10"—V-10-1123
    [Spross: Will o' the Wisp]
(Die) Schwestern, Op. 61, No. 1 (Mörike)
  (Duo for Soprano & Alto)
  Mmes. de Polignac & Irène Kedroff with
  Nadia Boulanger   12"—G-DB5060
    [Der Gang zum Liebchen; Klänge & Die Meere]
  Victoria Anderson, Viola Morris (in English) with Hubert Foss
    (in CM-234) 10"—C-DB1233
    [Auf dem Schiffe & Schumann: An den Abendstern & Du bist wie eine Blume]
    (in Col. History of Music, Vol. 4)
Serenade See: Ständchen, Op. 106, No. 1
(Ein) Sonett, Op. 14, No. 4 (Thibaut of Navarre, trans. Herder)
  Alexander Kipnis (bs) & Gerald Moore, in Brahms Song Society, Vol. I: VM-522
Sonntag, Op. 47, No. 3 (Folksong Text: aus Uhlands Volksliedern)
  Alexander Kipnis (bs) & Gerald Moore, in Brahms Song Society, Vol. I: VM-522
  Lotte Lehmann (s) & Paul Ulanowsky
    (in CM-453) 12"—C-71980D
    [O liebliche Wangen & Die Mainacht]
  Julius Patzak (t)   10"—PD-25014
    [Meine Liebe ist grün & O wüsst' ich doch]
So Willst du des Armen, Op. 33, No. 5
  Marjorie Lawrence (s) & Ivor Newton
                 10"—D-M598
    [Der Schmied & Nicht mehr zu dir zu Gehen]
Ständchen, Op. 106, No. 1 (Kugler) Eng. Serenade
  ("Der Mond steht über dem Berge")
  Alexander Kipnis (bs) & Gerald Moore, in Brahms Song Society, Vol. I: VM-522
  Lotte Lehmann (s) & Paul Ulanowsky
    [Wiegenlied]   10"—C-17300D
  Elena Gerhardt (s) & Conrad von Bos
                 12"—V-7793
    [Die Nachtigall & Feldeinsamkeit]
  Karl Schmitt-Walter (b) & Ferdinand Leitner   10"—T-A2539
    [Minnelied]
  Heinrich Schlusnus (b) & Franz Rupp
              10"—PD-90177
    [Minnelied]
  Leo Slezak (t)   10"—PD-21692
    [Hildach: Der Lenz]
Tambourliedchen, Op. 69, No. 5 (Candidus)
  Heinrich Schlusnus (b) 10"—PD-30004
    [Wenn du nur zuweilen lächelst & An die Tauben]
Therese, Op. 86, No. 1 (Keller)
  Lotte Lehmann (s) & Erno Balogh
    (in VM-292) 10"—V-1733
    [Meine Liebe ist grün & Der Tod, das ist die Kühle Nacht]
  Elena Gerhardt (ms) & Gerald Moore
    (Private recording—HMV)

Der Tod, das ist die kühle Nacht, Op. 96, No. 1 (Heine)
  Elisabeth Schumann (s) & Gerald Moore
             10"—G-DA1525
    [Schubert: An die Musik]
  Lotte Lehmann (s) & Erno Balogh
    (in VM-292) 10"—V-1733
    [Meine Liebe ist grün & Therese]
  Josef von Manawarda (b)
    [Auf dem Kirchhofe] 10"—PD-23158
  Elena Gerhardt (ms) & Gerald Moore
    (Private recording—HMV)
Der Ueberläufer, Op. 48, No. 2
  Alexander Kipnis (bs) & Ernst V. Wolff, in Brahms Song Society, Vol. II: VM-751
Vergebliches Ständchen, Op. 84, No. 4 (Zuccalmaglio) It. Serenata inutile
  Elisabeth Schumann (s) & George Reeves (G-DA1417) 10"—V-1756
    [Der Jäger; Die Nachtigall & Wiegenlied]
  Alexander Kipnis (bs) & Gerald Moore, in Brahms Song Society, Vol. I: VM-522
  Richard Tauber (t), (in English) & Percy Kahn   10"—P-RO20530
    [O wüsst' ich doch den weg zurück]
Verrath, Op. 105, No. 5 (Lemcke)
  Alexander Kipnis (bs) & Gerald Moore, in Brahms Song Society, Vol. I: VM-522
Von Ewiger Liebe, Op. 43, No. 1 (Slavonic Folksong Text)
  Alexander Kipnis (bs) & Gerald Moore, in Brahms Song Society, Vol. I: VM-522
  Heinrich Schlusnus (b) 12"—PD-67538
    [Regenlied]
  Tiana Lemnitz (s)   12"—G-DB5540
    [Immer leiser]
—In French "Amours éternelles" (trans. M. Kufferath)
  Pierre de Seyguières (b) & Yvonne Vallier   12"—C-DFX220
    [Fauré: Chant d'automne]
Vor dem Fenster, Op. 14, No. 1 (Folksong Text)
  Alexander Kipnis (bs) & Ernst V. Wolff, in Brahms Song Society, Vol. II: VM-751
Waltz in A flat (Vocal arr. by Moreno)
  See: Waltzes, Op. 39, No. 5
Ein Wanderer, Op. 106, No. 5
  Alexander Kipnis (bs) & Ernst V. Wolff, in Brahms Song Society, Vol. II: VM-751
Wenn du nur zuweilen lächelst, Op. 57, No. 2 (Daumer)
  Heinrich Schlusnus (b)
             10"—PD-30004
    [An die Tauben & Tambourliedchen]
Wenn ich mit Menschen See: Ernste Gesänge No. 4
Wie bist du, meine Königin? Op. 32, No. 9 (Daumer)
  Lotte Lehmann (s) & Paul Ulanowsky
    (in CM-453) 10"—C-17438D
    [Wir Wandelten]
  Heinrich Schlusnus (b) 12"—PD-35032
    [Ruhe, Süssliebchen]
  Gerhard Hüsch (b) & Hans Udo Müller
    [Feldeinsamkeit] 10"—G-EG3308
    [Hildach: Wo du hingehst, on G-EG6779]
  Emmi Leisner (c) & Berlin State Opera Orch—Melichar   12"—PD-27326
    [R. Strauss: Wiegenlied]

Wiegenlied, Op. 49, No. 4 (Folksong Text)
("Guten Aben, gut' Nacht")
Alexander Kipnis (bs) & Ernst V. Wolff,
in Brahms Song Society, Vol. II: VM-751
Elisabeth Schumann (s) & George Reeves
(G-DA1417)   10"—V-1756
[Der Jäger; Die Nachtigall; Vergebliches
Ständchen]
Lotte Lehmann (s) & Paul Ulanowsky
[Ständchen]   10"—C-17300D
Elisabeth Schumann (s) & Orch. acc.
[Immer leiser]   10"—G-DA1562
Beniamino Gigli (t) & Orch.—Oliveri
[Schubert: Ständchen] 10"—G-DA1657
Ria Ginster (s) & Paul Baumgartner
                      10"—G-DA6011
[Schumann: An die Sonnenschein]
DUPLICATIONS: Wolfgang Kieling
(treble), G-EG6488; Franz Völker, PD-
23084; Hulda Lashanska with cho.,
V-7085; Erna Sack, T-A2257; Erna
Berger, PD-47068; Giana Pederzini,
G-DA5426.
—In English
Helen Traubel (s)   12"—C-71872D
[Fraser-Simpson: Vespers]
Blanche Thebom (ms) 10"—V-10-1173
[Reger: Mariaewiegenlied]
—Instrumental versions
—Arr. Orch.
Boston Pops Orch.—Fiedler
                      10"—V-4435
[Waltz in A flat & Strauss: Perpetuum
mobile]
[Waltz in A flat & Cadman: At Dawning,
on G-B8599]
—Arr. Piano
Alfred Cortot   10"—V-1271
[Albéniz: Sous le palmier]
Artur Rubinstein
  (in VM-1149†)   12"—V-11-9731
[Schumann:Widmung]
[Schumann: Widmung & Träumerei, on
G-DB6532]
Arr. Instrumental Ensemble, on
V-22160

Wie Melodien zieht es mir, Op. 105, No. 1
(Groth)
Alexander Kipnis (bs) & Ernst V. Wolff,
Brahms Song Society, Vol. II: VM-751
Irène Joachim (s) & Ludwig Bergmann
                      12"—G-L1055
[Am Sonntag Morgen & O wüsst ich doch
den Weg zurück]

Wir Wandelten, Op. 96, No. 2 (Daumer)
Alexander Kipnis (bs) & Ernst V. Wolff,
Brahms Song Society, Vol. II: VM-751
Lotte Lehmann (s) & Paul Ulanowsky
      (in CM-453)   10"—C-17438D
[Die bist du, meine Königin]

Zigeunerlieder, Op. 103
(See also original version for vocal en-
semble under Z)
(1st seven and No. 11 of original eleven)
Lotte Lehmann (s) & Paul Ulanowsky
      2   10"—VM-1180†
Nancy Evans (a) & M. Foggin (pf)
[An die Nachtigall] 2   12"—D-X165/6

Walter Ludwig (t) & Ferdinand Leitner
      2   10"—PD-47310/1
Elena Gerhardt (ms) & Gerald Moore
(Private recording—HMV)

SYMPHONIES Orchestra
No. 1, C minor, Op. 68
  NBC Symphony—Toscanini
      5   12"—VM-875†
  (G-BD6124/8 in GM-376†)
  Philharmonic-Symphony Orch. of N. Y.—
  Rodzinski   5   12"—CM-621†
  Vienna Philharmonic Orch.—Walter
      5   12"—VM-470†
  (G-DB3277/81 in GM-288†)
  London Symphony Orch.—Weingartner
  (C-LX833/7†)   5   12"—CM-383†
  (C-GQX10594/8)
  Philadelphia Orch.—Stokowski
  (G-DB2874/8†)   5   12"—VM-301†
  Hollywood Bowl Orch.—Stokowski
  (Plastic discs)   5   12"—V-V4†
  Berlin Philharmonic Orch.—Abendroth
      6   12"—O-09122/7
  Berlin Philharmonic Orch.—Jochum
      5   12"—T-E2703/7
  Amsterdam Concertgebouw Orch.—van
  Beinum 5   12"—(in prep.) Dutch Decca
—3rd Mvt. only
  Amsterdam Concertgebouw Orch.—
  Mengelberg   12"—C-LWX247
  [Akademisches Festouvertüre, Pt. 3]
  (C-GQX10300)
—4th Movement (Abridged version)
  Victor Symphony Orch.—O'Connell, in
  V-G15
No. 2, D minor, Op. 73
  San Francisco Symphony—Monteux   ..
      4   12"—VM-1065†
  Philadelphia Orch.—Ormandy
      6   12"—VM-694†
  N. Y. Philharmonic-Symphony Orch.
  Rodzinski   5   12"—CM-725†
  N. Y. Philharmonic-Symphony Orch.—
  Barbirolli   5   12"—CM-412†
  London Symphony Orch.—Weingartner
  (C-LX899/903†)   5   12"—CM-493†
  London Philharmonic Orch.—Beecham
      5   12"—CM-265†
  (C-LX515/9†) (C-LWX124/8)
  Berlin Philharmonic Orch.—M. Fiedler
  (PD-516594/8)   5   12"—PD-95453/7
  [Trio, Op. 87—3rd Mvt., Bern Trio]
  Amsterdam Concertgebouw Orch.—
  Mengelberg   5   12"—T-SK3075/9
  Orch. of "Maggio Musicale"—Gui
      4   12"—CET-BB25171/4
  Danish State Broadcasting Symphony—
  Fritz Busch   4   12"—(in prep.) HMV
  Orch. of the Suisse Romande—
  Knappertsbusch
      5   12"—(in prep.) Swiss Decca
  Philadelphia Orch.—Stokowski
      6   12"—G-AW190/5
  New York Symphony Orch.—Damrosch
      5   12—C-GQX10849/53
No. 3. F major, Op. 90
  Philadelphia Orch.—Ormandy
      4   12"—CM-642†

Vienna Philharmonic Orch.—Walter
    4   12"—VM-341†
(G-DB2933/6 in GM-263†)
Boston Symphony—Koussevitzky
    4   12"—VM-1007†
London Philharmonic—Van Bienum
(D-K1488/52†)   5 12"—D-ED22†
London Philharmonic—Weingartner
    4   12"—CM-353†
(C-LX748/51†) (C-LFX563/6)
Chicago Symphony Orch.—Stock
    4   12"—CM-443†
Orch. of "Maggio Musicale"—Gui
    4 12"—CET-BB25163/6
Hamburg Philharmonic Orch.—Jochum
    4 12"—T-SK3024/7
Philadelphia Orch.—Stokowski
    5 12"—VM-42†
Amsterdam Concertgebouw Orch.—
Mengelberg   4 12"—C-GQX10688/91
No. 4, F minor, Op. 98
Boston Symphony—Koussevitzky
    5 12"—VM-730†
[Bach: Suite No. 2—Polonaise]
Saxon State Orch.—Böhm
(G-DB4684/9s)   6 12"—GM-342†
B. B. C. Symphony Orch.—Walter
    5 12"—VM-242†
(G-DB2253/7, in GM-218†)
Berlin Philharmonic—De Sabata
    6 12"—PD-67290/5s
[Chopin: Etude, Op. 10, No. 3, Brailow-sky, on CET-RR8000/5]
Philadelphia Orch.—Ormandy
    5 12"—CM-567†
Amsterdam Concertgebouw Orch.—
Mengelberg   5 12"—T-SK2772/7
London Symphony—Weingartner
(C-LX705/9)   5 12"—CM-335†
Berlin Philharmonic—M. Fiedler
    6 12"—PD-95356/61
[Quartet No. 2—3rd Mvt.—Buxbaum Quartet]
Lucerne Festival Orch.—Kletzki
    5 12"—C-LCX109/13
Leipzig Gewandhaus Orch.—Abendroth
    6 12"—O-9142/7
Tragische Ouvertüre, Op. 81 Orchestra
Eng. **Tragic Overture**
BBC Symphony—Toscanini
(in VM-507†)   2 12"—V-15386/7
[with Beethoven: Symphony No. 1, C major]
[Beethoven: Symphony No. 1—Minuet & Trio on G-DB3349/50]
Chicago Symphony—Stock
    2 12"—CX-214†
[Serenade No. 1—Minuet]
London Philharmonic—Beecham
    2 12"—CX-85†
[Mozart: Le Nozze di Figaro—Overture]
(C-LX638/9) (C-LFX502/3)
Amsterdam Concertgebouw Orch.—
Mengelberg 2 12"—T-SK3327/8

TRIOS—Violin, 'Cello, Piano

No. 1, B major, Op. 8
Jascha Heifetz, Emanuel Feuermann & Artur Rubinstein   4 12"—VM-883†

Elly Ney Trio   4 12"—PD-27316/9
No. 2, C major, Op. 87
Yelly D'Aranyi, Gaspar Cassadó & Myra Hess   4 12"—CM-266†
(C-LWX119/22)
Bern Trio   4 12"—PD-95286/9
[Mozart: Trio No. 8, G major, K. 564—Andante only]
A. Poltronieri, A. Bonucci & A. Casella
    3 12"—C-GQX10523/5
Santoloquido Trio 4 12"—PD-67670/3
—3rd Mvt. only
Bern Trio   12"—PD-95457
[Symphony No. 2, Pt. 9]
No. 3, C minor, Op. 101
Trieste Trio   3 12"—G-C3624/6†
Budapest Trio   3 12"—D-K828/30
(PD-516702/4)

TRIO—Clarinet, 'Cello, Piano, A minor, Op. 114

Reginald Kell, Anthony Pini & Louis Kentner   3 12"—C-DX1007/9†

TRIO—Violin, Horn, Piano, E flat major, Op. 40

Adolf Busch, Aubrey Brain & Rudolf Serkin   4 12"—VM-199†
(G-DB105/8 in GM-201†)
Ungarische Tänze See: Hungarian Dances

VARIATIONS

Variations on a Theme of Haydn, Op. 56a ("St. Antoni Chorale") Orchestra
N. Y. Philharmonic-Symphony Orch.—Toscanini   2 12"—VM-355†
(G-DB3031/2)
Minneapolis Symphony—Mitropoulos
    2 12"—CX-225†
London Philharmonic—Weingartner
(C-LX744/5)   2 12"—CX-125†
Hallé Orch.—Sargent
    2 12"—C-DX1105/6
Queen's Hall Orch.—Wood
(PD-516726/7)   2 12"—D-K763/4
Variations on a Theme of Haydn, Op. 56b 2 Pianos
Ethel Bartlett & Rae Robertson
    2 12"—CX-181†
Pierre Luboshutz & Genia Nemenoff
    2 12"—VM-799†
Variations & Fugue on a Theme on Handel, Op. 24 Piano
(This theme is the Aria in B flat major from Handel's Harpsichord Suite No. 1)
Solomon   3 12"—G-C3301/3†
Egon Petri   3 12"—CM-345†
Winfried Wolf 3 12"—G-DB5529/31
Variations on a Theme of Paganini, Op. 35 Piano
(The theme is Paganini's Caprice No. 24, A minor, for unacc. violin)
Egon Petri   2 12"—CX-80†
(C-LX628/9)
Aline van Barentzen
    2 12"—G-DB5181/2
Anna Antoniades 2 12"—PD-57094/5
Jacob Gimpel   2 12"—VOX-209

Moura Lympany (Book II only)
12"—G-C3697

Vier ernste Gesänge—See: Songs—Ernste Gesänge

Volkslieder See: Deutsche Volkslieder

WALTZES

Liebeslieder Waltzes, Op. 52 Vocal Quartet & Piano (4 Hands)
J. de Polignac, I. Kedroff, H. Cuenod, D. Conrad with Dinu Lipatti & Nadia Boulanger (pf) 3 12"—G-DB5057/9
Victor Chorale (12 voices) with Luboshutz & Nemenoff (2 Pfs.)—
Robert Shaw 3 12"—VM-1076†

—Arr. Orch. Friedrich Hermann
NBC String Symphony—Black
(in VM-455†) 3 12"—V-12229/31
[Sibelius: Rakastava, Pt. 1]

(16) Waltzes, Op. 39 Piano (4 Hands)
—Nos. 1, 2, 5, 6, 10, 14, 15 only
Nadia Boulanger & Dinu Lapatti
12"—G-DB5061

—Nos. 1, 2, 11, 14, 16 only
Vronsky & Babin 10"—C-17407D
—Arr. Piano solo

Complete recording
Wilhelm Backhaus
(in VM-321) 2 12"—V-14131/2
[Intermezzo No. 6, E major, Op. 116, No. 4]
Anatole Kitain 3 12"—CM-342†
(C-DX859/61)
[Ballade "Edward" D minor, Op. 10, No. 1]

—Nos. 1, 2, 4, 5, 6, 11, 14, 15 only
Walter Rehberg 10"—PD-25192

—No. 1
Galina Wershenskya (pf. solo)
12"—G-Z249
[Beethoven: Farewell to the piano; Schubert: Waltz, Op. 9a]

—(3) Waltzes (unidentified)
Stell Anderson 12"—PD-516782
[Intermezzo No. 10]

—Nos. 2 & 15
Dirk Schäfer (pf. solo) 12"—C-DHX15
Leo Nadelmann (pf. solo)
10"—G-DA6018

—No. 5 Arr. Violin & Piano
Siegfried Borries & pf. acc.
10"—G-DA4471
[Tchaikovsky: Romance, Op. 5]

—No. 15, A flat major

(This waltz, the most popular of the set—often labeled merely "Brahms Waltz" or "Brahms Waltz No. 15"—is often transcribed into A major, particularly in violin transcriptions.)

Elly Ney 10"—G-DA4438
[Intermezzo No. 1 & Romance No. 5]
France Ellegaard 10"—PD-62833

[Fauré: Romance sans paroles, Op. 17, No. 3]
Oscar Levant 12"—C-72372D
[Intermezzo No. 13 & Schumann: Träumerei]

—Arr. Violin
Ida Haendel (vl) & Adela Kolowska (pf)
10"—D-M495
[Dvořák-Kreisler: Slavonic Dance No. 2, E minor]
Erica Morini (vl) & M. Raucheisen (pf)
12"—PD-67023
[Hungarian Dance No. 8]
Fritz Kreisler (vl) & Franz Rupp (pf)
10"—G-DA1631
[Chopin: Mazurka No. 45, A minor, Op. 67, No. 4]
DUPLICATIONS: Jacques Thibaud, G-DA866; Bronislaw Hubermann, C-LX107: C-GQX10302; René Benedetti, C-D13037; L. Cesano, PAT-PA495; E. Telmanyi, TONO-A101; A-107; Mazzacurati (vlc) CET-CC220

—Arr. Orchestra
Boston "Pops" Orch.—Fiedler
10"—V-4435
[Wiegenlied & Strauss: Perpetuum mobile]
[Wiegenlied & Cadman: At Dawning on G-B8599]
Andre Kostelanetz & Orch.
12"—C-71491D
[Gershwin: Porgy & Bess—Summertime, with Lily Pons]
Salon Trio, ESTA-D2008

—Vocal Arrangement
Ninon Vallin (In French) & P. Darck (pf) 10"—O-281277
[Hungarian Dance No. 4, vocal arr.]

Misc. Waltzes   Arr. Orchestra

No. 1, 2, 9
Victor Orch. (in "Rhythms for children") 10"—V-20162

No. 5, 11
Victor Orch.—Reibold (in Brahms Medley) 10"—V-24799

Unspecified group of Waltzes
Symphony Orch.—Goehr 12"—G-C3011

Zigeunerlieder, Op. 103 Vocal Quartet & Piano
(See also under Songs for arr. for Solo voice & Piano)
(All 11 Songs in original version)
Madrigal Singers—Lehmann Engel
(D. Everett Roudebush, pf.)
2 12"—CX-88

BRASART, Johannes (early 15th Century)
A Flemish priest and one of the outstanding composers of the 15th century, ranking with Dufay, Dunstable and Binchois. He wrote many motets in 3 and 4 voices.

O Flos Flagrans Motet in Latin
Lina Dauby (c) & Trio of Medieval Viols (in Vol. III) 12"—AS-27
[Instrumental music of 16th century]

BRETON, Tomas (1850-1923)

An outstanding composer of "zarzuelas," Breton also attempted to help found a Spanish school of opera. There are probably other recordings listed in Spanish catalogues.

(LA) DOLORES   Opera in 3 Acts
In Spanish
Jota   Soloists, Chorus & Orchestra
—Arr. Orchestra
     Madrid Symphony—Arbós
          (in CM-331†)   12"—C-69201D
Madrigal: Henchido de amor santo   Tenor
     Miguel Fleta   12"—G-DB1483
     [Freire: Ay ay ay]

En la Alhambra—Serenata   Orchestra
     Madrid Symphony—Arbós
          (in CM-146†)   12"—C-67819D
Las Escenas Andaluzas—Polo Gitano
Orchestra
     Madrid Symphony—Arbós
          (in CM-146†)   12"—C-67820D
     [Albéniz: Pepita Jimenez—Intermezzo]

BREVILLE, Pierre de (1861-   )

A French critic and composer in all forms, Bréville is best known for his art songs which are comparable to those of Chausson and Duparc.

SONGS   In French
Prières d'enfant
     Yves Tinayre (t)   10"—LUM-30022
     [Bach: Komm, süsser Tod]

BREVAL, Jean Baptiste (1756-1825)

A French composer and 'cellist, Bréval composed operas, symphonies and string quartets.

Sonata, G major   'Cello & Piano
     Bernard Michélin & Tasso Janopoulo
          2 12"—C-LFX691/2
     [Francoeur: Sonata, E major—Adagio
     & Allegro]

BRIDGE, Frank (1879-1941)

A British viola-player and technically skilled composer who has written many works in the traditional idiom. He is best known in England.

(Two) Old English Songs
String Quartet, or String Orch.
Sally in Our Alley & Cherry Ripe
—Cherry Ripe only
     Prisca Quartet   10"—PD-10541
     [Grainger: Molly on the Shore]
—Sally in Our Alley only
     Boston "Pops" Orch.—Fiedler
          10"—V-4569
     [Foster-Shulman: Oh, Susannah!]
Phantasie in C minor
     Grinke Trio   2 12"—D-K945/6

SONGS
Come to me in my dreams (Matthew Arnold)
     John Charles Thomas (b) & Carol
     Hollister (pf)
          (in VM-966)   10"—V-10-1088
     [Tosti: Mattinata]
     Richard Tauber (t) & Percy Kahn (pf)
     [Ronald: Goodnight]   10"—P-RO20554

Love went a-riding
     Kirsten Flagstad (s) & Edwin
     McArthur (pf)   10"—V-2009
     [Drořák: Songs my mother taught me]
     Charles Kullman (t) & Fritz Kitzinger
     (pf)   10"—C-17242D
     [Rachmaninoff: In the silence of the
     night]
     Henry Wendon (t) & Gerald Moore (pf)
          10"—C-DB2083
     [Coleridge-Taylor: Elinor]
     DUPLICATION: Frank Titterton,
     D-F1648
Suite for String Orchestra
     Boyd Neel String Orch.—Neel
          3 12"—D-X250/2

BRITTEN, Benjamin (1913-   )

A controversial British composer who has succeeded in attracting attention and making a name for himself. Aware of the possibilities of contemporary modes of musical expression, he has written in all forms, including music for British films. His operas "Peter Grimes" and "The Rape of Lucretia" have met with outstanding success.

A Ceremony of Carols   Choir & Harp
Processional; Welcome Yule; There is no rose; That Yonge Child; Balulalow; As dew in Aprille; This little Babe; Interlude (Harp); In freezing winter night; Spring carol; Deo gratias; Recessional.
     Morriston Boys Choir—Ivor Sims, with
     Maria Korchinska (harp)
          3 12"—D-K1155/7
     [Kodalý: Ave Maria; Bartók: Enchanting song]
Hymn to St. Cecilia, Op. 27 (Auden)
     Fleet Street Choir—T. B. Lawrence
          2 12"—D-K1088/9
     [Holst: This have I done for my true love]
Introduction & Rondo alla Burlesca,
Op. 23, No. 1
Mazurka Elegiaca, Op. 23, No. 2
     Clifford Curzon & Benjamin Britten
     (2 Pfs.) (D-K1117/8) 2   12"—D-ED17†

PETER GRIMES   Opera
Four Sea Interludes   Orchestra
Dawn; Sunday morning; Moonlight; Storm
     London Symphony—Sargent
          2 12"—C-DX1441/2
     Amsterdam Concertgebouw Orch.—
     van Bienum   2 12"—D-K1702/3
Passacaglia
     Amsterdam Concertgebouw Orch.—
     van Beinum   12"—D-K1704
Serenade for Tenor, Horn & Strings, Op. 31
     Peter Pears (t), Dennis Brain (horn)
     & Boyd Neel String Orch.—Neel
     (D-K1151/3)   3 12"—D-ED7†
(7) Sonnets of Michelangelo   Voice & Piano
(Nos. XXIV; LV; XXXVIII; XXX; XVI; XXXII; XXXI)
     Peter Pears (t) & Benjamin Britten (pf)
          12" & 10"—G-C3312 & G-B9302

Simple Symphony

Boyd Neel String Orch.—Neel
3 12″—D-X245/7
[Bach: Fugue in A minor]

String Quartet No. 2, C major, Op. 36

Zorian String Quartet 4 12″—G-C3536/9
[Purcell: Fantasia on one note]

Variations on a Theme of Frank Bridge, Op. 10

Boyd Neel String Orch.—Neel
3 12″—D-X226/8

Village Harvest Music for the film

Irish Reel

Charles Brill Orch.   12″—D-K874
[Rossini-Britten: Soirées musicales, Pt. 3 —Tarantella]

Young Person's Guide to the Orchestra
Music for the educational film
(Variations and Fugue on a Theme of Purcell)

Liverpool Philharmonic—Sargent
3 12″—CM-702†
[Bach: Suite No. 3—Air]
(C-DX1307/9S†—last side blank)

ARRANGEMENTS

Soirées Musicales (from Rossini)

March; Canzonetta; Tyrolese; Bolero; Tarantella

Charles Brill Orch.   2 12″—D-K873/4
[Village Harvest—Irish reel]

Folk Songs (arrangements)

La Belle est au Jardin d'amour; Le Roi s'en va-t-en Chasse

Sophie Wyss (s) & B. Britten (pf)
10″—D-M568

The Foggy Dew; The Ploughboy; Come ye not from Newcastle?

Peter Pears (t) & B. Britten (pf)
10″—G-DA1873

Little Sir Williams; Oliver Cromwell

Peter Pears (t) & B. Britten (pf)
10″—D-M555
[Trad: The Sally gardens]

The Bonny Earl O'Moray; Heigh Ho! Heigh Hi!

Peter Pears (t) & B. Britten (pf)
10″—D-M594

BRIXI, Frantisek Xavier (1732-1771)

A Czechoslovakian composer of choral works, including masses, oratorios, requiems and litanies.

Pastoral Motet In Czech

Chorus & Ultraphon Orch.—
Smetacek   12″—U-G14019
[Linek: Pastorella]

BROLO, Bartolomeus (14th Century)

An early Italian composer of polyphonic music.

O celestial lume Song

(Modern notation by Stainer, in "Early Bodleian Music")
Max Meili (t) & Fr. Seidersbeck (viol)
(in Vol. I.) 12″—AS-1
(Anon: Lauda de Noël; Vincenzo da da Rimini; Ita se n'era; Giovanni da Cascia; Io son un pellegrin

BRUCH, Max (1838-1920)

A German romantic composer who was known chiefly during his day by his large choral works. Today he is remembered by various works for the violin.

CONCERTOS   Violin & Orchestra

No. 1, G minor, Op. 26

Yehudi Menuhin & San Francisco
Symphony—Monteux 3 12″—VM-1023†
Yehudi Menuhin & London Symphony
—Ronald   3 12″—G-DB1611/3†
Alfredo Campoli & Symphony Orch.
—Goehr   3 12″—C-DX807/9†
(C-DWX1604/6)   (C-GQX11039/41)
Nathan Millstein & Philharmonic-Symphony of N. Y.—Rodzinski
3 12″—CM-517†
Georg Kulenkampff & Berlin Philharmonic—Keilberth 3 12″—T-SK8172/4
Georg Kulenkampff & Zürich Tonhalle
Orch.—Schuricht   3 12″—D-K1603/5
H. Stanske & Berlin State Opera Orch.
Schuricht   3 12″—CET-RR8058/60

—2nd Mvt. (Adagio) only

Georg Kulenkampff & Berlin Philharmonic—Kempen   12″—T-E1492
L. Zimmermann & Pf. acc.
12″—C-DHX29

Jubliate Choir & Orchestra

Aachen Cathedral Choir & Prussian
State Orch.—Rehmann
[Brahms: Nänie, Pt. 3] 12″—G-DB7655

Kol Nidre, Op. 47 'Cello & Orchestra

Pablo Casals & London Symphony
—Ronald   2 12″—VM-680†
[Haydn: Minuet in C major, arr. Piatti]

—Arr. Violin & Piano

Bronislaw Hubermann & S. Schultze
[Schubert: Ave Maria] 12″—C-LFX314
(C-GQX10522)

Scottish Fantasy, Op. 46 Violin, Harp & Orchestra

Jascha Heifetz, Stanley Chaloupka &
Victor Symphony Orch.—Steinberg
3 12″—VM-1183†
(Also V-VII plastic pressing)

Ulysses, Op. 41 (Odysseus) Chorus & Orchestra

Prelude Orchestra

EIAR Orch.—Schuricht
[Zandonai: Trescone]   12″—CET-BB25091

BRUCK, Arnold von (early 16th century)

A composer of the early German lied and many choral works.

Aus tiefer Not 4-pt. Cho. in German

(from "Newe deudsche Geistliche
Gesenge" 1544)
Berlin State Academy Cho.—Kalt
10″—P-R1020
[Finck: Christ ist erstanden]
(in "2000 Years of Music" album)

BRUCKNER, Anton (1824-1896)

Ave Maria Chorus in Latin
Dresdner Kreuzchor-Mauersberger
10"—G-EG3568
[Isaac: Innsbruck, ich muss dich lassen]
Strasbourg Cathedral Choir—Hoch
12"—C-DFX71
[Josquin des Prés: Tu pauperum refugium]
Christus factus est Chorus in Latin
Paderborn Cathedral Cho.—Schaurte
12"—PD-27137
[Eberlin: Tenebrae factae sunt]
Herbstlied Chorus
Aachen Cathedral Choir
10"—G-EG6530
[Reger: Im Himmelreich ein Haus steht —Regensburger Domchor]
Locus iste (Graduale) Chorus in Latin
Regensburger Domchor-Schrems
10"—G-EG3903
[Liszt: Ave Maria]

MASSES

No. 2, E minor In Latin
Aachen Cathedral Choir, with Wind players of the Berlin State Opera Orch.
—Rehmann 6 12"—VM-596†
Hamburg State Opera Chorus & Orch.
—Thurn 5 12"—T-E2607/11
[Gloria slightly cut]
Os justi (Graduale) Chorus in Latin
Dresdner Kreuzchor-Mauersberger
[Virga Jesse] 10"—PD-10281
Overture in G minor
Queen's Hall Orch.—Wood
2 12"—D-X192/3
[Glinka: Russlan and Ludmilla—Overture]
Quintet in F major
Prisca String Quartet & S. Meincke (vla)
6 12"—PD-15165/70
[Haydn: Quartet, F major, Op. 3, No. 5—Serenade]
(D-X220/5) (CET-OR5117/22)
Strub Quartet & Münch-Holland (vla)
5 12"—G-DB5541/5

SYMPHONIES Orchestra

No. 4, E flat major ("Romantic") 1874
Saxon State Orch.—Böhm
(G-DB4450/7) 8 12"—VM-331†
Hamburg Philharmonic—Jochum
8 12"—T-SK3032/9
No. 5, B flat major 1876
Saxon State Orch.—Böhm
9 12"—G-DB4486/94
Hamburg Philharmonic—Jochum
9 12"—T-E2672/80
No. 7, E major 1883
Amsterdam Concertgebouw Orch.—van Beinum
8 12"—Dutch Decca (in prep.)

Vienna Philharmonic—Jochum
8 12"—T-SK3000/7
Berlin Philharmonic—Schuricht
8 12"—PD-67195/202
[Reger: Toccata in D minor: A. Sittard, organ]
Munich Philharmonic—Kabasta
8 12"—G-DB7684/91
—2nd Mvt. (Adagio) only
Berlin Philharmonic—Furtwängler
3 12"—T-SK3230/2
No. 9, D minor 1894
Munich Philharmonic—von Hausegger
(G-DB4515/21) 7 12"—VM-627†
Tota pulchra es Maria (Antiphon)
Tenor, Cho. & Organ in Latin
Munich Cathedral Cho.—Berberich
12"—PD-27119
[Anon: Klagelied des Propheten]
Virga Jesse floruit (Graduale)
Chorus in Latin
William Faure Kammerchor—Faure
[Anon: Transeamus] 10"—T-A10046
Dresdner Kreuzchor—Mauersberger
[Os justi] 10"—PD-10281

BRUMEL, Antoine (c.1480-c.1520)

A pupil of Ockeghem, Brumel was noted as being adept at writing in the canonic forms of the French-Flemish counterpoint.

Sicut Lilium Motet in Latin
La Manécanterie des Petits Chanteurs à la Croix de Bois 10"—G-K8108
[French Folk Song: Complainte de Notre Dame]
Mass "De beata Virgine" a Cappella in Latin
Vocal ensemble—Marcel Couraud
(DF-51/5) 5 12"—DF-A11

BRUNEAU, Alfred (1857-1934)

Synthesizing "verismo" and Wagnerianism, Bruneau wrote a number of operas based upon his friend, Zola's social novels.

OPERAS In French

(L') ATTAQUE DU MOULIN, Op. 22
4 Acts 1893
Les Adieux à la forêt Tenor
Georges Thill & Orch.—Bruneau
12"—C-LFX38
[Massenet: Sapho—Ah! qu'il est loin, mon pays]

BULL, Dr. John (1563-1628)

Probably the most outstanding member of the English virginal school, Bull himself was a virtuoso on the instrument. He took his musical doctorate at Dublin University.

Gigge: **"Dr. Bull's Myselfe"** Harpsichord
[Fitzwilliam Virginal Book No. 189]
George Dyson (pf) 12"—C-D40139
[in Illustrations for a Lecture on "Early Keyboard Music:" International Educational Society]

The King's Hunt Harpsichord (Virginals)
(*The two recorded performances below vary somewhat. The Dyson version is labelled "King's Hunting Jigg" and the Dolmetsch version is labelled "Variations on the King's Hunt"*)
George Dyson 12"—C-D40139
[in Illustrations for a lecture on "Early Keyboard Music:" International Educational Society]
Rudolph Dolmetsch 10"—C-5713
[Farnaby: His Toye, His Dreame, His Rest]
(in Columbia History of Music, Vol. I: CM-231)
—**Arr. Harp** Grandjany
Marcel Grandjany 10"—V-2095
[Trad: Le Petit Roi d'Yvetot & Et Ron ron ron, petit patapon]
—**Arr. 2 Pianos** Bartlett
Bartlett & Robertson
(in CX-256) 12"—C-72128D
(C-DX1341)
[Farnaby: His dreame; Tower Hill Jigge; Tune for Two Virginals; Peerson: The fall of the leafe]

BULL, Ole (1810-1880)

A Norwegian violinist profoundly influenced by Paganini, Bull played principally his own bravura compositions for the instrument. Very few, if any, have survived.

Saeterjentens Södag Song in Norwegian
Eng. The herd girl's Sunday
—**Arr. Chorus** Gilbert
Jenny Lind Chorus of the Augustana Choir, V-2052
—**Arr. Violin**
H. Fritz-Crone, G-X1658; Johan Nilsson, G-X2367
—**Arr. Orchestra** Svendsen
Göteborg Symphony Orch.—Tor Mann
12"—G-Z205
[Södermann: Jungfrau av Orleans—Overture]
[Svendsen: Festpolonais, on G-Z209]

BUONONCINI, Giovanni Battista (1672-1750)

An Italian composer, associated with Ariosti in London, who listed many sacred, secular and dramatic pieces among his works. His music has been greatly obscured by that of his contemporary, Handel.

Lungi da te
Roland Hayes (t) & R. Boardman (pf)
(in CM-393) 10"—C-17174D
[Monteverdi: Maledetto & Galuppi: Eviva Rosa Bella]
Pupille nere Song in Italian
Ezio Pinza (bs) & Fritz Kitzinger (pf)
(in VM-766) 12"—V-17916
[Sarti: Lungi dal caro bene & Giordani: Caro mio ben; Falconieri: O bellissimi capelli]
Vado ben spesso Cantata
Gaston Micheletti (t) & String Orch.—Curt Sachs (in Vol. VII) 12"—AS-64
[Rossi: Mitrane—Ah! rendimi]

BURIAN, Emil František (1904-)

An ardent modernist who has composed in all forms. A man of diverse talents, he works in many capacities in the production of his own and other modern works.

String Quartet No. 3
Czechoslovak String Quartet
2 12"—U-G14444/5
Sonata Romantica Violin & Piano
Josef Peska & Jan H. Tichy
2 12"—U-G14484/5

BURKHARD, Willy

A teacher of piano and composition at the Bern Conservatory, Burkhard is a Swiss composer of choral, chamber, symphonic and keyboard music.

Herbst, Op. 36 Cantata—Soprano, Violin, 'Cello & Piano
E. Scherz-Meister with trio
2 12"—ELITE-7018/9
String Quartet No. 2 (in one movement) 1943
Stefi Geyer Quartet 2 12"—C-LZX11/2

BURLEIGH, Harry Thacker (1866-)

An American composer and arranger of Negro spirituals, Burleigh was a friend of Dvořák and MacDowell. He is a well-known choir leader and has been connected with choirs in New York churches for many years.

Arrangements of Negro Spirituals
Balm in Gilead
Paul Robeson (bs) & pf. acc.
(in CM-610) 10"—C-17467D
[Go down, Moses]
By n' By
Paul Robeson (bs) & pf. acc.
[Were you there?] 10"—G-B4480
[Also on C-17468D in CM-610]
Deep River
Marian Anderson (c) & Kosti Vehanen (pf) 10"—V-2032
[Dere's no hidin' place; Every time I feel the Spirit]
[I don't feel no ways tired, on G-DA1676]
Paul Robeson (bs) & pf. acc.
10"—G-B2619
[Arr. Brown: I'm goin' to tell]
Ezio Pinza (bs) & Gibner King (pf)
10"—C-17383D
[MacGimsey: Thunderin']
Nelson Eddy (b)
(in V-C27) 10"—V-4371
[Fox: The hills of home]
[Cadman: At Dawning, on G-DA1585]
Go down, Moses
Marian Anderson (c) & Kosti Vehanen (pf) 10"—V-1799
[Arr. Price: My soul's been anchored]
Paul Robeson (bs) & pf. acc.
10"—G-B3381
[I stood on the ribber & Peter, go ring]
[Also on C-17467D in CM-610]
Heav'n, Heav'n (I got a robe)
Marian Anderson (c) & Kosti Vehanen (pf) 12"—V-8958
[Hayes: Lord, I can't stay away & Johnson: City called Heaven]

I don't feel no-ways tired
Marian Anderson (a) & Kosti Vehanen
(pf)   10"—G-DA1676
[Deep river]
I stood on de ribber
Paul Robeson (bs) & pf. acc.
                         10"—G-B3381
[Peter, go ring & Go down, Moses]
Peter, go ring dem bells
Paul Robeson (bs) & pf. acc.
                         10"—G-B3381
[I stood on de ribber; Go down, Moses]
Were you there?
Marian Anderson (a) & Kosti Vehanen
(pf) (G-DA1670)   10"—V-1966
[I can't stay away, arr. Hayes]
Paul Robeson (bs) & pf. acc.
[By n' By]   10"—G-B4480

BUS, Gervaise du

*An early Swiss polyphonist, Gervais du Bus
(or du Bos) was a composer of the period between the Ars Antiqua and the Ars Nova.*

Motet from Roman de Fauvel 3 Voices
Mme. Bonte, Demiau, Rousselon
            (in Vol. X)   12"—AS-91
[Beginnings of Swiss Polyphony; 14th
Century music of the Juggler & Scholar]

BUSCA, Padre Ludovico (Italy, 17th century)

*A monk of Turin, Padre Busca was one of the
early Baroque composers who continued to use
the Italian madrigal.*

Occhi belli
Bionda, bionda Clori
Max Meili (t) & Ruggero Gerlin (harp-
sichord)   (in Vol. VIII) 12"—AS-79
[Frescobaldi: Voi partite & Miniscalchi:
Non passo & Io tento invan]

BUSONI, Ferruccio (1866-1924)

*An internationally famous pianist and exponent
of Liszt and Wagner during his lifetime, Busoni was also known as a teacher and editor.*

Duettino Concertante
[After the Finale of Mozart Piano Con-
certo No. 19, F major, K.459] 1919
Astrid & Hans Otto Schmidt-Nauhaus
                         12"—PD-57101
(7) Elegien Piano
—No. 5, Die Nächtlichen only
Claudio Arrau   10"—PD-90025
[Stravinsky: Petrouchka—Russian
dance]
Indianisches Tagebuch Piano
Egon Petri   12"—C-LWX204
Valzer danzato
EIAR Symphony Orch.—Previtali
         2 12"—CET-CB20165/6
[Pick-Mangiagalli: Il carillon magico—
Intermezzo]
Transcriptions for Piano
See under—
[Bach: Chorale Preludes; Clavier Con-
certo Nos. 1 & 5; Sonata No. 3 for Unacc.
Violin—Chaconne; Toccata, Adagio &
Fugue.]

BUSSER, (Paul) Henri (1872-   )
*A French organist, conductor and composer in
many forms. He is known outside of France
by his songs.*

Pièce de Concert Harp & Orchestra
Lily Laskine & Orch.—Prüwer
                         12"—G-L1030
SONGS In French
Notre Père qui êtes aux cieux
Jane Laval (s)   10"—C-DF593
[Salutation angélique]
Jean Planel (t)   10"—PAT-X93111
[Franck: Panis Angelicus]
David Devriès (t)   10"—O-188773
[Salutation angélique]
(La) Salutation angélique
Jane Laval (s)   10"—C-DF593
[Notre Père qui êtes]
David Devriès (t)   10"—O-188773
[Notre Père qui êtes]
Le Sommeil de l'enfant Jésus (Raffaeli)
Jane Laval (s)   12"—C-BFX3
[Fauré: Requiem—Pie Jesu]
ORCHESTRATIONS
See under Debussy: Petite Suite

**BUTTERWORTH, George Santon Kaye (1885-
1916)**

*A friend of Vaughan-Williams and a collector
of British folksongs and dances and who composed in the style of this music. He was killed
in World War I.*

(The) Banks of Green Willow Orchestra
Philharmonia Orch.—Miles
                         12"—G-C3491
(A) Shropshire Lad Rhapsody for Orchestra
Hallé Orch.—Boult   12"—G-C3287

SONGS

(A) Shropshire Lad (Housmann)
Roy Henderson (b) & Gerald Moore (pf)
                    2 10"—D-M506/7

BUXTEHUDE, Dietrich (1637-1707)
*One of the great baroque organists whose
works influenced Johann Sebastian Bach, Buxtehude is too frequently dismissed as a "fore-
runner" of Bach. His music shows great power
and originality.*

NOTE: *The vocal works as far as possible, are
identified by their numbers in the complete
Ugrino edition of which seven volumes have
appeared so far. The organ works are numbered according to the Spitta-Seiffert edition.*

CANTATAS for one or more solo voices
Aperite mihi portas justitiae
[Ugrino No. 71]
Elsa Sigfuss (a), Aksel Schiøtz (t), Hol-
ger Nørgaard (bs) with 2 vlns., vlc. &
harpsichord   12"—G-Z292
Jubilate Domino
[Ugrino No. 19]
Lina Falk (c) with Viola da gamba &
harpsichord   12"—LUM-32050
O Fröhliche Stunden
[Ugrino No. 12]
Ethel Luening (s) & Instrumental En-
semble   12"—MC-1009

Singet dem Herrn ein neues Lied
[Ugrino No. 16]
Ethel Luening (s) & Instrumental Ensemble 12"—MC-1008

Was mich auf dieser Welt betrübt
[Ugrino No. 17]
Aksel Schiøtz (t) with 2 vls., vlc. & harpsichord 12"—G-DB5240
[Bach: Weihnachts Oratorium—No. 15, Frohe Hirten, eilt!]

CANTATAS for mixed chorus

Befiehl dem Engel, dass er komm'
(Dan. Send hid din Engel)
Copenhagen Boys' and Men's Choir (in Danish) with String Quintet & Finn Viderø (org.)—Mogens Wöldike
(C-LWX169) 12"—C-DDX10

Canzonetta, G major
(Vol. I, No. 23)
Finn Viderø (Gaveau harpsichord)
[Toccata in G major] 10"—G-DA5227

Chaconne, E minor
(Vol. I, No. 3)
—Arr. Chavez
Symphony Orchestra of Mexico City—
Chávez (in VM-503†) 12"—V-12340

CHORALE FANTASIES Organ

Ich dank' dir, lieber Herre Gott
(Vol. II, Pt. 1, No. 3)
Friedrich Mihatsch (Gonzalez Organ)
12"—PAT-PAT70
[Pachelbel: Toccata in C & Durch Adams Fall]
(in 3 Centuries of Organ Music)

Wie schön leuchtet der Morgenstern
(Vol. II, Pt. 1, No. 10)
Carl Weinrich (Praetorius Organ, Princeton, N. J.), in MC-40

CHORALE PRELUDES Organ

Ach Herr, mich armen Sünder
(Vol. II, Pt. 2, No. 1)

Nun bitten wir den heiligen Geist

Nun komm der Heiden Heiland
(Vol. II, Pt. 2, No. 25)

Vater unser im Himmelreich
Finn Viderø (Grundtvigskirken organ)
12"—G-DB5260

Ein' feste Burg ist unser Gott
(Vol. II, Pt. 2, No. 5)
Carl Weinrich (Westminster Choir School Organ, Princeton, N. J.), in MC-9

Ich ruf' zu dir, Herr Jesu Christ
(Vol. II, Pt. 2, No. 15)
Carl Weinrich (Praetorius Organ, Princeton, N. J.) in MC-40

In dulci jubilo
(Vol. II, Pt. 2, No. 17)
Finn Viderø (Christiansborg Slotskirke Organ) 10"—G-DA5223
[Toccata in F]

Lobt Gott, ihr Christen allzugleich
(Vol. II, Pt. 2, No. 21)
Carl Weinrich (Praetorius Organ,

Princeton, N. J.) in MC-40

Nun bitten wir den heiligen Geist
N. O. Raasted (Copenhagen Cathedral Organ) 12"—TONO-A116
[Prelude, Fugue & Chaconne, C major]

Von Gott will ich nicht lassen
(Vol. II, Pt. 2, No. 27)
Carl Weinrich (Westminster Choir School Organ, Princeton, N. J.) in MC-9

Magnificat Primi Toni
(Vol. II, Pt. 1, No. 5a)
Carl Weinrich (Praetorius Organ), in MC-40

Missa Brevis 5-pt. Choir
(Ugrino No. 42)
Motet Singers—Paul Boepple in MC-24
Also: In prep. Dan. H.M.V.

Passacaglia, D minor
(Vol. I, No. 1)
Finn Viderø (Christiansborg Slotskirke Organ) 10"—G-DA5222

PRELUDES & FUGUES Organ

E major (Vol. I, No. 8)
Finn Viderø (Grundtvigskirken Organ)
10"—G-DA5238

E minor (Vol. I, No. 6)
Carl Weinrich (Praetorius Organ)
in MC-40

F major (Vol. I, No. 15)
—Fugue only
Karl Matthaei (Winterthur Organ)
12"—G-FM23
[Pachelbel: Chorale-Preludes]

G minor (Vol. I, No. 14)
Finn Viderø (Christiansborg Slotskirke Organ) 12"—G-DB5248

Prelude, Fugue & Chaconne, C major
(Vol. I, No. 4)
N. O. Raasted (Copenhagen Cathedral Organ) 12"—TONO-A116
[Nun bitten wir den heiligen Geist]

Sonata, C major 2 Violins, Vla. d. g. & Figured Bass (D.D.T., Series I, Vol. II)
Elsa Marie Bruun, Julius Koppel (vlns)
Alberto Medici (vlc), Mogens Wöldike (harpsichord) 12"—G-DB5249
Suites in D minor & E minor
Harpsichord (recently discovered)
In Prep. Danish HMV

TOCCATAS

F major (Vol. I, No. 21)
Carl Weinrich (Praetorius Organ), in MC-40
Finn Viderø (Christiansborg Slotskirke Organ) 10"—G-DA5223
[Chorale-Prelude: In dulci jubilo]

G major (Vol. I, No. 22)
Finn Viderø (Gaveau harpsichord)
10"—G-DA5227
[Canzonetta in G]

Toccata & Fugue, F major
(Probably Vol. I, No. 21)
Hans Vollenweider (organ)
12"—G-HEX104
[Bach: Fugue, A major]

BYRD, William (1543-1623)

Considered by his contemporaries as the most outstanding composer of Elizabethan England, Byrd was for many years obscured by the fame of Purcelli; and it is only recently, with the renewed appreciation of Renaissance polyphony, that his true worth has been realized.

Ave Verum Corpus (Motet) Unacc. Chorus in Latin
Fleet Street Choir   12"—D-K1081
[Stanford: Heraclitus; & Coelus, Ascendit Hodie]

(The) Bells Virginals
[Fitzwilliam Virginal Book No. 69]
Pauline Aubert (in Vol. II)   12"—AS-14
[Farnaby: The new Sa-Hoo & A Toye; Peereson: The Fall of the Leafe]

—Transcribed Orchestra Gordon Jacob
Toronto Symphony—MacMillan
         12"—V-11-8726 (Canada)
[Haydn: Quartet in F, Op. 3, No. 5— Serenade]

Earl of Salisbury See: Pavane & Galliard

Earl of Oxford's March
—Transcribed Orchestra Gordon Jacob
Toronto Symphony—MacMillan
[Pavane]   12"—V-11-8725 (Canada)

Fantasia
Putnam Aldrich (harpsichord), in TC-T11

Galliard Harpsichord
(See also Pavane & Galliard: Earl of Salisbury)
Isabelle Nef   10"—OL-76
[Lulla]

Gigue Unidentified
—Arr. Orchestra Stokowski
Philadelphia Orch.—Stokowski
         10"—V-1943
[Pavane "Earl of Salisbury"]

I thought that love had been a boy 5-Pt. Madrigal
London Madrigal Group   10"—V-4316
[Morley: My bonny lass & Now is the month of maying; & Summer is icumen in]

Justorum animae
Harvard Glee Club & Radcliffe Choral Soc.
—Woodworth, in TC-T11

Lulla Harpsichord
Isabelle Nef   10"—OL-76
[Galliard]

MASS Five Voices

Fleet Street Choir—T. B. Lawrence
      3   12"—D-K1058/60

Miserere 4-Pt.
(Fitzwilliam Virginal Book No. 177)
Carl Weinrich (Westminster Choir School Organ)   in MC-9
Putnam Aldrich (harpsichord), in TC-T11

Non vos relinquam orphanos
Harvard Glee Club & Radcliffe Choral Soc.
—Woodworth, in TC-T11

Pavane & Galliard "Earl of Salisbury"
Virginals (from "Parthenia," 1611)
Rudolph Dolmetsch   10"—C-5712
[Palestrina: Missa Papae Marcelli—Sanctus & Hosanna, Chorus]
(Columbia History of Music, Vol. I: CM-231)
Alice Ehlers (Harpsichord) (D-F7726)
      (in D-A61)   10"—D-23089
[Bach: French Suite 5, G major— Gavotte; & Frescobaldi: Gagliarda; Lully: Courante]

—Pavane only Arr. Orchestra Gordon Jacob
Toronto Symphony—MacMillan
         12"—V-11-8725 (Canada)
[Earl of Oxford's March]

—Arr. Orchestra Stokowski
Philadelphia Orch.—Stokowski
[Gigue]   10"—V-1943

—Arr. 2 Pfs. Bartlett
Bartlett & Robertson (C-DX1340)
      (in CX-256)   12"—C-72127D
[Variations on John come kiss me & Farnaby: His conceit & A Toye]

Sacerdotes Domini
Harvard Glee Club & Radcliffe Choral Soc.
—Woodworth, in TC-T11

Sellinger's Round Harpsichord
(Fitzwilliam Virginal Book No. 64)
Erwin Bodky   10"—P-R1023
[M. Franck: Pavane & Hausmann: Tanz, Viol-Quintet]
(in "2000 Years of Music" album)

Suite (Selected from the Fitzwilliam Virginal Book)
(Freely transcribed for orchestra by Gordon Jacob)

1. **The Earl of Oxford's March**
2. **Pavane**
3. **The Bells**
Toronto Symphony—MacMillan
     2   12"—V-11-8725/6 (Canada)
[Haydn: Quartet in F major—Serenade]

Variations on "John come kisse me now"
(Fitzwilliam Virginal Book No. 10)
—Arr. 2 Pfs. Bartlett
Bartlett & Robertson (C-DX1340)
      (in CX-256)   12"—C-72127D
[Earle of Salisbury's Pavane & Farnaby: His Conceit & A Toye]

Variations on "O Mistress Mine" Harpsichord
(Fitzwilliam Virginal Book No. 66)
George Dyson (pf)   12"—C-D40137
(in illustrations to a lecture on "Early Keyboard Music"—International Educational Society)

(La) Volta
—Arr. Hunt Bamboo Pipes
Pipers Guild Quartet   10"—C-DB2282
[Rossiter: Ayre; Farnaby: Tower Hill, Jigs, etc.]

Wolsey's Wilde Harpsichord
(Fitzwilliam Virginal Book No. 157)
Wanda Landowska   10"—G-DA1014
[Bach: Gavotte in G minor]

CABANILLAS, Juan (1644-1712)

Organist of the Valencian Cathedral, whose compositions are reprinted in Pedrell's "Antologia de organistas clasicos espanoles," Vol. v.

Passacaille, D minor (Style Dorian)
Friedrich Mihatsch (Gonzalez Organ,
Paris) 12"—PAT-PAT65
[Cabezón: Tiento del primer tono]
(in 3 Centuries of Organ Music set)
Tiento
Joseph Bonnet (organ)
(in Vol. VII) 12"—AS-69
[Cabezón: Diferencias sobre El Canto del Caballero & Santa Maria: Clausula de octavo tono]

CABEZON, Antonio de (1510-1566)

A blind Spanish organist who served both Charles V and Philip II as a court performer upon the clavier. His keyboard style is remarkably advanced for his time and is believed to have influenced Sweelinck and the brothers Gabrieli.

Tiento del primer tono
André Marchal (Gonzalez organ, Paris)
12"—PAT-PAT65
[Santa Maria: Harmonization of a melody & Cabanillas: Passacaille, D minor]
(in 3 Centuries of Organ Music set)
Finn Viderø (Compenius organ, Fredriksborg Castle) 10"—G-DA5207
[N. de Begué: Les cloches & Santa Maria: Fantasia tertii toni]
Diferencias (Variations) sobre El Canto del Caballero
(Pedrell: Hispaniae Schola Musica Sacra, Vol. VIII)
Joseph Bonnet (organ)
(in Vol. VII) 12"—AS-69
[Cabanillas: Tiento & Santa Maria: Clausula de octavo tono]
Carl Weinrich (Praetorius organ, Westminster Choir School), **in MC-9**

CACCINI, Francesca (1581- ?)

Daughter of Giulio, Francesca was the composer of cantatas, ballets and one opera, "La Liberazione de Ruggiero." She was both a friend and rival of Peri.

Dispiegate, Guancie amato Aria in Italian
(Realization by Gerlin)
Yvon le Marc' Hadour (b) & Ruggero
Gerlin (harpsichord) 10"—PAT-PG86
[Strozzi: Amor dormiglione]

CACCINI, Giulio (1548-1618)

A well known singer and member of the Florentine "camerata," influential in the development of the "recitativo secco" and the "nuove musiche" which reached opera through the genius of Monteverde.

Amarilli Air (or solo madrigal) in Italian
Beniamino Gigli (t) 12"—G-DB6313
(G-DB3895)
[Donuady: O del mio amato ben]
Georges Thill (t) & Maurice Faure (pf)
12"—C-LFX507
[Marcello: Quelle fiamma]

Salvatore Salvati (t) & harpsichord
12"—MIA-1
[Fere selvagge & Peri: Belliasima regina & Euridice—Gioite al canto mio]
Lorri Lail (ms) 10"—G-X7173
[Martini: Plaisir d'amour]
Giuseppe De Luca (b) & pf. aac., **in D-U1**
DUPLICATIONS: Aubrey Panky, PAT-PG95; Elena Fava, G-HN1663; Claire Chalandon, G-DB5098
Fere selvage Solo Madrigal in Italian
Salvatore Salvati (t) with Harpsichord
12"—MIA-1
[Amarilli & Peri: Bellisima regina & Euridice—Gioite al canto mio]

CADMAN, Charles Wakefield (1881-1947)

A well known and well loved American composer who did considerable work with American Indian music, Cadman is widely known by the salon type of his compositions.

SONGS In English (See also current catalogues)
At Dawning (Eberhardt)
Richard Tauber (t) 10"—P-RO20524
[Geiger: Just for a while]
Nelson Eddy (b)
(in V-C27) 10"—V-4369
[Jacobs-Bond: Perfect Day]
[Arr. Burleigh: Deep river, on G-DA1585]
Paul Robeson (bs) 10"—G-B8731
[Jacobs-Bond: Just a-wearying for you]
Risë Stevens (ms) **in CM-654**
DUPLICATIONS: Alfred Piccaver, D-M419
—**Arr. Orchestra**
Boston "Pops" Orch.—Fiedler
(in VM-968) 10"—V-10-1092
[Guion: Sheep and Goat walking to the meadow]
[Brahms: Wiegenlied & Waltz in A flat major, on G-B8599]
—**Instrumental versions**
Fritz Kreisler (vl) & Carl Lamson (pf)
[Lemare: Andantino] 10"—V-1165
From the Land of the Sky-Blue Water
(Eberhart)
Jeanette MacDonald (s) & Giuseppe
Bamboschek (pf)
(in VM-642) 10"—V-2055
[Raymond: Let me always sing; Scott: Annie Laurie; Anon: Comin' thro' the rye]
—**Arr. Orchestra**
Andre Kostelanetz & his Orch., **in CX-284**
Also: Albert Sandler Trio, C-DB2129
—**Arr. Violin & Piano** Kreisler
Fritz Kreisler & Carl Lamson
10"—V-1115
[Liliuokalani: Aloha Oe]

CAGE, John

An experimental composer who follows the thematic style of Schönberg, using various percussive sounds instead of definite pitches, in the generally accepted sense of the word.

Amores I & IV Prepared Piano
Maro Ajemian, in   DISC-875
[with Hovhaness: Invocations to
Vahakn IV & V]
Three Dances 2 Prepared Pianos
Maro Ajemian & William Masselos
3   12"—DISC-877

CAILLIET, Lucien

*For many years bass-clarinet and saxophone
solo with the Philadelphia Orchestra, Cailliet
has done much clever and interesting arranging.*

Variations on "Pop Goes the Weasel"
Orchestra
Boston "Pops" Orch.—Fiedler
10"—V-4397
Carnegie "Pops" Orch.—O'Connell
10"—C-4368M
Orchestrations:
Bach: Chorale—Jesu Joy of Man's
Desiring
Unacc. Violin Sonata No. 6—Prelude
Mussorgsky: Pictures at an Exhibition

CAIX D'HERVELOIS, Louie de (c1670-c1760)

*A noted performer on the viola da gamba who
has left much literature for that instrument as
well as for the flute.*

La Napolitaine
—Arr. 'Cello & Piano De Béon
Maurice Maréchal & Jean Doyen
[Prélude & Plainte]   12"—C-D15221
Plainte
—Arr. 'Cello & Piano De Béon
Maurice Maréchal & Jean Doyen
[Napolitaine & Prélude]   12"—C-D15221
Prélude
—Arr. 'Cello & Piano De Béon
Maurice Maréchal & Jean Doyen
[Napolitaine & Plainte]   12"—C-D15221
Sarabande & Musette
Cecilie (Treb. viol), Nathalie (vla da
gamba) & Arnold Dolmetsch (harpsi-
chord)   10"—C-DB1062
[Anon: Greensleeves to a Ground, re-
corders & harpsichord]

CALDARA, Antonio (1670-1736)

*A member of the Venetian school of homo-
phonic opera composers who became assistant
to the imperial Kapellmeister in Vienna. He
composed nearly seventy operas, numerous
masses and oratorios.*

Come raggio del sol Aria in Italian
Yvon Le Marc'Hadour (b) with harpsi-
chord, vl. & vlc.   10"—PAT-PA83
[A. Scarlatti: Si si fedel & Pasquini:
Ermina in Riva]
A. Cravcenco (ms) & pf. acc.
10"—G-AV52
[Durante: Vergin tutt' amor]
Mirti jaggi Aria in Italian
Stella Tavarès (s) & R. Herbin (pf)
[Haydn: Pastorella]   12"—BAM-40
Selve Amiche Aria in Italian
Guiseppe De Luca (b), in   D-U1

CAMBINI, Giovanni Giuseppe (1746-c.1825)

*Associated for a time with Gossec's "Concerts
Spirituels" in Paris this Italian led a very adventurous life. He was a renowned chamber
music performer and an exceedingly prolific
composer.*

Quartet, D major Strings arr. Torrefranca
Roma String Quartet
3   12"—G-DB4447/9
[Paganini: Quartet in E major—Minuet,
arr. Zuccarini]

CAMPOS, Juan Morel (1857-1896)

*A very versatile Puerto Rican musician, an
organist, flutist and conductor, who was a most
prolific composer. He wrote in all forms and
left over two hundred original Puerto Rican
dance pieces, as well as many "zaruelas" performed while he was a director of a Spanish
musical-comedy company.*

Puerto Rican Danzas Piano
Felices Días; Maldito Amor; Alma Sublime;
Tormento; No me Toques; Vano Empeño;
Laura y Georgina; Buen Humor
Jesús María Sanromá 4 10"—VM-849

CAMPRA, André (1660-1744)

*A Frenchman of Italian descent, Campra for
many years was a musical director at the more
important French cathedrals including Notre-
Dame de Paris. Having also written ballet-
operas successfully published under his brother's name, he eventually lost his ecclesiastical
position. His music is frequently considered
superior to that of his predecessor, Lully, and
his successor, Rameau.*

Air de Musette
Jean Planel (t), fl., vlc. & harpsichord
(in Vol. X)   12"—AS-96
[Le Papillon]

L'EUROPE GALANTE Opera in French

Excerpts Arr. Désormière
**Marche des masques; Air à danser; Air
pour des Espagnoles; Passepied; For-
lane; Rondo**
Symphony Orch.—Roger Désormière
12"—OL-72
Le Papillon "Cantate"
Jean Planel (t) with vl., harpsichord
(in Vol. X)   12"—AS-96
[Air de Musette]
Rigaudon Arr. Virgil Fox
Virgil Fox (organ)   10"—V-10-1208
[Gigout: Toccata in B minor]

CANNABICH, Christian (1731-1798)

*A pupil of Stamitz, Cannabich was a noted
conductor at Mannheim. Both Mozart and Dr.
Burney praised the ensemble and expression of
his orchestra.*

Symphony, B major Orchestra
Berlin State Opera Orch.—W. Gmeindl
3   12"—PD-67549/51S
[Last side blank]

CAPLET, André (1879-1925)

Winner of the Prix de Rome in 1901, Caplet was more famous as a conductor than as a composer. His friendship with Debussy apparently influenced the style of his composition.

Epiphanie
Danse des petits nègres 'Cello & Piano
Maurice Màréchal & Robert Casadesus
12"—C-LFX86
[Debussy: Sonata No. 1, Pt. 3]

MASS 3 Voices
Female Choir (a cappella)—A. de Vallombrosá   2   12"—LUM-32067/8

SEPTET Sop. Mezzo, Alto, String Quartet
Marise Cottavoz, Natalie Wetchor, Marguérite Pifteau & Calvet Quartet
2   10"—G-DA4876/7

SONGS In French & Latin
Oraison Dominicale In Latin
Claire Croiza (s) & Pascal Quartet
[Salutation angélique] 10"—LUM-30008
Panis Angelicus In Latin
Marie E. Péhu (s) & Krettley Quartet
10"—LUM-30043
[Chausson: Ave Verum Corpus]
Les Prières
Hélène Bovier (ms)   12"—PAT-PDT79
Symbole des Apôtres Vocal trio
Doniau-Blanc, Arnaldez, Delmotte
12"—LUM-32004
[Saint-Saëns: Oratorio de Noël-Tecum Principum]
Miscellaneous Orchestration
See under Debussy: Children's Corner Suite

CARILLO, Julian (1875-   )

An experimenter in microtones, Carillo is a well known Mexican violinist.

Preludio à Cristobal Colon
(written in quarter, eighth and sixteenth tones for harp-zithera, octavina, 'cello, trumpet, horn & etc.)
13th Sound Ensemble of Havana—Angel Rayes (C-DFX62)   12"—C-7357M

CARISSIMI, Giacomo (1605-1674)

The teacher of Scarlatti, Cesti, Buononcini and many others who played an important part in the development of the oratorio and cantata. Unfortunately much of his music was destroyed at the time of the suppression of the Jesuits.

EZECHIAS Oratorio
Air d'Ezéchias
Jean Planel (t, in French) & Organ
12"—C-DFX43
[M. A. Charpentier: Dialogue entre Madeleine et Jésus]

Vittorio, mio core
Charles Kullman (t)   10"—C-DW3051
[Strauss: Rosenkavalier—Italian Serenade]

CARMICHAEL, Hoagy (1899-   )

An American pianist and composer of popular songs, a star of stage, screen and radio, Carmichael's "Stardust" and other melodies have become contemporary American light classics.

Collection "The Stardust Road"
Star Dust; Hong Kong Blues; Rockin' Chair; Riverboat Shuffle; The Old Music Master; Judy; Washboard Blues; Little Old Lady
Hoagy Carmichael (vocals & pf) with Glen Gray and the Casa Loma Orchestra
4   10"—D-A554
Stardust
Eleanor Steber (s)   10"—V-11-9186
[Gershwin: Porgy & Bess—Summertime]
—Arr. Orchestra
Andre Kostelanetz & his Orch.
(in CM-574)   12"—C-7428M
[Ellington: Mood Indigo, on C-DX1243]
See also current catalogues.

CARPENTER, John Alden (1876-   )

Adventures in a Perambulator Orchestra
—No. 3, Hurdy-Gurdy
Minneapolis Symphony Orch.—Ormandy
(in VM-1063)   12"—V-11-9231
[Tchaikovsky: Nutcracker Suite—Overture, Philadelphia Orch.]

QUARTET—Strings
A minor 1928
Gordon String Quartet   3   12"—SCH-4

SONGS

Gintanjali   Song Cycle
(Rabindranath Tagore)
No. 3, The sleep that flits on baby's eyes
Rose Bampton (s) & Wilfred Pelletier (pf)   10"—V-10-1118
[Hageman: Do not go, my love]
(The) Home Road
Ralph Crane (b) & Orch.   10"—V-22616
[Pitts: The little brown church; Foster: Oh! Susanna]
Two Night Songs
—Serenade (Sassoon)
Gladys Swarthout (ms) & Lester Hodges (pf)   (in VM-679)   12"—V-16780
[Anon, arr. Harty: My Lagan Love]
James Melton (t) & Robert Hill (pf)
(in VM-947)   10"—V-10-1051
[Hageman: Miranda]

CASADESUS, Francis

(La) Bergère aux champs (Bergèrette Limousine)
Les Chanteurs de Grenoble—Mixed Chorus—A. Clertant   10"—C-DF2285
[Ritz, harm. Edinger—La petite Marjolaine]
Coeur de Nenette Valse
Jean Vaissade & Ensemble musette
10"—G-K8094
[Grammon-Vàissade: Tu peux partir-tango]

CASADESUS, Henri (1879-   )

The founder of "La Société des Instruments Anciens" who is a famous member of the well-known family of French musicians.

Ballet de la Reyne
Pastorale; Passe Pied; Madrigal; Branle
Society of Ancient Instruments—H.
Casadesus   12"—C-LFX579

Ballet Divertissement
Introduction; Tambour; Carillon; Farandole
Society of Ancient Instruments—H.
Casadesus   12"—C-LFX578

Divertissement
Intermezzo & Tambourin et cortège
Quartet of Chromatic Harps
                   12"—G-L843

Le Jardin des Amours
Pavane; Passe Pied; Menuet tendre; Canarie
Society of Ancient Instruments—H.
Casadesus   12"—C-LFX547

Les Récréations de la Campagne
Sentier fleuri; Colin-Maillard; Menuet galant; La ronde des amours; Les blés d'or
Society of Ancient Instruments—H.
Casadesus   2 12"—C-LFX548/9

Suite Florentine
Introduction; Menuetto; Chaconne; Gigue
Society of Ancient Instruments—H.
Casadesus   12"—C-LFX561

CASADESUS, Robert (1899-   )

A noted French pianist whose interpretations of Chopin are considered definitive. His compositions are in the modern idiom.

SONATA Flute & Piano
René Le Roy & Robert Casadesus
    12" & 10"—C-LFX330 & C-LF147

CASCIA, Giovanni da (14th Century)

A minor Italian composer of popular "ballatas," typical of the musical pastimes mentioned in the "Decameron" of Boccaccio.

Io son un pellegrin Ballade in Italian
Max Meili (t) & Viol acc.
        (in Vol. I) 12"—AS-1
[Italian Ballades & Religious Songs of the 14th Century]

CASELLA, Alfredo (1883-1947)

Le Concert sur l'eau Commedia coregrafica
Orchestral Suite
—Pas de Vieilles Dames & Rondo d'Enfants only
La Scala Orch.—Panizza 12"—G-AW243
[Pick-Mangiagalli: Danza di Olaf]

LA DONNA SERPENTE Opera
Overture Orchestra
EIAR Symphony Orch.—La Rosa Parodi
        12"—CET-CB20266

La Giara Ballet 1 Act Eng. The Jar
Orchestral Suite, Nos. 2 (Tarantella "Il chiodo"), 7 (General Dance), 8 (Finale)
Milan Symphony—Molajoli
                   12"—C-D14467

Scarlattiana Divertimento for Piano & Orchestra
Hans Priegnitz & German Opera Orch., Berlin—Fritz Lehmann
        4 12"—O-9128/31

Serenata Small Orchestra
—Finale (Tarantella) only
Jean Pougnet (vl), Anthony Pini (vlc), Reginald Kell (cl), Paul Draper (bsn), George Eskdale (trp) 10"—C-DB1788
[Milhaud: Symphony No. 3]
(Col. History of Music Vol. V: CM-361)
Also: C. F. Cillario (vl), G-GW1703

Siciliana e Burlesca Trio (Vl., Vlc., Pf.)
Trio Italiana   12"—C-GQX10134

Undici pezzi infantili Piano
Eng. 11 Children's Pieces
Marcelle Barzetti
        2 10"—G-GW1966/7

ARRANGEMENTS See under
Bach: Das musikalische Opfer—Trio
Balakirev: Islamey

CASSADO, Gaspar (1898-   )

A famous Catalan 'cellist and son of an important Spanish church musician and composer, Cassadó studied with Casals. His compositions are not as well known as his playing.

Danse du diable vert 'Cello & Piano
André Navarra & pf. acc.
                   10"—O-188932
[Schumann: Träumerei]

Requiebros 'Cello & Piano
Fr. Les Compliments
Gaspar Cassadó & Michael Raucheisen
                   12"—T-E1820
[Tartini: 'Cello Concerto—Grave]
Edmund Kurtz & Artur Balsam
                   12"—V-11-9953
[Handel-Hubay: Larghetto]

Serenade
Gilberto Crépax (vlc) & pf. acc.
                   12"—C-D5830
[Saint-Saëns: Carnaval des Animaux-Le Cygne]

ARRANGEMENTS 'Cello
Granados: Goyescas-Intermezzo
Laserna: Tonadilla
Schubert: Arpegione Sonata

CASTELNUOVO-TEDESCO, Mario (1895-

An Italian composer and conductor who has spent much time recently in California writing for the films.

Captain Fracassa Violin & Piano
M. Abbado & Gavezzeni
                   10"—G-GW1062
[Falla: Canción & Mortari: Largo]

Deux études d'ondes (Sea Murmurs) Piano
1. Ondes courtes 2. Ondes longues
Mario Castelnuovo-Tedesco
12"—PD-516781
[Le Vieux Vienne—Fox Trot tragique]
—**Arr. Violin & Piano** Heifetz (labelled
"Sea Murmurs")
Jascha Heifetz & Emanuel Bay
10"—V-10-1328
[Rimsky-Korsakov: Flight of the Bum-
ble Bee & Sarasate: Zapateado]
Jascha Heifetz & Arpad Sandor
10"—V-1645
[Rimsky-Korsakov: Flight of the Bum-
ble Bee & Godowsky: Alt Wien]
Tango Arr. Heifetz
(Adaptation of "Two Maids Wooing"
from Shakespeare's "Winter's Tale)
Jascha Heifetz & Emanuel Bay
(in VM-1126) 10"—V-10-1293
[Bax: Mediterranean]
Le Vieux Vienne Piano
Fox Trot tragique; Valse; Nocturne
Mario Castelnuovo-Tedesco
2 12"—PD-561142 & 516781
[Deux études d'ondes, on PD-516781]
—**Valse only** Arr. Violin & Piano Heifetz
Jascha Heifetz & Arpad Sandor
10"—G-DA1377
[Moszkowski: Guitarre]
Vivo e energico
Andres Segovia (guitar)
12"—G-DB3243
[Mendelssohn: String Quartet, E flat
major, Op. 12—Canzonetta]

CARTUCCI, Pietro (1679-1752)
Sicilienne & Gavotte
Emma Boynet (pf) 12"—PD-561146
[Pasquini: Aria]

CATALANI, Alfredo (1854-1893)

OPERAS In Italian
EDMEA 3 Acts 1886
Prelude, Act I Orchestra
La Scala Orch.—Sabaino
12"—G-S10349
[La Wally—Walzer del bacio]

LORELEY 3 Acts 1890
Individual Excerpts
O forze recondite Soprano (Act I)
Bianca Scacciati 12"—C-GQX10213
[Verdi: Forza del Destino—Trio Finale,
with Scacciati, Merli, Pasero]
Walzer dei fiori Orchestra (Act II)
Milan Symphony—Molajoli
12"—C-GQX10517
[Wally—Walzer del bacio]
[Mancinelli: Ero e Leander—Selections,
on G-GQX10492]
Danza delle Ondine Orchestra (Act III)
Eng. **Dance of the waves** (or Water
spirits)
EIAR Orch.—Tansini
12"—CET-CB20261

La Scala Orch.—Sabajno
12"—G-S10043
La Scala Orch.—Guarnieri
12"—G-S10101
Milan Symphony—Molajoli
12"—C-GQX11072
[Mascagni: Amico Fritz—Intermezzo]
DUPLICATION: Marek Weber Orch.,
G-HN601
Nel verde Maggio Tenor
Beniamino Gigli 10"—G-DA586*
[Puccini: Tosca—O dolci mani]
Deh! vieni Soprano & Tenor (Act III)
Bianca Scacciati & Francesco Merli
12"—C-GQX10203

(LA) WALLY 1892
Orchestral selections
[Coro dei cacciatori, & Ebben? ne andro]
La Scala Orch.—Sabajno 10"—G-HN791
[Verdi: Ballo in Maschera—Fantasia]
Individual excerpts (in order they appear
in the opera)
Ebben? ne andro lontana Soprano
Maria Caniglia 12"—G-DB6351
[Mascagni: Cavalleria Rusticana—Voi lo
sapete]
N. V. Poggioli 12"—C-GQX11014
[Verdi: Forza del Destino—Pace, pace]
B. Scacciati 10"—C-DQ1060
[Ponchielli: Gioconda—Sucidio!]
C. Castellani 12"—G-DB11302
[Verdi: Trovatore—D'amor sull' ali
rosee]
Hini Spani 12"—G-DB1163
[Gounod: Faust—Il m'aime, Act III]
Maria Luisa Fanelli 12"—G-DB1508
[Puccini: Tosca—Te Deum, Franci]
Rosetta Pampanini 10"—C-GQ7068
[Puccini: Manon Lescaut—In quelle
trine morbide]
DUPLICATIONS: M. Farneti, C-GQX10491;
B. Scacciati, C-DQ1060; M. Zamboni,
C-DQ1122; Pacetti, C-DQ1158; Poli Ran-
dacio, G-DB182*
Prelude, Act III (A sera) Orchestra
EIAR Orch.—Votti 12"—CET-CB20156
[Mascagni: Salvani—Barcarolla]
La Scala Orch.—Guarnieri
12"—G-S10103
[Rossini: Semiramide—Overture, Pt. 3]
La Scala Orch.—Sabajno
12"—G-HN788
[Boito: Mefistole—Amore, misterio]
DUPLICATION: Milan Symphony Orch.
—Molajoli, C-GQ7193
Ne mai dunque avro pace Soprano
Gina Cigna 12"—C-GQX10663
[Bellini: Norma—Casta Diva]
Walzer del bacio Orchestra
Milan Symphony—Molajoli
12"—C-GQX10157
[Loreley—Walzer dei fiori]
La Scala Orch.—Sabajno
12"—G-S10349
[Edmea—Prelude, Act I]
T'amo ben io Baritone
Gino Bechi (b) 10"—G-DA5405
[Verdi: Trovatore—Il balen]

Prelude, Act IV Orchestra
La Scala Orch.—Sabajno
12″—G-S10046
Finale
M'hai salvato & O dolce incanto Soprano &
Tenor
Maria Vinceiguerra & Paolo Civil
12″—CET-CC2322
[Donizetti: Lucrezia Borgia—Di pesca-
tore, Civil]

CAURROY, François Eustace de (1549-1609)

*A contemporary of Palestrina and Orlando di
Lasso, a musician to the King of France. He
composed a "Missa pro defunctis" which was
performed at the funerals of the French kings
until the eighteenth century.*

Fantasie sur l'air "Une jeune fillette" (Arr.
Bonnet)
Joseph Bonnet (organ of Hammond Mu-
seum, Gloucester)   12″—V-18413
[Perotinus: Triplum; Anon: Le moulin
de Paris: Couperin: Chaconne]

CAVALLI, Francesco (1600-1676)

*The baroque operatic composer of the Vene-
tian school of Monteverdi who was partially
responsible for the spread of Italian opera to
France.*

Donzelle fuggite (trans. P. Floridia)
Ezio Pinza (bs) & Fritz Kitzinger (pf)
(in VM-766)   12″—V-17915
[Monteverdi: Incoronazione di Poppea—
Oblivion socave; Torelli: Tu lo sai &
Paisiello: La Molinara—Nel cor più non
mi sento]

OPERAS In Italian & French

GIASONE 1649 In Italian (Opera Oratorio)
Scene 2
Yvon le Marc'Hadour (b) & Pasquier
Trio, with Ruggero Gerlin (harpsichord)
12″—PAT-PAT89

SERSE 1654 In Italian
Beato chi puo Bass
Giuseppe Flamini, with harpsichord &
bass continuo   12″—MIA-4
[Marcello: Cantata for Bass]

CERTANI, Antonio (1879-   )

L'Isola del Garda Symphonic Poem
Orchestra
Milan Symphony—Molajoli
12″—C-GQX10729
Leggenda delle Dolomiti Orchestra
Milan Symphony—Ariani
12″—C-GQX10711
Serenatina
B. Mazzucurati (vlc) & Luigi Gallino (pf)
12″—CET-P56106
[Granados: Goyescas—Intermezzo]

CESTI, Marc'Antonio (1618-1669)

*A pupil of Carissimi, this Franciscan monk
contributed to the development of the baroque
opera.*

OPERAS In Italian

IL POMO D'ORO 1667
Ah quanto è vero, Act II Soprano
(Air de Venus)
Martha Angelici & Orch.—Gerlin, with
Pauline Aubert (harpsichord)
(in Vol. IX)   12″—AS-82
[Sacchini: Nitteti—In amor la gelosia è
follia & Puoi vantar le tue ritorte]

CHABRIER, Alexis Emmanuel (1841-1894)

*Hampered by desultory training and many mis-
fortunes, Chabrier wrote music of remarkable
rhythmic intensity and melodic verve.*

Bourrée Fantasque Piano 1891
Lucette Descaves-Truc   10″—G-DA4946
—Arr. Orchestra F. Mottl
Paris Symphony—Meyrowitz
10″—PAT-PD9
Colonne Orch.—Pierné
12″—O-123545
Lamoureux Orch.—Wolff
(PD-66950)   12″—PD-566003
[Marche Joyeuse]
Cotillon Ballet
**Menuet Pompeux; Scherzo-Valse; Idylle;
Danse Villageoise**
London Philharmonic—Dorati
(C-DX877/8)   2 12″—CX-113†
España-Rapsodie Orchestra 1883
London Philharmonic—Beecham
(C-LX880)   12″—C-71250D
Boston "Pops" Orch.—Fiedler
10″—V-4375
(G-B8713) (G-EG6308) (G-K8050)
Berlin Philharmonic—Schmidt-
Isserstedt (U-F18078)   12″—T-E2624
Lamoureux Orch.—Wolff
(PD-67040)   12″—PD-566133
Colonne Orch.—Pierné 12″—O-123666
DUPLICATIONS: Paris Symphony Orch.
—Coppola, G-L678; Symphony Orch, G-
L659; Symphony Orch., U-E462; La Scala
Orch.—Sabajno, G-S10042
—Arr. Band
Garde Républicaine Band—Dupont
12″—C-D11019
L'Etoile See under Operas
Gwendoline See under Operas
Habañera Orchestra (Originally Piano)
Lamoureux Orch.—Wolff
12″—PD-566019
[Falla: Amor Brujo—Danza ritual]
Paris Conservatory Orch.—Gaubert
[Marche Joyeuse]   12″—C-LFX174
Victor Orch.—J. P. Morel
(in VM-460†)   12″—V-14957
[Debussy: Iberia, New York Philharmonic
Symphony—Barbirolli]

Marche Joyeuse Orchestra
(Originally Piano—4 Hands)
Royal Philharmonic—Beecham
12″—G-DB6422
[Tchaikovsky: Romeo and Juliet, Pt. 5]
Cincinnati Symphony—Goossens
(in VM-1041†)   12″—V-11-9096
[Stravinsky: Chant du Rossignol, Pt. 5]
London Philharmonic—Lambert
12″—G-C3112
[Meyerbeer: Prophête—Coronation
March]
Lamoureux Orch.—Wolff
(PD-66950)   12″—PD-566003
[Bourrée fantasque]
Paris Conservatory Orch.—Gaubert
[Habañera]   12″—C-LFX174
Colonne Orch.—Pierné   12″—O-123539
[Berlioz: Symphonie Fantastique, Pt. 7]

OPERAS In French
L'ETOILE 1877
Selections
Soloists & Orch. of L'Opéra-Comique—
Désormière   5 10″—PAT-PD21/5

GWENDOLINE 3 Acts 1886
Overture Orchestra
Paris Conservatory Orch.—Bigot
2 12″—C-LFX685/6
[Suite Pastorale—Danse villageoise]
Colonne Orch.—Pierné
[Ronde villageoise] 2 12″—O-123675/6
Lamoureux Orch.—Wolff
12″—PD-566165

LE ROI MALGRE LUI 1887
Danse Slave Orchestra
Symphony Orch.—Lambert
12″—G-C3218
[Tchaikovsky: Romeo and Juliet, Pt. 5]
Fête Polonaise, Act II Orchestra
Berlin State Opera Orch.—
Melichar   12″—PD-516543
Orch. of the "Maggio Musicale"—
Markevitch   12″—CET-BB25160

(10) Pièces Pittoresques Piano 1880
—No. 4, Sous bois
Lazare-Lévy   12″—G-DB5049
[No. 6]
—Arr. Orchestra
Orch. of "Maggio Musicale"—Gui
12″—CET-BB25175
[Debussy-Ravel: Sarabande]
—No. 6, Idylle
Lazare-Lévy   12″—G-DB5049
[No. 4]
Gaby Casadesus, in VOX-163
—Arr. Orchestra Chabrier
See under Cotillon Ballet
—No. 7, Danse villageoise
—Arr. Orchestra Chabrier
See under Cotillon Ballet & Ronde
Villageoise
—No. 8, Improvisation (or, Impromptu)
Robert Casadesus   12″—C-LFX589
[No. 10]
—No. 9, Menuet Pompeux
—Arr. Orchestra Rieti
See under Cotillon Ballet

—No. 10, Scherzo—Valse
Robert Casadesus   12″—C-LFX589
[No. 8]
—Arr. Orchestra Chabrier
See also under Cotillon Ballet
Lamoureux Orch.—Wolff
(PD-566018)   12″—PD-66995
[Rachmaninoff: Prelude, C sharp minor]
Ronde villageoise Orchestra
(Orchestral version of "Dix pièces
pittoresques No. 7")
Colonne Orch.—Pierné   12″—O-123676
[Gwendoline—Overture, Pt. 3]

SONGS In French
Ballade des gros Dindons (Rostand) 1889
Pierre Bernac (b) & Francis Poulenc (pf)
[L'Isle heureuse]   10″—G-DA4892
L'Isle heureuse (Mikhaël) 1889
Pierre Bernac (b) & Francis Poulenc (pf)
10″—G-DA4892
[Ballade des gros Dindons]
Ninon Vallin (s) & pf. acc.
10″—O-166667
[Fontenailles: Les deux coeurs]
Reynaldo Hahn (b) & self pf. acc.
[Gounod: Aimons-nous] 10″—C-D2020
Villanelle des petits canards
Jean Planel (t)   10″—PAT-PG79
[Duparc: Lamento]
Sophie Wyss (s) & Josephine Southey-
John (pf)   10″—D-M529
[Fauré: Les Berceaux]
Suite Pastorale
Danse villageoise (Sous bois)
Paris Conservatory Orch.—Bigot
12″—C-LFX686
[Gwendoline—Overture, Pt. 3)
Trois Valses Romantiques 2 Pianos 1883
Robert & Gaby Casadesus
2 10″—CX-209†

**CHAMBONNIERES, Jacques Champion de
(1602-1672)**
*Regarded as the founder of the French harpsi-
chord school in both composition and execu-
tion, Chambonnières published two books of
"Pièces de clavecin" the first containing a table
of agréments.*
Chaconne & Rondeau Harpsichord
Wanda Landowska   12″—G-DB4973
[Daquin: L'Hirondelle & Lully: Les
Songes agréables]
Sarabande, D minor Harpsichord
Wanda Landowska
(in VM-1181) 12″—V-11-9998
[Rameau: La Dauphine; Couperin: Les
Barricades & l'Arlequine]
Volte Harpsichord
Eta Harich-Schneider   10″—G-DA4449
[Couperin: Chaconne; Daiquin: Guitarre;
Candrieu: Cascades]

CHAMINADE, Cecile (1861-1944)
*For many years one of the best known women
composers. She was an excellent pianist and her
"Scarf Dance" (from a ballet "Callirhoë) is
probably best known.*
Automne, Op. 35, No. 2 Piano
Mark Hambourg   12″—G-C2064
[Chopin: Prelude No. 17]

—**Arr. Orchestra** Melachrino
George Melachrino Orch. 12″—**G-C3570**
[Melachrino: First Rhapsody]
Also: Albert Sandler Trio, C-FB2172
Sérénade espagnole Arr. Vl. & Pf. Kreisler
Alfredo Campoli & acc. 10″—**D-F6179**
[Moskowski-Sarasate: Guitarre]
DUPLICATION: M. Quiroga, PAT-X98002

SONGS In French
L'Anneau d'argent (Gerard)
Eng. **The little silver ring**
Ninon Vallin (s) & pf. acc.
10″—**O-166666**
[Fontenailles: Sais-tu?]
John McCormack (t) (in English)
& pf. acc.   10″—**G-DA973**
[Coates: Bird songs at eventide]
DUPLICATIONS: André Baugé, PAT-PA972; Robert Couzinou, PD-522527;
L. Fugère, C-D13077; André Baugé,
PAT-X93080; Gordon, G-K6792
Ronde d'Amour (Fuster)
Lucien Fugère (b) & pf. acc.
10″—**C-D13044**
[Martini: Plaisir d'Amour]

CHARLES, Ernest
An American composer, whose songs and choruses are well known and often sung by leading singers and chorus groups.

SONGS
When I have sung my songs
Kirsten Flagstad (s) & Edwin
McArthur (pf)
(in VM-342) 10″—**V-1817**
[Scott: Lullaby]
Jeanette MacDonald (s) & G.
Bamboschek (pf)
(in VM-642) 10″—**V-2047**
[Hageman: Do not go my love]

CHARPENTIER, Gustave (1860-   )
Best known as a composer by his opera "Louise," Charpentier has also written orchestral works, songs and a cantata. He is also known as a conductor and operatic coach.
Impressions d'Italie Suite Orchestra
Sérénade; La Fontaine; A Mules; Sur les Cimes; Napoli
Symphony Orch.—Charpentier
3 12″—**PAT-X5477/9**
(Also C-D15071/3)
—**Nos. 3 & 5 only**
Lamoureux Orch.—Wolff
(PD-566114/5) 2 12″—**PD-67035/6**
—**No. 3 only**
Vocal arr. See: Songs—A Mules

OPERAS In French
JULIEN 4 Acts 1913
No actual excerpts from this opera have been traced on records. See "La Vie du Poète," which together with some thematic material from "Louise" furnished most of the score for "Julien."

LOUISE 4 Acts 1900
Abridged recording (Version arranged by Charpentier)
Soloists, Raugel Chorus & Orch.—Bigot
(C-RFX47/54)   8 12″—**C-OP12†**
The Cast:
Louise . . . . Ninon Vallin (s)
Julien . . . . Georges Thill (t)
Le Père . . . . . . André Pernet (b)
La Mère . . . . . . A. Lecouvreur (a)
Irma . . . . . Christiane Gaudel (s)
Orchestral Selections
Symphony Orch.—Gurlitt
12″—**PD-19944**
Individual Excerpts
ACT I
Depuis longtemps j'habitais cette chambre
Duo: Soprano & Tenor
Cesar Vezzani & Jean Guyla
12″—**G-DB4970**
[Massenet: Griselidis—La mer est sur les flots, J. Guyla]
ACT II
Depuis le jour où je me suis donnée Soprano
Ninon Vallin 12″—**C-LFX594**
[Chopin-DeBadet: Intime—Etude No. 3]
(Also on O-171033; PAT-X90029, earlier recording)
Eleanor Steber 12″—**G-DB6514**
[Bizet: Carmen—Je dis que rien]
Dorothy Maynor 12″—**V-17698**
[Debussy: L'Enfant prodigue—Air de Lia]
Joan Hammond 12″—**C-DX1135**
[Tchaikovsky: Eugene Onegin—Letter Scene, Pt. 3]
DUPLICATIONS: Grace Moore, V-17189:
G-DB6031; Jeanette MacDonald,
V-15850: G-DB3940; Helen Jepson,
V-14204 in VM-329; Gabrielle Ritter-Ciampi, PD-66840: PD-516691; Jeanne Guyla, G-DB4872; I. Jouglet, C-BFX7;
L. DuRoy, PD-521891; B. Delprat, PAT-PGT7; S. Dubost, PD-516501; Fanny Heldy, G-DB1304; In German: Felicie Hüni-Mihacsek, PD-66615
ACT IV
Les pauvres gens peuvent-ils être heureux?
Voir naître un enfant Baritone (Air du Père)
Lucien van Obbergh 12″—**PD-516733**
Julien Lafont 10″—**O-188538**
Etienne Billot 10″—**O-188745**
[Berlioz: Damnation de Faust—Song of the Flea]
Bonsoir, père—Louise! Louise! Recit.
Berceuse: Reste, repose-toi Bar.
L'enfant serait sage (Duo: Sop. & Bar.)
(The Vallin-Lafont disc omits the brief part for the Mother)
Julien Lafont & Ninon Vallin
12″—**O-123507**
—**Recit. & Berceuse only** Baritone
Vanni-Marcoux 12″—**G-DB4950**
[Mussorgsky: Boris Godunov—My heart is sad]
DUPLICATIONS: Robert Couzinou & Orch., PD-516570: PD-66965; M. Journet, G-DB1174

SONGS In French

Collections: 6 Mélodies de Charpentier
Germaine Féraldy, Jean Planel, Joseph
Lanzone, Women's Chorus & Orch.—
Charpentier   3 12"—**PAT-PAT26/5**
              & **PAT-35**

A Mules (after "Impressions d'Italie")
(J. Mery)
Jean Planel (t)   12"—**PAT-PAT26**
[Les Chevaux de Bois]

La Chanson du Chemin Scène lyrique
(C. Mauclair)
Jean Planel (t) & Joseph Lanzone (b)
           12"—**PAT-PAT25**
[Ronde des Compagnons, J. Lanzone,
Male Cho. & Orch.]

Les Chevaux de Bois (Verlaine)
Jean Planel (t)   12"—**PAT-PAT26**
[A Mules, Planel with Women's Cho.]

Ronde des Compagnons Impressions
Fausses (Verlaine)
Joseph Lanzone (b)   12"—**PAT-PAT25**
[La Chanson du Chemin, J. Planel, J.
Lanzone, Cho.]

Sérénade à Watteau (Clair de Lune)
(Verlaine)
Germaine Féraldy (s) 12"—**PAT-PAT35**
[Les Yeux de Berthe]

Les Yeux de Berthe (Baudelaire: Les
Fleurs de Mal)
Germaine Féraldy (s) & Pf. acc.
[Sérénade à Watteau]
           12"—**PAT-PAT35**

La Vie du Poète Symphonie-Drama 4 Acts
Soloists, Chorus & Orch.
(*This work, first performed in June 1892, pro-
fided much of the material for Charpentier's
opera "Julien"*)
Act I, **Enthousiasme**
Act II, **Doute**
Act III, **Désespérance**
Act IV, **Ivresse**
Anon. soloists, Chorus & Pasdeloup
Orch.—Charpentier
         4 12"—**G-DB4966/9**

CHAUSSON, Ernest (1855-1899)

*A pupil of Cesar Franck who wrote music of
sensuous melody and opulent harmony.*

Concerto, D major, Op. 21
Violin, Piano & String Quartet
Jascha Heifetz, J. M. Sanromá &
Musical Art. Qt.   4 12"—**VM-877†**
Jacques Thibaud, Alfred Cortot with
String Quartet   5 12"—**G-DB1649/53**
(Fauré: Berceuse)

Poème, Op. 25 Violin & Orchestra
Yehudi Menuhin & Paris Symphony
Orch.—Georges Enesco
(G-DB1961/2)   2 12"—**V-7913/4**
Georges Enesco & S. Schlussel (pf)
        2 12"—**C-DFX125/6**

Quartet, Strings, A major, Op. 30
No recordings available

(LE) ROI ARTHURS
Opera in French 3 Acts 1903

Prophétie de Merlin: Pommiers verts, Act II
Ne m'interroge plus, ô roi, Act II. Bar.
Arthur Endrèze   10"—**PAT-PD6**

SONGS In French

(L') Amour d'antan
Germaine Corney (s)   10"—**PD-561051**
[Le temps de lilas]

Ave Verum Corpus In Latin
André d'Akor (t)
(C-CQX16523)   12"—**C-BFX2**
[Franck: Panis Angelicus]
Marie Pehu (s)   10"—**LUM-30048**
[Caplet: Panis Angelicus]

Chanson Perpétuelle, Op. 37, (Cros)
Maggie Teyte (s), Gerald Moore (pf)
& Blech Quartet   12"—**G-DB6159**
Geori-Boué (s) & Pascal String
Quartet   12"—**O-123889**

Le Charme
Ninon Vallin (s) & P. Darck (pf)
        10"—**PAT-PG100**
[Les Papillons & Le Colibri]

Le Colibri (Lecomte de Lisle)
Maggie Teyte (s) & Gerald Moore (pf)
        10"—**G-DA1833**
[Bizet: Le Chanson d'Avril]
Pierre Bernac (b) & Francis Poulenc (pf)
[Duparc: Soupir]   10"—**G-DA4928**
Ninon Vallin (s) & P. Darck (pf)
        10"—**PAT-PG100**
[Le Charme & Les Papillons]

Dans la Forêt du Charme et de l'Enchante-
ment, Op. 36
Povla Frijsh (s) & Celius Dougherty (pf)
    (in VM-789) 12"—**V-18052**
[Duparc: Le Manoir de Rosemonde,
Hahn: Infidélité; Dupont: Mandoline]

Les Papillons (Chanson des heures)
Ninon Vallin (s) & Pierre Darck (pf)
        10"—**PAT-PG100**
[Le Charme & Le Colibri]

Les Temps de lilas (Boucher)
Charles Panzéra (b) & Orch.—Coppola
[Gounod: Soir]   12"—**G-DB4971**
Gladys Swarthout (ms) & Lester
Hodges (pf)
    (in VM-679) 12"—**V-16779**
[Pittaluga: Romance de Solita &
Granados: El Majo Discreto]
DUPLICATION: G. Corney, PD-561051;
Jane Laval, C-LFX35

Symphony, B flat major, Op. 20
Chicago Symphony Orch.—Stock
        4 12"—**VM-950†**
Paris Conservatory Orch.—Coppola
        4 12"—**G-DB4953/6**

CHAVEZ, Carlos (1899-   )

*Mexican composer and conductor who has made
fine collections of Indian and Mestizo folk-
music. His own compositions are based for the
most part on native Mexican thematic material.*

(Los) Cuatro Soles Ballet

Danza a Centeotl
Chorus & Orchestra—Chavez
    (in CM-414†) 12"—**C-70334D**
[Xochipili—Macuilxochitl]

Sinfonia de Antigona Orchestra
Symphony Orch. of Mexico—Chavez
     (in VM-503†) 2 12"—**V-12338/9**
[Sinfonia India—Pt. 3]

Sinfonia India Orchestra
Symphony Orch. of Mexico—Chavez
     (in VM-503†) 2 12"—**V-12337/8**
[Sinfonia de Antigona—Pt. 1]

Xochipili—Macuilixochitl (Music for pre-Conquest instruments)
Orch.—Chavez
     (in CM-414†) 12"—**C-70334D**
[Los Cuatro Soles—Danza]

ARRANGEMENTS

La Paloma Azul (Trad. arr. Cho. & Orch.)
Chorus & Orchestra—Chavez
     (in CM-414†) 12"—**C-70333D**
See also:
Buxtehude: Chaconne in E minor

CHERUBINI, Maria Luigi (1760-1842)

Ad Te Levavi Chorus
Julian Chapel Cro.—Boezi
          12"—**SEMS-42**
[Calzanera: O Jesu mi dulcissime]

OPERAS In French

(LES) ABENCERAGES 1813
Recit. & Air: Suspendez à ces murs
  Arr. Gevaert
  Georges Thill (t)   12"—**C-LFX274**
[Gluck: Iphigénie en Tauride—Unis dès
ma plus tendre enfance]

ANACREON 1803
Overture Orchestra
  Berlin State Opera Orch.—Von Karajan
          12"—**PD-67514**
  Amsterdam Concertgebouw Orch.—
  Mengelberg   2 12"—**C-GQX10460/1**
[Beethoven: Symphony No. 8, 2nd Mvt.]

(LES) DEUX JOURNEES 1800
Ger. Der Wasserträger It. Il portatore
  d'acqua
Eng. The Water Carrier
Overture Orchestra
  EIAR Symphony Orchestra—
  La Rosa Parodi   12"—**CET-CB20218**

MEDEE 1797
Overture Orchestra
  Milan Symphony—L. Molajoli
          12"—**C-GQX10015**
O Salutaris Hostia Chorus in Latin
  EIAR Chorus—Bruno Erminero
          12"—**CET-PE113**
[Handel: Sepulto Domino]
Symphony, D major Orchestra
  Chamber Orch. of Royal Conservatory,
  S. Pietro a Majella, Naples—Adriano
  Lualdi   4 12"—**G-DB5436/9**
[Cimarosa: I Traci Amanti—Overture]
  Leipzig Gewandhaus Chamber Orch.—
  Paul Schmitz   4 12"—**PD-67652/5**

Unspecified Scherzo, B flat
  Poltronieri Quartet   10"—**C-GQ7032**
[Schumann: Träumerei]

CHOPIN, Frederic-François (1810-1849)

As standard as the works of Bach and Bee-
thoven in the concert-pianist's repertory, the
works of Chopin are some of the most grateful
and pleasing piano pieces ever written. Chopin's
place as a developer of piano technique is
equally as important as that of his more bril-
liant colleague, Liszt.

COLLECTIONS

Chopin Piano Music
Andante Spianato & Grande Polonaise, Op.
  22; Valse No. 3; Polonaise No. 6
  Vladimir Horowitz 3 12"—**VM-1034†**
Music to Remember
Impromptu No. 4; Valses No. 6 & 7; Ma-
  zurka No. 5
  José Iturbi
  (G-DA1848/9)   2 10"—**VM-1110†**
Piano Music of Chopin
Mazurkas, B flat major (No. 2 of Posth.
  Series); No. 49; No. 43; No. 19; Noc-
  turnes No. 19 & No. 20; Valses No. 11 &
  No. 13; Polonaise No. 9
  Maryla Jonas   3 12"—**CM-626**
Oscar Levant Plays Chopin
Etudes No. 3, No. 4, No. 5 & No. 12; Noc-
  turnes No. 2 & No. 5; Polonaise No. 3;
  Berceuse; Valses No. 7 & No. 11
  Oscar Levant   4 12"—**CM-649**
Selections
Impromptu No. 4; Polonaise No. 6; Mazurka
  No. 5; Etude No. 12; Valse No. 7; Noc-
  turne No. 2
  Jakob Gimpel   4 10"—**VOX-604**
See also: Ballades, Etudes, Impromptus,
  Mazurkas, Nocturnes, Polonaises, Pré-
  ludes, Scherzos & Valses

Andante Spianato & Grande Polonaise,
  Op. 22
  See under Polonaises

(4) BALLADES Piano

Collections (The 4 Ballades)
  Alfred Cortot   4 12"—**VM-399†**
  (G-DB2023/6 in GM-198†)
  Jean Doyen   5 12"—**G-DB5145/9**
  [Valses No. 6 & 11]
  Raoul Koczalski 4 12"—**PD-67528/31**
  Robert Casadesus 5 12"—**C-D15076;**
          C-LFX166; C-LFX131;
  [Mazurka No. 13]   **C-LFX74/5**
  Anna Kremarova 4 12"—**ESTA-F5213/6**

Individual Ballades

No. 1, G minor, Op. 23
  Alfred Cortot (G-DB2023 in GM-198†;
    V-14651 in VM-399†)
  Jean Doyen   12"—**G-DB5145**
  Raoul Koczalski   12"—**PD-67528**
  Robert Casadesus   12"—**C-D15076**

Anna Kremarova   12"—ESTA-F5213
Eileen Joyce   12"—C-DX1084
Victor Schiøler   12"—TONO-A103
Benno Moiseiwitsch   12"—G-C3101
Louis Kentner   12"—C-DX1391
Julian von Karolyi   12"—PD-68089
Vladimir Horowitz
(in VM-1165†)   12"—V-11-9841
Alexander Brailowsky   12"—PD-95325
Samson François   12"—D-K1398

No. 2, F major, Op. 38
Alfred Cortot (G-DB2024 in GM-198†;
V-14562 in VM-399†)
Jean Doyen   12"—G-DB5146
Raoul Koczalski   12"—PD-67531
Robert Casadesus   12"—C-LFX166
Anna Kremarova   12"—ESTA-F5214
Benno Moiseiwitsch   12"—G-C3685

No. 3, A flat major, Op. 47
Alfred Cortot (G-DB2025 in GM-198†;
V-14563 in VM-399†)
Jean Doyen   12"—G-DB5147
Raoul Koczalski   12"—PD-67529
Robert Casadesus   12"—C-LFX131
Anna Kremarova   12"—ESTA-F5215
Eileen Joyce   12"—C-DX976
Benno Moiseiwitsch   12"—G-C3100
Claudio Arrau (O-9144) 12"—P-R20443
Leo Nadelmann   12"—G-DB10050
Guiomar Novaës   12"—C-72345D
C. M. Savery   12"—TONO-A124
—Arr. 2 Pfs., Rawicz & Landauer,
C-DB2293

No. 4, F minor, Op. 52
Alfred Cortot (G-DB2026 in GM-198†;
V-14564 in VM-399†)
Jean Doyen   2 12"—G-DB5148/9
[Valses Nos. 6 & 11]
Raoul Koczalski   12"—PD-67530
Robert Casadesus   C-LFX74/5
[Mazurka No. 13]
Anna Kremarova   12"—ESTA-F5216
Solomon   12"—G-C3403
Jacques Dupont   2 10"—PAT-X98015/6

Bacarolle, F sharp minor, Op. 60 Piano
Walter Gieseking
(C-LWX299)   12"—C-71026D
Louis Kentner   12"—C-DX1112
Benno Moiseiwitsch   12"—G-C3229
Carlo Zecchi   12"—CET-CB20349
Alexander Brailowsky   12"—PD-35014
Marguerite Long   12"—C-LFX325
Alfred Cortot   12"—G-DB2030
Artur Rubinstein   12"—G-DB1161

Berceuse, D flat major, Op. 57 Piano
Artur Rubinstein
(in VM-1012†)   12"—V-11-9408
[Concerto No. 2, Pt. 7]
Artur Rubinstein   12"—G-DB2149
[Mazurkas Nos. 23 & 39]
Alexander Brailowsky   12"—V-15382
[Ecossaises]
Yvonne Gellibert   12"—G-W1523
[Liszt: Liebestraum No. 3]
Walter Gieseking   12"—C-LWX304
[Mazurka No. 13] (C-GQX11049)
Eileen Joyce   12"—P-E11432
[Impromptu No. 4]
Solomon   12"—G-C3308

[Nocturne No. 8]
Wilhelm Backhaus   12"—G-DB1131
[Valse No. 1]
Suzanne Gyr   12"—G-DB10074
[Polonaise No. 3]
Arturo Benedetti Michelangeli
[Mazurka No. 25]   12"—T-SKB3289
Raoul Koczalski   12"—PD-95202
[Etude No. 19]
[Nocturne No. 2, on PD-67246]
DUPLICATIONS: Oscar Levant, on C-
72108D in CM-649; Cor de Groot,
O-8776; Carlo Zecchi, CET-CB20354
Bolero, C major, Op. 19 Piano
Lilly Dymont   12"—PD-27041
Chant Polonais
See under Songs

CONCERTOS Piano & Orchestra

No. 1, E minor, Op. 11
Artur Rubinstein & London Symphony
Orch.—Barbirolli
    4 12"—VM-418†
(G-DB3201/4 in GM-279†)
Edward Kilenyi & Minneapolis Sym-
phony Orch.—Mitropoulos
    4 12"—CM-515†
Alexander Brailowsky & Berlin Phil-
harmonic Orch.—Prüwer
(PD-66753/6)   4 12"—VOX-452

No. 2, F minor, Op. 21
Artur Rubinstein & NBC Symphony
Orch.—Steinberg
[Berceuse]   4 12"—VM-1012†
Artur Rubinstein & London Symphony
Orch.—Barbirolli   4 12"—GM-128†
[Valse No. 7] (G-DB1494/7)
Alfred Cortot & Orch.—Barbirolli
    4 12"—VM-567†
(G-DB2612/5 in GM-330†)
Marguerite Long & Paris Conservatory
Orch.—Gaubert   4 12"—CM-143†
[Mazurka No. 38] (C-D15236/9)
Malcuzynski & Philharmonia Orch.—
Kletzki   4 12"—C-LX1013/6†

(3) Ecossaises, Op. 72 Piano
Alexander Brailowsky   12"—V-15382
[Berceuse]
[Valse No. 1, on G-DB3706]
Raoul Koczalski   10"—G-DA4430
[Mazurka No. 48 & Nocturne No. 5]
Raymond Trouard   10"—O-188940
[Etude, G flat major]
Jacques Dupont   10"—PAT-PG21
[Nocturne No. 14]

ETUDES Piano

12 Etudes, Op. 10; 12 Etudes, Op. 25; 3
"Nouvelles" Etudes
Collections
Op. 10, Op. 25 & 3 "Nouvelles" Etudes
Complete
Alexander Brailowsky
    8 12"—VM-1171†
Robert Lortat   8 12"—C-LFX135/42
Raoul Koczalski
    7 12"—PD-67262/4 & PD-67242/5
Op. 10 & Op. 25 Complete
Alfred Cortot
    6 12"—G-DB2027/9 & G-DB2308/10

Alfred Cortot 6 12"—G-W1531/6
Edward Kilenyi
6 12"—CM-368 & CM-473
Op. 10 only
Alfred Cortot 3 12"—VM-398
Individual Etudes

No. 1, C major, Op. 10, No. 1
Alexander Brailowsky, on V-11-9885 in
VM-1171†
Alfred Cortot, on V-14558 in VM-398:
G-DB2027
Edward Kilenyi, on C-P72063D in CM-
368: PAT-PAT105
Raoul Koczalski, on PD-67263
DUPLICATIONS: Robert Lortat,
C-LFX135; Wilhelm Backhaus,
G-DB928: G-DB2059; Otakar Vondrovic,
ESTA-F5189; Jeanne-Marie Darré, PAT-
PDT93; M. de Salvo, C-DQ7223

No. 2, A minor, Op. 10, No. 2
Alexander Brailowsky, on V-11-9885 in
VM-1171†
Alfred Cortot, on V-14558 in VM-398:
G-DB2027
Edward Kilenyi, on C-P72063D in CM-
368: PAT-PAT105
Raoul Koczalski, on PD-67263
DUPLICATIONS: Robert Lortat,
C-LFX135; Backhaus, G-DB928; Raoul
Koczalski, PD-90030; Jeanne-Marie
Darré, PAT-PDT93

No. 3, E major, Op. 10, No. 3
Alexander Brailowsky, on V-11-9886, in
VM-1171
Alfred Cortot, on V-14559 in VM-398:
G-DB2028
Edward Kilenyi, on C-P72064D in CM-
368: PAT-PAT106
Raoul Koczalski, on PD-67262
Eileen Joyce 12"—C-DX1002
[Ravel: Jeau d'eau]
Solomon 12"—G-C3433
[Valse No. 5]
DUPLICATIONS: Robert Lortat,
C-LFX135; William Murdoch, D-K704;
Raymond Trouard, O-123844; I. J. Pad-
erewski, V-6628: G-DB1037; France Elle-
gard, PD-67919; Alexander Brailowsky,
PD-95323: CET-OR5111: CET-RR8005;
Oscar Levant, on C-72106D in CM-649;
Hans Leygraf, SON-K9516; O. Frugoni,
ELITE-7031

—Arr. Violin & Piano
Daniel Guilevitch & Lucien Petitjean
10"—PD-524611
[Tchaikovsky: Chanson Triste]
DUPLICATIONS: S. Filon, PD-522841;
Y. Curti, PAT-X98104

—Arr. Guitar & Orch.: Gino Bordin & Orch.
PD-47101; PD-524282

—Arr. Orch.—See La Nuit ensorcelée
Also: Orchestre Raymonde, C-DX907;
Albert Sandler Orch., C-FB2318

—Vocal arrangements
In English: **"So deep is the night"** (Melfi)
Webster Booth (t) & Ann Ziegler (s)
(G-B9247) 10"—V-10-1049

[Parr-Davis: My Paradise]
John McCormack (t) & acc.
10"—G-DA1730
[Lehar-Stothart: The Magic of Your
Love)
DUPLICATION: W. Midgley, C-DB1934
In French
Ninon Vallin (s) 12"—C-LFX338
[Hahn: Une Revue—Dernière Valse]
Tino Rossi (t) (arr. Marbot)
10"—C-DB1874
[Massenet: Pensée d'Automne]
Odette Moulin (s) 10"—PAT-PA1007
[Liszt: Hungarian Rhapsody No. 6,
vocal arr.]
Alba Mazzoni (s) 10"—PAT-PA1458
[Schubert: Serenade]
Richard Tauber (t) 10"—P-RO20484
[Herbert: Mlle. Modiste—Kiss me
again]
DUPLICATIONS: Germaine Lubin,
O-123641; A. de Busny, C-DF2158;L.
Bory, O-281279; L. Muratore, PAT-
X93079

No. 4, C sharp minor, Op. 10, No. 4
Alexander Brailowsky, on V-11-9886 in
VM-1171†
Alfred Cortot, on V-14558 in VM-398:
G-DB2027
Edward Kilenyi, on C-P72064D in CM-
369: PAT-PAT106
(Also on PAT-PG93)
Raoul Koczalski, on PD-67262
Vladimir Horowitz
(G-DB2788) 12"—V-14140
[No. 5, & Mazurka No. 32]
DUPLICATIONS: Robert Lortat,
C-LFX136; Alexander Brailowsky, PD-
35012; Oscar Levant, C-72109D in CM-
649; N. Orloff, D-K1426

**No. 5, G flat major, Op. 10, No. 5 "Black
Keys"**
Alexander Brailowsky, on V-11-9887 in
VM-1171†
Alfred Cortot, on V-14558 in VM-398:
G-DB2027
Edward Kilenyi, on C-P72065D in CM-
368: PAT-PAT107
Raoul Koczalski, on PD-67263
Vladimir Horowitz
(G-DB2788) 12"—V-14140
[No. 4 & Mazurka No. 32]
Ignace Jan Paderewski
[No. 12] (G-DA1047) 12"—V-1387
DUPLICATIONS: Vladimir de Pach-
mann, G-DA1302; Alexander Brailowsky,
PD-95140: CET-OR5082; Irene Scharrer,
G-D1303; Jeanne-Marie Darré, PAT-
PDT93; Oscar Levant, C-71890D; also on
C-72106D in CM-649; N. de Magaloff,
RAD-RZ3044

No. 6, E flat major, Op. 10, No. 6
Alexander Brailowsky, on V-11-9887, in
VM-1171†
Alfred Cortot, on V-14559 in VM-398:
G-DB2028
Edward Kilenyi, on C-P72065D in CM-
368: PAT-PAT107

Raoul Koczalski, on PD-67262
DUPLICATIONS: Robert Lortat,
C-LFX136; Raoul Koczalski, PD-90028

No. 7, C major, Op. 10, No. 7
Alexander Brailowsky, on V-11-9885 in
VM-1171†
Alfred Cortot, on V-14558 in VM-398:
G-DB2027
Edward Kilenyi, on C-P72063D in CM-
368: PAT-PAT105
Raoul Koczalski, on PD-67263
DUPLICATIONS: Robert Lortat,
C-LFX137; Wilhelm Backhaus,
G-DB929

No. 8, F major, Op. 10, No. 8
Alexander Brailowsky, on V-11-9888 in
VM-1171†
Alfred Cortot, on V-14560 in VM-398:
G-DB2029
Edward Kilenyi, on C-P72064D in CM-
368: PAT-PAT106
Raoul Koczalski, on PD-67264
Solomon 12"—C-DX669
[No. 15 & Fantasie, Pt. 3]
Vladimir Horowitz 10"—G-DA1305
[Mazurka No. 7]
Carlo Zecchi 10"—T-A1948
[Liszt: Paganini Etude No. 5]
DUPLICATIONS: Jakob Gimpel, in
VOX-164; N. de Magaloff, RAD-RZ3044;
N. Orloff, D-K1426; Robert Lortat,
C-LFX137

No. 9, F minor, Op. 10, No. 9
Alexander Brailowsky, on V-11-9886 in
VM-1171†
Alfred Cortot, on V-14560 in VM-398:
G-DB2029
Edward Kilenyi, on C-P72063D in CM-
368: PAT-PAT105
Raoul Koczalski, on PD-67264
Solomon 12"—G-C3345
[Nos. 14, 15 & Nocturne No. 2]
DUPLICATION: Robert Lortat,
C-LFX137

No. 10, A flat major, Op. 10, No. 10
Alexander Brailowsky, on V-11-9885, in
VM-1171†
Alfred Cortot, on V-14560 in VM-398:
G-DB2029
Edward Kilenyi, on C-P72065D in CM-
368: PAT-PAT107
Raoul Koczalski, on PD-67264
DUPLICATIONS: Robert Lortat,
C-LFX137; Otakar Vondrovic, ESTA-
F5188
—Arr. Vl. & Pf. Ricci
Ruggiero Ricci & Louis Persinger, in
VOX-196

No. 11, E flat major, Op. 10, No. 11
Alexander Brailowsky, on V-11-9888 in
VM-1171†
Alfred Cortot, on V-14559 in VM-398:
G-DB2028
Edward Kilenyi, on C-P72063D in CM-
368: PAT-PAT105
Raoul Koczalski, on PD-67263
DUPLICATIONS: Robert Lortat,
C-LFX138; Josef Lhevinne in DISC-774;
S. François, D-K1399

**No. 12, C minor, Op. 10, No. 12 "Revolu-
tionary"**
Alexander Brailowsky, on V-11-9888 in
VM-1171†
Alfred Cortot, on V-14560 in VM-398:
G-DB2029
Edward Kilenyi, on C-P72065D in CM-
368: PAT-PAT107
Raoul Koczalski, on PD-67264
Louis Kentner 12"—C-DX1083
[Polonaise, Pt. 3]
Emile von Sauer 10"—C-LW38
[Valse No. 4]
DUPLICATIONS: Robert Lortat,
C-LFX138; Wilhelm Backhaus,
G-DB928; I. J. Paderewski, V-1387:
G-DA1047; Jacob Gimpel, in VOX-604.
Oscar Levant, C-71890D, also on
C-72106D in CM-649; Ganto, G-GW1730;
Irene Scharrer, C-DX456
—Arr. Orch.—Rogal-Lewitzsky
Robin Hood Dell Orch.—Mitropoulos, in
CM-598

**No. 13, A flat major, Op. 25, No. 1
"Aeolian Harp"**
Alexander Brailowsky, on V-11-9888, in
VM-1171†
Alfred Cortot, on G-DB2308
(Also on G-DA691)
Edward Kilenyi, on C-72074D in CM-473
Raoul Koczalski, on PD-67243: PD-
566198
Solomon 12"—C-LX314
[Polonaise No. 6]
DUPLICATIONS: Jeanne-Marie Darré,
PAT-PDT92; Robert Lortat, C-LFX139;
Jacques Dupont, PAT-PG9; Otakar Von-
drovic, ESTA-F5188; Irene Scharrer,
C-DB1348; I. Ungar, RAD-RBM103

**No. 14, F minor, Op. 25, No. 2 "Les
Abeilles"**
Alexander Brailowsky, on V-11-9889 in
VM-1171†
Alfred Cortot, on G-DB2308
Edward Kilenyi, on C-72074D in CM-473
(Also on PAT-PG93)
Raoul Koczalski, on PD-67243: PD-
566198
Solomon 12"—G-C3345
[Etudes Nos. 9 & 15, Nocturne No. 2]
DUPLICATIONS: Robert Lortat,
C-LFX139; Alexander Brailowsky, PD-
95140: CET-OR5082; Colin Horsley,
D-K1405; M. de Salvo, C-DQ7223

No. 15, F major, Op. 25, No. 3
Alexander Brailowsky, on V-11-9889 in
VM-1171†
Alfred Cortot, on G-DB2309
Edward Kilenyi, on C-72074D in CM-473
Raoul Koczalski, on PD-67245: PD-
566200
Solomon 12"—G-C3345
[Nos. 9 & 14, Nocturne No. 2]
DUPLICATIONS: Robert Lortat,
C-LFX139; Wilhelm Backhaus, G-DB928;
Solomon, C-DX669; Alexander Brailow-
sky, PD-35012; Vladimir de Pachmann,
G-DB860

No. 16, A minor, Op. 25, No. 4
Alexander Brailowsky, on V-11-9889 in VM-1171†
Alfred Cortot, on G-DB2309
Edward Kilenyi, on C-72074D in CM-473 (Also on PAT-PG93)
Raoul Koczalski, on PD-67245: PD-566200
DUPLICATIONS: Robert Lortat, C-LFX139; Colin Horsley, D-K1405

No. 17, E minor, Op. 25, No. 5
Alexander Brailowsky, on V-11-9890 in VM-1171†
Alfred Cortot, on G-DB2309
Edward Kilenyi, on C-72075D in CM-473
Raoul Koczalski, on PD-67243: PD-566198
DUPLICATION: Robert Lortat, C-LFX140

No. 18, G sharp minor, Op. 25, No. 6
Alexander Brailowsky, on V-11-9890 in VM-1171†
Alfred Cortot, on G-DB2309
Edward Kilenyi, on C-72075D in CM-473
Raoul Koczalski, on PD-67245: PD-566200
DUPLICATIONS: Robert Lortat, C-LFX140; Jeanne-Marie Darré, PAT-PDT92; France Ellegard, PD-62839; Irene Scharrer, C-DB1348; Colin Horsley, D-K1405

No. 19, C sharp minor, Op. 25, No. 7
Alexander Brailowsky, on V-11-9891 in VM-1171†
Alfred Cortot, on G-DB2310
Edward Kilenyi, on C-72075D in CM-473
Raoul Koczalski, on PD-67242: PD-566197
DUPLICATIONS: Robert Lortat, C-LFX141; Raoul Koczalski, PD-95202; Otakar Vondrovic, ESTA-F5188; C. Chaillez-Richez, C-LFX734

No. 20, D flat major, Op. 25, No. 8
Alexander Brailowsky, on V-11-9889 in VM-1171†
Alfred Cortot, on G-DB2309
Edward Kilenyi, on C-72076D in CM-473
Raoul Koczalski, on PD-67243: PD-566198
Robert Lortat, on C-LFX140
DUPLICATIONS: Robert Lortat, C-LFX140; Jeanne-Marie Darré, PAT-PDT93; Colin Horsley, D-K1405

No. 21, G flat major, Op. 25, No. 9 "Butterfly"
Alexander Brailowsky, on V-11-9890, in VM-1171†
Alfred Cortot, on G-DB2310
Edward Kilenyi, on C-72076D in CM-473
Raoul Koczalski, on PD-67243: PD-566198
DUPLICATIONS: Robert Lortat, C-LFX138; Alexander Brailowsky, PD-90197; Colin Horsley, D-K405; Dirk Schäfer, C-DHX15; Myrtle C. Eaver, V-24796; I. J. Paderewski, G-DA470*; Josef Lhevinne in DISC-774; Jeanne-Marie Darré, PAT-PDT93; Irene Schar-

rer, C-DB1348; N. de Magaloff, RAD-RZ3044; I. Ungar, RAD-RBM103

No. 22, B minor, Op. 25, No. 10
Alexander Brailowsky, on V-11-9891 in VM-1171†
Alfred Cortot, on G-DB2308
Edward Kilenyi, on C-72076D in CM-473
Raoul Koczalski, on PD-67242: PD-566197
Robert Lortat, on C-LFX141
DUPLICATION: S. François, D-K1399

No. 23, A minor, Op. 25, No. 11 "Winter Wind"
Alexander Brailowsky, on V-11-9892 in VM-1171†
Alfred Cortot, on G-DB2310
Edward Kilenyi, on C-72076D in CM-473
Raoul Koczalski, on PD-67244: PD-566199
Jacques Dupont 10"—PAT-PG9 [No. 13]
DUPLICATIONS: Robert Lortat, C-LFX142; Alexander Brailowsky, PD-95323: CET-RR8029

No. 24, C minor, Op. 25, No. 12
Alexander Brailowsky, on V-11-9888 in VM-1171†
Alfred Cortot, on G-DB2308
Edward Kilenyi, on C-72074D in CM-473
Raoul Koczalski, on PD-67245: PD-566200
DUPLICATIONS: Robert Lortat, C-LFX142; Alexander Brailowsky, PD-95423; Dirk Schäfer, C-DHX15; Otakar Vondrovic, ESTA-F5185

No. 25, F minor (No. 1 of "3 Nouvelles Etudes") Piano
Alexander Brailowsky, on V-11-9892 in VM-1171†
Raoul Koczalski, on PD-67244: PD-566199
Harriet Cohen 12"—C-DX1231 [No. 27 & Nocturne No. 4]
DUPLICATION: Robert Lortat, C-LFX138

No. 26, D flat major
(This is No. 2 of "3 Nouvelles Etudes" but is given as No. 3 in some editions)
Alexander Brailowsky, on V-11-9892 in VM-1171†
Raoul Koczalski, on PD-67244: PD-566199
(older version, PD-90039)
DUPLICATION: Robert Lortat, C-LFX142

No. 27, A flat major (No. 3 of "3 Nouvelles Etudes")
(No. 26, or 2, in some editions)
Alexander Brailowsky, on V-11-9892 in VM-1171†
Raoul Koczalski, on PD-67244: PD-566199
Harriet Cohen 12"—C-DX1231 [No. 25 & Nocturne No. 4]
DUPLICATION: Robert Lortat, C-LFX140

Unspecified Etude, G flat Piano
Raymond Trouard 10"—O-188940 [Ecoissaises]

Fantasie, F minor, Op. 49 Piano
  Alfred Cortot   2   12″—G-DB2031/2
  [Tarantelle]
  Solomon   2   12″—C-DX668/9
  [Etudes Nos. 8 & 15]
Fantasie-Impromptu See: Impromptu No. 4
Funeral March See: **Sonata No. 2, B flat minor**

(4) IMPROMPTUS Piano

Collection (The 4 Impromptus)
  Alfred Cortot   2   12″—G-DB2021/2
No. 1, A flat major, Op. 29
  Alfred Cortot, G-DB2021
  Alexander Brailowsky   12″—V-11-8643
  [Liszt: Liebestraum No. 3]
  (older version, PD-95423)
  Louis Kentner   12″—C-DX1081
  [Valse No. 7]
  Ania Dorfmann
  (C-DWX1608)   12″—C-DX818
  [Valse No. 5]
  Hanna Schwab   12″—PD-15175
  [Polonaise No. 1]
  Irene Scharrer   12″—G-D1087
  [No. 4]
  Nicolas Orloff   12″—D-K1424
  [Mazurka No. 7 & Valse No. 4]
No. 2, F sharp major, Op. 36
  Alfred Cortot, G-DB2021
  Louis Kentner   12″—C-DX997
  [No. 4]
  Lili Kraus   12″—P-R20451
  [Prelude No. 4]
  Raoul Koczalski   12″—PD-67248
  [No. 4]
No. 3, G flat major, Op. 51
  Alfred Cortot, G-DB2022: V-8239
  Artur Rubinstein
      (in VM-1075†)   12″—V-11-9301
  [Rachmaninoff: Concerto No. 2, Pt. 9, with NBC Symphony]
No. 4, C sharp minor, Op. 66 "Fantasie-Impromptu"
  Alfred Cortot, G-DB2022: V-8239
  Eileen Joyce   12″—P-E11432
  [Berceuse]
  José Iturbi
      (in VM-1110)   10″—V-10-1283
  [Valse No. 6]
  Louis Kentner   12″—C-DX997
  [No. 2]
  Alexander Brailowsky   12″—V-12-0016
  [Nocturne No.2]
  [Mazurka No. 5 on PD-95324]
  Jacob Gimpel, in VOX-604

  DUPLICATIONS: Wilhelm Backhaus, G-DB2059; Irene Scharrer, C-DX456, also G-D1087; Magda Tagliaferro, PAT-PAT22; Dirk Schäfer, C-DHX12; Raoul Koczalski, PD-67248; Iris Loveridge, C-DX1239; D'Erasmo, G-S10118; Nicolas Orloff, D-K1425
Introduction & Polonaise Brillante, Op. 3
  Piano & 'Cello
  Gregor Piatigorsky & Valentine Pavlov-sky   12″—C-71889D
  Margaret Good & William Pleeth
      12″—D-K922

Emanuel Feuermann & Franz Rupp
      12″—G-DB6042

(55) MAZURKAS Piano
  (49 Mazurkas with opus numbers; 6 without)

Collections
51 Mazurkas
Vol. I—containing Op. 6, Nos. 1-4; Op. 7, Nos. 1-5; Op. 17, Nos. 1-4; Op. 24, Nos. 1-3; Op. 30, Nos. 1 & 3; Op. 41, Nos. 2 & 4.
  Artur Rubinstein   5   12″—VM-626
Vol. II—containing Op. 24, No. 4; Op. 30, No. 4; Op. 33, Nos. 2, 3, 4; Op. 41, Nos. 1 & 3; Op. 50, Nos. 1, 2, 3; Op. 56, No. 1; Op. 63, Nos. 1, 2, 3; Op. 68, No. 4
  Artur Rubinstein   5   12″—VM-656
Vol. III—containing Op. 30, No. 2; Op. 33; No. 1; Op. 56, Nos. 2 & 3; Op. 59, Nos. 1-3; Op. 67, Nos. 1-4 (complete); Op. 68, Nos. 1, 2, 3; A Minor (Posth.); A Minor ("Notre temps")
  Artur Rubinstein   4   12″—VM-691

The Rubinstein recordings have been released in England in 2 Volumes, GM-332 & 367. The European couplings vary from the American.

12 Mazurkas
  Nos. 5, 6, 7, 17, 23, 26, 31, 41, 44, 45, 47
  Ignaz Friedman   4   12″—CM-159
Individual Mazurkas
No. 1, F sharp minor, Op. 6, No. 1
  Artur Rubinstein
      (in VM-626)   12″—V-15779
  (G-DB3802, in GM-332)
Nos. 2, C sharp minor, Op. 6, No. 2
  Artur Rubinstein
      (in VM-626)   12″—V-15779
  (G-DB3802 in GM-332)
No. 3, E major, Op. 6, No. 3
  Artur Rubinstein
      (in VM-626)   12″—V-15779
  (G-DB3802 in GM-332)
No. 4, E flat major, Op. 6, No. 4
  Artur Rubinstein
      (in VM-626)   12″—V-15780
  (G-DB3803 in GM-332)
No. 5, B flat major, Op. 7, No. 1
  Artur Rubinstein
      (in VM-626)   12″—V-15781
  (G-DB3804 in GM-332)
  Ignaz Friedman, on C-72059D in CM-159
  José Iturbi
      (in VM-1110)   10″—V-10-1284
  [Valse No. 7] (G-DA1849)
  Alexander Brailowsky   12″—PD-95324
  [Impromptu No. 4]

  DUPLICATIONS: Jacob Gimpel, in VOX-604; France Ellegard, PD-62839; Oscar Levant, in CM-649
No. 6, A minor, Op. 7, No. 2
  Artur Rubinstein
      (in VM-626)   12″—V-15779
  (G-DB3802 in GM-332)
  Ignaz Friedman, on C-72059D in CM-159

No. 7, F minor, Op. 7, No. 3
Artur Rubinstein
        (in VM-626)   12″—**V-15780**
(G-DB3803 in GM-332)
Ignaz Friedman, on C-72059D in CM-159
Vladimir Horowitz   10″—**G-DA1305**
[Etude No. 8]
Nicolas Orloff   12″—**D-K1424**
[Impromptu No. 1 & Valse No. 4]
No. 8, A flat major, Op. 7, No. 4
Artur Rubinstein
        (in VM-626)   12″—**V-15780**
(G-DB3803 in GM-332)
No. 9, C major, Op. 7, No. 5
Artur Rubinstein
        (in VM-626)   12″—**V-15780**
(G-DB3803 in GM-332)
No. 10, B flat major, Op. 17, No. 1
Artur Rubinstein
        (in VM-626)   12″—**V-15781**
(G-DB3804 in GM-332)
No. 11, E minor, Op. 17, No. 2
Artur Rubinstein
        (in VM-626)   12″—**V-15781**
(G-DB3804 in GM-332)
No. 12, A flat major, Op. 17, No. 3
Artur Rubinstein
        (in VM-626)   12″—**V-15782**
(G-DB3805 in GM-332)
No. 13, A minor, Op. 17, No. 4
Artur Rubinstein
        (in VM-626)   12″—**V-15782**
(G-DB3805 in GM-332)
Edward Kilenyi
        (in CM-378)   12″—**C-P69671D**
[Sonata No. 2, Pt. 5] (PAT-PAT82)
Walter Gieseking   12″—**C-LWX304**
[Berceuse, Op. 57] (C-GQX11049)
Robert Casadesus, in CM-698
(Also on C-LFX75)

DUPLICATIONS: Marie Panthès,
C-DF1919; Mlle. Boutet de Monvel,
G-L1045; Carlo Zecchi, CET-CB20359
No. 14, G minor, Op. 24, No. 1
Artur Rubinstein
        (in VM-626)   12″—**V-15783**
(G-DB3806 in GM-332)
No. 15, C major, Op. 24, No. 2
Artur Rubinstein
        (in VM-626)   12″—**V-15783**
(G-DB3806 in GM-332)
No. 16, A flat major, Op. 24, No. 3
Artur Rubinstein
        (in VM-626)   12″—**V-15780**
(G-DB3803 in GM-332)
No. 17, B flat minor, Op. 24, No. 4
Artur Rubinstein
        (in VM-656)   12″—**V-15907**
(G-DB3807 in GM-332)
Ignaz Friedman, on C-72060D in CM-159
Malcuzynski   12″—**C-LX1028**
[No. 32]
Otakar Vondrovic   12″—**ESTA-F5186**
[Valse No. 9]
—**Arr. Orchestra** See: Miscellaneous—La
Nuit Ensorcelée
No. 18, C minor, Op. 30, No. 1
Artur Rubinstein
        (in VM-626)   12″—**V-15781**
(G-DB3804 in GM-332)

No. 19, B minor, Op. 30, No. 2
Artur Rubinstein
        (in VM-691)   12″—**V-17297**
(G-DB3807 in GM-332)
Maryla Jonas
        (in CM-626)   12″—**C-72099D**
[Nos. 43, 49, & B flat, Op. Posth.]
No. 20, D flat major, Op. 30, No. 3
Artur Rubinstein
        (in VM-626)   12″—**V-15783**
(G-DB3806 in GM-332)
No. 21, C sharp minor, Op. 30, No. 4
Artur Rubinstein
        (in VM-656)   12″—**V-15907**
(G-DB3808 in GM-332)
Vladimir Horowitz   10″—**V-1327**
[Bizet-Horowitz: Variations on themes
from Carmen]
DUPLICATION: Carlo Zecchi, CET-
CB20346
No. 22, G sharp minor, Op. 33, No. 1
Artur Rubinstein
        (in VM-691)   12″—**V-17298**
(G-DB3808 in GM-332)
No. 23, D major, Op. 33, No. 2
Artur Rubinstein
        (in VM-656)   12″—**V-15908**
(G-DB3839 in GM-367)
[Older version on G-DB2149 with No. 39
& Berceuse]
Ignaz Friedman, on C-72059D in CM-159
DUPLICATION: I. J. Paderewski,
G-DA1245
Arr. Orchestra See: Miscellaneous—Les
Sylphides
No. 24, C major, Op. 33, No. 3
Artur Rubinstein
        (in VM-656)   12″—**V-15908**
(G-DB3839 in GM-367)
No. 25, B minor, Op. 33, No. 4
Artur Rubinstein
        (in VM-656)   12″—**V-15909**
(G-DB3840 in GM-367)
Ignaz Friedman, on C-72060D in CM-159
DUPLICATIONS: A. Benedetti Michel-
angeli, T-SKB3289; Marie Panthès,
C-DFX216; Leonid Kreutzer, PD-90034;
Carlo Zecchi, CET-CB20359; R. Koczal-
ski, PD-90031
—**Arr. Orch.**
Robin Hood Dell Orch.—Mitropoulos, in
CM-598
Philadelphia Orch.—Stokowski, in
VM-841†
No. 26, C sharp minor, Op. 41, No. 1
Artur Rubinstein
        (in VM-656)   12″—**V-15909**
(G-DB3840 in GM-367)
Ignaz Friedman, on C-72061D in CM-159
No. 27, E minor, Op. 41, No. 2
Artur Rubinstein
        (in VM-626)   12″—**V-15783**
(G-DB3806 in GM-332)
Vladimir Horowitz   10″—**G-DA1353**
[Schumann: Traumeswirren]
No. 28, B major, Op. 41, No. 3
Artur Rubinstein
        (in VM-656)   12″—**V-15909**
(G-DB3840 in GM-367)

No. 29, A flat major, Op. 41, No. 4
Artur Rubinstein
    (in VM-626) 12"—**V-15780**
(G-DB3803 in GM-332)

No. 30, G major, Op. 50, No. 1
Artur Rubinstein
    (in VM-656) 12"—**V-15910**
(G-DB3841 in GM-367)

No. 31, A flat major, Op. 50, No. 2
Artur Rubinstein
    (in VM-656) 12"—**V-15910**
(G-DB3841 in GM-367)
Ignaz Friedman, on C-72061D in CM-159

No. 32, C sharp minor, Op. 50, No. 3
Artur Rubinstein
    (in VM-656) 12"—**V-15911**
(G-DB3842 in GM-367)
Vladimir Horowitz   12"—**V-14140**
[Etudes No. 4 & 5] (G-DB2788)
Otakar Vondrovic 12"—**ESTA-F5185**
[Etude No. 24]
Malcuzynski   12"—**C-LX1028**
[No. 17]
Nicolas Orloff   12"—**D-K1426**
[Etudes No. 8 & No. 4]
DUPLICATION: N. de Magaloff, RAD-RZ3031

No. 33, B major, Op. 56, No. 1
Artur Rubinstein
    (in VM-656) 12"—**V-15911**
(G-DB3842 in GM-367)

No. 34, C major, Op. 56, No. 2
Artur Rubinstein
    (in VM-691) 12"—**V-17295**
(G-DB3843 in GM-367)

No. 35, C minor, Op. 56, No. 3
Artur Rubinstein
    (in VM-691) 12"—**V-15295**
(G-DB3843 in GM-367)
[Older version on G-DB1462, with Granados: Goyescas—La maja y el ruiseñor]

No. 36, A minor, Op. 59, No. 1
Artur Rubinstein
    (in VM-691) 12"—**V-17295**
(G-DB3843 in GM-367)

No. 37, A flat major, Op. 59, No. 2
Artur Rubinstein
    (in VM-691) 12"—**V-17296**
(G-DB3844 in GM-367)

DUPLICATION: I. J. Paderewski,
G-DA1245

No. 38, F sharp minor, Op. 59, No. 3
Artur Rubinstein
    (in VM-691) 12"—**V-17296**
(G-DB3844 in GM-367)
Simon Barere   12"—**V-14263**
[Schumann: Toccata, Op. 7]
Marguerite Long
    (in CM-143) 12"—**C-67803D**
[Concerto No. 2, Pt. 7] (C-D15239)

No. 39, B major, Op. 63, No. 1
Artur Rubinstein
    (in VM-656) 12"—**V-15908**
(G-DB3839 in GM-367)
[Older version, G-DB2149, with No. 23 & Berceuse]

No. 40, F minor, Op. 63, No. 2
Artur Rubinstein
    (in VM-656) 12"—**V-15910**
(G-DB3841 in GM-367)

No. 41, C sharp minor, Op. 63, No. 3
Artur Rubinstein
    (in VM-656) 12"—**V-15910**
(G-DB3841 in GM-367)
Ignaz Friedman, on C-72062D in CM-159
Ignace Jan Paderewski 12"—**V-7416**
[Nocturne No. 2] (G-DB1763)
Edward Kilenyi   10"—**PAT-PG92**
[Valse No. 5]
DUPLICATION: Andor Földes, in CON-22

No. 42, G major, Op. 67, No. 1
Artur Rubinstein
    (in VM-691) 12"—**V-17296**
(G-DB3844 in GM-367)
Vladimir de Pachmann 10"—**G-DA1302**
[Prelude No. 6 & Etude No. 5]

No. 43, G minor, Op. 67, No. 2
Artur Rubinstein
    (in VM-691) 12"—**V-17297**
(G-DB3807 in GM-332)
Maryla Jones
    (in CM-626) 12"—**C-72099D**
[Nos. 19, 49, and B flat, Op. Posth.]

No. 44, C major, Op. 67, No. 3
Artur Rubinstein
    (in VM-691) 12"—**V-17297**
(G-DB3807 in GM-332)
Ignaz Friedman, on C-72062D in CM-159
—**Arr. Orch.** See: Miscellaneous—Les Sylphides

No. 45, A minor, Op. 67, No. 4
Artur Rubinstein
    (in VM-691) 12"—**V-17298**
(G-DB3808 in GM-332)
Ignaz Friedman, on C-72062D in CM-159
Jean Françaix   10"—**T-A2232**
[Debussy: Children's Corner Suite, No. 3]
—**Arr. Violin & Piano** Kreisler
Fritz Kreisler & Franz Rupp
        10"—**V-2164**
[Arr. Grainger-Kreisler: Londonderry Air]
[Brahms-Hochstein: Waltz, Op. 39, No. 15, on G-DA1631]
Miguel Candela & Maurice Faure
        10"—**C-LF32**
[Albéniz: Tango, D major]

No. 46, C major, Op. 68, No. 1
Artur Rubinstein
    (in VM-691) 12"—**V-17296**
(G-DB3844 in GM-367)

No. 47, A minor, Op. 68, No. 2
Artur Rubinstein
    (in VM-691) 12"—**V-17297**
(G-DB3845 in GM-367)
Ignaz Friedman, on C-72062D in CM-159
Solomon   12"—**G-C3509**
[Valse No. 14 & Daquin: Le Coucou; de Séverac: Musical Box]
Arturo Benedetti Michelangeli
[Valse No. 3]   10"—**G-DA5371**
John Hunt   12"—**G-C2567**
[Prélude No. 20, & Debussy: Clair de Lune]

Raoul Koczalski 10"—**PD-90040**
[Paderewski: Au soir]
No. 48, F major, Op. 68, No. 3
Artur Rubinstein
(in VM-691) 12"—**V-17298**
(G-DB3808 in GM-332)
Raoul Koczalski 10"—**G-DA4430**
[3 Ecossaises & Nocturne No. 5]
No. 49, F minor, Op. 68, No. 4
Artur Rubinstein
(in VM-656) 12"—**V-15908**
(G-DB3839 in GM-367)
Maryla Jonas
(in CM-626) 12"—**C-72099D**
[Nos. 19, 43, & B flat, Op. Posth.]
No. 50, A minor "Notre Temps"
Artur Rubinstein
(in VM-691) 12"—**V-17298**
(G-DB3845 in GM-367)
No. 51, A minor (Dedicated to Emile Gaillard)
Artur Rubinstein
(in VM-691) 12"—**V-17297**
(G-DB3845 in GM-367)
B flat major (No. 2 of Posthumous series) (1825)
Maryla Jonas
(in CM-626) 12"—**C-72099D**
[Nos. 49, 43, 19]
Unidentified: A minor
Lev Oborin 12"—**U-G14743**
[Rimsky-Korsakov; Flight of the Bumble Bee; Katchaturian: Toccata]
Also: Georgio Vidusso, ADAM-C111

(20) NOCTURNES Piano
(19 Nocturnes with Opus numbers and one additional Nocturne discovered in 1895)
Volume I—containing Nos. 1 to 8 and 13 to 19
Artur Rubinstein
(GM-284A) 6 12"—**VM-461**
Volume II—containing Nos. 9, 10, 11, 12, 14, 15, 19
Artur Rubinstein
(GM-284B) 5 12"—**VM-462**
12 Nocturnes
(Nos. 1, 2, 4, 5, 7, 8, 9, 11, 12, 14, 15, 19)
Leopold Godowsky 7 12"—**CM-112**
[With two sides of remarks by Ernest Newman on C-GQX10841/8]

No. 1, B flat minor, Op. 9, No. 1
Artur Rubinstein
(in VM-461) 12"—**V-14961**
(G-DB3186 in GM-284A)
Leopold Godowsky, in CM-112

No. 2, E flat major, Op. 9, No. 2 (The most popular Nocturne)
Artur Rubinstein
(in VM-461) 12"—**V-14961**
(G-DB3186 in GM-284A)
Leopold Godowsky, in CM-112
Solomon 12"—**G-C3345**
[Etudes No. 9, 14, 15]
Eileen Joyce 12"—**P-E11448**
[No. 9]

DUPLICATIONS: Benno Moiseiwitsch, G-C3197; Raoul Koczalski, PD-67246; Alexander Brailowsky, PD-95143; I. J. Paderewski, V-7416: G-DB1763; Sergei Rachmaninoff, V-6731; Leo Nadelmann, G-DB10073; Johanne Stockmarr, G-DB5261; Willi Stech, T-A1914; Alfred Cortot, G-DB1321; Mark Hambourg, G-C2587; Jacob Gimpel, in VOX-604; F. Rausch, U-G12943; Oscar Levant, on C-72107D in CM-649; G. Faragó, RAD-SP8029

—**Arr. Violin & Piano** Sarasate
David Oistrakh & Abram Makarov
12"—**U-G14742**
[Tartini-Kreisler: Variations on a theme of Corelli]
Ibolyka Zilzer & Michael Raucheisen
(Raff: Cavatina] 12"—**PD-27160**
DUPLICATIONS: Y. Curti, PAT-X9744; A. Abussi, C-CQ565
—**Arr. 'Cello & Piano** Popper
Gaspar Cassadó & pf. aac.
12"—**PD-95027**
[Schumann: Träumerei]
Maurice Maréchal & Maurice Faure
12"—**C-LFX319**
[Liszt: Liebestraum No. 3]
André Navarra & pf. 12"—**O-123850**
DUPLICATION: Pablo Casals, G-DB966
—**Miscellaneous transcriptions**
Squire Celeste Octet, C-DX362: C-DFX129
—**Vocal arrangement**
"Good-night, my beloved" (arr. Maurice Besly)
Anne Ziegler & Webster Booth (s & t)
[Liszt: Liebestraum] 12"—**G-C3460**

No. 3, B major, Op. 9, No. 3
Artur Rubinstein
(in VM-461) 12"—**V-14962**
(G-DB3187 in GM-284A)
DUPLICATION: Josef Lhevinne in DISC-774

No. 4, F major, Op. 15, No. 1
Artur Rubinstein
(in VM-461) 12"—**V-14962**
(G-DB3187 in GM-384A)
Leopold Godowsky, in CM-112
Harriet Cohen 12"—**C-DX1231**
[Etudes Nos. 25 & 27]

No. 5, F sharp major, Op. 15, No. 2
Artur Rubinstein
(in VM-461) 12"—**V-14963**
(G-DB3188 in GM-284A)
Leopold Godowsky, in CM-112
Alexander Brailowsky 12"—**V-11-9009**
[Rimsky-Korsakoff, arr. Rachmaninoff: Flight of the Bumble Bee & Liadov: Musical snuff box]
Raoul Koczalski 10"—**G-DA4430**
[3 Ecossaises & Mazurka No. 48]
Vladimir Horowitz
(in VM-1165†) 12"—**V-11-9842**
[Liszt: Au bord d'une source]

Malcuzynski 12"—C-LX975
[Valse No. 7]
DUPLICATIONS: I. J. Paderewski,
G-DB3711: older version, V-6825:
G-DB1167; also on G-DB375*; Levitzki,
G-D1721; Myra Hess, C-DB1232 in CM-
234; Jacques Dupont, PAT-PG21; Wil-
liam Murdoch, D-K704; Myrtle C. Eaver,
V-24796; Raymond Trouard, O-123844;
Oscar Levant, C-72107D in CM-649; I.
Ungar, RAD-RBM103

No. 6, G minor, Op. 15, No. 3
Artur Rubinstein
(in VM-461) 12"—V-14963
(G-DB3188 in GM-284A)

No. 7, C sharp minor, Op. 27, No. 1
Artur Rubinstein
(in VM-461) 12"—V-14964
(G-DB3189 in GM-284A)
Leopold Godowsky, in CM-112
Winfried Wolf 12"—G-DB7605
[Polonaise No. 3]
William Murdoch 12"—D-K691
[Mendelssohn: Songs without words,
Nos. 22 & 47]

—Arr. Violin & Piano
G. M. Guarino & Adelina Satamato
[Debussy: Minstrels] 10"—C-GQ7225

—Arr. 'Cello & Piano
André Navarra, O-123850: Gregor
Piatigorsky, G-DB2271

No. 8, D flat major, Op. 27, No. 2
Artur Rubinstein
(in VM-461) 12"—V-14965
(G-DB3190 in GM-284A)
Leopold Godowsky, in CM-112
Solomon 12"—G-C3308
[Berceuse]
Dinu Lipatti 10"—C-LB63
Yvonne Gellibert 12"—G-DB5159
[No. 16]
Vladimir de Pachmann 12"—G-DB860
[Etude No. 15 & Valse No. 7]
Raoul Koczalski 12"—PD-95172
[No. 17]

—Arr. Violin & Piano
Mischa Elman & pf. acc. 12"—G-DB1398
[Mendelssohn: Auf Flügeln des Ges-
anges]
René Benedetti & Maurice Faure
[Sarasate: Zapateado] 12"—C-LFX21

No. 9, B major, Op. 32, No. 1
Artur Rubinstein
(in VM-462) 12"—V-14967
(G-DB3192 in GM-284B)
Leopold Godowsky, in CM-112
Louis Kentner 12"—C-DX1147
[Polonaise No. 7, Pt. 3]
Raoul Koczalski 12"—PD-67534
[No. 13]
Eileen Joyce 12"—P-E11448
[No. 2]
T. van der Pas 12"—D-X10030
[No. 20]

No. 10, A flat major, Op. 32, No. 2

Artur Rubinstein
(in VM-462) 12"—V-14967
(G-DB3192 in GM-284B)
[No. 9]
France Ellegaard 12"—PD-67841
[Valse No. 5]

—Arr. Orchestra
See: Miscellaneous—Les Sylphides

No. 11, G minor, Op. 37, No. 1
Artur Rubinstein
(in VM-461) 12"—V-14964
(G-DB3189 in GM-384A)
Leopold Godowsky, in CM-112

No. 12, G major, Op. 37, No. 2
Artur Rubinstein
(in VM-461) 12"—V-14966
(G-DB3191 in GM-284A)
Leopold Godowsky, in CM-112
Mark Hambourg 12"—G-C2516
[Liszt: Liebestraum No. 3]

No. 13, C minor, Op. 48, No. 1
(in VM-462) 12"—V-14968
(G-DB3193 in GM-284B)
Raoul Koczalski 12"—PD-67534
[No. 9]

—Arr. Orch.—Rogal-Lewitzsky
Robin Hood Dell Orch.—Mitropoulos, in
CM-598

No. 14, F sharp minor, Op. 48, No. 2
Artur Rubinstein
(in VM-462) 12"—V-14968
(G-DB3193 in GM-284B)
Leopold Godowsky, in CM-112
Jacques Dupont 10"—PAT-PG21
[Ecossaises]
W. Worden 10"—D-F3053
[Liszt: Gnomenreigen]

—Arr. Orchestra
See: Miscellaneous—La Nuit Ensorcelée

No. 15, F minor, Op. 55, No. 1
Artur Rubinstein
(in VM-462) 12"—V-14969
(G-DB3194 in GM-284B)
Leopold Godowsky, in CM-112

No. 16, E flat major, Op. 55, No. 2
Artur Rubinstein
(in VM-462) 12"—V-14969
(G-DB3194 in GM-284B)
Ignaz Friedman 12"—C-DX781
[Impromptu No. 2]
Yvonne Gellibert 12"—G-DB5159
[No. 8]

No. 17, B major, Op. 62, No. 1
Artur Rubinstein
(in VM-462) 12"—V-14970
(G-DB3195 in GM-284B)
Erik Then-Bergh 12"—G-EH1306
Raoul Koczalski 12"—PD-95172
[No. 8]
Marie Panthès 12"—C-DFX216
[Mazurka No. 25]

No. 18, E major, Op. 62, No. 2
Artur Rubinstein
(in VM-462) 12"—V-14971
(G-DB3196 in GM-284B)

No. 19, E minor, Op. 72, No. 1
Artur Rubinstein
        (in VM-462)   12″—V-14971
(G-DB3196 in GM-284B)
Leopold Godowsky, in CM-112
Leo Nadelmann   12″—G-DB10056
[Valse No. 3]
Maryla Jonas
[No. 20] (in CM-626) 12″—C-72100D
DUPLICATION: D'Erasmo, G-S10118
—Arr. Violin & Piano Auer
Jascha Heifetz & Emanuel Bay
               12″—V-11-9573
[Sarasate: Romanza andaluza]
No. 20, C sharp minor (Posth.)
Maryla Jonas
[No. 19] (in CM-626) 12″—C-72100D
Marie Panthès   10″—C-DF1919
[Mazurka No. 13]
Theo van der Pas   12″—D-X10030
[No. 9]
—Arr. Violin & Piano
Ginette Neveu & Bruno Seidler—Winkler
[Suk: Appassionata] 12″—G-DB4514
—Arr. 'Cello & Piano
Gregor Piatigorsky & I. Newton
               12″—G-DB2271
[Scriabin: Romance & Tchaikovsky:
Valse sentimentale]
Camillo Oblach & Mario Salerno
             12″—CET-CC2119
[Schubert: Wiegenlied]
La Nuit Ensorcelée (Ballet based on Chopin
music)
See: Miscellaneous—La Nuit Ensorcelée

POLONAISES Piano

*In addition to the 12 Polonaise for piano solo
(10 with Opus numbers and 2 early Polonaises
without opus numbers) Chopin wrote an Introduction and Polonaise for 'Cello and Piano, Op.
3, and an Andante spianato and Grande Polonaise Brilliante for piano and orchestra, Op. 22.*

Collection
Andante Spianato & Grande Polonaise
Polonaises 1 to 7 inclusive
Artur Rubinstein
(GM-256A & B)   8 12″—VM-353†
Individual Polonaises
**Andante Spianato & Grande Polonaise, E
flat major, Op. 22**
For Piano & Orchestra
—Arr. Piano solo
Artur Rubinstein, on V-14287/8 in VM-
353†
(G-DB2499/500 in GM-256B)
Vladimir Horowitz
  (in VM-1034†) 2 12″—V-11-9043/4
[Valse No. 3]
No. 1, C sharp minor, Op. 26, No. 1
Artur Rubinstein, on V-14281 in VM-353†
(G-DB2493 in GM-256A†)
Hanna Schwab   12″—PD-15175
[Impromptu No. 1]
No. 2, E flat minor, Op. 26, No. 2 ("Serbian"
or "Revolt")

Artur Rubinstein, on V-14282 in VM-353†
(G-DB2494 in GM-256A†)
Ignace Jan Paderewski 12″—G-DB5897
[older version on G-DB1577]

No. 3, A major, Op. 40, No. 1
("Polonaise Militaire"—"Military
Polonaise")
Artur Rubinstein, on V-14283 in VM-353†
(G-DB2495 in GM-256A†)
Louis Kentner   12″—C-DX1083
[Etude No. 12]
Solomon   12″—C-DX441
[Liszt: Hungarian Rhapsody No. 15]
Suzanne Gyr   12″—G-DB10074
[Berceuse]
Iris Loveridge   12″—C-DX1239
[Impromptu No. 4]
DUPLICATIONS: Winifried Wolf,
G-DB7605; Mark Hambourg, G-C1292;
Raoul Koczalski, PD-90031; Oscar Le-
vant,, on C-72108D in CM-649; E. Hillel,
USSR-13298/9; I. J. Paderewski, G-
DB375*
—Arr. 8 Piano Ensemble, V-36140
(G-C2612)
—Arr. Orchestra Glazounov
(in "Chopiniana" Op. 46)
Boston "Pops" Orchestra—Fiedler
             12″—V-11947
[Mendelssohn: Octet, Op. 20—Scherzo]
[Tchaikovsky: Sleeping Beauty—Waltz
on G-C2892: G-EH1058]
Orchestra Raymonde—G. Walter
           10″—C-DB1401
[Weber: Invitation to the Dance]
(C-DQ1445]
—Arr. Band
Coldstream Guards Band, G-C3150;
also C-FB2956

No. 4, C minor, Op. 40, No. 2
Artur Rubinstein, on V-14283 in VM-353†
(G-DB2495 in GM-256A†)

No. 5, F sharp minor, Op. 44
Artur Rubinstein, on V-14284 in VM-353†
(G-DB2496 in GM-256A†)

No. 6, A flat major, Op. 53 ("Heroic")
Artur Rubinstein, on V-14285 in-VM-353†
(G-DB2497 in GM-256B†)
Vladimir Horowitz   12″—V-11-9065
(also on V-11-9045 in VM-1034†)
France Ellegaard   12″—D-K1600
(also on PD-67840)
Egon Petri   10″—C-17377D
Malcuzynski   12″—C-LX982
Yvonne Gellibert   10″—G-DA4932
Winfried Wolf   12″—G-DB7683
Ignace Jan Paderewski (G-DB3134)
      (in VM-748) 12″—V-14974
José Iturbi
(G-DB6288)   12″—V-11-8848
DUPLICATIONS: Raoul Koczalski,
G-DA4431; Alfred Cortet, G-DB2014;
Solomon, C-LX314; Mischa Levitzki,
G-DA1316; Alexander Brailowsky, PD-
90196: CET-LL3008; Paul Baumgartner,
G-DB10033; Jacob Gimpel, in VOX-604;
Victor Schiøler, TONO-A104

—**Arr. 2 pfs.** Hatzfield & Strong, D-F8208
—**Arr. 4 pfs.**
First Piano Quartet, V-46-0005
—**Arr. Orch.** Rogal-Lewitzsky
Robin Hood Dell Orch.—Mitropoulos, in CM-598

No. 7, A flat major, Op. 61 ("Fantasie Polonaise")
Artur Rubinstein, on V-14286/7 in VM-353† (G-DB2498/9 in GM-256B†)
Louis Kentner   2   12"—C-DX1146/7 [Nocturne No. 9]
Walter Rehberg   2   10"—PD-25137/8 [Liszt: Eclogue]

No. 8, D minor, Op. 71, No. 1
No recording available

No. 9, B flat major, Op. 71, No. 2
Benno Moiseiwitsch   12"—G-C3485 [Debussy: Clair de lune]
Mark Hambourg   12"—G-C2579 [Valses Nos. 6 & 11]
Maryla Jonas
        (in CM-626)   12"—C-72101D [Valses No. 11 & 13]

No. 10, F minor, Op. 71, No. 3
No recording available

(26) PRELUDES Piano

Collections
24 Preludes, Op. 28
Alfred Cortot (1934)   4   12"—VM-282 (G-DB2015/8 in GM-196)
Alfred Cortot (1943)
        4   12"—G-W1541/4
Egon Petri   4   12"—CM-523

No. 1, C major, Op. 28, No. 1
Alfred Cortot, on V-8813 in VM-282 (G-DB2015 in GM-196)
(also on G-W1541)
Wilhelm Backhaus   12"—G-DB2059 [Etude No. 1 & Impromptu No. 4]
Egon Petri, on C-71402D in CM-523
Andor Földes, in CON-22
DUPLICATION: Nicolas Orloff, D-K1425

No. 2, A minor, Op. 28, No. 2
Alfred Cortot, on V-8813 in VM-282 (G-DB2015 in GM-196)
(also on G-W1541)
Egon Petri, on C-71402D in CM-523
DUPLICATION: Nicolas Orloff, D-K1425

No. 3, G major, Op. 28, No. 3
Alfred Cortot, on V-8813 in VM-282 (G-DB2015 in GM-196)
(Also G-W1541)
Moritz Rosenthal   12"—G-DB2772 [Nos. 6 & 7 & Valse No. 5]
Alexander Brailowsky   12"—PD-95423 [No. 6, Etude No. 24 & Impromptu No. 1]
Egon Petri, on C-71402D in CM-543
DUPLICATION: Nicolas Orloff, D-K1425

No. 4, E minor, Op. 28, No. 4
Alfred Cortot, on V-8813 in VM-282 (G-DB2015 in GM-196)
(Also G-W1541)
Egon Petri, on C-71402D in CM-523
Lili Kraus   12"—P-R20451 [Impromptu No. 2]

DUPLICATION: Nicolas Orloff, D-K1425
—**Arr. 'Cello & Piano** Balzelaire
P. Tortelier & T. Janopoulo [Sarasate: Zapateado]   12"—G-DB11116

No. 5, D major, Op. 28, No. 5
Alfred Cortot, on V-8813 in VM-282 (G-DB2015 in GM-196)
(Also G-W1541)
Egon Petri, on C-71402D in CM-523

No. 6, B minor, Op. 28, No. 6
Alfred Cortot, on V-8813 in VM-282 (G-DB2015 in GM-196)
(Also G-W1541)
Egon Petri, on C-71402D in CM-523
Moritz Rosenthal   12"—G-DB2772 [Nos. 3 & 7 & Valse No. 5]
Edward Kilenyi   10"—PAT-PG93 [Etudes Nos. 4, 14, & 16]
Alexander Brailowsky   12"—PD-95423 [No. 3, Etude No. 24, Impromptu No. 1]
Vladimir de Pachmann   10"—G-DA1302 [Mazurka No. 42, & Etude No. 5]
DUPLICATION: I. Ungar, RAD-RBM104

No. 7, A major, Op. 28, No. 7
Alfred Cortot, on V-8814 in CM-282 (G-DB2016 in GM-196)
(Also G-W1542)
Egon Petri, on C-71403D in CM-523
Moritz Rosenthal   12"—G-DB2772 [Nos. 3 & 6 & Valse No. 5]
DUPLICATIONS: Raoul Koczalski, O-4761; I. Ungar, RAD-RBM104
—**Arr. Orchestra**
See: Miscellaneous—Les Sylphides

No. 8, F sharp minor, Op. 28, No. 8
Alfred Cortot, on V-8814 in VM-282 (G-DB2016 in GM-196)
(Also G-W1542)
Egon Petri, on C-71403D in CM-523

No. 9, E major, Op. 28, No. 9
Alfred Cortot, on V-8814 in VM-282 (G-DB2016 in GM-196)
(Also G-W1542)
Egon Petri, on C-71403D in CM-523
Raoul Koczalski   12"—PD-67506 [Nos. 10-14]
[Nos. 10, 11, & Valse No. 7, on PD-90038]

No. 10, C sharp minor, Op. 28, No. 10
Alfred Cortot, on V-8814 in VM-282 (G-DB2016 in GM-196)
(Also G-W1542)
Egon Petri, on C-71403D in CM-523
Raoul Koczalski   12"—PD-67506 [Nos. 9, 11-14]
[Nos. 9, 11, Valse No. 7, on PD-90038]
—**Arr. Orchestra**
See: Miscellaneous—La Nuit Ensorcelée

No. 11, B major, Op. 28, No. 11
Alfred Cortot, on V-8814 in VM-282 (G-DB2016 in GM-196)
(Also G-W1542)
Egon Petri, on C-71403D in CM-523
Raoul Koczalski   12"—PD-90038 [Nos. 9, 10, & Valse No. 7]
[Nos. 9, 10, 12-14, on PD-67506]

—**Arr. Orchestra**
See: Miscellaneous—La Nuit Ensorcelée
No. 12, G sharp minor, Op. 28, No. 12
Alfred Cortot, on V-8814 in VM-282
(G-DB2016 in GM-196)
(Also on G-W1542)
Egon Petri, on C-71403D in CM-523
Raoul Koczalski   12"—**PD-67506**
[Nos. 9-11, 13, 14]
[No. 20, Etude No. 2, Valse No. 6, on
PD-90030]
No. 13, F sharp major, Op. 28, No. 13
Alfred Cortot, on V-8814 in VM-282
(G-DB2016 in GM-196)
(Also on G-W1542)
Egon Petri, on C-71403D in CM-523
Raoul Koczalski   12"—**PD-67506**
[Nos. 9-12, 14]
No. 14, E flat minor, Op. 28, No. 14
Alfred Cortot, on V-8814 in VM-282
(G-DB2016 in GM-196)
(Also on G-W1542)
Egon Petri, on C-71403D in CM-523
Raoul Koczalski   12"—**PD-67506**
[No. 9-13]
No. 15, D flat major, Op. 28, No. 15
Alfred Cortot, on V-8815 in VM-282
(G-DB2017 in GM-196)
(Also on G-W1543)
Egon Petri, on C-71404D in CM-523
DUPLICATIONS: I. J. Paderewski,
V-6847: G-DB1272; Alexander Brailow-
sky, PD-35012; Mary-Jo Turner, D-K652;
Leo Nadelmann, G-DB10073
—**Arr. 'Cello & Piano** Gieseking
Pablo Casals & N. Mednikoff
[Nocturne No. 2]   12"—**G-DB966**
No. 16, B flat minor, Op. 28, No. 16
Alfred Cortot, on V-8815 in VM-282
(G-DB2017 in GM-196)
(Also on G-W1543)
Egon Petri, on C-71404D in CM-523
DUPLICATION: S. François, D-K1399
No. 17, A flat major, Op. 28, No. 17
Alfred Cortot, on V-8815 in VM-282
(G-DB2017 in GM-196)
(Also on G-W1543)
Egon Petri, on C-71404D in CM-523
DUPLICATIONS: I. J. Paderewski,
V-6847: G-DB1272; Mark Hambourg,
G-C2064; Raoul Koczalski, PD-95174; I.
Ungar, RAD-RBM105; S. François,
D-K1399
No. 18, F minor, Op. 28, No. 18
Alfred Cortot, on V-8815 in VM-282
(G-DB2017 in GM-196)
(Also on G-W1543)
Egon Petri, on C-71404D in CM-523
No. 19, E flat major, Op. 28, No. 19
Alfred Cortot, on V-8816 in VM-282
(G-DB2018 in GM-196)
(Also on G-W1543)
Egon Petri, on C-71405D in CM-523
No. 20, C minor, Op. 28, No. 20
Alfred Cortot, on V-8816 in VM-282
(G-DB2018 in GM-196)
(Also on G-W1543)
Egon Petri, on C-71405D in CM-523
Raoul Koczalski   12"—**PD-90030**
[No. 12, Valse No. 6, Etude No. 2]

DUPLICATIONS: John Hunt, G-C2567;
I. Ungar, RAD-RBM105
No. 21, B flat major, Op. 28, No. 21
Alfred Cortot, on V-8816 in VM-282
(G-DB2018 in GM-196)
(Also on G-W1544)
Egon Petri, on C-71405D in CM-523
No. 22, G minor, Op. 28, No. 22
Alfred Cortot, on V-8816 in VM-282
(G-DB2018 in GM-196)
(Also on G-W1544)
Egon Petri, on C-71405D in CM-523
—**Arr. Orchestra**
See: Miscellaneous—La Nuit Ensorcelée
No. 23, F major, Op. 28, No. 23
Alfred Cortot, on V-8816 in VM-282
(G-DB2018 in GM-196)
(Also on G-W1544)
Egon Petri, on C-71405D in CM-523
Walter Gieseking   10"—**C-17079D**
[Valse No. 6; Schubert: Moment Musical,
Op. 94, No. 3; Brahms: Intermezzo No.
18] (C-LW18) (C-GQ7208)
DUPLICATION: I. Ungar, RAD-RBM105
No. 24, D minor, Op. 28, No. 24
Alfred Cortot, on V-8816 in VM-282
(G-DB2018 in GM-196)
(Also on G-W1544)
Egon Petri, on C-71405D in CM-523
—**Arr. Orchestra** Stokowski
Philadelphia Orch.—Stokowski
[Stravinsky: Pastorale]   10"—**V-1998**
[Bach: English Suite No. 2—Bourrée No.
1, on G-DA1639]
No. 25, C sharp major, Op. 45
Raoul Koczalski   12"—**PD-95174**
[No. 17]
No. 26, A flat major
(A recently discovered Prelude, pub-
lished in the "Pages d'Art" Geneva, in
1918. The only recording was made by
Niedzielski, G-B8044—now discontinued,
and mislabelled No. 17)
Rondo, C major, Op. 73 2 Pianos 1828
Pierre Luboshutz & Genia Nemenoff
(in VM-1047†)   12"—**V-11-9137**
Rondo, F major, Op. 14 "Krakowiak"
Piano & Orchestra
—**Arr. Orchestra**
See: Miscellaneous—La Nuit Ensorcelée
(4) SCHERZOS Piano
Collection
Artur Rubinstein   4   12"—**VM-189†**
(G-DB1915/8 in GM-185†)
Individual Scherzos
No. 1, B minor, Op. 20
Artur Rubinstein
(in VM-189)   12"—**V-7855**
(G-DB1915 in GM-185†)
Anatole Kitain   12"—**C-DX885**
Cyril Smith   12"—**C-DX1382**
Raoul Koczalski   12"—**G-DB4474**
DUPLICATION: Niedzieldski,
G-K7797/8
No. 2, B flat minor, Op. 31
Artur Rubinstein
(in VM-189†)   12"—**V-7856**
(G-DB1916 in GM-185†)
A. Benedetti Michelangeli
     12"—**G-DB5355**

Marguerite Long	12"—C-LFX513
Raoul Koczalski	12"—G-DB4474
Hans Bund	12"—T-E2011
Irene Scharrer	12"—C-DX433
Marcel Ciampi	12"—C-D15225
Benno Moiseiwitsch	12"—G-D1065
Otakar Vondrovic	12"—ESTA-F5184

No. 3, C sharp minor, Op. 39
Artur Rubinstein
     (in VM-189†) 12"—V-7857
(G-DB1917 in GM-185†)
Claudio Arrau   12"—P-R20428
Jacques Dupont   12"—PAT-X98071
France Ellegaard   12"—PD-67918

No. 4, E major, Op. 54
Artur Rubinstein
     (in VM-189†) 12"—V-7858
(G-DB1918 in GM-185†)
Vladimir Horowitz   12"—V-14634
(G-DB3205)

SONATAS Piano

No. 2, B flat minor, Op. 35 (with the celebrated "Funeral March")
Artur Rubinstein 3 12"—VM-1082†
Edward Kilenyi 3 12"—CM-378†
[Mazurka No. 13] (PAT-PAT80/2)
Alfred Cortot 2 12"—G-DB2019/20
Alexander Brailowsky 2 12"—VOX-453
(PD-95480/1)
Robert Casadesus 3 12"—CM-698†
[Mazurka No. 13]
Robert Lortat 2 12"—C-D15092/3
[Valse No. 14]
Sergei Rachmaninoff 4 10—GM-151†
(G-DA1186/9)
Percy Grainger 3 12"—C-GQX10303/5
Paul Baumgartner
     3 12"—G-DB10026/8

—**3rd Mvt.** (Funeral March) only
William Murdoch   12"—D-K661
Leonid Kreutzer   12"—PD-95177
[Prelude No. 15]

—**3rd Mvt.** (Funeral March) only **Arr. Orchestra**
BBC Symphony—Boult 12"—G-DB1722
Lamoureux Orch.—Wolff
     12"—PD-566010
[Berlioz: Damnation of Faust—Rakoczy March]
DUPLICATIONS: Symphony Orch.—
Cloëz, O-170052; Berlin Philharmonic, Meyrowitz, U-B14499

No. 3, B minor, Op. 58
Dinu Lipatti 3 12"—C-LX994/6†
Alexander Brailowsky 3 12"—VM-548†
(G-DB3700/2)
Alfred Cortot 4 10"—G-DA1333/6

SONGS

(17) **Polish Songs, Op. 74** (Chants Polonais)

No. 1, The Maiden's Wish
Ger. Mädchens Wünsch Pol. Zyczenie
Fr. Souhaite d'une jeune fille

—**Arr. Piano** Liszt (No. 1 in Liszt series)
Sergei Rachmaninoff 12"—V-11-8593
[No. 15 & Schumann: Der Contrabandiste]
Margarita Mirimanowa
     12"—C-CQX16447
[Albéniz: Séguidillas]

No. 12, My Joys
Ger. Meine Freuden Pol. Moja Pieszczotka

—**Arr. Piano** Liszt (No. 5 in Liszt Series)
Bernhard Stavenhagen 10"—O-4751
[Carreno: Kleiner Walzer, Carreno]
[Grieg: Norwegian Bridal Procession, Grieg, on O-4785]

No. 15, The Return Home
Ger. Heimkehr Pol. Narzeczony

—**Arr. Piano** Liszt (No. 6 in Liszt Series)
Sergei Rachmaninoff 12"—V-11-8593
[No. 1 & Schumann: Der Contrabandiste]

(**Les**) **Sylphides** Ballet based on Chopin's music
See under Miscellaneous

Tarantelle, A flat major, Op. 43 Piano
Alfred Corot   12"—V-8251
(G-DB2032)
[Fantasie in F minor, Pt. 3]
[Valse No. 9, on G-DA1213]
Noel Mewton-Wood 12"—D-K1064
[Weber: Sonata No. 2, Pt. 7]

—**Arr. Orchestra** Glazounov (in "Chopiniana" Op. 46)
London Philharmonic Orch.—Ronald
     12"—G-C2639
[Mendelssohn: Songs Without Words—Spring Song & Spinning Song]

(14) **VALSES** Piano

Collections
Alfred Cortot 6 12"—GM-229
(G-DB2311/6)
Alfred Cortot   G-W1603/5
     3 12" & 3 10"—G-DA4962/4
Alexander Brailowsky
(Nos. 1 to 8)   VM-863
(Nos. 9 to 14) 7 12"—VM-864
Edward Kilenyi 5 12"—CM-390
Robert Lortat 5 12"—C-LFX214/8
Jacques Abram 3 12"—MC-76
(Nos. 1, 2, 3, 4, 6, 7, 8)

Individual Valses

No. 1, E flat major, Op. 18, ("Grande valse brillante")
Alfred Cortot, on G-DB2311 in GM-229
(See also Collections above)
Alexander Brailowsky, on V-18383 in VM-863
Edward Kilenyi, on C-72066D in CM-390
Robert Lortat   12"—C-LFX214
[No. 2]
DUPLICATIONS: A. Brailowsky,
G-DB3706; Lubka Kolessa, G-DB4654;
I. J. Paderewski, V-6877: G-DB1273;
Wilhelm Backhaus, G-DB1131; Robert
Goldsand, D-23191 in D-A185; Raoul
Koczalski, PD-95201: PD-67615; Otakar
Vondrovic, ESTA-F5187; Jacques
Abram, in MC-76

—**Arr. Orchestra**
See: Miscellaneous—Les Sylphides
No. 2, A flat major, Op. 34, No. 1 "Valse
Brillante"
Alfred Cortot, on G-DB2311 in GM-229
(See also Collections above)
Alexander Brailowsky, on V-18383 in
VM-863
Edward Kilenyi, on C-72066D in CM-390
Robert Lortat   12"—**C-LFX214**
[No. 1]
Artur Rubinstein   12"—**G-DB1160**
[Schubert: Impromptu, Op. 90, No. 4]
DUPLICATIONS: Rudolph Ganz,
V-7290; A. Brailowsky, PD-95143; Raoul
Koczalski, PD-67247; Jacques Abram, in
MC-76; Myrtle Eaver, on V-24796
No. 3, A minor, Op. 34, No. 2
Alfred Cortot, on G-DB2312 in GM-229
(See also Collections above)
Alexander Brailowsky, on V-18384 in
VM-863
Edward Kilenyi, on C-72067D in CM-390
Robert Lortat   12"—**C-LFX215**
[Nos. 4 & 14]
Vladimir Horowitz
     (in VM-1034†)   12"—**V-11-9044**
[Andante spianato & Grande Polonaise,
Pt. 3]
DUPLICATIONS: Leo Nadelmann,
G-DB10056; Raoul Koczalski, PD-
95201; PD-67515; Margarita Mirima-
nowa, C-GQX16448; Jacques Abram, in
MC-76
—**Arr. 'Cello & Piano**
Raya Garboursova & Erich-Itor Kahn
     (in VM-1017)   12"—**V-11-8869**
[Saint-Saëns: Le Cygne]
No. 4, F major, Op. 34, No. 3
Alfred Cortot, on G-DB2312 in GM-229
(See also Collections above)
Alexander Brailowsky, on V-18385 in
VM-863
Edward Kilenyi, on C-72067D in CM-390
Robert Lortat   12"—**C-LFX215**
[Nos. 3 & 14]
Emil von Sauer   10"—**C-LW38**
[Etude No. 12]
Nicolas Orloff   12"—**D-K1424**
[Impromptu No. 1; Mazurka No. 7]
DUPLICATIONS: R. Koczalski;
PD-67553; R. Trouard, O-188947;
J. Abram, in MC-76
—**Arr. Orch.**
See: Miscellaneous—La Nuit Ensorcelée
No. 5, A flat major, Op. 42
Alfred Cortot, on G-DB2313 in GM-229
(See also Collections above)
Alexander Brailowsky, on V-18385 in
VM-863
Edward Kilenyi, on C-72068D in CM-390
(Also on PAT-PG92)
Robert Lortat   12"—**C-LFX216**
[No. 7]
Solomon   12"—**G-C3433**
[Etude No. 3]
Moritz Rosenthal
(Preludes 3, 6, 7)   12"—**G-DB2772**
DUPLICATIONS: Ania Dorfmann,
C-DX818: C-DWX1608; Carlo Zecchi,

CET-CB20351; Simon Barere, G-DB2166;
France Ellegaard, PD-67841; I. J. Pad-
erewski, G-DB380*
No. 6, D flat major, Op. 64, No. 1 "Minute
Valse"
Alfred Cortot, on G-DB2313 in GM-229
(See also Collections above)
Alexander Brailowsky, on V-18385 in
VM-863
Edward Kilenyi, on C-72068D in CM-390
José Iturbi
     (in VM-1110)   10"—**V-10-1283**
[Impromptu No. 4] (G-DA1848)
Walter Gieseking   10"—**C-17079D**
[Prelude No. 23; Schubert: Moment Mu-
sical, Op. 94, No. 3; Brahms: Intermezzo
No. 18] (C-LW18) (C-GQ7208)
DUPLICATIONS: Robert Lortat,
C-LFX217; Raoul Koczalski, PD-90030;
also PD-67533; Jean Doyen, G-DB5149;
Robert Goldsand, D-23191 in D-A185;
Vladimir de Pachmann, G-DA761; Wil-
helm Backhaus, G-DB929; William Mur-
doch, D-K682; Mark Hambourg,
G-C2579; Michael von Zadora, PD-
22120; Otakar Vondrovic, ESTA-F5189;
Raymond Trouard, O-188949; Jacques
Abram, in MC-76; N. de Magaloff, RAD-
RZ3031
—**Arr. Orchestra**
Barnabas von Geczy Orch.
             10"—**G-EG3229**
[Godard: Jocelyn—Berceuse]
No. 7, C sharp minor, Op. 64, No. 2
Alfred Cortot, on G-DB2311 in GM-229
(See also Collections above)
Alexander Brailowsky, on V-18386 in
VM-863
Edward Kilenyi, on C-72069D in CM-390
Robert Lortat   12"—**C-LFX216**
[No. 5]
Malcuzynski   12"—**C-LX975**
[Nocturne No. 5]
Vladimir Horowitz   12"—**V-11-9519**
[Mendelssohn: Songs without words,
Nos. 30 & 40]
José Iturbi
     (in VM-1110)   10"—**V-10-1284**
[Mazurka No. 5] (G-DA1849)
DUPLICATIONS: Alfred Cortot,
G-DB1321; A. Brailowsky, CET-OR5077:
CET-OR5108; PD-95140; Robert Gold-
sand, D-23193 in D-A185; Louis Kentner,
C-DX1081; I. J. Paderewski, G-DB3711;
Sergei Rachmaninoff, V-1245; Cor de
Groot, O-8776; Vladimir de Pachmann,
G-DB860; William Murdoch, D-F7495;
Willi Stech, T-A1914; Raoul Koczalski,
PD-90038; Oscar Levant, on C-72109D in
CM-649; Mark Hambourg, G-B3798;
Margarita Mirimanowa, C-CQ102; Mich-
ael von Zadora, PD-22120; Johanne
Stockmarr, G-DB5261; Jacob Gimpel, in
VOX-604; Raymond Trouard, O-188950;
Jacques Abram, in MC-76; Artur Rubin-
stein, G-DB1495 in GM-128; Orazio
Frugoni, ELITE-7031
—**Arr. 2 Pianos**
Rawicz & Landauer, C-DB2338

No. 8, A flat major, Op. 64, No. 3
Alfred Cortot, on G-DB2314 in GM-229
(See also Collections above)
Alexander Brailowsky, on V-18386 in VM-863
Edward Kilenyi, on C-72067D in CM-390
DUPLICATIONS: Robert Lortat,
C-LFX218; Raoul Koczalski, PD-67533;
Sergei Rachmaninoff, V-1245; Jacques
Abram, in MC-76

No. 9, A flat major, Op. 69, No. 1 "L'adieu"
(Often called the Valse in F minor)
Alfred Cortot, on G-DB2315 in GM-229
(See also Collections above)
Alexander Brailowsky, on V-18367 in VM-864
Edward Kilenyi, on C-72069D in CM-390
Arturo Benedetti Michelangeli
[Mazurka No. 47]   10"—**G-DA5371**
DUPLICATIONS: Robert Lortat,
C-LFX217; Alfred Cortot, G-DA1213;
Robert Goldsand, D-23192 in D-A185; A.
Brailowsky, PD-90197; Raoul Koczalski,
PD-67247; Otakar Vondrovic, ESTA-
F5186; Raymond Trouard, O-188950
—Arr. Orchestra
See: Miscellaneous—Les Sylphides
—Vocal arrangement J. Darck (Text: Jean
Calmes)
Ninon Vallin (s) & P. Darck (pf)
                          10"—**O-281277**
[Brahms-Darck: Hungarian Dance No. 4,
vocal arr.]

No. 10, B minor, Op. 69, No. 2
Alfred Cortot, on G-DB2315 in GM-229
(See also Collections above)
Alexander Brailowsky, on V-18387 in VM-864
Edward Kilenyi, on C-72068D in CM-390
Robert Lortat   12"—**C-LFX217**
[Nos. 9 & 6]

No. 11, G flat major, Op. 70, No. 1
Alfred Cortot, on G-DB2316 in GM-229
(See also Collections above)
Alexander Brailowsky, on V-18388 in VM-864
Edward Kilenyi, on C-72070D in CM-390
DUPLICATIONS: Maryla Jonas,
C-72101 in CM-626; Robert Lortat,
C-LFX218; Robert Goldsand, D-23193 in
D-A185; Jean Doyen, G-DB5149; Mark
Hambourg, G-C2579; Vladimir de Pach-
mann, G-DA761; Raoul Koczalski, PD-
67533: PD-90029; William Murdoch,
D-K682; Wilfred Worden, D-F2708;
Otakar Vondrovic, ESTA-F5189; Ray-
mond Trouard, O-188951; Oscar Levant,
on C-72109D in CM-649
—Arr. Orchestra See: Miscellaneous—Les
Sylphides

No. 12, F minor, Op. 70, No. 2
Alfred Cortot, on G-DB2313 in GM-229
(See also Collections above)
Alexander Brailowsky, on V-18388 in VM-864
Edward Kilenyi, on C-72070D in CM-390
Robert Lortat   12"—**C-LFX218**
[Nos. 8, 11, 13]

No. 13, D flat major, Op. 70, No. 3
Alfred Cortot, on G-DB2316 in GM-229
(See also Collections above)
Alexander Brailowsky, on V-18389 in VM-864
Edward Kilenyi, on C-72070D in CM-390
Paul Baumgartner   12"—**G-DB10012**
[Liszt: Liebestraum No. 3]
DUPLICATIONS: Maryla Jonas,
C-72101D in CM-626; Robert Lortat,
C-LFX218

No. 14, E minor, Posthumous
Alfred Cortot, on G-DB2316 in GM-229
(See also Collections above)
Alexander Brailowsky, on V-18389 in VM-864
Edward Kilenyi, on C-72070D in CM-390
Solomon   12"—**G-C3509**
[Mazurka No. 47; Daquin: Le coucou; De
Severac: Music Box]
DUPLICATIONS: Robert Lortat,
C-LFX215; A. Brailowsky, PD-90174; F.
Rauch, U-G14121; Robert Goldsand,
D-23192 in D-A185; Leonid Kreutzer,
PD-90034; Raymond Trouard, O-188951;
Sergei Rachmaninoff, G-DA1189 in GM-
151; I. Ungar, RAD-RBM104
—Arr. Orchestra Rogal-Lewitzsky
Robin Hood Dell Orch.—Metropoulos, in
CM-598

No. 15, E major, 1829
No recording available

**Variations Brilliantes on "Je vends des
scapulaires" of Hérold** Piano
Wilfrid Maggiar   12"—**PAT-PDT101**

Variations on "La ci darem la mano," Op. 2
Piano & Orchestra
(The theme is that of the famous duet
from Mozart's "Don Giovanni")
No recording available

Waltzes See under Valses

MISCELLANEOUS

Chopiniana Orchestra arr. Glazunov
—Tarantelle only
London Philharmonic Orch.—Ronald
                          12"—**G-C2639**
[Mendelssohn: Spring Song & Spinning
Song]

Lecture on Chopin
(International Educational Society Lec-
ture No. 79)
Dr. E. Markham Lee
                    2   12"—**C-D40157/8**

(La) Nuit Ensorcelée Ballet **arr. Orchestra**
Aubert
Eng. **The Enchanted Night**
(Etude Nos. 3 & 14; Nocturne No. 14;
Preludes Nos. 10, 11 & 22; Mazurka No.
17; Valse No. 4; Rondo, F major, Op. 14)
Paris Conservatory Orch.—Münch
                    3   12"—**G-DB11100/2**
Symphony Orch.—Louis Aubert
(C-LFX223/4)   2   12"—**CX-76†**
[Adaptation by Vuillermoz]

(Les) Sylphides Ballet Orchestra
(Prélude No. 7; Nocturne No. 11; Mazurka Nos. 23 & 44; Valse Nos. 1, 7 & 9)

—**Arr.** Anderson & Bodge
Boston "Pops" Orchestra—Fiedler
3 12"—**VM-1119**†
—**Arr.** J Ainslie Murray & Felix White
London Philharmonic Orch.—Sargent
3 12"—**G-C2781/3**
—**Excerpts**
National Symphony Orch.—Fistoulari
2 12"—**D-K1487/8**
London Philharmonic—Goehr
12"—**C-69281D**
(C-DX844: C-LFX535)
Symphony Orch.—Goehr (in Nights of
the Ballet album) in **VC-30**
(G-C2915; G-C2914; G-2983)
Miscellaneous Selections
—**Arr. 2 Pianos**
Rawicz & Landauer, C-DB2079;
C-FB1469; C-DB2166
Selections from the film "Abschiedswalzer"
Polydor Orch. 2 10"—**PD-10260/1**
Chopiniana Arranged by Rogal-Lewitzky
(Etude No. 12; Nocturne No. 13; Mazur-
ka No. 25; Valse Brillante No. 14;
Polonaise No. 6)
Robin Hood Dell Orch.—Mitropoulos
3 12"—**CM-598**†

CHRISTENSEN, Bernhard

The 24 Hours Jazz Oratorio in Danish
Excerpts
—**At School; Food; Geography; Free!**
Aksel Schiøtz, the Three Rhythm Girls,
Asta Kordt, with pf. acc.
2 10"—**G-X4285** & **X-4363**
The School Turned Upside Down Jazz Ora-
torio in Danish
Excerpts
—**Natural History**
Copenhagen Boys' Choir—Wöldike
10"—**G-X6404**
—**The meeting of the Playground & Traffic
Regulations**
Copenhagen Boys' Choir—Wöldike
10"—**G-X6405**
The Trumpet Song Jazz Oratorio
Excerpts
—**Josephine's Ballad; Armstrong gets the
trumpet**
Inga Kordt, with the Jazz Society & Rich-
ard Johansen's Band 10"—**G-X4429**

CIAMPI, Legrenzio Vincenzo (1719-1773)

*Coming to London with an Italian singing
troupe in 1748, Ciampi produced many operas
on the English stage. He is remembered by
his "Tre giorni son che Nina" which is frequently erroneously attributed to Pergolesi.*

GLI TRE CICISBEI RIDICOLI Opera in
Italian
Tre giorni son che Nina (Siciliana)
(often labelled "Nina" or "Siciliana")
Mariano Stabile (b) 10"—**C-DQ701**
[Mozart: Nozze di Figaro—Aprite un po']
Gino Sinimberghi (t) & Luigi Scolari
(pf) 10"—**O-26285**
[Tosti: Ideale]
Tito Schipa (t) 10"—**G-DA974**

[Tosti: 'A vucchella]
—**Arr. 'Cello & Piano** Lier
Paul Grümmer & Bruno Hinze-Reinhold
[Valensin: Minuet] 10"—**PD-47122**
Arnold Földesy & W. von Vultee
10"—**PD-24366**
[Giordano: Caro mio ben]
—**Arr. Orchestra** Derksen
Bruno Saenges & his Orch., O-26515

CICONIA, Johannes

Cacciando un giorno vidi un Cervetto
Eng. Madrigal of the Hunt
S. Danco (s) & pf. acc. 10"—**G-HN1870**
[Anon. 15th Century: Amor, amore]

CILEA, Francesco (1866-   )

*An Italian composer of the school of "Verismo"
who was handicapped by poor librettos. His
work has not survived outside of Italy.*

OPERAS In Italian
ADRIANA LECOUVREUR 4 Acts 1902
Individual excerpts
Act I
Io sono l'umile ancella Soprano
Maria Caniglia 12"—**G-DB6356**
[Poveri Fiori]
Licia Albanese 12"—**G-DB5383**
[Puccini: Madama Butterfly—Un bel dì]
Augusta Oltrabella 10"—**G-DA1479**
[Puccini: Bohême—Addio]
Magda Olivero 12"—**CET-BB25028**
[Poveri fiori]
Adelaide Saraceni 12"—**G-S10243**
[Poveri fiori]
Salomea Krusceniski (Recorded 1908/9)
10"—**CRS-25*
DUPLICATION: G. Cigna, C-CQ7176
La dolcissima effigie Tenor
Galliano Masini 10"—**CET-TI7009**
Aureliano Pertile 10"—**G-DA1185**
[Giordano: Andrea Chénier—Come un
bel dì]
(Also on C-GQ7178)

Act II
O vagabonda stella d'oriente Mezzo-soprano
Cloe Elmo 12"—**CET-BB25033**
[Giordano: Fedora—O grandi occhi lu-
centi]
L'anima ho stanca Tenor
Galliano Masini 10"—**CET-TI7009**
[La dolcissima effigie]
Stefano Islandi 10"—**G-DA5202**
[Giordano: Fedora—Amor ti vieta]
Alessandro Granda 10"—**G-AV536**
[Oteo: Mi viejo amor]
DUPLICATION: A. Pertile, C-GQ7178
Io son sua per l'amore Soprano & Mezzo-
Soprano
Gina Gigna & Cloe Elmo
12"—**CET-BB25029**
[Ponchielli: Gioconda—L'amo come il
fulgor]
Intermezzo Orchestra
La Scala Orch.—Ghione 10"—**G-HN794**
[Giordano: Fedora—Interlude]

Act IV
Prelude Orchestra
La Scala Orch.—Ghione 10"—G-HN795
[Järnefelt: Praeludium]

Poveri fiori Soprano
Maria Caniglia 12"—G-DB6356
[Io sono l'umile ancella]
Claudia Muzio 10"—C-LC20
[Debussy: Beau soir] (C-BQ6001)
[Verdi: Trovatore—Tacea la notte, on
C-BQ6004]
Magda Olivero 12"—CET-BB25028
[Io sono l'umile ancella]
[Boito: Mefistofele—L'altra notte, on
CET-BB25049]
Gina Cigna 12"—C-GQ7176
[Io sono l'umile ancella]
Adelaide Saraceni 12"—G-S10243
[Io sono l'umile ancella]
DUPLICATION: R. Pampanini,
C-GQ7212

No, la mia fronte Soprano & Tenor
A. Saraceni & P. Pauli 12"—G-DB2012
[R. Strauss: Wiegenlied, Pauli]

L'ARLESIANA 3 Acts 1896

Esser madre e un inferno Soprano
Claudio Muzio
(in CM-259) 12"—C-9168M
[Boito: Mefistofele—L'altra notte]
[Giordano: Andrea Chênier—La mamma
morta, on C-LCX28: C-BQX2507]
Gianna Pederzini 12"—CET-BB25027
[Alfano: Risurrezione—Dio pietoso]

Lamento di Federico: E la solita storia
Tenor
Ferruccio Tagliavini 12"—CET-BB25056
[Wolf-Ferrari: I Quattro Rusteghi—
Lucretia è un bel nome]
[Puccini: Bohême—Che gelida manina,
on CET-BB25021 in CET-1]
(Also in VM-1191; V-V13)
Beniamino Gigli 12"—V-14312
[Franck: Panis Angelicus] (G-DB2914)
[Giordano: Andrea Chênier—Improvviso
di Chênier on G-DB4506]
[Mascagni: Cavalleria Rusticana—Addio
alla madre on G-DB3905]
Tito Schipa 12"—G-DB3461
[Donizetti: Elisir d'Amore—Una furtiva
lagrima]
[Different recording, G-DB1610, with
Schipa: Prece]
Giuseppe di Stefano 12"—G-DB6580
[Puccini: Tosca—E lucevan le stelle]
Richard Crooks
(in VM-585) 12"—V-15544
[Bizet: Pêcheurs de Perles—Je crois en-
tendre] (G-DB3926)
DUPLICATIONS: Galliano Masini,
C-CQX16524; Luigi Fort, C-CQX8000;
Piero Pauli, G-DB2013; Enzo de Muro
Lomanto, C-GQX10251; Roberto d'Ales-
sio, C-GQX10236

Racconto del Pastore Baritone
Mario Basiola 12"—C-GQX10978
[Ponchielli: Figliuol Prodigo—Raccogli
e calma]

Come due tizzi accesi Baritone
Tito Gobbi 12"—G-DB5400
[Verdi: Boccanegra—Il lacerato spirito,
with A. de Beuf]

CIMAROSA, Domenico (1749-1801)

*A pupil of Sacchini and Piccini, Cimarosa was
internationally famous as a composer of opera
buffa.*

CONCERTO—Oboe & Strings (arr. Arthur
Benjamin)
Leon Goossens & Liverpool Philharmonic
—Sargent 2 12"—C-DX1137/8
(Bach: Easter Oratorio—Sinfonia-
Adagio only]

Mattutino "Risveglio" Harpsichord
Corradina Mola 10"—G-DA5392
[G. B. Martini: Gavotte]

OPERAS In Italian

GIANNINA E BERNARDONE 1788
Overture Orchestra
EIAR Orch.—Tansini 12"—CET-PE101
[Paisiello: Il Barbiere de Siviglia—Over-
ture]

(IL) MATRIMONIO PER RAGGIRO

Overture Orchestra
Orch. of the "Maggio Musicale"—Mario
Rossi 10"—CET-TI7007

(IL) MATRIMONIO SEGRETO 1792
Ger. Die heimliche Ehe Eng. The Secret
Marriage
Overture Orchestra
EIAR Orch.—La Rosa Parodi
12"—CET-CB20216
Berlin Philharmonic—Blech
10"—G-DA4404
DUPLICATIONS: Milan Symphony Mo-
lajoli, C-D14462; Symphony Orch.—
Ruhlmann, PAT-X96063

Geronimo's Air: Udite tutti, udite Baritone
Fr. Venez qu'on vous révèle
A. Balbon (in French)
12"—PAT-X91023

Perdonate Signor mio Soprano
Liana Grani (s) 12"—C-GQX11097
[Verdi: Rigoletto—Caro nome]

(I) TRACI AMANTI
Overture Orchestra
Chamber Orch. of Royal Conservatoire,
Naples—Lualdi 12"—G-DB5439
[Cherubini: Symphony, D major, Pt. 7]

CLARKE, Robert Conningsby (1879-1934)

*An American organist who held a post at Trin-
ity College, Oxford. He is best known for his
songs.*

The Blind Plowman Song in English (Radcliffe Hall)
Norman Cordon (bs) & Archie Black (pf)
10"—V-10-1176
[Pinsuti: Bedouin Love Song]

Feodor Chaliapin (bs)   10″—**G-DA993**
[Malashkin: Oh, could I but express in song]
Nelson Eddy (b)   10″—**C-17292D**
[Keel: Tomorrow] (C-DB2114)

CLAUDE Le Jeune (c.1528-1600)

The great musical spokesman of the Huguenots, whose major works were his settings of the Psalms of David, although he wrote many secular choral works. Extolled by his contemporaries as the last great master of polyphony, he stands with Goudimel as one of the Franco-Flemish polyphonic giants. Psalm 69 is an excellent example of his art.

(La) Belle aronde Unacc. Cho. in French
Choeur de la Chanterie de la Renaissance
—Henri Expert   12″—**C-DFX54**
[Bertrand: Las, je me plainds]
Psalm 42: Ainsi qu'on oit le cerf
Psalm 69: Hélas! Seigneur Unacc. Cho. in French
Vocal Ensemble—Henry Expert
     (in Vol. II)   12″—**AS-12**
[Goudimel: Psalms 19 & 25]

CLEMENS, NON PAPA (Jacobus Clement c.1510-1556)

A member of the Franco-Flemish school of polyphony, supposed to have been the first Kapellmeister to the Emperor Charles V of Vienna. He left many vocal works in the complicated contrapuntal style of the period.

Aymer est ma vie Chanson in French
M. Vhita (c) & H. Leeb (Lute)
     (in Vol. IV)   12″—**AS-36**
[Nicolas de la Grotte: Je suis amour; Anon: Il me suffit & Besard: Lute Pieces]

CLEMENTI, Muzio (1752-1832)

One of the founders of the school of piano technique as separate from harpsichord, Clement was also a successful business man. His pupils included Kramer and Moscheles, and his works help set the sonata-form.

GRADUS AD PARNASSUM
Fugue, B major
Scherzo, A major
Allegretto B major
Ruggero Gerlin (pf)   10″—**G-DA5441**
SONATAS 2 Pianos
No. 2, B flat major
Gino Gorini & Sergio Lorenzi
     12″—**G-DB11310**
Sonata, A major, Op. 36, No. 2 Piano
Ruggero Gerlin   10″—**G-DA5442**

SONATINAS Piano
No. 13, E flat major
—1st Mvt. only
Harold Samuel   10″—**C-DB831**
[K. P. E. Bach: Rondo espressivo]
(in Columbia History of Music, Vol. III: CM-233)

CLERAMBAULT, Louis Nicolas (1676-1749)

A Parisian organist who wrote keyboard pieces and many cantatas.

Basse et dessus de trompette Organ
Fernando Germani   12″—**SEMS-1140**
[Schumann: Canon 5 & Pachelbel: Chaconne]

Dialogue & Caprice sur les grands jeux Organ
Joseph Bonnet (Gonzalez Organ)
     12″—**PAT-PAT68**
[Couperin: Récit. de Cromorne & Daquin: Noël sur les flûtes]
(in 3 Centuries of Organ Music album)
Edouard Commette (Lyon Cathedral)
     10″—**C-D19289**
Fernando Germani   12″—**SEMS-1138**
[Daquin: Noël III]

Largo on the G String arr. Dandelot
Jascha Heifetz (vl) & Arpad Sandor (pf)   12″—**G-DB2219**
[Wieniawski: Scherzo tarantelle]

Léandre et Héro Cantata
Martha Angelici (s) & Flute, Violin, Viola da Gamba & Harpsichord
     (in Vol. XI) 2 12″—**AS-105/6**

Recit de Nasarde Organ
Vignanelli   12″—**SEMS-1142**
[Dandrieux: Musette & Couperin: Cromorne]

Symphonia Quarta
Paris Conservatory Orch.—Fendler
     12″—**BAM-22**
[Lully: L'Amour Médecin—Overture: Chaconne]

COATES, Eric (1886-   )

A British composer and violist, Coates has written many songs and light symphonic works.

By the Sleepy Lagoon Orchestra
Symphony Orch.—Coates 12″—**C-7408M**
[Last Love]
[Cinderella, Pt. 3, on C-DX712]
[Calling all workers, on C-DB1945]
Albert Sandler Orch   10″—**C-DB1061**
[Payen: Under Heaven's Blue]
Also: Peter York Orch., C-DB2323;
Mantovani & Torch (organ) D-F7563

By the Tamarisk Orchestra
Symphony Orch.—Coates
     (in CX-102†)   12″—**C-69264D**
[London Again Suite, Pt. 3] (C-DX737)

Calling All Workers March
Symphony Orch.—Coates
     10″—**C-DB1945**
[By the Sleepy Lagoon]
Also: Royal Artillery Band, D-F7638

Cinderella—A Phantasy Orchestra
Symphony Orch.—Coates
     2   12″—**CX-239†**
[Footlights]
[By the Sleepy Lagoon, on C-DX711/2]

Dancing Nights Valse Orchestra
London Symphony Orch.—Coates
     10″—**C-DB2345**

Eighth Army March (arr. Duthoit)
H. M. Grenadier Guards Band—Harris
                    10"—C-DB2140
[Alwyn: Desert Victory March]

Footlights Concert Waltz Orchestra
Light Symphony Orch.—Coates
        (in CX-239†)   12"—C-7403M
[Cinderella, Pt. 3]
[Last Love, on C-DX966]

Four Centuries Suite Orchestra
    Prelude; Hornpipe, Pavane; Tambourine;
    Valse; Rhythm
National Symphony Orch.—Eric Coates
            2 12"—D-K1273/4†

Four Ways Suite Orchestra
    Northwards (March); Southwards
    (Valse); Eastwards (Eastern Dance);
    Westwards (Rhythm)
New Light Symphony—J. Lewis
        2   12"—G-C2665/6
[London Bridge March]

Last Love Romance Orchestra
Light Symphony Orch.—Coates
[By the Sleepy Lagoon]   12"—C-7408M
[Footlights, on C-DX966]

London Again Suite Orchestra
    Oxford Street (March); Langham Palace
    (Elegy); Mayfair (Valse)
Symphony Orch.—Coates
(C-DX736/7   2 12"—CX-102†
[By the Tamarisk]

London Bridge March Orchestra
Symphony Orch.—Coates
[Summer Afternoon]   10"—C-DB1382
New Queen's Hall Orch.—Wood
[London Suite, Pt. 3]   12"—D-K801
New Light Symphony Orch.—Lewis
[Four Ways Suite, Pt. 3] 12"—G-C2666

—Arr. Band: H. M. Grenadier Guards,
D-F5077

London Suite Orchestra
    Covent Garden (Tarantelle); Westminster
    (Meditation); Knightsbridge (March)
Symphony Orch.—Coates
                    12"—C-69399D
(C-DX470) (C-DWX1613)
New Light Symphony Orch.—Lewis
            2   12"—G-C2655/6
[Hayden Wood: Unforgotten Melody]
New Queen's Hall Orch.—Wood
            2   12"—D-K800/1
[London Bridge March]
Also: Grenadier Guards Band,
D-F5076/7

—Knightsbridge only
Tivoli Orch.—Jensen, TONO-X25009

—Arr. Piano duet
Rawicz & Landauer   10"—C-DB2088
[Scène du bal]

London Calling March
London Symphony—Coates
[Television March]   10"—C-DB2233

Miniature Suite Orchestra arr. Fletcher
Children's Dance; Intermezzo; Scène au bal

Light Symphony Orch.—Raybould
                    12"—C-DX380
Saxo-Rhapsody Saxophone & Orchestra
Sigurd Rascher & Symphony Orch.—
Coates   12"—G-C2891
Scène ad bal (Same as Scène au bal from
    Miniature Suite)
—Arr. Piano duet
Rawicz & Landauer   10"—C-DB2088
[London Suite—Knightsbridge March]

SONGS
Bird Songs at Eventide Fr. Les oiseaux dans
    le soir
John McCormack (t) & Edwin
Schneider (pf)   10"—G-DA1712
[Brahe: Bless this house]
[Earlier recording, G-DA973, with Cham-
    inade: Anneau d'argent]
Richard Crooks (t) & pf. acc.
                    10"—G-DA1714
[Phillips: Open your window]
[Earlier recording, G-DA1536, with Del
Riego: Green Hills of Ireland]
Richard Tauber (t)   10"—P-RO20200
[D'Hardelot: Because]
DUPLICATIONS: John McHugh,
C-FB2189; Alfred Piccaver, D-M413
In French: Georges Thill, C-LF110

The Green Hills o' Somerset
Joan Hammond (s)   10"—C-DB2015
[Lieurance: By the waters of Minne-
    tonka]

I Heard You Singing
Alfred Piccaver (t) & pf. acc.
[Gertner: Trusting Eyes]   10"—D-M456

Summer Afternoon Idyll Orchestra
Symphony Orch.—Coates
[London Bridge March] 10"—C-DB1382

Summer Days Suite Orchestra
In a Country Lane; On the Erge of the
    Lake; At the Dance
New Queen's Hall Orch.—Coates
[Wood Nymphs]   2 12"—C-9369/70
Light Symphony Orch.—Coates
                    12"—G-C2901

Symphonic Rhapsodies Orchestra
I heard you singing; Bird Songs at Even-
    tide; I Pitch my Lonely Caravan
Symphony Orch.—Coates 12"—C-DX454

Television March
London Symphony Orch.—Coates
[London Calling March] 10"—C-DB2233

The Three Bears Suite Orchestra
London Symphony Orch.—Coates
(C-DX1217)   12"—C-72237D
Hastings Municipal Orch.—Cameron
                    12"—D-K515
Plaza Theatre Orch.—Tours
                    12"—C-9499

The Three Elizabeths Orchestra
Halcyon Days (Elizabeth Tudor); Spring in
    Forfarshire (Elizabeth of Glamis);
    Youth of Britain (Princess Elizabeth)
National Symphony Orch.—Coates
(D-K1109/10†)   2   12"—D-ED8†

Wood Nymphs Valsette Orchestra
New Queen's Hall Orch.—Coates
12"—C-9370
[Summer Days Suite, Pt. 3]

COLEMAN, Ellen

Sonata, 'Cello & Piano
Jacques Serres & Ady Leyvastre
2   12"—G-L1051/2

COLERIDGE-TAYLOR, Samuel (1875-1912)

An English mulatto who was a prolific composer and a well known conductor. His music greatly resembles much of Elgar's work.

Hiawatha See: Song of Hiawatha
Petite Suite de Concert, Op. 77 Orchestra
Caprice de Nanette; Demande et Réponse; Sonnet d'Amour; Tarantelle Frétillante
London Symphony Orch.—Sargent
2   12"—G-C2372/3
Bournemouth Municipal Orch.—
Godfrey   2   12"—C-DX651/2
Royal Marines Orch.—Dunn
2   12"—C-DX1041/2
—Arr. 2 Pianos
Rawicz & Landauer
2   10"—C-DB2205/6
Song of Hiawatha, Op. 30
Trilogy for Soloists, Chorus & Orchestra
In English
I. Hiawatha's Wedding Feast II. The Death of Minnehaha III. Hiawatha's Departure
No. 1, Hiawatha's Wedding Feast
Walter Glynne (t) & Royal Choral Society with Albert Hall Orch.—Sargent
4   12"—G-C1931/4
[A. G. Thomas: Esmerelda—O vision entrancing, Glynne, on G-C1933]
—Onaway! Awake! beloved
Webster Booth (t) & Liverpool Philharmonic—Sargent   12"—G-C3407
[A. G. Thomas: Esmerelda—O vision entrancing]
Tudor Davies (t)   12"—G-DA1142
[Offenbach: Contes d'Hoffmann—Legend of Kleinzach]
Frank Titterton (t)   12"—D-K543
[Balfe: Bohemian Girl—When other lips]

SONGS In English

Eleanore, Op. 36, No. 6
Webster Booth (t) & Hubert Greenslade (pf)   10"—G-B9451
[Unmindful of the Roses; Life & Death]
Henry Wendon (t) & Gerald Moore (pf)
10"—C-DB2083
[Bridge: Love went a-riding]
Roy Henderson (b) & pf. acc.
[Cowan: Border Ballad]   10"—D-F1699
Life and Death
Webster Booth (t) & Hubert Greenslade (pf)   10"—G-B9451
[Unmindful of Roses; Eleanore]
Unmindful of the Roses
Webster Booth (t) & Hubert Greenslade (pf)   10"—G-B9451
[Life and Death; Eleanore]

Three-Fours Valse Suite, Op. 71
—Nos. 2 & 6 only
Albert Sandler & his Palm Court Orch.
10"—C-DB2212

COLLINS, Anthony

A Threnody for a Soldier Killed in Action
(Arranged, developed & orchestrated from material left by Michael Heming, a composer killed in the Battle of El Alamein)
Hallé Orch.—Barbirolli   12"—G-C3427

COMPERE, Loyset (d. 1518)

A Flemish contrapuntist, pupil of Okeghem, who was chorister, canon and chancellor of the Cathedral of St. Quentin.

Crucifige 4-Part Motet
Les Paraphonistes de St. Jean—G. de Van
(in Vol. VIII)   12"—AS-80
[Anon: Parce domine & Obrecht: 2 Versets]

COPLAND, Aaron (1900-   )

A pupil of Goldmark and Nadia Boulanger, this American composer from Brooklyn has written very brilliant music in many forms. His work in behalf of contemporary American composers (both in North and South America) is well known, and some of his best scores have been composed especially for the films and for the ballet.

A Lincoln Portrait Speaker & Orchestra
1942
Kenneth Spencer with Philharmonic-Symphony Orch. of N. Y.—Rodzinski
2   12"—CX-266†
Melvyn Douglas with Boston Symphony Orch.—Koussevitzky   2   12"—VM-1088†
[Lincoln: Gettysburg Address, Melvyn Douglas]
Appalachian Spring Suite from the Ballet Orchestra 1944
Boston Symphony Orch.—Koussevitzky
3   12"—VM-1046†
Danzón Cubano 2 Pianos
Aaron Copland & Leo Smit   12"—CH-AL
Music for the Theatre Orchestra 1925
Prologue; Dance Interlude; Burlesque; Epilogue
Eastman-Rochester Symphony Orch.—Hanson   3   12"—VM-744†
Our Town Three Pieces from the film score 1940
Story of Our Town; Conversation at the Soda Fountain; Resting Place on the Hill.
—Arr. Piano
Leo Smit   (Limited Edition)
12"—in CH-A2
[Sonata for Piano, 1941]
—Story of Our Town only
Andor Foldes (pf), in VOX-174
(The) Quiet City Orchestra
Janssen Symphony of Los Angeles—
Janssen, in   ARTIST-JS13
(El) Sálon México Orchestra 1936
Boston Symphony Orch.—Koussevitzky
(G-DB3812/3   2   12"—VM-546†
[Trad., arr. Stravinsky: Song of the Volga Boatman]

Sonata for Piano 1941
Leo Smit   4 12"—CH-A2
                          (Limited Edition)
[Our Town, 3 pieces from the film score]

CORBETT, Francisque (1620-1681)

A famous Italian guitarist of his day, Corbett (or Corbetti) traveled all over Europe.

Allemande; Folie; Prélude
Jean Lafon (guitar)
                    (in Vol. IX) 12"—AS-89

CORELLI, Arcangelo (1653-1713)

A contemporary and friend of Handel and Scarlatti, Corelli was doubly important as a violinist and as a composer. His playing laid the foundation for all future violin technique and the style of his writing for the instrument greatly influenced other composers.

CONCERTI GROSSI, Op. 6 Strings & Harpsichord

No. 1, D major
EIAR Orch.—Zecchi
          2 12"—CET-BB25125/6
Symphony Orch.—Francis Cébron
                    10"—LUM-30101

No. 7, D Major
Else Marie Brun & Julius Koppel (vls),
T. A. Svendsen (vlc), with Chamber
Orch. of Royal Palace, Copenhagen—
Wöldike   2 10"—G-DA5256/7

No. 8, G minor ("Christmas Concerto")
(Per le Notte di Natale)
London Symphony—Walter
(G-DB3639/40)   2 12"—VM-600†
Collegium Musicum—Diener
(G-HN2086/7)   2 10"—G-EG6502/3
Berlin State Opera Orch.—F. Lehmann
(O-50018/19)   2 12"—O-7985/6
Soloists: Rudolf Schulz & Franz Seiffert
(vls), Walter Lutz (vlc) & Harpsichord
String Orch.—Antonelli
          2 12"—SEMS-1149/50
[Suite for Strings]

CONCERTO—Oboe & Orchestra
Evelyn Rothwell & Hallé Orch.—Barbirolli   12"—G-C3540

La Follia, or Folies d'Espagne See: Sonatas, Op. 5, No. 12

Sarabande & Allegretto Arr. Kreisler
Poltronieri Quartet 12"—C-GQX10138
[Mozart: Quartet No. 13, D minor—
Minuet only]

(12) SONATAS (Sonate di chiesa) Trio
Sonatas, Op. 1
Strings (2 vls. & vlc.) with Organ

No. 1, F major
Arthur Fiedler's Sinfonietta, with E.
Power Biggs (organ of Germanic Museum, Cambridge)   10"—V-10-1105

(12) SONATAS (Sonate de camera) Trio
Sonatas, Op. 2
Strings (2vls. & vlc.) with Harpsichord
(or Organ)

No. 2, D major
E. Power Biggs (Germanic Museum Organ, Cambridge) & Arthur Fiedler's Sinfonietta
          (in VM-924†) 12"—V-11-8399
[Sonata, C major, Op. 5, No. 3]

(12) SONATAS—Violin & Figured Bass, Op. 5
No. 3, C major
—Arr. Organ & Strings Malipiero
E. Power Biggs (Germanic Museum Organ) with Arthur Fiedler's Sinfonietta
                    2 12"—VM-924†
[Sonata in D major, Op. 3, No. 2]

No. 5, G minor
—3rd Mvt. (Adagio) only Arr. Orchestra
Filippi
CBS Orch.—Barlow
          (in CX-139†) 12"—C-69633D
[Gluck: Iphigénie en Aulide Overture, Pt. 3]
St. Louis Symphony—Golschmann
          (in VM-1005†) 12"—V-11-8819
[Schönberg: Verklärte Nacht, Pt. 7]

No. 12, D minor "La Follia" or "Folies d'Espagne"
(Adagio & 23 Variations) (arr. Leonard)
Yovanovitch Bratza & Frederic Jackson
(harpsichord)   10"—C-DB501
(in Col. History of Music, Vol. II: CM-232)
Joseph Szigeti & Andor Farkas (pf)
                    2 12"—CX-202†
[Bach: Unacc. Vl. Sonata No. 2 in B minor—Bourrée]
Alfredo Campoli & Eric Gritton (pf)
(arr. Leonard)   2 12"—D-K1670/1
[Paganini-Kreisler: La Campanella]
Yehudi Menuhin & H. Giesen (pf)
                    12"—G-DB1501
—Arr. String Quartet Vincenzo Mortari
Roma String Quartet   12"—G-DB4511
—Arr. Violin & String Orchestra Rozzi
Romeo Scarpa & EIAR Orch.—Tansini
                    12"—CET-CB20177

Sonata, F major (Unidentified)
—Adagio (Preludio) Arr. Busch
Adolf Busch (vl) & Busch Chamber
Players (in CM-530†) 12"—C-11913D
[Bach: Vl. Concerto No. 2, E major, Pt. 5]

SUITE String Orchestra
Arranged from movements of Sonatas, Op. 5
1. Sarabande: 3rd Mvt. D minor Sonata, Op. 5, No. 7
2. Giga: 2nd Mvt. A major Sonata, Op. 5, No. 9
3. Badinerie: 3rd Mvt. (Gavotta) E major Sonata, Op. 5, No. 11
National Symphony Orch.—Kindler (arr. Kindler)   12"—V-11-8111
Madrid Symphony—Arbós (arr. Arbós)
(C-D41008)   12"—C-68811D
String Orch.—Antonelli
                    12"—SEMS-1150
[Concerto Grosso No. 8, Pt. 3]
EIAR Orch.—Tansini
                    12"—CET-CB20249

[Handel: Minuetto, Musette, Gavotta]
Angelicum String Orch.—Gerelli
10″—G-AV50
Radio Antwerp Orch.—Gason
10″—OLYMPIA-M2176
—Giga & Badinerie only
Berlin Philharmonic Chamber Orch.—
Benda   12″—T-E2537
[Respighi: Antiche Arie—Suite No. 3,
Pt. 5]
—Giga only Arr. Clarinet & Piano Kell
Reginald Kell & Gerald Moore
10″—C-DB2189
[Handel: Sonata, Op. 1, No. 5—Allegro]
Miscellaneous
Adagio (Unidentified)
Massimo Amfitheatroff (vlc) & Orch.
12″—G-DB5413
[Laserna: Tonadilla; Galuppi: Giga]

CORNELIUS, Peter (1824-1874)

*A member of the Weimar circle, Cornelius was
influenced by Wagner and Liszt. His work,
other than his songs, is little known outside of
Germany.*

OPERAS In German
DER BARBIER VON BAGDAD 2 Acts 1858
Eng. The Barber of Bagdad
Overture Orchestra
Berlin Philharmonic Orch.—Strauss
12″—PD-66936
ACT I
Ach, das Leid hab' ich getragen Tenor
Helge Roswaenge   10″—G-DA4465
[Strauss: Rosenkavalier—Arie des
Sängers]
ACT II
O holdes Bild (Dove Duo) Soprano & Tenor
Helge & Ilonka Roswaenge
12″—G-DB4495
[Verdi: Traviata—De' miei bollenti
spiriti, H. Roswaenge]
SONGS
Ave Maria
John McCormack (t)   10″—G-DA1177
[Speaks: The Prayer Perfect]
The Monotone
Roy Henderson (b) In English & Eric
Gritten (pf)   10″—D-M584
[Schubert: Who is Sylvia?]
Weihnachtsliedern (Christmas Songs)
Christbaum; Hirten; Könige
Gerhard Hüsch (b)   12″—G-EH944

COSTELEY, Guillaume (1531-1606)

*An Irish musician who settled in France as
organist to Henri II and Charles IX, Costeley
was the first president of the St. Cecilia Society.
He wrote many four and five part "chansons."*

Madrigals Unacc. Chorus in French
Allons, gay, gay, gay bergères
Chorale "Motet et Madrigal"—H. Opien-
ski   (in Vol. V)   12″—AS-45
[Mignonne, allons voir & Jannequin: Ce
moys de may & Au joly jeu]
Lyons Cathedral Children's Chorus
10″—C-D19114
[Dupont: La mère Jeanne, Sibert]

Je voy des glissantes eaux
Paris Teachers' Chorus—Ducasse
10″—PAT-X93085
[Lassus: Quand mon mary; Palestrina:
Madrigal; Bach: Chorale]
Mignonne, allons voir si la rose (Ronsard)
Chorale "Motet et Madrigal"—H. Opien-
ski   (in Vol. V)   12″—AS-45
[Allons gay, gay, gay bergères; Janne-
quin: Ce moys de may & Au joly jeu]

COTTRAU, Teodoro (1827-1879)

SONGS

Addio a Napoli in Neapolitan
Enrico Caruso
(G-DA1655)   10″—V-2212
[Gastaldon: Musica proibita]
Beniamino Gigli   10″—G-DA941
[Donaudy: O bel nini d'aurore]
Santa Lucia
Enrico Caruso   12″—G-DB2991
[Meyerbeer: Africana—O Paradiso]
[Tosti: Addio, on G-DB5387]
Beniamino Gigli   12″—G-DB1902
[Mascagni: Cavalleria Rusticana—Addio
alla madre]
Giuseppi di Stefano   12″—G-HEX115
[Gastoldon: Musica proibita]
See also Current Catalogues.

COUILLARD (16th Century)

Viri Galilaei—Extrait des "Motets d'At-
taingnant"
Strasbourg Cathedral Choir—A. Hoch
10″—OL-21

COUPERIN, François (Le Grand) (1668-1733)

*The most famous member of the French family
of harpsichordists, François Couperin "Le
Grand" (as he was called) was a favorite of
Louis XIV. His elegant, witty pieces for harpsichord have almost obscured his religious and
concerted works, which deserve to be ranked
among the greatest productions of French composers. Influenced by the Italian Corelli, Couperin in turn commanded the respect and emu-
lation of Bach, who in his "French Suites"
makes use of the rhythmically angular agréments the great French master explained and
codified in "L'Art de Toucher le Clavecin," the
standard treatise on ornamentation in the
Baroque period.*

COLLECTION: Miscellaneous Harpsichord
Works (H.M.V.)

Les Bergèries; Les Calotins et les Calotines;

La Commère, Le Dodo, La Favorite; Les
Folies françaises;

Le Gazouillement; Les Jongleurs etc.; Les
Langueurs tendres;

Les Moissonneurs; Le Moucheron; La Musette de Taverny;

La Passacaille, Soeur Monique; Les
Tambourins;

Les Vergers fleuris

Wanda Landowska
      6   12"—Couperin Society Set
(Individual records are not available separately)

COLLECTION: Miscellaneous Harpsichord Pieces

Le Dodo; Le Tic-Toc-Choc; Les Fauvettes plaintives; La Muse Plantine; L'Arlequine; Les Ombres errantes; Les Barricades mystérieuses; Les Folies françaises; La Passacaille
Marcelle Meyer (pf)
(DF-72/5)   4 12"—DF-A16

Air Sérieux (August 1701)
Lise Daniels (s) & Irène Aitoff (pf)
[Brunête]   10"—OL-10

Air Sérieux (March 1697)
Lise Daniels (s) & Irène Aitoff
                    10"—OL-19
[Rameau: Diane at Actéon—Air tendre]

Amour Harpsichord
Isabelle Nef   10"—OL-77
[L'Himen]

(L') Apothéose de Corelli See: Le Parnasse

(L') Apothéose de Lulli
Hewitt Chamber Orch, in DF-A3

(L') Arlequine
Wanda Landowska
    (in VM-1181†)   12"—V-11-9998
[Les Barricades mystérieuses; Chambonnières: Sarabande & Rameau: La Dauphine]
Marcelle Meyer (pf), in DF-A16

(Les) Barricades Mystérieuses
Harpsichord
Wanda Landowska
    (in VM-1181†)   12"—V-11-9998
[L'Arlequine; Chambonnières: Sarabande & Rameau: La Dauphine]
Ralph Kirkpatrick, in MC-25
Gaby Casadesus (pf) in VOX-163
Marcelle Meyer (pf), in DF-A16

(Les) Bergèries
Wanda Landowska, in Couperin Society Set

Brunête (Air) December 1711
Lise Daniels (s) & Irène Aitoff (pf)
[Air sérieux]   10"—OL-10

(Les) Calotins et les Calotines ou la pièce à tretous Harpsichord
Wanda Landowska, in Couperin Society Set

(Le) Carillon de Cythère Harpsichord
Ralph Kirkpatrick, in MC-25
Gaby Casadesus (pf), in VOX-163

Chaconne Harpsichord
Eta Harich-Schneider   10"—G-DA4449
[Daquin: Guitare; Chambonnières: Volte; Dandrieu: Cascades]

Chanson Louis XIII et Pavane Really by Kreisler
See under Kreisler

(La) Commère Harpsichord
Wanda Landowska, in Couperin Society Set

CONCERTOS

Pieces en Concert ('Cello & String Quartet)
(Realized by Bazelaire from Concertos Nos. 6 & 10)

Prélude; La Trombe; Plainte; Sicilienne; Air de diable
Pierre Fournier (vlc) & String Quartet
[Haydn: Adagio] 2   12"—G-DB5087/8

(4) CONCERTS ROYAUX 1722
No. 2 Strings & Harpsichord
Prélude, Allemande, Air tendre; Air contrefugue, Echos
Instrumental Ensemble—Curt Sachs
         (in Vol. II)   12"—AS-13

No. 4
Instrumental Ensemble—Désormière
           2   12"—OL-51/2

CONCERTS DANS LE GOUT THEATRAL
(Les Goûts Réunis)
Originally written for two violins & bass, 1724. This series was a continuation of the "Concerts royaux"—Nos. 1 to 4 inclusive. The "Goûts réunis" were numbered from 5 to 14 inclusive
No. 6 See "Piéces en Concerts" above
No. 8 (No. 4 of "Les Goûts réunis")
Overture; Ritournelle; Air; Air tendre; Air léger; Loure; Air animé;
Sarabande; Air léger; Air tendre; Air des Bacchantes
Paris Ecole Normale Chamber Orch.—
Alfred Cortot   2   12"—G-DB1767/8
Wiesbaden Collegium Musicum—Weyns
        2   12"—T-E2354/55

No. 9 "Ritratto dell'amore" (No. 5 of Les Goûts réunis)
Le Charme; L'Enjouement; Les Graces; Courante Française; Le je-ne-sçay-quoy; La Vivacité; La Noble Fièrté; Sarabandes; La Douceur; L'et Coetera ou Menuets
Henri Merckel (vl), A. Navarra (vlc), Goetghelück (ob), F. Oubradous (bsn), Isabelle Nef (harpsichord)—R. Désormière   2   10"—OL-73/4

—Le Charme, L'Enjouement & La Noble Fièrté only
G. Crunelle (fl), V. Clerget (vla da gamba) & Pauline Aubert (harpsichord)
    (in Vol. XII)   12"—AS-116
[Le Parnasse, Pt. 3]
No. 10 See "Piéces en concert" above
No. 13 Two 'celli unaccompanied
Mm. Frécheville & R. Ladoux
             12"—OL-59

(La) Convalescente Harpsichord
Pauline Aubert
       (in Vol. XI)   12"—AS-109
[Les Vieux Seigneurs, Les Jeunes Seigneurs; La Visionaire]

(La) Crouilli ou la Couperinète
Alice Merckel (vla), Morel (ob), Oubradous (bsn), Isabelle Nef (harpsichord)—
Désormière   10"—OL-56
[Musette de Taverni & Musette de Choisi]

(Le) Dodo, ou L'Amour au berceau Harpsichord
Wanda Landowska, in Couperin Society Set
Marcel Meyer (pf) in DF-A16
—**Arr. 'Cello & Harpsichord**
M. Frécheville & Isabelle Nef
[La Sultane, Pt. 3] 10″—OL-54
(L') Engageante
C. Guilbert (pf) 12″—CLFX606
[Rameau: 2 Rigaudons & Menuet en Rondeau]
(Les) Fastes de la grande et ancienne Menestrandise Harpsichord
—**Les Notables; Les Vielleux et les Gueux; Les Jongleurs avec les singes et les ours; Les Invalides; Déroute de la troupe**
Marcelle de Lacour 12″—OL-11
Sylvia Marlowe, in MC-84
—**Les Jongleurs & Les Vielleux only**
Wanda Landowska, in Couperin Society Set
(Les) Fauvettes plaintives Harpsichord
Marcelle Meyer (pf), in DF-A16
(La) Favorite (Chaconne) Harpsichord
Wanda Landowska, in Couperin Society Set
(Les) Folies françaises ou les Dominos Harpsichord
Wanda Landowska, in Couperin Society Set
Marcelle Meyer (pf), in DF-A16
Fugue on the Kyrie (sur les jeux d'anches)
Carl Weinrich (Westminster Choir School Organ), in MC-9
(Le) Gazouillement Harpsichord
Wanda Landowska, in Couperin Society Set
(L') Himen Harpsichord
Isabelle Nef 10″—OL-77
[Amour]
(L') Impériale
Hewitt Chamber Orch. 3 12″—in DF-A3
(Les) Jeunes Seigneurs Harpsichord
Pauline Aubert
(in Vol. XI) 12″—AS-109
[Les vieux Seigneurs, La Convalescent, La visionnaire]
(La) Julliet
R. Cortot (fl) & Isabelle Nef (harpsichord) 12″—OL-55
[La Létiville & Le Rossignol en amour]
(Les) Langueurs tendres Harpsichord
Wanda Landowska, in Couperin Society Set

LECONS DE TENEBRES (à une voix)
—**No. 2**
Lise Daniels (s), Maurice Duruflé (organ) & Fernand Lemaire (vlc)
2 10″—OL-43 & 47
—**No. 3** (for Wednesday of Holy Week)
(Arr. Arthur Hoerée)
Paul Derenne & Hughes Cuénod (tenors), Archimbaud (treble), N. Wetchor (s), Adriano (tr), Madeleine de Lacour (harpsichord), Bracquemond (Gonzalez organ), Y. Gouverné Chorus, Orchestre Feminin de Paris—Jane Evrard
(G-DB5010/1) 2 12″—V-12325/6

(La) Létiville
H. Merckel (vl), & Isabelle Nef (harpsichord) 12″—OL-55
[La Julliet & Le Rossignol en amour]
(Les) Moissonneurs Harpsichord
Wanda Landowska, in Couperin Society Set

MOTETS

Adolescentulus Sum
Erika Rokyta (s), Paul Brunold (organ), with Flutes & Strings 10″—OL-50
[Note sur la Musique Religieuse de François Couperin, spoken in French by Paul Brunold]
Ostende Domine (from Motets du Roy, 1704) In Latin
Yves Tinayre (t) 12″—LUM-32021
[Gombert: Confitemini Domino]
(in Yves Tinayre Album No. 2)
Venite Exultemus Domino
Erika Rokyta (s), Germaine Cernay (ms) & Paul Brunold (organ) 12″—OL-49
[Note sur la Musique Religieuse de François Couperin, spoken in French by Paul Brunold]
Quatre Versets d'un Motet
Adolescentulus sum; Qui dat nivem; Ignitum eloquium; Justitia tua
Erika Rokyta & Gisèle Peyron (sopranos), Yvonne Gouverné Chorus, Maurice Duruflé (organ) & Chamber Orch.—Cloëz 2 10″—OL-60 & 92
(Le) Moucheron Harpsichord
Wanda Landowska, in Couperin Society Set
(La) Muse plantine Harpsichord
Marcelle Meyer (pf), in DF-A16
(La) Musette de Choisi
(La) Musette de Taverni
M. Morel & L. Gromer (obs), F. Oubradous (bsn), & Isabelle Nef (harpsichord)
[La Crouilli] 10″—OL-56
—**(La) Musette de Taverni** only
Wanda Landowska, in Couperin Society Set
Offertoire sur les grands jeux
Joseph Bonnet (organ)
(in Vol. VIII) 12″—AS-75
[Sanctus; Grigny: Plein jeux]
(Les) Ombres errantes Harpsichord
Ralph Kirkpatrick, in MC-25
Marcelle Meyer (pf) in DF-A16
(Le) Parnasse ou L'Apothéose de Corelli
Chamber Orch. of the Société des Concerts de Versailles—Cloëz
(in Vol. XII) 2 12″—AS-115/6
[Concert No. 9—3 movements]
H. Merckel & G. Ales (vls), Frécheville (vlc), R. Gerlin (harpsichord)—Roger Désormière 12″ & 10″—OL-57/8
(La) Passacaille Harpsichord
Wanda Landowska, in Couperin Society Set
Marcelle Meyer (pf), in DF-A16
(Les) Petits moulins à vent
—**Eng. The Little Windmills**
—**Arr. Violin & Piano**

Jascha Heifetz & pf. acc.   12"—**G-DB945**
[Bach: 2 Minuets & Debussy: Valse—La
plus que lente]
—**Arr. Orchestra** Filippi
CBS Symphony Orch.—Barlow
(in CX-145†)   12"—**C-69686D**
[Le Trophée, Soeur Monique & Franck:
Les Eolides, Pt. 3]
Récit de Cromorne Organ
Joseph Bonnet (Gonzalez Organ)
12"—**PAT-PAT68**
[Clérambault: Dialogue sur les grands
jeux & Daquin; Noël sur les flûtes]
(in 3 Centuries of Organ Music album)
DUPLICATION: Vignanelli, SEMS-1142
Rigaudon en Rondeau, A minor Harpsi-
chord ("Les Vendangeuses")
Alice Ehlers, in D-A62
(Le) Rossignol en amour
Wanda Landowska (harpsichord)
[Scarlatti: Pastorale]   10"—**G-DA1130**
R. Cortet (fl), & Isabelle Nef (harpsi-
chord)—   12"—**OL-55**
[La Létiville & La Julliet]
Sanctus Organ
Joseph Bonnet
(in Vol. VIII)   12"—**AS-75**
[Offertoire & Grigny: Plein jeux]
Soeur Monique—Rondeau Harpsichord
Wanda Landowska, in Couperin Society
Set
Dirk Schäfer (pf)   12"—**C-DHX12**
[Chopin: Fantaisie—Impromptu]
—**Arr. Organ** Guilmant
Gustave Bret (Salle Pleyel)
[Daquin: Noël]   10"—**G-DA4839**
—**Arr. Orchestra** Filippi
CBS Symphony Orch.—Barlow
(in CX-145†)   12"—**C-69686D**
[Les Petits Moulins à vent; Le Trophée;
Franck: Les Eolides, Pt. 3]

SUITES Viola da Gamba & Harpsichord
No. 2, A major
Prélude, Fuguette, Pompe Funèbre, La
Chemise blanche
Alfred Zighera & Putnam Aldrich, in
TC-T9
[with Marais: Suite in D minor]
Suite du Sixième Ordre
Paul Loyonnet (pf)   4   12"—**CH-B14**
(Limited edition)
La Sultane—Sonade en quatuor
A. Merckel & Blampain (vlas), Fréche-
ville & Neilz (vlcs), Isabelle Nef (harp-
sichord)—Désormière
12" & 10"—**OL-53/4**
[Le Dodo ou l'amour au berceau]
—**Overture & Allegro** Arr. Milhaud
Minneapolis Symphony Orch.—Mitro-
poulos   12"—**C-12161D**
St. Louis Symphony Orch.—Golschmann
12"—**V-11-8238**
(Les) Tambourins Harpsichord
Wanda Landowska, in Couperin Society
Set
(Le) Tic-toc-choc, ou les maillotins Harp-
sichord
Sylvia Marlowe, in   **MC-84**
Marcelle Meyer (pf), in   **DF-A16**

(Le) Trophée
—**Arr. Orchestra** Filippi
CBS Symphony Orch.—Barlow
(in CX-145†)   12"—**C-69686D**
[Soeur Monique & Les Petits moulins à
vent; Franck: Les Eolides, Pt. 3]
(Les) Vendangeuses See Rigaudon en Ron-
deau, A minor
(Les) Vergers fleuris Harpsichord
Ralph Kirkpatrick, in   **MC-25**
(Les) Vieux Seigneurs Harpsichord
Pauline Aubert
(in Vol. XI)   12"—**AS-109**
[Les jeunes Seigneurs; La Visionnaire &
La Convalescente]
(La) Visionnaire Harpsichord
Pauline Aubert
(in Vol. XI)   12"—**AS-109**
[Les Vieux Seigneurs, Les Jeunes Seig-
neurs & La Convalescente]

COUPERIN, Louis (1626-1661)
A noted violist and organist, Louis Couperin
was the uncle of François "Le Grand." He was
a pupil of Chambonnières, as were his two
brothers.

Chaconne
Joseph Bonnet (organ)   12"—**V-18413**
[Perotin: Trio; Anon: Le Moulin de
Paris; Caurroy: Fantaisie sur l'air "Une
Jeune Fillette"]
Chaconne, Branle de basque, Pavane, Pas-
sacaille Harpsichord
Ruggero Gerlin
(in Vol. X)   12"—**AS-92**
Chaconne et Duo Harpsichord
Marcelle de Lacour   12"—**OL-12**
[Le Tombeau de M. de Blancrocher]
Le Tombeau de M. de Blancrocher Harpsi-
chord
Marcelle de Lacour   12"—**OL-12**
[Chaconne et Duo]

COUPERIN, Pierre-Louis (1755-1789)
A collateral descendant of Couperin "Le
Grand," Pierre-Louis was an organist, harpsi-
chordist and composer as was the rest of his
family.

Chaconne, D minor Harpsichord
Alice Ehlers (in D-A62   10"—**D-23113**
[Bach: English Suite No. 2—Bourrées 1
& 2]
Dans cet asile solitaire (Romance)
Villabella (t) with pf. acc.
10"—**PAT-PG11**
[Grétry: Amant Jaloux—Sérénade]

COWARD, Noel (1899-   )
A man of versatile talents, Coward is quite
well known as an actor, dancer, singer, composer
and playwright.

BITTER SWEET Operetta in English
Vocal & Orchestral Selections
Peggy Wood & George Metaxa
12"—**G-C1746**
(from the cast of original performance)
Columbia Light Opera Company
12"—**C-9900**
Jack Hylton Orchestra
(G-C1727)   12"—**V-36098**

I'll See You Again
Noel Coward (b) & pf. acc.
      10″—G-B8740
[Operette—Dearest love]
Richard Tauber (t)   10″—P-RO20533
[Casey: Maire, my girl]
Gladys Swarthout (ms) 10″—V-10-1044
[Romberg: My Maryland—Mother]
Lily Pons (s)
      (in CM-606)   12″—C-71732D
[I'll follow my secret heart]
Nelson Eddy (b)
(C-DB2022)   10″—C-4263M
[Tokay]
Evelyn Laye (s)   10″—C-DB1870
[Zigeuner]
DUPLICATION: Dorothy Kirsten & Robert Merrill, V-10-1398

Zigeuner
Evelyn Laye (s)   10″—C-DB1870
[I'll see you again]

If You Could Only Come With Me
Call of Life
Dear Little Café
Nelson Eddy (b)
(C-DB2023)   10″—C-4264M
Tokay
Nelson Eddy (b) & Chorus
(C-DB2022)   10″—C-4263M
[I'll see you again]

CONVERSATION PIECE Operetta in
English

I'll Follow my Secret Heart
Yvonne Printemps (s), Noel Coward (b)
      10″—G-DA1363
Lily Pons (s)
      (in CM-606) 12″—C-71732D
[I'll see you again]
Maggie Teyte (s)   10″—D-F3919
[Nevermore]
Nevermore
Maggie Teyte (s)   10″—D-F3919
[I'll follow my secret heart]
Imagine the Duchess's Feelings
Noel Coward (b) & Carroll Gibbons (pf)
[Gibbons: It's only you] 10″—G-B9210
Let's Not be Beastly to the Germans
Noel Coward (b) & Robb Stewart (pf)
      10″—G-B9336
[Dane: The Welcoming Land—Recitation]
London Pride
Noel Coward (b) & Orch.
      10″—G-B9198
[Kern: The last time I saw Paris]

OPERETTE 1938

The Stately Homes of England

Where are the Songs we Sung?
Noel Coward (b)   10″—G-B8722
Dearest Love
Webster Booth (t) & Anne Ziegler (s)
[Ronald: O lovely night] 10″—G-B9552

Noel Coward (b) & pf. acc.
      10″—G-B8740
[Bitter Sweet—I'll see you again]

PACIFIC 1860 Selections
Mary Martin, with cast and Orch.—Mantovani   6 12″—D-K1590/5
This is a Changing World; Uncle Harry;
Bright as the Day; His Excellency Regrets
Noel Coward (b) & Orch.
     2 10″—G-B9532/3

PRIVATE LIVES Stage Play
Love Scene, Act I; Scene, Act II
(Recitations and singing with Orch.)
Gertrude Lawrence & Noel Coward
      12″—G-C2043

WORDS AND MUSIC Revue in English
Let's Say Goodbye
Mad Dogs and Englishmen
Noel Coward (b)   G-B9433/5

SIGH NO MORE Revue in English
Sigh No More; I wonder what happened to
him?
Matelot and Nina; Never Again; Wait a bit,
Joe
Noel Coward (b) 2 10″—G-B9433/5

MISCELLANEOUS Medley of Coward's
Songs
Noel Coward (b)   12″—G-C2450
Anne Ziegler, Joyce Grenfell & Graham
Payn & Orch.—Harry Ayres
     2 12″—G-C3635/6
See current catalogues for additional listings

COWELL, Henry (1897-   )

An excellent musician himself, Cowell is an
ardent propagandist for the most advanced
American music. His experiments with tone-
clusters and unusual instrumental effects are
most interesting.

Ancient Desert Drone Orchestra
Janssen Symphony of Los Angeles—Janssen, in   **ARTIST-JS13**
Jig; Aeolian Harp; Advertisement Piano
Henry Cowell, in **CH-B9** (Limited Edition)
Movement for String Quartet
Dorian Quartet
     (in CM-388†) 12″—C-69747D
[Piston: Quartet No. 1, Pt. 5]
Tales of Our Countryside
Deep Tides; Exultation; The Harp of Life;
Country Reel
Henry Cowell (pf) & All American Orch.
—Stokowski   2 12″—CX-235†

CRESCENZO, Vincent de (1875-   )
SONGS In Italian
Notte d'amore
Beniamino Gigli (t)   12″—G-DB3815
[Tosti: Aprile]
Quanno'a femmena vo
Beniamino Gigli (t)   10″—G-DA763
[Di Capua: Mari, Mari]

Rondine al Nido
  Stefan Islandi (t)   10"—G-DA5242
  [Tosti: Melodie]
  Luigi Infantino   10"—C-DB2335
  [Cardillo: Core 'ngrato]

Tarantella sincera
  G. Micheletti (t)   10"—PD-166778
  [Fonzo: Comme! O Zuccaro]

Triste Maggio
  Beniamino Gigli (t)   10"—G-DA1307
  [Rimsky-Korsakov: Sadko—Song of
  India]

CRESTON, Paul (1906-   )

*A pupil of Pietro Yon and a Guggenheim Fel-
low (1938), Creston is one of the young American composers who has devoted himself also
to musicology.*

Symphony, Op. 20
—Scherzo only
  All American Orch.—Stokowski
                              12"—C-11713D
  [Gould: Latin-American Symphonette—
  Guaracho]

CRIST, Bainbridge (1883-   )

*An American composer, flutist and voice teach-
er, who has composed much vocal music.*

SONGS In French
C'est mon ami
  Claudio Muzio (s)
              (in CM-289)   12"—C-9171M
  [Delibes: Filles de Cadiz] (C-BQX2523)
  [Verdi: Traviata—Addio del passato, on
  C-LCX30: C-BQX2509]

CROCE, Giovanni Dalla (c.1557-1609)

*Maestro di capella of the famous cathedral of
Saint Mark in Venice, Croce wrote many sacred
and secular vocal works.*

Tristis est anima mea Motet Unacc. Cho.
  Lyons Cathedral Children's Chorus
                              10"—C-D19113
  [Bach: Chorale—Lobe den Herrn]

CROOK, John (d.1922)

PETER PAN Incidental Music from the Ed-
  ward Genn production
Selections
  George Baker, Nancy Evans & Italia Conti
  Children, with Orch.—Clifford Green-
  wood   3   10"—G-B9117/9

CROUCH, Frederick Nicholls (1808-1896)

*Born in London, where he was a 'cello virtuoso,
Crouch came to New York at the age of forty,
was an officer in the Confederate Army and
spent the remainder of his life as a singing-
teacher in Baltimore. He wrote many chamber
works and songs, but is remembered solely for
"Kathleen Mavourneen."*

Kathleen Mavourneen
  John McCormack (t) & Edwin Schneider
  (pf) (G-DB1200)   12"—V-6776
  [Molloy: Love's Old Sweet Song]
  (Also G-DB342*)

Richard Crooks (t)
  (G-DB2336)   12"—V-8454
  [Lehar: Merry Widow—I love you so]
  John Carter (t) & J. Quillan (pf)
                              10"—C-4274M
  [MacMurrough: Macushla]
  James Melton
              (in VM-1090)   12"—V-11-9401
  [Traditional: The Minstrel Boy]

CUI, Cesar Antonovich (1835-1918)

*A member of the Russian "Five," Cui is re-
membered today by a very few of his smaller
works.*

Berceuse Russe Violin & Piano
  Simone Filone & pf.   10"—PD-522839
  [Debussy: La plus que lente]

Kaleidoscope, Op. 50
  (24 Pieces for Violin & Piano)

—No. 9, Orientale
  Mischa Elman & Raymond Bauman
                              10"—V-1354
  [Drdla: Souvenir]
  Heinz Stanske & Michael Raucheisen
                              10"—PD-47414
  [D'Ambrosio: Canzonetta, Op. 6]

—Arr. 'Cello & Piano
  Gregor Piatigorsky & Ralph Berkowitz
              (in CM-684)   10"—C-17413D
  [Rimsky-Korsakov: Sadko—Song of
  India]
  Emanuel Feuermann & Gerald Moore
  (C-DB1860)   10"—C-17158D
  [Albéniz: Tango]

—Arr. 2 Pianos
  Pierre Luboshutz & Genia Nemenoff
                              10"—V-2084
  [Mussorgsky-Luboshutz: Boris Godunov
  —Coronation Scene]

Tarantelle, Op. 12 Orchestra 1859
  Lamoureux Orch.—Wolff
  (PD-566138)   12"—PD-67041
  [Glazounov: Rêverie for Horn]

CZERNY, Karl (1791-1857)

*A pupil of Beethoven and the teacher of Franz
Liszt, Czerny himself was an excellent pianist.
His compositions in all forms number more
than a thousand, but he is represented today
chiefly by his pedagogical works.*

Scherzo fantastique Piano
  Jacques Dupont   10"—PAT-X98176
  [Schubert: Minuet]

Variations on the Aria "La Ricordanza"
  Op. 33 Piano
  Vladimir Horowitz (G-DB6274)
              (in VM-1001)   12"—V-11-8777

DALAYRAC, Nicholas (1753-1809)

*An early composer of opéras-comiques, Dalayrac
also wrote chamber music. He was a Chevalier
in the Legion d'Honneur and a very successful
composer.*

QUARTETS Strings
D major, Op. 7, No. 3
Orchestre Féminin—Jeanne Evard
12″—G-W1595
E flat major, Op. 7, No. 5
Pascal Quartet
(in Vol. XIII) 12″—AS-127

DAMROSCH, Walter (1862-   )
An important conductor, Damrosch has con-
tributed much to the development of symphonic
and operatic music in America.
Danny Deever Song in English (Kipling)
Norman Cordon (bs) & Archie Black
(pf) (in VM-1030) 10″—V-10-1182
[Speaks: On the Road to Mandalay]

DANDELOT, Georges
Chansons de Bilitis Songs in French
(Pierre Loüys)
Berceuse; Les contes; La pluie au Matin;
Scène
Germaine Cernay (ms) & Georges
Dandelot (pf) 12″—C-RFX69

DANDRIEU, Jean-François (1684?-1740)
A lesser known contemporary of Couperin who
wrote clavier music and a treatise on accom-
paniment from a thorough-bass.
(Les) Caractères de la Guerre Harpsichord
Le boute-selle; La marche; Deux fanfares;
La charge; La mêlée; Les cris; Les plain-
tes; La victoire; Le triomphe
Pauline Aubert 12″—PAT-PAT51
(Les) Cascades Harpsichord
Eta Harich-Schneider 10″—G-DA4449
[Daquin: Guitare; Couperin: Chaconne;
Chambonnières: Volte]
Musette
Vignanelli (organ) 12″—SEMS-1142
[Clérambault: Récit de nasarde; Couper-
in: Cromorne]

DAQUIN, Louis Claude (1694-1772)
A child prodigy who became a famous organist
and harpsichordist. His music, with Couperin's,
forms some of the most charming examples of
the French Rococo.
(Le) Coucou Harpsichord
Eng. The Cuckoo
Wanda Landowska 10″—G-DA977
[Rameau: Tambourin; Mozart: Don
Giovanni—Minuet]
Corradina Mola 10″—G-DA5393
[La Guitare; Mozart: Rondo alla Turca]
Solomon (pf) 12″—G-C3509
[De Séverac: Music Box; Chopin: Mazur-
ka No. 47 & Valse No. 14]
(La) Guitare Harpsichord
Corradina Mola 10″—G-DA5393
[Le Coucou; Mozart: Rondo alla Turca]
Eta Harich-Schneider 10″—G-DA4449
[Dandrieu: Les Cascades; Couperin:
Chaconne; Chambonnières: Volte]
(L') Hirondelle Harpsichord
Wanda Landowska 12″—G-DB4973
[Lully: Songes agréables d'Atys;
Chambonniéres: Chaconne et Rondeau]

NOELS Organ
No. 3
Fernando Germani 12″—SEMS-1138
[Clérambault: Dialogue]
No. 10 "Noël grand jeu et duo"
E. Power Biggs (Germanic Museum or-
gan, Harvard)
(in VM-616) 12″—V-15730
[Noël sur les flûtes]
(Also with Handel: Concerto—No. 13, on
TC-1139)
Fernando Germani 12″—CET-PE89
[Cottone: Ninna Nanna]
(Also with Bach: Herzlich tut mich ver-
langen, on SEMS-1137)
Gustave Bret (Salle Pleyel organ)
10″—G-DA4839
[Couperin: Soeur Monique]
Noël sur les flûtes
E. Power Biggs (Germanic Museum or-
gan, Harvard)
(in VM-616) 12″—V-15730
[Noël No. 10]
Joseph Bonnet (Gonzalez organ)
12″—PAT-PAT68
[Couperin: Récit de Cromorne; Cléram-
bault: Dialogue]
(in 3 Centuries of Organ Music Set)

DARGOMIJSKY, Alexander Sergeivich (1813-
1869)
With Glinka, Dargomijsky was one of the
founders of the Russian school of composers
given such impetus by the "Five." His opera
"The Stone Guest," although never popular,
employed a mezzo-recitative style that affected
both Borodin and Mussorgsky in their work.

(THE) ROUSSALKA Opera in Russian
1856
Eng. The Water Witch, or The Mermaid
Individual Excerpts
Ballet Music (Danses slaves et Tziganes)
Orchestra
London Philharmonic—Dorati
12″—C-DWX1603
Cavatina Tenor
I. S. Koslovsky 10″—USSR—12540/1
Mad Scene & Death of the Miller, Act 3
Bass & Tenor
Feodor Chaliapin & G. M. Pozemkovsky
12″—V-11-8695
Miller's Aria, Act I Bass
Alexander Kipnis
(in VM-1073) 12″—V-11-9286
[Mussorgsky: Song of the Flea]
DUPLICATION: Feodor Chaliapin,
G-DB1530; also USSR-O12292
Olga's Aria: On our street Soprano
N. M. Vechor 10″—G-EK96
[Rimsky-Korsakov: Sadko—Song of the
Venetian Guest, Loukine]

SONGS In Russian
Darling Girl
Hélène Sadoven (s) 10″—G-EK106
[Vanka Tanka, Sadoven & Kaidanoff]
(The) Old Corporal Rus. Stary Kapral
Feodor Chaliapin 12″—G-DB1342
[Flégier: Le Cor]

(The) Storm Covers the Sky with Mist
Russian State Choir—A. V. Sveshnikov
USSR-13847

Vanka Tanka Duo: Soprano & Bass
Hélène Sadoven & C. E. Kaidanoff
10"—G-EK106
[Darling Girl, Sadoven]

DAVID, Félicien César (1810-1876)
Having traveled in the Levant, David's music shows the coloring of the East. Although later French composers treated the idea more effectively, their attention was probably drawn originally by the works of David.

OPERAS In French

LALLA ROUKH 2 Acts 1862

Ma Maîtresse a quitté la tente Tenor (Romance de Noureddin)

Si vous ne savez plus charmer Soprano (Couplets de Mirza)
Jean Planel & Solange Renaux
10"—PAT-PD11

(LA) PERLE DU BRESIL 1851

Charmant oiseau Soprano (Couplets du Mysoli)
Lily Pons
(in CM-582) **10"—C-17372D**
DUPLICATION: A. Galli-Curci, D-DB255*

La Ronde des Saints-Simoniens 1830
Chorale Populaire de Paris—Peters Rosset **10"—O-281085**
[Chant Populaire Russe: Hardi camarades]

DAVIDOFF, Carl (1839-1889)
A Russian 'cellist and composer of four 'cello concertos and a method for that instrument.

At the Fountain, Op. 20, No. 2
Ger. **Am Springbrunnen** 'Cello & Piano
Hans Bottermund & pf. acc.
10"—PD-23629
[Leoncavallo: Serenade, with harp acc.]

DAVIES, (Sir) Henry Walford (1869-1941)
An important organist and choral conductor, knighted in 1922 for his contribution to British music. His compositions, many of which are designed for the Angelican Church, show the influence of his training with Parry, Stanford and Rockstro.

Be Strong and play the man
Included in Coronation Service of George VI, **G-RG7**

O Little Town of Bethlehem Hymn in English
Dennis Barthel (treble) with organ
[Parry: Jerusalem] **10"—G-B4285**

Royal Air Force March Past Band
Royal Air Force Band—Amers
10"—C-DB1916
[We're on our way, March]
(Also on G-RAF2)
Coldstream Guards Band **10"—G-B8856**
[Hamm: The Coldstream March]

Solemn Melody Originally set for String Orchestra, 1908
Harold Dawber (org), Clyde Twelvetrees (vlc) with Hallé Orch.—Harty
(C-L1986) **12"—C-7136M**
[Purcell-Wood: Trumpet Voluntary]
New Light Symphony—Sargent
[Raff: Cavatina] **12"—G-C2176**
DUPLICATIONS: New Symphony— George Walter, G-C2897; Royal Artillery Band, D-F8035; Reginald Foort (org), G-BD670

DEBUSSY, Claude Achille (1862-1918)
The outstanding exponent of impressionism in music and a skilled composer in all forms. His respect of previous masters combined with his own talent for originality led him to compose fresh, interesting music at a time when slavish following of academic rules had greatly hindered the originality of French composers. His music is well represented on records and he himself at one time recorded as accompanist to several of his songs and for operatic excerpts.

(L') Après-midi d'un faune
See below: Prélude à l'après-midi d'un faune

(2) Arabesques Piano 1888
1, E major, **Andantino con moto**
2, G major, **Allegretto scherzando**
José Iturbi **12"—V-18237**
Walter Gieseking **10"—C-17145D**
(Older version on P-E11109)
Marguerite Long **10"—C-LF55**
Suzanne Gyr **10"—G-DA6031**
DUPLICATIONS: Oscar Levant, in CM-710; Gaby Casadesus, in DISC-DM103; G. Faragó, RAD-RZ3045

—**No. 1 (E major) only**

—**Arr. 2 Pianos**
Rawicz & Landauer, C-DB2324

—**Arr. Harp**
John Cockrell **12"—C-DX1311**
[Ravel: Introduction & Allegro, Pt. 3]
Luigi Maria Magistretti **12"—G-DB5363**
[Méditation]
DUPLICATION: D. Herbrecht, G-L904

—**No. 2 (G major) only**

—**Arr. 2 Pianos**
Rawicz & Landauer, C-DB2338

Cantata See below: L'Enfant prodigue

(La) Cathédrale engloutie See below: Preludes—No. 10

(3) Chansons de Charles d'Orléans 4-Pt. Unacc. Cho. 1908
1. **Dieu! qu'il la fait bon regarder**
2. **Quand j'ai ouy le tabourin**, (with Alto solo)
3. **Yver, vous n'estes qu'un villain**

—**Nos. 1 & 3 only**
Antwerp "Coecilia" Cho.—L. de Vocht
10"—C-D19215

(THE) CHILDREN'S CORNER Suite for Piano 1908

(The original titles were in English)

1. **Doctor Gradus ad Parnassum**
2. **Jimbo's Lullaby** (Berceuse des Eléphants)
3. **Serenade for the Doll** (Sérénade à la Poupée)
4. **The Snow is Dancing** (La Neige danse)
5. **The Little Shepherd** (Le petit Berger)
6. **Golliwogg's Cake-walk**
   Walter Gieseking
   (in CM-314)   12″ & 10″—C-68962D & C-17088D
   [Nos. 1, 4, 5, 6 on C-LX597]
   [Nos. 2 & 3 on C-GQ7202]
   (C-LFX473 & C-LF155)
   Alfred Cortot   2   12″—V-7147/8
   [Preludes Nos. 3 & 8] (G-DB1248/9)
—**Arr. Orchestra** André Caplet
   Paris Conservatory Orch.—P. Coppola
   (G-DA4860/2)   3   10″—VM-280†
—**Arr. Harp, Flute & 'Cello** Salzedo
   Carlos Salzedo, Georges Barrère & Horace Britt   3   10″—VM-639†
—**No. 3, (Serenade for the Doll)** only
   Vladimir Horowitz   10″—G-DA1160
   [Scarlatti: Capriccio]
   Alexander Brailowsky
   (PD-561107)   10″—PD-62756
   [Schumann: Faschingschwank—Intermezzo]
   Gaby Casadesus, in DISC-DM103
   Jean Françaix   10″—T-A2232
   [Chopin: Mazurka, Op. 67, No. 4]
   Oscar Levant, in   CM-710
—**No. 5 (The Little Shepherd)** only
   Hazel Gertrude Kinscella   10″—V-21945
   [No. 6, Golliwogg's Cake Walk; Goossens: Hurdy Gurdy]
   Oscar Levant, in   CM-710
—**No. 6 (Golliwogg's Cake-Walk)** only
   William Murdoch   10″—D-F7495
   [Chopin: Waltz, C sharp minor]
   Hazel Gertrude Kinscella
   10″—V-21945
   [No. 5 & Goossens: Hurdy Gurdy]
   Gaby Casadesus, in   DISC-DM103
   Oscar Levant, C-72080D in CM-560
   DUPLICATION: N. de Magaloff, RAD-RZ3034
—**Arr. Piano duet:** Rawicz & Landauer, C-DB2198
—**Arr. Band:** Grenadier Guards Band, C-DB1741
—**Arr. Violin & Piano:** Jacques Thibaud & pf. acc., G-DA758

Clair de lune See: Suite Bergamasque, No. 3
Cloches à travers les feuilles Piano
   (Images, Set II, No. 1)
   Walter Gieseking
   (C-LW32)   10″—C-17218D
   [Mouvement]
—**Arr. Orchestra** Coppola
   Paris Conservatory Orch.—P. Coppola
   (in VM-363)   12″—V-12054
   [Printemps, Pt. 3] (G-DB4986)

(La) Damoiselle Elue Poème lyrique 1887
   2 Sopranos, Women's Chorus & Orchestra
   Odette Ricquier, Jeanne Guyla, St. Gervais Women's Cho. & Pasdeloup Orch.—P. Coppola (G-DB4957/8)
   (in VM-363†)   2   12″—V-12051/2
—**Prélude only** Orchestra
   National Symphony Orch.—Enrique Jorda   (in D-ED16†)   12″—D-K1176
   [Dukas: L'Apprenti sorcier, Pt. 3]

Danse (Tarantelle styrienne) Piano 1890
   Gaby Casadesus, in VOX-617
(2) Danses Chromatic Harp & String Orchestra 1904
1. **Danse sacrée** 2. **Danse profane**
   Edna Phillips & Philadelphia Orch.—Stokowski
   (in VM-116†)   12″—V-7455/6
   [Thomas: Mignon—Gavotte]
   (G-DB1642/3)
   Lily Laskine & Orch.—Coppola
   12″—G-W1025
   Marcel Grandjany & Victor String Orch.—Levin
   (in VM-1021†)   2   12″—V-11-8918/9
   [Ravel: Introduction & Allegro, Pt. 1]

En blanc et noir 3 Pieces for 2 Pianos 1915
   Bartlett & Robertson   2   12″—CX-241†
(L') Enfant Prodigue Cantata (Scène lyrique)
   Soloists, Chorus & Orch. In French 1884
Individual Excerpts
Prélude Orchestra
   Opéra-Comique Orch.—Cloëz
   12″—P-E10776
   [Cortège & Air de danse]
—**Arr. Violin & Piano**
   Jascha Heifetz & Arpad Sandor
   10″—G-DA1376
   [Paganini-Kreisler: Caprice No. 13]
L'Année en vain—Recit.
Azraël! Pourquoi mas-tu quittée?—Air
   (Recit. & Air de Lia) Eng. The years roll on
   Dorothy Maynor (s) & Philadelphia Orch.—Ormandy   12″—V-17698
   [Charpentier: Louise—Depuis le jour]
   Rose Bampton (a) & Wilfred Pelletier (pf)   12″—V-7746
   [Handel: Atalanta—Care selve]
   Inès Jouglet (s)   12″—C-BFX7
   [Charpentier: Louise—Depuis le jour]
Cortège & Air de danse Orchestra
   Royal Philharmonic—Klenau
   [Ibéria, Pt. 5]   12″—C-GQX10472
Ces airs joyeux—Recit.
O temps à jamais effacé—Air Azraël Tenor
   Charles Friant & Orch.—Cloëz
   12″—O-171028
   [Bizet: Carmen—Air de la fleur]
(6) Epigraphes antiques Piano 4 Hands 1915
—**No. 3 (Pour que la nuit soit propice)** only
   Max Pirani & Eric Grant
   10″—C-DB1301
   [Ravel: Shéhérazade—Flûte enchantée, Rose Walter]
   (in Columbia History of Music, Vol. V: CM-361)

ESTAMPES Piano 1913
See under individual titles:
1. Pagodes
2. Soirée dans Grenade
3. Jardins sous la pluie

(12) Etudes Piano 1915 (To the memory of Chopin)
1. Five Fingers. 2. Thirds. 3. Fourths. 4. Sixths. 5. Octaves. 6. Eight Fingers. 7. Chromatic Intervals. 8. Grace Notes. 9. Reiterated Notes. 10. Contrasted Tone. 11. Extended Arpeggios. 12. Chords.
Adolph Hallis   6 12″—D-K891/6

—Nos. 1, 3, 4, 8, 10 & 11 only
Jacqueline Blancard
                     3 12″—PD-27297/9

—No. 1 only
Jakob Gimpel   10″—C-17305D
[Etude No. 7] (Also in VOX-164)

—No. 7 only
Jakob Gimpel   10″—C-17305D
[Etude No. 1] (Also in VOX-164)

—No. 11 only
Vladimir Horowitz   12″—G-DB2247
[Poulenc: Pastourelle & Toccata]
Marie Thérèse Fourneau
[Jardins sous la pluie] 12″—C-LFX693

(La) Fille aux cheveux de lin See under Preludes, No. 8

Gigues Images pour orchestre Set III, No. 1 1912
San Francisco Symphony Orch.—Monteux
    (in VM-954†) 12″—V-11-8520
(G-DB6182)

Golliwogg's Cake-Walk See under Children's Corner Suite, No. 6

Hommage à Haydn Piano 1909 (Sur le nom d'Haydn)
E. Robert Schmitz
    (in VM-1031†) 10″—V-10-1191
[Preludes, Bk. I, Pt. 11]

Hommage à Rameau Images pour Piano, Set I, No. 2
Artur Rubinstein
    (in VM-998) 12″—V-11-8774
[Reflets dans l'eau]
Jean Doyen   10″—G-DA4961

Ibéria Images pour Orchestre Set III, No. 2 1907
1. Par les rues et par les chemins
2. Les parfums de la nuit
3. Le matin d'un jour de fête
Philharmonic-Symphony of N. Y.—Barbirolli   3 12″—VM-460†
[Chabrier: Habanera, Victor Orch.—Morel]
Pittsburgh Symphony—Reiner
                   3 12″—CM-491†
[Berlioz: Damnation of Faust—Rakoczy March]
Colonne Orch.—Gaston Poulet
                   3 12″—C-LFX603/5
[La Cathédrale engloutie]
Paris Conservatory Orch.—Coppola
                   3 12″—G-DB4974/6
[Soirée dans Grenade]

Royal Philharmonic Orch.—Klenau
                   3 12″—C-GQX10470/2
[L'Enfant prodigue—Cortège & Air de Danse]

IMAGES See under individual titles
Set I Piano 1905
1. Reflets dans l'eau
2. Hommage à Rameau
3. Mouvement

Set II Piano 1907
1. Cloches á travers les feuilles
2. Et la lune descend sur le temple qui fut (Unrecorded)
3. Poissons d'or

Set III Orchestra
1. Gigues 1912
2. Ibéria 1907
3. Rondes de printemps 1909

(L') Isle joyeuse Piano 1904
Walter Gieseking (C-GQX11035)
                   12″—C-69841D
[Pagodes]
Lucette Descaves-Truc 10″—G-DA4966
Jacques Dupont   10″—PAT-PG8

—Arr. 2 Pianos
Jacques Fray & Mario Braggiotti
    (in D-A52) 10″—D-23087

Jardins sous la pluie Piano Estampes No. 3
Artur Rubinstein
    (in VM-998) 12″—V-11-8773
[Soirée dans Grenade]
Walter Gieseking   10″—C-17127D
[Minstrels] (C-LF163) (C-BQ6014)
Marie-Thérèse Fourneau
[Etude No. 11]   12″—C-LFX693
Marguerite Long   12″—C-LFX24
[Plus que lente—Valse]
Oscar Levant
    (in CM-508) 10″—C-17453D
[Prelude No. 5—Les Collines d'Anacapri]
Benno Moiseiwitsch   12″—G-C2998
[Poulenc: Mouvement perpétuel No. 1; Stravinsky: Etude, F sharp minor]

Lindaraja 2 Pianos 1901
Gino Gorini & Sergio Lorenzi
                   12″—G-DB11309
[Stravinsky: Sonata for 2 Pianos, Pt. 3]

(Le) Martyre de Saint-Sébastien 1911
(Incidental Music to D'Annunzio's Mystery Drama in 5 Acts)

Symphonic Fragments Orchestra
Le Cour des lys (Prelude); Danse extatique (Scene 3); Finale (Act 1); La Passion (Act 3, Scene 4); Le bon Pasteur (Prelude Act 4)
Paris Conservatory Orch.—Coppola
                   2 12″—G-DB4817/8

—Fanfare only
Debussy Festival Orch.—Inghelbrecht, PAT-PDT19, also in CM-344†

Méditation
Luigi Maria Magistretti (harp)
[Arabesque No. 1] 12″—G-DB5363

(La) Mer Orchestra 1905 (Trois esquisses symphoniques)
1. De l'aube à midi sur la mer
2. Jeux des vagues
3. Dialogue du vent et de la mer
Cleveland Orch.—Rodzinski
      3 12"—**CM-531†**
Orch. of Swiss Romande—Ansermet
      3 12"—**D-K1606/8**
Boston Symphony Orch.—Koussevitzky
      3 12"—**VM-643†**
(G-DB3923/5) (G-DB6025/7)
Paris Conservatory Orch.—Coppola
      3 12"—**G-DB4874/6**
Paris Conservatory Orch.—Münch
      3 12"—**G-W1500/2**

Mouvement (Images pour piano Set I, No. 3)
Walter Gieseking
(C-LW32)   12"—**C-17218D**
[Cloches à travers les feuilles]
Jean Doyen   12"—**G-W1593**
[Reflets dans l'eau]

Minstrels See: Prélude No. 12

Nocturnes Orchestra 1899
1. Nuages
2. Fêtes
3. Sirènes (with Women's Chorus)
Philadelphia Orch., with Women's Cho.—
Stokowski   3 12" & 10"—**VM-630**
[Last side blank]
Orchestre des Festivals Debussy—Inghelbrecht   4 12"—**CM-344†**
[Martyre de Saint Sébastien—Fanfare & Dukas: La Peri—Fanfare]
(PAT-PDT16; X96225; PDT17 & 19)
(C-GQX10883/5; 10910)
National Symphony Orch. & Luton
Choral Society—Sidney Beer
      3 12"—**D-K1344/6**
Paris Conservatoire Orch. & Cho.—
Coppola   3 12"—**G-DB5066/8**
—No. 1 (Nuages) only
Philadelphia Orch.—Ormandy
    (in CX-247†) 12"—**C-12110D**
Philadelphia Orch.—Stokowski
    (in VM-630) 12"—**V-15814**
(G-DB3596)
(Older version, on V-7453 in VM-116†:
G-DB1614)
Lamoureux Orch.—Albert Wolff
(PD-66989)   12"—**PD-566054**
—No. 2 (Fêtes) only See Collections above
Philadelphia Orch.—Ormandy
    (in CX-247†) 12"—**C-12111D**
Philadelphia Orch.—Stokowski
    (in VM-630) 10"—**V-2034**
(Older version on G-AV4) (G-DA6005)
EIAR Symphony Orch.—Ferrero
      12"—**CET-BB25014**
Lamoureux Orch.—Wolff
    (PD-66990) 12"—**PD-566055**
—No. 2 (Fêtes) only Arr. 2 Pianos Ravel
Jacques Fray & Mario Braggiotti
    (in D-A52) 10"—**D-23088**

ORCHESTRA

Collection of Miscellaneous Orchestral Works ("Selected Works")

Includes: Nocturnes No. 1 (Nuages), Prelude No. 10—La Cathédrale engloutie (Orch. Stokowski), Danses—Sacrée et Profane
Philadelphia Orch.—Stokowski
      4 12"—**VM-116†**
[Thomas: Mignon—Gavotte]

Pagodes Piano Estampes No. 1 1903
Walter Gieseking
(C-GQX11035)   12"—**C-69841D**
[L'Isle joyeuse]

PELLEAS ET MELISANDE
Opera in French 5 Acts (Maeterlinck)
1892-1902

Complete recording
Soloists, Yvonne Gouverné Chorus, with
Symphony Orch.—Roger Désormière
(Artistic director—Louis Beydts;
Chorus director—Georg Viseur)
    20 12"—**G-DB5161/80**
The Cast:
Mélisande .... Irène Joachim (s)
Pelléas .... Jacques Jensen (t)
Geneviève .... Germaine Cernay (ms)
Golaud .... H. B. Etcheverry (b)
Arkel .... Paul Cabanel (b)
Ynold .... Leila Ben Sedira (s)
Le Berger .... Emile Rousseau (b)
Le Medecin .... Narçon (bs)

Vocal & Orchestral Selections
Paris Opéra & Opéra-Comique Soloists,
with Symphony Orch.—Georges Truc
(C-D15021/7)   6 12"—**C-OP13†**
The Cast:
Mélisande ...... Marthe Nespoulous (s)
Pelléas .... Alfred Maguenat (b)
Geneviève .... Claire Croiza (s)
Golaud .... Hector Dufranne (b)
Arkel .... Narçon (bs)
This set includes the Opening Scene (Act I), the Letter Duo (Act I), The Fountain Duo (Act II), the Bedside Scene (Act II), the Tower Scene (Act III) and Arkel's solo in Act IV.

Individual Excerpts
A synopsis of the opera indicating the portions not included in the complete recording. All references are to the Durand vocal score.

Act I, Scene 1

Je ne pourrai plus sortir Duo
(Golaud & Mélisande, p. 2, bar 9 to p. 22, bar 4)
    H. Dufranne & M. Nespoulous
    (in C-Op 13†) 12"—**C-68518D**
(C-D15021)

Act I, Scene 2

Duo de la lettre: Voici ce qu'il écrit
(Geneviève & Arkel, p. 25, bar 10 to p. 35, bar 7)
    C. Croiza & Narçon (C-D15026)
    (in C-Op 13†) 12"—**C-68519D**
—Geneviève's part only:
Maggie Teyte (s) & Gerald Moore (pf)
    In Gramophone Shop Album **GSC-3**

Act II, Scene 1

Duo de la fontaine: Vous ne savez pas
(Pelléas & Mélisande, p. 55, bar 1 to p. 73, bar 3)
  A. Maguenat & M. Nespoulous
        (in C-Op 13†)   12"—**C-68520D**
(C-D15022)

Act II, Scene 2

Ah! ah! tout va bien (Bedside Scene)
(Golaud & Mélisande, p. 76, bar 5 to p. 94, bar 5)
  H. Dufranne & M. Nespoulous
        (in C-Op 13†)   12"—**C-68521D**
(C-D15025)

Act III, Scene 1

Scène des cheveux: Mes longs cheveux
(Tower Scene: Mélisande, Pelléas, Golaud, p. 115, bar 1 to p. 140, bar 3)
  André Gaudin, Simonne Berriau, José
  Beckmans   2 12"—**PD-566051/2**
[Prenez garde & Interlude, Scene 2]
  Maguenot, Nespoulous, Dufranne
        (in C-Op 13†)   12"—**C-68522/3D**
[Maintenant que le père de Pelléas est sauvé]
(C-D15024 & C-D15027)

Act III, Scene 2

Interlude Orchestra (P. 140, bar 4 to p. 141, last bar)
  Symphony Orch.—Albert Wolff
           12"—**PD-566052**
[Prenez garde & Scène des cheveux Pt. 3]

Prenez garde Vault Duo: Golaud & Pelléas, p. 142, bar 1 to p. 147, bar 6
  José Beckmans & André Gaudin
           12"—**PD-566052**
[Scène des cheveux, Pt. 3 & Interlude, Orch.]

Act IV, Scene 2

Maintenant que le père de Pelléas est sauvé
(Arkel's address to Mélisande, p. 197, bar 6 to p. 204, bar 3)
  Narçon (in C-Op 13†)   12"—**C-68523D**
[Scène des cheveux, Pt. 3]
(C-D15027)

Act IV, Scene 4

Duo de la fontaine (p. 243, bar 5 to p. 255, bar 2)
  This excerpt begins "Tu ne sais pourquoi il faut . . ."
  Maggie Teyte (s) & Gerald Moore (pf)
      In Gramophone Shop Album **GSC-3**
  NOTE: *Miss Teyte sings the music of both Pelléas and Mélisande.*

Petite Suite Piano 4 Hands 1889
1. En bateau 2. Cortège 3. Menuet
4. Ballet
—**Arr. Orchestra** Henri Büsser
  Symphony Orch.—Coppola
  (G-K5890/1)   2 10"— **G-B8116/7**
  Lamoureux Orch.—Albert Wolff
  (PD-566011/2)   2 12"—**PD-66958/9**
  DUPLICATION: Symphony Orch.—
  Büsser C-DF707/8
Individual pieces in miscellaneous arrangements

—**No. 1. (En bateau) only Arr. Violin & Piano** Fritz Kreisler & Carl Lamson
[Prelude No. 8, La fille] 10"—**G-DA1026**
  Ferenc Vecsey & G. Agosti
           10"—**PD-62716**
[Vecsey: Cascade, Caprice No. 2]
(PD-10306)
DUPLICATIONS: G. Bustabo, C-LW15; Y. Curti, C-DFX82

—**Arr. Harp**
Caspar Reardon   12"—**SCH-5507**
[Salzedo: Chanson dans la Nuit]

—**No. 3 (Menuet) only Arr.** S. Dushkin
G. Kulenkampff (vl)   10"—**PD-15095**
[Wagner: Albumblatt]

—**Arr. 'Cello & Piano**
Raya Garbousova & Artur Balsam, in
CH-A10 (Limited Edition)

—**No. 4 (Ballet) only Arr. Orchestra**
Philharmonic-Symphony Orchestra of New York—Barbirolli
      (in CX-207†)   12"—**C-11641D**
[Ravel: La Valse, Pt. 3]

PIANO MUSIC Collections

Prelude No. 10; La Cathédrale engloutie; Children's Corner Suite; Suite Bergamasque; Reflets dans l'Eau; La Soirée dans Grenade
Walter Gieseking
      2 10"— 4 12"—**CM-314**

Soirée dans Grenade; Jardins sous la pluie; Reflets dans l'eau; Hommage à Rameau; Poissons d'or; Le plus que lente—Valse
Artur Rubinstein   3 12"—**VM-998**

Arabesques 1 & 2; Serenade for the Doll; Golliwogg's Cake Walk; Fille aux cheveux de lin; Minstrels; Voiles; La Sérénade interrompue
Gaby Casadesus   4 10"—**DISC-DM103**

Reflets dans l'eau; La soirée dans Grenade; General Lavine-eccentric; Minstrels; La Cathédrale engloutie; Serenade for the doll; The Little Shepherd; La plus que lente; Arabesque 1 & 2
Oscar Levant   4 12"—**CM-710**

Images & Préludes, but no detailed information as to exact excerpts is available.
Marcelle Meyer
(DF-92/5)   4 12"—**DF-A21**
See also under individual titles.

(La) Plus que lente—Valse Piano 1910
Artur Rubinstein
      (in VM-998)   12"—**V-11-8775**
[Poissons d'or]
Marguerite Long   12"—**C-LFX24**
[Jardins sous la pluie]
Oscar Levant, in CM-710

—**Arr. Violin & Piano** Roques
Jascha Heifetz & Emanuel Bay
           12"—**V-11-9571**
[Schubert-Wilhelmj: Ave Maria]
[Achron: Hebrew Melody, on G-DB6469]
(older recording on G-DB945)
Jean Fournier & Pierre Capdevielle
[Sonata No. 3, Pt. 3] 12"—**PAT-PDT59**

Poissons d'or Piano Images, Set II, No. 3
Artur Rubinstein
(in VM-998) 12″—V-11-8775
[Le Plus que lente—Valse]
Carlo Zecchi 12″—CET-CB20354
[Chopin: Berceuse]
Walter Gieseking 12″—C-69020D
[Ravel: Ondine]
(C-LFX539) (C-LWX205)

Pour le piano—Suite Piano 1901
1. Prélude, A minor 2. Sarabande 3. Toccata, C sharp minor
Gaby Casadesus 2 12″—VOX-617
[Danse]
—**No. 1 (Prelude) only**
Artur Rubinstein 12″—G-DB2450
[Ravel: Tombeau de Couperin—Forlane]
—**No. 2 (Sarabande) only**
—**Arr. Orchestra** Ravel
Boston Symphony—Koussevitzky
(in VM-102†) 12″—V-7375
[Mussorgsky-Ravel: Pictures at an Exhibition, Pt. 7] (G-DB1893)
San Francisco Symphony Orch.—Monteux (in VM-1143†) 12″—V-11-9684
[Ravel: Daphnis et Chloé—Suite No. 1, Pt. 3]
Orch. of the Maggio Musicale—Gui
12″—CET-BB25175
[Chabrier: Sous bois]
—**No. 3 (Toccata) only**
Benno Moiseiwitsch 12″—G-C3487
[Ravel: Le Tombeau de Couperin—Toccata]
Eileen Joyce 12″—P-E11239
[Moszkowski: Waltz in E major]

Prélude à l'après-midi d'un faune 1893
Orchestra
(Eclogue for orchestra, after Mallarmé)
Eng. **Prelude to the Afternoon of a Faun**
Philadelphia Orch.—Stokowski
12″—V-17700
Philharmonia Orch.—Galliera
12″—C-DX1381
Amsterdam Concertgebouw Orch.—
Mengelberg 12″—T-SK2955
(U-G14208)
London Philharmonic—Beecham
(C-LX805) 12″—C-69600D
National Symphony Orch.—Beer
12″—D-K1037
Orchestra Stabile of the Academy of St.
Cecelia, Rome—Molinari
12″—CET-BB25012
Straram Orch.—Walter Straram
(C-CQX10638) 12″—C-LFX30
Lamoureux Orch.—Albert Wolff
(PD-566000) 12″—PD-66892
DUPLICATIONS: Symphony Orch.—Coppola, G-W1150: G-AW281; Colonne
Orch.—Pierné, O-123689

PRELUDES 2 Books Piano 1910/13
Collections
Book I (12 Préludes) (Préludes 1 to 12)
Walter Gieseking 6 10″—CM-352
(C-LF158/63) (C-BQ6008/14)
(C-LC24/9)
[Jardins sous la pluie: Estampes No. 3]

(This set does not include Prélude No. 10
—La cathédrale engloutie, previously recorded by Gieseking on C-17077D, for which an extra pocket is provided in the present album.)
Alfred Cortot 5 10″ & 1 12″—
G-DA1240/4 & G-DB1593
E. Robert Schmitz 7 10″—VM-1031†
[Sur le nom d'Haydn]

Book II (12 Préludes) (Préludes 13 to 24)
Walter Gieseking
(C-LZ3/8) 6 10″—CM-382
Robert Casadesus 6 10″—CM-644
E. Robert Schmitz 6 12″—VM-1138
Kathleen Long 5 12″—D-K1052/6

Individual Préludes
—**No. 1 (Danseuses de Delphes)** Book I, No. 1
Walter Gieseking, C-17122D in CM-352
(C-LF158; C-BQ6008)
Alfred Cortot, G-DA1240
E. Robert Schmitz, V-10-1185 in VM-1031
—**No. 2 (Voiles)** Book I, No. 2
Walter Gieseking, C-17122D in CM-353
(C-LF158; C-BQ6008)
Alfred Cortot, G-DA1240
E. Robert Schmitz, V-10-1185 in VM-1031
Gaby Casadesus, in DISC-DM103
Solomon 10″—G-B9561
[La fille aux cheveux de lin]

—**No. 3 (Le vent dans la plaine)** Book I, No. 3
Walter Gieseking, C-17123D in CM-352
(C-LF159; C-BQ6009)
Alfred Cortot, G-DA1241
(Also V-7148 & G-DB1249 with Children's Corner Suite, Pt. 3)
E. Robert Schmitz, V-10-1186 in VM-1031
Ignace Jan Paderewski 10″—G-DA1173
[Minstrels]

—**No. 4 (Les sons et les parfums tournent dans l'air du soir)** Book I, No. 4
Walter Gieseking, C-17123D in CM-352
(C-LF159; C-BQ6009)
Alfred Cortot, G-DA1241
E. Robert Schmitz, V-10-1186 in VM-1031

—**No. 5 (Les Collines d'Anacapri)** Book I, No. 5
Walter Gieseking, C-17124D in CM-352
(C-LF160; C-BQ6010)
E. Robert Schmitz, V-10-1187 in VM-1031
Alfred Cortot, G-DA1242
Oscar Levant
(in CM-508) 10″—C-17453D
[Jardins sous la pluie]

—**No. 6 (Des pas sur le neige)** Book I, No. 6
Walter Gieseking, C-17124D in CM-352
(C-LF160; C-BQ6010)
Alfred Cortot, G-DA1242
E. Robert Schmitz, V-10-1187 in VM-1031
Friedrich Gulda, in preparation (English Decca)

—**No. 7 (Ce qu'a vu le vent d'ouest)** Book I No. 7
Walter Gieseking, C-17125D in CM-352
(C-LF161; C-BQ6011)
Alfred Cortot, G-DA1243
E. Robert Schmitz, V-10-1188 in VM-1031

—**No. 8 (La fille aux cheveux de lin)** Book I, No. 8
Walter Gieseking, C-17125D in CM-352
(C-LF161; C-BQ6011)
Alfred Cortot, G-DA1243
(Also V-7148: G-DB1249 with Children's Corner Suite, Pt. 3)
E. Robert Schmitz, V-10-1188 in VM-1031
Solomon   10"—**G-B9561**
[Prelude No. 2, Voiles]
Theo van der Pas, in preparation (English Decca)
Oscar Levant
               (in CM-560)   12"—**C-72080D**
[Golliwogg's Cake Walk; Clair de Lune]
Suzanne Gyr   12"—**G-DB10046**
[Ravel: Sonatine, Pt. 3]
DUPLICATIONS: Gaby Casadesus, in DISC-DM101; Andor Foldes, in CON-22
—**Arr. Violin & Piano** Hartmann
Yehudi Menuhin & Adolph Baller
                           10"—**V-10-1220**
[Elgar: Salut d'amour, Op. 12]
[Dvořák-Persinger: Songs my mother taught me, on G-DA1499]
Jascha Heifetz & Emanuel Bay
                           10"—**V-10-1324**
[Falla: Jota]
[Grieg: Scherzo Impromptu & Mendelssohn: Auf flügeln des Gesanges, on G-DB1246]
Fritz Kreisler & Isidor Achron
(G-DA1026)   10"—**V-1358**
[Petite Suite—En bateau]
Grisha Goluboff & Ivor Newton
                           10"—**C-DW4529**
[Brahms-Joachim: Hungarian Dance No. 1]
DUPLICATIONS: J. Thibaud & H. Craxton, G-DA866; Zino Francescatti & M. Lanner, on C-17477D in **CM-660**
—**Arr. Harp**
Laura Newell
               (in CX-167†)   12"—**C-70083D**
[Ravel: Introduction & Allegro, Pt. 3]
—**No. 9 (La sérénade interrompue)** Book I, No. 9
Walter Gieseking, C-17126D in CM-352
(C-LF162; C-BQ6012)
Alfred Cortot, G-DA1244
E. Robert Schmitz, V-10-1189 in VM-1031
Gaby Casadesus, in DISC-DM103
—**No. 10 (La cathédrale engloutie)** Book I, No. 10
Walter Gieseking, C-17077D (also included in CM-314) (C-LF153)
(See note above) (C-BQ6013) (C-LB30)
Alfred Cortot, G-DB1593
E. Robert Schmitz, V-10-1190 in VM-1031
(Also on V-11-8240 with Clair de lune)
Paul Baumgartner   12"—**G-DB10034**
Artur Rubinstein
(G-DB1258)   12"—**V-36289**
[Brahms: Capriccio No. 2]
Oscar Levant, in CM-710
—**Arr. Orchestra**
Philadelphia Orch.—Stokowski
               (in VM-116†)   12"—**V-7454**
Colonne Orch.—Gaston Poulet
[Ibéria, Pt. 5]   12"—**C-LFX605**

—**No. 11 (La danse de Puck)** Book I, No. 11
Walter Gieseking, C-17126D in CM-352
(C-LF162; C-BQ6012)
Alfred Cortot, G-DB1593
E. Robert Schmitz, V-10-1189 in VM-1031
—**No. 12 (Minstrels)** Book I, No. 12
Walter Gieseking, C-17126D in CM-352
(C-LF163; C-BQ6014)
Alfred Cortot, G-DA1244
E. Robert Schmitz, V-10-1191 in VM-1031
Ignace Jan Paderewski
[Le vent dans la plaine] 10"—**G-DA1173**
Gaby Casadesus, in DISC-DM103
DUPLICATIONS: Eduard Erdmann, PD-90024; Oscar Levant, in CM-710
—**Arr. Violin & Piano** Hartmann
Zino Francescatti & Max Lanner, C-17477D in CM-660
Yehudi Menuhin & Arthur Balsam
                           10"—**G-DA1280**
[Rimsky-Korsakov: Flight of the Bumblebee & Falla: Danse espagnole]
Jacques Thibaud & Alfred Cortot
[Sonata No. 3, Pt. 3]   10"—**G-DB1323**
—**No. 13 (Brouillards)** Book II, No. 1
Walter Gieseking, C-17163 in CM-382
(C-LZ3)
E. Robert Schmitz, V-10-1317 in VM-1138
Robert Casadesus, C-17391D in CM-644
Kathleen Long, D-K1052
—**No. 14 (Feuilles mortes)** Book II, No. 2
Walter Gieseking, C-17163D in CM-382
(C-LZ3)
E. Robert Schmitz, V-10-1317 in VM-1138
Robert Casadesus, C-17391D in CM-644
Kathleen Long, D-K1052
—**No. 15 (La puerta del vino)** Book II, No. 3
Walter Gieseking, C-17164D in CM-382
(C-LZ4)
E. Robert Schmitz, V-10-1318 in VM-1138
Robert Casadesus, C-17392D in CM-644
Kathleen Long, D-K1053
—**No. 16 (Les fées sont d'exquises danseuses)** Book II, No. 4
Walter Gieseking, C-17164D in CM-382
(C-LZ4)
E. Robert Schmitz, V-10-1318 in VM-1138
Robert Casadesus, C-17392D in CM-644
Kathleen Long, D-K1053
—**No. 17 (Bruyères)** Book II, No. 5
Walter Gieseking, C-17165D in CM-382
(C-LZ5)
E. Robert Schmitz, V-10-1319 in VM-1138
Robert Casadesus, C-17393D in CM-644
Kathleen Long, D-K1054
Carmen Guilbert   10"—**PAT-X98135**
[Fauré: Barcarolle No. 6]
—**No. 18 (General Lavine—eccentric)** Book II, No. 6
Walter Gieseking, C-17165D in CM-382
(C-LZ5)
E. Robert Schmitz, V-10-1319 in VM-1138
Robert Casadesus, C-17393D in CM-644
(C-LB64)
Kathleen Long, D-K1052
Oscar Levant, in CM-710

—No. 19 (La terrasse des audiences du clair de lune) Book II, No. 7
Walter Gieseking, C-17166D in CM-382 (C-LZ6)
E. Robert Schmitz, V-10-1320 in VM-1138
Robert Casadesus, C-17394D in CM-644 (C-LB64)
Kathleen Long, D-K1054

—No. 20 (Ondine) Book II, No. 8
Walter Gieseking, C-17166D in CM-382 (C-LZ6)
E. Robert Schmitz, V-10-1320 in VM-1138
Robert Casadesus, C-17394D in CM-644 (C-LB61)
Kathleen Long, D-K1055
Eduard Erdmann   10"—PD-90024
[Minstrels]

—No. 21 (Hommage à S. Pickwick, Esq., P.P.M.P.C.) Book II, No. 9
Walter Gieseking, C-17167D in CM-382 (C-LZ7)
E. Robert Schmitz, V-10-1321 in VM-1138
Robert Casadesus, C-17395D in CM-644
Kathleen Long, D-K1055

—No. 22 (Canope) Book II, No. 10
Walter Gieseking, C-17167D in CM-382 (C-LZ7)
E. Robert Schmitz, V-10-1321 in VM-1138
Robert Casadesus, C-17395D in CM-644
Kathleen Long, D-K1055

—No. 23 (Les tierces alternées) Book II, No. 11
Walter Gieseking, C-17168D in CM-382 (C-LZ8)
E. Robert Schmitz, V-10-1322 in VM-1138
Robert Casadesus, C-17394D in CM-644 (C-LB61)
Kathleen Long, D-K1056

—No. 24 (Feux d'artifice) Book II, No. 12
Walter Gieseking, C-17168D in CM-382 (C-LZ8)
E. Robert Schmitz, V-10-1322 in VM-1138
Robert Casadesus, C-17394D in CM-644
Kathleen Long, D-K1056
Lucette Descaves-Truc
[Ravel: Jeux d'eau]   12"—G-DB5192
DUPLICATIONS: Marie-Thérèse Brazeau, PD-27094; N. de Magaloff, RAD-RZ3038

Printemps Symphonic Suite: Chorus & Orchestra 1886/7
(Revised as Orchestra alone, 1913)
Royal Philharmonic Orch.—Beecham
                   2   12"—G-DB6549/50
Paris Conservatory Orch.—Coppola
   (in VM-363†)   2   12"—V-12053/4
(Cloches à travers les feuilles, arr. orch. Coppola) (G-DB4985/6)

Quartet (String) G minor, Op. 10 1893
Budapest Quartet   4   12"—CM-467†
Pro Arte Quartet   4   12"—VM-186†
[Glazounov: Interludium]
Calvet Quartet   4   12"—C-LFX210/3
Gabriel Bouillon Quartet
                   3   12"—G-DB5109/11
DUPLICATIONS: New Italian Quartet, T-E9094/7

Reflets dans l'eau (Images pour Piano, Set I, No. 1)

Walter Gieseking
         (in CM-314   12"—C-68575D
(C-LX480) (C-LFX423) (C-GQX10816)
[Soirée dans Grenade]
Artur Rubinstein
         (in VM-998)   12"—V-11-8774
[Hommage à Rameau]
Ignace Jan Paderewski   12"—V-6633
[Stojowski: Chant d'amour]
Otakar Vondrovic   12"—ESTA-F5196
[Ravel: Jeux d'eau]
Jean Doyen   12"—G-W1593
[Mouvement]
Oscar Levant, in CM-710

Rêverie Piano 1890
Walter Gieseking   10"—C-17138D
[R. Strauss: Ständchen, arr. Gieseking]
E. Robert Schmitz   12"—V-12-0066
[Ravel: Pavane pour une Infante défunte]

Rhapsody Clarinet & Orchestra 1910
Benny Goodman & New York Philharmonic-Symphony Orch.—Barbirolli
                          12"—C-11517D

Rondes de printemps Images pour orchestre Set III, No. 3 1909
San Francisco Orchestra—Monteux
         (in VM-954†)   12"—V-11-8521
(G-DB6183)

Sarabande
See: Pour le piano, No. 2

(La) Soirée dans Grenade Piano Estampes No. 2
Walter Gieseking
         (in CM-314)   12"—C-68575D
(C-LX480) (C-LFX423) (C-GQX10816)
[Reflets dans l'eau]
Artur Rubinstein
         (in VM-998)   12"—V-11-8773
[Jardins sous la pluie]
DUPLICATION: Oscar Levant, in CM-710

—Arr. Orchestra Coppola
Paris Conservatory Orch.—Coppola
[Ibéria Pt. 5]   12"—G-DB4976

SONATAS (Pour divers instruments)
No. 1, 'Cello & Piano 1915 (Prologue, Sérénade, Finale)
Maurice Maréchal & Robert Casadesus
                   2   12"—C-LFX85/6
[Caplet: Epiphanie—Danse des petits nègres]
Raya Garbousova & Artur Balsam, in CH-A10 (Limited Edition)
(with Petite Suite—Minuet)

No. 2 (Trio) Flute, Harp, Viola, 1916
(Pastorale, Interlude, Finale)
John Wummer, Milton Katims & Laura Newell   2   12"—CX-282†
Marcel Moyse, Lily Laskine & Alice Merkel (G-L1066/7) 2 12"—VM-873†
A. Tassinari, C. Gandolfi & F. Mora
                   2   12"—C-CQX16491/2
[Tedeschi: 2 Pieces for Harp, Gandolfi]

No. 3 Violin & Piano 1916/17 (Allegro vivo, Intermède, Finale)
Zino Francescatti & Robert Casadesus
[Ravel: Berceuse]   2   12"—CX-280†

Joseph Szigiti & Andor Foldes
[Clair de lune] 2 12″—**CX-242**†
Mischa Elman & Leopold Mittman
2 12″—**VM-938**†
[Fauré-Elman: Après un rêve]
DUPLICATIONS: Alfred Dubois & Marcel Maas, C-DFX198/9; Jean Fournier & Pierre Capdevielle, PAT-PDT58/9; Jacques Thibaud & Alfred Cortot,
G-DB1322/3

SONGS

Collection

The Songs of Debussy (14 Songs)
Maggie Teyte (s) & Alfred Cortot (pf)
(G-DA1471/77) 7 10″—**VM-322**
(No records sold separately)
(Includes: Trois chansons de Bilitis—La Flûte de Pan; La Chevelure; Le Tombeau des Naïades. Le Promenoir de deux amants—Auprès de cette grotte sombre; Crois mon conseil, chère Climène; Je tremble en voyant ton visage. Fêtes Galantes—En sourdine; Clair de lune; Fantoches; Les Ingénus; Le Faune; Colloque sentimental, Proses Lyriques—De Gréve. Ballades de Villon—Des Femmes de Paris.)

Individual Songs

(L') Angélus (Le Roy) 1891
Claire Croiza (s) & Mlle. Meedintiano
(pf) 12″—**LUM-32045**
[Cloches & Ballade de Nostre Dame]
Ariettes Oubliées (Verlaine) 1888-1903
See individual titles:
1. C'est l'extase langoureuse
2. Il pleure dans mon coeur
3. L'ombre des arbres
4. Chevaux de bois
5. Aquarelles—Green
6. Aquarelles—Spleen
Aquarelles—Spleen (Ariettes oubliées No. 6) (Verlaine)
Lucienne Tragin (s) & Francis Poulenc
(pf) 12″—**C-LFX651**
[Aquarelles—Green & Chevaux debois]
Aquarelles—Green (Ariettes oubliées No. 5) (Verlaine)
Lily Pons (s) & Frank LaForge (pf)
(in VM-599) 10″—**V-1905**
[Mandoline & Benedict: La Capinera]
Lucienne Tragin (s) & Francis Poulenc
(pf) 12″—**C-LFX651**
[Aquarelles—Spleen & Chevaux de bois]
Auprès de cette grotte sombre (Le promenoir de deux amants No. 1)
(Tristan L'Hermite) (See also—Grotte)
Maggie Teyte & Alfred Cortot, in VM-322
Ninon Vallin (s) & pf. acc.
12″—**PAT-PDT82**
[Crois mon conseil, Chère Climène; Je tremble en voyant ton visage; Mandoline]
(3) Ballades de François Villon 1910
Orch. acc.
See individual titles:
1. Ballade de Villon à s'amye (Unrecorded)
2. Ballade que fait Villon à la requeste de sa mère, pour prier Nostre-Dame.

3. **Ballade des femmes de Paris**
Ballade que fait Villon à la requeste de sa mère, pour prier Nostre-Dame
Charles Panzéra (b) 10″—**G-DA4810**
[Ballade des femmes de Paris]
Claire Croiza (s) & Mlle. Meedintiano
(pf) 12″—**LUM-32045**
[Angélus & Les Cloches]
Ballade des femmes de Paris
Maggie Teyte (s) & Alfred Cortot (pf), in
VM-322
Charles Panzéra (b) 10″—**G-DA4810**
[Ballade que fait Villon]
Beau Soir (Paul Bourget) 1878
Maggie Teyte (s) & Gerald Moore (pf)
[Romance] 10″—**G-DA1838**
Claudia Muzio (s)
(in CM-289) 10″—**C-4398M**
[Delibes: Bonjour Suzon] (C-BQ6007)
[Cilea: Adriana Lecouvreur—Poveri fiori, on C-LC20; C-BQ6001]
—**Arr. Violin & Piano** Heifetz
Jascha Heifetz & Milton Kaye
(in D-A385) 10″—**D-23386**
[Gardner: From the Canebrake]
C'est l'extase langoureuse (Ariettes oubliées No. 1) (Verlaine)
Lucienne Tragin (s) & Francis Poulenc
(pf) 12″—**C-LFX650**
[Il pleure dans mon coeur]
Chansons de Bilitis (Pierre Loüys) 1898
See individual titles:
1. La flûte de Pan
2. La chevelure
3. Le tombeau des Naïades
(Trois) Chansons de France
See individual titles:
1. Rondel
2. La Grotte
3. Rondel
Chevaux de bois (Ariettes oubliées No. 4) (Verlaine)
Lucienne Tragin (s) & Francis Poulenc
12″—**C-LFX651**
[Aquarelles—Green & Spleen]
(La) Chevelure (Chansons de Bilitis No. 2) (Loüys)
Maggie Teyte (s) & Alfred Cortot (pf), in
VM-322
Jan Bathoiri (s) pf. acc.
[La flûte de Pan] 10″—**C-D13086**
Madeleine Dubuis (s) & Suzanne Gyr
(pf) 10″—**G-DA6012**
[La flûte de Pan]
—**Arr. Violin & Piano**
Jascha Heifetz & Emanuel Bay
(in VM-1126) 10″—**V-10-1295**
[Medtner: Fairy Tale, Op. 20, No. 1]
Clair de lune (Fêtes Galantes, Set I, No. 3) (Verlaine)
Maggie Teyte (s) & Alfred Cortot (pf), in VM-322
(Les) Cloches (Paul Bourget) 1887
Claire Croiza (s) & Mme. Meedintiano
(pf) 12″—**LUM-32045**
[Angélus & Ballade No. 2]

Colloque sentimental (Fêtes galantes, Set II, No. 3) (Verlaine)
Maggie Teyte (s) & Alfred Cortot (pf), in VM-322

Crois mon conseil, chère Climène (Promenoir de deux amants No. 2) (Tristan L'Hermite)
Maggie Teyte (s) & Alfred Cortot (pf), in VM-322
Ninon Vallin (s)   12"—PAT-PDT82
[Je tremble; Auprès de cette grotte sombre; Mandoline]

De Fleurs (Proses lyriques No. 3)
Maggie Teyte (s) & Gerald Moore (pf), in Gramophone Shop Album

De Grève (Proses lyriques No. 2)
Maggie Teyte (s) & Alfred Cortot (pf), in VM-322

De Rêve (Proses lyriques No. 1)
Maggie Teyte (s) & Gerald Moore (pf), in Gramophone Shop Album

De Soir (Proses lyriques No. 4)
Maggie Teyte (s) & Gerald Moore (pf), in Gramophone Shop Album

(L') Echelonnement des Haies (Trois Melodies, No. 3) (Verlaine) 1891
Lucienne Tragin (s) & Francis Poulenc (pf)   12"—C-LFX651
[Ariettes Oubliées, Pt. 3]

En sourdine (Fêtes galantes, Set I, No. 1) (Verlaine)
Maggie Teyte (s) & Alfred Cortot (pf), in VM-322

Fantoches (Fêtes galantes, Set I, No. 2) (Verlaine)
Maggie Teyte (s) & Alfred Cortot (pf), in VM-322
Madeleine Dubuis (s) & Suzanne Gyr (pf)   10"—G-DA6013
[Mandoline & Le Tombeau des Naïades]

(Le) Faune (Fêtes galantes, Set II, No. 2) (Verlaine)
Maggie Teyte (s) & Alfred Cortot (pf), in VM-322

Fêtes Galantes (Paul Verlaine) See individual titles:
Set I (1892)
1. En sourdine
2. Fantoches
3. Clair de lune
Set II (1904)
1. Les Ingénus
2. Le Faune
3. Colloque sentimental

(La) Flûte de Pan (Chansons de Bilitis, No. 1) (Loüys)
Maggie Teyte (s) & Alfred Cortot (pf), in VM-322
Jane Bathori (s) & pf. acc.
[Chevelure]   10"—C-D13086
Madeleine Dubuis (s) & Suzanne Gyr (pf)   10"—G-DA6012
[Chevelure]

Green See under Aquarelles (Ariettes oubliées No. 5)

(La) Grotte (Trois Chansons de France, No. 2) (Tristan L'Hermite) 1904
(This song is identical with "Auprés de cette grotte sombre" No. 1 in the series

"Le promenoir de deux amants" 1910. For a recorded version see above.)
Pierre Bernac (b) & Francis Poulenc (pf)   10"—G-DA4890
[Deux Rondels]

Il pleure dans mon coeur (Ariettes oubliées No. 2) (Verlaine)
Claire Croiza (s) & Francis Poulenc
[Roussel: Sarabande]   10"—C-D13084
Lucienne Tragin (s) & Francis Poulenc (pf)   12"—C-LFX650
[C'est l'extase langoureuse]
—Arr. Violin & Piano Hartmann
Jascha Heifetz & Emanuel Bay
           (in VM-1158)   10"—V-10-1341
[Poldowsky: Tango]

(Les) Ingénus (Fêtes galantes, Set II, No. 1) (Verlaine)
Maggie Teyte (s) & Alfred Cortot (pf), in VM-322

Je tremble en voyant ton visage (Le promenoir de deux amants No. 3) (Tristan L'Hermite)
Maggie Teyte (s) & Alfred Cortot (pf), in VM-322
Ninon Vallin (s)   12"—PAT-PDT82
[Auprès de cette grotte; Crois mon conseil; Mandoline]

(Le) Jet d'eau (Cinq poèmes No. 3) (Baudelaire) 1890
Maggie Teyte (s) & Gerald Moore (pf), in Gramophone Shop Album

Mandoline (Verlaine) 1880
Lily Pons (s) & Frank La Forge (pf)
           (in VM-599)   10"—V-1905
[Aquarelles—Green & Benedict: La Capinera]
Ninon Vallin (s)   12"—PAT-PDT82
[Promenoir de deux amants, Nos. 1, 2 & 3]
Madeleine Dubuis (s) & Suzanne Gyr (pf)   10"—G-DA6003
[Fantoches & 3 Chansons de Bilitis, Pt. 3]

Noël des enfants qui n'ont plus de maison 1915
Claude Pascal (tr) & pf. acc.
           10"—C-DF1343
[Grovlez: J'ai fait un trou]

(L') Ombre des arbres (Ariettes oubliées No. 3) (Verlaine)
Lucienne Tragin (s) & Francis Poulenc (pf)   12"—C-LFX650
[C'est l'extase langoureuse, etc.]

Paysages Belges
Lucienne Tragin (s) & Francis Poulenc (pf)   12"—C-LFX650
[L'Ombre des arbres; C'est l'extase langoureuse]

(Le) Promenoir de deux amants (Tristan L'Hermite) 1910
See individual titles:
1. Auprès de cette grotte sombre
2. Crois mon conseil, chère Climène
3. Je tremble en voyant ton visage

Proses Lyriques 1894
See individual titles:
1. De Rêve
2. De Grève

3. De Fleurs
4. De Soir
Romance (Paul Bourget) 1887
Maggie Teyte (s) & Gerald Moore (pf)
[Beau Soir] 10"—**G-DA1838**
—Arr. 'Cello & Piano
Gregor Piatigorsky & Valentin Pavlovsky
(in CM-501) 10"—**C-17447D**
[Fauré: Tarantelle]
(2) Rondels (Charles d'Orléans)
(Trois Chansons de France, No. 1 & No.
3) 1904
Pierre Bernac (b) & pf. acc.
[La Grotte] 10"—**G-DA4890**
Spleen See Aquarelles—Spleen
(Le) Tombeau des Naïades (Chansons de
Bilitis No. 3) (Loüys)
Maggie Teyte (s) & Alfred Cortot (pf),
in VM-322
Madeleine Dubuis (s) & Suzanne Gyr
(pf) 10"—**G-DA6013**
[Mandoline & Fantoches]
(La) Vièrge Erigone
Lucienne Tragin (s) & Francis Poulenc
(pf) 12"—**C-LFX650**
[Il pleure dans mon coeur]
Voici que le printemps Trois Mélodies, No.
2 1887
Povla Frijsh (s) & C. Dougherty (pf)
(in VM-789) 12"—**V-18053**
[Ravel: Le Paon]
Suite Bergamasque Piano 1890
**1. Prélude 2. Menuet 3. Clair de lune 4.
Passepied**
Walter Gieseking
(also in CM-314) 2 12"—**CX-8†**
(C-DX337/8) (C-DFX123/4)
(C-GQX11058/9) (C-DCX41/2)
—No. 1, Prélude
E. Robert Schmitz 12"—**V-11-8694**
[No. 2, Menuet]
—No. 2, Menuet
E. Robert Schmitz 12"—**V-11-8694**
[No. 1, Prélude]
—No. 3, Clair de lune
E. Robert Schmitz 12"—**V-11-8240**
[Prélude No. 10]
Benno Moiseiwitsch 12"—**G-C3485**
[Chopin: Polonaise No. 9]
José Iturbi 12"—**V-11-8851**
[Liszt: Liebestraum No. 3]
Oscar Levant, C-72050D in CM-560
DUPLICATIONS: Hans Leygraf, SON-
K9516; Harold Bauer, G-DB1390; John
Hunt, G-C2567
—Arr. Piano Duet
Rawicz & Landauer, C-DB2198
—Arr. Orchestra
Andre Kostelanetz and his Orch.
(C-DX1001) 12"—**C-7361M**
[Ravel-Schmid: Pavane pour une Infante
défunte]
Philadelphia Orch.—Stokowski
(G-DA1634) 10"—**V-1812**
Victor Orch.—Charles O'Connell
[Sibelius: Valse Triste] 12"—**V-36228**
Also: Mantovani & his Orch., D-F8528

—Arr. Violin & Piano Roelius
Joseph Szigeti & Andor Földes
(in CX-242†) 12"—**C-71591D**
[Sonata No. 3, Pt. 3]
**Suites: Children's Corner, Petite Suite,
Pour le piano**
See above under these titles
Toccata, C sharp minor See above Pour le
piano, No. 3
Trio See above—Sonata (Trio) No. 2
Miscellaneous Arrangements by Debussy
Satie: Gymnopédie No. 1 Arr. Orchestra
Boston Symphony Orch.—Koussevitzky
(G-D1860) (in VM-352) 12"—**V-7252**
[Ravel: Boléro, Pt. 3]

DELANNOY, Marcel (1898-)
*A pupil of Arthur Honegger whose composi-
tions include operas, symphonies and chamber
music, although he is best known for his highly
successful ballet scores.*
Dancéries pour violin et piano
Janine Andrade (vl) & Claude Delvin-
court (pf) 2 12"—**C-LFX643/4**
Jeunesse Valse pour orchestre et choeurs
Yvonne Gouverné Chorus & Orch.—
Maurice Jaubert 12"—**G-DB5112**

OPERAS
GINEVRA (Based on a Tale of Boccaccio)
1942
Selections
Irène Joachim, Eliette Schenneberg, H.
B. Etcheverry, with Orch. of Opéra-
Comique, Paris—Roger Désormière
3 12"—**PAT-PDT76/8**

PHILIPPINE (Text: G. Limozin)
**Complaintes de l'homme serpent; Le Fruit
défendu**
Paule Drevet, Y. Le Marc'hadour & H.
Cuénod, with Orch.—Maurice Jaubert
10"—**C-DF2280**
Le Coup de bambou; La lettre
Y. Le Marc'hadour 10"—**C-DF2281**
(La) Pantoufle de Vair Violin & Orchestra
Danse de négrillons & Apothéose
Henri Merckel (vl) & Paris Conservatory
Orch.—Münch 12"—**G-DB5186**
[Sérénade Concertante, Pt. 5]
**Petits Ballets pour les "Comédiens de Bois"
Marlbrough s'en va t'en guerre & Pas-
torale**
Orchestra—R. Desormière
2 10"—**FLOR-HP1201/2**
Quartet—String, E major
Calvet Quartet 4 12"—**PAT-PAT43/6**
Sérénade Concertante Violin & Orchestra
Henri Merckel & Paris Conservatory
Orch.—Münch 3 12"—**G-DB5184/6**
[La Pantoufle de Vair—Danse des Né-
grillons & Apothéose]

SONGS In French
Ah quil est bou!
Que chantes-vous si doux?
P. Derenne (t), C. Mauranc, P. Darian
(b) with pf. acc. 10"—**FLOR-CD406**

Chansons de Clarin (Tourterelle & Serpent)
Odette Ertaud (s) & pf. acc.
by composer   10"—C-DF1422
Le Galant Jardinier; Marine
Odette Ertaud (s) & pf. acc. by com-
poser   10"—C-DF67

FOLK SONG SETTINGS (Harmonization &
arrangement)
L'Amour de Moy (Chanson du XVeme
siécle)
Paul Derenne   10"—CdM-525
[Trad., arr. Jaubert: Fanfarneto, with
Marthe Brega]
(Le) Condamné à Mort (Angoumois)
J. Peyron & Yvonne Gouverné Chorus
with Orch.—Désormière
                        10"—CdM-513
[Trad., arr. Honegger: Le femme du
Marin]
(La) Mort de Jean Renaud (Normandie)
M. T. Holley, O. Ertaud, J. Peyron with
Yvonne Gouverné Cho. & Orch.—Désor-
mière   10"—CdM-511
[Trad., arr. Auric: Le fils du Cordonnier]

DELIBES, Léo (1836-1891)

*A pupil of Adam, Benoist, Bazin and others,
Delibes composed many operas, operettas, ballets and other works. He was director of the
Paris Conservatoire and a member of the Institut.*

Arioso: See under Songs
Ballets
See under: Coppélia; Corsaire; Lakmé;
Naïla; Le Roi s'amuse; Source; Sylvia
Boléro—Filles de Cadix See under Songs

COPPELIA Ballet 3 Tableaux 1870
Ballet Suites Orchestra
Prélude, Mazurka, Andante, Valse lente,
Ballade de l'épi, Scène et valse de la
poupée
Orchestre Symphonique de Paris—F.
Ruhlmann   2 10"—C-P17128/9D
(PAT-X96239/40)
Prélude, Mazurka, Swanhilda's Waltz, Czar-
das, Valse de la poupée, Boléro, Gigue,
Thème slav varié
Royal Opera House Orch., Covent Garden
—Lambert   2 12"—C-DX1371/2
Mazurka, Intermezzo, Valse lente, Valse de
la poupée, Czardas
Grand Symphony Orch.—Cloëz
               2 10"—O-165423/4
Excerpts (Act 3)
Marche de la cloche, La Prière; Danse des
heures; Danse villageoise; Pas de deux,
Les fileuses; Danse de fête; Galop final
Royal Opera House Orch., Covent Garden
—Lambert   2 12"—C-DX1429/30
Individual Excerpts Not included in collec-
tions above
Czardas (Danse hongrois)
Boston "Pops" Orch.—Arthur Fiedler
               12"—G-C3012
[Danse des Automates & Valse lente]
London Symphony Orch.—Goossens
[Mazurka]   10"—G-B3941

London Philharmonic Orch.—Efrem
Kurtz   12"—C-69323D
[Thème Slav varié & Sylvia—Prélude,
Valse lente & Pizzicati]
(with Entr'acte de Valse & Mazurka on
C-DX797)
DUPLICATIONS: Bournemouth Munici-
pal Orch.—Birch, D-F7812; Tivoli Orch.
—Jensen, TONO-X25061; National Sym-
phony—Fistoulari, D-K1294
Danse des Automates
Boston "Pops" Orch.—Arthur Fiedler
[Valse lente & Czardas]   12"—G-C3012
Entr'acte de Valse
London Philharmonic Orch.—Kurtz
                    12"—C-DX797
[Mazurka; Thème slav varié & Czardas]
Mazurka
Minneapolis Symphony Orch.—Ormandy
                    10"—V-1743
[Valse lente & Wolf-Ferrari: Jewels of
the Madonna—Intermezzo]
London Symphony Orch.—Goossens
[Czardas]   10"—G-B3941
DUPLICATIONS: Symphony Orch.—
Gaubert, C-LFX304; National Symphony
—Fistoulari, D-K1294; Berlin Philhar-
monic—Borchard, U-B18064; London
Philharmonic—Kurtz, C-DX797; Paris
Symphony—Ruhlmann, PAT-X96239;
C-P17128D; Bournemouth Municipal
Orch.—Birch, D-F7813; Tivoli Orch.—
Jensen, TONO-X25061
Thème slav varié
Symphony Orch.—Schmalstich
[Valse des heures]   12"—G-C1939
London Philharmonic Orch.—Kurtz
                    12"—C-69323D
[Czardas & Sylvia—Prélude, Valse lente
& Pizzicati]
[Entr'acte de valse & Mazurka on
C-DX797]
Valse des heures
Symphony Orch.—Schmalstich
[Thème slav varié]   12"—G-C1939
Valse lente
Boston "Pops" Orch.—Fiedler
                    12"—G-C2012
[Danse des Automates & Czardas]
Minneapolis Symphony—Ormandy
                    10"—V-1743
[Mazurka & Wolf-Ferrari: Jewels of
the Madonna—Intermezzo]
DUPLICATIONS: Symphony Orch.—
Gaubert, C-LFX304; Berlin Philhar-
monic—Borchard, U-B18064; Orch.,
V-36215 in V-C30: G-C2915
—Arr. Piano Dohnanyi
Erno Dohnanyi (pf)   12"—G-AN443
[Dohnanyi: Pastorale]
Also: Karcosch Singers (in German),
PD-25121
Selections (Fantasias, etc.)
London Ballet Orch.—Goehr
                    12"—C-DX899
Symphony Orch.—Szyfer   12"—G-L847
Berlin State Opera Orch.—Weissmann
                    12"—P-E10813

(Le) Corsaire—Ballet Orchestra 1870
This is an opera by Adolphe Adam for which (revival of 1870) Delibes was commissioned to write a "divertissement"—the "Pas des Fleurs" which is better known as the "Naïla Valse." For recordings see below under "Naïla Valse."

(Les) Filles de Cadix—Boléro See under Songs

LAKME Opera in 3 Acts In French 1883

Orchestral Selections (Fantasias, etc.)
Symphony Orch.—Weiss
(PD-516541)   12"—PD-27286
Symphony Orch.—Szyfer 12"—G-L866

Individual Excerpts

ACT I

Prélude Orchestra
Symphony Orch.—Cloëz   10"—O-165078
[Entr'acte, Act III]

A l'heure accoutumée & Blanche Dourge
(Prière & Choeur d'entrée) Soprano
Miliza Korjus (in Italian) 12"—V-12136
[Air des clochettes, Act II]
Marie-Thérèse Gauley   12"—O-171017
[Gounod: Mireille—O Magali, Gauley & Micheletti]
DUPLICATION: G. Féraldy, C-D13039

Viens, Mallaika , les lianes en fleurs
Sous le dôme épais Duo: 2 Sopranos
Lemichel du Roy & Jeanne Manceau
                              12"—PD-516564
[Lalo: Le Roi d'Ys—En silence, C. Tiraud & J. Manceau]

Prendre le dessin d'un bijou—Recit.
Fantaisie aux divins mensonges—Air Tenor
(Sometimes called "Fantaisie aux ailes d'or"; the 2nd verse begins "Au bras poli de la païenne")
Georges Thill   10"—C-LF13
Jean Planel   10"—PAT-PG33
DUPLICATIONS: M. Claudel, PD-524075; Vergnes, O-188899; C. Friant, O-171012; Villabella, PAT-X90050: O-123516; Lugo, PD-56110: also in VOX-176; G. Micheletti, O-123528

Mais je sens en mon coeur—Recit.
Pourquoi dans les grands bois Soprano
Lily Pons (in CM-505)   12"—C-17314D
Yvonne Brothier   12"—G-W879
[Sous le ciel étoile]
DUPLICATIONS: Clara Clairbert, PD-67792; Yvonne Gall, PAT-PAT33; G. Féraldy, C-D15029; M. T. Gauley, O-188504

D'où viens tu?
C'est le Dieu de la jeunesse Duo: Soprano & Tenor
Germaine Féraldy & Villabella
                              10"—PAT-PD13
—C'est le Dieu only
Yvonne Brothier & Marcelin
                              10"—G-P678
Miliza Korjus & Marcel Wittrisch (in German)   12"—G-DB4443
[Donizetti: La Zingara—Fra l'erbe cosparse, Korjus]

Marie-Thérèse Gauley & G. Micheletti
[Sous le dôme épais]   10"—O-188507

ACT II

Ballet (Danses des Bayadères) Orchestra
Entrée, Terana, Rektal, Persian, Echarpes, Les Ethiopiens, Coda
Symphony Orch.—Inghelbrecht
                2 10"—PAT-X96249/50
Lakmè, ton doux regard se voile (Stances)
Bar. or Bass
Willy Tubiana   10"—G-P714
[Berlioz: Damnation of Faust—Voici des rosès]
Robert Couzinou   12"—PD-516570
[Charpentier: Louise—Berceuse]
DUPLICATIONS: Louis Richard, C-D14243; L. van Obbergh, PD-566122; Guénot, C-D14219; E. Billot, O-171039; A. Arbeau, PD-522376; Endrèze, O-123802; A. Pernet, O-123693; R. Bourdin, O-171016

Air des clochettes
Où va la jeune Hindoue?
Là-bas, dans la forêt Soprano (Lakme)
It. **Dov' è l'Indiana bruna?** Eng. **Bell Song**
Lily Pons (C-LX940)
(in CM-561)   12"—C-71640D
(Also C-71973D in CM-676)
(Also on O-188641)
(Also on V-1502: G-DA1190)
Yvonne Brothier   10"—G-P814
DUPLICATIONS: Turba-Rabier, G-DB5001; M. T. Gauley, PAT-X90001: O-188509; C. Clairbert, PD-66791: G. Féraldy, C-D15042; In Italian: Miliza Korjus, V-12136: G-EH961; Mercedes Capsir, C-GQ857: C-GQ7151; Lina Pagliughi, P-DPX27; CET-T17002; A. Galli-Curci, G-DB263*; In English: Gwen Catley, G-B9541

Lakmé! c'est toi! (Gérald)
Dans le forêt près de nous Duo: Tenor & Soprano
Gaston Micheletti & Marie-Thérèse Gauley   12"—O-188515
Germaine Féraldy & Villabella
                              12"—PAT-PGT15
—Pt. 2 (Dans la forêt) Soprano only
Lily Pons & Orch.—Cloëz
                              10"—O-188640
[Pourquoi dans les grands bois?]
Clara Clairbert   12"—PD-566157
[Bizet: Pêcheurs de Perles—Cavatine]
DUPLICATIONS: Germaine Féraldy, C-D15029; Yvonne Gall, PAT-X90078; M. T. Gauley, O-188515

ACT III

Entr'acte (Prelude to Act III) Orchestra
Symphony Orch.—Cloëz   10"—O-165078
[Prelude to Act I]

Ah! Viens dans la forêt profonde Cantilène
Tenor (Gérald)
(or, **Ah! viens dans cette paix profonde**)
Marcel Claudel   12"—PD-524065
[Thomas: Mignon—Adieu]
DUPLICATIONS: Villabella, PAT-

X90051: O-188556; Vergnes, O-188891;
C. Friant, O-188503

Tu m'as donné le plus doux rêve Soprano
Germaine Féraldy   10″—**C-D13039**
[Blanche Dourge]
Yvonne Gall   10″—**PAT-X90078**
[Dans le forêt]
Marie-Thérèse Gauley   10″—**O-188504**
[Pourquoi?]
DUPLICATION: L. du Roy, PD-521893

Naïla valse—Pas des Fleurs Orchestra
This waltz was written as a divertisse-
ment for a revival of Adam's opera "Le
Corsaire" and is sometimes listed as "Le
Corsaire Ballet—Pas des Fleurs" or "In-
termezzo"
London Philharmonic Orch.—Kurtz
(C-DX787)   12″—**C-69080D**
[Tchaikovsky: Swan Lake—Waltz]
Berlin Philharmonic Orch.—Schmidt-Is-
serstedt (U-F14401)   12″—**T-E2247**
[Gounod: Faust—Valse]
Royal Opera Orch.—Collingwood
                        12″—**V-11442**
[Glazounov: Seasons Ballet—Bacchanale,
cond. Barbirolli]
DUPLICATIONS: Orch.—Ruhlmann,
PAT-X96205; Viennese Waltz Orch.—
G-C3029; Tivoli Orch.—Felumb, TONO-
L28005; Also: Albert Sandler Trio,
C-DB2192
—Arr. Piano Dohnanyi
Wilhelm Backhaus, G-DB926; Paul
Baumgartner, G-DB10031; Cyril Smith,
C-DX1159

(LE) ROI S'AMUSE Incidental music
(Scène de bal) to Hugo's drama
Pavane Orchestra 1882
(This Pavane is based on an old French
tune, taken from Arbeau's "'Orchésographie." It has also been set under the
original title of the tune "Pieds-en-l'air"
in Peter Warlock's "Capriol Suite"—
G-C2904; D-K576)

SONGS In French
Arioso (A. Sylvestre) in Mélodies, 1872
Charlotte Tirard   10″—**PD-524028**
[Chausson: Le Colibri]
DUPLICATIONS: M. Sibille, PAT-
X93071; Germaine Cernay, O-188611
Bonjour Suzon
Claudia Muzio (s)
        (in CM-289)   12″—**C-4398M**
[Debussy: Beau soir] (C-BQ6007)
[Puccini: Tosca-Vissi d'Arte, on C-LC19:
C-BQ6000]
(Les) Filles de Cadix—Boléro (Chanson
espagnole)
Ger. **Die Mädchen von Cadiz**
Lily Pons (s) & Frank LaForge (pf)
        (in VM-599)   10″—**V-1997**
[Fauré: Les Roses D'Ispahan]
Claudia Muzio (s)
        (in CM-289)   12″—**C-9174M**
[Crist: C'est mon ami] (C-BQX2523)
[Puccini: Bohème—Sì, mi chiamano
Mimì, on C-LCX29: C-BQX2508]

Jeanette MacDonald (s)
        (in VM-642)   10″—**V-2049**
[Gounod: Ave Maria] (G-DA6000)
Miliza Korjus (s) in German
(G-L1029)   12″—**G-EH973**
[Moszkowski: Serenata, vocal arr.]
Lily Pons (s) & Kostelanetz Orch. in CM-
720
DUPLICATIONS: Amelita Galli-Curci,
V-1524: G-DA1164; Mado Robin,
G-DA4939; Jane Powell, in CX-271
Sérénade à Ninon (Musset) "A quoi rêvent
les jeunes filles"
André Gaudin (b)   10″—**PD-524059**
[Duparc: Chanson triste]

(LA) SOURCE Ballet 1886
Orchestral Suite
**Pas des écharpes; Scène d'amour & Varia-
tions; Scherzo-Polka** (arr. Jüngnickel)
Minneapolis Symphony Orch.—Ormandy
        (in VM-220†) 2 10″—**V-1670/1**
[Sylvia—Pizzicati]

SYLVIA Ballet 3 Acts 1876
Orchestral Suite
**Prélude; Les Chasseresses; Intermezzo &
Valse lente; Pizzicati; Cortège de Bacchus
(Marche et Bacchanale)**
BBC Theatre Orch.—Robinson
(D-K1364/5)   2 12″—**D-ED5**†
Symphony Orch.—Barbirolli
                       2 12″—**G-C2695/6**
DUPLICATIONS: Berlin Philharmonic—
Melichar, PD-24960/2; British Sympho-
ny—Oskar Fried, C-LFX171/2; Opéra-
Comique Orch.—Cloëz, O-165074/5
Prélude only
London Philharmonic Orch.—Kurtz
(C-DFX215)   12″—**C-DX817**
[Intermezzo & Valse lente; Pizzicati]
[Coppélia—Thème slav varié & Czardas
on C-69323D]
Chasseresses only
Symphony Orch.—P. Gaubert
[Cortège de Bacchus]   12″—**C-LFX303**
Intermezzo & Valse lente only
London Philharmonic—Kurtz
                       12″—**C-69323D**
[Prélude & Piccicati; Coppélia—Thème
Slav varié & Czardas]
[Prélude, Pizzicati & Cortège on
C-DX817: C-DWX1609: C-DFX215]
DUPLICATIONS: Berlin Philharmonic—
Borchard, U-B18063; Symphony Orch.—
Cohen, C-D11037
Pizzicati only
London Philharmonic Orch.—Kurtz
                       12″—**C-69323D**
[Prélude & Intermezzo—Valse lente;
Coppélia-Thème Slave varié & Czardas]
[Prélude, Intermezzo & Valse lente; Cor-
tège on C-DX817: C-DWX1609:
C-DFX215]
DUPLICATIONS: Berlin Philharmonic—
Borchard, U-B18063; Symphony Orch.—
Cohen, C-D11037; Minneapolis Symphony
—Ormandy, V-1670, in VM-220

—**Vocal arrangement** Frank LaForge
Lily Pons (s) (in French)
(in CM-638) 12"—**C-71833D**
[Jacobson: Chanson de Marie Antoinette
& Lenoir: Parlez-moi d'amour]

—**Cortège de Bacchus** only
London Philharmonic Orch.—Kurtz
12"—**C-DX817**
(C-DWX1609: C-DFX215)
[Prélude; Intermezzo & Valse lente; Piz-
zicati]
Symphony Orch.—Gaubert
[Les Chasseresses] 12"—**C-LFX303**
Minneapolis Symphony Orch.—Ormandy
(in VM-220) 10"—**V-1670**
[Pizzicati; Source Ballet—Pas des
écharpes]

DELIUS, Frederick (1862-1934)

*A controversial composer, Delius was a cos-
mopolitan who wrote in all forms. Although
he stands apart from other styles, his treatment
of folk songs has apparently influenced such
composers as Vaughan Williams and Holst.
Festivals of Delius' music are frequently heard
in England (through the efforts of Sir Thomas
Beecham and others) and consequently much
of his music has been made available through
the recordings of the Delius Society.*

COLLECTION: The Delius Society
(Formed in May 1933: Columbia)
Volume I
(Single records not available separately)
Paris; Koanga—Closing Scene; Eventyr;
Hassan—Interlude and Serenade; Songs:
**To the Queen of My Heart & Love's
Philosophy**
Chorus & London Philharmonic—
Beecham; Heddle Nash (t) &
Gerald Moore (pf) 7 12"—**CM-305†**
Volume II
**Sea Drift; Over the Hills and Far Away;
In a Summer Garden; Intermezzo from
Fennimore and Gerda**
John Brownlee (b) & London Select
Choir, with London Philharmonic—
Beecham 7 12"—**CM-290†**
Volume III
**Appalachia; Hassan—Closing Scene;
Koanga—La Calinda; Irmelin—Prelude**
London Philharmonic Orch., B.B.C.
Chorus & Royal Opera Choir—Beecham;
Jan van der Gucht (t) 7 12"—**CM-355†**

Air and Dance String Orchestra
Boyd Neel String Orch.—Neel
12"—**D-X147**
[Two Aquarelles, arr. Fenby]
Appalachia—Variations on an Old Slave
Song Chorus & Orchestra 1903
B.B.C. Chorus & London Philharmonic—
Beecham
(in Delius Society, Vol. III: CM-355†)
(Two) Aquarelles (arr. Fenby, from 2
Unacc. Choruses)
Boyd Neel String Orch.—Neel
[Air and Dance] 12"—**D-X147**

Brigg Fair—An English Rhapsody
Orchestra 1907
Royal Philharmonic—Beecham
(C-L2294/5) 2 12"—**CX-30†**

CONCERTO—**Piano & Orchestra** Revised
version 1907
Benno Moiseiwitsch & Philharmonic Orch.
—Lambert 3 12"—**G-C3533/5S**
(Last side blank)
Betty Humby Beecham & Royal Phil-
harmonic—Beecham
(in VM-1185) 3 12"—**V-12-0028/30**
[March Caprice]

CONCERTO—**Violin & Orchestra** 1916
Albert Sammons & Liverpool Philhar-
monic Orch.—Sargent
(C-DX1160/2) 3 12"—**CM-672†**
Jean Pougnet & Royal Philharmonic
Orch.—Beecham 3 12"—**G-DB6369/71**
[Irmelin—Prelude, with Orch. only]

Eventyr ("Once upon a time") Ballade for
Orchestra 1917
(Based on Asbjornsen's fairy tales)
London Philharmonic Orch.—Beecham
(in Delius Society, Vol I:)
2 12"—**CM-305†**

FENNIMORE AND GERDA
Opera based on the novel "Niels Lynne" by
J. P. Jacobsen 1919
—**Intermezzo**
London Philharmonic Symphony Orch.
Beecham
(in Delius Society, Vol. II:CM-290†)
HASSAN Incidental music to James Elroy
Flecker's drama 1920
—**Entr'acte & Serenade** only Arr. Beecham
London Philharmonic—Beecham
(in Delius Society, Vol. I: CM-305†)
Hallé Orch.—Lambert
(G-C3273) 12"—**V-11-8644**
[Koanga—La Calinda, Act II]
—**Serenade** only
Albert Sandler Orch., C-DB1616
—**Closing Scene**
Chorus and London Philharmonic—
Beecham; Jan van der Gucht (t)
(in Delius Society, Vol. III: CM-355†)

In a Summer Garden Orchestral Fantasy
1908
London Philharmonic—Beecham
(in Delius Society, Vol. II: CM-290†)
London Symphony—Geoffrey Toye
2 12"—**G-D1696/7**
[Song Before Sunrise, cond. Barbirolli]
IRMELIN Opera 1890-92
—**Prelude**
London Philharmonic—Beecham
(in Delius Society, Vol. II: CM-290†)
Royal Philharmonic—Beecham
12"—**G-DB6371**
[Violin Concerto, with Pougnet, Pt. 5]
KOANGA Opera in English 1895/7
Based on G. W. Cable's "The
Grandissimes"
(First English performance in London
1935)

—**La Calinda,** Act 2 arr. Fenby
London Philharmonic—Beecham
(in Delius Society, Vol. III: **CM-355†**)
Hallé Orch.—Lambert
(G-C3273)
12"—**V-11-8644**
[Hassan—Intermezzo & Serenade]
—**Final Scene only** Chorus & Orchestra
London Select Choir with London Philharmonic—Beecham
(in Delius Society, Vol. I: **CM-305†**)
March Caprice
Royal Philharmonic Orch.—Beecham,
in VM-1185
On Hearing the First Cookoo in Spring 1912
(No. 2 of Two Pieces for Small Orch.)
Royal Philharmonic—Beecham
(C-L2096) (in CX-31) 12"—**C-67475D**
London Philharmonic Orch.—Lambert
(G-B8819) 10"—**V-4496**
National Symphony Orch.—Walter
Goehr 12"—**D-K1341**

OPERAS See Fennimore and Gerda; Koanga; A Village Romeo and Juliet
Over the Hills and Far Away Fantasia for
Orchestra 1895
London Philharmonic—Beecham
(in Delius Society, Vol. II: **CM-290†**)
Paris ("Ein Nachtstück") Orchestra
(Nocturne: The Song of a Great City)
1899
London Philharmonic—Beecham
(in Delius Society, Vol. I: **CM-305†**)
Sea Drift Baritone, Chorus & Orchestra
1904
(Based on Walt Whitman's "Out of the
Cradle endlessly Rocking")
John Brownlee (b) with London Select
Choir & London Philharmonic—Beecham
(in Delius Society, Vol. II: **CM-290†**)

SONATAS Violin & Piano
No. 3 1914/18 Completed 1930 Dedicated
to Eric Fenby
Albert Sammons & Kathleen Long
3 10"—**D-M557/9**
[Schubert: Sonatine, Op. 137, No. 3—
Menuetto]

SONGS In English
Indian Love Song (Shelley)
Irmelin Rose (Jacobsen)
Nancy Evans (a) & pf. acc.
10"—**D-F5707**
Love's Philosophy (Shelley)
To the Queen of My Heart (Shelley)
Heddle Nash (t) & George Reeves (pf)
(in Delius Society, Vol. I: **CM-305†**)
Love's Philosophy (Shelley)
Isobel Baillie (s) & Gerald Moore (pf)
10"—**C-DB2178**
[Harty: Land o'the Thrushes]

(A) Song Before Sunrise Orchestra 1918
New Symphony Orch.—John Barbirolli
12"—**G-D1697**
[In a summer garden, Pt. 3, cond. Toye]
(A) Song of the High Hills
Chorus & Orchestra
Royal Philharmonic Orch. & Luton

Choral Society—Beecham
(in VM-1185) 3 12"—**V-12-0031/3**
(G-DB6470/2)
Summer Night on the River 1911
(No. 2 of Two Pieces for Small Orch.)
London Philharmonic—Beecham
(C-LB44) 10"—**C-17087D**
(A) VILLAGE ROMEO AND JULIET
Opera in a Prologue and 3 Acts In English 1907
**Intermezzo: The Walk to the Paradise
Gardens** Orchestra
Hallé Orch.—Barbirolli 12"—**G-C3484**
Royal Philharmonic—Beecham
(C-L2087) (in CX-31†) 12"—**C-67474D**
Cincinnati Orch.—Goossens
12"—**V-11-9493**

DELLO-JOIO, Norman (1913-   )
*A pupil of Pietro Yon and Hindemith, who
attended Julliard School and Yale music department. The winner of many awards for composition, Dello-Joio has written many works
on special commission, and has twice been a
Guggenheim Fellow.*

(2) Préludes Piano
To a young musician
To a young dancer
Norman Dello-Joio, in CH-B9
(Limited Edition)
Trio Flute, 'Cello & Piano
Julius Baker, Daniel Saidenberg
& Leonid Hambro 4 12"—**CH-B13**
(Limited Edition)

**DELMAS, Marc (Maris Jean Baptiste)
(1885-   )**
Chansons Petites Russiennes 'Cello & Piano
Marix Loevensohn 10"—**O-238131**
[Bach: Largo, D major]

DEMENYI, Desiderius (1871-1937)
*Although esteemed in Hungary and Austria,
Demenyi is little known outside central Europe.
There are probably many recordings of his
works in Hungarian catalogues.*

Haragszik az édesanyám Song in Hungarian
József Cselény (b) & Gypsy Orch.,
G-AM3119
Szerenád; Busan bugo gerlice; Esik esö
Choruses in Hungarian
Budai dalárdo Chorus—Szeghö,
10"—**G-AM1722**
DES PRES
See under JOSQUIN

DESTOUCHES, André-Cardinal (1672-1749)
*A pupil of Campra who led a very adventurous life, having at different times gone to
Siam as a member of the King's Musketeers.
He wrote several operas which achieved much
popularity.*

CALLIRHOE Opera in French
**Overture; Air de la Dryade; Airs pour les
Faunes**
Mlle. Angelici & Orch. de la Société des
concerts de Versailles—Cloëz
(in Vol. IX) 12"—**AS-86**
[Colin de Blamont: Circé]

Menuet du pays du tendre
(Arr. H. Casadesus)
Paris Society of Ancient Instruments—
Henri Casadesus 12"—C-D15224
[Martini: Plaisir d'Amour]

DETT, Robert Nathaniel (1882-1943)
A prolific composer who studied with Nadia Boulanger. His work for the development of Negro music and musicians is well known.

In the Bottoms Suite
—Prélude (Night) Excerpts only Piano
Percy Grainger, in D-A586
—Juba Dance only
Victor Symphony Orch.—Bourdon
10"—V-21750
[Gardner: From the Canebrake]
Also RCA-Victor Orch., in V-E76
—Arr. Piano
Percy Grainger, in D-A586

DEWANGER, Anton
Marche Solenelle, Op. 67
Paris Radio Orch.—Dewanger
12"—C-LFX600

CLAUDIA Opera
—Ballet excerpts
Paris Radio Orch.—Dewanger
2 10"—C-RF86/7

DIAZ, (De La Pena) Eugene (1837-1901)
A French composer of operas and songs who is remembered today almost exclusively by the baritone arioso from his opera "Benvenuto Cellini."

OPERAS In French
BENVENUTO CELLINI 1890
Arioso: De l'art, splendeur immortelle
Baritone
Louis Musy 12"—G-W1176
[Offenbach: Contes d'Hoffman—J'ai des yeux]
Pierre Deldi 12"—C-DFX91
[Rossini: Barbiere—Largo al factotum]
DUPLICATIONS: L. van Obbergh, PD-524026; A. Endrèze, O-188064; A. Baugé, PAT-X90042

(LA) COUPE DU ROI DE THULE 1867
Hélas! il avait vingt ans Baritone
André Baugé 12"—PAT-PGT5
[Donizetti: Favorita—Viens Leonora]

DINICU
A contemporary Romanian violinist whose "Hora Staccato" arranged by Heifetz has become a standard encore piece for violinists.

Hora Staccato Arr. Violin Heifetz
Jascha Heifetz & Emanuel Bay
10"—V-1864
[Korngold: Holzapfel und Schlehwein, with A. Sandor, pf.]
[Bach-Heifetz: Gavotte and Musette, on G-DA1568]
[Ponce: Estrellita, on G-DA1702]
Ginette Neveu & Jean Neveu
[Falla: Danse espagnole] 10"—G-DA1865

C. F. Cillario 10"—G-DA5412
[Sammartini: Canto amoroso]
—Arr. Orchestra Schmid
Boston "Pops" Orch.—Fiedler
10"—V-4413
[Tchaikovsky: None but the Lonely Heart, arr. Cailliet]

DITTERSDORF, Karl Von (1739-1799)
A popular composer of operas who also wrote many chamber works and symphonies. He was a friend of Haydn and at times in great favor at the Viennese court.

Quartets—String
No. 6, A major
Perolé Quartet 2 12"—MC-45
Sonata Viola & Piano
Hans Riphahn & Eral Weiss
12"—PD-57092

DJABADANY
Rapsodie Grégorienne Piano & Orchestra
Jean Doyen & Opéra Orch.—Fourestier
2 12"—O-595100/1

DLUGORAJ, Adalbert (c.1550-c.1603)
Villanelle Arr. Besard
(10 Villanelles in Besard's Thesaurus Musicus, Köln, 1603)
Hermann Leeb (lute)
(in Vol. IV) 12"—AS-36
[Besard: Lute Pieces, Airs by Clemens non Papa, Grotte & Anon. Airs]

DOHNANYI, Ernest Von (Ernö) (1877-   )
An internationally known pianist and teacher who has composed in many forms. Showing the influence of Brahms and the Viennese composers more than the folk-melodies of his own country, Dohnányi, with Kodaly and Bartók, is a representative of Hungarian music.

Capriccio, F. minor Piano
Vladimir Horowitz 10"—G-DA1140
[Liszt: Valse oubliée]
Moura Lympany 10"—D-M556
[Poulenc: Novelette No. 1, C major]
Gavotte & Musette (Arr. Urai)
E. Zathureczky (vl) & O. Herz (pf)
12"—RAD-RBM107
[Gluck-Kreisler: Orfeo-Mélodie]
Hiszekegy Hungarian Hymn Orchestra
Budapest Philharmonic—Dohnányi
12"—G-AN149
[Egressy: Szozat & Berlioz: Rakoczy March]
(Also: G-AM1284 & G-AM1282)
Pastorale (Magyar karácsonyi ének) Piano
Ernö Dohnányi 12"—G-AN443
[Delibes-Dohnányi: Coppélia Valse]
Quartets—String
No. 2, D flat major, Op. 15
Roth Quartet 3 12"—CM-367†
Quintet—Piano & Strings
C minor, Op. 1
Edward Kilenyi & Roth Quartet
4 12"—CM-546†
[Ruralia Hungarica, Op. 32a—Presto ma non tanto]

(4) RHAPSODIES, Op. 11 Piano
—No. 3, C major
Eileen Joyce 12"—P-E11351
[Rachmaninoff: Prélude in E flat major,
Op. 23, No. 6 & Prélude in C minor, Op.
23, No. 7]
Johanne Stockmarr 10"—G-DA5247

RURALIA HUNGARICA, Op. 32 Suite
Orchestra
1. Presto 2. Gypsy Andante 3. Molto
Vivace
—Arr. Violin & Piano Kreisler
P. Nevini & J. Nevini 2 10"—C-LF184/5
—2nd Mvt. (Gypsy Andante) only
London Symphony Orch.—Dohnányi
(in VM-162†) 12"—V-11438
[Variations on a Nursery Tune, Pt. 5]
Jascha Heifetz (vl) & pf. acc.,
G-DB2220
—3rd Mvt. (Molto vivace) only
Budapest Philharmonic—Dohnányi
[Hiszekegy] 10"—G-AM1284

RURALIA HUNGARICA, Op. 32a Suite
Piano
No. 1, Presto ma non tanto
Edward Kilenyi
(in CM-546†) 12"—C-71654D
[Quintet, C minor, Op. 1, Pt. 7]

(Der) Schleier der Pierrette Ballet 1910
Eng. Pierrette's Veil
—Wedding Waltz
City of Birmingham Orch.—Weldon
10"—C-DB2188
Serenade, C major, Op. 10 Violin, Viola
& 'Cello
Jascha Heifetz, William Primrose &
Emanuel Feuermann 3 12"—VM-903†

SONGS In Hungarian
**Azok, ázok; Szrettelek álnok lékek; Valaki
jár udvaromon**
Imre Molnar & pf. acc. 10"—G-AM1683

Suite, F sharp minor, Op. 19 Orchestra
Philharmonic Orch. of Los Angeles—
Wallenstein 3 12"—D-DA433
Symphonic Minutes, Op. 36 Orchestra
Ger. Symphonische Minuten
Munich Philharmonic Orch.—
Kabasta 2 12"—G-DB5591/2
Queen's Hall Orch.—Wood
2 12"—D-X190/1
Variations on a Nursery Tune, Op. 25
Piano & Orchestra
Cyril Smith & Liverpool Philharmonic
—Sargent 3 12"—C-DX1148/50
—Slightly abridged version, includes:
Introduction—Theme: Ah! vous dirai-je
maman (Baa, baa, Black Sheep); 11 Va-
riations: No. 7, Waltz; No. 8, March; No.
9, Scherzo; No. 10, Passacaglia; No. 11,
Chorale—Finale
Erno Dohnányi & London Symphony
Orch.—Collingwood 3 12"—VM-162†
[Ruralia Hungarica—Finale]
(G-D2054/6) (G-AW270/2)

MISCELLANEOUS Piano Arrangements
See under:
Delibes: Coppélia—Valse lente: Naïla-Valse

DONATO (Donati) Baldassare (d.1603)
*An Italian singer, organist, choir master (con-
nected with San Marco of Venice all his life),
and a prolific composer of church music, madrigals, villotte, etc. The recorded example below,
one of his best known works, is taken from the
first book of Canzoni (1550) and is characteristic of the vivacity and grace of his secular
music.*

Chi li gagliarda Madrigal (Unacc.) in Ital.
Ger. Wenn wir hinausziehn
Regensburger Domchar (in German)—
Schrems 10"—G-EG3927
[Morley: Sing we and chant it]

DONAUDY, Stefano (1879-   )

SONGS In Italian
O del mio amato ben
Claudia Muzio (s)
(in CM-259) 12"—C-9169M
(C-BQX2524)
[Pergolesi: Se tu m'ami]
[Boito: Mefistofele—L'altra notte, on
C-LCX24: C-BQX2504]
Tito Schipa (t) 12"—G-DB2131
[Martini: Plasir d'amour]
Beniamino Gigli (t) 12"—G-DB6313
[Caccini: Amarilli] (G-DB3895)
Spirate pur, spirate
Claudia Muzio (s)
(in CM-289) 10"—C-4397M
[Reger: Mariä Wiegenlied]
[Verdi: Trovatore—Tacea la notte, on
C-LC21 & C-BQ6002]

DONIZETTI, Gaetano (1797-1848)
*Contemporary of Rossini and Bellini, Donizetti
wrote sixty-three operas, of which "Don Pasquale" and "Lucia di Lammermoor" are the
most outstanding examples of his style.*

OPERAS In Italian

DON PASQUALE 3 Acts 1843
Complete recording in Italian
Soloists, La Scala Chorus & Orchestra—
Carlo Sabajno
(G-C2519/33 in GM-177†)
15 12—VM-187†
(G-S10410/24)
The Cast:
Don Pasquale ...... Ernesto Badini (b)
Ernesto .... Tito Schipa (t)
Dr. Malatesta .... Afro Poli (b)
Norina .... Adelaide Saraceni (s)
Notary .... Giordano Callegari (bs)
(Vittore Veneziani, Chorus Master)
Abridged recording in Italian
Soloists, La Scala Chorus & Milan
Symphony Orch.—Molajoli
6 12"—C-GQX10100/5
The Cast:
Don Pasquale ...... Atillio Giuliani (b)
Ernesto .... Cristy Solari (t)
Dr. Malatesta ...... Lorenzo Conati (b)

Norina .... Ines Alfani Tellini (s)
(Vittore Veneziani, Chorus Master)

Individual Excerpts

Overture Orchestra
Dresden Philharmonic—Von Karajan
12″—CET-OR5029
Berlin State Opera—Oskar Fried
12″—PD-27003
La Scala Orch.—Sabajno
12″—G-S10188
DUPLICATION: Symphony Orch.—
Toscanini, G-DA376*

ACT I

Sogno soave e casto Tenor
C. Gero 12″—CET—IT7039
[Rossini: Barbiere—Se il mio nome]
Tito Schipa 10″—G-DA885
[Verdi: Rigoletto—Questa o quella]
DUPLICATIONS: D. Borgioli, C-DQ1107;
E. Lomanto, C-DQ1044: C-DQ2674

Quel guardo il cavaliere
So anch' io la virtù magica Soprano
Ger. Auch ich versteh' die feine Kunst
Lina Pagliughi
(CET-PP60000) 12″—P-DPX15
[Rossini: Barbiere—Una voce]
[Thomas: Mignon—Polonaise on O-9113]
Toti Dal Monte 12″—G-DB5396
[Mascagni: Lodoletta—Flammen
perdonami]
Erna Sack (in German) 12″—T-E1755
[Rossini: Barbiere—Cavatina]
DUPLICATIONS: A. Guglielmetti,
C-DQ1111; Elda Ribetti, G-AW321;
—So anch'io only
M. Gentile 10″—PD-10330
[Donizetti: Lucia—Quando rapito]
DUPLICATION: M. Tauberova (in Boh.),
ESTA-H5145

ACT II

Cercherò lontana terra Tenor
Cristi Solari 10″—C-DB5698
[Flotow: Marta—M'Apparì]

ACT III

Coro dei servitori: Che interminabile
(Servant's Chorus)
La Scala Chorus & Orch.—Molajoli
12″—C-GQX10265
[Ponchielli: Gioconda—Marinaresca]
(Also PD-95278)
Com' è gentil (Serenade) Tenor & Cho.
Gino Sinimberghi & Cho.
12″—PD-67536
[Tornami a dir, with Erna Berger]
C. Gero 12″—CET-TI7040
[Verdi: Traviata—De'miei bollenti]
DUPLICATIONS: Dino Borgioli,
C-D4963; L. Cecil, C-DQ251; E. Caruso,
G-DB159*
Tornami a dir che m'ami (Notturno)
Duo: Soprano & Tenor
Amelita Galli-Curci & Tito Schipa
10″—G-DA1161
[Verdi: Rigoletto—E il sol dell'anima]
Erna Berger & Gino Sinimberghi
12″—PD-67536
[Com' è gentil, Sinimberghi]

Toti Dal Monti & Tito Schipa
10″—G-DA1351
[Bellini: Sonnambula—Prendi l'anel]
DUPLICATIONS: A. Rettore & D. Bor-
gioli; C-DQ1107; E. O. Pedersen & O.
Svendsen, TONO-X25031

DON SEBASTIANO 5 Acts 1843
In terra solo Tenor
Enrico Caruso 12″—G-DB700*
[Giordano: Andrea Chênier—Un dì
all'azzurro spazio]

(IL) DUCA D'ALBA 1882
Angelo casto e bel Tenor
Enrico Caruso 12″—G-DB640*
[Gioe: T'm'arricordo e' Napule]

(L') ELISIR D'AMORE 2 Acts 1832
Fr. L'Elixir d'amour Ger. Der Liebestrank
Abridged recording in Italian
Soloists, La Scala Chorus & Orch.—
Molajoli 6 12″—C-GQX10093/8
The Cast:
Adina .... Ines Alfani Tellini (s)
Nemorino .... Cristy Solari (t)
Belcore .... Lorenzo Conati (bs)
Dulcamara .... Eduardo Faticanti (bs)
Gianetta .... Ida Mannarini (s)
(Vittore Veneziani, Chorus Master)

Individual Excerpts

ACT I

Quanto è bella! Tenor
Beniamino Gigli 10″—G-DA797
[Tagliaferri: Mandulinata]
C. Gero 12″—CET-IT7041
[Mascagni: Cavalleria Rusticana—
Siciliana]
Alessandro Bonci & pf. acc.
10″—ARIA-62123/39687*
[Rossini: Il Barbiere—Se il mio nome]
Udite, udite o rustici Bass & Cho.
Salvatore Baccaloni & Cho.
12″—C-71383D
(Older recording on C-CQX16451)
DUPLICATION: Antonio Gelli & Chorus,
G-S10163
Adina, credimi Tenor
Tito Schipa 10″—G-DA1016
[Favorita—Una vergine]
Nino Ederle 10″—C-DQ246
[Verdi: Rigoletto—Parmi veder]

ACT II

Venti scudi Duo: Tenor & Bass
Enrico Caruso & G. De Luca
12″—G-DM107*
[Verdi: Forza del Destino—Sleale!]
Una furtiva lagrima (Romanza) Tenor
Ger. Heimlich aus ihrem Auge
Fr. Une larme secrète
Eng. Down her pale cheek
Beniamino Gigli & Orch.—Barbirolli
[Handel: Serse—Largo] 12″—G-DB1901
(Different recording, with Ponchielli:
Gioconda-Cielo e mar, on V-7194)
[Flotow: Marta—M'apparì, on
G-DB4592]

[Gounod: Faust—Salut! demeure,
on G-DB3906]
Ferruccio Tagliavini
(in CET-2)   12"—CET-BB25058
[Verdi: Rigoletto—Parmi veder le
lagrime]
[Rossini: Barbiere—Ecco ridente,
on CET-BB25145]
(Also in VM-1191: V-V13)
Richard Crooks   12"—V-15235
[Mozart: Don Giovanni—Il mio tesoro]
Stefan Islandi   12"—G-DB5247
[Puccini: Bohême—Che gelida manina]
Enrico Caruso   12"—V-11-8112
[Verdi: Rigoletto—Ella mi fu]
(G-DB3903)
(Original recording on V-6016* &
G-DB126*)
Tito Schipa   12"—G-DB1387
[Mascagni: Ave Maria]
[Cilea: Arlesiana—E la solita storia,
on G-DB3461]
Giovanni Malipiero   12"—P-DPX24
[Favorita—Spirto gentil]
Luigi Infantino   12"—C-GQX11096
[Verdi: Rigoletto—Parmi veder]
DUPLICATIONS: K. von Pataky, RAD-
SP8015; Dino Borgioli, C-GQX10167; C-
D16379; Julius Patzak, PD-25011; Aure-
liano Pertile, G-DB1402; R. d'Alessio,
C-GQX10236; G. Manuritta, C-D14622;
Cristy Solari, C-D5699; Luigi Fort, C-
OQX8001; Nino Ederle, C-DQ245; Lion-
ello Cecil, C-DQ251; Sinimberghi, PD-
27433
In English: Heddle Nash, G-C3492
In French: André d'Arkor, C-RFX39
In German: Peter Anders, T-E3228;
Willy Tressner, G-EH1289
In Bohemian: Oldrich Kovar, U-G12828

ACT II

Prendi: per me sei libero Soprano
Lina Pagliughi
(CET-T17003)   12"—P-DPX26
[Verdi: Rigoletto—Tutte le feste al
tempio]

(LA) FAVORITA 4 Acts 1840

Fr. **La Favorite**   Ger. **Die Favoritin**
Abridged recording in Italian
Soloist, La Scala Chorus & Orchestra—
Molajoli   5 12"—C-GQX10064/8
The Cast:
Leonora ...... Giuseppina Zinetti (ms)
Fernando .... Cristy Solari (t)
Alfonso XI ...... Carmelo Maugeri (b)
Baldassarre ...... Corrado Zambelli (b)
Ines .... Ida Mannarini (s)
Don Gasparo ..... Giuseppe Nessi (t)
(Vittore Veneziani, Chorus Master)
Individual Excerpts
Overture Orchestra
(Not included in Columbia set)
La Scala Orch.—Sabajno
12"—G-S10169

ACT I

Romanza: Una Vergine, un angiol di Dio
Tenor Fr. **Une ange, une femme inconnue**

Tito Schipa   10"—G-DA1016
[Elisir d'amore—Adina credimi]
Aureliano Pertile   10"—G-DA1183
[Bellini: Puritani—A te, o cara]
DUPLICATION: M Fleta, G-DB1053; A.
Cortis, G-DA757; G. Voyer, C-CQ714
In French: C. Vezzani, G-DA4863; M.
Claudel, PD-524098; Villabella, PAT-
PGT6; Campagnola, G-P537*
Ah! mio bene Duo: Contralto & Tenor
Aurora Buades & R. D'Alessio
12"—C-CQX16449

ACT II

Vien Leonora a piedi tuoi Baritone
Fr. **Dans les Jardins d'Alcazar**
E. Mascherini   10"—C-GQ7219
[A tanto amor]
Riccardo Stracciari   10"—C-CQ692
[A tanto amor]
(Also ARIA-AD1/2*)
In French: A. Baugé, PAT-PGT5; En-
drèze, PAT-X90038
Quando le soglie paterne
In questo suolo Duo: Contralto & Baritone
G. Pederzini & B. Franci 12"—G-DB1748
[Verdi: Forza del Destino—Madre,
pietosa Vergine, with Fanelli]

ACT III

A tanto amor Baritone
Fr. **Pour tant d'amour**
Ger. **Teuer, dür dich**
E. Mascherini   10"—C-GQ7219
[Vien Leonora]
DUPLICATIONS: Mario Basiola,
C-GQX10967; Stracciari, C-CQ692; also
ARIA-AD1/2*; M. Ancona, CRS-13*;
M. Sammarco, CRS-14*; M. Battistini,
V-15-1010*
In French: A. Endrèze, PAT-X90038
Fia dunque vero—Recit. Contralto
O mio Fernando—Aria
Fr. **O mon Fernand**
NOTE: *The Stignani version contains the first
part of the aria only. All versions listed are
abbreviated in one way or another.*
Nan Merriman   12"—V-11-9793
Ebe Stignani
(CET-BB25006)   12"—P-DPX20
[Thomas: Mignon—Io concosco un
garzoncello]
Risë Stevens   12"—C-71440D
[Tchaikovsky: Jeanne d'arc—Adieu
forêts]
Fedora Barbieri   12"—G-AW324
[Verdi: Trovatore—Stride la vampa]
DUPLICATIONS: G. Besanzoni,
G-DB151*; I. Minghini-Cattaneo,
G-DB1441

ACT IV

Splendon più belle in ciel Bass & Chorus
Ezio Pinza & Metropolitan Opera Cho. &
Orch.—Setti   12"—V-7552
[Verdi: Ernani-Infelice] (G-DB1750)
T. Pasero & Chorus 12"—C-GQX10209
[Favorita—Spirto gentil, E. Lomanto]
Romanza: Spirto gentil Tenor
Fr. **Ange si pur**   Ger. **Engel so rein**

Giovanni Malipiero 12"—P-DPX24
[Elisir d'amore—Una furtiva lagrima]
[Different recording with Massenet:
Werther—O nature, on G-DB5405]
Tommaso Alcaide 12"—C-GQX10063
[Bizet: Pêcheurs de perles—Je crois]
DUPLICATIONS: Miguel Fleta,
G-DB1053; Pertile, G-DB1480:
G-DB1183; E. Lomanto, C-GQX10216:
C-GQX10209; Caruso, G-DB129*; B.
Gigli, G-DB273*; Borgioli, C-D16379
In French: M. Claudel, PD-524098;
Villabella, PAT-PG29; Campagnola,
G-P537*; Vezzani, G-DA4863
In English: Heddle Nash, G-C3409

Preghiera: Pietoso al par del nume
Vieni! Ah vien! Duo: Contralto & Tenor
I. Minghini-Cattaneo & L. Cecil
12"—G-DB1441
[O mio Fernando, Minghini-Cattaneo
only]
A. Buades & R. D'Alessio
12"—C-CQX16457
[Ponchielli: Gioconda—Cielo e mar, with
D'Alessio]

(LA) FILLE DU REGIMENT
2 Acts 1840
(First produced in French)
It. La Figlia del Reggimento
Ger. Die Regimentstochter
Eng. The Daughter of the Regiment
Orchestral Selections (Fantasias, etc.)
Republican Guard Band 10"—G-K5601

Selections:
Act I—Chaun le sait; Il faut partir
Act II—Et mon coeur va changer;
Salût à la France
Lily Pons (s) in French, with Metro-
politan Opera House Orch.—Pietro
Cimara 2 12"—CX-206
Overture Orchestra
Berlin Philharmonic—Prüwer
12"—PD-19899
Dresden Philharmonic—Van Kempen
(CET-OR5057) 12"—PD-15301
German Opera House Orch., Berlin—
Lutze (U-F18098) 12"—T-E3022
DUPLICATIONS: Symphony Orch.—G.
Amato, U-A478; Berlin Orch.—F. Leh-
mann, O-3601; Tivoli Concert Orch.—
Felumb, TONO-X25069

Individual Excerpts

ACT I
Chacun le sait Soprano & Chorus
It. Ciascun lo dice Eng. Song of the Regi-
ment
Lily Pons (in CX-206) 12"—C-72119D
[Il faut partir]
Toti Dal Monte & La Scala Chorus (in
Italian) 12"—G-DB1152
[Par le rang]
Il faut partir Soprano
It. Convien partir
Lily Pons (in CX-206) 12"—C-72119D
[Chacun le sait]
Lina Pagliughi (in Italian)

(CET-BB25001) 12"—P-DPX18
[Bellini: Sonnambula—Ah! non credea
mirarti]
Toti Dal Monte & La Scala Chorus (In
Italian) 12"—G-DB1040
[Lucia—Regnava del silenzio]

ACT II
Par le rang et par l'opulence Soprano
It. Le ricchezze ed il rango
Lily Pons (in CX-206) 12"—C-72120D
[Salût à la France]
(This is preceeded by the recitative: Et
mon coeur va changer)
Ninon Vallin 10"—PAT-PG36
[Salût à la France]
Toti Dal Monte (In Italian)
[Chacun le sait] 12"—G-DB1152
Tyrolienne Soprano
Erna Berger (In German)
10"—PD-10329
[Flotow: Marta—Last rose of summer]
Eva Marie Siefert (In German)
[Salût à la France] 12"—G-EH1305
Pour me rapprocher de Marie (Cavatine)
Tenor
It. Per viver vicino a Maria
John McCormack (In Italian)
12"—V-15-1015*
[Mozart: Don Giovanni—Il mio tesoro]
DUPLICATION: R. Gilles PD-23299:
PD-521542

Salût à la France (Finale) Soprano part only
Lily Pons (in CX-206) 12"—C-72120D
[Et mon coeur; Par le rang]
Clara Clairbert 12"—PD-66921
[Lucia—Spargi d'amore]
Ninon Vallin 10"—PAT-PG36
[Par le rang]
Eva Marie Siefert (In German)
[Tyrolienne] 12"—G-EH1305

LINDA DI CHAMOUNIX 3 Acts 1842
Individual Excerpts
Love Duet Soprano & Tenor
Linda! Carlo! Sei tu sola?
Da quel dì che t'incontrai
A consolarmi affrettisi
Lina Pagliughi & Franco Perulli
12"—CET-PP60011
Mad Scene Soprano & Mezzo-soprano
Linda! A che pensato
Lina Pagliughi & Rita Monticone
12"—CET-PP60012
[O luce di quest' anima, Pagliughi]

O luce di quest' anima Soprano
Lina Pagliughi 12"—CET-PP60012
[Mad Scene, with Monticone]
Toti Dal Monte 12"—G-DB1318
[Thomas: Mignon—Polonaise]
Erna Sack 12"—T-SK3242
[Puccini: La Bohème—Mi chiamano Mimì
Elda Ribetti 12"—G-C3587
[Verdi: Rigoletto—Caro nome]
Per sua madre andò una figlia (Pierotto's
Romanza) Mezzo-Soprano
Ebe Stignani (CET-BB25045)
(in P-P53) 12"—P-DPX23
[Saint-Saëns: Samson et Dalila—Amour
viens aider]

Se tanto in ira Tenor
Enzo de Muro Lomanto   10"—C-DQ2667
[Mozart: Don Giovanni—Il mio tesoro]

LUCIA DI LAMMERMOOR 3 Acts 1835

Complete recording in Italian
Soloists, Chorus & Orchestra of the EIAR
of Turin—Ugo Tansini
(O-8032/44)   13 12"—P-P31†
(CET-CB20078/90) (P-R20454/66)
The Cast:
Enrico Ashton Giuseppe Manacchini (b)
Lucia .... Lina Pagliughi (s)
Edgardo di Ravenswood
               Giovanni Malipiero (t)
Arturo Bucklaw .. Muzio Giovagnoli (t)
Raimondo Bidebent Luciano Neroni (bs)
Alisa .... Maria Vinciguerra (s)
Normanno .... Armando Giannotti (t)
   (Chorus master: Achille Consoli)

Complete recording in Italian
Soloists, La Scala Chorus & Orchestra—
Lorenzo Molajoli   13 12"—C-OP20†
(C-D14604/20)
The Cast:
Enrico Ashton .... Enrico Molinari (b)
Lucia .... Mercedes Capsir (s)
Edgardo di Ravenswood
            Enzo de Muro Lomanto (t)
Arturo Bucklaw .. Emilio Venturini (t)
Raimondo Bidebent
            Salvatore Baccaloni (bs)
Alisa .... Ida Mannarini (s)
Normanno .... Emilio Venturini (t)
   (Chorus master: Vittore Veneziani)
Individual excerpts

ACT I

Intermezzo Harp solo
Ines Rutalo & Orch.   12"—C-D16441
[Suppé: Donna Juanita—Intermezzo]
Ancor non giunse!—Recit.
Regnava nel silenzio—Cavatina Soprano
Quando rapita—Cavatina, Pt. 2
Lily Pons (in CM-505) 10"—C-17313D
Elda Ribetti   12"—G-C3616
DUPLICATIONS: M. Gentile, C-D1602;
Mercedes Capsir, C-GQ7153; N. Sanchi-
oni, C-DQ653
—**Regnava nel silenzio** (Part 1) only
Toti Dal Monte   12"—G-DB1040
[La Fille du Regiment—Il faut partir]
—**Quando rapita** (Part 2) only
Maria Gentile   10"—PD-10330
[Don Pasquale—So anch'io]
Sulla tomba che rinserra
Verranno a te sull' aure
Duo: Tenor & Soprano Eng.Love Duet
Aureliano Pertile & Anna Rozsa
               12"—G-DB1481
—**Verrano a te** only
G. Malipiero & Lina Pagliughi
[Sextet]   12"—CET-BB25127
DUPLICATIONS: A. Galli-Curci & Tito
Schipa, G-DB811*; Barrientos & Hackett,
C-D16393*

ACT II

Appressati, Lucia
Soffriva nel pianto Soprano & Baritone

Margherita Carosio & Carlo Tagliabue
               12"—G-DB6358
Par te d'immenso giubilo Tenor & Chorus
Emilio Venturini & Chorus
               10"—C-DQ7122
[Wagner: Lohengrin—Brautchor]
Dov' è Lucia? Quartet
Féraldy, Villabella, Lanzone & Balbon
(in French)   12"—PAT-PGT1
[Verdi: Rigoletto—Quartet]
Chi mi frena in tal momento? Sextet (the
celebrated "Lucia Sextet")
Mercedes Capsir, E. Molinari, L. Mannar-
ini, E. de Muro Lomanto, S. Baccaloni, E.
Venturini   12"—C-9145M
(Isolated recorded versions of the Sextet
usually contain only the first section, end-
ing before the Stretta, "T'allontana scia-
gurato," side 17 in the Columbia album
set)
Lina Pagliughi, G. Malipiero, G. Manac-
chini, M. Vinciguerra, M. Giovagnoli, L.
Neroni, with Chorus 12"—CET-BB25127
[Verrano a te, Pagliughi & Malipiero]
Galli-Curci, Homer, DeLuca, Pinza, Gigli
& Bada (G-DQ102)   12"—V-10012
[Verdi: Rigoletto—Quartet]
Gentile, Vanelli, Borgioli, Baccaloni,
Nessi, Mannarini, with Chorus
               10"—C-GQX10154
[Bellini: Sonnambula—D'un pensiero]
Galli-Curci, Egener, Caruso, DeLuca,
Journet, Bada   12"—V-10000*
[Verdi: Rigoletto—Quartet] (G-DQ100*)
Tetrazzini, Jacoby, Caruso, Amato, Jour-
net, Bada
(in VM-953) 12"—V-16-5000*
[Verdi: Un Ballo in Maschera—E scherzo
od è follia—Quintet]
Sembrich, Severina, Caruso, Scotti, Jour-
net, Daddi   12"—G-DQ101*
[Verdi: Rigoletto—Quartet]
Scena della pazzia Soprano Eng. Mad Scene
Il dolce suono mi colpi di sua voce—Recit.
Ardon gl' incensi; splendon le sacre faci
Spargi d'amaro pianto—Aria, Pts. 1 & 2
Fr. **L'autel rayonne & Je vais loin de la
terre** Ger. **Wahnsinns Szene**

NOTE: *Isolated recordings of the Mad Scene
usually omit the recitative and begin with
"Ardon gl' incensi," two bars later with "Splen-
dor le sacre faci," or several bars still later
with "Alfin son tuo." The brief parts, for
Raimondo and Enrico, are omitted, and Lucia's
own part is considerably cut. The two-sided
12" versions, usually begin on the second side
with Part 2 of the aria, "Spargi d'amara pianto," but all sorts of cadenzas, embellishments
and repeats are introduced, and the printed
score is seldom followed very closely.*

Lily Pons (Recit. included)
(in CM-561†) 2 12"—C-71641/2D
[Flute obb. Frank Versaci]
Lily Pons   12"—V-7369
[Flute obb. George Possel] (G-DB1504)
Toti Dal Monte
(G-DB1015)   12"—V-36285
Lina Pagliughi   12"—P-DPX16
(Also on G-S10376) (CET-PP60001)

DUPLICATIONS: Maria Gentile, C-GQX10163; Sanchioni, C-DQ654; Vina Bovy, G-DB4998; A. M. Guglielmetti, C-GQX10170
Recit. & Part 1 only
Miliza Korjus & Berlin State Opera Orch. —Seidler-Winkler (G-EH956)
(in VM-871) 12"—V-13808
Part 1 only (Ardon gl' incensi) only
Nellie Melba, V-18143* in VM-816; A. Galli-Curci, G-DB5384*: G-DB260*; L. Aimaro, C-GQX10983: G-DB5359
In French: Lucienne Jourfier, PAT-PDT111; Yvonne Brothier, G-W966; C. Clairbert, PD-66921
Part 2 only (Spargi d'amaro) only
Maria Galvany, G-DB400*
ACT III
Tombe degl'avi miei—Recit.
Fra poco a me ricovero—Aria Tenor
Giusto Cielo! rispondete Tenor, Bass & Chorus
Tu che a Dio spiegasti l'ali Tenor
Eng. **Tomb Scene** Fr. **Tombe de mex aieux**
Ger. **Grabstatte meiner Ahnen**
Complete recording
Jan Peerce & Arthur Kent, with Chorus & Victor Symphony Orch.—Pelletier
2 12"—VM-845†
Tombe degl' avi miei & Fra poco a me ricovero only
Aureliano Pertile, G-DB1412; E. de Muro Lomanto, C-DQ1123; Galliano Masini, C-CQ1062; Beniamino Gigli, G-DB1222: G-DB870; G-DB2235; L. Marini, C-DQ1094
Giusto Cielo! rispondete & Tu che a Dio spiegasti l'ali Tenor, Bass & Chorus
Beniamino Gigli, Ezio Pinza & Metropolitan Opera Chorus & Orch.—Setti
(G-DB1229) 12"—V-8096
Tu che a Dio only
G. Malipiero & L. Neroni
12"—CET-BB25106
[Verdi: Forza del Destino—Sulla terra, with Masini & Tagliabue]
B. Gigli, G-DB870; T. Schipa, G-DA365;* C. Solari, C-D5700; L. Marini; E. Lomanto, C-GQX10216
LUCREZIA BORGIA Prologue & 2 Acts 1833
Individual Excerpts
(in alphabetical order)
Brindisi: Il segreto per essere felice Act II (Orsini's Ballata) Contralto
Sigrid Onegin 10"—V-1367
[Mozart: Alleluia]
Ernestine Schumann-Heink (Recorded 1906) 12"—V-15-1012*
[Arditi: Bolero—Leggiero invisible]
Come è bello quale incanto Prologue
M'odi, ah! m'odi Soprano
G. Arangi-Lombardi
12"—C-GQX10703
Di pescatore ignobile Prologue Tenor
Paolo Civil 12"—CET-CC2322
[Catalani: La Wally—M'hai salvato, with M. Vinciguerra]
Cristy Solari 10"—C-CQ352
[Luisa Miller—Quando le sere]

LA ZINGARA 1822
Ger. **Die Zigeunerin**
Fra l'erbe cosparse Soprano & Male Chorus
Miliza Korjus (in German) & Chorus
12"—V-13826
[Adam: Variations on a Mozart Theme]
[Delibes: Lakmé—C'est le Dieu de jeunesse, with Wittrisch, on G-DB4443]

Quartet, D major Strings
Quartetto di Roma
2 12"—G-DB4649/50

DOPPER
Gothic Chaconne (Ciaconna Gotica) Orchestra
Amsterdam Concertgebouw Orch.—
Mengelberg 3 12"—T-SK3155/7
[Röntgen: Old Netherland Dances, Op. 46—Bergerette—Les grandes couleurs & Pavane]

DORNEL, Antoine (c. 1685-1765)
An excellent organist, having won the post of organist at the Madeleine from Rameau in 1706, Dornel was a minor French composer in the style of Couperin.

(La) Noce d'Auteuil
(La) Pendant d'Oreille Harpsichord
Pauline Aubert (in Vol. I) 12"—AS-8
[Jean Nicholas Geoffroy: Tombeau en forme d'Allemande]

DOURLEN, Victor Charles (1780-1864)
Renowned chiefly as a teacher at the Paris Conservatoire and a theorist in the field of harmony, Dourlen composed nine opéras-comiques, as well as a sizeable body of instrumental music. His vocal music suggests the influence of Rossini.

LES OIES DE FRERE PHILIPPE Opéra-comique in French
Je sais attacher des rubans Soprano
Maggie Teyte
(in VM-1169) 10"—V-10-1370
[Grétry: Zémire et Azor—Rose chérie]

DOWLAND, John (1563-1626)
One of the great song composers of all time, Dowland was an Englishman who spent much time on the Continent. A virtuoso on the lute, during his lifetime his fame as an instrumentalist eclipsed his genius as a composer.

AYRES In English
Awake, sweet love 1st Book of Ayres, 1597
Cecile Dolmetsch (s), with lute & bass viol acc. 10"—C-5715
[Sumer is icumen in]
(in Col. History of Music, Vol. I: CM-231)
Come again, sweet love 1st Book of Ayres, 1597
Max Meili (t) & F. Worshung (lute)
12"—G-DB5018
[Come heavy sleep; Willaert: Con lagrime & Morley: It was a lover]
Gladys Swarthout (ms) & L. Hodges (pf)
(in VM-679) 12"—V-16778
[Purcell: Nymphs & Shepherds & Handel: Rinaldo—Lascia]

Come, heavy sleep 1st Book of Ayres, 1597
Max Meili (t) & F. Worshung (lute)
12″—G-DB5018
[Come again; Willaert: Con lagrime &
Morley: It was a lover]
Fine nacks for ladies 2nd Book of Ayres,
1600
Anonymous Soprano with pf. acc.
12″—C-D40121
(in musical illustrations for Lecture 61
"The Progress of Music," George Dyson:
International Educational Society)
Flow, my tears 2nd Book of Ayres, 1600
Aksel Schiøtz (t) & Jytte Gorki Schmidt
(guitar) 12″—G-DB5270
[Shall I sue? & Now cease, my wandering
eyes]
Go crystal tears 1st Book of Ayres 1597
Motet & Madrigal Group—Opienski
(in Vol. VI) 12″—AS-58
[Jones: Farewell deare love & Morley:
Since my tears]
Now cease, my wandering eyes 2nd Book
of Ayres, 1600
Aksel Schiøtz (t) & Jytte Gorki Schmidt
(guitar) 12″—G-DB5270
[Shall I sue?; Flow, my tears]
Shall I sue? 2nd Book of Ayres, 1600
Aksel Schiøtz (t) & Jytte Gorki Schmidt
(guitar) 12″—G-DB5270
[Flow, my tears; Now cease, my wander-
ing eyes]
English Dance —Arr. Lute Besard
Hermann Leeb
(in Vol. IV) 12″—AS-36
[Besard: Lute Pieces & Airs by Clemens
non Papa, Grotte & Anon]
Galliard (Unidentified)
—Arr. Guitar Segovia
Andrés Segovia, in D-A596
Pavane (from "Lacrymae, or Seven Teares,
figured in Seven Passionate Pavans"
1604) Viols
—Arr. Piano
George Dyson 12″—C-D40138
(in illustrations for Lecture 69, "Early
Keyboard Music"—International Educa-
tional Society)
Süsse lieb (Unidentified)
Die Kantorei der Staatlichen Hochschule
für Musik, Berlin—Thomas
12″—T-E2926
[Hassler: Ach weh des leiden; Schein:
Wenn Philli ihre Liebestrahl & Mylius:
Ein Maeglein]

DUBENSKY, Arcady (1890-   )
*A violinist for many years with the Philhar-
monic-Symphony Orchestra of New York who
composes in traditional idioms.*
Fugue for 18 Violins 1932
Indianapolis Symphony Orch.—Sevitzky
(in VM-912†) 12″—V-11-8366
[Stephen Foster, Pt. 3]
Gossips String Orchestra 1930
—Arr. 2 Pianos Whittemore & Lowe
Arthur Whittemore & Jack Lowe
10″—V-10-1041
[Prokofiev: Love for Three Oranges—
March; Reger: Ballet Suite—Waltz]

Stephen Foster: Theme, Variations & Finale
Orchestra
Indianapolis Symphony Orch.—Sevitzky
[Fugue for 18 violins] 2 12″—VM-912†

DUFAY, Guillaume (c.1400-1474)
*Dufay was one of the greatest early members
of the Netherlands polyphonic school. Con-
sidering the prolific output of his composition,
much of which has survived, he is not too well
represented on discs at the present time.*
Alma Redemptoris Mater Air in Latin
(Anthem-motet)
La Société Pro Musica Antiqua of Brus-
sels (Unacc. Cho. in Latin)—Safford Cape
(in Vol. IV) 12″—AS-35
[Mass "Se la face ay pâle"]
Yves Tinayre (t) & String Orch.
[Paumann: Benedicite] 12″—LUM-32012
(in Yves Tinayre album No. 1)
Ave Maris Stella—See Hymns
Bon jour, bon mois (Tr. A. Stainer)
La Psallette Notre Dame (Choir in
French)—J. Chailley 12″—G-DB5117
(with recorders & viols)
[Omnes amici ejus & Anon. 15th Cen-
tury: L'Amour de moy]
(in French Masters of the Middle Ages
Set)
Christe Redemptor See also Hymns
Conditor Alme Siderum Chorus in Latin
(Plainsongs with Faburdens by Dufay)
Unacc. Cho.—Richard Terry
10″—C-5711
[Anon: Nunc Dimittis & Palestrina: Nunc
Dimittis]
(in Columbia History of Music, Vol. I:
CM-231)

Flos Florum Chorus in Latin
Choir of the Pius X School of Liturgical
Music (in VM-739) 12″—V-13557
[Anon: Descent of the Holy Ghost &
Obrecht: Qui cum patre]
Hymns: Christe Redemptor omnium;
Ave Maria stella; Tantum ergo
Les Paraphonistes de St. Jean-des-Matines
—G. de Van 12″—LUM-32054
[Palestrina: Lamentation]
(Le) Jour s'endort Chanson in French
Max Meili (t) (in Vol. I) 12″—AS-3
[Pourrai-je; Heinrich Isaac: Zwischen
Berg & Okeghem: Ma Maîtresse]
Mass "Ad Modum Tubae"—Gloria in Ex-
celsis Boys Choir & 2 Trumpets
Berlin State Academy Cho.—Kalt
10″—P-R1019
[Josquin des Prés: Et incarnatus]
(in "2000 Years of Music" Set—P-P11)
Mass "Se la face ay pâle"—Kyrie Unacc.
Cho. in Latin
La Société Pro Musica Antiqua of Brus-
sels—Cape (in Vol. IV) 12″—AS-35
[Anthem-Motet: Alma Redemptoris
Mater]
Omnes amici ejus (Complainte de Con-
stantinople) (Tr. J. Chailley)
La Psallette Notre Dame—J. Chailley
(with recorders & Viols)
12″—G-DB5117

[Bon jour, bon mois & Anon. 15th Century—L'Amour de moy]
(in French Masters of the Middle Ages Set)

Pourrai-je Chanson in French
Max Meili (t) (in Vol. I) 12"—**AS-3**
[Le jour s'endort; Isaac: Zwischen Berg; Okeghem: Ma Maîtresse]

Rondeau "Adieu m'amour"
Lina Dauby (c) & Frederic Anspach (t) with 3 Mediaeval Viols
(in Vol. V) 12"—**AS-43**
[Isaac: Chanson—Hélas que]

Salve quae fama—vos nunc—viri mendaces
Motet for 4 voices
Les Parphonistes de St.-Jean-des-Matines —G. de Van (in Vol. XIII) **AS-121**
Tantum ergo—See Hymns

Vergine Bella Air in Latin (Ed. van den Borren)
Yves Tinayre (t) with 3 Strings
12"—**LUM-32019**
[Anon 14th Century: Ave Mater]
(in Tinayre album No. 2)
Ernst Konrad Haase (b) (in German), with Fiedel Trio 12"—**PD-10751**
[Lapicida: Instrumental-satz über das Lied "Zu Andernach am Rheine": K. Lechner, blockflöte]

DUKAS, Paul (1865-1935)
A well known French composer, critic and editor who was a friend of Debussy and a very successful musician.

(L') Apprenti sorcier Scherzo for Orchestra (after Goethe's poem)
Eng. Sorcerer's Apprentice
National Symphony Orch.—Enrique Jorda 2 12"—**D-ED16†**
[Debussy: La Damoiselle Elue—Prélude] (D-K1175/6)
Philadelphia Orch.—Ormandy
12"—**C-12584D**
Philadelphia Orch.—Stokowski
2 12"—**VM-717†**
[Rimsky-Korsakov: Ivan the Terrible: Prelude, Act III]
(Sibelius: Tempest—Berceuse, on G-DB3533/4: G-DB6038/9)
N. Y. Philharmonic Orch.—Toscanini
12"—**V-7021**
(G-D1689) (G-W1114) (G-AW86)
Minneapolis Symphony Orch.— Mitropoulos 2 12"—**CX-212†**
[Rimsky-Korsakov: Coq d'Or—Bridal Procession]
Paris Conservatory Orch.—Gaubert
2 12"—**CX-75**
(C-LFX464/5) (C-LX653/4)
[Fauré: Shylock—Nocturne No. 5]
DUPLICATIONS: Lamoureux Orch.— Wolff, PD-66893/4: PD-566001/2; Pasdeloup Orch.—Ingelbrecht, PAT-X5484/5

(La) Péri—Poème dansé Dance Poem for Orchestra
Colonne Orch.—Gabriel Pierné
2 12"—**O-123750/1**

—Fanfare only
Orchestre des Festivals Debussy—Désiré Inghelbrecht
(in CM-344†) 12"—**C-P69318D**
[Debussy: Le Martyre de Saint-Sebastian-Fanfare; & Nocturnes Pt. 7]
(PAT-PDT19)

Variations, Interlude et Finale on a Theme by Rameau Piano
Yvonne Lefébre 2 12"—**G-L1009/10**
Villanelle French Horn & Piano
Jean Devemy & pf. acc.
10"—**PAT-X98067**

DUNSTABLE, John (c.1370-1453)
One of the earliest English contrapuntists, paralleling Dufay and Binchois, Dunstable was a composer of power and learning.

Hymn after Agincourt (with refrain "Deo gratias")
(attributed to Dunstable, 1415)
Winchester Music Club, unacc.
12"—**C-D40118**
(illustration for Lecture 61 "The Progress of Music," Dyson: International Educational Society)

Quam Pulchra es
Choir of the Pius X School of Liturgical Music (in VM-739) 12"—**V-13556**
[14th Cent: Flagellants' Hymn & 13th Century: O Miranda dei Caritas; Puellare Gremium]

DUPARC, Henri (1848-1933)
A pupil of César Franck, Duparc was compelled to give up music because of illness in 1885. A self-critical composer, he destroyed many of his manuscripts, and his fame lies chiefly in his songs.

SONGS in French
Chanson triste (J. Lahor)
Maggie Teyte (s) & Gerald Moore (pf)
(in VM-895) 10"—**V-10-1003**
[Paladilhe: Psyché] (G-DA1779)
Eleanor Steber (s) & J. Quillan (pf)
[Bachelet: Chère nuit] 12"—**V-18088**
Charles Panzéra (b) & Mme. Panzéra-Baillot (pf) 10"—**G-DA4880**
[Soupir]
John Charles Thomas 12"—**V-11-8568**
[Mattei: Non è ver]
André Gaudin (b) 12"—**PD-524059**
[Delibes: Sérénade à Ninon]
Ninon Vallin (s) 12"—**O-123562**
[Puccini: Madame Butterfly—Un bel di]
Sophie Wyss (s) & pf. acc. 10"—**D-M498**
[Arr. Ferrari: Auprès de ma Blonde]
DUPLICATION: Claire Croiza, C-LF59

Elégie (On the death of Robert Emmet)
Pierre Bernac (b) & Francis Poulenc (pf) 12"—**G-DB6312**
[Invitation au voyage]
Charles Panzéra (b) & Panzéra-Baillot (pf) 12"—**G-DB5075**
[Manoir de Rosemonde; Phidylé]

Extase (Jean Lahor)
Maggie Teyte (s) & Gerald Moore (pf)
[Szulc: Clair de lune] 12"—**G-DB5937**

Charles Panzéra (b) & Mme. Panzéra-
Baillot 12″—G-DB5084
[Sérénade Florentine; Lamento]
(L') **Invitation au voyage** (Baudelaire)
Maggie Teyte (s) & London Philhar-
monic—Heward (In Gramophone Shop
Album)
Charles Panzéra (b) & Mme. Panzéra-
Baillot 12″—V-18051
[Vie antérieure] (G-DB5000)
Pierre Bernac (b) & Francis Poulenc
(pf) 12″—G-DB6312
[Elégie]
Claire Croiza (s) & Francis Poulenc (pf)
[Poulenc: Le Bestaire] 12″—C-D15041
DUPLICATIONS: Paul Sandoz,
G-DB10035; Lily Pons, on C-72050D in
CM-689

Lamento (Gautier)
Charles Panzéra (b) & Mme. Panzéra-
Baillot 12″—G-DB5084
[Extase & Sérénade Florentine]
DUPLICATIONS: Jean Planel, PAT-
PG79; Claire Croiza, C-LF59

(Le) Manoir de Rosemonde (R. de Bon-
nières)
Charles Panzéra (b) & Mme. Panzéra-
Baillot (pf) 12″—G-DB5075
[Elégie & Phidylé]
DUPLICATIONS: Povla Frijsh, V-18052
in VM-789; Vanni-Marcoux, G-DA1123

Phidylé (Coppée)
Maggie Teyte (s) & London Philharmonic
—Heward (In Gramophone Shop Album)
Charles Panzéra (b) & Mme. Panzéra-
Baillot (pf) 12″—G-DB5075
[Elégie & Manoir de Rosemonde]
Georges Thill (t) & Maurice Faure (pf)
[La Vie antérieure] 12″—C-LFX491
Grace Moore (s)
(in VM-918) 12″—V-11-8258
[Massenet: Hérodiade—Il est doux]

Sérénade Florentine (Jean Lahor)
Charles Panzéra (b) & Mme. Panzéra-
Baillot 12″—G-DB5084
[Extase & Lamento]

Soupir (Prud'homme)
Charles Panzéra (b) & Mme. Panzéra-
Baillot 10″—G-DA4880
[Chanson triste]
Pierre Bernac (t) & Francis Poulenc (pf)
[Chausson: Le colibri] 10″—G-DA4928
Joseph Rogatchewsky (t) pf. acc.
[Koechlin: Si tu le veux] 10″—C-LF136

Testament (Sylvestre)
Charles Panzéra (b) & Mme. Panzéra-
Baillot (pf) 12″—G-DB5085
[La Vague et la cloche]

(La) Vague et la cloche (deLisle)
Charles Panzéra (b) & Mme. Panzéra-
Baillot (pf) 12″—G-DB5085
[Testament]

(La) Vie antérieure (Baudelaire)
Charles Panzéra (b) & Mme. Panzéra-
Baillot (pf) 12″—V-18051
[Invitation au voyage] (G-DB5000]
Georges Thill (t) & Maurice Faure (pf)
[Phidylé] 12″—C-LFX491

Paul Sandoz (b) & Paul Baumgartner
(pf) 12″—G-DB10035
[L'Invitation au voyage]

DUPHLY (Duflitz) (1716-1788)
A French composer and clavecinist.
(Les) Colombes Harpsichord
Pauline Aubert 12″—PAT-PAT50
[Jacques de la Guerre: Sarabande &
Rondo]

DUPONT, Gabriel (1878-1914)
*A pupil of Widor, Dupont was an operatic
composer whose works have attained success in
France, Italy and Belgium.*

(LA) FARCE DU CUVIER Opera in French
1912
Overture Orchestra
Lamoureux Orch.—Albert Wolff
(PD-566141) 12″—PD-67042
[Lalo: Scherzo]
SONGS
Mandoline—Mélodie
Povla Frijsh (s) & Celius Dougherty (pf)
(in VM-789) 12″—V-18052
[Duparc: Manoir de Rosemonde, etc.]

DUPRE, Marcel (1886-   )
(6) Choral Preludes Organ
8. De Profundis
19. Le jour qui est plein de joie
41. In dulci jubilo
64. Pare-toi, chère âme
74. Avec quelle beauté brille l'étoile du
matin
67. Notre Père qui êtes aux cieux
Marcel Dupré (Meudon organ)
12″—LUM-32010
Prelude & Fugue, G minor, Op. 7, No. 3
Organ
Virgil Fox (Hammond Museum Organ),
in VM-1177
Variations on a Noël Organ
E. Power Biggs (Memorial Church, Cambridge, Mass.) 12″—V-11-9329

DUPUY, Edouard (1770-1822)
*A Swiss singer and violinist who became direc-
tor of court music at Stockholm, Dupuy wrote
chamber music as well as operas.*

UNGDOM OG GALSKAB Opéra-Comique
1806
Eng. **Youth and Madness**
Overture Orchestra
Royal Orch., Copenhagen—J. Hye-
Knudsen 12″—G-Z268
Jeg er endnu; Livets Vaar Soprano & Tenor
Eng. **I am still in the springtime of life**
Edith Oldrup Pedersen, Paul Wiedemann
& Marius Jacobsen 12″—G-DB5246
[Heise: Drot og Marsk—2 Arias]
(G-Z284)

DURANTE, Francesco (1684-1755)
*A pupil of Scarlatti and a teacher of Pergolesi,
Piccini and Paisiello, Durante was known pri-
marily as a church composer.*
Concerto, G minor Arr. Lualdi
Chamber Orch. of the Royal Conservatory,
San Pietro a Majella, Naples—A. Lualdi
12″—G-DBO5354

Danza (unspecified) arr. Plectrum Quartet
Madami
Madami Plectrum Quartet
10"—C-D5630
[Scarlatti—Madami: Gavotte]

Misericordias Domini
Augustana Choir—Veld   12"—V-17633
[Palestrina: Ecce quomodo moritur]

Toccata (unspecified)
Pasquier String Trio   12"—PAT-PAT31
[Scarlatti: Toccata & Purcell: Fantasia
No. 3]

Vergin, tutto amor   Aria in Italian
Theodora Versteegh (c)   12"—C-D17183
[Gluck: Orfeo—Che farò]
Gino Sinimberghi (t) & Organ
10"—PD-62806
[Tosti: Ideale] (PD-25871)
A. Carvcenco (ms) & pf. acc.
10"—G-AV52
[Caldera: Come raggio del sol]

DUSSEK, Jan Ladislav (1761-1812)
Sonata No. 3, Op. 9   Piano
—Allegro Maestoso only
Jacques Fevrier (in Vol. VII) 12"—AS-62
[Schobert: Sonata, Op. 8—Allegro
moderato]

DVORAK, Antonin (1841-1904)
*With Smetana, Dvorák is probably the most
widely known Czechoslovakian composer of the
nineteenth century. His association with music
in America is widely known.*
Ballade, D minor, Op. 15   Violin & Piano
1885
Frederick Grinke & Gerald Moore
[Romantic Pieces, Pt. 3] 12"—D-K1017

Biblical Songs   See under Songs

Carnaval Overture, Op. 92   Orchestra 1891
Czech Philharmonic Orch.—Vaclav
Talich   12"—V-13710
Boston "Pops" Orch.—Fiedler
12"—V-12159
CBS Symphony—Howard Barlow
12"—C-70739D
Berlin Philharmonic—Schmidt-Isserstedt
(U-F14407)   12"—T-E3053
City of Birmingham Orch.—Weldon
12"—C-DX1235
National Symphony Orch.—Rankl
12"—D-K1316
DUPLICATION: Czech Broadcasting
Orch.—Jeremias, ESTA-H5013

Concerto—Piano & Orchestra, Op. 33   1876
Willy Stech & Berlin Philharmonic—
Schmidt-Isserstedt   4 12"—T-E3166/9

Concerto, A minor, Op. 53   Violin & Orches-
tra 1880
Yehudi Menuhin & Paris Conservatory
Orch.—Enesco   4 12"—GM-254†
[Paganini-Enesco: Caprice No. 6, Menu-
hin & Enesco, pf.] (G-DB2838/41)
Georg Kulenkampff & Berlin Philhar-
monic Orch.—Jochum
(U-G18033/6)   4 12"—T-SK3237/40

Concerto, B minor, Op. 104   'Cello & Orchestra 1895

Pablo Casals & Czech Philharmonic Orch.
—George Szell   5 12"—VM-458†
(G-DB3288/92 in GM-306†)
Maurice Gendron & London Philharmonic
Orch.—Rankl   5   12"—D-K1437/41
Gaspar Cassadó & Berlin Philharmonic
Orch.—Schmidt-Isserstedt
(U-F14392/6)   5   12"—T-E1893/7
Gregor Piatigorsky & Philadelphia Orch.
—Ormandy   5   12"—CM-658†

Dimitrij   See under Operas
Dumky Trio   See under Trios
Dumka & Furiant, Op. 12   Piano
—No. 1, Dumka (Elégie) only
Jan Herman   12"—G-AN348
[Humoresques Nos. 1 & 7]

Festival March, C major, Op. 54
Symphony Orchestra—Smetacek
12"—U-F12328
[Ten Legends, Op. 59, Pt. 11]
Symphony Orchestra—Sejna
12"—ESTA-H5059
[Scherzo capriccio, Pt. 3]

Goin' Home
*This is a vocal paraphrase by William Arms
Fisher, of the Largo (2nd) Movement of the
Symphony No. 5 in E minor (From the New
World") See Symphony—No. 5, Largo—Ar-
rangements.*

Gypsy Songs, Op. 55   See under Songs
Holoubka   See under The Wood Dove

HUMORESQUES, Op. 101   Piano 1894
Nos. 1 & 6
Jan Herman   12"—G-AN348
[Dumka, Op. 12]
No. 2
Jan Herman   12"—U-G14033
[No. 7 & Suk: Dumka]
No. 7 (The celebrated Humoresque)   Piano
Mark Hambourg   10"—G-B2685
[Schumann: Träumerei]
Jan Herman   12"—U-G14033
[No. 2 & Suk: Dumka]
—Arr. 2 Pianos
Rawicz & Landauer, C-FB2145
—Arr. Orchestra
FOK Symphony Orch.—Vaclav Smetacek
[Suk: Love Song]   12"—U-E12669
Berlin State Opera Orch.—Melichar
12"—P-R2536
[Tchaikovsky: Sleeping Beauty—Waltz]
DUPLICATIONS: New   Queen's   Hall
Orch.—Wood, D-K762; New Light Sym-
phony, G-B8129; Hastings Municipal
Orch.—Cameron, D-K568; Czech Sym-
phony—Parik, ESTA-D2004
—Arr. Violin & Piano
Fritz Kreisler & Franz Rupp
12"—V-15217
[Tchaikovsky: Andante cantabile, from D
major Quartet, Op. 11]
(G-DB3443) (Also on G-DB1091)
Mischa Elman & Leopold Mittman
12"—V-11-8950
[Massenet: Thaïs—Méditation]
Georg Kulenkampff & Franz Rupp
[Schubert: Ave Maria]   12"—PD-95074

Nathan Milstein & Artur Balsam
[Schumann: Träumerei] 10″—C-17337D
Jan Kubelik & A. Holacek
12″—U-G11386
[Fibich: Poem & Suk: Burleska]
DUPLICATIONS: Ida Haendel, D-M521;
Zino Francescatti, C-LF91; Siegfried Bor-
ries, G-DA4444; Vasa Prihoda, PD-30033;
PD-66885: CET-LL3003; Jascha Heifetz,
D-23384 in D-A385; Albert Sammons,
C-DB1008
Also: Isaac Stern, on C-71881D in CM-
657†
—**Arr. Viola & Orchestra** E. de Luca
William Primrose & Victor Symphony
Orch.—O'Connell 12″—V-18222
[Nevin: The Rosary]
—**Miscellaneous arrangements**
Squire Octet, C-3470; Inst. Ensemble,
ESTA-D2008
—**Vocal arrangement in English** ("Chris-
tina's Lament")
(Text by Creyke)
Maggie Teyte (s) & pf. acc.
10″—D-M444
[Songs my mother taught me]
—**Vocal arrangement in German** ("Eine
kleine Fruhlingsweise")
(Text by Lengsfelder)
Richard Tauber (t) 10″—P-RO20220
[Saint-Saëns: Le Cygne, vocal arr.]
DUPLICATION: Marius Jacobsen, in Dan-
ish, G-X4442

Hussite See under Overtures

In Nature's Realm See under Overtures

Indian Lament See under Sonatine, G major—2nd Mvt.

J. K. TYL Music from the play by Samberk
1891
Unspecified Excerpt
National Theatre Orch., Pregue—
Vasata 12″—U-G14295
[Rusalka—Polonaise]
(See also Overtures—My Home)

Jacobin See under Operas

Largo See Symphonies—No. 5, E minor,
2nd Mvt.

(10) Legends Orchestra Op. 59 1881
(Originally Piano 4 Hands: Orch.
Dvořák)
Symphony Orch.—Smetacek
6 12″—U-F12285/7 & F12326/8
[Festival March, Op. 54a]
—**No. 3, G minor**
London Philharmonic—T. Beecham
(in CX-55†) 12″—C-68387D
[Slavonic Rhapsody, Pt. 3]
[C-LWX144) (C-LFX542)

Lonely Sweetheart Boh. Milenka Travička
(No. 2 of 2 Choruses for Men's Voices,
1877)
Prague Teachers' Chorus
[Spilka: Koupim ja si] 10″—G-AM793
Bakule Chorus 10″—U-A12378
[Fibich: Stilly Night]

Mazurka, E minor, Op. 49 Violin & Or-
chestra 1879
Jarka Stepanek & Vera Repkova (pf)
10″—U-A12165
(13) Moravian Duets, Op. 32 Soprano &
Contralto 1876
Prague Teachers' Chorus & F. Maxian
(pf) 4 12″—U-F12374/7
"Negro Spiritual Melody"
*This is Kreisler's arrangement for Violin and
Piano of the theme from the Largo from the
Symphony No. 5, E minor ("From the New
World")*
Fritz Kreisler and Carl Lamson
10″—G-DA1120
[Song of the Volga Boatmen, arr. Kreis-
ler]
Yehudi Menuhin & Marcel Gazelle
12″—G-DB6158
[Schubert-Menuhin: Ave Maria]
—**Arr. Viola**
William Primrose & Franz Rupp
12″—V-11-8730
[Songs my mother taught me]
Notturno, B major, Op. 40 Strings 1870
Busch Chamber Players—A. Busch
10″—C-17513D

OPERAS In Bohemian

ARMIDA, Op. 115 4 Acts 1902/3·
Armida's Aria
Maria Podvalová (s) 12″—U-G12568
[Dimitrij-Dimitrij's Aria, J. Gleich]

(THE) BLOCKHEADS, Op. 19 Ger. Die
Dickschädel 1 Act 1874 Boh. Tvrdé palice
Overture Orchestra
National Theatre Orch. of Prague—
Charvat 12″—ESTA-H5138
Reřichy's Aria
Jaroslav Veverka 12″—U-G12567
[The Sly Peasant—Duet]

(THE) DEVIL AND KATE, Op. 112 Ger.
Der Teufel und die wilde Käthe 1898/9
Boh. Cert a Káča
Orchestral Selections (Fantasia)
National Theatre Orch. of Prague—
Jeremias 12″—ESTA-H5017
Vocal Selections
Lida Cervinkova, S. Stepanova, J. Kon-
stantin, J. Vojta with National Theatre
Chorus & Orchestra—Chalabala
3 12″—ESTA-H5174/6
Prelude, Act III
National Theatre Orch. of Prague—
Chalabala 12″—U-G12754
[Rusalka—Polonaise]
Czech Broadcasting Orch.—Smetacek
12″—ESTA-H5039
[Wood Dove—Wedding Dance]
Jak smutno v zámku
Maria Podvalová (s) 12″—U-G12569
[King and Collier—Jenik's Aria, Jin-
dřich Blažicek]

DIMITRIJ, Op. 64 4 Acts 1881/2
Dimitrij's Aria
Jaroslav Gleich (t) 12″—U-G12568
[Armida—Armida's Aria, Maria Podval-
ova]

(THE) JACOBIN, Op. 84 3 Acts 1889
Orchestral Selections (Fantasia)
National Theatre Orch. of Prague—
Jeremias **ESTA-H5016**
Burgrave's Aria, Act 1 Bass
Emil Pollert **10″—G-AM2176**
[Smetana: Dalibor—Aria, Act II]
Duo: **Julie & Bohuse, Act II** Soprano &
Bass
M. Kocova & H. Vavra **12″—G-AN321**
[Smetana: Two Widows—Karliny-Ane-
zky Duo, with Kocova & Nordenova]
DUPLICATIONS: S. Stepanova & Z.
Otava, ESTA-H5116; M. Podvalova & J.
Konstantin, U-G12570
Terinky's Aria Soprano
Boh. Na podzim v ořeší
Ota Horakova **12″—U-G12570**
[Duet: My cizenou jsme bloudili]
(Smetana: Bartered Bride—Marenka's
Aria, on U-F12336)

KING AND COLLIER, Op. 14 Ger. Der
König und der Köhler 3 Acts 1871 Boh.
Král a uhlíř
Jenik's Aria Tenor
Boh. O jak roužím k tobê
Jindrick Blazicek **12″—U-G12569**
[Devil and Kate—Jak smutno v zámku]
Kdyz tve dite roztomile
J. Ourednik **10″—U-C12998**
[The Sly Peasant—Kdo jest, H. Vavra]

RUSALKA 3 Acts 1900 Eng. **The Water
Witch**
Selections
Stepanka Jelinkova, Marta Krasova, Beno
Blachut, Eduard Haken, Josef Krikava,
with Chorus & National Theatre Orches-
tra—Zdenek Folprecht
8 **12″—ESTA-H5096/103**
Selections
Zofie Napravilova, Maria Tauberova,
Maria Podvalova, Milada Jiraskova, Dus-
ka Hanzalikova, Marie Vesala, Stepanka
Stepanova, Jindrich Blazicek, Karel
Kalas, Zdenek Otava, with National The-
atre Chorus & Orchestra—Rudolf Vasata
& Zdenek Chalabala
5 **12″—U-G12386 & 88/90 & U-G12653**
Orchestral Selections (Fantasia)
FOK Symphony Orch.—Jeremias
ESTA-H5011
Individual excerpts
Overture Orchestra
Orch. of the National Theatre—Chalabala
[Polonaise] **12″—U-G12400**
Alas, alas! (Air of the Water Fay) Act II
Bass
Boh. Arie Vodnika: Beda, beda
Emil Pollert
(G-AN323) **12″—G-AN530**
[Tchaikovsky: Eugene Onegin—Gremin's
Air]
I have golden hair (Air of the Water
Nymph) Act III Soprano
Boh. Mam zlate vlasky, mam
Jarmila Novotna & pf. acc.
10″—G-AM3783
[Flotow: Marta—Last rose of summer]

Jářku, klouče milé Act II
Maria Tauberova & Oldrich Kovar
12″—U-G12852
[Smetana: Dalibor—O jaké toužení, S.
Jelinkova & Jindrich Blazicek]
O lovely moon (Air of Rusalka) Act I So-
prano
Ada Sari & pf. acc. **12″—G-AN679**
[Smetana: Bartered Bride—Marie's Air,
Act I]
Ada Nordenova **12″—G-AN319**
[Smetana: Bartered Bride—Marie's Air,
Act II]
DUPLICATION: M. Kocova, U-A10650
O strange vision (Prince's Air) Tenor
Boh. Vím, že jsi kouzlo
Jindrich Blazicek **10″—U-C12500**
[Smetana: Libuse—O vy lipy]
Polonaise Orchestra
Czech Philharmonic—Talich
10″—G-DA5302
Orch. of the National Theatre of Prague
—Vasata **12″—U-G12400**
[Overture]
[Devil and Kate—Prelude, Act 3, on
U-G12754]
[J. K. Tyl—Excerpt on U-G14295]
White flowers along the way Bass & Chorus
Boh. Květiny bílé po cestě
Karel Kalas & Cho. **12″—U-G12431**
[Smetana: Bartered Bride—Opening
Chorus]

(THE) SLY PEASANT, Op. 37 Ger. Der
Bauer ein Schelm 2 Acts 1877
Boh. Selma Sedlák
Overture Orchestra
Czech Symphony Orch.—Sejna
12″—ESTA-H5051
National Theatre Orch. of Prague—
Charvat **12″—ESTA-H5139**
Duet: Jsme čeští sedláci
Oldrich Kovar & Ludek Mandus
12″—U-G12567
[The Blockheads—Rerichy's Aria, Jaro-
slav Veverka]
Kdo, jest, jenž slovy vypoví
Hilbert Vavra & pf. acc.
10″—U-C12998
[King and Collier—Když tvé dítě roz-
tomilé, J. Ourednik]
Prince's Aria Boh. Kdo jest, jenž slovy
vypovi
Zdenek Otava **12″—ESTA-H5116**
[Jacobin—Duet, with S. Jelinkova]
Duo: We shall find somewhere else a quiet
retreat Sop. & Ten.
Boh. Najdeme si jinde klidný útulek
Marie Budikova & Jindrich Blazicek
12″—U-G12986
[Kovarovic: Through the Window—About
the beautiful paradise of matrimony,
Jelinkova]
(Also on U-G12713)

VANDA, Op. 25 5 Acts 1875/6
Overture Orchestra
FOK Symphony Orch.—O. Parik
12″—ESTA-H5002

OVERTURES (Concert) Orchestra
Carnaval Overture, Op. 92 See under Carnaval Overture
Hussite, Op. 67 1883 Boh. **Husitská**
Boston "Pops" Orch.—Fiedler, in
VM-1210†
Symphony Orch.—Jeremias
2 10″—ESTA-D4009/10
In Nature's Realm, Op. 91 1891 Ger. **In der Natur**
Chicago Symphony Orch.—Stock
2 12″—VM-975†
[Suk: Fairy Tale Suite, Op. 16 No. 2—
Folk Dance & Polka]
Czech Philharmonic Orch.—Kubelik
2 12″—G-C3628/9
My Home, Op. 62
Boh. **Domov můj** Ger. **Mein Heim**
NOTE: *This is the overture from the incidental music to Sam Berk's play "J. K. Tyl."*
FOK Orch.—Jeremias
12″—ESTA-H5003
(13) Poetic Moods, Op. 85 Piano
—**No. 6, Sorrowful Reverie** Boh. **Vzpominani** Fr. **Cruelle souvenance**
Arr. Saxophone & Piano
Viard & Andolfi 10″—PAT-X98043
[Ravel: Five o'clock fox-trot]
—**No. 7, Furiant Arr. Saxophone & Piano**
Viard & Andolfi 10″—PAT-X98074
[Andolfi: Pitie]
Polonaise, E flat major Orchestra 1879
Czech Philharmonic—Talich
10″—G-DA5301
Czech Broadcasting Orch.—Jeremias
[Slavonic Dance No. 16] 12″—U-F12409
Prague Waltz Orchestra
FOK Symphony Orch.—Smetacek
12″—U-F12620

QUARTETS Strings
No. 3, E flat major, Op. 51 1879
Busch Quartet 4 12″—CM-480†
Léner Quartet 4 12″—C-GQX11010/3
—**2nd Mvt. (Dumka) only**
Bohemian (Suk) Quartet
12″—PD-95087
No. 4, C major, Op. 61 1882
Gordon Quartet 8 12″—CH-B12
(Limited Edition)
No. 6, F major, Op. 96 "American" 1893
Budapest Quartet 3 12″—VM-681†
Roth Quartet 3 12″—CM-328†
Ondricek Quartet
3 12″—U-G12559/61
Sevcikovo-Lhotskeho Quartet
3 12″—G-AN332/4
Poltronieri Quartet
3 12″—C-D14549/51
Röntgen Quartet
3 12″—ELITE-7038/40
No. 7, A flat major, Op. 105 1895
Quartetto di Roma
2 12″—G-DB5525/6
Ondricek Quartet 4 12″—PD-67775/8
No. 8, G major, Op. 106 1895
Isolde Menges Quartet
5 12—D-K1000/4

QUARTETS—Piano and Strings
No. 1, D major, Op. 23 1875
Silverman Piano Quartet
4 12″—D-K967/70
No. 2, E flat major, Op. 87 1889
Silverman Piano Quartet
4 12″—D-K971/4
QUINTET—Piano and Strings 1887
A major, Op. 81
J. Herman & Ondricek Quartet
4 12″—ESTA-H5027/30
—**2nd Mvt. (Dumka) only**
E. Calace & La Scala Quartet
12″—C-GQX11082
QUINTETS—Strings
No. 3, E flat major, Op. 97
Prague String Quartet & Richard Kosderka (2nd vla) 4 12″—VM-811†
Romantic Pieces, Op. 75 Violin & Piano 1887
Frederick Grinke & Gerald Moore
[Ballade, Op. 15] 2 12″—D-K1016/7
Rondo, Op. 94 'Cello & Orchestra 1891
G. Crépax & E. Calace (pf)
12″—C-GQX10099
L. Zelenka & Jan Herman (pf)
12″—U-G12396
Rusalka See under Operas
Scherzo Capriccioso, E minor, Op. 66 Orchestra
Minneapolis Symphony Orch.—Ormandy
12″—G-DB2520
Symphony Orch.—Sejna
2 12″—ESTA-H5058/9
[Festival March]
Berlin Philharmonic Orch.—Kleiber
12″—U-E655
Serenade for Strings, E major, Op. 22 1875
Boyd Neel String Orch.—Neel
4 12″—D-X214/7
German Opera House Orch.—Lehmann
(O-50015/7) 3 12″—O-7992/4
Berlin Philharmonic Orch.—von Benda
3 12″—T-E2650/2
Sextet, A major, Op. 48 1878
Budapest Quartet, with Watson Forbes (2nd vla) & John Moore (2nd vlc)
4 12″—VM-661†
Menges Sextet 4 12″—D-K963/6

SLAVONIC DANCES
Fr. **Danses slaves** Ger. **Slawische Tänze**
Originally for Piano 4-Hands, later orchestrated by the composer
Op. 46, Nos. 1 to 8 inclusive
Op. 72, (New Slavonic Dances), Nos. 1 to 8 incl.
NOTE: *Three Dances, Nos. 2, 10 & 16 have been transcribed for Violin & Piano by Kreisler. These are invariably mis-labelled Nos. 1, 2 & 3. When the composer orchestrated the complete set, the order of Nos. 3 & 6 was reversed.*
Collection: 16 Slavonic Dances, Complete
Czech Philharmonic Orch.—Vaclav Talich
5 10″ & 4 12″—VM-345 & VM-310

(G-AN832/5 & G-AM4606/10)
Czech Broadcasting Orch.—Jeremias
    9   12"—**U-F12401/9**
[Polonaise, E flat major]
FOK Symphony Orch.—Jirak
    9 12"—**ESTA-H5018/26**

Individual Dances (In order of their original publication for piano 4-hands)

No. 1, C major (Presto) Op. 46, No. 1
Myra Hess & H. Harty (pf.—4 hands)
    10"—**C-DB1235**
[MacDowell: A. D. 1620, Hess]
(in Col. History of Music, Vol. IV: CM-234)
Rawicz & Landauer (2 pfs.)
[No. 8]   10"—**C-DB2102**
Czech Philharmonic—Talich
(G-C2825) (in VM-310) 12"—**V-11925**
(G-L1019) (G-EH1180) (G-AN832)
[No. 2]
Czech Broadcasting Orch.—Jeremias
[No. 9]   12"—**U-F12401**
FOK Symphony Orch.—Jirak
[No. 9]   12"—**ESTA-H5018**
St. Louis Symphony Orch.—Golschmann
[No. 6]   12"—**V-11-8566**
Minneapolis Symphony Orch.—Mitropoulos   12"—**C-11645D**
[No. 6]
London Symphony Orch.—Olaf
[No. 10]   12"—**D-K1124**
N. Y. Philharmonic-Symphony Orch.—
Walter (in CX-211†) 12"—**C-11667D**
[Smetana: Moldau, Pt. 3]
DUPLICATIONS: Berlin State Opera Orch.—Kleiber, PD-66653: PD-516645; Prague Philharmonic, Jeremias, T-E3096

No. 2, E minor (Allegretto scherzando) Op. 46, No. 2
Czech Philharmonic Orch.—Talich
(in VM-310) 12"—**V-11925**
(G-C2835) (G-AN832) (G-L1019)
[No. 1] (G-EH1180)
Czech Broadcasting Orch.—Jeremias
[No. 10]   12"—**U-F12402**
FOK Symphony Orch.—Jirak
[No. 10]   12"—**ESTA-H5019**
DUPLICATION: Prague Philharmonic—Jeremias, T-E3096

—Arr. Violin & Piano
Paraphrase (No. 1) by Kreisler (Transcribed to G minor)
Joseph Szigeti & Andor Foldes
[No. 10] (in CM-513) 10"—**C-17338D**
(Older recording on C-GQX10931)
Yehudi Menuhin & M. Gazelle
    10"—**G-DA1506**
[Kreisler: Caprice Viennois]
Ida Haendel & Adela Kotowska
    10"—**D-M495**
[Brahms-Höchstein: Waltz, A major, Op. 39, No. 15]
Fritz Kreisler & Carl Lamson
    10"—**G-DA1057**
[Songs my mother taught me]
DUPLICATION: Albert Locatelli, C-DF2000

No. 3, D major (Allegretto scherzando) Op. 46, No. 3
(No. 6 in the orchestral set)
Czech Philharmonic—Talich
[No. 6]   (in VM-310) 12"—**V-11926**
(G-AN833) (G-C2831) (G-L1020)
[No. 12 on G-EH1182]
Czech Broadcasting Orch.—Jeremias
[No. 13]   12"—**U-F12406**
FOK Symphony Orch.—Jirak
[No. 13]   12"—**ESTA-H5023**
[Slavonic Rhapsody No. 1, Pt. 3, on ESTA-H5032]
DUPLICATION: Berlin Philharmonic Orch.—Schmidt-Isserstedt, T-E2829

No. 4, F major (Tempo di Minuetto) Op. 46, No. 4
Czech Philharmonic—Talich
(in VM-345) 10"—**V-4353**
(G-K7733) (G-EG6470)
Czech Broadcasting Orch.—Jeremias
    12"—**U-F12404**
FOK Symphony Orch.—Jirak
    12"—**ESTA-H5021**

No. 5, A major (Allegro vivace) Op. 46, No. 5
Czech Philharmonic—Talich
(in VM-345) 10"—**V-4354**
[No. 7] (G-EG6471) (G-AM4607)
Czech Broadcasting Orch.—Jeremias
[No. 12]   12"—**U-F12405**
FOK Symphony Orch.—Jirak
[No. 12]   12"—**ESTA-H5022**

No. 6, A flat major (Poco Allegro) Op. 46, No. 6
(No. 3 in orchestral set)
NOTE: *Invariably labelled No. 3.*
Czech Philharmonic—Talich
(G-C2831) (in VM-310) 12"—**V-11926**
[No. 3] (G-AN833) (G-L1020)
[No. 10 on G-EH967]
Czech Broadcasting Orch.—Jeremias
[No. 11]   12"—**U-F12403**
FOK Symphony Orch.—Jirak
[No. 11]   12"—**ESTA-H5020**
Minneapolis Symphony Orch.—Mitropoulos   12"—**C-11645D**
[No. 1]
St. Louis Symphony—Golschmann
[No. 1]   12"—**V-11-8566**
DUPLICATION: Prague Philharmonic—Jeremias, T-E3100

No. 7, C minor (Allegro assai) Op. 46, No. 7
Czech Philharmonic Orch.—Talich
(in VM-345) 10"—**V-4354**
[No. 5] (G-EG6471) (G-AM4607)
Czech Broadcasting Orch.—Jeremias
[No. 14]   12"—**U-F12407**
FOK Symphony Orch.—Jirak
[No. 14)   12"—**ESTA-H5024**
Prague Philharmonic—Jeremias
[No. 6]   12"—**T-E3100**

No. 8, G minor (Presto) Op. 46, No. 8
Rawicz & Landauer (2 pfs.)
[No. 1]   10"—**C-DB2102**
Czech Philharmonic Orch.—Talich
(in VM-310) 12"—**V-11927**

[No. 9] (G-C2852) (G-AN834)
(G-EH1185)
Czech Broadcasting Orch.—Jeremias
[No. 15] 12″—U-F12408
FOK Symphony Orch.—Jirak
[No. 15] 12″—ESTA-H5025
(Slavonic Rhapsody No. 2, Pt. 3 on
ESTA-H5034)
Danish Radio Orch.—Jensen
12″—TONO-X25042
[Smetana: Moldau, Pt. 3]
DUPLICATION: Chicago Symphony—
Stock, G-D1432

No. 9, B major (Molto vivace) Op. 72, No. 1
Czech Philharmonic Orch.—Talich
[No. 8] (in VM-310) 12″—V-11927
(G-C2852) (G-AN834) (G-EH1185)
Czech Broadcasting Orch.—Jeremias
[No. 1] 12″—U-F12401
FOK Symphony Orch.—Jirak
[No. 1] 12″—ESTA-H5018

No. 10, E minor (Allegretto grazioso) Op. 72, No. 2
Czech Philharmonic Orch.—Talich
(in VM-310) 12″—V-11928
[No. 12] (G-AN835) (G-C2859)
[No. 6 on G-EH967]
Czech Broadcasting Orch.—Jeremias
[No. 2] 12″—U-F12402
FOK Symphony Orch.—Jirak
[No. 2] 12″—ESTA-H5019
[Slavonic Rhapsody No. 3, Pt. 3, on
ESTA-H5036]
London Symphony Orch.—Olaf
[No. 1] 12″—D-K1124
Philadelphia Orch.—Ormandy
(in CM-588) 12″—C-12606D
[Smetana: Bartered Bride—Dance of the
Comedians]
Berlin Chamber Orch.—Hans von Benda
[Reger: Lyric andante] 12″—PD-67852

—Arr. Violin & Piano
Paraphrase (No. 2) by Kreisler
Josef Szigeti & Andor Foldes
[No. 2] (in CM-513) 12″—C-17338D
Yehudi Menuhin & Marcel Gazelle
(G-DB2922) 12″—V-14905
[Brahms-Joachim: Hungarian Dance No. 4, B minor]
Ida Haendel & pf. acc. 10″—D-M495
[Brahms: Waltz No. 15]
DUPLICATION: Vasa Prihoda, PD-57086: PD-66886: CET-OR5041

No. 11, F major (Allegro) Op. 72, No. 3
Czech Philharmonic Orch.—Talich
(in VM-345) 12″—V-4355
[No. 13] (G-EG6472) (G-AM4608)
Czech Broadcasting Orch.—Jeremias
[No. 6] 12″—U-F12403
FOK Symphony Orch.—Jirak
[No. 6] 12″—ESTA-H5020

No. 12, D flat major (Allegretto grazioso) Op. 72, No. 4
Czech Philharmonic Orch.—Talich
(in VM-310) 12″—V-11928
[No. 10] (G-C2859) (G-AN835)
[No. 3, on G-EH1182]

Czech Broadcasting Orch.—Jeremias
[No. 5] 12″—U-F12405
FOK Symphony Orch.—Jirak
[No. 5] 12″—ESTA-H5022

No. 13, B flat minor (Poco adagio) Op. 72, No. 5
Czech Philharmonic Orch.—Talich
(in VM-345) 10″—V-4355
[No. 11] (G-AM4608) (G-EG6472)
Czech Broadcasting Orch.—Jeremias
[No. 3] 12″—U-F12406
FOK Symphony Orch.—Jirak
[No. 3] 12″—ESTA-H5023

No. 14, B flat major (Moderato tempo di Minuetto) Op. 72, No. 6
Czech Philharmonic Orch.—Talich
(in VM-345) 10″—V-4356
[No. 15] (G-EG6473) (G-AM4609)
Czech Broadcasting Orch.—Jeremias
[No. 7] 12″—U-F12407
FOK Symphony Orch.—Jirak
[No. 7] 12″—ESTA-H5024

No. 15, C major (Allegro vivace) Op. 72, No. 7
Czech Philharmonic Orch.—Talich
(in VM-345) 10″—V-4356
[No. 14] (G-AM4609) (G-EG6473)
Czech Broadcasting Orch.—Jeremias
[No. 8] 12″—U-F12408
FOK Symphony Orch.—Jirak
[No. 8] 12″—ESTA-H5025
Prague Philharmonic Orch.—Jeremias
[No. 16] 12″—T-E3141

No. 16, A flat major (Grazioso, Lento, Tempo di Valse) Op. 72, No. 8
Czech Philharmonic Orch.—Talich
(in VM-345) 10″—V-4357
(G-AM4610) (G-EG6474)
Czech Broadcasting Orch.—Jeremias
12″—U-F12409
[Polonaise, E flat major]
FOK Symphony Orch.—Jirak
12″—ESTA-H5026
Prague Philharmonic Orch.—Jeremias
[No. 15] 12″—T-E3141

—Arr. Violin & Piano Paraphrase (No. 3)
Kreisler (Trans. G major)
Fritz Kreisler & Carl Lamson
(G-DB1445) 12″—V-7225
[Indian Lament]
(3) Slavonic Rhapsodies, Op. 45 Orchestra 1878
1. D major
2. G minor
3. A flat major
FOK Symphony Orch.—Jirak
6 12″—ESTA-H5031/6
[Slavonic Dances, Nos. 3, 8 & 10]

—No. 3 only
London Philharmonic—Beecham
2 12″—CX-55†
[Legend, Op. 59, No. 3] (C-LX402/3)
(C-LFX541/2) (C-LWX143/4)
Sonatina, G major, Op. 100 Violin & Piano 1893
Frederick Grinke & Kendall Taylor
2 12″—D-K1006/7

—2nd Mvt. Arr. Kreisler Entitled "Indian Lament"
Fritz Kreisler & Carl Lamson
(G-DB1445) 12"—V-7225
[Slavonic Dance No. 16, arr. Kreisler No. 3]
Lilia D'Albore & Herbert Giesen
[Veracini-Corti: Largo] 12"—PD-67681

—Arr. 'Cello Arr. Cassadó
Gaspar Cassadó & Gerald Moore
10"—C-LB66
[Cassadó: Danse du diable vent]
(Also on T-A2127)

SONGS

A-mowing stood a lovely maid, Op. 73, No. 2
(No. 2 of 4 Czech Folksongs, Op. 73)
Boh. Zalo dievca, zalo travu
Karla Ticha (s) & pf. acc.
[Grieg: Solvejg's Song] 10"—G-AM3846

(10) Biblical Songs, Op. 99 Boh.Biblické Pisen 1894
Marta Karsova (c) & J. Konstantin (b) & FOK Orch.—Jirak
5 10"—ESTA-D4001/5

—No. 2 Lord thou are my refuge and shield
Boh. Skryse ma a paveza ma ty jsi
Egon Fuchs (bs) 10"—G-AM2912
[No. 9]
DUPLICATION: Czech Chorus—Pecenka, U-B10658

—No. 3, Hear my Prayer, O Lord
Boh. Slyš ó Bože, slyš, modlitbu moje
Olga Valouskova (s) & pf. acc.
10"—U-C12997
[Smetana: Dalibor—Aria]
Jan Konstantin (b) 10"—U-C12922
[Biblical Song No. 4]

—No. 4, God is my shepherd
Boh. Hospodin jest můj pastýř
Egon Fuchs (bs) 10"—G-AM2912
[Biblical Song No. 5]
Jan Konstantin (b) 10"—U-C12922
[Biblical Song No. 3]

—No. 5, I will sing new songs of gladness
Boh. Bože, Bože, píseň novou zpívati budu
Egon Fuchs (bs) 10"—G-AM2911
[Biblical Song No. 4]
DUPLICATION: Czech Chorus—J. B. Pecenka, U-B10658

—No. 9, I will lift up mine eyes
Boh. Pozdvihuji očí tvých k horam
Egon Fuchs (bs) 10"—G-AM2912
[Biblical Song No. 2]

"Christina's Lament" See: Humoresque No. 7, vocal arr.

Cradle Song Boh. Ukolébavka
(One of 2 songs, no opus number, written in England, 1885)
Karla Ticha (s) & pf. acc.
[Tregler: Ave Maria] 10"—G-AM2298
Gabriela Horvatova (s) & pf. acc.
10"—U-C12999
[Smetana: Tajemství—Tak plane láska prava]

Death reigns in many a human heart, Op. 83, No. 2
Boh. V tak mnohém srdci (No. 2 of 8 Love Songs, Op. 83)
Amalie Bobkova & pf 10"—U-C14004
[Smetana: Spring Song, A. Slavikova]
DUPLICATION: Eva Markova, ESTA-D4017

Heimatslied sehnsuchtsschwer
Friedel Beckmann (a) 12"—G-EH1323
[Welter: Weit in die Welt]

(7) Gypsy Songs Op. 55
Else Fink (s, in German) & Suzanne Gyr (pf) 2 12"—G-DB10109/10

—No. 1, I chant my lay (or, I chant my hymn of love)
Boh. Ma píseň zas Ger. Mein Lied ertönt
Margherita Perras (s) (in German)
[No. 4] 10"—G-DA4419
Povla Frijsh (s) & Celius Dougherty (pf)
[Nos. 6 & 7] (in VM-789 10"—V-2158

—No. 4, Songs my mother taught me
Boh. Když mne stará matka
Ger. Als die alte Mutter
Fr. Chansons que ma mère m'a apprises
Karel Kalas (b) & R. Vasata (pf)
[Fibich: Song] 10"—U-C12897
Jarmila Novotna (s) 12"—V-11-9153
[Smetana: The Kiss-Cradle song]
Kirsten Flagstad (s) in English & Edwin McArthur (pf) 10"—V-2009
[Frank Bridge: Love went a'riding]
Maggie Teyte (s) in English & George Reeves (pf) 10"—D-M444
[Humoresque No. 7, voc. arr.]
Richard Crooks (t) in English & F. Schauwecker (pf) 10"—V-1806
[Tours: Mother o'mine]
Margherita Perras (s) in German
[No. 4] 10"—G-DA4419
DUPLICATIONS: (In English) Paul Robeson, G-B8830; G-K8243; David Lloyd, C-DB2131; In Bohemian: Marta Krasova, G-AM2909: G-AM2910; Ada Sari, G-AM3553

—Arr. Violin & Piano Kresiler
Fritz Kreisler & Carl Lamson
10"—G-DA1057
[Slavonic Dance No. 2]
Yehudi Menuhin & M. Gazelle
10"—G-DA1499
[Debussy-Hartmann: La fille aux cheveux de lin]
Ellen Birgithe Nielsen & Karl Browall
10"—G-DA5250
[Paradis: Sicilienne] (Arr. Hansen)
William Primrose (vla) & Franz Rupp
12"—V-11-9730
[Dvořák: Symphony No. 5—Largo, arr. viola]

—Arr. 'Cello & Piano Grünfeld
Pablo Casals & Blas-Net
(G-DB1399) 12"—V-7193
[Rimsky-Korsakov: Flight of the Bumblebee & Mendelssohn: Song without words]

—Arr. Orchestra
Marek Weber Orch., in C-C118
[Mendelssohn: Spring song, on
G-EG3102]
Frank Black String Ensemble
[Ponce: Estrellita]   10"—C-240M
—No. 5, Tune thy strings, O gypsy
Boh. Struna naladěna
H. Spani (s) in Italian   10"—G-DA1246
[No. 7 & Tirindelli: O Primavera]
—No. 6, Freer is the gypsy (or, In his wide
and ample airy linen vesture)
Boh. Siroke rukary
Ger. In dem seiten Breiten
Povla Frijsh (s) & Celius Dougherty
(pf)   (in VM-789)   10"—V-2158
[No. 1 & No. 7]
—No. 7, The cloudy heights of Tatra
Boh. Dejte klec jestra bu
Ger. Darl des falken schwinge
Povla Frijsh (s) & Celius Dougherty (pf)
(in VM-789)   10"—V-2158
[No. 1 & No. 6]
Hina Spani (s) in Italian
10"—G-DA1246
[No. 5, & Tirindelli: O Primavera]
Leave me alone, Op. 82, No. 1
Boh. Kez duch muj sam
Marta Krasova (s)   12"—G-AN528
[Blodek: In the Well—Young Love, with
Nordenova & Krasova]
When thy sweet glances on me fall, Op. 83,
No. 7
Boh. V te sladke moci oci tvych
(No. 7 of 8 Love Songs, Op. 83)
Marta Krasova (s) & Charvat (pf)
[Gypsy Songs, No. 4]   10"—G-AM2909
Suite, D major, Op. 39 "Czech"   Orchestra
—Polka & Neighbor's Dance
FOK Symphony Orch.—Smetacek
12"—U-G14118
Symphonic Variations, Op. 78   Orchestra
(Theme and 27 Variations: Originally Op.
40)
Queen's Hall Orch.—Henry Wood
3   12"—D-X182/4
[Handel: Rodrigo—Sailor's Dance & Al-
mira—Rigaudon, arr. Wood]

SYMPHONIES

No. 1, D major, Op. 60
Cleveland Orch.—Leinsdorf
5   12"—CM-687†
Czech Philharmonic Orch.—Talich
5   12"—VM-874†
(G-DB5932/6 in GM-363†)
No. 2, D minor, Op. 70
Czech Philharmonic—Talich
(G-DB3685/9)   5   12"—VM-663†
—3rd Mvt. (Scherzo) only
Czech Symphony Orch.—Sejna
12"—ESTA-H5044
No. 3, F major, Op. 76
City of Birmingham Orch.—Weldon
5   12"—C-DX1315/9
[Glinka: Russlan and Ludmilla Overture]
No. 4, G major, Op. 88
Czech Philharmonic Orch.—Talich
5   12"—VM-304†

(G-DB2691/5 in GM-248†)
National Symphony Orch.—Basil Cam-
eron   5   12"—D-K1263/7†
No. 5, E minor, Op. 95 ("From the New
World")
Czech Philharmonic Orch.—Szell
5   12"—VM-469†
(G-C2949/53 in GM-297†)
Philadelphia Orch.—Ormandy
5   12"—CM-570†
Philadelphia Orch.—Stokowski
5   12"—VM-273†
(G-DB2543/7 in GM-251†)
Philharmonia Orch.—Galliera
5   12"—C-DX1399/403
National Symphony Orch.—Karl Rankl
5   12"—D-K1357/61†
DUPLICATIONS: All American Orch.—
Stokowski, CM-416; Rochester Philhar-
monic Orch.—Iturbi, VM-899†; Amster-
dam Concertgebouw Orch.—Mengelberg,
T-SK3190/4: U-G14280/4; Berlin Phil-
harmonic Orch.—Karajan, PD-67519/24:
CET-RR8018/23; FOK Symphony Orch.
—Jeremias,   ESTA-H5077/81;   Berlin
State Opera Orch.—Kleiber, PD-
66909/13; Hallé Orch.—Harty, C-9770/4
—2nd Mvt. (Largo) only Arr. Romberg
Symphony Orch.—Romberg, V-11-9233
Also: (abridged) Victor Orch.—O'Con-
nell, in V-G15
—Paraphrase—"Goin' Home"—William
Arms Fisher
Lawrence Tibbett (b)   12"—V-15549
[Traditional: The Baliff's Daughter]
[Gershwin: Porgy & Bess—I got plenty
o'nuttin', on V-11-8860, in VM-1015]
[Speaks: On the Road to Mandalay, on
G-DB3036]
Also: In Czech: Ruzena Horakova,
ESTA-H5061
See also under "Negro Spiritual Melody"
arr. Kreisler

TRIO (2 Violins & Viola) Op. 74
F. Grinke, D. Martin, W. Forbes
3   12"—D-K891/3

TRIOS (Piano, Violin & 'Cello)
No. 3, F minor, Op. 65   1883
Budapest Trio   4 12"—D-X161/4
No. 4, E minor ("Dumky," or "Elegiac")
Op. 90
Prague Trio
3   10" & 2   12"—U-A & E-12156/60
Louis Kentner, Henry Holst & Anthony
Pini   4 12"—C-DX1017/20
Trio di Trieste   4   12"—T-E9147/50
(The) Wood Dove, Op. 110 Orchestra 1896
Boh. Holoubka   Ger. Die Waldtaube
—Wedding dance only
Boh. Svatebni   Ger. Hochzeitstanz
Berlin Philharmonic Orch.—Kleiber
12"—U-E10278
[Smetana: Triumphal Symphony—
Scherzo, Pt. 3]
Czech Broadcasting Symphony—Jeremias
12"—ESTA-H5039
[Devil and Kate—Prelude, Act III]

(8) Waltzes, Op. 54 Piano
—Arr. Orchestra Seidel
FOK Symphony Orch.—Jeremias
4 12″—ESTA-H5053/6
No. 1, A major Arr. String Quartet
Bohemian (Suk) Quartet
12″—PD-95083
[Suk: Quartet in B, Pt. 7]
Sevcikovo-Lhotskeho Quartet
10″—G-AM2221
—Arr. Orchestra
Czech Philharmonic Orch.—Talich
12″—G-DB5609
[Waltz No. 4, D flat major]
Prague Radiojournal Orch.—Tichy
10″—U-A10105
[Waltz No. 4, D flat major]
—Arr. Violin Prihoda
R. de Barbieri & G. Guastalla
12″—G-AW340
[Sarasate: Romanza Andaluza]
No. 4, D flat major Arr. Orchestra Leopold
Czech Philharmonic Orch.—Talich
[Waltz No. 1, A major] 12″—G-DB5609
Prague Radio journal Orch.—Tichy
[Waltz No. 1, A major] 10″—U-A10105
—Arr. String Quartet
Sevcikovo-Khotskeho Quartet
[Waltz No. 1, A major] 10″—G-AM2221

EBERLIN, Johann Ernst (1702-1762)
*A Bavarian organist and composer highly
esteemed in his day by Mozart. For many years
one of his fugues was attributed to Bach, dem-
onstrating the quality of his work.*

Tenebrae factae sunt Unacc. Chorus in
Latin
Basilica Cho.—Pius Kalt
12″—PD-27137
[Bruckner: Christus factus est, Pader-
born Cathedral Choir]

EGK, Werner (1901-   )
*A German composer of operas and ballet music
who has been conductor at the State Opera in
Berlin.*

Joan of Zarissa Ballet Suite
Orch. de l'Opéra—Egk
2 12″—G-W1517/8
Olympic Hymn
Berlin Cho. & Orch.—Seidler-Winkler
12″—G-EH982
[Strauss: Olympic Hymn & Winter:
Olympic Fanfares]

ELGAR, (Sir) Edward (1857-1934)
*Highly esteemed in England and Germany both
as a composer and conductor, Elgar is known
elsewhere chiefly by his lighter occasional
works.*

**(3) BAVARIAN DANCES, Op. 27 Orches-
tra**
1. The Dance (Sonnenbichl)
2. Lullaby (In Hammersbach)
3. The Marksmen (Bei Murnau)
National Symphony Orch.—Neel
[Dream Children] 2 12″—D-K1295/6

—Nos. 1 & 2 only
London Symphony Orch.—Elgar
12″—G-D1367
CANTATAS
See: Caractacus & Coronation Ode

(La) Capricieuse, Op. 17 Violin & Piano
Arnold Eidus & Gerald Moore
[Sarasate: Habañera] 12″—G-C3582
DUPLICATIONS: Vasa Prihoda, PD-
30034: PD-62672; A. Campoli, D-F3174

CARACTACUS, Op. 35 Cantata 1898

Lament—Oh! my warriors Bass
Peter Dawson 12″—G-C1579
[Mussorgsky: Song of the Flea]
Carissima Orchestra (No opus number)
New Symphony Orch.—Elgar
[Salut d'Amour] 10″—G-E547
Chanson de Nuit, Op. 15, No. 1
**Chanson de Matin, Op. 15, No. 2 Violin &
Piano**
Albert Catterall & Pf. acc.
12″—G-C1839
—Arr. Orchestra Elgar
City of Birmingham Orch.—Weldon
12″—C-DX1198
Royal Albert Hall Orch.—Elgar
12″—G-D1236
Boyd Neel String Orch.—Neel (arr. Reed)
12″—D-K1212
DUPLICATION: A. Sandler Orch.,
C-DB2203
**Cockaigne (In London Town) Concert
Overture, Op. 40 Orchestra**
BBC Symphony Orch.—Elgar
2 12″—G-DB1935/6
[Pomp and Circumstance March No. 4]

**CONCERTO—Violin & Orchestra, B minor,
Op. 61**
Yehudi Menuhin & London Symphony
Orch.—Elgar 6 12″—GM-164†
(G-DB1751/6)

**CONCERTO—'Cello & Orchestra, E minor,
Op. 85**
Pablo Casals & BBC Symphony—Boult
(G-DB6338/41S) 4 12″—GM-394†
**Contrasts (The Gavotte, 1700-1900) Op. 10,
No. 3**
London Philharmonic Orch.—Elgar
12″—G-DB2133
[Serenade, Op. 20, Pt. 3]
Coronation Ode, Op. 44 Cantata
—No. 6 (Finale), Land of Hope and Glory

*This is a vocal arrangement for alto, chorus
and orchestra, of the Trio of the Pomp and
Circumstance March No. 1. Used as the finale
of the Coronation Ode, it was originally issued
separately and has become a sort of unofficial
British national anthem. For recordings see:
Land of Hope and Glory.*

Dream Children, Op. 43, No. 2 Orchestra
National Symphony Orch.—Neel
12″—D-K1296

[Bavarian Dances, Pt. 3]
Hallé Orch.—Harty 12"—C-DX325
[Enigma Variations, Pt. 7]

DREAM OF GERONTIUS, Op. 38 Oratorio
Complete recording
Huddersfield Choral Society, Heddle Nash
(t), Gladys Ripley (ms), Dennis Noble
(b), Norman Walker (bs) & Liverpool
Philharmonic Orch.—Sargent
12 12"—G-C3435/46†
Elegy, Op. 58 String Orchestra
Hallé Orch.—Barbirolli 10"—G-B9567
[Fauré: Shylock—Nocturne]
Enigma Variations, Op. 36 Orchestra
BBC Symphony Orch.—Boult
(G-DB2800/2†) 3 12"—VM-475†
National Symphony Orch.—Sargent
4 12"—D-K1351/4†
[Pomp and Circumstance March No. 5]
Hallé Orch.—Harty
[Dream Children] 4 12"—C-DX322/5†
Falstaff, Op. 68 Symphonic Study Orchestra
London Symphony Orch.—Elgar
(G-DB1621/4) 4 12"—GM-155†
Idyll Organ
Herbert Dawson (Kingsway Hall)
[Martin: Evensong] 10"—G-B2263
Imperial March, Op. 32 Orchestra 1897
BBC Symphony Orch.—Boult
12"—G-DB3163
[Meyerbeer: Prophète—Coronation
March]
BBC Symphony Orch.—Boult
(in VM-929†) 12"—V-11-8415
[Holst: Planets, Pt. 7—Jupiter, Pt. 2,
Toronto Symphony—MacMillan]
Introduction & Allegro for Strings, Op. 47
BBC Symphony Orch.—Boult
[Sospiri, Op. 70] 2 12"—G-DB3198/9
String Orch.—Boyd Neel
2 12"—D-K775/6
Hallé Orch.—Barbirolli
2 12"—G-C3669/70
String Orch.—Barbirolli
2 12"—G-C1694/5

(THE) KINGDOM, Op. 51 Oratorio
The Sun goeth down. Sop.
Isobel Baillie & Philharmonia Orch.—
Sargent 12"—C-DX1443
Land of Hope and Glory Alto, Chorus &
Orchestra
*This vocal arrangement of the Trio of the
Pomp & Circumstance March No. 1 is also used
as the Finale of the Coronation Ode, Op. 44.*
Essie Ackland, Chorus, Organ & Band
12"—G-C1848
[Sullivan: Onward, Christian Soldiers]
Clara Butt, Chorus & Band
12"—C-DX730
[Foster: Old Folks at Home]
Dennis Noble & Massed Orch.
[England, my England] 12"—G-C2898
Nancy Evans & Cho. with Coldstream
Guards Band 12"—G-C3191
[Song of Liberty, Dennis Noble]

DUPLICATIONS: Jeanette MacDonald,
V-18317; Oscar Natzke & Chorus,
P-R2718; Astra Desmond, D-K1022; G.
Little, D-K738
Nursery Suite Orchestra
**Aubade; The Serious Doll; Busy-ness;
The Sad Doll; The Merry Doll; The Wagon Passes; Dreaming-Envoi (Coda)**
London Symphony Orch.—Elgar
2 12"—G-D1998/9
—No. 2 (The Serious Doll) only
Liverpool Philharmonic Orch.—Sargent
12"—C-DX1120
[Harty: A John Field Suite, Pt. 5]

ORATORIOS
See: Dream of Gerontius; The Kingdom

POMP AND CIRCUMSTANCE, Op. 39
(6) Military Marches Orchestra
No. 1, D major ("Land of Hope and
Glory")
Toronto Symphony Orch.—MacMillan
(in VM-911) 12"—V-11-8226
[No. 2] (G-C3328)
London Symphony Orch.—Braithwaite
[No. 2] 12"—D-K1140
BBC Symphony Orch.—Elgar
[No. 2] 12"—G-DB1801
CBS Symphony Orch.—Barlow
12"—C-71441D
[Trad.: Londonderry Air]
DUPLICATIONS: Boston "Pops" Orch.—
Fiedler, V-11885: G-C3236; London Philharmonic Orch.—Wood, C-70364D:
C-DX965; Berlin State Opera Orch.—
Melichar, PD-25070; Chicago Symphony
—Stock, V-6648; Tivoli Orch.—Jensen,
TONO-X25009; Coldstream Guards Band,
G-C3078 & C-9080; BBC Military Band,
C-DX589; RAF Band, C-DB1982:
G-RAF1
—Arr. 2 Pianos
Rawicz & Landauer, C-DB2066
No. 2, A minor
Toronto Symphony Orch.—MacMillan
(in VM-911) 12"—V-11-8226
[No. 1] (G-C3328)
London Symphony Orch.—Braithwaite
[No. 1] 12"—D-K1140
BBC Symphony Orch.—Elgar
[No. 1] 12"—G-DB1801
DUPLICATIONS: Berlin State Opera
Orch.—Melichar, PD-25070; BBC Military Band, C-DX589
No. 3, C minor
London Symphony Orch.—Braithwaite
[No. 4] 12"—D-K1141
London Symphony Orch.—Elgar
[No. 4] 12"—G-D1301
Toronto Symphony Orch.—MacMillan
[No. 4] (in VM-911) 12"—V-11-8227
DUPLICATION: BBC Military Band,
C-DX589
No. 4, G major (See also "Song of Liberty")
Toronto Symphony Orch.—MacMillan
[No. 3] (in VM-911) 12"—V-11-8227
London Symphony Orch.—Braithwaite
[No. 3] 12"—D-K1141

London Symphony Orch.—Elgar
[No. 3]   12"—**G-D1301**
DUPLICATIONS: BBC Sym. Orch.—El-
gar, G-DB1936; London Philharmonic
Orch.—Wood, C-70364D: C-DX965;
BBC Military Band, C-DX589; Cold-
stream Guards Band, G-C3078; RAF
Band, C-DB1982; Grenadier Guards
Band, D-K738
—**Arr. 2 Pianos**
Rawicz & Landauer, C-DB2066
No. 5, C major
National Symphony Orch.—Sargent
                                12"—**D-K1354**
[Enigma Variations, Pt. 7]
Salut d'amour. Morceau Mignon, Op. 12
Ger. **Liebesgrüss**
*(Originally for small orchestra, but also pub-
lished in many arrangements.)*
New Symphony Orch.—Elgar
[Carissima]   10"—**G-E547**
DUPLICATIONS: Light Symphony Orch.,
C-DB2082; Sandler Orch., C-5685; Marek
Weber Orch., in C-C115
—**Arr. Violin & Piano**
Yehudi Menuhin & Adolph Baller
                                10"—**V-10-1220**
[Debussy-Hartmann: La fille aux
cheveux de lin]
Vasa Prihoda & Otto Graef
                                12"—**PD-30033**
[Dvořák-Wilhelmj: Humoresque]
(Also on PD-95369)
DUPLICATIONS: Max Ladscheck, PD-
10239; Alfredo Campoli, D-F3174; A.
Sammons, D-F7530
Other Arrangements:
Gaspar Cassadó (vlc), T-A2083;
U-A14233
Vocal Arrangement
Jussi Björling (in Swedish), G-X3622

SEA PICTURES, Op. 37 Contralto & Orch.
1. **Sea Slumber Song**
2. **In Haven (Capri)**
3. **Sabbath Morning at Sea**
4. **Where Corals Lie**
5. **The Swimmer**
Gladys Ripley & Philharmonia Orch.—
Weldon   3 12"—**G-C3498/500**
[Haydn: Hark what I tell to thee—The
spirit song]
Serenade, E minor, Op. 20
String Orchestra 1890
London Philharmonic Orch.—Elgar
                        2 12"—**G-DB2132/3**
[Contrasts, Op. 10, No. 2]
Boyd Neel String Orch.—Neel
                        2 12"—**D-K1196/7**

SONGS In English
See also under: Caractacus; Salut d'-
amour (arr.); Sea Pictures
Is She Not Passing Fair?
David Lloyd (t) & Gerald Moore (pf)
                                10"—**C-DB2217**
[Young—arr. Wilson: Phyllis Has Such
Charming Graces]

Song of Liberty
(Pomp & Circumstance No. 4—Trio)
Dennis Noble, with Chorus and H. M.
Coldstream Guards Band
                                12"—**G-C3191**
[Land of Hope and Glory, Nancy Evans]
DUPLICATION: Astra Desmond,
D-K1022
Sospiri, Op. 70 String Orchestra 1914
BBC Symphony Orch.—Boult
                                12"—**G-DB3199**
[Introduction and Allegro, Pt. 3]
String Orchestra & Harp.—Goehr
                                10"—**C-DB1300**
[R. Strauss: Le Bourgeois Gentilhomme
—Intermezzo] (C-DB1784)
(in Columbia History of Music, Vol.
V: CM-361)

SUITES See: Nursery Suite & Wand of
Youth Suites

SYMPHONIES
No. 1, A flat major, Op. 55 Orchestra
No recording available
No. 2, E flat major, Op. 63 Orchestra
BBC Orch.—Boult   6 12"—**GM-378†**
(G-DB6190/5)
Wand of Youth Suites Orchestra
No. 1, Op. 1a
—**Fairy Pipers only**
Victor Orch., in V-E78
No. 2, Op. 1b
—**Moths and Butterflies & The Tame
Bears only**
Victor Orch., in V-E78

MISCELLANEOUS
See: Chopin: Sonata No. 2—Funeral
March (Arr. Elgar)

ELLINGTON, "Duke" (Edward K.)
(1889-   )
*A prolific composer and arranger of popular
songs.*
See current catalogues for listings

ENESCO, Georges (1881-   )
A Romanian violinist, pianist and conductor.
Poème roumain, Op. 1 Orchestra
Eng. **Romanian Poem**
Bucharest Philharmonic.—Georgescu
                                12"—**G-AN305**
Romanian Rhapsodies, Op. 11 Orchestra
No. 1, A major
Chicago Symphony Orch.—Stock
                        2 12"—**CX-203†**
[Reznicek: Donna Diana—Overture]
Philadelphia Orch.—Ormandy
        (in VM-830†) 12"—**V-18201**
(G-DB6130)
Symphony Orch.—Stokowski
                                12"—**V-12-0069**
Bucharest Philharmonic—Georgescu
                        2 10"—**G-AM1986/7**
DUPLICATION: Detroit Sym. Orch.—
Kolar, D-23172; D-M493
—**Arr. 2 Pfs.**
Arthur Whittemore & Jack Lowe
                                12"—**V-11-8515**

No. 2, D major
National Symphony—Hans Kindler
(in VM-830†) 12"—V-18202
Sonata No. 3, A minor, Op. 25
(On Romanian Themes) Violin & Piano
Yehudi Menuhin & Hepzibah Menuhin
3 12"—G-DB2739/41

ENGEL, Carl, (1883-1941)

The editor of "The Musical Quarterly," president of G. Schirmer, Inc., and former Chief of the Music Division of the Library of Congress, Carl Engel composed chamber music, songs and choral works.

Triptych Violin & Piano 1920
William Kroll & Frank Sheridan
3 12"—SCH-15

ENNA, August (1859-1939)

A prolific Danish composer, chiefly noted for his numerous operas, which have remained in the repertory of the Royal Theatre, Copenhagen.

(THE) LITTLE MATCH GIRL Opera in
Danish 1897
Dan. Den lille Pige med Svovlstikkerne
Vocal Selections
Edith Oldrup Pedersen (s) 12"—G-Z239
Overture Orchestra
Royal Theatre Orch., Copenhagen—
Hye-Knudsen 12"—G-Z240

ERBACH, Christian (1573-c.1628)

Successor to Hassler as town organist of Augsburg in 1602, Erbach was one of the lesser-known composers of motets in early 17th century Germany.

Canzone, G major Organ
Alfred Sittard (St. Michael's organ,
Hamburg) 10"—PD-10257
[Sittard: Chorale—Nun sich her Tag]

ERKEL, Franz (1810-1893)

One of the most renowned native composers, in Hungary, Erkel introduced the folk element into Hungarian opera. He composed the national anthem, and his "Hunyadi László" is the most frequently performed opera in Hungary. There are probably other recordings of his work in Hungarian catalogues.

Himnusz Hungarian National Hymn
Chorus & Orchestra
Palestrina Choir & Orch.—Rekai
10"—G-AM1786
[Sazbados: Hiszekegy]
—Arr. Orchestra
Budapest Philharmonic Orch.—
Dohnányi 10"—G-AM1283
[Egressy: Szozat]
(Also: G-AM1281)

OPERAS In Hungarian

BANK BAN 1861
Orchestral Selections (Fantasia)
Budapest Chamber Orch.—Komor
12"—G-AN444
Bordal Baritone
Imre Pallo 10"—G-AM2523
[Hunyadi László—Czardas, Orch.]

HUNYADI LASZLO 1844
Overture Orchestra
Budapest Chamber Orch.—Komor
2 10"—G-AM2520/1
Budapest Philharmonic Orch.—
Ferencsik 2 12"—RAD-SP8013/4
Dol Dauber Orch. 12"—G-AN474
Csardas Orchestra
Budapest Chamber Orch.—Komor
10"—G-AM2523
[Bank Ban—Bordal, I. Pallo]

ERLANGER, Baron Frederic d' (1868-1943)

An ecclectic composer best known for his melodious ballet scores.

(Les) Cent Baisers—Ballet Suite Orch.
Eng.: The Hundred Kisses
London Symphony Orch.—Dorati
2 12"—VM-511

ERLEBACH, Philipp Heinrich (1657-1714)

A German Kapellmeister at the court of Rudolstadt in 1697 and a composer of concerted music.

Harmonische Freude (Fragments)
(Airs in German, acc. pf., 2 or 3 Vls.,
Vla. & Vlc.: "realization" by Mlle. Claude
Crussard)
—Was quälet; Trocknet euch; Nur Getrost;
Schwaches Herz
Yvon Le Marc'Hadour (b) & Musique
Intime Ensemble 12"—BAM-2
Ouverturen—Suite in C major
(Arr. Max Seiffert)
Overture; Air-Trio; Air-Ballet; Air- Gavotte; Air-le sommeil; Air-la réjouissance
Scheck-Wenzinger Chamber Orch.
12"—G-EH1221

EULENBURG, Philipp (1847-1921)

A minor German composer, best known for his songs.

Rosenlieder Song Cycle in German
Marcel Wittrisch (t) 12"—G-EH1002

FALCONIERI, Andrea (c.1600-1650)

One of the Italian composers of villanelle, that early harmonic-type part-song that influenced the Elizabethan madrigal and the French chanson.

AIRS In Italian
Begli occhi lucenti
Bella fanciulla
Cara è la rosa
Salvatore Salvati (t) & guitar acc.
[Milanuzzi: Four Airs] 12"—MIA-3
—Bella fanciulla only
Giuseppe De Luca (b) & P. Cimara
(pf), in D-U1
O bellissimi capelli (Trans. P. Floridia)
Ezio Pinza (bs) & Fritz Kitzinger (pf)
(in VM-766) 12"—V-17916
[Giordani: Caro mio ben; Sarti: Lungi
dal caro bene; Buononcini: Pupille nere]

FALL, Leo (1873-1925)

A minor Austrian composer of popular operettas.

OPERETTAS In German

Bruderlein Fein
(Die) Dollar Prinzessin
(Der) Fidele Bauer
(Die) Kaiserin
(Die) Geschiedene Frau
(Der) Liebe Augustin
Madame Pompadour
(Die) Rose Von Stamboul
(Die) Spanische Nachtigall
See current catalogues for listings

FALLA, Manuel de (1876-1946)
*Like Albéniz and Granados a pupil of Pedrell,
Falla was the most distinguished Spanish composer of recent years. His operas and opera-
ballets are some of the most familiar of modern
music; and his concerto for harpsichord and
chamber ensemble has been called the connect-
ing link between contemporary Spanish music
and Victoria and Cabezón.*

(EL) AMOR BRUJO Ballet
Orchestra & Mezzo-soprano, in Spanish
Eng. Love the Sorcerer (Love the Magician, or Wedded by Witchcraft)
1. Introducción & escena 2. En la cueva
3. La noche 4. Canción del amor dolido
5. Los sortilegios 6. A media noche
7. Danza ritual del fuego 8. Escena
9. Canción del fuego fatuo 10. El aparecido
11. Danza del terror 12. El circulo magico
13. Romanza del pescador 14. Pantomima
15. Danza del juego de amor
16. Finale—Las Campanas del Amanecer

Complete recordings
Carol Brice (c) with Pittsburgh Sym-
phony Reiner   3 12"—CM-633†
Nan Merriman (c) with Hollywood Bowl
Orch.—Stokowski   3 12"—VM-1089†

—Selections
Including 1, 2, 4, 10, 11, 12, 7, 8, 9, 14, 15,
16 only
Argentinita (vocal) & Ballet Theatre
Orch.—Dorati   3 10"—D-A390
Orchestral Suite only (Vocal numbers
omitted)
Symphony Orch.—Pedro Morales
                       3 12"—CM-108
National Symphony Orch.—Jorda
                     3 12"—D-K1332/4†

Individual excerpts
No. 7, Danza ritual del fuego Orchestra
Eng. Ritual Fire Dance
Fr. Danse rituelle du feu
Boston "Pops" Orch.—Fiedler
                       12"—V-12160
[Gade: Jalousie—Tango tzigane]
[Ravel: Bolero, Pt. 3, on G-C2955]
All American Orch.—Stokowski
                       12"—C-11879D
[Novacek: Perpetual motion]
DUPLICATIONS: Andre Kostelanetz
Orch., C-7519M in CM-681; Guarino
Orch., G-AV684; Lamoureux Orch.—
Wolff, PD-566019: PD-566142; Sym-
phony Orch.—Coppola, G-D1453:
G-W891; EIAR Orch.—Ferrero,
CET-BB25016

—Arr. Piano
Artur Rubinstein   10"—V-10-1326
[No. 11, Danza del terror]
(Older recording, V-1596: G-DA1151)
José Iturbi   10"—V-10-1135
[No. 10, Danza del terror] (G-DA1853)
Roger Machado   12"—C-LFX675
[Granados: Spanish Dance No. 4]
Oscar Levant
         (in CM-560) 12"—C-72079D
[Lecuona: Malagueña & Poulenc:
Pastourelle]
DUPLICATIONS: France Ellegaard, PD-
67919; Alexander Brailowsky, PD-
95142; Z. Jilek, ESTA-F5198; G. de
Lausney, PAT-X5507; G. Werschenska,
TONO-A113

—Arr. 2 Pianos
Pierre Luboschutz & Genia Nemenoff
                       10"—V-2214
[Shostakovich: Age of Gold—Polka]
Rawicz & Landauer   10"—C-DB2324
[Debussy: Arabesque No. 1]

No. 11, Danza del terror Arr. Piano
Artur Rubinstein   10"—V-10-1326
[No. 7, Danza ritual del fuego]
(Older recording on V-1596: G-DA1151)
José Iturbi   10"—V-10-1135
[No. 7, Danza ritual del fuego]
(G-DA1853)

No. 13, Romanza del pescador Orchestra
—Arr. Piano
Harriét Cohen   12"—C-DX1131
[Andaluza & Sombrero de tres picos—
Danza de molinero]

No. 14, Pantomime Orchestra
—Arr. Violin & Piano Kochanski
Jascha Heifetz & E. Bay, in VM-1158
DUPLICATIONS: E. Telmanyi, TONO-
A102; G. Bustabo, C-LWX363

Andaluza Piano
Harriet Cohen   12"—C-DX1131
[Sombrero de tres picos—Miller Dance
& Amor Brujo—Fisherman's Tale]
Emma Boynet   10"—PAT-PG3
[Fauré: Impromptu, F minor]
DUPLICATIONS: A van Barentzen,
G-W940; W. Murdoch, D-F3584

—Arr. Castanets & Orchestra
La Argentina & Ballet Orch.
[Albéniz: Sevilla]   10"—O-188755

(7) Canciones Populares españoles
Voice & Piano
In Spanish (Blas de Laserna)
Eng. Seven Popular Spanish Songs
(The instrumental version of these songs
is called "Suite populaire espagnole")
1. El paño moruno
2. Seguidilla murciana
3. Asturiana
4. Jota
5. Nana (Berceuse)
6. Canción
7. Polo

Complete recordings
Conchita Supervia (ms) & F. Marshall
(pf) (P-PO153/5)   3 10"—P-P52
DUPLICATION: Nancy Evans,
D-X197/8

Individual numbers
No. 1, El paño moruno
  Supervia, P-PO153; Evans, D-X197
  Gina Bera (c) & pf. acc.
  [Nos. 3, 5, 7]   10″—PAT-PG97
No. 2, Seguidilla murciana
  Supervia, P-PO153; Evans, D-X197
  Ninon Vallin (s) & pf. acc.
  [Nos. 4 & 6]   10″—PAT-PG71
No. 3, Asturiana
  Supervia, P-PO154; Evans, D-X197
  Gina Bera (c) & pf. acc.
  [Nos. 1, 5, 7]   10″—PAT-PG97
No. 4, Jota
  Supervia, P-PO154; Evans, D-X198
  Gianna Pederzini (ms) & pf. acc.
                          10″—G-DA5425
  [Pieraccini: Beppino nubacuore]
  Ninon Vallin (s) & pf. acc.
  [Nos. 2 & 5]   10″—PAT-PG71
  DUPLICATION: Armand Crabbé,
  D-K994
—Arr. Violin & Piano Kochanski
  Jascha Heifetz & Emanuel Bay
                          10″—V-10-1324
  [Debussy: La fille aux cheveux de lin,
  trans. Hartmann]
  (Older recording on V-6858; with Grieg:
  Puck & Mendelssohn: Auf Flügeln des
  Gesanges)
  DUPLICATIONS: M. Quiroga, PAT-
  X9938; Fritz Kreisler, G-DA1157
No. 5, Nana French, Berceuse
  Supervia, P-PO155; Evans, D-X197
  Ninon Vallin (s) & pf. acc.
  [Nos. 2 & 4]   10″—PAT-PG71
  Gina Bera (c) & Lucien Petitjean (pf)
  [Nos. 1, 3 & 7]   10″—PAT-PG97
  Olga Coelho (s) & guitar acc. in
  Hargail-HN700
No. 6. Canción
  Supervia, P-PO155; Evans, D-X198
No. 7, Polo
  Supervia, P-PO155; Evans, D-X198
  Gina Bera (c) & Lucien Petitjean (pf)
  [Nos. 1, 3 & 5]   10″—PAT-PG97

CONCERTO—Harpsichord, Flute, Oboe,
  Clarinet, Violin & 'Cello
  Manuel de Falla, Moyse, Bonneau, Go-
  deau, Darrieux & Cruque 2 12″—CX-9†
Cubana Piano (from "Pièces espagnoles")
  Lucette Descaves-Truc
       (in VM-725)   12″—V-13515
  (G-DB5097)
  [Noches en los jardines de España, Pt. 5]
Jota See: Canciónes populares—No. 4
Homenaje (Homage for the Tomb of
  Debussy) Guitar
  Albert Harris   10″—C-DB1305
  [Hindemith: Scherzo for violin & viola]
  (in Columbia History of Music, Vol. V:
  CM-361)
  (C-DB1789)

NOCHES EN LOS JARDINES DE ESPANA
  (Impressiones sinfonicas)
  Piano & Orchestra
  Eng. Nights in the Garden of Spain

En el Generalife; Danza lejana; En los jar-
  dines de la Sierra de Córdoba
  Clifford Curzon & National Symphony
  Orch.—Jorda   3 12″—D-ED10†
  (D-K1158/60)
  Jacqueline Blanchard & Orchestre de la
  Suisse Romande—Ansermet
                       3 12″—O-8785/7
  Lucette Descaves-Truc & Paris Conserva-
  tory Orch.—Bigot   3 12″—VM-725
  [Cubana]   (G-DB5095/7)
  Manuel Navarra & Orquesta Betica da
  Camara—Halffter   3 12″—CM-156
  A. van Barentzen & Orch.—Coppola
                       3 12″—G-W938/40
Psyché Mezzo-Soprano, Flute, Harp,, Oboe,
  Clarinet, Violin & 'Cello 1924 In French
  Leila Ben Sedira & Jamet Instrumental
  Group   12″—G-W1507
  [Rameau: Hippolyte et Aricie—
  Rossignols amoureux]

(EL) RETABLO DE MAESE PEDRO
  Puppet Opera 1923
  No recordings traced

(EL) SOMBRERO DE TRES PICOS
  Ballet Orchestra
  Eng. The Three-Cornered Hat
  Fr. Le Tricorne
—Three Dances
1. Los Vecinos (The Neighbors)
2. Danza del molinero (The Miller's Dance)
3. Danza Final (Final Dance)
  National Symphony Orch.—Jorda
                       2 12″—D-K1335/6†
  Boston "Pops" Orch.—Fiedler
                       2 10″—VM-505†
  (G-B8887/8) (G-K8317/8)
  (G-EG6771/2)
  Philharmonia Orch.—Galliera
                       2 12″—C-DX1258/9
  Madrid Symphony—Arbós
                       2 12″—CX-38†
—Nos. 2 & 3 only
  EIAR Orch.—Ferrero
                       12″—CET-BB25023
—No. 2 (Danza del molinero) only
—Arr. Piano
  Harriet Cohen   12″—C-DX1131
  [Amor Brujo—Fisherman's Tale &
  Andaluza]
  Oscar Levant
       (in CM-560)   12″—C-72081D
  [Poulenc: Mouvements perpetuels;
  Albéniz: Tango, D major]
—Arr. Violin & Piano Szigeti
  Ida Haendel & Adela Kotowska
                       10″—D-M603
  [Ibert: Le petit ane blanc]
  Joseph Szigeti & pf. acc.
       (in CX-188)   12″—C-70744D
  [Milhaud-Lévy: Saudades do Brazil—
  Sumaré]

SONGS In Spanish
  See under: Amor Brujo; Canciones
  Populares

(LA) VIDA BREVE Opera 2 Acts 1913 (Composed 1905)

Interlude & Danza No. 1 Orchestra
EIAR Symphony—Ferrero
    12"—CET-BB25043
Berlin Philharmonic—Wolff
    12"—PD-66724

—Danza Nos. 1 & 2 (with chorus) Act II
Théatre de la Monnaie, Brussels, Cho. & Orch.—Bastin
   (in CM-146) 12"—C-67818D
(C-D11092)

—Danza No. 1 only
Eng. **Spanish Dance** Fr. **Danse espagnole**
St. Louis Symphony—Golschmann
    12"—V-11-8592
[Shostakovich: Age of Gold—Polka & Russian Dance]
Symphony Orch.—Coppola
    12"—G-D1453
[Amor Brujo—Danza ritual del fuego] (G-W891)
DUPLICATION: EIAR Orch.—Ferrero, CET-CB20179

—Arr. Violin & Piano Kreisler
Fritz Kreisler & Franz Rupp
    10"—V-1891
[Kreisler: Liebesfreud] (G-DA1630)
(Older recording on G-DA1009)
Jascha Heifetz & Emanuel Bay
    12"—V-14625
[Szymanowski: Le Roi Roger—Chant de Roxane]
[Bazzini: Ronde des Lutins, on G-DB3535]
Yehudi Menuhin & A. Balsam
    10"—G-DA1280
[Rimsky-Korsakov: Flight of the Bumblebee & Debussy: Minstrels]
Ginette & Jean Neveu 10"—G-DA1865
[Dinicu: Hora Staccato]
Jacques Thibaud & G. de Lausnay
    12"—G-DB1338
[Saint-Saëns: Le Déluge—Prélude]
DUPLICATIONS: René Benedetti, C-D13037; Ida Haendel, D-K1073; D-K1214

—Arr. Castanets & Orchestra
La Argentina & Ballet Orch.
    10"—O-188683
[Granados: Goyescas—Intermezzo]

—Arr. 2 Pianos Kovacs
Bartlett & Robertson
[Lecuona: Andalucia] 10"—C-17516D

FARMER, John (c.1565-c.1605)
An organist at Christ Church, Dublin, who composed many madrigals. He was also one of the most important contributors to Thomas East's "Whole Book of Psalms," 1592.

Fair Phyllis I saw thee sitting all alone
4-Pt. Madrigal
St. George's Singers, unacc.
    10"—C-5717
[Gibbons: Silver Swan & Weelkes: As Vesta was descending]
(in Columbia History of Music, Vol. 1: CM-231)

Fleet Street Choir—Lawrence
    12"—D-K1046
[Wood: Music when soft voices die; Tompkins: See, see the shepherds]

FARNABY, Giles, (c.1560-1600)
An adept composer of madrigals, rivaling Gesualdo in harmonic inventiveness, Farnaby was also one of the best writers of virginal music, being considered second only to William Byrd.

HARPSICHORD (VIRGINALS) PIECES
His Conceit (Fitzwilliam Virginal Book No. 273)
Bartlett & Robertson (Arr. 2 Pfs.))
  (in CX-256) 12"—C-72127D
[A Toye; Byrd: Earl of Salisbury's Pavane & Variations on John, come kiss me now] (C-DX1340)
His Dreame (Fitzwilliam Virginal Book No. 260)
Dolmetsch Group, Virginals
    10"—C-5713
[His Rest; A Toy; Bull: King's Hunt]
(In Col. Hist. of Music, Vol. I: CM-231)
Bartlett & Robertson (arr. 2 pfs.)
  (in CX-256) 12"—C-72128D
[Tower Hill Jigge; Tune for 2 virginals; Peereson: Fall of the leafe; Bull: King's Hunting Jig] (C-DX1341)
His Humor (Fitzwilliam Virginal Book No. 196)
George Dyson 12"—C-D40139
(in illustrations for lecture No. 29 "Early Keyboard Music"—International Educational Society series)
[Bull: King's Hunting Jig]
His Rest—Galiard (Fitzwilliam Virginal Book No. 195)
Dolmetsch Group, virginals 10"—C-5713
[A Toye; His dreame; Bull: King Hunt's]
(in Col. Hist. of Music, Vol. I: CM-231)
(The) New Sa-Hoo (Fitzwilliam Virginal Book No. 148)
Pauline Aubert
   (in Vol. II) 12"—AS-14
[A Toye; Byrd: The Bells; Peereson: The Fall of the Leafe]
A Toye (Fitzwilliam Virginal Book No. 270)
Dolmetsch Group, virginals 10"—C-5713
[His dreame; His rest; Bull: King's Hunt]
(in Col. Hist. of Music, Vol. I: CM-231)
Pauline Aubert
   (in Vol. II) 12"—AS-14
[The New Sa-hoo; Byrd: The Bells; Peereson: Fall of the Leafe]
Bartlett & Robertson (Arr. 2 Pfs.)
  (in CX-256) 12"—C-72127D
[His Conceit; Byrd: Variations on John, come kiss me now & Earl of Salisbury's Pavane] (C-DX1340)
Tower Hill Jigge (Fitzwilliam Virginal Book No. 245)
Bartlett & Robertson (Arr. 2 Pfs.)
  (in CX-256) 12"—C-72128D
[Tune for 2 virginals; His dreame; Peereson: Fall of the Leafe; Bull: King's Hunting Jigge] (C-DX1341)

—Arr. Pipes: Pipers Guild Quartet,
C-DB2282
Tune for 2 Virginals (Fitzwilliam Virginal
Book No. 55)
Bartlett & Robertson (Arr. 2 Pfs.)
(in CX-256) 12"—C-72128D
[His dreame; Tower Hill Jigge; Bull:
King's Hunting Jigge & Peereson: Fall
of the Leafe] (C-DX1341)

FAURE, Gabriel (1845-1924)

*One of the most sensitive French composers of
the turn of the century, Fauré was also important as a teacher of composition. His pupils include Maurice Ravel, Nadia Boulanger, Georges
Enesco and many others. Known outside of
France chiefly by his songs and chamber music,
Fauré also wrote incidental music for the theatre and religious choral works.*

Andante, Op. 75 Violin & Piano
Denise Soriano & M. Tagliafero
12"—PAT-PAT10
[Bach-Kreisler: Praeludium]
Après un rêve See under Songs
Ballade, Op. 19 Piano & Orchestra
Kathleen Long & National Symphony
Orch.—Boyd Neel 2 12"—D-K1130/1
Marguerite Long & Symphony Orch.—
Gaubert 2 12"—C-LFX54/5
G. Farago & Budapest Philharmonic
Orch.—Ferencsik
2 12"—RAD-SP8011/2

(13) BARCAROLLES Piano

No. 2, Op. 41
Kathleen Long 10"—D-M575
No. 3, Op. 42
M. T. Fourneau 10"—C-LF231
No. 6, Op. 70
Marguerite Long 12"—C-LFX567
[Nocturne No. 4]
Carmen Guilbert 10"—PAT-X98135
[Debussy: Bruyères]
Berceuse, Op. 16 Violin & Piano
Jacques Thibaud & Alfred Cortot
12"—G-DB1654
[Chausson: Concerto, Pt. 9]
DUPLICATIONS: Henry Merckel,
G-L1015; Lucien Schwartz, G-L881; J.
Gautier, O-166039; Y. Curti, PAT-PA283;
Denise Soriano, PAT-PAT155
Cantique de Jean Racine, Op. 11
Martha Angelici (s), Germaine Cernay
(ms), Pierre Giannotti (b), Julien Gio-
vanetti (t) with Noëlie Pierront (organ)
& Orch.—Cébron 10"—LUM-30080
Dolly, Op. 56 Suite for Piano—4 Hands
Berceuse; Mi-a-ao; Le Jardin de Dolly;
Kitty-Valse; Tendresse; Le Pas espagnol
Anita Siegal & Babeth Léonet
12"— & 10"—C-DFX193 & C-DF1665
Dolly See also under Songs
Elégie, Op. 24 'Cello & Piano
A. Navarra, O-188939; A. Lévy, O-166051
—Arr. 'Cello & Orchestra
Jean Bedetti & Boston Symphony Orch.
—Koussevitsky 12"—G-DB3210
Impromptu pour harpe, Op. 86
Lilly Laskine 12"—G-L993

(6) IMPROMPTUS Piano

No. 2, F. minor, Op. 31
Marguerite Long 10"—C-LF126
[Impromptu No. 5]
Emma Boynet 10"—PAT-PG3
[Falla: Andaluza]
Eileen Joyce 12"—P-E11372
[Liszt: Liebestraum] (O-123833)
Gaby Casadesus, in VOX-163
No. 5, Op. 102
Marguerite Long 10"—C-LF126
[Impromptu No. 2]
Robert Casadesus 12"—C-LFX401
[Prélude No. 5 & Séverac: Cerdaña]
No. 6, Op. 86 A piano version of the Im-
promptu for Harp.
Maria Mater Gratiae, Op. 47, No. 2
Motet 2 Sopranos & Chorus in Latin
Doniau-Blanc, Franck & Pascal Quartet
[Franck: Ave Maria] 10"—LUM-30009
Masques et Bergamasques, Suite, Op. 112
Symphony Orch.—M. F. Gaillard
2 10"—O-188929/30

(13) NOCTURNES Piano

No. 3, A flat major, Op. 33, No. 3
Carmen Guilbert 12"—PAT-PAT114
[Theme and Variations, Pt. 3]
Artur Rubinstein 12"—G-DB6467
[Poulenc: Mouvements perpetuels]
No. 4, E flat major, Op. 36 1885
Emma Boynet 10"—PAT-PG3
Marguerite Long 12"—C-LFX567
[Barcarolle No. 6, Op. 70]
No. 6, Op. 63
Kathleen Long 10"—D-M574
Suzanne Gyr 12"—G-DB10079
Jean Doyen 12"—G-DB5029
Marguerite Long 12"—C-LFX437
Carmen Guilbert 12"—PAT-PAT55
No. 7, Op. 74
Jacques Fevrier 12"—C-LFX652
Noël: Il est né, le divin enfant
S. Laydeker & J. Renault (sops.)
Organ & orch.—Andolfi
10"—PAT-PA987
Papillon 'Cello & Piano
B. Michelin & T. Janopoulo
[Après un rêve] 10"—C-LF241
André Navarra & pf. acc.
10"—O-188931
[Saint-Saëns: Le Cygne]
Pavane, Op. 50 Chorus & Orchestra
Philharmonia Chorus & Orch.—
Sargent 12"—C-DX1369
Paris Conservatory Orch.—Münch
(No Cho.) (in D-ED37†) 12"—D-K1644
[Roussel: Petite Suite, Pt. 3]

PELLEAS ET MELISANDE Orchestra
Op. 80
(Incidental Music to Maeterlinck's
Drama)
1. Prélude 2. Fileuse 3. Sicilienne
4. Death of Mélisande

Nos. 1, 2 & 4 only
  Boston Symphony Orch.—
  Koussevitzky   2 12"—VM-941†
  [Rimsky-Korsakov: Dubinushka, Op. 69]
Nos. 1, 2 & 3 only
  Berlin Philharmonic Orch.—Wolff
  [Ravel: Pavane]   2 12"—PD-66725/6
No. 3 only
  Berlin Philharmonic Orch.—Wolff
                           12"—PD-66727
  [Bizet: Carmen, Prélude to Act I]
  Chicago Symphony Orch.—Defauw
                           12"—V-11-9447
  [Stravinsky: Feu d'artifice]
Prélude No. 5, D minor
  Robert Casadesus   12"—C-LFX401
  [Impromptu No. 5; Séverac: Cerdaña
  No. 5]

QUARTET—String, Op. 121
  No recording available

QUARTETS—Piano & Strings
No. 1, C minor, Op. 15
  Robert Casadesus, J. Calvet, L. Pascal,
  P. Mas   4 12"—CM-255†
  (C-LFX380/3)
  DUPLICATION: H. & A. Merckel, G.
  Marchesini, E. Zurfluh-Tenroc, G-L973/6
No. 2, G minor, Op. 45
  Marguerite Long, Jacques Thibaud,
  Maurice Vieux & Pierre Fournier
                         4 12"—G-DB5103/6
  London Belgian Piano Quartet
                         4 12"—D-K1183/6†

QUINTET—Piano & Strings, D minor,
  Op. 89
  Emma Boynet & Gordon String Quartet
                           4 12"—SCH-9

REQUIEM Soloists, Chorus, Orchestra &
  Organ In Latin Op. 48 1887
Introit; Kyrie; Offertorium; Sanctus; Pie
  Jesu; Agnus Dei; Libera; In Paradisum
  Les Chanteurs de Lyon, Suzanne Dupont
  (s), M. Midier (bs), Edouard Commette
  (org.), Le Trigintuor Instrumental Lyon-
  nais—E. Bourmauck   5 12"—CM-354†
  (C-RFX63/7)   (C-LX773/7†)
  Les Disciples de Massenet, Marcelle Den-
  ya (s), Mack Harrell (b), Roland Roy
  (org) & Montreal Festivals Orch.—
  Pelletier   5 12"—VM-844†
  [Mozart: Ave Verum Corpus, K. 618]
  DUPLICATION: Malnory-Marseillac (s),
  L. Morturier (bs), Bach Society Cho.,
  Orch. & Organ—G. Bret, G-W1154/8
—Pie Jesu & In Paradisum only
  Doniau-Blanc (S) & St. Nocolas Cho.
                          10"—LUM-30003
—Pie Jesu only
  Jane Laval, C-BFX3
Romance, A major, Op. 69 'Cello & Piano
  Pierre Fournier & Babeth Lénoet
                          12"—G-DB11144
  [Schumann: Fantasiestücke, Pt. 3]
Romance sans Paroles, No. 3 Op. 17 Piano
  France Ellegaard   10"—PD-62833
  [Brahms: Waltz, Op. 39, No. 15]

—Arr. 'Cello & Piano
  Caponsacchi, PAT-X98124; A Lévy,
  O-166047

Salve Regina, Op. 67, No. 1
  Germaine Cernay (ms), organ & orch.
  —Cébron   10"—LUM-30085
  [En prière]

SHYLOCK Incidental Music to Ed. Harau-
  court's drama (after Shakespeare) 1889
Orchestral Suite, Op. 57
  Entr'acte; Epithalame; Nocturne; Final
—Nocturne only
  Paris Conservatory Orch.—Gaubert
              (in CX-75†) 10"—C-68960D
  [Dukas: Apprenti sorcier, Pt. 3]
  (C-LX654) (C-LFX465)
  Hallé Orch.—Barbirolli
  [Elgar: Elegy]   10"—G-B9567
—Chant de Shylock & Madrigal
  See under Songs
Sicilienne, Op. 78 'Cello & Piano
  (See also under Pelléas et Mélisande)
  Arnold Földesy & W. von Vultee
  [Popper: Tarantella]   10"—PD-24416

SONATAS—Violin & Piano
No. 1, A major, Op. 13
  Mischa Elman & Leopold Mittmann
                           3 12"—VM-859†
  Jascha Heifetz & Emmanuel Bay
                           3 12"—VM-328†
  Denise Soriano & Magda Tagliafero
                          3 12"—PAT-PAT3/5
  Jacques Thibaud & Alfred Cortot
                          3 12"—G-DB1080/2

SONATAS—'Cello & Piano
No. 2, Op. 117
  Maurice Gendron & Monique Haas
  [Après un rêve]   3 12"—D-K1374/6†

SONGS In French
Collection
  Charles Panzéra (b) & Magdeleine
  Panzéra-Baillot (pf)   5 12"—VM-478†
  (Includes: La Bonne Chanson—cycle; Au
  cimetière; En sourdine; L'Horizon
  chimérique—cycle)
(L') Absent, Op. 5, No. 3
  Jacques Bastard (b) & Joseph Bene-
  venuti (pf)   12"—C-LFX599
  [Nocturne]
Adieu See: Poèmes d'un jour—No. 3
Après un rêve, Op. 7, No. 1
  Maggie Teyte (s) & Gerald Moore (pf)
       (in VM-895)   10"—V-10-1002
  [Hahn: Si mes vers avaient des ailes]
  (G-DA1777)
  Charles Panzéra (b) & Mme. Panzéra-
  Baillot (pf)   10"—G-DA4911
  [L'Autome]
  Gerard Souzay (b) & Jean-Michel
  Damase (pf)   10"—D-M604
  [En sourdine]
  Ninon Vallin (s) & pf. acc.
                         10"—PAT-X93081

[Au bord de l'eau]
DUPLICATIONS: Georges Thill, C-
LF125; Pierre Bernac, G-DA4931; Lily
Pons, C-72050D in CM-689

—Arr. 'Cello & Piano Casals
Pablo Casals & N. Mednikoff
10″—V-1083
[Popper: Chanson villageoise]
Maurice Gendron & Monique Haas
[Sonata No. 2, Pt. 5]   12″—D-K1376
Cedric Sharpe & Gerald Moore
[Saint-Saëns: Le Cygne] 10″—D-F7630
DUPLICATIONS: Maurice Maréchal, C-
D13108; Gilberto Crepax, C-D5831; A.
Navarra, O-188937; B. Michelin, C-LF241

—Arr. Violin & Piano Mischa Elman
Mischa Elman & Leopold Mittman
(in VM-938†)   12″—V-11-8429
[Debussy: Sonata No. 3, Pt. 3]

Au bord de l'eau, Op. 8, No. 1
Ninon Vallin (s) & pf. acc.
[Après un rêve]   10″—PAT-X93081

Au cimetière, Op. 51, No. 2 (Richepin)
Charles Panzéra (b) & Mme. Panzéra-
Baillot (pf)
(in VM-478†)   12″—V-15036
[En sourdine] (G-DB4903)
Ninon Vallin (s) & Maurice Faure (pf)
[Les roses d'Ispahan] 10″—PAT-PD66
DUPLICATION: Alice Raveau, PAT-
X93077

Aurore, Op. 39, No. 1 (Silvestre)
Charles Panzéra (b) & Mme. Panzéra-
Baillott (pf)   10″—G-DA4913
[C'est l'extase]
Ninon Vallin (s) & Maurice Faure (pf)
[En sourdine]   10″—PAT-PD46
DUPLICATIONS: Ginette Guillamat,
C-DF2487; Sophie Wyss, D-M553

(L') Automme, Op. 18, No. 3
Charles Panzéra (b) & Mme. Panzéra-
Baillot   10″—G-DA4911
[Après un rêve]
Ninon Vallin (s) & pf. acc.
[La Rose]   10″—PAT-PG60
A. Endrèze (b) & Mme. Endrèze-
Krieger   10″—PAT-PA1586
[Les Berceaux]
Povla Frijsh (s) & Celius Dougherty
(pf)   (in VM-789) 12″—V-18053
[Ravel: Le Paon; Debussy: Voici que
le printemps]

Avant que tu ne t'en ailles
See: La Bonne Chanson—No. 6

(Les) Berceaux, Op. 23, No. 1
(Sully-Prud'homme)
Charles Panzéra (b) & Mme. Panzéra-
Baillot (pf)   10″—G-DA4909
[Chanson du Pêcheur]
Ninon Vallin (s) & M. Long (pf)
10″—C-LF125
[Après un rêve, Georges Thill]
Sophie Wyss (s) & Josephine Southey-
John (pf)   10″—D-M529
[Chabrier: Villanelle des petits canards]
DUPLICATIONS: Martha Angelici, LUM-
33191; Alice Raveau, PAT-X93120;

Roger Bourdin, O-188564; A. Endrèze,
PAT-PA1986

—Arr. Violin & Piano
Yvonne Curti & Andolfi
[Hahn: Si mes vers] 10″—PAT-X98156

(LA) BONNE CHANSON, Op. 61 Song
Cycle   (Verlaine)
1. Une sainte en son auréole
2. Puisque l'aube grandit
3. La lune blanche luit dans les bois
4. J'aillais par des chemins perfides
5. J'ai presque peur en vérité
6. Avant que tu ne t'en ailles
7. Donc, ce sera par un clair jour d'été
8. N'est-ce pas?
9. L'Hiver a cessé
Charles Panzéra (b) & Mme. Panzéra-
Baillot (pf)
(in VM-478†) 3 12″—V-15033/5
(G-DB5020/2)
Suzanne Stappen (s) & Orch.—
Coppola   5 10″—G-K7327;
G-K7368; G-K7458/60
[Roses d'Ispahan]

—Nos. 3 & 5 only
Maggie Teyte (s) & Gerald Moore (pf)
In Gramophone Shop Alb. GSC-3

C'est l'extase, Op. 58, No. 5 (Verlaine)
Charles Panzéra (b) & Mme. Panzéra-
Baillot (pf)   10″—G-DA4913
[Aurore]

Chanson de Shylock (from Incidental music
to "Shylock") Op. 57 (Haraucourt)
Pierre de Seyguières (b) & Orch.
10″—C-DF2542
[Madrigal & Parfum impérissable]
Yvon Le Marc'Hadour (b) & pf. acc.
[Prison & Cygne sur l'eau] 12″—BAM-31
Villabella (t) & pf. acc.
[Hahn: Paysage]   10″—O-188558

**Chanson du Pêcheur (Lamento) Op. 4,
No. 1** (Gautier)
Charles Panzéra (b) & Mme. Panzéra-
Baillot (pf)   10″—G-DA4909
[Les Berceaux]

Chant d'Automne, Op. 5, No. 1
(Baudelaire)
Pierre de Seyguières (b) & Yvonne
Vallier (pf)   12″—C-DFX220
[Brahms: Von ewiger Liebe]

Clair de Lune, Op. 43, No. 3 (Verlaine)
Maggie Teyte (s) & G. Moore (pf)
[Le Secret]   10″—G-DA1876
Charles Panzéra (b) & Mme. Panzéra-
Baillot (pf)   10″—G-DA4887
[En Prière]
Georges Thill (t) & Maurice Faure (pf)
[Sérénade toscane]   10″—C-LF154
DUPLICATIONS: Ninon Vallin, PAT-
PG101; Alice Raveau, PAT-X93120

Cygne sur l'eau (Mirages No. 1)
Yvon Le Marc'Hadour (b) & pf. acc.
12″—BAM-31
[Chanson de Shylock & Prison]

Dans la forêt de Septembre, Op. 85, No. 1
Noémie Perrugia (s) & I. Aitoff (pf)
[Le Don silencieux]   10″—G-DA5008

Dans les ruines d'une abbaye, Op. 2, No. 1
(Hugo)
Maggie Teyte (s) & Gerald Moore (pf)
10"—G-DA1810
[Martini: Plaisir d'amour]

Diane, Séléné
See: L'Horizon Chimérique—No. 3

Dolly (Berceuse) Op. 56, No. 1 (Hamelle)
(Arr. from No. 1 of Dolly Suite—
Piano: 4-Hands)
—**Arr. Violin & Piano**
Jacques Thibaud & Tasso Janopoulo
10"—G-DA4999
[Ravel: Pièce en forme de Habañera]

(Le) Don silencieux, Op. 92
Noémie Perrugia (s) & I. Aitoff (pf)
10"—G-DA5008
[Dans la forêt de Septembre]

Donc, ce sera par un clair jour d'été
See: La Bonne Chanson—No. 7

En prière (Stephen Bordese)
Charles Panzéra (b) & Mme. Panzéra-
Baillot (pf)
10"—G-DA4887
[Clair de Lune]
Germaine Cernay (ms) & orch. acc.
[Salve Regina] 10"—LUM-30085
Georges Thill (t) & Maurice Faure (pf)
[Noël] 10"—C-LF152
DUPLICATIONS: Ginette Guillamat,
C-DF2486; Janine Micheau, C-DF2260

En sourdine, Op. 58, No. 2 (Verlaine)
Charles Panzéra (b) & Mme. Panzéra-
Baillot (pf)
(in VM-478†) 12"—V-15036
[Au cimetière] (G-DB4903)
Ninon Vallin (s) & P. Darck (pf)
10"—PAT-PG102
[Aurore, on PAT-PG46] [Nell]
Gerard Souzay (b) & Jean-Michel
Damase (pf) 10"—D-M604
[Après un rêve]
Ginette Guillamat & Vlado Perlemuter
(pf) 10"—C-DF2485
[Tristesse]

Extase See: C'est l'extase

Fleur jetée, Op. 39, No. 2
Georges Thill (t) & Maurice Faure (pf)
[Poèmes d'un jour] 10"—C-LF157

(L') Hiver a cessé See: La Bonne Chanson
—No. 9

(L') Horizon Chimérique, Op. 113
(Song Cycle)
(Jean de la Ville de Mismont)
(Dedicated to Charles Panzéra)
1. La mer est infinie
2. Je me suis embarqué
3. Diane, Séléné
4. Vaisseaux, nous vous aurons aimés
Charles Panzéra (b) & Mme. Panzéra-
Baillot (pf)
(in VM-478†) 12"—V-15037
(G-DB5009)
Gerard Souzay (b) & J. M. Damase
12"—D-K1693

Ici-Bas! Op. 8, No. 3
Maggie Teyte (s) & Gerald Moore (pf)
[Hahn: En sourdine] 10"—G-DA1830

J'ai presque peur en vérité See: La Bonne
Chanson—No. 5

J'allais par des chemins perfides See: La
Bonne Chanson—No. 4

(Le) Jardin clos, Op. 106 (Song Cycle)
(8 songs)
Noémie Perrugia (s) & Joseph Benvenuti
(pf) 2 12"—G-DB5157/8
[Tristesse]

Jardin Nocturne, Op. 113, No. 3
(Mirages No. 3)
Pierre Bernac (b) & Francis Poulenc (pf)
[Prison] 10"—G-DA4889

Je me suis embarqué See: L'Horizon
Chimérique—No. 2

Lamento See: Chanson du Pêcheur

(La) Lune blanche luit dans les bois
See: La Bonne Chanson—No. 3

Lydia, Op. 4, No. 2 (de Lisle)
Maggie Teyte (s) & Gerald Moore (pf)
[Nell] 10"—G-DA1832
Pierre Bernac (b) & Francis Poulenc (pf)
[Après un rêve] 10"—G-DA4931
Charles Panzéra (b) & Mme. Panzéra-
Baillot (pf) 10"—G-DA4878
[Le Parfum impérissable]
DUPLICATION: Roger Bourdin,
O-188634

Madrigal (from "Shylock") Op. 57
(Haraucourt)
Pierre de Seyguières (b)
10"—C-DF2542
[Chanson de Shylock & Parfum
impérissable]

(La) Mer est infinie See: L'Horizon
Chimérique—No. 1

MIRAGES (Cycle) Op. 113
1. **Cygne sur l'eau**
2. **Reflets dans l'eau**
3. **Jardin Nocturne**
4. **Danseuse**
Lise Daniels (s) & J. Benvenuti (pf)
10" & 12"—OL-27/28
See under individual titles for isolated
recordings.

Nell, Op. 18, No. 1 (de Lisle)
Maggie Teyte (s) & Gerald Moore (pf)
[Lydia] 10"—G-DA1831
Ninon Vallin (s) & Maurice Faure (pf)
10"—PAT-PD51
[Le parfum impérissable]
[En sourdine, on PAT-PG102]

N'est-ce pas? See: La Bonne Chanson
—No. 8

Nocturne, Op. 43, No. 2
(Villiers de L'Isle Adam)
Charles Panzéra (b) & Mme. Panzéra-
Baillot (pf) 10"—G-DA4905
[Soir]
Jacques Bastard (b) & J. Benvenuti (pf)
[L'Absent] 12"—C-LFX599

Noël, Op. 43, No. 1 (Victor Wilder)
George Thill (t) & Maurice Faure (pf)
[En prière] 10"—C-LF152

(Le) Parfum impérissable, Op. 76 (de Lisle)
Charles Panzéra (b) & Mme. Panzéra-
Baillot (pf) 12"—G-DB4878

[Lydia]
Ninon Vallin (s) & Maurice Faure (pf)
[Nell] 10″—PAT-PD51
DUPLICATIONS: Ginette Guillamat,
C-DF2484; Pierre de Seyguières,
C-DF2542

POEMES D'UN JOUR, Op. 21
(Grandmougin)
1. **Rencontre**
2. **Toujours**
3. **Adieu**
Georges Thill (t) & Maurice Faure (pf)
[Fleur jetée] 10″—C-LF157
Ninon Vallin (s) & pf. acc.
10″—PAT-PG61
Eide Norena (s) & Orch.—
Coppola 10″—G-K7202
Prison, Op. 83, No. 1 (Verlaine)
Yvon Le Marc'Hadour (b) & pf. acc.
12″—BAM-31
[Chanson de Shylock; Cygne sur l'eau]
Pierre Bernac (b) & Francis Poulenc (pf)
[Jardin Nocturne] 10″—G-DA4889
DUPLICATION: G. Guillamat, C-DF2487
Puisque l'aube grandit See: La Bonne
Chanson—No. 2
(La) Rencontre See: Poèmes d'un jour
—No. 1
(La) Rose, Op. 51, No. 4
(Ode Acréontique) (de Lisle)
Ninon Vallin (s) & pf. acc.
[Automne] 10″—PAT-PG60
(Les) Roses d'Ispahan, Op. 39, No. 4
(Original orch. acc.) (de Lisle)
Maggie Teyte (s) & Gerald Moore (pf)
[Soir] 10″—G-DA1819
Lily Pons (s) & Orch.—Abravanel
(in CM-689) 12″—C-72048D
[Bachelet: Chère nuit]
Lily Pons (s) & Frank La Forge (pf)
(in VM-599) 10″—V-1997
[Delibes: Les Filles de Cadix]
Charles Panzéra (b) & Mme. Panzéra-
Baillot (pf) 10″—G-P852
[Soir]
Ninon Vallin (s) & pf. acc.
[Au cimetière] 10″—PAT-PD66
DUPLICATIONS: Sophie Wyss, D-M553;
Etienne Billot, O-123779; Suzanne Stap-
pen, G-K7460; Roger Bourdin,
O-188634;
(Une) Sainte en son auréole
See: La Bonne Chanson—No. 1
(Le) Secret, Op. 23, No. 3
Vanni-Marcoux (b) 10″—G-DA4814
[Tosti: Chanson de l'adieu]
Alice Raveau (ms)
[Au cimetière] 12″—PAT-X93077
Sérénade toscane, Op. 3, No. 2 (Bussine)
Georges Thill (t) & Maurice Faure (pf)
[Clair de lune] 10″—C-LF154
(Le) Soir, Op. 83, No. 2 (Samain)
Maggie Teyte (s) & Gerald Moore (pf)
[Les Roses d'Ispahan] 10″—G-DA1819
Ninon Vallin (s) & P. Darck (pf)
[Clair de lune] 10″—PAT-PG101
Charles Panzéra (b) & Mme. Panzéra-
Baillot (pf) 10″—G-DA4905
[Nocturne]

DUPLICATION: Ginette Guillamat,
C-DF2484;
Spleen, Op. 51, No. 3
Ginette Guillamat (s) & Vlado Perle-
muter (pf) 10″—C-DF2486
[En prière]
Tarantelle, Op. 10, No. 2 (Monnier)
—Arr. 'Cello & Piano
Gregor Piatigorsky & Valentin Pavlovsky
(in CM-501) 10″—C-17447D
[Debussy: Romance]
Toujours See: Poèmes d'un jour—No. 2
Tristesse, Op. 6, No. 2
Noémie Peruggia (s) & Joseph
Benvenuti (pf) 12″—G-DB5158
[Le jardin clos, Pt. 3]
Ginette Guillamat (s) & Vlado Perle-
muter (pf) 10″—C-DF2485
[En sourdine]
Vaisseaux, nous vous aurons aimés
See: L'Horizon Chimérique—No. 4
Theme and Variations, Op. 73 Piano
Kathleen Long 2 10″—D-M547/8
Carmen Guilbert 2 12″—PAT-PAT113/4
[Nocturne, Op. 33, No. 3]
Tu es Petrus Chorus in Latin
Delmotte (s) & St. Nicholas Choir
10″—LUM-30006
[Anon: Acclamations Carolingiennes]
FAURE, Jean-Baptiste (1830-1914)
*The leading French baritone of the mid-
nineteenth century who created roles in such
operas as "L'Africaine," "Faust," "Hamlet," and
"Don Carlos." He also composed songs, mostly
of a quasi-religious nature.*
SONGS For 1 & 2 voices In French
Charité
Robert Couzinou (b)
(PD-27227) 12″—PD-516520
[Gounod: Ave Maria, R. Gilles]
DUPLICATION: Lafont, O-188609
(Le) Crucifix Duo: Tenor & Baritone
(Prilleux)
César Vezzani & L. Casaux
[Les Rameaux, Casaux] 12″—G-L929
DUPLICATIONS: Richard & Dister,
C-D14255; Villabella & Baugé,
PAT-X93041; Gilles & Couzinou,
PD-521813; Caruso & Journet,
G-DB591*
O Salutaris
Jean Planel 10″—PAT-X93143
[Holmes: Noël]
(Les) Rameaux (J. Bertrand)
Eng. The Palms
Enrico Caruso (t) (in French) & re-
recorded orch. 12″—V-14744
[Franck: La Procession]
(Original recording: G-DB132*)
John McCormack (t) & Cho. (in English)
[Adeste Fideles] 12″—V-6607
Thomas L. Thomas (b) Cho. (in English)
[Schubert: Ave Maria] 12″—V-11-9109
DUPLICATIONS: Louis Cazaux & Cho.,
G-L929; Couzinou, PD-27211: PD-
516515; Franz, C-DF255; Lynel, O-
166176; Plançon, G-DB591*
Sancta Maria (J. Bertrand)
Pierre Giannotti (b) 12″—LUM-32061
[Bizet: Agnus Dei]

FELTON, William (1713-1769)

A well-known contemporary of Handel, Felton composed many works for the organ and harpsichord.

Concerto No. 3, B flat major Organ & Orch.
E. Power Biggs & Arthur Fiedler's
Sinfonietta   2 10"—VM-866†

FERGUSON, Howard (1908-   )

Born in Ireland, Ferguson went to London and became a pupil of Harold Samuel. He has composed piano music and scores for chamber ensembles and has made interesting arrangements of Irish folk tunes.

(5) Bagatelles Piano
Myra Hess   12"—G-C3423

OCTET—Clarinet, Bassoon, Horn, 2 Violins, Viola, Cello & Bass
Griller String Quartet, with Pauline Juler (cl), Cecil James (bsn), Dennis Brain (hn), James Merrett (bs)
                           3 12"—D-K1095/7
Sonata, F minor Piano
Myra Hess   3 12"—G-C3335/7†
[Purcell: Sarabande, Minuet & Air]

FERNANDEZ, Oscar Lorenzo (1897-   )

A native of Rio de Janeiro, Fernandez is a pupil of Braga and his compositions—flavored with Brazilian atmosphere—include ballets, an opera, several orchestral works and a "Trio Brasileiro."

Batuque Orchestra
Philadelphia "Pops" Orch.—Caston
        (in CM-588) 12"—C-12605D
[Gliere: Red Poppy—Russian Sailor's Dance]

FERNANDEZ-ARBOS, Enrique (1863-1939)

A Spanish conductor and violinist who attended the conservatories at Madrid and at Brussels and became a pupil of Joachim in Berlin. He is better known as a conductor, especially of the Madrid Symphony, although at one time he was concert-master of the Berlin Philharmonic and the Boston Symphony.

Noche de Arabia—Intermezzo Orchestra
Madrid Symphony Orch.—Arbós
                           12"—C-69203D
(in Spanish Album No. 2: CM-331)

FERROUD, Pierre (1900-1936)

A minor French composer, a pupil of Ropartz and Florent Schmitt.

Sonata—'Cello & Piano, A major
M. Maréchal & H. Pignari-Salles
                        2 12"—C-LFX355/6
Trio—Oboe, Clarinet & Basson, E flat major
Trio d'Anches de Paris
                        2 10"—PAT-PG84/5

FEVRIER, Henri (1876-   )

A pupil of Fauré and Massenet who wrote a number of operas, the best known being "Monna Vanna."

OPERAS-COMIQUES In French
AGNES, DAME GALANTE 1912

Doux propos Arr. Saxophones
Viard Saxophone Quartet
                           10"—PAT-PA286
MONNA VANNA Opera 1909
No recordings available
(Le) Récit de Djalmar Violin & Piano
Yvonne Curti & G. Andolfi
[Accordi: La Seduzione] 10"—PAT-PA31
SONGS In French
Au jardin charmant Duo: 2 Sops.
Hendes Højhed & Frøken Erika Raff
w. E. Selmar Saelges (pf)
[Tosti: Ave Maria]   10"—G-DA5214

FIBICH, Zdeněk (1850-1900)

A pupil of Moscheles and Jadassohn who was considered one of the prominent representatives in the renaissance of Bohemian music during the last half of the nineteenth century. Although quite prolific, he is remembered outside of Czechoslovakia today by his "Poème" (with its popular version "Moonlight Madonna.")

THE BRIDE OF MESSINA Opera in Czech
Orchestral excerpts
Symphony Orch.—Jeremias
                           12"—ESTA-H5057
Idyll Clarinet & Piano
Czech. Selanka
Milan Kostohryz & pf. acc.
                           12"—U-G14156
[Smetana: Remembrance]
Night in Karlstein Concert Overture Orch.
FOK Sym. Orch.—Parik
                           12"—ESTA-H5001
Quartet—String
—Polka only
Ondricek Quartet   12"—U-G12457
[Novak: Quartet, D major, Pt. 7]
Poème (from Idyll "In the Dusk")
—Arr. Violin & Piano Kubelik
Wolfi Schneiderhan   10"—C-DB1058
[Saint-Saëns: Le Cygne]
Jan Kubelik & pf. acc. 12"—U-G11386
[Dvořák: Humoresque & Suk: Burleske]
DUPLICATIONS: I. Kawaciuk, U-A12258; A. Sammons, D-F7950; H. Fritz-Crone, G-X4598; Chrystja Kolessa, G-EG7135
—Arr. Orchestra
Czechoslovak Broadcasting Orch.—
Jirak   12"—U-F12467
[Nedbal: Valse Triste]
Andre Kostelanetz & his Orch.
[Drigo: Sérénade]   12"—C-7294M
[Liszt: Liebestraum, on C-DX1163]
DUPLICATIONS: Melachrino Strings, G-B9554; Jack Hylton Concert Orch., D-K708; Campoli Orch., D-F3325; C. A. Hallgren, G-X6201; Sym. Orch.—Parik, ESTA-D2004
—Vocal arrangement "My Moonlight Madonna"
Helen Traubel (s), C-17510D
Slavonic Polonaise Violin & Orch.
Karel Sroubek & Orch.—O. Parik
                           12"—U-G12902

SARKA Opera 1897

Overture
  Symphony Orch.—Chalabala
                          12"—ESTA-H5112

Individual excerpts
How beautiful you are
  Czech. **Jak jsi krásná** Soprano & Tenor
  Marie Podvalova & Jaroslav Gleich
                          12"—U-G12798
  [Janáček: Jenufa—They went away]

I am not afraid of the cold death
  Czech. **Já nelekám se, smrti chladná** Tenor
  Josef Masak   12"—U-G12932
  [Smetana: Dalibor—O the unspeakable
  happiness of love]

You are beautiful like a summer night
  Czech. **Jsi krásná jako letní noc**
  Time moves like a blessed echo
  Czech. **Jako blahý ohlas doby zašlé**
  Soprano & Chorus
  Marie Reznickova w. Cho.
                          12"—U-G14114

Silent Night Chorus in Boh.
  Czech. **Ticha Noc**
  Prague Teachers Chorus 10"—G-AM794
  [Kricka: Drifting Waters]
  Bakule Cho.   10"—U-A12003
  [Dvořák: Lonely Sweetheart]
  (also on U-A12378)

Spring Symphonic Poem Orch.
  Czech. **Vesna**
  Czech Broadcasting Orch.—
  Jeremias   2 12"—U-E10255/6
  NOTE: *There are undoubtedly other recordings
  in Czech catalogues.*

FIELD, John (1782-1837)
  *An Irish pianist, pupil of Clementi, who spent
  most of his life in Russia. His "Nocturnes,"
  setting the form and style for these pieces, were
  the models Chopin used in developing his own
  popular works.*

NOCTURNES Piano
No. 4, A major
  Louis Kentner   12"—C-DX1129
  [No. 12]
  Myra Hess   10"—C-DB1232
  [Chopin: Nocturne, Op. 15, No. 2]
  (in Columbia History of Music, Vol. IV:
  CM-234)

No. 12, G major
  Louis Kentner   12"—C-DX1129
  [No. 4]
E major ("Midi" in Rondo form) (same as
  "Midi" in the "John Field Suite")

E minor
  Denis Matthews   12"—C-DX1228
Miscellaneous:
A John Field Suite Arr. Orchestra Harty
  1. **Polka**
  2. **Nocturne**
  3. **Slow Waltz (Remembrance)**
  4. **Rondo "Midi" (Nocturne, E major)**
  Liverpool Philharmonic—Sargeant
  [Elgar: Serious Doll] 12"—C-DX1118/20

FILTZ, Anton (1730-1760)
  *A German-Bohemian composer and 'cellist who
  became a pupil of Stamitz in Mannheim. He
  became celebrated for his symphonies, which
  belong to the most important achievements of
  the Mannheim school.*

Symphony, E flat major Orch.
  Boyd Neel String Orch.—Neel
                          12"—D-K1680

FINCK, Heinrich (1445-1527)
  *A Polish-German Kapellmeister who wrote both
  sacred and secular hymns of great beauty.*

Ach herzig's herz 4-Part Chorus in German
Wach auf 4-Part Chorus in German
  Basel Chamber Choir—Sacher
                  (in Vol. VI) 12"—AS-51
  [Senfl: Also heilig & Kling, klang]
Christ ist erstanden 5-Part Chorus in
  German
  State Academy Church & School Music
  Choir—Pius Kalt   10"—P-R1020
        (in 2000 Years of Music album)
  [Bruck: Aus tiefer Not]

FIOCCO, Gioseffo Hectore (fl.1729/37)
  *An Italian conductor and harpsichordist who
  composed pieces for that instrument and who
  became choirmaster at Antwerp Cathedral.*

Arioso Arr. Oboe & Piano Bent & O'Neill
  Leon Goossens & Gerald Moore
                          12"—C-DX1390
  [Marcello: Oboe Concerto, C minor, Pt. 3]
—Arr. Violin
  Yehudi Menuhin, G-DA1003
  Sandler, C-DB1038

FIORONI, Giovanni Andrea (1704-1778)
  *An Italian church composer who was choir-
  master of the Milan Cathedral for over thirty
  years.*

Angelus Domini descendit de Coelo
  5-Part Motet in Latin
  Milan Cathedral Choir & Organ
  (G-HN1381)   10"—G-EG6290

**FISCHER, Johann Kaspar Ferdinand
  (c.1650-c.1746)**
  *A German oboist who held important musical
  positions in various parts of Europe—in the
  court orchestra at Dresden, in the Queen's band
  in London, in the Vauxhall concerts in Dublin.
  Mozart wrote variations on his Minuet and
  J. S. Bach composed a quartet for him. He
  spent his last days in London and married the
  daughter of the painter Gainsborough.*

Suite No. 1, from "Le Journal de Printemps"
Overture, Marche, Menuet
  Chamber Orch.—Sachs
                  (in Vol. VI) 12"—AS-52
  [Rosenmüller: Suite, C major]
Passepied
  Alice Ehlers (harpsichord)
                  (in D-A61) 10"—D-23090
  [Bach: French Suite No. 1—Sarabande;
  Loeillet: Suite in G minor—Gigue]

FLAMENT, Edouard (1880-   )
*A French pianist and conductor of opera at
Algiers and at Lille who has composed sym-
phonic poems, chamber music and songs.*

Sextet, Op. 109
Bucolique; Villageoise; Arabesque; Blues;
Finaletto
Sextet—E. Flament
      3 10"—PAT-PG44/6
Préludes pour piano, Op. 114
 E. Flament (pf) 12"—PD-561120

FLOTOW, Friedrich von (1812-1883)
*A German nobleman and operatic composer
long associated with the musical life of Paris,
Flotow was the author of many works, the best
known being his opera "Martha." First produced in German in Vienna, this work has been
performed in every European language.*

OPERAS In German, French & Italian

**ALESSANDRO STRADELLA In German
1844**
Overture Orchestra
 German Opera House Orch.—Lutze
      12"—T-E3060
 DUPLICATIONS: Symphony Orch. Berlin
 —Heger, O-7880; Berlin State Opera
 Orch.—Zemlinsky, PD-66795
Alles theile unser Glück Sop.
 [Leonora's Air]
 Felicie Hüni-Mihacsek 12"—PD-66616
 [Adam: Postillon de Longjumeau—
 Je vais le revoir]

INDRA
Overture Orchestra
 German Opera House Orch.—Lutze
      12"—T-E3048

MARTHA 4 Acts 1847
 It. **Marta** Fr. **Marthe**
 (Inasmuch as the opera is best known in
 its Italian version, rather than the orig-
 inal German, the recorded excerpts are
 listed below by their Italian titles)
Vocal & Orchestral Selections
 Peter Anders, Hans Heinz Nissen, Carla
 Spletter, Else Tagetthoff, Chorus & Orch.
 —Schmidt-Isserstedt
 (In German) 12"—T-E2060
Orchestral Selections (Fantasia)
 Symphony Orch.—Gurlitt
      12"—PD-27087
 Grand Opera Orch.—Seidler-Winkler
 (G-EH1037) 12"—G-C3361
Overture Orchestra
 Berlin State Opera Orch.—
 P. van Kempen 12"—PD-15324
 (CET-OR5031)
 Berlin State Opera—Melichar
      12"—PD-27244
 Vienna State Opera Orch.—Reichwein
 (O-7878) 12"—P-E11392
 German Opera House, Berlin—Schmidt-
 Isserstedt 12"—T-E2228
 Berlin State Opera Orch.—
 Schmalstich 12"—G-EH420

State Orch., Berlin—Fritz Zaun
      12"—C-DWX1630
 DUPLICATIONS: Concert Orch.,
 G-S10030; National Theatre Orch.,
 Prague—Charvat, ESTA-H5136
Individual excerpts

ACT I
Solo, profugo, regetto Tenor & Baritone
Ger. **Ja, seit früher Kindheit Tagen**
 Caruso & Journet 12"—G-DM115*
 [Gounod: Faust—O merveille]
 Walther Ludwig & Wilhelm Strienz
 (in Ger.) 12"—G-EH1083
 [Auber: La Muette de Portici—
 Bacarolle]

ACT II
Qui sola, vergin rosa Soprano
 Eng. **The Last Rose of Summer**
 Ger. **Die letzte Rose**
 (A traditional Irish song-tune: "The
 Banks of Blarney" with words by Thomas
 Moore, interpolated into the opera)
 Mafalda Favaro 10"—C-DQ1070
 [Puccini: Madame Butterfly—Ancora
 un passo]
 Gwen Catley (in Eng.) 10"—G-B9574
 [Bishop: Home Sweet Home]
 A. Galli-Curci (in Eng.) & pf. acc.
      10"—V-1355
 [Bishop: Home Sweet Home]
 (G-DA1011)
 Ada Alsop (in Eng.) 12"—D-K1204
 [Bishop: Home Sweet Home]
 Lily Pons (in Eng.)
  (in VM-702) 12"—V-17231
 [Bishop: Pretty Mocking Bird]
 (also in CM-720)
 Margherita Perras (in German)
      12"—G-DB4438
 [Thomas: Mignon—Polonaise]
 Erna Berger (in German)
 [Grieg: Solvejg's Song] 10"—PD-47061
 [Donizetti: Fille du Régiment—
 Tyrolienne, on PD-10329]
 DUPLICATIONS: (in German) Helge
 Roswaenge, PD-10434; Wolfgang
 Kieling, G-EG6708
 In French: L. du Roy, PD-522588
 In Bohemian: S. Jelinkova, U-G12731;
 M. Jiraskova, U-G14151

T'ho raggiunta sciagurata!
Dormi pur Quartet
 Eng. **Goodnight Quartet**
 Caruso, Alda, Jacoby & Journet
  (in VM-953) 12"—V-16-5002*
 [Verdi: Lombardi—Qual volutta]

ACT III
Chi mi dira (Canzona del Portier) (Brindisi)
 Baritone & Cho.
 Ger. **Portierlied** Eng. **Porter's Song**
 Wilhelm Strienz (in German) & Cho.
      10"—G-EG6013
 [Fischer: Im tiefen Keller]
 Wilhelm Schirp (in German)
      10"—T-A10001
 [Nicolai: Lustigen Weiber—Als
 büblein klein]

DUPLICATIONS: Vittorio Arimondi &
Cho., CRS-27*; T. Ruffo, G-DA396*
In German: Ludwig Hoffman, PD-62686

M'apparì tutt' amor Tenor
Ger. **Ach, so fromm**
Eng. **Lionel's Air**
Fr. **Air des larmes—"A mes yeux
enchantés"**
Enrico Caruso & re-recorded Orch.
12"—V-7720
[Leoncavallo: Pagliacci—Vesti la giubba]
(G-DB1802)
(Original recording, G-DB159*)
Beniamino Gigli   12"—V-7109
[Meyerbeer: Africana—O Paradiso]
(G-DB1382)
[Verdi: Trovatore—Ai nostri monti, with
Elmo, on G-DB5385]
[Donizetti: Elisir—Una furtiva lagrima,
on G-DB4592]
Tito Schipa   12"—G-DB1064
[Handel: Largo]
Jussi Björling   12"—V-13790
[Gounod: Faust—Salut! Demeure]
(G-DB3887)
A. Salvarezza   12"—CET-BB25152
[Verdi: Luisa Miller—Quando le sere]
James Melton   10"—V-10-1329
[Bizet: Carmen—Air de la Fleur]
DUPLICATIONS: A. Pertile, G-DB1479;
A. Piccaver, PD-66890; R. D'Alessio,
C-DQ1129; C. Solari, C-D5698, Benton-
elli, C-DQ664
In German: Willy Tressner, G-DB5597,
Peter Anders, T-A2466; Helge Ros-
waenge, PD-10434; F. Wolff, PD-90171;
Patzak, PD-25012; K. von Pataky, RAD-
SP8018;
In French: Jan Kiepura, C-71397D;
Georges Thill, C-LF21; A. D'Arkor,
C-RF49; M. Claudel, PD-522588; G.
Micheletti, O-188813; Jean Planel,
PAT-X90037
In Russian: Sergei Lemeshev, D-F8145
In Danish: Marius Jacobsen, G-M113
In Swedish: Einar Andersson, G-X6015
In Czech: O. Kovar, U-G12974,
U-G14151

Ah! che a voi perdoni Iddio
Quintet & Chorus
Ger. **Mag der Himmel euch vergeben**
Wittrisch, Klose, Berger, Carli, Beck
& Chorus (in Ger.)   12"—G-DB4411
[Kienzl: Evangelimann—Selig sind]
Roswaenge, Leisner, Debicka, Watzke
& Chorus (in Ger.)   12"—PD-73093
[Verdi: Trovatore—Miserere]
—Tenor & Chorus only
J. Patzak (in German) PD-90180

ACT IV

(Den) Theuren zu versöhnen Soprano
(This Aria, omitted in the Italian score,
appears in German editions)
Erna Sack   12"—T-E1772
[Arditi: Parla' Valse]

Il mio Lionel perira Baritone
Mattia Battistini   12"—V-15-1010*
[Donizetti: Favorita—A tanto amor]

(L') OMBRE In French 1870

Lorsqu'à mes yeux le chère image, Act III
Tenor
Jean Planel   10"—PAT-X90037
[Adam: Si j'étais Roi—J'ignorais son
nom]

FOERSTER, Joseph Bohuslav (1859-   )

*A Bohemian composer, organist and music
critic and a teacher at the Hamburg Conservatory. He is noted for his choral music although
he composed in all forms.*

EVA, Op. 50 Lyric drama 1895/7
Vocal Excerpts
L. Cervinkova, M. Vesala, L. Hanzlikova,
O. Masak   2 12"—ESTA-H5109/10

Quintet, Op. 95
Prague Quintet   10"—U-B10572

SONGS In Czech

Love Song Cycle
Jara Pospisil & J. B. Foerster (pf.)
2 10"—U-B12238/9
Skrivankovi Eng. **Sky Lark**
Moravian Teachers Cho.
10"—U-C14007
Miscellaneous unidentified songs
Jara Pospisil & J. B. Foerster
12"— & 10"—U-E12631
U-B12632
Symphony No. 4, C minor, Op. 54
—Andante sostenuto only
Czech Broadcasting Orch.
12"—U-G12465

FONTENAILLES, H. de

A contemporary French composer of art songs.

SONGS In French

(Les) Deux Coeurs (H. Lucas)
Ninon Vallin (s) & pf. acc.
10"—O-166667
(Chabrier: L'Ile heureuse]
Jean Clement (b)   10"—C-DF769
[Delmet: La petite église]

Obstination (F. Coppée)
Maggie Teyte (s) & Gerald Moore (pf)
10"—G-DA1847
[Massenet: Elégie, with vlc. obb.]
Sais-tu?
Ninon Vallin (s) & pf. acc.
10"—O-166666
[Chaminade: Anneau d'argent]

FOOTE, Arthur (1853-1937)

*A Bostonian composer and organist, one of the
founders of the American Guild of Organists.
His compositions are in all forms except that of
the symphony.*

Suite for Strings, E major, Op. 63
Boston Symphony Orch.—
Koussevitzky   2 12"—VM-962†

FORD, Thomas (c.1580-1648)

A musician of the court of Charles I and an able lutenist, Ford composed homophonic ayres and lute pieces.

AYRE In English
There is a lady sweet and kind
  Stuart Robertson (b) & pf. acc.
                  10"—G-B4255
  [Woodgate: Bring us in good ale
  & Handel-Somervell: Silent Worship]

FORNEROD, Aloys (1890-   )

A contemporary Swiss composer, Fornerod is also known as a musicologist.

Concerto for 2 violins and piano
  Victor & George Desarzeu (vls) &
  Jules Godard (pf)   2 12"—C-DZX11/2

FORNSETE, John

A British monk, probably the copyist rather than the composer of the "Reading Rota" or "Sumer is icumen in." For many years the date of this prodigy has been accepted as early thirteenth century. Recently the date has been placed much later, but it still remains important for the reasons given in Groves: (1) It is the oldest known canon; (2) It is the earliest known harmonized music which is frequently performed and enjoyed by listeners today; (3) It is the oldest known six-part composition; (4) It is one of the oldest specimens of the use of what is now the major mode; (5) It is the oldest known specimen of a ground-bass; (6) It is the oldest known manuscript in which both secular and sacred words are written to the music. The International Educational Society recording of this work is interesting and valuable in that it contains several performances of the Rota giving an extremely clear idea of its construction.

Sumer is icumen in (The Reading Rota)
  1 Solo, 1 full canon
  Winchester Music Club   12"—C-D40119
  (Illustration for Lecture 60 "The Progress of Music," George Dyson)
  (International Educational Society Series)
  London Madrigal Group   10"—V-4316
  [Morley: Now is the month of maying & My bonnie lass; Byrd: I thought that love had been a boy]
  St. George's Singers   10"—C-5715
  [Dowland: Awake, sweet love, with Cecile Dolmetsch]
  (in Columbia History of Music, Vol. I: CM-231)

FOSS, Lukas (1922-   )
Dedication Violin & Piano
  Edgar Ortenberg & Lukas Foss,
  in **Hargail-MW300**

Rondo Fantasy Piano
  Lukas Foss, in **CH-B9** (Limited Edition)

FOSTER, Stephen Collins (1826-1864)

One of America's best loved composers whose numerous songs became very popular during and after his lifetime, and whose ballads, typical of his period, have taken on the character of folksongs with their simplicity and sentimentality.

Collections
(The) Music of Stephen Foster
  Arr. Orchestra
  (Includes: Old Black Joe; Oh! Susanna; My Old Kentucky Home; Beautiful Dreamer; Massa's in de Cold, Cold Ground; Come Where My Love Lies Dreaming; I Dream of Jeanie; Old Folks at Home; Camptown Races)
  Andre Kostelanetz & his Orchestra
                3 12"—CM-442

Stephen Foster Album
  (Includes: Old Folks at Home; Beautiful Dreamer; My Old Kentucky Home; Come Where My Love Lies Dreaming; Oh! Susanna; Old Black Joe; I Dream of Jeanie; Massa's in de Cold, Cold Ground; Ah! May the Red Rose Live Alway; Camptown Races)
  Richard Crooks (t), Balladeers Male Quartet, with Frank LaForge (pf) & Ralph Colicchio (banjo) 5 10"—VM-354
  (G-DA1578; G-DA1599)

Stephen Foster Melodies Arr. Shilkret
  (Includes: Open Thy Lattice Love; Uncle Ned; Village Maiden; Beautiful Dreamer; Ring de Banjo; Oh! Lemuel!; Nelly Bly; Oh! Boys Carry Me 'Long; Louisiana Belle; Camptown Races; Nelly Was a Lady; Jeanie with the Light Brown Hair; Oh! Susanna; Come Where My Love Lies Dreaming; Hard Times; Angelina Baker; Gentle Annie; Old Dog Tray; Some Folks; Old Black Joe; My Old Kentucky Home; Massa's in de Cold, Cold Ground; Old Folks at Home (Swanee River)
  Victor Salon Group & Orch.—
  Shilkret   4 12"—V-C2

Sixteen Songs
  (Includes: My Old Kentucky Home; Beautiful Dreamer; Old Folks at Home; I Dream of Jeanie; Old Black Joe; Camptown Races; Uncle Ned; Ring de Banjo; Come Where My Love Lies Dreaming; Oh! Boys Carry Me 'Long; Some Folks Do; Old Dog Tray; Massa's in de Cold; Cold Ground; Nelly Bly; Hard Times; Oh Susanna)
  Frank Luther & the Lyn Murray Quartet, with Piano, Violin, Guitar & Banjo
           5 10"—D-F6907/11

Stephen Foster Melodies
  (Arranged for String Quartet)
  (Includes: Oh Susanna; De Camptown Races; Old Folks at Home; Sweet Laura Lee; Beautiful Dreamer; Gentle Annie; Jeanie; Old Black Joe)
  London String Quartet   4 10"—D-A582

Individual Songs
  (See Collections for other recordings not listed)

Gentle Annie
  John Charles Thomas (b) & Carroll
  Hollister (pf)   10"—V-10-1023
  [Lohr: Where my caravan has rested]

I Dream of Jeanie with the Light Brown Hair
John McCormack   10"—V-1700
[Sweetly she sleeps]
DUPLICATIONS: S. MacEwan,
C-DB1980; C. Gibbons Orch., C-FB3055;
Karin Juel, C-X4945

My Old Kentucky Home
Marian Anderson (c)   12"—V-18314
[Bland: Carry me back to old Virginny]
Paul Robeson (bs)   10"—G-X3648
[Old Folks at Home]

Oh! Susanna
—Arr. Unacc. Choir Noble Cain
Augustana Choir—Veld   10"—V-1971
[Lassus: Echo Song; Russian Folksong:
Fireflies]
DUPLICATION: Madrigal Singers—
Engel, C-4402M in CM-329
—Arr. Orchestra Shulman
Boston "Pops" Orch.—Fiedler
                           10"—V-4569
[Arr. Bridge: Sally in our Alley]

Old Black Joe (See also under "Poor Old Joe")
Lawrence Tibbett (b) & Male Quartet
[Uncle Ned]   10"—V-1265

Old Folks at Home (Swanee River)
Helen Traubel (s) & Chorus
        (in CM-639)   12"—C-72104D
[Bland: Carry me back to old Virginny]
Paul Robeson (bs)   10"—G-B3664
[Poor Old Joe]
[My Old Kentucky Home, on G-X3648]
DUPLICATIONS: Clara Butt, C-DX730;
Ralph Crane, V-21050; Willy Schneider
(in German), PD-2605; K. Juel,
G-X4945
—Arr. Violin & Piano Kreisler
David Oistrakh & A. D. Makarov
                    10"—USSR-12457/9
[Sarasate: Zapateado]
DUPLICATION: Kreisler, V-1325,
G-DA975

Poor Old Joe (Old Black Joe)
Paul Robeson (bs)   10"—G-B3664
[Old Folks at Home]
[Kern: Show Boat—Old Man River, on
G-X4603]

Swanee River See: Old Folks at Home

Sweetly She Sleeps
John McCormack (t) & pf. acc.
[I Dream of Jeanie]   10"—V-1700

Uncle Ned
Lawrence Tibbett (b) & Male Quartet
[Old Black Joe]   10"—V-1265

Miscellaneous:
See under Morton Gould: **Foster Gallery**
(VM-727†); Arcady Dubensky: **Stephen
Foster—Theme, Variations and Finale
for Orchestra** (VM-912†)

FRANCAIX, Jean (1912-   )
*A gifted young French composer, pupil of
Nadia Boulanger, Françaix has written successfully in all forms, including ballet scores, and
has appeared as soloist in his own works for
the piano.*

Concertino Piano & Orchestra
Jean Françaix & Berlin Philharmonic
Orch.—Borchard   12"—T-E2175

Concerto Piano & Orchestra 1937
Jean Françaix & Paris Philharmonic
Orch.—Nadia Boulanger
                     2 12"—G-DB5034/5

Sérénade (for 12 Instruments)
Hamburg Chamber Orch.—Jochum
                     2 10"—T-A10037/8

Sérénade comique
Saxophone Quartet of Paris
                           10"—C-DF2239
[Bozza: Scherzo]   (C-DW4624)

Trio, C major Violin, Viola, 'Cello
Philharmonic String Trio
                     2 10"—D-F7053/4

FRANCHETTI, Alberto (1860-   )
*An Italian opera composer, sometimes known
as the "Italian Meyerbeer" who has also been
influenced by the realistic "verismo" school,
but whose works are seldom performed outside
his own country.*

OPERAS In Italian

CHRISTOFORO COLOMBO 4 Acts 1892
No recordings available

GERMANIA Prologue, 2 Acts & Epilogue
1902

Studenti! udite Prologue Tenor
**Ah! vieni qui & No' non chiuder gli occhi
vaghi, Act I**
Piero Pauli   10"—G-DA1332
DUPLICATION: Caruso G-DA543*

Ferito prigioner Baritone
Pasquale Amato   12"—V-15-1005*
[Verdi: I due Foscari—O vecchio cor]
(Recorded 1913]

FRANCK, César (1822-1890)
*The Belgian-French organist, teacher and com-
poser, esteemed as one of the great musicians
of the 19th century, wrote prolifically in almost
every form. Although a great many inferior
works are numbered among his compositions,
his best works have a unique individuality.*

(LES) BEATITUDES Oratorio In French
No. 4, Heureux les coeurs Tenor
Georges Thill   12"—C-D15121
[Wagner: Parsifal-Nur eine Waffe taugt]
No. 8, Mater Dolorosa Soprano
Germaine Martinelli
[Nocturne]   12"—PD-566044
(Le) Chasseur Maudit Symphonic Poem
Orchestra
London Philharmonic Orch.—Franz
André   2 12"—D-ED20†
(D-K1485/6)
Chicago Symphony Orch.—Désiré Defauw
   (in VM-1122†)   2 12"—V-11-9577/8
City of Berlin Orch.—Schuricht
                     2 12"—PD-68086/7
Lamoureux Orch.—A. Wolff
(PD-67002/3)   2 12"—PD-566047/8
[D'Indy: Fervaal—Prélude]

(3) CHORALES Organ

No. 1, E major
Albert Schweitzer (Ste.-Aurélie,
Strasbourg) 2 12″—**CX-100†**
(C-DWX1614/5)
—**Introduction only**
Charles Courboin (Academy of Arts &
Letters, New York)
(in VM-695†) 12″—**V-17321**
[Chorale No. 3, Pt. 1]

No. 2, B minor No recording available

No. 3, A minor
Fernando Germani (Westminster Cathe-
dral Organ) 2 12″—**G-C3580/1**
Charles Courboin (Academy of Arts &
Letters, New York)
(in VM-695†) 2 12″—**V-17321/2**
[with Chorale No. 1—Introduction only]
Charles Tournemire (Ste. Clotilde, Paris)
2 12″—**PD-66992/3**
[Tournemire: Cantilène Improvisation
No. 1] (PD-566057/8)

CONCERTOS Piano & Orchestra
See under Variations Symphoniques

(Les) Eolides (Poème Symphonique)
Orchestra 1876
Columbia Broadcasting Symphony Orch.
—Barlow 2 12″—**CX-145†**
[Couperin: Les Petits Moulins à vent;
Soeur Monique; Le Trophée—trans.
Filippi]

Grand Pièce Symphonique Organ 1862
—**Andante only Arr. Orch.** O'Connell
Philadelphia Orch.—Leopold Stokowski
12″—**V-14947**
[Tchaikovsky: Solitude, Op. 73, No. 6]

ORGAN MUSIC
Collection
(Pastorale, Op. 19, No. 4; Introduction—
Chorale No. 1, E major
Chorale No. 3, A minor; Pièce héroïque)
Charles M. Courboin (Academy of Arts
& Letters, New York)
4 12″—**VM-695†**
Offertoire: Dextera Domine
Schola de la Cathédrale de Périgueux-
Abbé Beleymet 12″—**LUM-32055**
[Psalm 150]

Panis Angelicus See under Songs

Pastorale, Op. 19 Organ
Charles M. Courboin (Academy of Arts
&Letters, New York)
(in VM-695†) 12″—**V-17320**
Fernando Germani (Westminster Cathe-
dral Organ) 12″—**G-C3672**
DUPLICATIONS: M. Dupré, G-W793;
E. Commette, C-D11029

Pièce Oboe & Piano
Leon Goosens & Gerald Moore
(in CX-160†) 12″—**C-69817D**
[Schumann: Romance, A minor, Op.
94, No. 3]
(C-DX937)

Pièce héroïque Organ
Charles M. Courboin (Academy of Arts &
Letters, New York)
(in VM-695†) 12″—**V-17323**

Edouard Commette (Lyons Cathedral)
12″—**C-DFX219**
—**Arr. Orchestra** O'Connell
San Francisco Orch.—Monteux
12″—**V-18485**

Prélude, Aria & Finale Piano
Lucienne Delforge 3 12″—**G-W1597/9**

Prélude, Choral & Fugue Piano 1884
Artur Rubinstein 2 12″—**VM-1004†**
Egon Petri 2 12″—**CX-176†**
Alfred Cortot 2 12″—**G-DB1299/300**
Lucienne Delforge 2 12″—**G-DB5195/6**
DUPLICATIONS: Mlle. Boutet de Monvel,
G-L1043/5; Blanche Selva,
C-GQX10750/2

Prélude, Fugue & Variations, Op. 18
Organ 1862
Marcel Dupré (Queen's Hall)
12″—**G-W1165**

Psalm 150 4-Part Chorus, with Organ
In French (or Latin)
Eng. **Sing Praise to God**
Lat. **Laudate Dominum**
Schola of Cathedral of Périgueux-
Abbé Beleymet (in French)
12″—**LUM-32055**
[Offertoire—Dextera Domine]

PSYCHE Symphonic Poem for Orchestra
& Chorus In French
1. **Sommeil de Psyché**
2. **Psyché enlevée par les Zéphyrs**
3. **Le jardin d'Eros**
4. **Psyché et Eros**

Symphonic Suite Orchestra only
(Nos. 1, 2, & 4)
Chicago Symphony Orch.—Désiré Defauw
(in VM-1122†) 2 12″—**V-11-9575/6**
Lamoureux Orch.—A. Wolff
2 12″—**PD-566159/60**
—**No. 1 (Le Sommeil de Psyché) only**
Orch. of the "Maggio Musicale"—
Gui 12″—**CET-BB25176**
—**No. 2 (Psyché enlevée par les Zéphyrs)**
only
Paris Conservatory Orch.—Coppola
[Redemption, Pt. 3] 12″—**G-P860**
—**No. 3 (Le jardin d'Eros) only**
Pasdeloup Orch.—Coppola
[Lalo: Scherzo] 12″—**G-AW280**
—**No. 4 (Psyché et Eros) only**
Brussels Royal Conservatory Orch.—
Defauw 12″—**C-D15197**
Amsterdam Concertgebouw Orch.—
Mengelberg 12″—**T-SK2463**
(U-G14279)
EIAR Symphony Orch.—Gui
12″—**CET-BB25117**

QUARTET—String, D major
Pro Arte Quartet 6 12″—**G-DB2051/6**
[Schubert: Quartet, Op. 125, No. 1—
Finale only]
London Quartet 6 12″—**CM-128†**

QUINTET—Piano & Strings, F minor
1878/9
Lucette Descaves-Truc & Gabriel
Bouillon Quartet
4 12″—**G-DB5123/6**

E. Robert Schmitz & Roth String
Quartet   5 12"—CM-334†
Marcel Ciampi & Capet Quartet
     5 12"—C-D15102/6
Alfred Cortot & International Quartet
     4 12"—G-DB1099/102
Chaillez-Richez Quintet
     5 12"—C-LFX730/4
[Chopin: Etude No. 19, Chaillez-Richez,
pf. solo]

REBECCA Biblical Scene for Soloists,
Chorus & Orch.
General Chorus
Schola St. Léon de Nancy—Gaudard
     12"—PAT-X93055
[Palestrina: Alma Redemptoris Mater &
Josquin: Ave Vera Virginitas]

REDEMPTION Symphonic Poem for So-
prano, Chorus & Orchestra
**—Symphonic Interlude (Prologue to Part
II)** Orchestra
Paris Conservatory Orch.—Coppola
     12" & 10"—G-W1159 & G-P860
[Psyché—No. 2, Psyché enlevée par les
Zéphyrs]
Lamoureux Orch.—A. Wolff
(PD-67005)   12"—PD-566020
—Les Rois dont vous vantez la gloire
Soprano
(1st Air of the Archangel)
Mme. Doniau-Blanc & A. Cellier
(organ)   12"—LUM-32008
[Accompaniment for study purposes,
A. Cellier]

SONATA—Violin & Piano, A major
Jascha Heifetz & Artur Rubinstein
(G-DB3206/8)   3 12"—VM-449†
Yehudi & Hephzibah Menuhin
(G-DB2742/5)   4 12"—GM-253†
Georg Kulenkampff & S. Schultze
     4 12"—T-E3268/71
G. Taschner & Cor de Groot
     4 12"—O-8793/6
J. Thibaud & A. Cortot
     4 12"—G-DB1347/50

SONGS In French
(L') Ange gardien Duo Soprano & Alto
Jo Vincent & Theodora Versteegh
[La Vierge à la Crèche] 10"—C-D10045
Ave Maria Soprano & Chorus in Latin
Mme. Doniau-Blanc 10"—LUM-30009
[Maria Mater]
(Le) Mariage des roses (E. David)
(from "3 Offertoires") 12"—C-LFX517
Georges Thill (t) & Maurice Faure (pf)
[S'il est un charmant gazon & Nocturne]
DUPLICATION: Mme. Marilliet,
C-D12057
Nocturne ("O fraîche Nuit") (Fourcaud)
Charles Panzéra (b) 12"—G-DB4868
[Séverac: Chanson de la nuit durable]
Georges Thill (t) & Maurice Faure (pf)
     12"—C-LFX517
[Mariage des roses & S'il est un charmant
gazon]

Germaine Martinelli (s)
[Béatitudes—No. 8] 12"—PD-566044
DUPLICATIONS: A. Endrèze, O-123726;
R. Couzinou, PD-522632
Panis Angelicus Tenor, Organ, Harp, Bass
in Latin
(from a Messe Solennelle, Op. 12)
Beniamino Gigli (t) & Cho.
     12"—V-14312
[Cilea: Arlesiana—Romanza di Federico]
(G-DB2914)
Richard Crooks (t)
[Massenet: Elégie] 12"—V-11-8490
Joan Hammond (s) 12"—C-DX1023
[Gounod: Ave Maria]
Richard Tauber (t) & Cho.
[Kahn: Ave Maria] 10"—P-RO20517
DUPLICATIONS: John McCormack,
V-6708; André d'Arkor, C-BFX2; Göta
Ljungberg, G-DB962; Jean Planel,
PAT-X93111; Theodora Versteegh,
C-D17216; Paul Payen, LUM-32007;
J. Lafont, O-123513
In Eng. Jeanette MacDonald, in VM-996
—Arr. Orchestra Stokowski
Philadelphia Orch.—Stokowski
     (in VM-300†) 12"—V-8964
[Franck: Symphony, Pt. 11]
[Sibelius: Valse Triste, on G-DB3318]
Boston "Pops" Orch.—Fiedler
[Schubert: Ave Maria, arr. Wilhelmj]
(La) Procession (Charles Brizeux)
Enrico Caruso (t) & re-recorded orch.
[Faure: Rameaux] 12"—V-14744
[Gounod: Reine de Saba—Prête moi,
on G-DB3078]
(original recording on G-DB145*)
Paul Sandoz (b) 12"—G-HEX103
[Widor: Non credo]
A. Endrèze 12"—O-123726
[Nocturne]
S'il est un charmant gazon (Hugo)
Georges Thill (t) & Maurice Faure (pf)
     12"—C-LFX517
[Le Mariage des roses & Nocturne]
(La) Vierge à la Crèche Duo (Daudet)
Suzanne Laydeker & Jeanne Renault
[Lacôme: Noël] 10"—PAT-PA747
Jo Vincent & Theodora Versteegh
[L'Ange gardien] 10"—C-D10045
Mme. Doniau-Blanc & Franck
     10"—LUM-32003
[Semain: Le Repos en Egypte]
Symphonic Variations—See: Variations
Symphoniques

SYMPHONY, D minor Orchestra
Philadelphia Orch.—Ormandy
     5 12"—CM-608†
San Francisco Orch.—Monteux
     5 12"—VM-840†
Philadelphia Orch.—Stokowski
     6 12"—VM-300†
[Panis Angelicus, arr. Stokowski]
(G-DB3226/31s—last side blank in
GM-285†)
London Philharmonic—Beecham
(C-LX904/8)   5 12"—CM-479†
Paris Conservatory Orch.—Münch
(D-K1639/42)   4 12"—D-ED36†

Minneapolis Symphony Orch.—
Mitropoulous   5 12"—CM-436†
DUPLICATIONS: Lamoureux Orch.—
Wolff, PD-566093/6; PD-69006/9:
PD-67028/31: PD-15062/5
TRIOS—Piano, Violin, 'Cello .
No recordings available
Variations Symphoniques
Piano & Orchestra 1885
Eng. Symphonic Variations
Alfred Cortot & London Philharmonic
—Ronald   2 12"—G-DB2185/6
Walter Gieseking & London Philharmonic
Wood   2 12"—CX-10†
(C-LX192/3) (C-LFX311/2)
(C-GQX10912/3)
Eileen Joyce & Paris Conservatory
Orch.—Münch   2 12"—D-ED35†
(D-K1587/8)
Myra Hess & City of Birmingham Orch.
Cameron   2 12"—G-C3237/8
Yves Nat & Colonne Orch.—Poulet
          2 12"—C-LFX608/9
Geza Anda & Amsterdam Concertgebouw
Orch.—Beinum   2 12"—PD-68132/3

FRANCK, J. W. (1641?-1696)

A predecessor of Keiser in the development of German opera, Franck was also a Kapellmeister at Hambourg.

SONGS In German
Passionlied: Jesu neight sein Haupt und stirbt
Yves Tinayre (t) & org. 12"—LUM-32014
[Albert: Festleid & Bach: Cantata
No. 85—No. 5]
(In Yves Tinayre Album No. 1)
Sei nur stille
A. Noordewier Reddingius (s) & org.
          12"—C-DHX39
[Old Netherland: Jesus en die Siele]

FRANCK, Melchior (1573-1639)

A Saxon Kapellmeister, composer of church music, known historically for his contribution to the development of German song, particularly with regard to elaboration of accompaniments. It is unfortunate that some of these examples are not available on discs at the present time.

Pavana (Newer Pavanen No. 19, 1603)
Tanz (Deutsche Weltliche Gesang & Dantze
No. 9, 1604)
Intrada (Neue Intraden No. 7, 1608)
Brass Ensemble—Sachs
          (in Vol. VI) 12"—AS-57
[Schein: Suite 14 from "Banchetto
Musicale," 1617]
—Pavana (Arr. Viols) only
Munich Viol Quintet   10"—P-R1023
[Hausmann: Dance; Byrd: Sellinger's
Round]
(in "2000 Years of Music" album)

FRANCISUS, Magister (14th Cent.)

De Narcisus Ballade for Flute, Trumpet,
& Viola
Instrumental Ensemble   10"—OL-102
[Don Paolo di Firenze: Fra Duri scogli
senz' Alcun Governo]

FRANCO, Magister (11th century)
(Franco of Cologne)

Author of treatises which were the first works to deal with the notation of measured music. The work listed below is attributed to him, but its authenticity is not definite.

Ave gloriosa Mater Salvatoris
Motet In Latin
(Attributed to Franco: transcribed by
Coussemaker)
Yves Tinayre (t) & Chorus
          12"—LUM-32018
[Anon—13th Century: Laudi a San
Lorenzo]
(in Yves Tinayre Album No. 2)

FRANCOEUR, François (1698-1787)

Chamber musician to the King and manager of the Opera, Francoeur composed violin sonatas, operas and ballets. The "Sicilienne et Rigaudon" attributed to him and which has become a popular standard work in violinists'. repertoire has been revealed as a composition of Fritz Kreisler.

Largo & Vivo (Unspecified) 'Cello & Piano
Gregor Piatigorsky & pf. acc.
[Weber: Adagio & Rondo]
          12"—G-DB2539
Sicilienne et Rigaudon See under Kreisler
Sonata, E major Cello & Piano
Adagio & Allegro vivo (This may be the
same as the unspecified Largo & Vivo
for 'Cello above)
Bernard Michelin & Tasso Janopoulo
          12"—C-LFX692
[Bréval; Sonata, G major, Pt. 3]
Sonata, G minor Violin & Basso continuo
Adagio & Allemande
J. Grabowski & P. Aubert
(harpsichord) (in Vol. VIII) 12"—AS-74
[Senaille: Sonata, E major]

FRANK, Alan

Suite for two clarinets
Frederick Thurston & Ralph Clark
          12"—D-K853
[Stanford: Clarinet Sonata—Caoine]

FRANKL, Ben (1912-   )

Sonata, Op. 13 Unaccompanied Violin
Max Rostal   2 12"—D-K1178/9
Toulon
Choir—Frankl   10"—D-M578
[Corbett: Raiders]

FRANZ, Robert (1815-1892)

A German composer who contributed to the "lied" and closely followed the style and purpose of Schubert, Schumann and Brahms, although his songs are extremely elegiac and contemplative.

Abends, Op. 16, No. 4 (Eichendorf)
Lorri Lail (ms) & Gerald Moore (pf)
          in Gramophone Shop Album GSC-4
**(Die) Blauen Frühlingsaugen, Op. 20,
No. 1** (Heine)
Lorri Lail (ms) & Gerald Moore (pf) in
Gramophone Shop Album GSC-4

Für Musik, Op. 10, No. 1
"Nun die Schatten dunkeln" (Geibel)
Lotte Lehmann (s) & Ernö Balogh (pf)
(in VM-419)   10"—V-1861
[Gute Nacht & Jensen: Lehn' deine
Wang']

Gute Nacht, Op. 5, No. 7
"Die Höh'n und Wälder schon steigen"
(Eichendorff)
Lotte Lehmann (s) & Ernö Balogh (pf)
(in VM-419)   10"—V-1861
[Für Musik & Jensen: Lehn' deine
Wang']

(Die) Helle Sonne leuchtet, Op. 42, No. 2
(Mizra Schaffy)
Lorri Lail (ms) & Gerald Moore (pf)
in Gramophone Shop Album GSC-4

Im Herbst, Op. 17, No. 6 (Müller)
Eng. **Autumn**
Margarete Klose (c)   10"—G-DA4482
[Mutter, o sing mich zur Ruh']
Margherite Teschemacher (s) & pf. acc.
10"—G-EG3896
[Mutter, o sing mich zur Ruh']

(Daz) Macht des Dunkelgrüne Laub,
Op. 20, No. 5 (Rognette)
Lorri Lail (ms) & Gerald Moore (pf)
in Gramophone Shop Album GSC-4

Ständchen, Op. 17, No. 2 (Ostenvald)
Lorri Lail (ms) & Gerald Moore (pf)
in Gramophone Shop Album GSC-4

Mutter, o sing mich zur Ruh', Op. 10, No. 3
Margherite Teschemacher (s) & pf. acc.
[Im Herbst]   10"—G-EG3896
Margarete Klose (c)
[Im Herbst]   10"—G-DA4482

Stille Sicherheit, Op. 10, No. 2
"Horch, wie still es wird im dunkeln
Hain" (Lenau)
Richard Crooks (t) (in English) &
pf. acc.   (in VM-846)   10"—V-2179
[Purcell-Fischer: Passing By]

Widmung, Op. 14, No. 1
"O danke nicht für diese Lieder"
(Müller)   Eng. **Dedication**
Richard Crooks (t) (in English) &
pf. acc.   (in VM-846)   10"—V-2176
[Handel: Parthenope—Se mia gioia &
& Pessard: L'Adieu du Matin]

FRASER-SIMPSON, Harold (1878-1944)
*A British composer best known for his faithful
settings of A. A. Milne's children's poems, and
for his songs from "Alice in Wonderland."*

(The) HUMS OF POOH
Poems by A. A. Milne
(Includes: **Isn't it funny; How sweet to
be a cloud; It's very very funny; Cottle-
ston Pie; Lines written by a bear; Sing
ho! for the life of a bear; They all went
off to discover the Pole; Three cheers for
Pooh; The more it snows; The butterflies are flying; If Rabbit was bigger;
Here lies a tree; Christopher Robin is
going**)
George Baker (b) & pf. acc.
3 10"—G-B3386/8

MAID OF THE MOUNTAINS
Operetta in English
Vocal & Orchestral Selections
Light Opera Company   12"—G-C2063
Columbia Light Opera Company
12"—C-DX81
Theatre Orchestra   12"—C-DX61
A. Welch, N. Collyer, V. Conway
10"—D-F1989
London Palladium Orch.   12"—G-C1881
Bachelor gay
Peter Dawson (bs), G-B3464
Love will find a way
Ina Souez (s), C-DB1226
Paradise for two
Anne Ziegler (s) & Webster Booth (t),
G-B8982

NOW WE ARE SIX   Poems by A. A. Milne
(Includes: **Sneezles; The friend; The Em-
peror's rhyme; Furry bear; The engineer;
Wind in the hill**)
Mimi Crawford (s) & H. Fraser-
Simpson (pf)   2 10"—G-B2678/9
[When we were very young—King's
breakfast]

SOUTHERN MAID   Operetta
Selections
Olive Groves & George Baker   D-K721

VERY YOUNG SONGS
(Including: **Market Square; Knights and
Ladies; Us Two; The End**)
Ann Stevens   10"—G-BD1178

WHEN WE WERE VERY YOUNG
Poems by A. A. Milne
First Series
(Includes: **Buckingham Palace; Three
foxes; Christening; Brownie, Halfway
down; Hoppity; Growing up; Happiness;
Missing; In the fashion; Politeness; Mar-
ket Square; Lines & Squares; Vespers**)
George Baker (b) & H. Fraser-
Simpson (pf)   3 10"—G-B2220/2
DUPLICATION: J. Dale Smith (b),
C-4104/7
Individual Songs
Down by the Pond
Webster Booth (t)
[Vespers]   10"—G-B9304
(The) King's Breakfast
Mimi Crawford (s) & H. Fraser-
Simpson (pf)   10"—G-B2679
[The engineer: Wind in the hill]
DUPLICATION: Dale Smith, C-4107
**Vespers (Christopher Robin is saying his
prayers)**
Helen Traubel (s)   12"—C-71872D
[Brahms: Wiegenlied]
Webster Booth (t)   10"—G-B9304
[Down by the pond]
**Selections ("When We Were Very Young" &
"Now We Are Six")**
**Hoppity, At the Zoo, Missing, In the Fash-
ion, Politeness, Sneezles, Halfway Down,
The Four Friends**
Gene Kelly   2 10"—C-J42

FRESCOBALDI, Girolamo (1583-1644)

An Italian organist, one of the first great virtuosos of that instrument, and a composer of choral and organ works that give him a sure ranking among the truly outstanding composers of all times. This superb music is seldom heard today and additions to this all too brief list of discs are badly needed.

Arietta
Edmund Kurtz (vlc) & Artur Balsam (pf)
[Milhaud: Elegie] 12"—V-11-9414
Gagliarda Orch. Stokowski
Philadelphia Orch.—Stokowski
[Bach: Fugue, C minor] 10"—V-1985
[Palestrina: Adoramus Te, on
G-DA1606]
Gagliarda Harpsichord
Alice Ehlers (in D-A61) 10"—D-23089
[Byrd: Earl of Salisbury Pavane; Lully:
Courante; Bach: French Suite No. 5—
Gavotte] (D-F7726)

LIBRO 2 DI INTAVOLATURE
Aria detta la Frescobalda
Quattro Gagliarde
Anne Linde (harpsichord) 12"—MIA-6
—**Aria only**
Vignanelli (org), SEMS-1141
(La) Mia pallida faccia
Non mi negate, ohimè Airs in Italian
Salvatore Salvati (t) acc. Harpsichord &
Basso continuo 12"—MIA-2
[Rasi: 3 Madrigals]
Prelude, G minor
String Orch.—Antonelli
12"—SEMS-1153
[Vivaldi: Concerto Grosso No. 8—
Larghetto]
Toccata Orch. Hans Kindler
National Symphony Orch.—Kindler
12"—V-17632
Toccata for the Elevation Organ
Marcel Dupré (in Vol. I) 12"—AS-4
[Gabrieli: Ricercare in the Tenth Tone]
Joseph Bonnet (Gonzalez organ)
12"—PAT-PAT64
[Padre Martini: Aria con variazione]
(in 3 Centuries of Organ Music)
DUPLICATION: Vignanelli, SEMS-1141
Toccata sopra i Pedali Organ
Finn Viderø (Compenius organ,
Frederiksborg Castle, Denmark)
12"—G-DB5214
[Sweelinck: Echo-Fantasia]
Toccata, A minor Arr. Respighi
Guido Agosti (pf) 12"—G-AW298
[Galilei: Gagliarda]
Voi partite mio sole Air
Max Meili (t) & R. Gerlin (harpsichord)
(in Vol. VIII) 12"—AS-79
[Miniscalchi: Non posso & Io tento;
Busca: Occhi belli & Bionda]

FRIEDRICH II of Prussia (1712-1786)
(Frederick the Great)

One of the best known music-sovereigns, Friedrich II was a good flutist, and composer of many works for that instrument and for other chamber ensembles. A pupil of Quantz and K. P. E. Bach, the King is best remembered

musically by his theme for J. S. Bach's "Das musicalische Opfer."

CONCERTOS Flute & Orchestra
No. 2—Largo only Arr. Müller
Georg Müller, Chamber Orch. & harpsichord—Melichar 12"—PD-27290
[Solo for Flute, Op. 122—Allegro]

SOLOS FOR FLUTE Chamber Orch. accs.
Op. 122—Allegro only
Arr. Müller
Georg Müller, Chamber Orch. & harpsichord—Melichar 12"—PD-27290
[Flute Concerto No. 2—Largo]

FRIML, Rudolf (1881-)

A Bohemian-American pianist and composer of highly melodious operettas and salon pieces, all of which are internationally known and frequently performed on stage, screen and radio.

Collections
Highlights from Operettas
(Including: Firefly: Sympathy; Giannina Mia; You're in Love: I'm only dreaming; Gloriana: I Love you, dear; Vagabond King: Valse Huguette; March of Vagabonds; White Eagle: Give me one hour; Katinka: Allah's holiday; High Jinks: The Bubble; Rose Marie: Rose Marie)
Rudolf Friml (pf) 4 12"—SCH-2
Moods and Fancies
(Including: Chanson; Valse poétique; Spanish Dance (Improvisation); Amour coquet—Vagrant love; Improvisation; Valse Lucille, Op. 85; No. 1; Adieux; Drifting, Op. 67; Egyptian Dance, Op. 41; Mélodie, Op. 27)
Rudolf Friml (pf) 4 12"—SCH-3

ORIENTAL SUITES
1. **Po Ling and Ming Toy** 1924
Po Ling and Ming Toy; Chinese Love Song; Time o'gloaming; Cometh as a birch
2. **Arabian Suite**
Call of the Desert; Bedouin dance; Mystic moonlight; Shiek's patrol
Rudolf Friml (pf) 4 12"—SCH-5
Individual Songs & Operettas
(L') Amour, toujours l'Amour Song
Eng. Love everlasting
Richard Crooks (t) 10"—V-1478
[Romberg: Student Prince—Serenade]
(G-DA1142)
Richard Tauber (t) 10"—P-RO20402
[German: Merrie England—English Rose]
Alfred Piccaver (t) 10"—D-M419
[Cadman: At Dawning]

(THE) FIREFLY Operetta & Film
(Text: Harbach)
Donkey Serenade (in film only)
Allan Jones (t) 10"—V-4380
[Giannina Mia] (G-B8714)
Also: Melachrino Strings: G-B9591
Giannina Mia
Allan Jones (t) 10"—V-4380
[Donkey Serenade] (G-B8714)

Richard Tauber (t)   10"—P-RO20381
[Pease: Command Performance—My
gypsy dream girl]
DUPLICATION: Joel Berglund (in Swed-
ish), G-X6008
Sympathy
H. Schymberg & Joel Berglund (in
Swedish)   10"—G-X6008
[Giannina Mia, Berglund only]

NORTHWEST OUTPOST—Film
Selections
Nelson Eddy (b) & Cho.   **CM-690**

ROSE MARIE Operetta & Film
Orchestral Selections
New Mayfair Orch.   12"—G-C1756
H. Finck Orch.   12"—C-DX309
Coldstream Guards Band 12"—G-C3096
Indian Love Call
Jeanette MacDonald (s) & Nelson
Eddy (b)   10"—G-DA1537
[Herbert: Naughty Marietta—Sweet
mystery of life]
Marcel Wittrisch (t) (in German)
[Rose Marie] (G-FKX9) 10"—G-EH115
Anne Ziegler (s) & Webster Booth (t)
                        10"—G-B9370
[Offenbach: Tales of Hoffmann—
Barcarolle]
Rose Marie
Nelson Eddy (b)   10"—V-4305
[The Mounties] (G-DA1464)
Marcel Wittrisch (t) (in German)
[Indian Love Call] (G-FKX9)
                      12"—G-EH115

(THE) WHITE EAGLE Operetta
Give me one hour
Gladys Swarthout (ms)
    (in VM-935)   10"—V-10-1038
[Schwartz: Band Wagon—Dancing in
the dark]

(THE) THREE MUSKETEERS Operetta
Ma Belle
Robert Merrill (b)   10"—V-10-1239
[Trad. Spanish: Juanita]

(THE) VAGABOND KING Operetta
Only a Rose
Richard Crooks (t)   10"—V-1448
[Romberg: Rio Rita—Rio Rita]

FRITZ (Friz), Gaspard (1716-1783)
*A Swiss violinist and composer who wrote six
symphonies and a great many chamber music
works, including twelve violin sonatas.*

SYMPHONIES Orchestra
No. 1, B flat
Winterthur Municipal Orch.—Herman
Scherchen   2 12"—G-DB6085/6

FROBERGER, Johann Jacob (1616-1667)
*A Saxon organist to the Court of Vienna, pupil
of Frescobaldi in Italy, who later became Court
Organist in London at Westminster Abbey. He
published many organ scores in Germany.*

Canzona, D minor (No. 4 of 6) Organ

Fantasia on "On freudt verzer" Organ
Carl Weinrich (Westminster Choir
School organ), in **MC-9**
Toccata, F major
Friedrich Mihatsch (Gonzalez Organ)
[Hanff: O Seigneur]   12"—PAT-PAT69
(in 3 Centuries of Organ Music)

FRUMERIE, Gunnar de (1908-   )
Piano Quartet 1941
Gunnar de Frumerie Quartet
                   3 12"—G-DB11016/8

FUENLLANA, Miguel de (16th century)
*A blind Spanish lutenist who published a fam-
ous collection of lute and vihuela pieces entitled "Orphenica Lyra" in 1554.*

Paseábase el Rey moro Romance in
Spanish from "Orphenica Lyra"
Maria Cid (s) & Emilio Pujol (vihuela)
        (in Vol. II)   12"—AS-17
[Luis Milan: Durandarte; Juan Vasquez:
Vos me metasteis; Diego Pisador: A las
armas moriscote]

FUNCK, David (1630-1689)
Suite, G minor
Ars Rediviva Ensemble   12"—BAM-10
[Bach: Fugue, G minor]

FURTWAENGLER, Wilhelm (1886-   )
*A German conductor in many opera houses
throughout Europe who has achieved an international reputation for his concert and opera
performances. His compositions are less known
and infrequently performed.*

CONCERTO Piano & Orch.
(Symphonic Dialogue in 2 parts)
—2nd mvt. only
Edwin Fischer & Berlin Philharmonic
Orch.—Furtwängler
(last side blank) 2 12"—G-DB4696/7s

GABRIELI, Andrea (c.1510-1586)
*A contemporary of Palestrina, organist at St.
Mark's in Venice, who is best remembered today as the teacher of Leo Hassler, Peter Sweelinck and his nephew, Giovanni Gabrieli.*

Canzona, F major (from the Canzoni
francese per l'organo)
Charles Hens (Gonzalez Organ)
                      12"—PAT-PAT63
[Landino: Questa fanciulla & Palestrina:
Ricercare]
(in 3 Centuries of Organ Music)

Pass'è mezzo antico variato in 5 modi
Anna Linde (harpsichord) 12"—MIA-5
[Anon: Pass'è mezzi]

GABRIELI, Giovanni (1557-1612)
*A nephew of Andrea Gabrieli, the teacher of
Schütz and Praetorius, and one of the greatest
contrapuntalists of all times, noted particularly
for his daring experiments in chromaticism.
The Anthologie Sonore examples, listed below,
are of unusual interest in that they are among
the earliest examples of music composed specifically for instruments.*

Benedictus Unacc. Chorus in Latin
Palestrina Cho.—Wöldike   12″—**G-Z187**
[Palestrina: Sicut cervus]
Benedixisti 7-Pt. Motet, Unacc. Chorus
in Latin
Berlin Akademie Cho.—Kalt
10″—**P-R1024**
[Monteverdi: Arianna—Lamento, Maria
Peschken]
(in 2000 Years of Music Set)
Canzona Brass & Strings ("Canzoni et
Sonate" Venice 1615)
Brass & String Ensemble—Curt Sachs
(in Vol. III)   12″—**AS-25**
[Sonata pian e forte]

**PROCESSIONAL AND CEREMONIAL
MUSIC** Voices, Organ & Brass
**Intonazione per organo, Tono IX—In
Ecclesiis benedicte Domino**
**Intonazione per organo, Tono X—
O Jesu mi dulcissime**
(from "Sacrae Symphoniae," Venice 1615)
**Intonazione per organo Tono XI—Jubilate
Deo** (from "Sacrae Symphoniae,"
Venice 1597)
Harvard Glee Club, Radcliffe Choral
Society, with Boston Symphony Orch.
Brass Choir & E. Power Biggs (org.)
—G. Wallace Woodworth
4 12″—**VM-928†**
Ricercare in the 10th Tone 4-Part Organ
Marcel Dupré   (in Vol. I)   12″—**AS-4**
[Frescobaldi: Toccata for the Elevation]
Sonata pian e forte Brass and Strings
(from "Sacre Symphoniae," Venice 1597)
Brass and String Ensemble—Sachs
[Canzona]   (in Vol. III)   12″—**AS-25**

GADE, Jacob (1879-   )

*A Danish conductor for theatres and the films
in Copenhagen, has composed much salon
music and is known here for his popular tango
"Jealousy."*

Jealousy Tango
Andre Kostalanetz & his Orch.
(in CM-681)   12″—**C-7517M**
[Rubinstein: Romance, E flat, Op. 44,
No. 1]
Boston "Pops" Orch.—Fiedler
12″—**V-12160**
[Falla: Amor Brujo—Danza Ritual
del Fuego]
Radio Symphony Orch., Copenhagen—
Emil Reesen (in preparation) English
Decca
See current catalogues for further
recordings

GADE, Niels W. (1817-1890)

*A Danish composer, friend and disciple of
Mendelssohn and Schumann, once highly pop-
ular but now almost forgotten except in the
Scandinavian countries.*

ELVERSKUD Cantata in Danish (B. G.
Ingemann)

I Osten stiger Solen Op
Copenhagen Men & Boy's Choir & Orch.
—Wöldike   12″—**G-Z261**
[Olufs Ballade, Aksel Schiøtz]

Olufs Ballade: Saa tit jeg rider mig under O
Aksel Schiøtz (t)   12″—**G-Z261**
[I Osten stiger Solen Op, Chorus]
DUPLICATION: Chr. Stage, G-X3796

(ET) FOLKSAGN Ballet
Ger. **Eine Volkssage**   Eng. **A Folk Tale**
—**Polonäs & Brudevals** Orchestra
Eng. **Polonaise & Wedding Waltz**
Royal Theatre Orch.—Hye-Knudsen
10″—**G-X6419**
Tivoli Orch.   10″—**TONO-L28003**
DUPLICATIONS: Danish Radio Orch.—
Reesen, C-J50; Royal Theater Orch.,
O-DO2006

NAPOLI Ballet
—**Galop**
Royal Theater Orch., Copenhagen,
10″—**O-DO7002**

OSSIAN, Op. 1
Ger. **Nachklänge von Ossian**
Eng. **Echoes of Ossian**
Overture Orchestra
Royal Theater Orchestra, Copenhagen—
G. Høeberg   2 12″—**G-Z252/3**
DUPLICATION: Copenhagen Philhar-
monic—Jensen, O-DXX8000/1

SONGS In Danish

Barn Jesus i en Krybbe laa
Aksel Schiøtz (t) & pf. acc.
[Grüber: Stille Nacht]   10″—**G-X6611**

Farvel lille Grethe
Marius Jacobsen (t) & pf. acc.
[Heise: Lille Karen]   10″—**G-X6868**

Hvorfor svulmer Weichselfloden
(C. Hausch)
Knud Lavard (C. Hausch)
Aksel Schiøtz (t) & pf. acc. 12″—**G-Z262**

TRIO—Violin, 'Cello, Piano F major,
Op. 42
Members of the Danish Quartet
2 12″—**G-DB5244/5**

GALILEI, Vincenzo (c.1533-1531)

*One of the most important of the Florentine
"Camerata," father of the great astronomer
Galileo Galilei, and in his own right an author
of significant treatises on music, a famous lutenist of his time, and a composer of madrigals,
lute pieces and works in other forms.*

Gagliarda Lute
—**Arr. Piano** Respighi
G. Agosti   12″—**G-AW298**
[Frescobaldi: Toccata, A minor]
Carlo Zecchi   12″—**CET-CB20352**
[Scarlatti: Sonata, C major & Anon.
Siciliana]
—**Arr. Orchestra** Respighi ("Antiche Danze
ed Arie" Suite 1, No. 2)
EIAR Orch.—Faillone
12″—**CET-BB25017**

GALLON, Noël (1891-   )

A French composer, of the Conservatoire, winner of many prizes including the Prix de Rome (1910) and known for his lyric dramas and ballet scores.

Récit and Allegro Bassoon & Piano
Fernand Oubradous & Noël Gallon
                        12″—OL-9
[Oubradous: Cadence et Divertissement pour clarinet]

GALLOT, Jacques de (fl.c.1670)

Known as Gallot of Paris, this seventeenth century French lutenist is the composer of "Pièces de Luth."

(La) Colombe Lute Eng. The Dove
—**Arr. Orchestra** Respighi
(in "Gli Uccelli")
Chicago Symphony Orch.—Defauw,
in VM-1112
EIAR Orch.—Ferraro 12″—CET-CC2195

GALUPPI, Baldassare (1706-1785)

A Venetian operatic composer who used several librettos by Goldoni. He is remembered today by his instrumental pieces, a few of which have been recorded but not properly identified.

Giga (Unspecified)
M. Amfitheatrof (vcl) & Orch.
                        12″—G-DB5413
[Corelli: Sonata No. 1—Adagio & Laserna: Tonadilla]

LA CALAMITA DEI CUORI
—**Eviva rosa bella** (Giacinto's Air)
Roland Hayes (t) & R. Boardman (pf)
(in CM-393)   12″—C-17174D
[Monteverdi: Maledetto; Buononcini: Lungi da te]

Largo & Allegro giocoso
Frederick Thurston (cl) & M. Foggin (pf)
                        12″—D-K858
[Browne: A Truro Maggot & Lloyd: Gigue]

Sonata, A major Harpsichord
Anna Linde   12″—MIA-7

Sonata, C minor Harpsichord
Rudolf Gerlin   12″—MIA-11

Sonata (Unspecified)
G. Crepax (vcl) & Pf. Acc.
                        10″—C-D5442
[Boccherini: Sonata No. 3—Excerpt]

GARDINER, Henry Balfour (1877-   )

A British composer who studied abroad, Balfour did much to promote important orchestral concerts of contemporary English music. He is known for his choral music, incidental and chamber music.

Shepherd Fennel's Dance Orchestra
(After an episode in Hardy's "Wessex Tales")
Liverpool Philharmonic Orch.—
Sargent   12″—C-DX1393

GARDNER, Samuel (1892-   )

A Russian born American violinist, pupil of Loeffler, Goetschius and others, who has played with leading orchestras and chamber music groups in this country. His string quartet won the Pulitzer Prize in 1918.

From the Canebrake, Op. 5, No. 1 Violin & Piano
Jascha Heifetz & Milton Kaye
(in D-A385)   10″—D-23386
[Debussy-Heifetz: Beau soir]
—**Arr. Orchestra**
Victor Orchestra—Bourdon
[Dett: Juba Dance]   10″—V-21750
DUPLICATION: Victor Orchestra, In V-E76

GARNIER   (16th century)

A French song-writer of the 16th Century.

Resveillez-moy, mon bel ami Song in French
Marcelle Gerer (s) with viols, flute & guitar acc.   (Vol. II) 12″—AS-15
[Gentian: La Loy d'honneur; Claudin de Sermisy: En entrant en un jardin; Jachet van Berchem: Jehan de Lagny & Que feu craintif; René: Gros Jehan menoit hors de Paris]

GASPARINI, Quirino (d.1788)

An Italian 'cellist and composer who was choirmaster at Turin.

Adoramus te Christe Motet in Latin
(Sometimes attributed to Mozart: K-327, Anh. 109)
Strasbourg Cathedral Choir & Organ—
Hoch   12″—C-69488D
(C-RFX59) (C-LWX295) (C-LX766)
[Mozart: Ave Verum Corpus]
(Josquin: Ave vera virginitas, on C-RFX68)

GAUDIOSI, Mario

Rosa d'Engaddy—Danza
EIAR Symphony Orch.—Parodi
                        12″—CET-CB20271
Sensazioni sinfoniche
EIAR Symphony Orch.—Parodi
[Sogno d'eroe, Pt. 3] 12″—CET-CB20260
Sogno d'eroe (Symphonic poem in 3 Episodes)
EIAR Symphony Orch.—Parodi
2   12″—CET-CB20259/60
[Sensazioni sinfoniche]
Sui Camaldoli—Visione sinfonico
EIAR Symphony Orch.—Parodi
                        12″—CET-CB20258

GEMINIANI, Francesco (1667-1762)

A pupil of Scarlatti and Corelli. His compositions, mostly for violin, were of less importance thin his own virtuosity and his books on violin technique.

Andante (Unspecified)
—**Arr. Strings, Harp & Organ** Marinuzzi
La Scala Orch.—Marinuzzi
                        10″—G-DA1566
[Wolf-Ferrari: Il Campiello—Ritornello]

DUPLICATIONS: (Same Andante?)
Royal Theater Orch., Copenhagen— Tango; TONO-X25032; Madami Plectrum
Quartet, C-D16419

Concerto Grosso, Op. 3, No. 2
EIAR String Orch.—Carlo Zecchi
2   12"—CET-BB25112/3

Sonata, C minor

—Siciliano Arr. Busch
Adolf Busch (vl) & Artur Balsam (pf)
(in CM-685)   12"—C-72005D
[Handel: Concerto Grosso No. 12—
Largo & Allegro]
Adolf Busch (vl) & Rudolf Serkin (pf)
[Vivaldi: Sonata]   12"—G-DB1524

GENTIAN   (16th Century)
A French song-writer of the 16th Century.

(La) Loy d'honneur Song in French
Marcelle Gerar (s) with viols, flute &
guitar acc.   (in Vol. II)   12"—AS-15
[Claudin de Sermisy: En entrant en un
jardin; Jachet van Berchem: Jehan de
Lagny & Que feu craintif; René: Gros
Jehan menoit hors de Paris; Garnier:
Resveillez-moy, mon bel ami]

GEOFFROY, Jean Nicolas (c. 1700)
*An organist of St. Nicolas du Chardonnet,
Geoffroy's harpsichord pieces are known today
as an example of early French keyboard music.*

Tombeau en forme d'Allemande Harpsichord
Pauline Aubert   (Vol. I)   12"—AS-8
[Dornel: Le Pendant d'Oreille & La Noce
d'Auteuil]

GERMAN, (Sir) Edward (1862-1936)
*A British composer, principally of light operas,
noted as the only man to attempt with any success to carry on the vogue of the Sullivan
operettas. His "Nell Gwyn" and "Henry VIII"
dances are probably the works for which he is
best known outside of England, although he
composed in all forms.*

HENRY VIII Incidental Music
(3) Dances Orchestra
**Morris Dance; Shepherd's Dance; Torch
Dance**
BBC Theatre Orch.—Stanford Robinson
12"—D-K1356
New Symphony Orch.—Sargent
10"—G-B2981
Bournemouth Municipal Orch.—Godfrey
10"—C-5577
City of Birmingham Orch.—Weldon
2 10"—C-DB2343/4
[Nell Gwyn: Pastoral Dance]
—Shepherd's Dance only
Victor Orch.—Reibold, V-22171

MERRIE ENGLAND Light Opera in English
1902
Abridged Recording
Columbia Light Opera Company
8 10"—C-DB478/83
(Recorded under supervision of the composer)

The Cast:
Earl of Essex .... George Baker (b)
Sir Walter Raleigh ...... Dan Jones (t)
Queen Elizabeth .. Edith Furmedge (a)
Maid of Honour .... Alice Lilley (s)
Jill-all-alone .... Nellie Walker (a)
Long Tom .... Robert Carr (b)
Clarence Raybould, conductor
Vocal & Orchestral Selections
Light Opera Company   12"—G-C2106
Light Opera Company   12"—C-9893
Orchestral Selections (Fantasias, etc.)
New Symphony Orch.—Sargent
12"—G-C2196
DUPLICATION: Grenadier Guards Band,
C-9607
**—Dances (Hornpipe, Minuet, Rustic Dance,
Jig)**
Bournemouth Municipal Orch.—Birch
10"—D-F7998
—Arr. 2 Pfs. Rawicz & Landauer
Rawicz & Landauer   10"—C-DB2305
Individual Excerpts
Chorus & Dance, Act II
Review Cho. & BBC Theater Orch.
12"—D-K844
[Love is meant to make us glad]
(The) English Rose Tenor
Webster Booth   10"—G-B8947
[Boughton: Immortal Hour—Faery
Song]
Richard Tauber   10"—P-RO20402
[Friml: L'amour, toujours L'amour]
DUPLICATIONS: Walter Midgley,
C-DB1899; David Lloyd, C-DB2109
Love is meant to make us glad Quintet
Review Cho. & BBC Theater Orch.
(Chorus & Dance, Act II)   12"—D-K844
O Peaceful England
Essie Ackland (c)   10"—G-B8537
[Braga: Serenata]
Gladys Ripley (c) & Light Opera Cho.
12"—G-C3490
[Yeomen of England—Dennis Noble]
(The) Yeomen of England Baritone
Dennis Noble & Light Opera Cho.
12"—G-C3490
[O Peaceful England, Gladys Ripley]
Peter Dawson   12"—G-B3111
[Sanderson: Drake goes west]
DUPLICATION: Vocal Quartet & Band,
D-F7286

NELL GWYN Incidental Music to a play by
Anthony Hope 1900
(3) Dances Orchestra
Country Dance; Pastoral Dance; Merrymaker's Dance
New Symphony Orch.—Sargent
2 10"—G-B2987 & G-B3036
Light Symphony Orch.
2 10"—C-DB2081/2
[Elgar: Salut d'Amour]
—Pastoral Dance only
City of Birmingham Orch.—Weldon
10"—C-DB2344
[Henry VIII Dances, Pt. 3]

ROMEO AND JULIET Incidental Music
Pavane Orchestra
   Hastings Municipal Orch.—Cameron
   [Welsh Rhapsody, Pt. 3]   12″—D-K518

SONGS In English
Glorious Devon
   Peter Dawson (b)   10″—G-B3280
   [Newton: Drum Major]

TOM JONES Light Opera in English 1907
Waltz Song Soprano
   Anne Ziegler   10″—G-B9241
   [Weber: Invitation to the Waltz, vocal
   arr.]

WELSH RHAPSODY Orchestra
1. Loudly proclaim o'er land and sea
2. Hunting the hare & The bells of Aber-
   dovey
3. David of the White Rock
4. Men of Harlech
   City of Birmingham Orch.—George
   Weldon   2 12″—C-DX1274/5
   Hastings Municipal Orch.—Cameron
                2 12″—D-K577/8
   [Romeo and Juliet—Pavane]
   London Symphony Orch.—Ronald
                2 12″—G-D1939/40

GERSHWIN, George (1898-1937)
*One of the most popular American composers,
Gershwin reached international fame before his
untimely death at the age of 40. He wrote many
"hit tunes" (composed with care and intelli-
gence) for musical comedies, "folk operas" (his
"Porgy and Bess" is perhaps now an American
classic) and will probably be best remembered
by his excursion into symphonic jazz, the
"Rhapsody in Blue."*

COLLECTIONS
(AN) ALBUM OF GEORGE GERSHWIN
   MUSIC
Including: Rhapsody in Blue; Second
   Rhapsody; Cuban Overture; An Ameri-
   can in Paris
   Roy Bargy & Rosa Linda (solo pianists),
   with Paul Whiteman and his Concert Or-
   chestra   5 12″—D-A31

JAZZ CONCERT
Including: 'S wonderful; Somebody loves
   me; My one and only; Oh, Lady be good;
   Someone to watch over me; The man I
   love; Swanee; I'll build a stairway to
   Paradise
   Eddie Condon, with Lee Wiley (vocal)
   and selected group of Jazz musicians
                4 10″—D-A23

MEMORIAL ALBUM
Including: Of Thee I sing—Excerpts; Girl
   Crazy—Excerpts, (V-12332); Rhapsody
   in Blue—Andante; The Man I Love
   (V-12333); Porgy and Bess—Excerpts
   (V-12334); Oh, Kay!—Excerpts; Med-
   ley: Swanee, South Sea Isle; That Cer-
   tain Feeling; Somebody Loves me

(V-12335); Lady Be Good!—Excerpts
Tip Toes—Excerpts; Medley: Oh, gee!
Oh, joy; 'S wonderful, Do It Again;
Strike up the Band (V-12336)
   Jane Froman (s), with Sonny Schuyler,
   Felix Knight & Victor Salon Group
   (chorus & orchestra)—Shilkret
             5 12″—V-C29

MUSIC OF GEORGE GERSHWIN
Including:· Embraceable you; Fascinatin'
   rhythm; The man I love; 'S wonderful;
   Maybe; Someone to watch over me; Oh,
   Lady be good; Soon
   Andre Kostelanetz & his Orchestra
            4 10″—CM-559

SELECTIONS Arr. Violin & Piano
Including: Porgy and Bess—Summertime;
   A woman is a sometime thing; My man's
   gone now; It ain't necessarily so; Bess,
   you is my woman now; Tempo di blues;
   Preludes 1, 2 & 3
   Jascha Heifetz & Emanuel Bay
          10″ & 3 12″—D-A435

SHOW TUNES
Including: Oh, Lady be good; Someone to
   watch over me; Maybe; Somebody loves
   me; Nice work if you can get it; It ain't
   necessarily so; They can't take that away
   from me; Do it again
   Billy Butterfield and his Orchestra
            4 10″—CAP-BD10

SPECIALS—George and Ira Gershwin
Including: By Strauss; Blah-Blah, Blah;
   Lorelei; Isn't it a pity; Three times a day;
   I love to rhyme; The half-of-it-dearie
   blues; The jolly tar and the milk maid
   George Byron (t) & Bobby Tucker (pf)
            4 10″—GEN-G14
(An) American in Paris Orchestra
   Philharmonic-Symphony of New York—
   Rodzinski   2 12″—CX-246†
   Paul Whiteman Concert Orch.—White-
   man, in D-A31†
   Victor Symphony—Shilkret
            2 12″—V-35963/4
Concerto, F major Piano & Orchestra
   Oscar Levant & Philharmonic-Symphony
   Orch. of New York—Kostelanetz
            4 12″—CM-512†
   Jesús María Sanromá & Boston "Pops"
   Orch.—Fiedler   4 12″—VM-690†
   Roy Bargy & Paul Whiteman Concert
   Orch.—Whiteman   2 12″—D-A57†
Cuban Overture Orchestra
   Paul Whiteman Concert Orch.—White-
   man, in D-A31†

PORGY AND BESS 3 Act Opera in English
   1935
Selections
Volume I: Overture; Summertime; I got
   plenty o'nuttin'; Buzzard Song; Bess, you
   is my woman now; It ain't necessarily so;
   The Requiem; Porgy's Lament and finale
Volume II: A woman is a sometime thing;
   It take a long pull to get there; What

you want wid Bess?; Strawberry woman's call and Crab man's call (Street cries); I love you, Porgy; There's a boat dat's leavin' soon for New York
Anne Brown (s), Todd Duncan (b), Eva Jessye Choir and members of the original New York production, with Decca Symphony Orch.—Smallens
      Vol. I 4 12"—**D-A145**
      Vol. II 3 10"—**D-A283**
Volume III: (In Dance Tempo) It ain't necessarily so; A woman is a sometime thing; Summertime; There's a boat dat's leavin' soon for New York; I got plenty o' nuttin'; Bess, you is my woman now.
Avon Long (b), Helen Dowdy (s) & Leo Reisman Orchestra 3 10"—**D-A351**

Selections
Including: It ain't necessarily so; The buzzard's song; Summertime; Crap Game; Bess, you is my woman now; I got plenty o' nuttin'; Where is my Bess?; Lullaby; My man's gone now
Helen Jepson (s), Lawrence Tibbett (b) with Orch.—Smallens (Recording supervised by Gershwin) 4 12"—**V-C25**

Individual Excerpts
I Got plenty o' Nuttin'
Lawrence Tibbett, (b)
   (in VM-1015) 12"—**V-11-8860**
[Dvořák-Fisher: Goin' Home]

It ain't necessarily so; A woman is a sometime thing
Paul Robeson (bs) 10"—**G-B8711**

Summertime
Lily Pons (s) 12"—**C-71491D**
[Brahms: Waltz, A flat, Op. 39, No. 15—Orch. only]
Eleanor Steber (s) 12"—**V-11-9186**
[Carmichael: Stardust]
DUPLICATION: Camilla Williams, V-46-0004

Where is my Bess?
James Melton (t) with duo-pfs
     12"—**V-11-9224**
[Kern: All through the day]

A Symphonic Picture
(from "Porgy and Bess")
Arranged for orchestra by Robert Russell Bennett
Pittsburgh Symphony Orch.—Reiner
     3 12"—**CM-572†**
Indianapolis Symphony Orch.—
Sevitzky 3 12"—**VM-999†**
Slightly abbreviated version
Philharmonic Orchestra of Los Angeles
—Wallenstein 2 12"—**D-DA397**

(3) Preludes Piano
No. 1, B flat major
No. 2, C sharp minor
No. 3, E flat major
George Gershwin 12"—**C-7192M**
[Rhapsody in Blue—Andante only]
Oscar Levant
   (in CM-508) 10"—**C-17452D**

—Arr. Violin & Piano
Jascha Heifetz & Emanuel Bay, in
D-A435

—No. 1, B flat major
Andor Foldes, in **CON-22**
—Nos 2 & 3 only
Oscar Levant
   (in CX-251†) 12"—**C-12125D**
[Rhapsody in Blue, Pt. 3] (C-DX1213)
—No. 2 only
Artur Rubinstein 12"—**V-11-9420**
[Milhaud: Saudades do Brazil—Nos. 5, 9, 11]

RHAPSODY IN BLUE Piano and Orchestra

Oscar Levant & Philadelphia Orch.—
Ormandy 2 12"—**CX-251†**
[Preludes Nos. 2 & 3, Levant only]
(C-DX1212/3)
Jesús María Sanromá & Boston "Pops" Orch.—Fiedler 2 12"—**VM-358†**
[Strike up the Band]
(G-C2806/7) (G-EH953/4)
(G-FKX46/7)
George Gershwin & Paul Whiteman Orch.—Whiteman 12"—**V-35822**
(G-C1395) (G-S10037) (G-L634)
Alec Templeton & Andre Kostelanetz & his Orch. 2 12"—**CX-196†**
(C-DX1045/6)
Roy Bargy & Whiteman Concert Orch.—Whiteman, in **D-A31†** (B-0140)
DUPLICATIONS: Vladimir Sokolov & Al Goodman Orch., V-46-0004; Earl Wild & Paul Whiteman Orch. w. Chorus, Signature-GP1
—Arr. 2 Pianos
Jose & Ampara Iturbi (Arr. Iturbi)
(G-DB6220/1) 2 12"—**VM-517†**
Rawicz & Landauer 10"—**C-DB2104**
Miscellaneous arrangements
Eight Piano Ensemble, V-36123:
G-C2616; Larry Adler (harmonica) & Orch., C-35513 in C-18; G. Binz & T. Thomassen (2 pfs.) & Orch., U-G18128
—Andante only Pf. solo
George Gershwin 12"—**C-7192M**
[3 Preludes]
Second Rhapsody Piano & Orchestra 1932
Roy Bargy & Whiteman Concert Orch.—Paul Whiteman, in **D-A31†**

Strike Up the Band Musical Comedy
Title song
Boston "Pops" Orch.—Fiedler
   (in VM-358) 12"—**V-11823**
[Rhapsody in Blue, Pt. 3: with Sanromá, pf.]
(G-C2807) (G-FKX47) (G-EH954)

The Man I Love
Gladys Swarthout (ms) 10"—**V-10-1039**
[Rodgers: Connecticut Yankee—My heart stood still]

See also domestic catalogues for more complete listings.

GERVAISE, Claude (16th century)
A French viol-player who published numbers of "Danceries" and chansons.

Danceries françaises Strings

Allemande, Pavane, Gaillarde, Branle simple, Branle de Bourgogne, Branle de Champagne
String Orch.—Curt Sachs
(in Vol. I)   12"—AS-6
—**Allemande only**
Margarete Riedel (harpsichord) & recorders   10"—G-EG6098
[Anon: Louven, 1571: Pavane "Lesquercardes"; Gaillarde "La Fanfare"; Fantasie & Passomezzo "La Doulce"]

Six Dances of the Renaissance (16th Century) Strings
(Revised and adapted by Rosario Scalero)

Branle de Bourgogne; Branle de Poitou; Branle de Champagne; Gaillarde; Branle Double; Branle Gay
Curtis Chamber Music Ensemble—Louis Bailly   10"—G-DA1555

Danses de la Renaissance
Quartet of Viols—Mme. H. Teysseire-Wuillemier   12"—G-W1594

GESUALDO, Don Carlo (Prince of Venosa) (c. 1560-1613)

One of the most fantastic figures in musical history (see Gray and Heseltine's "Gesualdo, Prince of Murderers") and one of the most original and radical composers of the Italian madrigal school during the Renaissance period.

Moro lasso Unacc. Madrigal in Italian
Passani Choir
(in Vol. XIII)   12"—AS-120
[Marenzio: Stridar faceva; Perchè la pioggia]

Resti di darmi noia Unacc. Madrigal in Italian
Thiel's Choir—Thiel   10"—P-R1022
[Hassler: Mein Lieb' will mit mir kriegen]
(in 2000 Years of Music Set)

GHERARDELLO (Ghirarellus de Florentia) (14th Century)

A Florentine composer of madrigals, best known today for his songs for two voices.

Caccia—Tosto che l'alba Voice & Trombone
Mertins Jacquier (t) & Society Pro Arte
(in Vol. VI)   12"—AS-59
[Jacopo da Bologna: Madrigal]

GHEYN, Matthias van den (1721-1785)

Member of a renowned Flemish family of bell-founders, Gheyn was an organist, carillonneur, and composer in the style of Handel and Arne.

Fugue, G major Organ
Alfred Sittard (St. Michael's organ)
12"—PD-95157
[Schmid: Galliarda & Boellmann: Toccata, C minor]

GHIZEGHEM, Hayne van (15th Century)

A Flemish singer and composer of many chansons and small instrumental pieces.

Les Grans Regrez Unacc. Chorus
Yvonne Gouverné Chorus   10"—OL-63

[Binchois: Filles à marier & Morton: Trois Chansons]
A la Audienche
Plus n'en aray
Violas, Trumpet & Trombone
12"—OL-136
[Grenon: Je ne requier de ma dame]
—**Plus n'en aray only**
Lavaillotte (fl), Lefèbvre (cl) & Oubradous (bsn)   12"—OL-61
[Morton: Mon bien ma joye & Grenon: Nova vobis Gaudia]

GIARDINI, Felice de (1716-1796)

An Italian violinist and singer of Turin, manager of Italian opera in London where he was very successful for many years. He composed many operas and over fifty sonatas for the violin together with other chamber music.

Sonata a Tre, E flat
—**Siciliana only**
Enzo Calace (pf) & La Scala Quartet
12"—G-AW291
[Montani: Concertino, E flat, Pt. 3]

GIBBONS, Orlando (1583-1625)

An important member of the Elizabethan school, known as one of the finest organists of his time and as a composer of church music, madrigals, keyboard works and fantasias for strings.

Ah, dear heart 5-Part Madrigal (John Donne)
London Madrigal Group   10"—V-4317
[Wilbye: Sweet honey sucking bees]

Amen (Threefold)
Westminster Abbey Choir (for Princess Elizabeth's Wedding Music, 1947),
12"—G-B9614
(Also included on Side 25 in Coronation Service of George VI, G-RG12)

Hosanna to the Son of David 6-Part Motet
Winchester Music Club, unacc.
12"—C-D40120
(illustration for Lecture 61 "The Progress of Music"—Dyson)
(International Educational Society Series)

(The) Lord of Salisbury—His Pavin; The Queen's Command (from "Parthenia" 1611)
Ralph Kirkpatrick (harpsichord), in MC-25

(The) Silver Swan 5-Part Madrigal
St. George's Singers, unacc.
10"—C-5717
[Farmer: Fair Phyllis & Weelkes: As Vesta was from Latmos Hill descending]
(in Columbia History of Music, Vol. I: CM-231)
Danish State Radio Madrigal Chorus—Wöldike   (in preparation)
Danish Columbia

GIBBS, Cecil Armstrong (1889-   )

A conservative, skillful British composer, principally of songs and chamber music.

Fancy Dress—Suite
—Dusk
   Melachrino Strings   10"—G-B9535
   [Melachrino: Vision d'amour]

GIGOUT, Eugène (1844-1925)

A French organist and composer of over 400 works, a pupil of Saint-Saëns, who became a teacher at the Conservatoire.

Toccata, B minor Organ
   Virgil Fox   10"—V-10-1208
   [Campra: Rigaudon]
   Édouard Commette (Cathédral St. Jean)
   [Boellmann: Toccata]   12"—C-D11026

GILBERT, Henry F. (1868-1928)

A New England composer, pupil of MacDowell, who made use of Negro themes for his work and is remembered by his symphonic ballet listed below.

Dance in the Place Congo Symphonic Ballet
Orchestra 1918
   Janssen Symphony of Los Angeles—Janssen, in ARTIST-JS13
   ["in Four American Landscapes" with music of Copland, Ives, & Cowell]

GIORDANI, Giuseppe (1744-1798)

An Italian composer of songs and operas who achieved success in England and Ireland. He devoted the last part of his life composing oratorios and other church music for his post as choirmaster at Fermo.

Caro mio ben Air in Italian
   Ezio Pinza (bs) & Fritz Kitzinger (pf)
       (in VM-766)   12"—V-17916
   [Falconieri: O bellissimi capelli & Sarti: Lungi dal caro bene; Buononcini: Pupille nere]
   Heinrich Schlusnus (b)   12"—PD-67250
   [Handel: Serse—Largo]
   Paul Sandoz (b) & H. Vollenweider
   (org)   12"—G-DB10043
   [Handel: Serse—Largo]
   Guiseppe De Luca (b) & Pietro Cimara (pf), in D-U1
   DUPLICATIONS: Karl Schmitt-Walter, T-E2234; Margarete Klose, G-EH993; Vaselli, G-HN1106; B. Saenger Orch. O-26515

GIORDANO, Umberto (1867-   )

A contemporary Italian opera composer, numbered among the Mascagni group in the "verismo" school, and best known for his "Andrea Chénier."

Crepuscolo triste Song in Italian
   Gianna Pederzini (ms) 10"—G-DA5385
   [Bizet: Carmen—Habañera]

Idyll Arr. Harpsichord Mola
   Corradina Mola (harpsichord)
   [Liadov: Music Box]   10"—G-DA5399

OPERAS In Italian

ANDREA CHENIER 4 Acts 1896

Complete recording
   La Scala Soloists, Chorus & Orchestra—
   de Fabritiis   13 12"—G-DB5423/35
   The Cast:
   Andrea Chénier .... Benimino Gigli (t)
   Maddalena .... Maria Caniglia (s)
   Gerard .... Gino Bechi (b)
   Countess .... G. Simionato (s)
   Madelon .... M. Palombini (s)
   Bersi .... Maria Huder (s)
   Mathieu .... Paci (b)
   Roucher .... I. Tajo (bs)
   Fouquier-Tinville ...... Taddei (bs)
   Maestro, Dumas, Schmidt ... Conti (bs)
   L'Abate, Spy, etc. ...... Zangonara (bs)
   (A. Consoli, Chorus master)

Complete recording
   Soloists, La Scala Chorus & Orchestra—
   Molajoli   13 12"—C-OP21†
   (C-GQX10106/18)
   The Cast:
   Andrea Chénier ...... Luigi Marini (t)
   Carlo Gerard .... Carlo Galeffi (b)
   Maddalena ...... Lina Bruna Rasa (s)
   Countess }
   Madelon } ....A. M. Bassi (s)
   Bersi .... Ida Conti (s)
   Roucher   }
   Fouquier-Tinville } ...S. Baccaloni (bs)
   Mathieu   }
   Il Romanziere }Aristide Baracchi (b)
   L'Abate & Spy ..... Giuseppe Nessi (t)
   Schmidt Dumas, etc. .. Natale Villa (bs)
   (Vitorre Veneziani, chorus master)

Fantasy Arr. Weniger
   Symphony Orch.   12"—C-CQX16468

Individual Excerpts

ACT I

Son sessant' anni Baritone
   Benvenuto Franci   10"—G-DA1093
   [Verdi: Ballo in Maschera—Alla vita]
   [Un dì m'era di gioia, on C-DQ1130]

Un dì all' azzurro spazio (Improvviso)
Tenor
   Beniamino Gigli   12"—G-DB5406
   [Cilea: L'Arlesiana—Lamento di Federico]
   [Ponchielli: Gioconda—Cielo e mar, on G-DB2234]
   Leonida Bellon   12"—CET-CC2205
   [Mascagni: Cavalleria—Addio, with Vinciguerra]
   Georges Thill   12"—C-D41012
   [Puccini: Turandot—Nessun dorma]
   DUPLICATIONS: R. Zanelli, G-DB1339; L. Marini, C-DQ1092; A. Pertile, G-DB1118; H. Lazaro, C-GQX10140; S. Rayner, D-K997; F. Merli, C-GQX10245; A. Lindi, C-DQ1100; G. Voyer, C-CQ266; Martinelli, G-DB1143; De Muro, G-DB553*, Caruso, G-DB700*; G. Lauri-Volpi, G-DB539: G-DB2263; Tamagno, G-DS101* & G-DR102*; A. Ferrauto, CET-CB20281

ACT III
Nemico della patria (Monologo di Gerard)
Baritone
Un dì m'era di gioia
> G. Manacchini   12″—CET-CC2158
> [Verdi: Rigoletto—Cortigiani]
> John Charles Thomas   12″—V-17639
> [Verdi: Otello—Credo]
> Robert Merrill   12″—V-11-9384
> [Meyerbeer: Africana—Adamastor, Re]
> Heinrich Schlusnus   12″—PD-67107
> [Verdi: Don Carlos—Per me giunto]
> [Tschaikovsky: Eugene Onegin—Onegin's
> Aria, on PD-67249]
> Enzo Mascherini   12″—C-GQX11084
> [Verdi: Don Carlos—O Carlo ascolta]
> DUPLICATIONS: Titta Ruffo,
> G-DB1397: G-DB5386; G-DB242*;
> Apollo Granforte, G-DB1453; M. Stabile,
> C-CQX16502; E. Molinari, C-D16425; B.
> Franci, C-DQ1130; R. Stracciari,
> C-CQX16488; U. Di Lelio, C-D16425; C.
> Maugeri, C-D16422; C. Galeffi, C-GQ7036
> In German: G. Hüsch, G-DB4510; S. O.
> Sandberg, O-9134

La mamma morta Soprano
Ger. **Von blut gerotet**
> Claudio Muzio
>   (in CM-259)   12″—C-9167M
> [Puccini: Bohême—Si, mi chiamano
> Mimì]
> (C-BQX2507) (C-LCX28)
> Rosa Raisa   12″—G-DB2123
> [Mascagni: Cavalleria—Voi lo sapete]
> Maria Caniglia   12″—G-DB5361
> [Verdi: Forza del Destino—Pace, pace]
> DUPLICATIONS: Maria Pedrini, CET-
> CC2324; Rosetta Pampanini,
> C-GQX10230: C-LWX251; Scacciati,
> C-CQX16502; Iva Pacetti, C-D14476;
> Gina Cigna, C-CQX10593; L. B. Rasa,
> C-GQX10256; M. Laurenti, C-CQX16456;
> In German: Maria Reining, G-DB7648

Si, fui soldato Tenor
> Beniamino Gigli   10″—G-DA1312
> [Leoncavallo: Pagliacci—No, Pagliaccio
> non son]
> Renato Zanelli   12″—G-DB1339
> [Un dì all'azzurro]
> DUPLICATIONS: Masini, CET-TI7010;
> Merli, C-GQX10245; Lindi, C-DQ1125;
> Fagoaga, C-D12311; A. Ferrauto, CET-
> CB20281; De Muro, G-DB553*

ACT IV
Come un bel dì di Maggio Tenor
> Jussi Björling   10″—V-10-1323
> [Verdi: Ballo in Maschera—Barcarola]
> [Fedora—Amor ti vieta, on G-DA1836]
> Tito Schipa   10″—G-DA5352
> [Marcella—Dolce notte]
> Giovanni Martinelli   12″—G-DB1143
> [Un dì all'azzurro]
> DUPLICATIONS: Aureliano Pertile,
> G-DA1185 & C-CQ968; Alfred Piccaver,
> PD-95354; G. Masini, CET-TI7010;
> Lazaro, C-CQX10140; A. Lindi,
> C-DQ1125; Marini, C-DQ1096; Pertile,
> C-CQ698; L. Bellon, CET-CC2213;
> Caruso, G-DA117*

Vicino a te Final Duo: Soprano & Tenor
La nostra morte
> Margherita Sheridan & A. Pertile
>   12″—G-DB1289
> B. Scacciati & F. Merli
>   12″—C-GQX10212

FEDORA   3 Acts 1898
Complete recording
> Soloists, La Scala Chorus & Orch.—
> Molajoli   11 12″—C-GQX10496/506
> [Siberia—Cena di Pasqua]
> The Cast:
> Fedora .... Gilda Dalla Rizza
> Loris .... Antonio Melandri
> De Siriex .... Emilio Ghirardini
> Olga .... Mirella Luba
> Grech .... Corrado Zambelli
> Cirillo .... Ernesto Dominici
> Dmitri .... Ebe Ticozzi
> Piccolo Savoiardo ...... Ida Mannarini
> Desiré & Barone Rouvel .. Piero Girardi
> Lorek & Borov .... Eugenio Dall'Argine
> Nicola .... Blando Giusti
> Boleslao Lazinski   Bernardo de Plaisant
> Sergio .... Antonio Alferi
> (Vittore Veneziani, chorus master)

Individual Excerpts

Act I
O grandi occhi Soprano
> Cloe Elmo (ms)   12″—CET-BB25033
> [Cilea: Adriana Lecouvreur—O vaga-
> bonda]

ACT II
Amor ti vieta Tenor
> Jussi Björling   10″—G-DA1836
> [Andrea Chénier—Come un bel dì]
> Beniamino Gigli   10″—G-DA5377
> [Pietri: Maristella—I' conosco un
> giardino]
> [Buzzi-Peccia: Lolita, on G-DA1722]
> DUPLICATIONS: Giovanni Malipiero
> G-DA5407; Stefan Islandi, G-DA5202;
> Alessandro Ziliani, G-DA1424; Martinelli,
> G-DA861; P. Civil, CET-CB20277; A.
> Pertile, C-GQ7177; Granda, C-DQ1109;
> Gigli, G-DA225*; L. Giudice, C-DQ271;
> Amadeo Bassi, CRS-29*; (Recorded
> 1906); Dino Borgioli, C-CQ695; Picca-
> luga, C-DQ692; Edward Johnson,
> G-DA116*
> In German: A. Piccaver, PD-90151

Intermezzo Orchestra
> La Scala Orch.—Ghione 10″—G-HN794
> [Cilea: Adriana Lecouvreur—Intermez-
> zo]

Mia Madre Duo: Soprano & Tenor
> Augusta Oltrabella & A. Ziliani
>   12″—G-DB5350
> [Puccini: Suor Angelica—Senza mamma,
> Oltrabella]
> (Wagner: Lohengrin—Act 1 Duo,
> Caniglia & Ziliani on G-DB2859)
> A. Oltrabella & P. Pauli
>   10″—G-DA1340
> [Verdi: Ballo in Maschera—Saper vor-
> reste, A. Saraceni]

—**Tenor part only**
Giovanni Martinelli   10″—**G-DA861**
[Amor ti vieta]
Vedi, io piango Tenor
Aureliano Pertile   10″—**C-GQ7177**
[Amor ti vieta]
DUPLICATION: B. Gigli, G-DA225*
—**Unspecified Excerpt** (Labelled "Elite Waltz")
Cincinnati Summer Opera Orch.—
Cleva, in **D-A491**

MARCELLA
Prelude to Scene 3 Orchestra
Romanza di Giorgio (Dolce notte misteriosa)
Tenor
Gino del Signore & EIAR Symphony
Orch.—Giordano   12″—**CET-P56096**
[Il Rè—Intermezzo]
—**Romanza only**
Tito Schipa   10″—**G-DA5352**
[Andrea Chénier—Come un bel dì]

MESE MARIANO
Racconto di Carmela
Augusta Oltrabella, Tegani (sopranos) &
Rita Monticone (c)   12″—**G-DB5382**
Intermezzo Orchestra
Milan Symphony Orch.—Olivero
    12″—**G-S10489**
[Jachino: Christmas pastorale]

(IL) RE
O Colombello, sposarti
Valzer (Brilla sulla mia fronte) Act 3 Soprano
Lina Pagliughi
(in CET-8)   12″—**CET-BB25093**
[Verdi: Falstaff—Sul fin d'un soffio etesio]
Mercedes Capsir   10″—**C-GQ7150**
Intermezzo
EIAR Orch.—Giordano
    12″—**CET-P56096**
[Marcella—Prelude & Romanza]

SIBERIA 1904
Cena di Pasqua Orchestra
Milan Symphony—Molajoli
    12″—**C-GQX10506**
[Fedora—Complete opera, Pt. 21]
La Scala Orch.—Marinuzzi
    12″—**G-DB3209**
[Rossini: Il Signor Bruschino—Overture]
DUPLICATION: EIAR Orch.—Tansini,
CET-P56091
Intermezzo, Act II
EIAR Orch.—Tansini 12″—**CET-P56091**
[Cena di Pasqua]
Qual vergogna tu porti, Act III
Maria Caniglia   10″—**G-DA1563**
[Puccini: Manon Lescaut—In quelle trine, M. Favero]
T'incontra per via Tenor
Amadeo Bassi & pf. acc.
(Recorded 1906)   10″—**CRS-29***
[Fedora—Amor ti vieta]

SONGS See Crepuscolo triste

GIULIANO, Maruto (c.1780-c.1840)
An Italian guitar virtuoso.
Grande Overture, Op. 61 Guitar
Julio Martinez Oyanguren 12″—**V-13673**

GLANVILLE-HICKS, Peggy (1911-   )
An Australian composer, pupil of Vaughan-Williams, Nadia Boulanger and others. She is known for chamber music and songs, as well as for an opera "Cadman."
Choral Suite Women's Voices, Oboe & String Orchestra
(5 Poems by John Fletcher, 1579)
Chorus & Orchestra   10″—**OL-100**

GLAZOUNOV, Alexander (1865-1936)
One of the older and more conservative contemporary Russian musicians, a pupil of Rimsky-Korsakov, a sound craftsman, and a prolific composer in many forms.
Ballets
See: Raymonda; Scènes de Ballet; The Seasons
Carnival, Op. 45 Overture for Orchestra
Chicago Symphony Orch.—Stock
    12″—**C-11771D**
Chant du ménestrel, Op. 71 'Cello & Piano
Edmund Kurtz & Emanuel Bay
    12″—**V-11-8815**
[Beethoven: Sonata, C minor, Groves 150]
Chopiniana, Op. 46
Suite for Orchestra
Orchestrations of Chopin piano pieces:
—**Tarantelle, Op. 42 only**
London Philharmonic Orch.—Ronald
(G-S10442)   2   12″—**G-C2639**
[Mendelssohn: Spring Song & Spinning Song]
Concerto—Violin & Orchestra, A minor, Op. 82
Jascha Heifetz & London Philharmonic—
Barbirolli   3   12″—**VM-218†**
[Méditation, Op. 32]
Miguel Candela & Colonne Orch.—
Désormière   3   12″—**C-LFX645/7**
Etude de concert, C major, Op. 31, No. 1
Piano
Alexander Borovsky
(PD-62761)   10″—**PD-561095**
[Prokofiev: Sarcasme No. 5]
From the Middle Ages, Op. 79 Orch. Suite
—**Scherzo**
EIAR Orch.—DeSabata
    12″—**CET-PP60009**
[Stravinsky: Feu d'artifice]
—**Troubadour's Serenade**
EIAR Orch.—DeSabata
    12″—**CET-PP60008**
[Mossolov: Steel Foundry]
Méditation, Op. 32 Violin & Piano
Jascha Heifetz & Arpad Sandor
(in VM-218†)   12″—**V-8298**
[Violin Concerto, Pt. 5]
(Wieniawski: Scherzo Tarantelle, on V-14323)
(Mozart: Duo for Violin & Viola, Pt. 5 on V-18197 in VM-831†)

Karel Sroubek & F. Maxian
                    12"—U-G14234
[Borodin: Nocturne & Rimsky Korsa-
kov: Flight of the Bumblebee]
(5) Novellettes, Op. 15 String Quartet
1. Allegretto alla spagnuola
2. Orientale
3. Interludim in modo antico
4. Waltz
5. Allegretto all' ungherese
—No. 3 (Interludium in modo antico) only
Calvet Quartet   12"—G-DB5028
[Ravel: Quartet, Pt. 7]
Poltronieri Quartet   12"—C-CQX10044
[No. 5, Allegretto]
DUPLICATIONS: Rome Quartet,
G-DB4699; Pro Arte Quartet, on V-8298
in VM-186†
—No. 5 (Allegretto all' ungherese) only
Poltronieri Quartet   12"—C-GQX10044
[No. 3, Interludium]
Overture on Greek Themes No. 1, Op. 3
Orchestra
Minneapolis Symphony Orch.—Mitro-
poulos   2 12"—CX-228†

QUARTETS—String
No. 3, G major ("The Slavonic") Op. 26
—Mazurka only
Rome String Quartet   12"—G-DB4653
Quartet—Theme & Scherzo Saxophone
Quartet
Quartet from La Garde Républicaine
Band   10"—C-DF1806
[Mendelssohn: Agitato]

RAYMONDA—Ballet, Op. 57 Orchestra
Excerpts
Including: Introduction; Opening Scene—
In the Castle; Dance of the Pages &
Young Girls; The Arrival of the Stranger;
Entrance of Raymonda; Moonlight; Pre-
lude and La Romanesca; Variations; Ray-
monda's Dream; Spanish Dance; Valse
Fantastique; Grand Adagio; Variation
Raymonda; Dance of the Arab Boys; En-
trance of the Saracens; Love Triumphant
and Wedding Feast
Boston "Pops" Orchestra—Fiedler
                    4 12"—VM-1133†
—Valse Fantasique & Spanish Dance only
Bolshoi Theatre Orch.—Freir
                    10"—USSR-12815/6
Rêverie, Op. 24 Horn & Piano (or Or-
chestra)
Jean Devemy & Lamoureux Orch.—A.
Wolff   12"—PD-67041
[Cui: Tarantelle] (PD-566138)

SCENES DE BALLET, Op. 52 Orchestra
—No. 5, (Dance Orientale) only
Philadelphia Orch.—Stokowski
                    10"—V-1335
[Ippolitov-Ivanov: Caucasian Sketches—
Procession of the Sardar]
(G-E521) (G-P802) (G-AV10)
—No. 2 (Marionnettes) only
Victor Concert Orch.—Bourdon
[Francis: Persiflage]   10"—V-20914

(THE) SEASONS—Ballet Orchestra
Winter (Introduction; The Frost; The Ice;
The Hail; The Snow)
Spring
Summer (Waltz of the Cornflowers & Pop-
pies; Barcarolle; Variation; Coda)
Autumn (Bacchanale: Petit Adagio; Finale
—Les Bacchantes & Apotheosis)
Dallas Symphony Orch.—Antal Dorati
                4 12"—VM-1072†
Symphony Orch.—Glazounov
                5 12"—C-GQX10289/93
[Delibes: Naila Valse, Lucerne Kursaal
Orch.]
—Bacchanale only
Royal Opera Orch.—Barbirolli
[Delibes: Naila Valse]   12"—V-11442
Sérénade espagnole, Op. 20, No. 2 'Cello &
Piano
Maurice Maréchal & J. Doyen
[Faure: Après un rêve]   10"—C-D13108
André Navarra & pf. acc.
                    10"—O-188923
[Granados: Spanish Dance No. 5]
—Arr. Violin & Piano
Fritz Kreisler   10"—G-DA1157
[Falla: Jota]

SONGS In Russian
Romance orientale (Pushkin)
Ada Sari (s) & pf. acc.   10"—G-AM3671
[Gretchaninov: Berceuse]
Spielmannslied
Chrystja Kolessa (vlc) & pf. acc.
                    12"—G-EH1293
[Schubert: Allegretto grazioso]
Stenka Razin, Op. 13 Symphonic Poem
Orchestra
Liverpool Philharmonic Orch.—
Lambert   2 12"—C-DX1107/8
Valse de Concert, No. 1, D major, Op. 47
Valse de Concert, No. 2, F major, Op. 51
Chicago Symphony Orch.—Stock
                2 12"—CX-232†
—No. 1 only
Berlin State Opera Orch.—Melichar
                    12"—PD-27279

MISCELLANEOUS—Orchestrations
See under:
Borodin: Prince Igor—Overture
Chopin: Tarantelle (Chopiniana, Op. 46)
Schumann: Carnaval

GLIERE, Reinhold (1874-   )
*A conservative Russian composer who was a
professor at the Moscow Conservatory under
the old regime. Glière has remained in Russia
and has taken a prominent part in the musical
promotional work carried on under the Soviet
government. There are probably many other of
his recordings listed in Soviet catalogues.*

CONCERTO Voice & Orchestra
N. A. Kazanova & Radio Orch.—
Golovanov   2 10"—USSR-13122/24
[Oh, do not wreathe]

(THE) RED POPPY—Ballet Orchestra
—Yablochko (Russian Sailor's Dance)
Philadelphia Orch.—Caston
(in CM-588) 12″—**C-12605D**
[Fernandez: Batuque]
Minneapolis Symphony Orch.—Mitro-
poulos (in CM-528†) 12″—**C-11905D**
[Borodin: Symphony No. 2, B minor,
Pt. 7]
Philadelphia Orch.—Stokowski
10″—**V-1675**
[Brahms-Stokowski: Hungarian Dance
No. 1]
National Symphony Orch.—Fistoulari
12″—**D-K1281**
[Berlioz: Hungarian March, Op. 24]
Unspecified Excerpts: USSR-271; 671; 831

SONGS In Russian
Oh, do not wreathe
N. A. Kozanova, on USSR-131215
Sladko pyel doosha Volovvoschka Song in
Russian
V. A. Sabinin (t) 10″—**G-EK56**
[Anon: Romance—Goree]

SYMPHONY—No. 3, B minor, Op. 42
"Ilya Mourometz"
Philadelphia Orch.—Stokowski
6 12″—**VM-841†**
[Chopin: Mazurka, B minor, trans.
Stokowski]
—Scherzo (Festival in the Palace) only
Chicago Symphony Orch.—Stock
12″—**C-11697D**

GLINKA, Michael (1803-1857)
*A significant influence in the development of
the Russian national school and upon the work
of Mussorgsky, Borodin and even later Russian
composers. He turned to folk music for his
own inspiration and his scores are filled with
the atmosphere of his country. He has been
called the founder of the Russian national
school of composers.*

(L') Alouette See under Songs—The Lark
Kamarinskaya Orchestra
(Fantasia on 2 Russian Folksongs—
Wedding Song & Dance Song)
Pittsburgh Symphony Orch.—Reiner
12″—**C-12715D**
London Symphony Orch.—Coates
12″—**G-AW180**
Berlin State Opera Orch.—Melichar
12″—**PD-27249**
[Mussorgsky-Ravel: Pictures at an Exhi-
bition, Pt. 7]
(Also on PD-24235)

OPERAS In Russian

(A) LIFE FOR THE CZAR 4 Acts 1836
(Ivan Sussanin)
Collection
(Including: **Polonaise; Krakoviak; Mazur-
ka; Sussanin's aria**)
Bolshoi State Theatre Orch.—Samosud,
with Mikhailov (bs)
4 10″—**STIN-S305**

(USSR: 7680/1; 9906/7; 7678/9;
11610/1)
Introduction
Kedroff Russian Vocal Quartet
10″—**C-4804**
[Trad: Church Bells of Novgorod]
Individual Excerpts
**Ballet Music: Polonaise, Krakowiak, Ma-
zurka**
Bolshoi Theatre Orch.—Samosud, in
STIN-S305

Cavatina & Rondo of Antonida, Act I
Soprano
V. V. Barsova 10″—**USSR-7769/70**
Jelna Svecova 10″—**U-C14476**

March & Mazurka
Anonymous Orchestra 10″—**G-EK36***

Boydan Sobinjin's Aria Tenor
Helge Roswaenge (in German)
12″—**G-DB5563**
[Sussanin's Aria, Strienz]

They guess the truth (Sussanin's Aria)
Bass
Mikhailov, in STIN-S305 (USSR-
11610/1)
Wilhelm Strienz (in German)
12″—**G-DB5563**
[Boydan Sobinjin's Aria, Roswaenge]

RUSSLAN AND LUDMILLA 5 Acts 1842
Collection
Including: **Bayan's Song "There's a desert
country" Persian Chorus; Gorislava's
Cavatina "Oh! my Ratmir!"**
Soloists & Orch. of Bolshoi Theatre,
USSR—S. Samosud 2 12″—**DISC-F751**

Overture Orchestra
Indianapolis Symphony—Sevitzky
(G-C3347) 12″—**V-17731**
[Rimsky-Korsakov: Dubinushka]
Boston "Pops" Orch.—Fiedler
(in VM-554) 10″—**V-4427**
Queen's Hall Orch.—Wood
12″—**D-X193**
[Bruckner: Overture, G minor, Pt. 3]
City of Birmingham Orch.—Weldon
12″—**C-DX1319**
[Dvořák: Symphony No. 3, Pt. 9]

ACT I
**Bayan's Song (Bard's Song) "There's a des-
ert country"** Tenor
Kromchenko
(D-X278) 12″—**DISC-F751**
[Persian Song, Act III, Chorus]

ACT II
Farlaf's Rondo (Patter Song) Bass
Jouravlenko 12″—**D-X279**
[Tchaikovsky: Eugene Onegin, Act II,
Scene 1, Trio]
C. E. Kaidanoff 12″—**G-EL9**
[Borodin: Prince Igor—No. 15: How goes
it Prince, with Yourenev]
DUPLICATION: Chaliapin, G-DB1530

ACT III

Persian Song. Soprano & Chorus
L. Stavrovskaya & Bolshoi Theatre Cho.
(D-X278) 12"— in DISC-F751
[Bayan's Song, Act I—Kromchenko]
—**Arr. Violin & Piano**
David Oistrakh & S. Topilin
[Hubay: Zephyr] 10"—USSR-10499/500
Gorislava's Cavatina "Oh! my Ratmir!"
Soprano
Slivinskaya 12"—in DISC-F751
Russlan's Air (unspecified) Baritone
G. M. Yourenev 12"—G-EL8
[Borodin: Prince Igor—No. 13, Igor's
Aria]
DUPLICATION: A. Pirogov, USSR-0750

SONGS In Russian
Do not sing
I remember
G. P. Vinogradov (t) & K. Vinogradov
(pf) 10"—ESTA-D2104
[Tchaikovsky: In moonlight night]
In my blood the fire of desire burns
G. P. Vinogradov (t) & K. Vinogradov
(pf) 10"—ESTA-D2103
[Tchaikovsky: If I could but express in
one word & Rimsky-Korsakov: Sadko—
Song of India]
(The) Lark Fr. **L'Alouette**
—**Arr. 2 Pfs.**
Luboschutz & Nemenoff 10"—V-17993
[Reigger: New Dance]
(The) North Star (or Siberian Star) Folk-
song arrangement
Rus. **Sievernaya Zviezda**
Ger. **Die Nordstern**
N. A. Bolshakoff (t) 10"—G-EK43
[Plotnikov: Sladkim zápakhom, A. M.
Karenzin]
Tarantella, A minor Piano
Shura Cherkassy, in **VOX-165**
Trio Pathétique Clarinet, Bassoon & Piano
P. Lefèbvre, Fernand Oubradous & Noël
Gallon 2 12"—OL-34/5
Valse-Fantasie
Bolshoi Theatre State Orch.—Pashayev
12"—D-X277

GLUCK, Christoph Willibald (1714-1787)

*One of the greatest of the many "reformers" of
opera, and one of the supremely great composers of dramatic music of all time. Gluck's
dramatic expressiveness was a tremendous influence on later composers, notably Richard
Wagner. Considering his musical output, Gluck
is sadly lacking recorded performances except
for some of the ballet music, a few arias, and
two abridged recordings of "Orfeo." It is hoped
that it will not be too long before this is rem-
idied and such works as "Alceste" or the
"Iphigénie" scores may find their way into the
catalogues.*

Andante & Allegretto Piano Arr. Wolf
NOTE: *The Allegretto is the familiar Air de
Ballet from "Alceste"*
Winfried Wolf 12"—G-EH1078
[Schubert: Impromptu, A flat major, Op.
142, No. 2]

Ballet Suites See under various operas, also
under Miscellaneous for the synthetic
groupings of ballet excerpts arranged by
Mottl & Gevaert
Caprice Arr. Saint-Saëns
See under Operas—Alceste
Concerto, G major Flute & Orchestra (Arr.
Scherchen)
Willi Urfer & Winterthur Municipal
Orch.—Scherchen 2 12"—G-DB6083/4
[Rameau: Platée—Minuet & Acanthe et
Céphise—Musette]
Don Juan—Ballet 1761 Selections
Chamber Orch.—Hans von Benda
12"—G-EH949
Elena e Paride See under Operas—Paride
ed Elena
Gavotte Arr. Brahms. See under Operas—
Iphigénie in Tauride
Mélodie
See under Operas—Orfeo: Ballet Music

OPERAS In French & Italian

ALCESTE 3 Acts In French 1776
(First produced in Italian, Vienna, 1767)
Overture Orchestra
Berlin Philharmonic—Furtwängler
12"—T-SK3266
Amsterdam Concertgebouw Orch.—Men-
gelberg (PD-516688) 12"—D-K771
Individual Excerpts
Ah, malgré moi, Act II Soprano
Rose Bampton 12"—V-18218
[Non, ce n'est point un sacrifice, Act I]
Air de Ballet (See also Andante & Allegret-
to, G-EH1078)
—**Arr. Piano solo** Saint Saëns (Edited by
Carl Dies) "Caprice on Airs de ballet
from Gluck's Alceste"
Guiomar Novaës 12"—C-71961D
Bannis la crainte, Act II Tenor (Air
d'Admète)
Georges Thill 12"—C-LFX39
[Wagner: Lohengrin—In fernem Land]
Divinités du Styx, Act I Soprano It.**Divinita
infernale** Ger. **Ihr Gotter we'ger nacht**
Helen Traubel 12"—V-17268
[Wagner: Tannhäuser: Introduction &
Dich, teure Halle]
Risë Stevens (ms) 12"—C-71486
[Meyerbeer: Prophète—Ah mon fils]
Ebe Stignani (ms) (in Italian)
[Orfeo—Che farò] 12"—CET-BB25094
Margarete Klose (in German)
12"—G-DB4532
[Paride ed Elene—O del mio dolce ardor]
Non, ce n'est point un sacrifice, Act I
Rose Bampton (s) 12"—V-18218
[Ah, malgré moi]

ARMIDE 5 Acts In French 1777
Musette (from Act IV, Ballet Music) Or-
chestra
(*Sometimes labelled "Gavotte" and included
in the Mottl and Gevaert arrangements*)
For recordings see under Miscellaneous
Sicilienne See under Miscellaneous: Ballet
Suite, arr. Mottl

IPHIGENIE EN AULIDE 3 Acts In French 1774

Ger. **Iphigénie in Aulis**

Overture Orchestra

NOTE: *Most versions use Wagner's concert ending.*

CBS Symphony Orch.—Barlow
                           2 12"—**CX-138**
[Corelli: Sonata, Op. 5, No. 5—Adagio, trans. Filippi]

Berlin State Opera Orch.—Abendroth
                              12"—**O-7894**

Berlin Philharmonic—R. Strauss
(PD-516625)   12"—**PD-66829**

Orch. of the Suisse Romande—Leo Blech
          (In preparation) Swiss Decca

DUPLICATION: Berlin Philharmonic—Klieber, U-E844

Individual Excerpts

Air gai & Lento

See under Miscellaneous—Ballet Suite, arr. Mottl

Chantons, célébrons notre Reine! Act II

Chorus Ger. **Festgesang**

Basilica Chorus—P. Kalt In German
[Weber: Die Sterne]   10"—**PD-62632**

Tambourin Orchestra

See under Miscellaneous—Ballet Suite, arr. Gevaert

IPHIGENIE EN TAURIDE 4 Acts 1779

Individual Excerpts

Gavotte (from Act II Ballet Music) Orchestra

—**Arr. Piano solo** Brahms

No recording available

—**Arr. 2 Pfs.** Doebber

Ethel Bartlett & Rae Robertson
                           10"—**C-17240D**
[Bach: Jesu, Joy of Man's Desiring]

Unis dès la plus tendre enfance Tenor

Georges Thill (arr. Gevaert)
                           12"—**C-LFX274**
[Cherubini: Les Abencérages—Suspendez à ces murs]

ORFEO ED EURIDICE In Italian 3 Acts 1762

(*Revised with additions in French in 1774 as ORPHEE ET EURIDICE*)

(*The following list follows the numbering in the Novello, Ricordi and B. & H. editions*)

Abridged Recording In Italian

Soloists, Glyndebourne Festival Chorus & Southern Philharmonic Orch.—Fritz Stiedry

(D-K1656/62)   7 12"—**D-ED39†**

The Cast:

Orfeo .... Kathleen Ferrier (c)

Euridice .... Anne Ayars (s)

Amor .... Zoe Vlachopoulos (s)

Abridged Recording In French

Soloists, Vlassoff Choir & Symphony Orch.—Henri Tomasi

(PAT-PDT20/7)   8 12"—**C-OP15†**

The Cast:

Orphée .... Alice Raveau (c)

Euridice .... Germaine Féraldy (s)

L'Amour .... Jany Delille (s)

Individual Excerpts

Since most performances are sung in the original Italian, the following excerpts are listed in Italian.

Overture Orchestra

La Scala Orch.—Jonel Perlea
                   In Prep. English Decca

NOTE: *This music is omitted in both sets listed above.*

ACT I

No. 1, Ah! se intorno a quest' urna funesta

Fr. **Ah! dans ce bois tranquille et sombre**

(Side 1 in both D-ED39† & C-OP15†)

No. 2, Amici, quel lamento

Fr. **Vos plaintes, vos regrets**

(Side 1 in D-ED39† & Side 2 in C-OP15†)

No. 3, Pantomime Orchestra

(Side 2 in C-OP15†)

No. 5, Restar vogl'io

Fr. **Eloignez-vous**

(Side 2 in C-OP15†)

Margarete Klose (in German)
[Nos. 7, 11 & 43]   12"—**G-DB4531**

No. 6, Ritornello Orchestra

(Side 2 in D-ED39†)

No. 7, Chiamo il mio ben così

Fr. **Objet de mon amour**

(Side 3 in C-OP15†)

Margarete Klose (in German)
[Nos. 5, 11 & 43]   12"—**G-DB4531**

No. 8, Euridice, ombra cara

Fr. **Euridice, ombre chère**

(Side 3 in C-OP15†)

No. 10, Euridice, ah questo nome sanno spiagge

(Side 2 in D-ED39†)

No. 11, Piango il mio ben così

(Side 2 in D-ED39†)

Margarete Klose (in German)
[Nos. 5. 7 & 43]   12"—**G-DB4531**

No. 12, O numi, barbari numi

Fr. **Divinités de l'Acheron**

(Sides 2 & 3 in D-ED39†; Side 4 in C-OP15†)

(Decca version abridged; also different text)

No. 13, Se il dolce suon de la tua lire

Fr. **Si les doux accords de la lyre**

(Side 3 in D-ED39†; Side 4 in C-OP15†)

No. 14, Ciel! rivedrarla potrò

Fr. **Dieux! je le reverrai**

(Side 3 in D-ED39†; Side 4 in C-OP15†)

No. 15, Gli sguardi trattieni

Fr. **Soumis au silence**

(Side 3 in D-ED39†; Side 5 in C-OP15†)

No. 16, Che disse

Fr. **Qu'entends-je**

(Side 3 in D-ED15†; Side 5 in C-OP15†)

ACT II, Scene 1

No. 18, Dance of the Furies Orchestra

(Side 4 in D-ED39†; Side 7 in C-OP15†)

No. 19, Chi mai dell' Erebo

Fr. **Quel est l'audacieux**

(Side 7 in C-OP15†; Introduction only on Side 5 in D-ED39†)

No. 20, Dance of the Furies. Orchestra

(Side 7 in C-OP15†)

No. 21, Chi mai dell' Erebo
Fr. Quel est l'audacieux
(Side 5 in D-ED39†; Side 7 in C-OP15†)
No. 22, Deh! placatevi con me
Fr. Laissez-vous toucher pas mes pleurs
(Side 5 in D-ED39†; Side 8 in C-OP15†)
No. 23, Misero giovine
(Side 6 in D-ED39†)
No. 24, Mille pene, ombre sdegnose
(Side 6 in D-ED39†)
No. 25, Ah, quale incognito
Fr. Par quels puissants accords
(Side 6 in D-ED39†; Side 9 in C-OP15†)
No. 26, Men tirane, ah, voi sareste
Fr. La tendresse qui me presse
(Side 6 in D-ED39†; Side 9 in C-OP15†)
No. 27, Le porte stridano
Fr. Quels chants doux et touchants
(Side 6 in D-ED39†; Side 9 in C-OP15†)
No. 28, Dance of the Furies Orchestra
(Side 6 in C-OP15†)
NOTE: *This music, added to the score for the Paris production, comes from Gluck's ballet "Don Juan."*
Symphony Orchestra—Tomasi
(PAT-PDT24)   12"—C-69250D
[Nos. 29 & 30]

ACT II, Scene 2

No. 29, Ballet Orchestra
No. 30, Ballet Orchestra
Eng. **Dance of the Blessed Spirits**
(Side 10 in C-OP15†; No. 30 only on Side 7 in D-ED39†)
See also Miscellaneous—Ballet Suite, arr. Mottl
Symphony Orch.—Tomasi
(PAT-PDT24)   12"—C-69250D
[No. 28]
N. Y. Philharmonic-Symphony Orch.—
Toscanini   (in VM-65†)   12"—V-7138
(G-D1784) (G-W1194) (G-AW113)
[Mozart: Symphony No. 35, Pt. 5]
NBC Symphony Orch.—Toscanini
(in VM-1172†)   12"—V-11-9903
[Mozart: Symphony No. 35, Pt. 5]
La Scala Orch.—Perlea
                In Prep. English Decca
DUPLICATION: German Symphony
Orch.—Kloss, PD-10627
—Arr. Violin Kreisler "Mélodie" (Second section—Andante—only)
Nathan Milstein & Arthur Balsam (pf)
                10"—C-17408D
[Kreisler: Rondino on a Theme of Beethoven]
DUPLICATIONS: Ginette Neveu, G-DA4453; E. Zathwieczky, RAD-RBM108
—Arr. 'Cello & Piano
G. Crepax, C-D16424
—Arr. Viola & Organ
Paul Godwin & P. Palla   12"—D-X10036
[Handel: Sonata, B minor]
No. 31, Ballet Orchestra
Chamber Orch. of the Paris Conservatory

—Cloëz   (in Vol. XI)   12"—AS-102
[Nos. 46, 49 & 52]
No. 32, E quest' asilo
Fr. Cet asile aimable
(Side 7 in D-ED39†; Side 11 in C-OP15†)
No. 33, Che puro ciel
Fr. Quel nouveau ciel
(Side 8 in D-ED39†; Side 12 in C-OP15†)
Risë Stevens   12"—C-71365D
[No. 43]
No. 34, Vieni ai regni del riposo
(Side 9 in D-ED39†)

ACT III

No. 38, Ah! Vieni o diletta
(Abridged on Sides 9 & 10 in D-ED39†)
No. 39, Vieni, appaga il tuo consorte
(Side 10 in D-ED39†)
No. 40, Qual vita è questa mai, che a viver incomincio
(Side 11 in D-ED39†)
No. 41, Che fiero momento
Fr. Fortune ennemie
(Side 11 in D-ED39†; Side 13 in C-OP15†)
No. 42, Ecco novel tormento
(Side 12 in D-ED39†: begins "Ah, per me il duol ricomincia")
No. 43, Che farò senza Euridice
Fr. J'ai perdu mon Euridice Ger. Ach, ich habe sie verloren
(Side 12 in D-ED39†; 1st half only on Side 14 in C-OP15†)
Alice Raveau (in French)
(Complete)   12"—PAT-PDT38
Ebe Stignani   12"—CET-BB25094
[Alceste—Divinités du Styx]
Nan Merriman   12"—V-12-0067
[Thomas: Mignon—Gavotte]
Kathleen Ferrier (in English)
                         12"—D-K1466
[Handel: Rodelinda—Art thou troubled]
Tito Schipa (t)   12"—G-DB1723
[A. Scarlatti: Sento nel cor]
DUPLICATIONS: Enid Szantho, G-DB6000
In German: Margarete Klose, G-DB4531; Friedel Beckmann, G-DB5627; Emmi Leisner, PD-66735
In Bohemian: M. Krasova, ESTA-H5118
No. 44, Ah! finisca e per sempre colla vita il dolor
(Side 13 in D-ED39†)
No. 45, Trionfi Amore
(Abridged on Side 13 in D-ED39†)
No. 46, Dance of the Heroes and Heroines Orchestra
Chamber Orchestra of the Paris Conservatory—Cloëz   (in Vol. XI)   12"—AS-102
[Nos. 31, 49 & 52]
No. 49, Minuet Orchestra
Chamber Orch. of Paris Conservatory—Cloëz   (in Vol. XI)   12"—AS-102
[Nos. 31, 46 & 52]
No. 50, Divo amore
Fr. Tendre amour
(Side 14 in D-ED14†; 1st half only on Side 15 in C-OP15†)

No. 52, Ballet Orchestra
Chamber Orch. of Paris Conservatory—
Cloëz   (in Vol. XI)   12"—AS-102
[Nos. 31, 46 & 49]

No. 53, Chaconne Orchestra
(Abridged on Side 4 of D-ED39†)
Chamber Orch. of Paris Conservatory—
Cloëz   (in Vol. XI)   12"—AS-101

Le Dieu de Paphos
(Side 16 in C-OP15†)
(*The first half of "Le Dieu de Paphos" from
"Echo et Narcisse" is used as the finale in the
French recording. It was first interpolated by
Berlioz in his arrangement of the score for
Mme. Viardot-Garcia*)

PARIDE ED ELENA In Italian 1770
Eng. Paris and Helen

O del mio dolce ardor Act I Tenor
Beniamino Gigli   12"—G-DB2531
[Bizet: Carmen—Air de la fleur]
Margarete Klose (ms)   12"—G-DB4532
[Alceste—Divinités du Styx]
Hedwig von Debicka (s) & pf. acc.
                           12"—PD-66924
[Bach: Cantata No. 209—Hort doch!]
Friedel Beckmann (s)   12"—G-DB5627
[Orfeo—Che farò senza Euridice]

(LA) RECONTRE IMPREVUE In French
3 Acts 1764
(or: Les Pèlerins de la Mecque)
Ger. Die Pilgrimme von Mekka

Un ruisseau bien clair Baritone
Ger. Einen Bach, der Fliesst
Lorri Lail (s) (in German) & Millicent
Silver (harpsichord)
       in Gramophone Shop Album—GSC-4

Sonata Flute, Violin, 'Cello & Piano
—Menuet only
Danish Quartet   12"—G-DB5243
[Handel: Sonata, C major, Op. 1, No. 7,
Pt. 3]

SONGS In German

Klopstock Odes
Die Sommernacht; Die Fruhen Gräber;
Der Jungling; Schlachtgesang—Marsch;
Die Neigung
Lorri Lail (ms) & Millicent Silver (harp-
sichord) in Gramophone Shop Album—
                                   GSC-4

MISCELLANEOUS

Ballet Suite Arr. Felix Mottl
Including: Orfeo—Dance of the Spirits;
Iphigénie en Aulide—Air gai & Lento
Armide—Musette & Sicilienne
Boston "Pops" Orch.—Fiedler
(G-C3420/1)   2 12"—VM-787†
—Excerpts only (Iphigénie & Orfeo)
Berlin State Opera Orch.—Blech
                           12"—G-EJ196

Ballet Suite Arr. Gevaert
Armide—Musette & Iphgénie en Aulide—
Tambourin only
Berlin Philharmonic Orch.—Schmidt—
Isserstedt   12"—T-E2080
[Bach: Italian Concerto, Pt. 3]

GODARD, Benjamin (1849-1895)
*A French romantic composer, influenced by
Schumann, who was very popular in his own
time. Except for his salon favorite, the "Berceuse" from "Jocelyn," he is heard less and less
frequently today.*

Adagio pathétique, Op. 128 No. 3 Violin
—Arr. String Orchestra
Victor String Orch.—Shilkret
                        12"—G-S10322
[Beethoven: "Moonlight" Sonata—
Adagio]

Berceuse See under Jocelyn

Chanson de Florian (Chanson d'Estelle)
(Gillington)
Maggie Teyte (s) & Gerald Moore (pf)
[Bizet: Pastorale]   10"—D-DA1840
Richard Tauber (t) in English
[Jocelyn—Berceuse]   10"—P-RO20529

JOCELYN Opera in French 1888
Berceuse: Cachés dans cet asile
Eng. Angels guard thee Ger. Ach, war es
nicht ein Traum
Richard Crooks (t) in English
(G-DB2093)   12"—V-8421
[Massenet: Manon—Le rêve]
Richard Tauber (t) in English
[Chanson de Florian]   10"—P-RO20529
Richard Tauber (t) in German
                          10"—P-RO20238
[Silesu: Un peu d'amour]
DUPLICATIONS: Ninon Vallin,
O-281032; Tino Rossi, C-4212M:
C-DB1765: C-BF31; Mimi Thoma, (in
Ger.) PD-10653; Planel, PAT-X90046;
G. Cernay, O-123544; M. Claudel,
PD-521948; A. d'Arkor, C-DF315
In English: John McCormack w. Kreisler,
V-8032*; G-DB577*; Bing Crosby &
Jascha Heifetz, D-40012

—Arr. Violin & Piano
Lucien Schwartz & L. Petitjean
[Fauré: Berceuse, Op. 16] 12"—G-L881
DUPLICATIONS: V. Prihoda, PD-95371;
P. Godwin, PD-19913; H. Fritz-Crone,
G-X4597; G. Serra (vla), G-HN455

—Arr. 'Cello & Piano
Pablo Casals, G-DB1039; A. Földesy,
PD-25060; A. Frézin, C-D19073; Mar-
celli-Herson, G-L932; Paul Grummer,
PD-47054; Cedric Sharpe, D-F7627
Also: Alfredo Campoli Orch., G-BD846;
Harry Horlick Orch., D-F7243
See current catalogues for miscellaneous
arrangements

(LA) VIVANDIERE Opéra-Comique 1895
Mon p'tit, si nous t'écrivons (La Lettre)
Viens avec nous, petit (Couplets de
Marion)
Alice Raveau (c)   10"—PAT-X91036

GODOWSKY, Leopold (1870-1938)
*A Polish born American pianist who was a
pupil of Saint-Saëns. He is well known as a
teacher and performer, although he also composed many piano works, made numerous*

transcriptions for that instrument and left a few orchestral and violin scores. His own performances are preserved and may be found listed under recordings of Chopin, Beethoven and others.

Alt Wien (Old Vienna)
Carl Tillius (pf) 10"—G-X7326
[Rimsky-Korsakov: Flight of the Bumblebee; Scriabin: Etude No. 1]

—Arr. Violin & Piano Heifetz
Jascha Heifetz & Emanuel Bay
[Drigo: Valse Bluette] 10"—V-10-1345
(Older version: V-1645)

Wienerisch (Viennese) Arr. Heifetz
Jascha Heifetz & Milton Kaye
(in D-A385) 10"—D-23385
[Benjamin: Jamaican Rhumba]

—Transcriptions and Arrangements
See under: Albéniz: Tango in D; Schubert: Songs—Gute nacht & Morgengrüss; J. Strauss: Waltz—Du und du

GOEHR, Walter
Great Expectations—Music from the film
Estella & Waltz
London Symphony Orch.—Goehr
12"—D-K1596

GOETZ, Hermann (1849-1878)

OPERA in German

DER WIEDERSPAENSTIGEN ZAEHMUNG 1874
Eng. The Taming of the Shrew
Die Kraft versagt Contralto
Eng. Katherine's Aria
Friedel Beckmann 10"—G-DA4480

GOLDMARK, Karl (1830-1915)
At one time a very popular composer, the Hungarian-Jewish Goldmark is heard today only in excerpts. He was a romantic of warmth and a careful and accomplished craftsman. His opera overtures and ballet music probably contain his best work.

CONCERTO—Violin & Orch., A minor, Op. 28
—Air (Andante) only
Vasa Prihoda & pf. acc.
[Eili, Eili, arr. Prihoda] 12"—PD-95370
Georginen Piano pieces
—Verloren only Arr. Orchestra
Dol Dauber Orch. 12"—G-AM1661
[Zemlinsky: Kleider Mächen Leute—Waltz]

Im Frühling—Overture. Op. 36 Orchestra
Eng. In Springtime
Vienna Philharmonic—Krauss
12"—G-AN438

OPERAS In German

(DAS) HEIMCHEN AM HERD 1896
Eng. The Cricket on the Hearth
Prelude to Act III Orchestra
Vienna Philharmonic—Krauss
12"—G-AN451

(DIE) KOENIGIN VON SABA
Op. 27 4 Acts 1875
Eng. The Queen of Sheba

Magische Töne Tenor
It. Magiche Note
Enrico Caruso (in Italian)
10"—G-DA122*

Sakuntala—Overture, Op. 13 Orchestra
Vienna Philharmonic—Krauss
2 12"—G-AN439/40

SYMPHONY "Die ländliche Hochzeit"
Op. 26
Eng. Rustic Wedding Symphony
Orchestra
CBS Symphony—Barlow
5 12"—CM-385
Vienna Philharmonic Orch.—Heger
5 12"—G-AN263/7

GOLESTAN, Stan (1876-   )
A Romanian composer who studied under d'Indy, Dukas and Roussel, who now lives in Paris, and whose works—principally chamber music—are generally grouped with those of the French school.

Ballade roumaine Harp solo
Lily Laskine 12"—G-L985
[Pierné: Impromptu Caprice]

Chanson du pays Bassoon & Piano
Fernand Oubradous & Mme. Ginisty-Brisson 10"—G-DA4920
[Petite Suite bucolique, Pt. 3]

Chant du berceau Violin & Piano
Lola Bobesco & Mme. Ginistry-Brisson
[Tzingarella] 12"—G-L1078

Intermezzo et Sicilienne
Lily Laskine & Chamber Orch.—
Oubradous 12"—G-DB11157

La Laotar 'Cello & Piano
Raya Garbousova & Mme. Ginisty-Brisson 10"—PD-524337
(PD-10919)
Lola Bobesco & Mme. Ginistry-Brisson
10"—G-K8422

Pastorale du Baragan Flute
René le Roy 12"—G-L1025
[Sonatine Pt. 3]

Petite Suite Bucolique Oboe, Clarinet, Bassoon
Trio d'Anches de Paris
2 10"—G-DA4919/20
[Chanson du Pays]

Romanesca Rhapsody Violin & Piano
Lola Bobesco & Mme. Ginisty-Brisson
12"—G-L1079

Sonatine Flute & Piano
René le Roy & Mme. Ginisty-Brisson
2 12"—G-L1024/5
[Pastorale du Baragan]

Tzingarella Violin & Piano
Lola Bobesco & Mme. Ginisty-Brisson
12"—G-L1078
[Chant du berceau]

GOMBERT, Nicolas (c.1495-1560)

A pupil of Josquin des Prés and a worthy successor to his teacher, making significant contributions to the development of secular vocal and chamber music.

Confitemini Domine   In Latin
(2nd half of a 5-Pt. Easter Motet)
Yves Tinayre (t) & Krettly String
Quartet   12"—LUM-32021
[Couperin: Ostende Domino]
[in Yves Tinayre Album No. 2]

In festis Beatae Mariae Virginis
(5-Pt. Motet in Latin)
Yves Tinayre (t) & Krettly String
Quartet   12"—LUM-32013
[Anon: Mélisme—Ille]
[in Yves Tinayre Album No. 1]

GOMEZ, Antonio Carlos (1839-1896)

A Brazilian composer trained at the Conservatory of Milan, remembered today for his opera "Il Guarany" (where he used Amazon Indian Indian themes) and a few excerpts from other scores.

OPERAS In Italian

(IL) GUARANY 1870
Orchestral Selections (Fantasia)
Paul Godwin Orch.   10"—PD-21359
Overture Orchestra
Boston "Pops" Orch.—Fiedler
                           12"—V-11-9112
La Scala Orch.—Molajoli
                           12"—C-D14457
La Scala Orch.—Sabajno
                           12"—G-S10083
Individual excerpts
Gentil di cuore, Act I   Soprano
Bidú Sayão   12"—G-DB2394
[C'era una volta un principe, Act II]
Sento una forza indomita, Act I Soprano &
Tenor
Bianca Scacciata & F. Merli
                           12"—C-GQX10201
DUPLICATION: Destinn & Caruso,
G-DB616*
C'era un volta un principe, Act II Soprano
Bidú Sayão   12"—G-DB2394
[Gentil di cuore, Act I]
O come è bello il ciel Ballata Soprano
Lina Pagliughi
(in CET-8)   12"—CET-BB25086

SALVATOR ROSA 1874
Di sposo di padre le gioie serene, Act III
(Duca d'Arcos) Bass
Luciano Neroni (bs)
                           12"—CET-BB25099
[Verdi: Simon Boccanegra—Il Lacerato
spirito]
Mia piccirella   Tenor
Enrico Caruso   12"—G-DB144*
[Verdi: Aida—Celeste Aida]

LO SCHIAVO
Quando nascesti fu Tenor
G. Lauri-Volpi   12"—G-DB1438
[Bellini: Puritani—A te o cara]

DUPLICATION: E. Caruso, G-DB137*
Quem sabe Sop. in Portuguese
Cristina Maristany (s) & pf. acc.
                           10"—PD-47231
[Braga: A Casinha pequenina]

GOMOLKA, Mikolaj (c.1539-1609)

A 16th century Polish composer of choral music.

Psalm 77   Chorus in Latin
Motet and Madrigal Group—Opienski
(in Vol. VI)   12"—AS-53
[Polish Choruses of the Renaissance]
There are undoubtedly more selections in
Polish catalogues.

GORDON, Gavin (1901-   )

A contemporary British composer.

(THE) RAKE'S PROGRESS Ballet Music
Orchestra

Excerpts: The Reception; The Pure Girl;
The Orgy
Royal Opera Orch., Covent Garden—
Lambert   2 12"—C-DX1249/50

GOSSEC, François Joseph (1734-1829)

Contemporary of Mozart and Cherubini, this Belgian-French composer was most important in the realm of symphonic music, particularly as an important influence in France. Today he is remembered by a few dance pieces.

Gavotte Arr. Violin & Piano Burmester
(from the opera "Rosina" 1786)
Vasa Prihoda & C. Cerné
[Volkmann: Walzer]   10"—PD-90164

—Arr. Orchestra
Symphony Orch.—Locatelli, C-DF2043

Hymne à la Nature
Choral Music School Cho. & Orch.—
Radiguer   10"—C-DF82
[French Revolutionary Songs: Ca ira &
La Carmagnole]

Hymne à la Victorie 1794 Chorus
Chorale Poplaire de Paris Cho. & Orch.—
Rosset   10"—O-281115
[Montéhus: Chant des Jeunes Gardes]

Ronde Nationale 1792 Chorus (Arr.
Sauveplane; Text—Chénier)
Chorale Populaire de Paris & Orch.—
Désormière   10"—CdM-503
[Hymne à la victoire 1792]

GOTTSCHALK, Louis Moreau (1829-1869)

A Creole-American virtuoso pianist who attained tremendous fame in his day, and a composer who was best known by such salon pieces as The Dying Poet.

(The) Banjo Arr. Orch. Maganini
Boston "Pops" Orch.—Fiedler
                           10"—V-10-1089
[Anderson: Jazz legato and Jazz pizzicato]

GOUBLIER, Gustave

SONGS In French

L'Angélus de la Mer
André Baugé (b) & Cho.
      12"—PAT-X93094
[Le Credo du Paysan]
Louis Guénot (b)   12"—C-D12053
[Dupont: Les Sapins]
Paul Sandoz (b)   12"—G-HEX109
[Le credo du Paysan]
Fred Gouin & Louis Zucca
[Fauré: Crucifix] 12"—O-166448

Le Credo du Paysan
André Baugé (b) & Cho.
[Angélus de la Mer] 12"—PAT-X93094
Paul Sandoz (b)   12"—G-HEX109
[Angélus de la Mer]
DUPLICATIONS: Louis Guénot,
C-DFX48; Carillon de la Ville de Nivilles,
L. Henry, C-DF91

La Croix du Chemin (R. Gaël)
René Hérent (b)   12"—LUM-33021
[Fragerolle: Grande amie]
DUPLICATION: Robert Couzinou, PD-
522701

Notre Dame de Paris (J. Messis)
Robert Couzinou (b) 12"—PD-522701
[Croix du Chemin]
André Gordon (b)   10"—G-K7250
(André: Le Clairon]

La Voix des chênes (S. & F. Borel)
Pierre Deldi (b)   10"—C-DF1000
[Doria: La chanson des peupliers]

(La) Vièrge à la crèche (Daudet)
Suzanne Feyrou (s) 10"—LUM-30062
[Métayer: Pluie de roses]

GOUDIMEL, Claude (c.1505-1572)

*Another pupil of Josquin des Prés, Goudimel
died in the Huguenot massacre at Lyons. His
settings for the Psalter are still in use in France
today.*

PSALM SETTINGS Unacc. Vocal Ensembles In French

Psalm 19, Les cieux en chacun lieu
(Coeli enarrant gloriam Dei) 4-Part

Psalm 25, A toi, mon Dieu (2 settings)
(Ad te Dominum levavi) 4-Part
Vocal Quartet—Henri Expert
     (Vol. II) 12"—AS-12
[Claude Le Jeune: Psalm 42 & Psalm 69]

Psalm: Hører ril I høje Himle Arr. Thomas
Kingo
(*This is probably either Psalm 19 or Psalm 123
sung in a Danish translation*)
Copenhagen Boys Choir—Wöldike
      10"—G-X6995
[Praetorius: Es ist ein Ros']
Palestrina Choir—Wöldike
      10"—G-X2834
[Praetorius: Es ist ein Ros']

GOULD, Morton (1913-)

*New York pianist and composer, a graduate of
the Julliard School, who has become popular
with his own radio programs.*

COLLECTION

Cowboy Rhapsody (Trail to Mexico; Little
Old Sod Shanty; Old Paint; Home on the
Range)

American Salute (based on "When Johnny
Comes Marching Home")

**Go Down Moses & Sometimes I Feel Like a
Motherless Child**
[Arr. of spirituals]

New China March

Red Cavalry March
Robin Hood Dell Orch.—Gould
     4 12"—CM-668†

American Concertette Pf. & Orch.
NOTE: *This score is used for the ballet "Interplay"*
Morton Gould & Robin Hood Dell Orch.
     2 12"—CX-289†

—Blues
José Iturbi (pf)
(G-B9466)   10"—V-10-1127
[Boogie Woogie Etude]

**American Salute—When Johnny Comes
Marching Home** Orch.
Boston "Pops" Orch.—Fiedler
      12"—V-11-8762
[Yankee Doodle Went to Town]

American Symphonette, No. 2
—Pavanne
Morton Gould & his Orch.
   (in C-C96) 12"—C-55030
[Friml: Donkey Serenade]
Boston "Pops" Orch.—Fiedler
[Scott: Toy Trumpet] 10"—V-4456

Boogie Woogie Etude Pf
José Iturbi (G-B9466) 10"—V-10-1127
[American Concertette—Blues]

Foster Gallery 1940 (13 movements based
on Stephen Foster Melodies)
Orch.
Boston "Pops" Orch.—Fiedler
     2 12"—VM-727

Interplay See American Concertette

Latin-American Symphonette
(Symphonette No. 4)
Rhumba; Tango; Guaracha; Conga
Rochester Philharmonic Orch.—
Iturbi   3 12"—VM-964†

—Guaracha only
All American Orch.—Stokowski
      12"—C-11713D
[Creston: Symphony, Op. 20—Scherzo]

—Arr. 2 pfs.
Arthur Whittemore & Jack Lowe
[Lecuona: Malagueña] 12"—V-11-9759

Minstrel Show
Minneapolis Orch.—Mitropoulos
      12"—V-11-9654

Yankee Doodle Went to Town
Boston "Pops" Orch.—Fiedler
      12"—V-11-8762
[American Salute—When Johnny Comes
Marching Home]

GOUNOD, Charles François (1818-1893)

The composer of "Faust" and other operas firmly entrenched in the international repertoire of the lyric stage. Still theatrically and musically effective if competently staged and sung, this composer's works remain extremely popular in his native France.

Adore te
A. Dadò (b)   10"—SEMS-56
[Somma: Salve Regina]
Ave Maria See under Songs
Faust See under Operas
Hymne à Sainte Cécile (Méditation religieuse)
V. Pascal (vlc) & D. Herbrecht
(harp)   12"—G-L919
[Massenet: Thaïs—Méditation]
(G-S10382)
Also: Louis Zimmerman (vl), C-DHX30

JEANNE D'ARC Incidental Music 1873
Vision de Jeanne d'Arc Orchestra
(Méditation)
—Arr. Violin & Piano
A. Locatelli & pf. acc.   10"—O-250499
[Massenet: Le dernier sommeil da la Vièrge]
Marche funèbre d'une Marionnette Orch.
Eng. **Funeral March of a Marionette**
London Philharmonic Orch.—Wood
(C-DX969)   12"—C-7374M
DUPLICATIONS: Lamoureux Orch.—
Wolff, PD-66856: PD-566016;
Also: BBC Band, C-DX269

MASSES

Messe à Jeanne d'Arc—Prélude
Chorus in French
St. Nicolas Choir, Organ & Trumpets
[Mors et Vita—Judex] 12"—LUM-32001
Messe Solennelle, G major In Latin
(St. Cecilia Mass)
—Sanctus, Benedictus, Agnus Dei
Catholic Church Music Concert Choir &
Organ—Baldwin   2 10"—C-DQ1201/2
NOTE: *The Sanctus only on C-4141M*

MORS ET VITA Oratorio in Latin 1885
Hosanna Chorus
St. Nicolas Choir—Lepage
[Alain: Tantum ergo] 10"—LUM-30007
Judex Chorus
St. Nicolas Choir, Organ & Trumpets
                             12"—LUM-32001
[Messe à Jeanne d'Arc—Prélude]
—Arr. Solo In Danish
Tenna Fredriksen (s)   12"—G-Z223
[Schubert: Ave Maria]
—Arr. Orchestra
New Symphony Orch.—Collingwood
                           12"—G-S10251
[Delibes: Naïla Valse]
DUPLICATIONS: Milan Symphony—
Molajoli, C-GQX10693; Symphony Orch.
& Organ, PD-35082; PD-516742; Symph.
Orch., G-Z162
OPERAS In French

CINQ-MARS 1877
No recordings available.

FAUST 5 Acts 1859
Ger. **Margarethe**
Complete Recording Sung in French
Paris Opéra & Opéra-Comique Soloists,
Chorus & Symphony Orch.—Henri Büsser
                20 12"—VM-105†
(G-C2122/41 in GM-115†)
(G-L806/25)
The Cast:
Marguerite .... Mireille Berthon (s)
Faust .... César Vezzani (t)
Méphisto .... Marcel Journet (b)
Siebel .... Marthe Coiffier (s)
Valentine .... Louis Musy (b)
Marthe .... Jeanne Montfort (a)
Wagner .... Michel Cozette (b)
Complete Recording Sung in English
Soloists, BBC Chorus & Symphony Orch.
—Sir Thomas Beecham
                16 12"—C-DX88/103†
The Cast:
Marguerite .... Miriam Licette (s)
Faust .... Heddle Nash (t)
Méphisto .... Robert Easton (bs)
Siebel .... Doris Vane (s)
Valentine .... Harold Williams (b)
Marthe .... Muriel Brunskill (c)
Wagner .... Robert Carr (b)
Abridged Recording Sung in French
Paris Opera Soloists, Chorus &
Lamoureux Orch.—Wolff
(PD-566070/74)   5 12"—PD-27382/6
The Cast:
Marguerite ...... Germaine Martinelli
Faust .... M. Lapelletrie
Méphisto .... José Beckmans
Valentin .... M. Cambon
Wagner .... M. Gaudin
Siebel .... Lemichel du Roy
Marthe .... Jeanne Montfort
Abridged Recording Sung in German
Berlin State Opera Soloists, Chorus
& Orchestra—Hermann Weigert
                5 12"—PD-27377/81
The Cast includes Hedwig von Debicka,
Helge Roswaenge, Eduard Kandl, Hedwig Jungkurth, Heinrich Schlusnus, Marie
Schulz-Dorenburg & Waldemar Henke.

Vocal & Orchestral Selections In English
Grand Opera Company 12"—G-C2290

Instrumental Selections (Fantasias, etc.)
Marek Weber Orch.   12"—G-L674
(G-S10461)
DUPLICATION: Goldstream Guards
Band, G-C1877
Individual Excerpts

ACT I

Act I (Complete version) Sung in Italian
A. Melandri, N. de Angelis, La Scala
Chorus & Orch.—Molajoli
                3 12"—C-D14586/8
Introduction Orchestra
Milan Symphony Orch.—Molajoli
[Valse, Act II]   12"—C-D16435
Berlin State Opera Orch.—Blech
[Valse, Act II]   12"—G-EJ180

Rien! En vain j'interroge
Salut! O mon dernier matin!
  Tenor & Chorus
  Eng. **Opening Scene**
  Georges Thill & Chorus
        12″—**C-LFX1431**
  Miguel Villabella & Chorus
        12″—**O-123681**

Salut! O mon dernier matin! only
  Kaisin, PD-27351: PD-516589; Lugo,
  PD-561106; also in VOX-176

Mais ce Dieu, que peut-il pour moi? Tenor
Me voici!   It. **Sono qui!**
  Eng. **Méphisto's Entry**
Ici je suis à ton service Duo: Tenor & Bass
O merveille! It. **O stupore**
  Georges Thill & Fred Bordon
        12″—**C-LFX150**
  Fernand Ansseau & Marcel Journet
        12″—**G-DB1364**

—**Me voici!** to end of scene
Pauli & Zambelli (in Italian)
        12″—**G-DB1637**

ACT II

La Kermesse: Vin ou bière Chorus
—**Abbreviated versions**
  Paris Opéra Chorus & Orch.—Szyfer
        12″—**C-D15046**
  [Choeur des soldats, Act V]
  La Scala Chorus (In Italian)
        12″—**C-GQX10267**
  [Leoncavallo: Pagliacci—Coro delle
  campane]
—**Unspecified excerpts** from the Kermesse
Scene
  Schlusnus, Debicka, Jungkurth,
  Roswaenge, etc. (In German)
        12″—**PD-27337**

Invocation: Avant de quitter ces lieux
  Baritone (Side 8 in VM-105)
  It. **Dio possente** Ger. **Valentins Gebet**
  Eng. **Even bravest heart**
  (This air, not in the original score, was com-
  posed by Gounod for a British production—
  with Santley in 1864)
  Leonard Warren   12″—**V-18420**
  [Offenbach: Contes d'Hoffman—
  Scintille diamant]
  Lawrence Tibbett   12″—**V-8452**
  [Wagner: Tannhäuser—O du mein
  holder Abendstern] (C-DB2262)
  Giuseppe De Luca (In Italian)
        12″—**V-7086**
  [Verdi: Traviata—Di Provenza il mar]
  (G-DB1340)
  Enzo Mascherini (in Italian)
        12″—**CET-BB25123**
  [Rossini: Barbiere—Largo]
  G. Manacchini (in Italian)
        12″—**CET-CC2150**
  [Bellini: Puritani—Suoni la tromba]
  DUPLICATIONS: A. Baugé PAT-
  X90055; A. Endrèze, PAT-X90054;
  C. Cambon, PD-522455
  In Italian: C. Galeffi, C-GQX10150; B.
  Franci, C-D5173; Mario Ancona,
  V-15-1002*; Ruffo, G-DB405*

In German: Karl Schmitt-Walter,
T-E2465; Heinrich Schlusnus, PD-
35027; Gerhard Hüsch, G-EG6136
In Swedish: H. Hasslo, G-Z309
In English: Dennis Noble, G-C3153;
P. Dawson, G-C1267
In Finnish: Oiva Soini, G-Z212

Le Veau d'or (Rondo) Bass & Ensemble
  It. **Dio dell'or** Eng. **The Calf of Gold**
  Ger. **Rondo dem goldene Kalb (Ja, das**
  Gold regiert die Welt)
  Chaliapin, Cozette & Chorus 12″—**V-7600**
  [Sérénade, Act IV] (G-DB1437)
  Pinza & Metropolitan Opera Chorus
        10″—**V-1753**
  [Bellini: Norma—Ah, del Tebro]
  André Pernet   12″—**O-188782**
  [Sérénade, Act IV]
  DUPLICATIONS: A. Endrèze, PAT-PG77
  Alexander Kipnis, C-5044; Van Obbergh,
  PD-524041; Huberty, PD-521895
  In Italian: Pasero, C-DQ1081; Zaccarini,
  G-HN779
  In German: Ludwig Hoffmann, PD-62685;
  Wilhelm Strienz, G-DA4485
  In Swedish: Joel Burglund, G-X6016

Choral des épées Bass & Chorus
  Eng. **Sword Scene**
  F. Bordon, C. Cambon & Cho.
  [Mort de Valentin]   12″—**C-D15181**

Valse: Ainsi que la brise Chorus
  BBC Theatre Chorus (In English)
        12″—**D-K1599**
  [Roméo et Juliette—Prologue]
  DUPLICATION: Paris Opera Chorus,
  C-D15180

—**Arr. Orchestra**
  Boston "Pops" Orch.—Fiedler
        10″—**V-10-1009**
  Berlin Orch.—Seidler-Winkler
        12″—**G-EH1130**
  [Strauss: Liebeslieder Waltz]
  (G-S10484)
  DUPLICATIONS: Berlin Philharmonic—
  Schmidt-Isserstedt, T-E2247: U-F14401;
  Berlin State Opera Orch.—Blech,
  G-EJ180; Berlin-Charlottenburg Opera
  Orch.—Oskar Fried, PD-19804; Berlin
  Opera Orch.—Melichar, PD-27220; Marek
  Weber Orch., G-B3894; G-EG2188; La
  Scala Orch.—Nastrucci, G-HN779; Cin-
  cinnati Summer Opera Orch.—Cleva in
  D-A491; Milan Symph. Orch.—Molajoli,
  C-D16435

—**Arr. Piano** Liszt
  Eileen Joyce   12″—**P-E11252**
  [Rachmaninoff: Prelude, G minor, Op. 23,
  No. 5]
  Egon Petri   12″—**C-69031D**
  Sigfrid Grundeis   12″—**O-7998**

—**Arr. Violin** Sarasate
  Erica Morini & Max Lanner (pf)
        10″—**V-10-1011**
  [Ravel: Pièce en forme de Habañera]

ACT III

Faites-lui mes aveux Tenor
  It. **Le parlate d'amore**

Eng. **Flower Song** Ger. **Blumlein traut**
(*This tenor air is often sung by sopranos.*)
Gladys Swarthout (ms)
    (in VM-925) 12"—**V-11-8280**
[Roméo et Juliette—Que fais-tu]
Marthe Nespoulous 10"—**C-RF61**
[Versez vos chagrins, Act IV]
DUPLICATIONS: Germaine Cernay,
O-188611
In German: Adele Kern, PD-25826;
Friedel Beckmann, G-EG6824

Quel trouble inconnu—Recit.

Salut! demeure—Cavatine Tenor
It. **Salve dimora** Ger. **Gegrüsst sei mir**
Eng. **All hail, thou dwelling**
Jussi Björling 12"—**V-13790**
[Flotow: Marta—M'appari] (G-DB3887)
Georges Thill 10"—**C-LF17**
Richard Crooks
    (in VM-585) 12"—**V-15542**
[Roméo—Ah, lève-toi]
Beniamino Gigli (in Italian)
    12"—**G-DB1538**
[Puccini: La Bohême—Che gelida
manina]
DUPLICATIONS: Georges Noré, PAT-
PD65; C. Rouquetty, G-DA4902; G. Lugo
in VOX-176; G. Micheletti, O-123650;
Villabella, PAT-X90010
In Italian: L. Fort, C-OQX8000; Salvar-
ezza, CET-BB25151; Schipa, G-DA365*;
Cortis, G-DB1468; Lazaro, G-DQ1134;
Gigli, G-DB273*; Borgioli, C-D5037
In German: Peter Anders, T-E2523; Helge
Roswaenge, G-DB4655: PD-66824
In English: Charles Kullman, C-DX442;
Heddle Nash, G-C3405; Webster Booth,
G-C3309; James Johnston, C-DX1455

Je voudrais bien savoir—Recit.

Ballade: Il était un roi de Thulé Soprano
It. **Come vorrei saper** (Sometimes labelled
"Aria dei gioielli, Pt. 1")
Ger. **Es war ein König in Thule**
Eng. **Ballad of the King of Thule**
Bidú Sayão
    (in CM-612) 12"—**C-72095D**
[Air des bijoux]
Ninon Vallin 12"—**PAT-X90084**
[Air des bijoux] (O-171031)
Yvonne Gall 12"—**C-D15127**
[Air des bijoux]
Eidé Noréna 12"—**G-DB4904**
(Air des bijoux]
Eleanor Steber 12"—**V-11-9838**
[Air des bijoux]
Elisabeth Rethberg 12"—**V-7179**
[Air des bijoux] (G-DB1456)
DUPLICATIONS: Mme. Géori-Boué,
O-123872; Ritter-Ciampi, PD-566062:
PD-516581; Beaujon, C-D15044; F.
Heldy, G-DA1250; Luart, O-123678; L.
du Roy, PD-521890; Belmas, PD-67000;
Balguerie, PD-524090; Jeannette Mac-
Donald, V-2050 in VM-642
In Italian: Pia Tassinari, G-DB1935;
Gina Cigna, C-GQX10014
In English: Joan Hammond, G-C3674

Les grands Seigneurs—Recit.
Air des bijoux Soprano
It. **I gran Signori & Air dei gioielli**
Ger. **Juwelen-Aria: Ach, welch ein Glück**
Eng. **Jewel Song**
Bidú Sayão
    (in CM-612) 12"—**C-72095D**
[Ballade de Thulé]
Eleanor Steber 12"—**V-11-9838**
[Ballade de Thulé]
Ninon Vallin 12"—**PAT-X90084**
[Ballade de Thulé] (O-171031)
Eidé Noréna 12"—**G-DB4904**
[Ballade de Thulé]
[Lalo: Roi d'Ys—Aubade, with Crooks,
on V-15821 in VM-633]
Elisabeth Rethberg 12"—**V-7179**
[Il était un roi de Thulé] (G-DB1456)
DUPLICATIONS: Mme. Géori-Boué,
O-123872; Yvonne Gall, C-D15127; Fan-
ny Heldy, G-DA1051; M. Beaujon,
C-D15044; Balguerie, PD-524090; Ritter-
Ciampi, PD-516581; Belmas, PD-67000;
Delmas, J. MacDonald, V-2050 in VM-
642; Blanche Arral, V-15-1016*; J. An-
toine, C-698131D
In Italian: Pia Tassinari, G-DB1933;
Gina Cigna, C-GQX10014
In Swedish: Hjördis Schymberg,
G-X6010
In English: Joan Hammond, G-C3674

Seigneur Dieu, que vois-je
(Quartuor du jardin)
Eng. **Garden Quartet**
Farrar, Gilibert, Caruso, Journet
    12"—**G-DM102***

Il était temps Bass
Il se fait tard —O nuit d'amour
Soprano & Tenor

Tête folle! —Elle ouvre sa fenêtre
Bass & Tenor

Il m'aime Soprano
Marthe Nespoulous (s), Georges
Thill (t) & Fred Bordon (bs)
    2 12"—**C-LFX182/3**

—**Unspecified Excerpt**
H. von Debicka, J. Jungkurth, H.
Roswaenge & E. Kandl (In German)
    12"—**PD-27338**

—**Il se fait tard —O nuit d'amour** only
It. **Tardi si fa & Sempre amor**
Eng. **Love Duet**
Ger. **Es is schon spät & O Mondenschein**
(or **Ewig dein**)
Farrar & Caruso 12"—**G-DM108***
Pia Tassinari & Piero Pauli
(In Italian) 12"—**G-DA1322**
Zamboni & Borgioli (In Italian)
    12"—**C-GQX10158**
Angerer & Piccaver (In German)
    12"—**PD-66858**
Margarete Teschemacher & Marcel
Wittrisch (In German)
    12"—**G-DB4459**
[Mascagni: Cavalleria Rusticana—
No, no, Turridu]

—**Elle ouvre sa fenêtre**
Farrar, Journet & Caruso
    12"—**G-DK106***

—Il m'aime only
H. Spani, (In Italian) G-DB1163

ACT IV

Versez vos chagrins Tenor
Eng. **When all was young**
(Scene 1 of Act IV (Siebel and Marguer-
ite) is omitted in VM-105, as in most
operatic performances. Siebel's Romance,
"Versez vos chagrins" is frequently sung
by women, as in the recorded version be-
low.)
Marthe Nespoulous   10"—C-RF61
[Faites-lui mes aveux, Act III]

Seigneur, daignez permettre
(Scène de l'Eglise)
Eng. **Church Scene** Soprano, Bass & Cho.
M. Beaujon, Fred Bordon & Chorus
                           12"—C-D15045
Florence Austral, F. Chaliapin & Cho.
                           12"—G-DB899
Charlotte Tirard, Etienne Billot & Cho.
                      2 10"—O-188703/4
Margarete Teschemacher & W. Streinz
(In German)   12"—G-DB4523
G. Cigna, N. de Angelis & Chorus
(In Italian)   12"—C-D14589

Choeur des Soldats Chorus
Eng. **Soldiers' Chorus**
Paris Opéra Chorus & Orch.—Szyfer
[La kermesse]   12"—C-D15046
Victor Chorale & Orch.—Shaw
        (in VM-1074)   12"—V-11-9289
[Bizet: Carmen-Habañera, with
Swarthout]
DUPLICATION: Dresden Opera Chorus &
Orch. (in German)—Böhm, G-DA4457

Sérénade: Vous qui faites l'enormie Bass
Eng. **Mèphisto's Serenade**
Feodor Chaliapin   12"—V-7600
[Veau d'or]   (G-DB1437)
Alexander Kipnis   10"—C-5044
[Veau d'or]
DUPLICATIONS: Fred Bordon,
C-D12033; L. van Obbergh, PD-524041;
A. Pernet, O-188782: G-DA4884; En-
drèze, PAT-PG77
In Italian: T. Pasero, CET-BB25059:
CET-BB25061: also G-DA11301:
C-DQ1081; N. de Angelis, C-GQX10183;
Vittorio Arimondi, CRS-27*; T. Ruffo,
G-DA360*
In German: W. Strienz, G-DA4485; Lud-
wig Hoffmann, PD-62685

Duel: Que voulez-vous, messieurs?
Trio.   Eng. **Duel Trio**
Billot, Rouard, Villabella
[Mort de Valentin]   12"—O-123680
DUPLICATION: Roger Bourdin, René
Maison & Lafont, O-123509

Mort de Valentin: Par ici Baritone &
Ensemble

Ecoute-moi bien
Eng. **Valentine's Death**
Ger. **Hore mich jetz an**
(Single-sided versions include only Val-
entine's final "Ecoute-moi bien" with
Chorus)

Charles Cambon & Chorus
                           12"—C-9091M
[Final Trio, w. Thill & Féraldy]
[Choral des épées on C-D15181]
A. Endrèze   12"—PAT-PDT51
[Thomas: Hamlet—Etre]
In German: K. Schmitt-Walter,
T-E2441; Heinrich Schlusnus, PD-73085
In Italian: Molinari, Cheni, Mannarini
& Cho., C-D14590

ACT V

Ballet Orchestra (Nuit de Walpurgis)
    Les Nubiennes; Adagio; Danse antique;
    Variations de Cléopatre; Les Troyennes;
    Variations du Miroir; Danse de Phryné
National Symphony Orch.—Fistoulari
(D-K1339/40)   2 12"—D-ED11
City of Birmingham Orch.—Weldon
                       2 12"—C-DX1247/8
Symphony Orch.—Melichar
[Valse, Act II]   3 12"—PD-27218/20
Royal Opera Orch.—Byng
                       2 12"—G-C1462/3
NOTE: *The 1st 4 mvts. are issued on* G-S10486
DUPLICATIONS: Opéra-Comique Orch.
—Cloëz, O-170003/4; Berlin State Opera
Orch.—Weissman, P-E11006/7
2 Sided Versions
Boston "Pops" Orch.—Fiedler
(G-C3268)   12"—V-13830
Berlin Philharmonic—Schmitt-Isserstedt
(U-F18071)   12"—T-E2150
Berlin State Opera Orch.—
Seidler-Winkler   12"—G-EH992
Berlin State Opera Orch.—Heger
(O-7843)   12"—P-E11376

Scène de la prison: Le jour va luire
Eng. **Prison Scene**

Alerte! Alerte! Trio

Anges purs

Apothéose

—**Complete**
C. Tirard, M. Villabella & E. Billot
                           12"—O-123679
M. Teschemacher, H. Roswaenge & W.
Strienz (In German)   12"—G-DB4507

—**Alerte & Anges purs** only
N. Vallin, J. Lafont & R. Maison
[Duel Trio, Act IV]   12"—O-123509
Farrar, Caruso & Journet
        (in VM-953)   12"—V-16-5003*
[Saint-Saëns: Samson et Dalila—Trio]
[Elle ouvre sa fenêtre, on G-DK106*]
In Italian: Cigna, Civil, Pasero,
C-D14582; Melba, McCormack, Sam-
marco, V-15-1019*
In English: Cross, Booth & Walker,
G-C3086

—**Anges purs et Apothéose**
Beaujon, Thill, Bourdon & Cho.
[Mort de Valentin]   12"—C-9091M
[Valse, Act II, on C-D15180]

(LE) MEDECIN MALGRE LUI

Opéra-Comique 1858
No recordings available

MIREILLE 3 Acts (Originally in 5 Acts)
1864
Individual Excerpts
Overture Orchestra
Vienna Symphony—Paul Kerby
12"—**C-69065D**
[Boïeldieu: Calife de Bagdad Overture]
Grand Symphony Orch. of Paris—Cloëz
10"—**O-165104**
Symphony Orch.—Weissmann
(PD-522183) 10"—**PD-24482**
Republican Guard Band
10"—**G-K5066**

ACT I

Chantez, chantez, Magnarelles Chorus
Opéra-Comique Chorus & Orch.
10"—**O-165170**
Valse: O légère hirondelle Soprano
It. O d'amor messagera
Ger. Vöglein Walzer
Lily Pons & Kostelanetz Orch.
(in CM-606) 12"—**C-71734D**
[Roméo et Juliette—Valse]
[Older Version: Offenbach: Contes
d'Hoffmann—Les oiseaux, on O-188642]
DUPLICATIONS: Yvonne Brothier,
G-P689; G. Myrris, PAT-X90067; C.
Clairbert, PD-66794
In German: Miliza Korjus, G-EH914

ACT II

La Farandole Chorus
Opéra-Comique Chorus & Orch.
10"—**O-165169**
[Choeur de Ste. Marie, Act III]
La brise est douce (Chanson de Magali)
Soprano & Baritone
G. Féraldy & E. Rambaud
12"—**C-LFX99**
[Foi de son flambeau, Act III]
DUPLICATIONS: Corney & Claudel,
PD-516559; Gauley & Micheletti,
O-171017
Trahir Vincent—Recit.
Mon coeur ne peut changer—Air Soprano
A toi mon âme—Non, jamais—Air (Part 2)
Mme. Géori-Boué 10"—**O-188945**
DUPLICATION: C. Clairbert, PD-66793
Si les filles d'Arles (Couplets d'Ourrias)
Baritone
L. Guénot 12"—**C-D14211**
[Bizet: Carmen—Chanson du Toreador]
DUPLICATION: Arbeau, PD-522376

ACT III

Le jour se lève (Chanson du berger) Con-
tralto
Germaine Féraldy (s) 10"—**PAT-PG63**
[Puccini: Bohème—Valse]
DUPLICATIONS: Myrris, PAT-X90067;
A. Vavon, C-D19182
Heureux petit berger Soprano
Germaine Féraldy 10"—**C-D13055**
[Massenet: Manon—Au cours la Reine]
DUPLICATION: G. Corney, PD-524097
Anges du Paradis (Cavatine) Tenor
Georges Thill 12"—**C-LFX324**
[Reyer: Sigurd—Esprits gardiens]
José de Trévi 10"—**G-P786**

[Lalo: Roi d'Ys—Aubade]
DUPLICATIONS: Paul-Henry Vergnes,
O-188891; A. d'Arkor, C-RF62; Claudel,
PD-524089; Micheletti, O-188510; Villa-
bella, PAT-X90059: O-123550; Genio,
G-K6633
Foi de son flambeau Duo: Sop. & Ten.
G. Féraldy & E. Rambaud
[Brise est douce, Act II] 12"—**C-LFX99**
Choeur de Sainte-Marie Chorus
Opéra-Comique Chorus & Orch.
[Farandole, Act II] 10"—**O-165169**

ACT IV (Original version)
Allons me voila reposée Soprano
*(This air, subtitled "Scène et vision" does not
appear in the libretto or vocal score of the re-
vised 3-Act version of the opera)*
Germaine Féraldy 12"—**C-LFX25**
[Bizet: Pêcheurs de Perles—Comme
autrefois]
Voici la vaste plaine Soprano
Mme. Géori-Boué 10"—**O-188946**

PHILEMON ET BAUCIS 3 Acts 1860
Individual excerpts
Au bruit des lourds marteaux Bass
Eng. Vulcan's Song
Marcel Journet (Recorded 1910)
12"—**V-15-1003***
[Meyerbeer: Huguénots—Piff! Paff!]
In English: Peter Dawson, G-B3464
O riante nature Soprano
Amelita Galli—Curci 12"—**G-DB1516**
[A. Scarlatti: Io vi miro ancor]

POLYEUCTE Opera 1878
Source délicieuse (Stances) Tenor
José Luccioni 12"—**G-DB11115**
[Roméo et Juliette—Ah lève toi]

(LA) REINE DE SABA 4 Acts 1862
Eng. The Queen of Sheba
Individual excerpts
Faiblesse de la race humaine—Recit. Act II
Inspirez-moi, race divine—Air Tenor
(or: **Prête-moi ton aide**) Eng. Lend me
your aid
Enrico Caruso & re-recorded orchestra
12"—**V-15732**
[Mascagni: Cavalleria—Addio]
[Franck: Procession, on G-DB3078]
[Original version on G-DB145*]
In English: Walter Widdop, G-D1742

ROMEO ET JULIETTE 5 Acts 1867
Orchestral Selections
Berlin Symphony—Gurlitt
12"—**PD-27088**
Individual excerpts
Prologue Chorus & Orchestra
BBC Theatre Chorus (in Eng.) & Orch.—
Goehr 12"—**D-K1599**
[Faust—Valse]

ACT I

Ballade de la Reine Mab Baritone
Martial Singher
(in CM-578) 12"—**C-72806D**

[Berlioz: Damnation of Faust—Chanson de la puce, Voici des roses & Sérénade]
DUPLICATIONS: Arthur Endrèze, O-123720; R. Couzinou, PD-516593

Valse: Je veux vivre dans ce rêve Soprano
Eng. **Juliette's Waltz Song**
Bidú Sayão   10″—C-17301D
[Massenet: Manon—Gavotte]
Lily Pons (in CM-606)   12″—C-71734D
[Mireille—O légère hirondelle]
Eidé Noréna   12″—V-14742
[Bizet: Carmen—Je dis que rien]
(G-DB4922)
DUPLICATIONS: Jeanette MacDonald, V-15850: G-DB3940; C. Clairbert, PD-66792; Fanny Heldy, G-DB1304
In Swedish: Hjördis Schymberg, G-X4776

—Arr. Orchestra
Cincinnati Summer Opera Orch.—Cleva, in D-A491

ACT II

L'Amour l'amour—Recit. Tenor

Ah! lève-toi soleil! Tenor Eng. **Romeo's Cavatina**
Jussi Björling   12″—G-DB6249
[Massenet: Manon—Ah, fuyez]
[Also: In Swedish, on G-X3628]
Richard Crooks
      (in VM-585)   12″—V-15542
[Faust: Salut! demeure]
José Luccioni   12″—G-DB11115
[Polyeucte—Source délicieuse]
Raoul Jobin
      (in CM-696)   12″—C-72140D
[Massenet: Manon—Ah! Fuyez]
Charles Dalmores (Recorded 1912)
          12″—V-15-1013*
[Bizet: Carmen—Air de la fleur]
DUPLICATIONS: César Vezzani, G-DB4931; Micheletti, O-171019; Sidney Rayner, D-K677; Villabella, PAT-X90041; Vergnes, O-123722;
In English: Heddle Nash, G-C3492

ACT III

Que fais-tu, blanche tourterelle Soprano
(Stephano)
Gladys Swarthout (ms)
      (in VM-925)   12″—V-11-8280
[Faust—Faites-lui mes aveux]

ACT IV

Va, je t'ai pardonné
Non, ce n'est-pas le jour Duo: Sop. & Ten.
Eng. **Chamber Duet**
Germaine Féraldy & Villabella
          12″—PAT-PGT8

Que l'hymne nuptial Bass (Capulet)
Arthur Endrèze   12″—O-123720
[Ballade de la Reine Mab, Act I]

ACT IV

Le Tombeau Eng. **Tomb Scene**
(*The Thill-Féraldy is recorded without cuts from Romeo's "Salut, tombeau!" to the end of the opera*)
Georges Thill & Féraldy
      2 12″—C-LFX1/2

—Tenor part only
Vezzani G-DB4931; Villabella, PAT-X90041

SAPHO 3 Acts 1851
No recordings available

Petite Symphonie pour instruments à vent
Eng. **Little Symphony for Wind Instruments**
Paris Wind Instrument Society—
Oubradous   2 12″—G-DB11107/8

SONGS In French

Aimons-nous
Reynaldo Hahn (b) & self piano acc.
          10″—C-D2020
[Chabrier: L'Ile heureuse]

Au printemps (Chanson du printemps)
Yvonne Brothier (s) & pf. acc.
[Sérénade]   10″—G-K7128
Ninon Vallin (s) & pf. acc.
          10″—PAT-PG81
[Roesgen-Champion: Mai & Secret]
In German: F. Hüni-Mihacsek, PD-66757; Franz Völker, PD-24200

Au Rossignol (Lamartine)
Pierre Bernac (b) & Francis Poulenc
(pf)   12″—G-DB6250
[Sérénade—Quand tu chantes]

Ave Maria In Latin
("Meditation" on the Bach Prelude in C major, Das Wohltemperierte Klavier, Book I, No. 1)
Beniamino Gigli (t) & Chorus
[Bizet: Agnus Dei]   10″—G-DA1488
Lily Pons (s)   10″—C-17376D
[Scott: Think of me]
Astra Desmond (c) with pf. & vlc.
[Bizet: Agnus Dei]   12″—D-K1014
Joan Hammond (s) with organ & vl.
          12″—C-DX1023
[Franck: Panis Angelicus]
DUPLICATIONS: Jeanette MacDonald, V-2049: G-DA6000; Richard Tauber & Cho., P-RO20452; Margherita Perras & Cho., G-DB4464; Webster Booth & Cho., G-DB8990; Rosa Ponselle, V-6599; Charles Kullman, (in Eng.) C-DX458: C-9143M; Heinrich Schlusnus, PD-30005; Göta Ljungberg, G-DB962; Gracie Fields, D-F8015; Ninon Vallin, O-281032: PAT-X93046; Isobel Baillie, (in Eng.), C-DX301; Ernest Lough, G-B8697; Enzo De Muro Lomanto, C-DQ2296; Erna Sack, T-A2219; D'Arkor, C-BFX1: C-CQX16530; Doniau-Blanc, LUM-32007; A. Baugé, PAT-X93117; Di Mazzei, O-188566; J. Laval, C-DF254; Gilles, PD-27227: PD-516520; Phelan, G-C2766; Alberti, G-S10159; I. Steffensen, C-DDX5; John McCormack & Fritz Kreisler, V-8032*: G-DB577*; John McHugh, C-FB2065; Tino Rossi, C-DB1841: C-BF41; Maria Tauberová, U-C12787; Melba & Kubelik (vl), G-DK112*; Orlandis, G-HN455

—Arr. Chorus
Don Cossack Cho., C-4278M; Quartet & Cho., LUM-32007

—**Arr. Orchestra**
Andre Kostelanetz & his Orch.
[Schubert: Ave Maria]   12"—**C-7416M**
DUPLICATIONS: Victor Concert Orch.—
Bourdon, G-Z221; Hastings Municipal,
D-K573; Dauber Orch., G-B4479:
G-GW618; Nastrucci Orch., G-HN487
—**Arr. Organ**
Charles O'Connell   10"—**V-21216**
[Nevin: The Rosary]
DUPLICATION: R. Foort, D-F5714
—**Arr. Violin**
DeGroot, G-HN451; Ferraresi, G-S10113;
Ranzato, G-HN475; Swaap, G-K5588
—**Arr. 'Cello**
Pascal, G-K6003; C. Sharpe, D-F7627;
Lopes, PAT-X98064
—**Miscellaneous Arrangements**
M. L. Goldis (viola d'amore), PD-22681;
Albert Sandler Trio, C-DB1981

Barcarolle See: Où voulez-vous aller?

Benedictus Duo
(Unspecified: possibly from a Gounod
Mass)
Jane Laval (s) & André d'Arkor (t)
(C-GQX16530)   12"—**C-BFX1**
(Ave Maria, d'Arkor]

(Le) Calvaire Eng. There is a green hill
far away
St. Martins Choral Society & Orch.—
Goldsborough   10"—**D-F2660**
[Tune Miles Lane: All hail the power]

Ce que je suis sans toi
Pierre Bernac (b) & F. Poulenc (pf)
[Prière]   10"—**G-DA4915**

(Le) Ciel a visité le terre (de Segur)
Jean Planel (t) & Chorus
10"—**PAT-X93106**
[Anon: Lauda Jerusalem]

Envoi des fleurs
Vanni-Marcoux (b) & pf acc.
[Priére]   10"—**G-DA4829**

Medjé (Chanson Arabe)
Georges Thill (t) & pf. acc.
(C-LFX333)   12"—**C-7326M**
[Liszt: Liebesträume]

Nazareth In English
Webster Booth   10"—**G-B9507**
[Traditional: Adeste Fideles]
Ernest Lough (b)   10"—**G-B8805**
[Schubert: Litany]
Richard Crooks (t)   10"—**V-1634**
[Nevin: The Rosary] (G-DA1288)

O Divine Redeemer See: Repentir

O ma belle rebelle
Georges Thill (t) & Joseph Benvenuti
(pf)   10"—**C-LF165**
[Lazari: Le cavalier d'Ormedo]

Où voulez-vous aller? (Barcarolle)
(Gauthier)
Ninon Vallin (s) & Pierre Darck (pf)
10"—**O-166804**
[Fortunio: La maison grise]
DUPLICATION: Tino Rossi, C-BF29

Prière
Pierre Bernac (b) & Francis Poulenc
(pf)   10"—**G-DA4915**

[Ce que je suis sans toi]
Vanni-Marcoux (b) & pf. acc.
[Envoi de fleurs]   10"—**G-DA4829**
Repentir Eng. O divine Redeemer
Clara Butt (c) (in Eng.) 12"—**C-DX755**
[Sullivan: Light of the World—God
Shall Wipe Away]
Sérénade: Quand tu chantes (Hugo)
Pierre Bernac (b) & Francis Poulenc
(pf.)   12"—**G-DB6250**
[Au rossignol]
DUPLICATIONS: Yvonne Brothier,
G-K7128; Ninon Vallin, PAT-X93046;
Josef Rogatchewsky, C-LF95; André
Baugé, PAT-PA973
In Italian: Ferrara, G-GW1065
(Le) Soir
Charles Panzéra (b)   12"—**G-DB4917**
[Bordes: Promenade matinale]
Mario Battistini, G-DB214*
There is a green hill far away See: Calvaire
(Le) Vallon (Lamartine)
Narçon (bs)   12"—**C-RFX32**
[Schumann: Die Beiden Grenadiere]
Venise (Alfred deMusset)
Ninon Vallin   10"—**PAT-PG82**
[Gretchaninov: Over the Steppe &
Rachmaninoff: Lilacs]

GRAENER, Paul (1872-1944)
*A German composer and conductor, who was
professor of composition at the Royal Academy
in London, the conservatories in Vienna, Salzburg, Munich, Leipzig and Berlin. He was an
excellent technician, whose music leaned toward the classico-romantic.*

Comedietta, Op 82
Berlin Symphony Orch.—Abendroth
12"—**O-7912**
(Die) Flöte von Sanssouci Suite Chamber
Orchestra
Berlin Philharmonic——(with flute solo,
Paul Bose)—Graener
2 12"—**PD-15011/2**

SONGS In German
Der alte Herr, Op. 43, No. 3 (Münch-
hausen)
Heinrich Schlusnus (b) & Sebastian
Peschko (pf)   10"—**PD-30019**
[Trunk: Vor Akkon, Op. 14, No. 1]
Paul Bender (bs) & Michael Raucheisen
(pf)   10"—**G-EG6107**
[R. Strauss: Traum durch die Däm-
merung]
(Der) Page sprach (Münchhausen)
Philantropisch—Palmström (Morgen-
stern)
Gerhard Hüsch (b) & U. Müller (pf)
10"—**G-EG3544**
(Der) König, Op. 71, No. 3
Heinrich Schlusnus (b) & Franz Rupp
(pf)   10"—**PD-62713**
[Winter]
Walter Ludwig (t) & pf. acc.
[Der Kuckuck]   10"—**G-EG3366**
(Der) Kuckuck
Walter Ludwig (t) & pf. acc.
[Der König]   10"—**G-EG3366**

Männertreu, Op. 71, No. 6
Maria Reiner (s)   10"—PD-47218
[Versprach]
Vale Carissima (Karl Stieler)
Heinrich Schlusnus (b) & Franz Rupp
(pf)   10"—PD-30002
[Wetzel: In Danzig]
Versprach, Op. 71, No. 9
Maria Reiner (s)   10"—PD-47218
[Männertreu]
Winter ("Uber die Heide geht mein
Gedenken")
Heinrich Schlusnus (b) & Franz Rupp
(pf)   10"—PD-62713
[Der König]
Swedish Dances, Op. 98 Orch.
Berlin State Opera Orch.—Graener
                               10"—PD-62811

GRAINGER, Percy (1882-   )

*The Australian-American pianist, composer and
arranger of folk tunes and dance settings, is
best known by these popular piano pieces. During the early part of this century he collected
hundreds of melodies from the people in various parts of the world, thus making an outstanding contribution to the preservation of
folklore.*

PIANO COLLECTION

Molly on the Shore; Irish Tune from
County Derry; Country Gardens; One
more day, my John
(the collection also includes music by
Dett & Cyril Scott)
Percy Grainger (pf)   3 10"—D-A586
(The) Arrival Platform Humlet Unaccom-
panied Viola
Watson Forbes   10"—D-M540
[Sussex Mummers' Christmas Carol]
Brigg Fair English Folksong Setting
Richard Dyer-Bennett (t) with guitar
acc., in DISC-609
Country Gardens English Morris Dance Set-
ting Piano
Percy Grainger, in D-A586
Cecil Dixon   10"—C-DB1713
[Shepherd's Hey]
—Arr. Orchestra
RCA Victor Orchestra, in V-E76 (Earlier
recording: V-20802)
Handel in the Strand Clog Dance for Or-
chestra
Boyd Neel String Orch.—Neel
                           12"—D-K1216
[Vaughan-Williams: Fantasia on Green-
sleeves]
New Light Symphony Orch.—Sargent
[Mock Morris]   12"—G-C2002
Londonderry Air Irish Folksong Setting
Percy Grainger (pf), in D-A586
Minneapolis Symphony Orch.—Ormandy
[Molly on the Shore]   12"—V-8734
DUPLICATIONS: Boyd Neel String Orch.,
D-M596; New Symphony—Sargent,
G-B2931; New State Symphony, D-F3104
Mock Morris Orchestra
Boyd Neel String Orch.—Neel
[Molly on the Shore]   12"—D-K1215

New Light Symphony Orch.—Sargent
[Handel in the Strand]   12"—G-C2002
Molly on the Shore Irish Reel
Percy Grainger, in D-A586
Minneapolis Symphony Orch.—Ormandy
[Londonderry Air]   12"—V-8734
Royal Opera Orch.—Collingwood
(G-B2641)   10"—V-4165
[Shepherds Hey]
Boyd Neel String Orch.—Neel
[Mock Morris]   12"—D-K1215
DUPLICATION: Prisca Quartet, PD-
10541
One More Day, My John Sea Shanty Setting
Percy Grainger, in D-A586
Shepherd's Hey English Morris Dance Set-
ting Piano
Cecil Dixon   10"—C-DB1713
[Country Gardens]
Percy Grainger, in D-A586
—Arr. Orchestra
Royal Opera Orch.—Collingwood
[Molly on the Shore]   10"—G-B2641
Also: Victor Orch., in V-E74; Older re-
cording on V-20802; Royal Artillery
Band, D-F7657
(The) Sussex Mummers' Christmas Carol
Unaccompanied Viola
Watson Forbes   10"—D-M540
[The Arrival Platform Humlet]

GRAM, Pider

Poème Lyrique
Danish Radio Symphony Orchestra, Copenhagen—Tuxen   NP-HM80011

GRANADOS, Enrique (1867-1916)

*Primarily a performer and composer of piano
music, Granados (one of the outstanding Spanish composers during recent times) is well
known for his major work, the opera "Goyescas." He is most popularly known for his
"Danzas Espanolas" for the piano.*

Allegro de Concierto Piano
Roger Machado   10"—C-LF246
Andaluza See: **Danza Española, No. 5**

(12) DANZAS ESPANOLAS Piano

Eng. Spanish Dances Fr. Danses espag-
noles
No. 4, 5 & 6 only
—Arr. Orchestra Sir Henry Wood
Queen's Hall Orch.—Wood
(PD-516787/8)   2 12"—D-X180/1
Individual recordings
No. 2, C minor (Oriental)
—Arr. 'Cello & Piano
Gregor Piatigorsky & Valentin Pavlovsky
(in CM-501)   10"—C-17446D
[Prokofiev: Romeo & Juliet—Masques]
No. 4, G major (Villanesca)
Roger Machado   12"—C-LFX675
[Falla: Amor Brujo—Ritual Fire Dance]
—Arr. Orchestra
New Queen's Hall Orch.—Wood
[No. 6]   12"—D-X180
No. 5, E minor (Andaluza or Playera)
(The celebrated "Spanish Dance")
A. Benedetti Michelangeli
                           12"—G-DB5354

[Marescotti: Fantasque]
Andor Földes, in CON-34
DUPLICATIONS: Janine Weill, D-M125;
Lydia Tartaglia Morichini, C-DQ2724;
José Iturbi, G-DB6573
—**Arr. Guitar**
Prof. Mozzani 10"—**G-GW1754**
[Albéniz: Granada]
Andrés Segovia, in D-A384
—**Arr. Orchestra**
Queen's Hall Orch.—Wood
12"—**D-X181**
—**Arr. Violin & Piano** Kreisler
Yehudi Menuhin & Ferguson Webster
12"—**G-DB3500**
[Brahms: Hungarian Dance No. 11]
Jacques Thibaud & pf. acc.
[No. 6] 12"—**G-DB1113**
[Falla: Jota, on G-DB1498]
DUPLICATION: Erica Morini, PD-66823
—**Arr. 'Cello & Piano**
M. Amfitheatrof & Arnella Paliti Santo-
liquido 12"—**G-DB5413**
[Veracini-Corti: Largo]
Pablo Casals & N. Mednikoff
[Schumann: Träumerei] 10"—**G-DA5402**
[Popper: Vito, on G-DA1015]
DUPLICATIONS: André Navarra,
O-188923; Caspar Cassadó, C-GQX10487
—**Vocal arrs.**
Margherita Carosio (s)
[Pedilla: Violetera] 10"—**G-DA5404**
Tito Schipa (t) 10"—**G-DA1132**
[Longas: Sevillana]
No. 6, D major (Rondalla Aragonesa)
Andor Földes, in CON-34
—**Arr. Orchestra**
New Queen's Hall Orch.—Wood
[No. 4] 12"—**D-X180**
Madrid Symphony—E. F. Arbós
[Goyescas—Intermezzo] 12"—**O-123849**
—**Arr. 'Cello & Piano**
André Navarra & Pf. acc.
12"—**O-123849**
[Goyescas—Intermezzo]
No. 10, G major
José Iturbi 12"—**G-DB6573**
[No. 5]
—**Arr. Guitar**
Andrés Segovia, in D-A384
—**Arr. Violin & Piano** Thibaud
Jacques Thibaud & pf. acc.
[No. 5] 12"—**G-DB1113**
—**Arr. Castanets & Orch.** Argentinita, in
D-A597

GOYESCAS 3 Acts Opera in Spanish 1916
(Originally a set of piano pieces)
Intermezzo Orchestra
Madrid Symphony Orch.—Arbós
(in CM-331) 12"—**C-68923D**
[Danza española No. 6]
Boston "Pops" Orch.—Fiedler
(G-C3230) 12"—**V-12429**
[Tchaikowsky: Eugene Onegin—Polon-
aise]
—**Arr. 'Cello & Piano** Cassadó
Pablo Casals & pf. acc.
12"—**G-DB1067**

[Bach: Toccata, C major—Adagio]
Gilberto Crépax & pf. acc.
12"—**C-D16424**
[Gluck: Orfeo—Mélodie]
André Navarra & pf. acc. 12"—**O-123849**
[Danza Española No. 6]
DUPLICATIONS: B. Michelin, C-LFX735;
B. Mazzacerati, CET-P51606
—**Arr. Castanets & Orch.**
La Argentinita in D-A597
Quejas o "La maja y el ruiseñor" (No. 4 of
Piano version)
Artur Rubinstein (pf) 12"—**G-DB1462**
[Chopin: Mazurka, C minor, Op. 56,
No. 3]
Roger Machado 12"—**C-LFX716**
[Rodrigo: La copla intrusa]
(Los) Requibros (No. 1 of Piano version)
Iris Loveridge (pf) 12"—**C-DX1456**
Oriental See Danza Española No. 2
Playera See Danza Española No. 5
Rondalla Aragonesa (Tonadilla) See Danza
Española No. 6

SONGS In Spanish
Amor y Odio
Conchita Supervia (ms) & Frank
Marshall (pf) 10"—**P-PO162**
[El Trá-lá-lá; El Majo Discreto; El
Majo Tímido]
Callejeo
Conchita Supervia (ms) & Frank Mar-
shall (pf) 10"—**P-PO161**
[Las Currutacas Modestas; La Maja
Dolorosa]
(Las) Currutacas Modestas
Conchita Supervia (ms) & Frank Mar-
shall (pf) 10"—**P-PO161**
[Callejeo; La Maja Dolorosa]
(La) Maja de Goya
—**Arr. Guitar** Segovia
Andrés Segovia, in D-A384
(La) Maja Dolorosa
Conchita Supervia (ms) & Frank Mar-
shall (pf) 10"—**P-PO161**
[Las Currutacas Modestas; Callejeo]
Jolanda di Maria-Petris (s) & Olav Roots
(pf) 12"—**G-DB6438**
[Respighi: Nebbie & Davico: Lune che fa
lume]
(El) Majo celoso
Christina Maristany (s) & G. Puchelt
(pf) 10"—**PD-47233**
[El Trá-lá-lá; Obradors: Cantar & Cora-
zón porque pasais]
(El) Majo Discreto
Conchita Supervia (ms) & Frank Mar-
shall (pf) 10"—**P-PO162**
[El Majo Tímido: Amor y Odio; El Trá-
lá-lá]
Gladys Swarthout (ms) & L. Hodges
(pf) (in VM-679) 12"—**V-16779**
[Pittaluga: Romance de Solita & Chaus-
son: Le temps des Lilas]
(El) Majo Tímido
Conchita Supervia (ms) & Frank Mar-
shall (pf) 10"—**P-PO162**
[Majo Discreto; Amor y Odio; El Trá-
lá-lá]

(El) Trá-lá-lá y cl puntcado
Conchita Supervia (ms) & Frank Marshall (pf)   10″—P-PO162
[Amor y Odio; El Majo Discreto; El Majo Tímido]
Cristina Maristany & G. Puchelt (pf)
    10″—PD-47233
[El Majo celoso; Obradors: Cantar; Corazón porque pasais]
Villanesca See: Danza Española No. 4

GRANDJANY, Marcel (1891-   )
French harpist and composer who received the Paris Conservatoire prize at the age of 13. He was professor of harp at the American Conservatory of Fontainebleau for several years.

Automne Harp
Marcel Grandjany   10″—V-10-1120
[Gretchaninoff: Allegro vivace, from Piano Sonata, G minor, arr. Grandjany]
Rhapsody (for the Harp)
Marcel Grandjany   10″—V-2060
Two Old French Folk Songs Arr. Harp—Grandjany
   1. Le bon petit Roi d'Yvetot
   2. Et ron ron ron petit patapon
Marcel Grandjany   10″—V-2095
[Bull: King's Hunt, arr. Grandjany]

GRAZIOLI, Giovanni B. (c. 1750-c. 1820)
Adagio Violoncello & acc.
Louis Jensen & Gerthe Louis Jensen (pf)   12″—G-DB5222
[Handel: Berenice—Largo]
Edmund Kurtz & Emanuel Bay (pf)
    12″—V-11-9024
[Rachmaninoff: Danse Orientale, Op. 2, No. 2]
Massimo Amphitheatroff & Orch.
[Albéniz: Malagueña]   12″—G-DB5414

GREBAN, Arnould (c. 1420-c. 1471)
Le Mystère de la Passion (Adaption by Henri Brochet)
Eng. Passion Play
L'Enseignement de Jésus
Les Paintes de Notre Dame
Les Filles de Jérusalem
La Mort de Jésus
Les Compagnons de Jeux
    2   12″—LUM-35011/2

GREEN, Maurice (c. 1695-c. 1755)
I will lay me down in peace
O praise the Lord
Kathleen Ferrier (c) & Gerald Moore (pf)   10″—C-DB2152

GREGORIAN CHANTS
COLLECTIONS
THE KYRIALE CHANTS
The Ordinary of the Mass and the Requiem Seminary and Monastic Choirs in the United States and Canada
    46   10″—KYR-1/10
Including:
Asperges me; Vidi aquam; Asperges (ad lib) No. 1 & 2; Mass I (Lux et origo); Mass II (Kyrie fons bonitatis)
St. Bernard's Seminary Choir, Rochester, N. Y.—Rev. Benedict A. Ehmann
    5   10″—KYR-1

Mass III (Kyrie Deus sempiterne); **Mass IV** (Cuncti potens Genitor Deus); **Mass V** (Kyrie magnae Deus potentiae)
Notre Dame Seminary Choir, New Orleans, La.—Rev. Robert Stahl, S.M.
    4   10″—KYR-2
Mass VI (Kyrie Rex Genitor); **Mass VII** (Kyrie Rex splendens); **Mass VIII** (De Angelis)
St. Meinrad Abbey Choir, St. Meinrad, Ind.—Dom Rudolph Siedling, O.S.B.
    5   10″—KYR-3
Mass IX (Cum jubilo); **Mass X** (Alme Pater); **Mass XI** (Orbis factor)
St. Mary's Seminary Choir, Roland Park, Baltimore, Maryland—Rev. John Selner, S.S.   4   10″—KYR-4
Mass XII (Pater cuncta); **Mass XIII** (Stelliferi Conditor orbis); **Mass XIV** (Jesu Redemptor)
Sulpician Seminary of Philosophy Choir, Montreal, P. Q.—Rev. Ethelbert Thibault, P.S.S.   4   10″—KYR-5
Mass XV (Dominator Deus); **Mass XVI; Mass XVII; Mass XVIII** (Deus Genitor alme)
St. Augustine's Seminary Choir, Toronto, Ont.—John E. Ronan, M.C.G.
    4   10″—KYR-6
Credos I-VI
St. John's Seminary Choir, Los Angeles, Calif.—Robert E. Brennan, Mus. D.
    5   10″—KYR-7
Ad libitum Kyries I-XI
St. John's Seminary Choir, Collegeville, Minn.—Dom Dominic Keller, O.S.B.
    5   10″—KYR-8
Ad libitum Glorias I, II, III; Ambrosian Gloria; Sanctus (ad lib) **I, II, III; Agnus Dei I, II; Responses at Mass**
Mount St. Mary Seminary Choir, Cincinnati, Ohio—Dr. John J. Fehring
    4   10″—KYR-9
Requiem Mass complete with **Subvenite; In paradisum; Libera me; Ego sum & Canticle Benedictus**
St. Charles Borromeo Seminary Choir, Overbrook, Philadelphia, Pa.—Dr. James A. Boylan   6   10″—KYR-10

GREGORIAN CHANTS Unacc. Unison Choir in Latin
Monks Choir of St. Pierre de Solesmes Abbey.—Dom J. Gajard, O.S.B.
    12   12″—VM-87
(G-W1115/26) (G-AW249/60)
Including:
Mass "Lux et Origo" (Ed. Vaticana No. I)
—Kyrie; Agnus Dei; Gloria & Sanctus
Mass for the Dead (Requiem)
—Introit: Requiem Aeternam
—Tract: Absolve Domine
—Offertory: Domine Jesu
Gradual: Christus factus est (Maundy Thursday)
Communion: Hoc Corpus (Passion Sunday)
vent)
Gradual: Dirigatur Oratio Mea (19th Sunday after Pentecost)
Gradual: Qui sedes (3rd Sunday after Advent)

Mass for Doctors
—Alleluia: Justus Germinabit
Communions: **Memento Verbi tui** (20th Sunday after Pentecost); **Quinque Prudentes** (from Mass for a Virgin not a Martyr); **Pascha nostrum** (Easter Sunday)
Offeratories: **Ad te levavi** (1st Sunday after Advent); **Meditabor** (2nd Sunday after Lent)
Antiphon: **Montes Gelboe** (1st Vespers of the 5th Sunday after Pentecost, from the Monastic Antiphonary)
Offertory: **Custodi me** (Tuesday in Holy Week)
Responsory: **Ecce quomodo moritur** (Holy Saturday Tenebrae)
Responsory: **Tenebrae factae sunt** (Good Friday Tenebrae)
Mass "Cum jubilo" (Ed. Vaticana No. 9)
—Sanctus & Agnus Dei
Hymn: **Adoro Te**
Antiphon: **Salve Regina** (Simple tone)
Introit: **Spiritus Domini** (Pentecost Sunday)
Communions: **Spiritus Sanctus Docebit Vos & Spiritus Qui a Patre** (Monday and Tuesday of Pentecost Week)
Introit: **Da Pacem** (18th Sunday after Pentecost)
Kyrie "Orbis Factor" (Ed. Vaticana No. 10 ad libitum)
Offertory: **Prescatus est Moyses** (12th Sunday after Pentecost)
Offertory: **Jubilate Deo** (2nd Sunday after Epiphany)
Responsory: **Descendit** (Christmas Matins)
Alleluias: **Ascendit Deus** (Ascension Day) & **Assumpta est Maria** (Feast of the Assumption)
Responsory: **Media Vita** (Septuagesima)
Responsory: **Christus Resurgens**
Antiphons: **Alleluia, Lapis Revolutus Est; Alleluia, Quem Quaeris; & Alleluia, Noli Flere Maria** (Easter Chants)
Hymn: **Urbs Jerusalem** (Dedication Feast)
Hymns: **Virgo Dei Gentrix & O Quam Glorifica** (Hymns to the Blessed Virgin)

RYTHMIQUE GREGORIENNE
Benedictine Monks Choir of Saint Benoit du Lac, Lac Memphremagog, P. Q.
6   10"—GRCH-1
Including:
Introit: **Exsurge** (Sexagesima Sunday)
Introit: **Cantate Domino** (Fourth Sunday after Easter)
Kyrie: **Clemens Rector**
Gloria (more Ambrosiano)
Gradual: **Haec Dies** (Easter)
Alleluia: **Emitte Spiritum**
Alleluia: **Veni Sancte Spiritus** (Whitsunday)
Tract: **Gaude** (Saturdays between Septuagesima and Easter)
Credo VI
Offertory: **Recordare** (Feast of Our Lady of the Seven Sorrows)
Sanctus: **Cum Jubilo**
Agnus Dei: **Dominator Deus**
Communion: **Videns Dominus**
Communion: **Spiritus**

Ite Missa Est: **Lux et Origo**
Hymn: **Creator Alme Siderum** (Advent)
Hymn: **Coelestis Urbs Jerusalem**
Anthem: **Ad Jesus Autem, and Magnificat** (Feast of the Sacred Heart of Jesus)
Anthem: **Salve Regina**
Hymn: **Tantum Ergo**

GREGORIAN CHANT
Maîtrise de la Cathédrale de Soissons—Abbé H. Doyen
12   12"—LUM-32031/42
Including:
La Classe de Chant; Commentaire d'un disque grégorien (Doyen)
Introït de la Toussaint: "Gaudeamus omnes in Domino"
Hymne de la Toussaint: "Placare Christe servulis" (1st strophe only)
Credo I—"Credo in unum Deum"
Mass IV "Cunctipotens Genitor Deus"—Kyrie & Sanctus, Gloria & Agnus Dei
Anthem "Lumen!" & Psalm "Nunc dimittis" (Day of Purification)
Prière du Soir Liturgique; (Début des Complies, incl. Benediction & Brief Lesson)
Aprés l'Elévation: **O Salutaris Hostia** (Motet)
Kyrie X "Alme Pater" (2nd Mass for Fêtes de la Sainte Vierge)
Hymne de la Pentecôte: "Veni, Creator Spiritus"
Mass IX "Cum Jubilio" (1st Mass for Fêtes de la Sainte Vierge)
—Kyrie, Sanctus, Gloria, Agnus Dei
Introït de Noël (Messe du jour) "Puer natus est nobis"
Introït (Messe de Minuit) "Dominus dixit"
Répons bref pour la fête de Noël "Verbum caro factum est"
Alléluia de Noël (Messe du jour) "Alleluia, Dies sanctificatus"
Bénédiction des Rameaux "Hosanna filio David" (Anthem)
Bénédiction "Pueri Habraeorum" (Anthem)
Gloria (Hymne de Theodulfe, evêque d'Orléans)
Puer natus in Bethleem (organ acc.); Isti sunt agni novelli (2 cantilènes: Temps de Noël & Temps Pascal)
"Haec Dies" de Pâques
"Sequence" de Pâques "Victimae paschali laudes"
Mass XVIII "Deus Genitor Alme"—Kyrie, Sanctus, Agnus Dei
Alléluia de la Fête des SS Apôtres Pierre et Paul "Tu es Petrus"
Asperges Me; Kyrie XII "Pater Cuncta"; Agnus Dei ad libitum
Introït "Dignus est Agnus"
Antienne du Magnificat "Habet in vestimento" de la Fête du Christ-Roi
Introït "Cogitationes"
Antienne du Magnificat "Ad Jesum autem cum venissent" de la Fête du Sacré-Coeur
Introït de l'Ascension "Viri Galilaei"
Alléluia de la Pentecôte "Veni Sanctus Spiritus"

Alléluia "Caro mea"; Introït "Cibavit eos" de la Fête du Très Saint-Sacrement
Mass XVII—Kyrie & Sanctus
Mass XVII—Agnus Dei; Hymne du Dimanche de la Passion "Vexilla Regis"; Hymne de la Fête du Très Saint-Sacrement—"Pange Lingua"

ORDINARY OF THE MASS Chorus & Organ in Latin
Pius X Choir, College of the Sacred Heart —Justine B. Ward   2   12"—VM-69
[Intonations: Rev. V. C. Donovan, O.P. Organist: Achille Bragers]
Including:
Kyrie—In Festis B.V.M. No. 2 (Alme Pater)
Gloria—In Festis B.V.M. No. 1 (Cum Jubilo)
Credo No. 1
Preface of the Mass (Praefatio Communis)
Sanctus & Benedictus—In Festis B.V.M. No. 2 (Cum Jubilo)
Pater Noster
Agnus Dei—In Festis B.V.M. No. 9 (Cum Jubilo)
Ite Missa Est—In Festis B.V.M. No. 2 (Cum Jubilo)

REQUIEM MASS (Missa pro Defunctis)
Antiphon: Si Iniquitates
Psalm: De Profundis
Responsory: Subvenite
Antiphon: Exsultabunt
Psalm: Miserere
Introit: Requiem Aeternam
Kyrie
Gradual: Requiem Aeternam
Tract: Absolve Domine
Sequence: Dies Irae
Offertory: Domine Jesu Christe
Responses: Preface, Sanctus, Pater Noster
Responses before Agnus Dei & Agnus Dei
Communion: Lux Aeterna
Responsory: Libera Me
Antiphon: Ego Sum & Canticle: Benedictus
Antiphon: In Paradisum
Pius X Choir, College of the Sacred Heart —Julia Sampson   5   12"—VM-177
[Celebrant's Chants: Rev. V. C. Donovan, O. P.; Organist: Achille Bragers]
Benedictine Monks Choir of Saint Benoît du Lac, Lake Memphremagog, P. Q.
4   12"—GRCH-2
DUPLICATION: St. Charles Borromeo Choir—Boylan, KYR-10

GREGORIAN CHANTS Unacc. Chorus in Latin
Vernay Monastery Choir—Dr. E. Brüning 2 10"— & 4 12"—C-DH42/3 & C-DHX6/9
(C-CQX16471/4 & C-CQ641/2)
Including:
Dominus dixit, In Splendoribus, Puer Natus Est, Spiritus Domini, Veni Sancti Spiritus, Rorate Coeli, Kyrie Eleison, Rorate Coeli, Ne Irascaris Domine, Christus Factus Est, Plange, Ecce Lignum Crucis, Agios o Theos, Alleluia, Confitemini Dom-ino, Alleluia, Laudate Dominum, Haec Dies, Victimae Paschali, Requiem Aeternam, Kyrie Eleison, Lux Aeterna, Ego Sum Ressurectio

GREGORIAN CHANTS Polyphonic Arrangements
Campanile Chorus, Notre-Dame d'Auteuil —Dom B. de Malherbe
3   12"—C-DFX155/6 & C-DFX184 (C-GQX16556/8)
Including:
Responsory: Christus Resurgens
Responsory: Media Vita (Unacc. Polyphonic Arr. by J. Noyon)
Kyrie: Lux et Origo
Gloria (Easter)
Introit (Pentecost)
Alleluia & Victimae Paschali
Magnificat & Montes Gelboe
(Polyphonic arr. & Org. acc. by J. Noyon)

INDIVIDUAL GREGORIAN CHANT RECORDINGS
Among the many other Gregorian and Plainsong recordings are those in the Columbia History of Music, Volume I (C-5710/1 in CM-231), in the Dijon Cathedral Album (VM-212; GM-189), in the Parlophone 2000 Years of Music Album (P-R1017), in the Anthologie Sonore (No. 34 in Volume IV) as well as those by the following organizations:
Choir of the Pius X School of Liturgical Music   (in VM-739) V-13560
Chorus of the Seminary of Metropolitan Turin   CET-DR105/7
Choir of S. Vittore, Milan G-HN1592/93 & HN1606
Beuron Cathedral Choir   G-K6958
Dortmund Town School of Music
PD-90054/7 & PD-95251
Notre-Dame Cathedral, Paris
LUM-30034/5
Paderborn Cathedral Choir
PD-22197/8 & PD-22646/7
Julian Chapel Cho.—Antonelli
2   12"—SEMS-1117/8
St. Eustache Choir School
10" & 12"—LUM-30040 & 32025
[Missa de Angelis]

GRENON, Nicolas (15th Century)
Early fifteenth century singer and composer.
Je ne requier de ma dame
Lise Daniels (s) & 2 vlas acc.
12"—OL-136
[Ghizeghem: A la Audienche & Plus n'en aray]
Nova vobis Gaudia
Lise Daniels & Simone Peneau (s) with flute and vlc. acc.   12"—OL-61
[Ghizeghem: Plus n'en aray & Morton: Mon bien ma joye]

GRETCHANINOV, Alexander (1864-   )
A conservative contemporary Russian composer (pupil of Rimsky-Korsakov) who writes in all forms but who is best known by many songs and choral works.

Cossack Cradle Song Unacc. Chorus in Russian
Don Cossack Cho.—S. Jaroff
12"—C-7226M
[Tchesnokov: Herr Gewahre]

(3) Cossack Songs Unacc. Chorus in Russian
Blow, oh blow
There's a cloud of dust
Little red berry
Don Cossack Cho.—S. Jaroff
[Trad: Red Sarafan] 12"—C-7250M

Credo (Liturgia Domestica) Bass, Chorus & Organ
Rus. Slava tiebe, Gospody
Eng. Litany of Supplication
F. Chaliapin & Metropolitan Church Choir & Organ—Afonsky
(G-DB1701) 12"—V-7715
[Archangelsky: The Creed]
Gen. Platoff Don Cossack Choir—
Kostnikoff 12"—V-11-8514
[N. Khadarick, bar. solo]
[Tchesnokoff: Save Thy People, O God!]
Maria Kurenko (s) & A. Grechaninoff
(pf) (in VM-862) 12"—V-18380
[The Wounded Birch & Snowflakes]

DOBRINYA NIKITICH Opera in Russian
1903

The Flowers were growing in the fields
(Song of Alesha)
(or, Gaily bloom the little flowers)
Sergei Lemeshev 10"—USSR-10513/4
[Rimsky-Korsakov: May Night—Aria]
—Arr. Unacc. Chorus Jaroff
Don Cossack Choir 12"—C-7342M
[Rimsky-Korsakov: Sadko—Song of India]

Liturgy of Saint John Chrysostom, No. 2, Op. 29
Russian Metropolitan Choir—Afonsky
4 12"—G-DB5187/90
—Credo only
General Platoff Don Cossack Choir
(in VM-768) 12"—V-17917
[Tchaikovsky: Blessed by the Lord]
Don Cossack Choir—Jaroff
(U-F14269) 12"—T-E1908
[Trad.: Lord, Open the Door for me]
Mme. Pavlenko & Metropolitan Church Cho.—Afonsky 12"—G-C2206
[Archangelsky: Lord, Hear My Prayer]
(G-L880)

(2) Old Wedding Songs Unacc. Chorus in Russian
Don Cossack Choir—Jaroff
12"—C-7220M
[Bortniansky: How Glorious]

Responsory XI Unacc. Chorus in Russian
Rus. Prositelnaja Ektenja
Don Cossack Choir—Jaroff
12"—C-7325M
[Bortniansky: Who can equal Thee]

Sonata, G minor Op. 129 Piano
Allegro vivace (Finale)

—Arr. Harp Grandjany
Marcel Grandjany 10"—V-10-1120
[Grandjany: Automne]

SONGS In Russian
Collection
Maria Kurenko (s) & A. Gretchaninov
(pf) 3 12"—VM-862
Including:
Credo (from "Liturgica Domestica");
The Wounded Birch, Op. 1, No. 2; Snowflakes, Op. 47, No. 1; Oh my country, Op. 1, No. 4; Over the Steppe, Op. 5, No. 4; Dewdrop, Op. 69, No. 2; Declaration of Love (from "Aux temps heureux") Op. 64, No. 1; Snowdrop, Op. 47, No. 9; Ai doudou (from "Children's Songs") Op. 31; Lullaby, Op. 1, No. 5; On the Mountain, Op. 77, No. 3 (arr. Folksong); I'll go, I'll come, Op. 91, No. 1 (arr. Folksong)

Individual songs
Berceuse (Cradle song) Rus. Kolibeljnaja
Paul Robeson (bs) & Lawrence Brown
(pf) 12"—C-71367D
[Mussorgsky: Within four walls]
DUPLICATIONS: Ada Sari, G-AM3671;
Betty Martin (in Eng.), in C-J17

The Captive, Op. 20, No. 4
Jacques Bastard (b) (in French) & pf. acc. 10"—PAT-PG53
[Mussorgsky: Song of the old man]
DUPLICATION: V. Slivinsky, USSR-527

Death Ger. Der Tod
Wilhelm Strienz (bs) (in German)
12"—G-EH1044
[My country & Over the Steppe]

(The) Dreary Steppe See: Over the Steppe

(The) Flowers were growing
See under Dobrinya Nikitich

My Country Ger. Heimat
See Collection above
Franz Völker (t) (in German)
12"—PD-19793
[Leoncavallo: Mattinata]
DUPLICATION: In German: Wilhelm Strienz, G-EH1044

Night Ger. Nacht
Heinrich Schlusnus (b) (in Ger.)
10"—PD-62798
[Tchaikovsky: Pilgrim's Song]

Over the Steppe, Op. 5, No. 1 (or, The Lonely Steppe)
See collection above
Alexander Kipnis (bs) & Celius Dougherty (pf) 10"—V-11-8595
[Rachmaninoff: Harvest of Sorrow]
G. M. Youreneff (b) 10"—G-EK112
[Karnavaloff: Bells of the Kremlin]
I. Akobtsev 10"—USSR-14276
[Varlamov: I'll saddle the horse]
In German: Wilhelm Strienz, G-EH1044;
Maria Basca, T-A2132
In French: Ninon Vallin, PAT-PG82

GRETRY, André (1741-1813)
*A brilliant Belgian-French composer, largely
of comic operas who has been called the Molière
of music. He is most often represented today
by ballet music from his many dramatic works.*

Danses Villageoises Orchestral Suite
*The six dances included in this suite are drawn
from five of Grétry's fifty-eight operas:*
Richard Coeur-de-Lion—Danse rustique;
Colinette à la Cour—Gavotte & Danse en
rond; L'Epreuve Villageoise—Gigue; La
Rosière de Salency—Entr'acte; L'Embar-
ras de Richesses—Contre-Danse
Symphony Orch.—F. Ruhlmann
        2 12″—PAT-X96133/4
[Mozart: Nozze di Figaro—Overture]

OPERAS & OPERAS-COMIQUES In French

L'AMANT JALOUX 3 Acts 1778
Sérénade: Les événements imprévus, Act II
Ten.
Miguel Villabella   10″—PAT-PG11
[P. L. Couperin: Romance]

CEPHALE ET PROCRIS 3 Acts 1775
Ballet Suite Orchestra Arr. Mottl
Tambourin, Minuet (Les Nymphes de
Diane), Gigue
Chicago Symphony Orch.—Defauw
          12″—V-11-8825

COLINETTE A LA COUR 3 Acts 1782
(or "La Double Epreuve")
Gavotte & Danse en rond Orchestra
See under: Danses Villageoises, PAT-
X96133

L'EMBARRAS DE RICHESSES 3 Acts 1782
Contre-Danse Orchestra
See under: Danses Villageoises, PAT-
X96134

L'EPREUVE VILLAGEOISE 2 Acts 1784
(or "Théodore et Pauline")
Gigue Orchestra
See under: Danses Villageoises, PAT-
X96133

RICHARD COEUR-DE-LION
Danse rustique Orchestra
See under: Danses Villageoises, PAT-
X96133

O Richard, O mon Roi! Baritone
Eng. Blondel's Air
Martial Singher
     (in CM-578)   12″—C-72085D
[Lully: Amadis—Bois épais]

LA ROSIERE DE SALENCY 3 Acts 1774
Entr'acte Orchestra
See under: Danses Villageoises, PAT-
X96134

LA ROSIERE REPUBLICAINE 1 Act 1793
(or "Le Fête de la Raison")

Ballet Suite Orchestra Arr. Meyrowitz
Including: Danse légère; Contre-Danse; In-
termezzo; Rondo; Romance; Furioso;
Gavotte; Carmagnole
Symphony Orch.—Meyrowitz
        2 10″—PAT-PD7/8

LE TABLEAU PARLANT 1769
Vous étiez, ce que vous n'êtes plus Sop.
Maggie Teyte
    (in VM-1169)   10″—V-10-1371
[Monsigny: Le Déserteur—Adieu chère
Louise]

ZEMIRE ET AZOR
La Fauvette Soprano
Lily Pons   (in VM-756) 10″—V-2149
A. Galli-Curci   12″—G-DB1144
[Proch: Air & Variations]
Air de Ballet
London Philharmonic—Beecham
    (in CX-215) 12″—C-71330D
[Rossini: Semiramide—Overture, Pt. 3]
(C-LX885)
Rose chérie Sop.
Maggie Teyte
    (in VM-1169)   10″—V-10-1370
[Dourlen: Les Oies de Frère Philippe—
Aria]

GRIEG, Edvard Hagerup (1843-1907)
*The best known Norwegian composer and prob-
ably the most significant figure in the devel-
opement of national Scandinavian music. Although he wrote in many forms, Grieg was essentially a lyricist and did his best work in
small pieces of a strong folksong cast. Linguistic
difculties have presented problems in compiling a list of Grieg's recordings, but English
titles have been used in most headings. Many
of these works are known by German titles, because in that country many of Grieg's compositions were first published.*

Album Leaf, A major, Op. 28, No. 3 Piano
(from "Four Album Leaves")
Harold Bauer   10″—V-10-1217
[Berceuse]
Arthur De Greef   12″—G-D1825
[Arietta, Butterfly & To Spring]
—Arr. Violin & Piano Hartmann
Mischa Elman & Leopold Mittman
[Schumann: Träumerei] 10″—V-10-1271
Arietta, Op. 12, No. 1 Piano
(from "Lyric Pieces, Book I")
Arthur De Greef   12″—G-D1825
[Album Leaf, Butterfly & To Spring]
Anitra's Dance See under Peer Gynt
Ase's Death See under Peer Gynt
Au Printemps See: To Spring
Aus Holberg's Zeit See: Holberg Suite
Ballade, G minor, Op. 24 Piano
Eileen Joyce   2 12″—C-DX1116/7
Cor de Groot   2 12″—O-8791/2
Berceuse, Op. 38, No. 1 Piano
(from "Lyric Pieces, Book II")
Harold Bauer   10″—V-10-1217
[Album Leaf, Op. 28, No. 3]

—**Arr. 'Cello & Piano** Stutschewsky-
Thaler
William Pleeth & Margaret Good
['Cello Sonata Pt. 7]   12"—**D-K1051**

Bergliot, Op 42 Melodrama—Poem by
Björnson
Augusta Blad (recitation) & Danish State
Radio Orch.—Martellius Lundqvist
               2 12"—**TONO-X25024/5**

Brooklet, Op. 62, No. 4 Piano
(from "Lyric Pieces, Book VII")
(or "Little Brook")
Eileen Joyce   12"—**P-E11411**
[Solitary Traveller, Butterfly & Melody]

Butterfly, Op. 43, No. 1 Piano
(from "Lyric Pieces, Book III")
Fr. **Papillon** Ger. **Schmetterling**
Jesús María Sanromá   12"—**V-18153**
[Sinding: Rustle of Spring & Wagner—
Sanromá: Walküre—Fire Music]
Eileen Joyce   12"—**P-E11411**
[Melody, Solitary Traveller & Brooklet]
Kathleen Long   10"—**D-M542**
[Peasant Song & Nocturne]
Walter Gieseking
(O-7804)   12"—**P-E11136**
[To Spring & Wedding Day at Trold-
haugen]
Ivor Johnsen   12"—**T-E3225**
[Puck Sinding: Frühlingsrauschen]
DUPLICATIONS: F. Backer-Grøndahl,
C-GN409; A. De Greef, G-D1825; W.
Murdoch, D-F7496

(The) Carnival, Op. 19, No. 3 Piano
Eva Knardahl   10"—**TONO-K8037**

CHORUS
See under: Great White Flock; Land
Sighting

CONCERTO, A minor, Op. 16 Piano and
Orchestra
Artur Rubinstein & Philadelphia Orch.—
Ormandy   3 12"—**VM-900†**
(G-DB6234/6†)
Moura Lympany & National Symphony—
Sidney Beer   4 12"—**D-K1134/7†**
Walter Gieseking & Berlin State Opera
Orch.—Rosbaud   4 12"—**CM-313†**
(C-LX647/50†) (C-LFX498/501)
(C-LWX210/3)
[Cradle Song; French Serenade]
Benno Moiseiwitsch & Hallé Orch.—
Heward   4 12"—**G-C3264/7†**
[Palmgren: Refrain de Berceau; West
Finnish Dance]
DUPLICATIONS: Wilhelm Backhaus &
New Symphony Orch.—Barbirolli,
G-DB2074/6†; Ivar Johnsen & German
Opera House Orch.—Schmidt-Isserstedt,
T-E3132/5: U-F14417/20; Arturo Bene-
detti-Michelangeli & La Scala Orch.—
Galliera, T-SKB3280/3

—**1st Mvt. only** Condensed version
Jesús Maria Sanromá & Orch.—O'Con-
nell   (in VM-818) 12"—**V-13758**
[Tchaikovsky: Concerto No. 1, 1st Mvt.]

Cradle Song, Op. 68, No. 6 Piano
(from "Lyric Pieces, Book IX")
Ger. **An der Wiege**
Walter Gieseking
               (in CM-313) 12"—**C-69090D**
[French Serenade & Concerto, Pt. 7]
(C-LX650) (C-LFX501) (C-LWX213)
A. Benedetti-Michelangeli
[Melancholy]   10"—**G-DA5379**
Den store hvide Flok See: The Great White
Host

(2) Elegiac Melodies, Op. 34 String Orch.
1. **Heart Wounds** (Nor. Hjärtesär)
2. **Last Spring** (Nor. Vären)
(*These two pieces are Grieg's own transcrip-
tions of two songs in Op. 33—The Wounded
Heart & Springtide. For vocal versions see these
titles under Songs.*)
London Philharmonic—Goossens
               12"—**G-C2935**
Minneapolis Symphony Orch.—Mitro-
poulos   12"—**C-11698D**
Boyd Neel String Orch.—Neel
               12"—**D-K1217**
DUPLICATIONS: Royal Opera Orch.—
Copenhagen—Hye-Knudsen, G-EH1318;
Berlin Philharmonic Orch.—Schmidt-Is-
serstedt, T-E2600: U-F18109; Symphony
Orch.—Järnefelt, O-D6034: O-7902; Am-
sterdam Concertgebouw Orch.—Mengel-
berg, C-LX168

—**No. 2 (Last Spring)** only
Boston Symphony Orch.—Koussevitzky
               12"—**V-11-8727**
[Tchaikovsky: Serenade—Waltz]
[Vivaldi: Concerto Grosso No. 11, Pt. 3,
on V-18528 in VM-886†]
[Rimsky-Korsakov: Invisible City of
Kitezh—Battle of Kershenetz, on
G-DB6136]

Erotic, Op. 43, No. 5 Piano
(from "Lyric Pieces, Book III")
Arturo Benedetti-Michelangeli
[Concerto, Pt. 7]   12"—**T-SKB3283**
M. Rytter   12"—**TONO-K8032**
[To Spring]

—**Arr. Ensemble:** Godwin Quintet, PD-
21699

(The) First Meeting See: (2) Melodies &
also Songs

French Serenade, Op. 62, No. 3 Piano
(from "Lyric Pieces, Book VII")
Ger. **Französische Serenade**
Walter Gieseking
               (in CM-313†) 12"—**C-69090D**
[Cradle Song & Concerto, Pt. 7]
(C-LX650) (C-LFX501) (C-LWX213)

(The) Great White Host, Op. 30, No. 1 Bar.
& Male Cho. in Nor.
Nor. **Den store hvide Flok**
Sigurd Hoff & Handelsstandens Chorus—
Halvorsen   10"—**G-AL2107**
[Reissiger: Høstandagt] (G-X2736)
DUPLICATION: E. Krogh, G-AL2164

Holberg Suite, Op. 40 String Orchestra
Ger. **Aus Holbergs Zeit**
Prelude; Sarabande; Gavotte; Air;

Rigaudon
Boyd Neel String Orch.—Neel
                         3 12″—D-X144/6
[2 Norwegian Melodies—Cowkeeper's Tune]
London String Orch.—Goehr
(G-C3059/60)   2 12″—VM-792†
Metropolitan Symphony Orch.—
Rudolph Ganz   4 10″—PILO-DA301
(Commentary by Deems Taylor, 2 sides)

Ich liebe dich See under Songs

I love thee See under Songs

In the Hall of the Mountain King
See under Peer Gynt

Land-Sighting, Op. 31
Baritone, Male Chorus & Orchestra
Nor. **Landkjenning**
John Neergaard, Handelsstandens Chorus
& Orch.—Halvorsen   12″—G-Z178
—Arr. Band
2nd Division Musikkorps—Hanssen
C-GN125: C-DN12

(The) Last Spring See under Elegiac
Melodies & also Songs

Little Bird, Op. 43, No. 4 Piano
(from "Lyric Pieces, Book III")
Ger. **Vöglen**   Fr. **Oisillon**
Fridtjof Backer-Grøndahl
[Butterfly & To Spring] 10″—C-GN409

Lyric Suite, Op. 54 Orchestra
*An orchestral version of the first four Lyric
Pieces, Op. 54. For recordings of the piano ver-
sions, see titles of Nos. 1 & 3.*

1. **Shepherd Boy**
2. **Norwegian Rustic March**
3. **Nocturne**
4. **March of the Dwarfs**
Liverpool Philharmonic Orch.—
Cameron   2 12″—C-DX1142/3
London Philharmonic—Ronald
                    2 12″—G-C2642/3
[Sigurd Jorsalfar—Homage March]
(G-EH894/5)
National Symphony—Sargent
                    2 12″—D-K1412/3
—Nos. 1 & 3 only
Reichs-Symphonic Orch.—Erich Kloss
                         12″—PD-15157
—No. 4 only
Victor Symphony, V-22177

March of the Dwarfs, Op. 54, No. 4 Piano
(from "Lyric Pieces, Book V")
See under "Lyric Suite" for orchestral
version

Melancholy, Op. 65, No. 3 Piano
(From "Lyric Pieces, Book VIII")
A. Benedetti-Michelangeli
[Cradle Song]   10″—G-DA5379

Melody, Op. 47, No. 3 Piano
(from "Lyric Pieces, Book IV")
Eileen Joyce   12″—P-E11411
[Butterfly: Solitary Traveller & Brooklet]

(2) Melodies (2 original songs orchestrated)
String Orchestra
Norwegian & The First Meeting
Boyd Neel String Orch.—Neel
                         12″—D-K957

Nocturne, Op. 54, No. 3 Piano
(From "Lyric Pieces, Book V")
See under "Lyric Suite" for orchestral
version
Kathleen Long   10″—D-M542
[Peasant's Song & Butterfly]

Norwegian See under (2) Melodies

Norwegian Bridal Procession, Op. 19, No. 2
Piano
(from "Pictures of the Folk Life")
Nor. **Brude fölget drager forbi**
(*A recording by Edvard Grieg, made from a
Welte Piano roll of April 1906, is still listed on
O-4748, O-4785*)
Hilding Domellöf   10″—G-X7163
[Sjögren: Erotiken, Op. 10, No. 3]
—Arr. Orchestra
Victor Concert Orch.—Bourdon, V-20805

(4) Norwegian Dances, Op. 35 Orchestra
(Also arranged by Grieg for Piano solo
& 4 Hands)
1. **D minor**   2. **A minor**
3. **G major**   4. **D major**
London Symphony—Blech
(G-DB1668/9)   2 12″—V-11456/7
City of Birmingham Orch.—Weldon
                    2 12″—C-DX1192/3
—Nos. 1 & 4
Paris Symphony Orch.—Ruhlmann
                         12″—PAT-PAT96
—No. 1
German Opera House, Berlin—
Schmidt-Isserstedt   12″—T-E3185
[Concerto, with Johnsen, Pt. 7]
—No. 2
Symphony Orch.—Cloëz 10″—O-165047
[Peer Gynt—Anitra's Dance]
DUPLICATIONS: Berlin Orch., Dobrindt,
O-26383; Paul Godwin Orch., PD-21714;
Victor Orch., V-22171; Knudsen & Rief-
ling, C-GN195
—No. 3
German Opera House Orch.—Grüber
[Symphonic Dance No. 3] 12″—O-3628
DUPLICATION: Paul Godwin Orch.,
PD-21714
—No. 4
Paris Philharmonic—Cloëz, O-250541

(2) Norwegian Melodies, Op. 63
String Orchestra
1. **In the Popular Style**
Boyd Neel String Orch.—Neel
                         12″—D-K954
2. **Cow-Keeper's Tune & Country Dance**
Boyd Neel String Orch.—Neel
[Holberg Suite, Pt. 5]   12″—D-X146

Norwegian Peasant Dances (from "Släter")
Piano
—Jon Vastavos Springdans, Op. 72, No. 2
Ingebjörg Gresvik   10″—G-X4062
[Sinding: Rustle of Spring]

Norwegian Rustic March, Op. 54, No. 2
Piano
(from "Lyric Pieces" Book V)
See under: "Lyric Suite" for orchestral
version

Once Upon a Time, Op. 71, No. 1   Piano
(from "Lyric Pieces" Book X)
Kathleen Long   10"—**D-M543**
[Summer's Eve & Puck]

Papillon   See under: Butterfly

Peasant's Song, Op. 65, No. 2   Piano
(from "Lyric Pieces" Book VIII)
Kathleen Long   10"—**D-M542**
[Nocturne]

PEER GYNT   Incidental Music to Ibsen's
Drama   1875
The music Grieg wrote for Ibsen's play, com-
prising 23 numbers, is best known by the two
orchestral suites, Op. 46 and Op. 55, although
Solvejg's Song from Act IV (transcribed for or-
chestra in the 2nd Suite) is frequently heard
in its original vocal version. The scheme of
listing the "Peer Gynt" records is as follows:

1. *Pieces from the original stage version—in-*
cluding Solvejg's Sunshine and Cradle Songs,
vocal versions.
2. *Orchestral Suite No. 1, Op. 46*
3. *Orchestral Suite No. 2, Op. 55 (including*
the orchestral version of Solvejg's Sunshine
Song)

1. Music from the original stage version,
Op. 23
Suite   Orchestra & Chorus
In the Hall of the Mountain King, Act II
Solvejg's Sunshine Song, Act IV
Ase's Death, Prelude to Act III
Morning Mood, Prelude to Act IV
Anitra's Dance, Act IV
Vienna Symphony Orch. & Chorus—
Paul Kerby   2 10"—**C-CQ1350/1**
(C-D1268/9)

Dramatic performance with Grieg's music.
(Text: Henrik Ibsen)
The pair of discs immediately below is pri-
marily a diction recording, but is of pertinent
interest here.
Morning Song, Act I
Ase's Death, Act III
Solvejg's Cradle Song, Act V
Suzanne Després (Ase) & Lugné-Poë
(Peer) Diction in French, with orchestral
background—Bigot   2 12"—**C-BFX5/6**

Ase's Death
Clara Pontoppidan & Mogens Wieth
(recitation) with Royal Theater Orch.,
Copenhagen—Hye-Knudsen
            12"—**TONO-X25033**

Solvejg's Song (Sunshine song) Act IV
Soprano
Edith Oldrup-Pedersen (In Danish)
            12"—**G-DB5278**
[Solvejg's Cradle Song]   (G-Z285)
In French: Amelita Galli-Curci, V-6924:
G-DB1278: also on G-DB263*; Ninon
Vallin, O-123665; Andrée Marilliet,
C-D12057; Germaine Cernay, O-250789;
Eidé Noréna, G-K6885; Mado Robin,
G-DA4940; Marthe Coiffier, G-L912;

Manécanterie des Petits Chanteurs,
G-K7891
In Italian: Dina Manucci-Contini,
C-CQX16619
In German: Elisabeth Schumann,
G-DA1544; Margherita Perras,
G-DB10112; M. Teschemacher,
G-DB5598; Erna Berger, PD-47061:
PD-10429; Tatiana Angelini, O-3630;
Aulikki Rautawaara, T-E1795
In English: Joan Taylor, D-K1202
In Bohemian: Z. Ziková, U-A11331; M.
Tauberová, U-C12817

Solvejg's Cradle Song (Berceuse) Act V
Soprano
Edith Oldrup-Pederson (in Danish)
            12"—**G-DB5278**
[Solvejg's Sunshine Song]   (G-Z285)
Margarete Teschemacher (in German)
[Sunshine Song]   12"—**G-DB5598**
Margherita Perras (in German)
[Sunshine Song]   12"—**G-DB10112**
DUPLICATIONS: Marthe Coiffier (in
French), G-L912; Tatiana Angelini,
O-3630; Aulikki Rautawaara, T-E1795

2. Suite No. 1, Op. 46   Orchestra
1. Morning
2. Ase's Death
3. Anitra's Dance
4. In the Hall of the Mountain King
London Philharmonic Orch.—
Beecham   2 12"—**CX-180**†
(C-LX838/9)   (C-LFX587/8)
London Symphony—Walter Goehr
            2 12"—**D-K1319/20**†
Cincinnati Symphony Orch.—
Goossens   2 12"—**VM-1100**†
Berlin Radio Orch.—Kretschmar
            2 12"—**C-DWX1632/3**
Dresden Philharmonic Orch.—
van Kempen   2 12"—**PD-11383/4**
Berlin Orch.—Heger   2 12"—**O-3623/4**
London Philharmonic Orch.—
Goossens   2 12"—**G-C2933/4**
(G-FKX50 & 66)
Philharmonic Orch., Paris—
Inghelbrecht   2 12"—**CX-110**†
(PAT-PGT10/1)
DUPLICATIONS: Berlin Philharmonic,
Schreker, PD-24627/8; Berlin Philhar-
monic—Borchard, T-A1726/7; Symphony
Orch.—Inghelbrecht, PAT-PGT10/1; Vi-
enna Symphony—Kerby, C-DFX165 &
C-DF1395; Berlin State Opera Orch.—
Weissmann, P-E11027/8; Berlin State
Opera Orch.—Fried, PD-516608/9;
Colonne Orch.—Pierné, O-123731/2;
Royal Opera Orch., Covent Garden—
Goosens, G-S8836 & G-S8838
Also: G. Thalben Ball (organ),
G-B4484/5; L. Stin (organ),
PD-521690/1

Individual excerpts from Suite No. 1
(*See above for complete recordings*)

No. 1 (Morning Mood) only
Symphony Orch.—Cloëz, O-170000;
Eight Piano Orchestra, C-DB1481

No. 2 (Ase's Death) only
Symphony Orch.—Cloëz, O-170000;
Godwin Quintet, PD-21700; A. Lévy
(vlc), O-166373

No. 3 (Anitra's Dance) only
Symphony Orchestra, U-B14390; Godwin
Quintet, PD-21700; William Murdoch
(pf), D-K661; A. Lévy (vlc), O-166373

3. Suite No. 2, Op. 55 Orchestra
1. Ingrid's Lament
2. Arabian Dance
3. Return of Peer Gynt
4. Solvejg's Song

Indianapolis Symphony Orch.—
Sevitzky   2 12"—VM-902†
London Philharmonic Orch.—
Cameron   2 12"—D-K1456/7†
New Light Symphony Orch.—
Goossens   2 12"—G-C1571/2
(G-L728/9) (G-S10013/4)
Berlin State Opera Orch.—Fried
                2 12"—PD-516610/1
Paris Philharmonic—Cloëz
                2 12"—O-123846/7
Berlin Radio Orch.—Kretzschmar
                2 12"—C-DWX1634/5
Berlin Orch.—Heger   2 12"—O-3625/6

No. 4 (Solvejg's Song) only
Instrumental version
(For original vocal version see under 1, Peer
Gynt Stage Version above.)
DUPLICATIONS: Bournemouth Munici-
pal Orch.—Godfrey, C-DF1053; C-DB810;
M. Weber Orch., G-EG1155: G-K5849;
G-HN612; Symphony Orchestra,
U-B14390; B. von Geczy Orch.,
G-HN2084
Arrangements:
Maurice Maréchal (vlc) & Yolanda
Kornhold (pf)   10"—C-LF150
[Pierné: Sérénade]

Puck, Op. 71, No. 3   Piano
(from "Lyric Pieces, Book X)
Ger. Kobold
Kathleen Long   10"—D-M543
[Once upon a time & Summer's Eve]
Ivar Johnsen   12"—T-E3225
[Butterfly & Sinding: Rustle of Spring]

—Arr. Violin & Piano   J. Achron
Jascha Heifetz & Isador Achron
                12"—V-6848
[Falla: Jota & Mendelssohn: Auf
Flügeln des Gesanges]

QUARTET—G minor, Op. 27   String
Budapest Quartet   4 12"—VM-465

Scherzo, Op. 54, No. 5   Piano
(from "Lyric Pieces," Book V)
Kathleen Long   10"—D-M544
[Shepherd's Boy]

Scherzo-Impromptu, Op. 73, No. 2   Piano
(from "Moods")
Eileen Joyce   12"—P-E11427
[To Spring, Summer's Eve & Sinding:
Rustle of Spring]

—Arr. Violin & Piano   J. Achron
Jascha Heifetz & Isadore Achron
                12"—G-DB1246
[Debussy: La fille aux cheveux de lin &
Mendelssohn: Auf Flügeln des Gesanges]

Shepherd's Boy, Op. 54, No. 1   Piano
(from "Lyric Pieces Book V")
Kathleen Long   10"—D-M544
[Scherzo]
(See under "Lyric Suite" for orchestral ver-
sion.)

SIGURD JORSALFAR Incidental Music for
Björnson's drama, Op. 56

Orchestral Suite
1. In the King's Hall (Prelude)
2. Borghild's Dream (Intermezzo)
3. Homage March (Triumphal March)
—No. 3 only
Hallé Orch.—Lambert, C-DX1037
Symphony Orch.—Barbirolli, G-C2711
Symphony Orch.—Gurlitt, PD-27042
Orchestra—Dobrindt, O-7920
Victor Concert Orchestra, G-X6074

(The) Solitary Traveller, Op. 43, No. 2
(from "Lyric Pieces Book III")
(or, "The Lonely Wanderer")   Piano
Eileen Joyce   12"—P-E11411
[Brooklet, Butterfly & Melody]

Solvejg's Song   See under Peer Gynt

SONATAS—Violin & Piano

No. 2, G major, Op. 13
Jascha Heifetz & Emanuel Bay
                3 12"—VM-735†
[Wieniawski: Polonaise Brilliante, D]
A. Sjøn & Hans Solum
                2 12"—T-E15070/1

No. 3, C minor, Op. 45
Georg Kulenkampff & Siegfried Schultze
                3 12"—T-E3284/6
Gunnar Knudsen & Robert Riefling
                3 12"—G-DB11900/2

SONATAS—'Cello & Piano

A minor, Op. 36
Raya Garbousova & Arthur Balsam
                3   12"—CH-AD
William Pleeth & Margaret Good
[Berceuse]   4 12"—D-K1048/51
William Van den Burg & Sara Compinsky
                3 12"—ALCO-AC201

SONGS

NOTE: As in most catalogues, the song titles in
the following list are largely given in English.

At the Brookside, Op. 33, No. 5
Nor. Tro—"Guds rike er et fredens rike"
Erling Krogh (t)   10"—G-X3041
[Nordraak: Maria Stuart-Taylors Sang]

(The) Autumn Storm, Op. 18, No. 4
Nor. Efteraarsstormen
Astra Desmond (c) (in Nor.) & Gerald
Moore (pf)   10"—D-M491
[A Swan]

(A) Boat is Rocking on the Waves, Op. 69, No. 1
Nor. **Der gynger en Baad paa Bolge**
Kirsten Flagsted, (s) (in Norwegian) &
Edwin McArthur (pf)
            (in VM-342)   10"—**V-1813**
[In the Boat]

(A) Dream, Op. 48, No. 6 (Bödenstedt)
Nor. **En Dröm**   Ger. **Ein Traum**
Kirsten Flagsted (s) (in German) &
Edwin McArthur (pf)   10"—**V-1804**
[I love thee]   (G-DA1505)
Richard Tauber (t) (In German)
[Eros]   10"—**P-RO20553**
Beniamino Gigli (t) (in Italian)
                    10"—**G-DA1504**
[Schumann: Lotosblüme]
Richard Crooks (t) (in English)
        (in VM-846)   10"—**V-2177**
[Schubert: Serenade]
H. E. Groh (t) (in German)
[I love thee]   10"—**O-26573**

Eros, Op. 70, No. 1 (Benzon)
("Hear me, ye frosty cold hearts")
Lauritz Melichior (t) (in Danish) &
Ignace Strasfogel (pf)
        (in VM-851)   10"—**V-2188**
[Til Norge; Hannikainen: Stille mit Hjaerte]
Richard Tauber (t) (in German)
[A Dream]   10"—**P-RO20553**
DUPLICATIONS: (in German) Karl
Schmitt-Walter, T-A2178; Walther Ludwig, G-EG3242

(The) First Meeting, Op. 21, No. 1
(Björnson)
Nor. **Det første Møte**
Ger. **Erstes Begenen**
Astra Desmond (c) (in Nor.) & Gerald
Moore (pf)   12"—**D-K962**
[There screamed a bird; I love thee; Love; Rock, O Wave]
Eidé Noréna (s)   10"—**G-DA4848**
[Lie: Sne]
See also: (2) Melodies

Fisherman's Song, Op. 61, No. 3
(Björnson)
Nor. **Lok**   Ger. **Lockweise**
Hulda F. Gran & pf.   10"—**C-DN217**

From Monte Pincio, Op. 39, No. 1
(Björnson)
Nor. **Fra Monte Pincio**
Eidé Noréna (s) (in Norwegian)
[Springtide]   12"—**G-DB4849**
Sophie Schonning (s) & Boyd Neel
String Orch.   12"—**D-K1208**
[Little Hut; Summer Eve]

Hear me, ye frosty cold hearts See: Eros

Heart Wounds See under: Wounded Heart
NOTE: *For orchestral transcription see: Elegiac Melodies*

Hope, Op. 26, No. 1
Nor. **Et Haab**
Kirsten Flagstad (s) (in Norwegian) &
Edwin McArthur (pf)
        (in VM-342)   10"—**V-1816**

[Alnaes: Lykken mellem to Mennesker]
(G-DA1516)

I love thee, Op. 5, No. 3 (Andersen)
Dan. **Jeg elsker Dig**   Ger. **Ich liebe dich**
Aksel Schiøtz (t) & F. Jensen (pf)
                    10"—**G-X7203**
[Two Brown eyes & A Poet's Last Song]
[Two Brown eyes & Wounded Heart, on G-X6924]
Kirsten Flagstad (s) (in Norwegian)
                    10"—**G-DA1520**
[Backer-Grøndahl: Mot Kveld]
Astra Desmond (c) (in Nor.) & Gerald
Moore (pf)   12"—**D-K962**
[Love; Rock, O Wave]
In German:
Kirsten Flagstad (s) & Edwin
McArthur (pf)   10"—**V-1804**
[A Dream]   (G-DA1505)
Karl Schmitt-Walter (b) &
Franz Rupp (pf)   10"—**T-A2040**
[Brahms: Feldeinsamkeit]
DUPLICATIONS: Friedel Beckmann,
G-DA4505; Franz Völker, PD-21041;
Rudolf Steiner, PAT-X93025
In English & Danish:
Lauritz Melchior (t) & Orch.
        (in VM-990)   10"—**V-10-1177**
[Hubay—Arr. Stoll: Lonely Night]
[Fain: Please Don't Say No, on G-B9446]
In English:
Marjorie Lawrence (s) & Ivor
Newton (pf)   10"—**D-M602**
[Rachmaninoff: Floods of Spring]
Richard Crooks (t) & Fred. Schauwecker
(pf)   (in VM-846)   10"—**V-2178**
[Anon: Have you seen but a whyte lillie grow]
[Tosti: Parted, on G-DA1394]
Webster Booth (t) & Gerald
Moore (pf)   10"—**G-B9497**
[Schumann: Widmung]
DUPLICATIONS: Charles Kullman,
C-DB1400; C-4143M; Frank Titterton,
D-F3195
In French: Lemichel du Roy,
PD-522633; R. Temps, PAT-PA287
In Italian: Cloe Elmo, CET-TI7011
In Bohemian: Z. Ziková, U-A11331;
M. Tauberová, U-C12817

Ich liebe dich See: I love thee

In the Boat, Op. 60, No. 3 (Krag)
Nor. **Mens jeg venter**   Ger. **Im Kahne**
Kirsten Flagstad (s) (in German) &
Edwin McArthur (pf)
        (in VM-342)   10"—**V-1813**
[A Swan]   (G-DA1513)
Friedel Beckmann (c) (in German)
[I love thee]   10"—**G-DA4505**
Heinrich Rehkemper (b) (in German)
& Raucheisen (pf)   10"—**PD-23150**
[St. John's Eve]

—**Arr. Victor Orchestra, in V-24789**

It was a lovely summer evening, Op. 26, No. 2 (Paulsen)
Nor. **Jeg Rejste En Delig Sommerkvaeld**

Sophie Schonning (s) & Boyd Neel
String Orch. 12"—D-K1208
[From Monte Pincio; Little Hut]
Randi Heide Stenn (s) & R. Levin (pf)
[Little Kirsten] 10"—G-AL2930

Kveldsang for Blakken (Rolfsen)
Randi Heide Stenn (s) & Robert
Levin (pf) 10"—G-AL2931
[Trad. arr., Alnaes: Anne Knutsdatter &
Backer-Grøndahl: Efter en sommerfugl]

Langs en å (Vinge)
Randi Heide Stenn (s) & Robert
Levin (pf) 10"—G-AL2929
[Alnaes: A leva]

Last Spring See under: Springtide
*The Last Spring is the title of the orchestral
transcription—Elegiac Melodies—of this song.*

Little Kirsten Op. 60, No. 1 (Krag)
Randi Heide Stenn (s) & Robert
Levin (pf) 10"—G-AL2930
[It was a lovely summer evening]

Love, Op. 15, No. 2 (Kjaerlighed)
Astra Desmond (c) (in Nor.) & Gerald
Moore (pf) 12"—D-K962
[Rock, O Wave & I Love Thee]

Mid en vanlije See: With a Waterlily

Med en primulavens See: With a Primrose

Outward Bound, Op. 9, No. 2
Dan. **Udfarten**
Aksel Schiøtz (t) & Folmer Jensen (pf)
[Springtide] 12"—G-Z279

(A) Poet's Last Song
Dan. **En Dikter sidste Sang**
Aksel Schiøtz (t) (in Dan.) & Gerald
Moore (pf) 10"—G-X7203
[Two Brown Eyes; I Love Thee]

Radiant Night, Op. 70, No. 3
Nor. **Lyse Nat** Ger. **Licht Nacht**
Kirsten Flagstad (s) (in Norwegian) &
Edwin McArthur (pf)
[A Swan] (in VM-342) 10"—V-1814

(The) Return, Op. 33, No. 9
(Ved Rundame)
(or, "On the way home")
Astra Desmond (c) (in Nor.) &
Harold Craxton (pf) 12"—D-M536
[Springtide]

Rock, O Wave, Op. 49, No. 2
Nor. **Vug o Vove**
(or, "Waft O Waters")
Astra Desmond (c) (in Nor.) & Gerald
Moore (pf) 12"—D-K962
[Love; I Love Thee]

Saint John's Eve, Op. 60, No. 5 (Krag)
(or, "Midsummer's Eve")
Nor. **Og jeg vil ha' mig**
Ger. **Zur Johannisnacht**
Kirsten Flagstad (s) (in Nor.) & Edwin
McArthur (pf) 12"—G-DB3392
[First Primrose & Hurum: Blonde
Naetter]

Solvejg's Song See under Peer Gynt

Spring Rain, Op. 49, No. 6 (or "Showers")
Nor. **Foraarsregn**
Astra Desmond (c) (in Nor.) &
Gerald Moore (pf) 10"—D-M492
[With a Primrose; Thanks for thy rede]

Springtide, Op. 33, No. 2 (Vinje)
Nor. **Varen** Ger. **Letzter Fruhling**
*(This song is the original version of Last
Spring"—No. 2 of the "Elegiac Melodies" for
string orchestra, Op. 34.)*
Eidé Noréna (s) (in Norwegian) &
Orch.—Coppola 12"—G-DB4849
[From Monte Pincio]
Richard Tauber (t) (in English)
[I love thee] 10"—P-RO20520
Astra Desmond (c) (in Nor.) &
Harold Craxton (pf) 10"—D-M536
[The Return]
Aksel Schiøtz (t) & Folmer Jensen (pf)
[Outward Bound] 12"—G-Z279

—**Arr. Violin & Piano**
H. Fritz-Crone, G-X4597

(A) Swan, Op. 25, No. 2 (Ibsen)
Nor. **En svan** Ger. **Ein Schwan**
Kirsten Flagstad (s) (in Nor.) &
Edwin McArthur (pf)
 (in VM-342) 10"—V-1814
[Radiant Night]
Astra Desmond (c) (in Nor.) & Gerald
Moore (pf) 10"—D-M491
[Autumn Storm]
Lorri Lail (ms) (in Norwegian) & Sven
Gunnar Andren (pf) 10"—G-X7172
[Sibelius: The first Kiss]

Thanks for Thy Rede, Op. 21, No. 4
(or, "Your advice is good")
Nor. **Tak for dit Raad**
Astra Desmond (c) (in Nor.) &
Gerald Moore (pf) 10"—D-M492
[With a primrose; Spring rain]

There Screamed a Bird, Op. 60, No. 4
(or, "A bird cried out")
Nor. **Der skreg en Fugl**
Astra Desmond (c) (in Nor.) & Gerald
Moore (pf) 12"—D-K962
[Rock, O Wave; Love; First Meeting]

To Norway, Op. 68, No. 1
Nor. **Til Norge**
Lauritz Melchior (t) & Ignace
Strasfogel (pf)
[Eros] (in VM-851) 10"—V-2188

(Ein) Traum See: A Dream
Two Brown Eyes Dan. **To Brune Ojne**
Aksel Schiøtz (t) (in Dan.) &
Folmer Jensen (pf) 10"—G-X7203
[I love thee & A Poet's Last Song]
[I love thee & The Wounded Heart, on
G-X6924]
DUPLICATION: Edi Laider (t) & Ole
Williamsen (pf), G-X6164

Våren See: Springtide

Verse for an Album, Op. 25, No. 3
(or, "Album Lines") Nor. **Stanbogerim**
Astra Desmond (c) & Gerald Moore (pf)
[With a waterlily] 12"—D-K961

With a Primrose, Op. 26, No. 4 (Paulsen)
Nor. **Med en Primula Veris**
Kirsten Flagstad (s) (in Nor.)
& Edwin McArthur (pf) 12"—**G-DB3392**
[St. John's Eve; Hurum: Blonde Naetter]
Astra Desmond (c) (in Nor.) &
Gerald Moore (pf) 10"—**D-M492**
[Thanks for thy Rede; Spring Rain]
Anna Howard (s) (in English) &
pf. acc. 12"—**V-36033**
[in "Songs for Children"]

With a Waterlily, Op. 25, No. 4
Nor. **Med en Vandlilje**
Astra Desmond (c) & Gerald Moore (pf)
[Verse for an album] 12"—**D-K961**

(The) Wounded Heart, Op. 33, No. 3
(Vinje)
Nor. **Ved Ronderne**
*This is the original version of "Heart Wounds,"
No. 1 of the "Elegiac Melodies" for string or-
chestra, Op. 34.*
Aksel Schiøtz (t) & pf. acc.
10"—**G-X6924**
[Two brown eyes & I love thee]
Erling Krogh (t) 10"—**G-AL2003**
[Sjöberg: Tonerne]

Summer's Eve, Op. 71, No. 2 Piano
(from "Lyric Pieces Book X")
Eileen Joyce 12"—**P-E11427**
[To Spring; Scherzo-Impromptu &
Sinding: Rustle of Spring]
Kathleen Long 10"—**D-M543**
[Once upon a time & Puck]

(4) Symphonic Dances, Op. 64 Orchestra
Indianapolis Symphony Orch.—
Sevitzky 3 12"—**VM-1066†**
[Liadov: Baba Yaga]
Berlin State Opera Orch.—
Van Kempen 2 12"—**CET-OR5114/5**
German Opera House Orch.—Grüber
3 12"—**O-3627/9**
[Norwegian Dance No. 3 on O-3628]

Nos. 1 & 4 only
Paris Conservatory Orch.—Coppola
12"—**G-DB4867**

No. 2 only
Symphony Orch.—Coppola
12"—**G-W978**
[Coppola: Scherzo fantastique]

To Spring, Op. 43, No. 6 Piano
(from "Lyric Pieces Book III")
Nor. **Til Varen** Fr. **Au Printemps**
Ger. **An den Frühling**
Walter Gieseking 12"—**P-E11136**
[Butterfly & Wedding Day at
Troldhaugen] (O-7804)
Eileen Joyce 12"—**P-E11427**
[Summer's Eve; Scherzo-Impromptu;
Sinding: Rustle of Spring]
DUPLICATIONS: Walter Rehberg,
PD-27229; De Greef, G-D1825; Fridt-
jof Backer-Grøndahl, C-GN409; William
Murdoch, D-F7499; M. Rytter,
TONO-K8032

—Arr. Orchestra
Berlin Orch.—Dobrindt, O-26383; Marek
Weber Orch., G-EG3174; J. Pinel Orch.,

G-K5785; P. Godwin Quintet, PD-21699;
Chamber Orch., G-GW1871; Ultraphon
Orch.—Vipler, U-B12960; Albert Sandler
Trio, C-FB2172

Wedding Day at Troldhaugen, Op. 65, No. 6
Piano (from "Lyric Pieces Book VIII")
Ger. **Hochzeitstag auf Troldhaugen**
Nor. **Brylluppet paa Troldhaugen**
Walter Gieseking 12"—**P-E11136**
[Butterfly & To Spring] (O-7804)
Walter Rehberg 10"—**PD-24989**
[Sinding: Frühlingsrauschen]
DUPLICATIONS: Percy Grainger,
C-7150M; Arthur deGreef, G-E529; Fridt-
jof Backer-Grøndahl; C-GN410; Hilda
Bor, C-FB2147; Eva Knardahl,
TONO-K8038
Also: Marek Weber Orch., G-EH97;
Symph. Orch., U-E416

MISCELLANEOUS:

SONG OF NORWAY An operetta arranged
from Grieg's music
(Robert Wright & George Forest)
Selections (Orchestral)
Palace Theatre Symphony Orch.—
Gideon Fagan 12"—**G-C3495**
Mantovani & his Orch. 10"—**D-F8645**
Selections (Vocal)
Irra Petina & Robert Weede, with Orch.
Sylvan Shulman 3 12"—**CM-562**
Strange Music
James Melton (t) 12"—**V-11-8746**
[Freed—There's beauty everywhere]
Nelson Eddy (b)
(in CM-571) 10"—**C-4318M**
[I love you] (C-DB2222)
Janet Hamilton-Smith (s) & John
Hargraves (b), with Chorus
[Three Loves] 10"—**G-B9479**
Medleys of Grieg Melodies
("Reminiscences of Grieg" "Golden
Memories of Grieg," etc.)
Berlin State Opera Orch.—Melichar
2 10"—**PD-25061 & PD-25117**
Marek Weber Orch. 12"—**G-C2374**
(G-EH693)
Berlin Philharmonic Orch. 12"—**T-E2406**

GRIFFES, Charles Tomlinson (1884-1920)
*A talented American composer of whom great
things were expected, but who died before he
had an opportunity to develop beyond a skillful
craftsman in the contemporary French idiom.
His well known orchestral poem "The Pleasure
Dome of Kubla Kahn" is no longer available
on recordings.*

Poem for Flute & Orchestra 1918
Joseph Mariano & Eastman-Rochester
Symphony Orch.—Hanson
12"—**V-11-8349**

(The) Pleasure Dome of Kubla Khan
Orchestra No recordings available

Roman Sketches, Op. 7 (after poems by
William Sharp) Piano

No. 1, The White Peacock
—Arr. Orchestra Griffes
CBS Symphony—Howard Barlow
10"—C-17140D
Eastman-Rochester Orch.—Howard
Hanson   (in VM-608)   12"—V-15659
[Kennan: Night Soliloquy]

By a Lonely Forest Pathway Song
(in English)
Eleanor Steber (s) & pf. acc.
[Sacco: Rapunzel]   10"—V-10-1071

GRIGNY, Nicolas de (1671-1703)
*French organist of Rheims Cathedral, whose
"Pièces d'Orgue" were published in 1711.*

Plein Jeu Organ
Joseph Bonnet
(in Vol. VIII)   12"—AS-75
[Couperin: Offertoire & Sanctus]

Récit de Tierce Organ
Joseph Bonnett (Gonzalez Organ)
12"—PAT-PAT67
[Marchand: Fond d'orgue en mi mineur
& Anon: Trois versets de Te Deum]
(in 3 Centuries of Organ Music Set)

GROFE, Ferde (1892-   )
*Well known arranger of modern American
works who has written many compositions in
the symphonic jazz idiom, mostly of a programmatic and highly descriptive nature.*

Grand Canyon Suite Orchestra
Sunrise; Painted Desert; On the Trail;
Sunset; Cloudburst
NBC Symphony—Toscanini
4 12"—VM-1038†
Andre Kostelanetz & his Orch.
4 12"—CM-463†
—On the Trail only
Andre Kostelanetz & his Orch.
12"—C-7390M

Mississippi Suite—A Tone Journey
Orchestra
Huckleberry Finn; Old Creole Days;
Mardi Gras
Andre Kostelanetz & his Orch.
2 12"—CX-284†
[Cadman: From the land of the sky-
blue water & Lieurance: By the waters
of Minnetonka]
Paul Whiteman's Concert Orch.
12"—V-35859

GROSSIN (Grossino de Jaris—Parisius)
(c.1400)
An early composer of church and secular songs.

Rondeaux: Va t'en soupir (Va-t'ent,
souspier) 3-Part
Mlle. H. Guermant & F. Anspach, with
Mediaeval viols, lute, little harp &
recorder—S. Cape
(in Vol. IV)   12"—AS-39
[Binchois: De plus en plus & Lantins:
Puisque je voy]

GROSSMAN, Sasha
Russian Dances Orchestra
No. 1, D minor
No. 3, C major
FOK Symphony Orch.—Vaclav
Smetacek   12"—U-F14758
Russian Songs
Zachem Ljubitj
Prosti Proschaj
Leonid Schulakowskij (vocal) & Bala-
laika Orch.   10"—U-A11292

GROTTE, Nicolas de la
*A French musician, organist to Henri III,
Grotte wrote chansons and pieces for lute and
organ.*

Je suis amour
M. Vhita (a) & H. Leeb (lute)
(in Vol. IV)   12"—AS-36
[Clemens non Papa: Aymer est ma vie;
Anon: Il me suffit; Besard: 4 Lute pieces]

GRUBER, Franz Xavier (1787-1863)
*A German organist, choirmaster and composer
who wrote "Silent Night, Holy Night" in 1818.*

Stille Nacht, Heilige Nicht Chorale
(Joseph Mohr)

Vocal versions in German Chorale
Basilica Chor-Pius Kalt
[O du fröhliche]   10"—PD-21696
Thomanerchor, Leipzig—Straube
10"—PD-24781
[Praetorius: Es ist ein' Ros'
entsprungen]

Vocal versions in German Solo Voice
Ernestine Schumann-Heink
12"—V-6723
[Humperdinck: Weihnachten]
Elisabeth Schumann (s)
[Anon: O du fröhliche] 10"—G-DA1666
DUPLICATIONS: Walter Ludwig,
PD-47257; Franz Marszalek, PD-10970;
Wolfgang Kieling (treble) with Chorus,
G-EG6280

Choral Versions in English
Madrigal Singers—Engel (with organ)
10"—C-322M
[Redner: O little town of Bethlehem]
Also: Baillie, Brunskill, Nash & Allin,
C-DB976

Vocal Versions in English Solo
John McCormack (t) & Gerald Moore (pf)
[Tchaikowsky: Legend] 10"—G-DA1755
Elisabeth Schumann (s) & Hugh
Dawson (organ)   10"—G-DA1667
[Trad: Coventry Carol]
Beniamino Gigli (t) & Cho.
[Trad. Adeste fideles] 10"—G-DA1874
James Melton (t)   10"—V-10-1356
[Trad. Adeste fideles]
Lotte Lehmann (s)   10"—V-10-1367
[Trad. Adeste fideles]
DUPLICATIONS: Hulda Lashanska,
V-1748; Paul Robeson, G-B8668;
Webster Booth & Anne Ziegler, G-B9598

Miscellaneous Arrangements
Mark Andrews (organ), V-20298;
Charles Courboin, in VM-1091

GRUENBERG, Louis, (1884-   )

A Russian-American composer known for his opera "Emperor Jones," based on the Eugene O'Neill play.

Concerto for Violin & Orchestra, Op. 47
1944
Jascha Heifetz & San Francisco Orch.—
Monteux   4 12"—**VM-1079**†
Emperor Jones Opera in English 1932
—**Standin' in the need of prayer** Baritone
Lawrence Tibbett   12"—**V-7959**
[Hanson: Merry Mount—'Tis an earth
defiled]

GUARNIERI, Camargo (1907-   )

A Brazilian modernist, trained in Europe after studying at the Sao Paulo Conservatory. Guarnieri's music is imbued with the folklore of his country. He is considered the "strongest polyphonic composer" in Brazil since he believes the dynamic force of folklore music in his country is such that one should avoid harmonization by chords. He has made frequent visits to the United States and has appeared as conductor and as piano soloist with leading orchestras. Guarnieri is a prolific composer in all forms.

SONGS In Portuguese
Quebra o coco menina
Dem Bau
Rei madou me chama
Bambalele
Olga Coelho (s) with guitar acc., in
Hargail-MW700

Toccata Piano
Guiomar Novaës
(in CM-692] 10"—**C-17487D**
[Villa-Lobos: Brazilian folk songs]

GUION, David W. (1895-   )

A contemporary American composer who has specialized in settings of native cowboy and hillbilly tunes, and in larger works based on their idioms.

All Day Long on the Prairie
(Setting by Guion from English
traditional)
James Melton (t)
(in VM-1060) 10"—**V-10-1237**
[Fox: The Hills of Home]
Arkansas Traveller (Setting by Guion)
Orchestra
Boston "Pops" Orch.—Fiedler
[Billings: Chester]   10"—**V-4502**
[Serradel: Golondrina, on G-B9388]
Home on the Range (Cowboy Song Setting)
John Charles Thomas (b) 10"—**V-1525**
[Rasbach: Trees]
Robert Merrill (b)   10"—**V-10-1273**
[Hill: Last Round-up]

Sheep and Goat Walkin' to Pasture Piano
(Cowboy breakdown setting)
Percy Grainger   12"—**C-7134M**
[Bach: Partita No. 1—Gigue & Liszt:
Liebestraum]
—**Arr. Orchestra**
Boston "Pops" Orch.—Fiedler
(in VM-968) 10"—**V-10-1092**
[Cadman: At dawning]
Turkey in the Straw Fiddle Tune Setting
Boston "Pops" Orch.—Fiedler
10"—**V-4390**
[Liadov: The Music Box, Op. 32]
Victor Concert Orch.—Bourdon
10"—**V-22131**
[Sowerby: Irish Washerwoman]
Also: Andre Kostelanetz & his Orch.,
C-35784: C-DB1821

HABA, Alois (1893-   )

A Czech composer, pupil of Novak, and proponent of quarter-tone music. He was appointed a professor at Prague Conservatory in 1924, where he wrote a harmony book based on his principals.

Duo—2 Violins in the Sixth Tone System,
Op. 49
—**1st Mvt. (Allegro moderato) only**
Weismeyer & Stein   10"—**C-DB1307**
[Varèse: Octandre, 3rd Mvt.]
(C-DB1791)
(in Columbia History of Music,
Vol. V: CM-361)
Fantasia for Unaccompanied Violin, Op. 9a
Josef Peska   10"—**U-B11067**
(10) Fantasias—Quarter-tone piano
—**No. 5**
Karel Reiner 2 12"—**ESTA-F5199/200**
[Suite No. 1]
—**No. 10**
Karel Reiner   12"—**ESTA-F5201**
Fantasia, Op. 15
Karel Reiner   12"—**ESTA-F5202**

MATKA, Op. 35 1931 Opera
—**Unidentified Vocal Quartet**
10"—**U-B11066**
[String Quartet No. 2—1st Mvt. only—
Andante]

QUARTETS—String In Quarter-tone
—**No. 1, Opus 7**
Haba Quartet   12"—**ESTA-F5205/6**
[Suite No. 1 for Quarter-tone Piano,
Karel Reiner]
—**No. 2, Op. 12**
Prague Quartet   10"—**U-B11065**
—**1st Mvt. (Andante) only**
Prague Quartet   10"—**U-B11066**
[Matka—Unidentified quartet from
opera]
Suites No. 1—for Quarter-tone Piano
Karel Reiner   12"—**ESTA-F5200**
[Fantasia No. 5, Pt. 3]
[Quarter-tone Quartet, Op. 7, Pt. 3,
on ESTA-F5206]
Suite for Quarter-tone Piano, Op. 11-b
Karel Reiner   10"—**U-B11064**

HAGEMAN, Richard (1882-   )
Dutch-American conductor and composer of operas and many art-songs.

SONGS

Christ went up into the Hills (Adam)
John McCormack (t) with Orch.
[Franck: Panis Angelicus] 12″—**V-6708**
Do Not Go, My Love (Rabindranath Tagore)
Rose Bampton (s) & Wilfred Pelletier
(pf)   10″—**V-10-1118**
[Carpenter: The sleep that flits on baby's eyes]
Jeanette MacDonald (s) & G. Bamboschek (pf)
        (in VM-642) 10″—**V-2047**
[Charles: When I have sung my songs]
DUPLICATION: Nancy Evans, D-K866
(The) Donkey
Joan Hammond (s) & Gerald Moore (pf)
                10″—**G-B9503**
[Lehmann: Magdalene at Michael's Gate]
Miranda (Belloc)
James Melton (t) & Robert Hill (pf)
        (in VM-947) 10″—**V-10-1051**
[Carpenter: Serenade]

HAHN, Reynaldo (1874-1947)
A French composer and music critic (born in Venezuela) who studied at the Paris Conservatoire, where he was a pupil of Massenet. His songs have enjoyed wide popularity and his music (in many forms) has considerable charm and elegance.

(Le) Bal de Béatrice d'Este Suite 14 Instruments
(Wood winds, Brass, Harps, Piano, Percussion)
Chamber Orch.—R. Hahn
        2 12″—**G-L990/1**
Concerto, E major Piano & Orchestra
Magda Tagliafero & Orch.—Hahn
        3 12″—**PAT-PAT86/88**
Concerto Provençal (Flute, Clarinet, Bassoon, Horn & Strings)
Chamber Orchestra—F. Oubradous
        3 10″—**G-DA4993/5**
Eglogue
Trio d'Anches de Paris
                12″—**PAT-PA929**
[Decruck: Vars on "P'tit Quinquin"]

OPERETTAS In French

CIBOULETTE 1923
Orchestral Selections (Fantasia)
Grand Symphony Orch.—Weiss
                10″—**PD-522163**
Individual Excerpts
C'était pas la peine Soprano & Tenor
Lemichel du Roy & Rozani
                10″—**PD-521670**
C'est sa banlieue Soprano
Lemichel duRoy, PD-521994
Chanson de route: Moi, je m'en fous Baritone & Soprano
Jeanne Perriat, O-166657
Edmée Favart & Chorus, PAT-X91034
Comme frère et soeur Soprano & Tenor
Favart & Burnier, PAT-X91055

Dans une charrette Soprano
Lemichel du Roy, PD-521994
Duo de la lettre Baritone & Tenor
Roger Bourdin & Victor Pujol, O-166657
Moi, je m'appelle Ciboulette Soprano
Edmée Favart & Chorus, PAT-X91034
Nous avons fait un beau voyage Soprano & Tenor
Favart & Burnier, PAT-X91055

MALVINA
Vocal excerpts
René Camia, Roger Bourdin & Théâtre Lyrique de la Gaîté Orch.
        3 10″—**O-166914/6**

(LE) MARCHAND DE VENISE
Vocal excerpts
Fanny Heldy, Martial Singher, André Pernet, R. Mahé & Le Clézio
        2 10″—**G-DA4871/2**

O MON BEL INCONNU 1933
Vocal & Orchestral Selections
Reynaldo Hahn, Arletty, H. Gregory, M. Muriel, G. Ferrant
        3 10″—**PAT-PA36, PA63/4**

MOZART
Air de la lettre, Act II Soprano
(Le) Petit Menuet, Act I Diction
Yvonne Printemps & S. Guitry
                10″—**G-P825**
Air des adieux, Act III Sop.
Maggie Teyte & Gerald Moore (pf)
        (In Gramophone Shop Album GSC-3)
Yvonne Printemps   12″—**G-W1044**
[Messager: Debrau—Scène de l'intervue, S. Guitry, diction]
Etre adoré, Act 1 Sop.
Maggie Teyte & Gerald Moore (pf)
        (in Gramophone Shop Album, GSC-3)

(UNE) REVUE
La dernière valse
Ninon Vallin (s), C-LFX338
Romance Violin & Piano
Denise Soriano & acc.
                12″—**PAT-PAT54**
[Kreisler: Minuet in the style of Porpora]
Sonatina, C major Piano
Magda Tagliaferro   12″—**PAT-PAT61**

SONGS

(L') Air (De Banville)
Ninon Vallin (s) & Reynaldo Hahn (pf)
[Le Printemps]   10″—**O-188739**
(La) Barcheta—Chanson vénitienne (Herra)
George Thill (t)   10″—**C-LF103**
[Lévadé: Enlèvement]
(Le) Cimetière de Campagne
Ninon Vallin (s) & P. Darck (pf)
[L'Heure exquise]   10″—**PAT-PG80**
D'une prison (Verlaine)
Ninon Vallin (s) & Hahn (pf)
[Infidélité]   10″—**O-188738**
DUPLICATIONS: Tino Rossi, C-DF1783: C-DB1864; Yvonne Gall, C-DF971; J. Planel, PAT-X93137; Roger Bourdin, O-188635; R. Burnier, G-K5899

(L') Enamourée
Elyane Celis (s)   10″—G-K7711
[Koechlin: Si tu le veux & Fontenailles:
Sais-tu]
Arthur Endrèze (b) & Hahn (pf)
[L'heure exquise]   10″—PAT-PG89
En sourdine
Maggie Teyte (s) & Gerald Moore (pf)
[Fauré: Ici-Bas]   10″—G-DA1830
(L') Heure exquise (Verlaine)
Maggie Teyte (s) & Gerald Moore (pf)
          (in VM-895)   10″—V-10-1004
[Offrande] (G-DA1821)
Ninon Vallin (s) & pf. acc.
[Si mes vers]   10″—O-188579
[Cimetière de Campagne, on PAT-PG80]
Arthur Endrèze (b) & Hahn (pf)
[L'enamourée]   10″—PAT-PG89
DUPLICATION: Edmond Rambaud,
C-DF97
(L') Incrédule (Verlaine)
Roger Bourdin (b) & pf. acc.
[D'une prison]   10″—O-188635
Infidélité (Gautier)
Povla Frijsh (s) & Celius Dougherty
(pf)   (in VM-789)   12″—V-18052
[Dupont: Mandoline—Mélodie]
Ninon Vallin (s) & R. Hahn (pf)
[D'une prison]   10″—O-188737
Je me mets en votre mercy
(Rondel of Charles d'Orléans)
Guy Ferrant (t) & Hahn (pf)
[Carmélite—Stances]   10″—C-DF2435
Vanni-Marcoux (bs)   10″—G-DA1201
[Offrande]
Mai (Coppée)
Ninon Vallin (s)   10″—PAT-X93082
[Rêverie]
Offrande (Verlaine)
Maggie Teyte (s) & Gerald Moore (pf)
          (in VM-895)   10″—V-10-1004
[L'Heure exquise] (G-DA1821)
DUPLICATIONS: Vanni-Marcoux,
G-DA1201; Jean Planel, PAT-X93137;
Louis Lynel, O-166156
Paysage (Theuriet)
Ninon Vallin (s)   10″—PAT-X93074
[Si mes vers]
DUPLICATIONS: Willy Tubiana,
G-P847; Tino Rossi, C-DF1783;
C-DB1864; R. Burnier, G-K6101; Guy
Ferrant, C-DF2305; E. Rambaud,
C-DF97
Paysage triste
Guy Ferrant & pf. acc.   10″—C-DF2305
[Le Plus beau présent]
Phyllis (from Etudes Latines)
A. Endrèze (b) & Hahn (pf)
[Paladilhe: Psyché]   10″—PAT-PG88
(Le) Plus beau présent
Guy Ferrant & pf. acc.   10″—C-DF2305
[Paysage triste]
(Le) Printemps (de Banville)
Ninon Vallin (s) & Hahn (pf)
[L'Air]   10″—O-188739
Rêverie
Ninon Vallin (s)   10″—PAT-X93082
[Mai]

Si mes vers avaient des ailes (Hugo)
Maggie Teyte (s) & Gerald Moore (pf)
          (in VM-895)   10″—V-10-1002
(G-DA1777)
[Fauré: Après un rêve]
Ninon Vallin   10″—PAT-X93074
[Paysage] (Also: O-188579)
Grace Moore (s) & Victor Symphony—
Pelletier (in VM-918)   10″—V-10-1018
[Paladilhe: Psyché]
DUPLICATION: Robert Burnier,
G-K5899

HALE (Halle), Adam de la (c.1230-1287)
See under **ADAM DE LA HALLE**

HALEVY, Jacques François (1799-1862)
Best known for his opera "La Juive," Halevy,
a prolific French composer of marked talent,
was influenced and overshadowed by Meyer-
beer.

OPERAS In French

(LA) JUIVE 5 Acts 1835
It. **L'Ebrea** Ger. **Die Jüdin** Eng. **The**
Jewess
Si la rigeur et la vengeance (Cavatine)
Act I Bass
Ezio Pinza   10″—G-DA907
[Vous qui du Dieu]
(Also in Italian on G-DB698*)
O Dieu, Dieu de nos pères Act II Tenor &
Chorus
Si trahison (Passover Music)
Jan Peerce (t) & Dorothy Sarnoff (s)
with Chorus & Orch.—Pelletier
          12″—V-18401
Dieu que ma voix tremblante (Cavatine)
Tenor
César Vezzani   12″—G-W846
[Rachel, quand du Seigneur]
DUPLICATION: Theo. Beets, PD-27350
Vous qui du Dieu vivant (Malediction) Act
III Bass
Ezio Pinza   10″—G-DA907
[Si la rigeur, Act I]
Rachel, quand du Seigneur Act IV Tenor
Beniamino Gigli   12″—G-DB6366
[Lalo: Le Roi d'Ys—Aubade]
Enrico Caruso (Recorded 1920)
          12″—V-15-1004*
[Massenet: Manon—Ah, fuyez, douce
image]
[Massenet: Le Cid—O Souverain, on
G-DB123*]
Georges Thill   12″—C-LFX111
[Meyerbeer: Huguenots—Plus blanche]
José de Trevi   12″—PAT-X90044
DUPLICATIONS: T. Beets, PD-27350;
C. Vezzani, G-W846

HALFFTER Escriche, Ernesto (1905-   )
A young Spanish conductor and composer who
was a pupil ow Manuel de Falla.

Danza de la Gitana (Halffter-Manso)
Jascha Heifetz & Emanuel Bay
          (in VM-1126)   10″—V-10-1296

[Rachmaninoff: Etude Tableau, Op. 39, No. 2]

Manuel Perediaz (vl) & Narciso Figueroa (pf) 12"—PAT-PAT83
[Sarasate: Romanza Andaluza]

Rhapsodie portugaise Piano & Orchestra
Marguerite Long & Paris Conservatory
Orch.—Münch 2 12"—C-LFX629/30

HALVORSEN, Johan (1864-1935)

A Norwegian violinist, conductor and composer, who wrote under the influence of Grieg.

Andante religioso Orchestra
Symphony Orch.—Grevillius
10"—O-D4817
[Petersen-Berger: Danslek]

Bojarenes Indtog—Marsj Orchestra
Eng. Entry of the Boyards, or March of the Bojaren
Boston "Pops" Orch.—Fiedler
(in VM-522†) 10"—V-12175
[Ravel: Bolero, Pt. 3] (G-FKX37)
[Gade: Jealousy—Tango Tzigane on G-C2861]
Symphony Orch.—Järnefelt
12"—O-D6031
[Söderman: Swedish Wedding March]

Passacaglia (Handel) Arr. Violin & Viola
NOTE: *Selection taken from Handel's Harpsichord Suite No. 7 in G minor.*
Jascha Heifetz & William Primrose
(G-DB6170) 12"—V-11-8151

Sarabande (Handel) Arr. Violin & Viola
NOTE: *The Sarabande comes from the Harpsichord Suite No. 11. Handel supplies the first two variations, Halvorsen the rest.*
Frederick Grinke & Watson Forbes
12"—D-K917

HAMURGER, Povl

A contemporary Scandinavian composer who has edited much organ and choral music.

SONGS In Danish
Limfjorden (E. Bertelsen)
Der Er Ingenting I Verden Saa Stille Som Sne (H. Rode)
Aksel Schiøtz (t) & Hermann Koppel
(pf) 10"—G-X6352

HAMERIK, (Sir) Asger (1843-1923)

A Danish composer, pupil of Gade, Berlioz and Bülow, who later came to America as head of the Peabody Institute at Baltimore.

Symphony No. 6, G major, Op. 38 "Spirituelle"
Boyd Neel String Orch.—Neel
4 12"—D-K1420/3

HAMMERSCHMIDT, Andreas (1612-1675)

A Bohemian-German composer, highly renowned in his day and of great historical importance in the development of Luthern Church music that culminated with Bach. His works include many motets, chorale tunes. concertos, etc.

Danklied: Sei nun wieder zufrieden
Song—from "Musikalische Andachten"
1639

Yves Tinayre (t) & Org. acc.
12"—LUM-32022
[Albert: Todeslied & Mozart: Laudate Dominum]
(in Yves Tinayre Album No. 2)

Machet die Tore weit Unacc. Motet
Basilica Choir—Pius Kalt
[Lassus: Tui sunt coeli] 12"—PD-66673

HANDEL, George Frederic (1685-1759)

With J. S. Bach, Handel was one of the twin giants of the early 18th century and one of the supreme musical geniuses of all time. Although German by birth, and composer of many operas and other works in Italian, Handel was associated so closely with England during the last two-thirds of his life that he is considered (at least in England) as an English composer.
In the following listings the recordings are catalogued in their original language—German, Italian, English, as the case may be. Of late there has been more attention given to the recording of Handel's music.

ACIS AND GALATEA Secular Oratorio
1720

Individual Excerpts

I rage, I melt, I burn—Recit.

O ruddier than the cherry—Air Bass
Peter Dawson 12"—G-C1500
[Samson—Honour and arms]

Love in her eyes sits playing

Love sounds the alarm Tenor
Walter Widdop (arr. Mozart)
12"—G-DB1566

O didst thou know?—Recit.

As when the dove Soprano
Isobel Baillie 12"—C-DX1158

Air & Variations See Suites (also Harmonious Blacksmith)

Air & Variations, B flat major
(*This is the subject of the Brahms' Variations*)
Wanda Landowska (harpsichord)
12"—G-DB3308
[Concerto, B flat major, Op. 4, No. 6, Pt. 3]

ALCINA Opera in Italian 1735
Orchestral Suite

Dream Music (Act II); Ballet Music (Act I); Entrance & Tamburino (Act III)
(Trans. Whittaker)
Paris Conservatory Orch.—Weingartner
(C-LX918/9) 2 12"—CX-164†

Orchestral Suite

Entrance Music Act III & Ballet Music, Act I
Berlin Philharmonic Orch.—Kleiber, with W. Drwensky, harpsichord
(U-F14383) 12"—T-SK1270

Tambourino only Arr. Beecham
This movement is included in Beecham's "Gods Go A-Begging" Ballet. For a recording see under that title (C-68202D in CM-194).

ALESSANDRO Opera 1726

Lusinghe più care
Lily Pons (s) & Renaissance Quintet
      (in VM-756) 10″—**V-2151**
[Floridante—Alma mia]

(L') ALLEGRO, IL PENSEROSO, ED IL MODERATO
Ode in English 1740

Individual Excerpts
Let me wander, not unseen (Siciliana)
Ger. **Lass mich wandern durch das Grün**
Blanche Thebom (ms) 10″—**V-10-1178**
[Purcell: Indian Queen—I attempt from love's sickness to fly]
Marian Anderson (c) (in German) &
Kosti Vehanen (pf) 10″—**V-1939**
[Bach: Komm, süsser Tod]

Sweet Bird (Penseroso's Air) Soprano, with flute obb.
Elisabeth Schwarzkopf 12″—**C-LX1010**
Margherita Perras (in German)
[Gounod: Ave Maria] 12″—**G-DB4464**
G. Ritter-Ciampi (in Italian)
      12″—**PD-66841**
[Mozart: Rè Pastore—L'amerò, sarò costante]

ALMIRA Opera in German 1704

Rigaudon Arr. Wood
Queen's Hall Orch.—Wood 12″—**D-X184**
[Rodrigo—Sailor's Dance & Dvořák: Symphonic variations, Op. 78, Pt. 5]

Angels ever bright and fair See under Theodora

Arioso: Dank sei dir, Herr See under Cantata con Stromenti

ATALANTA Opera in Italian 1736

Care selve Soprano Eng. **Come, beloved**
Eidé Noréna (in Italian)
      12″—**G-DB5054**
[Haydn: Die Schöpfung—Auf starkem Fittige schwingt]
Rose Bampton (c) (in English) & pf. acc.
      12″—**V-7746**
[Debussy: Enfant prodigue—Air de Lia]
Ada Alsop (in English) 12″—**D-K1164**
[Semele—Oh Sleep! why dost thou leave me?]
Friedel Beckmann (in German)
      12″—**G-DB7653**
[Giulio Cesare—V'adoro pupille]

Come alla tortorella langue Soprano
Eng. **Like as the love-lorn turtle**
Doris Owens (in English)
      10″—**C-DB503**
[Solomon—Nightingale Chorus]
(in Columbia History of Music, Vol. II: CM-232)

Awake my soul See under While Shepherds watched

BERENICE Opera in Italian 1737

Overture Orchestra Arr. Wood
Queen's Hall Orch.—Wood 12″—**D-K819**

Minuet (from the Overture) (Largo, E flat major)
Jacques String Orch. 12″—**C-DX868**
[Purcell: The Faery Queen—3 Dances]
Hastings Municipal Orch.—Harrison
(Arr. Best) 12″—**D-K578**
[Tchaikowsky: Eugene Onegin—Waltz]
Also: Victor Orch. (labelled Andante), V-24793; Sandler Orch. (in Minuet Medley), C-DX759

—Arr. 'Cello & Piano
Louis Jensen & Grethe Jensen, G-DB5222

—Arr. Organ
Reginald Foort (BBC Theatre Organ), G-BD578

Bourrés See under Fireworks Music, Origin of Design, Sonata—Flute, Water Music

Bourrées, A major (unidentified)
Hans Vollenweider (organ) 10″—**G-JK9**
[Bach: Prelude, C major, unidentified]
(2) **Bourrées** (unidentified) Arr. Shepperd
Pipers Guild Quartet, C-DB2278

Cantata for Solo Voice (Secular)—**Nell dolce dell' oblio**
(H. G. Vol. 52, No. 17)
Katherine Harris (s) with Alfred Mann & Anton Winkler (recorders), Edith Weiss-Mann (harpsichord) & Lucy Weiss (vla da gamba)
      12″—**Hargail—MW103**

Cantata con stromenti

Arioso: Dank sei dir, Herr Arr. Ochs
Eng. **Hymn of Praise**
The authenticity of this famous work is questionable. Recorded versions are usually labelled merely "Arioso."
Gerhard Hüsch (b) 12″—**G-EH925**
[Giulio Cesare—V'adoro, pupille]
Emmi Leisner (c) 12″—**PD-67792**
[Serse—Ombra mai fu]
[Older recording on PD-66736]
DUPLICATIONS: Heinrich Schlusnus, PD-95421; Paul Sandoz, G-DB10092; John McCormack (in English), G-DA1786

Cantata—Look down, look down, Harmonious Saint (with Recit.)
Max Meili (t) with harpsichord & Orch. —Curt Sachs
      (in Vol. VIII) 12″—**AS-70**

Caro Amore—See under Floridante

Chaconne, F major
Ruggero Gerlin (harpsichord)
      10″—**C-BQ6016**
[Purcell: Prelude, Ground & Minuet]

Chaconne, G major (No. 2 from 2nd Collection for Harpsichord)
Edwin Fischer (pf) (abridged)
      10″—**G-DA4401**
Adrian Aeschbacher (pf)
      12″—**PD-67650**

Chandos Anthems See under Overture, D minor & Psalms

CONCERTI GROSSI

(12) **Concerti Grossi, Op. 6** Strings & Harpsichord 1739

Complete recordings
Busch Chamber Players—Adolf Busch &
M. Horszowski (harpsichord)
25   12"—**CM-685**†
[Geminiani: Siciliana, arr. Busch, with
Adolf Busch, vl., & Artur Balsam, pf.]
Boyd Neel String Orch.—Boyd Neel &
Arnold Goldsbrough (harpsichord)
25   12"—**D-X119/143**

Individual Concerti

No. 1, G major
Busch Chamber Players, in CM-685†
Boyd Neel String Orch., D-X119/20: PD-
516716/7
Collegium Musicum—Hermann Diener
(in VM-808†)   2   12"—**V-13696/7**
(G-EH1127/8)

No. 2, F major
Busch Chamber Players, in CM-685†
Boyd Neel String Orch., D-X121/22:
PD-516718/9
German Opera House Orch.—F. Lehmann
2   12"—**O-7973/4**

No. 3, E minor
Busch Chamber Players, in CM-685†
Boyd Neel String Orch., D-X123/4: PD-
516720/1

**—1st (Larghetto) & 4th (Polonaise) Mvts.
only**
(Labelled "Concerto Grosso No. 14, Op. 6".)
Symph. Orch.—Beecham   12"—**C-L2345**
[Messiah—Pastoral Symphony]
(C-LFX228)

No. 4, A minor
Busch Chamber Players, in CM-685†
Boyd Neel String Orch., D-X124/26

No. 5, D major
Busch Chamber Players, in CM-685†
Boyd Neel String Orch., D-X126/9
London Philharmonic Orch.—Weingart-
ner   2   12"—**CX-142**†
(C-LX803/4)
Collegium Musicum—Hermann Diener
(in VM-808†)   2   12"—**V-13698/9**
(G-EH1202/3)

—6th (Minuet) Mvt. only
Vienna Philharmonic Chamber Orch.—
Jerger   12"—**G-EH1324**
[Paganini: Moto perpetuo]

No. 6, G minor
Busch Chamber Players, in CM-685†
Boyd Neel String Orch., D-X129/31
London Symphony Orch.—Weingartner
(C-LX831/2)   2   12"—**CX-154**†

No. 7, B flat major
Busch Chamber Players, in CM-685†
Boyd Neel String Orch., D-X132/3: PD-
516775/6

No. 8, C minor
Busch Chamber Players, in CM-685†
Boyd Neel String Orch., D-X134/5: PD-
51677/8

No. 9, F major
Busch Chamber Players, in CM-685†
Boyd Neel String Orch., D-X136/7: PD-
516779/80

No. 10, D minor
Busch Chamber Players, in CM-685†
Boyd Neel String Orch., D-X138/9

No. 11, A major
Busch Chamber Players, in CM-685†
Boyd Neel String Orch., D-X140/1

No. 12, B minor
Busch Chamber Players, in CM-685†
Boyd Neel String Orch., D-X142/3
Paris Conservatory Orch.—Walter
2   12"—**G-DB3601/2**

—3rd (Larghetto) Mvt. only
Boston Symphony Orch.—Koussevitzky
12"—**V-14231**
[Berlioz: Damnation de Faust—Minuet
of the Will of the Wisps]
[Berlioz: Damnation de Faust—Danse
des Sylphes on G-DB3010]
[Mozart: Symphony No. 34, Pt. 5, on
V-18067 in VM-795]
[Vivaldi: Concerto Grosso, Op. 3, No. 11,
Pt.3, on G-DB3669]

CONCERTOS

Oboe & Orchestra

No. 1, B flat major
(H. G. Vol. 21, p. 85)
Leon Goossens & London Philharmonic—
E. Goossens   12"—**G-C2993**
(G-FKX35)

No. 3, G minor
(H. G. Vol. 21, p. 100)
Leon Goossens & Liverpool Philharmonic
—Basil Cameron   12"—**C-DX1144**
Mitchell Miller & CBS Symphony—
Barlow   12"—**C-69660D**
Italo Toppo & EIAR String Orch.—Ralf
Rapp   12"—**CET-BB25129**

Organ (or Harpsichord) & Orchestra
*Handel wrote three sets of Organ Concerti, the
second of which consisted largely of arrangements of the Concerti Grossi. The best known
works are the 12 Concerti that make up Op. 4
& Op. 7; Op. 4 is subtitled "for Organ or Harpsichord" and one of these works, No. 6, is available in a harpsichord version.*

No. 1, G minor, Op. 4, No. 1

—1st (Adagio) & 2nd (Allegro) Mvts. only

—Arr. 'Cello & Piano Feuermann
Emanuel Feuermann & Fritz Rupp
12"—**V-18154**

**—2nd (Allegro) & 4th (Andante) Mvts.
only**
Alfred Sittard & Berlin Philharmonic
Orch.—Ludwig   12"—**PD-67257**
(PD-566195)

No. 2, B flat, Op. 4, No. 2
G. D. Cunningham & City of Birmingham
Orch.—Weldon   2   12"—**C-DX1358/59**†
[Concerto No. 4, F major, Pt. 1]
E. Power Biggs & Fiedler's Sinfonietta
(Edited by Max Seiffert)   12"—**G-FKX40**
E. Bullock (Westminster Cathedral Or-
gan) & String Orch. 2   10"—**G-B2890/1**
[Water Music—Allegro deciso]

—1st (Andante-Allegro) Mvt. only Solo arrangement
Paul Hebestreit (Paderborn Organ)
10″—PD-22721

No. 4, F major, Op. 4, No. 4
G. D. Cunningham & City of Birmingham Orch.—Weldon 2 12″—C-DX1359/60†
[Concerto No. 2, B flat, Pt. 3]
—1st Mvt. (Allegro moderato) only Solo arrangement
Alfred Sittard (St. Michael's Organ, Hamburg) 12″—PD-95426
[4th Mvt.]
[Saul—March, on PD-66554]
—2nd Mvt. (Andante Maestoso) only Solo arrangement
Paul Hebestreit (Paderborn Cathedral)
10″—PD-22592
—4th Mvt. (Allegro) only Solo arrangement
Alfred Sittard (St. Michael's Organ)
[1st Mvt.] 12″—PD-95426
[Hercules—March, on PD-95158]

No. 6, B flat major, Op. 4, No. 6
—Harpsichord & Orchestra version
Wanda Landowska & Orch.—E. Bigot
2 12″—G-DB3307/8
[Air & Variations, B flat major]
M. Roesgen-Champion & Orch.—Coppola
2 10″—G-K7392/3
[Suite No. 11—Sarabande & Gigue]

No. 7, B flat major, Op. 7, No. 1
—4th Mvt. (Bourrée) only
Herbert Dawson & London Symphony Orch.—Coates 10″—G-DA1261
[No. 13—Cuckoo & Nightingale]

No. 10, D minor, Op. 7, No. 4
E. Power Biggs & Fiedler's Sinfonietta
2 12″—VM-587
—1st (Adagio) & 2nd (Allegro) Mvts. only Arr. Seiffert
Alfred Sittard & Berlin Philharmonic Orch.—Ludwig 12″—PD-67258
(PD-566196)
—2nd Mvt. (Allegro) only
H. Vollenweider 12″—G-FKX69
[Bach: Fugue, G minor]

No. 11, G minor, Op. 7, No. 5
E. Power Biggs (Germanic Museum organ) & Fiedler's Sinfonietta
2 10″—G-JK2195/6

No. 13, F major—"The Cuckoo & the Nightingale"
E. Power Biggs (Germanic Museum organ) & Fiedler's Sinfonietta
2 12″—VM-733†
—2nd Mvt. ("Cuckoo & Nightingale") only
Herbert Dawson & London Symphony Orch.—Coates 10″—G-DA1261
[No. 7, Bourrée only]
E. Power Biggs (Germanic Museum)
(Solo arr.) 12″—TC-1139
[Daquin: Variations on a Noël]

CONCERTOS—Miscellaneous
(See also Fireworks Music & Water Music)
Concerto in F major Double Wind Choir & String Orch.
(H.G. Vol. 47, p. 1)

Berlin Philharmonic Orch.—Hans von Benda 2 12″—T-E2352/3
[Fireworks Music—Bourrée, Menuet, La Réjouissance]
Concerto à 4—No. 1, D minor Flute, Violin, 'Cello & Figured bass
(Edited by Fritz Zoberly)
NOTE: *Originally a trio-sonata, but reworked by Handel into a concerto, this composition was published by Schott in 1935.*
Danish Quartet 12″—G-DB5218
Concerto in D major Organ and Orchestra (*Concerto "B" in Handel Gesellschaft, Vol. 47*)
—Arr. Harty
London Symphony Orch., & Harold Dawber (organ)—Harty 12″—C-68256D
(C-LX341) (C-LFX367)
—Arr. Ormandy
Philadelphia Orch.—Ormandy
12″—C-12280D
Concerto Viola & Orchestra
(*The authenticity of this Concerto, recently discovered and edited by Henri Casadesus, is open to question.*)
William Primrose & Chamber Orch.—Goehr 3 12″—CM-295†
[Last side blank]
[Paganini: La Campanella on C-LWX189/91: C-GQX11023/5]
William Primrose & Victor Orch.—Weissmann 3 12″—VM-1131†
[Kreisler: Praeludium & Allegro in the Style of Pugnani, with Primrose, vla., & Franz Rupp, pf.]
(The) Cuckoo & the Nightingale
See under Concertos—Organ, No. 13
Dank sei dir, Herr See under Cantata con Stromenti—Arioso
"Dettingen" Te Deum—See under Te Deum

DRAMATIC PIECES See under Hercules, Semele; also under Operas
Entrance of the Queen of Sheba See under Solomon
(The) Faithful Shepherd See (Il) Pastor Fido
Fantasia, C major Harpsichord
Dirk Schäfer (pf) 12″—C-DHX11
[Beethoven: Andante favori]

FARAMONDO Opera 1738
Overture Arr. Rawlinson
Boyd Neel String Orch.—Neel
12″—D-K947
(Royal) Fireworks Music Wind Instruments & Drums
(H.G. Vol. 47, p. 99)
Overture; Largo alla Siciliana ("La Paix")
Allegro ("La Réjouissance"); Bourrée; Minuets 1 & 2
Radio Orch. of Brussels—Lehmann
(O-50231/2) 2 12″—O-9150/1
Overture, Largo alla Siciliana, Bourrée, Minuets 1 & 2 only
—Arr. Orchestra Harty
London Philharmonic Orch.—Harty
(C-LX389/90) 2 12″—CX-51†
National Symphony Orch.—Sargent
2 12″—D-K1414/5†

Bourrée (Allegro), Minuet No. 2 & Allegro
only
Berlin Philharmonic Orch.—von Benda
12"—**T-E2353**
[Double Orch. Concerto, F major, Pt. 3]

FLORIDANTE Opera in Italian 1721
Alma mia (Trans. F. Günther)
Ezio Pinza (bs) & Fritz Kitzinger (pf)
(in VM-766) 12"—**V-17914**
[Monteverdi: Arianna—Lasciatemi morire & Legrenzi: Eteocle—Che fiero costume; A. Scarlatti: Chi vuole innamorarsi]
Lily Pons (s) Renaissance Quintet
(in VM-756) 10"—**V-2151**
[Alessandro—Lusinghe più care]
Richard Crooks (t) & Fred Schauwecker (pf) (in VM-846) 10"—**V-2175**
[Arne: Comus—Preach me not; Haydn: Serenade]

Caro amore
John McCormack (t) 12"—**G-DB2867**
[Semele—Where'er you walk]

Gavottes See also under Alcina, Ottone, Suites

Gigues See under Sonatas & Suites

GIULIO CESARE Opera in Italian 1724
Eng. **Julius Caesar**
V'adoro, pupille (Act II, No. 14) Soprano
Ger. **Es blaut die Nacht**
NOTE: *Both versions listed below are sung in German.*
Friedel Beckmann (c) 12"—**G-DB7653**
[Atalanta: Care selve]
Gerhard Hüsch (b) 12"—**G-EH925**
[Cantata con Stromenti—Dank sei dir, Herr]
NOTE: *The "Battle Music" in Sir Thomas Beecham's ballet, "The Gods Go A-Begging" is a composite of the Battle Music in "Giulio Cesare" and "Rinaldo."*

(The) Gods Go A-Begging Suite de Ballet Orch.
Arranged by Sir Thomas Beecham from miscellaneous Handel pieces.
1. Introduction 2. Minuet 3. Hornpipe 4. Musette 5. Ensemble 6. Dream 7. Tamburino 8. Gavotte 9. Bourrée
—**No. 2** (Minuet) & **No. 3** (Hornpipe) only
London Philharmonic Orch.—Beecham
(in CM-360†) 12"—**C-69472D**
[Mozart: Symphony No. 31, Finale]
(C-LX756) (C-LFX560)
—**No. 4** (Musette) & **No. 7** (Tamburino) only
London Philharmonic Orch.—Beecham
12"—**C-68881D**
[Origin of Design—Minuet & Sarabande]
—**No. 4** (Musette) only
London Philharmonic—Beecham
(in CX-60†) 12"—**C-68475D**
[Origin of Design—Minuet & Rossini: Guglielmo Tell—Overture, Pt. 3]
(C-LX340) (C-LWX130) (C-LFX416)
—**No. 7** (Tamburino) only
London Philharmonic Orch.—Beecham
(in CM-194†) 12"—**C-68202D**

[Origin of Design—Sarabande; Mozart: Symphony No. 41 "Jupiter"—Finale]
(C-LX285) (C-LFX342)
(The) Great Elopement Ballet Suite arranged from miscellaneous Handel works by Sir Thomas Beecham
(*17 pieces were chosen from "Roderigo", "Il Pastor Fido", "Ariodante", "Il Parnasso in Festa", "Teseo" and posthumous suites for harpsichord. 13 are recorded.*)
London Philharmonic Orch.—Beecham
(G-DB6295/7) 3 12"—**VM-1093†**
(The) Harmonious Blacksmith
Harpsichord or Piano
(*This familiar piece is the Air and Variations Movement from the Harpsichord Suite No. 5, E major.*)
—**Harpsichord versions:**
Wanda Landowska 10"—**V-1193**
[Mozart: Rondo alla Turca] (G-DA860)
(Also by Landowska in Handel Harpsichord Suite Society, VM-592† & in VM-1181†
—**Piano versions:**
Walter Gieseking 12"—**C-68595D**
[Mozart: Rondo alla Turca]
(C-GQX11032) (C-LWX117)
Sergei Rachmaninoff 12"—**G-DB3146**
[Mendelssohn-Rachmaninoff: Midsummer Night's Dream—Scherzo]
DUPLICATION: William Murdoch, D-K682

HERCULES Dramatic Piece in English 1745
(*Handel also wrote a "Choice of Hercules" musical interlude 1750.*)
March Orchestra
—**Arr. Organ**
Alfred Sittard (St. Michael's Organ, Hamburg) 12"—**PD-95158**
[Organ Concerto No. 4, F major—4th Mvt.]

ISRAEL IN EGYPT Oratorio in English 1738
Individual Excerpts
No. 22, The Lord is a man of war 2 Basses
Malcolm McEachern & Harold Williams
12"—**C-DX585**
[Offenbach: Geneviève de Brabant— Gendarmes' Duet]

JEPHTHA Oratorio in English 1751
Deeper and deeper still—Recit.
Waft her angels—Aria Tenor
Webster Booth 12"—**G-C3414**
Heddle Nash 12"—**C-DX295**

JOSHUA Oratorio in English 1748
Oh! had I Jubal's lyre Soprano
Isobel Baillie 12"—**C-9697**
[Theodora—Angels ever bright]
Gwen Catley 10"—**G-B9138**
[Mozart: Alleluia]
Joy to the World! Hymn in English (Watts)
This familiar hymn is not an original composition by Handel, but a synthesis pieced together from themes from the "Messiah."

RCA Victor Chorale—Robert Shaw
(in VM-1077) 12"—**V-11-9313**
[with Christmas Hymns & Carols]
DUPLICATIONS: Lyn Murray Singers,
C-36655 in C-C94; in Christmas Hymn
Medleys, V-20993: V-26050 in V-P2

JUDAS MACCABAEUS Oratorio in English
1746
Individual Excerpts
No. 24, How vain is man Tenor
Heddle Nash 12"—**G-C3550**
[No. 28]
No. 28, Sound an alarm Tenor
Heddle Nash 12"—**G-C3550**
[No. 24]
Richard Crooks
(in VM-934) 12"—**V-11-8315**
[Mendelssohn: St. Paul—Be thou faith-
ful]
Walter Widdop 12"—**G-D1886**
[Messiah—Thou shalt break them]
**No. 35, March & See the Conquering Hero
Comes**
Ger. **Marsch & Seht den Sieger** ("Tochter
Zion, freue dich")
—**See the Conquering Hero Comes (Chorus)**
only
—**Arr. with French words:** A toi la gloire
(Psalm 104)
Paul Sandoz (b) 10"—**G-JK6**
[Mason: Nearer My God to Thee]
No. 66, O lovely peace (O lovely night)
Choristers of St. Nicolas' College
12"—**C-DX1032**
[Marosa: Brother James' Air]
Larghetto See Sonata, Op. 1, No. 9
Largo
*The Handel Largo is an aria for tenor (ar-
ranged and transcribed in many ways) from
the opera "Serse" ("Xerxes".) For recordings
see under Serse—Ombra mai fu.*

MESSIAH Oratorio in English 1742
Complete Recordings
Luton Choral Society, Special Choir &
Royal Philharmonic Orch.—Sir Thomas
Beecham, with Elsie Suddaby (s), Mar-
jorie Thomas (c), Heddle Nash (t),
Trevor Anthony (b)
21 12"—**VM-1194/5†**
[Side One contains an introductory talk
by Sir Thomas Beecham]
Huddersfield Choral Society (Herbert
Bardgett, Chorus Master) & Liverpool
Philharmonic—Sargent, with Isobel
Baillie (s), Gladys Ripley (c), James
Johnston (t) & Norman Walker (b)
19 12"—**CM-666†**
(C-DX1283/301†)
*(In this recording, Nos. 34-36, & Nos. 49-52 are
omitted. Mozart's additional scoring is used.)*
Abridged Recording
BBC Chorus & London Symphony Orch.
& Organ—Beecham, with Dora Labette
(s), Muriel Brunskill (c), Nellie Walker
(c), Hubert Eisdell (t) & Harold
Williams (b) 8 12"—**C-DX630/7**

Abridged Excerpts
Lura Stover (s), Lydia Summers (c),
Harold Haugh (t), J. Alden Edkins (b),
Augustana Choir—Henry Veld with
Boynolf Lundholm & Clarence Snyder
(organ) 4 10"—**BIBLETONE-T**
Individual Excerpts
NOTE: *The numbering in the following list fol-
lows that of the Schirmer vocal score. The
numbers in parentheses are those of the new
Carl Fischer score, edited by Dr. J. M. Cooper-
smith.*
No. 1, Overture Orchestra
London Symphony Orch.—Sargent
12"—**D-K1499**
[No. 13, Pastoral Symphony]
London Symphony Orch.—Maurice
Miles 12"—**C-DX1182**
[No. 13, Pastoral Symphony]
EIAR Symphony Orch.—La Rosa Parodi
12"—**CET-CB20187**
[Wagner: Tannhäuser—Overture, Pt. 3]
No. 2, Comfort ye, my people Tenor
Aksel Schiøtz & Orch.—Mogens Wöldike
[No. 3] 12"—**G-DB5239**
Heddle Nash 12"—**G-C3454**
[No. 3]
Webster Booth 12"—**V-12598**
[No. 3] (G-C3087)
Walter Widdop 12"—**G-D1620**
[No. 3]
Richard Crooks
(in VM-934) 12"—**V-11-8315**
[Samson—No. 14, Total eclipse]
No. 3, Ev'ry valley shall be exalted Tenor
Aksel Schiøtz & Orch.—Mogens Wöldike
[No. 2] 12"—**G-DB5239**
Webster Booth 12"—**V-12598**
[No. 2] (G-C3087)
Walter Widdop 12"—**G-D1620**
[No. 2]
Heddle Nash 12"—**G-C3454**
[No. 2]
No. 4, And the Glory of the Lord Chorus
Royal Choral Society—Sargent
[No. 44, Hallelujah] 12"—**V-11825**
(G-C2489) (G-FKX16)
DUPLICATION: BBC Choir, D-K805
No. 5, Thus saith the Lord—Recit.
No. 6, But who may abide the day?—Air
Baritone
Paul Sandoz (in German) & Karl
Matthaei (organ) 12"—**G-DB10097**
[Mendelssohn: St. Paul—O God, have
mercy]
No. 11, The people that walked in darkness
—Air Baritone
Paul Sandoz (in German) & Hans Vollen-
weider (organ) 12"—**G-DB10072**
No. 12, For unto us a Child is born Chorus
Philharmonic Choir—C. K. Scott
[No. 17, Glory to God] 12"—**G-D1876**
No. 13, Pastoral Symphony Orchestra
*(Sometimes known as the "Pifa" referring to
the old Chant of the Piferari on which the
melody is founded.)*
London Symphony Orch.—Sargent
[No. 1, Overture] 12"—**D-K1499**

London Symphony Orch.—Miles
[No. 1, Overture] 12"—C-DX1182
Philadelphia Orch.—Stokowski
12"—V-7316
[Bach: Wohltemperierte Clavier—Prelude, B minor, Book 1, No. 24]
(G-AW219)
Symphony Orch.—Beecham
12"—C-71606D
[Mozart: Nozze di Figaro—Overture]
[Concerto grosso, Op. 6, No. 3, 2 Mvts., on C-L2345] (C-LFX228)
London Symphony Orch.—Sargent
[No. 1, Overture] 12"—G-C2071
EIAR Symphony Orch.—La Rosa Parodi
12"—CET-CB20175
[Boccherini: Pastorale]
Symphony Orch.—Stokowski
12"—V-11-9837
[Trad: Russian Christmas Music]
No. 17, (No. 18), Glory to God Chorus
Royal Choral Society & London Philharmonic Orch.—Sargent
(G-C2548) 12"—V-11824
[No. 24, Behold the Lamb of God]
Philharmonic Choir—C. K. Scott
12"—G-D1876
[No. 12, For unto us a child is born]
No. 18, (No. 19), Rejoice greatly, O Daughter of Zion Soprano
Isobel Baillie 12"—C-DX1154
[No. 52, If God be for us]
Eleanor Steber
(in VM-927†) 12"—V-11-8406
[Haydn: The Creation—Nos. 7 & 8]
No. 19, (No. 20), Then shall the eyes—Recit. Contralto
No. 20, (No. 21a) He shall feed His flock—Air Contralto
(b) Come unto Him—Air Soprano
—No. 20a only
Marian Anderson
(in VM-850) 12"—V-18324
[No. 23, He was despised]
Gladys Ripley 12"—G-C3424
[No. 23, He was despised]
Lina Falk 12"—LUM-32053
[Te Deum—Dignare Domine & Serse-Ombra mai fù]
DUPLICATION: Margarete Matzenauer, V-6555
—No. 20b only
D. Middleton (treble) 10"—G-B4133
[Semele—Where'er you walk]
No. 22, (No. 23), Behold the Lamb of God Chorus
Sadler's Wells Chorus—Braithwaite
12"—V-11-8670
[No. 44, Hallelujah] (G-C3129)
Royal Choral Society—Sargent
12"—V-11824
[No. 17, Glory to God] (G-C2548)
(Older version, G-AW4296)
No. 23, (No. 24), He was despised and rejected Contralto
Elsa Sigfuss & Chamber Orch. of the Palace Chapel, Copenhagen—Wöldike
12"—G-Z293
Gladys Ripley 12"—G-C3424

[No. 20a, He shall feed His flock]
Marian Anderson
(in VM-850) 12"—V-18324
[No. 20a, He shall feed His flock]
No. 24, (No. 25a), Surely He hath borne our griefs Chorus
Royal Choral Society—Sargent
[No. 26, All we like sheep] 12"—V-9109
No. 26, (No. 25c), All we like sheep have gone astray Chorus
Royal Choral Society—Sargent
12"—V-9019
[No. 24, Surely He hath borne our griefs]
No. 29, (No. 28), Thy rebuke hath broken his heart—Recit.
No. 30, (No. 29), Behold and see—Air Tenor
No. 31, (No. 30), He was cut off—Recit.
No. 32, (No. 31), But Thou didst not leave his soul—Air Tenor
Webster Booth 12"—G-C3430
—Nos. 29 & 30 only
Yves Tinayre (in French)
12"—LUM-32029
No. 33, (No. 32), Lift up your heads Chorus
Royal Choral Society—Sargent
12"—G-D1057
[No. 53, Worthy is the Lamb]
No. 38, (No. 37a), How beautiful are the feet Soprano
Dorothy Maynor
(in VM-1043) 12"—V-11-9106
[Mendelssohn: Elijah—Hear ye, Israel]
No. 40, (No. 38), Why do the nations? Baritone
Peter Dawson 12"—G-C2694
[Stanford: Songs of the Fleet—Farewell]
Norman Cordon
(in VM-1094) 12"—V-11-9430
[Haydn: Creation—No. 22, Now Heaven in Fullest Glory Shone]
No. 42, (No. 40), He that dwelleth in heaven—Recit.
No. 43, (No. 41), Thou shalt break them—Air Tenor
Walter Widdop 12"—G-D1886
[Judas—Sound an alarm]
No. 44, (No. 42), Hallelujah Chorus
Sadler's Wells Chorus—Braithwaite
(G-C3129) 12"—V-11-8670
[No. 22, Behold the Lamb of God]
Royal Choral Society—Sargent
(G-C2489) (G-FKX16) 12"—V-11825
[No. 4, And the glory of the Lord]
(Older Version: G-AW4296)
DUPLICATIONS: Jubilee Thanksgiving Service Massed Choir & Band, C-DX693; Festival of English Church Music Choir of 4000 Voices—Nicholson, C-DB1170; Bruno Kittel Choir & Berlin Philharmonic Orch, (in German), PD-66896 & O-7913; Sheffield Choir—Coward, C-9068; BBC Choir & Organ, D-K805
—Arr. Orchestra
Boston "Pops" Orch.—Fiedler
12"—V-11-8985
[Mendelssohn: Athalie—War March of the Priests]

—Arr. Organ
Mark Andrews, G-S10016
No. 45 (No. 43), I know that my Redeemer liveth Soprano
Isobel Baillie   12"—C-DX1036
Ria Ginster (in German) & Hans Vollenweider (organ)   12"—G-DB10060
DUPLICATION: E. Lough (treble), G-B2656
No. 47 (No. 45) Behold, I tell you a mystery —Recit.
No. 48 (No. 46) The trumpet shall sound— Air Baritone
Arthur Fear   12"—G-C1786
[Mendelssohn: Elijah—Lord God of Abraham]
No. 52 (No. 49) If God be for us, who can be against us? Soprano
Isobel Baillie   12"—C-DX1154
[No. 19, Rejoice greatly]
No. 53a (No. 50a) Worthy is the Lamb Chorus
Royal Choral Society—Sargent
                            12"—G-D1057
[No. 35, Lift up your heads]
DUPLICATION: Sheffield Choir, C-9068
No. 53b (No. 50c) Amen Chorus
Royal Choral Society   12"—V-9125
[No. 4, And the glory]
Ode to St. Cecilia (But oh! what art can teach)
Ger. **Wer kündet deinen Preis**
Ria Ginster (s) (in German) & K. Matthaei (organ)   12"—G-DB10102
[Süsse stille, sanfte quelle]
Odes See under L'Allegro
Ombra mai fù See under Serse—Largo

OPERAS See under Alcina, Alessandro, Almira, Atalanta, Berenice, Floridante, Giulio Cesare, Ottone, Partenope, Pastor Fido, Radamisto, Rinaldo, Rodelinda, Rodrigo, Scipione, Serse, Siroe, Sosarme, Tolomeo (also under Dramatic Pieces)

ORATORIOS See under Acis and Galatea, Israel in Egypt, Jephtha, Joseph, Joshua, Judas Maccabaeus, Messiah, Samson, Saul, Solomon, Theodora, Triumph of Time and Truth

(The) Origin of Design Orchestra
A ballet, arranged and probably titled by Sir Thomas Beecham, for the Camargo Society. First performed, with settings by Inigo Jones, in 1932 (London.) This work, like the "Gods Go A-Begging" is made up of short pieces from the less familiar works of Handel. The recorded excerpts are unidentified, save for the "Battle Music" which is drawn from the operas "Rinaldo" and "Giulio Cesare." The Bourrée is the same piece of music as the Rigaudon in the suite of miscellaneous pieces arranged by Sir Hamilton Harty.

Orchestral Suite
Bourrée, Rondeau, Gigue, Musette, Battle, Finale
London Philharmonic—Beecham
(C-LX224) (C-LFX313) 12"—C-68156D
—Minuet
(Not included in the suite above)

London Philharmonic—Beecham
        (in CX-60†)   12"—C-68475D
[Gods Go A-Begging—Musette & Guglielmo Tell—Overture, Pt. 3]
(C-LX340) (C-LWX130) (C-LFX416)
[Sarabande & Gods Go A-Begging—Musette & Tamburino, on C-68881D]
—Sarabande
(Not included in the suite above)
London Philharmonic Orch.—
Beecham (in CM-194) 12"—C-68202D
[Minuet; Gods Go A-Begging—Tamburino & Mozart: Symphony No. 41, Pt. 7]
(C-LX285)   (C-LFX342)
[Minuet; Gods Go A-Begging—Musette & Tamburino on C-68881D]

OTTONE Opera in Italian 1723 Eng. **Otho**
Overture
—Gavotte only
Victor Orch.   10"—V-20451
[Dances by Corelli, Weber, Beethoven, etc.]
Aria di Gismonda (Unidentified) Soprano
Germaine Martinelli   12"—PD-566101
[Serse—Ombra mai fù]
La speranza è giunta in porto, Act I Soprano
Eng. (arr. Somervell) **Hope has come into harbor**
Kathleen Ferrier (c) (in English) & Gerald Moore (pf)   12"—C-DX1194
[Vieni o figlio caro e mi consola]
Vieni o figlio caro e mi consola, Act II Soprano
Eng. (arr. Somervell) **Come, dear son and comfort me**
Kathleen Ferrier (c) (in English) & Gerald Moore (pf)   12"—C-DX1194
[La speranza è giunta in porto]
Overture, D minor Organ
(Sinfonia from the Chandos Anthem "In the Lord put I my Trust")
—Arr. Orch. (freely) Stokowski
Philadelphia Orch.—Stokowski
                            10"—G-DA1556

PARTENOPE Opera in Italian 1730
Se mia gioia Tenor
Richard Crooks & Fred Schauwecker (pf)   (in VM-846)   10"—V-2176
[Franz: Widmung & Pessard: L'Adieu du Matin]
Passacaille (Passacaglia), G minor
(from Harpsichord Suite No. 7, G minor)
—Arr. Unaccompanied Violin & Viola Halvorsen
Jascha Heifetz & William Primrose
(G-DB6170)   12"—V-11-8151

(IL) PASTOR FIDO Opera in Italian 1712
Suite (Arr. Beecham)
Eng. **The Faithful Shepherd**
Overture; Adagio; Gavotte; Musette; Bourrée; Pastorale; Finale
London Philharmonic Orch.—Beecham
(C-LX915/7†)   3 12"—CM-458†
Sarabande & Musette
Included in Sir Thomas Beecham's Ballet Suite "The Gods Go A-Begging"

Pastoral Symphony See under Messiah

(Il) Penseroso See L'Allegro

Prelude and Fugue, F minor Organ
Fernando Germani 12"—CEMS-1139
[Bach: Chorale—"In dulci Jubilo"]

Psalm 100: O praise the Lord
Chorus & Orch.
(from the Chandos Anthem, Handel Gesellschaft, Vol. 36, No. 1)
Ger. O frohlocket dem Herrn

—**Finale** only
Copenhagen Academy Choir & Orch.—
W. Mayer-Radon 12"—PD-67061
[Bach: Cantata No. 6, Bleib hei uns]

Psalm 104 (Fr. A toi la gloire)
See under Judas—Hail the conquering
hero comes

RADIMISTO Opera in Italian 1720
Sommi dei Soprano
Winifred Cecil (s) & A. Simonetto (pf)
[Torelli: Tu lo sai] 10"—CET-TI7006

RINALDO Opera in Italian 1711

Battle Music Orchestra
Incorporated in Sir Thomas Beecham's Ballet
Suite "The Origin of Design"

Lascia ch' io pianga Soprano
Gladys Swarthout (ms) & L. Hodges (pf)
(in VM-679) 12"—V-16778
[Dowland: Come Again sweet love;
Purcell: Nymphs and Shepherds]
DUPLICATION: Victor Orch. (arr.), in
V-24793

RODELINDA Opera in Italian 1725

Dove sei amato bene, Act I Baritone
(Arr. with new words—"Art thou
troubled?")
Isobel Baillie (s) (in English)
12"—C-DX1022
[Bach: Cantata No. 68—Mein gläubiges
Herze]
Kathleen Ferrier (c) (in English)
[Gluck: Orfeo—Che farò] 12"—D-K1466

RODRIGO Opera in Italian 1707

Passacaglia Orchestra
Incorporated in Sir Hamilton Harty's Handel
Suite. See under Suites.

Sailor's Dance Arr. Wood
Queen's Hall Orch.—Wood 12"—D-X184
[Almira-Rigaudon & Dvořák: Symphonic
Variations, Pt. 5]

(The) Royal Fireworks Music See Fireworks Music

SAMSON Oratorio in English 1743

Overture Orchestra
Queen's Hall Orch.—Henry Wood
12"—D-K812

No. 14, Total eclipse Tenor
Webster Booth 12"—G-C3571
[Haydn: Creation—In native worth]
Richard Crooks
(in VM-934) 12"—V-11-8315
[Messiah—Comfort Ye]

No. 57, Honour and arms Bass
Peter Dawson 12"—G-C1500
[Acis and Galatea—I rage, I melt, I burn]
Oscar Natzke 12"—P-E11402
[Weiss: The Village Blacksmith]

No. 95, Let the bright seraphim Soprano
Isobel Baillie & Hallé Orch.—
Braithwaite with Arthur Lockwood,
trumpet 12"—C-DX1113

Sarabande (Unidentified)
String Quartet 12"—SEMS-1143
[Mattheson: Aria]

Sarabande with Variations Arr. Halvorsen
(from Harpsichord Suite No. 11, D minor)
Frederick Grinke (vl) & Watson
Forbes (vla) 12"—D-K917

SAUL Oratorio in English 1739

Death March (Largo, C major) Orchestra
The famous Death (or Dead) March from
"Saul" was often substituted for that originally
written for "Samson."

—**Arr. Organ**
Alfred Sittard (St. Michael's Organ,
Hamburg) 12"—PD-66554
[Organ Concerto No. 4, 1st Mvt.]

—**Arr. Band:** Regimental Band of H. M.
Grenadier Guards, C-7340M: C-DFX210

SCIPONE Opera in Italian 1726
Eng. Scipio

Triumphal March, Act I Orchestra
Victor Orch., V-24793

Hear me, ye winds and waves Bass
Oscar Natzke 12"—P-E11426
[Elliott: The Song of Hybias the Cretan]

SEMELE Dramatic Piece in English 1744

Oh, sleep! why dost thou leave me? Soprano
Ada Alsop & Boyd Neel String Orch.—
Neel 12"—D-K1164
[Atalanta—Care selve]
Dorothy Maynor & Boston Symphony
Orch.—Koussevitzky 12"—V-15826
[Mozart: Zauberflöte-Ach, ich fühls]

Where'er you walk Tenor
John McCormack 12"—G-DB2867
[Floridante—Caro Amore]
Lawrence Tibbett (b) & pf. acc.
12"—V-17456
[Theodora—Defend her! Heaven]
Webster Booth 12"—G-C3305
[Mendelssohn: Be thou faithful into
death]
DUPLICATIONS: Ria Ginster (in Ger-
man) G-DB10044; Derek Oldham,
G-C2146; Derek Middleton, G-B4133

SERSE Opera in Italian 1738
Eng. Xerxes

Largo: Ombra mai fu, Act I Tenor
Beniamino Gigli & Orch.—
Barbirolli 12"—G-DB1901
[Donizetti: L'Elisir d'amore—Una
furtiva lagrima]
Enrico Caruso & re-recorded organ
12"—V-8806
[Sullivan: The Lost Chord] (G-DB2073)
[Bizet: Carmen—Flower Song on
G-DB5388]

Tito Schipa 12"—G-DB1064
[Flotow: Marta-M'apparì]
Paul Sandoz (b) & Hans Vollenweider
(organ) 12"—G-DB10043
[Giordani: Caro mio ben]
Richard Tauber (t) 10"—P-RO20452
[Gounod: Ave Maria]
Ebe Stignani (ms) 12"—CET-CB20310
[Parelli: Gloria in excelsis Deo]
Marian Zygmunt Nowakowski (bs)
[Massenet: Elégie] 12"—D-K1207
DUPLICATIONS: Enid Szantho,
G-DB6000; Heinrich Schlusnus,
PD-66984; PD-67250; H. E. Groh,
O-4644; Emmi Leisner, PD-67792:
PD-66736; Richard Bonelli, C-17287D;
Leibenberg, T-A523; Germaine Marti-
nelli, PD-566101; E. de Muro Lomanto,
C-DQ2410
In English: Webster Booth, G-C3130;
Charles Kullmann, C-DX389: C-9143M;
Gladys Ripley (c) & Herbert Dawson
(org), G-C3549
In French: Lina Falk, LUM-32053
In German: K. Schmitt-Walter, T-E2234;
M. Klose & Cho. G-EH993

Instrumental Transcriptions

—Arr. Orchestra
Orch. Stabile of Acad. of St. Cecilia,
Rome—Molinari 10"—CET-TI7013
Boston "Pops" Orch.—Fiedler
12"—V-11887
[Massenet: Thaïs—Méditation]
(G-C2838) (G-EG870) (G-FKX28)
Chicago Symphony Orch. & Organ—
Stock 12"—V-6648
[Elgar: Pomp and Circumstance No. 1]
[Dvořák: Slavonic Dance No. 1, on
G-D1432: G-AW282]
DUPLICATIONS: Berlin State Opera
Orch.—Järnefelt, O-D6055; Bournemouth
Municipal Orch.—Godfrey, C-DX620:
C-7331M; Berlin State Opera Orch.,
Weissmann, P-E10701

—Arr. Organ
Feike Asma, PD-67717; Jens Laumann,
G-Z254; Mark Andrews, G-S10087; A.
Meale, G-C2493; H. Schimmelpfennig,
PD-10433; G. T. Ball, G-C1458; Donald
Thorne, D-F6847; Reginald Foort,
G-BD578: G-EG6526; H. R. Cleaver,
P-1594

—Arr. Violin & Piano
V. Prihoda, PD-25721: PD-90163:
PD-47030: CET-LL3001; A. Sandler,
with organ, C-FB1594; C-GN406; H.
Fritz-Crone, G-X2278; P. Godwin,
PD-1091

—Arr. 'Cello & Piano
Gaspar Cassadó, C-L2046: C-GQX10487;
Cedric Sharpe & Gerald Moore, D-F7628;
Paul Grümmer, PD-47059; Marcelli-
Herson, G-K5115; Lopes, PAT-X98064;
André-Lévy, O-166581

Miscellaneous arrangements
Massed Bands Aldershott Command,
G-C2251; Schmidt Band, G-EG2643;
Ensemble Gunther Schulz-Furstenberg,
G-K7777; Instr. Quartet, T-A2088

Sepulto Domino 4 Voices
EIAR Cho.—Erminero 12"—CET-PE113
[Cherubini: O Salutaris hostia]

Siciliana See L'Allegro—Let me wander

SIROE Opera in Italian 1728

Ch'io mai vi possa lasciar d'amare, Act III
Marian Anderson (c) & Kosti
Vehanen (pf) 10"—G-DA1480
[Te Deum]

SOLOMON Oratorio in English 1749

No. 22, With thee th' unsheltered moor
Isobel Baillie (s) 12"—C-DX1080
[Mozart: La Finta Giardiniera—Aria)

**No. 23, Nightingale Chorus: May no rash
intruder**
Bach Cantata Club—Kennedy Scott
10"—C-DB503
[Atalanta—Come alla tortorella, Doris
Owens]
(in Columbia History of Music, Vol. II:
CM-232)

No. 45, Entrance of the Queen of Sheba
(Sinfonia to Part III)
London Symph. Orch—Sargent
12"—D-K1503
[Haydn: Symphony No. 98, Pt. 7]
London Philharmonic—Beecham
(Arr. Beecham) 12"—C-9077M
[Rossini: Scala di Seta—Overture, Pt. 2]
(C-LX255: C-LFX429)
EIAR Orch.—Willy Ferrero
[Scarlatti: Burlesca] 10"—CET-TI7004

—Arr. 2 Pianos
Bartlett & Robertson 12"—C-69818D
[Bach: Sheep May Safely Graze]
(C-DX992)

SONATAS

*The Handel Sonatas are listed by Opus num-
ber, Op. 1, Op. 2, Op. 5 & by groups as they
were originally published—i.e. Trio Sonatas
for 2 Oboes & Bass & two isolated Sonatas. We
have listed all the Sonatas in Op. 1 by number, rather than instrument.*

OPUS 1

No. 5, G major Flute & Figured Bass

—2nd Mvt. (Allegro) only Arranged Kell
Reginald Kell (cl) & Gerald Moore (pf)
[Corelli: Gigue] 10"—C-DB2189

No. 7, C major Flute & Figured Bass
Danish Quartet (fl, vl, vlc, & pf)
2 12"—G-DB5242/3
[Gluck: Sonata for Flute & Figured Bass
—Menuet only]

No. 9, B minor Flute & Figured Bass
Jan Merry & Pauline Aubert
(harpsichord) 12"—PAT-PAT37
(6th Mvt.—Andante—omitted)

—6th Mvt (Andante) only

—**Arr. Violin** Hubay ("Larghetto")
This "Larghetto," a familiar recital piece, is published and recorded without reference to its actual source.
Edmund Kurtz (vlc) & Artur
Balsam (pf) 12"—V-11-9953
[Cassadó: Requiebros]
Erica Morini & Michael Raucheisen (pf)
12"—PD-67021
[Tartini: Variations on a Theme of Corelli]
[Mozart: Symphony No. 40, Pt. 7, with Berlin State Opera Orch.—Strauss, on PD-69872]
DUPLICATIONS: Jeno Hubay, G-AN418;
Emil Telmanyi, TONO-A101 & A108

No. 13, D major Violin & Figured Bass
(Violin Sonata No. 4)
Simon Goldberg & Gerald Moore (pf)
(P-PXO1043/4) 2 12"—P-P59†
Emil Telmanyi & Annette Telmanyi (pf)
2 12"—TONO-A126/7
Bernard Shore (vla) & Gerald Moore (pf)
2 10"—G-B9596/7
—**2nd Mvt. (Allegro)** only
Isaac Stern & Alexander Zakin (pf)
(in CM-604) 12"—C-71726D
[Beethoven: Violin Sonata No. 7, Pt. 7]

No. 14, A major Violin & Figured Bass
(Violin Sonata No. 5)
Carl Flesch & Felix Dyck (pf)
12"—PD-67178

No. 15, E major Violin & Figured Bass
(Violin Sonata No. 6)
Louis Gromer (oboe), Etienne Pasquier (vlc) & Marcelle de Lacour (harpsichord)
(in Vol. II) 12"—AS-11

OPUS 2 1733

No. 1, C minor Flute, Violin & Figured Bass
—**3rd Mvt. (Andante)** only
Luther & Strub, with Kruttge (harpsichord) 10"—G-EG2881
[Mozart: Jugendkonzert, D major, K.107—Minuet]

No. 2, G minor 2 Violins (or Flutes) & Figured Bass
Ars Rediviva Ensemble 12"—BAM-24
—**1st Mvt. (Andante)** only
Heinz Stopker & Hans Kruger (recorders), Georg Seegers (vlc) with Margaret Riedel (harpsichord) 10"—G-EG3976
[Sammartini: Trio Sonata No. 5—Grave & Allegro]

No. 9, E major 2 Violins & Figured Bass
—**1st Mvt. (Adagio)** only
Albert Spalding (vl) William Primrose (vla), with André Benoist (pf)
(in VM-838†) 12"—V-18241
(*Labelled: Op. 2, No. 8*)
[Mozart: Sinfonia Concertante, K.364, Pt. 7]

TRIO SONATAS 1696
2 Oboes or Violins, or Oboe & Violin, with Figured Bass

No. 3, E flat major
—**1st Mvt. (Adagio)** only
Blumensaat (ob), Geissmar (vl), Bodky (harpsichord) & Hermann (vlc)
10"—P-R1026
[Bach: Violin Sonata No. 2, 1st Mvt. only]
(in 2000 Years of Music Set.)

MISCELLANEOUS SONATAS

C major Viola da Gamba & Harpsichord
This isolated Sonata, written about 1705, is published in Vol. 48 of the Handel-Gesellschaft.
Antonio Tusa & Isabelle Nef
2 10"—OL-105/6
Eva Heinitz & Marcelle de Lacour
(in Vol V) 12"—AS-49
Sonata for 2 Flutes Authenticity doubtful
Marcel & Louis Moyse 12"—G-DB5080
[Neubauer: Adagio for Flute & Viola]

SUITES—Harpsichord (or Piano)
Collection: Handel Harpsichord Suite Society (Formed 1935 by HMV)
Contents: No. 2, F major; No. 5, E major; No. 7, G minor; No. 10, D minor; No. 14, G major
(NOTE: *Not available separately*)
Wanda Landowska 6 12"—VM-592†
NOTE: *A group of unidentified Suites played by Marcelle Meyer (piano) have been announced by Les Discophiles Françaises.*

Individual Harpsichord Suites
No. 2, F major
Wanda Landowska, in Handel Society Album: VM-592†
No. 3, D minor
—**1st, 5th, & 6th Mvts.** only
Edwin Fischer 12"—G-DB2378
No. 4, E minor
Erik Then-Bergh (pf) 12"—G-EH1307
No. 5, E major
Wanda Landowska, in Handel Society Album: VM-592†
—**4th Mvt. (Air & Variations)**
See under Harmonious Blacksmith for isolated recordings of this famous piece.
No. 7, G minor
Wanda Landowska, in Handel Society Album: VM-592†
—**6th Mvt. (Passacaglia)** only
Alice Ehlers
(in D-A61) 10"—D-23091
[Mozart: Sonata No. 11, A major—Rondo alla Turca]
—**Arr. Violin & Viola** Halvorsen
J. Heifetz & Wm. Primrose
(G-DB6170) 12"—V-11-8151
No. 8, F minor
—**3rd Mvt. (Allemande) & 4th Mvt. (Courante)** only
Rudolph Dolmetsch 10"—C-DB502
[Purcell: Suite No. 1]
(in Columbia History of Music, Vol. II: CM-232)
No. 10, D minor (No. 2 of 2nd Set)
Wanda Landowska, in Handel Society Album: VM-592†
No. 11, D minor (No. 3 of 2nd Set)

—3rd Mvt. (Sarabande) & 4th Mvt.
(Gigue) only
Roesgen-Champion (harpsichord) &
Orch.—Coppola   10"—G-K7393
[Harpsichord Concerto, B flat, Op. 4,
No. 6, Pt. 3]

—3rd Mvt. (Sarabande) only
—Arr. Violin & Viola Halvorsen
Frederick Grinke & Watson Forbes
12"—D-K917
(Handel supplied 1st 2 variations, Halvorsen
the rest.)

No. 14, G major (No. 6 of 2nd Set)
Wanda Landowska, in Handel Society
Album: VM-592†

SUITES Orchestra
See under Alcina, Fireworks Music,
Gods Go A-Begging (arr. Beecham), The
Great Elopement (arr. Beecham), Origin
of Design (arr. Beecham), Suite (arr.
Harty), Suite (arr. Martucci), Water
Music
Suite—Orchestra Arr. Hamilton Harty
*The Passacaglia is drawn from the Overture to
the opera "Rodrigo." The other pieces are un-
identified, except that the Arietta is tran-
scribed from a vocal air in one of the Handel
operas. The Rigaudon is the same piece of
music as the Bourrée in Beecham's "Origin of
Design" Suite.*
Introduction, Rigaudon, Polonaise,
Arietta, Passacaglia
London Symphony Orch.—Harty
2 12"—D-K795/6

Suite (Unidentified) Arr. Martucci
Minuetto, Musette, Gavotta
EIAR String Orch.—Tansini
12"—CET-CB20249
[Corelli: Sarabande, Giga, Badinerie]

Süsse Stille German Aria Soprano
(or Tenor) 1729
A. Noordewier-Reddingius (s) & Anton
van der Horst (org), with M.
Noordewier (fl)   12"—C-DHX37
[Bach: Cantata No. 39—Höchster was
ich habe]
Ria Ginster (s) & K. Matthei (org.)
12"—G-DB10102
[Ode to St. Cecilia—But oh! what art
can teach]

Te Deum ("Dettingen") In Latin 1743
Eng. Vouchsafe, O Lord Contralto
Lina Falk & String Orch.—Gerlin
12"—LUM-32053
[Serse-Recit. & Largo—Ombra mai fù;
Messiah—He shall feed His flock]
Marian Anderson & Kosti Vehanen (pf)
10"—G-DA1480
[Siroe—Ch'io mai vi possa]

THEODORA Oratorio in English 1750
Angels ever bright and fair Soprano
Isobel Baillie   12"—C-9697
[Joshua—Oh had I Jubal's lyre]
Defend her! Heaven
Lawrence Tibbett (b) & Stewart Wille
(pf)   12"—V-17456
[Semele—Where'er You Walk]

TOLOMEO Opera in Italian 1728
Non lo dirò col labbro, Act I
—Arr. Somervell in English: Silent Wor-
ship
Stuart Robertson (b) & pf. acc.
10"—G-B4255
[Ford: There is a lady sweet and kind &
Woodgate: Bring us in good ale]
Dennis Noble (b)   10"—C-DB1482
[H. Wood: I bless the dawn]

(THE) TRIUMPH OF TIME & TRUTH
Oratorio 1757
Ger. Der Sieg der Zeit und Wahrheit
Unspecified Duo Soprano & Tenor
*The English version (1757) contains no duet.
The Italian version (1737) contains two duets,
but neither is the movement here recorded.*
Jo Vincent & L. van Tulder (in Ger.) w.
pf. acc.   10"—C-DH37
[Mozart: Sub tuum praesidium]

(The) Water Music Orchestra
—Suite of 6 Movements Arr. Harty
Allegro, Air, Bourrée, Hornpipe, Andante,
Allegro deciso
London Philharmonic Orch.—Cameron
(D-K1582/3)   2   12"—D-ED38†
London Philharmonic Orch.—Harty
(C-DX538/9)   2   12"—CX-13†
(C-DFX167/8) (C-CQX16602/3)
Hallé Orch.—Sargent
2   12"—G-C3306/7
Philadelphia Orch.—Stokowski (Arr.
Stokowski)   2   12"—V-8550/1
(G-DB2528/9)
Philadelphia Orch.—Ormandy (Arr.
Ormandy)   2   12"—CX-279†
—Allegro deciso only Arr. Organ
E. Bullock (Westminster Abbey)
10"—G-B2891
[Organ Concerto No. 3, Pt. 3]

While Shepherds watched Hymn in English
Tate-Handel
*Arranged from an air, "Non vi piaque," From
Act II of Handel's "Siroe" with Tate's famous
Christmas hymn-poem. This is the same music
used with the words "Awake My Soul," but is
not the same as the best known setting—the
16th Century tune "Old Winchester." The
Ginster record has not been heard for positive
identification. It is merely listed as "Weih-
nacht."*
Ria Ginster (s) (in German) & K. Matthaei (organ)   10"—G-DA6021
[Old Carol Arr. Goehler: Es kam die
gnadenvolle Nacht]

Xerxes See under Serse
Zadok the Priest
Chorus written for the coronation of
George III
In Coronation Service of George VI

HANDL, Jacob (1500-1591)
*An old German Kapellmeister (also known as
Gallus) who composed much fine choral music,
but who is remembered today almost exclu-
sively by the 4-Pt. motet listed below. This
work was borrowed by Handel for his Funeral
Anthem for Queen Caroline, "The Ways of
Zion do mourn."*

Ecce quomodo moritur Unacc. 4-Part Motet in Latin
Amsterdam Bel Canto Chorus
12"—C-D17196
[Mozart: Ave Verum Corpus]
Dortmund Conservatory Choir
10"—PD-22757
[Nekes: O crux ave, Aachen Cathedral Cho.]

HANFF, Johann Nicolaus (1630-1706)

A German organist, teacher and choirmaster who composed chorales which influenced the writing of J. S. Bach's work in the same genre.

Ach Gott, vom Himmel sieh darein
Charles Hens (Gonzalez Organ)
12"—PAT-PAT69
[Froberger: Toccata, F major, with F. Mihatsch]
[in 3 Centuries of Organ Music Set]

HANSON, Howard (1896-)

An American conductor, director of the Eastman School of Music at Rochester, New York, a prolific composer of orthodox works in all forms, who has promoted contemporary Americans in festivals of their works given throughout the United States.

(The) Lament for Beowulf, Op. 25 Chorus & Orchestra
Eastman School Choir, Eastman-Rochester Symphony Orch.—Hanson
3   12"—VM-889†
[Norton: Dance Suite—Prologue]

MERRY MOUNT Opera in English 1933
Suite: Overture; Children's Dance; Love Duet; Prelude, Act III; Maypole Dances Arr. Hanson
Eastman-Rochester Symphony Orch.—Hanson   2   12"—VM-781†
'Tis an Earth Defiled Baritone
Lawrence Tibbett & Orch.—Pelletier
12"—V-7959
[Gruenberg: Emperor Jones—Standin' in the need of prayer]
[Taylor: King's Henchman—Nay, Maccus, lay him down, in V-11-8932, in VM-1015]

SYMPHONIES
No. 1, E minor, Op. 21 ("Nordic") 1922
Eastman-Rochester Symphony Orch.—Hanson   3   12"—VM-973†
No. 2, Op. 30 ("Romantic") 1930
Eastman-Rochester Symphony Orch.—Hanson   4   12"—VM-648†
No. 3, A Minor
Boston Symphony Orch.—Koussevitzky
5   12"—VM-1170†
[Sibelius: Swanwhite, Op. 54-Maiden with the Roses]

HARDELOT, Guy d' (1858-1936)

Pseudonym of Mrs. W. I. (Helen Guy) Rhodes, a French composer of songs, who attended the Paris Conservatoire. These compositions have attained great popularity and have been sung by leading singers over the world.

SONGS
Because (Teschemacher)
Jan Peerce (t) & Orch.—Levin
12"—V-11-9007
[Harmati: Bluebird of Happiness]
Lauritz Melchior (t) & Chorus
10"—V-10-1227
[Robinson: The House I Live In]
John Carter (t) & James Quillian (pf)
10"—C-4242M
[Foster: Beautiful Dreamer, arr. Howard]
Enrico Caruso & re-recorded Orch.
(G-DA1380)   10"—V-1688
[Tosti: La Mia Canzone]
DUPLICATIONS: Tauber, P-RO20200; Richard Crooks, V-1497

HARRIS, Roy (1898-)

One of the most significant of the younger contemporary composers and one of the most characteristically native American Americans, Harris has written much music of sturdy vitality and genuinely Yankee saltiness.

Quartet No. 3 1939
Roth String Quartet   4   12"—CM-450†
Soliloquy & Dance
William Primrose (vla) & Johanna Harris (pf)
(in VM-1061†)   2   12"—V-11-9212/3
[Benjamin: Elegy, Waltz & Toccata]

SYMPHONIES
No. 3
Boston Symphony Orch.—Koussevitzky
2   12"—VM-651†
Miscellaneous—Arrangement
See under: Bach—Kunst der Fuge, arr. Harris & Norton

HARTMANN, Johann Peter Emilius (1805-1900)

A Dane, who studied law, but turned to music at the advice of Weyse. Director of the Copenhagen Conservatory, he later became Royal Kapellmeister, composing in all forms. He is best recognized for his songs.

CHORAL WORKS In Danish

Frejas Stjerne (Arr. Molbech)
College Men's Choral Union—Hye-Knudsen, G-X6689

Rejsen til Vinland:
Vort Dagvaerk er til Ende
College Men's Choral Union—Hye-Knudsen, G-X6663

Slumrer sødt i Slesvigs Jord (H. P. Holst)
College Men's Choral Union—Hye-Knudsen, G-X6899
Aksel Schiøtz (t), G-X7209

Snart er Natten svunden (J. L. Heiberg)
College Men's Choral Union—Hye-Knudsen, G-X6344

Stundentersang: Vi er et lystigt Folkefaerd (Christian Richardt)
College Men's Choral Union—Hye-Knudsen G-X6663

LIDEN KIRSTEN Opera 1846 (Hans Christian Andersen)

Overture Orchestra
Danish Radio Orch., Copenhagen—Erik Tuxen 12″—NP-Z60216

Sverkels Romance: Langt, langt fra Hjemmets Tenor
Eng. **Far, far from Home**
Aksel Schiøtz & Orch.—Wöldike
(G-X6313) 10″—G-DA5226

Tavlebordsduetten Soprano & Tenor Duet
Eng. **The Drafting Table Duet**
Edith Oldrup-Pedersen & Aksel Schiøtz
12″—G-DB5237
[Nielsen: Maskarade—Magdelones Dansescene, Trio]

TRYMSKVIDEN

Gudernes Triumphal March
Copenhagen Philharmonic Orch.— Jensen, O-DX8001

SONGS in Danish

Den kedsom Vinter gik sin Gang (Ambrosius Stub)
Aksel Schiøtz (t) & guitar acc., G-X6268

Du som har sorg i sinde (Chr. Winther)
Aksel Schiøtz (t) & Herm. D. Koppel
(pf), G-X6350 (G-X6989)

Flyv Fugl, Flyv (Chr. Winther)
Lauritz Melchior (t) & Students' 100th Jubilee Cho.—Johan Hye-Knudsen, G-DB5233
Aksel Schiøtz (t) & H. D. Koppel (pf), G-X6604

Jeg synge skal en Vise (A. Stub)
Aksel Schiøtz (t) & guitar acc., G-X6268

Laer mig Nallens Stjerne (Chr. Richardt)
Aksel Schiøtz (t), G-X6637

HARTY, (Sir) Hamilton (1879-1941)
An Irish pianist and well-known conductor in England, Harty was a skillful composer of orchestral and chamber works, songs, and as an arranger brought out interesting concert versions of the works of Purcell, Handel and others.

(A) John Field Suite
Liverpool Philharmonic—Sargent
3 12″—C-DX1118/20
[Elgar: Serious Doll, No. 2 from Nursery Suite]

Lane o' the Thrushes Song
Isobel Baillie (s) & Gerald Moore (pf)
10″—C-DB2178
[Delius: Love's Philosophy]

Londonderry Air Arr. String Orchestra
Hallé Orch.—Harty 12″—C-9891
[Symphony—An Irish Symphony, Scherzo only]

My Lagan Love (From 3 Trad. Ulster Airs) Arr. Harty
Gladys Swarthout (ms) & L. Hodges
(pf) (in VM-679) 12″—V-16780
[Carpenter: Serenade]

Symphony—An Irish Symphony
—Scherzo only
Hallé Orch.—Harty 12″—C-9891
[Londonderry Air, arr. Harty]

Miscellaneous—Arrangements
See under Handel: (Royal) Fireworks Suite & Water Music Suite

HASSE, Johann Adolph (1699-1783)
Among the most prolific of eighteenth century operatic composers, Hasse wrote more than one hundred operas as well as prodigious quantities of church and instrumental music. He is today practically forgotten outside of the music history classes.

Sonata, D major Flute & Clavier
Hermann Kuttruff & Hans Vollenweider
(organ) 2 10″—G-JK10/11

HASSLER, Hans Leo (1564-1612)
One of the outstanding German organists and composers of choral music, a highly significant figure in the development of the German chorale and motet that culminated with Bach.

Ach weh des leiden Chorale
Kantorei der Staatlichen Hochschule für Musik, Berlin—Thomas 12″—T-E2926
[Schein: Wenn Philli ihre Liebesstrahl; Mylius: Ein Mägdlein; Dowland: Süsses Lieb]

All mein Gedenken
St. Thomas Choir, Leipzig—Ramin
10″—PD-47574
[Bach: Motet-Komm, Jesus, komm—Aria & Kommt Seelen, dieser Tag]

Christ ist erstanden Chorale
Berliner Solisten-Vereinigung
10″—G-EG3188
[Bach: O Haupt voll Blut]

Feinslieb, du hast mich g'fangen

Jungfrau, dein schön' Gestalt Chorale
Leipzig Conservatory Chorus
12″—PD-27312
[Schütz: O lieber Herre Gott]

Mein Lieb' will mit mir kriegen 8-Pt. Madrigal
Madrigal Choir—Thiel 10″—P-R1022
[Gesualdo: Resti di darmi noia]
(in 2000 Years of Music Set)

Meine Seel an meinem letzten End Chorale

Wenn mein Stündlein Motet
Basle Chamber Choir (unacc.)—Sacher
(in Vol. VIII) 12″—AS-72
[Praetorius: Beati omnes]

Vom Himmel hoch
Spieleinigung Berlin 10″—G-EG6116
[Praetorius: Es ist ein' Rös']

HAUSMANN, Valentin (16th Century)
Saxon organist and composer who wrote secular songs and church music, as well as the instrumental piece listed below.

Tanz Viols
Munich Viol Quintet 10″—P-R1023
[M. Franck: Pavane & Byrd: Sellinger's Round]
(in 2000 Years of Music Set)

HAYDN, Franz Josef (1732-1809)
The Austrian composer who, from comparatively meager beginnings, brought the symphony and its related forms in concerted and chamber music to a singular perfection. Ranked

*as one of the titans, he both influenced and was
influenced by his younger contemporary Mozart.*

Adagio (unidentified)
Pierre Fournier (vlc) & String Quartet
12″—**G-DB5088**
[Couperin: Pièces en Concert, Pt. 3]

Andante (unidentified) Arr. Tarrega
Prof. Mozzani (guitar) 10″—**G-GW1773**
[Mozart-Sor: Theme & Variations]

Austrian National Hymn See under
Oesterreichische Bundeshymne

Cassation, F major 1765
NOTE: *No. 2 of a series of 6 Cassations in the
B. & H. Archives.*
Chamber Orch.—E. Fendler
2 12″ & 1 10″—**OL-110/2**

CONCERTOS
'Cello & Orchestra

No. 1, D major, Op. 101
Emanuel Feuermann & Orch.—Sargent
4 12″—**CM-262†**
(C-LFX468/71) (C-LX472/5)
Gaspar Cassadó & Berlin Philharmonic
—Schmidt-Isserstedt
3 12″—**T-SK3222/4**

Clavier & Orchestra

D major, Op. 21 1767
Wanda Landowska (harpsichord) &
Orch.—Bigot   3 12″—**VM-471†**
(G-DB3293/5)
[Sonata No. 36—Minuet & German Ball]
Marguerite Roesgen-Champion (pf) &
Orch.—Marius-François Gaillard (ab-
breviated)   2 12″—**PAT-PGT27/8**
Edwin Fischer (pf) & Vienna Phil-
harmonic   2 12″—**G-DB7657/8**
—3rd Mvt. (Rondo all' ongarese) finale
only
Yvonne Arnaud & String Orch.
12″—**G-C2455**
[Saint-Saëns: Valse caprice—Wedding
Cake]

F major 1771
M. Roesgen-Champion (harpsichord) &
Orch.—Coppola   12″—**G-L966**

Violin & Orchestra

No. 1, C major 1769
Michele Auclair & Paris Conservatory
Orch.—Thibaud 2 12″—**G-W1579/80**
Simon Goldberg & Philharmonia Orch.—
Süsskind   2 12″—**P-P60†**

Trumpet & Orchestra

E flat major 1796
—2nd Mvt. (Andante) & 3rd Mvt. (Rondo)
only
George Eskdale & Symphony Orch.—
Goehr   12″—**C-70106D**
(C-DX933)

(THE) CREATION Oratorio Ger. **Die
Schöpfung**
*Based on a text by Lidley, derived from Mil-
ton's "Paradise Lost" with German translation
by van Swieten. Since the work is best known
in the English version and the majority of the*

*recorded excerpts are sung in that language, it
is catalogued here with English rather than
German titles.*

Individual Excerpts

PART I

No. 6, Rolling in foaming billows Baritone
Ger. **Rollend in schaümenden Wellen**
Nelson Eddy   12″—**C-71450D**
[No. 22, Now Heaven in fullest glory
shone]

**No. 7, And God said: Let the earth bring
forth grass**
Ger. **Und Gott sprach: Es bringe die Erde
Grass Hervor**

No. 8, With verdure clad Ger. **Nun beut' die
Flur das frische Grün**
Irmgard Seefried (in German) & Vienna
Philharmonic—Krips
(C-LCX114)   12″—**C-LX1011**
Eleanor Steber
(in VM-927†) 12″—**V-11-8405**

No. 8, With verdure clad only
Karin Munk (in German) & Orch.—
Wöldike   12″—**G-DB5271**
[No. 24, In native worth, A. Schiøtz]
Isobel Baillie & Hallé Orch.—Heward
12″—**C-DX1052**

No. 13, The heavens are telling Chorus
(Finale of Part I)
Ger. **Die Himmel erzählen die Ehre Gottes**
Royal Choral Society—Sargent
(G-C2513)   12″—**V-11960**
[No. 28, Achieved is the glorious work]

PART II

No. 15, And God said—Recit. Ger. **Und Gott
sprach: Es bringe das Wasser**

No. 16, On mighty pens—Aria Ger.
"Taubenarie"—Auf starkem Fittige
Soprano
Eleanor Steber
(in VM-927†) 12″—**V-11-8406**
[Handel: Messiah—Rejoice greatly]

No. 16, On mighty pens only
Isobel Baillie & Philharmonia Orch.—
Weldon   12″—**C-DX1392**
Eidé Noréna (in German)
12″—**G-DB5054**
[Handel: Atalanta—Care selve]

**No. 20, And God Said Let the Earth bring
forth a living Creature** (Recit.)

No. 21, Straight opening her fertile womb
(Recit.)

No. 22, Now Heav'n in fullest glory shone
(Aria) Bass
Ger. **Nun Scheint in vollem Glanz der
Himmel**
Norman Walker   12″—**C-DX1407**

No. 22, Now Heav'n in fullest glory shone
only
Nelson Eddy   12″—**C-71450D**
[No. 6, Rolling in foaming billows]
Norman Cordon
(in VM-1094) 12″—**V-11-9430**
[Handel: Messiah—No. 40, Why do the
Nations]

No. 24, In native worth Tenor
Ger. Mit Würd' und Hoheit
Aksel Schiøtz (in German) & Orch.—
Mogens Wöldike   12"—G-DB5271
[No. 8, With verdure clad, Karin Munk]
Webster Booth   12"—G-C3571
[Handel: Samson—Total eclipse]
Richard Tauber   12"—P-R20543
[Méhul: Joseph—Champs paternels]
Derek Oldham & Organ   12"—G-C2146
[Handel: Semele—Where'er you walk]
No. 28, Achieved is the glorious work
Chorus
Ger. Vollendet ist das grosse Werk
Royal Choral Society—Sargent
(G-C2513)   12"—V-11960
[No. 13, The heavens are telling]
Deutsche Tänze Orchestra 1792
—Nos. 2, 4 & 6 Arr. O. E. Deutsch
Berlin Philharmonic—Kleiber
10"—T-B1340
[Quartet, Op. 3, No. 5—Serenade only]
Divertimento (unidentified) Arr.
Piatigorsky
Adagio, Minuet, Allegro molto
Gregor Piatigorsky (vlc) & Valentin
Pavlovsky (pf)   12"—C-11830D
German Ball (Chain of Waltzes)
Wanda Landowska (harpsichord)
(in VM-471†)   12"—V-15015
(G-DB3295)
[Sonata No. 36, C sharp minor—Minuet
& Concerto, D major, Op. 21—Pt. 5]
Gypsy Rondo See under Trio No. 1, 3rd Mvt.
(L') Isola Disabitata See under Operas

(DIE) JAHRESZEITEN Oratorio in
German 1801
Eng. The Seasons   It. Le Stagione
Abridged recording in Italian
(Numbers refer to B. & H. score)
Gabriella Gatti (s) Francesco Albanese
(t), Luciano Neroni (bs) with EIAR
Chorus & Orch.—Vittorio Gui
(CET-SS1009/18)   10 12"—CET-6
(Sections included: Nos. 2, 4, 6, 7, 8, 13,
14, 15, 16, 17, 18, 22, 25, 26, 28, 29, 30,
34, 36, 38, 39.)
(Schirmer score: Nos. 3, 5, 7, 8, 9, 10, 17,
18, 19, 20, 21, 22, 27, 30, 31, 33, 34, 36,
40, 42, 44, 46.)
Individual Excerpts
NOTE: The numbers in parentheses refer to the
Schirmer score.
No. 2, (No. 3) Komm, holder Lenz Chorus
Berlin Singakademie—G. Schumann
12"—G-EH258
[Brahms: Requiem—Selig sind, Pt. 3]
No. 4, (No. 5) Schon eilet froh der Ackers-
mann Bass
Louis Mortourier (in French)
12"—G-W1137
[Berlioz: L'Enfance du Christ—Toujours
ce rêve]
No. 15, (No. 19) Welche Labung für die
Sinne Soprano
Eng. O how pleasing to the senses
Isobel Baillie (in English)
12"—C-DX1234
[Purcell: Fairy Queen—Hark the
echoing air]

No. 22, (No. 27) Ihr Schönen aus der Stadt
Soprano & Tenor
Jo Vincent & Louis Van Tulder
12"—C-DHX3

MINUETS
C major Arr. 'Cello & Piano Piatti
Pablo Casals & Blas-Net
(G-DB3064)   12"—V-14843
[Bruch: Kol Nidrei, Pt. 3]
[Cassadó: Requiebros, on G-DB1391]
E flat major (unidentified)
Leo Petroni (vl) & Michael Raucheisen
(pf)   12"—G-EH1236
[Tchaikovsky: Chant sans paroles]
Notturno VI, G major
(Identical with Entr'acte I & Ballet III from
"Il mondo della luna")
Chamber Orch. of Paris Conservatory—
Fendler   10"—G-DA4923
Oesterreichische Bundeshymne Eng.
Austrian National Hymn
There are many different versions of this fa-
mous hymn, including Haydn's own use of it
as the basis of the Theme and Variations (An-
dante) movement of the String Quartet in C
major, Op. 76, No. 3 ("Emperor" Quartet).
Besides the Austrian version with the words
"Gott erhalte Franz den Kaiser," there is the
German version "Deutschland, Deutschland,
über alles," and various English adaptations
for church use.
Deutschland, Deutschland über alles
Chorus
Erk Male Cho.—Kopsch 10"—PD-25184
[Von Baussnern: Deutschland]
DUPLICATIONS: Cho. & Band, PD-
23100 & G-EG2811
Arr. Band: T-A1556; G-EG2808; PD-
23194; PD-21749; C-DW3061; T-A2122

OPERAS

(LA) FEDELTA PREMIATA
Prelude, Act III See Symphony No. 73—4th
Mvt.

(L') ISOLA DISABITATA 1779 Eng. The
Uninhabited Isle
Overture
Indianapolis Symphony Orch.—Sevitzky
12"—V-11-8487

(IL) MONDO DELLA LUNA Dramma
giocoso 1777
Ger. Die Welt auf dem Monde Eng. The
World on the Moon
Suite—Including: Entr'acte; Presto; First
Minuet & Trio; Adagio; Second Minuet &
Trio; Presto finale
Charles Brill Orch.—Brill
2 12"—D-K877/8
See also under Notturno VI, G major

OVERTURES
No. 4, D major Orchestra After 1780
Paris Conservatory Orch.—Fendler
10"—G-DA4912
[Mozart: Marches K. 335 & K. 408]
No. 13, G minor See under Operas—(L')
Isola Disabitata

QUARTETS String

Collections

The Haydn Quartet Society (formed 1932 by HMV)

All performances are by the Pro Arte Quartet Each volume contains 7 12" records. Individual records are not sold separately.

Vol. I (not obtainable)
C major, Op. 20, No. 2
C major, Op. 33, No. 3 ("Bird")
G major, Op. 77, No. 1

Vol. II (not obtainable)
D major, Op. 33, No. 6
G major, Op. 54, No. 1
C major, Op. 54, No. 2
G minor, Op. 74, No. 3 ("Horseman")

Vol. III—VM-525†
F major, Op. 3, No. 5
E flat major, Op. 33, No. 2
E flat major, Op. 64, No. 6
B flat major, Op. 71, No. 1

Volume IV—VM-526†
E flat major, Op. 50, No. 3
C major, Op. 76, No. 3 ("Emperor")
F minor, Op. 20, No. 5

Vol. V—VM-527†
D major, Op. 20, No. 4
F major, Op. 74, No. 2
F major, Op. 77, No. 2

Vol. VI
C major, Op. 1, No. 6
E major, Op. 54, No. 3
A major, Op. 55, No. 1
G major, Op. 64, No. 4

Vol. VII—VM-689†
B flat major, Op. 3, No. 4
D major, Op. 50, No. 6 ("Frog")
B flat major, Op. 64, No. 3
C major, Op. 74, No. 1

Vol. VIII—VM-595†
B flat major, Op. 1, No. 1
E flat major, Op. 20, No. 1
B flat major, Op. 55, No. 3
B flat major, Op. 76, No. 4 ("Sunrise")

Individual Quartets

B flat major, Op. 1, No. 1
Pro Arte Quartet, in Society Vol. VIII: VM-595†

C major, Op. 1, No. 6
Pro Arte Quartet, in Society Vol. VI

B flat major, Op. 3, No. 4
Pro Arte Quartet, in Society Vol. VII: VM-689†

F major, Op. 3, No. 5 (With the famous Serenade: 2nd Mvt.)
Pro Arte Quartet, in Society Vol. III: VM-525†
Erling Bloch Quartet
                    2   10"—G-DA5244/5
Léner Quartet   2   12"—C-9658/9
Calvet Quartet   2   10"—T-A2176/7

—2nd Mvt. (Serenade—Andante cantabile) only
Poltronieri Quartet, C-GQX11065; Wendling Quartet, PD-95312; Prisca Quartet, PD-15170: PD-15230: CET-OR5122

—Arr Orchestra
Winterthur Municipal Orch.—
Scherchen   12"—G-DB6090
[Boccherini: Minuet]
Hollywood Bowl Orch.—Stokowski
                             12"—V-11-9419
[Purcell: Trumpet Voluntary, arr. Stokowski]
Toronto Symphony Orch.—MacMillan
        (Canadian) 12"—V-11-8726
[Byrd: Suite, Pt. 3]
Philadelphia Orch.—Stokowski
(G-AW181)   12"—V-7256
[Boccherini: Minuet]
[Bach: Prelude, B minor, Wohltemperiertes Clavier No. 24, on G-D1995]
DUPLICATIONS: Berlin Philharmonic—Kleiber, T-B1340; Willy Steiner Orch., PD-47130; Barnabas von Geczy & his Orch., G-EG6911

E flat major, Op. 20, No. 1
Pro Arte Quartet, in Society Vol. VIII: VM-595†

C major, Op. 20, No. 2
Pro Arte Quartet, in Society Vol. I: unobtainable

D major, Op. 20, No. 4
Pro Arte Quartet, in Society Vol. V: VM-527†

F minor, Op. 20, No. 5
Pro Arte Quartet, in Society Vol. IV: VM-526†
Roth Quartet   3   12"—CM-228†

E flat major, Op. 33, No. 2
Pro Arte Quartet, in Society Vol. III: VM-525†

C major, Op. 33, No. 3 ("Bird" Quartet)
Pro Arte Quartet, in Society Vol. I: unobtainable
Griller Quartet   2   12"—D-K1668/9†

D major, Op. 33, No. 6
Pro Arte Quartet, in Society Vol. II: unobtainable

E flat major, Op. 50, No. 3
Pro Arte Quartet, in Society Vol. IV: VM-526†

D major, Op. 50, No. 6 ("Frog" Quartet)
Pro Arte Quartet, in Society Vol. VII: VM-689†

The Seven Last Words, (Quartet version), Op. 51
Primrose Quartet   9   12"—VM-757†
[Schubert: Litanei]

G major, Op. 54, No. 1
Pro Arte Quartet, in Society Vol. II: unobtainable
Budapest Quartet   2   12"—VM-869†

C major, Op. 54, No. 2
Pro Arte Quartet, in Society Vol. II. unobtainable

E major, Op. 54, No. 3
Pro Arte Quartet, in Society Vol. VI

A major, Op. 55, No. 1
Pro Arte Quartet, in Society Vol. VI

B flat major, Op. 55, No. 3
Pro Arte Quartet, in Society Vol. VIII: VM-595†

B flat major, Op. 64, No. 3
Pro Arte Quartet, in Society Vol. VII: VM-689†

G major, Op. 64, No. 4
  Pro Arte Quartet, in Society Vol. VI
D major, Op. 64, No. 5 ("Lark" Quartet)
  Hungarian Quartet
                      2   12"—G-DB6390/1
  Riele Queling Quartet
                      2   12"—G-EH1248/9
  Calvet Quartet
    (T-A2243/5)   3   10"—U-C18023/5
E flat major, Op. 64, No. 6
  Pro Arte Quartet, in Society Vol. III:
  VM-525†
B flat major, Op. 71, No. 1
  Pro Arte Quartet, in Society Vol. III:
  VM-525†
C major, Op. 74, No. 1
  Pro Arte Quartet, in Society Vol. VII:
  VM-689†
—Minuet & Trio only
  Gertler Quartet   12"—D-K1436
  [Bartók: Quartet No. 6 Pt. 7]
F major, Op. 74, No. 2
  Pro Arte Quartet, in Society Vol. V:
  VM-527†
G minor, Op. 74, No. 3 ("Reiter"—"Horse-
  man")
  Pro Arte Quartet, in Society Vol. II: un-
  obtainable
  Budapest Quartet   2   12"—CX-274†
—2nd Mvt. only
  Guarneri Quartet, PD-67140
G major, Op. 76, No. 1
  Rome Quartet   2   12"—G-DB5631/2
  Poltronieri Quartet
                       2   12"—C-D14552/3
D minor, Op. 76, No. 2 ("Quinten")
  Poltronieri Quartet
                       2   12"—C-GQX10135/6
—2nd Mvt. (Andante) only
  Léner Quartet, C-68424D in CM-246†;
  C-LFX720; C-GQX10909
C major, Op. 76, No. 3 ("Kaiser"—
  "Emperor")
  Pro Arte Quartet, in Society Vol. IV:
  VM-526†
  Léner Quartet   4   12"—CM-246†
  (C-GQX10906/9) (C-LFX417/20)
  [Quartet in D minor, Op. 76, No. 2—
  Andante only]
  Röntgen Quartet
                       2   12"—ELITE-7033/4
—2nd Mvt. (Theme & Variations) only
  *The theme is that of the Austrian National
  Hymn. For recordings of this Hymn alone in
  its versions see under Oesterreichische Bundes-
  hymne.*
  Wendling Quartet, PD-27216; Riele
  Queling Quartet, G-EH1288
—Arr. String Orchestra
  Berlin Philharmonic Strings—Schmidt-
  Isserstedt   12"—T-E1828
B flat major, Op. 76, No. 4 ("Sunrise")
  Pro Arte Quartet, in Society Vol. VIII:
  VM-595†
  Prisca Quartet   3   12"—PD-10531/3
  (PD-524294/6)
D major, Op. 76, No. 5 (With the famous
  Largo: 2nd Mvt.)
  Roth Quartet   3   12"—CM-400†

G major, Op. 77, No. 1
  Pro Arte Quartet, in Society Vol. I: un-
  obtainable
F major, Op. 77, No. 2
  Pro Arte Quartet, in Society Vol. V: VM-
  527†
B flat major, Op. 103 ("Ultimo")
—Menuetto ma non troppo
  Busch Quartet
         (in CM-543†)   12"—C-71479D
  [Beethoven, Quartet, F major, Op. 59,
  No. 1, Pt. 11]
Quartet, D major Flute & Strings
  Jean Pierre Rampal & Pasquier Trio
                          12"—BAM-35
Rondo all' ongarese See Concerto, D major,
  Op. 21 & Trio No. 5
(Die) Schöpfung See under The Creation

(DIE) SIEBEN WORTE DES ERLOESERS
  AM KREUZE Oratorio
  Eng. The Seven Words of the Savior on
  the Cross
Complete recording:
  Soloists, Chorus & Orch. of Tokio
  Academy of Music—C. Lautrup
                      9   12"—CM-297†
  Soloists: T. Kurosawa (s), H. Tanji (c),
  S. Sonoda (t), T. Itch (bs)
—Arr. Haydn String Quartet
  *7 Quartets, Op. 51 Arr. from Good Friday
  music composed for Cadiz Cathedral, 1785*
  Primrose Quartet   9   12"—VM-757†
  [Schubert: Litanei, Primrose & organ
  acc.]
Sinfonia Concertante, Op. 84 Solo
  Violin, 'Cello, Oboe, Bassoon & Orch.
  Roland Charmy, André Navarra, Myrtil
  Morel, Fernand Oubradous w. Paris
  Conservatory Orch.—Charles Münch
                      3   12"—OL-83/5

SONATAS—Clavier (Breitkopf & Härtel
  numbering)
No. 3, C major
—Menuet only
  Alice Ehlers (harpsichord)
         (in D-A62)   10"—D-23114
  [Bach: French Suite No. 4—Allenmande
  & Purcell: Suite No. 7—Hornpipe]
No. 19, D major
—Adagio ma non troppo only
  Ruggero Gerlin (pf)
              (in Vol. IX) 12"—AS-83
No. 34, E minor
  M. Rytter (pf)   12"—TONO-K8029
No. 36, C sharp minor
—Minuet only
  Wanda Landowska (harpsichord)
         (in VM-471†)   12"—V-15015
  (G-DB3295)
  [Concerto, D major, Op. 21, Pt. 5]
No. 37, D major
  Solomon (pf)   12"—G-C3494
No. 49, E flat major
  Denis Matthews (pf)
                       2   12"—C-DX1374/5

—Menuet only
Charlotte Kaufmann (Mozart piano of 1790) 12″—PD-95224
[Beethoven: Clarinet Trio, Op. 11, Pt. 5]
No. 52, E flat major
Vladimir Horowitz
2 12″—G-DB1837/8
Sonata G major Flute & Piano
René Le Roy & Paul Loyonnet
(Limited Edition) 4 12″—CH-B8

SONATAS—Violin & Harpsichord
No recordings available

SONGS

My mother bids me bind my hair (Mrs. Hunter)
(from the 12 English Canzonettas)
Marian Anderson (c) & Franz Rupp (pf)
10″—V-10-1199
[She never told her love]
Pastorella
Stella Tavarès (s, in Italian) & R. Herbin (pf) 12″—BAM-40
[Caldara: Mirti faggi]
The Sailor's Song (Mrs. Hunter)
(from the 12 English Canzonettas)
Elisabeth Schumann (s) & Gerald Moore (pf) 10″—G-DA1850
[She never told her love]
Serenade
Richard Crooks (t) (in English) & Fred. Schauwecker (pf)
(in VM-846) 10″—V-2175
[Handel: Floridante—Alma mia & Arne: Comus—Preach me not]
She never told her love (Shakespeare)
(from the 12 English Canzonettas)
Elisabeth Schumann (s) Gerald Moore (pf) 10″—G-DA1850
[The Sailor's song]
Marian Anderson (c) & Franz Rupp (pf)
10″—V-10-1199
[My mother bids me bind my hair]
The Spirit Song ("Hark what I tell to thee")
Gladys Ripley (c) & Philharmonia Orch. —Geo. Weldon 12″—G-C3500†
[Elgar: Sea Pictures, Pt. 5]

SYMPHONIES Orchestra
The Breitkopf-Härtel (Mandyczewski) numberings are used. The old B. & H. numbering is indicated in parentheses.

No. 45, F sharp minor (Old No. 18)
("Abschieds"—"Farewell")
London Symphony Orch.—Henry Wood
(C-LFX364/6) 3 12″—CM-205†
Metropolitan Symphony Orch.—Leinsdorf
4 10″—PILO-DA302
[Commentary by Deems Taylor, 2 sides]
No. 49, F minor ("La Passione")
Chamber Orch. of Paris—Pierre Duvanchelle 2 12″—C-LFX676/7
No. 53, D major ("Imperial")
Paris Conservatory Orch.—Fendler
2 12″—G-DB5131/2
No. 73, D major ("La Chasse")
—4th mvt. only (Originally Prelude, Act III of "Fedelta Premiata")

Chamber Orch.—Hans von Benda
10″—G-EG3584
[Mozart: March, D major, K.249]
No. 86, D major (Old No. 10) (Paris No. 5)
Leipzig Gewandhaus Chamber Orch.—
Paul Schmitz 3 12″—PD-57107/9
(Fonit-91121/3)
No. 88, G major (Old No. 13)
NBC Symphony Orch.—Toscanini
(G-DB3515/7†) 3 12″—VM-454†
National Symphony Orch.—Jorda
3 12″—D-K1472/4†
Orch. Stabile of Academy of St. Cecilia, Rome—Molinari
3 12″—CET-BB25103/5
Vienna Philharmonic—Clemens Krauss
3 10″—G-AM2280/2
—4th Mvt. (Allegro) only
Berlin Philharmonic—Borchard
[Boccherini: Minuet] 10″—T-A1711
No. 91, E flat major (Old No. 28)
Berlin Philharmonic—Konoye
(PD-561135/7) 3 10″—PD-62792/4
No. 92, G major (Old No. 16) ("Oxford")
Paris Conservatory Orch.—Walter
(G-DB3559/61†) 3 12″—VM-682†
Berlin Philharmonic—W. Gmeindl
(Fonit-96089/92) 4 12″—PD-67562/5
No. 93, D major (Old No. 5) (Salomon No. 2)
London Philharmonic—Beecham
(C-LFX550/2) 3 12″—CM-336†
No. 94, G major (Old No. 6) (Salomon No. 3) ("Paukenschlag") ("Surprise")
Winterthur Municipal Orch.—Scherchen
3 12″—G-DB10000/2
Boston Symphony Orch.—Koussevitzky
3 12″—VM-1155†
(Older version in VM-55†; G-D1735/7†; G-DB5570/2)
Berlin Philharmonic—Schmidt-Isserstedt
3 12″—T-E2864/6
Orchestra of the Suisse Romande—Blech
In Prep. (English Decca)
CBS Symphony—Howard Barlow
3 12″—CM-363†
DUPLICATIONS: Berlin Philharmonic—
Knappertsbusch, G-DB5671/3; Berlin Philharmonic—Horenstein, PD-66914/6
No. 95, C minor (Old No. 9) (Salomon No. 5)
London Symphony Orch.—Harty
(PD-516689/90) 2 12″—D-K798/9
No. 96, D major (Old No. 14) (Salomon No. 6) ("Miracle")
Vienna Philharmonic—Walter
(G-DB3282/4†) 3 12″—VM-885†
Amsterdam Concertgebouw Orch.—Van Beinum In Prep. (English Decca)
No. 97, C major (Old No. 7) (Salomon No. 1)
London Philharmonic—Beecham
(G-DB6222/4†) 3 12″—VM-1059†
No. 98, B flat major (Old No. 8) (Salomon No. 4)
NBC Symphony Orch.—Toscanini
4 12″—VM-1025†
[Mendelssohn: Octet—Scherzo only]

London Symphony Orch.—Sargent
    4   12"—**D-K1500/3†**
[Handel: Salomon—Entrance of the
Queen of Sheba]

No. 99, E flat major (Old No. 3) (Salomon
No. 10)
London Philharmonic—Beecham
    3   12"—**CM-264†**
(C-LFX431/3) (C-LWX155/7)

No. 100, G major (Old No. 11) (Salomon
No. 12) ("Military")
Vienna Philharmonic Orch.—Walter
(G-DB3421/3)   3 12"—**VM-472†**
Vienna Philharmonic Orch.—Schüler
    3 12"—**IMP-014054/6**

No. 101, D major (Old No. 4) (Salomon No.
11) ("Clock")
N. Y. Philharmonic-Symphony Orch.—
Toscanini   4 12"—**VM-57†**
[Mendelssohn: Midsummer Night's
Dream—Scherzo] (G-AW77/80)
(G-D1668/71†) (G-W1070/3)
EIAR Symphony Orch.—La Rosa
Parodi   4 12"—**CET-CB20188/91**
[Mozart: Schauspieldirektor—Overture]
German Philharmonic Orch. of Prague—
Keilberth   3 12"—**T-E3233/5**
CBS Symphony—Howard Barlow
    4 12"—**CM-459†**
[Bach: Partita No. 6, E major—Prelude,
with New Queen's Hall Orch.—Wood]

No. 102, B flat major (Old No. 12)
(Salomon No. 9)
Boston Symphony Orch.—Koussevitzky
    3 12"—**VM-529†**

No. 103, E flat major (Old No. 1) (Salomon
No. 8) ("Paukenwirbel") ("Drumroll")
Hallé Orch.—Heward 3 12"—**CM-547†**
(C-DX1057/9†)
Berlin Philharmonic Orch.—Ludwig
    4 12"—**PD-67616/9**

—1st Mvt. only
Symphony Orch.—Raybould
    10"—**C-DB833**
(in Columbia History of Music, Vol. III:
CM-233)

No. 104, D major (Old No. 2) (Salomon
No. 7) ("London")
Philharmonia Orch.—Issay Dobrowen
    3 12"—**G-C3515/7†**
Edwin Fischer Chamber Orch.—Fischer
(G-DB4615/7)   3 12"—**VM-617†**
London Philharmonic—Beecham
(C-LX856/8†)   3 12"—**CM-409†**
Vienna Philharmonic Orch.—Weisbach
    3 12"—**IMP-014066/8**

"Toy" Symphony C major (Sinfonia
Berchtolsgadensis)
Winterthur Municipal Orch.—Scherchen
    12"—**G-DB6087**
Symphony Orch.—Weingartner
(C-DX311) (C-DFX116) 12"—**C-7274M**
Orch. Raymonde—G. Walter
    10"—**C-DF2290**
Victor Orch.   10"—**V-20215**
Orch.—Max Goberman
    10"—**YPR 1001/2**

TRIOS
Strings

D major, Op. 32
Pasquier Trio
    (in Vol. XIII) 12"—**AS-117**

G major, (3-Pt. Fugue) .1772
Minuet & Finale only
NOTE: *MS in B. & H. Archives*
Pasquier Trio   12"—**PAT-PAT30**
[Boccherini: Adagio, Op. 38]

Piano, Violin, 'Cello
Collections

The Haydn Trio Society (Parlophone)

Vol. I—No. 2, F sharp minor; No. 3,
C major; No. 5, E flat major
Lili Kraus, Simon Goldberg & Anthony
Pini   6 12"—**P-P35†**

Individual recordings

No. 1, G major
Eileen Joyce, Henry Holst & Anthony
Pini   2 12"—**C-DX1054/5**
[Mozart: Gigue, K.574; Minuet, K.355]
Cortot, Thibaud, Casals
    2 10"—**G-DA895/6**

—2nd Mvt. (Adagio cantabile) only
Weitzman Trio   10"—**O-25216**
[Schubert: Nocturne, E flat, Op. 148]

—3rd Mvt. (Finale: Rondo all' ongarese)
only
(*The celebrated "Gypsy Rondo"*)
Elly Ney Trio   12"—**PD-15090**
[Schumann: Quartet, Op. 47, Pt. 7]
[Beethoven: Piano Sonata, Op. 31, No. 3,
Pt. 5, with W. Kempff, on PD-67071]

—Arr. Kreisler ("Hungarian Rondo")
Fritz Kreisler (vl) & Victor Orch.—
Voorhees
    (in VM-1044) 10"—**V-10-1204**
[Trad. Arr. Kreisler: Londonderry Air]

No. 2, F sharp minor
Kraus, Goldberg & Pini, in Parlophone—
Haydn Trio Society, Vol. I; P-P35†

No. 3, C major
Kraus, Goldberg & Pini, in Parlophone—
Haydn Trio Society, Vol. I; P-P35†

No. 5, E flat major
Kraus, Goldberg & Pini, in Parlophone—
Haydn Trio Society, Vol. I; P-P35†
Jacques Février, Jean Fournier & Pierre
Fournier
    (in Vol. VI) 2 12"—**AS-55/6**
[F. X. Richter: Trio No. 3, A major—
Larghetto]

Variations (Andante) F minor (Andante
con variazioni) Piano
Lili Kraus   2 12"—**P-PXO1022/3**
Eduard Erdmann 2 12"—**PD-67727/8S**
Ignace Jan Paderewski
    (in VM-748) 12"—**V-14727**
(G-DB3183)
Clara Haskill   10"—**PD-522864**

HEISE, Peter Arnold (1830-1879)

*Although best known for his songs, Heise, a
Dane who was a pupil of Gade, also wrote ballet music. His opera "King and Marshall" is
one of the most popular stage works in Denmark.*

DROT OG MARSK Opera in Danish 1878
Eng. **King and Marshall**

Det var sig Humleranken
Eng. **It was the hop wine**

Jeg kender af Navn kun Guldet
Eng. **Gold I only know by name** Sop.
Edith Oldrup-Pedersen & Royal Theatre
Orch., Copenhagen—Hye-Knudsen
(G-Z284) 12"—**G-DB5246**
[Dupuy: Ungdom og Galskab—Trio]

SONGS In Danish

Aften paa Loggiaen (B. S. Ingemann)
Aksel Schiøtz (t), G-X6866
Helge Roswaenge (t), G-DA5224
Marius Jacobsen, G-X2917

Arnes Sang: Ornen løfter med staerke Slag
Aksel Schiøtz (t), G-X6866
Christian Stage (b), G-X3796

Dengang jeg var stor som saa ("Helligtre-
königersaften")
Eng. **When I was a tiny boy** ("Twelfth
Night") (Shakespeare)
Aksel Schiøtz (t), G-X6105

Der var en svend med sin pigelil ("Som man
behager")
Eng. **It was a lover and his lass** ("As You
Like It") (Shakespeare)
Aksel Schiøtz (t), G-X6105
Helge Roswaenge (t), G-DA5225

Det var paa Isted Hede (N.F.S. Grundtvig)
Aksel Schiøtz (t), G-X6240

Dyvekes Sange (Holger Drachmann) Song
Cycle
1. **Skal altid faeste mit Haar under Hue**
2. **Ak, Lvem der havde en Hue med Fjer**
3. **Hvad vil den Mand**
4. **Vildt suser Blaesten**
5. **Naeppi tør jeg tale**
6. **Det stiger herop**
Dorothy Lassen (s)
4 10"—**G-DA5233/6**
[Sol deroppe on G-DA5234]

Husker du i Høst (Carl Ploug)
Aksel Schiøtz (t), G-X6604

Hvor tindrer nu min stjerne
Marius Jacobsen (t), G-X2918

Jylland mellen tvende Have
(H. C. Andersen)
Aksel Schiøtz (t) & Royal Orch.,
Copenhagen, J. Hye-Knudsen, G-X6652

Kongesonnens Romance "Tornrose"
Helge Roswaenge (t), G-DA5225
Edi Laider (b), G-X6211

Lille Karen Eng. **Little Karen**
Lauritz Melchior (t), (in CX-233)
Marius Jacobsen (t), G-X2868

Skovensomhed: Igennen Bøgeskoven
(Emil Aarestrup)
Edith Oldrup-Pedersen (s), G-X4770
Aksel Schiøtz (t), G-X6867
Tenna Kraft (s), O-DO2001

Sol deroppe ganger under Lide
(Hans C. Andersen)
Edith Oldrup-Pedersen (s), G-X4770
Else Brems (ms), G-DA5228
Dorothy Larsen (s), G-DA5234

Til en Veninde
Aksel Schiøtz (t), G-X6867

Vildt fly ver Hog
Lauritz Melchior (t) & Ignace Stasfogel
(pf), C-17481D (in CX-233)

HEMING, Michael (1920-1942)

A Threnody for a Soldier killed in action
*(Arranged, developed, and orchestrated by
Antony Collins from material left by Michael
Heming, killed in the battle of El Alamein.)*
Hallé Orch.—Barbirolli 12"—**G-C3427**

HENRIQUES, Fini (1867-1940)

*A Danish violinist and composer of operas and
ballets, best known by his compositions for
children and a few virtuoso pieces for violin.*

Billedbogen (A Picture Book) Piano
**Bolden; Dukkens Vuggevise; Den lille
Jokey; Den lille Soldat; Sommerfuglen**
Fini Henriques 10"—**G-X4833**
Galina Werschenska 12"—**TONO-A117**
Folmer Jensen 10"—**O-DO2004**

(DEN) LILLE HAVFRUE (The Little
Mermaid) Ballet

—**Livsglaedens Dans** (Joy of Life Dance)
Orchestra
Royal Orch. Copenhagen—Joh. Hye-
Knudsen 10"—**G-X4740**
[Vølunds Smed—Alfedans]

Myggedansen (Dance of the Mosquitoes)
Violin & Piano
Fini Henriques (vl) & Borge
Rosenbaum (pf) 10"—**G-X4834**
[Vuggevise]

Varren er kommen Song in Danish
Else Brems (ms) & Folmer Jensen (pf)
[Heise: Sol deroppe] 10"—**G-DA5228**

VOLUND SMED Opera
Eng. **Vølund, the Smith**

Overture Orchestra
Royal Orch., Copenhagen—Joh. Hye-
Knudsen 12"—**G-Z235**

—**Alfedans** (Elf Dance) only
Royal Orch., Copenhagen—Joh. Hye-
Knudsen 10"—**G-X4740**
[Den Lille Havfrue: Livsglaedens Dans]

—**Scene**
Else Skonboe (recitation) with orch.
TONO-A109

Vuggevise (Lullaby) Violin & Piano
Fini Henriques (vl) & Borge
Rosenbaum (pf 10"—**G-X4834**
[Myggedansen]

HERBERT, Victor (1859-1924)

*An Irish-American 'cellist, conductor and com-
poser, who achieved his greatest successes in the
operetta field. His light operas were immensely
popular during his lifetime, then fell off in
favor. Today, however, several have been revived on stage and screen and have met with as
much success on radio programs.*

COLLECTIONS

VICTOR HERBERT MELODIES

Naughty Marietta—Ah! Sweet mystery of life; 'Neath the southern moon; I'm falling in love with someone; Italian street song (V-12589); The Fortune Teller—Gypsy love song; Romany life; Czardas; Mademoiselle Modiste—Kiss me again (V-12590); Badinage; Air de Ballet: Al Fresco (V-12591); Babes in Toyland—March of the Toys; In the Toymaker's workshop; Go to sleep; Never mind, Bo-Peep; Toyland; I can't do that sum (V-12591); Sweethearts—While on parade; For every lover; The Angelus; Pretty as a picture; Jeanette; Sweethearts waltz; The Red Mill— For every day is ladies' day; Isle of my dreams; When you're pretty; Whistling song; Moonbeams; Because you're you; Streets of New York (V-12593)
Anne Jamison & Gladys Rice (s), Jan Peerce (t), Thomas L. Thomas (b) with Victor Orchestra & Salon Group—Shilkret   5 10"—V-C33

VOL. II

Selections from Rose of Algeria; Eileen; Babette; Natoma; Enchantress; Princess Pat; Pan-Americana; Yesterthoughts; Punchinello; Only Girl; Fleurette; Under the Elms; 'Cello Suite—4th Mvt.— Serenade; It Happened in Nordland—Absinthe Frappé
Victor Salon Group, Light Opera Company & Orch.—Shilkret   5 12"—V-C11

SELECTED SONGS

Ah Sweet mystery of Life; A Kiss in the Dark; Thine Alone; When you're Away; Kiss Me Again; Sweethearts
Risë Stevens (ms) w. Male Chorus & Orch.—Shulman   3 12"—CM-682
Kiss me again; Moonbeams; Indian Summer; 'Neath a southern moon; A kiss in the dark; Romany life
Dorothy Kirsten (s) with Russ Cass and his Orch. & Cho.   3 12"—VM-1069

MUSIC OF VICTOR HERBERT   Orchestra

Ah! sweet mystery of life; Sweethearts waltz; March of the toys; Toyland; Streets of New York; Thine alone; Indian Summer; When you're away; Kiss me again; A kiss in the dark; Habañera (from Natoma); Sunset; For I'm Falling in love with someone; 'Neath the southern moon; Italian street song; Gypsy love song; Moonbeams; Gypsy love song; Czardas; Dream Girl
Andre Kostelanetz and his Orch.
                                4 12"—CM-415
Air de Ballet Orchestra
Victor Concert Orch.—Shilkret, on V-12591 in V-C33
Al Fresco . Orchestra
Victor Concert Orch., Shilkret, on V-12591, in V-C33
Badinage ("Sweethearts") Orch.
Victor Concert Orch.—Shilkret, on V-12591, in V-C33

Arr. Soprano & Orchestra (Stothart)
Jeanette MacDonald & Orch.—
Pilzer   10"—V-10-1134
[Naughty Marietta—Italian Street Song]
Fleurette Orchestra
Victor Concert Orch.—Shilkret, on V-9906, in V-C11
Foreign Children Song in English (Stevenson)
Anna Howard (s) & pf. acc.
[in Songs for Children]   12"—V-36032
Indian Summer (An American Idyll) Orch.
Dorothy Kirsten in VM-1069

OPERA In English
NATOMA
Orchestral Selections

Habañera, Vaquero's Song, Natoma Theme, Dagger Dance & Finale
Victor Concert Orch. & Salon Group—Shilkret, on V-9907, in V-C11
Dagger Dance
Boston "Pops" Orch.—Fiedler
                                12"—V-11932
[Tchaikovsky: Sleeping Beauty—Waltz]
Habañera
Andre Kostelanetz & his Orch.
            (in CM-415)   12"—C-7366M
[Sunset]

OPERETTAS In English
(See also above collections)

BABES IN TOYLAND 1903
Selections

Opening & Never mind; Floretta; I can't do that sum; Go to sleep; Hail to Xmas; Song of the poet; March of the Toys; Military Ball; Toyland; He won't be happy till he gets it; Finale
Kenny Baker (t) & Karen Temple (s) with Chorus & Orch.—Alexander Smallens   5 10"—D-DA419
Vocal & Orch. Selections
Victor Salon Group—Shilkret, on V-12592 in V-C33
March of the Toys
André Kostelanetz Orch., C-7364M in CM-415

BABETTE 1903
Vocal & Orch. selections, V-9905 in V-C11

EILEEN 1917
Selections

Overture; Free trade and a Misty moon; Thine alone; When love awakes; Eileen, Alanna Asthore; My little Irish rose; The Irish have a great day tonight; Finale
Frances Greer (s), Jimmie Carroll (t), Earl Wrightson (b) with the Guild Choristers & Orch.—Al Goodman
                                4 10"—V-K2

Vocal & Orch. Selections
in V-C11
Thine Alone
Dorothy Kirsten
            (in V-P133)   10"—V-27967
[Romberg: New Moon—Wanting you]
Igor Gorin (b)   10"—V-10-1201

[Youmans: Through the years]
Charles Kullman (t)   10"—**C-17141D**
[Naughty Marietta—I'm falling in love]

(THE) ENCHANTRESS 1911
Land of my own Romance
Victor Salon Group, on V-9907, in V-C11

(THE) FORTUNE TELLER 1898
Vocal & Orchestral selections, on
V-12590, in V-C33

Gypsy Love Song
Charles Kullman (t)   10"—**C-17135D**
[Penn: Smilin' Through] (C-DB1812)
Andre Kostelanetz & his Orch. in CM-415

Romany Life
Dorothy Kirsten (s)
     (in VM-1069)   12"—**V-11-9270**
[Kiss in the dark]

IT HAPPENED IN NORDLAND 1904
Absinthe Frappé
Victor Salon Group & Orch.—Shilkret,
on V-9907, in V-C11

MLLE. MODISTE 1905
Kiss me again
Dorothy Kirsten (s)
     (in VM-1069)   12"—**V-11-9268**
[Red Mill—Moonbeams]
Lily Pons (s)
     (in CM-606)   12"—**C-71731D**
[Bixio: Tell me that you love me tonight]
DUPLICATIONS: Victor Salon Group &
Orch.—Shilkret, on V-12590, in V-C33;
London Palladium Orch., G-B8189

NAUGHTY MARIETTA 1910
(Also film 1934)
Vocal & Orchestral selections, V-12589
in V-C33

Ah! Sweet Mystery of Life
Nelson Eddy (b)   10"—**V-4281**
['Neath the southern moon]
Charles Kullman (t)   10"—**C-4107M**
[Ravini: Serenade] (C-DB1340)
Jeanette MacDonald (s)   10"—**G-B8320**
[Italian Street song]
Richard Crooks (t)   10"—**V-1343**
[Moya: Song of songs]
Richard Tauber (t)   10"—**P-RO20345**
[Penn: Smilin' Thru]
Dorothy Kirsten (s)
     (in V-P133)   10"—**V-27966**
[Romberg: Maytime—Will you
remember]
Also: Jesse Crawford (organ),
V-22333

—Duet arrangement
Jeanette MacDonald (s) & Nelson
Eddy (b)   10"—**V-4323**
[Friml: Rose Marie—Indian Love Call]
(G-DA1537)

I'm Falling in Love with Someone
Nelson Eddy (b)   10"—**V-4280**
[Tramp, Tramp, Tramp] (G-DA1418)
Richard Crooks (t)   10"—**V-1371**
[Red Mill—Moonbeams] (G-DA1041)

Charles Kullman (t)   10"—**C-P17141D**
[Eileen—Thine Alone]
[Speaks: Road to Mandalay, on
C-DB1842]

Italian Street Song
Jeanette MacDonald (s) 10"—**V-10-1134**
[Sweethearts—Badinage]
[Ah! Sweet mystery, on G-B8320]
DUPLICATION: Jane Powell, C-4458M,
in CX-271

'Neath the Southern Moon
Nelson Eddy (b)   10"—**V-4281**
[Ah! Sweet mystery of life]
(G-DA1418)

Tramp, Tramp, Tramp along the Highway
Nelson Eddy (b)   10"—**V-4280**
[I'm falling in love with someone]
(G-DA1419)

(THE) ONLY GIRL 1914
Vocal & Orchestral selections, on V-9905,
in V-C11

When You're Away
Charles Kullman (t)   10"—**C-P17135D**
[Gypsy Love Song]
[Thine Alone, on C-DB1820]

ORANGE BLOSSOMS
Kiss in the Dark
Dorothy Kirsten (s)
     (in VM-1069)   12"—**V-11-9270**
[Fortune Teller—Romany Life]
Andre Kostelanetz & his Orch., in CM-415

PRINCESS PAT 1915
Vocal & Orchestral selections, on V-9906,
in V-C11

Neapolitan Love Song
Richard Crooks (t)   12"—**V-7745**
[Firestone: In my garden] (G-DB1876)

(THE) RED MILL
Selections—The Isle of Dreams; In Old
New York; When you're pretty; Every
Day is Ladies' Day; Moonbeams; I want
you to marry me; Because you're you;
Wedding Bells (Badinage)
Earl Wrightson (b), Donald Dame (t),
Mary Martha Briney (s), The Mullen
Sisters with Mixed Chorus & Orch.—
Al Goodman   4   10"—**V-K1**

Selections—Moonbeams; When you're pret-
ty; Everyday is Ladies' Day; Streets of
New York; Because you're you; In the
Isle of our dreams
Wilbur Evans (b), Eileen Farrell (ms),
Felix Knight (t) with Chorus & Orch.—
Jay Blackton   3 10"—**D-A411**
Vocal & Orchestral selections, on V-12593
in V-C33

(THE) ROSE OF ALGERIA 1908
Vocal & Orchestral selections, on V-9903,
in V-C11
The Rose of Algeria
James Melton (t)   12"—**V-18466**
[Strauss-Korngold: You haunt my heart]

SWEETHEARTS 1913
See also under Badinage

Selections—Sweethearts; Every lover;
Game of love; Angelus; Jeanette and her
wooden shoes; Pretty as a picture; To
the Land of my own romance; I might
be your once in a while.
Earl Wrightson (b), Frances Greer (s),
Jimmie Carroll (t), Christini Lind (s),
with the Guild Choristers & Orch.—
Al Goodman   4 10″—**V-P174**
Vocal & Orchestral selections, on V-12593,
in V-C33
Sweethearts Waltz
Dorothy Kirsten (s)
            (in V-P133)   10″—**V-27968**
[Romberg: Desert Song—One alone]

Pan-Americana Orchestra
Victor Orch.—Shilkret, on V-9903,
in V-C11
Punchinello Orchestra
Victor Orch.—Shilkret, on V-9904,
in V-C11
Suite—'Cello—4th Mvt. (Serenade) only
Victor Orch.—Shilkret, on V-9907,
in V-C11
Sunset
Andre Kostelanetz Orch., in CM-415
Under the Elms
Yesterthoughts
Victor Orch.—Shilkret, on V-9906,
in V-C11

WALTZES (arrs.)
A Kiss in the Dark; Absinthe Frappé;
Kiss Me Again; Fleurette; Sweethearts;
Love is a Tyrant; I'm Falling in Love
with Someone; When You're Away.
Paul Lavalle Orch.   4 10″—**MC-81**
There are further excerpts listed in cur-
rent catalogues

HERITIER, Jean L' (16th Century)
Beata es, Virgo Maria (Motet in Latin)
(from the "Motets d'Attaignant)
Strasbourg Cathedral Choir—Hoch
                          10″—**OL-23**

HEROLD, Louis, (1791-1833)
*A French opera composer, one of the leading
figures of the opéra-comique school, remembered today by his "Le Pré aux Clercs" and
by the overture to "Zampa."*

OPERAS-COMIQUES In French
(LE) PRE AUX CLERCS 1832
Individual Excerpts
Air de Nicette (unspecified) Soprano
Germaine Corney   10″—**PD-524097**
[Gounod: Mireille—Heureux berger]
Ce soir, j'arrive donc Tenor
M. Villabella   12″—**PAT-PGT6**
[Donizetti: Favorita—Una vergin]
(Les) Rendez-vous de noble compagnie
Charpini & Brancato   10″—**C-DF1392**

ZAMPA 1831
Eng. The Marble Betrothed
Overture Orchestra
N. Y. Philharmonic-Symphony—
Efrem Kurtz   12″—**C-12270D**
Boston "Pops" Orch.—Fiedler
(G-C3283)   12″—**V-13647**
Liverpool Philharmonic Orch.—
Sargent   12″—**C-DX1467**

London Philharmonic—Cameron
                          12″—**D-K1453**
DUPLICATIONS: Vienna Philharmonic
—Krauss, G-S10231; Ruhlmann Orch.,
PAT-X96030

HEUBERGER, Richard (1850-1914)
*German choirmaster, teacher, editor and music
critic who composed music in many forms. He
is known for his biography of Schubert and as
the editor of Cherubini's great work on counterpoint.*

OPERETTAS In German

EINE ENTZUECKEND FRAU
Overture Orchestra
Orch. of the Theaters des Volkes—Curt
Kretzechmar   12″—**C-DWX1621**
[Kunnecke: Coeur As—Overture]

(DER) OPERNBALL 1898
Eng. The Opera Ball
Querschnitt durch die Operetta
Hildegard Erdmann & Walter Ecosy, with
Chorus & Orch.   12″—**G-EH1294**
Overture Orchestra
Berlin Philharmonic—Kleiber
                          12″—**T-SK1195**
Berlin State Opera Orch.—Melichar
                          10″—**PD-47053**
Im Chambre séparée
Friedel Beckmann (c) & Wilhelm
Strienz (bs)   10″—**G-EG7070**
[Suppé: Boccaccio—Hab' ich nur deine
Liebe]
Erna Sack (s) & Max Lichtegg
                          12″—**D-K1578**
[Lehar: Zarewitsch—Hab' nur dich
allein]
DUPLICATIONS: Richard Tauber,
P-RO20175; Fritz Wolf, PD-25105;
R. Glawitsch, T-A10061
—Arr. Orch.
B. Von Geczy and his Orch., G-EG3510
Mitternachtsglocken
Eng. Midnight Bells
—Arr. Violin Kreisler
Fritz Kreisler, with Carl Lamson (pf)
[Kreisler: Old Refrain] 10″—**G-DA1138**
Fritz Kreisler & Victor Symphony—
Voorhees (in VM-1044) 10″—**V-10-1203**
[Kreisler: Rondino on a Theme of
Beethoven]
Also: A. Campoli, D-F5532

HICKS, Peggy Glanville
A contemporary English composer.
Choral Suite
Female Chorus, Oboe & Orch.
                          10″—**OL-100**

HILDACH, Eugen (1849-1924)
*A German baritone and composer of many
songs of the salon type.*

SONGS In German
(Der) Lenz, Op. 19, No. 5 (F. Dahn)
Franz Völker (t)   10″—**PD-21040**
[Strauss: Eine Nacht in Venedig—
Gondellied]

DUPLICATIONS: Karl Schmitt-Walter,
T-A2147; Marcel Wittrisch, G-EG1467;
Leo Slezak, PD-21692

Wo du hingehst, Op. 8
6-Part Chorus or Solo voice with organ
or harp acc.
Gerhard Hüsch (b) & pf. acc.
10"—G-EG6779
[Brahms: Wie bist du, meine Königin]

HIMMEL, Friedrich H. (1765-1814)
*As a composer of choral works, Himmel was a
musician of considerable distinction in his day.*

Gebet während der Schlacht
Baritone & Chorus in German
("Vater, iche rufe Dich") (Körner)
Wilhelm Strienz (bs) with Cho. &
Orch. 10"—G-EG7035
[Niel: Matrosenlied]
DUPLICATION: Wilhelm Rode & Berlin
Opera Cho.—Melichar, PD-25213

HINDEMITH, Paul (1895-   )
*A noted German viola player and one of the
most distinguished of contemporary composers.
A musician of marked intellectual attainments,
possessing a fluent but craftsmanly technique,
Hindemith is one of the outstanding contrapuntists of modern music. He was at one
time the leading proponent of "Gebrauchs-
musik," growing out of a theory that reacted
completely against art for art's sake. Now an
American citizen, he is on the faculty of Yale
University.*

(6) CHANSONS Unacc. Chorus in English
(R. M. Rilke)
The Roe; A Swan; Since all is passing;
Springtime; In Winter; The Orchard
Victor Chorale—Robert Shaw
12"—V-11-8868

Kleine Kammermusik, Op. 24, No. 2
Los Angeles Woodwind Quintet
2 10"—CX-149†

QUARTETS—String
No. 4, Op. 32
Guilet Quartet 6 12"—CH-B2
(Limited Edition)
Scherzo Viola & 'Cello
Paul Hindemith & Emanuel Feuermann
(C-DB1789) 10"—C-DB1305
[Falla: Homage, Albert Harris, guitar]
(in Columbia History of Music, Vol V,
CM-361)
(Der) Schwanendreher (Concerto for
Viola & Small Orchestra) 1935
Paul Hindemith & Arthur Fiedler's
Sinfonietta 3 12"—G-DB6028/30

SONATAS
Op. 25, No. 1, Unacc. Viola 1923
No recording available
Op. 25, No. 2, Viola d'amore & Piano
Milton Thomas & Sara Cominsky
2 12"—ALCO-AC204
Op. 25, No. 3, Unacc. 'Cello 1923
Kurt Reher 12"—ALCO-AR101/2
Violin & Piano, E major 1935
Edgar Ortenberg & Lukas Foss
2 12"—Hargail-MW300
[Foss: Dedication]

Ruggiero Ricci & Louis Persinger
12"—in VOX-603
Unacc. Violin, Op. 31, No. 2
Ruggiero Ricci 12"—in VOX-602

SYMPHONY "Mathis, der Mahler" Orch.
Eng. Matthias the Painter
Berlin Philharmonic—Hindemith
(U-F14386/8†) 3 12"—T-E1647/9
Philadelphia Orch.—Ormandy
3 12"—VM-854†

TRIOS—String Violin, Viola, 'Cello
No. 2 1933
S. Goldberg, P. Hindemith, E. Feuermann
3 12"—CM-209†

HOFHAIMER, Paul (1459-1537)
*A German Renaissance organist and humanist,
court musician of Kaiser Maximilian I.*

Fantasia on "On freudt verzer"
Carl Weinrich (Organ of Westminster
Choir School, Princeton) in MC-9

HOFFDING, Finn (1899-   )
Dialogues for oboe & clarinet Op. 10
Waldemar Wolsing & P. Allin Erichsen
12"—G-DB5274
Purpurprikken (Tom Kristensen)
College Men's Choral Union—Hye-
Knudsen 10"—G-X6689
[Bentzon: Lyse Land]
Det er ganske vist
Eng. It's Perfectly True
Symphonic Fantasy for Orch. after H. C.
Andersen
Tivoli Orch.—Jensen
12"—TONO-X25090

HOLBROOKE, Joseph (1878-   )
*A prolific and somewhat eccentric contemporary
British composer and propagandist. His enormous output is highly uneven and he is probably known best by the operas listed below.*

(THE) CHILDREN OF DON
Overture Orchestra
Symphony Orch.—Arthur Hammond
12"—D-X196
Noden's Song
Norman Walker (bs) 12"—D-X176
[Dylan—Sea King's Song]

DYLAN Opera
Prelude
Symphony Orch.—Raybould
2 12"—D-X194/5
[Symphony No. 3—Finale]
Sea King's Song
Norman Walker (bs) 12"—D-X176
[Children of Don—Noden's Song]

SYMPHONIES
No. 3—Finale (Ships)
Symphony Orch.—Raybould
[Dylan: Prelude, Pt. 3] 12"—D-X195

HOLMBOE, Vagn (1909-   )

One of the outstanding Danish composers, little known outside of his native country. He has written works in most forms—operas, symphonies, concertos, etc.

Music for Wind Instruments 1940
Wind Quintet of 1932: Johann Bentzon (fl); Waldemar Wolsing (ob); P. A. Erichsen (cl); Ingbert Mikkelsen (hn); Kjell Roikjer (bassoon)
2 10"—**G-DA5258/9**

HOLST, Gustave (1878-1934)

An English composer and pianist of Swedish descent, Holst developed several styles and wrote in all forms except chamber music. Many of his important works have now been recorded.

(The) Hymn of Jesus
(Apocryphal Acts of St. John) 1917
Huddersfield Choral Society & Liverpool Philharmonic—Sargent
(Last side blank)
3 12"—**G-C3399/401S†**

Hymn to the Waters (Choral Hymn)
(from the Rig-Veda)
Nottingham Oriana Choir—Roy Henderson, with Dennis Brain & Norman Del Mar (horns) & Gwendolene Mason (harp)
10"—**D-M560**
[Brahms: Whenever the sounding harp is heard]

Mid-Winter 4-Part Carol Unacc.
(Christina Rosetti)
Madrigal Singers—Lehman Engel
10"—**C-321M**
[Carol, arr. Smith: Sing we Noël once more]

(THE) PERFECT FOOL, Op. 39
Opera in English 1923

Ballet Music
Dance of the Spirits of the Earth
Dance of the Spirits of Water
Dance of the Spirits of Fire
London Philharmonic Orch.—Sargent
2 12"—**D-ED31†**
[Wagner: Walküre—Ride of the Valkyries, cond. de Sabata] (D-K1561/2†)

(THE) PLANETS, Op. 32 Orchestra
(Suite of Seven Tone Poems)
Mars, the Bringer of War
Venus, the Bringer of Peace
Mercury, the Winged Messenger
Jupiter, the Bringer of Jollity
Saturn, the Bringer of Old Age
Uranus, the Magician
Neptune, the Mystic (with Women's Chorus)
BBC Symphony Orch.—Boult
(G-DB6227/33S) 7 12"—**GM-387†**
London Symphony Orch. & Chorus—Holst 7 12"—**CM-359†**
[Song without words, No. 2]

—Nos. 1, 2, 3, & 4 only
Toronto Symphony Orch.—MacMillan
4 12"—**VM-929†**
[Elgar: Imperial March, BBC Symphony—Boult]

St. Paul's Suite String Orchestra 1913
Jacques String Orch.—Reginald Jacques 2 10"—**C-DB1793/4**
Boyd Neel String Orch.—Neel
2 10"—**D-F5365/6**

Songs Without Words, Op. 22

No. 2, Marching Song
London Symphony Orch.—Holst
(in CM-359†) 12"—**C-69526D**
[Planets—Mercury]

This Have I Done for My True Love
Fleet Street Choir—T. B. Lawrence
12"—**D-K1089**
[Britten: Hymn to St. Cecilia, Op. 27, Pt. 3]
BBC Chorus—Woodgate 12"—**D-K841**
[Wassail Song]

Wassail Song
BBC Chorus—L. Woodgate 12"—**D-K841**
[This Have I done for my true love]

Folksong Arrangement I Love my Love
Fleet Street Choir—T. B. Lawrence
12"—**D-K1021**
[Stanford: The Blue Bird]

HONEGGER, Arthur (1892-   )

A composer of Swiss parentage, one of the famous French "Six," Honegger is perhaps one of the outstanding contemporary masters of choral music. Recently he has written effective orchestral scores for films.

CONCERTO—'Cello & Orchestra

—Andante only
Maurice Maréchal & Paris Conservatory Orch.—Honegger 2 12"—**C-LFX676/7**

(LA) DANSE DES MORTS (Paul Claudel)
Eng. The Dance of Death

Dialogue; Danse des Morts; Lamento; Sanglots; La Réponse de Dieu; Espérance dans la Croix; Affirmation
Charles Panzéra (b), Mme. Turba-Rabier (s), Eliette Schennenberg (c), Jean-Louis Barrault (recitant), Chorale Yvonne Gouverné, Paris Conservatory Orch.—Charles Münch
3 12"—**G-DB5135/7**

JEANNE d'ARC AU BUCHER Oratorio
(Paul Claudel)
Eng. Joan of Arc at the Stake
Soloists, Antwerp Coecilia Cho., Cureghem Children's Choir, Belgian National Orch. (Brussels Philharmonic Society Orch.)—Louis de Vocht
9 12"—**G-W1546/54**

Jeunesse (P. Vaillant-Couturier)
Chorale de la Jeunesse & Orch.—Désormière 10"—**CdM-501**
[Auric: Chantons jeunes filles]

JUDITH 3 Act Opera in French 1925
Vocal & Orchestral Excerpts
Act. I: Cantique funèbre, Invocation
Act II: Fanfare (Prélude to Act II), Incantation

Act III: Interlude, Cantique des Vièrges, Cantique de la victoire
Claire Croiza (s), J. van Hertbruggen (s), Coecilia Chorus & Antwerp Orch.—
L. de Vocht 2 12"—C-D15240/1
Pacific 231—Symphonic Movement Orch.
Symphony Orch.—Honegger
12"—O-170111
Symphony Orch.—Coppola
(G-AW286) 12"—G-W870
Pastorale d'Eté Orchestra 1920
Orch. de la Suisse Romande—
Ansermet 12"—O-8788
Petite Suite en trois parties
L'Homme (sax), Manuel (pf), M. & L. Moyse (fl), Locatelli (vl), Hamélin (cl)
10"—CdM-519
Prelude, Arioso & Larghetto on the Name of BACH String Orchestra
Zürich Collegium Musicum—Paul Sacher 12"—C-LZX10

(LE) ROI DAVID Symphonic Psalm in French 1921 Eng. **King David**
Individual Excerpts
No. 5, Le Cortège
No. 8, Psaume—Ah, si j'avais des ailes
No. 23, Marche des Hébreux
No. 24, Psaume—Je t'aimerai, Seigneur
No. 26, Psaume—Loué soit le Seigneur
Swiss Romand Chorus & Orch.—
E. Ansermet 12"—C-8865
Sonata Clarinet & Piano
Louis Cahuzac & Folmer Jensen
In prep. Danish Col.

SONGS In French
Amour
Madeleine Martinetti (s) & Orch.—
Honegger 10"—C-LF237
[Flavio]
(4) Chansons pour voix grave
—Poème de Verlaine; Poème de William Aguet
Madeleine Martinetti & Orch.—Honegger
12"—C-LFX741
[Psaume 130—Mimaamaquin]
Le Grand Etang Chanson du XIV Siècle (Jean Tranchant)
Marianne Oswald (s) 10"—C-DF1114
[Weill: Surabaya-Johnny]
De l'Atlantique au Pacifique (J. Fetine)
Mme. Damia, with Chorus & Orch.—
Chagnon 10"—C-DF2287
[Pingault: Johnny Palmer]
Flavio—Air de Guido
Madeleine Martinetti (s) & Orch.—
Honegger 10"—C-LF237
[Amour]
Psaume 130—Mimaamaquin
Madeleine Martinetti (s) & Orch.—
Honegger 12"—C-LFX741
[Chansons pour voix grave]
(3) Psalms
(2) Chansons by Verlaine & Ronsard
Eliette Schennenberg (c) & A. Honnegger (pf) 12"—C-LFX690
(3) Poèmes de Claudel
Sieste; Le delphinium; Le rendez-vous
Elsa Scherz-Meister (s) & K. Rothenbühler (pf) 12"—G-DB10085

Saluste du Bartas
Le château du Bartas; Tout le long de la Baïse; Le départ; La promenade; Néras en fête; Duo
fête; Duo
Elsa Scherz-Meister (s) & K. Rothenbühler (pf) 12"—G-DB10086
SYMPHONIES
No. 1, String Orchestra
Paris Conservatory Orch.—Münch
3 12"—G-W1600/2
Toccata & Variations Piano
Jacqueline Potier 2 10"—PAT-PD52/3
ARRANGEMENTS
French Folksong Settings
(Harmonization & arrangement)
(La) Femme du Marin (Aunis)
Yvonne Gouverné Chorus & Orch.—
Désormière 10"—CdM-513
[Arr. Delannoy: Le Condamné à mort (Angoumois)]
(Les) Trois princesses au pommier doux (Franche—Comte)
Yvonne Gouverné Chorus & Orch.—
Désormière 10"—CdM-520
[Arr. Koechlin: Les Trente voleurs de Bazoges]

HOOK, James (1746-1827)
Bright Phoebus
Marian Anderson (c) & Fr. Rupp (pf)
10"—V-10-1300
[Thomas: O Men from the Fields]
Doun the Burn
Marjorie Lawrence (s) & F. Wolfes (pf)
[Lemon: My ain Folk] 10"—V-2147

HORNEMANN, Johan Ole Emil (1809-1870)
A Danish composer of vocal music.
Kongernes Konge
Lauritz Melchoir (t) & Orch.—Hye-Knudsen (in VM-851) 10"—V-2193
[Kroyer: Der er et yndigt Land] (G-DA5213)
DUPLICATIONS: Students Cho., G-X6899; Chr. Anthonsen, O-D175
Vort Hjem du danske Jord
Students Cho., G-X6900

HOVHANESS, Alan (1911-   )
A contemporary American composer of Scottish and Armenian parentage.
Invocations to Vahäkn IV & V
1 pf w. Chinese gong & drums
Maro Ajemian (pf) w. Alan Hovhaness (Chinese gong & drums)
2 12"—DISC-875
[Cage: Amores I & IV]
Mihr (2 pfs)
Maro Ajemian & Alan Hovhaness (in DISC-875)
Lousadzak (The Coming of Light)
(Concerto No. 1 for Piano and String Orchestra imitating the Tar, Kanoon, Oud and Saz)
Maro Ajemian & Orch.—Hovhaness
Tzaikerk (Evening Song)
Anahid Ajemian (vl), Philip Kaplan (fl), & Orch.—Hovhaness
3 12"—DISC-876

HOWELLS, Herbert (1892-   )
Elégie for Viola, String Quartet, &
String Orch.
Max Gilbert & the Boyd Neel String
Orch.—B. Neel   2 12″—D-M484/5
[Liadov: Fugue]
(A) Spotless Rose   Unacc. Cho. in Eng.
(A setting of a 14th Cent. Anthem)
St. Martins Cho., D-F2643

HSIAO-SHUSIEN
Chinese Dream Pictures
Ger. Chinesische Traumbilder
Winterthur Municipal Orch.—
Scherchen   2 12″—G-DB6088/9

HUBAY, Jenö (1858-1937)
A prominent Hungarian violinist, conductor
and teacher (of Szigeti and others), Hubay
wrote many scores for the violin, some of them
inspired by nationalistic and folk tendencies.

Hejre Kati
See: Hungarian Czardas Scenes No. 4

HUNGARIAN CZARDAS SCENES
Violin & Orchestra (or Piano)
No. 2, Op. 13
Emil Telmanyi & Budapest Municipal
Orch.—Fricsay   RAD-SP8028
No. 3 (Hungarian Rhapsody) Op. 18
Joseph Szigeti & Andor Földes
(in CM-513)   10″—C-17339D
No. 4 (Hejre Kati) Op. 32
Mischa Elman & Leopold Mittman
12″—V-11-9423
[Balakirev: Oh! Come to Me]
Emil Telmanyi & his Chamber Orch.
10″—TONO-L28014
Bernard Lessman & German Opera House
Orch. of Berlin—Lutze
10″—T-A10469
DUPLICATIONS: Ilja Livschakoff &
Orch., PD-10326: PD-47076; Alfredo
Campoli, D-F5532
No. 5 (Hullámazo Balaton) Op. 33
Hugo Kolberg & Wladiseroff (pf)
[Mozart: Minuet in D]   10″—PD-24307
DUPLICATION: V. von Géczy Orch.,
G-EG3294

SONGS (Unidentified)
Piroska Anday, RAD-RZ3012

(THE) VIOLIN-MAKER OF CREMONA
Opera 1893
Fr. Le Luthier de Crémone
Ger. Der Geigenmacher von Cremona
Intermezzo Violin & Piano
(This popular violin piece is almost always
given under the title of "The Violin-Maker of
Cremona" only.)
Francesca Asti & pf. acc.   10″—G-X3456
[Drigo: Serenade]
(The) Zephyr, Op. 30, No. 5 Violin & Piano
Joseph Szigeti & pf. acc.
12″—C-GQX10344
[Kreisler: Sicilienne et Rigaudon]
Jan Kubélik & A. Holeček
10″—U-C11384
[Kubélik: Canzonetta]

DUPLICATIONS: Feraresi, G-GW2015;
David Oistrakh, USSR-10499/500;
Tibor Varga, RAD-RBM159

HUBEAU, Jean (1918-   )
A contemporary French composer.
Concerto, C major Violin & Orchestra
Henri Merckel & Lamoureux Orch.—
Bigot   3 12″—G-W1503/5

HUE, Georges (1858-   )
A conservative French composer who succeeded
Saint-Saëns in the French Académie des Beaux-
Arts.
SONGS In French
A des Oiseaux
Lily Pons (s) & Frank LaForge (pf)
(in VM-599)   10″—V-1918
[Liadov: Une Tabatière & Liszt: Com-
ment disaient-ils?]
(L') Ane blanc
(Klingsor: Croquis d'Orient)
Jean Planel (t)   10″—PAT-PG15
[Sonnez les matines]
DUPLICATION: Germaine Cernay,
O-188765
Sonnez les matines
Jean Planel (t)   10″—PAT-PG15
[L'Ane blanc]

HUGHES, Herbert (1882-1937)
An Irish composer, organist and music critic
who specialized in folklore music and whose
arrangements of many songs are part of his
collection of Irish melodies adapted for concert
use.

ARRANGEMENTS Folk Songs
(A) Ballynure Ballad
James Melton (t) & Robert Hill (pf)
(in VM-947)   10″—V-10-1052
[Lover: Low Backed Car; Lohr: Little
Irish Girl; Kitty me love, will you marry
me?]
By the old Turf Fire
Christopher Lynch (t)   10″—V-10-1316
[Westendorf: I'll Take You Home Again,
Kathleen]
I Have a Bonnet Trimmed with Blue
I Know Where I'm Going
I Will Walk with My Love
(The) Next Market Day
Barbara Mullen (s) & Gerald
Moore (pf)   10″—G-B9132
Open the Door Softly
Christopher Lynch (t) & Gerald
Moore (pf)   10″—G-DA1859
[Kearney: Down by the Glenside]
Barbara Mullen (s) & Gerald
Moore (pf)   10″—G-B9148
[The Little Boats; & French, arr. Col-
lisson: Eileen Oge]
(The) Little Boats
Barbara Mullen (s) & Gerald
Moore (pf)   10″—G-B9148
[Open the door Softly: & French, arr.
Collisson: Eileen Oge]
She Moved Through the Fair
James Melton (t) with Orch.—Broekman
(in VM-1090) 12″—V-11-9400
[Rowe-MacMurrough: Macushla]

HUMMEL, Johann (1778-1837)

One of the outstanding pianists of the nine-teenth century, Hummel was a pupil of Mozart and Clementi. He devised and published the first useful system of piano fingering, although among his many compositions for the piano he is remembered only for a few short pieces such as the one listed below.

Rondo, E flat major, Op. 11
("Rondo favori") Piano
Lubka Kolessa 12"—G-DB5510
[Beethoven: Piano Concerto No. 3, Pt. 9]
—Arr. Violin & Piano Heifetz
Jascha Heifetz & Arpad Sandor
 12"—V-8420
[Schubert: Impromptu, G major, Op. 90, No. 3]
[Wieniawski: Concerto No. 2, Pt. 5, on G-DB2449]

HUMPERDINCK, Engelbert (1854-1921)

A disciple and friend of Wagner, whose fame rests almost entirely upon his opera "Hänsel and Gretel." Humperdinck wrote many other works, but nothing ever captured the world's imagination as this charming tonal expression of the purest German sentiment.

OPERAS In German

HAENSEL UND GRETEL 3 Acts 1893
Complete recording Sung in English
Soloists, Metropolitan Opera House
Chorus & Orchestra
Max Rudolf 12 12"—C-OP26†
The Cast:
Hänsel .... Risë Stevens (ms)
Gretel .... Nadine Conner (s)
Witch & Sandman .. Thelma Votipka (s)
Peter (Father) .... John Brownlee (b)
Gertrude (Mother) Claramae Turner (c)
Dewman .... Lillian Raymondi (s)

Abridged Recording sung in German
(Arr. Weigert & Maeder) ..
Soloists, Berlin State Opera Chorus &
Orch.—H. Weigert 4 12"—PD-27391/4
The Cast:
Hänsel .... Else Ruziczka (s)
Gretel .... Tilly de Garmo (s)
Witch ...... Marie Schulz-Dornburg (s)
Peter (Father) .... Eduard Kandl (bs)
Gertrude (Mother) Claramae Turner (c)
Sandman & Dewman
 Margarete Wagenar (s)

Musical-Dramatic Adaptation
In English (Ralph Rose)
Basil Rathbone & Jane Powell, with sup-
porting cast and Orch.—Carmen
Dragon 4 12"—CM-632†

Vocal & Orchestral Selections
Junior Programs Opera Company,
In English, directed by Saul Lancourt,
with Soloists, Chorus & Victor Orch.—
N. Shilkret 4 10"—V-P38
Die Duoptisten & Berlin State Opera
Orch.—C. Schmalstich
 3 10"—G-EG1611/3
A. Frind (s), E. Ruziczka (s), E. Fuchs
(b), with Chorus & Berlin Philharmonic
—Reuss 12"—T-E1508

H. Erdmann, Rut Berglund, Eva Marie
Siefert & W. Strienz, with Orch.
(G-HEX4) 12"—G-EH1304
Orchestral Suites
CBS Symphony—Barlow
 3 10"—CM-424†
Victor Orch.—B. Reibold
 2 10"—V-22175/6
Prelude (Overture) Orchestra
BBC Symphony—Boult
(G-DB1758) 12"—V-11929
Saxon State Orch.—Böhm
 12"—G-DB4648
Hallé Orch.—Barbirolli
 12"—G-C3623
Orch. of the Suisse Romande—Blech
 12"—(In Prep. Eng. Decca)
DUPLICATIONS: German Opera House
Orch.—Schmidt-Isserstedt, T-E3112;
Philharmonic-Symphony Orch. of New
York—Mengelberg, G-AW242; London
Symphony Orch.—Raybould, D-K1315

Individual Excerpts

ACT I
Suse, liebe Suse Duo
Brüderchen, komm tanz' mit mir Duo
(Included in orchestral suites above)
Elisabeth Schwartzkopf & Irmgaard
Seefried w. Philharmonia Orch.—
Krips 2 12"—C-LX1036/7
[Der kleine Sandmann & Abendsegen]
—Suse, liebe Suse only
2 Trebles of Regensburg Cath. Cho.—
Schrems 10"—G-EG2899
[Abensegen]
Besenbinderlied: Ach, wir armen, armen Leute
Eine Hex, steinalt, haust tief im Wald
Baritone (Peter)
Eng. Broom-Maker's Song & A Witch
Dwells in the Wood
Gerhard Hüsch, with Anon. soprano &
Orch.—Müller 12"—G-EH1024
[Königskinder: Verdorben-gestorben]

ACT II
Prelude (Hexenritt) Orchestra
Eng. Witch's Ride
(Included in orchestral suites)
(Ein) Männlein steht im Walde
Soprano (Gretel)
Eng. Folk Song—A Little Man Stands in the Wood
(Included in orchestral suites)
Elisabeth Schumann (s) & E. Lush (pf)
(G-DA1439) 10"—V-1948
[Der kleine Sandman bin ich &
Abendsegen]
(Der) Kleine Sandmann bin ich
Soprano (Sandman)
Abendsegen: Abends, will ich schlafen geh'n Duo
Eng. Sandman's Song & Evening Prayer
Elisabeth Schumann (s) & E. Lush (pf)
(G-DA1439) 10"—V-1948
[Ein Männlein steht]
(A trick recording in which Miss Schumann sings both parts of the Duet)

Elisabeth Schwartzkopf & Irmgaard
Seefried with Philharmonia Orch.—
Krips 12"—C-LX1037
[Duet, Act I]

Abendsegen (Evening Prayer) only
2 Solo Trebles of Regensburg Cathedral
Choir—Schrems 10"—G-EG2899
[Suse, liebe Suse]

—Arr. Chamber Orch: in C-J17

Dream Pantomime Orchestra
(Ballet of Angels)
National Symphony Orch.—Kindler
12"—V-11-8948

ACT III
Prelude (Das Knusperhäuschen) Orchestra
Eng. The Witch's House
(Included in orchestral suites)

Mir träumte, ich hört' ein Rauschen Duo
2 Solo Trebles of Regensburg Cathedral
Choir—Schrems 10"—T-A1507
[Mozart: Wiegenlied]

Hexenlied: Hurr, hopp, hopp, hopp
Soprano (Witch)

**Knusperwalzer: Juchhei! nun ist die
Hexe Todt** Duo
Eng. Witch's Song & Gingerbread Waltz
(Included in Telefunken Medley above)

Finale: Erlöst, befreit, für alle Zeit
Ensemble
(Included in Medleys and Suites above)

(DIE) KOENIGSKINDER 1910
Verdorben—Gestorben
Eng. Spielmann's Air Baritone
Gerhard Hüsch 12"—G-EH1024
[Hänsel und Gretel—Ach, wir armen]

SONGS In German
Am Rhein
Heinrich Schlusnus (b) & Franz
Rupp (pf) 10"—PD-62801
[Schumann: Wanderlied]
DUPLICATION: F. Völker, PD-19729

Weihnachten Eng. Christmas
Ernestine Schumann-Heink (a)
[Grüber: Stille Nacht] 12"—V-6723

HUSEN, (Graf) Friedrich von (d.c. 1196)
A German Minnesinger of the 12th century.

Minnelied In Mediaeval German
("Deich von der guoten schiet")
Eng. Because I left the good woman
Hans Joachim Moser (b) unacc.
10"—P-R1018
(Troubadour Songs & Minnesongs)
(in 2000 Years of Music Set)

IBERT, Jacques (1890-   )
*A skillful contemporary French composer, who
followed the impressionist school of Debussy
and Ravel and created unique and colorful
compositions striking an unmistakable note of
his own.*

Andantino et Allegro Marziale
Oboe, Clarinet, Bassoon
Trio d'Anches de Paris 12"—PAT-PG90
[Milhaud: Pastorale]

Aria 'Cello & Piano
G. Marchesini & M. Monard
['Cello Concerto, Pt. 3] 12"—G-DB11141

Berceuse du petit Zébu
Quatuor Vocal Féminin Seupel
10"—LUM-33140
[Tiersot: Berceuse provençale]

Concerto—'Cello & Wind Instruments
G. Marchesini & Wind Instrument
Society of Paris—Oubradous
2 12"—G-DB11140/1
[Aria for Vlc. & pf.]

Concerto—Flute & Orchestra
Marcel Moyse & Orch.—Bigot
2 12"—G-L1013/4

Concerto da Camera—Saxophone & Orch.
Marcel Mule & Orch.—Gaubert
(G-DB5062/3) 2 12"—VM-588
[Vellones: Rhapsody for Alto Saxophone]

Divertissement Chamber Orchestra
*(Suite from the musical comedy "Le Chapeau
de paille d'Italie")*
Cortège; Nocturne: Valse; Parade &
Finale
Boston "Pops" Orch.—Fiedler
2 12"—VM-1199†
Chamber Orch.—Ibert
2 10"—G-K7573/4

Entr'acte
Marcel Moyse (fl) & Jean Lafon
(guitar) 10"—CdM-518
[Sauveplane: Habañera, with Charmy
& Manuel]

Escales (Ports of Call) Orchestral Suite
Rome-Palermo; Tunis-Nefta; Valencia
San Francisco Symphony—Monteux
2 12"—VM-1173†
(Also on vinylite, V-V10†)
Philharmonic-Symphony of N. Y.—
Rodzinski 2 12"—CX-263†
Straram Orch.—Walter Straram
2 12"—C-LFX17/18

HISTOIRES 10 Pieces for Piano
No. 2, Le petit âne blanc only
Eng. Little White Donkey
Emma Boynet 10"—G-DA1501
[Le Marchand d'eau]

—Arr. Violin & Piano
Ida Haendel & Adela Kotowska
10"—D-M603
[Falla-Szigeti: Three Cornered Hat—
Miller's Dance]

No. 9, Le Marchand d'eau fraîche
Emma Boynet 10"—G-DA1501
[Le Petit âne blanc]

Piece pour flûte seule Unacc. Flute
Marcel Moyse 10"—C-DF1801
[Bach: Unacc. Flute Sonata, A minor—
Sarabande]

(3) Pièces brèves
Flute, Oboe, Clarinet, Bassoon, Horn
Garde Républicaine Quintet
12"—PAT-PAT11

Pièces en Trio Oboe, Clarinet, Bassoon
Trio d'Anches de Paris 12"—OL-5

ILLIASHENKO
Trois complaints russes
Maurice Maréchal (vlc) & H. Roget (pf)
10"—C-LF244

INDIA, Sigismondo d' (Early 17th Century)
See: Sigismondo

INDY, Vincent d' (1851-1931)
A pupil of César Franck and teacher of many of the younger French musicians, D'Indy was noted as an educator and critic. As a composer, his work is marked by considerable austerity, but also by great sincerity, strength, and skillful craftsmanship.

A la pêche des moules, Op. 3, No. 100
Chant populaire français
Manécanterie des Petits Chanteurs à la Croix de Bois, Unacc.   10"—**G-K8072**
[Perissas: Sur le pont d'Avignon—Variations]

En passant par la Lorraine
Manécanterie des Petits Chanteurs à la Croix de Bois, Unacc.   10"—**G-K8429**
[Renard: L'Enfant dormira bientôt]

FERVAAL, Op. 40 Opera in 3 Acts 1897
Introduction to Act I   Orchestra
San Francisco Orch.—Monteux
    (in VM-1113†)   12"—**V-11-9509**
[Istar, Pt. 3]
Paris Conservatory Orch.—Münch
                                  12"—**D-K1718**
[Mendelssohn: Symphony No. 5, Pt. 7]
Lamoureux Orch.—Wolff
                                  12"—**PD-67003**
[Franck: Le Chasseur maudit, Pt. 3]
(PD-566048)

Gentil Coqu'licot (Arranged)
Manécanterie des Petits Chanteurs à la Croix de Bois   10"—**G-K7708**
[Perissas: Il était un petit navire]

Istar, Op. 42 Symphonic Variations Orch.
San Francisco Symphony—Monteux
    2 12"—**VM-1113†**
[Ferval, Introduction to Act I]

QUARTETS—String
No. 2, E major, Op. 45
Gabriel Bouillon Quartet
    4 12"—**G-W1537/40**
(Le) Roi Loys unacc. Chorus in French
Manécanterie des Petits Chanteurs à la Croix de Bois   10"—**G-K7432**
[Trad: Harm. Marc de Ranse: Trois jeun' Tambours]

Sonata, C major, Op. 59
Violin & Piano   (1903/4)
Charles Bistesi & Mlle Andrée Vidal
    4 12"—**G-L1069/72**

SYMPHONIES
No. 1, G major, Op. 25 (Symphony on a French Mountain Air) Orch. & Piano
(Symphonie sur un chant montagnard français)
Maxim Shapiro & San Francisco Symphony—Monteux   3 12"—**VM-913†**
Marguerite Long & Colonne Orch.—
Paray (C-LFX352/4) 3   12"—**CM-211†**
Jeanne-Marie Darré & Lamoureux Orch.
Wolff   3 12"—**PD-566130/2**
(PD-67037/9)

No. 2, B flat major, Op. 57
San Francisco Symphony—Monteux
    5 12"—**VM-943†**

(Le) Vingt-Cinq d'Août (Unacc. Setting of an Old French Sea Song)
Manécanterie des Petits Chanteurs à la Croix de Bois   10"—**G-K7514**
[Trad: Tengo de subir al Puerto]

INGEGNERI, Marc Antonio (1545-1592)
An Italian Choirmaster, teacher of Monteverdi, and composer of church music. The selection below is often attributed to Palestrina.

Tenebrae factae sunt   Motet in Latin
Strasbourg Cathedral Choir—Hoch
                                  12"—**C-RFX56**
[Viadana: O Sacrum convivum;
Palestrina: O bone Jesu]

INGHELBRECHT, Désiré (1880-   )
A French conductor, noted for his sympathetic playing of Debussy and Ravel, and whose own compositions display a rich satirical humor. His "Nursery Suites" are charming modern harmonizations of French folk melodies.

(4) Fanfares   Brass
Pour une fête—Pour le Président—Funèbre (pour des mineurs ensevelis)—Dédicatoire
National Orch. Brass Choir—
Inghelbrecht   10"—**PAT-PG58**

(La) Légende du Grand Saint-Nicolas
(Vocal Duo with Orch. in French)
Jany Delille, René Barral & Debussy Festival Orch.—Inghelbrecht
                                  10"—**PAT-PD1**

(La) Nursery   Suites on French Nursery Songs   Orchestra
Set 3 (Dernières Nurseries)
Pasadeloup Orch.—Inghelbrecht
                                  12"—**PAT-PDT7**

IPPOLITOV-IVANOV, Michael (1859-1935)
A Russian music professor, pupil of Rimsky-Korsakov and an authority on Caucasian (particularly Georgian) folk music. He is best known by the "Caucasian Sketches" listed below.

Bless the Lord, O My Soul
Unacc. Chorus in Russian
De Paur's Infantry Chorus (in Eng.)
in **CM-709**

CAUCASIAN SKETCHES, Op. 10 Orchestra
1. In a Mountain Pass   2. In the Village
3. In the Mosque   4. Procession of the Sardar (or, March of the Caucasian Chief)
Boston "Pops" Orch.—Fiedler
    3 12"—**VM-797†**
[Rimsky-Korsakoff: Le Coq d'or—Bridal Procession]
Berlin Philharmonic Orch.—Melichar
    3 10"—**PD-24802/3 & PD-25027**
[Rimsky-Korsakoff: Czar Saltan—Flight of the Bumblebee]

No. 1 (In a Mountain Pass) only
Boston "Pops" Orch.—Fiedler
12"—**V-12460**
(Also on V-11-8507 in VM-797)
Berlin Philharmonic—Hans Bund
[No. 2 & No. 4] 12"—**T-E1605**

No. 2 (In the Village) only
Boston "Pops" Orch.—Fiedler
[No. 4] (G-EH1023) 12"—**V-11883**
(Also on V-11-8508 in VM-797)
Philadelphia Orch.—Stokowski
12"—**V-6514**
[Borodin: Prince Igor—Polovtsian
Dances]
Berlin Philharmonic—Hans Bund
[No. 1 & No. 4] 12"—**T-E1605**
N. Y. Philharmonic Symphony Orch.—
Stokowski 12"—in **CM-729**†
[Khachaturian: Masquerade Suite]

No. 3 (In the Mosque) only
Boston "Pops" Orch.—Fiedler,
V-11-8508 in VM-797
Berlin Philharmonic Orch.—
Melichar 10"—**PD-24803**

No. 4 (Procession of the Sardar) only
Boston "Pops" Orch.—Fiedler
[No. 2] 12"—**V-11883**
[Also on V-11-8509 in VM-797†, with
Rimsky-Korsakoff: Coq d'or-Procession]
[Verdi: Aida—March on G-C2849;
G-EH1023]
Chicago Symphony—Stock
12"—**C-11738D**
[Paganini: Moto perpetuo, Op. 11]
DUPLICATIONS: CBS Orch.—Barlow,
C-71464D; Philadelphia Orch.— Stokow-
ski, V-1335: G-E521: G-AV10; Berlin
Philharmonic—Hans Bund, T-E1605

Quartet—String, A minor, Op. 13
—Humoresca (Intermezzo) only
Poltronieri Quartet 12"—**C-GQX10045**

IRELAND, John, (1879-   )
*Even though he is best known by his songs and
smaller works, this British composer of good
craftsmanship and taste has written successful
orchestral scores and music for several motion
pictures.*

Concerto, E flat major Piano & Orchestra
Eileen Joyce & Hallé Orch.—Heward
3 12"—**C-DX1072/4**†

Concertino Pastorale
Boyd Neel Orch.—Neel
3 12"—**D-X253/55**
[Downland Suite—Minuet]

(A) Downland Suite Band
—Minuet only Arr. Orchestra
Boyd Neel Orch.—Neel 12"—**D-X255**
[Concertino Pastorale, Pt. 5]

(The) Holy Boy (Nativity Carol)
Piano Prélude 1917 (1 of 4 Préludes)
—Arr. 'Cello & Piano
Florence Hooton & Rose Pratt
12"—**D-K900**
[Phantasie Trio, A minor, Pt. 3]
—Arr. String Orchestra
Boyd Neel String Orch.—Neel
[Bach: Air, D major] 10"—**D-M595**

(A) London Overture 1936
Liverpool Philharmonic—Sargent
2 12"—**C-DX1155/6**
[Strauss: Radetzky March]

(The) Overlanders Music for the Film
(Arr. Ernest Irving)
London Symphony—Muir Mathieson
12"—**D-K1602**

SONATAS Violin & Piano
No. 1, D major
Frederick Grinke & John Ireland
4 12"—**D-K1400/3**†

SONGS
Sea Fever (Masefield)
Paul Robeson (bs) & pf. acc.
[Metcalf: Absent] 10"—**G-B9257**
DUPLICATIONS: Roy Henderson,
D-M526; Robert Irwin, G-B9073

The Soldier (Brooke)
Roy Henderson (b) & Ivor Newton (pf)
[Sea Fever] 10"—**D-M526**

Phantasie Trio, A minor (One movement)
Grinke Trio 12"—**D-K899/900**
[Holy Boy, Florence Hooton, vlc.]

Trio No. 3, E major
Grinke Trio 3 12"—**D-X242/4**

ISAAC, Heinrich (c.1450-1517)
*One of the earliest important German com-
posers, a friend of Lorenzo de' Medici, Isaac
adapted Flemish polyphony to a new German
idiom.*

"Hélas que deuera mon couer"
3 Mediaeval Viols
(in Vol. V) 12"—**AS-43**
[Dufay: Rondeau "Adieu m'amour"]

(Der) Hundt
Fiedel Trio 10"—**PD-10750**
[Torre: Spanischer Tanz; Lechner;
Provencalischer Tanz]

Innsbruck, ich muss dich lassen
(Isaac's setting of a folk tune for 4-Part Unacc.
Chorus)
Berliner Lehrergesangverein—Rüdel
12"—**PD-19882**
[Folksong, arr. Marschner: Trennung]
DUPLICATION: Dresdner Kreutschor—
Mauersberger, G-EG3568

Nun ruht die Welt
Ingelbrecht Church Choir—Ahlén
12"—**Swed. Radiotjanst-RA103**
[Söderman: Osanna]

Zwischen Berg 4-Part in German
(Tenor, Flute, Trombone & Viol)
Max Meili (t) with Ensemble—Curt
Sachs (in Vol. I) 12"—**AS-3**
[Franco-Flemish Chansons of the 15th
Century]

IVES, Charles (1874-   )
*Once thought the work of a complete eccentric,
Ives' music anticipated a great many modern
composers. Largely self-taught, he is one of the
most original and characteristically "American"
composers. There is music of great worth im-
bedded in his scores and Ives, whose technique*

and idiom spring from purely Yankee roots, has taken advantage of New England village bands, country dances and congregational singing.

Housatonic   Orchestra
Janssen Symphony of Los Angeles—
Janssen   **in ART-JS13**

QUARTETS—String
No. 2
Walden Quartet   **DISC-775**

SONATAS   Violin & Piano
No. 2
—2nd (In the Barn) & 3rd (The Revival) mvts. only
Sol Babitz & Ingolf Dahl
                    12″—ALCO-AR101/2

JACOPO DA BOLOGNA (14th Century)
A 14th century Italian composer of madrigals and other vocal works.

MADRIGALS
Fenice fu
E. Jacquier (t) & H. Guermant (s),
with Lute & Alto Viol acc.
           (in Vol. VI)   **12″—AS-59**
[The Chanson in the 14th Century, with examples from Ghirardellus, Molins]
Non al suo Amante
J. Archimbaud (treble) & R. Bonté (t)
w. trombone   **12″—OL-1**
[Matheus de Perusio: Gloria in Excelsis]

MOTETS
Lux purpurata radiis & Diligite justitiam
J. Archimbaud (treble) & R. Bonté
(t), w. trombone & viol   **12″—OL-2**
[Anon: 14th Century motets]

JACQUET, DE LA GUERRE, Elisabeth (c.1666-1729)
A French harpsichordist of the "Grand Siècle."
Allemande
Marcelle de Lacour (harpsichord)
[Gigue]   **10″—OL-75**
Gigue
Marcelle de Lacour (harpsichord)
[Allemande]   **10″—OL-75**
Sarabandes in D major & G major
Marcelle de Lacour (harpsichord)
                            10″—OL-13
Sarabande & Rondo
Pauline Aubert (harpsichord)
                         12″—PAT-PAT50
[Duphly: Les Colombes]

JAERNEFELT, Armas (1869-   )
A Finnish conductor, related to Sibelius by marriage, known internationally by smaller orchestral pieces, even though he has composed in all forms.

Ajan aalot   Chorus in Finnish
Eng. Waves of the Time
Chorus—H. Klemetti   **10″—G-X3139**
[Klemetti: Sinikellot; Finnish Folksong, arr. Madetoja; Läskin minä Kesäyonä Käymään]

Berceuse   Orchestra   Fin. Kehtolaulu
National Symphony—Kindler
[Praeludium]   **10″—V-10-1245**
Symphony Orch.—Barbirolli
[Praeludium]   **10″—G-B8112**
DUPLICATIONS: Symphony Orch.—
Järnefelt, O-D4714; Marek Weber Orch., G-EG1155
Also: Lessman (vl) & Orch., T-A10177;
H. Fritz-Crone (vl), G-X2278; Von Géczy, G-EG6326; V. Sola (t, in Finnish), G-X2370

Preludio funebre   Orchestra
Berlin State Opera—Järnefelt
(O-D6055)   **12″—P-E11147**
[Handel: Largo]
Praeludium   Orchestra
National Symphony Orch.—Kindler
[Berceuse]   **10″—V-10-1245**
Cleveland Symphony Orch.—Rodzinski
      (in CM-514†)   **12″—C-11835D**
[Sibelius: Symphony No. 5, Pt. 7]
Symphony Orch.—Barbirolli
[Berceuse]   **10″—G-B8112**
National Symphony—Victor Olof
                     12″—D-K1149
[Sibelius: Valse Triste]
La Scala Orch.—Ghione   **10″—G-HN795**
[Cilea: Adriana Lecouvreur—Prelude, Act IV]
DUPLICATIONS: Stockholm Sym. Orch.
—Järnefelt, O-26456: O-D4714; Queen's Hall Orch.—Wood, D-K766
Sangen Om Dent Elroda Blomann
Music for the Film Orchestra
Symphony Orch.—Järnefelt
      10″ & 12″—O-D1052 & O-D6061
Sirkka   Chorus in Finnish Eng. Grasshopper
Male Chorus—W. Rautawaara
                     10″—G-X2803
[Toruud: Kitkat-kat-kat & Palmgren: Tuutulaulv]
Sunnuntai   Song in Finnish   Eng. Sunday
Signe Liljequist (s) & pf. acc.
                     10″—G-X2828
[Merikanto: Pai, Paitaressu]

JANACEK, Leoš (1854-1928)
One of the most important modern Bohemian composers, Janáček was also a teacher, a writer on music, and a collector of folksongs. Very little of his music is known outside of his own country, but in recent years much of it has been recorded in Czechoslovakia and in 1948 (the twentieth year after his death) festivals of his compositions are being held throughout the world.

By Overgrown Tracks 10 Short Pieces Piano
Boh. Po zarotlem chodnicku
Josef Palenicek   3 **12″—U-G12889/91**
Concertino for Piano, Strings and Wind Instruments
Rudolf Firkusny (pf) & Ensemble
(Limited Edition)   4 **12″—CH-B10**
Diary of One Who Disappeared
(Daybook of one who vanished)
Boh. Zapisnik Zmizeleho   1916
R. Horakova (c), J. Valka (t) with Women's Choir & J. Páleníček (pf)
                   4 **12″—ESTA-H5158/16**

I.X. 1905 Piano
—Death Boh. Smrt
—Foreboding Boh. Predlucha
Zdenek Jilek 12"—ESTA-F5197
Female Evening Ghost Boh. Klekánica
Moravian Teacher's Choir—Soupal
10"—U-C12444
[When You Know & F. Vach: Let's
Drink, Boys]
In the Threshing House 1913 Piano
Boh. V mlhách
Joseph Páleníček
2 12"—ESTA-F5193/4
Labor Male Cho. Boh. Orání
Czech Cho.—Kovalsky
[Picha: Song] 10"—U-A12075
Lasské Tance Orchestra
(Old Bohemian Folk Dance Settings)
Eng. Lash Dances
Czech Broadcasting Orch.—R. Horakova
[Spring Song] 3 12"—ESTA-H5153/5
—No. 6 (Pilky) only Eng. Saws
Czech Broadcasting Orch.—K. B. Jirak
12"—U-G12617
[Novak: Slavic Suite, Op. 32, Pt. 7]
Nursery Tale 'Cello & Piano
Boh. Pohádka
Bohus Heran & Alfred Holecek
[Suk: Serenade] 12"—U-GI2667

OPERAS In Bohemian

JENUFA (JEJI PASTORKYNA)
Opera in 3 Acts
Eng. Her Step-Daughter
Orchestral Selections (Fantasia)
Dol Dauber Orch. 12"—G-AN188
Individual Excerpts
Every now and then Boh. Co chvila
Marie Podvalova (s) 12"—U-G12901
They Went Away—You go, too
Boh. Odešli—Jdi také
Stepanka Jelinkova (s) & Josef
Vojta (t) 12"—U-G12901
(U-G12798)

QUARTETS—String
No. 1
Ondricek Quartet 3 12"—PD-67782/4
No. 2 ("Confidential Letters")
Cerny Quartet 3 12"—U-G12968/70
Sinfonietta
Czech Philharmonic Orch.—
Kubelik 3 12"—G-C3573/5†
Spring Song
Czech Broadcasting Orch.—Horakova
[Lasské Tance, Pt. 5] 12"—ESTA-H5155
Sonata—Violin & Piano 1914
A. Polcek & Josef Páleníček
2 12"—ESTA-H5156/7

Suite—String Orchestra
—Scherzo only
Czech Broadcasting Orch.—Jirak
[Smetana: Fisherman] 12"—U-G12547
This, our Birch Tree Male Cho.
Boh. Což la naše bříza

Czech Chorus—Veselka
12"—U-F14838
[Blažek: Prayer]
When you Know Boh. Dež viš
Moravian Teacher's Choir—Soupal
10"—U-C12444
[Female Evening Ghost & Vach:
Let's Drink, Boys]
Youth Suite for Wind Sextet
Prague Wind Sextet—V. Kotas
2 12"—ESTA-E7125/6
NOTE: There are undoubtedly additional list-
ings in Czech catalogues.

JANNEQUIN, Clément (fl. 1529-1559)

An important adaptor of Netherland polyphony, a pupil of Josquin des Prés and at one
time attached to the Papal Court in Rome. Little is known of his life, but his music is unusually interesting by reason of its frequent ex-
perimentation in descriptive effects and program depiction.

Chansons Françaises
L'Alouette; Quand j'ay esté;
Las, povre coeur; Ce sont gallans;
L'amour, la mort et la vie;
Quand je boy; Petit jardin;
Puisque mon coeur; Du beau tetin;
A ce joly moys;
Au verd boys; Hellas mon Dieu;
Au premier jouer; Je suys à vous
Vocal Ensemble—Marcel Couraud
4 12"—DF-A12

MADRIGALS
Unacc. Choral Works in French
Au joli jeu
Ce moys de may
Motet & Madrigal Choir—Opienski
(in Vol. V) 12"—AS-45
[Costeley: Migonne, allons voir &
Allons, gay, gay]
(La) Bataille de Marignam
(Original title: "La Guerre")
Chanterie de la Renaissance Cho.—
H. Expert 12"—C-DFX19
Chanteurs de Lyon—E. Bourmauck
12"—C-RF84

(Le) Chant des Oyseaux 4-Part
Chanterie de la Renaissance—
H. Expert (in Vol. I) 12"—AS-7

JAUBERT, Maurice (1900-)

A contemporary French composer some of
whose works have been premiered in America
and who is known for his film scores and arrangements of folksongs.

(Le) Carnet de Bal Music for the Film
Valse Grise
Symphony Orch.—Cariven
10"—C-DB1767
[Lanner: Valse Romantique]
[Romberg: Maytime—Will you remem-
ber?—Sandler Orch. on C-DF2333]

(La) Chanson de Tessa (Giraudoux)
Irène Joachim (s) & Jean Germaine (pf)
12"—**BAM-48**
[Roussel: Réponse d'une épouse sage]

ARRANGEMENTS French Folk Songs
(Les) Cloches de Nantes (Bretagne)
Gouverné Chorus & Orch.—
10"—**CdM-512**
[Trad. arr. Auric: Le Roi a fait]
Fanfarneto (Provence)
Marthe Brega (s) 10"—**CdM-525**
[Chanson 15th Century, arr. Delannoy]
(Le) Soldat par Chagrin (Angoumois)
Y. Le Marc' Hadour (b) 10"—**CdM-515**
[Trad. arr. Bourgault-Ducoudray: Un jour sur le pont de Tréguier]

JELOBENSKY, Valery Viktorovich (1911-)

A young Soviet composer who studied at the Leningrad Conservatory, Jelobensky has written symphonies, operas and chamber music.

Etudes, Nos. 1 & 2, Op. 19 Piano
Oscar Levant
(in CM-508) 10"—**C-17454D**
[Shostakovich: Prelude, A minor, Op. 34, No. 2 & Age of Gold—Polka]

JENSEN, Adolf (1837-1879)

A composer of German lieder, influenced by Schumann, with considerable melodic gifts. He wrote songs principally, but also a few piano pieces.

SONGS In German
Lehn' deine Wang' an meine Wang' Op. 1, No. 1
Lotte Lehmann (s) & Erno Balogh (pf)
(in VM-419) 10"—**V-1861**
[Franz: Für Music & Gute Nacht]
Murmelndes Lüftchen (from "Spanisches Liederbuch" Op. 21)
Franz Völker (t) & pf. acc.
[Eulenberg: Seerose] 10"—**PD-23958**
(Der) Schmied
Waldesgesprach
Dusolina Gianini (s) 10"—**G-DA4451**

JENSEN, Irgens

Alter (Halldis Morea) Song in Norwegian
Eva Gustavson (ms) & Amund Rakserud (pf) 10"—**G-DA11901**
[Alnaes: Der du gjekk fyre]

JEREMIAS, Bohuslav (1859-1918)

Czech organist, teacher and composer who was director of the music school at Budejovice. He is the father of Jaroslav Jeremiás and grandfather of Otakar Jeremiás, both conductors and teachers of international renown.

Bohemian Polka Orchestra
FOK Symphony Orch.—Smetacek
10"—**U-A12299**
[Suk: Master of the Forest—Polka]

JERGER, Wilhelm
Salzburg Court and Baroque Music
Vienna Philharmonic Chamber Orch.—
Jerger 12"—**G-EH1325**

JOAO IV (John IV) (1604-1656)

The founder of a great music library and a serious student of music, this King of Portugal also composed religious choral music of distinction.

Crux fidelis Motet, Unacc. Chorus in Latin
Dijon Cathedral Choir—Samson
(in VM-212) 12"—**V-11679**
[Aichinger: Ubi est Abel]
(G-DB4895 in GM-189)

JONES, Robert (fl.1597-1617)

An important member of the Elizabethan school, probably better known for his Ayres with lute accompaniment than for his madrigals, although he wrote fine works in both forms. Jones published five books of Ayres, the last of which, "The Muses Gardin for Delights," has been re-printed under the editorship of Peter Warlock.

Farewell, dear Love (Shakespeare) (1st Book of Ayres, 1600)
Motet & Madrigal Group—Opienski
(in Vol. VI) 12"—**AS-58**
[Dowland: Go crystal tears & Morley: Since my tears]

JONGEN, Joseph (1873-)

Considered by conservative Belgian critics to be their country's outstanding modern composer, Jongen's work is little known in America. Called the spiritual successor to César Franck, he is a prolific writer and winner of many prizes.

Walloon Dance No. 2
Brussels Symphony Orch.—Franz André
12"—**U-E14230**
[Poot: Ouverture joyeuse]

JOSQUIN DES PRES (c.1445-1521)

Although for many years overshadowed by the fame of Lassus and Palestrina, the "marvelous Josquin" will be remembered as one of the greatest of the Flemish contrapuntalists. He was a prolific composer of Masses, motets and secular songs.

COLLECTIONS
(13) Chansons Françaises
Parfons regretz (5 voices)
Plaine de dueil (5 voices)
Ma bouche rit et mon coeur pleure (6 voices)
Allégez moy (6 voices)
Je me complains (5 voices)
Basiès moy (6 voices)
Incessament (5 voices)
Basiès moy (4 voices)
Tenez moy en vos bras (6 voices)
L'homme armé (4 voices)
Coeur Langoreulx (5 voices)
J'ay bien cause de lamenter (6 voices)
N'esse pas un grant desplaisir (5 voices)
Vocal Ensemble—Marcel Couraud
4 12"—**DF-A7**

(4) Motets
4 *Motets for which no detailed information is yet available.*
Vocal Ensemble—Marcel Couraud
4 12"—DF-A19

INDIVIDUAL WORKS

Ave Maria I & II
Julian Chapel Choir—Boezi
10"—SEMS-48

Ave vera Virginitas
St. Léon IX Cho.—Gaudard
12"—PAT-X93055
[Palestrina: Alma Redemptoris &
Franck: Rebecca-Chorus]
Strasbourg Cathedral Choir—Hoch
(C-LX767: C-LWX296) 12"—C-69693D
[Berlioz: Enfance du Christ—Adieu des
Bergers]
[Gasperini: Adoramus Te Christe, on
C-RFX59]

Ave coelorum Domina (from Ave Maria)
4-Part

Ave, verum corpus natum 5-Part
Dijon Cathedral Choir—Samson
(in VM-212) 12"—V-11677
(G-DB4893 in GM-189)

(2) Chansons (Vive le Roy & Se congié
prens de mes belles amours)
Instrumental Ensemble
(in Vol. XI) 12"—AS-108
[Miserere à 5, Pt. 3, Paraphonistes de St.
Jean des Matinés—de Van]

Et incarnatus est (from the Credo) 4-Part
State Academy Choir—Pius Kalt
[Dufay: Gloria] 10"—P-R1019
(in 2000 Years of Music Set)

Kyrie of the Missa Hercules
Les Paraphonistes de St. Jean-des-
Matines—G. de Van
(in Vol. VIII) 12"—AS-73
[Stabat Mater]

Miserere à 5
Les Paraphonistes de St. Jean-des-
Matines—G. de Van 2 12"—AS-107/8
[2 Chansons, Instrumental ensemble]

O Domine Jesu Christe (Passion Motet—
Male Voices)
Strasbourg Cathedral Cho.—Hoch
12"—C-RFX73
[Pierre de la Rue: O Salutaris Hostia]

Stabat Mater
Les Paraphonistes de St. Jean-des-
Matines—G. de Van 12"—AS-73
[Kyrie of the Missa Hercules]

Tu pauperum refugium
Strasbourg Cathedral Choir—Hoch
[Brückner: Ave Maria] 12"—C-RFX71

KABALEVSKY, Dmitri (1904-   )

*A product of the Moscow Conservatory where
he was a pupil of Miaskovsky, Kabalevsky is
becoming known outside of Russia through
performances and recordings of his major
works in England and America. He has composed several operas and scores for films made
in the Soviet.*

(The) Comedians, Op. 26 Suite
N. Y. Philharmonic-Symphony—
Kurtz 2 12"—CX-295†
State Orch.—Yuryev USSR-14139

COLAS BREUGNON Opera

Overture Orchestra
NBC Symphony—Toscanini
(in VM-1178†) 12"—V-11-9978
[Tchaikovsky: Romeo & Juliet, Pt. 5]
Pittsburgh Symphony—Reiner
(in CM-585†) 12"—C-122031
[Shostakovich: Symphony No. 6, Pt. 9]
(C-LX1002)
Magelot Symphony—B. Z. Khaikin
USSR-6587/8

Fête populaire
Santa Monica Symphony Orch.—
Rachmilovich in DISC-A800
[Khachaturian: Masquerade Suite]

Sonatina, C major, Op. 13, No. 1 Piano
Harriet Cohen 12"—C-DX1066
[Shostakovich: Prelude, Op. 34, No. 14]

KALINNIKOV, Vassili (1866-1901)

*An expressive, short-lived Russian composer
whose first symphony gave promise of a fresh
and fluent talent.*

Beatitudes—In Thy Kingdom Cho. in
Russian
Russian Metropolitan Church Cho., Paris
Afonsky 10"—G-EK97
[Gontcharoff: Thy Cross]

SYMPHONIES

No. 1, G minor
Indianapolis Symphony Orch.—Sevitzky
4 12"—VM-827†

KALMAN, Emmerich (1882-   )

*One of the most popular of the Central Euro-
pean operetta composers of the present century, Kalman is a master of pseudo-Viennese
sentiment. See current catalogues for listings of
the following German operettas.*

(DIE) BAJADERE

(DIE) CZARDASFURSTIN 3 Acts 1915
Eng. The Gypsy Princess Fr. La Princesse
Csardas

GRAFIN MARIZA Eng. Countess Mariza

TEUFELSREITER

(DAS) VEILCHEN VOM MONTMARTRE

(DER) ZIGEUNERPRIMAS Eng. Sari

(DIE) ZIRKUSPRINZESSIN Eng. The
Circus Princess

KAUDER, Hugo (1888-   )

**Sonata for English Horn & Piano & Impro-
visation for English Horn Alone**
Louis Speyer & Edwin Bodky
2 10"—NIGHT MUSIC-105

KAYSER, Leif (1919-   )

Birken: Maa vi (Ludwig Holstein)
College Men's Choral Union—Hye-
Knudsen   10"—G-X6689
[Høffding: Purpurprikken & Bentzon:
Lyse hand]

KELLER, Homer (1915-   )

*A California composer and teacher, a pupil of
Howard Hanson, whose chamber and orchestral scores have been heard over the air.*

Serenade Clarinet & Strings
Rufust Arey & Eastman-Rochester Sym-
phony—Hanson
         (in VM-802) 12"—V-18102
[Phillips: American Dance]

KENNAN, Kent (1913-   )

*A graduate of the Eastman School of Music,
Kennan won the Prix de Rome. His orchestral
and chamber works are heard frequently over
the major radio networks and his shorter
pieces are included in the repertory of several
American orchestras.*

Night Soliloquy Orchestra
Eastman-Rochester Symphony Orch.—
Howard Hanson
         (in VM-608) 12"—V-15659
[Griffes: The White Peacock]

KENNEDY-FRASER, Marjory (1857-1930)

*A Scottish singer and editor who collected and
arranged an extensive work "The Songs of the
Hebrides," published in several volumes from
1909-1921. These songs, comparable to the Cecil
Sharp Collection, have been sung by Mrs. Fraser
and her daughter in lecture recitals over the
world and many of them have been recorded.*

SONGS OF THE HEBRIDES Sung in
English

Ailite; The Wild Swan; The Mull Fisher's
Love Songs; Isle Reaper's Song; An Eris-
kay Love Lilt; The River Calleth; Land
of Heart's Desire; Bloweth the West
Wind; Sleeps the Moon; Kishmul's Gal-
ley; The Bens of Jura; A Fairy Love
Song
Astra Desmond (c) & Marie Korchinska
(harp)   3 12"—D-K977/9
An Eriskay Love Lilt
Isobel Baillie (s) & Gerald Moore (pf)
[A Fairy's Love Song] 10"—C-DB2239
Paul Robeson (bs)   10"—G-B8750
[Trad: Song of the Volga Boatman]
DUPLICATIONS: Polish Army Chorus,
G-BD968; Glasgow Orpheus Choir,
G-E409; Robert Wilson, G-BD1068;
Sydney MacEwan, C-DB1942
(A) Fairy's Love Song
Isobel Baillie (s) & Gerald Moore (pf)
[An Eriskay Love Tilt] 10"—C-DB2239
Land of Heart's Desire
Robert Wilson (t)   10"—G-B9626
[If I can help Somebody]

Mull Fisher's Love Song
Alexander Macrae (t) & pf. acc.
         10"—P-F3329
[Scotch, arr. Ricketts: Tog Orm Mo
Phiob]
DUPLICATION: N. McLean, P-F3190
(The) Road to the Isles (Macleod)
Stuart Robertson (b)   10"—G-B8260
[Trad: Skye Boat Song]
Robert Irwin (b) & Gerald Moore (pf)
[Ireland: Sea Fever]   10"—G-B9073
Henry Wendon (t)   10"—C-DB2058
[Come to the Fair]
DUPLICATIONS: Robert Wilson,
G-BD1059; Harry Lauder, G-D1085;
Sydney MacEwan & Trio, P-R2298;
Polish Army Choir, G-BD952
Sea Sorrow (Arr. Banrock)
Glasgow Orpheus Choir—Roberton
         12"—G-C3639
[Scottish Psalm Tune—Arr. Grant:
Crimond]

KERN, Jerome (1885-1946)

*Rivaling Irving Berlin and George Gershwin as
America's most successful composer of musical
comedies, operettas and reviews, Kern composed several scores that seem destined to en-
dure. See also current catalogues.*

COLLECTIONS

MUSICAL COMEDY FAVORITES

Showboat—Can't help lovin' dat man;
Girl from Utah—They didn't believe me;
Sally—Look for the silver lining; Ro-
berta—Smoke gets in your eyes & The
touch of your hand; Very Warm for May
—All the things you are; Music in the Air
—The song is you; Sweet Adeline—Don't
ever leave me
Risë Stevens (ms) & Orch.—Sylvan
Schulman   4 12"—CM-568

MUSIC OF JEROME KERN (Arr. Or-
chestra)

Smoke gets in your eyes; Yesterdays;
I've told every little star; The song is you;
The night was made for love; She didn't
say yes; All the things you are; Look for
the silver lining; They didn't believe me;
Long ago; I dream too much; Jockey on
the Carrousel; Why was I born; The way
you look tonight; Who; Only make believe; Bill; Why do I love you; You are
love; Ol' Man river
Andre Kostelanetz and his Orch.
         4 12"—CM-622

SIX SONGS

Smoke gets in your eyes; I've told every
little star; All the things you are; Why
was I born; Babes in the woods; They
didn't believe me
Irene Dunn (s) & Orch.—Victor Young
         3 10"—D-A484

JEROME KERN FAVORITES

I have the room above; Once in a blue
moon; She didn't say yes; One moment

alone; You never know about me; Go
little boat
George Byron (t) & Bobby Tucker (pf)
                    3   10"—GEN-G19

Mark Twain Portrait for Orchestra
Andre Kostelanetz & his Orch.
                    2   12"—CX-227†

Individual Musical Comedies and Films
See Collections above

CENTENNIAL SUMMER Film
All Through the Day
James Melton (t) with Sapertin & Shefter
(duo-pfs.)   12"—V-11-9224
[Gershwin: Porgy and Bess—Where is
my Bess?]

(THE) GIRL FROM UTAH
They Didn't Believe Me
Melanchrino Strs.—Melanchrino
                    10"—G-B9591
[Friml: Donkey Serenade]

I DREAM TOO MUCH Film 1936
I Dream too Much; I'm the Echo
Lily Pons (s) & Chorus
(G-DA1456)   10"—V-4304
MUSIC IN THE AIR
The Song is You
John Charles Thomas (b)
                    10"—V-11-8110
[Very Warm for May—All the things you
are]

ROBERTA—Selections
Overture; You're devastating; Yesterdays; Something had to happen; The
touch of your hand; Fashion Show;
Don't ask me not to sing; I'll be hard to
handle; Smoke gets in your eyes; Lovely
to look at; Let's begin; Finale
Kitty Carlisle; Kathryn Meisle; Alfred
Drake, Paula Lawrence with Jeffry Alexander Chorus & Orch.—Harry Sosnick
                    6   10"—D-DA374

Smoke Gets In Your Eyes
Gladys Swarthout (ms)
          (in VM-935)   10"—V-10-1037
[Youmans: Through the years]
(Also: Victor Orch., V-24609)

The Touch of Your Hand
Eleanor Steber (s)   10"—V-10-1248
[Kreisler: Stars in my Eyes]

SHOW BOAT 1926
Scenario for Orchestra on Themes from
"Show Boat"
Janssen Symphony of Los Angeles—
Janssen   3   12"—VM-906†
Cleveland Orch.—Rodzinski
                    3   12"—CM-495†

Selections
(with the cast of the 1946 revival)
Overture; Cotton Blossom; Only make be-
lieve; Ol' Man River; Can't help lovin'
dat man; Life upon the wicked stage;
You are love; Why do I love you?; Bill;
Nobody else but you
Carol Bruce, Jan Clayton, Charles Fred-
ericks, Helen Dowdy, Kenneth Spencer &
Show Boat Cho. & Orch.—Edwin Mc-
Arthur   5   12"—CM-611†

Selections
Tommy Dorsey and his Orch.
                    4   10"—V-P152
Ah Still Suits Me
Paul Robeson (bs), V-25376: G-B8497
(Also in CM-732)
Bill
Helen Morgan, in V-P102
Can't Help Lovin' Dat Man
Helen Morgan, in V-P102
Risë Stevens, in CM-568
Make Believe
James Melton (t)   10"—V-10-1236
[Swing Time—The way you look tonight]
Ol' Man River
Paul Robeson (bs), V-25376: G-B8497
(Also in CM-732)
Robert Weede (b) & Pablo Miguel (pf)
                    10"—C-17293D
[Anon: City called Heaven]

VERY WARM FOR MAY
All the Things You Are
John Charles Thomas (b)
                    10"—V-11-8110
[Music in the Air—The song is you]
Helen Traubel (s)
          (in CM-639)   12"—C-71839D
[Rodgers: Oklahoma!—Oh, what a beau-
tiful morning]

KETELBEY, Albert (c1885-   )
A British composer well known for his orchestral pieces written in a highly descriptive
pseudo-Oriental style.

Bells Across the Meadow
Concert Orch.—Ketelbey
[The Sacred Hour]   12"—D-F7618
[Sanctuary of the Heart, on C-DX775:
C-DFX211]
Also: London Palladium Orch., G-C1916:
G-S10341

Cockney Suite
—No. 5, Bank Holiday ('Appy 'Ampstead)
Concert Orch.—Ketelbey   10"—D-F7616
[In a Persian Market]

Gallantry
Concert Orch.—Ketelbey   10"—D-F7617
[Sanctuary of the Heart]

In a Chinese Temple Garden
Concert Orch.—Ketelbey   10"—D-F7619
[Jungle Drums]
International Concert Orch.
(G-C1304) (G-L867)   12"—V-35777
[In a Persian Market]
Also: Reginald Foort (org.), G-C1330

In a Monastery Garden
Andre Kostelanetz & his Orch., in CM-681
Concert Orch.—Ketelbey   12"—C-9403
[In the Moonlight, on D-F7615]
Victor Orch.   12"—V-35808
[Tchaikowsky: Romance]
DUPLICATIONS: Grand Symphony Orch.
& Chorus, P-E10646; Westminster Light
Symph., D-K604; Massed Bands,
G-B8217; Reginald Foort (org.),
V-35821: G-C1285: G-L617; Lew White
(org.), V-36209

In a Persian Market
Concert Orch.—Ketelbey   12"—**C-9404**
['Appy 'Amstead, on D-F7616]
International Concert Orch.—Shilkret
(G-C1304)   12"—**V-35777**
[In the Chinese Temple Garden]
Boston "Pops" Orch.—Fiedler
(G-K8065) (G-B8663)   10"—**V-4338**
DUPLICATIONS: Grand Symphony Orch.
& Chorus, P-E10646; Reginald Foort
(org.), V-35821: G-C1285: G-L617;
Comedian Harmonists, G-X4766:
G-K7906

In Holiday Mood
Hillingdon Orch.   10"—**D-F7850**
In the Moonlight
Concert Orch.—Ketelbey 10"—**D-F7615**
[In a Monastery Garden]
Jungle Drums
Concert Orch.—Ketelbey 10"—**D-F7619**
[In a Chinese Temple Garden]
(The) Sacred Hour
Concert Orch.—Ketelbey 10"—**D-F7618**
[Bells across the Meadow]
Sanctuary of the Heart
Concert Orch.—Ketelbey 12"—**C-DX775**
[Bells across the Meadow] (C-DFX211)
[Gallantry, on D-F7617]
Sunday Afternoon Reverie
Westminster Light Symph. 12"—**D-K604**
[In a Monastery Garden]
NOTE: *There are undoubtably additional re-
cordings in current catalogues.*

KHACHATURIAN, Aram (1904-   )
*Contemporary Russian-Armenian composer
who has suddenly become well known outside
his own country with recent performances of his
piano concerto and music composed for ballets.*

CONCERTOS
Piano & Orchestra 1936
William Kapell & Boston Symphony
Orch.—Koussevitsky   4 12"—**VM-1084†**
Moura Lympany & London Symphony—
Fistoulari   4 12"—**D-ED3†**
(D-K1145/8)
Violin & Orchestra 1941
David Oistrakh & USSR Symphony Orch.
—Hauk   5 12"—**USSR-No Data**
Louis Kaufman & Santa Monica Symph.
Orch.—Rachmilovich   4 12"—**CH-AN**
Danse Suite No. 5—Lezghinka only
Bolshoi Theatre Orch.—Nebolsin
in DISC-A753

GAYNE Ballet Suites
No. 1
Sabre dance; Dance of Ayshe; Dance of
the Rose Maidens; Dance of the Kurds;
Lullaby; Dance of the Young Kurds;
Armen's Variations; Lezghinka
N. Y. Philharmonic-Symphony Orch.—
Kurtz   3 12"—**CM-664†**
**Lullaby; Danse of the Young Maidens;
Sabre Danse** only
Philharmonia Orch.—Malko
12"—**G-C3572**
Lullaby only
Radio Orch.—Golovanov
10"—**USSR-12802/3**

Sabre Dance only
Chicago Symphony Orch.—Rodzinski
12"—**V-12-0209**
[Masquerade—Valse, Boston Pops Orch.
—Fiedler]
Oscar Levant (pf) & Col. Concert Orch.—
Bring   10"—**C-17521D**
Sabre Danse & Lezghinka
Symph. Orch.—Golovanov
10"—**USSR-12502/3**
No. 2
N. Y. Philharmonic-Symphony Orch.—
Kurtz   2 12"—**CX-292†**
Russian Dance (Unidentified)
Symphony Orch.—Golovanov
10"—**USSR-12804/5**

—Arr. Violin:
D. Oistrakh, USSR-14248/9

MASQUERADE Suite
**Valse; Nocturne; Mazurka; Romance;
Galop**
Santa Monica Symphony Orch.—
Rachmilovich   3 12"—**DISC-800**
[Kabalevsky: Colas Breugnon—Fête
populaire]
Boston "Pops" Orch.—Fiedler
2 12"—**VM-1166†**
N. Y. Philharmonic-Symphony Orch.—
Stokowski   3 12"—**CM-729†**
[Ippolitov-Ivanov: In the Village]
—Valse only
Boston "Pops" Orch.—Fiedler
12"—**V-12-0209**
[Gayne—Sabre Dance, Chicago Symphony
—Rodzinski]
Toccata Piano
Benno Moiseiwitsch   12"—**G-C3397**
[Medtner: Russian Fairy Tale, Op. 42,
No. 1]
Lev Oborin   12"—**U-G14743**
[Rimsky-Korsakov: Flight of the Bum-
blebee & Chopin: Mazurka, A minor]
Shura Cherkassky, in VOX-165
Zangezur
—March
USSR Orch.—Chernetzki
10"—**USSR-6990/91**
[Khait: Fighting Banners]

KHRENNIKOV, Tikhon (1913-   )
*A student at the Moscow Conservatory, Khren-
nikov has written piano pieces, songs, incidental
music for plays and operas. His symphony was
warmly received when performed in America a
few years ago. However his work is not often
programmed outside his own country.*

MUCH ADO ABOUT NOTHING
Incidental Music
Song of the Drunkard
The Night breeze rustles the leaves
A. Dolivo (b)   10"—**D-M533**
—Night Breeze only Arr. Orchestra
Bolshoi Theatre Orch.—Nebolsin, in
DISC-753

SYMPHONIES
No. 1, Op. 4
—3rd Mvt. only
USSR State Orch. in DISC-753

KIENZL, Wilhelm (1857-1941)

A disciple and friend of Wagner who was influenced by many of Wagner's techniques, Kienzl composed many operas but is remembered by his popular "Der Evangelimann."

Kahn—Scene, Op. 5

Neuer Walzer (from "Aus meinem Tagebuch, Op. 15)
Wilhelm Kienzl (pf) 12"—O-4780

OPERAS In German

(DER) EVANGELIMANN 2 Acts 1895
Eng. The Evangelist
Orchestral Selections (Fantasia)
Concert Orch. & Organ—Seidler-Winkler
12"—G-EH1050
Individual Excerpts
O schöne Jungendtage Contralto
Marieluise Schlip 12"—O-7988
Friedel Beckmann 10"—G-EG6824
[Gounod: Faust—Flower Song]
Selig sind, die Verfolgung leiden Tenor
Eng. Blessed are they who are persecuted
H. E. Groh & Children's Cho.
[Handel: Serse—Largo] 10"—O-4644
Walther Ludwig & Children's Chorus
12"—PD-57115
[Der Kuhreigen-Das Strassburglied]
Marcel Wittrisch & Children's Chorus
12"—G-DB4411
[Flotow: Marta—Ah! che a voi; with
Berger, Klose, Carli & Beck]
DUPLICATIONS: Peter Anders, T-E2523;
J. Patzak, PD-25012; Franz Völker, PD-95037

(DER) KUHREIGEN 3 Acts 1911
Lug', Dursel lug' Tenor Act I
Strassburg Lied—Zur Strassburg auf der
Schanz Tenor & Chorus
Herbert E. Groh 12"—O-3612
—Strassburg Lied only
Walther Ludwig & Children's Chorus,
PD-57115; H. E. Groh & Male Chorus,
O-7909

KILPINEN, Yrjö (1892-)

A Finnish music critic and composer who has devoted his talents largely to setting the Finnish poets to music. He is highly regarded in England, but little known in America. He has been considered one of the greatest song writers since Hugo Wolf and Moussorgsky. The Kilpinen Song Society was supervised by the composer and his wife is the piano accompanist.

SONGS In Finnish, German & Swedish

COLLECTION—Kilpinen Song Society
(H. M. V.)

LIEDER UM DEN TOD, Op. 62 (Morgenstern)
1. Vögelein Schwermut
2. Auf einem verfallenen Kirchof
3. Der Tod und der einsame Trinker
4. Winternacht
5. Der Säemann
6. Unverlierbare Gewähr

LIEDER DER LIEBE Op. 61 (Morgenstern)
1. Heimat
2. Kleines Lied
4. Uber die tausend Berge
5. Ammutiger Vertrag

SPIELMANNSLIEDER, Op. 77 (Sergel)
4. Tanzlied
5. Spielmannssehnen
8. Ich sang mich durch das deutsche Land
Mondschein (Jalkanen); Elegie an die
Nachtigall, Op. 21, No. 1; Der Skiläufer
(Jalkanen); Vergissmeinnichte; Venezianisches Intermezzo, Op. 79, No. 4 (V.
Zwohl); Marienkirche zu Danzig im
Gerüst, Op. 79, No. 7
Gerhard Hüsch (b) & Margaret Kilpinen
(pf) 5 12"—Society Set
(Not available separately)
Individual Songs In Finnish
Käköä Kuullessa, Op. 7, No. 2 Eng. The
Cuckoo Calls
Aulikki Rautawaara (s) 10"—T-A2542
[Trad. Finnish: Tulin onneni yrittitarhaan]
Kesäyö Eng. Summer Night
Oiva Soini (b) 10"—G-X3633
[Madetoja: Toisen oma]
Ruusu pieni, Op. 47, No. 15 Eng. Little Rose
Hanna Granfelt (s) 10"—G-X3134
[Hannikainen: Aiden silmät]

KINGO, Thomas (1634-1703)

Den klar Sol gaar ned
Det mulner mod den mørke Nat
(Both from "Aandelige Sjungekor,"
1674)
Erling Knudsen (treble) & Mogens
Wöldike (harpsichord) 10"—G-X6935
Arr. of Goudimel's Psalm: Hører til, i hoje
Himle
Copenhagen Boy's Choir—Wöldike
10"—G-X6995
[Praetorius: Es ist ein Ros' entsprungen]
DUPLICATION: Palestrina Cho.—
Wöldike, G-X2834

KJERULF, Halfdan (1815-1868)

A Norwegian composer and teacher, a friend of Grieg, who wrote fine piano music of strong Scandanavian character. His reputation rests upon his songs which were popularized by Jenny Lind, Nilsson and Sontag.

SONGS (in Norwegian)
Alt laegger for din Fod jeg ned (Thomas Moore)
Erling Krogh (t) & pf. acc.
[Svendsen: Kom Carina] 10"—G-X2720
Aksel Schiøtz & pf. acc. 10"—G-X6415
[Bendix: Hvor tindrer nu min Stjerne]
Blanchefleur
Marius Jacobsen (t) & pf. acc.
10"—G-X2918
[Heise: Hvor tindrer]
Elfenspiel
—Arr. Orch: Victor Orch., V-20399 (in
Rhythms for Children)
Lullaby, Op. 4, No. 3 Arr. Organ
Joseph Bonnet (Hammond Organ,

Gloucester, Mass.)
   (in VM-835) 12″—V-18213
[Aria Popolare del Paese di Ath,
Belgium]

KLEINSINGER, George (1914-)

*A contemporary American composer of stage
and choral works, whose musical scores (some
of them for children) have been broadcast and
filmed.*

I Hear America Singing Cantata in English
 (Walt Whitman)
 John Charles Thomas, with I. L. G. W. U.
 Radio Chorus & Victor Symphony Orch.
 —Shilkret 2 12″—VM-777†
Tubby the Tuba Musical Fable (Paul
 Tripp)
 Victor Jory (narrator) & Orch.
   2 10″—COSMO-101
 Danny Kaye (narrator) & Orch.
   12″—D-CU10

KODALY, Zoltan (1882-....)

*With Béla Bartók the two outstanding repre-
sentative composers of their native Hungary.
Like Bartók, Kodály has also arranged and collected folksongs, and he too is a composer in
his own right. Like many nationalists he has
been strongly influenced by the music and the
stories of his country's folk art.*

Ave Maria
 Morriston Boys Choir & Maria Korchinska
 (harp) 12″—D-K1157
 [Britten: A Ceremony of Carols, Part 3,
 & Bartók: Enchanting Song]
Dances of Marosszêk Piano
 Andor Földes 2 12″—VOX-609
 [Two pieces from Opus 11]
Dances from Galanta Orchestra
 Boston "Pops" Orch.—Fiedler
   2 12″—VM-834
 Berlin Philharmonic Orch.—deSabata
 (CET-RR8006/7) 2 12″—PD-67525/6

HARY JANOS Opera in Hungarian 1926

Orchestral Suite

 **Prelude—The Fairy Tale Begins; Vien-
 nese Musical Clock; Song; Battle and De-
 feat of Napoleon; Intermezzo; Entrance
 of the Emperor and his Court**
 Minneapolis Symphony Orch.—Ormandy
   3 12″—VM-197†
 German Opera House Orch.—Fritz
 Lehmann 3 12″—O-9118/20

Individual Excerpts

No. 7, Piros alma (Háry) Baritone Eng.
 Red Apple
 Imre Palló 12″—G-AN213
 [Nos. 22 & 29]

No. 8, Bordal—O, mely sok hal Baritone
 Eng. Drinking Song
 Imre Palló 10″—G-AM1687
 [Song: Tölem à nap, Mária, with
 Basilides & pf.]

No. 9, Tiszán innen, Dunán tûl Duo (Háry
 & Orzse) Baritone & Soprano

Eng. **This Side of the Tisza River**
 Imre Palló & Izabella Nagy
 [No. 10] 12″—G-AN208
—**Arr. Orchestra,** in VM-197

No. 10, Közjaték (Intermezzo) Orchestra
 Minneapolis Symphony Orch., in VM-197
 Budapest Opera Orch.—Rékai
 [No. 9] 12″—G-AN208

—**Arr. Violin** Szigeti
 Joseph Szigeti & Andor Földes (pf)
   (in CM-513) 10″—C-17340D
 [Brahms-Joachim: Hungarian Dance
 No. 5]

No. 13, Hogyan tudtál rózsám Eng. **How did
 you know?**

No. 14, Hej két tikom Eng. **Two hens of
 mine** Soprano
 Izabella Nagy 12″—G-AN212
 [No. 28]

No. 22, Toborzó (Háry) Baritone Eng.
 Enlistment
 Imre Palló 12″—G-AN213
 [Nos. 7 & 29]

No. 28, Szegeny vagyok (Orzse) Soprano
 Eng. **I am poor**
 Izabella Nagy 12″—G-AN212
 [Nos. 13 & 14]

No. 29, Felszantom a csaszar udvaret
 (Háry) Baritone
 Eng. **I am going to plow the Emperor's
 courtyard**
 Imre Palló 12″—G-AN213
 [No. 7 & 22]

Hungarian Songs

*It is not clear just which of the recorded songs
credited to Kodály are original compositions
and which are his settings of Hungarian folk
songs. Most, if not all of the short songs on
G-AM1671/7 are undoubtedly folksong settings. Quite possibly the longer songs on
G-AN209/10 & AN211 are wholly original
compositions. In any case the distinction is
rather an academic one: Kodaly's settings, like
Bartók's, are so ingenious, craftsmanly, and
skillful that one of them is superior in originality and musical value to a score of "original" songs by minor composers. For convenience, and inasmuch as several of the discs contain three or four short songs, each song is
listed in groups by the artists rather than separately in alphabetical order.*

**Három árva balladája (Ballad of the 3
 Orphans)** 12″—G-AN209
Mónár Anna (Ballad of Anna Monar)
   12″—G-AN210
Kitrákotty mese (Tale of the Clucking);
 Szomorú füzfának (Of the weeping willow) 10″—G-AM1672
Elkiáltom magamat (I yell out); **Egy
 nagyorrú bolha** (Big-nosed flea); **Rossz
 feleség** (Ballard of the Bad Wife)
   10″—G-AM1673
Kocsi szekér (The Hay Rack); **Asszony,
 asszony** (Woman, Woman); **Akkor szép
 az erdö** (The forest is beautiful)
   10″—G-AM1674

Körtefa (Pear tree); Virágos kenderem elázott ((My flax got wet); Meghalok (I shall die); Szölöhegyen keresztul (Throughout the wine hill)
10"—G-AM1675
The above 6 discs are all sung by Maria Basilides (s), with Béla Bartók (pf)

Tölem a nap (Magyar népdal) (For me the day)
Maria Basilides (s) & Otto Herz (pf)
10"—G-AM1687
[Háry Janos—Drinking song, with Palló]

Kádár Kata (Ballad) 12"—G-AN211

Zöld erdöben (In the green forest)
10"—G-AM1676
[Bartók: 3 Hungarian Folksongs]

A növérek (The sisters); Tücsöklakodalom (Wedding of the Cricket)
10"—G-AM1677

Most jöttem Erdélyböl (I have just come from Transylvania); Cigánynóta (Gypsy Song) 10"—G-AM1678
[Bartók: 2 Hungarian Folksongs]
The above 4 discs are all sung by Vilma Medgyaszay (s), with Béla Bartók (pf)

Kit kéne elvenni? (Whom ought one to marry?); Apró alma lehullott (The tiny apple has fallen); Ahol én elmegyek (Where I am passing by)
12"—G-AN214

Vasárbap bort inni (To drink wine on a Sunday); Puciné (Mrs. Puci); Egy kicsi madárka (A little bird)
10"—G-AM1688

Hej a Mohi hegy borának (Wine of the Mountain of Moh); Oreg vagyok (I am old) 10"—G-AM1689
The above 3 discs are all sung by Imre Palló (b), with Ottó Herz (pf)

Kádár István balladája 12"—G-AN215
[Bartók: 3 Hungarian Folksongs]

Szaladj kuruk (Labanc gúnydal a kurucra); Rákóczi kesergöje 12"—G-AN216

Siralmas volt nekem (Louis Kentner, pf. acc.); Verbunk, székely toborzó
10"—G-AM449

Megé gett Racorzag & Arrólalul; Katona vagyok én 10"—G-AM1690
The above 4 discs are all sung by Dr. Ferenc Szekelyhedy (t) with Béla Bartók (pf) (except as indicated in "Siralmas volt nekem.")

Méditation sur un motif de Debussy Piano
Louise Gargurevich 12"—OL-108
[Turina: Ritmos Pt. 3]

(2) Pieces, Opus 11 Piano
Il pleut dans la Ville; Székely Lament
Andor Földes, in VOX-609

KOECHLIN, Charles (1867-)
A pupil of Fauré and Massenet, this French composer of art songs shows no direct influence of either of his teachers.

Songs In French
Si tu le veux (Marsan)
Louis Bory 10"—O-281279
[Chopin: Tristesse arr. Litvinne]

Elyane Celis 10"—G-K7684
[de Fontenailles: Sais-tu; Hahn: L'enamourée]
DUPLICATION: Joseph Rogatchewsky, C-LF136

French Provincial Folk Songs (in modern arrangements)
En passant par la Lorraine (Lorraine)
La bourrée d'Auvergne (Auvergne)
An hini goz, "La Vieille" (Bretagne)
La fille du Maréchal de France (Ile de France)
Yvonne Gouverné Chorus & Orch.—
Désormière 3 10"—CdM-505/7
[With French Folksongs arranged by other composers]

KORNGOLD, Erich (1897-)
A conventional German opera composer, Korngold has turned in recent years to Hollywood and has written many film scores for Warner Brothers studios.

Holzapfel und Schlehwein Violin & Piano
Jascha Heifetz & Arpad Sandor
10"—V-1864
[Dinicu: Hora Staccato, arr. Heifetz]
[Elgar: Capricciosa, on G-DA1378]

Much Ado About Nothing
March only
—Arr. Violin & Piano
Jascha Heifetz & Emanuel Bay
10"—V-10-1314
[Ponce: Estrellita, trans. Heifetz]

OPERAS, OPERETTAS In German

(DAS) LIED DER LIEBE
(*Operetta based on Johann Strauss Melodies*)
Du bist mein Traum
James Melton (t) (in English)
12"—V-18466
[Herbert: Rose of Algeria—Rose of the world]

(DIE) TOTE STADT, Op. 12 Opera 1920
Marietta's Lied (Marietta's Lute Song) Act I Soprano
Polyna Stoska, in CX-294

KOTILAINEN, Otto (1868-1936)
A Finnish composer who studied at the Helsinki Conservatory and who has many songs, choral pieces and symphonic poems to his credit.

Kun joulu on (Kun maas' on hanki) Song in Finnish
Sulo Saarits (b) & Orch. 10"—G-X6339
[Sibelius: Jouluvirsi—En etsi valtaa loistoa]

KOVAROVIC, Karel (1862-1920)
A conductor of the National Opera, Prague, for twenty years, Kovarovic was also the accompanist for the violinist, Franz Ondricek. A nationalist composer, he was the disciple of Smetana, yet in his individualism he contributed much to the literature of chamber music, the orchestra and the opera.

Bergmannspolka
Czech Philharmonic Orch.—V. Talich
12″—**G-EH1315**
[Smetana: Nasim Devam—Polka]

OPERAS

CESTA OKNEM Eng. **Through the Window**
O manželském krásném ráji Soprano
Eng. **About the beautiful paradise of
matrimony**
Stepanka Jelinkova 12″—**U-G12986**
[Dvořák: Sly Peasant—We shall find
somewhere a quiet retreat, with Budi-
kova & Blazicek]

KOVEN, Reginald De (1859-1920)
*An American composer of light operas and
songs, best known of which is "Robin Hood"
and its perennial "Oh, promise me."*

Marching Song (Stevenson) Song in
English
Anna Howard (s) & pf. acc.
[In Songs for Children] 12″—**V-36032**

ROBIN HOOD Operetta in English 1890
O Promise Me! Soprano
Nelson Eddy (b)
(in V-C27) 10″—**V-4370**
[Nevin: The Rosary] (G-DA4441)

KREISLER, Fritz (1875-   )
*The noted violinist has composed many small
works, almost all for the violin, and has made
scores of violin transcriptions. Many of these
arrangements were long claimed to be the
work of Vivaldi, Corelli, Pugnani and other old
composers, but Kreisler has admitted that these
are his own compositions "in the style of"
these early masters.*

COLLECTIONS

My Favorites Violin & Orchestra
Caprice Viennois; Tambourin Chinois;
Liebesfreud; Liebesleid; Schön Rosmarin;
La Gitana
Fritz Kreisler & Victor Symphony Orch.
—Charles O'Connell 3 12″—**VM-910**
Kreisler Program (Arr. Kreisler)
The Old Refrain; Miniature Viennese
March; Rondino on a Beethoven Theme;
Midnight Bells (Heuberger); London-
derry Air; Hungarian Rondo (Haydn)
Fritz Kreisler & Victor Symphony Orch.
—Voorhees 3 10″—**VM-1044**
Music of Fritz Kreisler (Arr. Orchestra)
Caprice Viennois; Tambourin Chinois;
The Old Refrain; Stars in My Eyes;
Liebesleid; Liebesfreud
Andre Kostelanetz & his Orch.
3 12″—**CM-614**
(C-DX1306: C-DX1321: C-DX1395)
*(The English couplings are somewhat dif-
ferent)*
Allegretto in the Style of Boccherini
William Primrose (vla) & Joseph Kahn
(pf) 10″—**V-10-1098**
[K. P. E. Bach: Solfeggietto & Rameau:
Tambourin]
DUPLICATION: Georg Kulenkampff (vl),
PD-90017

APPLE BLOSSOMS Operetta in English
You are Free Baritone
Nelson Eddy 10″—**V-4285**
[Romberg: Night is Young—When I
grow too old to dream]

Caprice Viennois, Op. 2 Violin & Piano
(See also Collections above)
Fritz Kreisler & pf. acc.
12″—**G-DB3050**
[Tambourin Chinois, Op. 3]
[Dvořák: Humoresque, on G-DB1091]
Yehudi Menuhin & Marcel Gazelle
10″—**G-DA1506**
[Dvořák-Kreisler: Slavonic Dance No. 1]
[Ravel: Pièce en forme d'Habañera, on
G-DA1832]
DUPLICATIONS: Francescatti, G-L663;
Josef Hassid, G-C3208; Emil Telmanyi,
TONO-A107; Ida Haendel, D-M521

—**Arr. Orchestra**
Andre Kostelanetz & his Orch.
(Also in CM-614) 12″—**C-DX1306**
[The King Steps Out—Stars in your
Eyes]
DUPLICATION: San Francisco Orch.—
Hertz, G-D1272: G-AW204

—**Vocal arrangement:** Richard Tauber,
P-PO160

Chanson Louis XIII et Pavane Violin &
Piano
(in the style of Couperin)
Fritz Kreisler & Victor Orch.—Voorhees
(in VM-1070) 12″—**V-11-9265**
[Concerto, C major, Pt. 3]
[Brahms: Violin Concerto Pt. 9 in VM-
402]
Fritz Kreisler (vl) & M. Raucheisen (pf)
[Précieuse] 10″—**G-DA1139**

(La) Chasse (in the style of Cartier)
Yehudi Menuhin & Marcel Gazelle
10″—**G-DA1494**
[Beethoven-Auer: Turkish March]

Concerto C major Violin & Orchestra
(after Vivaldi)
Fritz Kreisler & Victor String Orch.—
Voorhees 2 12″—**VM-1070**
[Chanson Louis XIII et Pavane]
Isaac José Weinstein & Argentine Cham-
ber Orch. 2 12″—**V-11-9273/4**
(Argentine Victor]
Enrique Campajola & Chamber Orch.
2 12″—**C-D15502/3**
[Dvořák-Kreisler: Slavonic Dance No. 1]

(La) Gitana: Arabian-Spanish Song Violin
(See collections above)
Emil Telmanyi & pf. 12″—**TONO-A102**
[Falla: Amor Brujo—Pantomime]
Fritz Kreisler & pf. acc. 10″—**G-DA1629**
[Liebesleid]

(THE) KING STEPS OUT Film
(Based on the operetta "Sissy")

Stars in My Eyes
Eleanor Steber (s) 10″—**V-10-1248**
[Kern: Roberta—The touch of your
hand]
Fritz Kreisler (vl) 10″—**V-10-1395**
[Nevin: The Rosary]

—**Arr. Orchestra**
Andre Kostelanetz & his Orch.
[Caprice Viennois] 12"—**C-DX1306**
(*Also in* CM-614)

Liebesfreud ("Old Viennese Song") Violin
& Piano
(*See Collections*)
Fritz Kreisler & Franz Rupp
(G-DA1630) 10"—**V-1891**
[Falla-Kreisler: La Vida Breve—Danse
No. 1]
(Older Version: G-DB985)
DUPLICATIONS: Francescatti, C-LF44:
C-GN109: C-DC87; Vasa Prihoda, PD-
47036: PD-524191; E. Telmanyi, RAD-
RZ3043; H. Fritz-Crone, G-X3914

—**Arr. Orchestra**
Minneapolis Symphony—Ormandy
[Schumann: Träumerei] 12"—**G-DB2353**
Andre Kostelanetz & his Orch.
[Liebesleid] 12"—**C-DX1321**
(*Also in* CM-614)

—**Arr. Vocal Solo**, Richard Tauber, P-PO160

—**Arr. Piano** Rachmaninoff
Sergei Rachmaninoff 12"—**V-11-8728**
[Schubert: Ständchen]

—**Arr. 2 Pfs.**
Rawicz & Landauer, C-DB2011
Also: M. Mule (sax), C-DF1704

Liebesleid ("Old Viennese Song") Violin &
Piano
(*See Collections*)
Fritz Kreisler & pf. acc. 10"—**G-DA1629**
[La Gitana]
(Older version on G-DB985)
DUPLICATIONS: Francescatti, C-DC87:
C-GN109: C-LF44; Vasa Prihoda, PD-
47036: PD-524191; E. Telmanyi, RAD-
RZ3043; H. Fritz-Crone, G-X3914; L.
Schwarz, G-K5164

—**Arr. Orchestra**
Andre Kostelanetz & his Orch.
12"—**C-DX1321**
(*Also in* CM-614)
[Liebesfreud]

—**Arr. Vocal Solo**, Richard Tauber,
P-PO160
Also: Viard (sax), PAT-PA330

(The) Londonderry Air
(Old Irish Air: "Farewell to Cucullain")

—**Arr. Violin & Piano** Kreisler (See also
Collections)
Fritz Kreisler & Franz Rupp
10"—**G-DA1622**
[Poldini-Kreisler: La Poupée valsante]
Fritz Kreisler & Victor Symphony Orch.
—Voorhees
(in VM-1044) 10"—**V-10-1204**
[Haydn: Trio No. 1, Rondo]
DUPLICATION: Albert Sandler,
C-FB1594

Marche miniature viennoise Violin, 'Cello &
Piano
(*See also Collections*)
Lore Durante Trio 10"—**G-HE661**
[Braga: Serenata]

Menuet (In the style of Porpora) Violin &
Piano
Denise Soriano 12"—**PAT-PAT54**
[Hahn: Romance A Major]

(The) Old Refrain ("Viennese Song")
Violin & Piano
(*See Collections*)
(*Transcription of the popular Viennese song
"Du alter Stefensturm" by Johann Brandl,
1760-1837*)
Fritz Kreisler & M. Raucheisen
(G-DA1138) 10"—**V-1465**
[Heuberger-Kreisler: Opera Ball—Mid-
night Bells]
DUPLICATION: Erica Morini, PD-66822:
PD-62658

—**Arr. Orchestra**
Andre Kostelanetz & his Orch.
12"—**C-DX1395**
(*Also in* CM-614)
[Tambourin Chinois]

—**Vocal arrangements in English** (Mattul-
lath)
Beniamino Gigli (t) 10"—**G-DA1195**
[De Curtis: Carmela]
Grace Moore (s) 10"—**V-10-1152**
[Pestalozza: Ciribirbin]

Polichinelle Serenade Violin & Piano
Fritz Kreisler & M. Raucheisen
10"—**G-DA1215**
[Winternitz: Dance of the Marionnette]

Praeludium & Allegro (in the Style of
Pugnani) Violin & Piano
Yehudi Menuhin & Marcel Gazelle
12"—**G-DA1490**
Guila Bustabo & Gerald Moore
12"—**C-LCX35**
[Mendelssohn: Auf Flügeln des Ges-
sanges]
William Primrose (vla) & Franz Rupp
(in VM-1131†) 12"—**V-11-9614**
[Handel: Viola Concerto, Pt. 5]
DUPLICATION: E. Zathwieczky & O.
Herz, RAD-RBM108

—**Arr. 2 Pianos**
Rawicz & Landauer 10"—**C-DB2235**

(La) Précieuse (in the style of Couperin)
Violin & Piano
Fritz Kreisler & M. Raucheisen
10"—**G-DA1139**
[Chanson Louis XIII et Pavane]
Erica Morini & M. Raucheisen
10"—**PD-62657**
[Tchaikovsky: Chant sans paroles]
DUPLICATIONS: Costa Vladesco (cym-
balum), PAT-PA66; M. Mule (sax),
C-DF1741

Recitative and Scherzo-Caprice, Op. 6
Unacc. Violin
Yehudi Menuhin 12"—**G-DB1787**
[Tartini: Devil's Trill Sonata, Pt. 3]

Rondino on a Theme of Beethoven Violin &
Piano (See Collections)
Fritz Kreisler & pf. acc.
(G-DA1628) 10"—**V-10-1022**
[Bach: Gavotte from Partita No. 3, E
major]
(Older version on V-1386: G-DA1044)
Denise Soriano & pf. acc.
10"—**PAT-PG107**

[Paganini: Caprice No. 13]
Nathan Milstein & Artur Balsam
10"—C-17408D
[Gluck-Kreisler: Mélodie from "Orfeo"]
DUPLICATION: Quiroga, PAT-X98001

Schön Rosmarin Eng. **Fair Rosemary**
Violin & Piano
Fritz Kreisler & pf. acc.   10"—V-1386
(G-DA1044)
[Rondino on a Theme of Beethoven]
[Rimsky-Korsakov: Song of India, on
G-DA1627]
Ida Haendel & Adela Kotowska
[Tambourin Chinois]   10"—D-M520
Yehudi Menuhin & Marcel Gazelle
[Tambourin Chinois]   10"—G-DA1489
DUPLICATIONS: Erica Morini, PD-
62658; Campoli, D-F5192; A. Lindblom,
G-X1626
Also: M. Mule (sax), C-DF1704

Sicilienne et Rigaudon (in the style of
Francoeur) Violin & Piano
Yehudi Menuhin & A. Balsam
[Moszkowski: Guitare]   10"—G-DA1282
DUPLICATIONS: Alfredo Campoli,
D-F6594; Zilzer, PD-27159

SISSY Operetta in German Eng. **Cissy**
See under title of film version, "The King
Steps Out"; see also "Caprice Viennois"
& "Liebesleid," both of which are con-
tained in this operetta.

Tambourin Chinois, Op. 3 Violin & Piano
Eng. **Chinese Tambourine**
(See also under Collections)
Fritz Kreisler & Franz Rupp
[Caprice Viennois]   12"—G-DB3050
(Older version on V-6844: G-DB1207)
DUPLICATIONS: Ida Haendel, D-M520;
Francescatti, G-L663; Campoli, D-F2512;
Gautier, O-166038; Gulli, ADAM-C111;
Menuhin, G-DA1489

—**Arr Orchestra**
Andre Kostelanetz & his Orch.
[The Old Refrain]   12"—C-DX1395
(Also in CM-614)

—**Arr. 2 Pianos**
Luboshutz & Nemenoff   12"—V-11-8987
[Rossini: Barbiere—Largo al factotum]
Rawicz & Landauer   10"—C-DB2011
[Liebesfreud]

Viennese Rhapsodic Fantasietta Violin &
Orch.
Fritz Kreisler & Victor Orch.—Voorhees
12"—V-11-9952

KREMSER, Eduard (1838-1914)
*An Austrian choral conductor and composer of
operettas, part songs and vocal solos.*

Wir treten zum Beten Chorus in German
(Old Netherland Hymn of Thanksgiving)
Richard Tauber (t) with Chorus, Orch. &
Bells   10"—P-PO165
[Beethoven: Die Ehre Gottes]
Neuköln Lehrergesangverein
12"—PD-27147
[Beethoven: Die Ehre Gottes]
[Chorale: Ein feste Burg, on PD-19953]

DUPLICATIONS: Basilica Cho., PD-
66560; Stuttgarter Liederkranz,
G-EG3350
Also: Boston "Pops" Orch.—Fiedler,
V-4322; Band, PD-23194

KREUTZER, Konradin (1780-1849)
*A German composer of some thirty operas and
many choral works.*

**Das ist der Tag des Herrn (Schäfers Sonn-
tagslied)**
(Chorus in German)
Folksong Chorus—Kalt, PD-22689;
Double Quartet, G-EG1134

—**Arr. Baritone & Orchestra**
Karl Schmitt-Walter & Orch.—
Schultze, T-A2162; Gerhard Hüsch &
Chorus, G-EG3952; Heinrich Schlusnus,
PD-62788
Also: Paul Godwin Orch., PD-21706

OPERAS In German

(Das) NACHTLAGER IN GRANADA 1834
Overture Orchestra
Berlin State Opera Orch.—Lutze
12"—T-E2815

Individual Excepts

(Die) Nacht ist schön—Recit.

(Ein) Schütz bin ich—Air Baritone Eng.
Air of the Hunter
Theodor Scheidl   12"—PD-95368

(DER) VERSCHWENDER Fairy Opera
(Raimund) 1836

Hobelied: Da streiten sich die Leur'
Baritone
Willi Domgraf-Fassbaender
10"—G-EG2336
[Strauss: Zigeunerbaron-Werberlied]
DUPLICATIONS: Leo Slezak, PD-47168;
Gustav Waldau, T-A2648

KRIEGER, Johann Philipp (1649-1725)
*A German composer of "Singspiele" and chor-
uses, as well as instrumental chamber music.*

Cantata "Die Gerechten werden weggerafft"
Basel Chamber Choir—with Gamba, Bassoon & Organ—Sacher
(in Vol. VI)   12"—AS-60
[Schütz: Motet "Selig sind die Toten"]

Sonata, E minor 1688   Arr. Crussard
E. Ortmans-Bach & D. Blot (vls), Y.
Thibaut (vlc) & C. Crussard (pf)
12"—BAM-5

KROYER, H. E.

Der er et yndigt Land
Aksel Schiøtz (t)   10"—G-X6652
[Heise: Jylland mellem tvende]
Lauritz Melchior (t)
(in VM-851)   10"—V-2193
[Hornemann: Kongernes Konge]
(G-DA5213)

KUHLAU, Friedrich (1786-1832)

A German flutist and pianist who became court composer to the King of Denmark. He is remembered best for his flute pieces.

ELVERHOJ, Op. 100 Opera 1828 Eng. Elf Hill

Vocal Selections In Danish
Jonna Neiiendam, Margherita Flor, Einar Nørby, with Copenhagen Royal Opera Chorus & Orch.—Johan Hye-Knudsen
12″—C-DDX3

Overture Orchestra
Royal Theatre Orch., Copenhagen—Johan Hye-Knudsen 12″—G-Z228
(Earlier recording, G-Z175)
Royal Theatre Orch., Copenhagen—S. C. Felumb 2 12″—TONO-X25044/5
[Minuet]
Danish Radio Sym. Orch., Copenhagen— Erik Tuxen 2 12″—NP-Z60123/4
[Fairies' Dance]
DUPLICATION: Tivoli Orch., O-D6012

Ballet Music
Fairies' Dance; Menuet; Contradance; Polonaise; Children's Dance; Pas de nuit; Garlands-Dance; Eccossaise, Hunter's Chorus
Danish Radio Sym. Orch.—Erik Tuxen [Overture, Pt. 3] 2 12″—NP-Z60124/5

Agnetes Drøm; Fairies' Dream; Kranedans; Eccossaise
Copenhagen State Radio Orch.—Emil Reesen 10″—C-DD117

Minuet only
Copenhagen Royal Theatre Orch.— Felumb 12″—TONO-X25045
[Overture Pt. 3]

—Arr. Violin
Johann Nilsson & pf 10″—G-X2367
[Bull: Herd Girl's Sunday]

ROVERBORGEN Opera Eng. The Robber's Castle

Overture Orchestra
Tivoli Concert Orch.—Felumb
12″—TONO-X25076
[Riisager: Finale-Galop]

Sonatina, A minor, Op. 38, No. 3 Piano
Folmer Jensen 10″—O-DO2002

Trio, G major, Op. 119b Flute, Violin & Piano
Members of the Danish Quartet
12″—G-DB5226

Uber allen Gipfeln ist Ruh' (Goethe)
Bielefelder Kinderchor—Friedrich Oberschelp 10″—T-A2085
[Bortniansky: Vespergesang-Jubilate]

KUHNAU, Johann (1660-1722)

A Bohemian-German organist, choral director and composer (who preceded J. S. Bach as Thomascantor at Leipzig), most noted for his clavier pieces in which genre he was the outstanding German figure before the great Bach.

(The) Combat Between David and Goliath (Biblical Sonata) Clavichord
Erwin Bodky (in Vol. I) 12″—AS-5

LABROCA, Mario (1896-)

Italian composer, critic and a pupil of Resphighi and Malipiero.

Quartet No. 2 Strings
Bernardinelli Quartet
3 12″—G-AW311/3

LACOSTE, Louis de (c.1675-1754)

A French opera composer; also chamber musician at the French court.

J'ay surpris l'Amour
G. Micheletti (t) & R. Gerlin (harpsichord) (in Vol. X) 12″—AS-98
(in a collection of serious and drinking songs)

LALANDE, Michel Richard De (1657-1726)

Music teacher to the daughters of Louis XIV, and director of the Royal Chapel, LaLande wrote admirable church music, chamber music and ballets.

Benedictus Deus Tenor, Flute, Violin, Harpsichord
Deus in domibus Tenor, Strings, Oboe, Harpsichord
Jean Planel & Instrumental acc., with R. Gerlin (harpsichord)
10″—LUM-30078

De Profundis Psalm for Soli, Chorus & Orch.
Martha Angelici, (s), Eliette Schennenberg (c), Jean Planel (t), L. Noguera (bs), Y. Corke (ms), JMF Choir, H. Roget (organ), Colonne Orch.—L. Martini 5 12″—PAT-PDT139/43

Sinfonies pour les soupers du Roy
L'Oiseau Lyre Orch.—Désormière
2 12″—OL-141/2

LALO, Edouard (1823-1892)

A distinguished French composer of Spanish descent, best known for his opera "Le Roi d'Ys" and his violin concerto "Symphonie espagnole." Esteemed in his own country as one of the most purely French composers, Lalo's music is characterized by its grace, piquancy and facility.

CONCERTOS

Violin & Orchestra
(See also under "Symphonie espagnole")

G minor (Concerto russe) Op. 29
—2nd Mvt. (Chants russes, Lento) Arr. 'Cello
Madeleine Marcelli-Herson & pf.
12″—G-L837
[Popper: Tarantelle, Op. 33]
—3rd Mvt. (Intermezzo) only
Miguel Candela & pf. acc.
[Nin: Saeta & Granadina] 10″—C-LF145
Henri Merckel 12″—G-L1015
[Fauré: Berceuse]

'Cello & Orchestra, D minor
Maurice Maréchal & Orch.—Gaubert
(C-LFX282/4) 3 12″—CM-185†

Divertissement, A major—Andantino Orchestra
London Symphony—Coppola
12″—G-L864
[Roi d'Ys—Overture, Pt. 3]

NAMOUNA Ballet 1882
Suites Nos. 1 & 2
  Paris Opera Orch.—Fourestrier
                4 12″—**G-DB1116/4**
No. 1 only
  Prélude, Sérénade, Thème varié, Parades
  de foire, Fête foraine
  Lamoureux Orch.—Albert Wolff
  (PD-67032/4)   3 12″—**PD-566086/8**
—**2nd & 3rd Mvts.** only
  Paris Conservatory Orch.—Coppola
                   12″—**G-W1172**
Rhapsodie norvégienne. Orchestra Eng.
  Norwegian Rhapsody
  Lamoureux Orch.—Albert Wolff
                   12″—**PD-566158**
  Symphony Orch.—Pierre Chagnon
                   12″—**C-D11005**
  Conservatory Orch.—Bigot
                   12″—**G-DB5089**
(LE) ROI D'YS Opera in French 3 Acts
  1888 (Edouard Blau)
Overture Orchestra
  San Francisco Symphony—Monteux
                   12″—**V-11-8489**
  Symphony Orch.—Gaubert
                2 10″—**C-LF77/8**
  DUPLICATIONS: Colonne Concerts
  Orch.—Pierné, O-123704/5; London
  Symphony—Piero Coppola, G-L863/4;
  Berlin Philharmonic—Wolff, PD-
  66722/3

Individual Excerpts

ACT I
En silence pourquoi souffrir—Duo 2 So-
  pranos
  (Rozenn & Margared Duet)
  C. Tirard & J. Manceau
  (PD-66963)   12″—**PD-516564**
  [Delibes: Lakmé-Viens, Malika]

ACT II
(La) Salut nous est promis Tenor
  Villabella   10″—**PAT-X90064**
  [Bizet: Carmen—Air de la fleur]
  [Aubade, Act III, on O-188555]
Tais-toi! Margared! (Air de Rozenn)
  Soprano
  G. Corney   12″—**PD-516559**
  [Gounod: Mireille—Chanson de Magali]

ACT III
Aubade: Vainement, ma bien aimée Tenor
  NOTE: *The Choral part is usually omitted*
  Beniamino Gigli   12″—**G-DB6366**
  [Halévy: La Juive-Rachel, quand du
  Seigneur]
  Richard Crooks
          (in VM-585) 12″—**V-15543**
  [Massenet: Manon—Ah fuyez]
  [Gounod: Faust-Air des Bijoux, Noréna,
  on V-15821 in VM-633]
  Richard Tauber & Chorus
  [Tosti: Pour un baiser] 10″—**P-RO20546**
  César Vezzani   12″—**G-DB4854**
  [A l'autel, Act III]
  Tino Rossi   10″—**C-4185M**
  (C-DB1792: C-BF21)
  [Massenet: Manon—Le Rêve]

DUPLICATIONS: Joseph Rogatchewsky,
C-12527; J. Planel, PAT-X90036; J. de
Trévi, G-P786; A. D'Arkor, C-RF63; R.
Gilles, PD-52176; Micheletti, O-188654;
D. Devries, O-188505; Villabella,
O-188555: PAT-X90051; P. H. Vergnès,
O-188847

—**Arr. Violin & Piano**
  Joseph Szigeti & Andor Foldes
                   10″—**C-17311D**
  [Mussorgsky-Rachmaninoff: Hopak]

A l'autel j'allais rayonnant Duo Soprano &
  Tenor

Dans mon coeur enivré (Rozenn & Mylio
  Duet)
  Jany Delille & Jean Planel
                   10″—**PAT-PG40**
  Yvonne Brothier & C. Vezzani
                   12″—**G-DB4854**
  [Aubade, Act III, Vezzani]

Scherzo Orchestra
  Lamoureux Orch.—Albert Wolff
  (PD-566141)   12″—**PD-67042**
  [Dupont: La Farce du Cuvier—Overture]
  Pasdeloup Orch.—Coppola
                   12″—**G-AW280**
  [Franck: Psyché—Jardin d'Eros]

Symphonie Espagnole, Op. 21 Violin &
  Orchestra
  Yehudi Menuhin & Paris Symphony
  Orch.—Enesco   4 12″—**VM-136†**
  (G-DB1999/2002 in GM-195†)
  Zino Francescatti & Columbia Symphony
  Orch.—Cluytens   4 12″—**C-LFX723/6**
  [Bach: Vl. Sonata No. 6—Praeludium
  only]
  Lola Bobesco & Lamoureux Orch.—Bigot
                4 12″—**C-LFX610/3**
—**4 Mvts.** only
  (*Omitting the 3rd Mvt.—Intermezzo*)
  Ida Haendel & National Symphony—
  Jorda   3 12″—**D-K1275/7†**
  Nathan Milstein & Philadelphia Orch.—
  Ormandy   3 12″—**CM-564**
  Bronislaw Hubermann & Vienna Phil-
  harmonic—Szell 3 12″—**C-LFX370/2**

LAMBERT, Constant (1905-   )

  A noteworthy figure among contemporary Brit-
  ish composers, Lambert is a brilliant conductor,
  music critic and author of several books. See
  also under Purcell: "Comus."

Horoscope—Ballet Suite
  1. **Dance of the Followers of Leo**
  2. **Valse for the Gemini**
  3. **Invocation to the Moon and Finale**
  Liverpool Philharmonic—Lambert
                2 12″—**C-DX1196/7**

(The) Rio Grande Chorus in English, with
  Piano & Orch.
  (*Based on Sacheverell Sitwell's poem of the*
  same name in "The Thirteenth Caesar and
  Other Poems")
  St. Michael's Singers, Hamilton Harty,
  pf., and Hallé Orch.—Lambert
                2 12″—**C-L2373/4**

She is Far from the Land Song in English
(Moore)
John McCormack (t)   12″—V-14611
[Molloy: The Kerry Dance]
Webster Booth (t) & Gerald Moore (pf)
    12″—G-C3171
[Trad. The Snowy Breasted Pearl]

LANDINO (or Landini), Francesco (c.1325-1397)

As one of the leading musicians of the Ars Nova, Landino, a Florentine organist, composed madrigals, ballads, canzonas and secular songs.

Bench' ora piova Song in 2-Pt. Setting
(Published in modern notation in J. Wolf's Geschichte der Mensuralnotation, Vol. 3)
Carl Weinrich (Westminster Choir School Organ) in MC-9
Gram piant' agl'occhi 14th Century Ballad
H. Guermant (s) & F. Anspach (t), with
Pro Musica Ensemble
    (in Vol. VII) 12″—AS-63
[Mattheus de Perusio: Plus onques dame n'a mercy]
Questa fanciulla
André Marchal (Gonzalez Organ)
    12″—PAT-PAT63
[Palestrina: Ricercar; Gabrieli: Canzona]
(in 3 Centuries of Organ Music Set)

LANDRE, Guillaume (1905-   )

A contemporary Belgian composer, pupil of his father, William Landré (1874-) and composer of a large volume of instrumental music.

Suite
String Orchestra & Piano
    12″—OL-101

LANGE-MUELLER, Peter Erasmus (1850-1926)

The noted Danish composer of operas successfully produced at Copenhagen and Stockholm, best remembered today outside of Scandinavia for his songs. He also gained considerable distinction for his incidental music to a number of Danish plays.

DER VAR ENGANG Incidental Music from the play by Holger Drachmann
Eng. **Once upon a time**
Excerpts Orchestra
Prelude; Zigeunermusik; Aftenmusik; Jaegermusik; Kokkenmusik; Skumringsmusik
Royal Orch., Copenhagen—Joh. Hye-Knudsen   3 10″—G-DA5229/31
(The last two records are issued on G-X6992/3)
Excerpts
Mealtime & Wedding Music
Royal Opera House Orch., Copenhagen—
Hølberg   12″—NP-Z60121
[Serenade & Midsummer Song]
DUPLICATION: Andreas Thyregods Orch., G-AL1234
Vocal Selections in Danish
Einar Nørby & Marius Jacobsen
    12″—G-Z226
Karen Nellemose & Mogens Wieth
(recitation) w. Orch. 12″—TONO-A100

Midsommervise Eng. **Midsummer Song**
Serenade
Aksel Schiøtz (t) & Chorus
(G-Z256)   12″—G-DB5255
Marius Jacobsen (t)   10″—G-X3298
—Arr. Orch.
Royal Opera Orch., Copenhagen—
Hølberg   12″—NP-Z60121
[Mealtime & Wedding Music]

—Serenade only
Lauritz Melchior (t) & Chorus—
Knudsen   12″—G-DB5233
[Hartmann: Flyv, Fugl, Flyv]
DUPLICATION: Thyge Thygesen, O-D6016

RENAISSANCE Incidental Music from the play by Holger Drachmann

Prelude Orchestra
Copenhagen Royal Theatre Orch.—Hye-Knudsen   12″—G-Z237
[Nielsen: Moderen—Prelude, Act 2 & Faedrelandssang, with Chorus]
Berlin Philharmonic Orch.—Reesen
    12″—PD-15358
[Gade: Folk Tale Ballet—Polonaise & Wedding Waltz]
Danish Radio Sym. Orch., Copenhagen—
Tuxen   12″—NP-HM80010
[Nielsen: Maskerade—Overture]
DUPLICATION: Tivoli Orch.—Jensen, TONO-X25008

Serenade
Aksel Schiøtz (t)   12″—G-DB5241
[Nielsen: Moderen—Skjaldens Vise]
Lauritz Melchior (t) w. Cho. & pf.
    (in CX-233) 12″—C-17482D
[Skind ud du klave Solskin & Kommod glandsen]

SONGS In Danish

Aakande (Bergsøe)

Hojt oppe i Fjeldet (Thor Lange)
Ellen Munter Jessen (s) & Folmer Jensen (pf)   10″—G-X4848

Alle Klokker bringe fjernt (Drachmann)
Johannes Wahl (t) & Koppel (pf)
    10″—G-X6656
[Himlen ulmer svagt i flammerodt]

Gjenboens forste Vise (from the Bauditz play "I Mester Sebalds Have")
Else Brems (ms) & Folmer Jensen (pf)
    10″—G-DA5237
[Himlen ulmer svagt i flammerodt]

Himlen ulmer svagt i flammerodt (Thor Lange)
Johannes Wahl (t) & Herm. Koppel (pf)
    10″—G-X6656
[Alle Klokker bringe fjernt]
Else Brems (ms) & Folmer Jensen (pf)
[Gjenboens forste Vise] 10″—G-DA5237

I Würzburg ringer de Klokker til Fest
(Thor Lange)
Lauritz Melchior (t), Choir & pf.
(G-DA5211) (in VM-851) 12″—V-2191
[Rung: Hvor Nilen vander Aegypterens Jord]

Kommod glandsen Eng. **Summer Lightning**
Lauritz Melchior (t) & Ignace Strasfogel
(pf)   (in CX-233)   10"—**C-17482D**
[Renaissance-Serenade & Skind ud du
klave Solskin]

Kornmodsglansen
College Men's Choral Union—Hye-
Knudsen   10"—**G-X6662**
[Rung: Modersmaalet]

Lykken er ikke Gods eller Guld (Chas.
Gandrup)
Elsa Sigfuss (s) & V. Einarsson (pf)
                    10"—**G-X6389**
DUPLICATION: Tenna Kraft, O-DO2001

Skind ud du klave Solskin Eng. **Bright
Sunshine**
Lauritz Melchior (t) & Ignace Strasfogel
(pf)   (in CX-233)   10"—**C-17482D**
[Renaissance-Serenade & Kommod
Glandsen]

LANNER, Josef Franz Karl (1801-1843)

*One of the composers of Viennese dance music,
a rival of Johann Strauss. Lanner's music became popular in places of amusement and at
court balls.*

Abendsterne Walzer
Marek Weber Orch., G-EG2655:
G-HE2281; Barnabas von Géczy & his
Orch., G-EG7013

Alt Wien Walzer
Marek Weber Orch., G-EH390

Marien Walzer
Wiener Schrammel-Quartet—Lenz,
G-EG1769

Pesther Walzer
Philharmonic Orch.—Pfitzner, PD-
25274

(Die) Romantiker Walzer
Orchestre Raymonde, C-DB1767; Marek
Weber Orch., G-EG2655: G-HE2281;
Barnabas von Géczy, G-HE2192

(Die) Schöbrunner Walzer, Op. 200
German Opera House Orch.—Schultze,
T-A10128; Marek Weber Orch.,
G-EG1793; G-HE2275; State Symphony
Orch.—F. Adam, PD-15160; Sym. Orch.
—Seidel, ESTA-D2027

Steyrische Tänze
Barnabas von Géczy Orch., G-EG7230

LANTINS, Arnoldus De (Arnold) .. (fl.1431)

*A Netherland singer in the Papal Chapel known
for his sacred and secular songs.*

Rondeau: Puisque je voy
Lina Dauby (c) acc. 3 Mediaeval Viols—
S. Cape   (in Vol. IV)   12"—**AS-39**
[15th Century Rondeaux—Binchois &
Grossin]

LARSSON, Lars-Erik (1908-   )

*A Swedish composer who began his studies in
his own country and later became a pupil of
Alban Berg. He has composed in many forms
and is known outside of Scandinavian for his
songs and for his lyrical orchestral pieces.*

**Intimate Miniatures for String Quartet,
Op. 21**
Garaguly Quartet
                    2 12"—**G-DB11012/3**

Pastoral Suite
Symphony Orch.—Larsson
                    2 12"—**G-Z312/3**
[A Winter's Tale—Epilogue]
Göteborg Symphony—Eckerberg
                    2 12"—**T-E19009/10**
[Dag Wiren: Serenade for Orchestra—
March only]

Tills det blir sista gang Song
G. Kellertz (t) & acc.
[Berger: Boljebyvals]   10"—**G-X7307**

(A) Winter's Tale—Epilogue
Symphony Orch.—Larsson 12"—**G-Z312**
[Pastoral Suite, Pt. 1]

LASERNA, Blas de (1751-1816)

*A Spanish composer and conductor who wrote
short character pieces and several comic operas.*

Tonadilla (unspecified) Arr. 'Cello
G. Cassadó & Berlin Phil.—H. Schmidt-
Isserstedt   10"—**T-A1830**
[Tcherepnin: Ode]
M. Amphitheatrof   12"—**G-DB5413**
[Galuppi: Giga & Corelli: Adagio]
DUPLICATION: P. Casals, G-DA1118

LASSEN, Eduard (1830-1904)

*Successor to Liszt as opera director at Weimer,
Lassen, a Dane who received musical training
in Brussels, was a winner of the Grand Prix de
Rome. He is known for his operas and as court
music director at Weimer, where he spent the
greater part of his life.*

Ich hatte einst ein schönes Vaterland Song
in German
Heinrich Schlusnus (b) & pf. acc.
                    10"—**PD-62681**
[Radecke: Aus der Jungendzeit]

LASSUS, Orlando de (c.1530-1594)

(Also: Orlando di Lasso, Orlandus Lassus,
Roland de Lassus)
*The time has at last past when Palestrina is in-
correctly regarded as the only shining light of
the musical Renaissance. Lassus looms up as
one of the giants of the sixteenth century, and
it is not an exaggeration to say that in his
greater robustness and secularity, he more aptly
typifies the spirit of the Renaissance. His output is prolific to the point of being astonishing:
it totals some two thousand works.*

COLLECTIONS

Chansons Françaises
Dessus le marché d'Arras; O mère des
amours; O vin en vigne; Bon jour, bon
jour; Le nuit froide; Hélas! quel jour;
Suzanne un jour; Sçais tu dir L'Ave; Le
rossignol plaisant; Guérir ma douleur;
J'ay cherché la science; Toutes les nuits;
A ce matin; Amour, amour, donne-moy
payx; Margot, labourez les vignes
Vocal Ensemble—M. Couraud
                    4 12"—**DF-A8**

Unaccompanied Choral Works In Latin

(4) Motets (unspecified)
Vocal Ensemble—Couraud
(In Preparation) **DF-**
Justorum animae 5 Voices
Julian Chapel Choir—Boezi
10"—**SEMS-23**
[Capocci: Sacerdos in aeternum]
[Somma: Dirigatur, on SEMS-58]

MASSES In Latin

"Douce Mémoire"

—Benedictus only
Dijon Cathedral Cho.—J. Samson
12"—**G-DB4949**
[Bach: 2 Chorale-Preludes, Gustave Bret, org.]

"Super le Bergier et la bergière" 8-Part

—Sanctus & Agnus Dei
Les Paraphonistes de St. Jean—G. de Van
(in Vol.XI) 12"—**AS-104**
[Motet-Omnia tempus habent]

Missa pro Defunctis

—Benedictus
Choir of the Pius X School of Liturgical
Music (in VM-739) 12"—**V-13560**
[Taverner: Audivi; Gregorian: Pueri
Habraeorum; Palestrina: Pueri
Habraeorum]

Miserere Mei Deus (from 7 Penitential
Psalms)
Berlin Staats und Domchor—Rudel
10"—**P-R1021**
[Palestrina: Missa Papae Marcelli-
Sanctus]
(in 2000 Years of Music Set)

Nos, qui sumus in hoc mundo
Schola St. Léon IX Cho.—Gaudard
12"—**PAT-X93052**
[Victoria: O magnum misterium]

Ola! o che bon eccho!
("Echo" madrigal from "Libro di villa-
nelle")
Dresdner Kreuzchor—Mauersberger
(in German) 10"—**G-EG3545**
[Mendelssohn: Die Nachtigall]
[Schumann: Gute Nacht—Im Walde, on
G-EG6338]

Omnia tempus habent Motet for 2 Choirs
Les Paraphonistes de St. Jean—G. de Van
(in Vol. XI) 12"—**AS-104**
[Mass "Super le Bergier et la bergière"—
Sanctus & Agnus Dei]

Quand mon mary vient du dehors
Madrigal in French
Paris Teachers' Cho.—R. Ducasse
12"—**PAT-X93085**
[Palestrina: Madrigal; Costeley: Je voy
des glissantes; Bach: Choral—La brebis
égarée]

Surrexit pastor bonus
Munich Cathedral Cho.—Berberich
10"—**PD-22587**
[Trad: Christus ist erstanden, Paderborn
Cho.]

Tristis est anima mea 5 Voices
Munich Cathedral Cho.—Berberich
12"—**PD-27116**
[Hatzfeld: Ihr Felsen hart, Paderborn
Cho.]
Julian Chapel Choir—Boezi
[Somma: Pater noster] 12"—**SEMS-9**

Tui sunt coeli 8-Part
Basilica Cho.—Pius Kalt
12"—**PD-66673**
[Hammerschmidt: Machet die Tore]

Velociter exaudi 5 Voices
Julian Chapel Choir—Boezi
[Palestrina: Exaltabo te] 10"—**SEMS-54**

LAUB, Thomas (1852-1927)

SONGS in Danish

Aftensuk (Uffe Berkedal)
Aldrig Herre du forglemme (N. F. S.
Grundtig)
Aksel Schiøtz (t) & pf. acc.
10"—**G-X6863**

Gammel noker jeg nu blevet
Einar Nørby (b) & organ acc.
[Handel: Serse-Largo] 12"—**TONO-A115**

LAVAGNE, André

Concerto romantique 'Cello & Orchestra
Paul Tosteller & Lamoureux Orch.—
Bigot 3 12"—**PAT-PDT66/8**

LAZARUS, Daniel (1898-   )

*French pianist and composer, Lazarus is a prod-
uct of the Paris Conservatoire. His compositions include piano, chamber and orchestral
works.*

Carnaval héroïque Piano
D. Lazarus 3 12"—**C-LFX727/9**

LECLAIR, Jean-Marie (1697-1764)

*One of the greatest French violin virtuosos and
a composer of many works for that instrument.*

Concerto, F major, Op. 7, No. 4 Violin &
Orch.
D. Blot & Ars Rediviva Ensemble—
Crussard 2 12"—**G-DB5133/4**
Sicilienne
Ars Rediviva Ensemble
12"—**G-DB51082**
[Sonata, F major, Pt. 3]
Trio Sonata, D major
Flute, Gamba & Harpsichord 1725
G. Blanquart, Eva Heinitz & Marcelle de
Lacour (in Vol. V) 12"—**AS-48**
Sonata, F major
D. Blot & Ortmans-Bach (vls), Yvonne
Thibaut (vlc) Claude Crussard (harpsi-
chord)
[Sicilienne] 2 12"—**G-DB5107/8**

LECOCQ, Alexandre Charles (1832-1918)

*A prolific French composer of operettas in the
style of Offenbach, who was very popular in his
day.*

See current catalogues for recordings of:

LES CENT VIERGES 1872

LE COEUR ET LA MAIN 1882

LE FILLE DE MADAME ANGOT 1872

LE JOUR ET LA NUIT 1881

LE PETIT DUC 1878

LA PETITE MARIEE 1875

LECUONA, Ernesto (1896-   )

A popular contemporary Cuban pianist and composer who writes in the folk song style and whose dances for the piano (including the often played "Malaguena") are included in many concert pianists' repertoire.

Collection
Malagueña; Andalucía; Gitanerías; La Comparsa; Guadalquevir; Danza Lucumi; Cordoba
Erno Balogh (pf)   3   10″—**VOX-172**
Collection
Malagueña; Danza Negra; Danza Lucumi; Andalucía; Aragonesa; Danza de los Nanigos; La Comparsa
First Piano Quartet   3 12″—**V-C41**
Dame de tus Rosas Song in Spanish
Carlos Ramírez (b) & Victor Orch.—
Cibelli   10″—**V-10-1043**
[Domínguez: Mala noche]
Maria la O Eng. **Maria my own**
Decca Concert Orch.—Horlick
       12″—**D-29199**
[Malagueña, from "Suite Andalucía"]
Suite Andalucía
Malagueña only Piano
Francisco P. Cortes   10″—**C-379M**
[Andalucía]
Oscar Levant
      (in CM-560)   12″—**C-72079D**
[Falla: Fire Dance; Poulenc: Pastourelle]
[Poulenc: Pastourelle & Chopin: Etudes Nos. 5 & 12, on C-71890D]
Ivor Newton   10″—**D-M588**
[Anon: España Cani]
—Arr. 2 Pfs.
Arthur Whittemore & Jack Lowe
       12″—**V-11-9759**
—Arr. Orchestra
Boston "Pops" Orch.—Fiedler
        10″—**V-4330**
[Wolf-Ferrari: Jewels of the Madonna—Dance of the Cammorristi]
Decca Orch., D-29199
Andalucía only Arr. 2 Pfs.
Bartlett & Robertson, C-17516
Siboney
James Melton (t)
      (in VM-1060)   10″—**V-10-1238**
[Rodgers: State Fair—It's a grand night for singing]
DUPLICATION: Lecuona Cuban Boys, C-DF2265
See also current catalogues for other releases such as the recordings of the music for the film, "Carnival in Costa Rica."

LEE, Dai-Keong (1915-   )
A contemporary Hawaiian composer of short orchestral pieces.
Prelude and Hula Orchestra
National Symphony Orch.—Hans Kindler
       12″—**V-11-8452**

LEFEVRE, Joseph
Invocation à la nuit
String Quintet, with harp—Georges Briez
[Sous les Cyprès-Cortège] 12″—**G-L1080**
Sous les Cyprès Cortège
Grand Symphony Orch., with Chorus—
Briez   12″—**G-L1080**
[Invocation à la nuit]
A la gloire de Saint Christophe
(From the film "Christophe, géant de la route")
Cloches de France
Baldous & Chorus, with Symphony Orch.
—Briez   10″—**G-K8232**

LEGRENZI, Giovanni (c.1625-1690)
A Venetian composer and maestro di capella of St. Mark's who also organized the Orchestra of St. Mark's. He wrote many motets, church sonatas, masses, psalms as well as instrumental music of various kinds. His operas were produced with great success in his native city.

ETEOCLE E POLINICE Opera in Italian
Che fiero costume (Trans. P. Florinda)
Ezio Pinza (bs) & Fritz Kitzinger (pf)
      (in VM-766)   12″—**V-17914**
[Arias by Monteverdi, Handel and Scarlatti]
Expergiscere igitur Motet in Latin
Maria Castellazzi Bovy (s) & Ars Rediviva Ensemble   12″—**BAM-4**
[A. Scarlatti: Partirò, La tua pena, Speranza]

LEHAR, Franz (1870-   )
The Hungarian composer best known the world around for his dance music and highly successful operettas.
Musical Memories (Musikalische Memoiren)
Vienna Philharmonic—Lehar
      2   12″—**G-EH1300/1**

CLO CLO Film Music
Excerpts—Lina Pagliughi, CET-GP91960;
Mercedes Capsir, C-DQ1877

LES COMPAGNONS D'ULYSSE Roman musical de P. Benoit
Ma Rose Blanche—Romance
Tango d'amour
José Janson (t), PAT-PA1199; Pizella, C-DF2148

LA DANSE DES LIBELLULES
It. **La Danza delle Libellule**
Complete recording in Italian, C-OQ2042/59

EVA Operetta in German
Orchestral Selections
Symphony Orch.—Josef Snaga, PD-27025
Prelude
Vienna Philharmonic—Lehar, G-DA4499

Waltz
Berlin Philharmonic, T-A2556
War' es nicht ein Augenblick Soprano
E. Kochhann, PD-27181; A. Rautawaara,
T-E2496
Zwansinette
Orchestra—Otto Dobrindt, O-26494
Im heimlichen Dämmer
Maria Reining (s) & Vienna Philhar-
monic Orch.—Lehar, G-DB5694

FRASQUITA Operetta in German, Vienna,
1923
Orchestral Selections
Symphony Orch.—Snaga, PD-27025
Hab' ein blaues Himmelbett Tenor
Eng. **Frasquita Serenade**
Richard Tauber (t) (in German)
O-123551: (in English) P-RO20436;
Marcel Wittrisch, G-EH98; Georges Thill,
(in French) C-LF124
Also: Fritz Kreisler (vl), V-1158:
G-DA792; Marek Weber Orch., G-K6911;
Albert Sandler Orch., C-DX667; Harry
Horlick Orch., D-F6944

FRIEDERIKE Operetta in German **Eng.**
Frederica
Orchestral Selections
London Theatre Orch., C-DX132; Sym-
phony Orch.—Snaga, PD-27070: PD-
22235

O Mädchen, mein Mädchen
Sah' ein Knab' ein Roslein steh'n Tenor
Eng. **Wayside Rose**
Richard Tauber, P-RO20249; Marcel
Wittrisch, G-EH276; Franz Völker, PD-
21811; Peter Anders, T-E2830; Max
Lichtegg, D-K1563; H. Nash, (in Eng-
lish), C-DX115
Liebe, goldner Traum Tenor (Act II)
Marek Weber Orch., G-K6911
Warum hast du mich aufgewacht geküsst?
Maria Reining (s) & Vienna Philhar-
monic Orch.—Lehar, G-DB5694
Also: Marek Weber Orch., G-L779

GIUDITTA Operetta in German
Orchestral Selections
Paris Radio Orch.—Dewanger,
C-LFX601/2; Vienna Radio Orch.,
G-X4268
Vocal Selections
Richard Tauber (t) & Jarmila Novotna
(s) with Vienna Philharmonic—Lehar,
O-4535/7
Du bist meine Sonne Ten.
Helge Roswaenge, G-DB7664; Anton
Dermota, T-A10455; H. E. Groh, O-26316
Freunde das Leben ist lebenswert Tenor
Helge Roswaenge, G-DB7664; F. Völker,
PD-25368
Meine lippen sie küssen so heiss
Jarmila Novotna, O-26316; Esther Rethy
(s), G-DA4481
Gold und Silber Walzer, Op. 79 Orchestra
Eng. **Gold and Silver** Fr. **Or et Argent**
Sigmund Romberg and his Orch., V-11-
9221; Eugene's Viennese Orch., C-324M:

C-FB1648; Tivoli Orch., TONO-X25058;
Berlin State Opera Orch.—Beutler, PD-
15360; Marek Weber Orch., G-EG2091:
G-HN605; Concert Orch.—Seidler-Wink-
ler, G-EG6348
—Vocal arrangement R. Jilger
Erna Sack (s) & Berlin Philharmonic
Orch. & Cho., T-E2273

(DER) GOETTERGATTE Operetta
Was ich längst erträumte Tenor
Rupert Glawitsch, T-E3211; H. E. Groh,
O-26460

(DER) GRAF VON LUXEMBURG Operetta
in German 1909
Eng. **The Count of Luxemburg**
Vocal & Orchestral excerpts
Operetta Ensemble & Orch.—Agans, PD-
15045; Orch. & Vocalists, Grevillius,
G-Z215; Martina Wulf & Hugo Meyer-
Welfing, T-E2249; Johannes Heesters,
PD-47589: PD-57151
Waltz
International Orch.—Shilkret, G-C1392:
G-Z168: G-L647; Wiener Bohême Orch.,
O-31404; Marek Weber Orch., G-B8034:
G-EG2877: G-K7141; Geczy Orch.,
G-EG6418: G-HE2174

(DAS) LAND DES LAECHELNS Operetta
in German
Eng. **The Land of Smiles**
Orchestral Selections
Symphony Orch., G-EH401; I. Livschak-
off Orch., PD-23320; London Theatre
Orch., C-DFX130; Berlin State Opera
Orch.—Marszalek, PD-15172
Vocal Excerpts (Querschnitt)
E. Schwarzkopf & R. Glawitsch, T-E3115
Overture
Berlin State Opera Orch.—Hansgeorg
Otto, T-E2221: U-F18116
Dein ist mein ganzes Herz Tenor
Eng. **Yours is my heart alone**
Richard Tauber, P-RO20107: O-188051;
Anton Dermota, T-A10455; Franz Völker,
PD-62803: PD-22760; Marcel Wittrisch,
G-EG1583
In French: Georges Thill, C-LF110;
Micheletti, O-166646
In English: Max Lichtegg, D-K1560;
Richard Tauber, P-RO20284:
P-RO20467: P-RO20500; Richard
Crooks, V-1509: G-DA1207
—Arr. Orch.
Andre Kostelanetz & his Orch., (in CM-
681) C-7520M
Immer nur lächeln Eng. **Patiently smiling**
Richard Tauber, P-RO20107; R. Glaw-
itsch, T-A2965; Franz Völker, PD-62803
Von Apfelblüten einen Kranz
Wittrisch, G-EH1268; Peter Anders,
T-E2830
In English: Max Lichtegg, D-K1560
Wer hat die Liebe uns ins Herz gesenkt
Else Kochhann & Franz Völker, PD-
22843

LIED UND CZARDAS

Wien, du bist das Herz der Welt
Ester Rethy (s) & Vienna Phil. Orch.—
Lehar, G-DB5690

(DIE) LUSTIGE WITWE Operetta 3 Acts
Wien, 1905
Eng. The Merry Widow Fr. La Veuve
joyeuse
Selections (in English)
Overture; In Marsovia; Maxims; Finale,
Act I; Down in dear Marsovia; Vilia;
Women; Love in my heart; Finale, Act
II; Girls at Maxims; Merry Widow Waltz;
Finale, Act III
Kitty Carlisle (s), Wilbur Evans (b),
Felix Knight (t), Lisette Verca (c) with
Chorus & Orch.—Isaac van Grove
         6   10"—D-DA364

Abridged Version (in French)
Germaine Cernay, Hélène Régelly, Mm.
Duvaleix, Descombes, Gillard, Jugain,
Arnoult, Montigny, Dufont, Lumière,
with Chorus & Orch.—Minssart
         4   10"—O-250058/61

Vocal & Orchestral excerpts
Hildegard Erdmann (s) & Walter Eczy,
G-EH1244; Marcel Wittrisch, G-EH98;
Light Opera Company, (in Eng.)
G-C2585; A. Gura, Peter Anders with
Chorus & Orch., T-E1866; Berlin Opera
Orch.—Melichar, PD-15351; Marek
Weber Orch., C-36086: G-EH141:
G-EH884: G-FKX6; Symphony Orch.,
Snaga, PD-27002; Sidney Torch & his
Orch., P-E11455; Nils Grevillius Orch.,
G-Z207; Géczy Orch., G-EG6148; Berlin
State Opera Orch.—Lutze, T-E2718:
U-F18114

Overture
Vienna Philharmonic—Lehar, G-DB5579;
Berlin State Opera Orch.—Melichar, PD-
1535

Waltz Eng. I love you so Ger. Lippen
schweigen
Richard Tauber, P-RO20175; D. Giannini
& M. Wittrisch, G-DA4446; Johannes
Heesters, PD-47467
In English: Eleanor Steber, V-11-9218;
Jeanette MacDonald, V-24729: G-B8247:
G-K7362; Richard Crooks, V-8454
In Swedish: Zarah Leander & Oluf
Svendsen, O-D6063

—Instrumental arrangements
International Concert Orch., G-C1392:
G-L647: G-Z168; Marek Weber Orch.,
G-EG2877: G-EH54; Paul Whiteman
Orch., C-9460; Sandler Orch., C-DB1484

Vilja
H. Erdmann, G-EG7184; D. Giannini,
G-DA4446; A. Rautawaara, T-E2496;
Anni Frind, G-EG3640; Richard Tauber,
P-RO20188
In English: Eleanor Steber, V-11-9218;
J. MacDonald, V-24729: G-B8247:
G-K7262
In French: M. Beaujon, C-LF79; Ninon
Vallin, PAT-X90032

—Instrumental arrangements
Marek Weber Orch., G-K7141; Sandler
Orch., C-DB1484
Miscellaneous Selections: Fritzi Massari &
Walter Jankun, G-EH249; Comedian
Harmonists, G-EH432

PAGANINI

Potpourri (Vocal & Orchestral excerpts)
Elisabeth Schwarzkopf & Rupert Glaw-
itsch, T-E3041; Bruno Saenger Orch.,
O-7978; Anni Frind, Walther Ludwig,
Wilhelm Strienz, G-EH1046; Berlin State
Opera Orch.—Marszalek, PD-15164
Gern hab' ich die Frau'n geküsst Tenor
Max Lichtegg, D-K1564; Richard Tauber,
O-123551; Louis Graveure, PD-10474;
Peter Anders, T-E3131; Marcel Wittrisch,
G-EH98: G-EH1100: G-EH1268; H. E.
Groh, O-26272: P-R2651; André Baugé
(in French), PAT-PG-66

—Instrumental arrangement
L. Kiss Orch., T-A402

Liebe, du Himmel auf Erden
Eng. Love is like a breeze in May
Ester Rethy (s) & Vienna Philharmonic
—Lehar, G-DA4481; James Melton (t)
in English, V-11-8224; Maria Reining,
T-E3074

(DER) RASTELBINDER Operetta in German 1902

Wenn zwei sich liebe
A. Rautawaara & P. Anders, T-E2572;
W. Ludwig, G-EG3633

SCHOEN IST DIE WELT

Ich bin verliebt
Ester Rethy (s) & Vienna Phil. Orch.—
Lehar, G-DA4497

Liebste, glaub an mich
K. Friedrich, PD-47562

(DER) ZAREWITSCH Operetta in German

Einer wird kommen Soprano
Ester Rethy & Vienna Phil. Orch.—
Lehar, G-DA4497; Maria Reining,
T-E3074

Hab' nur dich allein Sop. & Tenor
Erna Sack & Max Lichtegg, D-K1578

Napoletana
Max Lichtegg, (in preparation, English
Decca); Karl Friedrich, PD-47562

Potpourri
Concert Orch.—Seidler-Winkler,
G-EH1126

Wolgalied Tenor
Marcel Wittrisch, G-EH619: G-EH1100;
also T-E2467; R. Glawitsch, T-E3057; F.
Völker, PD-15415; G. Treptow, PD-10809

ZIGEUNERLIEBE Operetta in German
1910
Eng. Gipsy Love
Vocal Selections
Hildegard Erdmann & Walter Eczy,
G-EH1263

Waltz
International Concert Orch., G-C1402:
G-Z174; Marek Weber Orch., G-EG3219;
Geczy Orch., G-EG7059; Richard Tauber,
P-PO159

Zorika, kehre zurück
R. Glawitsch, T-E3211

MISCELLANEOUS

Potpourris of Lehar Melodies
German Opera House Orch., Berlin—
Bund, PD-15393; Vienna Phil. Orch.—
Lehar, G-EH1300/1; M. Wittrisch (t) &
H. Jungkurth (s), G-EH955; Richard
Tauber (in English), P-R20493; A.
Rautawaara (s), P. Anders (t) & Berlin
Philharmonic—Schmidt-Isserstedt,
T-E1781; Symphony Orch., Snaga, PD-
27173; Marek Weber Orch., PD-
G-C2599; Peter Anders, T-E2400; Berlin
State Opera Orch.—Otto, T-E2194

NOTE: *See current catalogues for other Lehar
recordings since no attempt has been made to
classify and list all of the hundreds of discs
which have been made here and abroad.*

LEHMANN, Liza (1862-1918)
*A noted British soprano and composer, chiefly
of song cycles, the best known of which is "In
a Persian Garden."*

SONGS In English

(The) Cuckoo (W. B. Rand)
Marian Anderson (c) & Franz Rupp)pf)
(in VM-986) 12"—V-10-1125
[Old Scotch Air: Comin' Through the
Rye]

IN A PERSIAN GARDEN Song Cycle
(Omar Khayyam)

—Ah! Moon of my Delight
Webster Booth (t) 10"—G-B9069

—Myself when Young
Lawrence Tibbett (b)
(G-DA1383) 10"—V-1706
[Tchaikovsky: None but the lonely
heart]
Oscar Natzke (bs) & H. Greenslade (pf)
10"—P-E11397
[Tchaikovsky: Pilgrim's Song]

Magdalene at Michael's Gate
Joan Hammond (s) & Gerald Moore (pf)
[Hageman: The Donkey] 10"—G-B9503

**There are Fairies at the Bottom of our
Garden**
*(Although this song is generally known today
only in Miss Lillie's burlesque version, it was
originally written, and still is occasionally sung,
quite seriously.)*
Beatrice Lillie (s) & pf. acc.
10"—GSV-1002
[Kalmar-Ruby: Snoops the Lawyer]

LEKEU, Guillaume (1870-1894)
*A short-lived but highly promising Belgian
composer, a student of Franck and d'Indy, who
wrote a number of symphonic and chamber
works that are highly esteemed in France and
occasionally heard elsewhere.*

Adagio for String Orchestra, Op. 3
Boyd Neel Orch.—Neel 2 12"—D-X236/7
[Bach: Arioso, arr. Franko]

Quartet, B minor Piano & Strings
*(The 2nd Mvt., left unfinished at the com-
poser's death, was completed by d'Indy.)*
C. van Lancker, H. Koch, J. Rogister, L.
Rogister 3 12"—PD-516555/7

Sonata, G major Violin & Piano
Yehudi & Hepzibah Menuhin
4 12"—G-DB3492/5
Henri Koch & Charles van Lancker
4 12"—PD-516549/52

LEONCAVALLO, Ruggiero (1858-1919)
*An Italian operatic composer whose fame rests
almost exclusively on the undying popularity
of "Pagliacci."*

OPERAS In Italian

(LA) BOHEME 4 Acts 1897

Io non ho che una povera stanzetta Tenor
Enrico Caruso 12"—G-DB122*
[Testa adorata]

Testa adorata Act IV
Piero Pauli 10"—G-DA1331
[Wagner: Walküre—Winterstürme
wichen]
Enrico Caruso 12"—G-DB122*
[Io non ho che una povera stanzetta]

PAGLIACCI 2 Acts 1892
Fr. Paillasse Ger. Bajazzo

Complete recording in Italian (1934)
La Scala soloists, Chorus & Orch.—
Franco Ghione (G-DB2299/2307)
(in GM-244†) 9 12"—VM-249†
The Cast:
Canio .... Beniamino Gigli (t)
Nedda .... Iva Pacetti (s)
Tonio .... Mario Basiola (b)
Peppe .... Giuseppe Nessi (t)
Silvio .... Leone Paci (b)
Chorus Master: Vittore Veneziani

Complete recording in Italian (1930)
La Scala soloists, Chorus & Milan Sym-
phony Orch.—Molajoli
(C-GQX10016/24) 9 12"—C-OP22†
The Cast:
Canio .... Francesco Merli (t)
Nedda .... Rosetta Pampanini (s)
Tonio .... Carlo Galeffi (b)
Peppe .... Giuseppe Nessi (t)
Silvio .... Gino Vanelli (b)
Chorus Master: Vittore Veneziani

Vocal & Orchestral Selections
Richard Tauber & Orch.
2 10"—P-RO20329/30
*(From the film, in English translation by
Drinkwater & Weatherley.)*
Peter Anders, Karl Schmidt-Walter &
Carla Spletter (in German) w. Cho.
12"—T-E2034

Orchestral Selections (Fantasias, etc.)
German Opera House Orch.—Lutze
12"—T-E2687
Berlin State Opera Orch.—Melichar
12"—PD-57082

DUPLICATIONS: La Scala Orch.—Sabajno, G-HN789; Milan Symphony—Molajoli, C-GQX10701: C-DFX179; Teddy Petersen's Concert Orch., G-Z213

Prologue: Si può! (Prologo) Baritone
Un nido di memorie
Paolo Silveri (C-GQX11099)
12"—C-DX1304
Lawrence Tibbett (G-DB975)
12"—V-6587
Leonard Warren 12"—V-11-9790
[Ponchielli: Gioconda—Barcarola]
[Verdi: Aida—Ritorna vincitor, Milanov, on V-11-9288 in VM-1074]
DUPLICATIONS: Apollo Granforte, G-DB1044; Riccardo Stracciari, C-GQ7149: C-CQ706; Carlo Tagliabue, CET-BB25064; Robert Weede, C-71261D; Beniamino Gigli, G-DB7623: G-DBO5353; Dino Borgioli, C-D5825; E. Molinari, C-D5761; B. Franci, C-DQ1067; U. Urbano, PD-66773; F. Valentino, C-DQ720; C. Galeffi, C-GQ7043; T. Bayle, D-X10034; T. Ruffo, G-DB464*
In German: Karl Schmitt-Walter, T-E2119; Helge Roswaenge, G-DB5569; G. Oeggl, T-E3102; Heinrich Schlusnus, PD-35022; PD-35089; Hans Hotter, PD-67854; Hans Wocke, O-3620
In French: André Pernet, G-DB5019; P. Deldi, C-BFX16; A. Crabbé, G-DB1128; L. Richard, C-D14243; A. Baugé, PAT-PGT9; J. Beckmans, PD-566039; A. Endrèze, O-123802; Lovano, PD-521919
In English: Dennis Noble, G-C3141; Richard Tauber, P-RO20330
In Czech: Zdenek Otava, ESTA-H5127

ACT I

Un tal gioco, credetemi Tenor
Fr. Avec moi, vrai, tenter ce jeu Ger.
Scherzet immer
Aureliano Pertile 10"—C-CQ698
[Giordano: Andrea Chénier: Come un bel dì]
In German: Helge Roswaenge, G-DA4472; Louis Graveure, T-F1239; Franz Völker, PD-90166
In French: Georges Thill, C-LF94
In English: Richard Tauber, P-RO20330

Coro delle campane: Andiam! (Bell Chorus)
La Scala Cho.—Molajoli
12"—C-GQX10267
[Gounod: Faust—Kermesse]
DUPLICATION: La Scala Cho.—Sabajno, G-S5440
In German: Hamburg State Opera Cho.—Schmidt-Isserstedta, T-E3030

Ballatella: Qual fiamma avea nel guardo Soprano
Eng. Nedda's Bird Song Ger. Vogellied
Fr. Ah! de soleil
Licia Albanese 12"—V-11-9848
[Boito: Mefistole—L'Altra notte]
Eidé Noréna 12"—G-DB4892
[Verdi: Rigoletto—Caro nome]
DUPLICATIONS: M. Favero, C-D6123; X. Belmas, PD-67001
In Swedish: Hjördis Schymberg, G-X6009

Sei là? credea che te ne fossi andato Soprano & Baritone
(Duo: Nedda & Tonio)
Ger. Du sagest doch, du ginst zum Weine
H. von Debicka & T. Scheidl (in German)
12"—PD-95384
[Verdi: Rigoletto—V'ho ingannato]

Nedda! Silvio! a quest' ora Soprano & Baritone

No, più non m'ami Duo: Silvio & Nedda
R. Pampanini & G. Vanelli
12"—C-GQX10249
X. Belmas & W. Domgraf-Fassbaender
12"—PD-66847
In German: Hedwig Jungkurth & Arno Schellenberg, G-EH1045; F. Hüni-Mihacsek & W. Domgraf-Fassbaender, PD-95405

Recitar!—Vesti la giubba Tenor
Ridi, Pagliaccio
Fr. Arioso: Pauvre Paillasse, or Me grimer
Ger. Jetz spielen
(Lache Bajazzo)
Eng. On with the motley
Enrico Caruso & re-recorded orch.
(G-DB1802) 12"—V-7720
[Flotow: Marta—M'apparì]
[Original recording, on G-DB111*]
Giovanni Martinelli 12"—V-6754
[No Pagliaccio] (G-DB1139]
Beniamino Gigli 12"—G-DB3158
[Serenata d'Arlecchino]
[Bizet: Carmen—Flower Song, G-DB6307]
Jussi Björling 12"—V-11-9287
(G-DB6163)
[Mascagni: Cavalleria Rusticana—Addio alla madre]
DUPLICATIONS: Stefan Islandi, G-DA5218; Aureliano Pertile, G-DB1118: C-GQX10675: C-GQX10664; Alfred Piccaver, PD-66889; Alessandro Valente, G-Z172; M. Fleta, G-DB1034; F. Merli, C-GQ7120; F. Piccalugá, C-DQ693; M. Bruno, G-HN778; Edward Johnson, CRS-22*; Giovanni Breviario, CET-CB20298
In French: Georges Thill, C-7016; G. Lugo, PD-62709; C. Vezzani, G-P727; Micheletti, O-123528; Lens, PD-522030; Villabella, PAT-X90065; José Luccioni, G-DA4888
In Swedish: Jussi Björling, G-X4220
In German: Helge Roswaenge, G-DA4472; P. Anders, T-E2816; L. Slezak, PD-95162; Franz Völker, PD-90166: PD-67159
In English: Richard Tauber, P-RO20330; Webster Booth, G-C3379; B. Mummery, G-C2662; J. O'Sullivan, C-D1564; S. Rayner, D-K995
In Czech: B. Blachut, ESTA-H5127
Also: Lopes (vlc), PAT-X98031

Intermezzo Orchestra
State Orchestra, Berlin—Haarth
12"—PD-57171
[Puccini: Manon Lescaut—Intermezzo]
Saxon State Orch.—Böhm
12"—G-DB4556

[Mascagni: Cavalleria Rusticana—Inter-
mezzo]
DUPLICATIONS: Berlin Opera House—
Lutze, T-E3073; Sym. Orch.—Parik,
ESTA-D2014; Milan Symphony—Mola-
joli, C-D12296

Serenata: O Colombina Tenor (Recit.
Pagliaccio, mio marito)
Eng. **Harlequin's Serenade**
Beniminio Gigli & Iva Pacetti (s)
[Vesti la giubba]   12"—**G-DB3158**
James Melton   12"—**V-18365**
[Mascagni: Cavalleria Rusticana—
Siciliana]
DUPLICATIONS: Tito Schipa, V-1183:
G-DA875; Aureliano Pertile, G-DA1162:
C-CQ701: C-CQ7181; Gervasi, G-HN778;
Villabella, PAT-X90062: PAT-X704

No, Pagliaccio mon son! Tenor
Fr. Non! Paillasse n'est plus
Ger. Nein, biu Bajazzo nicht bloss
Eng. A clown no more
Giovanni Martinelli & Metropolitan Opera
Cho.—Setti   12"—**V-6754**
[Vesti la giubba]
Beniamino Gigli   10"—**G-DA1312**
[Giordano: Andrea Chénier—Sì fui
soldato]
DUPLICATIONS: A. Lindi, C-DQ1099;
F. Merli, C-GQ7120; Enrico Caruso,
G-DB111*
In French: Georges Thill, C-LF94;
Micheletti, O-188582
In German: Helge Roswaenge,
G-DB5569; Peter Anders, T-E2816

ZAZA 1900

Buno Zazà
Tito Gobbi   10"—**G-DA5429**
[Zazà, piccola zingara]
DUPLICATION: T. Ruffo, G-DA355*

O mio piccolo tavolo Tenor
Giovanni Martinelli   12"—**G-DB337***
[Mascagni: Serenata]

Zazà, piccolo zingara Baritone
Tito Gobbi   10"—**G-DA5429**
[Buono Zazà]
John Charles Thomas
            (in VM-645)   12"—**V-15859**
[Massenet: Hérodiade—Salomé]
DUPLICATION: T. Ruffo, G-DA355*

SONGS

Barcarolle
M. Villabella (t)   10"—**PAT-PA1471**
[Ackermans: La Chanson du muletier]

Mattinata Fr. Aubade Eng. 'Tis the day
Jan Peerce (t)
        (in VM-1099)   10"—**V-10-1275**
[de Curtis: Torna a Surriento]
DUPLICATIONS: Aureliano Pertile,
G-DB1008; B. Gigli, G-DA1454:
G-DA1713; Jussi Björling, G-DA1841;
Giorgio Sempri, G-DA4967; G. Lugo, PD-
25516: PD-522974; Sydney Rayner,
D-M437; A. Piccaver, PD-62674; E. Lo-
manto, C-DQ1102; C. Vezzani, G-K6545;
Villabella, PAT-PA1276; Gino Sinim-
berghi, PD-62805: PD-25872

In French: J. Planel, PAT-X93062
In German: Richard Tauber, P-RO20135;
Franz Völker, PD-15415: PD-19793;
Karl Schmitt-Walter, T-A2182
In English: Richard Tauber, P-RO20512
In Swedish: Jussi Björling, G-X3622

—**Arr.** Orchestra Ilja Livschakoff Orch.,
PD-22915

Sérénade francaise (No. 1) In French
(Au clair de lune, or Mon gentil Pierrot)
Villabella (t)   10"—**PAT-X93093**
[Massenet: Pensée d'automne]
DUPLICATION: Sydney Rayner, D-M433

LEONINUS, Magister Leo (12th Century)
*Maître Léonin, as he was also known, was one
of the most noted musicians of the 12th century,
a famous organist, and a Maître de Chapelle at
the church which occupied the site of the relatively modern Cathedral of Notre Dame at
Paris. He is credited with being one of the first
to mark the different time values of notes.*

Easter Gradual—"Haec Dies"
Choir of the Pius X School of Liturgical
Music   (in VM-739)   12"—**V-13555**
[Chartres: Alleluia & Anon: Hymn of St.
Adalbert]

**Organum duplum on Gregorian Chant
"Haec Dies"**
(from "Magnus Liber" c. 1160)
Yves Tinayre (t) & Unison Strings
[Pérotin: Conductus]   12"—**LUM-32011**
(in Yves Tinayre Album No. 1)

Organum duplum on "Deum Time" (from
"Magnus Liber")
Yves Tinayre (t) & Chorus
                           12"—**LUM-32017**
[School of Pérotin: Agnius Douz]
(in Yves Tinayre Album No. 2)
F. Anspach & Ensemble
            (in Vol. VII)   12"—**AS-65**
[Pérotin: Organun triplum "Diffusa est
gratia]

LIADOV, Anatol (1855-1914)
*A brilliant Russian composer, student of Rim-
sky-Korsakov, with a particular gift for the
smaller forms, best known by his piano works
and the little tone poems and folk settings for
orchestra.*

Baba Yaga (Tableau musical) Op. 56
Orch.
Indianapolis Symphony Orch.—Sevitzky
        (in VM-1066)   12"—**V-11-9247**
[Grieg: Symphonic Dances, Pt. 5]
Lamoureux Orch.—Albert Wolff
                           12"—**PD-66894**
[Dukas: L'Apprenti sorcier, Pt. 3]
EIAR Orch.—LaRosa Parodi
                        12"—**CET-CB20183**
[Music Box & Paganini: Moto perpetuo]

(The) Enchanted Lake, Op. 62 Orchestra
Boston Symphony Orch.—Koussevitzky
(G-DB2896)   12"—**V-14078**
Berlin Philharmonic Orch.—Schmidt-
Isserstedt   12"—**T-E3059**
Stor Symphony—Jarnefelt
(O-D6047)   12"—**O-7697**
[Glinka: Kamarinskaya]

Fuga
Max Gilbert (vla) & Boyd Neel String
Orch.—Neel   12"—D-M485
[Howells: Elegy, Pt. 3]

Kikimora (Legend for Orchestra) Op. 63
Symphony Orch.—Järnefelt
(O-7733)   12"—O-D6052
EIAR Symphony Orch.—Ferrero
                      12"—CET-BB25030

(The) Music Box, Op. 32 Piano (or, The
Musical Snuff Box)
Fr. Une tabatière à musique
Alexander Brailowsky   12"—V-11-9009
[Rimsky-Korsakov-Rachmaninoff: Flight
of the Bumblebee & Chopin: Nocturne
No. 5]
Shura Cherkassy, in VOX-165
Corradina Mola (harpsichord)
[Giordano: Idyll]   10"—G-DA5399
—Arr. Orchestra
Boston "Pops" Orch.—Fiedler
                          10"—V-4390
[Guion: Turkey in the Straw—Fiddle
Tune Setting]
London Symphony Orch.—Coates
                      12"—G-AW169
[Russian Folk Dances, Pt. 3]
DUPLICATIONS: Wood Wind Ensemble,
V-19923; EIAR Orch.—LaRosa Parodi,
CET-CB20183
—Arr. Voice
Lily Pons (s) & Frank LaForge (pf)
     (in VM-599)   12"—V-1918
[Huë: A des oiseaux & Liszt: Comment
disaient-ils?]

(8) Russian Folk Dances, Op. 58 Orchestra
*(These pieces, sometimes known as Eight Rus-
sian Fairy Tales or Folk Songs, are settings of
traditional Russian tunes.)*
1. Religious Chant 2. Christmas Song 3.
Plaintive Vilage Song 4. Humorous Song
—Dance of the Gnat 5. Legend of the
Birds 6. Lullaby (Cradle Song) 7. Village
Dance Song
Philadelphia Orch.—Stokowski
          12" & 10"—V-8491 & V-1681
London Symphony Orch.—Coates
[Music Box]   2 12"—G-AW168/9
EIAR Orch.—Vittorio Gui
          2 12"—CET-CB20238/9
[Scriabin: Rêverie, Op. 24]
—Nos. 5, 6, 7 only
Pasdeloup Orch.—Ingelbrecht
                      12"—PAT-X5522

LIEBESKIND, Joseph (1866-1916)
*A German writer and editor on musical sub-
jects, especially interested in the eighteenth
century. He was also a composer of much instrumental music.*
Symphony No. 1, A minor
Zurich Radio Orch.—Hans Haug
              5 12"—G-FKX501/5

LIEURANCE, Thurlow (1878-   )
*A collector of American Indian music and mu-
sical instruments, Lieurance is a song composer.
Many of his compositions are based on Indian*

melodies. *In earlier days he recorded these
songs and the cylinders now are a part of the
National Archives collection. His songs, however, are pseudo-Indian and sentimental in
character.*

SONGS Settings of Indian Folk Songs
Winnebago Love Song
Love With Tears (Cheyenne Song)
Pueblo Lullaby
Omaha Ceremonial
T. Lieurance (Indian flute) & Clement
Barone (Modern flute) (in V-E89)
By the Waters of Minnetonka (Indian love
song) (Cavanass)
Nelson Eddy (b) & Theodore Paxson (pf)
(G-DA1579) (in VM-C27) 10"—V-4366
[Rasbach: Trees]
—Arranged Orchestra
Andre Kostelanetz & his Orch., in CX-284

LINCKE, Paul (1866-   )
*German conductor, publisher and composer
whose compositions include several successful
operettas.*

FRAU LUNA
GRI GRI
IM REICHE DES INDRA
LISISTRATA
VENUS AUF ERDEN
See current catalogues.

LINEK, Jirik Ignac (1725-1791)
Pastorella (on the motif "Christ was born")
Svatojakubsky Cho. & Orch.—Smetacek
[Brixi: Pastoral Motet]   12"—U-G14019

LISZT, Franz (1811-1886)
*Born in Hungary, but closely connected with
the musical life and achievements of France and
Germany, Liszt had an astounding career as
virtuoso, composer, conductor, and propagandist for the "new music" of Wagner and other
younger men. For the most part his own compositions are of less significance than his per-
sonal influence on the musical trends of his
time.*

COLLECTIONS
Piano Music of Liszt
Fantasia quasi Sonate (2me Année de
Pèlerinage, No. 7)
Concert Etude No. 2, F minor, "La Leg-
gerezza"
Funérailles
Liebestraum No. 3
Hungarian Rhapsody No. 15
Gyorgy Sandor   4 12"—CM-602†
Années de Pèlerinage 3 Sets of Piano pieces
1st year (Switzerland); 2nd year (Italy);
3rd year (Posthumous grouping)
For recorded examples see:
Au bord d'une source; Eglogue; Fantasia
quasi Sonate-Après une lecture de Dante;
Les Jeux d'eaux à la Ville d'Este; Sonetti
del Petrarca; Venezia e Napoli

Au bord d'une source Piano
(Années de pèlerinage, 1st Year, No. 4)
Vladimir Horowitz
(in VM-1165†)   12"—V-11-9842
[Chopin: Nocturne No. 5]
Alexander Borovsky   12"—PD-516613
[Albéniz: Ibéria—Malaga] (PD-27343)
Edward Kilenyi   10"—PAT-PG105
[Mephisto Waltz, Pt. 3]

Ave Maria Piano (Grove's No. 33)
Walter Rehberg   12"—PD-95043
—**Arr. Chorus** Thiel
Regensburg Cathedral Cho.—Schrems,
G-EG3903

(La) Campanella See Transcriptions:
Paganini

Caprice poétique See Etude de Concert
No. 1

CHRISTUS Oratorio in Latin

Christus vincit Chorus & Orchestra
Basilica Choir—Pius Kalt
[Koch: Jubilate Deo]   12"—PD-27126

CONCERTOS Piano & Orchestra

No. 1, E flat major (Grove's No. 22)
Artur Rubinstein & Dallas Symphony—
Dorati   2 12"—VM-1144†
Emil Sauer & Paris Conservatory Orch.—
Weingartner   3 12"—CM-371†
Walter Gieseking & London Philharmonic
—Wood (C-LFX299/300)
                   2 12"—CX-17†
(C-LX181/2) (C-GQX10681/2)
DUPLICATIONS: Joseph Benvenuti &
Paris Conservatory Orch.—Münch, PAT-
PDT49/50; Mischa Levitzki & London
Symphony—Ronald, G-D1775/6; Alexan-
der Brailowsky & Berlin Philharmonic—
Prüwer, VOX-454: PD-66750/2

No. 2, A major (Grove's No. 23)
Emil Sauer & Paris Conservatory Orch.—
Weingartner   3 12"—C-LFX568/70
Egon Petri & London Philharmonic—
Heward   3 12"—CM-362†
[Schubert-Liszt: Gretchen am Spinnrade]
(C-LX737/9)
Raymond Trouard & Orch.—Cloëz
              3 12"—O-123855/7

(6) Consolations Piano (Grove's No. 39)
—**No. 3, D flat major**
Emil Sauer   12"—C-69688D
[Valse oubliée No. 1]
Artur Rubinstein   12"—G-DB3216
[Hungarian Rhapsody No. 10]
Marie-Aimée Warrot 12"—PAT-PDT131
[Paganini—Etude No. 6]

Dance of the Gnomes See Gnomenreigen

Dante Sonata See Fantasia quasi Sonate-
Après une lecture de Dante

Eglogue Piano (Années de pèlerinage,
1st Year, No. 7)
Walter Rehberg   10"—PD-25138
(Chopin: Polonaise No. 7, Pt. 3]

(3) Etudes de Concert (Grove's No. 30)
1. Il Lamento (Capriccio) A flat major
2. La Leggerezza (Caprice poétique) F
minor

3. **Un Sospiro** (Allegro affettuoso) D flat
major
Jean Doyen   2 12"—G-W1569/70

No. 1, A flat major (Capriccio) "Il Lamento"
Jean Doyen, G-W1569

No. 2, F minor (Caprice poétique) "La
Leggerezza"
Jean Doyen, G-W1570
Gyorgy Sandor
(in CM-602†)   12"—C-71716D
[Fantasia quasi Sonate, Pt. 3]
DUPLICATIONS: Carlo Zecchi,
O-9103: CET-CB20347; Simon Barere,
G-DB2166; Louis Kentner, C-DX960; A.
Cortot, G-DB1535; Alexander Borovsky,
PD-516612: PD-27342

No. 3, D flat major (Allegro affettuoso) "Un
Sospiro"
Jean Doyen G-W1560
Louis Kentner   12"—C-DX960
[No. 2]
Harold Bauer   12"—V-11-9113
[Waldesrauschen]
Ania Dorfmann   12"—V-11-9672
[Schumann: Aufschwung]
DUPLICATIONS: Frederic Lamond,
D-K1015: G-EH999; Mischa Levitzki,
G-D1721; Egon Petri, C-68982D in CX-
77†: C-LX603; Sigfrid Grundeis, O-7990

(2) Concert Etudes See Gnomenreigen &
Waldesrauschen

**Fantasia & Fugue on the Chorale "Ad nos,
ad salutarem undam"**
(from Meyerbeer's "Le Prophète")
Organ (Grove's No. 133)
Alfred Sittard (St. Michael's, Harburg)
              2 12"—PD-95255 & PD-66555
[Reger: Toccata, D minor]

Fantasia & Fugue on B-A-C-H Organ
(Originally written for piano—Grove's No. 43
—arranged by Liszt for organ)
Fernando Germani   12"—SEMS-1135

Fantasia on Beethoven's "Ruins of Athens"
Piano & Orchestra
Egon Petri & London Philharmonic Orch.
Leslie Heward
(C-LX752/3)   2 12"—CX-136†
[Schubert-Liszt: Der Lindenbaum, piano
only]

**Fantasia quasi Sonate—Après une lecture
de Dante** Piano
(Années de pèlerinage, 2nd Year, No. 7)
Gyorgy Sandor
(in CM-602†)   12"—C-71715/6D
[Etude de Concert No. 2]
—**Arr. Piano & Orchestra**—Constant Lam-
bert
(For a ballet by Frederick Ashton—"Dante
Sonata")
Louis Kentner & Sadler's Wells Orch.—
Lambert   2 12"—C-DX967/8

(A) Faust Symphony Orchestra (with
Tenor & Chorus)
1. Faust 2. Marguerite 3. Mephisto
Paris Philharmonic & Vlassoff Choir, with
Villabella (t) in French—Meyrowitz
              7 12"—CM-272†
(C-GQX10804/10) (PAT-PDT31/7)

Feux follets Piano
(Etudes d'exécution transcendante,
No. 5)
Jeanne Marie Darré 12"—PAT-PDT92
[Chopin: Etudes Nos. 13 & 18]
Anatole Kitain 12"—C-LFX438
[Sonetto del Petrarca, No. 123]

Funérailles. Piano
(Harmonies poétiques et religieuses
No. 4)
Gyorgy Sandor
(in CM-602†) 12"—C-71717D
Vladimir Horowitz 12"—G-DB1848

Gnomenreigen Piano
(Concert Etude No. 2, Grove's No. 32)
Fr. Ronde des lutins Eng. Dance of the
Gnomes
Paul Baumgartner 12"—G-DB10032
[Waldesrauschen]
Louis Kentner 12"—C-DX1038
[Liebestraum No. 3]
DUPLICATIONS: Frederic Lamond,
D-K1015; G-EH968; A. Brailowsky, PD-
90175; N. de Magalov, RAD-RZ3031

Harmonies du Soir Piano
(Etudes d'exécution transcendante,
No. 11)
Georges Boskoff 12"—G-DB5090

Hungarian Fantasia Piano & Orchestra
(Grove's No. 26)
This work is based on the same material as the
Hungarian Rhapsody No. 14 (Orch. Set No. 1)
Edward Kilenyi & Grand Orch. Paris—
Meyrowitz 2 12"—CX-120†
(PAT-PAT119/20)
Winfried Wolf & Berlin Philharmonic—
Weisbach 2 12"—G-EH1209/10
(G-S10480/1)
Benno Moiseiwitsch & London Philhar-
monic—Lambert 2 12"—G-C3132/3
DUPLICATIONS: Victor Schiøler & Ti-
voli Orch., TONO-X25000/1; Jacques Du-
pont & Ruhlmann Orch., PAT-PGT3/4;
L. Malpas & Solas Orch., PAT-PA421

Hungarian March See under Transcriptions:
Schubert; also under Hungarian Rhapsody No. 15

HUNGARIAN RHAPSODIES

Liszt wrote 15 Hungarian Rhapsodies for piano
solo (Grove's No. 94). In the posthumously
published works there are 4 others. The com-
poser and Franz Doppler arranged six for or-
chestra (Grove's No. 17), numbered as fol-
lows:

Orch. Version	Piano Version
1	14
2	12
3	6
4	2

(The great popularity of the second Hun-
garian Rhapsody had led to the orchestral
version also being known as No. 2)

5	5
6	9

Liszt also made an arrangement for Piano and
Orchestra of No. 14, known as "Hungarian
Fantasia." The lists below are given in the
original piano version numbers.

No. 1, E major
Alexander Borovsky
(PD-561111/2) 2 10"—PD-62769/70

No. 2, C sharp minor (the famous Second
Rhapsody)
Alexander Brailowsky 12"—V-11-9330
(Also on V-11-9228 in VM-1064)
(G-DB6414)
Paul Baumgartner 12"—G-DB10064
Jesús María Sanromá 12"—V-13831
DUPLICATIONS: Raymond Trouard,
O-123842; Benno Moiseiwitsch, G-C3192;
Alexander Borovsky, PD-566181: PD-
67171; Louis Kentner, C-DX777; Alexan-
der Brailowsky, PD-95424: CET-OR5053;
Alfred Cortot, G-DB1042; Jacques Du-
pont, PAT-PD10; Mark Hambourg,
G-C2508; Yves Nat, C-D15244; Orazio
Frugoni, ELITE-7032; Julius Katchen,
D-K1694; Wilhelm Backhaus, G-DB1013

—Arr. 2 Pfs.
Rawicz & Landauer, C-FB1772

—Orchestral Version
The orchestral version, properly No. 4, is al-
most invariably known & listed as "No. 2."
Philadelphia Orch.—Stokowski
(G-DB3086) 12"—V-14422
(Arr. Müller-Berghaus)
Philadelphia Orchestra—Ormandy
(C-LX1045) 12"—C-12437D
(Arr. Müller-Berghaus)
National Symphony—Goehr
(Arr. Müller-Berghaus) 12"—D-K1321
All American Orch.—Stokowski
12"—C-11646D
New Queen's Hall Orch.—H. Wood
2 12"—C-DX9/10
Berlin Philharmonic—Hans Bund
(U-F18072) 12"—T-E1505
DUPLICATIONS: Berlin-Charlottenburg
Opera Orch.—Kopsch, PD-19772; Phil-
harmonic Orch.—Weissmann, P-E10724:
O-170095; Berlin Philharmonic—Abend-
roth, O-7887: P-E11389; Berlin Philhar-
monic Orch.—Melichar, PD-15364; Bar-
nabas von Géczy & his Orch.—G-EH1295;
Radiola Sym. Orch.—Majorossy, RAD-
RBM168; Tzigane Orch.—PAT-X96118

No. 3, B flat major
Alexander Borovsky
(PD-67172) 12"—PD-566182
[No. 7]

No. 4, E flat major
Alexander Borovsky 10"—PD-561114
(PD-62777)

No. 5, E minor
Alexander Borovsky 10"—PD-561118
(PD-62778)
Shura Cherkassky in VOX-175

No. 6, D flat major
Alexander Borovsky 10"—PD-561115
(PD-62779)
Vladimir Horowitz
(in VM-1165†) 12"—V-11-9843
Winfried Wolf 12"—G-EH987
Alexander Brailowsky 10"—PD-90146
Raymond Trouard 12"—O-123852
Shura Cherkassky in VOX-175
Mischa Levitzky 12"—G-AW20

—Orchestral version (No. 3)
National Symphony Orch.—Kindler
                          12"—V-11-9154
Berlin Orch.—Dobrindt   10"—O-25574
No. 7, D minor
Alexander Borovsky
(PD-67172)   12"—PD-566182
No. 8, F sharp minor "Capriccio"
Alexander Borovsky
(PD-62781)   10"—PD-561116
Edward Kilenyi   10"—PAT-PG98
No. 9, E flat major "Carnaval de Pesth"
Alexander Borovsky
(PD-67176)   12"—PD-566185
—Orchestral version (No. 6)
Boston "Pops" Orch.—Fiedler
                          12"—V-11-9652
Berlin Philharmonic Orch.—Schmidt-
Isserstedt   12"—T-E2280
Symphony Orch.—Havemann
                          12"—PD-27301
No. 10, E major "Preludio"
Artur Rubinstein   12"—G-DB3216
[Consolation No. 3]
Alexander Borovsky
(PD-67177)   12"—PD-566184
[No. 11]
No. 11, A minor
Alexander Borovsky
(PD-67177)   12"—PD-566184
[No. 10]
Shura Cherkassky   in VOX-175
Raymond Trouard   12"—O-123877
DUPLICATION: J. Dupont, PAT-PG10
No. 12, C sharp minor   (Piano Version)
Alexander Borovsky
(PD-67209)   12"—PD-566183
Alexander Brailowsky   12"—PD-35015
DUPLICATION: W. Wolf, G-EH931
—Orchestral version (No. 2, D minor)
Hallé Orch.—Harty   12"—C-7243M
(C-LX132))
No. 13, A minor
Alexander Borovsky
(PD-67194)   12"—PD-566186
Jacques Dupont   10"—PAT-X98154
No. 14, F minor "Mohac's Field"
Alexander Borovsky
(PD-67210)   12"—PD-566187
—Orchestral Version (No. 1)
(See also Hungarian Fantasia)
Boston "Pops" Orch.—Fiedler
(G-C3235)   12"—V-13596
Berlin Philharmonic Orch.—Schmidt-
Isserstedt   12"—T-E2146
DUPLICATIONS: Berlin State Opera
Orch.—Melichar, PD-27253; Berlin State
Opera Orch.—Abendroth, O-170158:
O-7734
No. 15 (Rakóczy March)
Gyorgy Sandor
        (in CM-602†)   12"—C-71718D
[Liebestraum No. 3]
Alexander Borovsky
(PD-62780)   10"—PD-561113
Shura Cherkassky   in VOX-175
DUPLICATIONS: Edward Kilenyi,
C-DX799: PAT-PAT79; Solomon,
C-DX441
(Les) Jeux d'eaux à la Villa d'Este   Piano
(Années de pèlerinage, 3rd Year, No. 4)

Eng. Fountains at the Villa d'Este
Claudio Arrau   12"—O-6743
Lucienne Delforge   12"—G-DB5102

LEGENDES   Piano
No. 2—St. François de Paule marchant sur
les flots.
Eng. St. Francis Walking on the Water
Roger Machado   12"—C-LFX684
Marcel Ciampi   12"—C-LFX186
DUPLICATIONS: Alfred Cortot,
G-DB3269; Vlado Perlmutter,
LUM-35020
(La) Leggerezza
See: Etude de Concert No. 2

(3) LIEBESTRAEUME   Op. 62
Eng. Love Dreams   Fr. Rêves d'amour
*The "Liebesträume" of Liszt were written
originally as songs (Grove's No. 171) and later
on transcribed by the composer as piano solos
(Grove's No. 62). No. 3 is the celebrated
"Liebestraum" and when the "Liebestraum" is
mentioned, it is this No. 3, although the num-
ber is almost invariably omitted.*
No. 1 ("Hohe Liebe")
No. 2 ("Gestorben war ich") E major
No recordings available.
No. 3 ("O Lieb' ") A flat major Piano
(For vocal versions see—Songs: O Lieb')
Gyorgy Sandor
        (in CM-602†)   12"—C-71718D
[Hungarian Rhapsody No. 15]
Eileen Joyce   12"—P-E11372
[Fauré: Impromptu No. 2]
(O-123833)
José Iturbi   12"—V-11-8851
[Debussy: Clair de lune]
Artur Rubinstein   12"—V-36337
[Rubinstein: Valse Caprice]
(G-DB2702)
DUPLICATIONS: Frederick Lamond,
G-EH999; Percy Grainger, C-7134M;
Rudolph Ganz, V-7290; Alexander
Brailowsky, V-11-8643: older version,
PD-95203: CET-OR5045; W. Backhaus,
G-DB926; Louis Kentner, C-DX1038;
Benno Moiseiwitsch, G-C3197; France
Ellegaard, PD-67839; Yvonne Gellibert,
G-W1523; Raymond Trouard, O-123843;
Jeanne-Marie Darré, PAT-PDT109; Paul
Baumgartner, G-DB10012; Josef
Lhevinne, in DISC-774; Mark Hambourg,
G-C2516; Schendel, G-S10242; Frantisek
Rauch, U-G14121
—Arr. 2 Pianos
Ethel Bartlett & Rae Robertson
                          12"—C-71452D
[Liszt: Paganini: Etude No. 3]
Rawicz & Landauer   12"—C-FB2145
[Dvořàk: Humoresque]
DUPLICATION: Whittemore & Lowe,
V-28-0410
—Arr. Orchestra
André Kostelanetz & his Orch.
        (in CM-484)   12"—C-71304D
[Rachmaninoff: Prelude in C sharp
minor]
[Fibich: Poème, on C-DX1163]
DUPLICATIONS: Victory Symphony,
V-35820: G-C1352; Marek Weber Orch.,

G-C2948: G-EH892, earlier version,
G-EH51; Campoli Salon Orch.,
G-BD846; Von Stachow Orch., PD-25196;
Paul Whiteman Orch., C-9798
—Arr. Organ: Adolf Wolff, T-A2637
—Miscellaneous arrangements:
Lew White (org.) with vl., harp., Cho.,
V-36209; Ferraresi (vl), G-S10493; Al-
bert Sandler (vl), C-DX621:
C-CQX16581; Maurice Maréchal (vlc),
C-LFX319; Squire Celeste Octet,
C-DX362: C-DFX129; Master Sextet,
G-EG6683; Mario Traversa (vl),
PD-47438
See also current catalogues
Malédiction   Pianos & Strings
Franz Osborn & Boyd Neel String Orch.
—Neel   12″—D-K1194
Mazeppa   Piano
(Etudes d'exécution transcendante No. 4)
No recording available
Mazeppa—Symphonic Poem, No. 6
Orchestra
(*An enlarged and orchestrated version of the
piano etude above*)
Berlin Philharmonic—Oskar Fried
2 12″—PD-66787/8
Mephiso Waltz   (Der Tanz in der Dorf-
schenke)   Orchestra
(*No. 2 of the Two Episodes after Lenau's
"Faust"—also arranged by Liszt for piano*)
Boston Symphony—Koussevitzky
2 12″—VM-870†
[Rimsky-Korsakov: Tale of the Invisible
City of Kitezh—Battle of Kershenetz]
New York Philharmonic-Symphony
Orch.—Rodzinski   2 12″—CX-281†
[Wolf-Ferrari: Secrets of Suzanne—
Overture]
London Philharmonic—Weingartner
2 12″—C-LX897/8
[Beethoven: Ruins of Athens—Overture]
DUPLICATIONS: Orch. of "Maggio Mu-
sicale"—Markevitch, CET-BB25158/9;
Lamoureux Orch.—Wolff, PD-67043:
PD-566140
—**Arr. Piano**   Liszt
William Kapell   2 12″—VM-1101†
[Albéniz: Ibéria—Evocation]
DUPLICATIONS: Aline van Barentzen,
G-DB5183; Edward Kilenyi, PAT-
PG104/5; Geza Anda (arr. d'Albert),
PD-67934/5: CET-OR5090/1

MISSA CHORALIS, A minor   Chorus &
Organ in Latin
**Kyrie, Gloria, Credo, Sanctus, Benedictus,
Agnus Dei**
Paris Philharmonic Cho.—E. Lévy
5 12″—PD-516627/31
Orpheus   Symphonic Poem No. 4   Orchestra
1854
CBS Symphony—Howard Barlow
2 12″—CX-165†
(2) Polonaises   Piano   (Grove's No. 46)
No. 1, C minor
Louis Kentner   12″—C-DX986
No. 2, E major
Raymond Trouard   12″—O-123851
Winifred Wolf   12″—G-EH1049

(Les) Préludes   Symphony Poem No. 3
Orchestra
(*After Lamartine's "Méditations poétiques"*)
Philadelphia Orch.—Ormandy
(G-DB3690/1)   2 12″—VM-453†
Philadelphia Orch.—Ormandy
2 12″—C-LX1052/3
London Symphony Orch.—Weingartner
(C-LX877/8)   2 12″—CX-198†
DUPLICATIONS: Amsterdam Concertge-
bouw Orch.—Mengelberg, CX-29†:
C-L2362/3: O-8402/3; Czech Philhar-
monic—Kleiber, T-E2022/3;
U-F18069/70; Berlin Philharmonic—van
Kempen, PD-67174/5: PD-516754/5;
Berlin Philharmonic—Knappertsbusch,
G-DB5691/2; London Symphony Orch.—
Coates, G-W1005/6; Symphony Orch.—
Meyrowitz, PAT-PDT8/9
Rakóczy March   Overture (Grove's No. 19)
Lilly Gyenes Hungarica Orch.
12″—PD-27283
[Kalman: Gräfin Mariza—Komm,
Zigany]
See also under: Hungarian Rhapsody
No. 15
Rhapsodie Espagnole   Piano
(Grove's No. 48)
(Folies d'Espagne & Jota Aragonesa)
Claudio Arrau   12″—T-E1629
—**Arr. Piano & Orchestra**   Busoni
Egon Petri & Minneapolis Symphony—
Mitropoulos   2 12″—CX-163†
(C-LX891/2)
Ricordanza   Piano
(Etudes d'exécution transcendante No. 9)
Emil von Sauer   12″—C-LWX353
Sigfrid Grundeis   10″—PD-10384
Schönster Herr Jesu   Chorus
Regensburger Domchor—Schrems
10″—G-EG3902
[Wagner: Parsifal—Der Glaube lebt]
Sonata, B minor   (Grove's No. 45)
Vladimir Horowitz   3 12″—VM-380†
Cor de Groot   4 12″—O-8772/5
(3) Sonetti del Petrarca   Piano
(Années de pèlerinage, 2nd year,
Nos. 4/6)
—**No. 47**
No recording available
—**No. 104**
Clifford Curzon   10″—D-M527
Walter Rehberg   12″—PD-95203
[Liebestraum No. 3, Brailowsky]
—**No. 123**
Anatole Kitain   12″—C-LFX438
[Feux Follets]

SONGS
*Liszt used both French and German texts for
his songs, and we have followed the original
titles in listing the songs below, with occa-
sional cross-references where a song is well
known by both its German and French titles.*
Comment disaient-ils?   In French
(Cornelius)
Lily Pons (s) & Frank LaForge (pf)
(in VM-599)   10″—V-1918
[Huë: A des Oiseaux; Liadov: Une
Tabatière à Musique]

(Die) drei Zigeuner In German
(Grove's No. 43) (Lenau)
Heinrich Schlusnus (b) & S. Peschko (pf)
[Oh! quand je dors]   12"—**PD-35088**
DUPLICATION: Theodor Scheidl,
PD-27203

Es muss ein Wunderbares sein (Redwitz)
In German (Grove's No. 28)
Heinrich Schlusnus (b)   10"—**PD-90199**
[Im Rhein]
Karl Erb (t)   10"—**G-DA4425**
[Schumann: Abendlied]
Pierre Bernac (b) & Francis
Poulenc (pf)   10"—**G-DA4914**
[Freudvoll und leidvoll; Nimm einen
Stahl der Sonne]
DUPLICATIONS: Theodor Scheidl,
PD-23371; Ursula van Diemen, G-EG813;
Piroska Anday, RAD-RZ3011

Freudvoll und leidvoll In German
Pierre Bernac (b) & Francis
Poulenc (pf)   10"—**G-DA4914**
[Es muss ein Wunderbares sein; Nimm
einen Strahl der Sonne]

Im Rhein, im schönen Strome In German
Heinrich Schlusnus (b) & Orch.—
Melichar   10"—**PD-90199**
[Es muss ein Wunderbares sein]

Liebestraum No. 3 (original song version)
See below—O Lieb', so lang du leiben
kannst

Nimm einen Strahl der Sonne In German
Pierre Bernac (b) & Francis
Poulenc (pf)   10"—**G-DA4914**
[Es muss ein Wunderbares sein;
Freudvoll und leidvoll]

O komm im Traum See—Oh! quand
je dors

O Lieb', so lang du lieben kannst In German
*(The original song version of the Liebestraum
No. 3; for instrumental versions see under
Liebestraum No. 3)*
Fr. Aimez, pendant la vie entière
Eng. Love's dream
It. Notturno No. 3—Sogno d'amore
Richard Tauber (t)   10"—**P-RO20497**
[Massenet: Elégie]
In French: Georges Thill, C-7326M:
C-LFX333
In English: Webster Booth, G-C3139;
John McHugh & Cho. (arr. Schipa),
C-DX1224
In Italian: Tito Schipa, G-DB873; Alfred
Piccaver, D-F8153

Oh! quand je dors In French (Hugo)
Ger. O komm im Traum
Maggie Teyte (s) & Gerald Moore (pf)
in Gramophone Shop Album, **GSC-3**
Theodor Scheidl (b) in German
[Die drei Zigeuner]   12"—**PD-27203**
Heinrich Schlusnus (b) in German
& Peschko (pf)   12"—**PD-35088**
[Die drei Zigeuner]

Wieder möcht' ich dir begegnen In German
(Grove's No. 37)
Theodor Scheidl (b) & Franz Rupp (pf)
                      10"—**PD-23371**
[Es muss ein Wunderbares sein]

Tarantelle See under Venezia e Napoli

Todtentanz (Paraphrase on "Dies Irae")
Piano & Orchestra (Grove's No. 24)
Jesús María Sanromá & Boston "Pops"
Orch.—Fiedler   2 12"—**VM-392†**
(G-FKX48/9)
Edward Kilenyi & Orch. Symphonique
de Paris—Meyrowitz   2 12"—**CX-122†**
(PAT-PAT102/3)

Tarantelle See: Venezia e Napoli

Valse oubliée No. 1 Piano
(No. 1 of Trois valses oubliées—Posth.)
Artur Rubinstein   10"—**V-10-1272**
[Schumann: Vogel als Prophet]
Eileen Joyce   12"—**P-R2738**
[Albéniz: Tango, Op. 165, No. 2]
Raymond Trouard   12"—**O-123878**
[Die wilde Jagd]
Emil Sauer   12"—**C-69688D**
[Consolation No. 3]

Venezia e Napoli Piano
(Années de pèlerinage, 2nd Year,
Nos. 8/10)
Gondoliera: Canzone; Tarantelle
Sigfrid Grundeis   2 12"—**O-7996/7**
—**No. 1 (Gondoliera)** only
Edward Kilenyi   12"—**PAT-PAT79**
[Hungarian Rhapsody No. 15]
—**No. 3 (Tarantelle)** only
Edward Kilenyi   12"—**PAT-PAT116**
Yvonne Gellibert   12"—**G-DB5160**
—**Arr. Orchestra**
Berlin Philharmonic Orch.—Kleiber,
T-F1154: U-F18051

Waldesrauschen (No. 1 of 2 Concert Etudes)
(Grove's No. 32) Piano
Harold Bauer   12"—**V-11-9113**
[Etude de Concert No. 3]
Paul Baumgartner   12"—**G-DB10032**
[Gnomenreigen]
DUPLICATIONS: Mark Hambourg,
G-C2587; Jacqueline Potier, G-K7909;
Jakob Gimpel, in VOX-164; F. Rauch,
U-G12943

(Die) Wilde Jagd
(Etudes d'exécution transcendante
No. 9) Piano
Raymond Trouard   12"—**O-123878**
[Valse oubliée No. 1]

MISCELLANEOUS Potpourri of Liszt
Melodies

Komponisten Bildnis: Franz Liszt
Piano & Orchestra
W. Stech & Berlin Philharmonic—
Schmidt-Isserstedt   12"—**T-E1899**

TRANSCRIPTIONS
(Arranged alphabetically by composer)

BACH

Fantasia & Fugue, G minor
(originally for organ)
Alexander Borovsky, PD-516617:
PD-67074

Prelude & Fugue, A minor
(originally for organ)
Solomon, G-C3376; André Collard,
C-DFX212

BEETHOVEN

Fantasia on Beethoven's "Ruins of Athens"
Piano & Orchestra
Egon Petri & London Philharmonic—
Leslie Heward 2 12"—**CX-136**†
[Schubert-Liszt: Der Lindenbaum,
piano only] (C-LX752/3)

CHOPIN

Polish Songs (See also Chopin: Songs)
(Liszt arranged six of Chopin's 17 Polish Songs)
No. 1, The Maiden's Wish (Chopin No. 1)
Sergei Rachmaninoff 12"—**V-11-8593**
[No. 6 & Schumann-Liszt: Der
Contrabandiste]
Moritz Rosenthal
(in VM-338) 12"—**V-14300**
[Chopin: Prélude No. 3, 6 & 7]
Margarita Mirimanowa
[Albéniz: Seguidillas]12"—**C-GQX16447**
No. 5, My Joys (Chopin No. 12)
Bernhard Stavenhagen 10"—**O-4785**
[Grieg: Norwegian Bridal Procession]
No. 6, The Return Home (Chopin No. 15)
Sergei Rachmaninoff 12"—**V-11-8593**
[No. 1 & Schumann-Liszt: Der
Contrabandiste]

GOUNOD

Faust—Valse, Act II
(originally for Chorus & Orchestra)
Eileen Joyce, P-E11252; Egon Petri,
C-69031D; Sigfrid Grundeis, O-7998

PAGANINI

(6) Grandes études de Paganini
(originally for Violin)
No. 1, Tremolo, G minor
(Paganini Caprice No. 6)
No recording available
No. 2, Andantino capriccioso, E flat major
(Paganini Caprice No. 17)
Vladimir Horowitz 10"—**V-1468**
[Demeny-Horowitz: Danse excentrique]
(G-DA1146)
[Debussy: Serenade to the Doll, on
G-DA1160]
Claudio Arrau 12"—**PD-95110**
[No. 5]
DUPLICATION: N. de Magaloff,
RAD-SP8020
No. 3, La Campanella
["Rondo à la clochette" from Paganini's
Violin Concerto, B minor, Op. 7)
Alexander Brailowsky 12"—**V-11-9025**
[Valse impromptu, A flat]
France Ellegaard 12"—**PD-67839**
[Liebestraum]
Cyril Smith 12"—**C-DX1214**
[Albéniz: Ibéria—Triana]
DUPLICATIONS: Raymond Trouard,
O-123843; Paderewski, V-6825:
G-DB1167; older version, G-DB376*;
Geza Anda, PD-67935: CET-RR8017:
CET-OR5091; Jeanne-Marie Darré,
PAT-PDT109: PD-95440; Vidusso,
G-S10451; Emil Hillel, USSR-13232/3;
Josef Lhevinne, in DISC-774, N. de
Magaloff, RAD-SP8020
—**Arr. 2 Pianos:** Bartlett & Robertson,
C-71452D

No. 4, Arpège, E major
(Paganini Caprice No. 1)
Carlo Zecchi 12"—**O-9103**
[No. 5 & Concert Etude No. 2]
[No. 5 & Chopin: Valse No. 5 on CET-
CB20351]
No. 5, La Chasse, E major
(Paganini Caprice No. 9)
Carlo Zecchi 12"—**O-9103**
[No. 4 & Concert Etude, No. 2]
[No. 4 & Chopin: Valse No. 5, on
CET-CB20351]
Sigfrid Grundeis 12"—**O-7990**
[Concert Etude No. 3]
DUPLICATION: Claudio Arrau,
PD-95110
No. 6, Tema e variazioni, A minor
(Paganini Caprice No. 24)
Marie-Aimée Warrot
[Consolation No. 3] 12"—**PAT-PDT131**

SCHUBERT (Lieder)

Gretchen am Spinnrade
Egon Petri
(in CM-362†) 12"—**C-69554D**
[Concerto No. 2, Part 5]
Hark, Hark the Lark (Morgenständchen)
Wilhelm Kempff 10"—**PD-62746**
[Schumann: Aufschwung]
Alexander Brailowsky 10"—**PD-90175**
[Liszt: Gnomenreigen]
(Der) Lindenbaum
Raoul von Koczalski 12"—**PD-95349**
[Beethoven: Trio, Op. 70—No. 1, with
Bern Trio]
Egon Petri (C-LX753)
(in CX-136†) 12"—**C-69620D**
[Fantasie on "Ruins of Athens" Pt. 3]
Ständchen
Sergei Rachmaninoff 12"—**V-11-8728**
[Kreisler-Rachmaninoff: Liebesfreud]

SCHUBERT (other works)

Fantasia "The Wanderer" C major, Op. 15
(Grove's No. 27)
Clifford Curzon (pf) & Queen's Hall
Orch.—Wood 3 12"—**D-X185/7**
(PD-516739/41)
Edward Kilenyi & Orch.—Meyrowitz
(PAT-PAT136/8) 3 12"—**CM-426**†
Hungarian March No. 4
(Originally for Piano—4 hands) Orch.
Berlin-Charlottenburg Opera Orch.—
Melichar 12"—**PD-27213**
[Schubert: Marche Militaire]
Soirée de Vienne
(Originally Schubert: Deutsche Tänze)
(Grove's No. 72)
Egon Petri 12"—**C-LWX115**
DUPLICATION: Walter Rehberg,
PD-24993

SCHUMANN

(Der) Contrabandiste
Sergei Rachmaninoff 12"—**V-11-8593**
[Chopin-Liszt: Polish Songs Nos. 1 & 6]
Widmung (Dedication)
Artur Rubinstein
(in VM-1139†) 12"—**V-11-9731**
[Brahms: Wiegenlied & Schumann:
Widmung]

VERDI

RIGOLETTO Paraphrase de concert
(Based on the famous Quartet)
Egon Petri (C-LW21) 10"—C-17101D
Alfred Cortot 12"—G-DB1105
DUPLICATIONS: P. Eggart, PD-24597;
Alexis Kligerman, D-M531

WAGNER

(DER) FLIEGENDE HOLLAENDER—
Spinning Chorus
Alexander Brailowsky 10"—PD-90027

TANNHAEUSER—Overture
Alexander Brailowsky
  2 12"—PD-95419/20
[Schubert: Moment Musical & Mendelssohn: Spinning Song]

LITOLFF, Henry Charles (1818-1891)

*A noted pianist and composer of his day, Litolff
was a pupil of Moscheles. He traveled extensively in Europe as a conductor and pianist,
then settled in Braunschweig and took over the
publishing business of Meyer. Later, turning
over this firm to his adopted son, he retired to
Paris and devoted himself to composition.*

Concerto Symphonique No. 4, Op. 102
Piano & Orch.
—Scherzo only
Irene Scharrer & London Symphony
Orch.—Wood 10"—C-17043D
(C-DB1267)

LOCATELLI, Pietro (1693-1764)

*An Italian violin virtuoso and a pupil of Cor-
elli who traveled widely, finally settling in Am-
sterdam.*
Caprice—"Le labyrinthe" Violin & Piano
(Arr. von Reuter)
Florizel von Reuter & pf.
  12"—PD-95250
[Rossini-Paganini: Fantasia on the G-
String on "Moses in Egypt"]
Yehudi Menuhin & F. Webster
  10"—G-DA1636
[Brahms: Hungarian Dance No. 12]
Sonata, D major (Arr. Piatti)
André Navarra (vlc) & Josef
Benvenuti (pf) 2 12"—PAT-PDT114/5
Sonata da camera Violin & Piano
Louis Zimmermann & pf. 12"—C-DHX16

LOEFFLER, Charles Martin (1861-1935)

*The Alsatian Loeffler, for many years a resi-
dent of the United States (he was a member of
both the Theodore Thomas and Boston Symphony Orchestras) was a composer of no clearly
definable school. His music is sometimes lush
and elegant, sometimes brusque and consciously
"American."*

(A) Pagan Poem, Op. 14 (after Virgil)
Orchestra, with Piano, English Horn
& Three Trumpets obbligati
Irene Gedney (pf), Richard Swingly
(English horn), & Eastman-Rochester
Symphony Orch.—Hanson
  3 12"—VM-876†

Quintet—Strings One Movement
Gordon String Quartet, with Ray Rickert
(3rd vl.) 2 12"—SCH-13
(2) Rhapsodies Oboe, Viola & Piano
Bruno Labate, Jacques Gordon & Emma
Boynet 3 12"—SCH-10
[Adieu pour jamais, with Gordon &
Carl Deis (pf)]

LOEILLET, Jean-Baptiste (1653-1728)

*A Belgian flutist and composer of flute and
chamber music.*

Suite, G minor Harpsichord
Alice Ehlers 10"—D-23090
[Bach: French Suite No. 1—Sarabande;
Fischer: Passepied]
(D-M494) (in D-A61)

LOEWE, Karl (1796-1869)

*A German singer, conductor and teacher, a
prolific composer in many forms but best
known by his ballades for voice and piano.*

BALLADES In German
Archibald Douglass, Op. 128 (Fontane)
Gerhard Hüsch (b) & Hanns Udo
  Müller (pf) 12"—G-DB4669
Theodor Scheidl (b) & pf acc.
  12"—PD-95215

Edward, Op. 1, No. 1
Wilhelm Streinz (b) & M. Raucheisen
(pf) 12"—G-EH1328
[Odins Meeresritt]
Lawrence Tibbett (b) (in English) & pf.
(G-DB1684) 12"—V-7486
[Wolfe: Glory Road]
(Das) Erkennen (Vogl)
Heinrich Schlusnus (b) & Sebastian
Peschko (pf) 12"—PD-35041
[Die Uhr]
(Der) Erlkönig, Op. 1, No. 3 (Goethe)
Adolf Harbich (b) & S. Peschko (pf)
[Prinz Eugen] 10"—PD-48482
Des fremden Kindes heil'ger Christ,
Op. 33, No. 3
Karl Erb (t) & B. Seidler-Winkler (pf)
  10"—G-DA4426
[Adam: Cantique de Noël]
Fridericus Rex (Vogl)
Hans Hermann Nissen (bs)
[Odin's Meeresritt) 12"—G-DB4674
DUPLICATIONS: Theodor Scheidl,
PD-95214; Adolf Harbich, PD-47398
(Des) Glockentürmers Töchterlein, Op. 112a
(Rückert)
Wilhelm Rhode (b) & Karl Bergher (pf)
[Heinrich der Vogler] 10"—PD-25321
Heinrich der Volger, Op. 56, No. 1 (Vogl)
Eng. **Henry the Fowler**
Gerhard Hüsch (b) & pf. acc.
[Prinz Eugen] 12"—G-EG3207
Theodor Scheidl (b) & pf. acc.
  12"—PD-95213
[Schumann: Beiden Grenadiere]
Wilhelm Rhode (b) & pf. acc.
  10"—PD-25321
[Glockentürmers Töchterlein]
Der Nöck, Op. 129, No. 2
Heinrich Schlusnus (b) 10"—PD-67213

Odin's Meeresritt, Op. 118
(Schreiber) 1851
Hans Herman Nissen (bs)
[Fridericus Rex]   12″—G-DB4674
Wilhelm Strienz (b) & M. Raucheisen
(pf) [Edward]   10″—G-EG1328
DUPLICATION: Wilhelm Rhode,
PD-25381

Prinz Eugen, der edle Ritter, Op. 92
(Freiligrath)
Theodor Scheidl (b) & pf. acc.
[Fridericus Rex]   12″—PD-95214
Gerhard Hüsch (b) & pf. acc.
[Heinrich der Vogler]   10″—G-EG3207
Adolf Harbich (b) & S. Peschko (pf)
[Erlkönig]   10″—PD-47482
DUPLICATION: Harold Williams (in
Eng.), C-DB837 in CM-233

Der Schatzgräber (Arm am Beutel)
Heinrich Schlusnus (b) & Sebastian
Peschko (pf)   12″—PD-67212
[Tom, der Reimer]

Tom, der Reimer, Op. 135 (Rückert)
Heinrich Schlusnus (b) & Sebastian
Peschko (pf)   12″—PD-67212
[Der Schatzgräber]
DUPLICATIONS: Theodor Scheidl,
PD-90043; Karl Schmitt-Walter,
T-E2087; Franz Völker, PD-57061;
Cornelius Bronsgeest, T-E5065; Leo
Slezak, PD-19926

(Die) Uhr, Op. 123, No. 3 (Seidl)
Heinrich Schlusnus (b) & S. Peschko
[Das Erkennen]   12″—PD-35041
DUPLICATIONS: Karl Schmitt-Walter,
T-E2087; Franz Völker, PD-57061

(Der) Wirtin Töchterlein, Op. 1, No. 2
(Uhland)
Adolf Harbich (b) & S. Peschko (pf)
[Fridericus Rex]   10″—PD-47398

LOPEZ BUCHARDO, Carlos (1881-)
Director of the National Conservatory of Argentina at Buenos Aires, Lopez Buchardo has written works for orchestra, voice and piano.

Bailecto Piano
Ricardo Viñes   10″—G-DA4910
[Allende: Tonadas Chilenas & Troiani:
Milonga]

LORTZING, Gustav Albert (1801-1851)
A leading German composer of comic operas whose works are still highly popular in his own country.

OPERAS In German

UNDINE 1845

Instrumental Selections
Polydor Band, PD-997

Ballet Music Orchestra
German Opera House Orch., Berlin—
Lutze   12″—T-E3097
Dresden State Opera Orch.—
Böhm   12″—G-EH916
[Zar und Zimmermann—Holtzschuhtanz]
(G-FKX24)

Individual Excerpts

Im Wein ist Wahrheit Duo: Bass & Tenor

Ludwig Hoffman & A. Peters
    10″—PD-62686
[Flotow: Marta-Canzone del portier]

Nun ist's vollbracht Baritone
Heinrich Schlusnus   12″—PD-73086
[Bizet: Carmen—Toréador Song]
[Zar und Zimmermann—Sonnst spielt'
ich, on PD-67151]
Karl Schmitt-Walter   12″—T-E2441
[Gounod: Faust—Valentins Tod, with
Chorus]

Vater, Mutter, Schwestern, Brüdern Tenor
Franz Völker   10″—PD-24193
[Zar und Zimmermann—Lebe wohl]
DUPLICATIONS: Marcel Wittrisch,
G-EG2412; Peter Anders, T-A2405;
H. E. Groh, O-26254

(DER) WAFFENSCHMIED 1846
Eng. The Armorer

Overture Orchestra
Berlin Philharmonic—Prüwer
    12″—PD-19901
Deutschen Opernhaus Orch.—Schmidt-
Isserstedt   12″—T-E2118
Concert Orch.—Seidler-Winkler
    12″—G-EH1254
Berlin Philharmonic—Melichar
    12″—PD-15320

Auch ich war ein Jüngling
(Stadinger's Air) Bass
Wilhelm Schirp   12″—T-E3130
[Wagner: Fliegende Holländer—
Daland's Aria]
Wilhelm Strienz   10″—G-EG6139
[Der Wildschütz—ABCD Duet, with
T. Machula]
DUPLICATIONS: Willy Schneider,
PD-47435; Ludwig Hoffmann, PD-66927

(DER) WILDSCHUETZ 1842
Eng. The Poacher

Overture Orchestra
German Opera House Orch.—
Grüber   12″—O-3605
DUPLICATIONS: German Opera Orch.
Lutze, T-E3054; Orch.—Seidler-Winkler,
G-EG6166

Individual Excerpts

A. B. C. D. Duet
Baritone, Soprano, Chorus & Orch.
Wilhelm Strienz, Traute Machula & Cho.
    10″—G-EG6139
[Waffenschmied—Auch ich war ein
Jüngling]

Fünftausend Thaler (Arie des Baculus)
Bass
Wilhelm Strienz   12″—G-EH1018
[Millöcker: Bettelstudent—Ach, ich hab']
DUPLICATION: Leo Schützendorf,
T-E725

Heiterkeit und Fröhlichkeit Baritone
Heinrich Rehkemper   12″—PD-95350
[Abt: Soldatenart]

ZAR UND ZIMMERMANN 3 Acts 1837
Eng. Czar and Carpenter

Abridged recording (Arr. Weigert &
Maeder)

Berlin State Opera Soloists, Chorus
& Orch.—Weigert
4 12"—PD-27407/10
The Cast:
Peter I.. Willy Domgraf-Fassbaender (b)
Peter Iwanow .... Waldemar Henke (t)
Van Bett .... Eduard Kandl (b)
Marie .... Tilly de Garmo (s)
Admiral Lefort ...... Felix Fleischer-
Janczak (b)
Lord Syndham ...... Desző Ernster (b)
Marquis .... Willy Frey (t)
Witwe Browe .... Ida von Scheele-
Müller (c)

Vocal Excerpts
Berlin State Opera Soloists & Cho.
12"—PD-15225

Overture Orchestra
Berlin Philharmonic—Schmidt-
Isserstedt 10"—T-A2270
Grosses Symphonie-Orchester
10"—PD-15116
DUPLICATIONS: Berlin Philharmonic—
Melichar, PD-11058; Berlin State Opera
—Pfitzner, PD-27069

Individual Excerpts
Auf Gesellen, greift zur Axt Bar. & Cho.
Gerhard Hüsch & Cho. 12"—G-EH1069
[Sonst spielt' ich]
Heil sei dem Tag! Bass & Cho.
Wilhelm Strienz & Cho. 12"—G-EH1132
Holzschuhtanz
Dresden State Opera Orch.—
Böhm 12"—G-EH916
[Undine—Ballet music] (G-FKX24)
Berlin Philharmonic Orch.—Schmidt-
Isserstedt 10"—T-A2270
Lebe wohl, mein flandrisch Mädchen, Act II
Tenor
Franz Völker 10"—PD-24193
[Undine—Vater, Mutter]
DUPLICATION: P. Anders, T-A2405
O sancta justitia! Act I Bass
Wilhelm Strienz 12"—G-EH1260
Leo Schützendorf 12"—T-E221
Willy Schneider 10"—PD-47460
Sonst spielt' ich mit Szepter Act III
Baritone
(sometimes listed as "Einst spielt' ich!")
Karl Schmitt-Walter 12"—T-E2465
[Gounod: Faust—Valentine's Prayer]
Gerhard Hüsch 12"—G-EH1069
[Auf, Gesellen, greift zur Axt]
Heinrich Schlusnus 12"—PD-67151
[Undine—Nun ist's vollbracht]
[Nessler: Der Trompeter von Säkkingen
Behüt, on PD-67255]

MISCELLANEOUS Medleys of Lortzing
Melodies
T. Rudolph, M. L. Küster, B. Arnold,
H. H. Nissen, W. Hiller with Chorus &
Orch.—Schröder 12"—T-E1854
Berlin State Opera Orch.—Steeger
12"—PD-57105

LOTHAR, Mark (1902-)
*A contemporary German composer who has
written several operas, symphonies and chamber works.*

Mefisto's Songs (from "Faust") Goethe
G. Gruendgens (Recitation in German)
with music by Lothar 12"—G-DB5661
[Hamlet Monologue]
Hamlet Monologue (Shakespeare)
G. Gruendgens (Recitation in German)
with M. Lothar, harpsichord & F. Thöne,
spinetton 12"—G-DB5661
[Faust: Mefisto's Songs]
(Der) Pirol
Heinrich Schlusnus (b) & S. Peschko (pf)
10"—PD-62828
[Schillings: Wie wundersam]

LOTTI, Antonio (c.1667-1740)
*A teacher of many noted Italian composers, in-
cluding Marcello, Lotti was the composer of
both church music and operas.*

Crucifixus Unacc. 8-Part Chorus in Latin
Basilica Choir—Pius Kalt
12"—PD-27117
[Victoria: Popule meus] (PD-566179)
Miserere Chorus in Latin
Harvard University Choir—Davidson
10"—TC-T1634
[Byrd: Sing Joyfully unto God]
Pur diceste Arietta
Giuseppe De Luca (b) & Pietro Cimara
(pf), in D-U1
—Arr. Violin & Piano: Leo Petroni,
T-A1912

LUALDI, Adriano (1887-)
*A pupil of Wolf-Ferrari whose operas are sel-
dom performed outside of his native Italy.*

La Canzone di Fracisio
Gianna Pederzini 10"—G-DA5424
[Massenet: Werther—Air des larmes]
Le Furie d' Arlecchino—Intermezzo Giocoso
(Opera for marionettes) 1915
Enzo de Muro Lomanto & Maria
Zamboni with Orch. 3 10"—C-DQ1126/8
(C-GQ7140/2)

FIGLIA DI RE Opera 1917
Interludio del sogno Orchestra
EIAR Symphony Orch.—Parodi
2 12"—CET-CB20263/4
[Mancinelli: Scene Veneziane—Fuga
degli amanti]

LA GRANCEOLA Opera 1930
Overture Orchestra
Chamber Orch. of the Conservatory of
S. Pietro a Majella, Naples—Lualdi
12"—CET-CB20269
[Ravel: Tombeau de Couperin—
Rigaudon]
Inno all'aviatore
(in collaboration with Di Miniello)
Corpo Musicale della Regia Aeronautica
—Di Miniello 10"—C-DQ2692
[Vesella: Vecchia marcia militare]
Queen Proserpina Ballet
**Sotto gli alberi in fiore; Romanza;
Tamburino**
Chamber Orch. of the Conservatory of
S. Pietro a Majella, Naples—Lualdi
12"—CET-CB20270

LUCETTE, Jean
Senenade
En Barque
D'une Volupté   Piano
    Jean Lucette   12"—G-DB11118

LUIGINI, Alexander (1850-1906)
A French composer of operas and numerous ballets, Luigini is better known as a conductor of the Paris Opéra-Comique and as a teacher at the Lyons Conservatoire.
Ballet Egyptien   Orchestra
    BBC Theatre Orch.—Robinson
         2   12"—D-K1477/8
    Concert Orch.—Fletcher
         2   10"—G-C1254/5
    Opéra-Comique Orch.—Cloëz
         2   10"—O-165070/1
    Berlin Philharmonic Orch.—Melichar
         2   12"—PD-24638/9
    DUPLICATIONS: Marek Weber Orch., G-K6146/7: G-B3655/6; Paris Symphony —Chagnon, C-D11013/4: C-9566/7: C-CQX16614/5

LULLY, (Lulli), Jean Baptiste (1639-1687)
A French composer of Italian birth who is highly important in the history of music as the "first composer of legitimate French opera" and as one of the first to use and develop the form of the "French" or "Lully" overture. A great favorite of Louis XIV, Lully was a prolific composer of operas, ballets and incidental stage music (particularly of Molière's plays).
Au clair de la lune   Song in French
(Probably the most popular of all Lully's works and long since adopted as a French folk song. Most recorded versions are sung in an arrangement by de la Tombelle).
    Yvonne Printemps (s) with harpsichord
         12"—G-DB1625
    [Martini: Plaisir d'amour]
    Yves Tinayre (t)   10"—C-D6270
    [Trad: Légende de St. Nicolas]
    DUPLICATIONS: Marilliet & Caurat, C-DF944; Louis Chartier, D-23062 in D-A4
Courante
    Alice Ehlers (harpsichord)
    (D-F7726)   (in D-A61)   10"—D-23089
    [Byrd: Earl of Salisbury; Bach: French Suite No. 5—Gavotte; Frescobaldi: Gagliarda]
Gavotte (unspecified)
—**Arr. Violin & Piano**   Burmester
    Erica Morini & M. Raucheisen
         10"—PD-68519
    [Mozart: Minuet, D major]
    Georg Kulenkampff & Ferd. Leitner
    (U-B18052)   10"—T-A2625
    [Svendsen: Romance, Op. 26]

OPERAS & STAGE WORKS   In French

ALCESTE   Opera in 5 Acts   1674
Il faut passer dans ma barque   (Act IV)
    (Air de Caron)
    Charles Panzéra (b) & Mme. Panzéra-
    Baillot (pf)   10"—G-DA4924

[Cadmus et Hermione—Cantilène de Cadmus]
Jacques Bastard, with Yvonne Gouverné Chorus & Ars Rediviva Ensemble—
Crussard   12"—G-DB5191
[Bach: Gedenke doch, mein Geist & Anon. 17th Century— O nuit plus belle que le jour]

AMADIS DE GAULE   Opera in 5 Acts   1684
Bois épais, Act II   Tenor   (Air d'Amadis)
    Martial Singher (b)
        (in CM-578)   12"—C-72085D
    [Grétry: Richard Coeur-de-Lion—O Richard]
    Enrico Caruso   10"—G-DA1097
    [Crescenzo: Première caresse]
    Miguel Villabella   12"—PAT-PGT20
    [Armide—Plus j'observe]
Menuet   Orchestra
    Symphony Orch.—Cauchie
         10"—PAT-PG48
    [Atys—Air pour la suite de Flore & Proserpine—Menuet]

L'AMOUR MEDECIN
    Incidental Music to Molière's drama
Overture   (Chaconne)
    Paris Conservatory Orch.—Fendler
         12"—BAM-22
    [Clerambault: Symphonia Quarta]

ARMIDE ET RENAUD
    Opera in 5 Acts   1686
Plus j'observe, Act II   (Air de Renaud)
    Yves Tinayre (t)
        (in Vol. II)   12"—AS-20
    [Persée: Air, with Lina Falk]
    Miguel Villabella   12"—PAT-PGT20
    [Amadis—Bois épais]

ATYS   Opera in 5 Acts   1676
Air pour la suite de Flore (Gavotte)
    Orchestra
    Symphony Orch.—Cauchie
         10"—PAT-PG48
    [Amadis—Menuet & Prosperpine— Menuet des ombres]
Les Songes agréables   Arr. Harpsichord
    Wanda Landowska   12"—G-DB4973
    [Daquin: L'Hirondelle & Chambonnières: Chaconne & Rondeau]

LE BOURGEOIS GENTILHOMME
    (Incidental Music to Molière's comedy)
Cérémonie turque, Act IV
    (This "Turkish Ceremony" scene is spoken in French with Lully's incidental music performed by chorus & orchestra.)
    Denis d'Inès (recitation & singing) with Orch.—R. Charpentier   12"—G-DB4855
Exemples de danses, Act I   Orchestra
    (Each dance is announced by M. d'Inès)
    Comédie-Française Orch.—
    R. Charpentier   10"—G-P809
    [Menuet]
Menuet (Song of the Dancing Master)
    Denis d'Inès (recitation & singing) with Comédie-Française Orch.   10"—G-P809
    [Exemples de danses]

—Arr. Orchestra
Jean Ibos Quintet, PD-522420
*(Richard Strauss interpolated an orchestral
version of this Lully Menuet in his "Bürger als
Edelmann" Suite. For recordings see under
Richard Strauss.)*

CADMUS ET HERMIONE
Opera in 5 Acts 1673
Chaconne
Orch. of the Société des Concerts de
Versailles—Cloëz
(in Vol. XII) 12"—AS-114
[Phaeton—Overture & Entrée]
Cantilène de Cadmus
Charles Panzéra (b) & Mme. Panzéra-
Baillot (pf) 10"—G-DA4924
[Alceste: Il faut passer dans ma barque]

DIVERTISSEMENT DE CHAMBORD
Pageant
Ariette de Cloris: Que soupirer d'amour
(Molière)
Yvonne Printemps (s) & Henri Büsser
(pf) 10"—G-P835
[Offenbach: La Grande Duchesse de
Gérolstein—Dites-lui qu'on l'a remarqué]

LE MEDECIN MALGRE LUI
(Incidental Music to Molière's comedy)
*(Some of Lully's music is used in the back-
ground of this phonographic version of the
Molière play.*
Abridged presentation by Jean Variot—
spoken by artists of the Comédie-
Française) 4 12"—G-L994/7

PERSEE Opera in 5 Acts 1682
J'ay perdu la beauté—Recit. Contralto
(Méduse)
Je porte l'épouvante—Air, Act III
Lina Falk (in Vol. II) 12"—AS-20
[Air from Armide, with Yves Tinayre]
O Mort! Soprano (Air de Merope)
Solange Renaux 12"—PAT-PGT21
[Roland—Par le secours]

PHAETON 1683
Overture & Entrée de danse
Orch. of the Société des Concerts de
Versailles—Cloëz
(in Vol. XII) 12"—AS-114
[Cadmus et Hermione—Chaconne]

PROSPERINE Opera in 5 Acts 1680
Menuet des ombres heureuses Orchestra
Symphony Orch.—Maurice Cauchie
10"—PAT-PG48
[Amadis—Menuet & Atys—Air pour la
suite de Flore]

ROLAND Opera in 5 Acts 1685
**Par le secours Soprano (Air de le Fée
Logistille)**
Solange Renaux 12"—PAT-PGT21
[Persée—O Mort!]

LA TEMPLE DE LA PAIX Ballet 1685
Minuet (arr. Mottl)
Minneapolis Symphony Orch.—
Mitropoulos
(in CX-197†) 12"—C-11566D
[Mendelssohn: Capriccio Brilliant]

THESEE Opera in 5 Acts 1675
Overture & Marche des sacrificateurs
Symphony Orch.—Cauchie
10"—PAT-PG47
Revenez, amours, revenez Soprano
(Venus)
Jane Laval 10"—C-LF18
[Rameau: Castor et Pollux—Tristes
apprêts]
La puissance de Dieu (Trans. G. Renard)
Strasbourg Cathedral Choir—A. Hoch
12"—C-RFX74
[Maudit: En son temple sacré]

LUMBYE, Hans Christian (1810-1874)
*A Danish composer of marches and dance mu-
sic, Lumbye is often called the "Danish
Strauss."*

Amélie Waltz
Tivoli Concert Orch.—Jensen
[Queen Louise Waltz] 12"—G-Z267
Symphony Orch. 10"—G-X2432
[Gade: Folk Tale Ballet—Wedding
Waltz]
Bouquet Royal
Tivoli Concert Orch.—Jensen
[Columbine Polka] 10"—O-D884
Britta Polka
Royal Opera House Orch., Copenhagen—
Høeberg 12"—NP-Z60130
[Champagne Galop & Concert Polka]
Tivoli Orch.—Jensen 10"—O-D155
[Champagne Galop]
Champagne Galop
Tivoli Orch.—Jensen 10"—O-D155
[Britta Polka]
Royal Opera House Orch., Copenhagen—
Høeberg 12"—NP-Z60130
[Britta Polka & Concert Polka]
German Opera House Orch., Berlin—
Lutze 10"—T-A2635
[Strauss: Leichtes Blut, Polka]
(U-B18079)
Christian IX March
Royal Opera House Orch., Copenhagen—
Høeberg 12"—NP-Z60136
[Queen Louise Waltz]
Columbine Polka
Tivoli Concert Orch.—Jensen
[Bouquet Royal] 10"—O-D884
Concert Polka 2 vls & Orch.
Peder Lynged & Carlo Andersen
(vls) with Royal Opera House Orch.,
Copenhagen—Høeberg 12"—NP-Z60130
[Britta Polka & Champagne Galop]
Carlo & K. P. Andersen (vls) & Orch.
[Jernbanegalop] 10"—G-X4224
Dream Pictures
Dan. Drømmebilleder Ger. Träumbilder
Royal Opera House Orch., Copenhagen—
Knudsen 12"—G-Z229
Royal Opera House Orch., Copenhagen—
G. Høeberg 12"—NP-Z60129
DUPLICATIONS: Copenhagen Philhar-
monic Orch.—T. Jensen, O-D6013; Tivoli
Concert Orch.—Felumb, TONO-X25057

(An) Evening at the Tivoli
(*Orchestral Suite from the works of Lumbye arranged by S. C. Felumb.*)
Introduction & March, Waltz, Galop, Mazurka, Galop
Tivoli Concert Orch.—Felumb
2 12"—G-Z246/7
Also: Tivoli Concert Orch.—Felumb, TONO-X25070

Far away from Denmark Ballet
Dan. Fjernt fra Danmark
—American Indian War Dance
Dan. Indiansk Krigsdans
Royal Opera House Orch., Copenhagen—
Høeberg   10"—NP-X51186
[Railway Galop]

Good Night Polka
Tivoli Orch.—Jensen   12"—O-D6409
[Railway Galop]

Hesperus Waltz
Tivoli Orch.—Th. Jensen   12"—O-D6408
[Sophie Waltz]

Jernbanegalop
Carlo Anderson (vl) & Orch.
10"—G-X4224
[Concert Polka for 2 Violins]
DUPLICATION: Tivoli Concert Orch., O-6409

Kroll's Ballklänge
Tivoli Orch.—Th. Jensen   12"—O-D6401
Tivoli Orch.—Felumb
10"—TONO-L28007

(The) Mounted Guards of Amager
—Final Galop
Danish State Radio Orch.—Reesen
10"—C-J50
[Gade: A Folk Tale Ballet—Polonaise & Wedding Waltz]

Queen Louise Waltz
Royal Opera House Orch., Copenhagen—
Høeberg   12"—NP-Z60136
[Christian IX March]
Tivoli Orch.—Th. Jensen   12"—G-Z267
[Amélie Waltz]

Railway Galop
Royal Opera House Orch., Copenhagen—
Høeberg   10"—NP-X51186
[Far Away From Denmark—Indian War Dance]
Tivoli Orch.—Jensen   12"—O-D6409
[Good Night Polka]

Sophie Waltz
Tivoli Orch.—Th. Jensen   12"—O-D6408
[Hesperus Waltz]

LUTHER, Martin (1483-1546)

The great Reformer was an ardent music lover and an important figure in musical history. He edited, or assisted in editing, many collections of German hymns and chorales. These tunes usually credited to Luther are generally heard today in the Bach settings.

Away in a Manger Arr. Wasner
Trapp Family Choir—Wasner
[Wasner: Kindersegen]   10"—V-2118

(Ein') Feste Burg
(Luther's most famous chorale)
Eng. A Mighty Fortress, or A Stronghold Sure

Erk'scher Männergesangverein, PD-10066; Neukölln Chorus, PD-19953; Romand Chorus (in French), G-FK162

—Arr. Orchestra   (Bach-Stokowski)
Philadelphia Orch.—Stokowski
10"—V-1692
[Trad. Arr. Stokowski: Russian Christmas Music]
See also: Reger—Fantasia on Ein' feste Burg, Op. 27

Vom Himmel hoch, da komm' ich her
Basilica Choir—Pius Kalt
[Trad: O du Fröhliche]   10"—PD-21020

MacDOWELL, Edward (1861-1908)

The first American composer to achieve international fame. His music is purely traditional in form (with direct influences from Grieg, Schumann and Raff), is Celtic in color and in detail, rich in happy and original inspirations.

COLLECTION

To a Water Lily, Op. 51, No. 6
To a Wild Rose, Op. 51, No. 1
Scotch Poem, Op. 31, No. 2
Improvisation, Op. 46, No. 4
March Wind, Op. 46, No. 10
Rigaudon, Op. 49, No. 2
AD MDCXX (AD 1620), Op. 55, No. 3
Of Br'er Rabbit, Op. 61, No. 2
Rudolf Ganz (pf)   2 12"—D-A599

A. D. 1620 Piano
(Sea Pieces, Op. 55, No. 3)
Myra Hess   10"—C-DB1235
[Dvořák: Slavonic Dance No. 1, with Hess & Harty—Pf., 4-Hands]
(in Columbia History of Music, Vol. IV: CM-234)
Rudolf Ganz, in D-A599

(A) Deserted Farm Piano
(Woodland Sketches, Op. 51, No. 8)
Myrtle C. Eaver   10"—V-22161
[Of Br'er Rabbit, To a Water Lily, To a Wild Rose]

Fireside Tales, Op. 61 Piano Suite
See: Of Br'er Rabbit

From an Indian Lodge Piano
(Woodland Sketches, Op. 51, No. 6)
—Arr. Orchestra
Victor Orch., in V-E89

Improvisation, Op. 46, No. 4 Piano
Rudolf Ganz, in D-A599

"Indian" Suite—See Suite No. 2

Love Song—See Suite No. 2, 2nd Mvt.

March Wind, Op. 46, No. 10 Piano
Rudolf Ganz, in D-A599

Marionettes, Op. 38 Piano Suite
1. Prologue, 2. Clown, 3. Lover, 4. Soubrette, 5. Sweetheart, 6. Villain, 7. Witch, 8. Epilogue
Rudolf Ganz   2 10"—D-A576
—Nos. 7 (Witch), 2 (Clown), 6 (Villain), Arr. Orchestra
Victor Orch.—Reibold, in V-E79
(Earlier recording, V-22163)

Of a Tailor and a Bear Piano
Arr. Orchestra
Victor Orch. 10"—V-20153
(in "Rythms for Children")

Of Br'er Rabbit Piano
(Fireside Tales, Op. 61, No. 2)
Myrtle C. Eaver 10"—V-22161
[Deserted Farm, To a Water Lily, To
a Wild Rose]
Rudolf Ganz, in D-A599

Rigaudon, Op. 49, No. 2 Piano
Rudolf Ganz, in D-A599

Sea Pieces, Op. 55 Piano Suite
See: A.D. 1620

Scotch Poem, Op. 31, No. 2 Piano
Rudolf Ganz, in D-A599

SONGS In English

(The) Blue Bell, Op. 26, No. 5
Anna Howard (s) & pf. 12"—36032
(in "Songs for Children")

Thy Beaming Eyes, Op. 40, No. 3
(Gardner)
Nelson Eddy (b) 10"—V-4368
[Speaks: Sylvia] (in V-C27)

Suite No. 2 ("Indian") Op. 48 Orchestra
Columbia Broadcasting Symphony—
Howard Barlow 4 12"—CM-373

—2nd Mvt. (Love Song) only
RCA Victor Orch., in V-E89

—4th Mvt. (Dirge) only
Eastman-Rochester Symphony—
Howard Hanson
(in VM-608) 12"—V-15657

To a Water Lily Piano
(Woodland Sketches, Op. 51, No. 6)
Myrtle C. Eaver 10"—V-22161
[To a Wild Rose, Deserted Farm,
Of Br'er Rabbit]
Rudolf Ganz, in D-A599

—Arr. Orchestra
André Kostelanetz & his Orch., C-4279M;
Chicago Symphony-Stock, V-1152

To a Wild Rose Piano
Myrtle C. Eaver 10"—V-22161
[To a Water Lily, Deserted Farm,
Of Br'er Rabbit]
Rudolf Ganz, in D-A599

—Arr. Orchestra
Chicago Symphony-Stock, V-1152; André
Kostelanetz & his Orch., C-4279M

—Vocal Arrangement
Heddle Nash, C-DB1365

Witches' Dance, Op. 17, No. 2 Piano
Lydia Tartaglia Morichini
10"—C-DQ2723
[Massenet: Scènes pittoresques—Air de
Ballet]

Woodland Sketches, Op. 51 Piano Suite
1. To a Wild Rose 2. Will o' the Wisp
3. At an Old Trysting Place 4. In Autumn
5. From an Indian Lodge
6. To a Water Lily 7. From Uncle Remus
8. A Deserted Farm 9. By a Meadow-Brook
10. Told at Sunset
*For recording see under titles of Nos. 1, 5 ,6, &
8 only.*

MACHAUT, Guillaume de (c.1300-1377)
*An important French poet and composer known
for his motets and ballades.*

Ballades

Quant Theseus—Double Ballad
Je suis trop bien—Ballade
F. Mertens & E. Jacquier (tenors) with
Instr. Ensemble of Société Pro Musica
Antiqua Brussels—Cape
(in Vol. VII) 12"—AS-67
[Virelai, "De tout sui si confortée"]

Hoquetus David
Trumpet, Bass Trumpet, Trombone
Instrumental Group 12"—OL-3
[Anon. 14th Cent: Virelai—Or sus, vous
dormès trop]

MASS
*(Probably the first mass to embrace the entire
Ordinary of the Mass, it is said that it was sung
in 1364 at the Cathedral of Rheims for the
coronation of Charles V.)*

**—Credo, Sanctus, Agnus Dei, & Ite Missa
Est** only
Les Paraphonistes de St. Jean des Matines
& Brass Ensemble—Van
(in Vol. IV) 2 12"—AS-31/2

—Kyrie & Qui propter nos only
La Psallette de Notre Dame—
J. Chailley 12"—G-DB5118
[Pérotin: Salvatoris hodie]
(in French Masters of the Middle Ages)

Rose lys
Chanterelle (s), Clarinet, Flute & Basoon
12"—BAM-44
[Anon: Chansons of the 13th, 14th,
& 15th Centuries]

Virelai: De tout sui si confortée
H. Guermant (s) & Medieval harp
(in Vol. VII) 12"—AS-67
[Quant Theseus & Je suis trop bien]

MAHLER, Gustav (1860-1911)
*Mahler was one of the leading conductors at
the turn of the century. He conducted both for
the Metropolitan Opera and the New York
Philharmonic Society. Until recently his symphonies and songs have had only a small group
of ardent partisans, but during the last few
years his major works have had consistent hear-
ings and recordings of these works have won for
Mahler a wide audience.*

(Das) Lied von der Erde
Orchestra & Soloists 1908
(First performance 1911)
Charles Kullman (t) & Kerstin Thorborg
(c) with Vienna Philharmonic Orch.—
Bruno Walter 7 12"—CM-300†
(Recorded at an actual performance,
Vienna, May 24, 1936)

SONGS In German

Ich atmet' einen linden Duft
(Rückert) 1902
(No. 1 of Rückert songs)
Eng. I breathe the breath of blossoms
Charles Kullman (t) (in English)
(C-DB1787) 10"—C-DB1303
[Schönberg: Hängenden Gärten, Nos.
5 & 12, E. Storm]

(in Columbia History of Music Vol. V:
CM-361)

Kindertotenlieder—Song Cycle
(Rückert) 1902
1. Nun will die Sonn' so hell aufgehen
2. Nun seh' ich wohl, warum so dunkle
Flammen
3. Wenn dein Mütterlein
4. Oft denk'ich, sie sind nur ausgegangen
5. In diesem Wetter
Heinrich Rehkemper (b) & Orch.—
Horenstein 3 12"—**PD-66693/5**
Lieder eines Fahrenden Gesellen 1883
Eng. Songs of a Wayfarer
1. Wenn mein Schatz Hochzeit macht
2. Ging heut Morgen über's Feld
3. Ich hab' ein glühend Messer
4. Die zwei blauen Augen
Carol Brice (c) & Pittsburgh Symphony
Orch.—Reiner 2 12"—**CX-267†**
Eugenia Zareska (c) & London Phil-
harmonic—Van Beinum
2 12"—**D-K1624/5†**
Rheinlegendchen
(from "Des Knaben Wunderhorn")
Heinrich Schlusnus (b) 12"—**PD-95469**
[Tamboursgesell]
(Der) Tamboursgesell
(from "Des Knaben Wunderhorn")
Heinrich Schlusnus (b) 12"—**PD-95469**
[Rheinlegendchen]
Um Mitternacht Rückert
A. Noordewier-Reddingius (s)
& Org. 10"—**C-DH81**
Wer hat die Liedlein erdacht?
(from "Des Knaben Wunderhorn")
Elisabeth Schumann (s) & George
Reeves (pf) 10"—**G-E555**
[Mozart: Warnung & Wiegenlied]

SYMPHONIES

No. 1, D major (The "Titan") 1888
Minneapolis Symphony—Mitropoulos
6 12"—**CM-469†**
No. 2, C minor
("Auferstehungs"—"Resurrection")
Soloists & Chorus in German
(Poem by Klopstock)
Twin City Chorus & Minneapolis Sym-
phony Orch. & Organ—Ormandy
(Recorded at actual performance at the
University of Minnesota, Jan. 6, 1935,
with Ann O'Malley Gallogly, alto, Cor-
rine Frank Bowen, soprano, & Rupert
Sircum, chorus director)
11 12"—**VM-256†**
No. 4, G major
Philharmonic-Symphony Orch. of New
York—Bruno Walter (with Desi Halban,
soprano, in German) 6 12"—**CM-589†**
(C-LX949/54†)
No. 5, C sharp minor 1902
Philharmonic-Symphony Orch. of New
York—Bruno Walter 8 12"—**CM-718†**
—3rd Mvt. (Adagietto) only
Vienna Philharmonic—Bruno Walter
(G-DB3406) 12"—**V-12319**
No. 9, D major 1911
Vienna Philharmonic—Bruno Walter
(G-DB3613/22†) 10 12"—**VM-726†**

MAILLART, Louis, Aimé (1817-1871)
*A French composer (pupil of Halévy) of
operas and cantatas.*

(LES) DRAGONS DE VILLARS
Opéra-Comique 1856
Ger. **Das Glöckchen des Eremiten**
Vocal & Orchestral Selections
R. Revoil, A. Noël, with Chorus & Orch.—
Andolfi 10"—**PAT-PG23**
Overture Orchestra
Berlin State Opera—Zemlinsky
12"—**PD-66796**
Berlin State Opera Orch.—Lutze
12"—**T-E2909**
Individual Excerpts
Grâce à ce vilain Ermite (Couplets) Act 1
Soprano
Georgette Myriss, PAT-X91030
Ne parle pas, Rose (Romance) Act I Tenor
Villabella, PAT-PAT6; J. Planel,
PAT-X91053; M. Claudel, PD-62702;
PD-524064; Génio, G-K6633; Marcelin,
G-P592*
Soldatenart—Wenn Mann beim Wein sitz
Baritone
NOTE: *This is an air by Franz Abt interpolated
in the 3rd Act of some German versions of
"Les Dragons de Villars."*
H. Reimer, T-E1832; H. Rehkemper,
PD-96350

MALIPIERO, Francesco (1882-   )
*One of the most important contemporary Ital-
ian musicians, composer of many works in
modern idioms and the larger forms. Unfortunately none of the major works are yet represented on discs.*

Cantari alla Madrigalesca
String Quartet 1932
Rome Quartet 2 12"—**G-DB4512/3**
Impressioni dal vero
(Il capinero & Il cu-cu)
EIAR Symphony Orch.—Parodi
12"—**CET-CB20268**

MALOTTE, Albert Hay (1895-   )
(The) Lord's Prayer
John Charles Thomas (b) & Carroll
Hollister (pf) 10"—**V-1736**
[Partridge-Seaver: Just for Today]
Gladys Swarthout (ms) & L. Hodges (pf)
(In VM-679) 12"—**V-16781**
[Molloy: The Kerry Dance]
Nelson Eddy (b) 12"—**C-70369D**
[Sullivan: The Lost Chord]
Marjorie Lawrence (s) with Male
Quartet (in CM-579) 12"—**C-72090D**
[Trad: Danny Boy]
Conrad Thibault 10"—**D-24189**
[Dvořák-Fisher: Goin' Home]
Webster Booth (t) 10"—**G-B9201**
[Russell: When Big Ben Chimes]
Victor Choral & Orch.—Robert Shaw
12"—**V-11-9155**
[Adams: The Bells of St. Mary's]
DUPLICATIONS: Gracie Fields, D-F8763;
De Pauer Infantry Chorus, in CM-709;
Jesse Crawford (org), D-24191

Song of the Open Road
Igor Gorin (b)
    (in VM-1125)   10"—V-10-1179
[Kalman: Countess Maritza—Play Gypsies]

MANCINELLI, Luigi (1848-1921)
An Italian 'cellist, conductor and composer of operas and other dramatic music.

OPERAS In Italian
CLEOPATRA

Overture Orchestra
EIAR Symphony Orch.—Tansini
        12"—CET-CB20255
Intermezzo
La Scala Orch.—Panizza 12"—G-AW103
[Scene veneziane]

ERO E LEANDRO Orchestral Suite
Milan Symphony Orch.—Molajoli
        12"—C-GQX10492
[Catalani: Loreley—Waltz of the Flowers]

SUITES Orchestra
Scene veneziane
  Eng. Venetian Scenes
No. 3, Fuga degli amanti a Chioggia (Scherzo)
La Scala Orch.—Marinuzzi
        12"—T-SKB3267
[Marinuzzi: Rito nuziale]
EIAR Symphony Orch.—Parodi
        12"—CET-CB20264
[Lualdi: Figlia di Re—Interludio del sogno Pt. 3]
DUPLICATIONS: Milan Symphony—Serafin, C-GQX10494; La Scala Orch.—Panizza, G-AW103

MANZOLI, Domenico (17th Century)
Member of the school of Monteverdi, Manzoli composed operas, incidental music and airs. The examples listed below are from a volume of "Canzonette a una e due voci" published in 1623.

Quando tu mi guardi e ridi
Se vedeste la piaghe Canzonette in Italian
Max Meili (t) & Harpsichord
    (in Vol. III) 12"—AS-21
[Monteverdi: Ohimè, ch'io cado]

MARAIS, Marin (1656-1728)
A famous French gambist, Marais studied composition with Lully. He wrote operas, concerted chamber music, and religious works.

"Pièce" for 2 viols
Prélude, Allemande, Sarabande, Gigue
Eva Heinitz & M. Clerget (vlas da gamba) & Pauline Aubert (harpsichord)
    (in Vol. VIII) 12"—AS-78
Suite, A minor
Viola da Gamba & Harpsichord
Alfred Zighera & Putnam Aldrich, in TC-T9

MARCELLO, Benedetto (1686-1739)
A famous Italian composer, pupil of Lotti and Gasparini, who wrote many vocal and chamber works highly esteemed in their day and not frequently played nowadays.

Allegretto (from an unspecified Cello Sonata) arr. Barbirolli
Boyd Neel String Orch.   12"—D-X258
[Respighi: Suite No. 3, Pt. 5]

CANTATAS for Solo voice
Disciaglietevi in pianto—Recit.
Perchè mai non m'uccise il dolore—Air
Giuseppe Flamini (bs) & harpsichord
[Cavalli: Serse—Beato chi] 12"—MIA-4
Quella fiamma che m'accende
Recit. & Aria
Georges Thill (t) & Maurice Faure (pf)   12"—C-LFX507
[Caccini: Amarilli]
Concerto, C minor Oboe & Orchestra
Leon Goossens & Philharmonia Orch. —Süsskind 2 12"—C-DX1389/90
[Fiocco: Arioso, with pf. acc.]
—Arr. Harpsichord (Transposed to D minor) J. S. Bach
Ruggero Gerlin   12"—MIA-9
—Adagio only
Edwin Fischer (pf)   10"—G-DA1389
[Mozart: Minuet, K. 1]
Nino Rossi (pf)   12"—G-DB5353
[Bach: Prelude & Fugue in B minor]

SONATAS—Viola da Gamba & Harpsichord
F major Arr. Aubert & Cébron
E. Pasquier & Instr. Ensemble
    2 10"—LUM-30094/5
[Sonata, G major—Grave]
G major—Grave only Arr. Aubert & Cébron
E. Pasquier & Instr. Ensemble
    10"—LUM-30095
[Sonata, F major, Pt. 3]

MARCHAND, Louis (1669-1732)
Remembered principally because he challenged J. S. Bach to an organ-playing contest, and then defaulted, Marchand was the preeminent French organist of his time.

Fond d'Orgue, E minor
Joseph Bonnet (Gonzalez Organ)
    12"—PAT-PAT67
[Grigny: Récit de tierce en taille & Anon: Trois versets du Te Deum]
(in 3 Centuries of Organ Music set)

MARENZIO, Luca (1550-1599)
One of the most significant figures among the early Italian composers of vocal music. Marenzio wrote a number of motets and a mass, but his madrigals, finding their way to England, became very popular there and greatly influenced Elizabethan musicians.

Estate Fortes in Bello
Julian Chapel Cho.—Boezi
[Victoria: Animam meam]
        12"—SEMS-40
Perchè la pioggia
Passani Choir
    (in Vol. XII) 12"—AS-120
[Strider faceva & Gesualdo: Moro lasso]
Strider faceva
Passini Choir
    (in Vol. XII) 12"—AS-120
[Perchè la pioggia & Gesualdo: Moro lasso]

Innocentes
Julian Chapel Cho.—Boezi
10"—**SEMS-24**
[Caretto: Pater Noster, A. Dadò]
[Boezi: O Cor Amore, A. Dadò, on
SEMS-50]
O Rex gloriae
Julian Chapel Cho.—Boezi
10"—**SEMS-51**
[Somma: Ave Maria, A. Dadò]

MARESCOTTI, Arturo Ercole (1866-   )
*An Italian composer of operas, songs and piano
pieces.*
Fantasque   Piano
Arturo Benedetti Michelangeli
[Granados: Andaluza]   12"—**G-DB5354**

MARESCOTTI, André-François (1902-   )
L'Aubade   (Entrée, Cantilène & Marche)
Orch of the Suisse Romande—
Ansermet   2 12"—**G-HEX116/7**
Suite No. 3, B major
(Prélude, Aria, Toccata)
Lottie Morel (pf)   2 12"—**G-HEX117/8**

MARINI, Biagio (1595-1664)
*A Venetian violinist in the service of several
royal Italian families who was one of the earliest to publish concerted instrumental music
notable for the demands it made upon the
performers.*
Romance, Gaillarde, Courante
Ars Rediviva Quartet—Crussard
[Schmelzer: Pastorella]   12"—**BAM-3**

MARINUZZI, Gino (1882-   )
*An Italian conductor who has appeared in
many opera houses throughout the world,
Marinuzzi's compositions are mainly vocal. A
few of his operas and cantatas have met with
some success abroad.*
Rito Nuziale
La Scala Orch.—Marinuzzi
12"—**T-SKB3267**
[Mancinilli: Scene Veneziane—Scherzo]
DUPLICATION: La Scala Orch.—Marin-
uzzi, G-HN544
Suite Siciliana
Royal Opera Orch., Covent Garden—
Bellezza   12"—**G-S10226**

MARKEVITCH, Igor (1912-   )
*Born at Kiev, Markevitch has studied with
Nadia Boulanger. His works have been per-
formed primarily in Europe.*
(L') Envol d'Icare   Ballet Suite
Orchestre National Belge—
Markevitch   3 12"—**G-DB5069/71**
(Le) Nouvel Age   Orchestral Suite
Orchestre National Belge—
Markevitch   3 12"—**G-DB5072/4**

MARPURG, Friedrich Wilhelm (1718-1795)
*A Prussian theorist and critic, Marpurg lived
several years in Paris, where he met Rameau
and was influenced by his harmonic theories.
He published many theoretical works and some
pieces for cembalo, piano, and organ.*

Rondeau
Galina Werschenska (pf)
10"—**G-DA5200**
[Prokofiev: Suggestion Diabolique]

MARSCHNER, Heinrich (1795-1861)
*A self-taught German composer best known by
his operas, Marschner is a contemporary of
Weber and Spohr, a champion of German
Romantic opera.*

HANS HEILING
3 Act Opera in German   1833
Overture   Orchestra
German Opera House Orch., Berlin—
Lutze   12"—**T-E3272**
An jenem Tag, Act I   Baritone
Josef Hermann   12"—**G-DB5678**
[Bizet: Carmen—Toreador's Song]
Heinrich Schlusnus   12"—**PD-35027**
[Gounod: Faust—Avant de quitter]
(Also: PD-67191)

MARTIN, Frank (1890-   )
*A Swiss Composer, pianist, teacher and music
critic, founder of the well known school of
music "Technicum Moderne." He has com-
posed in all forms but is best known for his
chamber music and his stage works.*
Der Cornet   1942/3
Excerpts
Elsa Cavelti (a) & Zurich Collegium
Musicum—Paul Sacher
3 12"—**C-LZX15/7**
Trio on Popular Irish Tunes
Piano, Violin, 'Cello
Walter Lang Trio   2 12"—**C-DZX17/8**

**MARTINI (Padre) Giovanni Battista
(or Giambattista) (1776-1784)**
*The foremost Italian musicologist and musical
theorist of the eighteenth century. Among the
countless composers who sought advice and
training from him were Jomelli, J. C. Bach, and
Mozart.*
Allegro
Ruggero Gerlin (pf)
(in Vol. IX)   12"—**AS-95**
[Matielli: Adagio; Rutini: Andante]
Andantino   Arr. Violin & Piano
See under Kreisler
Aria con variazioni
(from the 4th Organ Sonata)
Joseph Bonnet (Gonzalez organ)
12"—**PAT-PAT64**
[Frescobaldi: Toccata for the Elevation]
(in 3 Centuries of Organ Music)
Gavotte
Corradina Mola (harpsichord)
10"—**G-DA5392**
[Cimarosa: Mattutino—"Risveglio"]

**MARTINI IL TEDESCO (1741-1816)
(Johann P. A. Schwartzendorf)**
*The German Martini (often confused with
Padre Martini) is known exclusively for his
charming and ever popular song "Plaisir
d'Amour." He spent most of his life in France
and wrote dramatic, church, chamber and vocal
music.*

Plaisir d'Amour Song in French (Florian)
Ger. Liebesfreud—Liebeslied
André Baugé (b) & Mme. Variven
(harp)   12"—**PAT-PAT1**
[Méhul: Ariodant—Femme sensible,
with orch. acc.]
Yvonne Printemps (s) & harpsichord
                          12"—**G-DB1625**
[Lully: Au clair de lune]
Maggie Teyte (s) & Gerald Moore (pf)
                          10"—**G-DA1810**
[Fauré: Dans les ruines d'une abbaye]
Lorri Lail (ms) & Instr. Ensemble
[Caccini: Amarilli]   10"—**G-X7173**
Ninon Vallin (s) & M. d'Aleman (pf)
                          12"—**O-123584**
[Jura: La Violette doublera: 18th
century French tambourin]
Beniamini Gigli (t)   12"—**G-DB2530**
[Massenet: Elégie]
John McCormack (t) & Gerald
Moore (pf)   10"—**G-DA1829**
[Malashkin: O could I in song tell my
sorrow]
Vanni-Marcoux (bs) & pf.
                          12"—**G-DB4916**
[Séverac: Ma poupée chérie]
Tito Schipa (t) & Orch.—Sabajno
                          12"—**G-DB2131**
[Donaudy: O del mio amato]
Marian Anderson (c)   12"—**G-C2065**
[Donizetti: La Favorita—O mio
Fernando]
DUPLICATIONS: Charles Panzéra,
G-W798; Luci Perelli, G-DB4810; Lucian
Fugère, C-D13044; Paul Robeson,
G-B9059: G-JK2229; Paul Sandoz,
G-JK2; Claudel, PD-521947;
Campagnola, G-P581*
In English: Richard Tauber, P-RO20532
Arrangements
Duos in French: Armand Crabbé & May
Rubia, G-K7546; Charpini & Brancato,
C-DF2294
Instrumental arrangements
Society of Ancient Instruments,
C-D15224; Dinicu (vl), C-D8414; Marek
Weber Orch., G-X4328

MARTINU, Bohuslav (1890-   )
*A contemporary Czech composer, associated
with the younger Parisian school, whose operas,
chamber music and symphonic poems have had
enormous popularity in Europe.*
Sonata Flute, Violin & Piano
Marcel Moyse, Blanche Honegger,
Louis Moyse   2 12"—**G-L1047/8**
Quartets—String
No. 2
Quartet of the National Theatre,
Prague   3 12"—**U-G14330/2**

MARTUCCI, Giuseppe (1856-1909)
*A noted Italian pianist, conductor and prolific
composer of orchestral, piano and chamber
works. He would be unknown in America but
for the inexplicable devotion of Arturo Toscanini to his orchestral pieces.*
Notturno, G flat major Orchestra
EIAR Symphony Orch.—Ferrero
                          12"—**CET-PP60005**

La Scala Orch.—Panizza
                          12"—**G-AW3986**
Noveletta Orchestra
EIAR Symphony Orch.—Ferrero
                          12"—**CET-BB25095**
Tarantella, Op. 44 Piano
Nino Rossi   10"—**G-DA5364**
Miscellaneous See under
Handel: Suite (Minuet, Musette &
Gavotte)

MARX, Josef (1882-   )
*Marx, for many years director of the Vienna
Academy of Music, is known almost exclusively
as a song composer. His originality, and his sen-
sitivity to the texts he chooses have led to his
being called the last of the great line of lyric
talents coming to prominence with Schubert
and leading through Brahms, Wolf and Franz
to our own day.*

Marienlied
Erna Sack (s)   10"—**T-AK2157**
[Reger: Mariä Wiegenlied]
Selige Nacht
Lotte Lehmann (s) & Erno Balogh (pf)
        (in VM-419)   10"—**V-1858**
[Pfitzner: Gretel]
Und gestern hat er mir Rosen gebracht
(Th. Lingen)
Venezianisches Wiegenlied (Nina)
(P. Heyse)
Hedwig Jungkurth (s)   10"—**G-EG3795**

MASCAGNI, Pietro (1863-1946)
*An Italian composer of many works whose fame
rests entirely upon one opera-"Cavalleria Rusticana"—one of the most popular in the world
and which seems likely to be Mascagni's endur-
ing work. This opera is an example of the late
nineteenth century school of realism—the "verismo"—which other composers (such as Leoncavallo) followed with some success. Some of
his other operas, such as "L'Amico Fritz" and
"Iris," contain delightful spots but are seldom
heard outside of Italy.*

Ave Maria
See under Operas—Cavalleria Rusticana:
Intermezzo (Vocal arr.)
Canto del Lavoro Chorus & Orch.
La Scala Chorus & Orch.—Mascagni
                          12"—**G-S6800**
(Side 2 is a version for orchestra alone for
accompaniment purposes)
Also: (Arr.): Royal Marine Band,
G-HN558
Cavalleria Rusticana See under Operas
Danza esotica Orchestra
La Scala Orch.—Sabajno 12"—**G-S10347**
Milan Symphony—Molajoli
                          12"—**C-GQX10025**
Barnabas von Geczy Orch.
                          12"—**G-EH1232**

OPERAS In Italian
(L') AMICO FRITZ 3 Acts 1891
Complete recording
Soloists, Chorus & EIAR Symphony
Orch.—Pietro Mascagni
(CET-CB20316/28)   13 12"—**CET-4**
The Cast:
Suzel .... Pia Tassinari (s)

Fritz Kobus ... Ferruccio Tagliavini (t)
David .... Saturno Meletti (bs)
Beppe .... Amalia Pini (ms)
Hanezo .... P. L. Latinucci (t)
Federico ...... Armando Giannotti (bs)
Caterina .... G. Abba'Bersone (s)

Individual Excerpts

ACT I

Son pochi fiori Soprano
Pia Tassinari 12"—CET-BB25037
[Non mi resta] (PD-68000)
[Puccini: Bohème—Addio, on
CET-BB25143 in CET-7]
Mafalda Favero 10"—G-DA1498
[Puccini: Turandot—Signore! ascolta]
DUPLICATIONS: Adriana Perris,
C-GQX11083; Amelia Armolli,
C-DQ2717; Lucrezia Bori, G-DA649*;
Favero, C-D6086

Laceri miseri Mezzo-soprano
Ebe Stignani 12"—CET-BB25041
[Thomas: Mignon—Non conosci il bel
suol]

ACT II

Duetto delle ciliege; Suzel, buon dì
Tutto tace Soprano & Tenor
Eng. **Duet of the Cherries**
Magda Olivero & Ferruccio Tagliavini
12"—CET-BB25050
Pia Tassinari & F. Tagliavini
[Intermezzo, Act III] 2 12"—CET-105
Mafalda Favero & Tito Schipa
12"—G-DB3067
R. Pampanini & Dino Borgioli
12"—C-GQX10282

ACT III

Intermezzo Orchestra
EIAR Orch.—Mascagni, in CET-105
Milan Symphony—Molajoli
12"—C-7200M
[Cavalleria Rusticana—Intermezzo]
[Catalani: Loreley—Danza, on
C-GQX11072]
DUPLICATIONS: La Scala Orch.— Saba-
jno, G-S10336; G-S10187; Berlin State
Opera—Mascagni, PD-66585; EIAR Orch.
Tansini, CET-CB20000

Ed anche Beppe amo Recit.

O Amore, o bella luce Aria Tenor
Ferruccio Tagliavini
(in CET-1) 12"—CET-BB25026
[Verdi: Lombardi—La mia letizia
infondere] (PD-67928)
Dino Borgioli 10"—C-DQ1068
[Non mi resta, Caniglia]
DUPLICATION: E. de Muro Lomanto,
C-DQ3317

Non mi resta che il pianto Soprano
Pia Tassinari 12"—CET-BB25037
[Son pochi fiori] (PD-68000)
Rina Lorenzelli Gigli 12"—G-DB6459
[Verdi: Vespri Siciliani—Mercè,
dilette]
DUPLICATIONS: Lucrezia Bori,
G-DA649; M. Favero, C-6086; M. Farneti,
C-GQ7170; M. Caniglia, C-DQ1068

CAVALLERIA RUSTICANA
One Act 1890
Eng. **Rustic Chivalry**

Complete Recording
Soloists, Chorus & Orch. of La Scala,
Milan—Pietro Mascagni
11 12"—G-DB3960/70†
The Cast:
Santuzza .... Lina Bruna Rasa (s) .
Turiddu .... Beniamino Gigli (t)
Alfio .... Gino Bechi (b)
Lola .... Mana Marcucci (s)
Mama Lucia .. Giulietta Simionato (ms)
Chorus Master: Achille Consoli

Complete Recording
Soloists, Chorus & Orch. of La Scala,
Milan—Molajoli
(C-D14623/32) 10 12"—C-OP7†
The Cast:
Santuzza
Giannina Arangi-Lombardi (s)
Lola .... Maria Castagna (s)
Turiddu .... Antonio Melandri (t)
Alfio .... Gino Lulli (b)
Lucia .... Ida Mannarini (ms)
Chorus Master: Vittore Veneziani

Complete Recording
Soloists, Chorus & Orch. of La Scala,
Milan—Carlo Sabajno 9 12"—VM-98†
(G-C1973/81) (G-EH580/8)
The Cast:
Santuzza .... Delia Sanzio (s)
Lola .... Mimma Pantaleoni (s)
Turiddu .... Giovanni Breviario (t)
Alfio .... Piero Biasini (b)
Lucia .... Olga de Franco (ms)

Abridged Recording (Sung in French)
Opéra-Comique Soloists, Chorus & Orch.
—G. Cloëz 6 12"—O-123817/22
The Cast includes: Germaine Cernay, Alice
Hena, Gaston Micheletti, Arthur Endrèze
& Mady Arty

Vocal & Orchestral Selections
Soloists, Chorus & Orch. (In German),
T-E1296

Orchestral Fantasias, Selections, etc.
Marek Weber Orch., G-C1736: G-L788:
G-EH286: G-FKX65; Milan Symphony—
Molajoli, C-DFX179: C-GQX10701; Sym-
phony Orch., G-L641; Berlin State Opera
Orch.—Melichar, PD-57069: PD-15386;
Berlin State Opera Orch.—Lutze,
U-F18106: T-E2871

Individual Excerpts
Prelude Orchestra
Siciliana: O Lola Tenor
Introduction
Berlin State Opera Orch. (with J.
Dworsky, in German)—Blech
12"—G-EJ135

—Prelude (excerpt only) & **Siciliana**
Tenor
Giovanni Martinelli 12"—V-8109
[Verdi: Trovatore—Di quella pira]
(G-DB1288)
DUPLICATION: C. Milona, P-DPX7

—**Siciliana** only Tenor & Harp acc.
Luigi Infantino 10"—**C-BQ6020**
[De Luca: Serenata a Manuzza]
James Melton 12"—**V-18365**
[Leoncavallo: Pagliacci—O Colombina]
DUPLICATIONS: Alfred Piccaver,
PD-62673: Antonio Cortis, G-DA1277;
Tommaso Alcaide, C-DQ1073; DiMazzei,
O-188501; Lugo, PD-561088; Pertile,
C-GQ7180; Parmeggiani, C-5625; C.
Gero, CET-TI7041; T. Schipa, G-DA364*;
E. Caruso, G-DA117*
In French: Villabella, PAT-X90062, C.
Vezzani, G-P727
In German: Richard Crooks, G-EW75;
Franz Völker, PD-90059; Patzak,
PD-24327; C. Andrijenko, T-E1920
In Hungarian: Koloman von Pataky,
RAD-SP8017
In Bohemian: Beno Blachut, U-C12740
In Danish: Folke Anderson, G-X3590
In Swedish: Jussi Björling, G-X4265

Opening Chorus: Gli aranci olezzano
Fr. **O doux parfum**
Ger. **Duftig erglühen Orangen**
Eng. **Blossoms of Oranges**
La Scala Chorus—Sabajno
(G-K5237) 10"—**G-S5440**
[Leoncavallo: Pagliacci—Coro della
campane]
La Scala Chorus 10"—**C-GQ7036**
[Giordano: Andrea Chénier-Undì, Galeffi]
DUPLICATIONS: La Scala Chorus,
PD-67096: PD-95278; Hamburg State
Opera Chorus (in German)—Schmidt-
Isserstedt, T-E3030

Il cavallo scalpita Baritone & Chorus
Fr. **Piaffe, mon cheval**
Ger. **Peitschenlied**
Roger Bourdin & Cho. in French
10"—**O-188614**
[Massenet: Werther—Werther est de
retour]
In German: T. Scheidl, PD-90165

**Regina coeli: Innegiamo, il Signor non
è morto** Soprano & Chorus
Eng. **Easter Hymn**
Ger. **Lasst uns preisen den Herrn**
G. Arangi-Lombardi & Chorus
12"—**C-GQX10169**
[Verdi: Traviati-Brindisi]
Sadler's Wells Chorus & Orch. (in Eng.)
—Braithwaite 12"—**V-13824**
[Offenbach: Tales of Hoffman—
Bacarolle] (G-C3126)
Saxon State Opera Cho., (in Ger.) &
Orch.—Böhm 12"—**G-DB5558**
[Verdi: Aida—Prélude]
DUPLICATIONS: Turchetti & Chorus,
G-HN775; Cho. & Orch. (in French),
O-123000

Voi lo sapete Soprano
Eng. **Now you shall know**
Fr. **Romance de Santuzza: Vous le savez**
Ger. **Als euer Sohn einst fortzog**
Zinka Milanov 12"—**V-11-8927**
[Verdi: Forza del Destino—Pace, pace]
Claudia Muzio 12"—**C-9084M**
[Buzzi-Peccia: Colombetta]

(C-BQX2501) (C-LCX20)
Eva Turner 12"—**C-L2118**
[Puccini: Tosca—Vissi d'arte]
Ebe Stignani 12"—**C-LX1049**
[Verdi: Trovatore—Condotta ell'era
in ceppi]
Ebe Stignani 12"—**CET-BB25055**
[Ponchielli: Gioconda—A te questo
rosario]
Gianna Pederzini 12"—**CET-BB25036**
[Mozart: Nozze di Figaro—Voi che
sapete]
Maria Caniglia 12"—**G-DB6351**
[Catalani: La Wally—Ebben? ne andro
lontano]
Helen Traubel
(in CM-675) 12"—**C-72112D**
[Ponchielli: Gioconda—Suicidio!]
DUPLICATIONS: Giannina Arangi-Lom-
bardi, C-GQX10277: C-GQ7048; Liliana
Cecchi, C-CQX16616; Iolanda Magnoni,
C-GQX10922; R. Pampanini, C-GQ7212;
B. Scacciati, C-GQX10252: C-CQ709; L.
B. Rasa, C-GQX10256; Caniglia,
C-GQX10092; Randacio, G-DB729*; R.
Raisa, G-DB2123
In French: Germaine Martinelli,
PD-66991: PD-566056; R. Visconti,
C-RF70; M. Sibille, PAT-PG65
In German: A. Rautawaara, T-E1807;
Hilde Singenstreu, PD-67992; Margarete
Teschemacher, G-EH1032
In English: Joan Taylor, D-K1087

Tu qui Santuzza? Duo—Soprano & Tenor

No, No, Turiddu
Eng. **Santuzza & Turiddu Duet**
Fr. **C'est toi, Santuzza & O mon Turridu**
(Most isolated recordings of this scene omit
the brief part for Lola—"Fior di giaggiolo")
Dusolina Giannini & Beniamino Gigli
(G-DB1790) 12"—**V-17697**
Giannina Arangi-Lombardi & F. Merli
12"—**C-GQX10155**
Madeleine Sibille, Villabella, Jany
Delille (in French) & Orch.
12"—**PAT-PG17**
DUPLICATIONS: Svilarova & Alabiso,
C-DQ655; Aulikki Rautawaara & Peter
Anders (in German) T-E1807

Ah! il Signore vi manda
Duo: Soprano & Baritone
Eng. **Santuzza-Alfio Duet**
Nadia Svilarova & G. Vanelli
10"—**C-DQ749**

Intermezzo Orchestra & organ
Boston "Pops" Orch.—Fiedler
10"—**V-4303**
[Rimsky-Korsakov: Sadko—Song of
India] (G-B8412)
BBC Theatre Orch.—Stanford
Robinson 12"—**D-K1363**
[Offenbach: Tales of Hoffman—
Barcarolle]
Saxon State Orch.—Böhm
12"—**G-DB4556**
[Leoncavallo: Pagliacci—Intermezzo]
Deutschen Opernhauses Orch.—
Lutze 12"—**T-E3073**
[Leoncavallo: Pagliacci—Intermezzo]

Berlin State Opera Orch.—Mascagni
12"—PD-66584
[Verdi: Aida—Ballet Music]
DUPLICATIONS: Milan Symphony—
Molajoli, C-7200M: C-D14463: C-DFX61;
Berlin Philharmonic—Meyrowitz,
U-F14411; Berlin Philharmonic—Melichar, PD-27234; La Scala Orch.—
Marinuzzi, G-DB2895; Symphony Orch.—
Wood, C-DX194; London Symphony—
Barbirolli, G-C2292; Victor Concert Orch.
—Bourdon, V-20011; Symphony Orch.—
Weissmann, P-E10701; La Scala Orch.
—Sabajno, G-S10437; Symphony Orch.—
Cloëz, O-165086; Ruhlmann Orch.,
PAT-X8680; New Light Symphony,
G-B2377: G-HE2301: G-K5177; Melachrino Strings, G-B9580; Czech Symphony Orch.—Parik, ESTA-D2014;
Ultraphon Symphony Orch., U-A337

—Arr. Violin: J. Gautier, O-166018; A.
Sammons, D-F7533

—Arr. Voice ("Ave Maria")
T. Schipa, G-DB1387; I. Baillie, C-DX230

Brindisi: Viva il vino Ten. & Cho.
Beniamino Gigli & Met. Opera Cho.
[Denza: Occhi turchini]   12"—V-8222
[Ponchielli: Gioconda—Cielo e mar, on
G-DB1499]
DUPLICATIONS: F. Merli, C-GQX10156;
A. Piccaver, PD-62673
In German: Peter Anders, T-E3338;
F. Völker, PD-90059
In French: G. Micheletti, O-188506

Addio alla madre

Mamma, quel vino è generoso Tenor
Eng. Turiddu's Farewell
Ger. Mutter, der Rote war allzu feurig
Enrico Caruso & re-recorded orch.
12"—V-15732
[Gounod: La Reine de Saba—Prête moi]
[Bizet: Carmen—Flower Song, on
G-DB3023]
(Original recording on G-DB118*)
Jussi Björling   12"—V-11-9387
[Leoncavallo: Pagliacci—Vesti la
giubba]   (G-DB6163)
Galliano Masini   12"—CET-BB25096
[Verdi: Aida—Celeste Aida]
(Also on C-CQX16526)
Mario Binci   12"—G-C3541
[Puccini: Bohème—Che gelida manina]
(G-S10499)
Beniamino Gigli   12"—G-DB1902
[Folksong: Santa Lucia]
[Cilea: L'Arlesiana—Lamento, on
G-DB3905]
DUPLICATIONS: Giovanni Martinelli,
G-DB1089; Francesco Merli,
C-GQX10156; Alfred Piccaver, PD-66890;
Leonida Bellon, CET-CC2205; A. Ferrauto, CET-CB20282; A. Pertile,
C-CQ696: C-GQX10675
In German: Peter Anders, T-E3228; A.
Seider, PD-10254; Willy Tressner,
G-EH1289; Franz Völker, PD-95233;
C. Andrijenko, T-E1920

GUGLIELMO RATCLIFF 1895
Individual Excerpts
E sempre il vecchio andazzo
Carlo Galeffi   10"—C-GQ7104
[Bellini: La Sonnambula—Prendi
l'anel, Borgioli]
Intermezzo "Il Sogno" Orchestra
Milan Symphony—L. Molajoli
[Intermezzo, Act IV] 12"—C-GQX10241
DUPLICATIONS: La Scala Orch.—
Sabajno, G-S10187; EIAR Symphony
Orch.—A. Votto, CET-CB20000
Intermezzo, Act IV Orchestra
La Scala Orch.—Sabajno
12"—G-S10368
[Puccini: Edgar—Intermezzo]
DUPLICATIONS: Milan Symphony—
Molajoli, C-GQX10241; Berlin State
Opera Orch.—Mascagni, PD-66580

IRIS 3 Acts 1898

ACT I
Introduction & Inno al sole
Arr. Orchestra only
EIAR Symphony Orch.—Parodi
12"—CET-CB20210
Berlin State Opera Orch.—Mascagni
2 12"—PD-66580 & PD-66583
[Guglielmo Ratcliff—Intermezzo]
DUPLICATION: La Scala Orch.—
Consoli, G-AW304/5
—Inno al sole only (shortened version)
Eng. Hymn to the Sun
La Scala Chorus & Orch.—Sabajno
12"—G-S5442
[Bellini: Norma—Casta Diva, Bardone]
DUPLICATION: Chorus & Orch.,
C-GQX10493
Apri la tua finestra! (Serenata) Tenor
Antonio Cortis   10"—G-DA1076
[Massenet: Werther—Pourquoi me
réveiller]
Aureliano Pertile   10"—C-GQ7180
[Cavalleria Rusticana—Siciliana]
[Leoncavallo: Pagliacci—Serenata, on
C-CQ701]
DUPLICATIONS: A. Granda, C-DQ1090;
Martinelli, G-DA330*
Danza delle quecas Orchestra
Covent Garden Orch.—Bellezza
12"—G-S10223
[Puccini: Suor Angelica—Intermezzo]
DUPLICATION: Milan Symphony—
Molajoli, C-GQX10679

ACT II
Io piango Soprano
Maria Farneti   12"—C-GQX10326
[Un dì—"La piovra"]
Un dì (Ero piccina) "La piovra" Soprano
Rosetta Pampanini 12"—CET-BB25035
[Puccini: Manon Lescaut—Sola
perduta abbandonata]
DUPLICATIONS: Maria Farneti,
C-GQX10326; A. Oltrabella, G-S10436
Or dammi il braccio tuo Tenor
A. Granda   10"—C-DQ1090
[Apri la tua finestra]

ISABEAU 3 Acts 1911

ACT I
Tu ch'odi lo mio grido Tenor
Bernardo De Muro, G-DB557*

ACT II
Or solo intorno (Canzone de Folco) Tenor
E passerà la viva creatura
Beniamino Gigli   12"—G-DB5407
[Non colombelle]
DUPLICATION: B. De Muro, G-DB557*

Non colombelle Tenor
Beniamino Gigli   12"—G-DB5407
[E passerà la viva creatura]
[Lodoletta—Ah! ritrovarla nella sua
capanna, on G-DB5408]

ACT III
Dormivi? Sognavo Duo: Soprano & Tenor
Bartolomasi & B. De Muro, G-DB556*

Fu vile l'editto Tenor
B. De Muro, G-DB558*

I suoi occhi Duo: Soprano & Tenor
Bartolomasi & De Muro, G-DB556*
Poli-Randaccio & Barbieri, O-F5613

LODOLETTA Operetta in 3 Acts 1917
Se Franz dicesse il vero, Act III

Ah! ritrovarla nella sua capanna Tenor
Beniamino Gigli   12"—G-DB5408
[Isabeau—Non colombelle]
Galliano Masini   12"—C-CQX16526
[Cavalleria Rusticana—Addio alla madre]

Flammen, perdonami Soprano
Mafalda Favero   12"—G-DB5397
[Verdi: Otello—Ave Maria]
Iris Adami Corradetti
[Puccini: Butterfly—Un bel dì]
Toti Dal Monte   12"—G-DB5396
[Donizetti: Don Pasquale—Quel guardo
il cavaliere]

(LE) MASCHERE 1901
Overture Orchestra
Royal Opera Orch., Covent Garden—
Bellezza   12"—G-S10222
EIAR Symphony Orch.—Tansini
12"—CET-CB20214
La Scala Orch.—Marinuzzi
12"—T-SKB3200
DUPLICATION: Milan Symphony Orch.
—Molajoli, C-D14468

(La) Pavana Orchestra
Milan Symphony—Molajoli
12"—C-GQX10679
[Iris—Danza delle quecas]

(IL) PICCOLO MARAT 1921
Gran Duetto, Act II Soprano & Tenor
M. de Voltri & H. Lazaro
2 12"—C-GQX10145 & GQX10142

—Last part (Va nella tua stanzetta) only
Vigano & De Muro, G-DB558*

(I) RANTZAU 1892
Overture Orchestra
Milan Symphony—Molajoli
12"—C-GQX10012
[Puccini: Suor Angelica—Intermezzo]

SILVANO 1895
Barcarola Orchestra
La Scala Orch.—Ghione
12"—G-S10437
[Cavalleria Rusticana—Intermezzo]
DUPLICATION: EIAR Orch.—Votto
CET-CB20156

(Il) Sogno Orchestra
Milan Symphony—Molajoli
12"—C-GQX10026
[Puccini: Villi—Prelude Act I]

Serenata Song in Italian (Stecchetti)
O. Fineschi (s)   10"—CET-TI7043
[Schubert: Serenade]
Alessandro Ziliani (t)   10"—G-DA1424
[Giordano: Fedora—Amor ti vieta]
DUPLICATIONS: Casavecchi, G-HN198;
Martinelli, G-DB337*

Stornelli marini Song in Italian (Menasci)
Beniamino Gigli (t)   10"—G-DA1052
[de Curtis: Canta pe'me]

Visione lirica Orchestra
Berlin State Opera Orch.—
Mascagni   12"—PD-66585
[Amico Fritz—Intermezzo]

MASON, Daniel Gregory (1873-)
Say a Little Prayer Song in English
John McCormack (t) & Gerald
Moore (pf)   10"—G-DA1820
[Leslie Smith: One love for forever]

MASSE, Felix Marie (called "Victor") (1822-1884)
*A pupil of Halévy and winner of the Prix de
Rome in 1844, Masse was a successful opera
composer. He taught at the Paris Conservatoire,
was a member of the "Institut," and an officer
in the Legion d'Honneur.*

OPERAS In French
LES NOCES DE JEANETTE
Fantasy
Odeon Orch., O-238203
Air de Jean Tenor
Pierre Deldi, C-DF750
Air du Rossignol
Germaine Féraldy, C-LFX247
Halte là, s'il vous plaît
Ah! Jarnique, ce n'est gai
Ninon Vallin & André Baugé, PAT-PD3
Parmi tant l'amoureux
Cours mon aiguille dans le laire
Germaine Féraldy, C-LF88; Marcelle
Ragon, G-P770

PAUL ET VIRGINIE
Chanson du Tigre
Jeanne Gerville-Reache (c)
12"—V-15-1008*
[Bizet: Carmen—Habañera]
(recorded 1911)

MASSENET, Jules 1842-1912)
*The most popular of French composers after
Gounod, Massenet supplied highly theatrical,
sentimental, and clever operas to several gen-
erations. His "Elégie" and the "Méditation"
(from "Thaïs") are popular all over the world,
and his operas, particularly "Manon" justifies
his bid for immortality.*

(LE) CID See under Operas

Clair de lune   See under Operas—
Werther, Act I

(Le) Dernier Sommeil de la Vierge
See under Operas—La Vierge

DON QUICHOTTE   See under Operas
Elégie   See under Songs

(LES) ERINNYES   Incidental Music to
Leconte de Lisle's drama   1873
1. Prélude   2. Scène religieuse
3. Invocation (Elégie)   4. Entr'acte
5. Danse grecque
6. La Troyenne regrettant sa patrie
7. Final (Santurnales)
Symphony Orch.—Cohen (M. Maréchal,
vlc. solo)   3 12"—C-DFX87/8 &
                               DFX92

—No. 3 (Invocation)
*This instrumental piece was later arranged by
the composer as a song with 'cello and piano
accompaniment: the famous "Elégie." For recordings of both vocal and instrumental versions see under Songs—Elégie.*

MANON   See under Operas

Méditation   See under Operas—
Thaïs, Act II Intermezzo

OPERAS   In French

ARIANE   5 Acts   1906

Unspecified Excerpt   Orchestra
*(This piece is labelled simply "Ariane" and
may possibly be the most popular air, the
"Thème des Roses" from Act IV.)*
Jean Lensen Orch., C-4483

(LE) CID   4 Acts   1885
Individual Excerpts

ACT I

O noble lame étincelante   Tenor
Georges Thill & Orch.—Bigot
                        12"—C-LFX309
[O Souverain! O Juge! Act III]

ACT II

Ballet Music   Orchestra
1. Castillane   2. Andalouse
3. Aragonaise   4. Aubade   5. Catalane
6. Madrilène   7. Navarraise
Boston "Pops" Orch.—Fiedler
(G-B9571/3)   3 10"—VM-1058†
—Nos. 1, 2, 4, 6 & 7
Grand Orchestre Symphonique—
Ruhlmann   2 10"—PAT-X96247/8
—Nos. 1, 2, 3, 4, 6 & 7
New Symphony Orch.—E. Goossens
                        2 12"—G-C1638/9

ACT III

Pleurez, pleurez, mes yeux
Soprano   (Air de Chimène)
Suzanne Sten (ms)   12"—C-71368D
[Hérodiade—Il est doux]
Ah! tout est bien fini—Recit.   Tenor
O Souverain! O Juge! O Père—Air (Prière)
Eng. Rodrigue's Prayer
Georges Thill & Orch.—Bigot
[O noble lame, Act 1]   12"—C-LFX309
DUPLICATION: Enrico Caruso,
G-DB123*

DON QUICHOTTE   5 Acts   1910
Individual Excerpts

ACT I

Quand apparaissent les étoiles (Serenade)
Bass & Soprano
André Balbon & Marcelle Mahieux
                        10"—PAT-X90076
[Puccini: Bohème—Vecchia zimarra]
Interlude (No. 2)   Orchestra with
'Cello Solo
("La Tristesse de Dulcinée")
Pasdeloup Orch.—Coppola
[Manon—Menuet]   10"—G-DA4869

ACT V

Mort de Don Quichotte
Bass, Baritone & Soprano
Feodor Chaliapin & Olive Kline
                        12"—G-DB1096
*(Sancho's part as well as Don Quixote's is
sung by Chaliapin)*
Vanni-Morcoux, Cozette & Odette
Ricquier   10"—G-DA4857
*(The above disc omits Sancho's opening air,
beginning with Don Quichotte's first words
"Ecoute, mon ami" but is otherwise complete
to the end of the opera.)*

(LES) ERINNYES
See: Les Erinnyes—Incidental Music

GRISELIDIS   3 Acts   1901
Individual Excerpts

ACT I

Oiseau, qui pars   Baritone
Robert Couzinou
(PD-516593)   12"—PD-66967
[Gounod: Roméo et Juliette—Ballade
de la Reine Mab]

ACT II

La Mer! et sur les flots—Recit.
Il partit au printemps—Aria   Soprano
Jeanne Guyla   12"—G-DB4970
[Charpentier: Louise—Depuis longtemps]
DUPLICATION: C. Tirard, PD-516646
Je suis l'oiseau   Tenor   (Air d'Alain)
Marcel Claudel   10"—PD-522908
[Jongleur de Notre-Dame— O liberté
ma mie]
DUPLICATION: Cazette, G-P436*

HERODIADE   4 Acts   1881
Individual Excerpts

ACT I

Il est doux, il est bon   Soprano
Suzanne Sten (ms)   12"—C-71368D
[Le Cid—Pleurez, pleurez, mes yeux]
Grace Moore   12"—V-11-8258
[Duparc: Phidylé]
Rose Bampton   12"—V-11-8237
[Puccini: Tosca—Vissi d'arte]
DUPLICATION: Ninon Vallin,
O-123530
Ne me refuse pas   Soprano
Germaine Cernay   10"—C-LF109
[Thomas: Mignon—Romance de Mignon]
Jean, je te revois   Duo: Soprano & Tenor
Jeanne Guyla & César Vezzani
[Quand nos jours]   12"—G-DB4907

ACT II

Ce breuvage—Recit.

Vision fugitive—Aria Baritone
Martial Singher
(in CM-578) 12″—**C-72087D**
[Thomas: Hamlet—Chanson Bachique]
Robert Merrill 12″—**V-11-9291**
[Thomas: Hamlet—Chanson Bachique]
DUPLICATIONS: John Charles Thomas,
V-1639; Nelson Eddy, C-70349D:
C-DX990; Arthur Endrèze, O-123725;
Pierre Deldi, C-DFX113; Luis Musy,
G-P762; Lovano, PD-521904; E. Billot,
O-188527
In Italian: M. Basiola, C-GQX10974

ACT III

Demande au prisonnier Baritone
Arthur Endrèze 12″—**O-123033**
[Thaïs: Voilà donc la terrible cité]

ACT IV

Ne pouvant réprimer les élans
Adieu donc, vains objets (Air de Jean)
Je ne regrette rien de ma prison Tenor
Raoul Jobin
(in CM-696) 12″—**C-72139D**
[Werther—Lied d'Ossian]
César Vezzani 12″—**G-DB4844**
[Manon—Ah! fuyez]
DUPLICATIONS: José Luccioni,
G-DB5036; G. Lugo, PD-566176; T.
Beets, PD-27349; Franz, C-LFX56; Thill,
C-L1964

Quand nos jours s'éteindront
Soprano & Tenor
(Duo de la prison)
Jean Guyla & César Vezzani
[Jean, je te revois] 12″—**G-DB4907**
—Tenor part only
F. Tamagno, G-DR101*

(LE) JONGLEUR DE NOTRE-DAME

3 Acts 1902
Individual Excerpts

ACT I

O Liberté ma mie Tenor
Marcel Claudel 12″—**PD-522908**
[Grisélidis—Je suis l'oiseau]

Pour le Vierge (Air de Boniface) Bass
Lucien Fugère 10″—**C-D13077**
[Chaminade: Anneau d'argent]

ACT II

Légende de la sauge: Le Vierge entend—
Recit.

Fleurissait une sauge—Air Bass
Lucien Fugère 12″—**C-D15119**
[Wagner: Lohengrin—Duo, Beaujon
& Thill]
Vanni-Marcoux 10″—**G-DA1159**
Marcel Journet 12″—**G-DB1174**
[Charpentier: Louise—Berceuse]
DUPLICATIONS: Louis Morturier,
G-P704; R. Couzinou, PD-516569; P.
Dupré, O-123707; J. Beckmans,
PAT-X7173; E. Billot, O-171039; R.
Bourdin, O-171016

MANON 4 Acts 1884

Complete recording
Opéra-Comique Soloists, Chorus & Orch.
—Elie Cohen 18 12″—**C-OP10†**
(C-D15156/73) (C-LCX84/101)
The Cast:
Manon Lescaut .. Germaine Féraldy (s)
Poussette .... Andrée Vavon (s)
Javotte .... Mlle. Rambert (s)
Rosette .... Mlles. A. Bernadet &
Fenoyer (s)
La Servante .... Mme. Julliot (s)
Le Chevalier des Grieux
Joseph Rogatchewsky (t)
Lescaut .... G. Villier (b)
Le Comte des Grieux . Louis Guénot (bs)
Guillot de Morfontaine . . M. de Creus (t)
De Brétigny .... A. Gaudin &
J. Vieuille (b)
L'Hôtelier .... M. Payen (b)

Orchestral Selections (Fantasias, etc.)
Arr. Tavan
Marek Weber Orch.
(G-L954) 12″—**G-S10299**
Symphony Orch.—Gurlitt
12″—**PD-19951**

Individual Excerpts

Prélude Orchestra
Symphony Orch.—G. Cloëz
[Minuet, Act III] 10″—**O-165084**

Je suis encore tout étourdie Soprano
It. Ancor son io tutta stordita
Eng. **Manon's Entrance**
Bidù Sayão
(in CM-612) 12″—**C-72094D**
[Adieu, notre petite table]
Ninon Vallin 10″—**PAT-X90052**
[Voyons, Manon, plus de chimères]
[Gavotte, Act III, on O-188863]
DUPLICATIONS: Mme. Géori-Boué,
O-188944; Fanny Heldy, G-DB1409; S.
Delmas, O-188736; G. Féraldy,
C-D15042; E. Luart, O-188571
In Italian: M. Zamboni, C-DQ1119

Regardez-moi bien les yeux—Recit. Baritone
Ne bronchez pas—Air
André Gaudin 10″—**PD-524006**
[A quoi bon l'économie]
DUPLICATION: R. Bourdin, O-188508

Restons ici, puisqu'il faut!—Recit.

Voyons, Manon, plus de chimères—Air
Soprano (Les regrets)
Ninon Vallin 12″—**PAT-X90052**
[Je suis encore tout étourdie]
[Adieu notre petite table, on O-188862]
DUPLICATIONS: G. Corney, PD-522561;
S. Delmas, O-188736; E. Luart,
O-188514
In Italian: M. Zamboni, C-DQ1119

J'ai marqué l'heure du départ
Soprano & Tenor

Non! Je ne veux pas croire
(Duo de la Rencontre)

Nous vivrons à Paris
Mary McCormick & Georges Thill
12″—**C-12509**
DUPLICATION: Luart & Friant,
O-123657

—Nous vivrons à Paris only
It. **A Parigi andrem**
Adelaide Saraceni & P. Pauli
(in Italian) 12″—**G-DB1648**
[Verdi: Falstaff—Dal labbro il canto]

ACT II

Duo de la lettre: J'écris à mon père
On l'appelle Manon
Vous aimer? Manon! Je t'adore!
Duo: Soprano & Tenor
Eng. **Letter Duet** Ger. **Briefduett**
Ninon Vallin & Villabella
[Gavotte] 12″—**PAT-X90034**
DUPLICATIONS: E. Luart & Micheletti,
O-123529; G. Farrar & E. Caruso,
G-DM110*

Enfin, les amoureux
Venir ici sous un déguisement Quartet
Luart, Friant, Bourdin, Vieuille
12″—**O-123581**

Adieu, notre petite table Soprano
It. **Addio nostro picciol desco**
Bidù Sayão (in CM-612) 12″—**C-72094D**
[Je suis encore tout étourdie]
Grace Moore
[Gavotte] (in VM-918) 12″—**V-11-8259**
Ninon Vallin & Orch.—Cloëz
12″—**PAT-X90053**
[Suis-je gentille ainsi?]
[Voyons, Manon, plus de chimères, on
O-188862]
[Gavotte, on P-RO20203]
DUPLICATIONS: Fanny Heldy,
G-DA1250; Germaine Féraldy,
C-D15034; Mme. Géori-Boué, O-188944;
G. Corney, PD-522561; E. Luart,
O-188571
In Italian: H. Spani, G-DB1503; M.
Zamboni, C-DQ1119

Le Rêve: C'est vrai!
—**Instant charmant—Recit.**
En fermant les yeux je vois—Air Tenor
It. **Il sogno: Chiudo gli occhi**
Ger. **Der Traum: Ich schloss die Augen**
Eng. **Des Grieux's Dream**
Georges Thill 12″—**C-LFX478**
[Ah fuyez]
Jussi Björling 12″—**G-DB3603**
[Bizet: Carmen—Air de la fleur]
James Melton
(in VM-1013) 12″—**V-11-8930**
[Ah! fuyez douce image]
DUPLICATIONS: Richard Crooks,
V-8421: V-14203: G-DB2093; Roland
Hayes, C-17176D in CM-393; José Jan-
son, PAT-PAT153; Jean Planel,
PAT-X90036; Tino Rossi, C-4185M:
C-DB1792: C-BF21; Campagnola,
G-P560; A. D'Arkor, C-RF63; G. Lugo,
PD-561099; Villabella, PAT-X90083:
O-188806; P. H. Vergnè, O-188847; E.
Di Mazzei, O-188868; K. von Pataky,
RAD-SP8015: SP8021; M. Claudel,
PD-524063; A. Delenda, PAT-X80105;
D. Devriès, O-188505; C. Friant,
O-188668; Micheletti, O-188655
In Italian: Ferrucio Tagliavini,
CET-BB25119 in CET-2; Giovanni Mali-
piero, P-DPX25: G-DB5362:

CET-BB25062; Beniamino Gigli,
G-DA1216; Dino Borgioli,
C-GQX10250; Tito Schipa, V-1183:
G-DA875; E. de M. Lomanto, C-DQ1101:
C-DQ3317; R. D'Alessio, C-GQX10225;
G. Manurita, C-D12323; E. Caruso,
G-DA125*
In German: Helge Roswaenge,
G-DB4655; Anton Dermota, T-E2910;
J. Patzak, PD-30031; A. Piccaver,
PD-90151
In English: Heddle Nash, C-DB961

ACT III

Entr'acte—Menuet
Pasdeloup Orch.—Coppola
10″—**G-DA4869**
[Don Quichotte—Interlude]
Symphony Orch.—Cloëz
[Prélude, Act I] 10″—**O-165084**
DUPLICATION: Royal Opera Orch.—
Bellezza, G-HN783

A quoi bon l'économie—Recit.
O Rosalinde—Air Baritone
André Gaudin 10″—**PD-524006**
[Ne bronchez pas]
DUPLICATION: R. Bourdin, O-188508

Suis-je gentille ainsi?—Recit.
Je marche sur tous les chemins—Air
Soprano
(Manon au Cours-la-Reine)
Ninon Vallin 12″—**PAT-X90053**
[Adieu notre petite table]
Germaine Féraldy 10″—**C-D13055**
[Gounod: Mireille—Heureux petit
berger]
DUPLICATIONS: C. Clairbert,
PD-66919; E. Luart, O-188514

Gavotte: Obéissons, quand leur voix appelle
Profitons bien de la jeunesse Soprano
Ger. **Nützet die schönen jungen Tage**
NOTE: *This famous Gavotte is often sung in
Act IV*
Bidù Sayão 10″—**C-17301D**
[Gounod: Roméo et Juliette—Valse]
Grace Moore
(in VM-918) 12″—**V-11-8259**
[Adieu, notre petite table]
Ninon Vallin & Orch.—Cloëz
12″—**PAT-X90034**
[On l'appelle Manon, with Villabella]
[Je suis encore tout étourdie, on
O-188863]
[Adieu notre petite table, on
P-RO20203]
In Italian: Xenia Belmas, PD-66636
—**Orch. only**
Royal Opera Orch.—Bellezza, G-HN783

Fabliau: Oui, dans les bois Soprano
*This air is printed in an appendix to the score
and may be sung by Manon in place of the
Gavotte above.*
Germaine Féraldy 12″—**C-D15034**
[Adieu notre petite table]

Pardon! Mais j'étais là
Duo: Soprano & Bass
(Duo du Cours-la-Reine)
Ninon Vallin & André Balbon
10″—**PAT-PG70**
[Thomas: Mignon—Hirondelles]

Les grands mots—Recit.
Epouse quelque brave fille—Air Bass
  Arthur Endrèze   10″—**O-188864**
  [Puccini: Bohème—Vecchia zimarra]
  DUPLICATIONS: Lovano, PD-521903; E.
  Billot, O-188527
Je suis seul enfin?—Recit.
Ah! fuyez, douce image—Air Tenor
  It. Ah! dispar vision
  Ger. Flieh, o flieh, holdes Bild
  Georges Thill   12″—**C-LFX478**
  [Le Rêve]
  Jussi Björling   12″—**G-DB6249**
  [Gounod: Roméo et Juliette—Cavatina]
  James Melton
        (in VM-1013) 12″—**V-11-8930**
  [Le Rêve]
  Richard Crooks
        (in VM-585) 12″—**V-15543**
  [Lalo: Roi d'Ys—Vainement]
  Raoul Jobin
        (in CM-696) 12″—**C-72140D**
  [Gounod: Roméo et Juliette—Cavatina]
  DUPLICATIONS: José Luccioni,
  G-DB5036; Sydney Rayner, D-K685;
  César Vezzani, G-DB4844; Giuseppe
  Lugo, PD-566176; José Janson,
  PAT-PAT153; P. H. Vergnès, O-188900;
  Campagnola, G-P560*; C. Friant,
  O-171012; Micheletti, O-188660;
  Villabella, O-123550
  In Italian: Beniamino Gigli, G-DB6346;
  Malipiero, G-DB5362; A. Salvarezza,
  CET-BB25151; Tito Schipa, G-DB2237;
  Enrico Caruso, V-15-1004* (recorded in
  1911); R. D'Alessio, C-GQX10225; A.
  Cortis, G-DB1363
  In German: Anton Dermota, T-E2910;
  Julius Patzak, PD-95267: PD-35083;
  H. Roswaenge, T-E2553; A. Piccaver,
  PD-95353
Toi! Vous! (Duo de Saint-Sulpice)
  Soprano & Tenor
N'est-ce plus ma main
  It. Tu! Voi! & La tua mano non è
  (The Vallin-Villabella disc below, labelled
  "Duo de Saint-Sulpice" begins somewhat earl-
  ier with "Magnificat anima")
  Ninon Vallin, Villabella & Chorus
              12″—**PAT-X90081**
  Mary McCormick & Georges Thill
              12″—**C-12508**
  Fanny Heldy & Fernand Ansseau
              12″—**G-DB1410**
  DUPLICATION: Luart & Friant,
  O-171029
  In Italian: Saraceni & Pauli, G-DB2013

ACT IV

Ce bruit de l'or
A nous les amours et les roses Soprano
  Ninon Vallin   12″—**PAT-X90082**
  [Offenbach: Contes d'Hoffman—Elle a
  fui la tourterelle]
  Clara Clairbert   12″—**PD-66919**
  [Suis-je gentille ainsi?]

ACT V

Ah! Des Grieux (Mort de Manon)
Le ciel lui-même te pardonne
  Duo: Soprano & Tenor
  Eng. **Manon's Death**

Emma Luart & Charles Friant
            12″—**O-123658**

MARIE-MAGDELEINE 3 Acts 1873
C'est ici même, à cette place Soprano
  (La Magdeleine à la fontaine)
  Germaine Martinelli 12″—**PD-566100**
  [O bien-aimé]
O bien-aimé (La Magdeleine à la croix)
  Soprano
  Germaine Martinelli 12″—**PD-566100**
  [C'est ici même, à cette place]

PANURGE 4 Acts 1913
Chanson de la Touraine:
Touraine est un pays Bass
  Vanni-Marcoux   10″—**G-DA1124**
  [Trad. French Chanson: Le beau séjour
  & Dans notre village]
(LE) ROI DE LAHORE 1877
Aux troupes du Sultan
Promesse de mon avenir (Arioso) Baritone
  It. O casto fior
  Arthur Endrèze   12″—**O-123021**
  [Verdi: Traviata—Di Provenza il mar]
  Mario Basiola (in Italian)
             12″—**C-GQX10974**
  [Hérodiade—Vision fugitive]
  DUPLICATIONS: C. Cambon, PD-522455;
  L. van Obbergh, PD-524026

SAPHO 5 Acts 1897
Individual Excerpts
Ah! qu'il est loin mon pays Act I
  Tenor (Jean)
  Georges Thill   12″—**C-LFX38**
  [Bruneau: Attaque du Moulin—Adieux]
Ce que j'appelle beau Act II Soprano
  Mireille Berthon   10″—**G-DA4801**
  [Puccini: Butterfly—Un bel dì]

THAIS 3 Acts 1894
Individual Excerpts

ACT I

Paix soit avec vous—Non, mon coeur
Hélas! enfant encore (Air d'Athanaël)
  Baritone
  Lucien van Obbergh 10″—**PD-524007**
  [Puccini: Tosca—Già, mi dicon venal]
Voila donc la terrible cité Baritone
  Arthur Endrèze   12″—**O-123033**
  [Hérodiade—Vision fugitive]
  DUPLICATIONS: L. van Obbergh,
  PD-566122; R. Couzinou, PD-516571;
  Lovano, PD-521904

Ah! je suis seule, enfin!—Recit. Soprano
Dis-moi que je suis belle—Air du miroir
Ah! tais-toi, voix impitoyable—Air, Part 2
  Eng. Mirror Song
  Fanny Heldy   12″—**G-DB1129**
  DUPLICATIONS: Charlotte Tirard,
  PD-524260; M. Nespoulous, C-D14207;
  L. du Roy, PD-521891
Méditation (Intermezzo) Orchestra
  (Violin & Harp)
  Prelude to Scene 2: the famous Méditation is
  also used as the accompaniment to Thaïs'
  death, Act III: "Tu souvient-il du lumineux
  voyage"

Boston "Pops" Orch.—Fiedler
(R. Runderson, vl.)   12"—**V-11887**
[Handel: Serse—Largo]
(G-C2838)   (G-EH970)
Robin Hood Dell Orch.—Kostelanetz
(in CX-257)   12"—**C-12163D**
[Ravel: Bolero, Pt. 3]
Paris Philharmonic Orch.—Defosse
                              12"—**O-170138**
[Wagner: Tannhäuser—Marche
Solennelle]
DUPLICATION: Hastings Municipal
Orch.—Harrison, D-K573

—Arr. Violin & Piano
Nathan Milstein & Arthur Balsam
                              12"—**C-71400D**
[Sarasate: Romanza Andaluza, Op. 22,
No. 1]   (C-LX993)
Josef Hassid & Gerald Moore
                              12"—**G-C3208**
[Kreisler: Caprice Viennois No. 2]
Ida Haendel & Adela Kotowska
                              10"—**D-F7659**
[Bazzini: La Ronde des Lutins]
Mischa Elman & Leopold Mittman
                              12"—**V-11-8950**
[Dvořák-Wilhelmj: Humoresque]
[Wieniawski: Légende, on G-DB1537]
Fritz Kreisler & pf. acc.   12"—**V-6844**
[Kreisler: Tambourin chinois]
(G-DB1207)
DUPLICATIONS: M. Darrieux, O-166491;
Albert Sandler, C-DX621: C-GQX16581;
L. Schwartz, G-L751; Ferraresi,
G-S10159; Armando Gramegna,
CET-CC2059; J. Gauthier, O-166019;
P. Godwin; PD-522688; V. Ranzato,
C-DQ428

—Arr. 'Cello
Victor Pascal & harp. acc., G-L919; A.
Földesy, PD-25026; A. Lévy, O-166202

ACT III

Prélude & Scène 1: Scène de l'oasis
(or: Duo de la source)
Soprano & Baritone

L'ardent soleil—De l'eau fraîche
O messager de Dieu (Soprano)
Baigne d'eau—Adieu, pour toujours!
—O massager de Dieu & Baigne d'eau only
Fanny Heldy & Marcel Journet
                              10"—**G-DA940**
Unidentified Excerpt
(labelled "Duo de l'oasis")
Yvonne Gall & Arthur Endrèze
                              12"—**PAT-X90072**

Mort de Thaïs Duo: Soprano & Baritone
Te souvient-il du lumineux voyage
Eng. **Death of Thais**
Dorothy Kirsten & Robert Merrill
                              12"—**V-11-9792**
[Puccini: Manon Lescaut—In quelle
trine, Kirsten only]

(LA) VIERGE Légende sacrée
4 Scenes 1880
(Le) Dernier sommeil de la vierge Orchestra
A. Locatelli (vl), O-250499; M. Marcelli-
Herson (vlc), G-K5114

WERTHER 4 Acts 1892
Complete recording
Paris Opéra & Opéra-Comique Soloists,
Chorus & Orch.—Elie Cohen
          15 12"—**C-LFX151/65**
(C-GQX10862/76)
The Cast:
Charlotte .... Ninon Vallin (s)
Sophie .... Germaine Féraldy (s)
Werther .... Georges Thill (t)
Le Bailli .... Narçon (b)
Albert .... Marcel Rocque (b)
Johann .... M. Guénot (b)
Schmidt .... H. Niel (t)
Les enfants .. Cantoria Children's Choir

Individual Excerpts

ACT I
Prélude Orchestra
Symphony Orch.—Coppola
                              12"—**G-S10228**
[Rachmaninoff: Prelude in C sharp
minor]
Je ne sais si je veille—Recit.
O nature, pleine de grâce—Air Tenor
(Invocation de la nature) It. **O Natura**
Georges Thill   12"—**C-12510**
[Berlioz: Damnation of Faust—
Invocation]
José Luccioni & Orch.—Bigot
                              12"—**G-DB5006**
[Bizet: Carmen—Air de la fleur]
Tito Schipa (in Italian) 10"—**G-DA5420**
DUPLICATIONS: G. Lugo, PD-27332:
PD-566171; Micheletti, O-188510
—O nature only
G. Malipiero (in Italian), G-DB5405

Oui, je veux que pour tous Baritone
Quelle prière de reconnaissance
(Air d'Albert)
(*The brief part of Sophie is omitted*)
André Baugé   10"—**PAT-X90015**
[Bizet: Carmen—Chanson du Toréador]
DUPLICATIONS: R. Bourdin, O-188518;
A. Gaudin, PD-524027

Clair de Lune (Intermezzo)
Orchestra: 'Cello solo
—Arr. 'Cello & Piano Adler
M. Marcelli-Herson & D. Herbrecht
                              12"—**G-L932**
[Godard: Jocelyn—Berceuse]
(G-S10382)
DUPLICATIONS: A. Lévy, O-166020;
Lopès, PAT-X9956; Instrumental Trio,
C-D19043

Clair de la Lune—Duo Soprano & Tenor
Il faut nous séparer—Vous avez dit vrai
Eng. **Garden Scene**
Germaine Cernay & Charles Friant
                              12"—**O-123556**
Ninon Vallin & Georges Thill
                              12"—**C-GQX10666**

ACT II
Un autre est son époux!
(Désolation de Werther)
J'aurais sur ma poitrine Tenor
Georges Thill   10"—**C-D1610**
[Leoncavallo: Pagliacci—Vesti la giubba]

[Wagner: Walküre—Winterstürme,
on C-7008]
DUPLICATIONS: José Luccioni,
G-DA4901; Sydney Rayner, D-K685; G.
Lugo, PD-27332: PD-566171: also in
VOX-176; R. Verdière, O-188670; Charles
Friant, O-188502; Lens, PD-521938;
Micheletti, O-188655; Villabella,
O-188816: O-188670: PAT-X90010;
Julius Patzak (in German), PD-35083

Oui, ce quelle m'ordonne—Recit.

Lorsque l'enfant revient d'un voyage—Air
Tenor
José Janson   10"—PAT-PG111
[Pourquoi me réveiller]
DUPLICATIONS: E. Di Mazzei, O-188868;
G. Lugo, PD-561099; F. Kaisin,
PD-524055; Micheletti, O-188654;
Charles Friant, O-188502

ACT III

**Air des lettres: Werther! Qui m'aurait dit
Des cris joyeux des enfants**   Soprano
It. **M'ha scritto che m'ama**
Bruna Castagna & Orch.—
Antonini   12"—C-71390D
[Saint-Saëns: Samson—Amour viens
aider]
Ninon Vallin & Orch.—Cloëz
                 12"—O-171022
DUPLICATIONS: Germaine Martinelli,
PD-524116; H. Bouvier, PAT-PD44;
J. Manceau, PD-524005; M. Sibille,
PAT-PD10
In Italian: Pia Tassinari, CET-BB25122
in CET-7; Cloe Elmo, CET-BB25009

Air des larmes: Va! laisse-les couler
Soprano
It. **Va, non è mal se piango**
Germaine Pape (ms)   10"—C-LF192
[Bizet: Carmen—Air des cartes]
DUPLICATION: Madeleine Sibille,
PAT-PG65
In Italian: Gianna Pederzini, G-DA5424

Lied d'Ossian: Pourquoi me réveiller?
Tenor
It. **Ah! non mi ridestar**
José Janson   10"—PAT-PG111
[Lorsque l'enfant revient]
DUPLICATIONS: Raoul Jobin, C-72139D
in CM-696; Richard Crooks, V-10-1093;
F. Kaisin, PD-524055; Charles Friant,
O-188503; Villabella, PAT-X90027:
O-188816; Nequecaur, P-29553; G. Lugo,
PD-561086; José Luccioni, G-DA4901;
Joseph Rogatchewsky, C-D13041
In Italian: Beniamino Gigli, G-DB6346;
A. Cortis, G-DA1076; A. Vesselovsky,
C-D5454; R. D' Alessio, C-DQ1129:
C-DQ1091; Tito Schipa, G-DB2237:
G-DB5351; Tomasso Alcaide, C-DQ1073;
M. Battistini, G-DB149*; M. Giovagnoli,
CET-CC2305
In German: J. Patzak, PD-30031;
Piccaver, PD-95353

Werther est de retour   Baritone
Roger Bourdin   10"—O-188614
[Mascagni: Cavalleria Rusticana—Il
cavallo scalpito]

Phèdre Overture   Orchestra
Grand Orchestre Symphonique—
Andolfi   12"—PAT-PGT22
Paris Philharmonic Orch.—
Cloëz   12"—O-170542
Colonne Orch.—Jean Fournet
            12"—PAT-PDT138
[Massager: Les Deux Pigeons—Ballet
Suite, Pt. 3]
Berlin Philharmonic—Schmidt-
Isserstedt   12"—T-E2399

Scènes Alsaciennes   Orchestral Suite No. 7
1. **Dimanche matin** (Sunday Morning)
2. **Au cabaret** (In the Tavern)
3. **Sous les tilleuls** (Under the Lindens)
4. **Dimanche soir: Air alsacien &
Retraite française**
(Sunday evening: Alsatian Air & Retreat)
Minneapolis Symphony Orchestra—
Mitropoulous   3 12"—CM-723†
Symphony Orch.—Chagnon
      2 10" & 2 12"—C-D19053/4,
            C-D11016, C-D11004
[Satie: Trois pièces montées]
London Symphony—Coppola
         2 12"—G-L901/2

Scènes Pittoresques   Orchestral Suite No. 4
1. **Marche**   2. **Air de ballet**   3. **Angélus**
4. **Fête bohème**
Berlin Philharmonic—Melichar
         2 10"—PD-24930/1
Symphony Orch.—P. Chagnon
         2 12"—C-D11007/8
—**No. 2, (Air de ballet)** only
—**Arr. Piano**
Lydia Tartaglia Morichini, C-DQ2723
—**No. 3 (Angelus)** only
Charles O'Connell (organ), G-S10016
See also under Songs—Nuit d'espagne

SONGS   In French
Elégie   E. Gallet
    Eng. **Song of Mourning**
*(Originally written as an "Invocation" in the
incidental music to "Les Erinnyes" and later
adapted by the composer as a song with 'Cello
& Piano accompaniment.)*
Maggie Teyte (s) w. Gerald Moore
(pf) & vlc.   10"—G-DA1847
[de Fontenailles: Obstination]
Marian Anderson (c) w. William
Primrose (vla) & Franz Rupp (pf)
(in VM-986)   10"—V-10-1122
[Rachmaninoff: When night descends]
James Melton (t) w. Jacques Zayde (vl)
& Karl Kritz (pf)   12"—V-13431
[Braga: Angel's Serenade]
Richard Crooks (t)   12"—V-11-8490
[Franck: Panis Angelicus]
DUPLICATIONS: Feodor Chaliapin (in
Russian), V-14902; G-DB1525; Rosa
Ponselle, V-6599; Guiseppe di Stefano,
G-HEX114; Georges Thill, C-LF104; B.
Gigli, G-DB2530; Ninon Vallin,
PAT-X93045: O-281030; Richard Tauber,
P-RO20497; Villabella, PD-524377;
Marcel Wittrisch, G-EG6104; X. Belmas,
PD-66716; Sidney Rayner, D-M433;
K. von Pataky (in German), PD-95375;
Caruso & Elman, G-DK103*
In English: Marian Z. Nowakowski,

D-K1207; Joan Hammond, G-B9486;
Webster Booth, G-B8843

Miscellaneous Instrumental Arrangements
*(See also under "Erinnyes" for recordings of
original version)*
—**Violin & Piano**
H. Fritz Crone, G-X1658
—**'Cello & Piano**
C. Sharpe, D-F7629; Victor Pascal,
G-K6003; A. Lévy, O-166020; A. Navarra,
O-188933
Also: Harry Horlick Orch., D-F6941
Enchantement
Ninon Vallin (s)　　10"—PAT-X93045
[Elégie]
Noël païen
Edmund Rambaud (t)　　10"—C-DF561
[Ouvre tes yeux bleus]
DUPLICATIONS: A. Gordon, G-K6684;
M. Sibille, PAT-X93071
Nuit d'Espagne
(Arr. from "Scènes pittoresques")
(L. Gallet)
Georges Thill (t)　　10"—C-LF118
[Bizet: Ouvre ton coeur]
Ouvres tes yeux bleus (Robiquet)
Edmund Rambaud (t)　　10"—C-DF561
[Noël païen]
DUPLICATION: J. Planel, PAT-X93099
Pensée d'automne (Silvestre)
Georges Thill (t)　　12"—C-LFX37
[Tosti: Ninon]
Tino Rossi (t)　　10"—C-DB1874
[Chopin: Etude, E major, Op. 10, No. 3—
Arr. Marbot]
DUPLICATIONS: Villabella,
PAT-X93093; O-281343; L. Lynel,
G-K6257; R. Bourdin, O-188551; G. Foix,
D-K511; C. Rouselière, PD-566065
**Sérénade du passant: Mignonne, voici
l'avril**
Ninon Vallin (s)　　10"—O-281031
[Levadé: Vieilles de chez nous]
Robert Marino　　10"—PAT-PA176
[Rabey: Tes yeux]
DUPLICATION: F. Gouin, O-166724

MATHEUS DE PERUSIO (fl. 1402-1415)
Gloria in Excelsis
J. Archimbaud (treble), R. Bonté (t) &
Lafosse (bass trumpet)　　12"—OL-1
[Jacopo da Bologna: Non al suo amante]
Plus onques dame n'a mercy
14th Century Ballade
Instrumental Ensemble
　　　　(in Vol. VII)　12"—AS-63
[Fourteenth Century Ballades by
Landino]

MATHIEU, André
Etudes Piano
Sur les Touches blanches
Sur les Touches noires
Dans la Nuit
Sur les Touches blanches et noires
Les abeilles piquantes
Dans sauvage
André Mathieu　　12"—BAM-26

MATIELLI, Giovanni Antonio
*An eighteenth century Italian composer and
harpsichordist and a pupil of Wagenseil at
Vienna.*
Adagio Piano
Ruggero Gerlin
　　　　(in Vol. X)　12"—AS-95
[Rutini: Andante & Martini: Allegro]

MATTHESON, Johann (1681-1764)
*A profound, and still valuable, musical theorist,
Mattheson was a respectable composer as well.
His works include eight operas, 24 oratorios
and cantatas and considerable chamber music.*
Air (unspecified)
Arr. Violin Burmester
Ruggiero Ricci　　10"—G-DA4467
[Suk: Burleske]
String Quartet　　12"—SEMS-1143
[Handel: Sarabande]

MAUDUIT, Jacques (1557-1627)
*A French lutenist and composer of chansons
and choral works, Mauduit was associated with
the poet Baïf in an attempt to bring about a
closer union between music and poetry.*
En son temple sacré Psalm No. 150
Unacc. Chorus in French
Dijon Cathedral Chorus—J. Samson
　　　　(in VM-212)　12"—V-11678
(G-DB4894 in GM-189)
[Victoria: Kyrie—"Orbis factor"]
Strasbourg Cathedral Chorus
　　　　　　12"—C-RFX74
[Lully-Renard: La Puissance de Dieu]
A la fontaine
Si d'une petite aïllade
Psaume 42
Emile Passani Cho.
　　　　(in Vol. XIII)　12"—AS-128

MAZELLIER, Jules
Complainte pour Noël
M. A. Chastil (pf)　　12"—PAT-PDT144
Nocturne
M. A. Chastil (pf)　　12"—PAT-PDT145
Poème lunaire (from "Esquisse")
André Baugé (b)　　10"—PAT-PA319
[Marcelin: Nocturne]

McBRIDE, Robert (1911-　　)
*A versatile young American composer who
divides his time between writing orchestral
music in the jazzy style and teaching.*
Mexican Rhapsody
Boston "Pops" Orch.—Fiedler
　　　　　　12"—V-13825

McDONALD, HARL (1899-　　)
*An active teacher, and manager of the Phila-
delphia Orchestra, Harl McDonald has been a
prolific composer. His larger orchestral works
are very elaborate, while some of his smaller
compositions are superior salon music of real
charm. McDonald's music is frequently played
by many American orchestras.*
(Two) Hebraic Poems
Philadelphia Orch.—Ormandy
　　　　　　12"—V-14903

(The) Legend of the Arkansas Traveller
Philadelphia Orch.—Stokowski
          12″—V-18069
[Novacek: Moto Perpetuo, trans.
Stokowski]

My Country at War   Symphonic Suite
1941; Bataan, Elégie; Hymn of the
People
Philadelphia Orch.—Ormandy
          3 12″—CM-592†

Suite—"From Childhood"
Harp & Orchestra
Edna Phillips & Philadelphia Orch.—
McDonald   3 12″—VM-839†

SYMPHONIES

No. 1—"The Santa Fe Trail"
Philadelphia Orch.—Ormandy
          3 12″—VM-754†

No. 3—Cakewalk (Scherzo) only
Philadelphia Orch.—Ormandy
          12″—V-15377
[Menotti: Amelia Goes to the Ball—
Overture] (G-DB5777)

MEDTNER, Nicolai (1879-   )
A Russian pianist and composer much influ-
enced by German romantic music. Before mov-
ing to England in 1936 he wrote little but piano
music, but since that time has completed several
orchestral scores. The recently formed Medtner
Society (by HMV in England) promises to in-
troduce many unfamiliar works to listeners via
recordings.

Collection

MEDTNER SOCIETY   VOL. I
Concerto No. 2   Piano & Orch.
N. Medtner & Philharmonia Orch.—
Dobrowen

Arabesque, Op. 7, No. 2   Piano

Fairy Tale, D minor, Op. 51, No. 1   Piano

Fairy Tale, F minor, Op. 26, No. 3   Piano
Nicholas Medtner

Spanish Romance, Op. 52, No. 5

Butterfly, Op. 28, No. 3
Patiana Nakushina (s) & N. Medtner (pf)

To a Dreamer, Op. 31, No. 1
Oda Slobodskaya (s) & N. Medtner (pf)
     7 12″—H.M.V. Medtner Society No. 1
(Not available separately)

Russian Fairy Tale, Op. 42, No. 1   Piano
Benno Moisewitsch   12″—G-C3397
[Khachaturian: Toccata]

Russian Fairy Tale, E minor   Piano
Shura Cherkassky, in VOX-165

Russian Fairy Tale, B flat minor, Op. 20,
No. 1
—Arr. Vl. & Pf.   Heifetz
Jascha Heifetz & Emanuel Bay
     (in VM-1126)   10″—V-10-1295
[Debussy-Heifetz: La Chevelure]

MEHUL, Etienne Henri (1763-1817)
A French dramatic composer, whose operas
carried on the work of Gluck, a contemporary
of Grétry and Cherubini, and one of the most
important French musicians of his time.

(Le) Chant du départ
Song in French (Chénier)
Georges Thill (t) & Band acc.
          10″—C-DF760
[Rouget de l'Isle: La Marseillaise]
Robert Couzinou (b)   10″—PD-521837
[Rouget de l'Isle: La Marseillaise]
(also on PD-521981)
DUPLICATION: André Baugé,
PAT-X93095
—Declamation & Orchestra
Robert Vidalin & Orch.—G. Tzipine,
PAT-PA1310
—Choral versions
Choir & Instrumental Ensemble of the
Red Army of USSR—A. V. Alexandroff
          10″—C-36266
[Rouget de l'Isle: La Marseillaise]
(C-DF2203)
[Rimsky-Korsakov: May Night—Song of
the Mayor on C-DB1763]
Also: Band, PAT-PA541, PAT-X8723
Gavotte (unidentified)
Gaspar Cassadó (vlc) & pf. acc.
          10″—T-A2083
[Elgar: Salut d'amour]   (U-A14233)

OPERAS   In French
ARIODANT   1799
Romance du barde: Femme sensible
Baritone
André Baugé   12″—PAT-PAT1
[Martini: Plaisir d'amour]

(LE) JEUNE HENRI   1797
Overture (La Chasse)   Orchestra
Lamoureux Orch.—A. Wolff
(PD-566105)   12″—PD-67026

JOSEPH   3 Acts   1807
Vainement Pharaon—Recit.
Champs paternels—Air de Joseph   Tenor
Georges Thill   10″—C-LF22
Richard Tauber (in German)
          12″—P-R20543
[Haydn: Creation—In Native worth]

MENDELSSOHN, Felix (1809-1847)
One of the most popular and successful com-
posers of the first half of the nineteenth century
and for decades the idol of the British musical
public, Mendelssohn is well represented on discs
and has been given prominent place on concert
programs during recent years, especially since
the observation of the centenary of his death.
As a conductor, Mendelssohn did great service
to the revival of earlier composers, especially in
performance of the works of J. S. Bach.

Allegro Brillant, Op. 92   2 Pianos
Luboshutz & Nemenoff
     (in VM-1047†)   12″—V-11-9138
Andante (unspecified)
Magda Tagliafero (pf)
          12″—PAT-PAT53
[Etude & Weber: Rondo brilliant]
Andante & Rondo Capriccioso
See: Rondo Capriccioso

ATHALIE, Op. 74—Incidental Music to
Racine's Drama
Overture   Orchestra
National Symphony—Heinz Unger
          12″—D-K1298

War March of the Priests   Orchestra
Boston "Pops" Orch.—Fiedler
           12″—**V-11-8985**
[Handel: Messiah-Hallelujah Chorus, orch. only]
National Symphony Orch.—Anatole
Fistoulari   (in D-ED1)   12″—**D-K1373**
[Symphony No. 4, Pt. 7, cond. Unger]
New York Philharmonic-Symphony—
Mengelberg   12″—**V-7104**
[Meyerbeer: Prophète—Coronation March]

Ave Maria, Op. 98 Soprano & Women's Cho.
(from an unfinished opera "Loreley")
Ursula van Diemen & Berlin Philharmonic Chorus—Ochs   12″—**G-C2736**
[Mozart: Laudate Dominum]
(G-EH173)

Beati Mortui, Op. 115, No. 1
Male Chorus in Latin
Haarlem Royal Cho.—L. Duvosel
          12″—**C-D17155**
[Handl: Ecce quomodo moritur]

Bees' Wedding
See under Song Without Words No. 34
(Spinning Song)

But the Lord is Mindful of His Own
See under St. Paul

Canzonetta   See under Quartets
(String), No. 1, 2nd Mvt.

Capriccio Brillant, Op. 22
Piano & Orchestra
Joanna Graudan & Minneapolis Symphony Orch.—Mitropoulos
        2 12″—**CX-197**
[Lully: La Temple de la Paix—Menuet]
Moura Lympany & National Symphony
Orch.—Boyd Neel   12″—**D-K1191**

Concerto No. 1, G minor, Op. 25
Piano & Orch.
Jesús María Sanromá & Boston "Pops"
Orch.—Fiedler   3 12″—**VM-780**†
[Songs without Words: No. 8 & 45, Sanromá pf. only]
Ania Dorfman & London Symphony Orch.
Goehr   2 12″—**CX-124**†
(C-DX893/4)
Eileen Joyce & London Symphony Orch.
—Fistoulari   2 12″—**D-K1687/8**†

Concerto, E minor, Op. 64
Violin & Orchestra
Ida Haendel & National Symphony—
Sir Malcolm Sargent   4 12″—**D-ED23**†
[Midsummer Night's Dream: Wedding March—dir. Fistoulari] (D-K1377/80)
Nathan Milstein & Philharmonic-Symphony of N. Y.—Walter 4 12″—**CM-577**†
[Midsummer Night's Dream—Scherzo]
Yehudi Menuhin & Orchestre des Concerts
Colonne—Enesco   4 12″—**VM-531**†
[Bach: Sonata No. 6—Praeludium]
(G-DB6012/5S—last side blank)
[Mozart: Sonata, K.378—Andantino sostenuto, on G-DB3555/8]
Joseph Szigeti & Royal Philharmonic—
Beecham   4 12″—**CM-190**†
[Chabrier-Loeffler: Scherzo-Valse]
[Paganini: Caprice No. 9, La Chasse, on
C-LX262/5: C-GQX10739/42:
C-LFX348/51]

Fritz Kreisler & London Philharmonic—
Ronald   3 12″—**VM-277**†
(G-DB2460/2)
Emil Telmanyi & Chamber Orch.—
Jensen   3 12″—**TONO-X25065/7**

ELIJAH, Op. 70   Oratorio   Ger. Elias
"Complete" recording in English
Soloists, Huddersfield Choral Society &
Liverpool Philharmonic Orch.—Sir
Malcolm Sargent   16 12″—**CM-715**†
Soloists: Isobel Baillie (s), Gladys
Ripley (c), James Johnston (t) &
Harold Williams (b) (C-DX1408/23†)

Individual Excerpts

No. 4, Ye People Rend Your Hearts—Recit.
If With all Your Hearts—Air   Tenor
Webster Booth   12″—**V-12609**
[No. 39, Then shall the Righteous Shine
Forth] (G-C3095)
Richard Crooks
    (in VM-934)   12″—**V-11-8317**
[No. 39, Then shall the Righteous Shine
Forth]

No. 14, Draw near—Recit.
Lord God of Abraham—Air   Bass
Roy Henderson   12″—**D-K1557**
[No. 26, It is enough]
Norman Cordon
    (in VM-1094)   12″—**V-11-9432**
[No. 26, It is enough]
DUPLICATION: Arthur Fear, G-C1786

No. 18, Woe unto them   Alto
Kathleen Ferrier & Boyd Neel String
Orch.   12″—**D-K1556**
[No. 31, O rest in the Lord]

No. 21, Hear ye, Israel!   Soprano
Ger. Höre Israel
Dorothy Maynor
    (in VM-1043)   12″—**V-11-9106**
[Handel: Messiah—How beautiful are
the feet]
DUPLICATION: Jo Vincent (in German),
C-D17212

No. 26, It is enough   Baritone
Ger. Es ist genug
Roy Henderson   12″—**D-K1557**
[No. 14, Lord God of Abraham]
Norman Cordon
    (in VM-1094)   12″—**V-11-9432**
[No. 14, Lord God of Abraham]
Paul Sandoz (in German) & Karl
Matthei (organ)   12″—**G-DB10095**
DUPLICATION: H. Rehkemper,
PD-66713

No. 31, O rest in the Lord   Alto
Margaret Matzenauer   12″—**V-6555**
[Handel: Messiah—He shall feed his
flock]
Marian Anderson
    (in VM-850)   12″—**V-18325**
[St. Paul—No. 13, But the Lord]
(G-DB10122)
Kathleen Ferrier & Boyd Neel String
Orch.   12″—**D-K1556**
[No. 18, Woe unto them]
DUPLICATIONS: Clara Butt, C-DX811;
T. Versteegh (in Dutch), C-D17169

No. 39, Then shall the righteous shine forth
Tenor
Webster Booth   12″—**V-12609**
[No. 4, If with all your hearts]
(G-C3095)
Richard Crooks
    (in VM-934)   12″—**V-11-8317**
[No. 4, If with all your hearts]
No. 42, O come, everyone that thirsteth
Quartet
E. Lough, R. Mallett (trebles) & Temple
Church Choir   12″—**G-C1398**
[Hymn of Praise—I waited for the Lord]

ETUDES Piano
F major, Op. 104, No. 2
Jakob Gimpel, in VOX-164
Etude (unspecified)
Magda Tagliafero   12″—**PAT-PAT53**
[Andante & Weber: Rondo brilliant]
Fingal's Cave See Hebrides Overture
Hark! the Herald Angels Sing
Chorus in English
This well-known Christmas chorus was orig-
inally Part 2 of Mendelssohn's "Festgesang" for
Male Chorus & Orchestra. It was adapted by
W. H. Cummings to Wesley's words.
BBC Choir & Organ, C-246M: C-DB1453;
Westminster Abbey Choir, G-B2385;
Westminster Central Hall Choir,
G-C1589; Choir, D-F3726; Fleet Street
Choir, D-F8235
See also current catalogues under Christ-
mas Music for other recordings.
Hear My Prayer Hymn in English
Soprano, Chorus & Organ
Oh! for the wings of a dove
(Part 2 of Hymn)
Ger. O könnt ich fliegen No opus number
Derek Barsham (treble) High Wycombe
Orpheus Male Voice Choir & Organ
         12″—**D-K1111**
E. Lough (treble) & Temple Church
Cho. & Organ   12″—**G-C1329**
—**Oh, for the wings of a dove** only
Isobel Baillie (s) & organ acc.
[Gounod: Ave Maria]   12″—**C-DX301**
—**Arr.** Violin & Piano Lucas
Mischa Elman & pf. acc. 12″—**G-DB1398**
[Chopin-Wilhelmj: Nocturne, D flat
major, Op. 27, No. 2]
(The) Hebrides (Fingal's Cave) Overture,
Op. 26 Orchestra
Ger. Die Hebriden (Fingalshöhle)
or Die einsame Insel
Boston "Pops" Orch.—Fiedler
         12″—**V-11-8745**
National Symphony Orch.—Unger
         12″—**D-K1120**
London Philharmonic Orch.—
Beecham   12″—**C-69400D**
(C-LX747)   (C-71621D in CM-552)
(C-LFX556)
BBC Symphony Orch.—Boult
(G-DB2100)   12″—**V-11886**
Hallé Orch.—Sargent   12″—**C-DX1053**
Berlin Philharmonic Orch.—
Furtwängler   12″—**PD-95470**
DUPLICATIONS: Berlin Philharmonic—
Pfitzner, PD-27292; La Scala Orch.
—Panizza, G-AW3984

Heimkehr aus der Fremde, Op. 89
See: Son and Stranger
Hymn of Praise, Op. 52
Symphony-Cantata in English
Ger. Lobgesang
No. 2, All men, all things Chorus
BBC Chorus & Organ—Woodgate
         12″—**C-DX576**
[St. Paul—Great is the depth]
Jubilee Choirs & Band   12″—**C-DX693**
[Handel: Messiah—Hallelujah]
No. 5, I waited for the Lord
2 Sopranos & Chorus
E. Lough, R. Mallet (trebles) & Temple
Church Choir   12″—**G-C1398**
[Elijah—No. 42, O come, everyone]
Immer wenn der Marzwind weht
(unidentified) Chorus
Dresdner Kreuzchor—Mauerberger
         10″—**PD-10282**
[Brahms: Fahr' wohl o Vöglein]
Introduction and Rondo Capriccioso
See: Rondo Capriccioso
Jerusalem See under Saint Paul
Lieder Ohne Worte
See: Songs Without Words
Lobgesang, Op. 52 See: Hymn of Praise
Loreley Unfinished opera See: Ave Maria
Meeresstille und glückliche Fahrt—
Overture
(D major) Op. 27 Orchestra
Eng. Calm Sea & Prosperous Voyage
No recording available
(A) Midsummer Night's Dream, Op. 21 & 61
Orchestra
(Incidental Music to Shakespeare's Play)
Collection
Overture, Scherzo, Intermezzo, Nocturne,
Wedding March only
Cleveland Orch.—Rodzinski
      4 12″—**CM-504†**
Individual Excerpts
Overture, E major, Op. 21
Cleveland Orch.—Rodzinski
    (in CM-504)   2   12″—**C-11782/3D**
[Scherzo]
Boston "Pops" Orch.—Fiedler
(G-C3004/5)   2   12″—**V-11919/20**
[Wedding March]
BBC Symphony Orch.—Boult
[Wedding March] 2 12″—**G-DDB6242/3**
DUPLICATIONS: Berlin Philharmonic
Orch.—Furtwängler, PD-66925/6; Ber-
lin State Opera—Blech, G-EH330/1:
G-S10224/5; New Queen's Hall Orch.—
Wood, C-9559/60
Scherzo, Op. 61, No. 1 (Prelude to Act II)
Cleveland Orch.—Rodzinski
    (in CM-504) 12″—**C-11783D**
[Overture, Pt. 3]
N. Y. Philharmonic-Symphony Orch.—
Walter   (in CM-577)   12″—**C-12145D**
[Violin Concerto, E minor, Pt. 7, with
Milstein]
Hallé Orch.—Barbirolli   12″—**G-C3426**
[Wagner: Rienzi Overture, Pt. 3]
DUPLICATIONS: N. Y. Philharmonic—
Toscanini, V-7080 in VM-57: G-D1671:
G-W1073: PD-595008; Amsterdam Con-

certgebouw—Mengelberg, C-9560; Berlin Philharmonic—Kleiber, PD-66731; London Symphony—Beecham, C-L1812; All-American Orch.—Stokowski, C-11983D; New Queens Hall Orch.—Wood, C-9560; Royal Theatre Orch., Copenhagen—Tango, TONO-25048
—**Arr. Piano** Rachmaninoff
Sergi Rachmaninoff, G-DB3146; Benno Moiseiwitsch, G-C3209
Victor Schiøler, TONO-A106
—**Arr. 2 Pianos** Isidore Phillipp
Luboshutz & Nemenoff, V-11-8455; Bartlett & Robertson, C-71398D; Rawicz & Landauer, C-DB2148
Intermezzo, Op. 61, No. 5
Cleveland Orch.—Rodzinski
(in CM-504) 12"—**C-11785D**
[Wedding March]
—**Final part only** (labeled "Clowns")
Victor Orch., in V-19882
Nocturne, Op. 61, No. 7 (with French Horn solo)
Cleveland Orch.—Rodzinski
(in CM-504) 12"—**C-11784D**
London Philharmonic Orch.—Beecham (C-LX574) 12"—**C-68888D**
[Wedding March]
BBC Symphony Orch.—Boult (A. Brain, solo (G-DA1318) 10"—**V-4312**
Berlin Philharmonic Orch.—Kleiber, 12"—**PD-66850**
N. Y. Philharmonic-Symphony—Toscanini 12"—**PD-595008**
[Scherzo]
Wedding March, Op. 61, No. 9
Ger. Hochzeitmarsch
Cleveland Orch.—Rodzinski
(in CM-504) 12"—**C-11785D**
[Intermezzo]
Boston "Pops" Orch.—Fiedler (G-C3005) 12"—**V-11920**
[Overture, Pt. 3]
BBC Symphony Orch.—Boult
[Overture, Pt. 3] 12"—**G-DB6243**
London Philharmonic Orch.—Beecham
[Nocturne]
(C-LX574) 12"—**C-68888D**
DUPLICATIONS: Royal Orch., Copenhagen—Tango, TONO-X25048; Berlin Philharmonic—Blech, U-F14384; Berlin Philharmonic Orch.—Kleiber, PD-66731; Berlin State Opera Orch.—Blech, G-EH331: G-S10224; London Symphony Orch.—Fistoulari, D-K1380 in D-ED23; Symphony Orch.—G-Z162
—**Arr. Organ**
Q. M. Maclean, C-361M: C-DF365; Eduard Commette, C-DFX93; Mark Andrews, V-20036; Hans Vollenweider, G-HEX113; Fred Feibel, C-7528M; Dr. O. H. Peasgood, G-B3690
—**Arr. Piano** Horowitz
(Mendelssohn's Wedding March & Variations after Liszt)
Vladimir Horowitz
(in VM-1121) 12"—**V-11-9564**
(Also on V-11-9693)
(Die) Nachtigall, Op. 59, No. 4 Partsong
("Die Nachtigall, sie war entfernt")
Basilica Choir—P. Kalt 10"—**PD-62631**

[Schumann: Im Walde]
Dresdner Kreuzchor—Rudolf Mauersberger 10"—**G-EG3545**
[Lasso: Echolied]
Neujahrslied, Op. 88, No. 1 Partsong
("Mit der Freude zieht der Schmerz")
St. Caecilia Cho.—P. Kalt
10"—**PD-23403**
[Schulz: Des Jahres letzte Stunde]
Octet, E flat major, Op. 20 Strings
—**Scherzo Mvt. only** String Orchestra Version
NBC Symphony Orch.—Toscanini
(in VM-1025) 12"—**V-11-8966**
[Haydn: Symphony No. 98, Pt. 7]
Boston "Pops" Orch.—Fiedler
12"—**V-11947**
[Chopin-Glazounov: Polonaise No. 3]
[Wagner: Lohengrin—Prelude Act III on G-C3234]
Minneapolis Symphony Orch.—Mitropoulos (C-LX924)
(in CX-166) 12"—**C-11239D**
[Prokofiev: Symphony No. 1—Classical, Pt. 3]
On Wings of Song See: Songs—Auf Flügeln des Gesanges
Paulus, Op. 36 See Saint Paul

PIANO
Collection
Variations Sérieuses, Op. 54, Songs without Words, Nos. 25 & 35; Horowitz-Mendelssohn: Wedding March & Variations after Liszt
Vladimir Horowitz 3 12"—**VM-1121†**

QUARTETS—String
No. 1, E flat major, Op. 12
—**2nd Mvt.** (Canzonetta) only
—**Arr. Guitar**
A. Segovia, G-DB3242
No. 3, D major, Op. 44, No. 1
Stradivarius Quartet 3 12"—**CM-304**
Rondo Capriccioso, E major, Op. 14 Piano
(*The Rondo is preceded by an Andante*)
Eileen Joyce 10"—**C-DB2179**
Mischa Levitzki 10"—**G-DA1317**
Ania Dorfmann 10"—**C-DB1776**
Irene Scharrer 10"—**C-DB306**
Ruy Blas—Overture, Op. 95 Orchestra
National Symphony Orch.—Heinz Unger
12"—**D-K1326**
City of Birmingham Orch.—Weldon
12"—**C-DX1223**
London Philharmonic Orch.—Beecham (C-LX879) 12"—**C-70352D**
BBC Symphony Orch.—Boult
12"—**G-DB2365**
Berlin State Opera Orch.—Prüwer
12"—**PD-19990**

SAINT PAUL, Op. 36 Oratorio Ger. **Paulus**
Individual Excerpts
No. 7, Jerusalem, thou that killest Soprano
Jo Vincent (in Dutch) & organ acc.
12"—**C-D17169**
[Elijah—O Rest in the Lord, T. Versteegh]
No. 11, Happy and blest are they
BBC Choral Society—Woodgate, w.

organ 12″—D-K806
[No. 26, How lovely are the messengers]
No. 13, And he journeyed—Recit. Alto
But the Lord is mindful of his own—Arioso
Marian Anderson
(in VM-850) 12″—V-18325
[Elijah—No. 31, O rest in the Lord]
(G-DB10122)
No. 18, O God, have mercy upon me Baritone
Ger. Gott, sei mir gnädig
Norman Cordon
(in VM-1094) 12″—V-11-9431
[Bach: Matthäus Passion—No. 51, Gibt
mir meinem Jesum wieder]
Paul Sandoz (in German) & K. Matthaei
(organ) 12″—G-DB10097
[Handel: Messiah—Thus saith the Lord]
DUPLICATION: Heinrich Rehkemper (in
German), PD-66713
No. 26, How lovely are the messengers
Chorus
BBC Choral Society—Woodgate, w. organ
12″—D-K806
[No. 11, Happy and blest are they]
Temple Church Cho. & Organ
10″—G-B3518
[Davies: Lord, it belongs not]
No. 40, Be thou faithful unto death Tenor
Ger. Sei getreu bis in den Tod
Richard Crooks
(in VM-934) 12″—V-11-8316
[Handel: Judas—No. 28, Sound an
alarm]
Webster Booth 12″—G-C3305
[Handel: Semele—Where'er you walk]
Scherzo a Capriccio, F sharp minor Piano
Edward Kilenyi 12″—C-71968D
[Beethoven: Polonaise, C major]
Scherzo, E minor, Op. 16, No. 2 Piano
Alexander Brailowsky 12″—V-18100
[Scriabin: Etude, D sharp minor, Op. 8,
No. 12]
[Older version with Schumann: Traume-
swirren, on PD-90173]

SON AND STRANGER, Op. 89 Singspiel
Ger. Heimkehr aus der Fremde
I'm a roamer bold Bass
Malcolm McEchern 10″—C-DB1465
[Chu Chin Chow—Cobbler's Song]

SONATAS Cello & Piano
No. 1, B flat major, Op. 41
William Pleeth & Margaret Good
3 12″—D-K914/6
No. 2, D major, Op. 58, No. 2
William Pleeth & Margaret Good
4 12″—D-K918/21
(6) Sonatas—Organ, Op. 65 1844/5
No. 5, D major
—Finale only
Hans Vollenweider 12″—G-HEX113
[Midsummer Night's Dream—Wedding
March]
No. 6, D minor
Virgil Fox (Hammond Museum organ,
Gloucester), in VM-1177
—3rd Mvt. (Allegro molto) only
Eduard Commette (Lyons Cathedral)
12″—C-DFX93

[Midsummer Night's Dream—Wedding
March]
—5th Mvt. (Andante) only
Eduard Commette (Lyons Cathedral)
10″—C-DF680
[Bach: Chorale-Prelude—Komm,
heiliger Geist]

SONGS
Vocal Duets Collection
Ich wollt' meine Lieb, Op. 63, No. 1
Abschiedslied der Zugvögel, Op. 63, No. 2
Grüss, Op. 63, No. 3
Herbstlied, Op. 63, No. 4
Sonntagsmorgen, Op. 77, No. 1
Lied aus Ruy Blas, Op. 77, No. 3
Abendlied, Drei Volkslieder, No. 2
Wasserfahrt, Drei Volkslieder, No. 3
Hulda Lashanska (s) & Kerstin Thorborg
(ms), with George Schick (pf)
2 12″—V-11-9021/2
Individual Songs (1 or 2 Voices) (in German)
Abschiedslied der Zugvögel, Op. 63, No. 2
Duet
Lashanska & Thorborg, on V-11-9021
Abendlied, Drei Volkslieder, No. 2 Duet
Lashanska & Thorborg, on V-11-9021
Auf Flügeln des Gesanges, Op. 34, No. 2
Eng. On Wings of Song
Elisabeth Schumann (s)
10″—G-DA1395
[Jos. Strauss: Sphärenklänge]
Lotte Lehmann (s) & Paul Ulanowsky
(pf) 10″—C-17344D
[Morgengruss]
Heinrich Schlusnus (b) & Franz Rupp
(pf) 10″—PD-90195
[Venetianisches Gondellied]
In English: Isobel Baillie, C-DX230;
Richard Crooks, V-11-8241; Webster
Booth, G-B9315; Thomas Criddle,
G-BD1046; Gwen Catley, G-B9222; Derek
Barsham, D-K1393; J. van der Gucht,
D-M512
Also: Webster Booth & Anne Ziegler,
G-B9627
—Arr. Violin & Piano J. Achron
Jascha Heifetz & I. Achron 12″—V-6848
[Falla: Jota]
[Debussy: Fille aux cheveux de lin &
Grieg: Scherzo-Impromptu on
G-DB1246]
Guila Bustabo & Gerald Moore
12″—C-LCX35
[Kreisler: Preludium & Allegro]
A. Campoli & Gerald Moore
[Schubert: Ave Maria] 12″—G-C3144
Also: Albert Sandler Trio, C-DB2122
(Der) Frohe Wandersmann, Op. 75, No. 1
("Wem Gott will rechte Gunst erveisen")
—Arr. Male Chorus
Berlin Teachers' Chorus—Rudel
12″—PD-19843
[Krause: Mädel, wie blüht's]
DUPLICATIONS: Potsdam Male Chorus,
G-EG1664; Male Quartet, PD-21144
Grüss, Op. 63, No. 3 Duet (Eichendorff)
Eng. Greeting
Isobel Baillie (s) & Kathleen Ferrier (c)

(in English) with Gerald Moore (pf)
10"—**C-DB2194**
[Ich wollt', meine Liebe]
Lashanska & Thorborg, on V-11-9021

Herbstlied, Op. 63, No. 4 Duet
Lashanska & Thorborg, on V-11-9022

Ich wollt', meine Liebe ergosse sich, Op. 63, No. 1 Duet (Heine)
Eng. **I would that my love**
Lashanka & Thorborg, on V-11-9021
Isobel Baillie (s) & Kathleen Ferrier (c) (in English), with Gerald Moore (pf)
[Grüss] 10"—**C-DB2194**

Lied aus Ruy Blas, Op. 77, No. 3 Duet
Lashanska & Thorborg, on V-11-9022

Morgengruss, Op. 47, No. 2 (Heine)
Lotte Lehmann (s) & Paul Ulanowsky (pf) 10"—**C-17334D**
[Auf Flügeln des Gesanges]

On Wings of Song See: Auf Flügeln des Gesanges

Sonntagsmorgen, Op. 77, No. 1 Duet ("Das ist der Tag des Herrn")
Theo. Versteegh & Jo Vincent
[Anon: In Sternennacht] 10"—**C-D10044**
Lashanska & Thorborg, on V-11-9022

Venetianisches Gondellied, Op. 57, No. 5 ("Wenn durch die Piazzetta")
Heinrich Schlusnus (b) 10"—**PD-90195**
[Auf Flügeln des Gesanges]

Wasserfahrt, Drei Volkslieder, No. 3
Lashanska & Thorborg, on V-11-9022

SONGS WITHOUT WORDS Piano
Ger. **Lieder ohne Worte**
(The "Spring Song" is No. 30; the "Spinning Song," or "Bees' Wedding" is No. 34)

No. 1 (Sweet Remembrance), E major, Op. 19, No. 1
Alfred Cortot 12"—**G-DB3267**
[Variations sérieuses, Pt. 3]

No. 18, (Duetto), E flat major, Op. 38, No. 6
Jesús María Sanromá
(in VM-780) 12"—**V-13615**
[No. 45 & Concerto No. 1, G minor. Pt. 5]

No. 22 (Sadness of Soul), F major, Op. 53, No. 4
William Murdoch 12"—**D-K691**
[No. 47 & Chopin: Nocturne, C sharp minor, Op. 27, No. 1]

No. 25 (May Breezes), G major, Op. 62, No. 1
Vladimir Horowitz
(in VM-1121) 12"—**V-11-9563**
[No. 35 & Variations sérieuses, Pt. 3]
—**Arr. Violin & Piano** (B major) Kreisler
Fritz Kreisler & Arpad Sandor
12"—**G-DB2117**
[Londonderry Air, arr. Kreisler]

No. 30, (Spring Song) A major, Op. 62, No. 6
Ger. **Frühlingslied**
Vladimir Horowitz 12"—**V-11-9519**
[No. 40 & Chopin: Waltz, C sharp minor]
William Murdoch 12"—**C-9274**
[Brahms: Waltz A flat & Rachmaninoff: Prelude C sharp minor]

DUPLICATIONS: Walter Rehberg, PD-27229; Francis Planté, C-D13058; Ida Perrin, PAT-X98153
—**Arr. Orchestra**
New Queen's Hall Orch.—Wood
12"—**C-DX579**
[No. 34 & Tchaikovsky: Chant sans paroles]
London Philharmonic Orch.—Ronald
12"—**G-C2639**
[No. 34 & Glazounov: Chopiniana, Pt. 3, Tarantelle]
DUPLICATIONS: New Light Symphony, G-B2819; G-K5583; Weber Orch., G-B8151; Locatelli Orch., O-238391
Also: Lore Durant Trio, G-HE662; Florentine Quartet, V-20195; Bohemian Salon Orch., C-FB1947; Alfredo Campoli (vl), D-F6836
—**Vocal arr.:** Odette Moulin, PAT-PA792

No. 34 (Spinning Song, or Bees' Wedding) C major, Op. 67, No. 4
Ger. **Spinnlied** Fr. **La Fileuse**
William Murdoch 12"—**D-F7499**
[No. 47 & Grieg: To Spring]
[Chopin: Sonata No. 2—Funeral March, on D-K661]
Sergei Rachmaninoff 10"—**V-1326**
[Rachmaninoff: Prelude, C sharp minor] (G-DA996)
DUPLICATIONS: Francis Planté, C-D13058; Irene Scharrer, G-D1303; Ida Perrin, PAT-X98153
—**Arr. 2 Pianos:** Rawicz & Landauer, C-DB2148
—**Arr. Orchestra**
New Queen's Hall Orch.—Wood
12"—**C-DX579**
[No. 30 & Tchaikovsky: Chant sans paroles]
London Philharmonic—Ronald
12"—**G-C2639**
[No. 30 & Glazounov: Chopiniana, Part 3—Tarantelle]
Lamoureux Orch.—Wolff
(PD-566017) 12"—**PD-66957**
[Saint-Saëns: Le Cygne]

No. 35 (The Shepherd's Complaint) B major, Op. 67, No. 5
Vladimir Horowitz
(in VM-1121) 12"—**V-11-9563**
[No. 25 & Variations sérieuses, Pt. 3]

No. 40, (Elégie) Op. 85, No. 4
Vladimir Horowitz 12"—**V-11-9519**
[No. 30 & Chopin: Waltz, C sharp minor]

No. 45 (Tarantelle) C major, Op. 102, No. 3
Jesús María Sanromá
(in VM-780) 12"—**V-13615**
[No. 18 & Concerto No. 1, G minor, Pt. 5]

No. 47 (The Joyous Peasant) A major, Op. 102, No. 5
William Murdoch 12"—**D-K691**
[No. 22 & Chopin: Nocturne C sharp minor, Op. 27, No. 1]
[No. 34 & Grieg: To Spring on D-F7499]

No. 49, D major, Op. 109 'Cello & Piano
(This is an additional Song without Words, written specifically for 'Cello & Piano)
Pablo Casals & Blas-Net
(G-DB1399) 12"—**V-7193**
[Dvořák: Songs my mother taught me &

Rimsky-Korsakov: Flight of the Bumble-
bee]
Spinning Song See: Songs without Words—
No. 34
Spring Song See: Songs without Words—
No. 30
SYMPHONIES
No. 3, A minor, Op. 56 ("Scotch") 1842
Liverpool Philharmonic Orch.—Sargent
4 12"—**C-DX1451/4**†
Minneapolis Symphony Orch.—Mitro-
poulos 4 12"—**CM-540**†
Rochester Philharmonic Orch.—Iturbi
4 12"—**VM-699**†
No. 4, A major, Op. 90 ("Italian")
National Symphony Orch.—Heinz Unger
(D-K1370/3) 4 12"—**D-ED1**†
[Athalia—War March of the Priests, dir.
Fistoulari]
N. Y. Philharmonic-Symphony Orch.—
Beecham 4 12"—**CM-538**†
Boston Symphony Orch.—Koussevitzky
(G-DB2605/7) 3 12"—**VM-294**†
DUPLICATIONS: Hallé Orch.—Harty,
C-DX342/4: C-DFX119/21; London
Symphony Orch.—Coates, G-AW245/8
—**4th Mvt. (Saltarello—Finale)** only
London Symphony Orch.—Blech,
G-DA1263
No. 5, D major, Op. 107 ("Reformation")
Paris Conservatory Orch.—Münch
4 12"—**D-K1715/8**
[d'Indy: Fervaal—Prelude, Act I]
London Philharmonic Orch.—Beecham
4 12"—**VM-1104**†
[Mozart: La Clemenza di Tito—Over-
ture]
(G-DB6316/9s, last side blank)
Columbia Broadcasting Symphony Orch.
—Barlow 4 12"—**CM-391**†
TRIOS—Violin, 'Cello, Piano
No. 1, D minor, Op. 49
Jacques Thibaud, Pablo Casals, Alfred
Cortot 4 12"—**G-DB1072/5**
—**3rd Mvt. (Scherzo)** only
—**Arr. Violin & Piano** Heifetz
Jascha Heifetz & Emanuel Bay, in VM-
1158
No. 2, C minor, Op. 66
William Murdoch, Albert Sammons, Ce-
dric Sharpe 4 12"—**D-K950/3**
Variations sérieuses, D minor, Op. 54 Piano
Vladimir Horowitz
(in VM-1121) 2 12"—**V-11-9562/3**
[Songs without Words, Nos. 25 & 35]
Ginette Doyen 2 12"—**G-DB11128/9**
[Weber: Sonata No. 1—Rondo]
Alfred Cortot 2 12"—**G-DB3266/7**
[Songs without Words, No. 1]
War March of the Priests See: Athalie
Wedding March See Midsummer Night's
Dream
**Wer hat dich, du schöner Wald, Op. 50,
No. 2**
("Der Jäger Abschied") Partsong
Berlin Teachers' Cho.—Rüdel
12"—**PD-19844**
[Schumann: Die Rose stand im Tau]
[Schubert: Der Lindenbaum, on PD-
27210]
(Also: G-EG749)

MENOTTI, Gian-Carlo (1911-   )
*Winning instantaneous acclaim with his two
operas "The Medium" and "The Telephone,"
Menotti is also known for other lyric works
now revived with much success.*

AMELIA GOES TO THE BALL Opera
Overture Orchestra
Philadelphia Orch.—Ormandy
(G-DB5777) 12"—**V-15377**
[McDonald: Third Symphony—Cakewalk
—Scherzo]

(The) MEDIUM Opera in English
Evelyn Keller, Marie Powers, Beverly Dame,
Catherine Mastico & Orch.—Balaban in
CM-726†
Sebastian Ballet Suite
Robin Hood Dell Orch.—Mitropoulos
2 12"—**CX-278**†

(The) TELEPHONE Opera in English
Marilyn Cotlow & Frank Rogier & Orch.
—Balaban in CM-726†

MERBECKE, John (d. c. 1585)
*A noted British church composer who was
the first to set the English language liturgy to
music.*

Pater Noster (1550)
In Coronation Service of George VI
(G-RG12)

MESOMEDES (2nd Century, B.C.)
*One of the few recorded examples of early
Greek music is attributed to Mesomedes.*

Hymn to the Sun God Solo & Chorus
Hans J. Moser & Chorus 10"—**P-R1016**
[Skolion of Seikilos & Early Jewish
Music]
(in 2000 Years of Music Set)

MESSAGER, André (1853-1929)
*A French organist and operatic and theatrical
conductor (he led the first performance of
Debussy's "Pelléas et Mélisande") whose fame
rests on several light operas.*

OPERAS-COMIQUES, etc. In French
(L') AMOUR MASQUE
Selections
Yvonne Printemps & Orch.
[Véronique—Selections] 12"—**G-DB5114**
(Also on G-P826)

COUPS DE ROULIS
Selections
Soloists, Cho. & Orch.
3 10"—**G-DA4951/3**

(LES) DEUX PIGEONS Ballet 1886
Ballet Suite Orchestra
Symphony Orch.—Bervily
2 12"—**G-L938/9**
Colonne Orch.—Fournet
3 12"—**PAT-PDT135/8**
[Massenet: Phèdre Overture]

FORTUNIO 1907

(La) Maison grise Tenor
Georges Thill   10″—C-LF104
[Massenet: Elégie]
Ninon Vallin (s)   10″—O-166804
[Gounod: Où voulez-vous aller?]
DUPLICATIONS: Marcel Claudel,
G-K5945; R. Buguet, G-K7230; Cozette,
G-P436
Si vous croyez (Chanson de Fortunio)
Tenor
Marcel Claudel   10″—G-K5945
[Maison grise]

ISOLINE 1888

Ballet Suite Orchestra
Symphony Orch.—Ruhlmann
    2 12″—PAT-X96206/7
Symphony Orch.—Lauweryns
    2 10″—G-K5979/80

MADAME CHRYSANTHEME 1893

Jour sous le soleil béni Soprano
Yoshito Miyakawa   12″—C-LFX167
[Puccini: Butterfly—Un bel dì]

VERONIQUE 1898

Vocal & Orchestral excerpts
Yvonne Printemps   12″—G-DB5114
[L'Amour masqué—Selections]
DUPLICATIONS: Lemichel du Roy (s)
& R. Burnier (b), PD-521509/10; M.
Coiffier (s) &. E. Rousseau (b), G-L870;
A. Baugé & S. Laydeker, PAT-PG67
Petite, Dinde, ah, quel outrage
Ma foi, pour venir de Provence Soprano
Maggie Teyte   12″—D-K993
[Offenbach: Périchole—Tu n'est pas
beau]
*See in French catalogues under the following
titles for other recordings: La Basoche; Coups
de Roulis; Debureau; La Fauvette du Temple;
François les Bas-Bleus; Monsieur Beaucaire;
Passionnément; Les Petites Michu; Sacha; Suite
Funambulesque.*

MESSIAEN, Olivier (1908-)

*French organist, composer, and pedagogue,
Messiaen writes music impregnated with Catholic mysticism.*

Preludes Piano
Les sons impalpables du rêve; La Co-
lombe; Le nombre léger
Yvonne Loriod   12″—PAT-PDT132
Vingt regards sur l'Enfant Jésus Piano
—No. 15, Le baiser de l'Enfant Jésus
Yvonne Loriod   12″—PAT-PDT113

MEYERBEER, Giacomo (1791-1864)

*The many shallow, and pompous pages of this
composer's "grand operas" are not very popular
today, but there are gems than can be culled
from his many works for the lyric stage, as even
Meyerbeer's arch-enemy, Richard Wagner, admitted.*

L' Africana: See under Operas—Africaine
Coronation March: See under Operas—
Prophète
Dinorah: See under Operas—Pardon du
Ploërmel
(3) Fackeltänze Brass Band or Orchestra
Eng. **Torch Dances**

No. 1 (B flat major) only
Berlin Philharmonic—Prüwer
    12″—PD-27033
No. 3 (C minor) only
Toulon Band   12″—G-L874
[Prophète—Marche du Sacre]

OPERAS In French

(L') AFRICAINE 5 Acts 1865
Ger. **Die Afrikanerin** It. **L'Africana**
Orchestral Selections (Fantasias, etc.)
Symphony Orch.—Gurlitt
    12″—PD-27012
Individual Excerpts

ACT II

Fille des Rois Baritone
Ger. **Dir, o Königin** It. **Figlia dei Rè**
Arthur Endrèze   10″—PAT-X90074
Theodor Scheidl (in German)
[Adamastor, Act III]   12″—PD-66777
Celestino Sarobe (in Italian)
    12″—PD-66899
[Verdi: Traviata—Di Provenza]

ACT III

Holà! matelots Baritone
It. **All'erta marinar**
Titta Ruffo (in Italian)   10″—G-DA164*
[Berlioz: Damnation de Faust—Séré-
nade]
Adamastor, roi des vagues (Ballade)
Baritone
Ger. **Hei Adamastor, König der Wellen!**
It. **Adamastor, re dell' onde profonde**
Robert Merrill (in Italian)
    12″—V-11-9384
[Giordano: Andrea Chenier—Nemico
della patria]
Titta Ruffo (in Italian)   12″—G-DB1397
[Giordano: Andrea Chenier—Nemico
della patria]
(Also: G-DB406*)
G. Mario Sammarco (in Italian)
(Recorded 1911)   12″—V-15-1018*
[Thomas: Hamlet—Brindisi]
In German: Theodor Scheidl, PD-66777

ACT III

O Paradis (Pays merveilleux) Tenor
It. **O Paradiso** Ger. **Land so wunderbar**
Georges Thill   10″—C-LF21
[Flotow: Marta—M'apparì]
César Vezzani   10″—G-P854
[Verdi: Trovatore—Ah sì, ben mio]
Raoul Jobin
    (in CM-696)   12″—C-72138D
[Berlioz: La Damnation de Faust—
Invocation à la Nature]
Jan Peerce (in Italian)   12″—V-11-9295
[Verdi: Ballo in Maschera—Ma se n'è
forza perderti]
Jussi Björling (in Italian)
(G-DB3302)   12″—V-12150
[Ponchielli: Gioconda—Cielo e mar)
Enrico Caruso (in Italian) & re-recorded
Orch.   12″—V-14234
[Bizet: Carmen—Air de la fleur]
[Santa Lucia, on G-DB2991]
(Original recording: G-DB117*)
Beniamino Gigli (in Italian)
    12″—V-7109

[Flotow: Marta—M'appari]
(G-DB1382)
In Italian: Nino Martini, C-71343D;
Giacomo Lauri-Volpi, G-DB2263; Alfred
Piccaver, PD-66769; Miguel Fleta,
G-DB1071; S. Rayner, D-M453
In German: Franz Völker, PD-95186

Conduisez-moi Tenor & Chorus
It. **Deh', ch'io ritorni**
Enrico Caruso (in Italian)
[Tosti: Addio] 12"—**G-DB1386**

(L') Avoir tant adorée Baritone
It. **Averla tanto amata**
Benvenuto Franci (in Italian)
12"—**G-DB1393**
[Rossini: Guglielmo Tell—Resta
immobile]

DINORAH
The title of an Italian version of "Le Pardon de Ploërmel." For recordings see under the latter title.

(L') ETOILE DU NORD 3 Acts 1854
It. **La Stella del Nord**

Là, là, là, air chéri Soprano & 2 Flutes
(Grand air de Catherine)
Amelita Galli-Curci (with 2 flute obb.)
(G-DB1477) 12"—**V-7655**
[Verdi: Rigoletto—Caro nome]

O jours heureux (Romance de Pierre) Bass
Narçon 10"—**C-RF17**
[Adam: Toréador—Oui la Vie]

(LES) HUGUENOTS 5 Acts 1836
It. **Gli Ugonotti** Ger. **Die Huguenotten**
Vocal & Orchestral Selections
H. Jungkurth (s), H. Roswaenge (t)
& Berlin State Opera Orch.—Melichar
(in German) 12"—**PD-27278**

Orchestral Selections (Fantasias, etc.)
Symphony Orch.—M. Gurlitt
12"—**PD-19889**

Overture Orchestra
Berlin Philharmonic Orch.—
Prüwer 12"—**PD-19898**

Individual Excerpts
ACT I
Non loin des vieilles & Ah! quel spectacle
Recit.
Plus blanche que le blanche hermine—Air
(Romance de Raoul) Tenor
Georges Thill (Viola: Ginot)
12"—**C-LFX111**
[Halévy: La Juive—Rachel, quand
du Seigneur]
César Vezzani (Viola: Quattrocchi)
12"—**G-W1087**
[Verdi: Aida—Celeste Aida]
DUPLICATION: A. d'Arkor, C-RFX22

Seigneur, rempart et seul soutien Bass
(Chorale de Luther—"Ein' feste Burg")
Narçon 10"—**C-RF7**
[Robert le Diable—Voici donc]

Eh! mais, plus je vois—Recit.
Piff, paff, piff, paff—Air Bass
(Scène et chanson huguenote)
Louis Morturier 10"—**G-P733**

[Bizet: Pêcheurs de Perles—Je crois
entendre encore, Vezzani]
Marcel Journet (Recorded 1910)
12"—**V-15-1003***
[Gounod: Philémon et Baucis—
Vulcan's Song]

Nobles Seigneurs, salut—Recit.
Soprano or Alto
Une Dame noble et sage—Air
(Cavatine du page)
Ger. **Ihr edlen Herrn allhier**
It. **Nobil Signori, saluta**
Xenia Belmas 12"—**PD-66715**
[Mascagni: Cavalleria—Voi lo sapete]
Louise Homer (c) (in Italian) &
pf. acc. 12"—**V-15-1011***
[Schubert: Die Allmacht]
(Recorded 1905)
In German: Adele Kern, PD-66946

ACT II
O beau pays de la Touraine Soprano
(Air de Marguerite)
Ger. **O glücklich Land**
Clara Clairbert 12"—**PD-66920**
[Proch: Air & Variations]

ACT IV
Conjuration, "Des troubles renaissants"
Bénédiction des Poignards (Gloire au grand
Dieu vengeur) Bass & Chorus
André Pernet, with M. Bassonnet,
Mme. Doniau-Blanc, M. Deleu, Chorus
& Orch.—Bigot 12"—**G-DB5044**

(LE) PARDON DE PLOERMEL
3 Acts 1859
It., Ger. & Eng. **Dinorah**
Individual Excerpts

ACT II
Ombre légère Soprano Eng. **Shadow Dance**
It. **Ombra leggiera** Ger. **Schattentanz**
Lily Pons (in CM-505) 10"—**C-17315D**
Lily Pons 12"—**V-11-8225**
Vina Bovy 12"—**G-DB4997**
[Verdi: Rigoletto—Caro nome]
Miliza Korjus (in German)
(in VM-871) 12"—**V-13807**
[Rossini: Barbiere di Siviglia—Una
voce poco fa]
[Offenbach: Contes d' Hoffman—Air de
la Poupée on G-C2770; G-EH905]
DUPLICATIONS: Clara Clairbert,
PD-67046; PD-566156; Galli-Curci (in
Italian), G-DB260*; Martha Mayo,
PAT-PGT16

ACT III
En chasse (Chant du chasseur) Bass
André Balbon 12"—**PAT-X90049**
[Rossini: Barbiere—La Calunnia]

(LE) PROPHETE 5 Acts 1849
It. **Il Profeta**
Individual Excerpts

ACT II
Pour Bertha moi je soupire
It. **Sopra Berta l'amor mio**
F. Tamagno (in Italian), G-DR104*

Ah! mon fils! Contralto
Risë Stevens   12"—C-71486D
[Gluck: Alceste—Divinités du Styx]
Margarete Matzenauer   12"—V-36287
[Saint-Saëns: Samson et Dalila—
Mon Coeur]

Prélude: Quadrille (Skating Scene)
Ballet Suite Orchestra
Arr. Lambert ("Les Patineurs")
Sadler's Wells Orch.—Lambert
     12"—G-C3105

Marche du couronnement
(Marche du Sacre) Orchestra
Eng. **Coronation March**
Ger. **Krönungsmarsch**
Boston "Pops" Orch.—Fiedler
    (in VM-968)   10"—V-10-1091
[Wagner: Lohengrin—Prelude Act III]
CBS Symphony—Barlow 12"—C-71287D
[Berlioz: Damnation of Faust—
Rakoczy March]
London Philharmonic—Lambert
     12"—G-C3112
[Chabrier: Marche Joyeuse]
DUPLICATIONS: BBC Symphony—
Boult, G-DB3163; N. Y. Philharmonic-
Symphony—Mengelberg, V-7104; Berlin
Philharmonic—Prüwer, PD-95254; Ber-
lin Philharmonic—Blech, U-F14384;
Bournemouth Municipal Orch.—Godfrey,
C-DX620: C-7331M; Berlin State Opera
Orch.—Blech, G-EJ190
Arr. Band: Republican Guard Band—
Dupont, C-DFX147; Toulon Band,
G-L874; Black Dyke Mills Band,
G-BD593

Roi du ciel (Hymne triomphale)
Tenor & Chorus
It. **Re del cielo** (Inno)
F. Tamagno (in Italian)
[Pour Bertha]   10"—G-DR104*

ACT V

O prêtres de Baal Alto
(Scène de la Prison: Cavatine de Fidès)
Jeanne Manceau   10"—PD-62698
[Reyer: Sigurd—Air d'Uta]

ROBERT LE DIABLE 5 Acts 1831
It. **Roberto il Diavolo**
Ger. **Robert der Teufel**

Voici donc les débris du monastère—Recit.
Act III

Nonnes, qui reposez—Evocation Bass
It. **Evocazione: Suore, che riposate**
Narçon   10"—C-RF7
[Huguenots—Choral de Luther]
Ezio Pinza (in Italian) 12"—G-DB1088
[Mozart: Die Zauberflöte—O Isis und
Osiris]

MEYTUSS, Julius (1903-)

Dnieprostroi (2nd Descriptive Suite) Orch.
Eng. **Dnieper Water Power Station**
—4th Part (Les premiers travaux sur le
Dnieper: Explosions, Pose des premiers
pilliers)
Paris Symphony Orch.—J. Erlich
    (in CM-347)   10"—C-P17416D
[Mossolov: Symphony of Machines—

Soviet Iron Foundry]
(C-LB17) (PAT-X96300)

**MIASKOVSKY, Nicolai Yakolevitch
(1881-)**
*An indefatigable composer of symphonies, hav-
ing produced some twenty in thirty-three years,
Miaskovsky studied with Rimsky-Korsakov, Liadov and Glière. His work shows a curious mix-
ture of German romanticism and Russian na-
tionalism. In his later works, as an honored
Soviet composer, he has returned to folk inspiration.*

Concerto, Op. 44 Violin & Orchestra
David Oistrakh & USSR Orch.—
A. Gauk   5 12"—D-X272/6

SYMPHONIES

No. 18, C major
State Orch.—Gauk
   3 12"—USSR-07773/4 & 05884/7

No. 21, Op. 51
USSR State Orch.—Rahklin
(D-M571/3)   3 10"—COMP-A103

MICA, František Vačlav (1694-1744)
Symphony, D major Orch.
—1st & 3rd Mvts. only
Czech Philharmonic Orch.—Kubelik
     12"—U-H18129

MIEG, Peter
Concerto for 2 pianos
N. Aesbacher & Peter Mieg
    2 12"—ELITE-7008/9

MIGNONE, Francisco, 1897-)
*With Villa-Lobos, Mignone has come to be the
best known of contemporary Brazilian composers. He has great melodic gifts and has composed operas, symphonic poems and many songs.*

Bella Granada Song
Cristina Maristany (s) (in Spanish)
& pf.   10"—PD-47229
[El Clavelito en Tos Lindos Cabellos]

Cantiga de Ninar Lullaby in Portuguese
Gladys Swarthout (ms), with Lester
Hodges (pf) & Lucien Schmit (vlc)
     10"—V-10-1181
[Anon.—Arr. Niles: I wonder as I
wander]
DUPLICATION: Cristina Maristany,
PD-47230

(El) Clavelito en Tos Lindos Cabellos
Song in Portuguese
Cristina Maristany (s) (in Spanish) & pf.
[Bella Granada]   10"—PD-47229

Collection of Dances Orchestra
Saltellando (Polka); Sempre più su
(Mazurka); **Mazurca dei campanelli**
(Mazurka); **C'invita la fisarmonica**
(Waltz)
Orchestrina "Gli allegri virtuosi"
    2 12"—PD-19441/2

Variations for soprano on the popular song:
"Luar do Sertão" (in Portuguese)
Cristina Maristany (s) & pf.
[Cantiga de Ninar]   12"—PD-47230

MIGOT, Georges (1891-   )

A prolific composer, Migot studied with Widor at the Paris Conservatory. He has written several books on musical aesthetics and is also a talented painter. Most of his work has been in chamber music.

(Le) Paravent de laque Ballet
Symphony Orch.—Francis Cébron
2 10″—LUM-30097/8
[Prélude No. 2 for Orchestra]
Prélude No. 2 for Orchestra
Symphony Orch.—Francis Cébron
10″—LUM-30098
[Le Paravent de laque, Pt. 3]

MILAN, Luis (c.1500-c.1561)

A composer for the vihuela (a type of large Spanish lute or guitar) Spanish musicologists regard Milan as one of the most important of their country's early musicians.

Durandarte Song in Spanish
Maria Cid (c) & Emilio Pujol (vihuela)
(in Vol. II) 12″—AS-17
[with Spanish Romances & Villancicos of the 16th Century]
Max Meili (t) & Fritz Worsching
(vihuela) 12″—G-DB5017
[Perdida tengo la color & Mudarra: Mañana de San Juan]
(3) Pavanes Vihuela Solo
Emilio Pujol (in Vol. IV) 12″—AS-40
[Ortiz: Ricercada for Viola da gamba & harpsichord]
Perdida tengo la color
Max Meili (t) & Fritz Worsching
(vihuela) 12″—G-DB5017
[Durandarte & Mudarra: Mañana de San Juan]

MILANUZZI, Fra Carlo (c.1600-c.1650)

An Italian Augustinian monk, organist and prolific composer of church music and secular songs.

(4) Ariosos (in Italian)
Ardo, ma sivelar; La notte sorge; Ora canusco (Aria Siciliana); Sì, sì, ch'io t'amo (Fedele amante)
Salvatore Salvati (t) & guitar
[Falconieri: 3 Ariosos] 12″—MIA-3

MILHAUD, Darius (1892-   )

Now living in the United States, Milhaud is one of the most vivid and versatile of contemporary French composers. A member of the "Six," he composes in a multiplicity of styles, manners and forms. Best known for his ballets and other orchestral scores, Milhaud has appeared in America as a conductor.

(L') Automne Suite for Piano
—No. 2, Alfama only
Marguerite Long 12″—C-LFX376
[Saudades do Brazil—Paysandu & Piano Concerto, Pt. 3]
(Le) Bal Martiniquais 2 Pianos
Robert & Gaby Casadesus
12″—C-71831D
(Le) Boeuf sur le Toit Pantomime
(Produced in London as "The Nothing-Doing Bar")

—Arr. Violin & Piano
(Cadenza by Honegger)
René Benedetti & Jean Wiener
2 12″—C-D15074/5
Concertino de Printemps
Violin & Orchestra
Yvonne Astruc & Orch.—Milhaud
(PD-67147) 12″—PD-516616
Concerto—Piano & Orchestra
Marguerite Long & Orch.—Milhaud
2 12″—C-LFX375/6
[Automne-Alfama & Saudades do Brazil —Paysandu]
(La) Création du Monde—Ballet Nègre
Orchestra
Eng. The Creation of the World
Symphony Orch.—Milhaud
(C-LFX251/2) 2 12″—CX-18
Elégie
Edmund Kurtz (vlc) & Arthur
Balsam (pf) 12″—V-11-9414
[Frescobaldi: Arietta]
Nothing-Doing Bar
See under Boeuf sur le Toit
(L') Orestie d'Eschyle Incidental Music
In French
Les Choréphores—Vocifération funèbre, Libation, Exhortation & Conclusion;
Les Euménides—Processional
Soloists, Antwerp Coecilia Chorus & Symphony Orch.—L. de Vocht
2 12″—CX-64
Pastorale Oboe, Clarinet, Bassoon
Trio d'Anches de Paris 10″—PAT-PG90
[Ibert: Andantino & Allegro marziale]
Protée Symphonic Suite No. 2
Overture, Prélude & Fugue; Pastorale; Nocturne
San Francisco Symphony Orch.—
Monteux 3 12″—VM-1027
Quartets—String
No. 7, B flat major
Galimir Quartet, dir. Milhaud
(PD-62767/8) 2 12″—PD-561100/1
Salade—Ballet chanté Duo & Tango
Mlle. Mahé & M. Rouquetty (in Duo)
Mme. Chastenet & M. Froumenty (in Tango) with Orch.—Milhaud
10″—G-DA4886
Saudades Do Brazil Suite
(An overture and 12 Dances were written originally for piano and later orchestrated by the composer.)
No. 5 (Ipanema)
Artur Rubinstein 12″—V-11-9420
[No. 9 & No. 11; Gershwin: Prelude No. 2]
No. 7, (Corcovado)
—Arr. Violin & Piano Claude Lévy
Jascha Heifetz & Emanuel Bay, in
VM-1158
No. 9 (Sumaré)
Artur Rubinstein 12″—V-11-9420
[No. 5 & No. 11: Gershwin: Prelude No. 2]
—Arr. Violin & Piano
Jascha Heifetz & A. Sandor
10″—G-DA1375

[Paganini-Kreisler: Caprice No. 20]
Joseph Szigeti & A. Farkas
       (in CX-188)   12"—C-70744D
[Falla: Miller's Dance & Bloch: Baal
Shem, Pt. 3]

No. 11 (Larenjeiras)
Artur Rubinstein   12"—V-11-9420
[No. 5 & No. 9; Gershwin: Prelude
No. 2]

No. 12 (Paysandu)
Marguerite Long   12"—C-LFX376
[Automne-Alfama & Piano Concerto,
Pt. 3]

Scaramouche   Suite for Two Pianos   1937
Darius Milhaud & Marcelle Meyer
             12"—G-DB5086
Ethel Bartlett & Rae Robertson
             12"—C-69835D
Vitya Vronsky & Victor Babin
             12"—V-12726

SONGS   In French

(Les) Amours de Ronsard
La Rose; l'Aubépine; Le Rossignol
R. Mahe (s), E. Schenneberg (c),
Rouquetty (t) & Froumenty (b) with
Orch.—Milhaud   12"—G-DB4999

Chansons de Ronsard
A une fontaine; Dieu vous garde; A
Cupidon; Tais-toi, babillarde
Lily Pons (s) & Orch.—Kostelanetz
      (in CM-689)   12"—C-72049D

Cinq Chansons   (Paul Vildrac)
Les quatres petits lions; La pomme et
l'escargot; La malpropre; Poupette et
Patata; Le Jardinier Impatient
Verna Osborne (s) & Lukas Foss (pf)
          2 10"—Hargail-HM650

La Tourterelle
Pierre Bernac (b) & F. Poulenc (pf)
           10"—G-DA4894
[Poulenc: Chansons gaillardes—La Belle
Jeunesse; Invocation aux Parques]

Suite d'apres Corrette
(Oboe, Clarinet, & Bassoon)
Trio d'Anches de Paris
          2 10"—OL-17/18

Suite Française   Orchestra
(Originally for band but later arranged for
orchestra by the composer)
N. Y. Philharmonic-Symphony Orch.—
Milhaud   2 12"—C-X268†

Suite Provençale   Orchestra
St. Louis Symphony Orch.—
Golschmann   2 12"—VM-951†
Grand Orchestre, Paris—Désormière
          2 12"—CdM-516/7

Symphony No. 3   (Sérénade)
Symphony Orch.—Goehr
(C-DB1788)   10"—C-DB1304
[Casella: Serenata—Tarantella]
(In Columbia History of Music, Vol. V;
CM-361)

Folksong Arrangements
Magali   (Provence)
Yvonne Gouverné Chorus & Orch.—
Désormière   10"—CdM-506
[Trad.—Arr. Koechlin: An Hini Goz]

Se Canto   (Langue 'oc)
Yvonne Gouverné Chorus & Orch.—
Désormière   10"—CdM-506
[Trad.—Arr. Koechlin: En passant par
la Lorraine]

MILLOECKER, Karl (1842-1899)
*Millöecker supplied the Austro-Hungarian thea-
tre with a new operetta annually for over thirty
years, and his works are still heard abroad. In
recent years a modern version of "La Dubarry"
was made by Theodore Mackeben and revived
with much success.*

OPERETTAS   In German
(DER) ARME JONATHAN
In der blauen Dämmerstunde
Barnabas von Geczy & his Orch.,
G-EG7047
Ich bin der arme Jonathan   Tenor
H. Roswaenge, PD-24418
—Arr. Orchestra
Barnabas von Geczy Orch., G-EG7047

(DER) BETTELSTUDENT   3 Acts   1882
Eng. The Beggar Student
Abridged Recording
Berlin State Opera Company.—
H. Weigert   4 12"—PD-27411/4
The cast includes Ida Perry, Eduard
Kandl, Julius Patzak, Else Ruzicka and
others.
Orchestral Selections (Fantasias, etc.)
Künstler Orch., PD-19742; Marek Weber
Orch., G-EH59; Nils Grevillius Orch.,
G-Z211
Vocal Excerpts
Anni Frind, Marcel Wittrisch, Wilhelm
Strienz, with Chorus & Orch.
          12"—G-EH1006
Peter Anders, Carla Spletter, Hanns Heinz
Nissen with Chorus & Orch.—Schultze
          12"—T-E2120
Also: Johannes Heesters, PD-47050;
Hans Fidesser, O-25764; Margarete
Slezak & H. E. Groh, O-26261; Franz
Völker, PD-27068; Leo Schützendorf,
T-E391; Wilhelm Strienz, G-EH1018;
Franz Völker, PD-10269; Peter Anders,
T-A2092
Ich setz den Fall   Duet   Act II
Walter Ludwig (t) & Hedwig Jung-
kurth (s), G-EH893; Jussi Björling (t)
& Hjördis Schymberg (s) (in Swedish),
G-X6146; Margarete Slezak & H. E.
Groh, O-26261

(LA) DUBARRY
Modern version by Theo. Mackeben
Vocal Selections
Jarmila Ksirova, G-EG6485
Orchestral Selections
Grand Orch.—Mackeben, G-EH1214
Dunkelrote Rosen
Wilhelm Strienz (bs) & Cho.,
G-EG7038

(DER) FELDPREDIGER
Traum-Walzer   Tenor   Eng. Dream Waltz
Franz Völker, PD-24177

—Arr. Orchestra
Marek Weber Orch., G-EH691; Viennese
Orch., PD-10198

GASPARONE
Vocal & Orchestral Selections
Operetta Ensemble   12"—G-EH389
Mrika Rokk & Rudi Schuricke
          10"—G-EG6205
Also: G-EG6185; G-EG3972; G-EG6356
Canzonetta: Komm, mia bella   Soprano
Erna Sack, T-A2035
O wen ich doch der Räuber wär'   Tenor
Helge Roswaenge, PD-24418
Julius Patzak, PD-10324; PD-90061
Marcel Wittrisch, G-EG3870
Dunkelrote Rosen bring' ich schöne Frau
Walter Ludwig, PD-15382; W. Schneider,
PD-11407
Glückswalzer
Beniamino Gigli (t) & Prussian State
Orch.—Seidler-Winkler   12"—G-DB7623
[Leoncavallo: Pagliacci—Prologue]
(Also G-DBO5353)

MINISCALCHI (XVII Century)
Io tento invan
Non passo piu soffrir
Max Meili (t) & R. Gerlin (harpsichord)
     (in Vol. VIII)   12"—AS-79
[Busca: Occhi Belli & Bionda, bionda;
Frescobaldi: Voi partite]

MOERAN, Ernest John (1894-   )
*A British composer of Irish extraction who has
collected much folk material, and whose works
bear the stamp of the influence of John Ireland.*
**Diaphenia (Constable); (The) Sweet o'
the Year (Shakespeare)—Songs**
Heddle Nash (t) & Gerald Moore (pf)
[R. Strauss: Ständchen]   10"—G-B9412
Symphony, G minor
Hallé Orch.—Leslie Heward
     6   12"—G-C3319/24†
[Rawsthorne: Four Bagatelles, Denis
Matthews]
Trio, G major
Jean Pougnet (vl); Frederick Riddle
(vla), Anthony Pini (vlc)
     3   12"—C-DX1014/6†

MOESCHINGER, Albert (1897-   )
*A Swiss composer of chamber music, concertos,
songs, and choral works.*
**Missa ad quatuor voces inaequates, organo
comitante, Op. 59**
Bern Radio Vocal Quartet w. O.
Schärrer (organ) 3 12"—ELITE-7015/7

MOLARSKY, Delmar
Quintet for String Quartet & Voice
Delmar Molarsky (b) & Cambourakis
String Quartet   2 12"—TC-T1105

MOMPOU, Frederico (1893-   )
*A Catalan composer who has studied in Paris,
Mompou has written in the style he chooses to
call "primitivista."*
Canción y dansa   Piano
A. Benedetti-Michelangeli
[Albéniz: Malagueña]   10"—G-DA5432

Jeunes Filles au Jardin   Piano
(from Scènes d'enfants)
Guiomar Novaës   10"—C-17522D
[Philipp: Feux follets]

MONIUSZKO, Stanislaus (1820-1872)
*A conductor at the Warsaw opera and professor
at the Conservatory, Moniuszko is thought of
as the father of Polish national opera and as
the chief exponent of the Polish art-song.*
HALKA   Opera   1846
Prayer Act IV
Stefan Schwer (t) (in German) &
Hamburg State Opera Cho. & Orch.—
Schmidt-Isserstedt   12"—T-E1934
[Mussorgsky: Boris Godunov—
Revolutionary Cho.]

STRASZNY DWOR
Mazurka
Sym. Orch.—G. Fitelberg   10"—C-DC344
[Polish National Anthem]

MONSIGNY, Pierre Alexandre (1729-1817)
*Although untrained in the modern systematic
sense, Monsigny had great melodic gifts. He
composed primarily for the subversive French
comic stage, the "opéra-comique."*
LE DESERTEUR
Adieu, chère Louise
Maggie Teyte, in VM-1169
Entr'acte
L'Oiseau-Lyre Orch.—Désormière
         12"—OL-144

ROSE ET COLAS
La Sagesse est un tresor
Maggie Teyte, in VM-1169

MONTANI, Pietro
Concertino, E major
Piano & String Quartet
Enzo Calace & La Scala Quartet
     2   12"—G-AW290/1
[Giordini: Sonata, E flat major—
Siciliana]
Carlo Bassotti & EIAR Chamber Orch.—
T. Petralia   2 12"—CET-IT891/2

MONTECLAIR, Michel Pignolet de (1666-1737)
*A French double-bass player and violinist who
composed operas and opera-ballets.*
Comme une hyrondelle
Micheletti (t) & R. Gerlin (harpsichord)
     (in Vol. X)   12"—AS-98
[Airs Sérieux et à Boire]
JEPHTE   1732
Entr'acte
L'Oisieau-Lyre Orch.—Désormière
         12"—OL-143
(Les) Plaisirs champêtres
—Arr. Viols Casadesus
Ritournelle; Passepied; Entrée des
Bergers; Cortège des Musettes et des
Vielles; Route du bonheur
Société des Instruments Anciens, Paris—
Henri Casadesus   2 12"—C-LFX19/20
Sombre forêts
Micheletti (t) & R. Gerlin (harpsichord)
     (in Vol. X)   12"—AS-98
[Airs Sérieux et à Boire]

MONTEMEZZI, Italo (1875-   )

*Well known for his opera "L'Amore dei tre re,"
Montemezzi followed the pattern set by his
veristic predecessors, Mascagni and Leoncavallo.*

(L) AMORE DEI TRE RE
Opera in Italian   1913
Eng. The Love of Three Kings
Prelude to Act III   Orchestra
Royal Opera Orch. Covent Garden—
V. Bellezza   12"—**G-S10224**
[Wolf-Ferrari: Jewels of the Madonna—
Intermezzo, No. 2]

MONTEVERDI, Claudio (1567-1643)

*The great Italian composer who forms the most
important link between the old and the new
musical styles. Monteverdi not only carried on
the old contrapuntal traditions of Gabrieli and
Palestrina in his church music and madrigals,
but also struck out in new and revolutionary
paths to lay the foundation for modern dramatic music and orchestration. His surviving
operas, though they can scarcely be widely performed, contain very great music.*

Collections

Madrigals & Selected Works
Amor; Ardo; Il ballo delle ingrate;
Chiome d'oro; Ecco mormorar l'onde;
Hor ch'el ciel e la terra; Lasciatemi
morire; Ohime dove il mio ben; Zefiro
torna
Mmes. J. de Polignac, I. & N. Kedroff,
Rauh, Mm. P. Derenne, H. Cuenod, D.
Conrad & Instrumental Ensemble—Nadia
Boulanger
(G-DB5038/42)   5 12"—**VM-496†**
(7) Madrigals a cappella unspecified
Vocal Ensemble—Marcel Couraud
(DF-88/91)   4 12"—**DF-A20**
Amor (Lamento della Ninfa)
Boulanger group, V-12304 in VM-496:
G-DB5042
Ardo
Boulanger group, V-12302 in VM-496:
G-DB5040
Arianna See under Operas
(Il) Ballo delle Ingrate
In genere rappresentativo—Ballet 1608
(8th Book of Madrigals, 1638)
—Excerpt: Boulanger group, V-12303 in
VM-496: G-DB5041
Chiome d'oro
Boulanger group, V-12302 in VM-496:
G-DB5040
Maria Castellazzi & Leïla ben Sedira (ss)
& Ars Rediviva Ensemble
                    12"—**G-DB5024**
[Maledetto: Ohimè, dov'è il mio ben &
Sigismondo: Lagrimo]
Ecco mormorar l'onde
5-Part Madrigal
Boulanger group, V-12304 in VM-496:
G-DB5042
Hor ch'el ciel e la terra
6-Part Madrigal
Boulanger group, V-12300 in VM-496:
G-DB5038
(L') Incoronazione di Poppea
See under Operas

Lagrime d'Amante al Sepolcro dell' Amata
(Madrigal—Sestina in Italian, from the 6th
Book of Madrigals)
1. Incenerite spoglie avara tomba
2. Ditelo voi o fiumi, e voi ch' udiste
Glauco
3. Darà anotte il sol lume alla terra
4. Ma te raccoglie, o Ninfa
5. O chiome d'or, neve gentil del seno
6. Dunque amate reliquie un mar di
pianto
Cantori Bolognesi Chorus—
Cremesini   3 12"—**C-D16436/8**
Lasciatemi morire 5-Part Madrigal
(6th Book of Madrigals)
Boulanger group, V-12300 in VM-496:
G-DB5038
See also Opera—Arianna
Lettera Amorosa Solo Madrigal
("Se i languidi miei sguardi")
Yvon Le Marc' Hadour (b) & R. Gerlin
(harpsichord)   10"—**BAM-6**
Inez Alfani Tellini (s) & M.
Favaretto (pf)   10"—**G-AV45**
Maladetto Air
Maria Castelazzi (s) w. "Ars Rediviva"—
Crussard   12"—**G-DB5024**
[Chiome d'oro & ohimè dov'è il mio ben;
Sigismondo: Lagrimo]
DUPLICATION: Roland Hayes,
C-17174D in CM-393
Ohimè, ch'io cado Air
Max Meili (t) & R. Gerlin (harpsichord)
             (in Vol. III) 12"—**AS-21**
[Manzoli: 2 Airs]
Ohimè, dov'è il mio ben Madrigal
Boulanger group, V-12302 in VM-496:
G-DB5040
Maria Castellazzi (s) & Leïla ben
Sedira (c)   12"—**G-DB5024**
[Maladetto & Chiome d'oro; Sigismondo:
Lagrimo]

OPERAS In Italian

ARIANNA 1608

Lasciatemi morire (Lamento d'Arianna)
(See also under Lasciatemi—Madrigal version)
Maria Peschken (t) with harpsichord
& Vlc. acc.   10"—**P-R1024**
[Gabrieli: Benedixisti, Chorus]
(in 2000 Years of Music Set)
Gabriella Gatti (s) & London Philhar-
monic Orch.—Bellezza 12"—**G-DB6515**
Gabriella Gatti (s) & EIAR Orch.—
Alfredo Simonetti   12"—**CET-BB25087**
(PD-67940)
Ezio Pinza (bs) & Fritz Kitzinger (pf)
             (in VM-766) 12"—**V-17914**
[Handel: Floridante-Alma mia; Legrenzi:
Eteocle & Polinice—Che fiero costume;
Al. Scarlatti: Chi vuole innamorarsi]
DUPLICATIONS: M. Voltolina,
CET-IT582; Louis Graveure, T-E977

(L') INCORONAZIONE DI POPPEA 1642

Oblivion soave (Trans. G. Benvenuti)
Eng. May sweet oblivion lull thee
Ezio Pinza (bs) & Fritz Kitsinger (pf)
             (in VM-766) 12"—**V-17915**

[Cavalli: Donzelle, fuggite & Torelli: **Tu lo sai**; Paisiello: La Molinara—Nel cor più non mi sento]
Doris Owens (c) in English, with Harpsichord acc. 10″—**C-DB500**
[Purcell: Bell Anthem, Chorus]
(in Columbia History of Music, Vol. II: CM-232)

Sento un certo non so che Soprano
Isabel French (s) & Harpsichord
10″—in **TC-T2**

(L') ORFEO—Favola Musicale 1607
Complete recording
Soloists, Chorus, with Harpsichord, Organ & Orchestra—F. Calusio
(MIA-14/25) 12 12″—**G-DB5370/81**
The Cast:
Orfeo .... E. de Franceschi (b)
1° Pastore .... E. Lombardi (t)
2° Pastore .... G. Manacchini (b)
Caronte }............A. Marone (bs)
Plutone }
Apollo .... G. Manacchini (b)
Euridice }............G. Vivante (s)
La Musica }
Ninfa .... V. Palombini (ms)
Messaggera .... E. Nicolai (ms)
Speranza }........V. Palombini (ms)
Proserpina }
Vittore Veneziani, Chorus Director
(Corradina Mola, harpsichord; Alceo Galliera, organ)

Individual Excerpts
Ahi sventurato amante, Recit., Act III
Lamenti d'Orfeo, Recit., Act II
Qual honor, Aria, Act IV
Yvon Le Marc'Hadour (b) & Pasquier Trio, with R. Gerlin (harpsichord) & Pierront (organ) 12″—**PAT-PAT76**
Sei canti guerri amorosi 3 voices
(Arr. Malipiero)
Roman Vocal Trio 10″—**G-HN1426**
Zefiro torna (Ciaconna) 2 Tenors
(Real: Boulanger)
Boulanger group, V-12301 in VM-496:
G-DB5039

MORLEY, Thomas (1557-1603)
Probably the best known and most popular of the Elizabethan madrigal composers, Morley was a pupil of William Byrd, and the composer of many "ballets" and canzonets as well as serious madrigals, motets and some instrumental music. He played a significant role as a writer as well. His "Plaine and Easie Introduction to Practicall Musike" gives a superb picture of musical life in England and the musical theories of the time.

Fire, fire, my heart 5-Pt. Madrigal
Danish Radio Madrigal Choir—
Wöldike In Prep. Danish Columbia
* **Goe from My Window**
Fitzwilliam Book No. 9 Virginal
Ralph Kirkpatrick (harpsichord), in MC-25
It was a lover and his lass Ayre
(Shakespeare)
Max Meili (t) & F. Worsching (lute)
12″—**G-DB5018**

[Willaert: Con lagrime e sospiro; Dowland: Come again & Come, heavy Sleep]
Elsie Suddaby (s) & Gerald Moore (pf)
10″—**D-M510**
[Arne: Where the Bee Sucks & Loch Lomond]

My bonnie lass she smileth 5-Part Madrigal
1595
London Madrigal Group—T. B. Lawrence 10″—**V-4316**
[Now is the month of maying; Fornsete; Sumer is icumen in; Byrd: I thought that Love had been a Boy]

Now is the month of Laying
5-Part Madrigal 1595
London Madrigal Group—T. B. Lawrence 10″—**V-4316**
[My bonnie lass; Fornsete; Sumer is icumen in; Byrd: I thought that Love had been a boy]
Danish Radio Madrigal Choir—
Wöldike In Prep. Danish Columbia

Since my tears and lamenting
4-Part Madrigal 1594
Motet & Madrigal Group—Opienski
(in Vol. VI) 12″—**AS-58**
[Jones: Farewell dear Love & Dowland: Go Crystal Tears]

Sing We and Chant It
5-Part Madrigal 1595
Ger. **Auf, lasst uns singen!**
St. George's Singers, unacc.
10″—**C-5716**
[Pilkington: Rest, Sweet Nymphs]
(in Columbia History of Music, Vol. I: CM-231)
Regensburg Cathedral Choir—Th. Schrems (in German) 10″—**G-EG3927**
DUPLICATION: Kilven Kouro
(in Finnish), G-X3138

Sweet Nymph 2-Part Canzonet, unacc.
Winchester College Quiristers
12″—**C-D40121**
[in examples for Lecture 61, "The Progress of Music" by George Dyson]
(International Educational Society Series)

MORTON (Mourton), Robert (15th Century)
Clerk of the chapel of Philipp the Good and Charles the Bold of Burgundy about 1464, Morton was a learned and highly esteemed musician in his time.

Trois Chansons
Vlas. & Trombone 10″—**OL-126**
[Binchois: Inter Natos Mulierum]
Trois Chansons
Three wind instruments 10″—**OL-63**
[Ghizeghem: Les Grans Regrez & Binchois: Files a marier]
Mon bien ma joyeux
Lavaillotte (fl), P. Lefebvre (cl) & F. Oubradous (bsn) 12″—**OL-61**
[Ghizeghem: Plus n'en aray & Grenon: Nova vobis Gaudia, with Daniels & Peneau (s)]

MOSSOLOV, Alexander (1900-   )

One of the younger and more radical contemporary Russian composers though he had most conservative training under Glière and Miaskovsky, Mossolov's works tend toward clever realism.

Berceuse Turkmène
La Chorale Populaire de Paris, unacc.
Chorus   10"—O-281086
[Dupont: Le Chant des Ouvriers]
Symphony of Machines Orchestra
—Steel Foundry
EIAR Symphony Orch.—Victor de
Sabata   12"—CET-PP60008
[Glazunov: Troubadour's Serenade]
Paris Symphony—J. Ehrlich
        (in CM-347)   10"—C-P17121D
[Meytuss: Dnieprostroi]
(C-LB17)   (PAT-X96300)

MOSKOWSKI, Moritz (1854-1925)

A Polish pianist and composer, largely trained in Germany, who wrote many highly popular piano pieces. He is known for his sentimental piano and orchestral music, a considerable portion of which is pseudo-Spanish.

BOABDIL Opera in German 1892
No recording available
Caprice espagnol, Op. 37 Piano
Eileen Joyce   12"—O-7741
[Schumann: Novelette, D major, Op. 21
No. 2]
Ermelinda Magnetti 10"—CET-TI7050
Danses Espagnoles See: Spanish Dances
From Foreign Lands, Op. 23
Piano 4-Hands
(Spain, Hungary, Germany, Italy)
Ger. **Aus aller Herren Länder**
—Arr. Orchestra
Philharmonic Orch., Berlin—Järnefelt
        10"— & 12"— O-D4895 & O-D6044
Guitarre, Op. 45, No. 2 Piano
—Arr. Violin & Piano Sarasate
Jascha Heifetz & A. Sandor
                        10"—G-DA1377
[Castelnuovo-Tedesco: Alt Wien]
Yehudi Menuhin & A. Balsam
                        10"—G-DA1282
[Kreisler: Sicilienne & Rigaudon]
Serenade (Serenata) Op. 15, No. 1 Piano
—Arr. Orchestra
Harry Horlick, D-F7242
—Vocal Arrangement in German
("Liebe kleine Nachtigall")
Miliza Korjus (s)   12"—G-EH973
[Delibes: Les filles de Cadix] (G-L1029)
Spanish Dances, Op. 12 Piano 4-Hands
Fr. **Danses espagnoles**
Rawicz & Landauer   10"—C-FB1872
[Nos. 1-5] (Arr. Orch.)
City of Birmingham Orch.—
Weldon   2 12"—C-DX1225/6
No. 2, G minor
Boston "Pops" Orch.—Fiedler
[No. 2]   10"—G-B9158
No. 5, D major
Boston "Pops" Orch.—Fiedler
[No. 2]   10"—G-B9158

Waltz, E major, Op. 34, No. 1 Piano
Eileen Joyce   12"—P-E11239
[Debussy: Toccata]
DUPLICATIONS: A. De Greef, G-E563;
Rawicz & Landauer (2 Pfs.), C-DB2262

MOURET, Jean Joseph (1682-1738)

A director of the "Concerts spirituels" in Paris, Mouret composed operas, ballets, motets and instrumental divertissements.

(Les) Festes de Thalie
2 Airs pour les jeux et les plaisirs
Air de Florine
Air de Nérine & Instrumental Music
Mlle. Epicaste, Martha Angelici &
Versailles Concert Orch.—Cloëz
        (in Vol. IX)   12"—AS-84

MOUTON, Jean (d.1522)

A pupil of Josquin, Mouton is an eminent exponent of the French Renaissance. His works include masses, motets and hymns.

Ave Maria
Strasbourg Cathedral Cho.—A. Hoch
[Victoria; Popule Meus] 12"—C-RFX72

MOZART, Leopold (1719-1787)

Author of a textbook on the technique of the violin, Leopold Mozart, the father of the famous Mozart, also wrote a considerable amount of church and instrumental music, seldom if ever heard today.

Divertimento militare sive Sinfonia,
D major 1756
Berlin State Orch.—Gmeindl
[Last side blank] 3 12"—PD-67557/9S

MOZART, Wolfgang Amadeus (1756-1791)

Despite the enormous recorded repertory of Mozart, there are still numerous and serious gaps. Important operas, sacred music, concertos and chamber works have yet to make their appearance on records, and too many fine recorded works have, for some reason, been deleted from both domestic and foreign catalogues.
In the list below, the Köchel catalogue numbers are given after each title. The number in parentheses represents the revised chronology of Alfred Einstein.

(4) Adagios & Fugues K.404a Strings
(*the Fugues, arr. Mozart, after J. S. & W. F. Bach*)
No. 1, D minor (w. Bach: Wohltemperiertes
Clavier—Fugue Vol. I, No. 8)
No. 2, G minor (w. Bach: Wohltemperiertes
Clavier—Fugue Vol. II, No. 14)
No. 3, F major (w. Bach: Wohltemperiertes
Clavier—Fugue Vol. II, No. 13)
No. 6, F minor (w. W. F. Bach: Fugue,
F minor)
Pasquier Trio   4 12"—DF-A4
(See also under BACH)

Adagio, E major, K.261
1776 Violin & Orchestra
(*An alternate slow movement for the Concerto
No. 5, A major, K.219 "Turkish"*)
Stefi Geyer & Zurich Collegium Musicum
Paul Sacher   12"—C-LZX7

Georg Kulenkampff & Orch—Schmidt-
Isserstedt 12"—T-E2021
[Beethoven: Violin Concerto, Pt. 11]
Georg Kulenkampff & Franz Rupp (pf)
(PD-566188) 12"—PD-67156
[Eine kleine Nachtmusik, pt. 1, dir.
Furtwängler]
[Quartet, C major, K.465, pt. 7, Deman
Qt., on PD-95304: PD-15026]
[Symphony No. 40, pt. 7, dir. Strauss,
on PD-95445]
Adagio, B major, K.411 (K.440a) 1783
*(An isolated Divertimento Movement for 2
clarinets and 3 basset horns, also arranged for
String Quartet.)*
—**Arr. Flute, Oboe, Clarinet, Bassoon, Horn**
Leipzig Gewandhaus Wind Quintet
12"—PD-95168
[Divertimento No. 16, K.289—Presto]
Adagio, B minor, K.540 1788 Piano
Lili Kraus 12"—P-R20445
Adagio and Fugue, C minor, K.546 1788
Strings (Quartet No. 22, Peters Edition)
Symphony Orch.—Münch 12"—OL-93
Busch Chamber Orch.—Busch
(G-DB3391) 12"—V-12324
Adagio and Rondo K.617
Glass Harmonica, Flute, Oboe, Viola,
'Cello
E. Power Biggs (celesta), Phillip Kaplan,
Louis Speyer, Emil Korrisand, Josef
Zimbler 12"—V-11-9570
Adoramus te Christe, K.327 (Anh. K.109)
*(Actually composed by Quirino Gasparini, but
often attributed to Mozart)*
Strasbourg Cathedral Choir—A. Hoch
(M. F. Rich, organ) 12"—C-69488D
[Ave, verum corpus, K.618]
(C-LX766) (C-LWX295)
[Josquin des Prés: Ave vera virginitas,
on C-RFX59]
Alleluja See Motet—Exsultate, K.165
(The) Alphabet K.Anh.294d
Quatuor Vocal A.B.C.D.
10"—LUM-33175
[Canteloube: Unidentified Selection]
Andante, C major, K.315 (K.285e)
1778 Flute & Orchestra
Lucien Lavaillotte & Paris Conservatory
Chamber Orch.—Fendler
10"—PAT-PA1832
[Vivaldi: Concerto for Flute, Op. 10,
No. 3, pt. 3]
ARIAS In Italian
(Isolated concert Arias for solo voice
& Orchestra)
(For other solo vocal arias see under:
Litaniae, Masses, Motets, Operas, Songs,
Vespers)
Collection
Mentre ti lascio, o figlia, K. 513
Un bacio di mano, Arietta, K. 541
Per questa bella mano, Aria, K. 612
Cosi dunque tradisci, Recit. & Aria,
K. 432 (K. 421a)
Rivolgete a lui lo sguardo, Aria, K. 584
Alcandro, lo confesso, Recit. & Aria,
K. 512
Italo Tajo (bs) 3 12"—CET-104
(CET-BB25186/8)

Alcandro, lo confesso Recit.
Non so d'onde viene K. 512 Aria
Bass 1787
Italo Tajo (abbreviated), on
CET-BB25188, also in CET-104
(Un) Bacio di mano, K. 541 Bass 1788
Italo Tajo, on CET-BB25186, also in
CET-104
Cosi dunque tradisci Recit.
Aspri rimorsi atroci K. 432 Aria
(K. 421a) Bass
Italo Tajo, on CET-BB25187, also in
CET-104
Mentre ti lascio, o figlia, K.513 Bass 1787
Ezio Pinza & Metropolitan Opera Orch.
—Walter (in CM-643†) 12"—C-71844D
Italo Tajo (abbreviated), on
CET-BB25186, also in CET-104
(Un) Moto di gioia, K. 579 1789 Soprano
*(An alternate aria for "Deh, vieni" in "Le
Nozze di Figaro")*
Martha Angelici & Jean Hubeau (pf)
(in Vol. X) 12"—AS-93
[Ridente le calma & Das Lied der
Trennung]
Leïla Ben Sedira & pf. acc.
10"—G-DA5014
[Ridente le calma & Oiseaux, si tous les
ans]
Oiseaux, si tous les ans K. 307 (K.284d)
Leila Ben Sedira (s) & pf. acc.
10"—G-DA5014
[Ridente la calma & Un moto di gioia]
Per questa bella mano, K. 612 Bass 1791
Italo Tajo (abbreviated), on
CET-BB35187, also in CET-104
Rivolgete a lui di sguardo, K. 584
Bass 1789
Italo Tajo, on CET-BB25188,
also in CET-104
Ave Maria, K.554 4-Part Canon in Latin
1788
St. Nicholas Choir 10"—LUM-30004
[Motet—Ave, verum corpus]
Ave, verum See Motets—Ave, verum corpus
**Bundeslied: Brüder, reicht die Hand
zum Bunde**
*(Originally Eine kleine Freimaurer-Kantate
"Laute verkünde unser Freude," K-623, arr.
4-Part Male Chorus)*
Berlin Teachers' Chorus—Rüdel
12"—PD-19878
[Kirchl: Die Weihnachtsglocken in
der Ostmark]
Neukölln Teachers' Chorus—Melichar
12"—PD-21881
[B. A. Weber-Melichar: Brüder, streckt
num die Gewehre]

CASSATIONS

No. 2, B flat major, K.99 (K.63a) 1769
(2 Violins, Viola, Bass, 2 Oboes, 2 Horns)
L'Oiseau Lyre Orch.—Oubradous
2 12"—OL-124/5
Concertantes
See under Concertos—Violin, Viola &
Orch., K.364; Concertos—Woodwinds &
Orch., K.Anh.9

CONCERTOS—Bassoon & Orchestra

No. 1, B flat major, K.191 (K.186e) 1774
Ferdinand Oubradous & Orch.—Eugène
Bigot (G-L1026/7) 2 12"—VM-704
Archie Camden & Hallé Orch.—
Harty 3 12"—CM-71†
[Senaillé: Allegro spiritoso]
(C-L1824/6)

No. 2, B flat major, K. Anh.230a 1775
*Edited Max Seiffert. Not Mozart, according to
Einstein*
Ferdinand Oubradous & Orch.—
Edvard Fendler 2 12"—OL-40/1

CONCERTO—Clarinet & Orchestra

A major, K. 622 1791
Reginald Kell & London Philharmonic
—Sargent 4 12"—VM-708†
[Schumann: Phantasiestücke, Op. 73
No. 1]
(G-C3167/70†) (G-FKX61/4)
F. Etienne & Orch. de Chambre—
Hewitt 3 12"—DF-A2
Luigi Amodio & Berlin State Orch.—
Galliera 4 12"—PD-68134/7
(Fonit-69010/3)
—2nd Mvt. (Adagio) only
Haydn Draper & Orch.—Raybould
10"—C-DB834
(in Columbia History of Music, Vol. III:
CM-233)

CONCERTOS—Flute & Orchestra

*(See also Andante, C major, K-315, for Flute
and Orchestra)*

No. 1, G major, K.313 (K.285c) 1776
Marcel Moyse & Orch.—Bigot
(G-L1021/3) 3 12"—VM-396†
(Taffanel cadanzas)

No. 2, D major, K.314 (K.285d) 1778
Marcel Moyse & Orch.—Coppola
2 12"—VM-589
(G-L835/6) (G-FKX41/2)
(Donjon cadenza)
(Finale abridged)

CONCERTO—Flute, Harp & Orchestra

C major, K. 299 (K.297c) 1778
Gaston Crunelle, Pierre Jamet & Orch.—
Cloëz (in Vol. XIII) 4 12"—AS-122/5
René Le Roy, Lily Laskine, & Royal
Philharmonic Orch.—Beecham
3 12"—G-DB6485/7†
Marcel Moyse, Lily Laskine & Orch.—
Coppola 3 12"—G-C2387/9†
(G-L876/8) (G-FKX43/5)
(Graener cadenza)
Harpsichord & Orchestra
See Concertos—Piano

CONCERTOS—Horn & Orchestra

No. 2, E flat major, K.417 1783
Dennis Brain & Philharmonia Orch.—
Süsskind 2 12"—C-DX1365/6

No. 3, E flat major, K.447 1783
Aubrey Brain & BBC Symphony Orch.
Boult 2 12"—VM-829†
(G-DB3973/4)
Max Zimolong & Saxon State Orch.—
Böhm 2 12"—G-DB5628/9
L. Trevet & Orch.—Oubradous
2 10"—G-DA4929/30

No. 4, E flat major, K.495 1786
Dennis Brain & Hallé Orch.
(C-DX1123/4) 2 12"—CX-285†

CONCERTOS—Organ & Orchestra
See Sonatas—Organ & Strings

CONCERTOS—Harpsichord w. 2 Violins
& 'Cello
(After the Sonatas of J. C. Bach)

No. 1, D major, K. 107 (K.216) 1765
(from J. C. Bach, Op. 5, No. 2)
—Minuet only
Kruttge, Strub, Mazurat, Schrader
10"—G-EG2881
[Handel: Trio Sonata, C minor, Op. 2,
No. 1—Andante]

CONCERTOS—Piano & Orchestra

No. 1, F major, K. 37 1767
(Harpsichord & Orch.)
(After Raupach, Schobert, & Honauer)
Marguerite Roesgen-Champion & Paris
Symphony Orch.—Gaillard
2 12"—PAT-PGT24/5
[J. C. Bach: Concerto No. 1, C major—
Rondo only]

No. 4, G major, K.41 1767
(Harpsichord & Orch.)
(After Honauer & Raupach)
Marguerite Roesgen-Champion (pf) &
Lamoureux Orch.—Wolff
2 12"—C-RFX75/6
[J. S. Bach: Concerto, F major, Op. 13,
No. 3—Rondo]

No. 9, E flat major, K.271 "Jeunehomme"
1777
Walter Gieseking & Berlin State Opera
Orch.—Rosbaud 4 12"—CM-291†
(C-LFX460/3) (C-GQX10818/21)
(Mozart cadenzas used except in last
mvt.)

No. 10, E flat major, K.365 (K.316a)
1779 (For 2 Pianos & Orchestra)
Artur & Karl Ulrich Schnabel with
London Symphony—Boult
(Mozart cadenzas used) 3 12"—VM-484†
(G-DB3033/5†)
Vitya Vronsky & Victor Babin with Robin
Hood Dell Orch.—Mitropoulos
(Babin cadenzas used) 3 12"—CM-628†
José & Amparo Iturbi with Rochester
Philharmonic—Iturbi 3 12"—VM-732†
(Iturbi cadenzas used)

No. 12, A major, K.414 (K.386a) 1782
(See Rondos for original last movement)
Louis Kentner & London Philharmonic—
Beecham 3 12"—CM-544†
(C-LX894/6) (Mozart cadenzas used)
Kathleen Long & Boyd Neel Orch.—
Neel 3 12"—D-K772/4
(PD-516685/7) (Mozart cadenzas used
in 2nd & 3rd mvts. only)

No. 14, E flat major, K.449 1784
Rudolf Serkin & Busch Chamber
Players—Busch 3 12"—VM-657†
(Mozart cadenzas used)
Kathleen Long & Boyd Neel Orch.—
Neel 3 12"—D-K784/6
(PD-516670/2)

No. 15, B flat major, K.450 1784
Kathleen Long & National Symphony
Orch.—Neel 3 12″—**D-ED25**†
(Mozart cadenzas in 1st & 3rd Mvts. only)
(D-K1121/3)

No. 17, G major, K.453 1784
Edwin Fischer & his Chamber Orch.
(G-DB3362/4) 3 12″—**VM-481**†
(Fischer cadenza in 1st, although first
few bars are from Mozart; Mozart's are
used in the 2nd Mvt.)

No. 18, B flat major, K.456 1784
Lili Kraus & London Philharmonic—
Goehr 4 12″—**P-P25**†
[Sonata No. 39, C major, K.404, with
Kraus & Simon Goldberg]
(P-R20404/7)
(Mozart cadenzas used)

No. 19, F major, K.459 1784
Artur Schnabel & London Symphony—
Sargent 4 12″—**GM-282**†
(G-DB3095/8s)
(Mozart cadenzas used)

No. 20, D minor, K.466 1785
Bruno Walter & Vienna Philharmonic—
Walter 4 12″—**VM-420**†
(Reinecke cadenzas used)
(G-DB3273/6, in GM-317†)
Edwin Fischer & London Philharmonic
—Fischer 4 12″—**GM-203**†
(Fischer cadenzas used)
(G-DB2118/21)
Wilhelm Kempff & Dresden Philharmonic
—Van Kempen 4 12″—**PD-67706/9S**
(Fonit-96083/6S) (PD-67687/90)
Jean Doyen & Paris Conservatory Orch.
Münch 4 12″—**G-W1524/7**
[Fantasia, D minor, K.397, Doyen solo]
DUPLICATIONS: Mitja Nikisch & Berlin
Philharmonic—Schultz-Dornburg,
T-E1643/6: U-F18037/40; José Iturbi
& Rochester Philharmonic—Iturbi,
VM-794† (Beethoven cadenzas used)

No. 21, C major, K.467 1785
Arthur Schnabel & London Symphony—
Sargent 4 12″—**VM-486**†
(Schnabel cadenzas used)
(G-DB3099/102, in GM-290†)

No. 22, E flat major, K. 482 1785
Edwin Fischer & Chamber Orch.—
Barbirolli 4 12″—**VM-316**†
(Fischer cadenzas used)
(G-DB2681/4, in GM-249†)

No. 23, A major, K. 488 1786
Denis Matthews & Liverpool Philhar-
monic—Weldon 3 12″—**C-DX1167/9**†
(Mozart cadenzas used)
Clifford Curzon & National Symphony
Orch.—Neel 3 12″—**D-K1394/6**†
Marguerite Long & Orch.—Gaubert
3 12″—**CM-261**†
(Pierné cadenzas used)
(C-LFX408/10) (C-LWX172/4)
(C-GQX11050/2)
Artur Rubinstein & London Symphony
Orch.—Barbirolli 3 12″—**VM-147**†
(Mozart cadenza used) (G-DB1491/3†)

No. 24, C minor, K. 491 1786
Edwin Fischer & London Philharmonic
Collingwood 4 12″—**VM-482**†
(Fischer cadenzas in 1st & 3rd Mvts.)

(G-DB3339/42, in GM-301†)
Robert Casadesus & Paris Symphony—
Bigot 4 12″—**CM-356**†
[Rondo, D major, K. 485, Casadesus solo]
(C-LX762/5†) (C-LFX543/6)
(C-LWX273/6)

No. 25, C major, K.503 1786
Kathleen Long & Boyd Neel Orch.—
Neel 4 12″—**D-X229/32**
(No cadenzas used)

No. 26, D major, K.537 "Coronation" 1788
Wanda Landowska & Chamber Orch.—
Goehr 4 12″—**VM-483**†
[Fantasia, D minor, K.397, Landowska
solo]
(Landowska cadenzas used)
(G-DB3147/50, in GM-276†)
Wilhelm Backhaus & Berlin State
Orch.—Zaun 4 12″—**G-DB5674/7**
(Backhaus cadenzas used)

No. 27, B flat major, K.595 1791
Artur Schnabel & London Symphony
Orch.—Barbirolli 4 12″—**VM-240**†
(Mozart cadenzas used)
(G-DB2249/52, in GM-221†)
Robert Casadesus & N. Y. Philharmonic-
Symphony—Barbirolli 4 12″—**CM-490**†
[Minuet, K.355 & Gigue, K.574,
Casadesus solo]
Herman Zilcher & Prussian State Orch.
—Heinz Gerhart-Zilcher
3 12″—**G-DB7641/3**

CONCERTO—2 Pianos & Orchestra
See Concertos (Piano & Orch.), No. 10,
E flat major, K.365

CONCERTOS—Violin & Orchestra
*See also Adagio K. 261 & Rondos, K. 269 &
K. 373*

No. 3, G major, K.216 1775
Yehudi Menuhin & Paris Symphony—
Enesco 3 12″—**VM-485**†
(Franko cadenzas used)
(G-DB2729/31)
Bronislaw Huberman & Vienna Phil-
harmonic—Dobrowen 3 12″—**CM-258**†
Denise Soriano & Orch.—Bouchert
3 12″—**PAT-PAT127/9**
—**2nd Mvt. (Adagio) only**
Yehudi Menuhin, G-DB1295

No. 4, D major, K.218 1775
Yehudi Menuhin & Liverpool Philhar-
monic—Sargent 3 12″—**G-DB6146/8**†
(Menuhin cadenzas used)
Fritz Kreisler & London Philharmonic—
Sargent 3 12″—**VM-623**†
(Kreisler cadenzas used)
Joseph Szigeti & London Philharmonic
—Beecham 3 12″—**CM-224**†
(Joachim cadenzas used)
(C-LX386/8†) (C-LFX390/2)
Heinz Stanske & Dresden Philharmonic
Orch.—van Kempen
3 12″—**PD-67888/90**

No. 5, A major, K.219 "Turkish" 1775
Jacques Thibaud & Orch.—Münch
3 12″—**G-DB5142/4**
Jascha Heifetz & London Philharmonic
—Barbirolli 4 12″—**VM-254**†
(Joachim cadenzas used)
(G-DB2199/2202†)
Jan Dahmen & Saxon State Orch.—

Böhm 4 12"—G-DB4578/81
Frederick Grinke & Boyd Neel Orch.—
Neel 4 12"—D-K1268/71†
Georg Kulenkampff & German Opera
House Orch.—Rother
4 12"—T-E3044/7
Adolf Busch & Busch Chamber
Players 4 12"—CM-609†
[Tartini-Busch: Sonata, G major, Op. 2,
No. 12—Air]

No. 6, E flat major, K.268 (K.365b) 1780/1
Alfred Dubois & Orch.—Defauw
(O-9405/7) 3 12"—C-LFX201/3
[Divertimento No. 17—Minuet]
(C-GQX10660/2)

No. 7, D major, K.217a (K.271i) 1777
Yehudi Menuhin & Orch.—Enesco
4 12"—VM-231†
[Bach: Sonata No. 2, A minor—Andante]
(Enesco cadenzas used)
(G-DB1735/8)
Denise Soriano & Orch.—Münch
4 12"—PAT-PAT143/6
[Divertimento No. 17—Minuet, A.
Lermyte, pf.]

"Adelaide" Concerto, D major K. Anh. 294a
(A recently discovered concerto of doubtful
authenticity, dedicated to Princess Adelaide.
The accompaniment was orchestrated by Ma-
rius Casadesus; the cadenzas are by Paul Hinde-
mith)
Yehudi Menuhin & Paris Symphony—
Monteux 3 12"—G-DB2268/70

CONCERTO—Violin, Viola & Orchestra

Sinfonia concertante, E flat major, K.364
(K.320d) 1779/80
Albert Spalding, William Primrose & New
Friends of Music Orch.—Fritz Stiedry
4 12"—VM-838†
[Handel: Trio Sonata, E major, Op. 2,
No. 9—Adagio, with Spalding, Primrose
& Benoist, pf.]
Albert Sammons, Lionel Tertis & London
Philharmonic—Harty
4 12"—C-DX478/81†
(C-DFX158/61) (O-9418/21)

CONCERTO—Woodwinds & Orchestra

Sinfonia concertante, E flat major,
K. Anh. 9 (K. 297b) 1778
Marcel Tabuteau (ob), Bernard Portnoy
(cl), Sol Schoenbach (bsn), Mason Jones
(horn) & Philadelphia Orch.—
Stokowski 4 12"—VM-760†
E. Venzke (ob), A. Bürkner (cl), O.
Rothensteiner (bsn), M. Ziller (horn) &
Berlin Philharmonic—Konoye
(abbreviated) 4 12"—C-LFX508/11

Contre-Tanz, D major, K. 534
("Das Donnerwetter")
Chamber Orch.—Fischer
(in VM-786†) 12"—V-18029
[Bach: Concerto No. 4, F minor, Pt. 3]
(G-DB4680)

De Profundis See: Psalm

DEUTSCHE TAENZE Orchestra
Eng. German Dances
(Arranged in order by Köchel numbers)

K. 509 1787
—No. 6 only
Berlin Philharmonic—Kleiber, PD-66730
K. 536 1788
—No. 1, only Arr. Harpsichord
Alice Ehlers (in D-A62) 10"—D-23112
[W. F. Bach: Polonaise IV; Rameau:
Suite in E minor—Musette en rondeau;
Couperin: Rigaudon en rondeau]
K. 571 1789
—No. 4 only
Berlin Philharmonic—Kleiber, PD-66730
—No. 6 only
Berlin Philharmonic—Kleiber, PD-66729
K. 600 1791
—Nos. 1-5 only Arr. Steinbach
Minneapolis Symphony—Ormandy
2 10"—G-DA6002/3
[with K. 602, No. 3; K. 605, Nos. 2 & 3]
—No. 3 only
Berlin Philharmonic Symphony Orchestra
—Kleiber, PD-66729
—Arr. Pf.
Raoul von Koczalski, O-25615
—No. 4 only
Berlin Philharmonic Orch.—Kleiber,
PD-66730
—Arr. Violin & Pf. Acc. Burmester
Leo Petroni, T-A1912
(No. 3 used as Trio)
K. 602 1791
—No. 3 ("Der Leiermann") only
Eng. The Organ Grinder
Minneapolis Symphony Orch.—
Ormandy, G-DA6003
K. 605 1791
Nos. 1-3 complete
Vienna Philharmonic—Walter
(G-DA1570) 10"—V-4564
Vienna Chamber Orch.—Jerger
10"—G-DA4503
—No. 2 only
Minneapolis Symphony—Ormandy,
G-DA6003
Berlin Philharmonic—Kleiber, PD-66730
—No. 3 ("Die Schlittenfahrt") only
Eng. The Sleigh Ride
Orch. of "Maggio Musicale"—
Markevitch 12"—CET-BB25159
[Liszt: Mephisto Waltz, Pt. 3]
Minneapolis Symphony Orch.—
Ormandy, G-DA6003

DIVERTIMENTI—Miscellaneous Instru-
mental Ensembles
No. 2, D major, K. 131 1772
(2 violins, 2 violas, bass, flute, oboe,
bassoon, 4 horns)
Paris Conservatory Chamber Orch.
(in Vol. XIV) 3 12"—AS-133/5
No. 3, E flat major, K. 166 (K. 159d) 1773
(2 Oboes, 2 Clarinets, 2 English Horns,
2 Horns, 2 Bassoons)
Chamber Ensemble—Oubradous
2 10"—O-188912/3
No. 8, F major, K. 213 1775
(2 Oboes, 2 Bassoons, 2 Horns)
—Arr. Flute, Oboe, Clarinet, Bassoon, Horn
Leipzig Gewandhaus Wind Quintet
12"—PD-95167

No. 10, F major, K.247 1776
(2 Violins, Viola, 'Cello, 2 Horns)
Philadelphia Orch.—Ormandy
12″— & 2 10″—**VM-603**
[Adagio & Menuetto II omitted]
No. 11, D major, K.251 1776
(2 Violins, Viola, Bass, Oboe, 2 Horns)
Berlin Chamber Orch.—von Benda
3 12″—**PD-67849/51**
—3rd Mvt. (Andantino) only
Hallé Orch.—Lawrence Turner
12″—**C-DX1128**
[Borodin: Symphony No. 2, B minor, Pt. 7]
No. 14, B flat major, K. 270 1777
(2 Oboes, 2 Horns, 2 Bassoons)
Danish Instrumental Sextet
2 10″—**G-DA5260/1**
—Arr. Flute, Oboe, Clarinet, Bassoon, Horn
Leipzig Gewandhaus Wind Quintet
12″—**PD-95166**
No. 15, B flat major, K.287 (K.271b) 1777
(2 Violins, Viola, Bass, 2 Horns)
Joseph Szigeti (vl) & Chamber Orch.—
Gobermann 4 12″—**CM-322†**
Pasquier Trio w. D. Blot (vl), Mignot,
Thevet (hns) In Prep. **DF**
No. 16, E flat major, K. 289 (K.271g) 1777
(2 Oboes, 2 Horns, 2 Bassoons)
—4th Mvt. (Presto) only
—Arr. Flute, Oboe, Clarinet, Bassoon, Horn
Leipzig Gewandhaus Wind Quintet
[Adagio, K.411] 12″—**PD-95168**
No. 17, D major, K. 334 (K. 320b) 1779
(2 Violins, Viola, Bass, 2 Horns)
Léner Quartet & Aubrey & Dennis
Brain (Horns) 5 12″—**CM-379†**
(C-GQX11044/8)
—1st, 2nd, 3rd & 6th Mvts. only
London Philharmonic—Harty
3 12″—**CM-207†**
(C-LX350/2†) (C-LFX377/9)
—3rd Mvt. (Minuet) only
NOTE: *This is perhaps the most famous of the many Mozart Minuets. Recordings are usually merely labelled Minuet or Minuetto*
Von Géczy Orch., G-EG6201; London
Mozart Orch.—Collins, D-K1251
—Arr. Violin & Piano
Alfred Dubois & F. Goeyens
12″—**C-LFX203**
[Violin Concerto No. 6, Pt. 5] (O-9407)
Yehudi Menuhin & Gerald Moore
(arr. Kross) 10″—**G-DA1861**
[Paganini-Green: Romance]
DUPLICATIONS: V. Ranzato, C-DQ429;
H. Stanske, PD-57106; Albert Sandler,
C-DX759
—Arr. Piano: A. Lermyte, PAT-PAT146
Also: A. Tassinari (fl), C-CQ750
(5) DIVERTIMENTI, K. Anh. 229 & 229a (K.439b)
(2 Clarinets (orig. Basset Horns) & Bassoon)
—Arr. Oubradous for Oboe, Clarinet, Bassoon
No. 1, B flat major
Trio d'Anches de Paris 2 10″—**OL-64/5**
No. 2, B flat major
Trio d'Anches de Paris
(Minuet II omitted) 2 10″—**OL-66/7**

No. 3, B flat major
Trio d'Anches de Paris
(Minuet II omitted) 2 10″—**OL-68/9**
No. 4, B flat major
Trio d'Anches de Paris 2 10″—**OL-15/6**
—Arr. Flute, Clarinet, Bassoon
Leipzig Gewandhaus Wind Trio
12″—**PD-66643**
No. 5, B flat major
Trio d'Anches de Paris 2 10″—**OL-36/7**

DIVERTIMENTI—String Quartets
No. 1, D major, K. 136 (K.125a) 1772
Boyd Neel String Orch.—Neel
2 12″—**D-K787/8**
[No. 3, F major, Pt. 1]
(PD-516728/9)
Zurich Collegium Musicum—
Paul Sacher 12″—**C-LZX6**
No. 3, F major, K. 138 (K.125c) 1772
Boyd Neel String Orch.—Neel
(PD-516729/30) 2 12″—**D-K788/9**
[No. 1, D major, Pt. 3]

DIVERTIMENTO—String Trio
E flat major, K. 563 1788
Violin, Viola, 'Cello
Pasquier Trio 5 12″—**CM-351†**
(PAT-PAT38/42)
Jascha Heifetz, William Primrose,
Emanuel Feuermann 4 12″—**VM-959†**

DUOS—Violin & Viola
No. 1, G major, K. 423 1783
Jean & Pierre Pasquier, in DF-A5
Frederick Grinke & Watson Forbes
2 12″—**D-K910/1**
[No. 2, B flat major, K. 424, Pt. 1]
No. 2, B flat major, K. 424 1783
Jean & Pierre Pasquier, in DF-A5
Frederick Grinke & Watson Forbes
2 12″—**D-K911/2**
[No. 1, G major, K. 423, Pt. 3]
Jascha Heifetz & William Primrose
3 12″—**VM-831†**
—2nd Mvt. (Andante cantabile) only
Paul Klinger & Fridolin Klinger
12″—**G-EH1031**
[Reger: Serenade, D major, Op. 77a, Pt. 5]
L'Epreuvre d'amour
Ballet Suite arr. Ludwig Seitz
Ger. Die Liebesprobe
K. Anh. 28 (K.416a)
London Philharmonic Orch.—
Kurtz 12″—**C-DZX19**
Exsultate jubilate See: Motets

FANTASIA—Organ
F minor, K. 608 1791
(*A transcription of a piece originally written for mechanical organ*)
Virgil Fox (Hammond Museum Organ,
Gloucester, Mass.) 2 12″—in **VM-1177†**

FANTASIAS—Piano
C minor, K. 396 (K.385f) 1782
(*Actually a sonata movement for violin and piano*)
Edwin Fischer 12″—**G-DB2377**

D minor, K. 397 (K.385g) 1782
Wanda Landowska
     (in VM-483†) 12″—V-15607
[Concerto No. 26, D major, K. 537, Pt. 7]
(G-DB3150)
Jean Doyen   12″—G-W1527
[Concerto No. 20, D minor, K. 466, Pt. 7]
Hans Leygraf   12″—G-Z311
[Rondo, D major, K. 485]
DUPLICATION: Emma Boynet, in
VOX-630
C minor, K. 475 1785
(Often associated with the Piano Sonata No.
14, C minor, K.457)
Lili Kraus   4 12″—P-P29†
[w. Sonata No. 14] (P-PXO1027/30)
Edwin Fischer   2 12″—G-DB5637/8
[Romance, A flat major, K. Anh. 205]
Suzanne Gyr   4 12″—G-DB10075/8
[w. Sonata No. 14]
Fantasia & Fugue, C major, K. 394
(K. 383a) 1782
Denis Mathews   12″—C-DX1095
Denise Lassimonne   12″—D-K1008
(La) Finta Giardiniera See under Operas
Gebet: "Auf der Andacht heil'gem Flügel"
(an arrangement of the "Secondate,
aurette amiche" from "Così fan tutte")
Regensburg Cathedral Choir
[Ave, verum corpus]   10″—G-EG6945

GIGUES—Piano

G major, K. 574 "Eine kleine Gigue"
Eileen Joyce   12″—C-DX1055
[Minuet K. 355 & Haydn: Trio No. 1,
G major, Pt. 3]
Robert Casadesus
     (in CM-490) 12″—C-11702D
[Minuet, K. 355 & Concerto No. 27, K.
595, Pt. 7]
—Arr. Orchestra Tchaikovsky
(Part I of Suite No. 4 "Mozartiana")
N. Y. Philharmonc-Symphony—
Rodzinski (in CX-248†) 12″—C-12114D
[Minuet, D major, K. 355 & Ave, verum
corpus, K. 618]
Idomeneo See under Operas
(Eine) kleine Nachtmusik, K. 525
See under Serenades—Eine kleine
Nachtmusik, K. 525
Litaniae de Venerabili Altaris Sacramento,
K. 243 1776
—Dulcissimum Convivium
Soprano in Latin
Yves Tinayre (t) w. Strings & organ—
A. Cellier   10″—LUM-32016
(The) Magic Flute
See under Operas—Die Zauberflöte

MARCHES

D major, K. 249 1776
(for the Haffner family)
Chamber Orch.—Hans von Benda
       10″—G-EG3584
[Haydn: Symphony No. 73, D major,
"La Chasse"—Finale]
D major, K. 335, No. 1 (K. 320a No. 1) 1779
D major, K. 408, No. 2 (K.385a) 1782
Paris Conservatory Orch.—Fendler
       10″—G-DA4912
[Haydn: Overture, D major]

MASSES
Soloists, Chorus & Orchestra in Latin

No. 3, C major, K. 66 (Dominicus Messe)
1769
—Et in spiritum sanctum only
Yves Tinayre (t) w. Orch. & Organ—
A. Cellier   12″—LUM-32043
[Motet: Regina Coeli, K. 108—Ora pro
nobis]
No. 17, C major ("Krönungs Messe")
K. 317 1779
—Agnus Dei only
Hedwig Jungkurth (s) & Orch.—
Seidler-Winkler   10″—G-EG6058
[Schumann: Zur Trauerfeier]
No. 19, C minor, K. 427 (K.417a)
1782/3 Unfinished
—Kyrie Eleison only Soprano & Chorus
Dora Labette, Leeds Festival Chorus &
London Philharmonic—Beecham
       10″—C-LF144
—Qui Tollis only Chorus
Leeds Festival Choir & London Phil-
harmonic—Beecham
     (in CX-54†) 12″—C-68385D
[Borodin: Prince Igor-Polovtsian
Dances, Pt. 3]
(C-LX370)   (C-LFX422)
—Et incarnatus est only Soprano
Erna Berger & Philharmonia Orch.—
Krips   12″—G-DB6536
Jo Vincent   12″—C-DHX5
[Schubert: Fischers Liebesglück]
—Agnus Dei only Soprano & Chorus
In the absence of an "Agnus Dei" composed
by Mozart, Dr. Alois Schmidt fitted the "Kyrie
Eleison" to the "Agnus Dei" text.
Marcella Denya, with Les Disciples de
Massenet & Montreal Festivals Orch.—
Pelletier   12″—V-18512
No. 20, Requiem, K. 626 1791
(Left unfinished at Mozart's death, the Re-
quiem was completed and edited by Süssmayr)
Pia Tassinari (s), Ebe Stignani (c),
Ferruccio Tagliavini (t), Italo Tajo (b)
with EIAR Orch. & Chorus—Victor de
Sabata (CET-SS1001/8) 8 12″—CET-5
Tilla Briem (s), Gertrude Freimuth (c),
Walter Ludwig (t), Fred Drissen (bs),
with Bruno Kittel Choir & Berlin Phil-
harmonic—Kittel   9 12″—PD-67731/9
NOTE: Alternate Nazi text is used in this record-
ing.
Barbara Thorne (s), Elsie MacFarlane
(c), Donald Coker (t), Lester Englander
(b) with Univ. of Pennsylvania Choral
Society & Philadelphia Orch.—Harl
McDonald   6 12″—VM-649†
Maurerische Trauermusik, C minor, K. 477
(K. 479a) 1785
Eng. Masonic Funeral Music
Orch. de Chambre—Hewitt
       12″—in DF-A2

MINUETS

G major, K. 1 1761 Piano
Edwin Fischer   10″—G-DA1389
[Marcello: Oboe Concerto—Adagio arr.
Bach]

D major, K. 355 (K. 594a) 1790 Piano
Eileen Joyce   12"—C-DX1055
[Gigue, K. 574; Haydn: Trio No. 1,
G major, Pt. 3]
Robert Casadesus
    (in CM-490†)   12"—C-11702D
[Gigue, G major, K. 574; Concerto No.
27, K. 595, Pt. 7]
Wanda Landowska (harpsichord), in
VM-1181†
—**Arr. Orchestra** Tchaikovsky
(Part II of Suite No. 4 "Mozartiana")
N. Y. Philharmonic-Symphony—
Rodzinski
    (in CX-248†)   12"—C-12114D
[Gigue, G major, K. 574 & Ave, verum
corpus, K.618]

Minuet, C major K. 409 (K.383f) Orch.
Cleveland Orchestra—Leinsdorf
    12"—C-12749D

(2) Minuets, K. 463 (K. 448c) Orch.
Symphony Orch.—Marius-François
Gaillard   10"—O-188917

Unspecified Minuet
Orch.—Willy Steiner, PD-47130

(16) Menuetti, K.176 1773 Orch.
—**Nos. 1-11 & 16**
Symphony Orch.—Fendler
    2 12"—OL-86/7
Vox Chamber Orch.—Fendler
    3 10"—VOX-166

MOTETS Soloists, 4-Part Chorus in Latin
Ave, verum corpus, K. 618 1791
4 Voices, Strings, Organ
Strasbourg Cathedral Choir, Orch. & F.
Rich (org.)—A. Hoch   12"—C-69488D
[Gasparini: Motet—Adoramus Te
Christe]
(C-LWX295)   (C-LX766)
[Berlioz: Enfance du Christ—Adieu des
Bergers, on C-RFX60]
Copenhagen Boy's Choir—Wöldike
(G-X6994)   10"—G-DA5246
[Exsultate, jubilate—Alleluja, Karen
Munk]
Les Disciples of Massenet (Goulet, dir.),
Roland Roy (organ) & Montreal Festi-
vals Orch.—Pelletier
    (in VM-844†)   12"—V-18300
[Fauré: Requiem, Pt. 9]
DUPLICATIONS: Regensburg Cathedral
Choir, G-EG6945; Basilica Choir &
Organ—Kalt, PD-66534: PD-15214:
PD-66863; Berlin Philharmonic Chorus
—Ochs, G-EH175; St. Nicholas Choir,
LUM-30004; Choir of All Saints' Church,
London, D-F7550
—**Vocal Quartet**
Mancini (s), Travaglia (c), Fantozzi (t),
Dos Santos (bs) with Antonelli (org)
    12"—SEMS-1111
[Antonelli: Benedicta et Venerabilis]
—**Arr. Solo Voice** Schmidt
Ingeborg Steffensen (ms) (in Danish)
& String Quartet   12"—C-DDX5
[Gounod: Ave Maria]
—**Instrumental Transcription**
Ensemble Günther Schultz-Furstenberg
[Handel: Serse—Largo] 10"—G-K7777

—**Arr. Organ** Courboin
Charles M. Courboin (St. Patrick's, New
York) (in VM-1091)   12"—V-11-9402
[Catholic Hymnal: Jesus, My Lord &
Holy God, We Praise Thy Name]
—**Arr. Orchestra** Tchaikovsky
(Part III of Suite No. 4 "Mozartiana")
*(Based on Liszt's piano transcription "A la
Chapelle Sixtine")*
N. Y. Philharmonic-Symphony—
Rodzinski
    (in CX-248†)   12"—C-12114D
[Gigue, G major, K. 574 & Minuet, D
major, K. 355]

Exsultate, jubilate, K. 165 (K-158a) 1773
Soprano, Orchestra & Organ
Erika Rokyta & Orch.—Felix Raugel
    2 12"—OL-38/9
—**Alleluja** only
Karin Munk & Orch.—Wöldike
(G-X6994)   10"—G-DA5246
[Ave, verum corpus, Copenhagen Boys'
Choir]
Gwen Catley   10"—G-B9138
[Handel: Joshua—Oh, had I Jubal's lyre]
Elisabeth Schumann   10"—G-DA845
[Don Giovanni—Vedrai carino]
Dorothy Maynor
    (in VM-1043)   12"—V-11-9107
[Bach: Matthäus-Passion—Blute nur]
Maria Stader & Winterthur Municipal
Orch.   12"—G-DB10111
[Rè Pastore—L'Amerò, sarò costante]
DUPLICATIONS: Martha Angelici,
LUM-32060; Lily Pons, C-17347D,
in CM-518; Sigrid Onegin, V-1367;
Maria Tauberova, U-C12787

Regina Coeli, K. 108 (K.74d) 1771
—**Ora pro nobis** only
Yves Tinayre (t) w. Orch. & Organ—
A. Cellier   12"—LUM-32043
[Mass No. 3, C major, K.66—Et in
spiritum sanctum]

**Offertorium, F major: Sub tuum praesidi-
um, K. 198 (K.158b)** 1773
(Soprano, Tenor, Orchestra & Organ)
In Latin
Jo Vincent & Louis van Tulder, with
Betsy Rijkens-Culp (pf)   10"—C-DH37
[Handel: Triumph of Time and Truth—
Duo]

OPERAS In Italian and German
*Title of the operas and of the individual re-
corded excerpts are catalogued in the language
in which the works were originally written. For
convenience, translations and cross-references
are also given wherever necessary. All excerpts
are listed in the order they occur in the opera
and numbered as in the Köchel Index.*

**BASTIEN UND BASTIENNE, K. 50
(K.46b)** I Act 1768
"Complete" recording Sung in French
Soloists & Paris Conservatory Orch.—
Cloëz with Pauline Aubert (harpsichord)
    6 10"—AS-801/6
The Cast:
Bastien .... Paul Derenne
Bastienne .... Martha Angelici
Colas .... André Mondé

(LA) CLEMENZA DI TITO (TITUS)

K.621 2 Acts 1791

Overture Orchestra
London Philharmonic—Beecham
(in VM-1104†) 12"—V-11-9470
[Mendelssohn: Symphony No. 5—
"Reformation," Pt. 5]
EIAR Symphony—La Rosa Parodi
12"—CET-CB20193
[Vivaldi: Concerto Grosso, Op. 3, No. 11,
D minor, Pt. 3]
Vienna Philharmonic—Walter
12"—G-DB6032
[La Finta Giardiniera, K. 196—Overture]
Berlin Philharmonic—Jascha Horenstein
12"—PD-516614
[Idomeneo—Overture, dir. Kleiber]

COSI FAN TUTTE, K. 588

2 Acts 1790

"Complete" recording Sung in Italian
Glyndebourne Festival Company—Fritz
Busch
(Mozart Opera Society, Vols. 4/6)
(3 vols.) 20 12"—VM-812/813/814†
The Cast:
Fiordiligi .... Ina Souez (s)
Dorabella ..... Luise Helletsgrüber (s)
Ferrando .... Heddle Nash (t)
Guglielmo .... Willi Domgraf-
Fassbaender (b)
Don Alfonso ...... John Brownlee (bs)
Despina .... Irene Eisinger (s)
Chorus & Orch. of Glyndebourne Festival, 1935

Overture Orchestra
N. Y. Philharmonic-Symphony—Walter
(in CM-565†) 12"—C-12073D
[Symphony No. 41, Pt. 7]
BBC Symphony—Boult
(in VM-794†) 12"—V-18084
[Concerto No. 20, Pt. 7]
[Brahms: Hungarian Dances, 19/21, on
G-DB3814]
National Symphony Orch.—Boyd
Neel 12"—D-K1297
[Nozze di Figaro—Overture]
Berlin Philharmonic—Schmidt-
Isserstedt 12"—T-E2522
[Entführung aus dem Serail—
Overture) (U-F18107)

DUPLICATIONS. Berlin State Opera
Orch.—Ludwig, PD-15224; Berlin State
Opera Orch.—Pfitzner, PD-27066; Berlin
State Opera Orch.—Blech, G-EJ57;
G-W884; Vienna Philharmonic Orch.—
Krauss, G-C2233: G-S10295; Berlin-
Charlottenburg Opera Orch.—Zemlinsky,
PD-57074; Berlin Philharmonic Orch.—
Furtwängler, PD-67184

Individual Excerpts

ACT I

No. 7, Al fato dan legge Ten. & Bar.
Omitted in Mozart Society Vols.
No recording traced
No. 14, Come scoglio immoto resta Soprano
Hjördis Schymberg 12"—G-DB2694
[Nozze di Figaro—No. 27, Deh, vieni]
Lina Pagliughi 12"—P-DPX17

[Rimsky-Korsakov: Coq d'or—Hymn to
the Sun]
[Thomas: Mignon—Polonaise, on
CET-BB25004]
Suzanne Danco 12"—D-K1732
[Nozze di Figaro—No. 11, Voi che sapete]
No. 17, Un aura amorosa Tenor
Ger. Der Odem der Liebe, or
Wie schön ist die Liebe
Aksel Schiøtz 12"—G-DB5265
[Zauberflöte—No. 3, Bildnisarie]
Julius Patzak (in German)
12"—PD-95437
[Zauberflöte—No. 3, Bildnisarie]

ACT II

No. 21, Secondate, aurette amiche
Duet w. Chorus
—Arr. Cho. w. new words "Auf der
Andacht heil'gen Flügel"
Regensburg Cathedral Cho.
[Ave, verum corpus] 10"—G-EG6945
No. 23, Il core vi dono Soprano & Baritone
Edith Oldrup-Pedersen & Einar Nørby
12"—TONO-X25104
[Nozze di Figaro—No. 16, Crudel!
perché finora]
No. 24, Ah! io veggio, quell' anima bella
Tenor
Omitted in Mozart Society Vols.
No recording traced
No. 25, Ei parte, senti Recit.
Per pieta, ben mio Aria (Rondo)
Eng. Ah, my love, forgive this madness
Felicie Hüni-Mihacsek (in German)
12"—PD-66613
Joan Cross (in English) 12"—C-DX1353
(without Recitative)
Suzanne Danco In Prep. English Decca
No. 26, Donne mie, la fate a tanti Baritone
Ger. Mädchen so triebt ihrs mit allein
Gerhard Hüsch (in Ger.) 10"—G-DA4463
[Don Giovanni—No. 12, Finch' han dal
vino & No. 17, Serenata]
No. 27, Tradito, schernito Tenor
Omitted in Mozart Society Vols.
No recording traced
No. 28, E Amore un ladroncello
Soprano (Dorabella)
Omitted in Mozart Society Vols.
No recording traced
Unidentified Aria of Despina
Edith Oldrup-Pedersen
12"—TONO-X25096
[Nozze di Figaro—No. 27, Deh, vieni]
Unidentified Aria of Guglielmo
Einar Nørby 12"—TONO-X25047
[Entführung aus dem Serail—Osmin's
Aria]

DON GIOVANNI, K. 527 2 Acts 1787

"Complete" recording Sung in Italian
Glyndebourne Festival Company—
Fritz Busch
(Mozart Opera Society, Vols. 7/9)
(3 Vols.) 23 12"—VM-423/424/425†
The Cast:
Don Giovanni ...... John Brownlee (b)
Donna Anna .... Ina Souez (s)
Donna Elvira .. Luise Helletsgruber (s)
Zerlina .... Audrey Mildmay (s)

Don Ottavio .... Koloman von
Pataky (t)
Leporello .... Salvatore Baccaloni (bs)
Commendatore .. David Franklin (bs)
Masetto .... Roy Henderson (b)
Chorus & Orch. of Glyndebourne Festival,
1936

Overture Orchestra
London Philharmonic—Beecham
12"—C-70365D
(C-LX893) (C-71620D in CM-552†)
London Symphony—Wood
(C-DFX189) 12"—C-DX587
Berlin Philharmonic—Schmidt-
Isserstedt 12"—T-E3072
(U-F18099)
DUPLICATIONS: Berlin State Opera
Orch.—Ludwig, PD-15171: PD-516766;
Berlin State Opera Orch.—Blech,
G-EW17; Symphony Orch.—Schmalstich,
G-HN800; Berlin-Charlottenburg Orch.
—Zemlinsky, PD-516725

Individual Excerpts

ACT I

No. 4, Madamina, il catalogo Bass
(Leporello)
Ger. Registerarie
Salvatore Baccaloni 12"—C-71048D
[No. 21, Ah, pietà signori miei]
Ezio Pinza & Metropolitan Opera Orch.
—Walter (in CM-643†) 12"—C-71842D
Joel Berglund (G-DA1866)
10"—V-10-1346
Tancredi Pasero 10"—G-DA5415
Feodor Chaliapin 10"—G-DA994
Oscar Natzke 10"—C-DB2291
Fed. Ollendorff, with M. Pistreich
(pf) 10"—O-15041
In French: Charles Panzéra, G-DA4858
In German: Alexander Kipnis, G-EW89;
Hellmut Schweebs, C-LW37

No. 7, Là ci darem la mano
Duet: Soprano & Baritone (Don &
Zerlina)
Ger. Reich mir die Hand
Fr. Viens, une voix t'appelle
Elisabeth Rethberg & Ezio Pinza
(in VM-783) 10"—V-2154
[Nozze di Figaro—No. 2, Se a caso
Madama]
Toti Dal Monte & Augusto Beuf
10"—G-DA5406
[Nozze di Figaro—No. 16, Crudel,
perchè finora]
Edith Oldrup-Pedersen & Einar
Nørby 12"—TONO-X25095
[Die Zauberflöte—No. 21,
Pa-Pa-Pa-Pa-Papagena]
Renata Villiani & Luigi Borgnovo
10"—G-HN358
[Nozze di Figaro—No. 11, Voi che sapete,
R. Villiani]
In German:
Margherita Perras & Gerhard Hüsch
(G-DA4408) 10"—V-4374
[Zauberflöte—No. 7, Bei Männern]
Erna Berger & Heinrich Schlusnus
10"—PD-62755
[Nozze di Figaro—No. 20, Che soave
zefiretto, Berger & Ursuleac]

[No. 17, Serenata, Schlusnus, on
PD-62760]
Felicie Hüni-Mihacsek & Willi Domgraf-
Fassbaender 10"—PD-62699
[Zauberflöte—No. 7, Bei Männern]
In French:
Solange Delmas & André Pernet
10"—G-DA4850
[No. 12, Finch' han dal vino & No. 17,
Serenata]
In English:
Gwen Catley & Dennis Noble
10"—G-B9338
[Zauberflöte—No. 7, Bei Männern]

No. 10, Don Ottavio, son morta Recit.
Soprano & Tenor
Or sai chi l'onore Aria Soprano
Eng. Donna Anna's Vengeance
Rose Bampton & Hardesty Johnson
12"—V-11-8466
[No. 25, Non mi dir, bell' idol mio,
Bampton]
NOTE: *Begins "Eragià alquanto avanz at a la
notte."*

—Or sai chi l'onore only
Helen Traubel
(in CM-675) 12"—C-72111D
[Puccini: Tosca—Vissi d'arte]

No. 11, Dalla sua pace Tenor (Ottavio)
Ger. Bande der Freunschaft, or
Nur ihrem Frieden
Fr. Ah! quand je suis loin d'elle
Eng. On her all joy dependeth
Aksel Schiøtz & Copenhagen Royal
Theatre Orch.—Tango 12"—G-DB2564
[No. 22, Il mio tesoro]
Richard Tauber 12"—P-R20444
[No. 22, Il mio tesoro]
Beniamino Gigli 12"—G-DB3809
[No. 22, Il mio tesoro]
DUPLICATIONS: Tito Schipa, G-DA963;
G. Gero, CET-TI7045
In German:
Julius Patzak 12"—PD-15080
[Entführung aus dem Serail, No. 4—
Constanze]
Peter Anders 12"—T-E1796
[No. 22, Il mio tesoro]
Anton Dermota 12"—T-E3162
[Zauberflöte—No. 3, Bildnisarie]
Hugo Meyer-Welfing 12"—C-DX1385
[Zauberflöte—No. 3, Bildnisarie]
In French: Miguel Villabella, PAT-PGT2
In English: Webster Booth, G-C3372

No. 12, Finch' han dal vino
Baritone (Don Giovanni)
Ger. Champagnerlied: Auf zu dem Fest
or Treibt der Champagner
Fr. Fête complète, or Pour cette fête
Eng. For a Carousal
Ezio Pinza 10"—V-1467
[No. 17, Serenata] (G-DA1134)
Umberto Urbano 10"—PD-62671
[No. 17, Serenata]
[Verdi. Ernani—Vieni, meco on
PD-66774]
Mariano Stabile 10"—C-DQ698
[No. 17, Serenata]
Ezio Pinza & Rosa Linda (pf)
(in CM-676) 12"—C-71975D

[No. 17, Serenata & Verdi: Simon
Boccanegra—Il lacerato Spirito]
In German:
Gerhard Hüsch   10"—G-DA4463
[No. 17, Serenata & Così fan tutte—No.
26,—Donne mie]
Karl Schmidt-Walter   10"—T-A2223
[No. 17, Serenata]
DUPLICATION: Sven-Olaf Sandberg,
O-9135
In French: André Pernet, G-DA4850

No. 13, Batti, batti, o bel Masetto
Soprano   (Zerlina)
Ger. Schmäle, tobe, lieber Junge, or
Schlage,schlage, dein' Zerlinchen
Bidù Sayão   12"—C-71577D
[No. 19, Vedrai, carino]
[with Recit.—"Ma se colpa"]
Elisabeth Schumann   12"—C-DB946
[Nozze di Figaro—No. 11, Voi che
sapete]
Lina Pagliughi   12"—P-DPX28
[Nozze di Figaro—No. 27, Giunse al fin]
(CET-TI7001)
Eleanor Steber   12"—V-11-9114
[Zauberflöte—No. 17, Ach, ich fühls]
In German:
Adele Kern   10"—PD-24798
[No. 19, Vedrai, carino]
Maria Cebotari   12"—PD-67686
[No. 19, Vedrai, carino]

No. 14, Presto, presto! pria ch' ei venga
(Finale, Act I)
—Minuet only (Arrangements)
Wanda Landowska (harpsichord) with
Orch.   10"—G-DA977
[Rameau: Tambourin & Daquin: Le
Coucou]
Also: Bells, V-20440; Band, V-21938:
V-20990

ACT II

No. 17, Serenata; Deh, vieni alla finestra
Baritone
Ger. Ständchen: Horch auf dem Klang
Fr. Parais à ta fenêtre
Ezio Pinza   10"—V-1467
[No. 12, Finch' han dal vino]
(G-DA1134)
Ezio Pinza
      (in CM-676†)   12"—C-71975D
[No. 12, Finch, han dal vino & Verdi:
Simon Boccanegra—Il lacerato spirito]
Paul Schoeffler   10"—D-M613
[Nozze di Figaro—No. 3, Se vuol ballare]
Tito Gobbi   10"—G-DA5430
[Puccini: La Fanciulla del West—
Minnie dalla mia casa]
DUPLICATIONS: Umberto Urbano,
PD-62671; Luigi Montesanto, C-DQ684;
Mariano Stabile, C-DQ698
In German:
Gerhard Hüsch   10"—G-DA4463
[No. 12, Finch' han dal vino & Così fan
tutte—No. 26, Donne mie]
Willi Domgraf-Fassbaender
                 10"—G-EG2906
[Nozze di Figaro—No. 3, Se vuol ballare]
Heinrich Schlusnus   10"—PD-62760
[No. 7, Là ci darem la mano, with Berger]

DUPLICATIONS: Arno Schellenberg,
G-EG6161; Karl Schmitt-Walter,
T-A2223; Sven-Olaf Sandberg, O-9135
In French:
André Pernet   10"—G-DA4850
[No. 12, Finch' han dal vino & No. 7,
Là ci darem, with Delmas]
André Baugé   10"—PAT-PA973
[Gounod: Sérénade: Quand tu chantes]

No. 19, Vedrai, carino—Aria   Soprano
(Zerlina)
Ger. Wenn du fein fromm bist
Bidù Sayão   12"—C-71577D
[No. 13, Batti, batti]
Mafalda Favero   12"—G-DB5446
[Bellini: Puritani—Son vergin vezzosa,
E. Ribetti]
Elisabeth Schumann   10"—G-DA845
[Motet—Exsultate—Alleluja]
In German:
Adele Kern   10"—PD-24798
[No. 13, Batti, batti]
Maria Cebotari   12"—PD-67686
[No. 13, Batti, batti]

No. 21, Ah! pietà, Signori miei   Aria
Bass   (Leporello)
Salvatore Baccoloni   12"—C-71048D
[No. 4, Madamina, il catalogo]

No. 22, Il mio tesoro   Tenor   (Ottavio)
Ger. Tränen, vom Freunde getrocknet;
Folget der Heissgeliebten; Trösten will
ich der Teuer
Eng. Speak for me; To her I love
Aksel Schiøtz   12"—G-DB5264
[No. 11, Dalla sua pace]
Richard Tauber   12"—P-R20444
[No. 11, Dalla sua pace]
Beniamino Gigli   12"—G-DB3809
[No. 11, Dalla sua pace]
Tito Schipa (abbrev.)   10"—G-DA963
[No. 11, Dalla sua pace]
Richard Crooks   12"—V-15235
[Donizeti: Elisir d'Amore—Una
furtiva lagrima]
John McCormack (recorded 1910)
              12"—V-15-1015*
[Donizetti: Fille du Régiment—
Pour vivre]
G. Gero   12"—CET-TI7045
[No. 11, Dalla sua pace]
James Melton
(in VM-1013)   12"—V-11-8929
[Zauberflöte—No. 3, Bildnisarie]
[Verdi: Traviata—Un dì felice, Albanese
& Peerce, on V-11-9290 in VM-1074]
Max Lichtegg   12"—D-K1565
[Zauberflöte—No. 3, Bildnisarie]
In German:
Peter Anders   12"—T-E1796
[No. 11, Dalla sua pace]
Julius Patzak   12"—PD-35029
[Entführung aus dem Serail—No. 15,
Wenn der Freude]
In English:
Webster Booth   12"—G-C3372
[No. 11, Dalla sua pace]
David Lloyd   12"—C-DX983
[Zauberflöte—No. 3, Bildnisarie]
In French: Miguel Villabella, PAT-PGT2

No. 22b, Per queste due manine, K. 540b
Soprano & Bass
NOTE: *This duet for Zerlina & Leporello was composed for the Viennese premiere of Don Giovanni. It is usually omitted in performances and is omitted in the Mozart Society Vols. No recording traced.*

No. 23, In quali eccessi Recit.
Mi tradì quell' alma ingrata Aria
Ger. Mich verlässt di undankbare
Eng. In what Abysses; & Cruel One!
Thou hast betrayed me!
Joan Hammond (in English)
     12"—C-DX1075
Felicie Hüni-Mihacsek (Aria only, in German) 12"—PD-66614
[No. 25, Non mi dir]

No. 25, Crudele? Ah no, mio bene! Recit.
Non mi dir, bell' idol mio Aria Soprano
Ger. Briefarie: Ueber alles bleibst du teuer
NOTE: *Both versions below omit the recit.*
Rose Bampton 12"—V-11-8466
[No. 10, Or sai chi l'onore]
Felicie Hüni-Mihacsek (in German)
     12"—PD-66614
[No. 23, Mi tradì quell' alma ingrata]

(DIE) ENTFUEHRUNG AUS DEM SERAIL, K. 384 3 Acts 1782
It. Il Ratto dal Serraglio
Fr. L'Enlèvement au Sérail
Eng. The Elopement from the Harem
Overture Orchestra
London Philharmonic Orch.—Beecham
(Arr. Wagner) 12"—V-11-9191
(G-DB6251)
Saxon State Orch.—Böhm
     12"—G-DB4692
[Nozze di Figaro—Overture]
Berlin Philharmonic—Schmidt-Isserstedt 12"—T-E2522
[Così fan tutte—Overture] (U-F18107)
German Opera House Orch.—Arthur
Grüber   12"—O-7980
[Der Schauspieldirektor—Overture]
National Symphony Orch.—Boyd Neel
     12"—D-K1323
Berlin Philharmonic—Furtwängler
     12"—PD-35013
[Nozze di Figaro—Overture]
Vienna Philharmonic—Krauss
     12"—V-11242
[Nozze di Figaro—Overture]
(G-S10290) (G-C2194)
[Symphony No. 41, Pt. 7, on V-12470 in VM-584†]
DUPLICATIONS: Berlin State Opera Orch.—Blech (Busoni version), G-EJ496; Berlin-Charlottenburg Opera Orch.—Zemlinsky, PD-57074; Symphony Orch., U-E396

ACT I

No. 1, Hier soll ich dich denn sehen
Tenor
Aksel Schiøtz & Copenhagen Royal Theatre Orch.—Egisto Tango
[No. 18, In Mohrenland] 10"—G-DA5253
Helge Roswaenge 10"—G-DA4417
[Weber: Oberon—Du, der diese Prüfung schickt]

Peter Anders 10"—T-A1874
[No. 18, In Mohrenland]

No. 2, Wer ein Liebchen hat gefunden
Bass (Osmin)
Alexander Kipnis 10"—V-1738
[Zauberflöte—No. 11, O Isis und Osiris]
(G-DA1218)
Wilhelm Strienz 10"—G-EG6347
[No. 14, Vivat Bacchus, with W. Ludwig]

No. 4, Constanze, Constanze, dich wiederzusehen Recit.
O wie ängstlich, o wie feurig Aria Tenor
Richard Tauber 12"—P-PXO1024
[Zauberflöte—No. 3, Bildnisarie]
(O-123834)
Julius Patzak 12"—PD-15080
[Don Giovanni—No. 11, Dalla sua pace]
Peter Anders 12"—T-E1867
[Zauberflöte—No. 3, Bildnisarie]
In English: Webster Booth, G-C3402

No. 6, Ach, ich liebte Soprano (Constanze)
It. Ah, che amando
Margherita Perras 12"—G-DB4439
[No. 11, Martern aller Arten]
Lily Pons (in Italian) & Orch.—Walter
  (in CM-518†) 10"—C-17346D
Lina Pagliughi (in Italian)
  (in CET-8) 12"—CET-BB25010
[No. 12, Welche Wonne]
In English: Gwen Catley, G-C3696

ACT II

No. 8, Durch Zärtlichkeit Soprano (Blonde)
It. Con vezzie
Lily Pons (in French)
  (in VM-702) 10"—V-2110
[Paradies: Quel ruscelletto]
Adele Kern 12"—PD-66945
[Nozze di Figaro—No. 27, Deh, vieni]

No. 9, Ich gehe, doch rate ich dir
Soprano & Baritone
Edith Oldrup-Pedersen & Einar
Nørby (in Dan.) 12"—TONO-X25097
[Zauberflöte—No. 7, Bei Männern]

No. 10, Welcher Kummer or
Welcher Wechsel Recit.
Traurigkeit ward mir zum Lose
Aria Soprano (Constanze)
Elisabeth Schwarzkopf 12"—C-LZX241
Margherita Perras 12"—G-DB4484
[Nozze di Figaro—No. 27, Deh, vieni]

No. 11, Martern aller Arten Soprano
Eng. Tortures unabating
NOTE: *Most versions are abbreviated.*
Erna Berger (complete) 12"—G-DB6619
Eleanor Steber (complete, in English)
  (in VM-1157†) 12"—V-11-9772
Felicie Hüni-Mihacsek 12"—PD-66758
Maria Cebotari 10"—O-25399
Miliza Korjus 12"—G-EH898
[Zauberflöte—No. 14, Der Hölle Rache]
Margherita Perras 12"—G-DB4439
[No. 6, Ach, ich liebte]

No. 12, Welche Wonne, welche Lust
Soprano
It. O che gioia, che piacer
Lina Pagliughi (in Italian)
  (in CET-8) 12"—CET-BB25010
[No. 6, Ach, ich liebte]
Lily Pons (in French) & Orch.—Walter
  (in CM-518†) 10"—C-17347D
[Motet—Exsultate—Alleluja]

No. 14, Vivat Bacchus, Bacchus lebe
Duet   Tenor & Bass
Walther Ludwig & Wilhelm Strienz
10″—G-EG6347
[No. 2, Wer ein Liebchen hat gefunden, Strienz]

No. 15, Wenn der Freude Tränen fliessen
Tenor
Julius Patzak   12″—PD-35029
[Don Giovanni—No. 22, Il mio tesoro]

ACT III

No. 18, In Mohrenland gefangen
(Romanze)   Tenor
Aksel Schiøtz & Royal Opera Orch., Copenhagen—Tango   10″—G-DA5253
[No. 1, Hier soll ich dich]
Peter Anders   10″—T-A1874
[No. 1, Hier soll ich dich]

No. 19, Ha! wie will ich triumphieren Bass
It. Ah che voglio trionfare
Ezio Pinza (in Italian) & Metropolitan Opera Orch.—Walter
(in CM-643)   12″—C-71843D
[Zauberflöte—No. 15, In diesen heil'gen Hallen]

No. 21, Nie werd' ich deine Huld verkennen
Quintet
Erna Berger, Adele Kern, Max Hirzel, C. Jöken, with Berlin State Opera Orch.—Blech   12″—PD-35005
[Zauberflöte—No. 5, Hm, Hm]

Unidentified **Aria of Osmin**
Einar Nørby   12″—TONO-X25049
[Così fan tutte—Guglielmo's Aria]

(LA) FINTA GIARDINIERA, K. 196
3 Acts   1775
Ger. **Die Gärtnerin aus Liebe**
Overture   Orchestra
Vienna Philharmonic—Walter
12″—G-DB6032
[Clemenza di Tito—Overture]
[Symphony No. 41, C major, Pt. 7, on G-DB3431 in GM-307†]

No. 4, Noi donne poverine Soprano
Eng. **A maiden's is an evil plight**
NOTE: *The translation by Blom is from an inaccurate 18th century German version of the Italian text.*
Isobel Baillie (in English)
12″—C-DX1080
[Handel: Solomon—With thee th' unsheltered moor]

No. 11, Geme la Tortorella Soprano
(Sandrina)
Ger. **Einsam in fernem Lande** (Trans. from original Ital. by S. Anheisser)
Elisabeth Reichelt (in German)
10″—G-EG3988
[No. 27, Lei mi chiama, with Ludwig]

No. 27, Dove mai son! Duet: Sop. & Ten. (Sandrina & Contino)
—**Lei mi chiama** only (Andantino section)
Ger. **Wie du riefst mich**
(Trans. from original Ital. by S. Anheisser)
Elisabeth Reichelt & Walther Ludwig (in Ger.)   10″—G-EG3988
[No. 11, Geme la tortorella, Reichelt]

IDOMENEO, RE DI CRETA K. 366 3 Acts 1781
(or, Ilia ed Idamante)
Overture Orchestra
EIAR Orch.—La Rosa Parodi
12″—CET-CC2177
[Rè Pastore—Overture]
National Symphony Orch.—Boyd Neel
12″—D-K1410
[Schauspieldirektor—Overture]
Dresden Philharmonic—Van Kempen
12″—PD-57188
[Nozze di Figaro—Overture]
DUPLICATIONS: Brussels Royal Conservatory Orch.—Defauw, C-D15231; Berlin Philharmonic Orch.—Kleiber, PD-66729: PD-516614

No. 19, Zeffiretti lusinghieri Soprano (Ilia)
Ger. **Sanfte Winde folgt dem Teuern** or **Zephyrtten leicht gefiedert**
Lea Piltti (in German)   12″—G-DB5668
[Verdi: Rigoletto—Caro nome]

Ballet Music, K. 367 Orchestra
No. 4 (Gavotte) only
Chamber Orch.—Von Benda
10″—G-EG3095
[Serenade No. 9, D major, K. 320—Posthorn Minuet]
Orch. of the "Maggio Musicale"—Rossi
12″—CET-BB25032
[Schumann: Manfred—Pt. 3, dir. Marinuzzi]

(LE) NOZZE DI FIGARO, K. 492 4 Acts 1786
Ger. **Die Hochzeit des Figaro**
Fr. **Les Noces de Figaro**
Eng. **The Marriage of Figaro**
Complete recording Sung in Italian
Glyndebourne Festival Company—Fritz Busch (Mozart Opera Society, Vols. 1/3)   17   12″—VM-313/314/315†
The Cast:
Susanna .... Aubrey Mildmay (s)
Countess ...... Aulikki Rautawaara (s)
Cherubino .... Luise Helletsgruber (s)
Marcellina ...... Constance Willis (s)
Barberina ...... Winifred Radford (s)
Figaro . Willi Domgraf-Fassbaender (b)
Count Almaviva ... Roy Henderson (b)
Bartolo . Norman Allin & Italo Tajo (bs)
Basilio .... Heddle Nash (t)
Antonio .... Fergus Dunlop (bs)
Curzio .... Morgan Jones (t)
Chorus & Orchestra of Glyndebourne Festival, 1935
NOTE: *The "secco" recitatives have been omitted in this recording.*

Overture Orchestra
London Philharmonic—Beecham
12″—C-71606D
[Handel: Messiah—Pastoral Symphony]
[Brahms: Tragic Overture, Pt. 3, on C-69058D in CX-85†: C-LX639: C-LFX503]
[Beethoven: Triple Concerto, Pt. 9, on C-GQX10919]
Vienna Philharmonic—Karajan
12″—C-LX1008
[Symphony No. 33, Pt. 5]

National Symphony Orch.—Boyd Neel
  12″—D-K1297
[Così fan tutte—Overture]
Saxon State Orch.—Böhm
  12″—G-DB4692
[Entführung aus dem Serail—Overture]
Dresden Philharmonic—van Kempen
[Idomeneo—Overture] 12″—PD-57188
[Pfitzner: Kathchen von Heilbronn—
Overture, Pt. 3 on PD-15242]
[Symphony No. 35, Pt. 5, EIAR Orch.—
Karajan, on CET-RR8037]
Vienna Philharmonic—Krauss
(G-S10290) (G-C2194) 12″—V-11242
[Entführung aus dem Serail—Overture]
Royal Theatre Orch., Copenhagen—
Tango 12″—TONO-X25022
[Les Petits Riens—Overture]
DUPLICATIOINS: Berlin Philharmonic
—Furtwängler, PD-35013; Berlin Phil-
harmonic—Schmidt-Isserstedt,
U-B18110: T-A2141; Minneapolis Sym-
phony Orch.—Ormandy, V-14325; Berlin
State Opera Orch.—Blech, G-EJ57:
G-W884; British Symphony Orch.—
Walter, C-LFX329; Berlin State Opera
Orch.—Pfitzner, PD-27066; Berlin State
Opera Orch.—Schmalstich, G-S10227;
Milan Symphony Orch.—Molajoli,
C-67947D in C-OP8†: C-D14579; Sym-
phony Orch.—Ruhlmann, PAT-X96134;
Sym. Orch., U-E396; EIAR Orch.—La
Rosa Parodi, CET-CB20241
—Arr. 2 Pianos Conus
Luboschutz & Nemenoff 12″—V-11-8455
[Mendelssohn: Midsummer Night's
Dream—Scherzo, arr. Philipp]

ACT I

No. 1, Cinque . . . dieci! Duo: Sop. & Bar.
  (Susanna & Figaro)
Josef Herrmann & Margarete Düren (in
German) 10″—G-DA4502
[No. 16, Crudel! perchè finora]
No. 2, Se a caso madama Duo: Soprano &
Baritone
Elisabeth Rethberg & Ezio Pinza
  (in VM-783) 10″—V-2154
[Don Giovanni-No. 7, Là ci darem la
mano]
No. 3, Se vuol ballare Bar. (Cavatina)
  (Figaro)
Ger. Will einst das Gräflein ein Tänzchen
wagen
Eng. If you are after a little amusement
Ezio Pinza & Metropolitan Opera Orch.—
Walter (in CM-643†) 12″—C-71845D
[No. 26, Aprite un po']
Paul Schoeffler 10″—D-M613
[Don Giovanni—No. 17, Serenata]
Nelson Eddy
  (in CM-507) 10″—C-17451D
[No. 9, Non più andrai]
In German:
Willi Domgraf-Fassbaender
  10″—G-EG2906
[Don Giovanni—No. 17, Serenade]
Gerhard Hüsch 10″—O-25092
[No. 9, Non più andrai]
In English:
Dennis Noble 10″—G-B9325

[Zauberflöte—No. 2, Der Vogelfänger
bin ich, ja]
No. 4, La Vendetta Bass (Bartolo)
Ger. Rache-Arie: Süsse Rache
Salvatore Baccaloni 12″—C-71193D
[Rossini: Il Barbiere di Siviglia—Un'
dottore della mia sorte]
A. Kipnis & E. Ruziczka (in Ger.)
  12″—G-DB1551
[Zauberflöte—No. 15, In diesen heil'gen
Hallen, Kipnis]
NOTE: *Preceded by a bit of the Recit: "Und Sie
konnten warten" for Bass and Soprano.*
No. 6, Non so più cosa son Sop. (Cherubino)
Ger. Neue Freuden, Neue Schmerzen, or
Weiss ich nicht
Fr. Je ne sais quelle ardeur
Bidù Sayão
  (in CM-612) 12″—C-72092D
[No. 11, Voi che sapete]
Elisabeth Schumann 10″—G-DA844
[No. 12, Venite inginocchiatevi]
Maria Stader 10″—G-DA6026
[No. 11, Voi che sapete]
Eleanor Steber
  (in VM-1157) 12″—V-11-9773
[No. 27, Deh vieni non tardar]
Conchita Supervia 12″—P-R20077
[No. 11, Voi che sapete]
Risë Stevens (ms) 10″—C-17298D
[No. 11, Voi che sapete]
In German:
Delia Reinhardt, PD-62650
In French:
Yvonne Brothier 10″—G-P698
[No. 11, Voi che sapete]
DUPLICATIONS: Germaine Corney, PD-
522582; Germaine Féraldy, C-LF99
No. 8, Giovani lieti Cho.
Omitted in Mozart Society Vols. No re-
cording traced
No. 9, Non più andrai Baritone
Ger. Dort vergiss leises Flehen
Eng. Now your philandering days are over
Ezio Pinza (in VM-783) 12″—V-18015
[No. 19, Dove sono, Rethberg]
Nelson Eddy
  (in CM-507) 10″—C-17451D
[No. 3, Se vuol ballare]
In German:
Gerhard Hüsch 12″—G-DB4681
[No. 17, Hai già vinta]
Willi Domgraf-Fassbaender
[No. 27, Aprite un po'] 10″—G-EG2323
Leo Schützendorf 12″—T-E725
[Lortzing: Wildschütz-Funftausend
Thaler]
DUPLICATIONS: Arno Schellenberg,
G-EG6161; Heinrich Rehkemper, PD-
24914; Gerhard Hüsch, O-25092
In English:
Dennis Noble 12″—G-C3304
[Verdi: Traviata-Di Provenza]
Peter Dawson 12″—G-C1401
[Verdi: Otello-Credo]
In Swedish: Joel Berglund, T-E19029

ACT II

No. 10, Porgi amor Soprano
Ger. Heil'ge Quelle

Eng. Love thou holy passion or Thou, O
Love
Tiana Lemnitz   12"—G-DB3462
[No. 19, Dove sono]
Gabriella Gatti   12"—CET-BB25088
[Weber: Oberon—Traure mein Herz]
[Verdi: Ballo in Maschera—Morrò ma
prima in grazia, on CET-BB25142]
Eleanor Steber   12"—V-11-8850
[No. 19, Dove sono]
Aulikki Rautawaara   12"—T-E2688
[Zauberflöte-No. 17, Ach ich fühl's]
Elisabeth Rethberg
        (in VM-783) 10"—V-2155
[No. 16, Crudel! perchè finora, Pinza]
In German:
Maria Reining   12"—G-DB7665
[No. 27, Deh vieni, non tardar]
Lotte Lehmann   12"—P-PXO1014
[Strauss: Rosenkavalier-Marschallin's
Monologue]
In English:
Joan Hammond   12"—C-DX1141
[Zauberflöte-No. 17, Ach, ich fühl's]

No. 11, Voi che sapete Soprano
Ger. Ihr, die ihr Triebe
Fr. Mon coeur soupire
Bidù Sayão
        (in CM-612) 12"—C-72092D
[No. 6, Non so più]
Elisabeth Schumann   12"—G-DB946
[Don Giovanni, No. 13, Batti, batti]
Conchita Supervia   12"—P-R20077
[No. 6, Non so più]
Suzanne Danco   12"—D-K1732
[Così fan tutte-No. 14, Come scoglio]
DUPLICATIONS: Gianna Pederzini,
CET-BB25036; Maria Stader, G-DA6026;
Luisa Tetrazzini, V-15-1001* (Rec.
1908); Risë Stevens, C-17298D; Rosetta
Pampanini, C-GQ7066; Renata Villani,
G-HN358
In German:
Delia Reinhardt   10"—PD-62650
[No. 6, Non so più]
In French:
Lily Pons (in CM-518) 10"—C-17345D
[Zauberflöte—No. 14, Der hölle Rache]
Lily Pons   10"—O-188644
[Zauberflöte—No. 14, Der hölle Rache]
DUPLICATIONS: Yvonne Brothier,
G-P698; Germaine Corney, PD-522582;
Germaine Féraldy, C-LF99; E. Celis,
G-K7658

No. 12, Venite, inginocchiatevi Soprano
Elisabeth Schumann   10"—G-DA844
[No. 6, Non so più cosa son]

ACT III

No. 16, Crudel! perchè finora & Mi sento
dal contento
Ger. So lang' hab' ich geschmachet
Soprano & Baritone
Elisabeth Rethberg & Ezio Pinza
        (in VM-783) 10"—V-2155
[No. 10, Porgi amor, Rethberg]
Toti Dal Monte & Augusto Beuf
                     10"—G-DA5406
[Don Giovanni-No. 7, Là ci darem la
mano]

Geraldine Farrar & Antonio Scotti
                     12"—G-DK118*
[Puccini: La Bohème-Mimì, è ver]
Edith Oldrup-Pedersen & Einar Nørby
                     12"—TONO-X25104
[Così fan tutte-No. 23, Il core vi dono]
In German:
Felicie Hüni-Mihacsek & Willi Domgraf-
Fassbaender   12"—PD-66861
[Zauberflöte-No. 8, Schnelle Füsse]
Margarete Düren & Josef Herrmann
                     10"—G-DA4502
[No. 1, Cinque . . . dieci]
No. 17, Hai già vinta & Vedrò mentr' io
Recit. & Aria Baritone
Ger. Der Prozess schon gewonnen & Ich
soll ein Glück
Tancredi Pasero   10"—G-DA5438
[Zauberflöte-No. 15, In diesen heil'gen
Hallen]
In German:
Gerhard Hüsch   12"—G-DB4681
[No. 9, Non più andrai]
Sven-Olof Sandberg   12"—O-9135
[Don Giovanni-No. 12, Finch' han dal
vino, & No. 17, Serenata]
No. 19, E Susanna non vien Recit.
Dove sono Aria Soprano
Ger. Und Susanna kommt nicht & Nur zu
flüchtig
Fr. Dois-je croire Susanne & Douce image
évanouie
Eng. Is Susanna not here? Golden mo-
ments
Complete versions:
Maria Cebotari & Philharmonia Orch.—
Krips   10"—G-DA1875
Joan Hammond (in English) & Hallé
Orch.—Heward   12"—C-DX1082
—Dove Sono only
Tiana Lemnitz   12"—G-DB3462
[No. 10, Porgi amor]
Eleanor Steber   12"—V-11-8850
[No. 10, Porgi amor]
Elisabeth Rethberg
        (in VM-783) 12"—V-18015
[No. 9, Non più andrai, Pinza]
In German:
Margarete Teschemacher
                     12"—G-DB4690
[No. 20, Sull' aria, with Beilke]
In French:
Ninon Vallin   10"—PAT-PD35
Germaine Féraldy   12"—C-LFX60
[Zauberflöte—No. 17, Ach, ich fühl's]
In English:
Joan Cross   12"—G-C3187
[Zauberflöte—No. 17, Ach, ich fühl's]
In Hungarian: E. Sandoz, RAD-RB13
No. 20, Sull' aria! Che soave zefiretto 2
Sopranos
Ger. Briefduett: Wenn de sanften Abend-
lüfte
Fr. Quand le soir entend ses voiles
Emma Eames & Marcella Sembrich
                     12"—G-DK121*
[Zauberflöte-No. 7, Bei männern, Eames
& Gogorza]
In French:
Yvonne Brothier & Jeanne Guyla
                     10"—G-P864

[Zauberflöte—No. 17, Ach, ich fühl's, Brothier]
In German:
Margarete Teschemacher & Irma Beilke
[No. 19, Dove sono] 12"—G-DB4690
DUPLICATION: Viorica Ursuleac & Erna Berger, PD-62755

ACT IV

No. 23, L'ho perduta, me meschina! Sop. (Barbarina)
Omitted in Mozart Society Vols. No recording traced

No. 24, Il capro e la capretta Sop. (Marcellina)
Omitted in Mozart Society Vols. No recording traced

No. 25, In quegl' anni Ten. (Basilio)
Omitted in Mozart Society Vols. No recording traced

No. 26, Tutto è disposto Recit.
Aprite un po' Aria Baritone
Ger. Ach, öffnet eure Augen
Ezio Pinza
(in CM-643†) 12"—C-71845D
[No. 3, Se vuol ballare]
Mariano Stabile 10"—C-DQ701
[Ciampi: Nina]
In German:
Willi Domgraf-Fassbaender
[No. 9, Non più andrai] 10"—G-EG2323
In Swedish: Joel Berglund, T-E19029

No. 27, Giunse alfin il momento Recit.
Deh vieni, non tardar Aria Soprano
Ger. Rosenarie: O säume länger nicht;
Endlich naht sich die Stunde
Fr. O nuit enchanteresse or Pourquoi te faire attendre & Viens cher amant
Eng. Now at last comes the moment
Pia Tassinari
(in CET-7) 12"—CET-BB25122
[Massenet: Werther-Letter aria]
Eleanor Steber
(in VM-1157†) 12"—V-11-9773
[No. 6, Non so più]
Hjördis Schymberg 12"—G-DB6294
[Così fan tutte-No. 14, Come scoglio]
Lina Pagliughi 12"—P-DPX28
[Don Giovanni-No. 13, Batti, batti]
(CET-TI7001)
DUPLICATIONS: Gabrielle Ritter-Ciampi, PD-66884; Toti Dal Monte, G-DB831*; Elda Ribetti, G-AW321; Martha Angelici, AS-118 in Vol. XII; E. Oldrup-Pedersen, TONO-X25096
In German:
Maria Reining 12"—G-DB7665
[No. 10, Porgi amor]
Margherita Perras 12"—G-DB4484
[Entführung aus dem Serail—No. 10, Welcher Kummer]
DUPLICATIONS: Adele Kern, PD-66945; Lotte Lehmann, P-PO158: O-4851

(IL) RE PASTORE, K. 208 2 Acts 1775

Overture Orchestra
EIAR Orch.—La Rosa Parodi
12"—CET-CB20209
[Idomeneo—Overture]

No. 10, L'Amerò, sarò costante Soprano (with Vl. obb.)
Ger. Dein bin ich
Lily Pons (Vl. obb. Michel Piastro)
12"—C-71696D
Maria Stader 12"—G-DB10111
[Exsultate jubilate-Alleluia]
Martha Angelici
(in Vol. XII) 12"—AS-118
[Nozze di Figaro-No. 27, Deh vieni, non tardar]
DUPLICATIONS: Gabrielle Ritter-Ciampi, PD-66841; Nellie Melba, with Jan Kubelik (vl), G-DK112*

(DER) SCHAUSPIELDIREKTOR, K. 486

1 Act 1786
It. & Eng. Impresario
Fr. Le Directeur de Théâtre
Overture. Orchestra
National Symphony Orch.—Boyd Neel
[Idomeneo—Overture] 12"—D-K1410
EIAR Orch.—La Rosa Parodi
12"—CET-CC2185
[Haydn: Symphony No. 101, Pt. 7]
German Opera House Orch.—Grüber
12"—O-7980
[Entführung aus dem Serail—Overture]
Vienna Philharmonic—Johannes
Schuler 12"—PAT-PDT75
[Symphony No. 35, D major, Pt. 5]

(DIE) ZAUBERFLOETE, K. 620 2 Acts 1791

It. Il Flauto Magico
Fr. La Flûte Enchantée
Eng. The Magic Flute
"Complete" recording Sung in German
Soloists & Chorus, with Berlin Philharmonic Orch.—Sir Thomas Beecham
(Mozart Opera Society, Vols. 10/13)
(2 Vols.) 19 12"—VM-541/542†
The Cast:
Sarastro .... Wilhelm Strienz (bs)
Tamino .... Helge Roswaenge (t)
Speaker ...... Walter Grossmann (bs)
Second Priest ...... Ernst Fabbry (t)
Queen of the Night .... Erna Berger (s)
Pamina .... Tiana Lemnitz (s)
First Lady .... Hilde Scheppan (s)
Second Lady ...... Elfride Marherr (s)
Third Lady ...... Rut Berglund (c)
Papageno .... Gerhard Hüsch (b)
Papagena .... Irma Beilke (s)
Monostatos ...... Heinrich Tessmer (t)
First Boy .... Irma Beilke (s)
Second Boy .... Carla Spletter (s)
Third Boy .... Rut Berglund (c)
First Armed Man . Heinrich Tessmer (t)
Second Armed Man ....
.... Walter Grossmann (bs)
NOTE: The spoken dialogue is omitted in this recording.
Vocal & Orchestral Selections (Querschnitt)
Peter Anders (t), Martina Wulf (s), Hans-Heinz Nissen (b), Wilhelm Hiller (bs) with Chorus & Orch.—Schultze
12"—T-E2133

Overture Orchestra
BBC Symphony Orch.—Toscanini
(G-DB3550) 12″—V-15190
Berlin Philharmonic—Schmidt-Isserstedt
(U-F18108) 12″—T-E2627
Berlin State Opera Orch.—Von Karajan
12″—PD-67465
Symphony Orch.—Bruno Walter
12″—C-67660D
(C-12549) (C-CQX16604)
National Symphony Orch.—Boyd Neel
12″—D-K1409
Berlin State Opera Orch.—R. Strauss
12″—PD-66826
Berlin State Opera Orch.—Blech
(G-P745) 10″—G-EW58
Berlin Orch.—Fritz Lehmann
12″—O-7944
Royal Theatre Orch., Copenhagen—
Tango 12″—TONO-X25015
Symphony Orch.—H. Rabaud
12″—PAT-5526

No. 2, Der Vogelfänger bin ich Bass
It. Gente, e qui l'uccellatore
Fr. Je suis le galant oiseleur, or C'est
l'oiseleur
Eng. A fowler bold
Gerhard Hüsch 12″—G-DB4682
[No. 20, Ein Mädchen]
Arno Schellenberg 10″—G-EG6140
[No. 20, Ein Mädchen]
Sven-Olaf Sandberg 10″—O-4638
[No. 20, Ein Mädchen]
In French:
Lucien Fugère, C-D13092
In English:
Dennis Noble 10″—G-B9325
[Nozze di Figaro-No. 3, Se vuol ballare]

No. 3, Dies Bildnis ist bezaubernd schön
Tenor
It. Oh! cara immagine
Eng. O loveliness beyond compare
Aksel Schiøtz 12″—G-DB5265
[Così fan tutte-No. 17, Un aura amorosa]
Richard Tauber 12″—P-PXO1024
(O-123834)
[Entführung aus dem Serail-No. 4, O wie
ängstlich]
Richard Tauber 12″—P-R20550
[Bizet: Carmen—Air de la fleur]
Hugo Meyer-Welfing 12″—C-DX1385
[Don Giovanni-No. 11, Dalla sua pace]
Anton Dermota 12″—T-E3162
[Don Giovanni-No. 11, Dalla sua pace]
Helge Roswaenge 12″—G-DB4637
[No. 17, Ach, ich fühl's, Lemnitz]
Franz Völker 12″—PD-67161
[No. 8, Flöten-Arie]
Max Lichtegg 12″—D-K1565
[Don Giovanni-No. 22, Il mio tesoro]
DUPLICATIONS: Julius Patzak, PD-
95437; Marcel Wittrisch, G-EH657;
Peter Anders, T-E1867
In English:
Webster Booth 12″—G-C3402
[Entführung aus dem Serail-No. 4,
Constanze]
David Lloyd 12″—C-DX983
[Don Giovanni-No. 22, Il mio tesoro]
James Melton
(in VM-1013) 12″—V-11-8929

[Don Giovanni-No. 22, Il mio tesoro]
Heddle Nash 12″—C-9228
[No. 8, Flöten-Arie]
No. 4, O zitt're nicht Recit.
Zum Leiden bin ich auserkoren Aria So-
prano
It. Non paventar; Infelice, sconsolata
Erna Berger & Berlin Philharmonic—
Beecham 12″—G-DB4645
[No. 14, Der Hölle Rache]
Elisabeth Reichelt 12″—PD-57117
[No. 14, Der Hölle Rache]
**No. 5, Hm, hm, hm! Der Arme kann von
Strafe sagen** Quintet
Erna Berger, Adele Kern, Elsa Ruziczka,
Max Hirzel, K. A. Newmann
12″—PD-35005
[Entführung aus dem Serail-No. 21, Nie
werd' ich deine Huld verkennen]
No. 7, Bei Männern Duo: Soprano & Bari-
tone
It. La dove prende Eng. Manly Heart
Tiana Lemnitz & Gerhard Hüsch
12″—G-DB4656
[No. 21, Klinget, Glöckchen, Klinget]
Margherita Perras & Gerhard Hüsch
(G-DA4408) 10″—V-4374
[Don Giovanni-No. 7, Là ci darem la
mano]
Felicie Hüni-Mihacsek & Willi Domgraf-
Fassbaender 10″—PD-62669
[Don Giovanni-No. 7, Là ci darem la
mano]
DUPLICATION: Die Duoptisten,
G-EG2019
In Italian:
Emma Eames & Emilio de Gogorza
12″—G-DK121*
[Nozze di Figaro-No. 20, Che soave
zefiretto, Eames & Sembrich]
In English:
Gwen Catley & Dennis Noble
10″—G-B9338
[Don Giovanni-No. 7, Là ci darem la
mano]
In Danish:
Edith Oldrup Pedersen & Einar Nørby
12″—TONO-25097
[Entführung aus dem Serail-No. 9, Ich
gehe]
No. 8, Finale
—**Wie stark ist doch dein Zauberton!**
(Flöten-Arie) Tenor
Eng. O voice of magic melody or Thy
magic tones
Walther Ludwig 12″—G-EH1020
[Nicolai: Lustige Weiber—Romanze des
Fenton]
Marcel Wittrisch 12″—G-EH657
[No. 3, Bildnisarie]
Franz Völker with Berlin State Opera
Orch.—Schmidt 12″—PD-67161
[No. 3, Bildnisarie]
In English:
Heddle Nash 12″—C-9228
[No. 3, Bildnisarie]
—**Schnelle Füsse, rascher Mut** Trio
—**Das klinget so herrlich** Trio & Chorus
Felicie Hüni-Mihacsek, Willi Domgraf-
Fassbaender, G. Witting & Cho.
12″—PD-66861

[Nozze di Figaro-No. 16, Crudel! perchè finora]

ACT II

No. 9, Marsch der Priester Orchestra
Berlin Philharmonic Orch.—Blech
10"—G-DA4405
[No. 18, O Isis und Osiris]

No. 10, O Isis und Osiris Bass & Chorus
It. **Possenti Numi** Eng. **Invocation** (Sarastro's Aria)
Alexander Kipnis & Cho.
(G-DA1218) 10"—V-1738
[Entführung aus dem Serail-No. 2, Wer ein Liebchen]
Wilhelm Schirp & Cho. 12"—T-E3049
[No. 15, In diesen heil'gen Hallen]
Wilhelm Strienz & Cho. 12"—G-DB5578
[No. 15, In diesen heil'gen Hallen]
[Older version, with pf. acc., on PD-19715]
Ivar Andrésen & Cho. 12"—G-EH121
[No. 15, In diesen heil'gen Hallen]
DUPLICATIONS: Ludwig Hoffmann, PD-62684; Oscar Natzke, P-E11423; Ezio Pinza (in Italian), G-DB5389: G-DB1088
In English:
Oscar Natzke & Cho. 12"—C-DX1370
[No. 15, In diesen heil'gen Hallen]
Norman Allin & Cho. 12"—C-9802
[No. 15, In diesen heil'gen Hallen]

No. 14, Der Hölle Rache (Rache-Arie)
Soprano
It. **Gli angui d'inferno**
Erna Berger & Berlin Philharmonic
Orch.—Beecham 12"—G-DB4645
[No. 4, O zitt're nicht]
Elisabeth Reichelt 12"—PD-57117
[No. 4, O zittre nicht]
Miliza Korjus 12"—V-11921
[Offenbach: Contes d'Hoffmann—Doll song]
[Entführung aus dem Serail-No. 11, Martern aller Arten, on G-EH898]
Anna M. Guglielmetti (in Italian)
12"—C-GQX10181
[Proch: Air & Variations]
Lily Pons (in French) & Orch.—Walter
(in CM-518) 10"—C-17345D
[Nozze di Figaro-No. 11, Voi che sapete]
(Older version on O-188644)

No. 15, In diesen heil'gen Hallen Bass
It. **Qui sdegno non s'accende** Eng. **Within these sacred walls**
Alexander Kipnis 12"—V-8684
[Verdi: Simon Boccanegra—Il lacerato spirito]
Wilhelm Strienz & Berlin Philharmonic
—Beecham 12"—G-DB5578
[No. 10, O Isis und Osiris]
Wilhelm Schirp 12"—T-E3049
[No. 10, O Isis und Osiris]
DUPLICATIONS: Ivar Andrésen, G-EH121; Ludwig Hoffmann, PD-66927
In Italian:
Ezio Pinza & Metropolitan Opera Orch.—
Walter (in CM-643†) 12"—C-71843D
[Entführung aus dem Serail-No. 19, Ha, ha!]
Tancredi Pasero 10"—G-DA5438

[Nozze di Figaro-No. 17, Vedrò mentr' io sospiro]
In English:
Oscar Natzke 12"—C-DX1370
[No. 10, O Isis und Osiris]
Norman Allin 12"—C-9802
[No. 10, O Isis und Osiris]

No. 17, Ach, ich fühl's Soprano
It. **Ah, lo so** Fr. **Ah! je le sais** Eng. **Ah, 'tis gone**
Tiana Lemnitz & Berlin Philharmonic
Orch.—Beecham 12"—G-DB4637
[No. 3, Bildnisarie, Roswaenge]
Dorothy Maynor & Boston Symphony—
Koussevitzky 12"—V-15826
[Handel: Semele—Oh Sleep, why dost thou leave me?]
Aulikki Rautawaara 12"—T-E2688
[Nozze di Figaro-No. 10, Porgi amor]
DUPLICATIONS: Felicie Hüni-Mihascek, PD-66615; Lotte Lehmann, P-PO157: O-4851
In French:
Gabrielle Ritter-Ciampi 12"—PD-566062
[Gounod: Faust—Roi de Thulé]
Lily Pons (G-DB2502) 12"—V-8733
[Bishop: Lo! here the gentle lark]
DUPLICATIONS: Germaine Féraldy, C-LFX60; Yvonne Brothier, G-P864
In English:
Joan Hammond 12"—C-DX1141
[Nozze di Figaro-No. 10, Porgi amor]
Joan Cross 12"—G-C3187
[Nozze di Figaro-No. 19, Dove sono]
Eleanor Steber 12"—V-11-9114
[Don Giovanni-No. 13, Batti, Batti]

No. 18, O Isis und Osiris (Priesterchor)
Hamburg State Opera Chorus & Orch.—
Schmidt-Isserstedt 12"—T-E2998
[Verdi: Aida—Act II, Final Chorus]
Berlin State Opera Chorus & Orch.—
Blech 10"—G-DA4405
[No. 9, Marsch der Priester]

No. 20, Ein Mädchen oder Weibchen Baritone
Fr. **C'est l'amour d'une belle**
Eng. **'Tis love they say** or **O maiden fair**
Gerhard Hüsch & Berlin Philharmonic—
Beecham 12"—G-DB4682
[No. 2, Der Vogelfänger]
Arno Schellenberg & Orch.—Seidler-
Winkler 10"—G-EG6140
[No. 2, Der Vogelfänger]
DUPLICATIONS: Sven-Olof Sandberg, O-4638; Heinrich Rehkemper, PD-66714
In French: Lucien Fugère, C-D13092
In English:
Dennis Noble 12"—G-C3520
[Verdi: Rigoletto—Pari siamo]

No. 21, Finale
—**Papagena! Weibchen! Taubchen!** Baritone
Heinrich Rehkemper 12"—PD-66714
[No. 20, Ein Mädchen oder Weibchen]

—**Klinget, Glöckchen, klinget**
I. Beilke, C. Spletter, R. Berglund, G. Hüsch with Berlin Philharmonic—
Beecham 12"—G-DB4656
[No. 7, Bei Männern, Lemnitz & Hüsch]

—Pa-Pa-Pa-Pa-Pa-Papagena Baritone & Soprano
Jane Laval & Fred Bordon (in French)
10"—C-LF52
[Berlioz: Damnation de Faust—Voici des roses, Bordon]
Edith Oldrup-Pedersen & Einar Nørby
(in Dan.)   12"—TONO-X25095
[Don Giovanni-No. 7, Là ci darem]

Overture, B flat major, K. Anh. 8 (K. 311a) 1778
Paris Conservatory Orch.—Fendler
12"—G-DB5050

Pastorale variée, K. Anh. 209b (K. Anh. 284n) Clavier
Marie Panthes (pf)   12"—C-DFX169
[Albéniz: Granada]

(LES) PETITS RIENS (Ballet Pantomime, K. Anh. 10 (K. 299b) 1778
(Overture & 13 Numbers)

—Unspecified excerpts
Winterthur Municipal Orch.—H.
Scherchen   2 12"—G-DB6080/1

—Overture, No. 6 (Gavotte joyeuse), No. 10 (Pantomime), No. 12 (Gavotte)
London Symphony Orch.—Blech
12"—G-DB1676

—Overture only
Royal Theatre Orch., Copenhagen—
Tango   12"—TONO-X25022
[Nozze di Figaro—Overture]

Psalm: De Profundis clamavi (Psalm 129) K. 93 1771
4-Part Chorus, 2 Violins & Organ
Chorale Félix Raugel-Raugel
12"—OL-48
[Vesperae-Laudate Dominum]

QUARTETS—String
NOTE: See also Divertimenti—String.

No. 11, E flat major, K. 171 1773
(No. 9 Peters Edition)
Loewenguth Quartet (PD-566207/8)
2 12"—VOX-183

No. 14, G major, K. 387 1782
(No. 1 Haydn Series; No. 12 Peters Edition)
Calvet Quartet (U-F18030/2)
3 12"—T-E2867/9
Griller Quartet (D-K1652/5)
4 12"—D-ED48†
Roth Quartet   3 12"—CM-374†
Wendling Quartet 3 12"—PD-95306/8
Belardinelli Quartet
4 12"—G-AW314/7

No. 15, D minor, K. 421 (K. 417b) 1783
(No. 2 Haydn Series; No. 13 Peters Edition)
Hungarian Quartet
3 12"—G-DB6445/7†
Budapest Quartet 3 12"—CM-462†
Griller Quartet 4 12"—D-K1719/22†
[Purcell-Warlock: 4 Part Fantasia No. 9]
Strub Quartet   3 12"—G-DB5603/5
Léner Quartet 3 12"—C-GQX10457/9
Blech Quartet   3 12"—D-K923/5
—2nd Mvt. (Andante) only
Léner Quartet, C-DB832 (in Columbia
History of Music Vol. III, CM-233)

—3rd Mvt. (Minuetto) only
Poltronieri Quartet, C-GQX11065

No. 16, E flat major, K. 428 (K. 421b) 1783
(No. 3 Haydn Series; No. 14 Peters Edition)
Busch Quartet   4 12"—CM-529†
Prisca Quartet (PD-62729/32)
4 10"—PD-10394/7

No. 17, B flat major, K. 458 ("Hunting") 1784
(No. 4 Haydn Series; No. 15 Peters Edition)
Budapest Quartet   3 12"—VM-763†
Philharmonia Quartet
3 12"—C-DX1025/7†
Roth Quartet   3 12"—CM-438†
Röntgen Quartet
3 12"—ELITE-7035/7
—2nd Mvt. (Menuet) only
Paganini Quartet (in VM-1151†)

No. 18, A major, K. 464 1785
(No. 5 Haydn Series; No. 16 Peters Edition)
Calvet Quartet   3 12"—T-E3014/6
Roth Quartet   4 12"—CM-222†

No. 19, C major, K. 465 1785
(No. 6 Haydn Series; No. 17 Peters Edition)
(The Quartet with the dissonant introduction)
Budapest Quartet (G-DB1863/5)
3 12"—VM-285†
Loewenguth Quartet
3 12"—G-DB11120/2
Pascal String Quartet
3 12"—O-123882/4
Kolisch Quartet   3 12"—CM-439†
DUPLICATIONS: Deman Quartet, PD-95301/4; Capet Quartet, C-D15110/3

No. 20, D major, K. 499 1786
(No. 18, Peters Edition)
Prisca Quartet   4 10"—PD-62725/8

No. 21, D major, K. 575 (" 'Cello") 1789
(No. 1, King of Prussia Series)
Honegger Quartet 3 12"—G-HEX110/2
Prisca Quartet   4 10"—PD-10398/401
Kolisch Quartet 2 12"—C-GQX10760/1
—3rd Mvt. (Minuetto) only
Paganini Quartet, in VM-1153†

No. 22, B flat major, K. 589 1790
(No. 2, King of Prussia Series)
Worthington Quartet
1 10" & 2 12"—TC-T4

No. 23, F major, K. 590 1791
(No. 3, King of Prussia Series)
Budapest Quartet   3 12"—VM-348†
Léner Quartet 3 12"—C-GQX11053/5
Vegh Quartet
In Preparation—Swiss Decca

G major, K. 525 ("Eine kleine Nachtmusik") 1787
(No. 19, Peters Edition)
See under Serenades

C minor, K. 546 1788
(No. 20, Peters Edition)
See under Adagio & Fugue, C minor

(4) QUARTETS ("Milanese" Quartets) Strings
(Schott Edition; of doubtful authenticity)
No. 1, A major, K. Anh. 212
Dessauer Quartet   12"—PD-67713
No. 2, B flat major, K. Anh. 210
Dessauer Quartet   12"—PD-67711

No. 3, C major, K. Anh. 211
  Dessauer Quartet 12"—PD-67712
No. 4, E flat major, K. Anh. 213
  Dessauer Quartet 12"—PD-67714

QUARTETS—Flute & Strings
No. 1, D major, K. 285
  J. P. Rampal & Pasquier Trio
    2 12"—BAM-33/4
No. 2, A major, K. 298
  René Le Roy & Pasquier Trio
    12"—G-DB3365

QUARTET—Oboe & Strings
F major, K. 370 (K. 368b) 1781
  Leon Goossens & Members of Léner
  Quartet 2 12"—CX-21†
  (C-LFX327/8)
  Wiesbaden Collegium Musicum
  (U-F18100/1) 2 12"—T-E3070/1

QUARTETS—Piano & Strings
No. 1, G minor, K. 478
  Artur Schnabel & Members of Pro Arte
  Quartet 4 12"—GM-213†
  (G-DB2155/8)
No. 2, E flat major, K. 493
  George Szell & Members of Budapest
  Quartet 3 12"—CM-669†

QUINTETS—String Quartet & 2nd Viola
C major, K. 515 1787
  Budapest Quartet & Milton Katims
    4 12"—CM-586†
  Pro Arte Quartet & A. Hobday
    4 12"—G-DB6043/6
G minor, K. 516 1787
  Budapest Quartet & Milton Katims
    4 12"—CM-526†
  Pro Arte Quartet & A. Hobday
    4 12"—VM-190†
  (G-DB2173/6 in GM-215†)
  Léner Quartet & L. D'Oliveira
    4 12"—C-GQX10552/5
D major, K. 593 1790
  Pro Arte Quartet & A. Hobday
    3 12"—VM-350†
  Budapest Quartet & Milton Katims
  (C-LX1046/8†) 3 12"—CM-708†
E flat major, K. 614 1791
  No recording traced

QUINTET—String Quartet & Double Bass
  See under Serenades: "Eine kleine Nachtmusik"

QUINTET—Horn, Violin, 2 Violas, 'Cello
E flat major, K. 407 (K. 386c)
  Dennis Brain, Sidney Griller, Phillip Bur-
  ton, Max Gilbert, Colin Hempton
    2 12"—D-K1138/9†

QUINTET—Clarinet & String Quartet
A major, K. 581 ("Stadler Quintet") 1789
  Reginald Kell & Philharmonia Quartet
  (C-DX1187/90†) 4 12"—CM-702†
  Benny Goodman & Budapest Quartet
    3 10" & 1 12"—VM-452†
  (Released in England on 3 12",
  G-DB3576/8†)

Luigi Amodio & Poltronieri Quartet
    4 12"—C-GQX11088/91
Simeon Bellison & Roth Quartet
    4 12"—CM-293†
Luigi Amodio & Strub Quartet
    4 12"—G-DB5683/6
C. Draper & Léner Quartet
    4 12"—C-GQX10957/60
Philipp Dreisbach & Wendling Quartet
    4 12"—PD-95309/12
[Haydn: Quartet, Op. 3, No. 5-Serenade]

QUINTET—Glass Harmonica, Flute, Oboe,
Viola, 'Cello
  See under Adagio & Rondo, C minor, K.
  617 1791

REQUIEM See under Masses, No. 20 (Requiem)

Romance (Rondo), A flat major, K. Anh.
205 Piano
  Edwin Fischer 12"—G-DB5638
  [Fantasia, C minor, K. 475, Pt. 3]
  Eileen Joyce 12"—C-DX1035
  [Sonata, F major, K. 332, Pt. 3]
  Lubka Kolessa 12"—G-DB4654
  [Chopin: Waltz, No. 1]

RONDOS—Piano Solo
D major, K. 485 1786
  Robert Casadesus
  (in CM-356†) 12"—C-69452D
  (C-LX765†) (C-LFX546) (C-LWX276)
  [Concerto No. 24, K. 491, Pt. 7]
  Hans Leygraf 12"—G-Z311
  [Fantasia, D minor, K. 397]
  Wanda Landowska (harpsichord)
    in VM-1181†
A minor, K. 511 1787
  Artur Schnabel 12"—G-DB6298
  Elly Ney 12"—G-DB4620
  Ignace Jan Paderewski 12"—V-15421

RONDOS—Piano & Orchestra
D major, K. 382 1782
  Edwin Fischer & his Chamber Orch.
    12"—G-DB3110
  Wilhelm Kempf & Dresden Philharmonic
  —van Kempen 12"—PD-67710
A major, K. 386 1782 (Originally for A
major Concerto, K. 414)
  Eileen Joyce & Orch.—Raybould
  (O-7683) 12"—P-E11292

RONDO—Horn & Orchestra
E flat major, K. 371
  William Valkenier & Reginald Boardman
  (pf) Night Music—101/2
  [Ravel: Pavane pour une Infante dé-
  funte]

RONDO—Violin & Orchestra
C major, K. 373 1781
  Jean Pougnet & Symphony Orch.—
  Walter 12"—C-DWX1607

SERENADES—See also Divertimenti
No. 6, D major, K. 239 ("Serenata Not-
turna") 1776
  Adolf Busch Chamber Players—Busch
    2 10"—G-DA1673/4
  Paris Conservatory Orch.—Fendler
    12"—BAM-23

Berlin State Opera Orch.—Fritz Lehman
(O-50027/8)   2 12"—O-7965/6
Vox Chamber Orch.—Fendler
               4   10"—VOX-161
[No. 9-Concertante & Rondo only]
Boyd Neel String Orch.—Neel
(PD-516731/2)   2 12"—D-K813/4
[Symphony No. 13, F major—Andante]
EIAR Orch.—Carlo Zecchi
               12"—CET-BB25124
—3rd Mvt. (Rondo) only
Munich Philharmonic—Kabasta
               12"—G-DB5651
[Symphony No. 41, C major, Pt. 7]
No. 7, D major, K. 250 (K. 248b) ("Haff-
ner" Serenade) 1776
—4th Mvt. (Rondo) only
—Arr. Violin & Piano Kreisler
Simon Goldberg & pf. 12"—P-PXO1037
Fritz Kreisler & Franz Rupp
               12"—G-DB3731
Jacques Thibaud & Tasso Janopoulo
               10"—G-DA1649
Blanche Tarjus & Mireille Monard
               10"—G-DA5003
No. 9, D major, K. 320 1779
("Posthorn Serenade")
—3rd Mvt. (Concertante & Rondo) only
Vox Chamber Orch.—Fendler
[Serenade No. 6]   4   10"—In VOX-161
—5th Mvt. (Posthorn Minuet) only
Chamber Orch.—Hans von Benda,
G-EG3095
No. 10, B flat major, K. 361 (K. 370a)
("Gran Partita") 1781
Hewitt Chamber Ensemble
               6 12"—DF-A9
—1st, 3rd, 4th, 6th, 7th Mvts. only
Chamber Orch.—Edwin Fischer
               3 12"—G-DB4693/5
—1st, 2nd, 6th, 7th Mvts. only
Berlin State Opera Orch.—Blech
               2 12"—G-DB4401/2
—Unidentified Mvts.
Paris Wind Instrument Society—
Oubradous   3 12"—G-W1575/7
No. 11, E flat major, K. 375 1781
Hewitt Chamber Ensemble, in DF-A10
Members of the Alumni Orch. of Natl.
Orchestral Assn.—Korn
               3 12"—VM-826†
No. 12, C minor, K. 388 (K. 384a) 1782
L'Oiseau Lyre Orch.—Oubradous
               2 12"—OL-128/9
Hewitt Chamber Ensemble, in DF-A10
G major, K. 525 ("Eine kleine
Nachtmusik") 1787 Strings
Vienna Philharmonic—Walter
(G-DB3075/6)   2 12"—VM-364†
Symphony Orch.—Walter 2 12"—CX-19†
London Symphony—Weingartner
(C-LX854/5)   2 12"—CX-187†
Boyd Neel String Orch.—Neel
               2 12"—D-K1219/20†
Saxon State Orch.—Böhm
               2 12—G-DB4548/9
Berlin Philharmonic—Furtwängler
(PD-566188/90)   3 12"—PD-67156/8
[Adagio, E major, K. 261, Kulenkampff
& Rupp]

[Così fan tutte—Overture, on
PD-67182/4]
London Philharmonic—Beecham
(G-DB6204/5)   2 12"—VM-1163†
Lewis Heward String Orch.—
Heward   2 12"—C-DX1063/4
DUPLICATIONS: Berlin Philharmonic—
Kleiber, T-E1669/70: U-F14424/5;
Berlin State Opera Orch.—Fried,
PD-516638/9; Berlin State Opera Orch.
—Blech, G-EJ326/7; Telmanyi Chamber
Orch., TONO-X25026/7; Symphony Orch.
M. François Gaillard, O-188914/6; Pro
Musica Orch.—Klemperer, VOX-169:
PD-566224/5
—4th Mvt. (Rondo) only
London Philharmonic—Beecham
(in VM-1014)   12"—V-11-8898
[Schubert: Symphony No. 6, Pt. 7]
[Die Zauberflöte, Pt. 37 on V-12569 in
VM-542†]
—String Quintet Version
Pro Arte Quartet & Claude Hobday
(double bass) (G-DB3381/2)
               2 12"—VM-428
—String Quartet Version
(Quartet No. 19, Peters Edition)
Léner Quartet   2 12"—C-GQX10313/4
Sinfonia Concertante
See under Concertos—Violin, Viola &
Orch.; Concertos—Woodwinds & Orch.

SONATAS—Bassoon & 'Cello
B flat major, K. 292 (K. 196c) 1775
Ferdinand Oubradous & Etienne Pasquier
               (in Vol. V.) 12"—AS-44

SONATAS—Piano (or Harpsichord)
No. 4, E flat major, K. 282 (K. 189g)
1773/4
Johanne Stockmarr   12"—G-DB5262
Cor de Groot   2 12"—O-50547/8
[Suite, K. 399—Andante]
No. 5, G major, K. 283 (K. 189h) 1774
Claudio Arrau
(in VM-842†)   2 12"—V-18279/80
[No. 17, D major, K. 576, Pt. 1]
No. 8, A minor, K. 310 (K. 300d) 1778
Denis Matthews   2 12"—C-DX1114/5
Jacques Abrams   in MC-89
[with Hindemith: Sonata No. 2]
No. 9, D major, K. 311 (K. 284c) 1777
Jacqueline Blancard
               2 10"—PD-561122/3
No. 10, C major, K. 330
Emma Boynet   2 12"—VOX-630
[Fantasia, D minor, K. 397]
No. 11, A major, K. 331 (K. 300i) 1778
Edwin Fischer   2 12"—G-DB1993/4
Elly Ney   3 12"—PD-67596/8
Wilhelm Kempff   2 12"—PD-67067/8
José Iturbi   2 12"—V-11593/4
—1st Mvt. (Theme & Variations,
abbreviated) & 2nd Mvt. (Minuetto) only
Hans Bastien Ensemble (arr.), G-EG2861
—3rd Mvt. (Rondo alla Turca) only
Wanda Landowska (harpsichord)
(G-DA860)   10"—V-1193
[Handel: Harmonious Blacksmith]
(also in VM-1181†)
Alice Ehlers (harpsichord)
(in D-A61)   10"—D-23091

[Handel: Suite No. 7—Passacaglia]
Corradina Mola (harpsichord)
10"—**G-DA5393**
[Daquin: Le Coucou & La Guitare]
DUPLICATIONS: (Piano) Franz Osborn,
G-EG2279; Sergei Rachmaninoff,
G-DA719; Walter Gieseking, C-68595D:
C-GQX11032: C-LWX117; N. de Maga-
loff, RAD-RZ3032; William Murdoch,
D-F7496

—Arr. Orchestra
(Some versions labelled "Turkish
March")
Vienna Philharmonic—Alwin
10"—**G-B3188**
[Beethoven: Ruins of Athens—Turkish
March] (G-K5848) (G-HN482)
Berlin State Opera Orch.—
Schmalstich 12"—**G-S10227**
[Nozze di Figaro—Overture]
Berlin Philharmonic Orch.—Schmidt-
Isserstedt 10"—**T-A2141**
[Nozze di Figaro—Overture]
(U-B18110)
DUPLICATION: Polydor String Orch.,
PD-2901

—Arr. Band: Royal Italian Marine Band,
G-HN561

No. 12, F major, K. 332 (K. 300k) 1778
Eileen Joyce 2 12"—**C-DX1034/5**
[Romance, A flat major, K. Anh. 205]
Robert Casadesus
(in CM-433) 2 12"—**C-70706/7D**
[No. 17, D major, K. 576, Pt. 3]
No. 14, C minor, K. 457 1784
Lili Kraus 4 12"—**P-P29†**
[with Fantasia, C minor, K. 475]
(P-PXO1027/30)
Walter Gieseking 2 12"—**CX-93†**
(C-LFX492/3) (C-LWX202/3)
(C-GQX11042/3)
Suzanne Gyr 4 12"—**G-DB10075/8**
[with Fantasia, C minor, K. 475]
No. 15, C major, K. 545 1788
Eileen Joyce 2 12"—**P-E11442/3**
[Suite—Allemande & Courante, K. 399]
Jacqueline Blancard 12"—**PD-516765**
No. 16, B flat major, K. 570 1789
Walter Gieseking
(C-LWX160/1) 2 12"—**CX-79†**
No. 17, D major, K. 576 1789
"Trumpet Sonata"
Robert Casadesus
(in CM-433†) 2 12"—**C-70705/6D**
[No. 12, F major, K. 332, Pt. 1]
Claudia Arrau
(in VM-842†) 2 12"—**V-18280/1**
[No. 5, G major, K. 283, Pt. 3]
—3rd Mvt. (Rondo) only
Lucie Caffaret, PD-66641
D major (unidentified)
France Ellegaard 12"—**PD-67838**
[Scarlatti: Sonatas in D minor & A
flat major]

SONATAS—2 Pianos
D major, K. 448 (K. 375a) 1781
Jean Wiener & Clement Doucet
2 12"—**PAT-PAT94/5**

**SONATAS—Piano (or Harpsichord) &
Violin**
Collections
The Mozart Chamber Music Society
Vol. I—No. 24, C major, K. 296
No. 35, G major, K. 379
No. 41, E flat major, K 481
Lili Kraus & Simon Goldberg
7 12"—**P-P18†**
Vol. II—No. 33, F major, K. 377;
No. 34, B flat major, K. 378;
No. 36, E flat major, K. 380
Lili Kraus & Simon Goldberg
7 12"—**P-P19†**
Sonatas for Harpsichord & Violin
No. 24, C major, K. 296;
No. 34, B flat major, K. 378;
No. 35, G major, K. 379
Ralph Kirkpatrick & Alexander
Schneider 6 12"—**CM-650†**

Individual Sonatas
No. 24, C major, K. 296 1778
Lili Kraus & Simon Goldberg, in Vol I:
P-P18†
Arthur Balsam & Nathan Milstein
2 12"—**CX-143†**
Ralph Kirkpatrick (harpsi.) & Alexander
Schneider
(in CM-650†) 2 12"—**C-71860/1D**
[with Sonatas No. 34 & 35]
No. 28, E minor, K. 304 (K. 300c) 1778
Nikita de Magaloff & Joseph Szigeti
12"—**C-69005D**
(C-LFX479) (C-LWX188)
No. 32, F major, K. 376 (K. 374d) 1781
Hepzibah & Yehudi Menuhin
(labelled No. 34) 2 12"—**VM-791†**
(G-DB3552/3)
No. 33, F major, K. 377 (K. 374e) 1781
Lili Kraus & Simon Goldberg, in Society
Vol. 2: P-P19†
No. 34, B flat major, K. 378 (K. 317d) 1781
Lili Kraus & Simon Goldberg, in Society
Vol. 2: P-P19†
Ralph Kirkpatrick (harpsi.) & Alexander
Schneider
(in CM-650†) 2 12"—**C-71862/3D**
[with Sonatas No. 24 & 35]
Emanuel Bay & Jascha Heifetz
(labelled No. 10)
(in VM-343†) 2 12"— **V-14326/7**
[with Sonata No. 40, B flat, K. 454]
(G-DB6050/1)
Corradina Mola (harpsichord) &
Carlo Felice Cillario
2 12"—**G-DB5364/5**
Felix Dyck & Carl Flesch
2 12"—**PD-67179/80**
—2nd Mvt. (Andantino) only
Yaltah & Yehudi Menuhin
12"—**G-DB3558**
[Mendelssohn: Violin Concerto, E minor,
Pt. 7]
Chamber Duo 12"—**U-F12512**
[von Hoop—Etude, E minor]
No. 35, G major, K. 379 (K. 373a)
Lili Kraus & Simon Goldberg, in Society
Vol. 1: P-P18†

Ralph Kirkpatrick (harpsi.) & Alexander
Schneider
  (in CM-650†) 2 12"—C-71864/5D
[with Sonatas No. 24 & 34]
No. 36, E flat major, K. 380 (K.374f) 1781
Lili Kraus & Simon Goldberg, in Society
Vol. 2: P-P19†
H. Lund-Christiansen & Erling Bloch
              2 12"—G-DB5258/9
No. 39, C major, K. 404 (K. 385d) 1782
Lili Kraus & Simon Goldberg
  (in P-P25†) 12"—P-R20407
[Mozart: Concerto No. 18, Pt. 7]
No. 40, B flat major, K. 454 1784
Jean Hubeau & Henri Merckel
  (in Vol. XII) 3 12"—AS-111/3
Emanuel Bay & Jascha Heifetz
(labelled No. 15)
  (in VM-343†) 3 12"—V-14328/30
[with Sonata No. 34, B flat major]
(G-DB6052/4)
Magda Tagliafero & Denise Soriano
             2 12"—PAT-PAT84/5
Howard Ferguson & Yfrah Neaman
             3 12"—D-K1417/9†
No. 41, E flat, K. 481 1785
Lili Kraus & Simon Goldberg, in Society
Vol. 1: P-P18†
Lucette Descaves-Truc & André Asselin
             2 12"—G-W1573/4
No. 42, A major, K. 526 1787
Hepzibah & Yehudi Menuhin
             2 12"—G-DB2057/8
Marguerite Long & Jacques Thibaud
             2 12"—G-W1571/2
C major—Andante & Allegro (unidentified)
Hubert Giesen & Lilia d'Albore
             12"—PD-67848
[Schubert: Sonatina, Op. 137, Pt. 3]

SONATAS—Organ & Orchestra

Collection
No. 4, D major, K. 144;
No. 10, F major, K. 244;
No. 11, D major, K. 245;
No. 14, C major, K. 278;
No. 16, C major, K. 328;
No. 17, C major, K. 336
E. Power Biggs & Arthur Fiedler's
Sinfonietta   3 12"—VM-1019
No. 1, E flat major, K. 67 (K. 41h) 1767
Gerald Bunk & Dortmund Conservatory
Orch.—Van Kempen 12"—PD-95290
[No. 17, C major, K. 336]
No. 4, D major, K. 144 (K. 124a) 1772
E. Power Biggs & Arthur Fiedler's
Sinfonietta, on V-11-8909, in VM-1019
No. 5, F major, K. 145 (K. 124b) 1772
Noëlie Pierront (Gonzalez organ) &
Orch.—Gerlin 12"—PAT-PAT74
[No. 15, C major, K. 329] (C-DZX16)
No. 10, F major, K. 244 1776
E. Power Biggs & Arthur Fiedler's
Sinfonietta, V-11-8909, in VM-1019
No. 11, D major, K. 245 1776
E. Power Biggs & Arthur Fiedler's
Sinfonietta, V-11-8910, in VM-1019
No. 14, C major, K. 278 (K. 271e) 1777
E. Power Biggs & Arthur Fiedler's
Sinfonietta, V-11-8910, in VM-1019

No. 15, C major, K. 329 (K. 317a) 1779
Noëlie Pierront (Gonzalez organ) &
Orch.—Gerlin 12"—PAT-PAT74
[No. 5, F major, K. 145] (C-DZX16)
No. 16, C major, K. 328 (K. 317c) 1779
E. Power Biggs & Arthur Fiedler's
Sinfonietta, V-11-8911, in VM-1019
No. 17, C major, K. 336 (K. 336d) 1780
E. Power Biggs & Arthur Fiedler's
Sinfonietta, V-11-8911, in VM-1019
Gerald Bunk & Dortmund Conservatory
Orch.—Van Kempen 12"—PD-95290
[No. 1, E flat major, K. 67]
SONGS In German
See also Arias
Als Luise die Briefe ihres ungetreuen
  Liebhabers verbrannte, K. 520 1787
  ("Unglückliche Liebe")
  (G. von Baumberg)
Erika Rokyta (s) & Noël Gallon (pf)
              10"—OL-29
[Der Zauberer & Das Traumbild]
An Chloe ("Wenn die Lieb' ") K. 524
  (J. G. Jacobi) 1787
Margherita Perras (s) & Paul
Baumgartner (pf) 10"—G-DA6028
[Warnung]
Irène Joachim (s) & Ludwig
Bergmann (pf) 10"—G-DA4917
[Dans un bois solitaire]
Lotte Lehmann (s) & Erno Balogh
  (in VM-292) 10"—V-1730
[Die Verschweigung]
Dans un bois solitaire, "Ariette" K. 308
  (K. 295b) (de la Motte) 1788
Irène Joachim (s) (in French) & Ludwig
Bermann (pf) 10"—G-DA4917
[An Chloe]
(Das) Lied der Trennung, K. 519
  (K. E. K. Schmidt) 1787
  ("Die Engel Gottes weinen")
Martha Angelici (s) & Jean Hubeau
(pf)   (in Vol. X) 12"—AS-93
[Un mota di gioia & Ridente la calma]
Ridente la calma, K. 152 (K. 210a)
1775 (Canzonetta)
Martha Angelici (s) & Jean Hubeau (pf)
      (in Vol. X) 12"—AS-93
[Un moto di gioia & Das lied der
Trennung]
Leïla Ben Sedira (s) & pf. acc.
             10"—G-DA5014
[Un moto di gioia & Oiseaux, si tous
les ans]
Sehnsucht nach dem Frühlinge, K. 596
  (Overbeck) 1791
  ["Komm lieber Mai"]
Wolfgang Kieling (treble) & Orch. with
Chorus 10"—G-EG6380
[Schubert: Heidenröslein]
(Das) Traumbild, K. 530 (Hölty) 1787
  ("Wo bist du, Bild")
Erika Rokyta (s) & Noël Gallon (pf)
[Als Luise & Der Zauberer] 10"—OL-29
Un moto di gioia, K. 579 1789
See under Arias
(Das) Veilchen, K. 476 (Goethe) 1775
  ("Ein Veilchen auf der Wiese stand")
Elisabeth Schumann (s) & Gerald
Moore (pf) 10"—G-DA1854
[Schubert: Dass sie hier gewesen]

Franz Völker (t) & Franz Rupp (pf)
10″—**PD-23468**
[Schumann: Die Lotusblume]
DUPLICATION: Jean Planel (in French),
PAT-PA841

(Die) Verschweigung, K. 518
(C. F. Weisse) 1787
("Sobald Damoetas Chloen sieht")
Lotte Lehmann (s) & Erno Balogh (pf)
[An Chloe] (in VM-292) 10″—**V-1730**
Irène Joachim (s) & Jean Germain (pf)
[Schubert: Litanei] 10″—**BAM-49**

Warnung, K. 433 (K. 416c) 1783
Originally Bass & Orchestra
("Männer suchen stets zu naschen")
Elisabeth Schumann (s) & George
Reeves (pf) (G-DA6006) 10″—**G-E555**
[Wiegenlied & Mahler: Wer hat das
Liedlein]
Margherita Perras (s) & Paul
Baumgartner (pf) 10″—**G-DA6028**
[An Chloe]
Erna Sack (s) & Wilhelm Czernik
(pf) 10″—**T-A10426**
[Schubert: Die Forelle]

Wiegenlied, K. 350 (K. Anh. 284f)
("Schlafe, mein Prinzchen")
(*Attributed to Mozart, this Lullaby is really
by Bernard Flies*)
Erna Berger (s) & Hans Altmann (pf)
[Brahms: Wiegenlied] 10″—**PD-47068**
Elisabeth Schumann (s) & Orch.—
Collingwood 10″—**G-E555**
[Warnung; Mahler: Wer hat das
Liedlein] (G-DA6006)
Gwen Catley (s) (in English) & Gerald
Moore (pf) 10″—**G-B9222**
[Mendelssohn: Auf Flügeln]
DUPLICATION: Erna Sack, T-A2257:
T-A10454; Wolfgang Kieling (treble)
with Chorus, G-EG6257; Felicie Hüni-
Mihacsek, PD-66757; Jo Vincent,
C-DH40; Jean Planel (in French),
PAT-PA841; Betty Martin (in English),
(in C-J17)

—**Arr. Chorus**
Dreising Children's Choir—Goedel,
PD-11535; Regensburg Cathedral Choir
—Schrems, T-A1552: T-A1507:
U-B18046
Also: Comedian Harmonists, G-EG2865;
Livschakoff Orch., PD-10090; Geczy
Orch., G-EG6201

(Der) Zauberer, K. 472 (C. F. Weisse) 1785
("Ihr Mädchen, flieht Damöten ja")
Erika Rokyta (s) & Noël Gallon (pf)
10″—**OL-29**
[Als Luise & Das Traumbild]
Suite, K. 399 (K. 385i) 1782 Piano
—**2nd Mvt. (Allemande) & 3rd Mvt.
(Courante) only**
Eileen Joyce 12″—**P-E11443**
[Sonata No. 15, C major, K. 545, Pt. 3]
—**Unidentified movement (Andantino)**
Cor de Groot 12″—**O-50548**
[Sonata No. 4, K. 282, Pt. 3]

SYMPHONIES Orchestra
No. 13, F major, K. 112 1771

—**2nd Mvt. (Andante) only**
Boyd Neel Orch.—Neel
(PD-516732) 12″—**D-K814**
[Serenade, K. 239, Pt. 3]
No. 20, D major, K. 133 1772
Vox Chamber Orch.—Edvard Fendler
2 12″—**VOX-171**
No. 25, G minor, K. 183 1773
Philharmonic-Symphony of New York—
Barbirolli 2 12″—**CX-217**†
No. 26, E flat major, K. 184 (K. 166a) 1773
Boston Symphony Orch.—
Koussevitzky 12″—**V-11-9363**
No. 28, C major, K. 200 (K.173e) 1773
Berlin Collegium Musicum—Fritz
Stein 2 12″—**G-EH1047/8**
No. 29, A major, K. 201 (K. 186a) 1774
London Philharmonic—Beecham
(C-LWX238/40) 3 12″—**CM-333**†
Boston Symphony Orch.—Koussevitzky
(in VM-795) 2 12″—**V-18063/4**
[with Symphony No. 34, C minor, K. 338]
(G-DB5957/8)
No. 31, D major, K. 297 (K. 300a)
("Paris") 1778
London Philharmonic—Beecham
3 12″—**CM-360**†
[Handel-Beecham: The Gods Go a-Beg-
ging—Minuet & Hornpipe]
(C-LX754/6) (C-LFX558/60)
No. 32, G major, K. 318 1779
BBC Symphony—Boult 12″—**G-DB6172**
Berlin Philharmonic—Hans von
Benda 12″—**T-E2317**
No. 33, B flat major, K. 319 1779
Vienna Philharmonic Orch.—Karajan
3 12″—**C-LX1006/8**†
[Nozze di Figaro—Overture]
London Mozart Orch.—Collins
3 12″—**D-K1249/51**†
[Divertimento No. 17—Minuet]
Chamber Orch.—Edwin Fischer
3 12″—**G-DB3083/5**
[Bach: Suite No. 3, D major—Air]
No. 34, C major, K. 338 1780
London Philharmonic—Beecham
(C-LX920/2†) 3 12″—**CM-548**†
Boston Symphony Orch.—Koussevitzky
(in VM-795†) 3 12″—**V-18065/7**
[Handel: Concerto grosso, No. 12—
Larghetto]
(G-DB5959/61S†—last side blank)
No. 35, D major, K. 385 ("Haffner") 1782
N. Y. Philharmonic-Symphony Orch.—
Toscanini 3 12″—**VM-65**†
[Gluck: Orfeo—Dance of the Blessed
Spirits]
(G-W1192/4) (G-D1782/4†)
(G-AW111/3)
London Philharmonic—Beecham
(C-LX851/3S†) 3 12″—**CM-399**†
(Last side blank)
EIAR Symphony—von Karajan
3 12″—**CET-RR8035/7**
[Nozze di Figaro-Overture, with Dresden
Philharmonic—van Kempen]
N.B.C. Symphony Orch.—Toscanini
3 12″—**VM-1172**†
[Gluck: Orfeo—Dance of the Blessed
Spirits]

Vienna Philharmonic Orch.—Böhm
    3 12"—G-DB7649/51
[Bach: Suite No. 3—Air]
Vienna Philharmonic Orch.—Schüler
    3 12"—PAT-PDT73/5
[Der Schauspieldirektor—Overture]

No. 36, C major, K. 425 ("Linz") 1783
  London Philharmonic—Beecham
    4 12"—CM-387†
  (C-LX797/800S†) (C-LWX300/3S)
  London Symphony—Jorda
    3 12"—D-K1538/40†
  Symphony Orch.—Marius-François
  Gaillard   4 10"—O-188918/21
No. 38, D major, K. 504 ("Prague") 1786
  Vienna Philharmonic—Walter
    3 12"—VM-457†
  London Philharmonic—Beecham
  (C-LX911/3†)   3 12"—CM-509†
  German Philharmonic Orch., Prague—
  Keilberth   3 12"—T-E3208/10
  Chicago Symphony Orch.—Stock
    3 12"—CM-410†
  St. Louis Symphony Orch.—Golschmann
    3 12"—VM-1085†
  Orch. of the Suisse Romande
    3 12"—In Prep. (Swiss Decca)

No. 39, E flat major, K. 543 1788
  BBC Symphony Orch.—Walter
  (G-DB2258/60†)   3 12"—VM-258†
  London Philharmonic Orch.—Wein-
  gartner   3 12"—C-GQX10928/30
  Winterthur Municipal Orch.—Scherchen
    3 12"—G-DB6097/9
  London Philharmonic Orch.—Beecham
  (C-LX927/9†)   3 12"—CM-456†
  National Symphony Orch.—Goehr
    3 12"—D-K1236/8†
  German Philharmonic Orch., Prague—
  Keilberth   3 12"—T-E3105/7
  Berlin Philharmonic Orch.—L. Ludwig
  (Fonit-91138/40) 3 12"—PD-67613/5
  Royal Theatre Orch., Copenhagen—
  Tango   3 12"—TONO-X25072/4
—3rd Mvt. (Menuet) only
  Tivoli Concert Orch.—Jensen, TONO-
  X25007

No. 40, G minor, K. 550 1788
  NBC Symphony Orch.—Toscanini
  (G-DB3790/2†)   3 12"—VM-631†
  Pittsburgh Symphony Orch.—Reiner
    3 12"—CM-727†
  (Also CMV-727: Vinylite)
  London Philharmonic Orch.—Beecham
  (C-LX656/8†)   3 12"—CM-316†
  (C-LWX214/6) (C-GQX10897/9)
  Orchestre de la Suisse Romande—
  Ansermet   3 12"—O-8782/4
  Berlin State Opera Orch.—R. Strauss
    4 12"—PD-95442/5
  [Adagio, K. 261, Kulenkampff]
  [Handel: Sonata, Op. 1, No. 9, Larghetto
  —Morini, on PD-69869/72]
  London Philharmonic Orch.—
  Koussevitsky   3 12"—VM-293†
  (G-DB2343/5)

No. 41, C major, K. 551 ("Jupiter") 1788
  NBC Symphony Orch.—Toscanini
    4 12"—VM-1080†
  [Bach: Suite No. 3—Air]

N. Y. Philharmonic-Symphony Orch.—
  Walter   4 12"—CM-565†
  [Così fan tutte—Overture]
  Vienna Philharmonic—Walter
    4 12"—VM-584†
  [Die Entführung aus dem Serail—
  Overture, dir. Krauss]
  [La Finta Giardiniera—Overture, on
  G-DB3428/31, in GM-307†]
  La Scala Orch.—Krauss
    In Prep. Eng. Decca
  Munich Philharmonic—Kabasta
    4 12"—G-DB5648/51
  [Serenade No. 6, K. 239—Rondo only]
  London Philharmonic—Beecham
    4 12"—CM-194†
  (C-LX282/5) (C-LFX339/42)
  [Handel: Sarabande & Tambourin]
  Orchestre de la Suisse Romande— An-
  sermet   4 12"—O-8778/81

TRIOS—Piano, Violin & 'Cello
B flat major, K. 502 1786
  Trio di Trieste   3 12"—G-AW326/8
  Munich Chamber Music Ensemble
    3 12"—PD-95230/2

TRIO—Clarinet, Viola & Piano
E flat major, K. 498 1786
  Reginald Kell, Frederick Riddle & Louis
  Kentner   3 12"—C-DX998/1000†
  Luigi Amodio, R. Nel, & S. Schultze
    3 12"—CET-OR5099/101

TRIO—String
See under Divertimenti

VARIATIONS—Piano
(12) Variations, C major, on "Ah! vous
  dirai-je, maman" K. 265 (K. 300e) 1778
—Arr. Soprano & Orchestra Adolphe Adam
  *Usually known as the Mozart-Adam Variations,
  this coloratura showpiece was introduced in
  Adam's opera "Le Toreador" and is frequently
  interpolated in the Lesson Scene of Rossini's
  "Il Barbiere di Siviglia."*
  Miliza Korjus (in German)
    12"—V-13826
  [Donizetti: La Zingara—Aria]
  [Rossini: Il Barbiere di Siviglia—Una
  voce poco, fà, on G-C2688]
  [Alabiev: Nightingale Song, on
  G-EH860]
  DUPLICATIONS: Galli-Curci, G-DB262*;
  Erna Sack, T-E3063
(10) Variations, G major, on a Theme by
  Gluck, K. 455 1784 Piano
  (Theme: "Unser dummer Pöbel meint"
  from "Die Pilger von Mekka")
  Lubka Kolessa   12"—G-DB4621
—Arr. Orchestra Tchaikovsky (Part IV of
  Suite No. 4 "Mozartiana")
  Philharmonic-Symphony Orch. of N. Y.—
  Rodzinski (in CX-248†) 12"—C-12115D
  *(Variations 6, 7, 8 omitted and 9, 10 cut in
  this performance)*
(12) Variations, B flat major, on an Alle-
  gretto, K. 500 1786 Piano
  Alexander Borovsky
  (PD-516640)   12"—PD-27341
(9) Variations, D major, on a Minuet of Du-
  port, K. 573 1786 Piano
  Dirk Schäfer   12"—C-DHX14

Vesperae solennes de confessore, K. 339

1780 In Latin
—No. 5, Laudate Dominum Soprano &
Chorus (old K. Anh. 115)
Ursula van Dieman, Berlin Philharmonic
Chorus & Orch.—Ochs
(G-EH173) 12″—G-C2736
[Mendelssohn: Ave Maria]
[Ave, verum, on G-FKX18]
[Verdi: Ave Maria—M. Perras & Chorus
on G-EH1223: G-S10478]
Erika Rokyta, Chorus & Orch.—Raugel
[Psalm: De Profundis] 12″—OL-48
Yves Tinayre (t) & Chorus
12″—LUM-33022
[Albert: Todeslied & Hammerschmidt:
Danklied]
(in Tinayre Album No. 2)

MUDARRA, Alfonso (Alonso de) (16th Century)

A Spanish lutenist who published a book of pieces for that instrument in 1546.

De la sangre de tus nobles
Max Meili (t) & Fritz Wörsching
(vihuela) 12″—G-DB5016
[Triste estaba & Valderrabano: Señora,
si te olvidare & Al monte sale]

La mañana de San Juan
Max Meili (t) & Fritz Wörsching
(vihuela) 12″—G-DB5017
[Milan: Perdida tengo & Durandarte]

Triste estaba el Rey David
Max Meili (t) & Fritz Wörsching
(vihuela) 12″—G-DB5016
[De la sangre & Valderrabanno: Señora &
Al monte sale]

MULE, Giuseppe (1885-)

An Italian composer, director of the Conservatory of Palermo, known mostly for his operas, although he has also composed orchestral and chamber music.

DAFNI Opera 1928
Danza Satiresca Orchestra
EIAR Symphony—La Rosa Parodi
10″—CET-TI7005
[Rozzi: Moto Perpetuo]
Largo Strings, Harmonium, Harps & Piano
EIAR Symphony—Tansini
12″—CET-CB20244
[Pizzini: Symphony, C minor—Scherzo]
Symphony Orch.—Dino Oliviero
12″—G-S10490
[Trentinaglia: L'Apparizione]
Vendemmia
EIAR Symphony—La Rosa Parodi
12″—CET-CB20300

MULET, Henri (1878-)

A French organist who is best known by the one work listed below.

Esquisses byzantines
No. 10, Toccata, F sharp minor, "Tu es
Petra"
Virgil Fox 12″—V-11-8467
[Vierne: Symphony No. 2—Scherzo]

MUSSORGSKY, Modeste (1835-1881)

Probably the greatest of the Russian nationalists, Mussorgsky was one of the most unusual examples of sheer genius in all art, tonal or otherwise. With a vividness of imagination, originality of technique and depth of compassion, his scores reflect the whole psychology of Russian life.

During the last few years more of his music has been added to record catalogues, especially in releases through the USSR. Larger excerpts of "Boris Godounov" have been made available, although there is a definite need for examples of the original scoring—not that edited by Rimsky-Korsakov.

Arise beautiful sun (Robber song) Chorus
Russian State Choir—Klimoff
[Leontovitch: Koliadka] 10″—G-EK59

Gopak (Hopak)
See under Operas—Fair at Sorochinsk,
also under Songs

(A) Night on Bald Mountain—Fantasia
Orchestra
Fr. Une Nuit sur le Mont Chauve
Pittsburgh Symphony—Reiner
12″—C-12470D
Philadelphia Orch.—Stokowski
(G-DB5900) 12″—V-17900
London Symphony Orch.—A. Coates
2 12″—D-K1317/8
[Fair at Sorochinsk—Gopak]
Orchestra of the "Maggio Musicale"—
Markevitch 12″—CET-BB25162
Berlin Philharmonic—Konoye
12″—PD-67259
La Scala Orch.—Ferrera 12″—G-AW307
DUPLICATIONS: London Symphony—
Coates, G-AW274; Colonne Orch.—Paray,
C-68305D: C-LX384: C-BFX14; Lamoureux Orch.—Wolff, PD-66952: PD-566006

OPERAS In Russian

BORIS GODUNOV Prologue & 4 Acts 1874
The order of items used here is that of the Rimsky-Korsakov version, on which all recordings are based.

Collection
Prelude, Opening Chorus; Coronation
Scene; Prelude to Scene 1, Act I; Varlaam's Song "In the Town of Kazan";
Boris' Monologue "I have attained the
highest power"; Duet—Boris & Prince
Shuisky; Clock Scene; Boris' Farewell
and Death
Alexander Kipnis (bs) with Chorus (dir.
Robert Shaw) & Victor Symphony Orch.
—Berezowsky 5 12″—VM-1000†

Collection
Prologue; Coronation Scene; Boris' Monologue "I have attained the highest power"; Clock Scene; Polonaise; Pimen's
Tale; Boris' Farewell & Death
Ezio Pinza (bs) in Italian, with Metropolitan Opera Chorus & Orch.—Cooper
5 12″—CM-563†

Orchestral Excerpts Arr. Stokowski
(Based on the original, not Rimsky-Korsakov's version)

Philadelphia Orch.—Stokowski
(G-DB3244/6)   3   12"—VM-391†
All American Orch.—Stokowski
    3   12"—CM-516†
Prologue—Scene 1
Prelude Orchestra
Opening Chorus: Why has thou abandoned
us? & Pilgrim's Chorus
It. Ma perchè tu ci abbandoni? & Boris è
inflessible!
Chorus (in Russian) & Victor Symphony
—Berezowsky, on V-11-8763 in VM-
1000†
Metropolitan Cho. (in Italian) & Orch.—
Cooper, C-71646D in CM-563†
DUPLICATION: La Scala Chorus,
C-GQX10264
Prologue—Scene 2
"Coronation Scene"—Bass & Chorus
Alexander Kipnis, & Cho. on V-11-
8763/4 in VM-1000†
Feodor Chaliapin (in Russian) & Chorus
(in Italian) (G-DB900)   12"—V-11485
Ezio Pinza & Cho. (in It.), C-71647D in
CM-563†
—Arr. 2 Pianos Luboshutz
Pierre Luboshutz & Genia Nemenoff
[Cui: Orientale]   10"—V-2084
—Boris' part only (My soul is sad) Bass
Vanni-Marcoux (in French), G-DB4950

ACT I
Scene I
Pimen's Monologue: Still one more page
M. Mikhailov (bs)   10"—USSR-12244/5
Scene 2
Introduction Orchestra
Victor Symphony—Berezowsky, on V-11-
8764 in VM-1000†
Varlaam's Song: In the Town of Kazan
Bass
Alexander Kipnis, on V-11-8764 in VM-
1000†
Feodor Chaliapin   10"—G-DA891
[Borodin: Prince Igor—Prince Galit-
zky's Song]
DUPLICATION: C. E. Kaidanoff,
G-EK93
Scene: Varlaam, Hostess, Gregory, Misail &
Guard
Eng. Come, now, comrades, fill your glasses
Alexander Kipnis (bs), Anna Leskaya
(c), Ilya Tamarin (t)
    (in VM-1073)   12"—V-11-9285
[Borodin: Prince Igor—Prince Galitzky's
Song]
ACT II
Song of the Gnat
Derek Barsham (treble) & Gladys Palmer
(c) (in English)   12"—D-K1601
[Song of the Parrot]
Monologue: I have attained the highest
power Bass
Fr. J'ai le pouvoir suprême It. Ho il
poter supremo
Alexander Kipnis, on V-11-8765 in VM-
1000†
Feodor Chaliapin   12"—V-14517
[Clock Scene, Act II] (G-DB1532)
In French: Vanni-Marcoux, G-DB1112;
José Beckmans, PD-516618

In Italian: Ezio Pinza, C-71648D in CM-
563†
Song of the Parrot
Derek Barsham (treble) & Norman
Lumsden (bs) (in English)
[Song of the Gnat]   12"—D-K1601
Duet: Boris & Prince Shuisky Bass & Tenor
Alexander Kipnis & Ilya Tamarin, on
V-11-8765/6 in VM-1000†
Clock Scene: Ah! I am suffocating Bass
Alexander Kipnis, on V-11-8766 in VM-
1000†
Feodor Chaliapin
(G-DB1532)   12"—V-14517
[Monologue, Act II]
In French: Vanni-Marcoux, G-DB1112
In Italian: Ezio Pinza, C-71648D in CM-
563†

ACT III
Scene 2
Polonaise Soprano, Chorus & Orchestra
Metropolitan Opera Chorus (in Italian) &
Orch.—Cooper
    (in CM-563)   12"—C-71649D
[Pimen's Tale, Pinza]
Oh! Czarevitch Duo: Soprano & Tenor
(Fountain, or Garden Scene)
Friedel Beckmann & Helge Roswaenge
(in German)   12"—G-DB5593
H. A. Sadoven & N. I. Nagachevsky
    10"—G-EK94
[Rimsky-Korsakov: Sadko-Chanson
Hindoue, Nagachevsky]
—Arr. Orch. Kindler
National Symphony Orch.—Hans
Kindler   12"—G-C3346
[Shostakovich: Age of Gold—Polka]

ACT IV
Scene 1
(*Scene 2 in original version*)
Revolutionary Scene Chorus only
La Scala Chorus (in Italian)
[Pilgrim's Chorus]   12"—C-GQX10264
Hamburg State Opera Chorus & Orch.—
Jochum (in German)   12"—T-E1934
[Moniuszko: Halka-Heut' ist Sonntag]
Scene 2
(*Scene 1 in original version*)
Pimen's Tale: A peaceful monk & One eve-
ning I was alone Bass
Ezio Pinza (in Italian) & Orch.—Cooper
    (in CM-563)   12"—C-71649D
[Polonaise]
Farewell, my son, I am dying Bass
Death of Boris: Hark the Passing Bell Bass
& Chorus
Alexander Kipnis & Cho., on V-11-8767
in VM-1000†
(Also on V-11-8925)
Feodor Chaliapin, Chorus & Orch.—
Goossens (G-DB934)   12"—V-6724
[With Royal Opera Chorus, Covent Gar-
den—Bellezza, V-15177: G-DB3464]
Ezio Pinza & Cho. (in Italian) on
C-71650D in CM-563†
Wilhelm Strienz & Cho. (in German)
    12"—G-DB5594
—Farewell only
Vanni-Marcoux (in French) G-DB1114

(THE) FAIR AT SOROCHINSK 3 Acts
1887
*Mussgorksky wrote only fragments of this
opera; it was completed by N. Tcherepnin.*
Individual Excerpts
Act III
Parissia's Song (Day Dream) Soprano
Xenia Belmas 12"—PD-66748
[Rimsky-Korsakov: La Rose et la Ros-
signol]
Ada Slobodskaya & pf. acc.
10"—G-EK113
[Rubinstein: The Rose & Rachmaninoff:
Lilacs]
Gopak (Hopak) Fr. **Danse petite russienne**
CBS Symphony Orch.—Barlow
12"—C-71464D
[Rubinstein: Melody in F; Ippolitov-
Ivanov: Caucasian Sketches—March of
the Sardar]
London Symphony Orch.—A. Coates
12"—D-K1318
[Night on Bald Mountain, Pt. 3]
London Philharmonic—Walter Goehr
12"—C-DX828
[Borodin: Prince Igor—Girl's Dance]
(C-DFX214)
DUPLICATIONS: London Symphony—
Coates, G-AW240; Lamoureux Orch.—
A. Wolff, PD-66968: PD-566026
—Arr. Volin: J. Szigeti, C-17311D

KHOVANTCHINA 4 Acts 1885
(Orchestrated by Rimsky-Korsakov)
Individual Excerpts
Prelude Orchestra
Boston Symphony Orch.—Koussevitzky
(G-DB3260) 12"—V-14415
Cleveland Orch.—Rodzinski
(in CM-478) 12"—C-11657D
[Tchaikovsky: Romeo & Juliet, Pt. 5]
Hallé Orch.—Harty
(C-9908) 12"—C-67743D
[Rimsky-Korsakov: Flight of the Bumble
Bee]
ACT III
Entr'acte Orchestra
EIAR Symphony—Willy Ferrero
12"—CET-PP60004
[Rimsky-Korsakov: Flight of the Bum-
ble Bee]
Shaklovitov's Aria Baritone
Eng. **The Streltsys are sleeping**
A. Ivanov 10"—USSR-12732/3

ACT IV
Dances of the Persian Slaves Orchestra
Royal Philharmonic—Beecham
(G-DB6450) 12"—V-12-0239
Columbia Broadcasting Symphony—
Barlow 10"—C-17286D
DUPLICATIONS: London Symphony—
Coates, G-AW179; Milan Symphony—
Molajoli, C-GQ7185
Pictures at an Exhibition Piano 1874
Benno Moisewitsch 4 12"—G-C3576/9†
Alexander Brailowsky 4 12"—VM-861†
—**The Great Gate of Kiev** only
C. Guilbert, C-LFX607
—**Arr. Orchestra** Maurice Ravel
New York Philharmonic-Symphony Orch.
—Rodzinski 4 12"—CM-641†

[Fair at Sorochinsk-Gopak]
Boston Symphony Orch.—Koussevitzky
(G-DB1890/3) 4 12"—VM-102†
Paris Conservatory Orch.—Giardino
4 12"—PAT-PDT84/7†
Berlin State Opera Orch.—Melichar
4 12"—PD-27246/9
[Glinka: Kamarinskaya]
—**Arr. Orchestra** Lucien Cailliet
Philadelphia Orch.—Ormandy
4 12"—VM-442†
—**Arr. Orchestra** Leopold Stokowski
*(Promenade, Tuileries & Market Place at Lim-
oges omitted)*
Philadelphia Orch.—Stokowski
(G-DB5827/30†) 4 12"—VM-706†
All American Orch.—Stokowski
4 12"—CM-511†

SONGS In Russian

Individual Songs
(In alphabetical order by English title)
Death's Lullaby See Songs & Dances of
Death No. 2
Death's Serenade See Songs and Dances of
Death No. 3
Elegy See Sunless Cycle No. 5
Evening Prayer. Nursery No. 5
Betty Martin, in English, in C-J14
Nelson Eddy (b) in English
[Song of the Flea] 10"—C-17312D
Field Marshall Death See Songs & Dances
of Death No. 4
Hopak (Gopak) (Cheftchenko-Mey)
Nelson Eddy (b) (in English)
10"—C-17366D
[Tchaikovsky: Legend—Christ had a
garden]
DUPLICATION: Alexander Koubitsky,
C-DF12
(See also under Fair at Sorochinsk for
different Hopak)
(The) Nursery Song Cycle (7 Episodes of
Child Life)
1. With Nanny 2. Go into the Corner 3.
The Beetle 4. Dolly's Cradle Song 5. Eve-
ning Prayer 6. The Hobby Horse 7.
Naughty Pussy (or, The cat and the bird
cage)
Betty Martin (s) (in English) & Sergius
Kagan (pf) 2 10"—C-J14
(No. 4 omitted in the above collection)
Song of the Flea (from Goethe's "Faust")
Fr. **Chanson de la Puce** Ger. **Flohlied**
Feodor Chaliapin (bs) 12"—V-14901
[Koenemann: Song of the Volga Boat-
men]
[Rossini: Barbiere di Siviglia—La
Calunnia, on G-DB932]
Alexander Kipnis (bs)
(in VM-1073) 12"—V-11-9286
[Dargomijsky: Russalka-Miller's Aria]
Marian Nowakowski (bs) 12"—D-K1172
[Koenemann: King went forth to war]
Nelson Eddy (b) (in English)
[Evening Prayer] 10"—C-17312D
Lawrence Tibbett (b) (in English)
12"—V-7779
[Tchaikovsky: Pilgrim Song]
DUPLICATIONS: Heinrich Schlusnus (in

German), PD-67057; C. E. Kaidanov, G-EK93

In French: José Beckmans, PD-516618; Etienne Billot, O-123779

In English: Peter Dawson, G-C1579; Oscar Natzke, C-DB2363

In Bohemian: D. Beljanin, ESTA-D2110

Song of the Old Man Fr. Chant du Viellard Jacques Bastard (bs) (in French)
10"—PAT-PG53
[Gretchaninov: The Captive]

(4) Songs and Dances of Death (Song Cycle) (Golenischtschew-Kutusow)
1. Trepak 2. Death's Lullaby 3. Death's Serenade 4. Field Marshal Death
Marko Rothmüller (b) (in German) & Suzanne Gyr (pf)
2 12"—G-DB10062/3

—**No. 1 (Trepak) only**
Feodor Chaliapin (bs) 12"—G-DB1511
[Serov: Hostile Power—Merry Butterweek]

—**No. 4 (Field Marshal Death) only**
Charles Soix (b) (in French) & pf. acc.
[Rubinstein: Extase] 12"—PAT-PDT112

Sunless (Song Cycle) 6 Songs 1874/5
1. Within Four Walls 2. In the Throng 3. The Idle Noisy Day is Over 4. Bored 6. Over the River

—**No. 1 (Within Four Walls) only**
Paul Robeson (bs) (in English) & Lawrence Brown (pf) 12"—C-71367D
[Gretchaninoff: Cradle Song]

Trepak See Songs & Dances of Death No. 1

MYLIUS

Ein Mägdlein stund
Die Kantorei der Staadlichen Hochschule für Musik, Berlin—Thomas
12"—T-E2926
[Dowland: Süsse Lieb; Hassler: Ach weh des luden; & Schein: Wenn Philli ihre Liebesstrahl]

MYSLEVICEK, Josef (1737-1781)

A Bohemian composer who studied in Italy, Myslevicek wrote operas, oratorios, symphonic and chamber works.

Divertimento for Cembalo
—Rondo only
J. Langer (harpsichord)
[Benda: Presto] 10"—U-B12385

NANINI (Nanino), Giovanni Maria (c.1545-1607)

An important leader of the Roman school of polyphonists.

Diffusa es Gratia Motet, Unacc. Chorus in Latin
Schola St. León IX—Gaudard
12"—PAT-X93053
[Aichinger: Regina coeli & Victoria: Vere languores]

NAPRAVNIK, Eduard (1839-1916)

A Bohemian composer closely associated with the musical scene in Russia, where he spent most of his life.

DON JUAN Op. 54 Incidental Music

Don Juan's Serenade Song in Russian
Adolf Katin (bs) & pf. acc.
10"—G-EV19
[Rimsky-Korsakov: Gonets]

NAUDOT, Jean Ch. (or Jaques) (18th Cent.)

A French composer who wrote for the vielle and flute.

Sonata for 2 Flutes
Marcel & Louis Moyse 10"—OL-26
[Bate: Sonata for Fl. & Pf., Pt. 3]

NEDBAL, Oskar (1874-1930)

A Czech composer, conductor and viola player, Nedbal was a pupil of Dvorák. He was well known as a conductor and his operas and operettas are often performed in his own country.

POLISH BLOOD Operetta in Czech
Selections
Vera Cechová, Jara Pospisil, Karel Leiss, Karel Kalaš (vocals) with Chorus & FOK Orch.—Rene Kubinsky
12"—U-F12471

Valse Triste
FOK Symphony Orch.—Vačlav Smetáček
12"—U-F12467
[Fibich: Poème, with Czech Broadcasting Orch.—Jirák]

NEGLIA, F. P.

Trio, Op. 54 Piano, Violin & Harp
Bolzano Trio 2 12"—G-S10497/8
[Idyll for Trio, Op. 42]

Il Saluto di Beatrice
Come quel fior
Giulietta Simionato (ms) & Renzo (pf)
10"—G-HN2145

NEKES, Franz (1844-1914)

A Rhenish priest and church musician, Nekes was the composer of many masses and motets.

O crux ave Motet in Latin
Aachen Cathedral Choir—Rehmann
10"—PD-22757
[Handl: Ecce quomodo, Dortmund Conservatory Choir]

Regina coeli Motet in Latin
Aachen Cathedral Choir—Rehmann
10"—PD-22593
[Freith: Freu' dich, Dortmund Conservatory Choir]

NESSLER, Victor E. (1841-1890)

A German opera composer, Nessler is remembered chiefly by the work listed below.

DER TROMPETER VON SAKKINGEN

Opera in German 1884
Behüt' dich Gott Bar.
Heinrich Schlusnus 12"—PD-35036
[Hermann: Die drei Wandern]
[Marschner: Hans Heiling—Am jenem tag, on PD-67191]
[Lortzing: Zar und Zimmermann—Sonst spielt ich, on PD-67255]
Willy Schneider 12"—PD-15352
[Pressel: An der Wesser]

Hans Reinmar 12″—T-E1832
[Abt: Das Glöcklein des Ermiten—Wenn man]
—Arr. Trumpet solo: Hans Bode, PD-11048

NEUBAUER, Franz Christoph (1760-1795)

Adagio Flute & Viola
Marcel Moyse & Blanche Honegger
12″—G-DB5080
[Handel: Sonata for 2 flutes]

NEVIN, Ethelbert (1862-1901)

An American composer of songs and piano pieces, Nevin is known for his two salon pieces, "The Rosary" and "Narcissus."

SONGS In English

Little Boy Blue (Field)
John McCormack (t) 10″—V-1458
[The Rosary]

Mighty lak' a Rose
Paul Robeson (bs) 10″—G-B3199
[Phillips: Just keepin' on]
—Arr. Violin: Fritz Kreisler, V-1320

(The) Rosary (Rogers)
Ger. **Der Rosenkranz**
John McCormack (t) 10″—V-1458
[Little Boy Blue]
Richard Crooks (t) 10″—V-1634
[Gounod: Nazareth] (G-DA1288)
Nelson Eddy (b)
(in V-C27) 10″—V-4370
[Koven: Robin Hood—O Promise Me]
[Bond: A Perfect Day on G-DA1589]
Risë Stevens, in CM-654
DUPLICATIONS: Thomas L. Thomas & Chorus, V-11-9190
In German: Wilhelm Strienz, G-EG6944
—Arr. Violin Kreisler
Fritz Kreisler & Carl Lamson (pf)
[Mighty lak' a rose] 10″—V-1320
DUPLICATION: S. Filon, PD-524017
—Arr. Viola
William Primrose & Victor Symphony
Orch.—O'Connell 12″—V-18222
[Dvořák: Humoresque]
—Arr. Orchestra
Andre Kostelanetz & his Orch., in CM-681; Livschakoff Orch., PD-23648

NICOLAI, Karl (1810-1849)

A German conductor and opera composer, Nicolai is remembered today for the overture to "Die lustigen Weiber von Windsor."

OPERA In German

(DIE) LUSTIGEN WEIBER VON WINDSOR 1849
Eng. **The Merry Wives of Windsor**
Abridged Recording Arr. Weigert & Maeder
Soloists, Berlin State Opera Chorus & Orch.—Weigert
4 12″—PD-27399/402
(The Cast includes: Else Ruziczka, Elfriede Maherr-Wagner, Eduard Kandl, Armin Weltner, etc.)

Vocal Selections (Potpourri)
Soloists, Chorus & Orch. of Berlin Opera House—Schüler 12″—T-E2361
Hildegard Erdmann, Arno Schellenberg & Wilhelm Strienz 12″—G-EH1298

Overture Orchestra
London Philharmonic—Beecham
12″—C-68938D
(C-LX596) (C-LFX540) (C-LWX168)
(Also C-71622D in CM-552†)
Liverpool Philharmonic—Maurice Miles
12″—C-DX1201
Berlin Philharmonic—Böhm
12″—G-DB4444
New Queen's Hall Orch.—Wood
12″—C-DX819
Boston "Pops" Orch.—Fiedler
(G-C3215) 12″—V-12533
B.B.C. Symphony—Boult
(G-DB2195) 12″—V-11836
National Symphony Orch.—Victor Olof
12″—D-K1303
Berlin Philharmonic—E. Kleiber
12″—T-E1713
Orch. of the Suisse Romande—Blech
In Prep. **Swiss Decca**
DUPLICATIONS: Vienna State Opera Orch.—Reichwein, O-7874; Berlin State Opera Orch.—Van Kempen, PD-15302; Berlin State Opera Orch.—Kleiber, PD-66556

Individual Excerpts
Als Büblein klein, Act II Bass
Wilhelm Schirp 10″—T-A10001
[Flotow: Marta-Porterlied]
DUPLICATION: Willy Schneider, PD-47435

Horch, die Lerche (Romanze) Act II Tenor
Peter Anders 10″—T-A2466
[Flotow: Martha-Ach, so fromm]
Walther Ludwig 12″—G-EH1020
[Mozart: Zauberflöte-Flötenarie]
Julius Patzak 12″—PD-30014
[Thomas: Mignon—Adieu, Mignon]
DUPLICATION: Koloman von Pataky, PD-66648

Nun eilt nerbei (Arie der Frau Fluth) Soprano
Eng. **Mistress Ford's aria**
Felicie Hüni-Mihacsek 12″—PD-66586

NIELSEN, Carl (1865-1931)

The foremost Danish composer of recent years. Nielsen, a pupil of Nils Gade in Copenhagen, is best known for his symphonic works and songs.

ALADDIN Incidental Music to the play by Adam Oehlenschläger
Suite
Negro Dance, Aladdin's Dream, Dance of the Morning Fog, The Market in Ispahan, Oriental Festival March, Hindu Dance
Tivoli Concert Orch.—Felumb
2 12″ & 10″—G-Z231/2 & X4676
[Maskarade—Prelude, Act II on G-Z232]
—**Oriental Festival March & Negro Dance** only
Royal Opera House Orch., Copenhagen—Hye-Knudsen 12″—NP-HM80014

Andante lamentoso
Danish State Radio Symphony Orch.—
Launy Grøndahl   12″—G-Z294
[Hartmann: Sørgemarsch for Bertel
Thorwaldsen]

Chaconne, Op. 32 Piano
Hermann D. Koppel   12″—G-DB5236
(Also G-DB5254)

Concerto, Op. 57 Clarinet & Orch.
Louis Cahuzac & Royal Theatre Orch.—
John Frandsen   3   12″—C-LDX7000/1

Concerto, Op. 33 Violin & Orchestra
Emil Telmanyi & Royal Opera House
Orch., Copenhagen—Tango
    5   12″—TONO-X25081/5
[Mozart: Serenade No. 7—Minuet]

Du danska Mand Chorus in Danish
Bel Canto Chorus   10″—G-AL1282
[Hornemann: Homas faste Stok]

En Sagadrøm Orchestra Eng. A Saga Dream
Royal Theatre Orch., Copenhagen—
Tango   12″—G-DB5263
Royal Theatre Orch., Copenhagen—Hye-
Knudsen   12″—NP-HM80013

Five Pieces, Op. 3 Piano
Galina Werschenska   12″—TONO-A123

FYNSK FORAAR Soloists, Cho. & Orch.
Eng. Funen Springtime
Den milde Dag er lys og lang
Aksel Schiøtz (t) & Copenhagen Philhar-
monic Orch.—Felumb   10″—G-X6612
[Moderen—Min Pige er saa lys som Rav]
(Also on G-X6311)

Helios Overture
Royal Theatre Orch., Copenhagen—Th.
Jensen   2   12″—O-DXX8002/3

Humoresque-Bagatelle, Op. 11 Piano
Galina Werschenska   10″—G-DA5203

Little Suite for Strings, Op. 1
Strings of the Royal Theatre Orch., Copenhagen—Thomas Jensen
        2   12″—G-DB5256/7

MASKARADE Opera
Overture & Hanedans (Cock Dance)
Copenhagen Theatre Orch.—Hye-Knud-
sen   12″—G-Z264
(Also on G-Z230)
Overture only
Danish Radio Symphony Orch.—Malko
        12″—G-Z296
[Svendsen: Carneval in Paris, Pt. 3]
Danish Radio Symphony Orch.—Tuxen
        12″—NP-HM80010
[Lange-Müller: Renaissance—Prelude]
Royal Opera House Orch., Copenhagen—
Tango   12″—TONO-X25077
[Flogging Court Scene]
Hanedans only
Tivoli Concert Orch.—Jensen
        12″—TONO-X25008
[Lange-Müller: Renaissance—Prelude]
Jeronimus Sang Bar.
Holger Byrding, O-D176; Einar Nørby,
C-J51: TONO-X25078
Flogging Court Scene Bar.
Einar Nørby   12″—TONO-X25077
[Overture, Royal Opera House Orch.]

Finale, Act I
Holger Byrding (b), Marius Jacobsen
(t), Einar Nørby (b), Poul Wiedemann
& Elith Foss (t)   12″—TONO-X25078
[Jeronimus Sang]
Prelude to Act II
Royal Theatre Orch., Copenhagen—Hye-
Knudsen   12″—G-Z232
[Aladdin—The Market in Ispahan, dir.
Felumb]
Magdelones Dansescene Eng. Magdelone's
Dancing Scene
Ingeborg Steffensen (s) Einar Nørby (b)
& Aksel Schiøtz (t)   12″—G-DB5237
[Hartmann: Liden Kirsten—Tavlebords-
duetten]

MODEREN Music for the Festival Play by
Helge Rode
Eng. The Mother
Prelude to Scene 7 & Faedrelandssang
(Patriotic Song)
Royal Theatre Orch. & Chorus, Copen-
hagen—Hye-Knudsen   12″—G-Z237
[Lange-Müller: Renaissance—Prelude]
Royal Theatre Orch., Copenhagen—Th.
Jensen   12″—O-DDX8003
[March]
Prelude only
Tivoli Orch.—Jensen
        12″—TONO-X25002
[Saul & David, Prelude to Act II]
Danish Radio Symphony Orch.—Tuxen
[March]   12″—NP-HM80012
Skjaldens Vise: Saa bittert var mit hjerte
Eng. Song of the Scald—So bitter was my
heart
Aksel Schiøtz (t) & Copenhagen Royal
Theatre Orch.—Hye-Knudsen
        12″—G-DB5241
[Lange-Müller: Renaissance—Serenade]
March
Royal Theatre Orch., Copenhagen—Th.
Jensen   12″—O-DDX8003
[Prelude to Scene 7 & Faedrelandssang]
Danish Radio Symphony Orch.—Tuxen
[Prelude to Scene 7]   12″—NP-HM80012
**Skjaldens anden Vise: Min Pige er saa lys
som Rav**
Eng. Second Song of the Scald—My girl
is as fair as amber
Aksel Schiøtz (t) & Royal Theatre Orch.
—Hye-Knudsen   10″—G-X6612
[Fynsk Foraar—Den milde Dag er lys og
lang]
Aksel Schiøtz (t) & Chr. Christiansen
(pf)   10″—G-X6065
[Jeg Baerer med Smil & I Solen gaar
bag min Plov]
DUPLICATION: Thyge Thygesen,
O-D834
Taagen letter Eng. The fog is lifting
Gilbert Jespersen (fl) & Valborg Paulsen
(harp)   12″—G-DB5203
[Quintet for Wind Instruments, Pt. 7]
Quartet, F major, Op. 44 Strings
Erling Bloch Quartet 3   12″—G-DB1/3
Quintet for Wind Instruments, Op. 43
Danish Quintet   4   12″—G-DB5200/3
[Taagen letter, Jespersen & Paulsen]

To Fantasistykker, Op. 2 Oboe & Piano
Eng. Two Fantasies
1. Humoresque 2. Romance
S. C. Felumb & Chr. Christiansen
10″—G-DA5204
—No. 2 (Romance) only
—Arr. Violin & Piano
Emil Telmanyi & Gerald Moore
12″—G-DB2503
[Sibelius: Romance, Op. 72, No. 2 &
Danse Champêtre, Op. 106, No. 2]

SAUL AND DAVID Opera 1902
Prelude, Act II
Tivoli Orch.—Jensen
12″—TONO-X25002
[Moderen, Prelude to Scene 7]
Danish Radio Symphony Orch.—Tuxen
12″—NP-HM80009
[Symphony No. 3, Pt. 9]
Serenata in vano
A. Oxenvad (cl), K. Lassen (bsn), Hans
Sørensen (horn), L. Jensen (vlc), &
Hegner (bs)   12″—G-DB5204

SONATAS—Violin & Piano
No. 1, A major, Op. 9
Emil Telmanyi & Chr. Christiansen
3 12″—G-DB2732/4
No. 2, G minor, Op. 35
Erling Bloch & Lund Christiansen
2 12″—G-DB5219/20

SONGS In Danish

Aebleblomsten, Op. 10, No. 1 (Ludv.
Holstein)
Else Ammentorp (s), G-X4574; Edith
Oldrup-Pedersen (s), G-DA5217
Aftenstemning (Carsten Hauch)
College Men's Choral Union—Hye-Knud-
sen, G-X6344
Den danske Sang (Kaj Hoffmann)
Edi Laider (b), G-X4657: G-X6657
Aksel Schiøtz (t) & H. D. Koppel
10″—G-X6605
[Havet omkring Danmark]
Farvel, min velsigneds Føderby (P. M.
Møller)
Aksel Schiøtz (t) G-G6988: G-X6257
**Genrebillede: Pagen højt paa Taarnet sad,
Op. 6, No. 1** (J. P. Jacobsen)
Aksel Schiøtz (t), G-X6606
Agnete Zacharias (ms), G-X4574
Grøn er Vaarens Haek (P. M. Møller)
Aksel Schiøtz (t), G-X6988: G-X6257
Havet omkring Danmark (L. C. Nielsen)
Aksel Schiøtz (t), G-X6605
Einar Nørby (b), G-X4573
Havren
Aksel Schiøtz, G-X6695; Edith Oldrup-
Pedersen, G-DA5219
Hymne til Danmark (V. Rørdam)
"Danmark i tusind Aar"
Aksel Schiøtz (t), G-X6631
I Aften, Op. 10, No. 5 (Ludwig Holstein)
Aksel Schiøtz (t), G-X6987
Irmelin Rose, Op. 4, No. 4 (I. P. Jacobsen)
Aksel Schiøtz (t), G-X6606
Einar Nørby (b), G-X4573
I Solen gaar bag min Plov (Ludv. Holstein)
Aksel Schiøtz (t), G-X6065: G-X6917

Jaegersangen (Ludv. Holstein)
Aksel Schiøtz (t), G-X6152
Jeg baerer med Smil min Byrde (Jeppe
Aakjaer)
Aksel Schiøtz (t), G-X6065: G-X6917
Thyge Thygesen, G-X6839
Jeg laegger mig saa trygt til Ro (Chr.
Winther)
Knud Eriksen (treble), G-X4807
Jens Vejmand (Jeppe Aakjaer)
Aksel Schiøtz, G-X6989; Edi Laider (b),
G-X4657; Marius Jacobsen (t), G-X3816
Kommer I snart, I Husmaend (Jeppe
Aakjaer)
Johannes Fønss (b), G-X6688
Min Pige er saa lys (Helge Rode)
See under Moderen
Nu er da Vaaren kommet (A. Oehlen-
schläger)
Thyge Thygesen (t), G-X6890
Pagen højt i Taarnet sad
Aksel Schiøtz (t), G-X6606; Agnete
Zacharias (ms), G-X4574
Saenk kun dit Hoved, from Op. 21 (J.)
Jørgensen)
Edith Oldrup-Pedersen (s), G-DA5217
Se dig ud en Sommerdag (J. Aakjaer)
Thyge Thygesen (t), G-X6890
Sommersang, Op. 10, No. 3 (Ludvig
Holstein)
Aksel Schiøtz (t), G-X6987: G-X6257
Underlige Aftenlufte (Adam Oehlen-
schläger)
Aksel Schiøtz (t), G-X6101: G-X6610;
Thyge Thygesen, O-D834
Vi Sletternes Sønner (Ludv. Holstein)
Aksel Schiøtz (t), G-X6152
Symphonic Suite, Op. 8 Piano
—Intonation only
Sejr Volmer-Sørensen   10″—G-DA5206
[Riisager: Four Epigrams—Capriccio
only]

SYMPHONIES

No. 2, "The Four Temperaments," Op. 16
Danish State Radio Symphony Orch.—
Thomas Jensen   4   12″—G-DB17/20†
(Also G-Z7000/3: automatic)
No. 3, "Sinfonia Espansiva," Op. 27
Danish State Radio Symphony Orch.—
Erik Tuxen   5   12″—NP-HM80005/9
(w. Inger Lis Hassing (s) & Erik
Sjoberg (b))
[Saul and David—Prelude, Act 2]
Theme & Variations, Op. 40 Piano
Hermann D. Koppel
2   12″—G-DB5234/5
(Also G-DB5252/3)

NIN, Josquin (1883-   )
*Best known for his songs, Nin is recognized as
an musicologist, and as a fine pianist.*

Cantilena Asturiana Violin & Piano
Jascha Heifetz & Emanuel Bay, in VM-
1158

SONGS In Spanish (Chants d'Espagne)
(El) Amor es como un niño
C. Baria (s) & D. O. Colacelli (pf)
(Argentine)   10″—V-10-1109
[El Vito; Vives: El retrato de Isabella]

Granadina (Andaluza)
Miguel Fleta (t) 10″—G-DA1037
[Gretchaninov: Berceuse]
—Arr. Violin & Piano Kochanski
Miguel Candela & J. Nin 10″—C-LF145
[Saeta & Lalo: Concerto russe—Inter-
mezzo]

Saeta (Prière)
—Arr. Violin & Piano Kochanski
Miguel Candela & J. Nin 10″—C-LF145
[Granadina & Lalo: Concerto russe—In-
termezzo]

NORCOME, Daniel (1576-c.1626)

*One of the minor members of the Elisabethan
madrigal school, Norcome also composed instrumental pieces.*

Divisions on a Ground Viol da Gamba &
Lute
Rudolph & Arnold Dolmetsch
(in CM-231) 10″—C-5714
[Weelkes: Fantasy for a chest of 6 viols]
(In Columbia History of Music, Vol. I)

NORTON, Spencer (1909-   )

Dance Suite
—Prologue only
Eastman Rochester Symphony Orch.—
Hanson (in VM-889†) 12″—V-11-8116
[Hanson: Lament for Beowulf, Pt. 5]

NOVACEK, Ottokar (1866-1900)

*Hungarian violinist, a well-known member of
orchestras and string quartets of his day, No-
váček wrote many works for piano and violin.
He is remembered today for the work listed below.*

Perpetuum mobile, Op. 5, No. 4 Violin &
Piano
Y. Menuhin & Paris Symphony Orch.—
Enesco (in VM-230†) 12″—V-8383
[Paganini: Concerto I, Pt. 9]
(G-DB2283)
Riccardo Odnoposoff & Otto Herz
10″—V-10-1228
[Villa-Lobos: O canto do cysno negro]
Y. Menuhin & pf. acc. 10″—G-DA1196
[Monsigny-Franko: Rigaudon]
Frederick Grinke & Ivor Newton
[Lili Boulanger: Nocturne] 10″—D-M570
—Arr. Orch. Stokowski
Philadelphia Orch.—Stokowski
12″—V-18069
[McDonald: Legend of the Arkansas
Traveler]
All-American Orchestra—Stokowski
12″—C-11879D
[Falla: Ritual Fire Dance]

NOVAK, Vitězslav (1870-   )

*One of the most influential teachers in Czecho-
slovakia, Novak is a prolific composer and the
editor of many volumes of Slovak folksongs.*

Exoticon Piano suite
—Ballade only
J. Paleniček 10″—ESTA-D4013
[String trio, No. 2, D minor, Part 5]

Majestic Night
Moravian Teachers' Choir
10″—U-C14867
[Suk: Fairies & Strange Water]

Mládí, Op. 55
—Certovska Polka only
Viktorie Svihlikova (pf)
12″—U-G12453
[Serenade, Op. 9—Ma sladka pani—
Sladka Dono]

QUARTET—Strings

No. 2, D major, Op. 35
Ondriček Quartet 4 12″—U-G12454/7
[Fibich: String Quartet, A major, Polka
only]

Serenade, Op. 9
—Má Sladká Paní, Sladká Doňo only
Viktorie Svihlikova (pf)
12″—U-G12453
[Mladi—Certovska Polka]

Slovak Suite, Op. 32 Orchestra
Czech Broadcasting Orch.—Jirak
4 12″—U-G12614/7
[Janáček: Lash Dances—No. 6, Pilky]
Czech Broadcasting Orch.—Sejna
4 12″—ESTA-H5046/9
—Zamilovaniý & U muziki only
Symphony Orch.—K. Sejna
12″—ESTA-H5045
FOK Symphony Orch.—Smetáček
12″—U-E11792

SONGS In Czech

Balada Dětská Op. 28, No. 1 (Jan Neruda)
Marta Krasova (s) & Orch.
12″—U-G12461

Balada Horská, Op. 28, No. 2 (Jan Neurada)
Marta Krasova (s) & Orch.
12″—U-G12462

In the Valley of a New Kingdom (Song
Cycle) In Czech
Z. Otava (b) & pf. acc.
2 10″—U-C12924/5

Išiel Macek do Mlacek

Pri Dunaji šaty perú
Marta Krasová (s) 10″—ESTA-B7692
[Janáček: Nejistota, Karafiat]

Spring (Song Cycle)
M. Dvořáková (s) & pf. acc.
4 12″—ESTA-K7944/7

TRIOS—Piano, Violin, 'Cello

No. 2, D minor
Smetana Trio 3 10″—ESTA-D4011/3
[Exoticon—Ballade only, J. Palenicek,
piano]

Twelve White Hawks Cho. in Czech.
Prague Smetana Choir—O. Hilmer
12″—ESTA-F5208
[Praus: Bohemian Chorale]

NYSTROEM, Goesta (1890-   )

SONGS In Swedish
Gubben och gumman (An old song)
Karleken visa (Love song)
Ute skaren (Among the rocks)
Maria Ribbing (s) & Stig Ribbing (pf)
12″—G-DB11020

OBOUSSIER, Robert (1901-   )

(6) Abbreviations Harpsichord
  E. Harich-Schneider   12"—**G-DB4597**
  [Klopstock Odes, Pt. 3]
(3) Klopstock Arias
Zeit, Verkündigerin der besten Freuden
Weine du nicht
Dein süsses Bild, Edone
  Erna Berger (s), E. Harich-Schneider
  (harpsichord) & H. Walter Schleif
  (oboe)   2 12"—**G-DB4596/7**
  [Six Abbreviations, Harpsichord solo]

OBRECHT, Jacob (c.1430-1505)

*One of the great Flemish contrapuntists of the
15th Century, Obrecht was a most prolific composer. He was one of many Lowland composers who exposed themselves to the influence of
the Italian humanistic spirit, and blended the
transalpine lyricism with their pithy polyphony.*

Missa Maria Zart
—Credo: Qui propter & Et incarnatus est
  Les Paraphonistes de St. Jean-des-Mat-
  ines—Van   (in Vol. IX) 12"—**AS-80**
  [with XV Cent. Penetential Motets]
Missa Sine Nomine
—Credo, Kyrie, Agnus Dei only
  Choir of the Pius X School of Liturgical
  Music   (in VM-739) 2 12"—**V-13558/9**
  [Anon. 13th Century: Alleluia-Psallat]
Qui Cum Patre
  Choir of the Pius X School of Liturgical
  Music   (in VM-739) 12"—**V-13557**
  [Dufay: Flos Florum; Anon: Descent of
  the Holy Ghost]
Tsat een meskin
  Pro Musica Antiqua Brussels—Safford
  Cape   (in Vol. III) 12"—**AS-27**
  [Rue: Autant en emporte le vent; Bras-
  sart: O Flos Flagrans]

OFFENBACH, Jacques (1819-1880)

*One of the most successful composers and pro-
ducers of comic operas of his time. Offenbach
wrote over 100 works for the stage which enjoyed enormous popularity. Although best
known for his "Les Contes d'Hoffmann," Offenbach is represented on discs by excerpts
from many of his scores. There has been no attempt to list these recordings in their entirety.*

Apache Dance Orchestra
  *The familiar so-called "Apache Dance" is
  based upon the main theme of the "Valse des
  Papillons" from Offenbach's "Le Roi Carotte."*
  Lew Stone Orch., D-F5167
Can-Cans See under Miscellaneous

OPERAS-COMIQUES In French
BARBE-BLEUE 3 Acts 1866
  Eng. Bluebeard Ger. Blaubart
Orchestral Selections
  Symphony Orch.—Gurlitt 12"—**PD-27080**

(LA) BELLE HELENE 3 Acts 1865
  Eng. Helen Ger. Die Schöne Helena
Orchestral Selections (Fantasias, etc.)
  Marek Weber Orch., G-B3996; Symphony
  Orch., PD-19760

Overture Orchestra
  Boston "Pops" Orch.—Fiedler
  (G-C3597)   12"—**V-11-9026**
  Studio Orch., Beromunster—Scherchen
                    In Prep. **Swiss Decca**
Invocation à Vénus: Dis-moi Vénus (or, On
me nomme Hélène)
  Jane Marnac, O-1667378
Le Jugement de Pâris Ten.
  Marcel Claudel   12"—**PD-522700**
  [Contes d'Hoffmann—Il était une fois]
Paris' Entrance Tenor
  Dan. Paris Dom Swedish: Paris
  entresång
  Jussi Björling (in Swedish)
                    10"—**G-X6090**
  [Millösker: Bettelstudent—Aria]
  Marius Jacobsen (in Danish)
                    10"—**G-X4012**
  [Strauss: Fledermaus—Selections]
Dream Duet
  Webster Booth (t) & Anne Ziegler (s),
  G-B9581

(LES) BRACONNIERS 3 Acts 1873
Duettino des époux
  Charpini & Brancato 10"—**PAT-X91011**
  [Lecocq: Fille de Mme. Angot—Duo
  politique]

(LES) BRIGANDS 3 Acts 1869
Orchestral Selections (Medleys, etc.)
  Andolfi Orch.   10"—**PAT-X96023**

(LES) CONTES D'HOFFMANN 3 Acts
1881
  (Completed & Revised by Ernest Giraud)
  Eng. The Tales of Hoffmann Ger. Hoff-
  manns Erzählung
Abridged Recording Sung in German
  Berlin State Opera Soloists, Chorus &
  Orch.—Melichar 3 10"—**PD-24969/71**
  (The soloists include Hedwig von
  Debicka, Else Ruziczka, Helge Ros-
  waenge & Karl August Neumann.)
Orchestral Selections (Fantasias, etc.)
  London Philharmonic Orch.—Beecham
  (C-LX530)   12"—**C-68692D**
  Berlin Philharmonic—Melichar
                    10"—**PD-24353**
  DUPLICATIONS: Marek Weber Orch.,
  G-EH209; Regal Cinema Orch.,
  C-DFX68; Cincinnati Summer Opera
  Orch.—Cleva, in D-A491
Waltz (arr. Waldteufel)
  Mayfair Orch.—Walter Goehr
                    10"—**G-B9521**
Individual Excerpts
ACT I (or Prologue)
Légende de Kleinzach: Il était une fois
  Tenor & Chorus
  Ger. Es war einmal ein Hofe
  Marcel Claudel & Chorus
                    10"—**PD-522700**
  [Belle Hélène—Jugement de Pâris]
  Richard Tauber & Chorus (in German)
                    12"—**P-PX01033**
  [O Dieu, de quelle ivresse]
  In German: J. Patzak, PD-66985
  In English: Tudor Davies, G-D1142

Entr'acte (Minuet) Orchestra
London Philharmonic Orch.—Beecham
(C-LX530) 12"—C-68692D
[Barcarolle & other excerpts]
Berlin Philharmonic Orch.—Weissmann
12"—P-E10725
[Entra'acte to Act III & Barcarolle]
DUPLICATION: Opéra-Comique Orch.—
Cloëz, O-165044

ACT II

Je me nomme Coppélius Recit.
J'ai des yeux Air Baritone or Bass
Louis Musy 12"—G-W1176
[Diaz: Benvenuto Cellini-De l'art]
DUPLICATIONS: José Beckmans, PD-524062; A. Pernet, O-188715; E. Billot,
O-188529
(Les) Oiseaux dans la charmille Soprano
(Air de la poupée) Eng. **Doll Song**
Ger. **Puppen-Arie: Phöbus stolz im Son-nenwagen**
Miliza Korjus (in German) 12"—V-11921
[Mozart: Zauberflöte—Rache-Arie]
[Meyerbeer: Dinorah-Ombra leggera, on
G-C2770: G-EH905]
Lily Pons 10"—O-188642
[Gounod: Mirielle—La Valse]
DUPLICATIONS: Yvonne Brothier,
G-P689; Andrée Vavon, C-D19182
In German: Hedwig von Debicka, PD-95463
In English: Isobel Baillie, C-DX165

ACT III

Entr'acte & Barcarolle
Belle nuit, o nuit d'amour
Soprano, Mezzo-Soprano & Cho.
Ger. **Schöne Nacht, du Liebesnach**
Germaine Féraldy & Germaine Cernay
10"—C-LF122
[Elle a fui, Finale, Act IV]
[Also on C-LF135]
Yvonne Brothier & G. Galland
10"—G-K6059
[Messager: Petites Michu—Blanche-Marie et Marie-Blanche]
DUPLICATIONS: M. Sibille & Ninon
Vallin, PAT-X90058; Germaine Cernay &
E. Luart, O-123678
Solo Version: Jarmilla Novotna,
V-11-9263
In German:
M. Teschemacher, M. Klose & Chorus
[Trio, Act IV] 12"—G-DB4410
Emmy Bettendorf & Karen Branzell
12"—P-DPX1
[Rimsky-Korsakoff: Sadko—Song of
India—Branzell]
In English:
Elisabeth Schumann (both voices)
12"—G-DB3641
[Böhm: Still wie die Nacht]
Jeanne Dusseau & Nancy Evans & Cho.
(G-C3126) 12"—V-13824
[Mascagni: Cavalleria Rusticana—Easter
Hymn]
DUPLICATION: Isobel Baillie & Nellie
Walker, C-8654
—**Miscellaneous vocal versions (in English)**
Lucrezia Bori (s) & Lawrence Tibbett
(b) 10"—G-DA912

[Goetze: Calm as the night]
Ann Ziegler (s) & Webster Booth (t)
10"—G-B9370
[Friml: Rose Marie—Indian Love Call]
—**Arr. Orchestra**
London Philharmonic—Beecham
(C-LX530) 12"—C-68692D
[Entr'acte, Duo, Intermezzo]
Sigmund Romberg & his Orch.
12"—V-11-9222
[Romberg: Faithfully yours]
Hollywood Bowl Symphony—Stokowski
(arr. Stokowski) 12"—V-11-9174
[Schubert: Moment Musical, F minor]
[Also on V-11-9226 in VM-1062]
DUPLICATIONS: Berlin Charlottenberg
—Fried, PD-19804; Symphony Orch.—
Weissmann, P-E10725; Victor Concert
Orch.—Bourdon, V-20011: G-B2377:
G-K5177; BBC Theatre Orch.—Robinson,
D-K1363; Opéra-Comique Orch.—Cloëz,
O-165044; Andolfi Orch., PAT-X8680;
Künstler Orch.—Godwin, PD-22735
Also: Livschakoff Trio, PD-23879

Scintille diamant Baritone
Ger. **Spiegel-Arie: Leuchte, heller Spiegel**
Eng. **Dapertutto's Air**
Martial Singher
(in CM-578) 12"—C-72088D
[Bizet: Carmen—Toreador's Song]
Leonard Warren 12"—V-18420
[Gounod: Faust—Avant de quitter ces
lieux]
DUPLICATIONS: Pierre Dupré,
O-188763; José Beckmans, PD-524062:
PD-561069; Etienne Billot, O-188836:
O-188529; André Pernet, O-188715
In German: Theodor Scheidl, PD-95463;
Heinrich Schlusnus, PD-35021
In Swedish: Joel Berglund, G-X6016;
Hugo Hasslo, G-Z309

O Dieux, de quelle ivresse Tenor
(*This is part of the Duo beginning "Mal-heureux!"*)
Ger. **Ha, wie in meiner Seele entbrennet**
Richard Tauber (in German)
12"—P-PXO1033
[Légende de Kleinzach]
DUPLICATION: Julius Patzak, PD-66985
—**Arr. Orchestra**
London Philharmonic—Beecham
(C-LX530) 12"—C-68692D
[Barcarolle & other excerpts]

ACT IV

Elle a fui, la tourterelle Soprano
[Romance d'Antonia]
Jarmila Novotna 12"—V-11-9263
[Barcarolle]
Ninon Vallin 12"—PAT-X90082
[Massenet: Manon—A nous les amours]
DUPLICATION: Germaine Féraldy,
C-LF122

C'est une chanson d'amour

J'ai le bonheur dans l'âme Soprano & Tenor
[Duo: Hoffmann & Antonia]
Ger. **Horst du es tönen** Eng. **O joy beyond
compare**
Hedwig von Debicka & Helge Roswaenge,
(in German) 12"—PD-95464

Tu ne chanteras plus? Trio: Soprano,
Mezzo-Soprano, Baritone
Antonia! Ciel! Ecoute!
(Chère enfant!)
Ger. **Antonia! Himmel! So höre**
M. Teschmacher, M. Klose, W. Domgraff-
Fassbaender (in German)
[Barcarolle] 12″—G-DB4410

(LA) FILLE DU TAMBOUR-MAJOR 3 Acts
1879
Orchestral Selections (Fantasias, etc.) Arr.
Tavan
Symphony Orch.—Snaga
10″—PD-27111
Vocal Excerpts
Victor Pujol, O-166121; André Noël,
PAT-X91019

**(LA) GRANDE DUCHESSE DE GEROL-
STEIN** 3 Acts 1867
Ger. **Herzogin von Gerolstein**
Dites-lui qu' on l'a remarqué Act 2 Soprano
Yvonne Printemps & pf. acc.
[Lully: Ariette de Cloris] 10″—G-P835
Galop Orchestra
Orchestre Raymonde—G. Walter
(C-DF2331) 12″—C-DB1752
[J. Strauss: Tritsch-Trasch Polka]

LISCHEN ET FRITZCHEN 1 Act 1863
Chanson d'Alsace Duo
Madeleine Renaud & Pierre Bertin
12″—LUM-35002
[Lemoine-Puget: La dot d'Auvergne]
DUPLICATION: Jany Delille & Reda
Caire, PAT-PG52

MADAME FAVART 3 Acts 1887
Ronde des vignes: Ma mere aux vignes Act
I Soprano
M. Denya, C-RF37; E. Favart, PAT-
PG30

(L') ORFEVRE DE TOLEDE
Eng. **The Goldsmith of Toledo Serenade**
Tenor & Chorus
Ger. **Lieblichste aller Frauen**
John McHugh & Chorus (in English)
12″—C-DX1224
[Liszt-Schipa: Liebstraum]
Julius Patzak & Chorus (in German)
10″—PD-23921
[J. Strauss: Nacht in Venedig—Gondel-
lied]

ORPHEE AUX ENFERS 2 Acts 1858
Eng. **Orpheus in Hades** (Orpheus in the
Underworld)
Ger. **Orpheus in der Unterwelt**
Orchestral Selections
Andolfi Orch., PAT-X96088
Overture Orchestra
Boston "Pops" Orch.—Fiedler
12″—V-12-0240
London Philharmonic—Lambert
(G-C3110) (G-FKX55) 12″—V-12604
Detroit Symphony Orch.—Krueger
(G-C3431) 12″—V-11-8761
London Symphony—Blech
12″—G-DB1673

National Symphony Orch.—Robinson
12″—D-K1302
DUPLICATIONS: Bournemouth Munici-
pal Orch.—Godfrey, C-DX593; Tivoli
Orch.—Felumb, TONO-X25055; Winter-
thur Municipal Orch.—Scherchen,
G-DB6092; Berlin State Opera Orch.—
Melichar, PD-24233; Symphony Orch.—
Schmalstich, G-EH339; Dajos Bela Orch.,
P-E10833; Lucerne Concert Orch.,
C-DFX110
—Arr. 2 Pianos: Rawicz & Landauer,
C-FB2071
Quadrille Orchestra
Orch. de Bals champêtres (arr. Sohier)
10″—G-K5558
DUPLICATION: Carnet de Bal, PAT-
PA962

(LA) PERICHOLE 3 Acts 1868
Vocal Excerpts:
Jany Delille, Reda Caire, Chorus & Orch.
10″—PAT-PG52
Air de la lettre: O mon cher amant Soprano
Fanély Revoil, G-K7556; Jane Marnac,
O-166738
Couplets des aveux: Tu n'es pas beau
Soprano
Maggie Teyte 12″—D-K993
[Messager: Véronique-Petite Dinde]
DUPLICATION: Fanély Revoil, G-K7556

(LE) ROI CAROTTE 4 Acts 1872
See under Apache Dance

(LA) VIE PARISIENNE 5 Acts 1866
Ger. **Pariser Leben**
Orchestral selections (Fantasias, etc.)
Theatre Mogador Orch.—Diot
10″—C-DF572
DUPLICATION: P. Godwin Orch., PD-
23900
Quadrille Orchestra
Theatre Mogador Orch.—Diot
10″—O-238377
DUPLICATION: Ferrero Orch.—PD-
522427

MISCELLANEOUS
Gaité Parisienne—Ballet
NOTE: *Arranged from Offenbach selections by
Manuel Rosenthal.*
Complete recording
Boston "Pops" Orchestra—Fiedler
4 12″—VM-1147†
[Also V-V9†: Vinylite]
—**Excerpts**
London Philharmonic Orch.—Kurtz
2 12″—CX-115†
(C-DX883/4) (C-DFX223/4)
Selection of Can-Cans
Light Symphony Orch. 12″—G-C2963
[Joseph Strauss: Polkas]

OKEGHEM, Jean De (c.1430-1495)
*One of the greatest of the early Flemish con-
trapuntal masters, the teacher of Josquin des
Prés, Okeghem was an outstanding composer of
church music. He is regarded as the founder of
the second Netherlander school. Recordings of
his larger choral works are badly needed.*

Ma Maîtresse 3-Part Chanson in French
Max Meili (t), R. Seidersbeck (viol) &
A. Lafosse (trombone)
(in Vol. I)   12"—AS-3
[Isaac: Zwischen Berg; Dufay: Pour-Maîtresse]

Mass "L'homme armé"
—Credo only
Les Paraphonistes de St.-Jean-des-Matines—G. de Van   12"—G-W1513
[Dufay: Mass "L'homme armé"—Kyrie]

ORR, Robin (1909-   )
Sonatine Violin & Piano
Max Rostal & Franz Osborn
12"—D-K1112

ORTIZ, Diego (16th Century)
An important early Spanish composer of Toledo, Ortiz's book of variations for bass viol and cembalo was published in Rome in 1553.

Ricercada Viola da Gamba & Harpsichord
Van Leeuwen Boomkamp & Erwin Bodky
(in Vol. IV)   12"—AS-40
[Milan: 3 Pavanes, E. Pujol, vihuela]

OUBRADOUS, Fernand
Contemporary French basoonist and teacher at the Paris Conservatoire, Oubradous has written and arranged music for woodwinds. He is also known as a conductor.

Cadence et Divertissment Clarinet & Piano
Pierre Lefèbvre & Noël Gallon
[Gallon: Récit & Allegro]   12"—OL-9

PACHELBEL, Johann (1653-1706)
A great German organist and composer who specialized in organ variations and preludes on choral themes.

Alein Gott in der Höh sei Ehr Chorale Prelude Organ
Karl Matthaei   12"—G-FM23
[Vom Himmel hoch & Buxtehude: Fugue, F major]

Canon, D major
Collegium Musicum—Hermann Diener
12"—G-EH1231
[Torelli: Concertino, D minor]
Arthur Fiedler's Sinfonietta
(in VM-969†)   10"—V-10-1095
[Reusner: Suite No. 1, Pt. 3]

Chaconne Organ
Fernando Germani   12"—SEMS-1140
[Clerambault: Basse et dessus de trompette & Schumann: Canon 5]

Durch Adams Fall ist ganz verdebt
Chorale Prelude Organ
Friedrich Mihatsch (Gonzalez organ)
12"—PAT-PAT70
[Toccata in C; Buxtehude: Fantasia on Ich dank dir lieber Herre]
(in 3 Centuries of Organ Music)
Fernando Germani   12"—SEMS-1154
[Vom Himmel hoch & Zipoli: Elevation]

Fugue, A minor Organ
Carl Weinrich (Westminster Choir School organ), in MC-9

(2) Magnificats
Wanda Landowska (harpsichord)
12"—G-DB5048
[Bach: Toccata & Fugue—D major, Pt. 3]

Toccata, C major Organ
Friedrich Mihatsch (Gonzalez organ)
12"—PAT-PAT70
[Durch Adams Fall; Buxtehude: Fantasia on Ich dank dir]
(in 3 Centuries of Organ Music Set)

Vater Unser im Himmelreich (Lord's Prayer) Organ
Marcel Dupré (in Vol. I)   12"—AS-10
[Scheidt: Fantasia on Credo]

Vom Himmel hoch da komm ich her Organ
Karl Matthei   12"—G-FM23
[Allein Gott in der Höh' & Buxtehude: Fugue, F major]
Fernando Germani   12"—SEMS-1154
[Durch Adams Fall & Zipoli: Elevation]

Wie schön leuchtet der Morgenstern Organ
Carl Weinrich (Westminster Choir School organ), in MC-9

PADEREWSKI, Ignaz Jan (1860-1942)
The most renowned pianist since the days of Liszt and Rubinstein, Paderewski was a world figure both in music and in politics. As a composer he is remembered today by a few small piano pieces frequently performed. His larger works are seldom heard.

Minuet, G major, Op. 14, No. 1 Piano
"Celebrated Minuet"
I. J. Paderewski   12"—V-16250
[Beethoven: Moonlight Sonata—1st Mvt. only]
(Also V-14374 in VM-349) (G-DB1090)
Suzanne Gyr   10"—G-DA6014
[Rachmaninoff: Prelude, C sharp minor]
Sergei Rachmaninoff   12"—V-6731
[Chopin: Nocturne, Op. 9, No. 2]
José Iturbi   12"—V-11-9514
[Rachmaninoff: Prelude in C sharp minor, Op. 3, No. 2] (G-DB6468)
DUPLICATION: Ignaz Friedman, C-68987D
—Arr. Orchestra
Andre Kostelanetz & his Orch.
(in CM-484)   12"—C-71306D
[Sibelius: Valse triste]
DUPLICATIONS: Victor Symphony—Bourdon, V-20169; Marek Weber Orch., G-K5714
—Arr. Violin & Piano Kreisler
Miquel Candela & Maurice Faure, C-LF82
—Arr. 'Cello & Piano Cassadó
Marcelli-Herson & pf. acc., G-K6425

PAGANINI, Niccolo (1784-1840)
One of the greatest violin virtuosos of all times, the Italian Paganini was successful both as performer and as composer.

A Paganini Recital
La Campanella (2nd Mvt., Concerto No. 2, B minor, Op. 7); Fantasia on G string, after Rossini; Caprices No. 13 & 20; Moto Perpetuo; Le Streghe, Op. 8
Ruggiero Ricci (vl) & Louis Persinger
(pf)   3   12"—VOX-614

(La) Campanella See: Concerto No. 2—2nd Mvt.

CAPRICES Unaccompanied Violin

NOTE: *Most recordings use arrangements with piano accompaniments.*

No. 1, E major (Arpeggio)
—Arr. Piano (Liszt: Paganini Etude No. 4)
Carlo Zecchi, O-9103: CET-CB20351

No. 2, B minor
Joseph Szigeti   12"—C-LX435
[Prokofiev: Concerto No. 1, Pt. 5]
(C-GQX10973) (C-LFX404)

No. 5, A minor
Endré Wolff   10"—G-X7378
[Falla: Amor Brujo—Pantomime]
—Arr. Viola
William Primrose (labelled No. 15)
                12"—C-7323M
[Caprice 13 & Tchaikovsky: Nur wer die Sehnsucht kennt]

No. 6, G minor (Tremolo)
Yehudi Menuhin & Georges Enesco
                12"—G-DB2841
[Dvořák: Violin Concerto, Pt. 7]
—Arr. Piano
(Liszt: Paganini Etude No. 1)
No recording available

No. 9, E major (La Chasse)
Joseph Szigeti   12"—C-LX263
[Mendelssohn: Concerto, Pt. 3]
(C-LFX349)
[Debussy: Minuet, on C-GQX11070]
—Arr. Piano
(Liszt: Paganini Etude No. 5)
Claudio Arrau, PD-95110; Carlo Zecchi,
O-9103: CET-CB20351

No. 13, G minor (Le rire du diable)
Jascha Heifetz & Arpad Sandor
(arr. Kreisler)   10"—V-1697
[No. 20] (G-DA1761)
[Debussy: Enfant prodigue—Prélude on G-DA1376]
DUPLICATIONS: Ruggiero Ricci & Louis Persinger, in VOX-614; Jean Fournier, PAT-PDT61; Ferenc Vecsey, & pf., CET-LL3004: PD-62720
—Arr. Viola
William Primrose, C-7323M

No. 17, E flat major
(Andantino Capriccioso)
—Arr. Piano
(Liszt: Paganini Etude No. 2)
Vladimir Horowitz, V-1468: G-DA1146:
G-DA1160; Claudio Arrau, PD-95110;
N. de Magaloff, RAD-SP8020

No. 20, D major
Jascha Heifetz & Arpad Sandor
[Caprice 13] (G-DA1761)   10"—V-1697
[Milhaud: Sumaré, on G-DA1375]
Ruggiero Ricci & Louis Persinger, in VOX-614
Sigmund Bleier   10"—PD-10979
[Tchaikowsky: Chant sans paroles]

No. 21, A major
Siegfried Borries & pf. acc.
(arr. Szymanowski)   10"—G-DA4440
[Rimsky-Korsakov: Sadko—Song of India]

No. 24, A minor (Tema con variazioni)
(*This caprice has served as the subject for the Brahms "Variations on a Theme by Paganini" and for the Rachmaninoff "Rhapsodie on a Theme of Paganini." For recordings of these works see under Brahms and Rachmaninoff.*)
C. F. Cillario   12"—G-DB5410
Yehudi Menuhin (Arr. Kreisler)
                10"—G-DA1281
—Arr. Violin & Piano Auer
Jascha Heifetz & Arpad Sandor
(G-DB2218)   12"—V-8828
—Arr. Viola & Piano
William Primrose & Joseph Kahn
                12"—V-15733
[Schubert-Wilhelmj: Ave Maria]
—Arr. Piano
(Liszt: Paganini Etude No. 6)
Marie-Aimée Warrot, PAT-PDT131

CONCERTOS Violin & Orchestra

No. 1, D minor, Op. 6
Yehudi Menuhin & Paris Symphony—
Monteux (Sauret cadenza)
                5 12"—VM-230†
[Nováček: Perpetuum mobile]
(G-DB2279/83, in GM-219†)
René Benedetti & Lamoureux Orch.—
Bigot   4 12"—PAT-PDT45/8
Guila Bustabo & Berlin State Orch.—
Zaun   2 12"—C-LWX354/5
—1st Mvt. Arr. Kreisler
Fritz Kreisler & Philadelphia Orch.—
Ormandy   2 12"—VM-361
(Kreisler cadenzas) (G-DB3234/5)

No. 2, B minor, Op. 7 ("La Campanella")
—2nd Mvt. (Rondo à la clochette) only
Richard Odnopousoff (vl) & Valentin
Pavlovsky (pf)   12"—V-11-8849
[Prokofieff: Peter and the Wolf—Theme, arr. Kochanski]
Alfredo Campoli & Eric Gritton
                12"—D-K1671
[Corelli: Sonata No. 12, La Folia, Pt. 3]
Yehudi Menuhin & pf. acc.
                12"—G-DB1638
[Rimsky-Korsakov: Czar's Bride—Song of the Bride]
[Schubert-Wilhelmj: Ave Maria, on G-DB5394]
Ruggiero Ricci (vl) & Louis Persinger (pf), in VOX-614
(Also older version, on G-DB4619)
—Arr. Viola & Piano Primrose
William Primrose, C-LWX191: C-GQX11025
—Arr. Piano Liszt ("La Campanella")
Paderewski, V-6825: G-DB1167:
(also G-DB376*); Kilenyi, G-69798D;
Brailowsky, V-11-9025; France Elle-
gaard, PD-67839; Cyril Smith, C-DX1214;
N. de Magaloff, RAD-SP8020; J. M.
Darré, PD-95440; etc.

Fantasia on the G String
(after Rossini's "Mosé in Egitto")
Yehudi Menuhin (vl) & Ferguson
Webster (pf)   12"—G-DB3499
Ruggiero Ricci (vl) & L. Persinger (pf), in VOX-614
(older version on G-DB4619)
DUPLICATIONS: Florizel von Reuter,

PD-95250; Luigi Silva (vlc), G-DA4450;
Walter Barylli, PD-10810

Moto perpetuo (Allegro di Concert), Op. 11
Violin
Yehudi Menuhin & pf. acc.
12"—**V-8866**
[Brahms: Hungarian Dance No. 6]
[Bazzini: Ronde des lutins, on
G-DB2414]
Ruggiero Ricci & Louis Persinger, in
VOX-614
Karel Sroubek & Frantisek Maxián
12"—**U-G14204**
[Smetana: Bartered Bride—Polka, arr.
Ondriček]

—Arr. Orchestra
NBC Symphony—Toscanini
(G-DB3858) (in VM-590) 12"—**V-15547**
[Beethoven: Quartet No. 16, Op. 131—
Scherzo]
Minneapolis Symphony—Ormandy
12"—**V-14325**
[Mozart: Nozze di Figaro—Overture]
[Gounod: Marche funèbre d'une
marionette, on G-DB2823]
DUPLICATIONS: Chicago Symphony
Orch.—Stock, C-11738D; Vienna Cham-
ber Orch.—Jerger, G-EH1324; EIAR
Orch.—La Rosa Parodi, CET-CB20183;
Louis Levy Orch., D-K1577

Quartet—Strings
E major—Minuet only (arr. Zuccarini)
Rome String Quartet 12"—**DB-4449**
[Cambini: String Quartet, D major, arr.
Torrefranca]

Sonatas, Op. 3 Violin & guitar
Arr. Violin & Piano

No. 12, E minor
Gerhard Taschner & Gerhard Puchelt
12"—**O-8766**
[Sarasate: Romanza Andaluza, Op. 22,
No. 1]
R. de Barbieri & G. Guastalla
[Tartini: Sonata, Pt. 3] 12"—**G-AW339**
DUPLICATION: Alexij Petr Madle &
Frantisek Maxián, U-B12793

Grande Sonatine—Romance
(Originally Guitar & Violin)
Ida Presti (guitar) 10"—**G-K8114**
[Torroba: Sonata No. 1, A major,
Allegro]

(Le) Streghe, Op. 8 Violin Arr. Kreisler
(Witches' Dance on air by Simon Mayr)
Ruggiero Ricci & Louis Persinger, in
VOX-614
Ferraresi & pf. acc. 12"—**G-S10113**
[Gounod: Ave Maria]

VARIATIONS
G String after Rossini's "Mosé in Egitto"
See: Fantasia on the G String

"Nel cor più non mi sento" Violin
(from Paisiello's opera "La Molinara")
Vasa Prihoda & Otto A. Graef
(CET-OR5098) 12"—**PD-35091**

PAINE, John Knowles (1839-1906)
OEDIPUS TYRANNUS, Op. 35
Music for Sophocles' tragedy
Prelude Orchestra
Eastman-Rochester Symphony Orch.—
Howard Hanson
(in VM-608†) 12"—**V-15658**

PAISIELLO, Giovanni (1740-1816)
*Paisiello, who began his career as a church
composer, became the most popular and prolific composer of opera in Italy. He served as
court conductor to Catherine the Great, and
later to Napoleon. Paisiello's fame has long
suffered eclipse, although his most successful
opera "Il Barbiere di Siviglia" was held in high
regard until it was finally overshadowed by the
even more popular score of Rossini on the same
subject.*

Lode al ciel Aria
Yvon le Marc' Hadour (b) & R. Gerlin
(harpsichord) 10"—**PAT-PG87**
[Paradies: Quel Ruscelletto]

OPERAS In Italian

(IL) BARBIERE DI SIVIGLIA 1782
Overture Orchestra
EIAR Orch.—Tansini 12"—**CET-PE101**
[Cimarosa: Giannina e Bernardone—
Overture]

(LA) MOLINARA 1788
Nel cor più non mi sento
Ezio Pinza (bs) & Fritz Kitsinger (pf)
(in VM-766) 12"—**V-17915**
[Torelli: Tu lo sai & Monteverdi:
Incoronazione di Poppea—Oblivion soave;
Cavalli: Donzelle, fuggite]
See under Paganini for variations on the theme

Unspecified excerpt
Prof. Mozzani (guitar) 10"—**G-GW1774**
[Schumann: Träumerei]

NINA (O LA PAZZA PER AMORE)
Overture Orchestra
EIAR Symphony Orch.—Tansini
12"—**CET-CB20215**
[Rossini: Il Signor Bruschino—Overture]

PROSERPINA 1803
Ballet music Arr. Lualdi
Nei giardini di Cerere; Sarabanda; Il
corteo di Plutone e delle Divinità infer-
nali; Marcia; Zefiro—Danza—Giga; Sot-
to gli alberi in fiore—Passapiede delle
Ninfe; Minuetto della Regina Prosper-
pina; Romanza; La raggiunta felicita;
Tamburino
Chamber Orch. of San Pietro a Majella di
Napoli—Lualdi 2 12"—**G-DBO5357/8**

**—Sotto gli alberi in fiore; Romanza; Tam-
burino only**
Chamber Orch. of San Pietro a Majella di
Napoli—Lualdi 12"—**CET-CB20270**

(LA) SERVA PADRONA 1769
Overture Orchestra
EIAR Symphony Orch.—Tansini
[Bolzoni: Minuet] 12"—**CET-CB20276**

PALADILHE, Emile (1844-1926)

A French composer, pupil of Halévy, and winner of the Prix de Rome, Paladilhe wrote many operas which have not held the stage. He is best known for his songs and a few arias.

LE PASSANT Opéra-Comique 1 Act 1872

La Mandolinata—Souvenir de Rome
Orchestral versions: Locatelli Orch., O-238303; Napolitain Orch., PAT-X96167

PATRIE Opéra 1886
C'est ici le berceau de notre liberté
Air de Rysoor
Robert Couzinou (b) 12"—**PD-516571**
[Massenet: Thaïs—Voilà donc la terrible cité]
Psyché (Pierre Corneille) Song in French
Maggie Teyte (s) & Gerald Moore (pf)
(in VM-895) 10"—**V-10-1003**
[Duparc: Chanson triste] (G-DA1779)
Grace Moore (s)
(in VM-918) 10"—**V-10-1018**
[Hahn: Si mes vers]
A. Endrèze (b) & R. Hahn (pf)
[Hahn: Phyllis] 10"—**PAT-PG88**

PALESTRINA, Giovanni Pierluigi da (1525-1594)

Universally regarded as the towering summit of sixteenth-century polyphony, Palestrina was one of the richest natural geniuses and one of the most accomplished technicians in the history of the art. It is, however, a mistake to regard him as the quintessence of the Renaissance spirit. So completely engrossed was Palestrina in the service of the Roman Church that it remained for his contemporaries, among others, Lassus and Monte, to express the secular spirit of the sixteenth century.

HYMNS In Latin
O crux ave 4-voice
Motet & Madrigal Group—H. Opienski
(in Vol. V) 12"—**AS-47**
[Secular Madrigals in Italian]
O felix anima 3-voice
Julian Chapel Choir—Boezi
12"—**SEMS-43**
[Moriconi: Ave verum Corpus]

LAMENTATIONS In Latin
Incipit Oratio Jeremiae Prophetae 6-voice
Paraphonistes de St. Jean-des-Matines
—G. deVan 12"—**LUM-32054**
[Dufay: Hymns—Christe Redemptor;
Ave Maria; Tantum ergo]
Roman Vatican Singers—L. Refice, in SEVA-19

MADRIGALS (Secular) In Italian
Alla riva del Tebro 4-voice
Motet & Madrigal Choir—H. Opienski
(in Vol. V.) 12"—**AS-47**
[La cruda mia nemica; O crux ave;
Motet—Vulnerasti]
I vaghi fiori e l'amorose frondi 4-voice
Madrigal Choir of the Schola Cantorum
Pontificale—Antonelli 12"—**SEMS-1119**
[Anon: Laude de l'Annunciazione—
XV Cent.]

La Cruda mia nemica 4-voice
Motet & Madrigal Choir—H. Opienski
(in Vol. V) 12"—**AS-47**
[Alla riva; O crux ave; Motet—
Vulnerasti]
Madrigal—Unspecified
Paris Teachers' Chorus—R. Ducasse
10"—**PAT-X93085**
[Lassus: Quand mon mary; Costely; Je voy des glissantes; Bach; La brébis égarée]

MASSES In Latin
Assumpta est Maria 6-voice
—Kyrie, Christe, Kyrie, Agnus Dei, Sanctus, Benedictus, & Hosanna only
Dijon Cathedral Choir—Samson
(in VM-212†) 2 12"—**V-11680/1**
(G-DB4896/7, in GM-189)
Jesu nostra Redemptio 4-voice
—Benedictus & Hosanna only
Amsterdam "Bel Canto" Choir—
Alphons Vranken 12"—**C-D17195**
[Motet—Hodie Christus natus est]
Lauda Sion 4-voice
—Benedictus only
Regensburg Cathedral Choir—
T. Schrems 10"—**G-EG3431**
[Wagner: Parsifal—Der Glaube lebt]
Papae Marcelli 6-voice
St. Eustache Singers—Père Martin
5 12"—**PAT-PDT95/9**
(*This set includes a record entitled "Prestige de la Messe," read by Rev. Father Samson, PAT PDT94.*)
Julian Chapel Choir—Boezi
5 12"—**SEMS-26/30**
—Sanctus only
Antwerp "Coecilia" Choir—de Vocht
12"—**C-D11053**
[Vocht: 2 Etudes for Chorus]
Regensburg Cathedral Choir—
T. Schrems 10"—**G-EG6812**
[Victoria: Popule meus]
DUPLICATIONS: Choir—Terry, C-5712
in Columbia History of Music, Vol. I;
CM-231; Staats und Domchor—Rüdel,
P-R1021 in "2000 Years of Music"
—Hosanna only
Choir—Terry, on C-5712 in CM-231
—Benedictus only
Lyons Cathedral Choir—L. Vietti
[Anon: Noël Bressan] 12"—**C-DFX180**

MOTETS In Latin
Adoramus te Christe 4-voice
Julian Chapel Cho.—Boezi
[Victoria: Ave Maria] 12"—**SEMS-16**
De Pauer's Infantry Chorus—De Pauer, in CM-709
—Arr. Orchestra Stokowski
Philadelphia Orch.—Stokowski
(in VM-963) 12"—**V-11-8576**
[Bach: Trio-Sonata No. 1, 1st Mvt.]
Philadelphia Orch.—Stokowski
[Frescobaldi: Gagliarda] 10"—**G-DA1606**
Alleluia! tulerunt Dominum 5-voice
Julian Chapel Choir—Boezi
[Laudate Dominum] 12"—**SEMS-31**

Alma Redemptoris Mater 4- or 8-voice
La Manécanterie des Petits Chanteurs à
la Croix de Bois   10"—**G-K7378**
[Victoria: Ave Maria]
St. Léon IX de Nancy Choir—
Gaudard   12"—**PAT-X93055**
[Josquin: Ave vera & Franck: Rebecca
—Chorus]
Exultate Deo 5-voice
Julian Chapel Cho.—Boezi
[Tota pulchra es]   12"—**SEMS-41**
Hodie Christus natus est 8-voice
Amsterdam "Bel Canto" Choir—
Alphons Vranken   12"—**C-D17195**
[Missa Jesu nostra redemptio—
Benedictus]
Introduxit me rex in cellam 5-voice
Julian Chapel Cho.—Boezi
    12"—**SEMS-38**
[Victoria: O Domine Jesu]
Laudate pueri Dominum
Julian Chapel Choir—Boezi
    12"—**SEMS-2**
[Victoria: Caligaverunt oculi mei]
Manus tuae Domine 5-voice
Julian Chapel Cho.—Boezi
[Paucitas dierum]   12"—**SEMS-35**
Nunc Dimittis 4-voice (with free Faburden)
Choir—Sir Richard Terry 10"—**C-5711**
[Anon: Nunc Dimittis; Dufay: Christe
Redemptor & Conditor alme]
(In Columbia History of Music, Vol.
I; CM-231)
O admirabili commercium 5-voice
Paderborn Cathedral Choir—
Schauerte   10"—**PD-22528**
[Dombrowski: Eja' so seht den
Rosenstrauch]
O bone Jesu 6-voice
St. Léon IX de Nancy Choir—
Gaudard   12"—**PAT-X93051**
[Viadana: Exultate justi; Tombelle:
Sinite parvulos]
Strasbourg Cathedral Choir—Hoch
    12"—**C-RFX56**
[Viadana: Sacrum Convivium; Ingegneri:
Tenebrae factae sunt]
De Pauer's Infantry Chorus—De Pauer,
in CM-790
Paucitas dierum 5-voice
Julian Chapel Choir—Boezi
[Manus tuae]   12"—**SEMS-35**
Peccavimus—Tribulationes civitatum
5-voice
Julian Chapel Choir—Boezi
    12"—**SEMS-11**
Regina Coeli 8-voice
Roman Vatican Choir—L. Refice, in
SEVA-18
Sicut cervus desiderat (42nd Psalm)
4-voice
Sistine Chapel Choir—A. Rella
(in GM-139)   12"—**G-DB1570**
[Arcadelt: Ave Maria]
Amsterdam "Bel Canto" Choir—Vranken
[Sweelinck: Psalm 138] 12"—**C-D17193**
Palestrina Choir—M. Wöldike
[Gabrieli: Benedictus]   12"—**G-Z187**
DUPLICATION: Manécanterie des petits
chanteurs, G-K7558

Stabat Mater dolorosa 12-voice
Posen Cathedral Choir—
W. Gieburoskiego 2 10"—**SYR-9743/4**
Tota pulchra es amica mea 5-voice
Julian Chapel Cho.—Boezi
[Exultate Deo]   12"—**SEMS-41**
Tribulationes civitatum
See Peccavimus
Vox dilecti mei 5-voice
Julian Chapel Choir—Boezi
    10"—**SEMS-44**
[Somma: Ave Spes nostra]
Vulnerasti cor meum 5-voice
Motet & Madrigal Group—H. Opienski
(in Vol. V)   12"—**AS-47**
[O crux ave; Secular madrigals in
Italian]

OFFERTORIES

Bonum est 5-voice
Julian Chapel Cho.—Boezi
    12"—**SEMS-13**
[Tavoni: Ecce Panis—A. Dadò]
Exaltabo Te, Domine 5-voice
Julian Chapel Cho.—Boezi 12"—**SEMS-54**
[Lassus: Velociter exaudi]
Improperium expectavit 5-voice
Julian Chapel Choir—Boezi 12"—**SEMS-8**
[Victoria: O vos omnes]
Laudate Dominum 5-voice
Julian Chapel Choir—Boezi
    12"—**SEMS-31**
[Motet—Alleluia! tulerunt Dominum]
Julian Chapel Choir—Antonelli
    12"—**SEMS-1157**
[Victoria: Caligaverunt oculi mei]
Super flumina Babylonis 5-voice
Sistine Chapel Choir—A. Rella
(in GM-139) 12"—**G-DB1571**
[Popule meus]
Julian Chapel Cho.—Boezi 12"—**SEMS-1**
[Victorio: Tenebrae factae sunt]
(Dir. Antonelli—SEMS-1156)

RESPONSES & ANTIPHONS

Ecce, quomodo moritur justus 4-voice
Augustana Choir—Henry Veld
    12"—**V-17633**
[Durante: Misercordias Domini]
Popule meus (Improperia) 5-voice
Sistine Chapel Choir—A. Rella
(in GM-139) 12"—**G-DB1571**
[Super fluminia]
Julian Chapel Choir—Boezi
    12"—**SEMS-1116**
Pueri Hebraeorum (Antiphon) 4-voice
Choir of the Pius X School of Liturgical
Music (in VM-739) 12"—**V-13560**
[Gregorian: Pueri Hebraeorum;
Taverner: Audivi; Lassus; Missa pro
Defunctis—Benedictus]

Ricercare Organ
André Marchal (Gonzalez organ)
    12"—**PAT-PAT68**
[Landino: Questa Fanciulla & Gabrieli:
Canzona]
(In 3 Centuries of Organ Music)

PALMGREN, Selim (1878-   )

A Finnish pianist, conductor and composer, specializing in piano works. He is best known by his smaller lyric pieces, some of which are internationally popular.

At the Charcoal Kiln   Chorus

Swed. **Vid milan**
Male Chorus, in Swedish   10"—G-X2799
[Pacius: Suomis säng]
Canzonetta, Op. 43, No. 3   Violin & Piano
F. Vecsey & G. Agosti   12"—PD-10686
[Sibelius: Nocturne, Op. 81, No. 3]
Evening Whispers   Piano
Iris Loveridge   10"—C-DB2304
[The Swan]
Finnish Romance   Violin & Piano
Arvo Hannikainen & pf. acc.
   10"—G-X3133
[Merikanto: Valse lente & Arr.
Hannikainen: Spring Wagon]
Havet, Op. 17, No. 12   Piano
Johanne Stockmarr   10"—G-V184
[Grieg: Norwegian Bridal Procession]
Lullaby   Chorus   Fin. **Tuutulaulu**
Male Chorus—V. Rautavaara
   10"—G-X2803
[Järnefelt: Stirkka & Törnudd:
Kitkat-kat-kat]
(Also on V-26-6012)
—Arr. Piano
Benno Moiseiwitsch   12"—G-C3267
[West-Finnish Dance & Grieg:
Concerto, Pt. 7]
—Arr. Violin & Piano
Anja Ignatius & Timo Mikkilä
[Sibelius: Mazurka]   10"—G-X6341
Paimenen Ilo
Helsinki University Chorus—
Turunen   10"—G-X6283
[Törnudd: Prokko & Madetoja: Suvi-
Illan Vieno Tuuli]
(also on V-26-6022)

SONGS & FOLKSONG SETTINGS
In Finnish

Kesäilta   Eng. **Summer evening**
Maikki Järnefelt (s) & S. Palmgren (pf)
[Kun ensi kerran]   10"—G-X3113
Helsinki University Cho.   (G-X6047)
[Soi Kaisla]   10"—V-26-6011
Kevätlaulu   Eng. **Spring song**
Maikki Järnefelt (s) & S. Palmgren (pf)
[Miss' on matkan pää]   10"—G-X3112
Kun ensi kerran
Eng. **When I first saw your eyes**
Maikki Järnefelt (s) & S. Palmgren (pf)
[Kesäilta]   10"—G-X3113
Joululaulu (Ja neitsyt pikku poijuttansa)
Sulo Saarits (b) & Orch.   10"—G-X6340
[Collan: Sylvian Joululaulu]
Laksin minä Kesayonä Kaymään
Eng. **Summer night (arr.)**
Marian Anderson (c) & K. Vehanen
(pf) (G-DA1523)   10"—V-1809
[Arr. Vehanen: Bergerette; Sibelius:
Come away death]
Miss' on matkan pää
Eng. **Where is the end of the road?**
Maikki Järnefelt (s) & S. Palmgren (pf)
[Kevätlaulu]   10"—G-X3112

Soi Kaisla
Helsinki University Cho.   (G-X6047)
[Kesäilta]   10"—V-26-6011
Song of the Hiisi Slaves   Chorus
Fin. **Hiiden orjien laulu**
Male Chorus—Rautavaara
   10"—G-X2802
[Törnudd: Loitsu, Kajanus: Sotamarssi,
Genetz: Terve]
(also on G-X6283: V-26-6030)

———

(The) Swan   Piano
Iris Loveridge   10"—C-DB2304
[Evening whispers]
West-Finnish Dance, Op. 31, No. 5   Piano
Benno Moiseiwitsch   12"—G-C3267
[Lullaby & Grieg: Concerto, Pt. 7]

PAOLO DA FINENZE, Don (14th Century)

Fra Duri scogli senz' Alcun Governo
2-voice madrigal
Lise Daniels (s) & R. Bonté (t)
   10"—OL-102
[Magister Franciscus: De Narcisus]

PARADIES (Paradisi), Pietro Domenico (1710-1792)

An Italian teacher and composer of harpsichord works and operas.

Quel ruscelletto   Arietta in Italian
Yvon le Marc' Hadour (b) & R. Gerlin
(harpsichord)   10"—PAT-PG87
[Paisiello: Lode al ciel]
Margherita Voltolina (s) & M. Salerno
(pf)   10"—CET-IT581
[Scarlatti: Le violette]
Lily Pons (s) & instr. acc.
   (in VM-702)   10"—V-2110
[Mozart: Entführung-Durch Zärtlichkeit]
Toccata, A major   Orig. Harpsichord
Kathleen Long (pf)   10"—D-M517
[Anon., arr. Resphigi: Siciliano, 16th
century lute air]
Eileen Joyce (pf)   12"—P-E11354
[Bach: Prelude & Fugue, A minor]

PARADIS, Marie Therese von (1759-1824)

A talented German blind pianist who composed both dramatic works and chamber music. Mozart wrote a concerto (K. 456) for her.

Sicilienne   Arr. Violin & Piano   Dushkin
Jacques Thibaud & T. Janopoulo
[Vivaldi: Adagio]   10"—G-DA1191
Ginette Neveu & pf. acc.   10"—G-DA4453
[Gluck: Orfeo—Mélodie]
Ellen Birgithe Nielsen & Karl Browall
   10"—G-DA5250
[Dvořák: Songs my mother taught me]
D. B. Shafran (vlc) & pf. acc.
[Ravel: Habañera]   10"—USSR-13202/3
DUPLICATION: D. Soriano, PAT-PG31

PARIBENI, Gulio Cesare (1881-   )

A teacher at the Milan Conservatory, Paribeni has written orchestral works, sacred and secular chamber music, choruses, and operas.

Momento Mistico   Harp, Strings, & Organ
String Orch. of the "Angelicum," Milan
—Gerelli   12"—G-AW303

PARKER, Clifton

Seascape Music for the film "Western Approaches" (or "The Raiders")
London Symphony Orch.—Muir Mathieson   12"—D-K1544
[Alwyn: Calypso music, from the film "The Rake's Progress"—or "The Notorious Gentleman"]

PARRY, (Sir) Charles Hubert Hastings (1848-1918)

A British composer who wrote conservatively in all forms, Parry is known outside England perhaps only as a provocative writer on music.

Coronation Anthem: I was glad
Chorus Op. 154 (Psalm 122)
Sides 1/2, in Coronation of George VI: G-RG1

England, Op. 219 (after Shakespeare)
Unison Song
Mary Jarred & Massed Choirs (Royal Command Concert)   12"—G-C3017
[Jerusalem & God save the King]
David Lloyd (t)   10"—C-DB1968
[Jerusalem]

Jerusalem, Op. 208 (Blake)
Choral song in Unison
Royal Choral Society—Sargent (with organ acc.)   10"—G-B3125
[Webber: Now once more]
Mary Jarred & Massed Choirs (Royal Command Concert, 1938) 12"—G-C3017
[National Anthem—England, final verse only]
DUPLICATIONS: BBC Chorus, C-4364; BBC Male Chorus, D-F5755
—Solo voice only
Peter Dawson, G-B8196; D. Barthel (treble), G-B4285; David Lloyd, C-DB1968; Paul Robeson, G-B9010

SONGS

Armida's Garden (Mary E. Coleridge)
Joan Taylor (s) & Ivor Newton (pf)
                              10"—D-M537
[Whether I live; The Maiden]
Nancy Evans (c)   10"—D-K860
[Bury: There is a ladye]

The Maiden (Mary E. Coleridge)
Joan Taylor (s) & Ivor Newton (pf)
                              10"—D-M537
[Armida's Garden & Whether I live]

Whether I live (Mary E. Coleridge)
Joan Taylor (s) & Ivor Newton (pf)
                              10"—D-M537
[Armida's Garden & The Maiden]

PASQUINI, Bernardo (1637-1710)

An Italian composer of harpsichord music, operas and oratorios, Pasquini was a pupil of Vittori and Cesti and a contemporary of Corelli.

Arietta
Quartet "In Cembalis Bene Sonantibus"
[Bach: Aria Religiosa] 12"—SEMS-1147
Aria
Emma Boynet (pf)   12"—PD-516146
[Castrucci: Sicilienne et Gavotte]

Con tranquillo riposo Recit.
Sussurrate intorno Aria
Guiseppe De Luca (b) & P. Cimara (pf), in D-U1

ERMINIA IN RIVA DEL GIORDANO
Cantata
Air
Yvon le Marc' Hadour (b), with harpsichord & instrumental ensemble
                              10"—PAT-PG83
[Caldara: Come raggio di sol; A. Scarlatti: Sì, sì, fedel]

Preludio Harpsichord
—Freely Transcribed Orch. Resphigi
See under Resphigi: (Gli) Uccelli Suite, VM-1112†

Toccata sul canto del Cuculo Harpsichord
Eng. Toccata on the song of the Cuckoo
Nino Rossi (pf) (arr. Boghen)
                              12"—G-DB5352
[Rossi: Toccata, G major]
—Freely Transcribed Orch. Resphigi
See under Resphigi: (Gli) Uccelli Suite, VM-1112†

PAUMANN, Konrad (c.1410-1473)

A blind German organist and composer associated with the art of "coloration," who edited and published "Fundamentum organisandi," believed to be the earliest organ book.

Benedicite: Allmechtger Got Her Jesu Cris
(This popular German song of the 15th Century was set by Paumann with organ accompaniment—No. 74 in the "Locheimer Liederbuch.")
Yves Tinayre (t) & organ
                              12"—LUM-32012
[Dufay: Alma Redemptoris Mater]
(in Yves Tinayre Album No. 1)

PEDERSEN, Mogens (c.1585-1623)

A Danish composer, pupil of Gabrieli, Pedersen wrote madrigals, motets, and psalms.

Nu bede vi den Hellegaard
Med Konning David klage
(from collection "Praetum Spirituale," 1620)
Copenhagen Boys Choir—Mogens Wöldike   10"—G-DB5249

Ad te levavi Motet
Easter Kyrie
Aleneste Gud i Himmerig
Copenhagen Boys Choir—Wöldike
                              12"—G-DB5283

PEDROTTI, Carlo (1817-1893)

A prolific composer of Italian opera buffa, Pedrotti is best known for "Tutti in Maschere."

TUTTI IN MASCHERE
Opera in Italian 1856
Overture Orchestra
Milan Symphony—**Molajoli**
                              12"—C-D14469
La Scala Orch.—Sabajno
                              12"—G-S10168

PEERSON, Martin (c.1580-1651)

An English church musician, serving for many years as choirmaster and organist of St. Paul's Cathedral. He is one of the minor Elizabethans who composed ayres, fantasias for viols, harpsichord works and church music.

(The) Fall of the Leafe Virginal
(Fitzwilliam Virginal Book No. 272)
Pauline Aubert (in Vol. II) 12"—AS-14
[Byrd: The Bells; Farnaby: The new Sa-Hoo & A Toye]
—Arr. 2 Pianos Bartlett
Ethel Bartlett & Rae Robertson
(in CX-256) 12"—C-72128D
[Farnaby: Tower Hill Jigge; Tune for 2 Virginals; His Dreame; Bull: The King's Hunting Jigge] (C-DX1341)

PEPUSCH, Johann Christoph (1667-1752)

A German composer who settled in England, Pepusch is famous for his connection with English bourgeois comic opera, locally called the "Ballad Opera." In the work listed below, his contribution was as much the arranging of popular tunes of the day, as composing new ones.

(THE) BEGGAR'S OPERA

Ballad Opera in English 1728
(Lyrics by John Gay)
Selections (Arr. Frederic Austen)
Glyndebourne Opera Company, with Chorus & Orch.—Michael Mudie
6 12"—VM-772†
The cast includes: Audrey Mildmay, Linda Gray, Alys Brough, Constance Willis, Ruby Gilchrist, Bruce Flegg, Michael Redgrave, Roy Henderson, Joseph Farrington

PERGOLESI, (Pergolese), Giovanni (1710-1736)

An Italian composer of operas and church music, whose "Stabat Mater" and "La Serva Padrona" are still performed and whose other surviving music shows the imprint of fresh genius.

Aria (unidentified)
Vasa Prihoda (vl) & O. Graef (pf)
10"—CET-LL8011
[Schumann: Träumerei]
Concertino No. 5, E flat major (attributed)
EIAR Symphony Orch.—Fighera
12"—CET-BB25212
Concertino, F minor
Boyd Neel String Orch.—Neel
2 12"—D-X148/9
[Vivaldi: Concerto, D minor, Op. 3, No. 11—Largo]
Concerto, B flat major (arr. Lualdi)
Violin & Orchestra
A. Pelliccia & Chamber Orch. of Conservatory of San Pietro à Majella, Naples,—A. Lualdi 2 12"—G-DBO5350/1
[Bonporti: Concerto, F major, Op. 10, No. 5—Recitativo]
Concerto, G major Flute, Strings & Bass
Scheck-Wenzinger Chamber Orch.
2 12"—G-EH1219/20
[Bach: Suite, A minor, for Flute, Strings & Bass—Sarabande only] (G-S10494/5)

Laudate Pueri Motet
—A Solis Ortu Tenor
Yves Tinayre with organ & strings—
Cellier 12"—LUM-32029
[Handel: Messiah—No. 32]
Nina See under CIAMPI: Gli tre cicisbei ridicoli—Siciliana, or Nina—sometimes attributed to Pergolesi
Ogni pena più spietata—Siciliana
Giuseppe De Luca (b) & Pietro Cimara (pf), in D-U1
ORFEO Cantata
Intermezzo (arr. Gui)
EIAR Symphony Orch.—Gui
12"—CET-BB25008
[Wagner: Parsifal—Good-Friday Scene, Pt. 3]
Se tu m'ami Arietta
Claudia Muzio (s)
(in CM-289) 12"—C-9169M
[Donaudy: O del mio amato ben] (C-BQX2524)
[Verdi: Forza del Destino—Pace, pace, on C-BQX2505; C-LCX26]
Lily Pons (s) & Renaissance Quintet
(in VM-756) 10"—V-2152
[Bach: Cantata—Phoebus and Pan-Air of Momus]

(LA) SERVA PADRONA

Opera in Italian 1733
Fr. La Servante Maîtresse
Vocal Selections Sung in French (with descriptive remarks)
Jeanne Gatineau & Geo. Serrano
12"—PD-516521
A Serpina penserte Soprano
Maggie Teyte (in French)
(in VM-1169) 10"—V-10-1369
[Monsigny: Rose et Colas—La sagesse est un trésor]

(6) SONATAS Harpsichord
C major (Duetto); G major (Tarantella & Scherzo); A major; B flat major; G major; G major (Tempo di Danza); C major (Aria)
Corradina Mola 3 10"—G-DA5373/5

STABAT MATER

Sop., Contralto, Cho. (in Latin) & Orch.
1. Stabat Mater; 2. Cujus animam; 3. O quam tristis; 4. Quae moerebat; 5. Quis est homo; 6. Vidit suum; 7. Eia mater; 8. Fac ut ardeat; 9. Sancta Mater; 10. Fac ut portem; 11. Inflammatus; 12. Quando corpus; Amen
Complete recording
Joan Cross & Kathleen Ferrier with Nottingham Oriana Choir & Boyd Neel String Orch.—Roy Henderson 5 12"—D-ED13† (D-K1517/21)
Abridged recording
Nos. 1, 2 (cut), 3, 5, 7 (cut), 8, 9 (cut), 11, 12
Vienna Choir Boys with String Orch. & Harpsichord—Gomboz 3 12"—VM-545†
Excerpts (Nos. 1, 3, 5, 6, 11, 12)
Regensburg Cathedral Choir & Orch.—Schrems 3 10"—G-EG7106/8 (G-HN1875/7)

No. 10, Fac ut portem Alto
Lina Falk with strings & Noëlie Pierront
(organ)—Gerlin 12″—**LUM-32052**
[Bach: Johannes-Passion—No. 58, Est
ist vollbracht]
Miscellaneous
See under
Stravinsky: Suite de Pulcinella
(after Pergolesi)
Stravinsky: Suite Italienne
(after Pergolesi)

PERI, Jacopo (1561-1633)
Peri's music has great historic interest. The so-called "first operas," "Dafne" and "Euridice" are still preserved and performed in their original editions.
Bellissima regina
Madrigal for 1 Voice In Italian
Salvatore Salvati (t) with harpsichord
& basso continuo 12″—**MIA-1**
[Euridice—Gioïte al canto mio &
Caccini: 2 Madrigals]

EURIDICE Opera in Italian 1600
Gioïte al canto mio (Canto d'Orfeo) Tenor
Salvatore Salvati, with harpsichord &
basso continuo 12″—**MIA-1**
[Bellissima Regina & Caccini: 2
Madrigals]

PEROSI, (Dom) Lorenzo (1872-   )
A modern Italian composer and choirmaster, Perosi was one of the important men in the musical reform of the Catholic liturgy. He has written a number of liturgical works, as well as many secular works for orchestra and chamber ensembles.
Benedictus
Tu es Petrus Motets A Capella
in Latin
Sistine Chapel Cho.—A. Rella
(in GM-139) 12″—**G-DB1569**
Cantate Domino
Mancini (s) & A. Fantozzi (t)
[Domine Salvum me fac] 10″—**SEMS-49**
Domine Salvum me fac
Mancini (s) & A. Fantozzi (t)
[Cantate Domino] 10″—**SEMS-49**
[Antonelli: O Salutaris, on SEMS-47]

PEROSI, Marziano (1875-   )
Brother of the preceding, composer, organist and choirmaster, his works include three symphonies for organ and orchestra, and some vocal works.
Resurrexit 4-pt. Liturgia Ambrosiana
Milan Cathedral Cho.—M. Perosi
(G-HN1380) 10″—**G-EG6289**
[Bernabet: Alma Redemptoris Mater]

PEROTINUS, Magnus (early 13th Century)
(Pérotin-Le-Grand)
A noted early French musician, successor to Léonin as maître-de-chapelle of Notre Dame Cathedral, and an important contributor to the development of counterpoint and musical notation.
Agniaus douz (attributed to Perotinus)
In French
Yves Tinayre (t) unaccompanied
12″—**LUM-32017**

[Léonin: Organum duplum]
(in Yves Tinayre Album No. 2)
Conductus: Beata viscera Mariae Virginis
(de Grève) (Song in Latin)
Yves Tinayre (t) unaccompanied
12″—**LUM-32011**
[Léonin: Organum Duplum]
(in Yves Tinayre Album No. 1)
Organum triplum "Difusa est gratia"
F. Anspach (triplum); E. Jacquier
(duplum); F. Mortens & M. Georges
(organum)—S. Cape
(in Vol. VII) 12″—**AS-65**
[Léonin: Organum duplum "Deum time"]
La Psallette de Notre Dame—
J. Chailley 12″—**G-DB5119**
[Ecole de Paris: Crucificat omnes]
(in French Masters of the Middle Ages
Set)
Organum Virgo Unacc. 3-pt. Motet in Latin
La Psalette de Notre Dame
[Gregorian: Te Deum] 12″—**LUM-32027**
Trio—Organum Triplex
Joseph Bonnet (Hammond Museum
Organ, Gloucester, Mass.) 12″—**V-18413**
[Couperin: Chaconne; Anon: Le moulin
de Paris: Caurroy: Fantaisie sur l'air
"Une Jeune Fillette"]
Conductus Triplum:
Salvatoris hodie (Transc. J. Chailley)
La Psallette de Notre Dame—J. Chailley
12″—**G-DB5118**
[Machault: Mass—Kyrie & Qui propter
nos]
(in French Masters of the Middle Ages
set)

PERRIN D'AGINCOURT (13th Century)
A French troubadour of the 13th Century.
Quand voi an la fin d'estey Song in French
Max Meili (t) with Fr. Seidersbeck
(viol) (in Vol. II) 12″—**AS-18**
[with examples of French Troubadours &
German Minnesänger of 12th & 13th
Centuries]

PESSARD, Emile (1843-1917)
A supervisor of vocal music in Paris schools, Pessard also composed operas, masses, orchestral works, piano pieces and songs.
L'Adieu du Matin
Richard Crooks (t) & Fr. Schauwecker
(pf) (in VM-846) 10″—**V-2176**
[Handel: Partenope—Se mia gioia;
Franz: Widmung]

PEZEL, (Pezelius), Johann (1639-1694)
An Austrian musician credited as an influence in the evolution of instrumental forms and the style of orchestral writing.
Fünff-stimmigte blasende Musik
Fr. Cortèges et Danses pour cuivres
Eng. **Music in 5 Voices for brass instruments**
Brass Ensemble from Republican Guard
Band (in Vol. I) 12″—**AS-2**

PFEIFFER, Johann (1697-1761)
Sonata—Viola da gamba & harpsichord
Eva Heinitz & Ruggero Gerlin
(in Vol. IX) 12″—**AS-90**

PFITZNER, Hans (1869-)

A conservative German composer in all the larger forms, Pfitzner's music has never enjoyed wide popularity outside Germany. However he is known elsewhere as a conductor, especially on recordings.

Duo for Violin, 'Cello & Orchestra
Max Strub, Ludwig Hoelscher & Berlin State Opera Orch.—Pfitzner
     2 12"—**G-DB4508/9**
Kätchen von Heilbronn, Op. 17a
Incidental Music
Overture
Berlin State Opera Orch.—Arthur
Grüber   2 12"—**O-50043/4**
Dresden Philharmonic Orch.—van
Kempen   2 12"—**PD-15241/2**
[Mozart: Nozze di Figaro—Overture]
[Rimsky-Korsakov: Sadko—Song of India, Prihoda, on CET-OR5058/9]

OPERAS In German

(DAS) CHRIST-ELFLEIN 1906
Eng. The Christmas Fairy
Overture Orchestra
Berlin State Opera Orch.—Pfitzner
    2 12"—**PD-66606/7**
[Wagner: Tristan und Isolde—Liebestod, dir. von Schillings]

(DAS) HERZ 1933
Liebesmelodie Orchestra
Berlin Philharmonic—Pfitzner
    10"—**PD-25273**

PALESTRINA 3 Acts 1917
Prelude, Act I Orchestra
German Philharmonic Orch. of Prague—
Keilberth 12"—**T-E3337**
Berlin Philharmonic—Knappertsbusch
    12"—**G-DB7677**
Berlin Philharmonic Orch.—Pfitzner
    12"—**PD-95459**
Preludes, Acts II & III Orchestra
Berlin State Opera Orch.—Pfitzner
    2 12"—**PD-95460/61**

(DIE) ROSE VON LIEBESGARTEN
Trauermarch
Berlin State Opera Orch.—Pfitzner
    12"—**PD-66557**

Sonata, F sharp minor, Op. 1
'Cello & Piano
Ludwig Hoelscher & Ludwig Funk
    3 12"—**G-DB4629/31**

SONGS In German
Collection
Hast du von den Fischerkinden, Op. 7, No. 1
Aum Abscheid meiner Tochter, Op. 10, No. 3
Der Gärtner, Op. 9, No. 1
Die Einsame, Op. 9, No. 2
Abitte, Op. 29, No. 1
In Danzig, Op. 22, No. 1
Nachts, Op. 26, No. 2
Michaelskirchplatz, Op. 19, No. 2
Gerard Hüsch (b) & Hans Pfitzner (pf)
    4 10"—**G-DA4475/8**

(Der) Gärtner, Op. 9, No. 1
See Collection above
H. H. Nissen (b) 10"—**G-DA4489**
[Schumann: Frühlingsfahrt]
Gretel, Op. 11, No. 5 (Carl Busse)
Lotte Lehmann (s) & Erno Balogh (pf)
  (in VM-419) 10"—**V-1858**
[Marx: Selige Nacht]
Ist der Himmel darum im Lenz so blau?
Friedel Beckmann (s) & Bruno Seidler-Winkler (pf) 12"—**G-EG6846**
[Brahms: Sapphische Ode]
Symphony, C major, Op. 46
Saxon State Orch.—Böhm
    2 12"—**G-DB5618/9**
Berlin Philharmonic Orch.—Pfitzner
[Last side blank] 3 12"—**PD-67604/6s**

PHILIDOR, Pierre (1681-1731)

A flute, as well as viol player, in the King's Band, Philidor composed many pieces for these instruments.

5th Suite Flute & Continuo
Jan Merry & Pauline Aubert
(harpsichord) 12"—**PAT-PAT36**

PHILIPS, Peter (d.1628)

Contributor to the "Fitzwilliam Virginal Book," Philips composed in instrumental music and many madrigals and motets.

Galliard Virginal
George Dyson (pf) 12"—**C-D40138**
[in a group of dances by Bull, Dowland, etc. illustrating "Early Keyboard Music" —Lecture No. 69 in the International Educational Series]

PHILLIPS, Burill (1907-)

A graduate of Eastman School of Music, Phillips has written for orchestra, piano, and chamber groups.

American Dance for Bassoon & String Orch.
V. Pezzi & Eastman-Rochester Sym. Orch.
—Hanson (in VM-802) 12"—**V-18102**
[Keller: Serenade]

PICK-MANGIAGALLI, Riccordo (1882-)

One of the most distinctive modern Italian composers (born in Bohemia), who in addition to operas and ballets, has produced a mass of instrumental music with programmatic titles, and is essentially a contrapuntist.

Ballata, Op. 66 Piano
R. Pick-Mangiagalli 12"—**G-AW300**
Burlesca
EIAR Symphony Orch.—Petralia
    10"—**CET-DD10100**
[Three Miniatures, Op. 4, Pt. 3]
(Il) Carillon Magico Ballet 1915
—Intermezzo delle Rose Orchestra
Milan Symphony—Serafin
    12"—**C-GQX10494**
[Mancinelli: Scene Veneziani]
EIAR Symphony Orch.—La Rosa Parodi
    12"—**CET-CB20257**
[Notturno Romantico—Walzer viennese]
[Busoni; Valser Danzato, Pt. 3, dir. Previtali, on CET-CB20166]

(La) Danza di Olaf, Op. 33
(from "Deux Lunaires")
—Arr. Orchestra
La Scala Orch.—Panizza 12"—G-AW243
[Casella: Couvent sur l'eau]
Leipzig Radio Orch.—Merten
12"—G-EH1312
[Bolart: Spanish Night—Overture]
Notturno, Op. 67 Piano
R. Pick-Mangiagalli 12"—G-AW302
[2 Waltz-Caprices, Op. 20]
Notturno & Rondò Fantastico, Op. 28
Orchestra
—Notturno only
La Scala Orch.—Panizza
[I Piccoli Soldati] 12"—G-AW3988
—Rondò Fantastico only
La Scala Orch.—Panizza
12"—G-AW3990

(IL) NOTTURNO ROMANTICO Opera
Viennese Waltz
EIAR Symphony Orch.—Parodi
12"—CET-CB20257
[Il Carillon Magico—Intermezzo delle
Rose]
(3) Miniatures, Op. 4, No. 1
Piano & Orchestra
Mario Salerno & EIAR Symphony Orch.
—Petralia 2 12"—CET-DD10099/100
[Burlesca]
(I) Piccoli Soldati Orchestra
La Scala Orch.—Panizza
12"—G-AW3988
[Notturno, from Op. 28]
Piccolo Suite See: La Danza di Olaf
Rapsodia epica, Op. 68 Piano
R. Pick-Mangiagalli 12"—G-AW301
(La) Ronde des Arlequins Piano
E. Bonzagni 10"—C-GQ7228
[Sinding: Rustle of Spring]
(La) Ronda di Ariele Piano
Nino Rossi 10"—G-DA5365
[Alfano: Nostalgie]
(2) Waltz-Caprices, Op. 20 Piano
R. Pick-Mangiagalli 12"—G-AW302
[Notturno]
Arrangements & Orchestrations
String Orchestra
See under
Bach: Prelude, from Unacc. Violin
Sonata No. 6 in E
Bach: Prelude, from Organ Prelude &
Fugue in D minor

PIERNE, Gabriel (1863-1937)
*A notable French organist and conductor who
is popularly known for his short orchestral
pieces and chamber music.*
Canzonetta Clarinet & Piano
Louis Cahuzac & Folmer Jensen
12"—C-LDX3
[Honegger: Sonatine in A major]
—Arr. Saxophone & Pf. M. Mule,
C-DF1557
Chanson d'Antrefois Saxophone Quartet
Chanson de la grand'maman
Members of La Garde Républicaine
Band 10"—C-DF1807

CYDALISE ET LE CHEVRE-PIED
Opera 2 Acts 1923
—Marche des petits faunes only
Eng. Entrance (or School) of the
Little Faunes
Boston "Pops" Orch.—Fiedler
(G-B8488) 10"—V-4319
[White: Mosquito Dance; J. Strauss:
Unter donner und blitz, polka]
Carnegie "Pops" Orch.—Hendl
12"—C-7591M
[Marche des petits soldats & Waldteufel:
España Waltz]
Jack Payne Orch. 12"—C-DX273
(C-DFX98) (C-DWX1596)
[Ravel: Boléro]
DUPLICATION: Victor Orch.—Reibold,
V-22163
—Arr. Violin & Piano Dushkin
Miguel Candela & M. Faure
10"—C-LF27
[Schubert: Moment Musical]
Etude de concert Piano
Lucette Descaves-Truc 12"—G-DB11138
[Roussel: Suite, Op. 14—Ronde only]
FRAGONARD Operetta in French
Miscellaneous vocal excerpts
André Baugé (b) & S. Laydecker (s)
2 10"—PAT-PA395/6
Giration Ballet I Act Chamber Orch.
(Composed expressly for the gramophone)
Ensemble from the Colonne Orch.—
Pierné 12"—C-LFX337
(C-GQX10726)
Impressions de Music-Hall Orchestra
Chorus Girls; L'excentrique (Little Tich);
Rideau—le numéro espagnol; Les clowns
musicaux (Les Fratellini)
—Arr. Violin & Piano
Henri Merckel & Mme. Pugnet-
Caillard 2 12"—G-DB11126/7
—L'excentrique & Le numéro espagnol only
Maria-Antonia de Castro (pf)
10"—PAT-PA1308
Impromptu Caprice, Opus 9 Harp
Lily Laskine 12"—G-L985
[Golestan: Ballade roumaine]
**Introduction et Variations sur un thème
populaire**
Saxophone Quartet of Paris
12"—G-L1033
Konzertstück for Harp & Orchestra
Lily Laskine & Pasdeloup Orch.—
Coppola 2 10"—G-K7621/2
Marche des petits soldats de plomb Orch.
*(Originally for piano in the "Album pour mes
petits amis")*
Eng. March of the Little Lead Soldiers
Boston "Pops" Orch.—Fiedler
(G-B8454) (G-K7735) 10"—V-4314
[Schubert: Marche Militaire]
Carnegie "Pops" Orch.—Hendl
12"—C-7591M
[Marche des petits faunes & Waldteufel:
España Waltz]
Lamoureux Orch.—Albert Wolff
12"—PD-66956
[Gounod: Marche funèbre d'une
Marionette]
DUPLICATION: Victor Orch., V-19730:
G-GW610

Pastorale, Op. 14 Wind Instruments
Société des Instruments à Vent—
Oubradous   12″—G-W1568
[Taffanel: Quintet for Wind Instruments,
Pt. 3]

**(Trois) Pièces en trio pour violon, alto
et violoncello**
Pasquier Trio
(PAT-PAT90/1)   2 12″—CX-153†

Prélude Organ
Eduard Commette (Lyons Cathedral)
           10″—C-DF682
[Boëllmann: Suite Gothique—Minuet]

Sérénade, Op. 7 Violin & Piano
Renée Chemet & pf. acc. 10″—G-DA955
[Toselli: Serenade]

—Arr. 'Cello & Piano
M. Maréchal & Y. Kornhold
[Grieg: Solvejg's Song] 10″—C-LF150
Cedric Sharp & pf. acc. 10″—D-F7681
[Tchaikovsky: Chant sans paroles]
—Arr. Sax: Viard, PAT-X98012

Sonata, D major, Op. 36 Violin & Piano
M. Candela & J. M. Darré
        3 12″—C-LFX758/60

PIERRE DE MOLINS (14th Century)

*A fourteenth century French musician, Pierre
de Molins was a friend of Jean II. The ballade
below illustrates a popular form of the "Ars
Nova."*

Ballade "De ce que fol pense"
H. Guermant (s) with lute, alto viol,
tenor flûte à bec acc.
      (in Vol. VI) 12″—AS-59
[with examples of the "Canon" in the
14th Century]

PIETRI, Giuseppe (1886-)

*A successful Italian operetta composer, Pietri
is little known outside of Italy.*

MARISTELLA Opera in Italian
**Qui dinanzi all'altare giuro
Io conosco un giardino** Tenor
A. Marcato   10″—C-GQ7191
—Io conosco only
Beniamino Gigli   10″—G-DA5377
[Giordano: Fedora—Amor ti vieta]
**Oh! la mia casa
Uno strano senso arcano** Soprano
R. Pampanini   10″—C-GQ7190

PILKINGTON, Francis (c.1562-1638)

*An English clergyman and madrigal composer
who also wrote for lutes and viols.*

Rest, sweet nymphs 4-pt. Ayre
(1st Book of Ayres, 1605)
St. George's Singers, unacc. 10″—C-5716
[Morley: Sing we and chant it]
(in Columbia History of Music, Vol. I:
CM-231)

PINTO, Octavio

*A contemporary Brazilian composer, husband
of Guiomar Novaës.*

Scenas Infantas Piano
Eng. Memories of Childhood
Guiomar Novaës
     (in CM-692†) 10″—C-17486D

PIPELARE, Matthias (End of 15th Century)

*A Netherlandish composer who composed nu-
merous masses, motets and songs. He used the
signature "Pipe" and the notes "la, re," whence
his name.*

Mass "L'homme armé"
—Credo only
Les paraphonistes de St. Jean-des-Matines
—G. de Van   12″—G-W1515

PISADOR, Diego (c.1508-c.1557)

*A noted Spanish lutenist author of one of the
most important collections of vihuela music—
"Libro de musica de vihuela"—containing original compositions and transcriptions of polyphonic works by Josquin, Morales and others.*

A las armas moriscote Song in Spanish
(from the above noted Collection)
Maria Cid (s) & Emilio Pujol (vihuela)
    (in Vol. II) 12″—AS-17
[with Spanish romances and villancicos
of the 16th Century]

PISTON, Walter (1894-)

*A versatile American composer who teaches
music at Harvard.*

(The) Incredible Flutist Ballet Suite
Boston "Pops" Orch.—Fiedler
        2 12″—VM-621†

Prelude & Allegro Organ & Orchestra
E. Power Biggs & Boston Symphony Orch.
—Koussevitzky   12″—V-11-9262

QUARTETS—Strings
No. 1
Dorian String Quartet 3 12″—CM-388†
[Cowell: Movement for String Quartet]
Suite for Oboe & Piano 1933
Louis Speyer & Walter Piston
        12″—TC-1561

PIZZETTI, Ildebrando (1880-)

*A conservative but individual and significant
Italian composer of marked lyric gifts.*

Aria, D major 1906 Violin & Piano
A. Poltronieri & I. Pizzetti
[Canti, Pt. 3]   12″—C-D14557

(Tre) Canti ad una giovane fidanzata
Violin & Piano
A. Poltronieri & I. Pizzetti
[Aria, D major] 2 12″—C-D14556/7

Phaedra Overture
La Scala Orch.—Marinuzzi
        12″—T-SKB3202

(LA) PISANELLA
Incidental music to d'Annunzio's drama
**Sul molo del porto di Famiagosta
La danza basso della Sparviero**
EIAR Symphony Orch.—Ferraro
        12″—CET-BB25083

SONATA—Violin & Piano, A major 1918
Yehudi & Hephzibah Menuhin
          4 12″—**G-DB3579/82**
[Mozart: Sonata, G major, K. 301—
Allegro only]

SONGS In Italian
I Pastori (d'Annunzio)
Margherita Carosio (s)   10″—**G-DA5403**
Ninna nanna di Uliva
Rosina Ziliani (s) & E. Magnetti (pf)
          10″—**CET-TI7053**
[Castelnuevo-Tedesco: Ninna nanna]

PIZZINI, Carlo Alberto

(Il) Poema delle Dolomiti Orchestra
EIAR Symphony Orch.—A. La Rosa
Parodi   2 12″—**CET-CB20251/2**
Symphony, C minor Orchestra
—Scherzo in Classical Style only
EIAR Symphony Orch.—Tansini
          12″—**CET-CB20244**
[Mulé: Largo for harp & Orch.]

PLANQUETTE, Robert (1848-1903)

*A French composer of over 20 successful oper-
ettas, Planquette is widely known for his often
performed "Chimes of Normandy."*

OPERETTAS In French
(LES) CLOCHES DE CORNEVILLE
2 Acts 1877
Eng. **The Chimes of Normandy**
Abridged recording
Soloists, Chorus & Orch.—Paul Minssart
        10 10″—**O-166407/16**
Vocal Selections
Soloists & Chorus, PD-516523
Fanléy Revoil & Chorus, PAT-PG17
Lemichel du Roy, PD-23299
Orchestral Potpourri
Orch. of German Opera House, Berlin—
H. Otto   12″—**T-E3154**
Overture Orchestra
Vienna Symphony Orch. 12″—**C-DFX80**
[Lecocq: Fille de Mme. Angot—Overture]
DUPLICATION: Symphony Orch.—Diot,
G-L640
See also French catalogues.
Valse
Marek Weber Orch., G-C2810: G-L1012

RIP RIP 1882 Eng. **Rip van Winkle**
Orchestral Selections: PD-27102: G-L914

POLDINI, Eduard (1869-   )

*Italian-Hungarian composer, Poldini wrote op-
eras, piano pieces, and vocal works. He is
known chiefly by the work listed below.*

Poupée valsante Piano
Ger. **Die tanzende Puppe**
Eng. **Dancing Doll**
Alexander Borowsky   10″—**PD-561127**
[Spindler: La fileuse]
—Arr. Violin & Piano Kreisler
Fritz Kreisler & Franz Rupp
          10″—**V-1981**

[Rimsky-Korsakoff: Sadko—Song of
India]
[Londonderry Air, on G-DA1622]
Miguel Candela & pf. acc.
          10″—**G-DA1339**
[Albéniz: Tango, D major]
Renée Chemet & pf. acc.
[Drdla: Souvenir]   10″—**G-DA811**
—Arr. Voice & Orch. La Forge
Lily Pons (s) & orch.—Kostelanetz
    (in CM-484)   12″—**C-71307D**
[Bishop: Home, Sweet Home]
—Arr. Orch & Misc.
Orchestre Raymonde, C-DB1563: A.
Sandler Trio, C-DB2004; A. Campoli
Orch., D-F3325

PONC, Miroslav (1902-   )

*A pupil of Alois Haba, Ponc has written quar-
ter-tone music.*

Wedding in the Eiffel Tower—Suite for
Cocteau's play (quarter-tone)
National Theatre Orch., Prague—Ponc
          12″—**ESTA-F5203**

PONCHIELLI, Amilcare (1834-1886)

*All that is left of Ponchielli in the active re-
pertoire is his opera "La Gioconda." He will
be remembered as one of the founders of the
Italian veristic opera.*

OPERAS In Italian

(IL) FIGLIOL PRODIGO 1880
Raccogli e calma Baritone
Mario Basiola   12″—**C-GQX10978**
[Cilea: L'Arlesiana—Racconto del Pas-
tore]

(LA) GIOCONDA 4 Acts 1876
Complete recording
Soloists, Chorus & Orch. of La Scala—
Molajoli   19 12″—**C-GQX10600/18**
The Cast:
Gioconda .... Giannina Arangi-
                    Lombardi (s)
Laura .... Ebe Stignani (ms)
La Cieca .... Camilla Rota (a)
Enzo Grimaldo .. Alessandro Granda (t)
Barnaba .... Gaetano Viviani (b)
Alvise Badoero .. Corrado Zambelli (b)
Isepo .... Giuseppe Nessi (t)
Zuane .... Aristide Baracchi (b)
Vittore Veneziani, Chorus master

Instrumental Selections
Royal Italian Marine Band—Aghemo
          12″—**G-S10026**
Individual Excerpts
ACT I
Feste! Pane! Opening Chorus
La Scala Chorus—Molajoli
          10″—**C-GQ7168**
[Puccini: Madama Butterfly—Humming
Chorus]
Figlia, che reggi il tremulo piè Trio
Minghini-Cattaneo, Granforte, Martis
[Voce di donna]   12″—**G-DB1448**

Voce di donna o d'angelo

A te questo rosario Alto & Ensemble
[La Cieca's Romanza]
Irene Minghini-Cattaneo, with Lucini
(s), Masini (b) & Chorus
[Figlia, che reggi]   12"—**G-DB1448**
Ebe Stignani, ensemble & chorus
[E un anatèma]   12"—**C-GQX10168**

—Solo versions
Ebe Stignani   12"—**CET-BB25055**
[Mascagni: Cavalleria Rusticana—Voi lo
sapete]
Blanche Thebom   12"—**V-11-9795**
[Wagner: Rheingold-Weiche, Wotan]
Bruna Castagna   12"—**C-71276D**
[Verdi: Don Carlos—O don fatale]
DUPLICATIONS: Aurora Buades,
C-CQ351; G. Zinetti, C-DQ1124; G. Bes-
anzoni, G-DA128*

Enzo Grimaldo, Principe di Santafior Tenor
& Baritone
Beniamino Gigli & Giuseppe de Luca
(G-DB1150)   12"—**V-8084**
[Bizet: Pêcheurs de Perles—Au fond du
temple saint]
[Donizetti: Lucia—Tombe degli avi miei,
on G-DB2235]

Maledici? sta ben Recit.

O monumento Monologue Baritone
Eng. **Barnaba's Soliloquy**
Leonard Warren   12"—**V-18293**
[Verdi: Falstaff—Monologo di Ford]
A. Reali   12"—**CET-BB25150**
[Verdi: Ernani—O de' verd'anni miei]
[Puccini: Fanciulla del West—Minnie
della mia casa, on CET-BB25128]
DUPLICATIONS: Benvenuto Franci,
G-DB1117; R. Stracciari, C-CQX16489

O Cuor! dono funesto Duo: 2 Sopranos &
Chorus
Arangi-Lombardi, Zinette & Chorus
          12"—**C-GQX10211**
[Così mantieni il patto]

ACT II

Marinesca—Ho! He! Ho! Chorus
La Scala Chorus—Molajoli
          12"—**C-GQX10265**
[Donizetti: Don Pasquale—Coro dei
servitori]

Barcarola: Pescator, affonda l'esca Bari-
tone & Chorus
Leonard Warren & Victor Chorale—
Morel   12"—**V-11-9790**
[Leoncavallo: Pagliacci—Prologue]
DUPLICATIONS: Giuseppe de Luca &
Metropolitan Opera Chorus, G-DB1436;
Riccardo Stracciari & chorus, C-D5043:
C-GQ7148; Benvenuto Franci & chorus,
G-DB1117

Cielo e mar Tenor

Eng. **Enzo's Romance**
Jussi Björling
(G-DB3302)   12"—**V-12150**
[Meyerbeer: Africana—O Paradiso]
[Puccini: Bohème—Racconto, on
G-DB5393]
Beniamino Gigli   12"—**V-7194**

[Donizetti: Elisir d'amore—Una furtiva
lagrima]
[Mascagni: Cavalleria Rusticana—Viva
il vino, on G-DB1499]
[Giordano: Andrea Chénier—Un dì, on
G-DB2234]
Giacomo Lauri-Volpi & Rome Opera
Orch.—Ricci   12"—**G-DB6352**
[Puccini: Turandot—Non piangere Liù]
Mario Binci   12"—**G-C3606**
[Verdi: Rigoletto—Ella mi fù rapita]
Richard Tucker   12"—**C-72399D**
[Meyerbeer: Africana—O paradiso]
DUPLICATIONS: G. Masini, CET-
BB25039; Augusto Ferrauto, CET-
CC2302; Alfred Piccaver, PD-66769;
Alessandro Granda, C-GQX10253; Fran-
cesco Merli, C-GQX10185; Aureliano
Pertile, G-DB1208; Antonio Melandri,
C-GQX10592; R. D'Alessio, C-CQX16457;
S. C. Lo Guidice, C-DQ272; Caruso,
G-DB113*: G-DB696*
In German: Willy Tressner, G-DB5597

Stella del marinar Mezzo-Soprano
Cloe Elmo   12"—**CET-BB25009**
[Massenet: Werther—Letter aria]

Laggiù nelle nebbie remote Duo: Soprano
& Tenor
I. Minghini-Cattaneo & L. Cecil
          12"—**G-DB1432**
[L'amo come il fulgor, Minghini-Cat-
taneo & DeMartis]

E un anatèma

L'amo come il fulgor del creato Duo:
Sopranos
Gina Cigna & Cloe Elmo
          12"—**CET-BB25059**
[Adriana Lecouvreur—Io son sua per
l'amore, Cigna]
Arangi-Lombardi & Ebe Stignani
[Voci di donna]   12"—**C-GQX10168**
I. Minghini-Cattaneo & De Martis
          12"—**G-DB1432**
[Laggiù nelle nebbie remote, with Cecil]

ACT III

Sì, morir ella de' Bass
Tancredi Pasero   12"—**C-GQX11069**
[Rossini: Barbiere di Siviglia—La Ca-
lunnia]

Qui chiamata m'avete? Duo: Soprano &
Bass
Ebe Stignani & Tancredi Pasero
          10"—**C-DQ1083**
Risë Stevens & Ezio Pinza
          12"—**C-72371D**
[Thomas: Mignon—Légères hirodelles]
Begins "Bella così, madonna"

Danza della ore Ballet Music
Eng. **Dance of the Hours**. Orchestra
National Symphony Orch.—Fistoulari
          12"—**D-K1119**
Chicago Symphony Orch.—Stock
          12"—**C-11621D**
Boston "Pops" Orch.—Fiedler
(G-C2812)   12"—**V-11833**
Hallé Orch.—Sargent   12"—**C-DX1029**
Tivoli Orch.—Thomas Jensen
          12"—**TONO-X25059**

DUPLICATIONS: Berlin Philharmonic Orch.—Weissmann, P-E10859; Berlin State Opera Orch.—Beutler, PD-15307; La Scala Orch.—Marinuzzi, G-DB2857; Milan Symphony Orch.—Molajoli, C-D14496; Melachrino Orch.—Melachrino, G-C3627; Bournemouth Municipal Orch.—**Birch, D-F8150**

ACT IV

Suicidio! Soprano
Zinka Milanov 12"—**V-11-9293**
[Bellini: Norma-Casta diva]
Emmy Destinn (Recorded 1914)
12"—**V-15-1014***
[Puccini: Madama Butterfly—Un bel dì]
Gina Cigna 12"—**C-GQX10593**
[Giordano: Andrea Chénier—La Mamma morta]
Helen Traubel
(in CM-675) 12"—**C-72112D**
[Mascagni: Cavalleria Rusticana—Voi lo sapete]
DUPLICATIONS: Rosa Raisa, G-DB2122; Bianca Scacciati, C-DQ1060; C. Boninsegna, CRS-11*; R. Ponselle, G-DB854*

Così mantieni il patto? Finale
Ebbrezza! Delirio! Duo: Soprano & Baritone
G. Arangi-Lombardi & E Molinari
12"—**C-GQX10211**
[O Cuor! dono funesto]
DUPLICATION: DeWitt & Battistini, G-DB216*

LINA

La madre mia Sop.
Margherita Carosio 12"—**G-DB6388**
[Bellini: Sonnambula—Ah! non credea mirarti]

POOT, Marcel (1901-   )
Ouverture Joyeuse
Brussels Symphony Orch.—Franz André
12"—**U-E14230**
[Jongen: Walloon Dance No. 2]

POPPER, David (1843-1913)
Popper wrote many works that are standard in the repertory of the 'cellist.
Chanson Villageoise Op. 62, No. 2
A. Földesy & pf. acc. 10"—**PD-24325**
[Spinnlied, Op. 55, No. 1]
Pablo Casals & pf. acc. 10"—**G-DA731**
[Fauré: Après un rêve]
Serenade, Op. 54, No. 2
A. Földesy & pf. acc. 10"—**PD-25060**
[Godard: Jocelyn—Berceuse]
Spinnlied, Op. 55, No. 1
Arnold Földesy & pf. acc.
[Chanson Villageoise] 10"—**PD-25325**
[Schubert: Ave María, on PD-24305]
Tarantella, Op. 33
A. Földesy & pf. acc. 10"—**PD-24416**
[Fauré: Sicilienne]
M. Marcelli-Herson & pf. acc.
[Lalo: Chants russes] 12"—**G-L837**
Vito, Op. 54, No. 5
Pablo Casals & pf. acc. 10"—**G-DA1015**
[Granados: Rondella Aragonesa]

PORPORA, Niccolò (1686-1767)
A well-known composer, conductor, and singing-teacher of his own time, Porpora outlived his own popularity. He wrote many operas, cantatas, and concerted chamber-music.
Aria
Luigi Chiarappa (vlc) & String Orch.
12"—**SEMS-1151**
[Bach: Suite No. 3—Air]
Fanfare regale Arr. Lualdi
Chamber Orch. of Conservatory of San Pietro a Majella, Naples—A. Lualdi
12"—**G-DBO5355**

PORRINO, Ennio (1910-   )
A pupil of Respighi, Porrino has written orchestral works and songs.

GLI ORAZI
Io per l'antico diritto; Ahi! che il littore lega le mani Bass
Tancredi Pasero 12"—**G-DB11305**
Sardegna Symphonic Poem
EIAR Symphony Orch.—A. La Rosa Parodi 2 12"—**CET-CB20274/5**

PORTER, Cole (1893-   )
COLLECTIONS
Songs of Cole Porter
Night & Day; Begin the Beguine; Ev'rything I love; What is this thing called love?; I've got you under my skin; In the still of the night
Risë Stevens (ms) 3 12"—**CM-630**
Night & Day—Collection of Song Hits
Night & day; I've got you under my skin; Begin the Beguine; Why shouldn't I?; What is this thing called love?; Rosalie; Easy to love; In the still of the night
Allan Jones (t) & Cho. 4 10"—**VM-1033**
Music of Cole Porter
In the Still of the Night; All Through the Night; I concentrate on you; I love you; I've got you under my skin; Blow, Gabriel, Blow
Andre Kostelanetz & his Orch.
3 12"—**CM-721**
Mexican Hayride—Selections
June Havoc, Wilbur Evans, Corinna Mura & Chorus of original production—Harry Sosnik 4 10"—**D-A372**
Panama Hattie—Selections
Ethel Merman & Orch.—Harry Sosnik
2 10"—**D-A203**
See domestic catalogues under the following titles of musical comedies and films for other recorded releases:
Anthing Goes; Born to Dance; Gay Divorcee; Jubilee; Leave it to Me; Let's Face It; The New Yorkers; Nymph Errant; Red, Hot & Blue; Rosalie; Seven Lively Arts; The Sun Never Sets; Wake Up and Dream; You Never Know

POULENC, Francis (1899-   )
One of the French "Six," Poulenc's works are mostly for the piano or small chamber ensembles. His songs are justly famous.

Aubade Concerto chorégraphique
Piano & Chamber Orchestra of 18 Instruments
Poulenc & Straram Orch.—Straram
       3   10"—C-LF33/5

(Les) Biches Ballet Orchestra & Chorus
1923
—No. 2 (Adagietto) & No. 3 (Rondeau)
—Arr. Piano
Francis Poulenc   12"—C-D15094

Mass in G major Unaccompanied Chorus in Latin
Les Chanteurs de Lyon—E. Bourmauck
       2   12"—C-RFX61/2

(3) Mouvements perpetuels Piano 1918
Eng. **Perpetual Motions**
Artur Rubinstein   12"—G-DB6467
[Fauré: Nocturne, A flat major, Op. 33, No. 3]
Oscar Levant
       (in CM-560)   12"—C-72081D
[Falla: Miller's Dance; Albéniz: Tango, D major]
—No. 1 only
Benno Moiseiwitsch   12"—G-C2998
[Debussy: Jardins sous la pluie; Stravinsky: Etude]

(2) Novellettes Piano
—No. 1, C major only
Moura Lympany   10"—D-M556
[Dohnanyi: Capriccio, F minor, Op. 28]

Pastourelle (L'Eventail de Jeanne, No. 8)
Piano
Oscar Levant
       (in CM-560)   12"—C-72079D
[Falla: El Amor Brujo—Ritual Fire Dance; Lecuona: Malagueña]
[Chopin: Etudes Nos. 5 & 12 & Lecuona: Malagueña, on C-71890D]
Vladimir Horowitz   12"—G-DB2247
[Toccata & Debussy: Etude No. 11]

Presto, B flat major
—Arr. Violin & Piano. Heifetz
Jascha Heifetz & Emanuel Bay
       (in VM-1126)   10"—V-10-1294
[Ravel: Valses Nobles et Sentimentales No. 6 & 7]

Sonata—Trumpet, Trombone & Horn
George Mager, Jacob Reichman & William Valkenier
       12"—NIGHT MUSIC-103/4

SONGS In French

(Le) Bestiaire—Six Poèmes (Apollinaire)
1918
Le Dromadaire; Le Chèvre du Tibet; La Sauterelle; La Dauphin; L' Ecrévisse; La Carpe
Pierre Bernac (b) & Francis Poulenc (pf)   12"—G-DB6299
[Montparnasse]
Claire Croiza (s) & Francis Poulenc (pf)
       12"—C-D15041
[Duparc: Invitation au voyage]

(Le) Chemin de l'amour
Yvonne Printemps (s)   10"—G-DA4927
[Yvain: Je chant de la nuit]

Dans le jardin D'Anna
Pierre Bernac (b) & Francis Poulenc (pf)   12"—G-DB6384
[Tel jour, telle nuit, Pt. 3]

Chansons gaillardes
La Belle Jeunesse & Invocation aux parques
Pierre Bernac (b) & Francis Poulenc (pf)   10"—G-DA4894
[Milhaud: Tourterelle]

Métamorphoses (de Vilmorin)
Reine des Mouettes; C'est ainsi que tu es; Paganini
Pierre Bernac (b) & F. Poulenc (pf)
       12"—G-DB6267
[2 Poems by Louis Aragon]

Montparnasse (Apollinaire)
Pierre Bernac (b) & F. Poulenc (pf)
[Le Bestiaire]   12"—G-DB6299

Nous voulons une petite soeur
Agnes Capri   10"—CdM-2001
[Satie: Je te veux]

Petites Voix
Victor Chorale—Shaw   10"—V-10-1409

(2) Poems by Louis Aragon
1. C   2. Fêtes Galantes
Pierre Bernac (b) & F. Poulenc (pf)
[Métamorphoses]   12"—G-DB6267

Tel jour, telle nuit (Paul Eluard)
(Cycle of nine songs)
Pierre Bernac (b) & F. Poulenc (pf)
       2   12"—G-DB6383/4
[Dans le jardin d'amour]

Toccata (Pièces pour le Piano, No. 2)
Piano
Vladimir Horowitz   12"—G-DB2247
[Pastourelle & Debussey: Etude No. 11]

PRAETORIUS, Michael (1571-1621)

A German theorist and a very prolific composer, entitled to a distinctive place in music history if only for his great work "Syntagma Musicum" (Musical Treatise).

Beati omnes 8-Part Chorus
Max Meili (t) with Basel Chamber Choir & 3 Trombones
       (in Vol. VIII)   12"—AS-72
[Hassler: Motet & Choral]

PART SONGS

Es ist ein Ros' entsprungen Christmas Song
Eng. **Lo, how a rose e'er blooming**
Dan. **En Rose saa jeg skyde**
St. Thomas Church Choir, Leipsig—Straube   10"—PD-24781
[Stille Nacht, arr. Schreck]
Copenhagen Boys' Choir—Wöldike (in Danish)   10"—G-X6995
[Goudimel—Arr. Kingo: Hører til, I høje Himle]
DUPLICATIONS: Spieleinigung Berlin, G-EG6116; Palestrina Choir (in Danish) —Wöldike, G-X2834; Wolfgang Kieling (treble) with Chorus & Organ, G-EG6280

Lobe den Herren alle Heiden
Chorale du Petit Séminaire de Paris (in French)—Vallet   10"—LUM-30053
[Bach: So gehst du nun]

Dans une étable obscure (unidentified)
Chorale du Petit Séminaire de Paris (in
French)—Vallet 10"—**LUM-30052**
[Trad. Le petit Jésus, sauveur adorable]

PRES, Josquin des See: Josquin

PROCH, Heinrich (1809-1878)

*A Viennese violinist, singing teacher and com-
poser of operas and lieder, best known by his
famous set of coloratura variations listed below.*

Air & Variations In Italian Soprano
(Variazioni di Proch)
Lily Pons (in CM-582) 10"—**C-17371D**
(Flute obb. Frank Versacci)
A. Galli-Curci 12"—**G-DB1144**
[Grétry: Zémire & Azor—La Fauvette]
Miliza Korjus (in German)
12"—**V-11831**
[Alabiev: The Nightingale]
[J. Strauss: Frühlingsstimmen, on
G-C2664: G-EH860]
DUPLICATIONS: C. Clairbert, PD-
66920; A. M. Guglielmetti, C-GQX10181

PROKOFIEFF, Serge (1891-   )

*One of the most accomplished, versatile and
talented of the Russian contemporary composers, Prokofieff has become well known for his
orchestral symphonic works, his ballets and for
his musical fairy tale "Peter and the Wolf." He
is well represented on discs and is heard as solo
performer on many of them.*

Collection

(18) Piano Works
Visions Fugitives, Op. 22; Suggestion diabolique, Op. 4, No. 4; Deuxième Conte de
la vieille Grand'mère, Op. 31; Sonatine
Pastorale, Op. 59; Troisième Conte de la
vieille Grand'mère, Op. 31; Deuxième, Gavotte, Op. 25; Etude, Op. 52; Paysage,
Op. 59; Andante, Op. 29; Troisième Gavotte, Op. 32
Serge Prokofieff (pf)
4 12"—**G-DB5030/3**

ALEXANDER NEVSKY Op. 78 Cantata
Philadelphia Orch., Westminster Choir
(in English & Latin) with Jennie Tourel
(ms)—Ormandy
(C-LX977/81†) 5 12"—**CM-580†**

Excerpts from the Film
Song of Alexander Nevsky; Arise, Ye
Russian People
USSR Cho. & Orch.—Orlov 10"—**D-M579**
(Also in DISC-754)

Andante, Op. 29 Piano (from Fourth
Sonata)
Serge Prokofieff 12"—**G-DB5033**
[Gavotte No. 3, Op. 32]

Children's Pieces, Op. 65 Piano
Morning; Promenade; Fairy Tale; Tar-
antelle; Regrets; Waltz; Grasshopper's
Parade; Rain and the Rainbow; Tag;
March; Evening; Moonlight Meadows
Ray Lev 3 10"—**CH-AC**
See also Summer Day Suite

CHOUT Op. 21, Ballet Suite No. 1 Orchestra
Danse des bouffons; Le bouffon travesti
en jeune fille; Danse des filles des bouffons; Dans la chambre à coucher du
marchand; La querelle du bouffon avec le
marchand; Danse finale
Lamoureux Orch.—Wolff
(PD-67059/60) 2 12"—**PD-516583/4**

CINDERELLA—Ballet Suite
—Prelude; Waltz
K. Erdeli (harp) & Bolshoi Theatre Orch.
—Freier **USSR-13496, 6381**
—Adagio
Bolshoi Theatre Orch.—Freier
10"—**USSR-13497/8**
"Classical" Symphony—See under Sym-
phonies

CONCERTOS—Piano & Orchestra
No. 3, C major, Op. 26
Serge Prokofieff & London Symphony—
Coppola
(G-DB1725/7†) 3 12"—**VM-176†**
Dmitri Mitropoulos & Robin Hood Dell
Orch.— 3 12"—**CM-667†**

CONCERTOS—Violin & Orchestra
No. 1, D major, Op. 19
Joseph Szigeti & London Philharmonic—
Beecham 3 12"—**CM-244†**
[Final side blank]
[Paganini: Caprice No. 2, on
C-LX433/5†: C-GQX10971/3]
No. 2, G minor, Op. 63
Jascha Heifetz & Boston Symphony—
Koussevitzky
(G-DB3604/6†) 3 12"—**VM-450†**
Contes de le vieille grand'mère, Op. 31
Piano
Eng. Tales of the Old Grandmother (4
Pieces)
—No. 2
Serge Prokofieff, G-DB5031
—No. 3
Serge Prokofieff, G-DB5032
Etude, Op. 52 (from Six Transcriptions for
Piano)
Serge Prokofieff, G-DB5032
Gavottes Piano
—No. 2, Op. 25 (Same as the Gavotte of
"Classical" Symphony)
Serge Prokofieff, G-DB5032
—No. 3, Op. 32 (from Four Pieces for
Piano)
Serge Prokofieff, G-DB5033

LIEUTENANT KIJE—Suite, Op. 60 Or-
chestra
(Music from the film "The Czar Wants to
Sleep")
Birth of Kije; Romance; Kije's Wedding;
Troika; Burial of Kije
Boston Symphony Orch.—Koussevitzky
3 12"—**VM-459†**
[Love for 3 Oranges—March & Scherzo]

**(THE) LOVE FOR THREE ORANGES, Op.
33** Opera in 4 Acts 1921

Symphonic Suite, Op. 33a Orchestra
No. 1, Les ridicules 2. Scène infernale
(Waltz-Scherzo) 3. Marche 4. Scherzo 5.
La prince et la princesse 6. La fuite

—Nos. 2, 3, 5
NBC Symphony—Stokowski
(G-DB6151)   12"—V-18497

—Nos. 3, 4
Boston Symphony Orch.—Koussevitzky
(in VM-459) 12"—V-14950
[Lt. Kije Suite, Pt. 5]
[Tchaikovsky: Romeo and Juilet, Pt. 5,
on G-DB3167]
[Sibelius: Pohjola's Daughter, Pt. 3, on
G-DB5723]
[Older version with Classical Symphony,
Pt. 3, on V-7197: G-D1858: G-AW174]

—No. 3
—Arr Piano
Andor Földes, in CON-22

—Arr. 2 Pianos
Arthur Whittemore & Jack Lowe,
V-10-1042

Mélodie, Op. 35, No. 3
Davis Oistrakh (vl) & Abram Makarov
(pf)   12"—U-G14741
[Scriabin: Nocturne, F sharp minor, Op.
5, No. 1]

Overture on Hebrew Themes, Op. 34 Clar-
inet, Piano & String Quartet
William Novinski & George Ockner
(vls), Bernard Milopky (vla), Milton
Forstat (vlc), David Weber (cl), Vivian
Rivkin (pf)   12"—DISC-4020

Paysage, Op. 59 Piano (from Three Piano
Pieces)
Serge Prokofieff, G-DB5032

Peter and the Wolf—An Orchestral Fairy
Tale, Op. 67
Boston Symphony Orch.—Koussevitsky
(Richard Hale, narrator)
(G-DB3900/2†)   3 12"—VM-566†
All-American Orch.—Stokowski (Basil
Rathbone, narrator) 3 12"—CM-477†
DUPLICATIONS: Orch. (Sterling Hol-
loway, narrator)—Charles Wolcott,
V-Y323; Decca Symphony (Frank
Luther, narrator)—Smallens, D-A130

—Arr. Narrator & Piano Prokofieff
Milton Cross & Mario Janero
4 10"—MC-65

—Theme & Processional
—Arr. Violin & Piano Grunes
Richard Odnoposoff & Valentin Pavlovsky
12"—V-11-8849
[Paganini-Kochanski: La Campanella]

Prelude, C major, Op. 12, No. 7 Piano or
Harp
(from Ten Pieces for Piano)
Alexander Borowsky (pf) (Argentine)
12"—V-11-8741
[Rachmaninoff: Preludes, G major & G
minor]

QUARTETS—String

No. 1, B minor, Op. 50
Stuyvesant String Quartet
3 12"—CM-448†

No. 2, F major, Op. 92
Gordon String Quartet
6 12"—CH-A1 (limited edition)

ROMEO AND JULIET—Ballet
1st Suite—Op. 64 bis
No. 1, Dance of the People; No. 2, Scene;
No. 3, Madrigal; No. 4, Minuet; No. 5,
Masques; No. 6, Romeo & Juliet; No. 7,
Death of Tybalt
Bolshoi Theatre Orch.—Feier
3 10"—USSR-13952/7

—No. 5 only
Gregor Piatigorsky (vlc) & Valentin
(Arr. Piatigorsky)
Pavlovsky (pf) (Arr. Piatigorsky)
(in CM-501) 10"—C-17446D
[Granados: Spanish Dance No. 2]
Jascha Heifetz (vl) & Emanuel Bay (pf)
(in D-A492) 10"—D-24130
[Gluck-Kreisler: Orfeo—Mélodie]

2nd Suite
No. 1, Montagues & Capulets; No. 2, Ju-
liet, the Maiden; No. 3, Friar Lawrence;
No. 4, Dance; No. 5, Parting of Romeo &
Juliet; No. 6, Dance of the West Indian
Slave Girls; No. 7, Romeo at Juliet's
Grave
Moscow State Philharmonic Orch.—
Prokofieff   6 10"—USSR-7754/65
NOTE: The American pressings (DISC-754, 6
12" records), omit the second half of No. 2,
Juliet the Maiden. The English pressings,
(D-Z1 & Z3/6, 5 10" records), omit No. 2 en-
tirely.

—Nos. 1, 2, 4 & 7 only
Boston Symphony Orch.—Koussevitzky
2 12"—VM-1129†

Sarcasm, Op. 17, No. 5 Piano
Alexander Borovsky   10"—PD-561095
[Glazunov: Etude de Concert, C major]
[Vision fugitive & Bach: Italian Con-
certo, Pt. 3, on Argentine V-10-1241]

Scythian Suite "Ala and Lolly" Op. 20
Chicago Symphony Orch.—Defauw
3 12"—VM-1040†

SONATAS—Piano
No. 3, "D'après les Vieux Cahiers"
Shura Cherkassy   2 12"—VOX-624
[Toccata]

No. 6, Op. 82
V. Merzhänov USSR-14100/2; 14105/9;
13745A/6A

No. 7, Op. 83
Vladimir Horowitz 2 12"—VM-1042†
Friedrich Gulda   In prep., Dutch Decca

SONATA Violin & Piano
D major, Op. 94a
Joseph Szigeti & Leonid Hambro
3 12"—CM-620†

Sonatine Pastorale, Op. 59 Piano (from 3
Piano Pieces)
Serge Prokofieff, G-DB5031

Suggestion diabolique, Op. 4, No. 4 Piano
(from 4 Pieces for piano)
Serge Prokofieff, G-DB5031
Galina Werschenska   10"—G-DA5200
[Marpurg: Rondeau]
Shura Cherkassky, in VOX-165

Summer Day—Suite
Orchestral version of Children's Pieces, Op. 65
Santa Monica Symphony Orch.—Rach-
milovich 2 12"—**DISC-803**
[Toccata]

SYMPHONIES Orchestra

No. 1, D major, Op. 25 "Classical"
Minneapolis Symphony—Mitropoulos
(C-LX923/4) 2 12"—**CX-166**†
[Mendelssohn: Octet, Op. 20—Scherzo]
St. Louis Symphony—Golschmann
(G-AW173/4) 2 12"—**VM-942**†
Boston Symphony Orch.—Koussevitzky
(G-D1857/8) 2 12"—**V-7196/7**
[Love for 3 Oranges—Scherzo & March]
(G-AW173/4)
Philadelphia Orch.—Ormandy
2 12"—**CX-287**†

—3rd Mvt. (Gavotte) only Arr. Grunes
Violin & Piano
Joseph Szigeti & Nikita de Magaloff
10"—**C-17130D**
[Stravinsky-Dushkin: Petrouchka-Danse
Russe; Lie-Szigeti: Snow]

No. 5, B flat major, Op. 100
Boston Symphony Orch.—Koussevitzky
5 12"—**VM-1095**†
New York Philharmonic-Symphony
Orch.—Rodzinski 5 12"—**CM-661**†

Toccata Piano
Shura Cherkassky, in VOX-624
Lillian Steuber, in DISC-803

(20) Visions Fugitives, Op. 22 Piano

—Nos. 3, 5, 6, 9, 10, 11, 16, 18
Serge Prokofieff, G-DB5030

—Unspecified excerpts
Alexander Borovsky (Argentine)
10"—**V-10-1241**
[Sarcasm, Op. 17, No. 5 & Bach: Italian
Concerto, Pt. 3]

PUCCINI, Giacomo (1858-1924)
*One of the most famous of near-modern Italian
opera composers, his works are performed more
frequently than those of possibly any other
dramatic composer save Verdi and Wagner.
His popular works are not necessarily his best
and even though we have complete recordings
of most of them, works such as "Gianni Schicchi" and "Turandot" are seldom performed.*

Inno di Roma Hymn in Italian (F. Salva-
tori)
Josef Hermann (b) w. Leipzig Radio
Chorus & Orch.—Merten
12"—**G-DB5642**
[Turandot—Invocation to the moon]
DUPLICATION: Symphony Orch. &
Chorus, C-DQ2402

OPERAS In Italian

(LA) BOHEME 4 Acts 1896
Fr. Le Vie de Bohême

Complete recording
La Scala Soloists, Chorus & Orchestra—
Berrettoni 13 12"—**VM-518/519**†
(G-DB3448/60 in GM-313†)
The Cast:
Rodolfo .... Beniamino Gigli (t)

Mimì .... Licia Albanese (s)
Musetta .... Tatiana Menotti (s)
Marcello .... Afro Poli (b)
Colline .... Duilio Baronti (bs)
Schaunard ...... Aristide Baracchi (b)
Benoit & Alcindoro . Carlo Scattola (bs)
Parpignol .... Nello Palai (t)
Chorus Master: Vittore Veneziani

Complete recording
La Scala Soloists, Chorus & Milan Sym-
phony Orch.—Molajoli 13 12"—**C-OP5**†
(C-D14515/27) (C-9846/58)
[Manon Lescaut—Intermezzo on Side 26]
The Cast:
Mimì .... Rosetta Pampanini (s)
Musetta .... Luba Mirella (s)
Rodolfo .... Luigi Marini (t)
Marcello .... Gino Vanelli (b)
Colline .... Tacredi Pasero (bs)
Schaunard ...... Aristide Baracchi (b)
Benoit ...... Salvatore Baccaloni (bs)
Parpignol .... Carlo Nessi (t)
Chorus Master: Vittore Veneziani

Complete recording
Metropolitan Opera House Soloists,
Chorus & Orchestra—Antonicelli
13 12"—**C-OP27**†
The Cast:
Rodolfo .... Richard Tucker (t)
Mimì .... Bidú Sayão (s)
Musetta .... Mimi Benzell (s)
Marcello ..... Francesco Valentino (b)
Colline .... Nicola Moscona (bs)
Schaunard .... George Chehanovski (b)
Benoit
Alcindoro
.............Salvatore Baccaloni (bs)
Parpignol ...... Ludovico Oliviero (t)

"Recordrama"—The Heart of "La Bohème"
[Extracted from above set VM-518/519]
5 10"—**VM-980**†

Abridged recording
La Scala Soloists & Chorus with Milan
Symphony Orch. 6 12"—**C-DX604/9**†
[Extracted from the above set C-OP5]

Abridged recording In French
Opéra-Comique Soloists, Chorus &
Lamoureux Orch.—Wolff
(PD-566077/81) 5 12"—**PD-27362/6**
The cast includes: Germaine Corney,
Madeleine Sibille, Marcel Claudel, André
Gaudin, Paul Payen, José Beckmans.

Abridged recording In German Arr.
Weigert & Maeder
Berlin State Opera Soloists, Chorus &
Orch.—Weigert 5 12"—**PD-27357/61**
The cast includes: F. Hüni-Mihacsek,
Hedwig Jungkurth, Helge Roswaenge,
Armin Weltner, Edwin Heyer, Gerald
Kasenow, Waldemar Henke.

ACT IV only Complete version For details
see under ACT IV

Orchestral Selections (Fantasias, etc.)
London Symphony—Richard Tauber
(arr. Godfrey) 12"—**C-72235D**
Berlin Concert Orch.—Seidler-Winkler
12"—**G-EH1076**
Marek Weber Orch.—(arr. Gauwin)
(G-FKX60) 12"—**G-EH91**
DUPLICATIONS: Berlin State Opera

Orch.—Melichar, PD-27270: PD-24441;
German Opera House—Schmidt-Isserstedt, T-E2289

Individual Excerpts

ACT I

Nei cieli bigi Tenor & Baritone
Dino Borgioli & G. Vanelli
                          10"—**C-DQ1104**
[O Mimì, tu più non torni, Act IV]

Che gelida manina (Racconto di Rodolfo)
Ger. **Wie eiskalt ist dies Händchen**
Fr. **Que cette main est froide**
Eng. **Your tiny hand is frozen**
Ferruccio Tagliavini
       (in CET-1)   12"—**CET-BB25021**
[Cilea: L'Arlesiana—Lamento di Fed-
erico]
Jussi Björling   12"—**V-12039**
[Verdi: Aida—Celeste Aida] (G-DB3049)
[Ponchielli: Gioconda—Cielo e mar, on
G-DB5393]
Beniamino Gigli   12"—**G-DB1538**
[Gounod: Faust—Salve dimora]
G. Malipiero   12"—**CET-BB25052**
[Boito: Mefistofele—Giunto sul passo
estremo]
Gino Sinimberghi   12"—**PD-27433**
[Donizetti: L'Elisir d'Amore—Una fur-
tiva lagrima]
Stefan Islandi   12"—**G-DB5247**
[Donizetti: L'Elisir d'Amore—Una
furtiva lagrima]
DUPLICATIONS: Alessandro Ziliani,
G-DB2521; Giovanni Martinelli,
G-DB979; Mario Binci, G-C3541:
G-S10499; Alfred Piccaver, PD-66889;
Nino Martini, C-71343D; Jan Kiepura,
O-123824; Giuseppe Lugo, G-DB5093:
G-DB3276; Aureliano Pertile,
G-DB-1479; Sydney Rayner,
D-K997; Miguel Fleta, G-DB1034;
Lionello Cecil, C-D16411; Alessandro
Granda, C-GQX10253; Enzo de Muro
Lomanto, C-GQX10251; Roberto d'Ales-
sio, C-GQX10226; Libero de Luca, In
prep., Swiss Decca; Caruso, G-DB113*;
G. Masini, C-CQX16524; A. Ferrauto,
CET-CC2049; A. Cortis, G-DB1468; A.
Valente, G-HN766; Otte Svendsen, TONO-
X25017
In French:
Georges Thill, C-LFX144; Giuseppe
Lugo, PD-95478: PD-566139; A. D'Ar-
kor, C-RFX39; Enrico di Mazzei,
O-123508; Miguel Villabella,
PAT-X90027: O-123516
In German:
Peter Anders, T-E2628; Marcel Wittrisch,
G-DB4408: T-E1495; Julius Patzak, PD-
90182; Helge Roswaenge, PD-66824
In English:
Webster Booth, G-C3030; Browning
Mummery, G-C2662; James Johnston,
C-DX1455
In Hungarian: K. von Pataky, RAD-
SP8017

Si, mi chiamano Mimì Soprano
Fr. **On m'appelle Mimi**   Ger. **Man nennt
mich jetz nur Mimi**
Eng. **My name is Mimi**
Claudia Muzio
            (in CM-259)   12"—**C-9167M**
[Mascagni: Cavalleria Rusticana—Voi lo
sapete]
[Delibes: Filles de Cadiz, on C-BQX2508:
C-LCX29]
[Boito: Mefistofele—L'altra notte in
fondo al mare, on C-BQX2519]
Margherita Carosio   12"—**G-DB6343**
[Verdi: Traviata—Addio del passato]
Bidú Sayão   12"—**C-71320D**
[Butterfly—Un bel dì]
Mafalda Favero   12"—**G-DB3200**
[Manon Lescault—In quelle trine]
Eidé Noréna   12"—**G-DB4924**
[Donde lieta usci]
Grace Moore
(G-DB6031)   12"—**V-17189**
[Charpentier: Louise-Depuis le jour]
Magda Olivero   12"—**CET-BB25053**
[Tosca—Vissi d'arte]
Dorothy Kirsten   12"—**V-11-9694**
[Donde lieta usci]
Judith Hellwig, In Prep. Swiss Decca
DUPLICATIONS: Lucrezia Bori, V-14206
in VM-329: V-6790: G-DB1644; Rosetta
Pampanini, C-GQX10247; Jeanette Mac-
Donald, V-11-9599; Mafalda Favero,
C-D6123; Mercedes Capsir, C-GQX10205;
Xenia Belmas, PD-66631; Arangi-Lom-
bardi, C-GQX10508; Bianca Scacciati,
C-GQX10231; R. Torri, G-S10467;
Laurenti, C-CQX16456; M. Sheridan,
G-DB988; M. Zamboni, C-CQ710,
C-DQ1120; M. Di Voltri, C-D5427; Marta
Eggerth, O-123823; Edith Oldrup-Peder-
sen, TONO-X25017
In German: Erna Sack, T-SK3242; Maria
Reining, G-DB7648; Erna Berger,
T-SK3113; Maria Cebotari, G-DB4415;
Hildegarde Ranczak, T-SK1197
In French: Lily Pons, O-123623; Ninon
Vallin, O-123508: PAT-X90028; Géori-
Boué, O-123871; Gabrielle Ritter-Ciampi,
PD-516691; Fanny Heldy, G-DB1513;
Germaine Féraldy, C-D15096; Jane La-
val, C-LFX64; Marthe Nespoulous,
C-RFX24; Bernadette Delprat, PAT-
PGT7
In English: Joan Cross, G-C2824; Joan
Hammond, C-DX1003

O soave fanciulla Duo: Soprano & Tenor
Ger. **O du süssestes Mädchen**
Eng. **Lovely maid in the moonlight**
Mafalda Favero & A. Ziliani
[Che gelida manina]   12"—**G-DB2521**
Maria Caniglia & Beniamino Gigli
                            12"—**G-DB3225**
[Verdi: Aida-Celesta Aida, Gigli]
Pia Tassinari & Piero Pauli
                            12"—**G-DB1932**
[Boito: Mefistofele—L'altra notte in
fondo, Tassinari]
Hjördis Schymberg & Jussi Björling
(G-DB6119)   12"—**V-11-8440**
[Verdi: Rigoletto—E il sol dell'anima]
DUPLICATIONS: Margit Angerer & A.
Piccaver, PD-66859; Rosetta Pampanini
& Dino Borgioli, C-GQX10182; A. Cipelli
& L. Marini, G-DQ1095; Gigli & Zam-
boni, G-DB271*; Edith Oldrup-Pedersen

& Otte Svendsen, TONO-X25031
In German: Maria Cebotari & Marcel
Wittrisch, G-DB4415
In English: Joan Cross & Webster Booth,
G-C3053; Joan Hammond & David
Lloyd, C-DX1039

ACT II

Questa è Mimì Quartet
Pauli, Palai, Masini, Basi
10"—**G-DA1204**
[Gianni Schicchi-Firenze è come un albero, Pauli]

—**Rodolfo's part** only Tenor
E. Parmeggiani, C-D5625

Quando me'n vo' soletta Soprano
Fr. D'un pas léger—**Valse de Musette**
Ger. Will ich allein—**Walzer der Musette**
Eng. **Musetta's Waltz Song**
Bidú Sayão   10"—**C-17515D**
[Gianni Schicchi—O mio babbino caro]
Lucrezia Bori
(G-DA981)   10"—**V-1333**
[Varney: Valse d'oiseau]
Conchita Supervia (in French]
10"—**P-RO20180**
[Gounod: Faust—Faites-lui mes aveux]
DUPLICATION: Edith Oldrup-Pedersen,
TONO-X25034
In French: Germaine Féraldy, PAT-
PG63; Yvonne Brothier, G-DA4805
In German: Marta Eggerth, O-123823;
Erna Berger, T-SK3113: PD-10267
In Danish: Tenna Frederiksen Kraft,
G-V194

O Marcello! Ensemble
Ger. **Marcell, da bist bu**
Hüni-Mihacsek, De Garmo, Roswaenge,
Scheidl (in German)   12"—**PD-66764**
[Addio dolce svegliare]

ACT III

Mimì? Son io Duo: Soprano & Baritone
Fr. Je comptais vous trouver ici
Germaine Féraldy & G. Villier (in
French)   12"—**C-D15096**
[Mi chiamano Mimì, Féraldy]

Mimì è una civetta Trio
Mimì è tanto malata!
—**Rodolfo's part** only Tenor
Antonio Cortis, G-DA757; L. Cecil,
C-DQ252

Addio di Mimì (Mimi's Farewell)
Donde lieta uscì Soprano
Fr. La chambre qu'autrefois j'avais
quittée
Pia Tassinari
(in CET-7) 12"—**CET-BB25143**
[Mascagni: L'Amico Fritz—Son pochi
fiori]
Bidú Sayão
(in CM-612)   12"—**C-72093D**
[Bellini: Sonnambula—Ah non credea]
Claudia Muzio
(C-LC22)   12"—**C-BQ6003**
[Tosca—Vissi d'arte]
[Reger: Mariä Wiegenlied on
C-BQ6006]
Lisa Perli (Dora Labette)
(in CM-274†)   12"—**C-68774D**

[Act IV, complete version, Pt. 7]
Eidé Noréna   12"—**G-DB4924**
[Mi chiamano Mimì]
Dorothy Kirsten   12"—**V-11-9694**
[Mi chiamano Mimì]
DUPLICATIONS: A. Oltrabella,
G-DA1479; M. Zamboni, C-DQ1120:
C-CQ710; Bianca Scacciati, C-GQ7069; M.
Favero, C-DQ1071; Laurenti, C-DQ658
In French: Yvonne Brothier, G-DA4805;
Ninon Vallin, PAT-X90028; Germaine
Féraldy, C-LF8; Germaine Corney, PD-
524074
In English: Joan Cross, G-B8666; Joan
Hammond, C-DX1039

Quartet

Addio dolce svegliare
Che facevi, che dicevi
Pia Tassinari, Ferrucio Tagliavini, M.
Huder, Enzo Mascherini
12"—**CET-BB25121**
Farrar, Caruso, Viofora, Scotti
(in VM-953) 12"—**V-16-5001***
[Verdi: Rigoletto—Quartet]
Pampanini, Borgioli, Rettorre, Vanelli
12"—**C-7307M**
[Verdi: Trovatore-Miserere, with Arangi-
Lombardi, Merli & Chorus]
[O soave fanciulla, on C-GQX10182]
In French: Vallin, Sibille, Baugé, Villa-
bella, PAT-X90056
In German: Hüni-Mihacsek, Tilly de
Garmo, Roswaenge, Scheidl, PD-66764
—**1st part** (Ci lascieremo alla stagion) only
Marini & Cipelli, C-DQ1095

ACT IV

Complete recording
Soloists & London Philharmonic Orch.—
Beecham   4 12"—**CM-274†**
[Addio, Act III, with Lisa Perli]
The Cast:
Mimì .... Lisa Perli (s)
Rodolfo .... Heddle Nash (t)
Musetta .... Stella Andreva (s)
Marcello .... John Brownlee (b)
Schaunard .... Robert Alva (b)
Colline .... Robert Easton (bs)

In un coupé
O Mimì, tu più non torni Duo: Tenor &
Baritone
Beniamino Gigli & Giuseppe De Luca
(G-DB1050)   12"—**V-8069**
[Verdi: Forza del Destino—Solenne in
quest'ora]
Jan Peerce & Leonard Warren
(in VM-1156†) 12"—**V-11-9767**
[Verdi: Forza del Destino—Solenne in
quest'ora]
Caruso & Scotti
(G-DM105*)   12"—**V-8000***
[Verdi: Forza del Destino—Solenne in
quest'ora]
John McCormack & M. Sammarco (Re-
corded 1910)   12"—**V-15-1009***
[Verdi: Traviata—Parigi o cara, McCor-
mack & Bori]
DUPLICATIONS: Luigi Fort & Leo Pic-
cioli, C-DQ1976; K. von Pataky & Hein-

rich Schlusnus, PD-73090; P. Civil & G.
Vanelli, C-DQ666
In French: Villabella & Baugé, PAT-
PGT14
In German: Marcel Wittrisch & Hans
Reinmar, T-E1756; Helge Rosenwaenge
& Gerhard Hüsch, G-DB4499
In English: Webster Booth & Dennis
Noble, G-C3369; Heddle Nash & Dennis
Noble, C-DX212

Vecchia zimarra Bass
Fr. O défroque si chère (Air de Colline)
Ezio Pinza   10″—G-DA908
[Tosti: L'Ultima canzone]
DUPLICATION: Tancredi Pasero,
C-DQ1086
In French: André Balbon, PAT-X90076;
Paul Dupré, O-188763; Arthur Endrèze,
O-188864

Sono andati?

Oh! Dio, Mimì (Death Scene)
Fr. Ils sont partis
Recorded versions of the final scene vary con-
siderably. That by Bori & Schipa includes only
the parts of Mimi & Rodolfo. The single-sided
versions contain the first section only (Sono
andati?) and those for soprano alone only
Mimi's part.
Lucrezia Bori & Tito Schipa
(G-DB911)   12″—V-8068

—**Sono andati?** only
Margit Angerer & A. Piccaver, PD-66859;
De Voltri & Polverosi, C-D5427
In French: Ninon Vallin & Villabella,
PAT-X90056
In German: Hedwig von Debicka & Helge
Roswaenge, PD-66881

—**Sono andati?** (Mimi's part only) Soprano
Xenia Belmas, PD-66631; Mafalda
Favero, C-DQ1071

EDGAR 1889

Intermezzo to Act III Orchestra
La Scala Orch.—Sabajno
                             12″—G-S10368
[Mascagni: Guglielmo Ratcliff—Inter-
mezzo to Act IV]

(LA) FANCIULLA DEL WEST 3 Acts 1910
Ger. Das Mädchen aus dem goldenen
Westen
Fr. La Fille du Far-West
Eng. The Girl of the Golden West

Individual Excerpts

ACT I

Minnie della mia casa Air of Rance Bari-
tone
Tito Gobbi   10″—G-DA5430
[Mozart: Don Giovanni—Deh vieni alla
finestra]
A. Reali   12″—CET-BB25128
[Ponchielli: Gioconda—O Monumento]

Laggiù nel Soledad Soprano
Gina Cigna   10″—C-GQ7186
[Bizet: Carmen—Scène des cartes,
Baudes]

ACT II
Or son sei mesi Tenor
Alessandro Valente   10″—G-HN764
[Ch'ella mi creda]
Bernardo De Muro   10″—G-DA997
[Ch'ella mi creda libero]
DUPLICATIONS: A. Lindi, C-DQ1118;
H. Lazaro, C-GQX10141; A. Melandri,
C-GQ7174

ACT III
Ch'ella mi creda libero Tenor
Fr. Qu'elle me croit en liberté Eng. Let
her believe me free Ger. Lasset sie
glauben
Jussi Björling
(G-DA1584)   10″—V-4408
[Tosca—E lucevan le stelle]
G. Lauri-Volpi   10″—G-DA5427
[Turnadot—Nessun dorma]
Alfred Piccaver   12″—PD-66768
[Butterfly—Non ve l'avevo detto, Picca-
ver & Scheidl]
DUPLICATIONS: Bernardo De Muro,
G-DA997; also G-DA171*; Alessandro
Ziliani, G-DA1483; Alessandro Valente,
G-HN764; Antonio Melandri, C-GQ7174;
H. Lazaro, C-GQX10141; A. Granda,
C-DQ1109; A. Lindi, C-DQ1118; Picca-
luga, C-DQ693; Edward Johnson,
G-DA166*
In German: Torsten Ralf, G-DB5620;
Julius Patzak, PD-90182
In French: José Luccioni, C-RF70

GIANNI SCHICCHI 1 Act 1918

Individual Excerpts

Firenze è come un albero fiorito Tenor
Piero Pauli   10″—G-DA1204
[Bohème-Questa è Mimì—Quartet with
Palai, Masini & Basi]

O mio babbino caro Soprano
Licia Albanese   12″—V-11-9115
[Tosca—Vissi d'arte]
Joan Hammond (in English)
[Tosca—Vissi d'arte]   10″—C-DB2052
Bidú Sayão   10″—C-17515D
[Bohème—Quando me'n vo soletta]

MADAMA BUTTERFLY 2 Acts 1904

Complete recording in Italian
Soloists, Chorus & Orch. of the Rome
Opera—Oliviero de Fabritiis
(G-DB3859/74 in GM-338†)
                        16 12″—VM-700/701†

The Cast:
Mme. Butterfly .... Toti Dal Monte (s)
Suzuki .... Vittoria Palombini (ms)
Kate Pinkerton ..... Maria Huder (ms)
B. F. Pinkerton ... Beniamino Gigli (t)
Sharpless .... Mario Basiola (b)
Goro .... Adelio Zagonara (t)
Yamadori .... Gino Conti (t)
Lo Zio Bonzo .... Ernesto Dominici (bs)
    Chorus Master: Giuseppe Conca

Complete recording in Italian
La Scala Soloists, Chorus & Milan Sym-
phony Orch.—Molajoli 14 12″—C-OP4†
(C-D14530/43) (C-9784/97)

The Cast:
Mme. Butterfly .. Rosetta Pampanini (s)
Suzuki .... Conchita Velasquez (s)
Kate Pinkerton .... Cesira Ferrari (s)
B. F. Pinkerton .. Alesandro Granda (t)
Sharpless .... Gino Vanelli (b)
Goro .... Giuseppe Nessi (t)
Yamadori ...... Aristide Baracchi (b)
Lo Zio Bonzo .. Salvatore Baccaloni (bs)
Il Commissario ...... Lino Binardi (b)
Chorus Master: Vittore Veneziani

Abridged recording in Italian
La Scala Soloists & Chorus w. Milan Symphony Orch.—Molajoli
6 12"—**C-DX500/5**†
(An abridged version of C-9784/97 above)

Selections
Un bel dì; Love Duet, Act I; Flower Duet; Addio
Licia Albanese (s), Lucielle Browning (ms), James Melton (t)
3 12"—**VM-1068**†

Orchestral Selections (Fantasias, etc.)
Concert Orch.—Seidler-Winkler
(G-EH1129) (G-S10479) 12"—**G-C3256**
German Opera House Orch.—Schmidt-Isserstedt
12"—**T-E2404**
DUPLICATIONS: Berlin State Opera Orch.—Melichar, PD-27267; Berlin Philharmonic—Reuss, T-E1588; Victor Symphony—Pasternack, G-L675: G-S8084; Columbia Symphony—Bowers, C-D16423; Marek Weber Orch., G-EH112; Berlin Philharmonic Orch.—Abendroth, P-E11369; Royal Air Force Orch.—G-RAF6

Individual Excerpts

ACT I

Amore o grillo Tenor & Baritone
E. Caruso & A. Scotti 12"—**G-DM113***
[Non ve l'avevo]

Dovunque al mondo Duo: Tenor & Baritone
Alessandro Ziliani & Alfro Poli
[Addio fiorito asil] 10"—**T-AK10499**

Ancora un passo

Spira sul mare Soprano (Butterfly's Entrance)
Ger. Bald sind wir auf der Höhe & Uber das Meer
Lotte Lehmann (in German)
10"—**P-PO157**
[Mozart: Zauberflöte—Ach, ich fühl's]
DUPLICATIONS: Mafalda Favero, C-DQ1070
In German: Margit Angerer, PD-95355;
Hilde Konetzni (with chorus), T-E2246

Duetto d'amore (Love Duet) Soprano & Tenor
The various versions of the Love Duet vary considerably. For convenience the side labellings are given above each version. The order in which the excerpts appear is as follows:

Quest' obi pomposa
Bimba dagli occhi
Ma intanto finor
Stolta paura
Vogliatemi bene

Dammi ch'io baci
Dicon ch'oltre mare
Io t'ho ghermita
Via dall' anima pena
O quanti occhi fisa
Quest'obi pomposa
Rosetta Pampanini & Francesco Merli
12"—**C-GQX10229**

Bimba dagli occhi & Io t'ho ghermita
Mafalda Favero & Alessandro Ziliani
12"—**G-DB2894**
Margherita Sheridan & Aureliano Pertile
(slightly abridged) 12"—**G-DB1119**
Aulikki Rautawarra & Peter Anders (in German) 12"—**T-E1853**
Hedwig von Debicka & Helge Roswaenge
(in German) 12"—**PD-66880**

Ma intanto finor & Dicon ch'oltre mare
Dusolina Giannini & Marcel Wittrisch
(in German) (G-DB1960) 12"—**V-8921**
(Also in Italian on G-DB1946)

Stolta paura & Dicon ch'oltre mare
Licia Albanese & James Melton
(in VM-1068†) 12"—**V-11-9255**

Vogliatemi bene & Io t'ho ghermita
Eng. Ah, love me a little & See, I have caught you
Joan Hammond & Webster Booth (in English) 12"—**G-C3378**

Vogliatemi bene & Via dall'anima pena
Eng. Ah, love me a little & Love, what fear holds you?
Joyce Gartside & James Johnston (in English) 12"—**C-DX1376**

Dammi ch'io baci
Eng. Give me your darling hands
Isobel Baillie & Francis Russel (in English) 12"—**C-9654**
[Offenbach: Tales of Hoffmann—Barcarolle, Baillie & Walker]

O quanti occhi fisi
Enrico Caruso & Geraldine Farrar
12"—**G-DM110***
[Massenet: Manon—On l'appelle Manon]

ACT II

Un bel dì, vedremo Soprano
Fr. Sur la mer calmée Ger. Eines Tages sehn wir Eng. One fine day
Licia Albanese
(in VM-1068†) 12"—**V-11-9254**
[Addio fiorito, Melton]
[Tosca—Vissi d'arte, on G-DB6479]
[Cilea: Adrianna Lecouvreur—Io son l'umile ancella, on G-DB5383] (different recording)
Emmy Destinn (Recorded 1908)
12"—**V-15-1014***
[Ponchielli: La Gioconda—Suicidio!]
Bidú Sayão 12"—**C-71320D**
[Bohème—Mi chiamano Mimì]
Dusolina Giannini 12"—**G-DB1264**
[Manon Lescaut—In quelle trine]
Geraldine Farrar
(in VM-816) 12"—**V-18141***
[Bizet: Carmen—Air de la fleur, Dalmores]

DUPLICATIONS: Grace Moore, D-29000, in D-A165; Lucrezia Bori, V-6790: G-DB1644; Jeanette MacDonald, V-11-9599; Adriana Perris, C-GQX11083; Iris Adama Corradetti, CET-CB20265; Maria Gentile, PD-10451; Margherita Sheridan, G-DB981; Pampanini, C-GQX10230; Xenia Belmas, PD-66636; Maria Farneti, C-GQX10491; De Voltri, C-D5426; Poli-Randacio, G-DB181*; A. Galli-Curci, G-DB261*; Edith Oldrup-Pedersen, TONO-X25034

In French: Mme. Géori-Boué, O-123871; Ninon Vallin, PAT-X90029: O-123562; Fanny Heldy, G-DB1513; Yoshiko Miya-kawa, C-LFX167; Yvonne Brothier, G-P687; Mireille Berthon, G-DA4801; Bernadette Delprat, PAT-PD5; Charlotte Tirard, PD-516646: PD-522599; Marise Beaujon, C-LFX76; Marthe Nespoulous, C-RFX24; Jane Laval, C-LFX64

In English: Joan Cross, G-C2824; Joan Hammond, C-DX1003

In Swedish: Hjördis Schymberg, G-X6009

In German: Margherita Perras, G-DB4473; Maria Markan, G-DB5217; Erna Berger, PD-10267

In Czech: S. Jelínková, ESTA-H5128

Il cannone del porto

Tutti i fior (Flower Duet)
Licia Albanese & Lucielle Browning
(in VM-1068†)   12″—**V-11-9256**
(G-DB6615)
DUPLICATIONS: (in German) Margherita Perras & Margarete Klose & Cho., G-DB4501; Hilde Konetzni & Marie Luise Schilp, T-E-2320; Margit Angerer & Else Ruziczka, PD-95355

Coro muto (Coro a bocca chiusa) (Humming Chorus)

Nello Shosi
La Scala Chorus—Sabajno
12″—**G-S10434**
[Turandot—Gira la cote! Royal Opera Chorus—Bellezza]
DUPLICATION: La Scala Chorus—Molajoli, C-GQ7168

Act II, Scene 2 (Sometimes called Act III)
Intermezzo Orchestra
German Opera House Orch.—Lutze
12″—**T-E3065**

Non ve l'avevo detto?

Addio, fiorito asil Duo: Tenor & Baritone
Fr. **Adieu, séjour fleuri** Ger. **Leb' wohl, du mein Blütenreich**
A. Ziliani & Afro Poli   10″—**T-AK10499**
[Dovunque al mondo]
G. Lauri-Volpi & Luigi Borgonovo
10″—**G-DA1385**
[Manon Lescaut—No! pazzo son!]
DUPLICATIONS: Alfred Piccaver & Theo. Scheidl, PD-66768; Caruso & Scotti, G-DM113*

—Addio fiorito
(Pinkerton's part only) Tenor
James Melton
(in VM-1068†)   12″—**V-11-9254**
[Un bel dì, Albanese]

Leonida Bellon   12″—**CET-CC2204**
[Manon Lescaut—Donna]
DUPLICATIONS: Giuseppe Lugo, PD-561088; Galliano Masini, C-D6008; F. Piccaluga, C-DQ692; A. Gentilini, C-DQ2967
In German: Julius Patzak, PD-24327; Helge Roswaenge, T-A1538
In French: Lens, PD-521937

Tu, tu piccolo Iddio! Soprano
(Death of Butterfly)
Adrianna Guerrini & Aldo Ferrauto
12″—**C-DX1431**
(begins "Con onor" & includes Pinkerton's brief lines)
[Manon Lescaut—Sola, perduta, abbandonata]
Onelia Fineschi   12″—**CET-BB25204**
[Manon Lescaut—In quelle trine morbide]
Hina Spani   10″—**G-DA1060**
[Tosca-Vissi d'arte]
DUPLICATIONS: Maria Farneti, C-GQ7170; Hilda Konetzni (in German), T-E2320

MANON LESCAUT 4 Acts 1893

Complete recording in Italian
La Scala soloists, Chorus & Milan Symphony Orch.—Molajoli
13 12″—**C-GQX10119/31**
The Cast:
Manon Lescaut .... Maria Zamboni (s)
Des Grieux .... Francesco Merli (t)
Un musico .... Anna Masetti Bassi (s)
Lescaut .... Lorenzo Conati (b)
Geronte .... Attilio Bordinali (b)
Edmondo
Maestro di ballo }....Giuseppe Nessi (t)
Lampionaio
L'oste
Sargente }.....Aristide Baracchi (b)
Commandante ...... Natalie Villa (b)
Chorus Master: Vittore Veneziani

Orchestral Selections (Fantasia)
Milan Symphony—Molajoli
12″—**C-GQX10693**
[Gounod: Mors et Vita—Judex]

Individual Excerpts

ACT I

Tra voi, belle, brune e bionde
Tenor & Chorus
Aureliano Pertile & Chorus
[Donna non vidi mai]   10″—**G-DA1105**
(Older version: C-CQ700)

Donna non vidi mai Tenor
Fr. **Romance de Des Grieux**
Ger. **Wo lebte wohl ein Wesen**
Beniamino Gigli   10″—**G-DA856**
[Tosca—Recondita armonia]
Alessandro Ziliani   10″—**G-DA1423**
[Turandot—Nessun dorma]
DUPLICATIONS: Francesco Merli, C-GQ7091; Aureliano Pertile, G-DA1105: C-GQ7179; Leonida Bellon, CET-CC2204; Masini, C-CQ1062; Giudice, C-DQ268; E. Caruso, G-DA106*

ACT II

Buon giorno, sorellina!

In quelle trine morbide
Duo: Soprano & Baritone

—In quelle trine morbide
(Manon's part only)   Soprano
Dorothy Kirsten   12"—**V-11-9792**
[Massenet: Thaïs—Death of Thaïs,
with Merrill]
Licia Albanese   10"—**G-DA5391**
[Fusco: Dicitencello vuje]
Onelia Fineschi   12"—**CET-BB25204**
[Madama Butterfly—Tu, piccolo iddio]
Dusolina Giannini   12"—**G-DB1264**
[Madama Butterfly—Un bel dì]
Mafalda Favero   12"—**G-DB3200**
[Bohème—Mi chiamano Mimì]
[Giordano: Siberia—Qual vergogna,
Caniglia on G-DA1563]
Sara Scuderi   10"—**G-DA5449**
[Tosca—Vissi d'arte]
DUPLICATIONS: Rosetta Pampanini,
C-GQ7068; Mafalda Favero, C-D6016; de
Voltri, C-D5426; L. Bruna Rasa,
C-GQ7103; Rosa Ponselle, CRS-15*

Tu, tu amore?   Duo: Soprano & Tenor

O tentatrice!
Margherita Sheridan & A. Pertile
12"—**G-DB1281**

Ah! Manon, mi tradisce   Tenor
Aureliano Pertile   10"—**G-DA1162**
[Leoncavallo: Pagliacci—O Colombina]
(also on C-CQ699)
Beniamino Gigli   10"—**G-DA5411**
[No! pazzo son, with Noto]
DUPLICATION: Edward Johnson,
CRS-22*

ACT III

Intermezzo   Orchestra
Royal Opera House Orchestra, Covent
Garden—Patanè   12"—**C-DX1472**
[Zandonai: Giulietta e Romeo—
Cavalcata]
National Symphony Orch.—Beer
(in D-ED42†)   12"—**D-K1280**
[Bizet: L'Arlesienne Suite No. 2—
Farandole]
Milan Symphony Orch.—Molajoli
12"—**C-67723D**
[Bohème, Pt. 25 in C-OP5†]
(C-9858)   (C-D14527)
DUPLICATIONS: La Scala Orch.—
Sabajno, G-S10045; La Scala Orch.—
Marinuzzi, G-DB2895

Ah! non v' avvicinate   Recit.

No! pazzo son! guardate   Aria   Tenor
Beniamino Gigli (with Noto, baritone)
10"—**G-DA5398**
[Verdi: Trovatore—Di quella pira]
[Ah, Manon mi tradisce, on G-DA5411]
Giacomo Lauri-Volpi   10"—**G-DA1385**
[Butterfly—Addio fiorito asil, Lauri-
Volpi & Borgonova]
DUPLICATIONS: Francesco Merli,
C-GQ7091; Aureliano Pertile, C-GQ7179:
C-CQ699; also on G-DB1111

ACT IV

Sola, perduta, abbandonata   Soprano
Rosetta Pampanini   12"—**CET-BB25035**
[Mascagni: Iris—Un dì ero piccina]
Adrianna Guerrini   12"—**C-DX1431**
[Madama Butterfly—Con onor]

(LA) RONDINE
No recordings available

SUOR ANGELICA   I Act   1918

Intermezzo   Orchestra
Milan Symphony—Molajoli
12"—**C-GQX10012**
[Mascagni: I Rantzau—Prelude]
Royal Opera Orch.—Bellezza
[Mascagni: Iris—Dance] 12"—**G-S10223**

Senza mamma   (Arioso)   Soprano
Augusta Oltrabella   12"—**G-DB5350**
[Giordano: Fedora—Vedi, io piango, Duo
with Ziliani]
DUPLICATION: Poli Randacio,
G-DB181*

(LA) TOSCA   3 Acts   1900

Complete Recording in Italian
Soloists, Chorus & Orch. of Rome Opera
House—de Fabritiis
14 12"—**VM-539/540†**
(G-DB3562/75, in GM-322†)
The Cast:
Floria Tosca . . . . . . Maria Caniglia (s)
Mario Cavaradossi . . Beniamino Gigli (t)
Barone Scarpia . . Armando Borgioli (b)
Angelotti . . . . . . Ernesto Dominici (bs)
Sacristan . . . . Giulio Tomei (b)
Sciarrone . . . . Gino Conti (bs)
Spoletta . . . . Nino Mazziotti (t)
Shepherd Boy . . . . Anna Marcangeli (s)
Chorus Master: Giuseppe Conca

Complete Recording in Italian
La Scala Soloists, Chorus & Milan Sym-
phony Orch.—Molajoli 14 12"—**C-OP6†**
(C-D14594/607)   (C-9930/43)
The Cast:
Floria Tosca . . . . . . Bianca Scacciati (s)
Mario Cavaradossi . . . . Alessandro
Granda (t)
Barone Scarpia . . . . Enrico Molinari (b)
Angelotti . . . . Salvatore Baccaloni (bs)
Il Sagrestano ⎤
Sciarrone   ⎬ . . . . Aristide Baracchi (b)
Carceriere   ⎦
Spoletta . . . . Emilio Venturini (t)
Pastore . . . . Tommaso Cortellino
Chorus Master: Vittore Veneziani

Abridged Recording in Italian
La Scala Soloists & Cho. w. Milan
Symphony Orch.—Molajoli
6 12"—**C-DX524/9†**
(An abridged version of C-9930/43
above)

Abridged Recording sung in French
Soloists & Orch.—G. Cloëz
7 12"—**O-123810/6**
The Cast includes: Ninon Vallin (s),
Enrico Di Mazzei (t), Arthur Endrèze (b)

Orchestral Selections (Fantasias, etc.)
German Opera House Orch.—Schmidt-
Isserstedt 12″—T-E2431
Berlin Philharmonic—Borchard
12″—T-E1714
DUPLICATIONS: Marek Weber Orch.,
G-EH883: G-L982: G-S10456; Berlin
State Opera Orch.—Melichar, PD-24799;
Dajos Bela Orch, O-170098
Also: A. Ranzato (vlc), C-DQ452

Individual Excerpts

ACT I

Recondita armonia Tenor
Fr. O de beautés égales
Ger. Wie sich die Bilder gleichen
Eng. Strange harmony of contrasts
Ferruccio Tagliavini
(in CET-1) 12″—CET-BB25040
[E lucevan] (PD-68001)
Jussi Björling 10″—V-4372
[Verdi: Rigoletto—La donna è mobile]
(G-DA1548)
Enrico Caruso & re-recorded orch.
12″—V-11-8569
[Bizet: Agnus Dei] (G-DB2644)
(Original version, G-DA112*)
Beniamino Gigli 10″—G-DA856
[Manon Lescaut—Donna non vidi mai]
DUPLICATIONS: Jan Kiepura,
C-17310D; Galliano Masini, C-D5980;
Anton Dermota, T-A10000; Joseph
Schmidt, P-DP25; Giuseppe Lugo,
G-DA4921; Antonio Cortis, G-DA1074;
Araldo Lindi, C-GQ1075; Augusto
Ferrauto, CET-CB20248; Alfred Piccaver,
PD-66770; Alessandro Valente, G-Z172;
Enzo de Muro Lomanto, C-DQ1061;
Joseph Hislop, G-DA1063; Aureliano
Pertile, C-GQ7183; Giorgini, G-HN774;
H. Lazaro, C-DQ1133; Alessandro
Granda, C-DQ1058; Luigi Marini,
C-DQ1096; D'Alessio, C-DQ1079;
Giudice, C-DQ269: C-DQ271; Martinelli,
G-DA285*
In French:
César Vezzani, G-P848; Giuseppe
Lugo, G-DA4922: PD-561086; Paul
Henri Vergnès, O-188901; Enrico Di
Mazzei, O-188501; Joseph Rogatchewsky,
C-LF36; Friant, O-188544; Lens,
PD-521937; Micheletti, O-188657; Villa-
bella, PAT-X90071: O-188556;
Campagnola, G-P538*
In English:
John McHugh, C-DB2234; Webster
Booth, G-B8803
In German:
Hugo Meyer-Welfing, O-7977; Helge
Roswaenge, G-DA4504: PD-66632; Peter
Anders, T-A2360; Marcel Wittrisch,
T-B1434; Richard Crooks, G-EW75;
Franz Völker, PD-90037; Julius Patzak,
PD-30035

Duo: Tosca & Cavaradossi
Soprano & Tenor
Since recordings of this duet vary consider-
ably, beginning and ending at different points
in the score, they are listed below with side
references.

Mario! Mario! Son qui! Perchè chiuso?
Fr. Mario! Tu t'enfermes
Bernadette Delprat & Georges Thill
(in French) 12″—C-LFX3150
Non la sospiri la nostra casetta
Fr. Notre doux nid
—**Tosca's part only** Soprano
Xenia Belmas 12″—PD-66747
[Vissi d'arte]
In French: Ninon Vallin, PAT-X90057;
Elen Dosia, G-DA4881; Yvonne Gall,
C-D15128
Ah! quegli oochi! Ger. Ach, die Augen
Aulikki Rautawaara & Peter Anders
(in German) 12″—T-E2654
[Bizet: Carmen—Duet, Act I]
Margherita Perras & Helge Roswaenge
(in German) 12″—G-DB4475
[Vissi d'arte, Perras]
M. Angerer & A. Piccaver
(in German) 12″—PD-95462
[Amaro sol per te]

Te Deum: Tre sbirri Baritone & Chorus
Ger. Drei Häscher mit einem Wagen
Lawrence Tibbett & Metropolitan Opera
Chorus—Setti 12″—V-8124
[Bizet: Carmen—Air du Toréador]
[Verdi: Ballo in Maschera—Eri tu, on
V-11-8861 in VM-1015]
Josef Hermann & Leipzig Radio Chorus
(in German) 12″—G-DB5647
[Verdi: Otello—Credo]
DUPLICATIONS: Riccardo Stracciari &
Chorus, C-GQX10176: C-CQX16488;
Benvenuto Franci, G-DB1508
In French: André Baugé & Chorus,
PAT-PGT9; Louis Musy & Chorus,
G-W958
In German: Gerhard Hüsch & Chorus,
G-DB4485

ACT II

Già! Mi dicon venal! —Se la giurata fede
Fr: Oui, l'on me dit vénal or
Si pour les beaux yeux
Ger: Auch mich berührte manchmal die
Liebe
Marko Rothmüller & Franca Sacchi
12″—G-C3689
[Verdi: Rigoletto—Pari siamo,
Rothmüller]
Antonio Scotti
(in VM-816) 12″—V-18142*
[Wagner: Tannhäuser—Dich teure halle,
Gadski]
DUPLICATIONS: Tita Ruffo, G-DA163*
In German: Gerhard Hüsch, G-DB4485
In French: Lucien van Obbergh,
PD-524007; José Beckmans, PD-566039

Vissi d'arte Soprano
Fr. D'art et d'amour
Ger. Nur die Schönheit
Licia Albanese 12″—V-11-9115
[Gianni Schicchi—O mio babbino caro]
[Butterfly—Un bel dì, on G-DB6479]
Maria Caniglia 12″—G-DB5360
[Verdi: Trovatore—Tacea la notte]
[also on C-DQ1138]
Claudia Muzio 10″—C-BQ6006
[Bohème—Addio di Mimì]

[Delibes: Bonjour Suzon, on C-BQ6000;
C-LC19]
Rosa Raisa 12"—**G-DB2122**
[Ponchielli: Gioconda—Suicidio!]
Eva Turner 12"—**C-L2118**
[Mascagni: Cavalleria Rusticana—Voi
lo sapete]
Sara Scuderi 10"—**G-DA5449**
[Manon Lescaut—In quelle trine]
Magda Olivero 12"—**CET-BB25053**
[Bohème—Mi chiamano Mimì]
Helen Traubel
    (in CM-675) 12"—**C-72111D**
[Mozart: Don Giovanni—Or sai chi
l'onore]
DUPLICATIONS: Grace Moore, D-29010,
in D-A165; Turchetti, G-HN774; Arangi-
Lombardi, C-GQX10508; Lina Bruna
Rasa, C-GQ7103; Scacciati, V-GQX10165;
C-CQ709; Zamboni, C-DQ1122; M.
Nemeth, PD-66622; Emmy Destinn,
CRS-16*; Hina Spani, G-DA1060; R.
Pampanini, C-GQ7211
In French: Ninon Vallin, PAT-X90057:
O-123530; Elen Dosia, G-DA4881;
Yvonne Gall, C-D15128; Marise Beaujon,
C-LFX76; Mireille Berthon, G-P687;
Germaine Martinelli, PD-524117;
Haramboure, PD-521892, Charlotte
Tirard, PD-522599; Bernadette Delprat,
PAT-PD5; M. Nespoulos, C-D14207
In German: Maria Markan, G-DB5217;
Viorica Ursuleac, PD-35033; Hildegarde
Ranczak, PD-68042; Margherita Perras,
G-DB4475; Hilde Konetzni, T-E2246
In English: Joan Cross, G-B8666; Joan
Hammond, C-DB2052

ACT III

Prelude Orchestra
Milan Symphony Orch. Molajoli
        10"—**C-D12298**

E Lucevan le stelle Tenor
Fr. Le ciel luisait d'étoiles
Ger. Und es blitzten die Sterne
Eng. The stars were brightly shining
Ferruccio Tagliavini
    (in CET-1) 12"—**CET-BB25040**
[Recondita armonia] (PD-68001)
Jussi Björling 10"—**V-4408**
[La Fanciulla del West—Ch'ella mi
creda libero] (G-DA1584)
Jan Kiepura 10"—**C-17310D**
[Recondita armonia]
Beniamino Gigli 10"—**G-DA1372**
[Verdi: Rigoletto—La donna è mobile]
[Older version w. Boito: Mefistofele—Se
tu mi doni, Scattola, on G-DA233*]
Giacomo Lauri-Volpi 10"—**G-DA983**
[Bellini: Norma—Meco all' altar]
Giovanni Martinelli 10"—**G-DA842**
[Verdi: Rigoletto—La donna è mobile]
Guiseppe Lugo 10"—**G-DA4921**
[Recondita armonia]
(In French, G-DA4922)
Anton Dermota 10"—**T-A10000**
[Recondita armonia]
Giovanni Malipiero 12"—**P-DPX29**
[Boito: Mefistofele—Guinto sul passo
estremo]

[Gounod: Faust—Mephisto's Serenata,
Pasero & Malipiero, on CET-BB25061]
DUPLICATIONS: A. Ferrauto,
CET-CB20248; John McCormack,
CRS-12*; Araldo Lindi, C-DQ1075;
Aureliano Pertile, C-GQ7181; Galliano
Masini, C-D5980; Joseph Schmidt,
P-DP25; A. Piccaver, PD-66770; Joseph
Hislop, G-DA1063; Miguel Fleta,
G-DA446: G-DA1087; Enrico Caruso,
G-DA125*: G-DA112*; Antonio Cortis,
G-DA1074; Alessandro Valente,
G-HN768; Enzo de Muro Lomanto,
C-DQ1061; G. Bentonelli, C-DQ664; A.
Wesselowsky, C-D5454; Hippolito Lazaro,
C-DQ1133; Alessandro Granda,
C-DQ1058; Roberto d'Alessio,
C-DQ1079; K. von Pataky,
RAD-RZ3016
In French: Georges Thill, C-7016;
Villabella, PAT-X90071: O-188638;
Micheletti, O-188657; Charles Friant,
O-188544; José Luccioni, G-DA4888;
César Vezzani, G-P848; Paul Henri
Vergnès, O-188901; Campagnola,
G-P538*; Kaisin, PD-524021
In German: Hugo Meyer-Welfing, O-7977;
Helge Roswaenge, G-DA4504:
PD-66632; Marcel Wittrisch, T-B1434;
Franz Völker, PD-90037; Peter Anders,
T-A2360; Julius Patzak, PD-30035
In English: Webster Booth, G-B8803;
John McHugh, C-DB2234
In Icelandic: Pjetur A. Jonsson, G-Z182

Ah! Franchigia a Floria Tosca
Soprano & Tenor

O dolci mani (Tosca & Cavaradossi Duet)
—**O dolci mani** only
Bianca Scacciati & A. Granda
[Amaro sol per te] 12"—**C-GQX10161**
—**O dolci mani** (Cavaradossi solo) Tenor
Fr. O douces mains
Ferruccio Tagliavini
    (in CET-2) 12"—**CET-BB25118**
[Rossini: Barbiere—Ecco ridente]
Enrico Di Mazzei 10"—**O-188500**
[E lucevan le stelle]
DUPLICATION: Beniamino Gigli,
G-DA586*
In French: Giuseppe Lugo, PD-62709;
Marcel Claudel, PD-524063; Micheletti,
O-188658; Joseph Rogatchewsky, C-LF36

Amaro sol per te Soprano & Tenor
Margit Angerer & Alfred Piccaver
[Ah! quegli occhi] 12"—**PD-95462**
Bianca Scacciati & Alessandro Granda
[O dolci mani] 12"—**C-GQX10161**

TURANDOT 3 Acts 1926

*This opera, left unfinished at the death of
Puccini, was completed by Alfano.*

Complete Recording in Italian
Soloists with EIAR Chorus & Orch.—
Franco Ghione 16 12"—**P-P26/27†**
(P-R20410/25) (O-8416/31)
(CET-CB20046/61)
The Cast:
Turandot .... Gina Cigna (s)
Il Principe Ignoto .. Francesco Merli (t)

Liù .... Magda Olivero (s)
Timur .... Luciano Neroni (bs)
Altoum .... Armando Gianotti (t)
Un Mandarino .. Giuseppe Bravura (b)
Ping .... Afro Poli (b)
Pang .... Adelio Zangonara (t)
Pong .... Gino del Signore (t)
Chorus Master: Achille Consoli

Orchestral Selections (Fantasias, etc.)
Royal Opera Orch.—Malcolm
Sargent   12″—G-S8848
La Scala Orch.—Sabajno
                       10″—G-HN789
[Leoncavallo: Pagliacci—Selections]

Individual Excerpts

ACT I

Gira la cote! Chorus
Royal Opera Chorus & Orch.—
Bellezza   12″—G-S10434
[Butterfly—Humming Chorus, La Scala
Chorus—Sabajno]
[O Giovanetto, on G-S10001]
DUPLICATION: La Scala Chorus—
Molajoli, C-GQX10266

Invocazione alla luna Chorus
Josef Herrmann (b) & Leipzig Radio
Chorus (in German)   12″—G-DB5642
DUPLICATIONS: La Scala Chorus—
Molajoli, C-GQX10266; EIAR Cho. &
Orch.—Ghione, CET-BB25108

O giovanetto! (Marchi funebre) Chorus
Royal Opera Chorus & Orch.—Bellezza
[Gira la cote]   12″—G-S10001

Signore, ascolta Soprano
Licia Albanese   10″—G-DA5390
[Death of Liù]
Mafalda Favero   10″—G-DA1498
[Mascagni: Amico Fritz—Son pochi
fiori]
(also on C-D5932)
DUPLICATIONS: Rosetta Pampanini,
C-GQ7062; Rosina Torri, G-HN773;
Maria Zamboni, C-DQ1078; Ada
Saraceni, G-HN769
In English: Joan Hammond, G-B9407

Non piangere, Liù! Tenor
Ger. O weine nicht Liu
Fr. Ne pleure pas
(Brief part of Liu omitted in solo versions)
Antonio Cortis   10″—G-DA1075
[Nessun dorma]
Giacomo Lauri-Volpi   12″—G-DB6352
[Ponchielli: La Gioconda—Cielo e mar]
Alessandro Valente   12″—G-HN763
[Nessun dorma]
Alessandro Ziliani   10″—G-DA1483
[Fanciulla del West—Ch'ella mi creda]
DUPLICATIONS: Hipolito Lazara,
C-GQX10139; Araldo Lindi, C-DQ1116;
A. Granda, C-DQ1063; Francesco Merli,
C-GQ7040; CET-BB25108; Galliano
Masini, C-D6008; Enzo Vizzoni,
C-GQ7224; S. Costa Lo Guidice,
C-DQ268; A. Ferrauto, CET-CB20248;
A. Piccaver, PD-95352
In German: Hugo Meyer-Welfing,

O-3609; Helge Roswaenge, PD-10447;
Charles Kullman, C-DW3068; Anton
Dermota, T-A10087
In French: G. Thill, C-D13042
In English: John McHugh, C-DB2328

ACT II

Terzetto delle maschere Ping-Pang-Pong
Trio
The 10″ disc below contains the first and sec-
ond sections of the trio.
Nessi, Venturini, Baracchi
(C-D12300)   10″—C-D1663

In questa Reggia Soprano

O Principi che a lunghe carovane
Ger. In diesem Schlosse
Eng. Turandot's Air
Bianca Scacciati (with F. Merli)
                       10″—C-GQ7038
Eva Turner
(C-GQ7102)   10″—C-D1631
In German: Viorica Ursuleac, PD-35033

ACT III

Nessun dorma Tenor
Ger. Keiner schlafe   Fr. Nul ne dort
Antonio Cortis   10″—G-DA1075
[Non piangere]
Jussi Björling   10″—V-10-1200
[Verdi: Rigoletto—Questa o quella]
[Leoncavallo: Mattinata on G-DA1841]
G. Lauri-Volpi   10″—G-DA5427
[Fanciulla del West—Ch'ella mi creda]
DUPLICATIONS: Alessandro Ziliani,
G-DA1423; Enzo Vizzoni, C-GQ7224;
Alfred Piccaver, PD-95352; Hipolito
Lazaro, C-GQX10139: C-D18000;
Alessandro Valente, G-HN763; Araldo
Lindi, C-DQ1116; Francesco Merli,
C-GQ7040; Georges Thill, C-D14544:
C-D41012; A. Granda, G-DQ1063;
A. Ferrauto, CET-CB20280
In German: Helge Roswaenge, PD-10447;
Charles Kullman, C-DW3068; Anton
Dermota, T-A10087
In English: John McHugh, C-DB2328
In French: G. Thill, C-D13042

Principessa, l'amore

Tanto amore segreto Soprano
Eidé Noréna   10″—G-DA4832
[Death of Liù]

Morte di Liù (Death of Liù)

Tu che di gel sei cinta Soprano
Ger. Du mit Eis umgürtet
Eng. You who with ice are girdled
Licia Albanese   10″—G-DA5390
[Signore ascolta]
Eidé Noréna   10″—G-DA4832
[Tanto amore]
DUPLICATIONS: Mafalda Favero,
C-D5932; Rosetta Pampanini, C-GQ7062;
Rosina Torri, G-HN773; M. Zamboni,
C-DQ1078; Ada Saraceni, G-HN769
In English: Joan Hammond, G-B9407

(LE) VILLI 2 Acts 1884

Intermezzo No. 1 (L'abbandono)
Act II Orchestra
Milan Symphony—Molajoli
12″—**C-GQX10026**
[Mascagni: Silvano—Il sogno]
La Scala Orch.—Sabajno
[Intermezzo No. 2]   12″—**G-S10216**

Intermezzo No. 2 (La tregenda) Orchestra
Eng. Witches' Dance
La Scala Orch.—Sabajno
[Intermezzo No. 1]   12″—**G-S10216**

Torna ai felici dì Tenor
Alessandro Bonci   12″—**C-GQX10224**
[Verdi: Ballo in Maschere—La rivedrò
nell' estasi, Bonci, Rettore, Baccaloni,
Menni & Chorus]

Miscellaneous (Potpourris, etc.)
Berlin State Opera Orch.—Reuss
2 12″—**T-E1408/9**
DUPLICATIONS: Marek Weber Orch.,
G-EH761; Carugati, Giorgiani with
Orch., G-S5004

PUGNANI, Gaetano (1731-1798)

*A celebrated Italian violinist who preserved and
carried on the traditional school of Corelli,
Tartini and Vivaldi. Although he was a prolific composer of violin pieces and chamber
music, he is remembered today almost exclusively by only a few short pieces, two of which
have been revealed as compositions of Fritz
Kreisler.*

Largo espressivo Violin & Piano
Arr. Moffat
Elèves de Marcel Chailley & organ acc.
[Desplanes: Intrada] 10″—**LUM-30063**

Praeludium & Allegro "Arr." Kreisler
*Actually a composition of Fritz Kreisler, see
under that name for recordings.*

PURCELL-COCKRANE, E.
(Edward C. Purcell)

*A contemporary British song composer who has
set several Elizabethan lyrics to music.*

Passing By Song in English (Herrick)
("There is a lady sweet and kind")
Richard Tauber (t) 10″—**P-RO20527**
[Ronald: Down in the forest]
Alvar Lidell (b) & pf. acc.
10″—**G-B9233**
[Lockton: I'll walk beside you]
Richard Crooks (t) & Fred. Schauwecker
(pf)   (in VM-846) 10″—**V-2179**
[Franz: Still Sicherheit]
DUPLICATIONS: John McHugh,
C-FB2929; Paul Robeson, G-B8541; A.
Endrèze, PAT-PA1377; Dennis Noble,
C-DB1016

PURCELL, Henry (1658/9-1695)

*One of the giants of all music and possibly the
greatest British composer next to William
Byrd, Purcell is comparatively well represented
on discs. With the collections of the English
Music Society and the excerpts from the operas,
ballets and masques, together with two recordings of his "Dido and Aeneas" we have a fairly
adequate representation of Purcell's genius.
However, considering his prolific musical output, much more could be added to this list of
discs.*

COLLECTION: The English Music Society
Vol. 1—Music of Henry Purcell
(9) 4-Part Fantasias for Strings;
Fantasia (5-Part) on One Note
International String Quartet
The Golden Sonata, F major (Set 2, No. 9)
William Primrose & Isolde Menges (vls),
Ambrose Gauntlett (gamba), John
Ticehurst (harpsichord)
The Aspiration—How Long, Great God;
If Music be the Food of Love; I Love and
I Must
Keith Falkner (b) with 'cello & harpsi.
(2) Catches: I gave her cakes & To thee
to thee and to a maid
Purcell Singers (unacc.)
3 10″ & 5 12″— **English Columbia**
*(Individual records are not available separ-
ately)*

Abdelazar
See under Operas and Stage Works

Ah, How Pleasant 'tis to Love
(Text from Milton's L'Allegro)
Air with Basso continuo
Astra Desmond (c) & Harold Craxton
(pf)   10″—**D-M550**
[Sweet, be no longer sad; The Rival
Sisters—Celia has a thousand charms]

Air, Gavotte & Minuet G major Harpsichord
Alfred Cortot (pf) 10″—**G-DA1609**
[Siciliana, G minor]

(The) Aspiration
("How long, great God")
Hymn in English (Norris)
Keith Falkner, in English Music Society
album Vol. I

Ayres for the Theatre
Orchestral Suite Arr. Bernard
Prelude ("The Virtuous Wife"); Minuet
("The Gordian Knot Untied"); Bourrée
("The Old Bachelor"); Overture ("The
Rival Sisters")
London Chamber Orch.—A. Bernard
12″—**D-K612**

Bell Anthem
See under Rejoice in the Lord Alway

Bess o'Bedlam (Mad Bess)
Song in Scena form
("From silent shades")
Astra Desmond (c) & Harold
Craxton (pf)   12″—**D-K1098**
[Evening Hymn]

(The) Blessed Virgin's Expostulation
(Nathan Tate)
("Tell me, some pitying Angel")
Isobel Baillie (s) & Arnold Goldsborough
(organ)   12″—**C-DX1031**

CATCHES AND ROUNDS
Unacc. Vocal Ensembles

I gave her cakes and I gave her ale

To thee to thee and to a maid
Purcell Singers, in English Music Society
album Vol. I

Chaconne, G minor Strings
(from Sonata No. 6) Arr. Whittaker
Philharmonic String Orch.—
Lambert 12″—C-DX1230

Comus—Ballet Suite Arr. Constant Lambert
The excerpts used by Lambert are:
Side 1—
Largo (Fairy Queen, Act 4); Hornpipe, D
minor (Married Beau, No. 3); Dance for
Green Men (Fairy Queen, Act 3); Hornpipe,
D minor (Fairy Queen, 3rd Act tune).
Side 2—
Adagio, D major (Fairy Queen, Act 4); Min-
uet (Gordian Knot Untied, No. 8); Section
following Overture (Indian Queen); (No. 9,
Virtuous Wife).
Side 3—
Dance of Devils (Tempest, Act 4); Adagio
from Symphony (Indian Queen, Act 2); "O
the sweet delights of love" (Dioclesian).
Side 4—
Opening of Symphony D major (Fairy Queen,
Act 4); Symphony, G minor (Indian Queen,
Act 3); Trumpet Overture (Indian Queen,
Act 3).
Hallé Orch.—Lambert
2 12″—C-DX1076/7

Dido and Aeneas
See under Operas & Stage Works

Evening Hymn (Grace)
Astra Desmond (c) & Harold
Craxton (pf) 12″—D-K1098
[Bess o'Bedlam]

FANTASIAS—Strings

(There are three fantasias in three parts, nine
in four parts, and one in five parts—the "Fan-
tasia on One Note." Warlock Edition used.)

(3-Pt.) Fantasia No. 2, F major
Pasquier Trio 12″—PAT-PAT126
[Bonnal: Trio, Pt. 5]

(3-Pt.) Fantasia No. 3, G minor
Pasquier Trio 12″—PAT-PAT31
[Scarlatti: Toccatina & Durante:
Toccata]

(4-Pt) Fantasias, Nos. 1—9 inclusive

(5-Pt.) Fantasia (Fantasia on One Note)
International String Quartet, in English
Music Society album, Vol. 1

(4-Pt.) Fantasia No. 6, A minor only
Zurich Collegium Musicum—
Sacher 12″—C-LZX9

(4-Part) Fantasia No. 9, E minor only
Griller Quartet 12″—D-K1722
[Mozart: Quartet No. 15, Pt. 7]

(5-Pt.) Fantasia (on One Note)
Zorian String Quartet, with Benjamin
Britten (vla) 12″—G-C3539†
[Britten: String Quartet No. 2, Pt. 7]

(The) Golden Sonata
See under Sonatas, Set 2, No. 9

Ground, C minor Harpsichord
Wanda Landowska, in VM-1181†
Sylvia Marlowe, in D-DAU4

Hear my prayer, O Lord 8-Pt. Anthem
in Coronation Service of George VI,
G-RG8

How long, great God
See under The Aspiration

I gave her cakes
See under Catches & Rounds

I love and I must Air in English
Keith Falkner, in English Music Society
album, Vol. 1

I see she flies from me (unidentified)
Astra Desmond (c) & Harold
Craxton (pf) 12″—D-K1397
[Sylvia now your scorn; Ode to Cynthia;
King Richard II—Retir'd from any
mortal's sight]

If Music be the food of Love Air
(2nd setting)
Keith Falkner, in English Music Society
album, Vol. I

Let us wander
(An adaptation by Moffat of "We are spirits
of the air" from Act III of "The Indian
Queen.")
Isobel Baillie (s) & Kathleen Ferrier (c)
w. Gerald Moore (pf) 10″—C-DB2201
[Sound the trumpet & King Arthur—
Shepherd, shepherd, cease decoying]

Lilliburlera Harpsichord
Ralph Kirkpatrick, in MC-25
Sylvia Marlowe, in D-DAU4

(An) Ode to Cynthia Walking on Richmond
Hill
("On the brow of Richmond Hill")
Astra Desmond (c) & Harold
Craxton (pf) 12″—D-K1397
[I see she flies; Sylvia now your scorn;
King Richard II—Retir'd from any
mortal's sight]

OPERAS & STAGE WORKS

ABDELAZAR, or the Moor's Revenge
Orchestral Suite
Overture, Rondeau, Airs I & II, Minuet,
Air III, Jig, Hornpipe, Air IV
VOX Chamber Orch.—Edward Fendler
3 10″—VOX-199

(NOTE: *The Rondeau from this suite is used as*
the theme for Benjamin Britten's "Young Per-
son's Guide to the Orchestra.")

—Air, G. minor
Identical with the "Air" from "Overture,
Air & Jig"
See under Suites—Orchestra
(arr. Barbirolli)

DIDO AND AENEAS 3 Acts 1689

Complete Recording
(Edited by E. J. Dent)
Soloists, Chorus & Philharmonic String
Orch.—Lambert
(G-C3471/7) 7 12″—GM-389†
(Harpsichord: Boris Ord)

The Cast:
Dido .... Joan Hammond (s)
Belinda .... Isobel Baillie (s)
Sorceress .... Edith Coates (c)
Aeneas .... Dennis Noble (b)
The Spirit .... Sylvia Patriss (s)
Second Woman .... Joan Fullerton (s)
First Witch .... Edna Hobson (s)
Second Witch ...... Gladys Ripley (c)
Sailor .... Trefor Jones (t)

Complete Recording
Soloists, Charles Kennedy Scott's A
Capella Singers & Boyd Neel String Orch.
—Clarence Raybould   7 12″—**D-X101/7**
(Harpsichord: Bernhard Ord)
The Cast:
Dido .... Nancy Evans (c)
Belinda .... Mary Hamlin (s)
Sorceress .... Mary Jarred (c)
Aeneas .... Roy Henderson (b)
The Spirit .... Oliver Dyer (s)
Second Woman ...... Gladys Currie (s)
First Witch .... Gwen Catley (s)
Second Witch ...... Gladys Currie (s)
Sailor .... Sydney Northcote (t)

Suite   (arr. Cailliet)
Overture; Act I, Scene 1; Lento, Allegro
moderato, Tempo di minuetto; Act I,
Scene 2: Lento—Prelude for the Witches,
Dance of the Furies; Act II: Ritornelle
(Prelude) ; Act III: Prelude, Recit.—Thy
hand, Belinda & Aria—When I am laid
to earth
Philadelphia Orch.—Ormandy
2 12″—**VM-647**

Overture
Winterthur Municipal Orch.—
Scherchen   12″—**G-DB6096**
[K. P. E. Bach: Symphony No. 1, D
major, Pt. 3]

When I am laid in earth, Act III
Contralto   (Dido's Lament)
Marian Anderson & Kosti Vehanen (pf)
(G-DB6019)   12″—**V-17257**
[A. Scarlatti: Se Florindo e fedele]
See also under Suites—Orchestra
(arr. Barbirolli)

DIOCLESIAN
Prelude, Act 3   Arr. Wood
See under Suites—Orchestra
Masques: Cannaries
Piper's Guild Quartet, C-DB2281
See also under Comus—Ballet Suite

DISTRESSED INNOCENCE
Minuet   (arr. Wood)
See under Suites—Orchestra

DON QUIXOTE
From rosy bow'rs   (Altisidora's Song)
Astra Desmond (c) & Harold
Craxton (pf)   10″—**D-M569**

(THE) DOUBLE DEALER
No. 3, Minuet
See under Harpsichord Suite No. 8

(THE) FAIRY QUEEN
Incidental Music   1692

(3) Dances: Hornpipe, Rondeau, Jig
(Arr. Jacques)
Reginald Jacques String Orch.
12″—**C-DX868**
[Handel: Berenice—Overture—Minuet]
See also under Comus—Ballet Suite

Hark, the echoing air   Soprano
Isobel Baillie (s)   12″—**C-DX1234**
[Haydn: The Seasons—O how pleasing
to the senses]
Astra Desmond (c) & Harold
Craxton (pf)   10″—**D-M549**
[Indian Queen—I attempt from love's
sickness to fly; The Libertine—Nymphs
and shepherds]
Also: Piper's Guild Quartet, C-DB2280

(THE) GORDIAN KNOT UNTIED   1691
Orchestral Suite
Overture, Air, Rondeau, Minuet, Air, Jig
Saidenberg Little Symphony—Saidenberg
(Limited Edition)   2 10″—**CH-A3**
Overture
See under Suites—Orchestra
(arr. Barbirolli)
Minuet
See under Ayres for the Theatre &
Comus—Ballet Suite

HENRY II   Incidental Music   1692
Hornpipe
Piper's Guild Quartet, C-DB2281

(THE) INDIAN QUEEN
See also under Comus—Ballet Suite
I attempt from Love's sickness to fly Act III
Blanche Thebom (c)   10″—**V-10-1178**
[Handel: L'Allegro—Let me wander]
Astra Desmond (c) & Harold
Craxton (pf)   10″—**D-M549**
[Fairy Queen: Hark, the echoing air; The
Libertine—Nymphs & Shepherds]
We are the spirits of the air   Act III
(New words, arr. Moffat: Let us wander not
unseen.)
Isobel Baillie (s) & Kathleen Ferrier
(c) w. Gerald Moore (pf)
10″—**C-DB2201**
[King Arthur—Shepherd, shepherd, cease
decoying & Sound the trumpet]
Hornpipe
Piper's Guild Quartet, C-DB2281

KING ARTHUR
Overture   See under Suites—Orchestra
(Arr. Barbirolli)
Fairest isle of all isles excelling   Act V
Maggie Teyte (s) & Gerald Moore (pf)
10″—**G-DA1790**
[Libertine—Nymphs & Shepherds, arr.
Cummings]
—**Arr. Barbirolli**   See Suites—Orchestra
Also: Piper's Guild Quartet, C-DB2279
Shepherd, shepherd, cease decoying Act II
Isobel Baillie (s) & Kathleen Ferrier (c)
with Gerald Moore (pf) 10″—**C-DB2201**
[Let us wander & Sound the trumpet]
Yellow Sands; Hornpipe
Piper's Guild Quartet, C-DB2279

KING RICHARD II 1681

Retir'd from any mortal's sight
Astra Desmond (c) & Harold
Craxton (pf)   12″—**D-K1397**
[I see she flies from me; On the brow of
Richmond Hill; Sylvia, now your scorn]

(THE) LIBERTINE 1692

Nymphs and Shepherds
Maggie Teyte (s) & Gerald Moore (pf)
     10″—**G-DA1790**
[King Arthur—Fairest Isle of all Isles]
Gladys Swarthout (ms) & L. Hodges (pf)
     (in VM-679)   12″—**V-16778**
[Dowland: Come again sweet love;
Handel: Rinaldo—Lascia]
Astra Desmond (c) & Harold
Craxton (pf)   10″—**D-M549**
[Fairy Queen—Hark, the echoing air:
Indian Queen—I attempt from love's
sickness to fly]
Also: Children's Cho. & Hallé Orch.—
Harty, C-9906

(THE) MARRIED BEAU 1694

(2) Hornpipes

No. 1, D minor
See Comus—Ballet Suite

No. 2, C major
Chamber Orch.—Barbirolli
     12″—**V-36284**
[Mozart: Eine kleine Nachtmusik, Pt. 4]

OEDIPUS 1692

Now for a while
Roy Henderson (b) & Eric Gritten (pf)
     12″—**D-K1198**
[Arne: Now Phoebus sinketh in the west]

(THE) OLD BACHELOR 1695
Bourrée See under Ayres for the Theatre

(THE) RIVAL SISTERS
Incidental Music 1695
Overture See under Ayres for the Theatre
Celia has a thousand charms Act II
Astra Desmond (c) & Harold
Craxton (pf)   10″—**D-M550**
[Sweet, be no longer sad & Ah, how
pleasant it is to love]

(THE) TEMPEST Incidental Music
See under Comus—Ballet Suite

TIMON OF ATHENS

Song of the Birds
See under Suites—Orchestra
(Arr. Wood)

(THE) VIRTUOUS WIFE

No. 5, Preludio
See under Ayres for the Theatre

No. 6, Minuet
See under Suites—Orchestra
(Arr. Barbirolli)

No. 8, Minuet
Pipers Guild Quartet, C-DB2281

No. 9
See under Comus—Ballet Suite

Passing By
("There is a lady sweet and kind")
(*This song, often erroneously ascribed to
Henry Purcell, is by Edward C. Purcell. See
under that name for recordings: Purcell-Cock-
rane, Edward.*)

Overture, Air & Jig
—**Air only**
(*Identical with the Air in G minor from "Ab-
delazar."*)
Myra Hess   12″—**G-C3337**
[Suite No. 1—Minuet; Suite No. 2—
Saraband; Ferguson—Sonata, F minor,
Pt. 5]

Rejoice in the Lord Alway (Bell Anthem)
Bach Cantata Club—Kennedy Scott, acc.
Strings & Harpsichord   10″—**C-DB500**
[Monteverdi: Ariana—May sweet
oblivion lull thee, D. Owens]
(in Columbia History of Music, Vol. II:
CM-232)

Sarabande See under Suite—Harpsichord,
No. 2

Siciliana, G minor Harpsichord
Alfred Cortot (pf)   10″—**G-DA1609**
[Air, Gavotte & Minuets]

SONATAS—String

G minor Violin & Figured Bass
(*From a manuscript in a private library dated
1691*) (*Pub. 1901.*)

**Adagio—Moderato; Adagio con espressione
—Vivace**
Stefan Frenkel (vl), Sterling Hunkins
(vlc) & Ernst Victor Wolff (harpsichord)
     12″—**MC-1023**
Frederick Grinke & Arnold Goldsborough
(pf)   12″—**D-K1404**

SONATAS—String

Set No. 1 12 Sonatas in Three Parts

No. 1, G minor Violin & Harpsichord
—**Vivace only**
See under Suites—Orchestra (Arr. Wood)

No. 5, A minor Violin & Harpsichord
—**Largo only**
See under Suites—Orchestra (Arr.
Wood)

Set No. 2 10 Sonatas in Four Parts
No. 3, A minor 2 Violins & Harpsichord
Jean Pougnet, Frederick Grinke & Boris
Ord   12″—**D-K809**
No. 6, G minor
—**Chaconne only**
See under Chaconne, G minor (Arr. Whit-
taker)
No. 9, F major ("Golden Sonata") 2 Violins
& Continuo
William Primrose, Isolde Menges, w. A.
Gauntlett (vla. da gamba) & J. Ticehurst
(harpsichord) in English Music Society
album, Vol. I
Jean Pasquier, P. Ferret (vls), E. Pas-
quier (vlc), R. Gerlin (harpsichord)
     (in Vol. III)   12″—**AS-22**
Jean Pougnet, Frederick Grinke & Boris
Ord (harpsichord)   12″—**D-K778**

Sound the Trumpet Vocal Duet Arr. Moffat
(*From Come ye Sons of Art, a group of 6 Odes
composed for Queen Mary, 1687.*)

Isobel Baillie (s) & Kathleen Ferrier (c)
w. Gerald Moore (pf)   10″—C-DB2201
[Let us wander & King Arthur—Shepherd, shepherd cease decoying]

(8) SUITES—Harpsichord

Complete recording
Sylvia Marlowe   5 12″—In Gramophone Shop Album GSC-2
(Recorded exclusively for the Gramophone Shop)

No. 1, G major
Rudolph Dolmetsch   10″—C-DB501
[Handel: 8th Harpsichord Suite—Allemande & Courante]
(in Columbia History of Music, Vol. II: CM-232)
Ralph Kirkpatrick, in MC-25
—Minuet only
Myra Hess (pf), on G-C3337
Alfred Cortot (pf) (with Minuet from Suite No. 8 as Trio) on G-DA1609

No. 2, G minor
Ralph Kirkpatrick, in MC-25
—Sarabande only
Myra Hess (pf), on G-C3337

No. 7, D minor
—Hornpipe only
Alice Ehlers (in D-A62)   10″—D-23114
[Bach: Fr. Suite No. 4—Allemande & Haydn: Sonata No. 3—Minuet]

No. 8, F major—Minuet only
See Suite No. 1 above
Same as Minuet in "The Double Dealer"

SUITES—Miscellaneous Orchestral

—Arr. Strings, Horns, Flutes & English .
Horn Barbirolli
Andante Maestoso; Allegro ("The Gordian Knot Untied"—Overture); Tempo di Minuetto ("The Virtuous Wife"—No. 6); Andantino ("King Arthur"—Fairest Isle, Act V); Largo ("Dido and Aeneas"—When I am Laid in Earth); Allegro ("King Arthur"—2nd Music Overture)
New York Philharmonic-Symphony Orch.—Barbirolli
(G-DB3729/30)   2 12″—VM-533

Suite in Five Movements Arr. Henry Wood
Prelude, Act III ("Dioclesian"); Minuet ("Distressed Innocence"); Largo from 5th Sonata for Strings; Song of the Birds ("Timon of Athens"); Vivace from 1st Sonata for Strings
Queen's Hall Orch.—Wood
                  2 12″—D-K975/6

Sweet, be no longer sad Air
Astra Desmond (c) & Harold Craxton (pf)   10″—D-M550
[Celia has a thousand charms & Ah, how pleasant it is to love]

Sylvia, now your scorn give over Air
Astra Desmond (c) & Harold Craxton (pf)   12″—D-K1397
[I see she flies from me; Ode to Cynthia; King Richard II—Retir'd from any mortal's sight]

To thee to thee and to a maid
See under Catches & Rounds

(A) Trumpet Voluntary, D major Organ
E. Power Biggs
          (in VM-961†)   12″—V-11-8562
[Reubke: Sonata, C minor, on 94th Psalm, Pt. 5]
—Arr. Orchestra Henry Wood
Alex Harris (tr), H. Dawber (org) & Hallé Orch.—Harty
(C-L1986)   12″—C-7136M
[Davies: Solemn Melody]
—Arr. Orchestra Stokowski
Hollywood Bowl Orch.—Stokowski
                  12″—V-11-9419
[Haydn: Quartet, F major, Op. 3, No. 5—Serenade]

Trumpet Tune & Air Organ
Charles Hens (Gonzalez Organ)
                  12″—PAT-PAT66
[Bach: Christ lag in Todesbanden]
(in 3 Centuries of Organ Music)
Reginald Foort (Giant Möller Concert Organ)   10″—G-BD1014
[Addinsell: Theme from Warsaw Concerto]

QUANTZ, Johann Joachim (1697-1773)

A celebrated German flutist and composer best remembered today as the teacher and court conductor of Frederick the Great of Prussia.

Trio, D major Arr. Pilney
R. Fritzsche (flute), K. H. Pilney (harpsichord), & K. M. Schwamberger (viola da gamba)   12″—O-7955

QUILTER, Roger (1877-   )

A British composer who has specialized in songs. Despite German training, he remains intensely English, and has succeeded best with settings of Shakespeare and Tennyson.

Children's Overture Orchestra
(Based on nursery tunes from "The Baby's Opera.")
London Philharmonic—John Barbirolli
                  12″—G-C2603
London Philharmonic—Henry Wood
          2 10″—C-DB951/2
New Light Symphony—Malcolm Sargent
          2 10″—G-B2860/1
H. M. Grenadier Guards Band—Miller
                  12″—D-K998

Damask Roses, Op. 12, No. 3
Astra Desmond (c) & Gerald Moore (pf)
                  10″—D-M524
[Love's philosophy & White: When swallows homeward fly]

It was a lover and his lass (Shakespeare)
Roland Hayes (t) & Reginald Boardman (pf)   (in CM-393) 12″—C-17177D
[Bach: Bist du bei mir]

Love's philosophy (Shelley)
Astra Desmond (c) & Gerald Moore (pf)
                  10″—D-M524
[Damask Roses & White: When the swallows homeward fly]

Now sleeps the crimson petal (Tennyson)
Paul Robeson (bs) & pf. acc.
10″—G-B9281
[Graves: Love at my heart]

To daisies (Herrick)
Isobel Baillie (s) & Gerald Moore (pf)
10″—C-DB2303
[Rachmaninoff: Lilacs & At the window]

To daffodils

To the virgins Unacc. Chorus
BBC Chorus—Leslie Woodgate
10″—D-K832

RABAUD, Henri (1873-   )
*For some years chief conductor of the Paris
Opera, Rabaud was also with the Boston Sym-
phony Orchestra. Later he succeeded Gabriel
Fauré as director of the Paris Conservatoire.
His only well known composition is his opera
"Marouf" heard some years ago at the Metro-
politan Opera House.*

MAROUF, SAVETIER DU CAIRE Opera 5
Acts 1914

Individual Excerpts

ACT I

Il est des Musulmans Tenor
Georges Thill   12″—C-D15035
[La Caravane, Act II]

ACT II

(La) Caravane: A travers le désert Tenor
Georges Thill   12″—C-D15035
[Il est des Musulmans, Act I]
DUPLICATION: A. Gaudin, PD-524060

ACT IV

Dans le jardin fleuri Tenor
André Gaudin (b)   10″—PD-524060
[La Caravane, Act II]

(La) Procession Nocturne, Op. 6 Orchestra
*(Symphonic poem after an episode in Lenau's
"Faust")*
Symphony Orch.—Rabaud
2 12″—C-D15078/9
Lamoureux Orch.—Albert Wolff
2 12″—PD-566163/4
[Saint-Saëns: Le Déluge—Prélude]

RACHMANINOFF, Sergei (1873-1943)
*Once considered one of the most promising
Russian composers associated with the less
strongly nationalistic group that included
Tchaikowsky, Rachmaninoff, in later years,
confined himself largely to a career as a virtuoso of the piano and continued to perform
until his death. His piano compositions—including the preludes and concertos—have become
internationally popular.*

Collections

(11) Piano Pieces
Mélodie, E major, Op. 3, No. 3
Humoresque, Op. 10, No. 5
Moment Musical, Op. 16, No. 2
Prelude, G flat major, Op. 23, No. 10
Prelude, E major, Op. 32, No. 3
Prelude, F major, Op. 32, No. 7
Prelude, F minor, Op. 32, No. 6
Etude, C major, Op. 33, No. 2

Etude, E flat major, Op. 33, No. 7
Daisies, Op. 38
Oriental Sketch
Sergei Rachmaninoff   5   10″—VM-722

Rachmaninoff Recital Piano
Piano Concerto No. 2 (excerpts)
Oriental Sketch
Rhapsody on a Theme of Paganini
(theme only)
Prelude, G sharp minor, Op. 32, No. 12
Prelude, C sharp minor, Op. 3, No. 2
Prelude, G major, Op. 32, No. 5
Prelude, G minor, Op. 23, No. 5
Jacob Gimpel   3   10″—VOX-608

Albumblatt See under—Marguerite

ALEKO One Act Opera in Russian 1892

No. 10, The moon is high in the sky Bass
(Cavatine of Aleko)
Feodor Chaliapin   12″—V-14902
[Massenet: Elégie]
I. Ivanov   10″—USSR-12730/1

No. 12, Romance of the young gypsy Tenor
S. Khromchenko & N. Parfenov (harp)
10″—USSR-4598/5746
[Rimsky-Korsakov: Czar's Bride—Lykov's Aria, N. Sereda]

(The) Bells Chorus & Orchestra 1913
Santa Monica Symphony—Jacques
Rachmilovich, w. Hollywood First Metho-
dist Church Chorus & Carmen Prietto
(s), Breece Westmoreland (t), Stephen
Kemalyan (b) in English
4   12″—DISC-804

CONCERTOS—Piano & Orchestra
(See also Rhapsody for Piano & Orchestra)

No. 1, F sharp minor, Op. 1 (1890/1)
Sergei Rachmaninoff & Philadelphia
Orch.—Ormandy
(G-DB5706/8†)   3   12″—VM-865†

No. 2, C minor, Op. 18
Sergei Rachmaninoff & Philadelphia
Orch.—Stokowski   5   12″—VM-58†
(G-DB1333/7 in GM-84†)
Artur Rubinstein & NBC Symphony—
Golschmann   5   12″—VM-1075†
[Chopin, Impromptu No. 3]
(Also V-V6†)
Gyorgy Sandor & N. Y. Philharmonic-
Symphony Orch.—Rodzinski
4   12″—CM-605†
Cyril Smith & Liverpool Philharmonic
Orch.—Sargent 5 12″—C-DX1424/8†
Eugene List & Philharmonic Orch., of
Los Angeles—Wallenstein
5   12″—D-DA465
Benno Moiseiwitsch & London Philhar-
monic Orch.—Goehr
(G-C2973/6)   4   12″—GM-302†
Eileen Joyce & London Philharmonic—
Leinsdorf
(D-K1545/9†)   5 12″—D-ED32†
[Humoresque, Op. 10, No. 5, Joyce only]

—Excerpts: Jacob Gimpel, (piano solo) in
VOX-608; Al Goodman & Orch., V-28-
0404; Jesús María Sanromá, V-13759
in VM-818; G-C3300

No. 3, D minor, Op. 30 1909
Sergei Rachmaninoff & Philadelphia
Orch.—Ormandy   5   12"—**VM-710**†
[Tchaikovsky: Solitude] (G-DB6033/7S)
(G-DB5709/3S in GM-347†)
Cyril Smith & City of Birmingham Orch.
—Weldon   5   12"—**CM-671**†
(C-DX1251/5†)
Vladimir Horowitz & London Symphony
Orch.—Coates   5   12"—**VM-117**†
(G-DB1486/90)
[Prelude, G minor, Op. 23, No. 5]

No. 4, G minor, Op. 40
Sergei Rachmaninoff & Philadelphia
Orch.—Ormandy   4   12"—**VM-972**†

Daisies, Op. 38 Piano
See also under songs
Sergei Rachmaninoff
            (in VM-722)   10"—**V-2127**
[Oriental Sketch]
Émil Hillel   10"—**USSR-13298/9**
[Chopin: Polonaise No. 3]

—Arr. Violin & Piano Heifetz
Jascha Heifetz & Emanuel Bay
            10"—**V-10-1355**
[Oriental Sketch & Prokofiev: Gavotte &
March]

Danse Orientale, Op. 2, No. 2 'Cello & Piano
Edmund Kurtz & Emanuel Bay
[Grazioli: Adagio]   12"—**V-11-9024**

Etudes Tableaux, Op. 33 & Op. 39 Piano

F minor, Op. 33, No. 1
Anatole Kitain   12"—**C-69569D**
[Prelude, Op. 32, No. 12, & Scriabin:
Etude & Prelude]

C major, Op. 33, No. 2
Sergei Rachmaninoff
            (in VM-722)   10"—**V-2126**
[Etude, E flat, Op. 33, No. 7]
Jacob Gimpel, in VOX-164

E flat major, Op. 33, No. 7
Sergei Rachmaninoff
            (in VM-722)   10"—**V-2126**
[Etude, C major, Op. 33, No. 2]

C major, Op. 39, No. 2

—Arr. Violin & Piano Heifetz
Jascha Heifetz & Emanuel Bay
        (in VM-1126)   10"—**V-10-1296**
[Halffter: Danza de la gitana]

Humoresque, Op. 10, No. 5 Piano
Sergei Rachmaninoff
            (in VM-722)   10"—**V-2123**
[Mélodie, E major, Op. 3, No. 3]
Eileen Joyce
        (in D-ED32†)   12"—**D-K1549**
[Concerto No. 2, Pt. 9, with London
Philharmonic]

(The) Isle of the Dead, Op. 29 Orchestra
(Symphonic Poem after Boecklin's
painting)
Boston Symphony Orch.—Koussevitzky
            3   12"—**VM-1024**†
Minneapolis Symphony Orch.—Mitro-
poulos   3   12"—**CM-599**†

Marguerite (Albumblatt) Arr. Violin &
Piano Kreisler
Fritz Kreisler & Carl Lamson
(G-DA815)   10"—**V-1170**
[Tchaikovsky: Humoresque]

Mélodie, E major, Op. 3, No. 3 Piano
Sergei Rachmaninoff
            (in VM-722)   10"—**V-2123**
[Humoresque, Op. 10, No. 5]

Moments Musicaux, Op. 16 Piano

No. 2
Sergei Rachmaninoff
            (in VM-722)   10"—**V-2124**
[Prelude, No. 11]

No. 4, E minor
Benno Moiseiwitsch   12"—**G-C3370**
[Preludes No. 16 & 23]

Oriental Sketch. Piano
Sergei Rachmaninoff
            (in VM-722)   10"—**V-2127**
[Daisies, Op. 38]
Jacob Gimpel, in VOX-608

—Arr. Violin & Piano Heifetz
Jascha Heifetz & Emanuel Bay
            10"—**V-10-1355**
[Daisies & Prokofiev: Gavotte & March]

Polka de W. R. (No opus number) Piano
Sergei Rachmaninoff   12"—**V-6857**
[Tchaikovsky: Troïka en traineaux]

(24) PRELUDES Piano

Complete recording
Moura Lympany   9   12"—**D-K1023/31**

Individual Recordings

No. 1, C sharp minor, Op. 3, No. 2
Moura Lympany, on D-K1023
Sergei Rachmaninoff
(G-DA996)   10"—**V-1326**
[Mendelssohn: Spinning Song]
Artur Rubinstein   12"—**V-14276**
[Schubert: Sonata, G major, Op. 78—
Minuet & Trio]
José Iturbi
(G-DB6468)   12"—**V-11-9514**
[Paderewski: Minuet, G major, Op. 14,
No. 1]
William Kapell   12"—**V-11-8824**
[Shostakovich: 3 Preludes]
DUPLICATIONS: Moiseiwitsch, G-C3184;
Jacob Gimpel, in VOX-608; Syzanne Gyr,
G-DA6014; Walter Rehberg, PD-27229;
Elvi Henriksen, TONO-A125; William
Murdoch, C-DX244: C-CQX16610; Mark
Hambourg, G-C1292; O. Vondrovic,
ESTA-F5195; Schendel, G-S10242
Also: Rawicz & Landauer (2 pfs),
C-DB2144; Eight Piano Ensemble,
G-C2612

—Arr. Orchestra
Boston "Pops" Orch.—Fiedler
(G-C2889) (G-EH1028)   12"—**V-11922**
[Prelude No. 6]
André Kostelanetz & his Orch.
        (in CM-484)   12"—**C-71304D**
[Liszt: Liebestraum No. 3]
London Symphony Orch.—Sargent
            12"—**G-C2292**

[Mascagni: Cavalleria Rusticana—Intermezzo]
DUPLICATIONS: Lamoureux Orch.—Wolff, PD-566018: PD-66995; Queen's Hall Orch.—Wood, D-K762: C-DX87: C-DFX65; Berlin Philharmonic—Orthmann, U-B14249; Marek Weber Orch., G-EH61; Symphony Orchestra—Coppola, G-S10228
See current catalogues for miscellaneous arrangements.

No. 2, F sharp minor, Op. 23, No. 1
Moura Lympany, on D-K1023

No. 3, B flat major, Op. 23, No. 2
Moura Lympany, on D-K1024

No. 4, D minor, Op. 23, No. 3
Moura Lympany, on D-K1024

No. 5, D major, Op. 23, No. 4
Moura Lympany, on D-K1025

No. 6, G minor (Alla marcia), Op. 23, No. 5
Moura Lympany, on D-K1025
Vladimir Horowitz
(in VM-117†) 12"—V-7466
[Concerto No. 3, Pt. 9] (G-DB1490)
Benno Moiseiwitsch 12"—G-C3184
[Prelude No. 1]
Alexander Borovsky (Argentine)
12"—V-11-8741
[Prelude No. 23 & Prokofiev: Prelude, C major]
Cyril Smith 12"—C-DX1279
[Prelude No. 16]
DUPLICATIONS: Jacob Gimpel, in VOX-608; Eileen Joyce, P-E11252; William Murdoch, C-DX244: C-CQX16610; Elvi Henriksen, TONO-A125

—Arr. Orchestra
Boston "Pops" Orch.—Fiedler
(G-C2889) (G-EH1028) 12"—V-11922
[Prelude No. 1]

No. 7, E flat major, Op. 23, No. 6
Moura Lympany, on D-K1026
Eileen Joyce 12"—P-E11351
[Prelude No. 8 & Dohnanyi: Rhapsody, C major]

No. 8, C minor, Op. 23, No. 7
Moura Lympany, on D-K1026
Eileen Joyce 12"—P-E11351
[Prelude No. 7, & Dohnanyi: Rhapsody, C major]

No. 9, A flat major, Op. 23, No. 8
Moura Lympany, on D-K1027

No. 10, E flat minor, Op. 23, No. 9
Moura Lympany, on D-K1026

No. 11, G flat major, Op. 23, No. 10
Sergei Rachmaninoff
(in VM-722) 10"—V-2124
[Moment Musical, Op. 16, No. 2]
[Prelude No. 14, on G-DA1772]
Moura Lympany, on D-K1027

No. 12, C major, Op. 32, No. 1
Moura Lympany, on D-K1026

No. 13, B flat minor, Op. 32. No. 2
Moura Lympany, on D-K1028

No. 14, E major, Op. 32, No. 3
Moura Lympany, on D-K1028
Sergei Rachmaninoff
(in VM-722) 10"—V-2125
[Preludes Nos. 17 & 18]
[Prelude No. 11, on G-DA1772]

No. 15, E minor, Op. 32, No. 4
Moura Lympany, on D-K1029

No. 16, G major, Op. 32, No. 5
Moura Lympany, on D-K1029
Benno Moiseiwitsch 12"—G-C3370
[Prelude 23, & Moment Musical, Op. 16, No. 4]
Cyril Smith 12"—C-DX1279
[Prelude No. 6]
Also: Jacob Gimpel, in VOX-608

No. 17, F minor, Op. 32, No. 6
Moura Lympany, on D-K1027
Sergei Rachmaninoff
(in VM-722) 10"—V-2125
[Preludes Nos. 14 & 18]

No. 18, F major, Op. 32, No. 7
Moura Lympany, on D-K1028
Sergei Rachmaninoff
(in VM-722) 10"—V-2125
[Preludes Nos. 14 & 17]

No. 19, A minor, Op. 32, No. 8
Moura Lympany, on D-K1030

No. 20, A major, Op. 32, No. 9
Moura Lympany, on D-K1030

No. 21, B minor, Op. 32, No. 10
Moura Lympany, on D-K1030
Benno Moiseiwitsch 12"—G-C3209
[Mendelssohn-Rachmaninoff: Scherzo from Midsummer Night's Dream Music]

No. 22, B major, Op. 32, No. 11
Moura Lympany, on D-K1031

No. 23, G sharp minor, Op. 32, No. 12
Moura Lympany, on D-K1031
Anatole Kitain 12"—C-69569D
[Etude Tableau, Op. 33, No. 1 & Scriabin: Etude & Prelude]
Benno Moiseiwitsch 10"—G-C3370
[Prelude No. 16 & Moment Musical Op. 16, No. 4]
Alexander Borovsky (Argentine)
12"—V-11-8741
[Prelude No. 6 & Prokofiev: Prelude, C major]
DUPLICATION: Jacob Gimpel, in VOX-608

No. 24, D flat major, Op. 32, No. 13
Moura Lympany, on D-K1031

Rhapsody on a Theme of Paganini, Op. 43
Piano & Orchestra
(*The theme is that of the Paganini Caprice No. 24—Op. 1—which also serves as the basis of Brahms' Variations on a theme of Paganini. For recordings see under Paganini: Caprice No. 24, and under Brahms: Variations.*)
Sergei Rachmaninoff & Philadelphia Orch.—Stokowski
(G-DB2426/8†) 3 12"—VM-250†
Artur Rubinstein & Philharmonia Orch.—Süsskind 3 12"—G-DB6556/8†
Benno Moiseiwitsch & London Philharmonic—Cameron 3 12"—VM-855†
(G-C3262/4†) (G-L1063/5)

—Excerpt only: Jacob Gimpel (Piano), in VOX-608

Serenade, Op. 3, No. 5 Piano
Sergei Rachmaninoff 10"—G-DA1522
[Borodin: Scherzo]

—Arr. Violin & Piano
Frederick Grinke & Ivor Newton
10"—D-M539
[Gurney: The Apple Orchard]
—Arr. Saxophone & Piano: Viard & Grant,
PAT-PA185

SONGS In Russian

Collection
All things depart
The answer
At my window
Floods of Spring
In the silent night
Lilacs
O Cease thy singing, maiden fair
The Drooping corn (O thou billowy harvest field)
The Soldier's bride
Sorrow in Springtime
Jennie Tourel (ms) & Erich Itor Kahn
(pf)   3   12"—CM-625

Collection
All things depart; Christ is Risen; Daisies; How fair this spot; In the silent night; The island; Lilacs; Nuit de Mai—Fragment; O, cease thy singing, maiden fair; To the children; When yesterday we met
Nina Koshetz (s) & Celius Dogherty
4   12"—SCH-16

All things depart, Op. 26, No. 15 (Rathaus)
Jennie Tourel, on C-72097D in CM-625:
C-LX1020
Nina Koshetz (s), in SCH-16

(The) Answer, Op. 21, No. 4 (Victor Hugo)
Jennie Tourel, on C-72097D in CM-625:
C-LX1038

At my window, Op. 26, No. 10 (Galina)
Jennie Tourel, on C-72097D in CM-625:
C-LX1020
Isobel Baillie (s) (in English) & Gerald
Moore (pf)   10"—C-DB2303
[Lilacs; Quilter: To Daisies]

At Night
See: In the silent night

Chanson georgienne
See: Oh, cease thy singing

Christ is risen, Op. 26, No. 6 (Mereshkovsky)
Nina Koshetz, in SCH-16
Peter Dawson (b) (in English)
[Parry: Jerusalem]   10"—G-B8196

Daisies, Op. 38, No. 3
Nina Koshetz, in SCH-16

Do not trust me, friend
V. V. Victorova (s) & A. B. Goldenweiser
(pf)   10"—USSR-13068/71
[Tchaikovsky: Disappointment, Op. 65, No. 2]

Dreams, Op. 38, No. 5 (Brussov)
Vera Davidova (ms) & Alexander
Jerochin (pf)
in Prep. Danish Columbia

(The) Drooping Corn
See: O thou billowy harvest field

Floods of Spring, Op. 14, No. 11
(or Spring Waters) Ger. Frühlingsflüten
Jennie Tourel, on C-72098D in CM-625:
C-LX1038
Marjorie Lawrence (s) & Ivor Newton
(pf)   10"—D-M602
[Grieg: I love thee]
—Arr. 2 Pianos: Vronsky & Babin,
V-13777 in VM-822†

Harvest of Sorrow
See: O thou billowy harvest field

How fair this spot, Op. 21, No. 7 (Galina)
Nina Koshetz, in SCH-16
—Arr. 2 Pianos: Vronsky & Babin,
V-13777 in VM-822†

In the silent night, Op. 4, No. 3 (Foeth)
(Other English titles include: In the silence of the night; At night; When night descends, etc.)
Marian Anderson, (c) (in English),
Franz Rupp (pf) & William Primrose
(vla)   (in VM-986)   10"—V-10-1122
[Massenet: Elégie]
Jennie Tourel, on C-72097D in CM-605:
C-LX1038
Nina Koshetz, in SCH-16
DUPLICATION: Charles Kullman,
(in Eng.), C-17242D

(The) Island, Op. 14, No. 2 (Balmont)
Nina Koshetz, in SCH-16

Lilacs, Op. 21, No. 5 (Beketova)
Jennie Tourel, on C-72098D in CM-625:
C-LX1038
Nina Koshetz, in SCH-16
Ada Slobodskaya (s) & pf. acc.
10"—G-EK113
[Mussorgsky: Fair at Sorochinsk—Parassia's Day Dream & Rubenstein: The Rose]
Ninon Vallin (s) (in French) & pf. acc.
10"—PAT-PG82
[Gretchaninov: Over the steppe; Gounod: Venise]
Isobel Baillie (s) (in English) & Gerald
Moore (pf)   10"—C-DB2303
[At the window; Quilter: To Daisies]

Nuit de Mai—Fragment (Musset)
Nina Koshetz, in SCH-16

O, Cease thy singing, maiden fair, Op. 4, No. 4 (Pushkin)
Jennie Tourel, on C-72096D in CM-625
Nina Koshetz, in SCH-16

O thou billowy harvest field, Op. 4, No. 5
(or, The drooping corn)
Jennie Tourel, on C-72098D in CM-625
Alexander Kipnis (bs) & Celius Dogherty (pf)   12"—V-11-8595
[Gretchaninoff: Over the steppe]

(The) Soldier's Wife, Op. 8, No. 4
(or, Bride)
Jennie Tourel, on C-72096D in CM-625:
C-LX1020

Sorrow in Spring, Op. 21, No. 12
Jennie Tourel, on C-72097D in CM-625:
C-LX1020

To the children, Op. 26, No. 7 (Khomyakov)
Nina Koshetz, in SCH-16
John McCormack (t) (in English) with
pf. acc. 10"—G-DA1112
[Tchaikovsky: None but the lonely
heart]

Vocalise, Op. 34, No. 14 (Wordless song)
—Arr. Orchestra Rachmaninoff
Boston Symphony Orch.—Koussevitzky
(in VM-1024†) 12"—V-11-8959
[Isle of the Dead, Pt. 5]
Philadelphia Orch.—Rachmaninoff
(in VM-712†) 12"—V-17430
[Symphony, No. 3, Pt. 9]
—Arr. Violin & Piano Press
Ruggiero Ricci, G-DB4622
—Arr. 'Cello & Piano
G. Piatigorsky & R. Berkowitz, in CM-
684; Pierre Fournier, G-W1578
—Arr. 2 Pianos: Vronsky & Babin, V-13563
in VM-741

When night descends See: In the silent
night

When yesterday we met, Op. 26, No. 13
(Polansky)
Nina Koshetz, in SCH-16

SUITES—2 Pianos
No. 1, Op. 5
Vitya Vronsky & Victor Babin
[Vocalise] 3 12"—VM-741†
No. 2, Op. 17
Vronsky & Babin 3 12"—VM-822†
[Floods of Spring & How fair this spot,
arr. Babin]

SYMPHONIES
No. 2, E minor, Op. 27 Orchestra 1906/7
N. Y. Philharmonic-Symphony Orch.—
Rodzinski 6 12"—CM-569†
Minneapolis Symphony Orch.—Mitro-
poulos 6 12"—VM-1148†
Minneapolis Symphony Orch.—Ormandy
6 12"—VM-230†
No. 3, A minor, Op. 44 1936
Philadelphia Orch.—Rachmaninoff
[Vocalise] 5 12"—VM-712†
Trio, D minor, Op. 9 ("Elegaic")
Compinsky Trio 4 12"—ALCO-A4
Vocalise, Op. 34, No. 14
See under Songs—Vocalise
We sing to Thee (Tebje Pojem) Hymn in
Russian
Don Cossack Choir.—S. Jarnoff
[Trad. Stenka Razin] 12"—C-7360M

MISCELLANEOUS—Transcriptions for
Piano
See under: Kreisler: Liebesfreud &
Liebesleid; Mussorgsky: Fair at
Sorotchinsk-Gopak; Schubert: Wohin
(The Brook)

RAFF, Josef Joachim (1822-1882)
*A Swiss-German composer of the romantic
school whose works once enjoyed considerable
popularity. He is remembered today almost
entirely by such slight pieces as the celebrated
Cavatina.*

Cavatina, A flat major, Op. 85, No. 3 Violin
& Piano
Mischa Elman & Josef Bonime
[Schubert: Serenade] 12"—V-7461
DUPLICATIONS: I. Zilzer, PD-27160; Y.
Curti, PAT-X98079; A. Sammons,
D-F7532
—Arr. Orchestra
New Light Symphony—Sargent
[Davies: Solemn Melody] 12"—G-C2176
DUPLICATIONS: Alfredo Campoli,
D-F6330; Royal Artillery String Orch.—
Geary, D-F7566
Also: Reginald Foort (org), D-F6720
(La) Fileuse, Op. 157, No. 2 Piano
Yvonne Arnaud, with String Orch.
12"—G-C2456
[Bach: Piano Concerto No. 5, F minor—
Allegro]

RAMEAU, Jean Philippe (1683-1764)
*The outstanding native French musician of
the eighteenth century, Rameau was among
the first to employ instrumental color in his
opera scores. The list of his recorded works is
growing, but has yet to include complete performances of his more important compositions.*

Collection
Pièces de Clavecin (Harpsichord Pieces)
Les Sauvages; Les Cyclopes; Les tendres
Plaintes; La Villageoise; Les Soupirs;
Gavotte et doubles; Fanfarinette; Le
Rappel des Oiseaux; L'Entretien des
Muses; La Livri; L'Egyptienne
Marcelle Meyer (pf) 4 12"—DF-A14
Allemande Harpsichord
Wanda Landowska, on V-15562 (in VM-
593†) (G-DB5077)
Castor et Pollux See under Operas
Clavecin en concert See under Pièces de
Clavecin en concert
Courante Harpsichord
Wanda Landowska, on V-15562 (in VM-
593†) (G-DB5077)
(La) Cupis See under Pièces de Clavecin
en concert, No. 5
(Les) Cyclopes
Marcelle Meyer (pf), in DF-A14
Monique Haas (pf) 12"—D-K1443
[Bach: Italian Concerto, Pt. 3]
Dardanus See under Operas
Diane Et Acteon Cantata
—Air tendre (unspecified)
Lise Daniels (s) & Irène Aitoff (pf)
[Couperin: Air sérieux] 10"—OL-19
Cortège d'Eglé
Maurice Maréchal (vlc) & Henriette
Roget (pf) 12"—C-LFX641
(L') Egyptienne Harpsichord
Marcelle Meyer (pf), in DF-A14
Entrée See under Operas—Dardanus
(L') Entretien des Muses Harpsichord
Marcelle Meyer (pf), in DF-A14
Fanfarinette Harpsichord
Marcelle Meyer (pf), in DF-A14
Fêtes d'Hébé See under Operas

(La) **Forqueray** See under Pièces de Clavecin en concert, No. 5

Gavotte et doubles Harpsichord
Marcelle Meyer (pf), in DF-A14

Gavotte (Unidentified)
Marcel Mule (saxophone) 10"—D-8239
[Beethoven: Minuet]

Gavotte variée Harpsichord 1736
(Theme, A minor, & 6 variations)
Sylvia Marlowe, in MC-84

Gigues en rondeau Harpsichord
Wanda Landowska, on V-15563 (in VM-593†) (G-DB5078)

Hymne à la nuit Unacc. Chorus in French
(This piece, based on a chorus from the opera "Hippolyte et Aricie" is sometimes entitled "La Nuit.")

—Arr. Noyen
La Manécanterie des Petits Chanteurs à la Croix de Bois 10"—G-K8497
[Anon., Arr. Philip: Les Danseurs Noyes]
Ste. Chapelle Chanteurs—Delépine
10"—C-DF62
[Anon., arr. Noyen: Il est né]

L'Impatience Cantata
Hugues Cuenod (t) with harpsichord & vlc., in TC-2

(Les) **Indes Galantes** See under Operas

(La) **Joyeuse** Harpsichord
Wanda Landowska 12"—G-DB4990
[La Poule; Les Sauvages; Menuet Majeur, Menuet Mineur; Les Tricotets]

Laboravi Chorus in Latin
St. Gervais Choir 12"—LUM-30002
[Van Berchem: O Jesu Christe]

(Le) **Lardon** Harpsichord
Li Stadelmann 10"—PD-47282
[Rigaudon & Triomphante; Telemann: Fantasia, B flat major]

(La) **Livri** Harpsichord
Marcelle Meyer (pf), in DF-A14

(La) **Marais** See under Pièces de Clavecin en concert, No. 5

Menuet majeur & Menuet mineur Harpsichord
Wanda Landowska 12"—G-DB4990
[La Joyeuse; La Poule; Les Sauvages; Les Tricotets]

Menuets See under Operas: Castor et Pollux; Platée

Menuet (unspecified) Arr. Violin & Piano
Ysaye
Blanche Tarjus & M. Monard
[Rappel des Oiseaux] 10"—G-DA5011

(La) **Nuit** See under Hymne à la Nuit

Musette en Rondeau Harpsichord
Wanda Landowska, on V-15564 (in VM-593†) (G-DB5079)
Alice Ehlers, in D-A62
Ralph Kirkpatrick, in MC-25
C. Guilbert (pf) 12"—C-LFX606
[2 Rigaudons & Couperin: L'engageante]

OPERAS In French

ACANTHE ET CEPHISE
Gavotte (Arr. Scherchen)
Winterthur Municipal Orch.—Scherchen
12"—G-DB6082
[Platée-Rigaudon et Tambourin]

Musette (Arr. Scherchen)
Winterthur Municipal Orch.—Scherchen
12"—G-DB6084
[Platée-Menuet & Gluck: Flute Concerto, Pt. 3]

CASTOR ET POLLUX 1737
Ballet Music Orchestra
Gavotte; Tambourin; Menuet; Passepied
Lamoureux Orch.—Albert Wolff
(PD-566144) 12"—PD-67044

Tristes apprêts, Act I (Air de Thélaïre)
Soprano
Jane Laval 10"—C-LF18
[Lully: Thésée—Revenez amours]

DARDANUS 5 Acts 1739
Air gai en rondeau, Act III
Chamber Orch.—R. Gerlin
(in Vol. IX) 12"—AS-81
[Excerpts from Hippolyte et Aricie; Platée; Les Indes Galantes]

Rigaudon
Jean Ibos Quintet 10"—PD-522420
[Lully: Bourgeois Gentilhomme—Menuet]
—Arr. Saxophone Quartet: PAT-PA286

(LES) **FETES D'HEBE** 1739
Musette & Tambourin (Arr. Weckerlin)
NOTE: *This famous Tambourin is also familiar as a harpsichord work. For recordings, see: Tambourin.*
Grand Orchestre Symphonique, Paris—Ruhlmann 10"—PAT-X96259
[Boccherini: Minuet]

HIPPOLYTE ET ARICIE 1733
NOTE: *See above: Hymne à la Nuit.*
March (Prologue)
Chamber Orch.—R. Gerlin
(in Vol. IX) 12"—AS-81
[Excerpts from Les Indes Galantes; Platée; Dardanus]

(LES) **INDES GALANTES** Opera ballet
Excerpts
Camille Mauranne, Irène Joachim, R. Malvisco (vocalists) with Yvonne Gouverné Chorus & Chamber Orch.—Hewitt
6 12"—DF-A6

Rondeau & Tambourins only
Chamber Orch.—R. Gerlin
(in Vol. IX) 12"—AS-81
[Excerpts from Hippolyte et Aricie; Platée; Dardanus]

(LES) **PALADINS** 1760
—**1st Suite** Arr. Désormière
Entrée très gaye des Troubadours; Air pour les Pagodes; Gavotte gaye; Gavotte un peu lente
L'Oiseau Lyre Orch.—Desormière
2 10"—OL-139/40

—2nd Suite. Arr. Désormière
Menuet, Sarabande, Gaiement
L'Oiseau Lyre Orch.—Désormière
2 10"—OL-71 a & b

PLATEE
Air, Act II (the 2nd Air); Menuets
Chamber Orch.—Gerlin
(in Vol. IX) 12"—AS-81
[Excerpts from Hippolyte et Aricie; Les
Indes Galantes; Dardanus]

Menuet Arr. Scherchen
Winterthur Municipal Orch.—Scherchen
12"—G-DB6084
[Acanthe et Céphise—Musette & Gluck:
Flute Concerto, pt. 3]

Rigaudon & Tambourin Arr. Scherchen
Winterthur Municipal Orch.— Scherchen
12"—G-DB6082
[Acanthe et Céphise—Gavotte]

(5) PIECES DE CLAVECIN EN CONCERT
1er Concert: La Coulicam; La Livri; Le
Vézinet
2e Concert: La Laborde; La Boucon;
L'Agaçante; 1er Minuet; 2eMinuet
3e Concert: La Pouplinière; La Timide—
1er & 2e Rondeau; 1er & 2e Tambourin
4e Concert: La Pantomime; L'Indiscrète
—Rondeau; La Rameau
5e Concert: La Forqueray—Fugue; La
Cupis; La Marais
Complete Recording
—**Arranged String Orchestra**
Chamber Orch.—Hewitt
(DF-1/6) 6 12"—DF-A1
—**4e Concert only**
Ars Rediviva Ensemble (Arr. Crussard)
12"—G-DB5055
—**5e Concert only**
Jean Pasquier (vl), Eva Heinitz (gam-
ba), Pauline Aubert (harpsichord)
(in Vol. III) 12"—AS-30
(La) Poule Harpsichord Eng. **The Hen**
Wanda Landowska 12"—G-DB4990
[La Joyeuse; Menuet; Les Sauvages; Les
Tricotets]
Erwin Bodky 10"—P-R1027
[Bach: 5th French Suite—Sarabande &
Gavotte]
(in 2000 Years of Music Set)
Sylvia Marlowe, in MC-84
—**Arr. Orchestra**
See under Respighi: Gli Uccelli Suite,
VM-1112†
Prélude Harpsichord
Pauline Aubert
(in Vol. XI) 12"—AS-103
[Les soupirs & Les Trois Mains]

QUAM DELECTA
Chorus in Latin Arr. Saint-Saëns
**Beati qui habitant & Laudate nomen
Domini**
St. Nicolas Choir—Lepage
10"—LUM-30021

(Le) Rappel des Oiseaux Harpsichord
Wanda Landowska, on V-15563 (in VM-
593†): G-DB5078

Ralph Kirkpatrick, in MC-25
Marcelle Meyer (pf), in DF-A14
Gaby Casadesus (pf), in VOX-163
—**Arr. Violin & Piano:** Blanche Tarjus,
G-DA5011
(2) Rigaudons Harpsichord
Wanda Landowska, on V-15563/4 (in
VM-593†) (G-DB-5078/9)
Ralph Kirkpatrick, in MC-25
Li Stadelmann 10"—PD-47282
[Le Lardon & Triomphante; Telemann:
Fantasia, B flat major]
Carmen Guilbert (pf) 12"—C-LFX606
[Musette en rondeau & Couperin: L'en-
gageante]
Rococo Dances (Arr. Scherchen) See under
Operas—Platée; Acanthe et Céphise
Rossignols amoureux Air in French
Leila Ben Sedira & Instrumental
Quartet 12"—G-W1507
[Falla: Psyché]
(Les) Sauvages. Harpsichord
Wanda Landowska 12"—G-DB4990
[La Joyeuse; Menuet; La Poule; Les
Tricotets]
Marcelle Meyer, (pf), in DF-A14
(Les) Soupirs Harpsichord
Pauline Aubert
(in Vol. XI) 12"—AS-103
[Prelude & Les Trois Mains]
Suite, E minor Harpsichord (Miscel-
laneous pieces from Vol. II, Pièces de
Clavecin) 1724
Allemande; Courante; Gigues en ron-
deau; Le Rappel des Oiseaux; 2 Riga-
dons; Musette en rondeau; Tambourin;
La Villageoise
Wanda Landowska
(G-DB5077/9) 3 12"—VM-593†
(Les) Surprises de l'amour—Excerpts
Maurice Maréchal (vlc) & Henriette
Roget (pf) 12"—C-LFX694
Tambourin
Wanda Landowska, on V-15564 (in VM-
593†): G-DB5079; also G-DA977
Ralph Kirkpatrick, in MC-25
—**Arr. Viola & Piano**
Wm. Primrose & J. Kahn, V-10-1098; W.
Forbes & D. Lassimonne, D-M567
—**Arr. Orch.** Rameau-Weckerlin See "Les
Fêtes d'Hébé"
Tambourins
See also Operas: Castor et Pollux; Platée
(Les) Tendres Plaintes Harpsichord
Marcelle Meyer (pf), in DF-A14
Theme & Variations A minor See under
Gavotte variée
Three Dances Arr. Viola & Piano Alan
Richardson
**Rigaudon (unidentified), Minuet (uniden-
tified), Tambourin**
Watson Forbes & Denise Lassimonne
10"—D-M567
(Les) Tricotets Harpsichord
Wanda Landowska 12"—G-DB4990
[La Joyeuse; Menuet; La Poule; Les
Sauvages]

(La) **Triomphante** Harpsichord
Li Stadelmann   10"—**PD-47282**
[Lardon & Rigaudon; Telemann; Fantasia, B flat major]

(Les) **Trois Mains** Harpsichord
Pauline Aubert
(in Vol. XI)   12"—**AS-103**
[Prélude & Les Soupirs]

(La) **Villageoise** Harpsichord
Wanda Landowska, on V-15564 (in VM-593†): G-DB5079
Ralph Kirkpatrick, in MC-25
Marcelle Meyer (pf), in DF-A14

RANGSTROEME, Ture (1884-   )

SONGS In Swedish
Avskedet (Farewell); Flicken under nymanan (The girl beneath the new moon); Rondeau; Vinden och Tradet (The wind and the tree)
Maria Ribbing (s) & Stig Ribbing (pf)
12"—**G-DB11019**

RASCH, Hugo (1873-   )

German music critic, voice teacher and composer of songs and chamber music.

SONGS In German
**Als ich dich kaum geseh'n
Der Mond ist aufgegangen**
Tiana Lemnitz (s) w. Max Saal (harp) & Bruno Saenger (vl)   10"—**G-DA4486**

Ich hab' mich ganz verloren Wenn ich dereinst
Gerhard Hüsch (b) & pf. acc.
10"—**G-EG6343**

RASI, Francesco (c.1580-c.1650)

A pupil of Caccini and a well known singer of his day, Rasi sang in Peri's "Euridice." He wrote songs and madrigals, and was one of the first to compose cantatas.

(3) **Madrigals for solo voice** In Italian
Filli mia; Occhi sempre sereni; Filli, tu vuoi partire
Salvatore Salvati (t) & continuo
12"—**MIA-2**
[Frescobaldi: La mia pallida faccia & Non mi negate]

RAVEL, Maurice (1875-1938)

Perhaps the master orchestrator of the early twentieth century, Ravel's music is noted for its stylistic finish, its clarity and grace and the virtuosity with which he manipulates orchestral timbres.

Alborado del Gracioso (Miroirs No. 4)
Piano
Walter Gieseking (C-LB53)
(C-GQ7205)   10"—**C-17137D**
Carmen Guilbert   12"—**PAT-PAT23**
Lucette Descaves-Truc   12"—**G-DB5115**
Marcelle Meyer, in DF-A25

—**Arr. Orchestra** Ravel
Cleveland Orch.—Rodzinski
12"—**C-11910D**
Minneapolis Symphony Orch.—Ormandy
12"—**G-DB2459**

Orchestra of the Suisse Romande—Ansermet   12"—**D-K1609**
Straram Orch.—W. Straram
12"—**C-LFX185**

A la manière de Borodin Piano
E. Passani   12"—**PAT-PDT157**
[Chabrier; Paraphrase sur un air de Gounod; & Piano Concerto, Pt. 5]

Berceuse sur le nom de Fauré Violin & Piano
Zino Francescatti & Robert Casadesus
(in CX-280)   12"—**C-72044D**
[Debussy: Sonata No. 3, Pt. 3]

Boléro Orchestra
Paris Conservatory Orch.—Münch
(D-K1627/8)   2 12"—**D-ED33**†
Boston Symphony Orch.—Koussevitzky
(G-D1859/60)   2 12"—**VM-352**†
[Satie-Debussy: Gymnopedie]
(G-AW175/6)
Boston "Pops" Orch.—Fiedler
(G-FKX36/7)   2 12"—**VM-552**†
[Halvorsen: Entry of the Boyards]
[Falla: El Amor Brujo—Ritual Fire Dance, on G-C2954/5] (G-EH1109/10)
Robin Hood Dell Orch.—Kostelanetz
2 12"—**CX-257**†
[Massenet: Thaïs—Méditation]
EIAR Symphony Orch.—Willy Ferrero
2 12"—**CET-BB25019/20**
DUPLICATIONS: All-American Youth Orch.—Stokowski, CX-174†; Lamoureux Orch.—Ravel, VOX-167: PD-566030/1: PD-66947/8; Belgian Radio Institute Symphony Orch.—André, T-E3165/6; Paris Conservatory Orch.—Jean Giardino, PAT-PDT71/2; Symphony Orch.— Coppola, G-W1067/8; Amsterdam Concertgebouw Orch.—Mengelberg, CX-22†: C-LX48/9: C-LFX90/1: C-GQX10639/40

—**Arr. R. Branga**
Paris Symphony—P. Minssart, O-250746; Jack Payne Orch., C-DX273: C-DFX98: C-DWX1596; Olivero Orch., G-HN1500

Chabrier Piano
E. Passani   12"—**PAT-PDT157**
[A la manière de Borodin; Paraphrase sur un air de Gounod; & Piano Concerto, Pt. 5]

(3) **Chansons** Unacc. Chorus in French 1915
Nicolette: Ronde; Trois beaux oiseaux de paradis
Chanteurs de Lyon—Léon Vietti
12"—**C-DFX181**
Chanteurs de Lyon—E. Bourmauck
12"—**C-RFX68**

Chansons Hébraïques See under Songs

Chansons Madécasses See under Songs

CONCERTO—Piano & Orchestra 1932

(Concerto for the left hand alone)
Alfred Cortot & Paris Conservatory Orch.
—Münch (G-DB3885/6) 2 12"—**VM-629**
Robert Casadesus & Philadelphia Orch.—
Ormandy   2 12"—**CX-288**†

J. Février & Paris Conservatory Orch.—
Münch   3   12"—**C-LFX631/3**
[Noctuelles]
Jacqueline Blancard & Paris Philhar-
monic Orch.—Münch 2 12"—**VOX-168**
(PD-67192/3) (PD-566192/3)

CONCERTO—Piano & Orchestra 1932
Marguerite Long & Symphony Orch.—
Ravel (C-LX194/6†)   3   12"—**CM-176†**
[Pavane pour une Infante défunte]
(C-LFX257/9) (O-9413/5)
(C-GQX10676/8)
Leonard Bernstein & Philharmonia Orch.
    3   12"—**VM-1209†**
[Bernstein: Seven Anniversaries]
Emile Passani & Colonne Orch.—Fournet
    3   12"—**PAT-PDT155/7**
[A la manière de Borodin; Chabrier;
Paraphrase sur un air de Gounod]

DAPHNIS ET CHLOE   Ballet
Orchestra 1910
Suite No. 1
Nocturne; Interlude; Danse Guerrière
Complete Recording
San Francisco Symphony Orch. & Chorus
—Monteux   2 12"—**VM-1143†**
[with Valses nobles et sentimentales &
Debussy: Sarabande]
—**Nocturne & Danse Guerrière** only
Paris Conservatory Orch.—Münch,
D-K1584 in D-ED29†
Suite No. 2
**Lever du jour; Pantomime; Danse
générale**
Complete Recordings
Paris Conservatory Orch.—Münch,
D-K1585/6 in D-ED29†
Boston Symphony Orch.—Koussevitzky
(G-DB6239/40)   2 12"—**VM-1108†**
(Older version on G-W1084/5)
Philadelphia Orch.—Ormandy
    2 12"—**G-DB5734/5**
Cleveland Orch.—Rodzinski
    2 12"—**CX-230†**
Straram Orch.—Gaubert
    2 12"—**CX-32†**
(C-GQX11076/7) (C-LFX41/2)

(L) ENFANT ET LES SORTILEGES
Opera 1925 (Colette)
Complete Recording
    (In Preparation) **French H.M.V.**
Foxtrot, "Five o'Clock"   Arr. Branga
Symphony Orch.—Coppola
(G-W871)   12"—**G-D1564**
[Pavane pour une Infante défunte]
—**Arr. Saxophone & Piano**
Viard & Andolfi, PAT-X98043

Gaspard de la Nuit
(d'apres Aloysius Bertrand)   Piano
Ondine; Le Gibet; Scarbo
Walter Gieseking   2 12"—**CX-141†**
Jean Doyen   2 10"—& 1 12"—
    G-DA4906/7 & G-DB5043
Marcelle Meyer   In Prep. Discophiles
Français

—**Ondine** only
Walter Gieseking
[Le Gibet] (in CX-141†) 12"—**C-69658D**
[Debussy: Poissons d'or, on C-69020D:
C-LFX539: C-LWX205]
Jean Doyen   10"—**G-DA4906**
Alexander Brailowsky   12"—**V-11-9260**

—**Le Gibet** only
Walter Gieseking
[Ondine] (in CX-141†) 12"—**C-68658D**
[Valée des cloches, on C-LFX580]
Jean Doyen   10"—**G-DA4907**
Leon Kartun   12"—**G-DB11175**
[Oiseaux tristes]

—**Scarbo** only
Walter Gieseking
    (in CX-141†) 12"—**C-69659D**
Jean Doyen   12"—**G-DB5043**

(L') HEURE ESPAGNOLE
Opera in French   1 Act   1911
Complete Recording
Soloists & Symphony Orch.—Truc
(C-D15149/55)   7 12"—**C-OP14†**
The Cast:
Concepción ...... Mme. J. Kreiger (s)
Gonzalve .... Louis Arnould (t)
Torquemada .... Raoul Gilles (t)
Ramiro .... I. Aubert (b)
Don Inigo ...... Hector Dufranne (b)

Histoires naturelles   See under Songs

Introduction & Allegro, G flat major
(Harp, String Quartet, Flute, Clarinet)
John Cockerill, Jean Pougnet, David
Martin, Frederick Riddle, James White-
head, Arthur Cleghorn, Reginald Kell
    2 12"—**C-DX1310/1**
[Debussy: Arabesque No. 1, Cockerill,
harpist]
Marcel Grandjany & Victor Chamber
Orch.—Levin   2 12" in **VM-1021†**
[with Debussy: Danses]
Laura Newell, Stuyvesant String Quartet,
John Wummer & Ralph McLean
    2 12"—**CX-167†**
[Debussy-Grandjany: Maid with the
Flaxen Hair, Laura Newell, harpist]
DUPLICATIONS: Lily Laskine with Cal-
vet Quartet, Marcel Moyse & Ulysse
Delecluse, G-K8168/9; Pierre Jamet &
inst. acc., G-W1562

Jeux d'eau   Piano   Eng. The Fountain
Eileen Joyce   12"—**C-DX1003**
[Chopin: Etude No. 3]
Lucette Descaves-Truc   12"—**G-DB5192**
[Debussy: Feu d'Artifice]
Alfred Cortot   12"—**G-DB1534**
[Sonatine, Pt. 3]
O. Vondrovic   12"—**ESTA-F5196**
[Debussy: Reflets dans l'eau]
Robert Casadesus   10"—**C-D13054**
Marie Thérèse Brazeau   12"—**PD-27094**
[Debussy: Prélude—Feu d'artifice]

MA MERE L'OYE   Suite   Orchestra
(Originally for Piano—4-Hands)
Eng. **Mother Goose Suite**

1. Pavane de la Belle au bois dormant;
2. Petit Poucet; 3. Laideronnette—
Impératrice des Pagodes; 4. Les
Entretiens de la Belle et de la Bête;
5. Le Jardin féerique
Paris Conservatory Orch.—Coppola
(G-DB4898/9)   2 12"—VM-693†
National Symphony Orch.—Sidney Beer
                      2 12"—D-K1342/3†
CBS Symphony—Barlow 2 12"—CX-151†
Lamoureux Orch.—Albert Wolff
(PD-566161/2)   2 12"—VOX-194
—Pavane de la Belle au bois dormant only
Pasdeloup Orch.—Inghelbrecht,
PAT-X5485
—Petit Poucet & Laideronnette only
Colonne Orch.—Pierné, O-123546
—Petit Poucet only
Paris Symphony—Monteux, G-W1108
—Arr. Violin & Piano
Jean Fournier & J. Vigue
                      12"—PAT-PDT61
[Tzigane, Pt. 3 & Paganini: Caprice
No. 13]
—Laideronnette only Arr. Piano
Galina Werschenska, TONO-A113
Menuet antique Orchestra
(Originally for Piano)
Lamoureux Orch.—Wolff
(PD-566032)   12"—PD-66972
Menuet sur le nom de Haydn Piano
Gaby Casadesus ,in VOX-163
Miroirs Suite of Piano Pieces
1. Noctuelles; 2. Oiseaux tristes;
3. Une barque sur l'océan;
4. Alborado del gracioso;
5. La vallée des cloches
For recordings see under titles of Nos. 1,
2, 4 & 5 only
Nicolette See under 3 Chansons
Noctuelles Piano (Miroirs No. 1)
J. Février   12"—C-LFX633
[Concerto for Left Hand, Pt. 5]
Oiseaux tristes (Miroirs No. 2) Piano
Leon Kartun   12"—G-DB11175
[Gaspard de la Nuit—Le Gibet]
Marcelle Meyer, in DF-A25
Ondine
See under Gaspard de la Nuit No. 1
Paraphrase sur un air de Gounod Piano
E. Passani   12"—PAT-PDT157
[A la manière de Borodin; Chabrier; &
Piano Concerto, Pt. 5]
Pavane pour une Infante défunte Piano
E. Robert Schmitz   12"—V-12-0066
[Debussy: Rêverie]
George de Lausnay   12"—PAT-X5507
[Falla: Ritual Fire Dance]
—Arr. Orchestra Ravel
Boston Symphony Orch.—Koussevitzky
                      12"—V-11-9729
Paris Conservatory Orch.—Münch
[La Valse, Pt. 3]   12"—G-W1558
Andre Kostelanetz & his Orch.
(Arr. Schmidt)   12"—C-7361M
[Debussy-Kostelanetz: Clair de lune]
(C-DX1001)

DUPLICATIONS: Colonne Orch.—
Pierné, O-123617; Symphony Orch.—
Freitas-Branco, C-68066D: C-LX196:
C-LFX259: C-GQX10678: O-9415;
Berlin Philharmonic—Wolff, PD-66726:
PD-516649; Symphony Orch.—Coppola,
G-D1564: G-W871
—Arr. Violin & Piano Kochanski
Yvonne Curti & G. Van Parys
                      12"—C-DFX82
[Debussy: Petite Suite—En bateau]
—Arr. Horn & Piano
William Valkeiner & Reginald Boardman
                      12"—NIGHT MUSIC-101/2
[Mozart: Rondo, E flat major, K. 371]
Pièce en forme de Habañera
(Originally a Vocalise)
—Arr. Violin & Piano
Ginette Neveu & Jean Neveu
[Scarlatescu: Bagatelle] 10"—G-DA1877
Erica Morini & Max Lanner
                      10"—V-10-1011
[Gounod-Sarasate: Faust Fantasie—
Waltz]
Jacques Thibaud & Tasso Janopoulo
                      10"—G-DA4999
[Fauré: Dolly—Berceuse]
Yehudi Menuhin & Marcel Gazelle
                      10"—G-DA1832
[Kreisler: Caprice viennois]
Jascha Heifetz & Milton Kaye, in D-A385
DUPLICATIONS: Leo Petroni &
Favaretto, G-AV44; Guarino,
G-GW1645; Ede Zathwieczky,
RAD-RBM108
—Arr. 'Cello & Piano
Gregor Piatigorsky & Valentin Pavlovsky
              (in CM-501) 10"—C-17445D
[Saint-Saëns: Le Cygne]
D. B. Shafran & pf. acc.
[Paridis: Siciliana] 10"—USSR-13202/3
Prélude Piano 1913
Gaby Casadesus, in VOX-163
Quartet—Strings F major
Budapest Quartet   4 12"—CM-425†
Gabriel Bouillon Quartet
                      3 12"—G-DB5154/6
Pascal Quartet   4 12"—O-123885/8
DUPLICATIONS: Calvet Quartet,
G-DB5025/8; Galimir Quartet, dir. Ravel,
VOX-180: PD-27329/31: PD-516578/80;
Lener Quartet, C-GQX10984/7; Capet
Quartet, C-D15057/60
—1st Mvt. (Allegro moderato) only
Guarneri Quartet, PD-67127
Rapsodie espagnole Orchestra
Eng. Spanish Rhapsody
Cleveland Orch.—Rodzinski
                      2 12"—CX-234†
Boston Symphony Orch.—Koussevitzky
                      2 12"—VM-1200†
Belgian National Radio Symphony Orch.
—André   2 12"—T-E2987/8
(U-E14231/2)
Philadelphia Orch.—Stokowski
(G-DB2367/8)   2 12"—V-8282/3

Lamoureux Orch.—Wolff
(PD-67052/3)   2 12"—PD-566166/7

Scarbo See under Gaspard de la Nuit No. 3

Septet See under Introduction & Allegro

Shéhérazade See under Songs

Sonata Violin & Violoncello
Oscar Shumsky & Bernard Greenhouse
(Limited Edition)   4 12"—CH-B4

Sonatine Piano
Alfred Cortot   2 12"—G-DB1533/4
[Jeu d'eau]
Robert Casadesus   2 10"—CX-179†
[Le Tombeau de Couperin—Menuet only]
Suzanne Gyr   2 12"—G-DB10045/6
[Debussy: La Fille aux cheveux de lin]

—**2nd Mvt. (Menuet) only**
Oscar Levant
(in CM-508)   10"—C-17455D
[Levant: Sonata—1st Mvt.]

SONGS

(D') Anne jouant de l'epinette (Marot)
(from "Deux Epigrammes")
Maggie Teyte (s) & Gerald Moore (pf),
in Gramophone Shop Album **GSC-3**

Asie See under Shéhérazade

(3) Chansons madécasses
(French text: E. Parny)
Nahandove; Aoua; Repos
Madeline Grey (s) & trio acc.—Ravel
(PD-561076/7)   2 10"—inVOX-186

(3) Chants hébraïques In Yiddish
Kaddisch; Mejerke; L'Enigme éternelle
Madeline Grey (s) & Ravel (pf)
(PD-561075)   10"—in VOX-186

—**Kaddisch only** Arr. Violin & Pf.
Yehudi Menuhin & pf. acc.
[Bloch: Abodah]   12"—V-15887

Don Quichotte à Dulcinée (Paul Morand)
**Chanson romantique; Chanson épique;
Chanson à boire**
Pierre Bernac (b) & Francis Poulenc
(pf)   10"—G-DA1869
Martial Singher (b) 2 10"—G-DA4865/6
[Ronsard à son âme]
Yvon le Marc' Hadour (b) &
Maroussia le Marc' Hadour (pf)
10"—BAM-32

(La) Flûte enchantée

(L') Indifférent
See under Shéhérazade

Histoires naturelles (J. Renard)
**Le Paon; Le Grillon; Le Cygne; Le
Martin-Pêcheur; La Pintade**
Suzanne Stappen (s) & Marius-François
Gaillard (pf)   3 10"—O-188903/5

—**Le Paon; Le Martin-Pêcheur; La Pintade
only**
Marguerite Pifteau (s), C-LF186

—**Le Paon only**
Povla Frijsh (s) & Celius Dougherty (pf)
(in VM-789)   12"—V-18053
[Fauré: Automne]

—**Le Martin-Pêcheur only**
Maggie Teyte (s) & Gerald Moore (pf)
In Gramophone Shop Album **GSC-3**

Ronsard à son âme (Ronsard)
Martial Singher (b)   10"—G-DA4866
[Don Quichotte à Dulcinée, Pt. 3—
Chanson à boire]

Sainte (Mallarmé)
Pierre Bernac (b) & F. Poulenc (pf)
[Sur l'herbe]   10"—G-DA4891

Shéhérazade (Tristian Klingsor) 1903
Asie; La Flûte enchantée; L'Indifférent
Janine Micheau & Lamoureux Orch.
Bigot   2 12"—G-W1584/5

—**No. 2 (La flûte enchanté) only**
Leila Ben Sedira with pf. & fl. acc.
[Boïeldieu: Boléro]   10"—G-DA4938
Rose Walter (s)   10"—C-DB1301
[Debussy: No. 3 of Six Epigraphes
antiques, Pirani & Grant—2 pfs.]
(C-DB1785)
(In Columbia History of Music, Vol. V:
CM-361)

Sur l'herbe (Verlaine)
Pierre Bernac (b) & F. Poulenc (pf)
[Sainte]   10"—G-DA4891

Vocalise en forme da habañera
Wordless Song
NOTE: *No recordings have been traced of the
original vocal version, but for recorded instrumental transcriptions see under Pièce en forme
de habanera.*

(Le) Tombeau de Couperin
Piano Version 1914
**Prélude; Fugue; Rigaudon; Menuet;
Forlane; Toccata**
Suzanne Gyr   3 12"—G-DB10065/7
Lucienne Delforge   3 12"—G-W1606/8

—**Prélude & Rigaudon**
Lucette Descaves   10"—D-121

—**Forlane only**
Artur Rubinstein, G-DB2450

—**Toccata only**
Alexander Borovsky, PD-516612:
PD-27342; Benno Moiseiwitsch,
G-C3487; Boris Zadri, PAT-PAT184

—**Menuet only**
Robert Casadesus, in CX-179

(Le) Tombeau de Couperin
Orchestral Version 1919
Prélude; Rigaudon; Menuet; Forlane
Minneapolis Symphony Orch.—
Mitropoulos   2 10"—CX-222†
Paris Conservatory Orch.—
Coppola   2 12"—G-W1163/4

—**Rigaudon only**
Chamber Orch. of the Conservatory of S.
Pietro a Majella, Naples—Lualdi
12"—CET-CB20269
[Lualdi: La Granceola—Overture]

Trio—Violin, 'Cello, Piano A minor
Joseph Benvenuti, Benedetti &
Navarra   3 12"—PAT-PGT37/9
Trio di Trieste   3 12"—G-C3607/9†

Tzigane (Rapsodie de Concert)
Violin & Piano (or Orch.)
Jean Fournier & Paris Radio Orch.
2 12"—PAT-PDT60/1
[Petit Poucet & Paganini: Caprice No.
13, Fournier with J. Vigue, pf.]

Ida Haendel & Ivor Newton
12"—D-K1013
Jascha Heifetz & Arpad Sandor
12"—V-8411
Yehudi Menuhin & A. Balsam
12"—G-DB1785
Ellen Birgithe Nielsen & Carl Browall
12"—G-DB5277

(La) Vallée des cloches (Miroirs No. 5)
Piano
Walter Gieseking 12"—C-LFX580
[Gaspard de la Nuit—Le Gibet]
Boris Zadri 12"—PAT-PAT184
[Toccata]
Marcelle Meyer, in DF-A25

(La) Valse Poème choréographique
Orchestra
San Francisco Symphony Orch.—
Monteux 2 12"—VM-820†
[Rimsky-Korsakov: Le Coq d'or—Bridal
procession] (G-DB5964/5)
N. Y. Philharmonic-Symphony Orch.—
Barbirolli 2 12"—CX-207†
[Debussy: Petite Suite—Ballet]
Orch. of the "Maggio Musicale"—
Markevitch 2 12"—CET-BB25156/7
[Berlioz: Damnation de Faust—Danse
des sylphes]
DUPLICATIONS: Boston Symphony Orch.
—Koussevitzky, G-DB1541/2; Paris
Conservatory Orch.—Gaubert,
C-12502/3; Paris Conservatory Orch.—
Münch, G-W1557/8; Lamoureux Orch.
—Wolff, VOX-182: PD-67016/7:
PD-566068/9; Paris Symphony Orch.—
Monteaux, G-W1107/8

Valses nobles et sentimentales
—Original Version Piano
Robert Casadesus 2 10"—CX-194†
Tristan Risselin 2 10"—C-JO54/5
Marcelle Meyer, in DF-A25

—Arr. Orchestra Ravel
San Francisco Symphony Orch.—
Monteux 2 12"—VM-1143†
[Daphnis et Chloe, Suite No. 1 &
Debussy: Sarabande]
Paris Conservatory Orch.—
Coppola 2 12"—G-DB4935/6

—Nos. 6 & 7 only
Arr. Violin & Piano Heifetz
Jascha Heifetz & Emanuel Bay,
V-10-1294 in VM-1126

Miscellaneous Orchestrations
See under Debussy: Sarabande; Mussorg-
sky: Pictures at an Exhibition; Debussy:
Fêtes (Arr. 2 Pianos)

RAWSTHORNE, Alan (1905-   )
*A British composer who has written mostly for
smaller instrumental groups and piano.*
(4) Bagatelles Piano
Denis Matthews 12"—G-C3324
[Moeran: Symphony, G minor, Pt. 11]
Street Corner—Overture Orchestra
Philharmonia Orch.—Constant
Lambert 12"—G-C3502
Symphonic Studies 1939 Orchestra
Philharmonia Orch.—Lambert
3 12"—G-C3542/4

Theme & Variations Two Violins
Kathleen Washbourne & Jesse
Hinchliffe 2 12"—D-K884/5
Three French Nursery Songs
Sophie Wyss (s) & pf. acc.
12"—D-K1065
[Arr. Tiersot: Noël provençal & Arr.
Vuillermoz: Ronde des Filles de
Quimperlé]

REESEN, Emil
*A contemporary Danish composer and conduc-
tor.*
Fantasia on South-Jutland Tunes
Danish State Radio Symphony Orch.—
Reesen In Prep., NP
Den som har Livets Mildhed søgt
Aksel Schiøtz (t), G-X6830
FARINELLI Opera in Danish
Der er en Sang; Livets Glaeden
Aksel Schiøtz, G-X6831
Sagen har Vinger
Aksel Schiøtz, G-X6830

REFICE, Licinio (1885-   )
*An Italian priest-musician who has held im-
portant positions in Roman churches.*
Acclamations
Roman Vatican Choirs—Refice, in
SEVA-18
Alma Redemptoris Mater
A. Dadò (b) 12"—SEMS-39
[Anerio: Factum est silentium, Julian
Chapel Cho.]
Amavit eum Dominus
Roman Vatican Choir—Refice, in
SEVA-19
Ave Maria Motet
Roman Vatican Choir—Refice, in
SEVA-18
Ave Maria
Claudia Muzio (s)
(in CM-289) 12"—C-9170M
[Umbra di Nube] (C-BQX2521)
[Bellini: Sonnambula—Ah, non credea
mirarti, on C-LCX27; C-BQX2506]
Ave Maria Coelorum
A. Dadò (b) 12"—SEMS-15
[Somma: O Salutaris Hostia]

CECILIA Opera in Italian
(L') Annuncio
Claudia Muzio (s)
(C-BQX2503) 12"—C-LCX19
(La) Morte di Cecilia
Claudia Muzio (s) & Cho.
(C-BQX2500) 12"—C-LCX24
Dormi, non piangere
Roman Vatican Choir—Refice, in
SEVA-20
Ecce sic benedictus
A. Dadó (b) 12"—SEMS-3
[Victoria: O quantus luctus—Julian
Chapel Cho.]
[Boezi: Miserere, Pt. 5, on SEMS-34]

REFICE

Lauda Jerusalem (Psalm 147)
Julian Chapel Choir & Organ—
Antonelli   12"—**SEMS-1130**

Salve Regina
A. Dadò (b)   12"—**SEMS-46**
[Tavoni: O sacrum convivium—Dadò &
Fantozzi]

Umbra di nube
Claudia Muzio
              (in CM-289) 12"—**C-9170M**
[Ave Maria] (C-BQX2521)
[Bellini: Norma—Casta Diva, on
C-LCX23: C-BQX2502]

REGER, Max (1873-1916)

*Reger's larger works are seldom heard but
short pieces (such as his works for the organ or
his "Mariä Wiegenlied") are quite popular.*

An die Hoffnung See under Songs

Aria
after the Bach Organ Chorale—Prelude
"O Mensch, bewein' dein Sunde Gross"
String Orch.—Edvard Fendler
                             12"—**G-L999**

Ballet Suite, Op. 130 Orchestra

—**No. 5 (Valse d'amour) only**
Berlin Opera Orch.—Melichar
                             12"—**PD-95396**
[R. Strauss: Bürger als Edelmann Suite,
Pt. 9]

Benedictus, Op. 59, No. 9 Organ
Paul Hebestreit (Paderborn Cathedral)
[Renner: Canzone]   12"—**PD-27063**

Comedy Overture, Op. 120
(Eine Lustspiel Ouverture)
Berlin Orchestra—Lehmann
                             12"—**O-9121**

Concerto in the Old Style
See under Konzert im alten Stil

Ein' feste Burg, Op. 27
Fantasia for organ
Alfred Sittard (St. Michael's, Hamburg)
                             10"—**PD-10068**

Gavotte, E flat major, Op. 82, No. 5 Piano
Friedrich Wührer   10"—**G-EG6122**
[Humoresque, C major, Op. 20, No. 4]

Gloria in Excelsis Deo, Op. 59, No. 8 Organ
Paul Hebestreit (Paderborn Cathedral)
                             12"—**PD-27127**
[Rheinberger: Miscellanen—Ricercare]

Humoreske, C major, Op. 20, No. 4 Piano
Friedrich Wührer   10"—**G-EG6122**
[Gavotte, E major, Op. 82, No. 5]

Im Himmelreich ein Haus steht
Regensburg Domchor   10"—**G-EG6530**
[Bruckner: Herbstlied, with Aachen
Domchor]

Konzert im alten Stil, Op. 123 Orchestra
(Concerto in the Old Style)

—**Allegro only**
Berlin State Opera Orch.—
Melichar   12"—**PD-27309**
[Bach: Brandenburg Concerto, No. 4,
Pt. 5]

Lyric Andante
Berlin Chamber Orch.—Hans von
Banda   12"—**PD-67852**
[Dvořák: Slavonic Dance No. 10]

Mariä Wiegenlied See under Songs

Praeludium
See under Suite—Violin & Piano

QUARTET—String

No. 4, E flat major, Op. 109
Strub Quartet   4 12"—**G-EH1264/7**
—**1st Mvt. (Allegro Molto) &**
2nd Mvt. (Quasi Presto) only
Strub Quartet, G-EH1205/6

Romantic Suite, Op. 125
(Eine romantische Suite)
Brussels Radio Orch.—Fritz Lehmann
(O-50214/7)   4 12"—**O-9136/39**

Serenade, D major, Op. 77a
Paul Klingler (vl), Fridolin Klingler
(vla), Gustav Scheck (fl)
                   3 12"—**G-EH1029/31**
[Mozart: Duo, K. 424—Andante only]

Silhouetten, Op. 53

—**Nos. 2 & 6 only**
Erik Then-Bergh   12"—**G-EH1252**

SONATAS—Violin Unaccompanied

No. 1, Op. 91

—**Andante sostenuto only**
Georg Kulenkampff, T-E2078

Sonatine, E minor, Op. 89, No. 1 Piano
Cor de Groot
(O-50529/30)   2 12"—**O-8789/90**

SONGS In German

Am Brünnele, Op. 76, No. 9 (Gersdorf)
Johanna Egli (c) & Richard Laugs (pf)
                           10"—**O-25841**
[Mit Rosen, Volkslied, Das Dorf]

(Das) Dorf, Op. 97, No. 1 (Boelitz)
Johanna Egli (c) & Richard Laugs (pf)
                           10"—**O-25841**
[Volkslied; Am Brünnele; Mit Rosen]

(Des) Kindes Gebet, Op. 76, No. 22
(L. Rafael)
Johanna Egli (c) & Richard Laugs (pf)
                           10"—**O-25839**
[Morgengesang & Mariä Wiegenlied]
Anni Frind (s) & chamber orch.
[Waldeinsamkeit]   10"—**G-EG3643**

Mariä Wiegenlied, from Op. 76
(Martin Boelitz)
("Maria sitz am Rosenhag" No. 52 of the
"Schlichte Weisen")
Eng. The Virgin's Slumber Song
NOTE: *This is a setting of the mediaeval Ger-
man Christmas carol tune "Joseph, lieber
Joseph mein" used by Brahms (for his "Geist-
liches wiegenlied") and many other composers.*
Blanche Thebom (ms) (in English)
[Brahms: Wiegenlied] 10"—**V-10-1173**
Kersten Thorborg (c) & Leo Rosenek
(pf)   10"—**V-1323**

[Lundvik: A Swedish Lullaby, Op. 31, No. 1]
DUPLICATIONS: Johanna Egli, O-25839; Erna Sack, T-AK2157; Erna Berger, PD-10429; Jo Vincent, C-D10038; Maria Markan, G-X6042
In Italian: Claudia Muzio, in CM-289: C-LC22: C-BQ6005: C-BQ6003

—Arr. Chorus
Regensburg Cathedral Choir—
T. Schrems   10"—G-EG6786
[Folksong: Kindelein zart & Mozart: Wiegenlied]
[Mozart: Wiegenlied, on T-A1552: U-B18046]
Wolfgang Kieling (treble) & Chorus
                    10"—G-EG6426
[Fr. Bach: Kein Halmlein]

—Arr. Violin & Piano
Ferenc Vecsey & Guido Agosti, PD-10413

—Arr. Orchestra
Ilja Livschakoff Künstler Orch., PD-10090: Barnabas von Géczy Orch., G-EG3493: G-HE2238

Mit Rosen bestreut, Op. 76, No. 12 (Bern)
Johanna Egli (c) & Richard Laugs (pf)
                    10"—O-25841
[Am Brünnele; Volkslied; Das Dorf]

Morgengesang, Op. 137 (E. Alberus)
Johanna Egli (c) & Richard Laugs (pf)
                    10"—O-25839
[Kindes Gebet & Mariä Wiegenlied]

Schnee Soprano & Alto Eng. Snow
Anna Howard, E. Brown, (in English)
& pf. acc.   12"—V-36033
(in Songs for Children)

Volkslied, Op. 37, No. 2 (Ritter)
Johanna Egli (c) & Richard Laugs (pf)
                    10"—O-25841
[Das Dorf; Am Brünnele; Mit Rosen]

Waldeinsamkeit, Op. 76, No. 3
Anni Frind (s) & chamber orch.
[Des Kindes Gebet]   10"—G-EG3643

Suites—Unaccompanied 'Cello
G major, Op. 131c
Emanuel Feuermann 2 12"—CX-152†
D Minor

—Praeludium & Gavotte only
Ludwig Hoelscher   10"—G-EH966

Toccata, D minor, Op. 59, No. 5 Organ
Alfred Sittard (St. Michaels, Hamburg)
                    12"—PD-95256
[Sittard: Chorale-Prelude—Wenn wir in höchsten Nöten sein]
(PD-66555)
[Bruckner: Symphony No. 7, Pt. 15, on PD-67202]

TRIO—Violin, Viola, 'Cello
A minor, Op. 77b
Klingler Trio   3 12"—G-EH950/2

Valse d'amour See under Ballet Suite

Variations on a Theme by Mozart, Op. 132
Orchestra
(The theme is taken from the A major Piano Sonata of Mozart)
Saxon State Orch.—Karl Böhm
               4 12"—G-DB4480/3
Symphony Orch.—Abendroth (abbr.)
               2 12"—G-DB5197/8

Miscellaneous Orchestrations
See under Schubert: Rosamunde

REISSIGER, Karl Gottlieb (1789-1859)
A Viennese opera composer and conductor, Reissiger was important in the musical life of Dresden.

(DIE) FELSENMUEHLE VON ETALIERES
Opera in German
Overture
Berlin Radio Orchestra—Melichar
                    12"—PD-57116

RENAULD (17th Century)
Amis, buvons nuit et jour
Gaston Micheletti (t) & R. Gerlin (harpsichord)   (in Vol. X) 12"—AS-98
[Airs sérieux et à boire]

RENE, N. (16th Century)
A sixteenth century composer of French chansons.
Gros Jehan menoit hors de Paris
French chanson
Marcelle Gerar (c) & viol, flutes & guitar acc.   (in Vol. II) 12"—AS-15
[with French Chansons of the 16th Century]

RENIE, Henriette (1876-   )
A noted French harpist and composer of harp and chamber music.
Concerto—Harp & Orchestra, C minor
Henriette Renié & Paris Philharmonic Orch.—G. Cloëz   2 12"—O-171076/7

RESPIGHI, Ottorino (1879-1936)
A pupil of Rimsky-Korsakov, his music is characterized by an elaborate and rich orchestral coloring. Respighi's fame in the United States is due primarily to the relatively large number of performances of his works by his friend, Arturo Toscanini.

Adagio e Variazioni 'Cello & Piano
Arturo Bonucci & Sandro Fuga
                    12"—CET-CC2058

Antiche Danze ed Arie per Liuto
Orchestral Suites
Eng. Old Dances & Airs for the Lute
(A group of 16th & 17th Century Dances freely transcribed for Orchestra by Respighi)
Suite No. 1
1) Balletto detto "Il Conte Orlando" (after Simone Molinaro, 1599)
2) Gagliarda (after Vincenzo Galilei)
3) Villanella (after an anonymous 16th Century composer)

4) **Passo mezzo e mascherada**   (after an
anonymous 16th Century composer)
EIAR Orchestra—Sergio Failoni
2 12"—CET-BB25017/8
—**No. 2 (Gagliarda)** only
—**Arr. Piano** Respighi
Carlo Zecchi   12"—CET-CB20352
[Scarlatti: Sonata, C major & Anon:
Siciliana]
Guido Agosti   12"—G-AW298
[Frescobaldi: Toccata, A minor]
—**No. 3 (Villanella)** only
Milan Symphony Orch.—Molajoli,
C-D12297
Suite No. 2
1) **Laura Soave; Balletto con Gagliarda,
Saltarello e Canario**
(after Farizio Caroso)
2) **Danza rustica**
(after Jean Baptiste Besard)
3) **(a) Campanae Parisienses**   (after an
anonymous 16th Century composer)
(b) Aria (attributed to Marin Mersenne)
4) **Bergamasca**
(after Bernardo Giononcelli)
No recording available
Suite No. 3
1) **Italiana**   (after an anonymous
16th Century composer)
2) **Siciliana**   (after an anonymous
16th Century composer)
3) **Arie di Corte**
(after Jean Baptiste Besard)
4) **Passacaglia** (after Lodovico Roncalli)
Berlin Philharmonic Chamber Orch.—
von Benda   1 10" & 2 12"—
T-A2535 & T-E2536/7
[Corelli: Suite for Orch.—Giga &
Badinerie]
Boyd Neel String Orch.—Neel
3 12"—D-X256/8
[Marcello-Barbirolli: Allegretto]
—**Arr. String Quartet** Respighi
Rome Quartet   2 12"—G-DB4441/2
(The) Birds See: Gli Uccelli
(La) Boutique Fantasque Ballet Suite
(after Rossini piano pieces)
London Philharmonic Orch.—
Goossens   3 12"—VM-415†
(G-C2846/8) (G-EH977/9)
(G-S10468/70)
—**Selections**
London Philharmonic—Goehr
(C-LFX534)   12"—C-DX848
—**Tarantella**   (after La Danza) only
Symphony Orch.—Goehr, on V-36214
in V-C30: G-C2914
Brazilian Impressions
See: Impressioni Brasiliane
Feste Romane Symphonic Poem 1928
Eng. **Roman Festivals**
1) **Circenses**   2) **Giubileo**
3) **L'Ottobrata**   4) **La Befana**
Berlin Philharmonic Orch.—Victor de
Sabata   4 12"—PD-67510/3S
[Paganini-Liszt: La Campanella, Geza
Anda (pf) on CET-RR8014/7]
Philadelphia Orch.—Ormandy
3 12"—CM-707†

—**3rd Mvt. (L'Ottobrata)** only
EIAR Orch.—Ferrero
12"—CET-BB25046
Milan Symphony Orch.—Molajoli
12"—C-GQX10710
(Le) Fontaine di Roma Symphonic Poem
Eng. **The Fountains of Rome**
1) **La Fontana di Valle Giulia all'alba**
2) **La Fontana del Tritone all mattino**
3) **La Fontana dei Trevi nel meriggio**
4) **La Fontana di Villa Medici al tramonto**
Symphony Orch. of the Augusteo, Rome—
De Sabata   2 12"—G-DB6448/9
N. Y. Philharmonic-Symphony Orch.—
Barbirolli   2 12"—VM-576†
Milan Symphony Orch.—Molajoli
3 12"—C-D14474/5
Impressioni Brasiliane
1) **Notte tropicale**   2) **Butantan**
3) **Canzone e Danza**
Munich Philharmonic Orch.—
Kabasta   2 12"—G-DB4643/4
(I) Pini di Roma Symphonic Poem
Eng. **Pines of Rome**
1) **I Pini di Villa Borghese**
2) **I Pini presso una Catacomba**
3) **I Pini del Gianicolo**
4) **I Pini della Via Appia**
Philadelphia Orch.—Ormandy
3 12"—CM-616†
Paris Conservatory Orch.—Coppola
(G-DB4991/2)   2 12"—V-11917/8
Milan Symphony—Molajoli
3 10"—C-D12292/4
Rossiniana Suite for Orchestra
(Freely transcribed by Respighi, from
"Les Riens" of Rossini)
1) **Capri & Taormina (Barcarolle &
Siciliana)**
2) **Lament** 3) **Intermezzo** 4) **Tarantella**
—**Nos. 1, 3 & 4** only
London Philharmonic—Beecham
2 12"—CX-56†
Siciliana 16th Century Lute Air
(Possibly same as Antiche Danze Suite
No. 3—No. 2)
Kathleen Long   10"—D-M517
[Paradies: Toccata, A major]
Sonata, B minor Violin & Piano
Oscar Shumsky & Artur Balsam
(Limited Edition)   3 12"—CH-B15

SONGS In Italian

Abbandono (Stornellatrice)
Alba Angellotti (s) & G. Favoretto (pf)
[Olivieri: La mamma povera]
10"—G-AV46
Nebbie (A. Negri)
Jolanda di Maria-Petris (s) & Olav
Roots (pf)   12"—G-DB6438
[Davico: Luna che fa lume; Granados:
La Maja Dolorosa, Nos. 1, 2 & 3, in
Spanish]
Alba Angellotti (s) & pf. acc.
[Nevicata & Pioggia]   10"—G-AV47
Nevicata
Alba Angellotti (s) & G. Favoretto (pf)
[Nebbie & Pioggia]   10"—G-AV47

Pioggia
 Alba Angellotti (s) & pf. acc.
 [Nebbie & Nevicata] 10″—G-AV47
 Rosina Ziliani (s) & E. Magnetti (pf)
 10″—CET-TI7054
 [Ferrari: Strambotto in Serenata]

(Gli) Uccelli Suite for Small Orchestra
 Eng. The Birds
 1) **Preludio** (after B. Pasquini)
 2) **La Colomba**
 (The Dove, after J. de Gallot)
 3) **La Gallina** (The Hen, after Rameau)
 4) **L'Usignuolo** (The Nightingale, after
 an anonymous English composer)
 5) **Il Cuccù**
 (The Cuckoo, after B. Pasquini)
 EIAR Symphony Orch.—Ferrero
 2 12″—CET-BB25080/1
 Chicago Symphony Orch.—Defauw
 2 12″—VM-1112†
 Brussels Royal Conservatory Orch.—
 Defauw 2 12″—C-GQX10636/7
Arrangements See Frescobaldi: Toccata,
 A minor (G-AW298)

REUBKE, Julius (1834-1858)

*A pupil of Kullak and Liszt, this composer,
who died at the early age of 24, is best known
for the one organ work listed below.*

**Sonata for Organ, C minor, on the 94th
 Psalm**
 E. Power Biggs (Memorial Church,
 Harvard) 3 12″—VM-961†
 [Purcell: Trumpet Voluntary]

REUSNER, Esajas (1636-1679)

*A native of Silesia, this seventeenth century
composer became a prominent court lutenist.
His works include dance suites and a large
number of transcriptions for his instrument.
In 1676, he published a volume of one hundred
sacred tunes transcribed for the lute.*

Suite No. 1 Arr. Johann Georg Stanley
 **Paduan; Allemande; Courante; Sara-
 bande; Gavotte; Gigue; Courante**
 Arthur Fiedler's Sinfonietta
 [Pachelbel: Canon] 2 10″—VM-969†

REYER, Ernest (1823-1909)

*Best known for his opera "Sigurd," Reyer also
wrote many songs, and was—in keeping with
the spirit of his times—also a prominent contemporary critic.*

OPERAS In French

SALAMMBO 1890
Air des Colombes Soprano
 Germaine Martinelli
 (PD-566056) 12″—PD-66991
 [Mascagni: Cavalleria Rusticana—Voi
 lo sapete]

SIGURD 4 Acts 1884
Overture Orchestra
 Paris Conservatory—Coppola
 12″—G-DB4947
Individual Excerpts

ACT II

Et toi, Freïa Baritone
 Arthur Endrèze 12″—PAT-X90035
 [Thomas: Hamlet—Monologue]
J'ai gardé mon âme ingénue Tenor
 César Vezzani 10″—G-P753
 [Esprits gardiens]
Esprits gardiens: Le bruit des chants Tenor
 Georges Thill 12″—C-LFX324
 [Gounod: Mireille—Anges du Paradis]
 César Vezzani 10″—G-P753
 [J'ai gardé mon âme]
 DUPLICATION: Franz, C-LFX56:
 PAT-X90048
Salut, splendeur du jour Soprano
 Marjorie Lawrence 12″—G-DB4937
 [O Palais radieux]

ACT IV

O Palais radieux Soprano
 Marjorie Lawrence 12″—G-DB4937
 [Salut, splendeur du jour]

REZNICEK, Emil von (1860-1945)

*Known primarily for his comic opera "Donna
Diana," Reznicek's output spans the complete
range of nineteenth century interest, including
sacred music, the symphony, the folk opera,
the string quartet and a large volume of assort-
ed chamber music.*

DONNA DIANA

 Comic Opera in German 1894
Overture Orchestra
 Chicago Symphony Orch.—Stock
 (in CX-203†) 12″—C-11606D
 [Enesco: Romanian Rhapsody No. 1,
 Pt. 3]
 Dresden State Orch.—Böhm
 12″—G-DB4560
 [J. Strauss: 1001 Nights—Waltz]
 Berlin State Opera Orch.—Ludwig
 12″—PD-15213
 [Weber: Abu Hassan—Overture]
 DUPLICATIONS: Berlin Philharmonic—
 Kleiber, T-SK1215; La Scala Orch.—Carl
 Schuricht, G-DB5402

RHEINBERGER, Josef (1839-1901)

*A prominent organist whose output as a com-
poser is more than merely substantial; his
works include operas, orchestral compositions,
chamber music, choral works, piano pieces as
well as the organ concertos and pieces for
which he is largely remembered.*

Meditationes, Op. 167 12 Pieces for Organ
 —Tema variato only
 Paul Hebestreit (Paderborn Cathedral)
 [Vision, from Op. 156] 12″—PD-27128
Miscellanen, Op. 174 12 Pieces for Organ
 —Ricercare only
 Paul Hebestreit (Paderborn Cathedral)
 12″—PD-27127
 [Reger: Gloria in Excelsis Deo]
(Der) Stern von Bethlehem, Op. 164
 Christmas Cantata

—Zug der heiligen drei Könige
Chorus in German
Basilica Chorus—Pius Kalt
12″—PD-27107
[Sweelinck: Hodie Christus natus est]
Vision, from Op. 156 Organ
Paul Hebestreit (Paderborn Cathedral)
12″—PD-27128
[Meditationes—Tema variato]

RICHARD COEUR-DE-LION (1157-1199)

*An English King who had ample time to write
some energetic verses while imprisoned in
France from 1193-1194, Richard the Lion-
Hearted is unfortunately better known to the
music appreciation student than to the amateur
lover of music.*

Ja nuns hons pris Song in French
Max Meili (t) & Fr. Seidersbeck (viol)
(in Vol. II) 12″—AS-18
[with examples of French Troubadours
& German Minnesänger of the 12th &
13th Centuries]

RICHARDSON, Clive

London Fantasia Piano & Orchestra
Clive Richardson & Columbia Light
Symphony Orch.—Williams
12″—C-DX1204
Clive Richardson with Sidney Torch &
his Orch. 12″—P-E11451
Monia Liter with Mantovani & his
Orch. 12″—D-K1173
Prelude to a Dream
Charles Shadwell & his Orch.
10″—G-B9586
[Beaver: Picture Parade]
Traditional folk song Arr. Richardson
Greensleeves
Webster Booth (t) 10″—G-B9585
[Martin: Everywhere I go]

RICHTER, Franz Xaver (1709-1789)

*A versatile member of the renowned Mann-
heim School, he wrote some sixty symphonies
and prodigious quantities of religious and
chamber music. He was a fine bass singer, a
conductor and a teacher as well.*

Quartet, C major Strings
Moravian String Quartet
2 12″—U-E11794/5
Trio, No. 3, A major
Violin, 'Cello & Piano
—Larghetto (F sharp minor) only
Jean & Pierre Fournier with Jacques
Février (in Vol. VI) 12″—AS-56
[Haydn: Trio No. 5, E flat, Pt. 3]

RIEGGER, Wallingford (1885-   )

New Dance 1934
Pierre Luboshutz & Genia Nemenoff
(2-pfs.) 12″—V-17993
[Glinka: The Lark]

RIISAGER, Knudage (1897-   )

*A modern Danish composer whose works in-
clude symphonies, a trumpet concerto and
chamber music as well as the items listed below.*

(4) Epigrams, Op. 11 Piano
—Capriccio only
Sejr Volmer-Sørensen 10″—G-DA5206
[Nielsen: Symphonic Suite—
Intonation only]
Finale Gallop
Tivoli Concert Orch.—Felumb
12″—TONO-X25076
[Kuhlau: The Robber's Castle—
Overture]
Fool's Paradise Ballet Suite
Dan. Slaraffenland
Prelude; Departure; The Royal Guards-
men; The Lazy Dog's Polka; Princess
Sweet; Procession of the Gluttons; Punc-
tum Finale
Copenhagen Philharmonic Orch.—
Thomas Jensen 2 12″—G-Z250/1
[Marche Tartare]
Royal Theatre Orch., Copenhagen
2 12″—O-DO7000/1
Marche Tartare
Copenhagen Philharmonic Orch.—
Thomas Jensen 12″—G-Z251
[Fool's Paradise—Ballet Suite, Pt. 3]
On account of— Dan. I Anledning af
Bro, bro brille; Poul sine Høns;
Tingelingelater
Copenhagen Philharmonic Orch.—
Thomas Jensen 10″—G-X6151
[Two Danish Disciple Songs]
Qarrtsiluni, Op. 36 (Greenland Ballet)
Copenhagen Royal Theatre Orch.—
J. Hye-Knudsen 12″—G-DB5250
Serenade Flute, Violin, 'Cello
Danish Trio 12″—G-DB5205

SONGS In Danish
Hyldestsang til det danske Klima;
Ork ja (Kai Munk)
Gunnar Lemvigh (t) & H. D. Koppel
(pf) 10″—G-X6274
Mor Danmark (M. Lorentzen)
Eng. Mother Denmark
Aksel Schiøtz (t) & H. D. Koppel (pf)
10″—G-X6610
[Nielsen: Underlige Aftenlufte]
Tolv med Posten Ballet Suite
Eng. Twelve with the Mail-Coach
Royal Theatre Orch., Copenhagen—
Jensen 12″—TONO-X25040
Two Danish Disciple Songs
Nu lader os sjunge; Fuglevisen
Copenhagen Philharmonic Orch.—
Jensen 10″—G-X6151
[On account of—]

RIMINI, Vincenzo Da (14th Century)

*A composer of the Italian "Ars Nova." One
finds in his works a rich blending of our heri-
tage from the Near East and the germinating
spirit of the Renaissance.*

Ita se n'era (Ballata) In Italian
Max Meili (t) & Fr. Seidersbeck (viol)
(in Vol. I) 12″—AS-1
[with Italian Ballades & Religious Songs
of the 14th Century]

RIMSKY-KORSAKOV, Nikolai (1844-1908)

One of the best known Russian composers, a member of the famous "Five," and the only one of the group to obtain (largely by himself) a complete orthodox musical education, Rimsky's skill and imagination as an orchestrator plus his enormous industry and craftsmanship give him a position of considerable importance. His major works, the operas, are seldom heard today, and he is best known by a few orchestral works, the flamboyant "Scheherazade" remaining an ever-popular favorite both on records and on programs of outdoor summer concerts. His efforts to arrange Mussorgsky's works was undoubtedly a labor of love but in recent years it has been realized that his "corrections" of Mussorgsky's "crudities" were aesthetically indefensible, an awkward and ill-becoming cloak of musical orthodoxy hiding the true stature of one of the most original geniuses of modern times.

Antar See under Symphony No. 2

Capriccio espagnol, Op. 34 Orchestra
Alborado; Variations; Alborado; Scena & Gypsy Song; Fandango asturiano
Danish Radio Symphony Orch.—N.
Malko 2 12"—**G-C3686/7**
N. Y. Philharmonic-Symphony Orch.—
Barbirolli 2 12"—**CX-185†**
Liverpool Philharmonic—Malcolm
Sargent 2 12"—**C-DX1180/1**
Boston "Pops" Orch.—Fiedler
2 12"—**V-11827/8**
National Symphony Orch.—B. Cameron
2 12"—**D-K1328/9†**
DUPLICATIONS: Lamoureux Orch.—
Wolff, PD-67009/10: PD-566049/50;
London Symphony Orch.—Coates,
G-D1861/2: G-W1098/9; Colonne Orch.
Pierné, O-123625/7

Dubinushka, Op. 69 1905
Russian folksong arr. Rimsky-Korsakov
Indianapolis Symphony Orch.—
Sevitzky 12"—**G-C3347**
[Glinka: Russlan and Ludmilla—
Overture]
London Symphony Orch.—Coates
12"—**G-DB1683**
[Borodin: Prince Igor—March]

(La) Grande Pâque Russe Overture, Op. 36 Orchestra
Eng. **Russian Easter Overture**
Philadelphia Orch.—Ormandy
2 12"—**CX-276†**
National Symphony Orch.—Jorda
(D-K1522/3) 2 12"—**D-ED28†**
NBC Symphony Orch.—Stokowski
2 12"—**VM-937†**
Philadelphia Orch.—Stokowski
(G-AW81 & 83) 2 12"—**V-7018/9**
—**Arr. Band**
Grenadier Guards Band—G. Miller,
D-K748

OPERAS In Russian

CHRISTMAS EVE

Unspecified Aria Soprano
Xenia Belmas 12"—**PD-66716**
[Massenet: Elégie]

(LE) COQ D'OR Opera in 3 Acts 1910
Eng. **The Golden Cockerel**

Orchestral Suite
Arr. Glazunov & Steinberg
1) **Introduction; Prologue; Slumber Scene; Warning of the Cockerel**
2) **Prelude to Act II; Arrival of King Dodon at the Scene of the Battle**
3) **Dance of King Dodon & The Queen of Schamakha**
4) **Prelude to Act III; Bridal March; Death of King Dodon**
London Symphony Orch.—Eugene
Goossens 3 12"—**VM-504†**
(G-C3013/5) (G-EH1241/3)

—**Nos. 1, 3 & 4** only
Minneapolis Symphony Orch.—
Mitropoulos 2 12"—**CX-254†**

Introduction Orchestra
(See also above album sets)
Lamoureux Orch.—Albert Wolff
12"—**PD-66953**
[Bridal Cortège, Act III] (PD-566007)
London Symphony Orch.—Coates
[Bridal Cortège, Act III] 12"—**D-K1330**
Orch. of the Suisse Romande—Ansermet,
In Prep. Swiss Decca

Hymne au soleil: Salut à toi, soleil Act II
NOTE: *Most versions are sung in French*
Eng. **Hymn to the Sun** Soprano
Lily Pons (in VM-702) 12"—**V-17232**
[Thomas: Mignon—Je suis Titania]
(also in CM-740)
Patrice Munsel 12"—**V-11-8886**
[Thomas: Mignon—Je suis Titania]
Lina Pagliughi (in Italian)
12"—**P-DPX17**
[Mozart: Così fan tutte—Come scoglio]
[Verdi: Rigoletto—Caro nome, on
CET-BB25002]
Miliza Korjus (in German)
12"—**V-12021**
[Czar's Bride—In Novgorod]
[Sadko: Chant hindou, on G-EG996]
DUPLICATION: A. Galli-Curci,
G-DA219*

—**Arr. Violin & Piano** Kreisler
Fritz Kreisler & Franz Rupp
(G-DB3444) 12"—**V-15487**
[Scott: Lotus Land, arr. Kreisler]
Jascha Heifetz & Emanuel Bay, in D-A592
DUPLICATION: Jacques Thibaud,
G-DB1017

—**Arr. 'Cello & Piano**
Pierre Fournier & pf. acc.
[Rachmaninoff: Vocalise] 12"—**G-W1578**

Cortège des Noces (Bridal Procession)
Act III (See also album sets above)
San Francisco Symphony Orch.—
Monteux (in VM-820†) 12"—**V-18161**
[Ravel: La Valse, Pt. 3] (G-DB5965)
London Symphony Orch.—Coates
[Introduction] 12"—**D-K1330**
Minneapolis Symphony Orch.—
Mitropoulos
(in CX-212†) 12"—**C-11672D**
[Dukas: Sorcerer's Apprentice, Pt. 3]

Boston "Pops" Orch.—Fiedler
(in VM-797†) 12"—**V-11-8509**
[Ippolitov-Ivanov: Caucasian Sketches, No. 1]
DUPLICATIONS: Lamoureux Orch.—
Albert Wolff, PD-67010: PD-566050:
PD-66953: PD-566007; Orch. of the
Suisse Romande—Ansermet, in Preparation Swiss Decca

(THE) CZAR'S BRIDE 4 Acts 1899
In Novgorod (Martha's Aria)
Act II Soprano
N. N. Vechor 10"—**G-EK95**
[Sadko—O yon dark forest, G. M. Pozemkovsky]
H. Schipper 10"—**USSR-12466/7**
Miliza Korjus (in German)
12"—**V-12021**
[Coq d'or—Hymn to the Sun]
[Verdi: Ernani—Ernani involami, on G-EH994]

Lykov's Aria Tenor
N. Sereda 10"—**USSR-4598/5746**
[Rachmaniniff: Aleko—Song of the young gipsy]
Since I cannot wed (Lubasha's Song)
Act I Soprano
—Arr. Violin & Piano Franko
Yehudi Menuhin & pf. acc.
12"—**G-DB1638**
[Paganini: La Campanella]

Ivan the Terrible See: Maid of Pskov
Kitezh See: Tale of the Invisible City of Kitezh

(THE) MAID OF PSKOV
(or, Ivan The Terrible)
Rus. **Pskovitianka** 3 Acts 1873
Fr. **La Pskovitaine**
Overture Orchestra
Liverpool Philharmonic—Lambert
12"—**C-DX1140**
Hunt & Storm Music Act III Orchestra
(Intermezzo sinfonico, or "Musical picture")
Philadelphia Orch.—Stokowski
(G-DB6039) (in VM-717) 12"—**V-17502**
[Dukas: L'Apprenti Sorcier, Pt. 3]
[Bloch: Schlelomo, Pt. 5, w. Feuermann, on G-DB6057]
London Symphony Orch.—Coates
12"—**G-DB1698**
[Snow Maiden—Dance of the Tumblers]

MAY NIGHT 3 Acts 1880
Russ. **Maïskaza Noch**
Fr. **La Nuit de Mai**
Overture Orchestra
London Philharmonic Orch.—
Beecham 12"—**G-DB6308**
Song of the Village Mayor Tenor **Chorus**
Joseph Laoute & Red Army Cho.
(in C-C68) 10"—**C-36267**
[Kolitchev: Boatmen of the Volga, arr. Alexandroff] (C-DF2205)
[Méhul: Le Chant du Départ, on C-DB1763]

Levko's Song
Sergei Lemeshev 10"—**USSR-13152/3**
[Verstonvsky: Askold's Grave—Toropa's Aria]

MLADA Fairy Opera-Ballet 1892
Cortège des Nobles Orchestra
Eng. **Procession of the Nobles**
London Symphony—Coates
12"—**G-AW240**
[Mussorgsky: Fair at Sorotchinsk—Gopak]

(A) Night in May See under May Night

Pskovitianka See under Maid of Pskov

SADKO 7 Scenes 1897
Individual Excerpts
Scene 1
O yon dark forest (Sadko's Air) Tenor
G. M. Pozemkovsky 10"—**G-EK95**
[Czar's Bride—Martha's Aria, N. N. Vechor]
Scene 4
Song of the Viking Guest Bass
Alexander Kipnis
(in VM-1073) 12"—**V-11-9284**
[Tchaikovsky: Eugene Onegin—Gremin's Aria]
DUPLICATION: F. Chaliapin, G-DB1104
Song of the Indian Guest
(Song of India) Tenor
Fr. **Chant hindou or Chanson hindoue**
Ger. **Hindu Lied**
N. I. Nagachevsky 10"—**G-EK94**
[Mussorgsky: Boris Godunov—Garden Scene w. Sadoven]
G. P. Vinogradov & pf. acc.
10"—**ESTA-D2103**
[Glinka: In my blood; Tchaikovsky: If I could express]
DUPLICATIONS: A. Koubitzky, C-DF12;
D. A. Smirnoff, G-DB581*
In French: Beniamino Gigli, V-1570:
G-DA1307; Lily Pons, C-71305D in
CM-484; Ninon Vallin, O-123664:
PAT-X93044; Amelita Galli-Curci,
V-1524: G-DA1164; Georges Thill,
C-LFX336; M. Claudel, PD-521946;
Richard Crooks, V-10-1093
In German: Miliza Korjus, G-EH996;
Franz Völker, PD-10270; Maria Basca,
T-A2132; Peter Anders, T-A2321;
Herbert E. Groh, O-26335; Karin
Branzell, P-DPX1
In English: Webster Booth, G-B8843;
Joan Cross, D-1272
In Swedish: Jussi Björling, G-X4723
—Arr. Chorus
Don Cossacks—Jaroff, C-7342M
—Arr. Orchestra
Boston "Pops" Orch.—Fiedler
10"—**V-4303**
[Mascagni: Cavalleria Rusticana—Intermezzo] (G-B8412)
Andre Kostelanetz & his Orch.
(in CX-264) 12"—**C-7445M**
[Scott: Lotus Land]
DUPLICATIONS: Hastings Municipal
Orch.—Cameron, D-K568; Géczy Orch.,

G-B8464: G-EG3569: G-GW1782: G-K7734; Lew Stone Concert Orch., D-F7784

—Arr. Violin & Piano Kreisler
Fritz Kreisler & Franz Rupp
10″—**V-1981**
[Poldini: Poupée Valsante, arr. Kreisler]
[Kreisler: Schön Rosmarin, on G-DA1627]
DUPLICATIONS: Vasa Prihoda, PD-62672: CET-OR5059; Yvonne Curti, PAT-X98138; Albert Sammons, D-F7530; S. Swaap, G-K5588; Siegfried Borries, G-DA4440; Y. Bratza, C-4823; H. Volant, C-DF958

—Arr. 'Cello & Piano
Gregor Piatigorsky & R. Berkowitz, in CM-684; Gilberto Crepax, C-D5831

—Arr. Saxophone: Viard, PAT-PA185
See current catalogues for other arrangements and recordings.

Song of the Venetian Guest Baritone
N. S. Lukine 10″—**G-EK96**
[Dargomijsky: Russalka—Olga's aria, Vechor]

Scene 7
Berceuse Soprano
—Arr. 2 Pianos Babin
Vronsky & Babin, C-72082D in CM-576

(THE) SNOW MAIDEN 4 Acts 1882
Rus. **Snegourotchka**
Dance of the Tumblers (or Buffoons)
Act III Orchestra
National Symphony—Coates
(in D-ED6†) 12″—**D-K1307**
[Tchaikovsky: Romeo and Juliet, Pt. 5]
Bournemouth Municipal Orch.—
Birch 10″—**D-F7885**
[Tchaikovsky: Chanson triste]
DUPLICATION: London Symphony—Coates, G-DB1698

—Arr. 2 Pianos Babin
Vronsky & Babin, C-72082D in CM-576

(THE) TALE OF THE CZAR SALTAN
4 Acts 1900
Suite, Op. 57
London Philharmonic Orch.—Fitelberg
2 12″—**D-K1534/5**
Introduction (Warrior's March)
Act II Orchestra
San Francisco Symphony—Monteux
(in VM-920†) 12″—**V-11-8384**
[Scheherazade, Pt. 1]
Lamoureux Orch.—Wolff
(PD-566083) 12″—**PD-95435**
[Borodin: Prince Igor, Polovtsian Dances, Pt. 3]
Flight of the Bumble Bee Act III Orch.
Fr. **Le vol du bourdon**
Ger. **Hummelflug**
Hallé Orch.—Hamilton Harty
12″—**C-67743D**
[Mussorgsky: Khovantchina—Prelude] (C-9908)
Berlin Philharmonic—A. Melichar
10″—**PD-25027**

[Ippolitov-Ivanov: Procession of the Sardar]
All-American Orch.—Stokowski
(Arr. Stokowski) 10″—**C-19005D**
[Tchaikovsky-Stokowski: Humoresque]
Carnegie "Pops" Orch.—Abravanel
12″—**C-7566M**
[Strauss: Tritsch-Tratsch Polka; Wolf-Ferrari: Jewels of the Madonna—Dance of the Cammoristi]
DUPLICATIONS: Lamoureux Orch.—Wolff, PD-66968: PD-566026; Chicago Symphony Orch.—Stock, G-AW273: G-D1284; EIAR Orch.—Ferrero, CET-PP60004; Symphony Orch.—Inghelbrecht, PAT-X5485

—Arr. Violin & Piano Hartmann
Nathan Milstein & Arthur Balsam
10″—**C-17352D**
[Brahms-Joachim: Hungarian Dance No. 2]
Joseph Szigeti & Nitika de Magaloff
12″—**C-7304M**
[Stravinsky: Pastorale; Szymanowski: Fountain of Arethusa]
Yehudi Menuhin & Arthur Balsam
10″—**G-DA1280**
[Debussy-Hartmann: Minstrels & Dvořák-Kreisler; Spanish Dance No. 1]
Jascha Heifetz & Emanuel Bay
(Arr. Heifetz) 10″—**V-10-1328**
[Castelnuovo-Tedesco: Sea Murmurs & Godowsky: Alt Wien]
DUPLICATIONS: I. Stern, in CM-657; M. Candela, C-LF138: C-LW13; Karel Sroubek, U-G14743

—Arr. Piano
Alexander Borovsky, G-DA1308; Alexander Brailowsky, V-11-9009; Lev Oborin, U-G14743; Carl Tillius, G-X7326

(THE) TALE OF THE INVISIBLE CITY OF KITEZH
—The Battle of Kershenetz
Boston Symphony Orch.—Koussevitzky
(in VM-870†) 12″—**V-18410**
[Liszt: Mefisto Waltz, Pt. 3]
[Grieg: Last Spring, on G-DB6136]
Oriental Romance See under Songs—
Rose and the Nightingale

SCHEHERAZADE, Op. 35 Symphonic Suite
1) **The Sea and Sinbad's Ship**
2) **The Tale of the Prince Kalender**
3) **The Young Prince and the Young Princess**
4) **The Festival at Bagdad**
San Francisco Symphony—Monteux
[Czar Saltan—March] 5 12″—**VM-920†**
Cleveland Orch.—Rodzinski
5 12″—**CM-398†**
Philadelphia Orch.—Stokowski
6 12″—**VM-269†**
(G-DB2522/7 in GM-232†)
London Philharmonic—Dorati
(G-C2968/72) 5 12″—**GM-303†**
EIAR Symphony Orch.—Ferrero
5 12″—**CET-BB25137/41**
DUPLICATIONS: Detroit Symphony—

Kolar, (abbr) D-A164; Symphony Orch.
—Cloëz, O-170054/8: O-170067
—Excerpts
Symphony Orch.—Goehr, G-C2983, also
in V-C30†
See also under Miscellaneous—
Song of Scheherazade (Film)
Serbian Fantasy, Op. 6
USSR National Symphony Orch.—
Orlov   10"—USSR-12084/5

SONGS   In Russian
Aimant la rose, le rossignol
See under Rose and the Nightingale
Gonets
Adolf Kaktin (b) & pf. acc. 10"—G-EV19
[Napravnik: Don Juan—Serenade]
It is not the wind blowing from the height
I. Kozlovsky (t) & M. Sakharov (pf)
                         10"—D-M554
[Tchaikovsky: The Nightingale]
[In the Silence of the night, on
USSR-6265/6]
G. P. Vinogradov (t) & K. Vinogradov
(pf)   10"—ESTA-D2101
[The Rose and the Nightingale & Oh, If
you could]
In the silence of the night
I. Kozlovsky (t) & M. Sakharov (pf)
[It is not the wind] 10"—USSR-6265/6
Oh, if you could
G. P. Vinogradov (t) & K. Vinogradov
(pf)   10"—ESTA-D2101
[The Rose and the nightingale & It is
not the wind]
(The) Prophet, Op. 49   (Pushkin)
Feodor Chaliapin (bs) 12"—G-DB1103
[Song of the Volga Boatmen]
(The) Rose and the Nightingale, Op. 2, No. 2
Fr. Aimant la rose, le rossignol
G. P. Vinogradov (t) & K. Vinogradov
(pf)   10"—ESTA-D2101
[It is not the wind & Oh, if you could]
Josephine Antoine (s) (in English),
with flute & pf.   10"—C-17285D
[Thayer: My Laddie]
DUPLICATIONS: Xenia Belmas,
PD-66748
In French: T. Schipa, G-DA1323;
R. Temps, G-K7112
—Arr. Violin & Piano
E. Masetti, G-AV723

SYMPHONIES   Orchestra
No. 2, "Antar" Op. 9
San Francisco Symphony Orch.—
Monteux   3 12"—VM-1203†
Paris Conservatory Orch.—Coppola
                     3 12"—G-DB4887/9

MISCELLANEOUS
"Song of Scheherazade" Film
(Score arranged by Miklos Rosza for film based
on Rimsky-Korsakov's life.)
Song of India (Sadko); Hymn to the Sun
(Coq d'or); Gypsy song (from Antar
Symphony); Fandango (Capriccio es-
pagnole)
Charles Kullman (t) & Orch.—Julius
Berger   2 10"—CX-272

RING, Oluf
SONGS   In Danish
Danmark, nu blunder den lyse nat
Aksel Schiøtz (t) & H. D. Koppel (pf)
                         10"—G-X6632
[Rung: Hvor Nilen vander Aegypterens
Jord]
Sig naermer Tiden, da jeg maa vaek
Aksel Schiøtz (t) & H. D. Koppel (pf)
                         10"—G-X6388
[Vad Thomsen: Til Glaeden]

RIQUIER, Guiraut (13th Century)
Chanson religieuse (Troubadour Song)
Simone Gebelin (unacc. s) 10"—BAM-45
[Bernard de Ventadour: Can, vei la
lauzeta & Rudel: Lanquan li Jonn &
Canto rossinhols]

RIVIER, Jean (1896-   )
Petite Suite   Oboe, Clarinet & Bassoon
Trio d'Anches de Paris 12"—G-DB5083

ROBERTON, (Sir) Hugh
Arrangements of Folksongs, Airs, Hymns
All in the April Evening   (Tynan)
Glasgow Orpheus Choir—Roberton
                         12"—G-C3462
[Webbe: Belmont Hymn—By cool
Chiloam's Shady Rill]
Eriskay Love Lilt
Glasgow Orpheus Choir—Roberton
[Scots wha' hae]   10"—G-E409
(The) Herdmaiden's Song (Old Gaelic)
Glasgow Orpheus Choir—Roberton
                         10"—G-B9501
[Arr. Shaw—I live not where I love]
(The) Isle of Mull
Glasgow Orpheus Choir—Roberton
                         12"—G-C1512
[Arr. Burleigh: Deep River]
Kedron
Glasgow Orpheus Choir—Roberton
                         10"—G-B9549
[Brahms: In stiller Nacht]
(The) Old Woman
Glasgow Orpheus Choir—Roberton
                         12"—G-C3463
[Joze: Far Away, arr. Londonderry Air;
Arr. Vaughan-Williams: The Turtle dove]
Westering Home
(from "Songs of the Isles")
Robert Wilson (t)   10"—G-BD1098
[Curran: Nocturne]

ROBINSON, Earl (1911-   )
Ballad for Americans (John LaTouche)
Paul Robeson (bs) & Cho.
(G-B9160/1)   2 10"—V-P20
John G. Baumgartner (b) & West-
minster Choir   2 10"—C-C49
A Man's a Man for a' That
Earl Robinson, with Guitar 10"—K-538
Joe Hill
Paul Robeson (bs) & Lawrence Brown
(pf)   (in CM-534)   10"—C-17457D
[Blitzstein: No For an Answer—The
purest kind of guy]

(The) House I Live In
Earl Robinson, with guitar 10″—K-538
[A man's a man for a'that]
Lauritz Melchior (t) & chorus
(in VM-1056) 10″—V-10-1223
[Romberg: Student Prince—Serenade]

(The) Lonesome Train A Musical Legend
(Millard Lampell)
Earl Robinson (narrator), Burl Ives,
(ballad singer), Raymond Edward John-
son (Lincoln) and supporting cast, with
Jeffry Alexander Chorus & Lyn Murray
Orchestra (directed by Norman Corwin)
3 12″—D-A375

The People, Yes (Carl Sandburg)
(with William White)

—In the folded and quiet yesterdays
Michael Loring & American People's
Chorus—Grennell 12″—K-1001

(A) Walk in the Sun Ballad
(Millard Lampell)
(featured in the film of the same name)
Earl Robinson (vocal) with guitar
3 10″—DISC-623

ROCCA, Lodovico (1895-   )
*A contemporary Italian opera composer, Rocca
is known chiefly by his opera listed below, "Il
Dibuk (or Dybbuk)."*

(IL) DIBUK Opera in Italian 1934
Ecotti, mia bella amica
Ma oratorno verso Duo, Sop. & Ten.
Augusta Oltrabella & Gino del Signore
12″—G-DB2828

IN TERRA DI LEGGENDA
Opera in Italian
Corsa alla preda
Corteo Notturno
EIAR Symphony Orch.—A. La Rosa
Parodi 12″—CET-CB20253

RODGERS, Richard
Collections (Films & Musical comedies)
Music of Richard Rodgers
My heart stood still; The most beautiful
girl in the world; It might as well be
Spring; Blue Moon; Johnny-one-note; If
I loved you; Where or when; The Girl
Friend; There's a small hotel; Lover;
Slaughter on Tenth Avenue
Andre Kostelanetz & his Orch.
4 12″—CM-655

ALLEGRO
Selections
John Battles, Annamary Dickey, John
Conte, Kathryn Lee, Lisa Kirk, and other
members of original cast and Orch.—
Dell'Isola 5 10″—V-K11

CAROUSEL
Selections
Original Cast 6 12″—D-DA400
Selections
Thomas L. Thomas & Nan Merriman
2 10″—V-10-1174/5
Soliloquy
James Melton 12″—V-11-9116
Frank Sinatra 12″—C-7492M

Waltz
Pittsburgh Symphony Orch.—
Reiner 12″—C-12322D

(A) CONNECTICUT YANKEE
Selections
Cast of revival production
Vivienne Segal, Dick Foran, Julie War-
ren, Vera-Ellen, and others with Orch.—
Hirst 5 10″—D-DA367

OKLAHOMA!
Selections (Hammerstein)
Alfred Drake, Joan Roberts, Celeste
Holm, etc. of the original cast
Vol. I (B-3713/8) 6 10″—D-DA359
Vol. II 2 10″—D-DA383
Selections
James Melton (t), Eleanor Steber (s),
John Charles Thomas (b)
3 10″—VM-988
Original cast from Drury Lane produc-
tion, London, G-C3595/6; Gracie Fields,
D-F8804
—Selections Arr. Orchestra
Boston "Pops" Orch.—Fiedler
12″—V-11-8742
André Kostelanetz & his Orch.
(C-DX1363) 12″—C-7417M
Philharmonic Orch. of Los Angeles—
Wallenstein 2 10″—D-A378

STATE FAIR (Film) Selections
Dick Haymes (vocal) 3 10″—D-A412
See current catalogues under the above
film and musical comedy titles for addi-
tional recordings, also under the follow-
ing:
All Points West; Slaughter on Tenth Ave-
nue; Babes in Arms; Blue Moon; The
Boys from Syracuse; Fools for Scandal;
I'd Rather Be Right; I Married An Angel;
On Your Toes, etc.

ROESGEN-CHAMPION, Marguerite
*A contemporary French composer known also
to record collectors as an able harpsichordist
and pianist.*

Cécile; Daniele
M. Roesgen-Champion & Jean Doyen
(2 pfs.) 10″—PAT-PA1921
Conte bleu et or Piano Duo
Marche royale; Le Prince amoureux; La
Belle fileuse; Le Maître à danser; Le
Mariage
Marguerite Roesgen-Champion & Jean
Doyen 12″—PAT-PAT56
Etoiles filantes
M. Moyse (fl), Bleuzet (ob), M. Roesgen-
Champion (pf) & Orch. Féminin—Jane
Evrard 12″—PAT-PAT141
[Jeunes Filles—Bavardes & A la danse]
Idylle & Passepied
Marguerite Roesgen-Champion (pf) &
Orch.—Gaillard 10″—G-DA4936
Jeunes Filles
—Excerpts: Bavardes & A la danse
M. Moyse (fl), Bleuzet (ob), M. Roesgen-
Champion (pf) & Orch. Féminin—Jane
Evrard 12″—PAT-PAT141
[Etoiles filantes]

Pastorale
  Pastorale, Introduction à la valse senti-
  mentale, Valse sentimentale, Ronde
  M. Roesgen-Champion (pf), M. Bleuzet
  (ob), M. Cruque (vlc)
                          12"—PAT-PGT74
Pièces
  Henri Merckel (vl) & M. Roesgen-
  Champion (pf)   10"—G-DA4937

SONGS In French
  (L') Annonciation & La visitation SATB
  Notick, Douls, Arnault, Morturier
                          10"—PAT-PA1176
Mai & Secret
  Ninon Vallin (s)   12"—PAT-PG81
  [Gounod: Au printemps]

ROGERS, Bernard (1893-   )
  *A teacher at the Eastman School of Music,
  Rogers was at one time associated with Musical
  America. He has written for orchestra, chorus,
  chamber groups, and the stage.*

Soliloquy 1922
  Flute & String Quartet (or Orchestra)
  Joseph Mariano & Eastman-Rochester
  Symphony Orch.—Hanson
            (in VM-802) 12"—V-18101
  [Barlow: Rhapsody—"The Winter's
  Past"]

ROMAN, Johan Helmich (1694-1758)
  *Called "the father of Swedish music," Roman
  studied under Ariosti and Pepusch in London.
  Most of his music remains in manuscript.*

Sonata da chiesa in G minor (Trio Sonata)
  Arr. H. Rosenberg
  Ingrid Kjellstrom & Rolf Lannerholm
  (oboes) & Arik Arnhom (harpsichord)
            2 12"—G-DB11000/1
  [Berwald: Quartet, E flat major, Pt. 1,
  Kyndal Quartet]

ROMBERG, Sigmund (1887-   )
  *A Hungarian-American composer in whose
  operettas—now well over seventy in number—
  the Viennese style of popular music is adapted
  to American taste.*

Collections (Operettas, Musical Comedies,
  Films)
Music of Romberg
  Will you remember; One kiss; Romance;
  Deep in my heart, dear; When I grow too
  old to dream; Auf wiedersehn; Song of
  love
  Andre Kostelanetz & his Orch.
            4 10"—CM-635
Sigmund Romberg Favorites
  Sigmund Romberg & his Orch., with so-
  loists & chorus   4 10"—VM-1051

BLOSSOM TIME
Selections
  Mary Martha Briney, Blanka Peric, Don-
  ald Dame, Earl Wrightson, Cho. & Orch.
  —Goodman   5 10"—V-K5

THE DESERT SONG
Selections
  Frances Greer, Earl Wrightson, Jimmy
  Carroll, Cho. & Orch.—Goodman
            4 10"—V-K12
  Dennis Morgan (t) with Chorus & Orch.
  —Roemheid   2 10"—CX-260
  Kitty Carlisle, Wilbur Evans, Felix
  Knight, with Jeffry Alexander Chorus &
  Orch.—Isaac van Grove
            5 10"—D-DA370

NEW MOON
Selections
  Stout Hearted men; Paree; Lover, come
  back to me; One kiss; Wanting you;
  Softly as in a morning sunrise
  Florence George, Frank Forest, Paul
  Gregory, Mixed Chorus & Decca Concert
  Orch.—Harry Sosnik   3 10"—D-A155

UP IN CENTRAL PARK
Selections
  Eileen Farrell, Celeste Holm, Wilbur
  Evans, Betty Bruce, Orch. & Chorus
            4 10"—D-A395
  Jeanette MacDonald (s) & Robert Mer-
  rill (b) with Orch.—Russell Bennett
            3 10"—VM-991

(THE) STUDENT PRINCE
Selections
  Mary Martha Briney, Frances Greer, Donald Dame, Earl Wrightson, Cho. & Orch.
            4 10"—V-K8
  See current catalogues under the titles of
  the above operettas for individual recordings.

RONALD, (Sir) Landon (1873-1938)
  *A prominent English conductor during the
  first part of the century, Sir Landon was also
  a composer of charming pieces.*

SONGS In English
Down in the Forest (No. 2, Cycle of Life)
  Richard Tauber (t) 10"—P-RO20527
  [Purcell: Passing By]
Good Night
  Richard Tauber (t) & Percy Kahn (pf)
            10"—P-RO20554
  [Bridge: Come to me in my dreams]
O lovely night (Teschemacher)
  Richard Tauber (t) 10"—P-RO20512
  [Leoncavallo: Mattinata]
  Webster Booth (t) & Anne Ziegler (s)
            10"—G-B9552
  [Coward: Operette—Dearest boy]

RONCALLI, Ludovico
Passacaglia 1692
  See under Respighi: Antiche arie, Suite
  No. 3

ROSENBERG, Hilding (1892-   )
  A Swedish "expressionist" composer.

Quartet No. 4, Op. 79
  Garaguly String Quartet
            3 12"—G-DB11004/6

ROSENMUELLER, Johann (c.1619-1684)

A Saxonian composer important in the history of music as being among the first to write suites containing free movements in addition to the expected dances. His music provides one of the links on the chain leading to the symphony.

Sonata da chiesa, E minor
E. Ortmans-Bach & D. Blot (vls), Marcelle de Lacour (harpsichord), &
Noëlie Pierront (organ) with Ars Rediviva Ensemble—Crussard
12"—**G-DB5064**

Suite, C major
String Orch. & Harpsichord—Curt Sachs
(in Vol. VI) 12"—**AS-52**
[Fischer: Suite from "Le Journal de Printems"]

ROSSI, Francesco (born c.1645)

An Italian monk, Rossi is known today for the aria listed below. He wrote both sacred and secular music.

MITRANE Opera In Italian

Ah! rendimi quel core
Gaston Micheletti (t)
(in Vol. VII) 12"—**AS-64**
[Buononcini: Vado ben spesso]

ROSSI, Michael Angelo (c.1620-c.1660)

An early Italian baroque composer, a pupil of Frescobaldi at Rome, Rossi is one of the many seventeenth century composers whose names are linked with the rise of opera. By the same token, Rossi is also important in the development of a freer keyboard style, as the Toccatas listed below clearly show.

Toccata (unspecified)
Fritz Heitmann 12"—**U-E815**
[Bach: Little Prelude & Fugue, B flat major]

Toccata, G major Arr. Pf. Aleco Toni
Nino Rossi 12"—**G-DB5352**
[Pasquini: Toccata sul canto del cuculo]

ROSSINI, Gioacchino (1729-1868)

"Il Barbiere di Siviglia" is but one of Rossini's many delightful comic operas. The fact that his other works have not kept the boards of contemporary opera houses is compensated for somewhat by the considerable body of music that is available on records.

Collection—Three Overtures
La Scala di Seta Overture
L' Italiana in Algeri Overture
Semiramide Overture
BBC Symphony Orch. & N. Y. Philharmonic-Symphony Orch.—Toscanini
4 12"—**VM-825†**

Collection—Rossini Overtures
Il Barbiere di Siviglia Overture
La Gazza Ladra Overture
La Cenerentola Overture
Il Signor Bruschino Overture
NBC Symphony Orch.—Toscanini
(Also V-V2†) 4 12"—**VM-1037†**
[with William Tell—Act I—Passo a sei]

Collection—Operatic Arias
Il Barbiere di Siviglia—Una voce poco fa;
Semiramide—Bel raggio; L'Italiana in
Algeri—Cruda sorte! Cenerentola—
Nacqui all' affano & Non più mesta
Jennie Tourel (ms) & Metropolitan Opera
Orch.—Pietro Cimara 3 12"—**CM-691†**

(The) Barber of Seville See under Operas
—Il Barbiere di Siviglia

(La) Boutique Fantasque
See under Miscellaneous

(La) Danza See under Songs

Matinées Musicales
See under Miscellaneous

OPERAS In Italian

(L') ASSEDIO DI CORINTO 1826
(Originally in French)
Eng. The Siege of Corinth
Ger. Die Belagerung von Corinth
Overture
La Scala Orch.—Marinuzzi
2 12"—**T-SKB3219/20**
[Guglielmo Tell—Ballet Music]
La Scala Orch.—Atillio Parelli
12"—**FONIT-35031**
EIAR Symphony Orch.—LaRosa Parodi
(CET-CB20240) 12"—**P-DPX30**
DUPLICATIONS: La Scala Orch.—Sabajno, G-S10041; Milan Symphony—Molajoli, C-D14473

(IL) BARBIERE DI SIVIGLIA 2 Acts 1816
Fr. Le Barbier de Séville Eng. The Barber of Seville
Complete recording
La Scala Soloists & Chorus, with Milan Symphony Orch.—Molajoli
(C-D14564/79) 16 12"—**C-OP8†**
[Mozart: Le Nozze di Figaro—Overture, on side 32]
The Cast:
Figaro .... Riccardo Stracciari (b)
Rosina .... Mercedes Capsir (s)
Il Conte d'Almaviva .. Dino Borgioli (t)
Don Basilio ...... Vincenzo Bettoni (b)
Dott. Bartolo .. Salvatore Baccaloni (b)
Berta .... Cesira Ferrari (s)
Fiorello .... Attilio Bordonali (b)
Un Ufficiale ..... Aristide Baracchi (b)
Chorus Master: Vittore Veneziani

Abridged Recording
La Scala Soloists & Chorus, with Milan Symphony Orch.—Molajoli
6 12"—**C-DX610/5†**
(An abridged version of C-OP8† above)

Abridged Recording (Adapted by R. Wise & G. Bamboschek)
Soloists with Victor Male Chorus & Symphony Orch.—Bamboschek
8 12"—**VM-898†**
The Cast:
Figaro .... Carlos Ramirez (b)
Rosina .... Hilde Reggiani (s)
Almaviva .... Bruno Landi (t)
Don Basilio ...... Lorenzo Alvary (bs)
Dott. Bartolo ...... John Gurney (bs)
Berta .... Lucielle Browning (ms)
Fiorello & Un Ufficiale .... Wilfred Engelman (b)

Abridged recording In German
Berlin State Opera Soloists, Chorus &

Orch.—Hermann Weigert
　　　　　4　12"—PD-27353/6
The Cast includes Armin Weltner, Sabine Meyen, Julius Patzak, Martin Abendroth, Eduard Kandl, Ida V. Scheele-Müller, Karl Anders, Waldemar Henke & Carl Walter

Vocal & Orchestral excerpts
S. Meyen, J. Patzak, K. Anders, A. Weltner, E. Kandl, etc. (in German)
　　　　　　　　　　　12"—PD-27340

Overture Orchestra
NBC Symphony Orch.—Toscanini
　(in VM-1037†)　12"—V-11-9066
　(V-18-0005 in V-V2†)
　(V-11-9229 in VM-1063)
　(Older version with NY Philharmonic-Symphony Orch. on V-7255: G-D1835:
　G-DB6004: G-AW171: G-W1139)
National Symphony Orch.—Rankl
　　　　　　　　　　　12"—D-K1125
Berlin State Opera Orch.—v. Kempen
　(CET-OR5047)　　　12"—PD-57152
Hallé Orch.—Sargent　12"—C-DX1033
La Scala Orch.—Marinuzzi
　　　　　　　　　12"—T-SKB3215
DUPLICATIONS: La Scala Orch.—Parelli, Fonit-35022; Royal Theatre Orch., Copenhagen—Tango, TONO-X25029; CBS Symphony—Barlow, C-70704D; Philharmonic Orch.—Mascagni, P-E11148; Berlin Philharmonic—Furtwängler, PD-35028; La Scala Orch.—Sabajno, G-S10044; Berlin State Opera Orch.—Weissmann, P-E10928; Symphony Orch., Paris—Coppola, G-L623; Milan Symphony—Molajoli, C-D14461; Opéra-Comique Orch.—Cloëz, O-165103; Symphony Orch.—Andolfi, PAT-PD14; Berlin Philharmonic Orch.—Schmidt-Isserstedt, T-E1933; Berlin State Opera Orch.—Weigert, PD-22601
Also: Comedian Harmonists, G-X4758: G-K7925: G-HN1469: G-EG6430

Individual Excerpts

ACT I

Ecco ridente in cielo Tenor
　NOTE: *Introduction often cut in recordings.*
　Eng. Dawn with her rosy mantle Fr. Des rayons de l'aurore Ger. Sieh', schon die Morgenrote
Ferrucio Tagliavini　12"—CET-BB25145
　[Donizetti: Elisir d'amore—Una furtive lagrima]
　[Verdi: Rigoletto—Parmi veder le lagrime, on CET-BB25058 in CET-2]
Tito Schipa　　　　10"—G-DA874
　[Se il mio nome]
DUPLICATIONS: Dino Borgioli, C-DQ1084; Roberto d'Alessio, C-DQ1080; G. Bentonelli, C-CQX16466; De Muro Lomanto, C-DQ1059; G. Manuritta, C-D14622; A. Lotti Camici, C-GQ7222
In French: Villabella, O-188599: PAT-X90026

Largo al factotum Baritone
Paolo Silveri　　　12"—C-DX1432
　[Verdi: Rigoletto—Corteggiani]
Gino Bechi　　　　12"—G-DB5441

[Verdi: Otello—Credo]
Carlo Tagliabue　　12"—G-DB11300
[Wagner: Tannhäuser—O du mein holder Abendstern]
Tito Gobbi　　　　12"—G-DB6626
[Verdi: Otello—Era la notte]
Leonard Warren　　12"—V-11-8744
[Bizet: Carmen-Chanson du Toréador]
John Charles Thomas
　　　(in VM-645)　12"—V-15860
[Verdi: Traviata—Di Provenza]
Lawrence Tibbett
　(G-DB1478)　　　　12"—V-7353
[Verdi: Ballo in Maschera—Eri tu]
[Bizet: Carmen-Chanson du Toréador on V-14202 in VM-329]
Riccardo Stracciari　12"—C-7299M
[Verdi: Otello—Credo]
[Bizet: Carmen—Toréador song, on C-L2129: C-GQX10174]
[Dunque io son, on C-D16382]
DUPLICATIONS: Igor Gorin, G-DB3836; Apollo Granforte, G-DB1221; Enzo Mascherini, CET-BB25123; Mario Basiola, C-GQX10967; Giovanni Inghillieri, G-D1698; Heinrich Schlusnus, PD-35021: PD-67012: PD-67261; L. Piccioli, C-DQ1977; C. Galeffi, C-GQX10150; T. Ruffo, G-DB405*; E. Molinari, C-D14558; C. Maugeri, C-D16422
In English: Dennis Noble, C-9556: G-C3141; P. Dawson, G-C1400
In German: Karl Schmitt-Walter, T-E1916; Arno Schellenberg, G-EH1212
In French: Willy Clement, G-DB11123; P. Deldi, C-DFX91; A. Crabbé, G-DB1043; A. Baugé, PAT-X90055
In Spanish: L. Sagi Vela, Argentine V-68-8000
In Bohemian: Josef Kríkavá, U-C12727: Z. Otava, U-B10654: ESTA-H5117

—Arr. Violin & Piano Castelnuovo-Tedesco
Jascha Heifetz & Milton Kaye, D-29153: B-0156

—Arr. 2 Pianos Kovacs
Luboshutz & Nemenoff, V-11-8987

Se il mio nome saper (Serenata) Tenor
　Fr. Silence à sa fenêtre
Tito Schipa　　　　10"—G-DA874
　[Ecco ridente in cielo]
G. Gero　　　　　10"—CET-TI7039
　[Donizetti: Pasquale—Sogno soave]
Dino Borgioli　　　12"—C-GQX10167
　[Donizetti: Elisir d'amore—Una furtiva lagrima]
DUPLICATIONS: De Muro Lomanto, C-DQ1059; Alessandro Bonci, ARIA DISC-62123/39687*; R. D'Alessio, C-DQ1080; G. Manuritta, PAT-X15755: C-DQ1069; C. Solari, C-D5700
In French: Villabella, O-188599

All' idea di quel metallo
Dunque? All' opera Duo: Tenor & Baritone
Numero quindici a mano manca
　Fr. D'un metal si précieux
　Eng. 'Tis the spring of all invention & Fifteen is my number
Bruno Landi & Benvenuto Franci
　　　　　　　　　12"—G-DB1433

Dino Borgioli & G. Vanelli
10″—C-DQ1106
In French: Villabella & Baugé, PAT-PGT13
In English: Webster Booth & Dennis Noble, G-C3398

—Numero quindici only
L. Fort & L. Piccioli, C-CQ1393

Una voce poco fa

Io sono docile (Rosina's Cavatina) Soprano
(Act I, Scene 2—sometimes called Act II)
Fr. Rien ne peut changer mon âme
Ger. Frag' ich mein beklommen Herz (Rosinenarie)
Eng. There's a voice within my heart
Conchita Supervia 12″—P-PXO1015
Lily Pons (G-DB2501) 12″—V-8870
(Also in CM-740)
Janine Micheau 12″—D-K1650
Jennie Tourel
(in CM-691†) 12″—C-72131D
DUPLICATIONS: Erna Sack, PD-35087:
PD-516738; Maria Gentile, PD-10494:
Fonit-61070; Anna Maria Guglielmetti,
C-GQX10172; Sanchioni, C-DQ651
In French: Lily Pons, O-188646; Ga-brielle Ritter-Ciampi, PD-66842; Yvonne Brothier, G-P679; Solange Delmas,
G-K7176; Germaine Féraldy, C-LFX302;
M. Mayo, PAT-PG39
In German: Adele Kern, PD-10303; Erna Sack, T-E1735; Elisabeth Reichelt,
PD-57110; Alda Noni, PD-68108
In English: Gwen Catley, G-C9323

—Abbreviated versions
Lina Pagliughi 12″—P-DPX15
[Donizetti: Don Pasquale—So anch'io la virtu] (CET-PP60000)
Ebe Stignani
(in CET-9) 12″—CET-BB25098
[Verdi: Trovatore—Condotta]
DUPLICATIONS: Galli-Curci, V-7110:
G-DB1355; older version, G-DB261*;
Tetrazzini & re-recorded orch., V-7883:
G-DB1979; Lina Aimero, C-GQX10982;
Toti Dal Monte, G-DB830*; T. Tashko,
C-DQ2367
In German: Miliza Korjus, V-13807 in
VM-871: G-C2688: G-EH867
In Czech: M. Krasova, ESTA-H5118

(La) Calunnia è un venticello Bass
Fr. Air de la calomnie Ger. Die Ver-leumdung
Feodor Chaliapin
(G-DB932) 12″—V-6783
[Mussorgsky: Song of the flea]
Oscar Natzke 12″—P-E11423
[Mozart: Zauberflöte—O Isis]
Luciano Neroni 12″—CET-BB25144
[Verdi: Boccanegra—Il lacerato spirito]
Tancredi Pasero 12″—G-DBO5356
[Gounod: Faust—Le Veau d'or]
Tancredi Pasero 12″—CET-BB25059
[Gounod: Faust—Le Veau d'or]
DUPLICATIONS: Tancredi Pasero,
C-GQX11069: C-GQX10231; N. De An-gelis, C-GQX10180; Umberto di Lelio,
C-D16425
In German: Wilhelm Tisch, G-DB10004;
Leo Schützendorf, T-E197
In French: André Pernet, G-DB5019; M.
Guénot, C-D14219; Etienne Billot,
O-171037; André Balbon, PAT-X90049;
Lucien Van Obbergh, PD-516647

Dunque io son Duo: Soprano & Baritone
Lily Pons & G. De Luca (G-DB5815)
(in VM-702) 12″—V-17233
[Verdi: Rigoletto—Il nome vostro ditemi]
Toti Dal Monte & Luigi Montesanto
12″—G-DB2125
[Bellini: Norma-Casta diva, Dal Monte only]
Margherita Carosio & Carlo Tagliabue
12″—G-DB6387
[Verdi: Rigoletto—Ah! Solo per me]
DUPLICATIONS: M. Barrientos & R.
Stracciari, C-D16382; B. Gheradi & B.
Franci, C-DQ1139; Galvany & Ruffo,
G-DB400*

Manca un foglio (Bartolo's Air) Bass
(Sometimes substituted for "A un dottor")
No recording available

A un dottor della mia sorte (Bartolo's Air)
Bass
(Occasionally replaced by "Manca un foglio")
Salvatore Baccaloni 12″—C-71193D
[Mozart: Nozze di Figaro—La Vendetta]
DUPLICATIONS: Louis Musy (in French), G-W1026; Leo Schützendorf (in German), T-E197

Scena della lezione (Lesson Scene) Soprano
(with Tenor)
Contro un cor che accende amore
Cara immagine ridente
Conchita Supervia & Giovanni Manuritta
12″—P-PXO1020

(LA) CENERENTOLA 2 Acts 1817
Eng. Cinderella Fr. Cendrillon Ger.
Aschenbrödel

Overture Orchestra
NBC Symphony—Toscanini
(in VM-1037†) 12″—V-11-9068
(Also V-18-0007 in V-V2†) (G-DB6368)
Milan Symphony—Molajoli
12″—C-GQX10753
EIAR Symphony Orch.—Tansini
12″—CET-CB20245
DUPLICATIONS: La Scala Orch.—
Sabajno, G-S10161; La Scala Orch.—
Parelli, FONIT-35032

Individual excerpts

Signore, una parola, Act I Quintet

—1st Part, Soprano & Bass only
Conchita Supervia & V. Bettoni
12″—P-PXO1021
[Italiana in Algeri—Per lui che adoro,
Quartet]

Nacqui all'affano e al pianto

Non più mesta
Aria & Rondo Finale (Act II) Soprano

Conchita Supervia 12"—P-PXO1018
Jennie Tourel (C-LX1003)
(in CM-691†) 12"—C-72129D
Rose Bampton 12"—V-18217
[Semiramide—Bel raggio lushinghier]

CIRO IN BABILONIA Opera 1812
Overture
EIAR Symphony Orch.—Tansini
12"—CET-CB20267

(LA) GAZZA LADRA 2 Acts 1817
Fr. La Pie voleuse Ger. Die diebische
Elster Eng. The Thieving Magpie
Overture
NBC Symphony—Toscanini
(in VM-1037†) 12"—V-11-9067
(Also V-18-0006 in V-V2) (G-DB6342)
London Philharmonic—Beecham
(C-LX353) (C-LFX374) 12"—C-68301D
La Scala Orch.—Marinuzzi
12"—T-SKB3216
Boston "Pops" Orch.—Fiedler
(G-C3271) 12"—V-13751
National Symphony Orch.—Rankl
12"—D-K1407
DUPLICATIONS: Berlin State Opera
Orch.—Seidler-Winkler, G-EH1256:
G-FKX32; Berlin Philharmonic—Furt-
wängler, PD-95427; Berlin Opera Orch.—
Schmidt-Isserstedt, T-E2814; Berlin
State Opera Orch.—Viebig, G-EH111;
Milan Symphony Orch., C-D12276/7

Di piacer mi balza il cor, Act I
Deh! Tu reggi in tal momento, Act II
Soprano
Lina Pagliughi
(CET-PP60003) 12"—P-DPX13

GUGLIELMO TELL 4 Acts 1829
(Originally in French)
Fr. Guillaume Tell Ger. Wilhelm Tell
Eng. William Tell
Overture Orchestra
Morning; The Storm; Pastorale—The
Calm; Finale—March
NBC Symphony Orch.—Toscanini
(G-DA1695/6) 2 10"—VM-605†
London Philharmonic—Beecham
(C-LX339/40) 2 12"—CX-60†
(C-LWX129/30) (C-LFX415/6)
[Handel—Musette & Minuet, arr.
Beecham]
Boston "Pops" Orch.—Fiedler
2 10"—VM-456†
(G-B8693/4) (G-EG6306/7)
National Symphony Orch.—V. Olof
2 12"—D-K1310/11†
Andre Kostelanetz & his Orch.
2 10"—CX-293†
DUPLICATIONS: Berlin State Opera
Orch.—Van Kempen, CET-OR5054/5:
PD-67581/2; Berlin Philharmonic—
Schmidt-Isserstedt, T-E1803; Milan Sym-
phony Orch.—Molajoli, C-D14454/5; De-
troit Symphony Orch.—Kolar, D-A157;
Berlin Volksoper Orch.—E. Orthmann,
G-DA4500/1; Paris Conservatory—Cop-
pola, G-DA4833/4; Berlin State Opera—
Melichar, PD-24155/6; La Scala Orch.—

Parelli, Fonit-35029/30; Victor Sym-
phony—Bourdon, V-20606; La Scala
Orch.—Panizza, G-HN792/3; Symphony
Orch.—Ruhlmann, PAT-Z96257/8;
Royal Theatre Orch., Copenhagen—
Tango, TONO-X25018/9
—Andante Pastorale only
Orchestra of violoncelli, C-DQ1547

Individual Excerpts

ACT I
Ah! Mathilde, io t'amo Tenor & Baritone
A. Pertile & B. Franci 12"—G-DB1480
[Donizetti: Favorita—Spirto gentil,
Pertile]
March of the Shepherds
Dance: Passo a sei
Symphony Orch. of Augusteo, Rome—
Serafin 12"—G-C3559
—Arr. Band: Creatore Band, G-S10459
—Passo a sei only
NBC Symphony—Toscanini (G-DB6345)
(in VM-1037†) 12"—V-11-9069
[Il Signor Bruschino—Overture]
(Also V-18-0008 in V-V2†)
Sadler's Wells Orch.—Lambert
2 10"—G-B8900/1
[With Ballet Music, Act III]
La Scala Orch.—Marinuzzi
12"—T-SKB3220
[Assedio di Corinto—Overture, Pt. 3]
London Philharmonic Orch.—Cameron
12"—D-K1454
[With Ballet Music, Act III]
Coro dell' Imeneo: Cinto il crine Chorus
La Scala Chorus—Molajoli
[Tirolese, Act III] 10"—C-GQ7138

ACT II
Selva opaca Soprano
Fr. Sombre forêt
Giannina Arangi-Lombardi
12"—C-GQX10281
[Boito: Mefistofele—Ridda e fuga,
Chorus]
Lina Pagliughi
(CET-BB25060) 12"—P-E11406
[Bizet: Pêcheurs de Perles—Comme
autrefois]
Maria Pedrini 12"—CET-CC2202
[Verdi: Trovatore—D'amore sull' ali
rosee]
DUPLICATIONS: Toti Dal Monte,
G-DB831*; R. Ponselle, CRS-15*

ACT III
Tirolese: Quel agil piè Chorus
Fr. Tyrolienne
La Scala Chorus—Molajoli
[Coro dell' Imeneo] 10"—C-GQ7138
DUPLICATION: Chorus (in French),
O-188041

Resta immobile, e ver la terra Baritone
Fr. Prière—Sois immobile, or Je te bénis
Alexander Sved 12"—CET-BB25203
[Verdi: Rigoletto—Cortigiani, vil razza]
(Different recording w. Verdi: Macbeth-
Pieta, rispetto, amore, on G-DB5366)
Benvenuto Franci 12"—G-DB1393

[Meyerbeer: Africana—Averla tanta
amata]
[Verdi: Ballo in Maschera—Eri tu, on
G-DB5390]
In French: Arthur Endrèze, PAT-
X90060; J. Beckmans, PD-516714

Ballet Music
Sadler's Wells Orch.—Lambert
[Passo a sei, Act I]
2 10"—G-B8900/1
London Philharmonic—Basil Cameron
2 12"—D-K1454/5†
[Passo a sei, Act I]

ACT IV

O muto asil del pianto Tenor
Fr. Asile héréditaire Ger. Du meiner
Väter Hütte
Francesco Merli 10"—C-GQ7145
[Verdi: Trovatore—Di quella pira]
DUPLICATIONS: H. Lazaro, C-DQ1135;
F. Tamagno, G-DR103*
In French: A. D'Arkor, C-RFX22; R.
Verdière, O-188041; L. Orliac, O-249003;
M. Gregoire, PD-522295; G. Thill,
C-LFX110

(L') ITALIANA IN ALGERI 2 Acts 1813
Overture Orchestra
New York Philharmonic-Symphony
Orch.—Toscanini 12"—V-14161
(V-11-8511 in VM-825†) (G-DB2943)
National Symphony Orch.—Fistoulari
12"—D-K1490
CBS Symphony—Barlow
12"—C-71364D
La Scala Orch.—Parelli
12"—FONIT-35027
EIAR Symphony—Previtali
12"—CET-CB20211
DUPLICATIONS: Berlin Philharmonic—
Schmidt-Isserstedt, T-E2745: U-F18080;
La Scala Orch.—Molajoli, C-D12279/80

Individual Excerpts

ACT I

Languir per una bella Tenor
Luigi Fort 10"—C-DC190
[Thomas: Mignon—Addio]

ACT II

Oh, che muso Soprano & Bass
Conchita Supervia & C. Scattola
12"—P-R20278
[Bizet: Carmen—Habañera, Supervia]

Per lui che adoro Aria & Quartet
Supervia, Ederle, Scattola, Bettoni
12"—P-PXO1021
[Cenerentola—Signore, una parola,
Supervia & Bettoni]

—Aria only
Gianna Pederzini 12"—CET-BB25092
[Cruda sorte, amor tiranno]

Cruda sorte, amor tiranno Soprano
Jennie Tourel (C-LX1054)
(in CM-691†) 12"—C-72130D
[Semiramide—Bel raggio]
Gianna Pederzini 12"—CET-BB25092
[Per lui che adoro]

MATILDA DI SHABRAN

Overture
EIAR Orch.—Tansini
12"—CET-PE102

MOSE IN EGITTO 2 or 4 Acts 1818 Eng.
Moses in Egypt

March on Motives from the Opera Arr.
Band
Royal Italian Marine Band—Aghemo
[Verdi: Ernani—March] 10"—G-HN560
DUPLICATION: Band, C-D5847

Invocazione Bass

Preghiera: Dal tuo stellato soglio Ensemble
& Chorus
N. De Angelis (bs) with E. Cheni, I.
Mannarini, E. Venturini & Chorus
12"—C-GQX10207
—Preghiera only: Turchetti, Pinza & Cho.,
G-DB698*
See also under Paganini: Fantasia on G
String arranged from the prayer.

OTELLO

Overture
EIAR Symphony Orch.—Tansini
12"—CET-CB20227

(LA) SCALA DI SETA 1812

Overture Orchestra
BBC Symphony Orch.—Toscanini
(G-DB3541) 12"—V-15191
(Also V-11-8510 in VM-825†)
London Philharmonic—Beecham
12"—C-9077M
[Handel: Solomon—Entrance of the
Queen of Sheba]
(C-LX255) (C-LFX429) (C-GQX10706)
EIAR Symphony Orch.—La Rosa Parodi
12"—CET-CB20219
Berlin State Opera Orch.—Schmidt-Isser-
stedt (U-F18077) 12"—T-E2717
Orch. Sinfonia Triennale—M. Toni
10"—G-GW1200

SEMIRAMIDE

Overture
N. Y. Philharmonic-Symphony Orch.—
Toscanini (G-DB3079/80)
(in VM-408†) 2 12"—V-14632/3
(Also V-11-8512/3 in VM-825†)
London Philharmonic—Beecham
(C-LX884/5) 2 12"—CX-215†
[Grétry: Zémire et Azor—Air de Ballet]
National Symphony Orch.—Sargent
2 12"—D-K1475/6†
DUPLICATIONS: La Scala Orch.—Parel-
li, FONIT-35025/6; Milan Symphony—
Molajoli, C-D14458/9; Victor Symphony
—Bourdon, G-HN469; La Scala Orch.—
Guarnieri, G-S10102/3

Ah, quel giorno ognor rammento Soprano
Ebe Stignani 12"—CET-BB25066
[Verdi: Ballo in Maschera—Re dell
abisso]

Bel raggio lusinghier Act I Soprano
Jennie Tourel (C-LX1054)
(in CM-691†) 12"—C-72130D

[L'Italiana in Algeri—Cruda sorte]
Lina Pagliughi
(in CET-8)   12"—CET-BB25110
[Bizet: Carmen—Micaela's Aria]
Rose Bampton   12"—V-18217
[Cenerentola—Nacqui all'affanno]
Celestina Boninsegna   12"—CRS-11*
[Ponchielli: La Gioconda—Suicidio!]

(IL) SIGNOR BRUSCHINO

Overture. Orchestra
NBC Symphony Orch.—Toscanini
(in VM-1037†)   12"—V-11-9069
(Also V-18-0008 in V-V2†) (G-DB6345)
[Guglielmo Tell—Passo a sei]
La Scala Orch.—Marinuzzi
12"—G-DB3209
[Giordano: Siberia—La Pasqua]
EIAR Symphony Orch.—Tansini
12"—CET-CB20215
[Paisiello: Nina, o la pazza per amore—
Overture]

TANCREDI 1813

Overture Orchestra
EIAR Orch.—La Rosa Parodi
(CET-CB20184)   12"—P-E11338
La Scala Orch.—Parelli
12"—FONIT-35033
National Symphony Orch.—Victor Olof
12"—D-K1324
Royal Opera Orch.—Bellezza
12"—G-C1998

(UN) VIAGGIO A REIMS (L'Albergo del Giglio d'Oro)

Overture
EIAR Symphony Orch.—Tansini
12"—CET-CB20223
La Scala Orch.—Ghione 12"—G-DB5403

Péchés de vieillesse
See under Miscellaneous: Matinées Musicales & Soirées Musicales

Quartet, F major Flute, Clarinet, Horn, Bassoon
Soloists of Vienna Philharmonic Orch.
2   10"—G-DA4483/4

Rossiniana—Ballet Suite
See under Miscellaneous

Soirées Musicales
See under Miscellaneous

SONG In Italian

(La) Danza Tarantella Napolitana (Pepoli)
Jan Peerce (t) (G-DA1856)
(in VM-1099)   10"—V-10-1274
[di Capua: O sole mio]
Beniamino Gigli (t)   10"—G-DA1650
[Tosti: Marechiare]
Gino Sinimberghi (t)   12"—PD-25888
[Tosti: Marechiare]
Richard Tauber (t) (in German)
[Cottrau: Santa Lucia] 10"—P-RO20474
Jan Kiepura (t) & W. Rebner (pf)
10"—C-17332D
[Wieniawski: Kujawiak, arr. of Mazurka, A minor, Op. 3]

Miliza Korjus (s)   12"—V-11-8289
(G-C2813) (G-EH937)
[Denza: Funiculì, Funiculà]
DUPLICATIONS: Jan Kiepura,
P-RO20201: O-166567; Joseph Schmidt,
P-DP8; L. Infantino, C-BQ6018; Giorgio
Sempri, G-DA4967; Heddle Nash,
C-DB961; Rosetta Pampanini,
C-GQ7066; Julius Patzak, PD-25011; E.
Caruso, G-DB141*

STABAT MATER In Latin

No. 2, Cujus animam Tenor
Jussi Björling
(G-DB3665)   12"—V-13588
[Verdi: Requiem—Ingemisco, tanquam reus]
Beniamino Gigli
(G-DB1831)   12"—V-8768
[Stradella: Pietà Signore]
DUPLICATIONS: A. Melandri,
C-GQX10092; Caruso, G-DB138*

William Tell See under Operas—Gugliemo Tell

MISCELLANEOUS

(La) Boutique Fantasque—Ballet Suite

—Arr. Respighi (from Rossini piano pieces, etc.)
London Philharmonic Orch.—Goossens
3   12"—VM-415†
(G-C2646/8) (G-EH977/9)
(G-S10468/70)

Selections
London Philharmonic Orch.—Goehr
(C-LFX534)   12"—C-DX848

Matinées Musicales

—Arr. Britten (Second Suite of Five Movements after Rossini)
(from "Guglielmo Tell" & "Péchés de vieillesse")

March; Nocturne; Waltz; Pantomime; Moto perpetuo
Boston "Pops" Orch.—Fiedler
3   10"—VM-1204†
[Soirées Musicales—Tarantella]

Rossiniana—Ballet Suite

—Arr. Respighi (from Rossini piano pieces, etc.)
London Philharmonic Orch.—Beecham
2   12"—CX-240†

Soirées Musicales

—Arr. Britten (First Suite of Five Movements after Rossini)
(from "Guglielmo Tell" & "Péchés de vieillesse")

March; Canzonetta; Tyrolese; Bolero; Tarantella
Charles Brill Orch.   2 12"—D-K873/4
[Britten: Village Harvest—Irish Reel]

—**Tarantella** only
Boston "Pops" Orch.—Fiedler
(in VM-1204†)   10"—V-10-1401
[Matinées Musicales, Pt. 5]

ROUSSEAU, Jean Jacques (1712-1778)

This Swiss-born, but very French "philosophe" whose musical training was of very slender proportions, was not reluctant to write volumes on musical theory and practice. "Le Devin du village" was only one of his many compositions and it was written, Rousseau tells us, to show composers the superior merit of the Italian as against the French style. A comic-pastoral opera, it held the boards for seventy-five years and deeply influenced the course of the French "opéra-comique."

LE DEVIN DU VILLAGE Opera in French 1752

Overture Orchestra
Winterthur Municipal Orch.
　　　　　　　　　12″—G-DB6094
[Tartini: Violin Concerto, E major, Pt. 3]

Airs de Collette Soprano
J'ai perdu mon serviteur
Si des galans de la ville
Avec l'objet de mes amours
Allons danser sous les ormeaux
Martha Angelici & Orch.—Curt Sachs
　　　　　(in Vol. VI)　12″—AS-54
—**Unspecified Air** Baritone
Reynaldo Hahn & self pf. acc.
　　　　　　　　　10″—C-D2022
[Offenbach: La Boulangère a des Ecus]

ROUSSEL, Albert (1869-1937)

A prolific composer in almost every form, Roussel was a mild modernist with catholic taste. Three chief influences—travel in the Far East, the teaching of D'Indy, and the music of Debussy—moulded his musical personality.

(Le) Festin de l'Araignée, Op. 17 Ballet
Symphony Orch.—Albert Roussel
　　　　　3　10″—PAT-X8829/31
(with "vocal autograph")
Straram Orch.—Walther Straram
　　　　　2　12″—C-LFX47/8
Joueurs de Flûte, Op. 27 Flute & Piano
1. Pan 2. Tityre 3. Krishna 4. M. de la Péjaudie
—**Nos. 1, 2 & 4 only**
Marcel Moyse & J. Benvenuti
　　　　　　　　　10″—C-DF1800

Petite Suite, Op. 39 Orchestra
Paris Conservatory Orch.—Charles
Münch　　　　　2 12″—D-ED37†
[Faure: Pavane, Op. 50] (D-K1643/4)
Quartet—Strings D major, Op. 45 1931/2
Roth Quartet　　　3　12″—CM-339†
Sérénade, Op. 30
Pierre Jamet Instrumental Quintet
　　　　　2　12″—G-DB11124/5
Sinfonietta 1934
NBC String Symphony—Frank Black
　　　(in VM-455†)　12″—V-12233
Orchestre Féminin—Evard
　　　　　　　　　12″—G-W1596
SONGS In French
Ciel aer et vens Old French Song Arr.
Roussel
A. Noordewier-Reddingius (s) & Organ
acc.　　　　　　12″—C-D15839
[Anon: Noël Provençal]

Coeur en péril (René Chalupt)
Pierre Bernac (b) & Francis Poulenc
(pf)　　　　　　10″—G-DA4918
[Le jardin mouillé]
(Le) Jardin Mouillé, Op. 3, No. 3
Pierre Bernac (b) & Francis Poulenc
(pf)　　　　　　10″—G-DA4918
[Coeur en péril]
Réponse d'une Epouse sage, Op. 35, No. 2
Irène Joachim (s) & Jean Germain (pf)
　　　　　　　　　10″—BAM-48
[Jaubert: La Chanson de Tessa]
Suite for Piano, Op. 14 Piano
—**Ronde only**
Lucette Descaves-Truc 12″—G-DB11138
[Pierné: Etude de concert]
Symphony No. 3, G minor, Op. 42
(Composed for the 50th Anniversary of the Boston Symphony Orch., 1930)
Lamoureux Orch.—Albert Wolff
　　　　　3　12″—PD-566126/8

ROZSA, Miklos

A contemporary composer for the film.

(THE) JUNGLE BOOK Music for the Film
(Kipling)
Sabu (narrator) & Victor Concert Orch.
—Rozsa　　　3　12″—VM-905†

(THE) RED HOUSE Music for the Film—
Selections
Symphony Orch.—Rozsa
　　　　　2　10″—CAP-CB48

SPELLBOUND Music for the Film
—**Excerpt only** Arr. Goodman
Al Goodman and his Orch.
　　　　　　　　　12″—V-28-0404
[Rachmaninoff: Concerto No. 2, arr. Goodman]
Queen's Hall Light Orch.—Charles Williams　　　　　12″—C-DX1264
[Spoliansky: A Voice in the Night]

RUBBRA, Edmund (1901-　　)

A modern English composer associated with the contemporary renaissance in British musical life.

Sonata No. 2, Op. 31 Violin & Piano 1932
Albert Sammons & Gerald Moore
　　　　　2　12″—G-C3547/8

RUBINSTEIN, Anton (1830-1894)

A keyboard virtuoso in the Lisztian tradition, Rubinstein was a prolific composer. His works range from salon pieces to rather ambitious compositions for the lyric stage.

Kamenoi-Ostrow, Op. 10
NOTE: *This opus is a set of 24 "Portraits" for piano solo, of which the best known is No. 22, titled variously "Rêve angelique" or "Kamenoï-Ostrow."*

—**No. 22** Arr. Orchestra Victor Herbert
Boston "Pops" Orch.—Fiedler
　　　　　　　　　12″—V-12191
Victor Symphony Orch.—Bourdon
(G-C1352)　　　　12″—V-35820
[Liszt: Liebestraum]

Melody in F, Op. 3, No. 1 Piano
 Mark Hambourg 10"—**G-B4385**
 [Schumann: Slumber Song]
 William Murdoch 10"—**D-F7497**
 [Sinding: Rustle of Spring]

—Arr. Orchestra
 CBS Symphony—Barlow 12"—**C-71464D**
 [Mussorgsky: Fair at Sorotchinsk-Hopak;
 Ippolitov-Ivanov: Procession of the Sar-
 dar]
 Victor Concert Orch.—Bourdon
 [Romance, Op. 44, No. 1] 10"—**G-B3783**
 Symphony Orch.—Melichar
 [Feramors-Lichtertanz] 12"—**PD-27183**
 DUPLICATIONS: Alfredo Campoli Salon
 Orch., D-F6836; Harry Horlick Salon
 Orch., D-F6942

—Arr. 'Cello & Piano Popper
 Pierre Fournier & Gerald Moore,
 G-DA1868; Casals & Mednikoff, V-1178:
 G-DA833; G. Piatigorsky, in CM-684; H.
 Bottermund, PD-23628

—Arr. Violin & Piano: Yvonne Curti, PAT-
 PA502
 See current catalogues for miscellaneous
 arrangements.

OPERAS In Russian & German

(THE) DEMON 3 Acts In Russian 1875
Do not weep, my child Act II
I am he whom you called Act III Baritone
 or Bass
 L. M. Sibiriakoff 10"—**G-EK52**

FERAMORS (LALLA ROOKH) 3 Acts In
 German 1863

Lichtertanz der Braute Orchestra
 Eng. **Candle-Dance of the Brides of
 Kashmir**
 Symphony Orch.—Melichar
 12"—**PD-27183**
 [Melody in F, arr. Melichar]

Rêve angelique See under Kamenoï-Ostrow

Romance, E flat, Op. 44, No. 1 Piano
 (from a set of 6 pieces, "Soirées de St.
 Petersbourg")
—Arr. Orchestra
 Andre Kostelanetz & his Orch., in
 CM-681; Victor Concert Orch.—Bourdon,
 G-B3783

SONGS In Russian or German

Come back my love (Miller)
 Richard Tauber (t) (in English)
 [Provost: Intermezzo] 10"—**P-RO20508**

Extases
 Charles Soix (b) (in French) & André
 Tournier (pf) 12"—**PAT-PDT112**
 [Mussorgsky: Field Marshal Death]

Gold rolls here below me, Op. 34, No. 9
 (Mirza-Schaffy)
 Feodor Chaliapin (bs) (in Russian)
 [Massenet: Elégie] 12"—**G-DB1525**

Persian Songs, Op. 34 (Mirza-Schaffy)
 See: Gold rolls here below me & The Rose

(The) Prisoner, Op. 78, No. 6
 Feodor Chaliapin (bs) (in Russian), &
 Jean Bazilevsky (pf) 12"—**V-15236**
 [Trad. Black Eyes] (G-DB3463)

(The) Rose, Op. 34, No. 4 (Mirza-Schaffy)
 Ada Slobodskaya (s) (in Russian) &
 Kahn (pf) 10"—**G-EK113**
 [Rachmaninoff: Lilacs & Mussorgsky:
 Fair at Sorotchinsk—Parassia's Day
 Dream]

Toréador et Andalouse, Op. 103, No. 7
 (from a set of 20 pieces, "Bal costumé,"
 originally for Piano 4-Hands)
—Arr. Orchestra
 Berlin Philharmonic—J. Prüwer
 12"—**PD-95254**
 [Meyerbeer: Prophète—Coronation
 March]
 DUPLICATION: Royal Artillery String
 Orch., D-F7463

Valse caprice Piano
 Artur Rubinstein 12"—**V-36337**
 [Liszt: Liebestraum] (G-DB2702)
 Ignace Jan Paderewski 12"—**V-6877**
 [Chopin: Waltz, E flat, Op. 18]
 (G-DB1273)
—Arr. Voice Brossement
 Adele Kern, PD-27287

Miscellaneous Transcriptions
 See under Beethoven: Ruinen von Athen
 Turkische Marsch

RUDEL, Jaufré (13th Century)

Canto rossinhols

Lanquan li Jonn
 Chanterelle (Simone Gebelin)
 (s, unacc.) 10"—**BAM-45**
 [Riquier: Chanson religieuse & Bernard
 de Ventadour: Can vei la lauzeta]

RUE, Pierre de la (d.1518)

*A contemporary of Josquin and Obrecht,
 Pierre de la Rue was in the service of the
 Burgundian Court.*

Autant en emporte le vent
 Ensemble of medieval viols, lute, harp
 and flutes
 Pro Musica Antiqua, Brussels—Cape
 (in Vol. III) 12"—**AS-27**
 [Obrecht: Tsat een meskin & Brasart: O
 Flos Flagrans]

O Salutaris Hostia
 Strasbourg Cathedral Choir.—
 A. Hoch 12"—**C-RFX73**
 [Josquin des Prés: O Domine Jesu
 Christe]

RUEGEN, (Prince) Wislaw von (fl.c.1280)

*A German prince who, in the best medieval
 tradition, was also a "Minnesinger."*

Wie ich han gedacht
 Minnelied in German
 Hans Joachim Moser (b) unacc.
 10"—**P-R1018**
 [Troubadour Songs & Minnelieder]
 (in 2000 Years of Music set)

RUMELANT, Meister (13th Century)

One of the many German Minnesänger of the twelfth and thirteenth centuries who followed the lead of the French Troubadours and Trouvères.

Ob aller mynne mynnen kraft
Minnesong in German
Max Meili (t) unacc.
(in Vol. II)   12″—AS-18

RUNG, Henrik (1807-1851)

A Danish conductor and composer who was, for many years, the chorus-master at the Copenhagen Royal Opera.

SONGS In Danish
Hvor Nilen Vander Aegypterens Jord
Lauritz Melchior (t) cho. & pf.
(G-DA5211) (in VM-851)   10″—V-2191
[Lange-Müller: I Würzburg Ringe der Klokker]
Aksel Schiøtz (t) & H. D. Koppel (pf)
10″—G-X6632
[Ring: Danmark, nu blunder den lyse Nat]
I Danmark er jeg født
Aksel Schiøtz (t)   10″—G-X7202
[Moders Navn er enhimmelsk Lyd]
[Tarp: Her ha Hjertet hjemme, on G-X6646]
Kimar I Klokker
Elsa Sigfuss
(also O-D910)   10″—G-X6174
Paaskeklokken kimed' mildt
Aksel Schiøtz   10″—G-X6240
[Heise: Det var paa Isted Hede]

RUTINI, Giovanni Marco (Placido)
(1723-1797)

Musical director at the Courts of Modena and Tuscany, Rutini composed operas, cantatas, church music and piano sonatas.

Andante Piano
Ruggero Gerlin
(in Vol. X)   12″—AS-95
[Matielli: Adagio & Martini: Allegro]
Minuet Piano
Emma Boynet   10″—PD-561145
[Vinci: Largo]
Sonata, A major
Ruggero Gerlin (harpsichord)
12″—MIA-12

RYYGAARD

SONGS In Danish
Danmark
Fliget
Lauritz Melchior (t)
(G-DA5212) (in VM-851)   10″—V-2192

SABATA, Victor de (1892-)

A pupil of Orefice, de Sabata is a well known conductor who has recorded for several European companies.

Juventus Symphonic Poem
EIAR Orch.—de Sabata
2 12″—CET-PP60006/7

SACCHINI, Antonio (1734-1786)

A native of Florence and a fellow pupil of Piccini in Durante's classes in Naples, Sacchini for a time went to England and thence to Paris where he was completely won over by the greatness of Gluck's "tragedies."

(LA) NITETTI Opera in Italian
Two Arias
Rondo di Nitetti: (Soprano)
"In amor la gelosia è follia del nostro ver"
Air d'Amagi: (Tenor)
"Puoi vantar le tue ritorte"
Martha Angelici (s), Yvon le Marc' Hadour (t), chamber orchestra—R. Gerlin
(Pauline Aubert, harpsichord)
(in Vol. IX)   12″—AS-82
[Cesti: Il Pomo d'oro—Air de Venus]
Sonata, F major Harpsichord
Ruggero Gerlin   12″—MIA-10

SAEVERUD, Harald (1797-)
A contemporary Norwegian composer.

Bruremarsj ("Peer Gynt")
Rondo Amoroso, Op. 14, No. 7
Robert Riefling (pf)   10″—G-DA11902
Bån-låt, Op. 21, No. 3
Små-Sveinsganger, Op. 14, No. 1
Kjaempevise-slåtten, Op. 22, No. 5
Robert Riefling (pf)   12″—G-DB11903

SAINT-SAENS, Camille (1835-1921)

A French composer who wrote music which, if seldom truly inspired, was always of impeccable craftsmanship.

Allegro Appassionato, Op. 43 'Cello & Piano
B. Michelin & T. Janopoulo
12″—C-LFX750
[Boccherini: 'Cello Concerto, B flat major—Adagio]

Allegro Appassionato, Op. 70 Piano
José Iturbi   10″—V-10-1315

Ave Verum, E flat major Chorus in Latin
Petit Séminaire Chorus—Abbé Vallet
[Laudate Dominum]   10″—LUM-30056

Caprice on the airs de ballet from Gluck's "Alceste" Piano
Guiomar Novaës   12″—C-71961D

(Le) Carnaval des Animaux
Orchestra & Pianos
Eng. The Carnival of the Animals
(Grand Zoölogical Fantasy)
**Introduction et Marche royale du lion;
Poules et coqs; Hémiones; Tortues;
L'Eléphant; Kangourous; Aquarium; Personnages à longues oreilles; Volière; Le Coucou au fond des bois; Pianistes; Fossiles; Le Cygne; Finale**
Philadelphia Orch.—Stokowski
(G-DB5942/4)   3 12″—VM-785†
(Earlier recording: G-AW261/3: G-W1184/6)
Symphony Orch.—Georges Truc
(C-9519/22)   4 12″—C-12504/7
—**Le Cygne only**   Eng. The Swan
'Cello & Piano
Pierre Fournier & Gerald Moore,
G-DA1868; Pablo Casals, V-1143:

G-DA776; Gregor Piatigorsky, C-17445D in CM-501; Raya Garbousova, V-11-8869 in VM-1017; André Navarra, O-188931; C. Sharpe, D-F7630; A. Földesy, PD-25026; Marcelli-Herson, G-K6472: G-K5234; Flachot, PD-521819; G. Crepax, C-D5830; G. Cassadó, C-D1600; F. Salmond, C-D16403; H. Bottermund, PD-23628; Krabansky, LUM-30092

—Arr. Violin & Piano
Mischa Elman, G-DA1143; W. Schneiderman, C-DB1058

—Arr. Organ
M. Dupré, G-P789

—Arr. Orchestra
Andre Kostelanetz & his Orch., in CM-681; Decca Salon Orch., D-F6941; Lamoureux Orch.—Wolff, PD-66957: PD-566017; Alfred Campoli Salon Orch., D-F6464
See current catalogues for miscellaneous arrangements

CONCERTOS　Piano & Orchestra

No. 2, G minor, Op. 22
Moura Lympany & National Symphony—Braithwaite　　　3 12"—D-ED24†
(D-K1161/3)
Benno Moiseiwitsch & Philharmonia Orch.—Cameron　　　3 12"—G-C3588/90†

No. 4, C minor, Op. 44
Robert Casadesus & N. Y. Philharmonic-Symphony—Rodzinski　3 12"—CM-566†
Alfred Cortot & Orch.—Münch
(G-DB2577/9)　　　　3 12"—VM-367†

CONCERTOS　Violin & Orchestra

No. 3, B minor, Op. 61
Henri Merckel & Symphony Orch.
　　　　　　　　　3 12"—G-L1000/2
Louis Kaufman & Santa Monica Symphony Orch.—Rachmilovich
　　　　　　　　　3 12"—DISC-805

CONCERTOS　'Cello & Orchestra

No. 1, A minor, Op. 33
Gregor Piatigorsky & Chicago Symphony Orch.—Stock　　2 12"—CX-182†
André Navarra & Colonne Orch.—J. Fournet　　　2 12"—G-DB11176/7

Danse Macabre, Op. 40 Symphonic Poem
(See also under Songs—Danse macabre)
Philadelphia Orch.—Stokowski
(G-DB3077)　　　　12"—V-14162
(Older version G-AW4182)
Chicago Symphony Orch.—Stock
(C-LX910)　　　　　12"—C-11251D
Paris Symphony—Gaubert
(C-DFX205)　　　　12"—C-DX121
DUPLICATIONS: Opéra-Comique Orch.—Cloëz, O-170027; Symphony Orch.—Coppola, G-L654; Berlin Philharmonic—Fried, PD-95204; Symphony Orch.—Ruhlmann, PAT-X96092

—Arr. Piano　Liszt-Horowitz
Vladimir Horowitz　(G-DB6275)
　　(in VM-1001†)　12"—V-11-8776

—Arr. 2 Pianos　Saint-Saëns
Pierre Luboshutz & Genia Nemenoff
　　　　　　　　　12"—V-18486

(LE) DELUGE, Op. 45
Poème biblique　1875
Oratorio for Soloists, Chorus & Orchestra

Prélude　Violin & Orchestra
Roland Charmy & Lamoureux Orch.—Wolff　　　　　　12"—PD-566164
[Rabaud: Procession Nocturne, Pt. 3]
Jacques Thibaud & De Lausney (pf)
　　　　　　　　　12"—G-DB1338
[Falla: Vida Breve—Danza Española No. 1]
DUPLICATION: H. Volant, C-DF958

Etude in forme de valse, Op. 52, No. 6
Alfred Cortot　　　12"—G-DB1535
[Liszt: La Leggerezza]

Fantasie pour Harpe, Op. 95
Lily Laskine　　　　10"—G-DA5010

Havanaise, Op. 83
Violin & Piano (or Orchestra)
Jascha Heifetz & London Symphony Orch.—Barbirolli　　12"—V-15347
(G-DB3211)
DUPLICATIONS: Jacques Thibaud & T. Janopoulo, G-DB1990; Miguel Candela & J. Benvenuti, C-LFX332

Introduction & Rondo capriccioso, Op. 28
Violin & Piano (or Orchestra)
Jascha Heifetz & London Philharmonic—Barbirolli　　12"—V-14115
(G-DB2580)
Ida Haendel & National Symphony Orch.—Cameron　　12"—D-K1171
Alfredo Campoli & London Philharmonic—Goehr (C-DX902)　12"—C-69640D

(La) Jeunesse d'Hercule, Op. 50
Lamoureux Orch.—E. Bigot
　　　　　　　　2 12"—PAT-PDT147/8

Laudate Dominum, F major
2-Part Chorus in Latin
Chorale du Petit Séminaire de Paris—Abbé Vallet　　10"—LUM-30056
[Ave Verum]

Marche héroïque, Op. 34　Orchestra
Colonne Orch.—Pierné　12"—O-123749
DUPLICATION: Ruhlmann Orch., PAT-X96228

OPERAS　In French

ETIENNE MARCEL　4 Acts　1879
No recordings available

HENRI VIII　4 Acts　1883

Jig & Finale (Ballet Divertissement)
National Symphony Orchestra—Walter Damrosch (in VM-878†)　12"—V-18426
[Shakespeare: Macbeth, Evans & Anderson, Pt. 9]

(LA) PRINCESSE JAUNE, Op. 30
1 Act　1872
Eng. The Yellow Princess

Overture   Orchestra
  Berlin Philharmonic—Melichar
  (PD-522687)   10″—PD-25189
  Paris Conservatory Orch.—Cluytens
                       10″—G-DA4965

SAMSON ET DALILA, Op. 47
3 Acts   1877
Complete recording
  Paris Opera Soloists, Chorus & Orch.—
  Louis Fourestier
              15 12″—PAT-PDT116/30
  The Cast:
  Dalila .... Hélène Bouvier (ms)
  Samson .... José Luccioni (t)
  Abimelech ...... Charles Cambon (b)
  Le Grand Prêtre .... Paul Cabanel (bs)
  Viellard Hébreu .... M. Médus

Individual Excerpts

ACT I

Arrêtez ô mes frères!   Tenor & Chorus
It. Figli miei, v'arrestate
—Tenor part only (in Italian)
  F. Tamagno, G-DR101*

Maudite à jamais soit la race   Bass
  (Air of the High Priest)
  Arthur Endrèze   12″—PAT-PDT18
  [Berlioz: Damnation de Faust—Voici
  des Roses]
  [Rossini: Guglielmo Tell—Prayer, on
  PAT-X90060]

Je viens célébrer la victoire   Trio
  Caruso, Homer, Journet
            (in VM-953)   12″—V-16-5003*
  [Gounod: Faust—Trio]
  [Verdi: Lombardi—Qual volutta, on
  G-DM126*]

Dance of the Priestesses
  Included on P-DPX21 in P-P53:
  CET-BB25005
  (See below: Printemps qui commence)

Printemps qui commence   Mezzo-soprano
It. Apriele foriero
Ger. Die Sonne, sie lachte
Eng. Fair Spring is returning
  Bruno Castagna   12″—C-71058D
  [Mon coeur s'ouvre]
  Eliette Schenneberg   12″—C-LFX642
  [Mon coeur]
  Ebe Stignani (in Italian)
            (in P-P53)   12″—P-DPX21
  [with Dance of the Priestesses]
  (CET-BB25005)
  (Different recording, G-DA5385)
  DUPLICATIONS: Sigrid Onegin, V-7320;
  Jeanne Montfort, PD-516620; Germaine
  Cernay, C-LFX262; Alice Raveau,
  PAT-X7222; Piroska Anday, RAD-
  SP8006
  In Italian: Aurora Buades, C-GQX10161
  In German: Friedel Beckmann,
  G-DB596
  In English: Gladys Ripley, G-C3404

ACT II

Samson, recherchant ma présence   Recit.
Amour! viens aider ma faiblesse
  Aria   Mezzo-Soprano

It. Amor! I miei sini proteggi
Eng. O love from thy power
Ger. O Liebe, meinem Hass steh zur Seite
  Gladys Swarthout   12″—V-14143
  [Mon coeur s'ouvre]
  Bruna Castagna   12″—C-71390D
  [Massenet: Werther—Ces lettres]
  Marian Anderson (in English)
  [Mon coeur] (G-C2047) 12″—V-18008
  In Italian: Ebe Stignani, CET-BB25045:
  P-DPX23 in P-P53

Mon coeur s'ouvre à ta voix
  Mezzo-soprano & Tenor
It. S'apre per te il mio cor
Ger. Sieh', mein Herz erschliesset sich
Eng. Softly awakes my heart (or, My
Heart at thy sweet voice)

Complete version
  Germaine Cernay & Georges Thill
  (C-LX385) (C-LFX310) 12″—C-9109M
  (C-GQX10854)
  DUPLICATION: Mme. Duchène & César
  Vezzani, G-DA4819

—Mon coeur s'ouvre
  (Dalila's aria only)
  Gladys Swarthout   12″—V-14143
  [Amour viens aider]
  Risë Stevens
            (in CM-676)   12″—C-71974D
  [Bizet: Carmen—Seguidilla, with Jobin]
  Eliette Schenneberg   12″—C-LFX642
  [Printemps qui commence]
  Bruna Castagna   12″—C-71058D
  [Printemps qui commence]
  DUPLICATIONS: Sigrid Onegin, V-7320;
  Marguerite Matzenauer, V-36287; Laure
  Tessandra, O-188030; Luci Perelli,
  G-P678; Alice Raveau, PAT-X7222;
  Piroska Anday, RAD-SP8006
  In Italian: Ebe Stignani, P-DPX22 in
  P-P53: CET-BB25044: C-LX976; Irene
  Minghini-Cattaneo, G-DB1303; Aurora
  Buades, C-CQ351
  In German: Friedel Beckmann, G-DB5596
  In English: Marian Anderson, V-18008:
  G-C2047; Muriel Brunskill, C-3328
  Also: Albert Sandler, C-DB14
  See current catalogues for other
  arrangements

Vois ma misère, hélas!   Tenor & Chorus
  (Air de le meule)
  Georges Thill & Cho.   12″—C-LFX430
  DUPLICATIONS: Franz, Chorus,
  PAT-X90043; E. Caruso, G-DB136*

L'Aube qui blanchit
  EIAR Chorus (in Italian)
            (in P-P53)   12″—P-DPX22
  (CET-BB25044)
  [Mon coeur s'ouvre à ta voix, Stignani,
  Pt 2.]

Bacchanale (Ballet Music)   Orchestra
  Boston "Pops" Orch.—Fiedler
                       12″—V-12318
  Philadelphia Orch.—Stokowski
                       12″—G-D1307
  [Berlioz: Rakoczy March] (G-AW160)
  Milan Symphony—Molajoli
                       12″—C-GQX10756

DUPLICATIONS: Lamoureux Orch.—
Wolff, PD-67013: PD-566015; Ruhlmann
Orch., PAT-X96109; La Scala Orch.—
Jonel Perlea, In Prep. (English Decca)

ORATORIO DE NOEL, Op. 12
Soloists, Chorus & Orchestra
Eng. **Christmas Oratorio** In Latin

Individual Excerpts

No. 2, Gloria in Altissimis Chorus
St. Nicolas Choir   10"—LUM-30005
[No. 5]

No. 5, Benedictus Soprano & Tenor
Doniau-Blanc & Payen
[No. 2]   10"—LUM-30005

No. 7, Tecum Principium Trio
Doniau-Blanc, Arnaldez, Delmotte
                        12"—LUM-32004
[Caplet: Symbole des Apôtres]
DUPLICATION: Cantorum Soloists,
PAT-X93039

No. 10, Tollite Hostias Chorus
Cantorum Choir—P. Fauchet
[No. 7]   10"—PAT-X93039

PARYSATIS
Incidental Music to Dieulafoy's Drama

Le Rossignol et la Rose Soprano
(Wordless vocalise from the Ballet
Music)
Eng. **The Nightingale and the Rose**
No recording available

Phaëton, Op. 39 Symphonic Poem
Paris Conservatory Orch.—Coppola
                        12"—G-DB4807
Symphony Orch.—Fournet
                        12"—PAT-PDT63

Prélude, E flat major, Op. 99 Organ
(from 3 Préludes & Fugues, Book 1)
Marcel Dupré (Queen's Hall Organ)
[Le Cygne]   10"—G-P789

Romance, F minor, Op. 36
French Horn & Orchestra
Jean Devemy & Lamoureux Orch.
                        12"—PD-66968
[Mussorgsky: Gopak & Rimsky-
Korsakov: Flight of the Bumble Bee]
(PD-566026)

(Le) Rouet d'Omphale, Op. 31
Symphonic Poem
Eng. **Omphale's Spinning Wheel**
Royal Philharmonic Orch.—
Beecham   12"—V-12-0152
National Symphony Orch.—
Kindler   12"—V-18358
Paris Conservatory Orch.—Münch
                        12"—D-K1695
Liverpool Philharmonic Orch.—
Sargent   12"—C-DX1151
Lamoureux Orch.—Bigot
                        12"—PAT-PDT134
DUPLICATIONS: Paris Conservatory
Orch.—Gaubert, C-D15017; Lamoureux
Orch.—Wolff, PD-66994: PD-566046

Samson et Dalila See under Operas

Scherzo for 2 Pianos, Op. 87
Mlle. Herrenschmidt & M. I. Philipp
                     2 12"—PD-561143/4

SONATAS—Violin & Piano
No. 1, D minor, Op. 75
André Pascal & Isidore Philipp
(PAT-PAT15/17)   3 12"—CM-471†

SONATAS—'Cello & Piano
No. 1, C minor, Op. 32
Paul Bazelaire & Isidore Philipp
                     3 12"—PAT-PAT12/4
No. 2, F major, Op. 123
—2nd & 3rd Mvts. only
(Romanza & Scherzo con variazione)
Paul Bazelaire & Isidore Philipp
                     2 12"—PAT-PAT92/3

SONGS In French
(Le) Bonheur est chose légère (Barbier)
Lily Pons (s), in CM-720
(La) Cloche (Victor Hugo)
Germaine Cernay (s)   12"—C-LFX262
[Samson—Printemps qui commence]
Danse macabre (Henri Cazalis)
Nelson Eddy (b)   10"—C-17309D
[Tchaikovsky: Don Juan's Serenade]
Norman Cordon (bs)   10"—V-2165
[Strauss: Traum durch die Dämmerung]
(Le) Pas d'armes du Roi Jean
(Victor Hugo)
Narçon (b)   12"—C-RFX8
[Berlioz: Enfance du Christ—O misère
des Rois]
La Rossignol et la Rose
See under Parysatis

Suite Algérienne, Op. 60 Orchestra
—No. 3 (Rêverie) & No. 4 (Marche) only
Symphony Orch.—Coppola, G-L718

Symphony No. 3, C minor, Op. 78
Organ, 2 Pianos & Orchestra
A. Cellier, Herbrecht, Petijean & Sym-
phony Orch.—Coppola   4 12"—VM-100†
(G-W1092/5) (G-AW220/3)

Variations on a Theme of Beethoven, Op 35
2 Pianos
(Minuet of Beethoven's Piano Sonata No.
18, E flat major, Op. 31. No. 3)
No recording available

Wedding Cake (Valse caprice) Op. 76
Piano & Strings
Yvonne Arnaud & Orch.—Barbirolli
                        12"—G-C2455
[Haydn: Piano Concerto, D major—
Rondo all' Ungarese]

SAMAZEUILH, Gustave (1877-   )
*One of the many Vincent d'Indy pupils at the
Schola Cantorum, Samazeuilh was both critic
and composer.*

(Le) Cercle des heures Contralto & Or-
chestra
Eliette Schenneberg & Paris Conservatory
Orch.—Samazeuilh   12"—G-W1564
Nuit Poem for Orchestra
Paris Conservatory Orch.—Samazeuilh
                        12"—G-W1563

SAMMARTINI, Giovanni (1700-1775)

Another eighteenth century Italian composer more honored in the history of music than in the music that reaches the contemporary audience. An organist and choirmaster in many Italian churches, his output was prodigious—said to exceed two thousand works.

Concerto No. 1
—Andantes I & II only
String Quartet   12"—SEMS-1148

Sonata, G major
—Arr. 'Cello & Piano J. Salmon
Florence Hooten & Ross Platt
           12"—D-K909

Trio Sonata, No. 5 2 Recorders & Harpsichord
Spieleinung, Berlin   10"—G-EG3976
[Handel: Sonata, G minor, Op. 2, No. 2—Andante]

SAMMARTINI, Giuseppe (c.1693-1750)

A brilliant oboe virtuoso and composer, Sammartini's main creative years were spent in London where he played in the opera orchestra, and was later musical director of chamber concerts to the Prince of Wales. He is often called "St. Martini of London" to distinguish him from his more celebrated brother, Giovanni.

Canto amoroso Arr. Violin
(Transcription of the 3rd Mvt.—Andante expressivo—of a violin sonata in A minor, edited by Moffat.)
C. F. Cillario   10"—G-DA5412
[Dinicu-Heifetz: Hora Staccato]

SANTA MARIA, Tomás de (d.1580)

A Spanish organist, lutenist and Dominican Monk, Santa Maria was a sixteenth century composer of instrumental music.

Clausula de octavo tono Organ
Joseph Bonnet
       (in Vol. VII)   12"—AS-69
[Cabanilles: Tiento; Cabezón: Differencias sobre el Canto del Caballero]

Fantasia Tertii Toni Organ
Finn Viderø (Compenius Organ, Frederiksborg Castle)   10"—G-DA5207
[Le Bégue: Les Cloches; Cabezón: Tiento del Primer Tono]

Harmonization of a Melody (unidentified)
André Marchal (Gonzalez organ)
       12"—PAT-PAT65
[Cabezón: Tiento del Primer Tono; Cabanilles: Passacaille, D minor, with F. Mihatsch, org.]
(in 3 Centuries of Organ Music)

SARASATE, Pablo De (1844-1908)

One of the most prominent nineteenth century virtuosos of the violin, Sarasate was also the composer of innumerable character pieces calculated to display his violinistic prowess and transfer into the violin literature the wealth of melody and rhythm of his native Spain.

Adios montañas mias, Op. 37 Violin & Piano
Ossy Renardy, in CX-134

Chant de Rossignol, Op. 29 Violin & Piano
Florizel von Reuter & pf. acc.
       12"—PD-95249
[Negro folk songs, arr. Reuter]

Danses Espagnoles Violin & Piano
No. 1 See: Malagueña, Op. 21, No. 1
No. 2 See: Habañera, Op. 21, No. 2
No. 3 See: Romanza Andaluza, Op. 22, No. 1
No. 4 See: Jota Navarra, Op. 22, No. 2
No. 5, Playera, Op. 23, No. 1 No recording available
No. 6 See: Zapateado, Op. 23, No. 2
No. 7, A minor, Op. 26, No. 1 No recording available
No. 8, C major, Op. 26, No. 2 No recording available

Habañera, Op. 21, No. 2 Violin & Piano
(Danse espagnole No. 2)
Riccardo Odnopousoff & Gregory Ashman
[Malagueña]   12"—V-11-9495
Arnold Eidus & Gerald Moore
[Elgar: La Capricieuse] 12"—G-C3582
Yehudi Menuhin & M. Gazelle
[Malagueña]   12"—V-15823
DUPLICATIONS: Guila Bustabo, C-LWX363; Miron Poliakin, USSR-8284/5; Ruggiero Ricci, G-DB4598

Introduction & Tarantella, Op. 43 Violin & Piano
Ruggiero Ricci & L. Persinger
[Habañera]   12"—G-DB4598

Jota Navarra, Op. 22, No. 2 Violin & Piano
(Danse espagnole No. 4)
C. F. Cillario & Simoncelli 12"—G-S10472
[Szymanowski: La fontana di Aretusa]
Vasa Prihoda & Michael Rauchiesen
(Earlier rec.: PD-66886) 12"—PD-68045
[Tchaikovsky: Romance]
Ossy Renardy, in CX-134
Bronislaw Gimpel, in VOX-616

Malagueña, Op. 21, No. 1 Violin & Piano
(Danse espagnole No. 1)
Riccardo Odnopousoff & Gregory Ashman
[Habañera]   12"—V-11-9495
Yehudi Menuhin & Marcel Gazelle (pf)
[Habañera]   12"—V-15823
[Bloch: Abodah, on G-DB3782]

Romanza Andaluza, Op. 22, No. 1 Violin & Piano
(Danse espagnole No. 3)
Nathan Milstein & Arthur Balsam
(C-LX993)   12"—C-71400D
[Massenet: Thaïs-Méditation]
Jascha Heifetz & Emanuel Bay
       12"—V-11-9573
[Chopin: Nocturne No. 19, E minor, Op. 72, arr. Auer]
Yehudi Menuhin & Marcel Gazelle
       12"—G-DB5395
[Bazzini: Ronde des Lutins]
DUPLICATIONS: Bronislaw Hubermann, C-GQX10298; Manuel Perediaz, PAT-PAT83; Gerhard Taschner, O-8766; Vasa Prihoda, PD-57086; Ossy Renardy, in CX-134; R. de Barbieri, G-AW340; Albert Locatelli, C-DF2062

Zapateado, Op. 23, No. 2 Violin & Piano
(Danse espagnole No. 6) Eng. **The Cobbler**
Jascha Heifetz & Emanuel Bay
10″—**V-10-1328**
[Castelnuovo-Tedesco: Sea Murmurs;
Rimsky-Korsakov: Tale of Czar Saltan—
Flight of the Bumble Bee]
Yehudi Menuhin & Marcel Gazelle
10″—**G-DA1482**
[Brahms-Joachim: Hungarian Dance
No. 7]
DUPLICATIONS: Ossy Renardy, in CX-
134; Guila Bustabo, C-LW36; David Ois-
trakh, USSR-12457/9; Heinz Stanske,
PD-57104; Ida Haendel, D-F7727
—**Arr. 'Cello & Piano:** Paul Tortelier,
G-DB11116

Zigeunerweisen, Op. 20, No. 1 Violin &
Piano (or Orchestra)
Fr. Airs bohèmiens Eng. **Gypsy Airs**
Jascha Heifetz & London Symphony
Orch.—Barbirolli
(G-DB3212)   12″—**V-15246**
Ruggiero Ricci & pf. acc. 12″—**G-DB4673**
B. Lessmann & Orch.—Lutze
12″—**T-E3127**
DUPLICATIONS: Zino Francescatti,
C-LFX43: C-DCX37; Henri Merckel,
PAT-X98187; Vasa Prihoda, PD-30016:
PD-524290: CET-LL3000; Isaac Stern, in
CM-657; Simone Filon, PD-522415;
Wandy Tworek & Danish State Radio
Symphony Orch.—Reesen, In Prep (NP)
—**Arr. Orchestra:** Barnabas von Géczy,
G-EG3295

Miscellaneous Arrangements
See under: Bizet: Carmen Fantasia
Chopin: Nocturnes, Op. 9, No. 2 & Op. 27,
No. 2
Leclair: Sarabande & Tambourin
Moszkowski: Guitare

SARTI, Giuseppi (1729-1802)
*An Italian Opera composer and conductor who
spent many years in Denmark and Russia. He
also made extensive acoustical studies, introducing the use of A' 436 as normal pitch.*

ARMIDA E RINALDO Opera in Italian
Lungi dal caro bene
Ezio Pinza (b) & F. Kitzinger (pf)
(in VM-766)   12″—**V-17916**
[Buononcini: Pupille nere; Giordani:
Caro mio ben; Falconieri: O bellissimi
capelli]
Angelo Parigi (t)   10″—**G-HN1817**
[Schubert: Wohin & Morgengrüss]

SATIE, Erik (1866-1925)
*A Frenchman of partly English extraction, the
spiritual father of the post-Debussyan school
known as "Les Six," Satie himself sought the
"new" in music, although the novelty and wit
he strove for manifested itself less in the music
itself than in the often fantastic titles he con-
cocted for his compositions.*

(3) Gnossiennes Piano 1890
No. 3 only
Gaby Casadesus, in VOX-183

(3) Gymnopédies Piano 1888
(Arr. Orchestra Debussy)
No. 1 & 2 (Nos. 3 & 2 of original piano
version)
Philadelphia Orch.—Stokowski
10″—**V-1965**
No. 1 (No. 3 of the original piano version)
Boston Symphony Orch.—Koussevitzky
(in VM-352†)   12″—**V-7252**
[Ravel: Bolero, Pt. 3] (G-D1860)

Parade Ballet Orchestra 1917
—**Arr. Piano 4-hands**
Georges Auric & Francis Poulenc
2 12″—**BAM-16/7**
[Deux morceaux en forme de poire]

(Deux) Morceaux en forme de poire
2 Pianos
Georges Auric & Francis Poulenc
[Parade, Pt. 3]   12″—**BAM-17**

(3) Petites pièces montées Orchestra
L'Enfance de Pantagruel, Marche de
Cocagne, Jeunesse de Gargantua (after
Rabelais)
Symphony Orch.—Chagnon
12″—**C-D11016**
[Massenet: Scènes alsaciennes—Sous les
tilleuls]

SONGS
(La) Statue de Bronze (L. P. Fargue)
(La) Chapelier (R. Chalupt)
Pierre Bernac (b) & F. Poulenc (pf)
[Auric: Le Gloxinia]   10″—**G-DA4893**

SAUGUET, Henri (1901-   )
*A modern French composer and a member of
the "Ecole d'Arcueil," a group of contemporary
composers brought together in 1923 under the
leadership of Erik Satie.*

Concerto, A minor Piano & Orchestra
Arnold de Gontaut-Biron & Paris Conservatory Orch.—Désormière
2 12″—**C-LFX648/9**

Petits Ballets pour les "Comédiens de Bois"
La Cigale et La Fourmi
Orch.—Désormière 10″—**FLOR-HP1204**

La Voyante Cantata 1938
Germaine Cernay (ms) 2 12″—**OL-137/8**

SAUVEPLANE, Henri (1892-   )
Habañera
Roland Charmy (vl) & Jean Manuel (pf)
10″—**CdM-518**
[Ibert: Entr'acte, Moyse & Lafou]

Quartet, F minor Strings
Ortambert Quartet
2 12″—**PD-516789/90**

FOLK SONG ARRANGEMENTS
(L') Adieu d'un soldat russe (Chinese)
Chorale Chant du Monde & Orch.—
Désormière   10″—**CdM-509**
[USSR: Le chant du Kolkhoz]

(La) Carmagnole 1792
Chorale Populaire de Paris—Rosset
10″—**O-281114**
[Rouget de Lisle-Berlioz: La Marseillaise]

(Les) Filles de La Rochelle (Saintonge)
O. Ertaud, J. Peyron, Y. Gouverné cho., &
Orch.—Désormière   10″—CdM-521
[Trad. arr. Koechlin: Jeanne d'Ayme]

(Le) Pauvre Laboureur (Savoie)
Male Cho.—Désormière   10″—CdM-507
[Trad. arr. Koechlin: La Fille du
Maréchal de France]

(Le) 31 du Mois d'Août (Chanson de bord)
J. Peyron, Yvonne Gouverné cho. & Orch.
—Désormière   10″—CdM-514
[Trad. arr. Laocheur: Le Jaloux]

SCARLATESCU

Bagatella
Ginette Neveu (vl) & Jean Neveu (pf)
                            10″—G-DA1871
[Ravel: Pièce en forme d'Habañera]
Gulli (vl) & Giorgio Vidusso (pf)
                            10″—ADAM-C112
[Dvořák-Kreisler: Indian Lament]
Giorgio Ciompi (vl) & Walter Baracchi
(pf)   10″—CET-TI7008
[Chopin: Nocturne, C sharp minor, Op.
Posth.]

SCARLATTI, Alessandro (1659-1725)

*Not only the father of a brilliant keyboard vir-
tuoso and composer, Alessandro Scarlatti was
also the true founder of the Neapolitan school
of opera, and a composer of unquestioned
merit. Of his some one hundred fifteen operas,
only fifty have been preserved in whole or in
part, but these contain arias of surpassing
beauty. In addition there is also a wealth of
vocal and instrumental music—oratorios, cantatas, and chamber works for soloists and small
orchestra—that has yet to make its appearance
on records.*

A chi sempre (from an unpublished Can-
tata) In Italian
Leïla Ben Sedira (s) & Ars Rediviva En-
semble   12″—BAM-20
[Diana ed Endimione—Recit. & Aria di
Diana]

Chi vuole innamorarsi
Ezio Pinza (bs) & F. Kitzinger (pf)
      (in VM-766) 12″—V-17914
[Legrenzi: Che fiero costume; Monteve-
di: Arianna—Lasciatemi morire; Handel:
Floridante—Alma mia]

Col dire a me cosi Arietta
Leïla Ben Sedira (s) & Ars Rediviva Ensemble   12″—G-DB5023
[Labbra gradite; Quanto e dolce quel
velen; & Anon: D'amor faran le pene]

Correa nel seno Cantata

—Ombre opache only
Yvon Le Marc' Hadour w. Pasquier Trio
& R. Gerlin (harpsichord)
                            12″—PAT-PAT89

Concerto, F major Strings (arr. G. Lenszew-
ski)
Chamber Orch. of Conservatory of San
Pietro a Majella, Naples—A. Lualdi
                            12″—G-DBO5352

Diana ed Endimione Cantata

Recit. & Aria di Diana only Arr. Crussard
Leïla Ben Sedira (s) & Ars Rediviva En-
semble   12″—BAM-20
[A chi sempre]

Fugue, D minor Harpsichord
Ruggero Gerlin (in Vol. V) 12″—AS-33
[With Italian Harpsichord Music after
1700]

Già, il sole del Gange Canzonetta
Aubrey Pankey & Orch.—Gaillard
[Caccini: Amarilli]   12″—PAT-PG95
DUPLICATION: Elena Fava, G-HN1663

Io vi miro ancor See under Solitude ameni

Labbra gradite Arietta
Leïla Ben Sedira (s) & Ars Rediviva Ensemble   12″—G-DB5023
[Col dire a me cosi: Quanto e dolce quel
velen; & Anon: D'amor faran le pene]

Ombre opache
See under Correa nel seno

OPERAS In Italian

(IL) CLEARCO IN NEGROPONTI

Adrasto's Air
Mascia Predit (s), G. Favaretto (pf) &
G. Tassinari (fl)   10″—G-DA5436
[Wolff: Verborgenheit]

(IL) PIRRO E DEMETRIO 1694

Rugiadose odorose ("Le Violette")
Tito Schipa (t)   10″—G-DA5362
[Son tutta duolo]
Margherita Voltolina (s) & M. Salerno
(pf)   12″—CET-IT581
[Paradies: Quel ruscelletto]

Partirò Arietta
Mme. Castellazzi-Bovy (s) & Ars Rediviva
Ensemble   12″—BAM-4
[Speranza & La tua pena; Legrenzi:
Motet]

Quanto e dolce quel velen Arietta
Leïla Ben Sedira (s) & Ars Rediviva En-
semble   12″—G-DB5023
[Col dire a me cosi; Labbra gradite; &
Anon: D' amor faran le pene]

Sè Florindo è fedele Aria
Marian Anderson (c) & K. Vehanen (pf)
(G-DB6019)   12″—V-17257
[Purcell: Dido and Aeneas—When I am
laid in earth]

Sento nel cor Cantata
Tito Schipa (t)   12″—G-DB1723
[Gluck: Orfeo—Che farò]

Sì, sì, fedel
Yvon Le Marc' Hadour & Musique intime
Ensemble   10″—PAT-PG83
[Caldara: Come raggio di sol & Pasquini:
Erminia in riva del Giordano]

Solitude ameni, apriche collinette Recit.

Io vi miro ancor vestite di flor Aria Cantata

—Aria only Arr. Van Leeuwen
Amelita Galli-Curci (s) 12″—G-DB1516
[Gounod: Philémon et Baucis—O riante
Nature]

Son tutta duolo Aria
  Tito Schipa (t)   10″—G-DA5362
  [Il Pirro e Demetrio—Rugiadose
  odorose]

Speranza Arietta
  Maria Castelazzi-Bovy (s), C. Crussard
  (harpsichord), & Yvonne Thibout (vlc)
            12″—BAM-4
  [Partirò & La tua pena; Legrenzi:
  Motet]

Tinto a note di sangue Cantata
—Tu mi chiami only
  Licia Albanese (s)   10″—G-DA5372
  [Buzzi-Peccia: Colombetta]

Toccata, D minor Harpsichord
  Ruggero Gerlin
      (in Vol. IV)   12″—AS-33
  [Fugue; Zipoli: Sarabande & Canzona]

(La) Tua pena Arietta
  Maria Castelazzi-Bovy (s) & Ars Redi-
  viva Ensemble   12″—BAM-4
  [Partirò & Speranza; Legrenzi: Motet]

Tu mi chiami See under Tinto a note di
  sangue

(Le) Violette
  See under Operas: Il Pirro e Demetrio—
  Rugiadose odorose

SCARLATTI, Domenico (1685-1757)

The famous son of an equally famous father, Domenico Scarlatti contributed over 600 "Sonatas" to the keyboard literature and wrote a considerable quantity of as yet unexplored operas, masses, cantatas and concertos as well. His harpsichord pieces are miniature in proportions, startling in their anticipation of later piano techniques, and most varied in form. Hence, although there are many links from Scarlatti to the Viennese Classicists, they are not sonatas in the formal sense of the word, but sound pieces. The numbering scheme herein employed follows the Longo edition of the composer's keyboard works.

Collections See under "Sonatas"
Capriccio
  See under "Sonata," E major, L.375 &
  "Pastorale & Capriccio"
(The) Cat's Fugue
  See under "Sonata," G minor, L.499
Gavotta (unidentified) Arr. Madami
  Madami Plectrum Quartet 10″—C-D5630
  [Durante: Danza]
Gavotte & Sarabande (unidentified)
Arr. Guitar: Andrés Segovia, in D-A596
(The) Good-Humored Ladies Ballet
  See under Miscellaneous—Le Donne di
  Buon Umore
Pastorale
  See under "Sonata," D major, L.413 &
  "Pastorale & Capriccio" below
Pastorale & Capriccio Arr. Piano Tausig
  NOTE: *The Pastorale is the "Sonata" in D minor, L. 413; the Capriccio is the "Sonata" in E major, L. 375. Recordings of the original versions are listed under those titles and only the recordings of Tausig's concert piano versions are listed below.*
  Alexander Brailowsky

(G-DB3705)   12″—V-15407
[Beethoven: Rondo a Capriccio, G major,
Op. 129]
(Earlier recording: PD-95141)
DUPLICATION: Gyorgy Farago, RAD-
RZ3038
—Pastorale only
  Johanne Stockmarr   10″—G-DA5248
  [Bach: English Suite No. 3, G minor—
  Prelude]
  A. Benedetti Michelangeli
  [L. 342]   10″—G-DA5380
  DUPLICATION: Madami Quintet,
  C-D5633
Scherzo (unidentified) Arr. Bossi
  Poltronieri Quartet   10″—C-GQ7199
  [Anonymous: Aria fiamminga]
Siciliana
  See under "Sonata," F major, Longo 443

"SONATAS" Harpsichord

COLLECTIONS

The Scarlatti "Sonata" Society: Vol. I
  (formed in 1935 by HMV)
  G major, L. 232; G minor (Pastorale),
  L. 488; C major, L. 104; F minor, L. 438;
  A major (Barcarolle), L. 182; F major,
  L. 384; F minor, L. 475; B minor, L.
  263; D major (Tempo di Ballo), L. 463;
  F sharp minor, L. 294; D major, L. 208;
  E major (Les Adieux), L. 257; C sharp
  minor, L. 256; E major, L. 375; G major
  (Les Cloches), L. supplement 27; G min-
  or, L. 338; E flat major, L. 142; E major
  (Cortège), L. 23; F minor, L. 474; F
  major, L. 479
  Wanda Landowska (not available separ-
  ately)   6   12″—Society set

(9) "Sonatas"
  G major, L. 126; G major, L. 127; E
  major, L. 321; E major, L. 466; C major,
  L. 457; C minor, L. 10; F major, L. 279;
  D major, L. 415; D major, L. 215
  Ralph Kirkpatrick (Limited Edition)
            3 12″—CH-B5

(9) "Sonatas"
  G major, L. 232; C major, L. 205; E
  major, L. 257; D major, L. 461; F major,
  L. 433; E major, L. 23; F major, L. 479;
  D minor, L. 413; D major, L. 463
  Sylvia Marlowe   3 12″—MC-72

(11) "Sonatas"
  D major, L. 465; E minor, L. 22; G ma-
  jor, L. 486; B minor, L. 449; G major, L.
  387; D minor (Pastorale), L. 413; G
  major, L. 487; D major, L. 463; A major,
  L. 395; D major, L. 411; B minor, L. 263
  Robert Casadesus (pf)   3 12″—CM-372
  (C-LFX514/6) (C-LWX292/4)

(14) "Sonatas"
  D major, L. 107; F major, L. 384; D
  minor, L. 108; C major, L. 218; G major,
  L. 129; B minor, L. 33; B flat major, L.
  327; D minor, L. 58; A major, L. 238;
  B flat major, L. 434; A minor, L. 243; G
  major, L. 490; C minor, L. 407; C major,
  L. 205
  Yella Pessl (harpsichord)
            6 10″—CM-298

(13) "Sonatas"
D minor, L. 423; A minor, L. 429; B minor, L. 449; G major, L. 487; G minor, L. 499; B minor, L. 33; E major, L. 23; D major, L. 463; A major, L. 344; D minor, L. 58; A major, L. 468; B flat major, L. 498; F minor, L. 475
Marcelle Meyer (pf)   4   12"—DF-A15

INDIVIDUAL "SONATAS" after the "Longo" Edition

L. 10, C minor
Kathleen Long (pf)   10"—D-M566
[L. 294]

L. 22, E minor
Robert Casadesus, on C-72339D in CM-372

L. 23, E major (Cortège)
Wanda Landowska, in Scarlatti Society: Vol. I
Sylvia Marlowe, in MC-72
Marcelle Meyer, in DF-A15

L. 24, E minor
Ruggero Gerlin   12"—MIA-13
[L. 79, 97, 103]

L. 33, B minor
Yella Pessl, on C-17493D in CM-298
Marcelle Meyer, in DF-A15
Vladimir Horowitz (pf) 12"—G-DB2847
[L. 487]
—Arr. Orchestra Tommasini
See under Miscellaneous—Le Donne di Buon Umore

L. 45, A major

L. 46, B flat major
Kathleen Long (pf)   10"—D-M581

L. 58, D minor
Yella Pessl, on C-17494D in CM-298
Marcelle Meyer, in DF-A15

L. 79, G major

L. 97, B flat major ("Minuetto")
Ruggero Gerlin (harpsichord)
[L. 24 & 103]   12"—MIA-13

L. 103, G major ("Minuetto")
Ruggero Gerlin   12"—MIA-13
[L. 24, 79, 97]

L. 104, C major
Wanda Landowska, in Scarlatti Society: Vol I
Lubka Kolessa (pf)   10"—G-DA4454
[B major]
Myra Hess (pf)   10"—C-4083M
[L. 352; Beethoven: Bagatelle, Op. 119, No. 11; Brahms: Intermezzo, Op. 119, No. 3]

L. 107, D major
Yella Pessl, on C-17491D in CM-298

L. 108, D minor
Yella Pessl, on C-17492D in CM-298

L. 119, F major
Kathleen Long (pf)   10"—D-M582
[L. 154]

L. 126, G major

L. 127, G major
Ralph Kirkpatrick, in CH-B5 (Limited Edition)

L. 129, G major
Yella Pessl, on C-17493D in CM-298
Kathleen Long (pf)   10"—D-M552
[L. 256]

L. 132, A major ("Barcarolle")
Wanda Landowska, in Scarlatti Society: Vol. I

L. 135, A major
Raymond Trouard (pf)   10"—O-188941
[L. 286]

L. 142, E flat major
Wanda Landowska, in Scarlatti Society: Vol. I

L. 154, G major
Kathleen Long (pf)   10"—D-M582
[L. 119]

L. 205, C major
Sylvia Marlowe, in MC-72
Yella Pessl, on C-17496D in CM-298

L. 208, D major ("Minuetto")
Wanda Landowska, in Scarlatti Society: Vol. I

L. 209, G major
—Arr. Orch. Tommasini
See under Miscellaneous—Le Donne di Buon Umore

L. 215, D minor
Ralph Kirkpatrick, in CH-B5 (Limited Edition)

L. 218, C major
Yella Pessl, on C-17492D in CM-298

L. 232, G major
Wanda Landowska, in Scarlatti Society: Vol I
Sylvia Marlowe, in MC-72

L. 238, A major
Yella Pessl, on C-17494D in CM-298

L. 243, A minor
Yella Pessl, on C-17495D in CM-298

L. 256, C sharp minor
Wanda Landowska, in Scarlatti Society: Vol I
Kathleen Long (pf)   10"—D-M552
[L. 129]

L. 257, E major ("Les Adieux")
Wanda Landowska, in Scarlatti Society: Vol I
Sylvia Marlowe, in MC-72

L. 262, D major
Ralph Kirkpatrick, in MC-25

L. 263, B minor ("Bourrée")
Wanda Landowska, in Scarlatti Society: Vol I
Robert Casadesus, on C-72341D in CM-372

L. 279, F major
Ralph Kirkpatrick, in CH-B5 (Limited Edition)

L. 286, G major
Raymond Trouard (pf)   10"—O-188941
[L. 135]

L. 294, F sharp minor
Wanda Landowska, in Scarlatti Society: Vol. I
Kathleen Long (pf)   10"—D-M566
[L. 10]

L. 321, E minor
Ralph Kirkpatrick, in CH-B5 (Limited Edition)

L. 327, B flat major
Yella Pessl, on C-17494D in CM-298

L. 338, G minor ("Burlesca")
Wanda Landowska, in Scarlatti Society: Vol I
—Arr. String Orchestra De Nardis
EIAR Symphony—Ferrero, CET-IT7004

L. 342, C minor
A. Benedetti Michelangeli (pf)
[Pastorale]   10"—G-DA5380

L. 344, A major
Marcelle Meyer, in DF-A15

L. 352, C minor
Myra Hess (pf)   10"—C-4083M
[L. 104; Beethoven: Bagatelle; Brahms: Intermezzo]

L. 361, D major
—Arr. Orchestra Tommasini
See under Miscellaneous—Le Donne di Buon Umore

L. 375, E major ("Capriccio")
Wanda Landowska, in Scarlatti Society: Vol. I
See also under "Pastorale & Capriccio"
Arr. Tausig

L. 384, F major
Wanda Landowska, in Scarlatti Society: Vol. I
Yella Pessl, on C-17491D in CM-298

L. 385, F major
—Arr. Orchestra Tommasini (Transposed to G major)
See under Miscellaneous—Le Donne di Buon Umore

L. 387, G major
Robert Casadesus, on C-72340D in CM-372
Myra Hess (pf)
(G-B9035)   10"—V-4538
[Bach: Jesu, joy of man's desiring, arr. Hess]

L. 388, G major
—Arr. Orchestra Tommasini
See under Miscellaneous—Le Donne di Buon Umore

L. 395, A major
Robert Casadesus, on C-72341D in CM-372

L. 407, C minor
Yella Pessl, on C-17497D in CM-298

L. 411, D major
Robert Casadesus, on C-72341D in CM-372

L. 413, D minor ("Pastorale")
NOTE: *For recordings of the Tausig concert piano arrangement see under Pastorale & Capriccio. Only recorded performances of the original version are listed below.*
Wanda Landowska   10"—G-DA1130
[Couperin: Le Rossignol en amour]
Sylvia Marlowe, in MC-72
Robert Casadesus, on C-72340D in CM-372

L. 415, D major
Ralph Kirkpatrick, in CH-B5 (Limited Edition)

L. 418, D major
Wanda Landowska
    (in VM-1181†)   12"—V-11-9997
[L. 423 & Bach: Prelude, Fugue & Allegro, Pt. 3]

L. 422, D minor ("Toccata")
—Arr. String Trio
Pasquier Trio   12"—PAT-PAT31
[Durante: Toccata; Purcell: 3-Part Fantasia, No. 3]

L. 423, D minor
Marcelle Meyer, in DF-A15
Wanda Landowska
    (in VM-1181†)   12"—V-11-9997
[L. 418 & Bach: Prelude, Fugue & Allegro, Pt. 3]

L. 429, A minor
Ralph Kirkpatrick, in MC-25
Marcelle Meyer, DF-A15

L. 433, F major
Sylvia Marlowe, in MC-72

L. 434, B flat major
Yella Pessl, on C-17495D in CM-298

L. 438, F minor
Wanda Landowska, in Scarlatti Society: Vol I

L. 449, B minor
Marcelle Meyer, in DF-A15
Robert Casadesus, on C-72340D in CM-372

L. 457, C major
Ralph Kirkpatrick, in CH-B5 (Limited Edition)

L. 461, D major
Sylvia Marlowe, in MC-72

L. 463, D major
Wanda Landowska, in Scarlatti Society: Vol I
Sylvia Marlowe, in MC-72
Robert Casadesus, on C-72341D in CM-372
Marcelle Meyer, in DF-A15
—Arr. Orchestra Tommasini
See under Miscellaneous—Le Donne di Buon Umore

L. 465, D major
Robert Casadesus, on C-72339D in CM-372

L. 466, E major
Ralph Kirkpatrick, in CH-B5 (Limited Edition)

L. 468, A major
Marcelle Meyer, in DF-A15
—Arr. Orchestra Tommasini
See under Miscellaneous—Le Donne di Buon Umore

L. 474, F major
Wanda Landowska, in Scarlatti Society: Vol. I

L. 475, F minor
Wanda Landowska, in Scarlatti Society, Vol.I
Marcelle Meyer, in DF-A15

L. 479, F major
Wanda Landowska, in Scarlatti Society: Vol. I
Sylvia Marlowe, in MC-72

L. 486, G major
Robert Casadesus, on C-72339D in CM-372

L. 487, G major
Robert Casadesus, on C-72340D in CM-372
Vladimir Horowitz (pf) 12″—G-DB2847 [L. 33]

L. 490, G major
Yella Pessl, on C-17495D in CM-298
Marcelle Meyer, in DF-A15

L. 488, G minor
("Bucolique," "Pastorale," or "Sarabande")
Wanda Landowska, in Scarlatti Society: Vol. I

L. 498, B flat major
Marcelle Meyer, in DF-A15

L. 499, G minor ("The Cat's Fugue")
Marcelle Meyer, in DF-A15

—Arr. Orchestra Tommasini
See under Miscellaneous—Le Donne di Buon Umore

L. (Supplement) 27, G major
("Les Cloches")
Wanda Landowska, in Scarlatti Society: Vol. I

INDIVIDUAL "SONATAS"

after the "Codice Veneziano."
Vol. 10, No. 8, G major
Vol. 10, No. 25, B flat major
Vol. 15, No. 19, C minor
Vol. 15, No. 35, C major
Ruggero Gerlin
(in Vol. X) 12″—AS-100

UNIDENTIFIED "SONATAS"

C major
Carlo Zecchi (pf), on CET-CB20352

C major ("La Caccia")
Corradina Mola, on G-DA5394

D major
Carlo Zecchi (pf), on CET-CB20348

D major
A. Benedetti Michelangeli (pf), on T-SKB3290

D minor
Liselotte Selbiger, on C-DD512

D minor
France Ellegaard (pf), on PD-67838

D minor
M. De Salvo (pf), on C-GQ7223

E major
Liselotte Selbiger, on C-DD512

G major
M. De Salvo (pf), on C-GQ7223

G major
Nikita de Magaloff (pf), on RAD-RZ3032

A flat major
France Ellegaard (pf), on PD-67838

A major
Nikita de Magaloff (pf), on RAD-RZ3032

B major
Lubka Kolessa (pf), on G-DA4454

B minor
A. Benedetti Michelangeli (pf), on T-SKB3290

"Minuetto"
Carlo Zecchi, on CET-CB20348

Sonata Arr. Guitar
Andrés Segovia, in D-A596

Tempo di Ballo
See under "Sonata," L. 463, D major

Toccata (or "Toccatina")
See under "Sonata," L. 422, D major

Miscellaneous Arrangements
(Le) Donne di Buon Umore Ballet Suite
Eng. The Good-Humored Ladies
NOTE: *The thematic material for this ballet suite is derived from a large number of Scarlatti "Sonatas" as scored for orchestra by Vincenzo Tommasini. The recorded versions have five numbers using in whole or in part the following Scarlatti "Sonatas": 1) L. 388; 2) L. 361; 3) L. 33, L. 209, L. 499; 4) L. 463; 5) L. 385. For recordings, as written by Scarlatti, see the Longo numbers indicated.*
London Philharmonic Orch.—
Goossens 2 12″—VM-512
(G-C2864/5)
London Symphony Orch.—Sargent
2 12″—D-K1497/8†

Suite for String Quartet Arr. Bastini
Quartetto di Roma 2 12″—G-DB4651/2

SCHEIDT, Samuel (1587-1654)

A pupil of Sweelinck, Scheidt was a member of a melifluous trio of seventeenth century German composers, Schütz, Schein & Scheidt. He codified what has come to be known as the "German-Italian" baroque style of organ composition.

Chorale-Paraphrase: "Credo" Organ
Marcel Dupré (in Vol. I) 12″—AS-10
[Pachelbel: Vater unser]

Variations on the Choral "Da Jesus an dem Kreuze stund"
Finn Viderø (Compenius Organ, Frederiksborg Castle) 12″—G-DB5213

SCHEIN, Johann Hermann (1586-1630)

One of Bach's most notable predecessors as "Thomaskantor" at Leipzig, Schein utilized but absorbed the Italian baroque style in his compositions. He is especially well-known for his vocal works.

CHORUSES AND MOTETS In German
Jelängerjelieber und Vergissmeinnicht
Die Macht der Phyllis
St. Thomas Choir—K. Straube
10″—PD-90159

Wenn Philli ihre Liebesstrahl
(Arr. Schwickerath)
Kantorei der Staatlichen Hochschule für Musik, Berlin—K. Thomas
12″—T-E2926
[Dowland: Süsses Lieb; Hassler: Ach weh des Leiden; Mylius: Ein Mägdlein]

Suite 14 from "Banchetto Musicale"
Paduana; Gagliarda; Courante; Alle-
mande; Tripla
Brass Ensemble—Curt Sachs
(in Vol. VI) 12"—AS-57
[M. Franck: Pavana, Tanz & Intrada]

SCHIASSI, Gaetano Maria (-d.1754)

*An Italian composer of the late Baroque, whose
instrumental style displays marked similarities
to Corelli.*

Christmas Symphony   Orchestra
(Edited Upmeyer)
Ger. Weihnachts-Sinfonie
Collegium Musicum—Herman Diener
12"—G-EH1211

SCHILLINGS, Max von (1868-1933)

*An accomplished pianist, Schillings belonged
to the great body of talented and erudite German composers who lived under the crippling
shadow of Richard Wagner.*

(Das) Hexenlied, Op. 15   Melodrama
(Wildenbruch)
Recitation with orchestral accompaniment
Ludwig Wüllner (speaker) & Berlin
Philharmonic—von Schillings
3 12"—PD-27429/31

Wie wundersam (Stieler)   Song in German
Heinrich Schlusnus (b) & Sebastian
Peschko (pf)   10"—PD-62828
[Lothar-Bischoff: Der Pirol]

**SCHMELZER, Johann Heinrich
(c.1630-1680)**

*A violin virtuoso at the Viennese court during
the latter part of the seventeenth century who
wrote concerted chamber music, operas, and
"scordatura" violin pieces.*

Pastorella
Ars Rediviva Ensemble   12"—BAM-3
[Marini: Romance, Gaillarde & Courante]

SCHMID, Bernhard (born 1548)

*A Strasbourg organ composer and performer &
son of a musician of the same name and calling (1520-c.1592). The "Gagliarda" below is
ascribed to the son of the basis of the date
(1607) on the record label.*

Gagliarda   Organ
Alfred Sittard (St. Michael's, Hamburg)
12"—PD-95157
[Gheyn: Fugue, G minor; Boellmann:
Toccata, C minor]

SCHMIDT, Franz

Toccata in D minor   Piano
Friedrich Wührer   12"—C-LWX346

Notre Dame

Zwichenspiel (Entr'acte)
Berlin Philharmonic—Schmidt-Isserstedt
[Sibelius: Valse Triste]   12"—T-E2908

SCHMITT, Florent (1870-   )

*A French composer of Alsatian descent and a
pupil of both Massenet and Fauré, Schmitt
never achieved any popularity outside Paris.
His own compositions were never strikingly
original but the composer was among the first
to recognize the genius of such diverse men as
Satie, Stravinsky and Schönberg.*

Rapsodie viennoise   Orchestra
Lamoureux Orch.—Wolff
(PD-67027)   12"—PD-566089

Reflets d'Allemagne—Valse, Op. 28   Orch.
—No. 7 (Nuremburg) & No. 8 (Munich)
Symphony Orch.—Schmitt
12"—PAT-X96093

Suite en rocaille, Op. 84
Flute, Violin, Viola, 'Cello, Harp
Quintette Instrumental de Paris
2 10"—G-DA4882/3

(La) Tragédie de Salomé, Op. 50
Choreographic Drama, 2 Acts, 1907
No recording available

Trio—Strings, Op. 105
Pasquier Trio   4 12"—PAT-PDT103/6

SCHOBERT, Johann (c.1720-1767)

*A Silesian keyboard composer and virtuoso who
in his late years resided at Paris, and one of the
earliest champions in France of the new forte-
piano. We have a detailed account of Schobert's
death by accidental poisoning, laudatory comments by Baron Grimm on his playing, but
know next to nothing about his life. Mozart
had a high regard for his compositions, and
there is more than a suggestion of Schobert in
the works of the young Mozart.*

Concerto No. 5, G major
Harpsichord & Orchestra
Ruggero Gerlin & Orch. de Chambre de
la Société du Conservatoire—Cloëz
(in Vol. IX)   2 12"—AS-87/8

Sonata, Opus 8   Piano
—Allegro moderato   only
Jacques Février (in Vol. VI.) 12"—AS-62
[Dussek: Sonata No. 3, Op. 9—Allegro
maestoso]

SCHOECK, Othmar (b.1886   )

*A Swiss composer and conductor, a pupil of
Max Reger, Schoeck has composed many songs,
song cycles, and large choral works. He has also
written four operas, and is generally looked
upon as one of the representative Swiss composers of today.*

SONGS   In German

Collection
Die drei Zigeuner   (Lenau)
Das bescheidene Wünschlein (Spitteler)
In der Fremde (Eichendorf)
Sommerabend (Heine)
Nachtlied (Eichendorf)
Margherita Perras (s) & O. Schoeck (pf)
2 12"—G-DB10089/90

Elegie, Op. 36   Song Cycle
Solo voice & Chamber Orchestra
(Texts by Lenau & Eichendorff)
F. Loeffel (bs) & Ensemble—
Rothenbühler   5 10" & 4 12"—
ELITE-4482/6 & 7020/3

Individual Songs

Herbstgefühl

Mit einem getmaten Bande
Ria Ginster (s) & Paul Baumgartner (pf)
10"—G-DA6009

Nachruf
Karl Erb (t) & B. Seidler-Winkler (pf)
10"—G-DA4448.
[Wolf: Auf ein altes Bild]

Reiselied, Op. 12, No. 1

Wanderlied der Prager Studenten, Op. 12, No. 2
Paul Sandoz (t) & Paul Baumgartner
(pf) 12"—G-DB10036

SCHOENBERG, Arnold (1874-   )
A thorough musician and an excellent teacher, Arnold Schönberg has been the musical mentor of such composers as Alban Berg and Paul Hindemith. His own compositions, save for the "Verklärte Nacht," a comparatively early work, have not achieved popularity, chiefly for their intellectual complexity and aural difficulties.

Pierrot Lunaire
Erika Stiedry-Wagner (recitation)
with chamber ensemble—Schönberg
4 12"—CM-461†

SONGS
Buch der Hängenden Gärten (Stefan Georg)
—Nos. 5 & 12
Erica Storm (s) (in German) & Mosco
Carner (pf) 10"—C-DB1303
[Mahler: I Breathe the Breath of Blossoms, Kullman]
(in Columbia History of Music, Vol. V,
CM-361) (C-DB1787)

Verklärte Nacht, Op. 4 String Orchestra
Eng. **Transfigured Night**
St. Louis Symphony—Golschmann
4 12"—VM-1005†
[Corelli: Sonata, Op. 5, No. 5—Adagio]
Minneapolis Symphony Orch.—
Ormandy 4 12"—VM-207†

Miscellaneous Arrangement
Bach: Prelude & Fugue in E flat major
(St. Anne)
—Arr. Orchestra
Berlin Philharmonic—Kleiber
2 12"—U-E463/4

SCHRADER, M.

SONGS
I de lyse maetter (D. Schrader)
Mod Efteraar (D. Schrader)
Aksel Schiøtz (t) (in Danish) &
H. D. Koppel (pf) 10"—G-X6349

Sommernatt
Jussi Björling (t) (in Swedish)
[Sjöberg: Tonerna] 10"—G-X4716

SCHREKER, Franz (1879-1934)
An Austrian composer who in 1920 became Director of the Berlin Academy of Music, his works include a number of operas, and about 50 songs.

(Der) Geburtstag der Infantin
Orchestral Suite
Eng. **Birthday of the Infanta**
Berlin State Opera Orch.—Schreker
3 12"—PD-66549/51

Kleine Suite Chamber Orchestra
1. Praeludium (omitted from recording)
2. Marcia.   3. Canon   4. Fughetto
5. Intermezzo   6. Capriccio
Berlin Philharmonic Orch.—Schreker
2 12"—PD-24972/3

SCHUBERT, Franz (or François) (1808-1878)
Concertmaster of the Dresden opera, Schubert composed many works for the violin. Of these, only the piece below is known today. He is not to be confused with the Viennese Schubert.

L'Abeille Violin & Piano Acc.
Ger. **Die Biene**   Eng. **The Bee**
B. Lessman, T-A10177; Alexander
Schmidt, V-20614; Denise Soriano,
PAT-PG31

SCHUBERT, Franz (1797-1828)
Well-represented on records, the works of this prolific Viennese melodist are so voluminous that there will always be a number of his lesser-known works which it would be desirable to have available.

(L') Abeille
Eng. **The Bee**   Ger. **Die Biene**
Often attributed to the great Schubert, this violin piece was composed by another Franz Schubert (1808-1878). See above for recordings.

Adagio (unspecified) 'Cello & Piano
Judith Bokor & pf. acc. 12"—C-D17178
[Chopin: Nocturne]

ALFONSO UND ESTRELLA, Op. 69
3 Act Opera In German

Overture Orchestra
NOTE: *Used at the first performance of the incidental music to "Rosamunde." The so-called "Rosamunde" Overture was originally written for "Die Zauberharfe."*
No recording available

Allegretto, C minor Piano
Ray Lev, in CH-B3 (Limited Edition)

Allegretto grazioso (unidentified)
'Cello & Piano
C. Kolessa & pf. acc. 10"—G-EH1293
[Glazunov: Chant du Ménestrel]

Andante, A major 1813
Eileen Joyce 12"—P-E11403
[Impromptu, E flat major, Op. 90, No. 2]

Andantino varié, B minor, Op. 84, No. 1
Piano—4-Hands
Artur & Karl U. Schnabel
12"—G-DB3518
Heinz Jolles & Bernard Schulé
12"—BAM-21

Ave Maria See under Songs

Ballet Music See under Rosamunde

Choral Works (Unspecified)
Vocal Ensemble—Marcel Couraud
In Prep. (DF)

Deutsche Messe See under Masses

Deutsche Tänze   Eng. Dances
NOTE: *Schubert wrote scores of little dance pieces (Ecossaises, Ländler, Minuets, Waltzes, etc.) grouped under the general title of "Deutsche Tänze," and it is exceedingly difficult to identify them properly. In addition to the discs listed below, see also under Soirée de Vienne and Waltzes.*

—Nos. 9a & 18a
Barnabas von Géczy & his Orch.,
G-EH1311

(5) Deutsche Tänze (Minuets)
—Arr. String Quartet
Deman Quartet   2 12"—PD-95220/1

Entr'actes See under Rosamunde

Fantasia, C major, Op. 15 "The Wanderer"
Piano
No recording of the original version available

—Arr. Piano & Orchestra Liszt
Edward Kilenyi & Symphony Orch.—
Meyrowitz   3 12"—CM-426†
Clifford Curzon & Queen's Hall Orch.—
Wood   3 12"—D-X185/7
(PD-516739/41)

Fantasia Violin & Piano
See under Sonatas—Violin, No. 4, Op. 159

Gott ist mein Hirt See under Psalm 23

IMPROMPTUS Piano
Collections

(8) Impromptus, Op. 90, & Op. 142
Edwin Fischer   6 12"—GM-314†
(G-DB3484/9)

(4) Impromptus, Op. 90
Clifford Curzon   3 12"—D-K1018/20

Individual Impromptu recordings

Op. 90, No. 1, C minor
Edwin Fischer, G-DB3484 in GM-314†
Clifford Curzon, D-K1018
Adrian Aaeschbacher   12"—PD-68097

Op. 90, No. 2, E flat major
Edwin Fischer, G-DB3485 in GM-314†
Clifford Curzon, D-K1019
Eileen Joyce   12"—P-E11403
[Andante, A major]
Adrian Aeschbacher   12"—CET-OR5088
[No. 3] (PD-67750)
Cor de Groot   12"—O-8777
[Moment musical, Op. 94, No. 5]

Op. 90, No. 3, G major
Edwin Fischer, G-DB3485 in GM-314†
Clifford Curzon, D-K1019
Walter Rehberg   12"—PD-57090
[No. 4]
Maryla Jonas   12"—C-72047D
[Waltzes]
V. Varler   12"—TONO-K8031
Adrian Aeschbacher   12"—PD-67750
[No. 2]   (CET-OR5088)
[Rosamunde Overture, on CET-OR5087]
[Schumann: Symphony No. 4, Pt. 7,
Dresden Philharmonic—Van Kempen, on
CET-OR5070]

—Arr. Violin & Piano Heifetz
Jascha Heifetz & Arpad Sandor
12"—V-8420
[Hummel: Rondo, A flat major]

Op. 90, No. 4, A flat major
Edwin Fischer, G-DB3486 in GM-314†
Clifford Curzon, D-K1020
Eileen Joyce   12"—P-E11440
Louis Kentner   12"—C-DX1093
Adrian Aeschbacher   12"—PD-67607
S. Schultze   12"—T-E3151
DUPLICATIONS: Walter Rehberg,
PD-57090; Artur Rubinstein, G-DB1160;
S. Grundeis, O-7910

Op. 142, No. 1, F minor
Edwin Fischer, G-DB3487 in GM-314†
Adrian Aeschbacher   12"—PD-67751

Op. 142, No. 2, A flat major
Edwin Fischer, G-DB3488 in GM-314†
Ignace Jan Paderewski   12"—V-6628
[Chopin: Etude, Op. 10, No. 3]
(G-DB1037)
Paul Baumgartner   12"—G-DB10008
[Beethoven: Sonata No. 14, "Moonlight,"
Pt. 3]
Adrian Aeschbacher   10"—PD-62823
DUPLICATIONS: Winfried Wolff,
G-EH1078; Sigfrid Grundeis, O-7910;
Leff Pouishnoff, C-9400

Op. 142, No. 3, B flat major
(Andante con Variazioni)
Edwin Fischer, G-DB3489 in GM-314†
Adrian Aeschbacher   12"—PD-68098
Wilhelm Kempff   10"—PD-62745
Yvonne Gellibert   12"—G-W1506
DUPLICATION: Emma Boynet,
PAT-PAT2

Op. 142, No. 4, F minor
Edwin Fischer, G-DB3488 in GM-314†
Elly Ney   12"—G-DB4432
[Moment musical, Op. 94, No. 4]

Unspecified Impromptu
M. Miramowa, C-CQX16488

LAENDLER Piano
(12) Ländler, Op. 171
Alfred Cortot   12"—G-DB3268
Suzanne Gyr   12"—G-DB10059

—Nos. 1, 3, 4, 5, 6, 7, 8, 11 only
Robert Casadesus (C-LFX586)
(in CX-236†) 12"—C-71466D
[Sonata, A major, Op. 120, Pt. 3]

—Unspecified Ländler, Op. 18
Lili Krauss, P-R20390

Marche militaire See under Marches—
Militärmarsch, D major, Op. 41, No. 1

MARCHES Originally Piano 4-Hands
Militärmarsch, D major, Op. 41, No. 1
—Arr. Piano solo Tausig
Alexander Brailowsky 12"—PD-95425
[Liszt: Valse Impromptu, A flat]
—Arr. Orch.
Boston "Pops" Orch.—Fiedler
10"—V-4314
[Pierné: Marche des petits soldats de
plomb]
(G-B8454) (G-G7735) (G-EG6887)
Saxon State Orch.—Böhm
12"—G-DB5559
[Berlioz: Rakoczy March]
DUPLICATIONS: London Philharmonic
—Harty, C-7322M: C-DX571: C-DFX182;

Berlin-Charlottenburg Opera Orch.—
Melichar, PD-27213; Orch. Symphonique
—Meyrowitz, PAT-PAT101: C-DX924;
New Symphony Orch.—Barbirolli,
G-C2637; Opéra-Comique Orch.—Cloëz,
O-170052; Royal Opera Orch.—Goossens,
G-C1279; Bournemouth Municipal Orch.,
D-F8203

Ungarischesmarsch, C minor
Eng. Hungarian March
—**Arr. Orchestra** Liszt
Berlin State Opera Orch.—Blech
　　　　　　　　　12"—**G-EJ387**
[Smetana: Moldau, Pt. 3] (G-AW284)
Berlin-Charlottenburg Opera Orch.—
Melichar　　　　　12"—**PD-27213**
[Militärmarsch]

MASSES
F major, Deutsche Messe In German
Eng. German Mass
—**Sanctus (Heilig, heilig) only**
Berliner Soloisten-Vereinigung,
V-25-4038
G major (Usually listed as No. 2) In Latin
—**Agnus Dei only**
Hildegard Erdmann (s) with Chorus &
Orch.　　　　　　12"—**G-EH1250**
[Schumann: Paradies und Peri—Nun
ruhe sanft]
Menuet, Minuetto, Minuet
*See under Sonatas—Piano, Op. 78, 3rd Mvt. for
the popular Schubert Minuetto in B minor.
Also under Deutsche Tänze, Arr. String Quartet.*
(5) Minuets & 6 Trios for String Orchestra
Orch. of Berlin College of Instrumentalists—Stein　　12"—**G-EH1285**

MOMENTS MUSICAUX, Op. 94 Piano
Complete Recordings
Artur Schnabel
(G-DB3358/60)　　　3 12"—**VM-684**
Leonard Shure　　　3 12"—**VOX-615**
Individual Recordings
No. 1, C major
Artur Schnabel, V-17021 in VM-684:
G-DB3358
Nikita de Magaloff, RAD-RZ3034
Leonard Shure, in VOX-615
No. 2, A flat major
Artur Schnabel, V-17021/2 in VM-684:
G-DB3358/9
Leonard Shure, in VOX-615
Ignace Jan Paderewski (G-DB3710)
　　(in VM-748) 12"—**V-17699**
No. 3, F minor
NOTE: *This famous work is usually listed on
labels and in catalogues without key or opus
number.*
Artur Schnabel, V-17022 in VM-684:
G-DB3359
Leonard Shure, in VOX-615
Walter Gieseking (C-LW18)
　　　　　　　　10"—**C-17079D**
[Brahms: Intermezzo; Chopin: Waltz &
Prelude]
DUPLICATION: Wilhem Kempff,
PD-62747

—**Arr. Violin & Piano**
Miguel Candela, C-LF27;
Lucien Schwartz, G-K5164
—**Arr. 'Cello & Piano** Becker
Pablo Casals, V-1143: G-DA776;
André Navarra, O-188933
—**Arr. Orchestra**
Hollywood Bowl Orch.—Stokowski
　　　　　　　　12"—**V-11-9174**
[Offenbach: Contes d'Hoffmann—
Barcarolle]
EIAR Orch.—Ferrero 10"—**CET-TI7000**
[Schumann: Träumerei]
No. 4, C sharp minor
Artur Schnabel, V-17022 in VM-684:
G-DB3359
Leonard Shure, in VOX-615
Elly Ney　　　　　12"—**G-DB4432**
[Impromptu, F minor, Op. 142, No. 4]
Wilhelm Kempff　　　10"—**PD-62747**
[Moment Musical No. 3]
No. 5, F minor
Artur Schnabel, V-17023 in VM-684:
G-DB3360
Leonard Shure, in VOX-615
Cor de Groot　　　　12"—**O-8777**
[Impromptu, E flat, Op. 90, No. 2]
William Murdoch　　12"—**D-F7496**
[Grieg: Papillons; Mozart: Rondo alla
Turca]
No. 6, A flat major
Artur Schnabel, V-17023 in VM-684:
G-DB3360
Leonard Shure, in VOX-615
Carlo Zecchi　　12"—**CET-CB20346**
[Chopin: Mazurka, Op. 30, No. 4]
Mondenschein
Paul Derenne (t) & Vocal Ensemble—
N. Boulanger　　　10"—**G-DA4925**
(Die) Nacht, Op. 17, No. 4
Unacc. Male Chorus (Matthison)
Reveille Chor der Basler Liedertafel
　　　　　　　　12"—**G-HEX101**
[Haeser: Wanderlied der Prager
Studenten]
Coro di Trento (in Italian)—Mingozzi
　　　　　　　　10"—**T-A9145**
[Beethoven: Hymne an die Nacht]
Nachtgesang im Walde, Op. 139b
Male Chorus & Horns (Seidl)
Neukölln Teachers' Chorus, with Horn
Quartet acc.　　　10"—**PD-22022**
Nachthelle, Op. 134
Male Chorus in German
Basler Liedertafel & pf. acc.
[Die Nachtigall]　　　12"—**G-FM16**
(Die) Nachtigall, Op. 11, No. 2
Male Chorus in German
Basler Liedertafel & pf. acc.
[Nachthelle]　　　　12"—**G-FM16**
Octette, F major, Op. 166
String Quartet, Double Bass, Clarinet,
Horn, Bassoon
Lener Quartet & Hobday, Draper, Brain,
Hinchcliffe
(C-GQX10961/6)　　6 12"—**CM-97**†
Schneiderhan Quartet & Leopold Wlach,
Godfried von Freiberg, Karl Ohlberger,
Otto Rühm　　　　6 12"—**C-LWX364/9**

Ora pro nobis   See under Songs—
Ave Maria (arr. Chorus)

Overture in the Italian Style, C major, Op. 170
Liverpool Philharmonic—Sargent
(C-DX1157)   12"—C-72464D
National Symphony Orch.—Unger
                        12"—D-K1327

Psalm 23, Op. 132 Women's Chorus in German
("Gott ist mein Hirt" or "Der Herr ist mein Hirt")
Regensburg Cathedral Choir—T. Schrems   10"—G-EG7192

(3) Piano Pieces (Posthumous) (unidentified)
Rudolf Firkusny   2 12"—VOX-629

QUARTETS—String

No. 4, C major 1813
Prisca Quartet   4 10"—PD-10406/9
[Schumann: Des Abends, Karl Delseit, pf.]

No. 10, E flat major, Op. 125, No. 1 (c.1817)
Guilet Quartet   3 12"—CH-AE
Calvet Quartet
(U-F18081/3)   3 12"—T-E2356/8

No. 12, C minor (Quartetsatz) 1820
NOTE: *This is an isolated quartet movement ("Satz") not a "Satz" Quartet.*
Erling Bloch Quartet   12"—G-DB5282
[Børresen: Quartet, C minor—Scherzo]

No. 13, A minor, Op. 29 1824
Philharmonia Quartet
                    4 12"—C-DX1349/52†
Budapest Quartet
(G-DB224/7)   4 12"—VM-225†
Vegh Quartet
                    4 12"—In Prep. (Swiss Decca)

No. 14, D minor "Der Tod und das Mädchen" (1826)
NOTE: *This work is so called because the theme of that song of the same name is used as the basis for the variations in the 2nd movement. In some editions this quartet is listed as No. 6.*
Philharmonia Quartet
                    4 12"—C-DX1089/92†
Busch Quartet   4 12"—VM-468†
(G-DB3037/40 in GM-298†)
Calvet Quartet   5 12"—C-LFX695/9
(Also on T-E2282/6)
Strub Quartet   4 12"—G-DB5564/7

No. 15, G major, Op. 161 1826
Busch Quartet   5 12"—G-DB3744/8
Strub Quartet   5 12"—G-EH1039/43

QUINTETS

C major, Op. 163 String Quartet & 2nd 'Cello 1828
Pro Arte Quartet & Anthony Pini
                    5 12"—VM-299†
(G-DB2561/5 in GM-239†)
Budapest Quartet & B. Heifetz
                    6 12"—CM-497†

A major, Op. 114 ("Forellen" Quintet)
Piano, Violin, Viola, 'Cello, Double Bass
Eng. Trout Quintet
NOTE: *So-called because the song, "Die Forelle" serves as the thematic basis for the fourth (variation) movement.*

Schnabel, Onnou, Prevost, Maas, Hobday
                    5 12"—VM-312†
(G-DB2714/8 in GM-259†)
Elly Ney, members of the Strub Quartet & double bass   5 12"—G-DB4533/7
[Trio, E flat major, Op. 100—Scherzo]
Marcel Gazelle, M. Raskin, L. Ardenois, R. Soiron, H. Lodge 4 12"—D-K1366/9
Adrian Aeschbacher & members of Hanke Quartet   5 12"—PD-67842/6
(FONIT—68012/6) (CET-OR5127/31)
DUPLICATIONS: Franz Rupp & Quartet, T-E2112/5; Leipzig Gewandhaus Quartet with M. Pauer, PD-95066/70; M. Raucheisen & Berlin Philharmonic Chamber Ensemble, O-7890/3

RONDOS

A major Violin & String Quartet
Henri Temianka & his Chamber Orch.
                    2 12"—P-DPX11/2
[Sibelius: Humoresque IV]

Rondo Brilliante, B minor, Op. 70 Violin & Piano
Yehudi & Hephzibah Menuhin
(G-DB3583/4)   2 12"—VM-901†
E. Pierangeli & A. Musato-Pierangeli
                    2 10"—CET-TI7020/1

ROSAMUNDE, Op. 26 Incidental Music 1823 (for a play by W. C. von Chezy)
Overture "Zauberharfe"; 1. Entr'acte No. 1; 2. Ballet No. 1, B minor & D major; 3a. Entr'acte No. 2; 3b. Romanza; 4. Geister Chor (Male chorus); 5. Entr'acte No. 3; 6. Hirtenmelodien ("Shepherd's Melody"); 7. Hirtenchor (chorus); 8. Jäger Chor (chorus); 9. Ballet No. 2, G major & B minor
NOTE: *Numbering used follows the B. & H. Edition.*

Excerpts

Overture, Nos. 1, 2, 3, 5, 6 & 9 only
Hallé Orch.—Harty   4 12"—CM-343†

Overture Orchestra
(*Originally the overture to "Die Zauberharfe."*)
Hallé Orch.—Harty
(in CM-343†)   12"—C-69309D
Amsterdam Concertgebouw Orch.—Mengelberg   12"—T-SK3008
Dresden Philharmonic—Kempen
[Last side blank]   2 12"—PD-67594/5s
[Impromptu, Op. 90, No. 3, Geza Anda, pf, on CET-OR5086/7]
Symphony Orch.—Sargent
                    2 12"—G-C1873/4
[Brahms: Hungarian Dance No. 6]
Berlin State Opera Orch.—Kleiber
                    2 12"—G-EJ359/60
[No. 5, Entr'acte No. 3]

No. 1, Entr'acte 1, B minor
Hallé Orch.—Harty
(in CM-343†)   12"—C-69310D

No. 2, Ballet 1, B minor & D major
Hallé Orch.—Harty
[No. 9] (in CM-343†)   12"—C-69311D

London Symphony Orch.—B. Walter
(G-DB3651)   12"—V-12534
[No. 9, G major]
No. 3a, Entr'acte 2, D major
Hallé Orch.—Harty
          (in CM-343†)   12"—C-69312D
[Nos. 5 & 6]
No. 3b, Romanze: "Der Vollmond strahlt aus Bergeshöhn"
Elisabeth Schumann (s) & Gerald Moore
(pf)   10"—G-DA1852
[Die Forelle]
No. 5, Entr'acte 3, B flat major
NOTE: *Often labelled "Entr-acte No. 2."*
Hallé Orch.—Harty
          (in CM-343†)   12"—C-69312D
[No. 3a & 6]
Berlin Philharmonic—Furtwängler
                           12"—PD-95418
[Bach: Brandenburg Concerto No. 3, Pt. 3]
[Bach: Suite in D—Air, on PD-66935]
[No. 9, Ballet Music No. 2, on PD-95458]
National Symphony Orch.—Fistoulari
[No. 9]   12"—D-K1304
Berlin Philharmonic—Schmidt-Isserstedt
[No. 9]   12"—T-E1902
Berlin State Opera Orch.—Kleiber
[Overture, Pt. 3]   12"—G-EJ360
No. 6, Hirtenmelodien ("Shepherd's Melody")
Hallé Orch.—Harty
          (in CM-343†)   12"—C-69312D
[Nos. 3a & 5]
No. 9, Ballet 2, G major
NOTE: *This familiar piece is often labelled "Ballet Music No. 2," or merely "Rosamunde Ballet Music."*
Hallé Orch.—Harty
[No. 2] (in CM-343†)   12"—C-69311D
London Symphony Orch.—B. Walter
(G-DB3651)   12"—V-12534
[No. 2]
Berlin Philharmonic—Schmidt-Isserstedt
[No. 5]   12"—T-E1902
National Symphony Orch.—Fistoulari
[No. 5]   12"—D-K1304
DUPLICATIONS: Berlin Philharmonic—Furtwängler, PD-66935: PD-95458; Vienna Philharmonic—Krauss, G-C2233: G-EH494: G-S10295; Symphony Orch.—Meyrowitz, PAT-PAT101: C-DX924; New Symphony Orch.—Barbirolli, G-C2637; Victor Salon Orch.—Shilkret, V-9307, in V-C3
—Arr. Violin & Piano Kreisler
Fritz Kreisler & M. Raucheisen,
G-DA1137; George Bouillon & M. Faure,
PAT-X98027
Serenade See under Songs—Ständchen
Soirée de Vienne (Valses Caprices) Arr. Piano Liszt
NOTE: *Based on Schubert's "Wiener Damen-Ländler," Op. 67. See also under Deutsche Tänze & Waltzes.*
—Set 1, No. 6
Walter Rehberg   10"—PD-24993
Egon Petri   12"—C-LWX115
DUPLICATION: Victor Salon Orch.—Shilkret, V-9307 in V-C3

SONATAS Piano
NOTE: *Numbering used is that of the Breitkopf & Härtel complete works edition. The supplementary volume contains seven additional sonatas not in this series. The Peters (& Schirmer) numbering has been indicated in parentheses.*

No. 6, A minor, Op. 164 1823
(Peters No. 7)
Kathleen Long   2   12"—D-K1067/8

No. 7, E flat major, Op. 122 1817
(Peters No. 4)
Kathleen Long
(D-K1180/2)   3   12"—D-ED26†

No. 8, A minor, Op. 143 1823
(Peters No. 5)
Lili Krauss (labelled No. 7)
                     3   12"—P-R20388/90†
[Ländler, Op. 18]

No. 10, A major, Op. 120 1825
(Peters No. 3)
Robert Casadesus (labelled No. 9)
[Ländler, Op. 171]   2 12"—CX-236†
(C-LFX585/6)

No. 11, D major, Op. 53 1825
(Peters No. 2)
Artur Schnabel (labelled No. 10)
[March, E major]   5   12"—VM-888†
—4th Mvt. (Rondo) only
—Arr. Violin & Piano Friedberg
Jascha Heifetz & Isidor Achron
[Ave Maria]   12"—G-DB1047
Jascha Heifetz & Emanuel Bay
                         12"—V-11-9572
[Achron: Hebrew Melody]
[Beethoven: Symphony No. 3, Pt. 9, with NBC Symphony Orch.—Toscanini, on G-DB11114]
Joseph Szigeti & Andor Foldes
          (in CX-238†)   12"—C-71488D
[Sonatina No. 1, D major, Pt. 3]
Jacques Thibaud & T. Janopoulo
                         12"—G-DB11104
[Sonata No. 3, G minor, Pt. 3]

No. 12, G major, Op. 78 1826
(Not in Peters)
Franz Josef Hirt   4   12"—PD-95206/9
Leff Pouishnoff   5   12"—C-9396/400
—3rd Mvt. (Minuet or Minuetto, B minor) only
Artur Rubinstein, V-14276; Jacques Dupont, PAT-X98176
—Arr. Orch.: Victor Salon Orch.—Shilkret, V-9308 in V-C3

No. 13, C minor, Op. Posth. 1828
(Peters No. 8)
No recording available

No. 14, A major, Op. Posth. 1828
(Peter's No. 9)
Artur Schnabel   5   12"—VM-580†
[Beethoven: Für Elise]

No. 15, B flat major, Op. Posth. 1828
(Peters No. 10)

No recording available

C major (unfinished) 1825
(Recording labelled No. 15)
NOTE: *Scherzo & Finale completed by Ernst Krenek*, 1921.

Ray Lev (Limited Edition)
            4   12"—CH-B3
[With Allegretto, C minor]

SONATAS—Violin & Piano

No. 1, D major, Op. 137, No. 1 ("Sonatine")
Joseph Szigeti & Andor Foldes
            2   12"—CX-238†
[Rondo from Piano Sonata, D major, Op. 53, arr. Friedberg]
Ida Haendel & Adela Kotowska
            2   12"—D-K1074/5

No. 3, G minor, Op. 137, No. 3 ("Sonatine")
Jacques Thibaud & Tasso Janopoulo
            2   12"—G-DB11103/4
[Rondo from Piano Sonata, D major, Op. 53, arr. Friedberg]

—3rd Mvt. (Menuetto) only
Albert Sammons & Kathleen Long
            10"—D-M559
[Delius: Violin Sonata No. 3, Pt. 5]

No. 4, C major, Op. 159 ("Grand Fantasia")
Erling Bloch & Holger Lund Christiansen
            3   12"—G-DB4/6
[Weber: Air Russe & Rondo]

No. 5, A major, Op. 162 ("Duo")
Fritz Kreisler & Sergei Rachmaninoff
            3   12"—G-DB1465/7

Sonata, A minor Arpeggione (or 'Cello) & Piano
Emanuel Feuermann (vlc) & Gerald Moore (pf)   3   12"—CM-346†
[Chopin: Nocturne, Op. 9, No. 2]
(C-LX717/9) (C-LFX536/8)
Pierre Fournier (vlc) & Jean Hubeau (pf)   2   12"—G-L1037/8
Watson Forbes (vla) & Myers Foggin (pf)   2   12"—D-K955/6

"Sonata" Movement, B flat major 1812
See under Trios—"Sonata"

SONGS (LIEDER) In German
Song Cycle Collections

(DIE) SCHOENE MUELLERIN, Op. 25
(Wilhelm Müller)
Eng. The Maid of the Mill Fr. Le Belle Meunière
1. Das Wandern 2. Wohin? 3. Halt! 4. Danksagung an den Bach 5. Am Feierabend 6. Der Neugierige 7. Ungeduld 8. Morgengruss 9. Des Müllers Blumen 10. Tränenregen 11. Mein! 12. Pause 13. Mit dem grünen Lautenbande 14. Der Jäger 15. Eifersucht und Stolz 16. Die liebe Farbe 17. Die böse Farbe 18. Trock'ne Blumen 19. Der Müller und der Bach 20. Des Baches Wiegenlied
Aksel Schiøtz (t) & Gerald Moore (pf)
(G-DB6252/9)   8   12"—GM-407†
Gerhard Hüsch (b) & H. U. Müller (pf) in Schöne Müllerin Society (Not available separately) 8   12"

Lotte Lehmann (s) (omitting No. 7 which is included in VM-292) & Paul Ulanovsky (pf)   7   12"—CM-615†
Germaine Martinelli (s) (in French) & Jean Doyen (pf)   4   12"—C-RFX43/6

Nos. 1, 2, 3, 7, 8, 13, 14, 15, 16, 17, 18, 19 only
Richard Crooks (t) & Frank La Forge (pf)   3   12"—VM-1067

SCHWANENGESANG (Rellstab, Heine, Seidl)
Eng. Swan Songs
1. Liebesbotschaft 2. Kriegers Ahnung 3. Frühlingssehnsucht 4. Ständchen 5. Aufenthalt 6. In der Ferne 7. Abschied 8. (Der) Atlas 9. Ihr Bild 10. (Das) Fischermädchen 11. (Die) Stadt 12. Am Meer 13. (Der) Doppelgänger 14. (Die) Taubenpost
See under titles of individual songs.

(DIE) WINTERREISE, Op. 89 (Wilhelm Müller)
Eng. The Wintry Road
1. Gute Nacht 2. Die Wetterfahne 3. Gefror'ne Tränen 4. Erstarrung 5. Der Lindenbaum 6. Wasserflut 7. Auf dem Flusse 8. Rückblick 9. Irrlicht 10. Rast 11. Frühlingstraum 12. Einsamkeit 13. Die Post 14. Der greise Kopf 15. Die Krähe 16. Letzte Hoffnung 17. Im Dorfe 18. Der stürmische Morgen 19. Täuschung 20. Der Wegweiser 21. Das Wirtshaus 22. Mut' 23. Die Nebensonnen 24. Der Leiermann
Gerhard Hüsch (b) & H. U. Müller (pf) in Die Winterreise Society 3 10" & 6 12" (Not available separately)
Marko Rothmüller (b) & Suzanne Gyr (pf)   2 10" & 6 12"—G-DA6023/4 &
                               G-DB10103/8
Lotte Lehmann (s) & Paul Ulanowsky (pf) as follows:
Nos. 1, 6, 16, 2, 7, 10, 11: 3 12"—CM-466
Nos. 13, 18, 23, 15, 19, 22, 5, 17, 8, 20, 21:   2 10" & 2 12"—VM-692
Nos. 3, 4, 9, 12, 14, 24: 3 10"—CM-587

Nos. 1, 5, 6, 8, 11, 13, 15, 18, 20, 21, 22, 24 only
Richard Tauber (t) & M. Spoliansky (pf)
(P-RO20037/42)   6   10"—P-P9

NON-CYCLIC COLLECTIONS

Selected Songs
Ave Maria; Litanei; Du bist die Ruh'; Gretchen am Spinnrade—
Elsa Alsen (s) & pf. acc.
Der Erlkönig; Der Tod und das Mädchen; Die junge Nonne; Die Forelle; Heidenröslein—
Sophie Braslau (c) & pf. acc.
Ständchen; Who is Sylvia (in English)—
Charles Hackett (t) & orchestral acc.
Am Meer; Aufenthalt; Der Wanderer; Der Doppelgänger Der Lindenbaum; Der Wegweiser—
Alexander Kipnis (b) & F. Bibb (pf)
                   8   12"—CM-89

INDIVIDUAL SONGS

Abschied: "Ade, du muntre, du fröliche Stadt"
(Schwanengesang No. 7) (Rellstab)
Max Lichtegg (t) & Georg Solti (pf)
In Prep. **Swiss Decca**

Abschied: "Lebe Wohl" Fr. **Adieu**
NOTE: *This is not an original Schubert song, but a synthetic work pieced together from various Schubert thematic tidbits by A. H. von Weyrauch.*
John McCormack (t) (in English), on V-6928 in V-C3
H. St. Criq (t) (in French), on PAT-X93035

(Die) Allmacht: "Gross ist Jehova" Op. 79, No. 2 (Ryrker)
Eng. **Great is Jehovah** or **The Omnipotence**
Kerstin Thorborg (c)   10″—V-2148
Louise Homer (c) (in English) (Recorded, 1909)   12″—V-15-1011*
[Meyerbeer: Les Huguenots—Noble Seigneurs]
Lawrence Tibbett (b) (in English)
(G-DB5762)   12″—V-15891
[Der Wanderer, Op. 4, No. 1]

Am Feierabend (Schöne Müllerin No. 5)
Aksel Schiøtz, on G-DB6253 in GM-407†
Gerhard Hüsch, in Schöne Müllerin Society Set
Lotte Lehmann, on C-71772D in CM-615†
Germaine Martinelli (in French), on C-RFX43

Am Grabe Anselmos
Tiana Lemnitz (s) & M. Raucheisen (pf)
[Wagner: Schmerzen]   12″—PD-57085

Am Meer (Schwanengesang No. 12) (Heine)
Eng. **By the Sea.**   Fr. **A la Mer**
Alexander Kipnis, on C-72056D in CM-89
Heinrich Schlusnus (b) & Franz Rupp
(pf)   10″—PD-62644
[An die Musik]
[Pressel: An der Weser, on PD-30000]
Paul Sandoz (b) & W. Marti (pf)
[Der Wanderer]   12″—G-HEX108
DUPLICATIONS: Franz Völker, PD-19912; Leo Slezak, PD-19925
In English: Richard Tauber, P-RO20499

Am See (Bruchmann)
Heinrich Schlusnus (b) & Franz Rupp
(pf)   12″—PD-90178
[Der zürnende Barde]
Karl Erb (t) & Bruno Seidler-Winkler
(pf)   10″—G-DA4422
[An die Laute]

An den Mond
("Füllest wieder Busch und Tal")
Erika Rokyta (s) & Noël Gallon (pf)
[Todtengräbers Heimweh]   12″—OL-33

An die Laute, Op. 81, No. 2 (Rochlitz)
Eng. **To the Lute**
Erika Rokyta (s) & Noël Gallon (pf)
          12″—OL-31
[Schwanengesang, An die Sonne, Ellens zweiter Gesang]

Karl Erb (t) & Bruno Seidler-Winkler
(pf)   10″—G-DA4422
[Am See]

An die Leier, Op. 56, No. 2 (Bruchmann)
Eng. **To the Lyre**
Jussi Björling (t) & Harry Ebert (pf)
          12″—G-DB5787
[Alfven: Skogen søver; Cholf: Morgen]
Marko Rothmüller (b) & Suzanne Gyr
(pf)   12″—G-DB10084
[Sei mir gegrüsst]
Heinrich Schlusnus (b) & Franz Rupp
(pf)   12″—PD-67252
[Der Wanderer]
Heinz Rehfuss (bs) & R. Spira (pf)
[Der Lindenbaum]   12″—ELITE-7044

An die Musik, Op. 88, No. 4 (Schober)
Gerhard Hüsch (b) & Hanns Udo Müller
(pf)   10″—G-DA4445
[Ständchen]
Heinrich Schlusnus (b) & Franz Rupp
(pf) [Am Meer]   10″—PD-62644
DUPLICATIONS: Karl Schmitt-Walter, T-A1885; Leo Slezak, PD-23018; Ursula van Dieman, G-EG271; Alexander Sved, G-DB5367
In English: Isobel Baillie, C-DB2067; Richard Tauber, P-RO20525

An die Sonne
Erika Rokyta (s) & Noël Gallon (pf)
          12″—OL-31
[Ellens sweiter Gesang; Schwanengesang; An die Laute]

An die Thüren (from "Gesänge des Harfners")
Gerhard Hüsch (b) & pf. acc.
[Dass sie hier gewesen] 10″—G-DA4466

An mein Klavier (Schubart)
Elizabeth Schumann (s) & Gerald Moore
(pf)   10″—G-DA1864
[Das Mädchen]

An Schwager Kronos, Op. 19, No. 1
(Gothe)
Heinrich Schlusnus (b) & M. Raucheisen
(pf)   10″—PD-30006
[Schumann: Der Soldat]

An Sylvia (Shakespeare) See under **Who is Sylvia?**

(Der) Atlas (Schwanengesang No. 8)
(Rellstab)
Heinrich Schlusnus (b) & Franz Rupp
(pf)   10″—PD-62643
[Der Doppelgänger]

Auf dem Flusse (Winterreise No. 7)
(Müller)
Lotte Lehmann, C-72072D in CM-466
Gerhard Hüsch, in Society Set
Marko Rothmüller, on G-DA6023

Auf dem Wasser zu singen (Von Stollberg)
Frida Leider (s) & M. Raucheisen (pf)
[Der Erlkönig]   12″—G-DB5625

Aufenthalt (Schwanengesang No. 5)
(Rellstab)
Marian Anderson (c) & K. Vehanen (pf)
[Ave Maria]   12″—G-DB3025
Marian Anderson (c) & Franz Rupp (pf)
[Ave Maria]   12″—V-11-9836

Marko Rothmüller (b) & Suzanne Gyr
(pf)   10"—G-DA6019
[Rastlose Liebe]
Alexander Kipnis, on C-72056D in CM-89
Heinz Rehfuss (bs) & R. Spira (pf)
[Doppelgänger]   12"—ELITE-7043

Auflösung (Mayrhofer)
Eleanor Steber (s) & James Quillon (pf)
                          10"—V-10-1099
[Cimara: Canto di Primavera]

Ave Maria: "Jungfrau mild" Op. 52, No. 6
NOTE: *The German text by P. A. Storck is
after a lyric in Sir Walter Scott's "Lady of the
Lake."*
Elisabeth Schumann (s) & Orch.—
Rosenek   12"—V-8423
[Bach: Bist du bei mir] (G-DB2291)
Marian Anderson (c) & K. Vehanen (pf)
[Aufenthalt]   12"—G-DB3025
Marian Anderson (c) & Franz Rupp (pf)
[Aufenthalt]   12"—V-11-9886
Karl Erb (t) & B. Seidler-Winkler (pf)
[Du bist die Ruh']   10"—G-EG3756
[Litanei, on G-JK2317]
Erna Sack (s)   12"—T-A2219
[Gounod: Ave Maria]
DUPLICATIONS: Elsa Alsen, on
C-7530M in CM-89; Marta Eggerth,
P-R1779: O-250567; Erna Berger, PD-
10098; Wolfgang Kieling, G-EG6708
In English: John McCormack, V-6927 in
V-C3: also G-DB578*; Charles Kullman,
C-9103M: C-DX435: C-DFX213; Nelson
Eddy, C-71786D; J. Phelan (treble),
G-C2766; Bobby Breen (treble), D-F7303
In French: Jean Planel, PAT-PG78;
Martha Angelici, LUM-32060; Jane La-
val, C-DF254;. Tino Rossi, C-BF41:
C-DB1841
In Danish: Tenna Frederiksen (s),
G-Z223
In Latin: Richard Tauber, PO20501;
Richard Crooks, V-11-8570; Risë Stev-
ens, C-7425M; Thomas L. Thomas, V-11-
9109; Jane Powell, on C-4457M in CX-
271; Rosetta Pampanini, CET-BB25084;
T. Schipa, G-DA1408; V. Poggioli,
C-DQ3043; B. Gigli, G-DB6619

—**Arr. Violin & Piano**
Yehudi Menuhin, G-DB1788: G-DB6158:
G-DB5394; Alfredo Campoli, G-C3144;
Bronislaw Hubermann, C-LFX314:
C-GQX10522; Jascha Heifetz, V-11-9571:
(older version), G-DB1047; Efrem Zim-
balist, C-7275M: C-9674; Mischa Elman,
V-7103; Georg Kulenkampff, PD-95229;
Siegfried Borries, G-DB5550; Ellen
Birgithe Nielsen, G-DB5284

—**Arr. Viola & Piano**
William Primrose, V-15733; (w. harp)
C-7378M

—**Arr. 'Cello & Piano**
Arnold Földesy, PD-24305; Marcelli-Herson, G-K5115

—**Arr. Organ**
Charles M. Courboin, V-14368; A. Walton, C-9229; F. Feibel, C-35751; H. Robinson Cleaver, P-F1594

—**Arr. Orchestra**
Boston "Pops" Orch.—Fiedler, V-13589:
G-C3239; Lamoureux Orch.—Wolff, PD-
67006: PD-566027; Victor Concert Orch.
—Bourdon, G-FKX1; Dauber Orch.,
G-B4479: G-GW618: G-HE2376; Andre
Kostelanetz & Orch., C-7416M
*See current catalogues for other recordings of
arrangements.*

(Des) Baches Wiegenlied (Schöne Müllerin
No. 20)
Aksel Schiøtz (t) & Gerald Moore (pf),
on G-DB6259 in GM-407†
[Also different recording on G-DB5238]
Gerhard Hüsch, in Society Set
Lotte Lehmann, on C-71777D in CM-615†
Germaine Martinelli (in French),
C-RFX46
Elisabeth Schumann (s) & George Reeves
(pf)   12"—G-DB3426
[Wiegenlied, Op. 98, No. 2 & Der Schmet-
terling, Op. 57, No. 1]

(Die) Böse Farbe (Schöne Müllerin No. 17)
Aksel Schiøtz (t) & Gerald Moore (pf),
on G-DB6258 in GM-407†
[Also, different recording, G-DA5216]
Gerhard Hüsch, in Society Set
Lotte Lehmann, on C-71776D in CM-615†
Germaine Martinelli (in French),
C-RFX46

Danksagung an den Bach (Schöne Müllerin
No. 4)
Aksel Schiøtz (t) & Gerald Moore (pf),
on G-DB6252 in GM-407†
Gerhard Hüsch, in Society Set
Lotte Lehmann, on C-71771D in CM-615†
Germaine Martinelli (in French),
C-RFX43

Dass sie hier gewesen, Op. 59, No. 2
Elisabeth Schumann (s) & Gerald
Moore (pf)   10"—G-DA1854
[Mozart: Das Veilchen]
Gerhard Hüsch (b) & pf. acc.
[An die Thüren]   10"—G-DA4466
Karl Erb (t) & B. Seidler-Winkler (pf)
[Wolf: Andenken]   10"—G-DA4423

Dithyrambe, Op. 60, No. 3 (Schiller)
Elena Gerhardt (ms) & Gerald Moore
(pf)   Private Recording-HMV

(Der) Doppelgänger (Schwanengesang No.
13)
Eng. The Wraith, or Phantom Double
(Heine)   Fr. Le Sosie
Lotte Lehmann (s) & Paul Ulanowsky
(pf)   12"—C-71509D
[Die junge Nonne]
Hans Hotter (b) & Hermann von Nord-
berg (pf)   12"—C-LX1004
[Der Wanderer]
Gerhard Hüsch (b) & pf. acc.
[Erlkönig]   12"—G-DB5523
Heinz Rehfuss (bs) & R. Spira (pf)
[Aufenthalt]   12"—ELITE-7043
Alexander Kipnis, on C-72057D in CM-89
DUPLICATIONS: Heinrich Schlusnus,
PD-62643; Louis Graveure, PD-10545;
Marko Rothmüller, G-DB10087
In French: Charles Panzéra, G-DB4948

Du bist die Ruh', Op. 59, No. 3 (Rückert)
Eng. Thou are repose
Elisabeth Schumann (s) & pf. acc.
12"—G-DB1844
[Heidenröslein & Lied im Grünen]
Karl Erb (t) 10"—G-EG3756
[Ave Maria]
[Nacht und Träume, on G-JK2318]
Erika Rokyta (s) & Othon Wetzel (pf)
10"—OL-24
[Jungling an der Quelle; Der Wanderers Nachtlied II]
Marko Rothmüller (b) & S. Gyr (pf)
[Erlkönig] 12"—G-DB10088
DUPLICATIONS: Heinrich Schlusnus, PD-95479; Karl Schmitt-Walter, T-A2130; A. Rautawaara, T-E1687; Elsa Alsen, C-7529M in CM-89; Leo Slezak, PD-19927
In French: Martha Angelici, LUM-30086

Eifersucht und Stolz (Schöne Müllerin No. 15)
Aksel Schiøtz (t) & Gerald Moore (pf), on G-DB6257 in GM-407†
[Also, earlier recording, G-DA5216]
Gerhard Hüsch, in Society Set
Lotte Lehmann, on C-71775D in CM-615†
Germaine Martinelli (in French), on C-RFX45

(Der) Einsame, Op. 41 (Lappe)
Karl Erb (t) & B. Seidler-Winkler (pf)
[Wegweiser] 12"—G-DB4465
Einsamkeit (Winterreise No. 12)
Gerhard Hüsch, in Society Set
Lotte Lehmann, on C-17465D in CM-587
Marko Rothmüller, on G-DA6024

Ellens zweiter Gesang
Elena Gerhardt (ms) & G. Moore (pf)
Private Recording-HMV
Erika Rokyta (s) & Noël Gallon (pf)
12"—OL-31
[An die Laute; An die Sonne; Schwanengesang]

(Der) Erlkönig, Op. 1 (Goethe)
Frida Leider (s) & M. Raucheisen (pf)
12"—G-DB5625
[Auf dem Wasser zu singen]
Alexander Kipnis (bs) & Celius Dougherty (pf) 12"—V-15825
[Schumann: Die Beiden Grenadiere] (G-DB6010)
Gerhard Hüsch (b) & pf. acc.
[Der Doppelgänger] 12"—G-DB5523
DUPLICATIONS: Alexander Kipnis, C-9128M: C-LX665: C-LFX512; Sophie Braslau, on C-72054D in CM-89; Heinrich Schlusnus, PD-67051; Marko Rothmüller, G-DB10088; Piroska Anday, RAD-SP8005
In English: Peter Dawson, G-C1327
In French: Charles Panzéra, G-DB4948; Georges Thill (t), M. Etcheverry (bs), C. Pascal (treble) & Orch.—Bigot (Trio Arr.), on C-LFX336
—Arr Piano Liszt
Jean Guitton, D-112

Erstarrung (Winterreise No. 4)
Lotte Lehmann, on C-17464D in CM-587
Gerhard Hüsch, in Society Set
Marko Rothmüller, on G-DA6023

(Das) Fischermädchen (Heine)
(Schwanengesang No. 10)
No recording available
(Des) Fischers Liebesglück (Leitner)
Karl Erb (t) & B. Seidler-Winkler (pf)
[Nacht und Träume] 10"—G-EG3611
Jo Vincent (s) 12"—C-DHX5
[Mozart: Mass, C minor—Et incarnatus est]

(Die) Forelle, Op. 32 (Schubert) Eng. The Trout Fr. La Truite
NOTE: The theme of this song is used in the 4th Mvt. of the "Forellen Quintet." For recordings see under Quintet, A major, Op. 114.
Marian Anderson (c) & K. Vehanen (pf) (G-DA1550) 10"—V-1862
[Der Tod und das Mädchen]
Erna Sack (s) & Wilhelm Czernik (pf)
10"—T-A10426
[Mozart: Warnung, K. 433]
Ria Ginster (s) & Paul Baumgartner (pf)
[Wohin?] 10"—G-DA6010
(Earlier recording on G-DB2481)
DUPLICATIONS: Sophie Braslau, on C-72055D in CM-89; Petre Monteanu, CET-AA468
In English: Dorothy Stanton, on C-DB837, in Columbia History of Music, Vol. III: CM-233
In French: Georges Thill, C-LF141; Vanni-Marcoux, G-P847; M. Darmancier, LUM-30030; Martha Angelici, LUM-30086

Frühlingsglaube, Op. 20, No. 2 (Uhland)
Karl Schmitt-Walter (b) & M. Raucheisen (pf) 10"—T-A10190
[Der Musensohn]
Richard Tauber (t) 10"—P-PO166
[Hark, Hark, the Lark]
DUPLICATIONS: Edi Laider, G-X6360; Heinrich Schlusnus, PD-62795
Frühlingssehnsucht (Rellstab)
(Schwanengesang No. 3)
No recording available
Frühlingstraum (Winterreise No. 11)
Marko Rothmüller, on G-DB10105
Gerhard Hüsch, in Society Set
Lotte Lehmann, on C-72073D in CM-466
Richard Tauber, on P-RO20039 in P-P9
In Italian: Angelo Parigi, G-HN1969

Gefror'ne tränen (Winterreise No. 3)
Lotte Lehmann, on C-17464D in CM-587
Gerhard Hüsch, in Society Set
Marko Rothmüller, on G-DB10103

Geheimes, Op. 14, No. 2 (Goethe)
Henrich Schlusnus (b) & F. Rupp (pf)
[Neugierige] 10"—PD-30001
Erika Rokyta (s) & Noël Gallon (pf)
12"—OL-30
[Meerestille; Nähe des Geliebten]

Gesänge des Harfners
See under An die Thüren; Wer nie sein Brot mit tränen ass; Wer sich der einsamkeit ergiebt

(Der) Greise Kopf (Winterreise No. 14)
Gerhard Hüsch, in Society Set
Lotte Lehmann, on C-17466D in CM-587
Marko Rothmüller, on G-DB10106

Gretchen am Spinnrade, Op. 2 (Goethe)
It. Margherita all' arcolaio Eng.

**Gretchen at the Spinning Wheel Fr.
Marguerite au rouet**
Lotte Lehmann (s) & Erno Balogh (pf)
[Wiegenlied] (in VM-419) 10"—**V-1856**
Kathleen Ferrier (c) & Phyllis Spurr (pf)
[Die Junge Nonne] 12"—**D-K1632**
DUPLICATIONS: Elsa Alsen, on
C-7529D in CM-89; Rosette Anday, PD-
95164
In English: Isobel Baillie, C-DB836 **in**
CM-233 (Columbia History of Music,
Vol 3)
In Italian: Augusta Oltrabella,
G-DA5355
In French: Germaine Martinelli,
C-LFX250
—**Arr. Piano Liszt**
Egon Petri, on C-69554D in CM-362†

Gute Nacht (Winterreise No. 1)
Gerhard Hüsch, in Society Set
Lotte Lehmann, on C-72071D in CM-466
Marko Rothmüller, on G-DB10103
Richard Tauber (t) & pf. acc.
(in P-P9) 10"—**P-RO20037**
[Lindenbaum]

Haidenröslein See under Heidenröslein

Halt! (Schöne Müllerin No. 3)
Aksel Schiøtz, on G-DB6252 in GM-407†
Gerhard Hüsch, in Society Set
Lotte Lehmann, on C-71771D in CM-615†
Germaine Martinelli (in French), on
C-RFX43

Hark, Hark, the Lark (Shakespeare)
Ger. Ständchen (Morgenständchen):
Horch, horch, die Lerch'!
Gerhard Hüsch (b) & pf. acc.
[Liebeslauschen] 12"—**G-DB5522**
Elisabeth Schumann (s) & G. Moore (pf)
[Brahms: Sandmännchen]
10"—**G-DA1526**
Kerstin Thorborg (c) & Leo Rosenek (pf)
12"—**G-DB5766**
[Brahms: Sapphische Ode; Wolf: Gesang
Weylas]
Richard Tauber (t) 10"—**P-PO166**
[Frühlingsglaube]
Karl Schmitt-Walter (b) & M. Rauch-
eisen (pf) 10"—**T-A10155**
[Ständchen]
DUPLICATION: Annie Would, C-DH93
In English: Elsie Suddaby, G-B2746; E.
Lough (treble), G-B2681
—**Arr. Piano Liszt** ("Morgenständchen")
Alexander Brailowsky, PD-90175; Wil-
helm Kempff, PD-62746; Wm. Murdoch,
D-F7498

Heidenröslein, Op. 3, No. 3 (Goethe)
Eng. The Rosebud, or Hedge Rose
Alexander Kipnis (bs) & Gerald Moore
(pf) 12"—**C-9128M**
(C-LX665) (C-LFX512)
[Ungeduld & Erlkönig]
Eilsabeth Schumann (s) & pf. acc.
12"—**G-DB1844**
[Lied im Grünen & Du bist die Ruh']
Richard Tauber (t) & P. Kahn (pf)
[Silcher: Die Lorelei] 12"—**P-RO20442**
DUPLICATIONS: Sophie Braslau,
C-72055D in CM-89; Treble of Regens-

burg Cathedral, G-EG3871; Edi Laider,
G-X6361; Comedian Harmonists,
G-K8073: G-HN1468: G-EG6509
In French: Manécanterie des Petits Chan-
teurs à la Croix de Bois, G-K7891
In English: Elsie Suddaby, G-B2746

(Der) Hirt auf dem Felsen, Op. 129
(Chezy)
Ria Ginster (s), E. Fanghänel (cl), &
Paul Baumgartner (pf) 12"—**G-DB10080**
Margaret Ritchie (s), Reginald Kell (cl),
Gerald Moore (pf) 12"—**G-C3688**
Isabel French (s), Paul Mimart (cl), &
R. Hughes (pf) 12"—**TC-1129**
Dorothy Maynor (s), D. Oppenheim (cl),
& G. Schick (pf) 12"—**V-12-0186**
Winifred Cecil (s) (in Italian), L. Amo-
dio (cl), & A. Simonetti (pf)
12"—**CET-CC2153**

Horch, horch, die Lerch'! See under Hark,
Hark, the Lark!

Ihr Bild (Rellstab)
(Schwanengesang No. 9)
No recording available

Ihr Grab (Stoll)
Karl Erb (t) & B. Seidler-Winkler (pf)
12"—**G-DB4467**
[Schumann: Wer machte dich so krank;
Alte Laute]

Im Abendroth (Lappe)
Ria Ginster (s) & Gerald Moore (pf)
12"—**G-DB2481**
[Die Forelle; Die Liebe hat gelogen]
Lotte Lehmann (s) & E. Balogh (pf)
[Ungeduld] (in VM-292) 10"—**V-1731**
Heinrich Schlusnus (b) & S. Peschko (pf)
[Liebesbotschaft] 10"—**PD-62829**
DUPLICATIONS: Leo Slezak, PD-21690;
Karl Erb, G-DA4459; A. Noordewier—
Reddingius, C-DHX35

Im Dorfe (Winterreise No. 17) Fr. Au
Village
Gerhard Hüsch, in Society Set
Lotte Lehmann, on V-17190 in VM-692
Marko Rothmüller, on G-DB10107

In der Ferne (Rellstab)
(Schwanengesang No. 6)
Max Lichtegg (t) & Georg Solti (pf)
In Prep. **Swiss Decca**

Irrlicht (Winterreise No. 9)
Gerhard Hüsch, in Society Set
Lotte Lehmann, on C-17465D in CM-587
Marko Rothmüller, on G-DB10105

(Der) Jäger (Schöne Müllerin No. 14)
Aksel Schiøtz, on G-DB6257 in GM-407†
Gerhard Hüsch, in Society Set
Lotte Lehmann, C-71775D in CM-615†
Germaine Martinelli (in French), on
C-RFX45

(Die) Junge Nonne, Op. 43, No. 1
(Craigher)
Lotte Lehmann (s) & Paul Ulanowsky
(pf) 12"—**C-71509D**
[Der Doppelgänger]
Kathleen Ferrier (c) & Phyllis Spurr (pf)
[Gretchen am Spinnrade] 12"—**D-K1632**
DUPLICATION: Sophie Braslau,
C-72055D in CM-89

(Der) Jüngling an der Quelle (Salis)
Erika Rokyta (s) & Othon Wetzel (pf)
10″—OL-24
[Wanderers Nachtlied II; Du bist die Ruh']
Heinrich Schlusnus (b) & Franz Rupp (pf) 10″—PD-90194
[Wanderers an den Mond]
Lore Fischer (c) & M. Raucheisen (pf)
10″—PD-11362
[Wanderers an den Mond]
(Der) Jüngling und der Tod
Karl Erb (t) & B. Seidler-Winkler (pf)
[Vor meiner Wiege] 12″—G-DB4466
(Die) Junge Schäferin ("La Pastorella")
Lea Piltti (s) 10″—G-EG7093
[Schumann: Mondnacht]
(Die) Krähe (Winterreise No. 15)
Gerhard Hüsch, in Society Set
Lotte Lehmann, on V-2109 in VM-692
Marko Rothmüller, on G-DB10106
Richard Tauber (t) & pf. acc.
(O-4911) (in P-P9) 10″—P-RO20040
[Stürmische Morgen]
Kriegers Ahnung (Rellstab)
(Schwanengesang No. 2)
Heinrich Schlusnus (b) & S. Peschko (pf)
[Nachtstück] 12″—PD-67537
Lachen und weinen, Op. 59, No. 4
(Rückert)
Fr. Les Rires et les Pleurs
Vanni-Marcoux (in French), G-DA989
(Der) Leiermann (Winterreise No. 24)
Eng. The Hurdy-Gurdy Man, or The Organ Grinder
Gerhard Hüsch, in Society Set
Lotte Lehmann, on C-17466D in CM-587
Marko Rothmüller, on G-DA6025
Richard Tauber, on P-RO20042 in P-P9
In Italian: Augusta Oltrabella,
G-DA5355
In English: John McCormack, V-6928 in V-C3
Letzte Hoffnung (Winterreise No. 16)
Gerhard Hüsch, in Society Set
Lotte Lehmann, on C-72072D in CM-466
Marko Rothmüller, on G-DB10106
Else Fink (s) & Suzanne Gyr (pf)
[Tod und das Mädchen] 10″—G-DA6022
(Die) Liebe Farbe (Schöne Müllerin No. 16)
Aksel Schiøtz, on G-DB6257/8 in GM-407†
Gerhard Hüsch, in Society Set
Lotte Lehmann, on C-71775D in CM-615
Germaine Martinelli (in French),
C-RFX45
(Die) Liebe hat gelogen, Op. 23, No. 1
(Platen)
Karl Erb (t) & B. Seidler-Winkler (pf)
10″—G-DA4424
[Schumann: Was soll ich sagen?]
Ria Ginster (s) & Gerald Moore (pf)
[Forelle; Im Abendroth] 12″—G-DB2481
Liebeslauschen
Gerhard Hüsch (b) & pf. acc.
12″—G-DB5522
[Hörch, hörch, die lerch']
Liebesbotschaft (Rellstab)
(Schwanengesang No. 1)

Karl Erb (t) & B. Seidler-Winkler (pf)
[Wanderer an den Mond]
10″—G-DA4421
Heinrich Schlusnus (b) & S. Peschko (pf)
[Im Abendroth] 10″—PD-62829
DUPLICATIONS: Julius Patzak, PD-25013; Dorothy Maynor, V-10-1372
In Italian: Angelo Parigi, G-HN1969
Lied eines Schiffers an die Dioskuren Op. 65, No. 1 (Mayrhofer)
Gerhard Hüsch (b) & H. U. Müller (pf)
[Widerschein] 10″—G-DA4452
(Das) Lied im Grünen, Op. 115, No. 1
(Reil)
Elisabeth Schumann (s) & K. Alwin (pf)
12″—G-DB1844
[Heidenröslein; Du bist die Ruh']
Karl Erb (t) & B. Seidler-Winkler (pf)
[Wolf: Frohe Botschaft] 10″—G-DA4420
(Der) Lindenbaum (Winterreise No. 5)
Eng. The Linden Tree Fr. Le Tilleul
Gerhard Hüsch, in Society Set
Marko Rothmüller, on G-DB10104
Lotte Lehmann, on V-17190 in VM-692
Alexander Kipnis, on C-72058D in CM-89
Karl Schmitt-Walter (b) & Raucheisen (pf) 10″—T-A2130
[Du bist die Ruh']
[Radecke: Aus der Jugendzeit, on T-A2690]
Richard Tauber, on P-RO20037 in P-P9
DUPLICATION: Heinz Rehfuss, ELITE-7044
In French: Vanni-Marcoux, G-DB4821;
Georges Thill, C-LF250
—**Arr. Male Chorus:** Berlin Teachers' Chorus—Rudel, PD-21415; Nebe Quartet, G-EG1898; Erk'scher Male Chorus, PD-27210
—**Arr Piano Liszt**
Raoul von Koczalski, PD-27264: PD-95349; Egon Petri, in CX-136
Litanei (auf das Fest Allerseelen) (Jacobi)
Karl Erb (t) & B. Seidler-Winkler (pf)
[Bach: O Jesulein süss] 10″—G-EG3184
[Ave Maria, on G-JK2317]
Elsa Alsen, on C-7530M in CM-89
DUPLICATIONS: Irène Joachim, BAM-49; Leo Slezak, PD-21690
—**Arr. Piano Cortot**
Alfred Cortot, G-DB3338
—**Arr. Violin**
Vasa Prihoda, PD-57030; Siegfried Borries, G-DB5550
—**Arr. Viola**
William Primrose & Vernon de Tar (Organ), V-11-9117
(Das) Mädchen (Schlegel)
Elisabeth Schumann (s) & Gerald Moore (pf) 10″—G-DA1864
[An mein Klavier]
(Das) Mädchens Klage, Op. 58, No. 3
(Schiller)
Rosette Anday (c) & F. Rupp (pf)
[Gretchen am Spinnrade] 12″—PD-95164
Meeresstille, Op. 3, No. 4
Erika Rokyta (s) & Noël Gallon (pf)
12″—OL-30
[Geheimes; Nähe des Geliebten]

Mein! (Schöne Müllerin No. 11)
Aksel Schiøtz, on G-DB6256 in GM-407†
(Also on G-X6387)
Gerhard Hüsch, in Society Set
Lotte Lehmann, on C-71774D in CM-615†
In French: Germaine Martinelli,
C-RFX45

Memnon, Op. 6, No. 1 (Mayrhofer)
Harold Williams (b) (in English) & pf.
acc.   10″—C-DB836
[Gretchen am Spinnrade, Isobel Baillie]
(in Columbia History of Music, Vol III:
CM-233)

Mit dem grünen Lautenbande (Schöne
Müllerin No. 13)
Aksel Schiøtz, on G-DB6257 in GM-407†
Gerhard Hüsch, in Society Set
Lotte Lehmann, on C-71774D in CM-615†
Germaine Martinelli (in French),
C-RFX45

Mondenschein
See under Mondenschein in alphabetical
listing.

Morgengruss (Schöne Müllerin No. 8)
Eng. **Morning Greeting**
Aksel Schiøtz, G-DB6254 in GM-407†
(also older recording, G-X6312)
Gerhard Hüsch, in Society Set
Lotte Lehmann, on C-71773D in CM-615†
In French: Germaine Martinelli, on
C-RFX44
In Italian: Angelo Parigi, G-HN1817

(Der) Müller und der Bach (Schöne Müllerin No. 19)
Aksel Schiøtz, on G-DB6259 in GM-407†
(also different recording, G-DB5238)
Gerhard Hüsch, in Society Set
Lotte Lehmann, on C-71777D in CM-615†
Germaine Martinelli (in French), on
C-RFX46

(Des) Müllers Blumen (Schöne Müllerin
No. 9)
Aksel Schiøtz, on G-DB6255 in GM-407†
Gerhard Hüsch, in Society Set
Lotte Lehmann, on C-71773D in CM-615†
Germaine Martinelli (in French), on
C-RFX44

(Der) Musensohn, Op. 92, No. 1 (Goethe)
Karl Schmitt-Walter (b) & M. Rauch-
eisen (pf)   10″—T-A10190
[Frühlingsglaube]
Gerhard Hüsch (b) & H. U. Müller (pf)
[Wanderer]   10″—G-EG3201
DUPLICATIONS: Heinrich Schlusnus,
PD-30029; Leo Slezak, PD-21689

Mut' (Winterreise No. 22)
Gerhard Hüsch, in Society Set
Lotte Lehmann, on V-2109 in VM-692
Richard Tauber, on P-RO20042 in P-P9
Marko Rothmüller, on G-DB10108

Nacht und Träume, Op. 43, No. 2 (Collin)
Karl Erb (t) & B. Seidler-Winkler (pf)
                                        10″—G-EG3611
[Des Fischers Liebesglück]
[Du bist die Ruh', on G-JK2318]
Heinrich Schlusnus (b) & S. Peschko (pf)
[Wohin?]   10″—PD-62821

Nachtstück
Heinrich Schlusnus (b) & S. Peschko
(pf)   12″—PD-67537
[Kriegers Ahnung]

Nähe des Geliebten, Op. 5, No. 2 (Goethe)
Erika Rokyta (s) & Noël Gallon (pf)
[Meeresstille & Geheimes]   12″—OL-30

(Die) Nebensonnen (Winterreise No. 23)
Gerhard Hüsch, in Society Set
Lotte Lehmann, on V-2108 in VM-692
Marko Rothmüller, on G-DB10108
Karl Schmitt-Walter (b) & M. Rauch-
eisen (pf)   10″—T-A10168
[Post]

(Der) Neugierige (Schöne Müllerin No. 6)
Aksel Schiøtz, on G-DB6253 in GM-407†
(Also on G-X6351)
Gerhard Hüsch, in Society Set
Lotte Lehmann, on C-71772D in CM-615†
Germaine Martinelli (in French), on
C-RFX44
Karl Schmitt-Walter (b) & M. Rauch-
eisen (pf)   10″—T-A10144
[Ungeduld]
DUPLICATIONS: Heinrich Schlusnus,
PD-30001

(La) Pastorella See Junge Schäferin

Pause (Schöne Müllerin No. 12)
Aksel Schiøtz, on G-DB6256 in GM-407†
Gerhard Hüsch, in Society Set
Lotte Lehmann, on C-71774D in CM-615†
In French: Germaine Martinelli, on
C-RFX45

(Die) Post. (Winterreise No. 13)
Gerhard Hüsch, in Society Set
Lotte Lehmann, on V-2108 in VM-692
Marko Rothmüller, on G-DB10106
Richard Tauber, on P-RO20039 in P-P9
Karl Schmitt-Walter (b) & M. Rauch-
eisen (pf)   10″—T-A10168
[Nebensonnen]
DUPLICATIONS: Leo Slezak, PD-21689;
Piroska Anday, RAD-RZ3011
In English: Richard Tauber, P-RO20525

Rast (Winterreise No. 10)
Gerhard Hüsch, in Society Set
Lotte Lehmann, on C-72073D in CM-466
Marko Rothmüller, on G-DA6024

Rastlose Liebe, Op. 5, No. 1 (Goethe)
Marko Rothmüller (b) & Suzanne Gyr
(pf)   10″—G-DA6019
[Aufenthalt]
DUPLICATION: Julius Patzak,
PD-25013

Rückblick (Winterreise No. 8)
Gerhard Hüsch, in Society Set
Lotte Lehmann, on V-17190 in VM-692
Richard Tauber, on P-RO20038 in P-P9
Marko Rothmüller, on G-DB10105

(Der) Schmetterling, Op. 57, No. 1
Elisabeth Schumann (s) & George
Reeves (pf)   12″—G-DB3426
[Baches Wiegenlied; Wiegenlied]

(Die) Schöne Müllerin, Op. 25 Song Cycle
For complete list of titles and recorded
collections see under Song Cycles above.

Schwanengesang, Op. 23, No. 3 (Senn)
Erika Rokyta (s) & Noël Gallon (pf)
12"—OL-31
[An die Laute; Ellens Zweiter Gesang;
An die Sonne]
See also under Song Cycles above.

Sei mir gegrüsst, Op. 20, No. 1 (Rückert)
Heinrich Schlusnus (b) & S. Peschko (pf)
[Ständchen] 12"—PD-67181
Marko Rothmüller (b) & Suzanne Gyr
(pf) 12"—G-DB10084
[An die Leier]
Arno Schellenberg (b) & Orch.
[Ständchen] 12"—G-EH1262

Serenade See under Ständchen

(Die) Stadt (Schwanengesang No. 11)
(Heine)
Elena Gerhardt (ms) & Gerald Moore
(pf) Private Recording—HMV
Marko Rothmüller (b) & Suzanne Gyr
(pf) 12"—G-DB10087
[Doppelgänger]

Ständchen—"Leise flehen meine Lieder"
(Schwanengesang No. 4) (Rellstab)
Eng. Serenade
NOTE: *This is the celebrated Schubert Serenade,
used in Berte's "Blossom Time," the film
"Unfinished Symphony" and in most miscel-
laneous Schubert Medleys and Fantasias.*
Jussi Björling (t) & Harry Ebert (pf)
[An Sylvia] (G-DB5759) 12"—V-12725
Heinrich Schlusnus (b) & S. Peschko (pf)
[Sei mir gegrüsst] 12"—PD-67181
Gerhard Hüsch (b) & H. U. Müller (pf)
[An die Musik] 10"—G-DA4445
Richard Tauber (t) 10"—P-RO20260
[Ungeduld]
Dorothy Maynor (s) & George Schick (pf)
[Liebesbotschaft] 10"—V-10-1372
DUPLICATIONS: Lauritz Melchior,
C-17509D; Leo Slezak, PD-19923; Karl
Schmitt-Walter, T-A10155; Paul Sandoz,
G-JK24; Arno Schellenberg, G-EH1262;
Marta Eggerth, P-R1779; Jo Vincent,
C-D17181; Erna Berger, PD-10098;
Louis Graveure, PD-10545; B. Gigli,
G-DA1657
In English: Richard Crooks, V-2177;
Nelson Eddy, C-71786D; Richard Tauber,
P-RO20499; Charles Kullman, C-9130M:
C-DX435; Charles Hackett, C-7531M in
CM-89; Elsie Suddaby, G-B2746; Alfred
Piccaver, D-M458; Webster Booth,
G-C3116; John McCormack, G-DA458*:
also V-6927 in V-C3; Grace Moore,
D-29010 in D-A165
In French: Jean Planel, PAT-PG78; M.
Villabella, PD-524377; Paul Sandoz,
G-JK25; Georges Thill, C-LF141; Roger
Bourdin, O-123614; Herri St.-Cricq,
PAT-X93035; Ninon Vallin, O-123665;
M. Darmancier, LUM-30030; Alba Maz-
zoni, PAT-PA1458
In Italian: Beniamino Gigli, G-DB1903;
Mascia Predit, CET-BB25155; Enzo de
Muro Lomanto, C-DQ2296; O. Fineschi,
CET-7043; O. Fineschi & Olga Manetti
(duo), C-CQX16618; N. Vera Poggioli,
C-DQ3043; Inez Maria Ferraris, CET-
C27572

—Arr. Piano Liszt
Sergei Rachmaninoff, V-11-8728
—Arr. Orchestra
Victor Salon Orch.—Shilkret, V-21253:
G-B2768: G-HE2271; Radio Antwerp
Orch.—Gason, OLY-CL2601; Paul God-
win Orch., PD-522688; Melachrino
Strings, G-B9580
—Arr. Violin & Piano
Mischa Elman, V-7461; Mario Traversa,
PD-47346; Albert Sandler, C-DB563;
Miguel Candela, C-LF82; Bruno Sanger,
G-EG7005
—Arr. Organ: Charles M. Courboin, V-1968
*See current catalogues for recordings of other
musical arrangements.*

(Der) Stürmische Morgen (Winterreise
No. 18)
Gerhard Hüsch, in Society Set
Lotte Lehmann, on V-2108 in VM-692
Richard Tauber, on P-RO20040 in P-P9
Marko Rothmüller, on G-DB10107

(Die) Taubenpost (Claudius)
(Schwanengesang No. 14)
No recording available

Täuschung (Winterreise No. 19)
Gerhard Hüsch, in Society Set
Lotte Lehmann, on V-2109 in VM-692
Marko Rothmüller, on G-DA6025

(Der) Tod und das Mädchen, Op. 7, No. 3
(Claudius)
Eng. Death and the Maiden
NOTE: *The melody of this song is used as the
basis of the theme and variations movement of
the String Quartet No. 14 in D minor.*
Marian Anderson (c) & Franz Rupp (pf)
[Wohin?] 10"—V-10-1327
(Earlier recording, w. Kosti Vehanen
(pf), on V-1862: G-DA1550)
Else Fink (s) & Suzanne Gyr (pf)
[Letzte Hoffnung] 10"—G-DA6022
A. Rautawaara (s) & Franz Rupp (pf)
[Du bist die Ruh'] 12"—T-E1687
DUPLICATION: Sophie Braslau, on
C-72054D in CM-89

Totengräbers Heimweh
Erika Rokyta (s) & Noël Gallon (pf)
[An der Mond] 12"—OL-33

Tränenregen (Schöne Müllerin No. 10)
Aksel Schiøtz, on G-DB6255 in GM-407†
(Also on G-X6387)
Gerhard Hüsch, in Society Set
Lotte Lehmann, on C-71773D in CM-615†
Germaine Martinelli (in French), on
C-RFX44

Trock'ne Blumen (Schöne Müllerin No. 18)
Aksel Schiøtz, G-DB6258 in GM-407†
Gerhard Hüsch, in Society Set
Lotte Lehmann, on C-71776D in CM-615†
In French: Germaine Martinelli, on
C-RFX46

(Dem) Unendlichen (Klopstock)
Ria Ginster (s) & Hans Vollenweider
(organ) 12"—G-DB10044
[Handel: Semele—Where'er you walk]
Heinrich Schlusnus (b) 12"—PD-67467
[Beethoven: Die Himmel rühmen]
[Earlier recording with Du bist die Ruh'
on PD-95479]

Ungeduld (Schöne Müllerin No. 7) Eng.
  Impatience
  Aksel Schiøtz, on G-DB6254 in GM-407†
  (Also different recording, G-X6351)
  Gerhard Hüsch, in Society Set
  Lotte Lehmann, on V-1731 in VM-292
  Alexander Kipnis (bs) & Gerald Moore
  (pf)   12"—**C-9128M**
  (C-LX665) (C-LFX512)
  [Heidenröslein; Erlkönig]
  Paul Sandoz (b) & W. Marti (pf)
  [Ständchen]   10"—**G-JK24**
  DUPLICATIONS: Leo Slezak,
  PD-19923; Emmy Bettendorf, O-7962;
  Marta Eggerth, O-250615; Karl Schmitt-
  Walter, T-A10144; Piroska Anday, RAD-
  RZ3011
  In English: Webster Booth, G-B9315;
  Richard Tauber, P-RO20260
  In French: Odette Moulin, PAT-PA899;
  Germaine Martinelli, C-RFX44

Vergissmeinnicht (Schober)
  Fr. **Le Myosotis**
  Vanni-Marcoux (b) (in French)
  [Lindenbaum]   12"—**G-DB4821**

Verklärung (Pope-Herder)
  A. Noordewier-Reddingius (s) & pf. acc.
  [Im Abendroth]   12"—**C-DHX35**

Vor meiner Wiege, Op. 106, No. 3
  Karl Erb (t) & B. Seidler-Winkler (pf)
  [Jüngling und der Tod] 12"—**G-DB4466**

(Der) Wanderer, Op. 4, No. 1 (Schmidt)
  Hans Hotter (b) & Herman von Nord-
  berg (pf)   12"—**C-LX1004**
  [Der Doppelgänger]
  Gerhard Hüsch (b) & H. U. Müller (pf)
  [Musensohn]   10"—**G-EG3201**
  Heinrich Schlusnus (b) & Franz Rupp
  (pf)   12"—**PD-67252**
  [An die Leier]
  Alexander Sved (b) & pf. acc.
  [An die Musik]   12"—**G-DB5367**
  DUPLICATIONS: Alexander Kipnis, on
  C-72057D in CM-89; Paul Sandoz,
  G-HEX108
  In English: Lawrence Tibbett, V-15891:
  G-DB5762

(Der) Wanderer an den Mond, Op. 80, No. 1
  (Seidl)
  Karl Erb (t) & B. Seidler-Winkler (pf)
  [Liebesbotschaft]   10"—**G-DA4421**
  Lore Fischer (c) & M. Raucheisen (pf)
  [Jüngling an der Quelle] 10"—**PD-11362**

  Heinrich Schlusnus (b) & F. Rupp (pf)
  [Jüngling an der Quelle] 12"—**PD-90194**

Wanderers Nachtlied I, Op. 4, No. 3
  (Goethe)
  Edi Laider (b) & H. Sigurdsson (pf)
  [Heidenröslein]   10"—**G-X6361**

Wanderers Nachtlied II, Op. 96, No. 3
  (Goethe)
  Karl Schmitt-Walter (b) & M. Rauch-
  eisen (pf)   10"—**T-A2178**
  [Wolf: Gesang Weylas; Grieg: Eros]
  Erika Rokyta (s) & Othon Wetzel (pf)
            10"—**OL-24**

[Du bist die Ruh' & Jüngling an der
  Quelle]
  Karl Erb (t) & B. Seidler-Winkler (pf)
  [Im Abendroth]   10"—**G-DA4459**

(Das) Wandern (Schöne Müllerin No. 1)
  Aksel Schiøtz, on G-DB6252 in GM-407†
  (Also on G-X6312)
  Gerhard Hüsch, in Society Set
  Lotte Lehmann, on C-71771D in CM-615†
  Sven-Olof Sandberg (b) &. M. Rauch-
  eisen (pf)   10"—**O-4640**
  [Wohin?]
  In French: Germaine Martinelli, on
  C-RFX43
  —Arr. Piano Liszt
  Sergei Rachmaninoff, V-1161
Was ist Sylvia?
  See under Who is Sylvia

Wasserfluth (Winterreise No. 6)
  Gerhard Hüsch, in Society Set
  Lotte Lehmann, on C-72072D in CM-466
  Richard Tauber, on P-RO20038 in P-P9
  Marko Rothmüller, on G-DB10104

(Der) Wegweiser (Winterreise No. 20)
  Gerhard Hüsch, in Society Set
  Alexander Kipnis, on C-72058D in CM-89
  Lotte Lehmann, on V-17191 in VM-692
  Richard Tauber, on P-RO20041 in P-P9
  Marko Rothmüller, on G-DB10107
  Karl Erb (t) & B. Seidler-Winkler (pf)
  [Einsame]   12"—**G-DB4465**

Wer nie sein Brot mit Tränen ass (from
  "Gesange des Harfners")
  Gerhard Hüsch (b) & pf. acc.
            12"—**G-DB5524**
  [Wer sich der Einsamkeit ergiebt]

Wer sich der Einsamkeit ergiebt (from
  "Gesange des Harfners")
  Gerhard Hüsch (b) & pf. acc.
            12"—**G-DB5524**
  [Wer nie sein Brot mit Tränen ass]

(Die) Wetterfahne (Winterreise No. 2)
  Gerhard Hüsch, in Society Set
  Lotte Lehmann, on C-72072D in CM-466
  Marko Rothmüller, on G-DB10103

Who is Sylvia? Op. 106, No. 4 (Shakespeare)
  Ger. An Sylvia: "Was ist Sylvia"
  Jussi Björling (t) & Harry Ebert (pf)
  [Ständchen] (G-DB5759) 12"—**V-12725**
  Karl Erb (t) & B. Seidler-Winkler (pf)
            12"—**G-EG3687**
  [Brahms: Lerchengesang]
  Heinrich Schlusnus (b) & pf. acc.
  [Frühlingsglaube]   10"—**PD-62795**
  DUPLICATIONS (in English): John Mc-
  Cormack, V-1306; Charles Hackett, on
  C-7531M in CM-89; E. Lough (treble),
  G-B2681; Thomas Criddle (treble),
  G-BD1046

Widerschein
  Gerhard Hüsch (b) & H. U. Müller (pf)
  [Lied eines Schiffers]   10"—**G-DA4452**

Wiegenlied, Op. 98, No. 2 (Anon.)
  "Schlafe, schlafe, holder, süsser Knabe"
  Erna Sack (s) & Willy Czernik (pf)
  [Mozart: Wiegenlied]   12"—**T-A10454**
  Elisabeth Schumann (s) & George
  Reeves (pf)   12"—**G-DB3426**

[Des Baches Wiegenlied; Der Schmet-
terling]
Lotte Lehmann (s) & E. Balogh (pf)
          (in VM-419)   10"—V-1856
[Gretchen am Spinnrade]
DUPLICATIONS: Kurt Otzelberger,
C-DV1367; Jo Vincent, C-DH40
In English: Betty Martin, C-35613 in
C-J17
In French: Martha Angelici, LUM-33191
—Arr. Violin & Piano Elman
A. Poltronieri, C-GQ7019; Alexander
Schmidt, in Medley on V-22160
—Arr. 'Cello & Piano: Camillo Oblach,
CET-CC2119
Wiegenlied, Op. 105, No. 2
Elena Gerhardt (ms) & Gerald Moore
(pf)   Private Recording—HMV
(Die) Winterreise, Op. 89 (Müller)
For complete list of titles and recorded
collections see under Song Cycles above.
(Das) Wirtshaus (Winterreise No. 21)
Gerhard Hüsch, in Society Set
Lotte Lehmann, on V-17191 in VM-692
Richard Tauber, on P-RO20041 in P-P9
Marko Rothmüller, on G-DB10108
Karl Erb (t) & pf. acc. 12"—G-DB5537
[Schumann: Meine Rose]
Wohin? (Schöne Müllerin No. 2)
Fr. Là-bas, or Le Ruisseau Eng. Whither?
or The Brooklet
Aksel Schiøtz, on G-DB6252 in GM-407†
Gerhard Hüsch, in Society Set
Lotte Lehmann, on C-71771D in CM-615†
Charles Panzéra (b) & M. Panzéra-Bail-
lot (pf)   10"—G-DA4856
[Forelle]
Ria Ginster (s) & Paul Baumgartner (pf)
[Forelle]   10"—G-DA6010
Marian Anderson (c) & Franz Rupp (pf)
[Tod und das Mädchen] 10"—V-10-1327
DUPLICATIONS: Heinrich Schlusnus,
PD-62821; Leo Slezak, PD-21691; Sven-
Olof Sandberg, O-4640
In French: Germaine Martinelli,
C-RFX43
In Italian: Angelo Parigi, G-HN1817
(Der) Zürnende Barde (Bruchmann)
Heinrich Schlusnus (b) & Franz Rupp
(pf)   10"—PD-90178
[Am See]

SYMPHONIES

No. 2, B flat major 1815
CBS Symphony Orch.—Barlow
          3 12"—CM-420†
No. 3, D major 1815
Munich Philharmonic—Kabasta
          3 12"—G-DB5575/7
No. 4, C minor 1816 "Tragic"
Philharmonic-Symphony of N. Y.—Bar-
birolli   4 12"—VM-562†
(G-DB3826/9, in GM-333†)
Symphony Orch.—M. F. Gaillard
          4 12"—PAT-PDT88/91
National Symphony Orch.—Rankl
          4 12"—D-K1252/5†
No. 5, B flat major 1816
London Philharmonic—Beecham
          4 12"—CM-366†

[Rosamunde—Entr'acte No. 2 & Shep-
herd's Melody, Hallé Orch.—Harty]
(C-LX785/8S† last side blank)
Berlin Philharmonic—von Benda
          3 12"—T-E2516/8
DUPLICATIONS: Berlin State Orch.—
Zaun, C-LWX360/2; Chamber Orch. of
Queen Elizabeth of Belgium—Houdret,
G-DB5099/101; Berlin Philharmonic—
Horenstein, PD-95402/4
No. 6, C major 1817
London Philharmonic—Beecham
          4 12"—VM-1014†
[Mozart: Serenade, "Eine Kleine Nacht-
musik"—Rondo]
(G-DB6200/3S, last side blank, in GM-
380†)
No. 8, B minor ("Unfinished")
Philadelphia Orch.—Walter
          3 12"—CM-699†
Boston Symphony—Koussevitzky
          3 12"—VM-1039†
London Philharmonic—Beecham
          3 12"—CM-330†
(C-LX666/8†) (C-LWX241/3)
Liverpool Philharmonic—Sargent
          3 12"—C-DX1266/8†
DUPLICATIONS: Vienna Philharmonic—
Walter, G-DB2937/9†; Vienna Philhar-
monic—Böhm, G-DB5588/90; National
Symphony—Fistoulari, D-K1114/6 in
D-ED14†; Philadelphia Orch.—Stokow-
ski, VM-16†: G-DB7/9; G-AW138/40:
G-W1128/30; Paris Philharmonic—Mey-
rowitz, PAT-PAT98/100; Berlin Philhar-
monic—Kleiber, PD-66717/9:
T-E1777/9; Berlin Philharmonic—Meli-
char, PD-62721/4; Budapest Philhar-
monic Orch.—Ferencsik, RAD-
SP8008/10; Berlin State Opera Orch.—
von Schillings, P-E10672/4; Dresden
Philharmonic—van Kempen, PD-
67575/7: CET-OR5032/4; All American
Orch.—Stokowski, CM-485†; Royal Opera
Orch.—Goossens, G-C1294/6†; EIAR
Symphony Orch.—Parodi, CET-
CB20162/4
—1st Movement only
Boston Symphony Orch.—Koussevitsky
          12"—V-14117
—Abridged by O'Connell
Victor Symphony—O'Connell, V-36329 in
V-G15
—Arr. Voice ("La Lettre retrouvée")
Odette Moulin (in French), PAT-PA899
No. 9, C major (B. & H. No. 7) 1828
NBC Symphony Orch.—Toscanini
          5 12"—VM-1167†
[Mendelssohn: Midsummer Night's
Dream—Scherzo]
N. Y. Philharmonic-Symphony Orch.—
Walter   6 12"—CM-679†
Amsterdam Concertgebouw Orch.—Men-
gelberg   6 12"—T-SK3341/6
London Symphony Orch.—Sargent
          6 12"—D-K1459/64†
London Symphony Orch.—Walter
          6 12"—VM-602†
(G-DB3607/12 in GM-318†)
DUPLICATION: Chicago Symphony
Orch.—Stock, CM-403†

TRIOS—Strings

B flat major (Vl., Vla., Vlc.) 1817
Pasquier Trio   2   12"—**G-DB3319/20**

TRIOS—Piano, Violin & 'Cello

No. 1, B flat major, Op. 99
Artur Rubinstein, Jascha Heifetz &
Emanuel Feuermann 4 12"—**VM-923†**
Cortot, Thibaud, Casals
(G-DB947/50)   4 12"—**GM-20†**
Elly Ney, Max Strub & Ludwig Hoelscher
(CET-OR5102/5)   4 12"—**PD-57045/8**
Benvenuti, Benedetti & Navarra
          4 12"—**PAT-PGT29/32**

No. 2, E flat major, Op. 100
Adolf Busch, H. Busch, Rudolf Serkin
          5 12"—**G-DB2676/80**
Munich Chamber Music Ensemble
          5 12"—**PD-95225/9**
[Ave Maria, G. Kulenkampff]
Alma Trio   5 12"—**AL-AR1**
—**3rd Mvt. (Scherzo) only**
Elly Ney Trio, G-DB4537

Valse sentimentale, from Op. 50 Piano
—**Arr. Violin & Piano**
Mischa Elman, V-1482: G-DA1144

(12) Valses Nobles, Op. 77 Piano
Lili Kraus   12"—**P-PXO1039**

WALTZES

NOTE: *Schubert wrote scores of little dance
pieces, Waltzes, Ländler, Deutsche Tänze, etc.,
and it is seldom possible to identify or even
classify them properly. In addition to the recordings listed below, see also "Deutsche
Tänze," "Soirées de Vienne," "Valses sentimentales," and "Valses nobles."*

Waltz Collection, including Op. 9a Piano
Maryla Jonas, C-72047D
Galina Werschenska, G-Z249

Waltz Collection Arr. Orchestra
Victor Salon Orch.—Shilkret, V-9307/8,
in V-C3
Symphony Orch.—Goehr, V-36292

(DIE) ZAUBERHARFE Melodrama, 3 Acts
(1820)

Overture Orchestra
NOTE: *The overture is the work now known as
the "Rosamunde" overture and the list of recordings will be found under that title. The
overture performed at the original performance of the "Rosamunde" music was however
that written for the opera "Alfonso und Estrella."*

(DIE) ZWILLINGSBRUDER Singspiel
1 Act (1819)
Eng. **The Twin Brothers**

Overture Orchestra
Berlin Charlottenburg Opera Orch.—
Melichar   12"—**PD-95404**
[Symphony No. 5, Pt. 5, dir. Horenstein]

Miscellaneous Arrangements—Fantasias,
Portpourri, etc.

Unidentified arrangements
Chorus & Orch.—Melichar, PD-19946;
Marek Weber Orch., G-EH597; La Scala
Orch.—Olivieri, G-HN719: G-HE2267

"Lilac Time" Arr. from Schubert's music
Clutsam
—**Selections: Light Opera Co., G-C1450**

"Das Dreimäderlhaus" Arr. from Schu-
bert's music Berté
—**Selections—Marek Weber Orch.,**
G-EH124: EH178

Schubert Melodies: Marek Weber Orch.,
C-C109

Collection: An Hour with Schubert Arr.
Shilkret
Victor Salon Group (with John McCormack)—Shilkret   4 12"—**V-C3**
*See current catalogues for arrangements used
in operettas and films based on the composer's
life and music.*

SCHUETZ, Heinrich (1585-1672)

*Born one century to the year before J. S. Bach,
Schütz was one of Germany's greatest composers. His exposure to Italy—on two separate occasions—no doubt enriched his technical powers, but did not dilute the intellectualism already present in German music. Hence it is a
great mistake to lump sixteenth and seventeenth century German composers into that
amorphous category so often labelled "Pre-
Bach." Hence also, the lack of a recorded performance of Schütz's a cappella St. Matthew Passion and the deletion without replacement of
many recordings from current catalogues is to
be deplored.*

Eile, mich, Gott, zu erretten Air
(Psalm 40 from the "Geistliche Kon-
zerte," 1636) Soprano
Max Meili (t) & A. Cellier (organ)
          (in Vol. III) 12"—**AS-28**
[Psalm 51 & Psalm 111]

Erhöre mich, wenn ich dich rufe Duo
(from "Geistliche Konzerte," 1636) 2
Sopranos
Fr. **Exauce-moi**
Marthe Angelici (s) & Germaine Cernay
(ms.) (in Fr.) with N. Pierront (organ)
          12"—**LUM-32059**
[Bach: Cantata No. 4—Den Tod]

(Die) Furcht des Herren
(Psalm 111 from "Geistliche Konzerte,"
1639)
Max Meili (t) & Yvon Le Marc' Hadour
(b) with A. Cellier (organ)
          (in Vol. III) 12"—**AS-28**
[Psalm 40 & Psalm 51]

Herr, unser Herrscher! Air (Soprano or
Tenor)
(from Symphonie sacrae, Pt. 2, 1647)
Yves Tinayre (t) & String Orch. with
organ acc.   12"—**LUM-32015**
(in Tinayre album No. 1)

Ich danke dem Herrn 4-Part Chorus
(Psalm 111 from the 12 "Geistliche
Gesänge," 1657)
Berlin Staats-und Domchor—Rudel
          10"—**P-R1026**
[Bach: Motet—Der Geist hilft unserer
Schwachheit—Fugue]
(in 2000 Years of Music set`

Ich werde nicht sterben
(from "Symphoniae sacrae" Pt. 2, 1647)
Hughes Cuénod (t) & Chamber Orch., in
TC-T2

O lieber Herre Gott, wecke uns auf
(originally for 2 Sopranos & continuo, in
the "Geistliche Konzerte" 1636)
Leipzig Conservatory Chorus—Thomas
12"—PD-27312
[Hassler: Jungfrau dein schön' Gestalt;
Feinslieb, du hast mich g'fangen]

Psalm 40 See: Eile, mich, Gott, zu erretten

Psalm 51 See: Schaffe in mir, Gott

Psalm 111 See: Furcht des Herren

Schaffe in mir, Gott, ein reines Herz Duo
Soprano & Tenor
(Psalm 51 from "Geistliche Konzerte,"
1636)
Mme. Suter-Moser (s) & Max Meili (t)
with A. Cellier (org)
(in Vol. III) 12"—AS-28
[Psalm 40 & 111]

Selig sind die Toten Motet (1648)
Basel Chamber Choir (unacc.)—Paul
Sacher (in Vol. VI) 12"—AS-60
[Krieger: Cantata "Die Gerechten werden
weggerafft"]

SCHULZ, Svend Simon (1913-   )
Concertino for Flute, Violin, 'Cello, & Piano
Danish Quartet 12"—G-DB5227
Une Amorette
E. Thomsen Wind Quintet
12"—TONO-A112

SCHUMAN, William (1910-   )
*A graduate of Columbia University, and a
prominent composer, Schuman is also president
of the Juilliard School of Music.*
American Festival Overture Orchestra
National Symphony Orch.—Hans Kindler
12"—V-18511
Quartet No. 3 (Strings) 1939
Gordon Quartet 3 12"—CH-AB
Symphony for Strings
Concert Hall Symphony Orch.—Edgar
Schenkman 4 12"—CH-A11
(Limited Edition)

**SCHUMANN, Clara Josephine Wieck (1819-
1896)**
*One of the first great women concert pianists,
Clara Schumann was a leading exponent of her
husband's works.*
Er ist gekommen Song
Yvon Le Marc' Hadour (b) & Claude
Crussard (pf) 12"—BAM-1
[Robert Schumann: Heiss' mich nicht
reden & Jeden Morgen]

SCHUMANN, Robert (1810-1856)
*One of the most original composers of the Ro-
mantics, Schumann was also a critic and teach-
er. He is particularly well represented on rec-
ords.*
Abegg-Variationen, F major, Op. 1 Piano
(Variations on the Name "Abegg")
Clara Haskil 10"—PD-561121

Abendlied, Op. 85, No. 12 Piano—4-Hands
Eng. **Evening Song** Fr. **Chant du Soir**
See also Songs
—**Arr. Violin & Orch.**
Georg Kulenkampff & Berlin Philhar-
monic—Schmidt-Isserstedt 12"—T-E1849
[Spohr: Violin Concerto No. 8, Pt. 5]
DUPLICATION: B. Lessmann, T-A10157;
Vasa Prihoda, CET-LL3011
—**Arr. 'Cello & Piano**
André Navarra 10"—O-188924
[Bach: Musette]
—**Arr. Orchestra: Boston "Pops" Orch.—**
Fiedler, V-12-0017

(Des) Abends, Op. 12, No. 1 Piano (from
"Fantasiestücke")
Eng. **At Evening**
Yves Nat 12"—C-LFX489
[Aufschwung & Warum?]
Karl Delseit 10"—PD-10408
[Schubert: Quartet, C major, Pt. 5,
Prisca Quartet]

ALBUM FUR DIE JUGEND, Op. 68 Piano
(40 Pieces)
Eng. **Album for the Young**
See under titles of recorded pieces—
Fröhlicher Landmann; Nordisches Lied;
Reiterstück; Rundgesang; Soldaten-
marsch; Wilder Reiter

Andante and Variations, B flat, Op. 46 2
Pianos
Ethel Bartlett & Rae Robertson
2 12"—CX-213†
[Etude in the Form of a Canon, Op. 56,
No. 4, arr. Debussy]
Luboshutz & Nemenoff
2 12"—in VM-1047†

Arabesque, Op. 18 Piano
Artur Rubinstein
(in VM-1149†) 12"—V-11-9730
[Träumerei]
Artur Rubinstein 12"—G-DB6492
Vladimir Horowitz 10"—G-DA1381
José Iturbi 10"—V-10-1325
Claudio Arrau, in CM-716

Aufschwung, Op. 12, No. 2 Piano (from
"Fantasiestücke")
Eng. **Soaring**
Ania Dorfmann 12"—V-11-9672
[Liszt: Etude de Concert No. 3]
Yves Nat 12"—C-LFX489
[Warum & Des Abends]
DUPLICATION: Wilhelm Kempff, PD-
62746

Canto del Natale Unidentified Chorus
EIAR Chorus—Bruno Erminero
[Zandonai: Ave Maria] 12"—CET-PE114

CARNAVAL, Op. 9 Piano
Préambule; Pierrot; Arlequin; Valse
noble; Eusebius; Florestan; Coquette;
Réplique; Sphinxes; Papillons; Lettres
dansantes; Chiarina; Chopin; Estrella;
Reconnaissance; Pantalon et Colombine;
Valse allemande; Paganini; Aveu; Prom-
enade; Pause; Marche des "Davids-
bündler"
Myra Hess
(G-C3008/10†) 3 12"—VM-476†

Claudio Arrau
(P-R20448/50)   3 12"—P-P30†
DUPLICATIONS: Alfred Cortot,
G-DB1252/4

—Arr. Orch. Glazunov, etc.
London Philharmonic Orch.—E. Goos-
sens   3 12"—VM-513†
(G-C2916/8) (G-EH1123/5)
London Symphony—Ronald
              3 12"—G-D1840/2

—Excerpts Arr. Douglas
London Philharmonic—Walter Goehr
              12"—C-DX889

Concerto—Piano & Orchestra, A minor, Op.
54
Myra Hess & Symphony Orch.—Goehr
              4 12"—VM-473†
(G-C2942/5, in GM-296†)
Artur Rubinstein & RCA Victor Orch.—
Steinberg   4 12"—VM-1176†
Claudio Arrau & Detroit Symphony
Orch.   4 12"—VM-1009†
(G-DB6373/6, in GM-402†)
Arturo Benedetti Michelangeli & La
Scala Orch.—Pedrotti
              4 12"—T-SKB3260/3
Walter Gieseking & Prussian State Orch.
—Böhm   4 12"—C-LWX356/9
DUPLICATIONS: Yves Nat & Paris
Symphony—Bigot, CM-196†:
C-LFX320/3: O-9401/4: C-GQX10721/4;
Alfred Cortot & London Philharmonic—
Ronald, G-DB2181/4 in GM-209†

Concerto—Violin & Orchestra, D minor
Yehudi Menuhin & N. Y. Philharmonic-
Symphony Orch.—Barbirolli
              4 12"—VM-451†
[Paganini: Caprice, Op. 1, No. 9]
[Schumann: Romance, Op. 94, No. 2, on
G-DB3435/8]
Georg Kulenkampff & Berlin Philhar-
monic—Schmidt-Isserstedt
              4 12"—T-E2395/8
[Bach: Unacc. Sonata No. 6—Rondo
Gavotte]

Concerto—'Cello & Orchestra, A minor, Op.
129
Gregor Piatigorsky & London Philhar-
monic—Barbirolli   3 12"—VM-247†
(G-DB2244/6) (Cadenza by Piatigorsky)
Ludwig Hoelscher & Berlin State Opera
Orch.—Keilberth 3 12"—G-DB4550/2
André Navarra & Lamoureux Orch.—
Bigot   3 12"—PAT-PDT42/4
Enrico Mainardi & Berlin State Opera
Orch.—Van Kempen
(CET-OR5092/4)   3 12"—PD-68052/4

(Die) Davidsbündlertänze, Op. 6 Piano
(18 Pieces)
No recording available

Etude in the Form of a Canon, Op. 56 1845
[Studien für den Pedal-Flügel]

—No. 4, A flat major (Arr. Debussy)
Ethel Bartlett & Rae Robertson
              (in CX-213†) 12"—C-71311D
[Andante & Variations, Op. 46, Pt. 3]

Etudes Symphoniques, Op. 13 Piano
Edward Kilenyi   2 12"—CX-162†

Paul Baumgartner
              3 12"—G-DB10009/11
Alfred Cortot   3 12"—G-DB1325/7
Jacques Dupont (Omitting Etudes 2 &
11)   2 12"—PAT-X98076/7

Fantasia, C major, Op. 17 Piano
Wilhelm Backhaus
              3 12"—G-DB3221/24
[Nachtstücke, Op. 23, No. 4]

Fantasiestücke, Op. 12 Piano
1. Des Abends 2. Aufschwung 3. Warum
4. Grillen 5. In der Nacht 6. Fabel 7.
Traumeswirren 8. Ende vom Lied
For recordings see under titles of Nos. 1,
2, 3 & 7.

Fantasiestücke, Op. 73 Clarinet or 'Cello &
Piano
Zart und mit Ausdruck; Lebhaft, leicht;
Rasch, mit Feuer
Pierre Fournier (vlc) & Babeth Lénoet
(pf)   2 12"—G-DB11143/4
[Fauré: Romance, A major, Op. 69]
—No. 1 only
Reginald Kell (cl) & Gerald Moore (pf)
          (in VM-708†) 12"—V-13488
(G-C3170) (G-FKX64)
[Mozart: Clarinet Concerto, K. 622, Pt. 7]

Fantasiestücke, Op. 88
Wurmser Trio   3 10"—O-188926/8

Faschingsschwank aus Wien, Op. 26 Piano
Fr. Carnaval de Vienne
Allegro; Romanze; Scherzino; Intermez-
zo; Finale
Suzanne Gyr   3 12"—G-DB10051/3
Yves Nat   3 12"—C-LFX553/5
[Brahms: Intermezzo, Op. 117, No. 2]
Magda Tagliafero
              3 12"—PAT-PAT19/21
[Romanze, Op. 28, No. 2]
—4th Mvt. (Intermezzo) only
Alexander Brailowsky, PD-561107: PD-
62756; M. Rytter, TONO-K8025

Humoreske, Op. 20 Piano
Paul Loyonnet   3 12"—CH-A1

Im Walde, Op. 75, No. 2 Unacc. Chorus in
German (Eichendorff)
Basilica Choir—Pius Kalt
              10"—PD-62631
[Mendelssohn: Die Nachtigall]

Kinderscenen, Op. 15 Piano (13 Pieces)
Eng. Scenes of Childhood
Von fremden Ländern und Menschen;
Curiose Geschichte; Hasche-Mann; Bit-
tendes Kind; Glückes genug; Wichtige
Begebenheit; Träumerei; Am Camin; Rit-
ter vom Steckenperd; Fast zu ernst;
Fürchtenmachen; Kind im Einschlum-
mern; Der Dichter spricht.
Walter Gieseking 2 12"—C-LWX342/3
Carlo Zecchi   2 12"—CET-CB20344/5
Suzanne Gyr   2 12"—G-DB10057/8
Elly Ney   2 12"—G-DB4471/2
Maryla Jonas   2 12"—CX-290†
Alfred Cortot   2 12"—G-DB2581/2
DUPLICATIONS: Johnny Aubert,
PD-27223/4; Yves Nat, O-4693/4:
C-LF70/1; Erno von Dohnanyi,
G-AN456/7

—**No. 7 (Träumerei) only**
Eng. **Dreaming** Fr. **Rêverie**
Artur Rubinstein
     (in VM-1149†)   12"—**V-11-9730**
[Arabesque]
Artur Rubinstein   12"—**G-DB6532**
[Widmung & Brahms: Wiegenlied]
Oscar Levant   12"—**C-12372D**
[Brahms: Intermezzo No. 12; Waltz,
Op. 39, No. 15]
Mark Hambourg   10"—**G-B2685**
[Dvořák: Humoresque]
DUPLICATION: Wilhelm Kempff,
PD-62762

—**Arr. Violin & Piano**
Mischa Elman & Leopold Mittman
     12"—**V-10-1271**
[Grieg: Album Leaf, Op. 28, No. 3]
Nathan Milstein & Artur Balsam
[Dvořák: Humoresque] 10"—**C-17337D**
Efrem Zimbalist & T. Saidenberg
[Drdla: Serenade]   10"—**C-17105D**
DUPLICATIONS: Vasa Prihoda,
CET-LL3001: CET-LL3009: PD-25721;
B. Lessmann, T-A10157; M. Darrieux,
O-166195; V. Ranzato, C-DQ431; Albert
Sammons, D-F7529

—**Arr. 'Cello & Piano**
André Navarra, O-188932; Chrystja
Kolessa, G-EG7103; Pablo Casals,
V-1178: G-DA833; Gaspar Cassadó,
PD-95027; Paul Grümmer, PD-47059:
PD-524257; A. Lévy, O-166024

—**Arr. Orchestra**
Minneapolis Symphony—Ormandy,
G-DB2353; All American Orch.
Stokowski, C-11982D; EIAR String Orch.
& Harp—Ferrero, CET-TI7000; Bourne-
mouth Municipal Orch.—Godfrey,
C-DB810; Boston "Pops" Orch.—
Fiedler, V-12-0017; Harry Horlick Salon
Orch., D-F6942; Orch. of violoncelli,
C-DQ1547
*See current catalogues for other miscellaneous
instrumental arrangements.*

Kreisleriana, Op. 16 Piano (8 Pieces)
Claudio Arrau   5 12"—**CM-716†**
[Arabesque, C major, Op. 18]
—**Nos. 1, 4, 6, 7 only**
Jean Hubeau, LUM-32025

MANFRED, Op. 115
Incidental Music to Byron's Drama
Overture Orchestra
EIAR Symphony Orch.—Marinuzzi
     2 12"—**CET-BB25032/3**
[Mozart: Idomeneo—Overture]

Märchenbilder, Op. 113
Viola (or Violin) & Piano (4 Pieces)
Etienne Ginot (vla) & Joseph
Benvenuti (pf)   2 10"—**G-K8096/7**

Papillons, Op. 2 Piano
Paul Baumgartner 2 10"—**G-DA6015/6**
Cor de Groot   2 12"—**O-8770/1**
Giorgio Vidusso 2 12"—**ADAM-C113/4**
Alfred Cortot   2 12"—**G-DA1442/3**
J. M. Damase   2 12"—**D-K1696/7**
[Chopin: Berceuse]

(Das) Paradies und die Peri, Op. 50
—**Nun ruhe sanft**
Hildegard Erdmann (s) with Chorus
& Orch.   12"—**G-EH1250**
[Schubert: Mass, G major—Agnus Dei]

QUARTETS—String

No. 1, A minor, Op. 41, No. 1
Roth Quartet   3 12"—**CM-454†**
No. 3, A major, Op. 41, No. 3
Léner Quartet
(C-GQX10827/30)   4 12"—**CM-319†**
Quartets—Piano & Strings
E flat major, Op. 47
Elly Ney & Ensemble
     4 12"—**PD-15087/90**
[Haydn: Rondo all' ongarese, Elly Ney
Trio]
Quintet—Piano & String Quartet
E major, Op. 44
Artur Schnabel & Pro Arte Quartet
(G-DB2387/90)   4 12"—**GM-265†**
Rudolf Serkin & Busch Quartet
     4 12"—**CM-533†**
Jesús María Sanromá & Primrose
Quartet   4 12"—**VM-736†**
Unidentified pianist & Gabriel Bouillon
Quartet   4 12"—**G-DB5138/41**
Reiterstück, Op. 68, No. 23
Piano (from "Album für die Jugend")
Eng. **Rider's Story**
—**Arr. Orchestra:** Victor Orch., on V-22162
Romanzen, Op. 28 Piano
—**No. 2, F sharp major**
Leo Nadelmann   10"—**G-DA6018**
[Brahms: Waltzes, Op. 39, Nos. 2 & 15]
Benno Moiseiwitsch   12"—**G-C3260**
[Beethoven: Sonata, Op. 27, No. 2, Pt. 3]
Artur Rubinstein   12"—**V-14946**
[Brahms: Rhapsody, G minor, Op. 79,
No. 2] (G-DB3217)
DUPLICATION: Magda Tagliafero,
PAT-PAT21
Romanzen, Op. 94
Oboe (or violin) & Piano
Leon Goossens (oboe) & Gerald Moore
     2 12"—**CX-160†**
[Franck: Pièce, No. 5] (C-DX936/7)
—**No. 2, A major only**
Yehudi Menuhin (vl) & F. Webster
[Violin Concerto, Pt. 7] 12"—**G-DB3438**
(Die) Rose stand im Tau, Op. 65, No. 1
Unacc. Male Chorus
Berlin Teachers' Chorus—Rudel
     12"—**PD-19844**
[Mendelssohn: Wer hat dich, du schöner
Wald]
[Krauss: Mädel, wie blüht's, on
PD-15161]
Schlummerlied, Op. 124, No. 16 Piano
(from "Albumblätter")
Eng. **Slumber Song**
Mark Hambourg   10"—**G-B4385**
[Rubinstein: Melody in F]
—**Arr. Violin & Piano**
Bruno Sanger, G-EG7005; Heinrich
Grünfelt (vlc), G-EG1998

Soldatenmarsch, Op. 68, No. 2 Piano
(from "Album für die Jugend")
Eng. Soldier's March
—Arr. Orch: Victor Orch., V-22168

SONATAS Piano
No. 2, G minor, Op. 22
  Erik Then-Berg   3 12"—G-EH1281/3
No. 3, F minor, Op. 14
  (Concert sans Orchestre)
  Leonard Shure   3 12"—VOX-189

SONATAS Violin & Piano
No. 1, A minor, Op. 105
  Adolf Busch & Rudolf Serkin
            2 12"—G-DB3371/2
  Leo Petroni & Michael Raucheisen
            2 12"—G-EH1237/8
No. 2, D minor, Op. 121
  Yehudi & Hephzibah Menuhin
  (G-DB2264/7)   4 12"—GM-225†

SONGS (LIEDER) In German
Song Cycles

DICHTERLIEBE, Op. 48 Heine) 16 Songs
  1. Im wunderschönen Monat Mai
  2. Aus meinem Tränen spriessen
  3. Die Rose, die Lilie, die Taube, die
    Sonne
  4. Wenn ich in deine Augen seh'
  5. Ich will meine Seele tauchen
  6. Im Rhein, im heiligen Strome
  7. Ich grolle nicht
  8. Und wüssten's die Blumen
  9. Das ist ein Flöten und Geigen
  10. Hör ich das Liedchen klingen
  11. Ein Jüngling liebt ein Mädchen
  12. Am leuchtenden Sommermorgen
  13. Ich hab' im Traum geweinet
  14. Allnächtlich im Traume seh' ich dich
  15. Aus alten Märchen winkt es
  16. Die alten, bösen Lieder
  Aksel Schiøtz (t) & Gerald Moore (pf)
          3 12"—G-DB6270/2†
  Charles Panzéra (b) & Alfred Cortot (pf)
  (G-DB4987/9)   3 12"—VM-386
  Lotte Lehmann (s) & Bruno Walter (pf)
          2 10" & 2 12"—CM-486
  Paul Sandoz (b) & Paul Baumgartner
  (pf)   3 12"—G-DB10037/9

FRAUENLIEBE UND LEBEN, Op. 42
(Chamisso)
Eng. Woman's Life and Love (8 Songs)
  1. Seit ich ihn gesehen
  2. Er, der Herrlichste von Allen
  3. Ich kann's nicht fassen
  4. Du Ring an meinem Finger
  5. Helft mir, ihr Schwestern
  6. Süsser Freund, du blickest
  7. An meinem Herzen
  8. Nun hast du mir den ersten Schmerz
    getan
  Lotte Lehmann (s) & Bruno Walter (pf)
          4 10"—CM-539†
  (older recording with Orch. O-188785/8)
  Helen Traubel (s) & Conraad V. Bos (pf)
          3 10" & 1 12"—VM-737
  Astra Desmond (c) & Phyllis Spurr (pf)
          3 12"—D-K1566/8†

[Der Himmel hat eine Thräne geweint &
O ihr Herren]
  Ria Ginster   3 12"—G-DB10047/9
  Isabel French   3 10" & 1 12"—TC-T5
In French: Germaine Martinelli,
C-RFX40/1

LIEDERKREIS, Op. 39 (Eichendorff)
  (Cycle of 12 Songs)
  1. In der Fremde ("Aus der Heimat")
  2. Intermezzo   3. Waldesgespräch
  4. Die Stille   5. Mondnacht
  6. Schöne Fremde   7. Auf einer Burg
  8. In der Fremde ("Ich hör' die
    Bächlein")
  9. Wehmut   10. Zwielicht
  11. Im Walde   12. Frühlingsnacht
  No complete recording available

Schumann Duets
  Er und Sie, Op. 78, No. 2; Familien-
  Gemälde, Op. 34, No. 4; Ich denke dein,
  Op. 78, No. 3; So wahr die Sonne scheinet,
  Op. 37, No. 12; Unter'm Fenster, Op. 34,
  No. 3
  Lauritz Melchior (t) & Lotte Lehmann
  (s) with Orch.—Reibold 2 10"—VM-560

Song Collection
  Melancholie; Er ist's; Zwei Lieder der
  Braut (Mutter, Mutter! & Lass mich ihm
  am Busen hangen); Der Sandmann; In's
  Freie; Der Himmel hat eine Thräne
  geweint; Lust der Sturmnacht
  (Sung in German with piano acc., William
  Hughes)
  Mein Herz ist schwer; Drei Gesänge (from
  Byron's Hebrew Melodies): Die Tochter
  Jephthas, An den Mond & Dem Helden
  (Sung in English with harp acc., Laura
  Newell)
  Blanche Thebom (ms) w. pf. & harp.
          4 10"—VM-1187

Individual Songs
  Abendlied (Heine)
  Karl Erb (t) with vl. & pf. acc.
          10"—G-DA4425
  [Liszt: Es muss ein Wunderbares sein]
  Jan van der Gucht (t) & Ivor Newton
  (pf)   10"—D-M512
  [Mendelssohn: On wings of song]

  Allnächtlich im Traume
  (Dichterliebe No. 14)
  Aksel Schiøtz, on G-DB6272†
  Charles Panzéra, on V-14492 in VM-386:
  G-DB4989
  Lotte Lehmann, on C-17441D in CM-486
  Paul Sandoz, on G-DB10039

  Alte Laute, Op. 35, No. 12 (Kerner)
  Else Sigfuss (c) & Folmer Jensen (pf)
          10"—G-X7208
  [Wer machte dich so krank]
  Lotte Lehmann (s) & Erno Balogh (pf)
       (in VM-419) 10"—V-1859
  [Du bist wie eine Blume: Frühlingsnacht]
  Hans Hotter (b) & Herman von
  Nordberg (pf)   12"—C-LX997
  [Wer machte dich so krank; Die beiden
  Grenadiere] (C-LCX116)

Karl Erb (t) & B. Seidler-Winkler (pf)
12"—G-DB4467
[Wer machte dich so krank; Schubert:
Ihr Grabe]

(Die) Alten, bösen Lieder
(Dichterliebe No. 16)
Aksel Schiøtz, on G-DB6272†
Charles Panzéra, on V-14492 in VM-386:
G-DB4989
Lotte Lehmann, on C-72078D in CM-486
Paul Sandoz, on G-DB10039

Am leuchtenden Sommermorgen
(Dichterliebe No. 12)
Aksel Schiøtz, on G-DB6271†
Charles Panzéra, on V-14491 in VM-386:
G-DB4988
Lotte Lehmann, on C-17441D in CM-486
Paul Sandoz, on G-DB10038
Arthur Endrèze (b) & pf. acc.
[Ich grolle nicht]   10"—PAT-PA1497

An den Abendstern, Op. 103, No. 4
(Kulmann)
Eng. **To the Evening Star**
Duo: Soprano & Alto
Victoria Anderson & Viola Morris
(in English) with H. J. Foss (pf)
10"—C-DB1233
[Du bist wie eine Blume; Brahms: Die
Schwestern & Auf dem Schiffe]
(in Columbia History of Music Vol. IV:
CM-234)

An den Mond, Op. 95, No. 2
(Hebrew Melodies No. 2)   (Byron)
Eng. **Sun of the Sleepless**
Blanche Thebom (in English) w. harp.
acc., on V-10-1390 in VM-1187

An den Sonnenschein, Op. 36, No. 4
(Rückert)
Ria Ginster (s) & Paul Baumgartner (pf)
[Brahms: Wiegenlied]   10"—G-DA6011

An meinem Herzen (Frauenliebe No. 7)
Lotte Lehmann, on C-17365D in CM-539
(Earlier version on O-188788)
Helen Traubel, on V-2140 in VM-737
Astra Desmond, on D-K1567†
Ria Ginster, on G-DB10046
Isabel French, in TC-T5
In French: Germaine Martinelli, on
C-RFX41

Aufträge, Op. 77, No. 5 (L'Egru)
Heinrich Schlusnus (b) & Franz
Rupp (pf)   10"—PD-62800
[Frühlingsfahrt]

Aus alten Märchen winkt es
(Dichterliebe No. 15)
Aksel Schiøtz, on G-DB6272†
Charles Panzéra, on V-14492 in VM-386:
G-DB4989
Lotte Lehmann, on C-72078D in CM-486
Paul Sandoz, on G-DB10039

Aus meinem Tränen spriessen
(Dichterliebe No. 2)
Aksel Schiøtz, on G-DB6270†
Charles Panzéra, on V-14490 in VM-386:
G-DB4987
Lotte Lehmann, on C-17440D in CM-486
Paul Sandoz, on G-DB10037
In Italian: A. Parigi, G-HN1968

Richard Tauber (t) & P. B. Kahn (pf)
10"—P-PO168
[Dichterliebe Nos. 1, 3 & 13]

(Die) Beiden Grenadiere, Op. 49, No. 1
(Heine)
Eng. **The Two Grenadiers**
Fr. **Les Deux Grenadiers**
Alexander Kipnis (bs) & Celius
Dougherty (pf)   12"—V-15825
[Schubert: Erlkönig]   (G-DB6010)
Hans Hotter (b) & Herman Von
Nordberg (pf)   12"—C-LX997
[Wer machte dich so krank; Alte Laute]
(C-LCX116)
Paul Sandoz (b) & W. Marti (pf)
[Wanderlied]   10"—G-JK29
DUPLICATIONS: Heinrich Schlusnus,
PD-95477; Theodore Scheidl, PD-95213
In French: Marcel Journet, G-DB924;
Narçon, C-RFX32; Roger Bourdin,
O-123614; Lovano, C-RFX42; Marex
Liven, PD-524029; Robert Couzinou,
PD-516157
In Russian: Feodor Chaliapin, V-6619
In Italian: Titta Ruffo, G-DB242*

(Der) Contrabandiste
(Spanisches Liederspiel appendix)
—Arr. Piano Tausig
Sergei Rachmaninoff   12"—V-11-8593
[Chopin-Liszt: Polish Songs, No. 1 & 15]

Das ist ein Flöten und Geigen
(Dichterliebe No. 9)
Aksel Schiøtz, on G-DB6271†
Charles Panzéra, on V-14491 in VM-386:
G-DB4988
Lotte Lehmann, on C-72077D in CM-486
Paul Sandoz, on G-DB10038

DICHTERLIEBE, Op. 48
Song Cycle   (Heine)
For complete list of titles and complete
recordings see above under Song Cycles

Du bist wie eine Blume, Op. 25, No. 24
(Heine)   Eng. **Thou art like a flower**
Lotte Lehmann (s) & Erno Balogh (pf)
(in VM-419)   10"—V-1859
[Frühlingsnacht & Alte Laute]
Dorothea Helmrich (s) (in English) &
pf. acc.   10"—C-DB1233
[An den Abenstern; Brahms: Auf dem
Schiffe & Die Schwestern]
(in Columbia History of Music, Vol. IV:
CM-234)

Du Ring an meinem Finger
(Frauenliebe No. 4)
Lotte Lehmann, on C-17363D in CM-539
(Earlier version on O-188786)
Helen Traubel, on V-2139 in VM-737
Astra Desmond, on D-K1567†
Ria Ginster, on G-DB10048
Isabel French, in TC-T5
In French: Germaine Martinelli, on
C-RFX40

Er, der Herrlichste von Allen
(Frauenliebe No. 2)
Lotte Lehmann, on C-17362D in CM-539
(Earlier version on O-188785)
Helen Traubel, on V-2138 in VM-737
Astra Desmond, on D-K1566†

Ria Ginster, on G-DB10047
Isabel French, in TC-T5
In French: Germaine Martinelli, on
C-RFX40

Er ist gekommen, Op. 37, No. 2 (Rückert)
*This song is one of several in Op. 37 that were
written by Clara Schumann*

Er ist's, Op. 79, No. 23 (Mörike)
Blanche Thebom & pf. acc., on V-10-1037
in VM-1187

Er und Sie, Op. 78, No. 2 Duo
Lotte Lehmann & Lauritz Melchior, on
V-1906 in VM-560

Familien-Gemälde, Op. 34, No. 4 Duo
Lotte Lehmann & Lauritz Melchior, on
V-1907 in VM-560

FRAUENLIEBE UND LEBEN, Op. 42
Song Cycle
For complete list of titles and recorded
sets see above under Song Cycles

Frühlingsfahrt, Op. 45, No. 2
(Eichendorff)
Heinrich Schlusnus (b) & S. Peschko (pf)
[Aufträge] 10"—PD-62800
Hans Hermann Nissen (bs) & pf. acc.
[Pfitzner: Der Gärtner] 10"—G-DA4489

Frühlingsnacht, Op. 39, No. 12
(Eichendorff) (from "Liederkreis")
Lotte Lehmann (s) & Erno Balogh (pf)
(in VM-419) 10"—V-1856
[Du bist wie eine Blume & Alte Laute]

Heiss' mich nicht reden
Yvon le Marc' Hadour (b) & Claude
Crussard (pf) 12"—BAM-1
[Jeden Morgen & Clara Schumann: Er
ist gekommen]

(Dem) Helden, Op. 95, No. 3
(Hebrew Melodies, No. 3) (Byron)
Eng. **Thy Days are done**
Blanche Thebom (in Eng.) & harp. acc.,
V-10-1390 in VM-1187

Helft mir, ihr Schwestern
(Frauenliebe No. 5)
Lotte Lehmann, on C-17364D in CM-539
(Earlier version on O-188787)
Helen Traubel, on V-2140 in VM-737
Astra Desmond, on D-K1567†
Ria Ginster, on G-DB10048
Isabel French, in TC-T5
In French: Germaine Martinelli, on
C-RFX41

(Der) Hidalgo, Op. 30, No. 3 (Geibel)
Heinrich Schlusnus (b) & Franz Rupp
(pf) 12"—PD-95477
[Beiden Grenadiere]

**(Der) Himmel hat eine Träne geweint,
Op. 37, No. 1** (Rückert)
Blanche Thebom & pf. acc., on V-10-1388
in VM-1187
Astra Desmond (c) & Phyllis Spurr (pf)
12"—D-K1568†
[O Ihr Herren; Frauenliebe und Leben,
Pt. 5]

Höchländisches Wiegenlied, Op. 25, No. 14
Mlle. Darmancier (in French)
[Nussbaum] 12"—LUM-30029
In English: Anna Howard, on V-20737

Hör ich das Liedchen klingen
(Dichterliebe No. 10)
Aksel Schiøtz, on G-DB6271†
Charles Panzéra, on V-14491 in VM-386:
G-DB4988
Lotte Lehmann, on C-72077D in CM-486
Paul Sandoz, on G-DB10038

Ich denke dein, Op. 78, No. 3 Duo
Lotte Lehmann & Lauritz Melchior, on
V-1906 in VM-560
Jo Vincent (s) & L. van Tulder (t)
10"—C-DH38
[So wahr die Sonne scheinet]

Ich grolle nicht (Dichterliebe No. 7)
Aksel Schiøtz, on G-DB6270†
Charles Panzéra, on V-14490 in VM-386:
G-DB4987
Lotte Lehmann, on C-72077D in CM-486
Paul Sandoz, on G-DB10037
DUPLICATIONS: Arthur Endrèze,
PAT-PA1497; Alexander Sved, G-DA5387
In French: Alice Raveau, PAT-X93121

Ich hab' im Traum geweinet
(Dichterliebe No. 13)
Aksel Schiøtz, on G-DB6271†
Charles Panzéra, on V-14491 in VM-386:
G-DB4988
Lotte Lehmann, on C-17441D in CM-486
Paul Sandoz, on G-DB10038
Richard Tauber (t) & P. Kahn (pf)
10"—P-PO168
[Dichterliebe Nos. 1, 2 & 3]
Arthur Endrèze (b) & pf. acc.
10"—PAT-PA1545
[Wenn ich in deine Augen seh']
In French: Alice Raveau, PAT-X93087

Ich kann's nicht fassen (Frauenliebe No. 3)
Lotte Lehmann, on C-17363D in CM-539
(Earlier version on O-188786)
Helen Traubel, on V-2139 in VM-737
Astra Desmond, on D-K1566†
Ria Ginster, on G-DB10047
Isabel French, in TC-T5
In French: Germaine Martinelli, on
C-RFX40

Ich will meine Seele tauchen
(Dichterliebe No. 5)
Aksel Schiøtz, on G-DB6270†
Charles Panzéra, on V-14490 in VM-386:
G-DB4987
Lotte Lehmann, on C-17440D in CM-486
Paul Sandoz, on G-DB10037

Im Rhein, im heiligen Strome
(Dichterliebe No. 6)
Aksel Schiøtz, on G-DB6270
Charles Panzéra, on V-14490 in VM-386:
G-DB4987
Lotte Lehmann, on C-72077D in CM-486
Paul Sandoz, on G-DB10037

Im wunderschönen Monat Mai
(Dichterliebe No. 1)
Aksel Schiøtz, on G-DB6270
Charles Panzéra, on V-14490 in VM-386:
G-DB4987
Lotte Lehmann, on C-17440D in CM-486
Paul Sandoz, on G-DB10037
Richard Tauber (t) & Kahn (pf)
10"—P-PO168
[Dichterliebe Nos. 2, 3 & 13]
In Italian: A. Parigi, G-HN1968

In der Fremde, Op. 39, No. 1 (Eichendorff)
(from "Liederkreis")
In French: Charles Panzéra, G-DA4809,
Alice Raveau, PAT-X93087

In's Freie, Op. 89, No. 5 (Neun)
Blanche Thebom & pf. acc., on V-10-1388
in VM-1187

Jeden Morgen, Op. 79, No. 7b. (Geibel)
Yvon Le Marc' Hadour (b) & Claude
Crussard (pf) 12″—BAM-1
[Heiss' mich nicht reden & Clara
Schumann; Er ist gekommen]

(Ein) Jüngling liebt ein Mädchen
(Dichterliebe No. 11)
Aksel Schiøtz, on G-DB6271†
Charles Panzéra, on V-14491 in VM-386:
G-DB4988
Lotte Lehmann, on C-17441D in CM-486
Paul Sandoz, on G-DB10038

(Die) Kartenlegerin, Op. 31, No. 2
Lotte Lehmann (s) & Erno Balogh (pf)
(in VM-292) 10″—V-1732
[Waldesgespräch]
Elisabeth Höngen (c) & Hans Zipper (pf)
10″—C-LB62
[Wolf: Nur wer die sehnsucht kennt]

**Lass mich ihm am Busen hangen, Op. 25,
No. 12** (Rückert)
(Zwei Lieder der Braut, No. 2)
Blanche Thebom & pf. acc., on V-10-1387
in VM-1187

Liebesgarten, Op. 34, No. 1 Duo
Eleanor Steele (s) & Hall Clovis (t)
w. pf. acc. 10″—PD-561138
[So wahr die Sonne scheinet]

(Die) Lotosblume, Op. 25, No. 7 (Heine)
Herbert Janssen (b) & Gerald Moore (pf)
[Widmung] 10″—V-1931
Franz Völker (t) & Franz Rupp (pf)
[Mozart: Veilchen] 10″—PD-23468
In Italian: Beniamino Gigli, G-DA1504

Lust der Sturmnacht, Op. 35, No. 1 (Kerner)
Blanche Thebom & pf. acc., on V-10-1388
in VM-1187

Marienwürmchen, Op. 79, No. 13
("Knaben Wunderhorn")
Frida Leider (s) & M. Raucheisen (pf)
12″—G-DB5626
[Widmung & Meine Rose]

Mein Herz ist schwer, Op. 25, No. 15
(Byron)
Eng. My heart is dark
Blanche Thebom (in English) & harp
acc., on V-10-1389 in VM-1187

Meine Rose, Op. 90, No. 2 (Lenau)
Frida Leider (s) & M. Raucheisen (pf)
10″—G-DB5626
[Widmung & Marienwürmchen]
Karl Erb (t) & pf. acc.
12″—G-DB5537
[Schubert: Das Wirtshaus]

Melancholie, Op. 74, No. 6
Blanche Thebom & pf. acc., on V-10-1387
in VM-1187

Mondnacht, Op. 39, No. 5 (Eichendorff)
(Liederkreis No. 5)
Heinrich Schlusnus (b) & S. Peschko (pf)
[Schubert: Musensohn] 10″—PD-30029
Paul Schoeffler (b) & E. Lush (pf)
[Brahms: Feldeinsamkeit] 12″—D-K16
Richard Tauber (t) & P. B. Kahn (pf)
[Nussbaum] 10″—P-PO169
DUPLICATIONS: Erna Sack, T-A2233;
Leo Slezak, PD-19924; Lea Piltti,
G-EG7093; Petre Monteanu, CET-AA468

Mutter, Mutter, Op. 25, No. 11 (Rückert)
(Zwei Lieder der Braut, No. 1)
Blanche Thebom & pf. acc., on V-10-1387
in VM-1187

Nun hast du mir den ersten Schmerz getan
(Frauenliebe No. 8)
Lotte Lehmann, on C-17365D in CM-539†
(Earlier version on O-188788)
Helen Traubel, on V-17634 in VM-737
Astra Desmond, on D-K1568†
Ria Ginster, on G-DB10049
Isabel French, in TC-T5
In French: Germaine Martinelli, on
C-RFX41

(Der) Nussbaum, Op. 25, No. 3 (Mosen)
Eng. The Nut Tree Fr. Le Noyer
Marian Anderson (c) & Franz Rupp (pf)
[Stille Tränen] 12″—V-11-9173
(Earlier recording on V-14610:
G-DB2957)
Richard Tauber (t) & P. Kahn (pf)
[Mondnacht] 10″—P-PO169
DUPLICATIONS: Erna Sack, T-A2233;
Leo Slezak, PD-19924
In French: Charles Panzéra, G-DA4809;
Vanni-Marcoux, G-DA1123; Mlle.
Darmancier, LUM-30029

O ihr Herren, O ihr werthen, Op. 37, No. 3
(Rückert)
Astra Desmond (c) & Phyllis Spurr (pf)
12″—D-K1568†
[Der Himmel hat eine Träne geweint;
Frauenliebe und Leben, Pt. 5]

Provenzalisches Lied, Op. 139, No. 4
(Uhland)
Heinrich Schlusnus (b) & F. Rupp (pf)
[Talismane] 10″—PD-30003

**Romanze: Flutenreicher Ebro, Op. 138,
No. 5** (Geibel)
Heinrich Schlusnus (b) & Franz Rupp
(pf) 12″—PD-67051
[Schubert: Erlkönig]

(Die) Rose, die Lilie, die Taube, die Sonne
(Dichterliebe No. 3)
Aksel Schiøtz, on G-DB6270†
Charles Panzéra, on V-14490 in VM-386:
G-DB4987
Lotte Lehmann, on C-17440D in CM-486
Paul Sandoz, on G-DB10037
Richard Tauber (t) & P. Kahn (pf)
10″—P-PO168
[Dichterliebe Nos. 1, 2 & 13]
In Italian: A. Parigi, G-HN1968

(Der) Sandmann, Op. 79, No. 12 (Kletke)
Blanche Thebom & pf. acc., on V-10-1388
in VM-1187

(Ein) Scheckiges Pferd—Pferdchen hopp-hopp
NOTE: *Not heard for identification.*
Wolfgang Kieling (treble)
          10″—**G-EG6989**
[Kucken: Wer will unter die Soldaten]

Seit ich ihn gesehn (Frauenliebe No. 1)
Lotte Lehmann, on C-17362D in CM-539†
(Earlier version on O-188785)
Helen Traubel, on V-2138 in VM-737
Astra Desmond, on D-K1566†
Ria Ginster, on G-DB10047
Isabel French, on TC-T5
In French: Germaine Martinelli, on
C-RFX40

So wahr die Sonne scheinet, Op. 37, No. 12
Duo
Lotte Lehmann & Lauritz Melchior, on
V-1907 in VM-560
Eleanor Steele (s) & Hall Clovis (t)
[Liebesgarten]   10″—**PD-561138**
DUPLICATION: Jo Vincent & L. van
Tulder, C-DH38

(Der) Soldat, Op. 40, No. 3 (Anderson)
Heinrich Schlusnus (b) & M. Raucheisen
(pf)   10″—**PD-30006**
[Schubert: An Schwager Kronos]

Stille Tränen, Op. 35, No. 10 (Kerner)
Marian Anderson (c) & Franz Rupp (pf)
[Der Nussbaum]   12″—**V-11-9173**

Süsser Freund, du blickest
(Frauenliebe No. 6)
Lotte Lehmann, on C-17364D in CM-539†
(Earlier version on O-188787)
Helen Traubel, on V-17634 in VM-737
Astra Desmond, on D-K1567†
Ria Ginster, on G-DB10038
Isabel French, in TC-T5
In French: Germaine Martinelli, on
C-RFX41

Talismane, Op. 25, No. 8 (Goethe)
Heinrich Schlusnus (b) & Franz Rupp
(pf)   10″—**PD-30003**
[Provenzalisches Lied]

(Die) Tochter Jephthas, Op. 95, No. 1
(Hebrew Melodies, No. 1) (Byron)
Eng. **Jephtha's Daughter**
Blanche Thebom (in English) & harp acc.,
on V-10-1389 in VM-1187

Unter'm Fenster, Op. 34, No. 3 Duo
Lotte Lehmann & Lauritz Melchior, on
V-1907 in VM-560

Und wüssten's die Blumen
(Dichterliebe No. 8)
Aksel Schiøtz, on G-DB6276†
Charles Panzéra, on V-14491 in VM-386:
G-DB4988
Lotte Lehmann, on C-72077D in CM-486
Paul Sandoz, on G-DB10038

Waldesgespräch, Op. 39, No. 3 (Eichendorff)
(Liederkreis No. 3)
Lotte Lehmann (s) & Erno Balogh (pf)
    (in VM-292) 10″—**V-1732**
[Kartenlegerin]
Lore Fischer (a) & W. von Vultee (pf)
[Wehmut]   10″—**PD-10554**

Wanderlied, Op. 35, No. 3 (Kerner)
Eng. **Wanderer's Song**
Heinrich Schlusnus (b) & S. Peschko
(pf)   10″—**PD-62801**
[Humperdinck: Am Rhein]
Wilhelm Strienz (bs) & Orch.—Dobrindt
[Bungert: Bonn]   10″—**O-26488**
DUPLICATIONS: Paul Sandoz, G-JK29;
Ludwig Hoffman, PD-90172; Franz
Völker, PD-23084

Wass soll ich sagen? Op. 27, No. 3
Karl Erb (t) & pf. acc. 10″—**G-DA4424**
[Schubert: Die Liebe hat gelogen]

Wehmut, Op. 39, No. 9 (Eichendorff)
(Liederkreis No. 9)
Lore Fischer (c) & W. von Vultee (pf)
[Waldesgespräch]   10″—**PD-10554**

Wenn ich in deine Augen seh'
(Dichterliebe No. 4)
Aksel Schiøtz, on G-DB6270†
Charles Panzéra, on V-14490 in VM-386:
G-DB4987
Lotte Lehmann, on C-17440D in CM-486
Paul Sandoz, on G-DB10037
Arthur Endrèze (b) & pf. acc.
    10″—**PAT-PA1545**
[Ich hab' im Traum geweinet]
In French: Alice Raveau, PAT-X93121

Wer machte dich so krank, Op. 35, No. 11
Else Sigfuss (c) & Folmer Jensen (pf)
[Alte Laute]   10″—**G-X7208**
Hans Hotter (b) & H. von Nordberg (pf)
    12″—**C-LX997**
[Alte Laute; Beiden Grenadiere]
(C-LCX116)   12″—**C-LX997**
Karl Erb (t) & B. Seidler-Winkler (pf)
[Alte Laute; Schubert: Ihr Grab]

Widmung—"Du meine Seele", Op. 25, No. 1
(Rückert)
Eng. **Dedication, or Devotion**
Risë Stevens (ms) & H. G. Schick (pf)
    10″—**C-17297D**
[Wolf: In dem Schatten meiner Locken;
[Mausfallen-Sprüchlein]
Alexander Sved (b)   10″—**G-DA5387**
[Ich grolle nicht]
Frida Leider (s) & M. Raucheisen (pf)
    12″—**G-DB5626**
[Meine Rose & Marienwürmchen]
Herbert Janssen (b) & Gerald Moore (pf)
[Lotosblume]   10″—**V-1931**
Paul Schoeffler (b) & E. Lush (pf)
[Wolf: Fussreise]   10″—**D-M612**
In English: Webster Booth, G-B9497
In French: Jean Planel, PAT-PG10
—Arr. Piano
Artur Rubinstein
    (in VM-1149†)   12″—**V-11-9731**
[Same, arr. Liszt & Brahms: Wiegenlied]
[Träumerei & Brahms: Wiegenlied, on
G-DB6532]
—Arr. Piano Liszt
Artur Rubinstein
    (in VM-1149) 12″—**V-11-9731**
[Brahms: Wiegenlied]

Wiegenlied, Op. 78, No. 4 Duo
Jo Vincent (s) & L. van Tulder (t)
    10″—**C-DH35**
[Anon: Du liegst mir im Herzen]

Onelia Fineschi (s) & Olga Manetti (ms)
(in Italian) 12"—C-CQX16618
[Schubert: Ständchen]

Zur Trauerfeier (Th. Rehbaum)
"Ruhe sanft in Gottes Frieden"
Hedwig Jungkurth (s) & Orch.—B.
Seidler-Winkler 12"—G-EG6058
[Mozart: Coronation Mass, K. 317—
Agnus Dei]

Stücke im Volkston, Op. 102
Violoncello & Piano
André Navarra & Gerald Moore
2 12"—C-LX1065/6

SYMPHONIES
No. 1 B flat major, Op. 38 ("Spring")
Boston Symphony Orch.—Koussevitzky
4 12"—VM-655†
Cleveland Orch.—Leinsdorf
4 12"—CM-617†
[Brahms-Leinsdorf: Choral Prelude—Es
ist ein Ros' entsprungen]

No. 2, C major, Op. 61
Minneapolis Symphony Orch.—
Mitropoulos 5 12"—CM-503†
Philadelphia Orch.—Ormandy
5 12"—VM-448†
Berlin State Opera Orch.—Pfitzner
5 12"—PD-95412/6

No. 3, E flat major, Op. 97 ("Rhenish")
N. Y. Philharmonic-Symphony Orch.—
Walter 4 12"—CM-464†
Minneapolis Symphony Orch.—
Mitropoulos 4 12"—VM-1184†

No. 4, D minor, Op. 120
London Symphony Orch.—Walter
3 12"—VM-837†
Cincinnati Symphony Orch.—
Goossens 3 12"—VM-1124†
Chicago Symphony Orch.—Stock
3 12"—CM-475†
Minneapolis Symphony Orch—
Ormandy 3 12"—VM-201†
Dresden Philharmonic Orch.—
van Kempen 4 12"—PD-67586/9S
(Last side blank)
[Schubert: Impromptu, Op. 90, No. 2,
Aeschbacher, on CET-OR5067/70]
German Philharmonic Orch., Prague—
Keilberth 3 12"—T-E3255/7

Toccata, C major, Op. 7 Piano
Simon Barère 12"—V-14263
[Chopin: Mazurka, Op. 59, No. 3]
Friedrich Wührer 12"—G-EH1291

Träumerei See under Kinderscenen, No. 7

Traumeswirren, Op. 12, No. 7 Piano
(from "Fantasiestücke")
Eng. **Dream Visions**
Alexander Brailowsky 10"—PD-90173
[Mendelssohn: Scherzo, E minor]

TRIOS—Violin, 'Cello, Piano
No. 1, D minor, Op. 63
Trio di Trieste 4 12"—T-E9151/4
Thibaud, Casals, Cortot
4 12"—G-DB1209/12
No. 3, G minor, Op. 110
Würmser Trio 3 12"—O-123858/60

Variations on the Name "Abegg"
See under Abegg-Variationen, Op. 1

Vogel als Prophet, Op. 82, No. 7 Piano
(from "Waldscenen")
Eng. **The Prophet Bird**
Artur Rubinstein 10"—V-10-1272
[Liszt: Valse oubliée]
—Arr. Violin & Piano
Zino Francescatti & Max Lanner, in
CM-660; Anja Ignatius & Timo Mikkilä,
G-X6342

Warum?, Op. 12, No. 3
(from "Fantasiestücke") Eng. **Why?**
Yves Nat 12"—C-LFX489
[Aufschwung; Des Abends]

Wilder Reiter, Op. 68, No. 8 Piano
(from "Album für die Jugend")
Eng. **Wild Horseman**
—Arr. Orchestra
RCA Victor Orch., in V-E77
(Earlier recording, in V-22162: V-20153)

SCHUTZ, Heinrich (1585-1672)
See SCHUETZ

SCOTT, Cyril, (1879-)
A prolific British composer, Scott has written
many small works for piano in the impression-
istic style.

Cherry Ripe Piano
Percy Grainger, in D-A586
Danse nègre, Op. 58, No. 5 Piano
Eileen Joyce 12"—P-E11333
[Lotus Land: Farjeon: Tarantella, A
minor]
Percy Grainger, in D-A586
Lento Piano
Percy Grainger, in D-A586
Lotus Land, Op. 47, No. 1 Piano
Eileen Joyce 12"—P-E11333
[Danse nègre; Farjeon: Tarantella, A
minor]
—Arr. Violin & Piano Kreisler
Fritz Kreisler & Franz Rupp
12"—G-DB3444
[Rimsky-Korsakov: Coq D'or—Hymne au
soleil]
—Arr. Orchestra Kostelanetz
Andre Kostelanetz and his Orch.
(in CX-264) 12"—C-7445M
[Rimsky-Korsakov: Sadko—Song of
India]
Lullaby, Op. 57, No. 2
Song in English (Rossetti)
Marian Anderson(c) & Franz Rupp (pf)
10"—V-10-1260
[Bucky: Hear the wind whispering]
Kirsten Flagstad (s) & Edwin McArthur
(pf) (in VM-342) 10"—V-1817
[Charles: When I have sung my songs]
[Ronald: O lovely night, on G-DA1512]

SCRIABIN, Alexander (1872-1915)
A Russian composer who, following in the wake
of other Romanticists, sought to escape from
the "confinement" of diatonic harmony.

ETUDES Piano

Op. 2, No. 1, C sharp minor
Anatole Kitain   12"—C-69569D
[Prelude, Op. 11, No. 2; Rachmaninoff:
Etude Tableau, Op. 33, No. 1 & Prelude,
G sharp minor]
Carl Tillius   10"—G-X7326
[Godowsky: Alt Wein; Rimsky-Korsakov:
Flight of the Bumble Bee]

Op. 8, No. 10, D flat major (Study in 3rds)
Jacob Gimpel, in VOX-164

—Arr. Violin & Piano
David Oistrakh & A. Giakov
[Nocturne, Op. 5, No. 1]   10"—D-M545

Op. 8, No. 11
Samuel Yaffe, on PAR-1

Op. 8, No. 12, D sharp minor
Alexander Brailowsky   12"—V-18100
[Mendelssohn: Scherzo, E minor, Op. 16,
No. 2]
(Earlier recording on PD-95142)
DUPLICATIONS: Friedrich Wührer,
G-EG6224; Robert Riefling, C-GN440

Op. 42, No. 5, C sharp minor
Samuel Yaffe, on PAR-1

Op. 65, No. 1 (Etude in 9ths)
Ida Krehm, on PAR-30

Op. 65, No. 2, G major Etude in Sevenths
Samuel Yaffee, on PAR-16
Jacob Gimpel, in VOX-164

"Guirlandes" Op. 73, No. 1
(Dance No. 1) Piano
Samuel Yaffe, on PAR-3

NOCTURNES, Op. 5 Piano

No. 1, F sharp minor
Friedrich Wührer   10"—G-EG6297
[Nocturne No. 2]

—Arr. Violin & Piano
David Oistrakh & A. Giakov
[Etude, Op. 8, No. 10]   10"—D-M545
[Prokofiev: Mélodie, Op. 35, No. 3, on
U-G14741]

No. 2, A major
Friedrich Wührer   10"—G-EG6297
[Nocturne No. 1]

Pièce, Op. 22, No. 3 Piano
Samuel Yaffe, on PAR-2

POEMS Piano

Op. 32, No. 1
Samuel Yaffe, on PAR-3

Op. 32, No. 2
Samuel Yaffe, on PAR-4

Op. 34 (Poème tragique)
Samuel Yaffe, on PAR-8

Op. 36 (Poème satanique)
Samuel Yaffe, on PAR-6

Op. 41
Samuel Yaffe, on PAR-9

Op. 44, No. 1
Samuel Yaffe, on PAR-9

Op. 51, No. 3 (Poème Ailé)
Samuel Yaffe, on PAR-3

Op. 61 (Poème-Nocturne)
Samuel Yaffe, on PAR-12

Op. 69, No. 2
Samuel Yaffe, on PAR-16

Op. 71, No. 1
Samuel Yaffe, on PAR-16

Poème d'Extase, Op. 54 Orchestra
Eng. Poem of Ecstasy
Philadelphia Orch.—Stokowski
(in VM-125†)   2 12"—V-7515/6
(G-DB1706/7)
(with "Prometheus")

PRELUDES Piano

Op. 11, No. 2
Anatole Kitain   12"—C-69569D
[Etude: Op. 2, No. 1; Rachmaninoff:
Etude Tableau, Op. 33, No. 1 & Prelude
G sharp minor]

Op. 11, No. 7
Samuel Yaffe, on PAR-2

Op. 11, No. 9
Eileen Joyce (C-DX1051)
(in CM-527†)   12"—C-71423D
[Prelude, Op. 11, No. 10; Shostakovich:
Concerto, Pt. 5]

Op. 11, No. 10
Eileen Joyce (C-DX1051)
(in CM-527†)   12"—C-71423D
[Prelude Op. 11, No. 9; Shostakovich:
Concerto, Pt. 5]

Op. 11, No. 14
Samuel Yaffe, on PAR-8

Op. 11, No. 17
Samuel Yaffe, on PAR-9

Op. 13, No. 2
Samuel Yaffe, on PAR-2

Op. 13, No. 4
Samuel Yaffe, on PAR-2

Op. 13, No. 5
Samuel Yaffe, on PAR-2

Op. 16, No. 2
Samuel Yaffe, on PAR-2

Op 17, No. 5
Samuel Yaffe, on PAR-8

Op. 17, No. 7
Samuel Yaffe, on PAR-2

Op. 22, No. 1
Samuel Yaffe, on PAR-9

Op. 22, No. 3
Samuel Yaffe, on PAR-2

Op. 27, No. 1 ("Patetico")
Samuel Yaffe, on PAR-8

Op. 33, No. 4
Samuel Yaffe, on PAR-14

Op. 45, No. 3
Samuel Yaffe, on PAR-14

Op. 59, No. 2
Yolanda Bolotine, on PAR-24

Op. 67, No. 2
Samuel Yaffe, on PAR-14

Op. 74, No. 2
Yolanda Bolotine, on PAR-24

Op. 74, No. 3
Samuel Yaffe, on PAR-6

Op. 74, No. 5
Samuel Yaffe, on PAR-14

Prometheus, Op. 60 Orchestra, Piano, Organ & Chorus
Eng. The Poem of Fire
Philadelphia Orch., S. Levin (pf), organ & Curtis Institute Chorus—Stokowski
    (in VM-125†) 2 12"—**V-7517/8**
(with "Poème d'Extase")

Rêverie, Op. 24
EIAR Symphony Orch.—Vittorio Gui
    12"—**CET-BB25075**
[Liadov: Eight Russian Folk Dances]

Romance (unspecified) 'Cello & Piano
Gregor Piatigorsky & Ivor Newton
    12"—**G-DB2271**
[Tchaikovsky: Valse sentimentale; Chopin: Nocturne, C sharp minor, Op. post.]

SONATAS . Piano

No. 3, F sharp minor, Op. 23
Yolande Bolotine   3 10"—**PAR-25/7**

No. 4, F sharp minor, Op. 30
Vladimir Drosdoff   10"—**PAR-10**

No. 5, Op. 53
Ida Krehm   3 10"—**PAR-28/30**
[Etude in 9ths]

No. 6, Op. 62
Emma Criscuolo Gagliardi
    2 10"—**PAR-19/20**

No. 7, Op. 64 (The White Mass)
Samuel Yaffe   2 10"—**PAR-17/18**

No. 8, Op. 66
Yolanda Bolotine   3 10"—**PAR-22/4**
[Preludes, Op. 59, No. 2 & Op. 74, No. 2]

No. 10, Op. 70 (The Black Mass)
Samuel Yaffe   2 10"—**PAR-15/6**
[Poème, Op. 69, No. 2]

Vers la flamme, Op. 72 Piano
Samuel Yaffe, on PAR-7

WALTZES Piano

F minor, Op. 1
Friedrich Wührer   10"—**G-EG6224**
[Etude, D sharp minor, Op. 8, No. 12]

SEIDEL, Jan

A contemporary Czech composer.

Old Women (Extract from a quarter-tone quartet to words by Fr. Halan)
Marie Buresova (sprechstimme) & string quartet   12"—**ESTA-F2504**

SEIBER, Matyes (1905-   )

A contemporary Hungarian composer, residing in England. The recorded work below shows the influence of Bartók.

Fantasy for 'Cello & Piano
William Pleeth & Margaret Good
    10"—**D-M565**

SENAILLE, Jean Baptiste (1687-1730)

A native Parisian who went to Italy to study under Vitali, Senaillé influenced the course of the French violin school by his adherence to the Italian style of composition and performance. Little more than a token sample of his some fifty violin sonatas have to the present appeared on records.

Allegro spiritoso Arr. Bassoon
Archie Camden (bn) & Orch.—Harty
    (in CM-71†) 12"—**C-67330D**
[Mozart: Bassoon Concerto, K. 191, Pt. 5]

Sonata, E major Violin & Basso continuo
J. Grabowska (vl) & Pauline Aubert (harpsichord)
    (in Vol. VIII) 12"—**AS-74**
[Francoeur: Sonata, G minor]

SENFL, Ludwig, (c.1492-c.1555)

A Swiss-born pupil of Heinrich Isaac, Senfl succeeded his teacher as Kapellmeister to Maximilian I. In addition to the sacred music expected of composers in service at court, his output includes secular songs.

Also heilig ist der Tag 6-Part

Kling klang (Kommt her, Leute all') 6-Part
Basel Chamber Choir (unacc.)—Paul Sacher   (in Vol. VI) 12"—**AS-51**
[Finck: Wach auf & Ach herzigs Herz]

SERINI, Giambattista

One of Italy's many galant-style composers of the first half of the eighteenth century.

Sonata, B flat major Harpsichord
Anna Linde   12"—**MIA-8**

SERMISY, Claudin De (c.1490-1562)

A pupil of Josquin des Prés, Claudin de Sermisy composed many chansons, motets, and masses.

En entrant en ung Jardin Chanson in French
Marcelle Gerar (s) with Viols, Flute, Guitar acc.   (in Vol. II) 12"—**AS-15**
[with French Chansons of the 16th Century]

SEVERAC, Déodat De (1873-1921)

One of the pupils of Vincent d'Indy, Séverac has written many songs, chamber music and several operas.

Baigneuses au Soleil Piano
Blanche Selva   12"—**C-D15142**

Où l'on entend une vielle boite à musique
Solomon (pf)   12"—**G-C3509**
[Daquin: Le Coucou; Chopin: Mazurka No. 47 & Waltz No. 14]

(Le) Retour des Muletiers (Cerdaña No. 5)
Robert Casadesus (pf) 12"—**C-LFX401**
[Fauré: Impromptu No. 5 & Prelude No. 5]

SONGS In French

Aubade (Marguerite de Navarre)
Claire Croiza (s) & pf. acc. 10"—**C-LF60**
[Ma poupée chérie]

Chanson de la nuit durable (E. Mongeret)
Charles Panzéra (b)   12"—**G-DB4868**
[Franck: Nocturne]

Chanson pour le petit cheval (Eslien)
Germaine Corney (s) & pf. acc.
[Ma poupée chérie]   10"—**PD-561013**

(Les) Hiboux (Baudelaire)
Marquise de Vesins (c) & Mme. Panzéra-Baillot (pf)   12"—**C-DFX118**
[Bach: Komm süsser Tod]

Ma poupée chérie (Séverac)
Vanni-Marcoux (bs) & pf. acc.
12"—G-DB4916
[Martini: Plaisir d'amour]
Claire Croiza (s) & pf. acc.
[Aubade] 10"—C-LF60
DUPLICATIONS: G. Corney, PD-561013;
H. Chardy, O-238247

Arrangements
See under Albéniz: Navarra (completed
by Séverac)

SHOSTAKOVICH, Dmitri (1906-)

Unquestionably a gifted composer, Shostako-
vich has seemed to vacillate between approval
of the "party line" and satire of it. Quite well
represented on records, his popularity was at
least partly enhanced by the friendly wartime
disposition of the western world towards Soviet
Russia.

(The) Age of Gold Ballet
—Polka & Russian Dance
St. Louis Symphony—Golschmann
12"—V-11-8592
[Falla: Vida Breve—Spanish Dance
No. 1]
Paris Symphony—Erlich
(in CM-347) 10"—C-P17415D
(C-LB16) (PAT-X96301)
—Polka only
National Symphony Orch.—Kindler
12"—G-C3346
[Mussorgsky: Boris Godunov—Love
Music]
—Arr. Piano
Dmitri Shostakovich 12"—U-G14919
[7 Children's Pieces; 3 Fantastic Danses,
Op. 5]
Oscar Levant, in CM-508
Andor Foldes, in CON-22
—Arr. 2 Pianos
Pierre Luboshutz & Genia Nemenoff
10"—V-2214
[Falla: Amor Brujo—Ritual Fire Dance]
—Arr. Violin & Piano
Zino Francescatti & M. Lanner, in CM-
660
(7) Children's Pieces Piano
Dmitri Shostakovich 12"—U-G14919
[3 Fantastic Dances; Polka from the
"Age of Gold"]

Concerto, Op. 35 Piano & Orchestra
Eileen Joyce (pf), Arthur Lockwood (tr)
& Hallé Orch.—Heward
(C-DX1049/51†) 3 12"—CM-527†
[Scriabin: Préludes Nos. 9 & 10, Joyce
solo]

(3) Fantastic Dances, Op. 5 Piano
Dmitri Shostakovich 12"—U-G14919
[7 Children's Pieces; Polka from the
"Age of Gold"]
—Selection (unidentified)
Andor Foldes, in CON-22

(The) Golden Mountain Film score
—Waltz
Uriev's Orch. 10"—USSR-13266/7
[Taiti Trot]

(24) Preludes, Op. 34 Piano
No. 2, A minor
Oscar Levant, in CM-508
No. 5, D major
William Kapell 12"—V-11-8824
[Nos. 10 & 24; Rachmaninoff: Prelude
No. 1]
Shura Cherkassy, in VOX-165
No. 8, F sharp minor
Dmitri Shostakovich
(in COM-C102) 10"—USSR-11992
[No. 22 & Trio, Op. 67, Pt. 9]
No. 10, C sharp minor
William Kapell 12"—V-11-8824
[Nos. 5 & 24; Rachmaninoff: Prelude
No. 1]
Shura Cherkassky, in VOX-165
—Arr. Violin & Piano
Jascha Heifetz & Emanuel Bay, in D-A592
No. 14, E flat minor
Harriet Cohen 12"—C-DX1066
[Kabalevsky: Sonatina, C major, Op. 13,
No. 1]
—Arr. Orchestra Stokowski
All American Orch.—Stokowski
(in CM-446†) 12"—C-11524D
Philadelphia Orch.—Stokowski
[Stravinsky: Fire Bird Suite, Pt. 5]
(G-DB2884) (in VM-291†) 12"—V-8928
[Stravinsky: Fire Bird Suite, Pt. 5]
[Symphony No. 1, Pt. 9, on V-7888 in
VM-192†]
No. 15, D flat major Arr. Violin & Piano
Jascha Heifetz & Emanuel Bay, in D-A592
No. 22, G minor
Dmitri Shostakovich
(in COM-C102) 10"—USSR-11992
[No. 8 & Trio, Op. 67, Pt. 9]
No. 24, D major
William Kapell 12"—V-11-8824
[Nos. 5 & 10; Rachmaninoff: Prelude
No. 1]
(14) Preludes, Op. 48 Piano
Dmitri Shostakovich 12"—U-G14920

Quartet, Op. 49 Strings
Stuyvesant String Quartet
2 12"—CX-231†

Quintet, Op. 57 Piano & String Quartet
Vivian Rivkin & Stuyvesant String
Quartet 4 12"—CM-483†

Sonata, Op. 40 'Cello & Piano
Gregor Piatigorsky & Valentin Pavlovsky
3 12"—CM-551†

SYMPHONIES Orchestra

No. 1, F major, Op. 10
Philadelphia Orch.—Stokowski
5 12"—VM-192†
[Prelude, Op. 34, No. 14 arr. Orch.]
Cleveland Orch.—Rodzinski
4 12"—CM-472†

No. 5, Op. 47
Philadelphia Orch.—Stokowski
6 12"—VM-619†
(G-DB3991/6, in GM-375†)
Cleveland Orch.—Rodzinski
5 12"—CM-520†
Leningrad Philharmonic Orch.—
Mravinsky 7 12"—USSR-06820/23

No. 6, Op. 35
Philadelphia Orch.—Stokowski
5 12"—VM-867†
[McDonald: Legend of the Arkansas
Traveler]
Pittsburgh Symphony—Reiner
(C-LX998/1002†) 5 12"—CM-585†
[Kabalevsky: Colas Breugnon—Over-
ture]

No. 7, Op. 60 (Leningrad Symphony)
Buffalo Philharmonic Orch.—Steinberg
7 12"—MC-83

No. 9, Op. 70
New York Philharmonic-Symphony Orch.
—Efrem Kurtz 4 12"—CM-688†
Boston Symphony Orch.—Koussevitzky
3 12"—VM-1134†

Taïti Trot (Paraphrase on "Tea for Two")
Uriev Orch. 10"—USSR-13266/7
[Golden Mountain—Waltz]

Trio, Op. 67 Piano, Violin, 'Cello
Dmitri Shostakovich, D. Tzyganov, & S.
Shirinsky 5 10"—COM-C102
(USSR-13160/8)
[With Preludes, Op. 34, G minor & F
sharp minor, Shostakovich, pf. solo]
D. Shostakovich, D. Oistrakh, & M. Sadlo
3 12"—U-G14927/9
Compinsky Trio 3 12"—ALCO-A3

The United Nations
Paul Robeson (bs) (in English) & Cho.
12"—K-1200
[Registan: Anthem of USSR]

SIBELIUS, Jean (1865-   )

*The prolific national composer of Finland,
whose merits have been hotly debated for years,
Sibelius is extremely well represented on records.*

THE SIBELIUS SOCIETY

NOTE: *Formed in 1932 by H. M. V., each volume consists of seven twelve-inch records. Individual works are not available separately.*

Vol. I:
**Symphony No. 5; Pohjola's Daughter;
Tapiola**
London Symphony—Robert Kajanus

Vol. II:
Symphony No. 3, C major, Op. 52
London Symphony—Robert Kajanus
Symphony No. 7, C major, Op. 105
BBC Symphony Orch.—Koussevitzky

Vol. III:
String Quartet "Voces Intimae" Op. 56
Budapest String Quartet
Symphony No. 6, D minor, Op. 104
Finnish National Orch.—Georg
Schneevoigt 7 12"—VM-344†

Vol. IV:
a. **Concerto, Violin & Orch., D minor,
Op. 47**
Jascha Heifetz & London Philharmonic—
Beecham 4 12"—VM-309†
b. **Night Ride & Sunrise, Op. 55 & The
Oceanrides, Op. 73**
BBC Symphony—Boult
(Part "B" in Society Set IV only)

Vol. V:
Symphony No. 4, A minor, Op. 63
The Return of Lemminkäinen (Legend)
Op. 22, No. 4; **The Tempest—1st Suite,**
Op. 109, No. 2: (The Oak Tree; Humor-
esque; Caliban's Song; Berceuse); **The
Tempest—2nd Suite, Op. 109, No. 3**
(Prospero & Miranda)
London Philharmonic Orch.—Beecham
VM-446†

Vol. VI:
En Saga—Tone poem for orchestra, Op. 9
**Incidental Music to Kuolema—Valse
Triste, Op. 44; Pelléas et Mélisande—
Suite for small orchestra, Op. 46:**
(Spring in the Park; Entr'acte; Death of
Mélisande); **In Memoriam—Funeral
March for Orch., Op. 59; The Bard—Tone
poem for orchestra, Op. 64; Incidental
Music to the Tempest—Prelude, Op. 109a**
London Philharmonic Orch.—Beecham
VM-658†

Collection—75th Anniversary Album
**Finlandia, Op. 26, No. 7; The Swan of
Tuonela, Op. 22, No. 3; Lemminkäinen's
Homeward Journey, Op. 22, No. 4**
Philadelphia Orch.—Ormandy
3 12"—VM-750†

Auf der Heide
Anja Ignatius (vl) & Timo Mikkilä (pf)
10"—G-X6342
[Schumann: Vogel als Prophet]

(The) Bard, Op. 64 1913
London Philharmonic—Beecham, in Society set VI: VM-658†

Belshazzar's Feast, Op. 51 1906
(Suite for Small Orchestra)
1. Oriental Procession 2. Solitude 3.
Night Music 4. Khadra's Dance
London Symphony Orch.—Robert
Kajanus 2 12"—VM-715†
(G-DB3937/8)

Berceuse See under The Tempest—Incidental Music

Canzonetta, Op. 62a String Orchestra
Curtis Chamber Music Ensemble—Bailly
(in VM-563†) 12"—V-12440
[Bloch: Concerto Grosso, Pt. 5]

Chanson de printemps, Op. 16 1894
Paul Godwin Orch. 12"—PD-27011
[Valse triste]

Concerto, D minor, Op. 47 Violin & Or-
chestra
Jascha Heifetz & London Philharmonic—
Beecham 4 12"—VM-309†
(In Society Set IV)
Ginette Neveu & Philharmonia Orch.—
Süsskind 4 12"—GM-390†
(G-DB6244/7)

Guila Bustabo & Berlin State Orch.—
Zaun 4 12″—**C-LWX372/5**
Anja Ignatius & Berlin State Opera
Orch.—Järnefelt 4 12″—**PD-68070/3**

(5) Danses champêtres, Op. 106 Violin &
Piano
—No. 1
Emil Telmanyi & G. von Vasarhelyi
12″—**G-DB2798**
[Brahms: Hungarian Dance No. 1]
—No. 2
Emil Telmanyi & Gerald Moore
12″—**G-DB2503**
[Romance, Op. 78, No. 2; Nielsen: Romance]

En Saga See (En) Saga

Festivo, Op. 25, No. 3 Orchestra
(No. 3 of Scènes historiques: Tempo di
Bolero)
London Philharmonic Orch.—Beecham
(C-LWX118) 12″—**C-LX501**

Finlandia, Op. 26 Symphonic Poem
London Philharmonic—Beecham
(C-LX704) (C-LFX533) 12″—**C-69180D**
Philadelphia Orch.—Ormandy
(in VM-750†) 12″—**V-17701**
Cleveland Orch.—Rodzinski
12″—**C-11178D**
National Symphony Orch.—Braithwaite
12″—**D-K1150**
EIAR Symphony Orch.—S. Failoni
12″—**CET-BB25013**
DUPLICATIONS: Göteborg Symphony
Orch.—Eckerberg, T-E3186; Philadelphia Orch.—Stokowski, V-7412:
G-DB1584; Tivoli Orch.—Jensen, TONO-
X25003; New Queen's Hall Orch.—Wood,
C-9655; Philharmonic Orch.—Weissmann, P-E11170; Berlin Philharmonic—
Melichar, PD-57068; Berlin State Opera
Orch.—Järnefelt, P-E10774; Berlin State
Opera Orch.—Abendroth, O-7896; Symphony Orch.—Sargent, G-C1827
—Arr. Band: Grenadier Guards—Miller,
D-K736

(4) Humoresques, Op. 89 Violin & Piano
—No. 4 only
Henri Temianka & Chamber Orch.
12″—**P-DPX12**
[Schubert: Rondo, A major, Pt. 3]

In Memoriam—Funeral March, Op. 59 1909
London Philharmonic—Beecham, in Society Set, Vol. VI: VM-658†

Karelia Suite, Op. 11 Orchestra
No. 1 (Intermezzo) & No. 3 (Alla marcia)
BBC Symphony Orch.—Beecham
(G-DB6248) 12″—**V-11-9568**
London Philharmonic Orch.—Goehr
(G-C2985) 12″—**V-12830**
Symphony Orch.—Kajanus
12″—**C-GQX16518**

King Christian II—Incidental Music Op. 27
1898
(for Adolf Paul's drama)
—No. 1, Elégie
Leslie Heward String Orch.
[Rakastava Suite, Pt. 3] 12″—**C-DX1005**

City of Birmingham Orch.—Weldon
[Musette] 12″—**C-DX1220**
—No. 2, Musette
City of Birmingham Orch.—Weldon
[Elégie] 12″—**C-DX1220**
—No. 5, Nocturne & No. 7, Ballade
Royal Opera Orch., Stockholm—
Järnefelt 12″—**O-D6051**

Kuolema Incidental Music, Op. 44
See under Valse Triste

Lemminkäinen Legends, Op. 22
See under The Swan of Tuonela & The
Return of Lemminkäinen

Malinconia, Op. 20 'Cello & Piano
Louis Jensen & Galina Werschenska
12″—**G-DB5223**

March of the Finnish Infantry, Op. 91a
Orchestra
Fin. Jääkärien Marssi
Suomen Valkoisen Kaartin Soittokunta-
Nare 10″—**G-X6338**
[Karjalan Jääkärien Marssi]
Helsinki Orch.—Kajanus
10″—**G-X2825**
[Anon, arr. Kajanus: Karjalan
Jääkärien Marssi]

Mazurka, Op. 81, No. 1 Violin & Piano
Mischa Elman & Leopold Mittman
12″—**V-11-9111**
[Achron: Hebrew Melody]
Anja Ignatius & Timo Mikkilä
[Palmgren: Berceuse] 10″—**G-X6341**

Night Ride and Sunrise, Op. 55 Symphonic
Poem
BBC Symphony Orch.—Adrian Boult,
in Society Set IV

Nocturne, Op. 81, No. 3 Violin & Piano
Ferenc Vecsey & G. Agosti
(CET-LL3012) 10″—**PD-10686**
[Palmgren: Canzonetta, Op. 43, No. 3]

(The) Oceanides, Op. 73 Tone Poem
BBC Symphony-Adrian Boult, in Society
Set IV

Pelléas et Mélisande Incidental Music
Suite for Small Orchestra, Op. 46 1905 (9
numbers)
—No. 2, Mélisande
New York Philharmonic-Symphony
Orch.—Beecham
(in CM-524) 12″—**C-11892D**
[Symphony No. 7, Pt. 5]
—No. 3, A Spring in the Park
—No. 7, Entr'acte
—No. 8, Death of Mélisande
London Philharmonic—Beecham, in Society Set VI: VM-658†

Pohjola's Daughter, Op. 49 Symphonic
Fantasy
Fin. Pohjolan tytär
London Symphony—Kajanus, in Society
Set I
Boston Symphony Orch.—Koussevitzky
(in VM-474†) 2 12″—**V-15022/3**
[Symphony No. 5, Pt. 7]
[Prokofieff: Love for 3 Oranges—March
& Scherzo, on G-DB5722/3]
Hannover Nedersachsen Orch.—Thierfelder 2 12″—**PD-57172/3**

Quartet, Op. 56, D minor 1908
"Voces Intimae"
Budapest String Quartet, in Society Set
III: VM-344†

Rakastava Suite, Op. 14 1893
The Lover; The Lover's Walk; The Farewell
Leslie Heward String Orch.
2 12"—C-DX1004/5
[King Christian Suite—Elégie]
NBC String Symphony—Frank Black
(in VM-455†) 2 12"—V-12231/2
[Brahms: Liebeslieder, Pt. 5]
Boyd Neel Orch.—Neel
2 12"—D-X174/5

(The) Return of Lemminkäinen, Op. 22,
No. 4
London Philharmonic Orch.—Beecham,
in Society Set Vol. V: VM-446†
Philadelphia Orch.—Ormandy
(in VM-750†) 12"—V-17703

Romance, Op. 24, No. 9
Salon Orch., G-B9142

Romance, C major, Op. 42 String Orchestra
BBC Symphony Orch.—Adrian Boult
12"—G-DB3972
Boyd Neel String Orch.
(PD-516705) 12"—D-K831

Romance, Op. 78, No. 2 Violin & Piano (or
Orch.)
Emil Telmanyi & Gerald Moore
12"—G-DB2503
[Danse champêtre; Nielsen: Romance]
Francesco Asti & Göteborg Symphony
Orch.—Tor Mann 12"—G-Z206
[Stenhammer: Sentimental Romance]

(En) Saga, Op. 9 Tone Poem Finn. Satu
London Philharmonic Orch.—Beecham,
in Society Set Vol. VI: VM-658†
London Philharmonic Orch.—Victor De
Sabata 3 12"—D-ED49†
[Valse triste] (D-K1504/6)
New Symphony Orch.—Goossens
2 12"—G-C1994/5
[Valse triste] (abbr.)

SONGS In Finnish & Swedish

Astray, Op. 17, No. 4 Swedish: Vilse
Florence Wiese (c) (in Swedish) &
Daniel Kelly (pf) 10"—D-M505
[But my bird is long in homing; Speedwell; Driftwood]

Belshazzar See Song of the Jewish Girl

Black Roses, Op. 36, No. 1 Swedish:
Svarta Roser
Aulikki Rautawaara (s) (in Swedish) &
F. Leitner (pf) 10"—T-A2543
[On a balcony by the Sea]
Joan Hammond (s) (in English) &
Gerald Moore (pf) 10"—G-B9445
[The Tryst]

(The) Broken Voice, Op. 18, No. 1 Chorus
Finnish: Sortunut ääni
Helsinki University Cho.
(G-X6046) 10"—V-26-6010
[Kuula: Tanssista Palatessa & Iltatunnelma]

But my bird is long in homing, Op. 36, No. 2
Swedish: Men min Fågel Marks dock
icke
Florence Wiese (c) (in Swedish) & Daniel Kelly (pf) 10"—D-M505
[Astray; Speedwell; Driftwood]

Come away, Death, Op. 60, No. 1 (Shakespeare)
Marian Anderson (c) (in Eng.) & K.
Vehanen (pf) (G-DA1523) 10"—V-1809
[Finnish folksong: Sommernatt, arr.
Palmgren; Bergerette, arr. Vehanen]

(The) Coming of Spring, Op. 86, No. 1
Swedish: Vår Förnimmelser
Florence Wiese (c) (in Swedish) &
Daniel Kelly (pf) 10"—D-M504
[Diamond in the Snow; The Question]

Diamonds on the March Snow, Op. 36, No. 6
Swedish: Demanten på Marssnön
Aulikki Rautawaara (s) (in Swedish)
[Säf, säf, susa] 10"—T-A2519
[In Finnish, with Song of the Jewish girl
on ELEC-3120]
Florence Wiese (c) (in Swedish) &
Daniel Kelley (pf) 10"—D-M504
[Coming of Spring; The Question]

Driftwood, Op. 17, No. 7
Swedish: Lastu lainehilla
Florence Wiese (c) & Daniel Kelly (pf)
10"—D-M505
[But my Bird; Astray; Speedwell]

(The) First Kiss, Op. 37, No. 1
Swedish: Den första Kyssen
Aulikki Rautawaara (s) (in German)
[The Tryst] 10"—T-A1900
Florence Wiese (c) (in Swedish) &
Daniel Kelly (pf) 10"—D-M503
[Spring is Fleeting; Säf, Säf, Susa]
Lorri Lail (ms) (in Swedish) & Sven-
Gunnar Andren (pf) 10"—G-X7172
[Grieg: A Swan]

Hymn to Thaïs the Unforgettable
Aulikki Rautawaara (s) (in Finnish)
10"—ELEC-3119
[On a Balcony by the Sea]

In the field a maiden sings, Op. 50, No. 3
(or, A maiden yonder sings)
Ger. Im Feld ein Mädchen singt
Aulikki Rautawaara (s) (in Finnish) &
F. Leitner (pf) 10"—T-A2520
[Melartin: Gib nur dein Herze]

O, wert thou here, Op. 50, No. 4
Ger. Aus banger Brust
Marian Anderson (c) (in German) & K.
Vehanen (pf) 10"—G-DA1580
[Slow as the colors]

On a balcony by the sea, Op. 38, No. 2
Swedish: Pa Verandan vid hafvet
Aulikki Rautawaara (s) (in Swedish)
[Hymn to Thaïs] 10"—ELEC-3119
[Black Roses, on T-A2543]

(The) Question, Op. 17, No. 1
Swedish: Se'n har jag ej frågat mera
Florence Wiese (c) (in Swedish) &
Daniel Kelly (pf) 10"—D-M504
[Coming of Spring; Diamond in the
March Snow]

Säf, säf, susa, Op. 36, No. 4 (Ingalill)
Eng. Sigh, sedges, sigh
Swedish: Schilfrohr, Saus'le
Marian Anderson (c) (in Swedish) & K.
Vehanen (pf) 10"—G-DA1517
[The Tryst]
Aulikki Rautawaara (s) (in Finnish)
10"—T-A2519
[Diamond on the March Snow]
Florence Wiese (c) (in Swedish) &
Daniel Kelly (pf) 10"—D-M503
[Spring is Fleeting; First Kiss]

Slow as the colors, Op. 61, No. 1
Swedish: Långsam som kvällskyn
Marian Anderson (c) & K. Vehanen (pf)
[O, wert thou here] 10"—G-DA1580

Song of the Jewish Girl
Aulikki Rautawaara (s)
10"—ELEC-3120
[Diamonds on the March Snow]

Speedwell, Op. 88, No. 1 (or, the Anemone)
Swedish: Blasippan
Florence Wiese (c) (in Swedish) &
Daniel Kelly (pf) 10"—D-M505
[But my bird; Astray; Driftwood]

(The) Spider Fin. Ristilukki
Väinö Sola (t) 10"—G-X2809
[Linsen: Ma Oksalla Ylimmalla]

Spring is fleeting, Op. 13, No. 4
Swedish: Varen flyktar hastigt
Florence Wiese (c) (in Swedish) &
Daniel Kelly (pf) 10"—D-M503
[The First Kiss; Säf, säf, susa]

(The) Tryst, Op. 37, No. 5
Swedish: Flickan kom ifrån sin älsklings
mote
Ger. Mädchen kam von Stelldichein
Marian Anderson (c) (in Swedish) & K.
Vehanen (pf) 10"—G-DA1517
[Säf, säf, susa]
Aulikki Rautawaara (s) (in German)
[First kiss] 10"—T-A1900
Joan Hammond (s) (in English) &
Gerald Moore (pf) 10"—G-B9445
[Black roses]

Folk Song Settings
Jouluvirsi—En etsi valtaa Loistoa
Sulo Saarrits (b) 10"—G-X6339
[Kotilainen: Kun Joulu On—Kun maas'
on hanki]

Sydameni laulu, Op. 18, No. 6
Eng. Song of my Heart
Finlandia Chorus of Helsinki
10"—V-26-6021
[Milloin Pohjolan Nähda Saan]
[Terva Kuu, on G-X6280: G-EG6913]

Terva kuu, Op. 18, No. 2
Eng. Hail Moon
Finlandia Chorus of Helsinki
10"—V-26-6030
[Palmgren: Song of the Slaves of Hiisi]
[Sydameni laulu, on G-X6280: G-EG6913]

(The) Swan of Tuonela, Op. 22, No. 3
Symphonic Poem
(Lemminkäinen Legend No. 3)
Fin. Tuonelan joutsen—Kalevalasta
Philadelphia Orch.—Ormandy
(in VM-750†) 12"—V-17702
(G-DB5832)

Chicago Symphony Orch.—Stock
12"—C-11388D
Philadelphia Orch.—Stokowski
(G-AW267) 12"—V-7380
Amsterdam Concertgebouw Orch.—E. van
Beinum (U-G18115) 12"—T-SK3236
Hanover Orch.—H. Thierfelder
(CET-OR5089) 12"—PD-57128

Swan White, Op. 54
Incidental Music to Strindberg's play
Fin. Svanehvit
—Maiden with the Roses only
Boston Symphony Orch.—Koussevitsky
(in VM-1170†) 12"—V-11-9879
[Hanson: Symphony No. 3, Pt. 9]
Boston Symphony Orch.—Koussevitzky
(in VM-347†) 12"—V-14355
[Tchaikovsky: Romeo & Juliet, Pt. 5]
[Symphony No. 2, Pt. 11, on V-8726 in
VM-272†]
[Symphony No. 5, Pt. 7 on G-DB3171]

SYMPHONIES Orchestra

No. 1, E minor, Op. 39 1899
Philadelphia Orch.—Ormandy
4 12"—VM-881†
N. Y. Philharmonic-Symphony Orch.—
Barbirolli 5 12"—CM-532†
Minneapolis Symphony Orch.—Ormandy
(G-DB2709/13) 5 12"—GM-264†

No. 2, D major, Op. 43 1902
Boston Symphony Orch.—Koussevitzky
6 12"—VM-272†
[Swan White—Maiden with the Roses]
(G-DB2599/602s, last side blank, in GM-
241†)
N. Y. Philharmonic-Symphony Orch.—
Barbirolli 5 12"—CM-423†
Stockholm Symphony Orch.—Tor Mann
5 12"—T-SK3322/6

No. 3, C major, Op. 52 1907
London Symphony Orch.—Kajanus, in
Society Set II

No. 4, A minor, Op. 63 1912
London Philharmonic Orch.
Beecham, in Society Set V: VM-446†
N. Y. Philharmonic-Symphony Orch.—
Rodzinski 4 12"—CM-665†
Philadelphia Orch.—Stokowski
4 12"—VM-160†

No. 5, E flat major, Op. 82 1915
London Symphony Orch.—Kajanus, in
Society Set I
Cleveland Orch.—Rodzinski
4 12"—CM-514†
[Järnefelt: Praeludium]
Boston Symphony Orch.—Koussevitzky
(in VM-474†) 4 12"—V-15019/22
[Pohjola's Daughter, Pt. 1]
[Swan White—Maiden with the Roses
on G-DB3168/71 in GM-337†]

No. 6, D minor, Op. 104 1923
Finnish National Orch.—Scheevoigt, in
Society Set III: VM-344†

No. 7, C major, Op. 105 1925
BBC Symphony Orch.—Koussevitzky, in
Society Set II

N. Y. Philharmonic-Symphony Orch.—
Beecham   3   12"—CM-524†
[Pelléas et Mélisande—Mélisande]
St. Louis Symphony Orch.—Golschmann
(G-DB6167/9†)   3   12"—VM-922†

Tapiola, Op. 112 Symphonic Poem
  London Symphony—Kajanus, in Society
Set I
Royal Philharmonic—Beecham
       2   12"—G-DB6412/3
Boston Symphony Orch.—Koussevitzky
(G-DB5992/3)   2   12"—VM-848†

(The) Tempest, Op. 109 Incidental Music
No. 1, Prelude
London Philharmonic—Beecham, in So-
ciety Set VI: VM-658†

Orchestral Suite No. 1, Op. 109, No. 2 (9
Pieces)
**—Nos. 1, The Oak Tree, 2, Humoresque, 3,
Caliban's Song, & 7, Berceuse** only
London Philharmonic Orch.—
Beecham, in Society Set V: VM-446†
—No. 7, Berceuse only
Philadelphia Orch.—Stokowski
(G-DB6009)   12"—V-14726
[Valse triste]
[Dukas: Sorcerer's Apprentice, Pt. 3, on
G-DB3534]

Orchestral Suite No. 2, Op. 109, No. 3 (8
Pieces)
—Nos. 4, Prospero & 6, Miranda only
London Philharmonic Orch.—
Beecham, in Society Set V: VM-446†

Valse triste Orchestra
(from "Kuolema"—Incidental Music, Op.
44)
London Philharmonic Orch.—
Beecham, in Society Set VI: VM-658†
London Philharmonic Orch.—de Sabata
    (in D-ED49†)   12"—D-K1506
[En Saga, Pt. 5]
Philadelphia Orch.—Stokowski
(G-DB6009)   12"—V-14726
[Tempest—Berceuse]
[Franck: Panis Angelicus, on
G-DB3318]
London Philharmonic Orch.—Harty
(C-DX571) (C-DFX182)   12"—C-7322M
[Schubert: Marche militaire]
DUPLICATIONS: Queen's Hall Orch.—
Wood, PD-524224; Berlin State Opera
Orch.—Järnefelt, P-E10774; New Sym-
phony—Goossens, G-C1995; Berlin Phil-
harmonic—Schmidt-Isserstedt, T-E2908;
Victor Concert Orch., V-36228: G-B9124;
Andre Kostelanetz & his Orch., in CM-
484; CBS Symphony—Barlow, in CX-240;
Radio Orch.—Failoni,   CET-BB25111;
Geczy Orch., G-B8464: G-EG3569:
G-K7734: G-GW1782: G-HN2085; Radio
Antwerp Orch.—Gason, OLYM-CL2602;
Chicago Symphony Orch.—Stock,
G-D1284: G-W930: G-AW273; National
Symphony Orch.—V. Olof, D-K1149;
Czech Symphony Orch.—Jeremiáš, ESTA-
E6012; Paul Godwin Orch.—PD-27011
*See current catalogues for miscellaneous ar-
rangements.*

Voces Intimae See under Quartet—String

SIEGMEISTER, Elie
*An American composer, teacher and editor of
folk songs, Siegmeister makes extensive use of
folk material in his compositions.*

American Legends Chorus
Johnny Appleseed; The Lincoln Penny;
Nancy Hanks; Lazy Afternoon; John
Reed; Paul Bunyan
American Ballad Singers
     3   10"—DISC-725

Funnybone Alley—Musical for American
Children (Alfred Kreymborg)
Funnybone Song; Dreamy Kid; Bailyboo
Lullaby; Funnybone Zoo; Mister Clock;
Enter the Cat; The Junk Man; The
Friendly Song
Robert Penn, Tom Glazer, Margaret
Tobias (vocals) with Alfred Kreymborg
(narration) & Elie Siegmeister (pf)
     3   10"—DISC-F606

Ozark Set Orchestra
Minneapolis Symphony Orch.—Mitropoulos   2   12"—CX-262†

Sonata—"American" Piano
Elie Siegmeister   2 12"—DISC-773

**SIGISMONDO D'INDIA, Cavaliere (b. end of
16th Cent.)**
*An Italian composer of motets, madrigals and
vilanelle who was in the service of the Cardinal
of Savoy.*

Lagrimo occhi miei
Maria Castellazzi (s) & C. Crussard
(harpsichord)   12"—G-DB5024
[Monteverdi: Ohiomè dov'è; Maladetto;
Chiome d'oro]

SILCHER, Philipp Friedrich (1789-1860)
*A German composer many of whose songs were
accepted into the nineteenth century folk music of his country.*

Es geht bei gedämpfter Trommel Klang
(Chamisso)
Wilhelm Rode (b) & Berlin State Opera
Orch., & Chorus—Melichar
       10"—PD-25213
[Himmel: Gebet während der Schlacht]

In der Ferne (Schlippenbach)
Richard Tauber (t)   10"—P-RO20245
[Folk Song: Treue Liebe]
Berlin Teacher's Choir—Rüdel
       10"—PD-19846
[Kalliwoda: Das deutsche Lied]

Jubilate (Folk Song Arrangement?)
Erna Sack (s) & cho.   12"—T-E3274
[Neuman: Nachtgebet]

(Die) Lorelei Song in German (Heine)
Richard Tauber (t) & P. Kahn (pf)
       10"—P-RO20442
[Schubert: Heidenröslein]
DUPLICATIONS: Berliner Arztechor—
Singer, G-EG1898; Teacher's Chorus—
Franz Baumann, PD-21590

SIMONETTI, Achille (1857-1928)
*An Italian violinist and teacher, who seems to
have spent large portions of his life in every
European country except his native land.*

Madrigale Violin & Piano
Vasa Prihoda & pf. acc.   10″—PD-30034
[Elgar: La Capricieuse]
[Kreisler: Liebeslied, on PD-90162]
Max Ladscheck & pf. acc.
10″—CET-LL3013
[Drdla: Ricordo, Prihoda]
Yvonne Curti & pf. acc.   10″—C-D19041
[Monti: Czardas] (C-5290)
S. Borries & inst. acc.   10″—G-EG6248
[Svendsen: Serenade]
DUPLICATION: New Mayfair St. Orch.,
G-B9005

Recitativo, Corale, & Cadenza Violin & Piano
E. Pierangeli & A. Musato-Pierangeli
10″—CET-TI7022

SINDING, Christian (1856-1941)

Wisely not attempting to be profound, this Norwegian composer has written pleasant, fluent, pastoral-like music. There are undoubtably other recordings of his works in Norwegian catalogues.

Rustle of Spring, Op. 32, No. 3 Piano
Ger. Frühlingsrauschen Fr. Gazouillement du Printemps
Jesús María Sanromá   12″—V-18153
[Grieg: Papillon; Wagner-Sanromá: Walküre—Magic Fire Music]
Eileen Joyce   12″—P-E11427
[Grieg: To Spring; Summer's Eve; Scherzo Impromptu]
Ivar Johnson   12″—T-E3225
[Grieg: Butterfly; Puck]
DUPLICATIONS: Walter Rehberg, PD-24989; E. Bonzagni, C-GQ7228; William Murdoch, D-F7497; Irene Scharrer, G-D1303; Una Bourne, G-B2141; Ingebjörg Gresvik, G-X4820: G-X4062; Natanal Broman, G-X2730
—**Arr. Two Pianos:** Rawicz & Landauer, C-DB2032
—**Arr. Orchestra**
Milan Symphony Orch.—Molajoli, C-GQ7193; Grand Symphony Orch.—Weissmann, P-R1632; Radio Antwerp Orch.—Gason, OLYM-M2177; Marek Weber Orch., G-EH90; von Geczy Orch., G-B8804: G-HE2169; Stockholm Symphony Orch.—Järnefelt, O-26456; Symphony Orch., U-E416; Czech Symphony Orch.—A. Klíma, ESTA-D2017

Also: Sandler Trio, C-GN496: C-FB1862; BBC Band—O'Donnell, C-DX269; Eight Piano Symphony, C-DB1481: C-DQ1585

SINIGAGLIA, Leone (1868-   )

An Italian composer, pupil of Bolzoni, Mandyczewski, Goldmark and Dvorák, Sinigaglia has followed their lead by falling back upon folk music for his thematic material.

Danza piemontese, A major, Op. 31, No. 1
Boston "Pops" Orch.—Fiedler
12″—V-11-9446

SJOEGREN, Emil (1853-1918)

A Swedish organist and composer of songs and chamber music.

Legend
R. Meimberg (organ)   12″—U-E649
[Boellmann: Suite Gothique—Prière à Notre Dame]

Erotikon, Op. 10, No. 3 Piano
Hilding Domellöf   10″—G-X7163
[Grieg: Norwegian Bridal Procession]

I Drömmen da är mig nära Song in Swedish
Jussi Björling (t)   10″—G-X3377
[Körling: Hvita Rosa]

SKILTON, Charles Sanford (1868-1942)

A conservative American composer, Skilton has used Amer-indian folk music and themes.

Deer Dance
RCA Victor Concert Orch.—Bourdon, V-22174

(2) Indian Dances 1915
—**No. 2 (War Dance)** only
Eastman Rochester Symphony Orch.—Hanson   12″—V-11-8302
[Suite Primeval—Sunrise Dance]
RCA Orch., in V-E89 (also on V-22144)

Shawnee Indian Hunting Dance Orchestra
RCA Victor Orch., in V-E89 (also on V-22144)

Suite Primeval Orchestra 1920
—**Sunrise Dance**
Eastman-Rochester Symphony Orch.—Hanson   12″—V-11-8302
[Indian War Dance]

SKROUP, Frantisek Jan (1801-1862)

The composer of the Czech anthem and the first national opera.

FIDLOVACKA Opera in Bohemian
Overture
FOK Symphony Orch.—V. Smetáček
10″—U-C12934

SLAVIK, Josef (1806-1833)

A romantic Czech composer, whose violin concerto somewhat resembles those of Spohr and Paganini.

Concerto, A minor Violin & Orch.
A. Ploček & Czech Broadcasting Orch.—Stupka   2   12″—U-G14206/7

SMETANA, Bedřich (1824-1884)

The founder of the national school of modern Czech music, Smetana was influenced by Liszt and Berlioz. In addition to being a prolific composer, he was also known as a teacher and pianist.
The recent discography of Smetana (in Czech) by Dr. Jaroslav Bartos has been of invaluable assistance in compiling this list. There are probably other recordings listed in Czech catalogues.

Astride Piano (Bohemian Dance No. 8)
Boh. Obkročák
František Maxián   12″—U-G12827
[Little Hen]

At the Seashore Op. 17a Piano 1862
Boh. Na Břehu Mořském
Otakar Vondrovic   12″—U-G14122
[Concert Etude, C major]

(The) Bartered Bride See under Operas

(The) Bear Piano (Bohemian Dance No. 4)
 Boh. Medvěd
 František Maxián   12″—U-G12826
 [Little Onion]

BOHEMIAN DANCES See under the follow-
ing titles—
(4) Polkas 1855
(10) Idealized Folk Dances 1878
 Furiant; Little Hen; Oats; Bear; Little
 Onion; Stamping Dance; Lancer; Astride;
 Hop Dance; Neighbor's Dance
 Miscellaneous pianists
 7 12″—U-G12826/7; U-G12938;
 U-G12945; U-G12948; U-G14004;
 U-G14034
 See under individual titles for details

Bohemian Fantasie See under From My
 Home

Concert Etude, C major Piano
 Zdeněk Jilek   12″—ESTA-F5198
 [Falla: Ritual Fire Dance]
 Otakar Vondrovic   12″—U-G14122
 [At the Seashore]

Concert Fantasy on Czech National Songs,
 Op. 17b Piano
 Marie Knotková   12″—U-G14005
 Liza Fuchsová   10″—G-JO31

Czech Festival Piano
 Liza Fuchsová   12″—G-JOX2
 [Oats]

(The) Czech Song Cantata for Mixed Voices
 & Orchestra 1868
 Boh. Ceská píseň
 Czech Broadcasting Choir & Orch.—
 Smetáček   2 12″—U-G12520/1
 [Libuše—Libuše's Judgment]
 Choir & Orch.—Jeremiáš
          2 10″—ESTA-D7936/7

Dedication (or, The Dower) Male Chorus
 1880
 Boh. Věno (or Odkaz)
 Prague Teachers' Chorus 10″—G-AM491
 [Pokorný: Tancuj, tancuj]
 Prague "Smetana" Cho.—Spilka
 [Suk: Varaždínský bán] 10″—U-A10777

Dr. Faust Overture to the puppet play of
 Matěj Kopecký
 FOK Symphony Orch.—Vaclav
 Smetáček   10″—U-B14189
 [Oldřich and Božena—Overture]
 [Minuet, on U-C14117]

(The) Farmer's Song Male Chorus
 Boh. Rolnická
 Moravian Teachers' Cho.—F. Vach
          12″—G-AN660

Fisherman Orchestra
 Boh. Rybář
 Czech Broadcasting Orch.—Jirak
          12″—U-G12547
 (Janáček: Suite for strings—Scherzo)

From My Home Violin & Piano (Bohemian
 Fantasie) 1880
 Boh. Z moji domoviny Ger. Aus der
 Heimat
 Ivan Kawaciuk & František Maxián
          12″—U-E12364
 Jiří Straka & Ljuba Straková
          2 12″—G-JX5/6

—No. 1 only
 Georg Kulenkampff & Franz Rupp
          10″—PD-62749
 Mischa Elman & W. Rose
          12″—V-12-0241
 [Dvořák: Slavonic Fantasia, B minor]
—No. 2 only
 Nathan Milstein & Leopold Mittmann
          12″—C-LCX34
 [Chopin: Nocturne, C sharp minor, Op.
 Posth.]
 Váša Příhoda & Otto Graef
          10″—PD-30038
 Josef Wolfsthal & Karel Szreter
          10″—G-AM1273

Furiant Piano (Bohemian Dance No. 1)
 (See also under operas—Bartered Bride)
 Jan Heřman   12″—U-G14004
 [Neighbor's Dance]
 Rudolf Firkušný   12″—G-DB5300
 [Lancers]

Hakon Jarl, Op. 16 Symphonic Poem Orchestra 1861
 Czech Philharmonic Orch.—Kubelik
          2 12″—U-G14054/5

Hop Dance Piano (Bohemian Dance No.
 10)
 Boh. Skočná
 Otakar Vondrovic   12″—U-G12938
 [Stamp Dance]

Lancers Piano (Bohemian Dance No. 7)
 Boh. Hulán
 Jan Heřman   12″—U-G12945
 [Oats]
 Rudolf Firkušný   12″—G-DB5300
 [Furiant]

Ländler See: Neighbor's Dance

Little Hen Piano (Bohemian Dance No. 2)
 Boh. Slepička
 František Maxián   12″—U-G12827
 [Astride Dance]
 Jan Heřman   10″—G-AM2245
 [Polka, No. 2, & Waltz]
 Walter Rehberg   10″—PD-47204
 [Schmalstich: Die Quelle]

Little Onion Piano (Bohemian Dance No. 5)
 Boh. Cibulička
 František Maxián   12″—U-G12826
 [Bear]

MARCHES

National Guard March

Student Legion March
 FOK Symphony Orch.—Vaclav
 Smetáček   10″—U-B14209

Shakespeare Festival March 1864
 FOK Symphony Orch.—V. Smetáček
          12″—U-H18132

Minuet 1842
 FOK Symphony Orch.—V. Smetáček
 [Suk: Rural Serenade] 10″—U-B14197
 [Dr. Faust—Overture, on U-C14117]

MY COUNTRY Symphonic Cycle Orchestra
 1874-1879
 Boh. Má Vlast Ger. Mein Vaterland
 1. The High Castle (Vyšehrad)
 2. The Moldau (Vltava)

3. Sárka
4. From Bohemia's Meadows and Forests
(Z českých luhů a hájů)
5. Tábor
6. Blaník
Czech Broadcasting Symphony Orch.—
Otakar Jeremiáš 10 12"—U-G12535/44
Czech National Opera Orch., Prague—
K. B. Jirák 10 12"—ESTA-H5062/71
Czech Philharmonic Orch.—V. Talich
10 12"—G-DB5312/21
(also: G-AN386/95)
No. 2 (The Moldau—Vltava) only
N. Y. Philharmonic-Symphony Orch.—B.
Walter 2 12"—CX-211†
[Dvořák: Slavonic Dance No. 1]
National Symphony Orch.—Kindler
2 12"—VM-921†
Boston "Pops" Orch.—Fiedler
2 12"—VM-1210†
[Dvořák: Hussite Overture]
Czech Philharmonic—R. Kubelík
(in VM-523†) 2 12"—V-12520/1
[From Bohemia's Meadows, Pt. 1]
(G-C2979/80: G-JX14/15:
G-EH1120/1)
[Tchaikovsky: Sleeping Beauty—Waltz,
Marek Weber's Orch., on G-L1049/50]
DUPLICATIONS: Berlin Philharmonic—
von Karajan, CET-RR8033/4: PD-
67583/4; Czech Philharmonic—V.
Talich, G-DB7681/2; Berlin State Opera
Orch.—Kleiber, PD-66652/3; Berlin
Philharmonic—Schmidt-Isserstedt,
T-E2828/9; Berlin Philharmonic—Zem-
linsky, U-E176 & U-E179; Danish Radio
Orch.—Jensen, TONO-X25041/2
No. 4 (From Bohemia's Meadows & Forests
—Z českých luhů a hájů only
Czech Philharmonic Orch.—Raphael
Kubelík
(in VM-523†) 2 12"—V-12521/2
(G-C2980/1: G-JX15/6: G-EH1121/2)
[Moldau, Pt. 3]
Fantasia Arr. E. Pour
Prague Symphony Orch.—Dol Dauber
12"—G-AN794
My Star Chorus
Boh. Má hvězda
Chorus—Lýsek 10"—ESTA-B7681
[Songs of the people]
DUPLICATION: Chorus, U-A12029
Našim děvám See: To Our Damsels
Neighbor's Dance Piano (Bohemian Dance
No. 9)
Boh. Sousedská
Jan Heřman 12"—U-G14004
[Furiant]
Oats Piano (Bohemian Dance No. 3)
Boh. Oves
Jan Heřman 12"—U-G12945
[Lancers]
Liza Fuchsová 12"—G-JOX2
[Czech Festival]
Oldřich and Božena Overture to the puppet
play of Matěj Kopecký
FOK Symphony Orch.—Smetáček
[Dr. Faustus—Overture] 10"—U-B14189
[Suk: Venetian Serenade, on U-B14197]
Dol Dauber & his Orch. 10"—U-A11507

OPERAS In Czech

(THE) BARTERED BRIDE 3 Acts 1866
Boh. Prodaná Nevěsta
Ger. Die verkaufte Braut Fr. La Fiancée
vendue
Complete recording Sung in Czech
Prague National Opera Company—
Otakar Ostrčil 15 12"—VM-193†
(G-AN801/15)
The Cast:
Krušina .... Jan Konstantin (b)
Ludmila .... Marie Pixová (s)
Mařenka (Marie) .. Ada Nordenová (s)
Mícha .... Zdeněk Otava (bs)
Háta .... Marta Krásová (ms)
Vašek .... Jaroslav Gleich (t)
Jeník .... Vladimír Tomš (t)
Kecal .... Emil Pollert (bs)
Komediantů .... Karel Hruška (t)
Esmeralda .... Ota Horáková (s)
Indian .... Václav Marek (t)
Abridged recordings Sung in Czech
Soloists, Chorus & National Theatre
Orch.—Rudolf Vašata & Zdeněk
Chalabala 8 12"—U-G14301/8
The cast: Miluše Dvořáková, Ota Horá-
ková, Marie Budíková, Stěpánka Stěpá-
nová, Jaroslav Gleich, Jindřich Blažiček,
Oldřich Kovář, Karel Hruška, Eduard
Haken, Luděk Mandaus, Stanislas Muž,
Zdeněk Otava.
Soloists, Chorus & Orchestra of the
Czech National Opera, Prague—Otakar
Jeremiáš 9 12"—ESTA-H5082/8
H5090 & H5093
The cast: Marie Budíková-Jeremiášová,
Stěpánka Stěpánová, Beno Blachut, Karel
Kalaš & Theodor Srubař.
Orchestral Selections (Fantasias)
Berlin State Opera Orch.—Seidler-Wink-
ler, G-EH1034; FOK Symphony Orch.—
O. Jeremiáš, ESTA-H5012; Dol Dauber
Orch., G-AN634
Fantasy for Violin and Piano (Ondříček,
Op. 9)
Vojtěch Frait & Vladimír Polívka
2 10"—ESTA-D4016/7
Overture Orchestra
London Symphony Orch.—Bruno Walter
12"—G-DB3652
N. Y. Philharmonic-Symphony Orch.—
Barbirolli 12"—C-19003D
Boston "Pops" Orch.—Fiedler
10"—V-4498
National Symphony Orch.—Karl Rankl
12"—D-K1331
Czech National Opera Orch.—Z. Chala-
bala 12"—U-G12493
Chicago Symphony Orch.—D. Defauw
12"—V-12-0018
Berlin State Opera Orch.—A. Melichar
12"—PD-15103
Berlin State Opera Orch.—van Kempen
12"—PD-67578
Dresden Philharmonic—van Kempen
12"—PD-15337
DUPLICATIONS: London Philharmonic
—Harty, C-7314M: C-DX562:
C-GQX16567: C-DWX1587; Chicago Sym-

phony Orch.—Stock, V-1555; Saxon State
Orch.—Böhm, G-DB5552; Berlin State
Opera Orch.—Schmalstich, G-B3501:
G-AM3307; Czech Symphony Orch.—K.
Sejna, ESTA-D4016

Individual Excerpts

ACT I

Opening Chorus: See the buds burst on the bush
Boh. Proč bychom se netěšili
Ger. Seht an Strauch die Knospen springen (Chorus, Soprano & Tenor)
Czech National Opera Cho. & Orch.—
Vašata   12"—U-F12438
[Oh, what sorrow, Horáková]
[Dvořák: Rusalka, Aria, on U-G12431]
[Gladly do I trust you, Dvořáková, on U-G14302]
[Sextet, on U-G12580]
Maria Wutz, Max Fischer & Cho. (in German)   12"—G-EH1033
[Polka & Chorus]
Berlin State Opera soloists, & Cho.—
Sieber   12"—O-3610

Gladly do I trust you Soprano (Mařenka)
Boh. Kdybych se co takového
Marie Budíková & Beno Blachut
                          12"—ESTA-H5084
[With my mother, Duo]
Miluše Dvořáková   12"—U-G14302
[Opening Chorus]
Milada Jirásková   10"—U-B12435
[With my mother, Duo]
Ada Nordenová   12"—G-AM2170
[Faithful love, Duo]
Hilde Singenstreue   10"PD-62834
[Alone at last]

With my mother Duo Sop. & Ten.
(Mařenka & Jeník)
Boh. Jako matka požehnáním
Budíková & Beno Blachut
                          12"—ESTA-H5084
[Gladly do I trust you]
Marie Budíková & Jindřich Blažíček
                          10"—U-B12435
[Gladly do I trust you, Jirásková]
[Brandenburgers in Bohemia—Duet,
Kejřová & Gleich, on U-B12295]
Veřa Manšingerová & Viktor Propper w.
pf.   10"—G-AM2180
[Faithful love]

Faithful love Duo: Sop. & Ten. (Mařenka & Jeník)
Boh. Věrné milování
Marie Budíková & Beno Blachut
                          12"—ESTA-H5085
[A proper young man]
Miluše Dvořáková & Jaroslav Gleich
[Trio, Act I]   12"—U-G14303
Ota Horáková & Jindřich Blažíček
                          10"—U-B12337
[How is it possible, Blažíček]
[The Devil's Wall: She is the only one,
Rujan, on U-C12568]
Míla Kočová & Otakar Mařák
                          10"—U-B10718
[How is it possible, Mařák]
Veřa Manšingerová & Viktor Propper w.
pf.   10"—G-AM2180
[With my mother]

Ada Nordenová & Miloslav Jeník
                          10"—G-AM2170
[Gladly do I trust you, Nordenová]
Margarete Teschemacher & Marcel Wittrisch (in German)   12"—G-DB4538
[My dearest love, just listen]

Everything is ready Bass (Kecal)
Boh. Jak vám pravím
Karel Kalaš   12"—ESTA-H5086
[Trio]
Emil Pollert   10"—G-AM2172
[A proper young man]

Trio
Boh. To se nedá provést
Eduard Haken, Marie Veselá, & Stanislav Muž   12"—U-G14303
[Faithful love, Dvořáková & Gleich]
Karel Kalaš, Stěpánka Stěpánová, &
Theodor Srubař   12"—ESTA-H5086
[Everything is ready, Kalaš]

A proper young man Trio
Boh. Mladík slušný
Karel Kalaš, Stěpánka Stěpánová &
Theodor Srubař   12"—ESTA-H5085
[Faithful love, Budíková & Blachut]
Pavel Ludikar, Marie Budíková &
Zdeněk Otava   12"—U-F12298
[The Secret: I am a beggar, Otava]
[Sextet, on U-F12437]

—Bass part only
Emil Pollert, G-AM2172

Polka Chorus & Orchestra
Boh. Pojď sem, holka Eng. Through the rows to fly
National Opera Cho., Prague—Vašata
[Duet, Act II]   12"—U-G14304
National Opera Cho., Prague—Jeremiáš
[Furiant]   12"—ESTA-H5087
National Opera Chorus, Prague—
Charvát   12"—G-AN346
[Blodek: In the Well—Chorus]
Berlin Volksoper Cho. (in German)—
Orthmann   12"—G-EH1033
[Opening Chorus, Act I]

—Arr. Orchestra only
Royal Philharmonic Orch.—Beecham
                          12"—G-DB6454
[Dance of the Comedians]
Czech National Opera Orch.—F. Skvor
                          12"—ESTA-H5108
[The Two Widows—Polka]
Minneapolis Symphony Orch.—Ormandy
                          12"—V-8694
[Dance of the Comedians, Act III]
CBS Symphony Orch.—Barlow
(C-DX1130)   12"—C-71049D
[Furiant & Dance of the Comedians]

—Arr. Violin & Piano Ondříček (labelled "Scočna")
Karel Sroubek & F. Maxián, U-G14204,
Vojtěch Frajt & V. Polívka, ESTA-H5041

ACT II

Drinking chorus Duet & Chorus
Boh. To pivečko
Beno Blachut & Karel Kalaš w. Cho.
                          12"—ESTA-H5088
[Everyone praises his own girl]
Jindřich Blažíček & Luděk Mandaus

[Polka] 12″—U-G14304
[Dalibor—Chorus]
Vladimír Tomš, Emil Pollert & Cho.
12″—G-AN799
[Kovařovic: Dog Heads—Raftsmen]

Furiant (Orchestral Interlude)
CBS Symphony Orch.—Barlow
(C-DX1130) 12″—C-71049D
[Polka & Dance of the Comedians]
National Theater Orch.—Vašata
10″—U-C14064
[Dance of the Comedians]
DUPLICATIONS: National Theatre Orch.
—Jeremiáš, ESTA-H5087; Berlin Phil-
harmonic Orch.—Schmidt-Isserstedt,
T-A2161

Ma-ma-mama so dear Tenor (Vašek)
Boh. **Ma-ma-matička**
Oldřich Kovář 10″—U-B12436
[Calm yourself, my lass, Blažíček]
[Blodek: In the well—Aria, on
U-B12297]
Mirko Stork 10″—G-AM2913
[Leoncavallo: Pagliacci—O Colombina]

I know a maiden fair Duet Soprano &
Tenor (Mařenka & Vašek)
Boh. **Známt já jednu dívčinu**
Marie Budíková & Oldřich Kovář
10″—U-B12260

Everyone praises his own girl

One I know who has money galore Duo: Bs.
& Ten. (Kecal & Jeník)
Boh. **Každý jen tu svou—Znám jednu
dívku**
Ger. **Wer in Lieb' entbrannt—Weiss ich
doch eine**
Eduard Haken & Jaroslav Gleich
12″—U-G14305
Pavel Ludikar & J. Blažíček
10″—U-B12296
—**In German**
Walther Schirp & Peter Anders
12″—T-E3114
Wilhelm Strienz & Walther Ludwig
12″—G-EH1036
Michael Bohnen & J. Schmidt
12″—U-F626

Everyone praises his own girl only
Karel Kalaš & Beno Blachut
12″—ESTA-H5088
[The ale we now enjoy]

Kecal's part only
Emil Pollert, G-AN323

One I know who has money galore only
Karel Kalaš & Beno Blachut
12″—ESTA-H5090
[How is it possible, Blachut]
Emil Pollert & Otakar Mařak
10″—G-AM2175
[Blodek: In the Well—Aria]
Eugen Fuchs & Charles Kullman (in
German) 12—C-DWX5037
[Sextet, Act III]

It must succeed Recit.

How is it possible Air Ten. Jeník
Boh. **Až užris—Jak možna věřit**
Jindřich Blažíček 10″—U-B12337
[Faithful love]

[The Two Widows—When May is near,
on U-C12587]
Beno Blachut 12″—ESTA-H5090
[One I know]
Jaroslav Gleich 12″—U-G14306
[Vašek's Aria]
Otakar Mařak 10″—U-B10718
[Faithful Love, Kočová & Mařak]
[The Kiss—If I knew how to wipe out
my fault, on U-B10719]
DUPLICATIONS: Richard Kubla,
G-AM799; M. Jeník, G-AM2169
In German: Julius Patzak, PD-95268
In English: James Johnston, C-DB2217

Vašek's Aria Tenor
Boh. **To mi v hlavě leží**
Oldřich Kovář 12″—U-G14306
[How is it possible, Gleich]
[Devil's Wall—Aria, on U-F12338]

ACT III

Dance of the Comedians (Scene of the
Comedians, or Ballet Music)
Boh. **Skočná**
Philadelphia "Pops" Orch.—Ormandy
(in CM-588) 12″—C-12606D
[Dvořák: Slavonic Dance No. 10]
Royal Philharmonic Orch.—Beecham
[Polka] 12″—G-DB6454
Czech Broadcasting Orch.—Jeremiáš
12″—ESTA-H5040
[The Two Widows—Polka]
National Theater Orch.—Jeremiáš
12″—ESTA-H5108
[Two Widows—Polka]
CBS Symphony Orch.—Barlow
[Polka & Furiant] 12″—C-71049D
Minneapolis Symphony Orch.—Ormandy
[Polka] 12″—V-8694
DUPLICATIONS: National Theater Orch.
Vasata, U-F14064; The Bohemians—
Walter, C-263M

Trio Sop., Ten., & Bs. (Esmerelda, Vašek)
Boh. **Milostné zvířátko** (Circus-Master)
Miluše Dvořáková, Karel Hruška & Old-
řich Kovář 12″—U-G14307
[Sextet]
[My dearest love, just listen, on
U-G12982]

Think it over, Mařenka Sextet
Boh. **Rozmysli si, Mařenko** Ger. **Noch ein
Veilchen, Marie**
Milada Jirásková, Marie Veselá, Stěpánka
Stěpánová, Zdeněk Otava, Stanislav Muž,
& Luděk Mandaus 12″—U-G14307
[Trio]
[A proper young man, Budíková & Otava,
on U-F12437]
[Opening chorus, Act I, on U-G12580]
A. Nordenová, B. Kozlíková, M. Krásová,
H. Vávra, S. Muž, E. Pollert
12″—G-AN322
[The Kiss—Smugglers' Chorus]
Erna Berger, Else Ruziczka, E. Zador,
W. Beck, E. Fuchs, W. Grossman (in Ger-
man) 12″—C-DWX5037
(Duo, Act II, Fuchs & Kullmann)

Alone at last Recit.
How strange and dead Air Soprano
  (Mařenka)
  Boh. **Ten lasky sen—Ach, jaky zal** Ger.
  Endlich allein & Wie Fremd und todt
  Ota Horáková   12"—**U-G14308**
  [My dearest love, just listen]
  [Opening Chorus, on U-F12438]
  [Dvořák: Jacobin—Aria, on U-F12336]
  Marie Budíková   12"—**ESTA-H5093**
  [Final trio]
  Ada Sari & C. Cerne (pf) 12"—**G-AN679**
  [Dvořák: Rusalka—O lovely moon]
  Margarete Teschemacher (in German)
                12"—**G-EH1032**
  [Mascagni: Cavalleria Rusticana—Voi lo
  sapete]
  DUPLICATIONS: Ada Nordenová,
  G-AN319; Vera Manšingerová, G-AN318
  In German: Hilde Singenstreu, PD-62834

My dearest love, just listen Duo: Sop. &
  Ten. (Mařenka & Jeník)
  Boh. **Jak tvrdošíjná, dívko, jsi** Ger. **Mein
  lieber Schatz**
  Marie Budíková & Jindřich Blažíček
                12"—**U-G14308**
  [How strange & dead, Budíková]
  [Trio, on U-G12982]
  [Dvořák: The Sly Peasant—Aria, on
  U-G12713]
  Margarete Teschemacher & Marcel Wit-
  trisch (in German)   12"—**G-DB4538**
  [Faithful love]

Be calm (Jeník)
  Boh. **Utiš se, dívko** Tenor
  Jindřich Blažíček   10"—**U-B12436**
  [Ma-ma-matička]
  Mirko Stork   10"—**U-C14000**
  [Dalibor: Oh, my Zdeněk]
  Jaroslav Jaroš & pf. acc. 10"—**U-A12171**
  [Dvořák: Rusalka—Aria]

Trio
  Boh. **Ted přivedu sem rodiče**
  Marie Budíková, Beno Blachut, Karel
  Kalaš   12"—**ESTA-H5093**
  [Alone at last! Budíková]

(THE) BRANDENBURGERS IN BOHEMIA
  1866
  Boh. **Braniboři v Cechách**

Orchestral Selections (Fantasia)
  Dol Dauber Orch. (arr. B. Leopold)
                10"—**G-AM3404**

Individual Excerpts
Uhodila naše hodina
  Josef Zižka, Jiří Joran & Cho., U-G14335

Pane, v prachu se kloníme
  Václav Nouzovský & Chorus, U-G14335

O, jak blahá, krásná tato chvíle
  Nada Kejřová & Jaroslav Gleich,
  U-B12585, U-B12295, U-B12484

Tvůj obraz, dívko
  Josef Křikava, U-B12595
  Zdeněk Otava, ESTA-H5115

DALIBOR 3 Acts 1868
Vocal Excerpts
  Soloists, Chorus & Orch. of National

Opera House, Prague—J. Charvát
        4 12"—**ESTA-H5169/72**
  The soloists include: Marie Budíková,
  Lída Cervinková, Beno Blachut, Eduard
  Haken, B. Chorovič
  Soloists, Chorus, & Orch. of National
  Opera House, Prague—Vašata & Fol-
  precht   6 12"—**U-G14351/6**
  The soloists include: Stanislav Muž,
  Marie Podvalová, Jindřich Blažíček,
  Stěpánka Jelínková, Josef Munchinger,
  Josef Masák, Lubomir Višegonov

Orchestral Selections (Fantasias)
  Dol Dauber Orch. (arr. B. Leopold)
                12"—**G-AN594**
  FOK Symphony Orch.—Smetáček
                12"—**U-G14036**

Individual Excerpts

Rek ten mne bídné, opuštěné dítě
  Vlasta Loukotková & R. Vašata (pf),
  U-C14002

King Vadislav: It is known to you Bar.
  Boh. **Vám známo** (Vy víte)
  Stanislav Muž, U-G12863

Pohasnul den Sop.
  Marie Podvalova, U-G12797

Zapírat nechci—Kydž Zdeněk můj Tenor
  Beno Blachut, ESTA-H5169
  Jindřich Blažíček, U-G14352
  Otakar Mařak, U-B10717, C-OC57

Dalibor: Didst thou hear it? Tenor
Slyšels to, příteli
  Jindřich Blažíček, U-G14352: U-G12581
  Roman Hübner, G-AN531
  Richard Kubla, G-AM797

Jaká to bouře 2 Sops.
  Marie Podvalová & Stěpánka Jelínková,
  U-G14353: U-G12797

Ba, nejveselejší je tento svět Sop., Ten. &
  Cho.
  Stěpánka Jelínková, Jindřich Blažíček &
  Cho., U-G14353: U-G12851: U-G12907

ACT II

Vitka & Vitek: O Soul, this longing Sop. &
  Ten.
  Boh. **Ta duše, ta touha—O, jaké toužení**
  Marie Budíkova & Bronislav Chorovič,
  ESTA-H5172
  Stěpánka Jelínková & Jindřich Blažíček,
  U-G14352: U-G12908: U-G12852
  Ada Nordenová & Miloslav Jeník,
  G-AM2169
  Karal Tichá & Miloslav Jeník,
  G-AM2924

Jailer: How hard is the jailer's life Bass
  Boh. **Ach, Jak těžký žalářníka život**
  Eduard Haken, ESTA-H5170
  Jiří Huml & M. Kamplesheimer (pf),
  U-C14001
  Josef Munclinger, U-G14354
  Emil Pollert, G-AM2176

Milada: How do I feel? Sop.
  Boh. **Jak je mí**
  Marie Podvalová, U-C12909: U-C12589:
  U-B12249: U-G14355
  Karla Ticha, G-AN533

Intermezzo: Dalibor's Vision Orch.
Boh. **Daliborův sen**
National Theater Orch., Prague—R.
Vašata, U-G14355: U-G12863

Dalibor: O my Zdeněk Tenor
Boh. **O Zdeňku můj**
Beno Blachut, ESTA-H5169
Roman Hübner, G-AN531
Richard Kubla, G-AM798
Antonín Lebeda & J. Krombholc (pf),
U-C14000
Josef Vojta, U-C12909
Franz Völker (in German), PD-67603

Milada & Dalibor: Duet
Boh. **Ty ptáš se**
Lída Cervinková & Beno Blachut, ESTA-
H5171

Oh, the unspeakable happiness of love Duet
Sop. & Ten. (Milada & Dalibor)
Boh. **O nevýslovné štěstí lásky** (O blaho
neskonalé lásky)
Lída Cervinková & Beno Blachut, ESTA-
H5171
Marie Podvalová & Jaroslav Jaroš,
U-G12907: U-F12654: U-F12262
Marie Podvalová & Josef Masák,
U-G14356: U-G12932
Karla Tichá & Roman Hübner, G-AM2925

Ctyřicet let (O pane můj) Bass (Jailer)
Eduard Haken, ESTA-H5170
Emil Pollert, G-AN529
Lev Uhlíř & pf. acc., U-A10016
Lubomir Višegonov, U-F12654:
U-G12908: U-G14356

Krásný to cíl
Zdenek Otava, ESTA-H5114

Ha, kým to kouzlem Ten.
Beno Blachut, ESTA-H5172
Franz Völker (in German), PD-67603

Nuž, bud si tak
Theodor Schütz & R. Vašata (pf),
U-C12997

(THE) DEVIL'S WALL 3 Acts 1882
Boh. **Certova Sténa** Ger. **Die Teufelswand**
Orchestral Selections (Fantasias)
FOK Symphony Orch.—Václav Smetáček
12"—**U-G12816**
Dol Dauber Orch. 12"—**G-AN658**
Individual Excerpts

ACT I

Happy I know Soprano (Katuška)
Boh. **Stastná vím**
Miluše Dvořáková, U-G12904
Věra Manšingerová & J. Singer (pf),
G-AM2293

Což pozbyla jsi ve mne víry Ten. (Jarek)
Jaroslav Gleich, U-G12983

Tak věčně k tobě lnout Sop. & Ten.
(Katuska & Jarek)
Miluše Dvořáková & Jaroslav Gleich,
U-G12983

She is the only one Baritone
Boh. **Jen jediná** (Vok)
Otakar Chmel & B. Brzobohatý (pf),
U-C14001
Stanislav Muž, U-G14111: G-AM2288

Zdeněk Otava, ESTA-H5115
Bořek Rujan, U-C12586: U-B12484:
U-B12284

ACT II
Kam prchnout Ten. (Jarek)
Jaroslav Gleich, U-G12982: U-G12584
Ach, zle se tomu přivyká Bar. (Míchálek)
Oldřich Kovář, U-F12338

ACT III
Tiše, kradmo Chorus
National Theater, Prague, Cho. & Orch.—
Vašata, U-G12984
O God of Love Soprano (Hedořka)
Boh. **O Bože lásky**
Marie Podvalova, U-G14111

(THE) KISS 2 Acts 1876
Boh. **Hubička** Ger. **Der Küss**
Vocal & Orchestral Selections
Soloists, Cho., & Orch. of the National
Theater, Prague—Zdeněk Folprecht
5 12"—**ESTA-H5072/6**
The soloists: Lída Cervinková, Milada
Jirásková, Beno Blachut, & Josef Křikava
Individual Excerpts
Overture Orchestra
Czech Symphony Orch.—K. Sejna
12"—**ESTA-H5052**
National Theater Orch.—Z. Folprecht
12"—**ESTA-H5072**
National Theater Orch., Prague—Z.
Chalabala 12"—**U-G12366**
National Theater Orch., Prague—J. Char-
vát 12"—**G-AN571**
(Folksong, arr. Hilmera: In the Valley,
Krizkovsky Chorus)
You are mine Duet: Sop. & Ten.
(Vandulka & Lukáš)
Boh. **Jsme svoji**
Lída Cervinková & Beno Blachut,
ESTA-H-5073
Miluše Dvořáková & Jaroslav Gleich,
U-G14293
Vera Manšingerová & Miloslav Jeník,
G-AM2924
Ada Nordenová & Jaroslav Gleich,
U-C12718: U-B12261
Jak jsem to řek
Eduard Haken, ESTA-H5976
Luděk Mandaus, U-G12714: U-G12651
Cradle Song Soprano (Vandulka)
Boh. **Ukolébavky**
Jarmila Novotna 12"—**V-11-9153**
[Dvořák: Songs my mother taught me]
Marie Budíková 12"—**U-G12582**
[Lark Song, Tauberová]
[Dalibor—Oh, the unspeakable happiness
of love, Podvalová & Janoš, on
U-F12262]
Lída Cervinková 12"—**ESTA-H5075**
[Lark Song]
Ada Nordenová 12"—**G-AN320**
[Lark Song]
Elisabeth Schumann (in German)
10"—**G-DA1544**
[Grieg: Peer Gynt—Solvejg's Song]
DUPLICATION: Veřa Manšingerová,
G-AM2162

ACT II

Chorus of Smugglers—Forward! On! Bass & Chorus
Boh. **Sbor Pašířů—Jen Dál**
Karel Kalaš & Cho., ESTA-H5076
Karel Kalaš & Cho., U-G12714
Emil Pollert & Cho., G-AN322

If I knew how to wipe out my fault Tenor (Lukáš)
Boh. **Kdybych věděl, Jak svou vinu smýt**
Beno Blachut, ESTA-H5073
Jaroslav Gleich, U-C12718: U-C12589: U-C12498
Richard Kubla, G-AM798
Otakar Mařák, U-B10717: U-B10719
M. Jeník, G-AM2950

Only beg for her pardon Ten. & Bar. (Lukáš & Tomáš)
Boh. **Jen odpros ji**
Beno Blachut & Josef Křikava, ESTA-H5074
Jaroslav Gleich & Zdeněk Otava, U-F12472: U-G12715
Miloslav Jeník & Stanislav Muž, G-AM2290

O, Jak jsem mohla věřit bláhová Trio
Marie Budíková, Stěpánka Stěpánová & Karel Kalaš, U-G12715

Lark Song Soprano (Barce)
Boh. **Skřivánčí Píseň**
Milada Jirásková   12″—ESTA-H5075
[Cradle Song]
Ada Nordenová   12″—G-AN320
[Cradle Song]
Marie Tauberová   12″—U-G12582
[Cradle Song, Budíková]
[Only beg for her pardon, Gleich & Otava, on U-F12472]
Míla Kočová, U-A10650
Ema Miřiovská & R. Vašata, U-C14002

LIBUSA 3 Acts 1881
Boh. **Libuše** Ger. **Libuschka**

Vocal Excerpts
Soloists, Cho. & Orch. of National Theatre, Prague—Jeremiáš & Vašata
5   12″—U-G14342/6
The soloists include Marie Podvalová, Lída Cervinková, Stanislav Muž

Overture Orchestra
Czech Philharmonic Orch.—V. Talich
12″—G-DB5305
National Theatre Orch.—Vašata
12″—U-G14341
FOK Symphony Orch.—O. Jeremiáš
12″—ESTA-H5007
National Theatre Orch., Prague—Charvát   12″—G-AN347
Fanfare only—arr. Band: U-B14319

Individual Excerpts

ACT I

Eternal Gods! Soprano (Libuše)
Boh. **Bohové věční**
Veřa Manšingerová, G-AM2293
Marie Podvalová, U-C12588: U-G12249: U-G14342

ACT II, Scene 1

Když v blahé touze lásky (Za politování tě prosím) Sop. (Krasava)
Lída Cervinková, U-G14342: U-G12985
Ota Horáková & F. Skvor (pf) U-A12049

ACT II, Scene 3

Již plane slunce Bar. (Premysl)
Stanislav Muž, U-G14343: U-G12985

O you linden trees Baritone (Premysl)
Boh. **O, vy lípy**
Jan Konstantin, U-C12588: U-C12500
Stanislav Muž, U-G14343
Zdeněk Otava, ESTA-H5114

ACT III

Bud vítána Soprano & Chorus
Marie Podvalova & Cho., U-G14112

Hoj, tvrdý Vyšehrad Duet (Libuše & Přemysl)
Marie Podvalova & Stanislav Muž, U-G14112

Libusa's Prophecy
Boh. **Libušino Proroctví: "Bohové mocní, za tento štastný den dík budiž vám"**
Marie Podvalová, Jarmila Malá, Marta Krásová, Josef Vojta, Stanislav Muž, Josef Celerin, Josef Křikava, & Jaroslav Veverka w. Cho. & Orch.—Jeremiáš
2   12″—U-G14345/6

Libusa's Judgment
Boh. **Libušin Soud**
Czech Broadcasting Orch.—Smetáček
[Czech Song, Pt. 3]   12″—U-G12521

(THE) SECRET 3 Acts 1878
Boh. **Tajemství** Ger. **Das Geheimnis**

Overture Orchestra
FOK Symphony Orch.—Smetáček
12″—ESTA-H5006
National Theater Orch.—Z. Folprecht
12″—U-G14901

O hear Tenor (Skřivánek)
Boh. **O, slyš mne, předaleký světe**
Oldřich Kovář, U-G14149
Ven z podzemí, ven
Karel Kalaš & Cho., U-G12984

ACT II

Kaliny's Aria—I am a beggar Baritone
Boh. **Jsem žebrák**
Zdeněk Otava, ESTA-H5111: U-G12583: U-F12298: U-F12341

Jak, mé potěšení Duet
Drahomíra Tikalová & Jindřich Blažíček, U-G14113

When I hear thy horn Soprano (Blaženka)
Boh. **Když slyším jen trochu trého pění**
Marie Budíková, ESTA-H5166
Ada Nordenová, G-AM2171
Drahomíra Tikalová, U-G14113

Tak plane láska pravá
Marta Krásová, G-AM2291: U-G12583
Marie Slechtová & J. Krombholc (pf), U-C12999

I am a soldier Bass (Bonifáce)
Boh. Jsem voják
Luděk Mandaus, U-C12973
Emil Pollert, G-AM2915

ACT III

How the water from the high slopes Soprano (Blaženka)
Boh. Což ta voda a výše strání
Marie Budíková, ESTA-H5166:
U-B12261
Ada Nordenová, G-AM2171

(THE) TWO WIDOWS 2 Acts 1874
Boh. Dvě Vdovy   Ger. Zwei Witwen

Vocal & Orchestral Excerpts
Soloists, Cho. & Orch. of National Theater, Prague—František Skvor
3   12"—ESTA-5105/7
The soloists include: Lída Cervinková, Stěpánka Jelínková, & Beno Blachut

Orchestral Selections (Fantasia)
Dol Dauber Orch.   12"—G-AN657

Individual Excerpts

ACT I

The beautiful morning Chorus
Boh. Jitro Krásné, nebe jasné kyne nám
National Theatre Chorus & Orch.—
Vašata, U-G12834: U-G12837

I rule independently Soprano (Karolina)
Boh. Samostatné vladnu
Stěpánka Jelínková, ESTA-H5107
Marie Tauberová, U-G12834: U-G12609

O, with what difficulties Quartet
Boh. O, jakou tíseň
Marie Tauberová, Marie Podvalová, (ss)
Jindřich Blažíček (t), & Luděk Mandaus (b), U-G12835: U-G12593;
U-G12502

Aj, vizte lovce tam Tenor (Ladislav)
Beno Blachut, ESTA-H5106
Jindřich Blažíček, U-B12284: U-B12833:
U-B12342

ACT II

When May is near Tenor (Ladislav)
Boh. Když zavítá máj
Beno Blachut, ESTA-H5106
Jindřich Blažíček, U-B12342: U-B12832:
U-C12587
Bronislav Chorovič, U-G14293
Jaroslav Jaroš & L. Holoubek (pf),
U-A12172

Decided, resolved 2 Sopranos (Karolina & Anežka)
Boh. Rozhodnuto, Uzavřeno
Stěpánka Jelínková & Lída Cervinková,
ESTA-H5107
Míla Kočová & Ada Nordenová, G-AN34
Marie Tauberová & Marie Podvalová,
U-G12836

Ach, jak to krutě souží Duet: Sop. & Tenor
(Anežka & Ladislav)
Marie Podvalová & Jindřich Blažíček,
U-C12503

Melodrama—Vision of Love
Boh. Vyznání lásky Sop. & Ten.
Marie Podvalová & Jindřich Blažíček,
U-C12503

O what a beautiful day Soprano (Anežka)
Boh. Aj, jaký to krásný den
Marie Podvalová, U-G12835: U-F12341:
U-G12584

Mumlal's Aria
Boh. Necht cokoliv mne zlobí
Luděk Mandaus, U-C12833: U-C12652
Emil Pollert, G-AM2915

Co to, holka, co to Trio
Marie Budíková, Oldřich Kovář & Luděk
Mandaus, U-G12836: U-G12499

Ballet Music: Sousedska (Ländler) & Polka
Czech Radio Orchestra—Smetáček
12"—ESTA-H5040
[Bartered Bride—Dance of the Comedians]
National Theater Orch., Prague—
Charvát   10"—G-AM2243
[Bartered Bride—Dance of the Comedians]
National Theater Orch., Prague—Skvor
12"—ESTA-H5108
[Bartered Bride—Dance of the Comedians]
National Theater Orch., Prague—Vašata
10"—U-C12832
[When May is near, Blažíček]

POLKAS Piano (Bohemian Dances)
Collection
Polka, E flat major
Sketches, Op. 5, No. 1—Scherzo-Polka
Jan Herman
Salon Polkas, Op. 7, No. 1, F sharp major; No. 2, F minor
Ludvík Kundera
Poetic Polkas, Op. 8, No. 1, E flat major;
No. 2, G minor
František Maxián
Remembering Bohemia, Op. 12, No. 1—
Polka, A minor & No. 2, Polka, E minor
Vladimír Polívka
Remembering Bohemia, Op. 13, No. 2—
Polka, E flat major & Poetic Polka, Op. 8,
No. 3, A flat major
Dana Setková   5   10"—U-C14028/32

(4) Polkas Piano (Bohemian Dances)
No. 1, F sharp minor, No. 2, A minor, No. 3,
F major, No. 4, B major
Františék Rauch
2   12"—U-G12948 & U-G14034
[with Salon Polka, Op. 7, No. 3, E major
&Remembering Bohemia, Op. 13, No. 1.—
Polka, G major]

Individual recordings not listed in the above
collections:

No. 2, A minor
Jan Heřman   10"—G-AM2245
[Waltz & Little Hen]
Rudolf Firkušný   10"—G-DA5300
[Suk: Idyll & Humoresque]

Prague Carnival—Introduction & Polonaise
Czech Broadcasting Orch.—Jeremiáš
10"—U-B14316

QUARTETS—String

No. 1, E minor "From My Life" 1876
Boh. Z meho zivota Ger. Aus meinem
Leben
Ondriček Quartet 4 12"—**U-G12610/3**
Primrose Quartet 4 12"—**VM-675**†
[Bach: Komm süsser Tod]
Curtis String Quartet: 4 12"—**CM-405**†
[Tchaikovsky: Quartet, E flat minor,
Scherzo only]
DUPLICATIONS: Sevcik-Lhotsky Quartet, G-AN326/9; Bohemian Quartet, PD-95076/9

No. 2, D minor 1882
Suk Quartet 4 10"—**U-B12233/6**
[Suk: Barcarolle]

Richard III, Op. 11 Symphonic Poem 1858
Czech Philharmonic—Kubelík
2 12"—**U-G14050/1**

Rybar See under Fisherman
Sea Song
Moravian Teachers' Chorus—Soupal
12"—**U-G14950**
Slepička See under Little Hen

SONGS In Bohemian

Evening Songs (Cycle of 5 Lyrics)
Boh. Večernich Pisni (Halek)
1. Who is master of the golden strings?
(Kdo v zlaté struny zahrat zná)
**2. Don't throw stones against the
prophets** (Nekamenujte proroky)
3. I dreamt once (Mně zdálo se)
4. Hej! What a joy in playing (Hej jaká
radost v kole)
5. Out of my songs I build you a throne
(Z svých písní trůn ti udělám)
Marta Krásová (ms), Karel Leis (t) &
Oldřich Kovař (t) with National Theatre
Orch.—Rudolf Vašata
3 12"—**U-G12987/9**

First Songs Boh. Prvnich Písní
1. My dear eyes (Oči mé milé)
2. Goodbye (S Bohem)
3. Sorrow of Departure (Zal vzdálené)
4. The Invitation (Pozvání)
5. Spring Song (Jaro lasky)
Marta Krásová (ms), Karel Leis (t) &
Oldřich Kovař (t) with National Symphony Orch.—Rudolf Vašata
3 12"—**U-G12987/9**

—No. 5 (Spring Song) only
Anna Slavíková, U-C14003

Stamp Dance Piano
(Bohemian Dance No. 6)
Otakar Vondrovic 12"—**U-G12938**
[Hop Dance]

To our Damsels Orchestra
Boh. Nasim devam (Polka)
FOK Symphony Orch.—Smetacek
[Venkovanka] 12"—**U-F12518**
Czech Philharmonic Orch.—Talich
12"—**G-EH1315**
[Kovarovic: Bergmannspolka]
Czech Philharmonic Orch.—Rídký
[Balling: Czech Polka] 10"—**U-A1195**

**TRIO—Violin, 'Cello & Piano, G minor
Op. 15**
A. Plocek (vl), M. Sadlo (vlc), J.
Palenicek (pf) 4 12"—**U-G14890/3**
Louis Kaufman, Willem van den Burg,
Rudolf Firkusny 3 12"—**VOX-628**

Triumphal Symphony Orchestra
—Scherzo only
Radiojournal Symphony Orch., Prague—
Jeremiáš 2 12"—**U-E10257 &
U-E10278**
[Dvořák: Waldtaube—Wedding Dance,
with Berlin Orch.—Kleiber]

Venkovanka (The Country Girl)
Orchestra (Polka)
FOK Symphony Orch.—Smetáček
[To Our Damsels] 12"—**U-F12518**

Wallenstein's Camp, Op. 14
Symphonic Poem
Czech Philharmonic—Kubelík
2 12"—**U-G14052/3**
Czech Broadcasting Orch.—Jeremiáš
2 12"—**ESTA-H5014/5**

Waltz Orchestra
FOK Orch.—Smetáček 10"—**U-B12728**

Waltz, A flat major Piano
Jan Heřman 10"—**G-AM2245**
[Polka & Little Hen]

**Waltzes, C minor, A flat major &
E flat major**
Marie Knotková 10"—**G-DA5303**
[Dvořák: 2 Silhouettes]

SMIT, Leo (1922-   )

A young American composer-pianist.

Toccata Breakdown
Rondel (for a young girl)
Leo Smit (pf), in CH-B9 (Limited Edition)

SODDU, U.

(La) Madre e il figlio Cantata
Cloe Elmo (ms) & Orch.—Oliveri
12"—**G-DB5357**

SOEDERMANN, August Johan (1832-1876)

*A Swedish composer, German trained at Leipzig under Richter and Hauptmann, Söderman
is noted for his ballads.*

Jungfrun av Orleans—Incidental Music to
Schiller's drama
Eng. The Maid of Orleans
Overture
Göteborg Symphony—Tor Mann
[Bull: Herdgirl's Sunday] 12"—**G-Z205**

Kung Heimer och Aslög Song in Swedish
Joel Berglund (b) 12"—**G-Z304**
[Hallen: Junker nils sjunger till lutan]

Liturgical Songs for Mixed Choir & Organ
Kyrie; Agnus Die; Jesus Christe; Domine; Benedictus; Virgo gloriosa; Ossana
Radio Choir—Mogens Wöldike
4 12"—**SWED. RJ-RA100/3**
[Isaac: Now rests the world]

(6) Songs in the Folk Style
Radio Choir—Mogens Wöldike
2 10"—**SWED. RJ-RA109/10**
[Wikander: King Lily of the Valley]

SOLER, (Padre) Antonio (1729-1783)

A Spanish composer and theorist, Soler wrote organ, chamber, church and dramatic music. In his harpsichord pieces he was a self-styled disciple of Domenico Scarlatti.

Concerto, G major Harpsichord & Organ
Ruggero Gerlin & Noëlie Pierront
12"—PAT-PAT75

SOMERVELL, (Sir) Arthur (1863-1937)

Commandant of the English Royal Military School of Music for many years, Sir Arthur did much to improve military music and to persuade composers to write for band.

MAUD Cycle of Songs (Tennyson)

I hate the dreadful hollow; A voice by the cedar tree; She came to the village church; O let the solid ground; Birds in the High Hall garden; Maud had a garden; Go not happy; I have led her home; Come into the garden, Maud; The fault is mine; Dead, long dead; O that 't were possible; Epilogue
Roy Henderson (b) & Eric Gritten (pf)
5 10"—D-M589/93

SOMMA, Bonaventura (1893-   )

An Italian organist and church composer who has also written an orchestral symphony and some songs.

Ave Maria
Julian Chapel Choir—Antonelli
12"—SEMS-1126
[Antonelli: Oremus Pro Pontifice]
A. Dadò   12"—SEMS-14
[Viadana: Exultate justi in Domino]
DUPLICATION: Sextet of the Sistine Chapel—Boezi, SEMS-4

Ave Spes Nostra
A. Dadò (b)   12"—SEMS-14
[Palestrina: Motet-Vox dilecti mei, Julian Chapel Choir]

Dirigatur Domine orate mea
A. Dadò (b)   10"—SEMS-58
[Lassus: Justorum Animae, Julian Chapel Choir]

Flores apperuerunt
Sistine Chapel Sextet   10"—SEMS-19
[Capocci: Nostra Signora, A. Dadò]

Nenia Pastorale
A. Dadò (b) (SEMS-502) 10"—SEMS-18
[Tavoni: Canzona Vespertina alla Beata Vergina]

O Salutaris Hostia
A. Dadò (b)   10"—SEMS-15
[Refice: Ave Regina Coelorum, Sistine Chapel Sextet]

Pater Noster
A. Dadò (b)   12"—SEMS-9
[Lassus: Triste est, Julian Chapel Choir]

Regina Coeli
A. Dadò (b)   10"—SEMS-53
[Meluzzi: O Memoriale Mortis, Sistine Chapel Sextet]

SOR, Fernando (1778-1832)

Thème varié Guitar
Andrés Segovia   12"—G-D1255
[Bach: Gavotte for Lute]

SOUSA, John Philip (1856-1932)

The famous American bandmaster and composer of marches who also wrote several text books on band music and composed a number of light operas.

MARCHES
Collections

Sousa Marches—Vol 1
The Stars & Stripes Forever; Semper Fidelis; Washington Post; Hands Across the Sea; The Thunderer; High School Cadet; El Capitan; King Cotton
American Legion Band of Hollywood—Colling   4 10"—D-A537

Sousa Marches—Vol 2
The Fairest of the Fair; Jack Tar; Sabre & Spurs; U. S. Field Artillery March; The Invincible Eagle; Nobles of the Mystic Shrine; The Picadore; The Free Lance
Decca Band—Colling   4 10"—D-A538

Individual Marches (See also current catalogues)

(El) Capitan
Philadelphia Orch.—Stokowski, V-1441; Sousa Band, V-20191; Boston "Pops" Orch.—Fiedler, V-4501; Coldstream Guards Band, G-B2941

Semper Fidelis
Boston Symphony—Koussevitzky, V-18-0053; Boston "Pops" Orch.—Fiedler, V-4392: G-B8817: G-JK2302; Carnegie Pops Orch.—Broeckman, C-71957D; Sigmund Romberg & his Orch., V-11-9221; U. S. Marine Band, V-20979; Coldstream Guards Band, G-B2647

Stars and Stripes Forever
NBC Symphony—Toscanini, V-11-9188; Boston Symphony Orch.—Koussevitzky, V-18-0053; Boston "Pops" Orch.—Fiedler, V-4392: G-B8817; Philadelphia Orch.—Stokowski, G-E556: V-1441; Sousa Band, V-20132; Philadelphia Orch.—Ormandy, V-11-8451: G-DA1845; Coldstream Guards Band, G-B8095

—Arr. 2 Pianos: Rawicz & Landauer, C-FB2117

Washington Post
Philadelphia Orch.—Ormandy, V-11-8451: G-DA1845; Royal Air Force Band, C-DB567; Boston "Pops" Orch.—Fiedler, V-4501: G-B8817: G-JK2302; Sousa's Band, V-20191; Coldstream Guards Band, G-B3787
See current catalogues under the following March titles:
Black Horse Troop
El Capitan
Crusaders
Century of Progress
The Diplomat
Fairest of the Fair
Golden Jubilee
Gladiator

Gridiron Club
Hands Across the Sea
Her Majesty the Queen
High School Cadets
Invincible Eagle
King Cotton
Liberty Bell
Manhattan Beach
Sabre and Spurs
Stars and Stripes Forever
Semper Fidelis
The Thunderer
Washington Post

SOWERBY, Leo (1895-   )

Organist, teacher, and a composer whose works give evidence of his quest for an indigenous "American" style.

(The) Irish Washerwoman
(Irish Folk Tunes enlarged by Sowerby for Orchestra)
Victor Orch.—Bourdon   10"—V-22131
[Turkey in the Straw, arr. Guion]

Comes Autumn Time Overture
Eastman-Rochester Symphony Orch.—
Hanson   10"—V-2058

Symphony, G major Organ
E. Power Biggs (Memorial Church, Harvard University)   4   12"—VM-894†

SPOHR, Louis (Ludwig) (1784-1859)

A very versatile figure of the Romantic Era, Spohr was a virtuoso violinist, composer, conductor, and writer. Extremely popular during his lifetime, all that remains in the modern repertoire are a few of his violin concertos, and some oratorio excerpts still performed in England.

Concertos—Violin & Orchestra

No. 8, A minor, Op. 47 ("In Form einer Gesangs-Scene")
Albert Spalding & Philadelphia Orch.—
Ormandy (G-DB3831/2) 2 12"—VM-544
Georg Kulenkampff & Berlin Philharmonic—Schmidt-Isserstedt
                          3   12"—T-E1847/9
[Schumann: Abendlied]

(THE) LAST JUDGMENT
Oratorio in English 1830
(originally "Die letzten Dinge")

Lord God of Heaven and Earth   Chorus
Temple Church Choir (in English) &
organ—Ball   10"—G-B8123
[Bach: Jesu, Joy of Man's Desiring]

SPONTINI, Gaspar Luigi (1774-1851)

An Italian opera composer who gave the Napoleonic Era its musical style by restoring pomp and ceremony to French opera.

(LA) VESTALE   Opera in French   1807
Overture
EIAR Symphony Orch.—La Rosa Parodi
                          12"—CET-CB20225
Milan Symphony Orch.—Molajoli
                          12"—C-D14494

STAINER, (Sir) John (1840-1901)

Sir John's interest in church music has resulted in several books on early music and in the composition by himself of a sizeable amount of religious music.

(The) Crucifixion Oratorio in English 1887
Richard Crooks (t), Lawrence Tibbett (b), Wilfred Glen (bs), & Frank Crixton (bs), with Trinity Choir & organ—Mark Andrews   6   12"—VM-64†

(The) Crucifixion Negro Spiritual
—Arr. Johnson
Edric Connor (bs)   10"—D-F8721
[Mister Banjo]

Arrangements by Stainer

Good King Wenceslas & The First Nowell
Nelson Eddy (b)   10"—C-4296M

STAMITZ, Johann (1717-1757)

The leader, and considered the founder of the "Mannheim School," Stamitz is a figure of prime importance in transformation of the Galant style into the Classic. Unfortunately only one of his many symphonies and trios for orchestras is available on records.

Symphony, Opus 4, No. 6, in E flat major
Berlin State Orch.—Gmeindl
(last side blank)   3 12"—PD-67554/6S

STAMITZ, Karl (1746-1801)

The son of Johann Stamitz, Karl left the Mannheim orchestra in 1770 and made his way to Paris and later to London. His works are many, and as yet little explored; while not profound, they are clean, straight-forward, and energetic—not unlike those of the young Haydn. Several excellent works have been deleted from modern catalogues.

Quartet   Viola da gamba & String Trio
Eva Heinitz, Jean Fournier, G. Figueroa, Pierre Fournier
                  (in Vol. IX)   12"—AS-85

STANFORD, (Sir) Charles Villers (1852-1924)

A conservative British composer of Irish birth and German training, Stanford may not be considered one of England's great composers, but he certainly can claim credit for a great part of the recent improvement in musical standards evident in English music and conservatories.

Coelos, Ascendit Hodie, Op. 38
Fleet Street Choir   12"—D-K1081
[Heraclitus & Byrd: Ave Verum Corpus]

Gloria in Excelsis
(for the Coronation of George V)
Included in George VI Coronation Service: G-RG12/3

Heraclitus, Op. 110, No. 4
Fleet Street Choir   12"—D-K1081
[Coelos, Ascendit Hodie, Op. 38; Byrd: Ave Verum]

Sonata, Op. 129 Clarinet & Piano
—Caoine only
Frederick Thurston & Myers Foggin
                           12"—D-K853
[Frank: Suite for 2 clarinets]

SONGS In English
  (The) Blue Bird, Op. 119, No. 3
  (Coleridge)
  Glasgow Orpheus Choir—Roberton
                              10″—G-B9464
  [Arr. Bantock: O can ye sew Cushions?]
  Fleet Street Choir—T. B. Lawrence
  [Holst: I love my love]   12″—D-K1021
  (The) Fairy Lough, Op. 77 (O'Neill)
  (The) Pilbroch, Op. 157 (MacLean)
  Roy Henderson (b) & Ivor Newton (pf)
                              10″—D-M535
  She is far from the land
  Paul Robeson (b)   10″—G-B8010
  [Parry: Jerusalem]
  (A) Soft Day, Op. 140, No. 3
  Roy Henderson (b) & Eric Gritten (pf)
                              10″—D-M563
  [Warlock: Milkmaids & Capt. Stratton's
  Fancy]
  Songs of the Fleet, Op. 117
  (Henry Newbolt)
  —Farewell only
  Peter Dawson (bs)   12″—G-C2694
  [Handel: Messiah—Why do the Nations?]
  Songs of the Sea, Op. 91 (Henry Newbolt)
  Devon, O Devon; The old Superb; Drake's
  Drum; Outward Bound
  Peter Dawson (bs), Chorus & Orch.
                          2 10″—G-B4482/3
  —Drake's Drum only
  Dennis Noble (b)   10″—G-B9125
  [Sanderson: Friend o' Mine]
  Tell me ye Flowerates
  (from the opera, "Veiled Pilgrim")
  David Lloyd (t) & Gerald Moore (pf)
                              10″—C-DB2159
  [Vaughan Williams: Silent Noon]

STEFFANI, Agostino (1654-1728)
  *Diplomat, priest and composer, Steffani was one
  of many Italian musicians who found profitable
  posts in Germany.*
  Occhi perchè piangete
  Duo: Soprano & Contralto
  Mme. J. Peretti & Mlle M. Vhita
  with R. Gerlin (harpsichord)
         (in Vol. III)   12″—AS-29

STEINBERG, Maximilian (1883-   )
  *A Russian composer, Steinberg is best known
  for his arrangements of which the recorded
  ones are listed below. See also under K. P. E.
  Bach—Concerto in D major.*
  Russian Folk Songs
  Plaint of Abdurachman;
  Turkistan Love Song;
  Altai (Siberian);
  Dudar-ai (Kasackschtan)
  Lydia Chaliapin (s) (in Russian) &
  Orch.—Ehrlich   2 10″—PAT-PG56/7

STENHAMMAR, Wilhelm, (1871-1927)
  *A leading Swedish pianist and composer, Sten-
  hammar's works are little known outside Scan-
  danavian countries.*
  Concerto No. 2, D major Piano & Orch.
  Hans Leygraf & Göteborg Radio Orch.—
  S. Eckerberg 4 12″—Swed. RJ-RE701/4

Fantasia, Op. 11, No. 1 Piano
  Carl Tillius   10″—G-X7320
  [Wicklund: Melody]
Sentimental Romance, Op. 28
  Violin & Orchestra
  Francesco Asti & Göteborg Symphony—
  Tor Mann   12″—G-Z206
  [Sibelius: Romance]
Serenade, C major, Op. 29
  (String Quartet No. 5)
  Garaguly Quartet 3 12″—G-DB11007/9
  [Wiren: String Quartet No. 2]
Sweden Song in Swedish
  Swed. Sverige
  Jussi Björling (t)   10″—G-X4777
  [Althen: Land, du välsingnade]
—Arr. Orchestra
  Symphony Orch.—Järnefelt
                              10″—O-D4758
  [Folksong: Du gamla, du fria, arr.
  Stenhammer]
  Symphony Orch., G-X2409

STEPHAN, Rudi
  Music for Orchestra
  Berlin State Opera Orch.—Fritz
  Lehmann   2 12″—O-9132/3

STILL, William Grant (1895-   )
  *An American negro who has written for Holly-
  wood, Still is a skillful orchestrator who has not
  allowed the vicissitudes of working in the Movie
  Capitol to infect his musical style.*
  Afro-American Symphony Orchestra
  —Scherzo only
  Eastman-Rochester Symphony Orch.—
  Howard Hanson   10″—V-2059
  [Vardell: Joe Clark Steps Out]
  All American Orch.—Stokowski
                              12″—C-11992D
  [Bach-Stokowski: "Little" G minor
  Fugue]
  Here's One
  (Negro Spiritual harmonized by Still)
  —Arr. Violin & Piano Kaufman
  Louis & Annette Kaufman, in VOX-627
  Lenox Avenue Suite
  —Blues only
  —Arr. Violin & Piano Kaufman
  Louis & Annette Kaufman, in VOX-627

STOJOWSKI, Sigismond (1870-1946)
  *A Polish-American pianist, writer, composer
  and for many years head of the piano department at the Institute of Musical Art, Stojowski
  was, in his youth, a keyboard protegy whose
  creativity was sustained throughout his lifetime.*
  Chant d'Amour Piano
  Ignace Jan Paderewski   12″—V-6633
  [Debussy: Reflets dans l'eau]

STRADELLA, Alessandro (c.1645-1682)
  *An Italian composer whose colorful life—the
  accounts are largely speculative—has obscured
  his many operas and his very moving church
  music. Unfortunately the only recorded work is
  the aria listed below, and this has been attributed to Rossini.*

Pietà, Signore Aria da chiesa In Italian
Beniamino Gigli (t)   12″—V-8768
[Rossini: Stabat Mater—Cujus animam]
(G-DB1831)
Eidé Noréna (s)   12″—G-DB5046
[Verdi: Ave Maria—Ave Regina]
Tancredi Pasero (b)   10″—G-DA5440
[Beethoven: In questa tomba oscura]
DUPLICATIONS: Giuseppe Danise,
PD-595013; E. Caruso, G-DB134*

—Arr. 'Cello Solo
E. Chiarappa, SEMS-1152

STRAUS, Oskar (1870-   )

*The operettas of this Viennese composer have
become very popular in the United States. See
current catalogues for additional recordings of
the following operettas: The Chocolate Soldier, Eine Frau, Die Weiss was Sie Will; Land
without Music (film); The Last Waltz; Mariette; Mother of Pearl; Teresina; Les Trois
Valses; (A) Waltz Dream.*

OPERETTAS (for stage & films)

(THE) CHOCOLATE SOLDIER 1908
Ger. Der tapfere Soldat

Excerpts (in English)
My Hero; Sympathy; Why My lady
Sleeps; Ti-ra-la-la; Chocolate Soldier:
Forgive!
Risë Stevens (ms) & Nelson Eddy (b)
with Chorus & Orch.—Armbruster
(C-DB2069/71)   3 10″—CM-482
Orchestral Selections:
London Theatre Orch., C-DX980; A.
Campoli Salon Orch., D-K598; Jack
Hylton Orch., D-K620; Marek Weber
Orch., G-C2822; G-L1008

Waltz—"My Hero"
Dorothy Kirsten (s), on V-27969 in
V-P133; John Charles Thomas & Hope
Manning, V-18061; Richard Tauber,
P-RO20436; Joan Taylor, D-M523;
International Orch.—Shilkret, G-C1838;
Paul Whiteman's Orch., C-9460

The Song in my Heart
John Charles Thomas (b), on V-11-8610

MARIETTE Operetta in French

Vocal Excerpts
Yvonne Printemps & Sasha Guitry,
G-W1045/6

LES TROIS VALSES Operetta in French
Eng. The Three Waltzes

Excerpts
Yvonne Printemps (s)
3 10″—G-DA4903/4; DA4908
Germaine Féraldy (s)
10″—PAT-PA1205
Evelyn Laye (s) (in English)
10″—G-B9414

(A) WALTZ DREAM Operetta 1907
Ger. Ein Waltzertraum
Fr. Rêve de Valse

Abridged Recording in French
Odeon Operetta Company—Minssart
5 10″—O-250231/5

Excerpts
Lena Dachary, Raymond Malvasio,
Willy Clement   2 10″—PAT-PD67/8
Orchestral Selections
Marek Weber Orch., G-EH855;
International Concert Orch., G-Z169

Waltz: Da draussen im duftenden Garten
Peter Anders, T-A1936; Richard Tauber,
P-RO20199; Richard Crooks (in
English)), G-DA1328

STRAUSS, Eduard (1835-1916)

*The youngest brother of Johann II, Eduard
took over the conductorship of the family orchestra in 1863.*

Aus Lieb' zu ihr
Symphony Orch.—Dobrindt 12″—O-3622
[Jos. Strauss: Frauenherz Polka]
Bahn frei (Galop, or Polka), Op. 45
Eng. Right Away, or Fast Track
Boston "Pops" Orch.—Fiedler
(in VM-1049)   10″—V-10-1207
[Joh. Strauss, Jr.: Annen Polka]
(G-B9528)
Cleveland Orch.—Leinsdorf
12″—C-12543D
[Joh. Strauss, Jr.: Ueber Donner und
Blitz; Perpetuum mobile; Joh. Strauss,
Sr.: Radetzky March]
Liverpool Philharmonic—Sargent
10″—C-DB2156
[Joh. Strauss, Jr.: Annen Polka]
Doctrinen (Waltz), Op. 79
Eng. Faith Waltz
Boston "Pops" Orch.—Fiedler
(G-C3186)   12″—V-12428
DUPLICATIONS: Johann Strauss 3rd
Orch., C-9234; London Philharmonic—
Goehr, on G-C2962

STRAUSS, Johann, (Sr.) (1804-1849)

*The Viennese dances of the father of the fa-
mous Johann have been obscured by the
greater popularity of those of his son.*

Donaulieder (Waltz), Op. 127
Eng. Songs of the Danube
No recording available
Lorelei-Rhein-Klänge (Waltz) Op. 154
Eng. Lorelei Rhine Songs
Symphony.—A. Melchiar 10″—PD-22429
[Lanner: Schönbrunner Waltz]
London Philharmonic—Goehr, on
G-C2962
Radetzky March, Op. 228
Cleveland Orch.—Leinsdorf
12″—C-12543D
[J. Strauss, Jr.: Ueber Donner und Blitz
& Perpetuum mobile; E. Strauss: Bahn
frei polka]
Liverpool Philharmonic—Sargent
12″—C-DX1156
[Ireland: London Overture, Pt. 3]
DUPLICATIONS: J. Strauss, 3rd Orch.,
C-9289; BBC Band, C-DB1087; Berlin
Philharmonic—Kreuder, T-A2504

—Arr. 2 pfs.
Rawicz & Landauer, C-DB2193

—Arr. Chorus
Vienna Choir Boys & pf. acc., on
V-1910 in VM-561

Sans Souci Polka
Boston "Pops" Orch.—Fiedler
(in VM-1049) 10"—V-10-1205
[J.Strauss, Jr.: Tik Tak Polka]
(G-B9478)

STRAUSS, Johann (1825-1899)

*With the second Johann Strauss, aptly called
the "Waltz King," the waltz, which had lowly
bourgeois origins, became the most popular
dance form of the Nineteeth Century, at home
either in the aristocratic balls of the Viennese
Emperor or in the street cafes of European
cities. See current catalogues for additional recordings and dance band arrangements.*

COLLECTIONS

Rediscovered Music of Johann Strauss
Vol. I—Serail Tanze; Explosions Polka;
Electrofor Polka; Festival-Quadrille;
Paroxysmen Walzer
Columbia Broadcasting Symphony Orch.
—Barlow 3 12"—CM-389†
Vol. II—Motoren Walzer; Ballg'schichten
Walzer; Telegraphische Depeschen;
Champagner Polka; Schnellpost Polka
Columbia Broadcasting Symphony Orch.
—Barlow 3 12"—CM-445†
Two Overtures & Two Waltzes
Die Fledermaus & Der Zigeunerbaron—
Overtures; Emperor Waltz & Blue Danube
Waltz
Vienna Philharmonic & London Sym-
phony—Walter & Szell 4 12"—VM-805†
Music of Johann Strauss
Blue Danube Waltz; Accelerationen;
G'schichten aus dem Wiener Wald; Over-
tures to Die Fledermaus & Zigeunerbaron
Minneapolis Symphony Orch.—
Ormandy 5 12"—VM-262†
Viennese Music of Johann Strauss
An den schönen, blauen Donau, Op. 314;
Kaiserwalzer, Op. 437; Pizzicato Polka;
Radetzky March (J. Strauss, Sr.); Die
Fledermaus—Brüderlein und Schwester-
lein; Kläng der Hiemat
Vienna Boys Choir & pf. acc.—V.
Gomboz 4 10"—VM-561
See also under Marches and Waltzes
(Le) beau Danube See under Waltzes and
for the ballet, under Miscellaneous
(The) Bat Fr. (Le) Chauve Souris
See under Operettas—(Die) Fledermaus

MARCHES Band or Orchestra

Collection—Marches of Johann Strauss
Egyptian March, Op. 335; Persian March,
Op. 289; Marches from "Indigo" & "The
Gypsy Baron"
Boston "Pops" Orch.—Fiedler
2 10"—VM-1137
See also among operettas
Egyptian March, Op. 335
Ger. Aegyptischer Marsch
Boston "Pops" Orch.—Fiedler
(in VM-1137) 10"—V-10-1019

[Persian March]
Vienna Philharmonic—Krauss
12"—T-SK3241
[Jos. Strauss: Feuerfest Polka, Op. 269]

Persian March, Op. 289
Ger. Persischer Marsch
Boston "Pops" Orch.—Fiedler
(in VM-1137) 10"—V-10-1019
[Egyptian March]

Radetzky March
See under Johann Strauss, Sr.

Vor—Jubelfestmarsch (unidentified)
Karlakor Reykjavikur (Chorus, in Ice-
landic) & F. Weissheppel (pf)—S.
Pordarson 10"—G-X6040

OPERETTAS In German

NOTE: *Only the authentic Johann Strauss operettas are listed below. For the many operettas, films and other stage works arranged
from his waltzes and original operettas by
other composers, see below under Miscellaneous.*

CAGLIOSTRO IN WIEN, Op. 370
See under Waltzes

(DIE) FLEDERMAUS, Op. 56
3 Acts 1874
Eng. The Bat Fr. La Chauve Souris
It. Il Pipistrello

Abridged recording Arr. Weigert & Maeder
Berlin State Opera Company Soloists,
Chorus & Orch.—Weigert
5 12"—PD-27415/9
The Cast includes Adele Kern, Else Ruzic-
zka, Margaret Pfahl, Hertha Klust, Franz
Völker, Willi Domgraf-Fassbaender, Wal-
demar Henke, Eduard Kandl, Leonard
Kern

Vocal & Orchestral Selections: Berger,
Frind, Müller, Anders, Fuchs, Berlin
Philharmonic Orch. & Chorus—Reuss,
T-E1456

Orchestral Selections (Fantasias, etc.)
Concert Orch., G-EH1270; Symphony
Orch.—Melichar, PD-25233; J. Strauss,
3rd Orch., C-9247; Marek Weber Orch.,
G-EG549; Concert Orch.—B. Seidler-
Winkler, G-FKX17
Also: Rawicz & Landauer (2 pianos),
C-FB2415

Overture Orchestra
Paris Conservatoire—Walter
(G-DB3536) (in VM-805†) 12"—V-13688
Saxon State Orch.—Böhm
12"—G-DB4638
Berlin Philharmonic—Heger
12"—O-3616
Berlin Philharmonic—Kleiber
(U-F18061) 12"—T-E1536
Boston "Pops" Orch.—Fiedler
12"—V-12-0189
Minneapolis Symphony—Ormandy
(in VM-262†) 12"—V-8651
Berlin Philharmonic Orch.—von
Karajan 12"—PD-68043
Berlin State Opera Orch.—Walter
(C-L2311) 12"—C-9080M

Vienna Philharmonic Orch.—Krauss
    12"—**T-SK3161**
Hallé Orch.—Heward 12"—**C-DX1065**
DUPLICATIONS: Vienna Philharmonic—
Krauss, G-L968; Berlin State Opera Orch.
—Bodanzky, P-E10775; Berlin Philhar-
monic—Furtwängler, PD-67121;
PD-566194; Berlin Philharmonic—
Melichar, PD-57029; Tivoli Orch.—
Felumb, TONO-X25056; Berlin State
Opera Orch., Viebig, G-C1414: G-EH17,
Palace Theatre Orch.—Tauber, C-DX1203
Also: Foden's Motor Works Band,
C-FB3112

Individual Excerpts

ACT I

No. 1, Täubchen, das entflattert ist
Marcel Wittrisch (t) & Anni Frind (s)
    10"—**G-EG3870**
[Millöcker: Gasparone—O dass ich
Räuber]

—**Tenor Part only**
Marius Jacobsen (in Danish) G-X4012

No. 3, Komm' mit mir zum Souper
 Eng. **Come with me**
Heddle Nash (t) & Dennis Noble (b)
(in English) 12"—**C-DX212**
[Puccini: Bohème—Ah Mimì]

No. 5, Trinke, Liebchen, trinke schnell
 Eng. **Drinking Song**
Else Kochhann (s) & Franz Völker (t)
    10"—**PD-22253**
[Zigeunerbaron—Ha 'seht, es winkt, with
Bassth]

—**Tenor part only**
Franz Völker, PD-19791; Koloman von
Pataky, PD-23471; Richard Singeleitner,
PD-10915; Marius Jacobsen (in Danish),
G-X4012

Mein Herr, was dächten Sie?
Lotte Lehmann (s) & Orch.—
Weissmann 10"—**P-PO163**
[Czardas—Klänge der Heimat]

ACT II

No. 8, Mein Herr Marquis Soprano
 Eng. **Laughing Song**
Elisabeth Schumann 10"—**G-E545**
[Spiel' ich die Unschuld]
Miliza Korjus (in Spanish)
    12"—**V-11-8579**
[Pardavé: The Nightingale]
DUPLICATIONS: Erna Berger,
PD-10169; Erna Sack, T-E2571
In English: Irene Ambus, C-DB2187

No. 10, Czardas: Klänge der Heimat
 Soprano
Lotte Lehmann 10"—**P-PO163**
[Mein Herr, was dächten Sie]
Maria Reining 12"—**T-E3055**
[Suppé: Boccacio—Hab' ich]
DUPLICATIONS: Maria Ivogün,
G-DB4412; Vienna Boys' Choir (choral
arr.) V-1911 in VM-561; Jarmila
Ksírová (in Czech), U-F12876

No. 11, Act II, Finale Ensemble
 **Im Feuerstrom der Reben; Herr Che-
valier, ich grüsse Sie; Brüderlein und
Schwesterlein**
Lotte Lehmann, Karin Branzell, Richard
Tauber, Grete Merrem-Nikisch, W. Stage-
mann & Berlin State Opera Chorus &
Orch.—F. Weissmann 12"—**P-PXO1032**
E. Kochhann, Franz Völker, I. Eisinger
& Cho. 10"—**PD-22173**
—**Brüderlein only** Choral Arrangement
Vienna Boys' Choir, on V-1911 in VM-561

ACT III

No. 12, Spiel' ich die Unschuld vom Lande
 Soprano
Elisabeth Schumann 10"—**G-E545**
[Mein Herr Marquis]
Erna Berger 10"—**PD-10169**
[Mein Herr Marquis]
DUPLICATIONS: Erna Sack, T-E2571;
Irene Ambus (in English), C-DB2187

Miscellaneous Excerpts
—**Quadrille:** Band-Snaga, PD-27022
—**Fantasy** Arr. La Forge
Lily Pons (in French), C-71733D in
CM-606: C-LX968

Waltzes
Hollywood Bowl Orch.—Stokowski
    10"—**V-10-1310**
See also under Waltzes—Du und Du, and
under Polkas—Tik, Tak

(The) Gypsy Baron
See under Operettas—Zigeunerbaron

INDIGO (1001 NACHT) 1871

Intermezzo Orchestra
Saxon State Orch.—Böhm
    12"—**G-DB4560**
[Reznicek: Donna Dianna—Overture]
Members of Stockholm Opera Orch.—
A. Axelson 10"—**SYM-B5001**
[Offenbach: Tales of Hoffmann—
Barcarole]
DUPLICATIONS: Berlin Philharmonic—
Reuss, T-E1622; Grand Symphony—
Dobrindt, P-R2206; Berlin Philharmonic
—Melichar, PD-15216: PD-15231;
Barnabas von Géczy Orch.—G-EH1261

Indigo March, Op. 349
Boston "Pops" Orch.—Fiedler
 (in VM-1137) 10"—**V-10-1020**
[Ziguenerbaron—March] (G-B9335)

Launisches Glück Tenor
 Eng. **Fickle Fortune**
(an interpolated song, arr. von Burger)
Friedrich Eugen Engels 10"—**PD-10999**
[Lehar: Merry Widor—Komm' in]
Charles Kullman, on C-DW3046

Waltz See under Waltzes—Tausend und
eine Nacht

(DER) LUSTIGE KRIEG 1881

Overture
Berlin State Opera Orch.—Melichar
    10"—**PD-47424**

Nur für Natur (Waltz)
Julius Patzak (t), PD-90061

Waltz See under Waltzes—Küss

(EINE) NACHT IN VENEDIG 1883
Eng. A Night in Venice
Fr. Une nuit à Venise
Vocal Excerpts
Friedrich E. Engels (t) with Berlin
Opera Chorus & Orch.,—Schüler
12"—T-E2322
H. E. Groh (t) & Chorus
2 10"—O-26157 & 26303
Also: Walther Ludwig (t), PD-47526;
Lizzi Waldmüller, G-EG7250
Overture Orchestra
Vienna Symphony—Paul Kerby
12"—C-DFX86
[Boieldieu: Calife de Bagdad—Overture]
DUPLICATION: Berlin Philharmonic—
Kreuder, T-A2258
Polka See under Polkas—Annen
Individual Excerpts
Annina! Caramello! Soprano & Tenor
Hor' mich, Annina & Komm' in die Gondel
Lotte Schöne & Marcel Wittrisch
10"—G-EG2166
Komm' in die Gondel Tenor
Franz Völker, PD-21040: PD-10443;
Karl Schmitt-Walter, T-A10281; Max
Lichtegg, D-K1564; H. E. Groh, O-26157;
Peter Anders, T-A1834: T-A10131; Mar-
cel Wittrisch, G-EG2545; Julius Patzak,
PD-23921; Walther Ludwig, PD-47526;
Marius Jacobsen (in Danish), G-X4442;
Oldřich Kovař, (in Czech), U-B14184
Sei mir gegrüsst, du holdes Venetia (Waltz)
Treu sein, das liegt mir nicht Tenor
Franz Völker, PD-21043; Marcel Wit-
trisch, G-EG2167
—Sei mir only
H. E. Groh, O-26303; Rupert Glawitsch,
T-A2943
—Treu sein only
H. E. Groh, O-26157; Peters Anders,
T-A1834
Lagunen Walzer See under Waltzes

PRINZ METHUSALEM 1877
Waltz See under Waltzes—O schöner Mai

RITTER PASMAN 1892
Czardas
Berlin State Opera Orch.—Ludwig
[Perpetuum Mobile]   12"—PD-15359

SIMPLIZIUS
Waltz See under Waltzes—Donauweibchen

(DAS) SPITZENTUCH DER KOENIGIN
1880
Eng. The Queen's Lace Handkerchief
Du Märchenstadt im Donautal
Karl Friedrich (t)   12"—PD-47554
[Künneke: Die lockende Flamme—Ich
träume mit offenen Augen]
Max Lichtegg   In Preparation—**Swiss
Decca**
Wo die wolde Rose erblüht
Else Kochhann (s), PD-25827
Waltz See under Waltzes—Rosen aus dem
Süden

WALDMEISTER 1895
Overture Orchestra
German Opera House Orch.—Walter
Lutze   12"—T-E3040
DUPLICATION: Orch.—Havemann, PD-
25216
(Die) Ganze Nacht durchschwarmt Tenor
Julius Patzak   10"—PD-10324
[Millöcker: Gasparone—O wenn ich doch
ein Räuber wär]

(DER) ZIGEUNERBARON 3 Acts 1885
Eng. The Gypsy Baron Fr. Le Baron
Tzigane
Vocal & Orchestral Selections
Marcel Wittrisch, W. Domgraf-Fass-
baender, I. Eisinger, Leo Schützendorf,
E. Ruziczka   12"—G-EH725
Anita Gura, Peter Anders with Chorus
12"—T-E1673
Julius Patzak & Maria Reining
12"—PD-15212
Slávka Procházková, Marie Vojtková,
Zdeněk Milavcová, Karel Leiss (in Czech)
2 10"—ESTA-D2012/3
Orchestral Selections (Fantasias, etc.)
Berlin State Opera Orch.—Melichar, PD-
27235: PD-23912; German Opera House
Orch.—Lutze, T-E2735
Also: Rawicz & Landauer, (2 pf.)
C-FB2415
Overture Orchestra
London Symphony—Bruno Walter
(in VM-805†)   12"—V-13689
(G-DB3650)
Boston "Pops" Orch.—Fiedler
12"—V-12-0188
Vienna Philharmonic Orch.—Karajan
12"—C-LX1009
Berlin Philharmonic Orch.—Karajan
(CET-RR8038)   12"—PD-67997
DUPLICATIONS: Berlin Philharmonic—
Kleiber, U-F18073: T-E1491; Symphony
Orch.—Walter, C-9083M; Minneapolis
Symphony—Ormandy, V-8654 in
VM-262; Berlin State Opera Orch.—Meli-
char, PD-57049; Orch. of the Theater des
Volkes—Kretzschmar, C-DWX1629
Individual Excerpts

ACT I

No. 2, **Als flotter Geist doch früh verwaist**
Tenor & Chorus
Ja, das Alles auf Ehr' Chorus
Eng. Song of Greeting: Such was life in
my youth
Richard Tauber   10"—P-PO159
[Lehar: Zigeunerliebe]
Charles Kullman & Berlin Opera Chorus
10"—C-DW3067
[Wer uns getraut, with Berger]
DUPLICATIONS: Franz Völker, PD-
19791; K. von Pataky, PD-23471; Rich-
ard Sengeleitner, PD-10915
In English: Max Lichtegg, D-K1563;
John Charles Thomas, V-16184

No. 3, Ja, da Schreiben und das Lesen

Ja, mein idealer Lebenszweck Bass
Leo Schützendorf   10″—T-A684
[Von des Tajos Strand]
DUPLICATIONS: A. Griebel, C-DW3064;
Willy Schneider, PD-11009

No. 6, Zigeunerlied: So elend und so treu
Eng. Gypsy Song
Else Kochhann (s)   12″—PD-27182
[Lehar: Zigeunerliebe—Nur die Liebe
hält]

No. 7, Finale Act I Ensemble
(Beginning with "Er ist Baron")
Lotte Lehmann, Karin Branzell, Richard
Tauber, G. Merrem-Nikisch, H. Lange, W.
Stagemann with Berlin State Opera
Chorus & Orch.—Weissmann (mislabeled
on the record: "Finale, Act II")
[Finale, Act II]   12″—P-PXO1034

ACT II

No. 8, Mein Aug' bewacht Trio
M. Düren, G. Siebert, Joop de Vries
[No. 9]   12″—G-EH1327
E. Kochhann, E. Bassth, Franz Völker
                    12″—PD-27072
[No. 12½ with Völker & Chorus]

No. 9, Ha, seht es winkt Trio
M. Düren, G. Siebert, Joop de Vries
[No. 8]   12″—G-EH1327
E. Kochhann, E. Bassth, Frank Völker
                    10″—PD-22253
[Fledermaus-Trinke, Liebchen—Koch-
hann & Völker]

No. 11, Wer uns getraut? Soprano, Tenor &
Chorus
Eng. Who tied the knot? (Song of the
Bull-Finch)
Else Kochhann & Helge Roswaenge
                    12″—PD-25105
[Lehar: Merry Widow—Song of the
Rider]
Erna Berger & Charles Kullman
[No. 2, Als flotter Geist] 12″—C-DW3067
A. Rautawaara & Peter Anders
                    12″—T-E2572
[Lehar: Rastelbinder—Wenn zwei sich
liebe]
In Swedish: Jussi Björling & H. Schym-
berg, G-X6146
—Tenor Part only: Richard Fritz Wolf, PD-
25105

No. 12½, Werberlied & Czardas Tenor &
Chorus
Eng. Counting Song
Franz Völker & Berlin Opera Chorus—
Snaga   12″—PD-27072
[No. 8, with Kochhann & Bassth]
—Werberlied only
Willi Domgraf-Fassbaender, G-EG2336;
Arno Schellenberg, G-EG7006

No. 13, Finale (Act II) Ensemble
(Beginning with "Ein Fürstenkind")
Lotte Lehmann, Karin Branzell, Richard
Tauber, G. Merrem-Nikisch, H. Lange,
W. Stagemann & Berlin State Opera
Chorus & Orch.—Weissmann
[Finale, Act I]   12″—P-PXO1034

ACT III

No. 16, Von des Tajos Strand Bass & Chorus
Leo Schutzendorf (without Chorus)
[Ja, das Schreiben]   10″—T-A684
DUPLICATION: August Griebel,
C-DW3064

No. 17, Einzugsmarsch Chorus & Orch.
—Arr. Orchestra only
Boston "Pops" Orch.—Fiedler
    (in VM-1137)   10″—V-10-1020
[Indigo March] (G-B9335)
DUPLICATIONS: Berlin State Opera
Orch.—Melichar, PD-11385; Berlin State
Opera Orch.—Otto, T-A2193

Waltz See under Waltzes—Schatz

Perpetuum mobile, Op. 257 Orchestra
Eng. Perpetual Motion
Cleveland Orch.—Leinsdorf
                    12″—C-12543D
[Ueber Donner und Blitz; E. Strauss:
Bahn frei Polka; Joh. Strauss, Sr.:
Radetzky March]
Boston "Pops" Orch.—Fiedler
                    10″—V-4435
[Brahms: Wiegenlied; Waltz, A flat]
Vienna Philharmonic—C. Krauss
[Annen Polka]   10″—G-B3149
Berlin State Opera Orch.—Ludwig
[Ritter Pasman-Czardas] 12″—PD-15359
DUPLICATIONS: Amsterdam Concertge-
bouw—Mengelberg, C-9076M: C-LX240;
Edith Lorand Orch., P-R1696; Künstler
Orch.—Schutze, PD-10144
Also: Rawicz & Landauer, (2 pfs.)
C-DB2193; Comedian Harmonists,
G-HN704

POLKAS

Polka Medley—Annen, Frauenherz (Jos.
Strauss) Leichtes Blut, Libelle, Mutig
Voran, Pizzicato
Light Symphony Orch.   12″—G-C2963
[Offenbach: Can-Can Medley]

Annen Polka, Op. 117
Boston "Pops" Orch.—Fiedler
    (in VM-1049)   10″—V-10-1049
(G-B9528)
[Eduard Strauss: Bahn Frei Polka]
Liverpool Philharmonic—Sargent
                    10″—C-DB2156
[Eduard Strauss: Bahn Frei Polka]
DUPLICATIONS: Vienna Philharmonic
—Krauss, G-B3149; FOK Symphony
Orch.—Dyk, ESTA-D2061

Champagner Polka
CBS Symphony Orch.—Barlow
    (in CM-445)   12″—C-71029D
[Schnellpost Polka & Telegrafischer
Depeschen Waltz]

Electrofor Polka, Op. 297
CBS Symphony—Barlow
    (in CM-389)   12″—C-69756D
[Explosions Polka; Festival Quadrille]

Explosions Polka
CBS Symphony Orch.—Barlow
    (in CM-389)   12″—C-69756D
[Electrofor Polka; Festival Quadrille]

Leichtes Blut, Schnell-polka, Op. 319
  Eng. High Spirits
  Boston "Pops" Orch.—Fiedler
        (in VM-1049)   10"—V-10-1206
  [Pizzicato Polka] (G-B9473)
  Vienna Philharmonic—Knappertsbusch
  [Pizzicato Polka]   10"—G-DA4487
  Berlin State Opera Orch.—Lutze
                          10"—T-A2635
  [Lumbye: Champagner-Galop]
  Symphony Orch.—Dobrindt
  [Lehar: Eva-Zwanzinetté] 10"—O-26511
  Also: Radio Sextet (in German, vocal
  arr.), G-HE653

Pizzicato Polka
  (written in collaboration with Jos.
  Strauss)
  Boston "Pops" Orch.—Fiedler
        (in VM-1049)   10"—V-10-1206
  [Leichtes Blut Polka] (G-B9473)
  Vienna Philharmonic—Knappertsbusch
  [Leichtes Blut Polka]   10"—G-DA4487
  DUPLICATIONS: Vienna Philharmonic—
  Szell, G-C2687; Berlin State Opera Orch.
  —Melichar, PD-15319; Künstler Orch.—
  Schutze, PD-10144; Minneapolis Sym-
  phony—Ormandy, V-1757; Berlin Phil-
  harmonic—Reuss, T-E1622
  Also: Vienna Boys Choir (vocal arr.)
  V-1910 in VM-561; Rawicz & Landauer,
  (2 pfs.), C-DB2184

Schnellpost Polka
  CBS Symphony—Barlow
        (in CM-445)   12"—C-71029D
  [Champagner Polka & Telegrafischer
  Waltz]

Tik-Tak Polka (from "Die Fledermaus")
  Boston "Pops" Orch.—Fiedler
        (in VM-1049)   10"—V-10-1205
  (G-B9478)
  [Joh. Strauss, Sr.: San Souci Polka]

Tritsch-Tratsch, Op. 214
  NBC Symphony Orch.—Toscanini
                          12"—V-11-9188
  [Sousa: Stars & Stripes Forever]
  Boston "Pops" Orch.—Fiedler
  (G-B9393)   10"—V-10-1058
  [del Castillo: Cuckoo Clock]
  Vienna Philharmonic—Szell
                          12"—G-C2687
  [Pizzicato Polka & Frühlingsstimmen
  Walzer]
  Carnegie "Pops" Orch.—Abravanel
                          12"—C-7566M
  [Rimsky-Korsakov: Flight of the Bum-
  ble Bee; Wolf-Ferrari: Jewels of the Ma-
  donna—Dance of the Camorristi]
  DUPLICATIONS: Grand Symphony
  Orch.—Dobrindt, P-R2206; Orchestre
  Raymonde, C-DB1752: C-DF2331
  Also: Rawicz & Landauer (2 pfs.),
  C-DB2184

Ueber Donner und Blitz—Schnell Polka, Op. 324
  Eng. Thunder and Lightning Polka
  Boston "Pops" Orch.—Fiedler
  (G-B8488)   10"—V-4319
  [Pierné: Entrance of the Little Fauns &
  Paul White: Mosquito Dance]

Cleveland Orch.—Leinsdorf
                          12"—C-12543D
  [Perpeteum mobile; E. Strauss: Bahn
  frei polka; Joh. Strauss, Sr.: Radetzky
  March]

QUADRILLES
Festival Quadrille
  CBS Symphony—Barlow
        (in CM-389)   12"—C-69756D
  [Explosions Polka: Electrofor Polka]

WALTZES
Collections
(4) Novelty Waltzes of Johann Strauss
  Loves of the Poet (Dichterliebe) Op. 38
  (Joh. Strauss III); New Vienna (Neu
  Wien) Op. 342; Cagliostro (from the Op-
  eretta: Cagliostro in Wien) Op. 370; La-
  goon (Lagunen) (from the Operetta:
  Nacht in Venedig) Op. 411
  Boston "Pops" Orch.—Fiedler
                       4   10"—VM-665†

Strauss Waltzes
  An der schönen blauen Donau; G'schich-
  ten aus dem Wiener Wald; Frühlingsstim-
  men; Künsterleben; Wiener Blut; Kaiser
  Waltz
  Andre Kostelanetz & his Orch.
                       3   12"—CM-481

Waltzes—Volume I
  Rosen aus dem Suden, Op. 388;
  G'schichten aus dem Wiener Wald, Op.
  325; Tausend und eine Nacht, Op. 346;
  Frühlingsstimmen, Op. 410
  Symphony Orch.—Bruno Walter & Felix
  Weingartner   4 12"—CM-364†

Strauss Waltzes
  An die schönen, blauen Donau; Wiener
  Blut; Künstlerleben; Du und du; Wiener
  Bonbons
  New Mayfair Orchestra; von Géczy &
  Marek Weber Orchestra 3   10"—V-P14

Strauss Waltzes
  Künstlerleben; Kaiser; Wiener Blut;
  Wein, Weib und Gesang
  Boston "Pops" Orch.—Fiedler
                       4   12"—VM-445†

Strauss Waltzes (Vocal Arrangements)
  An die schönen blauen Donau; Kaiser-
  walzer; Tausend und eine Nacht; Wein,
  Weib und Gesang
  Miliza Korjus (s) (in English)
                       2   12"—VM-1114

Individual Waltzes

Accelerationen, Op. 234 Eng. Acceleration Waltz
  Minneapolis Symphony—Ormandy
        (in VM-262†)   12"—V-8653
  (G-DB2624)
  Berlin Philharmonic—Kleiber
                          12"—T-E1156
  DUPLICATION: Orchestra Mascotte,
  P-F1775

An der schönen blauen Donau, Op. 314
  Eng. On the Beautiful Blue Danube
  Fr. Le Beau Danube bleu
  NBC Symphony—Toscanini
  (G-DB6171)   12"—V-11-8580

Vienna Philharmonic—Szell (G-C2686)
(in VM-805†) 12″—**V-13691**
(G-FKX26) (G-S10460)
Royal Philharmonic Orch.—Weingartner
12″—**C-69275D**
Minneapolis Symphony—Ormandy
(in VM-262†) 12″—**V-8650**
(G-DB2621)
Vienna Philharmonic—Krauss
12″—**T-SK3150**
National Symphony Orch.—Krips
12″—**D-K1725**
Berlin State Opera Orch.—Schönherr
12″—**PAT-PDT62**
DUPLICATIONS: (two sided versions)
Berlin State Opera Orch.—Mörike,
P-E10626; Berlin Philharmonic—Kleiber, U-E963: T-E963; Berlin Philharmonic
—Melichar, PD-10598: PD-524336; Berlin State Opera Orch.—Melichar,
P-E11370: O-7785; Berlin State Opera Orch.—Blech, G-EH374; Orch of "Maggio Musicale"—Markevitch, CET-BB25161; Berlin State Opera Orch.—
Keilberth, G-EH1204; A. Rode Orch.,
PAT-X98013; Géczy Orch., T-A1591;
Orch. Raymonde, C-DB1375
—**Single-sided orchestral versions**
(Abridged)
Philadelphia Orch.—Stokowski, V-15425:
G-DB3821; (older recording), G-D1218:
G-AW53: G-W965; Andre Kostelanetz
Orch., on C-7391M in CM-481; CBS Symphony—Barlow, on C-72121D in CX-240;
Symphony Orch.— Schutze, PD-524402;
Marek Weber Orch., G-B3726: G-HE2278;
Grosses-walzer Orch.—B. Seidler-Winkler, G-EG6814: G-HE2229; Cor de Groot
Orch., G-B2298; A. Campoli Orch.,
D-F2521; International Concert Orch.,
G-C1563; Orch. Mascotte, P-F1664; Hans
Bund Konzert-Orchester, PD-47650; New
Mayfair Orch., in V-P14: G-B8974
—**Arr. Piano** "Arabesques on the Blue
Danube" (Schulz-Evler)
Louis Kentner, C-DX1184
—**Arr. Voice**
In German: Erna Sack & Chorus,
T-E2039; Marta Eggerth, P-E11315;
Maria Ivogün, G-DB4414; Adele Kern,
PD-27287
In English: Miliza Korjus, V-11-9512 in
VM-1114; Richard Tauber, P-RO20503
In French: Lily Pons, V-15610 in VM-599: G-DB3939; also in CM-720; Villabella, PAT-PA93
—**Arr. Chorus**
In German: Vienna Opera Chorus—Kerby, C-DFX112: C-DVX12; Neukölln
Teachers' Chorus—Melichar, PD-27040;
Wiener Mozart-Knabenchor—Gruber,
G-EG6516; Vienna Choir Boys, V-1908 in
VM-561: also C-DV1047; Vienna Male
Chorus, G-FKX106; Vocal Quartet and
pf. acc., PD-23343; Meistersextet,
G-EG6683
In French: Odeon Operetta Chorus,
O-23895
In English: BBC Chorus—Robinson,
C-DB301

—**Novelty Arrangements:** Albert Sandler
Orch., C-DB2334; Massed Bands,
D-K710
See current catalogues for other arrangements.
Artists' Life See under Künstlerleben
Ballg'schichten Walzer
CBS Symphony—Barlow
(in CM-445) 12″—**C-71028D**
Bei uns z' Haus, Op. 361 Eng. **At Home**
—**Arr. Voice** B. Seidler-Winkler
Eva Maria Seifert, G-EH1314
Blue Danube See under An der schönen,
blauen Donau
Cagliostro (from the operetta "Cagliostro
in Wien")
Boston "Pops" Orch.—Fiedler
(in VM-665†) 10″—**V-4479**
Doctrinen See under Eduard Strauss
Donaulieder See under Johann Strauss, Sr.
Donauweibchen, Op. 427
Eng. **Danube Maiden**
(from the operetta "Simplizius")
Wiener-Bohème Orch. 10″—**O-31677**
[Millöcker: Laura-walzer]
—**Vocal arrangement** (arr. May)
Joseph Schmidt, P-DP7
Dorfschwalben aus Oesterreich See under
Joseph Strauss
Draussen in Sievering
See Miscellaneous: Die Tänzerin Fanny
Elssler
Du und Du, Op. 367 (from "Die Fledermaus")
Vienna Philharmonic—Kleiber
12″—**G-C1676**
Chicago Symphony Orch.—Stock
(G-AV28) 10″—**V-1481**
DUPLICATIONS: Orch.—B. Seidler-Winkler, G-EG6417: G-HE2232; London
Philharmonic—Goehr, on G-C2962;
Marek Weber Orch., G-B3898:
G-EG1695: G-HE2272: G-K6193:
G-HN622: also in V-P14; Rode Tzigane
Orch., PAT-X96117: D-F2569
Emperor See under Kaiser
Fledermaus See under Du und Du
Frühlingsstimmen, Op. 410
Eng. **Voices of Spring**
London Philharmonic Orch.—Beecham
(C-LX867) 12″—**C-70338D**
Symphony Orch.—Weingartner
(in CM-364†) 12″—**C-69564D**
(C-DX266)
Philadelphia Orch.—Ormandy
(G-DB5963) 12″—**V-18060**
[Wiener Blut, Op. 354]
Vienna Philharmonic—Szell
12″—**G-C2687**
[Pizzicato Polka; Tritsch-Tratsch Polka]
BBC Theatre Orch.—Robinson
12″—**D-K1526**
Boston "Pops" Orch.—Fiedler
(in VM-544†) 10″—**V-4387**
(G-B8786: G-GW1567)

Indianapolis Symphony—Sevitzky
12″—V-11-8609
[Weber-Dubensky: Waltz]
DUPLICATIONS: Berlin State Opera
Orch.—Melichar, PD-516758: PD-15177;
Andre Kostelanetz & his Orch., C-7392M
in CM-481: C-DX1263; Hans Bund Kon-
zert-Orchester, PD-47650; Boston Sym-
phony—Koussevitzky, V-6903: G-D1774:
G-AW119; Dajos Bela Orch., O-165669:
P-E10740; Johann Strauss 3rd Orch.,
C-9289; Géczy Orch., G-B3611:
G-EG3928: G-HE2198: G-K7970; Or-
chestre Raymonde, C-DF2304: C-DB1737;
Ferdy Kauffman Orch., G-EH57
—Arr. Piano: Walter Rehberg, PD-23737
—Arr. 2 Pianos: Rawicz & Landauer,
G-X3059: C-DB2026
—Arr. 3 Pianos: PD-10013: PD-25183
—Arr. Band: H. M. Grenadier Guards
Band, C-DB2051
—Vocal Arrangements
In German: Miliza Korjus, V-12829:
G-C3122: G-C2664: G-EH860; Adele
Kern, PD-24552; Erna Sack, T-E1774;
Marta Eggerth, P-E11315; Felicie Hüni-
Mihacsek, PD-66759
In Swedish: Hjördis Schymberg,
G-X4776
In French: Clara Clairbert, PD-561082;
Lily Pons, in CM-720
In English: Gwen Catley, G-C3638

G'schichten aus dem Wiener Wald, Op. 325
Eng. Tales from the Vienna Woods
NOTE: *The Melichar version contains the orig-*
inal zither solo and is probably the only com-
plete and authentic recorded performance
available.
Berlin Philharmonic—Melichar
2 12″—PD-15215/6
[1001 Nacht—Intermezzo]
Philadelphia Orch.—Stokowski
(G-DB3821)   12″—V-15423
[An der schönen, blauen Donau]
(older versions: G-D1218: G-AW53:
G-W955)
Berlin State Opera Orch.—Schönherr
12″—PAT-PDT57
Minneapolis Symphony Orch.—Ormandy
(in VM-262) 12″—V-8652
Symphony Orch.—Bruno Walter
(C-L2334) (in CM-364†) 12″—C-69562
DUPLICATIONS: J. Strauss 3rd. Orch.,
C-9280; Andre Kostelanetz & his Orch.,
C-7391M in CM-481: C-DX1263; CBS
Symphony—Barlow C-72122D in CX-240;
Berlin State Opera Orch.—Knapperts-
busch, G-C1828: G-EH120; Marek Weber
Orch., V-20915: G-B2406: G-K5222:
G-EG263; Gyenes Hungarian Girls Orch.,
PD-10108; Wiener Mascotte Orch.,
P-F1794; Rode Tzigane Orch., C-DQ1591:
C-FB1265: PAT-PA316; Orch.—Seidler-
Winkler, G-EG6412: G-HE2231; Orch.—
Hans Bund, PD-47590; Edith Lorand
Orch., P-E11126; Johann Strauss III
Orch., P-F863; Charley Fischer Orch.,
G-GW1415; Salon Orch.—J. Seidel,
ESTA-E6005

—Arr. 3 Pianos: on PD-25183
—Vocal Arrangements
In German: Erna Sack, In preparation,
Swiss Decca; Adele Kern, PD-27228;
Richard Tauber, P-RO20190; Felicie
Hüni-Mihacsek, PD-66759; Margarete
Düren, G-EG7263; Comedian Harmon-
ists, G-EH432; Vienna Choir Boys,
C-DC315
In English: Richard Tauber, P-RO20503:
P-RO20432; Miliza Korjus, G-B8862:
V-4410; BBC Chorus & Orch., C-DB694;
Anne Ziegler, G-B9122
See also under Miscellaneous—The Great
Waltz

Kaiser, Op. 437 Eng. Emperor
Vienna Philharmonic—von Karajan
(C-LCX108)   12″—C-LX1021
Vienna Philharmonic—Bruno Walter
(in VM-805†) 12″—V-13690
(G-DB3397)
N. Y. Philharmonic-Symphony—Walter
12″—C-11854D
Saxon State Orch.—Böhm
12″—G-DB5560
Philadelphia Orch.—Ormandy
12″—V-18220
National Symphony Orch.—Goehr
12″—D-K1408
Berlin Philharmonic—von Karajan
(FONIT-91136)   12″—PD-67649
Berlin Philharmonic Orch.—Ludwig
12″—PD-15199
Berlin Philharmonic—Kleiber
12″—T-E964
Tivoli Concert Orch.—Jensen
12″—TONO-X25064
Berlin State Opera Orch.—Blech
12″—G-EJ328
Boston "Pops" Orch.—Fiedler
(in VM-445†) 12″—V-12195
(G-C3177)
Winterthur Municipal Orch.—Scherchen
12″—G-DB6091
DUPLICATIONS: Andre Kostelanetz &
Orch., C-7393M in CM-481; Marek Weber
Orch., G-EH328: G-S10136; Concert
Orch.—Seidler-Winkler, G-EG6060;
Dajos Bela Orch., O-166079; London Phil-
harmonic—Goehr, on G-C2962; New
Mayfair Orch., G-B9227; International
Novelty Orch.—Shilkret, G-C1617
—Arr. 2 Pianos: Rawicz & Landauer,
C-DB2130
—Arr. Voice
In German: Erna Sack, T-E2495; Lea
Piltti, G-EG6481
In English: Miliza Korjus, V-11-9063 in
VM-1119
—Arr. Chorus: Vienna Choir Boys, V-1909
in VM-561

Künstlerleben, Op. 316 Eng. Artist's Life
Vienna Philharmonic—Karajan
12″—C-LX1013
Boston "Pops" Orch.—Fiedler
(G-C2919) (in VM-445†) 12″—V-12194
Berlin Philharmonic—von Karajan
(CET-DD8030)   12″—PD-67585
DUPLICATIONS: Dajos Bela Orch.,

O-165668: O-170107: O-279346:
P-E10824; J. Strauss 3rd Orch., C-9280;
Marek Weber Orch., G-C2267: G-EH405:
G-S10184: G-L794; Orchestre Raymonde-
Walter, C-DB1740: G-GN460; Géczy
Orch., G-EH6726: also in V-P14:
G-GW1783: G-B8874: G-HE2177; Andre
Kostelanetz Orch., C-7392M in CM-481:
C-DX1170; Charles Fischer Orch.,
G-GW1450; FOK Symph. Orch.—Dyk,
ESTA-D2063; Rode & his Gypsy Orch.,
D-F2569

—Choral arrangement: Meistersextett,
G-EH998

Küss, Op. 400 Eng. Kiss
(based on motives from the operetta
"Der lustige Krieg")
Johann Strauss III Orchestra
[Wein, Weib und Gesang] 12"—C-9224

Lagunen-Walzer, Op. 411
(from "Nacht in Venedig") Eng. Lagoon Waltz
Boston "Pops" Orch.—Fiedler
(G-B9286) (in VM-665†) 10"—V-4480

—Arr. Voice (in German): Julius Patzak,
PD-10251

Liebeslieder, Op. 114 Eng. Songs of Love
Vienna Philharmonic—Krauss
12"—G-S10377
DUPLICATIONS: Berlin Philharmonic—
Prüwer, PD-19950; Concert Orch.—B.
Seidler-Winkler, G-EH1130: G-S10484

—Arr. Voice (in German): Adele Kern,
PD-27228

Märchen aus den Orient, Op. 444 Eng.
Tales from the Orient
Marek Weber Orch. 12"—G-C2810
[Planquette: Cloches de Corneville—
Valse]

Morgenblätter, Op. 279 Eng. Morning
Papers
Berlin State Opera Orch.—Heger
12"—PD-15122
DUPLICATIONS: Vienna Symphony—
Kerby, C-DF426; New Mayfair Orch.,
G-B9227; Marek Weber Orch.,
G-HE2272: G-B3898: G-EG1695:
G-HN622: G-HE2272: G-K6193; J.
Strauss 3rd Orch., C-9218; Orch.—B.
Seidler-Winkler, G-EG6417: G-HE2232;
Wiener-Bohème Orch., O-279075; Géczy
Orch., T-A1489; Edith Lorand,
P-B6117; A. Rode Tzigane Orch.,
D-F3123

Motoren Walzer
CBS Symphony—Barlow
(in CM-445†) 12"—C-71027D

Neu Wien Walzer, Op. 342
Eng. New Vienna Waltz
Boston "Pops" Orch.—Fiedler
(G-B9113) (in VM-665†) 10"—V-4478

—Arr. Piano Dora Bright
Mark Hambourg, G-S10408

O schöner Mai, Op. 375
Eng. Beautiful Maytime
(from the operetta "Prinz Methusalem")
Berlin Philharmonic—Melichar
10"—PD-24364

Paroxysemen Walzer, Op. 189
CBS Symphony Orch.—Barlow
(in CM-389†) 12"—C-69757D

Rosen aus dem Süden, Op. 388
(from the operetta "Spitzentuch der
Königin")
Eng. Southern Roses, or Roses from the
South
Hallé Orch.—Barbirolli 12"—G-C3408
Boston "Pops" Orch.—Fiedler
12"—V-11-8986
Vienna Philharmonic—Krauss
12"—T-SK3187
Berlin Philharmonic—Bruno Walter
(C-LX28) (in CM-364†) 12"—C-69561D
DUPLICATIONS: Chicago Symphony—
Stock, V-6647: G-D1452; J. Strauss 3rd.
Orch., C-9238; Berlin State Opera Orch.
—Melichar, PD-15177: PD-516758; Lon-
don Philharmonic Orch.—Goehr, on
G-C2962; Dajos Bela Orch., O-165535;
Concert Orch.—B. Seidler-Winkler,
G-HE2229: G-EG6814; Ilja Livschakoff
Orch., PD-23626: PD-27180; Géczy
Orch., T-A2531; Marek Weber Orch.,
G-HN627: G-B3499: G-EG1718:
G-HE2274: G-EG264: G-K5967; E.
Stubbs du Perron & Orch., C-DF217; A.
Sandler Orch., C-DB2165; Orchestre Mas-
cotte, P-F1715; Paramount Theater
Orch., G-HE2020; Symphony Orch.—J.
Seidel, ESTA-D2024

—Arr. Chorus: Vienna Opera Chorus (in
German), C-DFX112: C-DVX12

—Arr. Voice (in German): Richard Tauber,
P-RO20432; Lea Piltti, G-EG6425; Erna
Sack, T-E2039; Else Kochhann, PD-
25827

Schatz-Walzer, Op. 418 (from "Der Zig-
eunerbaron")
Eng. My Darling, Sweetheart, or Treas-
ure Waltz
Pittsburgh Symphony—Reiner
12"—C-11800D
DUPLICATIONS: Berlin State Opera—
Melichar, PD-11046; Marek Weber Orch.,
G-B8235: G-K7407: G-EG3219:
G-HE2448; International Orch.—Shil-
kret, G-L677: G-C1402: G-Z174; Para-
mount Theater Orch., G-HE2020; Orch.
—Max Schönherr, G-HE2185; Wiener
Bohème Orch., O-250949; Géczy Orch.,
G-EG6787: G-HE2176

Seid umschlungen, Millionen, Op. 443
Concert Orch.—B. Seidler-Winkler
10"—G-EG6152
[Lohr: Im schönen Tal der Isar]
DUPLICATION: German Orch., PD-
11563

Serail Tänze
Columbia Broadcasting Symphony—
Barlow (in CM-389†) 12"—C-69755D

Southern Roses See under Rosen aus dem
Süden

Sphärenklänge See under Joseph Strauss

Tales of the Orient See under Märchen aus
dem Orient

Tales from the Vienna Woods See under G'schichten aus dem Wiener Wald

Tausend und eine Nacht, Op. 346
(from the operetta "Indigo" or "1001 Nacht")
Eng. A Thousand and One Nights
British Symphony—Weingartner
(C-LX133) (in CM-364†) 12"—**C-69563D**
Vienna Philharmonic—Krauss
             12"—**G-S10078**
Symphony Orch.—Dobrindt
             12"—**O-3613**
DUPLICATIONS: Marek Weber Orch., G-L1012; J. Strauss 3rd Orch., C-9226; I. Livschakoff Orch. PD-905; Rode & Tzigane Orch., D-F3123
—**Arr. Voice:** Miliza Korjus (in English), on V-11-9513 in VM-1114; in German on G-C2784

Telegrafischer Depeschen Eng. Telegraph Messages
Columbia Broadcasting Symphony—Barlow (in CM-445†) 12"—**C-71029D**
[Champagner and Schnellpost Polkas]

Ueber, or Unter Donner und Blitz
See under Polkas

Vienna Blood See under Wiener Blut

Vienna Bon Bons See under Wiener Bonbons

Voices of Spring See under Frühlingsstimmen

Wein, Weib und Gesang, Op. 333 Eng. Wine, Women and Song
Paris Conservatory Orch.—Weingartner
(C-LX909)   12"—**C-71210D**
Boston "Pops" Orch.—Fiedler
     (in VM-445†)   12"—**V-12192**
(G-C3036) (G-EH1096)
Philadelphia "Pops" Orch.—Ormandy
     (in CM-588)   12"—**C-12607D**
[Brahms: Hungarian Dance No. 5]
DUPLICATIONS: Berlin State Opera Orch.—Bodanzky, P-E10651; Chicago Symphony—Stock, V-6647: G-D1452; J. Strauss 3rd Orch., C-9224; Marek Weber Orch., G-C1407: G-EH55: G-S10383: G-L651; London Philharmonic —Goehr, on G-C2962; Wiener Bohème Orch., P-F1759: O-279042; Symphony Orch.—J. Seidel, ESTA-D2025; Rode Gypsy Orch., PAT-X96119; Carnet de Bal Orch., PAT-PA141; Lilly Gyenes Orch., PD-27272
—**Arr. Voice:** Miliza Korjus (in English), on V-11-9513 in VM-1114; Georges Thill (in French), C-RF77; Max Lichtegg, In Preparation, Swiss Decca
—**Arr. Chorus:** Vienna Male Chorus (in German), PD-27175

Wiener Blut, Op. 354 Eng. Vienna Blood
Pittsburgh Symphony Orch.—Reiner
             12"—**C-11579D**
Philadelphia Orch.—Ormandy
(G-DB5963)   12"—**V-18060**
[Frühlingsstimmen]
Boston "Pops" Orch.—Fiedler
     (in VM-445†)   12"—**V-12193**
(G-C3006) (G-EH1103)

DUPLICATIONS: Kostelanetz Orch., C-7393M, in CM-481: C-DX1170; Salon Orch.—J. Seidel, ESTA-E6006; Berlin State Opera Orch.—Melichar, PD-22361; Boston Symphony Orch.—Koussevitzky, V-6903: G-D1774: G-AW119; Concert Orch.—B. Seidler-Winkler, G-EG6060; Ilja Livschakoff Orch., PD-27180: PD-23647; Dajos Bela Orch., P-E10740; Wiener Bohème Orch., O-279209; J. Strauss 3rd. Orch., C-9238; Marek Weber Orch., G-FKX20: G-EH315: G-S10172; Géczy Orch., T-A2531: T-A1663; New Mayfair Orch., in V-P14: G-B8974; E. Stubbs du Perron Orch., C-DF217; Cor de Groot Orch., G-B2298: G-K3580; Bela Rex Orch., PAT-X96307; Charley Fischer, G-GW1450; Somers Band, C-FB2815
—**Arr. Voice** (in German): Marcel Wittrisch, G-EG2545; Erna Sack, In Preparation, Swiss Decca; E. Schwarzkopf, R. Glawitsch, chorus & orch.—Lutze, T-E3099

Wiener Bonbons, Op. 307
Eng. Viennese Bonbons
Dance Orch.—Melichar 12"—**PD-2236**
DUPLICATIONS: Dajos Bela Orch., O-165388; Géczy Orch., T-A1489; Marek Weber Orch., in V-P14: G-HE2274: G-B3499: G-EG1718: G-K5797: G-HN627; Concert Orch.—B. Seidler-Winkler, G-HE2227; New Mayfair Orch., G-B9316; Grand Symphony Orch., U-A12862
—**Arr. Voice:** Joseph Schmidt (in German): O-281237

Wo die Zitronen blühn, Op. 364
Eng. Where the Lemon Trees Bloom
Boston "Pops" Orch.—Fiedler
(G-C3175) (G-EH1001) 12"—**V-11894**
Berlin State Opera Orch.—Beutler
             10"—**PD-11296**
DUPLICATIONS: German Opera House Orch.—Otto, T-A2873; J. Strauss 3rd. Orch., C-9234

BALLETS ARRANGED FROM STRAUSS MUSIC

(Le) Beau Danube Arr. Roger Désormière
London Philharmonic—Dorati
         3 12"—**VM-414†**
(G-EH988/90) (G-C2869/71)

Graduation Ball Arr. Antal Dorati
Dallas Symphony Orch.—Dorati
         4 12"—**VM-1180†**

OPERETTAS & FILM SCORES ARRANGED FROM STRAUSS MUSIC

Casanova Arr. Benatzky

Nuns' Chorus & Spanish Romance
Anni Frind, Cho. & Orch., G-EH207: G-C3711

(The) Great Waltz Arr. Dimitri Tiomkin
—**Excerpt (Tales from the Vienna Woods)**
Miliza Korjus (in English) with Toscha Seidel (vl) & MGM Orch.—Finston
(G-B8862) (G-K8275)   10"—**V-4410**

—**Vocal Selections:** Richard Tauber (in English), P-RO20431

(Die) Tänzerin Fanny Elssler Arr. Leopold Weninger
Eng. The Dancer Fanny Elssler
Overture Arr. Oskar Stalla
Concert Orch.—Dobrindt, O-25946: CET-B71025

—**Draussen in Sievering blüht schon der Flieder**
Erna Sack   12″—T-E1774
[Frühlingsstimmen-Walzer]
Eva Maria Siefert   10″—G-EG7134
[Pestalozza: Ciribiribin]

MISCELLANEOUS ARRANGEMENTS

NOTE: *Listed below are potpourris of Johann Strauss melodies freely arranged and titled. Only the more important recordings are entered; see current catalogues for additional titles, and for popular and dance arrangements for Strauss' music.*

Vocal & Orchestral Medleys
A. Baugé, F. Revoil & G. Féraldy, (in French), PAT-PA78/9
Jany Delille, (in French), PAT-PA457

Orchestral Medleys
EIAR Symphony Orch.—Ferrero, CET-BB25015; Symphony Orch.—Snaga, PD-27097; Vienna Waltz Orch., G-C2882: G-C3058; Marek Weber Orch., G-EH616; Orch of the Theatre des Volkes—Kretzschmar, C-DWX1624; Deutsche Künstler Orch.—Melichar, PD-27016/7; London Philharmonic Orch.—Goehr, G-C2962; Orchestre Raymonde, C-DB1706; Ilja Livschakoff Orch., PD-47039: PD-524194; German Opera House Orch.—Lutze, T-E2498/9: U-F18090/1

Choral Arrangement
Vienna Choir Boys—Viktor Gomboz
                         4 10″—VM-561
Two-Piano Arrangement: Whittemore & Lowe, V-10-1362

STRAUSS, Johann III (1866-1939)

The third Johann Strauss is the son of Eduard, and hence nephew to the "Waltz King" and grandson of Johann Strauss, Sr.

Dichterliebe, Op. 38
Boston "Pops" Orch.—Fiedler
    (in VM-665†)   10″—V-4477

STRAUSS, Josef (1827-1870)

An architect by profession, Josef Strauss was yet able to offer healthy competition to his brothers in composing light Viennese music.

POLKAS (& POLKA-MAZURKAS)
Collection of Polkas
Light Symphony Orch.   12″—G-C2963
[Includes Polka selections by Johann Strauss]

Feuerfest, Op. 269 Eng. Fire Festival
Vienna Philharmonic Orch.—Krauss
                         12″—T-SK3241
[Joh. Strauss: Aegyptischer Marsch]

Frauenherz, Op. 166 (from the operetta)
German Orch., PD-11563; Sym Orch., G-C2963

Pizzicato
NOTE: *This Polka was written by Josef & Johann Strauss in collaboration. For recordings see under Johann Strauss: Polkas—Pizzicato.*

WALTZES
Dynamiden (Geheimne Anziehungskräfte)
Will's Orch., C-DW2208; Wiener Bohème Orch., O-279489; Otto Kermbach Orch., PD-11422

Flattergeister Eng. Restless Mind
Ilja Livschakoff Orch., PD-27174: PD-23049

(Die) Guten, alten Zeiten Eng. Good Old Times
Ilja Livschakoff Orch., PD-27174: PD-23049

Marienklänge, Op. 214 Eng. Recollections of Marie
(or, St. Mary's Chimes or Joy Bells)
Marek Weber Orch., G-EG2114: G-HN606: G-K6495; Lajos Kiss Orch., T-A10127; Wiener Bohème Orch., O-279489

Sphärenklänge, Op. 235
Eng. Music of the Spheres
Boston "Pops" Orch.—Fiedler
                         12″—V-12-0068
Cleveland Orch.—Leinsdorf
                         12″—C-12579D
Vienna Philharmonic—Krauss
(G-S10292)   12″—G-C2195
DUPLICATIONS: Berlin Philharmonic—Melichar, PD-15200; Wiener Bohème Orch., O-279315; Marek Weber Orch., G-EG2501; Ilja Livschakoff Orch., PD-10154; Concert Orch.—Max Schönherr, G-HE2184

—**Arr. Voice** Mittler
Elisabeth Schumann (s) (in German)
                         10″—G-DA1395
[Mendelssohn: Auf Flügeln des Gesanges]

STRAUSS, Richard (1864-   )

It is not a coincidence that the recorded works of Richard Strauss are those whose composition dates largely cluster about the turn of the century. (Shortly before 1900 there are the famous symphonic poems; shortly after, come the more popular operas.) In his early years, Strauss was formulating his extravagantly sensuous musical vocabulary; after about 1910, writers are fairly unanimous in holding that this vocabulary was being exploited in an over-extended and mechanical manner, and that the composer was grinding out synthetic scores that added little to his output. Considering these musical limitations, Strauss is extremely well represented on discs.

(Eine) Alpensimfonie, Op. 64 Orchestra
Bavarian State Orch.—Strauss
                    6 12″—G-DB5662/7s
Also sprach Zarathustra, Op. 30 Tone Poem 1896
Eng. Thus Spake Zarathustra

Boston Symphony Orch.—Koussevitzky
5 12″—VM-257†
[Bach: Unacc. Vl. Sonata No. 6—
Praeludium]
(G-DB2616/20s, last side blank)
Chicago Symphony Orch.—Stock
4 12″—CM-421†

Aus Italien, Op. 16 Symphonic Fantasy
—3rd section (On the Shores of Sorrento)
only
Chicago Symphony—Stock
12″—V-18535

(DER) BURGER ALS EDELMANN, Op. 60
(Incidental Music to Molière's comedy)
Fr. Le Bourgeois Gentilhomme
The opera "Ariadne auf Naxos" is also
a part of the music for Molière's "Bour-
geois Gentilhomme." For "Ariadne" re-
cordings see below under Opera.
—Orchestral Suite
Overture to Act I; Minuet; Fencing
Master; Entrance & Dance of the Tailors;
Minuet of Lully; Courante; Entrance of
Cléonte; Intermezzo-Prelude to Act II;
The Dinner
Pittsburgh Symphony—Reiner
5 12″—CM-693†
Berlin Opera Orch.—R. Strauss
5 12″—PD-95392/6
[Reger: Valse d'amour, dir. Melichar]
Straram Orch.—Straram
4 12″—C-LFX49/52
(No. 7 omitted) (C-GQX10577/80)
—No. 8 (Intermezzo) only
Symphony Orch.—Malcolm Sargent
(C-DB1784) 10″—C-DB1300
[Elgar: Sospiri, cond. Walter Goehr]
(in Col. History of Music Vol. V: CM-
361)

Burleske Piano & Orchestra 1886
Claudio Arrau & Chicago Symphony
Orch.—Rodzinski 2 12″—in VM-1216†
[with Weber: Konzertstücke]
Marcelle Meyer & Paris Conservatory
Orch.—André Cluytenn
2 12″—G-W1565/6
Elly Ney & Berlin State Opera Orch.—
Van Hoogstraten 2 12″—G-DB4424/5

Concerto No. 1, E flat major, Op. 11 Horn
& Orch.
Dennis Brain & Philharmonia Orch.—
Galliera 2 12″—C-DX1397/8

Concerto Oboe & Orch.
Leon Goossens & Philharmonia Orch.—
Galliera 3 12″—C-DX1444/6

Death and Transfiguration See Tod und
Verklärung

Don Juan, Op. 20 Tone Poem 1888
Philharmonia Orch.—Alceo Galliera
2 12″—C-DX1356/7
Pittsburgh Symphony—Reiner
2 12″—CX-190†
Amsterdam Concertgebouw—Mengelberg
2 12″—T-SK2743/4
Saxon State Orch.—Böhm
2 12″—G-DB4625/6
National Symphony Orch.—Sidney Beer
(D-K1347/8) 2 12″—D-ED15†

London Philharmonic—Fritz Busch
(G-DB2897/8) 2 12″—VM-351†
Amsterdam Concertgebouw Orch.—von
Karajan 2 12″—PD-68127/9S
Berlin State Opera Orch.—Strauss
2 12″—PD-66902/3
Orch of the Chapel of the Queen of Bel-
gium 2 12″—G-W1555/6

Don Quixote, Op. 35 Tone Poem Orchestra
(Fantastic Variations on a Knightly
Theme)
Philadelphia Orch.—Ormandy (Emanuel
Feuermann, vlc; Alex. Hilsberg, vl;
Samuel Lifschey, vla)
5 12″—VM-720†
Pittsburgh Symphony—Reiner (Gregor
Piatigorsky vlc; Henri Temianka, vl;
Vladimir Bakaleinikoff, vla)
5 12″—CM-506†
Bavarian State Orch.—Richard Strauss
Oswald Uhl, vlc; Moraseh, vl; Haass,
(vla) 5 12″—PD-67800/4
DUPLICATION: Berlin State Opera
Orch.—Strauss, PD-35007/11: PD-
27320/4

Festmusik zue Feier des 2600 jährigen
Bestehens des Kaiserreichs Japan
(Festival Music Commemorating the
2600th Anniversary of the Japanese Em-
pire)
Bavarian State Opera Orch.—R. Strauss
2 12″—PD-67599/600

(Ein) Heldenleben, Op. 40 Tone Poem
Eng. A Hero's Life
Royal Philharmonic Orch.—Beecham
5 12″—G-DB6620/4†
Philadelphia Orch.—Ormandy
5 12″—VM-610†
Cleveland Orch.—Rodzinski
5 12″—CM-441†
Amsterdam Concertgebouw Orch.—Men-
gelberg 5 12″—T-SK3181/5
Pittsburgh Symphony Orch.—Reiner
5 12″—CM-748†
Bavarian State Orch.—Strauss (FON-
96096/100) 5 12″—PD-67756/60

Intermezzo See under Operas

(2) Marches, Op. 57 Orchestra
1. Militärmarsch 2. Kriegsmarsch
Berlin State Opera Orch.—Melichar
10″—PD-25090
—No. 1 only
Berlin State Orch.—Mayer
[Uhl: Symphonic March] 12″—PD-57316

Morgen See under Songs

Olympische Hymne Chorus & Orchestra
(R. Lubahn)
Chorus & Orch.—Bruno Kittel
10″—O-4741
Berliner Solistenvereinigung & State
Orch.—B. Seidler-Winkler
12″—G-EH982
[Winkler: Olympic Fanfares & Egk:
Olympic Hymn]

OPERAS In German

(DIE) AEGYPTISCHE HELENA, Op. 75
1927/8
No recordings available

ARABELLA, Op. 79 1933

ACT I

Aber der Richtige—wenn's einen gibt für mich; Ich weiss nicht wie du blist 2 Sopranos
Margarete Teschemacher & Irma Beilke
12"—G-DB4675
[Das war sehr gut, Mandryka]
Marta Fuchs & Elsa Wieber
12"—T-E1477
[Love Duet, Act II, M. Fuchs & P. Schoeffler]
Viorica Ursuleac & Margit Bokor
10"—PD-62712
[Love Duet, Act. II, V. Ursuleac & A. Jerger]

Mein Elemer (Act I Finale)
Tiana Lemnitz (s)   12"—G-DB5606
[Love Duet, Act II, with G. Hüsch]

ACT II

So wie Sie sind, so hab' ich keinen Menschen; Und Du wirst mein Gebieter sein (Love Duet: Arabella & Mandryka)
NOTE: *The Polydor version begins "So wie Sie sind" and omits the orchestral conclusion. The Telefunken version begins somewhat later with "Und Du wirst mein" and includes the orchestral conclusion. The Electrola version has not been heard for identification.*
Viorica Ursuleac & Alfred Jerger
10"—PD-62712
[Aber der Richtige, Ursuleac & Bokor]
Marta Fuchs & Paul Schoeffler
12"—T-E1477
[Aber der Richtige, M. Fuchs & E. Wieber]
Tiana Lemnitz & Gerhard Hüsch
12"—G-DB5606
[Arabella's Monologue—Mein Elemer, Lemnitz]

ACT III

Das war sehr gut, Mandryka (Finale Act III)
Und diesen unberührten Trunk Sop. & Bar.
Viorica Ursuleac & Alfred Jerger
10"—PD-62711
—Das war (Arabella) only
Margarete Teschemacher 12"—G-DB4675
[Aber der Richtige, w. Beilke]

ARIADNE AUF NAXOS, Op. 60 1912 I Act
NOTE: *Originally part of the incidental music for Molière's "Le Bourgeois Gentilhomme." It was enlarged and revised in 1916 as a separate work in 2 acts.*

Grossmachtigste Prinzessin Recit. & Aria of Zerbinetta
Lea Piltti   12"—G-DB7606
Maria Ivogün   12"—G-DB4405
Adele Kern   12—PD-27310

Seien wir wieder gut (Aria of the Composer)
Polyna Stoska (s), in CX-294

CAPRICCIO 1942

Ihre Liebe schlägt mir entgegen
Du Spiegelbild der verliebten Madelaine Sop.
Viorica Ursuleac   12"—PD-68125

DAPHNE 1 Act 1938

Excerpts
Verwandlung der Daphne ("Wind—spiele mit mir")
O wie gerne blieb' ich bei dir - Soprano
Götter! Brüder im hohen Olympos! Tenor
Margarete Teschemacher & Torsten Ralf
2 12"—G-DB4627/8

ELEKTRA, Op. 58 1 Act 1909
No recordings available

FEUERSNOT, Op. 50 1 Act 1901
Love Scene Orchestra
Royal Philharmonic Orch.—Beecham
12"—V-12-0289

INTERMEZZO, Op. 72
Waltz Scene Orchestra
Berlin State Opera Orch.—Knappertsbusch   12"—O-6744
Vienna Philharmonic—Karl Alwin
12"—G-AN740

(DER) ROSENKAVALIER, Op. 59 3 Acts 1911
Eng. The Rose-Bearer (or, Knight of the Rose)
Fr. Le Chevalier à la Rose

Abridged recording
Soloists & Vienna State Opera Company, Chorus & Orch.—Robert Heger
13 12"—VM-196†
(G-DB2060/72, in GM-192†)
The Cast:
Fürstin (Feldmarschallin) ..... Lotte Lehmann (s)
Baron Ochs .... Richard Mayr (bs)
Oktavian ...... Maria Olczewska (ms)
Faninal .... Viktor Madin (b)
Sophie .... Elisabeth Schumann (s)
Marianne .... Anne Michalsky (s)
Valzacchi .... Herman Gallos (t)
Annina .... Bella Paalen (s)
Kommissarius .... Karl Ettl (bs)
Wirt .... William Wergnick (t)
NOTE: *While a little more than half of the extremely long score is recorded here, there are few excisions of really important material. Exact page references to the vocal score are given in the booklet accompanying the album so the principal cuts need only be roughly indicated below.*

ACT I: 3 pages between Sides 4/5; 20 pages between Sides 5/6 and 16 pages in Side 6 (Marschallin-Baron Scene); 31 pages between sides 6/7 (Hairdressing scene, from which the Italian Serenade is available on isolated discs). Brief cuts on sides 8 & 10.

ACT II: 4½ pages between Sides 10/1 (Prelude and part of opening scene); 33 pages between Sides 13/4 (Baron, Sophie, etc.; signing of the marriage contract); 55½ pages between Sides 14/5 (Duel and confusion).

ACT III: 60 pages between Sides 18/20 (the farce played on Ochs, entrance of the Police, Faninal, etc.)

Waltz Movements (Rosenkavalier Waltz)
Orchestra

NOTE: *The celebrated Rosenkavalier Waltz (or more correctly, Waltz Movements) is a concert work assembled from the various waltz passages running throughout the opera.*

Saxon State Orch.—Karl Böhm
               12″—G-DB4557
Philadelphia Orch.—Ormandy
               12″—V-18390
Cleveland Orch.—Artur Rodzinski
               12″—C-11542D
Minneapolis Symphony—Ormandy
          2 10″—V-1758/9
[Stix: Spielerei]
Bavarian State Orch.—Richard Strauss
(FON-96077)   12″—PD-67729
Berlin Philharmonic—Bruno Walter
(C-LX60) (C-LFX94) 12″—C-67892D
DUPLICATIONS: Berlin Philharmonic—
Kleiber, U-E853: T-E1688; Berlin State
Opera Orch.—Blech, G-C1819: G-EH350:
G-FKX12; Grand Symphony Orch.—
Heger, O-7782

—**Arr. 2 Pianos**
Vitya Vronsky & Victor Babin (duo)
               12″—V-13150
—**Arr. Violin**
Siegfried Borries, G-DB4591; Váša
Příhoda, PD-47185: CET-LL3002; Fer-
raresi, G-S10493

Orchestral Suite
Hallé Orch.—Barbirolli (Arr. Strauss)
         3 12″—G-C3556/8
[Wagner: Lohengrin, Prelude Act III]
Philadelphia Orch.—Ormandy
(Arr. Strauss)   3 12″—CM-742†
Cincinnati Orch.—Goossens
(Arr. Antal Dorati) 3 12″—VM-997†
Individual Excerpts

ACT I

Introduction Orchestra
(Sides 1 & 2 in VM-196)
Vienna Philharmonic—Heger
[Introduction, Act III] 12″—G-DB2143

Arie des Sängers: Di rigori armato Tenor
Eng. **Italian Serenade** (Omitted in
VM-196† between Sides 6 & 7)
(Sung in Italian, as called for in the
score)
Helge Roswaenge   10″—G-DA4465
[Cornelius: Barbier von Bagdad—Ach,
das Lied]
Peter Anders   10″—T-A2321
[Rimsky-Korsakov: Sadko—Song of
India]
Einar Andersson   10″—G-X6015
[Flotow: Marta—M'appari]
Herbert E. Groh   10″—O-26132
[Cornelius: Barbier von Bagdad—
Sanfter, Schlummer]

Monolog der Marschallin
(Sides 7/9 in VM-196)

Kann mich auch an ein Mädel erinnern

Die Zeit sie ist ein sonderbar Ding
Elisabeth Ohms (s)   12″—PD-66901

—**Die Zeit only** (Side 9 in VM-196)
Lotte Lehmann   12″—P-PXO1014
[Mozart: Nozze di Figaro—Porgi amor]

ACT II

Presentation of the Silver Rose 2 Sopranos
(Sides 12/3 in VM-196)
—**Arr. Orchestra**
Contained in orchestral suites above

Da lieg' ich Bass (Baron)

Wart', dich hau' i' z'samm

Herr Kavalier! Bass & Alto
(Baron & Annina)
Eng. **Letter Scene & Waltzes**
(Finale **Act II**)
A. Huberty & M. Ant Almona
(in French)   12″—PAT-PDT83
—**Herr Kavalier! only**
Alexander Kipnis & Else Ruziczka
               12″—V-7894
[Wagner: Meistersinger—Ansprache des
Pogner, Kipnis only]

ACT III

Introduction
Vienna Philharmonic—Heger
[Introduction, Act I] 12″—G-DB2143
Waltz Movements
Bavarian State Orch.—R. Strauss
             12″—PD-67729
Berlin Philharmonic—Melichar
(PD-513724)   12″—PD-57063

Trio (Side 24 in VM-196)

Ich weiss auch nix—Marie Theres'!

Hab' mir's gelobt, ihn lieb zu haben
Viorica Ursuleac, Erna Berger, Tiana
Lemnitz   12″—PD-67075
[Ist ein Traum, Act III]
Elisabeth Ohms, Adele Kern, Elfriede
Marherr   12″—PD-66931
[Ist ein Traum, Act III]

Ist ein Traum (Final Duet)
(Sides 25 & 26 in VM-196)
Esther Rethy & Elizabeth Höngen
             12″—G-DB5617
Tiana Lemnitz & Erna Berger
[Hab' mir's gelobt] 12″—PD-67075
Adele Kern & Elfriede Marherr
[Hab' mir's gelobt] 12″—PD-66931

SALOME, Op. 54 I Act 1905

Salomes Tanz der sieben Schleier Orch.
Eng. **Salome's Dance of the Seven Veils**
Amsterdam Concertgebouw Orch.—
von Karajan   12″—PD-68126
Cleveland Orch.—Rodzinski
             12″—C-11781D
Saxon State Orch.—Böhm
             12″—G-DB4639
Vienna Philharmonic—Krauss
             12″—T-SK3199
Philadelphia Orch.—Stokowski
        2 12″—V-7259/60
[Eicheim: Japanese Nocturne]
(G-AW207/8)

DUPLICATIONS: Berlin State Opera
Orch.—R. Strauss, PD-66827; Berlin
Philharmonic—Bruno Walter, C-67814D:
C-LX39: C-GQX10705; Pasdeloup Orch.
Orch.—Coppola, G-DB4932; Berlin State
Opera Orch.—Knappertsbusch, O-6788

**Final Scene: Salome und das Haupt des
Jokanaan**
(Salome and the Head of John) Soprano

**Ah! Du wolltest mich nicht deinem Mund
Fr. Tu n'as pas voulu**
NOTE: *The brief outcries of Herod are omitted
in both versions below. The endings are also
abbreviated.*
Liselotte Enck   2 12"—T-SK3348/9
Marjorie Lawrence (in French)
(G-DB4933/4)   2 12"—V-8682/3

SCHLAGOBERS, Op. 70 Ballet-Pantomime
Eng. Whipped Cream
Schlagoberswalzer

Einzug der Prinzessin Pralinée—March
Eng. Whipped Cream Waltz & Entry of
the Princess Pralinée—March
Berlin Philharmonic—Melichar
12"—PD-27300

In der Konditorküche Orchestra
Eng. In the Confectioner's Kitchen
Berlin Philharmonic—Melichar
12"—PD-27324
[Don Quixote, Pt. 9, dir. R. Strauss]

Sinfonia Domestica
See under Symphonia Domestica

Sonata, E flat major, Op. 18 Violin & Piano
Ginette Neveu & Gustav Beck
4 12"—G-DB4663/6
[Tartini: Variations on a theme of
Corelli]

SONGS (LIEDER) In German

Collection
Ständchen; Morgen; Allerseelen;
Zueignung
Lotte Lehmann (s) & Paul Ulanowsky
(pf)   2 10"—CX-270

Individual Songs

**Ach, Lieb', ich muss nun scheiden,
Op. 21, No. 5** (Dahn)
Helge Roswaenge (t) & B. Seidler-
Winkler (pf)   10"—G-DA4412
[Freundliche Vision]

Allerseelen, Op. 10, No. 8 (von Gilm)
Eng. All Soul's Day
Lotte Lehmann, in CX-270
Richard Tauber (t) & Percy Kahn (pf)
10"—P-RO20555
[Ich trage meine Minne]
Kirsten Flagstad (s) & pf. acc.
10"—V-1726
[Wagner: Walküre—Ho-Yo-To-Ho]
DUPLICATIONS: Karl Hammes,
G-EG6213; Franz Völker, PD-10305;
Nelson Eddy, C-17185D
In English: Webster Booth, G-B9502

Cäcilie, Op. 27, No. 2 (Hart)
Jussi Björling (t) & Harry Ebert (pf)
[Morgen]   10"—G-DA1704
DUPLICATIONS: Viorica Ursuleac,
PD-30017; Julius Patzak, PD-23923

Freundliche Vision, Op. 48, No. 1
(Bierbaum)
Paul Schoeffler (b) & E. Lush (pf)
10"—D-M601
[Traum durch die Dämmerung]
Elisabeth Schumann (s)
[Wiegenlied]   12"—G-DB1065
Helge Roswaenge (t) & B. Seidler-
Winkler (pf)   10"—G-DA4412
[Ach, Lieb' ich muss nun scheiden]
Franz Völker (t) & G. Steeger (pf)
10"—PD-62817
[Traum durch die Dämmerung]
Heinrich Schlusnus (b) & Franz
Rupp (pf)   10"—PD-90167
[Traum durch die Dämmerung]
DUPLICATION: Leo Slezak, PD-21849

Frühlingsfeier
Viorica Ursuleac (s)   10"—PD-30017
[Cäcilie]

Geduld, Op. 10, No. 5 (von Gilm)
Henrich Schlusnus (b) & Franz
Rupp (pf)   10"—PD-62714
[Morgen]

(Die) Georgine
Luise Willer (c)   12"—PD-67153
[Traum durch die Dämmerung]

Heimkehr, Op. 15, No. 5 (Schack)
Margherita Perras (s) & Paul
Baumgartner (pf)   10"—G-DA6027
[Ständchen]
Heinrich Schlusnus (b) & pf. acc.
[Ständchen]   10"—PD-30030

Heimliche Aufforderung, Op. 27, No. 3
(Mackay)
Peter Anders (t)   10"—T-A2684
[Ständchen]
Heinrich Schlusnus (b) & pf. acc.
[Wolf: Heimweh]   10"—PD-62789
DUPLICATIONS: Karl Schmitt-Walter,
T-A1931; Piroska Anday, RAD-SP8005
In French: Georges Thill, C-LF156

Ich liebe dich, Op. 37, No. 3 (Liliencrom)
Heinrich Schlusnus (b) & S. Peschko (pf)
[Zueignung]   10"—PD-62796

Ich trage meine Minne, Op. 32, No. 1
(Henckell)
Richard Tauber (t) & Percy Kahn (pf)
[Allerseelen]   10"—P-RO20555
Heinrich Schlusnus (b) & S. Peschko (pf)
[Wolf: Gebet]   10"—PD-62784
Peter Anders (t) & Berlin Philharmonic
—Lutze   10"—T-A2782
[Traum durch die Dämmerung]
DUPLICATION: Leo Slezak, PD-21848

Liebeshymnus, Op. 32, No. 3
(Karl Henckell)
Karl Hammes (b) & B. Seidler-
Winkler (pf)   10"—G-EG3953
[Schlechtes Wetter]

Morgen, Op. 27, No. 4 (Mackay)
Lotte Lehmann, in CX-270
Elisabeth Schumann (s) with Isolde
Menges (vl) & Orch. 12"—G-DB1010
[Ständchen]
Heinrich Schlusnus (b) & Franz
Rupp (pf) 10"—PD-62714
[Geduld]
Jussi Björling (t) & pf. acc.
[Cäcilie] 10"—G-DA1704
DUPLICATION: L. Slezak, PD-23017
In English: Webster Booth, G-C3418
In Italian: Cloe Elmo, CET-TI7011

Nachtgang, Op. 29, No. 3 (von Gilm)
Heinrich Schlusnus (b) & Raucheisen
(pf) 10"—PD-30007
[Winterliebe]
Ivar Andrésen (bs) & pf. acc.
[Ruhe, meine Seele] 12"—C-DWX1319

Ruhe, meine Seele, Op. 27, No. 1 (Henckell)
Ivar Andrésen (bs) & pf. acc.
[Nachtgang] 12"—C-DWX1319

Schlechtes Wetter, Op. 69, No. 5 (Heine)
Karl Hammes (b) & B. Seidler-
Winkler (pf) 10"—G-EG3953
[Liebeshymnus]

Ständchen, Op. 17, No. 2 (Schack)
Eng. Serenade
Lotte Lehmann, in CX-270
Elisabeth Schumann (s) 12"—G-DB1010
[Morgen]
K. Schmitt-Walter (b) 10"—T-A1946
[Wolf: Hiemweh]
Margherita Perras (s) & Paul
Baumgartner (pf) 10"—G-DA6027
[Heimkehr]
DUPLICATIONS: Gianna Pederzini,
G-DA5426; Peter Anders, T-A2684;
Heinrich Schlusnus, PD-30030; J. Patzak,
PD-23923; Leo Slezak, PD-23017
In French: Georges Thill, C-LF156
In English: Heddle Nash, G-B9412
—Arr. Piano
Walter Gieseking, C-17138D

Traum durch die Dämmerung, Op. 29, No. 1
(Bierbaum)
Eng. Dream in the Twilight
Paul Schoeffler (b) & E. Lush (pf)
[Freundliche Vision] 10"—D-M601
Heinrich Schlusnus (b) & Franz
Rupp (pf) 10"—PD-90167
[Freundliche Vision]
Franz Völker (t) & Gerhard Steeger (pf)
[Freundliche Vision] 10"—PD-62817
DUPLICATIONS: Peter Anders, T-A2782;
Paul Bender, G-EG6107
In English: Norman Cordon, V-2165
In Italian: Gianna Pederzini, G-DA5386

Wiegenlied, Op. 41, No. 1 (Dehmel)
Eng. Cradle song, or Lullaby
Elisabeth Schumann (s)
[Freundliche Vision] 12"—G-DB1065
Emmy Bettendorf (s) & Michael
Rauscheisen (pf) 12"—O-7962
[Schubert: Ungeduld]
Emmi Leisner (c) 12"—PD-27326
[Brahms: Wie bist du]
In Italian: P. Pauli, G-DB2012

Winterliebe, Op. 48, No. 5 (Henckell)
Heinrich Schlusnus (b) & M.
Raucheisen (pf) 10"—PD-30007
[Nachtgang]

Winterweihe, Op. 48, No. 4 (Henckell)
Franz Völker (t) & Franz Rupp (pf)
[Allerseelen] 10"—PD-10305
Karl Hammes (b) & B. Seidler-
Winkler (pf) 10"—G-EG6213
[Allerseelen]

Zueignung, Op. 1), No. 1 (von Gilm)
Eng. Devotion
Lotte Lehmann, in CX-270
Heinrich Schlusnus (b) & pf. acc.
10"—PD-62796
[Ich liebe dich]
[Wolf: Er ist's, on PD-62789]
DUPLICATIONS: Karl Schmitt-Walter,
T-A1931; Nelson Eddy, C-17185D; Leo
Slezak, PD-21848

Symphonia Domestica, Op. 53 Orchestra
Philadelphia Orch.—Ormandy
5 12"—VM-520†
La Scala Orch.—Schuricht
4 12"—G-DB5418/21S

Symphonic Poems
See under **Also sprach Zarathustra; Don
Juan; Don Quixote; Heldenleben; Till
Eulenspiegel; Tod und Verklärung**

Symphonies
See under **Alpensinfonie, Aus Italien,
Symphonia Domestica**

Thus Spake Zarathustra
See **Also Sprach Zarathustra**

Till Eulenspiegels lustige Streiche, Op. 38
Tone Poem
Cleveland Orch.—Rodzinski
2 12"—CX-210†
Boston Symphony Orch.—Koussevitzky
2 12"—VM-1029†
(G-DB6268/9) (Also V-V1†)
Orch. of the "Maggio Musicale"—Gui
2 12"—CET-BB25133/4
La Scala Orch, Milan—Clemens Krauss
2 12"—D-K1681/2
Saxon State Orch.—Böhm
2 12"—G-DB5621/2
Berlin Philharmonic—Furtwängler
2 12"—PD-95410/1
[Berlioz: Rakoczy March]
DUPLICATIONS: Vienna Philharmonic—
Krauss, T-SK3139/40; BBC Symphony
Orch.—Busch, V-11724/5: G-DB2187/8;
Berlin State Opera Orch.—R. Strauss,
PD-66887/8. PD-516633/4; Paris Con-
servatory Orch.— Giardino,
PAT-PDT69/70; Berlin Philharmonic—
Kleiber, U-E651/2

Tod und Verklärung, Op. 24 Tone Poem
Eng. Death and Transfiguration
Philadelphia Orch.—Ormandy
3 12"—CM-613†
New York City Symphony—Stokowski
3 12"—VM-1006†
All American Orch.—Stokowski
3 12"—CM-492†
Philadelphia Orch.—Stokowski
(G-DB2324/6) 3 12"—VM-217†
Berlin Philharmonic—de Sabata
(CET-RR8011/3) 3 12"—PD-67516/8

STRAVINSKY, Igor (1882-   )

Stravinsky's life-long stylistic experiments have seemingly halted in his present neo-classicism. His restless search is baffling only if we expect from this Russian contemporary, the straight-lined development and steady deepening of a musical personality that was common among eighteenth century composers.

The music of Stravinsky on records fairly thoroughly explores all areas of his various styles, save for those early works written under the influence of his first important teacher, Rimsky-Korsakov.

Apollon Musagète Ballet
Prologue; Apollo's Dance; Pas d'action; Calliope's Dance; Polyhymnia's Dance; Terpsichore's Dance; Apollo's Dance; Pas de Deux; Coda; Apotheosis
Boyd Neel String Orchestra—Neel
4 12"—**D-X167/70**

(Le) Baiser de la Fée
Ballet Allégorie en 4 Tableaux 1928
Divertimento: Sinfonia; Danses Suisses; Valse; Scherzo; Pas de Deux
Victor Symphony Orch.—Stravinsky
3 12"—**VM-1202†**
Symphony Orch. of Mexico—Stravinsky
(Mexican Victor)   3 12"—**VM-931†**

Capriccio Piano & Orchestra
Jesús María Sanromá & Boston Symphony Orch.—Koussevitzky   2 12"—**VM-685†**
Igor Stravinsky & Straram Orch.—Ansermet   3 12"—**C-GQX10519/20; GQX10556**

(Le) Chant du Rossignol
Symphonic Poem 1917
Eng. **The Song of the Nightingale**
(Arranged from the opera "The Nightingale" composed in 1914)
Cincinnati Symphony Orch.—Goossens
3 12"—**VM-1041†**
[Chabrier: Marche joyeuse]

Circus Polka
—Arr. 2 Pianos Babin
Vitya Vronsky & Victor Babin
[Tango] (in CM-576)   12"—**C-72084M**

Concertino for String Quartet 1920
Gordon Quartet, in CH-B6
(Limited Edition)

CONCERTOS

E flat major ("Dumbarton Oaks")
(for 16 Instruments)
Dumbarton Oaks Festival Orch.—Stravinsky   2 12"—**K-DM1**
Chamber Orch. of Hamburg State Philharmonic—Schmidt-Isserstedt
(U-F18092/3)   2 12"—**T-E2994/5**

Piano & Orchestra of Wind Instruments
Soulima Stravinsky & Paris Wind Instrument Society—Oubradous
2 12"—**G-DB11105/6**

Violin & Orchestra, D major
Samuel Dushkin & Lamoureux Orch.—Stravinsky   3 12"—**VOX-173**
(PD-95500/2) (PD-566173/5)

Ebony Concerto
Woody Herman Band—Stravinsky
12"—**C-7479M**

Etudes, Op. 7 Piano
—**No. 12, F sharp minor**
Benno Moiseiwitsch   12"—**G-C2998**
[Debussy: Jardins sous la pluie; Poulenc: Mouvement perpétuel No. 1]
—**(2) Etudes only**
(Numbering undetermined)
Soulima Stravinsky   12"—**BAM-27**
[Bach: Wohltemperiertes Clavier, No. 13]

Feu d' Artifice, Op. 4 Fantasy for Orchestra
Eng. **Fireworks**
N. Y. Philharmonic-Symphony Orch.—Stravinsky
(in CM-653†)   12"—**C-12459D**
[Oiseau de Feu, Pt. 7]
Chicago Symphony Orch.—Defauw
12"—**V-11-9447**
[Fauré: Pelléas et Mélisande—No. 3, Sicilienne]
EIAR Symphony Orch.—de Sabata
12"—**CET-PP60009**
[Glazunov: Medieval Suite—Scherzo]
Berlin Philharmonic—Kleiber
12"—**U-F14385**
[Berlioz: Racoczy March]
(also on T-E1205)

(The) Fire Bird See: Oiseau de Feu

Four Norwegian Moods
N. Y. Philharmonic-Symphony Orch.—Stravinsky   12"—**C-12371D**

(L') Histoire d'un Soldat Ballet
(C. F. Ramuz)
Eng. **The Soldier's Tale** Septet
—Concert Version
1) The Soldier's March; 2) Little Tunes beside a Brook; 3) Pastoral; 4) Royal March; 5) Little Concert; 6) Tango—Waltz—Ragtime; 7) The Devil's Dance; 8) Little Choral; 9) The Devil's Song; 10) Great Choral; 11) Triumphal March of the Devil
Members of Boston Symphony Orch.—Bernstein
(in VM-1197†)   3 12"—**V-12-0136/8**
[with Octet]
—**No. 3, 8 & 9 omitted**
Chamber Orch.—Stravinsky
(C-LFX263/5)   3 12"—**CM-184†**
(C-GQX10672/4)

Jeu de Cartes—Ballet in 3 Deals 1937
Eng. **The Card Party (Game)**
Ger. **Das Kartenspiel**
—Suite
Berlin Philharmonic Orch.—Stravinsky   3 12"—**T-SK2460/2**
(U-G14244/6)

(Les) Noces Ballet
Eng. **The Wedding** (Craig)
Soloists, Cho., & Orch.—Stravinsky
(C-LWX253/5)   3 12"—**CM-204†**
Soloists: Kate Winter (s), Linda Seymour (c), Parry Jones (t), Roy Henderson (b)
Pianists: B. Mason, L. Heward, E. Lush, C. E. Benbow

—**Part only**
(Excerpt from above recording)
10″—**C-DB1306**
(Columbia History of Music, Vol. V:
CM-361) (C-DB1790)

Octet Wind Instruments
Sinfonia: Theme & Variations: Finale
Members of the Boston Symphony—
Bernstein
(in VM-1197†) 2 12″—**V-12-0139/40**
[with Histoire d'un Soldat]
Moyse (fl), Godeau (cl), Dherin & Piard
(bns), Foveau & Vignal (trpts), Lafosse
& Delbos (tbns)—Stravinsky
2 12″—**CX-25**†
(C-LWX222/3) (C-GQX11086/7)

(**L'**) **Oiseau de feu** Ballet
Eng. **The Fire Bird** 1910
NOTE: *Stravinsky has released a total of three
suites from the ballet, "L'Oiseau de feu." The
first is elaborately scored for a large orchestra.
The second suite (the one usually recorded) is
somewhat simplified and can be performed
with a smaller orchestra; it omits two movements (the Supplication of the Fire Bird & the
Scherzo) but adds the Berceuse & Finale lacking in the first suite. The third suite contains
all of the music of the second suite, the two deleted movements, as well as short bridge passages. For convenience, we have listed them as
Suite III and then Suite II.*

—**Suite III** (New augmented version)
1) **Jardin enchanté de Kastcheï & Danse
de l'oiseau de feu;** 2) **Supplications de
l'oiseau de feu (Pas de Deux);** 3) **Jeu
des Princesses avec les pommes d'or
(Scherzo);** 4) **Ronde des Princesses
(Khorovod);** 5) **Danse infernale de tous
les sujets de Kastcheï;** 6) **Berceuse;** 7)
Finale
N. Y. Philharmonic-Symphony Orch.—
Stravinsky 4 12″—**CM-653**†
[Feu d'artifice]
Symphony Orch.—Stravinsky
(C-L2279/82) 4 12″—**CM-115**†
(C-GQX10581/4) (C-D15122/5)
(Older recording)

—**Suite II** . (Earlier version)
(Omitting Nos. 2 & 3 of above Suite)
London Philharmonic—Ansermet
(D-K1574/6) 3 12″—**D-ED30**†
NOTE: *This recording contains the Scherzo (No.
3) from the original version.*
Philharmonia Orch.—Galliera
3 12″—**C-DCX70/2**
Berlin Philharmonic—Fried
2 12″—**PD-516650/1**
NOTE: *All Stokowski versions cut the Finale.*
NBC Symphony Orch.—Stokowski
3 12″—**VM-933**†
[Tchaikowsky: Humoresque]
Philadelphia Orch.—Stokowski
(G-DB2882/4†) 3 12″—**VM-291**†
[Shostakovich: Prelude No. 14]
All American Orch.—Stokowski
3 12″—**CM-446**†
[Shostakovich: Prelude No. 14]
—**Berceuse only**
Colonne Orch.—Pierné, O-123525

Pastorale (Originally a vocalise with wind
quartet)
—**Arr. Orch.** Stokowski
Philadelphia Orch.—Stokowski
10″—**V-1998**
[Chopin-Stokowski: Prelude, D minor,
Op. 28, No. 24]
—**Arr. Violin**
Joseph Szigeti & Wind Quartet—
Stravinsky 12″—**C-72495D**
[Russian Maiden Song, Szigeti &
Stravinsky]
Samuel Dushkin & Wind Quartet—
Stravinsky 10″—**C-LF129**
[Petrouchka—Danse russe]
Joseph Szigeti & N. de Magaloff (pf)
12″—**C-7304M**
[Rimsky-Korsakov: Flight of the Bumble
Bee & Szymanowsky: Fontaine
d'Arethusa]

Petrouchka Ballet 1910/11
(Scènes burlesques en 4 Tableaux)
1) **The Shrove-Tide Fair;** 2) **Russian
Dance;** 3) **In Petrouchka's Room;** 4) **In
the Moor's Room;** 5) **Dance of the Bal-
lerina and the Moor;** 6) **Grand Carnival
Dances of Gypsies, Coachmen and Grooms,
The Maskers;** 7) **Death of Petrouchka**
Complete Recordings
Philadelphia Orch.—Stokowski
4 12″—**VM-575**†
(G-DB3511/4) in GM-328†)
London Philharmonic—Ansermet
(D-K1388/92) 5 12″—**D-ED2**†
Excerpts
—**Nos. 1, 2, 3, 4, 6 only**
Symphony Orch.—Stravinsky
3 12″—**C-GQX10278/80**
—**Nos. 1 (Part), 2, 3, 6 only**
N. Y. Philharmonic-Symphony Orch.—
Stravinsky 2 12″—**CX-177**†
DUPLICATION: Colonne Orch.—Pierné,
O-123577/9
—**Carnival & Showman and his Puppets**
Philadelphia Orch.—Stokowski
(in VM-1064) 12″—**V-11-9234**
—**Russian Dance only**
Symphony Orch.—Goehr, in V-C30:
G-C2925
—**Arr. Piano**
Claudio Arrau, PD-90025; Nikita de
Magaloff, RAD-RZ3033; Luboshutz &
Nemenoff (duo), V-2096
—**Arr. Violin & Piano**
Samuel Dushkin & Igor Stravinsky,
C-LF129; Joseph Szigeti & N. de Maga-
loff, C-LB38: C-17130D; Bronislaw Gim-
pel & Artur Balsam, in VOX-616

(3) **Pièces pour Quatour à Cordes**
Eng. **3 Pieces for String Quartet** 1920
Gordon Quartet, in CH-B6
(Limited Edition)
(5) **Pièces faciles** 1917 2 Pianos
Arthur Gold & Robert Fizdale, in CH-A6
(Limited Edition)
Pulcinella Ballet with Song
(after Pergolesi) Small Orch.
1) **Sinfonia;** 2) **Serenata;** 3) **Scherzino,**

Allegro, Andantino; 4) Tarantella; 5)
Toccata; 6) Gavotta con due Variazioni;
7) Duetto; 8) Minuetto and Finale
—Nos. 5 & 6 only
Symphony Orch.—Stravinsky
12"—C-GQX11064
—Arr. Violin & Piano
Stravinsky (as "Suite Italienne")
—Arr. 'Cello & Piano Piatigorsky
(Titled: Aria; Largo; Tarantella; Sere-
nata; Minuet & Finale)
Florence Hooten & Gerald Moore
2 12"—D-X263/4
Quartets Strings See: **Concertino** &
3 Pièces pour Quatuor à Cordes
Rite of Spring See: Sacre du Printemps

(LE) ROSSIGNOL Opera 3 Acts 1923

NOTE: *The second and third acts of this opera
furnished the material for the symphonic poem,
"Le Chant du Rossignol"—also staged as a ballet. For recorded excerpts see "Chant du Rossignol."*

Russian Maiden Song Violin & Piano
Joseph Szigeti & Igor Stravinsky
[Pastorale] 12"—C-72495D
(Le) Sacre du Printemps Ballet
(Pictures of Pagan Russia)
N. Y. Philharmonic-Symphony Orch.—
Stravinsky 4 12"—CM-417†
San Francisco Symphony—Pierre
Monteux 4 12"—VM-1052†
Philadelphia Orch.—Stokowski
(G-AW209/12) 4 12"—VM-74†
Symphony Orch.—Stravinsky
5 12"—C-LX119/23
(C-D152137) (C-GQX10284/8)
Amsterdam Concertgebouw Orch.— van
Beinum 4 12"—D-K1727/30†

Scènes de Ballet (from "Seven Lively Arts")
N. Y. Philharmonic Symphony Orch.—
Stravinsky 2 12"—CX-245†
Serenade, A major Piano
Hymne; Romanza; Rondoletto; Cadenza
(Finale)
Igor Stravinsky
(C-LW22/3) 2 10"—C-GQ7194/5
Sonata for Two Pianos 1943/44
Gino Gorini & Sergio Lorenzi
2 12"—G-DB11308/9
[Debussy: Lindaraja]
Arthur Gold & Robert Fizdale, in CH-A6
(Limited Edition)

Song of the Volga Boatmen
Arr. Orchestra Stravinsky
Boston Symphony Orch.—Koussevitsky
(in VM-546†) 12"—V-15364
[Copland: El Salón México, Pt. 3]

Suite Italienne Arr. from part of the
Pulcinella Suite
See under **Pulcinella**

Suite No. 2 pour petit orchestre
(Originally for Piano 4-Hands; arranged
for small orchestra by Stravinsky)
Marche; Valse; Polka; Galop
Danish State Radio Orch.—Nikolai
Malko 12"—G-Z297

SUITES
See also under **Oiseau de feu; Petrouchka;
Pulcinella**
Symphonie des Psaumes
Chorus & Orchestra In Latin 1930
Eng. **Symphony of Psalms**
(The text is taken from Psalms 39, 40
& 150)
Alexis Vlassof Choir & Straram Orch.—
Stravinsky 3 12"—CM-162†
(C-LFX179/81) (C-GQX10513/5)
Symphony in 3 Movements 1945
N. Y. Philharmonic-Symphony Orch.—
Stravinsky 3 12"—CM-680†
(C-LX1042/4)
Tango Voice & Piano
—Arr. 2 Pianos Babin
Vitya Vronsky & Victor Babin
(in CM-576) 12"—C-72084D
[Circus Polka]

STROZZI, Barbara (fl. c.1644-1664)
*However circumscribed by nature and social
conventions, woman composers pop up even in
the 17th century; the output of this adopted
daughter of the poet, Giulio Strozzi is considerable—madrigals, ariettas, duets, cantatas, and
sacred music.*
Amor dormiglione
Yvon Le Marc'Hadour (b) & R. Gerlin
(harpsichord) 10"—PAT-PG86
[F. Caccini: Dispiegate]

SUK, Josef (1874-1935)
*A Czech Romantic, celebrated both as violinist
and composer. Suk's compositions start under
the influence of Schubert, Brahms and his
teacher, Dvořák, but become progressively more
daring in harmony and more intricate in rhy-
thm.*
Appassionata, Op. 17, No. 2 Violin & Piano
Ginette Neveu & Jean Neveu
12"—V-11-9840
[Quasi Ballata] (G-DB6359)
Ginette Neveu & Bruno Seidler-
Winkler 12"—G-DB4514
[Chopin: Nocturne, C sharp minor, Op.
Posth.]
Jarka Stěpánek & Věra Repková
10"—U-A12166
[Ondříček: Humoresque-Idyll]
Barcarolle String Quartet
Suk Quartet 10"—U-B12236
[Smetana: String Quartet No. 2, D
minor, Part 7]
Burleska, Op. 17, No. 4
Violin & Piano
Ginette Neveu & Jean Neveu
12"—V-12-0154
[Un poco triste] (G-DB6260)
Nathan Milstein & Artur Balsam
12"—C-71498D
[Wieniawski: Scherzo Tarantelle]
Ruggiero Ricci & pf. acc. 12"—G-DA4467
[Mattheson: Suite in G—Air]
Guila Bustabo & Heinz Schröter
10"—C-LW36
[Sarasate: Zapateado]

Heinz Stanske & Gerhard Puchelt
10"—PD-47529
[Daquin-Manen: Le Coucou]

Elegy Vl., Vlc. & Pf.
Stanislav Novák, Ladislav Zelenka, & Jan
Heřmann 12"—U-G12397

Elegy, Op. 21, No. 3 Piano
Czech: **Dumka**
Jan Heřmann 12"—U-G14033
[Dvořák: Humoresque, Op. 101, No. 7]

Fairies Czech: **Víly**
Moravian Teachers' Chorus
10"—U-C14867
[Strange Water; Novák: Majestic Night]

Fairy Tales Suite, Op. 16 Orchestra
—**No. 2, Polka: "Play at Peacocks" only**
Chicago Symphony Orch.—Stock
(in VM-975†) 12"—V-11-8640
[Dvořák: In der Natur, Op. 91]

In Yearning
FOK Symphony Orch.
[Viennese Serenade] 10"—ESTA-B7750

Love Song, Op. 7, No. 1 Piano
Boh. **Píseň Lásky**
Jan Heřmann 10"—G-AM2244
Pavel Stěpán 12"—U-G14062
—**Arr. Orchestra**
FOK Symphony Orch.—Smetáček
12"—U-E12669
[Dvořák: Humoresque, Op. 101, No. 7]
Prague Symphony Orch.—Dol Dauber
12"—G-AN797
[Moravia—Fantasia on Dvořák Melodies,
Arr. B. Leopold]
Salon Orch.—J. Seidel
10"—ESTA-D2006
—**Arr. Violin & Piano**
Aldo Ferraresi & G. Favaretto
10"—G-GW2014
K. J. Zoubek & Fr. Holeček
10"—ESTA-B7168
[Zoubek: Valse Caprice]

March: "Into a New Life" Orchestra
Boh. **V Nový Zivot**
An entrance march written for the 7th "Sokol"
(National gymnastic federation) meet in
Prague, 1920.
Radio Journal Orch.—Jeremiáš
10"—U-A10425
[With chorus on U-A10486]

**Meditation on an old Bohemian Chorale,
Op. 35a**
Czech Broadcasting Symphony Orch.—
Jirák 12"—U-G12548
Ondřiček Quartet 12"—ESTA-E7130
Boyd Neel String Orch.—Neel
12"—D-K1218
(4) Pieces, Op. 17 Violin & Piano 1900
See: Appassionata, Burleska, Quasi Bal-
lata, Un poco triste

Quartet—String, No. 1, B major, Op. 11
Bohemian Quartet 4 12"—PD-95080/3
[Dvořák: Waltz, A major, Op. 54, No. 1]

Quasi Ballata, Op. 17, No. 1 Violin & Piano
Ginette Neveu & Jean Neveu
12"—V-11-9840
[Appassionata] (G-DB6359)

RADUZ AND MAHULENA
Intermezzo
Czech Philharmonic Orch.—Talich
12"—G-DB7682
[Smetana: The Moldau, Pt. 3]

Serenade, Op. 3, No. 2 'Cello & Piano
Bohuš Heran & Alfred Holeček
[Janáček: Fairy Tale] 12"—U-G12667

Serenade for String Orch., Op. 6
Boyd Neel String Orch.—Neel
3 12"—D-K1209/11†

Sorrow Chorus In Bohemian Boh. **Zal**
Bakule Chorus 10"—U-A12015
[Dvořák: The Ring]

Strange Water Chorus In Bohemian
Boh. **Divná Voda**
Moravian Teachers' Chorus
10"—U-C14867
[Fairies: Novák: Majestic Night]

Un poco triste, Op. 17, No. 3 Violin & Piano
Ginette Neveu & Jean Neveu
12"—V-12-0154
[Burleska] (G-DB6360)
Heinz Stanske & M. Raucheisen
12"—PD-57104
[Sarasate: Zapateado, Op. 23, No. 2]
Bedřiška Seidlová & Alfred Holeček
[Sarasate: Zapateado] 12"—U-G12666

Viennese Serenade
FOK Symphony Orch.
[In Yearning] 10"—ESTA-B7750

SUK, Váša (1861-1933)
MASTER OF THE FOREST Opera
Boh. **Lesův pán**
—**Polka only**
FOK Symphony Orch.—V. Smetáček
10"—U-A12299
[Jeremiáš: Czech Polka]

SULLIVAN, (Sir) Arthur (1842-1900)
Although he received in Germany the thor-
ough musical training of the Romantic school,
Sir Arthur Sullivan—now inseperable from his
collaborator, W. S. Gilbert—chose to confine his
major creative efforts to a genre that is strong
in the English bourgeois tradition and which
had its origins in the eighteenth century bal-
lad opera. Although Gilbert & Sullivan oper-
etta is inimitably English, its fundamental
cleanliness, and humorous satire have made it
popular the world over. It should be noted that
only the major works are herein listed; see cur-
rent catalogues for more detailed listings.

Di Ballo—Overture Orchestra
City of Birmingham Orch.—Weldon
12"—C-DX1200

(THE) LIGHT OF THE WORLD
Oratorio 1873
—**God shall wipe away all tears** Alto
Clara Butt & organ acc. 12"—C-DX755
[Gounod: O Divine Redeemer]
(The) Lost Chord See under Songs
Onward Christian Soldiers Hymn
Essie Ackland with Chorus & Organ,
G-C1848; Pryor's Band, V-35804; The

Cloister Singers, D-F6554; All-Girl Orch. & Cho.—Spitalny, in C-C108; Nelson Eddy (4-Pt. harmony), in CM-646; Grenadier Guards Band, D-F5279

OPERETTAS In English
(See excerpts in collections below)

(THE GILBERT & SULLIVAN OPERETTAS)

(THE) GONDOLIERS 1889
Complete recording
D'Oyly Carte Co. 12 12″—V-C16†
(G-D1334/45 in GM-48†)
The Cast includes: Bertha Lewis, Sybil Gordon, Beatrice Elburn, Winifred Lawson, Aileen Davies, Mavis Bennett, Derek Oldham, George Baker, Henry A. Lytton, Richard Walker, Arthur Hosking, Leo Sheffield, etc.

Abridged recording
D'Oyly Carte Co.—Malcolm Sargent
(G-B3866/71) 6 12″—GM-127†
The Cast: Phylis Evens, Derek Oldham, Leslie Rands, George Baker, Essie Ackland, A. Moxon, Nellie Walker, Webster Booth, B. Elburn, Muriel Dickson, etc.

Vocal & Orchestral Selections
Light Opera Company, V-36146 in V-C23: G-C3151; Columbia Light Opera Company, C-9565; A. Welch, N. Collyer, V. Conway, D-K609

Instrumental Selections
Court Symphony—Raybould, C-DX386; Coldstream Guards Band, G-C1273; Foden's Motor Works Band, C-FB2860

Take a pair of sparkling eyes Tenor
Webster Booth 12″—G-C3261
[Mikado—A wandering minstrel I]

H.M.S. PINAFORE
See under Pinafore

IOLANTHE 1882
Complete recording
D'Oyly Carte Co.—Malcolm Sargent
11 12″—V-C10†
(G-D1785/95 in GM-89†)
The cast: Bertha Lewis, Alice Moxon, Beatrice Elburn, Nellie Briercliffe, Winifred Lawson, Nellie Walker, George Baker, Leslie Rands, Derek Oldham, Darrell Fancourt, Sydney Granville, etc.

Abridged Version
Columbia Light Opera Company—Joseph Batten 6 10″—CM-422
The cast: Sophie Rowlands, Joan Cross, Nellie Walker, Dan Jones, Barrington Hopper, George Portland, etc.

Vocal & Orchestral Selections
Columbia Light Opera Co., C-DX17

Instrumental Selections
Coldstream Guards Band, G-C1368

Overture
Liverpool Philharmonic—Sargent
(C-DX1378) 12″—C-72526D

(THE) MIKADO 2 Acts 1885
Complete recording
D'Oyly Carte Co.—Isadore Godfrey
11 12″—V-C26†
(G-DB4038/48 in GM-260†)
The cast: Darrell Fancourt, Derek Oldham, Martyn Green, Sydney Granville, Leslie Rands, Radley Flynn, Brenda Bennett, Marjorie Eyre, E. Nickell-Lean, Josephine Curtis, etc.

Abridged recording
Columbia Light Opera Co.—J. Batten
6 10″—C-DB321/6
The cast: Nellie Walker, Alice Lilley, Joan Cross, Robert Carr, Dan Jones, Appleton Moore, etc.

Vocal & Orchestral Selections
Light Opera Co., V-36148 in V-C23†: G-C3128: also G-C1404; Columbia Light Opera Co., C-9581

Instrumental Selections
Court Symphony—Raybould, C-DX414; Künstler Orch., PD-21029; Coldstream Guards Band, G-C2602

A wandering minstrel I Tenor
Webster Booth 12″—G-C3261
[Gondoliers—Take a pair of sparkling eyes]
DUPLICATION: Kenny Baker, G-BD741

The Moon and I
Kenny Baker, G-BD741

PATIENCE 2 Acts 1881
Complete recording
D'Oyly Carte Co.—Malcolm Sargent
10 12″—V-C14†
(G-D1909/18 in GM-106†)
The cast: Nellie Briercliffe, Rita Mackay, Bertha Lewis, Winifred Lawson, M. Eyre, Darrell Fancourt, George Baker, Leslie Rands, Derek Oldham, Martyn Green, etc.

Overture Orchestra
Liverpool Philharmonic—Sargent
12″—C-DX1339
[Yeoman of the Guard—Overture]

(H.M.S.) PINAFORE 2 Acts 1878
Complete recording
D'Oyly Carte Co.—Malcolm Sargent
9 12″—V-C13†
(G-D1844/52 in GM-100†)
The cast: Nellie Briercliffe, Bertha Lewis, Elsie Griffin, Charles Goulding, George Baker, Henry S. Lytton, Sydney Granville, Stuart Robertson, Darrell Fancourt, etc.

Abridged recording
Victor Light Opera Co.—Emile Coté
4 10″—V-P120

Vocal & Orchestral Selections
Light Opera Co., C-DX205; D-K630

Instrumental Selections
Coldstream Guards Band, G-C1283; BBC Theatre Orch.—Robinson, D-K842

When I was a lad Baritone
John Charles Thomas 12″—V-18223
[O'Hara: There is no death)

(THE) PIRATES OF PENZANCE
2 Acts 1880

Complete recording
D'Oyly Carte Co.—Malcolm Sargent
(G-D1678/88 in GM-83†) 11 12"—**V-C6**†
The cast: Nellie Briercliffe, Nellie Walker,
Dorothy Gill, Elsie Griffin, George Baker,
Peter Dawson, Stuart Robertson, Derek
Oldham, Leo Sheffield, etc.

Vocal & Orchestral Selections
Light Opera Co., V-36144 in V-C23:
G-C2499; also C-9622

Instrumental Selections
Coldstream Guards Band, G-C1368

PRINCESS IDA 3 Acts 1884

Complete recording
D'Oyly Carte Co.—Malcolm Sargent
(G-DB4016/25) 10 12"—**GM-169**†
The cast: Muriel Dickson, Dorothy Gill,
Alice Moxon, Nellie Briercliffe, Derek Old-
ham, Henry Lytton, George Baker, Stuart
Robertson, Richard Watson, Darrell Fan-
court, Edward Holland, Charles Goulding,
etc.

RUDDIGORE 2 Acts 1887

Complete recording
D'Oyly Carte Co.—Malcolm Sargent
(G-DB4005/13) 9 12"—**GM-143**†
The cast: Muriel Dickson, Nellie Brier-
cliffe, Dorothy Gill, Alice Moxon, George
Baker, Derek Oldham, Sydney Granville,
Stuart Robertson, etc.

(THE) SORCERER 1877
No complete recording available

Vocal & Orchestral Selections
Light Opera Co., V-36147 in V-C23

TRIAL BY JURY 1 Act 1875

Complete recording
D'Oyly Carte Co.—Rupert D'Oyly Carte
(G-D1469/72 in GM-71†) 4 12"—**V-C4**†
The cast includes Winifred Lawson, Leo
Sheffield, George Baker, Derek Oldham,
Arthur Hosking, etc.

(THE) YEOMAN OF THE GUARD
2 Acts 1888

D'Oyly Carte Co.—Malcolm Sargent
(G-D1549/59 in GM-74†)
11 12"—**V-C17**†
The Cast includes Nellie Briercliffe, Doro-
thy Gill, Winifred Lawson, Elsie Griffin,
Derek Oldham, George Baker, Henry
Millidge, Walter Glynne, Peter Dawson,
Arthur Hosking, Leo Sheffield, etc.

Vocal & Orchestral Selections
Light Opera Co., V-36145 in V-C23†:
G-C1807; Light Opera Co., C-9554:
D-K599

Instrumental Selections
Coldstream Guards Band, G-C1289; BBC
Theatre Orch.—Robinson, D-K848;
Foden's Motor Works Band, C-FB2860

Overture Orchestra
Liverpool Philharmonic Orch.—Sargent
[Patience—Overture] 12"—**C-DX1339**

MISCELLANEOUS OPERETTA COLLECTIONS & MEDLEYS

Gems from Gilbert & Sullivan Operettas
Excerpts from Pirates of Penzance; Yeo-
men of the Guard; Gondoliers; Sorcerer;
Mikado
Light Opera Company & Orch.
5 12"—**V-C23**†
(G-C2499: G-C1807: G-C3151: G-C3128
& G-C1404)

Gilbert & Sullivan Favorites
Excerpts from Gondoliers, Iolanthe, Mik-
ado, Pinafore, Yeoman of the Guard
D'Oyly Carte Artists
(G-DB4029/32) 4 12"—**GM-244**†
Also: Harry Davidson Orch., C-DX1450;
Ye Band of Rustics, D-F2628/9

Patter Songs
Vol I—Mikado—My object all sublime;
Yeomen of the Guard—Oh! a private buf-
foon; Iolanthe—Lord Chancellor's Song;
The Sorcerer—My name is John Welling-
ton Wells; H. M. S. Pinafore—I am the
monarch of the sea & When I was a lad;
Pirates of Penzance—Major General's
Song
Nelson Eddy (b) with Chorus & Orch.—
Armbruster 3 10"—**CM-440**

Vol. II—Pirates of Penzance—When a fel-
on's not engaged in his employment &
When the foeman bares his steel; Patience—If you're anxious for to shine;
Trial by Jury—When I good friends; Rud-
digore—My boy you may take from me;
The Gondoliers—Rising early in the
morning; Princess Ida—If you give me
your attention & When'er I spoke
Nelson Eddy (b) with Chorus & Orch.—
Armbruster 3 10"—**CM-670**

SONGS In English
(The) Lost Chord (Proctor)
Enrico Caruso (t) & re-recorded organ
acc. 12"—**V-8806**
[Handel: Largo] (G-DB2073)
(original recording, G-DB133*)
Webster Booth (t) & H. Dawson (org)
[Handel: Largo] 12"—**G-C3130**
Charles Kullman (t) 12"—**C-9143M**
[Handel: Largo] (C-DX389)
Richard Crooks (t) & organ acc.
[Tosti: Goodbye] 12"—**V-8869**
[Adams: Thora, on G-DB2571]
DUPLICATIONS: Oscar Natzke,
P-E11430; B. Gigli, G-DB1526; Dennis
Morgan & Choir, C-7442M; Essie Ack-
land, G-C1599; Clara Butt, C-DX754;
Peter Dawson, G-C3038; Mary Jarred,
C-DX1013; John McCormack, G-DB328*
—**Arr. Chorus**
Associated Glee Clubs, C-7354M; Ken-
tucky Minstrels, G-C3001
See current catalogues for other miscel-
laneous arrangements.

SUPPE, Franz von (1820-1895)

*Born in Dalmatia of Belgian parents, von Sup-
pé studied in Italy and became a well-known
Viennese operetta conductor. He composed in*

all forms, but is best remembered by the overtures to his operettas.

OPERETTAS In German

BANDITENSTREICHE
Eng. **Jolly Robbers**
Overture Orchestra
Symphony Orch.—Melichar
12″—**PD-27194**
Berlin Philharmonic—Borchard
10″—**T-A1732**
Vienna Symphony—Reichberger
10″—**G-X4406**
Symphony Orch.—Dobrindt
10″—**O-26287**

BOCCACCIO 1879
Orchestral Selections (Fantasias, etc.)
Marek Weber Orch., G-EG1276:
G-HN608
Overture Orchestra
Berlin Philharmonic—Schmidt-
Isserstedt 10″—**T-A2403**
Kampfbund Orch.—G. Havemann
10″—**PD-25217**
Berlin State Opera Orch.—
Melichar 12″—**PD-57123**
Vocal Selections
Elisabeth Schwarzkopf (s) & Rupert
Glawitch (t) 12″—**T-E3029**
Anni Frind (s), Walther Ludwig (t)
& Wilhelm Strienz (b) w. Cho.
12″—**G-EH991**
Individual Excerpts
Hab' ich nur deine Liebe Duo
Friedel Beckmann & Wilhelm Strienz
10″—**G-EG7070**
[Heuberger: Der Opernball—Komm' zu
mir]
—Soprano part only
Maria Reining, T-E3055
—Tenor only
J. Patzak, PD-10284: PD-10251
Florenz hat schöne Frauen
E. van Endert (s) & R. Walter (s),
G-EG759; Lilie Claus (s) & Walther
Ludwig (t), PD-15382
Holde schöne
Marcel Wittrisch, G-EG3320
March
Berlin State Opera Orch.—Melichar,
PD-11385; Berlin State Opera Orch.—
H. Otto, T-A2193
Miscellaneous Vocal Excerpts
(Sung in Italian)
Poggianti, Ferlito, Bassi, G-GW767:
G-GW469

DICHTER UND BAUER
Eng. **Poet and Peasant**
Fr. **Poète et Paysan**
Overture Orchestra
Amsterdam Concertgebouw—
Mengelberg 12″—**C-9075M**
(C-LX179) (C-LFX290) (C-GQX10720)
National Symphony Orch.—Sargent
12″—**D-K1411**
Berlin State Opera Orch.—Melichar
10″—**PD-24234**

Boston "Pops" Orch.—Fiedler
(G-C2874) (G-EH1025)
(in VM-746†) 12″—**V-11986**
(G-L1032) (G-FKX29)
DUPLICATIONS: Victor Symphony Orch.,
G-S10432; Berlin Philharmonic—
Schmidt-Isserstedt, T-A2359; Berlin
State Opera Orch—Seidler-Winkler,
G-EH1097; Berlin State Opera Orch.—
Weissmann, P-E10650: P-9213; Symphony Orch.—Pitt, C-9760: C-DFX50;
Vienna State Opera Orch.—Reichwein,
O-7877: P-E11381; Dajos Bela Orch.,
O-171048: O-238904; Symphony Orch.—
Schmalstich, G-EH284; Columbia Salon
Orch.—Palitz, C-35883; Andolfi Orch.,
PAT-X96293; Berlin State Opera Orch.—
Steeger, PD-15228; Salon Orch.—J.
Seidel, ESTA-E6007
—Arr. Band
Band of Gold Coast Police—Stenning,
G-JZ282; Black Dyke Mills Band,
G-BD773; Polydor Band, PD-2367
—Miscellaneous Transcriptions
R. Foort (org), PD-524216; Rawicz &
Landauer (2-pfs), C-FB2246; Tollefsen
(Accordion), C-FB1986; G. Sellers
(Accordion), G-K6516

DONNA JUANITA
Intermezzo Harp & Orchestra
Ines Ruotolo & Orch. 12″—**C-D16441**
[Donizetti: Lucia di Lammermoor—
Harp solo]

FATINITZA
Overture Orchestra
Boston "Pops" Orch.—Fiedler
12″—**V-11-9261**

FLOTTE BURSCHE—Overture
Berlin Philharmonic Orch.—
Kreuder 10″—**T-A2288**
Berlin State Opera Orch.—Melichar
12″—**PD-11025**
DUPLICATION: Otto Kermbach Orch.,
PD-2508

LEICHTE KAVALLERIE 1886
Eng. **Light Cavalry**
Overture Orchestra
BBC Symphony—Boult (G-DB2362)
(in VM-746†) 12″—**V-11837**
EIAR Symphony Orch.—Gallino
12″—**CET-TI7029**
Boston "Pops" Orch.—Fiedler
12″—**V-11-9954**
National Symphony Orch.—Neel
12″—**D-K1300**
DUPLICATIONS: Lamoureux Orch.—
Cariven, PAT-PD70; Berlin Philharmonic
—Kleiber, T-F1322; Berlin-Charlottenburg Opera Orch.—Melichar, PD-23934:
PD-27179; Victor Symphony—Bourdon,
G-HN467: G-B2856; Columbia Symphony,
C-CQX16455; Symphony Orch.—Zweig,
P-E10589; Berlin State Opera Orch.—
Viebig, G-HN604: G-L660: G-EH48;
Court Symphony Orch.—Pitt, C-DFX58:
C-DX42; Andolfi Orch., PAT-X96288;
FOK Symphony Orch.—Dyk,
ESTA-D2056

—Miscellaneous arrangements
Coldstream Guards Band, G-C1335;
Polydor Band, PD-2366; C. Sellers
(accordion), G-K7284; Black Dyke Mills
Band, G-BD807

**(EIN) MORGEN, EIN MITTAG, EIN
ABEND IN WIEN**
Eng. Morning, Noon & Night in Vienna
Overture Orchestra
Boston "Pops" Orch.—Fiedler
(C-C3020) (G-EH1105)
              (in VM-746†)   12″—V-12479
National Symphony Orch.—Victor Olof
                          12″—D-K1293
EIAR Symphony Orch.—Gallino
                          12″—CET-TI7026
London Philharmonic Orch.—Beecham
(C-LX865)   12″—C-71439D
DUPLICATIONS: Berlin State Opera
Orch.—Melichar, PD-24595; Künstler
Orch.—Dobrindt, O-7897

PIQUE DAME—Overture
National Symphony Orch.—
Fistoulari   12″—D-K1283
Vienna Philharmonic—Robert Heger
                          12″—G-C1677
Berlin Philharmonic—Schmidt-
Isserstedt   10″—T-A2248

(DIE) SCHOENE GALATHEA
Eng. The Beautiful Galathea
Overture
Boston "Pops" Orch.—Fiedler
                          12″—V-11-9494
Orch. of the Theater des Volkes—
Kretzschmar   12″—C-DWX1622
Dresden Philharmonic—van Kempen
(CET-OR5116)   12″—PD-57126
DUPLICATIONS: CBS Symphony—
Barlow, C-71191D; Berlin Philharmonic
Orch.—Schmidt-Isserstedt, T-A2318;
Vienna State Opera Orch.—Reichwein,
O-7840; Berlin State Opera Orch.—
Melichar, PD-15210; Berlin Philharmonic
—Prüwer, PD-19903; Tivoli Concert
Orch.—Felumb, TONO-X25071; Sym-
phony Orch.—Seidel, ESTA-E6003
Orchestral Selections: Eugen Wolff Orch.,
(O-279416
Einmal möcht' ich so verliebt sein
Ja, wenn die Musik nicht war'
Iwa Wanja (s)   10″—G-EG7130
—Arr. Orchestra: Barnabas von Géczy &
his Orch.   10″—G-EG7139

SVENDSEN, Johan (1840-1911)
*A Norwegian violinist, conductor and com-
poser, who wrote largely for orchestra. His
works also include arrangements of folk-songs.*

Carnival in Paris, Op. 9 Orchestra
Nor. Karneval i Paris
Danish State Radio Symphony Orch.—
N. Malko   2 12″—G-Z295/6
[Nielsen: Masquerade overture]
Festival Polonaise, Op. 12 Orchestra
Royal Theatre Orch., Copenhagen—
H. Hye-Knudsen   12″—G-Z263

Göteborg Symphony Orch.—Tor Mann
                          12″—G-Z209
[Bull: Herdgirl's Sunday, arr. Svendsen]
[Alfven: Festspel, on G-Z203]
Tivoli Orch.—S. C. Felumb
                          12″—TONO-X25046
Norwegian Artists' Carnival, Op. 16
Orchestra
Nor. Norsk konstnärkarneval
—Waltz only
Symphony Orch.—A. Järnefelt
                          10″—O-D1011
Romance, G major, Op. 26
Violin & Orchestra
Carlo Andersen & Copenhagen Philhar-
monic—Jensen   12″—G-DB5232
Georg Kulenkampff & F. Leitner (pf)
[Lully: Gavotte]   10″—T-A2625
(U-B18052)
Venetian Serenade: "Kom Carina"
Song (Poulsen)
Vilhelm Herold (t) & pf. acc.
[Sinding: Rav]   10″—G-V116
DUPLICATIONS: M. Jacobsen, G-X2720;
Aage Juhl-Thomsen's Orch. w. vocal,
G-X6255
—Arr. Violin & Piano
Siegfried Borries, G-EG6248
Miscellaneous—Orchestrations
Swedish Folksongs; Allt under himmelens
fäste; Du gamla, du fria
Chamber Orch. of the Palace Chapel,
Copenhagen—Wöldike, G-X7207
String Orch.—Järnefelt, O-D1027

SWEELINCK, Jan Pieterzoon (1562-1621)
*A Netherland composer and organist of almost
legendary fame, Sweelinck is considered the
founder of the North German School of organ
playing. His pupil Scheidemann handed down
the tradition to Reincken from whom it was
transmitted to Johann Sebastian Bach. We are
fortunate in having one recording—Fantasia
No. 10—played on an organ constructed during
the composer's lifetime.*

Chorale-Preludes Organ
O Mensch bewein dein sunde gross
Mein junges Leben
André Marchal
          (in Vol. XIV)   12″—AS-131
Fantasias Organ
No. 10 (in echo style)
Finn Viderø (Compenius Organ, Fred-
eriksborg Castle, Denmark)
                          12″—G-DB5214
[Frescobaldi: Toccata sopra i Pedali]
No. 11 (in echo style)
Carl Weinrich (Westminster Choir
School Organ), in MC-9
Hodie Christus natus est
Unacc. Chorus in Latin
Basilica Choir—Pius Kalt
                          12″—PD-27107
[Rheinberger: Stern von Bethlehem—
Zug der heiligen drei Könige]
Psalm 138 Unacc. Chorus in Latin
Amsterdam Bel Canto Choir—Vranken
                          12″—C-D17193
[Palestrina: Psalm 42—Sicut cervus]

SZAMOTUL, (Szamotulski), Waclaw (c.1525-1572)

Born the same year as Palestrina, little is known of this composer's life other than the fact that contemporary editions of his works were well received not only in his native Poland, but in Germany as well.

Juz sje zmyerska Evening Prayer
Unacc. Chorus in Polish
Motet & Madrigal Group—H. Opienski
(in Vol. VI)   12"—AS-53
[with Polish Chorus of the Renaissance:
Gomolka & Zielenski]

SZULC, Joseph (1875-   )

A contemporary Polish composer of operettas, instrumental music and songs.

Clair de lune, Op. 83, No. 1   (Verlaine)
Maggie Teyte (s) & G. Moore (pf)
[Duparc: Extase]   12"—G-DB5937

SZYMANOWSKI, Karol (1883-1937)

A Polish nationalistic composer of Romantic leanings, Szymanowski visited the United States in 1921 at which time many of his works were introduced to American audiences by Leopold Stokowski.

Etude   (Unidentified)   Piano
Theo van der Pas
In Prep. (Dutch Decca)
(The) Fountain of Arethusa, Op. 30, No. 1
(from 3 Myths for Violin & Piano)
Joseph Szigeti & N. de Magaloff
12"—C-7304M
[Stravinsky: Pastorale & Rimsky-
Korsakov: Flight of the Bumble Bee]
Jacques Thibaud & T. Janopoulo
[Marsick: Scherzando]   12"—G-DB2006
DUPLICATION: F. Cillario, G-S10472

Mazurkas, Op. 50   Piano
—Nos. 1 - 4 only
Artur Rubinstein
(G-DB6347)   12"—V-11-9019
Notturno & Tarantella, Op. 28, No. 1 & 2
Violin & Piano
Arthur Grumiaux & Gerald Moore
12"—C-DX1199
Ida Haendel & Adela Kotowska
12"—D-K1651
Y. Menuhin & M. Gazelle
12"—G-DB2871

(LE) ROI ROGER   Opera   1926

Chant de Roxane

—Arr. Violin & Piano
Jascha Heifetz & Emanuel Bey
12"—V-14625
[Falla-Kreisler: Vida Breve—Danse
Espagnole]

Theme & 12 Variations, Op. 3   Piano
Malcuzynski   12"—C-LX1050
(Variation IX & X omitted)

TAFFANEL, Claude Paul (1844-1908)

A famous French flutist, and founder of the "Société des Instruments à Vent," Taffanel was the teacher of Gaubert and Georges Barrère.

Quintet for Wind Instruments
Paris Society of Wind Instruments—
Oubradous   2 12"—G-W1567/8
[Pierné: Pastorale]

TALLIS, Thomas (c.1520-1585)

One of the greatest of English Renaissance composers, and organist at the Royal Chapel jointly with William Byrd. To date, we can unfortunately list only one of an original Tallis work. However, a theme from a piece Tallis wrote for the metrical Psalter of Archbishop Parker— "Why fumeth in flight?"—was used by Ralph Vaughan Williams in his Fantasia on a Theme of Thomas Tallis. For a recording of this work see under Vaughan Williams.

Canon   4-Voice
Large Grammar School Chorus
12"—G-C3530
[Harris: O What their Joy]

TANSMAN, Alexander (1897-   )

A Polish-Parisian composer and pianist, Tansman has made his way to Hollywood where he is writing for the films.

Scherzo (from the film "Flesh and Fantasy")
Janssen Symphony of Los Angeles—
Werner Janssen   12"—V-11-8808
[Raksin: Theme from the film "Laura"]

TARP, Svend Erik (1908-   )

A contemporary Danish composer.

Concerto, C major, Op. 39
Piano & Orchestra
Egil Harder & Copenhagen Philharmonic
Orch.—Felumb   2 12"—G-X286/7
Her har Hjertet hjemme   Song in Danish
Aksel Schiøtz (t) & pf. acc.
10"—G-X6646
[Rung: I Danmark er jeg født]
Mosaik-Miniature Suite
Tivoli Orch.—Thomas Jensen
12"—TONO-X25010
Serenade, Op. 28b
Flute, Violin, Viola, 'Cello
Erik Thomsen Quartet
12"—TONO-A122

TARREGA, Francisco (1852-1909)

Professor of guitar at the Madrid Conservatory of Music, Tarrega composed and transcribed for his instrument.

Recuerdos de Alhambra
Tremolo Study for Guitar
Andrés Sevogia   12"—G-D1305
[Turina: Fandanguillos]

Tango Guitar
Mario Vozza   10"—CET-DC4600
[Mozzani: Feste Larlane]

TARTINI, Giuseppe (1692-1770)

A versatile eighteenth century musical figure, Tartini was a theoretician of real stature, one of the great violin virtuosos, the founder of a famous violin school, the sponsor of several improvements in violin and bow manufacture (hence anticipating François Tourte) and an imaginative composer generally remembered only for his novelty, the "Devil's Trill" Sonata.

CONCERTOS Violin & Orchestra

D minor Arr. Pente Revised Szigeti
Joseph Szigeti & Orch.
2 12"—C-LWX261/2
[Bach: Clavier Concerto No. 5, F minor—
Arioso, arr. violin, Szigeti]

E major Arr. Scherchen
A. de Ribaupierre & Winterthur Munici-
pal Orch.—Scherchen
2 12"—G-DB6093/4
[Rousseau: Le Devin du Village—
Overture]

Concerto, D major 'Cello & Orchestra

—3rd Mvt. (Grave ed espressivo) only
Pablo Casals & pf. acc. 12"—G-DB1400
[Bach-Siloti: Komm süsser Tod]
Gaspar Cassadó & Berlin Philharmonic
[Cassadó: Requiebros] 12"—T-E1820

Quartet—String, D major
"Sonata a quattro"

—Larghetto & Andante assai only
String Quartet 12"—SEMS-1145

SONATAS Violin

C major
Denise Soriano & pf. acc.
12"—PAT-PAT57

G major, Op. 2, No. 12
—Air only Arr. Busch
Adolf Busch & Busch Chamber Players
(in CM-609†) 12"—C-71752D
[Mozart: Violin Concerto No. 5, Pt. 7]

G major
Joseph Szigeti & Karl Ruhrseitz (pf)
2 10"—C-GQ7206/7
[Beethoven: Sonata Op. 30, No. 3, Finale]

G minor—Grave only
Miquel Candela & pf. acc. (C-LW13)
10"—C-LF138
[Fairchild: Moustiques & Rimsky-
Korsakov: Flight of the Bumble Bee]

Sonata: "Il Trillo del Diavolo"
Arr. Kreisler
Alfredo Campoli & Eric Gritton
2 12"—D-K1531/2
[Bach: Cantata No. 156—Arioso]
Yehudi Menuhin & Artur Balsam
2 12"—G-DB1786/7
[Kreisler: Recitative & Scherzo-
Caprice, Op. 6]
DUPLICATIONS: R de Barbieri & G.
Guastalla, G-AW338/9; Příhoda & Otto
A. Graef, PD-57099/100;
CET-OR5049/50; F. von Reuter & pf.
acc., PD-95183

Variations on a Theme of Corelli
Violin Arr. Kreisler
David Oistrakh & Abram Makarov
12"—U-G14742
[Chopin-Sarasate: Nocturne No. 2]

Ginette Neveu & Gustave Beck
12"—G-DB4666
[R. Strauss: Sonata, E flat major, Op. 18]
Zino Francescatti & M. Lanner, in CM-660
(Earlier recording on C-LF90)
Ruggiero Ricci & Louis Persinger, in
VOX-196
DUPLICATION: Alfredo Campoli,
D-F6594

TAUBERT, Karl (1811-1891)

A German composer whose early songs drew praise from Mendelssohn. His later works include symphonies, a large amount of chamber music, and five operas.

Der Vogel im Wald Arr. Alwin
Miliza Korjus (s) (G-EH997)
(in VM-871†) 12"—V-13806
[Benedict: Carnevale di Venezia]

TAVERNER, John (c.1495-1545)

The most notable English composer and organist of his time, Taverner carried on the traditions of the polyphonic style of the early Tudor school that can be traced back to Dunstable, not however, without adding a breath of the newer Renaissance spirit that Thomas Morley, for one, recognized in his music.

Audivi
Choir of the Pius X School of Liturgical
Music (in VM-739) 12"—V-13560
[Lassus: Missa pro Defunctis-Benedictus;
Gregorian: Pueri Habraeorum; Pales-
trina: Pueri Habraeorum]

Magnificat du 6e ton 4-voice a cappella
Mm. Bonté, Deniau, Rousselon, Bousquet
—dir. G. de Van
(in Vol. X) 12"—AS-97
[Quemadmodum]

Quemadmodum 6-voice Instrumental piece
Ensemble—dir. G. de Van
[Magnificat] (in Vol. X) 12"—AS-97

TAVONI

Canzone Vespertina
A. Dadò (b) & Antonelli (org)
10"—SEMS-502
[Somma: Nenia Pastorale] (SEMS-18)

Ecce Panis
A. Dadò (b) 10"—SEMS-13
[Palestrina: Bonum est, Julian Chapel
Choir]

Fourth word of the Passion
A. Dadò (b) & Antonelli (org)
12"—SEMS-1102
[Dadò: Second word of the Passion]

O Sacrum Convivium
A. Dadò (b) & A. Fantozzi (t)
10"—SEMS-46
[Refice: Salve Regina, A. Dadò]

Regina delle Rose
A. Fantozzi (t) 10"—SEMS-25
[Moriconi: O cor Voluptas, Sistine Chapel
Trio]

Vergin soave e bella
A. Fantozzi (t) 10"—SEMS-45
[Carnevali: A se macchia, A. Dadò]

TAYLOR, DEEMS (1885-   )

Deems Taylor's fame—through radio and the printed word—as a witty master of ceremonies, and as a music commentator and critic, has pushed his activity as a composer into the background. His musical output includes operas, songs, chamber music and incidental music for the theatre, little of which is available on records.

OPERAS In English

(THE) KING'S HENCHMAN 1927
Nay, Maccus, lay him down, Act III
Baritone & Chorus
Lawrence Tibbett, Metropolitan Opera
Chorus & Orch.—Setti
(in VM-1015) 12"—**V-11-8932**
[Hanson: Merry Mount—'Tis an earth defiled, Act I]

PETER IBBETSON 1931
Orchestral Suite
Waltzes, Act I; Inn Music; Prelude to Act II; Dream Music, Act III
CBS Symphony—Barlow 2 12"—**CX-204†**

THROUGH THE LOOKING GLASS
Orchestral Suite
CBS Symphony—Barlow
4 12"—**CM-350†**
—Dedication only Arr. Organ
Charles Courboin, V-10-1007

TCHAIKOVSKY, Peter Illich (1840-1893)

The ratio of Tchaikovsky's recorded works to his total output is higher than that of any other composer living or dead, and not without reasons which transcend the unquestionably lavish musical gifts that nature has bestowed upon the composer. His music represents perhaps the furthest extension to which artistic subjectivity, to the exclusion of a larger morality, has been pushed within the confines of the diatonic system. It is thus hardly coincidental that the popularity of Freudian thinking and Tchaikovsky's music go hand in hand.

Andante cantabile See Quartets—Strings, D major, Op. 11

Aurora's Wedding Ballet Suite
Fr. **Le mariage d'Aurore**
NOTE: *This ballet suite is an arrangement for the Ballet Russe of the music from the last act of "The Sleeping Beauty," Op. 66.*
London Philharmonic Orch.—Efrem Kurtz 3 12"—**VM-326†**
(G-C2853/5) (also on G-L1028)

Autumn Song (October) Op. 37a, No. 10
Piano (from "The Months" Op. 37a)
Fr. **Chanson d'Automne** Ger. **Herbstlied**
Shura Cherkassky, in VOX-165

—Arr. Violin & Piano
Vasa Prihoda, PD-66885

Barcarolle (June) Op. 37a, No. 6
(from "The Months" Op. 37a)
Jacob Flier (pf) 10"—**USSR-10551/2**
Jose Iturbi (pf) 12"—**V-12-0242**
[Troïka]

—Arr. 2 Pianos
Edna Hatzfeld & Mark Strong
[Troïka] 10"—**D-F8136**

—Arr. Orchestra
Andre Kostelanetz & his Orch.
(in CM-601) 12"—**C-12279D**
[Nutcracker Suite—Waltz of the Flowers]
[Quartet No. 1—Andante Cantabile, on C-DX1354]
Also: Cesano (vl), PAT-PA495

Capriccio Italien, Op. 45 Orchestra
N. Y. Philharmonic-Symphony Orch.—Beecham 2 12"—**CX-229†**
Boston "Pops" Orch.—Fiedler
(G-C3136/7)
(Also in VM-776†) 2 12"—**VM-632†**
BBC Symphony Orch.—Boult
2 12"—**G-DB3956/7**

DUPLICATIONS: Philadelphia Orch.—Stokowski, V-6949/50: G-DB6005/6: G-AW201/2; Berlin State Opera Orch.—Melichar, PD-27221/2; Saxon State Orchestra—Karl Böhm, G-DB4632 (abbreviated); Berlin Philharmonic—Kleiber, T-E1406: U-G14277; Berlin State Opera Orch.—R. Heger, O-7769/70: O-50039/40; Berlin State Opera Orch.—Böhlke, PD-57277/8

—Arr. 2 Pianos
Rawicz & Landauer, C-DB2126

Carnival (February), Op. 37a, No. 2 Piano
(from "The Months," Op. 37a)

—Arr. Violin & Piano ("Neapolitanisch")
Georg Kulenkampff & F. Rupp
[Albéniz: Tango in D] 10"—**T-A2551**

Casse-Noisette Suite
See under Nutcracker Suite

Chanson Triste, Op. 40, No. 2 Piano
Benno Moiseiwitsch
(in GM-399†) 12"—**G-C3470**
[Concerto No. 1, B flat minor, Op. 23, Pt. 7, with Philharmonia Orch.—Weldon]
William Murdoch 12"—**D-F7498**
[Schubert-Liszt: Hark, hark the Lark]

—Arr. Violin & Piano
Daniel Guilevitch, PD-524611

—Arr. 'Cello & Piano
Gregor Piatigorsky & R. Berkowitz, in CM-684
S. N. Knushevitsky & S. K. Stuchewski
10"—**USSR-10501/2**
[Valse Sentimentale]

—Arr. Orchestra
Boston "Pops" Orch.—Fiedler, V-4527: G-B9182; Bournemouth Municipal Orch.—Birch, D-F7885

Chant Sans Paroles Piano
Eng. **Song without words**
Ger. **Lied ohne Worte**

F major, Op. 2, No. 2 Arr. Orchestra
New Queen's Hall Orch.—Wood
12"—**C-DX579**
[Mendelssohn: Spring Song & Spinning Song]

DUPLICATIONS: Philadelphia Orch.—
Stokowski, G-AW263: G-W1186; Géczy
Orch., G-EG6422
—**Miscellaneous Arrangements**
Chrystja Kolessa (vlc), G-EG7135; Leo
Petroni (vl), G-EH1236; Cedric Sharp
(vlc), D-F7631

CHORAL WORKS
See also **Liturgy of St. John Chrysostom**
Blessed be the Lord
Gen. Platoff's Don Cossack Choir
      (in VM-768)   12"—**V-17917**
[Gretchaninoff: Credo—2nd Liturgy]
In the church Unacc. Chorus
(Cossack lullaby arranged from Children's
Album, Op. 39, No. 24)
Don Cossacks Chorus—Jaroff
(in Russian)   12"—**C-7333M**
[Volga Song, arr. Jaroff]
—Arr. Orch. B. Romanov Orch., U-B14249
Our Father Rus. Otche nash
Russian Metropolitan Church Choir—
Afonsky   10"—**G-EK91**
[Bortniansky: Hymn of the Cherubim
No. 7]

CONCERTOS—Piano & Orchestra
No. 1, B flat minor, Op. 23
Artur Rubinstein & Minneapolis Sym-
phony—Mitropoulos 4 12"—**VM-1159†**
Vladimir Horowitz & NBC Symphony—
Toscanini   4 12"—**VM-800†**
(G-DB5988/91 in GM-372†)
Nicolas Orloff & National Symphony
Orch. Fistoulari 4 12"—**D-K1167/70†**
Winifried Wolf & Czech Philharmonic—
Talich   4 12"—**G-DB5584/7**
Conrad Hansen & Berlin Philharmonic—
Mengelberg   4 12"—**U-G14273/6**
(T-SK3092/5)
Egon Petri & London Philharmonic—
Goehr   4 12"—**CM-318†**
(C-LX681/4) (C-GQX11060/3)
Artur Rubinstein & London Symphony—
Barbirolli   4 12"—**GM-170†**
(G-DB1731/4)
DUPLICATIONS: Kostia Konstantinoff
& Paris Conservatory—Münch
C-LFX595/8; Solomon & Hallé Orch.—
Harty, C-LX19/22†; Benno Moiseiwitsch
& Philharmonia Orch.—Weldon,
G-C3466/70 in GM-399†; Victor
Schiøler & Danish Radio Orch.—
Garaguly, TONO-X25051/4
—**Abbreviated version**
Jesús María Sanromá & Victor Orch.—
O'Connell (in VM-818) 12"—**V-13758**
[Grieg: Concerto, 1st Mvt. condensed]
(G-C3297)
Arthur Sanford & Debroy Somers Band
         12"—**C-DX567**
No. 2, G major, Op. 44
Benno Moiseiwitsch & Liverpool Philhar-
monic—Weldon 4 12"—**GM-398†**
(G-C3410/3)
Shura Cherkassky & Santa Monica Sym-
phony Orch.—Rachmilovich
         4 12"—**CH-AM**
Eileen Joyce & London Philharmonic—
Fitelberg   4 12"—**D-K1527/30†**

**CONCERTO—Violin & Orchestra, D major,
Op. 35**
Ida Haendel & National Symphony Orch.
Cameron   4 12"—**D-K1444/7†**
Jascha Heifetz & London Philharmonic—
Barbirolli   4 12"—**VM-356†**
(G-DB3159/62 in GM-277†)
Erica Morini & Chicago Symphony Orch.
—Defauw   4 12"—**VM-1168†**
Nathan Milstein & Chicago Symphony
Orch.—Stock   4 12"—**CM-413†**
DUPLICATIONS: Wolfi Schneiderhan &
Czech Philharmonic—Talich,
C-LWX349/52; Georg Kulenkampff &
Berlin State Opera Orch.—Rother,
T-E3010/3: U-F18094/7; David Oistrakh
& Moscow State Philharmonic—Gauk,
USSR-06451/6: 06463/6; Bronislaw
Hubermann & Berlin State Opera Orch.—
Steinberg, C-GQX10585/8
Dolly's Funeral, Op. 39, No. 7 Piano
(from Children's Album)
—Arr. Orchestra: Victor Orch., in V-E73
Dumka, Op. 59 Piano
(Russian Rustic Scene)
Vladimir Horowitz
      (in VM-1001†) 12"—**V-11-8778**
(G-DB6273)
"Eighteen-Twelve" Overture
See: **Overture solennelle "1812"**
Eugene Onegin See under Operas
Francesca da Rimini, Op. 32
Symphonic Fantasia
London Philharmonic Orch.—Beecham
(C-LX887/9†)   3 12"—**CM-447†**
Boston Symphony Orch.—Koussevitzky
         3 12"—**VM-1179†**
N. Y. Philharmonic-Symphony Orch.—
Barbirolli   3 12"—**VM-598†**
[Purcell-Barbirolli: Dido and Aeneas—
When I am laid in earth]
[G-DB3658/60S, last side blank]
Hamlet, Op. 67
Overture-Fantasia 1885
Hallé Orch.—Constant Lambert
(C-DX1101/2)   2 12"—**CX-243†**
Hamlet, Op. 67b Incidental Music 1891
Overture Orchestra
London Philharmonic—Antal Dorati
         12"—**G-C3176**
Liturgy of St. John Chrysostom, Op. 41
Russian Mass
Russian Cathedral Choir—Afonsky
         3 12"—**G-DB5120/2**
—**No. 11, He is worthy**
Rus. Dostino yest
D. Aristoff Cho.   10"—**G-EV13**
[Feofan: Glory to God in the Highest]
Manfred, Op. 58 Symphonic Poem
Indianapolis Symphony Orch.—
Sevitzky   7 12"—**VM-940†**
Humoresque, Op. 10, No. 2 Piano
—**Arr. Violin & Piano** Kreisler
Fritz Kreisler & Carl Lamson
         10"—**V-1170**
[Rachmaninoff: Marguerite]
[Lemare: Andantino, on G-DA803]

—**Arr. Orchestra** Stokowski
NBC Symphony—Stokowski
(in VM-933†) 12"—**V-11-8425**
[Stravinsky: Oiseau de feu, Pt. 5]
Hollywood Bowl Orch.—Stokowski
[Solitude] 12"—**V-11-9187**
All-American Orch.—Stokowski
10"—**C-19005D**
[Rimsky-Korsakov: Flight of the Bumble
Bee]
DUPLICATIONS: Victor Salon Orch.—
Shilkret, G-B9100; Bournemouth Muni-
cipal Orch.—Birch, D-F8203

Jeanne d'Arc See under Operas
Maid of Orleans

Legend See under Songs

MARCHES

Slavonic, Op. 31 (Marche slav)
National Symphony Orch.—Fistoulari
12"—**D-K1282**
Hollywood Bowl Orch.—Stokowski
12"—**V-11-9388**
Cleveland Orch.—Rodzinski
12"—**C-11567D**
Boston "Pops" Orch.—Fiedler
(G-C2911) (G-EH1052) 12"—**V-12006**
Symphony Orch.—Golovanov
(USSR-12349/52) 2 10"—**COMP-C105**
DUPLICATIONS: Orch.—Stokowski,
G-AW3998; Dresden Philharmonic—van
Kempen, PD-15190: PD-516784; BBC
Symphony—Boult, G-DB3971

Mélodie, E flat major, Op. 42, No. 3
Violin & Piano
(from Souvenir d'un lieu cher)
Ellen Birgithe Nielsen & Karl Browall
10"—**G-DA5251**
[None but the lonely heart]
Mischa Elman & Carol Hollister
[Saint-Saëns: Le Cygne] 10"—**G-DA1143**
DUPLICATIONS: Bronislaw Hubermann,
C-GQX10588; Heinz Stanske, PD-47433;
G. Dinicu, C-DV61

—**Arr. Orchestra**
Robin Hood Dell Orch.—Kostelanetz
(in CM-601) 12"—**C-12278D**
[String Quartet—Andante cantabile, arr.
Orch.]
[Nutcracker Suite—Waltz of the Flowers
on C-DX1373]

(The) Months, Op. 37a
(12 Characteristic Pieces) Piano
For recorded portions see under Autumn
Song (October), Barcarolle (June), Car-
nival (February), Troïka en traineau
(November)

Moscow Cantata composed for the corona-
tion of Alexander III 1883
Baritone, Mezzo-Soprano, Chorus &
Orchestra (6 Parts)

—**No. 5 (Arioso) only**
Gladys Swarthout (in English)
10"—**V-10-1166**
[None but the lonely heart]

Mozartiana See under Suite No. 4

Neapolitanisch See under Carnival

Nocturne, C sharp minor, Op. 19, No. 4
Piano
—**Arr. Violin & Piano** Hartmann
Heinz Stanske & M. Raucheisen
[Mélodie] 12"—**PD-47433**
—**Arr. 'Cello & Piano**
G. D. Tzomyk & L. Feinstein
10"—**USSR-10555/6**

(THE) NUTCRACKER, Op. 71 Ballet Suite
Fr. Casse-Noisette
Excerpts: Introduction; March; Dance of
the Buffoons; The Doll; The Negress;
Chocolate; Trépak; Waltz & Apothéose
Bolshoi State Theatre Orch.—
U. F. Faier 3 10"—**COMP-C106**
Excerpts (labeled "Suite No. 2"): Winter
Scene; Waltz of the Snowflakes; Pas de
Deux; Chocolate; Waltz Finale
Boston "Pops" Orch.—Fiedler
2 12"—**VM-1164†**

Orchestral Suite, Op. 71a
1. Ouverture miniature; 2. Danses carac-
téristiques: March, Danse de la Fée-
Dragée, Danse russe (Trépak), Danse
arabe, Danse chinoise, Danse des mirli-
tons; 3. Valse des fleurs
Philadelphia Orch.—Ormandy
3 12"—**VM-1020†**
N. Y. Philharmonic-Symphony
Orch.—Rodzinski 3 12"—**CM-627†**
(C-DX1342/4)
Philadelphia Orch.—Stokowski
(G-DB4590/1) 3 12"—**CM-627**
Chicago Symphony Orch.—Stock
3 12"—**CM-395†**
DUPLICATIONS: Andre Kostelanetz &
his Orch., CM-714†; Dresden Philhar-
monic—van Kempen, PD-67546/8; Lon-
don Philharmonic Orch.—Goossens,
G-C2922/4†; National Symphony Orch.—
Robinson, D-K1142/4: D-ED9†; Berlin
Philharmonic—Borchard, T-A1862/5:
U-B14252/5; Little Symphony Orch.—
Smallens, D-DA408; Berlin State Opera
Orch.—Heger, P-E11269/71: O-50036/8;
Berlin State Opera Orch.—Fried;
PD-516656/8

—**Arr. 2 Pianos**
Rawicz & Landauer 3 10"—**C-DB2154/5**
[Sleeping Beauty—Waltz] & **FB2188**

Individual Excerpts

Ouverture miniature
Philadelphia Orch.—Ormandy
(in VM-1063) 12"—**V-11-9231**
[Carpenter: Adventures in a Perambulator—Hurdy Gurdy]

Marche
Victor Orch., in V-E72
(Earlier recording on V-22168)

Danse de la Fée-Dragée
Symphony Orch.—Goehr, V-36214 in
VM-C30: G-C2914
—**Arr. Organ:** Quentin Maclean, C-FB1771

Trépak
Tivoli Concert Orch.—Jensen, on
TONO-X25060

Valse des fleurs
Symphony Orch.—Goehr, on V-36215 in
V-C30: G-C2915; Tivoli Concert Orch.—
Jensen, TONO-X25060; Symphony—Bar-
low, in CX-240; Robin Hood Dell Orch.
—Kostelanetz, on C-DX1373 in CM-601;
Lew White (org.), V-36225

OPERAS In Russian

Collection of Operatic Excerpts
Eugene Onegin: Introduction & No. 1—
Duet; Act II, First Tableau, No. 14—
Trio; Act III, First Tableau, No. 21—
Dialogue & Onegin's Aria; Pique Dame:
Act II, No. 12—Yeletsky's Aria; Iolanthe:
Scene 1, Iolanthe's Aria; Scene 4, King
René's Aria
E. Kurglikova (s), E. Antonova (s), I. S.
Kozlovsky (t), P. M. Nortsov (b), M.
Mikhailov (b), Shara-Talian (b) with
Bolshoi Theatre Orch., of USRR—Mal-
untsev & Melik-Pashayev
3 12"—DISC-752

(THE) ENCHANTRESS 4 Acts 1887

Love Duet, Act III Soprano & Tenor
Tiana Lemnitz & Helge Roswaenge
(in German) 12"—G-DB5624
Prince's Aria Baritone
A. Ivanov 10"—USSR-13268/9

EUGENE ONEGIN, Op. 24 3 Acts 1879

"Complete" recording (in Russian)
Soloists, Chorus & Orch. of USSR
17 12"—DISC-755
The Cast:
Eugene Onegin .... P. M. Norzoff
Tatjana .... E. D. Kurglikova
Olga .... E. I. Antonova
Lenski .... I. S. Kozlowsky
Prince Gremin .... M. D. Mihailov

Introduction Orchestra
No. 1, Didst thou not hear?
Duet (2 Sopranos)
E. Kurglikova & E. Antonova & Bolshoi
Theatre Orch.—A. Melik-Pashayev, in
DISC-752

No. 9, Letter Scene
Soprano (Tatiana's Aria)
Joan Hammond (in English)
2 12"—C-DX1134/5
[Charpentier: Louise—Depuis le jour]

No. 12, Written words
Baritone (Onegin's Aria)
Ger. **Sie Schrieben mir—Wenn mich für
Hauslichkeit auf Erden**
In Boh. Zdeněk Otava, ESTA-H5190
In German: Heinrich Schlusnus,
PD-35016: PD-67249

No. 13, Waltz Concert Version
(In the opera, the Waltz Scene includes
chorus & orchestra)
London Philharmonic—Beecham
[No. 19] (G-DB6266) 12"—V-11-9421
Boston "Pops" Orch.—Fiedler
(G-B9312) 10"—V-4565
Hallé Orch.—Sargent (C-DX1044)
[No. 19] 12"—C-71929D
National Symphony Orch.—Robinson
[No. 19] 12"—D-K1301

Indianapolis Symphony Orch.—Sevitsky
(in VM-1189†) 12"—V-12-0044
[Symphony No. 1, Pt. 9]
DUPLICATIONS: Berlin Philharmonic—
Schmidt-Isserstedt, T-E2231: U-G14213;
Hastings Municipal Orch.—Harrison,
D-K578; Symphony Orch., G-EK35;
Tivoli Concert Orch.—Jensen,
TONO-X25020

No. 14, Trio & Couplets
Soprano, Tenor & Baritone
E. I. Antonova, I. S. Kozlovsky & P. M.
Wortsov, with Bolshoi Theatre Orch.—
Melik-Pashayev, in DISC-752
(also on D-X279)

No. 17, Faint echo of youth Tenor
(Lenski's Aria)
Ger. **Wohin, wohin seid ihr entschwunden**
Vinogradov 10"—USSR-12769/70
Sergei Lemeshev 10"—D-F8154
D. A. Smirnoff 12"—G-DB581*
[Rimsky-Korsakov: Sadko—Song of
India]
Helge Roswaenge (in German)
12"—G-DB5580
[Verdi: Aida—Celeste Aida]
Charles Kullman (in German)
(C-GQX10914) 12"—C-LWX97
[Borodin: Prince Igor—No. 11,
Vladimir's Cavatina]
Peter Anders (in German)
12"—T-E1761
[Bizet: Carmen—Flower Song]
In Boh. Bronislav Chorovič, ESTA-H5191

No. 19, Polonaise Orchestra
(Prelude to Act III)
London Philharmonic—Beecham
[No. 13] (G-DB6266) 12"—V-11-9421
Boston "Pops" Orch.—Fiedler
(G-C3230) 12"—V-12429
[Granados: Goyescas—Intermezzo]
Hallé Orch.—Sargent
[No. 13] (C-DX1044) 12"—C-71929D
National Symphony Orch.—Robinson
[No. 13] 12"—D-K1301
DUPLICATIONS: BBC Symphony—
Boult, G-DB3132; Berlin Philharmonic—
Schmidt-Isserstedt, T-E2231: U-G14213;
Berlin State Opera Orch.—Melichar,
PD-27222; Milan Symphony—Molajoli,
C-DCX50: C-GQX10692; Tivoli Concert
Orch.—Jensen, TONO-X25020

No. 20, Prince Gremin's Aria Bass
Ger. **Die Liebe blüht—Ein Jeder kennt**
Alexander Kipnis
(in VM-1073) 12"—V-11-9284
Adolf Kaktin 12"—G-EL1002
[Mazeppa—The 3 Treasures]
Wilhelm Strienz (in German)
12"—G-EH1051
[Verdi: Simon Boccanegra—Il lacerato
spirito]
Walther Schirp (in German)
12"—T-E2928
[Verdi: Vespri Siciliani—O tu Palermo]
In Czech: Stanislav Muž, ESTA-H5190

No. 21, Trio Baritone, Soprano & Bass
Alas, there is no doubt Baritone (Onegin)
P. N. Nortsov, E. Kurglikova, M. Mik-

hailov & Bolshoi Theatre Orch.—Melik-
Pashayev, in DISC-752

(THE) GUARDSMAN See Oprichnik
IOLANTHE, Op. 69 1 Act 1892

Iolanthe's Aria, Scene 1 Soprano
Zhukovskaya & Bolshoi Theatre Orch.,
in DISC-752

Who can compare? (King René's Aria,
Scene 4)
Pirogov & Bolshoi Theatre Orch., in
DISC-752
Adolf Kaktin (b) 10"—**G-EV15**
[Pique Dame—Yeletsky's Proposal,
When you choose]

JEANNE D'ARC
See under **Maid of Orleans**

(THE) MAID OF ORLEANS 4 Acts 1881
Fr. Jeanne d'Arc
Ger. Jungfrau von Orleans

Farewell, forests Soprano (Joanna's Aria)
Fr. Adieu, forêts
Ger. Lebt wohl, ihr Berge
Risë Stevens (ms) (in French)
12"—**C-71440D**
[Donizetti: Favorita—O mio Fernando]

MAZEPPA 3 Acts 1884
Cossack Dance Orchestra
Liverpool Philharmonic Orch.—
Sargent 12"—**G-C3340**
[Suite No. 3, Theme & Variations, Pt. 5]
Hallé Orch.—Harty 12"—**C-9076M**
[J. Strauss: Perpetuum mobile, Amster-
dam Concertgebouw—Mengelberg]
(C-LX240)

(The) Three Treasures Baritone
Adolf Kaktin 12"—**G-EL1002**
[Eugen Onegin—Prince Gremin's Aria]

OPRICHNIK 1874 Eng. The Guardsman
Overture
National Symphony Orch.—Fistoulari
12"—**D-K1291**
[Bellini: Norma—Overture]

PIQUE-DAME, Op. 68 3 Acts 1890
Eng. Queen of Spades
Rus. Pikovaya Dama

Individual Excerpts
ACT I
No. 2, Forgive me, bright celestial visions
Tenor
Fr. Pitié, pitié pour ma souffrance
Eng. Hermann's Arioso
A. M. Davidoff 10"—**G-EK45***
[No. 14]

ACT II
No. 12, When you choose me for your
husband
Ger. Als du zum Gatten mich erkoren
Eng. Prince Yeletsky's Proposal
Shara Talian, in DISC-752
Heinrich Schlusnus (in German)
12"—**PD-35003**
[Verdi: Vespri Siciliani—In braccio
dovizie]
DUPLICATION: A. Kaktin, G-EV15

No. 14, My darling friend 2 Sopranos
(or, Love is waiting—Pastorale Duo)
M. Cherkasskaya & N. Panina
10"—**G-EK45***
[No. 2, Forgive me, Davidoff]

ACT III
No. 20, It is near to midnight
Soprano (Lisa)
Irra Petina
(in CM-712) 12"—**C-72359D**
[None but the lonely heart]
Xenia Belmas 12"—**PD-66883**
[Verdi: Ernani—Surta è la notte]

Ouverture Solennelle "1812", Op. 49
Orchestra
Cleveland Orch.—Rodzinski
(C-LX932/3) 2 12"—**CX-205†**
Boston "Pops" Orch.—Fiedler
(G-C3040/1) 2 12"—**VM-515†**
(also in VM-776†)
Philadelphia Orch.—Stokowski
(G-DB1663/4) 2 12"—**V-7499/500**
Amsterdam Concertgebouw Orch.—
Mengelberg 2 12"—**T-SK3080/1**
(U-G14271/2)
Philharmonia Orch.—Malko
2 12"—**G-C3617/8**
National Symphony Orch.—Reginald
Goodall 2 12"—**D-K1349/50†**
—Arr. Band: H. M. Grenadier Guards Band
Miller, C-GQX16490
—Arr. Chorus & Orchestra
Berlin Philharmonic & Ural Cossacks
Choir—Kitschin, PD-95054/5

Overtures
See under **Hamlet; Ouverture Solennelle
"1812"; Romeo and Juliet**

Pique-Dame See under Operas

Polonaise
See under Operas—Eugen Onegin

QUARTETS—String

No. 1, D minor, Op. 11
Roth String Quartet 4 12"—**CM-407†**
—2nd Mvt. (Andante cantabile) only
(The single-sided versions are
abbreviated)
Pasquier Quartet 12"—**LUM-35024**
Budapest Quartet 12"—**G-D1634**
Lener Quartet 12"—**C-LX393**
(C-LWX96) (C-GQX10350)
New Hungarian Quartet 12"—**G-C3106**
DUPLICATIONS: Riele Queling Quartet,
G-EG6889; Prisca Quartet, PD-15230;
Mischa Elman Quartet, V-6634:
G-DB1055; Poltronieri Quartet,
C-D14529
—Arr. Violin & Piano
Fritz Kreisler & Franz Rupp, V-15217:
G-DB3443
—Arr. String Orchestra
Leslie Heward String Orch., C-7389M:
C-DX996; Robin Hood Dell Orch.—
Kostelanetz, in CM-601: C-DX1354;
Orch. of the "Maggio Musicale"—Gui,
CET-BB25180; Minneapolis Symphony—
Ormandy, V-1719: G-DA1461

Queen of Spades
See under Operas—Pique-Dame

Rococo Variations—
See under Variations on a Rococo Theme

Romance, F minor, Op. 5 Piano

—Arr. Orchestra: Victor Salon Orch.,
V-35808: G-C1397

—Arr. Violin & Piano
Vasa Prihoda & M. Raucheisen
[Sarasate: Jota Navarra] 12"—**PD-68045**
Siegfried Borries & pf. acc.
10"—**G-DA4471**
[Brahms: Waltz, Op. 39, No. 5]

Romeo and Juliet Overture-Fantasia
NBC Symphony Orch.—Toscanini
3 12"—**VM-1178†**
[Kabalevsky: Colas Breugnon—
Overture]
Royal Philharmonic—Beecham
3 12"—**G-DB6420/2†**
[Chabrier: Marche Joyeuse]
National Symphony Orch.—Coates
(D-K1305/7) 3 12"—**D-ED6†**
[Rimsky-Korsakov: Snow Maiden—
Dance of the Tumblers]
Cleveland Orch.—Rodzinski
3 12"—**CM-478†**
[Mussorgsky: Khovantchina—Prelude]
Boston Symphony Orch.—Koussevitzky
3 12"—**VM-347†**
[Sibelius: Swan White—Maiden with the
roses]
[Prokofieff: Love for 3 Oranges—
March & Scherzo, on G-DB3165/7†]
Vienna Philharmonic—von Karajan
3 12"—**C-LX1033/5†**
(C-LCX105/7) (C-LFX720/2)
DUPLICATIONS: Symphony Orch.—
Lambert, G-C3216/8†; Amsterdam Con-
certgebouw Orch.—Mengelberg, CX-33†:
C-LX55/6; Berlin State Opera Orch.—
Melichar, PD-27251/2

Scherzo, Op. 42, No. 2
(Souvenir d'un lieu cher)
Nathan Milstein (vl) & Leopold
Mittmann (pf) 10"—**C-17115D**
[Stravinsky: L'Oiseau de feu—Berceuse]

Serenade, C major, Op. 48
String Orchestra
1. Pezzo in forma di sonatina
2. Walzer 3. Elegie
4. Finale (Tema Russo)
Philadelphia Orch.—Ormandy
3 12"—**CM-677†**
BBC Symphony—Boult
(G-DB3303/5†) 3 12"—**VM-556†**
Amsterdam Concertgebouw Orch.—
Mengelberg
(U-G14219/21) 3 12"—**T-SK2901/3**
String Orch.—van Kempen
3 10"—**PD-25365/7**
—2nd Mvt. (Waltz) only
Boston Symphony—Koussevitzky, in
VM-327†; also V-11-8727: G-DB2903;
Amsterdam Concertgebouw—Mengelberg,
C-GQX10942; Berlin State Opera Orch.—
Blech, G-C2257: G-EH351; Berlin
Philharmonic—Weisbach, G-DB4586;

Royal Theatre Orch., Copenhagen—
Jensen, TONO-X25039

—4th Mvt. (Finale) only
Berlin State Opera Orch.—Blech,
G-C2257: G-EH351; Berlin Philharmonic
Orch.—Weisbach, G-DB4586

Sérénade mélancolique, B flat minor, Op. 26
Violin & Orchestra
D. Oistrakh, in COMP-C202
Mischa Elman
(G-DB1470) 12"—**V-7744**
Naoum Blinder & pf. acc. 12"—**C-9692**
Enrico Campajola & E. Sarti (pf)
12"—**C-CQX16621**
K. Sroubek & F. Maxian (pf)
[Taneiev: Tarantella] 12"—**U-G14235**

(THE) SLEEPING BEAUTY, Op. 66
Ballet
Fr. **La Belle au Bois Dormant**
Ger. **Dornröschen**

Miscellaneous Excerpts
Introduction; Fairy Carabosse; Lilac
Fairy; Six Fairies (Variations 1-4);
Valse; Rose adagio; Puss in Boots;
Diamond & Silver Fairies; Mazurka &
Apotheosis
Sadler's Wells Orch.—Lambert
(G-C3081/3†) 3 12"—**VM-673†**

—Introduction; Adagio; Waltz only
Bolshoi Theatre Orch.—Faier
(USSR-9818/23) 3 10"—**COMP-C200**

**—Panorama; Page's Dance; Aurora's Solo;
Vision Scene I; Red Riding Hood; March
only**
Royal Opera House Orch., Covent Garden
—Lambert 2 12"—**C-DX1281/2**

**—Overture; Polonaise; Adagio; Variations;
Bluebird; Three Ivans; Adagio; Pas de
quatre & Mazurka only**
(Arranged as "Aurora's Wedding" for
Ballet Russe performances)
London Philharmonic Orch.—Kurtz
3 12"—**VM-326†**
(G-C2853/5) (G-EH984/6)

**—Introduction; Bluebird; Princess Florisse;
Panorama; Waltz only**
BBC Theatre Orch.—Robinson
(D-K1524/5) 2 12"—**D-ED18†**

—Waltz only
Boston "Pops" Orch.—Fiedler
(G-EH1058) 12"—**V-11932**
[Herbert: Natoma—Dagger Dance]
[Chopin: Polonaise militaire, G-C2892]
Hallé Orch.—Sargent 12"—**C-DX1079**
[Borodin: Prince Igor—Overture, Pt. 3]
Royal Opera Orch.—Sargent
(G-L672) 12"—**G-C1415**
[Brahms: Hungarian Dance No. 5]
Robin Hood Dell Orch.—Kostelanetz
(in CM-601) 12"—**C-12277D**
[None but the lonely heart]
(C-DX1278)

DUPLICATIONS: Berlin State Opera
Orch.—Melichar, P-R2536; Marek Weber
Orch., G-C2948: G-L1050; Dinicu Orch.,
C-DB1753

—Arr. 2 Pianos: Rawicz & Landauer,
C-FB2188

—Arr. Band: Coldstream Guards Band,
G-C3150

SONGS

NOTE: *Unless specified to the contrary, all songs
are sung in the original language (generally
Russian or French) although for convenience,
the titles are listed in English translations.*

Collection
It was Early Spring, Op. 38, No. 2; Where
Dancing was loudest (At the Ball), Op.
38, No. 3; Green Grass, (Complaint of
the Bride), Op. 47, No. 7; I Wish, Op. 38,
No. 4; In this moonlight night, Op. 73,
No. 3; Do not Doubt me Dear; None but
the lonely heart, Op. 6, No. 6; Whether
by Day, Op. 47, No. 6
Irra Petina (s) & Orch.—Hendl
3 12"—**CM-712**
[Pique-Dame: Liza's Aria]

Individual Songs

All for you, Op. 57, No. 6 (Kroutikoff)
Fr. Toi seul
Grace Moore (s) (in French)
12"—**V-11-8158**
[Paulin: Que deviennent les roses,
Op. 110]

At the Ball, Op. 38, No. 3 (Tolstoi)
Irra Petina, in CM-712
S. Lemeshev (t) & S. K. Stuchevski
(pf) 10"—**USSR-8548/9**
[If you would only know, Op. 60, No. 3]
(Also in STIN-S303)
Richard Tauber (t) (in English)
[Pimpinella] 10"—**P-RO20549**
G. P. Vinogradov (t) & K. Vinogradov
(pf) 10"—**ESTA-D2102**
[Pimpinella]

At the open window, Op. 63, No. 2
(Von Russland)
N. I. Nagatschewsky (t) & pf. acc.
10"—**G-EK125**
[Kaschewarow: Die Stille]

Children's Song, Op. 54, No. 16
("My Lisochek")
S. Lemeshev (t) & S. K. Stuckevski (pf)
10"—**USSR-9865/70**
[Cuckoo, Op. 54, No. 8]

Complaint of the Bride, Op. 47, No. 7
(Surikov)
(or, Wasn't I a hale and hearty blade of
grass . . .)
Irra Petina, in CM-712
Xenia Belmas (s) & pf. acc.
[If I had known] 12"—**PD-66999**

(The) Cuckoo, Op. 54, No. 8
S. Lemeshev (t) & S. K. Stuckevski (pf)
10"—**USSR-9865/70**
[Children's Song, Op. 54, No. 16]

Disappointment, Op. 65, No. 2
M. Maksakarov (s) & S. Pogrebov (pf)
10"—**USSR-10037/8**
[Song of the gypsy girl, Op. 60, No. 7]
V. V. Viktorova (s) & A. B. Golden-
weiser (pf) 10"—**USSR-13068/71**
[Rachmaninoff: Do not trust me, friend]

Don Juan's Serenade, Op. 38, No. 1
(Tolstoi)
Dennis Noble (b) (in English) &
Gerald Moore (pf) 12"—**G-C3637**
[To the Forests]
Aubrey Pankey (t) (in English)
[Légende] 10"—**PAT-PG94**
Raphael Arie (b) In Prep. **Swiss Decca**
Peter Dawson (b) (in English)
[Schubert: Erlkönig] 12"—**G-C1327**
Nelson Eddy (b) (in French)
10"—**C-17309D**
[Saint-Saëns: Danse macabre]
DUPLICATION: (in French) E. Caruso,
G-DA114*

I bless you forests
See under Pilgrim's Song

If I had known, Op. 47, No. 1 (Tolstoi)
Xenia Belmas (s) & pf. acc.
12"—**PD-66999**
[Complaint of the bride, Op. 47, No. 7]

If you would only know, Op. 60, No. 3
(Variant: If I could express in one word)
G. P. Vinogradov (t) & K. Vinogradov
(pf) 10"—**ESTA-D2103**
[Rimsky-Korsakov: Sadko—Song of
India; Glinka: In my blood the fire of
desire burns]
S. Lemeshev (t) & S. K. Stuchevski (pf)
10"—**USSR-8548/9**
[At the ball, Op. 38, No. 3]

In this moonlight night, Op. 73, No. 3
Irra Petina, in CM-712
G. P. Vinogradov (t) & K. Vinogradov
(pf) 10"—**ESTA-D2104**
[Glinka: Do not sing: I remember]

It was early in Spring, Op. 38, No. 2
Irra Petina, in CM-712
Mascia Predit (s) (in Italian) &
G. Favoretto (pf) 12"—**CET-BB25154**
[None but the lonely heart]

(Les) Larmes, Op. 65, No. 5
(Blanchotte) Eng. Tears
Maggie Teyte (s) (in French) & Gerald
Moore (pf)
In Gramophone Shop Album **GSC-2**

Legend—Christ had a garden, Op. 54, No. 5
Dennis Noble (b) (in Eng.)
10"—**G-B9625**
[None but the lonely heart]
John McCormack (t) (in Eng.) & Gerald
Moore (pf) 10"—**G-DA1755**
[Grüber: Stille Nacht]
Aubrey Pankey (t) (in Eng.)
10"—**PAT-PG94**
[Don Juan's Serenade]
DUPLICATION: Nelson Eddy (in Eng.),
C-17366D

Lullaby, Op. 16, No. 1
Mascia Predit (s) (in Italian) & B.
Favaretto (pf) 12"—**CET-BB25153**
[Song of the gypsy girl, Op. 60, No. 7]
Betty Martin (s) (in English)
(in C-J17) 10"—**C-35613**
[Mozart: Wiegenlied & Schubert:
Wiegenlied]

(The) Nightingale, Op. 57, No. 1
I. Kozlovsky (t) & pf. acc. 10"—**D-M554**
[Rimsky-Korsakov: It is not the wind]

No more I'll be singing, Op. 6, No. 2
See Speak not, O beloved

None but the lonely heart, Op. 6, No. 6
(Goethe)
Ger. **Nur wer die Sehnsucht kennt**
Irra Petina, in CM-712
Gladys Swarthout (ms) (in English)
10"—**V-10-1166**
[Moscow, No. 5-Prayer only]
Richard Tauber (t) (in English)
[Speak not, O beloved] 10"—**P-RO20518**
Joan Hammond (s) (in English) with
James Whitehead (vlc) & Gerald
Moore (pf)   10"—**G-B9486**
[Massenet: Elégie]
Dennis Noble (b) (in English)
[Legend]   10"—**G-B9625**
John McCormack (t) (in English) with
vlc. & pf. acc. 10"—**V-1306**
[Schubert: Who is Sylvia?]
[Rachmaninoff: To the children, on
G-DA1112]
Lawrence Tibbett (b) (in English)
(G-DA1383) 10"—**V-1706**
[Lehmann: Myself when young]
Mascia Predit (s) (in Italian) & G.
Favaretto (pf) 12"—**CET-BB25154**
[It was early in Spring, Op. 38, No. 2]
DUPLICATIONS: Nelson Eddy,
C-17171D: C-LB59; John McHugh,
C-FB2929; Leonard Warren, V-10-1406

—**Arr. Orchestra**
Boston "Pops" Orch.—Fiedler
[Dinicu: Hora Staccato] 10"—**V-4413**
Robin Hood Dell Orch.—Kostelanetz, in
CM-601: C-DX1278
DUPLICATIONS: Marek Weber Orch.,
V-25228: G-B8768: G-EG3609; Mario
Traverso Orch., PD-43343

—**Miscellaneous arrangements**
Gregor Piatigorsky (vlc) in CM-684;
Albert Sandler (vl) & Orch.,
C-DB1616; Lionel Tertis (vla),
C-D1628; Ellen Birgithe Nielsen (vl),
G-DA5251; William Primrose (vla),
C-7323M

Pilgrim's Song, Op. 47, No. 5 (Tolstoi)
(I bless the forests)
Ger. **Gesegnet sei mir, Wald und Au**
Lawrence Tibbett (b) (in English)
(G-DB1945) 12"—**V-7779**
[Mussorgsky: Song of the Flea]
Dennis Noble (b) (in English) & Gerald
Moore (pf) 10"—**G-C3637**
[Don Juan's Serenade]
Nelson Eddy (b) (in English)
(C-LB59) 12"—**C-17171D**
[None but the lonely heart]
Oscar Natzke (bs) (in English) & H.
Greenslade (pf) 12"—**P-E11397**
[Lehmann: Myself when young]
In German: Heinrich Schlusnus,
PD-62798

Pimpinella (Florentine Song) Op. 38, No. 6
G. P. Vinogradov (t) & K. Vinogradov
(pf)   10"—**ESTA-D2102**
[At the ball]
Richard Tauber (t) (in English)
[At the ball] 10"—**P-RO20549**

DUPLICATION: E. Caruso (in Italian),
G-DA119*

Solitude, Op. 73, No. 6 (Rathaus)
(Also called "Again as before")

—**Arr. Orchestra** Stokowski
Hollywood Bowl Orch.—Stokowski
12"—**V-11-9187**
[Humoresque, Op. 10, No. 3]
Philadelphia Orch.—Stokowski
12"—**V-14947**
[Franck: Grande Pièce symphonique—
Andante]
[Rachmaninoff: Concerto No. 3, Pt. 9, on
V-17485 in VM-710†]
[Wagner: Tannhäuser—Prelude to Act
III, on G-DB3255]
All-American Orch.—Stokowski
12"—**C-11982D**
[Schumann: Kinderszenen—Träumerei]

Song of the gypsy girl, Op. 60, No. 7
(Down in the brush . . .)
M. Maksakarov (s) & S. Pogrebov (pf)
10"—**USSR-10037/8**
[Disappointment, Op. 65, No. 2]
Mascia Predit (s) (in Italian) & G.
Favaretto (pf) 12"—**CET-BB25153**
[Lullaby]

Speak not, o beloved, Op. 6, No. 2
(Pleshayeff)
Richard Tauber (t) (in English)
10"—**P-RO20518**
[None but the lonely heart]

Tears See (Les) Larmes

'Twas you alone, Op. 57, No. 6
See **All for you**

SUITES Orchestra

No. 3, G major, Op. 55

—**4th Mvt. (Theme & Variations) only**
Liverpool Philharmonic Orch.—Sargent
3 12"—**G-C3338/40†**
[Mazeppa: Cossack Dance]
Philharmonic-Symphony of N. Y.—
Barbirolli 2 12"—**CX-226†**

—**Abbreviated version**
Bolshoi Theatre Orch.—S. A. Samosud
(USSR-9210/3) 2 10"—**COMP-C104**

No. 4, G major, Op. 61 "Mozartiana"
(Arrangements of 4 Mozart selections)
1. Gigue, G major, Op. 574
2. Minuet, D major, K. 355
3. Ave, verum corpus, K. 618
(based on Liszt's piano transcription "A
la Chapelle Sistine")
4. (10) Variations on a theme of Gluck,
K. 455
Philharmonic-Symphony of N. Y.—
Rodzinski 2 12"—**CX-248†**
NOTE: *In this recording Variations 6, 7, 8 are
omitted & 9, 10 badly cut.*

(THE) SWAN LAKE, Op. 20 Ballet
Fr. **Lac des Cygnes**
Orchestral Suite. (Excerpts)
Introduction; No. 2, Dance of the Prince;
No. 4, Waltz in A—Corps de Ballet; No.

13, Dance of the Queen of Swans; No. 14,
Dance of the Little Swans; Nos. 16 & 17,
Scene & Coda; No. 20, Scene & Waltz in
A flat; No. 22, Spanish Dance; No. 23,
Pas d'action; No. 24, Hungarian Dance—
Czardas; No. 25, Mazurka; No. 31, Dance
of the Cygnets; No. 33, Final Scene
St. Louis Symphony Orch.—Golschmann
           5 12"—VM-1028†

—Nos. 4, 23, & 24 omitted
London Philharmonic Orch.—Dorati
(C-DX869/72†)   4 12"—CM-349†

—No. 4, Waltz; No. 9, Introduction—Act
II; No. 13; Dance of the Queen of the
Swans; No. 14, Dance of the Little Swans;
No. 24, Hungarian Dance—Czardas
National Symphony Orch.—Sidney Beer
(D-K1308/9)   2 12"—D-ED12†
London Philharmonic—Barbirolli
         2 12"—G-C2619/20

—No. 12, Waltz only
London Philharmonic—Efrem Kurtz
(C-DX787)   12"—C-69080D
[Delibes: Naila Valse—Intermezzo]

—No. 13, Dance of the Queen of the Swans
only
Symphony Orch.—Goehr, on V-36214, in
V-C30: G-C2983

—No. 14, Dance of the Little Swans only
Symphony Orch.—Goehr, on V-36214, in
V-C30: G-C2914

SYMPHONIES Orchestra
No. 1, G minor, Op. 13 "Winter Daydreams"
Indianapolis Symphony Orch.—
  F. Sevitsky   5 12"—VM-1189†
[Eugene Onegin—Waltz]
Santa Monica Symphony Orch.—Jacques
Rachmilovich   4 12"—DISC-A801

No. 2, C minor, Op. 17 "Little Russia"
Minneapolis Symphony Orch.—
  Mitropoulos   5 12"—CM-673†
Cincinnati Symphony Orch.—Goossens
      4 12"—VM-790†
(G-DB5938/41 in GM-365†)

No. 3, D major, Op. 29 "Polish"
National Symphony Orch.—Hans
Kindler   5 12"—VM-747†
London Symphony Orch.—Fitelberg
     5 12"—D-K1479/83†

No. 4, F minor, Op. 36
Philadelphia Orch.—Ormandy
      5 12"—CM-736†
Boston Symphony Orch.—Koussevitzky
      5 12"—VM-327†
NOTE: 3rd Mvt. Cut.
[Serenade—Waltz]
(G-DB2899/903 in GM-258†)
NBC Symphony Orch.—Stokowski
      5 12"—VM-880†
Minneapolis Symphony Orch.—
  Mitropoulos   5 12"—CM-468†
Hallé Orch.—Lambert
     5 12"—C-DX1096/100†
National Symphony Orch.—Sargent
     5 12"—D-K1226/30†
Amsterdam Concertgebouw Orch.—
Mengelberg   5 12"—O-8404/8
(C-GQX10923/7)

—3rd Mvt. (Scherzo: Pizzicato ostinato)
Abridged
Victor Symphony Orch.—O'Connell, in
V-G15

No. 5, E minor, Op. 64
Philharmonia Orch.—Paul Kletzki
(C-LX869/74†)   6 12"—CM-701†
Boston Symphony—Koussevitzky
      6 12"—VM-1057†
Philadelphia Orch.—Ormandy
     5 12"—VM-828†
Cleveland Orch.—Rodzinski
     5 12"—CM-406†
London Philharmonic—Beecham
(C-LX869/73†)   5 12"—CM-470†
Philadelphia Orch.—Stokowski
  (in GM-235†) 6 12"—VM-253†
(G-DB2548/53)
National Symphony—Sidney Beer
     5 12"—D-K1032/6†
Berlin Philharmonic Orch.—Mengelberg
     6 12"—T-SK3086/91
DUPLICATIONS: London Philharmonic
—Lambert, G-C3088/92 in GM-327†;
Amsterdam Concertgebouw Orch.—
Mengelberg, C-GQX10936/42:
O-8357/63

—2nd Mvt. (Andante cantabile) only (arr.)
Symphony Orch.—Stokowski: V-11-9574;
Salon Orch.—Shilkret, G-B9094

—Excerpts (1st & 4th Mvts.)
Symphony Orch.—Goehr, V-36215 in
V-C30: G-C2915

—Excerpts (unspecified)
Royal Theatre Orch., Copenhagen—
Jensen   2 12"—TONO-X25038/9
[String Serenade—Waltz]

No. 6, B minor, Op. 74 ("Pathétique")
Berlin Philharmonic—Furtwängler
(G-DB4609/14)   6 12"—GM-323†
National Symphony Orch.—Coates
(D-K1243/8)   6 12"—D-ED18†
Philharmonia Orch.—Nicolai Malko
     5 12"—G-C3630/4†
Hollywood Bowl Symphony Orch.—
Stokowski   6 12"—VM-1105†
Concertgebouw Orch.—Mengelberg
(U-G14214/8)   5 12"—T-SK3176/80
Philadelphia Orch.—Ormandy
(G-DB6070/4)   5 12"—VM-337†
Paris Conservatory Orch.—Gaubert
     5 12"—CM-277†
(C-LFX450/4) (C-GQX10857/61)
N. Y. Philharmonic-Symphony Orch.—
Rodzinski   5 12"—CM-558†
(C-DX1205/9†)
London Symphony Orch.—Coates
     5 12"—G-AW148/52
Berlin Philharmonic—von Karajan
     6 12"—PD-67499/504
DUPLICATIONS: Boston Symphony—
Koussevitzky, VM-85†: GM-114†; All-
American Youth Orch.—Stokowski,
CM-432†

Trio, A minor, Op. 50
Violin, 'Cello, Piano
"To the memory of a great artist"
Yehudi Menuhin, Maurice Eisenberg,
Hephzibah Menuhin 6 12"—VM-388†
(G-DB2887/92)

Troïka en traineaux (November) Op. 37a,
No. 11
(from "The Months") Piano
Sergei Rachmaninoff 12"—V-6857
[Rachmaninoff: Polka de W. R.]
Edward Kilenyi 12"—C-69798D
[Liszt-Paganini: La Campanella]
Otakar Vondrovic 12"—ESTA-F5195
[Rachmaninoff: Prelude No. 1]
José Iturbi 12"—V-12-0242
[Barcarolle]
—Arr. 2 Pianos Strong
Edna Hatzfeld & Mark Strong, D-F8136

Valse des fleurs
See under Nutcracker Suite

Valse sentimentale, Op. 51, No. 6 Piano
—Arr. 'Cello & Piano
Gregor Piatigorsky & Ivor Newton
12"—G-DB2271
[Scriabin: Romance; Chopin: Nocturne,
C sharp minor, Op. post.]
DUPLICATION: S. N. Knushevitzky,
USSR-10501/2

Variations On a Rococo Theme, Op. 33
'Cello & Piano
Pierre Fournier & Lamoureux Orch.—
Bigot 2 12"—G-DB5152/3
Danya Shafran & Leningrad State
Philharmonic—Gauk 3 12"—D-X269/71
[Golt: Scherzo—Vladimir Sofronitsky,
pf.]

Waltzes
See under Nutcracker Suite—Waltz of
the flowers; Operas—Eugen Onegin,
Waltz: Serenade, Op. 48—2nd Mvt.;
Valse sentimentale

MISCELLANEOUS
Collections
The Music of Tchaikovsky
None but the lonely heart; Sleeping
Beauty—Waltz; Andante cantabile (from
String Quartet); Melody, E flat major;
Barcarolle (from The Months); Nut-
cracker Suite—Waltz of the flowers
Andre Kostelanetz & Robin Hood Dell
Orch. 3 12"—CM-601

Fantasias, Potpourris, etc. of
Tchaikovsky's music
Berlin Philharmonic Orch.—Melichar,
PD-25188: PD-57080/1; also in
VOX-458; Berlin Philharmonic, with
soloists—Schröder, T-E1888; Concert
Orch.—B. Seidler-Winkler, G-EH1224:
G-C3299; Mantovani Orch., D-F8264

TCHEREPNIN, Alexander (1889-)
The son of Nicolai Tcherepnin, Alexander
studied with his father, and came to America
via Paris with the outbreak of the Russian
Revolution.
Bagatelles, Op. 5 Piano
A. Tcherepnin 12"—G-DB4440
Ode 'Cello & Piano
G. Cassadó & M. Raucheisen
[de Laserna: Tonadilla] 10"—T-A1830

TCHEREPNIN, Nicolai (1873-)
A contemporary Russian composer, pupil of
Rimsky-Korsakov, Tcherepnin's music combines
the atmosphere of French impressionism with
the orchestral brilliance and daring of his Rus-
sion teacher.
(Le) Pavillon d'Armide Ballet 1903
—Waltz
Bolshoi State Theatre Orch.—
Faier 10"—USSR-13226/7

TELEMANN, Georg Philipp (1681-1767)
Although Telemann wrote a great deal of
church music—he was in fact one of the most
prolific composers of all time—his art breathes
the new robust secularity of the eighteenth century in sharp contrast to his more profound
contemporary and countryman, J. S. Bach. It is
hence no accident that the last few decades,
when neo-classicism (pretended, or rather
pseudo-classicism) has been the order of the
day, have seen growing interest in Telemann's
music.
Concerto, F minor Oboe & Orchestra
Waldemar Wolsing & Danish Orch.—
Wöldike 12"—C-LDX2
Concerto, G minor Violin & Orch.
—Arr. J. S. Bach Harpsichord
Ruggero Gerlin 12"—C-BQX2534
Don Quichotte Suite
Arthur Fiedler Sinfonietta (Erwin
Bodky, harpsichord) 2 12"—VM-945†
Fantasias (1e douzaine)
(harpsichord)
Nos. 2, D minor; 3, E minor! 4, E minor;
8, G minor
Edith Weiss-Mann 2 12"—AL-AR2
No. 6. B flat major
Li Stadelmann (harpsichord)
10"—PD-47282
[Rameau: Lardon, Rigaudon,
Triomphante]
Liebe, liebe
Aria from an unidentified opera
Isabel French (s) with harpsichord &
'cello acc., in TC-2
Quartet, E minor (Tafelmusik, 1733)
Marcel Moyse (fl), Jean Pasquier (vl),
Etienne Pasquier (vlc) Ruggero Gerlin
(harpsichord) (in Vol. III) 12"—AS-26
Quintet, D major Flute & Strings
Ars Rediviva Ensemble 12"—G-DB11137
Suite, A minor Flute & Strings
William Kincaid & Philadelphia Orch.—
Ormandy 2 12"—VM-890†
Suite (Tafelmusik)
Ouvertüre; Bergerie; Allegresse; Fla-
terie; Menuett
Wiesbaden Collegium Musicum—Weyns
4 10"—T-A2128; 2905/7
Trio, E minor (Tafelmusik, 1733)
Wiesbaden Collegium Musicum—
E. Weyns 12"—T-E2256
Trio-Sonata Flute, Violin, Piano
Marcel Moyse, Blanche Honegger, Louis
Moyse 10"—OL-20

THOMAS, André

Le Tombeau de Max Jacob   Piano
Madeleine de Valmalete
                              12"—PAT-PDT146

THOMAS, Charles Louis Ambroise
(1811-1896)

*A conservative French composer, Ambroise
Thomas devoted the major part of his musical
life to the Paris "Opéra-Comique," for which
theatre he composed some twenty stage works.
He is today however a one-work composer;
"Mignon" alone has remained on the boards.*

Autumn—Variations
Egle Jeronutti Rocchi (harp)
                              10"—G-GW1039

OPERAS   In French

(LE) CAID   2 Acts   1849

Air du Tambour-Major, Act I   Bass
("Le Tambour-Major tout galonné
d'or")
Pol Plançon
          (in VM-816)   **12"—V-18143***
[Donizetti: Lucia—Mad Scene, Nellie
Melba]

Marche—Arr. Band   PD-521982:
PAT-PA543: O-165730

(LE) CARNAVAL DE VENISE
3 Acts   1857

Overture   Ochestra
Symphony Orch.—Ruhlmann
                              12"—PAT-X96077

HAMLET   5 Acts   1868
It. **Amleto**

ACT II

Chanson Bachique: O vin dissipe la tristesse
Baritone
It. **Brindisi: O vin, discaccia la tristezza**
Ger. **Trinklied: O wein, zerstreu' unsere
Sorgen**
Martial Singher
          (in CM-578)   **12"—C-72087D**
[Massenet: Hérodiade—Vision fugitive]
John Charles Thomas   **10"—V-1639**
[Massenet: Hérodiade—Vision fugitive]
Robert Merrill   **12"—V-11-9291**
[Massenet: Hérodiade—Vision fugitive]
Titta Ruffo (in Italian)
          (in VM-816)   **12"—V-18140***
[Verdi: Traviata—Ah fors è lui,
Sembrich]
[Comme une pâle fleur, G-DB569*]
DUPLICATIONS: Armand Crabbé,
G-DB1043; P. Deldi, C-RF72
In German: Heinrich Schlusnus,
PD-66630: PD-67187; Arno Schellenberg,
G-EH1212
In Italian: Riccardo Stracciari, C-CQ784;
Giulio Fregosi, PAT-X15681; G. Mario
Sammarco, V-15-1018*

ACT III

J'ai pu frapper le misérable   Recit.

Etre ou ne pas être   Monologue   Baritone
A. Endrèze   **12"—PAT-PDT51**
[Gounod: Faust—Mort de Valentin]
[Reyer: Sigurd—Et toi Freïa, on
PAT-X90035]

ACT IV

Scène de Folie (Mad Scene)   Soprano
A vos jeux, mes amis   Recit.
Partagez-vous mes fleurs!   Valse
Et maintenant écoutez ma chanson
Ballade
Janine Micheau   **12"—G-W1592**

ACT V

La fatigue alourdit mes pas   Recit.
Comme une pâle fleur   Arioso   Baritone
It. **Come il romito fior**
A. Gaudin   **10"—PD-524027**
[Massenet: Werther—Air d' Albert]
In Italian: Riccardo Straciari, C-CQ784;
Titta Ruffo, G-DB569*

MIGNON   3 Acts   1866
Abridged recording
Soloists, Chorus & Orch. of the Théâtre
Royal de la Monnaie—
Maurice Bastin   5 12"—**C-OP19†**
Mignon .... Germaine Cernay (s)
Philine .... Lucienne Tragin (s)
Wilhelm .... André d'Arkor (t)
Lothario .... M. Demoulin (b)
Laërte .... Valère Mayer (t)
NOTE: *The original set, C-RFX33/8—6 12"
discs—contains two sides which are omitted
from the domestic release.*

Vocal & Orchestral Selections
Peter Anders, Hanns-Heinz Nissen, Ilse
Koegel, Susi Gmeiner & Chorus
(in German)   **12"—T-E2043**

Orchestral Fantasias
Berlin State Opera Orch.—Melichar,
PD-24443; Berlin State Orch.—Schmidt,
PD-57088

Overture   Orchestra
NBC Symphony Orch.—Toscanini
(G-DB6177)   **12"—V-11-8545**
National Symphony Orch.—
Fistoulari   **12"—D-K1166**
Boston "Pops" Orch.—Fiedler
(G-C2131)   (G-L1034)   **12"—V-12038**
DUPLICATIONS: Berlin State Opera
Orch.—Schmidt-Isserstedt, U-F18104:
T-E1882; Paris Symphony—Bigot,
C-DFX75; Berlin State Opera Orch.—
Melichar, PD-27158; Berlin State Opera
—Blech, G-AW269; Vienna State Opera
Orch.—Reichwein, O-7875; Berlin State
Opera Orch.—Fried, PD-19744; Berlin
State Opera Orch.—Schmalsitch,
G-EH283; Milan Symphony Orch.—
Molajoli, C-D14559

Individual Excerpts

ACT I

Fugitif et tremblant   (Air de Lothario)
Bass
Vanni-Marcoux   **10"—G-DA4867**
[Berceuse, Act III]

Connais-tu le pays?   Soprano
Ger. **Kennst du das Land?**
It. **Non conosci il bel suol**
Eng. **Knowest thou the land?**
Gladys Swarthout (ms)
          (in VM-925)   **12"—V-11-8281**
[Je connais un pauvre enfant]

Risë Stevens (ms)　　　12″—C-71192D
[Bizet: Carmen—Habañera]
Ninon Vallin　　　　　12″—O-171032
[Gounod: Faust—Air des bijoux]
Lucrezia Bori
(G-DA1017)　　　　　10″—V-1361
[Rondo—Gavotte, Act II]
DUPLICATIONS: Lucy Perelli, G-P762;
Germaine Cernay, C-LF109; Deva-Dassy,
G-DA4859; Germaine Corney,
PD-25830: PD-522559
In German: H. Ranczak, T-SK1324;
Friedel Beckmann, G-EG6424
In Italian: Ebe Stignani, CET-BB25041
in CET-9: also C-DQ1042; Pederzini,
G-S10258

Légères hirondelles　Duo: Soprano & Bass
Ger. **Schwalbenduet**
It. **Duetto delle rondinelle**
Ninon Vallin & André Balbon
　　　　　　　　　10″—PAT-PG70
[Massenet: Manon—Pardon, mais
j'étais là]
Ninon Vallin & Julien Lafont
[As-tu souffert?]　　　10″—O-188537
Risë Stevens & Ezio Pinza
　　　　　　　　　12″—C-72371D
[Ponchielli: La Gioconda—Bella cosi]
DUPLICATIONS: Germaine Cernay & P.
Dupré, O-188758; Farrar & Journet,
G-DO101*
In German: Friedel Beckmann & Arno
Schellenberg, G-DA4474; F. Hüni-
Mihacsek & W. Domgraf-Fassbaender,
PD-66862
In Italian: G. Zinetti & T. Pasero,
C-DQ1124

ACT II

Entr'acte (Gavotte)　Orchestra
Philadelphia Orch.—Stokowski
(G-DB1643) (in VM-116†) 12″—V-7456
[Debussy: Danses, Pt. 3]
Berlin State Opera Orch.—Melichar
　　　　　　　　　10″—PD-24442
[Mascagni: Cavalleria Rusticana—
Intermezzo]
Marek Weber Orch. (G-HE2305)
[Beethoven: Minuet in G] 10″—G-B4466
(G-K7174) (G-HN260)
DUPLICATION: Paul Godwin Künstler—
Orch., PD-22520

Styrienne: Je connais un pauvre enfant
Soprano
Ger. **Kam ein armes Kind von fern**
Gladys Swarthout (ms)
　　　　(in VM-925) 12″—V-11-8281
[Connais-tu le pays?]
Xenia Belmas　　　　12″—PD-66746
[Connais-tu le pays?]
Germaine Corney
(PD-25830)　　　　　10″—PD-522559
[Connais-tu le pays?]
In Italian: Ebe Stignani, P-DPX20:
CET-BB25006
In German: Freidel Beckmann, G-EG6424

Rondo-Gavotte: Me voici dans son boudoir
Lucrezia Bori (s)　　　10″—V-1361
[Connais-tu le pays?] (G-DA1017)
Nan Merriman (c)　　　12″—V-12-0067
[Gluck: Orfeo—Che farò]

Adieu, Mignon, courage　Tenor
Ger. **Leb' wohl, Mignon, o weine nicht**
It. **Addio, Mignon! fa core!**
Villabella　　　　　　10″—PAT-PG29
[Donizetti: Favorita—Spirto gentil]
Charles Richard　　　12″—G-DB11119
[Elle ne croyait pas]
DUPLICATIONS: Micheletti, O-188506;
M. Claudel, PD-524065
In German: J. Patzak, PD-30014
In Italian: Ferruccio Tagliavini,
CET-BB25119, in CET-2; Giovanni
Malipiero, G-DB5356; Giuseppe di Ste-
fano, G-DB11311; Beniamino Gigli,
G-DB1270; L. Fort, C-DC190; R.
D'Alessio, C-DQ1088; T. Schipa,
G-DB843*; Fernando de Lucia,
V-15-1024*

Elle est là, près de lui　Recit

Elle est aimée　Air　Soprano
Ger. **Dort bei ihn ist sie jetz**
Ninon Vallin　　　　　12″—O-171032
[Connais-tu le pays?]
DUPLICATION: Deva-Dassy, G-DA4859

As-tu souffert?　Duo: Soprano & Bass
Ninon Vallin & Julien Lafont
[Légères hirondelles]　10″—O-188537
In German: Friedel Beckmann & Arno
Schellenberg, G-DA4474

Polonaise: Je suis Titania　Soprano
It. **Io son Titania**
Ger. **Titania ist herabgestiegen**
Lily Pons (in VM-702)　12″—V-17232
[Rimsky-Korsakov: Coq d'or—Hymn to
the Sun]
DUPLICATIONS: Patrice Munsel,
V-11-8886; Josephine Antoine,
C-69813D; C. Clairbert, PD-66794;
In Italian: Toti Dal Monte, G-DB1318;
Galli-Curci, V-7110: G-DB1355; Lina
Pagliughi, CET-BB25004: P-E11324:
O-9113; Luisa Tetrazzini, V-15-1001*
In German: M. Perras, G-DB4438
In Boh. Maria Tauberová, U-B12335

ACT III

Berceuse: De son coeur j'ai calmé la fièvre
(Lothario's Lullaby)　Bass or Baritone
Ger. **Wiegenlied: Endlich kehrt die Ruhe
ihr wieder**
Vanni-Marcoux　　　　10″—G-DA4867
[Fugitif et tremblant]
DUPLICATIONS: A. Balbon,
PAT-X90075; E. Billot, O-171037; P.
Dupré, O-123707
In German: Gerhard Hüsch, G-EG6136
In Italian: T. Pasero, C-DQ1103
In Swedish: Ivar Andrésen, G-Z93*
—Arr. 'Cello
Lopes, PAT-X98094

Elle ne croyait pas Tenor
Ger. Wie ihre Unschuld
It.Ah! non credevi tu
Eng. Wilhelm's Romance
Villabella 10"—PAT-X90083
[Massenet: Manon—Le rêve]
Charles Richard 12"—G-DB11119
[Adieu, Mignon]
DUPLICATIONS: Micheletti, O-171019;
Franz Kaisin, PD-524021
In Italian: Giuseppe di Stefano,
G-DB11311; Giovanni Malipiero,
G-DB5356; CET-BB25062: P-DPX25;
T. Schipa, G-DB843*; R. D'Alessio,
C-DQ1088; B. Gigli, G-DB1270; M.
Giovagnoli, CET-CC2305

RAYMOND 3 Acts 1851
Overture Orchestra
National Symphony Orch.—Boyd Neel
12"—D-K1299
Berlin State Opera Orch.—van Kempen
12"—PD-15302
DUPLICATIONS: Victor Symphony—
Shilkret, G-C1564; Symphony Orch.—
Pitt, C-DX104; Berlin Philharmonic—
Prüwer, PD-27058; Hastings Municipal
—Cameron, D-K561; Bournemouth
Municipal Orch.—Birch, D-F7839

THOMPSON, Randall (1899-   )
*Like most American composers, Randall
Thompson has supported himself not by his
compositions but through a teaching career. His
works range from the sacred, through the customary programmatic, to music of a more indigenous American character. In this last category can be included his now famous "Testament of Freedom."*

Alleluia Chorus
Fleet Street Choir—Lawrence
10"—D-M541
(The) Testament of Freedom
(Thomas Jefferson) Chorus & Orchestra
Harvard Glee Club & Boston Symphony
Orch.—Koussevitzky 3 12"—VM-1054†

THOMSON, Virgil (1896-   )
*A most versatile American-born musical per-
sonality, Virgil Thomson is a fluent and facile
composer, a music critic, conductor, writer and
organist. His appointment, in 1940, as music
critic of the New York Herald Tribune (where
he reveals himself an ardent supporter of things
French) has not curtailed the rapid flow of
musical works from his pen, of which the most
recent is his much debated opera, "The Mother
of Us All," (1947) written to the text of Gertrude Stein.*

The Plow that Broke the Plains
Film Score Excerpts
Prologue; Grass; Cattle; Blues; Drought;
Devastation
Hollywood Bowl Symphony Orch.—
Stokowski 2 12"—VM-1116†
(Five) Portraits Orchestra
Bugles & Birds; Percussion Piece; Canta-
bile for Strings; Tango Lullaby; Fugue
Philadelphia Orch.—Thomson
2 12"—CX-255†

TICCIATI, Francesco (1893-   )
*A contemporary Italian composer and pianist,
who studied with Respighi and Busoni.*

Impresione dal Vero Orchestra
—Strapaese
EIAR Symphony Orch.—Ferrero
12"—CET-BB25085
[Masetti: Il Gioco del Cucù]

O Salutaris Hostia
Mancini (s) SEMS-21
[Antonelli: Factus est—vocal quartet]

Toccata Piano
Carlo Zecchi 12"—CET-CB20347
[Liszt: Etude, F minor]

TIERSOT, Julien (1857-1936)
*Julien Tiersot went through the mill of the
famous Paris "Conservatoire," but was aware of
his creative limitations and wisely did not attempt to go beyond them. Thus instead of
accumulating several hundred opus numbers,
he proceeded to contribute many useful volumes on various aspects of French music history and a good number of collections of
French Folk Songs.*

French Folk Songs Arranged by Tiersot
L'Amour de Moy
Roland Hayes (t) & R. Boardman (pf)
(in CM-393) 12"—C-17176D
[Massenet: Manon—Le rêve]

**Chanson populaire Bressane; Le pauvre
laboureur;**

**Chanson populaire Poitevine: Le retour du
marin**
Reynaldo Hahn, with self pf. acc.
10"—C-BF1

Noël Provençal
Sophie Wyss (s) & pf. acc. 12"—D-K1065
[Arr. Viullermoz: Ronde des Filles de
Quimperlé; Rawsthorne: 3 French
nursery songs]

Tambourin
Ninon Vallin (s) & Madeleine D'Aleman
(pf) 12"—O-123584
[Jura: La Violette doublera; Martini:
Plaisir d'Amour]

TIOMKIN, Dmitri
*One of the many composers of Hollywood film
scores.*

Duel in the Sun
Excerpts from the film score
Rio Grande; Orizaba; On the trail to
Spanish Bit; Rendezvous; Prairie Sky;
Trek to the sun; Duel at Squaw's Head;
Passional; Love eternal
Boston "Pops" Orch.—Fiedler
4 10"—VM-1083†
—**On the trail to Spanish Bit & Prairie Sky**
only
Boston "Pops" Orch.—Fiedler
10"—G-B9556
See under Strauss (Johann) for arrange-
ments for "The Great Waltz"—operetta
and film score

TITELOUZE, Jean (1563-1633)

Canon and organist of Rouen Cathedral throughout almost his entire adult life, Titelouze is the founder of the French school of organ music.

Ave Maris Stella 2nd verset
(Hymnes de l'Eglise, Paris, 1623)
Carl Weinrich, in MC-9

TOCH, Ernst (1887-   )

An Austrian composer and pianist now resident of the United States, Toch is an essentially self-taught musician, whose works however show careful study of the scores of Schönberg and Hindemith.

(The) Chinese Flute, Op. 29 (Early Chinese poems)
Alice Mock (s) (in English) & Pacific Sinfonietta—Compinsky
3 12"—ALCO-AC203
Etude allegro, Op. 56, No. 10 "The Top"
Piano
Jakob Gimpel, in VOX-164
Serenade ("Spitzweg"), Op. 25 2 Violins & Viola
L. Kaufman, G. Monasevitch, & Ray Menhennick   2 10"—VOX-177

TOFFT, Alfred (1865-1931)

A prominent figure in the musical life of Denmark, Tofft was a critic, composer and teacher. His works include chamber pieces, several operas, cantatas and many songs, one of which is listed below.

Der gaar Sagn om to Song
Edi Laider (t) & Ole Williamsen (pf)
10"—G-X6164

TOMASI, Henri (1901-   )

A contemporary French composer and conductor. Tomasi's "Tam-Tam" was written especially for radio.

Chants de Cyrnos
Cantu di Malincunia; U Marcante in fiera; Zilimbrina; Sirinatu; Lamentu serenata si spanettu
Martha Angelici (in Corsican)
2 10"—PAT-PA1045/6
(2) Geisha Songs
Martha Angelici (s) & Tomasi (pf)
10"—FLOR-HP2005
[Variations on a Corsican Theme, Pt. 3, Wind Quintet]
Mélodies Corses Corsican Songs (Lorenzi di Bradi)
Ninina & O Ciuciarella (2 Berceuses)
Alice Raveau (c) & Tomasi (pf)
10"—PAT-PG19
Tam-tam Symphonic Poem for Chorus, Soloists & Orchestra
(After a piece by Julien Maigret) (Music for Radio)
Chorus & Symphony Orch.—Tomasi
2 12"—PAT-PGT18/9
Variations on a Corsican Theme
Paris Wind Orch. Quintet
2 10"—FLOR-HP2004/5
[2 Geisha Songs, Angelici]

TOMMASINI, Vincenzo (1880-   )

The tasteful scoring of the transcribed work listed below (although badly cut and pieced together) has made this Italian composer famous the world over, but it contrasts strongly with his own scores which begin under the sway of German Romanticism and veer towards the barren neo-classicism of modern times.

(Le) Donne Di Buon Umore Ballet Suite (based on D. Scarlatti's "sonatas")
Eng. **The Good-Humored Ladies**
London Philharmonic Orch.—Eugene Goossens (G-C2864/5) 2 12"—VM-512

TORELLI, Giuseppe (1650-1708)

A great 17th century violin virtuoso and composer, Torelli is, with Stradella and Corelli, one of first to write Baroque concerti grossi.

Concertino, D minor, Op. 6, No. 11
Collegium Musicum—Diener
[Pachelbel: Canon]   12"—G-EH1231
Tu lo sai
Ezio Pinza (bs) &. F. Kitzinger (pf)
(in VM-766) 12"—V-17915
[Paisiello: La Molinara—Nel cor più & Monteverdi: L'Incoronazione di Poppea—Oblivion soave; Cavalli: Donzelle, fuggite]
Winifred Cecil (s) & A. Simonetto (pf)
10"—CET-TI7006
[Handel: Radamisto—Sommi dei]

TORRE, Ferdinando De La (16th Century)

A Spanish Renaissance composer.

Adoramus Te, Señor!
Yves Tinayre (t), Chorus & 3 Trombones
12"—LUM-32020
[Attey: Sweete was the song & Benet: Pleni sunt coeli]
(in Yves Tinayes album No. 2)
Spanish Dance, with prelude
Viol Trio   12"—PD-10750
[Isaac: Der Hundt; Lechner: Provencalischer Tanz]

TOSELLI, Enrico (1883-1926)

An Italian composer of light music, Toselli has, with a few exceptions (operettas and a symphonic poem for orchestra), held to the small forms of the Romantics. His works include short piano pieces, songs, romances and programmatic suites for string quartet.

Serenata (No. 1), Op. 6
Alfred Piccaver, D-M458; B. Gigli, V-6610; Anton Dermota, T-A10413; Giuseppe Lugo, PD-524252; Richard Tauber, P-RO20135; Tino Rossi, C-DB1832; Paul Sandoz, G-JK25; J. Björling (in Swedish), G-X3556; M. Jacobsen (in Danish), G-X3893
—Arr. Violin & Piano
Vasa Prihoda, CET-LL3009; H. Fitz-Crone, G-X4598
See current catalogues for other vocal and miscellaneous instrumental recordings.
Serenade (No. 2)
Royal Artillery String Orch.—Geary, D-F7514

TOSTI, Sir Francesco Paolo (1846-1916)

An Italian composer who settled in England and was knighted there in 1908, presumably in acknowledgment of his efforts as singing instructor to the Royal family. He composed many songs to English, French and Italian texts.

SONGS In Italian & English

Addio (Rizzelli) Eng. **Good-bye**
Richard Tauber (t) 10″—**P-RO20515**
[My dreams]
Enrico Caruso & re-recorded orch.
[Parted] 12″—**G-DB3327**
[Cottrau: Santa Lucia, on G-DB5387]
Richard Crooks (t) 12″—**V-8869**
[Sullivan: Lost Chord] (G-DB2337)
Beniamino Gigli (t) 12″—**G-DB1526**
[Sullivan: Lost Chord]
DUPLICATIONS: Webster Booth,
G-C3139; A. Piccaver, PD-90200; E.
Caruso, G-DB131*; Vanni-Marcoux,
G-DA4814

(L') Alba separa dalla luce l'ombra
Tito Schipa, on G-DA5358

Aprile
Beniamino Gigli (t) 12″—**G-DB3815**
[Notte d'amore]
DUPLICATIONS: R. Stracciari,
C-GQX10197; Pauli, G-DA1321

Ave Maria
Hendes Højhed, Princess Viggo of Denmark (s) & E. Selmar Saelges (pf)
10″—**G-DA5214**
[Février: Au jardin charmant]
DUPLICATION: Fernando Gusso,
D-M428

Dopo!
Pederzini (ms), on G-S10258

Ideale (Errica) Eng. **My Ideal** Ger.
Sehnsucht
Jussi Björling (t) 10″—**G-DA1582**
[di Capua: O sole mio]
Richard Tauber (t) 10″—**P-RO20511**
[Moszkowski: Serenata]
DUPLICATIONS: Tino Rossi, C-DB1872:
C-DW4846; Tito Schipa, G-DA1114; Alfred Piccaver, PD-90200; Gino Sinimberghi, PD-25871: PD-62806; F. Gusso,
D-M466; Martinelli, G-DA332*; E.
Caruso, G-DB129*

Luna d'estate
E. Caruso, on G-DA120*; F. Gusso, on
D-M443

Malìa (Fagliari) Eng. **Enchantment**
Tito Schipa (t) 10″—**G-DA5358**
[L'alba separa]
DUPLICATION: Ferrara, G-GW1064

Marechiare (Di Giacomo)
Beniamino Gigli (t) 10″—**G-DA1650**
[Rossini: Tarantella—La danza]
[Bixio: Desiderio on G-DA1654]
Tito Schipa (t) 10″—**G-DA1114**
[Ideale]
DUPLICATIONS: Titta Ruffo, G-DA748:
G-DB404*; Barberini, G-HN191; Gino
Sinimberghi, PD-25888; Rina Ketty,
PAT-PA1478; Ebe Stignani, CET-AA313
Also: Meister-Sextet, G-EG3965

Mattinata
John Charles Thomas (b) & Caroll Hollister (pf)
(in VM-966) 10″—**V-10-1088**
[Bridge: Come to me in dreams]

Mélodie
Stefan Islandi (t) 10″—**G-DA5242**
[Crescenzi: Rondine al Nido]

(La) Mia Canzone
Enrico Caruso & re-recorded Orch.
(G-DA1380) 10″—**V-1688**
[d'Hardelot: Because]
(Original recording, G-DA116*)

My Dreams (Weatherley)
Richard Tauber (t) 10″—**P-RO20515**
[Addio]

Ninon
Georges Thill (t) (in French) & M.
Faure (pf) 12″—**C-LFX37**
[Bruneau: L'Attaque au Moulin]
DUPLICATION: Vanni-Marcoux,
G-DB1515

Non t'amo più
A. Pertile (t), G-DA1008

Parted (Weatherley)
Beniamino Gigli (t) 10″—**G-DA1870**
[Murray: I'll walk beside you]
Webster Booth (t) 10″—**G-B9472**
[Adams: The Bells of St. Mary's]
DUPLICATIONS: Richard Crooks,
G-DA1394: V-1696; Derek Oldham,
G-B8266; Enrico Caruso, G-DB3327;
Sydney Rayner, D-F3133; Richard
Tauber, P-RO20496

Pour un baiser
Richard Tauber (t) 10″—**P-RO20546**
[Lalo: Roi d'Ys-Aubade]
Marcel Wittrisch (t) 10″—**G-EG6104**
[Massenet: Elégie]
DUPLICATION: A. Piccaver, PD-62674

(La) Serenata (Lesareo)
Ezio Pinza (bs) & Gebner King (pf)
[L'Ultima canzone] 12″—**C-71687D**
Beniamino Gigli (t) 10″—**G-DA1713**
[Leoncavallo: Mattinata]
[de Mari-Cinque: Mattinata Veneziana,
on G-DA1618]
Ebe Stignani (s) 10″—**CET-AA313**
[Marechiare]
Anton Dermota (t) 10″—**T-A10413**
[Toselli: Serenata]
DUPLICATION: Bertucco, G-HN1791

Sogno
Tancredi Pasero (bs) 10″—**G-DA5337**
[Carelli: Mefisto]
DUPLICATION: Fererra, G-GW1064

Tristezza (Mazzola)
Tagliabue (b), on G-HN11

(L') Ultima Canzone
Ezio Pinza (bs) & Gebner King (pf)
[Serenata] 12″—**C-71687D**
(Earlier recording, G-DA908)
B. Gigli (t) 12″—**G-DB3551**
[Denza: Occhi di fata]

Vorrei morire Ger. **Todessehnen**
Karl Schmitt-Walter (b) (in German)
10″—**T-E2521**
[Bizet: Agnus Dei, with organ acc.]

('A) **Vuchella** (G. d'Annunzio)
Enzo De Muro Lomanto (t)
10"—**C-DQ2123**
[Storaci: Colei che torna]
Tito Schipa (t)   10"—**G-DA974**
[Ciampi: Nina]
DUPLICATIONS: E. Caruso, G-DA103*;
Sydney Rayner, D-F3327

TOYE, Geoffrey (1889-   )

Known best through his brother, Francis, author of biographies of Verdi (1931) and Rossini (1934). Geoffrey is a conductor and composer whose works include many songs, a symphony and several ballets written for the Sadler's Wells Theatre.

The Haunted Ballroom Concert Waltz
Sidney Torch & his Orch. 12"—**P-E11454**
[Brynes: Destiny Waltz]
Orchestra Raymonde   10"—**C-DB1868**

TROIANI, Cayetano (1873-   )

An Argentine pianist and composer of Italian parentage, Troiani is also Italian-trained at Conservatory of Naples.

Milonga Piano
Ricardo Viñes   10"—**G-DA4910**
[Lopez-Buchardo: Bailecito & Allende: Tonadas Chilenas]

TURINA, Joaquín (1882-   )

Spanish pianist and composer, Turina never quite overcame the influences of Moszkowski, with whom he studied piano, Dukas, Ravel and Debussy, who aided him when he was in Paris. His works derive their inspiration from pastoral Spain, but abound in the flashy instrumental color that Turina absorbed from the French composers.

Andalouse sentimentale (from "Femmes d'Espagne")
La Argentina (castanets) & Orch.
[Tango Andalou]   10"—**O-188686**

Danzas fantasticas Orchestra
Exaltación, Ensueño, Orgia
National Symphony Orch.—E. Jorda
2 12"—**D-K1337/8†**
—Ensueño & Orgia only
Madrid Symphony—Arbós
(in CM-146†) 12"—**C-67822D**

Fandanguillo Guitar Solo
Andrés Segovia   12"—**G-D1305**
[Tarrega: Estudio de Tremolo]
(G-W953)

Femmes d'Espagne See under Andalouse sentimentale

(La) **Oración del Torero** Lute Quartet
(Arr. by Turina for String Quartet & Orchestra)
Poltronieri String Quartet
12"—**C-GQX10137**
EIAR Orch.—Willy Ferrero
12"—**CET-BB25024**

(La) **Procesión del rocio** Orchestra
Fiesta en Triana; La Procesión
Madrid Symphony Orch.—Arbós
(in CM-331†) 12"—**C-69202D**
Quartet—String See under La Oración del Torero

Rapsodia Sinfonica Piano & Orch.
Eileen Joyce & Orch.—Raybould
12"—**P-E11299**

Ritmos: fantasia coreagrafica Piano
Louise Gargurevich 2 12"—**OL-107/8**
[Kodalý: Méditation sur un motif de Debussy]

SONGS In Spanish

Cantares (Canción)
V. de Los Angeles   10"—**G-AA340**
[Saeta en forma de Salve]

Saeta en forma de Salve a la Virgen de la Esperanza
V. de Los Angeles   10"—**G-AA340**
[Cantares]

Tango andalou Castanets & Guitar
La Argentina & Montoya
10"—**O-188686**
[Andalouse sentimentale]

Trio No. 1, D minor Violin, 'Cello, Piano
Vautier, Ortambert & Ruyssez
3 12"—**BAM-13/15**

Zapateado (from "3 Andalusian Dances")
La Argentinita (castnets & heels) & Inez
Gomez Carrillo (pf), in D-A597

VALDERRABANO, Enriquez de (16th Cent.)

A Spanish lutenist who transcribed a good deal of sacred and secular music (madrigals, motets and villancicos) for his instrument, a portion of which appeared in print in 1547.

Al Monte Sale (Soneto)
Señora, si te olvidare
Max Mieli (t) & Fritz Worsching
(Vihuela)   12"—**G-DB5016**
[Mudarra: Triste estaba & De la sangre de tus]

VALVERDE, Quinto Joaquín (1846-1910)

Flutist, conductor, teacher, and composer of the Spanish form of lyric theatre called the zarzuelas.

Clavelitos Song in Spanish
Amelita Galli-Curci (s)   10"—**V-1440**
[Ponce: Estrellita & Alabieff: Russian Nightingale Song]
Miguel Villabella (t)   10"—**PAT-PA1**
[Freire: Ay, ay, ay]

VAQUEIRAS, Raimbaut De (12th Century)

A 12th century troubadour. The song listed below was based on a popular dance called the estampie.

Kalenda maya Troubadour Song
Hans Joachim Moser, unacc.
10"—**P-R1018**
[With a group of Troubadour Songs & Minnesongs]
(in 2000 Years of Music Set)

VARESE, Edgar (1885-   )

A native Frenchman, Varèse has been in the United States since 1910, where he has composed music in keeping with his notion that the traditional orchestra is not capable of expressing our modern age.

Octandre
—3rd Mvt. only
Instrumental Ensemble—W. Goehr
(C-DB1791)   10"—**C-DB1307**
(in Columbia History of Music, Vol. V: CM-361)

VASQUEZ, Juán (16th Century)

Vásquez was one of a great number of Spanish composers of the sixteenth century—Luis Milan is perhaps the greatest of them—whose secular outpourings via song and instruments greatly influenced other areas of Europe by the turn of the seventeenth century.

Vos me matasteis Villancico in Spanish
Maria Cid (s) & Emilio Pujol (vihuela)
        (in Vol. II)   12"—**AS-17**
[With Spanish Romances & Villancicos of the 16th Century—Luis Milan & Diego Pisador]

VAUGHAN WILLIAMS, Ralph (1872-   )

The oldest of the living English composers truly at home among young progressive British musicians precisely because he was among the first to establish the higher standards of musical composition, Vaughan Williams is very well represented on records.

Concerto, D minor Violin & String Orchestra
Frederick Grinke & Boyd Neel String
Orch.—Neel   2   12"—**D-X248/9**

Eventide (No. 1 from 2 Hymn Tune Preludes)
Frederick Grinke & Boyd Neel Orch.—
Neel   12"—**D-X260**
[The Lark Ascending, Pt. 3]

Fantasia on "Greensleeves" (Arranged from an Entr'acte in the opera "Sir John in Love") String Orchestra
Boyd Neel String Orch.—Neel
              12"—**D-K1216**
[Grainger: Handel on the Strand]
Hallé Orch.—Sargent   12"—**C-DX1087**
[Bizet: L'Arlésienne, Pt. 5]
Jacques Orch.—Reginald Jacques
(C-DX925)   12"—**C-69735D**
[Foulds: Keltic Lament]
Queen's Hall Orch.—Henry Wood
[Wasps—Overture, Pt. 3]   12"—**D-K822**

Fantasia on a Theme by Tallis
Double String Orchestra
BBC Symphony Orch.—Boult
(G-DB3958/9)   2   12"—**VM-769**†
Hallé Orch.—Barbirolli
         2   12"—**G-C3507/8**
Boyd Neel String Orch.—Neel
         2   12"—**D-K815/16**†

Flos Campi Viola, Chorus & Orchestra
1925

William Primrose, BBC Chorus & Philharmonia Orch.—Boult
         3   12"—**G-DB6353/5**†

Folk Song Suite Military Band
(Orchestrated and arranged by Gordon Jacob)
1. Seventeen come Sunday; 2. My bonny boy; 3. Folksongs from Somerset
CBS Symphony—Barlow
(C-DB1930/31)   2   10"—**CX-159**†

For All the Saints ("Sine Nomine") Hymn
Temple Church Choir & Organ—Ball
         10"—**G-B2615**
[Davies: Mine eyes have seen]
St. George's Chapel Choir
         10"—**C-DB1206**
[Wesley: The Church's One Foundation]

Job A Masque for Dancing
(founded on Blake's "Illustrations of the Book of Job")
BBC Symphony Orch.—Boult
(G-DB6289/93)   5   12"—**GM-392**†

(The) Lark Ascending Romance Violin & Orchestra
David Wise & Liverpool Philharmonic
Orch.—Sargent   2   12"—**C-DX1386/7**
Frederick Grinke & Boyd Neel String
Orch.—Neel   2   12"—**D-X259/60**
[Eventide—No. 1 of 2 Hymn-Tune Preludes]

(The) Loves of Joanna Godden Music from the film
Philharmonia Orch.—Ernest Irving
         12"—**C-DX1377**

Opening Flourish of Trumpets (For Folk Dance Society)
Morris Motors Band—S. V. Wood
         10"—**C-DB1671**
[God save the King & Norfolk Long dance]

Mass, G minor Chorus (Communion Service)
—Kyrie only
Westminster Abbey Choir—Bullock
         10"—**C-DB1302**
[Arnold Bax: Paean, Harriet Cohen, pf. solo]
(in Columbia History of Music, Vol. V: CM-361) (C-DB1786)

Serenade to Music (A Tribute to Sir Henry J. Wood)
BBC Symphony Orch., with 16 Soloists in English—Wood   2   12"—**CX-121**†
(C-LX757/8)

Sir John in Love Opera
See under—Fantasia on "Greensleeves"

SONGS In English

Bright is the ring of words (R. L. Stevenson)
(from "Songs of Travel")
Robert Irwin (b) & Gerald Moore (pf)
[The Vagabond]   10"—**G-B9504**

House of Life Song Cycle (Rosetti)
See under Silent Noon, No. 2

How can a tree but wither?
Nancy Evans (s) & pf. acc. 12"—**D-K862**
[The water mill]

Linden Lea (Barnes)
Astra Desmond (c) & Gerald Moore (pf)
[Bax: I heard a piper] 10"—D-M522
Robert Irwin (b) & Gerald Moore (pf)
[Roadside Fire] 10"—G-B9505
John McCormack (t) & Gerald Moore
(pf) 10"—G-DA1791
[Bax: The White peace]

On Wenlock Edge Song Cycle 1903
(Poems from Housman's "Shropshire
Lad" for Tenor, String Quartet & Piano)
On Wenlock Edge; From far, from eve
and morning; Is my team ploughing?;
Oh, when I was in love with you; Bredon
Hill; Clun
Peter Pears (t), Benjamin Britten (pf) &
Zorian String Quartet
3 10"—D-M585/7

Orpheus with his Lute
Roy Henderson (b) & Eric Gritton (pf)
10"—D-M583
[Boyce: Song of Momus to Mars]
DUPLICATION: English School Choirs,
on G-C3526

(The) Roadside Fire (R. L. Stevenson)
("Songs of Travel No. 3")
Robert Irwin (b) & Gerald Moore (pf)
[Linden Lea] 10"—G-B9505

Silent Noon (No. 2 from Rosetti's "House
of Life")
Roy Henderson (b) & Eric Gritten (pf)
[Dale: Come away death] 12"—D-K1199
David Lloyd (t) & Gerald Moore (pf)
10"—C-DB2159
[Stanford: Tell me ye flowerates]

Songs of Travel Song Cycle (R. L.
Stevenson)
See under Bright is the ring of words;
Roadside fire; Vagabond

(The) Water Mill
Nancy Evans (c) & pf. acc.
12"—D-K862
[How can the tree but wither?]

(The) Vagabond (R. L. Stevenson) (from
"Songs of Travel")
Robert Irwin (b) & Gerald Moore (pf)
10"—G-B9504
[Bright is the ring of words]
Peter Dawson (b) 10"—G-B2297
[Drummond: The gay highway]

FOLKSONG SETTINGS
*British folksongs set for unaccompanied vocal
ensembles unless otherwise noted.*

Just as the tide was flowing
Eton College Musical Society, on
G-C1322

Loch Lomond (Scotch)
Scottish Banks Male Choir, on C-DB1907

The Tempest Arr. Band
Folk Dance Band, on G-B8732

The Turtle Dove
Glasgow Orpheus Choir—Roberton
12"—G-C3463
[Trad. Londonderry Air & Roberton:
Old woman]

Withers Rocking Hymn
English School Choirs, on G-C3525

Suite for Pipes
Minuet, Valse, Jig
Pipers' Guild Quartet 12"—C-DX1345

SYMPHONIES Orchestra

No. 1, "London Symphony"
Cincinnati Symphony—Eugene Goossens
5 12"—VM-916†
[Bizet: L'Arlésienne Suite No. 2—No. 4]
Queen's Hall Orch.—Wood
5 12"—D-X114/8

No. 4, F minor
BBC Symphony Orch.—Vaughan Wil-
liams 4 12"—VM-440†
(G-DB3367/70 in GM-304†)

No. 5, D major
Hallé Orch.—Barbirolli
(G-C3388/92) 5 12"—GM-385†

Te Deum (from Coronation Service, May 12,
1937)
Westminster Abbey Service, on
G-RG13/4

(The) Wasps Incidental Music to Aristo-
phanes' Comedy 1909
Overture Orchestra
Hallé Orch.—Leslie Heward
(C-DX1088) 12"—C-71605D
Queen's Hall Orch.—Wood
2 12"—D-K821/2
[Fantasia on "Greensleeves"]

VECCHI

*This recording is not at hand for study, and
available catalogues do not identify which of
the many 16th and 17th century Vecchis is the
composer of this selection.*

(Il) Grillo (Musical Sketch)
Madrigal Choir of the Schola Cantorum
Pontificale—Antonelli 12"—SEMS-1120
[Anonymous: Canto dei flagellanti]

VELLONES, Pierre (1879-1937)

A mon fils Song
Pierre Bernac (b) 12"—G-W1516
[Toccata—Aline von Barentzen, piano]

(Une) Aventure de Babar Musical Comedy
L'Arivée de Babar; L'Evasion; La forêt
natale; Le Jugement
Théâtre de L'Oncle Sébastien
2 10"—G-K7907/8

Concerto, Saxophone & Orch.
Marcel Mule & Orch.—Cébron
10"—FLOR-HP2002

Deux Pièces pour Columbia
Split (Valse Tzigane) & Vitamines (Fox-
trot)
Les Ondes Musicales Martenot—Cariven
10"—C-DF1681

Karakoram Music for the film
Les Indes; La Mousson
Septuor d'Ondes Martenot & Percussion
10"—C-DF2310

(Le) Paradis d'Amitabha Tibetan Ballet
Symphony Orch.—M. Jaubert
2 12"—G-L1053/4

Toccata Piano
Aline von Barentzen 12"—G-W1516
[A mon fils, Bernac]

VENTADORN (Ventadour), Bernart (Bernhard) de (d.1195)

A 12th century French troubadour, some of whose melodies have been preserved.

Can vei la lauzeta
Simone Gebelin (Chanterelle) (s)
10"—BAM-45
[Rudel: Lanquan li Jonn & Canto rossinhols: Riquier: Chanson religieuse]

Pois preyatz me, senhor Eng. Because you ask me, sir
Hans Joachim Moser, unacc.
10"—P-R1018
[With Troubadour Songs & Minnesongs]
(In 2000 Years of Music set)

VENZANO, Luigi (1814-1878)

An Italian opera composer who also wrote many songs and some small pieces for piano.

Grand Waltz Song in Italian
Margherita Carosio (s)   10"—G-DA5378
[Pagans: Canto arabo]

VERACINI, Francisco Maria (1690-1750)

Regarded by the contemporary English historian, Dr. Charles Burney, as the "greatest violinist in Europe," and highly respected by Tartini, this Italian virtuoso was also a great composer in the baroque tradition of Corelli and Geminiani. Unfortunately modern performers are seldom content to execute his compositions as written and therefore the recorded selections listed below do not give an adequate sampling of his style.

Concerto, E minor Trans. Viola & Piano
Hermann
Largo, Allegro con fuoco, Giga
A. de Paulis (vla) & E. Calace (pf)
12"—C-GQX11085

Giga & Largo
Louis Jensen (vlc) & Gerthe Jensen (pf)
10"—G-DA5209

Largo Arr. Corti Violin & Piano
C. F. Cillario   12"—G-DB5409
[Bach: Sonata No. 6 for Unacc. vl.—Praeludium]
Guarino   10"—G-GW1645
[Ravel: Pièce en forme de Habañera]
Lilia d'Albore   12"—PD-67681
[Dvořák: Sonatine G major—Larghetto]

—Arr. 'Cello & Piano
Massimo Amfitheatrof & O. P. Santoloquido   12"—G-DB5413
[Granados: Andaluza]

Sonata, E minor Violin Arr. Salmon
Minuetto, Gavotte, Giga
Jacques Thibaud & pf. acc.
12"—G-DB3111

VERDI, Giuseppe (1813-1901)

Surrounded in time by the sentimentality of Bellini and the sensuality of Puccini, Verdi's almost obstinate quest for dramatic truth makes him a great, albeit a lonely figure in nineteenth century Italian opera. Even more alone in the Romantic century is he in the life-long steadiness of his purpose and the relentless drive for its fulfillment, a creative process that his biographer, Francis Toye can only liken (and this

with reservations) to that of Beethoven. The discography of Verdi contains the laudable efforts of most of the great singers, and includes a sizable part of the composer's operas in complete—or nearly so—performances. Unfortunately, many of these recordings are tinged with Post-Verdian performance traditions which do violence to the expressed intentions of the composer. All of which makes it the more lamentable that the greatest and most unbending of Verdi interpreters, Arturo Toscanini, has to date given us in more permanent form precisely none of his memorable readings of the Verdi operas. It is a situation that calls for remedial action—and soon.

Ave Maria (Ave Regina) Soprano (in Latin) & Strings 1880
Eidé Noréna   12"—G-DB5046
[Stradella: Pietà, Signore]
Dina Mannucci-Contini
12"—C-CQX16619
[Grieg: Peer Gynt—Solvejg's Song]

—Arr. Soprano, Chorus & String Orchestra
Margherita Perras, Berlin Opera Chorus & Orch.—B. Seidler-Winkler
(G-EH1223)   12"—G-S10478
[Mozart: Laudate Dominum]

OPERAS In Italian

AIDA 4 Acts 1871
Complete Recording
Soloists, Chorus & Orchestra of Rome Opera—Tullio Serafin
(G-DB6391/411)   21   12"—GM-413†
The Cast:
Aida .... Maria Caniglia (s)
Amneris .... Ebe Stignani (ms)
Radames .... Beniamino Gigli (t)
Amonasro .... Gino Bechi (b)
Ramfis .... Tancredi Pasero (bs)
Il Re .... Italo Tajo (bs)
Messaggero ...... Adelio Zagnara (b)
Priestess .... Maria Huder (s)

Complete Recording
Soloists, Chorus & Orchestra of La Scala Opera, Milan—Carlo Sabajno
(G-AW23/41)   19   12"—VM-54†
The Cast:
Aida .... Dusolina Giannini (s)
Amneris .. Irene Minghini-Cattaneo (ms)
Radames .... Aureliano Pertile (t)
Amonasro ...... Giovanni Inghilleri (b)
Ramfis .... Luigi Manfrini (bs)
Il Re .... Guglielmo Masini (bs)
Un Messaggero .... Giuseppe Nessi (t)

"Complete" Recording
Soloists, Chorus & Orchestra of La Scala, Milan—Molajoli   18   12"—C-OP3†
(C-9726/43†) (C-D14497/514)
The Cast:
Aida .... Giannina Arangi-Lombardi (s)
Amneris .... Maria Capuana (ms)
Radames .... Aroldo Lindi (t)
Amonasro ...... Armando Borgioli (b)
Ramfis .... Tancredi Pasero (bs)
Il Re .... Salvatore Baccaloni (bs)
Un Messaggero .... Giuseppe Nessi (t)
Chorus Master: Vittore Veneziani

Abridged Recording
La Scala Soloists, Cho., & Orch.—Molajoli
6 12"—**C-DX506/11**†
(A condensed version of C-OP3 above)

"Highlights from Aida"
A collection of previously issued H.M.V.
and Victor recordings and excerpts from
album VM-54† featuring Caruso, Ponselle, Giannini, Martinelli, La Scala Orch.
3 12" & 2 10"—**VM-303**

Vocal & Orchestral Selections
Vocal Ensemble with Orch. (in German)
12"—**T-E1475**

Orchestral Selections (Fantasias, etc.)
Marek Weber Orch., G-EH422:
G-FKX51; Symphony Orch.—Gurlitt,
PD-19886; La Scala Orch.—Semprini,
U-A11428

Individual Excerpts

ACT I

Prelude Orchestra
Berlin Philharmonic—Schmidt-Isserstedt
12"—**T-E2601**
[Dances of the Priestesses & of the
Slaves]
German Opera House Orch.—Grüber
12"—**O-3602**
[Ballo in Maschera—Prelude]
Saxon State Orch.—Böhm
12"—**G-DB5558**
[Mascagni: Cavalleria Rusticana—Easter
Hymn]
Berlin State Opera Orch.—Blech
12"—**G-EJ190**
[Meyerbeer: Prophète—Coronation
March]

Se quel guerriero io fossi Recit.

Celeste Aida Air Tenor
Ger. Holde Aida Fr. O celeste Aida
Enrico Caruso & re-recorded Orch.
(G-DB1875) 12"—**V-7770**
[Bizet: Pêcheurs de Perles—Je crois entendre encore]
[Also on V-8993 in VM-303]
[Gomez: Salvatore Rosa—Mia piccerella,
G-DB144*]
[Già i sacerdoti adunansi, Caruso &
Homer, on G-DK115*]
[Forza del Destino—O tu che seno agli'
angeli, on V-6000*]
Beniamino Gigli 12"—**G-DB3225**
[Puccini: Bohème—O soave fanciulla,
Jussi Björling (G-DB3049) 12"—**V-12039**
[Puccini: Bohème—Che gelida manina]
Giovanni Martinelli 12"—**G-DB979**
[Puccini: Bohème—Che gelida manina]
(Also V-14206 in VM-329)
Galliano Masini 12"—**CET-BB25096**
[Mascagni: Cavalleria Rusticana—Addio
alla madre, with Maria Vinciguerra]
[Ponchielli: Gioconda—Cielo e mar, on
CET-BB25039]
DUPLICATIONS: Jan Kiepura,
P-RO20235; F. Merli, C-GQX10185:
G-GQX11068; A. Valente, G-HN767; M.
Fleta, G-DB1053; Sydney Rayner,
D-K996; H. Lazaro, C-GQX11066; A.
Lindi, C-CQ690: C-CQ691; J. McCormack, CRS-12* (Recorded 1908)

In German: Hugo Meyer-Welfing,
O-3609; Helge Roswaenge, T-SK1427:
G-DB5580; Peter Anders, T-E2628; J.
Patzak, PD-90183; Charles Kullman,
C-DX822; Franz Völker, PD-67105
In English: Webster Booth, G-C3379
In French: C. Vezzani, G-W1087; T.
Beets, PD-27349; Georges Thill,
C-LFX110; P. H. Vergnes, O-123806

Ritorna vincitor

I sacri nomi di padre d'amante Soprano
Single-sided versions are invariably abbreviated.
Ger. Als Sieger kehre heim & Vater,
Geliebter, helige Namen
Fr. Reviens vers nous vainqueur
Eva Turner 12"—**C-L2150**
Ljuba Weltisch 10"—**C-LB65**
Zinka Milanov 12"—**V-11-9839**
[Trovatore—D'amor sull' ali Rosee]
[Leoncavallo: Pagliacci—Prologue,
Warren, on V-11-9288 in VM-1074]
Helen Traubel
(in CM-675) 12"—**C-72110D**
[Otello—Ave Maria]
Rosa Ponselle 12"—**V-7438**
[Traviata—Ah! fors' è lui, Bori]
(Also V-8993 in VM-303) (G-DB1606)
DUPLICATIONS: Liliana Cecchi,
C-CQX16616; Rosetta Pampanini,
C-CQX11056: CET-BB25054; B. Scacciati, C-DQ1132; Poli Randacio,
G-DB568*; X. Belmas, PD-66857
In German: Tresi Rudolph, O-3603;
Tiana Lemnitz, PD-30018; Margarete
Teschemacher, G-DB4554
In French: Germaine Martinelli, PD-566112
In English: Joan Hammond, C-DB2060
In Czech: Lída Cervínková, ESTA-H5183

Immenso Fthà Bass & Chorus

Nume, custode e vindice Bass, Tenor, Soprano & Chorus
(Temple Scene) (Ballet music omitted in
the recording listed below)
Ezio Pinza, Giovanni Martinelli, Grace
Anthony & Cho. 12"—**V-8111**
—**Nume, custode e vindice** only
T. Pasero, F. Merli & Cho.
[Trovatore—Miserere]
12"—**C-GQX10162**
—**Dance of the Priestesses** only Orchestra
Berlin Philharmonic Orch.—Schmidt-Isserstedt, T-E2601; Boston "Pops" Orch.
—Fiedler, on V-11985: G-C2899

ACT II

Scene I

Dance of the Moorish Slaves Orchestra
Boston "Pops" Orch.—Fiedler, on
V-11985: G-C2899

Fu la sorte dell' armi

Ebben, qual nuovo fremito

E ancor' mentir tu speri? 2 Sopranos
Gina Cigna & Cloe Elmo
(PD-67941) 12"—**CET-BB25038**
Margherita Perras & Margarete Klose
(in German) 2 12"—**G-DB4500/1**
[Puccini: Madama Butterfly—Tutti i
fiori]

Scene II

Gloria all' Egito Chorus & Orch.
(Grand March & Chorus)
Ger. **Heil dir, Aegypten**
La Scala Chorus & Milan Symphony Orch.
Molajoli   12"—**C-GQX10242**
DUPLICATION (in German): Berlin
State Opera Chorus & Orch.—Curth,
PD-66542
In French: Chorus & Orch.—Ruhlmann,
PAT-X5523; Chorus, Organ & Orch.,
O-123001
—**Grand March only** Orchestra
Boston "Pops" Orch.—Fiedler
   12"—**V-11885**
[Elgar: Pomp and Circumstance]
[Ipolitov-Ivanov: Caucasian Sketches—
Procession of the Sardar, on G-C2849]
[Ballabili on V-11897 in VM-303]
CBS Symphony—Barlow 12"—**C-71401D**
[Ballabili] (C-DX1111)
Vienna Philharmonic—Knappertsbusch
   12"—**G-DB5608**
[Wagner: Rienzi—Overture, Pt. 3]
DUPLICATIONS: Berlin Philharmonic—
Schmidt-Isserstedt, T-E2319; Berlin
State Opera Orch.—Melichar, PD-27234;
Berlin State Opera Orch.—Blech,
G-EJ189; BBC Orch.—Pitt, C-9259;
Creatore Band, G-S8420

Ballabili (Ballet) Orchestra
(Dance of the Moorish Slave Girls)
Boston "Pops" Orch.—Fiedler
(G-C2899) 12"—**V-11985**
La Scala Orch.—Sabajno, on V-11897
in VM-303
CBS Symphony—Barlow 12"—**C-71401D**
[Grand March] (C-DX1111)
DUPLICATIONS: Berlin State Opera—
Mascagni, PD-66584; Berlin Philharmonic
—Schmidt-Isserstedt, T-E2601: T-E2319;
Creatore Band, G-S8420

Finale (Act II)
Salvator della Patria
Che veggo! Egli? Mio padre
Quest' assisa ch' io vesto vi dica
Gloria all' Egitto, ad Iside
Franci, Lucini, Lois, Masini & Chorus
   12"—**G-DB1320**
[Ballo in Maschera—Eri tu]
DUPLICATIONS: Stabile, Pagilarini, etc.
& Cho., C-DQ697; Hamburg State Opera
Cho. & Orch., T-E2998
—**Quest' assisa ch' io vesto only** Bar.
L. Rossi Morelli, C-DQ259; B. Franci,
C-DQ1131; C. Galeffi & Cho., C-GQ7044;
Inghilleri & Ensemble, V-8994 in
VM-303

ACT III
Qui Radames verrà Recit.
O cieli azzuri (O patria mia) Sop.
Eng. **Nile Air** Fr. **Air du Nil**
Ger. **Nil-Arie: O Vaterland**
Elisabeth Rethberg
   (in VM-303) 12"—**V-8994**
[Quest' assisa ch' io vesto]
Eva Turner   12"—**C-L2156**
[Trovatore—D'amor sull' ali rosee]

Celestina Boninsegna (Recorded 1910)
   12"—**V-15-1006***
[Ballo in Maschera—Ma dall'arido stelo
divulsa]
Maria Pedrini 12"—**CET-CC2324**
[Giordano: Andrea Chénier—La mamma
morta]
[Bellini: Norma—Casta Diva on
CET-CC2214]
DUPLICATIONS: C. Castellani,
G-DB11301; E. Destinn, CRS-16*
(Recorded 1907); R. Ponselle,
G-DB854*; Maria Nemeth, PD-66622;
G. Arangi-Lombardi, C-GQ7048
In German: Margarete Teschemacher,
G-DB4554
In Bohemian: Zdenka Zíková & pf. acc.,
U-A12186

Ciel! mio padre
Rivedrai le foreste imbalsamate
Su, dunque! Duo: Soprano & Baritone
Elisabeth Rethberg & Giuseppe De Luca
   12"—**G-DB1455**
Xenia Belmas & W. Domgraf-Fassbaender
   12"—**PD-66849**
DUPLICATIONS: L. B. Rasa & C.
Galeffi, C-GQX10189; N. Svilarova & G.
Vanelli, C-DQ750

Pur ti reveggo (Nel fiero anelito)
Fuggiam gli ardori
La, tra foreste vergine
Sovra una terra estrania
Duo: Soprano & Tenor
(Nile Duet: Aida & Radames)
Elisabeth Rethberg & G. Lauri-Volpi
   12"—**G-DB1341**
DUPLICATIONS: Pertile, Giannini, etc.,
in VM-303; Giannina Arangi-Lombardi &
F. Merli, C-GQX10157; Vigano & De
Muro, G-DA171*
In German: F. Hüni-Mihacsek & H.
Roswaenge, PD-66766

Ah, no! fuggiamo! Duo: Soprano & Tenor
Ma dimmi Trio: Soprano, Tenor, Baritone
(Nile Duet concluded & Finale, Act III)
Ger. **Nein, nein, entfliehen wir** & **Dort
sagt, auf welchem Wege**
Elisabeth Rethberg, Giacomo Lauri-Volpi,
& Giuseppe de Luca 12"—**G-DB1458**
Margarete Teschemacher, Marcel
Wittrisch & Gerard Hüsch
(in German) 12"—**G-DB4431**

ACT IV (Scene I)
Già i sacerdothi adunansi
Morire! ah! tu dei vivere
Aida a me togliesti Duo: Alto & Tenor
(Amneris & Radames Duet)
Ger. **Schon sind die Priester** & **Was hab'
ich leiden mussen**
Fr. **Pour rendre ta sentence**
Louise Homer & Enrico Caruso
   12"—**V-15-1025***
(also on G-DM111* & DK115*)
Emmi Leisner & Helge Roswaenge
(in German) 12"—**PD-66819**
—**Part only:** Minghini-Cattaneo & Pertile,
in VM-303

Finale (Scene 2)

La fatal pietra   Tenor

Presago il core   Soprano & Tenor

Morir; si pura e bella

O terra, addio
Ger. **Ahnend im Herzen & Leb' wohl,
o Erde**
Rosa Ponselle, Giovanni Martinelli,
Metropolitan Opera, Cho. & Orch.
        (in VM-303)   2 10"—V-1744/5
(G-DA809/10)
Johanna Gadski & Enrico Caruso
                        12"—G-DM114*
Florence Austral, Miguel Fleta & E.
Thornton   12"—G-DB580*
In German: .M. Teschemacher & Marcel
Wittrisch with Chorus, G-DB4409; F.
Hüni-Mihacsek & Helge Roswaenge,
PD-66767

—**Morir! si pura**   Tenor part only
F. Merli, C-GQ7050

—**O terra, addio** only
G. Arrangi-Lombardi & F. Merli,
C-GQX10157

ATTILA 1846

Te sol quest' anima, Act III
Trio: Soprano: Tenor & Bass
Elisabeth Rethberg, Beniamino Gigli,
Ezio Pinza   12"—V-8194
[Lombardi—Qual voluttà trascorrere]
(G-DB1506)

(UN) BALLO IN MASCHERA
3 Acts 1859
Eng. **A Masked Ball**   Ger. **Ein Maskenball**
Fr. **Le Bal Masqué**

Complete recording
Soloists, Chorus & Orchestra of Rome
Opera House—Serafin
(33 sides)   17 12"—G-DMO100/16
The Cast:
Riccardo .... Beniamino Gigli (t)
Amelia .... Maria Caniglia (s)
Renato .... G. Bechi (b)
Ulrica .... Fedora Barbieri (ms)
Oscar .... Elda Ribetti (s)
Silvano .... N. Niccolini (s)
Samuel .... Tancredi Pasero (bs)
Tom .... Ugo Novelli (bs)
Un giudice .... Blando Giusti (t)
Chorus Master: Giuseppe Conca

Orchestral Selections
La Scala Orch.—Sabajno, G-HN791;
Symphony Orch.—Gurlitt, PD-19890

Individual Excerpts

ACT I, Scene 1

Prelude   Orchestra
German Opera House Orch.—Grüber
[Aida—Prelude]   12"—O-3602

La Rivedrà nell' estasi   Tenor & Ensemble
A. Bonci, A. Rettore, S. Baccaloni, G.
Menni & Chorus   12"—C-GQX10224
[Puccini: Villi—Torna ai felice]
E. Caruso, F. Hempel, Rothier, A. De
Segurola   12"—G-DM103*
[E scherzo od è follia, with Duchêne]

Alla vita che t'arride   Baritone
Ger. **Für dein Glück**
Benvenuto Franci   10"—G-DA1093
[Giordano: Andrea Chénier—Son
sessant' anni]
(Earlier recordings C-DQ1131 &
C-D5096)
DUPLICATIONS: R. Stracciari,
C-GQ7155; Alexander Sved, PD-35040
In German: Gerhard Hüsch, G-DA4488;
W. Domgraf-Fassbaender, G-EG2341;
Heinrich Schlusnus, PD-67012

ACT I, Scene 2

Re dell' abisso, affrettati   Contralto
E lui, è lui
Ger. **König des Abgrunds**
Irene Minghini-Cattaneo 12"—G-DB1403
Ebe Stignani   12"—CET-BB25066
[Rossini: Semiramide—Ah quel giorno]
In German: Margarete Klose:
G-DB4461; Karin Branzell, PD-62633

Di tu se fedele flutto   (Bacarola)
Tenor & Chorus
Ger. **O sag', wenn ich fahr'**
Jussi Björling (no cho.) 10"—V-10-1323
[Giordano: Andrea Chénier—Come un
bel dì]
[Rigoletto—Questa o quella, on
G-DA1837]
DUPLICATIONS: A. Bonci & Chorus,
C-GQX10148; Enrico Caruso, G-DA102*
In German: Helge Roswaenge, G-DB4445:
G-DB4646
In Boh. J. Gleich, ESTA-H5141

E scherzo od è follia   Quintet
Ger. **Nur Scherze sind's un Possen**
A. Bonci, A. Rettore, E. Rubadi, S.
Baccaloni, G. Menni & Chorus
                     12"—C-GQX10148
[Di tu se fedele, Bonci & Chorus]
A. Cavara, E. Kandl, F. Fleisher—
Janczak, E. Berger, E. Ruziczka & Chorus
(in German)   12"—PD-35004
[Rigoletto—Partite? Crudele!]
E. Caruso, F. Hempel, Rothier, A. De
Segurola, Duchêne   12"—V-16-5000*
[Donizetti: Lucia—Sextet] (in VM-953)
[La rivedrà nell'estasi, on G-DM103*]

ACT II

Ma dall' arido stelo divulsa   Soprano
Ger. **Wenn das Kraut** Eng. **Amelia's Air**
Elisabeth Rethberg   12"—G-DB1461
[Morrò, ma prima]
Maria Caniglia   12"—G-DB5398
[Otello—Ave Maria]
Gina Cigna   12"—C-GQX10599
[Morrò, ma prima]
Celistina Boninsegna
(Recorded 1906)   12"—V-15-1006*
[Aïda—O cieli azzuri]
DUPLICATIONS: G. Arangi-Lombardi,
C-GQX10704
In German: Margarete Teschemacher,
G-DB5574

Teco io sto   Love Duet

O qual soave brivido   Soprano & Tenor
M. P. Pagliarini & A. Bonci
                     12"—C-GQX10223

Ve' se di notte Ensemble
G. Arangi-Lombardi, E. Molinari, S.
Baccaloni, A. Bordonali & Chorus
12″—C-D14591

ACT III

Morrò, ma prima in grazia Soprano
Ger. Der Tod sie mir willkommen
Elisabeth Rethberg   12″—G-DB1461
[Ma dall' arido]
Maria Caniglia   12″—G-DB5404
[Traviata—E strano]
Gabriella Gatti   12″—CET-BB25142
[Mozart: Nozze di Figaro—Porgi amor]
Gina Cigna   12″—C-GQX10599
[Ma dall' arido]
DUPLICATIONS: G. Arangi-Lombardi,
C-GQX10704; B. Scacciati, C-GQX10165;
Iolanda Magnoni, C-GQX10922
In German: Margarete Teschemacher,
G-DB5635; Hildegard Ranczak,
PD-68042

Eri tu, che macchiavi Baritone
Ger. Ja, du warst's Fr. Oui, c'était toi
Eng. Was it thou?
Gino Bechi   12″—G-DB5369
[Rigoletto—Cortigiani, vil razza]
Paolo Silveri   12″—C-DX1367
[Otello—Credo]
Carlo Tagliabue   12″—CET-BB25051
[Trovatore—Il balen]
Leonard Warren   12″—V-11-9292
[Otello—Credo]
Lawrence Tibbett
(G-DB1478)   12″—V-7353
[Rossini: Barbiere di Siviglia—Largo al
factotum]
[Traviata—Ah fors' è lui, Jepson, on
V-15819 in VM-633]
[Puccini: Tosca—Te Deum on V-11-8861
in VM-1015]
Benvenuto Franci   12″—G-DB1320
[Aida—Quest' assisa]
[Rossini: Guglielmo Tell—Resta
immobile, on G-DB5390]
DUPLICATIONS: Carlo Galeffi,
C-GQX10151; Hugo Hasslo, G-Z308; R.
Stracciari, C-GQX10173; Umberto Ur-
bano, PD-35076; Mario Ancona (recorded
1907), V-15-1002*; B. Franci, C-D5069;
T. Ruffo, G-DB398*; Alexander Sved,
PD-35040: CET-BB25191
In German: Heinrich Schlusnus,
PD-35022; Gerhard Hüsch, G-DB4510;
Karl Schmitt-Walter, T-E2849
In Boh. Zdenek Otava, ESTA-H5141
In Hungarian: Miklós Wágner,
RAD-RB3007

Forse la soglia attinse Recit.

Ah, l'ho segnato—Ma se m'è forza Tenor
Ger. Doch heisst dich auch das Pflicht-
gebot
Jan Peerce   12″—V-11-9295
[Meyerbeer: L'Africana—O Paradiso]
DUPLICATIONS: E. Caruso, G-DB137*
In German: Helge Roswaenge, PD-67211

Saper vorreste Soprano (Air of the Page)
Ger. Pagenarie: Lasst ab mit fragen
Ada Saraceni   10″—G-DA1340
[Giordano: Fedora—Mia madre, la mia
vecchia madre, Oltrabella & Pauli]

DUPLICATIONS: L. Tetrazzini, G-DB539*
In German: Adele Kern, PD-25826

(LA) BATTAGLIA DI LEGNANO 1849

Overture Orchestra
Milan Symphony Orch.—Molajoli
2 12″—C-D12295/6
[Leoncavallo: Pagliacci—Intermezzo]

DON CARLOS 5 Acts 1867

Individual Excerpts

ACT II

Dio, che nell' alma infondere
Tenor & Bass
Enrico Caruso & Antonio Scotti
12″—G-DM111*
[Aïda—Aïda, a me togliesti, Caruso &
Homer]

ACT III

O don fatale (Eboli's aria) Mezzo-Soprano
Ger. O grausames Schicksal
(Verhängnis voll war das Geschick)
Ebe Stignani   12″—CET-BB25082
[Trovatore—Stride la vampa]
Bruna Castagna   12″—C-71276D
[Ponchielli: La Gioconda—Voce di
donna]
Marian Anderson   12″—G-C2065
[Martini: Plaisir d'amour]
DUPLICATION: Janet Spencer,
V-15-1022*
In German: Margarete Klose, G-DB4461;
G. Rünger, PD-67072
In English: Gladys Ripley, G-C3404

ACT IV

Ella giammai m'amò Recit. Bass

Domirò sol nel manto mio regal Aria
Ger. Schlaf' find' ich erst; Sie hat mich
nie geliebt
Raphael Arie   12″—D-K1618
Tancredi Pasero
(O-9110)   12″—CET-BB25078
(Older Version: C-GQX10239)
Augusto Beuf   12″—G-DB5399
Nazareno de Angelis 12″—C-GQX10178
Cesare Siepi   12″—CET-BB25214
In German: Wilhelm Strienz, G-DB7646
(Earlier recording: G-EG6578); Wilhelm
Schirp, T-E2831; Josef Greindl,
PD-67999
—Domiro sol only: Ezio Pinza, G-DB1087
In French: Franzini, PAT-PAT97
In Boh. Ed. Haken, ESTA-H5146

Per me giunto (Rodrigo's Death)
O Carlo, ascolta Baritone
Ger. Schon seh' ich den Tag (Posas Tod)
Tito Gobbi   12″—G-DB5447

—O Carlo, ascolta only
Heinrich Schlusnus   12″—PD-67107
[Giordano: Andrea Chénier—Monologo]
[Also in German, with Vespri Siciliani—
In braccio, PD-68119]
Umberto Urbano, PD-66740; E. Mas-
cherini, C-GQX11084; U. Berettoni,
C-GQX11084

ACT V

Tu che le vanità conoscesti del mondo
Soprano
(Elisabetta's aria)
Ger. **Du im irdischen Wahn**
Margherita Grandi   12"—G-DB6631
Margarete Teschemacher (in German),
                           12"—G-DB4691
In Bohemian: Marie Tauberová,
ESTA-H5147

(I) DUE FOSCARI 1845

O vecchio cor che batti Baritone
Pasquale Amato (Recorded 1913)
                           12"—V-15-1005*
[Franchetti: Germania—Ferito
prigioner]
DUPLICATION: E. Molinari, C-D6052
Questa dunque è l'iniqua mercede Baritone
E. Molinari   10"—C-D6052
[O vecchio cor]

ERNANI 4 Acts 1844

Abridged recording
Soloists, Chorus & Orchestra of La Scala
Opera, Milan—Molajoli
          5 12"—C-GQX10069/78
The Cast:
Elvira .... Iva Pacetti (s)
Ernani .... Antonio Melandri (t)
Don Carlo .... Gino Vanelli (b)
Don Ruy Gomez de Silva
                  Corrado Zambelli (bs)
Giovanna .... Ida Mannarini (ms)
Don Riccardo ...... Giuseppe Nessi (t)
Jago .... Aristide Baracchi (b)
Chorus Master: Vittore Veneziani

Individual Excerpts

Evvia! Beviam, beviam! Opening Chorus
La Scala Chorus   10"—G-HN782
[Si redesti il leon]
DUPLICATION: Chorus, C-GQ7165
Come rugiada al cespite Tenor
Giovanni Chiaia   10"—C-DQ263
[Trovatore—Di quella pira]
Giovanni Martinelli   10"—G-DA330*
[Mascagni: Iris—Apri la tua finestra]
Sorta è la notte Recit.
Ernani, involami Air Soprano
Tutto sprezza che d'Ernani
Ger. **Ernani, rette mich**
Rosa Ponselle   12"—G-DB1275
[Forza del Destino—Pace mio Dio]
—**Ernani, involami** only
Xenia Belmas, PD-66883
In German: Miliza Korjus, G-EH994
Fà che a me venga
Da quel dì che t'ho veduta
Duo: Soprano & Baritone
G. Arangi-Lombardi & E. Molinari
                           12"—C-GQX10210
Che mai vegg'io Recit.
Infelice, e tu credevi Air Bass
Ezio Pinza (G-DB1750)   12"—V-7552
[Donizetti: Favorita—Splendon più belle]
[Mozart: Zauberflöte—O Isis und
Osiris, on G-DB5389]

DUPLICATIONS: T. Pasero, C-DQ1086;
E. de Reszke, CRS-3*; Raphael Arie, in
Prep. Swiss Decca
In French: Franzini, PAT-PAT97

ACT II

Lo vedremo, o veglio audace
Duo: Baritone & Bass
—**Baritone part** only
R. Stracciari, CRS-20* (Recorded
1915/17)
Vieni meco, sol di Rose
Baritone & Ensemble
—**Baritone part** only
Umberto Urbano   12"—PD-35076
[Ballo in Maschera—Eri tu]
[Earlier recording with Mozart: Don
Giovanni-Finch' han dal vino, on
PD-66774]

ACT III

Gran Dio! Recit.
O de' verd' anni miei Air Baritone
Gino Bechi   12"—G-DB5368
[Rigoletto—Pari siamo]
Carlo Tagliabue   12"—G-DB11303
[Bellini: Puritani—Ah! per sempre]
Antenore Basile   12"—CET-BB25150
[Ponchielli: Gioconda—O monumento]
DUPLICATIONS: Benvenuto Franci,
G-DB1138; C. Galeffi, C-GQ7035; Titta
Ruffo, G-DB398*; R. Stracciari, CRS-20*
(Recorded 1915/17)
Si ridesti il leon di Castiglia Chorus
La Scala Chorus   10"—G-HN782
[Beviam, beviam, Act I]
O sommo Carlo Baritone & Ensemble
Giuseppe De Luca, A. Tedesco, G.
Anthony & Cho.   12"—G-DB1486
[Ponchielli: Gioconda—Barcarola, De
Luca & Chorus]
Battistini, Corsi, Colazza, Silich & Chorus
          (in VM-816)   12"—V-18144*
[Bizet: Carmen—Habañera, Calvé]
Battistini, DeWitt, Taccani & Cho.
                           12"—G-DB216*
[Ponchielli: Gioconda—Ebrezza, delirio]
DUPLICATIONS: R. Stracciari & Chorus,
C-GQX10176; C. Galeffi & La Scala
Chorus, C-GQX10151; Franci, Palet,
Urbine & Chorus, G-DB1138

FALSTAFF 3 Acts 1893

Complete recording
Soloists, Chorus & Orchestra of La Scala,
Milan—Lorenzo Molajoli
                   14 12"—C-OP16†
(C-LX241/54†) (C-GQX10563/76)
The Cast:
John Falstaff ...... Giacomo Rimini (b)
Alice Ford .... Pia Tassinari (s)
Nanetta .... Ines Alfani Tellini (s)
Quickly .... Aurora Buades (s)
Fenton .... Roberto D'Alessio (t)
Meg Page .... Rita Monticone (s)
Ford .... Emilio Ghirardini (b)
Pistola .... Salvatore Baccaloni (b)
Dr. Cajus .... Emilio Venturini (t)
Bardolfo .... Giuseppe Nessi (t)
Chorus Master: Vittore Veneziani

Individual Excerpts

ACT I

So, che se andiam, la notte
M'ardea l'estro amatorio Bar., Ten., Bass
M. Stabile, R. Boscacci, A. Baracchi
               10″—C-DQ696
L'Onore! Ladri! Baritone
Mariano Stabile   12″—T-SKB3277
[Ehi taverniere]
[Earlier recording with Quand'ero
paggio, on C-CQX16499]
Titta Ruffo   12″—G-DB402*
[Rigoletto—Pari siamo]

ACT II

Prima di tutto Duo: 2 Baritones
Mariano Stabile & Afro Poli
             12″—T-SKB3278
E sogno? o realtà? (Monologo di Ford)
Baritone
Leonard Warren   12″—V-18293
[Ponchielli: La Gioconda—O
monumento]
Quand'ero paggio Duet: Soprano & Baritone
Palombini & Mariano Stabile
             12″—T-SKB3279
N. de Santis & Mariano Stabile
[L'Onore!]   12″—C-CQX16499

ACT III, Scene 1

Ehi taverniere Baritone
Mariano Stabile   12″—T-SKB3277
[L'Onore! Ladri!]

ACT III, Scene 2

Dal labbro il canto estasiato Tenor
Eng. **Oberon's Song**
Ferruccio Tagliavini
  (in CET-1)   12″—CET-BB25022
[Bellini: Sonnambula—Prendi l'anel ti
dono]
Piero Pauli   12″—G-DB1648
[Massenet: Manon—Nous vivrons à
Paris, Pauli & Saraceni]
Sul fil d'un soffio etesio Soprano & Chorus
Eng. **Titania's Song**
Lina Pagliughi
  (in CET-8)   12″—CET-BB25093
[Giordano: Il Re—O Colombello,
sposarti]
Toti Dal Monte   12″—G-DB1317
[Bellini: Sonnambula—Ah! non credea
mirarti]

(LA) FORZA DEL DESTINO 4 Acts
1862, revised 1869
Ger. **Die Macht des Schicksals**
Fr. **La Force du Destin**
Complete recording
Soloists, EIAR Chorus & Orchestra—
Gino Marinuzzi   18 12″—CET-3
(CET-CB20104/121]
[with I Lombardi alla Prima Crociata—
O Signore dal tetto natio, EIAR Chorus
& Orchestra]
The Cast:
Leonora .... Maria Caniglia (s)
Don Alvaro ...... Galliano Masini (t)
Don Carlo .... Carlo Tagliabue (b)

Preziosilla .... Ebe Stignani (ms)
Padre Guardiano . . Tancredi Pasero (bs)
Fra Melitone ...... Saturno Meletti (t)
Orchestral Selections
Milan Symphony—Molajoli, C-GQX10046;
Symphony Orch.—Gurlitt, PD-19982

Individual Excerpts

ACT I

Overture Orchestra
NBC Symphony—Toscanini
  (G-DB6314)   12″—V-11-9010
La Scala Orch.—Ferrara 12″—G-AW306
Berlin Opera House Orch.—Grüber
               12″—O-7987
La Scala Orch.—Capuana 12″—D-K1698
Munich Philharmonic—Kabasta
               12″—G-DB4642
Beromunster Studio Orch.—
Scherchen   In Prep. (Swiss Decca)
DUPLICATIONS: La Scala Orch.—
Molajoli, C-D14453; Berlin State Opera
Orch.—von Karajan, PD-67466; Berlin
Philharmonic—Schmidt-Isserstedt,
T-E2230; La Scala Orch.—Sabajno,
G-S10039
Me pellegrina ed orfana Soprano
Ger. **Noch hegt mich**
Bianca Scacciati   12″—C-GQX10206
[Pace, mio Dio]
DUPLICATION: G. Cigna, C-D14621
In German: F. Hüni-Mihacsek, PD-66612

ACT II, Scene 1

Al suon del tamburo (E bella la guerra)
Soprano, Baritone & Chorus
G. Pederzini, Gelli & Chorus
[Rataplan Chorus]   12″—G-S10259
Son Pereda, son ricco d'onore
Baritone & Chorus
Ger. **Man nennt mich den Schwarzen
Studenten**
Josef Hermann (In German)
               10″—G-DA4498
[Weber: Freischütz—Heir in ird 'schen
Jammertal]
Scene 2

Son giunta! grazie, o Dio! Recit.
Madre, pietosa Vergine Air Soprano
Ger. **Hier bin ich & Jungfrau, Mutter**
Dusolina Giannini   12″—G-DB1217
DUPLICATIONS: G. Arangi-Lombardi,
C-GQX10220; G. Cigna, C-D14621; F.
Franchi, C-D5835; Maria Luisa Fanelli,
G-DB1748
In German: Maria Wuth, T-E3042
Maledizione: Il santo nome di Dio
Bass & Chorus
La Vergine degli Angeli Chorus & Soprano
Ger. **Des ewigen Gotes geheilger Name
Die Königen der Engel**
Cesare Palagi & La Scala Chorus
               12″—PD-95279
—**Il santo nome di Dio** only
Ezio Pinza & Metropolitan Opera Chorus
—Setti   12″—G-DB1203
[Bellini: Norma—Ite sul colle]

—La Vergine degli angeli only
Rosa Ponselle, Ezio Pinza & Metropolitan
Opera Chorus 12″—V-8097
[Trovatore—Miserere] (G-DB1199)
DUPLICATIONS: G. Arangi-Lombardi &
Chorus, C-GQX10220; I. Turchetti & Cho.,
G-HN776
In German: Margarete Teschemacher,
G-DB5635; M. Wuth & Hamburg State
Opera Chorus, T-E3042

ACT III

La vita è inferno Recit.
O tu che in seno agli angeli Air Tenor
Ger. **Die Welt ist nur ein Traum der
Holle & O du . . .**
Enrico Caruso 12″—V-6000*
[Aida—Celeste Aida]
[Trovatore—Ah si ben mio, on
G-DB112*]
Beniamino Gigli 10″—G-DA5410
Francesco Merli 10″—C-GQ7049
Aureliano Pertile 12″—G-DB1208
[Ponchielli: Gioconda—Cielo e mar]
DUPLICATIONS: Giovanni Martinelli,
G-DB1089; A. Piccaver, PD-66771; A.
Lindi, C-CQ691
In German: Helge Roswaenge, PD-67211

Solenne in quest' ora Tenor & Baritone
Ger. **In dieser heil'gen Stunde**
Enrico Caruso & Antonio Scotti
(G-DM105*) 12″—V-8000*
[Puccini: Bohème—O Mimì, tu più non
torni]
Beniamo Gigli & G. De Luca
12″—V-8069
[Puccini: Bohème—O Mimì]
(G-DB1050)
Jan Peerce & Leonard Warren
(in VM-1156†) 12″—V-11-9767
[Puccini: Bohème—O Mimì tu più]
Stefan Islandi & Henry Skjaer
12″—G-DB5268
[Bizet: Les Pêcheurs de Perles—Au fond
du temple saint]
G. Lauri-Volpi & Gino Bechi
12″—G-DB5449
[Luisa Miller—Quando le sere]
DUPLICATIONS: F. Merli & G. Vanelli,
C-GQ7155; F. Corbella & G. Vanelli,
C-D5614; Charles Hackett & Riccardo
Stracciari, C-D16393*; L. Fort & L.
Piccioli, C-DQ1976
In German: Helge Roswaenge & Gerhard
Hüsch, G-DB4499; Charles Kullman &
Walter Grossmann, C-DX822; K. von
Pataky & Heinrich Schlusnus, PD-73090;
Marcel Wittrisch & H. Reinmar, T-E1756
In Danish: Vilhelm Herold & Helge
Nissen, G-M59*

Morir! tremenda cosa! Recit.

Urna fatale del mio destino Air Baritone
Heinrich Schlusnus (in German)
12″—PD-67150
[Simon Boccanegra—Plebe!]

Compagne, sostiamo Chorus
La Scala Chorus 12″—C-GQX10261
[Rataplan Chorus]

Sleale! il segreto fu dunque violato?
Tenor & Baritone
E. Caruso & G. De Luca 12″—G-DM107*
[Donizetti: L'Elisir D'Amore—Venti
scudi!]

Rataplan, rataplan, della gloria
Soprano & Chorus
G. Pederzini & La Scala Chorus
[Al suon del tamburo] 12″—G-S10259
Ebe Stignani & La Scala Chorus
[Compagne, sostiamo]
12″—G-GQX10261

ACT IV, Scene 1

Invano Alvaro ti celasti al mondo
La minaccie, i fieri accenti
Una suora mi lasciasti
Duo: Tenor & Baritone
E. Caruso & P. Amato 12″—G-DM106*
Giovanni Martinelli & Giuseppe De Luca
12″—G-DB1172
Jan Peerce & Leonard Warren
(in VM-1156†) 12″—V-11-9768
Aureliano Pertile & Benvenuto Franci
12″—G-DB1219
G. Lauri-Volpi & Gino Bechi
12″—G-DB5448
F. Merli & G. Vanelli 12″—C-GQX10200
—**La minaccie** only
F. Corbella & G. Vanelli, G-D5614;
Izquierdo & Ruffo, G-DB177*
—**Beginning "Sulla terra l'ho adorata"**
G. Masini & Carlo Tagliabue
12″—CET-BB25106
[Donizetti: Lucia—Tu che a Dio,
Malipiero & Neroni]

Scene 2
Pace, pace, mio Dio! Soprano
Ger. **Friedensarie: Frieden, Ruhe**
Zinka Milanov 12″—V-11-8927
[Mascagni: Cavalleria Rusticana—Voi
lo sapete]
Maria Caniglia 12″—G-DB5361
[Giordano: Andrea Chénier—La Mamma
Morta]
[Bellini: Norma—In mia man, Cigna &
Breviario, on CET-BB25107]
Claudia Muzio
(in CM-259) 12″—C-9166M
[Traviata—Addio del passato]
[Bellini: Norma—Casta Diva, on
C-BQX2520]
[Pergolesi: Se tu m'ami, on C-BQX2505:
C-LCX26]
Rosa Ponselle 12″—G-DB1275
[Ernani—Ernani, involami]
DUPLICATIONS: Felicie Hüni-Mihacsek,
PD-66612; Iva Pacetti, C-D14476; B.
Scacciati, C-GQX10206; N. V. Poggioli,
C-GQX11014; R. Pampanini,
C-GQX11056
In German: Margarete Teschemacher,
G-DB5574

Io muojo
Non imprecare Trio: Sop., Ten., & Bass
Rosa Ponselle, Giovanni Martinelli,
Ezio Pinza 12″—G-DB1202
DUPLICATION: Scacciati, Merli &
Pasero, C-GQX10213

GIOVANNA D'ARCO 1845
Overture Orchestra
Milan Symphony—Molajoli
12"—C-GQX10680
La Scala Orch.—Sabajno 12"—G-S10348

(I) LOMBARDI ALLA PRIMA CROCIATA
1843 Fr. Jérusalem 4 Acts
Individual Excerpts
ACT I
Tu vergin santa invoco Soprano
Giannina Arangi-Lombardi
12"—C-GQX10702
[O madre del Cielo, Act II]
La mia letizia infondere Tenor
Ferruccio Tagliavini (PD-67928)
(in CET-1) 12"—CET-BB25026
[Mascagni: Amico Fritz—Ed anche
Beppe amo]

ACT II
O Madre, dal cielo Soprano
Giannina Arangi-Lombardi
12"—C-GQX10702
[Tu vergin santa invoco! Act I]

ACT III
Qui, posa il fianco Trio
Qual voluttà trascorrere
B. Scacciati, F. Merli, N. De Angelis
12"—C-GQX10521
—Qual voluttà only
Elisabeth Rethberg, Beniamino Gigli,
Ezio Pinza (G-DB1506) 12"—V-8194
[Attila—Te sol quest'anima]
Alda, Caruso, Journet
(in VM-953) 12"—V-16-5002*
[Flotow: Marta-Dormi pur]
[Saint-Saëns: Samson et Dalila—Je viens
célébrer, on G-DM126*]

ACT IV
Polonesa: Qual prodigio Sop.
Blanche Arral (in French) (Recorded
1909) 12"—V-15-1016*
[Gounod: Faust—Jewel Song]
O Signore, dal tetto natio Chorus
EIAR Chorus & Orch.—Tansini
12"—CET-BB25077
[Nabucco—Va pensiero]
[Forza del Destino, Pt. 35 on CET-
CB20121 in CET-3]
DUPLICATIONS: La Scala Chorus,
C-GQ7166; La Scala Chorus—Sabajno,
G-S10189; V-25-7071: G-HN781:
G-FKX105

LUISA MILLER 3 Acts 1849
Il mio sangue, la vita darei Bass
Tancredi Pasero 12"—G-DB5440
[Nabucco—Tu sul labbro]
Quando le sere al placido, Act II Tenor
G. Lauri-Volpi 12"—G-DB5449
[Forza del Destino—Solenne in quest'
ora, with G. Bechi]
Tito Schipa 12"—G-DB1372
[Rigoletto—Parmi veder le lagrime]
Giuseppe Lugo
(G-DB5093) 12"—G-DB3276
[Puccini: Bohème—Che gelida]

A. Salvarezza 12"—CET-BB25152
[Flotow: Marta—M'apparì]
DUPLICATIONS: Aureliano Pertile,
G-DB1111; C. Solari, C-CQ352

MACBETH 4 Acts 1847
Coro di Profughi Scozzesi: Patria opressa!
Berlin State Opera Chorus—Reuss (in
German) 12"—T-E1656
[Otello—Fuoco di gioia]
Ah! la paterna mano Ten.
E. Caruso, G-DB118*
Una macchia è qui tuttora Soprano
(Gran Scena del Sonnambulisma)
(Sleep Walking scene)
Gertrud Rünger (in German)
12"—PD-67072
[Don Carlos—O Don fatale]
Pieta, rispetto, amore Baritone
Alexander Sved 12"—G-DB5366
[Rossini: Guglielmo Tell—Resta immo-
bile]

NABUCODONOSOR (NABUCCO) 1842
Overture Orchestra
German Opera House Orch.—Lutze
12"—T-E3188
EIAR Orch.—Failoni
12"—CET-BB25011
DUPLICATIONS: La Scala Orch.—Sa-
bajno, G-S10160; Milan Symphony—
Molajoli, C-D12274/5
Coro di Leviti, Act II Ten. & Cho.
G. Voyer & Cho. 10"—C-GQ7188
[Bellini: Norma—Guerra, guerra]
Sperate, O figli, Act I Bass
Nazzareno De Angelis 12"—C-GQX10196
[Tu sul labbro]
Tu sul labbro de' veggenti, Act II Bass
Tancredi Pasero 12"—G-DB5440
[Luisa Miller—Il mio sangue, la vita
darei]
Nazzareno De Angelis 12"—C-GQX10196
[Sperate, o figli]
Va pensiero sull' ali dorate, Act III Chorus
EIAR Chorus & Orch.—Marinuzzi
12"—CET-BB25077
[Lombardi—O Signor che dal tetto natio]
[Bellini: Norma—Ah, del tebro, with
Pasero & Chorus on CET-BB25109]
DUPLICATIONS: La Scala Chorus—
Sabajno, G-S10189: G-HN781:
G-FKX105: V-25-7071; La Scala Cho.,
C-GQ7166

OTELLO 4 Acts 1887
Complete recording
Soloists, Chorus & Orchestra—Carlo
Sabajno 16 12"—VM-152†
(G-C2413/28 in GM-157†)
(G-S10350/65)
The Cast:
Otello .... Nicolo Fusati (t)
Iago .... Apollo Granforte (b)
Desdemona .... Maria Carbone (s)
Cassio .... Piero Girardi (t)
Roderigo .... Nello Palai (t)
Ludovico .... Corrado Zambelli (b)
Montano }
A Herald } .... Enrico Spada (b)
Emilia .... Tamara Beltacchi (s)
Chorus Master: Vittore Veneziani

Excerpts
Soloists & Metropolitan Opera Cho. &
Orch.—Pelletier   6   12"—VM-620†
The Cast: Giovanni Martinelli, Lawrence
Tibbett, Helen Jepson, Nicholas Massue,
Herman Dreeben

Excerpts In French
Soloists & Orchestra of l'Opéra, Paris—
Ruhlmann   5   12"—C-LFX654/8
The Cast: Georges Thill, José Beckmans,
Jeanne Segala, Madeleine Sibille

Love Duet, Willow Song & Ave Maria
Tiana Lemnitz & Torsten Ralf
    2   12"—VM-860

Individual Excerpts

ACT I

(Una) Vela! (Uragano & Esultate!) En-
semble & Chorus
Eng. **Storm & Entrance of Otello**
Zanelli, Roggio, Palai, Masini & La Scala
Cho.   12"—G-DB1439
[Ora e per sempre addio, Zanelli]
DUPLICATIONS: La Scala Chorus—
Erede, T-SKB3287; Milan Chorus,
C-GQX10240

—Esultate only
G. Lauri-Volpi   12"—G-DB5416
[Ora e per sempre & Si, pel ciel, with
Basiola]
DUPLICATIONS: De Muro, G-DB559; F.
Tamagno & pf., G-DR100*: G-DS101*

Fuoco di gioia! Chorus Ger. **Feuerchor**
La Scala Chorus—Erede
[Una vela]   12"—T-SKB3287
Milan Opera Chorus   12"—C-GQX10240
[Uragano]
In German: Berlin State Opera Chorus,
T-E1656

Brindisi: Inaffia l'ugola! Baritone & Chorus
Ger. **Trinklied**
G. Inghilleri, Dua, Cilla & Cho.
    12"—G-D1698
[Rossini: Barbiere—Largo al factotum]
Heinrich Schlusnus & Cho. (in German)
    12"—PD-67187
[Thomas: Hamlet—Brindisi]
Lawrence Tibbett & Cho. (in VM-620)
[Love Duet, pt. 1]   12"—V-15801
DUPLICATION: Stracciari, C-CQ704

Gia nella notte densa

Quando narravi Duo: Soprano & Tenor

Ed io vedea fra le tue tempie

Venga la morte
[Love Duet: Desdemona & Othello]
Ger. **Nun in der nächt'gen Stille & Da
brannt' im dunkeln Antlitz**
Claudia Muzio & Francesco Merli
(C-LFX466)   12"—C-BQX2510
(C-LCX31)
Helen Jepson & Giovanni Martinelli
    (in VM-620)   2   12"—V-15801/2
[Brindisi, on V-15801 & Credo, on
V-15802]
Tiana Lemnitz & Torsten Ralf (in Ger-
man) (G-DB4668)
    (in VM-860)   12"—V-18363
G. Lauri-Volpi & Maria Caniglia
    12"—G-DB5417

Margherita Sheridan & Renato Zanelli
    12"—G-DB1395
In German: Wieber & Wittrisch,
T-E1504
In French: Jeanne Segala & Georges
Thill, C-LFX653

ACT II

Credo in un Dio crudel Baritone (Iago's
Creed)
Paul Schoeffler   12"—D-K1664
[Era la notte]
Paolo Silveri   12"—C-DX1367
[Ballo in Maschera—Eri tu]
Leonard Warren   12"—V-11-9292
[Ballo in Maschera—Eri tu]
Gino Bechi   12"—G-DB5441
[Rossini: Barbiere—Largo al factotum]
Carlo Tagliabue   12"—CET-BB25102
[Bizet: Carmen—Toreador's Song]
John Charles Thomas   12"—V-17639
[Giordano: Andrea Chénier—Nemico
della patria]
Riccardo Stracciari
(C-GQX10175)   12"—C-7299M
[Rossini: Barbiere—Largo al factotum]
[Wagner: Tannhäuser—O du mein hold-
er, C-GQX11067]
[Ponchielli: Gioconda—O Monumento,
C-CQX16489]
Lawrence Tibbett
    (in VM-620)   12"—V-15803
[Love Duet, pt. 2]
DUPLICATIONS: Benvenuto Franci,
G-DB1154: C-CQ702; E. Molinari,
C-D14558; Titta Ruffo, V-8045*:
G-DK114*; C. Sarobe, PD-66898: PD-
66186
In German: T. Scheidl, PD-67186; Josef
Hermann, G-DB5647
In French: A. Endrèze, O-123777; José
Beckmans, C-LFX654
In English: Dennis Noble, G-C3153;
Peter Dawson, G-C1401
In Czech: Zdeněk Otava, ESTA-H5178:
ESTA-H5117

Non pensateci più & Ora e per sempre Duo
Lawrence Tibbett & Giovanni Martinelli
    (in VM-620)   12"—V-15803
[Era la notte]

Ora e per sempre addio only Tenor
Fr. **Tout m'abandonne**
G. Lauri-Volpi   12"—G-DB5416
[Esultate & Si pel ciel, with Basiola]
Renato Zanelli   12"—G-DB1439
[Una vela, with Chorus]
Francesco Merli   10"—C-GQ7069
[Puccini: Bohème—Donde lieta usci,
Scacciati]
DUPLICATIONS: S. Rayner, D-K996; De
Muro, G-DB559; Tamagno & pf.
G-DS100*: G-DR105*; Caruso, G-DA561*
In German: Franz Völker, PD-62776

Il Sogno: Era la notte Baritone
Ger. **Traumerzählung: Zur Nachzeit war
es** Fr. **Récit. du rêve**
Tito Gobbi   12"—G-DB6626
[Rossini: Barbiere—Largo al factotum]
Benvenuto Franci   12"—G-DB1154
[Credo]

Paul Schoeffler   12″—D-K1664
[Credo]
Lawrence Tibbett
          (in VM-620)   12″—V-15803
[Non pensateci]
DUPLICATIONS: M. Stabile, C-DQ702;
R. Stracciari, C-CQ704; U. Urbano, PD-
66740; T. Ruffo, G-DB404*: G-DK114*
In German: H. Reinmar, T-E1476; Ger-
hard Hüsch, O-25093
In French: A. Endrèze, O-123777

Si, pel ciel marmoreo giuro! Tenor & Bari-
tone
[Oath Duet: Othello & Iago]
Ger. **Bei des Himmels ehernem Dache**
G. Lauri-Volpi & Mario Basiola
                         12″—G-DB5416
[Esultate & Ora e per sempre]
Aureliano Pertile & Benv. Franci
                         12″—G-DB1402
[Donizetti: Elisir d'amore—Una furtiva
lagrima]
Giovanni Martinelli & Lawrence Tibbett
          (in VM-620)   12″—V-15804
[Dio! mi potevi]
DUPLICATION: E. Caruso & T. Ruffo,
V-8045*: G-DK114*
In German: Torsten Ralf & J. Herrmann,
G-DB5620; Marcel Wittrisch & Hans
Reinmar, T-E1476
In French: Georges Thill & José Beck-
mans, C-LFX654/5

ACT III

Dio ti giocondi Duo: Soprano & Tenor
Esterrefatta fisso
Claudia Muzio & Francesco Merli
                         12″—C-LCX32
(C-BQX2511) (C-LFX467)
In French: Georges Thill & Jeanne
Segala, C-LFX656

Monologo: Dio! mi potevi scagliar Tenor
Ger. **Gott! Warum hast du gehauft dieses
Elend** Fr. **Dieu! tu pouvais m'infliger
tous les maux**
G. Lauri-Volpi   12″—G-DB5415
[Niun mi tema]
Lauritz Melchior   12″—C-71389D
[Niun mi tema]
Giovanni Martinelli
          (in VM-620)   12″—V-15804
[Sì, pel ciel]
Renato Zanelli   12″—G-DB1173
[Niun mi tema]
DUPLICATIONS: F. Merli, C-GQX10776;
B. De Muro, G-DB560
In German: Torsten Ralf, G-DB5630;
Franz Völker, PD-62776
In French: Georges Thill, C-LFX657

Vieni, l'aula è deserta Trio: 2 Tenors & Bar.
L. Tibbett, G. Martinelli, N. Massue
[Salce]   (in VM-620)   12″—V-15805

Ballabili (Dances) Orchestra (Usually
omitted from performances)
(Written for Paris Premiere)
Milan Symphony—Molajoli
                         10″—C-GQ7187
A terra! Si nel livido fango Soprano
Eugenia Burzio (Recorded 1908/9)
[Salce]   10″—CRS-26*

ACT IV

**Canzone del Salce: Mia Madre aveva una
povera ancella** Sop.
Ger. **Weidenlied** Eng. **Willow Song** Fr.
Air du Saule
Elisabeth Rethberg   12″—G-DB1517
[Ave Maria]
Tiana Lemnitz (in German)
          (in VM-860)   12″—V-18364
[Ave Maria] (G-DB4595)
Helen Jepson
          (in VM-620)   12″—V-15805
[Trio, Act III]
Licia Albanese   12″—V-11-9957
[Ave Maria]
Dusolina Giannini   12″—G-DB1791
[Ave Maria]
Maria Pedrini   12″—CET-CC2201
[Ave Maria]
DUPLICATIONS: Eidé Noréna,
G-DB5051; Poli Randacio, G-DB182*;
Frances Alda, V-15-1000*; M. Zamboni,
C-GQX10260; Eugenia Burzio, CRS-26*;
Rosa Ponselle, G-DB807*
In German: Aulikki Rautawaara, T-E3258
In French: Mm. Géori-Boué, O-123870;
Jeanne Segala, C-LFX658; Germaine
Martinelli, PD-524118
In English: Joan Cross, G-C2932
In Czech: S. Jelínková, & L. Hanzalí-
ková, ESTA-H5179

Ave Maria Soprano
Elisabeth Rethberg   12″—G-DB1517
[Salce]
Tiana Lemnitz (in German)
          (in VM-860)   12″—V-18364
[Salce] (G-DB4595)
Maria Caniglia   12″—G-DB5398
[Ballo in Maschera—Ma dall' arido stelo]
Mafalda Favero   12″—G-DB5397
[Mascagni: Lodoletta—Flammen, per-
donami]
Helen Jepson
          (in VM-620)   12″—V-15806
[Niun mi tema]
Licia Albanese   12″—V-11-9957
[Salce]
Helen Traubel
          (in CM-675)   12″—C-72110D
[Aida—Ritorna vincitor]
Maria Pedrini   12″—CET-CC2201
[Salce]
Dusolina Giannini   12″—G-DB1791
[Salce]
DUPLICATIONS: Frances Alda, V-15-
1000*; Rosetta Pampanini, C-LWX251:
C-GQX10247; Eidé Noréna, G-DB5051;
M. Zamboni, C-DQ697; Poli Randacio,
G-DB182*; R. Ponselle, G-DB807*; M.
Sheridan, G-DB981
In German: H. Ranczak, T-SK1273;
Maria Wutz, G-EH1038; H. Singenstreu,
PD-67992
In French: Mm. Géori-Boué, O-123870;
Germaine Martinelli, PD-566112
In English: Joan Cross, G-C2932
In Czech: S. Jelinkova, ESTA-H5178

Mort d'Otello: Nium mi tema Tenor
Ger. Othellos Tod: Jeder Knabe Fr. La
  mort d'Othello: Quel nul ne craigne
G. Lauri-Volpi   12"—G-DB5415
[Dio! mi potevi]
Renato Zanelli   12"—G-DB1173
[Dio! mi potevi]
Lauritz Melchior   12"—C-71389D
[Dio! mi potevi]
Giovanni Breviario   12"—CET-CB20298
[Leoncavallo: Pagliacci—Vesti la
giubba]
Giovanni Martinelli
       (in VM-620)   12"—V-15806
[Ave Maria]
DUPLICATIONS: F. Merli, C-GQX10776;
E. Salazar, C-CQX16514; I. Fagoaga,
C-GQX10270; De Muro, G-DB560;
Tamagno & pf., G-DR100*: G-DS100*
In German: Torsten Ralf, G-DB5630;
Franz Völker, PD-67159; Helge Ros-
waenge, T-SK1427; L. Slezak, PD-95162
In French: Georges Thill, C-LFX657

RIGOLETTO 3 Acts 1851
"Complete" recording
  Soloists, Chorus & Orchestra of La Scala
  Opera, Milan—Carlo Sabajno
  (G-S9500/9528)   15 12"—VM-32†
  (G-C1483/97 in GM-60†)
The Cast:
Rigoletto .... Luigi Piazza (b)
Gilda .... Lina Pagliughi (s)
Duca di Mantova ...... Tino Folgar (t)
Sparafucile ... Salvatore Baccaloni (bs)
Maddalena .... De Cristoff (s)
Conte di Monterone }
Marullo   } ..A. Baracchi (b)
Borsa .... Giuseppe Nessi (t)
Conte di Ceprano .... Menni (b)
Contessa di Ceprano .... Brambilla (s)
  Chorus Master: Vittore Veneziani
"Complete" Recording
  Soloists & Chorus of La Scala Opera,
  Milan, with Milan Symphony Orch.—
  Lorenzo Molajoli   15 12"—C-OP18†
  (C-DX139/53†) (C-GQX10028/42)
The Cast:
Rigoletto ...... Riccardo Stracciari (b)
Gilda .... Mercedes Capsir (s)
Duca di Mantova .... Dino Borgioli (t)
Sparafucile .... Ernesto Dominici (bs)
Maddalena .... Anna Masetti Bassi (s)
Conte de Monterone .... D. Baronti (b)
Giovanna   }
Contessa di Ceprano } . Ida Mannarini (s)
Conte di Ceprano .. E. Dall' Argine (b)
Marullo .... Aristide Baracchi (b)
Borsa .... Guido Uxa (t)
Paggio .... Anna Novi (s)
  Chorus Master: Vittore Veneziani
Abridged Recording
  La Scala Soloists, Chorus & Milan Sym-
  phony—Molajoli   6 12"—C-DX530/5†
  (An abbreviated version of the Columbia
  set above)
Vocal & Orchestral Selections
  N. Bischof, E. Tagetthoff, P. Anders, H.
  Reinmar & Berlin State Opera Chorus—
  Reuss   12"—T-E1509

Orchestral Selections (Fantasias, etc.)
  Marek Weber Orch., G-L770: G-FKX11:
  G-EH297; German Opera House Orch.,
  Berlin—Lutze, T-E3083; Berlin State
  Opera Orch.—Melichar, PD-24270; Ger-
  man Opera House Orch.—Dobrindt,
  O-7961; Géczy Orch., G-EH1303; La
  Scala Orch.—Semprini, U-A11429;
  Royal Marine Band, G-S10127

Individual excerpts

PROLOGUE
Introduction: Della mia bella 2 Tenors
Ballata: Questa o quella Tenor
  Alessandro Granda & Giuseppe Nessi
                     12"—C-GQX10190
  [Quel vecchio, with C. Galeffi & E.
  Dominici]
—Ballata: Questo o quella only
  Ger. Freundlich blick' ich Fr. Qu'une
  belle (Ballade du Duc)
  Eng. When a charmer . . .
  Jussi Björling   10"—V-10-1200
  [Puccini: Turandot—Nessun dorma]
  [Ballo in Maschera—Di tu se fedele, on
  G-DA1837]
  G. Malipiero   10"—G-DA5381
  [Parmi veder le lagrime]
  G. Malipiero (older recording)
                     12"—CET-BB25063
  [La donna è mobile & Boito: Mefistofele
  —Giunto sul passo]
  Luigi Infantino   10"—C-DB2269
  [La donne è mobile] (C-GQ7229)
  DUPLICATIONS: Antonio Cortis,
  G-DA1153; Tito Schipa, G-DA885; Nino
  Martini, C-17191D; R. D'Alessio,
  C-DQ1057; De Muro Lomanto, C-5060:
  C-DQ1062; Giorgini, G-HN777; L. Cecil,
  C-DQ252; D. Borgioli, C-D4962:
  C-DQ1084; A. Gentilini, C-DQ2985; H.
  Lazaro, C-D5045; E. Caruso, G-DA102*;
  Martinelli, G-DA285*; K. von Pataky,
  RAD-RZ3016
  In German: J. Patzak, PD-30008; Helge
  Roswaenge, PD-62660; Franz Völker,
  PD-90058; Peter Anders, T-A2430
  In French: G. Thill, C-LF148; C. Vezzani,
  G-P801; G. Lugo, PD-25535: PD-561093;
  Villabella, PAT-X90033: O-188585; A.
  D'Arkor, C-RF50; P. H. Vergnes,
  O-188848; M. Claudel, PD-524076;
  Micheletti, O-188867
  In Swedish: Jussi Björling, G-X3628
  In Russian: Sergei Lemeshev, D-F8109:
  also in STIN-303
  In Czech: J. Gleich, ESTA-H5151
  In English: Webster Booth, G-B8829

Minuetto: Partite? Crudele!

Gran nuova (Tutto è festa) Ensemble &
  Chorus
  Ger. Sie flieh'n mich
  A. Cavara, K. A. Neumann, H. Batteux, F.
  Fleischer-Janczak, E. Kandl, E. Berger &
  Berlin State Opera Chorus (in German)
                     12"—PD-35004
  [Ballo in Maschera—E scherzo od è
  follia]

ACT I

Quel vecchio maledivami!

Signor—Va, non ho niente Baritone &
Bass
(Duo: Rigoletto & Sparafucile)
Gino Bechi & Tancredi Pasero
12″—**G-DB11306**
[Bellini: Sonnambula—Oh Ciel—che
tento]
Apollo Granforte & Zaccarini
[Pari siamo, Granforte] 12″—**G-DB1475**
Carlo Galeffi & E. Dominici
12″—**C-GQX10188**
[Trovatore—Act I, Finale with Galeffi,
Merli & Arangi-Lombardi]
[Introduction & Ballata, Granda & Nessi,
on C-GQX10190]

Monologue: Pari siamo! (Quel vecchio)
Baritone
Ger. **Gleich sind wir beide** Fr. **Tous deux
égaux** Eng. **Rigoletto's Monologue: Yon
assassin's my equal**
Leonard Warren 12″—**V-11-9413**
[Cortigiani]
Gino Bechi 12″—**G-DB5368**
[Ernani—O de' verd' anni miei]
Carlo Tagliabue 12″—**CET-BB25064**
[Leoncavallo: Pagliacci—Prologue]
[Trovatore—Il balen, on G-DA5448]
[Also: In Prep. English Decca]
Riccardo Stracciari 12″—**C-GQX10171**
[Cortigiani, vil razza]
[Ponchielli: La Gioconda—Barcarola, on
C-D5043]
Marko Rothmüller 12″—**G-C3689**
[Puccini: Tosca—Già! mi dicon venal,
with Franca Sacchi]
Paolo Silveri 12″—**C-DX1461**
[Trovatore—Tutte è deserto & Il balen]
DUPLICATIONS: Apollo Granforte,
G-DB1475; C. Galeffi, C-GQX10194:
C-GQX10149; C. Sarobe, PD-66897; A.
Borgioli, C-D5798; B. Franci, C-D5108;
L. Piccioli, C-DQ1977; Alexander Sved,
PD-35039: CET-BB25199; T. Ruffo,
G-DB402*; H. Schlusnus, PD-67160
In German: Georg Oeggl, T-E3189; Ger-
hard Hüsch, G-DB4539; Karl Schmitt-
Walter, T-E2849
· In English: John Hargreaves, D-K1203;
Dennis Noble, G-C3520
In Czech: Zdeněk Otava, ESTA-H5123

Figlia! Mio Padre!

Deh! non parlare al misero Soprano &
Baritone (Gilda & Rigoletto)
Ger. **Sprich nie mit einem Armen**
Nunu Sanchioni & Enrico Molinari
10″—**C-DQ652**
Hedwig von Debicka & Willi Domgraf-
Fassbaender (in German)
[Lassù in ciel] 12″—**PD-66879**
Lina Aimaro & Carlo Tagliabue, In Prep.
English Decca
Lina Pagliughi & Alexander Sved
12″—**CET-BB25199**
DUPLICATION: F. Magrini & T. Ruffo,
G-DB175*

Il nome vostro ditemi Recit.

Veglia, o donna Duet Sop. & Baritone
NOTE: *Recorded versions of this scene, a con-
tinuation of the Gilda-Rigoletto duet above,
usually omit the brief parts of the Duke and
Giovanna.*
Lily Pons & Giuseppe De Luca
(in VM-702) 12″—**V-17233**
[Rossini: Barbiere—Dunque io son]
(G-DB5815)
Lina Pagliughi & Alexander Sved
12″—**CET-BB25200**
—Duet only (omitting recitative)
A. Saraceni, I. Mannarini, A. Granforte
[Piangi, fanciulla] 10″—**G-DA1128**
A. Galli-Curci & Giuseppe De Luca
[Piangi, fanciulla] 10″—**G-DA1028**
DUPLICATIONS: E. de Veroli & E.
Molinari, C-DQ231; Galvany & Ruffo,
G-DA564*

T'amo! Ah inseparabile

E il sol dell' anima Soprano & Tenor (Duo:
Gilda & Duke)
Ger. **Liebe ist Seligkeit**
Lily Pons & Enrico Di Mazzei (in French)
12″—**P-PXO1036**
DUPLICATIONS: (In French) G. Fér-
aldy & Villabella, PAT-PG41; Eidé Nor-
éna & Villabella, O-123010
—E il sol dell' anima only
Jussi Björling & Hjördis Schymberg
(G-DB6119) 12″—**V-11-8440**
[Puccini: Bohème—O soave fanciulla]
A. Galli-Curci & Tito Schipa
10″—**G-DA1161**
[Donizetti: Don Pasquale—Tornami]
DUPLICATIONS: M. Gentile & D. Borgi-
oli, C-GQX10164; Barrientos & Hackett,
C-D16397*
In German: Erna Berger & Julius Pat-
zak, PD-67535; Miliza Korjus & Helge
Roswaenge, G-DB4445
In French: Vina Bovy & Georges Thill,
C-LFX472

Gualtier Maldè Recit.

Caro nome Air Sop. (Gilda)
Ger. **Teurer Name, dessen Klang**
Fr. **O doux nom**
Doux nom
Lina Pagliughi 12″—**P-E11324**
[Thomas: Mignon—Je suis Titania]
[Rimsky-Korsakov: Coq d'or—Hymn to
the Sun, on CET-BB25002]
[Bellini: Sonnambula—Ah! non credea,
on CET-BB25073]
[Quartet, w. Folgar, Piazza, De Cristoff,
on G-S10276]
Liana Grani 12″—**C-GQX11097**
[Cimarosa: Matrimonio Segreto—Per-
donate, Signor mio]
Lily Pons (in CM-582) 10″—**C-17370D**
[Earlier recording, with Tutte le feste,
on V-7383: G-DB1597]
[Also on V-14203 in VM-329]
[Also on O-123623]
Elda Ribetti 12″—**G-C3587**
[Donizetti: Linda di Chamounix—O luce
di quest' anima]
DUPLICATIONS: Lina Aimaro,

C-GQX10983: G-DB5359; Toti Dal
Monte, G-DB830*; Louisa Tetrazzini &
re-recorded Orch., V-7883: G-DB1979; A.
Galli-Curci, G-DB5384: G-DB1477:
V-7655; also G-DB257*; M. Gentile,
C-GQX10164: PD-25852; A. M. Guglielmetti, C-GQX10177; M. Capsir,
C-GQX10205
In German: Lea Piltti, G-DB5668; M
Korjus, G-EH867; Erna Berger, PD-10444; F. Hüni-Mihacsek, PD-66760; E.
Sack, T-E1755
In French: Vina Bovy, G-DB4997; C.
Clairbert, PD-66793; Yvonne Brothier,
G-W845
In English: Gwen Catley, G-C3369
In Czech: Marie Tauberová, ESTA-H5148

Zitti, zitti Ensemble & Chorus
Gina Cigna, E. Molinari & Chorus
12"—C-GQX10273
[Bellini: Sonnambula—O fosco cielo]

ACT II

Ella mi fu rapita! Recit.

Parmi veder le lagrime Air Tenor
Ger. **Sie wurde mir entrissen & Ich seh'
die heissen Zähren**
Eng. **Ah! cruel fate & Art thou weeping?**
Ferruccio Tagliavini
(in VM-1191) 12"—V-12-0070
[Donizetti: L'Elisir d'Amore—Una furtiva lagrima]
[Also V-18-0106 in V-V13]
[Also CET-BB25058, in CET-2]
Enrico Caruso & re-recorded Orch.
(G-DB3903) 12"—V-11-8112
[Donizetti: Elisir d'Amore—Una furtiva lagrima]
[Original recording, V-6016*: G-DB126*]
Jan Peerce 12"—V-11-8926
[Traviata—De' miei bollenti spiriti]
Mario Binci 12"—G-C3606
[Ponchielli: Gioconda—Cielo e mar]
Giovanni Malipiero 10"—G-DA5381
[Questa o quella]
Luigi Infantino 12"—C-GQX11096
[Donizetti: Elisir d'Amore—Una furtiva
lagrima]
Tito Schipa 12"—G-DB1372
[Luisa Miller—Quando le sere]
(Also G-DA366*)
DUPLICATIONS: G. Lauri-Volpi,
G-DA1384; A. Granda, C-GQX10194; A.
Cortis, G-DA1152; S. C. Lo Guidice,
C-DQ272; De Muro Lomanto, C-DQ1064;
R. D'Alessio, C-DQ1115; A. Wesselowsky,
C-D16416; N. Ederle, C-DQ246
In German: F. Wolf, PD-90171
In Czech: J. Gleich, ESTA-H5151

Scorrendo uniti remota via Chorus
La Scala Chorus 12"—PD-95277
[Trovatore—Gypsy Chorus]
—Arr. Band: C-D5846

Povero Rigoletto! (La rà) Recit. Ensemble

Cortigiani, vil razza dannata Air Baritone

Miei signori, perdono
Ger. **Feile Sklaven** Fr. **Courtisans, race
vile**
Giuseppe De Luca & Metropolitan Opera
Chorus—Setti 12"—G-DB1371

Apollo Granforte w. Palai, Menni, Ottavi
& Chorus 12"—G-DB1450

—**Cortigiani, vil razza** only
Leonard Warren 12"—V-11-9413
[Pari siamo]
Paolo Silveri 12"—C-DX1432
[Rossini: Barbiere—Largo al factotum]
Carlo Tagliabue 12"—G-DB6367
[Traviata—Di provenza]
Alexander Sved 12"—CET-BB25203
[Rossini: Guglielmo Tell—Resta immobile]
(Also: PD-35039)
Gino Bechi 12"—G-DB5369
[Ballo in Maschera—Eri tu]
Hugo Hasslo 12"—G-Z308
[Ballo in Maschera—Eri tu]
DUPLICATIONS: G. Manacchini, CET-CC2154; Riccardo Stracciari,
C-GQX10171: C-D16381; Robert Weede,
C-71261D; Carlo Morelli, C-DQ686; C.
Galeffi, C-GQX10192: C-GQX10149; A.
Borgioli, C-D5798; F. Valentino,
C-DQ719; C. Sarobe, PD-66897; A. Wesselowsky, C-D16416; Titta Ruffo,
G-DB175*; H. Schlusnus, PD-67160
In German: Heinrich Schlusnus, PD-67253: PD-67261: PD-66852; Hans
Wocke, O-3620; Gerhard Hüsch,
G-DB4539; G. Oeggl, T-E3102; Karl
Schmitt-Walter, T-E2195
In French: A. Endrèze, O-123725; J.
Beckmans, PD-516714
In English: John Hargreaves, D-K1203

—**Miei signori** only
T. Ruffo, G-DA165*; F. Valentino,
C-DQ718

Tutte le feste al tempio Soprano

Solo per me l'infamia Duo: Soprano &
Baritone

Piangi, piangi, fanciulla. (Gilda & Rigoletto Duet)
Ger. **Wenn ich an Festestagen & Ach
Gott, nur für mich erfleht' ich von dir**
Lina Pagliughi & Alexander Sved
12"—CET-BB25200
Hedwig von Debicka & Willi Domgraf-Fassbaender (in German)
12"—PD-66878
DUPLICATION: Barrientos & Stracciari,
C-D16381*

—**Tutte le feste** only Soprano
Lily Pons 12"—V-7383
[Caro nome] (G-DB1597)
Lina Pagliughi (O-7911) 12"—P-DPX26
[Donizetti: L'Elisir d'amore, Adina's air]
[Zandonai: Francesca da Rimini—Paolo
datemi pace on CET-TI7014]
DUPLICATIONS: A. M. Guglielmetti,
C-DQ1043; M. Gentile, C-DQ1064; E. Di
Veroli, C-DQ231; Olympia Boronat,
V-15-1023*; A. Galli-Curci, G-DB641*

—**Piangi, piangi, fanciulla** only
Margherita Carosio & Carlo Tagliabue
12"—G-DB6387
(*Beginning "Ah! solo per me l'infamia—"*)
[Rossini: Barbiere—Dunque io son]
Amelita Galli-Curci & Giuseppe De Luca
[Ah, veglia, o donna] 10"—G-DA1028

DUPLICATION: N. Sanchioni & A. Granforte, G-DA1128; Galvany & Ruffo, G-DB177*

Compiuto pur quanto Recit. Ensemble

Si, vendetta Duo: Soprano & Baritone
N. Sanchioni, A. Granforte, Masini
[Lassù in ciel]   12"—**G-DB1449**
Lina Pagliughi & Alexander Sved
                               12"—**CET-BB25201**
DUPLICATIONS: M. Gentile & C. Galeffi, C-GQX10192; E. Di Veroli & E. Molinari, C-DQ230; Surinach & B. Franci, C-D5108; Galvany & Ruffo, G-DA564*
In German: E. Berger, W. Domgraf-Fassbaender, W. Grossman, W. Beck, G-DB4414

ACT III

La donna è mobile Air Tenor
Ger. **Ach, wie so trugerisch** Fr. **Comme la plume au vent** Eng. **Woman is fickle**
Jussi Björling
(G-DA1548)   10"—**V-4372**
[Puccini: Tosca—Recondita armonia]
G. Lauri-Volpi   10"—**G-DA5413**
[Trovatore—Di quella pira]
G. Malipiero   12"—**CET-BB25063**
[Questa o quella & Boito: Mefistofele—Giunto sul passo]
Luigi Infantino
(C-GQ7229)   10"—**C-DB2269**
[Questa o quella]
Enrico Caruso & re-recorded Orch.
(G-DA1303)   10"—**V-1616**
[Capua: O sole mio]
Beniamino Gigli   10"—**G-DA1372**
[Puccini: Tosca—E lucevan le stelle]
DUPLICATIONS: Tito Schipa, V-1099: G-DA739; Nino Martini, C-17191D; Stefan Islandi, G-DA5218; A. Cortis, G-DA1153; E. Di Mazzei, O-188512; De Muro Lomanto, C-5060: C-DQ1062; Sidney Rayner, D-M453; Dino Borgioli, C-4962; R. D'Alessio, C-DQ1057; Giorgini, G-HN777; H. Lazaro, C-D5045; S. C. Lo Giudice, C-DQ269; T. Alcaide, C-DQ1138; M. Fleta, G-DA446*; E. Caruso, G-DA561*
In German: J. Patzak, PD-30008; Peter Anders, T-A2430; Helge Roswaenge, PD-62660; Franz Völker, PD-90058
In French: G. Thill, C-LF148; C. Vezzani, G-P801; Villabella, PAT-X90033: O-188806; G. Lugo, PD-25535: PD-561093; A. D'Arkor, C-RF50; M. Claudel, PD-524076; P. H. Vergnes, O-188848; Micheletti, O-188867
In Russian: Sergei Lemeshev, in STIN-S303: also D-F8109
In English: James Johnston, C-DB2217; Webster Booth, G-B8829
In Swedish: Jussi Björling, G-X4220
In Czech: Jaroslav Gleich. ESTA-H5148

Quartetto: Un dì, se ben rammentomi

Bella figlia dell' amore
Ger. **Holdes Mädchen, sieh mein Leiden**
The first part of the quartet is almost invariably omitted in recorded versions.

Gigli, De Luca, Galli-Curci, Homer
(G-DQ102*)   12"—**V-10012***
[Donizetti: Lucia—Sextet]
Hackett, Stracciari, Barrientos, Gordon
(C-D16397)   12"—**C-7180M**
[Donizetti: Lucia—Sextet]
[E il sol dell' anima, on C-D16397]
Caruso, Scotti, Sembrich, Severina
                          12"—**V-16-5001***
[Puccini: Bohème—Quartet, Act 3]
[Donizetti: Lucia—Sextet, on G-DQ101*]
Caruso, De Luca, Galli-Curci, Perini
(G-DQ100*)   12"—**V-10000***
[Donizetti: Lucia—Sextet]
Caruso, Amato, Tetrazzini, Jacoby
                          12"—**V-15-1019***
[Gounod: Faust—Trio, Melba, McCormack, Sammarco]
DUPLICATIONS: Folgar, Piazza, Pagliughi, De Cristoff, G-S10276; Caruso, Scotti, Abott, Homer, G-DO100*
In German: Helge Roswaenge, Reinmar, Yoder, Kindermann, T-SK1162; Wittrisch, Domgraf-Fassbaender, Berger, Klose, G-DB4414; Roswaenge, Scheidl, Hüni-Mihacsek, Leisner, PD-66765
In French: Villabella, Rouard, Noréna, Tessandra, O-123010; Villabella, Rousseau, Féraldy, Lanzone, PAT-PGT1; Vezzani, Mortourier, Brothier, Galland, G-DB4869
In English: Noel Eadie, Edith Coates, Webster Booth, Arnold Matters, G-C3086; Licette, Brunskill, Nash, & Noble, C-DX302

—Tenor Part only: L. Cecil, C-DQ253

V'ho ingannato (Lassù in ciel) Soprano & Baritone
(Duo: Gilda & Rigoletto) Ger. **Ich bin strafbar**
Toti Dal Monte & Luigi Montesanto
                          12"—**G-DB2124**
[Traviata—Ah! fors' è lui]
Nunu Sanchioni & Apollo Granforte
[Si, Vendetta]   12"—**G-DB1449**
Lina Pagliughi & Alexander Sved
                          12"—**CET-BB25202**
DUPLICATIONS: Pareto & T. Ruffo, G-DB176*
In German: H. von Debicka & T. Scheidl, PD-95384; H. von Debicka & W. Domgraf-Fassbaender, PD-66879

Miscellaneous Arrangements

Paraphrase de Concert Liszt Piano (Based on Quartet)
Egon Petri, C-17101D; Alexis Kligerman, D-M531; Alfred Cortot, G-DB1105; Paul Eggert, PD-24597; W. Rehberg, PD-47203

Grande fantasie variée sur "Rigoletto"—Luigi Bossi
Louis Cahuzac (cl) & Magda Lafleur (pf)   10"—**PAT-PA1212**

SIMON BOCCANEGRA 3 Acts 1857
A te l'estremo addio, Prologue Recit.
Chorus
Il lacerato spirito Air Bass & Chorus
Alexander Kipnis & Cho.   12"—V-8684
[Mozart: Zauberflöte—In diesen heil'gen
Hallen]
[Puccini: Bohème—Che gelida manina,
Björling, on V-15820 in VM-633]
Ezio Pinza & Cho.
          (in CM-676)   12"—C-71975D
[Mozart: Don Giovanni—Champagne Air
& Serenata]
Augusto Beuf (no cho.) 12"—G-DB5400
[Cilea: L'Arlesiana—Come due tizzi, T.
Gobbi]
Raphael Arie   In Prep. Swiss Decca
DUPLICATIONS: L. Neroni, CET-
BB25144: CET-BB25079
In German: Wilhelm Strienz, G-EH1051
Dinne' alcun Recit.
Figlia, a tal nome palpito, Act II Air &
Duo: Bar. & Sop.
Lawrence Tibbett & Rose Bampton
(G-DB3950)   12"—V-15642
[Plebe! Patrizi! Piango su voi, Ensemble]
Plebe! Patrizi! Act III Recit.
Piango su voi Ensemble Baritone, etc.
Lawrence Tibbett, Rose Bampton, Leon-
ard Warren, Giovanni Martinelli, Robert
Nicholson & Cho.
(G-DB3950)   12"—V-15642
[Dinne' alcun & Figlia, a tal nome pal-
pito]
Heinrich Schlusnus (in Ger) w. Ensem-
ble & Cho.   12"—PD-67150
[Forza del Destino—Morir, tremenda
cosa]

(LA) TRAVIATA 3 Acts 1853
"Complete" recording
Royal Opera soloists, chorus & orchestra
—Vincenzo Belleza
(C-DX1324/38†)   15   12"—C-OP25†
The Cast:
Violetta .... Adriana Guerrini (s)
Flora ⎱
Anina ⎰ .... Maria Huder (ms)
Alfredo .... Luigi Infantino (t)
Germont .... Paolo Silveri (t)
Gaston .... Adelio Zagonara (t)
Il Dottore .... Gino Conti (bs)
Il Barone .... Paolo Rakowska (b)
Il Marchese .... Carlo Platania (bs)
Giuseppe .... Blando Giusti (t)
"Complete" recording
Soloists, Chorus & Orchestra of La
Scala, Milan—Carlo Sabajno
                  14   12"—VM-112†
(G-C2214/26 in GM-130†)
(G-S10260/72) (G-EH700/12)
The Cast:
Violetta .... Anna Rosza (s)
Flora ⎱
Annina ⎰ .... Olga De Franco (s)
Alfredo .... Alessandro Ziliani (t)
Germont .... Luigi Borgonovo (b)
Gastone ...... Giordano Callegari (t)
Il Dottore ⎱
Il Marchese ⎰ .... Antonio Gelli (b)
Il Barone .... Arnoldo Lenzi (b)
Chorus Master: Vittore Veneziani

"Complete" recording
Soloists, La Scala Chorus & Milan Sym-
phony Orch.—Molajoli
(C-D14479/93)   15   12"—C-OP2†
The Cast:
Violetta .... Mercedes Capsir (s)
Flora ⎱
Annina ⎰ .... Ida Conti (ms)
Alfredo .... Lionello Cecil (t)
Germont .... Carlo Galeffi (b)
Gastone .... Giuseppe Nessi (t)
Il Dottore .... Salvatore Baccaloni (bs)
Il Barone ...... Aristide Baracchi (bs)
Il Marchese .... N. Villa (b)
Chorus Master: Vittore Veneziani
Vocal & Orchestral Selections
M. Pfahl, Peter Anders, Eugene Fuchs
with Berlin State Opera Chorus & Orch.—
Schmidt-Isserstedt (in German)
                      12"—T-E1733
Orchestral Selections (Fantasias, etc.)
German Opera House Orch.—Lutze
                      12"—T-E2964
Symphony Orch.—Melichar
                      12"—PD-27187
DUPLICATIONS: Dajos Bela Orch.,
O-171049; Marek Weber Orch.,
G-EH143: G-L724: G-C1937: G-FKK56;
Creatore Band, G-S8436

Individual Excerpts

ACT I
Prelude Orchestra
NBC Symphony Orch.—Toscanini
(G-DB5956)   12"—V-18080
[Prelude, Act III]
[Wagner: Lohengrin—Prelude, Act 3, on
V-11-9233 in VM-1064]
Berlin Philharmonic—Schmidt-Isserstedt
[Prelude, Act III]   12"—T-E1831
Berlin State Opera Orch.—H.Haarth
[Prelude, Act III]   12"—PD-57183
N. Y. Philharmonic-Symphony Orch.—
Toscanini   12"—G-DB6002
[Prelude, Act III]
(G-W1048) (G-AW82)
DUPLICATIONS: Milan Symphony Orch.
—Molajoli, C-69064D: C-D14456; EIAR
Symphony Orch.—Parodi, CET-CB20005:
CET-CB20262; Berlin State Opera Orch.
—Ludwig, PD-15194: PD-516767

O barone, ne un verso Recit. Ensemble

Brindisi: Libiamo, libiamo ne'lieti calici
Soprano, Tenor & Chorus   Ger. Trink-
lied: Auf, schlürfet, in durstigen Zügen
Anna Rosza, Alessandro Ziliani & La
Scala Chorus—Sabajno   12"—V-12832
[Ah si! che feci!]
M. Gentile, A. Granda & Chorus
(C-GQX10169)   12"—C-L2048
[Mascagni: Cavalleria Rusticana—Re-
gina coeli]
A. Guerrini & L. Infantino
[Parigi o cara]   12"—C-72529D
DUPLICATIONS: Gargiulo, Parmeg-
giani, Vanelli, C-D5612; Gluck & E.
Caruso, G-DJ100*
In French: Vina Bovy & Georges Thill,
C-LF94

In German: Marcel Wittrisch, Margarete
Teschemacher & Berlin State Opera
Chorus, G-DB4416; Patzak, Debicka &
Chorus, PD-90180

"Parisian Waltz" Orchestra
NOTE: *An orchestral arr. of the Waltzes from
Act I.*
Cincinnati Summer Opera Orch.—F.
Cleva, in D-A491

Un dì felice, eterea Duo: Soprano & Tenor
Ger. **So hold, so reizend und engelsmild**
Fr. **Un jour pour charmer ma vie**
Licia Albanese & Jan Peerce
      (in VM-1074)   12"—**V-11-9290**
[Mozart: Don Giovanni—Il mio tesoro,
Melton]
Maria Caniglia & Beniamino Gigli
[Parigi, o cara]   12"—**G-DB3811**
A. Galli-Curci & Tito Schipa
(G-DA1133)   10"—**V-1754**
[Parigi, o cara]
DUPLICATIONS: Surinach & D. Borgioli,
C-D5105
In German: Tresi Rudolph & Hugo
Meyer-Welfing, O-3611; Margherita
Perras & Helge Roswaenge, G-DB4458
In French: Vina Bovy & Georges Thill,
C-LFX472

E strano! Recit.
Ah! fors' è lui Air Soprano
Follie! Follie!
Sempre libera Air (Part 2)
   Ger. **'S ist seltsam & Er ist es; O Torheit
& Von der Freude Blumenkränzen**
Fr. **Quel trouble; Folie! & Pour jamais la
destinée**
Licia Albanese   12"—**V-11-9331**
Bidú Sayão   12"—**C-71451D**
Eidé Noréna   12"—**G-DB4870**
Lina Aimaro & Mercuriali (t)
                12"—**G-DB5358**
Dina Mannuci-Contini & A. Lotti-Camici
(t)   12"—**C-CQX16623**
Lily Pons (in CM-638) 12"—**C-71834D**
(C-LX1017)
Magda Olivero   12"—**CET-BB25034**
DUPLICATIONS: Gitta Alpar, P-PO148;
Helen Jepson, V-15819 in VM-633; Mar-
cella Sembrich, V-18140* in VM-816;
Luisa Tetrazzini, G-DB531*
In German: Erna Berger, T-SK3101
In French: Vina Bovy, G-DB5004; Fanny
Heldy, G-DB1271; M. Mayo, PAT-PG64;
Clara Clairbert, PD-66790; Carmen
Torres, C-DF2413
In English: Joan Hammond, G-C3486;
Gwen Catley, G-C3358
—**Ah! fors' è lui** (Air, Pt. 1) only
Maria Caniglia   12"—**G-DB5404**
[Ballo in Maschera—Morrò ma prima in
grazie]
Toti Dal Monte   12"—**G-DB2124**
[Rigoletto-Lassù in ciel, with Monte-
santo]
Lucrezia Bori (G-DB1606) 12"—**V-7438**
[Aida-Ritorna vincitor, Ponselle]
DUPLICATIONS: A. M. Guglielmetti,
C-DQ1043; M. Zamboni, C-DQ1113;
Galli-Curci, G-DB257*
In Hungarian: Erszi Sandor, RAD-RB13

—**Sempre libera** (Air, Pt. 2) only
Lucrezia Bori   12"—**V-11-8569***
[Puccini: Tosca—Recondita armonia,
Caruso]
Anna Maria Guglielmetti 10"—**C-DQ1110**
DUPLICATIONS: M. Zamboni,
C-DQ1065; T. Tashko, C-DQ2367; A.
Galli-Curci, G-DB216*
In German: Margherita Perras,
G-DB4473
In Czech: Milada Jirásková, U-G12712

ACT II
Scene 1
Lunge da lei per me non v'ha diletto!
Recit.
De' miei bollenti spiriti Air Tenor
   Ger. **Wenn sie nicht bei mir,** or **Entfernt
von ihr & Ach, ihres auges Zauberblick**
Fr. **Non, non, loin d'elle & Je suis aimé de
toi**
NOTE: *The Roswaenge recording listed below
omits the recit., but contains the second sec-
tion, "O mio rimorso," which is almost al-
ways omitted in performance and recordings.*
Giovanni Malipiero   10"—**G-DA5407**
[Giordano: Fedora—Amor ti vieta]
Jan Peerce   12"—**V-11-8926**
[Rigoletto—Parmi veder le lagrime]
Beniamino Gigli   12"—**G-DB1222**
[Donizetti: Lucia—Tombe degl' avi
miei]
Helge Roswaenge (in German)
                12"—**G-DB4495**
[Cornelius: Der Barbier von Bagdad—O
holdes Bild]
[Ballo in Maschera—Barcarola, on
G-DB4646]
[Also on T-A1538]
C. Gero   10"—**CET-TI7040**
[Donizetti: Don Pasquale—Com è gentil]
DUPLICATIONS: Dino Borgioli,
C-D5127: C-DQ1089; A. Pertile,
C-D4997; S. Rayner, D-K995; R.
D'Alessio, C-DQ1115
In French: Villabella, PAT-X90065;
Thill, C-L1964

Madamigella Valery?

Pura siccome un angelo Duo: Sop. & Bar.
Germaine Féraldy & André Baugé (in
French)   12"—**PAT-X90077**
Moscisca & Battistini 12"—**G-DB201***
[Di Provenza, Battistini]

Dite alla giovine Duo: Sop. & Bar.
Imponete
Licia Albanese & Robert Merrill
                12"—**V-11-9175**
A. Galli-Curci & G. De Luca
                12"—**G-DB1165**
Frieda Hempel & Pasquale Amato (Re-
corded in 1914)   12"—**V-15-1020***
Joan Hammond & Dennis Noble (in
English)   12"—**G-C3387**
—**Dite alla giovine** only
Anna Rosza & Apollo Granforte
                12"—**G-DB1453**
[Giordano: Andrea Chénier—Nemico
della Patria, Granforte]
DUPLICATION: Galvany & Ruffo,
G-DB176*

Amami Alfredo Soprano
M. Zamboni   **10"—C-DQ1065**
[Sempre Libera]

Di Provenza il mar, il suol Baritone
Ger. **Hat dein heimatlisches Land**
Fr. **Lorsqu'à de folles amours**
Carlo Tagliabue   **12"—G-DB6367**
[Rigoletto——Cortigiani]
John Charles Thomas   **12"—V-7605**
[Wagner: Tannhäuser—Du holder
Abendstern]
(Also on V-14205 in VM-329)
(Different recording on V-15860 in
VM-645)
Riccardo Stracciari   **12"—C-7298M**
[Rigoletto—Pari siamo]
[Ballo in Maschera—Eri tu, on
C-GQX10173]
DUPLICATIONS: Giuseppe De Luca,
V-7086: G-DB1340; G. Inghilleri,
G-AV27; F. Valentino, C-DQ718; C.
Sarobe, PD-66899; B. Franci, C-D5109;
T. Ruffo, G-DA165*; Battistini, G-DB201*
In German: Georg Oeggl, T-E3189; Karl
Schmitt-Walter, T-E2195; Heinrich
Schlusnus, PD-66762; Gerhard Hüsch,
G-DA4488; W. Domgraf-Fassbaender,
G-EG2341
In French: Willy Clement, G-DB11123;
P. Deldi, C-DFX113; A. Baugé,
PAT-X90042; A. Endrèze, O-123021
In English: Dennis Noble, G-C3304
In Czech: Zdeněk Otava, U-B10654;
Josef Křikava, U-C12727
In Hungarian: Miklós Wágner,
RAD-RB3007

Scene 2
Coro delle Zingarelle: Noi siamo zingarelle
Chorus
La Scala Chorus   **10"—C-4802**
[Boito: Mefistofele—Il bel giovanetto]
(C-GQ7165)
Also: Creatore Band, V-35938

Scene della Borsa Tenor
Aureliano Pertile   **10"—C-D4997**
[De' miei bollenti spiriti]

Ah, si, che feci Ensemble
Rosza, Ziliani & Chorus   **12"—V-12832**
[Brindisi, Act I]

ACT III
Prelude Orchestra
NBC Symphony Orch.—Toscanini
                12"—V-18080
[Prelude, Act I] (G-DB5956)
N. Y. Philharmonic-Symphony Orch.—
Toscanini   **12"—G-DB6002**
[Prelude, Act I] (G-W1048) (G-AW82)
Milan Symphony Orch.—Molajoli
                12"—C-69064D
[Prelude, Act I] (C-D14456)
Berlin State Opera Orch.—H. Haarth
[Prelude, Act I]   **12"—PD-57183**
DUPLICATIONS: Berlin Philharmonic—
Schmidt-Isserstedt, T-E1831; EIAR
Symphony Orch.—A. Votto, CET-CB2005;
La Scala Orch.—Parelli, FONIT-35026;
Berlin State Opera Orch.—Ludwig,
PD-15194: PD-516767

E tardi! Attendo, attendo Recit.
Addio del passato
Ger. **Leb't wohl jetzt**
Fr. **J'attends & Adieu tout ce que j'aime**
Licia Albanese   **12"—V-12-0014**
[Bizet: Carmen—Micaëla's Aria]
Margherita Carosio   **12"—G-DB6343**
[Puccini: Bohème—Mi chiamano Mimì]
Claudia Muzio
      (in CM-259)   **12"—C-9166M**
[Forza del Destino—Pace, pace, mio Dio]
[Crist: C'est non ami, on C-LCX30 &
C-BQX2509]
[Bellini: Sonnambula—Ah! non credea,
on C-BQX2522]
Augusta Oltrabella   **10"—G-DA5351**
[Boito: Mefistofele—Spunta l'aurora
pallida]
DUPLICATIONS: Maria Gentile,
PD-25852: C-DQ1089; M. Zamboni,
C-DQ1113; A. Armolli, C-DQ2717; A.
Galli-Curci, G-DA216*; L. Tetrazzini,
G-DB539*
In French: F. Heldy, G-DB1409; Clara
Clairbert, PD-66918
In German: Erna Berger, PD-10444; F.
Hüni-Mihacsek, PD-66760

Parigi, o cara, noi lasceremo
Soprano & Tenor
Duo: **Violetto & Alfredo**
Ger. **O lass' uns fliehen aus diesen Mauern**
Fr. **Loin de Paris**
Maria Caniglia & Beniamino Gigli
[Un dì felice]   **12"—G-DB3811**
Amelita Galli-Curci & Tito Schipa
(G-DA1133)   **10"—V-1754**
[Un dì felice]
A. Guerrini & L. Infantino
[Brindisi]   **12"—C-72529D**
DUPLICATIONS: Surinach & Borgioli,
C-D5105; Bori & McCormack,
V-15-1009*
In German: Erna Berger & Julius Patzak,
PD-67535; M. Perras & H. Roswaenge,
G-DB4458; Tresi Rudolph & Hugo Meyer-
Welfing, O-3611
In French: Vina Bovy & Georges Thill,
C-LF149

Prendi, quest' è l'immagine Trio
(Finale Act III)
A. Gargiulo, E. Parmeggiani, G. Vanelli
[Brindisi]   **10"—C-D5612**

(IL) TROVATORE 4 Acts 1853
Ger. **Der Troubadour** Fr. **Le Trouvère**
"Complete" Recording
Soloists, Chorus & Orchestra of La Scala
Opera, Milan—Carlo Sabajno
       15 12"—**VM-106†**
(G-D1952/66 in GM-117†)
(G-AW224/38)
The Cast:
Leonora . . . . Maria Carena (s)
Azucena . . Irene Minghini-Cattaneo (ms)
Manrico . . . . . . Aureliano Pertile (t)
Conte di Luna . . . . Apollo Granforte (b)
Ferrando . . . . Bruno Carmassi (b)
Ines . . . . Olga de Franco (s)
Ruiz }
Messo }   .Giordano Callegari (t)

Un vecchio zingaro .. Antonio Gelli (b)
Chorus Master: Vittore Veneziani

"Complete" Recording
Soloists, Chorus & Orchestra of La Scala
—Lorenzo Molajoli   14 12"—**C-OP9**†
(C-GQX10047/60) (C-DX172/85†)
The Cast:
Leonora .... Bianca Scacciati (s)
Azucena ...... Giuseppina Zinetti (ms)
Manrico .... Francesco Merli (t)
Conte di Luna .... Enrico Molinari (b)
Ferrando ...... Corrado Zambelli (b)
Ines .... Ida Mannarini (s)
Ruiz .... Emilio Venturini (t)
Un vecchia zingaro .. Enzo Arnaldi (b)
Chorus Master: Vittore Veneziani

Abridged Recording
Soloists, Chorus & Orchestra of La Scala,
Milan—Molajoli   6 12"—**C-DX486/91**†
(PAT-PDT1/6)
An abridged version of C-OP9 above.

Abridged Recording   In German
Soloists, Chorus & Orchestra of Berlin
State Opera—Herman Weigert
                    4 12"—**PD-27403/6**
The Cast includes: Hella Toros, Lotte
Dörwald, Franz Völker, Armin Weltner,
Felix Fleisher-Janczak, Hertha Klust,
Waldemar Henke
(also 2 12"—PD-27333/4)

Vocal & Orchestral Selections
A. Rautawaara, Margarete Klose, Peter
Anders, Eugen Fuchs with Chorus &
Orch.—Schmidt-Isserstedt
(in German)   12"—**T-E1715**
Grand Opera Company (in English)
                        12"—**G-C1692**
Soloists & Cho. (in German)—
Schütze   12"—**PD-27334**

Orchestral Selections (Fantasias, etc.)
Concert Orch.—Seidler-Winkler,
G-C3270: G-EH1131: G-S10485:
G-FKX5; Berlin State Opera Orch.—
Melichar, PD-27245: PD-24159; Marek
Weber Orch., G-C2481: G-EH692:
G-S10398: G-L952; German Opera House
Orch.—Lutze, T-E2997; New Light
Symphony, G-L736: G-Z179

Individual Excerpts

ACT I
Scene 1
Di due figli   Recit.

Abbietta zingara   Air   Bass & Chorus
Tancredi Pasero & Chorus
                    12"—**C-GQX10159**
[Bellini: Norma—Ite sul colle, o Druidi]
In Czech: Zdeněk Otava, ESTA-H5143
Scene 2
Tacea la notte placida   Soprano
Di tale amor   (Cabaletta)
Ger. **Es glänzte schon das Sternenheer**
NOTE: *Most single sided versions omit the
cabaletta.*
Adriana Guerrini   12"—**C-DX1468**
[D'amor sull' ali rosee]
Claudia Muzio   10"—**C-BQ6004**
[Cilèa: Adriana Lecouvreur—Poveri
fiori]

[Donaudy: Spirate pur, on C-LC21:
C-BQ6002]
Maria Caniglia   12"—**G-DB5360**
[Puccini: Tosca—Vissi d'arte]
M. Pedrini   12"—**CET-CC2151**
[Forza del Destino—Pace, pace, mio Dio]
DUPLICATIONS: C. Castellani,
G-DB11301; A. Galli-Curci, G-DB1474;
Xenia Belmas, PD-66635; Bianca Scac-
ciati, C-DQ1117; G. Arangi-Lombardi,
C-GQX10509: C-GQX10166; F. Franchi,
C-D5835; R. Pampanini, C-GQ7211
In German: Tiana Lemnitz, G-DB7656
In English: Joan Hammond, G-C3419
In Czech: S. Jelínková, ESTA-H5143

Deserto sulla terra (Serenata)   Tenor
Giuseppe Taccani   10"—**C-DQ716**
[Di quella pira]
DUPLICATIONS: De Muro (t), & Ba-
dini (b), G-DB644*; Tamagno, G-DR105*

Non m'inganno   Recit.

Di geloso amor   Trio (Finale Act I)
Ger. **Wilde Eifersucht im Herzen**
G. Arangi-Lombardi, F. Merli, C. Galeffi
                        12"—**C-GQX10188**
[Rigoletto—Quel vecchio, C. Galeffi & E.
Dominici]
In German: F. Hüni-Mihacsek, Helge
Roswaenge, T. Scheidl, PD-66765

ACT II
Vedi! le fasche notturne spoglie   Chorus
(Coro degli Gitani)
Eng. **Anvil** or **Gypsy Chorus**
Victor Chorale & Orch.—Robert Shaw
                        12"—**V-11-9294**
[Wagner: Lohengrin—Bridal Chorus]
La Scala Chorus   12"—**PD-95277**
[Rigoletto—Scorrendo uniti]
(Also on G-AW22: G-K5237: PD-67096)
DUPLICATIONS: Victor Chorus,
V-20127: G-B2376; BBC Theatre Chorus,
with Organ, D-K833
Also: Arthur Pryor's Band, V-19879

Stride la vampa!   Mezzo-Soprano or Alto
Ger. **Lodernde Flammen**
Fr. **La flamme brille**
Ebe Stignani   12"—**CET-BB25082**
[Don Carlos—O don fatale]
(Older recording on C-DQ1105)
Irene Mignhini-Cattaneo 10"—**G-DA1277**
[Mascagni: Cavalleria Rusticana—O Lola,
Antonio Cortis]
Fedora Barbieri   12"—**G-AW324**
[Donizetti: Favorita—O mio Fernando]
DUPLICATIONS: G. Besanzoni,
G-DA128*
In German: Margarete Klose, G-DB4502;
Karen Branzell, PD-62633
In French: L. Tessandra, O-188030

Condotta ell' era in ceppi   Mezzo-Soprano
Ger. **Die Hände in schweren Ketten**
Ebe Stignani
(in CET-9)   12"—**CET-BB25098**
[Rossini: Barbiere—Una voce poco fa]
[Also Mascagni: Cavalleria Rusticana—
Voi lo sapete, on C-LX1049]
(Earlier recording, C-DQ1082)
Cloe Elmo   12"—**CET-BB25098**

[Wagner: Tristan—Brangaene's
Warning]
In German: M. Klose, G-DB4502

Mal reggendo all'aspro assalto

O giusto cielo
Duet: Mezzo-Soprano & Tenor
Ger. **Dass noch einmal sie erschiene**
Louise Homer & Giovanni Martinelli
12"—**V-8105**
[Ai nostri monti] (G-DB1215)
Else Brems & Stefan Islandi
[Ai nostri monti] 12"—**G-DB5279**
DUPLICATION: L. Homer & E. Caruso,
G-DM112*
In German: J. Patzak & Gertrud Rünger,
PD-67106

Tutto è deserto Recit.

Il balen del suo sorriso Air Baritone
Ger. **Ihrer Augen himmlisch' Strahlen**
Fr. **Tout est désert & Son regard, son
doux sourire**
Eng. **The Tempest of the heart**
The Recitative is usually omitted.
Gino Bechi 10"—**G-DA5405**
[Catalani: La Wally—T'amo, vien]
Paolo Silveri 12"—**C-DX1461**
[Rigoletto—Pari siamo!]
Carlo Tagliabue 12"—**CET-BB25051**
[Ballo in Maschera—Eri tu]
[Rigoletto—Pari siamo, on G-DA5448]
Apollo Granforte 12"—**G-DB1220**
[Per me ora fatale]
Leonard Warren 12"—**V-11-9956**
[Per me ora fatale & Nun's Chorus]
DUPLICATIONS: R. Stracciari,
C-GQ7148; G. Inghilleri, G-AV27; **U.**
Urbano, PD-66739; C. Galeffi, C-GQ7035;
F. Valentino, C-DQ718; B. Franci,
C-D5109
In German: Heinrich Schlusnus,
PD-66762; K. Schmidt-Walter, T-E1916;
Alexander Sved, PD-67173
In English: Dennis Noble, C-9556

Qual suono! Recit. Baritone & Bass

Per me ora fatale Air Baritone & Chorus
Ger. **Was hör' ich & Ach, alle Qual des
Lebens**
Leonard Warren & Cho. 12"—**V-11-9956**
[Il balen & Nuns' Chorus]
Apollo Granforte, G. Masini & La Scala
Cho. 12"—**G-DB1220**
[Il balen, Granforte]
G. De Luca & Metropolitan Opera Cho.
10"—**G-DA1169**
[Wolf-Ferrari: Gioielli della Madonna—
Aprila bella]

Ah! sel' error t'ingombra (Nuns' Chorus)
Included on V-11-9956

ACT III

Or co' dadi (Coro dei gendarmi) Chorus

Squilli, echeggi la tromba guerriera
Eng. **Soldier's Chorus**
Metropolitan Opera Chorus—Setti
12"—**G-AW166**
[Bellini: Norma—Soldier's Chorus]
DUPLICATION: La Scala Chorus,
G-AW22

Scene 2

Amor sublime amore Recit.

Ah! sì, ben mio coll'essere Air Tenor
Ger. **Dass nur für mich dein Herz erbebt**
Fr. **O toi, mon seul espoir**
Jussi Björling (G-DA1701) 10"—**V-2136**
[Di quella pira]
Aureliano Pertile 12"—**G-DB1198**
[Di quella pira]
Alfred Piccaver 12"—**PD-66771**
[Forza del Destino—O tu che in seno
agli angeli]
DUPLICATIONS: A. Cortis, G-DA1155;
E. Caruso, G-DB112*
In German: Franz Völker, PD-95186;
Marcel Wittrisch, T-E1495; Helge Ros-
waenge, G-DB4524
In French: C. Vezzani, G-P854
—**Arr. Band**: C-D5846

Di quella pira (Stretta) Tenor
All' armi, all' armi! Chorus (Finale Act III)
Ger. **Lodern zum Himmel**
Fr. **Supplice infâme**
Giovanni Martinelli, Grace Anthony &
Cho. (G-DB1288) 12"—**V-8109**
[Mascagni: Cavalleria Rusticana—
Preludio & Siciliana]
Aureliano Pertile, with G. Nessi, E. Lat-
tuata & Chorus 12"—**G-DB1198**
[Ah! sì, ben mio, Pertile]
DUPLICATIONS: F. Merli, B. Scacciati,
E. Venturini & Chorus, C-GQ7145; De
Muro & Chorus, G-DB562*
In German: Helge Roswaenge & Chorus,
PD-67104; Peter Anders & Berlin Opera
Chorus, T-E3338

—**Di quella pira (Stretta) only** Tenor
Jussi Björling 10"—**V-2136**
[Ah! sì, ben mio] (G-DA1701)
Beniamino Gigli 10"—**G-DA5398**
[Puccini: Manon Lescaut—No, pazzo son,
with Noto]
G. Lauri-Volpi 10"—**G-DA5413**
[Rigoletto—La donna è mobile]
Antonio Cortis & Cho. 10"—**G-DA1155**
[Ah! sì, ben mio]
DUPLICATIONS: Jan Kiepura,
P-RO20235; H. Lazaro, C-DQ1135: also
CRS-18*; A. Lindi, C-DQ1099; G. Tac-
cani, C-DQ716; G. Chiaia, C-DQ263; E.
Caruso, G-DA113*; F. Tamagno,
G-DR102*
In German: Helge Roswaenge, G-DB4524;
Franz Völker, PD-24240; PD-62776

ACT IV

Scene 1

Timor di me? Recit.

D'Amor sull' ali rosee Air Soprano
Ger. **In deines Kerkers tiefe Nacht**
Zinka Milanov 12"—**V-11-9839**
[Aida—Ritorna vincitor]
Eva Turner 12"—**C-L2156**
[Aïda—O patria mia]
Adriana Guerrini 12"—**C-DX1468**
[Tacea la notte placida]
C. Castellani 12"—**G-DB11302**
[Calatani: La Wally-Ebben n' andro
lontana]
Maria Pedrini 12"—**CET-CC2202**
[Rossini: William Tell—Selva opaca]

Amelita Galli-Curci   12″—**G-DB1474**
[Tacea la notte]
DUPLICATIONS: H. Spani, G-DB1503;
G. Arangi-Lombardi, C-GQX10166
In German: Tiana Lemnitz, G-DB7656
In English: Joan Hammond, G-C3419
In Czech. M. Tauberová, ESTA-H5145

Miserere: Ah! che la morte ognora
Soprano, Tenor & Chorus
Zinka Milanov, Jan Peerce & Cho.
    12″—**V-11-8782**
[Ai nostri monti, Peerce & Thorborg]
Rosa Ponselle, Giovanni Martinelli &
Metropolitan Opera Chorus 12″—**V-8097**
[Forza del Destino—La Vergine]
(G-DB1199)
Giannina Arangi-Lombardi, Francesco
Merli & La Scala Chorus 12″—**C-7307M**
[Puccini: Bohème—Quartet]
[Aida—Nume custode, on C-GQX10162]
DUPLICATIONS: I. Minghini-Cattaneo &
A. Pertile, P-PXO1031; F. Austral & B.
Mummery, G-D1302; Roggero & De
Muro, G-DB644*; F. Alda & E. Caruso,
w. Cho., V-8042*; G-DK119*
In German: M. Teschemacher, M.
Wittrisch & Chorus, G-DB4416; H. von
Debicka & H. Roswaenge, PD-73093:
PD-67104
In French: Germaine Martinelli &
Verdière, O-188043; O. Ricquier & C.
Vezzani, G-DB4869
In English: Joan Cross & Webster Booth,
G-C3053; M. Licette & Heddle Nash,
C-DX302; M. Bennett & J. Turner,
G-C1692

Udisti? Come albeggi Recit.

Mira, di acerbe lagrime Duo
Soprano & Baritone

Vivra! contende il giubilo
Ger. **Vernahmt Ihr? Wenn es tagt; Sieh'
meiner hellen Tränen Flut & Befreit, o
welche Seligkeit**
G. Arangi-Lombardi & C. Galeffi
    12″—**C-GQX10184**
In German: H. Scheppan & K. Schmitt-
Walter, T-E3098; H. von Debicka &
Theodor Scheidl, PD-66864; Viorica Ur-
suleac & Alexander Sved, PD-67173

Scene 2

Se m'ami ancor (Sì, la stanchezza) Recit.
Ai nostri monti Duo
Mezzo-Soprano & Tenor
Cloe Elmo & Beniamino Gigli
    12″—**G-DB5385**
[Flotow: Marta-M'apparì, Gigli solo]
Kerstin Thorborg & Jan Peerce
    12″—**V-11-8782**
[Miserere, Peerce & Milanov]
Else Brems & Stefan Islandi
[Mal reggendo]   12″—**G-DB5279**
Louise Homer & Giovanni Martinelli
    12″—**V-8105**
[Mal reggendo] (G-DB1215)
DUPLICATIONS: F. Austral & B. Mum-
mery, G-D1302; A. Dal Monte & Giorgini,
G-HN776; Cassasa & B. De Muro,

G-DB562*; E. Schumann-Heink & E.
Caruso, V-8042*; G-DK119*; L. Homer &
E. Caruso, G-DM112*
In German: J. Patzak & Gertrud Rünger,
PD-67106

(I) VESPRI SICILIANI 5 Acts 1855
Ger. **Die sizilianische Vesper**
Fr. **Les Vêpres Siciliennes**

Individual Excerpts

Overture Orchestra
Symphony Orch. of the Augusteo, Rome
—De Sabata   12″—**G-DB6444**
Milan Symphony Orch.—Molajoli
    2 12″—**C-D12272/3**
[Brahms: Hungarian Dance No. 6]
EIAR Symphony Orch.—Parodi
    12″—**CET-CB20224**
La Scala Orch.—Sabajno 12″—**G-S10038**
Dresden Philharmonic—van Kempen
(PD-15247)   12″—**CET-OR5037**
Berlin State Opera Orch.—Mascagni
    12″—**PD-66581**
La Scala Orch.—Marinuzzi
    12″—**T-SKB3201**
La Scala Orch.—van Kempen
    In Prep. **English Decca**

ACT II

O tu, Palermo Bass Ger. **O du, Palermo**
Tancredi Pasero
(O-9109)   12″—**CET-BB25065**
[Bellini: Sonnambula—Vi ravviso, o
luoghi ameni]
Ezio Pinza   12″—**G-DB1087**
[Don Carlos—Dormirò sol
Wilhelm Schirp (in German)
    12″—**T-E2928**
[Tchaikovsky: Eugen Onegin—Prince
Gremin's Air]

ACT III

In braccio alle dovizie Baritone
Ger. **In Glanz und Macht gebiet' ich hier**
Heinrich Schlusnus (in German)
    12″—**PD-35003**
[Tchaikovsky: Pique Dame—Prince
Yeletzky's Air]
[Don Carlos—O Carlo, ascolta, on
PD-68119]

Sogno, o son desto? Recit.

Quando al mio sen per te parlava
Baritone & Tenor
Ger. **Als ich mein Herz dir zugewendet**
Heinrich Schlusnus & Helge Roswaenge
(in German)   10″—**PD-90204**

ACT IV

Giorno di pianto Tenor
Ger. **O Tag des Grames**
Helge Roswaenge (in German)
    12″—**T-E2553**
[Massenet: Manon—Ah, fuyez]

ACT V

Bolero (Siciliano): Mercè, dilette amiche
Soprano
Rina Gigli   12″—**G-DB6459**
[Mascagni: L'Amico Fritz—Non mi resta]

Miliza Korjus (in German)
                         12"—G-EH914
[Gounod: Mireille—Valse]

Miscellaneous Selections (Potpourris,
Fantasias, etc.) from Verdi's Operas
Vocal Soloists & Orch., G-S5000; Berlin
State Opera Orch.—Melichar, PD-27281;
Berlin Philharmonic Orch.—Orthmann,
T-E1455 & T-E1474: U-F18059/60

Quartet—String, E minor 1873
Roma String Quartet 3 12"—G-DB4427/9
Prisca Quartet   4 10"—PD-62737/40

Requiem (Missa da Requiem) In Latin 1873
Requiem & Kyrie; Dies Irae; Domine
Jesu; Sanctus; Agnus Dei; Lux Aeterna;
Libera me
Maria Caniglia (s), Ebe Stignani (ms),
Beniamino Gigli (t), Ezio Pinza (bs),
with Chorus & Orch. of Royal Opera,
Rome—Tulio Serafin 10 12"—VM-734†
(G-DB6210/9 in GM-388†)
(also G-DB3875/84)

—**Ingemisco (Dies Irae)** only Tenor
Jussi Björling
(G-DB3665)   12"—V-13588
[Rossini: Stabat Mater—Cujus animam]
John McHugh   12"—C-DX1469
[Handel: Serse—Ombra mai fù]
Alfred Piccaver   12"—PD-95354
[Giordano: Andrea Chénier—Come un
bel dì]
E. Caruso, G-DB138*

—**Sanctus:** Irmler Choir, PD-57132

VIADANA, Ludovico Grossi (1564-1645)

*The stylistic change from the community of
Renaissance vocal polyphony to the individuality of the Baroque solo voice made the un-
derpinning of the voice by harmonic means in-
evitable. The device thus called into existance
was the "basso continuo" and somewhere along
the line, its invention was attributed to Viadana. Modern research has shown this technique was the result of many, not one composer, and that Viadana had several predecessors in the application of the continuo prin-
ciple. No longer able to dismiss this composer
as an innovator to be confined to text books on
music history, we will perhaps now be able to
honor this composer's music the more.*

Exultate Justi in Domino
St. Léon IX Cho.—Abbé Gaudard
                        12"—PAT-X93051
[Palestrina: O bone Jesu & Tombelle:
Sinite parvulos]
Julian Chapel Choir—Boezi
                        10"—SEMS-14
[Somma: Ave Maria, A Dadò]
[Antonelli: O Salutaris, dir. Vitali, on
SEMS-57]

O Sacrum Convivium
Strasbourg Choir—A. Hoch
                        12"—C-RFX56
[Palestrina: O bone Jesu & Ingegneri:
Tenebrae factae sunt]

Jubilate Justi
Roman-Vatican Choir, in SEVA-19

VICTORIA, Tomás Luis de (c.1535-1611)

*That the names of Palestrina and Victoria have
been persistently linked together explains, in
part, the incorrect, however frequent Italian-
ized form—Vittoria—of his name. The truth
seems to be that the aesthetic gap between
these two composers is greater than generally
allowed, & that the mystic-ascetical spirit peculiar to Spain, was also peculiar to Spanish
composers. Sad to state, there is to date, no
complete recording of a Victoria mass.*

CHORAL WORKS
Unaccompanied in Latin

Collection of Motets
O Regem coeli; Sancta Maria; Vadam et
circuibe; Vere languores; Vidi speciosam
Vocal Ensemble—Couraud
                        5 12"—DF-A26

Animam meam dilectum 4 Voice
Julian Chapel Choir—Boezi
                        12"—SEMS-40
[Marenzio: Estate Fortes in Bello]

Ave Maria 4 Voice
La Manécanterie des Petits Chanteurs à
la Croix de Bois   10"—G-K7378
[Palestrina: Motet—Alma Redemptoris]
Julian Chapel Choir—Boezi
                        10"—SEMS-16
[Palestrina: Motet—Adoramus]

Caligaverunt oculi mei 4 Voice
Julian Chapel Cho.—Boezi
                        12"—SEMS-2
[Palestrina: Motet—Laudate pueri
Dominum]
(Dir. Antonelli, w. Palestrina: Offertory
—Laudate Dominum, on SEMS-1157)

Caudant in coelis
Roman Vatican Choir—Refice, in
SEVA-19

Domine, non sum dignus
4 Voice Motet for Communion
La Manécanterie des Petits Chanteurs
à la Croix de Bois   10"—G-K7155
[Aichinger: Factus est repente]
Basilica Choir—Pius Kalt
                        12"—PD-27123
[W. Berten: Komm, heil'ger Geist]

Missa Dominicalis

—**Kyrie: "Orbis factor"**
Dijon Cathedral Choir—J. Samson
(G-DB4894 in GM-189)
    (in VM-212†) 12"—V-11678
[Mauduit: En son temple sacré]

O Domine Jesu 5 Voice
Julian Chapel Choir—Boezi
                        12"—SEMS-38
[Palestrina: Motet—Introduxit me]

O magnum mysterium 4 Voice Motet
La Manécanterie des Petits Chanteurs
à la Croix de Bois   12"—G-L1017
[Fevin: Descende in hortum]
St. Léon IX Choir—Abbé Gaudard
                        12"—PAT-X93052
[Lassus: Nos qui summus]

O quam gloriosum 4 Voice Motet
Strasbourg Cathedral Choir—Hoch
                        12"—C-RFX57
[Berchem: O Jesu Christe]

O quantus luctus 4 Voice
Julian Chapel Choir—Boezi
12"—SEMS-3
[Refice: Ecce sic benedicitur, A. Dadò]

O Regem coeli
Vocal Ensemble—Couraud, in DF-A26

O vos omnes 4 Voice Motet
Julian Chapel Choir—Boezi
12"—SEMS-8
[Palestrina: Offertory—Improperium
Expectavit]
La Manécanterie des Petits Chanteurs
à la Crois de Bois   10"—G-K7205
[Aichinger: Regina coeli]
Saint-Chapelle Choir—Abbé Delépine
12"—C-DFX18
[Berchem: O Jesus Christe]

Popule meus
Regensburg Cathedral Choir—Schrems
10"—G-EG6812
[Palestrina: Missa Papae Marcelli—
Sanctus]
Strasburg Cathedral Chorus
12"—C-RFX71
[Mouton: Ave Maria]
DUPLICATION: Basilica Choir—Kalt,
PD-566179: PD-27117

Responses for Holy Wednesday
Nos. 4, 5, 6, 7, 8 & 9 only
Julian Chapel Choir—Antonelli
3 12"—SEMS-1113/5

Sancta Maria
Vocal Ensemble—Couraud, in DF-A26

Tantum ergo
La Scala Chorus—Veneziani
12"—G-HN570
[Gotta-Schinelli: XI Febbraio]

Tenebrae factae sunt 4 Voice
Sistine Chapel Choir—Perosi
(in GM-139) 12"—G-DB1572
[Anerio: Introitus]
Julian Chapel Choir—Antonelli
12"—SEMS-1156
[Palestrina: Offertory—Super flumina
Babylonis]
(dir. Boezi, same coupling, SEMS-1)

Vadam et circuibe Motet
Vocal Ensemble—Couraud, in DF-A26

Vere languores nostros 4 Voice Motet
St. Léon IX Choir—Abbé Gaudard
12"—PAT-X93053
[Nanini: Diffusa est & Aichinger: Regina
coeli]
Vocal Ensemble—Couraud, in DF-A26

Vidi languores Motet
Vocal Ensemble—Couraud, in DF-A26

VIDE, Jacques

A contemporary of Giles Binchois, Vide was a
15th century composer in the service of the
munificent Burgundian Court.

Las, jay perdu mon espincel

Vit encore ce faux dangier
Lise Daniels (s) & Pasquier Trio
10"—OL-42
[Binchois: Je loe amours]

VIERNE, Louis, (1870-1937)

A French organist and composer in the tradition of César Franck and Charles Widor.

Carillon de Longpont Organ
Edouard Commette (St. Jean de Lyon
Organ)   12"—C-DFX226
[Widor: Variations from 5th Symphony,
Pt. 3]

Messe Solennelle, C sharp minor
Chorus & Organ
—Kyrie Eleison only
Lyons Cathedral Choir—Lachasange
(Commette, organ)   10"—C-D19129

Symphony No. 2, Op. 20 Organ
—Scherzo only
Virgil Fox (Chapel Organ, Girard College,
Philadelphia)   12"—V-11-8467
[Mulet: Toccata—Thou art the Rock]

VIEUXTEMPS, Henri (1820-1881)

A pupil of Anton Reicha, Vieuxtemps was the
leader of the 19th century French violin school.
It is to his credit that the violin concertos contain something more than the usual collection
of loosely strung violinistic tricks, a common
failing among composer-virtuosos.

CONCERTOS Violin & Orch.
No. 4, D minor, Op. 31
Jascha Heifetz & London Philharmonic—
Barbirolli   3 12"—VM-297†
No. 5, A minor, Op. 37
Jascha Heifetz & London Symphony Orch.
—Sargent   2 12"—G-DB6547/8
Rêverie, Op. 22, No. 3 Violin & Piano
Louis Zimmermann & pf. acc.
12"—C-DHX25
Saltarelle Arr. Orchestra Godard
Symphony Orch.—Ruhlmann
[Delibes: Naïla Valse] 12"—PAT-X96205

VILLA-LOBOS, Heitor (1884-   )

Villa-Lobos drinks deeply at the wells of
French Impressionism and Brazilian folk music, but well mixed in his music are the evident impatience with tradition, and the in-
satiable curiosity of a musical mind that ever
seeks the new and more subtle in creative
techniques. Several recent releases have added
significantly to the discography of this prolific composer.

Collection
A Festival of Brazilian Music (Villa-Lobos)
Bachianas Brasileiras No. 1; Nonetto for
Chamber Orchestra & Chorus; Serestas
No. 8—Canção do Carreiro; Quatuor for
Harp, Celesta, Flute, Saxophone &
Women's Voices; Canção da Saudade
Brazilian Festival Orch.—Burle Marx,
with Schola Cantorum—Hugh Ross, Elsie
Houston (s) & Brazilian Festival Quartet
5 12"—VM-773†
Alegria na horta
(Part 3 of "Suite Floral" Op. 97)
Artur Rubinstein (pf)
(in VM-970) 12"—V-11-8600
[A Próle Do Bébé, Pt. 3]

Alma Brasileira See Chorus No. 5
A Prôle Do Bébé (The Child's Family)
2 Suites for Piano
No. 1 1917
  1. Branquinha (Little China Doll)
  2. Moreninha (Little Paper Doll)
  3. Caboclinha (Little Brazilian Doll)
  4. Malatinha (Little Black, or Wooden
    Doll)
  5. Negrinha (Gingerbread Doll)
  6. A Pobresinha (Poor Little Rag Doll)
  7. O Polichinello (Punch)
  8. Brucha (Little Witch Doll)
—Nos. 1, 2, 3, 5, 6, 7, 8, only
  Artur Rubinstein   2 12"—VM-970
  [Alegria na horta]
—Nos. 2, 6 & 7 only
  Artur Rubinstein   12"—G-DB1762
  [Albéniz: Triana]
—Nos. 1, 2, 6 only
  Guiomar Novaës   10"—C-17355D

Bachianas Brasileiras
No. 1 8 'Cellos
  Brazilian Festival Orch.—Burle Marx
    (in VM-773†)   2 12"—V-17966/7
No. 5 Soprano & 8 'Cellos (with Bass)
  In Portuguese
  Bidú Sayão & Ensemble—Villa-Lobos
  (Cello Solo, Leonard Rose)
    12"—C-71670D

Canção da Saudade Chorus a cappella
  Eng. Song of Longing
  Schola Cantorum—Hugh Ross
    (in VM-773†) 12"—V-17970
  [Quatuor, Brazilian Festival Quartet]
Carnaval das Crianças Piano
—O Ginete do Pierrozinho only
  Maria Antonia de Castra
    12"—PAT-PAT109
  [Choros No. 5 & Danças—Farrapos]
Choros No. 5 (from Suite "Alma
  Brasileira") Piano
  Maria Antonia de Castro
    12"—PAT-PAT109
  [Carnaval das Crianças & Danças—
  Farrapos]
(O) Canto do cysno negro Violin & Piano
  Eng. Song of the Black Swan
  Ricardo Odnoposoff & Otto Herz
    10"—V-10-1228
  [Nováček: Perpetuum mobile]
Danças Caracteristicas Africanas Piano
—Farrapos only
  Maria Antonia de Castro
    12"—PAT-PAT109
  [Choros No. 5 & Carnaval—O Ginete]
Folk Songs—Brazilian (from the School
  Collection)
  O' Ciranda, O Ciranda; Come here, Vitu;
  In Bahia; Garibaldi went to Mass;
  Throw the Ball; Blind Man's Buff; Let's
  go to Maneca; Pease Porridge Hot;
  Hurry to the Carnival; The Three Marias
—Arr. Piano Novaës
  Guiomar Novaës   3 10"—CM-692†
  (with Pnto: Scenas Infantas & Guarnieri:
  Toccata)

Nonetto Chamber Orchestra & Chorus
  Schola Cantorum & Brazilian Festival
  Orch.—Hugh Ross
    (in VM-773†) 2 12"—V-17968/9
  [Serestas No. 8, Elsie Houston]

Quartet Strings
No. 6, E major (Quartetto Brasileiro No. 2)
  Stuyvesant String Quartet
    3 12"—INT-IM301

Quatuor Harp, Celesta, Flute, Saxophone
  & Women's Voices
  Brazilian Festival Quartet & Schola
  Cantorum—Hugh Ross
    (in VM-773†) 12"—17970
  [Canção da Saudade, Chorus only]

Saudades das Selvas Brasileiras Piano
  1. Momo Precoce 2. Dois Trechos
—No. 2 only
  Erno Balogh, in CON-103

SONGS In Portuguese
Miniaturas
—No. 6, Sino de aldeia only
  Eng. The Village Bell
  Jennie Tourel (ms) & Orch.—Villa-Lobos
    (in CX-249) 12"—C-72124D
  [Serestas Nos. 8 & 10]

(14) Serestas 1925/6 Eng. **Brazilian
Serenades**
—Nos. 5, 6, 8, 9, 10 only
  Jennie Tourel (ms) & Orch.—Villa-Lobos
    2 12"—CX-249
  [Miniaturas No. 6—Sino de Aldeia]
—No. 8 (Canção do Carriero) only
  Elsie Houston (s) & Pablo Miguel (pf)
    (in VM-773†) 12"—V-17969
  [Nonetto for Chamber Orchestra &
  Chorus]

Suite Floral See under Alegria na horta

Folksong arrangement
Xango (a religious African chant of the
  Makumba)
  Roland Hayes (t) & Reginald Boardman
  (pf), C-17294D

VINCI, Leonardo (1690-1730)

*It is strange that a composer so highly praised
for his dramatic works by the eminent historian, Dr. Charles Burney, should be represented on records only by instrumental forms
he cultivated so little. It is to be hoped that
the future will bring to discs some operetic excerpts of this contemporary of Alessandro Scarlatti.*

Gavotte
  New Italian String Quartet
  [Debussy: Quartet, pt. 7] 12"—T-E9097

Largo
  Emma Boynet (pf)   12"—PD-561145
  [Rutini: Menuet]

Sonata, D major Flute & Clavier
  Hermann Kuttruff (fl) & Hans Vollen-
  wieder (org)   12"—G-HEX105
  [Bach: Sonata, E minor—Andante]

VISEE, Robert de (c.1650-c.1725)

With Francisque Corbett, the two leading guitarists in France. Visée had the added distinction of being the teacher of Louis XIV, to whom several "livres" of his compositions were dedicated.

Allemande; Bourrée; Menuet; Prélude
Guitar
Jean Lafon (in Vol. IX) 12"—AS-89
[F. Corbett: Prélude; Allemande, & Folie]

Menuets I & II; Bourrée; Gavotte Guitar
Ida Presti 10"—G-K7910
[J. S. Bach: Courante]

VITALI, Tommaso Antonio (c.1665-   )

Among the many composers by the name of Vitali, Tommaso and his father Giovanni Battista, are easily the most significant. Both were skillful violinists as well as composers, and it is unfortunate that only the "Ciaccona" of the younger Vitali has thus far appeared on records.

Ciaccona (Chaconne) Violin & Continuo
J. Thibaud & T. Janopoulo (pf)
12"—G-DB2799
—**Arr. 'Cello & Piano**
Luigi Silva & Erik Schonsee
12"—G-DB4647

VITTORIA See above: Victoria

VIVALDI, Antonio (c.1680-1743)

Vivaldi's place in music history has yet to be assessed. There is to date no biography in English, and no thorough study in any language. Only in this century have large quantities of his manuscripts been unearthed, although the chronology of these works have not been established and few have appeared in modern editions. Likewise there are several testimonies as to the greatness of his operas, but few scholars have examined these autographs. Whatever the eventual stature of the composer, his works were sufficiently interesting to stimulate the now famous Bach transcriptions of his violin concertos. While the Bach transcriptions require no comment from this humble editorial quarter, the same cannot be said for more recent arrangers, conductors and performers who evidently feel that they must "improve" on Vivaldi's compositions.

Andante (Unidentified) Violin & Piano
Zlatko Topolski & Aleksije Butakoff
12"—G-EH1292
[Misoieritsch: Serbischer Tanz]

CONCERTOS

Flute & Orchestra

D major, Op. 10, No. 3 "Il Cardellino"
Lucien Lavaillotte & Chamber Orch. of Paris w. Mme. Marcelle de Lacour (harpsichord)—Fendler
2 10"—PAT-PA1831/2
[Mozart: Andante, Fl. & Orch., K. 315]

Violin & Orchestra

A major ("L'Eco in lontano")
—**Arr. Solo Violin, String Orch., Harpsichord, Organ** Molinari

Armando Gramegna & E. Graccone (vls)
w. EIAR Orch.—Ferrero
2 12"—CET-BB25047/8
A minor (Attr. Vivaldi)
Dominique Blot & Ars Rediviva Ensemble
—Crussard 12"—G-DB5065
B minor (Sometimes attr. Vivaldi—actually an anon. concerto)
—**Arr. Harpsichord** Bach (Peters Vol. X, No. 8)
Ruggero Gerlin (harpsichord)
12"—LUM-35018
—**Arr. Piano & Orch.**—Tamburini (based on Bach transcription)
Mario Salerno & EIAR Orch.—A. La Rosa Parodi 2 12"—CET-CB20301/2

Clavier Solo

G major (unidentified)
Carlo Zecchi (piano) 12"—CET-CB20350
[Scarlatti: Sonatina, G major—Giga]

CONCERTI GROSSI

(12) Concerti Grossi, Op. 3 ("L'estro armonico")
(Violins, Violas, 'Cello & Continuo)
No. 2, G minor
—**Arr. Molinari**
La Scala Orch.—Guarnieri
2 12"—G-S10105/6
No. 5, A major
—**Arr. String Quartet** (Concerto a quatro)
Pro Arte Quartet 12"—G-DB2148
No. 8, A minor (2 Violins obbligato)
NOTE: *In place of the customary last movement, an unidentified piece has been substituted.*
Amsterdam Concertgebouw Orch.—Mengelberg 2 12"—T-SK2401/2
[Bach: Suite No. 3—Air]
—**Arr. Organ** Bach (Peters Vol. VIII, No. 2)
E. Power Biggs, in TC-T1
—**Larghetto** only
String Orch., SEMS-1153
No. 9, D major
Jean Fournier w. Orch. & Harpsichord—Sachs (in Vol. IV) 12"—AS-37
Denise Soriano & Orch.—Münch
2 12"—PAT-PAT154/5
[Fauré: Berceuse]
—**Arr. Harpsichord** Bach
(Peters Vol. X, No. 1)
Ruggero Gerlin, AS-38 (in Vol. IV)
Wanda Landowska, V-12-0001 in VM-1181†
Sylvia Marlowe, in D-DAU4
—**Arr. 'Cello & Piano** Dandelot
Maurice Maréchal & M. Faure
12"—C-LFX62
No. 10, B minor (with 4 solo violins)
—**Arr. 4 Harpsichords & Orch.** Bach
(*Transposed to A minor*)
Pignari, Leroux, Rolet & Coppola (pfs.)
w. Orch.—Bret 2 12"—G-L963/4
[Bach: Cantata No. 106—Sinfonia]
(G-S10447/8)
No. 11, D minor
Dumbarton Oaks Chamber Orch.—Schneider 12"—K-2003

Boston Symphony Orch.—Koussevitzky
(Arr. Siloti) 2 12"—VM-886†
[Grieg: Last Spring]
[Handel: Concerto Grosso No. 12—
Larghetto, on G-DB3668/9]
EIAR Symphony Orch.—A. La Rosa
Parodi (Arr. Siloti)
2 12"—CET-CB20192/3
[Mozart: La Clemenza di Tito—Overture]
Emil Telmanyi's Chamber Orch.
2 12"—TONO-L28000/1
Philadelphia Orch.—Stokowski (Arr.
Stokowski) 2 12"—G-DB6047/8
—Arr. Clavier Bach (Arr. also attr. to
W. F. Bach)
Alfred Cortot (pf) 2 12"—G-DB3261/2
[Bach: Concerto No. 5—Largo]
Alexander Brailowsky (pf)
2 12"—G-DB3703/4
—3rd Mvt. (Adagio) only
—Arr. Organ Middelschulte
Virgil Fox (Chapel Organ, Girard College,
Philadelphia) 12"—V-11-8236
[Bach: Cantata 156—Arioso]
—Arr. Violin & Piano
Jacques Thibaud & pf. acc.
[Paradis: Siciliana] 10"—G-DA1191
—Arr. 'Cello & Piano
Pablo Casals & Blas-Net 10"—G-DA1118
[Valentini: Gavotte & De Laserna:
Tonadilla]
—4th Mvt. (Allegro) only
—Arr. Organ Bach
Alfred Sittard (St. Michael's Hamburg)
12"—PD-66553
[Bach: Prelude, E minor]
[Bach: Brandenburg Concerto No. 5, pt.
1, on PD-15073]
(4) Concerti Grossi, Op. 8 ("Le Quattro
Stagioni")
Eng. The Four Seasons
(La primavera; L'estate; L'autunno;
L'inverno)
—Arr. Orchestra Molinari
Symphony Orch. of the Augusteo, Rome—
Molinari 6 12"—CET-BB25067/72
Concerto, F major (unidentified)
—Largo only
Boyd Neel String Orch.—Neel
12"—D-X149
[Pergolesi: Concertino, F minor]

OPERAS

(L') OLYMPIADE

Overture (Arr. Mortari)
EIAR Symphony Orch.—Rossi
12"—CET-BB25185

SONATAS Violin & Figured Bass

Opus 2

No. 2, A major

—Arr. Violin & Piano Busch
Adolf Busch & Rudolf Serkin
12"—G-DB1524
[Geminiani-Busch: Siciliano]
Jascha Heifetz & Arpad Sandor
10"—G-DA1370

No. 3, D minor

—Arr. Violin & Piano Crussard
Dominique Blot & Claude Crussard
12"—G-DB5056

No. 11, D major

—Gavotte only
Dominique Blot & Claude Crussard
(harpsichord) 10"—BAM-30
[Sonata No. 12—Prelude & Capriccio]

No. 12, A minor

—Prelude & Capriccio only
Dominique Blot & Claude Crussard
(harpsichord) 10"—BAM-30
[Sonata No. 11—Gavotte only]

C minor
(Recently discovered in Dresden Library)

—Arr. Violin & Piano Crussard
Andante, Allegro, Largo, Allegro
Dominique Blot & Claude Crussard
12"—G-DB5092

D major

—Arr. Violin & Piano Respighi
(No opus number. Published by Ricordi,
1928)
Moderato, Allegro Moderato, Largo,
Vivace
Erica Morini & Max Lanner
12"—V-11-8671
Nathan Milstein & Leopold Mittmann
12"—C-GQX10886

VLADIGEROV, Pantcho (1899-)
*A contemporary Bulgarian composer, much in-
fluenced by German Romanticism, who inserted
Bulgarian folk elements into his operas and instrumental works.*
(3) Bulgarian Folk-songs
J. Urban (b) & P. Vladigerov (pf)
10"—U-B14924

Melancholie; Petite Prélude; Danse, Op. 37

Danse des paysans; Little crab, Op. 29
Piano
Pantcho Vladigerov 10"—U-C14925

Berceuse; Boite à musique and Humoresque,
Op. 29 Piano
Pantcho Vladigerov 10"—U-C14926

VOGELWEIDE, Walther von der
See under Walther

VORISEK, Jan Hugo (1791-1825)
A Czech contemporary of Beethoven.
Symphony, D major
—2nd Mvt. (Andante) only
Orchestral Association of Prague—
Krejci 12"—U-G12704

VULPIUS, Melchior, (c.1560-1615)
*A German composer of sacred music best
known for his choral settings and a famous
Passion oratorio according to St. Matthew.*
The Strife is O'er
British School Children 12"—G-C3528
[Bach: Jesu, Joy and Treasure; Anon.:
All People that on Earth do Dwell; Jesus
Good above all others]

VYCPALEK, Ladislav (1882-   )

One of the most interesting of Czech contemporaries, Vycpalek has not turned out music factory style, as so many other modern composers. Dead set against materialism in art as well as in society, he has resisted the easy path of folk music on the one hand, and that of the arbitrary formulas of the atonalists on the other.

Czech Requiem
—Dies Irae only
Czech Philharmonic Choir & Orch.—R.
Kubelik   3 12"—U-H14958/60

VYSCHNEGRADSKY, Ivan (1893-   )

An experimenter in the field of quarter-tone music.

Ainsi Parlait Zarathoustra 4 Quarter-Tone Pianos
—3rd Mvt. (Lento) only
Monique Haas, Edward Staempfli, Ina Marika, Max Vredenburg (pfs.)—cond.
Vyschenegradsky   12"—OL-70

WAGENSEIL, Georg Christoph (1715-1777)

A Viennese musician of the Pre-Classic period, Wagenseil was a prolific composer and an excellent keyboard performer, but perhaps his greatest works were the instrumental symphonies and concertos, with which Mozart became familiar early in his life.

Symphony, D major 1746
Berlin State Orch.—Walther Gmeindl
(Last side blank) 2 12"—PD-67560/1S

WAGNER, Richard (1813-1883)

Whatever one may think of the merits or otherwise of Richard Wagner—and here is not the place for such a discussion—he is inadequately represented on records. Unfortunately too many existing recordings are merely orchestral snippets or short scenes. Older and more extended excerpts from his music dramas have been withdrawn and those that remain are, in general, quite out of date. The performances are not of the best either technically or musically, and the few replacements which have been added to catalogues are of the type that can only be deplored.

Albumblatt (Romanze) C major Piano
Eng. **Album Leaf** 1861
—Arr. Violin Wilhelmj
Rudolf Schone & Munich Philharmonic—
Kabasta   12"—G-DB5573
[Träume]
Robert Zeiler & Berlin State Opera Orch.
—Schmalstich   12"—G-C2185
[Tannhäuser—Overture, Pt. 3]
DUPLICATIONS: G. Kulenkampff, PD-15095; H. Kolberg, PD-24634

(Eine) Faust Ouvertüre Orchestra 1840
Eng. **A Faust Overture** (Revised 1855)
NBC Symphony Orch.—Toscanini
(in VM-1135†) 2 12"—V-11-9642/3
[Walküre—Walkürenritt]
(G-DB6545/6)
London Philharmonic—Beecham
(C-LX481/2)   2 12"—CX-63†
[Lohengrin—Prelude, Act III]
(C-LFX170/1)

OPERAS (MUSIC DRAMAS) In German

(DER) FLIEGENDE HOLLAENDER
3 Acts 1843
Eng. **The Flying Dutchman**
Individual excerpts
Overture Orchestra
London Philharmonic Orch.—Beecham
          2 12"—CX-107†
[Tannhäuser—Einzug der Gäst]
(C-LX732/3) (C-LWX266/7)
La Scala Orch.—Paul van Kempen
          2 12"—D-K1684/5†
[Tannhäuser—Overture, Pt. 3]
Saxon State Orch.—Böhm
          2 12"—G-DB5553/4
[Lohengrin—Prelude, Act III]
Dresden Philharmonic—Paul van
Kempen   2 12"—PD-57165/6
[Rheingold—Einzug der Götter]
[Walküre—Walkürenritt, Berlin Philharmonic—Knappertsbusch, on CET-OR5112/3]
Bayreuth Festival ('36) Orch.—Tietjen
          2 12"—T-SK2089/90
[Meistersinger—Am stillen Herd, Roswaenge]
DUPLICATIONS: Berlin State Opera Orch.—von Schillings, PD-67101; Berlin Philharmonic—Abendroth, P-E11422: O-7888; Berlin Philharmonic—R. Strauss, PD-66830; Berlin State Opera Orch.—Blech, G-EJ89; Berlin Philharmonic—Schuricht, U-E331; Symphony Orch.—Schmalstich, G-C1870; Symphony Orch., C-DFX217; Symphony Orch.—Neubeck, PD-27155; Berlin State Opera Orch.—Muck, G-AW61/2

ACT I

Matrosenchor: Ho jo he! (Sailor's Chorus)
Chorus of Hamburg Opera & Hamburg Philharmonic—Schmidt-Isserstedt
[Spinnchor]   12"—T-E3050

Steuermannslied: Mitt Gewitter und Sturm
Tenor [Steersman's Song]
Lauritz Melchior & Cho.
(in VM-749) 12"—V-17725
[Siegfried—Ho-ho! Schmiede]
[Also V-11-8678 in VM-979†]
Peter Anders & Cho.   12"—T-E3056
[Willst jenes Tag's]
DUPLICATION: Franz Völker, PD-95233

Die Frist ist um Recit.

Wie oft in Meeres tiefsten Schlund Air Baritone

Dich frage ich
Joel Berglund   12"—G-DB6378
Hans Hermann Nissen   12"—G-DB5538
Josef Herrmann   12"—G-DB7645
George Oeggl   12"—T-E3129
DUPLICATIONS: Theodor Scheidl, PD-95428; A. Endrèze (in French) PAT-PGT26; Air only: A. van Rooy, CRS-9*

ACT II

Spinnchor: Summ' und brumm' Contralto & Cho.
(Spinning Chorus)

Hamburg State Opera Chorus & Orch.—
Schmidt-Isserstedt 12″—T-E3050
[Matrosenchor]
Friedel Beckmann & Cho.
[Senta's Ballad] 12″—G-DB5595
DUPLICATIONS: Berlin State Opera
Chorus—Fried, PD-66518
In English: Nellie Walker & Cho.,
G-D1517

—Arr. Piano Liszt
Alexander Brailowsky, PD-90027

Jo-ho-hoe! Traft ihr das Schiff Soprano &
Chorus (Senta's Ballad)
Marta Fuchs & Chorus 12″—G-DB5595
[Spinning Chorus]
DUPLICATIONS: Elisabeth Ohms (no
cho.), PD-66928
In English: Florence Austral, G-D1517

Traumerzählung des Erik Tenor & Soprano

Fühlst du den Schmerz
Franz Völker & Irmgaard Langhammer
[Rienzi-Gebet, Völker] 12″—PD-67799

Mögst du, mein Kind (Daland's Aria) Bass
Wilhelm Schirp 12″—T-E3130
[Lortzing: Der Waffenschmeid—Auch
ich war ein Jüngling]
Georg Hann 12″—PD-67942
[Lohengrin—Königsgebet]

Wie aus der Ferne Baritone
Theodor Scheidl 12″—PD-95409
[Meistersinger—Verachter mir die
Meister nicht]
[Parsifal—Amfortas Klage, on PD-
67185]
In French: A. Endreze, PAT-PGT 26

Versank ich jetzt in wunderbares Träumen

Wirst Du des Vaters Wahl nicht schelten
Soprano & Baritone (Love Duet)
Elisabeth Ohms & Theodor Scheidl
12″—PD-66930

ACT III

He! Seeleut'! Chorus
(Chorus of Sailors & Girls)
Berlin State Opera Chorus & Orch.—
Heger 12″—O-7779
[Tannhäuser—Pilgerchor]

Willst jenes Tag's du nicht Tenor
(Erik's Cavatina)
Peter Anders 12″—T-E3056
[Mit Gewitter und Sturm]
Franz Völker 10″—PD-90051
[Lohengrin—Atmest du nicht]

(DAS) LIEBESVERBOT 1836

Overture Orchestra
Berlin State Opera Orch.—Melichar
12″—PD-27296

LOHENGRIN 3 Acts 1850

Abridged recording Arr. Weigert & Maeder
Berlin State Opera Soloists, Chorus &
Orch.—Weigert 4 12″—PD-27395/8
The Cast:
Heinrich der Volger .. Otto Helgers (bs)
Lohengrin .... Fritz Wolff (t)
Elsa .... Beata Malkin (s)
Friedrich .... Rudolf Watzke (b)
Ortrud .... Henriette Gottlieb (c)
Heerführer (Herald) Armin Weltner (b)

Excerpts (1936 Bayreuth Festival)
Gralserzählung (in fernem Land) ;
Königs Gebet; Gang zum Münster; Vor-
spiel, Act III; Brautchor; Das susses Lied
verhallt; Höchstes Vertrau'n; Lohengrins
Abschied (Mein lieber Schwan)
Maria Müller (Elsa), Margarete Klose
(Ortrud), Franz Völker (Lohengrin),
Jaro Prohaska (Telramund), Josef von
Manowarda (King), Bayreuth Festival
Chorus & Orch.—Heinz Tietjen
5 12″—T-SKB2049/53

Individual Excerpts

ACT I

Prelude Orchestra
NBC Symphony Orch.—Toscanini
12″—V-11-8807
N. Y. Philharmonic-Symphony Orch.—
Toscanini (in VM-308†) 12″—V-14006
[Also on V-11-9287 in VM-1074]
(G-DB2904)
Hallé Orch.—Barbirolli 12″—G-C3545
Berlin Philharmonic—Furtwängler
12″—PD-95408
Pittsburgh Symphony—Reiner
(in CM-549†) 12″—C-11986D
German Opera House Orch.—Jochum
12″—T-E3175
DUPLICATIONS: Philadelphia Orch.—
Stokowski, V-6791: G-W986

Scene 2

Elsas Traum: Einsam in trüben Tagen
Soprano
It. Sola ne' miei prim' anni Fr. Seule
dans ma misère (Rêve d' Elsa)
Eng. Elsa's Dream
Kirsten Flagstad 12″—V-14181
[Tannhäuser—Dich, teure Halle]
Tiana Lemnitz 12″—PD-35081
[Euch Lüften]
Lotte Lehmann 10″—P-PO152
[Euch Lüften]
Helen Traubel 12″—C-12321D
(C-LX1026)
Astrid Varnay 12″—C-71399D
[Tannhäuser—Elizabeth Gebet]
DUPLICATIONS: Maria Reining,
T-E3052; Maria Wutz, G-EH1038; Hilde
Scheppan, PD-67863
In Italian: Maria Caniglia, G-DB2827:
also C-DQ1072; Mafalda Favero,
C-D6015; Pia Tassinari, CET-BB25120 in
CET-7; M. Zamboni, C-DQ1121; Rosetta
Pampanini, CET-BB25084; Margaret
Sheridan, G-DB988
In English: Joan Hammond, G-C3562
In French: Ninon Vallin, O-171033; Su-
zanne Balguerie, PD-566104

Lohengrins Ankunft (Lohengrin's Arrival)

Sei gegrüsst, du gottgesandter Held Chorus

Nun sei gedankt, mein lieber Schwan Tenor
& Chorus

Heil, König Heinrich Trio & Chorus

Wenn ich im Kampfe für dich siege Duo
& Chorus
Marcel Wittrisch (t), Käte Heidersbach
(s), Willi Domgraf-Fassbaender (b) &
Cho. 12″—G-DB4400

—Abbreviated versions

NOTE: *The Widdop record begins somewhat earlier with "Seht! Seht!" and concludes just before "Heil, König Heinrich."*

Walter Widdop (t) & Cho. (in English)
12"—**G-AW4112**
[Tannhäuser—Einzug der Gäste]
F. Wolf (t), B. Malkin (s) w. Cho.
12"—**PD-27335**
(Same as Side 3 in Polydor set above)
[In fernem Land & Abschied]

—Nun sei gedankt, mein lieber Schwan only
It. **Mercè, mercè, cigno gentil!** Tenor & Chorus
In Italian: A. Pertile & La Scala Chorus, G-DB1107; Dino Borgioli, C-DQ1108; E. Parmeggiani, C-D5837; G. Voyer, C-CQ714

—Wenn ich im Kampfe für dich siege only Duo & Chorus
Margit Angerer & Alfred Piccaver (no cho.) 12"—**PD-66833**
[Das süsse Lied verhallt, Act III]

Königs Gebet—Mein Herr und Gott Bass
Du kündest nun dein wahr Gericht Unacc. Quintet
Des Reinen Arm gieb Heldenkraft Ensemble, Chorus & Orch.
Josef von Manowarda (bs), Jaro Prohaska (b), Franz Völker (t), Maria Müller (s), Margarete Klose (c) w. Bayreuth Festival ('36) Chorus & Orch. —Tietjen 12"—**T-SKB2050**
[Gang zum Münster, Act 2]

Gebet—Mein Herr und Gott only (without Chorus)
Alexander Kipnis, C-7280M; Ludwig Hoffmann, PD-62684; Georg Hann, PD-67942
In Italian: T. Pasero, C-DQ1087
In Swedish: Ivar Andrésen, G-Z93*

ACT II

Euch Lüften die mein Klagen Soprano
(Elsa)
It. **Aurette, a cui si spesso**
Eng. **Elsa's Song to the Breezes**
Kirsten Flagstad & Philadelphia Orch.— Ormandy 10"—**V-1901**
[Walküre—Du bist der Lenz]
Lotte Lehmann 10"—**P-PO152**
[Elsas Traum]
Tiana Lemnitz 12"—**PD-35081**
[Elsas Traum]
Astrid Varnay 10"—**C-17354D**
[Walküre—Du bist der Lenz]
DUPLICATIONS: Hilde Schippan, PD-67863; Maria Reining, T-E3052
In Italian: Pia Tassinari, CET-BB25120 in CET-7; Maria Caniglia, G-DB2827: also C-DQ1072; Maria Zamboni, C-DQ1121; Mafalda Favero, C-D6015

Gang zum Münster: Gesegnet soll sie schreiten
(Elsas Brautzug) Chorus Eng. **Procession to the Minster**
Bayreuth Festival ('36) Chorus & Orch. —Tietjen 12"—**T-SKB2050**
[Königs Gebet]

Saxon State Opera Chorus & Orch.— Böhm 12"—**G-DB5551**
[Tannhäuser—Pilgerchor]

ACT III

Prelude (Introduction) Orchestra
N. Y. Philharmonic-Symphony Orch.— Toscanini (in VM-308†) 12"—**V-14007**
[Götterdämmerung—Dawn & Siegfried's Rhine Journey, Pt. 1]
[Götterdämmerung—Rhine Journey, Pt. 3, on G-DB2861]
[Verdi: Traviata—Prelude, Act 1, on V-11-9233 in VM-1064]
London Philharmonic—Beecham
(in CX-63†) 12"—**C-68594D**
(C-LX482) (C-LWX171)
[Faust Overture, Pt. 3]
Bayreuth Festival ('36) Orch.—Tietjen
12"—**T-SKB2051**
[Brautchor—Treulich geführt]
Hallé Orch.—Barbirolli 12"—**G-C3558**
[R. Strauss: Rosenkavalier Suite, Pt. 5]
Philadelphia Orch.—Stokowski
(in VM-731†) 12"—**V-17568**
(G-DB6041)
[Meistersinger—Prelude, Pt. 3]
Boston "Pops" Orch.—Fiedler
(in VM-968) 10"—**V-10-1091**
[Meyerbeer: Prophet—Coronation March]
[Mendelssohn: Octet—Scherzo, on G-C3234]
Pittsburgh Symphony Orch.—Reiner
(in CM-549†) 12"—**C-11987D**
[Walküre—Walkürenritt]
German Opera House Orch.—Jochum
12"—**T-E3227**
[Parsifal—Prelude, Act I, Pt. 3]
DUPLICATIONS: Saxon State Orch.— Böhm, G-DB5554; EIAR Symphony Orch. —Failoni, CET-BB25111; Chicago Symphony—Stock, V-7386: G-DB1557; Symphony Orch.—Coates, G-AW4108: G-D1815; Berlin Philharmonic—Jochum, T-E1425; Berlin State Opera Orch.— Ludwig, PD-15203: PD-516769: PD-15193
Also: Foden's Motor Works Band, C-FB2956; Garde Républicaine, G-L693

Brautchor: Treulich geführt Chorus
It. **Coro nuziale: Lieti fedel** Fr. **Choeur des fiancailles** Eng. **Bridal Chorus** (or— incorrectly—**Wedding March**)
Chorus & Orch. of Bayreuth Festival ('36)—Tietjen 12"—**T-SKB2051**
[Prelude, Act III]
Victor Chorale & Orch.—Robert Shaw
12"—**V-11-9294**
[Verdi: Trovatore—Anvil Chorus]
Vienna Opera Chorus—Kerby
(C-DFX178) 12"—**C-7271M**
[Tannhäuser—Pilgerchor]
DUPLICATIONS: Berlin State Opera Chorus—Blech, G-EW60; Berlin State Opera Chorus—Fried, PD-66517; Saxon State Opera Cho.—Böhm, G-DA4456
In English: Chorus & Orch.—A. Coates, G-AW4108
In Italian: La Scala Chorus—Molajoli, C-GQ7122

—Arr. Orchestra only
Paris Conservatory Orch.—Gaubert,
C-D15019; Deutches Künstler Orch. &
Organ—Schutze, PD-10221

—Arr. Band
Garde Républicaine—Dupont, C-DFX148:
C-GQX16563

—Arr. Organ
Mark Andrews, V-20036: G-HN472; F.
Feibel, C-7528M; Quentin M. Maclean,
C-DF365: C-361M

Scene 2 (Bridal Chamber Scene)
Das süsse Lied verhallt Ten. & Sop.

"Complete" recordings
Kirsten Flagstad & Lauritz Melchior
2 12"—VM-897†
Helen Traubel & Kurt Baum
(C-LX991/2) 2 12"—CX-261†
Germaine Martinelli & Georges Thill
(in French) 2 12"—C-LFX455/6

—2 sided versions
Tiana Lemnitz & Torsten Ralf
12"—G-DB4667
Maria Müller & Franz Völker
12"—T-SKB2052
Beate Malkin & Fritz Wolff
12"—PD-27336
In Italian: A. Tellini & A. Pertile,
G-DB1218
In French: M. Beaujon & G. Thill,

1 Side Versions
M. Angerer & A. Piccaver, PD-66833; M.
Beaujon & G. Thill (in French) C-D15119

—Atmest du nicht only Tenor
Franz Völker, PD-90051
In Italian: Aureliano Pertile, C-GQ7182

—Höchstes Vertrau'n only Tenor
Franz Völker & Bayreuth Festival ('36)
Orch.—Tietjen 12"—T-SKB2053
[Lohengrins Abschied]
In Italian: Francesco Merli, C-GQX11068

Scene 3
Gralserzählung; In fernem Land Ten.
(Lohengrin)
It. Racconto: Da voi lontan
Fr. Récit du Graal: Aux bords lointains
Eng. Lohengrin's Narration: In distant
land
Franz Völker & Bayreuth Festival Cho.
& Orch.—Tietjen 12"—T-SKB2049
NOTE: *The second side of this record begins
"Nun höre doch" and contains a portion of
the score used in the Weimar premiere (1850),
but was subsequently cut out of the opera. The
first side is also pressed on T-SKB2047 with
"Walküre"—"Siegmund heiss' ich."*

Helge Roswaenge 12"—G-DB5698
[Lohengrins Abschied]
Lauritz Melchior
(in VM-749) 12"—V-17726
[Tannhäuser—Dir töne Lob]
(Also, V-11-8676 in VM-979†)
Torsten Ralf
(in CM-634†) 12"—C-71826D
[Lohengrins Abschied]

Charles Kullman 12"—C-9146M
[Meistersinger—Preislied]
Franz Völker 12"—PD-95038
[Meistersinger—Am stillen Herd]
[Lohengrins Abschied, on PD-67148]
(Also: PD-95182)
DUPLICATIONS: Richard Crooks, V-
7105: G-DB1598: also G-EJ133; James
Melton, V-11-8931 in VM-1013; Leo Sle-
zak, PD-95182; Alfred Piccaver, PD-
66891; Fritz Krauss, G-EJ140
In Italian: Aureliano Pertile, G-DB1107:
C-D4949: C-GQX10664; Miguel Fleta,
G-DB976; A. Mercato, CET-BB25183
In English: Joseph Hislop, G-DB1351
In French: Georges Thill, C-LFX39;
César Vezzani, G-DB4828; René Maison,
O-123502; R. Verdière, O-123020
In Icelandic: Pjetur A. Jonssen, G-Z183
Lohengrins Abschied (Lohengrin's Fare-
well)
Mein lieber Schwan! Tenor
O Elsa! Nur ein Jahr an deiner Seite
(Abschied von Elsa)
It. Cigno fedel Fr. Mon cygne aimé
Lauritz Melchior
(in VM-516) 12"—V-15213
[Parsifal—Nur eine Waffe taugt]
Torsten Ralf
(in CM-634) 12"—C-71826D
[In fernem Land]
Helge Roswaenge 12"—G-DB5698
[In fernem Land]
Franz Völker & Bayreuth ('36) Festival
Orch.—Tietjen 12"—T-SKB2053
[Höchstes Vertrau'n]
[Also: In fernem land on PD-95182: PD-
67148]
DUPLICATIONS: Alfred Piccaver, PD-
66891; Leo Slezak, PD-95182; Fritz
Krauss, G-EJ140
In Italian: Miguel Fleta, G-DB976
In French: Georges Thill, C-LFX144;
César Vezzani, G-DB4828

**(DIE) MEISTERSINGER VON NUERN-
BERG** 3 Acts 1868
Eng. The Mastersingers Fr. Les Maîtres
Chanteurs It. I Maestri Cantori
Orchestral Selections
Berlin Philharmonic—Melichar (arr.
Charmilé)
(PD-10001) 10"—PD-24800
Individual Excerpts
Prelude Orchestra
NOTE: *The three-sided and two-sided recorded
performances of the prelude are listed separ-
ately as they represent two quite different con-
ceptions of the music. Both types are com-
plete (i. e. there are no cuts), but the two-
sided versions are brisker in tempo and
brighter in spirit, the three-sided versions
broader.*
Three-sided versions
Philadelphia Orch.—Stokowski
(G-DB6040/1) 2 12"—VM-731†
[Lohengrin—Prelude to Act III]
Paris Conservatory Orch.—Gaubert
2 12"—C-15018/9
[Lohengrin—Brautchor]

Two-sided versions
NBC Symphony Orch.—Toscanini
12″—V-11-9385
Amsterdam Concertgebouw—Mengelberg
12″—T-SK3137
Berlin Philharmonic—von Karajan
12″—PD-67532
Saxon State Orch.—Böhm
12″—G-DB4698
London Philharmonic—Beecham
(C-LX557) 12″—C-68854D
London Philharmonic—Fitelberg
12″—D-K1484
London Philharmonic—Szell
12″—G-C2809
DUPLICATIONS: Berlin Philharmonic—
Havemann, T-E1349; Pittsburgh Sym-
phony Orch.—Reiner, C-11984D in CM-
549; Symphony Orch.—Meyrowitz,
PAT-PDT39; Berlin Philharmonic—
Knappertsbusch, PD-516663: PD-66698:
CET-RR8031; BBC Symphony Orch.—
Boult, G-DB1924

ACT I, Scene 1

Kirchenchor: Da zu dir der Heiland kam
Chorus
Eng. Chorale: As our Savior came to thee
Royal Opera Chorus & London Philhar-
monic Orch.—Beecham
(in CX-37†) 12″—C-69095D
[Wach auf!] (Recorded at actual per-
formance in 1936) (C-LWX220)
Berlin State Opera Chorus—Blech
[Wach' auf! Act III] 12″—G-EJ53

Scene 3

Ansprache des Pogner: Nun hört Recit.
Das schöne Fest, Johannistag Bass Eng.
Pogner's Address
Alexander Kipnis 12″—V-7894
[R. Strauss: Rosenkavalier—Letter
Scene & Waltz, Kipnis & Ruziczka]
Am stillen Herd Tenor (Walther)
(All versions omit the brief parts of
Sachs, and others)
Lauritz Melchior
[Preislied] (in VM-749) 12″—V-17728
Set Svanholm 12″—V-11-9791
[Preislied] (G-DB6537)
Torsten Ralf
(in CM-634†) 12″—C-71824D
[Parsifal—Nur eine Waffe taugt]
Helge Roswaenge 12″—T-SK2090
[Fliegende Holländer—Overture, Pt. 3,
dir. Tietjen]
[Prieslied, on T-SK1297]
DUPLICATIONS: Franz Völker, PD-
67102: also PD-95038; Max Lorenz,
G-DB4547; Lauritz Melchior, G-DA1227;
J. Patzak, PD-90181; Leo Slezak, PD-
95181; Richard Tauber, O-123506
Probelied: Fanget an! Tenor (Walther)
Eng. Trial Song: Now begin!
Torsten Ralf 10″—G-DA4492
[Walküre-Winterstürme wichen]
Torsten Ralf
(in CM-634) 12″—C-71825D
[Preislied]
DUPLICATION: Franz Völker, PD-95161

ACT II, Scene 3

Fliedermonolog: Wie duftet doch der
Flieder & Kein' Regel wollte da passen
Bass (Sachs)
Eng. The elder's scent floats around me
Paul Schoeffler 12″—D-K1731
Herbert Janssen
(in CX-269†) 12″—C-71819D
Hans Hotter 12″—PD-67855
Rudolf Bockelmann 12″—T-SK1323
Wilhelm Rode 10″—PD-62649
Josef Hermann 12″—G-DB5623
—Single-sided version
Theodor Scheidl, PD-66671: PD67103

Scene 5

Ja, ihr seid es Duo: Sop. & Ten.
Fr. Qui, c'est vous (Eva & Walther)
Germaine Martinelli & Georges Thill (in
French) 12″—C-LFX373
[Preislied, Act III, Thill]

Scene 6

Schusterlied: Jerum! Jerum! Bass (Sachs
with others)
Eng. Cobbling Song
—Sach's part only
Friedrich Schorr 12″—G-EJ566
[Tannhäuser—Blick' ich umher]
Nelson Eddy (in English)
12″—C-71189D
[Tannhäuser—O du mein holder Abend-
stern]

ACT III

Complete recording
Soloists, Chorus of the Dresden State
Opera with the Saxon State Orchestra—
Karl Böhm 15 12″—VM-537/8†
(G-DB4562/78 in GM-329†)
The Cast:
Hans Sachs .. Hans Hermann Nissen (b)
Walther .... Torsten Ralf (t)
Eva ...... Margarete Teschemacher (s)
Magdalena .... Lene Jung (c)
David .... Martin Kremer (t)
Beckmesser .... Eugen Fuchs (bs)
Pogner .... Sven Nilsson (bs)

Suite from Act III Orchestra
Prelude, Dance of the Apprentices, Pro-
cession of the Masters, Homage to Sachs
and Finale
Hallé Orch.—Barbirolli
2 12″—G-C3416/7
Three Excerpts from Act III
Prelude, Dance of the Apprentices, Pro-
cession of the Masters
Pittsburgh Symphony Orch.—Reiner
2 12″—CX-218†
Three Excerpts from Act III
Prelude, Dance of the Apprentices,
Sorgiam (Chorus)
Symphony Orch.—Bruno Walter & La
Scala Chorus & Orch. (in Italian)
(C-LFX329 & LFX292) 2 12″—CX-43†

Individual Excerpts (Act III)

Vorspiel (Prelude) Orchestra
Berlin State Opera Orch.—von Karajan
12″—PD-67527

Berlin Philharmonic—Böhm
12″—G-EH962
Berlin Philharmonic—Jochum
10″—T-A1658
DUPLICATIONS: Berlin Philharmonic—
Knappertsbusch, PD-66780: PD-516664;
British Symphony Orch.—B. Walter,
C-LFX292: C-68690D in CX-43†; Pittsburgh Symphony—Reiner, C-11739D, in
CX-218†; Hallé Orch.—Barbirolli,
G-C3416

Wahnmonolog: Wahn! Wahn! Ueberall
Wahn Bass (Sachs)
Herbert Janssen (C-LX947)
(in CX-269†) 12″—C-71820D
Wilhelm Rode 12″—PD-66781

Scene 2

Abendlich glühend Tenor & Bass (Walther
& Sachs)
NOTE: *The second verse of the Prize Song, but
without its later conclusion.*
Lauritz Melchior & Friedrich Schorr
12″—V-7681
[Aha! da streicht die Lene]

Scene 4

O Sachs! Mein Freund Sop.
Delia Reinhardt 12″—PD-66783
[Walküre—Du bist der Lenz]

Mein Kind Bass (Sachs)

Aha! Da streicht die Lene
Herbert Janssen 12″—C-72518D
[Quintet]
Friedrich Schorr (begins "Aha! Da
streicht . . .") 12″—V-7681
[Abendlich glühend]
[Quintet, on G-D2002: G-AW289]

Quintet: Selig, wie die Sonne (Eva, Sachs,
Walther, David, Magdalene)
Elisabeth Schumann, Friedrich Schorr,
Lauritz Melchior, Ben Williams, Gladys
Parr 12″—V-7682
[Euch macht ihr's leicht, Schorr]
[Aha! Da streicht die Lene, Schorr on
G-D2002: G-AW289]
P. Stoska, H. Janssen, T. Ralf, J. Garris,
H. Glaz 12″—C-72518D
[Mein Kind]
M. Teschemacher, H. H. Nissen, T. Ralf,
M. Kremer, L. Jung 12″—G-DB4636
[Wach' auf!]
P. Yoder, H. Reinmer, H. Roswaenge, M.
Kuttner, L. Kindermann 12″—T-SK1162
[Verdi: Rigoletto—Quartet]
E. Berger, K. A. Neumann, M. Hirzel, K.
Jöken, E. Ruziczka 12″—PD-35006
[Preislied, Völker]

Scene 5

Aufzug der Zünfte: Saint Crispin Cho. &
Orch.
Eng. **Procession of the Guilds**
It. **Coro delle corporazione**
Saxon State Opera Cho. & Orch.—Böhm
[Tanz der Lehrbuben] 12″—G-DB4678
La Scala Cho. (in Italian)
12″—C-GQX10262
[Silentium & Wach' auf]

—Arr. Orch.
Berlin State Opera Orch.—Ludwig
(PD-516772) 12″—PD-15198
[Tanz der Lehrbuben]

Tanz der Lehrbuben: Ihr tanzt? Ten. &
Cho.
Eng. **Dance of the Apprentices**
Martin Kremer, Cho. & Orch.—Böhm
[Aufzug der Zünfte] 12″—G-DB4678
—Arr. Orch.
Philadelphia Orch.—Ormandy
(G-DA1561) 10″—V-1807
[Aufzug der Meistersinger]
Berlin Philharmonic—Schmidt-Isserstedt
[Walküre—Walkürenritt] 12″—T-E2746
Berlin Philharmonic—Ludwig
(PD-516772) 12″—PD-15198
[Aufzug der Zünfte]
DUPLICATIONS: Symphony Orch.—B.
Walter, C-68691D in CX-43†: C-LX232;
Symphony Orch.—Coates, G-AW4300;
Berlin Philharmonic—Knappertsbusch,
PD-516665: PD-66705

Aufzug der Meistersinger Orchestra Eng.
Entrance of the Mastersingers
(See also Act III Collections above)
Philadelphia Orch.—Ormandy
(G-DA1561) 10″—V-1807
[Tanz der Lehrbuben]

Silentium! Chorus
Wach' auf! es nahet gen den Tag Chorus
It. **Sorgiam!**
Saxon State Opera Chorus—Böhm
[Quintet] 12″—G-DB4636
Berlin State Opera Chorus—Reuss
12″—T-E1609
[Euch macht ihr's leicht, Reinmar]
La Scala Cho. (in Italian)
(in CX-43†) 12″—C-68691D
[Tanz der Lehrbuben, dir. Walter]
[Aufzug der Zünfte, on C-GQX10262]
—Wach' auf! only
Royal Opera Cho., Covent Garden & London Philharmonic—Beecham
(in CX-87†) 12″—C-69095D
[Kirchenchor, Act I] (C-LWX220)
Berlin State Opera Cho. & Orch.—Blech
[Kirchenchor, Act I] 12″—G-EJ53
DUPLICATION: Berlin State Opera Cho.
—Curth, PD-66542

Euch macht ihr's leicht Bass (Sachs)
Friedrich Schorr 12″—V-7682
[Quintet, with E. Schumann, Melchior,
etc.]
Hans Reinmar 12″—T-E1609
[Silentium! & Wach' auf!]

Preislied: Morgenlich leuchtend im rosigen
Schien
Tenor (Walther) with Ensemble
Eng. **Prize Song: Morning was glowing**
Fr. **Air du Concours** It. **Canzone del concorso**
Torsten Ralf w. Bockelmann, Jones,
Lemnitz, Worthington, Devereux, Sale,
Lloyd, Hitchin, Horsman, Woodhouse,
Cho. & London Philharmonic—Beecham
(in CX-87†) 12″—C-69096D
(C-LWX221)
(Recorded at an actual performance,
Covent Garden, 1936)

—Preislied (Walther's part only)
Lauritz Melchior
      (in VM-749)   12"—V-17728
[Am stillen Herd]
(Earlier recording on G-DB1858)
Torsten Ralf
      (in CM-634†) 12"—C-71825D
[Fanget An!]
Set Svanholm
(G-DB6537)   12"—V-11-9791
[Am stillen Herd]
Franz Völker   12"—PD-67102
[Am stillen Herd]
[Quintet, on PD-35006]
(Earlier recording PD-95161)
Charles Kullman   12"—C-9146M
[Lohengrin—In fernem Land]
DUPLICATIONS: James Melton, V-11-
8931 in VM-1013; Helge Roswaenge,
T-SK1297; Richard Crooks, V-7105;
G-DB1598; G-EJ133; Leo Slezak, PD-
95181; J. Patzak, PD-90181; Richard
Tauber, O-123506
In French: Georges Thill, C-LFX373
In English: Webster Booth, G-C3309;
Joseph Hislop, G-DB1351
In Icelandic: Jjetur A. Jonssen, G-Z183
—Arr. Violin & Piano Wilhelmj
L. Zimmerman, C-DHX30
—Arr. 'Cello & Piano
Raya Garbousova, V-11-8870 in VM-
1017; Pablo Casals, V-6620: G-DB1012

Verachtet mir die Meister nicht Bass

Was deutsch und echt Bass & Chorus
Ansprache des Hans Sachs (Sachs'
Panegyric)
Hans Hermann Nissen, Torsten Ralf, etc.
(from Act III complete set)
          12"—G-DB4683
Hens Reinmar & Chorus 12"—T-E1610
—Sachs' part only (without Chorus)
T. Scheidl, PD-67103: PD-95409

PARSIFAL 3 Acts 1882

Collections

Miscellaneous Excerpts
(More complete details below)
Bayreuth Festival Co.—Muck
[Siegfried: Waldweben] 8 12"—CM-337†
(C-GQX10473/80) (C-LCX36/43)

Vorspiel (Prelude) Orch.
Berlin Philharmonic—Furtwängler
        2 12"—G-DB3445/6
[Charfreitagszauber, Pt. 1]
Boston Symphony Orch.—Koussevitzky,
           in VM-1198†
[with Charfreitagszauber]
Philadelphia Orch.—Stokowski
      2 12"—V-14728/9
[with Charfreitagszauber] (in VM-421†)
German Opera House Orch.—Jochum
        2 12"—T-E3226/7
[Lohengrin—Prelude to Act III]
DUPLICATION: Berlin State Orch.—von
Schillings, PD-66592/3

Individual Excerpts (Page references are
to the Schott vocal score)

ACT I

Transformation Scene Orchestra

Vom Bade kehrt der König heim
Bass & Tenor
—Orchestra only
NOTE: *The double-sided orchestral versions of
the music accompanying the changing of
scenes in Act I begin on page 63 with Gurnemanz's lines and end shortly before the entrance of the chorus of Knights: "Zum letzten
Liebesmahle," on page 69. The single-sided
versions usually begin later, on page 65, following Gurnemanz's "Du sieh'st mein Sohn,
zum Raun wird hier die Zeit," and end as do
the longer versions. The Muck disc below,
however, ends at the bottom of page 67 (the
pealing of the bells) only to resume without
cut on the first side of the "Grail Scene" records.*
Bayreuth Festival Orch.—K. Muck
(C-LCX36) (in CM-337†) 12"—C-67364D
Berlin Philharmonic—Knappertsbusch
           12"—PD-66700
DUPLICATIONS: Paris Conservatory
Orch.—Coppola, G-DB4918; Berlin State
Opera Orch.—Grüber, O-7954

Grail Scene Soloists, Chorus & Orchestra

Zum letzten Liebesmahle Chorus
NOTE: *The Muck recordings below, which omit
the soloists' parts, continue after the "Trans-
formation Scene" (q. v.) on page 68. Be-
tween sides 2 and 3 there is a cut of 9½ pages,
from 76 to 85, deleting Titurel's questions and
Amfortas' lament; resuming on side 3 with
"Durch Mitleid wissend," the recording con-
tinues uncut to the top of page 98, where the
Knights prepare to leave the hall. The final
five pages of the act are omitted.*
Bayreuth Festival Chorus & Orch.—
Muck (C-LCX37/9) (C-GQX10474/6)
(in CM-337†) 3 12"—C-67365/70D
—Der Glaube lebt (Boys' Cho.) only
Regensburg Cathedral Choir—
T. Schrems   10"—G-EG3431
[Palestrina: Missa Lauda Sion—
Benedictus]
[Liszt: Schönster Herr Jesu, on
G-EG3902]

—Des Weihgefässes göttlicher Gehalt
Baritone
(Amfortas' Lament, 2nd Part)
Theodor Scheidl   12"—PD-66671
[Meistersinger—Fliedermonolog]
[Fliegende Holländer—Wie aus der
ferne, on PD-67185]

ACT II

Klingsor's Magic Garden & Flower Maiden's
Scene
Women's Chorus & Tenor (Parsifal)
NOTE: *The Muck version (with chorus) below
omits Parsifal's part and the entire first section
of the scene, beginning with the waltz theme
on page 116 and continuing up to the entrance of Kundry on page 167. The orchestral
version begins where the Magic Garden rises
up (page 126), with the essential choral parts
transcribed to instruments.*

Bayreuth Festival Chorus & Orch.—
Muck, (C-LCX40) (C-GQX10477)
(in CM-337†) 12"—C-67368D
—Arr. Orchestra
Berlin State Opera Orch.—von Schillings
12"—PD-66595

Herzeleide Scene Duo: Tenor & Soprano
(Parsifal & Kundry)
NOTE: *The Flagstad-Melchior recording be-*
gins "Dies Alles Hab' ich nun geträumt, and
is complete to the end of the act. Gordon Dil-
worth (b) sings the few lines alotted to Kling-
sor.
Lauritz Melchior & Kirsten Flagstad
4 12"—VM-755†
[Siegfried—Hammerlied, Melchior]
—Ich sah' das Kind Kundry's part only
Kerstin Thorborg
(in VM-707) 12"—V-17223
[Tristan und Isolde—Einsam wachend]
—Amfortas! Die Wunde!
Parsifal's part only
Lauritz Melchior (G-DB3781)
(in VM-516) 12"—V-15212
DUPLICATION: Franz (in French),
PAT-X7238

ACT III

Symphonic Synthesis Arr. Stokowski
Philadelphia Orchestra.—Stokowski
2 12"—G-DB2272/3
Prelude Orchestra
Bayreuth Festival Orch.—Siegfried
Wagner (C-LCX41) (C-GQX10478)
(in CM-337†) 12"—C-67369D
Charfreitagszauber Eng. Good Friday Spell
Bass & Tenor
Alexander Kipnis, Fritz Wolff &
Bayreuth Festival Orch.—Siegfried
Wagner (C-LCX42/3) (C-GQX10479/80)
(in CM-337†) 2 12"—C-67370/1D
[Siegfried—Waldweben]
—Charfreitagszauber Orchestra only
Berlin Philharmonic—Furtwängler
[Prelude, Act I] 12"—G-DB3446/7
Boston Symphony Orch.—Koussevitsky
[with Prelude, Act I] in VM-1198†
Philadelphia Orch.—Stokowski
(in VM-421†) 2 12"—V-14730/1
[with Prelude, Act I] (G-DB3271/2)
EIAR Symphony Orch.—V. Gui
2 12"—CET-BB25007/8
[Pergolesi-Gui: Orfeo—Intermezzo]
DUPLICATIONS: Berlin State Opera
Orch.—von Schillings, PD-66594; Berlin
State Opera Orch.—Grüber, O-7953/4;
BBC Symphony Orch.—Boult, G-DB1677

Transformation Scene & Procession of the
Knights Orchestra, later Cho.
—Orchestra only
Paris Conservatory Orch.—Coppola
12"—G-DB4918
[Transformation Scene, Act I]

Nur eine Waffe taugt Tenor (Parsifal)
Fr. Une arme seul et sure
It. Invocazione
Lauritz Melchior
(in VM-516) 12"—V-15213
[Lohengrin—Abschied]

Torsten Ralf
(in CM-634†) 12"—C-71824D
[Meistersinger—Am stillen Herd]
In French: Georges Thill, C-D15121;
Franz, PAT-X7238
In Italian: I. Fagoaga, C-GQX10270
Finale: Höchsten Heiles Wunder
Chorus & Orchestra
—Arr. Orchestra
Berlin State Opera Orch.—von Schillings
[Prelude Act I, Pt. 3] 12"—PD-66593

RIENZI 5 Acts 1842
(Rienzi, der Letzte der Tribunen)
Individual Excerpts
Overture Orchestra
Vienna Philharmonic—Knappertsbusch
2 12"—G-DB5607/8
[Verdi: Aida—Grand March]
Paris Conservatory Orch.—Weingartner
(C-LX860/1) 2 12"—CX-169†
[Berlioz: Les Troyens—Marche Troy-
enne]
Boston "Pops" Orch.—Fiedler
(G-EH1101/2) 2 12"—VM-569†
[Tannhäuser—Einzug der Gäste]
Hallé Orch.—Barbirolli
2 12"—G-C3425/6
[Mendelssohn: Midsummer Night's
Dream—Scherzo]
DUPLICATIONS: Philadelphia Orch.—
Stokowski, V-6624/5: G-AW4028 &
AW4030: G-W1013/4; Berlin State
Opera Orch.—Ludwig, PD-15192/3:
PD-516768/9

ACT I

Erstehe, hohe Roma, neu! Tenor & Chorus
Franz Völker & Cho. 12"—PD-67100
[Allmächt'ger Vater, Act V]
[Verdi: Otello—Mort d'Otello, on
PD-27325]

ACT III

Gerechtige Gott Contralto
Piroska Anday 12"—RAD-SP8004
[Rheingold—Weiche, Wotan!]

ACT V

Rienzis Gebet: Allmächt'ger Vater, blick'
herab Eng. Rienzi's Prayer Tenor
Lauritz Melchior 12"—C-71388D
[Tristan—O König]
Franz Völker 12"—PD-67799
[Fliegende Holländer—Traumerzählung
des Erik]
(Earlier recording: PD-67100)

(DER) RING DES NIBELUNGEN
Music Drama Cycle
Eng. The Ring of the Nibelungs
1. Das Rheingold
2. Die Walküre
3. Siegfried
4. Götterdämmerung
(First complete performance 1876)
Leading Motives of "Der Ring"
Peter Latham (lecturer) with piano
illustrations 3 12"—C-D40196/8
(International Educational Society
Lecture No. 100)

(DAS) RHEINGOLD 4 Scenes 1869
Eng. **The Rheingold** Fr. **L'Or du Rhin**
Excerpts Arr. Orch. Stokowski
Philadelphia Orch.—Stokowski
(G-DB1976/8)   3 12"—**VM-179**†
*(Includes the Prelude, Rhinemaidens' Song,
Alberich–Nibelungen Scene with anvil rhy-
thm, Erda's Warning, Rainbow Music & En-
trance of the Gods into Valhalla)*

Individual Excerpts
Vorspiel (Prelude) Orchestra
Symphony Orch.—Albert Coates
(G-W762)   12"—**G-AW4118**
[Walküre—Walkürenritt]

Scene 4
Erdas Warnung: Weiche, Wotan, weiche!
Alto
Eng. **Erda's Warning**
(Wotan's brief part omitted)
Blanche Thebom   12"—**V-11-9795**
[Ponchielli: Gioconda—Voce di donne]
Kerstin Thorborg
          (in VM-707)   12"—**V-17221**
[Walküre—2 Fricka excerpts]
DUPLICATIONS: Emmi Leisner,
PD-66737; Piroska Anday, RAD-SP8004

Einzug der Götter in Walhall
Zur Burg führt die Brücke
Abendlich strahlt der Sonne Auge
Eng. **Entrance of the Gods into Valhalla**
—Orchestra & Rhinemaiden part only
(no soloists)
Bayreuth Festival Orch. & Trio—von
Hösslin (in CM-338) 12"—**C-67373D**
(C-LCX45) (C-GQX10482)
—Orchestra only
Berlin State Opera Orch.—Elmendorf
          12"—**PD-57166**
[Fliegende Holländer—Overture, Pt. 3,
with Dresden Philharmonic—van
Kempen]
Philadelphia Orch.—Stokowski, in
VM-179†: Also on V-11-9230 in
VM-1063
DUPLICATION: Berlin Philharmonic—
Schmidt-Isserstedt, T-E2783

Wotan's part only (Abendlich strahlt)
Rudolf Bockelmann   12"—**T-SK1342**
[Tannhäuser—Blick' ich umher]
Hans Hermann Nissen   10"—**G-DA4460**
[Siegfried—Auf wolkigen Höh'n wohnen
die Götter]
DUPLICATION: Wilhelm Rode,
PD-66782

(DIE) WALKUERE 3 Acts 1870
Eng. **The Valkyrie** Fr. **La Walkyrie**
Collections

ACT I Complete recording
Soloists & Vienna Philharmonic Orch.—
Bruno Walter   8 12"—**VM-298**†
(G-DB2636/43 in GM-237†)
(C-GQX10889/96)
The Cast:
Sieglinde .... Lotte Lehmann (s)
Siegmund ...... Lauritz Melchior (t)
Hunding .... Emanuel List (bs)

ACT II "Complete" recording
Soloists with Berlin State Opera Orch.—
Seidler-Winkler & Vienna Philharmonic
—Bruno Walter   10 12"—**VM-582**†
(G-DB3719/28 in GM-336†)
The Cast:
Sieglinde .... Lotte Lehmann (s)
Brünnhilde .... Marta Fuchs (s)
Fricka .... Margarete Klose (c)
Siegmund .... Lauritz Melchoir (t)
Wotan .... Hans Hotter (b)
Hunding .... Emanuel List (bs)
(In addition Ella Flesch & Alfred Jerger
sing the brief lines allotted to Brünn-
hilde & Wotan in Scene 5)

ACT III Complete recording
Soloists & N. Y. Philharmonic—Sym-
phony Orch.—Rodzinski
(C-LX955/62†)   8 12"—**CM-581**†
The Cast:
Brünnhilde .... Helen Traubel (s)
Sieglinde .... Irene Jessner (s)
Wotan .... Herbert Janssen (b)
Helmwige .... Doris Doree (s)
Gerhilde .... Maxine Stellman (s)
Ortlinde .... Irene Jessner (s)
Rossweisse .... Doris Doe (s)
Grimgerde .... Martha Lipton (s)
Waltraute .... Jean Palmer (s)
Siegrune .... Hertha Glaz (c)
Schwerleite .... Anna Kaskas (c)

Excerpts Arr. Orch. Stokowski
(including Wotans Abschied)
NOTE: *This Stokowski transcription includes
the orchestral interlude to Scene 4, Act II,
and the first part of this scene; the Walkürenritt; the conclusion of Scene 2 and the beginning of Act III, Scene 3 (Brünnhilde's Bitte)
(with all vocal parts transcribed for orchestral
instruments) and Wotan's Abschied & Feuerzauber with Tibbett singing the part of Wotan.*
Philadelphia Orch. (Lawrence Tibbett as
Wotan)—Stokowski
(G-DB2470/3)   4 12"—**VM-248**†

Individual Excerpts

ACT I, Scene 3
Ein Schwert verhiess mir der Vater
Was gleisst dort hell? Tenor
Eng. **Siegmund's Monologue**
Fr. **O glaive promis par mon père**
It. **Un brando il padre promise**
Franz Völker
(PD-566191)   12"—**PD-67142**
[Winterstürme wichen dem Wonnemond]
(Older recording on PD-27291)
DUPLICATION: Max Lorenz, G-DB4547
In French: Georges Thill, C-LFX220
In Italian: I. Fagoaga, C-GQX10269

Love Duet (Finale of Act I)
Soprano & Tenor
Complete recording
(beginning "Schläfst du Gast?")
Helen Traubel & Emery Darcy
          3 12"—**CM-618**†

—Der Männer Sippe   Soprano only
Delia Reinhardt   12"—PD-66868
[Tannhäuser—Dich, teure Halle]
Lotte Lehmann
            (in VM-329)   12"—V-14205
[Verdi: Traviata—Di Provenza, Thomas]

Winterstürme wichen dem Wonnemond

Du bist der Lenz   Wie dir die Stirn

Ein Minnetraum gemahnt auch mich

Siegmund heiss ich und Siegmund bin ich
Franz Völker & Maria Müller w. Bayreuth
Festival ('36) Orch.—Tietjen
            2 12"—T-SKB2047/8
[Lohengrin—Gralserzählung]

—Winterstürme wichen (Liebeslied)
Tenor only
Eng. Siegmund's Love (or Spring) Song
Fr. Chant du printemps
It. Canto della primavera (Cede il verno)
Franz Völker & Berlin State Orch.—
Schuler   12"—PD-67142
[Ein Schwert verhiess] (PD-566191)
Lauritz Melchior & Philadelphia Orch.—
Ormandy   10"—V-2035
[Siegfried—Nothung]
(Earlier recording on G-DA1227)
Lauritz Melchior & Lotte Lehmann
            (in VM-329)   12"—V-14204
(Begins "Dich selige Frau")
[Charpentier: Louise—Depuis le jour]
Torsten Ralf   10"—G-DA4493
[Meistersinger—Fanget an]
In French: Georges Thill, C-7008
In Italian: P. Pauli, G-DA1331; I.
Fagoaga, C-D12311; E. Parmeggiani,
C-D5837; G. Borgatti, C-D6073

—Du bist der lenz   Sop. only
Kirsten Flagstad & Philadelphia Orch.—
Ormandy   10"—V-1901
[Lohengrin—Euch Lüften]
Lotte Lehmann
            (in VM-633)   12"—V-15817
[Siegmund heiss' ich]
Astrid Varnay   10"—C-17354D
[Lohengrin—Euch Lüften die mein
Klagen]
DUPLICATIONS: D. Reinhardt,
PD-66783; Olive Fremstad, CRS-21*

—Siegmund heiss' ich und Siegmund bin ich
Lotte Lehmann & Lauritz Melchior
            (in VM-633)   12"—V-15817
[Du bist der Lenz]
G. Martinelli & Georges Thill
(in French)   12"—C-LFX220
[Ein Schwert]

ACT II

Complete recording
See Collections above: VM-582†:
G-DB3719/28†

Scene I

Ho-Jo-To-Ho!   Brünnhilde only
Kirsten Flagstad   10"—V-1726
[R. Strauss: Allerseelen]
Olive Fremstad (Recorded 1913)
[Du bist der Lenz]   10"—CRS-21*

Fricka-Wotan Duet

Der alte Sturm, die alte Müh'!
Soprano & Baritone
—So ist es denn aus mit den ewigen Göttern
& Deiner ew'gen Gattin heilge
(Fricka part only)
Blanche Thebom   12"—V-11-8928
[Tristan—Brangäne's Warning]
Kerstin Thorborg
            (in VM-707)   12"—V-17221
[Rheingold—Weiche, Wotan!]

ACT III

Complete recording
See Collections above: CM-581†:
C-LX955/62†

Scene I

Prelude (Walkürenritt) Chorus & Orch.
Eng. Ride of the Valkyries
Fr. La Chevauchée des Walkyries
Bayreuth Festival Chorus & Orch.—von
Hösslin (C-GQX10483)
            (in CM-338†) 12"—C-67374D
Paris Opera Chorus (in French)
& Pasdeloup Orch.—Coppola
                           12"—G-DB4905
—Arr. Orchestra
NBC Symphony Orch.—Toscanini
            (in VM-1135†) 12"—V-11-9643
[Faust Overture, Pt. 3] (G-DB6546)
Philadelphia Orch.—Stokowski, in
VM-248†
London Philharmonic—de Sabata
            (in D-ED31†) 12"—D-K1562
[Holst: The Perfect Fool—Ballet Music,
Pt. 3, dir. Sargent]
Berlin State Opera Orch.—Elmendorff
[Feuerzauber]   12"—PD-67642
Pittsburgh Symphony Orch.—Reiner
            (in CM-549†) 12"—C-11987D
[Lohengrin—Prelude, Act III]
DUPLICATIONS: Berlin Philharmonic—
Schmidt-Isserstedt, T-E2746; Berlin
Philharmonic—Knappertsbusch,
PD-516665: PD-66705: PD-66895:
CET-RR8009: CET-RRe8032:
CET-OR5113; London Symphony Orch.
—Coates, G-AW4118: G-D1815: G-W762;
Berlin State Opera Orch.—Weissmann,
O-170140; New Queen's Hall Orch.—
Wood, D-K761: PD-516680; EIAR Sym-
phony Orch.—Molinari, CET-PP60010
Also: Republican Guard Band—Dupont,
G-L693

Scene 3

Brünnhildes Bitte: War es so schmälich?
Soprano & Bass
Eng. Brünnhilde's Pleading
—Brünnhilde's part only
Marta Fuchs   12"—G-DB4555

Wotans Abschied & Feuerzauber (Finale)

Leb' wohl, du kühnes, herrliches Kind!
Baritone
Eng. Wotan's Farewell & Magic Fire
Music
Fr. Adieux de Wotan & Incantation du feu
It. Addio di Wotan & Incantesimo del
fuoco
Paul Schoeffler & London Symphony—
Rankl (D-K1597/8)   2 12"—D-ED46†

Josef Hermann & Vienna Philharmonic
—Moralt 2 12"—G-DB7675/6
Lawrence Tibbett & Philadelphia Orch.
—Stokowski, in VM-248†
Hans Reinmar & Berlin Philharmonic—
Borchard 2 12"—T-E1589/90
DUPLICATION: Wilhelm Rode,
PD-66871/2
In French: André Pernet, O-123727/8
In Italian: Luciano Neroni,
CET-CB20342/3

—**Wotans Abschied** only
Leb' wohl & Der Augen leuchtendes Paar
In French: A. Endrèze, PAT-PGT12
In Italian: N. de Angelis, C-GQX10208

Feuerzauber
Eng. Magic Fire Music

—**Arr. Orchestra** only
Berlin State Opera Orch.—Elmendorff
[Walkürenritt] 12"—PD-67642
Philadelphia Orch.—Stokowski
(G-DB3942) (G-DB6042) 12"—V-15800
DUPLICATION: London Symphony—
Coates, G-AW142

—**Arr. Piano**
Jesús María Sanromá 12"—V-18153
[Sinding: Rustle of Spring & Grieg:
Butterfly]
Julius Schendel 12"—G-S10021
[Debussy: Arabesque No. 1]

SIEGFRIED 3 Acts 1876

Collection

*Contents: Concluding Portion, Act I (4 sides);
Forest Murmurs Scene, Act II (4 sides); Mis-
cellaneous Excerpts, Act III (12 sides).*
Soloists, with Berlin State Opera Orch.—
Blech, London Symphony—Albert
Coates & Robert Heger & Vienna State
Opera Orch.—Karl Alwin
10 12"—VM-83†
The Cast:

Siegfried .... { Rudolf Laubenthal (t)
{ Lauritz Melchior (t)
Brünnhilde .... Frida Leider (s)
Wanderer.... { Emil Schipper (b)
(Wotan) { Rudolf Bockelmann (b)
Mime .... Albert Reiss (t)
Erda .... Maria Olczewska (c)
Waldvögel .... Nora Grühn (s)

Excerpts Arr. Stokowski
*Contents: Sword Forging Scene (Act I); Con-
cert Version of the Forest Murmurs Scene (Act
II) & The Siegfried-Brünnhilde Duet (Act III)*
Frederick Jagel (t) & Agnes Davis (s)
with Philadelphia Orch.—Stokowski
3 12"—VM-441†
[Götterdämerung—Closing Scene]

Individual Excerpts

ACT I, Scene 2

Auf wolkigen Höh'n Bass
Hans Hermann Nissen 10"—G-DA4460
[Rheingold—Abendlich strahlt]

Scene 3

Fühltest du nie? (Mime & Siegfried)
Reiss & Melchoir, on V-9805 in VM-83†

Schmelzlied & Schmiedelied
(Siegfried & Mime)
Eng. Forging & Hammer Songs
Melchior & Reiss, on V-9805/6 in VM-83†
(Side 2 only on G-DB1858)

—**Schmelzlied** only Eng. Forging Song
(Nothung! Nothung! Neidliches Schwert!)
Max Lorenz & Bayreuth Festival ('36)
Orch.—Tietjen 12"—T-SKB2054
[Schmiedelied]
Max Lorenz 12"—G-DB4470
[Schmiedelied]
Frederick Jagel, in VM-441†
Lauritz Melchior 10"—V-2035
[Walküre—Winterstürme]
DUPLICATIONS (In French): Franz,
C-LF45; R. Verdière, O-123020

—**Schmiedelied** only Eng. Hammer Song
(Ho-Ho! Schmiede, mein Hammer)
Max Lorenz & Erich Zimmermann w.
Bayreuth Festival ('36) Orch.—
Tietjen 12"—T-SKB2054
[Schmelzlied]

—**Siegfried's part** only
Lauritz Melchior
(in VM-979†) 12"—V-11-8678
[Fliegende Holländer—Mit Gewitter]
(Also V-17725 in VM-749)
Max Lorenz 12"—G-DB4470
[Schmelzlied]

ACT II, Scene 2

Dass der mein Vater nicht ist!

Du holdes Vöglein (Siegfried)
(1st part of "Forest Murmurs" scene)
Lauritz Melchior, on V-9807 in VM-83†
Max Lorenz & Bayreuth Festival ('36)
Orch.—Tietjen 12"—T-SKB2055
In French: Franz, PAT-X7235

Scene 3

Da lieg' auch du (Siegfried & Waldvögel)
Melchior & Grühn, on V-9808 in VM-83†

Waldweben
Eng. Forest Murmurs

—**Arr. Orch.** only
NOTE: *The concert version is assembled from
passages from both the second and third
scenes, ending with the finale of Act II.*
Pittsburgh Symphony Orch.—Reiner
(in CM-549†) 12"—C-11985D
Berlin State Opera Orch.—Blech
(G-AW44) 12"—G-D1631
Hollywood Bowl Orch.—Stokowski
12"—V-11-9418
Orch. of the "Maggio Musicale"—Gui
12"—CET-BB25167
DUPLICATIONS: Bayreuth Festival
Orch.—von Hösslin, C-67371D in CM-337:
C-LCX43: C-GQX10480; Berlin State
Opera Orch.—von Schillings, PD-66590;
Colonne Orch.—Pierné, O-123580; Phila-
delphia Orch.—Stokowski, on V-14845/6
in VM-441†

ACT III, Scene 1

Prelude Orch.

Wache, Wala! Wanderer (Wotan)
Schipper, on V-9809 in VM-83†

—**Arr. Orch. only**
Bayreuth Festival Orch.—von Hösslin, on
C-67372D in CM-338†: C-LCX44:
C-GQX10481
—**Wache, Wala!** only
Wilhelm Rode, PD-66782

Stark ruft das Lied (Erda & Wanderer)
Olczewska & Schipper, on V-9809/10
in VM-83†

Scene 2
Kenntest du mich? (Wanderer & Siegfried)
Bockelmann & Melchior, on V-9811 in
VM-83†
—**Interlude to Scene 3** only (Fire Music)
Bayreuth Festival Orch.—von Hösslin, on
C-67372D in CM-338†: C-LCX44:
C-GQX10481
London Symphony—Coates, on V-9811
in VM-83†

Scene 3
Selige Oede auf sonniger Höh'!
Was rugt dort schlummernd? (Siegfried)
Lauritz Melchior, on V-9812/3 in VM-83†
(G-EJ485 contains Sides 15 & 16 of
VM-83†)
Heil dir, Sonne! (Finale Act III)
(Brünnhilde & Siegfried)
Frida Leider & R. Laubenthal, on
V-9813/4 in VM-83† (abbreviated)

(DIE) GOETTERDAEMMERUNG
Vorspiel & 3 Acts 1876
Fr. **Le Crépuscule des Dieux**
Eng. **The Twilight of the Gods**
Excerpts
—**Arr. Soprano & Orch.** Stokowski
Contents: Siefgried's Rhine Journey, Sieg-
fried's Death Music & Brünnhilde's Immola-
tion.
Agnes Davis & Philadelphia Orch.—
Stokowski
(G-DB2126/30) 5 12"—VM-188†

Individual Excerpts

PROLOGUE
Daybreak Music Orch.
See Siegfrieds Rheinfahrt below
Zu neuen Thaten (Brünnhilde & Siegfried)
Kirsten Flagstad & Lauritz Melchior
(in VM-749) 12"—V-17729
Siegfrieds Rheinfahrt Orchestra
Eng. **Siegfried's Rhine Journey**
NOTE: *The concert versions of the Rhine*
Journey are made up of the Interlude (Day-
break Music) which precedes the Duet: "Zu
neuen Thaten," omit the Duet and continue
with the Rhine Journey. The Toscanini ver-
sions contain an orchestral transcription of a
portion of the duet. Most recordings use the
Humperdinck concert ending.
NBC Symphony Orch.—Toscanini
(in VM-853†) 2 12"—V-18318/9
[Funeral Music, Pt. 1] (G-DB5994/5)
N. Y. Philharmonic-Symphony Orch.—
Toscanini (G-DB2860/1)
(in VM-308†) 2 12"—V-14007/8
[Lohengrin—Prelude, Act III]

Paris Conservatory Orch.—Weingartner
(in CX-224†) 12"—C-71384D
(C-LX925)
National Symphony Orch.—S. Beer
12"—D-K1284
Berlin Philharmonic—Schmidt-
Isserstedt 12"—T-E2685
Berlin State Opera Orch.—Elmendorff
12"—PD-67641
Vienna Philharmonic—Knappertsbusch
12"—G-DB5699
Orch. of the "Maggio Musicale"—Gui
12"—CET-BB25168
Symphony Orch.—Bruno Walter
12"—C-LFX301
Berlin State Opera Orch.—von
Schillings 12"—PD-66591
Philadelphia Orch.—Stokowski
(in VM-188†) 2 12"—V-7843/4
(G-DB2126/7)

ACT I
Scene 2
Hagens Wacht: Hier sitz' ich zur Wacht
Eng. **Hagen's Watch**
Ludwig Weber (b) & London Philhar-
monic—Beecham
(in CX-83†) 12"—C-69048D
[Hagen's Ruf, Pt. 3]
(Recorded at an actual performance,
Covent Garden, 1936)
Ivar Andrésen 12"—C-DWX1308
[Meistersinger—Ansprach des Pogner]

Scene 3
Erzählung der Waltraute (Waltraute)
Höre mit Sinn Contralto
Seit er von dir geschieden
Eng. **Waltraute's Narrative**
NOTE: *All versions below contain Waltraute's*
part only.
Kerstin Thorborg
(in VM-707) 12"—V-17222
Blanche Thebom 12"—V-11-9296
Rosette Anday 12"—PD-66778

ACT II
Scene 3
Hagens Ruf: Hoi-ho! (Hagen & Vassals)
Eng. **Hagen Summons the Vassals**
Ludwig Weber (b) & Herbert Janssen
(b) w. cho. & London Philharmonic—
Beecham
(in CX-83†) 2 12"—C-69047/8D
[Hagens Wacht]
(Recorded at an actual performance,
Covent Garden, 1936)

ACT III
Prelude & Scene 1
Frau Sonne sendet lichte Strahlen
(Rheintöchter & Siegfried)
Eng. **Song of the Rhinedaughters**
—**Arr. Orch. only** (Concert Version) Wood
Queen's Hall Orch—Henry Wood
2 12"—D-K765/6
[Järnefelt: Praeludium]

Scene 2
Siegfrieds Erzählung
(Siegfried, Hagen, Günther & Vassals)
Mime heiss ein mürrischer Zwerg
In Leid zu den Wipfel
Eng. **Siegfried's Narration**
Lauritz Melchior, O. Helgers & Cho.
                12″—**V-7659**
DUPLICATION: I. Fagoaga (in Italian),
C-GQX10268
Siegfrieds Tod
Eng. **Death of Sigfried**
Brünnhilde! Heilige Braut! (Siegfried)
(Preceeding the Funeral Music)
—Arr. Orch.
NBC Symphony Orch.—Toscanini
      (in VM-853†)   12″—**V-18319**
[Rhine Journey, Pt. 3] (G-DB5995)
Philadelphia Orch.—Stokowski, in
VM-188
Siegfrieds Tod   Orchestra
Eng. **Siegfried's Death Music or Funeral Music**
NBC Symphony Orch.—Toscanini
(G-DB5996) (in VM-853†) 12″—**V-18320**
Paris Conservatory Orch.—Weingartner
      (in CX-224†)   12″—**C-71385D**
Symphony Orch.—Bruno Walter
(C-LFX246)   12″—**C-68044D**
Philadelphia Orch.—Stokowski, in
VM-188†
National Symphony Orch.—S. Beer
                12″—**D-K1285**
DUPLICATIONS: Berlin Philharmonic—
Furtwängler, PD-67054; Berlin State
Opera Orch.—Karl Muck, G-AW54;
German Opera House Orch.—Jochum,
T-E3128; Symphony Orch.—A. Coates,
G-W799; Milan Symphony Orch.—Serafin, C-GQX10507; Berlin State Opera
Orch.—von Schillings, PD-66540

Scene 3
Brünnhilde Schlussgesang (Finale)
Starke Scheite schichtet mir dort
Soprano   (Brünnhilde)
Eng. **Brünnhilde's Immolation**
Fr. **Qu'un bûcher s'élève là-bas**
Kirsten Flagstad & San Francisco Opera
Orch.—McArthur
      (in VM-664†)   2 12″—**V-15841/2**
(G-DB5008 & DB6011)
Helen Traubel & NBC Symphony Orch.—
Toscanini   3 12″—**VM-978†**
[Tristan—Liebestod, Orch. only]
Agnes Davis & Philadelphia Orch.—
Stokowski
      (in VM-188†)   3 12″—**V-7845/7**
Marjorie Lawrence (in French)
            2 12″—**G-DB4914/5**
DUPLICATION: A. Konetzni, T-F1362
—Finale only   Orch.
Philadelphia Orch.—Stokowski
[Rienzi—Overture, Pt. 3] 12″—**V-6625**
(G-W1014: G-AW4030)
(Also on V-14847 in VM-441†)

TANNHAEUSER   3 Acts   1845
(Revised 1861)
Slightly abridged recording
Bayreuth Festival performance 1930,
supervised by Siegfried Wagner

Soloists, Chorus & Orch.—Karl
Elmendorff   18 12″—**C-OP24†**
(C-LCX46/63: C-LFX112/29:
C-GQX10074/91)
The Cast:
Tannhäuser .... Sigismund Pilinsky (t)
Elisabeth .... Maria Müller (s)
Landgrave ... . Ivar Andrésen (bs)
Wolfram .... Herbert Janssen (b)
Venus .... Ruth Jost-Arden (s)
Biterolf. .G. von Tschurtschenthaler (b)
Heinrich .... Joachim Sattler (t)
Reinmar .... Carl Stralendorf (b)
Ein junger Hirte .... Erna Berger (s)
NOTE: *In this set the Paris version (1861) is used. Act I is recorded complete. Act II cuts: last part of Scene 2 and the brief Scene 3; the Landgrave's address, Pages 152 to 158, and 163 to 189 in Scene 4. Act III cuts: Prelude; the last page of Scene 1; the first 5½ pages of Scene C. Page references are to the Schirmer vocal score.*

Orchestral Selections
Berlin State Opera Orch.—Gurlitt
                12″—**PD-27106**
DUPLICATION: Berlin State Opera Orch.
Melichar, PD-25101

Individual Excerpts

ACT I

Overture & Bacchanale
Orchestra & Women's voices
(Paris Version)
Philadelphia Orch. & Women's Chorus
—Stokowski
      (in VM-530†)   3 12″—**V-15310/2**
(Earlier recording, without Chorus, on
G-D1905/7: G-AW213/5)

Overture only   (Concert Version)
London Philharmonic Orch.—Beecham
(C-LX768/9)   2 12″—**CX-123†**
[Borodin: Prince Igor—Prelude Act III,
March]
La Scala Orch.—van Kempen
          2 12″—**D-K1683/4†**
[Fliegende Holländer—Overture, Pt. 1]
EIAR Symphony Orch.—La Rosa Parodi
         2 12″—**CET-CB20186/7**
[Handel: Messiah—Overture]
Saxon State Orch.—Böhm
          2 12″—**G-DB5555/6**
Berlin Philharmonic—L. Ludwig
          2 12″—**PD-15222/3**
[Einzug der Gäste] (PD-516770/1)
DUPLICATIONS: Amsterdam Concertgebouw—Mengelberg, CX-27†:
C-GQX10328/9: C-LFX276/7:
C-LX170/1: O-8589/90; Berlin State
Opera—Muck, G-EJ335/6; Berlin Philharmonic—Jochum, T-E1424/5; Berlin
State Opera—Blech, G-D1317/8:
G-EJ521/2; Symphony Orch.—Coates,
G-AW4298/4300; Berlin State Opera
Orch.—Schmalstich, G-C2184/5
—Arr. Piano Liszt
Alexander Brailowsky, PD-95419/20

Bacchanale (Venusberg Music) only Orch.
NOTE: *The choral parts have been transcribed for strings.*
Pittsburgh Symphony Orch.—Reiner
          2 12″—**CX-193†**

DUPLICATION: Berlin Philharmonic
Orch.—Knappertsbusch, PD-66701/2

ACT I, Scene 2

Dir töne Lob! Tenor
(First stanza of the Hymn to Venus)
Lauritz Melchior
  (in VM-749)   12"—**V-17726**
[Lohengrin—In fernem Land]
(Also V-11-8676 in VM-979†)

Stets soll nur dir Tenor
(Third stanza of the Hymn to Venus)
Franz Völker   10"—**PD-24240**
[Verdi: Trovatore—Di quella pira]

Scene 4

Als du in kühnem Sange
Baritone   (Wolfram)
Gerhard Hüsch   12"—**G-EH1003**
[Wohl wusst' ich hier]
Heinrich Schlusnus   12"—**PD-561117**
(PD-30015)
[O Himmel, lass' dich jetzt erfleh'n]
In French: A. Endrèze, PAT-X90073

ACT II, Scene 1

Dich, teure Halle Soprano
(Elisabeth's Greeting)
Eng. **Hail, Hall of Song**
Kirsten Flagstad   12"—**V-14181**
[Lohengrin—Elsas Traum]
Tiana Lemnitz   12"—**PD-67058**
[Elisabeths Gebet]
Helen Traubel   12"—**V-17268**
[Gluck: Alceste—Divinités du Styx]
Lotte Lehmann   10"—**P-PO156**
[Elisabeths Gebet]
Hilde Konetzni   12"—**T-SK2151**
[Elisabeths Gebet]
DUPLICATIONS: Elisabeth Rethberg,
V-15818 in VM-633; Johanna Gadski,
V-18142* in VM-816; Delia Reinhardt,
PD-66868
In Italian: Gabriella Gatti, CET-BB25076
In English: Joan Hammond, G-C3562

Scene 2

O Fürstin (Tannhäuser & Elisabeth Duo)

Doch welch' ein seltsam neues Leben
Tenor & Soprano
Max Lorenz & Maria Reining
        12"—**G-DB7624**

Scene 4

Einzug der Gäste (Fest-Marsch)

Chor der Ritter: Freudig begrüssen
Orchestra & Chorus
Eng. **Entrance of the Guests**
(Grand March & Chorus—Hail bright
abode)
NOTE: *All versions are abbreviated.*
Hamburg State Opera Chorus & Orch.—
Schmidt-Isserstedt   12"—**T-E3009**
[Pilgerchor]
Berlin State Opera Chorus & Orch.—
Melichar   12"—**PD-516713**
[Pilgerchor]   (PD-57042)
DUPLICATIONS: Berlin State Opera
Chorus—Blech, V-9161: G-D1292:
G-DB10126: G-EJ44
In English: Chorus & Orch.—Coates,
G-AW4112; BBC Chorus & Orch.—Pitt,
C-9826

In Italian: La Scala Chorus—Molajoli,
C-GQX10283

—Einzug der Gäste (Grand March)
Orchestra only
London Philharmonic—Beecham
(C-LX733) (in CX-107†) 12"—**C-69327D**
[Fliegende Holländer—Overture, Pt. 3]
Boston "Pops" Orch.—Fiedler
  (in VM-569†)   12"—**V-12448**
[Rienzi—Overture, Pt. 3] (G-EH1102)
DUPLICATIONS: Berlin Philharmonic—
Ludwig, PD-15223: PD-516771: Chicago
Symphony Orch.—Stock, V-7386:
G-DB1557; Berlin Philharmonic—
Knappertsbusch, PD-66702; Symphony
Orch.—Coates, G-AW4112

—Arr. Band
Republican Guard Band—Dupont,
C-DFX148: C-CQX16563; Black Dyke
Mills Band, G-DB593

**Ansprache des Landgrafen: Gar viel und
schön** Bass Eng. **Landgrave's Address**
No recording available. Omitted in
C-OP24†

Blick' ich umher Baritone (Wolfram)
Fr. **Air de concours: En contemplant
cette assemblée**
Eng. **Wolfram's Eulogy of Love: Gazing
around upon this fair assembly**
Joel Berglund   12"—**V-12-0185**
(G-DB6377)
[O du mein holder Abendstern]
Friedrich Schorr   12"—**G-EJ566**
[Meistersinger—Schusterlied]
Gerhard Hüsch   12"—**G-EH983**
[O du mein holder Abendstern]
DUPLICATIONS: Heinrich Schlusnus,
PD-35023; Karl Schmitt-Walter,
T-E2271; Rudolph Bockelmann,
T-SK1342; Paul Schoeffler, In Prep.
Swiss Decca
In French: C. Panzéra, G-DB4906; A.
Endrèze, PAT-X90040; L. van Obbergh,
PD-516709

O Himmel, lass' dich jetzt erflehen Bari-
tone (Wolfram)
NOTE: *Omitted in C-OP24†*
Heinrich Schlusnus   12"—**PD-561117**
[Als du in Kühnem Sange] (PD-30015)

ACT III

Prelude (Tannhäusers Pilgerfahrt)
NOTE: *Omitted in C-OP24†*
Eng. **Tannhauser's Pilgrimage**
Paris Conservatory Orch.—Weingartner
(C-LX868: C-LFX576) 12"—**C-69793D**
Philadelphia Orch.—Stokowski
(in VM530†)   2 12"—**V-15313/4**
[Bach-Stokowski: Ich ruf' zu dir]
[Tschaikovsky-Stokowski: Solitude, on
G-DB3254]

Scene 1

Wohl wusst' ich hier sie im Gebet zu finden
Baritone (Wolfram)
NOTE: *The Domgraf-Fassbaender—Heidersbach
version also includes the first part of the Pil-
grims' Chorus and the brief parts for Wolfram
and Elisabeth; the other discs contain only
Wolfram's solo that prefaces the Pilgrims'
Chorus.*

Herbert Janssen   12"—C-71694D
[O du mein holder Abendstern]
(C-LX948)
Willi Domgraf-Fassbaender, Käte Heid-
ersbach & Cho.   12"—G-EH724
[O du mein holder Abendstern]
(G-FKX94)
Gerhard Hüsch   12"—G-EH1003
[Als du in kühnem Sange]
Pilgerchor: Beglückt darf nun dich Chorus
Eng. **Pilgrims' Chorus**
(Isolated recordings usually cut the brief
parts of Wolfram & Elisabeth)
Dresden State Opera Chorus & Orch.—
Böhm   12"—G-DB5551
[Lohengrin—Gang zum Münster]
Hamburg State Opera Chorus & Orch.—
Schmidt-Isserstedt   12"—T-E3009
[Einzug der Gäste]
Vienna State Opera Chorus—Kerby
(C-DFX178)   12"—C-7271M
[Lohengrin-Brautchor]
DUPLICATIONS: Berlin State Opera
Chorus & Orch.—Melichar, PD-57042:
PD-516713; Berlin State Opera Chorus &
Orch.—Heger, O-7779; Berlin State
Opera Chorus & Orch.—Blech, V-9161:
G-D1292: G-DB10126: G-EJ44: G-EJ522
In Italian: La Scala Chorus—Veneziani,
C-GQX10283: C-GQX10493
In English: BBC Chorus—Pitt, C-9826;
Victor Chorus, V-20127: G-B2376
**Elisabeths Gebet: Allmächt'ge Jungfrau,
hör mein Flehen!**
Soprano
Eng. **Elisabeth's Prayer**
NOTE: *A brief cut of some 24 bars from the
middle of the prayer is usually made in most
recordings. It is complete, however, in C-OP24†
and in the Flagstad version.*
Kirsten Flagstad   12"—V-8920
Tiana Lemnitz   12"—PD-67058
[Dich, teure Halle]
Lotte Lehmann   10"—P-PO156
[Dich, teure Halle]
Hilde Konetzni   12"—T-SK2151
[Dich, teure Halle]
Astrid Varnay   12"—C-71399D
[Lohengrin—Elsas Traum]
In Italian: Gabriella Gatti, CET-BB25076
In French: S. Balguerie, PD-566104

Scene 2
Wie Todesahnung Recit.
O du mein holder Abendstern Air Baritone
(Wolfram)
Fr. **Mortel présage & Romance à
l'étoile**
It. **O tu bell' astro** Eng. **Evening Star**
Joel Berglund (G-DB6377)
[Blick' ich umher]   12"—V-12-0185
Gerhard Hüsch   12"—G-EH983
[Blick' ich umher]
Herbert Janssen   12"—C-71697D
[Wohl wusst' ich hier] (C-LX948)
Lawrence Tibbett (G-DB2262)
     12"—V-8452
[Gounod: Faust—Avant de quitter]
[Also on V-11-8862 in VM-1015 with
Speaks: On the road to Mandalay]
Alexander Kipnis   12"—C-7280M
[Lohengrin—Königsgebet]

DUPLICATIONS: John Charles Thomas,
V-7605: V-15818 in VM-633; Heinrich
Schlusnus, PD-35023; A. van Rooy, CRS-
29*; W. Domgraf-Fassbaender, G-EH724:
G-FKX94; Karl Schmitt-Walter,
T-E2271; Dezső Kovacs, RAD-A19428;
Paul Schoeffler, In Prep. Swiss Decca
In French: Charles Panzéra, G-DB4906;
L. van Obbergh, PD-516709; Lovano,
C-RFX42; A. Endrèze, PAT-X90040
In Italian: Carlo Tagliabue, G-DB11300;
R. Stracciari, C-GQX11067; A. Granforte,
G-DB1221
In English: Peter Dawson, G-C1267; H.
Williams, C-9873; Nelson Eddy,
C-71189D
In Finnish: Oiva Soini, G-Z212
In Hungarian: Dezső Kovacs, RAD-
A19427
—Arr. **'Cello & Piano**
Pablo Casals, V-6620: G-DB1012; A.
Lévy, O-166024; Raya Garbousova,
V-11870 in VM-1017
—Arr. **Organ:** Charles Courboin, V-1968

Scene 3
Inbrunst im Herzen
Da sah ich ihn (Romerzählung) Tenor
Eng. **Rome Narrative**
Lauritz Melchior & London Symphony
Orch.—Coates   12"—V-9707
Lauritz Melchior & Victor Symphony
Orch.—McArthur
    (in VM-749)   12"—V-17727
(Also on V-11-8677 in VM-979)
Max Lorenz   12"—G-DB7602
[Also on T-E2091 & G-DB4553]
DUPLICATIONS: Franz Völker, PD-
516746: PD-67141
In French: Franz, PAT-X7237
In Italian: I. Fagoaga, C-GQX10269; E.
Salazar, C-CQX16512; A. Marcato, CET-
CC2249

TRISTAN UND ISOLDE 3 Acts 1865
Abridged recording
Soloists, Chorus & Orchestra of Bay-
reuth Festival, 1928—Elmendorff (Super-
vised by Siegfried Wagner)
     19   12"—C-OP23†
(C-LCX64/83: C-GQX10532/51)
The Cast:
Isolde ...... Nanny Larsen-Todsen (s)
Tristan .... Gunnar Graarud (t)
Brangäne .... Anny Helm (s)
Kurwenal .... Rudolph Bockelmann (b)
König Marke ...... Ivar Andrésen (b)
Melot .... Joachim Sattler (t)
Junger Seemann ..... Gustav Podin (t)
Ein Hirt .... Hans Beer (t)
NOTE: *The British set, C-LCX64/83, contains
two additional sides devoted to an explanation
and to illustrations of the motives by Ernest
Newman. Acts I and II are recorded in nearly
complete form, but Act III is seriously abbre-
viated.*
Collections
**Prelude, Act I; Isolde's Narrative; Pre-
lude, Act III; Liebestod**
Helen Traubel (s) & N. Y. Philharmonic-
Symphony Orch.—Rodzinski
(C-LX941/5†)   5   12"—CM-573†

Symphonic Synthesis—arr. Orch. Stokowski
Prelude, Liebesnacht, Liebestod
Philadelphia Orch.—Stokowski
5 12"—VM-508†
[Palestrina-Stokowski: Adoramus te,
Christe]
(older recording on G-DB1911/4)

Love Music (Act II) & Liebestod Arr.
Orch.—Stokowski
All American Orch.—Stokowski
3 12"—CM-427†

Excerpts—Arr. Violin, Piano & Orch.
Waxman
(from the film "Humoresque")
Isaac Stern, Oscar Levant & Orch.—
Waxman, in CM-657†

Individual Excerpts

ACT I

Prelude Orchestra
N. Y. Philharmonic-Symphony Orch.—
Rodzinski, on C-12132/3D in CM-573†
Berlin Philharmonic Orch.—Furtwäng-
ler, on V-14934/5 in VM-653†:
G-DB3419/20
[Liebestod, Pt. 1]
Philadelphia Orch.—Stokowski, in VM-
508†
EIAR Symphony Orch.—A. La Rosa
Parodi 2 12"—CET-CB20220/1
[Liebestod, Pt. 1]
Berlin Philharmonic Orch.—Jochum
[Liebestod, Pt. 1] 2 12"—T-E2715/6
DUPLICATIONS: BBC Symphony Orch.
—Boult, G-DB1757; Berlin Philharmonic
—Furtwängler, PD-95438/9; Berlin
State Opera Orch.—Muck, G-AW60/1;
Berlin Philharmonic—R. Strauss, PD-
66832; Berlin State Opera Orch.—Klem-
perer, G-AV4223 & AV4225; Berlin Phil-
harmonic—De Sabata, PD-67496/7;
CET-RR8008/9

Scene 3
Isolde's Narrative & Curse
Helen Traubel & N. Y. Philharmonic-
Symphony Orch.—Rodzinski, in CM-573†
NOTE: Begins "Erfuhrst du meine Schmach."
Brangäne's brief part is omitted.

ACT II

Scene I

Prelude
—Part only Arr. Stokowski
Philadelphia Orch.—Stokowski, in VM-
508†

Scene 2 (Liebesnacht) Duo: Soprano &
Tenor

Isolde! Tristan! Geliebter

O sink' hernieder (Isolde & Tristan) (Love
Duet)
NOTE: The Leider-Melchior version begins
with the orchestral interlude to Scene 2 and
the meeting: "Isolde!" "Tristan! Geliebter!"
There is a cut of some 16 pages between Sides
1 & 2. Side 2 begins with "Doch es rächte sich"
(Page 157, 4 bars from end); Side 3 with "O
sink' hernieder"; Side 4, after a cut of some 11
pages (Brangäne's Warning,) begins with

"Soll' ich lauschen?" (Page 181, bar 1.) There
is a cut of some 24 bars in this side (page 185,
bar 6 to page 187, bar 6) and the record ends
at the beginning of Scene 3 (page 196, bar 1.)
Both the Flagstad—Melchior and the Trau-
bel—Ralf sets begin "O sink' hernieder" and
continue to the end of the scene. Each is
slightly abbreviated. Brangäne's Warning is
sung by Flagstad in the Victor set and by
Hertha Glaz in the Columbia.
Frida Leider & Lauritz Melchior
2 12"—V-7273/4
(G-AW287/8) (G-W1148/9)
Kirsten Flagstad & Lauritz Melchior
(G-DB6016/7) 2 12"—VM-671†
(Also on V-11-8674/5 in VM-979†)
(Also on V-15828/9 in VM-644†)
Helen Traubel, Torsten Ralf & Hertha
Glaz 2 12"—CX-286†

—Arr. Orch. Stokowski
Philadelphia Orch.—Stokowski, in VM-
508†
All American Orch.—Stokowski, in CM-
427†

—Einsam wachend only Soprano (Bran-
gäne)
(Brangäne's Warning)
Kirsten Flagstad, in VM-671†, VM-664†,
& VM-979†
Hertha Glaz, in CX-286†
Blanche Thebom 12"—V-11-8928
[Walküre—2 Fricka excerpts]
Kerstin Thorborg
(in VM-707) 12"—V-17223
[Parsifal—Ich sah das kind]
DUPLICATIONS: Emmi Leisner, PD-
66737; Eva Liebenberg, T-SK1163
In Italian: Cloe Elmo, CET-BB25057

Scene 3
O König, das kann ich dir nicht sagen
Recit.

Wohin nun Tristan scheidet Air Tenor
(Tristan)
Lauritz Melchior 12"—C-71388D
[Rienzi—Prayer]

ACT III

Excerpts from Scenes 1 & 2
NOTE: There are three brief cuts in this set,
which concludes at bar 20, page 277.
Lauritz Melchior (t) & Herbert Janssen
(b) 5 12"—CM-550†

Prelude Orchestra
Paris Conservatory Orch.—Weingartner
12"—C-69805D
(R. Lamorlette, English horn)
(C-LX866: C-LFX577)
N. Y. Philharmonic-Symphony Orch.—
Rodzinski, in CM-573†

Scene 3
Liebestod: Mild und leise Soprano
Eng. Isolde's Love death Fr. Mort
d'Yseult
Kirsten Flagstad (G-DB6007)
(in VM-644†) 12"—V-15840
(Earlier recording on G-DB2746)
Helen Traubel 12"—C-12212D
(Also in CM-573†)

DUPLICATIONS: Elisabeth Ohms, PD-66928; Gertrud Bindernagel, T-SK1163
In French: Suzanne Balguerie, PD-524022

—Arr. Orchestra
NOTE: *The Furtwängler and La Rosa Parodi recordings include the last few bars of the Prelude to Act I.*

NBC Symphony Orch.—Toscanini
(in VM-978†)   12″—**V-11-8666**
[Götterdämmerung—Finale, with Traubel]
Berlin Philharmonic—Furtwängler,
V-14935 in VM-653†: G-DB3420
Berlin Philharmonic—Furtwängler
[Prelude, Pt. 3]   12″—**PD-95439**
Berlin State Opera Orch.—von Schillings
12″—**PD-66607**
[Pfitzner: Christ Elflein—Overture,
Pt. 3]
Philadelphia Orch.—Stokowski, in VM-508†
DUPLICATIONS: Berlin Philharmonic—Jochum, T-E2716; EIAR Symphony
Orch.—La Rosa Parodi, CET-CB20221;
Berlin Philharmonic Orch.—V. De. Sabata, PD-67498: CET-RR8010; San
Francisco Orch.—Hertz, G-AV3999; All
American Orch.—Stokowski, in CM-427†

Siegfried Idyll Orchestra
N. Y. Philharmonic-Symphony Orch.—
Toscanini (G-DB2920/1)
(in VM-308†)   2   12″—**V-14009/10**
N. Y. Philharmonic-Symphony Orch.—
Rodzinski   2   12″—**CX-265†**
NBC Symphony Orch.—Toscanini
(in VM-1135†) 2   12″—**V-11-9640/1**
Vienna Philharmonic—Walter
2   12″—**G-DB2634/5**
London Philharmonic—Weingartner
(C-LX801/2)   2   12″—**CX-139†**
Symphony Orch.—Bruno Walter
(C-LFX145/6)   2   12″—**CX-26†**
Dresden Philharmonic Orch.—van
Kempen   2   12″—**PD-57102/3**
(CET-OR5035/6)
Paris Symphony Orch.—Meyrowitz
(C-GQX10774/5) 2 12″—**PAT-PDT28/9**
La Scala Orch.—Schuricht
In Prep. **English Decca**

SONGS in German & French

Attente (Hugo) In French 1840
Lorri Lail (ms) & Gerald Moore (pf)
In Gramophone Shop Album **GSC-4**

Dors mon enfant (unknown) In French
1840
Lorri Lail (ms) & Gerald Moore (pf)
In Gramophone Shop Album **GSC-4**

Mignonne (Ronsard) In French 1840
Lorri Lail (ms) & Gerald Moore (pf)
In Gramophone Shop Album **GSC-4**

(Der) Tannenbaum In German 1838/40
Lorri Lail (ms) & Gerald Moore (pf)
In Gramophone Shop Album **GSC-4**

(5) Wesendonck Gedichte (Mathilde Wesendonck) 1862
1) **Der Engel** 2) **Stehe still** 3) **Im Treibhaus** 4) **Schmerzen** 5) **Träume**

Tiana Lemnitz (s) & Michael Raucheisen
(pf)   3 12″—**PD-57084/5 & PD-57028**
[Schubert: Am Grabe Anselmos, on PD-57085]

—Nos. 3, 4, 5 only
Helen Traubel & Philadelphia Orch.—
Stokowski   2   12″—**VM-872†**

Individual songs in the cycle (See also collections above)

No. 2, Stehe still
Serafina di Leo (s)
[No. 5]   12″—**G-AW294**
[Also in Italian on G-AW293]

No. 3, Im Treibhaus
Lotte Lehmann (s) & Paul Ulanowsky
(pf)   12″—**C-71469D**
[No.5]
DUPLICATIONS: Serafina di Leo,
G-HN1844 (In Italian on G-HN1824)

No. 4, Schmerzen ("Sonne, weinest jeden
Abend")
Elisabeth Ohms (s)   12″—**PD-66929**
[No. 5]

No. 5, Träume ("Sag', welch' wunderbare
Träume")
Lotte Lehmann (s) & Paul Ulanowsky
(pf)   [No. 3]   12″—**C-71469D**
DUPLICATIONS: Elisabeth Ohms, PD-66929; Serefina di Leo, G-AW294 (In
Italian on G-AW293)

—Arr. Violin
Rudolf Schone & Munich Philharmonic—
Kabasta   12″—**G-DB5573**
[Albumblatt]

MISCELLANEOUS COLLECTIONS

Operatic Excerpts
Tannhäuser—Rome Narrative; Parsifal-Nur eine Waffe Taugt; Meistersinger-Am stillen Herd, Fanget an! & Preislied;
Lohengrin—In fernem Land & Lohengrins Abschied
Torsten Ralf (t) & Metropolitan Opera
Orch.—Fritz Busch   4 12″—**CM-634**

A Wagnerian Program
Siegfried Idyll; Eine Faust Ouvertüre; Die
Walküre—Walkürenritt
NBC Symphony—Toscanini
4   12″—**VM-1135†**
Selections from 6 Operas
Fliegende Holländer—Mit Gewitter und
Sturm; Lohengrin—In fernem Land;
Meistersinger—Am stillen Herd & Preislied; Tannhäuser—Dir töne Lob! &
Rome Narrative; Siegfried—Ho-Ho!
Schmiede, mein Hammer; Götterdämmerung—Zu neuen Thaten, Prologue
Lauritz Melchior (t) & Kirsten Flagstad
(s) with Philadelphia Orch.—Ormandy &
San Francisco Opera Orch.—McArthur
5   12″—**VM-749†**
Scenes from Wagner Operas
Tristan und Isolde—Love Duet; Lohengrin—In fernem land; Tannhäuser—Dir
töne Lob! & Romerzählung; Siegfried—
Ho-Ho! Schmiede, mein hammer; Der
Fliegende Holländer—Steuermannslied

Lauritz Melchior & Kirsten Flagstad with
Philadelphia Orch.—Ormandy & San
Francisco Opera Orch.—McArthur
5 12"—VM-979†

Wagnerian Characterizations
Rheingold-Weiche, Wotan!; Walküre—
So ist es denn aus mit den ewigen Göttern
& Deiner ew'gen Gattin heilige; Götter-
dämmerung—Höre mit Sinn; Parsifal—
Ich sah' das Kind; Tristan und Isolde—
Einsam wachend in der Nacht
Kerstin Thorborg (c) & Victor Symphony
—Riedel 3 12"—VM-707

Arias from Parsifal & Lohengrin
Parsifal—Amfortas! Die wunde! & Nur
eine waffe taugt; Lohengrin—Abschied
Lauritz Melchior (t) & Philadelphia
Orch.—Ormandy 2 12"—VM-516

(A) Wagnerian Concert
Meistersinger—Prelude; Siegfried—
Waldweben; Lohengrin—Prelude to Act
I & III; Walküre-Walkürenritt
Pittsburgh Symphony—Reiner
4 12"—CM-549†

(3) Famous Scenes
Tristan und Isolde—Love Duet & Lieb-
estod; Götterdämmerung—Brünnhilde's
Immolation
Lauritz Melchior (t) & Kirsten Flagstad
(s) with San Francisco Opera Orch.—
McArthur 5 12"—VM-644†

Toscanini Wagnerian Album
Lohengrin—Prelude to Act I & Act III
Götterdämmerung—Dawn & Siegfried's
Rhine Journey; Siegfried Idyll
N. Y. Philharmonic-Symphony Orch.—
Toscanini 5 12"—VM-308†

Bayreuth Festival Recordings
1st Series, 1927
Parsifal—Transformation Scene, Grail
Scene, Flower Maidens Scene, Prelude to
Act III & Good Friday Spell Siegfried—
Forest Murmurs; Prelude Act III; Fire
Music; Rheingold—Entry of the Gods in-
to Valhalla; Walküre—Ride of the Valky-
ries
Soloists, Bayreuth Festival Cho. & Orch.
—Karl Muck, F. von Hösslin & Siegfried
Wagner (C-LCX36/45—without Walküre
selection)
11 12"—CM-337† & CM-338†

2nd Series, 1936
Walküre—Winterstürme wichen dem
Wonnemond & Siegmund heiss' ich
(Franz Völker & Maria Müller); Lohen-
grin—Gralserzählung—In fernem Land;
Königsgebet—Mein Herr und Gott;
Gang zum Münster—Gesegnet sollst du
schreiten; Prelude to Act III; Brautchor
—Treulich geführt; Das süsse Lied ver-
hallt & Höchstes Vertrau'n; Lohengrin's
Abschied (Maria Müller, Margarete
Klose, Franz Völker, Jaro Prohaska and
Josef von Manowarda); Siegfried—
Schmelzlied & Schmiedelied; Wald-
weben "Dass der mein Vater nicht ist"
(Max Lorenz & Erich Zimmermann)
Specified Soloists with Bayreuth Festival
(1936) Orchestra—Heinz Tietjen
9 12"—T-SKB2047/55

WAGNER, Siegfried (1869-1930)
The only son of Richard Wagner became a
conductor and supervisor of his father's music
dramas, & also the composer of about fifteen
operas & a number of symphonic poems.

(DER) SCHMIED VON MARIENBURG
Opera 1920
Overture
Bayreuth Festival Orch.—Tietjen
[Last side blank] 2 12"—T-SK2110/1

WALDTEUFEL, Emil (1837-1915)
Born in Strasbourg, Waldteufel was a pianist
and composer, French-trained at the Paris
"Conservatoire," who popularized the Viennese
waltz at the French court. See current Euro-
pean catalogues for additional listings.

WALTZES Orchestra
Acclamations, Op. 223 (Hoch lebe der
Tanz)
Horlick Orch., PD-524490: D-F7006;
Grenadier Guards Band, C-DX335

A toi, Op. 150 Ger. An dich
Symphony Orch.—Marcel Cariven
[Herbstweisen] 12"—PAT-PDT102

Braun oder Blond
P. Godwin Orch., PD-21711; Marek
Weber Orch., G-EG2090: G-HE2277:
G-HN638: G-K6402

Dolores, Op. 170
Horlick Orch., PD-524494; Marek Weber
Orch., G-EG2349: G-HE2280
—Arr. voice: Ninon Vallin (s), PAT-X93134

España, Op. 236
(Waltz after Chabrier's celebrated
Rhapsody)
Boston "Pops" Orch.—Fiedler
(G-B9099) 10"—V-4461
Berlin State Opera Orch.—Melichar
10"—PD-24149
Philharmonic Orch.—Weissmann
12"—P-E10998
DUPLICATIONS: Géczy Orch.,
G-EG3296; Carnegie "Pops" Orch.—
Hendl, C-7591M; A. Campoli Orch.,
D-F2566; H. Horlick Orch., PD-544490

Estudiantina, Op. 191
Boston "Pops" Orch.—Fiedler
(G-B9330) 10"—V-10-1024
Berlin State Opera Orch.—Melichar
10"—PD-24148
DUPLICATIONS: Symphony Orch.—
Weissmann, P-E10998; International
Concert Orch., V-35798: G-C1326:
G-S8844: G-L633; Marek Weber Orch.,
G-AN626: G-EH90: G-EG1717:
G-HE2273; Orch. Mascotte, P-F1664;
Godwin Orch., PD-21003; Andolfi Orch.,
PAT-X96034

Frühlingskinder, Op. 148 Fr. Les Violettes
Kermbach Orch., PD-2397

Ganz allerliebst, Op. 159 Fr. Très jolie
Marek Weber Orch., G-EH636: G-EH97;
Edith Lorand Orch., P-E10874; Wiener
Bohème Orch. Mascotte, O-279257

Goldregen, Op. 160 Fr. Pluie d'or
Marek Weber Orch., G-B3894:
G-EG2188: G-HE2439: G-HN616:
G-K6908; D. Bela Orch., O-171062

Herbstweisen (Pomone) Op. 155
Symphony Orch.—Cariven, PAT-
PDT102; Paul Godwin Orch., PD-21707;
Marek Weber Orch., G-EG2090:
G-HE2277: G-X3733: G-K6402

Immer oder Nimmer, Op. 156
Eng. Ever or Never Fr. Toujours ou
jamais
Wiener Bohème Orch. Mascotte,
O-279205: P-F1794; Locatelli Orch.,
O-165965

Liebe und Frühling Eng. Love and Spring
Locatelli Orch., O-165965

Mein Traum, Op. 151 Eng. My Dream
Fr. Mon Rêve
Marek Weber Orch., G-EG1674:
G-HE2447: G-HN621: G-K5844; Paul
Godwin Orch., PD-21031

(Die) Schlittschuhläufer, Op. 183
Eng. The Skaters Fr. Les Patineurs
NBC Symphony Orch.—Toscanini
12"—V-11-8949
(Also on V-11-9227 in VM-1062)
Boston "Pops" Orch.—Fiedler
(G-B8665) (G-K8023) 10"—V-4396
Carnegie "Pops" Orch.—Broeckman
12"—C-71957D
[Trad: Arkansas Traveler & Sousa:
Semper Fidelis]
DUPLICATIONS: Paramount Theater
Orch., G-HE2028; A. Campoli Orch.,
D-F2566; Vienna Symphony Orch.,
C-DB1064: C-DF1268; International
Concert Orch., V-35798: G-C1326:
G-L533: G-S8844; Edith Lorand Orch.,
P-E10874; Marek Weber Orch.,
G-EG1717: G-HN626: G-HE2273

Sirenzauber, Op. 154 Eng. Sirens
Fr. Les Sirènes
Marek Weber Orch., G-HE2447:
G-EG1674: G-K5844

—Arr. Voice: Ninon Vallin (s), PAT-
X93134

Skaters See under Schlittschuhläufer
Solitude
Lamoureux Orch.—M. Cariven, PAT-
PDT151

(Ein) Sommerabend, Op. 188
Eng. A Summer Evening Fr. Soirée
d'Eté
Marek Weber Orch., G-EG2114:
G-K6495; Wiener Bohème Orch. Mas-
cotte, O-279042: P-F1742; Horlick
Orch., PD-524494; Paul Godwin Orch.,
PD-21173

Très Jolie See Ganz Allerliebst

Untern Regenbogen, Op. 237 Fr., Arc-en-
ciel
Wiener Bohème Orch. Mascotte,
O-279132

Violettes
Lamoureux Orch.—M. Cariven, PAT-
PDT151

WALLACE, William Vincent (1812-1865)
*An Irish pianist and composer who followed
the John Field-Frederic Chopin tradition in his
keyboard music. His English light opera,
"Maritana," was an immediate and lasting success.*

MARITANA Light Opera in English 1845
Overture
Berlin State Opera Orch.—Beutler
12"—PD-15245
German Opera House Orch.—Schmidt-
Isserstedt 12"—T-E2180

WALTHER, Johann Gottfried (1684-1748)
*A relative and good friend of Johann Sebas-
tian Bach, Walther was highly esteemed as a
composer by so exacting a critic as Mattheson,
but the most lasting contribution was his
"Musikalische Lexicon . . .," a dictionary,
that greatly faciliated the compilation of Ger-
ber's "Lexicon" some sixty years later.*

Meinen Jesum lass ich nicht
Jens Laumann (Compenius Organ, Fred-
eriksborg Castle, Denmark)
[Bach: In dulci Jubilo] 10"—G-X4975

WALTHER VON DER VOGELWEIDE (12th-
13th Centuries)
*In the courtly art of the German Minnesinger,
where music was the handmaid of poetry,
Walther von der Vogelweide is perhaps the
most renowned figure. Only five or six of his
many melodies have survived.*

Kreutzfahrerlied 1228 (Crusader's Song)
"Nu alerst leb ich mir werde"
Max Meili (t) unacc.
(in Vol. II) 12"—AS-18
[with French Troubadour & German
Minnesänger songs]
Hans J. Moser (b) unacc. 10"—P-R1018
[with French Troubadour & German
Minnesänger songs]
(in 2000 Years of Music set)

WALTHEW, Richard Henry (1872-   )
*A student of Parry, Walthew is a contemporary
English composer of conservative bent. Most of
his compositions remain in manuscript, and
he is better known as a teacher & conductor.*

Sonata, D major Viola & Piano
Mosaic in four pieces Viola & Piano
Watson Forbes & Meyers Foggin
2 12"—D-K897/8

WALTON, William (1902-   )
*One of the most original and powerful of mod-
ern British composers and unquestionably a
prime figure in the recent renaissance of English music. Recording companies are according Walton recognition at last, and are finding
that competently written modern music is a
profitable investment.*

Belshazzar's Feast
Dennis Noble (b), Huddersfield Choir,
Liverpool Philharmonic Orch.—William
Walton 5 12"—VM-974†
(G-C3330/4 in GM-382†)

Concerto, Viola & Orchestra
William Primrose & Philharmonia Orch.
Walton 3 12"—G-DB6309/11†
Frederick Riddle & London Symphony—
Walton 3 12"—D-X199/201

Concerto, Violin & Orchestra
Jascha Heifetz & Cincinnati Symphony
Orch.—Goossens 3 12"—VM-868†
(G-DB5953/5†)

Crown Imperial Coronation March 1937
BBC Symphony Orch. (Berkeley Mason, organ)—Boult 12"—G-DB3164
FACADE Melodrama for Voice & Chamber Orch. 1926
(Poems by Edith Sitwell)
Black Mrs. Behemoth; Jodelling Song; Long Steel Grass; A Man from a Far Countree
(recited by Edith Sitwell)
Polka; Fox-trot; Tango; Scotch Rhapsody; Tarantella; Valse; Popular Song
(recited by Constant Lambert)
Edith Sitwell & Constant Lambert with Chamber Orch. 2 12"—D-K991/2
—Arr. Orchestra Walton
Suite No. 1 1937
1) Polka; 2) Valse; 3) Swiss Jodelling Song; 4) Tango—Paso-Doblé; 5) Tarantella Sevilliana
Suite No. 2 1938
1) Fanfare; 2) Scotch Rhapsody; 3) Country Dance; 4) Noche Española; 5) Popular Song; 6) Old Sir Faulk

Suite No. 1 (complete) & Suite No. 2—Nos. 1, 2, 3 & 5
London Philharmonic Orch.—Walton
2 12"—G-C2836/7
Suite No. 2—Nos. 4 & 6 only
London Philharmonic Orch.—Walton
[Siesta] 12"—G-C3042
Suite No. 1—Valse only
Louis Kentner (pf) 12"—C-DX932
[Liapounov: Berceuse]

Suite No. 1—Nos. 1, 4 & 5 and Suite No. 2—No. 5 only
Orchestre Raymonde—Goehr
12"—C-DX938
HENRY V Music from the Film
Excerpts
Laurence Olivier (reader) with Philharmonia Orch. & Chorus—William Walton
(G-C3583/6†) 4 12"—VM-1128†

Death of Falstaff; Touch her sweet lips and part
(Not included in VM-1128, above)
Philharmonia String Orch.—William Walton 12"—G-C3480
[Sinfonia Concertante, Pt. 5, with Phyllis Sellick, pf., & City of Birmingham Orch.]

Overture "Portsmouth Point" 1925
(after Rowlandson's print of the same name)
BBC Symphony Orch.—Boult
10"—G-DA1540
Minneapolis Symphony Orch.—Mitropoulos 12"—C-12755D

Quartet, Piano & Strings 1918/9
Reginald Paul Piano Quartet
4 12"—D-X238/41
[Beethoven: Piano Quartet, D major, No. 2—Rondo]

Scapino A Comedy Overture (after an etching from Jacques Callot's "Balli di Sfessania")
Chicago Symphony Orch.—Stock
(C-LX931) 12"—C-11945D

Siesta
London Philharmonic Orch.—Walton
12"—G-C3042
[Façade Suite No. 2—Nos 4 & 6]

Sinfonia Concertante Piano & Orchestra
Phyllis Sellick (pf) & City of Birmingham Orch.—Walton
3 12"—G-C3478/80†
[Henry V—2 Excerpts, with Philharmonia String Orch.]

"Spitfire" Prelude & Fugue
Music from the film
Laurence Turner (vl) & Hallé Orch.—Walton 12"—G-C3359

Symphony Orchestra
London Symphony—H. Harty
6 12"—D-X108/13
Where does the uttered music go?
(Masefield)
BBC Choir (unacc.)—Leslie Woodgate
12"—G-C3503
(The) Wise Virgins Ballet Suite
(Arranged from the cantatas of J. S. Bach)
Sadler's Wells Orch.—Walter
(G-C3178/9) 2 12"—VM-817†

WARLOCK, Peter (1894-1930)

The composer of music issued under the name of Peter Warlock is Philip Heseltine, the critic and writer, who has studied and written on such diverse figures as Gesualdo, Delius and Bernard van Dieren. Warlock was, according to his friend Cecil Gray, a dual personality, and it is Gray's opinion that this and the composer's dissatisfaction with his own works, caused his death by suicide at the young age of thirty-six.

Capriol Suite String Orchestra
Basse Danse; Pavane; Tordion; Bransles; Pieds-en-l'air; Mattachins
The Capriol Suite comprises settings of 6 tunes from the famous treatise on dancing, published in 1588 by "Thoinot Arbeau"—Jehan Tabourot. Attention might be called to the record of "French Dances of the 16th Century" in the 1st volume of "L'Anthologie Sonore" a group of similar tunes played by a string group of viols, gambas and basses in authentic 16th century settings. The tune of "Pieds-en-l'air" used in the Capriol Suite was also used by Delibes for the "Pavane" in his incidental music to "Le Roi s'amuse."

Constant Lambert String Orch.—Lambert
12"—G-C2904
London Chamber Orch.—Anthony Bernard 12"—D-K576

SONGS In English

(The) Birds (Belloc) (Carol arr. for Childrens' Chorus)
North Midlands Primary School Chorus
12"—G-C3637
[with folk song arrangements, etc.]

Captain Stratton's Fancy (Masefield)
Roy Henderson (b) & Eric Gritten (pf)
10"—D-M563
[Milkmaids & Stanford: A soft day]

(A) Cornish Christmas Carol
Corpus Christi Unaccompanied Chorus
BBC Chorus—Leslie Woodgate
12″—**D-K827**

Fair and True (Breton)
Roy Henderson (b) & Gerald Moore (pf)
10″—**D-M519**
[Piggesnie & My own country]

Milkmaids
Roy Henderson (b) & Eric Gritten (pf)
10″—**D-M563**
[Captain Stratton's Fancy & Stanford: A soft day]

My own country (Belloc)
Roy Henderson (b) & Gerald Moore (pf)
10″—**D-M519**
[Fair and true & Piggesnie]

Passing By
Roy Henderson (b) & Gerald Moore (pf)
10″—**D-M514**
[Sigh no more & Pretty ring time]

Piggesnie
Roy Henderson (b) & Gerald Moore (pf)
10″—**D-M519**
[Fair and true & My own country]

Prayer to St. Anthony of Padua
John Runge (t) & pf. acc. 10″—**PAR-53**
[The Sick Heart & Parrott: I heard a linnet courting]
Nancy Evans (c) 12″—**D-K866**
[Rest, Sweet Nymphs & Hageman: Do not go, my love]

Pretty Ring Time
Roy Henderson (b) & Gerald Moore (pf)
10″—**D-M514**
[Passing by: Sigh no more]

Rest, Sweet Nymphs
Nancy Evans (c) 12″—**D-K866**
[Prayer to St. Anthony of Padua & Hageman: Do not go, my love]
DUPLICATION: English School Choirs, G-C3527

(The) Sick Heart
John Runge (t) & pf. acc. 10″—**PAR-53**
[Prayer to St. Anthony of Padua & Parrott: I heard a linnet courting]

Sigh no more
Roy Henderson (b) & Gerald Moore (pf)
10″—**D-M514**
[Passing by & Pretty ring time]

WEBER, Carl Maria von (1786-1826)

The founder of German nationalistic opera, Weber is also the first prominent musical figure of German Romanticism. His operas no longer hold the boards today although their overtures and the "Konzertstück" remain staples of the concert repertoire. The recordings available greatly supplement these few works.

Adagio e Rondo Arr. 'Cello & Piano
Piatigorsky
NOTE: *This Adagio is a movement from the Sonatina No. 2, G major for Piano and Violin obbligato; and the Rondo is from the Sonatina No. 3, D minor, for Piano and Violin obbligato.*
Gregor Piatigorsky & I. Newton
12″—**G-DB2539**
[Francoeur: Largo & Vivo]

Adagio e Rondo Ungarese, C minor, Op. 35
Bassoon & Orch. 1813
Fernand Oubradous & Paris Conservatory
Orch.—Désormière 12″—**OL-14**
William Gruner & Orch. (Abridged)
10″—**V-20525**
[Kranz: Tourbillon—C. Barone, fl.]

Air Russe & Rondo Violin & Piano
Erling Bloch & H. Lund Christiansen
12″—**G-DB6**
[Schubert: Violin Sonata No. 4, Pt. 5]

Andante e Variazioni 'Cello & Orchestra
1810

No. 2, F major
Emanuel Feuermann & Gerald Moore
(pf) (in CM-312†) 12″—**C-69083D**
[Beethoven: Sonata, A major, Op. 69, Pt. 5, Feuermann & Myra Hess] (C-LX643)

Aufforderung zum Tanz, Op. 65 Piano
(Rondo Brilliant, D flat major, 1814)
Fr. L'Invitation à la Danse (or Valse)
Eng. Invitation to the Dance (often incorrectly as Waltz)
Artur Schnabel 12″—**G-DB6491**
Benno Moiseiwitch (arr. Tausig)
(G-C3140) 12″—**V-18050**
Alfred Cortot 10″—**G-DA855**
DUPLICATION: Walter Rehberg, PD-47131

—**Arr. Piano, 4-Hands:** J. Dupont & G. Andolfi, PAT-PG12; Rawicz & Landauer, C-FB1872

—**Arr. Orchestra** Berlioz 1918
NOTE: *The name of the orchestrator is seldom stated, but the Berlioz is used more often than not. Exceptions are the Weingartner and Stokowski transcriptions as listed below.*
BBC Symphony Orchestra—Toscanini
(G-DB3542) 12″—**V-15192**
National Symphony Orch.—Fistoulari
12″—**D-K1108**
Orch. of Maggio Musicale—Markevitch
12″—**CET-BB25155**
Berlin Philharmonic Orch.—Knappertsbusch 12″—**G-DB7647**
Berlin Philharmonic Orch.—Furtwängler
12″—**PD-67056**
Berlin Philharmonic—Kleiber
(U-E10276) 12″—**T-E988**
Tioli Orch.—Jensen 12″—**TONO-X25062**
Berlin State Opera Orch.—Melichar
12″—**P-E11379**
Berlin Philharmonic Orch.—Weissmann
12″—**P-E10927**
Symphony Orch.—Cloëz 12″—**O-170035**
Ruhlmann Orchestra 12″—**PAT-X5531**
DUPLICATIONS: Orchestre Raymonde, C-DB1401: C-DQ1445; Republican Guard Band, C-D11040

—**Arr. Orchestra** Weingartner
London Philharmonic Orch.—Weingartner 12″—**C-LX890**
London Philharmonic Orchestra—Goehr
12″—**G-C2984**

—**Arr. Orchestra** Miscellaneous
Philadelphia Orchestra—Stokowski
(G-DB3699) 12″—**V-15189**
(Older version: G-AW4043: G-W954)

All American Orch.—Stokowski
                  12"—**C-11481D**
Philadelphia Orch.—Ormandy
                  12"—**C-12750D**
—Arr. Voice
Miliza Korjus (s) (in German)
(G-C3122)   12"—**V-12829**
Helene Regelly (s) (in French) (Arr.
André)   10"—**O-250438**
Anne Ziegler (s) (in English)
                  10"—**G-B9241**
Bauerntanz
Barnabas von Géczy & his Orch.
[Favoriten Walzer]   10"—**G-EG7159**

CHORUS Miscellaneous Choral Works in
German
See also under Leyer und Schwert, Op. 42.
Brüder steckt nun die Gewehre Arr.
Melichar
Neukölln Teachers Chorus, Organ &
Orch.—Melichar   10"—**PD-21881**
[Mozart: Brüder reicht die Hand]
Drei Sterne
Basilica Choir—Pius Kalt
                10"—**PD-62632**
[Gluck: Iphigénie en Aulide—Festal
Song]

CONCERTOS (or CONCERTINOS)
Bassoon & Orchestra, F major
—Adagio only
Fernand Oubradous & Noël Gallon (pf)
                12"—**OL-80**
[Beethoven: Duo No. 1, Pt. 3]
Clarinet & Orchestra, C minor, Op. 26
Reginald Kell & Symphony Orch.—
Walter Goehr   12"—**C-69869D**
(C-DX942)
Also: Garde Républicaine Band,
C-D11010
Clarinet & Orch. (unidentified)
Luigi Amodio & S. Schultz (pf)
      2 12"—**CET-OR5109/11**
[Chopin: Etude, Op. 10, No. 3, Brailow-
sky]
Conzertstück See under Konzertstück
Country Dance See under Waltz, E flat
Euryanthe See under Operas
Favoriten-Walzer
Barnabas von Géczy Orch.
[Bauerntanz]   10"—**G-EG7159**
(Der) Freischütz See under Operas
Grand Duo concertant, B flat major, Op. 48
Clarinet & Piano 1816
Ulysse Delecluse & Joseph Benvenuti
      2 10"—**PAT-PD19/20**
Invitation to the Dance See under Auf-
forderung zum Tanz
Jubel-Ouvertüre, E major, Op. 59 1818
Dresden Philharmonic—van Kempen
              12"—**CET-OR5030**
DUPLICATION: Berlin Philharmonic—
Pfitzner, PD-19858
Konzertstück, F minor, Op. 79 Piano &
Orch.
Robert Casadesus & Orch.—Bigot
(C-LWX113/4)   2 12"—**CX-59†**
(C-LX470/1) (C-LFX384/5)

Claudio Arrau & Chicago Symphony
Orch.—Rodzinski 2 12"—in **VM-1216†**
[With R. Strauss: Burleske]
Larghetto Arr. Violin & Piano Kreisler
NOTE: *The original source of this Larghetto is
not specified, but it resembles the 2nd Mvt.
("Schäfers Klage") of the Trio, G minor, Op.*
63.
Fritz Kreisler & M. Raucheisen
              10"—**G-DA1137**
[Schubert-Kreisler: Rosamunde—Ballet
Music]
Leyer und Schwert, Op. 42 (Körner)
NOTE: *Of these 10 songs, four are for single
voice with piano, the others for unaccompanied
male chorus.*
No. 2, Lützows wilde Jagd Male Chorus
("Wie glänzt dort im Walde")
Regensburg Cathedral Choir—Th.
Schrems   10"—**G-EG3835**
[Folk melody before 1700: Prinz Eugen]
Cologne Cho.—Papst   10"—**T-A2192**
[Silcher: Nun leb' wohl, du kleine Gasse]
No. 6, Schwertlied Male Chorus
("Du Schwert an meiner Linken")
—Arr. Baritone, Chorus & Orch.
Wilhelm Rode & Chorus 10"—**PD-25214**
[Methfessel: Vaterlandslied]
Oberon See under Operas

OPERAS In German
ABU HASSAN Singspiel 1 Act 1811
Overture Orchestra
German Opera House Orch.—Jochum
              12"—**T-E3153**
[Euryanthe—Overture, Pt. 3]
Berlin State Opera Orch.—Ludwig
              12"—**PD-15224**
[Mozart: Così fan tutte—Overture]
[Reznicek: Donna Diana—Overture, on
PD-15213]

(DER) BEHERRSCHER DER GEISTER
See Rübezahl

EURYANTHE 3 Acts 1823
Overture Orchestra
Hallé Orch.—Barbirolli 12"—**G-C3560**
National Symphony Orch.—Rankl
              12"—**D-K1154**
Chicago Symphony Orch.—Stock
(C-LX926)   12"—**C-11179D**
EIAR Symphony Orch.—Tansini
           12"—**CET-CB20283**
German Opera House Orch.—Jochum
    2 12"—**T-E3152/3**
[Abu Hassan—Overture]
DUPLICATIONS: Dresden Philharmonic
—van Kempen, PD-15232: CET-OR5028;
Amsterdam Concertgebouw Orch.—Men-
gelberg, C-GQX10994: C-LFX249; Berlin
Philharmonic—R. Strauss, PD-66828

(DER) FREISCHUETZ 3 Acts 1821
Eng. The Freeshooter, or The Seventh
Bullet
It. Il Franco Cacciatore
Abridged recording Arr. Weigert—Maeder
Soloists, Chorus & Orchestra of Berlin
State Opera—Hermann Weigert
        4 12"—**PD-27387/90**

The Cast:
Ottokar .... Armin Weltner (b)
Kuno ....Deszö Ernster (b)
Agathe .... Elfriede Marherr (s)
Aennchen .... Tilly de Garmo (s)
Caspar .... Eduard Kandl (b)
Max .... Fritz Soot (t)
Samiel .... Waldemar Henke (bs)
Ein Eremit .... Rudolf Watzke (b)
Kilian .... Albert Reiss (t)
Brautjungfer .... Herta Klust (s)

Vocal & Orchestral Selections
Ilse Koegel, Carla Spletter, Peter Anders,
Hanns Heinz Nissen with Berlin Opera
Chorus & Philharmonic—Schmidt-Isser-
stedt   12"—T-E1943
Elly Völkel, Hilde Scheppan, Günther
Treptow, Franz Wolf with Berlin Opera
Chorus & Orch.—Schütze
           12"—PD-15173

Individual Excerpts

Overture Orchestra
NBC Symphony Orch.—Toscanini
           12"—V-11-9172
London Philharmonic—Beecham
(C-LX601) (C-LWX187) 12"—C-68986D
Philharmonia Orch.—Süsskind
           12"—C-DX1244
Philadelphia Orch.—Ormandy
           12"—C-12665D
London Philharmonic—Leinsdorf
           12"—D-K1589
Cleveland Orch.—Rodzinski
           12"—C-11817D
DUPLICATIONS: Berlin State Opera
Orch.—van Kempen, CET-OR5056: PD-
15308; Orch. Maggio Musicale—Rossi,
CET-CB20148; Boston "Pops" Orch.—
Fiedler, V-12040: G-C3375; Saxon State
Opera Orch.—Böhm, G-DB4561; Paris
Conservatory—Bruno Walter,
G-DB3554; Berlin Philharmonic—Furt-
wängler, PD-67108/9: PD-566177/8;
BBC Symphony—Boult, G-DB1678; Am-
sterdam Concertgebouw—Mengelberg,
C-GQX10728; Royal Orch., Copenhagen
—Tango, TONO-X25043; Berlin Philhar-
monic—Jochum, T-E1493; Berlin State
Opera—Weigert, PD-27153; Symphony
Orch.—Gaubert, C-LFX173; Berlin
State Opera—Blech, G-W855: G-EJ520

ACT I, Scene 4

Nein, länger trag' ich nicht die Qualen
Recit.
Durch die Wälder, durch die Auen Air
Tenor
Jetzt ist wohl ihr Fenster offen (Arie des
Max)
Richard Tauber   10"—P-RO20551
Helge Roswaenge   10"—G-DA4418
Franz Völker   12"—PD-67260
(Earlier recording: PD-19683)
Peter Anders   12"—T-E2287
Horst Taubman   12"—PD-67998

Scene 5
Hier im ird'schen Jammerthal (Trinklied)
Bass
Eng. **Caspar's Drinking Song**

Josef Hermann   10"—G-DA4498
[Verdi: Forza del Destino—Son Pereda]
In Italian: Adamo Didur, CRS-28*; N. De
Angelis, C-GQX10180

ACT II, Scene 2

Agathes Gebet
Wie nahte mir der Schlummer Recit.
Leise, leise, fromme Weise Air (Part 1)
Alles pflegt schon längst der Ruh! (Part 2)
  Eng. **Agathe's Prayer: Softly sighs**
Tiana Lemnitz   12"—G-DB5549
Lotte Lehmann   12"—P-PXO1016
Polyna Stoska, in CX-294
Hilde Konetzni   12"—T-SK2160
D. Reinhardt   12"—PD-66949
Joan Hammond (in English)
           12"—G-C3510
—**Recit. & Part 1 only**
Tiana Lemnitz   12"—PD-15081
[Und ob Wolke sie verhülle]
Trude Eipperle   12"—PD-67853
[Und ob Wolke sie verhülle]

ACT III

Prelude
Berlin Philharmonic Orch.—Furt-
wängler   12"—PD-67109
[Overture, Pt. 3] (PD-566178)

Scene 1
Und ob die Wolke sie verhülle Soprano
(Agathe)
Tiana Lemnitz   10"—G-DA1881
Tiana Lemnitz   12"—PD-15081
[Agathes Gebet]
Trude Eipperle   12"—PD-67853
[Agathes Gebet]

Scene 3
Einst träumte meiner sel'gen Base Soprano
Trübe Augen, Liebchen, taugen (Aennchen)
Irma Beilke   10"—G-DA4495
Erna Sack   10"—T-A1771

Scene 4
Wir winden dir den Jungfernkranz (Brides-
maids' Chorus)
—**Arr. Orch.** Symphony Orch.—Kunz, PD-
10221

Scene 6
Jägerchor: Was gleicht wohl auf Erden
(Hunting Chorus)
Dresden State Opera Chorus & Saxon
State Orch.—Böhm 10"—G-DA4457
[Gounod: Faust—Soldiers' Chorus]
DUPLICATION: Erk'scher Male Chorus
—Kopsch, PD-10289

INEZ DE CASTRO, Op. 51 Incidental
Music for a drama

Scena & Aria In Italian

**Non paventar mia vita & Come tradir
potrei** Soprano
Erna Berger   12"—PD-57083

OBERON 3 Acts 1826
(or "The Elf King's Oath")

Overture

London Philharmonic Orch.—Beecham
12″—C-69410D
(C-LX746) (C-LWX281) (C-LFX557)
Saxon State Orch.—Böhm
12″—G-DB5557
Boston "Pops" Orch.—Fiedler
(G-C3111) (G-EH1104) 12″—V-12043
National Symphony Orch.—Braithwaite
12″—D-K1322
Boston Symphony Orch.—Koussevitsky
12″—V-11-9951
Amsterdam Concertgebouw Orch.—Mengelberg
2 12″—O-8397/8
[Beethoven: Symphony No. 8—Allegretto scherzando only]
London Philharmonic Orch.—Szell
12″—G-L1007
German Opera House Orch.—Jochum
12″—T-E3142
Orch. of the Suisse Romande—Blech
In Prep. Swiss Decca
DUPLICATIONS: Berlin Philharmonic—Ludwig, PD-15197; Philharmonic Orch.—Meyrowitz, PAT-PDT30; Berlin Philharmonic—Schuricht, U-E656; EIAR Symphony Orch.—A. La Rosa Parodi, CET-CB20180; London Symphony Orch.—Blech, G-DB1675

Individual Excerpts

ACT I

Arie des Hüon: Von Jugend auf in dem Kampfgefild Tenor
Helge Roswaenge . 10″—G-DA4416

ACT II

Gebet des Hüon: Du, der diese Prüfung schickt
(Prayer of Huon)
Helge Roswaenge 10″—G-DA4417
[Mozart: Entführung aus dem Serail—No. 1, Hier soll ich]

Ozean, du Ungeheuer (Rezia's Aria)
Eng. Ocean, thou mighty monster!
Kirsten Flagstad
(G-DB3440) 12″—V-15244
Margarete Teschemacher
12″—G-DB5568
DUPLICATION: Elisabeth Ohms, PD-66900
In English: Joan Hammond, G-C3493

ACT III

Traure, mein Herz Soprano
It. **Piangi mio cuor**
Gabriella Gatti (in It.)
12″—CET-BB25088
[Mozart: Nozze di Figaro—Porgi amor]

PETER SCHMOLL UND SEIN NACHBARN
1801

Overture, Op. 8 Orchestra (Revised 1807)
German Opera House Orch.—Beutler
12″—PD-15310

PRECIOSA See under Preciosa Incidental Music

RUEBEZAHL (or "Der Beherrscher der Geister")
Eng. **Ruler of the Spirits**

Overture
Philharmonia Orch.—Süsskind
12″—C-DX1262
Berlin State Orch.—Fritz Zaun
10″—C-DW4905

PRECIOSA Incidental Music
Overture
Dresden Philharmonic—P. van Kempen
12″—CET-OR5046

Rondo brillant, E flat, Op. 62 Piano
("La Gaité")
Emma Boynet 12″—PAT-PAT2
[Schubert: Impromptu, B flat major]
Magda Tagliaferro 12″—PAT-PAT53
[Mendelssohn: Andante & Etude]

SONATAS Piano
No. 1, C major, Op. 24
Noel Mewton-Wood
3 12″—D-K1038/40†
—**4th Mvt. (Rondo) only** ("Perpetual Motion")
Ginette Doyen, G-DB11129; Alexander Brailowsky, PD-95420: PD-95141

—**Arr. Violin & Piano**
Heinz Stanske & Hellmuth Hidegheti
12″—PD-57106
[Mozart: Minuet, D major]

No. 2, A flat major, Op. 39
Noel Mewton-Wood 12″—D-K1061/4†
[Chopin: Tarantelle]

SONATINAS—Piano with Violin obbligato
No. 3, D minor—Rondo only
—**Arr. 'Cello & Piano**
Gregor Piatigorsky & Ivar Newton
12″—G-DB2539
[Francoeur: Largo & Vivo]
Camillo Oblach & Mario Salerno
12″—CET-CC2120
[Rossellini: La fontana malata]

No. 5, A major, Op. 10, No. 5
—**Arr. 'Cello & Piano** Piatigorsky
G. Piatigorsky & Ivor Newton
12″—G-DB2248
NOTE: *The 1st Mvt.—Air & Variations, is based on a theme from Weber's opera "Silvana."*

Trio, G minor, Op. 63 Flute, 'Cello & Piano
René Le Roy, Janos Scholz & Ernö Balogh 2 12″—VOX-605

Waltz, E flat major Arr. Dubensky
Indianapolis Symphony Orch.—Sevitzky
12″—V-11-8609
[Strauss: Frühlingsstimmen]

WEBERN, Anton von (1883-1945)

A conductor and composer who studied with Schönberg, von Webern also did research under the direction of Guido Adler.

Trio, Op. 21 Violin, Viola, & 'Cello 1927
Kathleen Washbourne String Trio
12″—D-K904

WECKERLIN, Jean Baptiste Théodore (1821-1910)

Weckerlin has written several oratorios and other works for voice and orchestra, but he is best known as a writer and for the volumes of old French songs he collected, edited and published.

Aminte (18th Century Tambourin)
Roger Bourdin, O-188768

Chanson Normande (18th Century)
Vanni-Marcoux, G-DA4804

Entendez-vous le carillon de verre!
Vocal Quintet, PAT-PA1155

L'Etoile du matin (Chanson alsacienne)
Vanni-Marcoux, G-K6955

Bergère Légère (18th Century)
Roger Bourdin, O-188768

Jeunes filettes (18th Century)
Vocal quintet, PAT-PA1155

Lison dormait
Roger Bourdin, O-188768

Menuet d'Exaudet
Roger Bourdin, O-188768

Pastourelle
Pantofel-Nechestzkaia (in Russian),
USSR-10035/6

Pêche des moules (Chant de la Saintonge)
Vanni-Marcoux, G-K6955

Trop aimable Sylvie (18th Century)
Vanni-Marcoux, G-K6955

WEDEL, Artemi (1767-1806)

Russian born composer of church music and a well-known choral director who was a pupil of the Italian, Sarti, when the latter was in Russia (1784-1802).

Open to me the Gates of Repentance
Don Cossack Choir—Jaroff (U-F14269)
[Gretchaninov: Credo] 12"—T-E1908

WEELKES, Thomas (c.1575-1623)

With Wilbye the greatest of the later Elizabethan madrigalists. Weelkes also left large quantities of instrumental and sacred music, little of which has been accorded modern performances. We must report that the list of available recordings of this composer's works has shrunk to shameful proportions.

As Vesta was from Latmos Hill Descending
6-Voice Madrigal
(from "The Triumphs of Oriana")
St. George Singers 10"—C-5717
[Gibbons: The Silver Swan; Farmer:
Fair Phyllis]
(in Columbia History of Music, Vol. I:
CM-231)

Fantasy for a Chest of Viols
Dolmetsch Family Group 10"—C-5714
(in Columbia History of Music, Vol. I:
CM-231)

On the Plains 5-Voice Madrigal
Winchester Music Club 12"—C-D40122
(in illustrations for Lecture No. 61, "The
Progress of Music," George Dyson: International Educational Society)

WEILL, Kurt (1900-   )

A native of Germany, Kurt Weill's operatic experiments have aroused wide interest. His most successful work was his setting of John Gay's historic "Beggar's Opera" text. For a comparison with the original eighteenth century music of this ballad opera, see under Pepusch.

AUFSTIEG UND FALL DER STADT MAHAGONNY

Opera in 21 Episodes In German &
English 1929

Vocal & Orchestral Selections (Querschnitt)
Lotte Lenja (s) & Kurfürstendam Theatre Chorus & Orch.—Somer
12"—G-Z224

(DIE) DREIGROSCHENOPER

Eng. The Three-Penny Opera
(Beggar's Opera)
Fr. L'Opéra de Quat'sous

Abridged recording In German
Overture; Moritat; Ballade vom angenehmen Leben; Liebeslied; Kanonensong;
Die Seeräuberjenny; Finale Act I; Barbarasong; Eifersichtduett; Abschied; Finale Act II; Zuhälter-Ballade; Lied von
der Unzulängichkeit des menschlichen
Lebens; Moritat; Schluss-Choral (with
spoken narration by Kurt Gerron)
Lotte Lenja, K. Gerron, W. Trenk-Trebitsch, E. Helmke, E. Ponto, Lewis
Ruth Band—Theodor Mackeben
4 10"—T-A752/5

Vocal & Orchestral Selections
(Querschnitt)
Carola Neher, Kurt Gerron & A.
Schroeder 12"—G-EH301
Margo Lion & Albert Prejean
(in French) 2 10"—U-A717/8
Florelle (in French)
2 10"—PD-522171/2

Instrumental Selections
—"Kleine Dreigroschenmusik"
Brass & Woodwinds
Berlin State Opera Orch.—Klemperer
(PD-24172/3) 2 10"—VOX-451

—**Dance Potpourri**
Marek Weber Orch., G-K6406

Individual Excerpts (in French)

Chant des Canons
M. Oswald, C-DF1115

Chant de Barbara
La Fiancée du Pirate
Lys Gauty, C-DF873

KNICKERBOCKER HOLIDAY
(Maxwell Anderson)

September Song
Walter Huston, D-40001; Gladys
Swarthout, in VM-1127

LADY IN THE DARK (Ira Gershwin)

Selections
Hildegarde, with Cho. & Orch.
3 10"—D-A208

MARIE GALANTE Incidental Music
Vocal Selections
Le Grand Lustucru; J'attends un navire; Le Roi d'Aquitaine; Les Filles de Bordeaux
Florelle (s) 2 10"—PD-524011/2
J' attends un navire only
Lys Gauty, PD-524196

MINE EYES HAVE SEEN THE GLORY
Settings by Weill of Battle Hymn of the Republic (Howe); Star-Spangled Banner (Key); America (Smith); & Beat! Beat! Drums! (Whitman).
Helen Hayes (recitation) & Victor Orch.—Shields 2 12"—VM-909

ONE TOUCH OF VENUS (Ogden Nash)
Selections
Mary Martin, Kenny Baker w. Cho. & Orch.—Abravanel 5 10"—D-DA361

STREET SCENE
(from the play by Elmer Rice)
(Adapted by Langston Hughes)
Excerpts
Anne Jeffreys, Polyna Stoska, Brian Sullivan w. original cast & Orch.—Abravanel 6 12"—CM-683†

SONGS
Complainte de la Seine
Je ne t'aime pas
Lys Gauty 10"—PD-522988
Songs to Poems of Walt Whitman
William Horne (t)
2 12"—CH-B7 (Limited Edition)

WEINBERGER, Jaromir (1896-   )
The famous Bohemian composer of "Schwanda," who was at one time a professor of music in the Ithaca Conservatory, New York.

Czech Rhapsody Orchestra
National Symphony Orch.—Kindler
12"—V-11-8297

SCHWANDA, DER DUDELSACKPFEIFER
Opera
Fr. Schwanda, le Joueur de Cornemuse
Eng. Schwanda, the Bagpipe Player
Orchestral Selections
Introduction, Polka, Furiant, Ballad, Song of Dorotka, Entrance of Schwanda, Interlude, Finale
Berlin-Charlottenburg Opera Orch.—Melichar 12"—PD-27157
Individual Excerpts
Ich bin der Schwanda Baritone & Chorus
Wie kann ich denn vergessen? Baritone
Theodor Scheidl with Chorus
12"—PD-66937
Polka & Fugue Orchestra & Organ
Philadelphia Orch.—Ormandy
(C-LX1005) 12"—C-12372D
London Symphony Orch.—H. Harty
(C-LX293) 12"—C-68311D
Minneapolis Symphony—Ormandy
(G-DB2223) 12"—V-7958
(Also V-11-9225 in VM-1062)
Minneapolis Symphony Orch.—
Mitropoulos 12"—V-12-0019

—Arr. 2 Pianos Weinberger
Vronsky & Babin, V-11-8189
Polka & Furiant Orchestra
Berlin State Opera Orch.—Blech
10"—G-B8173
Under the Spreading Chestnut Tree 1939
(Variations and Fugue on an old English Tune)
Cleveland Orch.—Rodzinski
2 12"—CX-161†

WEINGARTNER, Felix (1863-1942)
Felix Weingartner's is a name respected the world over as one of the great conductors. He wrote several books, orchestrated many works (including Beethoven's "Hammerklavier" Sonata), and composed a great deal of original music.

SCHNEEWITTCHEN Opera
(based on themes of Franz Schubert's operas)
Vocal Excerpts
E. Gehri (c), Wilhelm Tisch (bs), Z. Wozniak (t) 4 12"—G-DB10003; G-DB10005/6; G-DB10013
SONGS In German
Liebesfeier, Op. 16, No. 2 (Lenau)
("An ihrem bunten Liedern")
Heinrich Schlusnus (b) 10"—PD-90201
[Hermann: Mahnung]
DUPLICATION: J. Patzak, PD-10325
—Arr. Orchestra: Paul Godwin Orch., PD-21708
Miscellaneous—See Weber: Aufforderung zum Tanz

WEIS, Flemming (1898-   )
A contemporary Danish composer of orchestral and chamber music.

Serenade without Serious Intentions
Dan. Serenade uden seele Hensigter
Wind Quintet of 1932 12"—G-DB5276

WERNER, Fritz (1898-   )
A German-born contemporary conductor, composer, pianist and choral director.

Theme & Variations on a Breton Melody
Paris Conservatory Orch.—Werner
2 10"—G-DA4949/50

WEYSE, Christoph Ernst Friedrich (1774-1842)
The most important Danish composer of the classical period and the father of the Danish Romance (lied). German born, he came to Denmark when 16 years old and studied with J. A. P. Schulz, who was at this time a conductor in the service of the King of Denmark. Only a few of his comic operas (after the French manner) are still alive on the stage, but his ballads and songs form the basis of a Danish musical tradition. Their latent warmth, smiling simplicity and purity of expression make them the noblest representatives of that tone and attitude in music which, by the Danes, is felt to be their own.

Allegro di Bravura, D minor
Holger Lund Christiansen
10"—G-DA5240
[Sonata, G minor—Finale only]

Etudes: C minor, Op. 51 & E major, Op. 60
Holger Lund Christiansen
10"—G-DA5239

OPERAS

ET EVENTYR I ROSENBORG HAVE
(Heiberg) 1827
En Elskovserklaering
Edith Oldrup-Pedersen (s), G-DA5221

FESTEN PAA KENILWORTH
(H. C. Anderson) 1836
Hyrden graesser sine Faar
Edith Oldrup-Pedersen, G-X6991:
G-DA5220

LUDLAMS HULE (Oehlenschläger) 1816
Der er en O i Livet
Edith Oldrup-Pedersen (s), G-DA5219
Vil du vaere staerk og fri
Thyge Thygesen (t), G-X6889

SOVEDRIKKEN (Oehlenschläger) 1809
Skøn Jomfru, luk dit Vindu op.
Aksel Schiøtz (t), G-X6637: G-X6165
De klare Bølger rulled
Edith Oldrup-Pedersen (s), G-DA5219
Sonata, G minor Piano
—Finale (Allegro assai) only
Holger Lund Christiansen
10"—G-DA5240
[Allegro di Bravura, D minor]

SONGS In Danish

Bliv hos os, naar Dagen haelder
Aksel Schiøtz (t), G-X6624
College Mens' Choral Union, G-X6664
Dagen gaar med raske Fjed
Christian, G-X6655
Den korte Sommernat
Copenhagen Boys Choir—Wöldike,
G-DA5255
Der staar et Slot i Vesterled
Aksel Schiøtz (t), G-X6624
Marius Jacobsen (t), G-X2270
Paul Pedersen (treble), G-X4601
Det er saa yndigt at følges ad
Teddy Petersen Orch., G-X3973
Duftende Enge
Aksel Schiøtz (t), G-X6631
En Skaal for den Mø
Aksel Schiøtz (t), G-X6651
Edi Laider (t), G-X6211
Gud ske Tak og Lov
Aksel Schiøtz (t), G-X6623
Hellige Flamme
College Men's Choral Union, G-X6664:
G-X6395
Hvor Bølgen larmer
Thyge Thygesen (t), G-X6889
I fjerne kirketaarne hist
Aksel Schiøtz (t), G-X6416: G-X6920
Anker Blüme, G-X6241
I Osten stiger Solen op
Marius Jacobsen (t), G-X2270
Anker Blüme, G-X6241
I skovens dybe, stille ro
Elsa Sigfuss (ms), G-X6390

Julen har bragt velsignet Bud
Aksel Schiøtz (t) & Cho., G-X6172
Thyge Thygesen (t), G-X6806
Marius Jacobsen (t), G-X2576
Kommer hid, i Piger smaa
Aksel Schiøtz (t), G-X6651
Lysets engel gaar med glans
Aksel Schiøtz (t), G-X6416: G-X6920
Natten er saa stille
Aksel Schiøtz (t), G-X6631
Elsa Sigfuss (ms), G-X6390
Copenhagen Boys Choir—Wöldike,
G-DA5255
Knud Eriksen (treble), G-X4807
Nu ringer alle klokker mod sky
Paul Pederson (treble), G-X4601
Nu vaagne alle Guds Fugle smaa
Aksel Schiøtz (t), G-X6623
Pigen paa gaerdet
Elsa Sigfuss (ms), G-X6390
Teklas Sang
Edith Oldrup-Pedersen (s), G-DA5220:
G-X6991
Til vor lille Gerning ud
Christian, G-X6655
Velkommen igen, Guds Engle smaa
Copenhagen Boys Choir—Wöldike,
G-DA5255

WHITE, PAUL (1895-   )
An American composer and conductor on the faculty of the Eastman School of Music.
(5) Miniatures for Orchestra
By the Lake; Caravan song; Waltz of a
Teenie doll; Hippopotamus dance; Mos-
quito dance
Boston "Pops" Orch.—Fiedler
(in VM-554) 10"—V-4429
—Mosquito Dance only
Boston "Pops" Orch.—Fiedler, on V-4319
Levee Dance
Jascha Heifetz (vl) & Milton Kaye (pf),
in D-A385
Sea Chanty for Harp & Strings
Edna Phillips (harp), A. Hilsberg & S.
Ruden (vls), S. Roens (vla), S. Mayes
(vlc), A. Torello (bs)—Ormandy
2 12"—CX-259†

WIDOR, Charles Marie (1845-1937)
*The Toccata from the fifth Organ Symphony has been a favorite war horse for concert or-
ganists for many years. It is in a way typical of Widor and of the Romantic Organ School in general. Hence, as the baroque style of organ playing comes once more into prominence, it becomes clear that Widor's contribution of greatest value today is the excellent edition he prepared (jointly with Schweitzer) of the Bach organ works.*

Fantasie pour Piano et Orchestre
Mlle. Herrenschmidt & Paris Philhar-
monic—Münch 2 12"—PD-566205/6
Non Credo Air in Latin
Paul Sandoz (b) & W. Marti (pf)
12"—G-HEX103
[Franck: La procession]
Jo Vincent (s) 12"—C-D17214
[Saint-Saëns: La Cloche]

SYMPHONIES Organ
No. 5, F minor, Op. 42, No. 1
—1st Mvt. (Variations) only
Edouard Commette, C-DFX225/6
—5th Mvt. (Toccata) only
Charles Marie Widor (St. Sulpice Organ),
G-DB4856
Edouard Commette (Lyon Cathedral),
C-D19198
Fernando Germani, CET-PE88
No. 9 (Symphonie Gothique), Op. 70
Charles Marie Widor (St. Sulpice Organ),
G-DB4864/5

WIENIAWSKI, Henri (1835-1880)
*A Polish violin virtuoso and composer, trained
at the Paris "Conservatoire" whose two con-
certos and short violin pieces have held on in
the fiddler's repertoire as excellent show pieces.*
Capriccio-Valse, Op. 7 Violin & Piano
Erica Morini & Max Lanner
12"—V-11-8731
[Concerto No. 2—Romance]
Blanche Tarjus & M. Monard
10"—G-DA5006
Erica Morini & M. Raucheisen
12"—PD-66823
[Granados: Danza española No. 5]
Caprice, A minor Violin & Piano
Zino Francescatti & M. Lanner, in
CM-660

CONCERTOS—Violin & Orchestra
No. 2, D minor, Op. 22
Isaac Stern & N. Y. Philharmonic-
Symphony Orch.—Kurtz 3 12"—CM-656†
Jascha Heifetz & London Philharmonic—
Barbirolli 3 12"—VM-275†
[Scherzo Tarantelle]
[Hummel—Heifetz: Rondo, E flat, Op. 11,
on G-DB2447/9]
Wandy Tworek & Danish State Radio
Orch.—Tuxen 3 12"—NP-HM80015/7
[Kujawiak]
—2nd Mvt. (Romance) only
Nathan Milstein & Leopold Mittman (pf)
12"—C-69032D
[Polonaise brilliante No. 1] (C-LFX529)
Erica Morini & Max Lanner (pf)
[Capriccio-Valse] 12"—V-11-8731
DUPLICATION: L. Zimmermann,
C-DHX27

Légende, Op. 17 Violin & Orchestra
Yehudi Menuhin & Colonne Orch.—
Enesco 12"—G-DB3653
Mischa Elman & C. Hollister (pf)
12"—G-DB1557
[Massenet: Thaïs-Mediation]

MAZURKAS Violin & Piano
Dudziarz, D major, Op. 19, No. 2
B. Gimpel & A. Balsam, in VOX-616
Kujawiak, A minor, Op. 3
Wandy Tworek & Esther Vagning
12"—NP-HM80017
[Concerto No. 2, Pt. 5]
—Vocal arr. Kiepura in Polish
Jan Kiepura (t), & Otto Herz (pf),
C-17332D

Obertass, G major, Op. 19, No. 1
Ibolyka Zilzer & M. Gurlitt, PD-22860
Polonaise Brillante, D major, Op. 4 Violin
& Piano
Jascha Heifetz & Emanuel Bay
12"—V-15813
[Bazzini: La Ronde des Lutins]
[Schubert: Impromptu, Op. 90, No. 3 on
G-DB3215]
[Grieg: Sonata No. 2, Pt. 5, on V-17613
in VM-735†]
Nathan Milstein & Leopold Mittman
(C-LFX529) 12"—C-69032D
[Concerto No. 2—Romance]
Polonaise Brillante (No. 2) A major, Op. 21
Ida Haendel & Adela Kotowska
12"—D-K1213
Romance See under Concerto No. 2, 2nd
Mvt.
Scherzo Tarantelle, Op. 16 Violin & Piano
Nathan Milstein & Artur Balsam
[Suk: Burleska] 12"—C-71498D
Jascha Heifetz, on V-8759 in VM-275†:
V-14323: G-DB2219: also in VM-856†
Yehudi Menuhin & Artur Balsam
[Schubert: Ave Maria] 12"—G-DB1788
Ida Haendel & Adela Kotowska
[Achron: Hebrew Melody] 12"—D-K1047
Walter Barylli & Otto A. Graef
12"—PD-15202
[Chopin: Nocturne, E flat major]
Souvenir de Moscou (Airs russes) Op. 6
Violin & Piano
Arnold Eidus & Colonne Orch.—Fournet
12"—G-DB11142
Staccato Study Violin & Piano
R. Ricci & L. Persinger, in VOX-196

WILBYE, John (1574-1638)
*A great Elizabethian composer who, unlike
Byrd and many others, confined himself almost
entirely to the composition of madrigals. Only
two madrigals are now available on records.*
Adieu, sweet Amaryllis 4-Voice Madrigal
Winchester Music Club, unacc.
12"—C-D40122
(in illustrations for Lecture No. 61, "The
Progress of Music," George Dyson—In-
ternational Educational Society)
Sweet honey sucking bees. 5-Voice Madrigal
London Madrigal Group 10"—V-4317
[Gibbons: Ah, dear heart]

WILLAERT, Adriano (or Adrian) (c.1480-
c.1562)
*One of the many fifteenth and sixteenth cen-
tury Flemings who dispersed themselves
throughout Europe and in so doing profoundly affected "cinquecento" musical style.
Willaert landed at St. Mark's in Venice, and is
considered the founder of the Venetian school.
Three of his famous pupils were Zarlino, the
elder Gabrieli and Cypriano da Rore. Unfortunately little of his madrigal and church music has yet appeared on records.*
Con lagrime e sospir 1536
Max Meili (t) & F. Worshing (vihuela)
12"—G-DB5018
[Morley: It was a lover; Dowland:
Come again & Come heavy sleep]

WILLE, Rudolf

KOENIGSBALLADE
Ewig muss ich Dein gedenken
Euren König will ich preisen
Helge Roswaenge (t) 12"—G-DB4623

WILLIAMS, Ralph Vaughan
See Vaughan Williams, Ralph

WIREN, Dag (1905-   )
A contemporary Swedish composer of French training.

Quartet No. 2, Op. 9
Kyndel String Quartet
3   12"—G-DB11007 & DB11010/1
[Stenhammer: Serenade, C major, Pt. 1
Garaguly Quartet]

Serenade for Orchestra
—March only
Unspecified Orchestra   12"—T-E19010
[Larsson: Pastoral Suite, Pt. 3]

WOLF, Hugo (1860-1903)
A very substantial portion of Hugo Wolf's lieder have been recorded in the six volumes (Volume I has been out of print since the late 1930's) of the H.M.V. Society, and this portion is augmented by many single records as listed below. There are those who, in their enthusiasm, clamor for more, but it is only fair to observe that if other equally important composers were at all as well represented on records as Hugo Wolf, there would be little need for the frequent critical editorial comments inserted in this volume.

Italienische Serenade, G major String
Quartet or Chamber Orchestra
Eng. **Italian Serenade**
Budapest Quartet   10"—G-DA1304
—Orchestral Version Edited by Reger
Philharmonia Orch.—Süsskind
12"—C-DX1236
German Opera House Orch.—Lehmann
12"—O-3604
Leipzig Gewandhaus Chamber Orch.—
Schmitz   12"—PD-67656
German Philharmonic Orch., Prague—
Keilberth   12"—T-E3158

SONGS (LIEDER) In German
Collections: The Hugo Wolf Society
NOTE: *Formed in 1931 by His Master's Voice, each volume contains six twelve inch records. Single records are not obtainable separately, and volume I, having been oversubscribed, is no longer available.*

Volume I (19 Songs)
(Mörike, Eichendorff, Paul Heyse: Spanish & Italian Song Books)
Begegnung; Lied vom Winde; Auf einer Wanderung; Rat einer Alten; Heimweh; Gesang Weylas; Das verlassene Mägdlein; Ständchen; Herr was trägt der Boden hier; Auch kleine Dinge; Und steht ihr früh am Morgen auf; Ihr jungen Leute; Du denkst mit einem Fädchen; Nein, junger Herr; In dem Schatten meiner Locken; Die ihr schwebet; Ach des Knaben Augen; Nun wandre Maria; Wenn du zu den Blumen gehst.
Elena Gerhardt (s) & C. van Bos (pf)

Volume II (16 Goethe Songs)
Prometheus; Ganymed; Beherzigung; 3 Harfenspieler Lieder (Wer sich der Einsamkeit ergibt; An die Türen will ich schleichen; Wer nie sein Brot mit Tränen ass); Cophtisches Lied II; Anakreons Grab; Epiphanias; Genialisch Treiben; Der Rattenfänger; Die Spröde; Die Bekehrte; Gleich und gleich; Blumengruss; Frühling übers Jahr.
Freidrich Schorr (b) & London Symphony Orch.
John McCormack (t) & Edwin Schneider (pf)
Herbert Janssen (b), Gerhard Hüsch (b) & Alexandre Trianti (s) with C. van Bos (pf)

Volume III (17 Songs) (Goethe, Mörike, Michelangelo, Eichendorff: Spanish & Italian Song Books)
Wohl denk' ich oft; Alles endet; Fühlt meine Seele; Um Mitternacht; Grenzen der Menschheit; Erstes Liebeslied eines Mädchens; Nixe Binsefuss; Mogen alle bosen Zungen; Köpfchen; Klinge, klinge mein Pandero; Bitt' ihn o Mutter; Wer rief dich denn; Mein Liebster hat zu Tische mich geladen; Schweig' einmal still; Benedeit die sel'ge Mutter; Der Mond hat eine schwere Klag' erhoben, Schon streckt' ich aus im Bett.
Alexander Kipnis (bs), Alexandra Trianti (s), Gerhard Hüsch (b) with C. van Bos (pf)

Volume IV (30 "Italiensches Liederbuch") (Paul Heyse)
Was soll der Zorn; Ich esse nun mein Brot; Wie soll ich fröhlich sein; Wie lange schon war immer mein Verlangen; Du sagst mir; Ich liess mir sagen; Wohl kenn' ich Euern Stand; Man sagt mir; Wenn du, mein Liebster; Mein Liebster singt am Haus; O wär' dein Haus durchsichtig; Gesegnet sei das Grün; Mir ward gesagt; Mein Liebster ist so klein; Ich hab' in Penna; Gesegnet sei durch den die Welt entstand; Ihr seid die Allerschönste; Hoffärtig seid ihr; Dass doch gemalt all' deine Reize; Und willst du deinen Liebsten sterben sehen; Wenn du mich mit den Augen streifst; Heut' Nacht erhob' ich mich; Ein Ständchen Euch zu bringen; Nun lass uns Frieden schliessen; Wir haben beide lange Zeit geschwiegen; Geselle woll'n wir uns in Kutten hüllen; Heb' auf dein blondes Haupt; Sterb' ich; Wie viele Zeit verlor' ich; Was für ein Lied
Elisabeth Rethberg (s) & C. van Bos (pf)
Ria Ginster (s) & Michael Raucheisen (pf)
Gerhard Hüsch (b) & Hanns Udo Müller (pf)
Alexander Kipnis (bs) & C. van Bos (pf)

Volume V (20 Songs) (Goethe, Eichendorff, Heyse, Mörike, Keller, and Schaffel)
Mühvoll komm' ich; Auf dem grünen Balkon; Triebe nur; Trau' nicht der Liebe; Sie blasen zum Abmarsch; Biterolf; Seufzer; Gebet; Auf ein altes Bild; An die Geliebte; Verborgenheit; Dank'

es o Seele; Bei einer Trauung; Ein
Stündlein wohl vor Tag; Elfenlied; Wie
glänzt der helle Mond; Cophtisches Lied
I; Der Musikant; Der Soldat I; Der
Schreckenberger
Elisabeth Rethberg (s), Gerhard Hüsch
(b), Ria Ginster (s), Herbert Janssen
(b) & Alexander Kipnis (bs) with pf.
acc.

Volume VI (16 Songs) (Mörike, Rob Rein-
ick, Goethe, Heyse, Geibel, Just, Kerner
& Spanish Song Book)
Der Feuerreiter; Gesellenlied; Mignon I
—Heiss mich nicht reden; Mignon III—
So lasst mich scheinen; Neue Liebe;
Storchenbotschaft; An den Schlaf; Lebe
wohl; Ach, im Maien war's; Herz, ver-
zage nicht geschwind; Dereinst, dereinst;
Alle gingen, Herz, zur Ruh'; Tief im
Herzen; Komm, O Tod; Zur Ruh', zur
Ruh'; Wiegenlied im Sommer.
Helge Roswaenge (t) & Gerald Moore
(pf) Marta Fuchs (s) with Gerald Moore
(pf) & Michael Raucheisen (pf)
Karl Erb (t) & Gerald Moore (pf)
Herbert Janssen (b) & Gerald Moore (pf)
Tiana Lemnitz (s) & Michael Rauch-
eisen (pf)

Collection: (5) Songs
Benedeit die Sel'ge Mutter; Der Jäger;
Frage und Antwort; Jägerlied; Fussreise
Paul Matthen (b) & Bertha Melnick (pf)
2   12″—Hargail-MW-HN800

Individual Songs In German

Abschied (Mörike)
Heinrich Schlusnus (b) & pf. acc.
[Anakreons Grab]   10″—PD-30010

Ach des Knaben Augen (Spanisches Liederbuch)
Elena Gerhardt in Society Set I (unobtainable)

Ach, im Maien war's (Spanisches Lieder-
buch)
Karl Erb, in Society Set VI
Lore Fischer (s) & Hermann Reuter (pf)
10″—G-DA4935
[In dem Schatten meiner Locken]
Mark Raphael (b) & pf. acc. (in English)
10″—C-DB1234
[Gesegnet sei & Nachtzauber]
(in Columbia History of Music, Vol. IV:
CM-234)

Alle gingen, Herz, zur Ruh (Spanisches
Liederbuch)
Herbert Janssen, in Society Set VI

Alles endet, was entsteht (Michaelangelo)
Alexander Kipnis, in Society Set III

An den Schlaf (Mörike)
Karl Erb, in Society Set VI

An die Geliebte (Mörike)
Herbert Janssen, in Society Set V
Heinrich Schlusnus (b) & pf. acc.
[Dass doch gemalt]   10″—PD-90179

An die Türen (Goethe) (Harfenspieler Lied
No. 2)
Herbert Janssen, in Society Set II

Anakreons Grab (Goethe)
Herbert Janssen, in Society Set II
Heinrich Schlusnus (b) & Orch.—
Steeger   12″—PD-67593
[Der Rattenfänger] [Earlier recording:
PD-30010 w. Abschied]
Lotte Lehmann (s) & Erno Balogh (pf)
(in VM-292)   10″—V-1734
[In dem Schatten]

Andenken (Matthison)
Karl Erb (t) & B. Seidler-Winkler (pf)
10″—G-DA4423
[Schubert: Dass sie hier]

Auch kleine Dinge (Italienisches Liederbuch, No. 1)
Elena Gerhardt, in Society Set I (unobtainable)
Elisabeth Schumann (s) & Gerald Moore
(pf)   10″—G-DA1860
[Und willst du deinen Liebsten sterben
sehen]
Heinrich Schlusnus (b) & S. Peschko
(pf)   10″—PD-62820
[Der Gärtner & Fussreise]

Auf dem grünen Balkon (Spanisches
Liederbuch)
Gerhard Hüsch, in Society Set V

Auf ein altes Bild (Mörike)
Herbert Janssen, in Society Set V
Karl Erb (t) & B. Seidler-Winkler (pf)
[Schoeck: Nachruf]   10″—G-DA4448

Auf einer Wanderung (Mörike)
Elena Gerhardt, in Society Set I (unob-
tainable)
Karl Schmitt-Walter (b) & Ferd.
Leitner (pf)   10″—T-A2540
[Der Gärtner]

Auftrag (Mörike)
Heinrich Rehkemper (b) & pf. acc.
[Der Rattenfänger]   10″—PD-23149

Bedeckt mich mit Blumen (Spanisches
Liederbuch)
Lore Fischer (s) & Hermann Reutter
(pf)   10″—G-DA4934
[Sie blasen zum Abmarsch]

Begegnung (Mörike)
Elena Gerhardt, in Society Set I (unobtainable)

Beherzigung (Goethe)
John McCormack, in Society Set II

Bei einer Trauung (Mörike)
Herbert Janssen, in Society Set V

(Die) Bekehrte (Goethe)
Alexandre Trianti, in Society Set II
Tiana Lemnitz (s) & M. Raucheisen (pf)
[Die Spröde]   10″—G-DA4469

Benedeit die sel'ge Mutter (Italienisches
Liederbuch)
Gerhard Hüsch, in Society Set III
Paul Matthen, in Hargail MW-HN800
Karl Schmitt-Walter (b) & Ferd.
Leitner (pf)   10″—T-A2541
[Dass doch gemalt]

Biterolf (Von Schaffel: Kampfmüd' und
sonverbrannt)
Herbert Janssen, in Society Set V
Heinrich Schlusnus (b) & pf. acc.
[Tambour]   10″—PD-62678

Bitt' ihn, o Mutter (Spanisches Lieder-
buch)
Alexandre Trianti, in Society Set III
Blumengruss (Goethe)
Alexandre Trianti, in Society Set II
Erika Rokyta (s) & Noël Gallon (pf)
10″—OL-46
[Elfenlied & Wiegenlied im Sommer]
Cophtisches Lied 1 (Goethe)
Alexander Kipnis, in Society Set V
Cophtisches Lied 2 (Goethe)
Herbert Janssen, in Society Set II
Dass doch gemalt all'deine Reize wären
(Italisches Liederbuch)
Gerhard Hüsch, in Society Set IV
Karl Schmitt-Walter (b) & Ferd. Leitner
(pf) 10″—T-A2541
[Benedeit die sel'ge Mutter]
Heinrich Schlusnus (b) & pf. acc.
[An die Geliebte] 10″—PD-90179
[Frühling übers Jahr, on PD-62799]
Denk' es, o Seele (Mörike)
Herbert Janssen, in Society Set V
Dereinst, dereinst, Gedanke mein (Span-
isches Liederbuch)
Herbert Janssen, in Society Set VI
Die ihr schwebet um diese Palmen (Span-
isches Liederbuch)
Elena Gerhardt, in Society Set I (unob-
tainable)
Du denkst mit einem Fädchen (Italienisches
Liederbuch)
Elena Gerhardt, in Society Set I (unob-
tainable)
Lotte Lehmann (s) & Erno Balogh (pf)
(in VM-419) 10″—V-1860
[Der Gärtner & Storchenbotschaft]
Du milchjunger Knabe (Keller)
Elena Gerhardt, in Society Set I (unob-
tainable)
Du sagst mir, dass ich keine Fürstin sei
(Italienisches Liederbuch)
Elisabeth Rethberg, in Society Set IV
Elfenlied (Mörike: Bei Nacht im Dorf)
Ria Ginster, in Society Set V
Erika Rokyta (s) & Noël Gallon (pf)
10″—OL-46
[Blumengruss & Wiegenlied im
Sommer]
Petre Monteneau (t) & Favoretto (pf)
12″—CET-PE128
[Der Gärtner & Brahms: Feldeinsam-
keit]
Epiphanias (Goethe: Die heiligen drei
Könige)
Gerhard Hüsch, in Society Set II
Heinrich Schlusnus (b) & pf. acc.
12″—PD-67254
[Brahms: Wie bist du, meine Königin?]
Er ist's (Mörike) (Frühling lässt sein
blaues Band)
Heinrich Schlusnus (b) & Franz Rupp
(pf) 10″—PD-62655
[Verschwiegene Liebe]
Erstes Liebeslied eines Mädchens
(Mörike)
Alexandre Trianti, in Society Set III

(Der) Feuerreiter (Mörike)
Helge Roswaenge, in Society Set VI
Heinrich Rehkemper (b) & M. Rau-
chiesen (pf) 12″—PD-27186
[Storchenbotschaft]
Frage und Antwort (Mörike)
Paul Matthen, in Hargail-MW-HN801
(Der) Freund (Eichendorff) (Wer auf den
Wogen)
Hans Hermann Nissen (b) & pf. acc.
[Fussreise] 10″—G-DA4458
Frohe Botschaft (Reinick)
Karl Erb (t) & B. Seidler-Winkler (pf)
10″—G-DA4420
[Schubert: Lied im grünen]
Frühling übers Jahr (Goethe)
Alexandre Trianti, in Society Set II
Heinrich Schlusnus (b) & Franz Rupp
(pf) 12″—PD-90203
[Der Schreckenberger]
[Dass doch gemalt on PD-62799]
Fühlt meine Seele (Michelangelo)
Alexander Kipnis, in Society Set III
Fussreise (Mörike) (Am frischgeschnitt'nen
Wanderstab)
Heinrich Schlusnus (b) & Sebastian
Peschko (pf) 10″—PD-62820
[Auch kleine Dinge & Der Gärtner]
Paul Matthen, in Hargail-MW-HN801
Hans Hermann Nissen (b) & pf. acc.
[Der Freund] 10″—G-DA4458
Josef von Manowarda (b) & pf. acc.
[Verborgenheit] 10″—PD-23160
Paul Schoeffler (bs) & E. Lush (pf)
[Schumann: Widmung] 10″—D-M612
Ganymed (Goethe)
John McCormack, in Society Set II
(Der) Gärtner (Mörike) (Auf ihrem Leib-
rosslein)
Lotte Lehmann (s) & Erno Balogh (pf)
(in VM-419) 10″—V-1860
[Du denkst & Storchenbotschaft]
Heinrich Schlusnus (b) & S. Peschko
(pf) 10″—PD-62820
[Auch kleine Dinge & Fussreise]
Karl Schmitt-Walter (b) & Ferd.
Leitner (pf) 10″—T-A2540
[Auf einer Wanderung]
Petre Monteneau (t) & Favoretto (pf)
12″—CET-PE128
[Elfenlied & Brahms: Feldeinsamkeit]
Gebet (Mörike) (Herr sende was du willst)
Herbert Janssen, in Society Set V
Karl Erb (t) & pf. acc. 10″—G-EG3591
[Verborgenheit]
Heinrich Schlusnus (b) & S. Peschko
(pf) 10″—PD-62784
[R. Strauss: Ich trage meine Minne]
Josef von Manowarda & pf. acc.
[Gesang Weylas] 10″—PD-23159
Genialisch Treiben (Goethe)
Gerhard Hüsch, in Society Set II
Gesang Weylas (Mörike) (Du bist Orplid,
mein Land)
Elena Gerhardt, in Society Set I (unob-
tainable)
Kerstin Thorborg (c) & pf. acc.
12″—G-DB5766
[Brahms: Sappnische Ode & Schubert:
Hark, Hark, the Lark]

Karl Schmitt-Walter (b) & M. Rauch-
eisen (pf)   10″—T-A2178
[Schubert: Wanderers Nachtlied & Grieg:
Eros]
Heinrich Schlusnus (b) & pf. acc.
                             10″—PD-30009
[Brahms: Feldeinsamkeit]
Paul Schoeffler (bs) & pf. acc.
[Verborgenheit]   10″—D-M600
DUPLICATION: Josef von Manowarda,
PD-23159

Gesegnet sei das Grün (Italienisches Liederbuch)
Ria Ginster, in Society Set IV

Gesegnet sei, durch den Welt entstund
(Italienisches Liederbuch)
Gerhard Hüsch, in Society Set IV
Mark Raphael (b) & pf. acc. (in English)
                             10″—C-DB1234
[Ach, im Maien war's & Nachtzauber]
(in Columbia History of Music, Vol. IV:
CM-234)

Geselle, woll'n wir uns in Kutten hüllen?
(Italienisches Liederbuch)
Alexander Kipnis, in Society Set IV

Gesellenlied (Reinick)
Helge Roswaenge, in Society Set VI

Gleich und gleich (Goethe)
Alexandra Trianti, in Society Set II

Grenzen der Menschheit (Goethe)
Alexander Kipnis, in Society Set III

(3) Harfenspieler Lieder (Goethe)
See also under 1. Wer sich der Einsamkeit er-
gibt; 2. An die Türen will ich schleichen; 3.
Wer nie sein Brot mit Tränen ass.
Herbert Janssen, in Society Set II

Heb' auf dein blondes Haupt (Italienisches
Liederbuch)
Alexander Kipnis, in Society Set IV

Heimweh (Eichendorff) (Wär' in die
Fremde)
Heinrich Schlusnus (b) & S. Peschko
(pf)   10″—PD-62789
[R. Strauss: Heimliche Aufforderung]
Karl Schmitt-Walter   10″—T-A1946
[R. Strauss: Ständchen, Op. 17, No. 2]

Heimweh (Mörike) (Anders wird die Welt)
Elena Gerhardt, in Society Set I (unobtainable)

Herr, was trägt der Boden hier (Spanisches
Liederbuch)
Elena Gerhardt, in Society Set I (unob-
tainable)
Mark Raphael (b) & Gerald Moore (pf)
[Nun wandre, Maria]   12″—G-C3591

Herz verzage nicht geschwind (Spanisches
Liederbuch)
Karl Erb, in Society Set VI

Heut' Nacht erbhob' ich mich um Mitternacht (Italienisches Liederbuch)
Gerhard Hüsch, in Society Set IV

Hoffärtig seid Ihr, schönes Kind
(Italienisches Liederbuch)
Gerhard Hüsch, in Society Set IV

Ich esse nun mein Brot nicht trocken mehr
(Italienisches Liederbuch)
Elisabeth Rethberg, in Society Set IV

Ich hab' in Penna
(Italienisches Liederbuch)
Ria Ginster, in Society Set IV

Ich liess mir sagen
(Italienisches Liederbuch)
Elisabeth Rethberg, in Society Set IV

Ihr jungen Leute (Italienisches Liederbuch)
Elena Gerhardt, in Society Set I (unobtainable)

Ihr seid die Allerschönste (Italienisches
Liederbuch)
Gerhard Hüsch, in Society Set IV

In dem Schatten meiner Locken
(Spanisches Liederbuch)
Elena Gerhardt, in Society Set I (unob-
tainable)
Elisabeth Schumann (s) & Gerald Moore
(pf)   10″—G-DA1862
[In der Frühe & Mausfallen-sprüchlein]
Lore Fischer (s) & Hermann Reutter
(pf)   10″—G-DA4935
[Ach, in Maien war']
Lotte Lehmann (s) & Erno Balogh (pf)
         (in VM-292)   10″—V-1734
[Anakreons Grab]
Risë Stevens (ms) & H. G. Schick (pf)
                             10″—C-17297D
[Mausfallen-sprüchlein & Schumann:
Widmung]

In der Frühe (Mörike)
Elisabeth Schumann (s) & Gerald Moore
(pf)   10″—G-DA1862
[In dem Schatten meiner Locken & Maus-
fallen-sprüchlein]
Erika Rokyta (s) Noël Gallon (pf)
                             10″—OL-44
[Der Knabe und das Immelein]

(Der) Jäger (Mörike)
Paul Matthen, in Hargail-MW-HN800

Jägerlied (Mörike)
Paul Matthen, in Hargail-MW-HN800

(Die) Kleine (Eichendorff)
Tiana Lemnitz (s) & M. Raucheisen (pf)
[Nachtgruss]   10″—G-DA4491

Klinge, klinge, mein Pandero
(Spanisches Liederbuch)
Alexandre Trianti, in Society Set III

(Der) Knabe und das Immelein (Mörike)
Erika Rokyta (s) & Noël Gallon (pf)
[In der Frühe]   10″—OL-44

Komm, O Tod, von Nacht umgeben
(Spanisches Liederbuch)
Herbert Janssen, in Society Set VI

Köpfchen, Köpfchen, nicht gewimmert
(Spanisches Liederbuch)
Alexandre Trianti, in Society Set III

Lebe wohl (Mörike)
Karl Erb, in Society Set VI

Lied vom Winde (Mörike)
Elena Gerhardt, in Society Set I (unobtainable)

Man sagt mir, deine Mutter wollt' es nicht
(Italienisches Liederbuch)
Elisabeth Rethberg, in Society Set IV

Mausfallen-sprüchlein (Mörike)
Elisabeth Schumann (s) & Gerald Moore
(pf) 10″—G-DA1862
[In dem Schatten meiner Locken & In
der Frühe]
Erika Rokyta (s) & Noël Gallon (pf)
[Zitronenfalter im April] 10″—OL-45
Risë Stevens (ms) & H. G. Schick (pf)
10″—C-17297D
[In dem Schatten meiner Locken & Schu-
mann: Widmung]

Mein Liebster hat zu Tische mich geladen
(Italienisches Liederbuch)
Alexandre Trianti, in Society Set III

Mein Liebster is so klein (Italienisches
Liederbuch)
Ria Ginster, in Society Set IV

**Mein Liebster singt am Haus im Monden-
schein** (Italienisches Liederbuch)
Ria Ginster, in Society Set IV

Mignon Ballads (Goethe)

—**No. 1—Heiss mich nicht reden**
Marta Fuchs, in Society Set VI

—**No. 2—Kennst du das Land**
No recording available

—**No. 3—So lässt mich scheinen**
Marta Fuchs, in Society Set VI

Mir ward gesagt, du reisest in die Ferne
(Italienisches Liederbuch)
Ria Ginster, in Society Set IV

Mögen alle bösen Zungen
(Spanisches Liederbuch)
Alexandre Trianti, in Society Set III

(Der) Mond hat eine schwere Klag' erhoben
(Italienisches Liederbuch)
Gerhard Hüsch, in Society Set III
Elena Gerhardt (s) & Gerald Moore (pf)
(Private recording—HMV)

Mühvoll komm' ich (Spanisches Liederbuch)
Elisabeth Rethberg, in Society Set V

(Der) Musikant (Eichendorff)
Alexander Kipnis, in Society Set V

Nachtgruss
Tiana Lemnitz (s) & M. Raucheisen (pf)
[Die Kleine] 10″—G-DA4491

Nachtzauber (Eichendorff)
Mark Raphael (b) & pf. acc. (in English)
10″—C-DB1234
[Ach, im Maien & Gesegnet sei]
(in Columbia History of Music, Vol. IV:
CM-234)

Nein, junger Herr (Italienisches Liederbuch)
Elena Gerhardt, in Society Set I (unobtainable)

Neue Liebe (Mörike)
Marta Fuchs, in Society Set VI

Nixe Binsefuss (Mörike)
Alexandre Trianti, in Society Set III

Nun lass uns Frieden schliessen
(Italienisches Liederbuch)
Alexander Kipnis, in Society Set IV

Nun wandre Maria (Spanisches Liederbuch) ("Der heilige Josef singt")
Elena Gerhardt, in Society Set I (unobtainable)

Mark Raphael (b) & Gerald Moore (pf)
12″—G-C3591
[Herr, was trägt der Boden hier]
Karl Erb (t) & pf. acc. 10″—G-EG3498
[Schlafendes Jesuskind]

Nur wer die sehnsucht kennt (Goethe)
Elisabeth Höngen (c) & Hans Zipper (pf)
10″—C-LB62
[Schumann: Die Kartenlegerin]

O wär' dein Haus durchsichtig wie ein Glas
(Italienisches Liederbuch)
Ria Ginster, in Society Set IV

Prometheus (Goethe)
(*Wolf scored this song with orchestral accompaniment the year following its composition in
1889*).
Friedrich Schorr (b) & London Symphony Orch.—Heger, in Society Set II

Rat einer Alten (Mörike)
Elena Gerhardt, in Society Set I (unobtainable)

(Der) Rattenfänger (Goethe)
Gerhard Hüsch, in Society Set II
Heinrich Schlusnus (b) 12″—PD-67593
[Anakreons Grab]
Heinrich Rehkemper (b) & M. Rauch-
eisen (pf) 10″—PD-23149
[Auftrag]

St. Nepomuks Vorabend (Goethe)
Antonio Crohen Kubizki (b) & G. Con-
falonieri (pf) 10″—G-HN2187
[Schlafendes Jesuskind]

Schlafendes Jesuskind (Mörike) ("Sohn
der Jungfrau")
Karl Erb (t) & pf. acc. 10″—G-EG3498
[Nun wandre Maria]
Antonio Crohen Kubizki (b) & G. Con-
falonieri (pf) 10″—G-HN2187
[St. Nepomuks Vorabend]

**Schon streckt' ich aus im Bett die müden
Glieder** (Italienisches Liederbuch)
Gerhard Hüsch, in Society Set III

(Der) Schreckenberger (Eichendorff)
Alexander Kipnis, in Society Set V
Heinrich Schlusnus (b) & Franz Rupp
(pf) 10″—PD-90203
[Frühling über's Jahr]

**Schweig' einmal still, du garst'ger
Schwätzer dort!**
(Italienisches Liederbuch)
Alexandre Trianti, in Society Set III

Seufzer (Mörike)
Herbert Janssen, in Society Set V

Sie blasen zum Abmarsch (Spanisches
Liederbuch)
Ria Ginster, in Society Set V
Lore Fischer (s) & Hermann Reutter
(pf) 10″—G-DA4934
[Bedeckt mich mit Blumen]

(Der) Soldat I (Eichendorff)
Alexander Kipnis, in Society Set IV

(Die) Spröde (Goethe)
Alexandre Trianti, in Society Set II
Tiana Lemnitz (s) & M. Raucheisen (pf)
[Die Bekehrte] 10″—G-DA4469

Ständchen (Eichendorff)
Elena Gerhardt, in Society Set I (unobtainable)

Heinrich Schlusnus (b) & S. Peschko
(pf) 10"—PD-30028
[Storchenbotschaft]

(Ein) Ständchen Euch zu bringen
(Italienisches Liederbuch)
Gerhard Hüsch, in Society Set IV

Sterb' ich, so hüllt in Blumen meine Glieder
(Italienisches Liederbuch)
Alexander Kipnis, in Society Set IV

Storchenbotschaft (Mörike)
Marta Fuchs, in Society Set VI
Lotte Lehmann (s) Erno Balogh (pf)
(in VM-419) 10"—V-1860
[Du denkst mit einen Fädchen & Der
Gärtner]
Heinrich Schlusnus (b) & S. Peschko
(pf) 10"—PD-30028
[Ständchen]
Heinrich Rehkemper (b) & M. Rauch-
eisen (pf) 12"—PD-27186
[Der Feuerreiter]

(Ein) Stündlein wohl vor Tag (Mörike)
Ria Ginster, in Society Set V

(Der) Tambour (Mörike) (Wenn meine
Mutter hexen könnt')
Heinrich Schlusnus (b) & Franz Rupp
(pf) 10"—PD-62678
[Biterolf]

Tief im Herzen trag' ich Pein
(Spanisches Liederbuch)
Herbert Janssen, in Society Set VI

Trau' nicht der Liebe (Spanisches Liederbuch)
Ria Ginster, in Society Set V

Treibe nur mit lieben Spott (Spanisches
Liederbuch)
Gerhard Hüsch, in Society Set V

Tretet ein, hoher Krieger (Keller)
Erika Rokyta (s) & Noël Gallon (pf)
10"—OL-22
[Wie glänzt der helle Mond]

Ueber Nacht (Sturm)
Richard Tauber (t) (in English)
[Verborgenheit] 10"—P-RO20536

Um Mitternacht (Mörike)
Alexander Kipnis, in Society Set III

Und steht ihr früh em Morgen auf
(Italienisches Liederbuch)
Elena Gerhardt, in Society Set I (unob-
tainable)

Und willst du deinen Liebsten sterben sehen?
(Italienisches Liederbuch)
Gerhard Hüsch, in Society Set IV
Elena Gerhardt (s) & Gerald Moore (pf)
(Private Recording—HMV)
Elisabeth Schumann (s) & Gerald Moore
(pf) 10"—G-DA1860
[Auch kleine Dinge]

Verborgenheit (Mörike) (Lass, o Welt)
Eng. Secrecy
Herbert Janssen, in Society Set V
Paul Schoeffler (bs) & Ernest Lush (pf)
[Gesang Weylas] 10"—D-M600
Margarete Teschemacher (s) & B. Seid-
ler-Winkler (pf) 10"—G-EG6153
[Wiegenlied]
Karl Erb (t) & pf. acc. 10"—G-EG3591
[Gebet]

Richard Tauber (t) (in English)
[Ueber Nacht] 10"—P-RO20536
Mascia Predit (s) (in Italian) & G.
Favaretto (pf) 10"—G-DA5436
[A. Scarlatti: Il Clearco in Negroponti—
Adrasto's Air]
DUPLICATIONS: Leo Slezak, PD-21847;
J. von Manowarda, PD-23160

(Das) verlassene Mägdlein (Mörike)
Elena Gerhardt, in Society Set I (unob-
tainable)
DUPLICATION: Josef von Manowarda,
PD-23160

Verschwiegene Liebe (Eichendorff) (Ueber
Wipfeln und Saaten)
Heinrich Schlusnus (b) & Franz Rupp
(pf) 10"—PD-62655
[Er ist's]
DUPLICATION: Leo Slezak, PD-21847

Was für ein Lied soll dir gesungen werden
(Italienisches Liederbuch)
Alexander Kipnis, in Society Set IV

Was soll der Zorn, mein Schatz
(Italienisches Liederbuch)
Elisabeth Rethberg, in Society Set IV

**Wenn du, mein Liebster, steigst zum Him-
mel auf**
(Italienisches Liederbuch)
Elisabeth Rethberg, in Society Set IV

Wenn du mich mit den Augen streifst
(Italienisches Liederbuch)
Gerhard Hüsch, in Society Set IV

Wenn du zu den Blumen gehst (Mörike)
(Spanisches Liederbuch)
Elena Gerhardt, in Society Set I (unob-
tainable)

Wer nie sein Brot mit Tränen ass (Goethe)
(Harfenspieler Lied No. 3)
Herbert Janssen, in Society Set II

Wer rief dich denn? (Italienisches Liederbuch)
Alexandre Trianti, in Society Set III

Wer sich der Einsamkeit ergibt (Goethe)
(Harfenspieler Lied No. 1)
Herbert Janssen, in Society Set II

Wie glänzt der helle Mond (Keller)
Alexander Kipnis, in Society Set V
Erika Rokyta (s) Noël Gallon (pf)
[Tretet ein, hoher Krieger] 10"—OL-22

**Wie lange schon war immer mein Ver-
langen** (Italienisches Liederbuch)
Elisabeth Rethberg, in Society Set IV

Wie soll' ich fröhlich sein (Italienisches
Liederbuch)
Elisabeth Rethberg, in Society Set IV

Wie viele Zeit verlor' ich (Italienisches
Liederbuch)
Alexander Kipnis, in Society Set IV

Wiegenlied im Sommer (Reinick) (Vom
Berg hinauf)
Tiana Lemnitz, in Society Set VI
Margarete Teschemacher (s) & B. Seid-
ler-Winkler (pf) 10"—G-EG6153
[Verborgenheit]
Erika Rokyta (s) & Noël Gallon (pf)
[Elfenlied & Blumengruss] 10"—OL-46

Wir haben beide lange Zeit geschwiegen
(Italienisches Liederbuch)
Alexander Kipnis, in Society Set IV

Wohl denk' ich oft (Michaelangelo)
Alexander Kipnis, in Society Set III

Wohl kenn' ich Euern Stand (Italienisches Liederbuch)
Elisabeth Rethberg, in Society Set IV

Zitronenfalter im April (Mörike)
Erika Rokyta (s) & Noël Gallon (pf)
[Mausfallen-sprüchlein] 10″—OL-45

Zum neuen Jahr (Mörike)
Karl Erb (t) & B. Seidler-Winkler (pf)
10″—G-EG3499
[Zilcher: Ein gar alt frohlich]

Zur Ruh', zur Ruh' (Kerner)
Herbert Janssen, in Society Set VI

WOLF-FERRARI, Ermano (1876-1948)

An Italian operatic composer of part German parentage and a pupil of Rheinberger in Munich, Wolf-Ferrari's most successful works are those in which he borrowed old styles and treated them in the contemporary veristic manner.

OPERAS In Italian

IL CAMPIELLO
Ritornello Act III
La Scala Orch.—Marinuzzi
10″—G-DA1566
[Geminiani: Andante for Strings, Harp & Organ]

(LE) DONNE CURIOSE 3 Acts 1903
Ger. Neugierigen Frauen
Il cor nel contento Duo: Soprano & Tenor
Geraldine Farrar & Herman Jadlowker
12″—G-DK124*
[Segreto di Susanna—Il dolce idillio, Farrar & Amato]
Menuet & Furlana
Zurich Tonhalle Orch.—Wolf-Ferrari
In Prep. Swiss Decca

(I) GIOIELLI DELLA MADONNA 3 Acts 1811
Ger. Der Schmuck der Madonna
Eng. The Jewels of the Madonna
Individual Excerpts

ACT II
Intermezzo Orchestra (Intermezzo No. 1)
Minneapolis Symphony Orch.—Ormandy
10″—V-1742
National Symphony Orch.—Boyd Neel
[Intermezzo No. 2] 12″—D-K1290
London Symphony Orch.—Bellezza
[Intermezzo No. 2] 12″—G-C3673
German Opera House Orch.—Lutze
[Intermezzo No. 2] 12″—T-E3143
DUPLICATIONS: Milan Symphony Orch.—Molajoli, C-GQX10744: C-68372D; Victor Symphony Orch.—Bourdon, G-S10239

Serenata: Aprila, o bella Baritone
Giuseppe De Luca 10″—G-DA1169
[Verdi: Trovatore—Per me ora fatale]

ACT III
Intermezzo, G major Orchestra (Intermezzo No. 2)
London Symphony—Bellezza
[Intermezzo No. 1] 12″—G-C3673

National Symphony Orch.—Boyd Neel
[Intermezzo No. 1] 12″—D-K1290
Minneapolis Symphony—Ormandy
10″—V-1743
[Delibes: Coppelia—Valse & Entr'acte]
Milan Symphony—Molapoli
(C-GQX10755) 12″—C-68372D
[Intermezzo No. 1]
Zurich Tonhalle Orch.—Wolf-Ferrari
In Prep. Swiss Decca
DUPLICATIONS: Victor Symphony—Bourdon, G-S10239; Covent Garden Orch.—Bellezza, G-S10224; German Opera House Orch.—Lutze, T-E3143

Dance of the Camorristi Orchestra
Boston "Pops" Orch.—Fiedler
[Lecuona: Malagueña] 10″—V-4330
Carnegie "Pops" Orch.—Abravanel
12″—C-7566M
[Strauss: Tritsch-Tratsch Polka & Rimsky-Korsakov: Flight of the Bumble Bee]

(I) QUARTRO RUSTEGHI 1906
Ger. Vier Grobiane

Intermezzo Orchestra
La Scala Orch.—Antonicelli
(G-GW1242) 10″—G-HN2112
[Segretto di Susanna—Overture]
Milan Symphony Orch.—Molajoli
12″—C-GQX10754
[Zandonai: Giulietta e Romeo—La Cavalcata]
Zurich Tonhalle Orch.—Wolf-Ferrari
In Prep. Swiss Decca

Lucretia è un bel nome Tenor
Ferrucio Tagliavini
12″—CET-BB25056
[Cilea: L'Arlesiana—E la solita storia]

(IL) SEGRETO DI SUSANNA 1 Act 1909
Eng. The Secret of Susanna
Ger. Susannens Geheimnis

Overture Orchestra
N. Y. Philharmonic-Symphony Orch.—Rodzinski (in CX-281†) 12″—C-12581D
[Liszt: Mefisto Waltz, Pt. 3]
Boston "Pops" Orch.—Fiedler
10″—V-4412
[Dvořák: Slavonic Dance No. 15, C major]
[Rimsky-Korsakov: Coq d'or—Cortège, on G-B8633: G-EG6176]
DUPLICATIONS: La Scala Orch.—Antonicelli, G-HN2112: G-GW1242; Theater des Volkes Orch.—Kretzschmar, C-DW4889; EIAR Symphony Orch.—Molinari, CET-PP60010; Zurich Tonhalle Orch.—Wolf-Ferrari, In Prep., Swiss Decca

Intermezzo
Theater des Volkes Orch.—Kurt Kretzschmar 10″—C-DW4889
[Overture]

SLY 3 Acts 1928
Non sono un buffone
Canzone dell 'orso Tenor
Francesco Merli 12″—C-GQX10244

YRADIER, Sebastian (1809-1865)
A Spanish composer, best known for the song listed below.
La Paloma (Habañera)
In Spanish: A. Galli-Curci, V-1338:
G-DA1002; G-DA5400; E. de Gogorza,
V-1141; Rosita Serrano, T-A2563:
U-B18117; Ninon Vallin, O-166669;
Marcel Wittrisch, G-EG7053
In German: R. Tauber, P-RO20247; P.
Anders, T-A2093
In English: R. Tauber, P-RO20514
Arr. Orch. Boston "Pops" Orch.—Fiedler,
V-4434
See also current catalogues

ZANDONAI, Riccardo (1883-   )
A contemporary Italian operatic composer.
Colombina—Overture on a popular Venetian theme
Berlin Radio Orch.—Schultz-Dornburg
12"—G-EH1321
EIAR Symphony Orch.—Tansini
12"—CET-CB20256
OPERAS In Italian
(I) CAVALIERI DI EKEBU 1925
Vocal & Orchestral Selections (In Swedish)
Kerstin Thorborg (s), D. Hertzberg (s),
I. Bjorck (s) E. Beyron (t)
3 10"— & 2 12"—O-D4730/1; O-D4737;
O-D6029/30
Orchestral Selections
Symphony Orch.—Grevillius, O-D6028

FRANCESCA DA RIMINI 4 Acts 1914
(Gabriele d'Annunzio)
Orchestral Selections (Fantasia) Arr. Tavan
La Scala Orch.—Sabajno 12"—G-S10288
Paolo datemi pace Sop.
Iris Adami-Corradetti 10"—CET-TI7014
[Verdi: Rigoletto—Tutte le feste,
Pagliughi]
Duo (Gianciotto & Malatestino) Act IV
Mariano Stabile & G. Nessi
12"—C-CQX16504
GIULIANO 1928
(La) Dolce madre che mi benedisse Tenor
F. Merli   12"—C-GQX10243
[La nenia del vago, Pampanini]
Duetto d'amore Soprano & Tenor
Rosetta Pampanini & F. Merli
(C-LWX345)   12"—C-GQX10238
(La) Nenia de vago usignolo Soprano
R. Pampanini   12"—C-GQX10243
[La dolce madre, Merli]

GIULIETTA E ROMEO 1921 Eng. **Juliet and Romeo**
Episodio sinfonico Orchestra
Il gioco del Torchio, Act II
Cavalcata di Romeo (Intermezzo)
Eng. Torch Dance & Romeo's Ride
La Scala Orch.—Bellezza 12"—G-S10141
EIAR Symphony Orch.—Erede
12"—CET-CB20361
—**Cavalcata only**
Royal Opera House Orch., Covent
Garden—Patanè   12"—C-DX1472
[Puccini: Manon Lescaut—Intermezzo]

Milan Symphony Orch.—Molajoli
12"—C-GQX10754
[Wolf-Ferrari: Quattro Rusteghi—Inter-
mezzo, Act II]
Giulietta, son io Tenor
M. Fleta   12"—G-DB524*
[Bizet: Carmen—Air de la fleur]

(LA) VIA DELLA FINESTRA
Tressone (Popular Tuscan Dance) Or-
chestra
EIAR Symphony Orch.—Schuricht
12"—CET-BB25092
[Bruch: Ulysses—Prelude]
Serenata Medioevale 'Cello & Orch.
E. Martinenghi & La Scala Orch.—
Schuricht   2 12"—G-DB5401/2
[Rezniček: Donna Diana—Overture]

ZELLER, Karl (1842-1898)
An Austrian composer of operettas.

OPERETTAS In German
(DER) KELLERMEISTER
Lass dir Zeit Tenor
Franz Völker   12"—PD-19908
[Vogelhändler—Wie mein Ahn'l]
Karl Schmitt-Walter   12"—T-E2251
[Abt: Gute Nacht, du mein herziges
Kind]

(DER) OBERSTEIGER 1894
Vocal & Orchestral Selections
Else Kochhann & Helge Roswaenge with
Orch.—Melichar   12"—PD-27195
Orchestral Selections (Fantasias)
Marek Weber Orch., G-EH267; Berlin
State Opera Orch.—Melichar, PD-23315
Sei nicht bös' (Wo sie war, die Müllerin)
Eng.**Don't be cross**
Elisabeth Schumann (s)   10"—G-E552
[Vogenhändler—Wie mein Ahn'l]
Karl Schmitt-Walter (b)
10"—T-A10012
[Vogelhändler—Wie mein Ahn'l]
Peter Anders (t)   10"—T-A2546
[Kunneke: Der Vetter aus Dingsda—Ich
bin nur]
DUPLICATIONS: Julius Patzak, PD-
23922
In English: R. Tauber, P-RO20477

(DER) VOGELHAENDLER 1891
Eng. **The Bird Catcher**
Vocal & Orchestral Selections
Erna Berger (s), Julius Patzak (t),
with Chorus & Orch.—Melichar
10"—PD-10248
Anita Gura (s), Anna Frind (s), Willy
Wortle (t), with Chorus & Orch.—Reuss
12"—T-E1614
Soloists, Chorus & Orch., G-FKX33
Orchestral Selections
Symphony Orch.—Melichar, PD-10248:
PD-25100; P. Godwin Orch., PD-19288;
F. Kauffmann Orch., G-EH117:
G-S10385
Ich bin die Christel von der Post
Elisabeth Reichelt   10"—G-EG3972
[Millöcker: Gasparone-Tarantella]

Als geblüht der Kirschenbaum
Hildegard Erdmann (s) with Chorus &
Orch. 10"—G-EG7184
[Lehar: Die lustige Witwe-Viljalied]

Schenkt man sich Rosen in Tirol, Act I
Ensemble
Walther Ludwig (t) & Lilli Claus (s)
with Berlin State Opera Chorus & Orch.
12"—PD-15338
[Lehar: Paganini—Niemand liebt dich]
DUPLICATIONS: Richard Sengeleitner
(t), PD-10599; Louis Graveure, PD-
10474; Else Kochhann, E. Bassth, I.
Eisinger, F. Völker, etc., PD-27068

Wie mein Ahn'l zwanzig Jah'r Eng. **Night-
ingale Song**
Elisabeth Schumann (s) 10"—G-E552
[Obersteiger—Sei nicht bös']
Karl Schmitt-Walter (b) 10"—T-A10012
[Obersteiger—Sei nicht bös']
DUPLICATIONS: U. Berner, T-A2547;
J. Patzak, PD-23922; Franz Völker, PD-
19908
In Italian: Fiore (t) & Ferlito (s),
G-GW464

ZICH, Otakar (1879-)

*A twentieth-century Czech operatic composer,
whose realistic dramas aroused a great deal of
controversy.*

At Heart Song Cycle (J. Nerudy)
Karel Leiss (t) & Orch.—Zich
2 12"—U-F50032/3

ZIEHRER, Carl Michael (1843-1922)

*An Austrian composer and conductor of light
music, Ziehrer wrote over six hundred marches
and waltzes, and over twenty operettas.*

Faschingskinder (Waltz)
Schrammel Quartet, PD-21981; Max
Schonherr Orch., G-HE2185

(DER) FREMDENFUEHRER Operetta in
German
Samt und Seide (Waltz)
Marek Weber Orch., G-EG1793:
G-HE2275; Schrammel Quartet, PD-
21919; Max Schonherr Orch., G-HE2186

(DER) LANDSTREICHER Operetta in
German
In lauschiger Nacht (Waltz)
Schrammel Quartet, PD-21981
Sei gepriesen, du lauschige Nacht Tenor
J. Patzak, PD-24326

(DER) SCHATZMEISTER
Hereinspaziert (Waltz)
Marek Weber Orch., G-EG2501; Schram-
mel Quartet, PD-21914; Max Schonherr
Orch., G-HE2184

Wiener Burger (Waltz)
Wiener Bohème Orch. Mascotte,
O-279315; Marek Weber Orch.,
G-EG1794: G-HE2276; B. Seidler-Wink-
ler & Orch., G-HE2231

Wiener Mad'ln (Waltz)
Berlin State Opera Orch.—Beutler, PD-
15360; Vienna Philharmonic Orch.—
Knappertsbusch, G-EH1299; Vienna
Philharmonic Orch.—Krauss, G-C2195;
Schrammel Quartet, PD-15104: PD-21221

Miscellaneous Medley of Ziehrer Melodies
Hans Bund Orch., T-A2001

ZIELENSKI, Nikolaus (Mikolaj) (17th century)

*A Polish church composer of the 16th and 17th
centuries, Zielenski was the leading exponent of
what may be called the Italo-Polish Renaissance style. The influence of Palestrina can be
observed in his works.*

In monte Oliveti
Per signum crucis
Motet & Madrigal Group—Opienski
(in Vol. VI) 12"—AS-53
[with Polish Choruses of the Renais-
sance]

ZIMBALIST, Efrem (1889-)

*This renowned violinist is also the composer
of a symphonic poem, a violin and piano sonata, an operetta and many small pieces for
the violin.*

String Quartet, E minor 1932
Gordon String Quartet 4 12"—SCH-6
[Kroll: Little March]

ZIPOLI, Domenico (c.1675-c.1726)

*An Italian keyboard composer and performer,
writing at a time when music was performed
interchangeably on the organ and the harpsichord.*

Elevazione
String Orch. 12"—SEMS-1154
[Pachelbel: Two Chorals—Durch Adams
fall & Von Himmel hoch]
Sarabande & Canzona
Ruggero Gerlin (harpsichord)
(in Vol. IV) 12"—AS-33
[A. Scarlatti: Toccata & Fuga, D minor]
Suite B minor—Air & Gavotte
Suite, G minor—Prelude & Giga
Guido Agosti (pf) 12"—G-AW299
Suite, G minor
—Arr. 2 Pianos Bormioli
Bormioli & Semprini 12"—CET-GP92880

COLLECTIONS

In this section are assembled the various collections which display aesthetic and historical unity. Eschewed are those collections which do not go beyond the scope of an individual composer or performer. (The former category is included in the composer section of this volume; the latter is adequately disposed of by the performer index.) Hence here is the place where the recordings of many composers, easily passed by in the main body of the Encyclopedia, can be seen listed together with other examples of a special period or field of musical endeavor. The enterprising record collector will find that a perusal of this section can expose new horizons of musical experience. All entries below are duplicated under the names of the individual composers concerned together with listings of such other examples of their music as is available on records.

As we go to press, news has come from abroad of an important addition to the historical collections of music on records. A fifty-record anthology of the music of Bohemian composers has been recorded under the artistic direction of Dr. Ladislav Vachulka. The collection contains examples dating from the eleventh to the middle of the nineteenth centuries, and includes such leading figures in western music as Johann Stamitz, Anton Reicha, Jacob Handl (Gallus), Leopold Kozeluch and Franz Anton Richter. Detailed information as to the contents and availability of this anthology will be promptly announced in *The Gramophone Shop Record Supplement*.

L'ANTHOLOGIE SONORE

Special mention must be made of the *Anthologie Sonore*, not alone because of the general musical excellence of its products, but especially because the avowed purpose of this society is to make available in permanent form the music that is almost always by-passed by the major recording companies, and which similarly is almost never heard in the concerts of symphony orchestras, quartets, and soloists. The attempt is made—and happily, it is a continuing process—to record with the originally intended scoring and proportions, representative examples of the music of all periods of western culture. In the difficult task of selecting the best possible works and transferring them to records, the directors of the *Anthologie Sonore* have been both wise and fortunate in obtaining, at its inception in 1933, the services of Dr. Curt Sachs as artistic director. Other scholars have assumed this responsibility since Dr. Sachs came to the United States, but all of these gentlemen stand as a comforting guarantee of the meticulous fidelity of these recordings to the intentions of the composer and to the historical period to which he belongs. Thus the *Anthologie Sonore* represents a unique kind of recording enterprise in which an ideal, but all too rare, team work is maintained between the executives and technicians of a recording society, the artist, and the scholar—all uniting in the service of the composer and his music.

To date the *Anthologie Sonore* has recorded at Paris, France, over thirteen volumes of records, each containing, as indicated below, ten twelve-inch records. In the United States, these records are manufactured by the sole American representative, *The Gramophone Shop*, and are available either singly or by volume. Each volume contains carefully written program notes by eminent authorities such as Dr. Sachs. Universally recognized by educators as indispensable to any school music library, the *Anthologie Sonore* has found its way into the homes of discriminating music lovers everywhere.

VOLUME I

Italian Ballades and Religious Songs of the 14th Century. Vincenzo da Rimini: Ita se n'era; Giovanni da Cascia: Io son un pellegrin: Anon.: Lauda de Noel (Gloria in cielo); Bartolomeo Brolo: O celestial lume.
Max Meili (t) & Fr. Seidersbeck (viol)   **AS-1**

German Municipal Music of the Late 17th Century. Johann Pezel (1639-1694); Fünffstimmigte blasende Musik—Intrade, Allemande, Courante, Allemande, Gigue.
E. Foveau, A. Adriano, H. Couillaud, A. Lafosse, R. Tudesq (brass ensemble)   **AS-2**

Franco-Flemish Chansons of the 15th Century. Heinrich Isaac: Zwischen Berg; Guillaume Dufay: Pourrai-je & Le jour s'endort; Jan Okeghem: Ma Maîtresse.

Max Meili (t) in German, with Jan Merry (fl), Fr. Seidersbeck (viol), & A. Lafosse (tromb) **AS-3**

Italian Organ Music of the 16th and 17th Centuries. Giovanni Gabrieli (1557-1613): Ricercare in the Tenth Tone & Girolamo Frescobaldi (1583-1643): Toccata for the Elevation.

Marcel Dupré (organ) **AS-4**

Johann Kuhnau (1660-1722): Biblical Sonata for Clavichord (1700), "The Combat between David and Goliath."

Erwin Bodky (clavichord) **AS-5**

French Dances of the 16th Century. Bassedanse, Toudrion, Allemande, Pavane-Gailliard-Pavane, Branle simple, Branle double, Branle de Bourgogne, Branle de Champagne.

String Orch. (Vls., Vlas., Gambas, Basses) —Curt Sachs **AS-6**

Clément Jannequin (1st half of 16th Century): Le Chant des Oyseaux.

La Chanterie de la Renaissance Française (unacc. chorus in French)—Henry Expert **AS-7**

French Harpsichord Music of Couperin's Time. Jean Nicolas Geoffroy (c. 1700): Tombeau en forme d'Allemande & Antoine Dornel (c.1685-1765): Le Pendant d'Oreille & La Noce d'Auteuil.

Pauline Aubert (harpsichord) **AS-8**

Michel Blavet (1700-1768); Sonata (Flute & Harpsichord) No. 2, "La Vibray"

Marcel Moyse (fl) & Pauline Aubert (harpsichord) **AS-9**

German Organ Music of the 17th Century. Johann Pachelbel (1653-1706): Chorale-Prelude "Vater Unser" & Samuel Scheidt (1587-1654): Chorale-Paraphrase "Credo."

Marcel Dupré (organ) **AS-10**

VOLUME II

George Frederic Handel (1685-1759): Sonata (Oboe & Basso Continuo) in E major, Op. 1, No. 15.

Louis Gromer (ob), Marcelle de Lacour (harpsichord), Etienne Pasquier (vlc) **AS-11**

The Huguenot Psalter (16th Century). Claude Goudimel (1505-1572): Psalm 25 (2 versions) & Psalm 19; Claude Le Jeune (1528-1600): Psalm 42 & Psalm 69.

Vocal Quartet & Quintet—Henry Expert **AS-12**

François Couperin (1668-1773): "Concert Royal" No. 2.

Ensemble of Viols & Harpsichord—Curt Sachs **AS-13**

English Virginalists (c.1600). William Byrd (1542/3-1623): The Bells; Giles Farnaby (c.1560-1600): The New Sa-Hoo & A Toye; Martin Peerson (c.1580-1650/1): The Fall of the Leafe.

Pauline Aubert (virginals) **AS-14**

French Chansons of the 16th Century. Garnier: Resveillez-moy; Gentian: La loy d'honneur; Claudin de Sermisy: En entrant dans ung jardin; Jachet van Berchem: Jehan de Lagny

& Que feu craintif; René: Gros Jehan menoit hors de Paris.

Marcelle Gérar (s) in French, with Viols, Flutes & Guitar **AS-15**

Dances of the Middle Ages (13th & 14th Centuries). English Dance, French Dance, English "Stantipes," French "Estampie," Italian "Ballo"—"Il lamento di Tristano."

Crunelle (piccolo), Debondue (musette), Clayette (tambour) **AS-16**

Spanish Romances & Vilancicos of the 16th Century. Luis Milan: Durandarte; Miguel de Fuenllana: Paseabase el Rey moro; Juan Vasquez: Vos me matasteis; Diego Pisador: A las armas moriscote.

Maria Cid (s) in Spanish & Emilio Pujol (vihuela) **AS-17**

French Troubadours and German Minnesänger (12th & 13th Centuries). Blondel de Nesles: A l'entrant d'esté; Perrin d'Agincourt: Quand voi an la fin d'estey; Richard Coeur-de-Lion: Ja nuns hons pris; Walther von der Vogelweide: Kreusfährerlier (1228); Meister Rumelant: Ob aller mynne.

Max Meili (t) in French & German & Fr. Seidersbeck (viol) **AS-18**

Anonymous (Second Half of the 17th Century): Sonata (Violin, Viole d'Amour & Bass).

Ensemble of Viols & Harpsichord—Curt Sachs **AS-19**

Jean Baptiste Lully (1632-1687) Opera Airs. Armide—Act II: Air de Renaud ("Plus j'observe ces lieux"); Persée—Act III: Récit. & Air de Méduse ("J'ay perdu la beauté" & "Je porte l'épouvante").

Yves Tinayre (b) in French; Lina Falk (c) in French; both with String Orch.—Alexander Cellier **AS-20**

VOLUME III

Italian Monodies c. 1625. Claudio Monteverdi (1567-1643): Ohimè, ch'io cado; Domenico Manzoli: Quando tu mi guardi & Se vedeste le piaghe.

Max Meili (t) in Italian, Ruggero Gerlin (harpsichord) & A. Mosser (vlc) **AS-21**

Henry Purcell (1658/9-1695): The Golden Sonata (2 Violins) in F major

Jean Pasquier & P. Ferret (vls), Ruggero Gerlin (harpsichord) & Etienne Pasquier (vlc) **AS-22**

Johann Sebastian Bach (1685-1750): Cantata No. 189, "Meine Seele rühmt und preist."

Max Meili (t) in German, L. Moyse (fl), L. Gromer (ob), J. Pasquier (vl), R. Gerlin (harpsichord) & A. Mosser (vlc) **AS-23**

Karl Philipp Emanuel Bach (1714-1750): Abschied von meinem Silbermannischen Claviere in einem Rondeau; Johann Sebastian Bach: Five Pieces for the Clavichord—Menuet, Polonaise, Menuet, March, Chorale.

Erwin Bodky (clavichord) **AS-24**

Giovanni Gabrieli (1557-c.1612): Music for Brass Instruments—Sonata pian e forte & 6-part Canzona.

Ensemble of Cornets, Trombones, Violins & Violas—Curt Sachs **AS-25**

Georg Phillip Teleman (1681-1767): Quartet in E minor (from the "Tafelmusik").

Jean Pasquier (vl), Marcel Moyse (fl), Etienne Pasquier (vlc), Ruggero Gerlin (harpsichord)   AS-26
Johannes Brasart: O Flos Flagrans
Lina Dauby (c) & viols—S. Cape
Instrumental Music c.1500. Pierre de la Rue: Autant en emporte le vent & Jakob Obrecht: Tsat een meskin.
"La Société Pro Musica Antiqua" (Ensemble of Mediaeval Viols, Lute, Mediaeval Harp & Flutes) of Brussels—Safford Cape AS-27
Heinrich Schütz (1586-1672); Drei Geistliche Konzerte—Psalm 40, "Eile, mich, Gott, zu erretten."
Max Meili (t)
—Psalm 51, "Schaffe in mir, Gott."
Mme. Suter-Moser (s) & Max Meili
—Psalm 111, "Die Furcht des Herren."
Max Meili & Yvon Le Marc' Hadour (b). All with organ accompaniment by Alexander Cellier   AS-28
Agostino Steffani (1654-1728): Duo "Occhi perchè piangete."
J. Peretti (s), M. Vhita (c) in Italian & Ruggero Gerlin (harpsichord)   AS-29
Jean Philippe Rameau (1683-1764): Fifth "Pièce de Clavecin en Concert"—La Forqueray, La Cupis & La Marais.
Jean Pasquier (vl), Eve Heinitz (viola da gamba), Pauline Aubert (harpsichord)
AS-30

VOLUME IV

Guillaume de Machault (c.1300-1377): Credo, Sanctus, Agnus Dei & Ite Missa Est from the Mass said to have been composed for the Coronation of Charles V (1364).
Les Paraphonistes de St.-Jean-des-Matines (Chorus in Latin) & Brass Ensemble—Guillaume de Van.   AS-31/2
Italian Harpsichord Music after 1700. Alessandro Scarlatti (1659-1725): Toccata & Fuga in D minor; Domenico Zipoli (born c.1675): Sarabanda & Canzona.
Ruggero Gerlin (harpsichord)   AS-33
Gregorian Chant Before the Year 1000. Respond-Gradual (originally for the Festival of Saint Agatha) & Easter Alleluia.
Agop Agopian & Les Paraphonistes de St-Jean-des-Matines—Guillaume de Van AS-34
Guillaume Dufay (c.1400-1474): Mass "Se la face ay pale"—Kyrie & Anthem-Motet "Alma Redemptoris Mater"
"La Société Pro Musica Antiqua" of Brussels (Unacc. Chorus in Latin)—Safford Cape   AS-35
16th Century Court Airs and Songs. Nicolas de la Grotte: Je suis amour; Clemens non Papa: Aymer est ma vie: Anon.: Il me suffit.
M. Vhita (c) in French & H. Leeb (lute)
—16th Century Lute Music. Jean-Baptiste Besard (c.1565-c.1625): Villanelle by A. Dlugoraj; Branle gay; Les Cloches de Paris; English Dance after John Dowland.
Herman Leeb (lute)   AS-36
Antonio Vivaldi (c.1678-1783): Concerto (Violin) in D major, Op. 3, No. 9.
Jean Fournier (vl) with Orchestra & Harpsichord   AS-37
The Same Vivaldi Concerto Transcribed for Harpsichord by Johann Sebastian Bach.
Ruggero Gerlin (harpsichord)   AS-38

15th Century Rondeaux. Arnold de Lantins: puisque je voy.
Lina Dauby (c) in French, with 3 Mediaeval Viols
—Gilles Binchois: De plus en plus & Grossin de Paris: Va t'en soupir.
H. Guermant & F. Anspach (in French) with Mediaeval Viols, Lute, Little Harp & Recorder—Safford Cape   AS-39
16th Century Spanish Instrumental Music: Luis Milan: 3 Pavanas.
Emilio Pujol (vihuela).
—Diego Ortiz: Ricercada.
Van Leeuwen Boomkamp (viola da gamba) & Erwin Bodky (harpsichord)   AS-40

VOLUME V

Johann Sebastian Bach: Concerto (2 Harpsichords) in C major.
Ruggero Gerlin & Marcelle Charbonnier (harpsichords) with String Orchestra—Curt Sachs   AS-41/2
Guillaume Dufay (c.1400-1474): Rondeau, "Adieu m'amour."
Lina Dauby (c) & Frédéric Anspach (t) with 3 Mediaeval Viols
—Heinrich Isaac (c.1450-1517): Chanson, "Hélas que deuera mon cuer."
Marcus (c), Bauwens (c), Dusêche (t) with 3 Mediaeval Viols—Safford Cape
AS-43
Wolfgang Amadeus Mozart (1756-1791): Sonata (Bassoon & Violoncello) in B flat major, K. 292.
Fernand Oubradous & Etienne Pasquier
AS-44
Chansons of Jannequin & Costeley. Clément Jannequin (1st Half of 16th Century): Ce moys de may & Au joly jeu; Guillaume Costeley (c.1530-1609): Mignonne, allons voir si la rose & Allons, gay, gay bergères.
"Motet et Madrigal" Group (Unacc., in French)—Heinrich Opienski   AS-45
Evaristo Felice Dall'Abaco (1675-1742): Sonata (2 Violins & Basso Continuo) in F major, Op. 3, No. 2.
J. Fournier & J. Pasquier (vls), E. Pasquier (vlc) & Ruggero Gerlin (harpsichord) AS-46
Giovanni Pierluigi da Palestrina (c.1525-1594): Hymn "O crux ave"; Motet "Vulnerasti"; Secular Madrigals, "La cruda mia nemica" & "Alla riva del Tebro."
"Motet et Madrigal" Group (Unacc., in Latin & Italian)—Heinrich Opienski AS-47
Jean Marie Leclair (1697-1764): Trio Sonata (Flute, Gamba, Harpsichord) in D major.
Gaston Blanquart, Eva Heinitz & Marcelle de Lacour   AS-48
George Frederic Handel (1685-1759): Sonata (Viola da Gamba & Harpsichord) in C major.
Eva Heinitz & Marcelle de Lacour.   AS-49
Johann Christian Bach (1735-1782): Quintet No. 6 in D major.
G. Grunelle (fl), L. Gromer (ob), J. Fournier (vl), P. Villain (vla), P. Fournier (vlc)   AS-50

VOLUME VI

German Songs c.1500. Heinrich Finck (1455-1527): Wach auf & Ach herzigs Herz; Ludwig Senfl (c.1492-1555): Also heilig ist dieser Tag & Kling klang (Kommt her, Leute all').
Basel Chamber Choir (Unacc., in German) Paul Sacher   **AS-51**

The Orchestral Suite Toward the End of the Seventeenth Century. Johann Kaspar Ferdinand Fischer (1650-1746): Suite from "Le Journal de Printems"—Overture, March, Menuet.
String Orchestra with Harpsichord & 2 Trumpets—Curt Sachs

—Johann Rosenmüller (c.1620-1684): Suite in C major—Grave-Allegro, Ballo, Sarabanda, Correnta.
String Orchestra with Harpsichord—Curt Sachs   **AS-52**

Polish Choruses of the Renaissance. Mikolaj Gomolka (c.1539-1609): Psalm 77 "Pana ja wzywac"; Waclaw Szamotulski (c.1525-1572): Evening Prayer "Juz sje zymerska"; Mikolaj Zielenski (fl.1611): In monte Oliveti & Per signum crucis.
"Motet et Madrigal" Group (Unacc., in Polish & Latin)—Heinrich Opienski   **AS-53**

Jean Jacques Rousseau (1712-1778): Airs from the Interlude "Le Devin du Village"—J'ai perdu mon serviteur, Si des galans de la ville, Avec l'object de mes amours, Allons danser sous les ormeaux (Airs de Collette).
Martha Angelici (s) in French with Orchestral accompaniments—Curt Sachs **AS-54**

Trios for Piano, Violin & Violoncello. Franz Josef Haydn (1732-1809): Trio No. 5 in E flat major (3 sides) & Franz Xavier Richter (1709-1789): Trio No. 3 in A major—Larghetto in F sharp minor (1 side).
Jacques Février (pf), Jean Fournier (vl), Pierre Fournier (vlc)   **AS-55/6**

The Instrumental Suite at the Beginning of the Seventeenth Century. Melchior Franck (c.1573-1639): Pavana, Tanz, Intrada; & Johann Hermann Schein (1586-1630): Suite No. 14 "Banchetto Musicale" (1617)—Paduana, Gagliarda, Courante, Allemande, Tripla.
Brass Ensemble—Curt Sachs   **AS-57**

English Madrigals (c.1600). Thomas Morley (1558-1603): Since my tears; Robert Jones (fl.1597-1617): Farewell, deare love; John Dowland (1562-1626): Go, crystal tears.
"Motet et Madrigal" Group (Unacc., in English)—Heinrich Opienski   **AS-58**

The "Canon" in the Fourteenth Century—Chace and Caccia. Pierre de Molins: Ballade, "De ce que fol pense."
H. Guermant (s) in French, with Lute, Alto Viol, Tenor Flute à Bec.

—Anonymous: Chace, "Se je chant mains que ne suel."
F. Anspach & E. Jacquier (tenors) in French

—Jacopo da Bolognia: Madrigal "Fenice fu."
H. Guermant (s) & E. Jacquier (t) in Italian, with Lute & Alto Viol

—Ghirardellus: Caccia, "Tosto che L'alba."
F. Mertens & E. Jacquier (tenors) in Italian, with Trombone

(Members of "La Société Pro Musica Antiqua" of Brussels—Safford Cape)   **AS-59**

Seventeenth Century "Trauermusik." Heinrich Schütz (1585-1672): Motet, "Selig sind die Toten" & Johann Philipp Krieger (1649-1727): Cantata, "Die Gerechten werden weggerafft."
The Basel Chamber Choir (in German)—Paul Sacher (Unacc. in the Schütz Motet; with Gamba, Bassoon & Organ in the Krieger Cantata)   **AS-60**

VOLUME VII

Johann Sebastian Bach (1685-1750): Cantata No. 65: "Sie werden aus Saba alle kommen."
Max Meili (t), Basle Chamber Choir & Orchestra—Paul Sacher   **AS-61**

Music for Piano. Johann Schobert: Sonata No. 8—Allegro moderato & Jan Ladislav Dussek: Sonata No. 3, Op. 9—Allegro maestoso.
Jacques Février (pf)   **AS-62**

Ballads of the Fourteenth Century. Francesco Landino: Gram piant' agl' occhi.
H. Guermant (s), F. Anspach (t) with Alto Viol, Mediaeval Harp, Soprano Flute à bec—Safford Cape

—Matheus de Perusio: Plus onques dame n'a mercy.
Trio of Viols—Safford Cape   **AS-63**

Italian Opera and Cantatas c.1700. Francesco Rossi: Mitrane—Ah! rendimi quel core & Giovanni Battista Buononcini: Vado ben spesso.
Gaston Micheletti (t) & String Orch.—Curt Sachs   **AS-64**

Organa of the School of Notre-Dame of Paris c.1200. Leoninus: Organum duplum "Deum time."
F. Anspach (duplum), E. Jacquier & F. Mertens (organum)—Safford Cape

—Perotinus: Organum triplum "Diffusa est gratia."
F. Anspach (triplum), E. Jacquier (duplum), F. Mertens & George (organum)—Safford Cape   **AS-65**

Boccherini: Sonata No. 2 in C major for 'Cello & Piano.
Pierre Fournier (vlc) & Ruggero Gerlin (pf)   **AS-66**

Guillaume de Machault (c.1330-1377): Double Ballade "Quant Theseus."
E. Jacquier & F. Mertens (tenors) with tenor Flute à bec, Alto Viol, Lute, Tenor Viol

—Ballade "Je puis trop bien."
F. Mertens (t) with Lute, Soprano Flute à bec, Tenor Viol

—Virelai "De tout sui si confortée."
H. Guermant (s) with Mediaeval Harp (Société Pro Musica Antiqua, Brussels)—Safford Cape   **AS-67**

Johann Christian Bach (1735-1782): Sonata in E flat major.
Jacques Février (pf)   **AS-68**

Spanish Organ Music. Antonio de Cabezón: Diferencias sobre el canto del Cabellero; Fray Thomas de Sancta Maria; Clausula de octavo tono; Juan Cabanilles: Tiento.
Joseph Bonnet (organ)   **AS-69**

George Frederic Handel: Cantata—Praise of Harmony (Look down, look down, harmonious Saint).

Max Meili (t) in English, & String Orchestra—Curt Sachs, with Ruggero Gerlin (harpsichord) **AS-70**

VOLUME VIII

Little Forms of the Ars Antiqua (13th Century). Gymel-Conductus—Alleluia; Motet Sacré —A la clarte; Adam de la Halle:Rondeau— Li dous regards de ma dame; Instrumental Trio; Motet Profane; Adam de la Halle: Virelai.

La Société Pro Musica Antiqua, Brussels— Safford Cape **AS-71**

Michael Praetorious (1571-1621): Beati omnes.

Basle Chamber Choir, Max Meili (t) & 3 Trombones

—Hans Leo Hassler (1564-1612): Motet— Wenn mein Stündlein & Chorale—Mein Seel an meinem letzten End.

Basle Chamber Choir (unaccompanied)— Paul Sacher **AS-72**

Josquin des Prés (1450-1521): Stabat Mater & Kyrie from the Missa Hercules.

Les Paraphonistes de Saint-Jean-des-Matines—Guillaume de Van **AS-73**

French Violin Music at the Beginning of the 18th Century. François Francoeur: Sonata in G minor (Violin & Basso continuo) & Jean Baptiste Senaillé: Sonata in E major (Violin & Basso continuo).

J. Grabowska (vl) & Pauline Aubert (harpsichord) **AS-74**

French Organists c. 1700. Nicolas de Grigny: Plein Jeu; François Couperin: Offertoire sur les grands jeux & Sanctus.

Joseph Bonnet (organ) **AS-75**

Johann Sebastian Bach: Suite No. 6 in D major for "violoncello piccolo à cinq cordes."

Van Leeuwen Boomkamp. **AS-76**

Popular Fifteenth Century Frottole. Dal letto levava; Rusticus; Rende l'arme al fiero amore. Fifteenth Century Italian Laude. Sancta Maria; Anima Christi; Poiche.

Les Paraphonistes de Saint-Jean-des-Matines—Guillaume de Van **AS-77**

Marin Marais (1656-1728): Piece for 2 Viols (Prelude, Allemande, Sarabande, Gigue)

Eva Heinitz & M. Clerget (Violas da Gamba) & Pauline Aubert (Harpsichord) **AS-78**

Italian Songs of the Seventeenth Century. Frescobaldi: Voi partite mio sole; Miniscalchi: Non passo più soffrir & Io tento invan; Padre Ludovico Busca: Occhi belli & Bionda, bionda, Clori.

Max Meili (t) & Ruggero Gerlin (harpsichord) **AS-79**

Pentential Motets of the Fifteenth Century. Anonymous: Parce domine; Loyset Compère: Crucifige; Jacob Obrecht: 2 Versets for 3 voices—Qui propter & Et incarnatus est.

Les Paraphonistes de Saint-Jean-des-Matines—Guillaume de Van **AS-80**

VOLUME IX

Jean Philippe Rameau (1683-1764): Airs de Ballet. Marche (Hippolyte et Aricie), Air gai en rondeau (Dardanus), Tambourines (Les Indes Galantes), Menuets (Platée), Rondeau (Les Indes Galantes), Air (Platée).

Orchestra & Harpsichord—Ruggero Gerlin **AS-81**

Evolution of Italian Opera. Marc' Antonio Cesti: Il Pomo d'Oro—Air de Venus; A. M. G. Sacchini: La Nitteti—Rondo di Nitteti.

Martha Angelici (s) & Orchestra—Ruggero Gerlin

—Air d'Amagi.

Yvon Le Marc' Hadour (b) & Orchestra— Ruggero Gerlin **AS-82**

Franz Joseph Haydn:: Sonata No. 19 in D major—Adagio ma non troppo.

Ruggero Gerlin (pf) **AS-83**

Jean Joseph Mouret (1682-1738): Les Festes de Thalie—2 Airs pour les jeux et les plaisirs, Forlane, Air de Nerine.

Martha Angelici (s)

—Rigaudon, Air en Rondeau, Air de Florine.

G. Epicaste (s)

—Entrée des matelots.

Orchestra of the Société des Concerts de Versailles—Gustave Cloëz **AS-84**

Karl Stamitz (1746-1801): Quartet for Viola da Gamba, Violin, Viola & 'Cello.

Eva Heinitz (viola da gamba), J. Fournier (vl), G. Figueroa (vla), P. Fournier (vlc) **AS-85**

André Cardinal Destouches (1672-1749): Callirhoè—Overture, Air de la Dryade, 2 Airs pour les Faunes.

Martha Angelici (c)

—François Colin de Blamont (1690-1760): Cantate—Circé—2 Récits et Air.

G. Epicaste (s) & Orchestra of the Société des Concerts de Versailles—Gustave Cloëz **AS-68**

Johann Schobert (d.1767): Concerto in G major (Harpsichord & Orchestra).

Ruggero Gerlin (harpsichord) & Chamber Orchestra of the Société des Concerts de Versailles—Gustave Cloëz **AS-87/8**

The Guitar in France in the 17th Century. Francisque Corbett: Prelude, Allemande, Folie & Robert de Visée: Prelude, Sarabande, Menuet, Bourrée.

Jean Lafon (guitar) **AS-89**

Johann Pfeiffer (1697-1761): Sonata a viola da gamba e cembalo concertato.

Eva Heinitz (viola da gamba) & Ruggero Gerlin (harpsichord) **AS-90**

VOLUME X

Juggler's Music & Learned Music (13th Century). En may la rosée.

Mairy Kuhner (Mediaeval Harp)

—Motet sacré (3 voices a cappella)

F. Anspach, E. Jaquier, F. Merten—Safford Cape

Beginning of Swiss Polyphony (14th Century). Benedicamus tropé (for 2 voices) & Motet for 2 voices.

Bousquet & Rousselon

—Motet du Roman du Fauvel.

Bonté, Deniau, Rousselon—Guillaume de Van **AS-91**

Louis Couperin (1626-1661): Chaconne, Branle de Basque, Pavanne, Passacaille.
Ruggero Gerlin (harpsichord)   AS-92

Mozart: Das Lied der Trennung, K. 519; Un moto di gioia, K. 579; Ridente la calma, K. 152.
Martha Angelici (s) & Jean Hubeau (pf)   AS-93

Heinz Ignaz Franz von Biber (1644-1704): Sonata in C minor (Violin & Harpsichord).
G. Strauss (vl) & Pauline Aubert (harpsichord)   AS-94

The Piano in Italy in the 18th Century. Giovanni-Antonio Matielli: Adagio; Giovanni-Placido Rutini: Andante; Padre Giovanni-Battista Martini: Allegro.
Ruggero Gerlin (pf)   AS-95

André Campra (1660-1744): Air de Musette & Cantata—La Papillon.
Jean Planel (t) & Flute, Violin, 'Cello & Harpsichord   AS-96

John Tavener (16th Century); Quemadmodum (Instrumental piece for 6 voices); Magnificat in the 6th Tone.
Bonté, Deniau, Rousselon, Bousquet—Guillaume de Van   AS-97

Serious and Drinking Songs. Monteclair: Sombre Forests & Comme une Hyrondelle: L'Affilards: Iris; Michel de la Barre: Bien que l'amour; Louis de Lacoste: J'ay surpris l' Amour; Anon: Le bon vin chasse le chagrin; Renauld: Amis buvons jour et nuit.
Gaston Micheletti (t) & Ruggero Gerlin (harpsichord)   AS-98

Music in the Time of Saint Louis: Conductus of Saint Louis—Tranfretasse (2 voices & 2 instruments); Conductus-Deus Misertus (4 voices a cappella).
Bonté, Deniau, Rousselon, Bousquet—Guillaume de Van

—Instrumental Music of the 13th Century. 2 Melisimas; Estampie.
2 Instruments—Guillaume de Van   AS-99

Domenico Scarlatti (1685-1757): Sonatas in C major, G major, E minor, B flat major.
Ruggero Gerlin (harpsichord)   AS-100

VOLUME XI

Christoph Willibald Gluck (1714-1787): Orfeo ed Euridice—Ballet Music—Chaconne, Menuet, Airs in C major, D major, A major.
Chamber Orchestra of the Société des Concerts de Versailles—Gustave Cloëz   AS-101/2

Rameau: Pièces pour clavecin—Prélude, Les Trois Mains, Les Soupirs.
Pauline Aubert (harpsichord)   AS-103

Orlando de Lassus (c.1532-1594): Mass (Super "Le bergier et la bergière")—Sanctus & Agnus Dei; Omnia tempus habent (Motet).
Choir—Guillaume de Van   AS-104

Nicolas Clérambault (1676-1749): Cantata—Léandre et Hero.
Martha Angelici (s) with Flute, Violin, Viola da Gamba, Harpsichord   AS-105/6

Josquin des Prés (c.1450-1521): Miserere for Five Voices (Choir a cappella) & Two Chansons (Instrumental ensemble).

Les Paraphonistes de Saint-Jean-des-Matines—Guillaume de Van   AS-107/8

François Couperin: 4 Portraits—Les Vieux Seigneurs; Les Jeunes Seigneurs; La Visionnaire; La Convalescente.
Pauline Aubert (harpsichord)   AS-109

French Chansons of the 14th Century for Six Instruments.
Les Paraphonistes de Saint-Jean-des-Matines—Guillaume de Van   AS-110

VOLUME XII

Mozart: Sonata No. 40 in B flat major, K. 454 (Piano & Violin).
Jean Hubeau (pf) & Henri Merckel (vl)   AS-111/113

The Orchestra in the Operas of Lully. Cadmus et Hermione—Chaconne & Phaeton—Overture & Entrée de Danse.
Orchestra of the Société des Concerts de Versailles—Gustave Cloëz   AS-114

François Couperin (1668-1733): La Parnasse ou l' Apothéose de Corelli.
Chamber Orchestra of the Société des Concerts de Versailles—Gustave Cloëz
—Les goûts réunis: La charme—La noble fierté—L'enjouement.
Gaston Crunelle (fl), V. Clerget (Viola da gamba), Pauline Aubert (harpsichord)   AS-115/6

Haydn: Trio in D major, Op. 32
Pasquier Trio   AS-117

Mozart: Le Nozze di Figaro—No. 27, Deh! vieni, non tarder & Il Rè Pastore—No. 10, L'Amerò sarò costante.
Martha Angelici (s) & Orchestra—Francis Cébron (with Jean Pasquier, violin)   AS-118

Luigi Boccherini (1743-1805): Sixth Trio Concertant (Violin, Viola & 'Cello).
Pasquier Trio   AS-119

Italian Madrigalists. Luca Marenzio: Strider & Perchè la pioggia & Don Carlo Gesualdo: Moro lasso.
Emile Passani Chorus   AS-120

VOLUME XIII

Guillaume Dufay (c.1400-1474): Motet for Four Voices
Les Paraphonistes de Saint-Jean-des-Matines—Guillaume de Van   AS-121

Mozart: Concerto in C major, K. 299 (Flute, Harp & Orchestra)
Gaston Crunelle (fl), Pierre Jamet (harp) & Orch.—Gustave Cloëz   AS-122/5

Polyphony at the Court of Cyprus (c.1420): Conductus—Gloria for 4 Voices; Ballade—"Le point agu"—for 3 Voices.
Les Paraphonistes de Saint-Jean-des-Matines—G. de Van   AS-126

Nicolas Dalayrac (1753-1809): String Quartet, E flat major, Op. 7, No. 5.
Léon Pascal Quartet   AS-127

Jacques Mauduit (1557-1627): Psalm XLII—"Juge le droit da ma cause" & Chansonettes mesurées à l'antique—A la fonteine & Si d'une petite oeillade.
Emile Passani Choir   AS-128

Luigi Boccherini (1743-1805): String Quartet, Op. 1, No. 2.
Léon Pascal Quartet   AS-129/30

VOLUME XIV

Jan-Pieter Sweelinck (1562-1621): Canzon—"O Mensch Bewein dein sünde gross" & Choral—"Mein junger leben hat ein' end."
André Marechal (org.)   AS-131

Swiss Mountain Songs: Benedictus d'Alpe—"O lobä" & Chant de Minnesänger—"Iche sezte minen vuoz."
Max Meili (t)   AS-132

W. A. Mozart (1756-1791): Divertimento No. 2, D major, K. 131, for 2 Violins, 2 Violas, Bass, Flute, Oboe, Bassoon, & 4 Horns.
Members of the Paris Conservatory Orch.—A. Goldschmidt   AS-133/5

ALSO

Mozart: "Bastien et Bastienne"
Comic Opera in One Act 1768
Complete recording: Paul Derenne, Martha Angelici, André Monde with Paris Conservatory Orch.—Gustave Cloëz, with Pauline Aubert (harpsichord) 6 10"—AS-801/6

COLUMBIA HISTORY OF MUSIC BY EAR AND EYE

VOLUME I—CM-231

Veni Sancte Spiritus—Plainsong with Organum
Mira Lege—Plainsong with Counterpoint
                                       C-5710

Dufay: Christe Redemptor & Conditor Alme Siderum
Anonymous: Nunc Dimittis & Palestrina: Nunc Dimittis   C-5711

Palestrina: Missa Papae Marcelli—Sanctus & Hosanna
Choir—Sir Richard Terry

Byrd: Earl of Salisbury—Pavane & Galliard for Virginals   C-5712

Bull: King's Hunt for Virginals
Farnaby: His Toye; His Dreame; His Rest—for Virginals
Rudolph Dolmetsch   C-5713

Norcombe: Divisions on a Ground—for Viola da Gamba & Lute
Rudolph & Arnold Dolmetsch

Weelkes: Fantasy for a Chest of Six Viols
Arnold, Cecile, Nathalie, Carl, Mabel & Rudolph Dolmetsch   C-5714

Dowland: Awake, Sweet Love—Ayre
Cecile Dolmetsch (s) & Arnold & Rudolph Dolmetsch (viol & lute)

Sumer is i-Cumen In   C-5715
Pilkington: Rest, Sweet Nymphs—Ayre
Morley: Sing we and Chant it—Ayre   C-5716
Weelkes: As Vesta was Descending
Gibbons: The Silver Swan & Farmer: Fair Phyllis
St. George's Singers—Rev. Dr. E. H. Fellowes   C-5717

VOLUME II—CM-232

Monteverdi: Oblivion Soave
Doris Owens (c) (in English) & Frederic Jackson (harpsichord)

Purcell: Rejoice in the Lord Alway
Bach Cantata Club of London—Kennedy Scott   C-DB500

Corelli: Violin Sonata XII—"La Follia"
Y. Bratza (vl) & Frederic Jackson (harpsichord)   C-DB501

Purcell: First Harpsichord Suite, G major
Handel: Harpsichord Suite VIII—Allemande & Courante
Rudolph Dolmetsch (harpsichord) C-DB502

Handel: Atalanta—Come alla tortorella langue
Doris Owens (c) (in English)
Solomon—May no Rash Intruder ("Nightingale Chorus")
Bach Cantata Club of London—Kennedy Scott   C-DB503

Bach: Concerto, E major, Violin & Orch.—1st Mvt.
Y. Bratza & String Orch.—Kennedy Scott   C-DB504

Bach: Wohltemperiertes Clavier—Prelude & Fugue No. 1, C major & No. 21, B flat major
Arnold Dolmetsch (clavichord)   C-DB505

Cantata No. 156, "Ich steh' mit einem Fuss im Grabe"—Sinfonia
Leon Goossens (ob) & String Orch.—Kennedy Scott

Chorales: Vater Unser in Himmelreich & Herzlich Tut Mich Verlangen
Bach Cantata Club of London—Kennedy Scott   C-DB506

Cantata No. 147, "Herz und Mund"—No. 10, "Jesu bleibet meine Freude"
Choir (in English) & Orch. of the Bach Cantata Club of London—Kennedy Scott

Suite No. 2, B minor, Flute & Strings—Rondeau & Badinerie
Robert Murchie & String Orch.—Kennedy Scott   C-DB507

VOLUME III—CM-233

K. P. E. Bach: Sonata, F minor—1st Mvt.
J. C. Bach: Sonata, E major, Op. 5, No. 3—Mvt. only   C-DB830

C. P. E. Bach: Sonata, G major (No. 3 of first Collection)—Slow Mvt. only
Clementi: Sonata XIII, E flat major—First Mvt.
Harold Samuel (pf)   C-DB831

Mozart: Quartet, K. 421, D minor—Andante
Léner String Quartet   C-DB832

Haydn: Symphony No. 103, E flat major ("Mit Paukenwirble")—1st Mvt.
Symphony Orch.—C. Raybould   C-DB833

Mozart: Concerto, Clarinet & Orch., A major, K. 622—2nd Mvt. (Adagio)
Haydn Draper & Symphony Orch.—C. Raybould   C-DB834

Beethoven: Fidelio, Op. 72—Overture
Symphony Orch.—C. Raybould   C-DB835

Schubert: Gretchen am Spinnrade
Isobel Baillie (s) (in English) & C. Raybould (pf)
Schubert: Memnon
Harold Williams (b) (in English) & Herbert Dawson (pf)   C-DB836

Schubert: Die Forelle
Dorothy Stanton (s) (in English) & Gerald Moore (pf)

Loewe: Prinz Eugen, der edle Ritter
Harold Williams (b) (in English) & Herbert Dawson (pf)   **C-DB837**

VOLUME IV—CM-234

Berlioz: Romeo and Juliet—Romeo's Rêverie & Fête Chez Capulet
London Philharmonic Orch.—Harty
C-DB1230/1

Field: Nocturne, A major, No. 4

Chopin: Nocturne, Op. 15, No. 2, F sharp major
Myra Hess (pf)   **C-DB1232**

Schumann: Du bist wie eine Blume, Op. 25, No. 24

Brahms: Auf dem Schiffe, Op. 97, No. 2
Dorothea Helmrich (s) (in English) & Hubert Foss (pf)

Schumann: An den Abendstern, Op. 103, No. 4

Brahms: Die Schwestern, Op. 61, No. 1
Victoria Anderson & Viola Morris (s) & Hubert Foss (pf)   **C-DB1233**

Wolf: Nachtzauber; Ach, im Maien;& Gesegnet sei, durch den die Welt entstund
Mark Raphael (b) (in English) & Joan Singleton (pf)   **C-DB1234**

MacDowell: Sea Pieces, Op. 55—A.D. 1620
Myra Hess (pf)

Dvořák: Slavonic Dance, Op. 46—No. 1
Myra Hess & Hamilton Harty (2-Pfs.)
C-DB1235
Balakirev: Russia (Symphonic Poem)
London Philharmonic—Harty **C-DB1236/7**

VOLUME V—CM-361

Elgar: Sospiri, Op. 70
String Orch. & Harp—Goehr

R. Strauss: Der Burger als Edelmann, Op. 60 —Intermezzo
Symphony Orch.—Sargent
C-DB1784: C-DB1300

Debussy: Six Epigraphes Antiques—No. 3
Max Pirani & Eric Grant (2-Pfs.)

Ravel: Shéhérazade—La Flûte Enchantée
Rose Walter (s) (in English)
C-DB1785: C-DB1301
Vaughan Williams: Communion Service, G minor—Kyrie
Westminster Abbey Choir—E. Bullock

Bax: Paean
Harriet Cohen (pf) **C-DB1786: C-DB1302**

Mahler: Ich atmet' einen Linden Duft
Charles Kullman (t) (in English)

Schönberg: Buch der Hängenden Gärten— Nos. 5 & 12
Erica Storm (s) & Mosco Carner (pf)
C-DB1787: C-DB1303
Milhaud: Symphony No. 3
Symphony Orch.—Goehr

Casella: Serenata—Tarantella
Jean Pougnet (vl), Anthony Pini (vlc), Reginald Kell (cl), Paul Draper (bn), George Eskdale (trpt)
C-DB1788: C-DB1304

Hindemith: Scherzo for Viola & 'Cello
Paul Hindemith & Emanuel Feuermann

De Falla: "Homenaje" from "Le Tombeau de Debussy"
Albert Harris (guitar)
C-DB1789: C-DB1305

Stravinsky: Les Noces—Excerpt
Soloists & Orch.—Stravinsky

Bartók: Mikrokosmos—Staccato & Ostinato
Béla Bartók (pf)   **C-DB1790: C-DB1306**

Varese: Octandre—3rd Mvt.
Instrumental Ensemble—Goehr

Haba: Duo for Two Violins in the Sixth-Tone System, Op. 49—1st Mvt.
Wiesmeyer & Stein **C-DB1791: C-DB1307**

EARLY CANTATAS AND SONGS

Schütz: Cantata—Ich werde nicht sterben
Hugues Cuénod (t), and Chamber Orch.

Telemann: Liebe, liebe (Aria from an unidentified Opera)
Isabel French (s) & Continuo

Monteverdi: L'Incoronazione di Poppea— Sento un certo non so che
Isabel French (s) & Continuo

Anon: Pavane—Belle qui tient ma vie (from "L'Orchesographie"—Arbeau)
Isabel French (s) & C. J. Chiasson (harpsichord)

Rameau: Cantata—L'Impatience
Hugues Cuénod (t) & Continuo

Arne: Suleiman and Zaide—Oh! the transport of possessing
Isabel French (s) & Hugues Cuénod (t) & Orch.—Chiasson (harpsichord)
3 10" & 2 12"—TC-T2

EARLY ORGAN MUSIC

Landino; Bench' ora piova

Froberger: Canzona, D minor

Hofhaimer: Fantasia on "On freudt verzer"

Fridolin Sicher's Tablature Book: Resonet in laudibus & In dulci jubilo

Cabezón: Diferencias sobre "El Canto del Caballero"

Couperin: Fugue on the Kyrie
Byrd: Miserere

Sweelinck: Fantasia in Echo Style

Titelouze: Ave maris stella

Pachelbel: Chorale-Prelude—"Wie schön leuchtet der Morgenstern"

Buxtehude: Chorale-Preludes—"Von Gott will ich nicht lassen" & "Ein' feste Burg ist unser Gott"
Carl Weinrich (Organ of the Westminster Choir School, Princeton)   4 12"—MC-9

ENGLISH MADRIGALS (1st Set)
(Edited by E. H. Fellowes)

NOTE: *Announced too late for inclusion in the main body of the Encyclopedia.*

Contents:

Bennet: All creatures now

Byrd: This sweet and merry month; Though Amaryllis dance in green

Dowland: Say, Love, if ever thou didst find

Gibbons: What is our life? & The Silver Swan

Morley: Shoot, False Love, I care not & Fire! Fire!

Tomkins: Oyez! Has any found a lad?

Weelkes: As Vesta was from Latmos Hill descending; Say dear, when will your frowning; On the plains Fairy Trains

Wilbye: Draw on Sweet Night; Lady when I behold; & Stay Corydon, thou swain
  The Cambridge University Madrigal Society
  —Boris Ord   5 12″—G-C3739/44

FRENCH MASTERS OF THE MIDDLE AGES
Contents:

Anonymous (XIII Cent.): Belle Ysabelot—Motet

Adam de la Halle (XIII Cent.): Rondeau—Je meurs, je meurs d'amourette & Virelai—Fines amourettes ai

XV Cent.: L'Amour de Moy

G. Dufay (c.1400-1474): Complainte de Constantinople—"Omnes amici ejus" & Bon jour, bon mois

G. Machaut (c. 1300-1377): Mass (composed for the coronation of Charles V)—Kyrie & Qui propter nos

Pérotin: Salvatoris hodie & Organum tripla—"Diffusa est"

School of Notre-Dame de Paris: (XIII Cent.): Conductus triplum—"Crucificat omnes"

  La Psallette Notre-Dame—Jacques Chailley
                     4 12″—G-DB5116/9

HARPSICHORD RECITAL

Gibbons: The Lord of Salisbury—His Pavin & The Queen's Command

Morley: Goe from my Window

Purcell, Suite No. I, G major; Suite No. II, G minor; Lilliburlero

Couperin: Les Vergers Fleuris: Le Carillon de Cithère; Les Ombres Errantes; Les Baricades Mistérieuses

Rameau: La Villageoise; Le Rappel des Oiseaux; Rigaudons; Musette en Rondeau; Tambourin

Bach: Chromatic Fantasy and Fugue
Scarlatti: Sonatas—D major (L. 262) & A minor (L. 429)
  Ralph Kirkpatrick (harpsichord)
                     6 12″—MC-25

LITURGICAL MUSIC OF THE CATHOLIC CHURCH
(Sistine Chapel Album)

Perosi: Tu es Petrus & Benedictus

Palestrina: Sicut cervus, Super Flumina & Improperia

Arcadelt: Ave Maria

Victoria: Tenebrae Factae sunt

Anerio: Missa pro Defunctis—Introitus
  Sistine Chapel Cho.—Perosi
  (G-DB1569/72   4 12″—GM-139†

LITURGICAL MUSIC OF THE CATHOLIC CHURCH
(Dijon Cathedral Album)
Contents:

Josquin des Prés: Ave Verum & Ave Coelorum Domina

Victoria: Missa Orbis Factor—Kyrie

Mauduit: Psalm CL

João IV: Crux Fidelis

Aichinger: Ubi est Abel

Palestrina: Missa Assumpta Est Maria
  Dijon Cathedral Cho.—J. Samson
                     5 12″—VM-212†
  (G-DB4893/7 in GM-189)

MONUMENTS OF THE "ARS NOVA"
(Fourteenth Century)

Jacobo da Bologna; Non al suo amante; Motet—Lux purpurata radiis—Diligite justicam

Anon: Motet—A vous Vierge de doucour—Ad te Virgo clamitans venio

Matheus de Perusio: Gloria in Excelsis

Guillaume de Machaut: Hoquetus David

Anon: Virelai—Or sus, vous dormes trop
  J. Archimbaud (treble), R. Bonté (t), A. Lafosse (bass trumpet), E. Foveau (trpt.), R. Tudesq (tbn), & Brunold (viol)
                     3 12″—OL-1/3

MUSIC OF THE ORIENT

Native Songs and Dances of Japan, China, Java, Bali, Siam, India, Persia, Egypt, & Tunis
  Native Artists   12 10″—P-P10
  (P-MO100/11)

MUSIC OF THE RENAISSANCE

Mudarra: Triste estaba el Rey David; De la sangre de tus nobles; La mañana de San Juan

Valderrabano; Señora, si te olvidare & Al monte sale amor (Soneto)

Milan: Durandarte & Perdida tengo la color

Dowland: Come heavy sleep & Come again

Willaert: Con lagrime e sospir

Morley: It was a lover and his lass
  Max Meili (t) & Fritz Wörsching (lute & vihuela)   3 12″—G-DB5016/8

MUSICHE ITALIANE ANTICHE

Contents:

J. Peri: Euridice—Gioite al canto mio; Madrigal—Bellissima regina

G. Caccini: Madrigals—Amarilli—Fere selvagge

F. Rasi: Madrigals—Filli mia—Occhi sempre sereni—Filli tu vuoi partire

G. Frescobaldi: Arias—La mia pallida faccia—Non mi negate, ohimè

A. del Falconiere: Arias—Cara è la rosa—Bella fanciulla—Begli occhi lucenti

F. C. Milanuzzi: Arias—Sì, sì che io t'amo—Ora canusco (alla siciliana)—Ardo ma rivelar—La notte sorge
  Salvatore Salvati (t) Continuo

B. Marcello: Cantata—Disciogletevi in pianto

F. Cavalli: Serse—Beato chi può
  Giuseppe Flamini (b) & Continuo

"Intabolatura Nova"—Pass'e Mezzi

A. Gabrieli: Pass'e mezzo antico variato in 5 modi

G. Frescobaldi: Aria detta la Frescobalda; & 4 Galliards

B. Galuppi: Sonata, A major

G. Serini: Sonata, B minor
  Anna Linde (Harpsichord)

B. Marcello: Concerto, D minor, Trans. J. S. Bach

A. Sacchini: Sonata, F major

B. Galuppi; Sonata, C minor

G. P. Rutini: Sonata, A major

D. Scarlatti: Sonatas—B flat major (L. 97); G major (L. 79); E minor (L. 24); G major (L. 103)
  Ruggero Gerlin (Harpsichord)
  13   12"—MIA-1/13

PARLOPHONE 2000 YEARS OF MUSIC ALBUM

(Edited by Prof. Curt Sachs)

Contents:

Early Greek music: Skolion of Seikilos; Mesomedes: Hymn to the Sun

Jewish music: Kaddisch for the Passover; Abodah for the Day of Atonement; Extract from the Book of Esther

Gregorian Chant: Gradual "Misit Dominus verbum suum" (2nd Sunday after Epiphany)

Minnesänger & Troubadours—Walther von der Vogelweide: Palestine Song; Satire against Rüdolf of Hapsburg; Prince Wizlaw von Rügen: Minnesong; Raimbaut de Vaqueiras: Kalenda maya; Bernard de Ventador: Pois preyatz me, senhor; Graf Friedrich von Hüsen: Pois preyatz me, senhor (Paraphrase in German)

Santiago de Compostella: Congaudeant Catholici

G. Dufay: Gloria

Josquin des Prés: Et incarnatus est

Heinrich Finck: Christ ist erstanden

Arnoldus de Bruck: Aus Tiefer not'

Palestrina: Missa Papae Marcelli—Sanctus

Orlando di Lasso: Penitential Psalms—Miserere

Hans Leo Hassler: Mein Lieb' will mit mir Kriegen

Gesualdo da Venosa: Resta di darmi noia

Melchior Franck & Valentin Hausmann: German dances c.1600

William Byrd: Sellinger's Round

Giovanni Gabrieli: Benedixisti

Claudio Monteverdi: Arianna—Lamento d'Arianna

Heinrich Schütz: Psalm CXI

J. S. Bach: Motet "Der Geist hilft unserer Schwachheit auf"—Fugue only; Sonata No. 2, Violin & Harpsichord—1st Mvt. only; French Suite No. 5—Sarabande & Gavotte

G. F. Handel: Trio-Sonata No. 3, E flat major—1st Mvt. only

J. P. Rameau: La Poule
  Various Artists   12   10"—P-11
  (P-R1016/27)

SEVEN CENTURIES OF SACRED MUSIC
(1st Set)

(Yves Tinayre Album No. 1)

Contents:

Léonin: Organum Duplum

Pérotin: Conductus

Dufay: Alma Redemptoris Mater

Paumann: Benedicite

Anon.: Melisma—"Ille"

Gombert: In Festis Beatae

J. W. Franck: Passionlied

Albert: Festlied

Bach: Cantata No. 85—Seht, was die Liebe tut'!

Schütz: Her, unser Herrscher (Psalm VIII)

Mozart: Litaniae—Dulcissimum Convivium
  Yves Tinayre, etc.   6   12"—LUM-32011/6

SEVEN CENTURIES OF SACRED MUSIC
(2nd Set)

(Yves Tinayre Album No. 2)

Contents:

Léonin: Organum Duplum

School of Pérotin: Agniaus douz

Francon: Ave gloriosa Mater

Anon.: Laudi a San Lorenzo

Dufay: Vergine Bella

Anon.: Ave Mater

Benet: Pleni sunt coeli

Attey: Sweet was the song

Torre: Adoramus te, Señor!

Gombert: Confitemini Domino

Couperin: Ostende, Domine

Albert: Todeslied

Hammerschmidt: Danklied

Mozart: Vespers—Laudate Dominum
  Yves Tinayre, etc.   6   12"—LUM-32017/22

THREE CENTURIES OF ORGAN MUSIC SET
Miscellaneous organists

11 12"—PAT-PAT63/73

(Gonzalez Organ, Salle de Musique of Mme. Henri Gouin, Paris)

Landino: Questa Fanciulla; Palestrina: Ricercare
André Marchal

Gabrieli: Canzona
Charles Hens   PAT-PAT63

Frescobaldi: Toccata per l'elevazione; Padre Martini: Aria con variazioni
Joseph Bonnet   PAT-PAT64

Cabanilles: Passacaglia, D minor
Friedrich Mihatsch

Cabezón: Tiento in the first mode

Sancta Maria: Harmonization of a melody
André Marchal   PAT-PAT65

Purcell: Trumpet Tune & Ayre; J. S. Bach: Christ lag in Todesbanden
Charles Hens   PAT-PAT66

Grigny: Récit de tierce en taille; Anonymus: Three versets on Te Deum; Marchand: Fond d'orgue in E minor
Joseph Bonnet   PAT-PAT67

Couperin "Le Grand": Récit de Cromorne; Clérambault: Dialogue sur les Grands Jeux; Daquin: Noël sur les flûtes
Joseph Bonnet   PAT-PAT68

Hanff: Ach Gott, von Himmel seih darein
Charles Hens

Froberger: Toccata, F major
Friedrich Mihatsch   PAT-PAT69

Buxtehude; Fantasia on "Ich dank' dir, Gott;" Pachelbel: Toccata, C major & Choral-Prelude: "Durch Adams Fall"
Friedrich Mihatsch   PAT-PAT70

J. S. Bach: Toccata, Adagio & Fugue, C major & Chorale-Prelude: "Nun freut euch, liebe Christen g'mein"
André Marchal   PAT-PAT71/2

J. S. Bach: Chorale-Preludes—Liebster Jesu, wir sind hier & Jesu Christe, unser Heiland
Friedrich Mihatsch   PAT-PAT73

In addition to the above, there is also a record (PAT-PAT62) containing a lecture (in French) commenting upon the music.

A TREASURY OF HARPSICHORD MUSIC

Bach: Prelude, Fugue and Allegro, E flat major; Fantasia, C minor

Vivaldi-Bach: Concerto, D major

D. Scarlatti: Sonatas—D major (L. 418) & D minor (L. 423)

Chambonnières: Sarabande, D minor

Rameau: La Dauphine

Couperin: Les Barricades Mystérieuses; L'Arlequine

Purcell: Ground, C minor

Anon: The Nightingale

Handel: "The Harmonious Blacksmith"

Mozart: Rondo, D major (K. 485); Sonata, A major (K. 331)—Rondo alla Turca; Menuetto, D major (K. 355)
Wanda Landowska (harpsichord)

6 12"—VM-1181†

PERFORMER INDEX

When page reference is followed by "a" entry is in left-hand column; when followed by "b" entry is in right-hand column; when followed by "ab" there are entries in both columns.

Martinelli, Germaine, 63a, 193b, 195b, 218b, 250b, 252a, 318b, 324b, 326a, 405a, 427a, 460b, 461a, 462a, 463a, 464ab, 465a, 466ab, 467b, 468ab, 469a, 474b, 475ab, 476ab, 477b, 478a, 546b, 555b, 565a, 574a, 575b, 580a
Martinelli, Giovanni, 206b, 207ab, 208a, 297b, 298a, 317b, 319b, 320b, 398a, 404a, 405a, 541a, 546ab, 548a, 550a, 554ab, 552ab, 555a, 556ab, 560a, 564ab, 565a
Martini, Nino, 336a, 398a, 556b, 559a
Mascagni, Pietro, 316b, 317ab, 318b, 319b, 320b, 436a, 547a, 553a, 565b
Mascherini, Enzo, 161b, 207a, 219a, 399b, 436b, 549b
Masini, Galliano, 129b, 130a, 207a, 392ab, 398a, 399a, 402b, 404a, 405b, 406a, 546a, 551a, 552b, 559a, 564a
Masselos, William, 105a
Massia, Joan, 32b, 52b
Massini, Galliano, 164a, 319a, 320a
Mathieson, Muir, 3a, 7a, 74b, 75a, 274b, 385a
Matthei, Karl, 53b, 248b, 250a, 254ab, 329b, 332a, 379ab
Matthen, Paul, 15a, 25ab, 600ab, 601b, 602b
Matthews, Dennis, 31b, 44a, 53b, 56b, 57a, 188a, 260b, 346a, 349a, 363b, 423a
Matzenauer, Margarete, 249a, 329b, 337a, 445b
Mauersberger, 34b, 35a, 84b, 99ab, 274b, 292a, 330b, 331b
Maugeri, C., 436b
Maynor, Dorothy, 15a, 25b, 29a, 111b, 143b, 249b, 251b, 329b, 350b, 360b, 464b, 465b, 467a
Mayr, Richard, 56a, 513b
Mazzei, Enrico Di, 403b, 404a, 405b, 557b, 559a
Mazzoni, Alba, 467a
McArthur, Edwin, 7a, 54a, 97b, 111a, 174b, 236ab, 237ab, 238a, 280a, 464b, 479b, 583a, 585b, 587b, 588a
McCormack, John, 41ab, 43b, 83b, 111a, 115b, 132b, 135a, 140a, 162b, 187b, 193a, 195b, 214b, 221b, 223b, 239b, 241a, 244b, 247a, 251b, 290a, 316a, 320b, 353b, 372a, 399b, 405b, 416a, 461a, 462a, 465a, 467a, 468b, 470b, 522b, 533b, 534a, 544a, 546b, 599b, 600b, 601b
McCormick Mary, 322b, 324a
McDonald, Harl, 328a, 349b
McKnight, Anne, 25b
Medtner, Nicolas, 51b, 328a
Meili, Max, 8a, 14b, 16a, 76a, 98a, 101a, 107a, 164b, 165ab, 166a, 198a, 244b, 274b, 314a, 338a, 340a, 341b, 342a, 368a, 379a, 387b, 394b, 428ab, 443a, 470b, 471a, 542b, 589a, 598b
Meisle, Kathryn, 280a
Melandri, Antonio, 71a, 78b, 79ab, 207b, 218b, 392b, 400b, 440b, 550a
Melba, Nellie, 164a, 221b, 223b, 358b
Melchior, Lauritz, 236ab, 237b, 255b, 256a, 263ab, 269b, 287b, 290b, 291a, 433a, 443a, 467a, 474b, 476ab, 478a, 555a, 556a, 571b, 574ab, 575a, 576a, 577a, 578ab, 579ab, 580a, 581ab, 582a, 583a, 584a, 585b, 586b, 587b, 588a
Melichar, Alois, 2a, 11b, 12a, 21ab, 28a, 29a, 38a, 46b, 78a, 81a, 93b, 110a, 155b, 168b, 177b, 190a, 209b, 210a, 219b, 221b, 238b, 266b, 267a, 273b, 274a, 295a, 296b, 301b, 302a, 304a, 305b, 307a, 308a, 309a, 317b, 326b, 336a, 344b, 370b, 376b, 378b, 398a, 401a, 404a, 424a, 425b, 431b, 438a, 442a, 445a, 457a, 469b, 470a, 484a, 487b, 490b, 501b, 502b, 503ab, 504b, 505b, 506a, 507a, 508a, 509ab, 510b, 511ab, 512b, 514ab, 515a, 523ab, 524a, 527b, 530b, 532ab, 536a, 537b, 538a, 547a, 556b, 563a, 566a, 572a, 574b, 583b, 584a, 585a, 588b, 592a, 596a, 606b
Melnick, Bertha, 600a
Melton, James, 71a, 83a, 106b, 140b, 191a, 204a, 238b, 239b, 240a, 241a, 265b, 270b, 280ab, 284b, 293a, 295b, 298a, 318a, 323a, 324a, 326b, 353b, 359a, 401ab, 402a, 433b, 574b
Mengelberg, Willem, 13a, 36ab, 45b, 46a, 47b, 49b, 54b, 55ab, 56a, 62ab, 80a, 83b, 94b, 95a, 113a, 147a, 164a, 175b, 194b, 211b, 232b, 271b, 303b, 329a, 331a, 337a, 419b, 458b, 469b, 505b, 512ab, 523a, 528a, 531b, 532a, 535ab, 569b, 575a, 583b, 592b, 593a, 594a
Menges, Isolde, 407b, 410b, 516a
Menuhin, Hephzibah, 32b, 49a, 52a, 53a, 56b, 89a, 179a, 195a, 296b, 364b, 365a, 391a, 458b, 474a, 535b
Menuhin, Yaltah, 364b
Menuhin, Yehudi, 22b, 23a, 31ab, 32b, 36b, 42ab, 43b, 45a, 49ab, 52b, 53a, 56b, 75b, 85ab, 86ab, 89a, 98b, 112a, 134b, 148ab, 168a, 169b, 172a, 173a, 174b, 176b, 178a, 179a, 182a, 189b, 195a,

226a, 285b, 286b, 287a, 289b, 296b, 306a, 329a, 343a, 346b, 347a, 348a, 364b, 365b, 375a, 380ab, 381a, 391a, 421b, 422a, 423a, 430a, 431b, 447b, 448a, 458b, 462a, 472a, 473b, 474a, 525a, 526a, 535b, 598ab
Menz, Julia, 24b, 29b
Merckel, Alice, 136b, 138a, 149b, 184a
Merckel, Henri, 13a, 31a, 32a, 45a, 83a, 136b, 137b, 152b, 183a, 184a, 270b, 288b, 365a, 389b, 434a, 444a, 448a
Merli, Francesco, 58a, 71a, 108b, 206b, 207ab, 216a, 296b, 297b, 298a, 318b, 319a, 392b, 401b, 402b, 403a, 405b, 406ab, 439a, 546ab, 547b, 548a, 552ab, 553a, 554ab, 555a, 557a, 563ab, 564b, 565a, 574a, 605b, 606a
Merrem-Nikisch, Grete, 503b, 505a
Merrill, Robert, 68b, 139a, 199a, 207a, 240a, 322a, 325a, 335b, 434b, 537a
Merriman, Nan, 65a, 161b, 180a, 213b, 433b, 538b
Metropolitan Opera Chorus, 57b, 58a, 59b, 68b, 70a, 161b, 164a, 219b, 271a, 298a, 341b, 352a, 368b, 369ab, 392a, 397b, 404b, 527a, 548a, 551b, 552a, 554a, 558a, 564a, 565a
Metropolitan Opera Orchestra, 57b, 58a, 62b, 63a, 68b, 161b, 162a, 164a, 271a, 355a, 356a, 360a, 368b, 369ab, 397b, 435b, 527a, 548a, 554ab, 587b
Metz, Lucius, 14b, 25b
Meudon Organ, 167b
Mewton-Wood, Noel, 52b, 126b, 594b
Meyen, Sabine, 436a
Meyer, Marcelle, 20b, 23ab, 24ab, 27b, 28a, 37a, 136a, 137ab, 138a, 146b, 339a, 416b, 417a, 418b, 419a, 420a, 421a, 423a, 451a, 452ab, 453a, 512a, 546b
Meyer-Welfing, Hugo, 6a, 294b, 352b, 359a, 404a, 405b, 406a
Meyrowitz, Selmar, 50b, 64a, 109b, 126a, 231b, 300b, 301a, 303b, 304b, 305b, 319a, 456a, 457a, 459a, 469b, 575a, 587b, 594a
Micheau, Janine, 422b, 437a, 537b
Michelangeli, Arturo Benedetti, 4b, 50a, 114b, 119b, 120b, 125b, 128a, 225b, 232ab, 233a, 315a, 340a, 450b, 453ab, 472a
Micheletti, Gaston, 3a, 9a, 42a, 70ab, 71ab, 72a, 73a, 100a, 140a, 154ab, 191a, 220a, 222ab, 223a, 288b, 289a, 294b, 297b, 298a, 317b, 323a, 324a, 325b, 326a, 340b, 404a, 405b, 425b, 435a, 538b, 539a, 556b, 559a
Mihatsch, Friederich, 19a, 102a, 104a, 199b, 379ab
Milan Cathedral Chorus, 64b, 189b, 387a
Milan Symphony Orchestra, 12a, 57b, 68b, 69a, 85b, 86a, 107b, 108ab, 109a, 113a, 130b, 159b, 203a, 218ab, 219b, 296b, 297a, 298a, 314a, 317ab, 318b, 319ab, 320a, 356a, 370a, 385b, 393a, 402b, 403ab, 405a, 407a, 426ab, 435b, 436a, 437b, 438a, 439b, 446a, 488a, 499a, 530b, 537b, 547a, 549b, 551b, 553b, 555a, 560b, 562a, 565b, 583a, 605ab, 606b
Milanov, Zinka, 58a, 318a, 393a, 546b, 552b, 564ab
Mildmay, Audrey, 351b, 355b, 386a
Miles, Maurice, 248b, 149a, 372b
Milhaud, Darius, 338b, 339a
Miller, Mitchell, 245b
Milstein, Nathan, 31b, 52b, 85b, 98b, 169a, 213a, 287a, 289b, 325a, 329a, 364b, 431b, 447b, 473a, 489b, 519b, 528b, 532a, 570b, 598ab
Minghini-Cattaneo, Irene, 58a, 69b, 161b, 162a, 391b, 392ab, 445b, 545b, 548ab, 563b, 565a
Minneapolis Symphony Orchestra, 20b, 24a, 37b, 45b, 47a, 55b, 82a, 86b, 95b, 106b, 114b, 138a, 153b, 155b, 156a, 166a, 171b, 172ab, 196a, 209a, 210a, 217b, 225ab, 232b, 283ab, 286a, 303b, 310a, 313a, 319a, 326b, 329a, 331b, 334a, 347b, 356a, 381a, 388b, 397a, 413a, 416a, 419a, 422b, 429b, 455a, 473a, 479a, 486b, 491b, 492b, 502ab, 504b, 506ab, 507a, 508a, 514a, 528a, 531b, 535a, 590a, 596a, 605ab
Mirella, Luba, 397b
Mitropoulos, Dimitri, 20b, 24a, 37b, 45b, 47a, 55b, 82a, 95b, 114b, 116b, 119b, 122b, 124a, 128b, 129a, 138a, 166a, 172ab, 196a, 209a, 210a, 217b, 232b, 303b, 310a, 313a, 326b, 329a, 331b, 334ab, 345b, 395b, 397a, 413a, 416a, 422b, 429b, 479a, 487b, 528a, 535a, 590a, 596a
Mittman, Leopold, 1a, 41a, 150a, 168b, 184b, 185a, 231b, 270a, 325a, 473a, 484b, 489b, 532a, 570b, 598ab
Miyakawa, Yoshito, 335a, 402a
Moiseiwitsch, Benno, 45a, 49a, 50b, 51b, 114a, 121b, 124a, 126a, 144b, 147a, 152a, 156b, 232a, 281b, 301ab, 302b, 328a, 331a, 370a, 384ab, 394a, 412b, 413b, 414ab, 422b, 444a, 473b, 517b, 527b, 528a, 591b

239a, 249a, 257b, 280a, 285b, 295a, 353a, 354b, 356b, 357ab, 358a, 360b, 433b, 462a
Steeger, Gerhard, 515b, 516a, 523b
Steele, Eleanor, 477a, 478a
Stefano, Giuseppe di, 135b, 326b, 538b, 539a
Steffensen, Ingeborg, 34b, 35a, 223b, 350a, 373b
Steinberg, 98b, 114b, 472a, 483a
Stellman, Maxine, 579b
Sten, Suzanne, 321ab
Stenn, Randi Heide, 6b, 7a, 40a, 237a
Stern, Isaac, 52b, 72a, 169a, 253a, 431b, 448a, 586a, 598a
Stevens, Risë, 68b, 69b, 70a, 104b, 161b, 211b, 213b, 271a, 279b, 280b, 337a, 356b, 357a, 372a, 392b, 393b, 445b, 462a, 478b, 501a, 531a, 538a, 602b, 603a
Stiedry, Fritz, 22ab, 212a, 347a
Stiedry-Wagner, Erika, 455a
Stignani, Ebe, 57b, 58a, 69b, 71b, 161b, 162b, 211b, 213b, 252a, 317a, 318b, 349b, 391b, 392ab, 437a, 439b, 445ab, 538a, 541ab, 545b, 548b, 551b, 552a, 563b, 566a
Stock, Frederick, 30a, 44b, 61a, 89a, 95a, 112b, 171a, 173a, 177b, 178b, 208b, 209b, 210a, 252a, 274a, 312a, 367a, 381a, 392b, 427b, 431b, 444a, 469b, 479a, 486b, 487a, 491a, 507b, 509b, 510a, 512a, 520a, 528b, 529b, 573b, 584b, 590a, 592b
Stockholm Radio Orchestra, 65b
Stockholm Royal Opera Orchestra, 65b, 503b
Stockholm Symphony Orchestra, 6b, 276b, 486b, 488a
Stockmarr, Johanne, 35b, 44a, 50b, 51b, 121b, 127b, 159a, 363b, 384a, 450b
Stokowski, Leopold, 13b, 15b, 16b, 17b, 18ab, 19b, 20b, 21a, 22a, 24ab, 26b, 27a, 28ab, 29b, 30b, 31ab, 32a, 33ab, 34b, 35ab, 36b, 37b, 38ab, 39a, 55b, 56a, 62b, 67b, 68b, 69ab, 70a, 71a, 75b, 76a, 80b, 81ab, 85a, 94b, 95a, 103ab, 125b, 139b, 140a, 143b, 145ab, 147a, 148a, 152a, 166a, 175b, 178b, 180a, 194a, 195b, 198a, 209a, 210a, 217b, 249a, 250b, 254b, 259b, 274a, 281b, 299a, 301b, 311b, 328a, 331a, 347a, 368b, 369a, 370b, 375a, 377b, 382b, 396a, 411b, 412b, 414b, 419b, 421b, 429a, 430a, 431b, 443b, 444a, 445b, 448b, 457b, 469b, 480b, 481a, 482b, 483a, 484a, 486b, 487a, 498b, 500b, 503b, 507a, 508a, 514b, 516b, 518ab, 519a, 527b, 528a, 529ab, 531b, 534b, 535ab, 538a, 539a, 570a,572b, 573b, 574b, 577a, 578ab, 579ab, 580b, 581ab, 582ab, 583ab, 586ab, 587ab, 591b, 592a
Stoska, Polyna, 284b, 513a, 576a, 593b, 596a
Stracciari, Riccardo, 70b, 161b, 207a, 297a, 392a, 404b, 435b, 436b, 437b, 537ab, 541a, 548b, 549a, 550b, 554ab, 555a, 556a, 557a, 558b, 559a, 562a, 564a, 585a
Stradivarius Quartet, 331b
Straram, Walter, 147a, 272a, 394a, 419b, 441a, 512a
Straram Orchestra, 147a, 272b, 394a, 419b, 420a, 441a, 512a, 517a, 519b
Strasbourg Cathedral Choir, see Chorale de la Cathédrale de Strasbourg
Strassfogel, Ignace, 54b, 236a, 237b, 263b, 291a
Straube, K., 26a, 34a, 77a, 86b, 92b, 394b, 453b
Strauss, Richard, 55b, 135a, 212a, 253a, 359a, 367a, 511b, 512ab, 514ab, 515a, 516b, 571b, 586a, 592b
Stravinsky, Igor, 517ab, 518ab, 519ab
Stravinsky, Soulima, 39a, 517ab
Strienz, Wilhelm, 12a, 53b, 54a, 74b, 190b, 191a, 210b, 219b, 221ab, 230b, 266b, 267a, 271b, 295b, 306b, 307ab, 308a, 339b, 354b, 355a, 358b, 360a, 369b, 372ab, 478b, 492a, 523a, 530b, 549b, 560a
Stross Quartet, 47b, 48a
Strub, Max, 22b, 45a, 345b, 388a, 424a, 425a, 470a
Strub Quartet, 48a, 99a, 361a, 362b, 424b, 458ab
Stuyvesant Quartet, 57b, 396a, 420b, 482b, 568b
Suddaby, Elsie, 10b, 28b, 248a, 342a, 464ab, 467a
Summers, Lydia, 25b, 248b
Supervia, Conchita, 69b, 70ab, 71ab, 72a, 73b, 74a, 180b, 181a, 226b, 227a, 356b, 357a, 399a, 437ab, 438a, 439a
Süsskind, 22a, 23a, 71b, 257a, 314b, 345a, 414b, 483b, 593a, 594b, 599a
Svanholm, Set, 575a, 577a
Sved, Alexander, 62b, 63a, 74a, 438b, 461b, 468a, 476b, 478b, 548b, 549a, 553a, 557ab, 558b, 559ab
Swarthout, Gladys, 44a, 68a, 69b, 70a, 72b, 106b, 112b, 139a, 164b, 199a, 204b, 220a, 223a, 226b, 251a, 256a, 280a, 313b, 337a, 410a, 445b, 529a, 534a, 537b, 538a, 595b
Symphony Orchestra of Mexico, 102a, 113a, 517a

Szantho, Enid, 56a, 213b, 252a
Szell, George, 45a, 55a, 84a, 168b, 175a, 289b, 502a, 506a, 507ab, 575a, 594a; as pianist, 362a
Szigeti, Joseph, 22ab, 23a, 31a, 42ab, 45a, 52ab, 64a, 75a, 84ab, 86a, 89a, 134b, 150a, 152b, 172a, 173a, 181b, 270a, 283b, 289b, 339a, 346b, 348a, 364b, 380a, 395b, 396b, 397a, 431b, 459b, 460a, 518b, 519a, 525a, 526a

Tabuteau, Marcel, 347a
Tagliabue, Carlo, 58b, 70b, 73b, 163b, 297a, 436b, 437b, 549a, 550b, 551a, 552b, 554b, 557a, 558b, 562a, 564a, 585a
Tagliafero, Magda, 5a, 31b, 118a, 183a, 184b, 241ab, 328b, 330a, 365a, 472b, 473b, 594b
Tagliavini, Ferruccio, 59a, 130a, 161a, 316b, 317a, 323a, 349b, 398a, 399b, 404a, 405ab, 436a, 538b, 551a, 553a, 558a, 605b
Tajo, Italo, 206b, 344ab, 349b, 355b, 545b
Talich, Vaclav, 168a, 170b, 171ab, 172ab, 173ab, 175a, 176a, 285a, 490a, 495a, 497a, 520b, 528ab
Tamagno, Francesco, 206b, 322a, 336b, 337a, 439a, 445a, 554ab, 556a, 563b, 564b
Tamarin, Ilya, 369ab
Tango, Egisto, 361a, 367a, 373a, 436a, 438b, 593a
Tansini, Ugo, 41b, 58ab, 59a, 79b, 108a, 130b, 134b, 163a, 208a, 254a, 314a, 317a, 320a, 368a, 381b, 391a, 437b, 438a, 439b, 440a, 592b, 606a
Tarjus, Blanche, 417a
Taschner, Gerhard, 31b, 195a, 381a, 447b
Tassinari, A., 21b, 36a, 149b, 348a, 573a
Tassinari, Pia, 79a, 220ab, 316b, 317a, 326a, 349b, 358a, 398b, 399ab, 550b, 572b
Tauber, Richard, 54a, 70b, 74a, 92b, 93b, 97a, 104b, 115b, 132b, 139a, 169a, 195b, 198b, 199a, 202b, 214b, 223b, 236a, 237b, 252a, 255b, 258a, 265a, 266b, 285b, 286a, 287a, 289a, 294ab, 295ab, 296ab, 297ab, 298b, 304a, 316a, 326b, 328b, 352b, 353b, 354b, 359a, 376b, 377b, 407a, 434b, 440a, 442a, 460b, 461ab, 462a, 463b, 464a, 465ab, 466ab, 467ab, 468ab, 469a, 475b, 476b, 477b, 487b, 501ab, 503b, 504b, 505a, 507a, 508b, 509b, 515ab, 533a, 534ab, 540b, 604ab, 606ab; (as conductor), 397b, 503a, 541ab, 575a, 593a
Taylor, Joan, 71b, 234b, 318b, 385a, 501a
Taylor, Kendall, 56b, 173b
Tcherepnin, Alexander, 436a
Telmanyi, Emil, 37a, 49a, 53a, 85a, 86a, 89ab, 96b, 180b, 253a, 270a, 285b, 286a, 329b, 363b, 373a, 374a, 484a, 485a
Telva, Marian, 58a
Temianka, Henri, 10a, 458b, 484a, 512b
Temple Church Choir (London), 15b, 88b, 330ab, 332a, 499a, 543b
Tertis, Lionel, 347a, 534a
Teschemacher, Margaret, 56a, 197a, 220b, 221ab, 318b, 357b, 358a, 377a, 378a, 491a, 493a, 513ab, 546b, 547b, 548ab, 549a, 550a, 552ab, 561a, 565a, 575b, 576a, 594a, 604ab
Tessandra, Laure, 445b, 559b, 563b
Tetrazzini, Luisa, 59b, 163b, 357a, 437a, 538b, 549b, 558a, 559b, 561a, 562b
Teyte, Maggie, 63b, 74a, 112b, 139a, 145b, 146a, 150ab, 151ab, 152a, 164b, 166b, 167a, 169a, 174b, 184b, 185b, 186ab, 187a, 191b, 214b, 231b, 241b, 242ab, 304a, 315b, 326b, 335a, 340b, 378b, 382a, 386b, 409b, 410a, 422a, 525a, 533b
Theatre de la Monnaie Chorus, Brussels, 182a, 537b
Theatre de la Monnaie Orchestra, Brussels, 182a, 537b
Thebom, Blanche, 25a, 94a, 244a, 392a, 409b, 424b, 474b, 475a, 476a, 477a, 478a, 579a, 580b, 582b, 586b
Then-Bergh, Erik, 31b, 44a, 52a, 122b, 253b, 424b
Thibaud, Jacques, 4b, 5b, 21b, 37a, 49a, 53a, 56b, 84b, 96b, 112a, 143a, 148ab, 150a, 182a, 183a, 184ab, 186a, 195a, 226a, 257a, 262b, 334a, 346b, 363a, 365a, 384b, 421b, 429b, 444b, 459b, 460a, 470a, 479a, 525a, 545a, 569a, 570a
Thibault, Conrad, 313b
Thibout, Yvonne, 33b, 292b, 450a
13th Sound Ensemble of Havana, 106a
Thill, Georges, 1b, 25b, 64b, 68b, 74a, 99b, 104a, 111b, 113a, 132b, 154a, 167a, 185ab, 186ab, 187a, 191a, 193b, 195ab, 206b, 211b, 212a, 219a, 220ab, 221b, 222a, 223a, 224a, 241b, 242b, 294ab, 297ab, 298a, 304a, 314b, 321a, 322ab, 323a, 324ab, 325b, 326b, 327a, 328b, 335ab, 336a, 398a, 404b, 405b, 406b, 412a, 427b, 430b, 439a, 445b, 463ab, 465b, 467a, 510a, 515b, 516a, 541b, 546b, 554ab, 555a, 556ab, 557b, 559a, 560b, 561a, 562b, 574ab, 575b, 577a, 578b, 579b, 580a